Tender Expectations

Kathleen and Roman have always had strong feelings
for each other, and when a baby enters the picture
they are forced to deal with them. Will their love
for each other and the baby win out in the end?
Jule McBride, *Baby Trap*

Beth and Nathan have a few things in common—
including a baby on the way and a forbidden
attraction. Can love help them overcome their fears
and insecurities to find their happily-ever-after?
Janice Kay Johnson, *The Miracle Baby*

JULE McBRIDE

received the *Romantic Times* Reviewer's Choice Award for Best First Series Romance in 1993. Since then she has penned thirty more heartwarming love stories that have met with strong reviews, been nominated for awards and made repeated appearances on romance bestseller lists. A three-time Reviewer's Choice nominee for Best American Romance, Jule has also been nominated for two Lifetime Achievement awards in the category of Love and Laughter.

JANICE KAY JOHNSON

The author of more than forty published or forthcoming books, Janice Kay Johnson has a B.A. in history and a master's degree in librarianship and worked as a librarian for two years before selling her first book. When she isn't chauffeuring her youngest daughter to play rehearsals or staying in touch by e-mail with her oldest daughter, now in college, Janice enjoys gardening, quilting and opening and closing doors for her many cats. Ms. Johnson currently lives and works in rural Arlington, Washington.

Tender Expectations

Jule McBride

Janice Kay Johnson

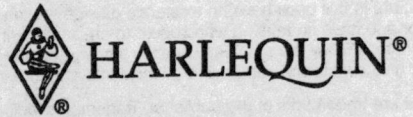

HARLEQUIN®

TORONTO • NEW YORK • LONDON
AMSTERDAM • PARIS • SYDNEY • HAMBURG
STOCKHOLM • ATHENS • TOKYO • MILAN • MADRID
PRAGUE • WARSAW • BUDAPEST • AUCKLAND

HARLEQUIN BOOKS

by Request—TENDER EXPECTATIONS

Copyright © 2002 by Harlequin Books S.A.

ISBN 0-373-21733-1

The publisher acknowledges the copyright holders of the individual works as follows:
BABY TRAP
Copyright © 1994 by Julianne Randolph Moore
THE MIRACLE BABY
Copyright © 1997 by Janice Kay Johnson

This edition published by arrangement with Harlequin Books S.A.

Visit us at www.eHarlequin.com

Printed in U.S.A.

CONTENTS

BABY TRAP
Jule McBride

Prologue

"Now, now, Kathleen, sweetheart," Malcolm Van Ness said in a silky voice. He edged toward where she was teetering on the starboard side rail of his forty-foot Sport Fisherman like a man used to dealing with hysterical, pregnant women. "Don't do anything crazy."

"Get back, Van Ness," Kathleen said coolly, thinking that this had to be the worst New Year's Eve of her life. She hooked her ankle through the boat's railing for balance, then crossed her fingers in front of her, as if he were a vampire. "Back!" Her green eyes met his baby blues with levity. "If you think I'd even *consider* drowning myself over a self-centered cretin like you, *you're* the crazy one!"

Van Ness now stood stock-still, his expression as dead calm as the gulf waters off Little Torch Key where they were anchored. Only the full moon and the dim headlights of the boat illuminated the silent waters, hinting at the silver-backed fish that darted through the coral. On the deck an ice bucket glistened with condensation. So did a still-corked bottle of champagne, two untouched shining crystal flutes and two foil party hats.

"Kathleen, I know you're a little high-strung—"

"Try unstrung! I'm jobless, homeless and ten weeks pregnant, Van Ness."

"Look," he began, "it's not my fault you're preg—"

"Oh, no? Just what do you think I am? Some self-reproducing sea creature?" Kathleen's voice rose in fury. "An amoeba, maybe?" In her outburst, she lost her footing. She swung for the rail, grabbed it tightly with one hand, then gathered the slit skirt of her long ruby silk dress in the other.

Van Ness's sun-streaked blond hair, navy-and-white nautical shirt and blousy Armani slacks blew in the slight coastal breeze, making him look every bit the two-timing playboy.

"Kathleen, I'm sure we can work out this misunderstanding...."

"Misunderstanding?" she returned in shock. "I understand perfectly. I am going to have a baby. And unfortunately the poor little thing's already cursed with your miserable genes!"

Kathleen bit back her tears and tried not to feel the weight of the gargantuan, four-carat, emerald-cut diamond on her ring finger. She'd found it in a big black velvet box in the captain's cabin. She'd thought the ring meant Van Ness had intended to ask her to marry him tonight, even before he found out she was pregnant. But the diamond belonged to his mother! "Damn my romantic soul," she muttered.

Van Ness slithered toward her. He was still a good ten feet away, which meant he was far too close. Oh, how she hated him! And the fact that they were anchored right in sight of Lawrence Island made things worse...so much worse.

"Sweetheart, we can't just stand here like this all

night,'' Van Ness said. ''And—I know this is terribly delicate—but I need the ring. My mother will kill me. She just wanted me to have it reset, before she auctions it—''

''I'm *pregnant* and you want to talk about jewelry!'' Kathleen tossed her head regally, then glared down at the ring on her finger. The diamond glinted back from its plain, heavy gold setting, and seemed to wink at her. Well, she thought, if it was winking, the joke was certainly on her.

Just moments before, she'd been so relieved. She didn't love Van Ness, even if she was willing to marry him for the sake of the baby.

But he had no intention of marrying her!

She turned abruptly and climbed over the rail of the boat.

''Kathleen!''

''Don't you dare come near me, you viper.'' She sent Van Ness a steely stare, then wrenched the ring from her finger. ''I ought to throw this ring right in your face,'' she managed to say.

''Oh, please, Kathleen…don't throw it.'' Van Ness's brows drew together in horror. ''Honey, that ring was part of an Austrian royal collection. Kathleen, I know you must be a little upset, but please don't throw that ring.''

Oh, yes, she wanted to throw the ring in his face, but that gesture just didn't seem extreme enough.

''Happy New Year, Van Ness,'' she snapped. She jiggled the heavy stone in her palm for a moment, feeling its weight. She took a deep breath—and then threw it overboard.

''That ring's worth in the seven figures,'' Van Ness screamed, completely losing his composure.

"As in one million dollars?" Kathleen echoed numbly. Van Ness gasped, and then she heard a very loud plunk.

She quickly twirled her slit silk dress to her waist, flung the skirt over her shoulder and dived.

In midair she remembered she was in the Florida Keys. The water was usually so shallow she could stand in it. If she didn't land in the channel that had been dug for boat traffic, she was in trouble.

She was so frightened at the prospect of cracking her skull, she barely felt the cool rush of the water against her skin. Someone was on her side—she'd hit the boat lane! She opened her eyes, fighting the sting of the salt water. She didn't know what came over her then, but she had to try to find the ring....

A glimmer of light flashed in the murky beams of the Sport Fisherman's dimmed headlights. She swiftly swam toward where the diamond's glinting rays spiraled through the coral and sank downward toward the murky sand. Just before the ring was lost forever, she thrust her open hand beneath it. The diamond circled in the water, looking weightless for a moment, then landed in her palm. She curled her fingers around it in a tight little fist.

But what now? Kathleen twisted in the water, her long ruby dress whirling in the slight current. The dark underbelly of Van Ness's boat was hardly inviting; the humiliation of having mistaken his mother's diamond for her own engagement ring was far worse. If this was the beginning of the new year, she thought wryly, she wasn't at all sure she wanted to see the rest of it.

No, she couldn't face Van Ness. Not now...perhaps not ever. Like it or not, there was only one thing to do.

Kathleen shoved the ring on her finger, forced herself to forget that barracuda were notorious for their attraction to flashy jewelry and then, with all her strength, started swimming for that oh-so-distant shore.

Chapter One

"Did you have a fight, sir?"

"Nope." Roman Lawrence smiled rakishly and continued to strip. "I think it was called a date."

Flanders gathered Roman's dusty tuxedo trousers and ripped jacket from the bed and grinned. "I see," he teased, intentionally emphasizing his own British accent, as if to point out the impropriety of Roman's behavior.

Roman shrugged out of his white pleated shirt and tossed it to Flanders. Then he crossed the room, flinging open the French doors that led to the terrace outside his bedroom suite. Far downward, past the garden, past where the old stone wall of his château opened in an archway that led to the calm dark gulf waters around his island, a pelican waded, then took flight beneath the date palms.

"The jacket caught on a hood ornament." Roman chuckled softly. "But it was a nice hood ornament. A Rolls, I think."

"Sounds enjoyable. I'll assume you weren't alone on that hood?"

"Hardly." Roman strolled in from the terrace, headed to his closet, walked inside, found his favorite

robe and shrugged into it, then stepped out of his briefs
and returned. He shot Flanders an apologetic grin.
"Sorry I picked the only car that wasn't so waxed you
could deliver babies on it."

"The jacket *is* a bit dusty," Flanders said. "But was
this one marriage material?"

Roman took enough flak from his mother for not
having yet produced an heir. He'd figured when he'd
gotten married that would appease his mother, but it
hadn't. He was now divorced. And he hardly needed
Flanders to start harping. "Afraid not. Her name was
Alexandra. She claimed she wanted just a moment
alone with Rodeo Roman. Then she attacked me." Roman smiled with feigned innocence.

"She's not the same woman you took to the New
Year's party?"

Roman shrugged. "Never saw her before."

Flanders leaned casually against the wall. He was in
his late forties, over ten years Roman's senior, and had
been with the Lawrence household forever. "I thought
they were calling you Lawrence of Arabia these days."

"True," Roman said. That had been the case since
he'd won a hefty purse in a Texas cutting horse futurity
the year before with an Arabian horse. Cutting horses
had long been his passion, but quarter horses were usually used to cut calves from herds, for branding. Roman
had been among the first to introduce Arabians, rather
than quarter horses, into the cutting horse circuit.

He still loved his quarter horses, though. Pirate's
Legacy, his most prized cutter, was the most beautiful
black stallion he'd ever trained. "Rodeo Roman,
Lawrence of Arabia..." Roman flashed Flanders a
playful smile. "But where's the one who's going to
call me plain old Romeo?"

"Oh, poor you," Flanders said, his voice dripping with irony. "But, seriously, you should watch out for fortune hunters."

Roman merely nodded and ran both his hands through his thick black hair. Glancing in the mirror, he touched his silver streak. It shot through the right side of his hair like a lightning bolt.

"Even so," Roman finally said, glancing from the mirror. "The night was a disaster."

"Even with Alexandra?"

"Especially with Alexandra." Had that really been the woman's name? Roman wasn't so sure now. All he knew was that he was sick of playing games with women. At first he always wanted them. He pursued them, too, but sooner or later they soured on him. He hadn't even slept with Alexandra, and she'd wanted him to usher in the New Year with her, right on the hood of a car.

"Yeah," Roman murmured. "The charms of Alexandra notwithstanding. I'm going skinny-dipping," he added. "Like to join me?"

Flanders rolled his eyes. "No, thanks."

Roman sent him a last wry glance, then headed for the terrace. He crossed the length of it and followed the long, winding stairs downward to the flagstone patio below. He felt his tensions ease when he reached the path that snaked around his raised flower beds and pool. He knew every inch of the island instinctively, from his stables and horse-training arena to the old family graveyard far behind him, with its crazed twining vines that grew up around the crumbling, tumbledown tombstones.

He took a deep breath, letting the scent of hibiscus and flowering cacti fill his lungs. There was nothing better than January in southernmost Florida, he thought, moaning aloud when his bare feet finally touched the brownish, gleaming, night-cooled ground of the marly shore.

When he reached the water he slipped out of his robe and tossed it to the ground. Then he stretched, naked, in the low, soft light of the moon, rolling the rounded muscles of his shoulders. He threaded his raised hands through his hair and stepped into the water, feeling good for the first time that night.

No doubt he was brooding and wild, the way people said he was, but he didn't care. He just wished all things were the way they were on his own private island. The place held the weight of history for him, dating back nearly two hundred years to when his Spanish ancestors had first settled in the Florida Keys. Wind, water, sand, salt. Nothing more, nothing less. The place seethed with primitive, raw, elemental life. *Earth, air, wind...*

But where was the fire? he wondered, walking slowly into the water until he was submerged to his neck. The fire that was fated to meet his fire?

He dipped beneath the water, which at its deepest, outside his canal, was only fifteen feet. His hair tightened to his scalp as he surfaced. He opened his eyes. *Impossible.*

"Fire..." he whispered, a teasing smile lifting his wide, expressive mouth at the corners.

A woman was floating toward him. She was still far out, drifting on her back. He should have noticed her before because the water was calm. Dead calm. Now a long, slender, very pale arm lifted and fell in the moonlight, as if she could barely be bothered to propel herself.

A snowbird. Yes, light skinned as she looked from
here, she was definitely a wintering tourist from up
north. After a long moment her other arm rose and fell,
bringing her magically toward him.

"You're a ship to my shore, darlin'," he whispered.
"My mermaid."

He pushed off, treading into the water, moving
slowly toward her, figuring he might as well seize the
mysterious moment. Whoever she was, she was given
to lonely, brooding, late-night swims, just the way he
was. Maybe she preferred the gritty scent of salt to wild
New Year's parties, too. Maybe she craved the soft
touch of seaweed when it lightly grazed her skin like
fingers and the danger of the forbidden that lurked in
the dark, secretive oceanic waters....

Roman swam silently until he was nearly beneath
her, so close he could almost see her eyes, mouth and
nose—the only parts of her not submerged. He concentrated on making no sounds, not wanting to say anything, not wanting to interrupt her.

He thought briefly of his pirate ancestry, of his very
distant grandfather, Fabian D'Agonistio. How would
old Fabian have handled this situation? He who had
purposely caused ships to wreck off what was now
Lawrence Island, just so he could steal all the cargo....

No doubt old Fabian would have laid immediate
claim to the woman. He would have called her *wench*
and, knowing the tales about his great-great-
grandfather, Roman felt sure he would have sold her
into white slavery right after that.

"Happy New Year, darlin'," Roman drawled.

Then everything happened in split seconds.

The woman screamed.

She wrenched violently and turned to her stomach

in a belly splash that would have made Moby Dick proud. One of her madly flailing hands shot downward like a hammer and smacked his shoulder smartly, as if it was driving a nail. But it was the palest, softest clenched fist he'd ever felt.

Roman grasped her arm just to steady her, but she struggled. Her small, firm breasts heaved against his arms when they encircled her from behind. Her head plunked under water. Then it bobbed back up like a buoy.

He wrestled back, trying not to feel her straining muscles against his naked skin, knowing he should never have startled her. "I meant to swim with you, like sea nymphs, not drown you," he muttered. Somehow he managed to pull her upward, grasping her waist even more firmly from behind, and still tread water.

"Would you please quit acting like a damn drowning rat?" he managed to say. "I really didn't mean to scare you." Hell, he'd been fantasizing about making love. The woman in his arms only gagged and sputtered. He pounded her back until she choked some water from her lungs. "You all right?"

All that met Roman's ears was a soft, strangled sighing sound. Then her body went limp. Apparently their tussle had taken all the fight out of her. From the pruney look of her fingers, she'd been in the water for some time. Roman squinted into the distance. Far off he could make out the silhouette of a yacht. She hadn't swum that far. Had she?

He turned her carefully to her side, slid closer behind her, rested a hand under her chin, then began hauling her to shore. "You'll be fine, darlin'," he whispered, unable to stop himself from nuzzling his own chin against the top of her short, white-blond hair. The woman's breath was shallow, and she was wearing a long, ruby-red silk dress that clung to her skin. "Did you fall overboard?" She was apparently too water-logged to respond.

Even though the woman had clearly almost drowned, her brief struggle had ensured him she'd be fine. She had rubbed and twisted and writhed against him like a wildcat. He just wished he could turn her over and see her face because, in his arms, she still felt every inch the fantasy woman he'd first thought her to be.

Her softer contours were molding perfectly to his harder nakedness in a way that felt nearly painful. His fingertip just touched the pounding pulse point in her throat and his arm that lay squarely between those round firm breasts tingled with pinpricks of awareness. Her heart was thudding so hard that it felt as if it was going to leap out of her skin. His own heart was beginning to thunder, too, with a storm of desire.

He nuzzled against her salty-smelling hair again. She felt so good he wished it was 1750…back when dashing adventurers with swords took women at their will. "The twentieth century be damned," he whispered.

He had no choice but to swim sidestroke, and his legs kept tangling between hers in the worst possible way. Hers drifted down. His kicked between. And at every touch he had to force himself not to moan. If she was conscious, she was feeling his growing arousal, and there wasn't a blessed thing he could do about it.

Alexandra what's-her-name had bored him to distraction, but he was going to take this mystery woman. Right here, right now and even in her half-drowned state. Whoever she was, he knew just through the feel of her that she belonged to him.

But was that good fortune or a curse? He tried to

remind himself that he was merely saving her life, but the more he tried to concentrate on swimming, the worse it got. Every thrusting kick and every even stroke brought him right against her. He knew he would have to take her in his arms on the marly sand, under the waving fronds of the palms and...

He was still swimming when he realized that he could have stood some time ago. Rising from the water, he gently lifted her in his arms so that she stretched over his shoulder. The wet fabric of her ruby dress was hiked high on her thighs; it nestled against him while her perfectly pale, long legs trailed down the deep bronze of his chest. She weighed next to nothing. He carried her out of the water, her breasts pressing sweetly against his shoulder.

When he reached the shore he brought her down slowly, laying her on the sand inch by inch. He teased himself, his eyes only starting at the pink painted toes and her delectable, slender feet. Then his gaze trailed upward, over her perfect legs, her full hips, her gently rounded stomach and her firm breasts. His breath caught, seeing the taut hardness of her nipples against the ruby silk. And he raised his gaze again, all with increasing anticipation of seeing her face.

Roman groaned out loud when he saw that part of her.

It was hardly from pleasure.

"Damn," he cursed in a low, lethal voice. It was a good thing she was already lying down. Otherwise he would have dropped her.

In an instant her legs became too damn skinny. The woman was practically flat chested, with way too much weight in her hips. And what woman would paint her toenails that horrendous color?

Baby Trap

"Tell me this ain't happening," he drawled.

But no. It was his stepsister, Kathleen Cannon. He hadn't seen her for twelve years, not since her sweet-sixteen party. He was sure he would have recognized her if she hadn't hacked off all her hair. Even though she looked like something the cat dragged in, his response to her was unfortunately just the same as it had been back then, when the Lawrences' maid—her mother—had managed to break up his parents' marriage.

What was she doing on *his* island? *Besides ruining New Year's,* he thought grimly.

Watching her lashless-looking eyelids flutter, he tried not to remember their last encounter. She'd caught him in the buff and had offered herself to him pretty boldly. Of course, he'd flatly rejected her. Well, not before he'd kissed her senseless, just to prove to her what she'd be missing. Now, taking in the way her wet dress clung to her curves, he wished, as he had many times, that he'd done the deed.

She opened her mean little green eyes and stared at him. He wasn't sure whether her slack-jawed look of horror was due to the fact that she'd just recognized him or because—as he now suddenly remembered, himself—he was standing there naked as a jaybird.

"What are you doing?" Kathleen sputtered.

"Saving your life," Roman returned. "Like a fool." He was hardly going to act as if she'd never seen him naked before. As he sauntered casually toward his robe he glanced over his shoulder just once, long enough to say, "Good to see you, too, Kathleen."

And then he began humming "Auld Lang Syne."

GRANTED, WHEN SHE'D BEGUN swimming she'd decided that it was high time she confront Roman and contest his father's will, so that she'd have money for her baby. After all, it was rightfully her money. But she hadn't counted on seeing Roman tonight…or on the effect of seeing him in the flesh again.

Naked, Kathleen reminded herself now. If she hadn't felt so sick to her stomach she would have realized who he was. But when she'd felt those strong arms encircle her waist and when she'd realized the man was naked, she'd completely lost her capacity to think. She'd meant to keep her eyes shut long enough for him to cover himself. But, of course, he hadn't bothered.

"This just isn't my day," Kathleen whispered. She huddled farther into a corner of the limo, wrapped in a blanket that Flanders had brought out for her. It didn't help matters that she hadn't been to Lawrence Island for so many years, either. As they headed through the archway in the high stone wall that encircled the château proper and drove away from the water toward the far end of the island and the road access to Little Torch Key, she had to fight not to look around to see if anything had changed.

But she ignored the urge to peer through the palms on either side of the road, not about to let Roman know she'd felt homesick. Instead she stared right at him. Thankfully, he'd thrown on cowboy boots, worn-out jeans and a white shirt. Still determined to show off his well-endowed body, he hadn't bothered to button the shirt.

"I don't need to go all the way to the hospital in Key West, and I certainly don't need you to accompany me," Kathleen huffed as the car approached the far end of the island. Jenkenson, the driver, stopped when he reached the high, curling, wrought-iron gates, and got out to open them.

"You damn near drowned," Roman said gruffly. "And you threw up on the beach." Past the leathery smell of the dark, enclosed car's upholstery, he could still smell the fresh salty scent of her skin. Why was it that the one woman whom he absolutely didn't want in his life had always been the one who most aroused him?

Not that Roman felt the least bit embarrassed about how the exposed parts of his anatomy had made her pale skin flush bright red. He was pretty sure he still held a physical power over her, as she did over him. He slouched in the car seat, stretched out his long legs and casually let his shirttails fall fully open, baring his chest, as if in testament to that fact.

"I was simply taking a swim," she finally said as Jenkenson got back in the car. She concentrated on not looking the least bit vulnerable. Around Roman, vulnerability could be lethal. She'd escaped Van Ness only to swim right into Roman. And Roman was definitely the worst of two evils. Then she'd gotten sick. Why couldn't she have *morning* sickness, like everybody else?

She realized Roman was staring right through her with those flashing, fierce dark eyes of his. She looked out the window. They were on the access road between Lawrence Island and Little Torch Key, so there wasn't much to see, just the narrow strip of roadway and the calm bay water on either side.

"So, do you always go swimming in a party dress, darlin'?" Roman finally asked in a deceptively casual tone. What could have possessed Kathleen to swim in such a state toward a house she hadn't visited in twelve years? He lowered his voice. "Not that I care. I'm just curious."

She turned and glared at him. Yes, his eyes were every bit as dark as they used to be. Dark as moonless midnight, but still as brightly intense as a roaring, stoked-up fire. His thick, dark brows were drawn up and the jagged streak of premature silver in his hair made him look dangerous. Like a fallen angel.

"At least I wear clothes," she finally returned as coolly as possible, though the last thing she wanted to remember was the way his body had looked...so powerfully naked and dripping wet, with every inch of his tanned silken skin gleaming in the moonlight.

"It's my beach," he said, wishing again that there wasn't so much bad blood between them. If there wasn't, he knew he'd admit his attraction to her. Then she would be his. "So," he continued, "I guess I can skinny-dip if I choose."

"That's the problem with you," Kathleen replied hotly. "You pretty much do anything you choose. Wherever, however, with whomever. But since you're not on your blessed little beach anymore, why don't you button your shirt? You're indecent."

Roman shrugged and smiled. "Sorry, but I'm a bit warm, Kathleen. Hot, even. Besides, I'm now in my—" he paused for effect "—blessed little car." He leaned forward, opened a small refrigerator and took out a bottled beer. He didn't bother to offer her anything.

"Only *you* would call a limo a little car." She forced herself to snap the words, hoping her voice wouldn't go all soft and sweet, the way other parts of her did when she looked at him.

"Honey," he said, "if we're going to discuss personalities, yours is hardly stellar."

She shot him a long, hard, level look. Her dress was nearly dry and the car *was* warm, but she wasn't about to lower the blanket around her shoulders and expose the clinging silk of her dress to his roving eyes. "Roman, I didn't say a word about your personality and there is not, nor has there ever been, anything wrong with mine."

"Right," Roman said. Yes, Kathleen was still every bit as dramatic and flighty as she used to be. Only some impulsive action on her part could have landed her in the middle of his ocean in a dress. And even though she'd seemed ill on the beach, she now seemed right as rain. *Make that crashing thunderstorm,* he thought. "But you clearly do think there's something wrong with *my* personality. Now don't you, Kathleen?"

Kathleen merely shrugged, her own light-colored brows drawing up in little points, as if that were for him to decide. Fortunately Roman seemed to have run out of things to say, and they fell silent until they reached the end of the access road.

Jenkenson electronically opened the gate that led onto Little Torch Key. Glancing across the highway, Kathleen saw that the sign marking the Krause residence was still in place. That meant that the family still helped Roman train horses when he brought them down to the Keys.

"At least I have a job," Roman said as Jenkenson pulled out onto A-1-A, heading for Key West. Roman took a sip of his beer, then rested the neck of the bottle between his pectorals and against the thick dark hair on his chest. New Year's night was sure becoming interesting. He draped his free arm over the back of the car seat so that his fingers dangled downward and nearly touched Kathleen's shoulder.

Kathleen flinched from both the comment and his physical nearness. She'd hardly call training horses a job. It was more a pastime for spoiled rich men, as far as she was concerned. She trained her gaze away from a glimmering droplet of condensation that dripped onto his skin and snaked downward, rolling toward his black leather belt and to where his dark, curling chest hairs narrowed and swirled beneath the waistband of his pants. Suddenly she wished the back seat wasn't so dark. "How did you find out—"

"That you got fired?"

"Laid off," Kathleen said quickly. She kept her eyes straight forward, on the highway. To the left was the Atlantic, to the right the bay waters.

"Whatever." He took another sip of his beer, feeling the cool liquid slide down his throat. It was a good thing there was beer in the car, he thought, since his throat grew dry every time he looked at her. Why, he didn't know. She was hardly beautiful, never had been. Her body was small and muscular and pale, the kind that could only be called scrappy. Her little green, lashless eyes were flecked with yellow. And she'd cut her hair very short, where once it had been long and, he'd thought, her only decent feature.

No, Kathleen Cannon was more like a small exotic tiger than a statuesque beauty. He smiled. Well, if she was a small white tiger, he'd certainly be glad to play the dark panther. Remembering how her paleness had looked curved against his own dark chest, he edged closer to her in the seat.

"Oh, I know all sorts of things about you, Kathleen," he said softly.

She scooted back, away from him. "Oh? Like what?" she asked lightly.

"Like the newspaper cut back on staff and you're out of a job," he said, his eyes never leaving her face. "And your string of boyfriends has been even less satisfactory lately."

"A lot of newspapers have had layoffs!" It was hardly her fault that the Boston weekly she'd worked with since college didn't need her now. No one had been more apologetic than her boss. Roman didn't know anything about her. Oh, he thought he did, but he was wrong. She tossed her head defiantly.

Roman smiled the smile of a shark coming in for its prey. "But you won't defend yourself on the boyfriend score?" he finally asked. "Dear Lord, darlin', I even heard you took up with that worthless character Malcolm Van Ness."

She turned abruptly and stared out the window again. Took up with him? She wished it was only that bad. Well, her relationship with Van Ness was something Roman would never find out about. "I didn't *take up* with Van Ness," she said. "He was my boyfriend for eight months." She blew out what she hoped was a bored-sounding sigh and turned back to Roman.

"Let's see," he said. "There was a florist named Joe Evans, some fellow named Jackson Rivers…"

Kathleen watched Roman's wry smile curl farther upward. He ran his tongue over his upper teeth, as if to taunt her. Good old Roman was certainly enjoying himself. She didn't want to appear defensive, but she snuggled farther back in the seat and crossed her arms over her chest. Joe, the florist, had been good with flowers but bad with emotions. And Jackson Rivers had worn plaids. Not that there was anything wrong with plaids, except his hadn't matched.

Suddenly she drew in a sharp breath. Roman didn't think she slept with all her boyfriends, did he? *Well, let him.* She told herself that there was nothing wrong with not having found Mr. Right. Now all she wanted was a secure future for her baby, with whom she intended to share all the warmth and love that she had missed in life.

"Now, which one, I wonder, gave you that rock on your finger?" Roman was saying now. "It's on your right hand so it can't be an engagement present."

Kathleen glanced down. In all the excitement—if one could call it that—she'd completely forgotten about the Van Ness diamond. But Roman had noticed it. And who could miss it? She had to be wearing the largest diamond in existence. And, she thought, if a barracuda hadn't attacked her in the water because of it, one was certainly attacking her now.

Roman's dangling hand dropped a notch so that it grazed her shoulder. "Maybe that was a little New Year's gift from Françis D'Vonlier...."

Françis. The chef had made such lovely dinners...right up until his visa ran out and immigration had deported him. Roman was baiting her, and she'd been trying to ignore him, but she couldn't help but sink her teeth in now, since poor Françis could never have afforded such a ring.

"And what exactly bothers you about Françis, Roman? The fact that he's a chef? A lowly cook? A member of what you think of as the servant class, like my mother? Like me?"

"Oh, Kathleen," Roman returned. "You don't really think I'm a snob, do you?"

Her mouth dropped. "You're saying you're not?"

"That's exactly what I'm saying. I never minded the fact that your mother worked for us. Just that she was a home wrecker."

That was one argument Kathleen didn't intend to have. "Well," she said, "I may not have had lasting relationships with my boyfriends, but I'm not the only one who's suffered relationship difficulties. For every Tinker Bell, I'm sure you'll find a Peter Pan." Roman may have been keeping tabs on her somehow, but she'd followed his latest lovers, not to mention his divorce. His checkered career was public.

He leaned so close his mouth almost touched her ear. "I didn't realize you thought we were close enough for this kind of conversation. I mean, intimate…like about my wife, who could hardly be called some flighty Tinker Bell."

"Ex-wife," Kathleen snapped. She edged backward, but there was nowhere to go. "Let's just change the subject, then," she said, still trying to ignore his physical nearness. "Perhaps you'd like to explain why you've been spying on me? I honestly didn't realize you'd missed me all that much."

"Just looking out for my family name," Roman said, thinking that Tinker Bell more aptly described Kathleen herself. "You're my little stepsister, after all."

His long-suffering tone implied that she was an embarrassment. "Hardly," she returned. "We've laid eyes on each other about ten times in our lives."

Exactly seventeen, Roman thought, but he was hardly going to correct her and let her know he'd counted. He remembered each and every time and he'd

wager she did, too. No other encounters had ever been
so intense. Most were fumblingly awkward and many
were as mundane as accidentally brushing arms in the
kitchen, but they'd always been charged. "Well, darlin', I guess this makes eleven," Roman finally said.

"And don't call me darlin'," she said.

He grinned and merely said, "Darlin'."

Things had happened so quickly this night that Kathleen had barely had time to gather her wits about her,
but now, looking at Roman's self-satisfied, if good-
looking figure, which was taking up practically the
whole seat, she wondered if her pregnancy was really
enough to make her stoop low enough to demand her
portion of the Lawrence inheritance. But she wanted
her child to have every possible advantage. Didn't she?

Roman, to her relief, leaned back in the seat. "Now,
do you mind telling me why you decided to usher in
the year by swimming the great blue oceans?"

"Green," she countered. "The oceans here look
green."

"Don't sidestep," he returned in a soft, almost singsong voice.

She sighed. "Just thought I'd visit. Okay?"

He chuckled in a way that more than annoyed her.
"You were swimming over to visit me? From Boston?
And in a dress?" Roman's eyebrows drew upward.
"Why, that's funny, seeing as how you haven't visited
for ten or so years." *Exactly twelve.* "In fact," he continued, "from what I recall, you didn't even bother to
show up at our parents' funeral."

"Don't you dare start that with me," she said flatly.
She forced herself to tamp down her anger. She hadn't
even had the money for a train ticket and she definitely
hadn't wanted to see Roman. The day of the funeral

and the next year had been the worst of her life. She'd walked away, only knowing that she held dear memories of both her mother and Roman's father to sustain her. And she had not looked back.

"So, why are you here?" Roman repeated.

"To contest your father's will." Kathleen could hardly believe she'd said it. But it was the best thing for her to do. With some money, she could spend time with her baby before she had to find work again.

She realized Roman was staring at her. Other than the whirring turn of the tires and the soft purr of the motor, the car was silent for a long moment. "Well," she said, staring right back, "you asked." She flashed him a smile. "And now you know."

"My, my, this is an interesting turn of events," Roman said. "But why, after all these years, have you suddenly decided to come backstroking home?" He paused, a faint smile suddenly lifting the corners of his mouth. "You must be in some kind of a bind, Kathleen." And looking into her face, Roman knew she was. There was just no way that Kathleen Cannon would come crawling back his way, not unless she was in trouble. So deep he couldn't even fathom it.

"Contest all you want," he said. "It doesn't mean you'll see a dime."

She half chuckled, half moaned. "You *know* I will," she said. "Miles Higgenbothem was drawing up the new will when..." For some reason she just couldn't bring herself to say "when our parents died."

Roman didn't respond. Kathleen was right, of course. She'd have no trouble at all getting the money. He'd seen the will his father had intended to leave. In fact, he'd hardly meant to squabble over it like cats and dogs. He just wasn't going to track her down and offer to give it to her personally. If she wanted it she'd just have to contest, like anyone else would.

"So, you *swam* all the way from Boston to Key West this evening, to start a long, drawn-out and very tiring legal battle?" He sighed, trying to sound bored, but somehow, anytime Kathleen was within ten feet of him, every sinew in his body seemed tuned countless notches higher. Boredom was the one thing that never entered the picture.

"Believe me, I'll only stay as long as I have to," she said curtly.

"I suppose you'll want your old room, then?" he asked, knowing he half wanted her to stay on the island. During the brief two years of her mother's marriage to his father, he'd been away at prep school and college, and then he'd run off to work for a rancher in Wyoming, but he could still remember the holidays…how he'd lain awake, sensing her far down the hallway, remembering her come-hither glances, wishing she would creep down the hall to his room. And knowing that when she did he'd somehow force himself to reject her.

"So nice of you to offer," she finally said, cringing. Unfortunately she had no choice. Her clothes, purse and credit cards were on Van Ness's boat, and her other things were in storage in Boston. *Because between jobs I'm supposed to be on a New Year's cruise with Van Ness.* All she had to her name at the moment was the now mildewy-smelling evening gown she was wearing.

"I take it that's a yes?" Roman made damn sure there was no hint of hopefulness in his voice.

She only nodded slightly. Roman watched her face turn wan and pale again. It was just that look that had made Flanders insist on the trip to the hospital.

Suddenly she doubled. "Pull over," she said levelly.

Roman glared at her for a split second, wondering what trick she had up her sleeve this time. But she *had* turned dead white. Roman hit the intercom button at his side. "Jenkenson, pull over, please."

As soon as the car ground to a halt Kathleen flung open the door and leaned outside, feeling the warm rush of air on her face.

"Are you all right?"

"Is that concern I hear in your voice?" she muttered.

Was it? If so, Kathleen thought it was nice, but she hardly wanted to feel the way Roman's broad, exposed chest now pressed against her back. He leaned farther over her shoulder. "Just leave me alone," she snapped, half turning her head.

He retreated to his side of the car seat. "Fine," he said gruffly.

And then she vomited.

Roman came back to her side, waving a white handkerchief over her shoulder like a flag of surrender. She yanked it from his hand, wiped her mouth and then took a sip from the bottle of Perrier water he offered. Being sick really wasn't so bad, she told herself. She was actually getting sort of used to it. She scooted back in the seat and sat upright.

"Now, are you ready to tell me what's wrong with you?" Roman demanded. He leaned forward so that his face was only inches from hers. "Why were you swimming in that dress? And what's made you so sick?"

Somehow, Kathleen wanted to smile. Roman actually looked concerned, even a little frightened, if such a thing could be imagined. But the last thing she intended to discuss was her supposed sickness. And the last person she intended to discuss it with was Roman.

"Going soft on me?" she taunted.

"You're one woman I could never go soft on," he nearly whispered.

The air seemed suddenly charged with the unintentional sexual connotation of what he'd said. Kathleen flushed and groped madly for the door. She slammed it shut and was thankful when the overhead car light snapped out.

Roman's expression hardened and his eyes turned a shade darker. "What's wrong with you?"

"I never felt better," she said.

Roman pushed the intercom button again. "Go straight to the emergency room."

"Don't be ridiculous!" Kathleen exclaimed. For the first time it occurred to her that Roman might find out about her pregnancy at the hospital. "I'm not sick!"

"Right," he muttered. "I always throw up when I feel fabulous." He tossed his empty beer bottle in a trash container and began buttoning his shirt.

Kathleen pulled her blanket tightly around her shoulders. "A little sick," she finally conceded.

THE ER WAS CROWDED because it was New Year's, and Kathleen had been with the doctor forever. Now Roman thought he could hear a rising argument in the examination room. He glanced at Jenkenson, who was beside him, then stared at the partially open door. As near as he could tell, some woman—maybe Kathleen— was mumbling in barely audible tones, while another voice was protesting.

Suddenly a man said loudly, "You've got to tell

relatives about something like this. What about your husband? Is that him out there waiting?''

Roman chuckled. Kathleen's husband? Now, that would be a cold day in hell. But what was she obligated to tell him? Was the doctor even talking about Kathleen? He rose and ambled stealthily toward the door. Just as he leaned beside it, it slammed shut in his face. He placed his ear as close to the crack as he could without looking like a fool. What exactly was scrappy little Kathleen trying to hide from him?

And what was it about her that always turned his mind to mush? Every time he saw her, he ended up doing foolhardy things…like eavesdropping through doors.

"Before long, everybody is going to notice," a woman was saying shakily. Again, was it Kathleen? He thought it was, but he couldn't be sure, and there *were* other women in the room with her. "When this happens, you can't exactly hide it." There was a long pause. "It's only a matter of time until—I'm already feeling so sick that I—I—"

The poor lady was crying. He'd never heard Kathleen cry before, but it sure sounded like her. Maybe there weren't really cutbacks at her newspaper. Was his information wrong? Was she on sick leave? *Damn.* He should have just given her her money ten years ago. Heaven knew, she'd had too much pride to come and ask him for it. His father was undoubtedly turning over in his grave at the moment.

Kathleen had become entirely self-supporting at eighteen. She'd dropped out of the Ivy League school where his father had sent her and bartended to put herself through a Boston community college. Roman had definitely made life rougher on her than it had to be.

But then, why did he have to be the one to crawl back to her, offering her the money, as if in apology?

"My dear, a young woman like yourself needs support...needs family," the doctor was saying. "Certainly, there are people who care...."

"Nobody cares!" the woman screamed.

It was definitely Kathleen. Roman was sure of it. There was more quiet mumbling. *What is wrong with her?* Why wouldn't someone say it outright? Roman felt as if *he* was going to scream.

"I know sometimes you feel your family doesn't care," the doctor said. "But they won't feel burdened. You'd be amazed at how I've seen families come together in a crisis."

Roman leaned even closer to the door. He gingerly tried the knob, but the door had locked when it shut.

After some time the doctor said, "Well, the bottom line is that you have no insurance. And you're going to need regular medical attention from here on out."

Medical attention? Roman blew out a sigh. Kathleen *was* sick. And it was all his fault.

"Well, you've got a little time left, dear."

"Not much! And I don't have insurance. There must be agencies...."

Roman froze. No person associated with the Lawrence family had ever had to resort to public assistance. And there was no denying the raw fear in her voice. No ignoring that he—well, it wasn't love, but it was something. A feeling so laced with resentment that he couldn't pursue it. Ever.

And now Kathleen might be dying. Losing her seemed too difficult to face now. He couldn't do anything about her health but maybe he could mend their differences.

Hearing footsteps inside the examining room, Roman ambled back and took his seat. He slouched, mustering a look of pure, unmitigated boredom. If Kathleen didn't want him to know she was sick, he'd pretend he didn't. Kathleen could have her way. *From here on out.* The ominous phrase played in his mind.

The door swung open. Kathleen's eyes were red rimmed and her cheeks were tear streaked. Roman had never seen her in such a state, but it was enough to convince him that she'd been the one doing the talking. Almost against his will he rose to his feet to help her, but she squared her shoulders regally.

"I'm absolutely fine," Kathleen announced.

"But the vomiting?" Jenkenson asked.

Kathleen shrugged. "Clearly caused by the way Roman took it upon himself to save my life." She glared at him. "After all, it was *quite* a trauma." With that she turned on her heel and strode toward the exit doors.

"Go ahead and indulge her," Roman muttered. "Give her everything she wants. No matter what she says or what she does or however rudely she acts." It was as much an instruction to himself as it was to Jenkenson.

"Are you serious?" the chauffeur managed to say. Like everyone in the house, Jenkenson was no stranger to the battle of wills that was fought every time Roman and Kathleen saw each other.

"Dead serious," Roman finally said.

Chapter Two

"Roman, are you sure about this?" Miles Higgenbothem asked. Kathleen paused outside the upstairs library in the southwest corner of the château and cocked her head toward the lawyer's hushed voice. "Kathleen'll get the money eventually, but the longer you hang on to it, the more money we can make investing it." It sounded as if Higgenbothem clapped Roman's shoulder. "Money making money, right?"

"Don't argue," Roman said crossly.

What did Roman have up his sleeve now? It was difficult enough dealing with how he looked—with his searing, devilish, dark-eyed gaze and his powerfully endowed body. She wasn't in the mood for any of his tricks.

To make matters worse, her only clothes were the ones in her old bedroom closet, and they were too small. She didn't want to ponder why Roman hadn't converted her old bedroom suite into something more useful. She'd found the room exactly as she'd left it; her canopied four-poster bed, brightly printed, country-style pillows and pink comforter were untouched.

She glanced down, wishing her taste in high school had been different. The sundress and beaded sandals were far too flowery for her current taste, which ran to deep natural colors—olives, crimsons and sandy beiges—and also too tight, so that what breasts she had spilled out the top. She couldn't find a bra, either. She'd thrown a mottled cotton sweater over the hideous ensemble, to cover herself. Not that that would keep Roman from continually daring her with his smoldering, heated glances.

She had been sure that her New Year's with Van Ness would constitute the worst possible moment in her life, but sitting in the back of the limo the night before and sleeping down the hall from Roman had told her otherwise. It was clear from the way his eyes and body taunted her that he wasn't through with leading her on the way he had all those years ago.

Then, on the way home, he'd fallen into one of his nasty, sullen, brooding moods. She had no idea why. She never did. Not that she'd ever forgotten how raw energy could radiate from the man. Somehow, it was as if all their encounters took place in an overheated steam room.

Well, regardless of what had caused his moodiness, this time she wasn't about to give in to his come-ons. Especially not now, when she wanted to spend her time preparing for her baby. Never again would Roman have the pleasure of knowing that she had craved his kiss. His game was to taunt her until she couldn't stand it any longer, until she could think of nothing but him, until she came to him…just so he could have the pleasure of rejecting her.

Roman and Higgenbothem were finished their conversation, so she couldn't eavesdrop anymore. Why had Roman called her to the library? She rapped on the door, then entered the room. There were subtle changes in the library. There was still an ocean view from the window, of course, the room itself was paneled and the floor-to-ceiling shelves were lined with books. But now, in addition to the old Spanish nautical maps on the walls, there were photographs of Roman and his horses. In the corner a new telescope perched by the rounded window of the turret.

Roman reclined in a deep red leather armchair, looking every bit as masculine as the room. The streak in his jet-black hair looked pure, silvery white in the natural light, and his hand rested idly on top of an old globe beside the chair, as if to say he could rule continents and seas at will. The whole world seemed to shrink beneath that large, tanned, muscular hand.

Just looking at his hands reminded her of his success with horses. No wonder he could move those animals at will with nothing more than a flick of his wrists. He finally glanced at her from beneath his heavy eyelids with a look that said she was in his domain now. And that he ruled everything in it…including her.

Kathleen fought not to pull the ugly old sweater around herself in self-protection. "Morning," she said with feigned lightness. "So, what can I do for you?" Kathleen glanced from Roman to the roundish, balding figure of Higgenbothem, who was leaning against the desk with a file folder in his hand.

"Roman's going to settle with you," Higgenbothem began.

Kathleen's eyes shot to Roman. He stared right into her with that fierce gaze of his. She felt more sure than ever that he was toying with her. What was his ulterior motive? She was far more interested in whatever game he was playing than in how he intended to "settle" with her.

Kathleen gazed thoughtfully from Roman through the wide window. And then she took a sharp breath. Far out in the ocean she saw Van Ness's Sport Fisherman. Abruptly she turned her full attention back to Higgenbothem. As he continued speaking, her lips parted in disbelief. Roman wasn't only giving her her rightful portion of her inheritance, but also half of the island. She spied a hefty pile of credit cards…with her name on them.

"Roman, what's gotten into you?" Kathleen pried her eyes away from how his lean, long legs straddled and stretched over the Oriental carpet. Away from how the heels of his black boots dug into a patch of red. Somehow she managed to keep her voice level.

"That's exactly what I'd like to know," Higgenbothem said. "No offense, Kathleen."

"None taken," Kathleen said.

Kathleen stared into the mesmerizing darkness of Roman's eyes again. Even though she felt herself falling right into their depths, she couldn't trust him, not one bit. Hot spots of color began to emerge on her pale, ill-covered chest.

"Well, darlin'—" He flashed her a smile. Against his tan, between his wide, expressive lips, his teeth gleamed like diamonds. "I know you think horse training's just a sport, but the National Cutting Horse Association gave out over sixteen million in prize money last year—"

His voice lowered, becoming silky and persuasive. "And since a fair portion of that went to me, and I've already made more money than I need, I've decided to just let bygones be bygones. You can also have a job over at Dad's shipping yards." Roman raised one hand in a negotiating gesture. "Name only, if you'd like, but I've had them put you on salary."

A name-only salary? Had Roman remembered that she'd hoped to work for his father once she'd graduated from college? She squinted at him. It was as if some other personality had entered Roman's body during the night. "Did you suddenly become possessed by an angel rather than a devil?" Kathleen finally managed to ask.

"Again, no offense, Kathleen," said Higgenbothem. "But that's what I said. I mean, your portion, the one we were always prepared to give, was a little less—"

"It's what I want," Roman said. When he stood, he was a full head taller than Higgenbothem. "And, as you all know, I always get what I want." He turned to Kathleen. "Wherever, however and with whomever." He shoved his hands into his pockets and left the room, without so much as a backward glance.

"I guess you can sign here, then," Higgenbothem said, offering her a pen.

Kathleen hastily signed the papers. And then she followed Roman.

She caught up to him in the upstairs east-wing hallway that separated their bedrooms. She knew he heard her approaching from behind, and she was just as sure he wasn't going to turn around. Without forethought she grabbed him by the bicep. She swallowed, feeling a thousand tough, hardened, cordlike muscles strain beneath her grasp. If there was one thing horse training had done for him, it was to delineate muscles most men didn't even have.

His body really was the most perfectly shaped male one she'd ever seen. And no man had the right to lay claim to both a body like that and the kind of face he possessed. His nose was so straight and strong and patrician between his damnably high cheekbones that it nearly inspired awe. One look at his full lips was enough to tell anyone that he'd been born with a silver spoon in his mouth. *Make that a ladle.*

"Mind telling me what's going on, Roman?"

He turned very slowly and then gazed deeply into her eyes. They stood only inches apart, and he cocked his head to the side and lowered his face toward hers in a way that made her feel completely breathless. She fought the urge to shudder, but she was powerless to move. Even when he raised his hand and lifted a lock of her bangs from her forehead.

"I just want to give you everything you need." His voice was the lowest of whispers. His mouth curled in the faintest teasing smile. "Or maybe devilish old me really has been possessed by an angel, darlin'."

"Right," she said weakly. She'd never seen eyes contain that many warring emotions in her life. She told herself to step back, but she was still rooted to the spot. Now one of his long, tanned fingers grazed the side of her face.

"Oh, Kathleen," he murmured.

We're supposed to spar with each other. It's the unwritten rule of our relationship. It's the law. "You've gone out of your mind," she whispered. She released his arm and turned away quickly.

She'd managed to flee two paces before he caught her wrist and turned her back to face him. He looked as if there was something he desperately wanted to say, but couldn't. "Kathy, I—"

"Kathy?" Only her mother and his father called her that. He pulled her wrist closer. Her body followed, as if by magic.

"Kathleen," he said, correcting himself. "Darlin', I, I just—"

She should have seen it coming, but she didn't. His

mouth covered hers, and for an instant his lips just rested lightly on hers. She could have moved. She knew she should have, knew she *had* to, but she simply couldn't. Not when that beautiful mouth rested on hers. Not when his lips turned featherlike and nuzzled her own open.

And especially not when the tip of his warm tongue darted between the very lips he'd just teased apart. He bit at her bottom lip almost vengefully, just before his whole mouth closed on hers with intense pressure. Her heart thundered beneath her ribs, and with every blessed second that passed he became more demanding.

Just for a second she'd respond, she told herself, allowing her own tongue to come into play with his. But with that one second long gone, she pushed upward on her toes, straining to meet him. Everything seemed so unfair.... How could she resist Roman?

His arms wrapped tightly around her waist, and he turned her quickly, expertly backing her against the wall with the force and expertise of a man well used to seducing women. His sheer weight pressed so hard against her that it lifted her so her feet weren't even touching the floor.

Had she lost her mind? She placed both hands on his shoulders and pushed, but not before she'd felt him press the most intimate part of himself against her. Not before she'd felt the length of him rest at the juncture of her thighs. She gasped. She shoved his shoulders again, as hard as she could. He stepped backward so quickly she nearly fell in a limp heap on the floor.

She tried to gather her rational senses. "Is that what this is about," she said flatly. "Your same old game? Roman plays the tease, coming on to poor Kathleen, maid's daughter, who's so naive and impressed that she just won't be able to resist the spoiled little rich boy?"

She felt a sudden flare of very harsh temper. "Go find yourself one of your own kind," she said. "They're always willing."

She almost felt guilty, since he actually looked as if she was getting under his skin, but her guilt quickly passed. His dark eyes turned a shade darker, as black as his hair, and the lightning streak that ran through his raven waves seemed to flash in his gaze, as well.

"Oh, I don't know, Kathleen," Roman said breathlessly. "You seemed pretty willing to me." He shoved his hands deep in the pockets of his tight, well-worn jeans, in a way that only accented his arousal. "Felt pretty willing, too," he added.

"Looks like the devil in you just took possession again," Kathleen responded hotly. "And, as far as I'm concerned, you can just rot in you-know-where."

With that Kathleen whirled around, fled to her room and slammed the door. She had half a mind to shove the chest of drawers in front of it, too.

GABRIELLA LAWRENCE LEANED back in her office chair and scrutinized her son as if she was still a new mother counting his fingers and toes. "Have you forgotten that your father left me for *her* mother, who I'll now remind you was our maid? I shouldn't even bother to forewarn you that she'll take full advantage, just like her mother did. Fortune hunters—the both of them. Have you gone mad?"

Still tasting the searing-hot, salty flavor of Kathleen Cannon's lips, Roman was sure he had. That ridiculous old floral dress had driven him crazy. She had gained weight and filled out and the dress was so tight that he could see every inch of her skin beneath it.

He shook his head as if to clear it of the confusion

he felt every time she was around. The woman was sick and he'd come on to her like a needy racehorse just put to stud. The thought should have sickened him, but all he wanted to do was kiss her again.

Wondering what was wrong with her was driving him just as mad as her kiss. What other help should he provide? He'd meant the inheritance to make her trust him, so that she'd tell him what was going on, but it had had the exact opposite effect. The fact that he'd kissed her had been the icing on the cake. Trust him? She wouldn't even look at him.

"Roman? Are you even listening to me?" Gabriella continued to stare at her son. "I demand to know why you're doing this instead of forcing her to contest! And why did you give her half the island?"

"Mother," he finally said, "I think Kathleen's very sick."

"Dying?" she managed to ask.

Roman shrugged. "I don't know." *Yet.*

She sent him a long, assessing gaze. "So you intend to get all your money back when she dies and assuage your guilt, all at the same time?"

"Mother." He lowered his voice in censure. That was hardly what had motivated him, though he could believe his mother—who had become hard as nails after her divorce from his father—would say such a thing.

Still, he couldn't help but wonder if Kathleen was really sick. Just a mere week after starting work, she was nearly running his father's shipping office. She was on a strict, healthy diet, and her meals were served up by the overly indulgent members of the house staff, who adored her. She looked so healthy she actually glowed.

Roman stood abruptly and headed for the door, suddenly determined to confront her, once and for all.

"I thought we were going to lunch!" Gabriella exclaimed.

"Sorry, changed my mind," he said.

Roman walked right out the door, leaving Gabriella with her hands planted on her hips. She blew out a long sigh. And then she told herself, as she had many times, that what Roman didn't know about her divorce from his father wouldn't hurt him.

KATHLEEN FULLY INTENDED to play the opportunistic, rich maid's daughter to the hilt since Roman had always pegged her that way. While Jenkenson opened the trunk of the car, she shifted from one new Versace boot to the other. They were awfully uncomfortable. They were open from ankle to thigh and threaded like sandals, but with hard-feeling cordish strips of leather that cut right into her calves. The leather strips were strewn with bright gold coins, too, which left painful, round, red imprints on her flesh. Still, the boots alone had sent one of her new credit cards up to the max. Sooner or later Roman was bound to realize that his ulterior game plan, whatever it was, had failed.

"Sure I can't carry these things in for you?" Jenkenson asked.

"Of course not, Mr. Jenkenson," Kathleen said, smiling into the man's weathered, tanned face. She drew the line at having people wait on her hand and foot. She tried to tug her microminiskirt down with one hand as she lifted the packages out of the trunk with the other. Short skirts always bothered her. Every time she bent or lifted, she felt as if her whole backside was exposed. Thankfully, her wild print top was nearly as long as the skirt.

"If you'd just loop that final bag over my arm,

please," she said, squinting at Jenkenson. The low, late-afternoon sun was setting over the water in bright strips of purplish red, orange and blue that seemed every bit as garish as her outfit.

Jenkenson smiled as he looped another bag over her arm. The handle tangled in one of her many new jangling, bangled bracelets. "Kathleen, Roman said we were supposed to help—"

"No, thanks." Laden down with her many new purchases, Kathleen waddled up the stone steps to the arched clay-colored door of the château. Unfortunately she couldn't buy anything she really wanted to, but she'd browsed in children's boutiques and toy stores for hours.

Kathleen glanced around the entrance hall expecting to see Roman's housekeeper, Ms. Rodriguez. A pair of Roman's boots were shoved beneath a hand-carved bench, an antique German saddle rested on the bench for show and an old iron blacksmith's shop sign hung on the wall. "Hello!" Kathleen called as she walked toward the stairs. "Ms. Rodriguez?"

"Shopping again?"

Kathleen turned toward the voice and wished she hadn't. Roman was standing in front of an open French door, his legs splayed and his hands in the back pockets of his worn-out jeans. He was shirtless, and the jeans—the knees of which were out—were tucked into boots that were as black as his hair. His head was tilted back and his longish, thick jet waves grazed his shoulders. A long white drape billowed right over one of his rounded, bronzed shoulders. Even from here she could see a drop of sweat roll downward, into the tangle of his chest hairs. As much as she didn't want to admit it, she could almost taste the saltiness of it, too.

"Something wrong with shopping?" she finally called out.

"Sorry, didn't hear you," Roman said, though she knew that was a lie. Slowly and stealthily he came toward her with even-paced steps. The closer he got, the more she became aware of just exactly how uniquely beautiful he was.

"I've been shopping," Kathleen managed to say. "So what?"

Roman shrugged and looked her over from head to toe. His gaze stopped at her legs. "Just making conversation."

She smiled tightly and headed for the stairs again. Her flashy, almost garish outfit had been calculated to let him know she didn't care what he thought of her. So why was she suddenly sure her little plan had backfired?

She'd made it up the first stair when Roman's fingers tangled in her bracelets, turning her. The weight of her many bags, in concert with his grasp, made her swing forward and down so that her nose nearly touched the hairs on his chest. She jerked her face back, set her bags on the first stair, then righted herself.

"So, are you going to tell me why you decided to settle with me?" She could smell the musky, animal scent of sun, oil and, beyond that, the masculine, sun-warmed scent of Roman's skin. He still held her wrist, where her pulse was beating out of control.

"What makes you sure I've got some ulterior motive?" He relaxed his arm, but didn't release her hand. The effect was to bring her skin right into contact with his thigh. Against her knuckles and wrist, the worn denim of his jeans was as soft as silk. *As soft as his lips.*

She forced herself not to look away from his eyes. He could never know that every time she looked deep into them, past his defenses, she could swear she saw a raw desire so intense that her whole body froze in a state of half-terror. "Because you *always* have some ulterior motive," she said. She smiled sweetly.

"Ah." Roman edged even closer. "And so do you, darlin'."

Unfortunately the added height of the step only meant that they were at exact eye level. "I don't know what you're talking about," she managed to say. Her mouth felt parched and she quickly licked her lips. "I just got my due and that's that. For heaven's sake, Roman, you gave me the money."

"That I did," he said softly. When he dropped her hand, she couldn't have felt more relieved.

"And if you're changing your mind now, you shouldn't have acted so impulsively in the first place," she continued, finding it much easier to talk once he'd let go of her. Unfortunately he now took a handful of her shirttail and lightly lifted it. In a flash she imagined her top going right up, over her head, and being tossed to the breeze.

"It wasn't impulse," Roman countered, letting the silk of the shirt rest ever so lightly between his fingers. "I just couldn't take another day of you wandering around my house in those frumpy old, ill-fitting, tattered little dresses." Everything in his voice said he couldn't approve more of the way she was dressed now.

Kathleen wasn't running. She was standing stock-still, but she still couldn't manage to catch her breath. She forced herself to smile. "My house now," she said. "Or have you forgotten that for some unfathomable reason you insisted on signing half the deed over to me?"

"Oh, but darlin'," he drawled. "I don't think I need to remind you that possession's nine-tenths of the law."

His voice was such a whisper that she had to fight not to scream. He dropped her shirttail. "And," he added, "you seem to have guessed that I like to see women with a lot of leg exposed." His eyes traveled downward.

"Why don't you just leave me alone?" Kathleen snapped.

Roman only chuckled. "And why don't you just tell me why you swam over here in a dress? We still haven't discussed that to my—" Roman leaned still closer "—satisfaction."

Kathleen leaned backward, feeling as if her vertebrae were going to snap, one by one, with her efforts to keep her lips out of his reach.

"I want to know just exactly what kind of trouble you're in, Kathleen."

"It's none of your business." The huskiness in her voice unnerved her every bit as much as Roman's nearness.

"Ah, so you *are* in trouble, though I doubt we really needed to establish that. And it is my business," he continued. "Or at least, I've decided to make it so. I'll find out what I want to know." Roman's gaze drifted slowly over her upper body. "One way or another."

"You think you are so hot," she said, feeling the heat in her own cheeks and on her chest even as she said it.

Roman's tongue grazed his upper teeth and his lips curved into a wry half smile. "Hot?" His face came so close to hers that she was sure he was going to kiss her again.

She was hardly one to confront matters of a sensual nature head-on, especially when it came to Roman, but she was just as determined not to let him think he had any effect on her now. "You think you can get things you want by seducing them out of people," she said curtly. She squared her shoulders. "But not me, Roman."

"I hate to tell you this," he said, his features breaking into a full, teasing smile. "But if I ever seduced you, I wasn't even trying. And, sweetheart, it ain't me who's walking around in strips of leather and what could hardly be called a skirt. I may have misunderstood, but from the looks of it, I'd say you were asking for my attention."

He brought his lips right next to hers and then slowly drew away. He was taunting her again. And it made her feel mad enough to kill. More than anything, she wanted to deny what happened to her every time he got this close.

He turned on his heel and headed back toward the French doors. She had half a mind to point out that he never bothered to wear a shirt, but thought better of it.

"Don't you dare flatter yourself by thinking my wardrobe has anything to do with you," she called after him. The man really was pushing her to the outer limits of her endurance. She tried to forget now that her choice of outfit had had everything to do with Roman. But that wasn't the sort of effect she'd intended, she reminded herself firmly. Was it her fault that such a garish outfit would attract him?

Roman leaned casually against a wall and smiled. "I'm not sure it's in your best interest to dare me, Kathleen," he finally said flirtatiously.

"I'll wear whatever I choose," she snapped. Every inch of her seemed to burn as his eyes traveled down her body and then back up. She felt as if she was going to catch fire, right there on the stairs, leaving behind nothing but a puff of smoke and a singed place on the red runner where her feet had been.

The man had the audacity to laugh. "Well, in some things, we do seem to have similar tastes."

She hated him, she thought as she gathered her bags. She really did. Even if every time he was near she had to fight not to fall into his arms. She was unable to think of any appropriate comeback. He turned again and headed outside.

"You wish," she finally countered, aiming the comment at Roman's now retreating back. She didn't head up the stairs as she had planned, but right back out to the car. She intended to return every single thing she'd bought.

She'd buy some nice floral print dresses, the kind he would hate. Very long ones that completely concealed her legs, with huge lace collars that covered her chest. She'd get one-piece pajamas, too, the kind with feet. And maybe she *would* buy some baby things, even if she had to hide them.

"WHERE'S THE LIMO?" Roman had thrown on a shirt—in fact, he'd only taken it off for Kathleen's benefit—and now he was staring at the dented jalopy Jenkenson had brought around for him. "And where did we get this..." He couldn't think of a word negative enough to describe the old four-door in the driveway.

"It's my personal car, Roman," Jenkenson managed to say after a long moment.

"Sorry," Roman said weakly, making a mental note to give Jenkenson a raise. He'd meant to take a very long ride, in order to clear Kathleen from his mind. He considered taking his Lamborghini but, given his foul humor, he figured he'd only wreck it. "So, where's the limo?" he repeated.

"Last I saw, Kathleen jumped in the front seat of it and headed out."

Roman stared at Jenkenson. "Kathleen was driving?"

Jenkenson nodded, an equal look of horror on his concerned face. "I tried to stop her. That woman has just never understood that…well, she doesn't need to do such things for herself."

Roman decided against a ride and headed back inside. "Flanders," he yelled. He hit the intercom in the entrance hall. "Flanders?"

"Right here." Flanders appeared from the direction of the kitchen.

"Bring a case of compuesto to the library." There was nothing like a Havana cigar or Cuban white lightning to make a man forget the world. And compuesto—which was nothing more than pure cane sugar, orange peels and anisette—was about as lethal as one could get.

"Compuesto? A whole case?"

Roman dared the protesting Flanders with his eyes. "Round me up a cigar, too," he added.

"Sure." Flanders sighed, as if realizing it was going to be a long night.

In the library Roman jerked the cords to the curtains that covered the turret window, shutting them tight against the lousy sunset. He lit the lamp by his favorite red leather armchair and then slouched into it, placing his hand on top of the old globe.

He hadn't drunk himself senseless since after his last fight with his ex and after he'd asked her to leave the house. How could a fool maid's daughter get him so damn upset? Just a week before, he hadn't had much on his mind. He had to run up to his farm in West Virginia some time this month, since all but four of his horses were there….

Now he could think of nothing but Kathleen Cannon. *Again.* Somehow he very much doubted that she was sick. She looked too healthy. Really healthy. She kissed healthy, too. Every curve of her—and she *was* getting delicious curves—seethed with life and passion. She wasn't going to tell him what was wrong, and seducing it out of her would be next to impossible.

If she was sick, then that only explained the look of trouble in her eyes. But why had she been swimming around in that fool dress? After he got himself good and drunk—which was necessary, since otherwise he'd never get one single moment's respite from thinking about her—he really would get to the bottom of the whole mess.

"Is there anything else I can do, Roman?" Flanders set a box of compuesto bottles at his feet. He glanced from Roman to the box and then back to Roman. "I suppose you'll need a glass?" he asked hopefully.

"That won't be necessary," Roman said more curtly than he intended. He immediately felt guilty. He was sure he hated his own moodiness as much as everyone else did. "Thanks," he said more gently.

"Are you all right?"

"Fine." And he was. He just wished he could stop wanting Kathleen. He wished he'd quit remembering that night, years ago, when he'd nearly made love to her.

As angry as he had been about his father marrying her mother, he'd flirted with her relentlessly all through the night at her sixteenth birthday party. He'd been barely twenty and, just looking at her, he'd felt as if he'd been plugged right into some high-voltage current.

After the party he'd gone to his room and lain awake, tossing and turning. And each second of every hour he'd felt her presence exactly ten doorways away…with no one on the second floor but the two of them.

He'd never really expected her to come. But she had. Right before dawn he'd heard her stealthy steps in the hallway…. What a fool he'd been for pushing her away. But his family had been torn asunder, and he'd wanted to punish her for it. Hell, maybe he still did.

"Roman?"

"Yeah?"

"Are you *sure* you're all right?"

He nodded. "I'm going to lock the door and get drunk. Do me a favor and don't let anyone in."

"Do you really think Kathleen's sick? I mean, really ill?"

Roman didn't say anything.

"I know how upset you are about Kathleen," Flanders said gently, making Roman mad again. If he only knew what was wrong with her and could fight his attraction….

"Well, don't tell her I'm upset," Roman said.

"Do you think she'd believe it?" Flanders said thoughtfully.

Chapter Three

Kathleen heaved her packages onto her hips. They were full of floral print dresses and solid-colored, practical tent dresses that could double as maternity outfits. Hidden beneath the clothes was a Mickey Mouse mobile.

She didn't want to see Roman. Still, he *had* given her her share of the inheritance and more. For that, she should have acted grateful. After all, it was possible—not probable—that Roman wanted to make amends. If so, she hadn't made it easy for him. Maybe his kiss and the way he'd taunted her today had just been a way of reasserting his fool masculine pride.

Besides, her own reaction to him was undoubtedly due to her pregnancy; she'd never felt quite so conscious of herself as a woman before. And if Roman was attempting to make amends, she could *try* to meet him halfway. The kiss, she told herself, meant absolutely nothing.

She left her packages by the stairs and headed for the kitchen. Like most rooms in the old château it had an eclectic feel, since much of the decor had been salvaged from ships aeons back. One of the two stoves had a fire grate beneath the burners, and old mosaic tiles covered a wall and the counters.

"Mr. Flanders?"

Flanders, who was seated at the Cuban cedar refectory table, glanced up. "Miss Kathleen!"

"You know you always just call me Kathleen.... I mean, you've been acting a little strange." And it wasn't just Flanders. No one looked her straight in the eye lately.

Flanders materialized beside her as if by magic. He placed his hand gingerly beneath her elbow, guided her to the table, seated her as carefully as if she were made of fragile glass, then peered into her face, his brows furrowing with concern. "What can I get for you? Your usual late-night skimmed milk and vitamins? Or maybe you'd just like to rest a bit before you tackle the stairs?"

"I can *tackle* the stairs just fine, and everyone need not wait on me hand and foot," Kathleen insisted. Mr. Flanders flew around the kitchen with the speed of a hurricane; the dried herbs and flowers suspended between the old fireplace and the modern oven swayed in his wake.

"In fact," she continued, "it makes me feel uncomfortable."

"I just don't want you to strain yourself, Kathleen."

"Getting a glass of milk would hardly strain me," she said. "And you know that even after Mama married Augustine, I didn't want to be treated like an overly pampered Lawrence prima donna."

Kathleen took a sip of the milk Flanders served her, instinctively licking the resulting mustache from her upper lip. "Would you please tell me what's gotten into you?"

"Gotten into me?" he echoed. "I don't know quite what you mean."

"Well..." Kathleen could think of no delicate way to point out that his watery brown eyes looked red rimmed. She lowered her voice. "Did Roman do something mean to you?" Had he taken his anger at himself out on Flanders? "What did Roman do?" she demanded.

"Roman wouldn't hurt a fly," Flanders declared.

Kathleen merely raised her brows. "Let's just put everything out on the table, can we?"

"Could we? Roman said we shouldn't say a word... but we're all just so damned sorry about your health, if you'll pardon my language. I mean, I couldn't not tell Jenkenson and Ms. Rodriguez. Why, you know how they feel about you. It's simply a crime, when you're so young. I knew your mother, you know, for many years. Back when she was Mr. Lawrence's housekeeper at his cabin in West Virginia, I used to accompany him there...."

Kathleen listened in horror as Mr. Flanders sorrowfully detailed how he had met her mother. He talked about what a pretty little girl Kathleen had been at ten, and how he'd been so pleased when Augustine and her mother had announced their marriage and the decision to move to the island together.

"How did you find out about my, uh, health?" Kathleen finally interjected. Did Roman know she was pregnant? Had Van Ness contacted him? Roman's mother and Van Ness's mother both mingled in Key West society circles. Had Malcolm told his mother about the baby, so that word had gotten back to Roman? She glanced downward at the Van Ness diamond. She didn't like wearing it, but was afraid to take it off for fear of losing it.

Flanders blew out a long sigh. "Roman overheard

the doctor at the hospital. He's convinced that you're...
My dear, when he realized that you just wanted to
come home to us, where you belong...'' Mr. Flanders
lifted his head and looked her right in the eye. "Roman's not a bad man, Kathleen, even though both you
and I know he blames your mother for the divorce, long
ago as it was. But he does want to do everything he
can to ensure that you're comfortable. And you need
not worry yourself with any details,'' he continued.
"There's long been a space reserved for you beside
your mother and stepfather right here on the island—''

"Please stop,'' Kathleen finally managed to say. "I
think I've got the picture.'' What in thunder had Roman *thought* he'd overheard?

"I'm so sorry, I—oh, dear—the last thing I'd meant
to do was upset you.''

"I'm not the least bit upset,'' she reassured him. She
considered setting Flanders straight, but she was so
mad all she could think of was Roman. "Where is
he?''

"Roman?''

"Who else?''

"He's so distraught that he's locked himself in the
library, and he won't let anyone come in. I'm fairly
sure he's drinking himself into oblivion. He asked for
a whole case of compuesto.''

She rose and patted Flanders on the back. "Where's
the key?''

"Kathleen, he said not to—''

"Please,'' she said sweetly.

Flanders handed over the key. "Just speak with
him.''

"Oh, I intend to speak with him, all right,'' she replied.

When she reached the stairs she gathered her bags, then took the steps two at a time. She felt so angry she was half sure steam was coming out of both her ears. To have upset Mr. Flanders like that!

And she'd thought Roman had finally overcome his pride enough to admit that he cared about her. But he'd just given her her inheritance because he'd thought she was sick. It seemed too crazy to even be true. She dumped her new belongings in her room, then headed down the hall.

Inside the library she shut the door and leaned against it, crinkling her nose against the smell of cigar smoke. Roman was fast asleep. *Good. I'd like to catch him off guard, just once.* A partially empty bottle was on the table and his hand rested on his thigh, the long fingers trailing over his threadbare jeans. She tried not to notice how even the large, imposing red leather chair did absolutely nothing to diminish his muscular body.

Or how his jeans were unsnapped for comfort and his long legs stretched out and straddled apart, in a way she could only see as inviting. Or how he'd stripped off his shirt. For a long time she stared at his chest and at how the many curling, dark hairs seemed to glisten in the soft, low lamplight with each even rise and fall of his breath. The hairs seemed to rush over each other in tiny waves as if in a race downward.

His hair fell over half his face, and wisps of his silver streak cast shadows over the planes beneath his cheekbones. As angry as she was, it was difficult not to want him. *I'll never stop wanting him.* But what did want have to do with love?

And what was going to happen when he found out she wasn't sick! He'd be furious, and take back every dime he'd just given her…the money that was for her baby. She couldn't leave the island, either. She'd already found an obstetrician, Dr. Peteck, whom she'd already seen.

She was three months pregnant now, and liking her doctor meant everything in the world.... Although no one else would notice, she could already feel how tight her jeans had become and see the way her stomach was molding outward from her hipbones. In another month or two her condition would be unmistakable.

Her eyes still roving over Roman's rounded shoulders, she decided there was only one thing she could do. It was despicable, the kind of thing women she didn't respect did in the movies. But if she did it, she could both maintain her silence and get Roman out of the house. If it worked.

She left the library, went to her own bedroom, changed blouses, dug in her bags and found a lacy bra and panty set. Back in the library she quietly flung the items on the floor. Then she found a pen and piece of paper and sat at the desk. She glanced from the paper to Roman and back again.

Roman stirred in the chair.

Kathleen gasped. What in the world was she doing? Had her battle of wills with Roman gone too far this time?

Roman settled back in, nestling his head into his shoulder. His eyelashes were so luxuriously thick that they cast shadows on his cheeks. Just glancing at him made a warm flush creep into her cheeks. She needed time to think! She should have known that only some mortal disaster could make Roman turn nice.... She really didn't want him to realize she was pregnant, did she?

With firm resolve she wrote a brief note.

Roman,
As you know, I am very ill, and I'm appalled at
the way you took advantage of me. I don't want
apologies. It's way too late for them. Drinking is
never an excuse, and if you don't leave this house,
I will call the authorities.

Just looking at the deceitful note made her shudder.
If Roman figured out her little ploy, she'd truly be in
trouble. She crept over and laid the note on top of her
bra. She didn't breathe until she'd locked the library
door behind her again.

If Roman knew her frailties like the back of his hand,
she knew his, too. And she knew, deep down, he was
honorable. Of course, that was *very* deep down. But
with any luck he'd be long gone by the time she got
up.

"WOULD YOU CARE FOR a cocktail, sir?"

"Never again in my life," Roman muttered. Then,
feeling guilty, he smiled at the stewardess. She was tall,
leggy and blond. Under other circumstances he'd undoubtedly flirt with her, but today he could only think
about Kathleen Cannon. "Could I please have juice?"

"Sure. We'll be in West Virginia in another half
hour."

"Thanks," Roman said, taking the cup. He downed
the contents in a gulp, then squinted out the window.
Every ray of sun seemed like a needle piercing his skin,
and his throat still burned from the fool cigar.

Had he really sunk so low that he'd taken advantage
of Kathleen? Surely he would remember a night of
love? Had he really been all that soused? But the worst

thing was that her note confirmed the fact that she was sick.

He could have stayed and confronted the situation, but for some reason—why, he'd never know—he wanted to just let her have her way, if only this once. So he was self-exiled, with no one to blame but himself. He'd had every intention of having George Roy and Johnny Walker drive Pirate's Legacy down to the Keys for the rest of the winter, the way he always did. Between Gee-Roy, Johnny and the Krauses they'd have enough riders to train for the Miami Futurity.

Now Roman was going to be stuck in an indoor arena, or else outside in thirty-degree weather. Not that being in West Virginia was all bad. He'd also just bought two miniature ponies to breed, in the hopes of showing them.

Outside, a blanket of white clouds lay between him and the ground, and the mountains below were covered with snow, making him want to be in Florida more than ever. And even though it was hard to admit, he wanted to be there because of Kathleen. Just to keep an eye on her, of course.

The great mounds of the mountains reminded him of a pale woman's body. White-covered hills rolled and undulated. They crested, opened to flat planes, then rose to peaks and dipped to valleys. But the illusion was nothing compared to the remembrance of one particular woman's body.

As much as he tried to convince himself that he'd acted like a cad by taking advantage of her when she was sick, he had only one honest regret—that he couldn't remember their night together in every single blessedly naked glorious detail.

KATHLEEN SET HER NOTEPAD on her lap while she waited for Dr. Peteck and glanced out the window at all the boats on the ocean. She'd just left Lawrence Shipping and she'd meant to take notes from a book on oil shipping policies while she waited for her sonogram, but she couldn't concentrate.

No matter how hard she tried to force her mind back to her shipping book, she only found herself imagining what a perfect pirate Roman would have been. It was easy enough to picture him in blousy white, unbuttoned shirts, since he wore them all the time, and with his hair blowing wildly, and a gold ring in his ear...

Did she have some kind of screwball gene that made her need around-the-clock excitement? As much as she wished she didn't need drama in her life, she knew she did. And Roman, with his wry, teasing smiles and sexy dare-you gazes, had been the only man who could provide it. From the moment she'd first laid eyes on him, she'd felt that only he could move her to the kind of passion she hoped she was capable of.

Van Ness sure hadn't done a thing for her. She'd thought he might, which is why she'd tried, but he simply hadn't. Why was it that only Roman truly excited her?

Briefly she considered alternatives. There was hang gliding, bungee jumping, skydiving, snorkeling in shark-infested waters.... Unfortunately none of them was as adventurous as hoping that Roman would try to really understand her one of these days. None were as daring as the thought of him kissing her again. Or of her kissing him back in such a way that would finally force him to admit that he longed for her. She couldn't fight the occasional fantasies that flitted into her mind, either…where she and Roman were a couple, expecting a child.

Kathleen snapped to attention. "Yes?"

"Dr. Peteck's ready for you now," the receptionist said.

Kathleen rose and followed the woman into the interior office.

Dr. Peteck, like many Key West natives, looked more like a fisherman than anything else. He was deeply tanned and wore a baseball cap, and Kathleen liked him immensely. She was even enrolling in the birthing classes that his wife taught.

He grinned. "So, do you want to know the sex of your child today? If so, I can even provide you with a videotape of the sonogram."

Kathleen bit her lower lip. Knowledge about her baby was right here, within reach. "No," she said softly. "I want to be surprised."

Dr. Peteck smiled back. "Sometimes the sonogram's hard to read. If we can't tell, do you want to see the tape?"

Tears almost sprang to her eyes. *My baby. Moving and growing…a real, living being inside me.* Suddenly everything seemed so real. She was going to be a mother. And she hoped with all her heart she would be a good one. A great one. She rubbed her stomach slowly. "Oh, yes," she murmured.

ROMAN SLAPPED HIS GLOVES against his chaps to shake the snow from them, put them back on, then shifted in his saddle, glancing at the fifteen head of cattle that crowded against the fence. He felt just as bored as the fool cows looked. Johnny Walker was working out Darlin', Roman's favorite Arabian, and Roman was riding turn-back on Pirate's Legacy. Johnny would walk Darlin' into the cattle and cut a calf from the herd. Once the calf was separated, Darlin' and the calf went head-to-head, dodging and bolting, until the calf gave up.

Then, thankfully, Roman got to drive the calf back into the herd. Training cutters was the most exciting thing he'd ever done, but riding turn-back bored him half to death. He'd felt especially antsy since Flanders's call this morning. Flanders had tracked down the emergency room doctor. And the man had sworn on his life that Kathleen wasn't sick.

"Lighten up on those reins, Johnny," Roman suddenly said. "You're gettin' in Darlin's mouth. The bit's chafing."

"Sorry." Johnny tipped his Stetson in Roman's direction.

Roman nodded, thinking Kathleen had played him for a fool. She'd had the nerve to mention her "illness" in the note she'd left him. Roman could kill Flanders for telling Kathleen he'd thought she was sick.

"Give Darlin' a rest," Roman called. "I'll give Pirate a run."

Johnny trotted the Arabian over to Roman and Roman walked his stallion into the cattle. "You're a feisty one," he whispered, riding out a Hereford calf. When the brown-and-white calf made his run, veering back toward the other cows, Roman sat back in the saddle, giving Pirate's Legacy full rein.

The stallion was good. The best. He bent back on his haunches and down on his forelegs to a near-kneel, daring the calf with his eyes, his head shaking back and forth and his tail swishing madly. Roman took the horse two steps back, turned quickly, then twisted to the right, turned again, then twisted to the left. The horse met each of the calf's moves as if he was a mirror.

Grabbing the saddle horn, Roman felt a rush of pure vertigo, the kind he lived for. Bucking around in the saddle was the only excitement he'd had in the past ten weeks since he'd left Kathleen. Mostly he'd felt restless and irritable, as if he'd just as soon kick something as look at it.

Pirate's Legacy missed a turn and the calf bolted toward the herd. Roman kicked in his heels and chased the calf two paces. The horse and calf faced off again in a series of moves and counter moves that forced a wry smile to Roman's lips. The way the horses and calves went at one another reminded him of his relationship with Kathleen.

He almost felt angry when the calf gave up. It suddenly stood upright, broke its gaze from that of the horse and stared toward the fence. And that was the difference between Kathleen and a cow, Roman thought. She never gave up…always fought him to the death.

"Until death do us part," he muttered. "Don't worry," he said to the calf. "You ain't gonna get branded. This is just a practice session."

When Roman turned around he couldn't believe who he saw. "Van Ness?" Roman reined in Pirate's Legacy and trotted toward the fence.

Van Ness had been a grade behind him in prep school, he ran into him at parties occasionally in the Keys and their mothers moved in the same circles, yet they weren't friends. But there was no mistaking him, looking like a fish out of water. He was deeply tanned,

had on a down coat that looked brand-new and was
sidestepping frozen cow dung in boat shoes.

"Tell me Kathleen didn't really go out with this
man," Roman muttered as he dismounted and tossed
his reins over a fence post. He hopped the fence and
leaned his elbows on the rail just as Van Ness arrived
breathlessly at his side.

"What in the world brings you out this way?" Roman asked after they'd shaken hands.

"Actually," Van Ness said nervously, "I was looking for you. It's about Kathleen."

As far as Roman's sources had informed him, Kathleen and Van Ness had broken up months ago. If Van
Ness meant for him to play conciliatory go-between,
he had another think coming. "What about her?"

Van Ness cleared his throat. "Well, it's a small matter, but..." He swallowed, glanced at Roman and then
at Pirate's Legacy. The horse ambled close, trying to
nuzzle him, but Van Ness leaped back a pace. So did
the horse.

"I let Kathleen, uh, borrow a ring," he said.

At least that solved the mystery of where she had
gotten the diamond she was wearing. But why would
Van Ness lend Kathleen a piece of jewelry? "She
didn't return it?" A persuasive smile played on Roman's lips. This was sure getting interesting.

"Oh, I'm sure she tried...."

Van Ness was incredibly nervous and he looked as
if he was lying. Had Kathleen stolen the diamond? Roman couldn't imagine her doing such a thing, but he
could hardly forget that she'd managed to get him to
deed over everything *he* owned.

"I'm sure she's got the ring," Roman said with a

calmness he didn't feel. "Gold set. Looks like it weighs a ton?"

"That's it! Could you possibly get it back to me? I know she's not feeling well now…"

Roman almost groaned. He'd just gotten the information that Kathleen was fine. But apparently something *was* wrong with her. Whenever the woman walked into his life she stirred up nothing but misinformation in her wake. "What's wrong with her, Van Ness?"

Van Ness swallowed. "She's staying with you now, right? I mean, you'd know better than I would. And I haven't actually seen her for some time," he said. "A *long* time…but, well, she said she was ten weeks pregnant and—"

"Pregnant?" Roman interjected hoarsely. "You spoke to her recently?"

Van Ness gulped audibly. "Oh, sure," he said. "Just the other day."

Ten weeks. Two and a half months. That was exactly how long it had been since they'd slept together. Roman stared at Van Ness for a long moment, then managed to lean and shake Van Ness's hand. "I'll get the ring to you," he said gruffly.

He turned and headed for the cabin. The same cabin that Loretta Cannon had cleaned for his father, right up until she'd married him. Well, Kathleen Cannon was one more fortune hunter who wasn't going to get the best of him.

"Johnny Walker," Roman yelled over his shoulder. "Get Darlin' and Pirate's Legacy ready for transport."

So sweet Kathleen had meant to keep this secret under wraps. She was pregnant with *his* child and hadn't told him. No wonder Van Ness had kept looking at him with that nervous expression. He thought Roman had done the deed, then taken off without a backward glance.

A baby. For so long he'd imagined having a son, and not because of his mother's harping about how he needed an heir, either. He wanted an heir, but he also wanted the opportunity to be the kind of father his own had been. Augustine Lawrence had been kind and gentle, yet formidable and successful. And really, he thought, he wouldn't mind a little girl....

As long as she turned out like him, not Kathleen.

He shook his head as if to clear it of thoughts, knowing full well that anytime Kathleen entered his life he was stripped of his rational instincts. If Kathleen had lied about being sick—which she obviously had—then maybe she'd lied about being pregnant, too.

When was the damnable woman going to grow up and give him peace of mind? Besides, he'd only slept with her once. Or had he? His hazy recollection of the event hardly amounted to cold, hard fact. But no, he thought, there was no use denying it. Every time he saw or touched her, his whole world went out of whack. If there was one woman he'd get pregnant on a first try, it was definitely Kathleen.

And if she was lying about the pregnancy, time would tell the truth. As he neared his cabin, thoughts of his child took a back seat to his anger. Then his anger began to rise to the level of pure fury.

He'd given Kathleen a fortune! He'd signed over half the deed to his very own house! He simply couldn't believe it. How could one woman drive him so crazy?

Before he had seen Van Ness he'd meant to have it

out with her. Now he intended to get absolute, sweet revenge.... And his baby.

"SOME HORSE TRAILERS just arrived," Ms. Rodriguez called from the flagstone porch.

"Horse trailers!" Kathleen was out of the pool in a flash. She fled for the house, dripping wet and still in her bikini. Where there were horses, Roman was sure to follow.

As Kathleen fled toward the stairs, Ms. Rodriguez shoved a bowl into her hand. "Great," Kathleen managed to say. "My afternoon snack." The last thing she needed right about now was the proverbial three scoops of ice cream with a pickle on the side.

She had to clean her room! She'd told Ms. Rodriguez that a friend of hers was expecting a baby and now... Oh, why had Roman decided to come back after all this time?

"Oh, no," she murmured feebly when she reached the room. It was completely strewn with new baby clothes and toys. A car seat and stroller in boxes sat on the floor. Glancing down, she knew that anyone with an astute eye would know full well she was pregnant. At over five months she'd already gained fifteen pounds. She hastily shrugged into a beach cover-up before she realized it was of white muslin and nearly transparent.

"Action mode," she whispered.

She slammed the bowl down on her dresser. She hauled the boxes across the carpet and crammed them beneath her bed. When the stroller box didn't fit, she shoved with both her hands and then covered what was left of the box with her spread.

She winced. It was all so obvious. "The clothes,"

she murmured. The clothes! Her hand flew upward to the bedspread. She'd laid out all the baby's clothes in complete sets, with socks and shoes and moccasins and hats.... Oh, why had she indulged herself by laying out the outfits and imagining how cute her baby was going to look in each and every one?

It would take a full year to de-baby her room!

She snatched the clothes from the bed by the handful, ran to her closet, shoved them inside and slammed the door.

The books! *How to Breast Feed, The Single Mom, Making Labor Easy...* Kathleen swept them into a drawer at her bedside. She glanced around and heaved a breath of relief.

Just in the nick of time. After one quick rap, the door swung open wide. Roman waltzed in, stopping right in front of her. *In his full glory,* she thought.

She was breathless and frazzled from hiding all the baby's things, and he looked as cool and calm as the cove waters outside the house. Her tanning skin was turning bright red in splotches. His was as coppery bronze as a new penny.

"Roman!" Kathleen tugged her cover-up tightly across her stomach. Guiltily glancing down, she saw that her ice cream had melted into a puddle. Roman was frowning into the murky mess.

"You shouldn't be eating that," he muttered. Then his eyes traveled slowly downward over her stomach. Or was that just her imagination? She tried to force herself to relax, but every muscle and sinew felt strained to breaking.

Her swimsuit was skimpy and the now wet, see-through muslin cover-up clung to her like a second skin. Whether she actually felt his gaze or just imagined it, her nipples beaded against the suit. She told herself it was the air-conditioning in the room, but she felt just as hot as she did cold. She felt as if she'd been immersed in both fire and ice at the same time.

The crib! She'd set it in a corner of the room...all made up with Disney sheets! A Daffy Duck outfit was laid out in the crib, with the hood positioned on the pillow, where the baby's head would be. Above it hung the Mickey Mouse mobile.

Your Baby was still on the dresser.

The crib was a dead giveaway.

And Roman was staring right at her stomach.

He flashed her a quick, teasing grin, then ambled across the room, every step of his long, lean-legged gait seeming to say he had the upper hand. She watched with horror as he lay across her bed, the heels of his boots hovering right over the box that contained the hidden stroller.

"Don't put your dirty boots on my bed," she said flatly.

Roman lifted his boots lightly, one by one, the inner muscles of his thighs straining against his jeans. One of his large, nimble-fingered hands ran slowly back and forth over the spread. Then he patted the space beside him.

"You certainly don't expect me to sit down, do you?" she managed to say, wishing he'd stop staring at her stomach.

"We need to have a talk, darlin'," he said in a playful tone that hardly inspired comfort. He stretched on her bed, as if he'd never felt more comfortable. "Whether you sit down or not."

"Not," she said curtly, fighting the wave of heat that seemed to wash over her. She breathed in sharply. Was

Roman taking the liberty of lounging on her bed because he thought they had become lovers? Wasn't that
what she'd wanted him to think, so he'd leave? But
now he was back, she thought grimly.

"I'd hoped you weren't still mad at me," he said
softly. His voice, when it went all low and persuasive
like that, sent shivers down her spine.

"I'm not mad," she replied. She glanced over his
shoulder at the crib and swallowed.

"Could have fooled me," he nearly whispered, with
no hint of annoyance in his voice.

One of his tanned arms raised in an arc as he reached
behind himself for a pillow. He found one and shoved
it beneath his arm. The girlish floral print of the throw
only made him look ten times more male.

"Make yourself comfortable, why don't you?" she
asked sweetly, wishing he'd decided to park himself
somewhere other than on her bed.

He flashed her a smile. "Why, thanks, darlin', I intend to."

She turned on her heel and headed for her closet,
not about to stand there one more second in her cover-
up. The swimsuit had once been too large, but now it
barely covered her breasts. The bottoms were indecent,
even by bikini standards. And the cover-up covered up
zilch, especially now that it was wet. When Kathleen
turned her back she could feel Roman's eyes burning
into her. Those two pinpoints of heat hit her neck, the
space between her shoulder blades and then her backside.

When she opened the closet door the wadded-up
bunch of baby clothes tumbled outward. She found a
long terry-cloth robe, shrugged it over the cover-up she
was already wearing, then casually nudged the baby

clothes back inside the closet with her foot. Then she slammed the closet door. She sat in the farthest chair from the bed—a rocker—and stared at Roman.

He simply gazed at her, long and steady, as if he had all the time in the world.

"So what is it we need to talk about?" No matter how hard she tried, she couldn't break their gaze.

"A lot," he said. "After all, I've been gone for... months."

Was it just her imagination, or did he really emphasize *months?* The word rang in her ears.

"Like what?" she finally blurted out.

He smiled. "Well, we could start with your pregnancy."

Kathleen gasped.

"I talked to Van Ness," he continued.

She crossed her hands more tightly over her stomach. "Van Ness told you?" If the man wasn't going to marry her, he could at least have kept his mouth shut. "He told you *everything?*" she squeaked.

"Every single detail." Judging from the knowing smile on Roman's please-touch-me lips, Van Ness truly had told him details. Kathleen's mouth went dry and she couldn't think of a thing to say.

"Van Ness was probably just worried about his mother's ring," she finally managed to say, trying to sound utterly bored by the conversation.

Roman merely chuckled softly. "Actually," he said, "that *was* the main purpose of his visit."

Van Ness was even more despicable than she'd thought. Roman was even worse for pointing that fact out. She forced herself to smile. "Well, it is a nice piece of jewelry," she said as casually as she could.

"And I said you'd return it, Kathleen," he said.

"Of course," she returned coolly. He scooted upward in her bed, rebunched the pillows, then turned his head toward her. This time he did put his feet on the bed.

"Your feet," she said, inadvertently looking over the length of him. His stomach was as flat as the mattress itself and his jeans, though they weren't particularly tight, packed a clearly perceptible bulge. She blinked and then swallowed.

Roman edged his ankles over the side. His boot heel nearly touched her stroller box. "I don't know why Van Ness didn't just ask for the ring when he talked to you," Roman continued.

When Van Ness had talked to her? She hadn't seen hide nor hair of him since she'd dived off his boat. "Who knows?" she responded. She flashed Roman a smile, determined to let him know that she didn't mind being an unwed mother.

"Look, Kathleen," Roman began, his voice lowering and becoming as gentle as a breeze. "Ever since you came—" he paused as if the words were somehow difficult to say "—came *home,* I've tried, in every way I know how, to make things right. As soon as you said you were going to contest the will, I turned over everything that was rightfully yours, and more. Now didn't I?"

"Only because you thought I was sick," she countered. She noted with satisfaction that his darkly tanned face turned even darker with what might have been a flush. If so, it was the first time she'd ever seen Roman color with embarrassment.

"Now, darlin'," he said, his voice dropping a notch so that it sounded even huskier and, she had to admit, sexy. "That had nothing to do with it."

She drew her brows upward in points, half wishing they were lovers, as her note had said. Half wishing that she could crawl right next to him in the bed. "Right," she finally said.

He shook his head, just enough so that the tendrils of his waving hair now fanned on her pillow. "It really didn't," he said in a near whisper. "Kathleen, won't you ever trust me?"

Roman looked so sincere that it was hard not to believe him. Was it possible that he had truly meant to do right by her?

"And I didn't have to arrange a job for you or give you half the deed to the house."

Kathleen felt her heart sinking. She had never felt this guilty in her life. As sure as she was that he had had some ulterior motive, maybe he hadn't.

"All that was very nice of you, Roman," she said. The words came out a little more curtly than she'd intended. No matter how she tried, she couldn't force herself to trust him. "But where are you leading with all this?" After all, he wouldn't bother to mention all his little kindnesses unless he wanted something. Would he?

"Leading?" He took on another one of those overly innocent expressions. How somebody as jaded as Roman could make himself look like a choirboy she'd never know.

"Yes, Roman." She was sure he wasn't on the level. "What is it you want?"

"Oh," he said, flashing her his most perfect smile. "That's easy."

"It is?" Everything about that smile said he was about to throw her a shocker. She gripped the armrests of the rocker and braced herself.

"Yes," he said, his voice becoming as soft and inviting as silk.

"So what is it?"

"Why, darlin'," Roman said smoothly. "I want to marry you."

Chapter Four

"Are you crazy?" Kathleen shot up from the rocking chair, feeling as if all the wind had just been knocked out of her. For a moment she just stood there trembling.

"That's about the strangest reaction to a proposal I've ever seen," Roman said casually.

"Get the hell out of my room, Roman Lawrence," she said.

"Can't we discuss this?"

She stared at him in horror. Then she stalked close to the bed, stood right over him with her hands on her hips and glared downward. She shook her head. "No!"

A droplet of water from her wet hair hit his cheek and he flinched as if he'd been burned. Something in his eyes made her think he was going to pull her down on the bed, right on top of him. But he only wiped the drop from his skin in a gesture that was almost a caress, his eyes never leaving hers.

She started when he rose lithely from her bed and ambled toward her bedroom door. When he reached it, he turned and leaned against the jamb. She followed him, too furious to worry about whether or not she was keeping at a safe distance.

"Kathleen," he said, "I don't want to bring up the

past. I don't want to remind you that my family has been through a lot of embarrassment—" He leaned downward, as if trying to meet her at eye level.

"Embarrassment!" she exclaimed. "Your fool family has its roots in piracy and salvaging and rum-running and—"

"That's enough," Roman said, leaning even closer and suddenly sounding a little angry himself.

He blew out a long sigh as if she were being completely irrational. "Sorry," he said, his voice becoming calm again.

It was only then that she realized their faces were mere inches apart. "You should be," she returned. She could have killed herself for sounding so breathless. Had Roman really just asked her to marry him?

"I realize that a lot of couples get divorced these days," he continued, still sounding like the voice of reason. "People just like my mother and father. It happens and it's really no one's fault."

"And a lot of women are home wreckers like my mother. Right?" she managed to say.

"Now, Kathleen, I didn't say that. You did." Roman sent her a censuring glance. "But like I said, I'm willing to put that behind us. And if you married me, our baby would have many more advantages."

"I already have plenty of money," she said. She couldn't help but let her expression soften. "And I thank you for that." She meant it from the bottom of her heart.

"But the Lawrence name—"

"Would undoubtedly open a lot of doors," she finished.

"And with that, the baby would stand to inherit anything I have, too," he said.

Her mouth dropped open. Roman was serious. He wanted to use her baby as his heir. She simply couldn't believe it. It was such a crazy proposal that she almost laughed. "No way," she said in shock.

"Kathleen, how could you deprive the baby of—"

The mere thought of depriving her baby of anything made her heart break. "Roman, you know we can barely stand to be in the same room without fighting," she said. *And without falling into each other's arms.* She swallowed and forced herself to smile lightly. "And being married would undoubtedly cramp your style."

Kathleen saw all those warring emotions in his eyes again. He leaned yet another inch closer and a playful smile touched his lips. "Now how could being married cramp my style?"

"You know exactly what I mean."

That all-too-innocent expression took possession of his face again. "Why, I don't have a clue," he whispered.

"Then let me spell it out for you," Kathleen said flatly, her voice rising again. "How do you expect to *womanize* once you're wearing a wedding band?"

He leaned so close that Kathleen stepped back a pace. He caught her hand and held it loosely. His skin felt dry and warm and smooth. Her own palms had turned clammy. He was so near that his breath whispered right by her ear. "Well, Kathleen," he said. "I had no intention of *sleeping* with you."

Kathleen felt her face grow hot with a flush. She was sure her cheeks were turning bright red.

"And I didn't intend to wear a ring, either," he continued. "It would be purely a legal proposition. But of course, if you're offering—"

"I didn't mean that!" she said quickly. She told herself she wouldn't sleep with Roman if he were the last man on earth.

"I guess you were thinking about that kiss I gave you in the hallway a few months back," Roman said amiably.

"Believe me," she said, jerking her hand from his, "it never crossed my mind." No, it had crossed and recrossed it so many times it zigzagged.

Kathleen realized he was watching her every expression. "Well, that's good," he finally said. "Because that kiss hasn't crossed mine, either. And you know how I get. I was all cooped up here on the island, and you were just the first woman I'd seen in a while and—"

"Can we please not discuss this?"

He shrugged. "Sure. I mean, it's hardly worth discussing, other than to say I lost my head and that it won't happen again."

"Ever?" she asked curtly, as if daring him.

"Never," he responded.

"That's good," she said. But the emotion in his eyes told her that he was lying through his teeth.

He nodded. "It truly is."

She had to force herself not to glare doubly hard at him. He'd wanted her, even if it was obvious that he'd never love her. She smiled sweetly. "Well, I'm glad you've decided to leave me alone. Finally."

"Anyway," he continued casually, "the marriage thing was just a thought."

"Marriage *thing*," she scoffed. "What an unfeeling way of putting it."

Roman threw up his hands, as if she was simply too irrational to argue with. "Look," he said. "I was trying to do you a favor. Even if people realize that our marriage is a farce, they'll know that I cared enough to give this baby a name. And they'll respect us both for it.''

He sighed, then continued. "And the kid'll have everything. Including a family name, and an inheritance. Since I never plan on getting really married again, it only seems natural that this child should be brought into the family through marriage, which will make his or her claim to everything we both have uncontestable.''

His voice became even lower. "My father would have wanted this. And…well, your mother would have wanted it, too.''

Kathleen could tell that the mention of her mother had cost him.

"And I want it,'' he said.

"I really don't think it would work,'' she managed to say, unable to believe Roman wanted to become involved with her baby. "But it's a nice thought.'' She forced herself to reach downward, grasp his hand and squeeze it quickly before she let it drop. "And anyway, these days, people are pretty accustomed to seeing single moms. Everything'll be okay.''

He shrugged casually. "That's fine.'' He sounded as if he meant it. "Like I said, it was just an offer to cover legalities.'' He flashed her a quick smile. "Besides, it would get my mother off my back. She wants and deserves a grandchild.''

Kathleen's body tensed at the mention of his mother. She very much doubted any woman would want to see her son married to her ex-husband's second wife's daughter. Or to be a grandma to a baby fathered by someone other than her son, in such circumstances. What a nightmare!

"I just wanted you to know that she'd be pleased at the idea."

"I somehow doubt that," Kathleen returned. Her voice held an odd combination of huskiness and disbelief.

"Well, it's a moot point. Isn't it?" Roman shoved himself off the doorjamb with his shoulder. "But why you insist on depriving a defenseless baby of a good life, I'll never know."

With that, Roman leaned agilely around the doorway. He bent and lifted something from a shopping bag and pressed it against her stomach. Kathleen reached for the object instinctively, then glanced downward. She was squeezing the softest, cutest, fuzziest little stuffed dolphin she'd ever seen.

"Think about it." Roman said the words with the same intonation Clint Eastwood had used when he'd said, "Make my day." It was hardly comforting.

And then he turned on his heel lightly and ambled down the hall toward his own room. The hallway was long enough that he actually seemed to grow smaller with the distance. That unnerving, ambling gait of his never once faltered. He walked along as if he didn't have a care in the world.

She went back inside her room, shut the door and leaned against it, clutching the dolphin. Then she stared, openmouthed, at the crib, as if her baby were already sleeping there.

"Oh, darlin'," she finally said in shock, barely noticing that she'd picked up the usage of Roman's favorite endearment. "I think Roman Lawrence just asked if he could be your daddy."

ROMAN FELL ONTO his own bed on his stomach, letting his boots dangle over the side. He stared out the window, through the blowing fronds of palms, at the red bark of a gumbo-limbo tree, and the pink-and-white vines that grew up around the château walls. The muscles of his backside tightened involuntarily. He groaned and rolled to his back.

"What that woman doesn't do to me," he muttered.

If there had been any doubt in his mind that she was pregnant, he sure knew the truth now. Her scrappy little body had filled out in ripe, luscious-looking curves that were already costing him his sanity. He hadn't been able to help staring at her full hips or at the way her stomach was now rounding ever so gently over them.

He didn't know a blessed thing about pregnant women, but it sure seemed amazing, if not impossible, that a woman's body could transform that much in just ten weeks.

He clasped his hands behind his neck and sighed with contentment. Kathleen was having *his* baby. It had been damn difficult not to touch her stomach. Hell, he thought now, he had every right to. Didn't he? After all, it was his child.

And lying in her bed...

He groaned again and rolled onto his side. Her pillows had carried the faintest scent of paprika, cinnamon and mangoes. That only meant that Ms. Rodriguez had been bringing her her meals. But beneath those hints of scents, he had also smelled the fresh-washed, salty, apricot soap smell of Kathleen's skin.

He wanted her. More now than ever. He'd have her, too. He'd nearly choked on half of what he'd said. He suddenly chuckled. His mother would be pleased by the idea. Hardly. His mother would die. But then, he figured what his mother didn't know wouldn't hurt her.

And had he really referred to Lawrence Island as Kathleen's *home?* That had been hard to swallow. Lawrence Island belonged to him. He didn't care about what the legal deed said at the moment, either.

He reached for the nightstand, picked up the phone and dialed Miles Higgenbothem. When the lawyer came on the line, Roman explained the basic scenario.

"Yes," Roman continued, twining the phone cord around his fingers, "I know it's the last thing you would have ever expected, but it's true. Can you start drawing up some divorce papers? No, I haven't married her yet, but I'm going to, and I intend to have custody of the baby after the divorce."

There was a long pause. Then Higgenbothem said, "But, Roman, the baby needs its mother."

Roman frowned, having to admit that Higgenbothem had a point. "Can't we just give her weekends or something?" he asked gruffly. Somehow the suggestion made him feel guiltier than he ever had in his life.

"I suppose so," Higgenbothem finally said. There was another long pause. "Anyway, Roman, you're not even married."

"Leave that to me," Roman said.

He would marry Kathleen, he thought after he'd hung up. The more he fantasized about it, the more he knew that fatherhood would suit him, even if marriage wouldn't. He thought about the things he'd do with his kid. For one, he would train one of his miniature ponies, so he could teach his son or daughter to ride. Of course, that wouldn't be for a while....

He just hoped he'd made Kathleen feel guilty

enough to think about his proposal. Yes, if he knew Kathleen, she wouldn't deprive her child of anything.

And now all Roman had to do was to kill her with kindness. It was going to be hard. But he could do it.

"BREAKFAST IN BED?" Kathleen asked softly the next morning.

Roman merely shrugged as if serving her in bed were the most natural thing in the world. He nestled the legs of a silver standing tray on either side of her lap, then admired his handiwork. He'd even put a vase on the tray, with a single white rose.

"It looks beautiful," Kathleen murmured, still too sleepy to feel shocked. She kept expecting to get the third degree, or at least questions about the baby's father...but what she'd got was breakfast.

And she looks beautiful, Roman thought. He tried to tell himself that the way his heart suddenly ached for her was simply due to the baby. Still, Kathleen really did look fabulous, all rumpled in the covers, with her short hair mussed. He realized that maybe it wouldn't be so hard to be nice to her, after all.

She smiled. "No coffee?"

He stood over her, crossing his arms. "You've been drinking coffee? Coffee can't be good for the baby."

She flushed guiltily. He made it sound as if she'd been smoking cigarettes or drinking alcohol. "I can't wake up without a little coffee," she said defensively.

"Well, don't worry about it, darlin'," he said, softening his voice. "But why don't you have a little orange juice, instead?" He leaned forward, lifted a glass from the tray and handed it to her.

Kathleen sipped it contritely and said, "Thanks." She glanced over the tray and blinked. Granted, she was eating more now than ever, but there was enough food on the tray for an active army.

"I didn't know if you wanted toast, a bagel, or an English muffin," Roman said, suddenly feeling a little embarrassed. He shrugged. "So I just brought all three."

She chuckled and picked up a slice of toast. "Oh, the way I've been scarfing food down, I'll probably eat all three." It was hardly true, but the tray looked so thoughtfully presented and Roman was acting so sweet that she felt compelled to say it. He wasn't even flirting with her, the way he usually did, but only watching her calmly. She felt a sudden rush of relief and happiness. She no longer had to hide her pregnancy, and Roman was actually going to be helpful.

"Have you been exercising?" Roman asked out of the blue.

"Well," she managed to say between crunchy bites of a diced apple, "I'm not supposed to strain myself, but I do have a recommended exercise program."

"Recommended by whom?" he asked gruffly.

Kathleen watched him reach down and take a mango slice from her plate. The fruit left a juicy sheen on his lips, which he promptly licked off. Realizing she'd been staring at his mouth, she blinked. "Uh…by my doctor. Dr. Peteck."

"Peteck," Roman echoed, making a mental note to check on the physician and make sure he was a good one. The best.

Suddenly Kathleen crinkled her nose. "Do I smell paint?"

"I'm having some work done in my bedroom," Roman said casually. He'd really hoped the painters would be finished by the time Kathleen got up. But they hadn't been. He told himself that was the main reason he had brought Kathleen breakfast, besides wanting to ensure that the baby was well fed. No, he didn't exactly want her to know that he was transforming his office into a nursery…not until she'd agreed to marry him, anyway.

"As a matter of fact," he continued, "I should probably go check on their progress." He forced himself to keep his eyes on her face, suddenly wanting to let them drift over the length of her. She really did look beautiful. Too appealing. He turned abruptly and headed for the door.

"Roman?" He turned toward the sound of Kathleen's voice.

"Yes?"

"Thanks for breakfast."

"Sure," he said, somehow wishing as he left the room that she didn't sound quite so surprised that he'd done something nice.

Kathleen stared at the door for a long moment. Maybe when it came to pregnant women, Roman really did have a soft spot in his heart.

"HEY, KATHLEEN, how're you feeling today?" Lately the drawling rasp of Roman's voice had been replaced by a brisk, concerned tone. And she was beginning to hate it. Not that he wasn't kind as could be. He made sure she ate well, did her exercises and took her vitamins. Her heart swelled with an almost undefinable happiness every time he pampered her…but he no longer really seemed to see her as a woman.

She didn't even bother to respond, only glanced downward over her one-piece bathing suit to make sure all her straps were in place. Not that it mattered. Roman couldn't have been less interested in her if she were a piece of furniture.

"Fine," she finally muttered, glancing up as he pulled a deck chair next to her. Her expression softened when she saw that he was carrying a small, unfinished wooden rocking horse. He unfolded a newspaper, spread a sheet at his feet, sat the horse on top of it, then opened a pint-sized can of paint.

"Are you sure?" he asked, glancing at her. "I mean, you sound a little sulky. Not that I mind it when you're sulky of course. I mean, pregnant women are rumored to have moods...."

"I really am fine," she said, thinking it was awfully sweet of Roman to buy a gift for her baby.

He stirred the paint, then picked up a brush and began to cover the horse with quick, bold strokes. He glanced at her again. "Just a base coat," he explained. "And don't worry, the paint's nontoxic. I figured the horse might dry more quickly in the sun...and besides, I wanted your company."

"Where did you find it?" she asked, suddenly smiling.

"Hansel and Gretel's on Key West," he said, not looking at her but concentrating on his work.

"I love it," she said. The horse's features weren't very detailed. It was a country-style toy, simple in its design, made of roundish tube shapes. The legs looked good and sturdy.

Roman flashed her a grin. "I hoped you'd like it."

"You did?"

Roman nodded. He was barefoot and wearing a pair of silky red short swim trunks that annoyed her all of a sudden. Since when did Roman care if she liked something or not? Oh, maybe Roman was right. She was getting awfully moody.

And yet, suddenly she felt angry with him, even though the man hadn't done anything wrong. He wasn't a criminal just because his gaze had stopped roving over every blessed inch of her, the way it used to.

When he was finished painting, he laid his brush to the side and smiled at her indulgently. And then he began rubbing sun oil over his chest and stomach. She watched his hands move over his gleaming skin in slow circles. He rustled up a sheet of newspaper from beside the rocking horse, then leaned back in his chair and began to read.

Kathleen leaned back and shut her eyes, determined to ignore him. But even with her eyes shut she could see how his washboard flat stomach looked, all shining and glistening with oil. Usually she'd be on pins and needles if he was seated next to her, especially if he was wearing nothing but that skimpy pair of trunks.

She crossed her arms over her chest. Were pregnant women unappealing to him? If so, that really made her angry. She liked the way her body looked now. On the other hand, when he'd served her breakfast she'd still seen his desire for her in his eyes. Hadn't she?

He'd only been acting this way for a few weeks, but it felt like years. She was so sick of it that she didn't even bother to deny her pique. Not that anything would ever come of the energy that used to radiate between them.

The newspaper crinkled as he turned the page. And she knew very well he was really reading it. Maybe he really had asked her to marry him just to help her and the baby.

A mosquito whirred by her face and she fanned it away. She half wished she had on her bikini. At least that had seemed to get his attention. She simply couldn't help but feel irritated. The one thing Roman had never done was ignore her. And it was driving her crazy.

Maybe she should just say yes, she suddenly thought. If he wasn't serious, she would call his bluff, which, she decided, would be satisfying. If he was serious, her child would be deprived of nothing the world could offer. Either way she looked at it, she came out the winner. And besides, she thought, she wanted nothing more than to shock him out of his newfound complacency.

Kathleen took a deep breath and rolled onto her side. "Roman?"

Seconds passed. Then he glanced over at her and blinked, as if he'd been so engrossed in the news that he hadn't heard her.

"Yeah?"

"You know that proposal you made the other day?"

He cocked his head as if trying to remember. "Oh," he said after a moment. "You mean about that legal—"

"Yeah," Kathleen forced herself to say casually. Suddenly she wished she hadn't reopened the subject. Why in the world was she doing this? Why was *he* doing it?

"Don't worry about it, darlin', you don't need to do anything you don't want to."

Darlin'. It was the first time he'd called her that in days. "Oh, I'd never do anything I didn't want to," she said coyly.

His eyes suddenly flashed like the devil. "Of course not," he drawled.

"Well," she said lightly as her heart started to pound in her chest. "I do believe I've changed my mind."

He was staring at her as if he'd already forgotten what they were talking about. He was supposed to back out! She was supposed to be calling his bluff!

"About getting married," she managed to say, her eyes dropping to the freshly painted rocking horse.

"That's good." Roman turned back to his paper. Then, as if in an afterthought, he flashed her another quick smile. Then he stuck his perfect patrician nose right back in the paper.

She forced herself to lean back in her chair and shut her eyes again. Her heart was hammering wildly beneath her ribs. There was something about Roman's smile—a certain sly curve to it—that made her feel very nervous.

She heard him rise from his chair. Her skin went cool where his body cast a shadow over hers.

"And about the date, darlin'…"

Her eyes flew open. For a second all she saw was his glistening, oiled thigh. She raised her gaze quickly. "What?" she asked in a strangled voice.

"Tomorrow, all right?"

Roman waited a moment for a response. When there was none, he simply walked away. Kathleen whirled in her chair and watched him saunter toward the house.

"I take it that's a yes," he called over his shoulder.

"Yes," she called back with a lightness she didn't begin to feel. Was she really going to marry Roman Lawrence? "If I don't kill him first," she suddenly muttered in shock.

And yet, glancing at the rocking horse again, she couldn't help but realize that Roman would probably make a wonderful father, even if it *was* in name only.

Chapter Five

"You're not wearing that!" Ms. Rodriguez's eyes flashed as she marched into Kathleen's bedroom.

Kathleen glanced downward. She was just signing a few legal documents, and her choice of jeans and a T-shirt was to show Roman that she wasn't taking their marriage seriously. Besides, it was only late afternoon, and she wasn't supposed to meet Roman and Higgenbothem until evening.

"Roman's already sent Mr. Flanders to the tailor in Key West to retrieve his tux," Ms. Rodriguez continued. "I believe the jacket was torn."

"Roman's wearing a tux?" Kathleen whirled toward Ms. Rodriguez. She smiled slowly. If Roman was dressing up, then she could, too. She had wanted to wear something special. After all, it was her wedding day. It might be the only one of her life....

Ms. Rodriguez rifled through her closet and pulled out a blousy white silk dress. "I can hardly wear white," Kathleen murmured, glancing downward at her stomach.

"You can and will!" Ms. Rodriguez spun toward Kathleen in protest. Her long black braid flew over her shoulder and the skirt of the silk dress fluttered in her wake like butterfly wings. Ms. Rodriguez's dark eyes were lit up and shining with excitement. "Now hand me those horrible clothes you've got on."

Kathleen tugged off her T-shirt obediently. There was no way she was going to look like a frumpy fool in jeans while Roman looked like the cat's meow in a tux, she told herself. "Forget that dress," Kathleen said. "Toward the back of the closet there's a pale peach cocktail dress. It's silk and chiffon."

"You intend to get married in a cocktail dress?"

Kathleen grinned. "Believe me, it doesn't look like a cocktail dress." She'd bought the dress on one of her trips to Key West. The bodice tucked in just beneath her breasts, the skirt was multilayered and swaths of chiffon crisscrossed over the shoulders, then trailed down her back, nearly touching her knees.

The inner skirt was a pale peach sheath that became filmier the longer it got. Over the sheath hung those countless layers of chiffon. It was a maternity dress, but it definitely didn't look like one.

"Oh, yes," the housekeeper murmured when she saw the dress. "He won't know what hit him."

When Kathleen realized the dress might throw Roman off balance, she began putting her whole heart into dressing. Ms. Rodriguez insisted that Kathleen bathe again, with some special bath oils she just happened to have in the kitchen. She pressed the dress—which Kathleen thought already looked fine—into absolute perfection, then returned to supervise how Kathleen should hold her curling iron and apply her makeup.

At one point Ms. Rodriguez cupped Kathleen's chin and turned her face from side to side. Then she sighed and said, "Shut your eyes."

Kathleen did, and felt the dabs of various makeup

brushes on her skin. She felt as though she were seated in the makeup chair at a cosmetics counter. For once she didn't fight the discomfort she usually felt at having someone pamper her. Her wedding might be a charade, but it was her special day nonetheless.

"I'm so glad we're doing this," Ms. Rodriguez said.

"What?"

"Don't move your mouth," the woman responded. "I'm going to fix your lips. All I meant was that I just couldn't be happier for you. Why, I knew as soon as I saw you that you were pregnant. Everybody else is just as excited as I am."

Kathleen's eyes flew open. "Everybody else?"

"Shut your eyes," Ms. Rodriguez commanded. "You'll ruin your liner."

Kathleen shut her eyes again. "Everybody who?"

"Well, Mr. Flanders and Mr. Jenkenson. And the Krauses—Jerry and Inge—who help out with the horses, you know. And then there're those extra hands Roman brought down—George Roy and his wife, Kelly, and that sweet fellow Johnny Walker and—"

Kathleen's eyes opened wide. "They're coming to my wedding?"

Ms. Rodriguez smiled down at her. "Why, I'd expect so."

With that, Ms. Rodriguez marched her to a mirror. Kathleen turned toward the housekeeper, meaning to tell her in no uncertain terms that this marriage was one of legal convenience and nothing more. But somehow, she couldn't.

Ms. Rodriguez was dressed for the wedding, too. Kathleen's own mother could not have been more excited. And anyway, once bedtime came, there'd be no doubt in anyone's mind that she was going straight to her own room while Roman went to his, Kathleen thought with a twinge of sadness.

"You look positively gorgeous, Kathleen."

Kathleen was sure she looked more beautiful than she ever had. The dress hung perfectly, accentuating all her new curves, and her skin glowed with health. The curls framing her face made her look more mature and more womanly. At twenty-eight, with her short hair and small-boned body, she generally looked even younger than she really was. Now no one, not even Roman, would dare call her cute. Ms. Rodriguez was probably right when she'd said that Roman wouldn't know what had hit him.

A knock sounded at the door. Kathleen gulped nervously. Was it Roman?

"Ms. Rodriguez," Mr. Flanders called from the hallway. "I must speak with you immediately."

"Everything will be ready in fifteen more minutes. I'll be back for you." She glanced toward the door. "I'm coming Mr. Flanders."

"He's giving you away," Ms. Rodriguez explained to Kathleen. "We have chairs for the guests arranged and your bouquet's downstairs in the fridge."

"What's going on here?" Kathleen managed to say as she watched the housekeeper head for the door. It had been her understanding that she and Roman were to meet Miles Higgenbothem in the library just as soon as the blood tests were okayed by a lab in Key West. And then, they were only going to put their John Hancocks on a couple of sheets of paper.

"You're getting married at sunset," the woman called over her shoulder. "By the ocean."

IN THE HALLWAY, FLANDERS pulled the housekeeper toward an alcove. Her hands immediately flew upward and encircled his neck. He brushed a stray lock of hair from her forehead and said, "You look bloody fabulous, Angelina." Then he lowered his head and planted a soul-searing kiss on her lips.

When he leaned back he whispered conspiratorially. "So, my dear, did you manage to get Kathleen in some kind of dress?"

"Oh, Colin, I did!" she said, squeezing his shoulder. "Did you get that fool Roman into his tux?"

He laughed. "My dear, that was simple. I merely told him that Kathleen was dressing to the nines. He hopped in that tux faster than you could say boo. And really, I think he was just looking for an excuse to wear it."

He swung her around so that she faced him. "So, when are you going to marry me? I mean it, Angel."

She tossed her head and her eyes flashed. "I'll let you know when I'm ready," she returned playfully.

He smiled. "Well, in the meantime, would you like to spend our next day off bird-watching on Marathon Key?"

"Sure," she said, placing her hand beneath his elbow and pulling him toward the other end of the hall. "Oh!" she said suddenly. "I made Kathleen bathe in a love potion. It contained special spices and oils and—"

He chuckled. "Angelina," he said, "it astounds me that you actually believe in such things."

"One of my grandmothers was Bahamian," she said a little huffily. "And she swore by it." She clucked her tongue. "I told you she wasn't sick and that she was pregnant, now, didn't I? A name-only marriage," she continued. "I never heard of such a thing."

''I've heard of it,'' he offered. ''But I think it's ridiculous.'' He paused. ''Did Kathleen tell you they weren't *really* getting married?''

''No, of course not.''

''Did you get rid of all the extra linens and beds you could?''

''I had all the mattresses hauled away from the guest rooms this morning,'' she said. ''I told Roman they were in terrible condition and had to be replaced. And as soon as Kathleen leaves her room, I'm going to strip her bed.''

Mr. Flanders grinned at her and released her arm when he reached Roman's door. ''Bye, Angel,'' he whispered.

''Do you, Kathleen, take Roman to be your lawful wedded husband?''

Something has gone terribly wrong. Everything about Roman told her she'd been had. The teasing glint was back in his eyes, the lopsided smirk didn't once leave his face, and even if his shining dare-you-to-touch-me hair was combed to perfection, the man was wearing bright red high-topped sneakers with his tux. *Roman never wears sneakers!*

She felt him elbow her side. She heard the minister clear his throat. And she couldn't say a word, not to save her life.

She stared at Roman. He smiled back in a way she couldn't quite interpret. Did he assume she'd lost her nerve? Wasn't *she* calling *his* bluff?

Roman turned to the minister. ''She does,'' he said confidently.

The minister lowered his voice. ''*She* has to say so,'' he whispered.

Kathleen felt the eyes of the guests, who were congregated behind her. They were seated on lovely white benches, the ends of which were tied with large white bows. The sunset really was perfect, too, setting in strips of otherworldly color.

Suddenly Kathleen felt as if she was falling into some deep abyss. They'd all gone mad! What in the world was happening here? But no...she was standing in front of a podium, a minister was behind the podium and Roman was beside her.

She clutched her bouquet so tightly that a petal fell off and drifted to the ground.

"Do you take Roman to be your husband?" the minister whispered more insistently.

No! She wanted to say that this marriage to Roman was such a complete mockery that she couldn't go through with it. She wanted to continue to dream that she'd find a real soul mate, a man with whom she could spend her entire life.

The minister raised his voice and repeated himself, as if she hadn't heard. "Do you, Kathleen, take Roman to be your law—"

"Yes," she managed to interject. The word quivered with uncertainty. She forced herself to steady her voice, adding, "I do." *Why does the woman always have to answer first? Now I'm at his mercy!* The minister continued speaking.

Roman's luscious mouth curved in a soft, sweet smile. Suddenly he didn't look rascally at all...just kind and almost loving.

The kiss, she thought as she stared at those wide, full lips.

Strategy. She would dip in quickly and smack him with a cheek peck. Such a maneuver would let him know that she had the upper hand once again. And that whatever sensual mischief she saw in his eyes would fail.

"Do you, Roman, take Kathleen to be your lawful wedded wife?"

Kathleen was thoroughly unprepared when Roman turned her. His lips were slightly parted and looked a little dry. He licked them lightly.

"Roman?" the minister asked.

He's going to reject me. Again. As embarrassing as it would be, she nearly sagged against him in sheer relief.

Suddenly, for the briefest hint of a moment, his features relaxed even more. He looked just a tad less reckless, just a touch less cavalier. He merely gazed at her, deep into her eyes, with a look of pure long-suffering caring and desire. And then it vanished without a trace.

"I do," he said, not even bothering to hide the irony that crept into his voice.

"The ring," the minister said.

Roman reached down slowly and disengaged her left hand from the bouquet of roses. His hand was deeply tanned and so large that, for an instant, she lost sight of her own.

What ring? she wondered.

In a swift movement Roman slid a band of gold on her finger. It was just a whisper-thin slender band, with no adornment. Glancing down at it, though, Kathleen thought it was beautiful. Roman, no matter what his real feelings for her had given it to her. He was really her husband now. For better or for worse.

Had she gone completely crazy? Was she really waxing romantic over Roman Lawrence again? She hazarded a glance into his eyes. They were the same old eyes that she'd seen exactly seventeen times before she'd returned to Lawrence Island. They were as dark as the deepest ocean…just as unfathomable and a little scary. And yet, they were as enticing and exciting as the sea, too, inviting adventure.

"You may kiss the bride."

Neither of them moved. Why had she agreed so rashly to this foolhardy marriage? Kathleen wondered. Had it been to call Roman's bluff? Had it been to find a father for her baby, even when she knew she was perfectly capable of raising a child on her own? Had it been to shock him into noticing her again, after he'd ignored her for mere weeks? Suddenly she knew all those reasons were ridiculous.

I'm marrying him because I want to. Because I have always wanted to marry Roman Lawrence! The thought shot through her mind and her mouth dropped open in shock.

The minister cleared his throat. "Please kiss the bride."

Now, she thought. She was supposed to hop up and kiss him quickly on the cheek, just to get it over with.

But she couldn't move. *I have always wanted to marry Roman Lawrence!*

His arm snaked behind her back. One of his hands fluttered across the layers of chiffon. The warmth of his fingers and palms increased their pressure at the small of her spine.

Her gaze flew upward, toward his eyes, but made no contact. She glanced toward Ms. Rodriguez, as if the woman might help her, but she just beamed her thousand-watt smile back at Kathleen. Then Roman nestled one of his legs in between hers and bent her swiftly backward. Kathleen gasped.

I'm marrying him simply because I love him. Or could…if he was just a little kinder. And yet, the fact that he was thinking about her baby *was* kind. Wasn't it? Her mouth remained slightly ajar, since she was still attempting to swallow that fact. The members of the small group of assembled guests began to applaud.

She glanced into Roman's face at the exact moment his mouth covered hers. The second their lips met, all preliminaries ended. She was bent over backward, with her eyes wide open. She was thoroughly pinned between the hard, solid, well-muscled lengths of his lean, strong thighs, and his tongue thrust her mouth open with a heat and fury so intense that she couldn't respond. And then he continued to seek out all the flavor of her with a kiss that was every bit as naughty as it was sweet and every bit as sinful as it was soft.

We're married! The phrase played over and over in her mind, while his free hand moved to support her head. As he drew her closer, his thigh fell at the juncture of her legs, and her back naturally arched upward. Her soft stomach pressed against the taut hardness of his.

And all the while, he intensified the pressure of his kiss, his tongue warming her mouth. The taste of him reminded her faintly of salt and oranges and hot honey. He explored every inch of her lips, her teeth, her tongue…as if he were already attuned to every nuance of her body, and as if his total possession of her was so assured that no one could ever contest it.

Kathleen wanted to say that she couldn't breathe. She wanted to say that her heart was thudding inside her. Instead, a moan rose in her throat and his lips, racing over her own, caught the sound. *My husband is kissing me,* she thought. She tried to remember how to breathe as she shut her eyes.

When she opened them again, the whole world had gone white. There was no Ms. Rodriguez, no Mr. Flanders, no guests. Only bright white light and the faraway sense that Roman was holding her as if he'd never let her go.

And then, while the onlookers still applauded, Kathleen fainted in Roman's embrace.

ROMAN SWEPT HIS NEW BRIDE into his arms, the soft chiffon of her dress teasing his skin. Kathleen looked so lovely that she had taken his breath away completely. He wanted nothing more than to slide his hands upward through all those sheer, filmy layers of fabric and touch her skin. He wanted to take off her sparkling beaded flats, one by one, and cup her slender feet in his hands. Instead he strode swiftly toward the benches and laid Kathleen gingerly on her back.

"Oh, darlin', what did I just do?" he murmured. "Are you all right?"

He was only vaguely aware that Ms. Rodriguez had leaned over him and begun to treat Kathleen with some Bahamian version of smelling salts that she had handy, just as if she'd expected this to happen.

Was Kathleen all right? Was the baby? What had just come over him? He'd intended to take full advantage of the ceremony in order to kiss her as she'd never been kissed before, but he hadn't expected to completely forget his surroundings. For a moment, though, he had actually felt as if they were absolutely alone. They'd gone to some never-never land of half sleeping and half waking, where there were no thoughts and where all his most daring dreams about Kathleen were coming true.

He told himself it was only because of the baby, but he could swear it had something to do with her skin, too. Its scent reminded him of spices, tropical flowers and saffron. Every time he'd leaned toward her, those scents had driven him wild.

Her dress had made him just as crazy. She was so incredibly unpredictable. That she would faint was the very last thing he'd ever suspected. He leaned closer and softly rubbed Kathleen's forehead. Why wasn't she coming around? In spite of her newly achieved suntan, she was still as white as a ghost.

His eyes traveled down the length of her body and rested on her legs. Her beautiful dress was hiked up, exposing the creamy inner skin of one of her thighs. Since she was lying on her back, the dress molded gently against the growing curve of her stomach. He felt his mouth go dry and he swallowed. Hard.

Suddenly he hoped it took her a good few minutes to come to, long enough for him to regain his own equilibrium. Hell, he'd shocked her so badly that she hadn't even resisted. Nor had she responded. He'd kissed her before, but never like that. In fact, as many women as he'd kissed, he'd never kissed *anybody* like that. He swallowed again.

Just as Kathleen's eyelids started to flutter, Flanders clapped him on the back. "Jolly good, sir!" he exclaimed. "As soon as Kathleen, uh, recovers, you two are to go to the west side of the patio. We all have a surprise waiting for you."

Roman glanced at the man quickly, too worried about Kathleen to give him his full attention. "That's awfully nice of you, Flanders, but—"

"No buts."

That figured. Flanders hadn't allowed him a single protest all day. And Roman knew very well that this whole charade—the perfect dress, the bouquet, the minister and the ring—was hardly Kathleen's idea.

When Roman turned back to Kathleen, Ms. Rodriguez was helping her to a sitting position. Why did the mother of his child have to look so damnably, beautifully bewildered? Her birdlike hands fluttered downward, looking for the bench, her heavy-lidded eyes blinked slowly and her sparkling beaded flats toed at the ground.

Briefly he wondered at how juvenile they could act when they were around each other. It was as if every time he saw her, he regressed. He had had countless mature relationships with women, including his ex-wife, but when it came to Kathleen he felt like a taunting, teasing, naughty little schoolboy…the kind who put mean surprises in a girl's lunch box and then went home and dreamed about her all night long. And this time the effect had been to make her pass out.

Kathleen had come around enough to start glaring at him. And her look made it pretty clear that both she and the baby were fine. Realizing that, he couldn't help but chuckle. After all, he'd gotten her pregnant on a first try and when he kissed her, the woman fainted. He felt a pure rush of male ego, even though her flashing eyes had narrowed to slits. His chuckle tempered to a lopsided grin.

For the first time he realized that the wedding guests were disappearing. Probably part of the surprise to which Flanders had referred. Undoubtedly a reception. Even Ms. Rodriguez had bolted the moment Kathleen opened her eyes, as if she had something important to do.

He hooked his hand beneath Kathleen's elbow and helped her to her feet. She stumbled into him and he took advantage of the situation by putting his arm around her. The shapely curve of her shoulder molded perfectly to the cup of his hand. She backed away until he squeezed, stopping her.

"I don't need your help, Roman." There was more spicy sauce in that voice than could be found in whole bottles of salsa.

"Why, I'm just concerned about you, darlin'," he managed to return playfully, wishing that she wasn't mad at him. He leaned toward one of the dangling white pearls that swung from her ear by a delicate chain. He wanted nothing more than to catch that pearl between his teeth and tug ever so lightly.

"But I think we should call Dr. Peteck. I mean, passing out like that might not be good for the baby."

"My baby's fine," she returned, shrugging out of his near embrace. Her rejection stung far more than he wanted to admit.

"*Our* baby," he said, shoving his hands deep into the pockets of his trousers. He was going to be a father now, and he couldn't allow Kathleen to take that from him, not even verbally.

He ignored her when she sent him a pert, pursed-lip stare, and nodded toward the château. "Flanders says we're supposed to go to the west patio." He started walking away from the floodlights on the beach, toward the darkness of the trees. She could follow him if she wanted.

"Don't try to change the subject."

He glanced over his shoulder, seeing that she'd begun walking, too. "What was the subject?"

She didn't reply at first, just smoothed that fabulous dress she was wearing. "I suppose you feel proud of yourself!"

He turned around. It was nearly full dark, and the sun was down, but he could see how her green eyes lit up and flashed. They looked more yellow than green, as if they were reflecting the light from her now golden, tanned skin.

He forced his hands deeper into his pockets. He hoped he looked casual, since everything about her— her passionate anger, her delicate dress, her lively eyes—was turning him on. She started walking. And she walked right past him.

"You mean, proud of myself for making you pass out with my overpowering…" His mouth went dry and he let his words trail off, knowing Kathleen could fill in the blanks. He didn't want to talk. He wanted to stare at the tiny bones of her back. The two long swaths of chiffon hung over either shoulder and sashayed, just sweeping at the soft-looking skin at the backs of her knees. He followed her into the ever-thickening darkness of the trees.

She suddenly stopped dead in her tracks. "Roman Lawrence, I passed out because it was hot," she called haughtily over her shoulder. She started walking again. Those two long, seductive-looking chiffon trailers started sashaying in time with her hips again.

Sure was hot, he thought as he followed her. "Regarding the weather, it's ten at night," he said aloud, his voice rising, just like the temperature he felt deep in his bones. "And only seventy-five degrees."

"Seventy-five's pretty hot," she called coyly. "And

if you're so concerned about my condition, you should never have…" He could almost hear her gulp.

"Kissed you?" *Go ahead and say it, Kathleen. I kissed you, and it felt right. We feel so right together.*

"Yes." She glanced over her shoulder and speeded her steps.

"Are you going to insist on being snappish all night?" he asked, hurrying his own steps and still taking in that gorgeous back of hers.

"Like you said," she finally responded. "It's ten o'clock."

"And?" He was hardly going to run, but he was now catching up to her and he lowered his voice. He winced when it came out raspier than he'd intended.

"And the night's over," she said. She speeded her steps again, outdistancing him by a few paces.

"Now, Kathleen—" Before he even realized he was going to do it, he leaned agilely and caught an end of a chiffon swath. In his hand the fabric felt as light as air and as sensually soft on his skin as a light spring rain. She simply stood still for a moment, her head tilting ever so slightly on her long slender neck, as if she might turn around.

She glanced over her shoulder at where he wrapped the edge of the trailer around his hand, then she turned and kept walking until it was pulled taut and she had to stop. The chiffon created a bridge of peachy gauze between her shoulder and his hand.

She smiled tightly over her shoulder. He wondered if she knew how that particular saucy smile both annoyed and invited him.

He grinned recklessly, daring her with his eyes, and looped the filmy, transparent trailing swath over his palm a second time, wishing she'd let him keep looping

it, again and again, until she was in his arms. But she
wouldn't. Not that he wouldn't do it, anyway, but it
would be so much sweeter if she let him…when she
let him.

"Now, darlin'," he said persuasively. "We can't
disappoint everybody."

"Everybody?"

He took a gamble and looped the trailer in his hand
yet again, this time forcing her to turn. She took a tiny
step toward him. He could hear hard-edged desire in
his own voice. He had no trouble admitting that he
wanted her, but suddenly what he felt was a little more
complex.

"I think they're having—" he slowly twisted the
fabric again, turning it over with the same dexterity he
exercised on reins when he rode "—a party for us."
Another of those beaded flats rose and fell in a step.
And then he wound the fabric over his hand…again
and again.

She was just two paces from him now, beneath a
gumbo-limbo tree that grew up against the outer stone
wall of the château. His nostrils flared slightly. Twining
flowering vines grew against the stone wall, too, and
their pungent odor combined with the wafting scent of
her perfume and the sumptuous beauty of her dress
were too much for him.

He tugged the trailer of the chiffon, not stopping
until her face was nearly pressed to his pleated white
shirtfront.

What exactly was he doing? Days before, he'd had
such a clear idea. It had seemed like such a rational
plan. It had something to do with marrying this woman
just so he could divorce her, something to do with seducing her as some kind of payback, and then taking

their baby away from her. Looking at her now, he couldn't imagine doing so. Now the whole plan seemed so crazy that he couldn't believe he'd actually thought it up. He lowered his face toward hers. His lips were just the merest whisper away from hers.

"I'll be civil if you will," she said, her voice sounding raspy and low. "But only because I have no intention of upsetting our guests," she added quickly. "I'll even momentarily forget the way you took it upon yourself to ignore our whole agreement."

"I married you," he replied, thinking that was more than a lot of men would have done under the circumstances. "So what exact part did I ignore?"

"The hands-off part."

"Did you really expect me not to kiss you?" With her so close he was half sure he was about to do it again. "I mean, there were all those people…"

"Well…" She paused as if considering. "I guess you had to."

Good, he thought, trying to tell himself that her rejection didn't sting at all. He really did hope that she thought that was why he'd kissed her the way he had. Almost against his will he dropped the chiffon trailer in his hand, hooked his fingers beneath her elbow again and began leading her to the patio.

"I really didn't see any way out of it, Kathleen. I mean, once we go our own ways, then people will get the general idea. But we don't want them to think things aren't working out right off. When I start seeing other women…"

Her mouth was slowly dropping. "Once you start seeing other women? I mean, am I keeping you from seeing someone right now?"

He threw his arms out carelessly in a gesture of

devil-may-care knavery. "Oh, c'mon, Kathleen. You really don't expect me to live the rest of my life without making love. Do you?"

It was dark, but he was fairly sure she'd colored at that.

"Of course not," she said quickly. She paused. "No more than I intend to live without…paramours."

"Para-what?" He threw his head back and laughed. "Is that kind of like paralegals? As in not ready for the full job?"

"No," she snapped. "Para as in parachute. As in something very exciting."

"Sorry I'm not more exciting, darlin'," he drawled, feeling more than a little offended.

"Why did we even stop out here?" she asked. She sighed softly. "So that we could bait each other and trade snide remarks?"

His laughter tempered to a wry chuckle. No, they'd stopped out there because he wanted to kiss her. Because he wanted to feel her kissing him back. "I guess we don't have to stop for that," he finally said.

"Oh, no," she remarked. "Now that we're married we've got a whole lifetime of it ahead of us."

In the darkness of the night a scowl suddenly replaced Roman's smile. *Don't forget that you're divorcing her.* With that knowledge firmly in mind again, he breathed a sigh of relief. No, they wouldn't fight all the time. He wouldn't fall in love with her, either. And it was only a matter of time until she gave in to his kisses. He could feel it in his bones. He had that to look forward to, even though his loving would only be temporary.

In spite of those thoughts, he turned her to face him again. "Kathleen," he said seriously. "Couldn't we try to get along?'' Her lips parted and her eyes grew wide, making him wish she didn't look so shocked. What kind of monster did she think he was?

"Do you really mean that, Roman?" she asked softly.

He nodded. "Yeah, I do."

"I think I'd like that," she nearly whispered.

He smiled and cocked his head toward the soft lights of the patio. And when he put his arm around her shoulder and headed in that direction he noted with satisfaction that she didn't try to move away.

Chapter Six

They were the only people at the party, and the patio looked so wonderfully romantic that Kathleen sucked in a quick, quavering breath.

Roman simply smiled and said, "We may as well eat, darlin'. After all, everybody's gone to a lot of trouble on our account."

"I suppose we may as well," Kathleen agreed as Roman seated her.

And they did. Salmon steaks, cooked to perfection in a light mustard sauce and served with wild rice and crisp green beans. Arugula and endives lightly tossed with spiced oil. Everything was served at a small table for two that had been laid on the white-columned, pavilioned area of the west patio, lit only by romantic candles and five-foot brass torches whose flames were fueled by kerosene, while a ten-piece orchestra played softly from the shadows.

The meal had mellowed Kathleen, and she felt relaxed. "That was so good." She stretched in her chair just as Flanders took away her plate.

Roman's breath caught in his throat. "Sure was." He watched her hands clasp lightly behind her slender neck, then break apart again as her arms stretched heavenward. Her breasts heaved when she sighed contentedly. Behind her, fireflies sparked, nestled in the island trees.

"Incredibly delicious, darlin'," he said gently, referring to her figure, as much as the meal. Her body was becoming so lusciously womanly during her pregnancy that he couldn't help but wonder how she'd look months from now. "More sparkling apple juice?"

"Sure." Kathleen proffered her champagne flute, thinking it was sweet of Roman not to indulge in wine at dinner, since she herself had none.

"A toast," he said, filling her glass and then his own. A smile he could only construe as seductive played at her lips. His gaze followed hers over the table's centerpiece. Hard, round brown coconuts sat in the center of a flower-and-fruit arrangement. Small green Annonas, brown sapodillas, red mangoes and pink West Indian cherries were punctuated by sprigs of coconut blossoms.

Kathleen lifted her glass and her gaze. During dinner she'd let her mind run wild. It was so easy to pretend that this was a real honeymoon night. Roman was her new, loving husband, and she was a woman in love. They were slowly gearing up for a night of lovemaking, where she would feel—really feel—what it was like to respond completely to a man.

"So, what should we toast to?" she asked, lowering her voice to a soft whisper.

"To a new mother," he said, his own voice gentling to an almost rasp.

Kathleen watched the tux sleeves tighten over his muscular arms as he leaned forward and rested his elbows on the table. The shadows shifted with the candle flames, moving delicately over the planes and hollows

of his face and making the silver streak in his raven
hair shine with light. Beautiful wasn't usually a term
used to describe men, but Roman—with his jet-black
hair and bronzed, sculptured-looking features—was
certainly that.

"To you, Kathleen…" He lifted his glass and leaned
forward. Even though the orchestra was playing softly,
the clink of their glasses seemed to be the only sound.
They sounded like bells…wedding bells.

"To you…" Roman's lips parted lightly. His gaze
lowered from her eyes and boldly took in her breasts.
She'd grown heavy and full and so undeniably touch-
able.…

"Thank you, Roman," she managed to say just before she brought her glass to her lips. Lights from the
flaming candles literally danced across his lips. The
lights made his black hair look even darker and the
streak look even more silver so that it almost appeared
pure white. And his eyes, she thought. *Those eyes.*
Large and round and fringed with dark, thick, luscious
lashes. His pupils were so black that they nearly
gleamed blue.

"To the mother of my child," Roman continued,
before sipping from his crystal flute.

Kathleen smiled back at him weakly. His child?
Could things possibly work out between them? "To
us," she said softly, trying to tell herself that Roman
didn't really mean *his child* in any significant way. It
was his child, as in his heir.

She was gazing so deeply into Roman's eyes that
she barely realized she'd placed her glass on the table-
cloth again, or that Flanders had placed cups of strong
Cuban coffee in front of them both. Kathleen managed
to ignore hers, knowing that Roman wouldn't want her

to have it. Besides, as good as it might taste, it wasn't the best thing for the baby. Somehow, the way Roman was watching over her lately made it easy to do all the right things.

Roman cleared his throat, took a sip of his steaming coffee and fought back the shudder that crept up his back and neck. He'd heard the phrase *trembling with longing,* but he'd never actually felt such a sneaking tingle of awareness. He took yet another sip as if to dispel the effect Kathleen was having on him. Still, each of her gestures—whether she sighed or leaned forward or stretched or merely gazed at him—seemed fraught with meaning. Every blessed movement said, *Make love to me, Roman.*

He cleared his throat again, enjoying the heady, sensually charged feeling that permeated all his limbs, but wanting the feelings to leave him nonetheless. This was all just a ploy to get his island back and get custody of his child.

"I told Van Ness I'd give him the ring," Roman said, hoping against hope that the topic would break his mood.

He still wasn't sure how he meant to play the end of this evening. Should he seduce her? Lead her to the edge of longing, then retreat? Either way, looking at her muddled his mind. Why did dealing with the woman make him try tactical strategies even Machiavelli would have shunned? He wanted to seduce her, all right. But, somehow, at the prospect—even if he could coerce her to agree—he felt incredibly guilty.

At the moment he didn't want to get back at her or hurt her. He just wanted her. And he couldn't imagine taking their child from her. Just the day before, he'd watched her study a dietary information pamphlet as if she were studying for the Florida bar exam. She'd been reading so intently that she hadn't even noticed him watching her. She loved their child so much that he knew what he was planning would break her heart... and he was becoming sure he couldn't do it.

"You'll return the ring for me?" Kathleen finally asked. She glanced down at the diamond on her finger. The Van Ness jewel was gorgeous. *So much for wishing for a real husband and ring.* Of course, she still had Roman's wedding band, even if it didn't signify a real marriage. She slid off the Van Ness diamond.

"I was afraid to take it off, for fear I'd lose it," she said.

Roman watched the various expressions cross her face as she handed him Van Ness's ring. For a second she looked so sad he wanted to hold her tightly in his arms.

"I'd appreciate it if you'd give it back to him," she said. "I really—" She'd meant to say that she didn't want to talk to Van Ness personally, but cut off her words. Van Ness was a touchy subject for her, and she didn't want to ruin her evening—her fantasies—by discussing him.

When Mr. Flanders set two tiny glass bowls of gleaming Italian ices in front of Kathleen and Roman, Roman gave him the ring. "Here, could you put this in the library safe?"

Roman turned back to Kathleen, who was daintily eating her dessert. For the first time he wondered if the ring signified a broken engagement. Van Ness had said Kathleen had borrowed it, but the look on her face said otherwise. *Heaven help me if she loves that fool Van Ness.* He shoved the thought away, desperately trying to deny how he was beginning to feel about her.

Vaguely Roman wondered what Kathleen's taste in men really was. If there was some connection between French chefs, florists and playboys, Roman couldn't fathom it.

He began to eat his own dessert, while the silence stretched between them. As nice as their dinner had been once they'd established an unspoken truce, he half wished they were trading barbs. The spark in her eyes when she was mad was preferable to this awkward silence.

Hell, there were other kinds of quiet he would gladly share with Kathleen. Like the kind of relaxed, satisfied contentment he felt after making love...when nothing else in the world seemed to matter except the woman by his side. Staring at the top of her head, into the soft curls that framed her forehead, he watched her sip her juice then polish off the last of her ice cream.

She even turned up her spoon when she was finished, and her tongue darted out to lick the tip of it, as if just to send him straight into agony again.

"C'mon, darlin'," he said suddenly. "Let's lighten up."

"I'm fine," she murmured. Oh, why couldn't every evening between them be this pleasant? If only she could trust him....

"You look like you lost your best friend," he teased. When she laughed, her voice sounded like a million tinkling bells.

"C'mon, let's dance." He knew it wasn't wise, not with the way she was making him feel. He hadn't wanted to start feeling as if he was falling in love, he'd just wanted to seduce her. He tried to tell himself he wouldn't be feeling this way if she wasn't pregnant with his child.

"They're playing a waltz now." She smiled. "Who do you think I am? Ginger Rogers?"

He raised a brow flirtatiously. "You don't have to be."

"Why's that?" Her white-blond brows arched.

"Because—" He lifted one of his red-sneaker-clad feet. "There's enough Fred Astaire in these shoes for the both of us."

Kathleen glanced down at the red high top. "The sneakers are a little...flamboyant." She fought it, but a flush crept over her cheeks. Damn Roman's capacity for being so dangerously romantic, she thought as he rose lithely, came to her side of the table and bent to a near kneel, proffering his hand in a mock-courtly gesture. With just one gesture he could make her feel like the lady of the realm—when he wanted to, anyway.

She placed her hand in his, unable to wipe the silly smile from her face. If she could trust the man, believe that he really wanted her and her baby as much as his actions said he did, then she could really fall in love with him.

He led her to an open space of the pavilioned patio and whirled her to face him in front of the orchestra. He lightly touched a layer of the chiffon that formed her skirt, then nestled his palm against her waist, his hand molding perfectly against her hip. She smiled shyly and placed a hand on his shoulder. When their free hands met she breathed in sharply. Rather than let her hand rest in his palm, Roman twined his fingers tightly in hers.

Her heart began to pound. Her skin began to color. She forced herself to smile broadly, in what she hoped was a merely friendly fashion. When it came to actually touching Roman, she assured herself that her little fantasies about him as husband had to come to an end.

"So now what?" she asked lightly. "You know I don't have a clue about how to waltz." *No, I was nothing more than a maid's daughter, except the two years my mother was married to Augustine.*

"Just stand on my feet, darlin'." His lips were dangerously close to her cheek.

"You've got on sneakers. I'll crush—"

Roman pulled her forward slightly, so that she nearly fell off balance. She clutched his shoulder. He chuckled, his eyes twinkling with mischief. "Somehow I don't think you're going to crush me."

"But I've gained—" She gulped, suddenly feeling far too physically close to him. She could smell the fresh, clean traces of soap and shampoo and feel the quivering strains of muscles in his hands.

"The weight looks good on you." *Damn good.* More than he could even find the words to say it with. He felt driven to hold her, to touch every blessed new curve of her flesh. His desire for her kept coming in pulling waves, like a relentless tide.

"Thank you," she managed to say. Her mouth went dry and she swallowed. Not knowing what else to do, she stepped her beaded flats, one by one, onto the tops of his feet. The movement unbalanced her even more but not nearly as much as the pure masculine scent of his skin. To maintain her stance she pressed her cheek lightly against his chest and clutched his shoulder more tightly.

Step, one-two. Step, one-two, she thought illogically as he began to waltz in circles. He stepped and whirled her in movements more graceful than any man's had a right to be. How could a man who was so broad in the chest, so muscular and tall, move so lithely? She told herself not to forget, not even for an instant, that his movements were graceful...the way a panther's were.

He leaned closer, right by her ear, and whispered, "Not bad, huh?" He nestled his cheek against hers, wanting just for a second to feel the softness of her glowing skin against his.

"Oh, no," she breathed, deeply wishing that some other man, some other time, had guided her body with such gallant expertise, just so that she wouldn't sound quite so overwhelmed now.

Roman wondered again what undefinable scent it was that she was wearing. Whatever it was could drive him mad even if her enticing body wasn't pressed so close to his. He lengthened his strides, in time with the quickening music, and drew her even closer. He could swear he felt her thighs quiver against his as he stepped backward, simultaneously pulling her forward, so that her body nearly stretched over the length of him.

Roman was spinning her too fast! He stepped and turned and dipped in ever wider circles. She was sure she'd faint again. Her breath came in small, quiet gasps. The long transparent trailers of chiffon over her shoulders had blown outward with vertigo, so far that she could catch glimpses of them wafting around his shoulders.

"We should stop," she finally said breathlessly. The words were barely audible. "I'm getting winded."

"One more spin and we'll stop," he murmured, his arm tightening around the line of her growing waist. His hand had become warm, his whole body heated by the feel of her and by exertion. Layers of chiffon lifted and fell and whirled, the transparent film teasing his skin.

"Stop," she whispered.

The emotion in her voice was unmistakable.

Roman heard it.

Kathleen heard it.

He spun into a last, graceful dipping arc, but it never ended. Kathleen only felt herself spiral like a feather. She was whirling in the circle, following his lead, but her feet had magically disconnected. She simply floated upward in space, turning in weightless circles like an astronaut. Gravity ceased to exist...and the sensation was positively surreal.

What was happening? She was caught in an envelope of chiffon, and she felt as if she was on a cloud! And then she realized that Roman had lifted her into his arms...and that he was swiftly carrying her from the room.

"Roman, this has gone too far," she managed to say in a small voice when they'd reached the stairs.

He felt a tiny rush of temper. Did the woman think he'd make love to her if she didn't want him to? He took the steps two at a time, Kathleen feeling as light as air. Her head curled into his shoulder and his cheek rested against her curls.

"That's more like it," he whispered.

"More like what?" she breathed.

"Nothing," he said gruffly.

"*Roman,*" Kathleen whispered censoriously. In spite of her tone she couldn't help but shut her eyes. She forgot the hand-carved wood of the banister and the red runner that covered the steps and gave into her fantasies. For a second. Because this was just exactly how things were meant to be. She was supposed to be lifted gently into a man's strong arms and carried up a staircase....

In the hallway she opened her eyes again, just in time to see Roman kick in the door to the bedroom. *His bedroom.* "No!" Her voice gained resolve.

Unfortunately she was serious, Roman thought, involuntarily tightening his arm beneath her knees. He heard that just as clearly as he'd sensed the breathless desire in her voice before. Perhaps if he hadn't wanted her so badly he wouldn't have cared. But he wasn't about to start acting like a man begging for what he wanted. Like a man who cared too much. Like a man in love.

He spun her around, then plopped her unceremoniously onto the bed. He headed straight for his closet, glancing briefly over his shoulder. "That show ought to appease everybody downstairs," he said hoarsely.

When she didn't respond he sent her a wry half smile. She looked as if she wanted to kill him. He rifled through his closet. Finally he found what he was looking for—a peignoir set he'd once bought for his ex-wife but had never given her. The set was as black-lace sexy as it was beautiful and had just been too expensive to throw away.

"Here." He tossed it into Kathleen's lap. "Somebody left it."

She stared at him openmouthed, fighting the urge to ask just exactly who. "I'm not sleeping in here!" she exclaimed.

Roman stared right back at her, placing his hands on his hips. "Fine," he said. "But I didn't want everyone to know—"

"I don't care who knows," she managed.

He didn't either, really. He pointed to a door that led from his room and that was slightly ajar. "I figured we could set you up in my old office. We could put the crib and a cot for you in there.''

She scrutinized him from head to toe. Then she glanced toward the room. Her mouth dropped and she hopped off the bed, half-staggering toward the door, as if propelled by something outside herself. She switched on the light, then blinked, since her eyes stung a little. ''This is so…so wonderful.''

The room was empty of furniture, but it had recently been painted. The ceiling was midnight blue, and covered with bright yellow stars and constellations and planets, as if it were the sky. The walls were white but midway down became pale blue. Waves crested against the white at eye level and fish swam in the painted ocean. On one wall, beside the window, a small oasis had been painted, and a large palm tree swayed, as if it were bending in the breeze.

Why had Roman done such a thing? Did he really mean for her and the baby to sleep here? Was he really hoping he'd truly become her husband? She simply couldn't believe it. She cleared her throat and turned.

''Like it?''

''It's the most beautiful thing I've ever seen.'' Not trusting what was happening, not wanting to look too overwhelmed, Kathleen continued, ''You mean, it'll look like we've set the cot by the crib so that when the baby's born and we can't sleep, one of us can go in there, while the other gets some rest?'' Had Roman only done this for propriety's sake? So people would *think* they were really married and preparing for the baby's arrival?

Roman leaned against the closed French doors that led to his terrace, trying not to feel pleased that she liked the nursery. He shrugged as she turned off the light.

"Well…all right," she said a little shakily. "Later, you can do whatever you want, but tonight I think I should sleep in my room." She vaguely wondered at the fact that she'd conceded to move next door to him and to share a bathroom, but told herself she was just using that as leverage until she was safely in her own bedroom. Tonight. And yet, the nursery was so perfect and so inviting.

"Thank you for the offer of your girlfriend's nightgown, though," she forced herself to continue lightly as she headed for the door. She turned and glanced again at the gown, which she'd left on the bed. She had to admit that it was just as tastefully glamorous as it was risqué. "But it's a little skimpy for my taste."

"I'm sure you've got plenty of flannel in your own closet," he returned. "Floor length, with lots of buttons that go right up to your—" he shot her an unnerving grin "—chinny-chin-chin."

Kathleen felt a flash of temper. Everything had been so wonderfully romantic. Why did Roman have to go and ruin it all? Then there was the obvious statement that he thought she was a prude. "All right." She smiled sweetly. "The gown's not too skimpy for my taste, but I am picky about when and where I wear such things. And, of course, for whom."

"Of course." He was starting to feel downright surly. He watched her leave, her hips twitching and the chiffon trailers still sweeping the backs of her knees.

Moments later she was in his doorway again. "Roman?"

He merely raised his eyebrows.

"My mattress is standing against the wall." She turned on her heel and headed back to her room.

"Oh, really," he muttered, wanting to kill Ms. Rodriguez. He knew very well that she had something to do with Kathleen's mattress being moved.

She was at the doorway again. "Aren't you going to help me move it?"

"Why don't you ask Flanders?" Roman turned on his bedside lamp, stepped past her and turned off the overhead. He shrugged off his tux jacket and tossed it onto the sofa beside his closet.

"Fine," Kathleen said.

Roman watched in amazement as she crossed the room, pulled back the covers of his bed and got in it. She was still fully dressed. After a second her little beaded shoes popped out from the covers, one by one, and then she kicked them off. Her slender feet raced under the covers again.

"Don't undress and you sleep on top," she said. "I'm really tired. So good night."

Her eyes snapped shut.

Roman stared at her face for a long moment. "Don't act like such a virgin," he muttered. He'd wanted her to sleep here, but not like this. He kicked off his sneakers and began unbuttoning his shirt.

"I am not acting like a virgin," she said. The lights in the room were dim, but she couldn't have felt more self-conscious if he'd been staring at her under interrogation lights. She knew she should have asked Flanders for help, but just moments before, it had somehow seemed just as easy to lie here fully dressed and go right to sleep. She heard the snappy sound of cotton.

He's taking off his shirt! Soon he'll be taking off his pants! Suddenly she admitted that one of the main reasons she didn't want to sleep with Roman Lawrence was that she'd just die if he guessed how inexperienced she really was....

"You're still undressing," she managed to say haughtily, keeping her eyes squeezed shut.

"Kathleen," he said flatly, "I can't sleep in a tux. Besides, darlin', you've seen men's bodies before."

But she'd never done more than look when it came to a man's body like his. As well endowed as he was, making love with him might not even work. She kept her eyes squeezed tightly shut, hoping he'd get the point, that she merely intended to sleep. She even curled into a little ball on the edge of the bed as if to better make her position known.

She didn't hear a zipper, but she did hear something else coming off...socks? "Roman, most adult women have seen men's bodies. That doesn't give you license to strip. I mean, if everybody thought the way you do, half the human race would be walking around stark naked." She was pleased to note that she sounded far more calm than she felt. If not at all sleepy.

Roman chuckled. "Everybody walking around stark naked," he murmured. "Why, Kathleen, there's an idea."

Her eyes flew open. She turned in the bed, just enough to look over her shoulder. He was wearing only his trousers. "Just go to sleep, Roman," she snapped. "Please."

He smiled playfully as he stalked toward the bed. As she turned back around and shut her eyes, she felt the mattress depress on the opposite side. He lay flat on his back on top of the covers.

"'Night, darlin'." He switched off the lamp and the room was thrown into darkness.

"'Night," she mumbled, opening her eyes. After a few moments she could make out the door to the hallway. If she had any common sense she'd head right out and find somewhere to sleep. She shifted her gaze to the door of the nursery. Her eyes were adjusting, and she could make out the beautiful mural. She'd never seen such a lovely baby room, and more than anything she wanted to be able to fill it...with toys and lots of love. And with her baby.

Kathleen sighed and punched her pillow. She sure wasn't going to get any sleep tonight!

ROMAN WAS DREAMING of the seventeenth century. He was himself but also Fabian D'Agonistio, calling out to his mates, commanding them to lower the sails.

"Aye, aye, captain," his first mate called.

Roman braced his thigh against the rail of the ship and adjusted the lens of his telescope. The wind was so strong that his hat blew from his head and his white shirt billowed, flapping above his breeches like the sails overhead.

"Ye gods," he said. "It's a lass in the water." He pressed his thigh harder against the rail for support and twined his ankle around a rope.

Kathleen sucked in a sharp breath when she felt Roman's ankle twine around hers. Soft warmth pressed against her cheek and curled into her lower body. She raised one brow and squinted into the first light of dawn that shone through the curtains over the French doors.

She felt so sleepily warm that she hardly cared that her head was curved into the crook of Roman's shoulder or that her cheek was pressed against his naked chest. One of his arms lay over her shoulder and down her back, the hand curving around her hip. He was still on his back, but he'd turned slightly toward her. One of his long, lean, well-muscled legs lay between her own. Roman shifted, nuzzling against her hair. Glancing at his face, Kathleen smiled. It was clear that he was dreaming, and she wondered about what.

Roman sighed deeply and snuggled even closer to Kathleen.

"You won't leave a lass to float, will ye, sir?" his mate was asking in his dream.

"Certainly not this lass," Roman replied, seeing her long, slender arm rise and fall in the water. He tightened the grip of his hand on the ship's rail.

"But, sir, those are shark-infested waters!" his mate was protesting.

Roman stripped to the waist. "Chilly, too, sir, but I do intend to save the wench. Lay down the plank."

When the plank was laid, Roman ran the length of it and dived.

Still gazing at Roman's face, Kathleen felt the warmth of his hand press more tightly against her waist. During the night she'd gotten used to it. She had awakened countless times, carefully scooting away from him, gently lifting one of his arms. Or she'd awaken, becoming vaguely aware that he was surreptitiously moving his hand from her waist and shoving it beneath his pillow. No matter which way they'd moved, they'd ended up in each other's arms again. Now she wondered if whatever he was dreaming was connected to the way he moved against her and held her.

Kathleen raised herself gently on her elbow to begin the work of disentangling herself. She glanced into his face again and stopped moving. His eyelids were twitching but his face was so relaxed and his thickly lashed eyes so gently closed that she couldn't help but stare.

Her eyes moved over the long, straight bridge of his nose and the flat, strong, high cheekbones to the shallows of his evenly bronzed cheeks, then lingered on his lips. In sleep his lips formed a slight smile. Whatever he was dreaming, it was something truly wonderful. His grasp on her hip tightened again.

In his dream Roman breathed in the salty scent of the woman's skin.

"Don't worry, my lass, and don't struggle. I have you. I'll swim you to my ship."

The razor-sharp blade of a shark's fin surfaced. "And swim fast, I will."

Kathleen chuckled softly. Clearly Roman had no idea what he was doing. His hand gently rubbed back and forth on her hip and Kathleen's eyes trailed downward, over the glowing skin of his chest. The black curling hairs looked so soft she wanted nothing more than to reach out and touch them. When her gaze reached the waistband of his trousers she breathed in sharply. Her lips remained parted and her mouth became dry. She licked her lips lightly and swallowed.

Sometime during the night he'd unsnapped the trousers, and though the fly remained zipped, she could make out the gleaming white edge of his briefs. Her gaze dropped a notch lower and her mouth fell full open.

The most intimate part of Roman was outlined by the pull of the tux pants over his hips. Her heart began to thud in her chest, and a languid liquid heat coursed through her. She couldn't believe she was looking at him....

She forced her gaze down the lengths of his legs, but her eyes immediately trailed back upward, as if they had a mind of their own, and she gazed long and hard at where the sleek, expensive fabric of his pants tightened against him, showing off every blessed contour. She simply couldn't stop looking. And fantasizing…wondering if making love could really work between them. She'd had only one other lover. She found herself blushing bright red. Malcolm Van Ness simply wasn't built the way Roman was.

In his dream Roman held the woman close. *The ship was in sight.*

In their water tussle, her muslin bodice had come untied. Her large pale breasts spilled outward, crushing against his chest, accentuating the cleavage. Through the wet, transparent material he had seen the darker color of her nipples. In his arms she was breathless.

"You've saved me, sir. But I do hope you've done so…only out of…out of the goodness of your heart."

"My good woman, do you attribute ulterior motives of some sort to me?" His mates sent a ladder downward, and he carried her up.

When they reached the deck she flung her arms around his neck and pressed his face against her breasts. Looking down, he realized that the woman was pregnant. And then he kissed her.

Roman sighed deeply and opened his eyes, feeling disoriented for the briefest second, a smile playing on his lips. *What a dream.*

And then he realized the woman from his dream was staring at him. Not at his face. Not at his chest. But at his trousers. Her eyes were feasting on him and her lips were slightly parted.

Kathleen felt Roman's hand leave her side and she glanced quickly toward his face. By the time her gaze met his, his fingers were touching a lock of her hair. Then he trailed a single finger over her forehead and brow, to her temple.

"Don't pretend," he whispered, wishing he'd managed to get more than an hour's worth of sleep. This time he meant to be fully conscious...if anything happened, that was.

She swallowed and licked her dry lips. "Pretend?"

"Don't pretend you don't want me, Kathleen," he whispered.

She opened her mouth to protest, but couldn't say a word. Just one time she did want to know what making love was really supposed to feel like.

"You do want me?" It was less a question than a statement.

Kathleen simply couldn't bring herself to voice a denial. She did want him. But was he going to lead her on and then reject her again? The silky touch of his finger moved downward, burning a trail from her cheek to her chin. It dropped from her chin right onto her breast, making her gasp. She bit her lower lip. Hard.

"You're beautiful, Kathleen," he said gently. He said it so easily she was sure he'd said it to a thousand women. Could she make love to him just once, and yet hide her vulnerability?

He flattened his palms against the filmy fabric of the dress she'd slept in, touching her softly until her breasts, which had become so sensitive with her pregnancy, strained against the cloth. She dipped her head toward his mouth, thinking she'd kiss him first. She'd play the aggressor and he wouldn't guess at her inexperience. She brushed his lips lightly.

He rolled toward her, shifted his weight and slid the flat of his palm inside the bodice of her dress to cup the soft, sweet mound of her breast. His other hand curved around her head. Was Kathleen really going to let him love her?

His hand dropped, molding itself over the curve of her stomach. He felt no movement, but it was enough to know that the baby was there...so close between them. He moaned, thinking about that, and tongued tiny fluttering kisses over her chest, her neck and her cheeks.

"You feel so good, darlin'," he murmured, his hands fighting up through what felt like miles of chiffon. He let out a shaking breath against her lips, wondering again just what the hell Van Ness had been doing with her. She felt a little tense, as if she were frightened.

He felt the scared little movements of her hands as she trembled with uncertainty. And each untutored touch nearly sent him into oblivion. The vibrations of her shaking fingers on his back and shoulders made him want to take her in an absolute fury. He kissed her more deeply, rubbing her stomach slowly as he did so, until she began to relax and become languid in his arms.

When he dropped his hand to touch the silk of her panties, she froze again. Her hands played on his back as if she was bracing herself. And then, as he touched her, her fingers fluttered every which way. They fumbled awkwardly at his thigh and then raced back upward again in the sweetest way, as if she wanted to touch him but just couldn't bring herself to.

"Relax, Kathleen," he whispered. "It's okay." He moaned softly as he caught her hand. As badly as he wanted her to touch the most intimate part of him, he wanted to reassure her, too. He uncurled her fingers, kissed her palm and then placed her hand over his heart and covered it with his own. He deepened the kiss again, touching her until she began to arch against him.

"Roman, just go ahead and..." she gasped.

Why did she sound so nervous? He glanced up, wanting to tell her she made it sound like a fate worse than death. But the look on her face stopped him. She was breathing in soft sighs but clearly trying not to. And she looked a little bewildered. She looked exactly the way she had when she'd fainted...all rumpled and sexy and confused to the point of befuddlement. He didn't say anything. Just started kissing her again, his hand nestling deep in the chiffon, touching every part of her.

Kathleen clutched at his shoulders. Roman's touches were building a slow, languid heat within her. Every sweet butterfly kiss, every deepening hot kiss, every gentle exploring kiss had made her more ready than she'd ever thought she could be.

Buried in the delicious scent of her skin, breathing in and tasting the honey-salt flavor of her, Roman was sure he'd never wanted a woman so much. When he released her so that he could remove her dress, he couldn't take his eyes off her face. Or her breasts.... He rubbed his hand gently over her stomach, feeling that he was touching not only her, but their baby.

"I've never made love to a pregnant woman before," he said, his own breath quickening. And he wanted to, he thought as he dipped his hand still lower. He touched her again until her lips parted in a gasp that he captured with a kiss.

He paused briefly, only to strip out of his own

clothes and take off the rest of hers. Then he moved on top of her and, with a moan that sounded other-worldly in its raw, primitive desire, he began to sink into her slowly, until his head rested between her breasts.

Suddenly Kathleen seemed incredibly tiny and delicate. He told himself to move slowly. He wanted it to be good for her, to last. He tried to concentrate on something other than her and the baby. Fishing or sailing or training horses. But he simply couldn't.

Kathleen moaned, feeling new waves of need and longing sweep over her with each of his movements. She fluttered kisses over his cheeks and lips. "Roman," she breathed. "Oh…Roman."

Kathleen moaned again just before his mouth crushed against hers with a power that was beyond anything she'd ever felt. He seemed to bite and tug and press against her lips all in one motion.

"C'mon, sweetheart," he whispered against her lips, his very words seeming to urge her on.

Suddenly her body arched against his again and she lost consciousness of the fact that he was above her. She clutched him tightly, feeling the ferocity of her body's relief. When she opened her eyes he was poised above her. He sighed over and over, lowering himself with each sound, to rest his head against her.

Slowly their hearts quieted and their breathing began to even.

"Roman?" she said, gently turning to disentangle from their embrace.

He rolled to his side and then ran a finger from her shoulder over her stomach and all the way down her side. He smiled. "Yeah, darlin'?"

She reached over the side of the bed for her dress, and then pulled it over her chest. "This isn't right."

"This?" He knew just exactly what she was going to say. And he wished the woman could give it a rest for a second. At least until he caught his breath.

"You and me," she said, pressing the dress closer against her. Suddenly she actually felt naked. Exposed.

"C'mon, darlin'. Making love was great." His smiled broadened.

"It's not that," she said quickly, causing tiny lights of mischief to spark in his eyes. "But our situation is more complex than—"

"We don't have to sleep together all the time, Kathleen," he said.

"Just sometimes?" she asked, feeling a small flare of temper. She wrapped her dress completely around her, like a towel. Outside, the dawn had given way to the full light of day. She was glad they'd made love, but this was certainly the most complex situation in which she'd ever been involved.

Roman sent her a long, hard stare. "It just sort of happened, Kathleen," he finally said.

"I realize that," she returned. She hopped out of bed and headed for his bathroom, hoping her dress covered her backside. She glanced quickly into the nursery. In the daylight the whole room seemed to sparkle. It made her heart ache for Roman...for the kind of man he could be.

She turned at the bathroom door. Roman had sat upright in the bed. He looked marvelous, too. His skin all coppery and his hair all rumpled, with sheets twined around his legs.

When she found her voice again, she said, "We're married. But it has to be in name only." At that she stopped, as if the words should explain everything. And then she shut the bathroom door quietly.

If she had a million years, she thought, she couldn't begin to explain everything. She had no illusions that Roman would want to make a real marriage out of this, or truly become the baby's father. If they weren't married, well, then, maybe they could make love again. Mere moments had passed and, heaven knew, she already wanted to.

But this was not going to turn into a nebulous or strange situation where she was a single mother, married to a man with whom she had a sometimes casual affair.

Kathleen sat on the cold, uninviting edge of the tub and blew out a sigh, feeling suddenly very confused. "Oh, no," she muttered. "What have I just done?" *And what in the world am I going to do now?*

Chapter Seven

There she is. Finally. Roman was lounging on the window seat, in front of the turreted window of the library. He'd found the parts to his boyhood train set in the attic, and the tracks and cars now sat in a paper bag at his feet. He dipped a rag in polish and began rubbing yet another one of the cars while he watched Kathleen. She skipped down the length of the patio, then disappeared between the columns of the pavilioned section, looking as mysteriously sexy as a wood nymph. She was waving tentatively at someone.

"Van Ness," Roman muttered. After all, he'd just returned the man's ring.

Just looking at Kathleen, even from this distance, Roman could still feel her warm body and the soft tremors of her fingertips against his skin. As she greeted Van Ness, Roman suddenly felt jealous and wondered if Kathleen still had feelings for the man.

She just might. No matter how he'd tried to talk to her over the past week, she'd made it clear that they were going nowhere together. Not as friends. Not as a couple. Not as anything.

Roman pulled another train car from the bag—this time the little red caboose—and began to polish it.

Kathleen was driving him crazy. He had done nothing but think about her since they'd made love. And every last scintilla of his resentment toward her had vanished.

He didn't care that her mother had run off with his father…didn't care about whether or not her name was on the deed to his island. He didn't even care if Kathleen was a fortune hunter, either. Or if his mother was going to be upset about his marriage to her.

Absolutely none of it mattered. He set the caboose beside him on the window seat. It gleamed a bright red. Glancing at it, Roman decided that the train set could go in the far corner of the nursery.

"Go ahead and have your little tryst with Van Ness," Roman said softly, watching the two head for the dock.

While she did, he could move the crib into the nursery. For the past few days she'd been hiding in her room, but she had agreed to move in next door to him. Now, hadn't she?

"And when you get back," he muttered to himself, "we'll talk, darlin'. Again."

KATHLEEN SKIPPED UP the stairs, thinking she'd never felt so relieved. She had dreaded seeing Malcolm for so long, but the meeting had actually gone well. Oh, she harbored some sadness, since the man's heart wasn't large enough to include his child, but she still felt happy. Van Ness had made it clear that he didn't mean to interfere with her life or the baby's. He'd only offered to help her financially, if she ever needed him to do so. Which, she thought with satisfaction, she wouldn't.

When she reached the top stair she stopped in her tracks. Roman was wearing only threadbare jeans and his boots, and he was trying to fit the crib through her bedroom doorway. "Roman?"

"Hey, there, Kathleen," he said, and grinned. "Mind giving me a hand?"

"Sure," she replied, wishing he didn't look quite so good. Every shirtless inch of him reminded her of how it had felt to be held in his arms, her cheek nuzzled against those soft, curling hairs on his chest. She cleared her throat. "The side rails of the crib come down and you can angle it around the corner of the doorway, on its side. But what are you doing?"

"Well, you did say you'd move into the nursery, didn't you?"

Kathleen managed a nod. After all, she had agreed, she thought, as she took down the side rails of the crib. *But only because of dire circumstances.* She had been trying to ensure that she'd leave Roman's room without making love to him. Which she hadn't. He turned the crib in the doorway, and she instinctively took the other end.

"Nope," he said as she prepared to pick up her end of the baby's bed. "I don't want you lifting anything, darlin'." He shot her another one of his sexy grins. "I just needed help with the logistics."

She found herself smiling back at him, in a way she knew had to look a bit silly. Why in the world did Roman want her and the baby next door? Even if he meant to make their marriage a real one—which he undoubtedly did not—how could he be so accepting of another man's child? Lord knew, Malcolm wasn't accepting, and he was the biological father. But Roman seemed to be so excited. As he eased the crib into the hallway the muscles of his back and shoulders rippled.

"Well," she said, unable to help the flirtatious tone

that crept into her voice, "maybe you'll at least let me help push." He glanced at her quickly, looking a little bewildered.

"The crib has rollers," she explained.

He chuckled. "Well, darlin', that's what I mean about needing help with logistics."

She arched her brows in question.

"I carried it all the way across your room," he explained. "On my shoulders."

She giggled, then suddenly sobered, half-wishing she'd seen him do so, just to watch all his well-defined muscles in action again. She placed her hands on the headboard. Together they began pushing the crib toward his room.

"Fortunately your door's a little wider," she said as they pushed the crib through it.

"And so's the one between my room and the nursery," he said agreeably.

When they reached the nursery her mouth dropped. Roman had already set her bed in the corner of the room farthest from the window. Now he positioned the crib on the other side.

It was really true, she thought, her breath catching in her throat. She was going to move in right next door to him. She knew she could forget about getting a good night's sleep...for the rest of her life. "My bed's in here," she finally managed to say aloud.

Not about to miss an opening, Roman said softly, "Would you prefer to sleep with me?"

Her mouth went dry and she drew in a quick breath. More than anything, Roman's simple acceptance of her pregnancy and how much he seemed to want to be involved with her and the baby made him dangerous. It was so easy for her to fall for him...and to be desperately hurt. There was just no way she could have a casual affair with a man who was legally her husband.

"Well?" Roman prompted.

He was so close that his breath fanned against her cheek. Kathleen reached out and touched his arm, lightly running her finger over the bicep. His skin was soft and cool and dry, even after the exertion of moving the furniture. "Roman, I don't mean to deny that I appreciate everything you're doing for the baby and that I enjoyed...the night we spent together. It was..."

Roman smiled playfully, rested an elbow on the rail of the crib, then reached over and touched her shoulder. "Do tell, darlin'."

"Well, it was..."

"I'm waiting," he nearly whispered.

"Roman, it was wonderful," she said in a quick rush.

"Oh, Kathleen," he whispered. He tilted his head, lowered his mouth and brushed her lips with his own.

His mouth felt and tasted so sweet that she wanted nothing more than to curl into the crook of his shoulder and keep kissing him. She forced herself to lean back after a moment. "We just can't..."

He looked at her long and hard, then shrugged. "I kissed you. So what?"

"So what?" she echoed. How could she explain that if this continued she'd really want him to act as the father of her baby? In fact, she already did. And Roman was going to break her heart.

"I like kissing women," he teased.

"Women," she repeated.

"No," he said softly. "You, Kathleen. I like kissing you."

She realized that this was the kind of moment she

had always hoped to reach with Roman Lawrence. And now that it had happened there wasn't a blessed thing she could do about it. Except say no. Yes, somehow or other, she had to resist him. "No," she said with resolve.

"You really mean it, Kathleen."

"I do," she said.

"All right."

Her brows drew upward. "You'll accept that, even though I'm going to sleep in here?"

"Sure." He suddenly flashed her a teasing grin. "For now, anyway."

His whole demeanor—from the playful curve of his lips, to his casual leaning posture against the crib, to his mischievous eyes—was so full of fun that she couldn't help but smile back.

"So—" He glanced quickly around the nursery. "It looks like we need some stuff."

At the very same time, both of them said, "Wanna go shopping?"

Roman chuckled. Kathleen grasped his hand and held it so that their pinkie fingers met. "Make a wish," she said, and then she ran another finger between their smallest fingers, sealing their wishes as surely as if it had been done with a kiss.

"LOOK AT THIS!" Kathleen exclaimed as she pulled him down the aisle of Hansel and Gretel's in Key West. She suddenly bent and lifted a set of sheets from the shelf. They were a yellow-and-blue print, with stars and planets, and matched the theme of the nursery perfectly. In fact, they were the very sheets that had prompted the idea for the ceiling mural in the first place. Roman just hadn't come back to buy them yet.

"Perfect," Roman said, taking the sheets and placing them in their cart. "You may as well get two sets."

"You really think so?" she asked.

The excitement in her voice made him feel as if he'd just accomplished some great and daring feat for her. His gaze roved over her olive tent dress, then traveled to her face. Her skin was flushed and her eyes sparkled. He'd never seen her look so happy or excited before. "Well," he said, smiling, "if it makes you that happy, we'll get three. I think we can afford it," he continued wryly as he picked up a whole stack of sheets.

She skipped ahead of him again, now heading for the clothes racks. When he reached her, she was holding a tiny baseball cap and making small cooing sounds. He took the cap from her, scrutinized it as if he wasn't sure whether or not it would be a wise purchase, then put it on his head.

She looked at him for a long moment, then laughed. "I don't think it fits," she finally teased.

He mustered his best puppy-dog look. "Well," he said with mock chagrin, "I guess we'll just have to buy it for the baby, then." He lifted the cap from his head and laid it gingerly in the baby-seat section of the cart. "But what if the baby's a girl?" he asked as Kathleen tossed a pair of pint-sized athletic socks on top of the cap.

She tossed her head and grinned saucily. "Are you saying you're sexist, Roman?"

"Well, yeah," he teased. "I think a woman's place is in..."

She laughed. "The kitchen?"

Quick as a flash he reached around the cart and hauled her against him. "Nope," he said, his lips so close that he could feel her breath.

"Barefoot and pregnant?" she guessed again with a smile.

"Yeah," he said, pulling her closer against his shoulder. "And in my arms."

Behind them, two of the teenage salesclerks had begun to giggle. Still smiling, he released Kathleen and nodded toward the toy section. "I have something to show you," he said.

"What?"

He whirled the cart around, then glanced over his shoulder and wiggled his brows at her. "You'll just have to follow me," he said playfully.

"I'm following you," she said from behind him, in a singsong voice.

"Bet you can't catch me," he said, pushing the cart down the aisle just a little faster.

"Bet I can," she returned.

He fought the urge to glance over his shoulder at her again, and when he felt her come close, he pulled abruptly to a halt. "I bet you can, too," he said, laughing as she crashed into him.

And then—he couldn't quite believe it—her arms snaked around his waist from behind. She squeezed him quickly before coming around beside him. He looped his arm around her shoulder. She might not want to sleep with him, but she did want to get to know him—not the baiting, snide side of him, either, but the real him, the side that could be kind and fun to be around. And suddenly, that seemed like enough.

He stopped the cart again, then headed for one of the floor-displays items and leaned against it. "So, what do you think?"

"About what?"

He chuckled as Kathleen glanced around. "Can't see

the forest for the trees?'' he teased. "Or maybe you just can't see the horse for the good-looking man in front of it.''

Her mouth dropped and then she shot him a lopsided grin. "You can't be serious.''

Granted, the stuffed horse was every bit as big as a real one, but Roman liked it. A lot. And he'd already checked to see if the store was willing to sell it, and they were. "This horse has been here ever since I was a kid,'' he said. "When I was little—''

"Roman Lawrence was once little?'' she interjected coyly.

"I know it's hard to believe that a virile man like me was once a kid,'' he said. "But it's true, Kathleen.''

She smiled and her eyes lit up. "And?''

"And when we used to come in here to shop, I wanted this horse more than anything in the world.''

"And you didn't get it?'' she prompted, the teasing glint still in her eyes. "I always thought you got everything you wanted.''

He looked into her face for a long moment. Her skin glowed as if there were light rays inside her that made it beam. "Not everything,'' he said softly, his voice growing husky.

Kathleen's smile vanished and she licked her lips, as if she knew full well that he was now thinking about wanting her…and not having her. "Did you ask for it?''

"The horse?'' he managed to say.

"Yeah,'' she said, smiling again. "The horse.''

"Oh, about a thousand times, darlin'.'' He chuckled. "But who would buy something like this?''

"You,'' she said softly, meeting his gaze. "The nursery's pretty big. I think it will fit.''

"Really?" His grin broadened. "Why do I feel like I'm suddenly regressing?"

"Because you're about to buy the toy of your childhood dreams," she said, laughing.

"I feel like I'm five again…and somebody just gave me my own gold card," he returned.

"Well, I hope the baby doesn't have some kind of horse phobia," she teased.

"Impossible," he said levelly. A love of horses was in the genes.

"Do you think they deliver?"

"Every bit as well as Dr. Peteck," he said. "I already checked."

"On Hansel and Gretel's ability to deliver or Dr. Peteck's?"

"Both," he said, his voice becoming husky again. Even though he'd told himself to try not to touch her, to give her all the space she needed, he now found himself looping his arm around her shoulder again. This time, as they headed toward the cash register, she nestled softly against him.

Once they'd reached the cash register, he said, "If we're having the horse delivered, we may as well have them bring everything else." Kathleen was watching him closely, in a way that made him want to bring her even closer and kiss her.

"Okay," she said. "And maybe we could take a walk down the boardwalk?"

Roman realized the clerk was glancing between them and smiling. "You two can go ahead," the teenager said. "I already ran your card through."

"Thanks," Roman said.

Once they were outside, he snaked his arm around Kathleen's waist and breathed in the salty scent of the air. Occasionally he glanced into the gleaming store-front windows along the promenade. After a few moments Kathleen's arm crept around him, too. They were walking in perfect step, and he couldn't quite get over how easily they moved together. Not here and not in bed. No woman had ever felt so right against him.

Suddenly he realized that Kathleen had come to a standstill. He glanced over her shoulder and found himself looking into a jewelry-store window.

"Sorry," she said, flushing guiltily. She started walking again, but before she was out of his grasp he pulled her against him again.

"Nothing to be sorry about," he said, rubbing his cheek against her hair. "So, which ring were you looking at?"

Kathleen pointed at a gold band set with four diamonds. It was simple, but extremely well crafted. "Isn't that just beautiful?"

"Yeah," he agreed. It was obviously a good ring, but then jewelry was…well, jewelry. He tried to sound excited for Kathleen's sake. After all, she had liked his horse. "Really gorgeous," he added.

Kathleen giggled, then shot him a wry glance, as if she knew window-shopping for jewelry wasn't exactly his cup of tea. "C'mon," she said, tugging him forward. "Let's go look at the ocean."

They walked to the end of the row of shops and boutiques, rounded a corner, then crossed to the pier. When they reached it, Kathleen leaned against the rail and looked out, over the blue expanse of water.

Roman moved behind her, his arms circling her waist. He pressed the flat of his palms over her stomach and rubbed her gently. Then he leaned down, nuzzling his face against her neck. She turned slowly in his arms until she was facing him, rested her palms against his chest and gazed up into his eyes.

"Roman, I really meant what I said...."

"I know," he said gently, not bothering to hide the raspiness of his voice. "But it's been such a nice day." He shrugged. "Shopping for the baby...taking a walk. And—"

"And you want to kiss me," she murmured.

He made a soft humming sound and drew her close in a hug. "That's about the size of it," he whispered. "And the sun's starting to set..."

She chuckled. "And the birds are singing in the trees..."

"And you're so close beside me." He cupped his hands around her neck and tilted her head back, looking into her eyes. Nothing could feel better to him, he thought, than the way her hands now crept upward on his chest, toward his shoulders.

"I'm just worried about where this might be going," she said softly.

"For just a minute...for just right now, why don't you forget to worry?" he asked.

"At moments like this," she said, "it's pretty easy to."

He smiled. "Good." He brushed her lips very softly with his own, again and again. He did nothing more until she herself deepened their kiss, her tongue lightly bringing his into play with hers. Between them he could feel the soft curve of her stomach pressing against him, arousing him.

After a long moment she drew back. "We better head back home," she said a little shakily.

He didn't move, only held her. "All right," he said,

looking at her glistening, well-kissed mouth. "But what did you wish for?"

"Wish for?"

"In the nursery, earlier today?"

Her green, lashless eyes brightened with mischief. "I'll never tell," she teased archly. "What did *you* wish for?"

A real wife and family. You and me and the baby...together, he thought, still not wholly believing he had wished for that. He assured himself that his newfound feelings for Kathleen were simply due to the baby. Roman forced himself to wiggle his brows playfully, and match her teasing tone. He leaned right by her ear, as if he meant to tell her. "Why, darlin'," he finally whispered, "only my hairdresser knows for sure."

Kathleen laughed. But before she released him she reached on her tiptoes and kissed him again. Lightly. And right on the lips.

KATHLEEN HAD BEEN SURE she'd never actually be able to sleep in the room next to Roman's. Boy, had she been wrong, she thought now, sleepily stretching her toes in the bed. The past few nights she'd slept like the dead.

Undoubtedly it was due to immense relief. Deep down, in her subconscious, she had been terrified that Van Ness would try to get custody of her baby...but he wasn't going to. Only now could she admit that she'd had nightmares and fantasies where Van Ness had wrenched her child from her arms. Now a great burden had been taken from her shoulders. That and the fact that she was having such fun preparing for the baby with Roman's help had freed her to sleep as she never had.

All at once she heard a strange raking sound. She bolted upright. "Roman?"

What was he doing in her new room? In her closet? It sounded as if Roman was shoving back all the clothes in her closet with one great sweep of his arm. The hangers rattled and clanked. She blinked, glanced at the crib in the corner, then smiled sleepily. The giant stuffed horse they'd bought stood in a corner.

"Mind telling me what you're doing?" she asked, rubbing her eyes.

Roman was removing the plastic dry-cleaner wrap from the silk-and-chiffon dress she'd worn for their wedding. He tossed the plastic in a waste can, then whirled around. The dress swung outward from its hanger, and one of the swaths of chiffon trailed over Roman's shoulder.

"Rise and shine, darlin'," he said, laying the dress on her bed. "And put on this dress."

With that he headed for the door, then disappeared. Kathleen was left staring groggily down at the dress. She blinked again, suddenly realizing that Roman had been wearing his tuxedo. What in the world was going on?

With one quick sweep of her arm she pulled back her covers, leaped out of bed and headed for the shower. What did he have up his sleeve? And why was he being so kind to her and the baby? Was he really beginning to have feelings for her? Within what felt like minutes she was all dressed up and headed downstairs.

"We've been waiting for you," a man teased once she'd reached the patio.

"Sorry I'm late," Kathleen responded, wondering just what she was late for. The man was heavy, with thinning wisps of hair combed over his scalp. No, she thought, she didn't recognize him.

She felt Roman's arms suddenly circle her waist from behind. She gasped. He'd been so quiet that she hadn't even heard him approach. He looked devilishly delightful in his tuxedo. She glanced downward. He even had on the red sneakers.

"Surprise," he said.

"Are you ready to start?" the man asked.

"Start what?" Kathleen whispered to Roman.

Roman grinned and pointed in the general direction of the ocean. Her gaze followed his fingertip and her lips suddenly parted. The man was a photographer! A large patterned screen and standing lights had been set up in the corner of the patio. She would have noticed them before, but she'd been looking in the wrong direction. And, of course, Roman's hands gently curving around her stomach had caused her to stop looking altogether.

"You called a photographer?" It was such a sweet gesture that she really didn't know what to say. She'd been so caught up with thinking about the baby that she hadn't thought to have pregnancy pictures taken.

"We'll want photos," he said. "Don't you think?"

"Oh, yes…" she breathed. But had he really said *we'll*…as in, he wanted memories, too?

"Go on, Kathleen," he said gently, releasing her from his arms and giving her a tiny, playful push in the direction of the screen.

At first she felt slightly embarrassed, a little exposed and on display when she had her picture taken. But trust Roman to find the best. Within minutes the pho-

tographer had helped loosen her up. She found herself
laughing and posing in a way that made her feel like
a professional model.

Not that the man's jovial good humor could make
her forget that Roman was watching from the sidelines.
Every time she glanced at him, she found him staring
at her intently. And then, when he caught her gaze, his
face would break into a smile.

"Get some more with her pulling the dress over her
stomach," Roman said at one point.

Kathleen flushed.

"You heard what the man said," the photographer
teased.

Kathleen glanced at Roman, then posed again. She
placed her palms beneath her breasts and slowly let
them drop downward, smiling all the while. When her
hands had slid all the way down over the soft chiffon
and reached the bottom of her stomach, she paused and
smiled again for the camera.

"Just one more," Roman said.

Kathleen flushed again and glanced at Roman. She
was trying to look somewhat reserved for the picture—
smiling but not laughing—but Roman was so sweet
and wonderful to do this that she inadvertently grinned.
And then she laughed.

"Perfect!" the photographer exclaimed. "What a
good shot! Now, let's get some couple pictures."

Couple pictures?

Sure enough, Roman ambled over and stood beside
her as if it were the most natural thing in the world.
She felt a sudden, undeniable twinge of fear. Was he
becoming *too* involved with her baby? She shook her
head as if to dispel the feeling. Roman had been kind

enough to think of the photographer. And he was her legal husband, after all.

"Let's see some poses," the photographer said.

The next thing she knew, Roman had seemed to take command of her body. He nestled his arms around her waist, moved his own palms over her dress to accentuate the curve of her stomach, and trailed kisses up and down her neck.

"Great," the photographer said again. "Just great. Kathleen, put your hands over his."

Kathleen covered Roman's arms with her own, placed her palms on top of his hands, then twined her fingers in his.

"These are going to be fantastic," the photographer murmured. "Nestle farther down on her shoulder, Roman, and kiss her."

Kathleen cleared her throat and swallowed. More and more, it really seemed that Roman wanted to be a father...and more and more, she was beginning to wonder what he felt about *her*. Every move he made stoked up the heat that was beginning to build within her. Every touch felt so good—the soft, featherlike kisses he was trailing down her neck, the way he lifted her hand, uncurled her fingers one by one and kissed her palm...the way his breath fanned against her cheek, smelling of peppermint and coffee. And her heart ached with each new, sweet thing he did for the baby.

He held her more tightly, and she wasn't sure but thought she felt the beginnings of his arousal against her. Her mouth went dry. She tried to swallow and couldn't. She turned her head to the side, meaning to tell him that they should stop. *Now*.

His lips met hers just as she turned her head. She leaned back in the crook of his arm, unable to resist kissing him back. His tongue darted between her lips as he slowly turned her to face him. Against her will her limbs relaxed as he leaned her gently backward in his arms.

Somewhere, far off, she thought she could hear the photographer muttering words like "perfect," "fantastic," and "fabulous," but she wasn't sure. She was only truly aware of how Roman's kiss affected her. Each touch of his lips and tongue made her heart pound and her pulse skip and her nerves quiver.

Slowly he lightened his kiss. He drew back from her, pulling her upward and against him as he did so. His beautiful dark eyes twinkled and he winked. "I'd love to keep going, darlin'," he said. "But we have company."

The photographer took another picture of them. Inadvertently she licked her lips. As the camera buzzed and whirred she could still taste the delicious flavor of Roman's mouth.

"At least I didn't faint this time," she finally quipped.

"That must mean you're getting used to me," Roman said with satisfaction.

And she was, she thought. *But what does it mean? And where are we going with it?*

Chapter Eight

"Pant, one-two. Pant, one-two..." Dr. Peteck's wife, Wendy, instructed over the snappy rhythm of a pop song. "Now a long breath...push!"

"Are you sure you really want to do this?" Kathleen glanced over her shoulder at Roman, then down the long line of expectant fathers who were positioned in a neat row behind their wives on the exercise mat. Kathleen and Roman were the only couple in the class who weren't married. *But we are married,* she thought.

Roman's legs trailed down either side of hers and he snuggled closer, his arms tightening around her thickening waist. "I definitely want to do this," he said. "Besides, I'm not the one really doing it, darlin'." His sugary drawl lowered another notch. "You are."

Between breaths she whispered, "Well, it's really nice of you to fill in for Ms. Rodriguez and come to class tonight."

"I *want* to come to class," he said huskily. "And anyway, are you saying I'm usually not nice?" he teased, sounding so prankishly naughty that a shiver zigzagged down her spine. Kathleen pushed out the long series of pants that was now required, feeling his breath tickle her neck. Her whole body flushed with the warmth of it.

"If I was nice all the time, I'd just bore you, Kathleen," he continued playfully.

If you were nice all the time I'd fall in love with you. If she hadn't done so already, she thought. Kathleen's breaths were turning less into the long, pushing variety that Wendy Peteck was asking for now, and more into piqued sighs. As nice as it was for Roman to offer to attend the class tonight, it was sure hard to concentrate when he was so close.

He began breathing in exact time with her. He was so good at it she half wished he was the one who was going to go into labor. Now he was panting right by her ear. The skin on her chest and cheeks started to tingle with little red pinpricks.

After long moments he whispered, "Are you afraid of your feelings for me?"

Absolutely, yes. "That's just a little presumptuous," she managed to whisper in a light tone, in the beat between songs. But she *was* afraid. Just what did Roman want from her? Every passing second she spent with him, she felt herself wondering how she could live without him. The days when they used to trade barbs and bait each other seemed light-years away.

Practically every day he helped her with some small, new addition to the nursery. They'd set up his boyhood train set, hung bright yellow curtains and found a rug that was woven with brightly colored threads in the shapes of fish. They'd also put the finishing coat on the rocking horse he'd bought. And the pictures the photographer had taken were beautiful.

Now she leaned far back in his arms and then forward again, panting in short, rhythmic breaths and trying, with all her might, to concentrate. She wished Ms. Rodriguez hadn't suddenly become so damnably unavailable. Lately the woman seemed to have more appointments than the president.

And Roman was driving Kathleen crazy. *He's breathing in my ears,* she thought. *And whispering oh, so softly. And rubbing my stomach. And hiring photographers. And, for all practical purposes, becoming a dad....* The closer she felt to him emotionally, the more she feared that things between them wouldn't last.

Thankfully, the music ended and the instructor pulled a towel over her shoulders. "Tonight we're watching a movie. So everybody can get a cup of water, then head into the TV room."

Roman stood, then came around to face her, towering over her. Like everyone, he was in his stocking feet in deference to the mats, and dressed in sweats. The baggy, soft red pants tightened over his waist and—at eye level—Kathleen could make out the outline hint of his lower body. She sucked in a breath as he reached down, grasped one of her hands and pulled her upward. Right into his arms.

Was he using this very public forum to hold her close again? A public place where she wouldn't remind him that she had mixed feelings about pursuing their relationship? *But I didn't back away last time you kissed me, Roman....*

He grabbed his boots and her shoes, which had been left by the cooler, and handed her a cup of water as they headed to the projection room. Kathleen was so lost in thought that she only vaguely realized Roman had draped his arm over the back of her chair and was now introducing himself to the other members of the group.

"We didn't want to ask," a woman named Angie was saying. "But...well, we're just so glad to meet Kathleen's husband."

Husband! It was the first time she'd ever heard Roman referred to as her husband by a third party. Somehow, the words made her feel desirable and cherished and loved. *I'm married.*

The feeling quickly passed as Roman explained how he'd been unfortunately away on a business trip, and how he couldn't be sorrier about all the classes he'd already missed. She fought not to roll her eyes at all the lies he was telling, and sent him a quirky, knowing smile when he pulled his boots on over his sweats. The outfit was ridiculous—as bad as Jackson Rivers's mismatched plaids—and yet it was the kind that men like Roman could get away with.

"Good," Angie's husband was saying, clapping Roman on the back. "So you'll be a part of our group, too."

Roman grinned. "Every week."

Every week! He had some nerve, ingratiating himself before she had invited him. She sighed. What if Roman was truly becoming too involved...wanting the baby, but not her?

"You're only filling in for Ms. Rodriguez," Kathleen whispered gently as Wendy began checking the VCR. She rubbed his shoulder briefly, to lessen the blow. And it was a blow, even to her. After all, she wanted him with her. He seemed as genuinely happy about the baby as she did. His presence felt right.

"Angelina Rodriguez is an employee," he returned after a long moment.

"And what exactly are you, when it comes to me?" It was the question that had been uppermost in her mind. *Husband? Boyfriend? Friend? Sometimes lover? Possible father to my baby? Man with ulterior motive?*

"A very interested party," he said softly.

Before the lights were dimmed, Wendy stood directly behind Kathleen and addressed the group, introducing Roman and saying that, although they would miss Ms. Rodriguez, she always felt that a husband's presence was the best.

"And some husband!" Wendy exclaimed, winking at Kathleen and patting Roman on the shoulder.

Kathleen felt a sharp twinge of unexpected jealousy, even though Wendy's remark could hardly be construed as a come-on. She managed a weak smile. It looked as if Roman really would be coming with her every week. Even though she didn't fully trust his change in attitude toward her, she had to admit that coming to class with him would be fun.

"You do seem to take to this rather well, Roman," Wendy said brightly. "Not all men do, you know."

"Real well." Roman's eyes twinkled, as one of the group members stood and began to dim the lights. "I figure having babies is just about the most natural thing in the world...not to mention the most pleasurable."

It was pretty clear he was referring to making babies, rather than having them. Everybody laughed in a way that suddenly annoyed Kathleen. How could she help but feel defensive? They weren't really married, even if he was choosing, for some unfathomable reason, to *act* as if he loved her and the baby. Vaguely she wondered if her hormones had kicked in and if she was being unnecessarily moody. Suddenly she wanted to cry. *Roman is going to break my heart. Again.*

Wendy was laughing. "Having babies certainly is pleasurable!" she was saying.

While the tape began to hum, Angie's husband leaned forward to offer Kathleen and Roman an open invitation to coffee after any of their classes. And he asked Roman, not her. She reminded herself that Angie *had* invited her before, but Roman's surefire charm still made her feel somehow angry. But really, beneath the anger, what she felt was scared. There was just no way she could fight her growing feelings for Roman.

Thankfully, the movie began before Roman could charm the rest of the class. The arm draped along the back of her chair shifted to her shoulders. More and more people, she realized, were beginning to see her and Roman as a couple—and she was, too. Perhaps she should just have it out with him, she thought. Or she should just ask him what his intentions were, toward both her and the baby. Was he beginning to love her? His every glance said that was the case.... But could he love another man's child? Probably so, she told herself, given the way he'd become involved.

Kathleen shook her head as if to clear it of confusion and turned her gaze to the film trailers that preceded the film they were to watch.

The movie was a documentary that followed a woman all through her pregnancy, right through labor and to the birth of her little girl. Kathleen had actually seen it before, since it was available at her video store. She wasn't even sure she could watch it again. Not that it wasn't beautiful—she had cried through much of it— but the screams of the woman during labor, even though they were muted by the soundtrack, were hardly something she could forget. Or look forward to, she thought grimly.

The only moment of comic relief came after the woman's first shriek. Her husband—an obviously sweet, supportive man—was busy signing her in at the hospital. When she screamed, his gaze shot up. "What in the world was that?" He looked shocked to his toes.

The duty nurse surveyed him a long time. "I hate to tell you this, sir," she finally managed to say, "but that was your wife."

"Most natural thing in the world," Kathleen whispered as the credits began to roll, and as she braced herself for what was to come.

Beside her, she felt Roman shrug. "Piece of cake, darlin'," he whispered with complete confidence.

"WHY DON'T YOU just drive, Kathleen?" Roman asked gruffly once they were in the dark parking lot. He pressed the keys into her hand forcibly. His palm, usually so dry and cool, felt a little damp.

"You want me to drive your Lamborghini?" Kathleen came to a full stop in the lot and stared down at the keys. Roman didn't respond, but just kept walking. He opened the passenger door, not even bothering to mention that she'd forgotten to lock it. His tall, broad-shouldered frame curled into the seat. And then the door swung shut.

She was still squinting at his already-shut door when she reached the driver's side and got in. "Are you all right?"

His arms were folded over his chest, pulling his tight black T-shirt taut over his ribs, and his expression was unreadable. He slicked back his hair, accentuating his high forehead, then flashed her a smile that didn't reach his eyes.

"Just watch the speed," he said hoarsely. "This baby goes from zero to ninety in less than ten seconds."

Kathleen turned toward the wheel, looked over the myriad high-tech gages below the dashboard and sighed. "Zero to ninety," she echoed. "Why don't you just drive?"

"Basically, it's just a regular stick shift," he said. He stretched his legs as far as they could go over the floor mat in the attitude of a man who had been waiting for a long time to go somewhere. "You can drive a stick, can't you, Kathleen?"

Of course she could drive a stick. She quickly turned the key in the ignition. She'd thought he'd enjoyed the class, but now it seemed as if he hadn't. Had all that charm and panache just been for the benefit of the group? As she pulled out of the lot, she could feel the hyperfast engine straining, as if the car wanted to leap out of her control.

The polished black racemobile was definitely a car custom-made for Roman. It was too dangerously fast, too sleekly dark and too wildly uncontrollable! The many gages, like his eyes, were so annoyingly unreadable! Why was he in a bad mood?

They'd gone a ways before he leaned toward her. When his hand darted over her lap and between her legs, she nearly jumped out of the seat. Was Roman coming on to her on the main drag of Key West? While she was driving one of the most powerful cars in the world?

She gasped when he just flicked on the headlights.

"Oh," she said weakly as he leaned back in his seat. "I knew I forgot something." She waited for his response—any response—and when none was forthcoming, she said, "I hate it when you get this way."

She kept her eyes glued to the road, but felt him turn toward her in the seat. Suddenly the car felt too small, too intimate and far too dark. She didn't like the fact that he could gaze at her like this when she had to look at the road.

"What way?" He pushed a button and his window went down. A rush of wind blew into the car.

"Like Mr. Strong and Silent," she said, turning onto A-1-A. "Silent," she repeated a good twenty minutes later.

He didn't say a word.

At the turnoff from A-1-A, onto the road access to the island, Roman reached above her and pulled the remote from the visor. He opened the gate and they passed through. They drove all the way down the access road, and when they reached the gate to the island proper, he opened and shut it.

It wasn't until she'd made it halfway down the dark, palm-lined road to the house that she hit the brakes and threw the car into Park.

"Do you mind telling me what's wrong with you?" For one blessed time, she intended to get to the bottom of his unnerving little silences. He hadn't acted moody like this for some time, and she wasn't going to stand for it. The last thing she wanted to see happen was their relationship to turn sour again.

Her glance caught his eyes and stopped there. They were far from the house and the island road was completely dark. The palms even shut out the moon. Shadows flickered across his features and his eyes were so dark that she couldn't tell the pupils from the irises under those luxurious lashes. They were just the kind of eyes every man should have, and that few actually did. He looked a tad ashen, in spite of his suntan.

"Roman? Are you all right?"

He rested his elbow in the open window and turned

fully toward her. Almost against her will, her gaze traveled over him slowly. He was wearing red and black—his colors—and the taut-fitting shirt stretched over him, leaving nothing to her imagination...nor did the sweatpants. Her gaze returned to his eyes. "Are you sick or something?"

"I can't believe you're going to do it," he finally said, shifting a little uncomfortably in the seat, as if this was a discussion he really didn't want to have. The movement brought him even closer. He looped a hand over the back of her seat, so that he held her headrest.

"Do what?" She stared at him quizzically.

"Oh, Lord, darlin'," he said a little shakily. "Have a baby."

"Roman," she managed to say, "you've known I was pregnant almost since the beginning." She hoped he didn't start in with some kind of propriety business. There was nothing wrong with being an unwed... She gulped in midthought, since actually she was wed. He'd wedded her. And bedded her. She gulped again, wishing she hadn't stopped the fool car.

"And I...I couldn't be happier about that fact," he finally said softly. "But, darlin'," he finally continued gruffly, "I mean *having* the baby."

Her mouth dropped and she turned in the seat, fully facing him. When she did, she wished he wasn't quite so good-looking. *Bronzed skin. Sleek black, shining waves of hair streaked with that otherworldly silver.*

Finally Kathleen managed a smile. "Pregnant women usually *have* babies," she said. "It's just one of those little ole piece-of-cake kind of things we do." Her voice, she realized, sounded husky.

He chuckled. "That movie..."

"What?" She leaned forward as if urging him to

continue. When he didn't, she said, "Roman, people can't read your mind. I can't." No matter how much she wished she could. "How are we supposed to really get along with each other if we don't talk?"

He flashed her a quick smile. "Oh," he said playfully. "I believe you've read my mind on occasion."

It had hardly been her intention to stop the car in the dark and remember how easily they could sometimes anticipate each other's needs.

"If I've ever read your mind, I'm not doing it now," she said gently.

His eyes went all squinty and sparkly. He shrugged, waving one of his hands in the air, as if something—she still had no idea what—was simply beyond belief. Or as if he were conjuring up something magical.

"I mean, in that movie, it was just awful," he said. "You have to put your feet in those metal…"

"Stirrups, Roman?" she asked. "Are you upset because of the movie? You mean, that's why you didn't want to drive?" She couldn't quite believe it. *Piece of cake, my foot,* she thought, with the realization.

He shook his head. "Well, honestly, for a moment there I felt just a tad squeamish, so I didn't want to talk." He quickly held up his hand. "But it won't happen again. I promise. I'm used to the idea now. By the next class I'll be completely prepared." He smiled and shook his shoulders in a teasing, mock shudder. "Stirrups."

Kathleen smiled. "Now, you can't tell me a seasoned horse trainer like yourself is going to get squeamish over silly old stir—"

"That's *horses,* Kathleen."

"Yeah," she teased. "Flanders said you were actually beginning to breed horses now, too. I mean, horses and people do work on the same basic, fundamental principles. And you're not going to have much success if you don't understand those basic—"

In a flash he pulled her across the seat, so that she stretched over his lap. He smiled down at her, still looking a little ashen. The movie had apparently affected him much the same way it had affected her the first time she'd seen it. Which meant it had scared the hell out of him.

"Kathleen—" He flashed her another grin. "I mean, I understand how it works, but that…that poor woman." One of his hands moved to his chest, over his heart. "No offense to your sex or anything, Kathleen," he continued. "But I am damn glad I'm a man. I simply can't imagine having to…"

Snuggling against his shoulder, Kathleen couldn't fight back her laughter. Tears of it suddenly sprang to her eyes. "Never in a million years would I have guessed that one day you and I would be having this kind of discussion," she managed to say. It was suddenly just too much for her.

"It really is a strange turn of events, isn't it?" he asked.

"Yeah," she said, giggling.

He chuckled in response. "You laugh—" he continued in mock censure, even as the corners of his mouth began to twitch. "But that baby weighed nearly nine pounds and she had it naturally."

The way he choked on the word *naturally* sent her into a gale of uncontrollable giggles. Her shoulders shook with laughter. She nuzzled her face against his shirt while she giggled, breathing in the heady scent of his skin. Kathleen knew exactly what he was trying to say—that the act of actually giving birth to a baby seemed too incredible to really be possible.

As true as that was, she couldn't stop laughing to save her life. It was all so incredible and touching…Roman, their marriage, the baby, and how involved he wanted to be in her pregnancy. And part of the laughter was serving to release her sheer near-hysterical anxiety over the fact of labor, too. But the worst thing was the hint of true bewilderment in Roman's eyes. Was this really Roman Lawrence? Could it be?

And the more she laughed, the more he tried to explain, between his own deep chuckles.

After a few moments Kathleen found herself wrapping her arms around his neck. They were both laughing and stopping and starting again, with a wicked case of the giggles. Every time they hazarded glances at each other, they'd just start laughing again, even though nothing funny had really been said…and even though their laughter signified amazement over their changed feelings toward each other.

After a while there was silence punctuated only by occasional shaking quick breaths or sighs or giggles, the kind of silence that just threatened to make them start all over again. Kathleen pressed her face against his T-shirt and shut her eyes.

Finally Roman said, "Darlin', the poor woman's screams didn't even sound human. It nearly broke my heart. I honestly don't think I could listen to you scream like that."

His words sobered her completely. The impulse to laugh totally vanished. Roman really was going to be there when it happened! He was imagining how he was going to handle her cries when she went into labor. He was going to class with her every week. She swallowed. Hard. He began to rub soft, slow circles over her back.

"It really is amazing," he said gently.

"Babies?" she asked, feeling suddenly breathless.

"Yeah," he said. "But I was talking about you and me."

Her mouth went dry. "I'm glad we're...together."

"Me, too," he said. Their eyes met and held for a moment. "Are you scared?"

"About labor?"

He nodded.

She knew she should move to her side of the seat, but she simply couldn't, not when Roman had admitted that he meant to be there for her, at least until she went into labor. She pressed her cheek against his shirt again, relaxing against him, and tried to force herself to sound practical.

"By then you're in so much pain and so anxious to have the baby born that you really don't have time to process it all until later," she finally said.

She glanced up at him and her breath caught in her throat. He was staring at her so long and so hard that she felt the cramped confines of the car closing in around her again. Like a vise.

"So you're not scared?" he finally asked.

"Oh, Roman," she whispered. "I'm scared to death."

He tilted his head downward, cupped her face with one of his hands and kissed her. It was the tenderest, softest kiss she'd ever felt.

"I'll do anything I can to help," he said softly.

"Thank you so much, Roman," she whispered.

"I mean it," he said after a moment. "Anything."

Kathleen's hand dropped to her stomach and rested there. She felt her eyes sting a little as she touched the life inside her. It was the most amazing thing in the world. Still looking into his eyes, she found herself whispering, "I never knew how kind you could be."

His hand moved gently down the length of her side and back up again. "Things have changed," he said gently.

"Yeah," she said, wishing that things would always be as they were at this moment. "They sure have."

After a moment she forced herself to tear her eyes from his and clear her throat. The heaviness she felt in the car suddenly felt oppressive. Perhaps he was beginning to love her and the baby, but she wasn't about to start truly believing he did. And yet she did believe it. Didn't she?

"We better go," she whispered.

He leaned and lightly brushed her lips with his again. Then he nodded.

She scooted back across the seat, took the car out of Park and continued driving toward the house.

"Wonder if it's a boy or a girl?" Roman asked thoughtfully as she pulled in front of the château.

"I don't know," she said, half wishing they were still parked on the roadway, beneath the palms. She wanted nothing more than to relax in Roman's arms, just to sit there quietly like that for a while. *For the rest of my life.* "I had a sonogram," she said as she parked and got out of the car. "But they couldn't tell the sex. And anyway, even if they could have told me, I didn't want to know."

He caught her wrist when she'd reached his side of the car. "A what?"

She realized she felt a little bereft when he dropped

her wrist nearly as quickly as he'd lifted it. "They take pictures of the baby. They have this wand they rub over your stomach, after they put jelly on it."

Roman leaned close. "Strawberry, I hope," he whispered in her ear.

"You would," she returned. She shot him a wry smile. "More like petroleum."

"Are you sure it's safe?"

"Of course."

He nodded. "Dr. Peteck has a great reputation."

"I can't believe you checked his background," she said.

He smiled and put his arms around her shoulders. "I want the best for you," he laughed softly. "And the baby."

Suddenly she laughed. "Have I got a surprise for you...."

She stepped lightly in front of Roman, preceding him through the door, then shot a very coy glance over her shoulder.

"Now what are you up to?" he called after her in a low teasing singsong.

"I'm not telling...." She singsonged back.

"OUR DEN IS HARDLY a surprise," Roman said, putting his hands on his hips and only vaguely noting that he'd referred to a room in his house as jointly belonging to them.

Just what did Kathleen have up her sleeve? She was rifling through drawers as if she'd lost something. Watching her move through the room, he felt a rush of pride. As far as he was concerned, she'd been the most beautiful expectant mother in the class. Of course, every other father undoubtedly felt the exact same way about *his* wife.

If Roman had always felt a little overwhelmed by his desire for her, and if he'd felt that desire even more during her pregnancy, he felt it tenfold since seeing that film. He'd never expected the effect of seeing that little head appear....

Something about it still seemed so strange and unbelievable and magical that every time he looked at Kathleen now, he could only think, *She's going to do that.* Somehow, when it came to labor, fathers didn't seem to matter quite so much. He'd be there, of course, but Kathleen was undoubtedly the principal player. And their baby.

Watching her backside twitch as she rifled through some more drawers, he grinned. He sat on the sofa and swallowed suddenly. He wasn't about to tell Kathleen, but there was a distinct possibility that he'd pass out when the baby was born. His brows furrowed. He wasn't about to tell her that he'd asked Miles to draw up divorce papers, either.

He made a mental note to call the lawyer. With every passing day he became more and more convinced that a divorce might not be necessary. Not that he was ready to make a lifelong commitment, he thought, but at moments, he sure felt close to it. He only hoped Kathleen was feeling the same way.

"If you told me what you were looking for, I could help you find, it darlin'," he drawled, as if to dispel his thoughts.

"Don't try to bribe me," she said over her shoulder. "Ah ha!"

It was a videotape. He watched her shove it in the player, thinking he'd seen enough movies for one night, and yet wondering what this one was about. Then she came toward him.

She leaned a hand toward the sofa seat, as if to better turn herself to sit on it. Before he even thought it through, he caught her wrist and turned her, so she plopped right in his lap. Then he gave her a quick, playful kiss.

"Surprise."

"This was suppose to be my surprise," she said a little weakly.

"And if you don't hurry up, I intend to seduce the secret out of you," he teased. He threw his head back and laughed when she playfully jumped off his lap. Her mind hadn't quite caught up to the changes in her body. She always began to move like her scrappy former self, and always seemed to be reminded, midmovement, of her additional weight.

The way she moved was so damnably adorable that he smiled. Then, feeling the warm tug of arousal that followed in her wake, he sobered. He was beginning to think that things really would work out between them. Perhaps they really could be a family.

She hit a button on the remote, forcing his attention to the television. "Nice surprise," he finally teased. "But what is it?"

He glanced at Kathleen. She was looking at him with an unnervingly knowing glance.

"Kathleen, if you don't tell me what this is, you're going to be sorry." He wiggled his brows.

That got her hopping. She jumped off the sofa, went all the way to the TV and knelt beside it. She started tracing lines on the screen with her fingers. "This is an arm," she began, her voice rising with excitement.

"This is the other one and here—see!—here's the baby's backside."

Roman squinted. "It's a baby?" he muttered as the picture slowly began to make sense.

Kathleen's hand shot to her stomach, and she patted herself with a hearty, self-satisfied gesture. "This one," she said with the biggest, silliest grin he'd ever seen.

"No," he finally whispered throatily, vaguely aware that he, himself, had slid off the sofa and was scooting toward Kathleen. His child! He got close to the screen, stared at it, then unceremoniously took the remote from her. The tape wasn't even over, but he rewound and started it again. The way the baby curled in a little knot made it very difficult to figure out exactly what was going on.

"Now where's the head?" He felt Kathleen take his remote-free hand and guide it along her stomach.

"Right there," she said softly.

His hand squeezed from beneath hers so he could slide it under her T-shirt. Feeling the soft warmth of her skin was pure torture. His palm moved upward. He forced himself to stop it where she'd said the head was, even though her breasts were just inches away. Kathleen was just so beautiful. *My wife is beautiful,* he thought. *And so is the baby I've fathered.*

"So its feet are about here," he said, his palm sliding downward again, over the silken curve of her stomach.

"Not even born and he's a star," Kathleen teased. "Lionized by his adoring public."

"Or *her* public," Roman corrected gently.

"Are you going to watch the whole tape? Or are you

just going to keep rewinding?'' she asked in a near whisper.

As much as he felt like teasing her back, he turned his attention to the set instead, determined to watch to the very end. Roman tried to fight it and couldn't. He hit Stop, Rewind, and Play over and over. His hand began to draw soft circles on her stomach. ''Well, this is just incredible.'' Midgesture his hand froze and he gasped.

''He moved,'' he said flatly.

''Or she,'' Kathleen said softly. ''All the time,'' she continued, pressing his hand against her. Whether it was so he'd feel the baby better or so his palm would stop creeping downward, he wasn't sure.

His eyes shot to Kathleen's again. She was looking at him as if he were as cute as a newborn, himself. He tried to temper the awed expression on his face, but couldn't.

''Well—'' He rolled full to the floor, lay on his back and looked up at her, hitting Rewind as he moved. ''You know how we always used to fight?'' he asked, feeling glad that they no longer did.

She nodded. ''Where it's always like one or the other of us is trying to get the upper hand?'' She flashed him a smile. She was trying to tease him, but her smile only looked sweet. ''And where I always win?''

''You only wished you won,'' he said, smiling back. Noting yet again how full her breasts had become, he sighed. She was one brave woman, too. After all, if he hadn't married her, it was clear she'd meant to have the baby alone. Leave it to Kathleen to take on such a responsibility all by herself.

"So?" she finally prompted, getting up from the floor.

He blinked. He'd been so immersed in thinking about Kathleen that he'd forgotten the topic. "Oh...so, even I'll admit you just won our latest round," he said, stretching his arms behind him and clasping his hands behind his neck. "Cause, lady, there's just some things even I can't do."

She smiled. "Now that I've won, I'm going to bed."

"With or without me?" He couldn't help but ask.

"Alone."

He watched her turn and head for the door. When she reached it he said, "That still doesn't answer my question. After all, you could certainly be alone with me." How could he even begin to try to make this marriage truly work without having a physical relationship? he wondered.

"Alone as in by myself," she called over her shoulder.

"Aren't you coy," he said, though not loudly enough that she would hear.

And she was. She teased and toyed with him at every turn, she fired him up and then she turned him off cold. And, after twelve years, he still had no clue about what to do about it.

He wanted her in the worst way...in every way. He wanted her playfully, wanted her tenderly.... *And, damn it,* he thought, *she is my wife. And the mother of my child.*

Roman's mouth stretched into a thinning line, recalling how she'd jumped from the bed they'd shared...as if their lovemaking were just some mistake she'd made. Every untutored touch and gasp of her breath had said otherwise, of course, but she'd still hopped off the bed like a scared rabbit. And yet, lately he'd been sure her feelings toward him had changed. He knew his had toward her.

He groaned and rolled to his stomach. For a long moment he gazed at the blank television screen. And then he hit the Play button on the remote again.

Chapter Nine

Kathleen heard footsteps pounding on the diving board behind her. She turned in the pool just in time to see Roman's body arch in another of his perfect swan dives. The board vibrated in his wake. He turned gracefully in the air, nearly touching his toes as he turned, then he shot into the water with barely a splash.

It was dark and the floodlights created wavering thin blue rays of light on the pool's bottom. Kathleen rested her hand in the indented gutter that ran around the pool's perimeter, kicked her legs slowly in the water and watched Roman swim toward her. His hair fanned out before each of his strokes, then slicked against his head when he kicked. She smiled when he surfaced right beside her and hooked his fingers into the gutter.

"I brought a snack when I came back outside," he said, nodding toward the deck. His glance skimmed over her black maternity suit; it was his favorite. Unlike some of the others, it lacked the addition of a skirted front that hid her stomach.

"Fruit?" she asked, smiling.

He nodded, taking her hand. "C'mon, let's get to where we can stand."

With that, he dunked under the water, pulling her

with him. She took a quick breath before she immersed her head, then swam toward the shallow end with him. She only kicked, allowing him to pull her forward by the hand.

"Much better," he said when they resurfaced.

She leaned against the side of the pool. The water eddied right below her breasts and the cooler air wafted against her upper body. "We're here," she said playfully. "Now what?"

"Oh, I don't know," he said softly. He placed his hands on either side of her, hooking his fingers in the drainage gutter, then glancing down at her stomach. He couldn't help but slide one of his hands just beneath her breasts and over it.

Seeing her nipples grow taut against the tight, wet black nylon of her suit, he felt his own blood quicken and his groin tighten. "I had a good time in class tonight." He smiled.

She nodded. "I did, too." It had been Roman's third class. Ever since he'd started the Lamaze classes, she'd enjoyed them twice as much. "I'm so glad you're coming with me," she added softly. Roman's hand rose just a notch on her stomach, and she sucked in her breath.

"Roman…"

"Yeah?" His huge dark eyes glanced into hers and he smiled, continuing to rub his palm over the curve of her stomach.

She placed her hand over his, stopping him. "Roman…"

"I think you already said that, darlin'," he teased.

"I—I want to be with you," she began. "But this really is all just more complex than I can handle right now. I'm going to be a mother—"

"I know," he interjected, smiling. "And I'm going to be a father."

Her brows furrowed. "But the relationship between us is just changing too fast," she protested. How could he accept fatherhood so easily, when he wasn't the biological father?

He leaned so close he could smell the scents of her skin and the chlorine. He lifted a wet lock of hair from her forehead and gently held it for a moment between his fingers before he let it drop. "No change is too fast," he said softly, "when it's a good change."

She blew out a soft sigh. He was so close that their bodies met at many points. One of his hands still rubbed her stomach. His other grazed her shoulder for a brief second, then his elbow touched hers. Their bare toes were touching on the pool floor. She had never felt more aware of his presence, and she reached out, almost against her will, and touched his lips.

He grasped her hand and pressed it against his mouth, kissing each of her fingers, one by one. Then he drew her hand over his shoulder, so that her arm curled around his neck. He tilted his head and swept his lips over hers.

When she leaned back she said, "I know what's happening between us is a good change, but..."

"But?" he prompted gently.

"But...well, for instance, there's Malcolm Van Ness..."

The last thing Roman wanted to discuss right about now was Van Ness. What did he have to do with anything? "I know you were involved, but I also know you don't love him, Kathleen," Roman managed to say, forcing down any jealousy he was feeling. Of course, he didn't know it for sure, but this was at least one way of getting at the truth.

She shook her head. "No, I don't."

Roman had never felt more relieved. "But could you love me?" He flashed her a lightning-quick grin. "That's the real question." He'd said it a bit flirtatiously, but he couldn't believe he'd actually voiced it at all. It was as if it had come from outside himself...or from very deep within him, from his most secret longing.

"I...I think I could," she said slowly, dropping her gaze shyly from his eyes to his chest. She lifted her other arm and twined both her hands behind his neck.

"I've thought long and hard about the past, Kathleen."

Her eyes shot to his. "You have?"

He nodded, cupping her chin in his fingers. "And I really don't harbor any more resentments."

"Really?"

"Really," he said. When she didn't say anything, he pulled her closer. "C'mon, let's have our snack."

They walked to the very end of the pool together and up the steps. When they reached the spot where their cover-ups were, he held hers out for her. As she slid into it, he rubbed the thick terry cloth vigorously against her, drying her with the robe. Then he leaned for the table where he'd put their fruit, and pulled a cluster of grapes from the tray. "Open up, Cleopatra," he teased.

Kathleen opened her mouth, shut her eyes and allowed him to feed her a half dozen of the grapes, one by one.

"Well, Caesar," she said after a moment. She opened her eyes and smiled at him.

"Marc Antony," he corrected. "He was Cleopatra's lover."

"Oh, right," she replied, wondering if, perhaps, it wasn't time that she and Roman became lovers again…and if it could mean forever. "Who was Brutus?"

"The bad guy," Roman said. "The traitor." He leaned against the table and pulled Kathleen in front of him, his arms circling her waist. She smelled of chlorine and soft, just-laundered terry cloth. Talking about bad guys made him think of Van Ness.

Vaguely he wondered why Van Ness and Kathleen had broken up…and he hoped again there was no chance of their feelings for each other being rekindled. After all, she had implied that Van Ness had something to do with why she wanted to take more time with their relationship now. Had he hurt her that much emotionally?

"So let's talk about you and me," he said softly, leaning to nuzzle his cheek against her neck. He couldn't help but add, "And not Malcolm Van Ness."

Kathleen sighed and turned in his arms to face him. She trailed her fingers over his cheek. Her gaze dropped to his chest. "Roman," she said gently, "you have to be realistic. Malcolm doesn't ever intend to be a real father to this child. He's made that clear. But he is the real father."

She could feel Roman tense against her, but she forced herself to continue. "As much as I respect and admire you for being able to accept this situation so easily, I'm not sure that I can do so quite as—" She glanced up. When she saw the look on Roman's face, she stopped talking.

"Roman?" she said.

He wanted to kill her, he thought. His arms had been circling her waist and now they shot away from her sides, and he managed to take a fast step backward. He moved so quickly from their embrace that she nearly lost her balance. Not that he cared if she did, he told himself. He stared at her for a long moment. Had Kathleen just said that Malcolm Van Ness was the biological father of his child? *His child.* Please, let there be some mistake.

"Repeat that, would you?" he said, his voice low and lethal.

Her mouth dropped in shock. What had she said? What was wrong? "Which part? What did I say?" she asked, her words sounding strangled, as if they were trapped in her throat and fighting to get out.

She had never seen Roman look so angry. His skin had turned a shade darker and his eyes had turned a flat, formidable black. He grasped her elbow, twisting her toward him, then leaned, staring deep into her eyes.

"Roman," she said in censure. He wasn't hurting her, but his grasp on her arm pinched.

"The father," he said, his voice dropping another notch. "Who is the father of the baby?"

"Roman, let go of my—"

"Who?" he demanded.

She managed to shrug. What in the world had gotten into Roman? Why did he suddenly look as if he was about to go crazy? "Malcolm is," she managed to say. "You said you talked to him and he told you everything…you knew…."

Roman dropped her elbow and his hand flew to his own stomach. He felt as if he'd been sucker punched and he felt a little sick. Kathleen was merely staring at him, openmouthed.

"Isn't that what he told you?" she asked. Her mouth went dry and she swallowed. What was happening? "What did he tell you?" she demanded. Roman was looking at her as if he hated her. But he couldn't. He didn't. Just moments before they'd been swimming, eating fruit, kissing...they'd just come from their birthing class....

Now he was slowly raising his finger and pointing it at her face. "Stay the hell away from me," he was saying flatly.

She reached out, almost instinctively, and grabbed his finger, trying to pull him toward her. It was a mistake. He flinched and pushed her hand away. Tears sprang to her eyes. "Roman?"

"I never want to see your face again," he said. "Do you hear me? Never."

With that he turned on his heel and strode quickly for the house.

AFTER A LONG, SHOCKED moment Kathleen ran after him. She'd seen Roman look a million ways—playfully innocent, darkly seductive, deeply suspicious, completely impassioned...and even angry as sin. But she had never seen the kind of look that had just crossed the man's dangerously handsome features. Roman looked furious...and hurt. Had Van Ness lied to him? What had he said?

She hadn't bothered to find her sandals, and as she fled toward the house, pebbles and twigs dug into her feet. She ran straight for the stairs, and didn't stop until she had reached his room. She leaned breathlessly inside the doorway, and stared at the bed. A suitcase was already lying on top of it. It was open, and she could hear Roman rummaging around inside his walk-in closet.

"Oh, no," she whispered, staring at the suitcase. "You're not leaving, are you? You can't be...." She glanced toward the closet door.

He emerged, carrying handfuls of socks and underwear. He tossed them into the open suitcase, not seeming to mind that they had all come unfolded. And then, as if only now becoming aware of her, he turned and stared. He looked as if he'd just seen a ghost.

"I thought I just told you to get the hell out of my life," he said. His voice was full of so much restrained emotion that Kathleen suddenly felt cold.

"Just whose baby did you think it was?" she managed to ask. "What in the world did Van Ness tell you?"

"Don't push your luck," he said, heading back inside his closet. He came back out and paused in front of the bed with a stack of folded blue jeans in his arms. He dropped the stack from nearly shoulder level, and they hit the bottom of the suitcase with a thud. He turned and stared at her for a long moment. "If I were you, darlin', I'd get out of here."

It was definitely a threat, but she couldn't force herself to walk away. "Whose?" she repeated.

He pulled a pair of jeans on, over his swim trunks, and then he sat on the bed and pulled on his socks and boots. Already the damp trunks were seeping through; wet spots formed on his jeans. Finally he looked at her.

Kathleen's mouth went dry and she swallowed. His dark eyes looked almost vulnerable and his wet hair was arranged in wild strands around his cheeks. She wanted to pull him into her arms and take away the hurt he was clearly feeling.

"Please, Roman," she said. "Whose?"

"Whose do you think?" he said flatly. Each word sounded like a threat.

"I don't know," she managed to say, both her own voice and her sense of foreboding rising.

"Mine," he said fiercely.

Then he leaped from the bed so fast she flinched. He only stalked past her to the bathroom, and came back out carrying a toiletry bag and an electric razor. He tossed the items into the suitcase.

Kathleen's hand moved down to her stomach, both as if her baby could comfort her and because she, too, was now feeling a little sick. Her eyes stung with tears that threatened to spill as she watched Roman head for the closet again. This time he returned with shirts. He dumped them into the suitcase without bothering to remove them from the hangers.

"Yours?" she finally asked weakly.

"Of course I thought it was mine," he said, his voice dropping another notch.

If it hadn't been for the look on his face, if it hadn't been for all the hurt he was feeling, her spirits would have soared. Roman had thought the baby was his...and he'd wanted it and her. She couldn't let him leave her now. "How did you come to that—"

"You left me that fine little note," he snarled as he ripped one of the shirts in the suitcase from a hanger. He turned toward her as he shrugged into it. "Or don't you remember it? White, green-bordered stationery...."

Her hand flew to her mouth, and the tear that had been wavering on her lower eyelash fell. She remembered it, all right. But she'd never have believed that it could have made events become so misconstrued.

How could the damnable thing cause so much damage? He was supposed to think he'd slept with her, not fathered her baby.

"Remember it?" he demanded as he slowly buttoned his shirt. His voice became lower, more lethal sounding. "You know, the one where mean old Roman took advantage of you...slept with you, even though you were so horribly, desperately ill? And you were so steamed you were calling the authorities?" The cotton of his shirt snapped as he tucked it in.

"Roman, I—I'm so sorry. So..." The skin around her eyes had grown terribly tight. Another tear splashed against her cheek, but for the first time in her life she didn't care if Roman saw her cry. She leaned back against the wall, not knowing what to do.

"Were you really so drunk you thought that..." She glanced at him.

His mouth dropped open and he gazed at her for a long moment. His eyes flashed like lightning. "This is my fault now?" he nearly yelled. He quickly pursed his lips, glanced down and began buckling his belt. "I was in my library, behind a damn locked door. I hardly invited you inside, darlin'."

He turned from her, leaned down and began zipping the suitcase. When he finished, he stalked toward her until he was standing right in front of her. "And if you must know," he continued, "I was pretty sure I wasn't all that soused."

"Well, then, why did you believe—"

"Hell if I know," he said, enunciating each word. "Maybe because I wanted to."

She reached out to touch him, but he stepped back, and she felt another tear splash at her cheek.

"Maybe I wanted to *then,*" he said. "But I sure don't want to *now.*"

She knew that was calculated to break her heart, and told herself not to give in...not to let him leave without a fight. "Roman," she ventured, "I know this is the worst imaginable misunderstand—"

"We really didn't sleep together." It was a statement, not a question. His eyes were still flashing and he was so close she could feel the angry heat radiate from his body.

"No," she forced herself to say.

"And you were sick at the hospital because you were pregnant, even then?" He spat the words out like curses.

She could only nod. She brushed the back of her hand against her cheek to wipe away her tears.

"And when was the last time you saw Van Ness before he came over for the ring?"

She sucked in a breath, feeling that she was under bright fluorescent lights.

"When, Kathleen?" he said.

"When I dived off his boat. The night you found me swimming," she said in a rush.

In other circumstances the cynical sound he made could have passed for a chuckle. "And I bet you'd just told him you were pregnant," he said.

She nodded again.

"And you never talked to him on the phone after that?"

"No," she answered, thinking that at least they were talking now. Maybe he wouldn't leave, after all. "Did Malcolm say—"

"Malcolm didn't say anything," Roman said gruffly. "He *lied.* And so did you, Kathleen."

"Please don't...don't leave, Roman," she said as calmly as she could. The words sounded strangled.

He leaned forward, so close his breath whispered by her cheek. "You really expect me to *stay?*"

"I don't expect anything," she said. "But I want you to stay. Oh, I *want*..."

Something flickered in his eyes—it looked like longing and desire and love—and for that second, she was sure that he'd unpack and that they could work things out. His lips parted and he inadvertently licked them. His eyes relaxed and seemed to have a million questions written inside them.

"Please, Roman?" *Oh, please.*

He didn't say anything.

Another tear teetered on her lash and fell. "It's been so good between us lately," she continued, a pleading tone creeping into her voice. She cleared her throat. "Please stay."

"No way." He turned quickly on his heel and headed for the closet again.

"Are you coming back?" The words came out in a gasp as he returned, shrugging into a jean jacket.

He placed his hand around the handle of the suitcase. Then he looked at her for a long moment and his gaze shot, seemingly inadvertently, toward the nursery. He stared into the room for a long time, then shut his eyes, turned his face and looked at her again.

"Roman, I'll do anything in the world to make this up to you," she managed to say, fighting how her voice wanted to break.

"Oh, I'm sure you would," he said levelly. "If I ever gave you the chance."

With that he heaved the suitcase off the bed. It

swung around to his side. Then he strode past her with even-paced steps and through the doorway.

"Roman!" She started out to the hallway, but stopped when he turned and glanced at her over his shoulder.

"Don't even bother," he said. He turned his back to her and continued walking.

He meant it. And she knew it. She watched him until he was gone...watched him walk down the hallway, turn and descend each stair and then walk across the tiled floor. The last thing she saw was his boot heel disappear around the doorway to the foyer. And then, after a long moment, she heard the front door slam shut.

Somehow she managed to make it to her bed. She flung herself across it, grabbed a pillow and wrapped her arms as tightly around it as if it were Roman.

Roman...who was never coming back. Roman... whom she would never see again.

Chapter Ten

Kathleen's gaze shot upward when she heard the doorbell. But Roman wouldn't ring his own doorbell, would he? Still, she thought, rising from the kitchen table and heading for the door, maybe it was a telegram. Or something...anything. She hadn't heard from him for two weeks. Would he ever give her the chance to make things up to him? And even if he did, could such a horrible thing ever truly be made right?

She opened the door slowly. *Please be Roman.*

It wasn't. Kathleen peered at each face in the small crowd that was assembled on the porch.

"Surprise!" the people shouted in unison.

"Tamara," Kathleen murmured, nodding at Inge Krause's teenage daughter. Inge herself held out a wrapped box with a thick, shining silver bow. The paper was white, printed with tiny adorable puppies. Her husband, Jerry, pushed a baby carriage past Kathleen across the threshold.

"Thank you," Kathleen managed to say as Johnny Walker filed through carrying another package, this one wrapped in yellow-and-pink paper with an A-B-C building-block print. "Dr. Peteck?" Kathleen said. Not only was her doctor here, but Wendy had come, too.

"And this must be Alicia," Kathleen continued, looking for a long moment at the two-year-old in Wendy's arms.

George Roy wiped his cowboy boots on the welcome mat and his wife, Kelly, smiled at Kathleen. She, too, came bearing a gift.

Too overwhelmed to know what to say, Kathleen murmured her thanks while she led her guests to the château's spacious living room. The last thing she'd expected was for people to bring gifts for the baby.

"So where's the expectant father?" Tamara asked shyly, glancing around.

"I know he called to say he couldn't be in class with you last week," Wendy piped in, "but he's been planning your little surprise shower for weeks. I figured he'd be back for the party."

"His invitations were so cute," Kelly said.

Kathleen felt the skin around her eyes grow tight and forced herself to smile. She couldn't have felt more glad to see Flanders at that moment. He entered the room swiftly, leaned by her ear and said, "We do have some refreshments. Roman had things ordered."

"Thank you so much," she whispered back, managing to smile at the guests. She could almost have kissed Flanders for the reassuring way he squeezed her shoulder.

"Roman's still…away," she managed to say in answer to all the questions. All along, Roman had been planning this surprise party for her…and it nearly broke her heart. The last thing she needed right now was such a sweet reminder of how kind and thoughtful he could be, and of what a wonderful father he would make.

"Well, it's such a shame he couldn't be here, too,"

George Roy finally said. "He was awfully excited about the party."

"I'm sorry he's not here, too," Kathleen responded, in what she thought had to be the greatest understatement of her life. She vaguely realized that someone had put on some music.

Within moments Flanders and Ms. Rodriguez had returned with a tray on rollers. It was laid with a fruit plate, small fruit tarts, slices of cake and assorted beverages. Fortunately most of the guests knew one another and busied themselves by filling their dessert plates; they all fell into immediate conversation.

That was good, Kathleen thought, because she was sure she couldn't exactly play the happy hostess...or the happy wife. She wasn't even sure she could play the happy mother-to-be. Kathleen followed the small talk as best she could, and even felt herself relaxing somewhat after a while. As much as she missed Roman, and as much as she longed for him to come back, seeing people was making her feel better than she had in days.

"When *is* Roman coming back, Kathleen?" Johnny Walker asked as he polished off a second slice of cake. "We've got to finish training for the Miami Futurity and, well...cutting out like this just isn't like Roman." Johnny Walker frowned. "Not even if it's to go over his quarterly earnings with the accountant."

"Quarterly earnings..." Kathleen echoed. Was that what Roman had told everyone? She supposed so, even if Kathleen knew he wasn't with the accountant or anyone else she had contacted. And no member of the household staff had any idea where he'd gone. Flanders, usually Roman's confidant, was just as worried about his whereabouts as Kathleen.

"Ready to open your gifts?" Inge asked. The jovial woman seated herself next to Kathleen and placed the package she'd brought in Kathleen's lap.

A genuine smile peeped through Kathleen's false one. "Sure," she said. These days, only thinking about the baby really softened the blow of Roman's departure. She slowly removed the ribbon and paper.

"It's lovely," she said breathlessly, holding up a plate and cup set. Tamara's package contained a matching bib and cap.

For the briefest moment, while she unwrapped those beautifully presented packages, Kathleen almost forgot about Roman. There were so many wonderful things for the baby—bunting outfits, building blocks, handcrafted wooden toys and a play seat....

"How can I ever thank you all enough?" she finally found herself saying.

"The baby's thanks enough," Johnny Walker said, grinning.

And yet, glancing down, she felt a sharp twinge of sadness. These were Roman's friends, too, and the party was his idea. The gifts were for him, as sure as they were for her and the baby. And she wanted him to have been here with her tonight.

"We've got to get going," Inge said a little later. Jerry nodded and stood. Everybody else soon followed, making Kathleen wish they'd all stay. Company seemed so preferable to being alone in a house that now seemed too big and too empty. She walked everyone to the door, murmuring her thanks again, and hoping everyone had had a good time.

"Don't you worry about any of this," Ms. Rodriguez said when Kathleen returned to the living room. "Go on up to bed."

Watching the woman arrange the baby's new things neatly in the boxes, Kathleen wanted to protest, but she only nodded and headed upstairs.

Even though everything in the nursery reminded her of Roman, she hadn't been able to bring herself to move into her old room. Now she glanced at the suitcase by her door, which she'd packed and repacked, although the hospital trip was still two long months away, and then she walked into Roman's bedroom.

She slowly drew her tent dress over her head and let it drop to the floor. She drew back his covers, slid beneath them, then kicked off her underwear. His sheets were sexy, of black silk, and as soft as his skin. She rubbed her hands over them, wishing that so many things were different…wishing that Roman might happen to come home and find her in his bed…wishing that he would become the father of her child…just wishing.

Outside, through the sheer curtains over the French doors, she could see a sliver of moon. She shut her eyes, imagining that a door downstairs had closed. She imagined that she heard soft, quiet footsteps ascending the stairs, and then the door to the hallway creaking just a bit as it opened…in both warning and a promise.

And then she rolled over, the cool silk sheets sliding over her skin as she turned, and he was there, standing in the doorway in a long black silk robe. He was walking toward her, so ready…so very ready…to make love to her again.

She didn't sleep. But in the early morning she felt even more determined to find him.

She had to find him.

A plan began to form in her mind. It was a last resort, but she knew what she had to do.

"MRS. LAWRENCE?" Kathleen clasped her hands in front of her and tried to steady her nerves. The secretary at Lawrence Realty had directed Kathleen to the construction site of a new hotel where Roman's mother could be found. "Are you Mrs. Lawrence?"

Gabriella turned and squinted at the young woman. In Gabriella's view she looked just lovely, and as pregnant as could be. But something about her seemed familiar. Terribly familiar. And the associations weren't good.

"What can I do for you?" she asked.

Kathleen couldn't say a word. Just what had she meant to do? She'd hoped Roman might have told his mother where he was, and yet Gabriella Lawrence was the last person she wanted to see. Ever.

"Speak up," Gabriella said, smiling at her again. She hated clichés about pregnant women, but it was simply true that they sometimes glowed. This one certainly did, and she was wearing one of the most tasteful, well-styled maternity dresses Gabriella had ever seen.

"You look a little peaked," Gabriella suddenly said.

"Really, I'm fine," Kathleen muttered. Peaked was an understatement. Confronting Gabriella Lawrence was making her quake in her sandals. Oh, why couldn't she say anything!

The next thing Kathleen knew, she found herself seated in a chair. Gabriella pressed an ice-cold glass of water in her hand, and then sat down, too. Things weren't going at all as Kathleen had planned. She'd meant to introduce herself and ask Gabriella directly if she knew where Roman was...but now his mother was pampering her.

"It's been absolute years since my son was born,

but I remember that peaked feeling well," Gabriella was saying. "What are you? About six months?"

"Seven," Kathleen managed to say. "And...thanks for the water. It *is* a little hot today."

"I was pregnant in the summer, too." Gabriella beamed at her. "Now, what can I do for you?"

"Uh, well, I..." Kathleen suddenly wondered if she should lie about who she was, and yet she didn't really want to. After all, in some deep part of herself she wanted Gabriella to accept her as a daughter-in-law. If Roman ever came back...if Roman ever loved her... *If, if, if...*

"Are you sure you're not too overheated?" Gabriella murmured, feeling concerned. Even though the woman was very tanned and thus, Gabriella thought, probably a native, she was starting to flush noticeably.

"No!" Kathleen gasped, thinking she had to be really in love with Roman to do such a crazy thing as visit his mother. *Just say it!* She cleared her throat. "Mrs. Lawrence, I—I'm Kathleen Cannon."

Gabriella Lawrence only stared at her.

Kathleen rushed on. "And I'm looking for Roman."

"Roman?" Gabriella repeated. "As in my son?"

"Yes," Kathleen said as levelly as she could. Gabriella had said "my son" as if every third man in America was named Roman.

"Why?" Gabriella asked in a strangled voice.

Kathleen bit back her temper, but her lip quivered with it. Gabriella made it sound as if Kathleen had absolutely no right to look for Roman. And she did have a right, didn't she?

"Why?" Gabriella asked again.

"Well, because...because he's my husband," Kathleen finished in a rush. She couldn't believe she'd said

it, but she'd felt nearly compelled to. Roman *was* her
husband. She *wanted* him to be a father to her baby.
And that, potentially, made Gabriella her mother-in-
law. In fact, Gabriella *was* already her mother-in-law,
if only legally.

"Husband?" Gabriella finally echoed.

"And if you see him—" The stunned look on Gabriella's face forced Kathleen to rise to her feet.
"Please tell him I'm looking for him." With that,
Kathleen headed down the steps, wishing for the ump-
teenth time that day that her ankles weren't quite so
swollen. And wishing that her visit to Gabriella had
rendered something concrete. At the moment the
woman was in such shock that she undoubtedly
couldn't talk.

Kathleen had made it to the car and Mr. Jenkenson
when she thought she heard Gabriella yelling at her.
She turned.

"I haven't heard from him for weeks," Gabriella
yelled. The woman's voice still sounded strangled.

Kathleen's mouth dropped in shock. "Thank you,"
she finally managed to yell back. As Kathleen got in
the car, she watched Gabriella disappear through a
doorway, clearly not willing to discuss the matter further.

Inside the building Gabriella leaned against a door
and blew out a shaky breath. So that was Kathleen
Cannon. Gertrude Van Ness had told her that Kathleen
was pregnant with Malcolm's child, though he intended
to make no claim on the baby. After all, rumors ran
around Key West just the way the waters of the ocean
did. But Roman had married Kathleen?

"I have a daughter-in-law, even if my son seems to
have disappeared," she murmured. "A *pregnant*

daughter-in-law." And suddenly Gabriella was sure there'd been far too many divorces in the Lawrence family. She was just going to have to do the responsible thing…and tell Roman that her divorce from his father had been entirely *her* fault.

"WELL, IN TERMS of the divorce, the baby's a key player," Miles Higgenbothem was saying. He was preparing for a lengthy vacation cruise in the Bahamas, and drinking a cold beer on the deck of his still-anchored boat at the Key West yacht club.

"But I don't just want a divorce," Roman said. "I want that baby." Roman sat on the closed lid of the beer cooler, then leaned back against the deck rail. He twined an arm through it as he stretched his long legs over the wood of the freshly washed deck.

"It's not your baby, Roman," Higgenbothem replied.

Roman merely shrugged. "But I *thought* it was."

Higgenbothem sighed. "Well, maybe we can get some kind of custody rights," he finally said, sounding none to happy about it.

"How's that?" Roman returned, sitting upright again long enough to pull his dark, waving hair back in a short ponytail with a coated elastic band. He knew he needed a haircut, but it had been a bad few weeks and he really didn't care how he looked. Who was looking, anyway? No one in the Miami Beach hotel where he'd been hiding out. And not Kathleen.

"Well, she deceived you," Higgenbothem said slowly.

Roman sighed. "Well, she didn't really…." After all, she hadn't intended to. And didn't intention count when it came to the law? *Why in thunder do I spend half my time taking her side in the matter?*

"I mean for argument's sake, in court," Higgenbothem said. "I mean, you thought it was your baby when you married her, right?"

"Right."

Higgenbothem sat opposite him in a deck chair, and placed his can of beer beside him on the deck. "That's deception, Roman."

"True," Roman muttered, still feeling angry with Kathleen even though the misunderstanding about the baby wasn't really her fault. When she'd realized what had happened she'd looked just as terrible as he'd felt.

Roman glanced over the rail at the calm green water that eddied around the dock. Higgenbothem acted as if he was crazy for wanting some rights to the child. But how could Higgenbothem know of the nights Roman had lain awake dreaming about his impending fatherhood...only to have the ground snapped right out from beneath him?

And how could he explain why he'd so desperately wanted to believe the baby was his? *What man would think he'd gotten a woman pregnant, on a first try...and without even remembering it? And then what man would marry her, to boot?*

Him. Because every single time he'd so much as glanced at her, she did an absolute number on his usually logical brain. Because he'd had more fun shopping for the baby with her than he'd ever had in his life.

Not that he hadn't had a grand old time in Miami Beach, he told himself. It was chic these days, with plenty of interesting passers-through and one of the best stretches of sand he'd found anywhere in the world. *Right, Roman. Face it, it was miserable.*

"You're going to have to divorce her on the grounds of mental cruelty, since, in court, it will look like she let you think you were the father of the baby. It's pretty solid," Higgenbothem was saying slowly. "But it's too soon."

Roman lifted himself up long enough to reach inside the cooler for a beer before he sat down again. "What do you mean? Soon?" he asked, cracking the tab.

How could Higgenbothem understand that Roman didn't even really want to divorce Kathleen, even though he didn't have much of another choice? What all those lonely Miami Beach nights had confirmed was that he wanted his marriage to Kathleen to eventually work out and to have their baby…his baby.

"I mean it's in your best interest to play the loving husband and father for the next couple of months," Higgenbothem was saying. "It'll really strengthen your case against her."

Roman rested his beer can against his thigh, feeling the cool condensation seep through his jeans. "Miles," he said, "I figure I'm just a little too angry to carry on that kind of charade."

"Do you want the baby or not?" Higgenbothem asked. He sighed. "Do you know how that will look in court? Fortune hunter takes man who was madly in love for the ride of his life. He loved her so much he even tried to reconcile after he found out the truth, that the child he thought was his really wasn't his own. And as hard as he tried, he couldn't reconcile because he was so deeply hurt? I wish you wouldn't pursue this, but if it's what you want, this line of argument is your best shot."

Roman wanted to protest and say that Kathleen wasn't devious enough to intentionally pretend that the baby was his, when it wasn't. But why was he taking Kathleen's side in the matter? he wondered again. Roman gulped down less than half his beer, then tossed the can to a trash container, hitting it right on. The can thudded in the bottom. "I'm supposed to go back and play the loving husband?"

"That's right," said Higgenbothem. "Loving husband."

THE FIRST MOMENT ROMAN saw her, he really did feel like a man in love. It was nearly midnight when he crept inside and stealthily ascended the stairs. He entered his bedroom just as quietly, the door creaking just a bit. His room was pitch-dark and, standing in the shadows, he could see her in the nursery.

Her back was toward him, a radio was on and she was doing stretch-and-breathe exercises, with her pale blue nightgown hiked to her thighs and her legs stretched wide apart. She leaned first toward one leg and then toward the other, stretching over her stomach, trying with all her might to reach the pink painted toes of her delectably slender feet...the same feet that had felt so right cupped in his hands.

You're divorcing her and don't forget it. "Loving husband," he muttered. "Kiss and make up."

He went toward the interconnecting door and leaned against the jamb. "Need someone to practice those exercises with, darlin'?"

Kathleen whirled around. She was on her feet faster than he would have imagined possible, given how large she was getting. "Roman!" She skipped to the doorway and stopped right in front of him.

Breathlessly in front of him. The blue gown had tiny spaghetti straps. Two triangular V-shaped bits of material barely covered her breasts. His gaze dipped into the cleavage and he audibly drew in his breath. He just couldn't help it.

"Roman?" she repeated.

"Expecting someone else?" he finally managed to tease. He reached upward lightly to graze a lock of her hair with his fingertips. He hoped the gesture was a little rascally, indicating sheer flirtatiousness, not the deep longing he actually felt…the feeling he meant to pursue, he thought now, right up until their divorce. "Been entertaining other men up here, in my absence?"

"No!" she said quickly. More quickly than she'd apparently intended because spots of color appeared on both her cheeks. "Where have you been?"

Her concern made him feel a little less exposed. After all, she knew how hurt he was…and how much he had wanted the baby. Still wanted the baby. "That's for me to know and you to find out, darlin'," he managed to say.

She took another step closer, leaning in the opposite side of the doorway, so that the toe of his boot nearly touched one of her perfectly pedicured feet. Her skin was flushed from exercise and when she clasped her hands in front of her, her gown pulled taut, right over her stomach. It was big. It reminded him of ripe, luscious, tasty fruits…and he wanted nothing more than to sink his face against her.

A slow-building languid heat pulsed through him. Every time he saw her stomach—every time he even thought about it—he felt that pull. Not that he was sexist. Not that he thought women *should* be pregnant. But, in her condition, every inch of her made him confront the intense, indescribable mystery of women…of her. Even if it *wasn't* his child.

She looked so big now he couldn't believe there were still two more months to go. And it was two months, not four, as he had thought. His shoulders were pressed against the jamb and his hips swung toward her just perceptibly. *Damn.* The movement was wholly involuntary.

He heard her quick intake of breath. That pointed little tongue of hers darted out and licked quickly at her lip. "Since where you've been is for me to find out, then why don't you just tell me, Roman?" she finally said, clearly barely able to match his playful tone.

Yes, her attempt at coyness fell flat. Her chest was starting to flush that splotchy red, too. He'd noticed the exact second it started to happen, since he'd barely bothered to take his eyes from her breasts. And she had no control over *her* eyes, either. They'd dipped down below his belt more times than he could count.

He tried his sexiest smile on her, and judging from her strangled-sounding little gasp, he figured it had worked. When he caught those green eyes dipping again, he whispered, "Guess you missed me, Kathleen."

"Yes," she said simply. She cleared her throat. "And I wish you had been here for the party." Her voice was thick and raspy with emotion. "It was so wonderful and kind of you," she finished in a rush.

"Missed you, too, darlin'," he said gruffly, feeling a twinge of temper at the mention of the shower that he'd so lovingly planned for *his* baby. The coarse sound of his voice made him feel even surlier. He'd missed her, all right, but he didn't exactly want her hearing how much.

"I'm glad you're back...really." Kathleen smiled at him—really smiled—and then rubbed her stomach softly, as if she wasn't even thinking about it, the way many pregnant women did.

He'd never really noticed that until lately. He'd never really noticed just how many pregnant women there were, walking around, either. But sure enough, he'd seen more pregnant women in Miami Beach than he'd noticed in his life. And for just an instant he'd thought every blessed one of them was Kathleen. Kathleen...who was supposed to be carrying *his* child.

He wished she'd say something else. The way her long blue gown rose and fell with each movement of her hand was making him long for her. In fact, the front of his jeans was starting to tighten and get a little uncomfortable. Next thing he knew, he'd probably be turning all motley, with those embarrassing splotches she got during awkward conversations.

"I'm so sorry..." she began. Her eyes looked all sleepy and sincere. "I don't want to talk about this...misunderstanding about the baby...not if you don't—"

Roman lifted his hand, resting his fingers lightly along the line of her jaw. He'd meant to just touch her lips with his thumb to silence her, but now, in spite of his anger, he found his thumb moving, tracing the lines of her lips. When she didn't protest, he pushed himself off the jamb with his shoulder and closed the foot of space between them.

Kathleen's arms quickly encircled his neck and Roman wrapped his around her waist in a tight hug. In the way she held him, he could feel just what kind of hug it was, too. It was far more than friendly but much less than sensual. She was simply saying with her body what she didn't want to say with words. She had seen the shock he'd felt when he'd realized she wasn't carrying his child. And she was sorry.

Her perfunctory little hug rankled. "I hardly want your sympathy, Kathleen," he said huskily. Her eyes widened slightly.

"I—I just wanted you to know that I mean to make things up to you, if you'll give me half a chance," she said. A hint of raspiness crept into her voice, as if she'd suddenly become aware that she was enclosed in his embrace.

Roman brought his lips close to hers, so they hovered right above her mouth, close enough that he could feel her trembling lower lip, far enough away that he could still gaze into her eyes. "Then make things up to me," he whispered.

"How?"

"Don't play dumb," he whispered. "Like this." He pressed his lips hard against hers, bending against her at the same time, feeling the soft roundness of her stomach press against his.

She responded, but not with any real passion. She took his lead, but only followed. He suddenly wanted to wrench her more aggressive side from her, to make her release it when she kissed him. He hadn't seen her in such a long time. Holding her, he tried to tell himself that this was all a charade. He was only *playing* the loving husband.

Roman's hands slid downward, over her shoulders. The callused flatness of his palms curved, molding along the silky lines of her gown, following the curves of her body, right down her sides. He nearly moaned when he discovered that she didn't have any waistline left.

The intimate aroused part of him strained against his own stomach through his clothes, begging to touch the heavy full weight of her stomach, even as his tongue thrust deeper, demanding every drop of her taste. Kathleen sank below him while his palms dipped past what used to be her waist and curled over her hips. Her gown strap slipped downward, following the pull of his hands. And yet, she was withholding herself. Why? he wondered. Hadn't she missed him?

She pulled away from him. Their lower lips just touched. He leaned again, unable to stop from pressing his lips softly to hers, feeling that wet, luscious pressure time and time again. When he felt her head strain even farther backward, he tongued a slow, heated, wet trail all the way down her long, slender neck.

"Darlin', that sound you're making is part sigh, part laugh and part moan. Mind telling me what it means?" He lifted his eyes.

"That felt pretty good," Kathleen whispered. "And I've missed you so much. I thought you were never coming back."

Roman simply held her, moving his hands to her waist, feeling when the warmth of her stomach suddenly left the heat of his own. What was he doing? He wanted her, of course, but things were so complex now. "But I did come back," he found himself murmuring.

Her hand crept upward and settled on his chest. "I'm still confused," she whispered. "Are you really not ~~~ry with me?"

"~~~~s," he managed to whisper back. He was furi- ~~~~ yet he had missed her.

~~~~ 're not, or yes, you're angry?" she asked.

Roman shot her a wry smile. "Just yes," he said. He leaned forward again, pressed his lips lightly to hers, then gazed into her eyes. *Those damnable eyes.* The flecks of yellow made them sparkle like green fire. She looked more passionately alive than any other woman he had ever seen.

She looked as if she only now realized how close they were to making love again. He had half a mind to just start kissing her, knowing that would weaken her will. But he didn't want her this way, not really. Not when so much was unresolved between them with regard to the baby.

"Why are you looking at me like that?"

"Like what, darlin'?" he managed to tease. "Or are you just begging me for compliments?" He eyed the strap that had fallen from her shoulder, noting how the triangular cloth over her breast had lowered. He decided not to replace the strap for her.

"I'm not sure," she finally murmured. "You're just looking at me like…I…I'm still confused about us."

"So there's still an us?"

"Roman," she said. "There's always been an us."

Her voice had steadied. It wasn't trembling anymore, wavering with questions about what their relationship could mean now.

"So come to my bed."

"Maybe…"

"Some other time?"

Kathleen nodded slowly. "Some other time… maybe."

"We can't be friends, Kathleen," he managed to say, his gaze dropping from her eyes to her well-kissed mouth. Her lips looked like the dew-drenched bulb of some wild red flower.

He watched those lips purse. "And why not, Roman?"

"Because nothing between us has ever been about being just friends." He flashed her a quick smile. "And anyway, the way I want you now has nothing to do with the way I used to want you."

For a second she looked scared. And suddenly he felt glad. God help him, but he half wanted to punish her for the unconscionable note she'd left him...the one that had made him think she was pregnant with his baby.

She cleared her throat. Her voice was still nearly a croak. "And how do you—" she turned bright scarlet "—uh, want me now?"

His heart twisted again. Kathleen was worried that he'd stopped wanting her altogether. "Oh, fiercely," he forced himself to say. *And that much is true.*

He brought his face an inch closer to hers, staring at her as if he could capture the moment forever. "With more than tenderness," he continued, covering yet another inch between them. "With such an intense appetite that I'm sure it has less to do with sweetness and caring and more to do with my more carnal, animal desires." He leaned just a fraction closer, hoping to taunt her, since she'd hurt him so much.

"I need to be loved," she murmured as his lips dipped toward hers.

The idea that the baby needed to be loved, too, hung between them, even though she hadn't said it. "Kathleen, you asked me how I wanted you and I'm just telling you the truth."

He brought his lips so near that barely a breath could pass between them. "But I don't want you..."

Her eyes grew wide.

"Until you want me in the very same way."

And suddenly he realized he wasn't toying with her anymore. He breathed in sharply and leaned to cover the space between their lips again. At the last second, just before he kissed her again, he forced himself not to.

To hell with letting her know how much I've missed her. "I'm always there," he whispered in her ear, as casually as he could. "Right on the other side of your doorway."

Her eyes were now as big as bright green saucers.

"Good night, Kathleen," he said softly.

When she didn't respond, he nodded and quietly closed the door that lay between them. Once it was shut, he leaned against it and blew out a long breath in the dark room. His heart was pounding and he could still feel her, right there, within his arms' reach, just on the other side of that door. He hadn't taunted her in quite that way for a long time, he thought.

And it was getting hard to do. It left him in a very foul mood. Stalking toward the bed, he began to strip, ripping his clothes off and leaving a trail between himself and Kathleen. By the time he reached the bed, he was fully nude and he slid between the sheets, wondering just how much Higgenbothem's game plan had to do with the way he'd come on to her. He hoped a lot.

What had he expected? he wondered as he stretched beneath the sheets. *I expected her to feel guilty and to have missed me, and to want to make love. I hoped she'd say that she wanted me to be the father of the baby.* Even though, within the next months, they were going to be divorced.

"The last thing you need is Kathleen," he muttered, hearing the radio next door snap off.

That deceitful note she'd left in the library proved just exactly how irresponsibly immature she could be.

He sighed, wondering why Kathleen had broken their kiss. After all, he was the injured party here. Although she had kissed him, it was clear she was very wary about pursuing their relationship now. He could hardly blame her for that. He was going to divorce her and take the baby.

When he stretched again, his foot caught at something beneath the sheets. His hand slid downward, seeking out whatever was there. Small, silky and lacy.

He pulled them from beneath the covers. In the moonlight, with his eyes adjusting to the dark, he could make them out. A pair of dark, solid-colored silk panties with lacy leg elastic.

"Someone's been sleeping in my bed," he muttered. As angry as he still felt, his heart skipped a beat. She had missed him…and not just out of guilt for what had happened. Almost against his will, he felt a little bit of the big bad wolf returning to his spirit.

Chapter Eleven

"Where are you taking me?" At the crack of dawn Kathleen had been hustled out the door, with barely enough time to dress. Then, in the back seat of the car, Roman had put a bandanna blindfold on her, folding it so no light could creep through at all, and knotting it at the back of her head.

"I'll never tell." His lips were right by her ear. "But I'm sorry I was so mad at you, and I'm trying to make it up."

Could things really be as simple as that? "May I please take this thing off?" she asked, unable to keep herself from smiling. As much as she hated to admit it, there was something tantalizing about having her eyes covered.

Roman was so close—but she didn't know just exactly where—and his breath lightly fluffed the hair by her ears when he talked. She could hardly believe how nicely he was treating her. It was almost as if he had never left. She wished he would talk more about the baby, but he didn't. Yet, he did seem to be trying to forgive her. And he had gone to the class with her since his return.

"Now, do you really want to take the blindfold off

and ruin your surprise, Kathleen?'' She felt him edge nearer on the seat of the car, and she caught a whiff of his subtle spiced cologne. The tiny hairs on her neck raised, and she somehow felt her back had gone up like a wary cat's, though she hadn't actually moved a muscle. The effect he was having on her was so dangerously exciting she couldn't stand it.

''No,'' she found herself saying just as the car pulled to a stop. She felt Roman slide across the seat again, this time away from her, and get out and slam the door. She had half a mind to remove her blindfold now, but decided to let him lead her wherever he was taking her...not that she really trusted him, of course. The way he was treating her, after all that had happened between them, seemed too good to be true. She'd seen how upset he had been, and that kind of hurt didn't just vanish.

Yes, he was nice, she thought now. *Too nice.* Pride went before a fall—she knew that well, and so did Roman Lawrence. Somehow, today felt like the beautiful calm that always preceded a crashing storm. Somehow, today felt like the old days, when they had spent all their time trading barbs.

Now, as the door beside her opened, she wondered if she wasn't being played for a fool. But how could she stay defensive when Roman had become so thoughtful and caring again?

''Come along, my pretty,'' Roman teased, singsonging his low-voiced words. He was nearly purring...and somehow it made her feel every bit like the proverbial toyed-with mouse. He leaned in the door, grasped her hand and pulled her from the passenger seat. The soft, cool dryness of his large hand covered hers, holding it tight. He was leading her forward.

Kathleen stopped in her tracks. "I won't take another step until you tell me where we're headed," she threatened.

She wondered again why she was letting him do this to her when, with every fiber of her being, she wanted to rip the bandanna from her eyes.

"Now, be a sport, darlin'," he said, his voice coming closer.

"But I don't trust you," she returned.

He only tugged her forward, so that she ran right into his chest. The cotton of it felt so neatly pressed and cleanly starchy smelling that she wanted nothing more than to rub her cheek against it.

"I don't blame you for not trusting me," he whispered. The whisper tickled a little, even if the way he said the words bothered her. But then his tongue darted quickly inside her ear, slightly dampening it. And then he blew against the wet spot. A tingle went through her whole body. She giggled, making him laugh. It was so good to hear him happy again, she thought.

"See," she declared, "even you know I shouldn't trust you."

"Just think of all the places I could be taking you." His voice had grown even huskier.

"Where *are* you taking me?"

He chuckled softly. "It could be a lion's den...." He began slowly luring her forward again.

"Lovely," she said. She'd meant it ironically, but her voice sounded low and raspy. She was just too affected by this little game he was playing to really tease him back. Did his flirtation mean that he wanted to get their relationship back on track...that he meant to try to make her his real wife? And what did he feel about the baby now?

He continued to pull her along. "Or I could be taking you to a volcano...." He suddenly laughed. "As a virgin sacrifice."

"I am not a virgin," she huffed a little defensively.

He laughed. It was a genuine, throaty laugh that rose and fell on her ears, seeming to touch them as he had with his tongue, though he hadn't really touched her at all.

"Since you're not a virgin, then maybe I'm taking you...to a deep, dark cave in the wilderness."

"The wilderness of Little Torch Key?" she asked, glad to hear the irony creeping back into her voice.

He didn't respond but only led her up a flight of steps. She could hear other people nearby. Where in the world was she? Was this the final destination? She hoped so. She didn't want to tell Roman, but her ankles were swollen and felt painfully tight. At the top of the steps—she counted eleven of them—she ran into him again.

"Or perhaps I'm taking you to my own private lair," Roman whispered. "Where I'll—"

"Where you'll what?" she asked, keeping her voice as flat and practical as she could.

"Oh, you know, darlin'." He was bending toward her; she could feel a lock of his hair fall against her cheek.

"Make me cook meals and do your laundry?" she asked, still trying to sound much more confident than his presence was making her feel.

He bent so close that his nose grazed along the line of her own, and his voice dropped to a whisper again. "No," he said. "After all, I'd hate to put Ms. Rodriguez on the bread line. I was thinking more in terms of..."

His lips skated across her cheek, making goose bumps rise on her flesh. More than ever she wanted to pull the bandanna off. She wanted to see exactly how playful or how serious he was. She didn't want him flirting with her—not anymore.

"Along the lines of ravishing you."

"Ravish is something they do in historical novels," she said levelly.

"Ravish works just fine for the twentieth century, darlin'," he murmured back. He dipped his lips lower and brushed her lips softly.

When he drew back, he pulled her with him, turned her expertly and seated her. Now, she thought, I'll finally figure out where he's taking me.

In a quick motion he drew off the bandanna. She was in a private airplane. And at the moment she opened her eyes the engines started. They began taxiing down the runway.

"So where are we going?" She couldn't help it. Her voice was a near wail of either desire or panic, and she didn't quite know which. Illogically, she felt that wherever it was, she might never be coming back. There would be no return from there at all.

Roman only smiled. It was a knowing smile, too. Was there anything the man couldn't guess about her? He knew just exactly which buttons to press...and how hard. Everything about his smirk said he knew just how much surprises fired her up.

"Don't worry." He leaned toward her. "I've got another surprise for the road."

Kathleen stared at him while he playfully fished in his pockets for something. Finally he found it, and pressed a box into her hand. The box was small, round and velvet.

It was a…ring!

A thick gold band studded with four diamonds. The very same one they'd seen in the jewelry store in Key West, when they'd gone shopping.

"What's this for?" she asked cautiously as he draped his arm around her.

"I decided that the ring I gave you is a little…" His voice trailed off and then he shrugged. "Frankly, Kathleen, I don't really know," he said with a trace of curtness in his voice. "You wanted it and that's all."

"It's beautiful, Roman," Kathleen managed to say as she slipped the slender band he'd given her when they'd married off her finger. Roman might still be a little testy, but he had come back home. She placed the new ring on her ring finger first, then slid the slender band on top of it.

"The idea was that the new ring should replace the old one," Roman said, his dark eyes suddenly twinkling again. "I mean, don't you want a more expensive ring…"

Kathleen pointed at the slender band. "This is my real wedding ring, the one you gave me when we got married," she said, coloring slightly when she said it, wishing he'd raise the topic of both their marriage and her baby. "I intend to keep wearing it."

"Women and rings," Roman muttered, as if the issue were simply beyond his comprehension. Nonetheless, the hand on her shoulder tightened perceptibly.

Kathleen allowed herself to sink farther into the seat, against Roman's shoulder. That this was too good to be true no longer mattered, she told herself. For just today she'd pretend that she could trust him because it felt so good…so right to be snuggled against his shoulder. Perhaps the ring did signify a willingness to try to work things out, even if Roman wouldn't say so.

She cleared her throat. "So where are we going, Roman?"

But it wasn't really a question now. She didn't care if he was taking her to a lion's den or to be sacrificed—which, one way or another, he probably was—or to be a prisoner in his private lair. She suddenly didn't care where she was going at all...just as long as Roman Lawrence was there.

"WHAT ARE YOU DOING HERE?" Roman croaked. This was his domain. And Roman was staring right at the one person he never wanted to see again. Ever.

Van Ness looked a little taken aback. "Well, Roman, when I saw your horse farm, I was pretty impressed. And then I started reading about how big the purses are, and it started to look like a decent investment."

Roman turned from the crowded concessions line. He'd just bought himself and Kathleen bottles of sparkling water. He'd wanted a cola, but changed his mind. Purified water would be better for the baby and if Kathleen couldn't have a soda, he'd decided he wouldn't, either. And now he felt like a fool. After all, it was Van Ness's baby, not his.

I'm only feeling guilty because the ring made her so happy. Hell, I was just trying to play the part of loving husband, the way Higgenbothem told me to. Wasn't I? Can I help it if a couple of diamonds make her go all gooey eyed and soft looking? It isn't my fault that the ring business made her curl against me like a furry little kitten....

"It is a good investment," Roman finally forced himself to say. Apparently Van Ness had no idea that he'd married Kathleen. If the man did, he probably wouldn't look so self-satisfied. Or would he? Roman wondered. He couldn't believe Van Ness hadn't even bothered to inquire about Kathleen's welfare.

While Van Ness rambled on about his recent researches into cutting horses, Roman only nodded at intervals, both unable and unwilling to force himself to concentrate on what the man was saying. Van Ness was the father of *his* baby, he kept thinking. It was totally illogical.

Still, *he* was the one who had gone to birthing classes. And he'd started back this week, too. *He* was the one who had watched the videotape more times than he'd ever admit to. *He* was the one who'd bought that cute hand-carved rocking horse. *He* was the one who watched Kathleen's diet, only ate what she could eat and had helped decorate the nursery....

And *he* was also the one who was divorcing Kathleen and attempting to get custody of the baby, he suddenly thought guiltily. He wondered if he should try to track Higgenbothem down in the Bahamas. Not to call off the divorce, of course, but just to buy a little time. Every time he looked at Kathleen her eyes seemed to say, "Forgive me, love me." And, at moments, he really wanted to. He just wasn't sure he could.

"What?" Apparently Van Ness had asked something that required more than a nod. Roman raised his glance, forcing himself to look at the man. *The real father of my baby.* And, he thought, looking at Van Ness he had to accept it. When he'd seen Higgenbothem he was still reacting as if the baby really was his own. Now, looking at Van Ness, he wondered if he could love another man's child. Would he really fight for custody of Van Ness and Kathleen's baby?

"Do you think it's feasible?" Van Ness was asking.

"That you train cutters?" Roman finally managed to say. Just looking at him was making his blood run cold.

"Yeah." Van Ness nodded.

"No," Roman said flatly.

Van Ness laughed. "I wouldn't train them myself. Just finance it."

No doubt, Roman thought. Otherwise Van Ness would more than likely get himself killed. *Now there's a thought.* "I think it might work great," Roman said, not bothering to hide the irony in his voice.

"John Walker says you've got to come back and—"

Roman turned. It was Kathleen. She looked breathless, her cheeks rosy from exertion...and she looked beautiful. "You're supposed to be riding pretty soon."

Roman watched carefully the way she said hello to Van Ness. It was amiable, at best anyway, and that was all. Then she looked around, clearly embarrassed by the situation, yet still enjoying the energy in the arena. Her eyes flitted over the people in the crowd, many of whom had turned out in full Western regalia.

"Cindy!" Van Ness suddenly called out.

Van Ness sure has some nerve, Roman thought. A bright-eyed young woman in a tight miniskirt bounced up to them. She had huge breasts, a teensy tiny waist and the kind of legs that went on forever. Her hair was pulled back in a ponytail and a big blue bow that fanned over half her head held it up. From the way they interacted it was clear that Cindy was Van Ness's date.

For the first time since he'd seen Van Ness, Roman stopped thinking about the baby and started thinking about Kathleen. How had she stood it? Being ditched by a playboy and facing motherhood alone? She probably felt so unwanted and unloved....

Roman dipped his head, nuzzled it against the top of Kathleen's, into her sweet-smelling hair, then kissed her cheek softly, and glared at Van Ness.

"John Walker said you really have to get back," Kathleen murmured gently. When she glanced at Van Ness, her face colored perceptibly.

Roman's glance shifted from Van Ness to Cindy to Kathleen. And then he eyed Kathleen's stomach. *The baby,* he thought. How had his life become so complicated? How was he going to ride in the middle of this madness?

"We've got to go," he muttered.

"Have a great time!" Van Ness shouted when Roman and Kathleen were nearly out of earshot.

He yelled it as if nothing more complex than bumping into each other had just occurred. "What a jerk," Roman muttered.

"You don't need to tell me that," Kathleen said tightly.

Roman couldn't help but rub her shoulder. "But the baby's not a mistake," he found himself saying. "And anyway, everybody makes mistakes now and then."

Feeling Kathleen so comfortably pressed against him, Roman wondered if *he* was making a mistake. He hated Kathleen for having acted so impulsively and for hurting him so much. And the more it sank in that the baby wasn't his, the more inclined he felt to tell Higgenbothem to drop the custody fight. They also couldn't continue in this nebulous, half-married state...and yet divorcing her felt all wrong...as if it might be the largest mistake of his life.

"I'm glad you don't think the baby's a mistake," Kathleen said softly after a long moment.

IT WAS ANOTHER ROMAN Kathleen didn't know. She'd seen him in tack rooms, in barns, in outdoor arenas, but Kathleen had never seen him sit a horse. He'd made it through three cuts and his next ride was for the first-place purse.

Roman walked Pirate's Legacy into the center of the pen. Against the far side of it, fifteen head of cattle huddled, all nosing toward the middle of their herd. Kathleen sucked in a breath. Roman wore a tall black Stetson. His hair was tightly bound back in a ponytail that did nothing to detract from his masculinity but only added to it, accentuating his bronzed skin, his high patrician forehead and the long, strong line of his nose.

As he circled the wall of the pen, she found herself staring at his mouth. The full, expressive lips were set in an attitude of almost contemptuous control. They were pulled into a half snarl, half smile, as if he were preparing for a battle, and as if he already knew that he'd won it. Everything about him said he would win— that he always won—no matter what the prize, no matter what the cost.

He rode to the center of the ring, and the referee's pistol sounded. Roman's lean, well-muscled thighs squeezed the horse, so that she could see every tremor in the shifting strength of his straddled legs, where the fringed chaps fell away from his waist.

He'd driven a calf from the herd and now he and the horse were facing off with it. Roman bucked in the saddle, forcing Pirate's Legacy to bend and twist and turn. And when the foolhardy calf attempted a run back to the herd, Roman brought the horse nearly to its knees, straining on its haunches, until it was eye level with the calf.

Roman was merciless. Neither he nor Pirate's Legacy gave quarter. Together, they only ran, backed up and twisted again. Roman's hair flew behind him, the same raven black as the horse's mane, and the horse's tail swished madly.

"He looks so…magnificent," Kathleen whispered. She glanced around quickly, but no one had heard her. Everybody was watching Roman.

She could feel the control he exercised over the animals deep in her bones as he expertly moved the horse. One flick of his wrists, one tap of the reins and the horse would dodge the calf again. Pirate's Legacy shook his powerful head, like a dog with a bone, but as powerful as the fury of the horse was, it was nothing compared to the intensity of its rider.

She knew Roman could move her like that horse. He could command…control…make her turn toward him with the merest flick of his wrist. But she couldn't let him, she thought, feeling her resolve weaken as she watched him ride. Not unless he could love her and her baby.

The calf suddenly stood still, stared at the horse for a long moment and then averted its gaze. Breathlessly Kathleen watched Roman ride the calf back into the herd. Just as he did so, another gun sounded, ending his time. All around her the crowd surged to its feet—people screamed and yelled and waved hats in the air.

Kathleen could only swallow. She had seen enough rides to know that his had been the best. And if she had not, the reaction of the crowd made his success clear. Yes, she knew that Roman had won…but had she and the baby won his heart? Was that really why he'd come back?

She felt something being thrust into her hands, and looked down. It was large, gold and cup shaped. And it took her a full minute to realize it was his trophy. She turned without even looking into his eyes, reached her arm around his neck and pulled his face to hers.

Then she kissed him. As hard as she could. She bit at his lips, darted her tongue between them, shoved her hand beneath his hat. She barely registered the fact that it fell right off his head, because she was tugging that silly band out of his hair. She raked her fingers through his now-loosened hair, twining the wavy darkness of it into a fist as she pressed the back of his head, demanding his response. She told herself she could be as powerful as he was...she could make him love both her and the baby.

She felt his hands twine through her hair with equal strength, his tongue straining against hers, meeting her every demand with one of his own. And then he leaned her head back and looked at her.

He didn't say anything, just stared. His mouth was wet and glistening, his dark eyes burning from within like hot coals. After a moment he attempted a smile, but it didn't quite reach his eyes.

"Ought to bring you to more of these things, darlin'," he teased. His voice was nothing more than a hoarse rasp.

"Sorry," she said weakly.

He chuckled. "Nothing to be sorry about. It just caught me a little off guard."

"Me, too." She laughed nervously. What had she done? What were *they* doing? What was happening to her? She'd told herself to back off and then she'd kissed him as if there was no tomorrow. Suddenly her growing stomach felt as if it had all the wobbly consistency of jelly.

"Nothing like that will ever happen again," she said, her voice gaining conviction.

"Why not?" He looked genuinely shocked.

"Because I—I fear the power you have over me, Roman," she managed to say, though her breath hadn't yet evened. "I always have. And I fear it more now than ever. And...I want to talk about the baby," she finished in a rush. "How do you feel about the baby now?"

He draped an arm around her shoulder. "I don't really know," he said gently. And then, under his breath, he said, "Can't say as I blame you for being scared of me, Kathleen."

Something in his tone sent a near shiver down her back. "Why?" she asked, lowering her voice. "What have you done?"

"Nothing." He managed a shrug. "Nothing at all."

Chapter Twelve

"Following me?" Roman tossed a towel on the marly sand of the shore. He was wearing only his silky red trunks, and in the rosy light of dusk, with the setting sun in her eyes, his bronzed golden chest seemed awash with pale rose. Kathleen dipped beneath the water and surfaced, her hair slicking back against her scalp.

"I was here first," she called out playfully.

"Hardly," he returned as he walked toward the water. "It's my island."

"Which means you were here first, I suppose?" She pushed off from the ocean bottom with her toes and began to float on her back. She wanted him to join her in an evening swim. And then she didn't. She'd come here to be alone, to think about their relationship and to soothe her tight, taut, swollen skin.

She was just about to right herself and head for the house when she felt his palm slide beneath her back, offering support. Just feeling his fingertips, falling on either side of her spine, she knew that she could drift like that indefinitely. She shut her eyes, telling herself that she could enjoy his touch for just a moment....

She rolled off his palm, dived into the shallow water,

turned and began swimming for the shore. After a moment she stood in the shoulder-deep water and began walking, her feet sinking in the sandy bottom, the water eddying around her breasts.

"Did I say something wrong darlin'?"

"No, Roman," she called over her shoulder. Everything he said was fine; it was all he didn't say that bothered her. The closer the baby came to being born, the more she felt as if time was somehow running out. They simply couldn't continue in their strange half-married state. She needed a man who loved her. And she needed a father for her baby. Since his return, Roman had been kind, but the only thing he had said about her baby was that it wasn't a mistake.

She could feel his dark, dangerous eyes searing two burning points between her shoulder blades. Without even turning, she could see him. Even with her eyes shut, she could see him. Even if she were on another planet, she could see him.

His broad, rosy-golden shoulders were glistening and wet, and droplets snaked downward over the curving indentions of his biceps and over his collarbone. Rivulets twined through the dark, curling, soft hairs, making them shimmer in the very last light of the fast-sinking sun.

Behind her she heard a near-silent splash as he entered the water. Seconds passed before she felt him grasping her ankles beneath the water. He swam effortlessly between her legs, making the water flow and push around her thighs. The hands holding her ankles moved upward slowly. His palms molded over her legs—from her ankles to her calves to her thighs—as he surfaced, sliding up right against her stomach from the water.

"I've got to go in, Roman," she said, keeping her voice level. Or at least attempting to.

He only dunked her lightly, knocking her off balance just enough that she fell into his arms when she surfaced. "No time for a little water sport?" he teased, daring her with a squinty, twinkling flash of his eyes.

Suddenly she couldn't resist. Without even thinking, she found herself leaping upward. She managed to place her hand on the top of his head so that she could dunk him back. It didn't work. She found herself merely suspended in midair with her hand planted on the middle of his head and her fingers all tangled in his hair.

His arms caught her around her waist and her legs fell on either side of him, her ankles naturally locking around his back. As large as she was, she could barely believe such a position was possible, but Roman held her as if she were light as air.

"Why are you going inside?" It was a question, but somehow censuring in its tone.

"I'm getting a little cold," she lied. How had the man so dexterously gotten her into this position? There was only a slight late-evening breeze, just enough that his male nipples had grown hard, contracting when his wet chest hit the air.

"I feel like you really don't want to spend time with me lately," Roman said gently. "And I don't understand it."

"In a few weeks I'm going to be having a baby, Roman, and I just feel so unsure about...everything," she said, gazing into his eyes.

Kathleen unlocked her ankles behind his back, but his hands only shot downwards cupping her thighs, leaving her no recourse but to clutch his shoulders for support. What woman would leave such a man alone in the water? His face could only be called beautiful. His lips—so full and wide and expressive—begged to be kissed. What woman would leave?

This one. Kathleen forcibly kicked from his grasp, turned with no explanation and splashed toward shore.

She'd just reached her towel when he caught her wrist from behind. Then he walked right into her and held her close, his arm circling her waist, the flat of his palm running over her full, rounded stomach.

"Roman, I need to go in," she said. Her voice was low and it sounded almost like a plea. "I have a whole future to think—"

"There's one other thing, darlin'," he whispered, cutting her off.

"What?" she managed to ask.

"As far as I'm concerned—" his voice grew huskier by the second "I—I want to make a real marriage of this."

Kathleen turned slowly in his arms and looked up into those round globes of shining eyes. In their intense darkness they reminded her of the fire that was said to burn at the center of the earth.

"Roman—" Her voice was shaking, but nearly flat with the seriousness it communicated. "Do you love me?"

He only stared back with those eyes.

"Do you?"

He didn't kiss her. He didn't lift a finger to her cheek or trace the line of her brow with his thumb. He just stared at her for a moment that seemed to stretch to eternity. Then he said, "Yes."

Yes. Her expression gentled and she cupped his face with her hand. "I love you, too," she murmured.

"You do?"

She nodded, then cleared her throat. "But could you love another man's child?"

Roman sighed softly. "At first I really thought so...but then I was still reacting as if the baby were mine. I wanted the baby, even if I never had you." He tilted his head and continued looking into her eyes.

"And then?" she asked anxiously.

"And then, when I saw Van Ness, it really sank in. I mean, it really is another man's child." He reached and brushed a lock of hair from her forehead. "And, for just a moment, I honestly felt that I didn't ever want to see the baby."

Kathleen swallowed. Her heart ached for how honestly he was trying to love the baby. "And now?"

"And now, darlin'," he said, "I'm still a little confused."

Kathleen turned quickly away from him. She bolted. She forgot her sandals and her towel and her cover-up. She was so heavy it felt difficult to run, but she somehow managed it. She fled barefoot over the briars, feeling the stinging harsh switches of the bushes catching at her calves.

"Kathleen—" he called after her.

She didn't turn, only ran as if the demons of hell were on her heels. Or as if Roman Lawrence was.

ROMAN STIFLED A GROAN by pressing his lips deep against one of his many tapestried pillows. Thoughts and images of Kathleen raced through his mind with the speed and intensity of light. He wished he hadn't told her the truth about his feelings, but wasn't honesty the basis for any good relationship? And had she really

expected him to accept the situation any more easily
than he was?

He had come up via the stairs to the terrace and
hadn't bothered to shut the terrace doors. He knew he
couldn't have entered the house through the hallway.
Because he might have seen her. And he wasn't ready
to. Ever since he'd taken her to the Miami Futurity he'd
become more and more convinced that he couldn't divorce her.

But could I love another man's child?

Even the night breeze that blew in and lifted the
filmy white curtains of the French doors did nothing to
cool him tonight. Roman forcibly threw back his
covers, then stood quickly, pulling his black silk robe
from the floor. He bounded toward the doors and
slipped on the robe.

He leaned against one of the doors and brooded, his
eyes piercing the darkness...staring at the door between their rooms. He started forward, stopped, forced
himself to lean again. He had no right to go to her, not
unless he was ready to commit himself to this situation.
There was no crack of light beneath the door. Kathleen
was sleeping. And he wanted nothing more than to
fling open that door, burst through it and make love to
her.

She'd bolted away from him when he'd said he
loved her. And he did love her. He loved her more than
he'd ever imagined himself capable of loving. And the
wildness of her green eyes—how they'd looked so vulnerable and yet so full of want—had made him feel a
sharp, twisting pang in his heart.

But could I love another man's child?

He could still teach the baby about the things he,
himself, loved—how to ride, sail, fish...and when there

were troubles, at school or with friends, he could offer the kind of sage advice his own father had.

Could I truly love another man's child?

"Yes," he said softly. *Of course I could.*

He began to walk slowly toward that distant shut door. But before he even reached his bed, the door swung open. And she was there.

"MARRY ME," HE WHISPERED huskily.

Kathleen was speechless. Her breath caught in her throat. Her mouth felt parched. She wasn't even sure why she'd opened the door. She only knew she meant to convince him—somehow—to love the baby, too.

"We are married," she finally managed to say, not caring how disheveled she looked or that her voice trembled and her eyes roved over every inch of him. A shaft of light seemed to glimmer on his chest in a triangle, but it was only the deep V of his dark silk robe, which closed only where he had loosely tied it around his slender hips. Moonlight shone over his shoulder. It seemed to illuminate only him and leave everything else in darkness as if nothing else in the world could matter.

"No, Kathleen," Roman said more softly, his eyes moving slowly over her. She was still standing there, leaning forward breathlessly, as if she might run away again...or else right into his arms. The same almost-stricken look was in her green eyes, and her filmy white muslin nightgown seemed to billow around her.

"Kathleen," he said gently, "I want you and I want to be a father."

"Just like that?"

He shook his head. "No, it's taken me some time... to feel sure."

"Marry you?" she repeated huskily.

He nodded.

The next moment was the slowest she had ever lived. He unloosed his robe and slightly moved his rounded, beautiful shoulders. The silk slid over his body and to the floor, leaving him stark naked in the moonlight. To her, he looked as vulnerable as he was powerful, as desirable as he was dangerous, and as calm as he could be volatile. She began to walk slowly toward him, allowing his eyes time to savor every second, every nuance of her movement.

"Oh, Kathleen," he whispered. Her body, even with the baby, *his* baby, was so fluid and so graceful that he felt his heart was full to breaking, just from looking at it.

She watched him slowly lift his powerful arms upward and outward, waiting silently for her embrace. The corded muscles of his arms rippled like water, each nerve and sinew seemingly stretched to breaking.

He looks so magnificent. So statuesque and majestic in the moonlight. The muscles in his arms flexed again, as if he already held the weight of her, and his hair, which rested on his shoulders, made him look timeless…like a man who had been born an eternity ago.

He swallowed against the dryness of his mouth when she stopped in front of him. He'd held his arms out to welcome her inside them, but now he couldn't move. He moaned when she ran her fingertips from his waist, over his chest and to his shoulders.

"So, will you marry me?" he whispered, his low voice catching. "You and me, together…with a family?"

Her gaze lifted almost shyly from his chest to his eyes, while her trembling fingers continued to trace soft circles on the silken bronzed skin of his shoulders. In the tiny vibrations of her fingertips he could feel the pure need racing through her, coursing like lightning just beneath her skin, and her attempt to disguise her own want with the deceptive softness of her touch.

"Marry you forever?" she finally whispered, her voice catching and ending on a throaty rasp. "For real?"

"Forever, sweetheart," he whispered, pulling her close against his nakedness, losing himself in the filmy fabric folds of her gown. He held her tightly in his embrace, wrapping his arms around her, knowing he would never let her go.

After a moment he leaned slightly and gazed into her eyes. Then he sighed softly and leaned downward and brushed her lips, the softness and lightness of the kiss as tender as it was intense.

"Forever." He brushed her lips again. "Beyond forever." He grazed her lips a third time, feeling the damp, burning hot sensation of her mouth…her own feverish desire so like his own. "For eternity, Kathleen."

The last taste of her spurred him on and he deepened the kiss, loving the heated spear of her darting tongue as it met his. With each touch of their lips, their teeth, their tongues, his mind blacked further out, his thoughts giving way to sensations. Within moments he couldn't speak. His every word was a kiss. And he couldn't breathe…because his every breath was a sigh.

While her back arched, bringing her full stomach gently against him, his lips trailed fire over her shoulders and the fullness of her breasts, his tongue reaching and stretching and straining for her. His hands strained, too, moving over her, until he caught the bottom of her filmy white gown.

"Oh, darling," he managed to whisper as he stepped quickly back and swiftly drew the gown over her head. The wide arc of his arm never stopped. The trailing gown left his fingertips and spiraled to the floor as if it were nothing more than airy mist. And then the arc of his arm completed itself, his hand coming back to rest on her heated skin.

She is so beautiful. Her breasts were large and full, growing so taut. Her stomach felt both soft and tight when his hands rounded to the naked curves of it. With every touch, he felt he was touching the very mystery of life itself...of love.

She kissed him again, deeply, as he flattened his palm over the lacy triangle of her underwear. He hooked his fingers through the lace and rolled the panties clear downward, his ears straining toward the moan of pleasure sounding so far above him.

As she stepped from the last remaining band of elastic, he lifted her into his arms, and she wrapped around him, her ankles locking at his back. With a surety of heart, he knew that she wouldn't run away this time...that she'd never run away again.

"I want all of you," he whispered shakily against her lips. He moved against her without entering her, only kissing her more deeply, until her tongue grew wild. When she began to move, he helped her, her weight in his arms the sweetest burden he had ever carried. He held her close, until her whole body convulsed gently against him.

"Oh, Roman." Her voice was a whimper that shot through him. "I—"

"Darlin'," he whispered softly, cradling her in his

arms and carrying her toward his bed. He knew from her voice that she'd never experienced pleasure in that way before. "Between us, there's no right way or wrong way to make love," he said gently. "I want to make you so happy."

"You do make me happy," she whispered.

And everything is perfect. It was perfect to feel how softly he'd held her, how he'd kept kissing her, how he let her body take what it needed from his strength. He laid her down softly and she clung to him, unwilling to let him go. And when he did, she gasped.

He leaned far over her, sliding his hand over her stomach again. Then he kissed her deeply, making her want him more.

"I'm so in love with you," he whispered. "And with the baby."

"It's really our baby?" she murmured.

"Yours and mine."

Her heart, which had begun to slow, suddenly beat double time again. She felt the trembling of her own hands as they crept downward. When she touched him, he moaned softly. And then his hips drove forward against her touch. "Oh, Kathleen…" He lowered his mouth and pressed against her lips with a soul-searing kiss.

Each touch was surely far more torturous than anything he'd ever felt. He loved her and wanted her so much. He finally drew back, knowing if he gave in to this, the sweetest thing he'd ever felt, that he would never last. And, tonight, the love they shared meant everything…because now she really was his wife and the mother of the child who would become his.

He caught her wrists lightly and raised them above her head. He knew how ready she was and so he sank into her slowly, loosening a soft moan. He felt he was entering the mystery of the universe itself…with his wife and their baby. His heart thundered with a fury that was almost terrifying.

"Oh, Roman, I love you," she murmured over and over again. "I love you. I—" Her fingers pressed into his shoulders and she pulled him close and wrapped her arms tightly around him.

With relief and desire he sank full into her again, over and over and over, conscious of himself…of her…of their baby. All of them bound together in love and longing and mystery.

Each movement brought him ever closer, until he thought he couldn't last another moment…until his whole body was taut with the desire he was fighting not to release…and until he filled her for what felt like forever. He rolled onto his back, pulling her with him, feathering soft kisses over her skin.

"Oh, Kathleen," he whispered, his voice still ragged. "Kathleen, darlin'." He raised up on an elbow and gazed down into her face.

"What?" she managed to say, blowing out a shaky sigh.

He shrugged and smiled. "Nothing…just Kathleen." As breathless as he was, he chuckled softly.

"Do you—do you really love me and the baby, Roman?"

He sat up in the twisting, rumpled covers and pulled her up with him. He cupped her cheeks in his hands. "Kathleen, I love you both more—" He shrugged, then sighed in another effort to even his breathing, not even knowing where to begin. "I don't even have the words to say how much."

"I'll remember this moment for the rest of my life," she said, still trying to even her breathing.

He smiled, and then a frown crossed his brow. "Are you sure you're all right? I mean, I was so afraid that it might be a little uncomfortable for you...with the baby."

"It was fine, Roman," she said softly. "Not uncomfortable at all." She sank against his shoulder, molding her body against his in a way that caused him to fall downward again, onto his back, pulling her with him.

She cuddled against him, both of her legs trailing on either side of one of his. Her hands tucked into the curves of his chest as if those curves had formed a pocket, and his cheek rested on the top of her head. He nuzzled into her hair, smelling the damp sweetness of the white-blond strands.

One day, he thought, they'd talk about all the craziness that had brought them together—all his past resentments, all his unwanted desire, about how he'd thought she was mortally ill, and how he'd thought he'd gotten her pregnant. One day...

Now, feeling her in his arms this way, glancing from the top of her hair out to the moon that was so kindly lighting their night of love, he simply felt happier than he ever had.

"Kathleen?"

"Hmm?"

"I know men don't generally say this," he whispered, "but this is really my favorite part."

She moved to look up at him, but he pressed her head softly against his chest again. She snuggled her face in his chest hairs. "You mean just lying here?"

"Yeah." After a few moments he said, "Well, maybe it used to be my favorite part."

"Before what?"

"Before you."

She chuckled and snuggled closer against him. After a long moment she said, "I can't wait until the baby's born."

"Me, neither," he said and sighed.

"If it's a boy, what do you think about naming him Augustine, after your dad?"

Roman could feel her lips curve in a smile against his skin. "Are you serious?" he asked softly. He lifted her hand to his lips and kissed her palm.

She turned and gazed into his eyes. "My dad died when I was young and your father was so kind to me. I mean, even though our parents were only married two years, he sort of took me under his wing and..."

"And," Roman said gently, "I'll only consider it under one condition."

"What's that?" she asked, tracing small circles on his chest with her fingertip.

"That if it's a girl we name her Loretta."

Kathleen's breath caught in her throat. Would Roman really name their baby after her mother? Her mother the home wrecker? A hint of tears stung her eyes. "You'd really do that?"

"I would," he said gently, pulling her on top of him and wrapping his arms tightly around her.

"Roman?" she said after a moment.

"Hmm?"

"I feel like everything is right with the world," she murmured.

"That's because it is, darlin'," he whispered back.

Chapter Thirteen

Silk sheets twined and twisted around Roman's ankles, making the bronzed tan of his skin gleam a deep copper. Kathleen took in his long, lean legs, his slender torso and the relaxed muscles of his arms that had held her so lovingly through the night.

"Hmm," she hummed. She'd seen him as she never had, his eyes brilliant and fixed on her, his body moving with a passion that seemed to know no bounds. Now his breathing was even, and he was smiling in his sleep. The morning breeze wafted through the still-open doors to the terrace, and the soft, pale rosy fingers of the sun just touched at the sky.

Her sleep had been completely deep and dreamless as if she had no more dreams left because they had all come true, with Roman. The way he'd gentled toward her during her pregnancy had touched her deeply, and now his ability to love the baby as his own made her heart swell with loving him. She smiled, suddenly realizing that she was hungry. Starved.

Kathleen rose from the bed quietly and tiptoed into the nursery. She glanced happily around at all the baby's things. Now when Roman looked at the nursery, she knew he'd view it as he had initially—as the room he'd painted for their child. *His child.* She donned a sundress and flats, and then headed downstairs, still humming.

Ms. Rodriguez was nowhere in sight, which was good, since Kathleen wanted to fix a tray for Roman, herself. She found a tray and pulled a large china platter from the cabinet. Rummaging through the refrigerator, she pulled out all the juicy, ripe fruits she could find.

She began to slice mangoes, kiwis and bananas, arranging them attractively on the platter. She added apricots and a persimmon. Then she cocked her head, glanced at the platter and rearranged the slices, placing the kiwis by the mangoes for the sake of how good the oranges and greens looked together.

She'd forgotten coffee! She half smiled, thinking that that's what she got for mentally going over every blessed detail of her life since she'd returned to Lawrence Island. She'd never known that such loving was possible. And while he'd held her the previous night, Roman had made clear that every single inch of him belonged to her now…there was nowhere she couldn't touch or kiss, no spot of him against which she couldn't murmur encouragements or endearments.

While her mind continued to replay every moment, she got down one large, heavy mug for Roman, and placed the sugar and filled creamer on the tray. She sliced some cheese, too, and found a hunk of fresh Italian bread.

By the time she'd finished arranging the tray, the coffee was done. The strong, harsh scent of it smelled more intense than it ever had. She poured Roman's coffee and had just replaced the pot when Miles Higgenbothem rapped on the back door and entered the kitchen.

"Morning," Kathleen said. She opened her mouth to offer him coffee, as she usually would, but realized she didn't really want him to stay. After all, Roman was still sleeping and she wanted him all to herself.

"Kathleen," Higgenbothem said after a long moment.

Something about his tone and seeming nervousness made her eyes drop downward. His hands were fidgety and he was holding a large yellow legal-style envelope. On it, someone—probably Higgenbothem himself—had written in bold black ink, "For Roman. Re: Kathleen/baby."

She smiled and stepped forward. "For me?"

"Uh—no," Higgenbothem said quickly, his hand tightening on the envelope.

Her gaze roved over him warily. "What is it?" She glanced at the envelope again.

Higgenbothem sighed and shook his head. "Frankly, Kathleen, I'd just as soon go ahead and tell you. I mean, I'm not your lawyer, I'm Roman's, and yet I know you and I've felt so bad about this...."

Kathleen's smile suddenly vanished, and now she held out her hand.

"At least you'll have some forewarning," Higgenbothem murmured as he handed her the envelope.

She opened it carefully, then looked over the papers inside. Her heart dropped to her feet. She couldn't believe it! She carefully flattened the papers on the countertop, as if that might change their contents. It didn't.

No, it was all true. They were divorce papers. But worse was that some of the documents said Roman wanted custody of the baby. She pressed her hand to her heart, feeling more terrified than she ever had. She knew very well that he had enough power to do such a thing. *To take my baby! The child that's supposed to be ours.*

"Sorry," Higgenbothem muttered. "If it helps, I actually want him to lose."

She gasped. "How long's he been planning this?" Hadn't they just shared one absolutely perfect night where all was right between them? Weren't they a real family now? Kathleen reached for the counter, for support.

Higgenbothem cleared his throat. "He's been planning the divorce since before your marriage. The custody fight, too," Higgenbothem said levelly.

"Before our marriage," she echoed in a whisper. How could Roman do such a thing? "Why?"

"When he found out you weren't sick, he wanted to get his island back during the divorce proceedings," Higgenbothem said gruffly. "And when he found out the baby wasn't his, he made it clear he wants to fight for custody, anyway."

"And you let him?" she asked, her voice rising.

"Kathleen," Higgenbothem began, looking nearly as upset as she felt, "I'm his lawyer and it's my job. I'm telling you now, so that you can be better prepared." He gazed at her for a long moment. "So that you can *win,* Kathleen."

"And do you expect me to thank you for that?" she retorted, not really expecting any response. Her mind was reeling. Her heart was broken. And her baby was in danger of being taken from her. "What should I do?" she murmured, talking to herself as much as Higgenbothem.

"Leave immediately," he said. "In court it will be

clear that you had no idea what Roman was planning…and that when you found out, your first thoughts were for keeping your baby. These divorce papers are ready to be signed but don't sign them until you get another lawyer. I highly recommend Stanley Bernstein. He's in the book.''

"Thank you,'' Kathleen finally managed to say. Higgenbothem nodded slowly, then headed out the door.

Kathleen stared down at the papers again. *Leave immediately.* Panic shot through her, and she bolted for the stairs. When she reached the top, she slowed her footsteps. And then she tiptoed into the nursery via the doorway in the hall. She didn't have much time. *Roman is going to take the baby!* And because he was in the next room, she was going to have to be very quiet.

Her hands mechanically packed a small carryon. When she carefully placed the stuffed dolphin Roman had bought the baby inside, she felt tears sting at her eyes. He had acted as if he couldn't accept the baby as his own, while all along he was planning to take the child. And he had only married her to get his fool island back.

She whirled around, looking for anything she might need, telling herself to take only essentials. She grabbed her shoulder bag, the carryon and her second small suitcase, the one she kept packed for the hospital.

She glanced over her shoulder, through the crack in the nursery door, and her breath caught in her throat. Roman was still sleeping…and she loved him so much. If it wasn't for the threat of the custody suit she was sure she'd wake him and have it out with him. Hadn't he meant just one of those things he'd said when they'd made love? Weren't they truly married now?

Leave the house! She headed back out into the hallway then carried her belongings down the steps, her temper beginning to mount with every breath. Even if he had decided to play her for a fool, he'd acted as if he loved her.

Hadn't he perhaps changed his mind after talking to Higgenbothem and begun to really love her? What had been lies? What had been truth?

Once she was in the kitchen, she put her bags down beside the table, where she'd left the wretched yellow envelope, and heaved a sigh. It hardly helped matters much that she was as big as a house. She swung her shoulder bag upward, nearly dumping its contents on the table in the process. She rifled through her wallet and pulled out every blessed credit card he'd given her. In a drawer she found the scissors. She cut up every last card, watching the bits of plastic scatter on the envelope.

Don't cry. She had to be strong. She had to do everything she could to ensure that Roman couldn't take the baby. She wiggled both her wedding bands on her finger. Her hands were so swollen it was nearly painful to take them off. Once she had, she laid them on top of the envelope. She might not be able to sign those divorce papers, but leaving her rings was statement enough.

She righted her bag on her shoulder, picked up her suitcases with either hand and went through the kitchen's screen door, hearing it snap tightly shut behind her.

And then she began walking down the road.

ROMAN'S HANDS ROVED OVER the sheets, but the other half of the bed was unoccupied. Where was his wife? "Kathleen?" he murmured.

When there was no response, he managed to sit upright and glance at the clock. It was nearly noon! He'd slept hours later than he usually did. He half smiled, thinking that was no wonder. But where was Kathleen? "Kathleen?" he called more loudly.

He got up, found his robe, which was on the floor by the French doors, and slipped into it. It was sweet of her to let him sleep, he thought, but he'd much rather have been awake and spending time with her. "Kathleen?" he yelled, walking toward the bathroom. He opened the door. She wasn't there.

"Oh, Kathlee—een," he called in singsong, this time pushing the door to the nursery full open. His lips parted slightly, and he leaned against the doorjamb for support. Her belongings were strewn everywhere. Her hospital suitcase, which always sat by the door, was gone.

"Oh, no!" he said in shock. "She's had the baby!" He shook his head quickly, as if to clear it of confusion. Kathleen wouldn't have the baby without him, would she?

No, she would certainly have awakened him. And she wasn't due for three more weeks. Glancing around the nursery again, he realized that some of the baby's things were gone, too—a mobile, the stuffed dolphin, the outfit that always stayed in the crib as if the baby were already in it.

A tiny jolt of fear shot through him. "Kathleen!" he yelled, heading for the hallway. He took the steps down, two at a time.

When he reached the kitchen he came to a complete standstill beside the counter. Surveying the beautifully arranged tray of fruit, he gasped. He dunked his finger in the coffee. It was cold! He blinked slowly, pulled a chair out from the table and forced himself to sit down. He carefully lifted Kathleen's wedding rings, which rested on top of the envelope, and placed them to the side. When he lifted the envelope, bits of her credit cards scattered across the table.

He pulled out the papers and glanced at them. Sure enough, they were divorce and custody papers. Why had he acted so impulsively? More than at any other time in his life, he wished he wasn't so moody and volatile. "Tell me this is a dream, darlin'," he said. "Nightmare," he amended.

The phone rang. He was on his feet and cradling the receiver in his hands in a heartbeat. "Kathleen? Kathleen, this is not what you think—" But it was exactly what she thought.

"Roman? This is your mother."

His heart fell. "Sorry, I can't talk right—"

"I know you're married, Roman, and I'm not upset about it."

He sighed, needing to get off the phone so he could start searching for Kathleen. Nonetheless, he couldn't quite believe his mother's reaction...or lack of it. "You don't mind that Kathleen and I are married?" he managed to say.

"No," she said. "Not at all."

He coiled the phone cord around his hand. What could have caused his mother's change of heart? "I would have thought you'd be furious. I mean, you sure acted mad when I settled with her over Dad's will."

"There are some things I have to tell you," his mother said after a moment. "Some things about your father and me. And I was hoping we could—"

As curious as he was about the matter, and as glad as he was that his mother would seemingly have no difficulty accepting Kathleen as his wife, he *had* to get off the phone. His mother had called at an incredibly inopportune moment. "Look, mother. I've really got to go. Kathleen just left me and I've got to find—"

"Left you?" Gabriella gasped.

"It's my fault," Roman said quickly, afraid his mother would find Kathleen at fault and begin disliking her all over again.

"I'll be right over," his mother said in a shocked voice. And then the phone went dead.

"Great," Roman said, hanging up his end of the line. "Just great."

WHERE WAS SHE? Roman had looked everywhere. The first day, he'd driven up and down streets, since Kathleen had seemingly walked wherever she'd gone. Since then he'd checked with everyone they knew. He'd checked hospitals, in case something had happened to her.

Finally Dr. Peteck had heard from her. He'd called as soon as Kathleen had contacted him, but only to let Roman know she was all right. Kathleen hadn't told him where she was staying.

Now Roman slouched farther down in the red leather armchair in the library. One of his hands was tightly wrapped around an untouched shot glass of compuesto, as if it could anchor him to the chair. His other rested on the phone, as if willing it to ring. "Kathleen," he murmured. "Please come home."

He shook his head. The baby was due any day now, and he couldn't believe that he might not be there for the event. Every time he thought of Kathleen—somewhere, out there, all alone—he felt his chest constrict. He'd spent every waking hour going over the time they'd spent together…remembering the feisty way she'd dived from Van Ness's yacht and how he'd saved her, remembering how her face lit up every time she so much as glanced into the nursery. Did she really believe that he could have wrenched their baby from her arms, after all they'd been through? He had forgiven her for writing the note that had led him to believe he'd fathered the baby. Couldn't she forgive him this?

"Roman?"

Roman started and glanced up. His heart sank again. It wasn't Kathleen. "Hi, Mother," he said.

Gabriella was breathless, but she didn't bother to sit down. "Roman," she said, "we need to talk."

They'd done nothing but talk for weeks now. And Roman wanted action. Especially when it came to finding Kathleen. He mustered a smile. After all, his mother had been incredibly helpful. She'd driven as many streets and made as many calls as he had. As shocked as he'd been by that turn of events, he was hardly going to look a gift horse in the mouth.

"Talk away," he finally managed to say.

His mother stared at him for a long moment. "Roman," she said. "I have to say this now, or I'm afraid I'll never say it." She crossed her arms over her waist.

Roman sighed. He was fairly sure this was the topic she'd alluded to weeks before on the telephone. Whatever it was, it sounded serious. As curious as he'd been, he hadn't asked her about it. He figured he had enough problems right now. For all he knew, Kathleen was having the baby at this very moment. "I'm listening," he said.

Gabriella cleared her throat. "I'm telling you this now because…I want you to be happy. I don't want a cloud hanging over our relationship. From now on, I want the past to be behind us, so we can concentrate on the future.''

What future? Kathleen's gone and she isn't coming back. Roman forced himself to sit straight in his chair. His mother was clearly having difficulty saying whatever it was she wanted to say.

"What, Mother?"

"Roman…" She cleared her throat. "Roman, I was entirely responsible for my divorce from your father."

That got his attention. He stared at her for a minute. "I can't believe you," he finally muttered. "All that time you let me think—"

"Let everybody think," she said. "But I left your father. He didn't leave me, and when things didn't work out for me, the way they did for him, I—" She shrugged. "I wanted to hide my wounded pride. And so I went out of my way to let people think…"

"That my father was a two-timing…"

"He was happy," she said simply.

When Roman only returned her comment with shocked silence, she continued. "I was having an affair with another man, who I thought was going to marry me, after I left your father."

Roman glanced at the floor. Was his mother really telling him about an extramarital affair? "And I guess this man didn't?" Roman asked, nearly choking on the words.

Gabriella shook her head. Her eyes looked a little sad.

"How could you lie to me?" he finally asked.

She shrugged. "I know I let people think that Loretta and your father had been carrying on for years, when they hadn't been. But I was younger and far more foolish and full of pride. I—'' Her voice suddenly broke. ''I didn't want you to hate me.''

Roman blew out a long breath. It was a strange revelation, odder still since it came so many years after their divorce. ''I could never hate you, Mother.''

Gabriella cleared her throat again. ''Do you see why I'm saying this?'' she asked, gazing into his face. ''I want to be a good grandma to Kathleen's baby. And I want to make friends with her in good faith.''

''I really am glad about that,'' Roman managed to say after another long moment. ''But, Mother, Kathleen left me.'' *And with good reason.* He tilted his head and scrutinized his mother's face. ''Why are you telling me this now?''

''Because I just found her,'' Gabriella said.

''THERE, THERE, HONEY,'' Inge Krause was saying. ''Everything's going to be just fine.'' She shook a bottle of lotion.

Kathleen nestled down in the bed in Inge's guest room, her back supported by myriad pillows. She tried to cross her legs Indian-style, but couldn't because her ankles were too swollen. They were even tighter than the day she'd walked all the way down the access road, and nearly collapsed at Inge and Jerry's house. Kathleen burst into tears. Again.

Inge rubbed more lotion on her ankles and calves. ''Why don't you call Roman?'' she prodded gently. ''I know he's looking for you.''

Kathleen glanced through a window. Far off, through the trees and over the water, she could just see a glimmer of light from the château. ''Because he's—he's going to take away the baby,'' Kathleen replied.

"Honey," Inge said, "he's looking for you, and I know he doesn't mean to do any such thing."

"Well, I can't call, because I'm going to have my, my—" She hiccuped. "My baby." Her gaze suddenly shot to Inge's face. "You didn't tell Roman where I am, did you, Inge?"

"You told me not to tell him," Inge said, now rubbing the lotion over Kathleen's feet. "So I most certainly did not. But he's called countless times, and he's really worried."

"Well, I don't care," she said, feeling tears well in her eyes again. What was wrong with her? Her whole system was going bonkers. Crying jags had become her middle name. She suddenly pressed a hand to her stomach and gasped.

Inge's head shot up. "More contractions?"

Kathleen managed a nod. She'd been having contractions off and on for two days now. She'd called Dr. Peteck so many times that she figured she might as well move next door to him. Thinking that made her tear up again. *I don't have a home anymore, and the baby's perfect nursery is in Roman's château.*

She sniffed. The worst thing was that Dr. Peteck just kept saying not to come to the hospital until the contractions were sustained for three hours. It had been only two, even though it felt like forever. And they hurt. She hiccuped again and a tear rolled down her cheek.

"And—and—and I don't think the baby is ever going to come." Why hadn't she just confronted him? Why hadn't she fought for her love for him? Didn't he know how much she needed him, especially now? "And now I—I'm too pregnant to go to the château, and I can't go anywhere except…"

"Except where?" Inge asked when she didn't continue.

"Except the hospital," Kathleen choked out. "Oh, Inge, what if I don't ever have this baby?"

Inge had the nerve to chuckle softly. "Oh, you'll have it, all right, sweetheart."

But I can't have Roman. She could never forgive what he'd done. Kathleen choked back another onslaught of throaty cries, and glanced toward his house again.

The bright headlights of a speeding car beamed back at her. And, through Inge's window, it looked as if the maniac driver was headed straight for her.

ROMAN SLAMMED his Lamborghini into Park in Inge's driveway. Then he leaped out of it, went up and rang the bell. He could kill Inge for lying to him, and yet he could understand it. After all, Kathleen was upset and pregnant. And anyway, Inge had finally given in and told his mother where she was.

"Is she really here?" Roman managed to say when Inge opened the door.

"She sure is," Inge said softly, nodding toward a hallway. "And as in love with you as ever, I think." She smiled and squeezed his arm. "She's in the back bedroom."

He found her with no trouble. Propped in bed in a blue tent dress, big as a house, and crying as if to save her life. He'd meant to be kind, but he was still mad at her for worrying him so much, and for believing that he really could have taken the baby away from her.

"Where have you been!" he found himself exclaiming.

"Here, obviously," she shot back, her tears drying

up in an instant. She sniffed and swiped her cheek with the back of her hand.

"With Inge?"

"Obviously," Kathleen said again. She glanced pointedly down at her stomach as if to say she was in no shape to go anywhere else. "I'm allowed to have friends," she added.

She scooted toward the edge of the bed and stood, arching her back and wincing as if each movement was causing her distress. She hiccuped. "And I can't *believe* Inge let you in here."

She said it almost as if she no longer counted Inge as one of her friends. And then her nose crinkled as if she was going to start crying again. Roman blew out a sigh. So this was what was meant when people talked about a pregnant woman's moods, he thought. He'd seen her surly, but never like this.

"No one, including Inge, could have stopped me from trying to find you, Kathleen," he managed to say gently. Staring at her stomach, he absolutely couldn't believe she hadn't had the baby yet. Looking at her, so full and round with the child—their child—softened him. He went to her swiftly, placed a steadying hand beneath her elbow and began to guide her toward the hallway.

She was apparently finished with her weeping. Whatever she'd been crying about had been forgotten the second he entered the room. She wasn't even hiccuping anymore.

"What do you think you're doing?" She snapped the words in such a way that made him think he preferred her crying. At least she seemed sweet and vulnerable that way.

She tried to wrench from his grasp. "Where do you think you're taking me!"

"Home," he said, trying to ignore the fact that she made him sound like an ax murderer, rather than her husband. He forced himself to keep his voice level. "We're going home, darlin'."

"I don't have a home," she said.

Roman took a deep breath and said nothing.

When they reached the front door he nodded at Inge. "Could you grab her bags?" If the situation hadn't seemed so dire—if Roman hadn't been so anxious to get Kathleen home—he would have gotten them himself.

Kathleen's body had gone nearly lax. She didn't protest, and that bothered Roman more than a little. It meant she was storing up energy for the battle that was to come, he thought as he gingerly seated her in the passenger seat of the car. Kathleen merely stared through the windshield, with her arms crossed defiantly over her chest.

"I love you," he managed to say before he turned and headed back to the porch for her bags.

KATHLEEN FOUGHT BACK her tears with all her might. *Home. Roman has come to take me home.* Why wasn't she happier? Was it hormones? Fear about having the baby? That she still hated him for lying to her? That she couldn't forgive him?

"Well, hurry up," she suddenly muttered.

And he did. Within moments all her belongings were behind the driver's seat and they were headed to the château. In silence.

"At least talk to me, Kathleen," Roman finally said.

"Don't drive so fast," she snapped. "I'm pregnant."

He was driving well under the speed limit, but he slowed the car to a complete crawl and stared forward, not about to make her talk if she didn't want to. She was pregnant and having a hard time, judging by her tear-stained cheeks, and he sure didn't want to make things worse for her.

After a few moments she hazarded a glance in his direction. Why did he have to look so damnably beautiful? His window was down and his long hair was blowing back in the wind. His full lips were pursed in a way that looked less angry and more kissable. How could a man who looked so nice have planned to take a baby away from its mother?

And why had she told him to slow down? Even though it was a short ride, she didn't want to be trapped in the little car with him any longer than necessary. And then she did. *I want every day of my life to be like our last night together.*

She gasped and her face contorted.

He nearly stopped the car. "What's wrong? Are you all right, Kathleen?"

"Fine," she snapped, even though the concern in his voice made her want to reach over and give him a hug. "Just fine." Her eyes started to tear up again.

"Could've fooled me," he muttered. "I'm sorry," he immediately added. "I just hoped you'd be happy to see me."

"Why didn't you tell me you were divorcing me?" she suddenly snarled.

"I didn't want to hurt your feelings." He managed to keep his voice gentle. "I mean, I was going to do it. Divorce you," Roman said. "But the more time I spent with you, the more I fell in love and…well, I liked being married—"

"Liked," she said and sniffed.

"Loved," he countered quickly, gripping the wheel more tightly. "No, love, Kathleen," he quickly corrected again, "as in the present tense. And Miles was on a vacation cruise and couldn't be reached."

Tears were welling in her eyes again but she fought them down. "But you were going to take the baby," she wailed.

He swallowed. "I couldn't have really done that, Kathleen," he said. "I couldn't have gone through with it. You've got to believe me."

"But you would have divorced me and gotten your island back! You are so petty!"

"I admit it," he said. Beginning to feel a little angry, Roman buzzed them through the gates and pulled the car up in front of the château. He reached behind the seat for her bags and hauled them onto the driveway. Then he leaned over, fighting his anger, and cupped her face. "And I'll do anything I can to make up for it. Anything in the world."

"You were going to take my baby," Kathleen said again. She got out, slammed her door and headed for the house.

"I wouldn't have done it," he called after her. What was he going to do? He watched her back as she went inside. His poor, sweet wife was walking as if every step was torture. He picked up her suitcases and followed her.

When she reached the kitchen, Kathleen leaned against the doorjamb, pausing for breath. She was just too pregnant to be having hysterical scenes like this. Why was her mind in such a muddle? She hadn't wanted to be in the car with Roman, and now she could kill him for not running right after her.

If there was anything she hated, it was talk about feminine hormones. She usually wanted to kill people who even suggested that female hormones could cause strange behavior in women. But she had to admit that hers were going haywire.

Roman had come to take her home. He'd said he loved her, he'd said he loved being married and he'd said he could never have taken the baby away from her. She shook her head in confusion.

When Roman found her in the kitchen, he leaned against the doorjamb opposite her and shoved his hands deep into the pockets of his well-worn jeans. He smiled at her gently.

"So, what's it gonna be, Kathleen?" he asked, his voice a little playful…as if they hadn't even been fighting.

"What do you mean?" she replied. Was this another Roman-style trick? She knew darn well he knew she was mad.

"I mean, I love you, Kathleen," he said. He leaned his head just slightly to the side. His eyes roved over every inch of her as though he hadn't seen her for years, rather than weeks.

Another contraction racked her body, but she managed to fight back a groan. She took a few practice breaths. *Pant, one-two; pant, one-two.*

Suddenly this just didn't seem like the time to be having an argument. "I love you, too, Roman," she said weakly.

He chuckled softly. "Think you could put a little emotion into it?"

She really wasn't sure she could at the moment. She

looked into his eyes and managed to smile. "I love you, Roman. I really do." She took in every plane and contour of his angelic face as he began leading her toward the table. He seated her, then pulled out the chair next to her and sat down.

"And from now on, when there's a problem, you'll come talk to me first?"

"Yes," she said softly.

Their thighs and knees touched, sending those age-old sparks of longing through her. His hand crept from her knee to her thigh and rested there. And then he kissed her softly.

"So what's it gonna be?" he murmured again, his lips still against her cheek. He leaned back just a fraction and nodded at the table.

When she looked down, she winced. The divorce and custody papers were still on the table.

A pen was neatly resting on the papers, right by the big *X* beside the signature line.

He slowly lifted the sheets from the table, taking one side and offering her the other. "Whaddaya say? We both pull on the count of three, darlin'." He smiled. "One...two...three."

They both tugged, and the papers ripped down the middle.

"Will you marry me, darling?"

For a moment all the odd pangs in her abdomen were forgotten. "Haven't we been through this before?"

He smiled, but the smile didn't quite reach his eyes. "No," he said. "We've never been here before. It's new. Every moment I spend with you always feels new."

"I'll marry you," she said. Another pain shot through her stomach and she winced.

He turned dead white in spite of his tan. "Kathleen, if you really don't want to—" he began quickly. "I don't know how I can live without you, darlin'. These weeks without you have been so miserable."

"No, it's all right," she said. Her face twisted into a grimace.

"If you don't want to live with me, I just—I mean, we just have to be together."

"It's not that, Roman," she said shakily.

"Whatever problems there are, I'm sure we can work them out, all of them. Every last—"

"Look, Roman, it's not—" she managed to say again.

"Kathleen, if you've changed your mind about loving me back, if you need more time to try and forgive me... Well, I'll try to give it to you, but I can't bear one more night without you in my arms, Kathleen."

"Roman, please, just—"

"Anything you want from me, I'll give—"

"It is not that!" she wailed.

"Then what is it, darlin'?"

And then a shriek hit the air. It sounded just like the one in the movie they had seen.

"Oh, dear heaven," he whispered. "You're in labor."

"YOU'RE DOING JUST FINE, darlin'," Roman murmured, pressing a dry white cloth against Kathleen's forehead. Her thin white cotton hospital gown was damp with perspiration. So was his own shirt. He glanced at the clock. *Twelve-fifty-nine.* She had been in labor now for over six hours.

"Just breathe, Kathleen," Dr. Peteck said.

"Everything's fine. You're doing so well...." Roman continued to murmur endearments as he had all night. He glanced at the clock again. "It's 1:04 now." He smiled down at Kathleen, pressing the soft cloth against her forehead again. "Guess our son or daughter's a night owl, huh, sweetheart?"

Kathleen tried to smile back, but her face contorted with pain again and she gasped. "Are you sure it's all right?" she asked, her voice rising in a wail. "It hurts so much. It can't be right if it—"

"It really is all right," Roman whispered.

"This is it," Dr. Peteck said, his voice as calm as could be. "Roman, do you want to head down to this end of the table?"

Roman gazed into Kathleen's frightened eyes just as her face contorted into a knot. When he sucked in a quick breath, his mouth went fully dry. He swallowed. "Oh, darlin', you're really okay," he soothed, feeling a little shaky himself for the first time. He winced when a high-pitched, strangled sound caught in Kathleen's throat.

"Roman, do you want to come down here?" Dr. Peteck asked again.

Roman glanced toward Dr. Peteck, wanting to see the baby come more than anything in the world, but feeling just as determined not to leave his position. He meant to stay right beside Kathleen where she could see him, and offer any comfort he could. How could a mere five feet of space suddenly seem such worlds apart? He looked at Kathleen again.

She choked on a scream. "Don't worry, I'm right here," Roman said. He somehow managed to start breathing with her, the way they had in class.

"Roman, get down here," Dr. Peteck said, his voice turning demanding.

Kathleen's mouth was contorted in so much pain that she couldn't talk. "I won't leave you, darlin'," Roman whispered.

She cried out, and Roman sucked in another quick breath.

"Roman, I *can't* go, so you have to," she managed to say. Her arm flew outward and she shoved him forcibly in the direction of Dr. Peteck.

"Go," she wailed.

When he was halfway down the table, she groaned. "Oh, my—"

Roman headed right back for her head, but Dr. Peteck jerked on his sleeve, stopping him.

"Roman, stand still and look over my shoulder," Doctor Peteck said calmly.

Roman blew out a shaky breath. He glanced quickly at the clock again. *One-oh-eight.*

Looking over Dr. Peteck's shoulder, he wished with all his life there was something he could do to ease Kathleen's pain. And that he could be in two places at once. Kathleen was beginning to breathe with fast, rhythmic pushes. That, he knew, was good.

Please hurry, Roman thought, just as Kathleen unleashed a heartrending wail that made him feel his heart would break.

And then Roman saw it—the most glorious, mysterious, beautiful thing in the world. The tiny little bulb of the baby's head appeared. Roman didn't remember ever crying in his adult life, but his eyes suddenly stung. One more push and the baby was squirming and wriggling in Dr. Peteck's hands like a wildcat.

"It's a boy," Dr. Peteck said. "Roman, cut the cord."

"It's a boy?" Kathleen called.

Roman was aware that she was struggling to sit, so that she could see. "It's a boy, sweetheart," he called.

"It's a boy," she said again.

"Born at 1:09," Dr. Peteck said efficiently.

Roman leaned forward, touching their son for the first time. He held his breath for fear he'd hurt the baby or Kathleen, and cut the cord.

"Congratulations, this little fellow's truly in the world now," Dr. Peteck said.

Yes, with that one gesture, their baby was truly in the world. Living and breathing…and crying, Roman thought, smiling.

Roman returned to Kathleen's side. He helped her move upward so that she could gaze at the baby, who was now kicking and flexing his arms and crying in long wails while Dr. Peteck patted him dry.

"It's really a boy?" she asked, even though she could see the truth of it from where she was. She stared at the baby with her lips parted in absolute wonderment.

"A boy," Roman repeated proudly. He smoothed a tangled hair by Kathleen's eyebrow and smiled gently. "And you're a mother, my darling."

Epilogue

"Now, don't you cry," Kathleen murmured. She cradled Augustine in her arms. The tiny bundle of her son quavered as she ever-so-gently rocked him to silence. He weighed nine and a half pounds, had measured in at nineteen inches and had a tuft of white-blond hair right in the middle of his scalp. And he was the most amazing thing she had ever seen. On New Year's night she'd been so unsure about her future, but this had turned out to be the best year of her life.

Kathleen glanced up and smiled at Roman, barely aware of the other people who crowded the room. Roman smiled back at her, his eyes slits of twinkling, shining black. He had just relinquished the baby, and was now lounging on the bed at her feet, his elbows on either side of her ankles. He rubbed Kathleen's calves through the light, pale pink hospital blanket.

Kathleen smiled down at Augustine again, and shifted her hand to offer his head more support. One of his arms stretched upward and she dipped so that he could touch her face. Then Kathleen forced herself to glance around the room, even though she only wanted to attend to her baby…and Roman.

"Mr. Flanders, we better get going," Ms. Rodriguez

murmured, catching Kathleen's eye. The woman nodded toward the baby wistfully.

"I have to get going, too," Gabriella said. She walked toward Kathleen, leaned and kissed Augustine. "It's so nice of you to name him for Roman's father," she said gently, meeting Kathleen's gaze.

As Inge leaned to kiss both Kathleen and the baby, Kathleen whispered, "Thank you for lying to me."

"About what?" Inge asked, letting Augustine grasp one of her fingers in his fist and hold it tight.

"About not telling Roman where I was," Kathleen said, smiling.

"I didn't tell Roman," Inge returned, gently prying Augustine's fingers from her own. Inge chuckled. "I told Gabriella." Then the woman squeezed Kathleen's shoulder quickly, glanced for a moment at Augustine again and headed for the door. "But—ahem—Ms. Rodriguez, can't we just ask Roman…" Flanders was protesting somewhere in the background.

"That can wait."

Far down, at the other end of the bed, Roman managed to tear his eyes away from Kathleen and the baby. "Ask Roman what?"

"Well," Flanders began, "Angelina and I want to request a joint two-week vacation."

As content as she was, just looking at the top of Augustine's tiny soft head and the tuft of hair on his scalp, Kathleen raised her eyes.

"At the same time?" she asked softly, hoping that Ms. Rodriguez wasn't going to leave just yet, not while Augustine was so tiny. All the books in the world couldn't have prepared her for her new responsibility. But Roman would help, she told herself now. Gabriella would, too.

"We're getting married," Flanders said happily. "And I think she deserves a little honeymoon. Don't you?"

"Married?" Kathleen said, glancing down at Augustine again, then back up at Flanders.

"Not immediately. But when Angelina saw you and Roman together—and the baby—well, she finally agreed—"

"You're really getting married?" Roman reached and squeezed Ms. Rodriguez's hand. That's wonderful. Congratulations, Flanders. And take all the time you want."

"The baby's beautiful," Ms. Rodriguez said in a small, reverent voice, before pushing her husband-to-be from the room.

"He really is," Gabriella said just as softly from the doorway. "I think he's going to look just like you, Kathleen."

"Thank you, Gabriella," Kathleen said.

Looking up at Kathleen from the foot of the bed, his hands still roving over her calves, Roman smiled. "He already does look like you," he said when everybody had left the room. "And I really hope his eyes turn green, like yours. You have the most beautiful eyes."

Roman began to inch upward, toward Kathleen and Augustine, his hands curling tighter around Kathleen's legs. His palms roved up from her calves, stretching for her thighs, knowing they were every bit as soft as the blanket that covered them.

"I'm coming to kiss you both," he singsonged. His smile was teasing and playful, and the brightness of his eyes said he had only one thing on his mind—loving her and Augustine. He inched up, just another fraction, his hands now rubbing over her hips.

"My, my, you are skinny, darlin'," he said when his hands reached the softness of her stomach.

"Are you saying you don't like me thin?" she teased.

"I *love* you just fine," he said. "But didn't you kind of hate being an only child?"

"Yeah," she said, gazing down again into her son's face. "I kind of did."

Roman inched ever closer, stopping only when his fingertips grazed Augustine's feet through the blanket. "Well," he said gently, "I don't think we should subject our son to the same fate."

She smiled, her brow suddenly furrowing as she looked at Augustine. "I just wish Mama had been here to see him." She glanced at Roman. "Your dad, too."

Roman grazed his hand softly over Augustine's head. "Yeah," he said gently.

"But your mother's here," Kathleen said, smiling again.

Roman chuckled. "And I'm getting the impression she may be around more than we want." His voice said he didn't really mean it.

"Well, I think she'll be a help." Kathleen suddenly grinned as Roman inched so dangerously close that he could trace the lines of her collarbone.

Roman chuckled again. "But I want to do all the help." He gazed at the baby for a long moment.

When he glanced at Kathleen again, his dark eyes were all lit up, like twin dark moons in a daytime sky. "Darlin'," he whispered. "You're both really mine now, no matter what."

"So would you like to kiss us, Roman?" she asked softly.

He leaned and kissed his son's forehead. And then

his lips pressed against hers. His tongue followed, gently, slowly, languidly seeking out hers. After a moment Augustine began to cry.

"I think he wants his daddy," Kathleen whispered.

Roman gazed deeply into her eyes, smiled and then gently lifted the baby from her arms. He leaned next to Kathleen in the bed and began to rock him.

"That kiss was only a promise," he said after a moment, cuddling Augustine closer and glancing at Kathleen. "Because I'm going to be kissing you for a long time."

Kathleen nuzzled against Roman's shoulder, listening contentedly to how Augustine's wailing cries tempered to shuddering sighs once he was in his father's arms. "A real long time, darlin'," Kathleen whispered in return.

THE MIRACLE BABY
Janice Kay Johnson

CHAPTER ONE

"ARE YOU MR. NATHAN McCABE?"

The man who stood on Nathan's front porch was young, sandy-haired, a little soft around the middle. His face was unfamiliar, but pleasant enough. Your average Joe.

"That's right," Nathan agreed a little warily, his hand gripping the open door. Salesmen didn't know your name.

The man extended a card. "Richard Clayton, private investigator."

Nathan took the card. It was plain, but the paper was heavyweight, expensive, the print engraved. His wariness edged into apprehension.

"What can I do for you?" he asked.

The P.I. cleared his throat. "Mr. McCabe, did you have a brother named Robin?"

Rob. Sometimes he could almost forget the part of himself he'd lost with the estrangement. Being reminded was a jolt.

"I have a brother named Robin." What could admitting that much hurt? "Did he hire you?"

The first real emotion showed on that bland face. "Hire me? You're not aware...?"

"Aware of what?" Nathan asked sharply.

Unexpected compassion added a few lines to the man's face. "I'm sorry, Mr. McCabe. It's your brother's widow who hired me to find you. I'm afraid he's dead.''

Dead? Rob? Shock held Nate still, unseeing. Dead? How could his brother be dead without his knowing?

Images flashed through his mind with scattergun speed: the boy, cheeks still childishly round, beguiling their kindergarten teacher; Rob, maybe ten, on the pitcher's mound; hanging upside down from the top bunk in their bedroom, tongue out and eyes crossed; lounging against his locker in high school, grinning lazily at some girl; the twenty-one-year-old, wiping blood from his nose and snarling. This last image was sharp, though fifteen years old. They hadn't seen each other since. Fifteen years, and Nathan didn't have to wonder what his brother had looked like before he died. All he had to do was glance in a mirror.

"How long ago?" he asked numbly.

"Three years. I'm sorry. I—"

"How?" Nathan's teeth were set. "How did he die?"

"I…" The P.I. retreated a step. "I'm not quite sure. Mrs. McCabe didn't say."

Mrs. McCabe. Rob had married and Nathan had never known. He couldn't picture his brother standing at the altar, gaze held by one woman. Couldn't imagine him saying, "I do," and meaning it. Lifting the veil and kissing her, sweeping her across a threshold, staying faithful, maybe changing diapers or coaching a Little League team. Making a marriage work, when Nathan couldn't.

Fifteen years. He kept bumping up against it. A big chunk of his lifetime. They'd been so young when he'd broken his brother's nose and walked away without looking back. Their parting wasn't supposed to be permanent, whatever he'd said at the time. Nathan had always figured Rob would give him some time to cool off, then come find him. Alone on Christmas Eve this year, Nathan had started thinking maybe it was time *he* did the finding. But even then, it had been too late.

Nathan closed his eyes for a moment, let the pain rip open a wound he'd thought long healed. He rubbed a hand over his face.

"If he died three years ago, why does she want to find me now?"

The P.I.'s unmemorable face would be forever engraved in Nathan's memory, stuck in his mental photo album. The poor SOB hadn't even known he was to be the bearer of the worst tidings.

He was talking, and with difficulty Nathan latched on to his words. A daughter. Something about a daughter, eleven years old. *Rob's daughter.*

He interrupted. "Do you have a picture?"

He'd caught the P.I. off guard. "Yes, I... Right here." He groped in one pocket of his jacket, then the other. "Mrs. McCabe thought..."

"A picture would soften me?"

"Yes. No. That is..."

Nathan took the photo and tuned the man out. It was a school picture, like those that came with Christmas cards, friends showing him in the faces of their children how quickly the years were passing. The girl wore a denim dress with an embroidered neckline and she was smiling uncertainly. Nathan knew her eyes, big and dark; they were Rob's—and his own.

But, good God, her hair wasn't an inch long, dark and fine, revealing the shape of her skull. And she was ghost pale, and thin. He was reminded of pictures he'd seen of concentration-camp survivors.

He lifted a shocked gaze to Richard Clayton, P.I. "What's wrong with her?"

"Leukemia," Clayton said bluntly. "She needs a bone-marrow transplant. Mrs. McCabe isn't a suitable donor, and the National Bone Marrow Donor Registry hasn't found one. Because you and Amanda's father were twins, the chances are excellent that your tissue is a match."

As he absorbed the news, Nathan lowered his gaze to the picture again. Rob's daughter. His niece. Maybe dying for lack of her father.

"What do I need to do?" he asked simply.

BETH RAN the vacuum cleaner down the hall. Ahead of her, bobtailed Calvin, an orange kitten, darted into Mandy's bedroom and no doubt under the bed. Behind Beth, Calvin's sister Polly chased the vacuum cord. From the same litter, with the same upbringing, and one was terrified by the vacuum cleaner while the other apparently thought it was just a big noisy mouse. Was there a gene for courage?

Was there one for leukemia?

She turned into her daughter's bedroom and ran the vacuum over the carpet while she tried not to look around, not to think. But her effort was as useless today as it was every other day. Mandy was doing well right now, to all appearances a normal preteen. In front of her, Beth pretended; alone, she had no defense against her fear. With a sigh she switched off the vacuum cleaner.

In the sudden silence Beth stood in the middle of Mandy's bedroom and gave way to the knowing, to the terror. The room was too neat—books in alphabetical order, spines perfectly lined up, dresser drawers and closet doors shut. And Beth knew that inside them the shoes and the socks and dresses and jeans would be stacked and hung in order just as perfectly, sorted by color or sometimes by a mysterious system all Mandy's own. Even her bulletin board was ordered: school pictures of her friends marching along the bottom, all held in place by the same-color thumbtacks; awards and ribbons just above them held by tacks of a different color; and in the upper third of the board a tidy line of odd tidbits—a dried bunch of flowers, a piece of lace, one earring, a newspaper photo of the middle-school boys' soccer team and a Garfield cartoon. It was as though Mandy thought she could save herself by imposing order on her world.

Exactly at the center of her desk was her journal, the cover marbled paper, the spine navy blue leather. Mandy left it there every day, never hiding it as Beth suspected most girls did with their diaries. Was her openness an act of trust? Or a way of begging her mother to peek into her heart and see her fears?

So far, Beth hadn't let herself. Every day, she resisted the terrible temptation. A girl's diary should be private. If Mandy handed it to her, she'd read it. Until then, she had to give her daughter the freedom to confide the unspeakable.

Beth blinked hard to clear the mist from her eyes. When she realized her nose was running, too, she mumbled, "Oh, damn. Why did I have to start?"

She was in the bathroom blowing her nose when a knock sounded on the front door. Her forehead crinkled. Funny, she hadn't heard the UPS truck pull in. Oh, well, maybe she'd still had the vacuum running. Fortunately she had the half-dozen shipments of jam packed and ready to go. She tossed the tissue into the wastebasket and hurried to answer the door.

"Hi, I'm all set—" When she saw the tall dark-haired man standing on her porch, shock snatched her breath and her voice with it. Rob. Oh, God, her dead husband was within arm's reach. Clutching the door frame, she whispered his name.

He moved his shoulders uncomfortably. "No, I'm Nathan McCabe. Rob's brother."

Still she sagged against the door, staring. She'd known Rob had a twin, had even hired the private investigator to find him, but somehow she'd never dreamed that he would *be* Rob all over again. The hair, wavy and short and silky, those prominent cheekbones, the dark slash of brows over brown eyes, the thin hard mouth. Her unbelieving gaze searched his face for some difference, anything she could fasten on to convince herself that he wasn't Rob, that Rob hadn't found a way to come back to her.

He flushed under her stare, something her supremely confident husband would never have done. But still...

His clothes. She seized on it. Rob would never have chosen anything as conservative as a gray suit, white shirt and narrow maroon tie. Yet that suit jacket would have hung just the same way from her husband's shoulders had he worn it. Even this man's hands, tanned, large and half-curled into fists, could have been Rob's. She made another strangled sound.

"I'm sorry," he said quietly. "I didn't think. I should have let Clayton warn you."

She lifted her gaze back to his face. "He found you?"

"Yeah. I thought you'd be pleased."

GET 2

HOW TO GET YOUR
2 FREE BOOKS AND FREE GIFT!

1. Peel off the MIRA sticker on the front cover. Place it in the space provided at right. This automatically entitles you to receive two free books and an exciting surprise gift.

2. Send back this card and you'll get 2 "The Best of the Best™" novels. These books have a combined cover price of $11.98 or more in the U.S. and $13.98 or more in Canada, but they are yours to keep absolutely FREE!

3. There's <u>no</u> catch. You're under <u>no</u> obligation to buy anything. We charge nothing – ZERO – for your first shipment. And you don't have to make any minimum number of purchases – not even one!

4. We call this line "The Best of the Best" because each month you'll receive the best books by some of today's most popular authors. These authors show up time and time again on all the major bestseller lists and their books sell out as soon as they hit the stores. You'll like the convenience of getting them delivered to your home at our special discount prices . . . and you'll love your *Heart to Heart* subscriber newsletter featuring author news, horoscopes, recipes, book reviews and much more!

5. We hope that after receiving your free books you'll want to remain a subscriber. But the choice is yours – to continue or cancel, anytime at all! So why not take us up on our invitation, with no risk of any kind. You'll be glad you did!

6. And remember...we'll send you a surprise gift ABSOLUTELY FREE just for giving "The Best of the Best" a try.

SPECIAL FREE GIFT!

We'll send you a fabulous surprise gift, absolutely FREE, simply for accepting our no-risk offer!

Visit us online at
www.mirabooks.com

® and TM are trademarks of Harlequin Enterprises Limited.

BOOKS FREE!

The Best of the Best™ — Here's How it Works:

Accepting your 2 free books and gift places you under no obligation to buy anything. You may keep the books and gift and return the shipping statement marked "cancel." If you do not cancel, about a month later we will send you 4 additional novels and bill you just $4.49 each in the U.S., or $4.99 each in Canada, plus 25¢ shipping & handling per book and applicable taxes if any.* That's the complete price and — compared to cover prices of $5.99 or more each in the U.S. and $6.99 or more each in Canada — it's quite a bargain! You may cancel at any time, but if you choose to continue, every month we'll send you 4 more books, which you may either purchase at the discount price or return to us and cancel your subscription.

*Terms and prices subject to change without notice. Sales tax applicable in N.Y. Canadian residents will be charged applicable provincial taxes and GST.

If offer card is missing write to: The Best of the Best, 3010 Walden Ave., P.O. Box 1867, Buffalo, NY 14240-1867

BUSINESS REPLY MAIL

FIRST-CLASS MAIL   PERMIT NO. 717-003   BUFFALO, NY

POSTAGE WILL BE PAID BY ADDRESSEE

THE BEST OF THE BEST
3010 WALDEN AVE
PO BOX 1867
BUFFALO NY 14240-9952

NO POSTAGE
NECESSARY
IF MAILED
IN THE
UNITED STATES

"Pleased." She sounded and felt blank, too stunned for rational thought.

He made that uneasy movement with his shoulders again. "Clayton said you needed me."

Understanding flooded back and with it embarrassment. She pressed hands to her hot cheeks. "Nathan. Your name's Nathan."

His eyes met hers. "Rob called me Nate."

"I know." Of course she did. "Is...is that what you go by?"

"Rob and our parents were the only ones who called me that."

"Family," she said softly.

The grooves on each side of his mouth deepened. "Yeah."

"We would have been family."

"We *are* family," he said with quiet intensity.

Beth shook her head, not in rejection of the idea, but in astonishment. He was here because she needed him. He was family.

She let out a long breath. "I'm sorry. Come in. I've been rude. It's just..."

"We look so much alike. I understand. I suppose it's...unnerving."

He stepped past her and she gave a small shiver. "He said you were identical twins. But somehow I thought after all these years there would be differences."

"There probably are. Were." Just inside the living room he stood silent for a moment, his back to her. "I didn't know he was dead."

"I'm sorry," Beth said again. "I should have tried to find you then. But that's when Mandy got sick. I...I just couldn't deal with everything. It was easy to convince myself you wouldn't care.''

"We were twins. A lot came between us, but no matter what, we were tied together.'' He faced her and his mouth twisted. "I can't believe he's dead.''

"Please, sit down.'' She moved to the couch and curled up on one end, watching him sit stiffly in the worn wing chair she kept meaning to reupholster.

"How?'' His voice was hoarse. "How did he die?''

She looked down at her hands. "A car accident. He always drove too fast. He had this red Corvette he really loved.''

"He always wanted one.'' Nathan's dark eyes became unfocused as he saw a past that Rob hadn't shared with her.

She nodded, even though he probably didn't see her. "I was glad when we could afford it. We don't get to fulfill that many dreams. Now I'd give anything to take it back. Maybe if he'd been driving a different car he wouldn't have been going so fast. All he was doing was coming home from work. Just a normal commute.'' She fell silent, remembering that night.

In January darkness fell early. The roads had been icy, but Rob was such a good driver, even if he did go too fast sometimes. His reflexes were quick, his instincts sure. Though he'd promised to be home by five o'clock, she hadn't worried until six came and went. She'd called his office and gotten only a recording. She'd been standing at the front window, looking at the dark driveway, willing Rob to appear, when a pair of headlights turned in. A giddy burst of relief had told her how worried she'd been. And then fear had trickled into her chest, for almost immediately she'd realized that the headlights weren't right, didn't look like the

Corvette's. She'd moved out onto the porch, hugging herself against the cold, and it was then she'd seen it was a police car. The trooper had climbed out and come slowly, heavily, toward her.

Remembering, Beth gave another small shiver and heard her husband's brother say, "Are you all right?"

She shook her head, attempting to clear it of memories. "Our insurance rates were horrendous. When I asked Rob to slow down, he'd just laugh. He'd never had an accident, just tickets for speeding. I told him if he needed an adrenaline rush, he should take up skydiving. It would have been safer."

"Did he..." Nathan cleared his throat. "Did he hit anybody else?"

"Oh, yeah." She was staring straight ahead, that video still playing for her. "A van driven by a mother with her two kids. The road was icy and the Corvette apparently went into a skid and crossed the center line. Rob died instantly. The mother had some broken bones, but thank God she recovered. The kids were in car seats and weren't hurt at all. If they had been..." She pressed her lips together.

"It wouldn't have been your fault," he said quietly.

"Maybe not, but it felt like it was."

Their eyes met, held; for a second she'd have sworn the world narrowed to the two of them. Then she squeezed her eyes shut just long enough to blot out the memories.

Almost composed, Beth looked from his hands, spread on the smooth gray fabric of his slacks, back to his face. *Don't think about Rob,* she told herself. *He's here because of Mandy; nothing else matters.* "Mr. Clayton told you about my daughter?"

Nathan leaned forward. "He said she has leukemia. He showed me a picture."

"Yes." She bit her lip. "She's doing fine right now, but doctors give her only two or three years unless she has a bone-marrow transplant. We can't find a donor who matches. Would you be willing?"

"That's why I'm here." He frowned. "Isn't hers the usual childhood leukemia? I thought doctors were doing wonders with chemotherapy."

"They are." Her throat wanted to close, which surprised her. She and Mandy had lived with the bogeyman for so long now; she'd explained the illness over and over again to teachers and principals and the parents of Mandy's friends. Why was it hard now to describe the monster inside her child?

Somehow she kept her voice steady. "Mandy—Amanda—has a more unusual form of leukemia for children, called chronic myelogenous leukemia. It was such a shock. She started having stomach cramps. We thought she had the flu. A week later she felt better and went back to school. But then the cramps started again. She was in agony. Of course, I took her to the doctor." Beth looked down to find that she was wringing her hands. With an effort she separated them.

"That must have been frightening."

She let out a breath in a laugh that held no humor. "Terrifying is a better word. When I was a child, my best friend died of leukemia. They couldn't do anything then. She just…came home until she was too sick, then went into the hospital to die. To have Mandy get it, too…" *Why?* she cried inside. *Dear God, why her?*

Nathan stirred, as though he would have liked to come over to her. Or was he longing to bolt, instead?

Beth had discovered that many people were so uncomfortable with the subject they avoided her.

"Mandy had lumps, too, around her ankles. She'd noticed them and just…shrugged them off, I guess. She was only eight. As soon as she was diagnosed, they started chemotherapy. She lost all her hair and was horribly sick. She responded well, though. But the doctors warned us that this form of leukemia is essentially incurable without a transplant. All they could do was buy time."

"When was this?"

She scrubbed at suddenly wet cheeks. "Three years ago."

"Then Rob was alive…?"

"No." Oh, how angry she'd been at him! "He'd been dead a month when she got sick."

He made a sound in his throat. "Did you have anyone to…?"

"Friends." She tried to smile. "Strangers. People were wonderful. I don't think I cooked a meal for six months. Casserole dishes just…appeared."

His dark eyes didn't waver. "Then what happened?"

"We couldn't find a donor. I have such a small family, and none of us comes close. The donor registry hasn't found anyone. A year and a half ago, Mandy got really sick again." Beth fought for composure. "This time the doctors used both chemotherapy and radiation. If…if she gets that sick again, she might be too weak to survive the procedure. She desperately needs the bone-marrow transplant."

"Was she sure to match either Rob or you?"

"No." Did she sound as helpless as she felt? Beth wondered. "A patient can have a large family and not be a close enough match with any of them. But the odds are a lot better with you than they would be with someone unrelated. Then the odds become something like one in twenty thousand.''

He rose as though he couldn't bear to sit any longer. "I'll do anything.''

She stood slowly, her eyes blurred. "Thank you,'' she whispered.

He came around the end of the coffee table, this man who looked so much like her husband. There he stopped, as though unsure what to do or uncertain of her reaction. If he'd opened his arms, she would have stepped into them, laid her head against his chest, accepted his strength and comfort. It was disquieting to know how easily she could have accepted almost anything from him, a total stranger. She didn't like to think she would have pretended he was Rob.

This man's eyes were unreadable, dark, but he lifted a hand and carefully brushed away the tears from her cheek. The gesture was heart-stoppingly intimate, and yet innocent. Any adult might do the same to a hurt child.

"I…'' Her voice was high, breathless. "I'd better call the hospital. Make…make arrangements.''

He cleared his throat and stepped back. "I can go anytime.''

She blinked at the reminder of everyday details, and was a little ashamed she hadn't asked any questions about his life. Not even where he lived.

"Do you live around Seattle? Or did you fly in?''

"Flew. I'm from Portland.''

"Maybe they could still do the blood test today. You haven't checked into a hotel already, have you? I have an extra bedroom.''

He shook his head immediately. "I'm afraid I can't stay overnight. Not this time. I have an early-morning meeting back in Portland."

She wondered if he'd planned it that way to give himself an escape. Would they ever see him again after the procedure? Did it matter? she asked herself impatiently. He was here now; that was what counted.

"Um…would you like a cup of coffee? Or anything else?"

"Thank you," he said, "but no."

"Then excuse me for a moment."

"Mrs. McCabe?" His voice stopped her in the doorway.

She turned. "Yes?"

"Clayton didn't tell me your name. He kept calling you the widow."

"Beth." She actually smiled, if tremulously. "I'm Beth McCabe."

The touch of his dark eyes was as palpable as a knuckle brushing her cheek. "Beth. Beth and Mandy."

"Does it feel strange?" She flattened her hand against the door frame. "To be here like this when you didn't even know we existed?"

"Very strange," he admitted, "but right."

She gave a small nod and left him in her living room. In her office she sat down at the enormous rolltop desk, reached for the phone—and suddenly felt herself trembling all over. She squeezed her hands into fists and closed her eyes. It was just reaction—the shock of finding her husband's double on her doorstep and the knowledge that he could be the gift of life to Mandy.

She knew she was crying again, but didn't care. He'd come without hesitation. He was willing. For the first time in a long while, she had hope.

THE HOUSE WAS too silent after his brother's widow left the room. Feeling the tension in his neck and back, Nathan listened for her footsteps or her voice. Nothing. It was as though she'd never existed, as though he'd imagined finding her. He began to pace.

A few strides took him from the Oriental rug onto hardwood floor. The old-fashioned, high-ceilinged parlor had the tall sashed windows typical of the time the house was built—between 1910 and 1920, he guessed. Lacy curtains hung open. He glanced out one side window at fields of some kind of vine—probably berry— twining along wire supports. A handsome wooden sign out at the road had said Tillicum Creek Farm. He supposed the fields went with the house. But surely, he thought, frowning, Beth wasn't farming alone.

All the while, he knew his speculation was no more than an attempt to distract himself from the framed photographs lovingly displayed on the fireplace mantel. He'd noticed them the moment he stepped in the room. They exerted a force that both repelled and drew him. It was the pull that was winning.

He had pictures of Rob, too, a couple of boxes of albums that had been faithfully kept by his mother, stashed in a seldom opened closet. He'd gone straight to the closet when he closed the door on Richard Clayton, P.I. When he pulled the albums out of the box and flipped them open, he'd found only the kid his brother had been: cheeky, smart-mouthed, too charismatic for his own damned good. His twin. That part of himself he'd savagely excised. None were of the man Rob had become. He had cried finally, howls of agony he'd kept corked tightly inside for too many years. With the knowledge of Rob's death, the seal had failed, and the poison of his bitterness and loneliness poured out. It was the most terrible night of his life, worse than discovering how his brother had betrayed him, worse than their fight, worse than losing his parents or his wife's leaving him.

And now he would be confronted with the man his brother had become. Bracing himself, Nathan approached the fireplace. Rob was there all right, in half-a-dozen photos, grinning in that crooked lazy way women always had found irresistible. Nathan gripped the edge of the mantel, feeling as though the wind had been kicked out of him. Bracing himself hadn't worked. He tried to look away from the photographs until he could control his reaction, but his hunger to see his brother's face was too great. In the sea of pain, Nathan was vaguely aware of surprise: Rob hadn't changed very much from Nathan's memory of him, which didn't gibe with Rob's having been a married man with a child. Maybe the change was all on the inside.

In only a couple of the photos was he alone; the others were either family portraits or home snapshots. In one he had a dark-haired toddler on his shoulders. She was clutching Daddy's hair and grinning, heels drumming his chest, if Nathan was any judge. In another Rob wore a suit, the solemnity spoiled by the tie, which sported a bold Van Gogh sunset. This time Amanda must have been seven or eight; she stood proudly beside him in patent-leather shoes and a pretty dress with a pleated skirt and a big fat bow on one shoulder. They looked uncannily alike, despite the gender and age difference. They *belonged* together. How could Rob be gone?

But the ones he found himself most reluctant to look at were those that included Beth, the studio portraits.

In them, they were the perfect family: broad-shouldered handsome man hovering protectively over his delicate wife and cute daughter. Rob's expression seemed to hold a little smugness; *I've got it all,* Nathan imagined him saying. As a kid Rob would have added, *And you don't.*

Nathan swore under his breath and muttered, "Grow up." He wasn't talking to his brother. He was shocked to discover how much competitiveness he still felt, even amidst his grief. No wonder he'd been a failure as a husband! No wonder he couldn't bring himself to forgive the person who had once been the most important in the world to him. He was corroded inside by the acid of his resentment.

Right now most of it had to do with Beth McCabe, the woman Rob had married. Didn't it figure that, at least in the looks department, she was exactly what had always attracted Nathan more than his brother? Curly blond hair—not the gold of a shiny new wedding ring, but something paler, softer, a shimmer instead of a glitter. Creamy skin with a few unexpected freckles on her small nose. Mist gray eyes that were candid and uncomfortably perceptive. A small-boned build that looked fragile but probably wasn't. He'd noticed her short unpainted nails, seen a few scratches on her hands. Her clothes didn't match the china-doll image, either: she wore snug, faded denim jeans with a Madras cotton shirt knotted around her slender waist, outlining small but shapely breasts.

Rob had always liked flashier women, ones with big tits and pouty lips and invitation in their eyes. Which hadn't stopped him from pursuing the ones with a quieter kind of beauty once he'd noticed his brother's interest. It had been his life's work to demonstrate that anything Nathan could have or do, he could have or do, too.

Nathan focused on his brother's grin again and could have sworn it had become a taunt from the past.

"What the hell is the matter with me?" he said aloud, backing away from the mantel. Good God, did he still hate Rob after all this time? Maybe his brother never had been the one with the problem. Maybe *he* was.

Before he had a chance to pursue the disquieting thought he heard the front door slam, quick footsteps and a girl's voice. "Hey, Mom, what are you doing—" She broke off suddenly, obviously noticing there was a man in the living room. His back was still to her. "Oh, sorry. I didn't know anybody was here."

Nathan turned to face her with damn near as much reluctance as he'd approached the family portrait gallery. He shouldn't have come like this, taken them by surprise.

He got what he expected and deserved. The skinny curly-haired girl first flushed, then paled. In a clogged voice she said, "Daddy?"

He felt lower than lice. Nothing like replaying this scene, and with a child even more vulnerable than her mother.

"No," he said quickly. "No, I'm not your father. I know I look like him. We were twins. I'm his brother."

She did nothing but stare from those huge dark eyes for a long unnerving moment. Then she said tentatively, "Are you Uncle Nate?"

He wasn't sure which part hit him harder, the "Uncle" or the "Nate." Rob's name for him.

"Yeah. That's me."

"Daddy..." She pressed her lips together. "Daddy used to talk about you sometimes."

"Did he have anything good to say?" Nate cringed inwardly at his question. Did he sound like he was begging? *Throw me a crumb. Tell me my brother remembered me with some affection.*

"Well, of course!" Her smile was unexpectedly merry in that solemn little face. "He used to tell me about things you guys did together. You know. Pranks." The smile dimmed a little. "He said he hadn't had as much fun since."

That part had hurt her feelings, Nathan could tell. He wanted to tell her the pranks hadn't been fun at all, though probably they'd started out that way. But he could hardly say, "Your dad lied. He liked cruel pranks."

He settled for, "Twins can pull things off that no one else can."

"I wish I had one," she said wistfully.

This pang was closer to a knife stabbing in his chest. If she had a twin, she could be cured of leukemia. She had to be thinking that.

"It has its down side. Sometimes..." He hesitated, then said what he'd never admitted aloud, "...sometimes you're not sure whether you exist at all alone."

Her eyes were disconcertingly intense. It was a relief when, after a moment, she ducked her head and hunched her shoulders awkwardly. "Uh, do you know where my mom is?"

"She went off to make a phone call."

"Oh." Her head lifted and she offered him a polite smile. "Excuse me. I'll go tell her I'm home."

"Sure."

She turned and walked right into her mother, who

came through the doorway. Amanda gasped, and Beth gave her a hug. "Sorry. I sneaked up on you." Though her tone was light, Beth's gaze went straight to him, and he saw the wariness in it. "Did you meet your uncle Nathan?"

"Uncle Nate. That's what Daddy always called him."

Always. Had Rob talked about him often? Missed him? Nathan had a disorienting sense of the ground shifting under his feet. All these years he'd done his damnedest not to think about his brother. Someday they'd forgive and forget. But what was the hurry? Apart from Nathan, his mirror image, maybe Rob would quit feeling as if he had to prove himself over and over. Maybe he'd find contentment.

Well, to all appearances he had. With luck he'd been freed to remember Nathan with fondness.

Mother and daughter were staring at him, he realized suddenly. He'd been silent too long, missed something. "I'm sorry," he said.

Nobody repeated whatever it was. Amanda suddenly frowned. "Why is Uncle Nate here now?"

The alarm in Beth's eyes was clear, as was her dilemma. Did she tell the truth and, perhaps falsely, raise her daughter's hopes? Or lie?

He had no idea how much his niece knew about her illness. *His niece.* Already he couldn't bear to think of her dying. If he hadn't seen that school picture, which must have been taken a few months ago, he might not have believed in her illness. Her hair was several inches longer now and curly, a halo surrounding a piquant face that was all cheekbones and high forehead and big eyes. She was thin, but no more so than many girls her age who had barely begun developing. Her mother had probably looked much the same, only her curls would have been silky pale, instead of fine and dark.

If she'd meant to lie, Beth shouldn't have hesitated as long as she did.

Amanda stepped away from her and lifted her chin. "It has something to do with my leukemia, doesn't it?"

Beth visibly gathered herself. "Yes," she said gently. "He's here to have his blood tested to find out whether he might be a suitable bone-marrow donor."

Mandy went completely still, unblinking. Then she focused on his face, gave a small nod and said politely, "Thank you." She turned to her mother. "May I get a snack?"

"Of course you can." Lines formed on Beth's brow as she watched her daughter leave the room, composure undented.

Nathan waited for a moment. Then he asked in a low voice, "Is she afraid of the transplant?"

He had never seen a woman look as vulnerable as Beth McCabe did at that moment. "Do you know," she said, "I don't have the slightest idea?"

"She doesn't talk to you?" he asked incredulously.

She clasped her hands together as though she was praying. "On any other subject, yes. On this one…she listens and nods and asks questions when she doesn't understand something. Usually she answers a direct question. But as close as we've always been, I truly don't know how frightened she is. I think…" Her voice broke. "It's as if she senses my fear and doesn't want to burden me with hers."

He nodded and shoved his fisted hands into his pants pockets. It was the only way he could figure to keep himself from pulling her into his arms. They didn't know each other well enough for that, even if he felt as though they did. Or maybe he only wished they did.

"When do they want me at the hospital?" he asked with unplanned brusqueness.

She gave her head a shake, as though she could rid herself of sad thoughts like a dog shaking off water droplets. "Now, if you want to go. It's in Seattle, at Children's Hospital. At least you're going against rush-hour traffic. You can make it in forty-five minutes."

"How long until they know whether I'm a match?"

"A while, unfortunately. Next week sometime. The doctor guessed Thursday." Beth smiled wanly. "You wouldn't believe how slowly time can crawl. Or how little sleep you can exist on."

He knew damn well that he wouldn't sleep much tonight, either. No more than he had last night. Then he'd had only his brother's ghost to torment him. Now, Amanda, slender and too grave, would stand beside her father to stare reproachfully at him in his waking nightmares.

She and her mother needed him, and he hated like hell knowing that his ability to play the hero was no more in his control than tomorrow's weather.

Yeah, he told himself, *and if you do turn out to be the hero, it's only because you're a carbon copy of Rob.* A humbling thought.

"I'm on my way, then," he said.

"We...we'd really like to get to know you." Her gray eyes were anxious. "Will you come for a longer visit soon? As I said, I have an extra bedroom. Maybe you could spend a weekend."

"You're sure? It wouldn't upset Amanda?"

"Are you kidding?" Beth actually reached out and

squeezed his arm. "You're the next best thing to having her dad back again. You'd be good for her."

He almost wished he hadn't given himself an out, that he *was* coming back here tonight. But he'd figured it would be easier for everyone if he didn't have the option of hanging around.

"If you mean it, I could come next week. Say, Thursday morning." He'd rather be here when she got the news, good or bad. Maybe especially if it was bad. "I could stay until Friday afternoon."

She smiled, for a fleeting moment radiant, letting him glimpse what she would look like freed from her ever-present fear. "Bless you. We'll look forward to it. It'll give Mandy something to think about." Something besides the blood test was what she meant.

He nodded and let Beth walk him to his rental car. On the way down the long bumpy lane, he allowed himself a wry smile. They needed him, all right. He was "the next best thing" to having Rob back again.

He guessed his little brother by one minute had won another round.

But when Nathan glanced in his rearview mirror, he saw that the smaller figure of Rob's daughter had come out onto the porch to join her mother in staring after his car. He was instantly ashamed of the pettiness of his thoughts.

Only one person counted here. Amanda McCabe. Rob's daughter and his niece. Whatever anger had lain between the brothers, on this they'd be united, Nathan felt suddenly sure. He hoped there was somebody up there listening when he prayed that his blood was Mandy's salvation, since Rob couldn't be here.

CHAPTER TWO

NATHAN WAS virtually useless at work that week. All the memories he'd repressed these past fifteen years stole back one at a time. They came at unexpected moments, one catching at him like a sharp nail tearing skin, another poking like a little boy jabbing him with a stick, yet another making him smile before he clenched his teeth in agony. The memories slipped into his dreams, and he woke twice with a face wet with tears. Moments of distraction, of real attention to the life taking place right in front of him, were sliced short by the knife edge of a name, a face. He jogged each morning from habit, but even then the pain of his brother's death gripped him like a side ache.

He didn't understand the extent of his grief. He hadn't seen Rob for so many years, hardly even thought of him. He'd even believed he hated his brother. Curiously, terrifyingly, his dreams filled in those lost years. He was at Rob's wedding, watching his brother lift the veil, kiss his bride. Somehow, Amanda was the flower girl. Another night, Rob drove up in his brand-new red Corvette, eager to show it off. They went for a drive, and the road was icy. In the middle of a long skid, Nathan woke up to his own muffled shout. God almighty. He'd seen through the windshield of the van they were about to hit head-on.

Beth was driving and Amanda was in the passenger seat.

There were other, more innocuous dreams. Rob sitting beside their parents at Nathan's college graduation. At the other end of the rope, belaying Nathan, on a climb up Three Fingers.

Under the onslaught only one thought held Nathan together: Rob's daughter needed him.

And Beth was right. Nathan hadn't known time could slow down to the point where waiting for the clock to move forward a minute was like waiting for the next drip from a leaky faucet. He'd sneak glances at his watch during meetings, then find out he'd missed half of what went on. As Monday passed, then Tuesday, his tension rose, like the jagged energy too much caffeine gave to an exhausted man. Finally, Tuesday evening he couldn't stand it. He called.

"No word yet," Beth told him in an upbeat voice, which meant her daughter was nearby. "But Mandy's doing great. She got straight A's this quarter."

"Hey." He felt absurdly pleased, as though his genes had helped make her smart. "Can I talk to her?"

"You bet."

A second later, "Uncle Nate?"

"Congratulations on the 4.0. You and your mom celebrating?"

"She took me to Baskin Robbins for an ice-cream sundae. It was really good."

"You deserved it." When she didn't say anything, he continued, "May I speak to your mom again?" After Beth came back on, Nathan asked, "Any chance I can move my visit up to tomorrow? I have to see some people at the Recreational Cooperative. It'd be late afternoon, probably just in time for dinner. I'd like to take you and Mandy out.''

Her voice warmed even further. ''Tomorrow would be great. Mandy keeps asking about you, and I have to admit how little I know. But why don't we plan on eating here? You won't want to turn around and head back into the city. We can go out another time. Thursday, if you can stay that long.''

''Done,'' he agreed. They broke off the connection, and he immediately dialed another number. Maybe he really should try to set up a meeting at R.E.I.

''DO YOU HAVE FAMILY, Beth?'' Though he was speaking to her mother, Nathan smiled across the dinner table at Amanda, who ducked her head shyly.

''A brother, but we're not close. He's a geologist for a petroleum company. He's been in Saudi Arabia for a couple of years, although he did fly home...'' She hesitated and glanced at her daughter.

Nathan could finish the sentence. *He did fly home when Mandy got sick the last time.* His blood must not have been a match, either.

''I still see my stepfather occasionally and we talk often,'' she continued, ''but my mother passed away some years ago. Lung cancer. She smoked.''

Nathan grunted. ''My father, too. Emphysema got him.''

''Yes, Rob mentioned it.'' Her gaze flitted nervously from his and she made a production out of buttering a roll.

Mandy announced suddenly, ''I want to be a doctor when I grow up.'' Her tone was defiant and he knew why. Unlike most kids, she had no certainty that she would grow up.

"Good for you," Nathan said. "I used to say the same, until I discovered how much I hated my college chemistry course."

Beth's eyes met his. "So what did you do?"

"Majored in business, worked a few years for Eddie Bauer, then I started my own company, Mount Hood Sporting Goods. We manufacture small tents, sleeping bags, climbing equipment. Stuff for serious outdoorsmen."

"Why, we have a couple of your sleeping bags." Expression arrested, Beth let her fork clatter onto her plate. "One of them was Rob's! Did he know...?"

Grief, sudden and strangling, tightened around his chest. What if Rob had known? What if he'd bought the sleeping bags *because* he'd known? As a—oh, hell—a kind of connection to his lost brother?

"I don't suppose he did." Beth wasn't the one Nathan was trying to convince. "We're based in Portland. Unless he read about the company in the business section of the newspaper, I can't imagine how he would have stumbled on my name."

"He talked about you quite a bit, you know." She hadn't picked up her fork. Tiny creases formed between her brows. "Didn't you ever...oh, wonder about him? What he was doing?"

"Of course I wondered." Anger edged his tone, though it wasn't directed at her. "I even thought... Damn." He swallowed hard. "Lately I'd been thinking I ought to try to find him." And kept putting it off. Now to learn Rob had been dead these last few years...

"Rob talked about hunting for you, too."

"It wouldn't have been hard," he said shortly. "I didn't hide."

Her voice cooled. "I encouraged him. But he didn't think you'd want to see him."

She didn't like him because he'd hurt her husband. He couldn't blame her. At the moment, knowing what his temper and pride had cost him, he didn't like himself, either.

It was sure as hell too late to discover he missed his twin.

Out of his peripheral vision, Nathan saw Amanda watching him anxiously. He laid down his knife and fork. Curiosity provoked the question, but a desire to reassure the girl made him school his voice to be pleasantly inquiring—no more, no less.

"What did Rob do? He always intended to go to law school. Said he had a golden tongue, could talk anybody into anything."

Beth wrinkled her nose. "He talked me into marrying him, and we'd only met a month before."

A bitter memory surfaced briefly before Nathan could shove it under again. His tone was sardonic. "He'd have been another Clarence Darrow if juries were all made up of women."

"Because we're all open to suggestion?" she asked tartly.

"Only Rob's."

Amanda was turning her head to follow the conversation as though it were a tennis match. "Who's Clarence Darrow?"

"A famous trial lawyer."

"Oh." She thought it over. "You mean, Dad talked women into—" She broke off abruptly, her cheeks flushing crimson.

"In high school, your father always dated the prettiest girls,'' Nathan said, smiling at her. ''I never could figure out where I went wrong.''

''Maybe he dressed cooler.'' Amanda sounded teen-age-wise, although she was only eleven. ''Or hung out with more popular kids. Sometimes girls like guys for really dumb reasons.''

His grin this time was genuine. ''Right. It had to have been his clothes. Or maybe because he wore his hair longer. I had to cut mine to be on the wrestling team.''

''Like Slater in 'Saved by the Bell.'''

Nathan knew vaguely it was a TV show. ''Yeah,'' he agreed.

''Dad was really cool, though,'' Amanda said. ''He drove a red Corvette. All my friends wished *their* dads were like him.''

Nathan glanced at the girl's mother, catching a flash of pain in her eyes, but she hid it quickly.

Before Amanda could remember that her father's red Corvette had killed him, Nathan said, ''You look like him. Especially when he was your age. Except we were both shrimps.''

''You mean, you were shorter than all the girls in fifth grade?'' she asked incredulously.

''Yep. My ego has never recovered.''

She digested that. ''But if I look like Dad, that must mean I look like you, too.''

He exchanged a silent glance with her mother. This time Beth said easily, ''I really can see a resemblance to your uncle Nathan.''

''Uncle Nate,'' Amanda corrected her.

Beth looked from his face to her daughter's and back again. ''It's partly your coloring, but...oh, there's something about the shape of your face. And your nose.''

''But I look kind of like you, too, don't I?'' Amanda sounded suddenly anxious.

Nathan gave her a teasing smile. ''The pretty part comes from your mom.''

''But I'm not pretty,'' she said gloomily. ''I'm shaped like a stick and my hair's so dumb and short, and Mom says I have to get glasses.''

''By the time the boys are worth looking at,'' Beth said, ''I promise I'll let you get contacts.''

He felt another twist in his gut. Having a conversation with his niece was like crossing an unstable snowfield. The future was everything to most kids Amanda's age, but she had to live with the knowledge that she might not have one.

How the hell did Beth manage to talk about next year and the year after and the one after that as though they were certainties? If he hurt for Amanda, what must her mother feel? Yet she was able to quietly express her faith over and over again, just by assuming that Amanda would be around to need contacts and braces and a bra. Someday Amanda would know how lucky she had been.

If she had that someday.

Had Rob known how lucky he was? Nathan tried to imagine his brother sitting in this chair, presiding over the family dinner, listening to Amanda chatter about school, then his wife relating tidbits of her day. The picture just wouldn't develop, like a Polaroid snapshot still murky.

Maybe she saw his discomfort, because Beth steered the conversation to generalities. Next thing he knew, mother and daughter both stood and started clearing the table. "Coffee?" Beth asked.

He pushed back his chair. "Thanks. Can I help?"

"Your next visit." Her smile looked a little forced. "Tonight you're a guest."

By the time the coffee was ready, Amanda had gone upstairs to do her homework. Beth brought his cup and a mug of herbal tea for herself out to the living room. She kicked off her shoes and curled up on one end of the sofa.

Before she could think up yet another innocuous topic, he asked, "What kind of work *did* Rob do?"

"Sales. He was a regional sales rep for an electronics company. He majored in business, too."

Damned if Nathan didn't feel a surge of resentment. One more thing he hadn't been permitted to do alone. His twin had echoed him in that, too.

But the resentment was mild, a shadow of the raw fury that had driven them apart. Rob couldn't possibly have copied him deliberately. The fact that they'd taken the same path in the last two years of college was just another reminder of how much a person's nature was determined by genes. He and his brother had been alike because they couldn't help it; hell, maybe he was attracted to Rob's widow because he was programmed to be just like his twin. Maybe their lifelong battle to be unique individuals had been doomed from the beginning, because physiologically they *were* identical.

Her soft voice interrupted his brooding. "Why does that upset you?"

He became aware that he was frowning in Beth's general direction, his coffee untouched. He raked his fingers through his hair. "Was I glowering at you? Sorry."

"Actually I had the sense you'd forgotten I was here."

He grimaced. "That's even worse."

"I don't take offense so easily." Her gaze was serene, though he wondered how much effort it took for her to give that impression. "I know this isn't easy for you. I'm all the more grateful that you were willing to come."

"How could I not?" He resisted the urge to stand up and pace. "She's my niece, for God's sake."

"But you didn't know her."

"I wish I had. I wish meeting her hadn't taken something like this." It swamped him then, a fact he couldn't quite believe. Couldn't quite accept. His throat closed and his eyes burned.

Dead. His brother was dead. They were part of each other, however far separated. Rob couldn't be dead.

Her voice entered his grief like a gentle touch. "He was a wonderful father. Silly sometimes. Like a little boy. He'd play games for hours with Mandy, give her rides on his back. He coached her soccer team, even took off work sometimes to go on school field trips. The mothers teased him, because he was usually the only father." She fell silent then, and he looked up expecting to see tears, but instead, she was smiling, her thoughts obviously faraway.

So Rob had grown up. Or else his boyishness had let him do one thing—maybe the most important thing—right: be a loving father.

Beth was still gazing at a past he couldn't see, and now he saw the shimmer in her eyes though she still smiled. His own grief eased even as he saw hers and realized that Rob had done more than one thing right. If he hadn't, his wife wouldn't still mourn him. Funny,

Nathan thought, how he could feel such pride at the same time jealousy ground a hole in his chest, like a piton pounded into rock.

Beth suddenly stood, blinking rapidly. "I...I'd better check on Mandy. If you want to watch TV..."

She needed to get away. He was just as eager to gain some breathing space to try to understand all these emotions buffeting him. Grief should be simple. Why the hell did everything feel so complicated?

"No," he said, rising, too. "I think I'll just read in bed for a while, if that's all right."

"Really, you don't have to hurry." But she didn't quite manage to hide her relief.

"It's been a long day," he said.

She half turned, head bowed, so that he saw only the curve of her cheek and the long graceful line of her neck below curls bundled into a knot at her nape. "And tomorrow..." Her voice ached. "Oh, tomorrow will seem endless. Until they call."

And he'd thought the last week was bad. "You've gone through this before." Why hadn't he realized what an agony his appearance was putting her through?

She gave him one haunted look. "Each time I really believe..." The words caught on a hiccuping breath. "And each time it's harder."

"I understand."

She looked so damned fragile that primitive urge to shelter her grabbed him by the throat again. Once more, he had to remind himself he was the last man who ought to take her into his arms, even if comfort was his only objective. How must she feel looking at him, seeing her husband and knowing what her eyes told her was only an illusion?

But Beth stunned him. "Thank you again," she

whispered. So quickly he might almost have imagined it she came to him, brushed her lips against his cheek and hurried from the room.

He stood stock-still, breathing in an insubstantial scent that reminded him of ripe berries in the sun, and cursed the fact that she was his brother's widow.

MANDY SAT on her bed, legs crossed, and listened to the murmur of voices drifting upstairs. She knew they must be talking about her, and about Dad.

It was so bizarre that Dad and Uncle Nate had gotten so mad at each other they didn't want to be brothers anymore. And they were twins! One of Mandy's friends, April, had an identical twin sister. Even though April and Samantha had other friends, it was obvious they were always each other's best friend. In the cafeteria once, April got really upset, and it turned out that at that exact same moment Samantha, who'd gone ahead out to recess, had broken her arm jumping from a swing. Everybody thought it was really weird, but cool. Mandy wondered if Uncle Nate and her dad had ever felt each other's pain like that. When Dad died, had Uncle Nate hurt without knowing why?

What would it be like to have someone who knew you that well? She dropped her binder on the floor and flopped on her stomach on the bed. She dreamed sometimes that she had a twin. It wasn't just that her twin would have the right blood antigens to save her. What she wanted most was someone who could understand how *she* felt. For a while she did; her first time in the hospital for chemo, she'd shared a room with another girl her age who had leukemia, too. After the nurses turned the lights out, they'd talk, not having to see each other's faces or put on any kind of act. They'd won-

dered whether death would hurt, whether there really
was heaven or hell. They promised each other that if
one died, she would try to come back long enough to
tell the other.

"Unless—" Jessica's voice had come from the darkness "—it's really awful. Then I don't think I want to
know ahead."

"Me, neither," Mandy said.

Jessica left the hospital two weeks before Mandy.
She lived in eastern Washington, so they couldn't see
each other, but they wrote and phoned. Then Jessica
got sick again and came back to Children's Hospital.
Mandy saw her once. Jessica had IVs and oxygen and
she was bruised-looking, and Mandy knew she was dying. Jessica grabbed her hand and said, "I'll keep my
promise if I can. So if you get a note or dream about
me or something, it's really me. Okay?"

Jessica died the next day, but she never came to
Mandy, unless it was in a dream Mandy didn't remember when she woke up. That scared her, because it
meant either that dying really was horrible, or that Jessica was just gone—that there wasn't any soul or spirit
or anything left that could keep a promise. It scared
Mandy most that there might be nothing at all left of
her when she died.

Her next time in the hospital, her roommate was only
six, and Mandy had to reassure her. She couldn't talk
about dying. Now she was really alone. Children's
Hospital had counselors, but they didn't really know
her. Mom always pretended that things would be fine.
Once, a long time ago, when Mandy asked her what
she thought dying would be like, Mom jumped to her
feet and said, "You're not dying! I won't let you!"

She'd sounded mad, but she'd also had tears sparkling in her eyes. Mandy hadn't asked her again.

Now she rolled onto her back and gazed up at the poster of Christian Slater she had taped to her ceiling. Maybe Uncle Nate's blood would turn out to be right. Before, they hadn't had anybody from Dad's side of the family to test. And he was Dad's twin. The odds must be pretty good, right? She examined her feelings and discovered she was hopeful. She pictured the feeling as a little bubble lodged in her chest. A bubble, because it was shimmery and iridescent and it wanted to float upward where she couldn't ignore it. But also a bubble because it could be popped so easily. The tiniest pinprick and it would be gone—snap!—just like Jessica was gone.

She sniffed and realized her cheeks were wet. She never cried anymore. She never let herself think about Jessica, either.

Footsteps on the stairs warned her that Mom was coming. Mandy sat up quickly, wiped her eyes, then bent over and grabbed her binder and pencil. By the time Mom stepped into her bedroom, Mandy was studying the next math problem.

"How's it going, kiddo?" her mother asked.

"Okay."

"Need any help?"

Mandy shrugged. "Not really."

Mom sat on the edge of the bed and pushed her bangs back from her forehead. "Are you almost done? It's bedtime."

"I don't really have to do this. I can finish it in class. I'll go brush my teeth now." She jumped up. "Will you tuck me in?"

"You bet." Mom smiled at her. "So what do you think of your uncle?"

Mandy sat back down. She didn't mind talking about him. "I like Uncle Nate." She thought for a moment. "He listens when you talk to him. You know what I mean?"

"Uh-huh. He's quieter than your father. Not really like him, if you can forget his looks."

Mandy frowned. "Do you think we'll ever see him again? I mean, now that they've tested his blood?"

"He did come back. I'll bet he does again. Anyway, if he matches, you'll see him in the hospital." Mom smiled, like she was suggesting a trip to the zoo or something. "Maybe you could share a room."

"They wouldn't let me." Mandy knew Mom was just joking, but she argued, anyway. "In case he had a cold or something."

"They won't let me touch you, either." Mom reached out and gave her a quick fierce hug.

Mandy didn't draw back. With her face buried in the crook of Mom's shoulder, she mumbled, "Do you think he *will* match?"

"The chances are pretty good, but...you know he may not, don't you?" Mom kissed the top of her head.

"Yeah, it's okay. I know."

They didn't talk any more about it. Mom didn't say whether she thought Uncle Nate would want to come back just to visit, whether he really felt like her uncle. She thought maybe he would. He smiled at her like he meant it, not fakey like some adults. Mandy wished she knew what they'd said downstairs.

After Mom tucked the covers around her and turned out the light, leaving only the soft glow from the hall,

Mandy thought, *I don't want to die. Please, God, make Uncle Nate be right. Make him my miracle.*

WAITING WAS THE WORST part. Each time they had hope of a close match, Beth wished she could just *know*, even if the news was bad. She'd rather not be given hope at all if she was always to be disappointed.

In the morning she woke Mandy, then got herself dressed. The house was quiet, the door to the spare bedroom closed. She'd awakened once during the night and seen light under his door. Maybe he'd read late. She assumed he was still asleep, but downstairs she found a note on the kitchen counter. "Gone jogging," it said in bold script. "N."

Mandy ate her usual breakfast of cold cereal with a sliced banana, got dressed, grabbed the lunch Beth had made and started out the front door. Halfway down the porch steps, she turned.

"Mom, will you call me at school if...if..."

"Of course I will!" Beth set her cup of coffee down on the porch railing and moved to Mandy to give her another hug. "But we may not hear until late afternoon."

"Okay." Her daughter looked unnaturally mature and solemn again. "I know that."

"Mandy—" She heard the squeal of brakes and looked up. Through a stand of alders clothed in spring green she saw the yellow of the school bus. "There's the bus. You'd better run."

Mandy did, her book bag bumping on her back. Like everything else she did, it was enough to send a shaft of "what if" deep into her mother's heart. She'd played soccer before she became sick the first time. At least she could run now, but the doctor had vetoed sports. He didn't want her to get that tired.

Even after the school bus had lumbered down the road, belching exhaust, and disappeared around a curve, Beth stayed on the front porch. She sat down on the top step, sipped her coffee and gazed at her kingdom.

The fields were weeded and the canes pruned and tied up. They'd be blooming soon, and the sunny acres would hum from the bees feasting. Then the berries would form, small and green, growing and blushing until they were fat and red or blue and sweet. That was when the hard work started.

In just five years she'd built this run-down farm into a business—Tillicum Creek Jams and Preserves. She grew most of her own raspberries and strawberries and blueberries, the last on huge bushes that grew happily in the low wet land down by the creek. She bought blackberries, boysenberries and gooseberries from other local farmers. The barn, now bright red with white trim, housed the kitchen where the jam was made and the shelves where sugar and pectin and empty jars were replaced by labeled jam, stored until shipped to gourmet kitchen shops and fine restaurants. Just last year she'd added a mail-order business that was more successful than her most optimistic projections and made tiny inroads on her mounting debt to hospitals and doctors and pharmacies. Thank God for Rob's life insurance, and for the increasing popularity of her jam. The first few years she'd managed mostly alone, with some seasonal help. Now she had one full-time employee year-round. Several others signed on to prune and weed and, during the season, make three to four thousand pounds of jam a week.

The business was to have been hers and Rob's together. Her skill in the garden and kitchen was to be allied with his in marketing. Someday he'd be able to quit his job, they'd dreamed. Because he traveled so much, she'd done most of what it took to start Tillicum Creek Jams herself, from designing a distinctive label to contacting potential outlets.

Now she was glad she'd proved herself before he died, that she hadn't lost a business partner, as well as a husband. Her ability to cope on her own had been tested severely enough by Mandy's illness. For a short while it had even turned her mourning into bitterness, because Rob's cocky refusal to admit he was mortal meant he wasn't here now that he was really needed.

But Rob's brother was. As though her thoughts had summoned him, she caught a flash of color through the alders and made out the figure of a man running along their country lane. A moment later he turned into her long driveway and slowed to a walk, head down as he shook his arms to loosen tight shoulders.

Despite the chilliness of the morning, he wore a bright red basketball jersey that bared broad shoulders, tanned and muscular. Sacky black sweatpants rode low on his hips. His dark hair was damp and matted to his head. While she watched, he lifted the hem of the jersey and wiped beads of sweat from his face. She caught a glimpse of flat stomach and reacted on some visceral level. Only because he reminded her of Rob, she told herself, and was uncomfortable with that realization.

Or perhaps her sexual awareness had more to do with the last-ditch plan she'd had in mind from the moment she'd hired the private investigator.

Nathan lifted his head and saw her sitting on the

porch steps. His eyes narrowed for a flicker, but his face remained impassive.

Some days she'd still have been in her bathrobe. But today, in his honor she'd showered and dressed before she'd even gone downstairs. One of the pleasures of the self-employed was that dressing meant jeans, no socks and an oversize flannel shirt with the too-long sleeves rolled up. She'd used a clip to confine her hair, although she could feel escaped curls on her neck.

"Morning," he said. "They haven't called?"

She shook her head. "It's a little early. If I don't hear from them by late afternoon, I'll phone them."

He grunted and bent over to do some stretches.

"What would you like for breakfast?" she asked.

"I can make my own." He began rolling his upper body from the waist.

"I don't mind."

He stopped, hands on his hips, and lifted a dark brow. "I'm still a guest?"

"Until your next visit."

"Ah. In that case, I'll take hash browns, an omelet, English muffins." He smiled, deepening the crease in one cheek. "Actually, I usually have cold cereal at home."

"I haven't eaten yet myself," Beth said. "I was thinking of making scrambled eggs and toast. You can try out my jam."

He nodded toward the field. "These are yours, then?"

"Uh-huh. Those are raspberries. Strawberries beyond the barn, blueberries down by the creek."

"Do you sell them?" he asked, contemplating the acres of vines tied to wires strung between split-wood supports.

"I make jam." She smiled at his expression. "It's a business. Tillicum Creek Jams and Preserves. We're small still, but doing well. I don't suppose you've heard of us..."

"Actually, I buy your jam. Usually the raspberry. Beats the hell out of the grocery-store brands. I should have caught on when I saw your sign." He nodded toward the road, his eyes holding new respect. "Was Rob involved?"

"He gave me advice. We had in mind that eventually, if the business took off the way we hoped, he'd be able to quit his job and take over the sales part of Tillicum Creek."

"I take it that didn't happen soon enough."

"No." She watched him walk in a circle to cool off, her thoughts casting circles of their own. "It occurs to me," she said, "that I didn't ask much about your life. My only excuse is that having a sick child makes you single-minded. Are you...are you married? Do you have kids of your own?"

"No, and no. I was married once, divorced after a couple of years. Fortunately we didn't have children."

Words came she hadn't intended to say. "Do you ever miss...?"

"Yeah." Nathan shot her an unreadable look. "I always pictured myself with a wife and a house and children by this age. It's...ironic that Rob had it all and I didn't."

She smiled a little wryly. "Yes, he always said he hadn't planned to marry. We laughed about it."

Something flashed in his eyes and then was gone. "Well—" Nathan wiped his forehead again "—let me take a quick shower, and then breakfast sounds great."

The meal was oddly companionable. They talked

about the news on the front page of the *Seattle Times*, argued amiably about a few recent movies and avoided the painful subject that had brought him here: Amanda.

After breakfast Beth gave him a tour of the barn, from the commercial kitchen where she sterilized jars and boiled jam in thirty-gallon steel vats, to the workbench where labels were wrapped around the distinctively designed jars.

"My office is in the house. That's where I make my phone calls and do correspondence. I have one full-time person, but Julie's on vacation right now. We're in the lull before summer. During berry season I have a couple of extra employees."

He studied her catalog and they compared experiences in their respective businesses. It was all so pleasant, so involving, she could almost forget what they were waiting for.

Twice the phone rang and her heart jumped sickeningly, but neither call was from the hospital. Aloud, Beth considered going grocery shopping, although the truth was that nothing short of a tow truck could have hauled her out of earshot of the telephone. Nathan insisted on taking a list and going for her, which left her with nothing to do but dust bookcases that didn't need it and scrub a bathtub that already sparkled. She knew she couldn't concentrate on work; if she'd tried, she would have fouled up orders. And she couldn't do nothing; she'd go crazy. She kept reminding herself that the call might not come today at all. It might be tomorrow or even, conceivably, not until Monday.

Nathan was back, still carrying grocery bags into the kitchen, when the phone rang again. Beth glanced at the clock. Two.

She felt dizzy when she picked up the receiver. Her voice cracked. "Hello?"

"Mrs. McCabe? This is Dr. Simonson at Children's."

"Yes?" If her life had depended on it, she couldn't have gotten more than that one word out.

Across the kitchen, her eyes met Nathan's. Somehow she communicated her panic and hope, because he came to her side, reached out and gripped her shoulder. The warmth and strength of his hand were obscurely comforting, although her entire being was focused on the voice in her ear.

"My news isn't good, Mrs. McCabe. I'm sorry. We were all hopeful, but I'm afraid not enough markers in Mr. McCabe's blood match Amanda's to make him a potential donor. We'll have to continue our hunt through the registry."

She said something—she hoped it was appropriate—before gently replacing the receiver in its cradle. Her breath came out in a long trembling sigh, and the hand on her shoulder tightened.

"No?" he asked roughly.

She closed her eyes and shook her head. His arms came around her, and she laid her cheek on his chest. For a moment all she could do was lean against him, hear the thud of his heart, feel his chest rise and fall with each breath, feel his arms holding her tightly.

Oh, God, she couldn't bear it. To have found someone so closely related to Amanda, to have hoped again... In anguish her mind skipped to the thought of her daughter bounding off the school bus and running down the driveway. How would she tell Mandy? Could she sound cheerful and promise that chemotherapy and radiation would be enough? Would she be doing

Mandy any favor when they both knew that Nathan McCabe might have been her last chance?

No, she thought, going very still. Not her last chance. Mandy had one other. If her Uncle Nate would agree.

Beth straightened and stepped back; Nathan released her, his hands falling to his sides.

"There's one other thing you could do," she said, hearing as if from a distance her own calmness and determination. "If you would."

"Name it." His eyes were dark and intense, his mouth set grimly.

"Father a baby for me."

CHAPTER THREE

NATHAN STARED at Beth. Good God, had she just suggested they have sex? He couldn't have heard right. "What did you say?"

She clasped her hands before her and said in the tone of one who'd memorized a speech, "If Rob and I'd had another child, the odds are one in four that he or she would be a match for Mandy. Normally—" she drew a deep breath "—I couldn't change the fact that we didn't have another baby. But because you and he were identical twins, I can."

He dug his fingers into his hair and gave it a yank. Maybe a little pain would wake him up.

"Let me get this straight. You want me to pretend I'm Rob and provide some sperm."

Her teeth worried her lower lip. "Well, I...I wouldn't have put it that way, but...yes."

He swore and turned his back to her. Hands flat on the tiled kitchen counter, he leaned on braced arms, shaking his head. God almighty. It was crazy. *She* was crazy.

And he was scum to have felt a knife-thrust of pure sexual longing at the very idea.

He was breathing as if he'd just finished a ten-kilometer race. Clenching his teeth, he slowed his breathing and blanked out the image of Beth McCabe, ripe with his child. Then he turned and faced her.

"My…participation aside, you can't have thought this through. In the first place, the odds are three to one that the baby *won't* be a match. Then what? Do you try again?"

Her face was so white the scattering of freckles stood out. "If I have to," she said steadily.

"What about the baby?" He made his tone brutal. "Do you discard him because he didn't measure up and hope for more success the next time?"

She flinched, but her voice was fierce. "I would love any baby of mine no matter what! Do you think I'd even suggest this if I wasn't sure of that? If…if I lose Mandy, another child would give me a reason to live. And for her sake, how can I not try? What kind of mother would I be?"

He didn't want to be impressed by her arguments, to feel himself swayed. He wanted to keep thinking she was crazy. Most of all, he didn't want to envy his brother all over again for having been lucky enough to have her.

Hoarsely he said, "How the hell would we handle custody?"

"We wouldn't." Her gray eyes glittered. "I'm not asking you to be a real father. We don't even know each other! All I'm asking is that you donate sperm. I don't expect anything else from you. You can walk away. I'm perfectly capable of supporting two children."

He stared incredulously. "You want me to have a baby and take no responsibility?"

"These are hardly normal circumstances."

"You can say that again," Nathan muttered. "Lady, you're nuts."

Her chin came up another notch. "Because I'm willing to do anything to save my daughter's life?"

If Amanda were his, wouldn't he do the same? He shook his head again. "I can't believe we're even talking about this."

"Other people have done it." She was pleading now. "They've done it and succeeded. And you can't tell me it's any worse than a lot of the other reasons people have children."

He'd heard some of those reasons. His administrative assistant had had a baby because she thought it would bring her and her husband closer together. They were divorced now and she was raising her son alone. Or how about the people who wanted to make sure someone would take care of them in their old age? Or the ones who just loved babies, forgetting that they become teenagers? At least Beth McCabe's motives were unselfish.

But what would his be?

If he'd thought things were complicated before, he hadn't known what complicated was.

"I have to think about this," he said.

"That's all I'm asking right now." Her voice had softened; she stretched a hand out to him. "Will you stay tonight?"

For a stunned second he thought again that she was inviting him into her bed. And, God help him, he didn't know if he could have refused her. She was beautiful: slim and strong, with emotional depths that darkened the mist gray of her eyes to the deep shades of dusk. Her curls looked as silky fine as her daughter's, completely suited to the delicacy of her cheek and jaw and sweep of throat. Under that shirt she'd be as delicate.

For the first time in his life, Nathan wanted something that had belonged to his brother.

Before he could do anything incredibly stupid, reason asserted itself. He was a goddamned fool. She didn't want him under her covers; she wanted him to stay as a guest. She wanted him to have time to learn to love her daughter, so it would become impossible for him to deny mother and child the one thing they needed of him.

And that sure as hell wasn't her husband's double mounting Beth in bed.

His voice sounded like gravel scraping a metal surface. "What time is it?"

"Um…" She looked oddly dazed, and he realized this conversation was as bizarre for her as it was for him. "Three-thirty. Mandy'll be home anytime." That note of pleading was in her voice again.

If he left now he could probably get a commuter flight for the short hop from Seattle to Portland. But he wouldn't be home until late. His secretary had cleared his calendar. Why not stay another night and satisfy his hunger to learn more about Rob and his family?

"I'll stay." He cleared his throat. "If I won't be inconveniencing you."

"Don't be silly." Her cheeks were pink now and she was suddenly bustling around, putting away groceries, which meant her eyes didn't have to meet his. "Even if…if nothing comes of it, Mandy and I are delighted to have had a chance to get to know you. Maybe, wherever Rob is, he sees you here."

Nathan almost laughed, although the sound would have been harsh. Rob wasn't smiling down from heaven or scowling up from hell. No, if he knew, he'd manage to come back one way or another so he could make damn sure he wasn't one-upped. Rob had never let Nathan get the last word in, throw the longest pass, buy the best gift. It didn't require any stretch to figure out how he would have felt about his brother being the last one to impregnate his wife. He'd accomplish an immaculate conception before he'd let Nathan's sperm reach her womb.

But this wasn't the time to remind Beth McCabe that her husband hadn't just loved his brother, he'd hated him.

Nathan made a noncommittal noise in his throat. "Why don't I take you two out to dinner tonight? I'd like to return your hospitality."

She turned to face him, back against the tile edging of the countertop. "My hospitality is nothing—nothing!—compared to what you were willing to do for Mandy."

"Willing doesn't cut it," he said roughly. "I can't help her."

"Yes, you can."

He couldn't look away from Beth, even though he knew he was being reeled in. "If I agreed, you'd have to share custody. I wouldn't disappear."

The pause was infinitesimal before she nodded. "That's fine. We'll make it work somehow."

"We'll *be* family. You won't be able to change that."

He heard the change in verb tense; he wasn't talking if anymore, but will.

She gazed back at him, not with the intensity of a hypnotist, but with the unwilling fascination of the one *being* hypnotized. "I understand," she whispered.

"The baby will be mine, not Rob's."

She wrenched her gaze away and he saw her mouth tremble. "I never—" She broke off, took a deep breath, controlled her voice. "I never was going to pretend the baby was Rob's. Those are your words, not mine."

"All right." He hated the hard edge to his voice. "I'll do it, so long as you understand my conditions."

Now her eyes were huge. "I do."

"Then how do you want to go about it?"

She opened her mouth—and then shut it when they both heard the sound of the front door opening and slamming, and Mandy's call, "I'm home!"

"We're in the kitchen!" Beth called back. She lowered her voice. "I don't want her to hear anything about this."

He saw her gird herself and wondered, like a coward, whether he should leave her alone to give the bad news to Mandy. But it was too late; the skinny eleven-year-old already stood in the kitchen doorway, her gaze darting from her uncle to her mother and back again.

"It was no, wasn't it?"

Her mother took a couple of quick steps, but Mandy retreated, vanishing from his sight into the front hall. "Just tell me," the girl said.

From where he stood, Nathan could only see Beth's back, but the compassion and pain in her voice sliced into his chest like a surgeon's scalpel. "It was no. He doesn't match. We're back where we started. Just remember that you're feeling well. One of the drugs they used on you is a new one. Who knows? Maybe you won't even need the transplant. And we still have time."

He expected an outburst of emotion: angry words, sobs, feet thundering up the stairs. But Mandy spoke with the quiet resignation of someone three times her age. "Right, Mom. I might be that one in a hundred or whatever it was. Or maybe they will find somebody. Don't worry."

"Sweetheart—"

"I have homework. I'd better get started."

He caught a glimpse of her trudging up the stairs, a small figure who couldn't even cry about her own fate.

Beth turned to face him, her mouth trembling. "Can we…can we talk about this later? After Mandy's gone to bed? Right now I just want…" She pressed her hands to her cheeks. "I just want…" Her voice shattered.

He took a step toward her, ready to draw her back into his arms, but she retreated, just as her daughter had done from her.

"I'm sorry," she whispered. "I just…I need to be alone." And she turned and fled.

Nathan waited until she was out of sight, then swore bitterly. Some savior *he* was. They'd have been better off if he hadn't appeared in their lives to give them hope.

Unless, a voice in his head reminded him, he was more of a success as a father than he'd been as a brother.

AMANDA WAITED until she heard her mother's bedroom door shut, then she crept down the stairs. Uncle Nate was still in the kitchen, but his back was to her and she was sure he didn't hear the creak of that second-to-the-bottom step, or else he would have turned. She slipped out the front door, then hurried around the house and down the sloping field toward the creek. She crossed it by stepping on the flat rocks Dad had set in place to form a small dam, which made a deep enough water hole to wade and splash in. On the other side was her refuge: a huge old weeping willow. The branches parted like lace curtains to let her inside.

Her heart was slamming against her ribs. She huddled with her back to the trunk, surrounded by pale wavering green light.

Mom had said she and Dad bought the house because of this tree. When Mom was a little girl, she'd had a willow tree, and the room inside its green walls was her special place. She wanted that for Mandy.

Nobody ever bothered her here. She didn't even know if Mom knew she came here.

Mandy stared sightlessly at the shifting curtain of long narrow leaves, thinking about the conversation she'd overheard. She hadn't meant to eavesdrop, but she'd come into the house from school so quietly they hadn't known she was there until she tiptoed back to the door and opened and shut it again, this time noisily.

What if Mom really had a new baby? Would Mandy have to share her willow tree?

Babies couldn't even walk until they were a year old, she knew from seeing her friend Kayla's baby brother. So it would be a long time before she had a sister or brother toddling behind her, demanding to be included.

That part didn't sound so bad, anyway. What really scared her was the reason Mom wanted to have the baby. She'd never wanted another kid before. Mandy bet Mom had told Uncle Nate they should have the baby so it could become a donor. But what if that was a lie? Or at least, kind of a lie? What if Mom really wanted the baby to replace her, Mandy, because she was going to die?

Her chin rested on her knees and she felt the hot

tears running down her cheeks. She hardly ever cried anymore! She should be happy, instead of sad that Mom might not have to be lonely when she died!

It was just… She sniffed and wiped her nose on her sleeve. She'd discovered there was something worse than leaving an empty space when you were gone, worse than there being *nothing* where you'd been. It was that space being filled by someone else, so you weren't only gone, pretty soon you were forgotten. Maybe not *totally*—after all, she still thought about Sylvester, their gray cat who'd died last summer of old age. But not very often, especially not since she and Mom had brought home Calvin and Polly from the animal shelter. Already sometimes she'd be snuggling Polly under the covers, the warm furry body curled against hers, and she'd try to remember whether Sylvester felt any different or maybe what his purr sounded like, and she couldn't, because her memories had gotten all tangled up with the present. Had his fur been softer? Had he rubbed his face hard against hers the way Calvin did? It bothered her that she wasn't sure.

That was partly what she was crying about right now. Because if she couldn't remember, maybe her mother wouldn't be able to, either. Maybe babies all felt the same in your arms; maybe Mom would forget what Mandy's laughter sounded like, because she was hearing her new little girl's.

If only, Mandy thought, she had someone to talk to! "Jessica," she whispered, "where are you?"

IN THE DARK BEDROOM, Beth stood for a moment above her sleeping daughter, listening to the quiet even breathing. In the crook of Mandy's knees, their black-

and-white kitten slept, as well. Beth knew that some-times Mandy pretended to be asleep when she checked on her. But tonight was the real thing: her face was utterly relaxed, her fingers that had started the night clutching her beloved blanket were uncurled now. She looked so peaceful, so defenseless. Beth leaned over and very softly kissed her daughter's temple.

Then she stroked her fingers down Polly's thin back and heard the astonishingly powerful purr start auto-matically. Perhaps it would give Mandy sweet dreams.

She slipped out of the room and pulled the door almost closed behind her, leaving a crack for Polly to escape if she needed her litter box or was in the mood for a midnight wrestle with her brother.

Downstairs, Beth stopped in the living-room door-way. Nathan was sprawled in the wing chair, feet on the ottoman. From this angle, she couldn't see his face, only the unruly dark hair and the bulk of his shoulder and those long lean legs. How many times had she seen the same scene?

Something in her went very still as past overlaid present. If she took a step forward, he'd turn his head and smile, that lazy charming smile that had never failed to soften her heart. "How's Sleeping Beauty?" he'd ask. "Do I need to go give her a kiss?"

How like him that was! He was forever magical to his daughter.

She took a step into the living room, then another, and he turned his head, but not lazily as Rob would have. Instead, the movement was sharp, contained, and the dark eyes that focused unerringly on her face were wary and penetrating. The anxiety that had coiled in-side her relaxed, leaving her feeling foolish; this wasn't Rob, however much they looked alike. She knew that.

"Asleep?" Nathan asked, his deep voice a little rougher than his brother's, making her wonder how his unshaven chin would feel under her palm.

"Uh-huh." She sat on one end of the couch and curled her legs beneath her. She hardly ever sat any other way. But tonight the outward relaxation was a pose. *Can we talk about this later?* she'd said. *After Mandy's gone to bed?* Well, now was later.

Beth looked with near envy at the mug of steaming coffee he cradled in his big hands. She had enough trouble sleeping these days without having tea or coffee so late, but she could have made herbal tea. If nothing else, it would have given her something to do with her hands.

"Have you, um, thought any more about it?" she asked. "I mean, about—"

"I know what you mean." He sounded abrupt. No longer looking at her, he leaned his head against the high back of the chair. "Hard not to."

"Yes." She studied her hands, traced a scratch across the palm of one with a finger. "I suppose it's...a little unusual."

"Yeah, you could say that."

When he didn't add more, she sneaked a glance at him. He was watching her now, and her own gaze nervously flitted away. "You haven't...changed your mind?" Beth was exasperated to hear how timid she sounded. She'd asked him boldly enough in the first place; why was she so nervous now?

He muttered something under his breath that she suspected was an obscenity. "No," he finally said, voice flat. "Good God, how can I look at Amanda and not do anything I can?"

"I'm glad you don't still think I'm nuts."

For the first time a hint of humor entered his dark eyes. "Did I say that?"

She found herself smiling. "Well, maybe I am, but I'm willing to do it, anyway."

"Yeah, me, too, I guess." He took his feet from the ottoman and planted them on the floor, then leaned forward. "Have you talked to the doctor about this?"

"You mean, Mandy's doctor? No."

"I meant yours."

In her heart, she'd known exactly what he meant. *Then how do you want to go about it?* His words, spoken earlier in the kitchen, were felt and heard more powerfully now, like an earthquake that rolled underground to tremble the earth far from its point of origin.

"No," she said carefully, not looking at him. "I haven't yet."

"Will your insurance pay for this?"

Still she evaded his gaze. "I doubt it. It's not medically necessary—not for me, anyway."

He sat silent for a moment. "Is the expense a problem?"

Did he sound annoyed? "I wasn't asking you to pay for it," she said quickly. "I just thought..." Oh, God, why was this so hard to say? But she didn't need to ask God. She knew the answer, and she finished in a rush, "I just thought maybe we could do it the old-fashioned way. If we slept together just once, at the right time of the month..." She trailed off again, unable to complete the sentence. *Slept together.* What a terrible euphemism.

The stirring in her belly when she looked at him, as she couldn't help doing, the way her mind kept flashing on images of the two of them in her big soft bed upstairs, made her wonder: was she really suggesting this only to be thrifty?

"The old-fashioned way?" he repeated, staring at her with utter blankness, as though what she had just suggested was unthinkable. Repugnant.

Her words tumbled over themselves. "Not if you don't find me at all attractive, of course. I mean, I know it wouldn't work if you didn't..." Oh, Lord, now she was bright red. And she was trying so hard to sound as if she didn't mind an admission that he found her physically unappealing!

Emotion flashed in his eyes, clenched the muscles of his jaw. If he'd been Rob, she would have known what he was thinking. But this man was a stranger, however familiar that face.

"Damn it!" He rose to his feet and glared down at her. "Are you imagining that you can have Rob back for a night or two? Well, get this straight, lady! I'm not Rob! Summon a ghost if you want him back! Just don't expect me to be it!"

Angry, she stood, too. With an effort she kept her voice down. "I have never for a minute pretended you were Rob, and I never will! All right, it was a dumb suggestion, but it didn't have anything to do with him!" Didn't it? she had to ask herself, only to decide she'd have to think about it later. "I only wanted—" to have someone hold her close? "—to avoid a ridiculous charge for something so easy. That's all." *Yeah, right!* murmured a mocking voice from her subconscious.

He frowned at her again, and she could see that she'd caught him off guard. "Isn't Mandy's illness covered by insurance?"

"Not all of it. Not at first." Damn it, this wasn't any

of his business. Or was it, considering the link they would now have? "We'd just switched medical plans," she explained reluctantly. "They covered most of her care, but not some of the first bills. The worst part is, they won't pay for the bone-marrow transplant. Fortunately Rob had life insurance, enough for us to squeak through, but I have to save it all for that. And when Rob died, my business hadn't reached a point where it could support us."

"They'd let a kid die rather than cover something that's done as routinely as bone-marrow transplants?" Nathan sounded as incredulous as she'd felt when her insurance agent first rendered the company's decision.

"They said they couldn't make an exception for one child. They said the plan would have to be more expensive to the insured if it covered extras like that. *Extras.*" She uttered the word with loathing. "They pointed out that I knew what was covered and what wasn't when I chose their plan."

He swore.

She gave a twisted smile. "I'm lucky, because I *can* pay for the procedure. Most people can't. You hear those pleas for donations and I always wonder if they got enough. Can you imagine seeing your child die because you're lacking forty thousand dollars? Or twenty, or even five? It must happen."

The compassion in his eyes was almost more than she could bear.

"So you see," Beth said, "why I suggested something so crazy. But you're right." She tried hard to sound brisk, positive. "The doctor it is." She started toward the doorway.

"Beth—"

"No." She barely glanced over her shoulder. "We should keep it impersonal."

"We can't keep a baby impersonal. *Our* baby."

She stopped, one hand on the cool wood of the door frame. "That's a little different."

"Is it?" His tone was odd, confusing her.

She couldn't afford to be confused. Only the goal was allowed to count: Mandy's salvation.

"Yes," she said firmly. "People do it all the time, after divorces. They share a child and both love him or her without feeling anything for each other. We can do it, too."

He didn't agree or argue; he just watched her with an expression as odd as his tone. What was he thinking?

"Good night," she said briskly. "Feel free to watch TV if you'd like, or raid the refrigerator."

"I have to leave first thing in the morning."

She'd almost whisked out of sight. Now she had to pause again, look back. "I know."

He cleared his throat. "You'll let me know when you need me? When the, uh, best time is?"

Best time. When she was most fertile. When his seed, implanted in her womb, would find an egg ready to receive it. At the thought, yearning, warm and exciting, spread throughout her belly. It was maternal, not sexual, she tried to tell herself, but it felt uncomfortably the same.

She imagined herself on the examining table at the doctor's office, thighs parted to receive some cold instrument. And how must Nathan feel, knowing he had to arouse himself sexually to provide the seed? Somehow, she hadn't realized quite what she was asking.

"I think..." She groped for a date, feeling absurdly

self-conscious to be discussing something so intimate. "Maybe two weeks from now? If…if that's good for you?"

His look held irony. "I'll make it good for me."

The double meaning, which she suspected he'd used deliberately, made her cheeks hotter.

"I'll call after I talk to the doctor."

"You do that."

She fled then, after murmuring something about seeing him in the morning. She peeked at Mandy once more, then went on to her own bedroom, where she got ready for bed in a flurry. Once she was curled alone in the queen-size bed, she squeezed her eyes shut and willed sleep to come.

It absolutely refused. All she could think about was how she'd feel right this minute if Nathan McCabe *had* agreed to father her child "the old-fashioned way." It wasn't something they could have done quickly and put behind them. Tonight wasn't the right time of the month. No, she would have had the next two weeks to anticipate his visit, to imagine over and over what it would be like, making love—no, having sex—with the stranger who lived in a body she knew so well.

But the quality of sex, she guessed, wasn't determined by the shape or size of any part of a man's body. No, it was determined by his sensitivity, his kindness, his sense of humor. *And* by the depth of feeling he had for the woman. Which was where she would have lost out.

Obviously he hadn't been interested at all, or he wouldn't have turned her down flat. She ought to be glad he had, glad that their future relationship wasn't to be complicated as it would inevitably have been if they'd shared a bed.

But, staring into the darkness, she had to admit the truth: she had wanted to find out whether it would be different with him. Maybe whether what she'd had with Rob was once in a lifetime for her. Did that make her despicable?

And most of all, she had wanted their baby to be conceived in the warm dark intimacy of her bed, in a moment of real emotion, even if it was only passion. Not with her staring up at a fluorescent light, the paper on the examining table crinkling under her, her feet held awkwardly in cold metal stirrups.

Could a miracle happen that way? she wondered with a shiver.

CHAPTER FOUR

LEFT ALONE in a somewhat unusual examining room, Nathan looked with distaste at the TV and VCR. A selection of ten pornographic movies was available for his…viewing pleasure. Should he prefer it, several copies of popular magazines containing pictures of naked women were neatly stacked on a shelf. Everything a man should need to get aroused.

Then, of course, there was the cup in which he'd been instructed to deposit the semen. Assuming he could get inspired to produce any. The nurse, a heavy cheerful woman, had told him not to worry if he had trouble; sometimes men needed to come back several times before they could relax enough to perform. Her word, not his.

"There is something just a tiny bit intimidating about this, isn't there?" she'd added with a chuckle just before she shut the door, leaving him alone.

Intimidating. Good God. He prowled across the room and back, the tiny, starkly lit confines making him feel claustrophobic. Hell, he'd never been interested in pornography. Photographs of naked women whose breasts looked like they'd been pumped full of helium left him cold. The women who attracted him had little in common with the nude models in those magazines, and they sure as hell wouldn't be appearing in any X-rated movie.

Take Beth McCabe. Her combination of delicacy and toughness had an allure that could captivate a man both in the bedroom and outside it. He could as easily picture her pruning vines in the fields as he could lying back against her pillows in a cotton nightgown all the more seductive for its simplicity.

He almost groaned at the last image. If he wasn't such a damned fool, he would know exactly what her gown hid, and whether her sheets were plain cotton or printed with dainty flowers. She'd be waiting for him, the bedclothes clutched to her chin, her eyes huge and apprehensive. That soft mouth might be trembling as he gently pried the covers from her grasp and peeled them back to allow his hands to cup her pretty breasts. He would bend forward and capture her mouth, stilling the trembling. He'd coax a response until she shyly reached for him, until her legs parted and she made soft needy sounds....

He did groan this time and then glanced ruefully down to see that his fantasy had done what no erotic video could accomplish: aroused him until he ached with wanting.

He wanted to smash his fist against something in anger and frustration. He could have had her. It didn't have to be a fantasy.

Sure, he could have had her. But what he never would have known was whom *she* was having: him or Rob. And damned if he was going to play his brother in any woman's sex games, even Beth McCabe's.

But that didn't mean he couldn't dream a little. He closed his eyes and reached for his zipper.

BETH TRIED TO READ the murder mystery she'd brought, but comprehension eluded her. After a while she set it down and picked up a magazine from the selection fanned open on an end table in the waiting room. She'd only been here an hour, but it felt like forever. Other women sat briefly on the soft teal armchairs, then were ushered by the nurse into examining rooms. After a while, they left. Beth just sat.

Not that she was bored. How could she be? Her heart took a little jump every time the nurse appeared, then sank like a rock when another name was called; her palms were so damp she had to wipe them surreptitiously on her jeans every few minutes. Her stomach seemed to have climbed into her throat, where it lodged uncomfortably. She felt as if she was in an airplane, ready to leap out and parachute down for the first time.

She must be certifiably nuts, she decided. What had seemed like a good idea was appearing more and more bizarre. She hardly knew this man, and here she was waiting to be impregnated with his sperm? All this, because the baby might—might!—have bone marrow compatible with Mandy's?

Twice she opened her wallet and flipped through several photos of her daughter, to remind herself of what was important. In one, Mandy was pale, her hair cropped, her eyes huge and dark in that white face. Both times, Beth felt steadied; her heartbeat calmed, her stomach settled, tension leached out of her muscles.

Five minutes later she was as scared as ever.

She knew Nathan had showed up; she'd asked when she got here. So now he was in some room trying to do his part. The part he refused to accomplish with her, because she didn't attract him.

She tried not to think about him or what he was doing right this minute. But images kept creeping into her mind, like tiny movements in her peripheral vision.

If she lowered her guard, they assumed the impact of the huge screen in a movie theater. The trouble was, his resemblance to Rob allowed her mind to fill in the details. She *knew* what Nathan McCabe looked like nude, plus or minus a tan or a scar.

And she hated the idea of him turned on by watching some big-busted bimbo on a TV screen, when she left him cold.

The violence of her feelings didn't make sense. He was a stranger. Why did she care what turned him on?

Well, duh, she thought, in imitation of her daughter. He *did* look just like Rob. Sure, she'd been a widow for three years. But Nathan's looks had brought back fading images of Rob, sharpening them. Like any other woman, she would have been jealous if she'd found out her husband was having an affair. That was all that was wrong today. She was transferring rational feelings about Rob to his lookalike brother.

Only…she didn't buy it.

She *knew* Nathan wasn't Rob. Their facial features might be alike, but the moment Nathan moved or spoke, the resemblance faded. He was quieter, more intense, more perceptive. And it had stung more than she liked to admit to know that, even in a good cause, he couldn't bring himself to share her bed.

"Mrs. McCabe."

Her heart jumped again. She let the magazine drop from nerveless fingers and rose to her feet.

The nurse was smiling. "We're ready for you now."

Oh, God. That meant he'd… She shied away from this particular image, but even in absentia, it sent an odd quiver from her heart down to her belly. Beth was honest enough with herself to acknowledge that the feeling was sexual, as were the shivery yearning cramps between her legs. However clinical the method, his seed was about to impregnate her. Her body knew it on a level that was purely sexual.

If all went well, she would soon be carrying Nathan McCabe's child in her womb.

Please, God, she thought, *never let me regret what I'm doing.* She clutched her purse and book so tightly her fingers hurt and followed the nurse.

"CONGRATULATIONS, Mrs. McCabe." Her doctor, an attractive black woman close to her own age, beamed at her. "You're definitely pregnant."

Relief made Beth dizzy. She hadn't been wrong. "Thank God!" she breathed.

But right behind was a wave of apprehension. There was no getting out of this now. She couldn't change her mind. And she especially couldn't change it when, at five months, an amniocentesis would be performed and the baby's tissue typed. She would know then whether the baby she carried could save Mandy. And if it couldn't...well, she'd promised herself she would welcome this second child no matter what. Now she silently renewed the vow, her hand splayed protectively over her belly.

The doctor was glancing through her chart. "You're not a smoker, I see, so we don't have to worry about that. I recommend you avoid alcohol altogether, even a glass of wine or a beer."

Beth nodded dutifully.

Dr. Williams wrote her out a prescription for prenatal vitamins and they discussed diet. It was all so ordinary—so much like the last time she'd gotten pregnant, when she had a husband. Not, however, at her side, Beth recalled; she'd wanted to surprise him.

She drove home almost in a dreamlike state. She would have to tell Mandy, of course. The cowardly side of her wanted to wait until her pregnancy became obvious. Or perhaps it was her compassionate side. This time they didn't have a week or ten days to wait before they would find out whether the news was good or bad; they'd have four more months. Wouldn't it be cruel to tell Mandy about the pregnancy now and give her hope?

She'd have to tell Nathan, too. He wouldn't be needed again. He would surely be pleased about that, at least.

Almost home, Beth felt her exhilaration ebb, leaving an emotion she couldn't name. Her stomach felt hollow, her chest squeezed by an invisible hand. It wasn't nervousness, not quite. After all, what did she have to be nervous about? No matter the outcome, she would do the same thing again, make the same decision. Nor was what she felt the tension of waiting; she knew it well, that sense of time blockish and slow, like a river jammed by chunks of ice.

She turned the van into her driveway, past the sign that usually gave her a flash of pride. Today she hardly saw it. Outside the barn she stopped the van, but didn't get out.

Damn it, she wanted to cry and she didn't even know why! She gripped the steering wheel and breathed slowly, in through her nose, out through her mouth.

For a woman, finding out she was pregnant was a momentous occasion. That was all that was wrong with her, she decided. That, and the sudden awareness of how alone she was. She didn't have the excitement ahead of breaking the news to her husband, of rejoicing and planning and dreaming with someone else who cared as much as she did. Even if she decided to tell her daughter, Mandy was too young to lean on. Beth knew she would battle her queasy stomach alone, nap alone, go to the hospital alone when the time came.

She was lonely.

She sighed, thought about lunch, decided against it when her stomach lurched uncertainly. She'd known she was pregnant two days ago when she poured her morning bowl of cereal, took one mouthful and had to run to the bathroom. Beth only hoped her stomach tolerated the smell of jam cooking. Otherwise, she'd be in big trouble.

THROUGH THE INTERCOM, his secretary announced crisply, "Mrs. McCabe is on line one."

"Thanks," Nathan said, wondering briefly whether Beth's last name had Jennifer speculating about the caller's identity. He picked up the phone and punched in the line.

"Beth. Nathan here."

"Hi." She sounded faraway, uncertain. "Is this a bad time?"

"No. I'm just doing paperwork."

"Oh." She drew an audible breath. "I wanted to call you while Mandy was at school. I'm pregnant."

The bluntness of it crushed the breath from his chest. He just sat there, receiver in hand, and waited to get his wind back. She was pregnant. Beth McCabe, with the silky curls, the soft mouth, the uncomfortably perceptive eyes, carrying a baby. His baby. Not Rob's, as she probably wished. In one way it didn't seem real. In another... He gritted his teeth on the jolt of sexual hunger she had a talent for awakening.

"Congratulations." His voice came out harsh, abrupt. "That was quick."

"Yes." A pause. "I'm due February fifth."

"And you won't know until then."

"Actually, I will. The doctor will do an amniocentesis at five months. She can do tissue typing at the same time."

Because of her age, his secretary had had the procedure, to make sure her baby didn't have Down syndrome. They had told Jennifer then that her child would be a boy. Beth would learn not just if she carried a healthy boy or girl, but whether he or she would be Mandy's savior.

If Nathan had any say in it, she wouldn't be alone when she found out.

"Does Mandy—?" He stopped. "You wouldn't be calling me while she's in school if she knew."

"I'll have to tell her eventually, of course, but…" Beth went quiet, then said in a voice so low he barely heard her, "I don't want her to hope too much. If I can wait until almost five months…"

"You can get the news over with, good or bad." He made a rough sound in his throat. "How is she?"

"She's doing fine. She ought to be able to hold out."

"I hope so." The words weren't a platitude. Although not a churchgoing man, he was praying.

"Yes. Well. I won't keep you."

She was trying to end the conversation. His hand tightened on the receiver. "How are you feeling?"

"Good. Just a little tired, which is perfectly normal."

"No morning sickness?"

"A little. But it doesn't last long."

"You're not going to be able to work as many hours,

are you?'' He didn't like the picture he suddenly saw of her slaving over those stainless-steel vats, the jam bubbling and the kitchen hot. How heavy were the flats of berries and the boxes of jam ready for shipment? Would she pick berries out in the summer sun?

"Women generally do,'' Beth said tartly.

"You mean, the European serfs did. Women who put in long hours now are usually in an office, not doing farm work and heavy lifting.'' He was scowling. "You should hire an extra employee.''

She didn't answer for a moment; he was afraid she'd hung up on him. But finally she said evasively, "I'll think about it.''

She probably couldn't afford another employee. Would she take money from him? Nathan had a pretty good idea what the answer to that question was.

"I'll be up in Seattle again next week.'' It was news to him; impulse seemed to have taken over. "I'll get a hotel room, but I was hoping to see you and Mandy.''

"You're welcome to stay with us if you'd like.''

He scowled again, hearing the change in her tone. He hadn't realized how slow and heavy her voice had been until he heard it lighten.

"You're sure?''

"We'd love to have you.'' If she didn't mean it, she was a hell of a liar. "Mandy talks about you a lot.''

What about you? he wanted to ask. Did she think about him? Look forward to seeing him again? Or did he remind her too much of Rob?

"Great,'' he said too heartily. "I'll plan on it. Uh, let's see…'' He reached for his date book, deciphered his brief scrawls. What could be jettisoned? "Tuesday through Thursday?''

"Wonderful,'' she said. "You can see Tillicum

Creek Jams in full operation. Strawberries and blueberries are both ripening now."

"Maybe I should stay longer. I could pick berries."

Unexpectedly she laughed, the sound unfettered, a child's giggle. "The owner of Mount Hood Sporting Goods picking strawberries? Do you have any idea how backbreaking it can be?"

"Yeah, I picked berries summers when I was a teenager. You'll be getting experienced help."

"You *must* have better things to do!"

"Like?"

"Ohh…" She drew the word out, and he pictured her pursed lips. "Make important decisions. Plan advertising campaigns. Glare at incompetent employees. Talk about quality assurance and employee morale."

"We just finished planning our upcoming advertising campaign. I have no incompetent employees, morale is just fine, thank you, and I've already assured quality." Damn, but he was enjoying himself. "Did I forget anything?"

"Important decisions." Laughter rippled through her voice.

"I can make them in Seattle."

"Oh, in that case, I'll be sure we save a few rows of berries just for you." That voice, a little husky, amused, intimate, made him crave her presence.

"Then I'll see you Tuesday afternoon."

He hung up and punched the intercom. "Jennifer, will you come in here?"

His secretary was going to love juggling his schedule yet again.

BETH STRAIGHTENED and pressed one hand to her lower back. She blinked sweat from her eyes and looked down at her basket, only half-full with fat red berries. She'd finish filling it and then stop for lunch.

On this June day no leaves stirred on the alders that fronted the road; the air, sharp with the scent of crushed berries, hung still and warm over the fields. A lawn mower growled, the sound muted by distance. Closer was the hum of bees pollinating the raspberries.

Reluctantly Beth crouched again and began deftly plucking the ripe strawberries from the plants. The ache in her lower back intensified, but when Evan, a college boy who worked here summers, paused in the next row and asked if she was okay, she managed an almost convincing "Sure. It's just so darned humid I feel like I'm working in slow motion."

She didn't remember this back ache from her first pregnancy. Of course, then she hadn't done farm labor. She and Rob had lived in a condo in Edmonds, north of Seattle on Puget Sound. She'd been an administrative assistant at a software manufacturer. Even minor manual tasks like copying were done by someone lower in the hierarchy. What's more, she'd been eleven—no, twelve—years younger.

Making herself continue picking, Beth wondered if she could somehow afford another worker. She hadn't taken Nathan's suggestion seriously before. She was used to hard work. But now...

She hardly saw the level rising in her basket, so preoccupied was she by her review of her mental spreadsheet. Expenses here, income there. There ought to be some extra in late June— No, she remembered another bill. She couldn't possibly pay another wage, she thought, feeling the familiar spurt of panic. Her business had gotten where it was because she'd been willing to put long hours into it. Anything she couldn't afford to pay someone else to do, she did herself. With no cushion of savings and a baby on the way, this was hardly the moment for her to become a lady of leisure. If only she didn't feel so tired!

She straightened again and wiped sweat from her forehead, her hands stained red. The sound of a car engine, rare on her quiet country road at this time of day, made her turn. An unfamiliar blue sedan had slowed and was pulling into her driveway. Hope, even excitement, tingled through her veins.

Heaving her now full basket to her hip, she carried it to the pickup truck that was parked between the fields. Beth set it on the tailgate and followed the dusty footpath between rows of raspberry vines, which seemed to vibrate, so covered were they with bees.

As she approached, a man got out of the car and stretched. Nathan. Beth was astonished and disquieted by the strength of her pleasure. He was visiting for a few days. So what? He was her brother-in-law; the only thing really personal between them was the baby.

But when he smiled at her, the slow quiet grin that didn't remind her at all of Rob, her heart lightened and she felt better than she had all day.

"I didn't expect you so early."

"I had no reason to go into the office." His broad shoulders moved in an easy shrug. "Caught a nine-o'clock flight."

"I was just going to stop for lunch." With his gaze moving over her, Beth was suddenly, acutely aware of how filthy she was. And how little she wore. As the day warmed, she'd rolled her khaki shorts up as high as they'd go and tied her sleeveless cotton shirt under her breasts. Her hair was bundled back in a red scarf, which she'd yanked off a couple of times to wipe the sweat from her eyes. It would be silly to take a shower, then go back out and get dirty all over again, but she was tempted.

"I'll make lunch." Darned if he wasn't frowning at her. "You should rest."

"I'm not sick, you know."

"You may not show yet—" his gaze touched her bare midriff "—but that doesn't mean you shouldn't take care of yourself."

It was childish to feel rebellious, but she couldn't seem to help it. Who the heck was he to approve or disapprove of how she ran her life?

"You're not my father." At least she didn't stick out her tongue at him.

"No, but I am the baby's father," he said sharply.

Just the reminder was enough to make her feel warmth and tingling between her legs. She'd never imagined that carrying Nathan's baby would make her body so determined to know him sexually. She could only hope the reaction disappeared as time went on. Otherwise, how could she stand the next twenty years?

She crossed her arms, half-protectively. "You aren't really worried about him. Her."

"No." This time his dark eyes didn't waver from hers. His voice had softened. "It's you I'm worried about."

Her defiance evaporated. "I'm fine. Just a little tired."

"You're sure?" He searched her face and she saw something unexpected in his eyes. Something vulnerable.

She felt a guilty twinge. "Sometimes my back aches," she admitted.

His frown returned. "Go wash up and sit down. I'll make sandwiches, or whatever you want."

"Thank you." She felt absurdly shy. "I might take a shower."

"Go ahead." He jerked his head toward the house. "I'll grab my suitcase and follow."

"I was going to make an egg-salad sandwich. I hard-boiled some eggs. If you'd like something else..."

"This time I'm not a guest." He went around to the trunk. "I like egg salad. I know how to make it. It'll be waiting when you come down."

She looked back toward the field, where her workers were heading toward their cars or the shade of the big maple to have their lunches. They didn't need her standing over them. This afternoon, she'd cook jam, instead of picking strawberries. At least then she wouldn't have to bend over.

The trunk of the car slammed. Nathan held a suitcase and a smaller traveling bag. "Why are you still standing here?" he asked gruffly.

Beth held up both hands. "I'm going, I'm going."

THREE-QUARTERS OF AN HOUR later Nathan had begun to worry. He'd heard the shower turned off twenty-five minutes ago. It had been followed by the hum of a hair dryer. Since then...nothing. What the hell was she doing?

Maybe she'd slipped on the wet floor. Or fainted. Did pregnant women faint? He had no idea.

The sandwiches were made, sliced in half diagonally and stacked artistically on a plate. He'd poured himself juice and Beth milk—he had the vague idea that pregnant women were supposed to drink plenty of milk.

Okay. He'd go find out what was keeping her. All

he had to figure out was which door led to her bedroom.

In the upstairs hall, he hesitated. The guest room, where he'd earlier dumped his suitcases and changed clothes, was the first on the left. He knocked on the door across the hall. When no one answered, he cautiously opened it. Stuffed animals and dolls were packed cozily on a shelf above a white-painted student desk. Posters of teen idols masked a good part of the floral wallpaper. Mandy's room.

His knock on the next door brought no response, either. This time when he opened it a crack, he saw Beth right away. She lay curled on her side on the bed, head on her lace-edged pillow, eyes closed. A fuzzy blue robe gaped open at her neck.

Alarm pulsed through him. Maybe she *had* fainted. Soundlessly he pushed the door all the way open and crossed the carpeted floor to the bed, one of those affairs with posts that tapered gracefully to finials near the ceiling. He gave a wild glance through another door, which stood open to a bathroom. Beside the clawfooted tub, surrounded by a shower curtain, was a heap of clothes.

Holding his breath, he listened for hers. It came, a deep sigh, then a resumption of even slow breaths. The strength of his relief made him feel like an idiot. What—had he really thought she was dead?

But why hadn't she let him know she was going to take a nap?

She murmured just then and rolled onto her back. He stood transfixed, feeling like a lecher but unable to look away from the curve of a creamy breast and the shadow of a nipple almost exposed. He was sweating as he stared down at her. With a near physical effort, he wrenched his gaze inch by inch from her breast, but nothing else he saw made him cool down any. Her throat was pale and graceful. This close, he could see every tiny freckle on her nose and cheeks. Her mouth was soft, the lower lip full. Her lashes were fans of spun gold against her delicate skin. She *had* dried her hair; the curls looked so springy he was sure a lock would curl around his finger if he just reached out. One arm was flung above her head in a pose of innocent abandon. The sleeve of the robe had fallen back to reveal a narrow wrist, veined in blue.

Nathan groaned, the sound recalling him to some sense of decency. What was he—a peeping Tom? Good God, what if she woke up and found him gaping at her?

With another painful effort, he stepped back. His palms tingled. He could *feel* her breast, just rounded enough to fill his hand, the skin softer than anything he'd ever touched. The bones of her shoulder would be fragile, her waist slender. If that robe fell all the way open, would he see curls as gold as those on her head? The image had him clenching his teeth and backing up another few steps until he bumped into the open door.

At least from here he couldn't see her breast anymore. He finally noticed that one of her feet, pink and clean from the shower, touched the carpet. It was as though she'd sat on the edge of the bed, then thought, *I'll just put my head down for a minute.*

"I'm fine. Just a little tired," she'd said.

More than a little, he thought now. She'd needed a nap and been too stubborn to take one. She was the boss here; who was going to tell her what to do, even if it was for her own good? Mandy? One of her seasonal berry pickers?

And he'd bet his next year's company profits that she hadn't told a soul but him she was pregnant. She wouldn't want someone to let it slip to Mandy. No, she'd forge on, pretending nothing was any different. She'd only told him because she'd had to! Otherwise, he'd have shown up at that damn clinic again to put himself through the humiliation of coming in a cup.

For now, Nathan decided, he'd let her sleep, even if she was annoyed at him later. But he didn't like the idea of not being here in the future, especially these next couple of months, when berry season would be at its height and she was bound to push herself beyond any sensible limits.

Downstairs he ate two sandwiches and gulped the juice before heading outside. He'd take her place picking this afternoon and maybe tomorrow. After that... well, hell, maybe he could get up here for a couple days every week or so.

Or— He stopped dead, aware that the other workers, gathering again after the break, had turned to stare at him. Or why not rent a place up here? He could do a good part of his business on the computer and by e-mail and fax. What traveling was required he could do just as well out of SeaTac Airport as he could from Portland International. Maybe every other week he could go to Portland for two or three days.

Beth would try to talk him out of it, he knew. She'd regard his presence as interference. But damn it, he had rights and responsibilities as the father of the child she carried. A baby was a pretty abstract idea. At the moment he was more concerned about Beth. But he didn't have to tell her that.

Yeah. He liked it. He had confidence he could arrange things so that he was around enough to make life easier on Beth.

For the moment Nathan shoved the more mundane concerns—how to handle specific obligations—out of the way and headed toward the pickers.

"Hi," he said, nodding. "I'm Nathan McCabe, Beth's brother-in-law. She's not feeling too well, so I'm going to help out."

The pause was noticeable. Most of them, if not all, hadn't known she *had* a brother-in-law. Two looked startled; they must have been around long enough to have met Rob. But none of them would quibble as long as he was ready to work.

A chorus of names came back at him. A college-age stud looked him over. "You ever done this before?"

"Yeah, summers when I was your age."

The kid nodded, as though begrudging him any credit, and pointed to one row. "She left off about halfway down. Take a basket and go for it."

He'd do that. Now and for as many days as he could manage. It was the least he owed the mother of his unborn son or daughter, even if the circumstances were a little bizarre.

CHAPTER FIVE

WHEN MANDY ARRIVED HOME on the school bus, she dropped her book bag on the front porch and went out to the field. She automatically scanned the pickers. No Mom. Maybe she was making jam. Mandy was about to turn back when she saw Uncle Nate. Cool!

He was pretty grungy, and his dark hair, a little longer than hers, was matted with sweat. Even so, she thought he was really cute.

When he heard her coming, he looked up with one eyebrow raised, like Keanu Reeves in *Speed*. Then he grinned, this flash of white teeth in a dirty face streaked with strawberry juice.

"How come you're working?" Mandy asked, squatting next to him. She plucked a big fat berry and bit it off just below the stem. Her tongue caught a squirt of juice trying to trickle down her chin.

"Your mom won't let me stay unless I earn my keep."

She gave him a look. "Yeah, right."

He grimaced. "Actually, I'm hiding out here because she's mad at me."

"What did you do?" she asked with interest. Mom hardly ever got mad at her.

He kept picking, his hands quick and sure. "When she came in for lunch, she fell asleep. I didn't wake her up. Mea culpa."

"What's that mean?"

She liked the way the crease in his cheek got deeper when he smiled. "I'm at fault. Guilty as charged."

Mandy frowned. "But *she's* the one who fell asleep."

"Try telling her that," Uncle Nate muttered.

"You're kidding, aren't you?" It wasn't quite a question. She frowned again. "Why did she fall asleep?"

He paused, still squatting, and rested his elbows on his knees. "Would you believe she was so excited about my visit she couldn't sleep last night?"

Mandy thought about it. "No."

He pretended she'd stabbed him, clasping his hand to his heart. "Are you telling me you slept like a baby, too? You weren't the slightest bit excited, either?"

Mandy didn't see any reason not to tell the truth. "I was kind of," she admitted. "I like having you here."

His smile was different this time. Not teasing at all. "I like being here. I wish I'd known about you and your mom a long time ago. I...feel like I've missed out. Your dad and I were idiots."

"What did you fight about?"

He picked without speaking for a minute. Then he paused and looked up at her. "I can't tell you about our last fight. It's...adult. But really, it was just the last straw. We'd spent years competing. I used to tell myself it was all your dad, that he'd never let me succeed at anything without him doing it, too, and better if he could. But I guess maybe I was doing the same without realizing it. Probably both of us were uncomfortable with the fact that we looked so much alike and had similar abilities. You get to be a teenager and you need to know who you are, what makes you special. We'd look at each other, and we weren't sure.''

Mandy listened, frowning. ''I can see why you'd feel that way,'' she said gravely. ''I'm not a teenager yet, but already everything seems really confusing, you know? But at least I don't have a…'' She'd been going to say ''twin,'' but she changed her mind. ''An echo.''

''An echo,'' he repeated, and she could tell he was thinking about it. ''Yeah. Our trouble was, we both wanted to know who was making the original sound and who was only echoing it.''

''Dad was really competitive.'' She wrinkled her nose. ''I remember Mom getting mad at him in the car. He acted like he thought all the other drivers were racing him. He always had to get away from stoplights before the other cars. Or be the fastest on the freeway.''

His face was fading from her memory—or it had been until Uncle Nate came—but most of what she did remember about her father was good. Comforting. So it was hard to think back to something that had scared her a little, like him driving too fast.

''Yeah, he was always kind of a show-off,'' Uncle Nate said. ''I wasn't. But then I resented it when he got more attention. What we should have done was go in different directions—me into something where I'd get attention without asking for it, Rob into drama or radio or car racing.'' He grinned. ''He should have been an Indy 500 driver.''

''Maybe that was your parents' fault.''

He shot her a look of surprise. ''Maybe.''

''What were they like?'' When Dad died, she was too young to care much about grandparents who were already dead and whom she'd never met. And now Dad wasn't around to ask.

Somebody shouted a question and Uncle Nate waved a hand. To her he said, "How about we talk about them this evening? Right now, I'm falling behind."

"Okay," Mandy agreed. "I'd better go do my homework. Is Mom in the house?"

"No, she's making jam in the barn."

Mandy nodded. "Bye."

"Hey," he called after her. "I like your glasses."

She made a face over her shoulder. She *hated* wearing glasses.

Pushing them up on her nose, she went to the barn so Mom would know she was home. The whole barn smelled sweet, like the taste in Mandy's mouth. Mom was in the kitchen ladling jam from a huge vat into jars. She was frowning and muttering to herself, and jam dripped down the side of the jar in her hand.

She *was* mad.

"Hi, Mom," Mandy said carefully, pretending she hadn't noticed.

"Sweetie." Her mother smiled and blew upward to puff her bangs from her damp forehead. "Have a good day?"

It was so hot in here Mandy was already backing toward the door. "Sure. Did you remember I have drama tonight?"

Mom's eyes widened. "Drama? Oh, Lord. Dinner should already be on. I'll finish up here as quick as I can."

"If I'm late or can't go, that's okay." Mandy didn't want to sound disappointed. Because of being sick, she knew she took more of her mother's time and energy than most kids did. But she really loved her drama class. It was the only time she could completely forget herself and, for a little while, be someone else. Maybe she was a show-off, too, like her dad.

She didn't mind being like him.

"No, we'll manage." Mom wiped off the jam jar and grabbed an empty one, then the ladle. "Your uncle Nate's here."

"I know. I talked to him." Mandy shifted her backpack from one shoulder to the other. "Maybe he could take me tonight."

Mom glanced at her. "Would you like that?"

"He could watch for the last half hour."

"I'll bet he'd enjoy that."

"Will you let me ask him?" Mandy bit her lip. "That way, I can tell if he doesn't really want to."

Mom tried to smile. "Okay."

"I could have told him and Dad apart right away," Mandy said. She wasn't exactly sure what she meant by that, but it seemed important to say.

Her mother only nodded. "Me, too. It seems funny when they look so much alike, doesn't it?"

AT THE DINNER TABLE, Beth could hardly bring herself to meet Nathan's eyes. She'd thrown a temper tantrum today, something she didn't remember ever doing before.

She'd awakened feeling drugged, her arms heavy, her eyelids leaden. Her thoughts moved as slowly as her body. Why was she lying on the bed in her robe? She rolled to one side and stared without understanding at the clock. Three. In the morning? But she had her robe on. Sunlight lay in a warm golden band across the floor.

And then she remembered. She'd come in for lunch,

taken a shower and laid down for just a minute. Three hours ago.

But surely Nathan would have woken her up. He knew she had to be back out to work.

She dressed and hurried downstairs to find a note on the kitchen table. *Sandwich and milk in the fridge. I'm out picking.*

Beth had stormed out to the field and told him he had no business deciding whether or not she would put in a full day of work. She'd all but stamped her foot and yelled, "So there!"

Dark eyes opaque, he'd listened until she wound down, then said tersely, "You wouldn't have fallen asleep if you hadn't needed the extra rest. If you're going to do this, you can't afford to be a fool."

Flushed, she looked around to see that they had an audience, although, thank God, she doubted anyone could have caught their words. She set her teeth and marched back to the barn, where one of her helpers was already rinsing berries.

She hadn't seen Nathan since, although half an hour ago she'd heard him come into the house and then the shower running. Now they sat across the table from each other, Mandy serving as a buffer.

He wasn't looking at Beth, either. He listened as Mandy told him about her drama class, offered by the Seattle Children's Theatre Drama School.

"My teacher is in a production right now at the Seattle Rep. It's not a play for kids, so I haven't seen it, but she thinks she's going to be in *Peter Pan* at the Intiman. Mom says we can go to that."

Beth hadn't heard Mandy chatter with such animation in a long while. Nathan was making all the appropriate responses and looking like he meant them.

"Anyway, my class is tonight, and I wondered if, um, you could take me. The teacher lets parents watch the last half hour." All of a sudden she was fiddling with her fork and only stealing sidelong glances at him.

Beth was going to kill him if he said no.

He offered her daughter one of those quick rare smiles. "I'd like that—if your mom doesn't mind."

"I'd be delighted," Beth said offhandedly. "If you can take her, I'd have some extra time to catch up on laundry and clean the kitchen."

His eyes met hers. "Don't you ever sit down and relax? Watch TV? Read?"

"Of course I do!" she snapped.

Mandy's anxiety showed in her too-thin face.

Nathan noticed, too, because he smiled again at Mandy. "Your mom makes me feel lazy. I can't keep up with her."

"You mean, you couldn't nap for three hours like I did?" Beth could have kicked herself the minute the words were out. She sounded so petty, so unpleasant. It was that damn smile that had done it, she acknowledged unhappily. She was jealous of her own daughter.

He gave Beth a brief unreadable look, then said, "Everybody's entitled."

She hated that deliberately courteous tone, which made it plain who interested him: Mandy. He had to get along with her to be allowed to visit her daughter.

Enjoying feeling sorry for yourself? her inner voice asked.

Yes! she answered, before a spark of humor let her see the idiocy of her pique. Nathan had been just as nice to her as he'd been to Mandy until she indulged in her little fit today. The funny thing was, she didn't even know why she'd been so angry. For Pete's sake, the man had gone out and done her job so she could sleep!

She automatically put a bite of lasagna into her mouth, tuning out whatever Nathan and Mandy were talking about.

She always woke up grumpy from naps, one reason she never took them. But still... Beth thought back to the way her heart had cramped in anger when she read the note. No, she amended slowly, not anger. Panic. She hadn't liked the idea that he was taking care of her. That implied a loss of control, which was scary. She didn't want to depend on anyone. She wanted to cope all on her own.

Why? she asked herself, but this time she had no answer.

"Cool!" Mandy bounced in her chair. "You're really moving?"

Moving? Beth turned a wary gaze on Nathan. "What did you say?"

"Would you please pass the garlic bread?" he asked Mandy before glancing at Beth with that same courteous blank expression. "I'm going to rent a place up here. Probably a little south, closer to the airport, but near enough to you so that I can be here if you need me."

Once again irrational panic fluttered in her chest. "But your office is in Portland."

If he noticed the way her voice rose, he ignored it. "I only go in a day or two a week, anyway. The rest of the time I'm either traveling or I work from home. Between fax machines and computers, I can get almost anything done long-distance."

"You must have friends, a health club, favorite restaurants.'' Beth tried hard to think of everything he might miss. ''Why uproot yourself?''

Betrayingly his gaze shifted lower to where he might have seen her belly if the table hadn't blocked his view. ''I don't know that I have roots there.'' He shrugged, meeting her eyes again. ''Seattle will be just as convenient.''

Given her daughter's presence, what could she say but ''Just so you don't feel some kind of...obligation. We've been doing fine on our own.''

One of his dark brows rose, the merest twitch, but enough to signal his skepticism and arouse her rage. She'd hit the nail on the head: he'd decided they needed him. She was working too hard, and poor sick little Mandy was languishing for lack of a father figure. He was some kind of demi-God, condescending to sweep in and save them.

Just wait until Mandy goes to bed, Beth thought, lips tightening. Then she'd tell him what he could do with his patronage.

Too bad she couldn't tell him what to do with his sperm. Yet even as she had the thought, her hand moved to her abdomen. Even if this child did entitle Nathan to some rights she'd rather deny him, she wouldn't change what she'd done. The baby they would share had restored her hope.

NATHAN PUT THE LAST PAN in the oak-veneer cupboard beside the built-in range and closed the door. The kitchen still looked uninhabited. The whole place did. He'd rented the town house furnished, the mostly neutral colors obviously chosen to be acceptable to any tenant, even if they didn't excite anyone. He'd brought some stuff from Portland, but not everything, because he'd decided to keep his condo there. He'd be spending nights down there often enough to make it handy. And while this seemed like a good idea right now, he could easily find himself unwelcome at Beth McCabe's. Regular reminders that this residence was temporary might not be a bad idea.

After all, she'd made it plain enough that she didn't want him around as often as he had in mind. The minute Mandy had gone to bed, she'd told him so. One remark struck below the belt.

"You're the one who suggested I was inviting you to stand in for Rob. Isn't that what you're trying to do?"

Was it? Hell, yeah, he intended to help out his brother's widow and daughter. If he'd known about their existence and Rob's death sooner, Beth wouldn't have had to struggle alone these past three years.

But was he, on another level, trying to step into his brother's shoes? The question made him uncomfortable. Rob might even consider that Nathan was evening the score, tit for tat. Nathan wanted to believe his motives were nobler than that, but how could he be sure?

He muttered a curse and headed into the spare bedroom, which he was converting to an office. With his things just half-unpacked, it bore more of his stamp than the rest of the town house. The computer was already set up, the fax machine waiting for a second phone line. On the white walls, he'd hung a couple of favorite photos, blown up and framed simply in black metal. One showed autumn leaves, pale yellow and vivid gold, lingering on an aspen tree. Those already fallen floated in a small stream and clogged a natural dam of tumbled boulders. The other photograph was the classic of Mount Shuksan, with its reflection cast on the still lake. Not original, but evocative. He could almost smell the huckleberries, feel the sharp chill of the water, breathe the crisp air.

It had been too long since he'd done any climbing. Even hiking. He thought back to the previous summer. He'd climbed Mount Hood a couple of times. He and his buddy Matt had vowed to climb Constance in the Olympic Mountains, but their free weekends never co-incided. He couldn't even remember the last time he'd talked to Matt. It had been weeks. Hell, probably months. Too long. And Nathan considered Matt his best friend.

Remembering Beth's mock concern about his pull-ing up roots, Nathan snorted. He hadn't put any down. If he were honest with himself, his condo in Portland was damn near as arid as this rented place. Did he ever really think of it as home? "My place," he tended to call it, which was even how he thought of it. He owned it, he lived there, but when he thought *home,* what flashed in his mind was the neat white bungalow where he'd grown up, not so far from here. Home had been Bremerton, on the other side of the sound. It was a navy town; his dad had been a welder working on de-stroyers and the occasional aircraft carrier. Dad had been a beer-drinking, chain-smoking veteran, proud be-cause his boys were smarter than he was. Mom had never worked—Dad wouldn't let her—for dinner might not have been on the table every day at five-thirty when he walked in the door.

Funny that in the light of memory, Mom's person-ality had a clarity and individuality Dad's didn't. Vol-unteering was okay with Dad, and by God she volun-teered. Friends of the Library, Room Mother, PTA. When she joined an organization, she ended up running it. She ran her household just as efficiently. She'd have made a hell of a CEO, something Dad's ego could never have stood.

Nathan sat down in his padded office chair and stared unseeingly at the blank computer screen. Mom would have been disgusted if she'd known he and Rob had let a quarrel end their relationship. "Remember," she used to tell them, with a brisk nod, "nobody will ever know you or understand you the way your brother does."

But then, he'd long ago realized Mom was partly responsible for the way things had turned out. She had believed in competition. She was constantly pitting her twin sons against each other. He could see her now, in her housedress, arms crossed. "Which one of you can fold the laundry the fastest?" She'd be sure to add, "And do it right."

They'd done it fast and right, but one of them would end up humiliated. He had to win back his self-esteem doing the next chore. Neighbors must have wondered why their lawn was always the most closely mowed, the most neatly raked. And in the meantime those McCabe boys had maintained straight A's and gone out for baseball, football and basketball. Always the same sports, except for the one spring when Nathan tried wrestling, instead of baseball.

They'd parted ways only when Rob stuck his head under the hood of a car and when Nathan swung a fifty-pound pack on his back and headed up into the Olympic Mountains. Some of the sense of freedom and joy he found there, he'd come to realize, was from the severing of the bond, which sometimes felt like the physical joining of Siamese twins. Probably Rob's pleasure in fast cars was partly made up of the same relief.

Nathan swore again and pushed back his chair. Hell. Wasn't it enough that he grieved for his brother? Did he have to understand the past, too? What was done was done. They'd each made a life separate from the other. Rob's had ended sooner than it should have. Nathan was doing what his mother had taught him was right: fulfilling the responsibility one brother had taken on. But he wasn't trying to do it better. Even if he'd wanted to, he couldn't. Beth McCabe had loved Rob, and no gratitude she came to feel for Nathan would ever equal that.

Sometimes she wanted to scream at him to stay away, if only his being here wasn't, God help her, such a relief. She was so *tired* this time around. The nausea, too, wore her down. There were days she didn't think she could bear the smell of cooking jam another minute. That rich sweet smell had always meant success to her, security, strength. The recipes were hers, the result of endless experimenting. When she tasted a batch of raspberry jam, the experience was sensual. But now...now, it was just work.

The summer was already setting heat records for the Northwest. That was good for the berries, which were ripening early and sweet. For a pregnant woman, it was sheer misery. She had two fans set up in the barn kitchen, but all they did was stir the muggy air around. She took showers twice a day, but she was sweating before she could even towel-dry.

She wanted to blame the heat for her insomnia, too, but was too honest. Heat did rise, making the upstairs of the old house too warm even after night fell. But with her windows flung open and the ceiling fan whirling, cooler air soon whispered over her skin as she lay sprawled on the crisp cotton sheet, covers flung to one side.

It was other things keeping her awake. Things like her conscience, which had stayed silent until she'd made an irrevocable decision but now was whispering questions.

Won't you be angry at this baby if he's not a close enough match to Mandy? How can you be sure you'll really love him, no matter what?

Firing up at someone else was easy enough; being one-hundred-percent, never-look-back sure in her own heart and mind was another matter. She lay in bed and splayed her hands over her belly. It was flat and smooth, without even a small swelling to convince her that she was really pregnant, that this wasn't all a dream or a nightmare. She touched her breasts, too, but even they weren't more sensitive yet.

"I'm pregnant," she whispered, and didn't altogether believe it. Except for the tiredness. And the nausea. And the confirmation from the doctor. But she needed that flutter inside, that shiver of life separate from herself, to settle her internal debate.

Of course she'd done the right thing. How could she have done less? But Beth wanted desperately to feel an attachment to the baby she carried, a love as powerful and protective as that she felt for Mandy. Only then could she silence the voices that expressed her deepest fears.

NATHAN INSISTED on accompanying her the next time she saw her obstetrician. Half a dozen times she tried telling him he really didn't need to come. She was fine;

the appointment was routine; even most husbands didn't go in the early months.

"Maybe so," he'd agree, "but their responsibility is pretty firmly established. Mine isn't. I'm here for you, and I'm here for my son or daughter. I want you to be sure of that."

I don't care! she wanted to cry, but it was a lie. She was scared of being alone this time around. Probably every parent fouled up sometimes, but when you were all your child had, panic was never very far away. She blamed herself for those times when Mandy looked at her with eyes older than her own, when Mandy said, "I'm fine, Mom. No, I don't want to talk about it. Really. Don't worry." When had her own daughter quit telling her what she felt? If only she knew what she'd done or said that was wrong, she could undo it. But she had no idea. And now she was proposing to raise another child, as though she'd become an expert. What if Mandy fell ill again while she had a baby crying nights? She was doing this for Mandy, but who would she choose then? Without Nathan, she might have to leave the baby with a hired sitter while she spent nights at the hospital. Or stay home with the baby, leaving Mandy alone in the hospital.

She needed him, but that didn't have to mean she gave up all her privacy. He wasn't her husband, even if he looked like he was.

She had to keep reminding herself of that, because when she lay in bed drifting toward sleep, she'd find herself reaching out for Rob, a pleasant ache between her thighs. They hadn't made love in such a long time. But he was here now, his weight settling on the edge of the bed. Surely he was as hungry for her as she was for him—

Beth jolted awake. Almost awake. *Rob,* she cried inside, and then knew. He was dead. Oh, God. She wasn't dreaming about Rob at all. The man sitting on the side of the bed wasn't smiling insouciently, his teeth flashing white even in the moonlight; the line of his mouth was grim. As he pulled his sweater over his head, she saw that the puckered scar bisecting her husband's belly, a legacy of a motorcycle accident, was missing.

She shot bolt upright and he faded. But she'd *seen* him! Beth squeezed her eyes shut and tried to slow her breathing. No. Nathan McCabe hadn't been in her bedroom only a moment ago, any more than he'd been there the other nights she'd had similar dreams. Her subconscious was confused, that was all. Thank God he didn't know. And thank God, she thought guiltily, Rob couldn't know.

In the morning Beth felt heavy-eyed and sluggish. Leaning against the counter as she waited for water to boil, wanting coffee and knowing she'd settle for herbal tea, she watched Mandy eat her cereal at the kitchen table. Jean shorts showed long legs so skinny the knees were knobby. Her elbows stuck out awkwardly. Despite the sun, she was still too pale. Fear cramped in Beth, as familiar as every other daily emotion. Even if your child was cured, how long did it take until the dread and fear quit stabbing a reminder of your helplessness, of what you might lose? Or did they ever?

Mandy looked up. If she saw what her mother tried to hide, she didn't comment. "When are you going to take me to Kayla's? I should call her."

Last week Beth had asked Kayla's mother if she'd have Mandy over today.

Mandy had no idea her mother had a doctor appointment. Now Beth said, "As soon as I've had breakfast."

"Okay." Mandy set her cereal bowl in the sink. "I have to go get my swimsuit and put sunscreen lotion on and stuff."

Mandy swung between awkwardness and grace. Today she pounded up the stairs, sounding like a teenage boy in size-twelve Reeboks.

The phone rang just as Beth was sitting down with her toast and tea, all her stomach seemed able to handle these days.

"Hello?"

"What time shall I pick you up?" Nathan asked without preamble.

A flash of anger had her saying more sharply than she normally would have allowed herself, "You shouldn't. You're not my husband. Please quit acting as if you are." *Please quit encouraging me to dream about you as if you are.*

The silence was long enough, thick enough, to have her opening her mouth to apologize. She didn't have a chance.

"I've been having trouble believing I'm really going to be a father." His voice was toneless. "I thought, if I heard the heartbeat…" He didn't finish. "It had nothing to do with you."

There was a soft click and Beth realized he'd hung up. She slammed down the receiver and fought the urge to burst into tears. She would not feel guilty. He was the one trying to take Rob's place, and she wouldn't let him! Next thing she knew he *would* be sitting on the edge of her bed looking at her, not tenderly, but grimly, as though she was a burden.

No, she thought, staring blindly at her dry toast. He

would never sit on the edge of her bed. She'd offered him the chance and he'd refused. He didn't want what had been Rob's. Didn't want her. She was the one confused, not him.

She should apologize at least. Maybe let him go with her to the doctor. What would it hurt? But she didn't reach for the telephone. Her emotions were too muddled for her to deal with his, as well. Later, she decided. They had time enough to come to terms—seven months, to be exact. And by then surely—please, God!—this child inside her would be real, a person, and she would be able to look at her baby's father and know he wasn't Rob.

CHAPTER SIX

DAMNED IF HE WASN'T going to cry. Nathan blinked hard and inhaled through his mouth. Around him other adults, probably all parents, stirred. A baby started to babble and the mother murmured nonsense in a singsong voice. But he didn't look away from the pale, dark-eyed girl sitting facing the audience, hands clasped in her lap.

Mandy was doing a monologue from *The Diary of Anne Frank*. It was a poignant little speech in which she was wishing herself out of the attic that had hidden the family for two long years. Soft, wistful, her voice ached with youth and dreams and resignation. Mandy *was* Anne, the Jewish girl who would die of fever in a concentration camp.

When she finished and bowed her head, the long moment of silence told Nathan he wasn't alone in being moved by her performance. Then the small audience erupted into applause. The teacher of the drama class rushed forward.

"Amanda, that was wonderful. I almost cried."

Nathan gave a quick surreptitious swipe to the corners of his eyes. The power of her performance and the sting her illness gave it was being supplanted by pride, enough to clog his throat.

Mandy quietly crossed to the chairs at the side of the room where the other members of the class awaited their turns. A younger boy had collected some props and taken her place. Just before she sat down, she put her glasses back on and looked toward Nathan. It both hurt and gratified him to see the need for approval in her eyes. His approval.

He grinned and offered her a thumbs-up, and was warmed by the quick smile that gave her face an elfin charm.

The woman beside him leaned over and whispered, "Your daughter is very talented. Does she have an agent?"

"She hasn't done that much acting yet," he returned in a low voice. He ought to tell her that Mandy wasn't his daughter, but he allowed himself the indulgence of pretending, if only for the evening.

After the class was over, he hugged Mandy. "You're incredible," he told her. "The woman who sat beside me thinks you ought to have an agent."

"Really?" Mandy brightened. "You mean, so I can do commercials and stuff?"

"I guess."

"That'd be cool." She thought about it. "Except this kid who was in my class last year went to lots of auditions. He said you'd sit for hours sometimes, and then you could tell they weren't even listening to you when it was your turn. He got one or two parts, but it didn't sound worth it. I mean, he couldn't play soccer or baseball or anything because of auditions."

Nathan breathed in the night air and opened the passenger door for her. Other car doors were slamming, taillights flashing. "You'd have to want it pretty bad."

She plopped inside and reached for the seat belt. "Yeah." Face dimly illuminated by the roof light and the yellow parking-lot lamps, she was quiet long enough that he almost closed the door. But suddenly she added in a false bright tone, "Maybe someday I'd like to do it. I don't know."

His heart contracted. He'd discovered that what he wanted most in life was for Mandy to be able to talk about the future with real hope, to believe that she *had* a future. He'd have given her his own if he could. Maybe, in a way, that was what he was doing, becoming a father for her sake.

Rob, he thought again, *did you know how lucky you were?*

He was beginning to suspect that his brother had indeed known. Nathan was spending a hell of a lot of night hours wishing he could do it all differently, have a chance to see Rob as a man he would have liked.

But then came an insidious thought. He would also have had to see Beth happily married to his brother.

By the time he'd reached his own side of the car, he had squelched his turmoil, shoved it back down and slammed the lid, like a hamper full of dirty laundry that had to be washed sooner or later, but not now.

Trouble was, now never seemed like the right time.

He and Mandy chatted on the way home, just an easy conversation with comfortable silences, as though they'd known each other all their lives. It was August, and tonight was her second-to-last acting class of the summer session. Next week was the final performance of the monologues they'd worked on all summer; tonight had been a rehearsal. Parents could come to either or both. Mandy had decided he could come tonight, her mom next week. He could go next week, too, she'd added hopefully.

Unspoken was what they all knew or at least suspected: Beth would rather he didn't. She was avoiding

him. Even Mandy had to have noticed. Oh, he saw
Beth, but mostly in passing. She'd suggest someplace
he might take Mandy. An errand he could do for them,
since he was determined to be helpful. Sometimes she
took naps when he was there.

Damned if that wasn't worse torture than her presence. She'd go up the stairs and close her door, and
eventually only silence would come from up there. Nathan would picture himself climbing the stairs the way
he had the other time, easing open her bedroom door,
stepping inside. She'd be curled on her side as she'd
been that afternoon, her fuzzy blue gown gaping open.
Below the golden tan of her throat, her breasts would
be pale. If he slipped a finger into the opening of the
gown, he'd be able to ease it aside. Just another inch,
and he'd see her nipple. And, God, he wanted to see
it, as he'd never wanted anything in his life. Almost,
he amended. Next to Mandy being cured.

When Beth was awake, her face held so much wariness he clung to the vision of it in sleep. Gold lashes,
tiny freckles, mouth soft. It looked younger than she
must be. Sweet. Pretty. Kissable.

And she was probably dreaming about Rob. The
knowledge was like an icy clump of snow falling on
his head. She had loved his brother. Still loved his
brother. Nathan looked just like Rob. Wasn't Rob.

He knew he couldn't have her, tried to make himself
quit dreaming he could. Good God, even if by some
miracle she claimed to fall in love with him, how
would he ever know whom she imagined she was going to bed with?

Tonight he almost didn't go in with Mandy, but
when he failed to turn off the ignition, she grabbed his

hand and begged, "Will you come and tell Mom how I did? Please?"

What could he say? "You just want me to puff up your ego," he grumbled, but in a way that let her know he was kidding. He turned off the car and got out, looking across the roof at her. "Next week, your mother'll see for herself that you're the next Claire Danes. Assuming she's never noticed any dramatics around the house."

Mandy dragged him up the porch steps. "You mean, like me pretending I hate something I really don't?"

"Yeah. Like that."

"You mean, like lie?"

"Uh—" he held open the front door for her "—exaggerate."

"Would I do that?" She raised shocked eyes to him.

"Yeah." He poked her. "You're pretty good, too."

Her grin was unaffectedly childlike, a couple of crooked front teeth making him think about braces and contact lenses to replace those detested glasses. God willing, she'd need both.

"Mom!" she bellowed.

Her mother appeared from the kitchen, a half-grown black-and-white cat draped over her shoulder. "Polly is determined to help me wash the dishes."

Damn, she looked good. Three months pregnant, and still she could wear snug jeans and a sleeveless shirt knotted at her waist. Her hair was held up by a clip, but pale curls were slipping out all around her face.

Mandy took the seemingly boneless animal from her mother. "She likes water."

Beth wrinkled her nose at the cat. "There's something about her staring in the toilet every time I flush it..."

"That shows she's intelligent," Mandy said confidently. "I mean, just think, she's trying to figure out where all that water is going and then why it comes rushing back."

So far Beth had ignored Nathan, but now her eyes met his in amusement over her daughter's head. For just a second she'd forgotten he threatened her. Upset her.

"Yeah, well," he drawled, "if Polly has an IQ of 150, Calvin's is about eighty-five. The other day, he was so busy watching a bird he fell off the porch railing into a lilac bush. Should've seen him slink away."

Eyes alight with laughter, Beth said, "It could have been worse. He might have fallen in a rosebush. Then more than his dignity would have been damaged."

Nathan tried for an easy grin. "I don't think he has any dignity."

"Of course he does!" Mandy declared indignantly. "He's like a little kid, that's all. Kids aren't supposed to be dignified."

"More like a teenager," her mother muttered.

"Speaking of teenagers," Nathan said, "I seem to remember that somebody around here has a birthday coming up."

"Two somebodies, actually," his niece told him with a sly look at her mother. "My birthday is on the twentieth, Mom's on the twenty-fourth."

Beth rolled her eyes at Mandy. "I'm doing my best to forget it."

"Oh, come on," Nathan said, "it can't be that bad." He leaned an elbow on the stair banister. "What is it? Thirty-three? Thirty-four?"

The scrunched-up nose reminded him of a nearly identical expression Mandy sometimes made.

"Thirty-five."

"Hey, I'll hit the big four-0 long before you will."

She blinked; a shadow crossed her face. "You will, won't you?"

Damn it, he'd screwed up. His birthday meant Rob's birthday. But Rob wouldn't make the big four-0.

"By the time you're forty," he said lightly, "you may have a famous actress for a daughter. She's dynamite."

The shadow disappeared. As clear as a high mountain stream, Beth's eyes fastened on his. "She's good, isn't she?"

She hadn't asked him to come any farther into the house and sit down, but at least they were talking. Well, he might kill it here, but one reason for his involvement in their lives was to share remembrances of his brother. "Yeah. Did you know Rob was in high-school drama? He wasn't half-bad."

"Really?" Mandy's eyes widened.

"Darn right. Let's see. He played Scrooge in *A Christmas Carol* in our senior year and, um, the King of Siam in *The King and I.* He was a real ham."

"You know, he never said." Beth's voice was soft. "I suppose the subject didn't come up. Mandy wasn't acting yet—" She stopped. "What are we standing here for? Would you like a cup of coffee?"

"Wouldn't mind," he agreed casually.

Of course that meant he had to continue to talk about Rob, dredging up every memory of those three or four high-school plays that had given his brother another chance to be the center of attention. Rob wouldn't have acted if he couldn't have had the starring roles. Nathan didn't tell Beth or Mandy that. The second he ran out of recollections, Mandy popped to her feet. "I'm gonna get ready for bed. Thank you for taking me tonight, Uncle Nathan. Night, Mom.''

Two-thirds of his coffee was left. Nathan hesitated, then put his cup down and started to get to his feet.

Beth's glance shied away from him, but she said, ''You don't have to hurry off.''

He raised an eyebrow. One surprise after another. He'd have sworn Mandy was trying to leave them alone, except he couldn't figure why she'd do that. Now Beth wasn't politely pushing him out the door as she normally did, either.

When she didn't say anything, he did. ''You've raised a nice kid.''

''She is, isn't she?'' Beth's eyes, shimmering with emotion that needn't be named, met his. ''Have you noticed she's developing?''

Developing? Blankly, Nathan thought, developing what? Then it clicked. ''Oh. Yeah.'' Mandy's breasts weren't much yet, but he had noticed her self-consciousness. ''That's normal, isn't it?'' he asked. ''She's almost twelve.'' Fifth, sixth grade, he seemed to remember that was when he really became aware of breasts, presumably because that was when the girls began to get them. His awareness had fueled a few wet dreams.

Unconscious of his detour into personal history, Beth nodded. ''Uh-huh. One of her friends is already—'' Beth's hands sketched a somewhat improbable Playboy-bunny bosom ''—and she's been menstruating for ages.'' She closed her eyes with a snap, and a tinge of pink ran along her cheeks. ''I'm sorry. I forget, you haven't had kids or... Am I embarrassing you?''

''Nah.'' He let his amusement show, not the clutch of longing her friendliness awakened. ''I do know the facts of life. Even if my one venture into parenthood didn't require a hell of a lot of knowledge.''

Now she was truly blushing. Primly she said, ''I'm sure the nurse must have given you instructions.''

''I think she did.'' A grin pulled at the corner of his mouth. ''I just didn't take them in. I was too stunned by the, uh, circumstances.''

''Well, I did give you an alternative...'' Horror made her mouth form an O. She hadn't meant that to slip out.

He rubbed the back of his neck. ''You know why I turned you down.''

She didn't seem to have heard him. ''It was dumb of me.'' She was trying to sound cheerful, uncaring, but her tone was forced. ''I don't even know what kind of woman attracts you! Maybe it's buxom redheads. I mean, if you'd agreed to my proposition just to be kind, think how humiliating it could have been for both of us.''

His eyes narrowed. Damned if she hadn't decided that he couldn't have gotten it up. Since she was so unattractive. The irony made him franker than he should have been for his self-preservation.

''Actually Rob and I had pretty similar tastes in women.'' More irony. Which wasn't why his voice roughened. ''Under other circumstances, I'd have given a lot to go up to your bedroom with you.''

She looked shocked and...flattered? Good God, had she really believed he'd turned her down because he didn't find her sexy?

Her tongue touched her lips. Nervously, no doubt, but he felt a jolt of pure hunger. She spoke gravely. ''Did anybody ever tell you you're chivalrous?''

He swore and stood up, looming over her. ''I didn't

say that to be nice. I said it because it's the truth. You're Rob's widow. If you weren't—'' His turn to put the brakes on. Probably too late.

She rose to her feet, too, slowly, never looking away from him. ''If…if it weren't for Rob, maybe…''

He sucked in a breath and squeezed his eyes shut. ''I shouldn't have said that.''

''No.'' She was being painfully honest. He wished she'd quit. ''I've been thinking the same thing. I'm confused. It's just…I can't be sure which of my feelings are for Rob and which are for you.''

Nathan forced himself to open his eyes and say levelly, ''A little confusion is natural. I make you think about him.''

''Sometimes—'' she bowed her head, exposing the long line of her neck ''—I have dreams…''

He had a feeling he knew what kind. God, why was she telling him this? He'd started it, he thought, appalled. Why hadn't he kept his damned mouth shut? He'd been better off not guessing that she felt some of the same turmoil he did. Now he'd lie awake nights wondering if she was thinking about him, dreaming about him, her nipples hardening for him.

Or for Rob.

''I'd better go.'' He blundered backward. ''I hope I haven't made you more uncomfortable around me.''

''No.'' Her sigh sounded unconscious. ''I think maybe it needed to be said. I've been rude. Hiding because I didn't know how to deal with the things I've felt.''

Things. Like what? he wanted to ask. Did her heart speed up when he was around? Did she feel a quiver in her belly? Did she have to busy her hands to keep from touching him? Or was she just talking about dreams of Rob, only she wasn't sure it wasn't him, instead?

He shrugged. "We're in a strange spot. Not just because of Rob. Because of…" He gestured at her belly.

Her hands spread protectively over it. The sight sent a lurch of pure desire through him.

"That's true." Her eyes were softer than he'd seen them in weeks. "Maybe we've cleared the air."

Had they? Oh, hell, maybe he could pretend. Maybe pretense would even become reality. Maybe eventually he could feel brotherly toward her.

Yeah, an inner voice mocked, *not in* your *dreams.*

"Are you feeling okay?" he asked awkwardly.

"Still nauseated," she admitted. "But it ought to pass soon. Otherwise, I'm fine."

He nodded. She didn't mention the tiredness, but he knew she still battled that, too. At least she'd listened to common sense and took naps when she could manage it. And berry season was winding down.

She seemed to be eyeing him carefully. "I…I have a doctor's appointment tomorrow."

Surprise coursed through him. He schooled his voice to be noncommittal. "Yeah?"

"If you'd like to come…"

Only the gravel in his voice betrayed his emotions. "Do you mean that?"

"I was a pig last month."

"This isn't exactly a toy we have to share."

"That's probably not a half-bad description," Beth said wryly. "We do need to learn to share. Or maybe *I* need to learn."

"We'll work it out." He cleared his throat. "What time?"

THE NIGHT WAS COOLER. In her dark bedroom Beth stood at the window looking out at the fields. A cloud cover—maybe rain tomorrow?—hid the moon. She couldn't see anything. Still, she let the air drift over her body until she felt goose bumps rise. Then she slipped into bed, poking a cat—Calvin, she decided, from the sound of the purr—out of the way with one foot.

Surely she would sleep better tonight. She almost hugged herself with pleasure because of her talk with Nathan. They should have done that long ago. She'd let her belief that he didn't want her rankle, had resented it for some absurd reason. Because of Rob, she supposed; it was as though Rob had reappeared and didn't want her anymore.

Everything was because of Rob, including her reawakened sexual longings. But maybe those would fade, if she could get to be friends with Nathan. They'd move past any stirrings between them. They were a man and a woman, so it was confusing to be thrust so much together, to be bound the way they would be forever by their child.

But she felt optimistic tonight. He'd go to the doctor with her tomorrow, and she'd feel nothing inappropriate. She had been selfish. He, too, should have the thrill of hearing their baby's heartbeat.

She closed her eyes and pictured him—Nathan, not Rob. A tanned strong neck. Lean forearms with prominent veins and tendons and only a light dusting of hair. Though not bulky, big-shouldered. Leaner than her husband, she thought; Rob had thought running was boring.

Immediately she realized she was comparing them again, standing one beside the other, hunting for differences. Tonight she wouldn't do it. *Picture Nathan alone,* she told herself.

Heavy brows, and eyes that were a little hooded. Cheekbones to die for, and a mouth that was all the sexier for being rather unsmiling. Beth felt a pang of guilt, because Rob had always been grinning and teasing and flirting, but she ignored it. *Nathan,* she reminded herself. Not Rob.

Short wavy hair he did his best to subdue. Steady quiet eyes. Emotions suppressed, ghosts behind those eyes, flickering sometimes in a cheek muscle, but rarely overt. She tried to imagine him angry, really angry, or shouting with laughter or—

A wave of heat washed through her. "Oh, God," she moaned. "What am I doing?"

Arousing herself apparently. Forgetting they were going to be friends. Remembering the grit in his voice when he'd said, "Under other circumstances, I'd have given a lot to go up to your bedroom with you." And, "You're Rob's widow. If you weren't..."

If she wasn't, she'd want him. She *did* want him. She admitted that much to herself. No question, no hesitation. He turned her on.

But how much was memory, because her husband had turned her on, too, and how much was the present? How much was Nathan?

She was terribly afraid that sooner or later she'd have to find out. But how?

As it turned out, she didn't sleep better tonight, not with such thoughts tumbling about in her head. Her unease wasn't improved by having to lie to Mandy come morning about what she'd be doing while Mandy went swimming with her friend Barbara.

"Oh, just a pile of paperwork..." She pretended to

think. "I might run to the grocery store, so if you call and can't reach me, don't worry."

Mandy gazed at her without blinking for a moment that stretched a little too long, then gave a small nod. "Okay." She cocked her head. "I hear a car. That must be Barbara's mom."

Don't let it be Nathan, Beth prayed. *Don't let him have decided to come early.* "Sunscreen lotion," she said. "If you stay long, don't forget to put more on."

Her daughter curled her lip. "Mom, I'm not dumb."

A glance out the window reassured Beth that the car in front was indeed Barbara's mother's station wagon. "No, you're just a kid." Mandy accepted Beth's hug with more grace than she sometimes did. "Kids are dumb. They don't get smart until they turn twenty-five."

Real indignation sounded this time. "Mom!"

She laughed. "Just kidding. Have fun."

Not until Mandy darted out the door, slamming it behind her, did Beth let out a sigh. How would Mandy feel when she learned Beth had been hiding something as central to their lives as a pregnancy? Would she ever trust her again?

Nathan showed up precisely on time, which she should have expected. He was well aware, after all, that Mandy wouldn't know where her mother was going today. Beth had offered to meet him at the doctor's office, but he'd shaken his head.

"I'd rather drive you. It'll give us time to talk."

She'd agreed; after all, they were going to be friends, right? Maybe, she thought hopefully, there was something to the saying that familiarity breeds contempt. She'd rather feel contempt than...whatever it was she did feel.

She couldn't quite work up anything approaching contempt this morning, however, not with him looking as good as he did in faded jeans, boots and a cream-colored, pearl-snapped cowboy shirt. He paused beside his car and gazed up at the house, that brooding face unreadable. Nor did his expression change when she came out onto the porch, though he nodded and said, "'Morning."

Beth felt unaccountably shy. "Hi. I'm all set."

He came around and opened her car door. "Where's Mandy?"

"Swimming with a friend."

He frowned. "She's taken lessons?"

Touched rather than offended by his concern, she smiled. "Yes. She won't drown."

He slammed the door, came around and got in behind the wheel. He reached for the keys, then turned to look at her, instead. "It's just that she's so frail."

"I know," Beth said softly.

"You're better at this than I am."

"No. I worry all the time."

He saw in her eyes that it was the truth, and he nodded. A moment later he started the engine.

They didn't talk about Mandy again, or last night's conversation, or their dreams, or even the baby. She was grateful when he said, "Looks like we're getting a big order from a sporting-goods chain back East. We're going to have to bump up production."

She congratulated him, encouraged him to talk, even discussed some marketing efforts of her own. All the while, she couldn't seem to tear her eyes from his hands. At the moment they were competently wrapped around the steering wheel. Every once in a while, as traffic slowed or sped up, he'd reach over to change gears, nearly brushing her thigh.

His hands were large, tanned, the nails clipped short. Pure male in their size and strength and bluntness, they made her feel safe.

Startled by the thought, she wondered where it had come from. Safe? She wasn't exactly in danger. Mandy was, but Nathan McCabe couldn't save her with brute strength or gentleness or determination.

Maybe not, but something in the sight of his hand every time he rested it on Mandy's thin shoulder cramped Beth's heart. She could easily picture him cradling a baby in those hands, too, dwarfing the small body even as he protected it. He'd scarcely touched her, yet Beth knew in every fiber what his hands would feel like on her.

And not because she knew Rob's touch. His had been different, she thought, looking away at last, gazing blindly out her side window as the car crossed the Evergreen Point Bridge. Rob hadn't been physical the way his brother was. His hands had been thinner, better cared for, the nails smooth, his fingertips uncallused. He'd hated the hard labor when she'd coaxed him to help tie up the long whippy canes of the raspberries or plant rows of strawberries. Only under the hood of a car was he willing to get really dirty or take a chance of scraping a knuckle.

More differences. She might end up like the mother of twins she knew who'd confessed that her two girls hardly looked alike to her and was always surprised when others confused them. Beth was pretty sure that if Nathan and Rob were both standing in front of her, she'd know one from the other immediately. So why was her dreaming mind so muddled?

She started to give Nathan directions to the clinic before remembering that he'd been there, and why. If he noticed her embarrassment, he didn't comment.

Her doctor's office was situated just off Broadway on Capitol Hill in Seattle. It was an area of trendy shops, busy sidewalks and scant parking. Fortunately the clinic had its own small lot. Inside, the middle-aged receptionist, Margaret, was saying hello to Beth when her eyes traveled to Nathan. They widened and she sucked in a breath.

"Mr. McCabe?" she whispered.

Oh, Lord. Dr. Williams had delivered Mandy, and the receptionist had worked here then. She'd known Rob. Beth recalled that she *wasn't* here the day the sperm was implanted. Without knowing the circumstances, no wonder she looked so shocked.

"My brother-in-law," Beth said hastily. "He's Mr. McCabe, too."

"Nathan." He held out a hand. "We were twins."

Margaret shook it, while she pressed her other hand to her chest. "I'm terribly sorry! I thought I was seeing a ghost!"

"No problem." But the crease between his brows had deepened, and Beth had the impression he was bothered by being mistaken even momentarily for Rob.

The nurse who called Beth's name was new, so she chatted under the apparent impression that they were married as she ushered them in. She checked Beth's weight and blood pressure—"Just dandy!" she chirped—before leaving them in an examining room and promising that Dr. Williams would be in shortly.

Beth would have sworn the room had shrunk since she was last here. Waiting alone was one thing; who cared if there wasn't space to do a pirouette? The stark decor and lack of window always had her feeling vaguely claustrophobic, but nothing like today. Today she wanted to bolt. Nathan's shoulders seemed several inches wider even than usual; he towered over her as she perched on the end of the examining table. What on earth had possessed her to invite him?

Maybe her panic showed on her face, because he turned abruptly away. She sensed, though, that his reason for retreating was instantly forgotten when he noticed a chart on the wall showing the fetus at different stages.

"He looks like a baby," he said suddenly.

"He? Oh." She touched her stomach. "You mean ours."

"Yeah. That picture says three months. That's what you are, right?"

"Yes," she told his back.

"Somehow I didn't think—" He stopped.

She had to swallow to hold down a tide of emotion. "It's…it's hard to believe, isn't it?"

He turned toward her again. She wanted to launch herself into his arms, cry a few tears against his chest; she didn't know why. She was actually scooting forward when the door swung open and Dr. Williams hustled in.

"Sorry to keep you waiting." Her dark eyes studied Nathan. "Mr. McCabe, good to meet you. I'm glad to see you here."

"Why?" he asked.

Another doctor might have been taken aback by his blunt question; Dr. Williams just raised an eyebrow and replied with equal bluntness, "Because it bodes well for your involvement once the baby is born."

His mouth lifted in a half smile. "I'll be there."

"Good." The doctor turned to Beth. "How're you feeling?"

Beth answered the usual questions while she lay back on the crinkly paper and let Dr. Williams lift her shirt. She had a flashback to the insemination, when she had stared at the same poster on the ceiling and imagined the man who now stood only a few feet away, his eyes fixed with seeming fascination on her bare belly.

The doctor's hands deftly probed. "The fetus should be about three inches long at this stage," she said. "Weighing maybe an ounce. Fingers and toes all formed. A twelve-week fetus even has fingerprints. If we could look, we'd see what sex your baby is."

Nathan hadn't moved, just stared. He didn't even appear to notice that Beth was watching him, not the doctor.

"Well, let's find that heartbeat," Dr. Williams announced, pulling her stethoscope from around her neck.

Listening intently, she paused, moved the bell-shaped diaphragm a few inches on Beth's abdomen, paused again. At last she smiled. "There we go. Steady and brisk. Mr. McCabe, would you care to hear your child's heartbeat?"

"Yeah." His voice was gravelly, as Beth was learning it always was when he felt a powerful emotion. "I'd care to."

He took a couple of steps forward and bent his head to place the tips of the stethoscope in his ears. He was so close Beth could see the blunt dark fan of his lashes against his cheeks, a tic at the corner of his mouth, the whorls of his ear and the lines beside his eyes. He went completely still, not even breathing.

At last he lifted a stunned gaze. "Incredible," he murmured.

"It is, isn't it?" Dr. Williams matter-of-factly took the stethoscope from him and pulled Beth's shirt down over her midriff. "Well, Beth, I'll see you in another month. Looks like things are going just as they should be. You ought to find the nausea disappearing in these next few weeks."

She nodded. "It did last time."

From the corner of her eye, she saw Nathan step back. The doctor breezed out a moment later and Beth sat up.

"That's it?" Nathan asked, voice still husky.

"I told you it was routine."

"Maybe for you. Not for me."

"Well…it's not as if I've been through this half-a-dozen times." Glad it was over, she retrieved her purse and slipped by him when he held open the door for her.

He waited while she made another appointment, then suggested, "How about some lunch?"

"I should get home.…"

"Why? Mandy's not due back yet, is she?"

"Well, no."

"Then?"

A date. It felt like a first date, and with the father of her unborn baby. *Stop this!* Beth told herself sharply. He was being polite. They were supposed to become friends.

Nonetheless, when she agreed with a casual-sounding "Why not?" she felt reckless, a little excited. And when his hand, steering her out the door, touched her lower back, heat settled between her legs.

She couldn't regret having been married to Rob, she

thought desperately. She'd loved him. They'd had good years together, and Mandy. She *was* his widow. So how could she be letting herself feel these things for Rob's brother?

CHAPTER SEVEN

"HAPPY BIRTHDAY, dear Amanda," everyone sang, "happy birthday to you!"

Mandy's tears blurred the faces around the table; she had to sniff. The five friends she'd invited to her party grinned at her. Uncle Nate was snapping pictures while Mom, who'd carried the cake from the kitchen, stood beaming to one side.

Gazing down at the twelve flickering candles, Mandy took a deep breath, made her wish and then blew. Everybody clapped because she'd blown them all out. That meant her wish would come true, right?

Maybe. The hope was like the wisps of smoke still rising from the candles even as Mom pulled them from the cake. Her wishes other years hadn't exactly come true, but they hadn't *not* come true, either. She was alive, wasn't she? Maybe Mom was right and the last chemotherapy really *had* made her better. Maybe the baby... She wouldn't let herself think about that.

"Big piece?" Mom asked her. She held the knife poised above the lemon yellow cake.

"Yeah, and I want lots of ice cream," Mandy said.

Uncle Nate put down the camera and started scooping vanilla ice cream onto the plates as Mom handed them to him. For a second he looked just like Dad. Well, she guessed he always looked like Dad, but just not quite as much as now, or at least she wasn't aware of it. But she'd sat in this same chair her last birthday that Dad was alive——her eighth, she decided, counting back. She squinted until today's party almost blended into the one she remembered, when Dad had teased her friends and slapped big helpings of ice cream onto their slices of cake. Pink cake; she'd been really into princesses and fairies and stuff like that then. Kid stuff. Kayla and April and Samantha had been at that party, too, she was pretty sure. They'd been friends a long time.

By her ninth birthday, Dad was dead and Mandy was in the hospital. The doctors had let Mom bring a cake in, and they'd all gathered around and sung "Happy Birthday" to her. Her only friend there was Jessica, in the next bed. She had a piece of birthday cake, too.

Mandy shook away the memories. She wouldn't think about Jessica, not today. This was her birthday, for Pete's sake! She was celebrating. Now she was a teenager. Well, almost a teenager.

Uncle Nate left after he'd had a piece of cake. She gave him a hard squeeze around the waist and whispered, "Thank you." His present had been tickets to a Broadway musical coming to the Fifth Avenue Theatre in Seattle. Four tickets, so she could take a friend and Mom could come, too.

He gave her a big smile and said, "Happy birthday, kiddo."

She and her friends spread their sleeping bags on blown-up air mattresses in front of the TV in the family room. She'd chosen two movies, which happened to have cute boys in them. The girls whispered and giggled, and later Mom brought them popcorn and soda.

At first, after the lights went off, they talked about starting middle school and what it would be like to have so many different teachers and classrooms and whether the eighth-grade boys would be any more grown-up than the ones their own age that they'd been stuck with forever.

It was later, when the whispers were getting further apart, that Barbara's voice came softly to Mandy. "You're not sick anymore, right?"

Mandy hadn't told her friends that her leukemia was incurable without the transplant. "I guess not," she said, trying to sound careless. "I might still have that bone-marrow transplant, if the doctors can ever find anyone whose blood matches mine."

"Why?" Kayla asked.

Mandy gave the easiest answer. "Just to be sure."

"Oh," another girl murmured.

Into the silence Mandy said, "Do you ever think about dying? I mean, just not being here? Like not ever turning thirteen?"

An answer was a long time coming. Finally April said sleepily, "I don't like to think about it. That'd mean I'd never be able to date, or drive a car, or kiss a boy, or…"

Barbara flopped over onto her stomach. "I don't want to kiss a boy. If anyone ever kissed me, it'd probably be somebody like Brian Robb."

They all squealed. Brian was this total nerd. He practically fell over his feet he was so big and clumsy. Mandy guessed he wasn't dumb or anything, but he always tried to be funny and he wasn't. Besides, he had big lips. She shuddered.

Somehow the other girls were talking about boys again and especially about kissing. Death wasn't real to them, not the way it was to her. They didn't know about the plaques lining the hallway at Children's Hospital, each with the name of a child who'd died. She couldn't talk to any of them, any more than she could to Mom.

Jessica popped into her mind again and she knew why. One night in the hospital Jessica had whispered to Mandy, "I used to say I never wanted to get breasts."

"They're gross, aren't they?" Mandy had agreed. She'd only been eight years old then; she couldn't imagine wanting blobs bobbing up and down on her chest when she ran or jumped.

After a long pause Jessica said in a low voice, "Yeah, but I really, really didn't want them. I think I was trying to give God an order."

"I bet he doesn't take that kind of order." Mandy frowned, staring at the light showing under the door. "Or maybe any kind of order."

Jessica was silent a long time. She sounded funny, kind of choked up, when she whispered, "I hope not."

I hope not? It took Mandy a second to realize what Jessica was afraid of. She was afraid she'd wished so hard not to get breasts God was giving her that wish. The only way He could keep her from getting the breasts was not to let her grow up.

"I bet lots of girls wish they wouldn't get breasts," she'd told Jessica. "God doesn't pay any attention to dumb little-kid wishes like that."

Jessica hadn't said anything else. Mandy'd almost forgotten the conversation. It had come back to her one day not very long ago when she'd been staring at her naked body in the mirror after her shower. She was getting hair and boobs and everything. It partly *was* gross and partly kind of exciting. Life *had* to be more exciting when you got to be a real teenager. And she wanted to grow up. She didn't just assume she would, like most kids probably did. She wanted it with an active passionate hunger that beat along with her heart. She wished Jessica had made it to being twelve years old, too. That she'd gotten breasts, so she could see that God wouldn't be so cruel.

Only, He *had* been, because Jessica didn't get to grow up. What Mandy didn't understand was why. Why Jessica? Why did some of the kids leave the hospital and never look back? Why was she still alive?

She wished she knew if there was a God at all.

"Jessica," she whispered, but nobody answered. Her friends were asleep, and Jessica never *had* answered once she was gone.

"COOL! WE NEVER COME to the zoo," Mandy exclaimed in satisfaction.

"Now that's not true," Beth protested. "We just haven't come *this* summer." Or last summer, she remembered; Mandy had been too sick.

Nathan eased the car into a slot in the zoo parking lot and turned off the engine. "I haven't been to a zoo in years."

"They've changed," Beth told him. "The animals aren't in little cages looking miserable anymore. Wait'll you see the lion enclosure and the elephants. Oh, and the wolves."

"I like the prairie dogs," Mandy contributed, already out of the car. In defiance of her mother's insistence that she wear a hat to keep from getting sunburned, her baseball cap was on backward. She looked boyish and gangly and cute.

Beth decided not to make an issue of the hat for now. After all, her daughter, like herself, was slathered with sunscreen. And she had to be protective about some things. It was just hard knowing when to quit.

They paid and entered. Mandy stopped immediately. "Can I climb the tree?"

Other kids already were. The huge fir spread its wide ancient branches parallel to the ground. A toddler bounced delightedly on one thick branch crying, "Giddyap, giddyap!" while her father supported her. Boys dared each other to go higher.

Nathan said, "Sure. Want a boost?"

Beth opened her mouth automatically to argue, then shut it. Right now Mandy was as well as she might ever be. No reason she couldn't climb a tree.

Beth reached out and touched a branch, the bark worn smooth by the scrape of countless jeans and tennis shoes. Helped up by her uncle Nate, Mandy clambered gingerly around, her smile as joyous as the toddler's. Suddenly she jumped, hitting the ground hard and falling to her hands and knees.

Beth gasped, but Mandy hopped up and said, "Come on. I want to see the giraffes."

They wandered from the African safari, where giraffes, antelopes and zebras grazed together, to the glass-fronted enclosure where lions sunned themselves on rocks only feet away. One lioness prowled at the edge of a pool, her eyes on something beneath the water's surface. She moved much like Calvin and Polly, with that boneless grace, yet each enormous paw was bigger than either kitten's whole body.

Mandy reached out and squeezed Beth's hand. Beth felt Nathan standing behind her, so close his warmth enfolded her. It took her back, this tableau.

Family. She and Rob and Mandy used to come to the Woodland Park Zoo three or four times a year, sometimes even in the winter, and wandered just like this. Coming here was never Rob's idea. He'd always groan and say, "But we were just there!" But if she and Mandy decided to go alone, he'd be waiting at the car, and once here he'd always be standing just behind her or boosting Mandy onto his shoulders so she could see better.

"Look!" Mandy cried now.

Beth's attention returned abruptly to the lioness. She caught the animal in midleap, then watched as it hit the water with a huge splash. As quickly, the lioness vaulted back onto the bank, a large fish flopping in her great jaws. The lioness gave her head a shake, the fish went still, and she crouched with her back to the glass to devour her prey.

Mandy chattered excitedly about the successful hunt even as they moved on to see the otters and the mountain goats, the elk and timber wolves. As Beth strolled across the grass, she watched Mandy and Nathan up ahead. Her daughter's cap was still on backward, her legs long and skinny beneath her cutoffs. Beside her, Nathan wore faded denim jeans and a dark green T-shirt that emphasized the breadth of his shoulders. Dark glasses partly masked his expressions.

They reached the enclosure with the wallaroos, and he and Mandy propped their elbows on the low fence. He threw back his head and laughed at something she said, the flash of teeth awakening his guarded face to a charm that matched Rob's. Maybe that was why Beth felt the odd lurch in the vicinity of her heart.

Or maybe not, she admitted with a private sigh. The sight of him had been giving her pleasure all morning; he moved with a grace as contained as the big cats', as sure and even arrogant. She imagined him in the

mountains, hefting a heavy pack easily or feeling his
way surefootedly up a rock face. She was agonizingly
conscious of the play of muscles and tendons when he
lifted a hand to snatch off Mandy's hat and ruffle her
hair. A play of muscles and tendons so like Rob's.

Or was it?

She shook her head, annoyed at her confusion. At
first, she'd seen Nathan as a reflection of her husband,
a shadow. When he lifted an eyebrow, she'd see Rob
doing the same. Now she'd find herself thinking, *Rob
did that,* and then wasn't positive he had. Maybe she'd
seen the same expression on Nathan's face before and
was mixing that up with her memories of her husband.

She reached them, and they both turned naturally to
include her. "Slowpoke," Nathan teased. When
Mandy hurried inside to see the wallaroos more
closely, he lowered his voice. "Feel okay?"

"Yep. Except I'm as hungry as that lion."

"You want sushi, too?"

She made a face at him, her dark mood vanishing.
"A hot dog will do very nicely, thank you. And a snow
cone. I saw someone with one."

His smile this time was lazy and more than charming. Sexy. "You're a cheap date."

"We'll make you take us someplace really expensive for dinner before that Fifth Avenue musical," she
promised, feeling suddenly lighthearted. "I'll show
you how cheap I am."

As casually as though he did it every day, Nathan
laid an arm across her shoulders. "Is that a threat?"

She caught a scent of pure male, felt the weight of
his arm, the heat of his body. Her voice sounded a little
husky to her ears. "Depends on how prosperous you're
feeling."

"I've never had a family to spend money on before. You know I'd be willing to help with everyday expenses."

She was both touched and made uneasy. He'd inserted himself so deftly, so relentlessly, into their lives she could scarcely turn around anymore without finding him there, or some reminder of him. What if she decided she didn't *want* him around all the time? What if these confusing feelings really began to frighten her? How would she say, *Go away?* How would she keep Mandy from being hurt?

He must have felt her stiffen, because his arm dropped and he gave her an unreadable look before moving ahead to rejoin Mandy. Beth was annoyed with herself to realize she felt bereft, even a little jealous again of Mandy's easy relationship with him. And his with her. Beth wondered whether Mandy, too, was seeing her father in him. Did she ever get at all confused, or did she, because of her age, just not remember Rob as well as her mother did?

"I see a concession stand," Nathan said. "How about if we eat in the shade of that tree?" He pointed.

"Yeah, and then we can go in the nocturnal house," Mandy replied eagerly. "The snakes are in there, too."

"And the cockroaches." Beth shuddered.

"They have a display of cockroaches?" Nathan sounded incredulous.

"Behind glass." She couldn't help another shudder. "Heaps and heaps of them. Huge ones. They give me the creeps. I'll take a rattlesnake any day."

"I'm not too crazy about snakes," he confessed. "I, uh, hike reluctantly in rattlesnake country."

A crafty look crossed Mandy's face.

"No," Beth told her. "Don't even think it."

Nathan turned. "Think what?"

"Mo-om. I wouldn't do something like that."

"Like what?" he asked again.

Beth ignored him. "If you hadn't been thinking it, Amanda McCabe, you wouldn't know what I'm talking about."

"I wouldn't have *really* scared him," Mandy said sulkily.

"You have a snake," he said.

"Just a pretend one."

"And it's extraordinarily realistic," Beth said severely. "This charming child put it in the vat where I make jam, out in the barn. I just about had a heart attack."

"I'd have had one." He proceeded to poke fun at himself as he told a story about meeting an enormous rattlesnake on a trail in Baja California. "A cliff going up on one side, dropping into the ocean on the other," Nathan said. "No way around. He was all coiled up, his tail rattling."

"Maybe it was *her* tail," Beth said.

"Nasty as it sounded, you're probably right," he agreed, then grinned as she poked him.

They took their hot dogs and pop to a shady spot and sprawled on the grass, Nathan on his side, head propped on his hand. Beth's gaze kept wandering down his body to places where his jeans were especially worn, and she had to repeatedly yank herself in. Damn it, she wished he'd sit up, not loll there like a man lazily lying on his bed watching a woman undress.

She swallowed hard. Where had *that* come from? All he was doing was relaxing and telling a story. About snakes.

"I waited all afternoon," he told them. "Once I tried

poking it with a stick, but all it did was coil tighter and rattle until it sounded like a tornado whipping the sagebrush. So I just moseyed back a little, gave him—her—plenty of space, but it just kept those cold eyes fixed on me.''

Her own eyes wide, Mandy leaned forward. ''So what'd you *do?*''

''Retraced my steps, walked a couple of miles across rough country until I hit a road and hitched a ride with a truckload of Mexican laborers.''

Amused, Beth asked, ''And did you admit to them why you were on the road with your thumb out?''

There was that smile again, the one that sent a shiver down her spine. ''You kidding? I implied, in my limited Spanish, that a bandit had held me up. Even though I'd been lucky enough to get away, I figured he'd be waiting for me down the trail.''

His story ended, Mandy began crumbling her bun and feeding the birds waiting for handouts. Nathan rolled onto his back and closed his eyes. Contentedly Beth watched her daughter. Mandy looked as happy as she'd ever seen her.

In part that was because of the man whose breaths slowed and deepened even as the tension left his face. His forearms were lean and brown; his fingers were splayed on his flat belly. Beth let herself look her fill, from his strong brown neck to his crossed ankles and the worn running shoes on his size-eleven feet.

She was amused and intrigued by the shoes. Nathan ran a sporting-goods manufacturing company; shouldn't he always wear the latest in high-tech, gel-filled running shoes, spandex and breathable PolarTec? His business suits looked well made and pretty sharp, but most of the clothes she'd seen him in appeared to be old friends, far from the cutting edge of sporting apparel.

She was glad. As uninterested as she was in fashion, she wouldn't have felt comfortable with a man who blow-dried his hair and showed off sculpted thigh muscles in shiny spandex. She found more than enough to enjoy in the way the faded denim hugged his narrow hips and long legs.

Beth wanted, with a fierceness that shook her, to sit astride his hips. She wanted him to roll over and pin her down, take off those dark glasses so she could see the intensity in his eyes. She wanted that big hand on her breast, that grim mouth to capture hers. She wanted—

With a near physical wrench, she closed her eyes and averted her face. Why him? she wondered in despair. Why not one of the other men who, in the past couple of years, had suggested dinner or dancing or a show? Why the one man for whom her emotions would inevitably be so complicated?

Damn you, Rob, why did you have to die? She struggled to picture her husband. A moment of passion, tenderness, the kind of intensity with which Nathan would make love to a woman. She saw Rob bending his head, but he was laughing, teasing, coaxing. All she could remember was lighthearted lovemaking. Had he ever slammed into her, his emotions raw? Had he ever completely lost control? Had she ever *wanted* him to? Why was she wondering now why she hadn't felt a bone-deep need to see him utterly vulnerable to her alone?

Her memory had to be faulty. She'd loved Rob. She was happy with him. She'd enjoyed his touch, his teasing, the way he made everything fun. She must have seen stark emotion on his face, heard aching need in his voice. She was just forgetting, which gave her a panicky sense that she had to scrabble for everything she did remember, clutch it tight or else it, too, would be gone.

That had to be the need that drew her to Rob's brother. *Just be smart,* Beth told herself. *Now that you recognize these feelings for what they are, you can ignore them. They'll go away.*

She opened her eyes, faced him. He had rolled onto his side again, his head propped on his elbow, and was watching her.

She said the first thing that came to mind. "Rob…" Her voice died.

His mouth hardened. "I'm not Rob."

"I know. I didn't mean…"

"What did you mean?"

Beth had no idea. "I don't know," she admitted. "I was…thinking about him."

He grunted and rose fluidly to his feet. "I suppose I stepped into his shoes today."

"No." Less gracefully she scrambled up. "No, it's not the same at all. I… I've been doing a lot of thinking lately. Maybe because…" Mandy was coming toward them, so Beth made a quick gesture toward her belly. "Just don't confuse us."

The grit in his voice reminded her of how bitterly the brothers had once quarreled. She'd give a great deal to know what they'd fought about. She knew better than to ask right now.

"Look, they're giving pony rides," Mandy said, bouncing on her toes when she reached them. "I wish I weren't too big."

"I'd forgotten how much you loved them." Beth didn't look toward Nathan. "Do you remember the neighbor who had a horse? They were always offering you rides, but you were scared to be so high off the ground. The ponies here are such miniature ones.''

"It embarrassed Dad when I got scared," Mandy blurted. Her eyes widened, as though the memory took her by surprise. "I guess…I guess he was so brave he wanted me to be, too.''

"Reckless, you mean," Beth muttered. "It was some kind of macho thing. I'm glad he didn't infect you with it.''

"Can girls be macho?" her daughter asked.

"Darn right! Some women seem determined to be as stupid as men.''

The clearing of a masculine throat reminded her of Nathan's presence.

"Present company excepted," Beth added, flushing a little.

"Thank you," he said dryly. "But, Mandy, let me tell you something I've realized recently. Your dad was like that because our mother pushed us to be competitive. We always had to do everything better than everybody else, faster. We had to win. She didn't want to hear excuses. We weren't allowed to cry. So, yeah, women can be like that. And it wasn't your dad's fault he was.''

Mandy's gaze was grave. "But you're not."

"Yeah." A muscle in his jaw worked. "Yeah, I am. Just in a different way. I don't speed behind the wheel of a car. Instead, I've been a workaholic the past fifteen years. Success was more important than anything. And, uh—" he moved his shoulders uneasily "—your dad and I wouldn't have stayed mad at each other so long if we weren't both stubborn. If he'd admitted he was wrong, or if I had, that would have meant losing. Neither of us could do that.''

Mandy's brow creased beneath the backward baseball cap. "But—" She stopped.

"Yeah. It was stupid as hell, wasn't it?"

"I think it was sad," she told him.

He grimaced. "Just remember, you never embarrassed your dad. Not really. He wasn't that big an idiot. I'll bet you were the sun and moon to him."

"He said I was his princess."

Nathan smiled crookedly. "Same thing."

"Has anybody ever been *your* sun and moon?" she asked artlessly.

He was silent for a moment as they walked, his face closed. "Oh, a time or two I thought a woman was," he finally said. "There was a girl in college." The memory didn't seem to be a happy one. "And I was married some years ago. Not for long. Julianne got tired of my schedule and my—" He broke off abruptly.

"Did you call her darling?" Mandy asked next. She'd been listening avidly. "Or...or baby or sweetie?"

"Mandy!" Beth gave her daughter a quelling look.

"It's okay." Nathan grinned at Mandy. "Maybe a man'll call you 'nosy babe' someday."

Unrepentant, she made a face. "Nobody tells me anything if I don't ask."

"True enough. Okay. I seem to recall referring to my wife as Jewel. That's as romantic as I got."

"That's not bad," Mandy told him kindly.

His tone was dry. "Thank you."

"Daddy called Mom—"

"Don't you dare," Beth interrupted.

"Berry pie," her indiscreet daughter continued

blithely. "He used to call her sugar pie, but then after she started making jam, he changed it."

Beth poked Mandy with her elbow. "It was a joke. He didn't call me that..."

"...at more romantic moments?" Nathan suggested when she didn't finish.

She flushed.

"Shall we let your mom off the hook?" he asked Mandy.

"Or out of the pie!" She giggled hysterically and scampered ahead when Beth made a lunge for her.

Nathan said quietly, "You're not upset with her, are you?"

Beth assumed an air of dignity. "I'd put up with any humiliation to see her laugh like that."

"Good." The smile he gave her was warm, friendly, uncomplicated. He reached out and took her hand. "Let's go see the gorillas."

Sweetness pierced her at the feel of that big hand enveloping hers, tugging her along. If only his gesture were more than friendly—

No! She clamped down on the thought. Thank God his gesture was only friendly. Because if Nathan ever laid a hand on her in passion, she had no idea how she would react.

CHAPTER EIGHT

NOBODY HAD COME in response to the doorbell. Nathan lifted his hand and knocked firmly. Mandy must be home; he'd passed the school bus out on the road.

The knock echoed. He repeated it. Still no one came. His anticipation seeping into disappointment, Nathan turned and surveyed the fields, as tidy as when he'd first seen them last spring. The raspberries had already been pruned and tied up. He'd helped with the job, which had proved simple enough, but damned unpleasant. This year's canes, drying up, had to be unwound from the wire supports and cut off at the base, then hauled in bundles to a low spot behind the barn where Beth let them compost. It had been hot and airless between the rows when he crouched to snip canes. Sweating more than he did in a ten-K race, he couldn't bear to wear a long-sleeved shirt, which meant he'd ended up with scratches all over his forearms.

He loosened his tie. Maybe Beth and Mandy were in the barn. He crossed the yard and entered the shadowy stuffy interior through the half-open door. A rustle came from a heap of straw to one side, which Beth used for mulching. Polly was flinging around an already dead mouse and then pouncing on it again. She snatched it up and uttered a small growl when she saw him looking.

"It's all yours," he told her. He raised his voice. "Anyone here?"

Silence. He found the kitchen dim and still, everything spotlessly clean. The back of the barn was lined with rows of shelving units, filled to near capacity now with the summer's bounty. Some of the jars were boxed, others still single, the distinctive shape and the labels too classy for the concrete floor and open rafters and scent of hay and long-aged manure.

Well, hell. He'd made a trip out here for nothing. He should have called. He'd come on impulse after flying in to Sea-Tac Airport. He'd been away for almost a week on business, the longest he'd gone without seeing Beth and Mandy since the P.I. had found him. On the road he'd caught himself thinking about them all the time, wondering what they were doing that minute, how Mandy liked middle school now that the first week's excitement had worn off, whether Beth ever thought about him. At night especially, trying to sleep in hotel beds, he pictured her curled up in hers, hair tousled, bare arms and shoulders golden from the sun, her window flung wide to let in the quiet sounds of night in the country. Sometimes his imagination left him more restless; other times it soothed him to sleep, as though he'd had to see them vividly to be sure Beth and Mandy would still be there, waiting when he got home.

When he'd pulled in, he'd half expected the front door to crash open and Mandy to pelt down the porch steps to fling herself into his arms. Beth would be close behind, shyly welcoming. Right. Father coming home from work, circa 1950s, he told himself dryly. Norman Rockwell. Only, he wasn't the father. This wasn't his home.

Even if it felt like it.

Nathan wandered out of the barn, then on impulse went around to the back. From here a dirt track led down to the creek. Mandy had dragged him down there once. At this time of year, the water must be low, maybe only deep enough for wading. Between blueberry bushes whose leaves were turning yellow, he caught a glimpse of green coolness: a sparkle of water, alder leaves flashing green-silver in a faint breeze, lush tangled grass. And something else: a red shirt, a shimmer of pale gold hair. Beth.

Nathan moved without thinking, each step kicking up a puff of dust. A hot summer had stretched into a dry autumn. School had started two weeks ago. On the trees along the road, leaves were turning color already. They'd be falling, brittle and brown, in no time.

He didn't call out a greeting. Mandy would probably see him coming, anyway. If not, he wouldn't mind a moment to savor the sight of Beth before she spotted him. Maybe that made him a voyeur, but what the hell. He seldom saw her completely relaxed, unguarded. He made her wary, just as she made him.

Beth stood in the middle of the creek. She wore khaki shorts, rolled up several times and just showing beneath a sacky red T-shirt. The water rippled around her calves. Her legs, slim and tanned, seemed to go on forever. That was about all he could see of her. Her back was to him, her head bowed as she stared down into the water with great concentration, like a child hunting for pollywogs.

"Hi," he said at last, huskily.

She whirled and slipped, just catching herself from falling. Her mouth trembled, and either she'd splashed herself in the face, or she was on the verge of tears.

Tears, Nathan decided, seeing the strain in her wide gray eyes.

"You...you scared me."

"I'm sorry. I knocked and, uh, nobody came, and then I saw a flash of red down here." He felt as though he were walking on loose talus, the boulders rocking under his feet. They'd made progress, he'd have sworn they had, and yet now she radiated distress at the sight of him.

"It's...it's okay." She hugged herself. "I, um, I was just thinking. Pretty hard, I guess. I should've heard you coming."

Not for the first time, he wished she had a dog, instead of two half-grown cats. With her and Mandy here alone...

"Where's Mandy?" he asked, looking around.

"Oh—" Beth's smile was forced "—she went to a friend's place. Barbara's. Barbara just got a puppy. Mandy'll be home by five. I can have her call you."

Nathan nodded.

"Did you have a good trip?"

So, she'd noticed he was gone. But she wasn't suggesting he stay for dinner.

"Yeah," he said quietly. *No,* he wanted to tell her, *I was homesick.* He nodded toward a sort of pool where the water was deeper. "Were you going swimming?"

She bent over and trailed her fingers in the ripples. The curve of her neck and cheek moved him almost unbearably. "I don't know." This smile wasn't any better. "It's hot in the house. I just thought... I come down here sometimes. It's sort of Mandy's place. She doesn't know I use it, too."

"The creek?"

"And under the willow. In there, I feel…enfolded by the tree. Did she show you?"

"No. The creek was higher, and I was dressed about like I am today."

He had the sense she was really looking at him for the first time. "You're a stick-in-the-mud. Why don't you take off your shoes and come in?"

What the hell. He sat down on the grass and unlaced his dress shoes, pulled off his socks, started rolling up his slacks. Knowing Beth was watching him was enough to make his fingers fumble.

"All right." He wriggled his toes in the grass, then stood. "Ready or not."

"Not." She said it so softly he knew he wasn't meant to hear.

He didn't have to hear it. He'd already known. Nonetheless, he stepped into the chill water and waded gingerly toward her. He hadn't rolled his pants up far enough. They were already wet.

When he was an arm's reach from her, Nathan said quietly, "Mandy's not sick, is she?"

"No." She put up a hand and pushed at her hair, tumbling as always from the giant clip on the back of her head. "Nothing's wrong. Not really."

"Not really?"

Beth sucked in a breath, closed her eyes. Her lashes sparkled like rays of sunlight, and he realized tears trembled on them.

"I don't know what's wrong with me," she whispered. "I'm strong. I've always been strong." Her lashes abruptly swept upward, and she stared fiercely at him. "I've started a business and done a damn good job. Rob died and I didn't fall apart. Mandy got sick and I coped. I've done just fine! So what is it now? Why do I keep crying?''

''Hormones—''

''It's not hormones!'' she snapped. ''It's…it's you!''

His brows drew together. ''What the hell are you talking about?''

''You'd make it easy for me to be weak, wouldn't you? You'd offer your strong shoulder, take care of Mandy, probably run my business. Well, I don't like it!''

She might as well have slugged him in the stomach. Numbly he said, ''You don't want me here at all.''

''I didn't say that!'' Her eyes glittered up at him.

''Then what did you say?'' Feeling sick, he hung on to an even tone by his fingernails.

Her face worked. ''I'm just… I'm afraid sometimes.''

''Of me.'' He ran a hand over his face. ''God.''

''No.'' Beth scrubbed her own cheeks. ''I didn't mean it.''

''Didn't you?''

Beneath the tan and the sprinkling of freckles, her face was pale. ''I'm afraid of myself.''

He swore softly. ''Because you want to lean your head on my shoulder.''

She gave a quick nod.

His throat damn near closed. ''I'm here.''

''Yes. I know.'' She didn't move.

He didn't dare. Could only wait her out.

''This morning…'' Beth's voice faltered. ''I was getting dressed. Mandy walked in on me.''

What the hell…? Then he understood. ''You're starting to show.''

Wordlessly she lifted her shirt. She hadn't been able

to get her shorts zipped all the way up or buttoned. The gentle swell of pale belly was another kick in his gut.

"She...she looked straight at my stomach."

"Did you say anything?"

Beth let the shirt fall. "Something dumb about eating too much. And I laughed! Oh, God. What's she going to say when I tell her?"

"You're doing it for her!"

"Yes." Beth swallowed a sob. "Yes, of course I am."

"Then what are you so worried about?"

Beth gave him an incredulous look. "Oh, only ten or twelve things. What do you *think* I'm worried about?"

He didn't let her divert him. "Telling Mandy. You're afraid she's going to feel angry or threatened or..." He spread his hands. "But I don't get it. She's a sensible kid. Why would she feel more threatened than any other child who finds out she's going to have a baby brother or sister?"

Beth closed her eyes. "Because I'm not married. Because I lied to her. Because this all might be pointless."

He got it at last. "Because you might have to say, 'I'm pregnant and I did it for you, but the baby's blood isn't compatible with yours.'"

"Yeah." Her mouth twisted and she looked away.

"Why don't you just tell her now?" he suggested gently. "Before she figures it out herself. Before you have the amniocentesis."

A distinct sniff came from Beth's direction. "I know you're right. It's just that I want to save her from..."

"Hope?"

"False hope."

"Maybe she doesn't need protecting. Maybe it

scares her more when you try to pretend everything is great.''

Her gaze sliced like a switchblade. ''You think I should take her down to the funeral home and let her choose her own casket?''

''Damn it,'' he said, ''you know that's not what I meant! But do you ever talk about the possibility that everything might *not* be great?''

''She's too young to think about death!''

''But not too young to die.''

He felt like a bastard when she clapped a hand to her mouth and he heard the tearing sound of a suppressed sob. He took a step toward her and brought his foot down on a sharp rock. He muttered a curse. ''Can we get out?''

He half expected her to suggest he depart and never come back. Instead, her shoulders slumped, and she turned and waded toward the far bank, where the strands of narrow green willow leaves hung like a curtain. Beth parted them and stepped onto the grassy bank. Nathan followed, unsure if he was expected to, but knowing he didn't want to leave Beth alone right now.

Inside was another world, a cavern under the sea, washed in pale green light that eddied like water chased by golden fingers of sunlight. But for the ripple of the creek and the whisper of breeze in the willow, the silence was near complete, the sense of separation and security curiously comforting.

''Like a womb,'' he murmured.

He hadn't meant her to hear him, but she nodded. ''It is, isn't it? I know Mandy spends hours here.''

''And you?''

''Oh, I come down once in a while.'' Her voice was

hushed. "I grew up on a farm. We had a tree and a creek just like this. It was my hideaway. I wanted Mandy to have one."

"Rob and I had a treehouse," Nathan offered. "Nothing fancy. Dad helped a little, but we did most of the work ourselves. We used to look down on people's heads and think they didn't know we were there. There's something...godlike about that."

"And kids feel so powerless."

"Yeah."

Beth's eyes met his directly. "Mandy most of all. How can she help it when she's so vulnerable?"

He let out a breath. "I was wrong, what I said out there. I'm sure you've talked to her about being sick and dying and everything else. I shouldn't assume, just because you're usually upbeat—"

"I haven't." Abruptly she sat, wrapping her arms around her knees. Her bent head muffled her words.

He stared at her. "Never?"

Beth shook her head without lifting it. She was barely audible. "At first I just couldn't! She wanted to, but it seemed...oh, like acknowledging it might really happen." She looked up at last, eyes damp and beseeching. "And then later...Mandy wouldn't talk to me. I mean, I haven't sat down and said, 'We're going to talk about dying.' But when I try to find out what she's worrying about or thinking, she puts me off. She does see a counselor at the hospital, and I've assumed..."

He dropped to his knees in front of her. "Quit blaming yourself," he said almost harshly. "Your reaction was normal. You probably didn't want to start crying in front of her."

"I should have pushed the issue later," she said dully. "I should have insisted she talk to me."

His mouth twisted. "Remember what you said about kids feeling powerless? If you'd intruded on her privacy, Mandy would have lost what little control over her life she has."

"Yes, but—"

"Mandy loves you. When she really needs to talk, she'll come to you."

Her eyes glistened like windowpanes on a rainy day. "You sound so sure."

Nathan gently wiped tears from her cheek. "She teases you. That's when I really hear her love."

She tilted her head to press her cheek against the back of his hand. "You always know what to say, don't you?"

His laugh grated. "You and I would've gotten along better if I were so damned tactful."

"I think," Beth whispered, "our troubles have more to do with…with *this*—" she touched her open mouth to his hand "—than with anything either of us has said."

He groaned and with both hands cupped her face, his touch rough. "Beth…"

Her gray eyes were hauntingly beautiful, her lips trembling. "Would you…would you kiss me?"

A surge of near agonizing hunger rocked him. He didn't give himself time to think. He pulled her up to meet him and crushed her mouth with his. She came eagerly, her lips parting, her breath warm and taste sweet.

Exhilaration rushed through him and he lost the power to think, could only feel. Her shoulders were as fine-boned as he'd dreamed, her back as narrow and supple. Her mouth was so damned soft, her throaty murmur intoxicating. He plunged his fingers into her hair, and the silky curls wrapped around them as though unwilling to release him.

His tongue plunged into her mouth, and hers met it. She nipped at his lower lip as he growled words of praise and desire and coaxing. His hands shook as he lifted that oversize T-shirt and pulled it over her head. He didn't give her time to react to the air on her skin, to protest. His mouth captured hers again and he bore her backward until she lay beneath him in the long grass.

He felt like a madman, need shoving him along as if he had a hand planted in the middle of his back. He'd die if he wasn't inside her in the next minute. She was his woman. She grew his seed, carried his baby. He undid the catch of her bra as he strung kisses down her throat, feeling the frenzied beat of her pulse. For one moment he lifted his head to gaze hungrily at her breasts, as pale as milk and delicately veined in blue. Her nipples were swollen, peaked for him to draw into his mouth.

Her skin was as soft as it looked. She gave a small cry when he kissed her breast, rubbed his cheek against her nipple, then stroked it with his tongue. She reached up and gripped his hair as he drew her nipple into his mouth and sucked strongly.

His loosened tie fell across her other breast. He ripped it from his neck, tore open the front of his shirt. He laid his hand over the mound of her belly and remembered the quick fluttering heartbeat. *His child.* Carried in her womb.

Beth's hands flattened on his bare chest; for a moment, stunned, he thought she was pushing him away.

But then she made a wondering sound in her throat and her hands slipped higher to knead his shoulder muscles. *Ah, God.*

He lifted his head again to look at her, neck arched, eyes foggy with passion, lips curved softly, curls loose and shimmery as the slender tree branches swayed and parted to let in narrow bands of sunlight. She was the picture of sensuality. Wanton. So why the hell did his chest tighten?

Because he wanted her eyes focused on *him*. Not gazing dreamily at nothing as her breasts rose and fell enticingly with each breath. Damn it, he wanted to know who she saw in her mind's eye!

"Beth…" he said huskily.

She made a murmured response.

Rob. Had she said Rob's name? His skin chilled and he rolled away from her, swearing.

Beth sat up, crossing her arms over her breasts. "What…what's wrong?"

He clenched his teeth and stared straight up at the canopy of willow. "I'm not Rob."

"I know you're not!" Her cheeks flushed.

"You just said 'Rob.'" His brother's name scraped his throat.

"I didn't!" She shot to her feet, Botticelli's Venus stepping from a seashell, curls tumbling around her white shoulders, arms protecting her bare breasts. "I didn't say anything! I just made a noise!"

He laid his forearm across his face. "It sure as hell sounded like—"

"It wasn't! But you can think what you damn well please!"

The rustle of clothing as she pulled on her T-shirt, the swish of branches, a splash and one muttered profanity, and she was gone. He lay there, eyes closed, and imagined her snatching up her sandals from the bank and then stalking up the hill without putting them on. That straight slender back, the proud angle of her head, those shining curls... His whole body clenched in anguish. God, he'd had her beneath him, skin as silky as he'd dreamed, breasts small but soft, her hips pushing up against his hand. And he'd blown it.

A groan tore from his chest. Why the hell couldn't he just have taken what was offered? She probably *hadn't* said "Rob." The sound had been rough and throaty, maybe no more than a wordless response to her own name. And he'd gone off the deep end. If she'd been any other woman...

But she wasn't. She was his brother's widow. He would not, could not, play Rob in her fantasies. Anyone else, but not Rob. Not his brother, who one too many times had played him, Nathan.

He had to know. He wanted Beth as he'd never wanted a woman in his life. He might even love her. But his instincts had been right from the beginning. He wasn't his brother. Until he was sure she knew that, he had to do a better job of keeping his hands off her.

WHAT HAD SHE ALMOST DONE? Beth curled into a ball on her bed, knees drawn up and arms squeezing herself. Oh God, oh God. *Had* she said "Rob"?

But she hadn't been *thinking* about Rob! She hadn't been thinking anything, only feeling.

Feeling a familiar rush of desire, the melting warmth running to her toes and fingers, the deep sense of urgency, the sweet tightening in her belly. But it wasn't familiar, she realized in shock, her eyes snapping open. Not familiar at all. The hunger in her blood was stronger, more desperate, than anything she'd felt before.

Yes, but maybe that was only because she'd been celibate for more than three years. She'd missed the closeness and gentle satisfaction of making love with her husband. Oh, how often she'd reached for him at first! Half-asleep, she couldn't understand why his side of the bed was empty. But as the months had stretched into a year, she'd become accustomed to being alone at night; after so long, she'd hardly been consciously aware of her loneliness. But surely, surely, her fierce response to Nathan's kisses and touch today could be explained by all those empty nights.

She made a small whimpering sound. Did she *want* that to be the explanation? Nathan hadn't mattered, only her own need?

And—oh, Lord, this was the part that really mattered—had she been pretending he was Rob?

But how could she have when Nathan's kisses and touch were so different? She had felt that difference with every fiber. It had excited her, she admitted, his intensity firing the urgency that had made her so quickly want sex, not just delicious foreplay. She had wanted him inside her right then. She had *needed* him.

And it wasn't Rob she needed. Not then, not now.

But she'd loved Rob! Beth thought in panic. How could she feel these things for his brother? She moaned again. What if Nathan had come into their lives when Rob was still alive? Would she still have been attracted, betraying her husband secretly, in thought if not in action?

Stiffly she uncurled herself and rolled onto her back,

staring up at the ceiling as she faced the bleak knowledge that she would almost rather have discovered she was pretending today. For that, she could have forgiven herself.

CHAPTER NINE

MANDY GAVE the glider a push and turned the page of her book. It was a second before she realized she'd heard a footstep. She looked up to find Mom had just come out onto the porch.

"I need to talk to you." Her mother sounded totally serious, the way she did when something bad had happened.

As quickly as her heartbeat sped up, fear raced through Mandy. She'd been for her regular checkup last week. The weird white blood cells must be multiplying again, shutting out the red ones. Her feet quit pushing and the glider stilled. She gave a small nod. "Okay."

Mom crossed the porch and sat down beside her. Calvin stood up on the railing, arched his back and stretched like a Halloween cat, then hopped onto Mom's lap. Somehow he'd become Mom's cat, and Polly was Mandy's.

Stroking Calvin's back as though unaware she was doing it, Mom gave a push and they began to swing. But she didn't say anything, and when Mandy stole a glance at her, her lips were tight.

After a moment she sighed. "Maybe I should have told you this a long time ago. I hope you'll understand why I didn't."

"But I only went…" Mandy trailed off, puzzled.

"Went?"

"Well, I thought… I mean, I did just have the blood test."

Mom gave a soft cry. "No, no. I haven't heard results. And you're feeling fine, aren't you? It's nothing like that. I'm sorry, I didn't think."

"That's okay." Mandy shrugged awkwardly. "But if you don't want to talk about me being sick…" Then it hit her. She'd wondered how long her mother thought she could hide her stomach. Jeez, even Mandy's friends were going to notice pretty soon.

"This is something else." Mom nibbled on her lower lip. "Although I'm doing it because of you."

"I know."

"The thing is…" Mom had continued talking as though she hadn't heard Mandy, but suddenly her head shot up. "You know what?"

"I know you're pregnant," Mandy said calmly. "And I know why. I heard you and Uncle Nate talking about it."

"When?"

"I don't know." She shrugged again, looking down at the book that still lay open in her lap. "A long time ago. When you were trying to get him to be the father."

Mom's breath whooshed out of her. "You've known since last spring?" she whispered.

Mandy pushed her glasses up. "Yeah."

"And you didn't say anything?"

She told the truth. "I figured if you didn't, I wouldn't."

"Oh, honey…" Mom moved to put an arm around her. Mandy stiffened and Mom's arm dropped. "You don't understand why I didn't tell you."

"I guess you didn't think it was my business."
Some of her resentment leaked into her voice.

"Of course it's your business!" Mom sounded indignant.

Yeah, right, Mandy thought. *Then why didn't you tell
me?*

As though she'd heard her, Mom said, "I didn't
want you to worry. Or...or hope. Like you did when
we found Uncle Nate and thought he might have the
right kind of blood."

Mandy didn't believe her. Hoping for something
wasn't that bad. It was better than *not* hoping. What
she thought was that Mom had given up after Uncle
Nate wasn't a match. If Mom thought she, Mandy, was
going to die, then it made sense for her to have another
baby, didn't it? That way she wouldn't be left all alone.

Mandy tried not to mind. Or not too much, anyway.
She didn't doubt her mother's love. Mom had loved
Dad, too. Think how awful it would be for her, with
Dad and her only kid both dead. So if Mom had another baby, it wouldn't be as bad for her. She wouldn't
be as lonely.

Only, Mandy felt even lonelier and more frightened
to know that her mother wouldn't miss her as much,
that she'd be busy cooing at some baby and teaching
him his colors and to read and to swing. Maybe the
willow tree would be his.

Knowing how much Mom would grieve for her had
been one way Mandy reassured herself that dying
wouldn't be like God zapping her and saying, "You're
gone. You never existed." If she was really, really
missed, that meant some part of her spirit was still here,
right? But if she wasn't really, really missed...

Mandy's stomach clenched. She didn't want to talk about it. She just nodded. "It's okay," she said again.

"The thing is, I'll have an amniocentesis in about a month. That's when they stick a needle into my stomach and take out some of the fluid. They can tell if the baby is healthy then. But they can also do tissue typing."

Interested for the first time, Mandy frowned. "You mean, we'll know then? A long time before the baby is born?"

"Yes."

"The baby might not be right."

"No. The chances are one in four. But those aren't bad odds."

"I guess not." Mandy hesitated. She felt like her mother was waiting for something. Finally, using her most polite voice, she said, "It's cool you'd do this for me. Thank you."

Mom's hands were wringing together in her lap. "I'd do anything for you."

Mandy's heart cramped. *Then don't have this baby.* "I know."

Although her face was averted, she felt her mother's searching look. "You won't worry too much?" Mom asked.

"No." She pretended to find her place in her book. "I just don't let myself think about stuff like that."

"Smart girl." Mom kissed her cheek and stood up, dumping Calvin off her lap. "I go to bed worrying about whether I'll remember in the morning to cut my toenails or buy peanut butter at the store. I'm glad you didn't inherit my neurotic tendencies."

Mandy watched Calvin hop back up on the porch

railing and begin cleaning himself. "Maybe I'm like Dad."

"He certainly didn't worry," Mom agreed dryly, and left her alone.

Mandy closed her book, not even glancing to see what page she was on.

I worry, too, she'd wanted to say to Mom. *I worry all the time. I'm scared.* She couldn't figure out why she didn't say it. If only she could, Mom would hold her tight and promise she'd get better. She could cry, and feel her tears wetting someone else's skin. She wouldn't be so terribly alone, the way she was when she cried into her pillow at night.

But the words just wouldn't come out. She'd trained them so well to stay unsaid that they didn't even struggle to say themselves anymore. It was easier to keep things to herself. Probably, she reminded herself, it wouldn't do any good to say those things, anyway. She made people uncomfortable. Or angry, like Mom had been that once. Jessica was the only one who'd understood.

After a long while Mandy sighed. Maybe this baby brother—she didn't know why, but she thought it was a boy—*would* be compatible. She'd rather hope than not. It wasn't *impossible* that he could save her.

If he did, just think how awful she'd feel for ever having hated his guts.

IF NATHAN HAD BEEN any other man, Beth knew darn well she'd have done the cowardly thing and called to tell him she didn't want to see him again. Given who he was, she couldn't do that. Mandy needed him.

But she couldn't imagine what they'd say to each other the next time he came over. Especially if Mandy was there. How could they pretend nothing had happened?

The day after her talk with Mandy—no, not with— the day after she'd talked *to* Mandy, Beth went to Nathan's condominium. She'd never been there; he always came to see them, not the other way around. But they needed to be alone if they were to be honest with each other, and she'd rather be away from the house she'd shared with Rob. Away from the photographs on the mantel, the stool he'd sat on in the kitchen to watch her cook, the porch glider he'd bought for Beth's thirtieth birthday. Nate's place would be...neutral.

She called and asked if he'd be home and have time for her to stop by. Sounding only momentarily surprised and then matter-of-fact, he suggested eleven o'clock. Now, she was here on his doorstep, hand raised to press the bell.

She felt a little queasy for the first time in at least a month. Not morning sickness. Nervousness. Taking a deep breath, she rang the doorbell.

He opened the door so quickly she wondered if he'd seen her park in front and been waiting. His hair was damp from the shower, and he wore charcoal gray slacks and a white shirt, unbuttoned at the collar and cuffs. The sight of the dress shirt and the tanned V at his neck sent a quiver through her. The last time she's seen him, he'd worn a white shirt just like that one. When he'd pulled it open, she'd laid her hands against the hard muscles of his chest, felt the heavy pounding of his heart, the warmth of his skin.

Don't think about it, she told herself. *Block it out.*

His dark gaze flicked to her stomach before returning to her face. He did that every time he saw her, she realized with some remote part of her mind. It was as though he was checking to make sure she was still pregnant. Apparently reassured, he nodded and stood back.

The condo—well, really a town house—was upscale, from its elegant tiled entry to thick blond carpet in the living room and a bay window in the dining room. For all that, it was lifeless, she saw in one surprised look. Colors were neutral, the furniture could have come from a hotel room, and the walls were undecorated. He hadn't troubled to make it a home. He obviously felt as if he was just passing through. Her stomach took a panicky dip. She'd become used to his presence in their lives! Did he intend to disappear again, once he was satisfied she could manage?

"Would you like coffee? Tea?" The groove in one of his cheeks deepened. "No, you've given up caffeine, haven't you? Can I get you something else?"

"No. Thank you. I just thought—" she hesitated "—we ought to talk."

His gaze lowered for an instant again. "You're all right?"

Beth nodded. "I, um, told Mandy." Now, where had that come from? She wasn't supposed to be here to confide in him. But when he relaxed perceptibly, she thought her instinct had been sound. *Instinct?* an inner voice murmured. *Try cowardice.*

"And?" He gestured her toward a seat on the leather sofa, sinfully soft and pale gold. She wasn't quite the shape of a hippopotamus yet, but she was still going to have to struggle to get up again. In the matching chair, he leaned back, his pose relaxed. Nevertheless, she felt the tension radiating from him. If she touched him—

Don't you dare think it.

"She already knew." Beth smiled, one of those smiles that hid painful emotions. "She overheard us talking last spring. She's known all along."

"And she didn't say anything?" He sounded incredulous.

"She figured if I didn't, she wouldn't. I quote."

He shook his head. "She's twelve going on thirty."

Beth squeezed her hands together. "You'd be justified in saying I told you so."

His eyes met hers. "You had good cause for keeping quiet."

"Maybe not so good."

"Hindsight is easy."

If only he wouldn't be so decent, so uncritical, so...sexy. Unreasonably annoyed, she stiffened her resolve.

"I really came about what happened at the creek. It wasn't such a good idea."

He closed his eyes for a moment and kneaded the back of his neck. "I was a jerk. I suppose I'm paranoid."

"I didn't say 'Rob.'" It seemed important to convince him.

He grimaced. "Yeah. Later I realized—"

"I wasn't thinking 'Rob,' either."

"Weren't you?" He sat forward, elbows braced on his knees. The intensity in his eyes cut through any pretense.

"No." She had to look away. "At least... No. I couldn't have been."

"But you're not sure." His tone was hard.

Her chin shot up. "I was married for ten years. I haven't made love to a man since Rob died. Is it unnatural that he'd come to mind the first time I..." Her throat clogged.

He swore under his breath. "Put that way, no. God. No, of course it isn't."

"Are you the kind of man who only wants a woman who's untouched?" She said it acidly, refusing to acknowledge the sharp pain lodged behind her breastbone. "Or is it only being untouched by your brother that matters?"

Nathan rose to his feet and crossed to the window to stare out at the parking lot. His neck and back were rigid. "I knew Mandy wasn't an immaculate conception."

Her question came without conscious thought. "Why do you hate Rob so much?" She knew suddenly, with some shock, that this was why she'd come. To hear the answer to this one question.

"Does it matter?"

"Yes." She looked down to where her hand stroked the buttery soft leather. "I assume, because of Mandy and the baby, you and I will have a relationship of sorts for a long time to come. It's obviously complicated by your feelings for Rob."

How stiff she sounded! Even stuffy. But how else could she have phrased it? What else could she have said? *Sometimes I think I'm falling in love with you, and I need to know whether you feel anything for me, or whether it all has to do with Rob.*

With a rough sound, Nathan turned to face her. His face, usually imperturbable, showed harshness and sorrow and a thousand other tangled emotions.

"All right. We competed." He chopped off each word. "Everything—every goddamned thing—was a competition. Our mother encouraged it. But Rob—"

Nathan closed his eyes momentarily "—Rob had this incredible compulsion to best me at everything we did. Nothing could be mine alone. If I did it, he did it, too. Preferably better. If I had one, he had to have one, too." His eyes burned into hers. "I'm not trying to excuse myself, Beth. Maybe I was just as bad. Maybe if I'd *let* him beat me often enough, he'd have been satisfied. But I was too driven to do that."

"You were twins," she whispered. "Didn't you love each other?"

His face worked. "Yeah. Of course we did. We always knew what the other one was thinking. We stuck together. Other people never would have guessed—"

"That you were both fighting so hard to be individuals," Beth said softly. "Separate."

Composed again, he looked at her without expression. "Got it in one." He shrugged. "That's the story."

She ached with a terrible muddle of feelings: sadness at what they'd lost, at what *all* of them had lost, regret that it was too late to mend the brothers' rift, and most of all, anger at their mother, who, whatever her intentions, had sown such bitterness.

"No," she said. "You didn't tell me the ending. Something must have happened. Something more."

"It was a long time coming."

"I want to know."

He swore and turned away again, then abruptly swung back to face her. His face held, not the anger she'd expected to see, but an expression more akin to pity. "You don't. It'll taint your memory of Rob."

The queasiness returned full force. Her husband had had his flaws; he was sometimes lazy, content to coast on his charm, maybe even a little selfish. She knew he wasn't perfect. But what could he have done that was so terrible even his twin brother wanted nothing to do with him?

"You've already tainted it," she said flatly. "If I don't know, I'll always wonder. That's worse."

The lines carved in Nathan's cheeks and forehead aged him, made him look weary. "I never intended—"

"I know. But it's too late to go back."

"Maybe it wasn't even so bad. Rob thought it was a joke. I'd been packing away resentment for years. His little joke brought it to a head."

Joke? She stared at him. "He didn't…murder somebody or rape a woman or…"

"Murder, no. Rape, maybe." Nathan let out a heavy breath. "Oh, hell. It's just a sordid episode I've never told anyone about. I had a girlfriend in college. I was pretty serious about her. One day she mentioned how wild the sex had been the night before." He paused. "Trouble was, I hadn't been with her. Rob knew I was busy."

"Oh, no," Beth breathed. She saw it with stark clarity, Rob borrowing one of his brother's shirts or jackets—or had they dressed enough alike he hadn't even had to do that? Knocking on the girl's door, playing a game. Only, he should have been old enough to know it wasn't a game.

"Oh, yeah." Nathan sat back down. With a grimace he continued, "I confronted Rob. He admitted it was him. Turned out, he'd pretended to be me half-a-dozen times. She never had a clue. He was damned good at it. To him, it was a grand joke. When we were kids, we thought it was funny to trick people. What was any different about this?"

Shock made her voice thin, thready. "What did you do?"

"I punched him. He broke my nose. I transferred to another college. I never saw him again."

"Did you...did you tell *her?*"

He shook his head. "What was the point? She took birth-control pills. Rob was healthy. We broke up not too much later."

"Because of what happened?"

Nathan looked away. "Yeah. I'm not proud of myself. I couldn't quit wondering which of us she'd preferred."

"What he did...it was *sick.*" She spoke with astonishment and loathing. Nathan was right. Her memory of Rob *would* be tainted. It *was* tainted. How could he have?

"We'd both asked her out. She turned him down. But if I had something, he had to have it, too. Most twins are fulfilled by the relationship. Rob was tormented by it."

"Thanks to your mother."

"Maybe." Nathan let out a long breath. "But maybe not. Maybe it was innate. Kids are born with needs their parents haven't created. Hell, maybe I took up too much space in her womb, and he hated me by the time we were born." He laughed without humor. "I beat him at that, too. I was born one minute ahead of him. When we were about eight, I made a big deal out of being the *older* brother. I had all the sensitivity of a rockfall."

"According to Mandy, no boys have any sensitivity."

His smile was wry. "She's probably right."

"Thank God boys grow up," Beth said thoughtfully.

"Some boys."

"Would you ever have forgiven him?" She flushed at her abruptness. "If...if he had called you when I told him he should?"

"I hope so." He eyes held bleak honesty. "I don't know."

"I think...I think he changed."

Roughly Nathan said, "I have no doubt he did. All I have to do is look at you and Mandy. He made you happy. Somehow he learned to deserve you."

"I wish..."

"I wish, too." He cleared his throat.

For a moment they sat in silence. Beth wondered why she hadn't doubted Nathan's story. Shouldn't she have automatically leapt to Rob's defense? Couldn't Nathan have gotten it wrong, somehow misunderstood? What if the girl had thought it was kinky fun to have sex with both brothers and had slipped up talking to Nathan? Rob might have been trying to shield Nathan from the hurt....

But she didn't believe it. Nathan's story rang true. And she had always known that Rob felt guilty for whatever had happened. He'd missed his brother desperately, but he'd steadfastly refused to try to find him. Shame, she thought, had made him feel he deserved a loneliness she'd never altogether understood, because she didn't have a twin. Rob hadn't believed Nathan would forgive him. And she knew now why he'd refused to tell her about the fight.

Feeling numb, she stood up. "I should go now. But first—" she bit her lip "—first I have to say what I came to say."

He stood, too, and she had the sense of him bracing himself, although he only waited.

"I sort of...came on to you the other day." Her cheeks warmed. "I know it was my fault. I also know that for us to act on...on any kind of attraction we feel would be a big mistake. For Mandy, you've taken her dad's place. She needs you. So if things didn't work out between us, that might make it impossible for us to all be together. I don't want that to happen." She hesitated, nibbling again on her lip. "Can...can we just be friends?"

"Friends." He repeated the word with no intonation, as though he didn't understand its meaning.

Anxiously she said, "Like we have been."

Nathan took a step toward her. "My feelings are a little more than friendly."

Beth retreated. "We've been doing just fine. Until the other day."

"And that was so bad?"

"No." She pressed her lips together. "No, of course not. But you don't believe I'm not seeing Rob every time I look at you, and I'm..." She hesitated.

"You're not sure." He'd made it not a question. His expression had closed. Shutters down.

Well, to hell with him. She lifted her chin. "All right. I'm not sure."

"Then *friends* it'll be." The sardonic emphasis told her what he thought of their chances of being buddies, but she couldn't blame him. She *was* the one who'd ignited the bonfire the other day.

He escorted her to the door, nodded goodbye and was already buttoning his cuffs as he shut it. While walking to her car and then driving home, Beth reminded herself over and over again of all the good reasons they shouldn't make love, shouldn't risk falling in love, shouldn't risk a blowup that would break Mandy's heart.

Friends. We can be friends.

THEY TRIED. They even succeeded up to a point.

Nathan came over nearly as often as before. Mandy seemed not to notice any special tension between her mother and her uncle. Maybe, Beth thought ruefully, that was because it had been there from the very beginning.

The last weekend in September Nathan took Beth and Mandy on a short hike to the ice caves at the foot of Big Four, a magnificent mountain with small, easily accessible glaciers. The trail, just over a mile long, crossed a crystal-clear river tumbling over rocks, then rose on switchbacks through deep woods. Moss coated tree trunks and draped from branches. Ferns, their fronds edged with brown after the hot summer and dry September, clambered over decomposing stumps and brushed the trail.

Mandy skipped ahead, her skinny legs letting her bound like a fawn. Around every turn of the trail, she'd either wait impatiently or start back to meet them.

"Look!" she said. "That whole line of trees is growing out of the one that fell down."

"It's called a nurse log," Nathan told her. "As it rots and crumbles, seeds take root and it provides the nutrients they need to grow. Eventually it composts altogether and enriches the forest floor. That's why a forest that's logged every fifty years is so much poorer."

"This is cool!" Mandy declared, and hurried ahead again.

"Well, she's sure got energy," Beth said, half rueful. This pregnancy was still making her tired, although she'd gotten over the worst of it along the nausea.

"Yeah. You've never taken her hiking before?"

"We did some when she was younger, but after she got sick…"

"This one is short enough not to tire her."

She made a face. "Or me?"

His mouth tilted into a genuine smile. "Or you."

The rest of the day was more relaxed. They ate their picnic lunch sitting on a huge rock. Mandy ran and slid on the snowfields, falling and giggling as she soaked her jeans. The sun warm on her face, Beth watched with the most positive feeling of contentment she'd known in a long time. Mandy looked so healthy, so *normal*. It was hard to imagine that she could be sick. But maybe, just maybe, this pregnancy would provide the insurance she needed. As though the baby had read her mind, Beth felt fluttery movements in her abdomen.

Eventually they scrambled up over a narrow rocky ridge and stood in the mouth of a cave formed by melting glacier ice. The air was frigid, and the only sound was the dripping of water. Toward the back of the cool dark natural cathedral, sunlight fell through an opening in the ice as if through a stained-glass window.

"Oh, it's so beautiful!" Mandy cried. "Can we go in?"

"You read the signs." Beth nodded toward one posted at the opening. "It's not safe. I remember reading just last year about a couple of guys who got trapped when a cave collapsed."

"Oh, poop." Mandy wrinkled her nose. "It looks safe."

"It probably is, but why take a chance?"

Mandy gave her a look that previewed the teenage

years. "Sometimes," she said, as though her mother were an idiot, "it's worth taking risks." She turned and walked away.

Beside her Nathan said nothing, and Beth could only pray he hadn't noticed the double meaning in Mandy's words.

Sometimes it is worth taking risks, Beth silently agreed. *But sometimes they're too great.*

Or had she been turned into a coward because she had to live constantly with the fear of losing her daughter?

She followed Nathan out of the mouth of the cave, picking her way carefully on the water-slick rocky footing. Internally she continued the debate. She had someone else to think about, too, she reminded herself, a baby whose face and personality and name she didn't know, but who was becoming increasingly real to her nonetheless.

She touched her stomach and wondered what the child would think, when he or she was Mandy's age, about the admittedly bizarre conception and the arrangement between the mother and father. Or would Nathan still be around?

But she knew the answer to that. Nathan took his responsibilities seriously. He'd be a good father, even if it meant she had to share custody.

Think how easy it would be, an insidious voice murmured, *if you got married. Mandy would be thrilled, and your financial problems would be at an end. And it isn't as though you aren't attracted to each other.*

Ahead of her Nathan paused just then and held out a hand to help her down a short scramble. Right, Beth thought, looking from his big brown hand to his broad shoulders and his face, handsome and somehow quite different from Rob's, it wasn't as though she wasn't attracted to him.

But children and good sex weren't basis enough for a marriage. Children grew up. Sex with any one person lost its novelty. Look at celebrities. As soon as the excitement wore off, they got divorced. No, there had to be more: real liking, a shared sense of humor, commitment. And love.

But love could only come when they exorcised Rob's ghost. As Nathan's hand closed on hers and she accepted its support, she suddenly saw his face, not courteous and even friendly as it was now, but contorted with emotion as he told her what his brother had done to him. Her heart squeezed painfully with the loss of the hope she must secretly have been nursing. What were the chances Nathan could ever forget that she had loved Rob first?

CHAPTER TEN

"DAMN IT!" Nathan exclaimed. Didn't that woman have any sense? Five months pregnant, and she was hefting boxes heavy enough to break her back!

He leapt out of his car and covered the fifty yards to the barn in long strides. "Let me take that."

"It's okay," she said blithely. "I've got it. If you want to help, there's more—"

He snatched the box from her arms and almost sagged under the weight of it. Straightening, he growled, "Where to?"

"Front porch steps." She rushed after him. "I'm perfectly capable of carrying it!"

Nathan didn't say a word until he'd set the box down on the bottom step as carefully as though it contained eggs. Then he straightened to face her.

"You're pregnant," he said tautly. "You shouldn't be lifting or carrying anything heavy."

Her cheeks flushed with indignation. "I have a business to run! What's more, five months pregnant does not constitute a disability! Lots of pregnant women work, not all at desk jobs."

His jaw muscles ached. "But you have more at stake than most. Or have you forgotten?"

Her eyes narrowed and she snapped, "Don't be insulting. If that's all you came for..."

"It's not." He rubbed a hand over the back of his

neck, belatedly recognizing that she had reason to be annoyed, however stupid her insistence on playing part-time longshoreman. "I'm sorry. I didn't mean to sound dictatorial."

"How *did* you mean to sound?" she asked tartly.

"Concerned."

"Concern duly noted." Her gaze didn't soften. "Why *are* you here?"

Because I didn't want to go home. Because this is home. "To finish my Monopoly game with Mandy. Is she here?"

"She's in her bedroom." Obviously grudging, Beth said, "I guess you can stay for dinner if you'd like."

"How about if I go pick up a pizza?"

She planted her hands on her hips. "Are you trying to appease me?"

Standing there like that, eyes sparking and chin defiant, she looked cute. Pretty. Sexy. Her pale curls were even more tousled than usual, as they might be when she awakened mornings. The pink in her cheeks was flattering to the delicate lines of her face. Her combative stare meant he didn't dare lower his gaze, but he was acutely aware of the ripe swell of her belly and the fact that her breasts were fuller than they used to be. Her position thrust them out.

Hell, these days, he was *always* acutely aware of her belly and breasts and long graceful neck and the softness of her lower lip. Every time he saw her—and all too often when he didn't—he remembered her taste and feel and small muffled sounds.

Appease her? He couldn't afford not to.

"Yep," he admitted, trying to sound a hell of a lot more free and easy than he felt with his groin tightening.

She thought about it. "Okay," she said at last. "And I'll let you help carry some of the boxes."

He had no intention of allowing her to pick up even one. On her long packing table in the barn he found a dozen ready to go.

"Do you ship every day?" he asked.

"More like twice a week. And Julie is usually here to help." She wrinkled her nose. "She's almost as bad as you are."

"You told her you're pregnant."

She glanced down at her stomach. "This is one secret that's impossible to keep."

"Good."

She sealed a box with packing tape, then pushed it at him. "Let me finish with these last couple, then I'll help you. The UPS truck should be here any minute."

Orders didn't work. He'd try begging. "Let me carry them. Please. I'd feel better."

Her eyes met his gravely. After a moment she nodded. "Okay. This time." She reached for the tape again, but her hand stilled. "Thank you."

"No problem."

"I wouldn't say that." Her lashes lowered and she stared fixedly at the brown carton she made no move to tape closed. "You're here so often. You must have given up vacations and time with friends and..." She let out a small sigh and her lashes swept up so that she could search his face with disquieting intensity. "You must have had a life before us."

Pride or truth? It was no contest. "Not much of one," he admitted gruffly. "Yeah, I have friends, but hell, most of 'em are married and too busy coaching their kids' Little League teams to be free to climb Mount Olympus. I, uh—" he rotated his shoulders uneasily ''—mostly worked. Seventy, eighty hours a week sometimes. When I was in Portland the other day, my secretary congratulated me for loosening up. I have you and Mandy to thank for that.''

Her brow creased. ''I think you're trying to make me feel better.''

''I enjoy being here.'' His sincerity sounded closer to fervency.

Her eyes, shadowed here in the barn, contemplated him for another long moment. ''Okay,'' she said at last with a nod, ''I'll let it slide. Probably because I'm too glad you're here to be noble.''

His heart lifted like a kite catching the wind. He felt foolish to be as excited as he'd been at the age of ten when his parents announced the family was going to Disneyland. But Beth had never before come right out and said she was happy he was around. He'd guessed she was when he showed up with dinner and saw her tiredness washed away by relief, or when she asked him to drive Mandy somewhere and he agreed, or even, sometimes, when he and Mandy were goofing around and Mandy's laugh rang out, clear and uncomplicated. But she hadn't *said* it, and the words felt good.

Now, he thought wryly, if only she'd confess that she wanted him to kiss her and needed him desperately! He grunted. In his dreams. Hoisting the next box of jam destined for—he glanced at the label—a gourmet-food store in San Rafael, California, he said, ''Be right back.''

Done packaging, she closed up the barn and they walked to the house together, Nathan with the last box on his shoulder. The brown UPS truck was just pulling into the driveway at a speed that sent dust billowing.

In seconds the driver had sunnily greeted them,

slapped on labels, loaded the pile into the truck and was tearing back down the driveway.

Nathan shook his head in admiration. "I should hire him."

"They're always in a hurry. And he already had the shipping info. I'm hooked up by computer."

"Still…" The truck was gone.

She gave a sudden mischievous smile. "I offered him a job last year. He turned me down. The pay I offered was lousy."

He grinned. "Lucky he didn't report you to his bosses. Maybe they'd have refused to ship your merchandise."

Her smile deepened. "I'm afraid he thought I was joking. You should have heard him laugh. Minimum wage sounds so puny it *is* a joke."

On the porch she sank onto the glider, instead of continuing into the house. He didn't push his luck by plunking himself down next to her. Instead, he half sat on the railing, watching as she idly swung. Her lips still curved; even her eyes held a smile. He wanted her with sudden ferocity. He did his damnedest to hide the way his muscles clenched.

But still she saw enough to make her smile fade and her gaze become wary. He was silently cursing himself when her expression changed yet again.

"Oh!" she exclaimed, her mouth rounding in surprise. She laid her hands over her belly and pressed.

He shot to his feet. "Is something wrong?"

"No. Oh, no." This smile was incredibly gentle and her eyes had softened. "He—she—just did some gymnastics. A tumbling run, I think."

His hunger found a new channel. He couldn't tear his eyes from her belly where her slender hands were splayed. He wanted to feel the life inside her. His seed. His baby. He wanted to lift her shirt out of the way and lay his own hand there, or even his cheek, until his son or daughter stirred again. He wanted to say, "Hi, kid. This is your dad. Hope it's going okay in there."

He swallowed hard, the silence roaring in his ears. He was probably scaring her again. Here they'd finally laughed together, and he was ruining it because he wanted more.

"Nathan." She spoke just above a whisper. "Would you, um, would you like to feel him move? I think you can if you put your hand here."

He wrenched his gaze up. "Do you mean it?" he asked hoarsely.

"Well, of course!" She took a deep breath. "If you won't be embarrassed."

She stopped the glider and he sat next to her, so close his thigh pressed hers. He reached out a hand that shook, and she took it in hers and spread it on her belly. Nathan closed his eyes, all his concentration focused on the point of contact. He felt the slight rise and fall as she breathed, but nothing else.

After a moment he cleared his throat. "Nothing's happening."

"It will."

He waited. Still no movement.

"Over here," she murmured, taking his hand again. She lifted her shirt and this time laid his hand on her bare skin.

Silk and warmth and unexpected firmness. She was so close he felt her breath. He could have bent his head and kissed her breast. Hammered by a barrage of sensations, he wondered how he could bear this.

And then her belly jumped under his hand. Astonished, he lifted his gaze. Beth was smiling. "You felt him?"

More movement shivered beneath the surface, like a fish disturbing a quiet pool.

"Later," she said softly, "little knobs will poke out. Fingers or toes or elbows. Or I'll be able to feel his hiccups. And he'll be able to hear our voices."

"Amazing." Incredible joy expanded like a helium balloon. "He's really in there. Alive."

"Already a person." The gentle curve of her mouth, the misty softness of her eyes, almost undid him. "Our son or daughter."

Her stomach jerked again and she laughed with quiet pleasure. He was going to kiss her. He had to kiss her. He couldn't survive another moment without touching and tasting her mouth, sharing her breath.

Her eyes widened, her smile faded, but he saw no wariness, no pulling back. She studied him solemnly as he bent his head, brushed her tremulous lips with his own, groaned—

A huge sob erupted behind him. "Please!" Mandy cried from only feet away. "Please don't have a baby!"

EARLIER, BEFORE UNCLE Nate had come by, Mandy was lying facedown on her bed trailing her fingers along the floor for Polly to pounce on. She didn't feel very good; her nose was stuffed up and she was tired. She should tell Mom; both times when she'd gotten sick with leukemia, it had started with stomachaches. For Jessica, it had been a runny nose and fever. The first time it had happened, nobody had guessed anything was wrong for weeks and weeks, because everyone thought she just had a cold. Of course, she and Jessica had different kinds of leukemia, but maybe this time Mandy's was showing itself with different symptoms. At the very least, the doctors would put her on an antibiotic, so she wouldn't get an infection. The maintenance drugs she took weakened her immune system.

But she didn't want to tell Mom. Mandy rolled onto her back and stared up at the ceiling. Her mother already thought she was dying. Maybe if she didn't tell anybody, it would all be over quicker. Mom could feel sad for a while, then be happy with the new baby.

But Mandy bet Uncle Nate would miss her. He came mostly to see her. She was almost sure he did. Two nights ago they'd played Monopoly for *hours* and still weren't finished the game. She had hotels on Boardwalk and Park Place, and he had them on the green Pacific, Pennsylvania and North Carolina Avenues. Plus, she owned Marvin Gardens and Atlantic and Ventnor Avenues. He was really cool to play with. Most of her friends sulked when they were losing and they wanted to give up right away. Or, if *she* was losing, they'd feel sorry for her and want to excuse rent she owed so she wouldn't have to drop out of the game. Either way was no fun. Uncle Nate was like a shark. She bet he'd take her last penny without feeling the least bit apologetic. But he also just got more determined when things didn't look good for him. Now that they were evenly enough matched, she bet this game would go on for days. Maybe, she thought hopefully, he'd come over this evening, although he hadn't promised to.

Tires crunched in the gravel out front, and she rolled off her bed to peer out the window. It *was* him. She was about to race downstairs to meet him, but he'd jumped out of his car and was heading toward the barn, not the house. He grabbed this big box out of Mom's hands even though Mom didn't want him to, and she trailed after him looking irritated. Mandy couldn't hear what they were saying, but they seemed to be arguing. After a moment, though, they went back to the barn.

She stayed at the window, watching as Uncle Nate carried a whole bunch of boxes of jam to the front. When he was done, he'd come in. She knew he would. Usually he came in first to say hi to her, even if he had to talk to Mom about something.

But the UPS truck came and went, and she didn't hear the screen door slam. What were they *doing?* She blew her nose, so he and Mom wouldn't be able to tell she was congested. Then she sat on the edge of her bed again and stroked Polly, who blinked sleepily up at her. Polly's eyes glowed emerald green, even when they were half-closed. Mandy could stare into them for ages they were such an incredible color, and so deep, like this fishing pool on the Sauk River that Mandy remembered seeing with her dad. Sometimes she almost thought she could tip forward and fall into Polly's unblinking cat eyes and sink without a trace. Sometimes she almost wanted to.

The house was completely quiet. No voices floated up the stairs, no doors slammed, no footsteps creaked on the stairs or in the hall downstairs. What were they doing?

Finally she had to find out, even though she was hurt that Uncle Nate hadn't come in. Had Mom been really mad at him? Maybe he'd left. But Mandy looked and saw his car still sitting right in front of the house. So she gave Polly one last stroke and slipped out of her room and down the stairs.

The living room and kitchen were empty. Mom's study was, too. Maybe they were still out in the barn. Mandy was hesitating in the hall when she heard the rumble of a man's voice. On the porch, then.

She opened the screen so quietly they didn't hear her come out. They didn't see her, either. Uncle Nate sat right next to Mom on the glider. As Mandy watched, Mom lifted his hand under her shirt, onto her stomach. A second later his head shot up.

"You felt him?" Mom was talking like it was the most incredible thing on earth. "Later," she said, "little knobs will poke out. Fingers or toes or elbows. Or I'll be able to feel his hiccups. And he'll be able to hear our voices."

"Amazing. He's really in there. Alive." Uncle Nate's voice had a wondering note. He'd never sounded that way about anything Mandy had done. And it wasn't like the baby had *done* anything yet, Mandy thought resentfully.

"Already a person," Mom said. "Our son or daughter."

What am I? Mandy wanted to wail. *Just some kid who won't be around to be a bother much longer?* Her fingers curled into fists so tight they hurt. Look at them! They were…they were like a family, only without her. They had a baby—together—and Uncle Nate was going to kiss Mom. Pain burned in Mandy's chest. He was here to see Mom. Probably he never *had* come to see her.

"Please!" The words were torn from her. "Please don't have a baby!"

Uncle Nate swung to face her; Mom, hand pressed to her mouth, half rose to her feet. "Mandy!"

"I won't leave you!" Hot tears poured down her face and she could hardly see Mom and Uncle Nate. "I promise I won't die! I promise, I promise, I promise! We don't need any baby!"

Uncle Nate got to her first. His arms crushed her into a hug and she sobbed against his stomach. Then she felt Mom's hands on her shoulders, turning her.

"Sweetheart!" Mom framed Mandy's face with her hands and tilted it up. "Of course you won't die! We're not having a baby to *replace* you! Is that what you think?"

She nodded dumbly, tears running down her cheeks and mucus down her upper lip.

"Amanda McCabe, I love you more than anything or anybody in the world." Mom's voice broke. "Don't you know that?"

She did, kind of. But the baby would be Mom's, too, and she'd love him more than anything or anybody in the world, too, wouldn't she? More than *anybody* might mean more than her, Mandy.

"We don't need him," she mumbled, sniffing.

"Mandy..." Mom looked so...so hopeless, as though she didn't know what to say or do. Mandy had never seen her like that before. Mom *always* said positive things and acted as if she was never out of control. A big sigh made her shoulders sag. "I think we'd better talk."

Mandy couldn't quit crying. Tears rolled down her cheeks and into her mouth and dripped off her chin. She nodded convulsively and hiccuped. Behind her the screen door slammed and a second later Uncle Nate thrust a tissue at her.

Mandy snatched the tissue and buried her face in it. The horrible snuffling sounds that came out humiliated her. She'd made such a fool of herself! She'd never done anything like this!

She found herself ensconced on the glider with Mom. A few feet away Uncle Nate leaned against the porch railing, arms crossed, his brows drawn ferociously together. He was so tall, rearing over them. Mandy couldn't meet his eyes. He must think she was some kind of idiot.

Mom spoke in her gentlest voice. "Mandy, love, why didn't you *say* anything before?"

Through the humiliation and the terror and the tears, her original resentment lifted its head. "What good would it have done?" she cried. "You didn't give *me* any choice! You just went and did it. So why should we talk about it?"

"Sometimes parents have to make decisions their kids don't agree with. But when I have to do that, I always hope you'll listen to my reasons. Don't I listen to you?"

"Only when you want to." Mandy blew her nose again. "Otherwise, you don't ask my opinion so you don't have to listen."

Mom flinched. "Okay, you're scared I'll love this baby more than I love you. That's not…unnatural. Most only children feel that way when they find out they're going to have a brother or sister. But do any of your friends' mothers love them less because there're other kids in the family?"

Mandy hunched her shoulders wretchedly. "Kayla couldn't take that art class, even though she's a really great artist and she desperately wanted to, because her brother already had football. Remember?"

"That's time, not love."

"If you really love somebody, you'd have time for them."

"There are parents who work two jobs just to pay the bills. Does that mean they don't love their children?"

Misery burned in Mandy's chest. "No," she whispered.

"Mandy," her mother said, "I love you. I promised I wouldn't let you die. I'll do anything to keep that promise. One thing I can do, thanks to your Uncle Nate, is give you one more good chance to have a bone-marrow donor." Her eyes were fierce, unblinking. "This baby—" she put her hand on her belly "—is your best chance yet. If he's not compatible, I'll get pregnant again." She spaced the next words out, her intensity making each hard and pure. "I will do anything for you."

Mesmerized by her mother's glittering eyes, Mandy felt shame flush her cheeks. She did know that. She always had. She opened her mouth and tried to speak, but her mother swept on.

"I will do this even if it makes you jealous. I'll do it even though I know I'll love this baby just as passionately as I love you, and that might hurt you. But I will *never*—" her voice shook "—love you any less than I did the day you were born, and any less than I do today. Do you understand?"

Fresh tears gushed so fast Mandy thought her body must be wringing itself out. "Yes!" she wailed.

"Oh, honey." Mom wrapped her arms around her. "Oh, honey, I'm so sorry you've been feeling this way. I was an idiot for not telling you. I was trying to save you from worrying, and look what I did! Shh, don't cry so hard. You'll make yourself sick. Shh.'' She kept murmuring as Mandy sobbed. Mom's arms were tight, and the glider began a gentle movement that was obscurely comforting.

It seemed like forever before her tears slowed and finally stopped. Mom's shirt under her cheek was soaked. Mandy knew what she looked like when she'd been crying: her face blotched red, her nose running, her eyes swollen practically shut. She couldn't lift her head, not with Uncle Nate still standing there watching. He must despise her!

After a moment her mother murmured something and handed Mandy some more tissues. He must have got them from the house, she realized. Turned away from him, she blew her nose again and mopped her cheeks and then defiantly looked up.

He was smiling at her, his mouth kind of crooked so she could tell he was sad underneath. ''You know,'' he said, ''the only reason *I* agreed to have this baby was you. I guess I'm starting to like the idea of being a father, but no more than I like the idea of…well, standing in for Rob with you. This sister or brother you're going to have can't take your place with me. By the time he's old enough to take me on in Monopoly, you'll be grown-up and off at college.''

It was true the baby wouldn't be able to do stuff like play games. A little bit cheered, Mandy mumbled, ''It's okay if you don't like me as much. I mean, he *will* be yours.''

This time he grinned, and she could see that what she'd guessed was true, it really was. He did love her. Even if he hadn't come into the house today to say hello to her first. He reached out and ruffled her bangs.

"As far as I'm concerned, kiddo," he said gruffly, "you're mine, too."

"Oh," she said shyly. "I...I'm glad you're here, Uncle Nate."

After that he insisted he had to go. Mom didn't argue and even Mandy didn't. She felt shaky and clingy and...oh, about five years old, not twelve. Just for now, she wanted her mother and nobody else.

She laid her head against her mother's breast and closed her eyes. Neither of them moved until after Uncle Nate's car was gone.

Then Mom let out a little puff of breath against Mandy's hair. "Do you worry all the time about dying?"

Mandy didn't say anything for a long time. It was hard to. She was out of practice. Would Mom get mad again? Or tell her she was silly? But all the tears had left her feeling weak and oddly calm.

"Pretty much." She rubbed her cheek against her mother. She loved her mother's softness and smell and the quiet beat of her heart. "Well, not all the time. Not so much in the day. I mean, mostly I'm busy. But at night..." She let her words hang.

Mom's breath caught raggedly. "But why, *why,* haven't you ever said anything? To think of you alone in your bedroom worrying about dying..."

"I guess I thought—" Mandy hesitated "—you wouldn't understand if I asked you about dying. Or—" she tried not to sound as though she minded "—you'd get mad and tell me I'm not going to die."

Mom was silent for a few heartbeats. Then her arms tightened convulsively and she bowed her head against Mandy's. "I did that once, didn't I?" she asked, choking up.

Mandy didn't answer. Mom distinctly sniffed before answering her own question. "I did. I...I just wasn't ready. I couldn't bear to think..." Her voice broke.

Tears had begun to seep from Mandy's eyes onto Mom's shirt again. "I know," she whispered.

"But that was so long ago." Mom straightened, taking her arms from around Mandy and turning her to face her. Her face was wet, too. "I've tried to talk to you, over and over. Hundreds of times! Did you really think I'd get mad if you asked again?"

Had she? Confusion momentarily clouded Mandy's thoughts. That was what she'd always told herself—that Mom would get mad. But it wasn't really true, she saw now. "I guess," she said slowly, "I didn't want to tell you how scared I was. I didn't want you to tell me you were scared, too."

Brow wrinkling, Mom stared at her. "It made you feel safer if I didn't admit I was scared? I don't understand."

Mandy looked down. In a rush she said, "Because if you weren't scared, I didn't really have to be. Even if sometimes I was."

Mom made a little gasping sound. Her fingers squeezed Mandy's upper arms. Then she hugged her again. Against Mandy's hair she murmured, "You're braver than I'll ever be. You've been afraid for *years,* and you kept quiet." Mandy felt her swallow. "Oh, honey."

Not now, but tonight when she went to bed, Mandy thought, she would talk to her mother about dying and whether there would be heaven or nothingness, or maybe you got reincarnated as a person or a cat or a bug. Some gross bug. She'd thought about that before. She never stepped on even an ant if she could help it.

But right now she felt too much at peace to talk about dying.

She lay quietly against her mother for a long while, until her neck started to hurt from being in such an awkward position. When she stirred, Mom let her go.

Mandy sat up. "Mom. Can *I* feel the baby move?"

Mom looked so surprised Mandy hunched her shoulders. "It's okay. It's no big deal. I just…I heard you talking and—"

"Of course you can!" Mom laughed, although her eyes were puffy, too, and she had to sniff again. "I never suggested it because I thought you were happier pretending I wasn't pregnant. But…oh, it's such a funny feeling. Let's see." She jiggled a little and then sat still, an inward-looking expression on her face. "Is he still— There!" She gripped Mandy's hand and laid it on her stomach under her shirt. Her stomach felt hard. And then it jerked, went still, then rippled, all without Mom moving a muscle. Mandy pulled her hand back.

"Hey!"

"You just met your brother or sister," Mom said solemnly.

Mandy got goose bumps. "Weird," she whispered.

"Yeah, it is, when you think about it." Mom's expression changed. "Kiddo, you need a bath. Your face is a mess. Look at you, your nose is still running! Come on." She eased to her feet, drawing Mandy with her.

"Mom—"

"We can talk more later, can't we? Aren't you starved? Why don't I put on dinner while you—"

"Mom, listen to me for a minute!"

Her mother froze, her mouth still forming an O.

Mandy took a deep breath. "Mom, I've got a cold.

Or something.'' She waited for the panic, the dread, the rush for a thermometer and a warm sweater and the car keys.

But Mom only reached out and touched her forehead and frowned slightly. ''So you do! Oh, dear, it'll mean an antibiotic. Heck, I'll go see if whoever's on call at the hospital can phone one to Howard's Drugs.''

Mom was pretending. She must be. Because she, Mandy, had told her she didn't want to know when Mom was scared.

''But they'll have to see me...''

''Oh, I doubt it.'' Mom gently pushed her to go ahead. ''Remember, you just had your blood workup. And *everybody* gets colds.''

The knot in Mandy's chest loosened. ''But...but when I got sick...''

''I know.'' Mom kissed her on top of her head and let the screen door close behind them. ''But you get colds, too. I used to always get scared. I guess you noticed, huh? But I don't think this time the leukemia could possibly have come back that fast. And don't I remember you saying something about Barbara missing school because she had a cold?''

''Oh, yeah. Yeah!'' Mandy bounced on her toes, then gave a hop. ''Cool! I thought...''

''...you were dying.''

Mandy realized Mom was teasing her. Incredible! Her giggle felt good. ''Yeah! Thanks, Mom.'' She bounced again. ''I'm gonna go take a bath, okay?''

''Okay.''

Mandy poured bubble bath under the running water. When the tub was full, she sank into the hot water feeling as light and shimmery as the bubbles. It wasn't dying she thought about or her throat getting raw, but the funny way her mother's stomach had shifted under her hand. She closed her eyes and pictured a baby—a really tiny baby—doing a somersault. Or maybe finning around inside Mom like she was doing now in the bathtub.

She smiled and sank lower in the water until the bubbles tickled her chin.

CHAPTER ELEVEN

BETH HATED hospital waiting rooms. They smelled alike. They *felt* alike, however homey the decor. Dozens of magazines through which people leafed without ever taking in a word. A television that chattered on one wall, unheard. A view of a parking lot. Comfortable chairs that nobody relaxed in. Tension, fear, like the fume rising from new carpeting.

This time, Beth thought semihysterically, at least she hadn't a child dying down the hall. She was only waiting to hear the result of her amniocentesis. Only a verdict on her unborn baby's health—and Mandy's future. That was all.

She drummed her fingers on the smooth oak arm of her chair, then rose to gaze out the window at the people hurrying to and from cars. Her appointment had been twenty minutes ago. Why the delay? Did it mean bad news?

Of course it didn't! Doctors were *always* behind. There'd been times she'd had the first appointment of the day and found the doctor already late. They had emergencies. Patients in hospital beds. Rounds. Consultations. Her appointment was routine. It could wait.

She crumpled back into the chair. *But I can't wait!* she cried inside. If the doctor had a grain of sensitivity, he had to know how anxious she was! Anxious. What a mild word. One was anxious about going to the dentist. Anxious when a distributor called to complain that a major order was overdue. Anxious for a check to arrive.

No, she was flat-out terrified.

"Mrs. McCabe?"

She shot to her feet, clutching her purse. "Yes?"

The nurse smiled pleasantly. "Dr. Simonson is ready to see you."

Beth's feet rooted to the floor. *But I'm not ready!* she thought in panic, fully aware of the absurdity of her reaction. He was going to steal her hope and present her with the truth, however crushing, instead.

"Oh. Fine." She shifted her purse unnecessarily from hand to hand, touched one palm to her stomach in an instinctive need for reassurance and was answered by a stir within.

The nurse waited in the doorway. "If you'll follow me?"

"Yes. Of course." She must look like an idiot, standing here frozen. Somehow her feet came unstuck; she was walking down the wide hospital corridor, into his office.

How the man could make a career of treating young cancer patients, she had never understood. Despite advances in treatment, he must lose so many! But Dr. Simonson was perhaps forty and had specialized in juvenile oncology from the beginning. When he was ten, his brother died of leukemia, he had told her once. The loss had fired him to devote his life to defeating that particular enemy. He was big, with hands that should have been clumsy. Carrot red hair was receding without it appearing to trouble him. His blue eyes usually twinkled, although she had seen him cry once. She and

Mandy both loved him, as much as you can love someone with such terrible power.

White lab coat rumpled as always, he leapt up, smiling, to shake her hand. She sank again into a chair, this time in front of his desk. He perched on the edge of it and started talking immediately. Things looked good with the baby, he said; she heard him from some great distance. Did she want to know if it was a girl or boy?

Beth stared mutely up at him. He understood, for the impish twinkle in his eyes blazed into wholehearted joy.

"The baby is going to be compatible," Dr. Simonson said quietly. "I think we have a perfect, six-out-of-six, bone-marrow-antigen match."

Compatible. He'd said compatible. She couldn't have misunderstood, could she?

He seized her hands. "Did you hear me, Beth? I had questions in my mind about your doing this, but damned if it wasn't justified. This baby is going to be Mandy's miracle."

The first tears rolled down her cheeks. Otherwise, she seemed paralyzed. "Dear God," she whispered. "You're *sure?*"

"Sure as we can be." He snatched up a lab report from his desk and began talking, but not a word penetrated.

She'd won. She'd kept her promise to Mandy. This child inside her was Mandy's miracle. Suddenly she had to bury her face in her hands. Tears dripped between her fingers.

Thank you. If You're listening, thank you.

SHE COULD, of course, have had company during her torturous wait. Nathan would have come with her; in fact, lately he'd been asking with exasperating insistence when she was to have her amniocentesis. She had managed to be vague without exactly refusing to answer.

She hardly even knew why she had been so fixed on coming alone. She'd known only that, if the news was bad, she wanted to crawl into hiding all by herself. She didn't want comfort, not even a shoulder to cry on. She alone had fought to conceive this baby; if the baby's tissue had proved not to be compatible with Mandy's, Beth needed to deal alone with the knowledge before she accepted or gave sympathy.

But, oh, he was compatible. *He.* She knew that now, too; her baby was a boy. She wanted suddenly, desperately, not to be standing alone in a hospital corridor.

Other people passed without even glancing at her, some with an air of urgency and tension, others, like a pair of off-duty nurses, laughing. An orderly pushing an empty wheelchair gave her a vague smile and she almost grabbed him and said, "I'm going to have a baby boy! And he's going to save my daughter's life!" But she saw that his mind was somewhere else and she let him pass.

She wished she could tell Mandy, but she'd have to wait until four, when her daughter got home from school. Her watch said one fifty-three. Two hours and seven minutes seemed like forever.

Nathan. Beth's mind fastened onto the name and the image of the man, tall, quiet, dark. Nathan would want to know almost as much as she had. He might be angry because she'd come alone, but he'd forget it quickly enough. Eager now, Beth hurried toward the exit.

Behind the wheel of her car she sat for a moment, imagining the moment when she told Mandy. It was tempting to call her at school, but some news was too emotionally laden to hear in a crowd. Only two hours.

How would Mandy react? Beth wondered. Before the explosion a week ago, she probably would have given a small collected nod, then retreated to her room. Now? If her daughter tried, Beth knew better than to let her get away with it. They would talk, even if that meant crying, too.

Beth drove to Nathan's in a daze. She glanced at herself in the rearview mirror and saw her own foolish smile. Amazingly, unbelievably, Mandy actually had a donor. All she had to do was stay healthy until he was old enough. The impossible, the bucket of gold at the end of the rainbow, the Holy Grail, was theirs. She'd hoped so many times. Prayed. Railed at God. And now… She touched her stomach and laughed out loud.

His car was in its slot, thank heaven. What if she'd had to go home and contain herself for the entire two hours, not having a soul to tell? She might have had to wake her brother up in the middle of the night in Saudi Arabia.

When Nathan flung the door open, he had a cell phone to one ear and was shoving his free hand through his hair. "Yeah?" he snapped, before he saw who was on his doorstep. "No, no, not you," he said into the phone as his gaze and Beth's held. "Listen," he added brusquely, "something's come up. I'll get back to you." Without waiting for a reply, he turned the phone off and pushed down the antenna.

"Is something wrong?" Nathan asked.

She was taking in the sight of him in those same, baggy black sweatpants—she recognized the tear in one knee—and a Stanford University T-shirt.

"Stanford. You transferred to Stanford after you and Rob fought."

"Huh?" He glanced down at his T-shirt. "Oh. Yeah. What difference does it make?"

When he backed up she stepped over the threshold.

"What?" he asked roughly. "You have news. Damn it, is it good or bad?"

"I had my amniocentesis." Inexplicably, tears ran down her face again. "It's a boy. The baby, I mean."

"A boy." Wonder showed briefly in his eyes. It was chased away almost immediately. "He doesn't match. Oh, my God, Beth..." He reached clumsily for her.

"No! Wait!" She held out both hands to fend him off. "He does! Dr. Simonson says he's almost certainly a match!"

Nathan froze. "Then why are you crying?"

"I don't know!" she wailed, and tumbled into his arms.

He laughed and swung her off her feet. "Damn, Beth! You're sure? *They're* sure?"

Through her tears, she told him, "They can't guarantee, but Dr. Simonson seemed positive. He called the baby Mandy's miracle."

Nathan's arms loosened and he stilled. "Mandy's miracle. Incredible." Voice ebullient, he added, "You were right. *You're* the miracle worker."

"Without you..."

"My part was pretty minor," he said dryly. "Stud service."

She looked up into his face, her eyes drenched with tears but her gaze grave. "Only you would have done. If you hadn't come when I contacted you, and if you hadn't agreed to become a father..."

He didn't seem to be listening. "Have you told Mandy yet?"

She shook her head. "You're first."

"What's she going to say?"

"I don't know." Beth was silent for a moment, suddenly aware that Nathan's arms were still around her, that if only he tipped his head, their mouths could meet. "Last week Mandy admitted that she thinks about dying all the time. Especially at night."

His hands reached up and threaded through her hair. "Now she can quit."

The skin on his neck was smooth and brown, his jaw clean-shaven. Swallowing, Beth said, "This isn't as easy as a pill she can pop. Ideally the transplant shouldn't be done until the baby is at least six months old. That's almost a year away. She has to stay strong that long. Even if we get that far, there are still risks. They have to kill all her bone-marrow cells, you know. And then sometimes the body rejects a transplant."

Silent for a long moment, his emotions plain in his eyes, he said at last, "How have you stood it all these years?"

"What else could I do?" she asked simply.

"I wish I'd been here." His jaw worked. "You shouldn't have been alone."

Now that she wasn't, Beth couldn't understand why she'd wanted to be today. Nathan would have held her hand in the waiting room. His strength might have lessened her fear.

"You don't have to be alone," he murmured, uncannily echoing her thoughts. "Not again."

A second later his mouth touched hers, as delicately as if he was handling a ripe tender berry. She closed her eyes and felt the sweetness burst inside her, freeing a tide of longing and gratitude and— No, not love, surely not love! But, oh, his lips were so gentle, so affectionate, coaxing her to feel impossible things. His big hands framing her face were just as gentle, his thumbs drawing circles on her temples and cheekbones and over her closed eyes. Passion was curiously absent from this kiss; with his mouth, Nathan conveyed admiration and congratulation and joy. Friendship.

The wrench in her heart told her she wanted more.

Abruptly his mouth left hers and he turned her in his arms, until they wrapped around her from behind. He pressed her to him; she discovered that passion had not, after all, been altogether absent, because he was aroused. But he didn't cup her breasts or nibble her neck. Instead, his hands splayed open over her belly.

"A boy," he murmured against her hair, and she heard again that wonder. But there was something more. He sounded choked, as though... A tear, wet and hot, slid down her neck, and she understood that he hadn't wanted her to see him cry. "Thank God. Without Mandy—" He stopped, audibly swallowed, continued in a painfully gritty voice, "I was afraid he couldn't help her, and we'd love him, but we'd blame him, too."

Her eyes burned with new tears. "No. We wouldn't have. We'd have loved him for what he was, just like I love Mandy. Nathan McCabe, you're not the kind of man who'd ask a baby to be responsible for someone else's fate."

"He is, though."

"Inadvertently. But it's a...a blessing." She struggled to explain. "A gift. Not something he had to be."

"I hope you're right." Nathan was silent for a moment. "Are you going to name him after Rob?"

"No. Oh, no!" The idea was instantly repugant to her. "He's not Rob's baby. He's yours. I...I thought of Patrick, after your father." It was hard to speak at all normally with his body and hands on her so intimately. "What do you think?"

"I like Patrick," Nathan said huskily. "What was *your* father's name?"

"Joe. Joseph."

"Patrick Joseph McCabe. Has a nice ring to it."

"Mmm-hmm." She could hardly think with his hands still wrapped around her waist.

"I don't feel him moving."

"No. I think he sleeps when I'm up and around."

"The better to plague you at night."

"Yes."

Nathan took a deep breath and lifted his hands from her belly. They shook, and he curled them into fists as he stepped back from her.

Beth sniffed and slowly turned to face him. He'd swiped away any betraying tears, but his eyes were reddened. He didn't seem to have any more idea what to say than she did. They looked at each other, Beth feeling as awkward as a fifteen-year-old alone for the first time with the boy she had a crush on.

"I...I'd better go." She took a step toward the door, assuming Nathan would move out of her way. "Mandy will be home soon."

He stayed blocking her path. "Can we celebrate? How about dinner tonight? Somewhere really fancy. Or would Mandy hate that?"

Beth seized on the subject of her daughter. "Are you kidding? She's twelve. Twelve-year-olds like to feel glamorous. She'll be sure she looks at least fourteen."

His mouth tilted into that heart-stopping smile. "I'll

tell her so. Six o'clock?'' Some of the emotion left his face. "Unless you'd rather be alone with her this evening. It's your celebration.''

"Ours," she said firmly. "Six sounds great.''

He walked her out to her car and opened the door for her, as if she was too fragile to make it on her own. Beth slipped in behind the wheel. Hand still on the door, Nathan gazed down at her.

"You know I'd have gone with you.''

She stared fixedly ahead. "Yes. You offered.''

"Then why the hell go through it alone?'' Suddenly he was scowling. "Don't you have a friend who'd have gone with you if you didn't want me?''

"I didn't want anybody.'' It was Nathan she'd thought of first after Mandy. She had never considered asking anyone else.

"You can be damned stubborn," he informed her.

"I know," Beth said with unaccustomed meekness. "I felt...like *I* should take responsibility. It was my idea, such a drastic step, and the chances still only one in four. I thought... I was afraid...''

A thoughtful scrutiny had replaced the scowl. "Afraid he wouldn't be compatible.''

"Yes.'' Now she stared down at her lap. "I was so scared. Sometimes it's easier to pretend to yourself than to other people.''

"I'm sorry.'' His voice held that husky note again. "I shouldn't chew you out. It was your decision.''

But she'd hurt him, she guessed, by leaving him out. "I came straight here," she said.

He only raised an eyebrow. "Would you have, if the news had been bad?'' Without waiting for her answer he nodded goodbye and slammed her door.

She almost rolled down her window and lied. ''Yes.

Of course I would have." Or was it a lie? But she didn't know, hadn't the slightest idea what she'd have done, where she'd have gone. The willow tree? Her bed, like a child who had no place else as refuge? Or maybe she would have gone to Nathan, who'd have understood as no one else could. Who, she saw now, loved Mandy. Perhaps not quite with a mother's ferocity, but with nearly a father's.

She made it home with fifteen or twenty minutes to spare before Mandy arrived. Not that she could make any use whatsoever of the time. She tried sitting on the glider and found herself jumping back to her feet. She sat on the railing and swung her legs, moved to the porch steps, paced. Finally she grabbed her garden gloves and cleaned up the flower beds to each side of the steps, deadheading October asters and gathering armfuls of brown foliage from earlier perennials. The rose was past; already it was forming hips that by Christmas would be glossy ornaments hanging from the bare thorny arms of the climber.

The rumble of the school bus in the distance brought her to her feet. It squealed to a stop down the road where the Jameson kids got off, lumbered to a start again and finally appeared through the alders, which had lost most of their leaves. She waited in unbearable suspense as the bus slowed and stopped again, the doors opened, and Mandy finally hopped out, turning to wave at her friends as the bus struggled up to speed again. Then Mandy began poking her way down the driveway, kicking at yellow leaves.

Beth couldn't stand it. She moved to meet her daughter, first strolling as though she had no particular reason, then faster and faster until she was running.

Mandy lifted her head. "Mom?"

Beth reached her like a whirlwind. Thank God she was laughing instead of crying, as she grabbed Mandy's shoulders and twirled her around until they were both dizzy.

Mandy pulled away and backed up, staggering a little when her foot hit uneven ground, but not seeming to notice. "Mom?" Her voice was thready. "Why are you acting like this?"

"He matches." Beth began to tremble all over. "You finally have a donor."

"He…" Her daughter's gaze darted to her stomach. "You mean, *him?*"

"Your brother. Patrick Joseph McCabe."

"It's a boy?" Mandy stared at her mother, eyes wide and dark. Stunned.

"Yep. And Dr. Simonson says he's an almost certain match. Six-out-of-six antigens, he thinks. A miracle."

"You…you'd tell me the truth if he didn't match, wouldn't you?" Mandy's face was too old. "You wouldn't lie to make me feel better?"

"I have never lied about your illness," Beth said with quiet intensity. "I never will. We have our miracle."

Mandy's tears came with a child's suddenness, belying her too-wise eyes. Her backpack dropped with a thud to the ground, and she sobbed against her mother's shoulder as though hope had been snatched away, not given to her. But with the memory of her own tears, Beth understood.

They dried up eventually, with sniffles, blown nose and a few fresh bursts. Beth carried Mandy's pack and they walked slowly up the drive, brown leaves crackling and disintegrating underfoot. Soon it would be raining, and then snow might come, and Christmas, and a new year. And in February, a baby. A miracle.

"Mom?"

"Mmm?"

"Will it hurt?" Mandy's voice was small.

"You mean, hurt the baby? When they take the bone marrow?" At her daughter's nod, Beth gave her a quick hug. "No. Actually, when he's born, the doctors will collect stem cells from his umbilical cord, instead of just tossing it. Your health permitting, the doctors will store those cells until Patrick is about six months old, when they'll use a long needle and take additional bone marrow cells from his hip and mix them with the stem cells. They tell me the pain is slight and the risks for him minimal."

Mandy nodded. They reached the porch steps and she plopped down. Beth followed suit and waited.

"Does this mean I'll get well for sure?"

If Beth hadn't sworn always to be honest, she might have lied now. But Mandy had faced too much unblinkingly not to deserve the truth.

"Well, first you have to stay healthy until Patrick's old enough to do the transplant. And then Dr. Simonson says the chances of a cure are about seventy percent. You know that the radiation needed to kill your own cells is risky, and there's always a small chance your body will reject the transplanted marrow."

Mandy stared ahead, thinking it over. After a moment she nodded. "You won't blame Patrick if it doesn't work, will you?"

Somebody might just as well have chopped Beth's heart in two. "No," she said tremulously. "We'll love him no matter what, I promise. He's…he's already a person to me."

Mandy scooted over a few inches until her hip bumped her mother's. "I'm going to be a good big sister. He'll never be sorry for what he had to go through for me."

"No." Beth could just get the words out. "No, I don't think he'll ever be sorry."

Mandy laid her head against her mother's shoulder. "He might hate knowing you had him only for...for some cells. Maybe you should lie."

"I don't like to lie," Beth said, "but this time you might be right."

They sat in peaceful silence. After a while Beth said lazily, "Nathan is going to take us out to dinner. To celebrate."

"Cool." Mandy didn't move. "Mom?"

"Mmm?"

"Can I buy a bra?"

"A bra?" Eyebrows lifted, Beth turned her head. "What on earth does that have to do with anything?"

"It's just that...well, you can see my nipples. When I wear anything tight. It's embarrassing!"

"Then I guess it's time," Beth agreed. "To tell you the truth, I'd noticed."

"Bras must be awfully uncomfortable." Mandy scrunched up her nose. "Why do we have to hide our breasts? *Boys* don't hide their chests."

"No, and very nice they are to look at, too."

"Mo-om!"

"Hey, I'm single. I can look, can't I?"

Mandy rolled her eyes. "Just don't look when my friends can see you, okay?"

"Deal." Beth stood up. "Whaddaya say we start gussying ourselves up? We're going fancy tonight."

"Can I wear that dress?" her daughter asked eagerly.

"That dress" was a hand-me-down from Beth's brother's daughter. Apparently their social circles and private schools in Saudi required even preteens to dress to the nines. This particular dress was black and gold and...well, sexy. Mandy had been praying for an appropriate occasion to wear it; Beth had been praying she'd get too tall before one arose. But seeing the hope in her daughter's dark eyes, she didn't have a qualm about capitulating.

"Why not?"

Mandy let out an ecstatic breath. "Thank you, thank you, thank you!"

"Just don't outshine me, okay?"

On her feet Mandy gazed critically at her mother. "But do you have anything really pretty that fits? I mean, since you're pregnant?"

Beth's eyes widened and she looked down at herself. "I don't know! I didn't think... Oh, no, what'll I do?"

"Uncle Nate will understand," her daughter said kindly.

"I don't want understanding!" Beth wailed, scrambling to her feet.

Mandy eyed her with a peculiar expression. "What *do* you want?"

Beth gulped. With what she considered quick wits, she said haughtily, "Admiration. Adulation. Awe would be okay. But I'd settle for not sticking out like a sore thumb."

"Oh." Mandy's face cleared. "Well, you're not *that* fat yet. You must have something."

She did, thank God, she found after an investigation of her closet. When she tugged the slinky teal sheath on, it fit all too snugly over her breasts and belly, but the black velvet jacket hid the overabundance of some parts of her body. And her legs still looked good, she decided, pirouetting in front of her mirror.

Half an hour later she opened the door to Nathan. He, of course, was heart-stoppingly handsome in a dark suit. The severity of the white shirtfront was the right foil for the angular, almost harsh lines of his face.

"Beautiful," he murmured to Beth, his eyes warm. His gaze went past her at the sound of Mandy clattering down the stairs. Beth, too, turned to look. The little girl wasn't quite gone, but close enough. The dress enhanced her slight curves and plunged at the neck, leaving a long sweep of white neck. Her dark hair was fastened on the crown of her head with a gold clip. Her eyes shone, her cheeks bloomed, and she was both ungainly and astonishingly graceful. Duckling and swan at the same time. Growing up, the way Beth had dreamed she would.

Beth couldn't have said a word to save her life. Fortunately Nathan said it for her.

"Sweetheart, what happened to your thirteenth and fourteenth birthdays? You decide to bypass them? You're going to break all the boys' hearts."

Mandy grinned, though she sounded anxious. "I really and truly look okay?"

"You take my breath away." He added quietly, "I'm glad for you, kiddo. I cried when your mom told me."

"Did you really?" She blinked as though to prevent new tears. "I did, too."

"Come here." He held out his arms.

Mandy launched herself into them. After a second

he held out an arm for Beth, and blinking fiercely to save her makeup, she went.

When they separated a moment later, they all had the same foolish smiles on their faces.

"Group hugs," Mandy said with satisfaction, "are the best kind."

"That was my first, but I think I'd have to agree." Very formally Nathan held out one elbow for Beth, the other for Mandy. "Ladies, shall we?"

Beth had never been happier than she was that evening. Only once did they put into words the source of the wellspring of joy that had them all laughing at next to nothing, that made the food ambrosia and the surroundings perfection.

Nathan made a toast, his glass of champagne gently touching theirs of sparkling cider. "To Mandy," he said. "And Patrick."

"To miracles," Beth said, her eyes meeting first Mandy's, then his.

"To Mom," Mandy contributed solemnly. "And to Uncle Nate."

They all drank, equally solemnly. And then Mandy said, "Just think. If Patrick was already born, we couldn't have brought him tonight. We'd have had to leave him with a baby-sitter! So this is best, huh?"

"Darn right," Nathan said. "Anyway, once he's born, we probably won't want to go anywhere. We'll be too busy sitting around the crib or cradle or whatever at home, exclaiming about how cute he is when he cries or spits up his milk or does something incredible like roll over."

From the experience of friends having little brothers and sisters, Mandy informed him how long it was before Patrick would roll over or do anything else really interesting. "They don't even *smile* for, like, six weeks or something. Babies are really pretty boring."

"But this one will be ours," Nathan pointed out.

Ours. Her heart ought to be numb by now, Beth thought, but the sharp stab she'd just felt showed that it wasn't. *Home.* He'd said *we'll* all sit around at home, hadn't he?

Today she'd been given what she wanted most in the world. Maybe it was selfish to ask for more, and so soon. But she couldn't seem to help it.

For the first time she let herself dream. Was it possible they could be a family? That Nathan could love her, as well as Patrick and Mandy? That it could quit mattering to all of them that he and Rob had been twins?

CHAPTER TWELVE

IN THE NEXT TWO and a half months, Beth's optimism wilted. Not that Nathan wasn't there, wasn't solicitous, wasn't friendly. He was. They had Thanksgiving together, celebrated Christmas as a family. Nathan found out when she regularly sent shipments of jam and managed to be around to carry the boxes. He called, he stopped by, he brought dinner, took them out to dinner, drove Mandy to drama and attended her school play. He was a devoted uncle/father figure. He was Beth's best friend. But that was all.

Occasionally she imagined she saw heat in his eyes when she touched him casually or looked up to find him watching her across a room. But he never, not once, acted on his desire—if he still felt any and she wasn't just seeing things.

And they never talked about Rob.

As far as the desire went…well, she didn't *feel* very desirable. Somehow with this pregnancy, she'd expanded faster and farther than when she carried Mandy. Now, at eight months along, she couldn't decide whether she more closely resembled a whale or a hippopotamus. Probably a hippo, she thought ruefully, looking at her bulging white stomach rising above the bubbles in her bath. Hippos didn't float. She was pretty sure she wouldn't, either. Who could blame a man for not lusting after this body?

The business about Rob, though, was something else again. It had taken her a while to notice that Rob's name rarely came up anymore. Those first few months, Nathan had made a point of talking about his brother, especially for Mandy's benefit. When Mandy asked questions, he still answered them without seeming uncomfortable, but he never spontaneously reminisced as he once had. *Did you know Rob was the quarterback of our high-school football team?* Or, *Did Rob ever tell you about the time he backed the car into the neighbor's fence, and we propped it up until a winter storm blew it over? Did you know Rob had childhood asthma?*

Just the other night Mandy was insisting she'd been really, really ugly in about fourth grade, and she dragged Uncle Nate to the fireplace mantel to see her school picture from that year. Out of curiosity Beth had followed them. Nathan looked at Mandy's photo, but his eyes never strayed to any of the other framed pictures standing along the mantel. He had to have *worked* at not looking.

Apparently he'd decided that the way to deal with his feelings about his brother was to pretend Rob never had existed. Beth couldn't imagine that, in the long term, his avoidance would work. One of these days that buried resentment was going to boil over. And there was no way they could have any kind of romantic relationship without him accepting that she'd once loved and been married to his brother.

Not, she had to admit, that Nathan gave any sign of *wanting* a romantic relationship. Beth made a face and slumped lower in the tub.

A moment later she sighed, reached for the towel and carefully got to her feet. She dried her arms and breasts and back, then lifted one foot to the rim of the bathtub and bent over to pat her leg dry.

That was when she saw the blood trickling down her thigh and staining the bathwater.

SOME DAYS he figured he was a gutless wonder. On others Nathan convinced himself he was being sensible, maybe even gentlemanly. Hell, noble.

Wait until she had the baby, he told himself. Five, six, eight months pregnant, she couldn't possibly be interested in love and marriage. She was dealing with enough already. Let her have the baby, see that he really would be a devoted father, get used to the idea that he *was* Patrick Joseph McCabe's father. By that time, maybe she wouldn't see Rob anymore when she looked at him.

Then a bad day, like today, would come, and he'd know in his heart that he wasn't waiting for Beth. His feelings were the stumbling block. He didn't have the guts to put her to the test. Looking up at him that day back in September, her eyes cloudy with passion, she probably hadn't said "Rob." But what if the next time she did? What if she was *thinking* Rob? Damn. What if she still wanted Rob? Nathan shoved his chair back from his computer and squeezed his eyes shut. How would he ever know?

How could he stand not knowing?

When the phone rang he didn't pick it up. Let the machine handle the call. He kept the answering machine in the living room so his concentration wouldn't be broken when he was involved in something. This time, ignoring the murmur of his own voice from the other room, he rubbed his temples and tried to focus on the columns of figures on the screen.

He was damned lucky he'd built a strong company and had people working for him who knew what the hell they were doing. He'd sure as God left them alone to do it lately. He should be traveling more than he was, but every time he got on an airplane, he felt uneasy. What if something went wrong with the pregnancy? What if Beth went into labor early? What if Mandy got sick? He didn't like knowing that no neighbor was within shouting distance, didn't like the narrow winding road separating their house from the nearest medical clinic. It was January now, and thus far the winter had been relatively dry for the Pacific Northwest, but what if a storm dumped eight inches of snow on the ground? Or the rain froze into black ice? He'd seen to it that Beth had snow tires on her car, but he still wasn't happy. He could have concentrated a hundred times better if he'd been there instead of—

A tremulous quality to the voice murmuring in place of his own on the answering machine wrenched Nathan from his brooding. Swearing, he snatched up the receiver.

"Beth?"

"Nathan?" She gave a sobbing breath that sounded like relief. "You *are* home."

"I was working." Alarm masqueraded as brusqueness. "What's wrong? You're not in labor, are you?"

She seemed to withdraw. "No, I... Oh, I can manage alone. I just..."

Manage alone. He gritted his teeth. Her confidence in him overwhelmed him. Brusque this time from irritation—or was it hurt?—he said shortly, "You don't have to. If you need me, I can come right away."

The tremble returned to her soft voice. "Are you sure?"

He surged to his feet and roared, "Goddamn it, Beth, what's wrong?"

Silence chastened him. And then, shakily, she said, "I'm bleeding." A sniffle came over the line. "Nathan, I'm scared. What if…?"

Pure terror tore a hole in his stomach like an ulcer. With an effort he spoke gently. "Have you called the doctor?"

"She wants me to come in. I…I was just getting dressed."

Nathan gave a wild glance at his watch as he groped for his car keys in his pocket. "I'm twenty-five minutes away. Shouldn't you have an ambulance?"

"My bleeding isn't that heavy. She wants to see me, but she said it's not necessarily an emergency."

He could tell Beth didn't believe the reassurance any more than he did. "I'm going out the door right now," he said steadily. "You know my cell-phone number if you need me. If things get worse, you call an ambulance. I'll be there as quick as I can." And to hell with any speed traps along the way.

Every traffic light turned red just as he got to it. Every grandfather out to drive the little woman to the grocery store cruised down the road at twenty-five miles an hour. Kids on bikes swerved from the shoulder into lanes of traffic. Nathan's knuckles were white on the steering wheel. He used language he'd forgotten he knew. He was saved only by frequent desperate looks at his watch, which told him he was making good time, despite everything. He took the swooping curves of her country road as if behind the wheel of a sports car. The tires skidded and spit out gravel when he accelerated down her driveway and slammed to a stop.

He half expected to find her lying in a pool of blood

on the kitchen floor. Relief uncramped a fraction of his
tension when she opened the front door before he could
mount the stairs. She wore thick leggings and a denim
jumper over a pink turtleneck. Her curly hair was dis-
ciplined with a clip. She looked composed, pretty. She
even wore makeup, for God's sake. The contrast to the
nightmarish images that had kept his foot heavy on the
accelerator couldn't have been greater. Why the hell
had she scared him?

Then he noticed her pallor, the shadows beneath her
eyes, the fear in her eyes. And he saw the bag she
carried.

Her gaze followed his. "I packed a few things just
in case..."

He nodded tightly and took it from her. Although
she moved confidently, he held her elbow as she de-
scended the porch steps. Normally, as he opened the
passenger-side door of the car and eased her in as carefully as he might have a new piece of furniture he
didn't want to scratch, she would have been protesting
that she didn't break. Today, she only gave him a shaky
smile. Now she knew that she did break.

He broke more speed records getting her to the
clinic. The nurse whisked Beth right in. When he
started to follow, the nurse said, "Why don't you wait
here, sir. The doctor will do an examination, then we'll
come get you. I promise."

So he had to suffer the agony of watching Beth disappear through the door. Then he looked helplessly
around. What was he supposed to do? Chat with another restless father-to-be? Trip the five-year-old who
was running laps and zooming like an airplane? Sit and
read *People* magazine? He didn't give a damn which
celebrity was divorcing her husband. Right this minute

he didn't give a damn about the budget crisis, either, which was featured on the cover of *Newsweek*. He made himself sit down, but he didn't even reach for a magazine.

What were they doing to her? How heavily was she bleeding? Would they hospitalize her? God, was she losing the baby? A fierce protest rose in his throat, had him gripping the arms of the chair until his hands ached.

His son. And what if Beth was in danger? And Mandy—how could they tell Mandy if the worst happened?

Mandy. Nathan looked at his watch again with new alarm. No, they were okay. It'd be two hours until she got off the school bus. They'd know something by then. If necessary, he would leave Beth to go pick up Mandy.

The nurse appeared and smiled at him. As he shot to his feet, she said, "Mr. McCabe? You can come back now."

She showed him into an empty room. Briskly she bundled up the crumpled paper on the examining table, but not before he saw some bright red bloodstains.

"Mrs. McCabe has gone downstairs to have an ultrasound," she said brightly. "Dr. Williams wanted to speak to you briefly, and then perhaps you'd prefer to wait out in front. It may be half an hour. You could even go get a cup of coffee."

He didn't say anything. She bustled out as cheerily as she'd led him in, leaving the door open. Fortunately Dr. Williams entered almost immediately.

Without preamble she said, "I suspect a condition called *placenta previa,* in which the placenta is partially over the cervix. Bleeding at this stage can signal the separation of the placenta, which is far more serious, but Mrs. McCabe has no tenderness, no rigidity in her abdominal wall. We're taking a closer look right now with an ultrasound.''

"Is she losing the baby?" he asked hoarsely.

"I don't believe so." Compassion made the doctor's tone less brisk than the other times he'd come here with Beth. "Besides, if necessary, we can do a cesarean section at this point. I'd prefer she hold on for at least another couple weeks, though."

Hold on. Nathan felt even more helpless. "How?"

"Bed rest," she said succinctly. "Maybe hospitalization. Home if she has enough help."

"She's got it."

"That's what I wanted to hear." Dr. Williams gave him a rare approving smile. "Would you prefer to wait in here?"

"Thanks."

The moment she quietly closed the door behind her, his legs collapsed, dumping him in the hard plastic chair. He was glad to be alone.

The half hour he waited was the longest of his life. Up to this point, he thought grimly. Beth hadn't asked him to take childbirth classes with her, which meant he'd be excluded when she had the baby. What if she was in labor for twelve hours? Would he have to pace a waiting room? The prospect was so appalling he gritted his teeth. He'd rather be the one suffering in the delivery room.

When the door opened, Nathan got to his feet. Dr. Williams and Beth came in together. Beth's face was pale and solemn, her eyes still frightened. When he reached out a hand, she slipped hers into it and squeezed back when he gripped tightly. Together they faced the doctor.

"My guess was right," she said. "The placenta is only partially blocking the cervix. It does mean we'll have to do a C-section when the time comes. When the cervix dilates, the placenta separates from the uterus, depriving the baby of oxygen. What we need to focus on now is sustaining your pregnancy as long as possible, Beth. Your bleeding is relatively minor and intermittent. I think, if you're willing to go to bed for the next few weeks, you can make it close to full term."

The shock on Beth's face told Nathan she hadn't been forewarned.

"Weeks?" she repeated. "Spend almost a *month* in bed?"

"You can get up. We won't tie you down. Bed *rest* is what we call it. But no lifting, no housework, no shopping, no jogging. For the most part I want you resting in bed. Indulge yourself. Read, watch TV, snooze. If you do too much and start bleeding again, I'll have to hospitalize you."

"A month?"

"If all goes well." Dr. Williams's tone wasn't without sympathy, but she was still matter-of-fact. "The indulgence doesn't carry over to food unfortunately. No heart-shaped boxes of chocolate. Weight gain hasn't been a problem for you, but without exercise, you'll have to be especially careful."

Beth dropped into a chair as abruptly as Nathan had earlier, her legs apparently giving way. She still held on to his hand.

"But...I can't do nothing! Mandy's only twelve." Beth looked from the doctor to Nathan and back as she begged for understanding. "She can't clean house and cook dinner and do the laundry and… I do have an assistant who I guess can handle the business for a few weeks, but… I have a life!'' she wailed.

Nathan figured it was time to contribute to this discussion. ''I'll clean house and cook dinner and do the laundry. I can give Julie a hand with the jam, too, if she needs it.''

Beth stared at him. ''But how can you? You have your own business! This is crazy.'' She turned beseeching eyes on the doctor. ''There has to be another way.''

''There isn't.'' The doctor's warm brown eyes didn't waver. ''The baby's welfare has to come first, however tough that is for a while.''

Beth was still in shock when Nathan ushered her out to the car a few minutes later after having agreed to bring her back in a couple of days. Sooner, if she began bleeding again or had any discomfort.

''We'll keep a close watch on her,'' had been Dr. Williams's last words.

Damn right they would. He'd take her home, wait until Mandy was there, then go to his condo and pack. He could use Beth's computer to keep in touch with his office, but somebody else would have to handle the trip to Arizona and New Mexico scheduled for the week after next. Already mentally shuffling schedules and duties, he only listened with half an ear to Beth's desperate objections.

''You're going to move *in?*''

''Mmm,'' he agreed absently.

''But…but…''

Waiting at a red light, Nathan turned his head. ''You have a problem with that?''

''I can hire someone.'' She waved her hands. ''You don't have to drop everything.''

"I won't. I'll use your office if that's okay. I presume the housework isn't a full-time job."

"You may be surprised. Especially—" she scrunched up her nose "—if you have to wait on me hand and foot."

"Are you going to be demanding?" he asked, feeling his first trace of amusement that day.

"What I'm going to do is go nuts," she said gloomily.

"You can keep up on paperwork."

"There's hardly any at this time of year." Beth sounded as sulky as Mandy in a bad mood.

"Hey, look on the bright side. What if this were June?"

She moaned and flopped back against the headrest. He let her brood the rest of the way home.

She didn't, however, take it well when he tried to help her up the front porch steps. "I can walk!" she snapped.

"Oh, this is going to be a fun month," he muttered, releasing her elbow.

In front of him Beth abruptly stopped. He waited a couple of steps below her. She was entitled to be angry, he figured; fear often came out that way. And she sure as hell had plenty to be afraid of.

She took a deep breath and turned to face him. No anger. Instead, tears streaked her cheeks. "I'm sorry. I'm being awful." Her voice rose into a wail. "And you're being so nice!"

"Ah, damn," he said, taking that next step and wrapping his arms around her. She stood enough higher that her face ended up buried in the crook of his neck and shoulder, instead of leaning against his chest. He felt the tears, hot and wet, against his bare skin; felt the quivers of sobs shake her swollen body.

When at last she looked up, her eyes were red and puffy and her nose was running. Which was a hell of a time for him to feel love rock him so hard he'd have stepped backward into space if he hadn't still been holding her.

"I *am* sorry," Beth repeated. "I'll be good. Dr. Williams was right. Nothing matters but the baby. And here I am sulking because I have to laze around. You're the one who's giving up everything to take care of us!"

"I'm not giving up anything," he said roughly. "For now, you guys are my only family. I've been worrying about you, anyway. Now I have an excuse to be right here where I want to be."

She sniffed one more time, then flung her arms around him again and gave him a quick hard hug. He felt her lips move against his neck, heard a murmur, but his ears wouldn't take in what she said. It couldn't have been "I love you." Or if it was, she didn't mean it the way he wanted her to. Friends loved each other. Family members loved each other. She was just grateful to Mandy's uncle Nate for being a good guy and helping out. She didn't mean "I love you" the way he felt it.

And that hurt like nothing had since his brother's betrayal.

MANDY THOUGHT it was cool having Uncle Nate living with them.

At first she'd been scared about Mom's losing the baby. Here she'd gotten used to the idea of having a brother. Patrick Joseph McCabe. Patrick. That was what she planned to call him. Not Pat or Joey or anything else cutesy. Patrick. She could close her eyes and picture him, dark-haired and dark-eyed like her, toddling after her like Kayla's little brother followed his big sister. Mandy could hold him, chunky and round, and he'd grin up at her without teeth. Eventually she'd teach him stuff. Like how to whistle and how to read and how to pump on the swing. She didn't want him never to be.

Even as frightened as she was, Mandy didn't let herself think about the other reason she desperately wanted him to be born. It seemed so selfish, as if she was the only one who mattered. So she just blanked her mind to it. Only, that didn't completely work. She knew that underneath, the selfish motive was still there.

But after a few days, when Mom and the baby seemed okay, Mandy started thinking how much fun it was to have Uncle Nate here. He made easy dinners, like pancakes, or macaroni and cheese, or sloppy joes. Mom rolled her eyes and asked how anyone could have lived alone all these years and not learned to cook. Mandy liked the dinners better than some of the stuff Mom got out of cookbooks, but she didn't say so where Mom could hear.

Uncle Nate teased Mandy a lot, and he played games with her and helped her with her homework. Once her social-studies teacher got mad because nobody was paying attention, and she said that everyone in the class had to write, "I will be courteous and listen to Mrs. Curtis when she speaks" three hundred times as homework. But Mandy *had* been listening! It was so unfair. And humiliating, treating them like little kids. Uncle Nate agreed, and he copied her handwriting and wrote half the sentences for her. How many parents would have done that?

Sometimes they all played a game together, Mom propped against pillows and Uncle Nate sitting on one side of her on the bed and Mandy on the other. They'd open the game board on Mom's lap—well, really her legs, since she didn't exactly have a lap anymore. That worked okay until she got up to go to the bathroom, which she had to do *constantly*. Uncle Nate teased her that it would be easier to wear a diaper. He was funny lots of the time. He made Mom laugh.

It was while they were playing TriBond one night that Mandy got her idea. Mom was scowling as she tried to decide what Superfly, The Body and The Macho Man had in common. Mandy happened to look at Uncle Nate, who was watching Mom. His mouth had this little smile, and his eyes were sort of soft and moony, and it hit Mandy: he was in love with Mom!

"Japanese horror movies," Mom finally decided.

"Nope," Uncle Nate said. "Professional wrestlers."

Mom made this awful face. "Superfly?"

"Yup. Dignity is not a component of professional wrestling."

"I guess not," Mom mumbled. "Okay, Mr. Know-it-all, it's your turn."

Mandy read the three things that had something in common. "A map, a fish and a weight-loss clinic."

"I know that one!" Mom gave a little bounce, which made their markers on the board slide. "Sorry, sorry." She put them all back in place.

"A map and a fish." Uncle Nate stared into space.

This time, Mom watched *him*. Mandy couldn't quite decide whether she was looking moony, too, or just normal. He *was* really cute. Mom must have been in love with Dad long time ago. And since Uncle Nate looked a lot like Dad, why couldn't she fall in love with him, too?

If they got married, Uncle Nate would stay, always and always. He'd be Mandy's stepfather.

"Scales!" he suddenly said triumphantly.

"Huh?" Mandy looked down at the card in her hand. "Oh. Yeah. You get to roll again."

Later she kept thinking about them, married. She could be a bridesmaid, or maybe even the maid of honor, if kids were allowed. Mom could wear white lace, and Uncle Nate a black tuxedo, and Mandy wouldn't even mind if they went away for a honeymoon, not when it meant Uncle Nate would come back with Mom forever. What would she call him? she wondered dreamily that night as she waited to fall asleep. Would she still call him Uncle Nate? Or just his first name, like some kids did with stepparents? Or... Well, not Dad. Somehow that seemed disloyal, even if she was having a harder and harder time remembering her father. Uncle Nate's face had gotten in the way. It was him she saw now when she tried to picture Dad.

Sometimes that made her feel guilty, too, just like her secret thoughts about Patrick, but then she remembered how much Dad had talked about Uncle Nate, and she convinced herself Dad would like knowing his twin brother was here, doing things with her and helping Mom out. And if Mom married him, it wasn't like she'd *chosen* Uncle Nate, instead of Dad. Dad was *dead*. Gone. All her friends thought it was romantic that Mom never dated; they said it must mean she was mourning him still. Probably, they thought, she'd mourn him for the rest of her life, and he'd be waiting for her up in heaven. But Mandy wasn't so sure. Mom didn't *act* like she was still grieving. Once, about a year ago, Mandy had asked her why she didn't date, and Mom had looked surprised.

"I don't know anybody I want to date." She'd shrugged. "And I'm busy. I don't feel the need."

Mandy had nodded. That was kind of what she'd guessed. She and Mom were okay by themselves, except for when Mandy was really sick. Why would they want some strange man around?

But Uncle Nate was different. Mandy wanted him around. What she couldn't figure was any way to push things along, except for thinking of reasons—like playing games—for him to be in Mom's bedroom every evening. Or keeping him away from Mom when she started to get grumpy about having to lie there and do nothing. Or, once in a while, when Mom was depressed and didn't want to bother doing anything to her hair or putting makeup on, Mandy encouraged her. If he saw her looking really awful, Uncle Nate might lose interest.

Mandy wouldn't have minded if these weeks could have gone on and on. She knew Uncle Nate was taking Mom to see the doctor really often, and that Mom would have to be cut open to have the baby out, instead of having him the normal way. But she thought Mom or Uncle Nate would at least give her some notice.

Instead, she was called from her prealgebra class to the office one day. The vice principal was waiting for her.

He smiled. "Amanda, I have good news for you."

She thought about an essay she'd entered in a national contest. But hers wasn't that good. It couldn't have won, could it?

"Your uncle Nathan just called. He wanted you to

know your mom has had her baby. He's a boy, and they're both doing fine.''

Mandy just stared. Patrick was already born? Had Mom and Uncle Nate known last night that today was the day? Why hadn't they told her?

''Your uncle says he'll pick you up from school, so you can go directly to the hospital. He guessed you might want to meet your new brother.''

Her new brother. Excitement suddenly fizzed through Mandy. Maybe she could hold him today. And she already knew how to change diapers and that you had to support a baby's head. Kayla had shown her. She could take care of Patrick while Mom napped and stuff. This was going to be so cool!

Uncle Nate came really fast. Mandy was waiting just inside the door. She wanted to run out and hop in the car, but, no, he had to come in and fill out a stupid form releasing her. By that time, she was practically hopping up and down.

''Let's go!''

He grinned when she grabbed his hand and tugged him toward the door. ''You're the one who told me babies don't do anything exciting for at least six weeks.''

''Yeah, but I want to see if he looks like me. And if he has all his toes, and what color his eyes are.'' She swallowed. ''And if Mom's okay.''

Uncle Nate's arm snaked out to give her a boa-constricting hug. ''Your mother is doing just great. She looks as proud as if she'd just painted a masterpiece.''

''Well, she kind of did.''

''Hey.'' He pretended to be offended. ''*I* wielded a brush, too, you know.''

"Yeah," Mandy said interestedly, "I've been wondering about that. I mean, *how*..."

"Don't ask."

Mandy had the feeling he meant it. He had a weird expression on his face, like he was remembering something really depressing. She was pretty sure he and Mom hadn't had sex, so how had they done it? It couldn't have been much fun. Maybe she could ask her health teacher how people make babies if they didn't want to go to bed together.

Once they got to the hospital, all she could think about was her brother. Patrick Joseph McCabe. She knew he couldn't smile, but maybe he'd—well, *look* at her at least, as though he knew they meant something to each other.

She kept having to hurry Uncle Nate, and the elevator took forever. But at last the doors crept open, and ahead was a sign that said Maternity.

"Shall we go by the nursery first?" Uncle Nate suggested.

It turned out to be this bright room surrounded with glass. Inside were rows of bassinets. Most were empty. Only a few babies slept in theirs, and she could hardly see them. The littlest ones had tiny knit caps covering most of their heads, and they were all swaddled up in blankets so she could just barely see their red, scrunched faces in between.

"Where is he?" she whispered.

"Not here," Uncle Nate said. "He must be up with your mom."

Mandy bounced on the balls of her feet. "Where's *she*?"

"Just down the hall."

Mandy was dying to see Patrick. And Mom. But

when Uncle Nate turned into one of the rooms down the hall, Mandy hesitated on the threshold. She felt...shy. Maybe a little scared. What if Mom had changed? This was a big deal, having a baby. And what if she, Mandy, thought Patrick was ugly, or hated him on sight? What if he was going to save her life, and she didn't like him?

The first bed was empty. Beyond the curtain, Mom called, "Mandy? Where are you?"

She edged around it. The head of Mom's bed was lifted, so she could sit up and still lean against the pillows. She wore a flannel nightgown that Mandy had never seen before. But she was smiling, and her cheeks were pink, and she held out her arms.

"I could hardly wait until you got here!"

Mandy flew over and closed her eyes against sudden tears while Mom hugged her.

"So, what do you think?" Mom asked.

Mandy opened her eyes and eased back. Patrick was nestled against Mom's side. He wasn't quite asleep, but almost, his fist pressed against his mouth. He definitely had ten fingers, though they were really, really tiny. And his eyes—well, she couldn't tell what color they were. They had a vague look, as if he couldn't see much of anything.

She bent over and touched the back of his hand. He jerked and rocked his head toward her. "Hi, Patrick," she whispered. "I'm Mandy."

He frowned, but instead of being offended, she giggled. He was a person, not a doll. Eventually he'd learn to like her, and do what she told him to do.

Suddenly she had the strangest feeling in her chest, as though she could hardly breathe. It was partly a good feeling, and partly a scary one.

He was a real person, not just an idea. Her little brother. And he was going to have to do something that, no matter what Mom said, would hurt. What if later, when he found out what they'd made him do, he was mad at her?

Mandy took a deep breath. *I'll make it up to you,* she told him silently. *I'll be the best big sister ever. I promise.*

CHAPTER THIRTEEN

WHEN NATHAN BROUGHT Mandy, Patrick and Beth home, he had every intention of staying. He wondered how long it would be before Beth noticed he still occupied the spare bedroom. Even as he carried her suitcase up the stairs, he waited for her to ask why his wasn't packed. She'd say thanks and goodbye nicely and send him on his way. But instead, right behind him, she paused in the doorway of her bedroom. "Oh! The crib looks beautiful! You even set up the bumper pads."

The white-painted crib stood within a few feet of Beth's bed. The crib's bedding, in sunshine yellow and sky blue, added a vivid note to her pale yellow bedroom, cheerful despite February's gray light coming through the windows.

"I did that part," Mandy told her, crowding in, too. "Uncle Nate couldn't figure out where the ties went."

Beth flashed him a teasing smile. "And this is the man responsible for manufacturing mountain tents. Can you set up your own?"

"I could have figured out how it worked," he said with dignity. "Mandy just beat me to it."

"I put the sheet on, too," the twelve-year-old said. "I thought that was the cutest one."

"Me, too." Her mother smiled at her. Then she glanced down at the small bundle in her arms. "Well.

Shall we try it out? It looks like Patrick has no intention of waking up.''

Nathan held out his arms. "Let me. You shouldn't bend over for a few days."

He had to give her credit. However she felt about him, she'd so far been unstintingly generous in sharing their son. She handed Patrick to him without hesitation.

Nathan eased the receiving blanket back from Patrick's face, set in the fierce scowl that appeared to be his usual sleeping—and often waking—expression. Despite the fact that his scrunched-up face was also red and wrinkly and flaking, and that his dark hair stuck up in sweaty tufts like marsh grass, Nathan was immediately pierced by a love so sweet it made his chest hurt. He was still baffled by the powerfully protective, triumphant, tender feelings that had gripped him from the moment he first saw his son.

Gently Nathan laid him in the crib on his back and tucked the thin blanket around him. Then, like idiots, they all stood around the crib and raptly watched Patrick Joseph McCabe sleep.

After a moment Nathan looked up. Beth's fingers were curled around the top rail as she smiled softly down at her newborn. She was as achingly beautiful as a Renaissance Madonna, if more fragile. No woman who'd just had surgery ought to be so clear-eyed, so glowing. Pale hair curled around her face, creamy with only a hint of the gold the summer sun had lent her. Her breasts were fuller, although her neck and arms were as slender as ever.

It had been bad enough remembering the shadowy cleft of her breasts from that day he'd come on her napping. Bad enough to remember the way she'd shuddered when he'd kissed them. It was far worse now that he was forced several times a day to see the ripe pale swell of one, even the brown aureole and nipple before she deftly slipped it into Patrick's mouth. Lucky Patrick.

Good God, he thought, half ruefully and half grimly, this was hardly the time to be getting sexually stimulated. What if Mandy noticed? He wrenched his gaze from Beth's breasts to her face—only to find that she was watching him now, not Patrick. Her eyes had darkened and her cheeks flushed a delicate pink. They stared at each other for an endless moment during which he cursed himself for giving her good reason not to want him living in her house.

But she could only be guessing about his thoughts. *Say something*, Nathan told himself. *Make her wonder.*

He had to clear his throat first. "Shall we let him sleep?"

Her eyes flickered at the distraction. "I suppose we should."

Nobody moved except Patrick, who grunted and jerked and frowned more fiercely.

"Do you want me to close the blinds?" Mandy whispered.

"It doesn't look like *he* cares." Her attention no longer on Nathan, Beth wrinkled her nose. "Besides, I don't know if I want him to sleep that well. I'm afraid he envisions being nocturnal."

"You mean, he'll scream all night," Mandy said knowledgeably.

"Right." Her mother made another face. "Last night the nurses helped out. Tonight I can't push a button and summon someone who's being paid to be wide awake and cheerful."

To hell with it. He might as well declare his intentions right now. "I'll get up with him, too," Nathan said, as though his presence were a given. "Surely he doesn't need to be fed every time he wakes up."

Beth's eyes widened. But before she could say anything, Patrick grunted again and squirmed deeper under his blanket. Beth made shooing motions at his audience. They all tiptoed out into the hall.

She turned to him and said quietly, "You mean, you haven't already gratefully packed your suitcase?"

"You just had surgery. You still need help."

Her chin was up, her gaze level. "We could manage."

Mandy was watching them anxiously, he noted out of the corner of his eye. To her mother he said evenly, "You shouldn't have to manage. Mandy and I can handle the meals and housework for a while. You should rest."

Her favorite word. "All I've done is rest!"

Mandy jumped in. "Yeah, but staying in bed makes a person weak, Mom. You always told me that when I couldn't figure out why I was so shaky. And you've been in bed for *weeks*."

One second the issue hung in the balance, their gazes warring and her pride on the line; the next she blinked and held up both hands. "So I have. Okay, okay! Pamper me. Adore me. I don't mind."

Wouldn't he like to, Nathan thought. But unfortunately she wasn't looking at him, and her tone was teasing.

"How about a cup of tea right now?" he asked.

Her laughing eyes met his, jolting him back into a heightened—no pun intended—state of physical awareness. "Certainly, sir. You may serve it in the parlor."

"Come into my parlor, said the spider to the fly," Nathan murmured.

Her mouth remained curved, but her eyes had gone serious on him. "Now's your chance to run away," she suggested for all the world as though she was still teasing.

Another anxious glance from Mandy told Nathan that *she* wasn't fooled, either.

"I'll worry about the sticky web when it wraps around me," he said, holding Beth's gaze just long enough to see how she reacted. Then, satisfied, he draped an arm around Mandy's shoulder. "Come on, kiddo. A life of service awaits us."

SHE OUGHT TO BE GRATEFUL he'd stayed.

She *was* grateful. Sometimes. Like this morning, when her son's fire-engine wail dragged her eyes open to the murky gray light of dawn, and a bleary glance at her clock told her she'd only been asleep for an hour this time. She thought she might die if she couldn't sleep just a little longer, but the wailing went on and she was just bracing herself to get out of bed no matter how wretched she felt when Patrick abruptly quit crying. She didn't even have to hear the soft creak of the rocking chair to know Nathan had come. She *felt* him in the room, no matter how silently he moved. Prying open leaden eyelids again, she could just make him out, bare-chested, cuddling their son and humming so low that it was no more than a murmur to her ears. His presence, that hum, the creak of the chair, all soothed her as much as they did Patrick, and she slept again for a few more precious hours.

But when she awoke later, she couldn't believe that she was letting this man wearing nothing but pajama bottoms come into her bedroom during the night whenever he pleased, and that she slept right through his visits. Or, worse, was comforted by them.

During the day she'd become absurdly shy with him. In return he was formal, even distant. Gone were the laughter and easiness of the last weeks of her pregnancy, when he'd sat on her bed and played board games on her lap. Letting it get to her now made her feel like a fool; okay, he'd been almost a total stranger when she asked him to father her baby, but he wasn't anymore. They were friends, at least, weren't they?

They'd be better friends if he wouldn't watch so fixedly when she nursed Patrick. Like now. She sat on one end of the couch, legs curled under her, Patrick lying lengthwise along her arm, mouth firmly attached to her breast. Nathan sat on the other end of the couch. Because he was so close, she was being as discreet as she could manage; she'd arranged her shirt so that he couldn't possibly have caught more than a fleeting glimpse of her breast before Patrick latched on. He wouldn't have seen even that much if he'd really been watching the TV news, his ostensible reason for lounging only a few feet away from her. But he wasn't, any more than she was. She could feel his eyes on her, and she knew that if she looked up she would see them, narrowed, intense, dark. Disquieting, making it hard, suddenly, for her to breathe.

What was she supposed to do? Cry, "Don't look at me that way?" Lurk behind closed bedroom doors every time she nursed Patrick? Damn it, this was her own home, and she was sick to death of her bedroom!

Besides… *Okay, admit it,* she ordered herself, pretending to watch Peter Jennings chat about a stalemated

Congress. *You like knowing Nathan's watching you. It turns you on.*

That was what was really getting to her. It wasn't him, it was *her*. She wanted him. Fiercely, hungrily, sweetly. Every nerve in her body seemed to be aware of him, like a radio tuned to only one airwave.

She sighed and felt Nathan stir two cushions down the couch from her. And no wonder. Congress might have warranted the sigh; the bouncy commercial currently on for dishwashing detergent didn't. She transferred her gaze from the television to the fuzzy top of Patrick's head. His sucking was slowing, his eyes had drifted shut. Soon his mouth would slip from her breast, and she would have to ease him up to her shoulder and refasten her bra at the same time. In her heart, she knew she might dawdle just the tiniest bit with the bra clasp.

She was pathetic. A woman who'd had a baby only three weeks before—and had a fresh incision in her stomach—shouldn't be, however subtly, trying to seduce a man. Or letting herself be seduced. She wasn't sure which was happening. All she knew was, if Nathan beckoned, she'd want to go more than she'd ever wanted anything.

With momentary humor Beth amended the thought: she'd go during those rare times she'd had enough sleep to feel human. In the murky light of dawn, even Nathan's bare chest didn't incite passion, only... comfort. Beth frowned a little. There was that word again, an odd one to use to describe your feelings for a man you were in love with.

And, oh, she was in love with him. For the first time she admitted it, knew it, accepted it. She loved Nathan McCabe. Not Rob. She no longer thought of him when she looked at Nathan; Nathan didn't even remind her of Rob anymore. In fact, the other day when she'd glanced at the photographs on the mantel, for a second she'd been startled, not because Nathan looked like Rob, but because Rob looked like Nathan.

When she thought about Rob at all, it was with fondness, a pallid emotion. What had once been love had eroded, the edges worn away until it was like a small smooth stone she carried in her pocket and ran her fingers over once in a while. She would never throw the stone away, but neither would it ever preoccupy her the way these disturbing, rough-edged feelings for Nathan did. Falling in love with Rob had been easy, fun; she'd been at an age when everyone was pairing up, and he was handsome, intelligent, made her laugh.

Why did it have to be so difficult this time around?

Patrick was asleep. She gently touched the furrows between his brows. Then, before she moved him, she sneaked a glance at Nathan. As she'd known he would be, he was looking at Patrick, too. Or at her breast. When he lifted his gaze to her face, his mouth had a twist she couldn't interpret, and his eyes smoldered with dangerous emotions.

Just like that a question popped into her mind: what if, back when she'd met Rob, Nathan had been there, too? Which brother would she have fallen in love with?

The answer was one of those rough edges. It came without a trace of doubt, leaving guilt in its wake. Worse yet, what if she'd met Nathan while Rob was still alive? What if the two had reconciled? How would she have reacted to Nathan?

Her hands shook a little as she lifted Patrick to her shoulder and then reached to fasten the flap on her nursing bra. Nathan's eyes, unwavering, held a molten glow; tension came from him in waves. Fumbling, she lowered her shirt and patted her son's back until a small burp rewarded her. With a jerk, Nathan turned his head to stare at the TV. Otherwise, he was so still it was unnatural.

Her legs trembled when she stood. "I'm going to put him to bed and see what Mandy's up to."

He didn't even look at her. "I'll clean the kitchen as soon as the news is over."

She nodded meaninglessly and fled.

Another week passed in much the same way. She needed Nathan, wanted him, didn't know if she could bear to go on this way. She could hardly talk to him anymore. What was he thinking? She couldn't be imagining the way he looked at her! Why didn't he say something? *Do* something?

Like kiss her. They were both single. Unattached. Together they'd created a baby. She knew he loved Mandy, as well as Patrick. So why couldn't they fall into each other's arms, get married and go off into the sunset hand in hand?

There wasn't a reason in the world. Which meant she *was* imagining things. He was here out of a sense of obligation. He wanted to prove he really intended to be a parent to Patrick. Maybe he was fascinated by the sight of his son nursing. Maybe his expression didn't have anything at all to do with her.

As the next week went by and March arrived, her thoughts circled around and around. He wanted her; he wasn't the slightest bit interested. Typical was one afternoon when Beth had just convinced herself of his indifference for the tenth or twelfth time. She went down to the kitchen for a before-dinner glass of juice. Nathan was there chopping green pepper on the cutting board with unnecessary ferocity. He looked up and his eyes pinned her.

She almost took a step back. "I, um, just came down to get something to drink."

"I'll pour it for you." He set down the knife.

"I'm not helpless," she said mildly. "It's nice enough that you're making dinner. Why don't you let me do it tomorrow night?"

His jaw muscles flexed and he picked up the paring knife again. "Fine," he said curtly.

She had to pass him to get to the refrigerator. The quarters seemed too close, even though the kitchen was a good size. Belatedly Beth wished she had let him pour the juice for her.

As she opened the cupboard and reached for a glass, she momentarily closed her eyes. If he didn't either move out of her house or kiss her in the next hour, she would go crazy. Stark raving mad.

"Excuse me," she murmured on the way back.

He seemed not to hear her, turning suddenly so that his denim-clad shoulder bumped her just as she passed, sloshing the juice. "Damn," he muttered, and grabbed her with his free hand.

A meaningless touch. And he'd been this close to her dozens of times. Hundreds of times. So why did pure longing shoot like a drug through her bloodstream? Why were her knees buckling?

Nathan froze, still gripping her upper arm. His eyes sharpened like a camera lens focusing and zeroed in on her mouth. She stared up at him, mesmerized. His throat vibrated as he growled something, and then his head bent slowly. Her eyelids sank shut, her lips parted and she tilted her head back.

The next thing she knew, he released her so quickly

he might as well have shoved her away. When she opened her eyes, she was looking at his back. After a second the chop, chop, chop resumed as he turned the diced green pepper into unusable shreds. Beth fled. Again. Running away was getting to be a habit.

HAD MOM AND UNCLE NATE had a fight or something? They hardly talked at all or looked at each other, except sometimes when he sat staring at Mom like…like he was mad at her. Except that wasn't quite right. Mandy didn't know *what* he was thinking. She only knew that things weren't going the way she wanted them to.

Mandy sat brooding on her bed. Calvin and Polly wrestled around her, tumbling and squeaking when teeth sank in too far. Sometimes she'd reach out and stroke one of them, and they'd pause for a second before springing back into battle.

She'd been so sure Patrick would be fun, even though she should have remembered that little babies weren't. He was kind of cute—well, cuter than he'd been at first, anyway. Not so red. When he grabbed her finger and held it tightly, his own so incredibly tiny but really strong, she felt a surge of sisterly pride. He liked holding on to *her* better than anyone.

She might have enjoyed helping with his baths, except he hated them and screamed and screamed. Inside the bathroom with its tiled walls, his crying hurt Mandy's ears. At first she felt important when she changed his diaper, but when he'd pooped, it was gross. Other times the diaper was so soggy she hated to touch it. And, since Mom was nursing, Mandy couldn't even give Patrick a bottle. Mom said she'd introduce one soon, so other people could take care of him sometimes, but she hadn't yet. So what use was a big sister?

Uncle Nate didn't ignore her just because he had his own kid now, but he wasn't fun like he used to be, either. For one thing, he and Mom were always tired. Patrick slept more during the day than he did at night. And he really could yell. Mandy knew that both Uncle Nate and Mom napped when she was at school, but it didn't seem to help that much. Maybe not enough sleep explained why they were both grumpy. And when Uncle Nate wasn't mopping the kitchen or making dinner, he was in Mom's office working. The fax machine clattered practically nonstop. If she had a question about her homework, he'd answer it, and she helped him with dinner and did more chores than usual, but he never wanted to play games or just tell jokes and be dumb like he did before.

Sometimes she almost wished Patrick had never been born. Except…she had that selfish reason to be glad he had been. And if it hadn't been for him, Uncle Nate wouldn't have been living here at all. Mandy kept wondering if he was going to stay for good, even if he and Mom didn't fall in love and get married like she'd dreamed they would. But she didn't ask; she was afraid she'd remind him that he really ought to go. Because she *liked* having him here. She just wished he'd lighten up.

By the time she heard Patrick awaking from a nap and then her mom's murmurs, the cats had worn themselves out and were curled together sleeping. She bent down and kissed Polly's white tummy and Calvin's creamy yellow one. Then she went into the hall and knocked on Mom's bedroom door.

"Come in," her mother called.

She sat cross-legged in the middle of the bed, Patrick lying on his back in front of her. She was changing his diaper and tickling his toes. When Mandy stopped beside the bed, she saw that his eyes were a little wider and brighter than usual. At least he looked interested, even if he didn't know how to smile yet.

"He's still so little." She dropped to her knees and rested her elbows on the bed so she was eye level with her baby brother.

"He *was* a little premature. He weighed almost two pounds less than you. He's just barely catching up." Mom bent over and blew on his toes. Patrick's eyes got even wider and his arms waved.

"Are you enjoying him?" Mandy asked dubiously.

"Enjoying?" Mom laughed. "Yes. Except at certain interludes in the middle of the night."

"What's to enjoy?"

Mom took the question seriously, tilting her head to one side as she fastened the tapes on the diaper. "When you have your own baby, it's…special. He needs me. That makes me feel all mushy inside. And…oh, it's exciting, the way he changes every day. The first few years are like a race. If I look away for even a minute, I miss some of it."

"I'm changing every day, too," Mandy said, trying to sound gloomy but not sure she meant it. Having her body change so fast sometimes scared her, but sometimes made her feel like she was really grown-up. Just yesterday she'd noticed Colin Hillman staring at her chest. He'd turned bright red when he realized she'd seen him.

"Changing… Oh." Mom smiled. "How's the leg shaving going?"

"It's okay. I don't cut myself very often." Mandy

hesitated. "Do you think my breasts will get very big?" It was weird thinking about stuff like that now that there was a good chance she might not die.

Mom buzzed her lips against Patrick's bare tummy. All his limbs waved again, like sea anemones on the bottom of the ocean. "Hard to say," Mom admitted. "Mine aren't especially large. And Grandma wasn't busty. Look at pictures of your other grandmother. I think maybe she was. But since you get genes through your grandfathers, too... Heck, who knows? Will you mind if you do?"

"I'd hate it!" Mandy said vehemently. "Krystal Peters at school already wears a C cup—she *brags* about it—and she bounces up and down every time she moves. You ought to see her in PE. The boys can hardly takes their eyes off her, but even if she likes having big boobs, *I* think they'd be uncomfortable."

Mom made a face. "Maybe a little. Besides, I had a buxom friend in college who swore she'd marry the first guy who looked at her face before her chest."

"And did she?"

"If she didn't change her criteria, it took her a while to find him. She didn't get married until she was thirty."

"Oh." Mandy thought about it. "Is there anything I can *do?* Like exercises, or...or..."

"Sorry." Mom grinned and leaned over to kiss her nose. Patrick gurgled, as if the attention should all be his. "How about keeping your fingers crossed?"

"Yeah, like that's going to help," Mandy grumbled. But she supposed if God let her live but made her have big boobs, she shouldn't complain too much. And she *had* sort of liked it when Colin noticed she was...well, a girl.

Mom just smiled again. "Can you reach that sleeper?"

Patrick was so little Mom didn't put him in real clothes yet. He always wore those knit one-piece pajamas with feet. This one was bright blue and had an elephant embroidered on the front. "Cute," Mandy said, handing it over.

Patrick didn't want to get dressed. He kicked and wriggled and arched his back and even screeched when Mom insisted. "Silly boy," she cooed. "It isn't warm enough to stay naked. Wait'll summer. Then you can sleep in nothing but your diaper. I promise." His face just scrunched up like a troll's. Mom laughed softly.

"When I was a baby, did I look like him?" Mandy hoped not.

Mom finished snapping up the front of the sleeper. "A little. Prettier, though. You seemed to be more cheerful about life."

"You said I was your sunshine." Mom wouldn't forget stuff like that now that she had another baby, would she?

Her mother immediately began caroling, "'You are my sunshine, my only sunshine!'" Mandy joined her for the rest.

When they'd finished and were smiling at each other, Mom added, "Actually I think you looked more like pictures of me when I was a baby, even though you have your dad's coloring. If he'd ever quit frowning, I suspect Patrick looks more like baby pictures of your dad. And your uncle, of course."

From the doorway Uncle Nate said, "Considering he's my son, not Rob's, it's nice of you to tack me on."

Mom's head shot up. "It's Rob's baby pictures I have in an album, not yours."

He stayed in the doorway. "We were together in most of them."

"Probably, but nonetheless they were my husband's. The last time I looked at them, I didn't know you. I didn't think, oh, Nathan's eyes aren't shaped like Mandy's. It was her dad's face I paid attention to."

Feeling anxious, although she wasn't sure why, Mandy tried to distract him. "You looked exactly alike, anyway, didn't you?"

His eyes didn't waver from Mom's. "We may have looked alike. But we weren't alike."

"Mandy." Mom sounded pleasant, as though there wasn't anything wrong. But there was. "Will you take Patrick downstairs? You can put him in the bassinet if you want. Just keep an eye on him. I'd like to talk to your uncle for a minute."

"Okay." Her chest tight, Mandy picked up her brother, carefully supporting his head. Neither adult said a word until she'd left the room and closed the door behind her. She thought she could hear Mom's voice as she started down the stairs.

A sick feeling in Mandy's stomach told her that, if Mom and Uncle Nate hadn't had a fight yet, they were having one right now.

CHAPTER FOURTEEN

THE MOMENT THE DOOR quietly shut behind her daughter, Beth asked, "Was what I said that offensive?"

"It didn't strike you as a little strange?" Nathan asked, teeth gritted. Maybe he was overreacting by making such an issue of this, but finding out she saw Rob even in Patrick's face had played into all his worst fears. "Comparing our son to your first husband, instead of his father?"

Beth scrambled off the bed to face him. "You were identical twins! All I was doing was comparing Mandy, who looks more like me, with Patrick who I think is going to look like you and Rob. Where's the harm in that?"

"Goddamn it, he's *my* son! Not Rob's!" With shock, Nathan realized he'd shouted.

She planted her hands on her hips and shouted back, "I know he is!"

"Do you?" he asked more quietly.

Beth gasped. From rage, hurt, he didn't know. "You still think I see Rob every time I look at you, don't you?"

He swore. "I don't know."

"I'll take that as a yes."

He slapped a hand down on the crib rail. The whole crib jumped and the mobile hanging above it swung wildly. "Take it any damn way you want!"

She backed up a step and stared at him with huge eyes. In contrast, her tone was almost musing when she said, "The question is, why do you care? What difference does it make to you whether your brother's widow is still pining for him?"

All that rage and anguish bottled inside him broke free and he stalked forward. "You're playing games. You know why."

She could have retreated a few more steps, but didn't. "Do I?"

Throwing his own questions back in his face wasn't calculated to soothe the wild beast she'd unchained. He swore again, took one more stride, snatched her into his arms and captured her mouth with his. He'd quit thinking, was blind with desperate hunger and bone-deep hurt. The kiss wasn't gentle; but, oh God, she was so soft, her taste as potent and smooth as fine scotch, the small sounds she made driving his frenzy.

Even in his mindless state, he slowly noticed that she did no more than stand passive in his embrace. Her lips were parted, her breath came quickly, her eyes had fallen closed, but she wasn't kissing him back. Her arms stayed at her sides.

A groan tore its way from his throat, which felt raw. He pushed her away and backed up until his legs hit the bed, where he stood swaying, rubbing his face with his hand.

"You didn't really answer my question," she said in a voice that would have sounded composed had it not been for a husky note.

He looked up incredulously. "What question?"

"Why do you care how I feel about Rob?" She paused. "Or you?"

Now he knew he was going crazy. Maybe the kiss

hadn't happened. He'd imagined it. He shook his head, trying to clear it. "You can't tell?"

"I can tell you want me." For the first time her gaze lowered, her lashes shielding her expression. "Is that all there is to it?"

He muttered a profanity and sank onto the edge of the bed, burying his face in his hands. How had he blown it so badly? He'd wandered into a nightmare. No, he'd created his own nightmare.

The only thing good about it was that he had nothing to lose now.

He looked up again, eyes painfully dry and jaw clenched. "I love you."

Her lashes swept up and, pupils dilated, she stared at him. For a moment he'd have sworn her mouth softened, and emotion deepened the gray of her eyes. An instant later her face twisted and she turned away. She was drawing deep ragged breaths, her head bent, and all he could look at was the slender line of her neck and the heavy weight of pale hair carelessly knotted above it. He wanted to put his lips against that soft skin, nuzzle her curls. He wanted...

His fists knotted and he closed his eyes. Waiting.

He didn't open them until she spoke, voice firm, unrevealing. "You need to move out, Nathan."

He nodded dumbly.

"Of course you can visit Patrick and Mandy."

But not her. She would take care to be elsewhere. He knew it.

"I wish..." Her voice faltered the tiniest bit. "I wish you'd find some way to forgive Rob. Or yourself."

"For what?" He sounded hard. Unforgiving.

"I don't know." Her breath came out in a sigh.

"Him for being too much like you. For being jealous of you. Yourself for cutting him off."

"You don't think he deserved it?"

"I don't know," Beth said again, face sorrowful. "What I do know is that he was a good man. Not perfect. But who is? And he loved you."

Intense grief hit Nathan with all the force of the head-on collision that had killed his brother. A part of him looked on in astonishment as a huge sob convulsed his chest. He fought it, throwing back his head and clenching his teeth and thinking about anything—everything—but Rob. His other half.

A gentle hand touched his arm. "Nathan—"

"No," he said harshly. "Leave it."

Beth took her hand back. Her magnificent eyes sparkled with hurt and pride. "That's your philosophy, isn't it?"

"What the hell is that supposed to mean?"

"You've just…shut away whatever it is you feel for Rob. Until you open that door and take a good long look, you aren't going to be ready to love anyone else. Especially not someone he loved. You need to resolve your feelings for him."

He got up and paced away from her, swung back and said bitterly, "You're a psychologist now? You're sure there's some deep meaning to the fact that we competed and ended up hating each other's guts? Life can be that simple, you know."

Her knot of hair slipped when she shook her head. "I don't think so. Not when you were twins. Each half of a single egg."

He uttered an obscenity.

Her eyebrows rose. "Fine," she said tartly. "Go wallow in hate. But don't do it here. I won't have you glaring at me because you *imagine* I'm being sick enough to pretend my dead husband is alive in your body!''

''I never said—''

''Yes, you did!'' Flat-out anger flushed her cheeks and glittered in her eyes. ''And you call what you feel for me *love?*'' She said it with loathing.

''Yes.'' He'd make her believe that much. ''I love you. Heart and soul.'' He gave a bitter laugh. ''I guess it goes to show that you're right. Even our damned brain cells were identical. Rob and I couldn't help loving the same woman. All I want to know is that I'm not second-best. That he's gone and it's me you see.''

''Not second-best? What you mean is, you want to be sure you came out first. Won the blue ribbon. Beat out brother Rob.''

She was wrong. He'd never been the one who cared about winning. ''Your opinion of me is heartwarming. I don't even know why we're having this discussion.'' His jaws ground together. ''Why didn't you just say you don't love me? Never will?''

Her gaze fell from his. ''Because,'' she said softly, ''I do.''

He quit breathing.

Her lashes lifted again to reveal eyes as clear as the purest mountain lake and utterly honest. ''I haven't been able to figure out why we didn't just fall into each other's arms. Go off into the sunset.'' She made a small helpless gesture. ''Now I know.''

Fear clawed at his chest. ''I love you.''

''Love,'' she said unhappily, ''makes you so terribly vulnerable. It can't work unless you trust each other. Because of Rob, you can't trust me.''

He felt as if he'd chosen to climb a mountain unroped, and now his fingers were slipping from holds on a steep rock face. Hoarsely he said, "I know you'd never betray me!"

"Except in my heart, where you think I'm betraying you every day." She shook her head hard when he took a step toward her. "No. Go back to your condo. Or...or even to Portland. Figure out why you can't believe that I've let Rob go. Figure it out for your own mental health, if nothing else. But, please—" her voice shattered "—go. Today. Now."

He went, blundering from her room to his, throwing his things in his suitcases, forcing them shut. He walked straight out of the house without looking into the living room where he knew Patrick and Mandy were. And he drove away, not knowing whether he'd ever be able to come home again.

THE DOOR CREAKED open. "Mom." Mandy's voice came hesitantly. "Uncle Nate...Uncle Nate *left*. He took all his stuff."

Beth should have been sobbing. Instead, she stood in the exact same spot she'd been when he walked out of the room. Lot's wife, turned to a pillar of salt. Her eyes were gritty and her insides were as arid. She scarcely felt anything. She had to be numb. Surely it would hurt later.

"I know." The words scraped out. "I asked him to go."

Mandy's face crumpled in shock. "You *asked* him?"

Pity was the first emotion to trickle through the crystalline salt that was her heart. "Honey—"

"I liked having him here!" her daughter cried. "He liked me!"

"I know." She should have hugged Mandy, held her, comforted her. Instead, Beth sank onto the edge of the bed and sighed so deeply she felt hollow. She patted the spot beside her. "Come here."

Mandy sniffled. "I left Patrick."

"In the bassinet?"

A nod.

"Then he'll be okay. He can't exactly climb out and toddle off."

"But if he gets unhappy…"

"We'll hear about it."

"Oh. Yeah. I guess so." Still Mandy didn't come. "I need to blow my nose."

"Go get a box of tissues."

Mandy nodded again and went. Beth wondered if she would come back or go hide out, maybe at the willow tree or in the barn. She undoubtedly didn't *want* to be held, not by her mother the betrayer, who had driven away the man who was her father in all but name.

Dear God, did I do the right thing? Beth asked, but got no reply. Maybe all Nathan had needed was time. Reassurance. Hadn't she herself been confused early on? She'd admitted as much. And it wasn't as if she'd ever announced one day, "I'm over Rob. When I'm having erotic dreams, I no longer get confused over which man I'm dreaming about."

But how could Nathan not have known? Her confusion had been shortlived. He *wasn't* at all like Rob, not in any of the ways that counted except being a good parent. He must know that. Did he think that she was an idiot, that she couldn't distinguish between the two of them?

No, her brains had nothing to do with it, she thought

unhappily. Nathan was so wrapped up in his own jealousy he'd never see her straight. Or was it guilt that made him unable to believe in her love? Did it matter which it was? She wasn't going to walk into a relationship where the man suspected her of infidelity, even if it was with a ghost.

She'd done the right thing.

Maybe for herself, but not necessarily for Mandy. Never mind little Patrick, who was going to have to do with one even wearier, crankier parent.

Mandy appeared in the bedroom doorway, box of tissues in hand. She stood there uncertainly until Beth patted the bed again.

"I put Patrick's little mirror in with him. He's looking at himself."

"Vain already."

Mandy's glasses rose high on her scrunched-up nose. "How could he be?"

"Give him a month or two. He'll be beautiful." She hesitated. "Mandy—"

At the precise same moment her daughter said, "Mom—"

They both stopped. Beth squeezed Mandy's hand. "You first."

"He did *everything*. I mean, he cooked and washed clothes and drove me and... I can't cook. And I'm always forgetting to take stuff out of the dryer, so it's wrinkled, and—"

"Sweetie." Not quite daring to test their relationship with a hug yet, Beth squeezed Mandy's hand again. "I'm healthy. I can do most everything I used to do. We've managed fine all these years, haven't we?"

"Yeah, but..." Mandy ducked her head.

"But what?"

"It was cool with him here!" she burst out. "More like a real family!"

Knife to the heart. "Yeah, it was, wasn't it?"

"*Why* did you ask him to go? I don't understand."

Only for a second did she consider...well, not lying, but telling less than the truth. She and Mandy had finally learned to be honest with each other. She wasn't going to risk that gain because it was hard talking about her feelings, not to mention adult love and sexual attraction.

"It's complicated."

Mandy waited, that too-old expression on her face.

"He thinks he's in love with me."

Shock replaced the skepticism on the twelve-year-old's thin face. "And you don't love him?"

"I do love him. No—" she held up her hand "—listen. You know he and your dad got angry enough at each other not to speak for fifteen years."

Mandy nodded.

"Well, as far as I can tell, Nathan still resents your dad or feels guilty because they didn't make up or something. Have you noticed how he doesn't talk about your father anymore?"

Her daughter's brow creased as she thought about it. "I guess," she finally said. "I mean, I hadn't noticed, but—"

"It took me a while, too. Anyway..." One more hesitation. This was the hard part. "He's convinced that I still love your dad and that I'm attracted to him because he looks like your dad. He thinks he's a substitute."

Mandy's mouth opened in a circle. "But...but..."

"My reaction exactly. The thing is, I can't convince him. So I told him to resolve his feelings about Rob and in the meantime I didn't want him around the house glaring at me.''

"Oh.''

"Do you think I was wrong?''

Her daughter gave a small, "I don't know.''

She shouldn't have asked. She was the adult. "You'll still be seeing him,'' Beth said bracingly. "Just because he moved out doesn't mean he won't be here often.''

"He didn't even say goodbye!'' Mandy flung herself into her mother's arms, sobbing.

If she'd been made of salt, she'd have dissolved like the Wicked Witch of the West, because the next thing Beth knew, she was crying, too. Her grief was almost as terrible as when she'd lost Rob. She'd only loved two men in her life. One was dead and now she'd driven the other away.

Mandy's shoulders quit shaking at last; she rubbed her tear-streaked face on Beth's shirt. Beth gave a choked laugh and wiped her own tears on Mandy's curly hair. But still they held each other.

"Do you think he'll really come back to see me?''

"Yes,'' Beth said with certainty, "I do. He wouldn't desert you or Patrick.''

Under her mother's chin, Mandy nodded. "But what about you? Will he ever see that you love him, not Dad?''

She hadn't thought she could cry another drop, but tears burned again in her eyes. "I haven't a clue.'' She blinked hard. "I did love your father, you know.''

"I know.'' Mandy, her face blotchy, pulled back to look up at her mother. "But Dad's been gone a long time. I mean, I loved him, but that doesn't mean I can't love Uncle Nate, does it? So why can't you, too?''

Why indeed?

"Kiddo," Beth said on a sigh, "you're smarter than he is."

FOR THE FIRST WEEK, he was angry. She'd sent him away because she *loved* him? Apparently she didn't want honesty from him; if he'd kept his fears to himself, he'd be putting a ring on her finger right now. But no, she wanted him to enter therapy to "resolve" his feelings for his brother so he didn't have to wonder anymore whether Rob's widow might be just a little confused, when she woke up in the middle of the night, about which brother's head rested on the pillow next to hers. Was that so unreasonable?

The next week he was so goddamned depressed he could hardly make himself roll out of bed every morning and stumble to the shower. For the first time since college, he got falling-down drunk one night, but instead of anesthetizing him, the booze made him maudlin. Beth was the love of his life; he'd lost his little boy; Mandy would die and never know that he felt like her father. He even dialed their number with the intention of drunkenly telling them how devoted he was. Thank God he dialed the wrong number and reached some total stranger's answering machine.

The third week he pulled himself together enough to call Mandy and offer to drive her to drama class. She accepted with such pathetic eagerness he hung up feeling like a crud. Big man, sulking for two weeks.

As he'd expected, Beth was nowhere to be seen when he picked up Mandy. His niece did take him into the living room to visit Patrick, who was awake in his bassinet. The dark hair was fluffy now, the cheeks plump and pink, the brown eyes bright and focused.

Seeing how much Patrick had changed was like a fist in Nathan's stomach. He was missing his son's life. But obviously Patrick was thriving. He didn't need his father.

Beside him, Mandy bounced. "Tickle his tummy. He really likes that."

"Okay." Hiding his gloom, he forced a grin and trailed his fingers over a stomach almost as round as the cheeks.

Patrick wriggled, his arms and legs waved, and then his mouth opened in a huge toothless smile.

"He's smiling," Nathan said foolishly.

Mandy bounced again. "Isn't it cool? He smiled for the first time a week or so ago. Mom screamed and I came running into her bedroom. Of course he wouldn't do it again, and I didn't believe her, but then in the morning, the second he saw me he smiled. It was, like, the most exciting thing ever!"

He should have been here. He hid his pain and swung Patrick up in his arms, tickling and grinning until he'd earned enough smiles to store away for the lonely evenings at his condo.

At least Patrick's achievement had kept any awkwardness from developing between him and Mandy. They talked like always during the drive each way. It was another evening where he got to watch part of the class, but this time he felt like a fraud among the parents.

He didn't come into the house with Mandy when he took her home, even though she invited him. What would have been the point? All he'd have achieved would be to make Beth uncomfortable—assuming she didn't see him coming and go into hiding first.

Sometime after that night Nathan started having

dreams about Beth and the kids that were vivid enough to stay with him when he woke up. At first the dreams were innocuous, just little snippets of him rocking Patrick while Mandy chattered, or of Beth breastfeeding Patrick, or of all of them wading in the stream by the willow tree in some sort of perpetual summer.

But after a few nights the dreams started getting weird. He'd be staring at Patrick feeling hostile because his son looked like Rob, instead of him. Once, Rob was there, and Nathan knew himself to be invisible, watching his brother with his family. The kicker was the night *he* was Rob, feeling smug as all get-out about his beautiful wife and cute kids.

That time, Nathan's eyes shot open and he stared uncomprehendingly into the darkness. He swore and sat up, putting his feet on the floor. What the hell had *that* been all about?

Beth's accusation, he thought grimly, running his hands through his hair. He'd hardly thought about Rob in the past three or four months, and then she'd decided he was obsessed with his brother. Now, courtesy of her, he apparently was.

Yeah, but what did the dream mean? He wanted to *be* Rob? On some level he and Rob were one and the same?

The thought was less than comforting.

Nathan wished he had a really close friend he could talk to. If it'd been summer, he'd have called Matt and suggested they swing their packs onto their backs and head into the Alpine Lakes. On a two- or three-day hiking trip you found yourself talking, maybe with the sun hot on your back while you put one foot in front of the other and felt the peace of the high mountain country, or maybe when you were sprawled on your sleeping bag staring at the fire as it died into coals and left such pure darkness the stars shone brighter than city lights. But it wasn't summer. It was March and raining like a son of a bitch.

Finally, out of desperation, he picked up the phone, anyway. His friend, home in Beaverton, Oregon, sounded glad to hear from him. They talked about work for a minute, then Matt's wife and kids.

Out of the blue Nathan said, "You knew I had a brother."

He could almost see the raised eyebrows. Then, "Yeah. A twin, wasn't he?"

Nathan grunted. "Turns out he's dead. Killed in a car accident three years ago. Left a wife and daughter."

Silence. "You didn't know?"

"I last saw him fifteen years ago. We had a hell of a fight, and…time passed." Even to him, that sounded weak.

"Fifteen *years?*"

"His, uh, widow tracked me down. Their daughter, Mandy, has leukemia. She needs a bone-marrow donor."

"Are you a match?"

"No. That's when I got myself into kind of a mess. The donor registry couldn't find anyone, either, and they were about giving up hope. Other relatives didn't work, and Mandy had no sisters or brothers, which are the best bet. So I, uh, fathered a son. Genetically he could be Rob's."

"And?"

"He matches. Mandy can have the transplant in about five months, when Patrick's old enough."

"But you're not celebrating," his friend said shrewdly.

"About that, I am. It's… Oh, hell. You don't want to hear this." He was suddenly sorry he'd called. What good would it do to dump all this on someone else?

"Yeah, I want to hear it. What are friends for?"

Nathan pictured Matt, relaxed in the leather chair in his home office, size-twelve feet in battered running shoes on his desk, which would be overflowing with undone paperwork, as usual. He might have his glasses on, which vanity made him reluctant to wear in public. Given that it was Sunday, he'd be wearing rumpled khakis and a University of Oregon Ducks sweatshirt over a brawny chest and a waistline that was getting just a little soft.

"I'm in love with Rob's widow," Nathan said baldly.

"Yeah?" Matt's voice sounded genuinely perplexed. "So what's the problem? There isn't any kind of law against marrying her, you know. In fact, it used to be tradition for a man's brother to marry his widow. He was taking care of her."

"The problem isn't one of legalities." Nathan swiveled his chair to gaze, unseeing, at the framed photograph of dead leaves clogging a stream. "It's the fact that Rob and I were identical twins that bothers me. What if it isn't me she wants? What if through me she's recapturing her relationship with Rob?"

A long silence was followed by the rumbling sound that indicated Matt was thinking seriously. "Do you have any reason to think that's what she's doing? What—did she blow it, call you by his name in a moment of passion?"

Which moment of passion? Their one and only?

"I thought she did. She denies it, and… Oh, hell, I'm undoubtedly being paranoid. She probably didn't.

She thinks—'' he had to force it out "—she thinks I have, quote, unquote, unresolved feelings for Rob. She doesn't want to see me until I do something about them.''

"Ah. Is it true?"

He swore. "I don't know."

"You plan to find out?"

"How? Spend ten years in therapy?"

"A few sessions might not hurt."

"You think she's right."

"I think it's a little strange that you've hardly mentioned your twin brother to me in all our years of being friends. That you didn't even know he'd gotten married, had a kid, died. I mean, are you still angry with him, or what?"

Nathan squeezed the bridge of his nose. "No. Not angry. I just... Hell. I don't want to find out I'm not enough on my own." He heard himself with shock.

This time the silence fairly vibrated. "Not enough *what?*" Matt finally asked.

Still stunned, but thinking hard, Nathan said, "As a kid I felt that way. I would have sworn I didn't anymore." He stopped, blank for a moment. "I don't. I'm a successful businessman, I managed to get married and divorced on my own, I have a decent life."

"But now you feel linked to your brother again because this woman loved him and now she loves you, too."

Nathan made a rough sound in his throat. "You're in the wrong business."

"You kidding? Lawyers are glorified therapists."

"Okay. I'm afraid of being lumped with Rob again. 'The twins.'"

"Not the worst thing in the world to have someone

who'll go back-to-back with you, knows what you're thinking, always cares.''

"And screws your girlfriend because he thinks it's funny she can't tell the difference between you. Or maybe because he doesn't like your having something he doesn't have, too."

"Ah," his friend said again. "Yeah, that's pretty crappy. It'd make me mad. But what was he? Twenty? Twenty-one? A kid. Both of you were. Kids do dumb unthinking things."

Blind to his surroundings again, Nathan saw the scene when he'd confronted Rob. Saw that face, handsome but still unfinished. No lines carved by experience. A boy's face. They'd done two years at the local community college, so that junior year at the university he and Rob had been away from home for the first time. Nathan's nature was the steadier, more earnest, Rob's the more reckless. He'd partied more than Nathan thought smart, drove faster, dated more women. No, not women. Girls. Rob had mocked him sometimes when he chose the library over a fraternity party. That had irritated him. But, God almighty, why had the one stupid stunt lit such a fuse?

Because he was looking for an excuse to shed his twin brother, find out if he could stand alone?

"Including me, apparently," Nathan said dryly. "Do dumb unthinking things, that is."

"Yeah, well, think about it now," his friend advised. "Maybe that's all this woman you love is asking."

Nathan hung up in a daze. Maybe Beth was right. Maybe he was overdue coming to terms with everything his anger at Rob had cost him.

Like a brother. Someone who'd always stood back-to-back with him. Family.

Oh, yeah, he'd found out he could be self-sufficient. He'd learned that so well he had damn near forgotten that he'd once feared he alone was incomplete, that without Rob to drive him, to provide the qualities he didn't have, he'd be inadequate. What he'd never noticed, until he'd found Beth and Mandy, was that self-sufficiency was damned lonely.

Would it be so bad to go back to being one-half of the McCabe boys? To guess that, once in a while, Beth saw them in double exposure?

To know that she'd loved Rob, too?

CHAPTER FIFTEEN

HE HADN'T BEEN HERE in fifteen years, and it was all as familiar as if he drove by it every day. Except that changes kept jumping out at him: the Murrays' house on the corner was gone, replaced by a convenience store. Somebody had added on to the Howards' place— an awkward second story. They should have hired an architect. The streets were still too narrow and lined with parked cars. Bicycles lay in the one-car drive-ways, which were cracked with age. Basketball hoops hung on the small detached garages. When Nathan was a kid, people stayed their whole lives in this neighbor-hood. He was willing to bet that now, these were "starter" homes, that families moved when their in-comes rose.

He took the last turn, seeing nothing but the house in the middle of the block. A bungalow, still white, with a deep front porch. The boxwood hedge wasn't as neatly trimmed as Dad had insisted on keeping it; shoots straggled out. Paint on the house peeled. Dad would roll over in his grave.

He had died soon after Rob and Nathan had left for college. With a speed that had taken them aback, Mom sold the house they'd grown up in and bought a condo out Wheaton Way that let her walk or take a bus ev-erywhere she wanted to go. It had a spare bedroom; they'd been able to come home for Christmas, but it wasn't really *home*. And then Mom had died, too, quickly and unexpectedly. No longer bound to Rob by anything but blood, Nathan had been able to walk away from his brother without weekly letters or phone calls from Mom keeping him up-to-date, without having to hide his enmity over Christmas holidays.

If Mom had still been alive, he suspected, the quarrel would never have solidified into permanent silence. Chances were, he'd have been there at Rob's wedding, held Mandy when she was tiny, carried one corner of his brother's casket.

Hated Rob anew for having the woman he wanted.

Or maybe he never would have let himself realize that he wanted her. He hoped not.

He stopped the car at the curb right in front of the house and sat there, wondering what in hell he was doing here. How was looking at the house he'd grown up in going to resolve anything? Last night, after talking to Matt, the idea seemed to make sense; if he physically went home, perhaps emotionally he could, too. Tap into something deeper. Pull up memories he'd repressed.

Now he sat here behind the wheel of his car and felt...old. Incredibly remote from the boy who had lived here, mowed that lawn, sheared the hedge once Dad deemed him responsible enough.

At that thought a wry smile twisted his lips. Rob had been really steamed when Dad handed the shears to Nathan one day and said, "You've seen me do it enough times, boy. Go for it."

"What about me?" Rob had asked.

Dad had shaken his head. "No matter how often your mother asks you to use a cutting board in the kitchen, you can't be bothered. You've ruined the Formica. So, first you have to prove you're ready for a job with sharp tools.''

Face flushed dark, Rob had stomped off. Of course, later he'd come out to mock Nathan for being stuck with a sweaty tedious chore he'd avoided.

He'd even succeeded in making Nathan feel he'd gotten the short end of the stick. Rob had been good at that.

By the next summer, they'd sheared the hedge together, each starting on one end and meeting in the middle. The first time they'd tried it that way, they'd met to find that Rob's half was cut more ruthlessly. There'd been a three-inch difference. But he'd helped Nathan go back and trim some more, until it came out even. Actually they hadn't made a bad team.

Nathan's fingers tightened on the steering wheel. Good God, he hadn't thought about that in years. Hadn't remembered...

Hell, maybe there was something to this, after all. But what did he do now? Go knock on the door and ask if he could wander through the house? Right.

Still, he did get out of the car and slam the door. Leaning against the fender, he gazed at the house. Behind the dormer window up above had been their bedroom. As teenagers he and Rob might have gotten along better if they hadn't had to share. In college Nathan had had a different roommate. Except for nights spent at friends' houses or in hotels when the football or track team was on the road, it was the first time in his life he hadn't fallen asleep to the sound of his twin's breathing. Somehow his roommate's was different. He'd told himself it was liberating. All the same, he hadn't slept well at first.

"Hey." A kid's voice jarred him out of his memories. "You want something, mister?"

Holding a basketball, a boy, maybe eleven or twelve, stood in the driveway by the end of the hedge. Blond hair was cut in the bowl shape boys currently favored. He wore jeans and a No Fear T-shirt.

"Not really." Nathan smiled crookedly. "Sorry. I must've looked strange. You live here?"

"Yeah." He sounded pugnacious. "My brother and me. With our mom."

"I grew up here." Nathan nodded toward the house. "I haven't been back in years. I was just...curious."

"Really?" Interest wiped out the edginess. "You mean, when you were a kid you lived here?"

"Yup. My brother and I shared the bedroom upstairs. Dad built in bunkbeds."

"Hey." The boy's eyes widened. "They're still there. My brother and me share 'em."

"How old's he?"

"He's ten. I'm twelve. Next week."

"Rob and I were twins," Nathan offered. "He died a few years ago. Car accident. It's him I was thinking about."

"Oh." The kid dribbled the ball a few times. "Do you miss him?"

For the first time, even to himself, Nathan admitted, "Yeah. Every day."

After a moment of silence, presumably to respect Nathan's grief, the boy asked, "Was it you who built the tree house?"

"In back?" Nathan found himself grinning. "In the big maple? Yeah. Jeez. Is it still there?"

"It was kind of rotting, but when we rented the

house, Mom bought some lumber and nails and stuff and let my brother and me work on it. It's really cool!''

"Do you sleep out there sometimes?"

The boy nodded. "You want to see it?"

"Would your mother mind?"

"She's not home right now." A belated recollection of safety lectures must have struck him, because he added hastily, "The neighbors are home. In case I need something."

Nathan nodded solemnly. "Sure. I'd like to see it."

As they circled the house, the boy asked, "Did you put that big hole in the floor of the tree house? I wondered what it was for."

"The pipe's gone?"

"Like a fireman's pole or something?" Satisfaction flitted across his face. "That's what I figured. My brother thought maybe you had a rope you swung from."

"Nah, we slid down a metal pipe." Looking up at the circle cut in the tree-house floor, he could still feel the texture as his hands slid down the cold pipe, the thud as his feet hit ground, the thrill.

"Must've rusted. Maybe we could get a new one. How'd you get it to stay there?"

At the boy's invitation, Nathan scrambled up into the tree house. His size made it feel cramped, but when he closed his eyes, he was ten again, swelled with pride because he and Rob had built it with hardly any help from Dad. In summer you could be up here without anybody knowing since the broad maple leaves grew so thick. It was quiet and green and secret. They'd hauled their sleeping bags up and stayed out here almost every summer night that year, then the next and the next. They could say anything they wanted, make up gory stories and plan pranks and, later, talk about girls and wet dreams and feeling like shrimps. He and Rob had talked about things other boys kept to themselves. Sharing something with Rob wasn't really like telling another person; it was more like *thinking* it. In those days they were that inseparable.

Nathan showed the boy how they'd drilled a hole just big enough for the pipe to slip into in the big branch above their heads; it was no more than a scar now. He explained how deep they'd sunk the pipe into the ground, and how they'd tamped around the base until the pole didn't even quiver when they swung onto it.

The boy listened raptly and finally nodded. "Cool! I bet Mom'll let us do that, too."

"Don't take shortcuts. Make sure it's rock solid."

The boy nodded again and walked him back to his car. "I guess you could come in," he said doubtfully, "if you want to see the house and all."

"Thanks." Nathan smiled. "But that's okay. Your mother wouldn't like it, and… I don't need to go inside. I found what I came for."

"What's that?"

"Memories." He opened his car door. "Rob and I as kids."

"I bet you had fun. I wish my brother was my age."

"Sometimes it was great. Sometimes not so great. But having a brother is special."

The boy made a face. "I guess."

"Someday you'll appreciate him."

"Yeah, sure."

Nathan laughed, started the engine and with a wave pulled away from the curb. He took one last look in his rearview mirror.

"'ROCK-A-BYE BABY, in a treetop,'" Beth sang softly, for the fifteenth or twentieth time. Patrick liked to fall asleep to soothing repetition, not a variety show. "'When the wind blows, the cradle will rock.'" A peek showed her that his mouth had gone slack around his thumb, and she didn't finish the lullaby, instead rising to put him in his crib. She tucked the blanket around her infant son, lingered for a moment to watch him sleep, then turned off the lamp and left the bedroom.

He usually napped for a couple of hours in the afternoon. Time for her to do laundry and put in an hour or so preparing the Tillicum Creek tax return. "Oh, joy," she muttered. "Maybe I should take a nap, too."

The idea was seductive, but... No. She was trying to get out of the habit. Patrick was eight weeks old now and sleeping through the night, if you could call midnight until six in the morning a night's sleep. It was now spring. In the next few weeks she would have to be out in the fields weeding and mulching, not snoozing away her afternoons. She'd already arranged for a half-day baby-sitter, a nice woman in her sixties who watched two grandchildren, too.

The phone rang before Beth had done more than throw the first load in the washer. Her heart stilled when she heard Nathan's voice.

"Beth, I'd like to talk to you." He didn't give the impression of being angry or upset. Nor was his tone demanding. Still...

"All right," she said warily. "Now's okay."

"May I come over?"

She hadn't seen him for a month, except for stolen looks between the curtains. A coward, she'd hidden every time he visited the kids. Dumb, considering they'd have to see each other regularly for the next eighteen years or so. But she hadn't been sure she could bear to exchange a few pleasant words, watch him snuggle Patrick, laugh with Mandy, nod a cool goodbye. Not when she missed him so terribly.

"I...can you tell me what you want to talk about?"

"I'd rather do that in person." He sounded so calm, noncommittal. What if he wanted to see more of Patrick, maybe intended to discuss getting a court order setting out visitation?

She licked dry lips. "All right."

"Mandy's not home?"

"No, she's at school."

"I'll see you in half an hour, then." Click. He was gone.

She had thirty minutes—forever—to wait and wonder. What did he want? It frightened her that he preferred not to say whatever it was in front of Mandy. Unless... She pressed her fingers to her mouth. Oh, God. Was there any chance he'd decided to file for joint custody, take Patrick away from her half the time?

She was shaking. She made it to a kitchen chair before her legs collapsed. Her eyes sought the kitchen clock. Twenty-five more minutes.

What if that was it? He'd loved being with Patrick, and when she'd asked him to leave, he'd probably felt as if she was taking his son away, too. She'd never intended... But how could she go on living with him almost as though they were husband and wife, when all the time he thought she was pretending he was Rob reincarnated?

He'd gone away so angry. She couldn't even kid herself that there was any hope he'd do as she'd asked and deal with his feelings for Rob. Why should he? He thought it was normal still to be painfully jealous of a brother who'd been in his grave for three years. Nathan probably figured *she* was the one with a problem. If he had ever really loved her, she doubted he did anymore. This could end up like the most bitter of divorces, with them fighting over the children.

And they had been so happy. Could be so happy...

"Don't think about it," she said aloud. In these last painful weeks she'd grieved, just as she had for Rob. She'd admitted no hope, didn't dare let herself feel any, because then it would mean starting all over with tear-soaked pillows and sleepless nights. She'd almost gotten numb, except those times when she knew he was coming, or could hear him downstairs, or waited for him to bring Mandy home. And then she felt the slicing agony of having to share a part of her life with the man she loved and couldn't have.

But if he took Patrick from her... Suddenly she leapt to her feet and began to pace. What would she do? Could she afford to fight him in court? Did she have any chance of winning? Did he want Patrick that badly? He claimed to love her—how could he do something like this?

The doorbell chimed and her heart took a sickening jump. He was here.

"Calm. You can be calm." Her fingers writhed together. She took long deep breaths, willed her heartbeat to slow down. And then she went to the door and opened it.

She had a flash of déjà vu: opening the door that first day to find a man on her doorstep who could have been Rob.

And now she saw only Nathan, dark, broad-shouldered, intense.

He shoved his hands in his pockets and nodded. "Beth."

"Hello, Nathan." She hesitated, then stood back. "Come in."

In the hallway his head turned. "Patrick asleep?"

"He naps every afternoon about this time."

"Am I keeping you from *your* nap?"

Oh, how polite they were being! "No," she said, leading the way into the living room. "I've given them up. I'm working on my taxes and I've arranged for half-day baby-sitting starting next week. I've got to be outside—we're setting out new strawberries and expanding our raspberry fields, and everything has to be weeded and mulched. Anyway, I figure for part of the day he can be in a playpen in the shade or in the barn with me, but we're going to try having him go to Mrs. Heyer's, two properties down, just for three hours to start with."

"You're giving him bottles now."

"Mandy feeds him once a day. He doesn't mind." Nathan seemed to be waiting for something. She looked around vaguely and realized they were standing in front of the couch. More politeness. "Please, sit down."

He nodded, waiting only until she'd chosen the wing chair facing the couch. He didn't lounge the way he had when he lived here; he sat more like a businessman biding his time.

Civilities were over; they looked at each other.

What he said was unexpected. "I've missed all of you."

Beth focused on her hands, folded on her lap as though she were a little girl at a tea party. "We've missed you, too."

"Patrick seems to be doing fine without me."

She lifted her head in surprise. "The fact that he's healthy doesn't mean—"

"I want to be here with him."

Her heart began to drum. "What do you propose? A separate apartment for you—"

"I want to marry you." His voice lowered a notch, acquired a hint of huskiness. "Live happily ever after."

"Mandy and Patrick will grow up. Leave home."

"Not for them. For us."

Abruptly she was trembling again. She stood, went behind the chair, gripping the back to hide the tremor in her hands. "I can't," she said desperately.

He rose to his feet, too, although he didn't come toward her. Thank God—she'd have crumpled. As it was, the hunger in his eyes shook her to her core.

"I've been thinking about what you said."

"Nathan—" His name caught in her throat.

"The other day I visited the house where Rob and I grew up. In Bremerton." Mouth wry, he looked away from her toward the fireplace. "A couple of boys live there now. I talked to one of them for a while. He let me go up in the tree house Rob and I built."

"You mentioned the tree house."

"Seeing it brought back the damnedest memories. You know, I don't think we ever went up in it again after we turned...oh, fourteen, fifteen. Partly because we'd physically outgrown it." The wryness became more pronounced. "And partly because we couldn't share it anymore. Good God. I don't know where we went wrong."

She was almost afraid to breathe, but she had to say something. "Hormones?"

"Yeah. Hormones and Mom." He fell silent for a

moment. "She loved us so much. She was so proud of us. I think...she was trying to encourage us to develop individual identities. I don't know, maybe she was afraid we'd wear matching business suits when we were forty if she didn't drive some kind of wedge between us. I guess we were pretty close when we were little. Must have scared her. We actually had our own language for a while. Rob ever tell you that?"

Beth shook her head.

If Nathan saw, it was out of his peripheral vision, because he was still looking the length of the room toward the photographs on the mantel. Toward his brother.

"Mom couldn't have afforded a psychologist, so she used a little old-fashioned competition. You notice I don't say 'healthy.'"

Beth wanted to wrap her arms around him, feel his control break. "No," she said. "Not healthy."

"By the time we were in college I hated him. It was like—" his jaw muscles knotted "—he was me. The side of me I didn't like. Dr. Jekyll and Mr. Hyde. I was the classic good kid by then. He was the screwup. Only, I had more stake in his screwups than a brother usually would. He was me. I was him." Nathan laughed humorlessly. "He must have resented the hell out of me. No wonder—" He stopped abruptly.

Her fingers bit into the chair upholstery. "No. There's no excuse for what he did. It wasn't funny, or even just careless and insensitive."

Nathan turned his head and his eyes, dark with emotion, met hers. "Rob was angry. He must have been."

"You know," Beth said quietly, "maybe each of you going your own way was best. When I knew Rob, he was...oh, sometimes a little lazy, sometimes unthinking, but good. Mostly he was funny and sweet. He adored Mandy. If he just hadn't been so sure he was immortal…''

''He was always reckless. That made him a better athlete than I was.'' Creases between his brows, Nathan was silent for a long time, seemingly thinking. ''For years I told myself it was best. We were better apart. But hell, all I was doing was justifying my own rigid unwillingness to forgive.'' He gave another bark of grim laughter. ''Ironic if I was right.''

She came to him at last, stopping a few feet away. ''Does it matter anymore either way?''

The creases came back. ''Matter? You're the one who was saying it did.''

''No.'' She drew a painful breath. ''How you remember Rob matters, not whether you were able to forgive him.''

Nathan's voice was harsh. ''You're saying that what can't be changed should be shrugged off?''

''No. Only that it's done. Over. And you know…'' Was she foolish to remind him? But she must. For their sake. ''Rob and I had a good marriage. He cherished his daughter. In fact—'' one last hesitation ''—I suspect he was happier than you've been.''

Nathan looked at her, layers of protection suddenly stripped away to reveal heartbreaking vulnerability. ''I suspect you're right.''

Her heart increased its drumbeat until it filled her ears. ''We could change that.'' Did she sound as odd to him?

''Oh, God, Beth…'' His voice broke and he had to clench his teeth. ''Can you believe that I love you?''

''If…'' She had to stop, press tremulous lips together, try again. "If you can truly believe that I love *you*."

Still several feet separated them.

The love and fear in his eyes nearly undid her. "I've been an idiot."

Oh, damn, she was crying.

One step closed the distance between them. His arms engulfed her with bruising force, as though he was afraid she'd slip away. She leaned her cheek against his chest and wept. Only a few tears, these ones of happiness.

"I can't promise I'll never be a jackass again." He moved his mouth against her hair. "Just...slap me down and forgive me?" When he heard his own choice of words, his muscles went rigid. "God. Who am I to ask anyone for forgiveness when I denied it for so long?"

Beth drew away, meeting his eyes squarely. "Rob didn't look for you, either. Remember that. He talked about you, he missed you, but... I think he was just as afraid as you were of starting the whole vicious cycle over. Maybe, for both of you, self-preservation didn't allow forgiveness."

His mouth twisted. "Now you sound like me. Sugar-coating it."

She'd gained enough confidence to add a hint of tartness to her voice. "Are you going to torture yourself for the rest of your life?"

"Just as long as I don't torture you." If he'd meant the words to sound light, he'd failed; he was raw, stripped bare for her.

No more talk of forgiveness. "I love you," she said shakily.

He snatched her to him again. Under her hands, she

felt his heart slamming against the wall of his chest. Her own raced so hard she was dizzy. She expected a kiss of passion, desperation; she got one so achingly tender her knees buckled. Nathan didn't just hold her up, he lifted her into his arms.

She clutched his shoulders.

The light that flared in his eyes warmed any chill left from her lonely nights. "I don't think I can wait any longer," he said roughly. "Do you have any idea how hard it was to turn down the chance you gave me last year to make a baby with you in that bed upstairs?"

"No," she whispered.

"I've been cursing myself ever since." He carried her into the hall. "When I had to produce sperm in that damn clinic…"

"I had to sit in the waiting room imagining you fantasizing about busty love goddesses. I hated them."

He set her down on the stairs, wrapping his hands around her hips. "Do you know who I fantasized about?"

Beth leaned forward and kissed the base of his throat. "Do I want to know?"

"You." His eyes smoldered. "All I could think about was what it would have been like with you."

Her breath came out on a sigh that he drank in with a second kiss, this one urgent and devastatingly sexy. Her lips parted, she tasted his tongue, felt his arousal pressing against her belly. She gasped for breath when he took his mouth from hers only to string kisses down her throat and along her collarbone. Her back arched, her head fell back, and her fingers twined in his hair.

"Nathan."

In response he unbuttoned her flannel shirt, unhooked the catch of her bra, groaned when he cupped her breasts in his hands.

"God, you're beautiful. I loved watching Patrick nurse."

She gave a faint laugh. "You looked like you hated watching. You glowered."

A reluctant grin caught his mouth. Freed from its reserve, his face was wickedly sensual. "Oh, I liked watching. But there's something a little cruel about making a man watch his son suckle on breasts *he's* never touched, don't you think?"

"I seem to remember you touching them."

"Like this?" His thumbs flicked her nipples, traced taunting circles around them.

"No," she whispered, remembering the tug of his mouth. "Not exactly."

His hands gripped her waist and lifted her up a step. He leaned forward and kissed her breast, teased it with his tongue, and then he moved up one step, too. This time he peeled her shirt and bra off altogether and tossed them. One more step up, and his attentions turned to her other breast. They were so sensitive heat coiled between her legs with stunning speed.

By the time Nathan and Beth had reached the top, she'd pulled his shirt over his head and discarded it, too, only a small part of her mind shocked by the sight of her bra dangling from the banister.

He backed her against the wall and kissed her deeply, grinding his hips against hers. A dark flush ran across his cheekbones, and the look in his eyes was molten.

"Am I dreaming?"

"No," she whispered. "If you were, we could use

my bed. As it is, I'm afraid a twin bed will have to do.''

"Oh, my God. Patrick. I forgot him.'' The dismay was curiously gratifying. "What if he wakes up?''

"Let's just be very quiet,'' she suggested. She wanted Nathan *now*, not tonight, not tomorrow when they could be alone together again. Right this second she didn't think she'd ever forgive their son if he kept Nathan from finishing what he'd begun—or had she begun it?—that day last summer under the willow tree.

They made it into the spare bedroom before they shed the rest of their clothes. The twin bed there looked so narrow, so prim, a gurgle of laughter lodged in her throat. The next second Nathan bore her down onto it, and the laughter died in a rush of need so intense she forgot where they were and what had come before. All that existed were his broad shoulders above her, his weight pressing her down, his mouth, damp and hot, moving on her breast.

She wrapped her legs around him, felt the muscles in his back bunch as he began a maddeningly slow thrust.

"If only,'' he said in a voice barely recognizable, "we'd made Patrick this way.''

"Yes.'' She sucked in breath as he filled her completely. "Oh, yes.''

What they did together on that narrow bed was glorious. He plunged and withdrew and she followed him, led him, coaxed him. They kissed and whispered and she looked up at Nathan's face, altered by passion, the angles of cheek and jaw sharper, the shadows more exaggerated. And, oh, the way he looked back at her, with tenderness and desire and love, made her hurt inside even as his every touch, every shift of weight, felt incredible, like nothing she'd ever known.

As he thrust harder, faster, as the rhythm became a frantic dance, the bed squeaked and Beth heard whimpers and words that could only be coming from her. She was pleading and promising and demanding. It was nothing like her—nothing, but wonderful. At the end, he smothered his own ragged bellow and her cries with his mouth. It was a kiss that didn't end even as his muscles went slack, and then he rolled onto his back and pulled her atop him.

At last he cradled her face and lifted it enough for her to see his lopsided smile. He looked…boyish, she realized in astonishment.

"Will you marry me?"

"Sir," she said in mock outrage, "I assumed I'd already been asked."

The smile deepened. "Let's make it official."

He'd slipped out of her. She scrambled away and sat up, clutching a pillow to hide her nakedness. Nathan rolled onto his side and braced his head on his hand. He looked older, apprehensive.

"I didn't think about Rob," she said.

He swore. "Damn it, Beth, I didn't ask!"

"No." She smiled tenderly. "But let me say this, just once. Rob and I had a good marriage. A *nice* marriage. But…I never felt anything like I just did. I love you, completely and utterly. Which is probably redundant, but that's okay." It was harder to smile this time. "Rob is a memory. You're my life."

He wasn't taking it well. His eyes frowned and his voice was taut. "Believe it or not, it never occurred to me that you were thinking about Rob." He muttered another obscenity. "Is this going to hang over us forever?"

"Nope." She grinned, letting him see her joy. "I would love to marry you, father of my son. I just thought that, once, you ought to know you did win the blue ribbon."

The warring emotions on his face would have been comical if they hadn't moved her nearly to tears. "Damn it, woman." He wrapped a hand around the back of her neck and pulled her close for another kiss, as sweet and lasting as a marriage vow.

She came away from it, laughing. "And by the way, father of my son. You're being called."

Nathan went still, listening to the grumble that preceded Patrick's piercing siren wail. Then he cocked an eyebrow at her. "What are you going to be doing while I'm performing diaper duty?"

"Picking up the clothes littering the hall before Mandy gets home."

"Jeez Louise." He erupted from bed. "Get a move on, woman!"

She watched as he yanked on his jeans. "We can work anything out, can't we?"

"Like diaper duty?"

"No, I mean..." She didn't know what she meant, except in an inchoate way.

But he did, because he gave another crooked grin. "Yeah. We can work it out. How can we fail? We're a family. And I never make the same mistake twice."

Family. Treasuring a last hard kiss, Beth collected the pieces of clothing littering the staircase and hall, then slipped into her bedroom past Nathan, who was now changing Patrick's diaper on the bed. He was cooing, and Daddy was cooing back. Unseen, she stood in

the bathroom doorway and watched them. Father and
son.

Her heart cramped. Oh, yes. They could be happy.
They would be.

She could hardly wait until Mandy came home.

EPILOGUE

MANDY SWALLOWED a sudden surge of nausea and clutched her middle. The sun didn't feel warm, although it was August and Mom wore a sleeveless dress. They all sat out on the front porch steps pretending they were soaking up the sun, pretending they weren't going anywhere important. A baseball cap shaded Patrick's eyes. He bounced on Mom's knee, laughing, his chubby legs kicking. On Mandy's other side, Uncle Nate gently squeezed the back of her neck with his big hand when he saw her double over.

"It'll get better," he said quietly. "Even if you are facing a cruddy few weeks."

She nodded, wordless. The strange thing was, she ought to be dreading those weeks. And she wasn't.

Today was the big day. Mom and Uncle Nate and Patrick—her *family*—were delivering her to the Fred Hutchison bone-marrow-transplant unit on one of the top floors of Swedish Hospital. Because her immune system had already given up, she'd be placed in sterile isolation for six days of chemotherapy and six more of radiation to kill her existing bone marrow. That meant she wouldn't be able to touch anybody for a long time. Mom and Uncle Nate and Patrick would be able to see her, but only through a transparent wall. No hugs or kisses, no hand holding hers. She knew how sick she'd be. She could even die there behind that clear wall.

What the doctors would be doing to her could damage her organs, or she could get an infection no matter how careful they were. Or, once Patrick's cells had been introduced into her, they might reject and attack her body. And she'd be alone in a way she'd never been. Always she'd had Mom beside her, holding the basin when she threw up, washing her face afterward, massaging her back, laying a hand over hers. But not this time.

The pain in her stomach eased and she lifted her face, despite her shivers feeling the sun's warmth. For a second she leaned against Uncle Nate, and his arm came around her in silent support. She turned her head and saw that Mom was watching her, this incredible love in her eyes. And even Patrick grinned at her. Mom was right, Mandy thought; he *was* cute. Except when applesauce dribbled back out of his mouth.

What had she been thinking about? she wondered vaguely. Oh, yeah—the fact that she wasn't really scared. And she didn't feel alone. She knew she wouldn't be even if nobody could touch her. Because she had more than Mom now. She had a whole family. Including a brother whose gift of life she absolutely, positively would not waste by dying. Besides, he needed her. Neither Mom nor Uncle Nate knew what life was like for a kid these days. She had to be around to teach Patrick.

And at the end of school last May, when everyone knew she was going to have the bone-marrow transplant this summer, Colin Hillman had come up to her and asked her to go out with him. To be his girlfriend. So *he* would be waiting for her to come back, too.

Nope. She knew she was going to get better, this time once and for all. What she had was faith. Knowing people loved you enough gave that to you.

"Okay," she said. "I'm ready to go."

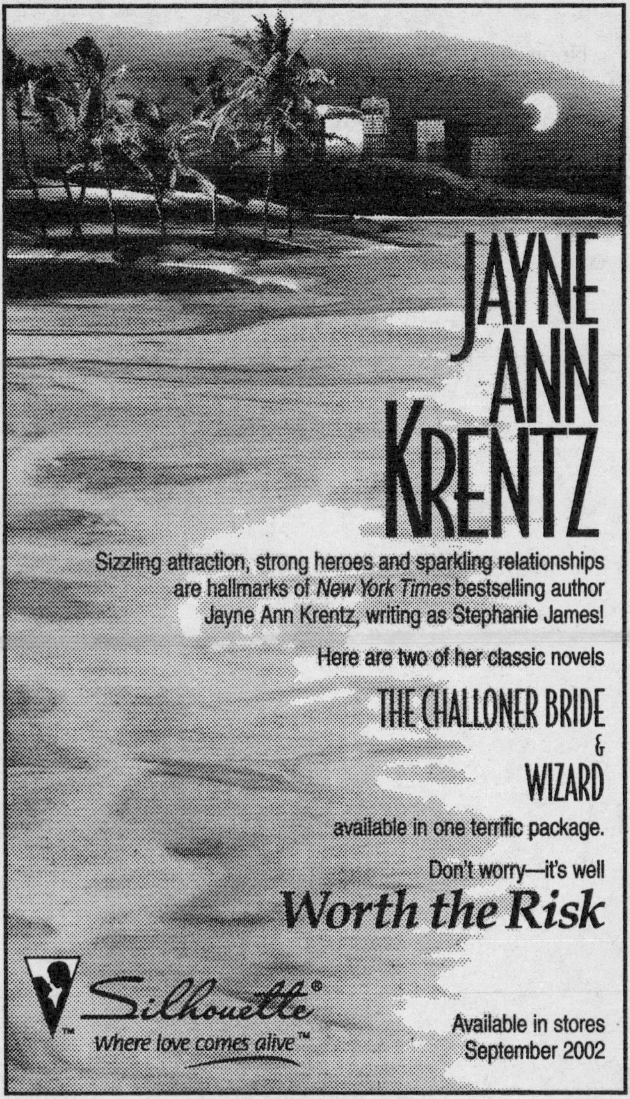
JAYNE ANN KRENTZ
Sizzling attraction, strong heroes and sparkling relationships are hallmarks of *New York Times* bestselling author Jayne Ann Krentz, writing as Stephanie James!
Here are two of her classic novels
THE CHALLONER BRIDE
&
WIZARD
available in one terrific package.
Don't worry—it's well
Worth the Risk
Silhouette®
Where love comes alive™
Available in stores September 2002

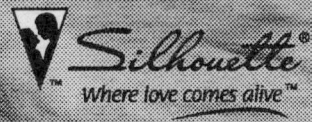

New York Times bestselling author

LINDA HOWARD

tells an incredible story!

Readers have always clamored for Chance Mackenzie's
story. Now the brooding loner, welcomed into the
Mackenzie family but never quite at home, is on a
desperate assignment. He'll take any risk, tell any lie,
do whatever is necessary. But when fiery, independent
and yet vulnerable Sunny Miller becomes the one in
danger, can Chance take the final gamble?

Don't miss

*A Game
of Chance*

Coming this September from Silhouette Books!

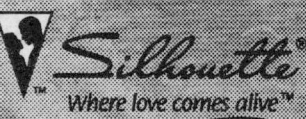

Silhouette®

Where love comes alive™

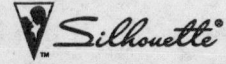

GUIDE TO USING
the Prentice Hall Health Professional's Drug Guide 2007–2008

Classifications and Prototype Drugs

The classifications used in this book are based on the system used by the American Hospital Formulary Service (AHFS). This book further classifies drugs by therapeutic uses, enabling the health professional to identify drugs in the same class that have similar indications for use. Thus, the book provides a framework for understanding

AMIODARONE HYDROCHLORIDE ⓟ
(a-mee′oh-da-rone)
Cordarone, Amio-Aqueous, Pacerone
Classifications: ANTIARRHYTHMIC, CLASS III
Therapeutic: ANTIARRHYTHMIC, CLASS III
Pregnancy Category: D

how drugs in a given class are used in clinical practice. The pharmacologic classification appears immediately after the Classification heading, followed by the Therapeutic classification. In general, all drugs in a class will have similar actions, uses, adverse effects, and clinical implications. Therefore, we have selected certain drugs that are representative of a class— **prototype drugs**—and discuss them in more detail than the other drugs in that class. Throughout the book, prototype drug monographs are identified with a small icon. The user can refer to the prototype drug to obtain in-depth information on those drugs in the class that may not be as extensively discussed in their monographs. When a drug belongs to a classification that has a designated prototype drug, that prototype is identified directly below the therapeutic classification. The table on pages xi–xviii outlines the classification scheme and lists the drug prototype considered to be representative of each class. All prototype drugs are highlighted in **bold** type in the index for quick identification. Finally, not every drug has a prototype. Some drugs have a unique mechanism of action or therapeutic effect. In these cases, no prototype drug will be identified.

Pregnancy Category

Drugs may be described as category A, B, C, D, or X according to the risk–benefit ratio for the mother and the fetus, with A being the lowest and X the highest risk. If the FDA pregnancy category is known, it is indicated after the classifications and prototype in each monograph. Refer to Appendix C, FDA Pregnancy Categories, for a more complete description of each category.

Controlled Substances

In the United States, controlled substances, such as narcotics, are classified as belonging to one of five schedules (I to V) according to abuse potential. Schedule I has the highest, and Schedule V has the lowest potential for abuse. Refer to Appendix B, U.S. Schedules of Controlled Substances, for a more complete description of each schedule.

Availability

Because drugs come in a variety of dosages and forms, the authors include a section devoted to Availability in each monograph. This section identifies the available forms (e.g., tablets, capsules) and the available dosage amounts for every drug.

> **AVAILABILITY** 200 mg tablets; 50 mg/mL injection

Action and *Therapeutic Effect*

Each monograph describes the mechanism by which the specific drug produces physiologic and biochemical changes at the cellular, tissue, and organ levels. This information helps the user understand how the drug works in the body and makes it easier to learn its side effects, adverse reactions, and cautious uses. The *therapeutic effects*, which are set in italics for maximum clarity and ease of use, are the reasons why a drug is prescribed. Therapeutic effectiveness of the drug can be determined by monitoring improvement in the condition for which the drug is prescribed.

> **ACTION & *THERAPEUTIC EFFECT***
> Class III antiarrhythmic; also has antianginal and antiadrenergic properties. Acts directly on all cardiac tissues by prolonging duration of action potential and refractory period without significantly affecting resting membrane potential. *By direct action on smooth muscle, decreases peripheral resistance and increases coronary blood flow. Blocks effects of sympathetic stimulation.*

Uses and Unlabeled Uses

The therapeutic applications of each drug are described in terms of approved, or FDA-labeled, uses and unlabeled uses. An unlabeled use is literally one that does not appear on the drug label or in the manufacturer's literature on the use of the drug. Although currently supported by medical literature, unlabeled uses are those that are not currently approved by the FDA. The unlabeled use is, nevertheless, an accepted use for the drug supported by the medical literature.

USES Prophylaxis and treatment of life-threatening ventricular arrhythmias and supraventricular arrhythmias, particularly with atrial fibrillation.
UNLABELED USES Treatment of nonexertional angina, conversion of atrial fibrillation to normal sinus rhythm, paroxysmal supraventricular tachycardia, ventricular rate control due to accessory pathway conduction in pre-excited atrial arrhythmia, after defibrillation and epinephrine in cardiac arrest, AV nodal reentry tachycardia.

Contraindications and Cautious Use

Many drugs have contraindications and therefore should not be used in specific conditions, such as during pregnancy, or with particular drugs or foods. In other cases, the drug should be used with great caution because of a greater than average risk of untoward effects.

CONTRAINDICATIONS Hypersensitivity to amiodarone, or benzyl alcohol; cardiogenic shock, severe sinus bradycardia, advanced AV block unless a pacemaker is available, severe sinus-node dysfunction or sick sinus syndrome, bradycardia, congenital or acquired QR prolongation syndromes, or history of torsade de pointes; severe liver disease, pregnancy (category D), lactation.
CAUTIOUS USE Hepatic disease, cirrhosis; Hashimoto's thyroiditis, goiter, thyrotoxicosis, or history of other thyroid dysfunction; CHF, left ventricular dysfunction; hypersensitivity to iodine; older adults; Fabry disease, especially with visual disturbances; electrolyte imbalance, hypokalemia, hypomagnesemia, hypovolemia; preexisting lung disease, COPD; open heart surgery.

Route and Dosages

Route of administration is specified as SC, IM, IV, PO, PR, nasal, ophthalmic, vaginal, topical, aural, intradermal, or intrathecal. Dosages are listed according to indication, or use. One of the hallmarks of this drug guide is the comprehensive dosage information it provides. The guide includes adult, geriatric, and pediatric dosages, as well as dosages for neonates and infants. This section also indicates dosage adjustments for renal impairment (based on creatinine clearance), clients undergoing hemodialysis, hepatic impairment, and obese clients (based on ideal body weight) whenever applicable. In all monographs, the routes and dosages are highlighted in a gray box to facilitate quick reference.

ROUTE & DOSAGE

Arrhythmias

Adult: **PO Loading Dose** 800–1600 mg/d in 1–2 doses for 1–3 wk **PO Maintenance Dose** 400–600 mg/d in 1–2 doses **IV Loading Dose** 150 mg over 10 min followed by 360 mg over next 6 h **IV Maintenance Dose** 540 mg over 18 h (0.5 mg/min), may continue at 0.5 mg/min **Convert IV to PO** Duration of infusion <1 wk use 800–1600 mg PO, 1–3 wk use 600–800 mg PO, >3 wk use 400 mg PO

Child: **PO Loading Dose** 10–15 mg/kg/d or 600–800 mg/1.73 m^2/d, in 1–2 divided doses for 4–14 d cycle or until adequate control of arrhythmia **PO Maintenance Dose** 5 mg/kg/d or 200–400 mg/1.73 m^2/d once daily, may be able to reduce to 2–5 mg/kg/d 5 d per week **IV Loading Dose** 5 mg/kg over 30 min **IV Maintenance Dose** 2–20 mg/kg/d

Hepatic Impairment

Adjustment only suggested in severe hepatic impairment.

ADMINISTRATION

- Note: Correct hypokalemia and hypomagnesemia prior to initiation of therapy.

Oral

- Give consistently with respect to meals.
- Note: Only a physician experienced with the drug and treatment of life-threatening arrhythmias should give loading doses.
- Note: GI symptoms commonly occur during high-dose therapy, especially with loading doses. Symptoms usually respond to dose reduction or divided dose given with food, including milk.

Administration

Organized by different routes, the drug administration section lists comprehensive instructions for administering, handling, and storing medications.

Intravenous Drug Administration

Within the Administration section of appropriate monographs, the authors highlight intravenous drugs, indicated by a vertical red bar. This section provides users with comprehensive instructions on how to **Prepare** and **Administer** direct, intermittent, and continuous intravenous medications. It also includes **Solution/Additive** and **Y-Site** incompatibility for every monograph, where appropriate, to indicate which drugs and solutions should not be mixed with the intravenous drug. This is crucial information for drug administration. Additionally, a chart for Y-Site compatibility for common intravenous drugs is located inside the back cover of this drug guide.

Intravenous

PREPARE: **IV Infusion: First rapid loading dose infusion:** Add 150 mg (3 mL) amiodarone to 100 mL D5W to yield 1.5 mg/mL. **Second infusion during first 24 h (slow loading dose and maintenance infusion):** Add 900 mg (18 mL) amiodarone to 500 mL D5W to yield 1.8 mg/mL. **Maintenance infusions after the first 24 h:** Prepare concentrations of 1–6 mg/mL amiodarone. Note: (Use central line to give concentrations >2 mg/mL).

ADMINISTER: **IV Infusion:** Rapidly infuse initial 150 mg dose over the first 10 min at a rate of 15 mg/min. Over next 6 h, infuse 360 mg at a rate of 1 mg/min. Over the remaining 18 h, infuse 540 mg at a rate of 0.5 mg/min. After the first 24 h, infuse maintenance doses of 720 mg/24 h at a rate of 0.5 mg/min.

INCOMPATIBILITIES **Solution/additive: Nitroprusside sodium, sodium bicarbonate. Y-site: Aminophylline, ampicillin/sulbactam, cefamandole, cefazolin, ceftazidime, ceftizoxime, ceftriaxone, cefuroxime, digoxin, heparin, imipenem/cilastatin, magnesium sulfate, piperacillin, potassium phosphate, sodium bicarbonate, sodium phosphate.**

Adverse Effects

Virtually all drugs have adverse side effects that may be bothersome to some individuals but not to others. In each monograph, adverse effects with an incidence of ≥1% are listed by body system or organs. The most common adverse effects appear in *italic* type, whereas those that are life-threatening are underlined. Users of the drug guide will find a key at the bottom of every page as a quick reminder.

ADVERSE EFFECTS (≥1%) **CNS:** Peripheral neuropathy (*muscle weakness,* wasting numbness, tingling), *fatigue,* abnormal gait, dyskinesias, *dizziness,* paresthesia, headache. **CV:** Bradycardia, *hypotension* (IV), sinus arrest, cardiogenic shock, CHF, arrhythmias; AV block. **Special Senses:** *Corneal microdeposits,* blurred vision, optic neuritis, optic neuropathy, permanent blindness, corneal degeneration, macular degeneration, photosensitivity. **GI:** *Anorexia, nausea, vomiting, constipation,* hepatotoxicity. **Metabolic:** Hyperthyroidism or hypothyroidism; may cause neonatal hypo- or hyperthyroidism if taken during pregnancy. **Respiratory:** (Pulmonary toxicity) Alveolitis, pneumonitis (fever, dry cough, dyspnea), interstitial pulmonary fibrosis, *fatal gasping syndrome* with IV in children. **Skin:** Slate-blue pigmentation, *photosensitivity,* rash. **Other:** With chronic use, angioedema.

Diagnostic Test Interference

This section describes the effect of the drug on various diagnostic tests and alerts the health professional to possible misinterpretations of test results when applicable. The specific altered element is highlighted in ***bold italic*** type.

Interactions

Whenever appropriate, this section lists individual drugs, drug classes, foods, and herbs that interact with the drug discussed in the monograph. Drugs may interact to inhibit or enhance one another. Thus, drug interactions may improve the therapeutic response, lead to therapeutic failure, or produce specific adverse reactions. Only drugs that have been shown to cause clinically significant and documented interactions with the drug discussed in the monograph are listed in this section. Note that generic drugs appear in **bold** type, and drug classes appear in SMALL CAPS.

> **INTERACTIONS Drug:** Significantly increases **digoxin** levels; enhances pharmacologic effects and toxicities of **disopyramide, procainamide, quinidine, flecainide, lidocaine, lovastatin, simvastatin;** anticoagulant effects of ORAL ANTICOAGULANTS enhanced; **verapamil, diltiazem,** BETA-ADRENERGIC BLOCKING AGENTS may potentiate sinus bradycardia, sinus arrest, or AV block; may increase **phenytoin** levels 2- to 3-fold; **cholestyramine** may decrease amiodarone levels; **fentanyl** may cause bradycardia, hypotension, or decreased output; may increase **cyclosporine** levels and toxicity; **cimetidine** may increase amiodarone levels; **ritonavir** may increase risk of amiodarone toxicity, including cardiotoxicity. **Herbal: Echinacea** possible increase in hepatotoxicity.

Pharmacokinetics

This section identifies how the drug moves throughout the body. It lists the mechanisms of absorption, distribution, metabolism, elimination, and half-life when known. It also provides information about onset, peak, and duration of the drug action. New information has been added for protein-binding and CYP450 where appropriate.

> **PHARMACOKINETICS Absorption:** 22–86% absorbed. **Onset:** 2–3 d to 1–3 wk. **Peak:** 3–7 h. **Distribution:** Concentrates in adipose tissue, lungs, kidneys, spleen; crosses placenta. **Metabolism:** Extensively in liver; undergoes some enterohepatic cycling; via CYP2C8 and 3A4. **Elimination:** Excreted chiefly in bile and feces; also in breast milk. **Half-Life:** Biphasic, initial 2.5–10 d, terminal 40–55 d.

Clinical Implications

The Clinical Implications section of each drug monograph is formatted in an easy-to-use manner so that all the pertinent information that health professionals need is listed under two headings: **Assessment & Drug Effects** and **Patient & Family Education.** Under these headings, the user can quickly and easily identify needed information and incorporate it into appropriate decision making.

Therapeutic Effectiveness

Therapeutic effectiveness of the drug can be determined by monitoring improvement in the condition for which the drug is prescribed, and by using the Assessment & Drug Effects section of the Clinical Implications. Drugs have multiple uses or indications. Therefore, it is important to know why a drug is being prescribed for a specific client. In the italicized sentences at the end of the Action & *Therapeutic Effect* section in all monographs, specific indicators of the effectiveness of the drug are provided. Additionally, in the Route & Dosage table for each drug, the dosages are listed according to the indications for use of the drug.

CLINICAL IMPLICATIONS

Assessment & Drug Effects

- Monitor BP carefully during infusion and slow the infusion if significant hypotension occurs; bradycardia should be treated by slowing the infusion or discontinuing if necessary. Monitor heart rate and rhythm and BP until drug response has stabilized; report promptly symptomatic bradycardia. Sustained monitoring is essential because drug has an unusually long half-life.

Patient & Family Education

- Check pulse daily once stabilized, or as prescribed. Report a pulse <60.
- Take oral drug consistently with respect to meals.
- Become familiar with potential adverse reactions and report those that are bothersome to the physician.

PRENTICE HALL
HEALTH
PROFESSIONAL'S
DRUG GUIDE
2007-2008

Margaret T. Shannon, RN, PhD

Professor Emeritus of Nursing
Our Lady of Holy Cross College
New Orleans, Louisiana

Billie Ann Wilson, RN, PhD

Professor of Nursing
School of Nursing
Loyola University New Orleans
New Orleans, Louisiana

Kelly M. Shields, PharmD

Assistant Professor of Pharmacy Practice
Director of Drug Information Center
Raabe College of Pharmacy
Ohio Northern University
Ada, Ohio

Carolyn L. Stang, PharmD

Vice President, Clinical Program Development
Caremark Inc.
Northbrook, Illinois

PEARSON
Prentice
Hall

Upper Saddle River, New Jersey 07458

Copyright © 2008 by Pearson Education, Inc.,
Upper Saddle River, NJ 07458

www.prenhall.com/drugguides

07   08 / 10   9   8   7   6   5   4   3   2   1

Pearson Education Ltd.
Pearson Education Australia Pty, Limited
Pearson Education Singapore, Pte. Ltd.
Pearson Education North Asia Ltd.
Pearson Education Canada, Ltd.
Pearson Educación de Mexico, S.A. de C.V.
Pearson Education—Japan
Pearson Education Malaysia, Pte. Ltd.
Pearson Education, Upper Saddle River, New Jersey

Pearson Prentice Hall™ is a trademark of Pearson Education, Inc.
Pearson® is a registered trademark of Pearson plc
Prentice Hall® is a registered trademark of Pearson Education, Inc.

ISBN 0-13-513408-0/978-0-13-513408-5

PRINTED IN THE UNITED STATES OF AMERICA

CONTENTS

To

Alvin, Theresa, Ellen, and

Michael, Rick, Kris, and Leah

without whom this work would not have been possible

♦

ABOUT THE AUTHORS

Margaret T. Shannon is Professor Emeritus of Nursing at Our Lady of Holy Cross College, New Orleans, Louisiana. She holds a BS and an MS in Chemistry, both from Saint Louis University; an MA in Teaching Biology from Saint Mary's College, a BS in Nursing from Northwestern State University of Louisiana, an MSN from Louisiana State University Health Sciences Center, and a PhD in Curriculum and Instruction from the University of New Orleans. Prior to entering nursing, she taught physical science, natural science, and mathematics at the secondary and collegiate levels.

Billie Ann Wilson is currently Professor of Nursing at the School of Nursing at Loyola University in New Orleans, Louisiana. Prior to entering nursing, she taught natural and physical sciences at the secondary and collegiate levels. She holds a BS in Biology from Boston College, an MS in Biology from Purdue University, a BS in Nursing from Northwestern State University of Louisiana, an MSN from Louisiana State University Health Sciences Center, and a PhD in Curriculum and Instruction from the University of New Orleans.

Kelly M. Shields is currently Assistant Professor of Pharmacy Practice at Ohio Northern University's Raabe College of Pharmacy. She holds a Doctor of Pharmacy from Butler University, and completed a fellowship in Natural Product Information and Research at University of Missouri-Kansas City. She has practiced pharmacy in retail, community, and academic settings and has worked as a freelance medical writer.

Carolyn L. Stang is currently Vice President for Clinical Program Development at Caremark Inc. She has worked in hospital and community pharmacies, home health care, and the pharmaceutical industry. She holds a BS in Pharmacy from The Ohio State University, and a Doctor of Pharmacy from the University of Tennessee, Memphis, and completed a fellowship in Family Medicine at the Medical University of South Carolina, Charleston.

EDITORIAL REVIEW PANEL

We wish to thank the following individuals for conducting thorough reviews of the drug information in this book for its accuracy, currency, relevance, presentation, accessibility, and use.

EDITORIAL CONSULTANT

A special acknowledgment to **Marc Harrold, PhD, RPh,** Professor of Medicinal Chemistry at Duquesne University in Pittsburgh, Pennsylvania, who was a tremendous addition to the author team as a contributor for all of the monographs for the new drugs in this edition. We are grateful for his expertise and for his input.

PREFACE

Prentice Hall Health Professional's Drug Guide 2007–2008 is a current and reliable reference designed to provide comprehensive information needed to make appropriate decisions regarding drug administration. This new edition includes 43 monographs for new drugs recently approved by the Food and Drug Administration (FDA). Several drugs removed from the market have been eliminated and archived on the Companion Website accompanying this handbook. On pages xi–xviii, the user will find a current listing of drug classifications and their associated drug prototypes. Prototype drugs are representative of all drugs in a particular classification. The classification list serves as a valuable tool, especially to students learning pharmacology and familiarizing themselves with drug families and prototypes.

Each drug monograph provides the necessary information for safe and effective drug administration. The user should read all the information provided. Occasionally, the user will be referred to Appendix F, Glossary of Key Terms, Clinical Conditions, and Associated Signs and Symptoms. This unique glossary provides valuable information regarding common assessment findings related to therapeutic effectiveness or ineffectiveness of specific drugs.

The authors recognize that the decision-making process related to drug administration is a cyclical one. For example, assessments are made both prior to and after drug administration. Thus, clinical interventions may change as a result of an *achieved therapeutic effect, therapeutic failure, manifestation of an adverse effect,* or *demonstration of a learning need.* The authors believe that the users of this drug reference will find that the clear and logical design of the drug monographs facilitates decision making and supports the nursing process.

Although some advanced practice nurses and other health professionals now have prescriptive privileges, the term *physician* is used throughout this book to designate the prescriber of medications.

ORGANIZATION

The ***Prentice Hall Health Professional's Drug Guide 2007–2008*** is user friendly. Health professionals, pharmacists, and students from across the country reviewed the content of this handbook and provided helpful suggestions on how it could be made more useful. Based on these comments, the authors updated and added new information to every monograph in this book. To help readers better understand how to use the drug guide, the authors illustrate and describe all the components of a drug monograph in the next section.

In this drug guide, all drugs are listed alphabetically according to their generic names. However, each drug is indexed by both its generic and trade names in the back of the guide to make it easier for the user to locate individual drug monographs. Trade names followed by a maple leaf indicate that brand of the drug is available only in Canada. If a drug is not listed in the alphabetical section, it may be a combination drug, which is a drug made up of more than one generic component. These combination drugs are listed under their trade names in the index and in Appendix E, Prescription Combination Drugs. The appendix identifies the generic components and the amount of each generic drug contained in the combination. Users of this drug guide will find the page numbers for monographs of the component drugs in this appendix to make access to this information easier and faster.

Appendixes

This drug guide includes several helpful tables and charts in the appendixes, including Appendix A, Ocular Medications, Low Molecular Weight Heparins, Inhaled Corticosteroids, and Topical Corticosteroids; Appendix B, U.S. Schedules of Controlled Substances; Appendix C, FDA Pregnancy Categories; Appendix D, Oral Dosage Forms That Should Not Be Crushed; Appendix E, Prescription Combination Drugs; Appendix F, Glossary of Key Terms, Clinical Conditions, and Associated Signs and Symptoms; Appendix G, Abbreviations; and Appendix H, Herbal and Dietary Supplement Table. Appendix H is a new feature the authors have added. This appendix identifies name, use, and safety issues associated with herbal products, such as potential drug interactions and side effects.

Index

The index in the **Prentice Hall Health Professional's Drug Guide 2007–2008** is perhaps the most often-used section in the entire book. All generic, trade, and combination drugs are listed in this index. Whenever a trade name is listed, the generic drug monograph is listed in parentheses. Additionally, classifications are listed and identified in SMALL CAPS, whereas all prototype drugs are highlighted in **bold** type. Drugs belonging to various classifications and subclassifications, including therapeutic uses, are also cross-referenced in this index. As a special new feature, the index now includes entries for combination drugs (e.g. Tylenol with Codeine) with index references to component drugs.

Companion Website – www.prenhall.com/drugguides

The Companion Website for the **Prentice Hall Health Professional's Drug Guide 2007–2008** is a *bonus* online resource that offers additional information and is updated periodically. It includes access to drug updates, links to drug-related sites, drug-related tools, medication administration techniques, drug classifications, principles of pharmacology, common herbal remedies, archived drug monographs for rarely used and discontinued drugs, and more. You can also send the authors your feedback about the drug guide through this website.

ACKNOWLEDGMENTS

We wish to express our appreciation to our past and present students who have provided the inspiration for this work. It is for these individuals and all who strive for excellence in patient care that this work was undertaken.

Margaret T. Shannon, RN, PhD
Billie Ann Wilson, RN, PhD
Kelly M. Shields, PharmD
Carolyn L. Stang, PharmD

Classifications	Prototype

ANTIGOUT AGENT.................................. Probenecid

ANTIHISTAMINES
ANTIHISTAMINES (H₁-RECEPTOR
    ANTAGONIST) .... Diphenhydramine HCl
        NON-SEDATING................................. Loratadine
ANTIPRURITIC .... Hydroxyzine HCl
    ANTIVERTIGO AGENT .... Meclizine HCl

ANTIINFECTIVES
ANTIBIOTICS
    AMEBICIDE .... Paromomycin Sulfate
    ANTHELMINTIC.. Mebendazole
    AMINOGLYCOSIDES................................ Gentamicin Sulfate
    ANTIFUNGALS .... Amphotericin B
    AZOLE ANTIFUNGAL .... Fluconazole
    ALLYLAMINE ANTIFUNGAL...................... Terbinafine
    ECHINOCARDIN ANTIFUNGAL .... Caspofungin
    BETA-LACTAM... Imipenem-Cilastatin
    CEPHALOSPORIN
        FIRST GENERATION .... Cefazolin Sodium
        SECOND GENERATION......................... Cefaclor
        THIRD GENERATION............................. Cefotaxime Sodium
    CLINDAMYCIN .... Clindamycin HCl
    MACROLIDES.. Erythromycin
    PENICILLIN
        AMINOPENICILLIN .... Ampicillin
        ANTIPSEUDOMONAL PENICILLIN .... Piperacillin
        NATURAL PENICILLIN .... Penicillin G Potassium
    QUINOLONES.. Ciprofloxacin HCl
    SULFONAMIDES...................................... Sulfisoxazole
    TETRACYCLINE.. Tetracycline HCl
ANTILEPROSY (SULFONE) AGENT .... Dapsone
ANTIMALARIAL... Chloroquine HCl
ANTIPROTOZOAL.. Metronidazole
ANTITUBERCULOSIS AGENTS............................ Isoniazid
    ANTITUBERCULOSIS AGENT,
        ANTIMYCOBACTERIAL .... Rifampin
ANTIVIRAL AGENTS .... Acyclovir
    ADAMANTANES...................................... Amantadine

*Based on the American Hospital Formulary Service Pharmacologic–Therapeutic Classification.
†Prototype drugs are highlighted in tinted boxes in this book.
Complete list of drugs for each classification found in classification index starting on p. 1783.

Classifications	Prototype

ANTIRETROVIRAL AGENTS
NUCLEOSIDE REVERSE TRANSCRIPTASE
INHIBITOR...Lamivudine
NONNUCLEOSIDE REVERSE
TRANSCRIPTASE INHIBITOR ....Efavirenz
PROTEASE INHIBITOR ....Saquinavir
URINARY TRACT ANTIINFECTIVE.........................Trimethoprim
VACCINE..Hepatitis B

ANTINEOPLASTICS
ALKYLATING AGENT....................................Cyclophosphamide
ANTIANDROGEN ....Flutamide
ANTIBIOTIC ....Doxorubicin HCl
ANTIMETABOLITES
ANTIMETABOLITE (ANTIFOLATE) ....Methotrexate
ANTIMETABOLITE (PURINE ANTAGONIST) 6-Mercaptopurine
ANTIMETABOLITE (PYRIMIDINE) 5-Fluorouracil
CAMPTOTHECIN ....Topotecan HCl
AROMATASE INHIBITOR.................................Anastrozole
EPIDERMAL GROWTH FACTOR RECEPTOR
INHIBITOR ....Gefitinib
HORMONE, ANTIESTROGEN ....Tamoxifen Citrate
MITOTIC INHIBITOR ....Vincristine Sulfate
TAXANE...Paclitaxel

ANTITUSSIVES, EXPECTORANTS, & MUCOLYTICS
ANTITUSSIVE ....Benzonatate
EXPECTORANT ....Guaifenesin
MUCOLYTIC...Acetylcysteine

AUTONOMIC NERVOUS SYSTEM AGENTS
ADRENERGIC AGONISTS
(SYMPATHOMIMETICS)
ALPHA-ADRENERGIC AGONIST......................Methoxamine HCl
ALPHA- & BETA-ADRENERGIC AGONIST ....Epinephrine
BETA-ADRENERGIC AGONIST ....Isoproterenol HCl
ADRENERGIC ANTAGONISTS
(SYMPATHOLYTICS)
ALPHA ANTAGONISTS (BLOCKING
AGENT) ....Prazosin HCl
BETA ANTAGONISTS ....Propranolol HCl
ERGOT ALKALOID ....Ergotamine Tartrate
5-HT$_1$ SEROTONIN AGONISTS......................Sumatriptan

Classifications	Prototype

ANTICHOLINERGICS
  (PARASYMPATHOLYTICS)
  ANTIPARKINSON AGENTS............................ Levodopa
  CATECHOLAMINE O-METHYL
      TRANSFERASE (COMT) INHIBITOR.............. Tolcapone
  ANTIMUSCARINIC .... Ipratropium Bromide
CHOLINERGICS (PARASYMPATHOMIMETICS)
  CHOLINESTERASE INHIBITOR .... Neostigmine
  CENTRAL-ACTING .... Donepezil
  DIRECT-ACTING CHOLINERGIC .... Bethanechol Chloride
AUTONOMIC DRUGS, MISC .... Nicotine

BENZODIAZEPINE ANTAGONIST .... Flumazenil

BIOLOGIC RESPONSE MODIFIERS
IMMUNOSUPPRESSANT.................................. Cyclosporine
IMMUNOGLOBULIN .... Immune Globulin
TUMOR NECROSIS FACTOR MODIFIER.................. Etanercept
FUSION PROTEIN .... Alefacept
MONOCLONAL ANTIBODY............................... Basiliximab

BLOOD DERIVATIVE, PLASMA VOLUME,
   EXPANDER... Normal Serum Albumin

BLOOD FORMERS, COAGULATORS, &
   ANTICOAGULANTS
ANTICOAGULANT .... Heparin Sodium
  DIRECT THROMBIN INHIBITOR .... Lepirudin
  LOW MOLECULAR WEIGHT HEPARIN .... Enoxaparin
ANTIPLATELET AGENTS................................... Clopidogrel
  GLYCOPROTEIN IIb/IIIa INHIBITOR .... Abciximab
HEMATOPOIETIC GROWTH FACTOR.................... Epoetin Alpha
HEMOSTATIC (COAGULATOR) .... Aminocaproic Acid
IRON PREPARATION....................................... Ferrous Sulfate
THROMBOLYTIC ENZYME .... Alteplase

BRONCHODILATORS (RESPIRATORY SMOOTH
   MUSCLE RELAXANT)
BETA-ADRENERGIC AGONIST .... Albuterol
XANTHINE... Theophylline
LEUKOTRIENE INHIBITOR................................ Zafirlukast

Classifications	Prototype

CARDIOVASCULAR AGENTS

ANGIOTENSIN II RECEPTOR
  ANTAGONISTS .... Losartan Potassium
ANGIOTENSIN-CONVERTING
  ENZYME INHIBITORS .... Enalapril
ANTIARRHYTHMIC AGENTS
  CLASS IA .... Procainamide HCl
  CLASS IB .... Lidocaine HCl
  CLASS IC .... Flecainide
  CLASS II .... Propranolol HCl
  CLASS III .... Amiodarone HCl
ANTILIPEMICS
  BILE ACID SEQUESTRANT .... Cholestyramine
  FIBRATES .... Fenofibrate
  HMG-CoA REDUCTASE INHIBITOR (STATIN) .... Lovastatin
CALCIUM CHANNEL BLOCKERS
  1,4 DIHYDROPYRIDINE .... Nifedipine
  MISCELLANEOUS .... Verapamil
CARDIAC GLYCOSIDE .... Digoxin
CENTRAL-ACTING ANTIHYPERTENSIVE .... Methyldopa
INOTROPIC AGENT .... Inamrinone
NITRATE VASODILATOR .... Nitroglycerin
NONNITRATE VASODILATOR .... Hydralazine HCl
RAUWOLFIA ALKALOID .... Reserpine

CENTRAL NERVOUS SYSTEM AGENTS

ANALGESICS, ANTIPYRETICS
  NARCOTIC (OPIATE) AGONISTS .... Morphine
  NARCOTIC (OPIATE) AGONIST-ANTAGONIST ..... Pentazocine HCl
  NARCOTIC (OPIATE) ANTAGONIST .... Naloxone HCl
  NONNARCOTIC ANALGESICS .... Acetaminophen
  NONSTEROIDAL ANTI-INFLAMMATORY
    DRUGS (NSAIDS)
      COX-1 .... Ibuprofen
      COX-2 .... Celecoxib
  SALICYLATE .... Aspirin
ANESTHETIC
  GENERAL .... Thiopental Sodium
  LOCAL (ESTER TYPE) .... Procaine HCl
  LOCAL (AMIDE TYPE) .... Lidocaine HCl
ANTICONVULSANTS
  BARBITURATE .... Phenobarbital

Classifications   ## Prototype

BENZODIAZEPINE	Diazepam
GABA INHIBITOR	Valproic Acid Sodium
GABA ANALOG	Gabapentin
HYDANTOIN	Phenytoin
SUCCINIMIDE	Ethosuximide
SULFONAMIDE	Zonisamide
TRICYCLIC	Carbamazepine

ANXIOLYTICS, SEDATIVE-HYPNOTICS

BARBITURATE	Secobarbital
BENZODIAZEPINE	Lorazepam
NONBENZODIAZEPINE	Zolpidem
CARBAMATE	Meprobamate

PSYCHOTHERAPEUTIC

ANTIDEPRESSANTS

SELECTIVE SEROTONIN-REUPTAKE INHIBITORS (SSRI)	Fluoxetine HCl
SEROTONIN NOREPINEPHRINE REUPTAKE INHIBITORS	Venlafaxine
MONOAMINE OXIDASE (MAO) INHIBITORS	Phenelzine Sulfate
TETRACYCLIC ANTIDEPRESSANTS	Mirtazapine
TRICYCLIC ANTIDEPRESSANTS	Imipramine HCl

ANTIPSYCHOTIC AGENT

BUTYROPHENONE	Haloperidol
PHENOTHIAZINE	Chlorpromazine
ATYPICAL	Clozapine
MOOD STABILIZER	Lithium Carbonate

CEREBRAL STIMULANT

AMPHETAMINE	Amphetamine Sulfate
XANTHINE	Caffeine

ELECTROLYTIC & WATER BALANCE AGENTS

DIURETIC

LOOP	Furosemide
OSMOTIC	Mannitol
POTASSIUM-SPARING	Spironolactone
THIAZIDE	Hydrochlorothiazide
PHOSPHATE BINDER	Sevelamer HCl
REPLACEMENT SOLUTION	Calcium Gluconate

ENZYMES

ENZYME REPLACEMENT	Pancrelipase
ENZYME INHIBITOR	Alpha$_1$-Proteinase Inhibitor

Classifications	Prototype

EYE, EAR, NOSE, & THROAT (EENT) PREPARATIONS

ANTIHISTAMINE, OCULAR ....Emedastine
CARBONIC ANHYDRASE INHIBITOR....................Acetazolamide
CYCLOPLEGIC ....Cyclopentolate HCl
MIOTIC (ANTIGLAUCOMA AGENT) ....Pilocarpine HCl
MYDRIATIC..Homatropine HBr
PROSTAGLANDIN...Latanoprost
VASOCONSTRICTOR, DECONGESTANT ....Naphazoline HCl

GASTROINTESTINAL AGENTS

ANORECTANT..Diethylpropion HCl
ANTACID, ADSORBENT....................................Aluminum Hydroxide
ANTIDIARRHEAL..Loperamide
ANTIDIARRHEAL, ADSORBENT ....Bismuth Subsalicylate
ANTIEMETIC ....Prochlorperazine
ANTIEMETIC (5-HT₃ ANTAGONIST)......................Ondansetron HCl
ANTISECRETORY (H₂-RECEPTOR
    ANTAGONIST) ....Cimetidine
BULK LAXATIVE ....Psyllium Hydrophilic Mucilloid
MUCOUS MEMBRANE
    ANTIINFLAMMATORY...................................Mesalamine
PROKINETIC AGENT (GI STIMULANT)....................Metoclopramide HCl
PROTON PUMP INHIBITORS ....Omeprazole
SALINE CATHARTIC ....Magnesium Hydroxide
STIMULANT LAXATIVE......................................Bisacodyl
STOOL SOFTENER..Docusate Calcium

GOLD COMPOUND ....Auranofin

HORMONES & SYNTHETIC SUBSTITUTES

ADRENAL CORTICOSTEROID
    GLUCOCORTICOSTEROID ....Prednisone
    MINERALOCORTICOID..................................Fludrocortisone Acetate
ANDROGEN/ANABOLIC STEROIDS ....Testosterone
ANTIANDROGENS
    5-ALPHA REDUCTASE INHIBITORS ....Finasteride
ANTIDIABETIC AGENTS
    ALPHA-GLUCOSIDASE INHIBITOR....................Acarbose
    BIGUANIDES...Metformin
    INSULIN ....Insulin Injection
    MEGLITINIDES ....Repaglinide

Classifications	Prototype
SULFONYLUREAS	Glyburide
THIAZOLIDINEDIONES	Rosiglitazone
ESTROGENS	Estradiol
GONADOTROPIN-RELEASING HORMONE ANALOGS	Leuprolide Acetate
GONADOTROPIN-RELEASING HORMONE ANTAGONIST	Ganirelix Acetate
GROWTH HORMONE	Somatropin
OXYTOCIC	Oxytocin Injection
PITUITARY (ANTIDIURETIC)	Vasopressin Injection
PROGESTINS (ORAL PRODUCTS)	Norgestrel
PROGESTINS (INJECTABLE PRODUCTS)	Progesterone
THYROID AGENTS	
ANTITHYROID AGENT	Propylthiouracil
THYROID	Levothyroxine Sodium
VITAMIN D ANALOG	Calcitriol

IMMUNOMODULATORS

INTERFERONS	Interferon Alfa-2a

IMPOTENCE AGENT

PHOSPHDIESTERASE INHIBITOR	Sildenafil

LUNG SURFACTANT ... Beractant

MAST CELL STABILIZER ... Cromolyn Sodium

PROSTAGLANDIN ... Epoprostenol

BISPHOSPHONATE (REGULATOR, BONE METABOLISM) ... Etidronate Disodium

SKIN & MUCOUS MEMBRANE AGENTS

ANTIACNE (RETINOID)	Isotretinoin
ANTI-INFLAMMATORY STEROID	Hydrocortisone
PEDICULICIDE	Permethrin
PSORALEN	Methoxsalen
SCABICIDE	Lindane

Classifications	Prototype

SOMATIC NERVOUS SYSTEM AGENTS

SKELETAL MUSCLE RELAXANTS
    CENTRAL-ACTING....................................Cyclobenzaprine HCl
    DEPOLARIZING ....Succinylcholine Chloride
    NONDEPOLARIZING..................................Atracurium

ABACAVIR SULFATE

(a-ba′ca-vir)

Ziagen

Classifications: ANTIVIRAL AGENT; ANTIRETROVIRAL AGENT; NUCLEOSIDE REVERSE TRANSCRIPTASE INHIBITOR (NRTI)

Therapeutic: ANTIVIRAL; ANTIRETROVIRAL

Prototype: Lamivudine

Pregnancy Category: C

AVAILABILITY 300 mg tablets; 20 mg/mL oral solution

ACTION & THERAPEUTIC EFFECT Abacavir is a synthetic nucleoside analogue with inhibitory activity against HIV. It inhibits the activity of HIV-1 reverse transcriptase (RT) both by competing with the natural DNA nucleoside and by incorporation into viral DNA. *Abacavir prevents the formation of viral DNA replication. Therefore the viral load decreases as measured by an increased CD_4 lymphocyte cell count and suppression of HIV RNA, indicated by decreased HIV RNA copies, in HIV-positive individuals with little or no exposure to zidovudine (AZT).*

USES Treatment of HIV infection in combination with other antiretroviral agents.

CONTRAINDICATIONS Hypersensitivity to abacavir (fatal rechallenge reactions reported); lactic acidosis; creatinine clearance of <50 mL/min; severe hepatomegaly; pregnancy (category C); lactation.

CAUTIOUS USE Prior resistance to another nucleoside reverse transcriptase inhibitor (NRTI); hepatic dysfunction; older adults.

ROUTE & DOSAGE

HIV Infection

Adult: **PO** 300 mg b.i.d.
Child: **PO** 3 mo–16 y, 8 mg/kg b.i.d. (max: 300 mg b.i.d.)

Hepatic Impairment

Mild (Child-Pugh score 5–6): 200 mg b.i.d.

ADMINISTRATION

Oral

▪ Tablets & oral solution are interchangeable on a mg-for-mg basis.
▪ Store tablets and liquid at 20°–25° C (68°–77° F). Liquid may be refrigerated.

ADVERSE EFFECTS (≥1%) **Body as a Whole:** Hypersensitivity reactions (including fever, skin rash, fatigue, nausea, vomiting, diarrhea, abdominal pain); malaise; lethargy; myalgia; arthralgia; paresthesia; edema; shortness of breath. **CNS:** Insomnia, *headache, fever.* **CV:** Hypotension (associated with hypersensitivity reaction). **GI:** <u>Hepatomegaly</u> with steatosis, *nausea, vomiting, diarrhea, anorexia,* pancreatitis, increased GGT, increased liver function tests. **Skin:** *Rash.* **Other:** Lactic acidosis, renal insufficiency.

INTERACTIONS Drug: Alcohol may increase abacavir blood levels.

PHARMACOKINETICS Absorption: Rapidly absorbed, 83% bioavailable. **Distribution:** Distributes into extravascular space and erythrocytes; 50% protein bound. **Metabolism:** Metabolized by alcohol dehydrogenase and glucuronyl transferase to inactive metabolites. **Elimination:** 84% in urine, primarily as inactive metabolites; 16% excreted in feces. **Half-Life:** 1.5 h.

Common adverse effects in *italic*, life-threatening effects <u>underlined</u>; generic names in **bold**; classifications in SMALL CAPS; ✦ Canadian drug name; ⊘ Prototype drug

1

CLINICAL IMPLICATIONS
Assessment & Drug Effects
- Monitor for S&S of hypersensitivity: fever, skin rash, fatigue, GI distress (nausea, vomiting, diarrhea, abdominal pain). Withhold drug immediately & notify physician if hypersensitivity develops.
- Lab tests: Periodically monitor liver function, BUN and creatinine, CBC with differential, triglyceride levels, and blood glucose, especially in diabetics.
- Withhold drug & notify physician for S&S of acidosis, hepatotoxicity, or renal insufficiency.

Patient & Family Education
- Take drug exactly as prescribed at indicated times. Missed dose: Take immediately, then resume dosing schedule. Do not double a dose.
- Withhold drug immediately & notify physician at first sign of hypersensitivity reaction (see Assessment & Drug Effects).
- Carry Warning Card provided with drug at all times.

ABATACEPT
(a-ba-ta′sept)
Orencia

Classifications: BIOLOGIC RESPONSE MODIFIER; FUSION PROTEIN; DISEASE-MODIFYING ANTIRHEUMATIC DRUG (DMARD)
Therapeutic: DMARD; BIOLOGIC RESPONSE MODIFIER
Pregnancy Category: C

AVAILABILITY 250 mg lyophilized powder for injection

ACTION & *THERAPEUTIC EFFECT*
Abatacept inhibits T-cell (T lymphocyte) proliferation and inhibits production of tumor necrosis factor (TNF)-alpha, interferon-gamma, and interleukin-2. It suppresses inflammation, decreases anticollagen antibody production, and reduces antigen-specific production of interferon-gamma. *Abatacept is used to reduce the number of activated T lymphocytes found in synovial fluid of RA patients. It relieves symptoms of RA and slows progression of structural damage. It improves physical function in adults with active RA who have had an inadequate response to other drugs.*

USES Treatment of moderate to severe rheumatoid arthritis in patients with an inadequate response to one or more disease-modifying antirheumatic drugs (DMARDs). It may be used as monotherapy or in combination with other DMARDs, with the exception of TNF antagonists.

CONTRAINDICATIONS Known hypersensitivity to abatacept; live vaccines; active infections; co-administration with anakinra; pregnancy (category C); lactation.
CAUTIOUS USE COPD, RA; malignancies.

ROUTE & DOSAGE

Rheumatoid Arthritis
Adult: **IV** <60 kg, 500 mg; 60–100 kg, 750 mg; >100 kg, 1000 mg q2wk × 2, then q mo.

ADMINISTRATION
Intravenous

PREPARE: **IV Infusion:** Use the supplied silicone-free disposable syringe with an 18–21 gauge needle to reconstitute the vial. Add 10 mL sterile water to yield 25 mg/mL. To avoid foaming, gently swirl until completely dissolved. Do not shake or vigorously agitate. After dissolving, vent the vial with a needle to dissipate any foam. The reconstituted solution must be further diluted to a total of 100 mL as follows: from a 100 mL NS IV bag remove a volume equal to the total volume of abatacept in the reconstituted vials (e.g., for 2 vials, remove 20 mL). Using the supplied silicone-free syringe, slowly add the reconstituted abatacept to the IV bag and gently mix. The final concentration of the IV solution will be approximately 5, 7.5, or 10 mg/mL, depending on whether 2, 3, or 4 vials are used. Discard any unused abatacept. *ADMINISTER:* **IV Infusion:** Use a 0.2–1.2 micron low-protein-binding filter. Infuse over 30 min. *INCOMPATIBILITIES* **Solution/Additive:** Should not be infused in the same intravenous line with other agents. **Y-site:** Should not be infused in the same intravenous line with other agents.

▪ Store at 2°–8° C (36°– 46° F).

ADVERSE EFFECTS (≥1%) **Body as a Whole:** Infusion-related reactions, malignancies, cough, hypersensitivity reactions. **CNS:** *Headache,* dizziness. **CV:** Hypertension. **GI:** *Nausea,* dyspepsia. **Musculoskeletal:** Back pain, pain in extremity. **Respiratory:** *Upper respiratory tract infection, nasopharyngitis,* sinusitis, influenza, bronchitis. **Skin:** Rash. **Urogenital:** Urinary tract infection.

INTERACTIONS Drug: TNF ANTAGONISTS increase the risk of serious infections.

PHARMACOKINETICS Half-Life: 13.1 d.

CLINICAL IMPLICATIONS
Assessment & Drug Effects
▪ Prior to initiating treatment with abatacept, screen for latent TB infection with a TB skin test.
▪ Monitor for S&S of hypersensitivity (e.g., hypotension, urticaria, and dyspnea); discontinue infusion and notify physician if any of these occur.
▪ Monitor for S&S of infection. Withhold drug and notify physician if patient develops a serious infection.
▪ Monitor for deterioration of respiratory status in patients with COPD.

Patient & Family Education
▪ Report any of the following to a health care provider: any type of infection, a positive TB skin test, a recent vaccination, a persistent cough, unexplained weight loss, fever, sore throat, or night sweats.
▪ Report S&S of an allergic reaction that may develop within 24 h of receiving abatacept (e.g., hives swollen face, eyelids, lips, tongue, throat, or trouble breathing).
▪ Do not accept immunizations with live vaccines while taking or within 3 mo of discontinuing abatacept.
▪ Taking abatacept with TNF-blocker medications [etanercept (Enbrel), adalimumab (Humira), infliximab (Remicade)] is not recommended.

ABCIXIMAB ⊕

(ab-cix'i-mab)
ReoPro
Classifications: PLATELET AGGREGATION INHIBITOR; GLYCOPROTEIN IIB/IIIA INHIBITOR; ANTITHROMBOTIC
Therapeutic: PLATELET AGGREGATION INHIBITOR; ANTITHROMBOTIC
Pregnancy Category: C

Common adverse effects in *italic*, life-threatening effects underlined; generic names in **bold**; classifications in SMALL CAPS; ♣ Canadian drug name; ⊕ Prototype drug

3

AVAILABILITY 2 mg/mL in 5 mL vials

ACTION & *THERAPEUTIC EFFECT*

Abciximab is a human–murine monoclonal antibody Fab (fragment antigen binding) fragment that binds to the glycoprotein IIb/IIIa (GPIIb/IIIa) receptor sites of platelets. *Abciximab inhibits platelet aggregation by preventing fibrinogen, von Willebrand's factor, and other molecules from adhering to GPIIb/IIIa receptor sites of the platelets.*

USES Adjunct to aspirin and heparin for the prevention of acute cardiac ischemic complications in patients undergoing percutaneous transluminal coronary angioplasty (PTCA).

CONTRAINDICATIONS Hypersensitivity to abciximab or to murine proteins; active internal bleeding; GI or GU bleeding within 6 wk; history of CVA within 2 y or a CVA with severe neurologic deficit; administration of oral anticoagulants unless PT <1.2 times control; thrombocytopenia (<100,000 cells/mL); recent major surgery or trauma; intracranial neoplasm, aneurysm, severe hypertension; history of vasculitis; use of dextran before or during PTCA.

CAUTIOUS USE Pregnancy (category C); lactation; patients weighing <75 kg; older adults; history of previous GI disease; recent thrombolytic therapy; PTCA within 12 h of MI; unsuccessful PTCA; PTCA procedure lasting >70 min.

ROUTE & DOSAGE

PTCA
Adult: **IV** Start 10–60 min prior to angioplasty, 0.25 mg/kg bolus over 5 min followed by continuous infusion of 0.125 mcg/kg/min (up to 10 mcg/min) for next 12 h

ADMINISTRATION

Intravenous

Do not shake vial. Discard if visible opaque particles are noted.

- Use a nonpyrogenic low protein-binding 0.2- or 0.22-μm filter when withdrawing drug into a syringe from the 2 mg/mL vial and when infusing as continuous IV.

PREPARE: **Direct:** No dilution required. **Continuous:** Inject 4.5 mL of drug into 250 mL of NS or D5W. *ADMINISTER:* **Direct:** Give undiluted bolus dose over 5 min. **Continuous:** Infuse at no more than 17 mL/h (10 mcg/min) via an infusion pump; add no other drugs to the solution or IV line. *INCOMPATIBILITIES* **Solution/additive:** Infuse through separate IV line. **Y-site:** Infuse through separate IV line.

- Discard any unused drug at the end of the 12-h infusion as well as any unused portion left in vial. ▪ Store vials at 2°–8° C (36°–46° F).

ADVERSE EFFECTS (≥1%) **Hematologic:** *Bleeding*, including intracranial, retroperitoneal, and hematemesis; thrombocytopenia.

INTERACTIONS Drug: ORAL ANTI-COAGULANTS, NSAIDs, **dipyridamole, ticlopidine, dextran** may increase risk of bleeding.

PHARMACOKINETICS Onset: >90% inhibition of platelet aggregation within 2 h. **Duration:** Approximately 48 h. **Half-Life:** 30 min.

CLINICAL IMPLICATIONS

Assessment & Drug Effects

- Monitor for S&S of: bleeding at all potential sites (e.g., catheter insertion, needle puncture, or cutdown

Common adverse effects in *italic*, life-threatening effects underlined; generic names in **bold**; classifications in SMALL CAPS; ✦ Canadian drug name; ✪ Prototype drug

sites; GI, GU, or retroperitoneal sites); hypersensitivity that may occur any time during administration.

- Lab tests: Monitor Hgb, Hct, platelet count, PT, APTT, INR, and activated clotting time, every 2–4 h during first 24 h.
- Avoid or minimize unnecessary invasive procedures and devices to reduce risk of bleeding.
- Elevate head of bed ≤30° and keep limb straight when femoral artery access is used; following sheath removal, apply pressure for 30 min.
- Stop infusion immediately & notify physician if bleeding or S&S of hypersensitivity occurs.

Patient & Family Education
- Report any S&S of bleeding immediately.

ACAMPROSATE CALCIUM

(a-cam-pro′sate)
Campral
Classifications: SUBSTANCE ABUSE DETERRENT
Therapeutic: SUBSTANCE ABUSE INHIBITOR
Pregnancy Category: C

AVAILABILITY 333 mg delayed-release tablets

ACTION & THERAPEUTIC EFFECT
May interact with CNS glutamate and GABA neurotransmitter systems and help restore normal balance between neuronal excitation and inhibition. Acamprosate is a neurotransmitter analog. *Reduces craving for alcohol intake due to chronic use, but does not cause alcohol aversion or a disulfiram-like reaction as a result of ethanol ingestion.*

USES Maintenance of abstinence from alcohol in patients with alcoholism

CONTRAINDICATIONS Hypersensitivity to acamprosate calcium or any of its components; suicidal ideation; pregnancy (category C). Safety and efficacy in patients with severe renal impairment (Cl_{cr} <30 mL/min) have not been established.

CAUTIOUS USE Moderate renal impairment; depression; lactation. Safety and efficacy of acamprosate have not been established in adolescents or children <18 y.

ROUTE & DOSAGE

Maintenance of Alcohol Abstinence
Adult: **PO** 666 mg t.i.d.
Renal Impairment
Adult: **PO** Cl_{cr} 30–50 mL/min: 333 mg t.i.d.; Cl_{cr} <30 mL/min: do not use

ADMINISTRATION

Oral
- Ensure that the drug is not chewed or crushed. It must be swallowed whole.
- Store at 15°–30° C (59°–86° F).

ADVERSE EFFECTS (≥1%) **Body as a Whole:** Flu syndrome, chills. **CNS:** Depression, anxiety, insomnia, asthenia, dizziness, paresthesia, headache, somnolence, decreased libido, amnesia, abnormal thinking, tremor. **CV:** Palpitation, syncope. **GI:** *Diarrhea,* nausea, vomiting, anorexia, flatulence, dry mouth, abdominal pain, dyspepsia, constipation, increased appetite. **Metabolic:** Peripheral edema, weight gain. **Musculoskeletal:** Musculoskeletal pain. **Respiratory:** Rhinitis, cough, dyspnea, pharyngitis, bronchitis. **Skin:** Pruritus, diaphoresis, rash. **Special Senses:** Abnormal vision, taste perversion. **Urogenital:** Impotence.

Common adverse effects in *italic*, life-threatening effects <u>underlined</u>; generic names in **bold**; classifications in SMALL CAPS; ♣ Canadian drug name; ⊘ Prototype drug

INTERACTIONS Drug: None reported.

PHARMACOKINETICS Absorption: 11% bioavailability. **Metabolism:** Not metabolized. **Elimination:** Renal. **Half-Life:** 20–33 h.

CLINICAL IMPLICATIONS

Assessment & Drug Effects

- Monitor for S&S depression or suicidal thinking.
- Monitor for dizziness or impaired judgment, thinking, and motor skills; take appropriate protective measures.

Patient & Family Education

- Report any alcohol consumption while taking acamprosate.
- Report promptly any of the following: unusual anxiousness or nervousness; depression or suicidal thoughts; burning or tingling sensations in arms, legs, hands, or feet; chest pains or palpitations; difficulty urinating.
- Do not drive or engage in other hazardous activities until reaction to the drug is known.

ACARBOSE ℗

(a-car'bose)

Precose

Classifications: ANTIDIABETIC AGENT; ALPHA-GLUCOSIDASE INHIBITOR
Therapeutic: ANTIDIABETIC
Pregnancy Category: B

AVAILABILITY 50 mg, 100 mg tablets

ACTION & *THERAPEUTIC EFFECT*
Acarbose is an oral alpha-glucosidase inhibitor. It inhibits or delays the absorption of sugars from the intestinal tract. The inhibitory effect of acarbose varies according to

which enzymes are involved; from most to least inhibited are glucoamylase, sucrase, maltase, and isomaltase. Lactase is not affected by acarbose. *Acarbose reduces blood sugar by interfering with carbohydrate absorption from the GI tract.*

USES As monotherapy or in combination with a sulfonylurea in patients with type 2 diabetes mellitus.
UNLABELED USES In combination with insulin and metformin in patients with type 1 diabetes mellitus.

CONTRAINDICATIONS Inflammatory bowel disease, colon ulcers, partial bowel obstruction, predisposition for obstruction; patients <18 y; lactation.
CAUTIOUS USE GI distress or liver disorders, pregnancy (category B).

ROUTE & DOSAGE

Diabetes Mellitus

Adult: **PO** Start with 25 mg daily to t.i.d. with meals, may increase q4–8wk up to 50–100 mg t.i.d. with meals (max: 150 mg/d for ≤60 kg, 300 mg/d for >60 kg)

ADMINISTRATION

Oral

- Remove drug from foil wrapper immediately before administration.
- Give drug with first bite at each of the three main meals.
- Do not store above 25° C (77° F). Keep tightly closed and protect from moisture.

ADVERSE EFFECTS (≥1%) **CNS:** Sleepiness, weakness, dizziness, headache, vertigo (may be due to poor diabetic control). **Endocrine:** Hypoglycemia (especially in combination with sulfonylureas and insulin). **GI:** *Diarrhea, flatulence, ab-*

dominal distention, borborygmi, increased liver function tests. **Hematologic:** Anemia (especially iron deficiency). **Skin:** Erythema, exanthema, urticaria.

INTERACTIONS Drug: SULFONYL-UREAS may increase hypoglycemic effects. Drugs that induce hyperglycemia (e.g., THIAZIDES, CORTICO-STEROIDS, PHENOTHIAZINES, ESTROGENS, **phenytoin, isoniazid**) may decrease effectiveness of acarbose. **Herbal: Garlic, ginseng** may increase hypoglycemic effects.

PHARMACOKINETICS Absorption: 0.5–2% is absorbed intact from GI tract. After degradation by intestinal bacteria, up to 35% of dose may be absorbed. **Peak:** Peak blood glucose reduction approximately 70 min after dose. **Metabolism:** In GI tract by intestinal bacteria and digestive enzymes. **Elimination:** 35% in urine, 51% in feces, 5% in air as CO_2. **Half-Life:** 2 h.

CLINICAL IMPLICATIONS

Assessment & Drug Effects
- Lab tests: Periodically monitor blood glucose, HbA_{1C} liver, enzymes, Hct and Hgb.
- Treat hypoglycemia with dextrose; not with sucrose (table sugar).

Patient & Family Education
- Note: Acarbose prevents the breakdown of table sugar. Have a source of dextrose, such as dextrose paste, available to treat low blood sugar.
- Monitor closely blood glucose especially following dosage changes.
- Report abdominal distress; dietary adjustment or dosage reduction may be warranted.
- Monitor weight and report significant changes.

ACEBUTOLOL HYDROCHLORIDE

(a-se-byoo-toe′lole)
Monitan ♦, Sectral

Classifications: BETA-ADRENERGIC ANTAGONIST; ANTIHYPERTENSIVE; ANTIARRHYTHMIC, CLASS II AGENT
Therapeutic: ANTIHYPERTENSIVE; ANTIARRYTHMIC, CLASS II
Prototype: Propranolol
Pregnancy Category: B

AVAILABILITY 200 mg, 400 mg capsules

ACTION & *THERAPEUTIC EFFECT*
Beta$_1$-selective adrenergic blocking agent with mild sympathomimetic activity (partial beta-agonist activity). Produces negative chronotropic and inotropic activity (i.e., decreases exercise-induced heart rate, inhibits reflex orthostatic tachycardia, and decreases cardiac output at rest and during exercise). *Decreases both systolic and diastolic BP at rest and during exercise. Exhibits antiarrhythmic activity (class II antiarrhythmic agent).*

USES Treatment of mild to moderate hypertension. Management of recurrent stable ventricular arrhythmias.
UNLABELED USES Supraventricular arrhythmias, chronic stable angina pectoris.

CONTRAINDICATIONS Overt CHF, second- or third-degree AV block, severe bradycardia, cardiogenic shock; acute bronchospasm, pulmonary edema; lactation; children <12 y.
CAUTIOUS USE Impaired cardiac function, well-compensated CHF, mesenteric or peripheral vascular disease; cerebrovascular disease;

Common adverse effects in *italic*, life-threatening effects underlined; generic names in **bold**; classifications in SMALL CAPS; ♦ Canadian drug name; ☻ Prototype drug

7

patients undergoing major surgery involving general anesthesia; renal or hepatic impairment; labile diabetes mellitus; hyperthyroidism; bronchospastic disease (asthma, emphysema); avoid abrupt withdrawal; pregnancy (category B).

ROUTE & DOSAGE

Hypertension
Adult: **PO** 400–800 mg/d in 1–2 divided doses (max: 1200 mg/d)
Geriatric: **PO** 200–400 mg/d (max: 800 mg/d)

Ventricular Arrhythmias
Adult: **PO** 200 mg b.i.d. increased to 600–1200 mg/d

Angina Pectoris
Adult: **PO** 300–400 mg t.i.d.

Renal Impairment
Cl_{cr} <50 mL/min: reduce dose by 50%; <25 mL/min: reduce dose by 75%

ADMINISTRATION

Oral
- Check apical pulse before administration. If <60 bpm or other ordered parameter, consult physician.
- Discontinue gradually over a period of 2 wk.
- Store at 15°–30° C (59°–86° F).

ADVERSE EFFECTS (≥1%) **Body as a Whole:** *Fatigue.* **CNS:** Dizziness, insomnia, drowsiness, confusion, fainting. **CV:** *Bradycardia,* hypotension, CHF. **GI:** Nausea, *diarrhea, constipation,* flatulence. **Hematologic:** Agranulocytosis, *antinuclear antibodies (ANA).* **Metabolic:** hypoglycemia (may mask symptoms of a hypoglycemic reaction). **Respiratory:** Bronchospasm, pulmonary edema, dyspnea. **Urogenital:** Decreased libido; impotence.

DIAGNOSTIC TEST INTERFERENCE False-negative test results possible (see **propranolol**).

INTERACTIONS Drug: Other HYPOTENSIVE AGENTS, DIURETICS increase hypotensive effect; with **albuterol, metaproterenol, terbutaline,** or **pirbuterol,** there is mutual antagonism with acebutolol; NSAIDs blunt hypotensive effect; decreases hypoglycemic effect of **glyburide;** increases bradycardia and sinus arrest with **amiodarone**.

PHARMACOKINETICS Absorption: Well absorbed after PO administration; undergoes extensive first-pass metabolism in liver with an average bioavailability of 40%. (In geriatric patients, bioavailability increases twofold). **Peak:** 3 h. **Distribution:** Minimally into CSF; crosses placenta; is excreted in breast milk. **Metabolism:** In liver to diacetolol with activity equipotent to parent compound. **Elimination:** Metabolite 8–13 h; 50–60% via bile into feces, 30–40% in urine. **Half-Life:** 3–4 h.

CLINICAL IMPLICATIONS

Assessment & Drug Effects
- Monitor BP and cardiac status throughout therapy. Observe for and report marked bradycardia or hypotension, especially when patient is also receiving a catecholamine-depleting drug (e.g., reserpine).
- Monitor I&O ratio and pattern and report changes to physician (e.g., dysuria, nocturia, oliguria, weight change).
- Monitor for S&S of CHF, especially peripheral edema, dyspnea, activity intolerance.
- Lab tests: Monitor for drug-induced positive ANA titer during long-term therapy, especially in women and older

adults; periodic CBC with long-term therapy.

Patient & Family Education

- Know parameters for withholding drug (e.g., pulse less than 60).
- Note: Common adverse effects include insomnia, drowsiness, and confusion.
- Do not drive or engage in potentially hazardous activities until response to drug is known.
- Do not increase, decrease, omit, or discontinue drug regimen without advice from the physician. Abrupt withdrawal may worsen angina or precipitate MI in patient with heart disease.
- Contact physician promptly at the first signs or symptoms of CHF (see Appendix F).
- Report muscle and joint pain to physician. Discontinuation of drug therapy usually reverses these adverse effects.
- Monitor for loss of glycemic control if diabetic.
- Note: Drug may mask symptoms of hypoglycemia (see Appendix F) and potentiate insulin-induced hypoglycemia in diabetics.
- Avoid use of OTC oral cold preparations and topical nasal decongestants unless approved by the physician.

ACETAMINOPHEN, PARACETAMOL ℗

(a-seat-a-mee′noe-fen)
Abenol ✦, A'Cenol, Acephen, Anacin-3, Anuphen, APAP, Atasol ✦, Campain ✦, Dolanex, Exdol ✦, Halenol, Liquiprin, Panadol, Pedric, Robigesic ✦, Rounox ✦, Tapar, Tempra, Tylenol, Tylenol Arthritis, Valadol

Classifications: NONNARCOTIC ANALGESIC, ANTIPYRETIC

Therapeutic: NONNARCOTIC ANALGESIC; ANTIPYRETIC
Pregnancy Category: B

AVAILABILITY 80 mg, 120 mg, 125 mg, 300 mg, 325 mg, 650 mg suppositories; 80 mg, 160 mg, 325 mg, 500 mg tablets/caplets; 650 mg extended release tablets/capsules; 80 mg/0.8 mL, 80 mg/2.5 mL, 80 mg/5 mL, 120 mg/5 mL, 160 mg/5 mL, 500 mg/5 mL liquid

ACTION & *THERAPEUTIC EFFECT*
Produces analgesia by unknown mechanism, but it is centrally acting in the CNS by increasing the pain threshold by inhibiting cyclooxygenase. Reduces fever by direct action on hypothalamus heat-regulating center with consequent peripheral vasodilation, sweating, and dissipation of heat. Unlike aspirin, has little effect on platelet aggregation, does not affect bleeding time, and produces no gastric bleeding. *It provides temporary analgesia for mild to moderate pain. In addition, acetaminophen lowers body temperature in individuals with a fever.*

USES Fever reduction. Temporary relief of mild to moderate pain. Generally as substitute for aspirin when the latter is not tolerated or is contraindicated.

CONTRAINDICATIONS Hypersensitivity to acetaminophen or phenacetin; use with alcohol.
CAUTIOUS USE Repeated administration to patients with anemia, G6PD deficiency, renal or hepatic disease; arthritic or rheumatoid conditions affecting children <12 y; alcoholism; malnutrition; thrombocytopenia; bone marrow depression, immunosuppression; pregnancy (category B).

Common adverse effects in *italic*, life-threatening effects underlined; generic names in **bold**; classifications in SMALL CAPS; ✦ Canadian drug name; ℗ Prototype drug

ROUTE & DOSAGE

Mild to Moderate Pain, Fever

Adult: **PO** 325–650 mg q4–6h (max: 4 g/d) **PR** 650 mg q4–6h (max: 4 g/d)
Child: **PO** 10–15 mg/kg q4–6h **PR** 2–5 y, 120 mg q4–6h (max: 720 mg/d); 6–12 y, 325 mg q4–6h (max: 2.6 g/d)
Neonate: **PO** 10–15 mg/kg q6–8h

ADMINISTRATION

Oral

- Administer tablets or caplets whole or crushed and give with fluid of patient's choice.
- Chewable tablets should be thoroughly chewed and wetted before they are swallowed.
- Do not coadminister with a high carbohydrate meal; absorption rate may be significantly retarded.
- Store in light-resistant containers at room temperature, preferably between 15°–30° C (59°–86° F).

Rectal

- Insert suppositories beyond the rectal sphincter.

ADVERSE EFFECTS (≥1%) **Body as a Whole:** Negligible with recommended dosage; rash. **Acute poisoning:** Anorexia, nausea, vomiting, dizziness, lethargy, diaphoresis, chills, epigastric or abdominal pain, diarrhea; onset of <u>hepatotoxicity</u>—elevation of serum transaminases (ALT, AST) and bilirubin; hypoglycemia, <u>hepatic coma, acute renal failure</u> (rare). **Chronic ingestion:** Neutropenia, pancytopenia, leukopenia, thrombocytopenic purpura, *hepatotoxicity in alcoholics,* renal damage.

DIAGNOSTIC TEST INTERFERENCE False increases in **urinary 5-HIAA** (5-hydroxyindoleacetic acid) byproduct of serotonin; false decreases in **blood glucose** (by **glucose oxidase–peroxidase procedure**); false increases in **urinary glucose** (with certain instruments in glucose analyses); and false increases in **serum uric acid** (with *phosphotungstate method*). High doses or long-term therapy: hepatic, renal, and hematopoietic function (periodically).

INTERACTIONS Drug: Cholestyramine may decrease acetaminophen absorption. With chronic coadministration, BARBITURATES, **carbamazepine, phenytoin,** and **rifampin** may increase potential for chronic hepatotoxicity. Chronic, excessive ingestion of **alcohol** will increase risk of hepatotoxicity.

PHARMACOKINETICS Absorption: Rapid and almost complete absorption from GI tract; less complete absorption from rectal suppository. **Peak:** 0.5–2 h. **Duration:** 3–4 h. **Distribution:** In all body fluids; crosses placenta. **Metabolism:** Extensively in liver. **Elimination:** 90–100% of drug excreted as metabolites in urine; excreted in breast milk. **Half-Life:** 1–3 h.

CLINICAL IMPLICATIONS

Assessment & Drug Effects

- Monitor for S&S of: hepatotoxicity, even with moderate acetaminophen doses, especially in individuals with poor nutrition or who have ingested alcohol over prolonged periods; poisoning, usually from accidental ingestion or suicide attempts; potential abuse from psychological dependence (withdrawal has been associated with restless and excited responses).

Patient & Family Education

- Do not take other medications (e.g., cold preparations) containing acetaminophen without medical advice; overdosing and chronic

Common adverse effects in ITALIC, life-threatening effects <u>underlined</u>; generic names in **bold**; classifications in SMALL CAPS; ✢ Canadian drug name; ⊙ Prototype drug

use can cause liver damage and other toxic effects.

- Do not self-medicate adults for pain more than 10 d (5 d in children) without consulting a physician.
- Do not use this medication without medical direction for: fever persisting longer than 3 d, fever over 39.5° C (103° F), or recurrent fever.
- Do not give children more than 5 doses in 24 h unless prescribed by physician.

ACETAZOLAMIDE ℗ⓡ

(a-set-a-zole′a-mide)

Acetazolam ✦, Apo-Acetazolamide ✦, Diamox Sequels

ACETAZOLAMIDE SODIUM

(a-set-a-zole′a-mide)

Diamox Parenteral

Classifications: EYE PREPARATION; CARBONIC ANHYDRASE INHIBITOR; DIURETIC; ANTICONVULSANT

Therapeutic: DIURETIC; ANTICONVULSANT

Pregnancy Category: C

AVAILABILITY 125 mg, 250 mg tablets; 500 mg sustained-release capsules; 500 mg powder for injection

ACTION & *THERAPEUTIC EFFECT*
The mechanism of anticonvulsant action is unknown but thought to involve inhibition of CNS carbonic anhydrase, which retards abnormal transmission from CNS neurons. Diuretic effect is due to inhibition of carbonic anhydrase activity in proximal renal tubule, preventing formation of carbonic acid, and therefore the formation of H^+ and HCO_3^-. Inhibition of carbonic anhydrase in eye reduces rate of aqueous humor formation with consequent lowering of intraocular pressure. *Reduces seizure activity and intraocular pressure. Additionally, it has a diuretic effect.*

USES Treatment of seizures: absence or petit mal, generalized tonic-clonic (grand mal), and focal; reduction of intraocular pressure in open-angle glaucoma and secondary glaucoma; preoperative treatment of acute closed-angle glaucoma; drug-induced edema and as adjunct in treatment of edema due to congestive heart failure; acute high-altitude sickness.

UNLABELED USES Prevent uric acid or cystine renal calculi; to treat acute pancreatitis, premenstrual syndrome (PMS), metabolic alkalosis, and hypokalemic and hyperkalemic forms of familial periodic paralysis; to increase secretion of phenobarbital or lithium; hydrocephalus.

CONTRAINDICATIONS Hypersensitivity to carbonic anhydrase inhibitors, marked renal and hepatic disease; Addison's disease or other types of adrenocortical insufficiency; hyponatremia, hypokalemia, hyperchloremic acidosis; prolonged administration to patients with hyphema; chronic noncongestive angle-closure glaucoma.

CAUTIOUS USE Hypersensitivity to sulfonamides and derivatives (e.g., thiazides), history of hypercalciuria; diabetes mellitus, elderly, gout, patients receiving digitalis, obstructive pulmonary disease, respiratory acidosis; pregnancy (category C).

ROUTE & DOSAGE

Glaucoma

Adult: **PO** 250 mg 1–4 times/d, 500 mg sustained release b.i.d. **IM/IV** 500 mg, may repeat in 2–4 h

---

Common adverse effects in *italic*, life-threatening effects <u>underlined</u>; generic names in **bold**; classifications in SMALL CAPS; ✦ Canadian drug name; ⓪ Prototype drug

11

Child: PO 8–30 mg/kg/d in 3 doses IM/IV 5–10 mg/kg q6h

Epilepsy
Adult/Child: PO 8–30 mg/kg/d in 1–4 doses

Edema
Adult: PO 250–375 mg every AM (5 mg/kg)
Child: PO/IM/IV 5 mg/kg or 150 mg/m²/every AM

High Altitude Sickness
Adult: PO 250 mg q8–12h or 500 mg sustained release q12–24h, starting 24–48 h before climb and continuing for 48 h at high altitude

Treatment Hydrocephalus
Neonate/Infant: PO/IV 20 mg/kg/d in divided doses q8–12h (max: 100 mg/kg/d)

Renal Impairment
Cl$_{cr}$ 10–50 mL/min: dose q12h; <10 mL/min: use not recommended

ADMINISTRATION

Oral

- Administer diuretic dose in morning to avoid interrupted sleep.
- Give with food or meals to minimize GI upset.
- Note: If tablet(s) cannot be swallowed, soften tablet(s) (not sustained release form) in 2 tsp of hot water and add to 2 tsp of honey/syrup to disguise bitter taste; avoid syrups containing alcohol or glycerin, or crush tablet(s) and suspend in syrup (250–500 mg/5 mL syrup). Prepare just before administration. Drug does not dissolve in fruit juices.
- Store oral preparations at 15°–30° C (59°–86° F) unless otherwise directed.

Intramuscular

- Reconstitute as for IV administration. See PREPARE Direct.
- Give IM for rapid lowering of intraocular pressure or in patients unable to take oral dosage.
- Note: The intramuscular dosage is not the route of choice because the alkalinity of the solution makes the injection painful.

Intravenous

IV administration to neonates, infants, and children: Verify correct IV concentration and rate of infusion/injection with physician.

PREPARE: **Direct:** Reconstitute each 500 mg vial with at least 5 mL of sterile water for injection. **IV Infusion:** Reconstituted solution may be further diluted with DSW or NS. Use within 24 h of reconstitution.

ADMINISTER: **Direct:** Give at a rate of 500 mg or fraction thereof over 1 min. **IV Infusion:** Give as a continuous infusion over 4–8 h.

ADVERSE EFFECTS (≥1%) **CNS:** Paresthesias, sedation, malaise, disorientation, depression, fatigue, muscle weakness, flaccid paralysis. **GI:** Anorexia, nausea, vomiting, weight loss, dry mouth, thirst, diarrhea. **Hematologic:** Bone marrow depression with agranulocytosis, hemolytic anemia, aplastic anemia, leukopenia, pancytopenia. **Metabolic:** Increased excretion of calcium, potassium, magnesium, and sodium; metabolic acidosis; hyperglycemia; hyperuricemia. **Ocular:** transient myopia. **Urogenital:** Glycosuria, urinary frequency, polyuria, dysuria, hematuria, crystalluria. **Other:** Exacerbation of gout, hepatic dysfunction, Stephen-Johnson syndrome.

DIAGNOSTIC TEST INTERFERENCE Monitor for false-positive *urinary protein* determinations; falsely high values for **urine urobilinogen;** depressed **iodine uptake** values (exception: hypothyroidism).

INTERACTIONS Drug: Renal excretion of AMPHETAMINES, **ephedrine, flecainide, quinidine, procainamide,** TRICYCLIC ANTIDEPRESSANTS may be decreased, thereby enhancing or prolonging their effects. Renal excretion of **lithium** is increased. Excretion of **phenobarbital** may be increased. **Amphotericin B** and CORTICOSTEROIDS may accelerate **potassium** loss. DIGITALIS GLYCOSIDES may predispose persons with hypokalemia to **digitalis** toxicity; puts patients on high doses of SALICYLATES at high risk for SALICYLATE toxicity.

PHARMACOKINETICS Absorption: Well absorbed from GI tract. **Onset:** 1 h regular release; 2 h sustained release; 2 min IV. **Peak:** 2–4 h reg; 8–18 h sustained; 15 min IV. **Duration:** 8–12 h reg; 18–24 h sustained; 4–5 h IV. **Distribution:** Distributed throughout body, concentrating in RBCs, plasma, and kidneys; crosses placenta. **Elimination:** Primarily in urine. **Half-Life:** 2.4–5.8 h.

CLINICAL IMPLICATIONS

Assessment & Drug Effects

- Establish baseline weight before initial therapy and weigh daily thereafter when used to treat edema.
- Monitor for S&S of: mild to severe metabolic acidosis; potassium loss which is greatest early in therapy (see hypokalemia in Appendix F).
- Monitor I&O especially when used with other diuretics.
- Lab tests: Blood pH, blood gases, urinalysis, CBC, and serum electrolytes (initially and periodically during prolonged therapy or concomitant therapy with other diuretics or digitalis).

Patient & Family Education

- Maintain adequate fluid intake (1.5–2.5 L/24 h; 1 liter is approximately equal to 1 quart) to reduce risk of kidney stones.
- Report any of the following: numbness, tingling, burning, drowsiness, and visual problems, sore throat or mouth, unusual bleeding, fever, skin or renal problems.
- Eat potassium-rich diet and take potassium supplement when taking this drug in high doses or for prolonged periods.

ACETOHEXAMIDE

(a-seat-oh-hex′a-mide)
Dimelor ♦

Classifications: HORMONE; SULFONYLUREA; ANTIDIABETIC AGENT
Therapeutic: ANTIDIABETIC; SULFONYLUREA
Prototype: Glyburide
Pregnancy Category: C

AVAILABILITY 250 mg, 500 mg tablets

ACTION & *THERAPEUTIC EFFECT*
Lowers blood glucose by stimulating pancreatic beta cells to secrete insulin. *Promotes increased effectiveness of endogenous insulin in type 2 diabetes mellitus.*

USES Mild to moderately severe stable type 2 diabetes mellitus. Preferred by some clinicians for patients who also have gout.

CONTRAINDICATIONS Hypersensitivity to sulfonylureas; severe impairment of hepatic, renal, thyroid, or other endocrine function; type 1 diabetics, diabetic ketoacidosis; renal failure, renal impairment; lactation. Safety and effectiveness in children have not been established.

Common adverse effects in *italic*, life-threatening effects <u>underlined</u>; generic names in **bold**; classifications in SMALL CAPS; ♦ Canadian drug name; ❷ Prototype drug

13

CAUTIOUS USE Renal insufficiency, hepatic impairment, history of hepatic porphyria, elderly, pregnancy (category C).

ROUTE & DOSAGE

Diabetes

Adult: **PO** 250 mg/d before breakfast, may be increased by 250–500 mg q5–7d (max: 1.5 g/d); may be dosed b.i.d.

ADMINISTRATION

Oral

- Administer daily dose before breakfast.
- Divided doses are given before breakfast and dinner.
- Store at 15°–30° C (59°–86° F), unless otherwise directed.

ADVERSE EFFECTS (≥1%) **Body as a Whole:** Generally dose-related. Erythema, urticaria, pruritus, rash, photosensitivity. **GI:** Nausea, vomiting, epigastric fullness, anorexia, stomach pain or discomfort, heartburn, diarrhea. **Hematologic:** Agranulocytosis, aplastic anemia, severe hypoglycemia, thrombocytopenia. **CNS:** Headache, dizziness.

DIAGNOSTIC TEST INTERFERENCE *Serum uric acid* levels may be appreciably reduced.

INTERACTIONS Drug: Alcohol may elicit **disulfiram** reaction; **warfarin, aspirin** and other SALICYLATES, **chloramphenicol, clofibrate, fenfluramine, guanethidine,** MAO INHIBITORS, **oxytetracycline, phenylbutazone, probenecid, sulfinpyrazone,** and SULFONAMIDES may enhance hypoglycemic effects; with **diazoxide** there is mutual antagonism and effects of both drugs are reduced; THIAZIDE DIURETICS may exacerbate hyperglycemia, resulting in need for increased acetohexamide doses; **phenytoin** may decrease effects of acetohexamide; BETA-ADRENERGIC BLOCKERS may mask symptoms of hypoglycemia. **Herbal: Garlic, ginseng** may increase hypoglycemic effects.

PHARMACOKINETICS Absorption: Rapidly from GI tract. **Onset:** 1 h. **Peak:** 2–4 h. **Duration:** 12–24 h. **Distribution:** Breast milk. **Metabolism:** In liver to active metabolite. **Elimination:** 80–95% in urine; 15% in bile. **Half-Life:** 5–6 h.

CLINICAL IMPLICATIONS

Assessment & Drug Effects

- Monitor blood glucose levels closely during first 24–48 h after therapy is initiated or the dose is changed.
- Monitor for S&S of hypoglycemia/exaggerated hypoglycemic response, particularly in older adults, malnourished, and debilitated patients or those with impaired hepatic, renal function, adrenal, or pituitary insufficiency.
- Lab tests: Periodic blood glucose, hemoglobin A_{1C}, and liver functions.

Patient & Family Education

- Ingest some form of sugar (e.g., orange juice, dissolved table sugar, corn syrup, honey) if symptoms of hypoglycemia develop, and seek medical assistance.
- Check blood glucose as prescribed.
- Do not take any other medication unless approved by physician.
- Alcoholic beverages may produce a disulfiram-type reaction (see Appendix F).
- Avoid prolonged direct exposure to sun to prevent photosensitivity reaction.

- Report dermatologic reactions such as rash or itching.

ACETYLCYSTEINE ⊕

(a-se-til-sis'tay-een)

Airbron ♣, Mucomyst, Mucosol, N-Acetylcysteine, Acetadote, Acys-5

Classifications: MUCOLYTIC AGENT; ANTIDOTE

Therapeutic: MUCOLYTIC; ANTIDOTE

Pregnancy Category: B

AVAILABILITY 10%, 20% solution for inhalation; 20% solution for injection

ACTION & *THERAPEUTIC EFFECT*
Acetylcysteine probably acts by disrupting disulfide linkages of mucoproteins in purulent and nonpurulent bronchial secretions. In acetaminophen overdose, it helps to prevent hepatotoxicity by serving as a substrate for the toxic metabolites of acetaminophen. *Lowers viscosity and facilitates the removal of secretions.*

USES Adjuvant therapy in patients with abnormal, viscid, or inspissated mucous secretions in acute and chronic bronchopulmonary diseases, and in pulmonary complications of cystic fibrosis and surgery, tracheostomy, and atelectasis. Also used in diagnostic bronchial studies and as an antidote for acute acetaminophen poisoning.

UNLABELED USES As an ophthalmic solution for treatment of dry eye (keratoconjunctivitis sicca); as an enema to treat bowel obstruction due to meconium ileus; prevention of radiocontrast-induced renal dysfunction.

CONTRAINDICATIONS Hypersensitivity to acetylcysteine; patients at risk of gastric hemorrhage.

CAUTIOUS USE Patients with asthma, older adults, severe hepatic disease, esophageal varices, peptic ulcer disease; debilitated patients with severe respiratory insufficiency, pregnancy (category B), lactation.

ROUTE & DOSAGE

Mucolytic

Adult: **Inhalation** 1–10 mL of 20% solution q4–6h or 2–20 mL of 10% solution q4–6h **Direct Instillation** 1–2 mL of 10–20% solution q1–4h

Child: **Inhalation** 3–5 mL of 20% solution or 6–10 mL of 10% solution 3–4 times/d

Infant: **Inhalation** 1–2 mL 20% solution or 2–4 mL of 10% solution 3–4 times/d

Acetaminophen Toxicity

Adult/Child: **PO** 140 mg/kg followed by 70 mg/kg q4h for 17 doses (use a 5% solution)

Adult/Adolescent: **IV** 150 mg/kg infused over 60 min, followed by 50 mg/kg over 4 h, then 100 mg/kg over 16 h

ADMINISTRATION

Inhalation and Instillation

- Prepare dilution within 1 h of use; drug does not contain an antimicrobial agent. A light purple discoloration does not significantly impair drug's effectiveness.
- Dilute the 20% solution with NS or water for injection. The 10% solution may be used undiluted.
- Give by direct instillation into tracheostomy (1–2 mL of 10–20% solution).
- Instruct patient to clear airway, if possible, coughing productively

---

Common adverse effects in *italic*, life-threatening effects underlined; generic names in **bold**; classifications in SMALL CAPS; ♣ Canadian drug name; ⊕ Prototype drug

15

prior to aerosol administration to ensure maximum effect.

- Store opened vial in refrigerator to retard oxidation; use within 96 h.
- Store unopened vial at 15°–30° C (59°–86° F), unless otherwise directed.

Oral

- Dilute the 20% solution 1:3 with cola, orange juice, or other soft drink to make a 5% solution. If administered via a gastric tube, water may be used as the diluent.
- Freshly prepare all diluted solutions and use within 1 h of preparation.

Intravenous

PREPARE: **IV Infusion:** Acetylcysteine reacts with certain metals and rubber; use IV equipment made of plastic or glass. Dilute all required doses in D5W as follows: for loading dose, add a dose equal to 150 mg/kg to 200 mL; for first maintenance dose, add a dose equal to 50 mg/kg to 500 mL; for second maintenance dose, add a dose equal to 100 mg/kg to 1000 mL. Note: The total IV volume should be reduced for patients <40 kg and for those with fluid restriction. In small children, individualize the total IV volume to avoid water intoxication and hyponatremia.
ADMINISTER: **IV Infusion:** Give loading dose over 15 min, maintenance dose 1 over 4 h, maintenance dose 2 over 16 h.

- Store reconstituted solution for up to 24 h at 15°–30° C (59°–86° F).

ADVERSE EFFECTS (≥1%) **CNS:** Dizziness, drowsiness. **GI:** Nausea, *vomiting,* stomatitis, hepatotoxicity (urticaria). **Respiratory:** <u>Bronchospasm</u>, rhinorrhea, burning sensation in upper respiratory passages, epistaxis.

PHARMACOKINETICS Onset: 1 min after inhalation or instillation. **Peak:** 5–10 min. **Metabolism:** Deacetylated in liver to cysteine.

CLINICAL IMPLICATIONS

Assessment & Drug Effects

- During IV infusion, carefully monitor for fluid overload and signs of hyponatremia (i.e., changes in mental status).
- Monitor for S&S of aspiration of excess secretions, and for bronchospasm (unpredictable); withhold drug and notify physician immediately if either occurs.
- Lab tests: Monitor ABGs, pulmonary functions and pulse oximetry as indicated.
- Have suction apparatus immediately available. Increased volume of respiratory tract fluid may be liberated; suction or endotracheal aspiration may be necessary to establish and maintain an open airway. Older adults and debilitated patients are particularly at risk.
- Nausea and vomiting may occur, particularly when face mask is used, due to unpleasant odor of drug and excess volume of liquefied bronchial secretions.

Patient & Family Education

- Report difficulty with clearing the airway or any other respiratory distress.
- Report nausea, as an antiemetic may be indicated.
- Note: Unpleasant odor of inhaled drug becomes less noticeable with continued use.

ACITRETIN

(a-ci-tree′tin)
Soriatane
Classifications: ANTIACNE; RETINOID

Common adverse effects in *italic*, life-threatening effects <u>underlined</u>; generic names in **bold**; classifications in SMALL CAPS; ◆ Canadian drug name; ☉ Prototype drug

Therapeutic: ANTIACNE
Prototype: Isotretinoin
Pregnancy Category: X

AVAILABILITY 10 mg, 25 mg capsules

ACTION & *THERAPEUTIC EFFECT*
Acitretin binds to the retinoic acid receptors in the skin, thus modifying gene expression, epithelial cell growth, and cell differentiation. *Acitretin is a highly toxic metabolite of retinol (vitamin A).*

USES Treatment of severe, recalcitrant psoriasis in adults.

CONTRAINDICATIONS Pregnancy (category X) for at least 3 y after use, sensitivity to parabens, lactation; papilledema, severe renal impairment or renal failure.

CAUTIOUS USE Patients with impaired hepatic function, hepatitis, diabetes mellitus, obesity, alcoholism, history of pancreatitis, hypertriglyceridemia, hypercholesterolemia, coronary artery disease, retinal disease, degenerative joint disease.

ROUTE & DOSAGE

Psoriasis
Adult: **PO** 25–50 mg q.d. with main meal

ADMINISTRATION
Oral
- Administer as single dose with main meal because food enhances absorption.
- Store at 15°–25° C (59°–77° F) and protect from light. After opening, avoid exposure to high temperatures and humidity.

ADVERSE EFFECTS (≥1%) **Body as a Whole:** *Hyperesthesia, paresthesias, arthralgia, progression of existing spi-* *nal hyperostosis, rigors,* back pain, hypertonia, myalgia, fatigue, hot flashes, increased appetite. **CNS:** Headache, depression, aggressive feelings and thoughts of self-harm, insomnia, somnolence. **CV:** Flushing, edema. **GI:** *Dry mouth, increased liver function tests, increased triglycerides and cholesterol,* hepatitis, gingival bleeding, gingivitis, increased saliva, stomatitis, thirst, ulcerative stomatitis, abdominal pain, diarrhea, nausea, tongue disorder. **Special Senses:** Blurred vision, blepharitis, conjunctivitis, decreased night vision/night blindness, eye pain, photophobia; earache, tinnitus; taste perversion. **Respiratory:** Sinusitis. **Skin:** *Alopecia, skin peeling, dry skin, nail disorders, pruritus, rash, cheilitis, skin atrophy, paronychia,* abnormal skin odor and hair texture, cold/clammy skin, increased sweating, purpura, seborrhea, skin ulceration, sunburn. **Other:** *Rhinitis, epistaxis, xerophthalmia.*

INTERACTIONS Drug: Combination with **ethanol** can create **etretinate,** which has a significantly longer half-life than acitretin; interferes with the contraceptive efficacy of **progestin**-only ORAL CONTRACEPTIVES. Use with **methotrexate** increases the risk of hepatitis. **Food:** Avoid excess vitamin A.

PHARMACOKINETICS Absorption: Rapidly from GI tract, optimal absorption when taken with food. **Peak:** 2–5 h. **Distribution:** Crosses placenta, distributed into breast milk. **Metabolism:** Active metabolite, *cis*-acitretin. **Elimination:** In both urine and feces. **Half-Life:** 49 h acitretin, 63 h *cis*-acitretin.

CLINICAL IMPLICATIONS
Assessment & Drug Effects
- Monitor for S&S of pancreatitis or loss of glycemic control in diabet-

Common adverse effects in *italic*, life-threatening effects <u>underlined</u>; generic names in **bold**; classifications in SMALL CAPS; ♣ Canadian drug name; ⊙ Prototype drug

17

ics. Report either condition immediately to physician.

- Lab tests: Before initiating therapy and at 1- to 2-wk intervals until response to drug is known, do lipid profile and liver function tests. Monitor blood glucose and HbA_{1C} periodically.

Patient & Family Education

- Note: Transient worsening of psoriasis may occur during early therapy.
- Review common adverse effects of drug; lag time of 2–3 mo may be necessary before drug effect is evident.
- Discontinue drug and report immediately to physician if visual problems develop.
- Note: Dry eyes with decreased tolerance for contact lenses may occur.
- Do not drink alcohol while taking this drug; it increases risk of hepatotoxicity and hypertriglyceridemia; females should avoid alcohol during and for 2 mo following therapy.
- Do not donate blood for 3 y following therapy.
- Avoid excessive exposure to sunlight or UV light.
- Use two forms of effective contraception for 1 mo before and at least 3 y following therapy because of the serious risk of fetal deformities that could result from exposure to this medication.

ACRIVASTINE/ PSEUDOEPHEDRINE

(a-cri-vas′teen)

Semprex-D (combination with pseudoephedrine)

Classifications: H_1-RECEPTOR ANTAGONIST; DECONGESTANT

Therapeutic: ANTIHISTAMINE; DECONGESTANT

Prototype: Diphenhydramine

Pregnancy Category: B

AVAILABILITY Acrivastine 8 mg/ pseudoephedrine 60 mg capsules

ACTION & *THERAPEUTIC EFFECT*

Acrivastine is an H_1-receptor histamine antagonist that controls histamine-mediated symptoms and acts on sympathetic nerve endings. Pseudoephedrine shrinks swollen nasal mucous membranes and reduces nasal congestion of the mucosa. *It is effective in allergic rhinitis by reducing nasal congestion and decreasing respiratory mucosa swelling.*

USES Seasonal and perennial allergic rhinitis with nasal congestion.

CONTRAINDICATIONS Hypersensitivity to acrivastine, triprolidine, pseudoephedrine, or ephedrine; severe hypertension or severe coronary artery disease; patients on MAO inhibitor drugs; uncontrolled hypertension; tachycardia, acute cardiac arrhythmias; closed-angle glaucoma.

CAUTIOUS USE Renal insufficiency, hypertension, DM, ischemic heart disease, increased intraocular pressure, hyperthyroidism, BPH, GI disorders, older adults, pregnancy (category B), lactation. Safety and effectiveness in children <12 y is not established.

ROUTE & DOSAGE

Allergic Rhinitis

Adult: **PO** 1 tab (8 mg acrivastine/60 mg pseudoephedrine) t.i.d.

Common adverse effects in *italic*, life-threatening effects underlined; generic names in **bold**; classifications in SMALL CAPS; ♣ Canadian drug name; ⊘ Prototype drug

ADMINISTRATION

Oral

- Do not give to patients with a creatinine clearance of 48 mL/min or less.
- Store at 15°–25° C (59°–77° F); protect from light and moisture.

ADVERSE EFFECTS (≥1%) CNS:
Headache, vertigo, dizziness, insomnia, jitteriness, *drowsiness*. GI: Nausea, diarrhea, dry mouth, dyspepsia.

INTERACTIONS Drug: Alcohol may increase psychomotor impairment.

PHARMACOKINETICS Absorption:
Rapidly from GI tract. Onset: 1 h. Duration: Approximately 12 h. Metabolism: In liver. Elimination: Approximately 65% excreted unchanged in urine. Half-Life: 1.5 h.

CLINICAL IMPLICATIONS

Assessment & Drug Effects

- Monitor for dizziness, sedation, urinary obstruction, and hypotension, especially in older adults.
- Assess for significant drowsiness, which may necessitate drug discontinuation.

Patient & Family Education

- Do not use this drug in combination with other OTC antihistamines or decongestants.
- Do not drive or engage in potentially hazardous activities until response to drug is known.
- Do not take alcohol or other CNS depressants while taking this drug.

ACYCLOVIR, ACYCLOVIR SODIUM ⊕

(ay-sye'kloe-ver)

Zovirax

Classifications: ANTIVIRAL
Therapeutic: ANTIVIRAL
Pregnancy Category: B

AVAILABILITY
200 mg capsules; 400 mg, 800 mg tablets; 200 mg/5 mL suspension; 50 mg/mL injection; 5% ointment, cream

ACTION & *THERAPEUTIC EFFECT*
Acyclovir is a synthetic nucleoside analog of guanine. Acyclovir preferentially interferes with DNA synthesis of herpes simplex virus types 1 and 2 (HSV-1 and HSV-2) and varicella-zoster virus, thereby inhibiting viral replication. *Acyclovir reduces viral shedding and formation of new lesions and speeds healing time. It demonstrates antiviral activity against herpes virus simiae (B virus), Epstein-Barr (infectious mononucleosis), varicella-zoster and cytomegalovirus, but does not eradicate the latent herpes virus.*

USES
Parenterally for treatment of initial and recurrent mucosal and cutaneous herpes simplex virus (HSV-1 and HSV-2) infections in immunocompromised adults and children and for severe initial episodes of herpes genitalis in immunocompetent (normal immune system) patients. Treatment of herpes encephalitis or neonatal herpes infection. Used orally for treatment of initial episodes of genital herpes, for management of selected patients with severe recurrent episodes, and for prophylaxis to reduce frequency and severity of recurrent infections. Used topically for herpes labialis (cold sores), initial episodes of herpes genitalis and in non-life-threatening mucocutaneous herpes simplex virus infections in immunocompromised patients.

UNLABELED USES
Treatment of eczema herpeticum caused by HSV localized and disseminated herpes zoster. Prevention of CMV in transplant patients. Prevention of HSV

Common adverse effects in *italic*, life-threatening effects underlined; generic names in **bold**; classifications in SMALL CAPS; ◆ Canadian drug name; ⊕ Prototype drug

19

in immunosuppressed HSV-sero-positive patients.

CONTRAINDICATIONS Hypersensitivity to acyclovir and valacyclovir. **CAUTIOUS USE** Pregnancy (category B), renal insufficiency, dehydration, seizure disorders, or neurologic disease.

ROUTE & DOSAGE

Cold Sores

Adult/Adolescents: **Topical** ≥12 y
Apply 5 times/d for 4 d

Genital Herpes Simplex

Adult: **PO** 200 mg q4h 5 times/d, 400 mg t.i.d. for 7–10 d cycle **IV** 5 mg/kg q8h **Topical** Apply q3h 6 times/d for 7 d
Child: **IV** <12 y, 250 mg/m² q8h, 80 mg/d in 2–5 doses

Herpes Simplex Immunocompromised Patient

Adult: **IV** 5 mg/kg/d q8h × 7 d
Child: **IV** 10 mg/kg q8h × 7 d

Prophylaxis for Genital Herpes Simplex

Adult: **PO** 200 mg 2–5 times/d, 400 mg t.i.d., 800 mg b.i.d.
Child: **PO** 80 mg/kg/d in 2–5 divided doses

Severe Genital Herpes

Adult/Adolescent: **IV** 5 mg/kg over 1 h q8h × 5 d

Herpes Zoster

Adult: **PO** 800 mg q4h 5 times/d
Child: **PO** 80 mg/kg/d in 5 divided doses

Herpes Simplex Encephalitis

Adult: **IV** 10 mg/kg q8h × 10 d
Child (3 mo–12 y): **IV** 20 mg/kg q8h × 10 d
Neonate (<3 mo): **IV** 10 mg/kg/d divided q8h × 10 d

Varicella Zoster

Child/Adolescent: **PO** 20 mg/kg (max: 800 mg) q.i.d. for 5 d cycle initiated within 24 h of onset of rash
Adult: **IV** 10 mg/kg q8h × 7 d
Child: **IV** 20 mg/kg q8h × 7 d

Obesity

Patient dose should be calculated using IBW

Renal Impairment

Cl_{cr} 25–50 mL/min: same dose q12h; 10–25 mL/min: same dose q24h
Hemodialysis: Administer dose after dialysis.

ADMINISTRATION

Oral

- Shake suspension well prior to use.
- Store capsules in tight, light-resistant containers at 15°–30° C (59°–86° F) unless otherwise directed.

Topical

- Wash hands thoroughly before and after treatment of lesions and after handling and disposition of secretions.
- Apply approximately $1/2$ inch of cream or ointment ribbon for each 4 square inches of surface area. Use sufficient ointment or cream to completely cover lesions.
- Apply topical preparation with finger cot or surgical glove.
- Store at 15°–25° C (59°–78° F) unless otherwise directed.

Intravenous

Verify correct IV concentration and rate of infusion with physician for neonates, infants, children.

- Note: Solutions containing benzyl alcohol are toxic to neonates.
- Directions for administration to adults follow.

PREPARE: **Intermittent:** Reconstitute by adding 10 mL sterile water for injection to 500-mg vial to yield 50 mg/mL. Shake well. ▪ Use reconstituted solution within 12 h. ▪ Dilute to ≤7 mg/mL to reduce risk of renal injury and phlebitis. Example: Add 1 mL of reconstituted solution to 9 mL of diluent to yield 5 mg/mL. ▪ Use standard electrolyte and glucose solutions (e.g., NS, RL, D5W) for dilution. Diluted solution should be used within 24 h. *ADMINISTER:* **Intermittent:** Administer over at least 1 h to prevent renal tubular damage. Rapid or bolus IV administration must be avoided. ▪ Monitor IV flow rate carefully; infusion pump or microdrip infusion set preferred. *INCOMPATIBILITIES* **Solution/additive: Bacteriostatic water for injection, albumin, hetastarch, dopamine, dobutamine**. **Y-site: Foscarnet, TPN.**

▪ Refrigerated reconstituted solution may precipitate; however, crystals will redissolve at room temperature. ▪ Store acyclovir powder and reconstituted solutions at controlled room temperature preferably at 15°–30° C (59°–86° F) unless otherwise directed by manufacturer.

ADVERSE EFFECTS (≥1%) **Body as a Whole:** Generally minimal and infrequent. **CNS:** *Headache,* lightheadedness, lethargy, fatigue, tremors, confusion, seizures, dizziness. **GI:** *Nausea, vomiting, diarrhea.* **Urogenital:** Glomerulonephritis, renal tubular damage, acute renal failure. **Skin:** Rash, urticaria, pruritus, burning, stinging sensation, irritation, sensitization. **Other:** Inflammation or phlebitis at IV injection site, sloughing (with extravasation), thrombocytopenic purpura/hemolytic uremic syndrome.

INTERACTIONS Drug: Probenecid decreases acyclovir elimination; **zidovudine** may cause increased drowsiness and lethargy.

PHARMACOKINETICS Absorption: Oral dose is 15–30% absorbed. **Peak:** 1.5–2 h after oral dose. **Distribution:** Into most tissues with lower levels in the CNS; crosses placenta. **Metabolism:** Drug is primarily excreted unchanged. **Elimination:** Renally eliminated; also excreted in breast milk. **Half-Life:** 2.5–5 h.

CLINICAL IMPLICATIONS

Assessment & Drug Effects

▪ Observe infusion site during infusion and for a few days following infusion for signs of tissue damage.
▪ Monitor I&O and hydration status. Keep patient adequately hydrated during first 2 h after infusion to maintain sufficient urinary flow and thus prevent precipitation of drug in renal tubules. Consult physician about amount and length of time oral fluids need to be pushed after IV drug treatment.
▪ Monitor for S&S of: reinfection in pregnant patients; acyclovir-induced neurologic symptoms in patients with history of neurologic problems; drug resistance in immunocompromised patients receiving prolonged or repeated therapy; acute renal failure with concomitant use with other nephrotoxic drugs or preexisting renal disease.
▪ Lab tests: Monitor baseline and periodic renal function studies, particularly with IV administration. Elevations of BUN and serum creatinine and decreases in creatinine clearance indicate need for dosage adjustment, discontin-

Common adverse effects in *italic*, life-threatening effects underlined; generic names in **bold**; classifications in SMALL CAPS; ♣ Canadian drug name; ● Prototype drug

21

uation of drug, or correction of fluid and electrolyte balance.

- Monitor for adverse effects and viral resistance with long-term prophylactic use of the oral drug.

Patient & Family Education

- Start therapy as soon as possible after onset of S&S for best results.
- Do not exceed recommended dosage, frequency of drug administration, or specified duration of therapy. Contact physician if relief is not obtained or adverse effects appear.
- Cleanse affected areas with soap and water 3–4 times daily prior to topical application; dry well before application. With application to genitals, wear loose-fitting clothes over affected areas.
- Note: Even after HSV infection is controlled, latent virus can be activated by stress, trauma, fever, exposure to sunlight, sexual intercourse, menstruation, treatment with immunosuppressive drugs.
- Refrain from sexual intercourse if either partner has S&S of herpes infection; neither topical nor systemic drug prevents transmission to other individuals.
- Avoid topical drug contact in or around eyes. Report unexplained eye symptoms to physician immediately (e.g., redness, pain); untreated infection can lead to corneal keratitis and blindness.

ADALIMUMAB (D2E7)

(a-da-lim'u-mab)
Humira
Classifications: BIOLOGIC RESPONSE MODIFIER; TUMOR NECROSIS FACTOR MODIFIER
Therapeutic: ANTIRHEUMATIC AGENT
Prototype: Etanercept
Pregnancy Category: B

AVAILABILITY 40 mg/0.8 mL injection

ACTION & *THERAPEUTIC EFFECT*
Adalimumab is a human recombinant IgG1 monoclonal antibody. It neutralizes the effects of tumor necrosis factor (TNF)-alpha, a cytokine, by blocking its interaction with cell surface TNF receptors. This mechanism blocks the normal inflammatory and immune responses controlled by TNF-alpha. In the presence of complement, adalimumab may also lyse TNF-expressing cells. *Reduces the levels of acute phase inflammatory reactants (C-reactive protein, ESR, interleukin-6) thus decreasing overall joint inflammation; also reduces levels of enzymes that produce tissue remodeling responsible for cartilage destruction. In RA, adalimumab reduces the numerous inflammatory events of polyarthritis. It reduces the overproduction of TNF-alpha principally by macrophages in rheumatoid joints.*

USES Treatment of moderate to severe rheumatoid arthritis or psoriatic arthritis and to reduce progression of the disease in patients with or without a disease-modifying antirheumatic drug (DMARD).
UNLABELED USES Treatment of Crohn's disease.

CONTRAINDICATIONS Hypersensitivity to adalimumab or mannitol; active infection, either chronic or acute; neoplastic disease; sepsis; lactation. Safe use in children has not been established.
CAUTIOUS USE History of recurrent infection or conditions predisposing to infection; recurrent history of sensitivity to monoclonal antibodies; cardiovascular disease; neurological disease; patients residing in areas with endemic TB or histoplasmosis; active or latent TB infection

prior to therapy; demyelinating disorders; concurrent administration of immunosuppressants; surgery; pregnancy (category B).

ROUTE & DOSAGE

Rheumatoid Arthritis
Adult: SC 40 mg every other wk (may use 40 mg every wk if not on concomitant methotrexate)

ADMINISTRATION
Subcutaneous
- Do not administer to persons with active infections. Evaluate for latent TB with TB skin test prior to initiation of therapy.
- Inspect prefilled syringe for particulate matter and discoloration prior to SC injection.
- Rotate injection sites and do not inject into skin that is red, bruised, tender, or hard. After injecting the drug, do not rub the site.
- Discard any remaining solution in prefilled syringe, as it contains no preservatives.
- Store in original carton at 2°–4° C (38°–48° F). Protect from light. Do not use beyond the expiration date.

ADVERSE EFFECTS (≥1%) **Body as a Whole:** Infections (especially reactivation of latent tuberculosis), sepsis, may see increase in malignancies (lymphoma), back pain, fever, allergic reactions (including <u>anaphylactic shock</u>), *flu-like symptoms, fatigue.* **CNS:** *Headache.* **CV:** Hypertension. **GI:** *Nausea, vomiting,* abdominal pain. **Hematologic:** Development of ANA antibodies. **Respiratory:** *Upper respiratory infection, sinusitis.* **Skin:** *Injection site reactions (erythema, itching, hemorrhage, pain, swelling), rash,* urticaria, fixed drug reaction. **Urogenital:** Urinary tract infection.

INTERACTIONS Drug: Do not give LIVE VIRUS VACCINES to patient on adalimumab; not recommended for use with other TNF BLOCKERS (**etanercept, infliximab, anakinra**).

PHARMACOKINETICS Absorption: 64% absorbed from SC injection site. **Peak:** 131 h. **Distribution:** Minimal beyond vascular/synovial space. **Elimination:** Higher clearance in presence of anti-adalimumab antibodies, lower clearance with increasing age. **Half-Life:** 11.8 d (10–20 d).

CLINICAL IMPLICATIONS
Assessment & Drug Effects
- Monitor for and report lupus-like syndrome (e.g., joint pain, rash on cheeks or arms that is sensitive to sun).
- Monitor for and report promptly S&S of infection.
- Monitor neurological status closely. Report any change in status such as blurred vision or paresthesia.

Patient & Family Education
- Live vaccines should not be accepted by persons taking this drug.
- Report promptly any of the following to the physician: unexplained joint pain, rash on cheeks or arms, fever, sore throat or other signs of infection, changes in vision, numbness or tingling in extremities.

ADAPALENE
(a-da'pa-leen)
Differin
Classifications: ANTIACNE; RETINOID
Therapeutic: ANTIACNE
Prototype: Isotretinoin
Pregnancy Category: C

Common adverse effects in *italic*, life-threatening effects <u>underlined</u>; generic names in **bold**; classifications in SMALL CAPS; ✦ Canadian drug name; ☺ Prototype drug

23

AVAILABILITY 0.1% gel

ACTION & *THERAPEUTIC EFFECT*
Adapalene is a topical retinoid-like compound that modulates cellular differentiation, keratinization, and inflammatory processes related to the pathology of acne vulgaris. Topical adapalene may normalize the differentiation of epithelial follicular cells. *Adapalene decreases the inflammatory process and acne formation.*

USES Topical treatment of acne vulgaris.

CONTRAINDICATIONS Hypersensitivity to adapalene or any of the components of the gel, irritating topical products, and sunburn; skin abrasion, eczema, seborrheic dermatitis.

CAUTIOUS USE Pregnancy (category C), lactation. Safety and effectiveness in children <12 y is not established.

ROUTE & DOSAGE

Acne
Adult: Apply once daily to affected areas in evening

ADMINISTRATION
Topical
- Apply a thin film to clean skin, avoiding eyes, lips, mucous membranes, cuts, abrasions, eczematous or sunburned skin.
- Do not apply to skin recently treated with preparations containing sulfur, resorcinol, or salicylic acid.
- Store at 20°–25° C (68°–77° F).

ADVERSE EFFECTS (≥1%) **Skin:** *Erythema, scaling, dryness, pruritus, burning,* skin irritation, stinging, sunburn, acne flares.

PHARMACOKINETICS Absorption: Minimal through intact skin. **Elimination:** Primarily in bile.

CLINICAL IMPLICATIONS
Assessment & Drug Effects
- Monitor therapeutic effectiveness, which is indicated by improvement after 8–12 wk of treatment; early therapy may be marked by apparent worsening of acne.
- Note: Cutaneous reactions (e.g., erythema, scaling, pruritus) are common and normally diminish after first month of therapy.

Patient & Family Education
- Apply only as directed; excessive application will not result in faster healing but will cause marked redness, peeling, and discomfort.
- Minimize exposure to sunlight and sunlamps, and use sunscreen and protective clothing as needed.

ADEFOVIR DIPIVOXIL
(a-de′fo-vir)
Hepsera
Classifications: ANTIVIRAL AGENT; NUCLEOTIDE ANALOG
Therapeutic: ANTIVIRAL
Pregnancy Category: C

AVAILABILITY 10 mg tablets

ACTION & *THERAPEUTIC EFFECT*
Inhibits human hepatitis virus (HBV) DNA polymerase (reverse transcriptase) by competing with its DNA and by causing DNA chain termination after its incorporation into viral DNA. This results in inhibition of HBV DNA replication. *A nucleotide analog with activity against human hepatitis B virus (HBV).*

Common adverse effects in *italic*, life-threatening effects <u>underlined</u>; generic names in **bold**; classifications in SMALL CAPS; ◆ Canadian drug name; ❿ Prototype drug

USES Treatment of chronic hepatitis B.

CONTRAINDICATIONS Hypersensitivity to adefovir; untreated or unknown human immunodeficiency virus (HIV); exacerbations of hepatitis B, especially in patients who have discontinued anti-hepatitis B therapy; lactation. Safety and efficacy in children are not established.

CAUTIOUS USE Decreased cardiac function due to concomitant disease or other drug therapy; elderly; pregnancy (category C); concomitant use of highly nephrotoxic drugs; renal dysfunction; co-administration with drugs that reduce renal function or compete for active tubular secretion. Appropriate infant immunizations should be used to prevent neonatal acquisition of the hepatitis B virus.

ROUTE & DOSAGE

Hepatitis B
Adult: **PO** 10 mg q.d.
Renal Impairment
Cl$_{cr}$ 20–49 mL/min: 10 mg q48h; 10–19 mL/min: 10 mg q72h *Hemodialysis:* 10 mg q7d following dialysis

ADMINISTRATION

Oral

- Note that the dosing interval of adefovir should be adjusted in patients with baseline creatinine clearance <50 mL/min.
- Store in original container at 15°–30° C (59°–86° F).

ADVERSE EFFECTS (≥1%) **CNS:** *Asthenia,* headache. **GI:** Abdominal pain, nausea, flatulence, diarrhea, dyspepsia, exacerbation of hepatitis after discontinuation of therapy, hepatomegaly. **Metabolic:** *Increased ALT, AST,* increased creatine kinase, amylase, lactic acidosis. **Urogenital:** *Hematuria,* glycosuria, increased serum creatinine, nephrotoxicity. **Other:** HIV resistance in patient with unrecognized HIV, hematuria.

INTERACTIONS Drug: Risk of lactic acidosis when used with NUCLEOSIDE ANALOGS. **Ibuprofen** increases bioavailability of adefovir.

PHARMACOKINETICS Absorption: Adefovir dipivoxil is a prodrug. 59% of dose is absorbed as active drug. **Peak:** 1–4 h. **Distribution:** Minimal protein binding. **Metabolism:** Adefovir dipivoxil is rapidly converted to active adefovir. **Elimination:** Primarily in urine. **Half-Life:** 7.5 h.

CLINICAL IMPLICATIONS

Assessment & Drug Effects

- Lab tests: Monitor baseline and periodic renal function tests (monitor more often with pre-existing impairment or other risk factors for renal impairment); monitor periodic liver function tests, creatinine kinase, serum amylase, and routine blood chemistries including serum electrolytes.
- Withhold drug and notify physician if lactic acidosis is suspected [e.g., hyperventilation, lethargy, plasma pH <7.35 and lactate >5–6 mol/L (mEq/L)].

Patient & Family Education

- Report any of the following to physician: blood in urine, unexplained weakness, or exacerbation of S&S of hepatitis.
- Patients who discontinue adefovir should be monitored at repeated intervals over a period of time for hepatic function.

ADENOSINE

(a-den'o-sin)
Adenocard, Adenoscan
Classifications: ANTIARRHYTHMIC AGENT
Therapeutic: ANTIARRHYTHMIC
Pregnancy Category: C

AVAILABILITY 3 mg/mL

ACTION & *THERAPEUTIC EFFECT*

Slows conduction through the atrioventricular (AV) and sinoatrial (SA) nodes. Can interrupt the reentry pathways through the AV node. *Restores normal sinus rhythm in patients with paroxysmal supraventricular tachycardia.*

USES Conversion to sinus rhythm of paroxysmal supraventricular tachycardia (PSVT) including PSVT associated with accessory bypass tracts (Wolff-Parkinson-White syndrome). "Chemical" thallium stress test.

UNLABELED USES Afterload-reducing agent in low-output states; to prevent graft occlusion following aortocoronary bypass surgery; to produce controlled hypotension during cerebral aneurysm surgery.

CONTRAINDICATIONS AV block, preexisting second- and third-degree heart block or sick sinus rhythm without pacemaker, since a heart block may result. Ineffective for atrial flutter, atrial fibrillation, and ventricular tachycardia.

CAUTIOUS USE Asthmatics, pregnancy (category C), unstable angina, stenotic valvular disease, hypovolemia; hepatic and renal failure.

ROUTE & DOSAGE

Supraventricular Tachycardia
Adult: **IV** 6 mg rapid IV bolus (over 1–2 s); may repeat in 1–2 min with 12 mg IV push, 2 times (total of 3 doses with max: 12 mg dose)
Neonate/Infant/Child: **IV** 0.05–1 mg/kg; may increase dose by 0.05 mg/kg q2 min (max: 12 mg/dose)

Stress Thallium Test
Adult: **IV** 140 mcg/kg/min × 6 min (max: 0.84 mg/kg total dose)

ADMINISTRATION

Intravenous

Make sure solution is clear at time of use.

- Discard unused portion (contains no preservatives).

PREPARE: **Direct:** No dilution is required.
ADMINISTER: **Direct:** Administer directly into vein as a rapid bolus over 1–2 s. If given by IV line, administer as proximally as possible, and follow with a rapid saline flush.

- Note: If high-level block develops after one dose, do not repeat dose.

- Store at room temperature 15°–30° C (59°–86° F). Do not refrigerate, as crystallization may occur. If crystals do form, dissolve by warming to room temperature.

ADVERSE EFFECTS (≥1%) **CNS:** Headache, lightheadedness, dizziness, tingling in arms (from IV infusion), apprehension, blurred vision, burning sensation (from IV infusion). **CV:** *Transient facial flushing,* sweating, palpitations, chest pain, atrial fibrillation or flutter. **Respiratory:** Shortness of breath, transient *dyspnea,* chest pressure. **GI:** Nausea, metallic taste, tightness in throat. **Other:** Irritability in children.

INTERACTIONS Drug: Dipyridamole can potentiate the effects of adenosine; **theophylline** will block the electrophysiologic effects of adenosine; **carbamazepine** may increase risk of heart block.

PHARMACOKINETICS Absorption: Rapid uptake by erythrocytes and vascular endothelial cells after IV administration. **Onset:** 20–30 s. **Metabolism:** Rapid uptake into cells; degraded by deamination to inosine, hypoxanthine, and adenosine monophosphate. **Elimination:** Route unknown. **Half-Life:** 10 s.

CLINICAL IMPLICATIONS

Assessment & Drug Effects

- Monitor for S&S of bronchospasm in asthma patients. Notify physician immediately.
- Use a hemodynamic monitoring system during administration; monitor BP and heart rate and rhythm continuously for several minutes after administration.
- Note: Adverse effects are generally self-limiting due to short half-life (10 s).
- Note: At the time of conversion to normal sinus rhythm, PVCs, PACs, sinus bradycardia, and sinus tachycardia, as well as various degrees of AV block, are seen on the ECG. These usually last only a few seconds and resolve without intervention.

Patient & Family Education

- Note: Flushing may occur along with a feeling of warmth as drug is injected.

AGALSIDASE BETA

(a-gal'si-dase)
Fabrazyme
Classifications: ENZYME; ENZYME REPLACEMENT
Therapeutic: ENZYME REPLACEMENT
Prototype: Pancrelipase
Pregnancy Category: B

AVAILABILITY 35 mg/vial injection

ACTION & *THERAPEUTIC EFFECT*
Fabry disease is caused by a deficiency of alpha-galactosidase A resulting in accumulation of glycosphinolipids in body tissues causing cardiomyopathy, renal failure, and CVA. Agalsidase beta provides an exogenous source of K-galactosidase A that catalyzes the breakdown of glycosphingolipids including GL-3. *Reduces globotriaosylceramide (GL-3) deposition in capillary endothelium of the kidney and certain other cell types.*

USES Treatment of Fabry disease.

CONTRAINDICATIONS Safety and efficacy in children <16 y have not been established. Lactation.
CAUTIOUS USE Hypersensitivity reaction to agalsidase beta or mannitol; compromised cardiac function; mild to severe hypertension; renal impairment; pregnancy (category B).

ROUTE & DOSAGE

Fabry Disease
Adult: **IV** 1 mg/kg q2wk

ADMINISTRATION

Intravenous
Give antipyretics prior to infusion.

PREPARE: **Infusion:** Bring Fabrazyme vials and supplied sterile water for injection to room tem-

---

Common adverse effects in *italic*, life-threatening effects <u>underlined</u>; generic names in **bold**; classifications in SMALL CAPS; ♣ Canadian drug name; ⊘ Prototype drug

27

perature prior to reconstitution. Reconstitute each 35 mg vial slowly injecting 7.2 mL of sterile water for injection down inside wall of vial. Roll and tilt vial gently to mix but do not shake. Reconstituted vial contains 5.0 mg/mL of clear, colorless solution. Do not use if there is particulate matter or if discolored. Further dilute in NS to a final total volume of 500 mL; prior to adding the volume of reconstituted Fabrazyme required for the dose, remove an equal volume of NS from the 500 mL infusion bag.

ADMINISTER: **Infusion:** Initial rate should not exceed 0.25 mg/min (15 mg/h; give more slowly if infusion-associated reactions occur). After tolerance to infusion is established, may increase rate in increments of 0.05–0.08 mg/min (increments of 3 to 5 mg/h) for each subsequent infusion.

INCOMPATIBILITIES **Solution/additive:** Do not infuse with other products.

▪ Store refrigerated until needed. Vials are for single use. Discard any unused portion. Do NOT use after expiration date.

ADVERSE EFFECTS (≥1%) **Body as a Whole:** *Fever, skeletal pain, pallor, rigors, temperature change sensation,* ataxia, stroke. **CNS:** *Dizziness, headache, paresthesia, anxiety, depression,* vertigo. **CV:** *Chest pain, cardiomegaly, hypertension, hypotension, dependent edema,* bradycardia, heart failure, exacerbation of preexisting arrhythmias. **GI:** *Dyspepsia, nausea, abdominal pain.* **Metabolic:** *Antibody development.* **Musculoskeletal:** *Arthrosis, skeletal pain.* **Respiratory:** *Bronchitis,* bronchospasm, laryngitis, *pharyngitis, rhinitis,* sinusitis, dyspnea. **Skin:** Pruritus, urticaria. **Special Senses:** Hearing loss. **Urogenital:** Testicular pain, nephrotic syndrome.

INTERACTIONS Drug: Coadministration with **amiodarone, chloroquine, hydroxychloroquine, gentamicin** is not recommended due to potential of decreased response to agalsidase beta therapy.

PHARMACOKINETICS Metabolism: Degraded through peptide hydrolysis. **Elimination:** Renal elimination expected to be a minor pathway. **Half-Life:** 45–102 min.

CLINICAL IMPLICATIONS

Assessment & Drug Effects

▪ During infusion, monitor for infusion-related reactions such as hypertension or hypotension, chest pain or chest tightness, dyspnea, fever and chills, headache, abdominal pain, pruritus and urticaria.

▪ Slow infusion and notify physician immediately if infusion reaction occurs. Note that additional antipyretic and/or an antihistamine and oral steroid may reduce the symptoms.

▪ Monitor cardiac status closely, especially with preexisting heart disease.

Patient & Family Education

▪ Notify physician if you have experienced an unusual reaction to agalsidase beta, agalsidase alfa, mannitol, other drugs, foods, or preservatives.

▪ Report any of the following to physician immediately: chest pain or chest tightness, rapid heartbeat, shortness of breath or difficulty breathing; depression; dizziness; skin rash, hives or itching; throat tightness; swelling of the face, lips, neck, ears, or extremities.

▪ Do not drive or engage in other hazardous activities until reaction to drug is known.

Common adverse effects in *italic*, life-threatening effects <u>underlined</u>; generic names in **bold**; classifications in SMALL CAPS; ♣ Canadian drug name; ❿ Prototype drug

ALBENDAZOLE

(al-ben′da-zole)

Albenza

Classifications: ANTHELMINTIC AGENT

Therapeutic: ANTHELMINTIC

Prototype: Mebendazole

Pregnancy Category: C

AVAILABILITY 200 mg tablets

ACTION & *THERAPEUTIC EFFECT*

A broad-spectrum oral anthelmintic agent. It is the only anthelmintic drug active against all stages of the helminth life cycle (ova, larvae, and adult worms). Its mechanism of action is unclear, but it appears to cause selective degeneration of cytoplasmic microtubules in the intestinal cells of the helminths and larvae. *Albendazole ultimately causes decreased ATP production in the helminths, resulting in energy depletion, which kills the worms.*

USES Treatment of neurocysticercosis caused by the larval form of pork tapeworm (*Taenia solium*), hydatid disease caused by the larval form of dog tapeworm (*Echinococcus granulosus*).

CONTRAINDICATIONS Hypersensitivity to the benzimidazole class of compounds or any components of albendazole.

CAUTIOUS USE Retinal lesions, pregnancy (category C), lactation.

ROUTE & DOSAGE

Neurocysticercosis

Adult/Child: **PO** >6 y, weight <60 kg, 15 mg/kg/d divided b.i.d. for 8–30 d cycle (max: 800 mg/d); weight ≥60 kg, 400 mg b.i.d. for 8–30 d cycle

Hydatid Disease

Adult/Child: **PO** >6 y, weight <60 kg, 15 mg/kg/d divided b.i.d. (max: 800 mg/d); weight ≥60 kg, 400 mg b.i.d. for 28 d cycle (then 14 d without drug & repeat regimen for 3 cycles)

ADMINISTRATION

Oral

- Give with meals. Absorption is significantly increased with a fatty meal.
- Do not exceed maximum total daily dose of 800 mg.
- Store at 20°–25° C (68°–77° F).

ADVERSE EFFECTS (≥1%) **Body as a Whole:** Hypersensitivity reactions. **CNS:** *Headache,* dizziness, vertigo, increased intracranial pressure, meningeal signs, alopecia (reversible), fever. **GI:** *Abnormal liver function tests,* abdominal pain, nausea, vomiting. **Hematologic:** (Rare) Reversible leukopenia, granulocytopenia, pancytopenia, agranulocytosis. **Skin:** Rash, urticaria.

INTERACTIONS Drug: **Cimetidine, dexamethasone, praziquantel** increase albendazole levels.

PHARMACOKINETICS Absorption: Poorly absorbed from GI tract, absorption enhanced with a fatty meal. **Peak:** 2–5 h. **Distribution:** 70% protein bound; widely distributed, including cyst fluid and CSF; secreted into animal breast milk. **Metabolism:** In liver to active metabolite, albendazole sulfoxide. **Elimination:** In bile. **Half-Life:** 8–12 h.

CLINICAL IMPLICATIONS

Assessment & Drug Effects

- Lab tests: Monitor WBC count, absolute neutrophil count, and liver

Common adverse effects in *italic*, life-threatening effects underlined; generic names in **bold**; classifications in SMALL CAPS; ♣ Canadian drug name; ☺ Prototype drug

29

function tests at start of each 28-d cycle and q2wk during cycle.

▪ Withhold drug and notify physician if WBC count falls below normal or liver enzymes are elevated.

▪ Note: Patients should be concurrently treated with appropriate steroid and anticonvulsant therapy.

Patient & Family Education

▪ Take with meals (see ADMINISTRATION).

▪ Do not become pregnant during or for at least 1 mo after therapy.

ALBUTEROL ⓟ

(al-byoo′ter-ole)
Accuneb, Novosalmol ♦, Pro-Air HFA, Proventil, Proventil HFA, Ventolin, Ventolin HFA, VoSpire ER
Classifications: BETA-ADRENERGIC AGONIST; BRONCHODILATOR (RESPIRATORY SMOOTH MUSCLE RELAXANT)
Therapeutic: BRONCHODILATOR (RESPIRATORY SMOOTH MUSCLE RELAXANT)
Pregnancy Category: C

AVAILABILITY 2 mg, 4 mg tablets; 4 mg, 8 mg, extended-release tablets; 2 mg/5 mL syrup; 200 mcg capsules for inhalation; 0.083%, 0.5% solution for inhalation

ACTION & *THERAPEUTIC EFFECT*
Moderately selective beta$_2$-adrenergic agonist with comparatively long action. Acts prominently on beta$_2$ receptors (particularly smooth muscles of trachea, bronchi, uterus, and vascular supply to skeletal muscles). Inhibits histamine release by mast cells. Produces bronchodilation by relaxing smooth muscles of bronchial tree. *Bronchodilation decreases airway resistance, facilitates mucous drainage, and increases vital capacity.*

USES To relieve bronchospasm associated with acute or chronic asthma, bronchitis, or other reversible obstructive airway diseases. Also used to prevent exercise-induced bronchospasm.
UNLABELED USES Adjunct in treatment of refractory heart failure and to stimulate intracellular transport of potassium in hyperkalemic familial periodic paralysis.

CONTRAINDICATIONS Lactation; albuterol or levalbuterol hypersensitivity; congenital long QT syndrome. Use of oral syrup in children <2 y.
CAUTIOUS USE Cardiovascular disease, renal impairment, hypertension, hyperthyroidism, diabetes mellitus, elderly, history of seizures; hypersensitivity to sympathomimetic amines or to fluorocarbon propellant used in inhalation aerosols; pregnancy (category C).

ROUTE & DOSAGE

Bronchospasm

Adult: **PO** 2–4 mg 3–4 times/d, 4–8 mg sustained release 2 times/d **Inhaled** 1–2 inhalations q4–6h
Child: **PO** 2–6 y, 0.1–0.2 mg/kg t.i.d. (max: 4 mg/dose); 6–12 y, 2 mg 3–4 times/d **Inhaled** 6–12 y, 1–2 inhalations q4–6h

ADMINISTRATION

Oral

▪ Do not crush extended release tablets. Scored tablets may be broken in half.

▪ Note: An initial dose of 2 mg t.i.d. or q.i.d. is recommended for older adult patients.

- Store tablets and syrup between 2°–25° C (36°–77° F) in tight, light-resistant container.

Inhalation

- Administer albuterol 20–30 min before concomitant beclomethasone (Vanceril) inhalation treatments to allow deeper penetration of beclomethasone into lungs, unless otherwise directed by physician.
- Store canisters between 15°–30° C (59°–86° F) away from heat and direct sunlight.

ADVERSE EFFECTS (≥1%) **Body as a Whole:** Hypersensitivity reaction. **CNS:** *Tremor,* anxiety, nervousness, restlessness, convulsions, weakness, headache, hallucinations. **CV:** Palpitation, hypertension, hypotension, bradycardia, reflex tachycardia. **Special Senses:** Blurred vision, dilated pupils. **GI:** Nausea, vomiting. **Other:** Muscle cramps, hoarseness.

DIAGNOSTIC TEST INTERFERENCE Transient small increases in *plasma glucose* may occur.

INTERACTIONS Drug: With **epinephrine,** other SYMPATHOMIMETIC BRONCHODILATORS, possible additive effects; MAO INHIBITORS, TRICYCLIC ANTIDEPRESSANTS potentiate action on vascular system; BETA-ADRENERGIC BLOCKERS antagonize the effects of both drugs.

PHARMACOKINETICS Onset: Inhaled: 5–15 min; PO 30 min. **Peak:** Inhaled: 0.5–2 h; PO 2.5 h. **Duration:** Inhaled: 3–6 h; PO 4–6 h (8–12 h with sustained release). **Metabolism:** In liver by CYP3A4; may cross the placenta. **Elimination:** 76% of dose eliminated in urine in 3 d. **Half-Life:** 2.75 h.

CLINICAL IMPLICATIONS
Assessment & Drug Effects
- Monitor therapeutic effectiveness which is indicated by significant

subjective improvement in pulmonary function within 60–90 min after drug administration.

- Monitor for: S&S of fine tremor in fingers, which may interfere with precision handwork; CNS stimulation, particularly in children 2–6 y, (hyperactivity, excitement, nervousness, insomnia), tachycardia, GI symptoms. Report promptly to physician.
- Lab tests: Periodic ABGs, pulmonary functions, and pulse oximetry.
- Consult physician about giving last albuterol dose several hours before bedtime, if drug-induced insomnia is a problem.

Patient & Family Education

- Review directions for correct use of medication and inhaler (see ADMINISTRATION).
- Avoid contact of inhalation drug with eyes.
- Do not increase number or frequency of inhalations without advice of physician.
- Notify physician if albuterol fails to provide relief because this can signify worsening of pulmonary function and a reevaluation of condition/therapy may be indicated.
- Note: Albuterol can cause dizziness or vertigo; take necessary precautions.
- Do not use OTC drugs without physician approval. Many medications (e.g., cold remedies) contain drugs that may intensify albuterol action.

ALCLOMETASONE DIPROPIONATE

(al-clo-met′a-sone)
Aclovate
Pregnancy Category: C
See Appendix A-4.

Common adverse effects in *italic*, life-threatening effects <u>underlined</u>; generic names in **bold**; classifications in SMALL CAPS; ♣ Canadian drug name; ⊘ Prototype drug

31

ALEFACEPT ⊕

(a-le'fa-cept)

Amevive

Classifications: BIOLOGIC RESPONSE MODIFIER; FUSION PROTEIN
Therapeutic: IMMUNOSUPPRESSANT
Pregnancy Category: B

AVAILABILITY 15 mg vials

ACTION & *THERAPEUTIC EFFECT*

Activation of T cells plays a role in chronic plaque psoriasis. Alefacept is thought to bind to CD2 receptors found on all peripheral T cells and to immunoglobulin receptors on cytotoxic cells, such as natural killer cells. Alefacept blocks further activation of T cells and reduces cellular-mediated apoptosis of T cells. *Alefacept modulates the immune response by decreasing activation of T cells that are believed to be the key mediators of psoriasis.*

USES Treatment of moderate to severe chronic plaque psoriasis.
UNLABELED USES Treatment of psoriatic arthritis.

CONTRAINDICATIONS Hypersensitivity to alefacept; CD4+ T lymphocyte count below normal; patients with HIV, history of systemic malignancies; patients with a clinically important infection; serious infections; live or attenuated vaccines; lactation.
CAUTIOUS USE Patients at high risk for malignancies; pregnancy (category B); elderly.

ROUTE & DOSAGE

Chronic Plaque Psoriasis

Adult: **IM** 15 mg once/wk × 12 wk, may repeat course after 12 wk off therapy **IV** 7.5 mg once/wk × 12 wk, may repeat course after 12 wk off therapy

Psoriatic Arthritis

Adult: **IV** 7.5 mg once/wk × 12 wk

ADMINISTRATION

- Administer only if CD4+ T lymphocyte count is ≥250 cells/microliter.
- Reconstituted alefacept should be clear and colorless to slightly yellow.

Intramuscular

- Reconstitute the 15 mg vial IM administration with 0.6 mL of the supplied diluent to yield 15 mg/0.5 mL. Gently swirl vial for about 2 min to mix, but do not shake.
- Rotate the injection sites and space at least 1 inch from an old site.
- Never inject into areas where the skin is tender, bruised, red, or hard.

Intravenous

PREPARE: Direct: Reconstitute the 7.5 mg vial for IV administration with 0.6 mL of the supplied diluent to yield 7.5 mg/0.5 mL. Gently swirl vial for about 2 min to mix, but do not shake.

ADMINISTER: Direct: Prime supplied infusion set with 3.0 mL of supplied diluent and insert into vein. Give reconstituted solution over ≤5 sec and do not use a filter. Follow with flush using 3 mL of supplied diluent.

INCOMPATIBILITIES Solution/additive: No data available at this time.

- Store vials of powder away from light at 15°–30° C (59°–86° F).
- Store reconstituted solution for up to 4 h between 2°–8° C (36°–46° F); discard solution not used within 4 h of reconstitution.

ADVERSE EFFECTS (≥1%) **Body as a Whole:** Secondary malignancies, serious infections, chills, *injection site pain,* injection site inflamma-

Common adverse effects in *italic*, life-threatening effects underlined; generic names in **bold**; classifications in SMALL CAPS; ♣ Canadian drug name; ⊕ Prototype drug

tion. **CNS:** Dizziness, headache. **GI:** Nausea, vomiting. **Hematologic:** *Lymphopenia,* alefacept antibody formation. **Musculoskeletal:** Myalgia. **Respiratory:** Pharyngitis, increased cough. **Skin:** Pruritus.

INTERACTIONS Drug: Additive immunosuppression with other immunosuppressant drugs (e.g., CORTICOSTEROIDS); LIVE VACCINES increase risk of secondary transmission of infection.

PHARMACOKINETICS Absorption: 63% from IM injection. **Metabolism:** Presumed to be broken down in plasma. **Half-Life:** 270 h after IV.

CLINICAL IMPLICATIONS

Assessment & Drug Effects
- Discontinue drug immediately and institute supportive measures if a serious hypersensitivity reaction occurs.
- Note: Drug should be discontinued if CD4+ T lymphocyte counts remain below 250 cells/microliter for one month.
- Lab tests: Weekly WBC with differential during 12-wk dosing period; periodic liver enzymes.
- Monitor for and promptly report S&S of infection.

Patient & Family Education
- Report any of the following promptly: chest pain or tightness, rapid or irregular heart beat; difficulty breathing or swallowing; swelling of face, tongue, hands, feet or ankles; rapid weight gain; signs of infection (e.g., fever, chills, cough, sore throat, pain or difficulty passing urine); skin rash or itchy skin; severe stomach pain.
- Do not accept live or live-attenuated vaccines while taking this drug.
- Notify physician if you become pregnant while taking this drug or within 8 wk of discontinuing drug.

ALEMTUZUMAB

(a-lem'tu-zu-mab)
Campath
Classifications: ANTINEOPLASTIC; MONOCLONAL ANTIBODY
Therapeutic: ANTINEOPLASTIC; MONOCLONAL ANTIBODY
Prototype: Basiliximab
Pregnancy Category: C

AVAILABILITY 30 mg/mL injection

ACTION & THERAPEUTIC EFFECT
Monoclonal antibody that attaches to CD52 cell surface antigens expressed on a variety of leukocytes, including normal and malignant B and T lymphocytes, monocytes, and some granulocytes. Proposed mechanism of action is antibody-dependent lysis of leukemic cells following binding to cell surface antigens. *Initiates antibody dependent cell lysis, thus inhibiting cell proliferation in chronic lymphocytic leukemia.*

USES Treatment of B-cell chronic lymphocytic leukemia in patients who have failed fludarabine therapy. **UNLABELED USES** Treatment of mycosis fungoides, non-Hodgkin's lymphoma.

CONTRAINDICATIONS Type I hypersensitivity to alemtuzumab or its components, hamster protein hypersensitivity; serious infection or exposure to viral infections (i.e., herpes or chickenpox), HIV infection, dental work; infection; lactation. **CAUTIOUS USE** History of hypersensitivity to other monoclonal antibodies; ischemic cardiac disease, angina, coronary artery disease; dental disease; history of varicella disease; pregnancy (category C), females of childbearing age. Safety

Common adverse effects in *italic*, life-threatening effects underlined; generic names in **bold**; classifications in SMALL CAPS; ♣ Canadian drug name; ⑩ Prototype drug

33

and efficacy in children are not established.

ROUTE & DOSAGE

B-Cell Chronic Lymphocytic Leukemia

Adult: IV Start with 3 mg/d infused over 2 h; when 3 mg/d is tolerated, increase dose over next 3–7 d to 10 mg/d, when 10 mg/d is tolerated, increase to maintenance dose of 30 mg/d (give 30 mg/d 3 times/wk). Single dose should not exceed 30 mg; cumulative dose should not exceed 90 mg/wk.

ADMINISTRATION

▪ Note: Premedication with antihistamines, acetaminophen, antiemetics, and corticosteroids prior to infusion may reduce the severity of adverse side effects.

Intravenous

PREPARE: **IV Infusion:** Do NOT shake ampule prior to use. Withdraw required dose into a syringe and filter with a sterile, low-protein binding, non-fiber releasing 5 micron filter prior to dilution. Inject into 100 mL NS or D5W. Gently invert bag to mix. Infuse within 8 h of mixing. Protect from light. Discard any unused solution.

ADMINISTER: **IV Infusion:** Infuse each dose over 2 h. Do NOT give single doses >30 mg or cumulative weekly doses >90 mg.

INCOMPATIBILITIES **Solution/additive:** Do not infuse or mix with other drugs.

▪ Store at 2°–8° C (36°–46° F). Discard if ampule has been frozen. Protect from direct light.

ADVERSE EFFECTS (≥1%) **Body as a Whole:** *Infusion reactions (rig-*

ors, fever, nausea, vomiting, hypotension, rash, shortness of breath, bronchospasm, chills), fatigue, pain, sepsis, asthenia, edema, herpes simplex, myalgias, malaise, moniliasis, temperature change sensation, coma, seizures. **CNS:** *Headache, dysesthesias, dizziness, insomnia,* depression, tremor, somnolence, cerebrovascular accident, subarachnoid hemorrhage. **CV:** *Hypotension, tachycardia, hypertension,* cardiac failure, arrhythmias, MI. **GI:** *Diarrhea, nausea, vomiting, stomatitis, abdominal pain, dyspepsia, anorexia,* constipation. **Hematologic:** *Neutropenia, anemia, thrombocytopenia,* purpura, epistaxis, pancytopenia. **Respiratory:** *Dyspnea, cough, bronchitis, pneumonia, pharyngitis,* bronchospasm, rhinitis. **Skin:** *Rash, urticaria, pruritus, increased sweating.* **Other:** Risk of opportunistic infections.

INTERACTIONS Drug: Additive risk of bleeding with ANTICOAGULANTS, NSAIDS, PLATELET INHIBITORS, SALICYLATES increased risk of opportunistic infections with **fludarabine.** **Herbal:** **Feverfew, garlic, ginger, ginkgo** may increase risk of bleeding.

PHARMACOKINETICS Peak: Steadystate levels in approximately 6 wk. **Half-Life:** 12 d.

CLINICAL IMPLICATIONS

Assessment & Drug Effects

▪ Monitor for acute infusion-related events, including hypotension, rigors, fever, shortness of breath, bronchospasm, chills, and/or rash. If such a reaction occurs, the infusion should be discontinued and the physician notified.

▪ Withhold drug and notify physician if absolute neutrophil count

<250/microliter or platelet count ≤25,000/microliter.

- Monitor BP closely during infusion period. Careful monitoring of BP and hypotensive symptoms is especially important in patients with ischemic heart disease and those on antihypertensives.
- Discontinue infusion and notify physician immediately if any of the following occurs: hypotension, fever, chills, shortness of breath, bronchospasm, or rash.
- Withhold drug during any serious infection. Therapy may be reinstituted following resolution of the infection.
- Lab tests: CBS with differential and platelet counts weekly or more frequently in the presence of anemia, thrombocytopenia, or neutropenia; periodic blood glucose, serum electrolytes, and alkaline phosphatase.
- Monitor diabetics closely for loss of glycemic control.
- Monitor for S&S of dehydration especially with severe vomiting.

Patient & Family Education

- Do not accept immunizations with live viral vaccines during therapy or if therapy has been recently terminated.
- Use effective methods of contraception to prevent pregnancy during therapy and for at least 6 mo following therapy.
- Report any of the following to physician immediately: unexplained bleeding, fever, sore throat, flu-like symptoms, S&S of an infection, difficulty breathing, significant GI distress, abdominal pain, fluid retention, or changes in mental status.
- Diabetics should monitor blood glucose levels carefully since loss of glycemic control is a possible adverse reaction.

ALENDRONATE SODIUM

(a-len'dro-nate)

Fosamax, Fosamax D (with 2800 IU Vitamin D3)

Classifications: BISPHOSPHONATE; REGULATOR, BONE METABOLISM

Therapeutic: BONE METABOLISM REGULATOR

Prototype: Etidronate

Pregnancy Category: C

AVAILABILITY 5 mg, 10 mg, 35 mg, 40 mg, 70 mg tablets; 70 mg/75 mL oral solution

ACTION & *THERAPEUTIC EFFECT*
A bisphosphonate that inhibits osteoclast-mediated bone resorption. Antiresorption mechanism is not fully understood. It localizes to resorption sites of active bone turnover and has minimal to no interference with bone mineralization. *Alendronate decreases bone resorption, thus minimizing loss of bone density.*

USES Prevention and treatment of osteoporosis in postmenopausal women, Paget's disease. Treatment of glucocorticoid-induced osteoporosis.

CONTRAINDICATIONS Hypersensitivity to alendronate or other bisphosphonates; achalasia, esophageal stricture, severe renal impairment (Cl_{cr} <35 mL/min); hypocalcemia; abnormalities; lactation.

CAUTIOUS USE Renal impairment, CHF, hyperphosphatemia, liver disease, fever or infection, active upper GI problems; pregnancy (category C).

ROUTE & DOSAGE

Treatment of Osteoporosis

Adult: **PO** 10 mg once/d (max: 40 mg/d) or 70 mg q wk

Common adverse effects in *italic*, life-threatening effects underlined; generic names in **bold**; classifications in SMALL CAPS; ♦ Canadian drug name; ☻ Prototype drug

35

Prevention of Osteoporosis, Treatment of Steroid-induced Osteoporosis

Adult: **PO** 5 mg q.d. or 35 mg q wk

Treatment of Paget's Disease

Adult: **PO** 40 mg once/d for 6 mo

Renal Impairment

Cl_{cr} <35 mL/min, use not recommended

ADMINISTRATION

Oral

- Correct hypocalcemia before administering alendronate.
- Administer in the morning at least 30 min before the first food, beverage, or medication. Do not administer within 2 h of calcium-containing foods, beverages, or medications. At least 30 min should elapse after alendronate dose before taking any other drugs.
- *Oral Solution:* Use oral syringe for accurate dosage. Give with at least 60 cc (2 oz) of plain water.
- *Tablet:* Give with 8 oz of plain water.
- Keep patient sitting up or ambulating for 30 min after taking drug.
- Store according to manufacturer's directions.

ADVERSE EFFECTS (≥1%) **Endocrine:** Hypocalcemia, hypophosphatemia. **GI:** Esophageal irritation and *ulceration, nausea, vomiting, abdominal pain, dyspepsia,* diarrhea, constipation, flatulence. **Other:** Arthralgias, myalgias, headache, rash.

INTERACTIONS Drug: Ranitidine increases alendronate availability. **Food: Calcium** and food (especially dairy products) reduce alendronate absorption.

PHARMACOKINETICS Absorption: 0.5–1% from GI tract (absorption significantly decreased by calcium and food). **Onset:** 3–6 wk. **Duration:** 12 wk after discontinuation. **Distribution:** Rapid skeletal uptake. **Metabolism:** Not metabolized. **Elimination:** Up to 50% excreted unchanged in urine. **Half-Life:** Up to 10 h.

CLINICAL IMPLICATIONS

Assessment & Drug Effects

- Lab tests: Monitor albumin-adjusted serum calcium, serum phosphate, serum alkaline phosphatase, fasting and 24 h urinary calcium, and serum electrolytes. Periodically monitor renal and liver functions.
- Diagnostic test: Bone density scan every 12–18 mo.
- Discontinue drug if the Cl_{cr} <35 mL/min.

Patient & Family Education

- Review directions for taking drug correctly (see ADMINISTRATION).
- Report fever, especially when accompanied by arthralgia and myalgia.

ALFENTANIL HYDROCHLORIDE

(al-fen'ta-nill)

Alfenta

Classifications: NARCOTIC (OPI-ATE AGONIST) ANALGESIC; GENERAL ANESTHETIC

Therapeutic: NARCOTIC ANALGESIC; GENERAL ANESTHETIC

Prototype: Morphine

Pregnancy Category: C

Controlled Substance: Schedule II

AVAILABILITY 500 mcg/mL injection

ACTION & *THERAPEUTIC EFFECT*

Alfentanil is a narcotic agonist analgesic with rapid onset and short duration of action. CNS effects appear to be related to interaction of drug with opiate receptors. *Analgesia is mediated through changes in the perception of pain at the spinal cord and at higher levels in the CNS. Brief duration of action is advantageous for short surgical procedures, but necessitates incremental injections or continuous infusion for long operations.*

USES Major component of balanced anesthesia; analgesic, analgesic supplement, and primary anesthetic for induction of anesthesia when endotracheal and mechanical ventilation are required.

CONTRAINDICATIONS Safety in lactation or in children <12 y is not established. Coagulation disorders, bacteremia, infection at injection site. **CAUTIOUS USE** Older adults, history of pulmonary disease; pregnancy (category C).

ROUTE & DOSAGE

Anesthesia Induction

Adult: **IV** 8–20 mcg/kg for surgery lasting <30 min, maintenance anesthesia can be maintained with incremental doses of 3–5 mcg/kg, continuous infusion of 0.5–1 mcg/kg/min (total dose of 8–40 mcg/kg)

ADMINISTRATION

Intravenous

PREPARE: **Direct or Continuous:** Alfentanil is available in concentrations of 500 mcg/mL. ▪Add 20 mL of alfentanil to 230 mL of compatible IV solution to yield 40 mcg/mL. Compatible IV solutions include NS, D5/NS, D5W, and RL. ▪Note: Alfentanil may be diluted to concentrations of 25–80 mcg/mL.

ADMINISTER: **Direct:** Administer over at least 3 min. Do not administer more rapidly. **Continuous:** Administer at a rate of 0.5–1 mcg/kg/min. Note: Dose may be individualized.
INCOMPATIBILITIES **Y-site: Amphotericin B, thiopental.**

▪Store at 15°–30° C (59°–86° F). Avoid freezing.

ADVERSE EFFECTS (≥1%) **Body as a Whole:** Thoracic muscle rigidity, flushing, diaphoresis; extremities feel heavy and warm. **CNS:** Dizziness, euphoria, drowsiness. **CV:** Hypotension, hypertension, tachycardia, bradycardia. **GI:** *Nausea,* vomiting, anorexia, constipation, cramps. **Respiratory:** Apnea, respiratory depression, dyspnea.

INTERACTIONS Drug: BETA-ADRENERGIC BLOCKERS increase incidence of bradycardia; CNS DEPRESSANTS such as BARBITURATES, TRANQUILIZERS, NEUROMUSCULAR BLOCKING AGENTS, OPIATES, and INHALATION GENERAL ANESTHETICS may enhance the cardiovascular and CNS effects of alfentanil in both magnitude and duration; enhancement or prolongation of postoperative respiratory depression also may result from concomitant administration of any of these agents with alfentanil.

PHARMACOKINETICS Onset: 2 min. **Duration:** Injection 30 min; continuous infusion 45 min. **Distribution:** Crosses placenta. **Metabolism:** In liver by CYP3A4. **Elimination:** Excreted in breast milk. **Half-Life:** 46–111 min.

CLINICAL IMPLICATIONS
Assessment & Drug Effects
▪ Monitor for S&S of increased sympathetic stimulation (arrhythmias) and evidence of depressed postoperative analgesia (tachycar-

Common adverse effects in *italic*, life-threatening effects underlined; generic names in **bold**; classifications in SMALL CAPS; ♣ Canadian drug name; ⊚ Prototype drug

37

dia, pain, pupillary dilation, spontaneous muscle movement) if a narcotic antagonist has been administered to overcome residual effects of alfentanil.

- Evaluate adequacy of spontaneous ventilation carefully during postoperative period.
- Monitor vital signs carefully during postoperative period; check for bradycardia, especially if patient is also taking a beta blocker.
- Note: Narcotic effects wear off quickly with negligible residual effects.
- Note: Dizziness, sedation, nausea, and vomiting are common when drug is used as a postoperative analgesic.

Patient & Family Education
- Report unpleasant adverse effects when drug is used for patient-controlled analgesia.

ALFUZOSIN

(al-fuz'o-sin)
UroXatral, Xatral ♦
Classifications: ALPHA-ADRENERGIC ANTAGONIST
Therapeutic: ANTAGONIST OF ALPHA-1 RECEPTORS
Prototype: Prazosin
Pregnancy Category: B

AVAILABILITY 10 mg extended-release tablet

ACTION & *THERAPEUTIC EFFECT*
Alfuzosin is a short-acting, selective antagonist at alpha-1 receptors with a low incidence of hypotension and sexual dysfunction at therapeutic doses. Alpha-1 receptors cause contraction of smooth muscle in the prostate, prostatic capsule, prostatic urethra, bladder base, and bladder neck. Both alpha-1a (70%)

and alpha-1b receptors exist in the prostate. *Blockade of alpha-1 receptors by alfuzosin causes smooth muscles in the bladder neck and prostate to relax, thereby reducing pressure on the urethra and improving urine flow rate. This results in a reduction in BPH symptoms.*

USES Treatment of symptomatic benign prostatic hypertrophy (BPH).

CONTRAINDICATIONS Hypersensitivity to alfuzosin; severe hepatic insufficiency; concurrent treatment with potent CYP3A4 inhibitors (e.g., ketoconazole, itraconazole, and ritonavir); angina; QT prolongation. **CAUTIOUS USE** Pregnancy (category B); coronary artery disease, cardiac arrhythmias; hepatic disease; dizziness, light-headedness, orthostatic hypotension.

ROUTE & DOSAGE

Benign Prostatic Hypertrophy
Adult: **PO** 10 mg q.d.

ADMINISTRATION

Oral
- Give immediately after same meal each day.
- Ensure that extended-release tablet is not crushed or chewed. It must be swallowed whole.
- Store at 15°–30° C (59°–86° F). Protect from light and moisture.

ADVERSE EFFECTS (≥1%) **Body as a Whole:** Fatigue, pain. **CNS:** Dizziness, headache. **GI:** Abdominal pain, dyspepsia, constipation, nausea. **Respiratory:** Upper respiratory infection, bronchitis, sinusitis, pharyngitis. **Urogenital:** Impotence, priapism.

INTERACTIONS Drug: Increased risk of hypotension with other ANTIHYPERTENSIVE AGENTS or **sildenafil, vardenafil,** and **tadalafil; keto-**

conazole, itraconazole, PROTEASE INHIBITORS may increase alfuzosin levels and toxicity.

PHARMACOKINETICS Absorption: 49% when taken with food. **Peak:** 8 h. **Metabolism:** In liver by CYP3A4. **Elimination:** 69% in feces, 24% in urine. **Half-Life:** 10 h.

CLINICAL IMPLICATIONS

Assessment & Drug Effects

- Monitor CV status and BP, especially if on concurrent treatment with antihypertensive drugs or inhibitors of CYP3A4. See INTERACTIONS.
- Check postural vital signs to evaluate for orthostatic hypotension within a few hours following administration.
- Withhold drug and report new or worsening angina to physician.
- Lab tests: Baseline and periodic LFTs.

Patient & Family Education

- Inform physician about all other prescription, nonprescription, or herbal drugs being taken.
- Make position changes slowly to minimize dizziness.
- Do not drive or engage in other hazardous activities until reaction to drug is known.
- Moderate or eliminate grapefruit juice consumption while on this drug.

ALITRETINOIN (9-*cis*-RETINOIC ACID)

(a-li-tre'ti-noyne)

Panretin

Classifications: ANTIACNE (RETINOID)

Therapeutic: ANTIACNE
Prototype: Isotretinoin
Pregnancy Category: D

AVAILABILITY 0.1% gel

ACTION & *THERAPEUTIC EFFECT*
Naturally occurring retinoid that binds to and activates all known retinoid receptors in cells, which regulate cellular differentiation and proliferation in both healthy and neoplastic cells. *Inhibits the growth of Kaposi's sarcoma (KS) in HIV patients. It does not prevent the development of new KS lesions.*

USES Treatment of cutaneous lesions of AIDS-related Kaposi's sarcoma.
UNLABELED USES Cutaneous T-cell lymphomas.

CONTRAINDICATIONS Hypersensitivity to alitretinoin or other retinoids including vitamin A; when systemic anti-KS therapy is required; pregnancy (category D), lactation.
CAUTIOUS USE Safety & efficacy in children <18 y, or older adults ≥65 y are unknown; cutaneous T-cell lymphoma.

ROUTE & DOSAGE

Cutaneous Kaposi's Sarcoma

Adult: **Topical** Apply sufficient gel to cover lesions b.i.d., may increase application to 3–4 times daily if tolerated

ADMINISTRATION

Topical

- Apply gel liberally over lesions; avoid unaffected skin and mucus membranes.
- Dry 3–5 min before covering with clothes. Do not cover with occlusive dressing.
- Store at 15°–30° C (59°–86° F).

ADVERSE EFFECTS (≥1%) **Skin:** Erythema, edema, vesiculation, *rash, burning pain,* pruritus, exfo-

Common adverse effects in *italic*, life-threatening effects underlined; generic names in **bold**; classifications in SMALL CAPS; ♣ Canadian drug name; ⊙ Prototype drug

39

liative dermatitis, excoriation, paresthesia.

INTERACTIONS Drug: Increased toxicity with insect repellents containing DEET.

PHARMACOKINETICS Absorption: Minimal.

CLINICAL IMPLICATIONS

Assessment & Drug Effects
- Monitor for S&S of dermal toxicity (e.g., erythema, edema, vesiculation).

Patient & Family Education
- Allow up to 14 wk for therapeutic response.
- Avoid exposure of medicated skin to sunlight or sun lamps.
- Contact physician if inflammation, swelling, or blisters appear on medicated areas.

ALLOPURINOL

(al-oh-pure′i-nole)
Alloprin A ◆, Alloprin, Apo-allopurinol-A ◆, Lopurin, Novopurinol A, Zyloprim
Classifications: ANTIGOUT AGENT
Therapeutic: ANTIGOUT
Pregnancy Category: C

AVAILABILITY 100 mg, 300 mg tablets; 500 mg vial

ACTION & *THERAPEUTIC EFFECT*
Allopurinol reduces endogenous uric acid by selectively inhibiting action of xanthine oxidase, the enzyme responsible for converting hypoxanthine to xanthine and xanthine to uric acid (end product of purine catabolism). Has no analgesic, antiinflammatory, or uricosuric actions. *Thus, urate pool is decreased by the lowering of both se-rum and urinary uric acid levels, and hyperuricemia is prevented.*

USES To control primary hyperuricemia that accompanies severe gout and to prevent possibility of flare-up of acute gouty attack; to prevent recurrent calcium oxalate stones; prophylactically to reduce severity of hyperuricemia associated with antineoplastic and radiation therapies, both of which greatly increase plasma uric acid levels by promoting nucleic acid degradation.

UNLABELED USES To reduce hyperuricemia secondary to Lesch–Nyhan syndrome, polycythemia vera, G6PD deficiency, sarcoidosis, and therapy with thiazides or ethambutol.

CONTRAINDICATIONS Hypersensitivity to allopurinol; as initial treatment for acute gouty attacks; idiopathic hemochromatosis (or those with family history); children (except those with hyperuricemia secondary to neoplastic disease and chemotherapy).

CAUTIOUS USE Impaired hepatic or renal function, history of peptic ulcer, lower GI tract disease, bone marrow depression; pregnancy (category C).

ROUTE & DOSAGE

Treatment of Hyperuricemia
Adult: **PO** 100 mg/d, may increase by 100 mg/wk (max: 800 mg/d), divide doses >300 mg/d **IV** 200–400 mg/m²/d (max: 600 mg/d) in 1–4 divided doses
Child: **PO** ≤10 y, 10 mg/kg/d in 2–3 divided doses (max: 800 mg/d) **IV** 200 mg/m²/d in 1–4 divided doses

Treatment of Secondary Hyperuricemia

Adult: **PO** 200–800 mg/d for 2–3 d or longer, divide doses >300 mg/d
Child: **PO** 6–10 y, 100 mg t.i.d., <6 y, 50 mg t.i.d.

Renal Impairment

Cl_{cr} 10–20 mL/min: 200 mg/d; 3–10 mL/min: 100 mg qd.
Dialysis: Administer dose after dialysis.

ADMINISTRATION

Oral

- Give after meals for best toleration; tablet may be crushed and taken with fluid and with food.
- Store at 15°–30° C (59°–86° F) in a tightly closed container.

Intravenous

PREPARE: Intermittent: Reconstitute a single dose vial (500 mg) with 25 mL of sterile water for injection to yield 20 mg/mL. ▪Further dilute with NS or D5W to a concentration of ≤6 mg/mL. ▪Note: Adding 2.3 mL of diluent yields 6 mg/mL.

ADMINISTER: Intermittent: Usually administered over 30–60 min.

INCOMPATIBILITIES Solution/Additive: Amikacin, amphotericin B, carmustine, cefotaxime, chlorpromazine, cimetidine, clindamycin, cytarabine, dacarbazine, daunorubicin, doxycycline, droperidol, floxuridine, gentamicin, haloperidol, hydroxyzine, idarubicin, imipenem-cilastatin, mechlorethamine, meperidine, metoclopramide, methylprednisolone, minocycline, nalbuphine, netilmicin, ondansetron, prochlorperazine, promethazine, sodium bicarbonate, streptozocin, tobramycin, vinorelbine.

ADVERSE EFFECTS (≥1%) **CNS:** Drowsiness, headache, vertigo. **GI:** Nausea, vomiting, diarrhea, abdominal discomfort, indigestion, malaise. **Hematologic:** (Rare) <u>Agranulocytosis, aplastic anemia, bone marrow depression</u>, thrombocytopenia. **Skin:** Urticaria or pruritus, pruritic maculopapular rash, toxic epidermal necrolysis. **Other:** <u>Hepatotoxicity</u>, renal insufficiency.

DIAGNOSTIC TEST INTERFERENCE

Possibility of elevated blood levels of *alkaline phosphatase* and *serum transaminases (AST, ALT)*, and decreased blood *Hct, Hgb, leukocytes.*

INTERACTIONS Drug: Alcohol may inhibit renal excretion of uric acid; **ampicillin, amoxicillin** increase risk of skin rash; enhances anticoagulant effect of **warfarin;** toxicity from **azathioprine, mercaptopurine, cyclophosphamide, cyclosporin** increased; enhances hypoglycemic effects of **chlorpropamide**; THIAZIDES increase risk of allopurinol toxicity and hypersensitivity (especially with impaired renal function); ACE INHIBITORS increase risk of hypersensitivity; high dose vitamin C increases risk of kidney stone formation.

PHARMACOKINETICS Absorption:

80–90% from GI tract. **Onset:** 24–48 h. **Peak:** 2–6 h. **Metabolism:** 75–80% to the active metabolite oxypurinol. **Elimination:** Slowly excreted in urine; excreted in breast milk. **Half-Life:** 1–3 h; oxypurinol, 18–30 h.

CLINICAL IMPLICATIONS

Assessment & Drug Effects

- Monitor for therapeutic effectiveness which is indicated by normal

Common adverse effects in *italic*, life-threatening effects <u>underlined</u>; generic names in **bold**; classifications in SMALL CAPS; ♣ Canadian drug name; ⓟ Prototype drug

41

serum and urinary uric acid levels usually by 1–3 wk (aim of therapy is to lower serum uric acid level gradually to about 6 mg/dL), gradual decrease in size of tophi, absence of new tophaceous deposits (after approximately 6 mo), with consequent relief of joint pain and increased joint mobility.

- Monitor for S&S of an acute gouty attack which is most likely to occur during first 6 wk of therapy.
- Lab tests: Monitor serum uric acid levels q1–2wk to check adequacy of dosage. Perform baseline CBC, liver and kidney function tests before therapy is initiated and then monthly, particularly during first few months. Check urinary pH at regular intervals.
- Monitor patients with renal disorders more often; they tend to have a higher incidence of renal stones and drug toxicity problems.
- Report onset of rash or fever immediately to physician; withdraw drug. Life-threatening toxicity syndrome can occur 2–4 wk after initiation of therapy (more common with impaired renal function) and is generally accompanied by malaise, fever, and aching, a diffuse erythematous, desquamating rash, hepatic dysfunction, eosinophilia, and worsening of renal function.

Patient & Family Education

- Drink enough fluid to produce urinary output of at least 2000 mL/d (fluid intake of at least 3000 mL/d). (Note that 1000 mL is approximately equal to 1 quart.) Report diminishing urinary output, cloudy urine, unusual color or odor to urine, pain or discomfort on urination.
- Report promptly the onset of itching or rash. Stop drug if a skin rash appears, even after 5 or more wk (and reportedly as long as 2 y) of therapy.

- Minimize exposure of eyes to ultraviolet or sunlight which may stimulate the development of cataracts.
- Do not drive or engage in potentially hazardous activities until response to drug is known.
- Remain under medical supervision while taking allopurinol (generally continued indefinitely); drug can cause severe adverse reactions.

ALMOTRIPTAN
(al-mo-trip'tan)
Axert
Classifications: ADRENERGIC AGONIST; SEROTONIN 5-HT$_1$-RECEPTOR AGONIST
Therapeutic: ANTIMIGRAINE
Prototype: Sumatriptan
Pregnancy Category: C

AVAILABILITY 6.25 mg, 12.5 mg tablets

ACTION & THERAPEUTIC EFFECT
Selective agonist that binds with high affinity to serotonin receptors found on extracerebral and intracranial blood vessels. Due primarily to its effects on 5-HT$_{1D}$ and 5-HT$_{1B}$ serotonin receptors on cranial blood vessels, it causes vasoconstriction and decreases inflammation and neurotransmission. *Deactivation of the serotonin receptors results in constriction of cranial vessels that become dilated during a migraine attack and reduces signal transmission in the pain pathways.*

USES Treatment of migraine headache with or without aura.

CONTRAINDICATIONS Hypersensitivity to almotriptan malate. Significant cardiovascular disease such as ischemic heart disease, coronary artery vasospasms, MI, angina, arteriosclerosis, cardiac arrhythmias, diabetes mellitus, colitis, history of cerebrovascular events, or uncontrolled hypertension; stroke, smoking, Wolff-Parkinson-White syndrome, within 24 h of receiving another 5-HT$_1$ agonist or an ergotamine-containing or ergot-type drug; basilar or hemiplegic migraine.

CAUTIOUS USE Significant risk factors for coronary artery disease unless a cardiac evaluation has been done; hypertension; risk factors for cerebrovascular accident; peripheral vascular disease, impaired liver or kidney function, Raynaud's disease, children, elderly, pregnancy (category C), lactation.

ROUTE & DOSAGE

Migraine Headache
Adult: **PO** 6.25–12.5 mg. If headache returns, may repeat after at least 2 h (max: 2 tabs/24 h)
Renal Impairment
Cl$_{cr}$ <10 mL/min: 6.25 mg (max: 12.5 mg/d)
Hepatic Impairment
6.25 mg (max: 12.5 mg/d)

ADMINISTRATION

Oral

- Do not give within 24 h of an ergot-containing drug.
- Administer any time after symptoms of migraine appear.
- Do not administer a second dose without consulting the physician for any attack during which the FIRST dose did NOT work.
- Give a second dose if headache was relieved by first dose but symptoms return; however, wait at

least 2 h after the first dose before giving a second dose.
- Do not give more than two doses in 24 h.
- Store at 15°–30° C (59°–86° F).

ADVERSE EFFECTS (≥1%) **Body as a Whole:** Flushing. **CNS:** Drowsiness, headache, paresthesia. **CV:** Palpitations, tachycardia, serious cardiac events (including <u>MI</u>) have been reported within a few hours after administration. **GI:** Nausea, vomiting, dry mouth.

INTERACTIONS Drug: Dihydroergotamine, methysergide, other 5-HT$_1$ AGONISTS may cause prolonged vasospastic reactions; SSRIS, **sibutramine** have rarely caused weakness, hyperreflexia, and incoordination; MAOIS should not be used with 5-HT$_1$ AGONISTS.

PHARMACOKINETICS Absorption: Well absorbed, 70% reaches systemic circulation. **Peak:** 1–3 h. **Distribution:** 35% protein bound. **Metabolism:** 27% metabolized by monoamine oxidase. **Elimination:** 75% renally, 13% in feces. **Half-Life:** 3–4 h.

CLINICAL IMPLICATIONS

Assessment & Drug Effects

- Monitor cardiovascular status carefully following first dose in patients at relatively high risk for coronary artery disease (e.g., postmenopausal women, men over 40 years old, persons with known CAD risk factors) or who have coronary artery vasospasms.
- Report to physician immediately chest pain or tightness in chest or throat that is severe or does not quickly resolve following a dose of almotriptan.
- Pain relief usually begins within 10 min of ingestion, with com-

Common adverse effects in *italic*, life-threatening effects <u>underlined</u>; generic names in **bold**; classifications in SMALL CAPS; ✦ Canadian drug name; ◐ Prototype drug

43

plete relief in approximately 65% of all patients within 2 h.

- Monitor BP, especially in those being treated for hypertension.

Patient & Family Education

- Review patient information leaflet provided by the manufacturer carefully.
- Notify physician immediately if symptoms of severe angina (e.g., severe or persistent pain or tightness in chest, back, neck, or throat) or hypersensitivity (e.g., wheezing, facial swelling, skin rash, or hives) occur.
- Do not take any other serotonin receptor agonist (e.g., Imitrex, Maxalt, Zomig, Amerge) within 24 h of taking almotriptan.
- Advise physician of any drugs taken within 1 wk of beginning almotriptan.
- Check with physician regarding drug interactions before taking any new OTC or prescription drugs.
- Report any other adverse effects (e.g., tingling, flushing, dizziness) at next physician visit.

ALOSETRON

(a-lo'se-tron)

Lotronex

Classifications: SEROTONIN 5-HT₃ RECEPTOR ANTAGONIST

Therapeutic: SEROTONIN RECEPTOR ANTAGONIST; GI ANTIMOTILITY

Pregnancy Category: B

AVAILABILITY 1 mg tablets

ACTION & *THERAPEUTIC EFFECT*

Potent and selective serotonin (5-HT₃) receptor antagonist. Serotonin 5-HT₃ receptors are extensively located on enteric neurons of the GI tract. Activation of these receptors affects amount of visceral pain experienced, transit time in the colon, and GI secretions. *Blockage of the serotonin 5-HT₃ receptors by alosetron results in significant control of GI pain, and severe diarrhea related to irritable bowel syndrome.*

USES Treatment of severe irritable bowel syndrome (IBS) in women whose predominant symptom is diarrhea and whose symptoms have lasted >6 mo and have failed to respond to conventional therapy.

CONTRAINDICATIONS Constipation, ischemic colitis, development of ischemic bowel symptoms such as sudden onset of rectal bleeding, bloody diarrhea, new or sudden worsening of abdominal pain; history of chronic or severe constipation, intestinal obstruction, toxic megacolon, GI adhesions, GI perforation, active diverticulitis, history of, or current Crohn's disease or ulcerative colitis; hypersensitivity to alosetron; thrombophlebitis, hypercoagulable state, inability to comply with Patient–Physician Agreement.

CAUTIOUS USE Hepatic insufficiency, renal impairment; pregnancy (category B), lactation; elderly. Safety and efficacy in children are not established.

ROUTE & DOSAGE

Irritable Bowel Syndrome

Adult: **PO** Start with 1 mg q.d. for 4 wk, may increase to 1 mg b.i.d. if tolerated

ADMINISTRATION

Oral

- Ensure that the patient has signed the Patient–Physician Agreement prior to administering alosetron.
- Do not give this drug if the patient has constipation.

Common adverse effects in *italic*, life-threatening effects underlined; generic names in **bold**; classifications in SMALL CAPS; ♣ Canadian drug name; ⊙ Prototype drug

- Review the contraindications for this drug and ensure that the patient has none of the conditions for which the drug is contraindicated.
- Store at 25° C (77° F).

ADVERSE EFFECTS (≥1%) **Body as a Whole:** Malaise, fatigue, cramps, pain. **CNS:** Anxiety. **CV:** Tachyarrhythmias. **GI:** _Constipation_, abdominal pain, nausea, distention, reflux, hemorrhoids, hyposalivation, dyspepsia, ischemic colitis. **Skin:** Sweating, urticaria. **Urogenital:** Urinary frequency.

INTERACTIONS Drug: Fluvoxamine increases alosetron serum level.

PHARMACOKINETICS Absorption: Rapidly absorbed, average bioavailability of 50–60%. **Peak:** 1 h. **Distribution:** 82% protein bound. **Metabolism:** Extensively in liver by CYP2C9. **Elimination:** 73% in urine, 24% in feces. **Half-Life:** 1.5 h.

CLINICAL IMPLICATIONS
Assessment & Drug Effects
- Monitor for and report immediately signs of ischemic colitis such as new or worsening abdominal pain, bloody diarrhea, or blood in the stool.
- Withhold drug and notify physician if patient has not had adequate control of IBS symptoms after 4 weeks of treatment with 1 mg twice a day.
- Monitor carefully patients who have decreased GI motility (e.g., older adults, persons receiving other drugs which may decrease GI motility) as they may be at greater risk of serious complications of constipation.
- Monitor carefully patients with any degree of hepatic insufficiency as they may be more susceptible to adverse drug effects.

- Monitor periodically for cardiac arrhythmias, especially with preexisting cardiovascular disease.

Patient & Family Education
- Read the Medication Guide before starting alosetron and each time you refill your prescription.
- Do not start taking alosetron if you are constipated.
- Discontinue alosetron immediately and contact your physician if you experience any of the following: constipation, new or worsening abdominal pain, bloody diarrhea, or blood in the stool.
- Contact your physician immediately if constipation does not resolve after discontinuation of alosetron. Resume alosetron again only if constipation has resolved and your physician directs you to begin taking the medication again.
- Stop taking alosetron and contact your physician if IBS symptoms are not adequately controlled after 4 wk of taking 1 tablet twice a day.

ALPHA₁-PROTEINASE INHIBITOR (HUMAN) ℗

(pro'ten-ase)

Prolastin, Aralast, Zemaira
Classifications: ENZYME INHIBITOR
Therapeutic: ENZYME INHIBITOR
Pregnancy Category: C

AVAILABILITY Prolastin: 25 mg/mL; **Aralast:** 16 mg/mL; **Zemaira:** 50 mg/mL

ACTION & _THERAPEUTIC EFFECT_
Alpha₁-proteinase inhibitor (alpha₁-PI; alpha₁-antitrypsin) is extracted from plasma and used in patients with panacinar emphysema who have alpha₁-antitrypsin deficiency. Alpha₁-antitrypsin deficiency is a chronic, hereditary, and usually fa-

Common adverse effects in _italic_, life-threatening effects underlined; generic names in **bold**; classifications in SMALL CAPS; ♣ Canadian drug name; ℗ Prototype drug

45

tal autosomal recessive disorder that results in a slowly progressive, panacinar emphysema. *Prevents the progressive breakdown of elastin tissues in the alveoli, thus slowing panacinar emphysema progression.*

USES Indicated for chronic replacement therapy in patients with alpha₁-antitrypsin deficiency and demonstrable panacinar emphysema.

CONTRAINDICATIONS Individuals with selective IgA deficiencies; lactation.

CAUTIOUS USE Patients with significant heart disease or other conditions that may be aggravated with slight increases in plasma volume; pregnancy (category C). Safety and efficacy in children are not established.

ROUTE & DOSAGE

Panacinar Emphysema
Adult: **IV** 60 mg/kg once/wk administered at a rate of ≥0.08 mL/kg/min

ADMINISTRATION

Intravenous
Give hepatitis B vaccine prior to utilizing this drug.

PREPARE: **IV Infusion:** Warm unopened diluent and concentrate to room temperature. ▪ Reconstitute with sterile water for injection supplied by manufacturer to yield a concentration of 20 mg/mL.

ADMINISTER: **IV Infusion:** Give within 3 h after reconstitution. ▪ Give alone, without mixing with other agents. ▪ Administer at rate of at least 0.08 mL/kg/min. ▪ Note: The recommended dosage takes about 30 min to administer to a 70 kg person.

▪ Store unreconstituted drug at 2°–8° C (35°–46° F). Do not refrigerate after reconstitution. Discard unused solution.

ADVERSE EFFECTS (≥1%) **Hematologic:** Leukocytosis. **CNS:** Dizziness, fever (may be delayed). **Respiratory:** Upper and lower respiratory tract infections. **Other:** Hepatitis B if not immunized.

PHARMACOKINETICS Distribution: Crosses placenta; distributed into breast milk. **Metabolism:** Undergoes catabolism in the intravascular space; approximately 33% is catabolized per day. **Half-Life:** 4.5–5.2 d.

CLINICAL IMPLICATIONS

Assessment & Drug Effects
▪ Administer with caution in patients at risk for circulatory overload. Monitor cardiac status.
▪ Monitor respiratory status (rate, dyspnea, lung sounds) throughout therapy.
▪ Lab tests: Monitor serum alpha₁-PI level (minimum serum concentration level should be 80 mg/mL); periodic pulmonary functions and ABGs.

Patient & Family Education
▪ Avoid smoking and notify physician of any changes in respiratory pattern.

ALPRAZOLAM

(al-pray′zoe-lam)
Niravam, Xanax, Xanax XR
Classifications: ANXIOLYTIC; SEDATIVE-HYPNOTIC; BENZODIAZEPINE
Therapeutic: ANTIANXIETY; SEDATIVE-HYPNOTIC
Prototype: Lorazepam
Pregnancy Category: D
Controlled Substance: Schedule IV

Common adverse effects in *italic*, life-threatening effects underlined; generic names in **bold**; classifications in SMALL CAPS; ♣ Canadian drug name; ⓟ Prototype drug

AVAILABILITY 0.25 mg, 0.5 mg, 1 mg, 2 mg tablets; 0.5 mg, 1 mg, 2 mg, 3 mg sustained-release tabs; 0.5 mg/5 mL, 1 mg/mL oral solution; 0.25 mg, 0.5 mg, 1 mg, 2 mg orally disintegrating tabs

ACTION & *THERAPEUTIC EFFECT*

A CNS depressant that appears to act at the limbic, thalamic, and hypothalamic levels of the CNS. *Has antianxiety and sedative effects with addictive potential.*

USES Management of anxiety disorders or for short-term relief of anxiety symptoms. Also used as adjunct in management of anxiety associated with depression and agitation, and for panic disorders, such as agoraphobia.
UNLABELED USES Alcohol withdrawal.

CONTRAINDICATIONS Sensitivity to benzodiazepines; acute narrow angle glaucoma; pulmonary disease; use alone in primary depression or psychotic disorders, bipolar disorders, organic brain disorders; myasthenia gravis; pregnancy (category D), lactation; children <18 y.
CAUTIOUS USE Impaired hepatic function; history of alcoholism; renal impairment, hepatic disease; geriatric and debilitated patients. Effectiveness for long-term treatment (>4 mo) not established.

ROUTE & DOSAGE

Anxiety Disorders
Adult: PO 0.25–0.5 mg t.i.d. (max: 4 mg/d)
Geriatric: PO 0.125–0.25 mg b.i.d.

Panic Attacks
Adult: PO 1–2 mg t.i.d. (max: 8 mg/d); sustained release: initiate with 0.5 mg to 1 mg once/d.

Depending on the response, the dose may be increased at intervals of 3 to 4 days in increments of no more than 1 mg/d. Target range 3–6 mg/d (max: 10 mg/d).
Hepatic Impairment
Reduce dose by 50% in hepatic impairment. Do not discontinue abruptly.

ADMINISTRATION

Oral
- Reduce drug gradually when discontinuing drug.
- Store in light-resistant containers at 15°–30° C (59°–86° F), unless otherwise directed.

ADVERSE EFFECTS (≥1%) **CNS:** *Drowsiness, sedation,* light-headedness, dizziness, syncope, depression, headache, confusion, insomnia, nervousness, fatigue, clumsiness, unsteadiness, rigidity, tremor, restlessness, paradoxical excitement, hallucinations. **CV:** Tachycardia, hypotension, ECG changes. **Special Senses:** Blurred vision. **Respiratory:** Dyspnea.

INTERACTIONS Drug: Alcohol and other CNS DEPRESSANTS, ANTICONVULSANTS, ANTIHISTAMINES, BARBITURATES, NARCOTIC ANALGESICS, BENZODIAZEPINES, compound CNS depressant effects; **cimetidine, disulfiram, fluoxetine,** [TRICYCLIC ANTIDEPRESSANTS] increase alprazolam levels (decreased metabolism); ORAL CONTRACEPTIVES may increase or decrease alprazolam effects. **Herbal: Kava-kava, valerian** may potentiate sedation; **St. John's wort** decreases serum level of alprazolam. Cigarette smoking may decrease serum level of alprazolam by 50%.

PHARMACOKINETICS Absorption: Rapidly absorbed. **Peak:** 1–2 h. **Distribution:** Crosses placenta. **Metabo-**

Common adverse effects in *italic*, life-threatening effects underlined; generic names in **bold**; classifications in SMALL CAPS; ✦ Canadian drug name; ❂ Prototype drug

lism: Oxidized in liver to inactive metabolites by CYP3A4. **Elimination:** Renal elimination. **Half-Life:** 12–15 h.

CLINICAL IMPLICATIONS

Assessment & Drug Effects

- Monitor for S&S of drowsiness and sedation, especially in older adults or the debilitated; they may require supervised ambulation and/or side rails.
- Lab tests: Monitor periodic blood counts, urinalyses, and blood chemistry studies, particularly during continuing therapy.

Patient & Family Education

- Note: Adverse reactions that may occur during early high-dose therapy. These usually disappear with continuing therapy, but dosage adjustments may be indicated.
- Make position changes slowly and in stages to prevent dizziness.
- Do not use alcohol, other CNS depressants, or OTC medications containing antihistamines (e.g., sleep aids, cold, hay fever, or allergy remedies) without consulting physician.
- Do not drive or engage in potentially hazardous activities until response to drug is known.
- Taper dosage following continuous use; abrupt discontinuation of drug may cause withdrawal symptoms: nausea, vomiting, abdominal and muscle cramps, sweating, confusion, tremors, convulsions.

ALPROSTADIL (PGE₁)

(al-pross′ta-dil)
Prostin VR Pediatric, Caverject, Muse, Edex
Classifications: PROSTAGLANDIN
Therapeutic: PROSTAGLANDIN
Prototype: Epoprostenol
Pregnancy Category: C

AVAILABILITY 500 mcg/mL injection; 5 mcg/mL, 10 mcg/mL, 20 mcg/mL, 40 mcg/mL powder for injection; 125 mcg, 250 mcg, 500 mcg, 1000 mcg pellets

ACTION & *THERAPEUTIC EFFECT*

Preserves ductal patency by relaxing smooth muscle of ductus arteriosus. Alprostadil induces penile erection by relaxing the smooth muscles of the corpus cavernosum and dilating the cavernosal arteries and their penile arterioles. Sufficient rigidity of the penis also requires increased venous outflow resistance. *Preserves ductal patency by relaxing smooth muscle of ductus arteriosus. It induces penile rigidity and erection by penile blood engorgement.*

USES Temporary measure to maintain patency of ductus arteriosus in infants with ductal-dependent congenital heart defects until corrective surgery can be performed. Also used in erectile dysfunction.

CONTRAINDICATIONS Ductus arteriosus respiratory distress syndrome (hyaline membrane disease); neonates with respiratory distress syndrome; hypersensitivity to alprostadil; patients with penile implants. *Muse, Edex:* Women, children, and newborns; lactation. *Muse:* Patients with urethral stricture, inflammation/infection of glans of penis, severe hypospadias, acute or chronic urethritis; sickle cell anemia or trait, thrombocytopenia, thrombocytosis; polycythemia, multiple myeloma.

CAUTIOUS USE Ductus arteriosus; bleeding tendencies; cardiovascular disease; erectile dysfunction; hypersensitivity to alprostadil; leukemia;

Common adverse effects in *italic*, life-threatening effects <u>underlined</u>; generic names in **bold**; classifications in SMALL CAPS; ♣ Canadian drug name; ⊕ Prototype drug

penile anatomic deformations; patients on anticoagulants, vasoactive or antihypertensive drugs.

ROUTE & DOSAGE

To Maintain Patency of Ductus Arteriosus

Neonate: **IV/Intraarterial/ Intraaortic** 0.05–0.1 mcg/kg/ min, may increase gradually (max: 0.4 mcg/kg/min if necessary)

Erectile Dysfunction of Vasculogenic, Psychogenic, or Mixed Etiology

Adult: **Intracavernosal** initiate with 2.5 mcg; if inadequate response, increase dose by 2.5 mcg. May then increase dose in 5- to 10-mcg increments until a suitable erection occurs, not exceeding 1 h in duration. Doses >60 mcg not recommended

Erectile Dysfunction of Pure Neurogenic Etiology

Adult: **Intracavernosal** initiate with 1.25 mcg; if inadequate response, increase dose by 1.25 mcg, then increase by 2.5 mcg, may then increase dose in 5 mcg increments until a suitable erection occurs, not exceeding 1 h in duration. Doses >60 mcg not recommended

ADMINISTRATION

Intracavernosal Injection

- Administer only after proper training in the penile injection technique. Refer to information on administration provided to the patient by the manufacturer.
- Use reconstituted solutions immediately.
- Store dry powder at or below 25° C (77° F) for up to 3 mo. Do not freeze.

Transurethral Insertion

- Refer to information on insertion into the urethra provided to the patient by the manufacturer.

Intravenous

PREPARE: **Continuous:** Dilute 500 mcg alprostadil with NS or D5W to volume appropriate for pump delivery system. ▪ Prepare fresh solution q24h. Discard unused portions. ▪ A 500 mcg ampule diluted in 250 mL yields a concentration of 2 mcg/mL.

ADMINISTER: **Continuous:** Infuse at rate of 0.05–0.1 mcg/kg/min up to a maximum of 0.4 mcg/kg/min. Reduce infusion rate immediately if arterial pressure drops significantly or if fever occurs. ▪ Discontinue promptly, if apnea or bradycardia occurs.

- Store at 2°–8° C (36°–46° F) unless otherwise directed by manufacturer. Protect from freezing.

ADVERSE EFFECTS (≥1%) **CNS:** *Fever,* seizures, lethargy. **CV:** *Flushing,* bradycardia, hypotension, syncope, tachycardia; CHF, <u>ventricular fibrillation, shock</u>. **GI:** Diarrhea, gastric regurgitation. **Hematologic:** <u>Disseminated intravascular coagulation</u> (DIC), thrombocytopenia. **Respiratory:** Apnea. **Urogenital:** Oliguria, anuria. *Penile pain,* prolonged erection, priapism, penile fibrosis, injection site hematoma/ecchymosis, penile rash and edema, prostatitis, perineal pain. **Skin:** Rash on face and arms, alopecia. **Other:** Leg pain.

INTERACTIONS Drug: May increase anticoagulant properties of **warfarin;** ANTIHYPERTENSIVE AGENTS increase risk of hypotension.

PHARMACOKINETICS Onset: 15 min to 3 h. **Metabolism:** Rapidly in lungs. **Elimination:** Through kidneys. **Half-Life:** 5–10 min.

Common adverse effects in *italic*, life-threatening effects <u>underlined</u>; generic names in **bold**; classifications in SMALL CAPS; ◆ Canadian drug name; ☻ Prototype drug

49

CLINICAL IMPLICATIONS

Assessment & Drug Effects

Ductus Arteriosus

- Monitor therapeutic effectiveness which is indicated by increase in blood oxygenation (P_{O_2}), usually evident within 30 min, in infants with cyanotic heart disease (restricted pulmonary blood flow). Normal P_{O_2} for neonates is 60–70 mm Hg. Indicated by increased pH in those with acidosis, increased systemic BP and urinary output, return of palpable pulses, and decreased ratio of pulmonary artery to aortic pressure in infants with restricted systemic blood flow.
- Monitor for arterial pressure, ECG, heart rate, BP, respiratory rate, and rectal temperature, intermittently throughout the infusion.
- Lab tests: Monitor arterial blood gases and arterial blood pH intermittently throughout the infusion.
- Monitor: Systemic BP, pulmonary artery and descending aorta pressures, femoral pulse, and urinary output.

Patient & Family Education

Erectile Dysfunction

- Follow carefully directions for penile injection provided by the manufacturer.
- Do not change dose without consulting the physician.
- Do not use intracavernosal injection more often than 3 times/wk; allow at least 24 h between uses.
- Do not use more than 2 urethral suppository systems in a 24 h period.
- Report nodules or hard tissue in penis; penile pain, redness, swelling, tenderness; or curvature of the erect penis to the physician as soon as possible.
- Seek immediate medical attention if an erection persists longer than 6 h.

ALTEPLASE RECOMBINANT ⓟ

(al'te-plase)

Actilyse, Activase, Cathflo Activase

Classifications: THROMBOLYTIC ENZYME

Therapeutic: THROMBOLYTIC AGENT

Pregnancy Category: C

AVAILABILITY 50 mg, 100 mg vials

ACTION & *THERAPEUTIC EFFECT*

This recombinant DNA-derived form of human tissue-type plasminogen activator (t-PA) is a thrombolytic agent. The agent t-PA promotes thrombolysis by forming the active proteolytic enzyme plasmin. *Plasmin is capable of degrading fibrin, fibrinogen, and factors V, VIII, and XII.*

USES Indicated in selective cases of acute MI, preferably within 6 h of attack for recanalization of the coronary artery; lysis of acute pulmonary emboli; acute ischemic stroke or thrombotic stroke (within 3 h of onset); treatment of acute coronary artery thrombosis in the setting of percutaneous coronary intervention (PCI); reestablishing patency of occluded IV catheter.

UNLABELED USES Lysis of arterial occlusions in peripheral and bypass vessels; DVT.

CONTRAINDICATIONS Active internal bleeding, history of cerebrovascular accident, aneurysm, recent (within 2 mo) intracranial or interspinal surgery or trauma, intracranial neoplasm, increased intracranial pressure; arteriovenous malformation, bleeding disorders, severe uncontrolled hypertension, likelihood of left heart thrombus, acute pericarditis, bacterial endocarditis, severe liver or renal dys-

Common adverse effects in *italic*, life-threatening effects underlined; generic names in **bold**; classifications in SMALL CAPS; ♣ Canadian drug name; ⓟ Prototype drug

function, septic thrombophlebitis, current use of oral anticoagulants.

CAUTIOUS USE Recent major surgery (within 10 d), cerebral vascular disease, recent GI or GU bleeding, recent trauma, renal impairment, hypertension, pregnancy (category C), lactation, hemorrhagic ophthalmic conditions; age >75.

ROUTE & DOSAGE

Acute MI

Adult: **IV** ≥65 kg: 60 mg over first hour, with 6–10 mg infused over first 1–2 min; then 20 mg/h over the second hour and 20 mg over the third hour (100 mg over 3 h); <65 kg: Infuse 1.25 mg/kg over 3 h (60%, h1; 20%, h2; 20%, h3) *accelerated schedule (with heparin and aspirin),* 15-mg bolus, then 50 mg over 30 min, then 35 mg over 60 min

Acute Ischemic Stroke/Thrombotic Stroke

Adult: **IV** 0.9 mg/kg over 60 min with 10% of dose as an initial bolus over 1 min (max: 90 mg)

Pulmonary Embolism

Adult: **IV** 100 mg infused over 2 h
Child: **IV** 0.1–0.6 mg/kg/h × 6 h

Reopen Occluded IV Catheter

Adult/Child: **IV** >30 kg: Instill 2 mg/2 mL into dysfunctional catheter for 2 h. May repeat once if needed.
Child: **IV** >2 y, 10–29 kg: Instill 110% of internal lumen volume with 1 mg/mL concentration (max 2 mg). May repeat if function not restored within 2 h. **IV** <2 y, <10 kg: 0.5 mg diluted in a volume to fill the lumen of the catheter.

ADMINISTRATION

Intravenous

PREPARE: **IV Infusion:** Reconstitute the 50-mg vial as follows: Do not use if vacuum in vial has been broken. Use a large-bore needle (e.g., 18 gauge) and do not prime needle with air. ▪ Dilute contents of vial with sterile water for injection supplied by manufacturer. ▪Direct stream of sterile water into the lyophilized cake. Slight foaming is usual. Allow to stand until bubbles dissipate. Resulting concentration is 1 mg/mL. ▪Reconstitute the 100-mg vial as follows: The 100-mg vial does not contain a vacuum. Use supplied transfer device for reconstitution and follow manufacturer's directions.

ADMINISTER: **IV Infusion:** Start IV infusion as soon as possible after the thrombolytic event, preferably within 6 h. ▪Administer drug as reconstituted (1 mg/mL) or further diluted with an equal volume of NS or D5W to yield 0.5 mg/mL. **Acute MI:** Administer 60% of total dose in the first hour for acute MI, with 6–10% given as a bolus dose over 1–2 min and remainder of first dose infused over hour 1. Follow with second dose (20% of total) over hour 2, and third dose (20% of total) over hour 3. ▪For patients weighing <65 kg calculate dose using 1.25 mg/kg over 3 h. See accelerated schedule under Route & Dosage. **Pulmonary embolism:** ▪ Administer entire dose over a 2 h period. **Acute ischemic stroke:** Give 5 mg as an initial bolus over 1 min, then give the remainder of the 0.75 mg/kg dose over 60 min. ▪Do not exceed a total dose of 100 mg. Higher doses have been

Common adverse effects in *italic*, life-threatening effects underlined; generic names in **bold**; classifications in SMALL CAPS; ♣ Canadian drug name; ♦ Prototype drug

51

associated with intracranial bleeding. ▪Follow infusion of drug by flushing IV tubing with 30–50 mL of NS or D5W. ▪Reconstituted drug is stable for 8 h in above solutions at room temperature (2°–30° C; 36°–86° F). Since there are no preservatives, discard any unused solution after that time.

▪ Store above reconstituted solutions at room temperature 2°–30° C (36°–86° F) for no longer than 8 h. Discard any unused solution after that time.

ADVERSE EFFECTS (≥1%) **Hematologic:** Internal and superficial bleeding (cerebral, retroperitoneal, GU, GI).

PHARMACOKINETICS Peak: 5–10 min after infusion completed. **Duration:** Baseline values restored in 3 h. **Metabolism:** In liver. **Elimination:** In urine. **Half-Life:** 26.5 min.

CLINICAL IMPLICATIONS

Assessment & Drug Effects

▪ Monitor for S&S of excess bleeding q15min for the first hour of therapy, q30min for second to eighth hour, then q8h. Monitor neurological checks throughout drug infusion q30min and qh for the first 8 h after infusion.

▪ Protect patient from invasive procedures because spontaneous bleeding occurs twice as often with alteplase as with heparin. IM injections are contraindicated. Also prevent physical manipulation of patient during thrombolytic therapy to prevent bruising.

▪ Lab tests: Coagulation tests including APTT, bleeding time, PT, TT, INR, must be done before administration of drug. Also check *baseline* Hct, Hgb, and platelet counts, in case of bleeding. Draw

Hct following drug administration to detect possible blood loss.

▪ Keep patient in bed while receiving this medication.

▪ Check vital signs frequently. Be alert to changes in cardiac rhythm.

▪ Stop therapy immediately if dysrhythmias occur.

▪ Report signs of bleeding: gum bleeding, epistaxis, hematoma, spontaneous ecchymoses, oozing at catheter site, increased pain from internal bleeding. Stop the infusion, then resume when bleeding stops.

▪ Use the radial artery to draw ABGs. Pressure to puncture sites, if necessary, should be maintained for up to 30 min.

▪ Continue monitoring vital signs until laboratory reports confirm anticoagulant control; patient is at risk for postthrombolytic bleeding for 2–4 d after intracoronary alteplase treatment.

Patient & Family Education

▪ Report immediately a sudden severe headache.

▪ Report blood in urine and bloody or tarry stools.

▪ Report any signs of bleeding or oozing from cuts or places of injection.

▪ Remain quiet and on bedrest while receiving this medicine.

ALTRETAMINE, HEXAMETHYLMELAMINE

(al-tre′ta-meen)

Hexalen

Classifications: ANTINEOPLASTIC; ALKYLATING AGENT

Therapeutic: ANTINEOPLASTIC

Prototype: Cyclophosphamide

Pregnancy Category: D

AVAILABILITY 50 mg capsules

ACTION & *THERAPEUTIC EFFECT*

Altretamine is a synthetic cytotoxic antineoplastic drug. It is metabolized to metabolites with cytotoxic properties. *Altretamine has demonstrated neoplastic activity in patients resistant to alkylating agents.*

USES Ovarian cancer.
UNLABELED USES Breast, cervical, colon, endometrial, head, and neck cancer; small-cell lung cancers and lymphomas.

CONTRAINDICATIONS Hypersensitivity to altretamine, severe bone marrow depression, neurologic toxicity, neurologic disease; intramuscular injections, pregnancy (category D), lactation.
CAUTIOUS USE Safety and efficacy in children are not established. History of viral infections, i.e., herpes simplex; radiation therapy.

ROUTE & DOSAGE

Ovarian Cancer
Adult: **PO** 260 mg/m²/d for 14 or 21 consecutive d in a 28-d cycle

ADMINISTRATION

Oral
- Give only under supervision of a qualified physician experienced in the use of antineoplastics.
- Give in 4 divided doses after meals and at bedtime.
- Discontinue altretamine for 14 d or longer and restart at 200 mg/m²/d if any of the following occur: severe GI intolerance; WBC count <2000/mm³, granulocyte count <1000/mm³; or progressive neurotoxicity.
- Store at room temperature, 15°–30° C (59°–86° F).

ADVERSE EFFECTS (≥1%) **CNS:** *Paresthesias, hyporeflexia, muscle weakness, peripheral numbness, ataxia, Parkinson-like tremors.* **GI:** *Nausea, vomiting.* **Hematologic:** Leukopenia, thrombocytopenia. **Urogenital:** Slight increase in serum creatinine. **Skin:** Alopecia and eczema.

INTERACTIONS Drug: Concomitant administration of altretamine and TRICYCLIC ANTIDEPRESSANTS (**imipramine, amitriptyline**), MONOAMINE OXIDASE INHIBITORS, or **selegiline** have been reported to result in incapacitating dizziness and syncopal episodes during the first week of altretamine treatment. Patients became asymptomatic 24–96 h after discontinuing ANTIDEPRESSANTS.

PHARMACOKINETICS Absorption: Rapidly from GI tract. Approximately 25% reaches systemic circulation due to extensive hepatic first-pass metabolism. **Metabolism:** Rapidly demethylated in the liver. **Elimination:** 62% of the dose is excreted in the urine in 24 h. A small amount is excreted through the lungs. **Half-Life:** 13 h.

CLINICAL IMPLICATIONS

Assessment & Drug Effects
- Lab tests: Monitor blood counts at least monthly and prior to each course of therapy.
- Perform a neurologic examination regularly; question patient about the presence of: paresthesias, hypoesthesias, muscle weakness, peripheral numbness, ataxia, decreased sensations, and alterations in mood or consciousness.
- Withhold medication if neurologic symptoms fail to resolve with dose reduction. Notify physician.
- Monitor for nausea and vomiting, which are related to the cumula-

---

Common adverse effects in *italic*, life-threatening effects <u>underlined</u>; generic names in **bold**; classifications in SMALL CAPS; ♣ Canadian drug name; ⊕ Prototype drug

tive dose of altretamine. After several weeks some patients develop tolerance to the GI effects. Antiemetics may be required to control GI distress.

Patient & Family Education

▪Taking altretamine after meals or with food or milk may decrease nausea.

▪Report symptoms indicative of neurotoxicity to physician (paresthesias, hypoesthesias, muscle weakness, peripheral numbness, ataxia, decreased sensations, and alterations in mood or consciousness).

▪Note: GI, hematologic, and neurologic adverse effects may be severe.

ALUMINUM HYDROXIDE ℗ℛ

(a-lu′mi-num)
ALternaGEL, Alu-Cap, Alugel, Alu-Tab, Amphojel, Dialume

ALUMINUM CARBONATE, BASIC

Basaljel

ALUMINUM PHOSPHATE

Phosphaljel

Classifications: ANTACID; ADSORBENT
Therapeutic: ANTACID
Pregnancy Category: C

AVAILABILITY Aluminum Hydroxide: 300 mg, 400 mg, 500 mg, 600 mg tablets; 300 mg, 400 mg, 500 mg, 600 mg capsules; 320 mg/5 mL, 450 mg/5 mL, 600 mg/5 mL, 675 mg/5 mL suspension **Aluminum Carbonate, Basic:** 608 mg tablets; 608 mg capsules; 400 mg/5 mL suspension **Aluminum Phosphate:** 608 mg tablets; 608 mg capsules; 400 mg/5 mL suspension

ACTION & *THERAPEUTIC EFFECT*

Nonsystemic antacid with moderate neutralizing action. Reduces acid concentration and pepsin activity by raising pH of gastric and intraesophageal secretions. *Reduces gastric acidity by neutralizing the stomach acid content. Aluminum carbonate lowers serum phosphate by binding dietary phosphate to form insoluble aluminum phosphate, which is excreted in feces.*

USES Symptomatic relief of gastric hyperacidity associated with gastritis, esophageal reflux, and hiatal hernia; adjunct in treatment of gastric and duodenal ulcer. More commonly used in combination with other antacids. Aluminum carbonate is used primarily in conjunction with a low phosphate diet to reduce hyperphosphatemia in patients with renal insufficiency and for prophylaxis and treatment of phosphatic renal calculi.

CONTRAINDICATIONS Prolonged use of high doses in presence of low serum phosphate.
CAUTIOUS USE Renal impairment; pregnancy (category C); gastric outlet obstruction; older adults; decreased bowel activity (e.g., patients receiving anticholinergic, antidiarrheal, or antispasmodic agents); patients who are dehydrated or on fluid restriction.

ROUTE & DOSAGE

Antacid (hydroxide & phosphate)
Adult: **PO** 600 mg t.i.d. or q.i.d.
Antacid (carbonate)
Adult: **PO** 10–30 mL of regular suspension or 5–15 mL of extra strength suspension or 2 capsules or tablets q2h

Common adverse effects in *italic*, life-threatening effects underlined; generic names in **bold**; classifications in SMALL CAPS; ♣ Canadian drug name; ℗Prototype drug

Phosphate Lowering (carbonate)

Adult: **PO** 10–30 mL of regular suspension or 5–15 mL of extra strength suspension or 2–6 capsules or tablets 1 h p.c. and h.s.

ADMINISTRATION

Oral

- Tablet must be chewed until it is thoroughly wetted before swallowing.
- Note for antacid use: Follow well-chewed tablet with one-half glass of water or milk; follow liquid preparation (suspension) with water to ensure passage into stomach. For phosphate lowering: follow tablet, capsule, or suspension with full glass of water or fruit juice.
- Store between 15°–30° C (59°–86° F) in tightly closed container.

ADVERSE EFFECTS (≥1%) **GI:** *Constipation*, fecal impaction, intestinal obstruction. **CNS:** Dialysis dementia (thought to be due to aluminum intoxication). **Metabolic:** Hypophosphatemia, hypomagnesemia.

INTERACTIONS Drug: Aluminum will decrease absorption of **chloroquine, cimetidine, ciprofloxacin, digoxin, isoniazid,** IRON SALTS, NSAIDS, **norfloxacin, ofloxacin, phenytoin, phenothiazines, quinidine, tetracycline, thyroxine. Sodium polystyrene sulfonate** may cause systemic alkalosis.

PHARMACOKINETICS Absorption: Minimal absorption. **Peak:** Slow onset. **Duration:** 2 h when taken with food; 3 h when taken 1 h after food. **Elimination:** In feces as insoluble phosphates.

CLINICAL IMPLICATIONS

Assessment & Drug Effects

- Note number and consistency of stools. Constipation is common

and dose related. Intestinal obstruction from fecal concretions has been reported.

- Lab tests: Monitor periodic serum calcium and phosphorus levels with prolonged high-dose therapy or impaired renal function.

Patient & Family Education

- Increase phosphorus in diet when taking large doses of these antacids for prolonged periods; hypophosphatemia can develop within 2 wk of continuous use of these antacids. The older adult in a poor nutritional state is at high risk.
- Note: Antacid may cause stools to appear speckled or whitish.
- Report epigastric or abdominal pain; it is a clinical guide for adjusting dosage. Keep physician informed. Pain that persists beyond 72 h may signify serious complications.
- Seek medical help if indigestion is accompanied by shortness of breath, sweating, or chest pain, if stools are dark or tarry, or if symptoms are recurrent when taking this medication.
- Seek medical advice and supervision if self-prescribed antacid use exceeds 2 wk.

AMANTADINE HYDROCHLORIDE ℗

(a-man′ta-deen)
Symmetrel

Classifications: ANTIVIRAL; ANTICHOLINERGIC; ANTIPARKINSON AGENT
Therapeutic: ANTIVIRAL; ANTIPARKINSON AGENT
Pregnancy Category: C

AVAILABILITY 100 mg capsules; 50 mg/5 mL syrup

Common adverse effects in *italic*, life-threatening effects underlined; generic names in **bold**; classifications in SMALL CAPS; ♣ Canadian drug name; ❷ Prototype drug

55

ACTION & *THERAPEUTIC EFFECT*
Because it does not suppress antibody formation, it can be administered for interim protection in combination with influenza A virus vaccine until antibody titer is adequate or to augment prophylaxis in a previously vaccinated individual. Mechanism of action in parkinsonism may be related to release of dopamine and other catecholamines from neuronal storage sites. *Active against several strains of influenza A virus; not effective against influenza B infections.*

USES In initial therapy or as adjunct with anticholinergic drugs or levodopa in treatment of all forms of parkinsonism (arteriosclerotic, idiopathic, postencephalitic) and for relief of drug-induced extrapyramidal reactions and symptomatic parkinsonism caused by carbon monoxide poisoning. Also used for prophylaxis and symptomatic treatment of influenza A infections.

UNLABELED USES Primary enuresis, pseudosclerosis, neuroleptic malignant syndrome (NMS), management of cocaine dependency and withdrawal.

CONTRAINDICATIONS Safety in children <1 y is not established. Lactation; amantadine or rimantadine hypersensitivity, closed angle glaucoma; suicidal ideation.

CAUTIOUS USE History of epilepsy or other types of seizures; CHF, peripheral edema, orthostatic hypotension; recurrent eczematoid dermatitis; psychoses, severe psychoneuroses; hepatic disease; renal impairment; pregnancy (category C); older adults with cerebral arteriosclerosis.

ROUTE & DOSAGE

Influenza A
Adult: **PO** 200 mg once/d or 100 mg q12h
Child: **PO** 1–9 y, 4.4–8.8 mg/kg in 2–3 equal doses (max: 150 mg/d)

Parkinsonism
Adult: **PO** 100 mg 1–2 times/d, start with 100 mg/d if patient is on other antiparkinsonism medications

Drug-Induced Extrapyramidal Symptoms
Adult: **PO** 100 mg b.i.d. (max: 400 mg/d if needed)

Renal Impairment
Cl_{cr} 40–60 mL/min: 100 mg/d; 30–40 mL/min: 200 mg 2 times/wk; 10–20 mL/min: 100 mg 3 times/wk

ADMINISTRATION

Oral
▪ Give with water, milk, or food.
▪ Use supplied calibrated device for measuring syrup formulation.
▪ Influenza prophylaxis: Drug should be initiated when exposure is anticipated and continued for at least 10 d.
▪ Note: Used in conjunction with influenza A vaccine (generally in high-risk patients who have not been vaccinated previously) until protective antibodies develop (10–21 d) after vaccine administration.
▪ Schedule medication in the morning or, with q12h dosing, schedule 2nd dose several hours before bedtime. If insomnia is a problem, suggest patient limit number of daytime naps.
▪ Store in tightly closed container preferably at 15°–30° C (59°–86° F) unless otherwise directed by manufacturer. Avoid freezing.

Common adverse effects in *italic*, life-threatening effects underlined; generic names in **bold**; classifications in SMALL CAPS; ✚ Canadian drug name; ❂ Prototype drug

ADVERSE EFFECTS (≥1%) **CNS:** *Dizziness, light-headedness,* headache, ataxia, irritability, anxiety, *nervousness, difficulty in concentrating,* mood or other mental changes, confusion, visual and auditory hallucinations, *insomnia,* nightmares, convulsions. **CV:** Orthostatic hypotension, peripheral edema, dyspnea. **Special Senses:** Blurring or loss of vision. **GI:** Anorexia, *nausea,* vomiting, dry mouth. **Hematologic:** Leukopenia.

INTERACTIONS Drug: Alcohol enhances CNS effects; may potentiate effects of ANTICHOLINERGICS.

PHARMACOKINETICS Absorption: Almost completely absorbed from GI tract. **Onset:** Within 48 h. **Peak:** 1–4 h. **Distribution:** Through body fluids. **Metabolism:** Not metabolized. **Elimination:** 90% unchanged in urine. **Half-Life:** 9–37 h (prolonged in renal insufficiency).

CLINICAL IMPLICATIONS

Assessment & Drug Effects

- Monitor effectiveness. Note that with parkinsonism, maximum response occurs within 2 wk–3 mo. Effectiveness may wane after 6–8 wk of treatment; report change to physician.
- Monitor and report: Mental status changes; nervousness, difficulty concentrating, or insomnia; loss of seizure control; S&S of toxicity, especially with doses above 200 mg/d.
- Establish a baseline profile of the patient's disabilities to accurately differentiate disease symptoms and drug-induced neuropsychiatric adverse reactions.
- Monitor vital signs for at least 3 or 4 d after increases in dosage; also monitor urinary output.
- Lab tests: pH and serum electrolytes.

- Monitor for and report reduced salivation, increased akinesia or rigidity, and psychological disturbances that may develop within 4–48 h after initiation of therapy and after dosage increases with parkinsonism.

Patient & Family Education

- Note: For influenza take within 24 h but no later than 48 h after onset of symptoms for effective response and continue for 24–48 h after symptoms disappear; contact physician if no improvement within this time.
- Make all position changes slowly, particularly from recumbent to upright position, in order to minimize dizziness.
- Report any of the following to physician: Shortness of breath, peripheral edema, significant weight gain, dizziness or light-headedness, inability to concentrate, and other changes in mental status, difficulty urinating, and visual impairment.
- Do not drive and exercise caution with potentially hazardous activities until response to the drug is known.
- Note: People with Parkinson's disease should not discontinue therapy abruptly; doing so may precipitate a parkinsonian crisis with severe akinesia, rigidity, tremor, and psychic disturbances. Adhere to established dosage regimen.

AMBENONIUM CHLORIDE

(am-be-noe′nee-um)

Mytelase

Classifications: CHOLINESTERASE INHIBITOR

Therapeutic: CHOLINESTERASE INHIBITOR

Prototype: Neostigmine

Pregnancy Category: C

Common adverse effects in *italic*, life-threatening effects <u>underlined</u>; generic names in **bold**; classifications in SMALL CAPS; ♣ Canadian drug name; ❷ Prototype drug

57

AVAILABILITY 10 mg tablets

ACTION & *THERAPEUTIC EFFECT*
Inhibits destruction of acetylcholine (ACh) by cholinesterase, thereby prolonging effects of ACh (neurotransmitter) at postsynaptic receptor sites. Has direct stimulant effect on striated muscles. *Improves the muscular strength in myasthenia gravis.*

USES Symptomatic treatment of myasthenia gravis for patients who cannot tolerate neostigmine bromide or pyridostigmine bromide because of bromide sensitivity. Has been used in conjunction with corticosteroids, ephedrine sulfate, and potassium chloride to increase muscle strength.

CONTRAINDICATIONS Intestinal or urinary tract obstruction; patients receiving mecamylamine; lactation. **CAUTIOUS USE** Epilepsy, bradycardia, cardiac arrhythmias, recent coronary occlusion; bronchial asthma; hyperthyroidism; older adults; pregnancy (category C); vagotonia; peptic ulcer, megacolon.

ROUTE & DOSAGE

Myasthenia Gravis
Adult: **PO** 2.5–5 mg t.i.d. or q.i.d., may increase q1–2d to 50–75 mg t.i.d. or q.i.d. if necessary
Child: **PO** 0.3 mg/kg/d in 3–4 divided doses, may need up to 1.5 mg/kg/d in 3–4 divided doses

ADMINISTRATION

Oral
- Give with food or milk to minimize adverse effects.
- Schedule larger doses when patient experiences the most fatigue or muscle weakness; to improve ability to eat, give drug 30–45 min before meals.
- Store at 15°–30° C (59°–86° F) unless otherwise directed.

ADVERSE EFFECTS (≥1%) **CNS:** Exaggerated cholinergic (muscarinic) effects; muscle cramps, headache, confusion, dizziness, incoordination, fasciculations, agitation, restlessness, muscle weakness, paralysis, slurred speech, convulsions, respiratory depression. **CV:** Bradycardia. **GI:** Nausea, vomiting, diarrhea, abdominal cramps, excessive salivation. **Special Senses:** Blurred vision, lacrimation. **Respiratory:** Bronchospasm, increased bronchial secretions, dyspnea. **Other:** Diaphoresis.

INTERACTIONS Drug: Demecarium and other CHOLINESTERASE INHIBITORS possibly compound toxicity; **mecamylamine, succinylcholine, procainamide, quinidine,** AMINOGLYCOSIDES increase neuromuscular blocking effects with possibility of respiratory depression; atropine antagonizes effects of ambenonium.

PHARMACOKINETICS Absorption: Poorly absorbed from GI tract. **Onset:** 20–30 min. **Duration:** 3–8 h.

CLINICAL IMPLICATIONS

Assessment & Drug Effects
- Therapeutic effect may not be apparent for several days after initiation of therapy.
- Keep atropine sulfate immediately available to treat severe cholinergic reactions.
- Monitor for S&S of overdosage (muscle weakness within 1 h; headache, weakness of muscles of neck, chewing, and swallowing, increased salivation) and inadequate ventilation (unusual apprehension, restlessness, rapid pulse and respirations, rising BP).

- Monitor vital signs during dosage adjustment periods.
- Note: Muscle weakness beginning 3 h or more after drug administration is probably due to underdosage or drug resistance.

Patient & Family Education
- Follow directions for taking this drug (see ADMINISTRATION).
- Learn to recognize adverse effects, how to modify the doses accordingly, and when to take atropine.
- Note: During long-term therapy the drug may become ineffective; responsiveness usually returns when dosage is reduced or drug is withdrawn for several days.
- Carry medical identification indicating medical diagnosis and medication(s) being taken.

AMCINONIDE

(am-sin′oh-nide)
Pregnancy Category: C
See Appendix A-4.

AMIFOSTINE

(am-i-fos′teen)
Ethyol
Classifications: CYTOPROTECTIVE AGENT
Therapeutic: CYTOPROTECTIVE AGENT
Pregnancy Category: C

AVAILABILITY 500 mg vial

ACTION & *THERAPEUTIC EFFECT*
Amifostine reduces cytotoxic damage induced by radiation or antineoplastic agents in well-oxygenated cells. Protective effects appear to be mediated by the formation of a metabolite of amifostine that removes free radicals from normal cells exposed to cisplatin. *Amifostine is cytoprotective in the kidney, bone marrow, and GI mucosa, but not in the brain or spinal cord. The cytoprotection results in decreased myelosuppression and peripheral neuropathy.*

USES Reduction of the cumulative renal toxicity associated with cisplatin, xerostomia.
UNLABELED USES Reduction of paclitaxel toxicity.

CONTRAINDICATIONS Sensitivity to aminothiol compounds or mannitol, patients with potentially curable malignancies, hypotensive patients or those who are dehydrated, lactation; exfoliated dermatitis.
CAUTIOUS USE Patients at risk for hypocalcemia, cardiovascular disease (i.e., arrhythmias, CHF, TIA, CVA); pregnancy (category C), radiation therapy; renal disease.

ROUTE & DOSAGE

Renal Protection
Adult: **IV** 910 mg/m^2 once daily
Reduction of Xerostomia
Adult: **IV** 200 mg/ m^2 prior to therapy

ADMINISTRATION

Intravenous
Give antiemetics, adequately hydrate, and defer antihypertensives for 24 h prior to administration.

PREPARE: **IV Infusion:** Reconstitute IV solution by adding 9.7 mL of NS injection to a single-dose vial.
ADMINISTER: **IV Infusion:** Infuse over no more than 15 min, beginning 30 min before chemotherapy; place patient in supine position prior to and during infusion.

Common adverse effects in *italic*, life-threatening effects underlined; generic names in **bold**; classifications in SMALL CAPS; ♣ Canadian drug name; ❷ Prototype drug

59

INCOMPATIBILITIES **Solution/Additive:** Do not mix with any solutions other than NS.

▪ Store reconstituted solution at 15°–30° C (59°–86° F) for 5 h or refrigerate up to 24 h.

ADVERSE EFFECTS (≥1%) **CV:** *Transient reduction in blood pressure.* **GI:** *Nausea, vomiting.* **Other:** Infusion reactions (flushing, feeling of warmth or coldness, chills, dizziness, somnolence, hiccups, sneezing), hypocalcemia, hypersensitivity reactions.

INTERACTIONS Drug: No clinically significant interactions established.

PHARMACOKINETICS Onset: 5–8 min. **Metabolism:** In liver to active free thiol metabolite. **Elimination:** Renally excreted. **Half-Life:** 8 min.

CLINICAL IMPLICATIONS

Assessment & Drug Effects

▪ Monitor for S&S of hypocalcemia and fluid balance if vomiting is significant.

▪ Monitor BP every 5 min during infusion. Stop infusion if systolic BP drops significantly from baseline (e.g., baseline[drop]: <100[20], 100–119[25], 120–139[30], 140–179[40], >180[50]) and place patient flat with legs raised. Restart infusion if BP returns to normal in 5 min.

Patient & Family Education

▪ Know and understand adverse effects.

AMIKACIN SULFATE

(am-i-kay′sin)
Amikin
Classifications: AMINOGLYCOSIDE ANTIBIOTIC
Therapeutic: ANTIBIOTIC
Prototype: Gentamicin
Pregnancy Category: C

AVAILABILITY 250 mg/mL, 50 mg/mL injection

ACTION & *THERAPEUTIC EFFECT*
Appears to inhibit protein synthesis in bacterial cells and is usually bactericidal. *Effective against a wide range of gram-negative bacteria, including many strains resistant to other aminoglycosides. Also effective against penicillinase- and non-penicillinase-producing* Staphylococcus.

USES Primarily for short-term treatment of serious infections of respiratory tract, bones, joints, skin, and soft tissue, CNS (including meningitis), peritonitis burns, recurrent urinary tract infections (UTIs).

UNLABELED USES Intrathecal or intraventricular administration, in conjunction with IM or IV dosage.

CONTRAINDICATIONS History of hypersensitivity or toxic reaction with an aminoglycoside antibiotic; lactation.

CAUTIOUS USE Impaired renal function; eighth cranial (auditory) nerve impairment; preexisting vertigo or dizziness, tinnitus, or dehydration; fever; older adults, premature infants, neonates and infants; pregnancy (category C); myasthenia gravis; parkinsonism; hypocalcemia.

ROUTE & DOSAGE

Moderate to Severe Infections
Adult: **IV/IM** 5–7.5 mg/kg loading dose, then 7.5 mg/kg q12h
Child: **IV/IM** 5–7.5 mg/kg loading dose, then 5 mg/kg q8h or 7.5 mg/kg q12h
Neonate: **IV/IM** 10 mg/kg loading dose, then 7.5 mg/kg q12–24h
Uncomplicated UTI
Adult: **IV/IM** 250 mg q12h
Obesity
Calculate dose based on IBW.

Renal Impairment
Extend the interval: 40–60 mL/min q12h; 20–40 mL/min q24h; *Dialysis:* Administer dose post-dialysis

ADMINISTRATION

Intramuscular
- Use the 250 mg/mL vials for IM injection. Calculate the required dose and withdraw the equivalent number of mLs from the vial.
- Give deep IM into a large muscle.

Intravenous
Verify correct IV concentration and rate of infusion with physician for neonates, infants, and children.

PREPARE: Intermittent: Add contents of 500 mg vial to 100 or 200 mL D5W, NS injection, or other diluent recommended by manufacturer. ▪ For pediatric patients, volume of diluent depends on patient's fluid tolerance. ▪ Note: Color of solution may vary from colorless to light straw color or very pale yellow. Discard solutions that appear discolored or that contain particulate matter.

ADMINISTER: Intermittent: Give a single adult dose (including loading dose) over at least 30–60 min by IV infusion. ▪ Increase infusion time to 1–2 h for infants. ▪ Monitor drip rate carefully. A rapid rise in serum amikacin level can cause respiratory depression (neuromuscular blockade) and other signs of toxicity.

INCOMPATIBILITIES **Solution/additive: Aminophylline, amphotericin B,** CEPHALOSPORINS, **chlorothiazide, erythromycin, heparin, oxytetracycline,** PENICILLINS, **phenytoin, thiopental, vitamin B complex with C, warfarin. Y-site: Amphoteri-**

cin B, azithromycin, heparin, phenytoin, thiopental.
- Store at 15°–30° C (59°–86° F) unless otherwise directed.

ADVERSE EFFECTS (≥1%) **CNS:** Neurotoxicity: drowsiness, unsteady gait, weakness, clumsiness, paresthesias, tremors, convulsions, peripheral neuritis. **Special Senses:** *Auditory–ototoxicity,* high-frequency hearing loss, complete hearing loss (occasionally permanent); tinnitus; ringing or buzzing in ears; *Vestibular:* dizziness, ataxia. **GI:** Nausea, vomiting, hepatotoxicity. **Metabolic:** Hypokalemia, hypomagnesemia. **Skin:** Skin rash, urticaria, pruritus, redness. **Urogenital:** Oliguria, urinary frequency, hematuria, tubular necrosis, azotemia. **Other:** Superinfections.

INTERACTIONS Drug: ANESTHETICS, SKELETAL MUSCLE RELAXANTS have additive neuromuscular blocking effects; **acyclovir, amphotericin B, bacitracin, capreomycin, cephalosporins, colistin, cisplatin, carboplatin, methoxyflurane, polymyxin B, vancomycin, furosemide, ethacrynic acid** increase risk of ototoxicity and nephrotoxicity.

PHARMACOKINETICS Peak: 30 min IV; 45 min to 2 h IM. **Distribution:** Does not cross blood–brain barrier; crosses placenta; accumulates in renal cortex. **Elimination:** 94–98% renally in 24 h, remainder in 10–30 d. **Half-Life:** 2–3 h in adults, 4–8 h in neonates.

CLINICAL IMPLICATIONS

Assessment & Drug Effects
- Baseline tests: Before initial dose, C&S; renal function and vestibulocochlear nerve function (and at regular intervals during therapy; closely monitor in the older adult,

---

Common adverse effects in *italic*, life-threatening effects underlined; generic names in **bold**; classifications in SMALL CAPS; ✚ Canadian drug name; ⦿ Prototype drug

61

patients with documented ear problems, renal impairment, or during high dose or prolonged therapy).

- Monitor peak and trough amikacin blood levels: Draw blood 1 h after IM or immediately after completion of IV infusion; draw trough levels immediately before the next IM or IV dose.
- Lab tests: Periodic serum creatinine and BUN, complete urinalysis. With treatment over 10 d, daily tests of renal function, weekly audiograms, and vestibular tests are strongly advised.
- Monitor serum creatinine or creatinine clearance (generally preferred) more often, in the presence of impaired renal function, in neonates, and in the older adult; note that prolonged high trough (>8 mcg/mL) or peak (>30–35 mcg/mL) levels are associated with toxicity.
- Monitor S&S of ototoxicity [primarily involves the cochlear (auditory) branch; high-frequency deafness usually appears first and can be detected only by audiometer]; indicators of declining renal function; respiratory tract infections and other symptoms indicative of superinfections and notify physician should they occur.
- Monitor for and report auditory symptoms (tinnitus, roaring noises, sensation of fullness in ears, hearing loss) and vestibular disturbances (dizziness or vertigo, nystagmus, ataxia).
- Monitor & report any changes in I&O, oliguria, hematuria, or cloudy urine. Keeping patient well hydrated reduces risk of nephrotoxicity; consult physician regarding optimum fluid intake.

Patient & Family Education

- Report immediately any changes in hearing or unexplained ringing/roaring noises or dizziness, and problems with balance or coordination.

AMILORIDE HYDROCHLORIDE

(a-mill′oh-ride)
Midamor

Classifications: DIURETIC, POTASSIUM-SPARING
Therapeutic: DIURETIC, POTASSIUM-SPARING; ANTIHYPERTENSIVE
Prototype: Spironolactone
Pregnancy Category: B

AVAILABILITY 5 mg tablets

ACTION & *THERAPEUTIC EFFECT*
Potassium-sparing diuretic with mild diuretic and antihypertensive action. Diuretic action is independent of aldosterone and carbonic anhydrase. *Induces urinary excretion of sodium and reduces excretion of potassium and hydrogen ions by direct action on distal renal tubules, thus lowering blood pressure.*

USES Potassium-sparing effect in prevention or treatment of diuretic-induced hypokalemia in patients with CHF, hepatic cirrhosis, or hypertension. Also used in management of primary hyperaldosteronism. Usually combined with a potassium-wasting (kaliuretic) diuretic such as a thiazide or loop diuretic.

UNLABELED USES With hydrochlorothiazide for recurrent calcium nephrolithiasis, lithium-induced polyuria.

CONTRAINDICATIONS Elevated serum potassium (>5.5 mEq/L), concomitant use of other potassium-sparing diuretics; anuria, acute or chronic renal insufficiency; evidence of diabetic nephropathy; type 1 diabetes mellitus; metabolic or respiratory acidosis; lactation. Safety in children is not established.

CAUTIOUS USE Debilitated patients; diet-controlled or uncontrolled diabetes mellitus; cardiopulmonary disease; pregnancy (category C); hepatic disease; older adult.

ROUTE & DOSAGE

Diuretic

Adult: **PO** 5 mg/d, may increase up to 20 mg/d in 1–2 divided doses

ADMINISTRATION

Oral
- Give once/d dose in the morning and schedule the second b.i.d. dose early to avoid interrupting sleep.
- Give with food to reduce possibility of gastric distress.
- Store at 15°–30° C (59°–86° F) in a tightly closed container unless otherwise directed.

ADVERSE EFFECTS (≥1%) **Body as a Whole:** Generally well tolerated. **CNS:** *Headache,* dizziness, nervousness, confusion, paresthesias, drowsiness. **CV:** Cardiac arrhythmias. **Metabolic:** Hyperkalemia, hyponatremia, positive Coombs' test. **Hematologic:** <u>Aplastic anemia</u>. **Special Senses:** Tinnitus; nasal congestion. Visual disturbances, increased intraocular pressure. **GI:** *Diarrhea* or constipation, anorexia, *nausea,* vomiting, abdominal cramps, dry mouth, thirst. **Urogenital:** Polyuria, dysuria, bladder spasms, urinary frequency, impotence, decreased libido. **Respiratory:** Dyspnea, shortness of breath. **Skin:** Rash, pruritus, photosensitivity reactions. **Other:** Weakness, fatigue, muscle cramps.

DIAGNOSTIC TEST INTERFERENCE

Manufacturer advises discontinuing amiloride in patients with dia-

betes mellitus at least 3 d before *glucose tolerance* test.

INTERACTIONS Drug: Blood from blood banks, ACE INHIBITORS (e.g., **captopril**), **spironolactone, triamterene,** POTASSIUM SUPPLEMENTS may cause hyperkalemia with cardiac arrhythmias; possibility of increased **lithium** toxicity (decreased renal elimination); possibility of altered **digoxin** response; NSAIDs may attenuate antihypertensive effects. **Food:** POTASSIUM-CONTAINING SALT SUBSTITUTES or foods high in potassium increase risk of hyperkalemia.

PHARMACOKINETICS Absorption: 50% from GI tract. **Onset:** 2 h. **Peak:** 6–10 h. **Duration:** 24 h. **Elimination:** 20–50% unchanged in urine, 40% in feces. **Half-Life:** 6–9 h.

CLINICAL IMPLICATIONS

Assessment & Drug Effects
- Monitor for S&S of hyperkalemia and hyponatremia (see Appendix F). Hyperkalemia occurs in about 10% of patients receiving amiloride and serum potassium can rise suddenly and without warning. It is more common in older adults and patients with diabetes or renal disease.
- Lab tests: Serum potassium levels, particularly when therapy is initiated, whenever dosage adjustments are made, and during any illness that may affect kidney function. Intermittent evaluations of BUN, creatinine, and ECG for patients with renal or hepatic dysfunction, diabetes mellitus, older adults, or the debilitated.

Patient & Family Education
- Learn S&S of hyperkalemia and hyponatremia (see Appendix F) and report to physician immediately.
- Do not take potassium supplements, salt substitutes, high intake

Common adverse effects in *italic,* life-threatening effects <u>underlined</u>; generic names in **bold**; classifications in SMALL CAPS; ✚ Canadian drug name; ⊕ Prototype drug

63

of dietary potassium unless prescribed by physician.
- Do not drive or engage in potentially hazardous activities until response to drug is known.

AMINOCAPROIC ACID ℗

(a-mee-noe-ka-proe'ik)
Amicar
Classifications: COAGULATOR; HEMOSTATIC
Therapeutic: COAGULATOR; ANTIHEMORRHAGIC; ANTIFIBRINOLYTIC
Pregnancy Category: C

AVAILABILITY 250 mg/mL injection; 500 mg tablets; 250 mg/mL syrup

ACTION & *THERAPEUTIC EFFECT*
Synthetic hemostatic with specific antifibrinolysis action. Inhibits plasminogen activator substance, and to a lesser degree plasmin (fibrinolysin), which is concerned with destruction of clots. *Acts as an inhibitor of fibrinolytic bleeding.*

USES To control excessive bleeding resulting from systemic hyperfibrinolysis, a pathologic condition that may accompany heart surgery, portocaval shunt, abruptio placentae, aplastic anemia, and carcinoma of lung, prostate, cervix, and stomach. Also used in urinary fibrinolysis associated with severe trauma, anoxia, shock, urologic surgery, and neoplastic diseases of GU tract.

UNLABELED USES To prevent hemorrhage in hemophiliacs undergoing dental extraction; as a specific antidote for streptokinase or urokinase toxicity; to prevent recurrence of subarachnoid hemorrhage, especially when surgery is delayed; for management of amegakaryocytic thrombocytopenia; and to prevent or abort hereditary angioedema episodes.

CONTRAINDICATIONS Severe renal impairment; active disseminated intravascular clotting (DIC); upper urinary tract bleeding (hematuria); hemophilia; benzyl alcohol hypersensitivity, especially in neonates; paraben hypersensitivity; lactation.
CAUTIOUS USE Cardiac, renal, or hepatic disease; renal impairment; history of pulmonary embolus or other thrombotic diseases; hypovolemia, pregnancy (category C).

ROUTE & DOSAGE

Hemostatic
Adult: **PO/IV** 4–5 g during first hour, then 1–1.25 g qh for 8 h or until bleeding is controlled (max: 30 g/24h)
Child: **PO/IV** 100 mg/kg during first hour, then 33.3 mg/kg qh (max: 18 g/m²/24 h)

ADMINISTRATION

Oral
- Note: May need to give patient as many as 10 tablets or 4 tsp for a 5 g dose during the first hour of treatment (each tablet contains 500 mg, syrup contains 250 mg/mL).

Intravenous

***PREPARE:* IV Infusion:** Dilute parenteral aminocaproic acid before use. Each 4 mL (1 g) is diluted with 50 mL of NS, D5W, or RL.
***ADMINISTER:* IV Infusion:** Physician orders specific IV flow rate. • Usual rate is 5 g or a fraction thereof over first hour (5 g/250 mL). • Give each additional gram over 1 h. Avoid rapid infusion to prevent hypotension, faintness, and bradycardia or other arrhythmias.

- Store in tightly closed containers at 15°–30° C (59°–86° F) un-

Common adverse effects in *italic*, life-threatening effects underlined; generic names in **bold**; classifications in SMALL CAPS; ♣ Canadian drug name; ℗ Prototype drug

less otherwise directed. Avoid freezing.

ADVERSE EFFECTS (≥1%) **CNS:** Dizziness, malaise, headache, seizures. **CV:** Faintness, orthostatic hypotension; dysrhythmias; thrombophlebitis, thromboses. **Special Senses:** Tinnitus, nasal congestion. Conjunctival erythema. **GI:** Nausea, vomiting, cramps, diarrhea, anorexia. **Urogenital:** Diuresis, dysuria, urinary frequency, oliguria, reddish-brown urine (myoglobinuria), acute renal failure. Prolonged menstruation with cramping. **Skin:** Rash.

DIAGNOSTIC TEST INTERFERENCE *Serum potassium* may be elevated (especially in patients with impaired renal function).

INTERACTIONS Drug: ESTROGENS, ORAL CONTRACEPTIVES may cause hypercoagulation.

PHARMACOKINETICS Absorption: Rapidly from GI tract. **Peak:** 2 h. **Distribution:** Readily penetrates RBCs and other body cells. **Elimination:** 80% as unmetabolized drug in 12 h.

CLINICAL IMPLICATIONS
Assessment & Drug Effects
- Check IV site at frequent intervals for extravasation.
- Observe for signs of thrombophlebitis. Change site immediately if extravasation or thrombophlebitis occurs (see Appendix F).
- Monitor & report S&S of myopathy: muscle weakness, myalgia, diaphoresis, fever, reddish-brown urine (myoglobinuria), oliguria, as well as thrombotic complications: arm or leg pain, tenderness or swelling, Homan's sign, prominence of superficial veins, chest pain, breathlessness, dyspnea. Drug should be discontinued promptly.

- Monitor vital signs and urine output.
- Lab tests: with prolonged therapy, monitor creatine phosphokinase activity and urinalyses for early detection of myopathy.

Patient & Family Education
- Report difficulty urinating or reddish-brown urine.
- Report arm or leg pain, chest pain, or difficulty breathing.

AMINOGLUTETHIMIDE

(a-mee-noe-gloo-teth′i-mide)
Cytadren
Classifications: ANTINEOPLASTIC AROMATASE INHIBITOR
Therapeutic: ANTINEOPLASTIC
Prototype: Anastozole
Pregnancy Category: D

AVAILABILITY 250 mg tablets

ACTION & *THERAPEUTIC EFFECT*
Blocks adrenal corticosteroid biosynthesis by inhibiting enzymatic conversion of cholesterol to precursors of cortisol and aldosterone in the adrenal glands. Also blocks aromatase, thereby preventing conversion of androgens to estrogens in peripheral tissues. *Because estrogens are supplied principally by the adrenals in postmenopausal and oophorectomized women, aminoglutethimide-induced lowering of plasma estrogen levels (by adrenal suppression) is reportedly as effective as that produced by surgical adrenalectomy.*

USES Temporary treatment of selected patients with Cushing's syndrome associated with adrenal carcinoma, ectopic ACTH-producing tumors, or adrenal hyperplasia.
UNLABELED USES To produce medical adrenalectomy in postmen-

Common adverse effects in *italic*, life-threatening effects underlined; generic names in **bold**; classifications in SMALL CAPS; ♣ Canadian drug name; ● Prototype drug

65

opausal women with positive estrogen receptor test, metastatic breast cancer, or who fail or relapse with tamoxifen, and for patients with prostatic carcinoma.

CONTRAINDICATIONS Hypothyroidism; infection. Safety during pregnancy (category D), lactation, and in children is not established. **CAUTIOUS USE** Older adults.

ROUTE & DOSAGE

Cushing's Disease
Adult: **PO** 250 mg q6h, may be increased 250 mg/d q1–2wk if needed (max: 2 g/d)

Breast Cancer
Adult: **PO** 250 mg b.i.d. and hydrocortisone 60 mg h.s., 20 mg in a.m., and 20 mg at 2 p.m. daily for 2 wk, then 250 mg q.i.d. and hydrocortisone 20 mg h.s., 10 mg in a.m., and 10 mg at 2 p.m. thereafter

ADMINISTRATION
Oral
- Note: For breast cancer, 40 mg of hydrocortisone daily, in divided doses is usually ordered to be given concurrently.
- Store at 15°–30° C (59°–86° F) in tightly closed containers unless otherwise directed.

ADVERSE EFFECTS (≥1%) **CNS:** Lethargy, drowsiness, *dizziness,* uncontrolled eye movements (dose related); clumsiness, *headache.* **CV:** *Hypotension, tachycardia.* **Endocrine:** Masculinization. **GI:** Nausea, vomiting, anorexia, hepatotoxicity. **Hematologic:** (Rare) Neutropenia, leukopenia, thrombocytopenia, pancytopenia, agranulocytosis, decreased Hgb and Hct, anemia, Coombs' negative hemolytic anemia. **Skin:** *Measles-like (morbilliform) rash,* pruritus.

INTERACTIONS Drug: Dexamethasone decreases pharmacologic effects of aminoglutethimide; decreases anticoagulant response to **warfarin**.

PHARMACOKINETICS Onset: 3–5 d. **Distribution:** Crosses placenta. **Metabolism:** In liver. **Elimination:** By kidneys; recovery of adrenal responsiveness to stress occurs 36–72 h after discontinuation. **Half-Life:** 13 h (7 h with long-term use).

CLINICAL IMPLICATIONS
Assessment & Drug Effects
- Monitor & report S&S of: Adrenal insufficiency or hypothyroidism (see Appendix F); in older adults, CNS effects (e.g., lethargy, ataxia, orthostatic dizziness, lightheadedness).
- Lab tests: Baseline & periodic fasting plasma cortisol levels, periodic CBC with differential, serum electrolytes, serum alkaline phosphate, liver functions, and thyroid function.
- Monitor BP in the recumbent and upright positions to evaluate fluid volume status and presence of orthostatic hypotension.
- Note: Dose reduction or temporary discontinuation may be indicated by: extreme drowsiness, severe skin rash, extremely low cortisol levels.
- Note: Patients with Cushing's syndrome may show reduced effect with continuing therapy and generally are not treated beyond 3 mo with this drug.

Patient & Family Education
- Change positions gradually, pausing between each change. Do not stand still for prolonged periods.

- Note: Lethargy, drowsiness, dizziness, and other adverse effects often disappear during the first few weeks of therapy. Inform physician if adverse effects persist or become bothersome.
- Report skin rash that persists beyond 5–8 d.
- Contact physician immediately in times of physical and emotional distress (e.g., acute illness, dental work). Steroid supplements may be indicated.
- Do not drive or engage in potentially hazardous activities until response to drug is known.
- Carry medical identification indicating medical diagnosis, medication(s), physician's name, address, and telephone number.
- Notify physician immediately if pregnancy is suspected.

AMINOPHYLLINE (theophylline ethylenediamide)

(am-in-off'i-lin)

Corophyllin ♦, Paladron ♦, Truphylline

Classifications: BRONCHODILATOR; XANTHINE

Therapeutic: BRONCHODILATOR (RESPIRATORY SMOOTH MUSCLE RELAXANT)

Prototype: Theophylline

Pregnancy Category: C

AVAILABILITY 100 mg, 200 mg tablets; 105 mg/5 mL oral liquid; 25 mg/mL injection; 250 mg, 500 mg suppositories

ACTION & *THERAPEUTIC EFFECT*

A xanthine derivative that relaxes smooth muscle in the airways of the lungs and suppresses the response of the airways to stimuli that constrict them. Aminophylline is a salt of theophylline with effects similar to those of other xanthines (e.g., caffeine and theobromine). Action is dependent on theophylline content (approximately 80%) and is measured as theophylline in the serum. *It is a respiratory smooth muscle relaxant that results in bronchodilation.*

USES To prevent and relieve symptoms of acute bronchial asthma and treatment of bronchospasm associated with chronic bronchitis and emphysema.

UNLABELED USES As a respiratory stimulant in Cheyne-Stokes respiration; for treatment of apnea and bradycardia in premature infants; as cardiac stimulant and diuretic in treatment of CHF.

CONTRAINDICATIONS Hypersensitivity to xanthine derivatives or to ethylenediamine component; cardiac arrhythmias; lactation.

CAUTIOUS USE Severe hypertension, cardiac disease, arrhythmias; impaired hepatic function; diabetes mellitus; hyperthyroidism; glaucoma; prostatic hypertrophy; fibrocystic breast disease; history of peptic ulcer; neonates and young children, patients over 55 y; pregnancy (category C); COPD, acute influenza or patients receiving influenza immunization.

ROUTE & DOSAGE

Bronchospasm

Adult: **IV Loading Dose** 6 mg/kg over 30 min **IV Maintenance Dose** *nonsmoker,* 0.5 mg/kg/h; *smoker,* 0.8 mg/kg/h; *CHF or cirrhosis,* 0.1–0.2 mg/kg/h **PO** *nonsmoker,* 0.5 mg/kg/h times 24 h in 4 divided doses; *smoker,* 0.75 mg/kg/h times 24 h in 4 divided doses; *CHF or cirrhosis,*

Common adverse effects in *italic*, life-threatening effects underlined; generic names in **bold**; classifications in SMALL CAPS; ♦ Canadian drug name; ⊙ Prototype drug

67

0.25 mg/kg/h times 24 h in 4 divided doses
Child: **IV Loading Dose** 6 mg/kg IV over 30 min **IV Maintenance Dose** 1–9 y, 1 mg/kg/h; >9 y, 0.8 mg/kg/h **PO** 1–9 y, 1 mg/kg/h times 24 h in 4 divided doses; >9 y, 0.75 mg/kg/h times 24 h in 4 divided doses
Infant: **PO/IV** 6–11 mo, 0.7 g/kg/h; 2–6 mo, 0.5 mg/kg/h

Neonatal Apnea
Neonate: **PO/IV Loading Dose** 5 mg/kg **PO/IV Maintenance Dose** 5 mg/kg/d divided q12h

ADMINISTRATION

▪ Note: All doses based on ideal body weight.

Oral

▪ Give with a full glass of water on an empty stomach ($\frac{1}{2}$–1 h before or 2 h after meals) for faster absorption, which is delayed but is not reduced with food.

▪ Minimize GI symptoms by taking immediately after a meal or with food.

▪ Do not chew or crush extended (controlled) release preparations before swallowing; however, if tablet is scored, it can be broken in half, then swallowed.

▪ Do mix contents of extended release capsules with soft, moist food to promote swallowing.

Suppository

▪ Note: Rectal preparations may be ordered when patient must fast or cannot tolerate the drug orally; absorption is enhanced if rectum is empty.

Intravenous

Verify correct IV concentration and rate of infusion with physician for neonates, infants, and children.

PREPARE: **IV Infusion:** Dilute loading dose in 100–200 mL NS, D5W, D5/NS, or RL. For continuous or intermittent infusion dilute in 500–1000 mL. ▪ Do not use aminophylline solutions if discolored or if crystals are present.

ADMINISTER: **IV Infusion:** Infuse at a rate not to exceed 25 mg/min.

INCOMPATIBILITIES Solution/additive: **amikacin, bleomycin,** CEPHALOSPORINS, **chlorpromazine, ciprofloxacin, clindamycin, codeine phosphate, dimenhydrinate, dobutamine, dopamine, doxapram, doxorubicin, epinephrine, hydralazine, hydroxyzine, insulin, isoproterenol, levorphanol, meperidine, methadone, methylprednisolone, morphine, nafcillin, norepinephrine, oxytetracycline, papaverine, penicillin G, pentazocine, procaine, prochlorperazine, promazine, promethazine, tetracycline, verapamil, vitamin B complex with C.** Y-site: **amiodarone, codeine phosphate, ciprofloxacin, clindamycin,** PHENOTHIAZINES (**chlorpromazine, prochlorperazine,** etc.), **epinephrine, dobutamine, dopamine, levorphanol, morphine, meperidine, methadone, norepinephrine, verapamil.**

▪ Store at 15°–30° C (59°–86° F) in tightly closed containers unless otherwise directed. ▪ Follow manufacturer's directions regarding storage of suppositories; some can be stored at room temperature; others must be refrigerated.

ADVERSE EFFECTS (≥1%) CNS:
Nervousness, restlessness, depression, insomnia, irritability, head-

ache, dizziness, muscle hyperactivity, convulsions. **CV:** Cardiac arrhythmias, tachycardia (with rapid IV), hyperventilation, chest pain, <u>severe hypotension, cardiac arrest</u>. **GI:** *Nausea, vomiting, anorexia,* hematemesis, diarrhea, epigastric pain.

INTERACTIONS Drug: Increases **lithium** excretion, lowering **lithium** levels; **cimetidine,** high-dose **allopurinol** (600 mg/d), **ciprofloxacin, erythromycin, troleandomycin** can significantly increase **theophylline** levels.

PHARMACOKINETICS Absorption: Most products are 100% absorbed from GI tract. **Peak:** IV 30 min; uncoated tablet 1 h; sustained release 4–6 h. **Duration:** 4–8 h; varies with age, smoking, and liver function. **Distribution:** Crosses placenta. **Metabolism:** Extensively in liver; by CYP1A2. **Elimination:** Parent drug and metabolites excreted by kidneys; excreted in breast milk. **Half-Life:** 3.7 h (child); 7.7 h (adult).

CLINICAL IMPLICATIONS

Assessment & Drug Effects

- Monitor for S&S of toxicity (generally related to theophylline serum levels over 20 mcg/mL). Observe patients receiving parenteral drug closely for signs of hypotension, arrhythmias, and convulsions until serum theophylline stabilizes within the therapeutic range.
- Note: High incidence of toxicity is associated with rectal suppository use due to erratic rate of absorption.
- Monitor & record vital signs and I&O. A sudden, sharp, unexplained rise in heart rate may indicate toxicity.

- Lab tests: Monitor serum theophylline levels.
- Note: Older adults, acutely ill, and patients with severe respiratory problems, liver dysfunction, or pulmonary edema are at greater risk of toxicity due to reduced drug clearance.
- Note: Children appear more susceptible to CNS stimulating effects of xanthines (nervousness, restlessness, insomnia, hyperactive reflexes, twitching, convulsions). Dosage reduction may be indicated.

Patient & Family Education

- Note: Use of tobacco tends to increase elimination of this drug (shortens half-life), necessitating higher dosage or shorter intervals than in nonsmokers.
- Report excessive nervousness or insomnia. Dosage reduction may be indicated.
- Note: Dizziness is a relatively common side effect, particularly in older adults; take necessary safety precautions.
- Do not take OTC remedies for treatment of asthma or cough unless approved by physician.

AMINOSALICYLIC ACID (PARA-AMINOSALICYLIC ACID)

(a-mee-noe-sal-i-sil'ik)
Paser
Classifications: ANTITUBERCULOSIS AGENT
Therapeutic: ANTITUBERCULOSIS AGENT
Prototype: Isoniazid
Pregnancy Category: C

AVAILABILITY 4 g packets

ACTION & THERAPEUTIC EFFECT
Aminosalicylic acid and salts are

Common adverse effects in *italic*, life-threatening effects <u>underlined</u>; generic names in **bold**; classifications in SMALL CAPS; ♣ Canadian drug name; ⊕ Prototype drug

69

highly specific bacteriostatic agents that suppress growth and multiplication of *Mycobacterium tuberculosis* by preventing folic acid synthesis. Their mechanism of action resembles that of sulfonamides. Aminosalicylates also reportedly have potent hypolipemic action. *Aminosalicylates are an effective antiinfective alone or in combined therapy and reduce serum cholesterol and triglycerides by lowering LDL and VLDL.*

USES With streptomycin or isoniazid or both in treatment of pulmonary and extrapulmonary tuberculosis to delay drug resistance.
UNLABELED USES Documented for lipid-lowering effect.

CONTRAINDICATIONS Hypersensitivity to aminosalicylates, salicylates, or to compounds containing *para*-aminophenyl groups (e.g., sulfonamides, certain hair dyes), G6PD deficiency, use of the sodium salt in patients on sodium restriction or CHF; lactation.
CAUTIOUS USE Impaired renal and hepatic function; pregnancy (category C), blood dyscrasias; goiter; gastric ulcer.

ROUTE & DOSAGE

Tuberculosis
Adult: **PO** 10–12 g/d in 2–3 divided doses
Child: **PO** 150–300 mg/kg/d in 3–4 divided doses

ADMINISTRATION

Oral
- Give with or immediately following meals to reduce irritative gastric effects. Physician may order an antacid to be given concomitantly. Generally, GI adverse ef-

fects disappear after a few days of therapy.
- Store in tight, light-resistant containers in a cool, dry place, preferably at 15°–30° C (59°–86° F), unless otherwise directed.

ADVERSE EFFECTS (≥1%) **Body as a Whole:** Fever, chills, generalized malaise, joint pain, rash, fixed-drug eruptions; pruritus; vasculitis; Loeffler's syndrome. **CNS:** Psychotic reactions. **GI:** *Anorexia, nausea, vomiting, abdominal distress, diarrhea,* peptic ulceration, acute hepatitis, malabsorption. **Hematologic:** Leukopenia, <u>agranulocytosis</u>, eosinophilia, lymphocytosis, thrombocytopenia, <u>hemolytic anemia</u>; (G6PD deficiency), prothrombinemia. **Urogenital:** Renal (irritation), crystalluria. **Other:** With long-term administration, goiter.

DIAGNOSTIC TEST INTERFERENCE
Aminosalicylates may interfere with urine **urobilinogen** determinations (using **Ehrlich's reagent**), and may cause false-positive **urinary protein** and **VMA** determinations (with **diazoreagent**); false-positive **urine glucose** may result with **cupric sulfate tests,** e.g., **Benedict's solution,** but reportedly not with **glucose oxidase reagents,** e.g., **TesTape, Clinistix.** Reduces **serum cholesterol,** and possibly **serum potassium, serum PBI,** and 24-hour **I-131 thyroidal uptake** (effect may last almost 14 d).

INTERACTIONS Drug: Increases hypoprothrombinemic effects of ORAL ANTICOAGULANTS; increased risk of crystalluria with **ammonium chloride, ascorbic acid;** decreased intestinal absorption of **cyanocobalamin, folic acid, digoxin;** ANTIHISTAMINES may inhibit PAS absorption; may increase or decrease

Common adverse effects in *italic*, life-threatening effects <u>underlined</u>; generic names in **bold**; classifications in SMALL CAPS; ✦ Canadian drug name; Ⓟ Prototype drug

phenytoin levels; **probenecid, sulfinpyrazone** decrease PAS elimination.

PHARMACOKINETICS Absorption:
Almost completely from GI tract; sodium form more rapidly absorbed than the acid. **Peak:** 1.5–2 h. **Duration:** 4 h. **Distribution:** Well distributed to tissue and body fluids except CSF unless meninges are inflamed. **Metabolism:** In liver. **Elimination:** >80% in urine in 7–10 h. **Half-Life:** 1 h.

CLINICAL IMPLICATIONS

Assessment & Drug Effects
- Monitor for abrupt onset of fever, particularly during the early weeks of therapy, and clinical picture resembling that of infectious mononucleosis (malaise, fatigue, generalized lymphadenopathy, splenomegaly, sore throat), as well as minor complaints of pruritus, joint pains, and headache, which strongly suggest hypersensitivity; report these symptoms promptly.
- Monitor I&O and encourage fluids. High concentrations of drug are excreted in urine, and this can cause crystalluria and hematuria.
- Note: To minimize crystalluria, keep urine neutral or alkaline with adjunctive drugs, such as antacids or with diet.

Patient & Family Education
- Rinse mouth with clear water or chew sugar-free gum or candy to relieve the mildly sour or bitter aftertaste of aminosalicylic acid.
- Note: Hypersensitivity reactions may occur after a few days, but most commonly in the fourth or fifth week; report promptly.
- Notify physician if sore throat or mouth, malaise, unusual fatigue, bleeding or bruising occurs (symptoms of blood dyscrasia).

- Note: Therapy generally lasts about 2 y. Adhere to the established drug regimen, and remain under close medical supervision to detect possible adverse drug effects during the treatment period. Resistant TB strains develop more rapidly when drug regimen is interrupted or is sporadic.
- Note: Urine may turn red on contact with bleach used in commercial toilet bowl cleaners.
- Do not take aspirin or other OTC drugs without physician's approval.
- Discard drug if it discolors (brownish or purplish); this signifies decomposition.

AMIODARONE HYDROCHLORIDE 🅟

(a-mee′oh-da-rone)
Cordarone, Amio-Aqueous, Pacerone
Classifications: ANTIARRHYTHMIC, CLASS III
Therapeutic: ANTIARRHYTHMIC, CLASS III
Pregnancy Category: D

AVAILABILITY 200 mg tablets; 50 mg/mL injection

ACTION & *THERAPEUTIC EFFECT*
Class III antiarrhythmic; also has antianginal and antiadrenergic properties. Acts directly on all cardiac tissues by prolonging duration of action potential and refractory period without significantly affecting resting membrane potential. *By direct action on smooth muscle, decreases peripheral resistance and increases coronary blood flow. Blocks effects of sympathetic stimulation.*

USES Prophylaxis and treatment of life-threatening ventricular arrhyth-

Common adverse effects in *italic*, life-threatening effects underlined; generic names in **bold**, classifications in SMALL CAPS; ◆ Canadian drug name; 🅟 Prototype drug

71

mias and supraventricular arrhythmias, particularly with atrial fibrillation.

UNLABELED USES Treatment of nonexertional angina, conversion of atrial fibrillation to normal sinus rhythm, paroxysmal supraventricular tachycardia, ventricular rate control due to accessory pathway conduction in pre-excited atrial arrhythmia, after defibrillation and epinephrine in cardiac arrest, AV nodal reentry tachycardia.

CONTRAINDICATIONS Hypersensitivity to amiodarone, or benzyl alcohol; cardiogenic shock, severe sinus bradycardia, advanced AV block unless a pacemaker is available, severe sinus-node dysfunction or sick sinus syndrome, bradycardia, congenital or acquired QR prolongation syndromes, or history of torsade de pointes; severe liver disease, pregnancy (category D), lactation.

CAUTIOUS USE Hepatic disease, cirrhosis; Hashimoto's thyroiditis, goiter, thyrotoxicosis, or history of other thyroid dysfunction; CHF, left ventricular dysfunction; hypersensitivity to iodine; older adults; Fabry disease, especially with visual disturbances; electrolyte imbalance, hypokalemia, hypomagnesemia, hypovolemia; preexisting lung disease, COPD; open heart surgery.

ROUTE & DOSAGE

Arrhythmias

Adult: **PO Loading Dose** 800–1600 mg/d in 1–2 doses for 1–3 wk **PO Maintenance Dose** 400–600 mg/d in 1–2 doses **IV Loading Dose** 150 mg over 10 min followed by 360 mg over next 6 h **IV Maintenance Dose** 540 mg over 18 h (0.5 mg/min), may continue at 0.5 mg/min **Convert IV to PO** Duration of infusion <1

wk use 800–1600 mg PO, 1–3 wk use 600–800 mg PO, >3 wk use 400 mg PO
Child: **PO Loading Dose** 10–15 mg/kg/d or 600–800 mg/1.73 m²/d, in 1–2 divided doses for 4–14 d cycle or until adequate control of arrhythmia **PO Maintenance Dose** 5 mg/kg/d or 200–400 mg/1.73 m²/d once daily, may be able to reduce to 2–5 mg/kg/d 5 d per week **IV Loading Dose** 5 mg/kg over 30 min **IV Maintenance Dose** 2–20 mg/kg/d

Hepatic Impairment

Adjustment only suggested in severe hepatic impairment.

ADMINISTRATION

- Note: Correct hypokalemia and hypomagnesemia prior to initiation of therapy.

Oral

- Give consistently with respect to meals.
- Note: Only a physician experienced with the drug and treatment of life-threatening arrhythmias should give loading doses.
- Note: GI symptoms commonly occur during high-dose therapy, especially with loading doses. Symptoms usually respond to dose reduction or divided dose given with food, including milk.

Intravenous

PREPARE: IV Infusion: First rapid loading dose infusion: Add 150 mg (3 mL) amiodarone to 100 mL D5W to yield 1.5 mg/mL. **Second infusion during first 24 h (slow loading dose and maintenance infusion):** Add 900 mg (18 mL) amiodarone to 500 mL D5W to yield 1.8 mg/mL. **Maintenance infusions after the**

first 24 h: Prepare concentrations of 1–6 mg/mL amiodarone. Note: (Use central line to give concentrations >2 mg/mL).

ADMINISTER: **IV Infusion:** Rapidly infuse initial 150 mg dose over the first 10 min at a rate of 15 mg/min. Over next 6 h, infuse 360 mg at a rate of 1 mg/min. Over the remaining 18 h, infuse 540 mg at a rate of 0.5 mg/min. After the first 24 h, infuse maintenance doses of 720 mg/24 h at a rate of 0.5 mg/min.

INCOMPATIBILITIES **Solution/additive: Nitroprusside sodium, sodium bicarbonate. Y-site: Aminophylline, ampicillin/sulbactam, cefamandole, cefazolin, ceftazidime, ceftizoxime, ceftriaxone, cefuroxime, digoxin, heparin, imipenem/cilastatin, magnesium sulfate, piperacillin, potassium phosphate, sodium bicarbonate, sodium phosphate.**

■ Store at 15°–30° C (59°–86° F) protected from light, unless otherwise directed.

ADVERSE EFFECTS (≥1%) **CNS:** Peripheral neuropathy (*muscle weakness,* wasting numbness, tingling), *fatigue,* abnormal gait, dyskinesias, *dizziness,* paresthesia, headache. **CV:** Bradycardia, *hypotension* (IV), sinus arrest, cardiogenic shock, CHF, arrhythmias; AV block. **Special Senses:** *Corneal microdeposits,* blurred vision, optic neuritis, optic neuropathy, permanent blindness, corneal degeneration, macular degeneration, photosensitivity. **GI:** *Anorexia, nausea, vomiting, constipation,* hepatotoxicity. **Metabolic:** Hyperthyroidism or hypothyroidism; may cause neonatal hypo- or hyperthyroidism if taken during pregnancy. **Respiratory:** (Pulmo-

nary toxicity) Alveolitis, pneumonitis (fever, dry cough, dyspnea), interstitial pulmonary fibrosis, *fatal gasping syndrome* with IV in children. **Skin:** Slate-blue pigmentation, *photosensitivity,* rash. **Other:** With chronic use, angioedema.

INTERACTIONS Drug: Significantly increases **digoxin** levels; enhances pharmacologic effects and toxicities of **disopyramide, procainamide, quinidine, flecainide, lidocaine, lovastatin, simvastatin;** anticoagulant effects of ORAL ANTICOAGULANTS enhanced; **verapamil, diltiazem,** BETA-ADRENERGIC BLOCKING AGENTS may potentiate sinus bradycardia, sinus arrest, or AV block; may increase **phenytoin** levels 2- to 3-fold; **cholestyramine** may decrease amiodarone levels; **fentanyl** may cause bradycardia, hypotension, or decreased output; may increase **cyclosporine** levels and toxicity; **cimetidine** may increase amiodarone levels; **ritonavir** may increase risk of amiodarone toxicity, including cardiotoxicity. **Herbal: Echinacea** possible increase in hepatotoxicity.

PHARMACOKINETICS Absorption: 22–86% absorbed. **Onset:** 2–3 d to 1–3 wk. **Peak:** 3–7 h. **Distribution:** Concentrates in adipose tissue, lungs, kidneys, spleen; crosses placenta. **Metabolism:** Extensively in liver; undergoes some enterohepatic cycling; via CYP2C8 and 3A4. **Elimination:** Excreted chiefly in bile and feces; also in breast milk. **Half-Life:** Biphasic, initial 2.5–10 d, terminal 40–55 d.

CLINICAL IMPLICATIONS

Assessment & Drug Effects

■ Monitor BP carefully during infusion and slow the infusion if significant hypotension occurs;

Common adverse effects in *italic*, life-threatening effects underlined; generic names in **bold**; classifications in SMALL CAPS; ✦ Canadian drug name; ⊙ Prototype drug

73

bradycardia should be treated by slowing the infusion or discontinuing if necessary. Monitor heart rate and rhythm and BP until drug response has stabilized; report promptly symptomatic bradycardia. Sustained monitoring is essential because drug has an unusually long half-life.

- Monitor for S&S of: Adverse effects, particularly conduction disturbances and exacerbation of arrhythmias, in patients receiving concomitant antiarrhythmic therapy (reduce dosage of previous agent by 30–50% several days after amiodarone therapy is started); drug-induced hypothyroidism or hyperthyroidism (see Appendix F), especially during early treatment period; pulmonary toxicity (progressive dyspnea, fatigue, cough, pleuritic pain, fever) throughout therapy.
- Lab tests: Baseline and periodic assessments should be made of liver, lung, thyroid, neurologic, and GI function. Drug may cause thyroid function test abnormalities in the absence of thyroid function impairment.
- Monitor for elevations of AST and ALT. If elevations persist or if they are 2–3 times above normal baseline readings, reduce dosage or withdraw drug promptly to prevent hepatotoxicity and liver damage.
- Auscultate chest periodically or when patient complains of respiratory symptoms. Check for diminished breath sounds, rales, pleuritic friction rub; observe breathing pattern. Drug-induced pulmonary function problems must be distinguished from CHF or pneumonia. Keep physician informed.
- Anticipate possible CNS symptoms within a week after amiodarone therapy begins. Proximal muscle weakness, a common side effect, intensified by tremors pre-

sents a great hazard to the ambulating patient. Assess severity of symptoms. Supervision of ambulation may be indicated.

Patient & Family Education

- Check pulse daily once stabilized, or as prescribed. Report a pulse <60.
- Take oral drug consistently with respect to meals.
- Become familiar with potential adverse reactions and report those that are bothersome to the physician.
- Use dark glasses to ease photophobia; some patients may not be able to go outdoors in the daytime even with such protection.
- Follow recommendation for regular ophthalmic exams, including funduscopy and slit-lamp exam.
- Wear protective clothing and a barrier-type sunscreen that physically blocks penetration of skin by ultraviolet light (e.g., titanium oxide or zinc formulations) to prevent a photosensitivity reaction (erythema, pruritus); avoid exposure to sun and sunlamps.

AMITRIPTYLINE HYDROCHLORIDE

(a-mee-trip'ti-leen)

Amitril, Apo-Amitriptyline ♦, Emitrip, Endep, Enovil, Levate ♦, Meravil, Novotriptyn ♦, SK-Amitriptyline

Classifications: PSYCHOTHERAPEUTIC; TRICYCLIC ANTIDEPRESSANT
Therapeutic: ANTIDEPRESSANT
Prototype: Imipramine
Pregnancy Category: C

AVAILABILITY 10 mg, 25 mg, 50 mg, 75 mg, 100 mg, 150 mg tablets; 10 mg/mL injection

ACTION & *THERAPEUTIC EFFECT*

A tricyclic antidepressant (TCA) that inhibits the reuptake of serotonin (5-HT) and norepinephrine from the synaptic gap; also inhibits norepinephrine reuptake to a moderate degree. Restoration of the levels of these neurotransmitters is a proposed mechanism of its antidepressant action. *Interference with the reuptake of serotonin and norepinephrine results in the antidepressant activity of amitriptyline.*

USES Endogenous depression.

UNLABELED USES Prophylaxis for cluster, migraine, and chronic tension headaches; intractable pain, peptic ulcer disease, to increase muscle strength in myotonic dystrophy, to treat pathologic weeping and laughing secondary to forebrain disease, for eating disorders associated with depression (anorexia or bulimia), and as sedative for nondepressed patients.

CONTRAINDICATIONS TCA hypersensitivity; acute recovery period after MI, cardiac arrhythmias, AV block, long-QT prolongation; suicidal ideation; history of seizure disorders, lactation, children <12 y.

CAUTIOUS USE Prostatic hypertrophy, history of urinary retention or obstruction; angle-closure glaucoma; diabetes mellitus; history of hematologic disorders; history of alcoholism; GERD, BPH; hyperthyroidism; patient with cardiovascular, hepatic, or renal dysfunction; patient with suicidal tendency, electroshock therapy; elective surgery; schizophrenia; respiratory disorders; Parkinson's disease; seizure disorders; older adults, adolescents, pregnancy (category C).

ROUTE & DOSAGE

Antidepressant

Adult: **PO** 75–100 mg/d, may gradually increase to 150–300 mg/d (use lower doses in outpatients) **IM** 20–30 mg q.i.d. until patient can take PO
Adolescent: **PO** 25–50 mg/d in divided doses, may gradually increase to 100 mg/d (max: 200 mg/d)
Geriatric: **PO** 10–25 mg h.s., may gradually increase to 25–150 mg/d

ADMINISTRATION

Oral

- Give with or immediately after food to reduce possibility of GI irritation. Tablet may be crushed if patient is unable to take it whole; administer with food or fluid.
- Give increased doses preferably in late afternoon or at bedtime due to sedative action that precedes antidepressant effect.
- Give as single dose at bedtime to promote sleep or for patients with dizziness or when daytime sedation interferes with work productivity.
- Note that dose is usually tapered over 2 wk at discontinuation to prevent withdrawal symptoms (headache, nausea, malaise, musculoskeletal pain, panic attack, weakness).

Intramuscular

- Reserve IM injections for patients unable or unwilling to take oral drug.
- Inject deep IM into a large muscle.
- Store drug at 15°–30° C (59°–86° F) and protect from light unless otherwise directed by manufacturer.

ADVERSE EFFECTS (≥1%) **CNS:** *Drowsiness, sedation, dizziness,*

Common adverse effects in *italic*, life-threatening effects <u>underlined</u>; generic names in **bold**; classifications in SMALL CAPS; ♣ Canadian drug name; ⊙ Prototype drug

75

nervousness, restlessness, fatigue, headache, insomnia, abnormal movements (extrapyramidal symptoms), seizures. **CV:** *Orthostatic hypotension*, tachycardia, palpitation, ECG changes. **Special Senses:** Blurred vision, mydriasis. **GI:** *Dry mouth*, increased appetite especially for sweets, *constipation*, weight gain, sour or metallic taste, nausea, vomiting. **Urogenital:** *Urinary retention*. **Other:** (Rare) <u>Bone marrow depression</u>.

INTERACTIONS Drug: ANTIHYPERTENSIVES may decrease some antihypertensive response; CNS DEPRESSANTS, **alcohol,** HYPNOTICS, BARBITURATES, SEDATIVES potentiate CNS depression; ANTICOAGULANTS, ORAL, may increase hypoprothrombinemic effect; **ethchlorvynol,** transient delirium; **levodopa,** SYMPATHOMIMETICS (e.g., **epinephrine, norepinephrine**), possibility of sympathetic hyperactivity with hypertension and hyperpyrexia; MAO INHIBITORS, possibility of severe reactions, toxic psychosis, cardiovascular instability; **methylphenidate** increases plasma TCA levels; THYROID DRUGS may increase possibility of arrhythmias; **cimetidine** may increase plasma TCA levels. **Herbal:** Ginkgo may decrease seizure threshold, **St. John's wort** may cause serotonin syndrome.

PHARMACOKINETICS Absorption: Rapidly from GI and injection sites. **Peak:** 2–12 h. **Distribution:** Crosses placenta. **Metabolism:** In liver to active metabolite; by CYP2D6. **Elimination:** Primarily in urine; enters breast milk. **Half-Life:** 10–50 h.

CLINICAL IMPLICATIONS
Assessment & Drug Effects
- Monitor therapeutic effectiveness. It may take 1–6 wk to reduce attacks when used for migraine prophylaxis.
- Monitor for S&S of drowsiness and dizziness (initial stages of therapy); institute measures to prevent falling. Also monitor for overdose or suicide ideation in patients who use excessive amounts of alcohol.
- Lab tests: Baseline and periodic leukocyte and differential counts; renal and hepatic function tests; eye examinations (including glaucoma testing); recommended particularly for older adults, adolescents, and patients receiving high doses/prolonged therapy.
- Monitor BP and pulse rate in patients with preexisting cardiovascular disease. Assess for orthostatic hypotension especially in older adults. Withhold drug if there is a rise or fall in systolic BP (by 10–20 mm Hg), or a sudden increase or a significant change in pulse rate or rhythm. Notify physician.
- Monitor I&O, including bowel elimination pattern.

Patient & Family Education
- Monitor weight; drug may increase appetite or a craving for sweets.
- Understand that tolerance/adaptation to anticholinergic actions (see Appendix F) usually develops with maintenance regimen. Keep physician informed.
- Relieve dry mouth by taking frequent sips of water and increasing total fluid intake.
- Make position change slowly and in stages to prevent dizziness.
- Do not drive or engage in potentially hazardous activities until response to drug is known.
- Do not use OTC drugs without consulting physician while on TCA therapy; many preparations contain sympathomimetic amines.
- Note: Amitriptyline may turn urine blue-green.

AMLEXANOX

(am-lex′a-nox)

Aphthasol, OraDisc A

Classifications: ANTIINFLAMMATORY AGENT

Therapeutic: ANTIINFLAMMATORY

Pregnancy Category: B

AVAILABILITY 5% paste; 2 mg mucoadhesive disc

ACTION & *THERAPEUTIC EFFECT*

Amlexanox is a potent inhibitor of inflammatory mediators (e.g., leukotrienes, IgE, IgG). Its mechanism of healing is unknown. *Amlexanox reduces healing time and pain related to aphthous ulcers or canker sores.*

USES Treatment of aphthous ulcers in patients with normal immune systems.

CONTRAINDICATIONS Sensitivity to amlexanox or benzyl alcohol.

CAUTIOUS USE Pregnancy (category B), lactation; immunosuppressed patients. Safety and efficacy in children are not established.

ROUTE & DOSAGE

Aphthous Ulcers

Adult: **Topical** Apply $^1/_4$ in. (0.5 cm) to finger and dab onto each mouth ulcer q.i.d. (after oral hygiene p.c. and h.s.) for 10 d cycle; apply disc to each mouth ulcer and allow to dissolve

ADMINISTRATION

Topical

- Apply after oral hygiene following each meal and before bedtime.
- Avoid prolonged contact with skin and wash off skin if contact occurs.

- Store at 15°–30° C (59°–86° F) away from heat and moisture. Do not freeze.

ADVERSE EFFECTS (≥1%) **Body as a Whole:** Transient pain, stinging, or burning at application site.

PHARMACOKINETICS Absorption: Minimally absorbed through ulcer. **Onset:** Approximately 3 d. **Elimination:** 17% in urine. **Half-Life:** 3.5 h.

CLINICAL IMPLICATIONS

Assessment & Drug Effects

- Discontinue use if rash or inflamed membranes develop.

Patient & Family Education

- Use at first sign of canker sore. Wash hands before and immediately after application.
- Flush eyes immediately with large amount of cold water if paste accidentally comes in contact with eyes or eye area.
- Contact physician if healing does not result after 10 d of therapy.

AMLODIPINE

(am-lo′di-peen)

Norvasc

Classifications: CALCIUM CHANNEL BLOCKER; ANTIHYPERTENSIVE AGENT

Therapeutic: ANTIHYPERTENSIVE; CALCIUM CHANNEL BLOCKER

Prototype: Nifedipine

Pregnancy Category: C

AVAILABILITY 2.5 mg, 5 mg, 10 mg tablets

ACTION & *THERAPEUTIC EFFECT*

Amlodipine is a calcium channel blocking agent that selectively blocks calcium influx across cell membranes of cardiac and vascular

Common adverse effects in *italic*, life-threatening effects underlined; generic names in **bold**; classifications in SMALL CAPS; ♣ Canadian drug name; ⊘ Prototype drug

77

smooth muscle without changing serum calcium concentrations. It decreases peripheral vascular resistance, increases oxygen delivery to myocardial tissue, and increases cardiac output. *Amlodipine reduces systolic, diastolic, and mean arterial blood pressure.*

USES Treatment of mild to moderate hypertension and angina.

CONTRAINDICATIONS Hypersensitivity to amlodipine; hypotension; severe obstructive coronary artery disease; severe aortic stenosis.

CAUTIOUS USE Liver disease; concomitant use with hypotension; CHF, ventricular dysfunction; lactation; older adults; children <6 y, GERD; hepatic disease; pregnancy (category C).

ROUTE & DOSAGE

Hypertension

Adult: **PO** 5–10 mg once daily
Geriatric: Start with 2.5 mg, adjust dose at intervals of not less than 2 wk

Hepatic Impairment

Start with 2.5 mg, adjust dose at intervals of not less than 2 wk

ADMINISTRATION

Oral

- Give drug without regard to meals.
- Prescribed initial dosages of 2.5 mg daily are common if added to a regimen including other antihypertensive drugs.
- Note: Doses are usually titrated over a period of 14 d or more rapidly if warranted.
- Store at 15°–30° C (59°–86° F).

ADVERSE EFFECTS (≥1%) **CV:** Palpitations, flushing tachycardia, *peripheral or facial edema*, bradycardia, chest pain, syncope, postural hypotension. **CNS:** Light-headedness, fatigue, *headache*. **GI:** Abdominal pain, nausea, anorexia, constipation, dyspepsia, dysphagia, diarrhea, flatulence, vomiting. **Urogenital:** Sexual dysfunction, frequency, nocturia. **Respiratory:** Dyspnea. **Skin:** Flushing, rash. **Other:** Arthralgia, cramps, myalgia.

INTERACTIONS Drug: Adenosine may increase the risk of bradycardia; **bosentan** may decrease efficacy of amlodipine; additive hypotensive effects with other ANTIHYPERTENSIVE AGENTS; AZOLE ANTIFUNGALS (e.g., **fluconazole, itraconazole**) may inhibit metabolism of amlodipine; **itraconazole** may increase edema. **Food: Grapefruit juice** may increase amlodipine levels. **Herbal: Ephedra, Ma Huang, melatonin** may antagonize antihypertensive effects.

PHARMACOKINETICS Absorption: >90% absorbed from GI tract. **Onset:** Gradual. **Peak:** 6–9 h. **Duration:** 24 h. **Distribution:** >95% protein bound. **Metabolism:** Extensively in the liver to inactive metabolites; via CYP3A4. **Elimination:** Inactive metabolites primarily excreted in urine (<5–10% excreted unchanged), 20–25% in feces. **Half-Life:** <45 y: 28–69 h; >60 y: 40–120 h.

CLINICAL IMPLICATIONS

Assessment & Drug Effects

- Monitor BP for therapeutic effectiveness. BP reduction is greatest after peak levels of amlodipine are achieved 6–9 h following oral doses.
- Monitor for S&S of dose-related peripheral or facial edema that may not be accompanied by weight gain; rarely, severe edema may cause discontinuation of drug.

- Monitor BP with postural changes. Report postural hypotension. Monitor more frequently when additional antihypertensives or diuretics are added.
- Monitor heart rate; dose-related palpitations (more common in women) may occur.

Patient & Family Education
- Report significant swelling of face or extremities.
- Take care to have support when standing & walking due to possible dose-related light-headedness/dizziness.
- Report shortness of breath, palpitations, irregular heartbeat, nausea, or constipation to physician.

AMMONIUM CHLORIDE

(ah-mo′ni-um)
Classifications: ELECTROLYTIC BALANCE AGENT
Therapeutic: ACIDIFIER; ELECTROLYTE REPLACEMENT
Pregnancy Category: B

AVAILABILITY 26.75% or 5 mEq/mL solution; 500 mg tablets; 486 mg enteric-coated tablets

ACTION & THERAPEUTIC EFFECT
Acidifying property is due to conversion of ammonium ion (NH_4^+) to urea in liver with liberation of H^+ and Cl^-. Potassium excretion also increases acid, but to a lesser extent. *Effective as a systemic acidifier in metabolic alkalosis by releasing H^+ ions which lower pH.*

USES Treatment of hypochloremic states and metabolic alkalosis. Diuretic or urinary acidifying agent.

CONTRAINDICATIONS Severe renal or hepatic insufficiency; primary respiratory acidosis.

CAUTIOUS USE Cardiac edema, cardiac insufficiency, pulmonary insufficiency; pregnancy (category B), lactation.

ROUTE & DOSAGE

Urine Acidifier, Diuretic
Adult: **PO** 4–12 g/d divided q4–6h
Child: **PO** 75 mg/kg/d in 4 divided doses

Metabolic Alkalosis and Hypochloremic States
Adult/Child: **IV** Dose calculated on basis of CO_2 combining power or serum Cl deficit, 50% of calculated deficit is administered slowly

ADMINISTRATION

Oral
- Give after meals for best tolerance or use enteric-coated tablets. Tablets should be swallowed whole.
- Store in airtight container.

Intravenous
Check with physician for slower rate for infants.

PREPARE: Intermittent: Dilute each 20 ml vial in 500 mL NS. Do not exceed a concentration of 1%–2%.

ADMINISTER: Intermittent: Give slowly to avoid serious adverse effects (ammonia toxicity) and local irritation and pain. Give at a rate not to exceed 5 mL/min.

INCOMPATIBILITIES Solution/additive: Codeine phosphate, levorphanol, methadone, nitrofurantoin, warfarin.

- Avoid freezing. ■ Concentrated solutions crystallize at low temperatures. ■ Crystals can be dissolved by placing intact container in a warm water bath and warming to room temperature.

Common adverse effects in *italic*, life-threatening effects underlined; generic names in **bold**; classifications in SMALL CAPS; ♣ Canadian drug name; ⊕ Prototype drug

79

ADVERSE EFFECTS (≥1%) **Body as a Whole:** Most secondary to ammonia toxicity. **CNS:** Headache, depression, drowsiness, twitching, excitability; EEG abnormalities. **CV:** Bradycardia and other arrhythmias. **GI:** Gastric irritation, nausea, vomiting, anorexia. **Metabolic:** Metabolic acidosis, hyperammonia. **Respiratory:** Hyperventilation. **Skin:** Rash. **Urogenital:** Glycosuria. **Other:** Pain and irritation at IV site.

DIAGNOSTIC TEST INTERFERENCE Ammonium chloride may increase *blood ammonia* and *AST,* decrease *serum magnesium* (by increasing urinary magnesium excretion), and decrease *urine urobilinogen.*

INTERACTIONS Drug: Aminosalicylic acid may cause crystalluria; increases urinary excretion of AMPHETAMINES, **flecainide, mexiletine, methadone, ephedrine, pseudoephedrine;** decreased urinary excretion of SULFONYLUREAS, SALICYLATES.

PHARMACOKINETICS Absorption: Completely absorbed in 3–6 h. **Metabolism:** In liver to HCl and urea. **Elimination:** Primarily in urine.

CLINICAL IMPLICATIONS
Assessment & Drug Effects
- Assess IV infusion site frequently for signs of irritation. Change site as warranted.
- Monitor for S&S of: metabolic acidosis (mental status changes including confusion, disorientation, coma, respiratory changes including increased respiratory rate and depth, exertional dyspnea); ammonium toxicity (cardiac arrhythmias including bradycardia, irregular respirations, twitching, seizures).

- Monitor I&O ratio and pattern. The diuretic effect of ammonium chloride is compensatory and lasts only 1–2 d.
- Lab tests: Baseline and periodic determinations of CO_2 combining power, serum electrolytes, and urinary and arterial pH during therapy to avoid serious acidosis.

Patient & Family Education
- Report pain at IV injection site.

AMOXAPINE

(a-mox'a-peen)
Classifications: PSYCHOTHERAPEUTIC; TRICYCLIC ANTIDEPRESSANT
Therapeutic: ANTIDEPRESSANT
Prototype: Imipramine
Pregnancy Category: C

AVAILABILITY 25 mg, 50 mg, 100 mg, 150 mg tablets

ACTION & *THERAPEUTIC EFFECT*
Tricyclic antidepressant (TCA) with mixed antidepressant and tranquilizing properties. Antidepressant activity is thought to be due to reduced reuptake of norepinephrine and serotonin at the cell membrane of the neuron, thus increasing the level of both neurotransmitters. *Enhancement of neurotransmitters results in its antidepressant activity.*

USES Neurotic and endogenous depression accompanied by anxiety or agitation.

CONTRAINDICATIONS Hypersensitivity to other tricyclic compounds; acute recovery period after MI; AV block; MAOI therapy, QT prolongation, lactation, children <16 y of age, suicidal ideation.
CAUTIOUS USE History of convulsive disorders, schizophrenia,

manic depression, electroshock therapy; alcohol abuse; history of urinary retention, benign prostatic hypertrophy; angle-closure glaucoma or increased intraocular pressure; cardiovascular disorders; impaired renal or hepatic function; elective surgery, pregnancy (category C).

ROUTE & DOSAGE

Antidepressant

Adult: PO Start at 50 mg b.i.d. or t.i.d., may increase on third day to 100 mg t.i.d. Maintenance doses ≤300 mg/d as single dose at bedtime
Geriatric: PO 25 mg h.s., may increase q3–7d to 50–150 mg/d in divided doses (max: 300 mg/d)

ADMINISTRATION

Oral

- Give with or after food to reduce GI irritation; tablet may be crushed and taken with fluid or mixed with food.
- Give maintenance dose as a single dose at bedtime to minimize daytime sedation and other annoying drug adverse effects.
- Do not abruptly discontinue drug. Doses should be tapered over 2 wk.
- Store at 15°–30° C (59°–86° F) in tightly closed container unless otherwise directed.

ADVERSE EFFECTS (≥1%) CNS:
Drowsiness, dizziness, headache, fatigue, *sedation,* lethargy; extrapyramidal effects (acute dystonic reactions, panic attacks, parkinsonism, tardive dyskinesia), seizures (overdosage). CV: Orthostatic hypotension; arrhythmias. GI: Constipation,

diarrhea, flatulence, *dry mouth,* peculiar taste, nausea, heartburn. Special Senses: Blurred vision, dry eyes. Urogenital: Nephrotoxicity (overdosage).

INTERACTIONS Drug: May decrease response to ANTIHYPERTENSIVES; CNS DEPRESSANTS, alcohol, HYPNOTICS, BARBITURATES, SEDATIVES potentiate CNS depression; may increase hypoprothrombinemic effect of ORAL ANTICOAGULANTS; ethchlorvynol, transient delirium; with levodopa, SYMPATHOMIMETICS (e.g., epinephrine, norepinephrine), possibility of sympathetic hyperactivity with hypertension and hyperpyrexia; with MAO INHIBITORS, possibility of severe reactions: toxic psychosis, cardiovascular instability; methylphenidate increases plasma TCA levels; thyroid drugs may increase possibility of arrhythmias; cimetidine may increase plasma TCA levels. Herbal: Ginkgo may decrease seizure threshold, St. John's wort may cause serotonin syndrome.

PHARMACOKINETICS Absorption: Rapidly absorbed. Peak: 1–2 h. Distribution: Probably crosses placenta; distributed into breast milk. Metabolism: Via CYP2D6; active metabolite. Elimination: 60% in urine in 6 d; 7–18% in feces. Half-Life: 8 h parent drug, 30 h metabolite.

CLINICAL IMPLICATIONS

Assessment & Drug Effects
- Monitor therapeutic effectiveness. Initial antidepressant effect (mild euphoria, increased energy) may occur within 4–7 d; however, in most patients clinical response does not occur until after 2–3 wk of drug therapy.

Common adverse effects in *italic*, life-threatening effects underlined; generic names in **bold**; classifications in SMALL CAPS; ♣ Canadian drug name; ⊘ Prototype drug

81

- Supervise patient closely during therapy for suicidal ideation and potential serious adverse effects.
- Report immediately signs of neuroleptic malignant syndrome: fever, sweating, rigidity (catatonia), unstable BP, rapid, irregular pulse; changes in level of consciousness, coma. Although rare, it can be life-threatening if drug is not stopped immediately. Death can result from acute respiratory, renal, or cardiovascular failure.
- Report immediately the onset of signs of tardive dyskinesia (see Appendix F); careful observation/reporting may prevent irreversibility.
- Monitor I&O ratio and bowel elimination pattern. Report continuing constipation.

Patient & Family Education
- Follow directions for taking this drug (see ADMINISTRATION).
- Do not abruptly discontinue drug. Dosage should be tapered over 2 wk. Maintain established dosage regimen. Do not skip, reduce, or double doses or change dose intervals.
- Minimize alcohol intake as it may potentiate drug effects, thus increasing the dangers of overdosage or suicidal ideation.
- Drink at least 2000 mL (approximately 2 qts) fluid daily and eat foods with high fiber content (if allowed) to provide needed roughage.
- Monitor weight at least weekly and report significant weight gain.
- Do not drive or engage in potentially hazardous tasks until response to drug is known.
- Rinse mouth frequently with clear water, especially after eating, to relieve mouth dryness.

- Do not take any prescription or OTC drugs without consulting physician.

AMOXICILLIN

(a-mox-i-sill'in)

Amoxil, Apo-Amoxi ◆, Larotid, Novamoxin, Trimox, Disper-Mox

Classifications: ANTIBIOTIC; AMINOPENICILLIN
Therapeutic: ANTIBIOTIC
Prototype: Ampicillin
Pregnancy Category: B

AVAILABILITY 125 mg, 250 mg, 500 mg tablets; 250 mg, 500 mg capsules; 50 mg/mL, 125 mg/5 mL, 250 mg/5 mL powder for suspension; 200 mg, 400 mg, 600 mg dispersible tablets

ACTION & *THERAPEUTIC EFFECT*
Broad-spectrum semisynthetic aminopenicillin and analogue of ampicillin. Like other penicillins, amoxicillin inhibits the final stage of bacterial cell wall synthesis by binding to specific penicillin-binding proteins (PBPs) located inside the cell wall of rapidly multiplying bacteria. It results in bacterial cell lysis and death. *Active against both aerobic gram positive and aerobic gram negative bacteria.*

USES Infections of ear, nose, throat, GU tract, skin, and soft tissue caused by susceptible bacteria. Also used in uncomplicated gonorrhea.

CONTRAINDICATIONS Hypersensitivity to penicillins; infectious mononucleosis.
CAUTIOUS USE History of or suspected atopy or allergy (hives, eczema, hay fever, asthma); history

of cephalosporin or carbapenem hypersensitivity; colitis, dialysis, diarrhea, GI disease; infants, neonates; viral infection, syphilis, renal impairment or failure, diabetes mellitus, leukemia, pregnancy (category B).

ROUTE & DOSAGE

Mild to Moderate Infections

Adult: **PO** 250–500 mg q8h
Child: **PO** 25–50 mg/kg/d (max: 60–80 mg/kg/d) divided q8h or 200–400 mg q12h

Gonorrhea

Adult: **PO** 3 g as single dose with 1 g probenecid
Child: **PO** ≥2 y, 50 mg/kg as single dose with probenecid 25 mg/kg

ADMINISTRATION

Oral

- Ensure that chewable tablets are chewed or crushed before being swallowed with a liquid.
- Place reconstituted pediatric drops directly on child's tongue or add to formula, milk, fruit juice, water, ginger ale, or other soft drink. Have child drink all the prepared dose promptly.
- Store in tightly covered containers at 15°–30° C (59°–86° F) unless otherwise directed. Reconstituted oral suspensions are stable for 7 d at room temperature.

ADVERSE EFFECTS (≥1%) **Body as a Whole:** As with other penicillins. Hypersensitivity (rash, <u>anaphylaxis</u>), superinfections. **GI:** Diarrhea, nausea, vomiting, <u>pseudo-membranous colitis</u> (rare). **Hematologic:** Hemolytic anemia, eosinophilia, <u>agranulocytosis</u> (rare). **Skin:** Pruritus, urticaria, or other skin erup-

tions. **Special Senses:** Conjunctival ecchymosis.

INTERACTIONS : TETRACYCLINES may inhibit activity of amoxicillin; **probenecid** prolongs the activity of amoxicillin.

PHARMACOKINETICS Absorption: Nearly complete absorption. **Peak:** 1–2 h. **Distribution:** Diffuses into most tissues and body fluids, except synovial fluid and CSF (unless meninges are inflamed); crosses placenta; distributed into breast milk in small amounts. **Metabolism:** In liver. **Elimination:** 60% of dose in urine in 6–8 h. **Half-Life:** 1–1.3 h.

CLINICAL IMPLICATIONS

Assessment & Drug Effects

- Determine previous hypersensitivity reactions to penicillins, cephalosporins, and other allergens prior to therapy.
- Lab tests: Baseline C&S tests prior to initiation of therapy, start drug pending results; periodic assessments of renal, hepatic, and hematologic functions should be made during prolonged therapy.
- Monitor for S&S of an urticarial rash (usually occurring within a few days after start of drug) suggestive of a hypersensitivity reaction. If it occurs, look for other signs of hypersensitivity (fever, wheezing, generalized itching, dyspnea), and report to physician immediately.
- Report onset of generalized, erythematous, maculopapular rash (ampicillin rash) to physician. Ampicillin rash is not due to hypersensitivity; however, hypersensitivity should be ruled out.
- Closely monitor diarrhea to rule out pseudomembranous colitis.

Common adverse effects in *italic*, life-threatening effects <u>underlined</u>; generic names in **bold**; classifications in SMALL CAPS; ✤ Canadian drug name; ⊕ Prototype drug

83

Patient & Family Education

- Take drug around the clock, do not miss a dose, and continue therapy until all medication is taken, unless otherwise directed by physician.
- Report onset of diarrhea and other possible symptoms of superinfection to physician (see Appendix F).

AMOXICILLIN AND CLAVULANATE POTASSIUM

(a-mox-i-sill′in)

Augmentin, Augmentin-ES600, Augmentin XR, Clavulin ♦

Classifications: BETA-LACTAM ANTIBIOTIC; AMINOPENICILLIN

Therapeutic: ANTIBIOTIC

Prototype: Ampicillin

Pregnancy Category: B

AVAILABILITY 250 mg, 500 mg, 875 mg tablets; 125 mg, 200 mg, 400 mg chewable tablets; 125 mg/5 mL, 200 mg/5 mL, 250 mg/5 mL, 400 mg/5 mL, 600 mg/5 mL oral suspension; 1000 mg amoxicillin/62.5 mg clavulanate sustained-release tablets

ACTION & *THERAPEUTIC EFFECT*

As a beta-lactam antibiotic, amoxicillin is bactericidal. It inhibits the final stage of bacterial cell wall synthesis by binding with specific penicillin-binding proteins (PBPs) that are located inside the bacterial cell wall that leads to bacterial cell lysis and death. *Clavulanic acid in combination with ampicillin inhibits enzyme (beta-lactamase) degradation of amoxicillin and by synergism extends both spectrum of activity and bactericidal effect of amoxicillin against many strains of beta-lactamase-producing bacteria resistant to amoxicillin alone.*

USES Infections caused by susceptible beta-lactamase-producing organisms: lower respiratory tract infections, acute bacterial sinusitis, community acquired pneumonia, otitis media, sinusitis, skin and skin structure infections, and UTI.

CONTRAINDICATIONS Hypersensitivity to penicillins; infectious mononucleosis; patient with previous history of drug-induced cholestasis, jaundice, or other hepatic dysfunction.

CAUTIOUS USE Allergic disorders; cephalosporin hypersensitivity; GI disorders; hepatic or renal disease; elderly; pregnancy (category B), lactation.

ROUTE & DOSAGE

Mild to Moderate Infections

Adult: **PO** 250 or 500 mg tablet (each with 125 mg clavulanic acid) q8–12h; Sustained-release tabs: 2 tablets (2000 mg amoxicillin/125 mg clavulanate) q12h × 7–10 d

Child: **PO** <40 kg, 20–40 mg/kg/d (based on amoxicillin component) divided q8–12h; >3 mo, 90 mg/kg/d of 600 ES divided q12h × 10 d

Neonate/Infant: **PO** <3 mo, 30 mg/kg/d (amoxicillin) divided q12h

ADMINISTRATION

Oral

- Give at the start of a meal to minimize GI upset and enhance absorption.
- Note that both 250- and 500-mg tablets contain the exact amount of clavulanic acid (125 mg and potassium salt); therefore, two 250-mg tablets are not equivalent to one 500-mg tablet.

Common adverse effects in *italic*, life-threatening effects <u>underlined</u>; generic names in **bold**; classifications in SMALL CAPS; ♦ Canadian drug name; ⦿ Prototype drug

- Reconstitute oral suspension by adding amount of water specified on container to provide a 5 mL suspension. Tap bottle before adding water to loosen powder, then add water in 2 portions, agitating suspension well before each addition.
- Agitate suspension well just before administration of each dose.
- Give dialysis patient an additional 2 doses on the day of dialysis; one dose before and another dose after dialysis.
- Store tablets in tight containers at <24° C (71° F). Reconstituted oral suspension should be refrigerated at 2°–8° C (36°–46° F), then discarded after 10 d.

ADVERSE EFFECTS (≥1%) **GI:** *Diarrhea,* nausea, vomiting. **Skin:** Rash, urticaria. **Other:** Candidal vaginitis; moderate increases in serum ALT, AST; glomerulonephritis; <u>agranulocytosis</u> (rare).

DIAGNOSTIC TEST INTERFERENCE May interfere with *urinary glucose* determinations using *cupric sulfate, Benedict's solution, Clinitest;* does not affect *glucose oxidase methods* (e.g., Clinistix, TesTape). Positive direct *antiglobulin (Coombs')* test results may be reported, a reaction that could interfere with *hematologic studies* or with *transfusion cross-matching* procedures.

INTERACTIONS Drug: TETRACYCLINES may inhibit activity of amoxicillin; **probenecid** prolongs the activity of amoxicillin.

PHARMACOKINETICS Absorption: Nearly complete absorption. **Peak:** 1–2 h. **Distribution:** Diffuses into most tissues and body fluids, except synovial fluid and CSF (unless meninges are inflamed); crosses placenta; distributed into breast milk in very small amounts. **Metabolism:** In liver. **Elimination:** 50–73% of the amoxicillin and 25–45% of the clavulanate dose excreted in urine in 2 h. **Half-Life:** Amoxicillin 1–1.3 h, clavulanate 0.78–1.2 h.

CLINICAL IMPLICATIONS

Assessment & Drug Effects

- Determine previous hypersensitivity reactions to penicillins, cephalosporins, and other allergens prior to therapy.
- Lab tests: Baseline C&S tests prior to initiation of therapy; start drug pending results.
- Monitor for S&S of an urticarial rash (usually occurring within a few days after start of drug) suggestive of a hypersensitivity reaction. If it occurs, look for other signs of hypersensitivity (fever, wheezing, generalized itching, dyspnea), and report to physician immediately.
- Note: Generalized, erythematous, maculopapular rash (ampicillin rash) is not due to hypersensitivity. It is usually mild, but can be severe. Report onset of rash to physician, since hypersensitivity should be ruled out.

Patient & Family Education

- Female patients should report onset of symptoms of *Candidal vaginitis* (e.g., moderate amount of white, cheesy, nonodorous vaginal discharge; vaginal inflammation and itching; vulvar excoriation, inflammation, burning, itching). Therapy may have to be discontinued.
- Note: Use Clinistix or TesTape when monitoring urinary glucose to avoid false readings with diabetes mellitus.

Common adverse effects in *italic,* life-threatening effects <u>underlined</u>; generic names in **bold**; classifications in SMALL CAPS; ♣ Canadian drug name; ⊕ Prototype drug

85

AMPHETAMINE SULFATE (Pr)

(am-fet'a-meen)

Adderall, Adderall XR

Classifications: CEREBRAL STIMULANT; ANOREXIANT

Therapeutic: CEREBRAL STIMULANT

Pregnancy Category: C

Controlled Substance: Schedule II

AVAILABILITY 5 mg, 10 mg tablets; Adderall 5 mg, 10 mg, 20 mg, 30 mg tablets; 5 mg, 15 mg, 20 mg, 25 mg, 30 mg sustained release capsules

ACTION & *THERAPEUTIC EFFECT*

Marked stimulant effect on CNS thought to be due to action on cerebral cortex and possibly the reticular activating system. Acts indirectly on adrenergic receptors by increasing synaptic release of norepinephrine in the brain and by blocking reuptake of norepinephrine at presynaptic membranes. *CNS stimulation results in increased motor activity, diminished sense of fatigue, alertness, wakefulness, and mood elevation. Anorexigenic effect thought to result from direct inhibition of hypothalamic appetite center, as well as mood elevation.*

USES Narcolepsy, attention deficit disorder in children and adults (hyperkinetic behavioral syndrome, minimal brain dysfunction). Use as short-term adjunct to control exogenous obesity not generally recommended because of its potential for abuse.

CONTRAINDICATIONS Hypersensitivity to sympathomimetic amines; history of drug abuse; severe agitation; hyperthyroidism; diabetes mellitus; moderate to severe hypertension, advanced arteriosclerosis, angina pectoris or other cardiovascular disorders; Gilles de la Tourette disorder; glaucoma; during or within 14 d after treatment with MAOIs; lactation.

CAUTIOUS USE Pregnancy (category C); mild hypertension.

ROUTE & DOSAGE

Narcolepsy

Adult: **PO** 5–60 mg/d divided q4–6h in 2–3 doses

Child: **PO** >12 y, 10 mg/d, may increase by 10 mg at weekly intervals; 6–12 y, 5 mg/d, may increase by 5 mg at weekly intervals

Attention Deficit Disorder

Adult/Adolescent: **PO** 10 mg extended release once daily in a.m.; may increase by 5–10 mg at weekly intervals if needed to max 30 mg/d.

Child: **PO** 6 y, 5 mg 1–2 times/d, may increase by 5 mg at weekly intervals (max: 40 mg/d); 3–5 y, 2.5 mg 1–2 times/d, may increase by 2.5 mg at weekly intervals; 10 mg extended release once daily in a.m.; may increase by 5–10 mg at weekly intervals if needed to max of 30 mg/d.

Obesity

Adult: **PO** 5–10 mg 1 h before meals

ADMINISTRATION

Oral

- Give first dose on awakening or early in a.m. when prescribed for narcolepsy.
- Give last dose no later than 6 h before patient retires to avoid insomnia.
- Ensure that sustained release capsules are not crushed or chewed.

- Give drug on an empty stomach 30–60 min before meal to suppress appetite when prescribed for obesity.
- Store at 15°–30° C (59°–86° F) unless otherwise directed.

ADVERSE EFFECTS (≥1%) **Body as a Whole:** Allergy, urticaria, <u>sudden death</u> (reported in children with structural cardiac abnormalities). **CNS:** *Irritability,* psychosis, *restlessness,* nervousness, headache, *insomnia,* weakness, *euphoria,* dysphoria, drowsiness, trembling, hyperactive reflexes. **CV:** *Palpitation,* elevated BP; tachycardia, vasculitis. **Urogenital:** Impotence & change in libido with high doses. **GI:** Dry mouth, anorexia, unusual weight loss, nausea, vomiting, diarrhea, or constipation.

DIAGNOSTIC TEST INTERFERENCE Elevations in *serum thyroxine (T₄)* levels with high amphetamine doses.

INTERACTIONS Drug: **Acetazolamide, sodium bicarbonate** decrease amphetamine elimination; **ammonium chloride, ascorbic acid** increase amphetamine elimination; effects of both amphetamine and BARBITURATE may be antagonized if given together; **furazolidone** may increase BP effects of amphetamines, and interaction may persist for several weeks after furazolidone is discontinued; **guanethidine, guanadryl** antagonize antihypertensive effects; because MAO INHIBITORS, **selegiline** can precipitate hypertensive crisis (fatalities reported), do not administer amphetamines during or within 14 d of these drugs; PHENOTHIAZINES may inhibit mood elevating effects of amphetamines; TRICYCLIC ANTIDEPRESSANTS enhance amphetamine effects through

increased **norepinephrine** release; BETA AGONISTS increase cardiovascular adverse effects.

PHARMACOKINETICS Absorption: Rapid. **Peak effect:** 1–5 h. **Duration:** Up to 10 h. **Distribution:** All tissues, especially CNS. **Metabolism:** In liver. **Elimination:** Renal; excreted into breast milk. **Half-Life:** 10–30 h.

CLINICAL IMPLICATIONS

Assessment & Drug Effects

- Monitor for therapeutic effectiveness. Tolerance to the mood-elevating effects commonly occurs within a few weeks. Drug is usually discontinued when tolerance develops. Generally, tolerance does not occur when used for attention deficit disorder or narcolepsy.
- Monitor for S&S of toxicity in children. Response to this drug is more variable in children than adults; acute toxicity has occurred over a wide range of dosage.
- Monitor for S&S of insomnia or anorexia. Report complaints to physician. Dosage reduction may be required.
- Monitor diabetics closely for loss of glycemic control.
- Monitor growth in children; drug may be discontinued periodically to allow for normal growth.
- Note: Drug's excitatory and euphoric effects are associated with a high abuse potential.

Patient & Family Education

- Keep physician informed of clinical response and persistent or bothersome adverse effects. This drug exerts a stimulating effect that masks fatigue; after exhilaration disappears, fatigue and depression are usually greater than before, and a longer period of rest is needed.

Common adverse effects in *italic,* life-threatening effects <u>underlined;</u> generic names in **bold;** classifications in SMALL CAPS; ♣ Canadian drug name; ⊘ Prototype drug

87

- Report insomnia or undesired weight loss.
- Do not drive or engage in potentially hazardous tasks until response to drug is known.
- Rinse mouth frequently with clear water, especially after eating, to relieve mouth dryness; increase fluid intake, if allowed; chew sugarless gum or sour-balls.
- Note: Meticulous oral hygiene is required because decreased saliva encourages demineralization of tooth surfaces and mucosal erosion. Use of a commercially available oral lubricant, such as Moi-Stir or Xero-Lube, can relieve soft tissue problems and reduce the potential of tooth decay.
- Note: Appetite suppression usually lessens within a few weeks and appetite increases; dose increase is not indicated.
- Avoid caffeine-containing beverages because caffeine increases amphetamine effects.
- Note that drug is usually tapered gradually following prolonged administration of high doses. Abrupt withdrawal may result in lethargy, profound depression, or other psychotic manifestations that may persist for several weeks.

AMPHOTERICIN B ℗

(am-foe-ter′i-sin)

Amphocin, Fungizone

AMPHOTERICIN B LIPID-BASED

Abelcet, Amphotec, AmBisome

Classifications: ANTIFUNGAL
Therapeutic: ANTIFUNGAL
Pregnancy Category: B; C (oral suspension)

AVAILABILITY Abelcet: 100 mg/ 20 mL suspension for injection; **Amphotec:** 50 mg, 100 mg powder for injection; **AmBisome:** 50 mg powder for injection; **Fungizone:** 50 mg powder for injection; 100 mg/ mL suspension; 3% cream, lotion, ointment

ACTION & *THERAPEUTIC EFFECT*

Fungistatic antibiotic produced by *Streptomyces nodosus*. Exerts antifungal action on both resting and growing cells at least in part by selectively binding to sterols in fungus cell membrane. *Fungicidal at higher concentrations, depending on sensitivity of fungus.*

USES Used intravenously for a wide spectrum of potentially fatal systemic fungal (mycotic) infections including aspergillosis, blastomycosis, coccidioidomycosis, cryptococcosis, disseminated candidiasis, histoplasmosis, paracoccidioidomycosis, sporotrichosis, and others. Has been used to potentiate antifungal effects of flucytosine (*Ancobon*) and to provide anticandidal prophylaxis in certain susceptible patients receiving immunosuppressive therapy. Used topically for cutaneous and mucocutaneous infections caused by *Candida* (monilia). *Abelcet:* aspergillosis.

UNLABELED USES Treatment of candiduria, fungal endocarditis, meningitis, septicemia; fungal infections of urinary bladder and urinary tract; amebic meningoencephalitis, and paracoccidioidomycosis.

CONTRAINDICATIONS Hypersensitivity to amphotericin; lactation.
CAUTIOUS USE Severe bone marrow depression; renal function impairment; anemia; pregnancy (category B), oral supsension (category C).

Common adverse effects in *italic*, life-threatening effects underlined; generic names in **bold**; classifications in SMALL CAPS; ♦ Canadian drug name; ℗ Prototype drug

ROUTE & DOSAGE

Systemic Infections [Amphocin, Fungizone]

Adult: **IV Test Dose** 1 mg dissolved in 20 mL of D5W by slow infusion (over 10–30 min) **IV Maintenance Dose** 0.25–0.3 mg/kg/day infused over 4–6 h, may gradually increase by 0.125–0.25 mg/kg/d up to 1–1.5 mg/kg/d
Child: **IV Test Dose** 0.1 mg/kg up to 1 mg dissolved in 20 mL of D5W by slow infusion (over 10–30 min) **IV Maintenance Dose** 0.4 mg/kg/d infused over 4–6 h, may increase by 0.25 mg/kg/d to target dose of 0.25–1 mg/kg/d infused over 2–6 h

[Abelcet]

Adult/Child: **IV** 3–5 mg/kg/d infused at 2.5 mg/kg/h

[Amphotec]

Adult/Child: **IV Test Dose** 10 mL (1.6–8.3 mg) of initial dose infused over 10–30 min **IV Maintenance Dose** 3–4 mg/kg/d (max: 7.5 mg/kg/d) infused at 1 mg/kg/h

[AmBisome]

Adult/Child: **IV** 3–5 mg/kg/d infused over 1–2 h

Cryptococcal Meningitis in HIV [AmBisome]

Adult: **IV** 6 mg/kg/d infused over 2 h

Leishmaniasis

Adult: **IV** 3 mg/kg/d days 1–5, 14, and 21

Candiduria [Amphocin, Fungizone]

Adult: Irrigation 5–50 mg/1000 mL sterile water instilled continuously into the bladder via a 3-way closed drainage catheter system at a rate of 1000 mL/24 h

Oral Candidiasis [Fungizone]

Adult/Child: **PO** 100 mg swish & swallow q.i.d.

Cutaneous Candidiasis [Fungizone]

Adult/Child/Infant: **Topical** apply to lesions 2–4 times/d for 1–4 wk

ADMINISTRATION

Oral

- Instruct patient not to swallow drug immediately, but swish carefully to coat lesions.
- Store according to manufacturer's recommendations.

Topical Application

- Do not cover with plastic wrap, plastic cloth, rubber, or other occlusive dressings. Ask physician to specify when and how lesions are to be washed.
- Discontinue topical treatment promptly if signs of hypersensitivity, irritation, or worsening of lesions occurs.
- Store topical forms in well-closed containers at room temperature, 15°–30° C (59°–86° F), unless otherwise directed.

Intravenous

PREPARE: Each brand of amphotericin is prepared differently according to manufacturer's directions. Refer to specific manufacturer's guidelines for preparation of IV solutions.
ADMINISTER: Abelcet Intermittent: Flush existing IV line with D5W before infusion. • Use 5 micron in-line filter. Infuse total daily dose at 2.5 mg/kg/h. • Shake IV bag at least q2h to evenly mix solution.

Common adverse effects in *italic*, life-threatening effects <u>underlined</u>; generic names in **bold**; classifications in SMALL CAPS; ♣ Canadian drug name; ⊕ Prototype drug

Amphotec Intermittent: Do not use an in-line filter. ▪ Infuse total daily dose at 1 mg/kg/h. Infusion time may be shortened but should never be <2 h. Infusion time may also be extended for better tolerance.

AmBisome Intermittent: Do not use an in-line filter. ▪ Infuse total daily dose over 2 h. Infusion time may be shortened but should never be <1 h.

Fungizone Intermittent: Use a 1-micron filter. ▪ Infuse total daily dose over 2–6 h. Use longer infusion time for better tolerance. ▪ Alert: Rapid infusion of any amphotericin can cause cardiovascular collapse. If hypotension or arrhythmias develop interrupt infusion and notify physician. ▪ Protect IV solution from light during administration. ▪ Note incompatibilities. When given through an existing IV line, flush before and after with D5W. ▪ Initiate therapy using the most distal vein possible and alternate sites with each dose if possible to reduce the risk of thrombophlebitis. ▪ Check IV site frequently for patency.

INCOMPATIBILITIES **Solution/additive:** Any **saline**-containing solution (precipitate will form), PARENTERAL NUTRITION SOLUTIONS, **calcium chloride, calcium gluconate, cimetidine, edetate calcium disodium, metaraminol, methyldopa, polymyxin, potassium chloride, ranitidine, verapamil**. **Y-site:** AMINOGLYCOSIDES, PENICILLINS, PHENOTHIAZINES, **clindamycin, cotrimoxazole, diphenhydramine, dopamine, dobutamine, heparin** (flush lines with D5W, not NS), **lidocaine, procaine, tetra**cycline, **fluconazole, vitamins, TPN.**
▪ Do not mix Abelcet or Amphotec with any other drugs.

▪ Store according to manufacturer's recommendations for reconstituted and unopened vials.

ADVERSE EFFECTS (≥1%) **Body as a Whole:** Hypersensitivity (pruritus, urticaria, skin rashes, fever, dyspnea, anaphylaxis); *fever, chills.* **CNS:** Headache, sedation, muscle pain, arthralgia, weakness. **CV:** Hypotension, cardiac arrest. **Special Senses:** Ototoxicity with tinnitus, vertigo, loss of hearing. **GI:** nausea, vomiting, diarrhea, epigastric cramps, anorexia, weight loss. **Hematologic:** Anemia, thrombocytopenia. **Metabolic:** *Hypokalemia, hypomagnesemia.* **Urogenital:** Nephrotoxicity, urine with low specific gravity. **Skin:** Dry, erythema, pruritus, burning sensation; allergic contact dermatitis, exacerbation of lesions. **Other:** Pain; arthralgias, thrombophlebitis (IV site), superinfections.

INTERACTIONS Drug: AMINOGLYCOSIDES, **capreomycin, cisplatin, carboplatin, colistin, cyclosporine, mechlorethamine, furosemide, vancomycin** increase the possibility of nephrotoxicity; CORTICOSTEROIDS potentiate hypokalemia; with DIGITALIS GLYCOSIDES, hypokalemia increases the risk of **digitalis** toxicity.

PHARMACOKINETICS Peak: 1–2 h after IV infusion. **Duration:** 20 h. **Distribution:** Minimal amounts enter CNS, eye, bile, pleural, pericardial, synovial, or amniotic fluids; similar plasma and urine concentrations. **Elimination:** Excreted renally; can be detected in blood up to 4 wk and in urine for 4–8 wk after discontinuing therapy. **Half-Life:** 24–48 h.

CLINICAL IMPLICATIONS

Assessment & Drug Effects

- Lab tests: Baseline C&S tests prior to initiation of therapy; start drug pending results. Baseline and periodic BUN, serum creatinine, creatinine clearance; during therapy periodic CBC, serum electrolytes (especially K⁺, Mg⁺⁺, Na⁺, Ca⁺⁺), and liver function tests.
- Monitor for S&S of local inflammatory reaction or thrombosis at injection site, particularly if extravasation occurs.
- Monitor cardiovascular and respiratory status and observe patient closely for adverse effects during initial IV therapy. If a test dose (1 mg over 20–30 min) is given, monitor vital signs every 30 min for at least 4 h. Febrile reactions (fever, chills, headache, nausea) occur in 20–90% of patients, usually 1–2 h after beginning infusion, and subside within 4 h after drug is discontinued. The severity of this reaction usually decreases with continued therapy. Keep physician informed.
- Monitor I&O and weight. Report immediately oliguria, any change in I&O ratio and pattern, or appearance of urine [e.g., sediment, pink or cloudy urine (hematuria)], abnormal renal function tests, unusual weight gain or loss. Generally, renal damage is reversible if drug is discontinued when first signs of renal dysfunction appear.
- Report to physician and withhold drug, if BUN exceeds 40 mg/dL or serum creatinine rises above 3 mg/dL. Dosage should be reduced or drug discontinued until renal function improves.
- Consult physician about the appearance of mild erythema surrounding topical application to skin lesions. This may be an indication to reduce frequency of topical application.
- Consult physician for guidelines on adequate hydration and adjustment of daily dose as a possible means of avoiding or minimizing nephrotoxicity.
- Report promptly any evidence of hearing loss or complaints of tinnitus, vertigo, or unsteady gait. Tinnitus may not be a complaint in older adults or the very young. Other signs of ototoxicity (i.e., vertigo or hearing loss) are more reliable indicators of ototoxicity in these age groups.

Patient & Family Education

- Notify physician if improvement does not occur within 1–2 wk or if lesions appear to worsen. Nail infections usually require several months or longer to improve.
- Wash towels and clothing that were in contact with affected areas after each treatment.
- Note: Topical cream slightly discolors the skin. Generally, lotion and ointment do not stain skin when rubbed in, but nail lesions may be stained.

AMPICILLIN ⓟ

(am-pi-sill′in)

Novo-Ampicillin ♦, Principen

AMPICILLIN SODIUM

Ampicin ♦, Penbritin ♦

Classifications: ANTIBIOTIC; AMINOPENICILLIN

Therapeutic: ANTIBIOTIC

Pregnancy Category: B

AVAILABILITY 250 mg, 500 mg capsules; 125 mg/5 mL, 250 mg/5 mL oral suspension; 125 mg, 250 mg, 500 mg, 1 gm, 2 gm vials

Common adverse effects in *italic*, life-threatening effects <u>underlined</u>; generic names in **bold**; classifications in SMALL CAPS; ♦ Canadian drug name; ⓟ Prototype drug

91

ACTION & *THERAPEUTIC EFFECT*

A broad-spectrum, semisynthetic aminopenicillin that is bactericidal but is inactivated by penicillinase (beta-lactamase). Like other penicillins, ampicillin inhibits the final stage of bacterial cell wall synthesis by binding to specific penicillin-binding proteins (PBPs) located inside the bacterial cell wall. This results in lysis and death of bacteria. *Effective against gram-positive bacteria as well as some gram negative.*

USES Infections of GU, respiratory, and GI tracts and skin and soft tissues; also gonococcal infections, bacterial meningitis, otitis media, sinusitis, and septicemia and for prophylaxis of bacterial endocarditis. Used parenterally only for moderately severe to severe infections.

CONTRAINDICATIONS Hypersensitivity to penicillin derivatives; infectious mononucleosis.

CAUTIOUS USE History of hypersensitivity to cephalosporins; GI disorders; renal disease or impairment; pregnancy (category B) or lactation.

ROUTE & DOSAGE

Systemic Infections

Adult: **PO** 250–500 mg q6h **IV/IM** 250 mg–500 mg q6h
Child: **PO** 25–50 mg/kg/d divided q6–8h **IV/IM** 25–100 mg/kg/d divided q6h
Neonate: **IV/IM** ≤7 d & ≤2000 g, 50 mg/kg/d divided q12h; ≤7 d & >2000 g, 75 mg/kg/d divided q8h; >7 d, 50–100 mg/kg/d divided q6–12h

Meningitis

Adult/Child: **IV** 150–200 mg/kg/d divided q3–4h

Neonate: **IV/IM** ≤7 d & ≤2000 g, 100 mg/kg/d divided q12h; ≤7 d & >2000 g, 150 mg/kg/d divided q8h; >7 d, 100–200 mg/kg/d divided q6–12h

Gonorrhea

Adult: **PO** 3.5 g with 1 g probenecid times 1 **IV/IM** 500 mg q8–12h

Bacterial Endocarditis Prophylaxis

Adult: **IV** 2 g 30 min before procedure
Child: **IV** 50 mg/kg 30 min before procedure (max: 2 g)

Group B Strep Prophylaxis

Adult: **IV** 2 g, then 1 g q4h until delivery

Renal Impairment

Cl$_{cr}$ 10–30 mL/min: give q6–12h; <10 mL/min: give q12h.
Dialysis: Dose should be given after dialysis.

ADMINISTRATION

Oral

- Give with a full glass of water on an empty stomach (at least 1 h before or 2 h after meals) for maximum absorption. Food hampers rate and extent of oral absorption.

Intramuscular

- Reconstitute each vial by adding the indicated amount of sterile water for injection or bacteriostatic water for injection (1.2 mL to 125 mg; 1 mL to 250 mg; 1.8 mL to 500 mg; 3.5 mL to 1 g; 6.8 mL to 2 g). All reconstituted vials yield 250 mg/mL except the 125 mg vial which yields 125 mg/mL. Administer within 1 h of preparation.
- Withdraw the ordered dose and inject deep IM into a large muscle.

Intravenous

Verify correct IV concentration and rate of infusion with physician for administration to neonates, infants, and children.

PREPARE: **Direct/Intermittent:** Reconstitute each 500 mg or less with at least 5 mL of sterile water for injection. Final concentration must be ≤30 mg/mL; thus may be further diluted in 50 mL or more of NS, D5W, D5/NS, D5W/0.45NS, or RL. ▪ Stability of solution varies with diluent and concentration of solution. Solutions in NS are stable for up to 8 h at room temperature; other solutions should be infused within 2–4 h of preparation. Give direct IV within 1 h of preparation. ▪ Wear disposable gloves when handling drug repeatedly; contact dermatitis occurs frequently in sensitized individuals.

ADMINISTER: **Direct/Intermittent:** Slowly over at least 15 min. ▪ With solutions of 100 mL or more, set rate according to amount of solution, but no faster than direct IV rate. ▪ Convulsions may be induced by too rapid administration.

INCOMPATIBILITIES **Solution/additive:** Do not add to a **dextrose**-containing solution unless entire dose is given within 1 h of preparation. **Y-site: Amiodarone.**

▪ Store capsules and unopened vials at 15°–30° C (59°–86° F) unless otherwise directed. Keep oral preparations tightly covered.

ADVERSE EFFECTS (≥1%) **Body as a Whole:** Similar to those for penicillin G. Hypersensitivity (pruritus, urticaria, eosinophilia, hemolytic anemia, interstitial nephritis, <u>anaphylactoid reaction</u>); superinfections. **CNS:** Convulsive seizures with high doses. **GI:** *Diarrhea,* nausea, vomiting, <u>pseudomembranous colitis</u>. **Other:** Severe pain (follow-

ing IM); phlebitis (following IV). **Skin:** *Rash.*

DIAGNOSTIC TEST INTERFERENCE Elevated ***CPK*** levels may result from local skeletal muscle injury following IM injection. ***Urine glucose:*** high urine drug concentrations can result in false-positive test results with ***Clinitest*** or ***Benedict's*** (enzymatic ***glucose oxidase methods,*** e.g., ***Clinistix, Diastix, TesTape,*** are not affected). ***AST*** may be elevated (significance not known).

INTERACTIONS Drug: Allopurinol increases incidence of rash. Effectiveness of the AMINOGLYCOSIDES may be impaired in patients with severe end-stage renal disease. **Chloramphenicol, erythromycin,** and **tetracycline** may reduce bactericidal effects of ampicillin; this interaction is primarily significant when low doses of ampicillin are used. Ampicillin may interfere with the contraceptive action of oral contraceptives (**estrogens**). Female patients should be advised to consider nonhormonal contraception while on antibiotics. **Food:** Food may decrease absorption of ampicillin, so it should be taken 1 h before or 2 h after meals.

PHARMACOKINETICS Absorption: Oral dose is 50% absorbed. Peak effect: 5 min IV, 1 h IM, 2 h PO. **Duration:** 6–8 h. **Distribution:** Most body tissues; high CNS concentrations only with inflamed meninges; crosses the placenta. **Metabolism:** Minimal hepatic metabolism. **Elimination:** 90% in urine; excreted into breast milk. **Half-Life:** 1–1.8 h.

CLINICAL IMPLICATIONS

Assessment & Drug Effects
▪ Determine previous hypersensitivity reactions to penicillins,

Common adverse effects in *italic*, life-threatening effects <u>underlined</u>; generic names in **bold**; classifications in SMALL CAPS; ♣ Canadian drug name; ◎ Prototype drug

93

cephalosporins, and other allergens prior to therapy.

- Lab tests: Baseline C&S tests prior to initiation of therapy; start drug pending results. Baseline and periodic assessments of renal, hepatic, and hematologic functions, particularly during prolonged or high-dose therapy.
- Note: Sodium content of drug must be considered in patients on sodium restriction.
- Inspect skin daily and instruct patient to do the same. The appearance of a rash should be carefully evaluated to differentiate a nonallergenic ampicillin rash from a hypersensitivity reaction. Report rash promptly to physician.
- Note: Incidence of ampicillin rash is higher in patients with infectious mononucleosis or other viral infections, *Salmonella* infections, lymphocytic leukemia, or hyperuricemia or in patients taking allopurinol.

Patient & Family Education

- Note: Ampicillin rash is believed to be nonallergenic and therefore its appearance is not an absolute contraindication to future therapy.
- Report diarrhea to physician; do not self-medicate. Give a detailed report to the physician regarding onset, duration, character of stools, associated symptoms, temperature and weight loss (if any) to help rule out the possibility of drug-induced, potentially fatal pseudomembranous colitis (see Appendix F).
- Report S&S of superinfection (onset of black, hairy tongue; oral lesions or soreness; rectal or vaginal itching; vaginal discharge; loose, foul-smelling stools; or unusual odor to urine).
- Notify physician if no improvement is noted within a few days after therapy is started.

- Take medication around the clock; continue taking medication until it is all gone (usually 10 d) unless otherwise directed by physician or pharmacist.

AMPICILLIN SODIUM AND SULBACTAM SODIUM

(am-pi-sill′in/sul-bak′tam)
Unasyn
Classifications: ANTIBIOTIC; AMINOPENICILLIN
Therapeutic: ANTIBIOTIC
Prototype: Ampicillin
Pregnancy Category: B

AVAILABILITY 1.5 gm, 3 gm vials

ACTION & *THERAPEUTIC EFFECT*
Ampicillin inhibits the final stage of bacterial cell wall synthesis by binding to specific penicillin-binding proteins (PBPs) located inside the bacterial cell wall. This results in bacteria cell wall lysis and death. Sulbactam inhibits beta-lactamases, most frequently responsible for transferred drug resistance. Thus the spectrum of drugs affected by the combination of the two is increased. *Effective against both gram-positive and gram-negative bacteria including those that produce beta-lactamase and nonbeta-lactamase producers. Ampicillin without sulbactam is not effective against beta-lactamase producing strains.*

USES Treatment of infections due to susceptible organisms in skin and skin structures, intraabdominal infections, and gynecologic infections.

CONTRAINDICATIONS Hypersensitivity to penicillins; mononucleosis.
CAUTIOUS USE Hypersensitivity to cephalosporins; GI disorders; renal

disease or impairment; pregnancy (category B) or lactation.

ROUTE & DOSAGE

Systemic Infections

Adult/Child: **IV/IM** ≥*40 kg*, 1.5 (1 g ampicillin, 0.5 g sulbactam) to 3 g (2 g ampicillin, 1 g sulbactam) q6h (max: 4 g sulbactam/d) *Child:* **IV** ≥*1 y*, 300 mg/kg/d (200 mg/kg ampicillin and 100 mg/kg sulbactam) divided q6h

Renal Impairment

Cl_{cr} 10–30 mL/min: give q6–12h; <10 mL/min: give q12h. Dialysis: give dose after dialysis.

ADMINISTRATION

Intramuscular

▪ Reconstitute solution with sterile water for injection by adding 6.4 mL diluent to a 3 g vial. Each mL contains 250 mg ampicillin and 125 mg sulbactam.

▪ Give deep IM into a large muscle. Rotate injection sites.

Intravenous

PREPARE: **Direct/Intermittent:** Reconstitute each 1.5 g with 3.2 mL of sterile water for injection to yield 375 mg/mL (250 mg ampicillin/125 mg sulbactam); further dilute with NS, D5W, D5/NS, D5W/0.45NS, or RL to a final concentration within the range of 3–45 mg/mL.

ADMINISTER: **Direct/Intermittent:** Give slowly over at least 15 min. With solutions of 100 mL or more, set rate according to amount of solution but no faster than direct IV rate. ▪ Convulsions may be induced by too rapid administration. ▪ Use only freshly prepared solution; administer within 1 h after preparation.

INCOMPATIBILITIES **Solution/additive:** Do not add to a **dextrose**-containing solution unless entire dose is given within 1 h of preparation. **Y-site: Amiodarone.**

▪ Store powder for injection at 15°–30° C (59°–86° F) before reconstitution. Storage times and temperatures vary for different concentrations of reconstituted solutions; consult manufacturer's directions.

ADVERSE EFFECTS (≥1%) **Body as a Whole:** Hypersensitivity (rash, itching, anaphylactoid reaction), fatigue, malaise, headache, chills, edema. **GI:** *Diarrhea, nausea,* vomiting, abdominal distention, candidiasis. **Hematologic:** Neutropenia, thrombocytopenia. **Urogenital:** Dysuria. **CNS:** Seizures. **Other:** Local pain at injection site; thrombophlebitis.

INTERACTIONS Drug: Allopurinol increases incidence of rash; effectiveness of the AMINOGLYCOSIDES may be impaired in patients with severe end stage renal disease; **chloramphenicol, erythromycin, tetracycline** may reduce bactericidal effects of ampicillin—this interaction is primarily significant when low doses are used; ampicillin may interfere with the contraceptive action of ORAL CONTRACEPTIVES—female patients should be advised to consider nonhormonal contraception while on antibiotics.

PHARMACOKINETICS Peak: Immediate after IV. **Duration:** 6–8 h. **Distribution:** Most body tissues; high CNS concentrations only with inflamed meninges; crosses placenta; appears in breast milk. **Metabolism:** Minimal hepatic metabolism. **Elimination:** In urine. **Half-Life:** 1 h.

Common adverse effects in *italic*, life-threatening effects underlined; generic names in **bold**; classifications in SMALL CAPS; ✦ Canadian drug name; ⊘ Prototype drug

95

CLINICAL IMPLICATIONS

Assessment & Drug Effects

- Determine previous hypersensitivity reactions to penicillins, cephalosporins, and other allergens prior to therapy.
- Lab tests: Baseline C&S tests prior to initiation of therapy; start drug pending results.
- Report promptly unexplained bleeding (e.g., epistaxis, purpura, ecchymoses).
- Monitor patient carefully during the first 30 min after initiation of IV therapy for signs of hypersensitivity and anaphylactoid reaction (see Appendix F). Serious anaphylactoid reactions require immediate use of emergency drugs and airway management.
- Observe for and report symptoms of superinfections (see Appendix F). Withhold drug and notify physician.
- Monitor I&O ratio and pattern. Report dysuria, urine retention, and hematuria.

Patient & Family Education

- Report chills, wheezing, pruritus (itching), respiratory distress, or palpitations to physician immediately.

AMPRENAVIR

(am-pre'na-vir)

Agenerase

Classifications: ANTIVIRAL AGENT; ANTIRETROVIRAL AGENT; PROTEASE INHIBITOR
Therapeutic: ANTIRETROVIRAL; PROTEASE INHIBITOR
Prototype: Saquinavir
Pregnancy Category: C

AVAILABILITY 50 mg capsules; 15 mg/mL oral solution

ACTION & *THERAPEUTIC EFFECT*

Amprenavir inhibits the activity of HIV-1 protease enzyme and thus prevents the cleavage of viral polyproteins essential for the maturation and proliferation of the HIV-1 virus. Amprenavir results in reduction of the viral load (HIV-RNA) in the plasma and an increase in the CD4 lymphocyte cell count. *The protease inhibitor activity results in the formation of immature, noninfectious viral particles. Effectiveness is measured by reduced viral particle count.*

USES Treatment of HIV infection in combination with other antiretroviral agents.

CONTRAINDICATIONS Prior sensitivity to amprenavir; lactation, oral solution in children <4 y, infants, neonates; renal failure.
CAUTIOUS USE History of hypersensitivity to other protease inhibitors (e.g., indinavir, ritonavir, saquinavir); hypersensitivity to sulfonamides; hepatic dysfunction; diabetes mellitus; diabetic ketoacidosis, hemophilia A and B; vitamin K deficiencies; anticoagulant therapy; oral contraceptives; coadministration with rifampin or sildenafil; antimicrobial resistance, hypercholesterolemia, hypertriglycerides, hyperglycemia, females, children, hepatic or renal impairment; pregnancy (category C).

ROUTE & DOSAGE

HIV Infection

Adult/Adolescent: **PO** 1200 mg capsules b.i.d.
Child: **PO** 4–12 y or <50 kg, 20 mg/kg b.i.d. capsules or 15 mg/kg t.i.d. capsules (max: 2400 mg/d); 22.5 mg/kg b.i.d. oral solution or 17 mg/kg t.i.d. oral solution

Common adverse effects in *italic*, life-threatening effects underlined; generic names in **bold**; classifications in SMALL CAPS; ✦ Canadian drug name; ❷ Prototype drug

ADMINISTRATION

Oral

- Give without regard to food, BUT not with high fat meal.
- Capsules & oral solution are not interchangeable on mg-for-mg basis.
- Give 1 h before/after antacid.
- Store tablets at 20°–25° C (68°–77° F). Do not refrigerate.

ADVERSE EFFECTS (≥1%) **CNS:** *Oral/perioral paresthesia,* peripheral paresthesia, depression, mood disorders. **GI:** *Nausea, vomiting, diarrhea,* taste disorders, increased triglycerides, hyperglycemia. **Skin:** *Rash,* Stevens-Johnson syndrome.

INTERACTIONS Drug: Administration with **amiodarone, bepridil, dihydroergotamine, ergotamine, lidocaine, midazolam, quinidine, triazolam,** and TRICYCLIC ANTIDEPRESSANTS may cause life-threatening reactions; **rifampin, rifabutin,** ORAL CONTRACEPTIVES, **phenobarbital, phenytoin, carbamazepine** decrease **amprenavir** concentrations; **amprenavir** may increase **dihydroergotamine, ergotamine sildenafil** concentrations and toxicity; **amprenavir** may decrease **methadone** levels; monitor INR with **warfarin; oral solution** may cause antabuse reaction with **disulfiram, metronidazole. Food:** Decreased absorption with high-fat meal. **Herbal: St. John's wort** may decrease antiretroviral activity.

PHARMACOKINETICS Absorption: Oral solution is less absorbed than capsules. **Peak:** 1–2 h. **Distribution:** 90% bound to plasma proteins. **Metabolism:** In liver by CYP3A4. **Elimination:** 14% in urine, 75% in feces as metabolites. **Half-Life:** 7.1–10.6 h.

CLINICAL IMPLICATIONS

Assessment & Drug Effects

- Monitor for therapeutic effectiveness which is indicated by elevated CD_4 count & decreased HIV RNA copies.
- Monitor for & promptly notify physician of severe skin rash.
- Lab tests: Monitor blood glucose & HbA_{1c}, Hgb & Hct, and lipid profile at periodic intervals.
- Note: Monitor blood levels for coadministered drugs including amiodarone, lidocaine, phenobarbital, phenytoin, quinidine, tricyclic antidepressants; monitor PT and INR with warfarin.

Patient & Family Education

- Follow directions for taking this drug (see ADMINISTRATION).
- Take drug exactly as prescribed at the indicated times. Missed dose: if less than 4 h, wait until the next scheduled dose; otherwise, take immediately.
- Do not take supplemental vitamin E with this drug unless approved by physician.
- Notify physician promptly about skin rash, nausea, vomiting, diarrhea, numbness or tingling around mouth or hands & feet.
- Inform physician of all other prescription/nonprescription drugs being taken. Serious interactions can occur.
- Use alternative barrier contraceptives rather than hormonal contraceptives while taking this drug.
- Note: Redistribution/accumulation of body fat may occur.
- Note: Diabetics may experience loss of glycemic control.

Common adverse effects in *italic*, life-threatening effects underlined; generic names in **bold**; classifications in SMALL CAPS; ♣ Canadian drug name; ● Prototype drug

97

AMYL NITRITE

(am'il)
Amyl Nitrite
Classifications: NITRATE VASODI-
LATOR; ANTIDOTE
Therapeutic: ANTIDOTE; NITRATE
VASODILATOR
Prototype: Nitroglycerin
Pregnancy Category: X

AVAILABILITY 0.3 mL ampules

ACTION & *THERAPEUTIC EFFECT*
Short-acting vasodilator and
smooth muscle relaxant. It is converted to nitric oxide, which
causes the vasodilation. Action in
treatment of cyanide poisoning is
based on ability of amyl nitrite to
convert hemoglobin to methemoglobin, which forms a nontoxic
complex with cyanide ion. *Effective for immediate treatment of cyanide poisoning.*

USES As an adjunct antidote in the
immediate treatment of cyanide
poisoning. (Because of adverse effects, unpleasant odor, and expense, infrequently used to treat
angina pectoris.)
UNLABELED USES Change intensity
of heart murmurs.

CONTRAINDICATIONS Hypersensitivity to nitrites or nitrates; severe
anemia; uncontrolled hyperthyroidism; acute alcoholism; pregnancy (category X).
CAUTIOUS USE Lactation; children;
elderly; recent increase in intracranial pressure; cerebral hemorrhage,
head trauma; hypotension; glaucoma; recent MI.

ROUTE & DOSAGE

Acute Angina
Adult: Inhalation 0.18–0.3 mL prn

Cyanide Poisoning
Adult/Child: Inhalation 0.3 mL
perle crushed every minute and
inhaled for 15–30 s until sodium
nitrite infusion is ready

ADMINISTRATION

Inhalation

- Crush ampule between fingers to
  prepare (amyl nitrite is available
  in 0.18 mL and 0.3 mL perles,
  which are thin, friable glass ampules enveloped with woven fabric cover).
- Instruct patient to sit a while immediately after drug is administered.
- Note: Amyl nitrite is volatile and
  highly flammable; when mixed
  with air or oxygen, it forms a mixture that can explode if ignited.
- Store at 8°–15° C (46°–59° F), unless otherwise directed. Protect
  from light.

ADVERSE EFFECTS (≥1%) **Body as
a Whole:** Transient flushing, weakness. **CV:** Orthostatic hypotension,
palpitation, <u>cardiovascular collapse</u>,
tachycardia. **GI:** Nausea, vomiting.
Hematologic: <u>Methemoglobinemia</u>
<u>(large doses)</u>. **CNS:** *Headache*, diz-
ziness, syncope. **Respiratory:** <u>Res-</u>
<u>piratory depression</u>.

PHARMACOKINETICS Absorption:
Rapidly from mucous membranes.
Onset: 10–30 s. **Duration:** 3–5 min.

CLINICAL IMPLICATIONS

Assessment & Drug Effects

- Monitor for S&S of syncope, due
  to a sudden drop in systolic BP,
  which sometimes follows drug inhalation, particularly in older
  adults.
- Monitor vital signs until stable.
  Rapid pulse, which usually lasts

for a brief period, is an expected response to the fall in BP produced by the drug.

- Chart length of time required for pain to subside after administration of drug.
- Note: Tolerance may develop with repeated use over prolonged periods.

Patient & Family Education

- Note: Drug has a strongly fruity odor.
- Go to the emergency room immediately or consult physician if no relief from angina is experienced after 3 doses 5 min apart.

ANAGRELIDE HYDROCHLORIDE

(a-na'gre-lyde)
Agrylin
Classifications: ANTICOAGULANT; ANTIPLATELET AGENT
Therapeutic: ANTIPLATELET; ANTI-THROMBOLYTIC
Pregnancy Category: C

AVAILABILITY 0.5 mg, 1 mg capsules

ACTION & *THERAPEUTIC EFFECT*
Anagrelide action appears to be related to a selective inhibition of platelet production. It inhibits platelet aggregation by affecting several aggregating agents (e.g., thrombin and arachidonic acid, ADP, and collagen). *Anagrelide is associated with significant decreases in platelet counts and is thought to prevent early changes in shape of platelets.*

USES Essential thrombocythemia.
UNLABELED USES Polycythemia vera.

CONTRAINDICATIONS Pregnancy (category C), lactation; hypotension, severe hepatic impairment, females of childbearing age.
CAUTIOUS USE Cardiovascular disease, renal and hepatic function impairment, jaundice. Safety and efficacy in patients <16 y are not established.

ROUTE & DOSAGE

Essential Thrombocythemia
Adult: **PO** ≥*16 y*, start with 0.5 mg q.i.d. or 1 mg b.i.d. times 1 wk, may increase by 0.5 mg/d qwk until platelet count is <600,000/mcL (max: 10 mg/d)

Hepatic Impairment
0.5 mg q.d. for 1 wk

ADMINISTRATION

Oral

- Make sure dosage increments do not exceed 0.5 mg/d in any 1 wk.
- Store at 15°–25° C (59°–77° F) in a light-resistant container.

ADVERSE EFFECTS (≥1%) **Body as a Whole:** *Asthenia, pain, edema (general)*, paresthesia, back pain, malaise, fever, chills, photosensitivity. **CNS:** Headache, *dizziness*, CVA, syncope, seizures. **CV:** *Palpitations,* chest pain, tachycardia, peripheral edema, CHF, MI, cardiomyopathy, heart block, atrial fibrillation, pericarditis, arrhythmia, hemorrhage. **GI:** *Diarrhea, abdominal pain, nausea,* flatulence, vomiting, dyspepsia, anorexia, pancreatitis, constipation, GI hemorrhage, and ulceration. **Hematologic:** Anemia, thrombocytopenia, ecchymoses, lymphedema. **Respiratory:** *Dyspnea,* pulmonary infiltrates, pulmonary fibrosis, pulmonary hypertension. **Skin:** Rash, urticaria. **Other:** Dysuria.

Common adverse effects in *italic*, life-threatening effects underlined; generic names in **bold**; classifications in SMALL CAPS; ◆ Canadian drug name; ◎ Prototype drug

99

PHARMACOKINETICS Absorption: 70% from GI tract. Food reduces bioavailability. **Onset:** 7–14 d. **Duration:** increased platelet counts were observed 4 d after discontinuing drug. **Metabolism:** Extensively metabolized. **Elimination:** Primarily in urine as metabolites. **Half-Life:** 1.3–1.8 h.

CLINICAL IMPLICATIONS

Assessment & Drug Effects

- Monitor for therapeutic effectiveness which is indicated by reduction of platelets for at least 4 wk to ≤600,000/mcL or 50% from baseline.
- Monitor for S&S of CHF or myocardial ischemia.
- Monitor for S&S of renal toxicity in patients with renal insufficiency (creatinine ≥2 mg/dL).
- Monitor for S&S of hepatic toxicity in patients with liver functions >1.5 times upper limit of normal.
- Lab tests: Monitor platelet count q2d for first wk, weekly thereafter until maintenance dose reached; closely monitor Hgb, WBC count, liver function tests, and BUN and creatinine while platelet count is being lowered.

Patient & Family Education

- Contact physician if palpitations, fluid retention, breathing difficulty, or any other distressful symptoms develop.
- Avoid excessive exposure to sunlight or UV light.

ANAKINRA

(an-a-kin′ra)
Kineret
Classifications: IMMUNOMODULATOR; INTERLEUKIN-1 RECEPTOR ANTAGONIST
Therapeutic: ANTIRHEUMATIC
Pregnancy Category: B

AVAILABILITY 100 mg prefilled syringes

ACTION & *THERAPEUTIC EFFECT*
Anakinra is a recombinant human interleukin-1 (IL-1) receptor antagonist (IL-1R1). It blocks the biologic activity of IL-1 by inhibiting it from binding to interleukin receptors that are present in both bone and cartilage as well as other kinds of tissues. Interleukin-1 is produced in response to inflammation. It mediates various responses of tissues, including inflammatory and immunologic responses. *Anakinra competes with interleukin-1 (IL-1) by inhibiting it from binding to its receptor sites in tissues.*

USES Treatment of rheumatoid arthritis in patients failing other disease modifying antirheumatic drugs (DMARDs). Usually given in combination with another DMARD.

CONTRAINDICATIONS Hypersensitivity to anakinra, *E. coli* derived products, latex; active infections; live vaccines.

CAUTIOUS USE Pregnancy (category B), lactation; neutropenia, immunosuppressed patients, or patients with frequent, serious infections; asthmatics; elderly; renal impairment; children; concomitant use of tumor necrosis factor blocking agents (TNF), etanercept, or infliximab.

ROUTE & DOSAGE

Rheumatoid Arthritis
Adult: **SC** 100 mg daily

ADMINISTRATION

Subcutaneous

- Do not give anakinra if the patient has an active infection.
- Note that anakinra should not ordinarily be given with tumor

necrosis factor (TNF) blocking agents.

- Discard any unused portions as the drug contains no preservative.
- Check expiration date and do not use if expired.
- Store in the refrigerator at 2° to 8° C (36° to 46° F). DO NOT FREEZE OR SHAKE. Protect from light.

ADVERSE EFFECTS (≥1%) **Body as a Whole:** *Bacterial infections (URI,* sinusitis, flu, *other).* **CNS:** Headache. **GI:** Nausea, diarrhea, abdominal pain. **Hematologic:** Decreased neutrophil count, antibody formation. **Other:** *Injection site reactions (erythema, ecchymosis, edema, inflammation, pain).*

INTERACTIONS Drug: Increased risk of infection with live virus vaccine, **etanercept, infliximab.** Increase risk of neutropenia as well as infection with **etanercept** and **infliximab.**

PHARMACOKINETICS Absorption: 95% absorbed SC site. **Peak:** 3–7 h. **Elimination:** In urine. **Half-Life:** 4–6 h.

CLINICAL IMPLICATIONS

Assessment & Drug Effects

- Monitor for S&S of infection (e.g., pneumonia or other URI, cellulitis). Withhold drug and notify physician if these appear.
- Lab tests: Monitor absolute neutrophil count (ANC) prior to initiating anakinra, monthly for 3 mo, and q3mo thereafter for 1 y; monitor periodically WBC and platelet counts.
- Monitor closely patients with impaired renal function for S&S of adverse drug reactions.
- Assess for injection site reactions manifested by erythema, ecchymosis, inflammation, and pain.

Patient & Family Education

- Review carefully the "Information for Patients and Caregivers" leaflet for detailed instructions on handling and injecting anakinra.
- Give the injection at approximately the same time every day.
- Administer only 1 dose (the entire contents of 1 prefilled glass syringe) per day. Discard any unused portions as the drug contains no preservative. Do not save unused drug.
- Do not permit vaccination with live vaccines while taking anakinra.
- Withhold drug and notify physician for S&S of upper respiratory, skin, or other infection(s).

ANASTROZOLE ℗

(a-nas'tro-zole)
Arimidex
Classifications: ANTINEOPLASTIC; NONSTEROIDAL AROMATASE INHIBITOR
Therapeutic: ANTINEOPLASTIC
Pregnancy Category: D

AVAILABILITY 1 mg tablets

ACTION & THERAPEUTIC EFFECT
Anastrozole is a potent and selective nonsteroidal aromatase inhibitor that converts estrone to estradiol. It lowers serum estrogen levels in postmenopausal women without interfering with adrenal steroid synthesis. *Inhibiting the biosynthesis of estrogens is one way to deprive tumors of estrogens, and thus restrict tumor growth.*

USES Early and advanced breast cancer in postmenopausal women.

CONTRAINDICATIONS Pregnancy (category D), lactation, premenopausal women, postmenopausal

Common adverse effects in *italic*, life-threatening effects underlined; generic names in **bold**; classifications in SMALL CAPS; ♣ Canadian drug name; ℗ Prototype drug

101

hormone replacement therapy; severe hepatic disease, children. **CAUTIOUS USE** Mild to moderate hepatic disease.

ROUTE & DOSAGE

Breast Cancer
Adult: **PO** 1 mg once daily

ADMINISTRATION

Oral

▪ Give on an empty stomach, 1 h before or 2 h after meals, because food affects extent of absorption.

▪ Store at 20°–25° C (68°–77° F).

ADVERSE EFFECTS (≥1%) **CNS:** Asthenia, headache, hot flushes, pain, dizziness, depression, paresthesia, malaise, insomnia, confusion, anxiety, nervousness. **CV:** Chest pain, hypertension, thrombophlebitis, edema. **GI:** *Diarrhea,* nausea, vomiting, constipation, abdominal pain, anorexia, dry mouth, increased liver function tests (ALT, AST, GGT). **Respiratory:** Dyspnea, cough, pharyngitis, bronchitis, rhinitis, sinusitis. **Other:** Rash, peripheral edema, pelvic pain, flu-like syndrome.

PHARMACOKINETICS Absorption: Rapidly absorbed from GI tract. **Distribution:** 40% protein bound. **Metabolism:** 85% metabolized in liver to inactive metabolites. **Elimination:** 10% excreted unchanged; 60% as metabolites in urine. **Half-Life:** 50 h.

CLINICAL IMPLICATIONS

Assessment & Drug Effects

▪ Lab Tests: Monitor periodically liver enzymes, CBC with differential, alkaline phosphatases, total cholesterol, and lipid profile.

▪ Assess for hypertension, complications of edema, thrombotic events, and signs of liver toxicity.

Patient & Family Education

▪ Recognize common adverse effects and seek information on measures to control discomfort.

▪ Seek medical attention if you experience chest pain, calf pain, or shortness of breath; unexplained loss of appetite or nausea; jaundice.

ANIDULAFUNGIN

(a-ni-dul′a-fun-gin)
Eraxis

Classifications: ANTIBIOTIC; ECHINOCANDIN ANTIFUNGAL
Therapeutic: ANTIFUNGAL ANTIBIOTIC
Prototype: Caspofungin
Pregnancy Category: C

AVAILABILITY 50 mg powder for injection

ACTION & *THERAPEUTIC EFFECT* Anidulafungin is a semisynthetic echinocandin with antifungal activity. It inhibits glucan synthase, an enzyme present in fungal cells. Glucan is an essential component of the fungal cell wall; therefore, anidulafungin causes fungal cell death. *Anidulafungin interferes with reproduction and growth of susceptible fungi.*

USES Treatment of candidemia and other *Candida* infections caused by *C. albicans, C. glabrata, C. parapsilosis,* and *C. tropicalis.* Treatment of esophageal candidiasis.

UNLABELED USES Fungal prophylaxis in immunocompromised children who are hospitalized with neutropenia.

CONTRAINDICATIONS Hypersensitivity to anidulafungin or another echinocandin antifungal agent; pregnancy (category C), lactation.

CAUTIOUS USE Hepatic impairment. Safety and efficacy in children have not been established.

ROUTE & DOSAGE

Candidemia and Other *Candida* Infections

Adult: **IV** 200 mg loading dose on day 1, then 100 mg IV daily for at least 14 d after last positive culture

For the Treatment of Esophageal Candidiasis:

Adult: **IV** 100 mg loading dose on day 1, then 50 mg IV daily for at least 14 d (and for at least 7 d after resolution of symptoms)

ADMINISTRATION

Intravenous

PREPARE: IV Infusion: Reconstitute each vial with the supplied single-use 15 mL vial of diluent (20% [w/w] dehydrated alcohol in water) to yield 3.33 mg/mL. Each 50 mg reconstituted vial must be further diluted with NS for D5W to a total infusion volume of 100 mL with a concentration of 0.5 mg/mL.

- For a 50 mg dose, dilute 15 mL reconstituted solution in 100 mL of IV fluid to yield 0.43 mg/mL.
- For a 100 mg dose, dilute 30 mL reconstituted solution in 250 mL of IV fluid to yield 0.36 mg/mL. ▪For a 200 mg dose, dilute 60 mL reconstituted solution in 500 mL of IV fluid to yield 0.36 mg/mL.

ADMINISTER: IV Infusion: Give at a rate **no greater** than 1.1 mg/min. DO NOT give a bolus dose.

INCOMPATIBILITIES Y-site: **Amphotericin B, ertapenem, sodium bicarbonate.**

- Store unreconstituted vials, reconstituted vials, and companion diluent vials at 15° to 30° C (59°–86° F). Reconstituted vials must be further diluted and administered within 24 h.

ADVERSE EFFECTS (≥1%) **Body as a Whole:** Hypersensitivity. **CNS:** Headache. **GI:** Diarrhea, nausea. **Hematologic:** Neutropenia. **Metabolic:** Increased alkaline phosphatase, increased ALT, increased gamma-glutamyl transferase, hypokalemia. **Skin:** Rash.

INTERACTIONS Drug: Cyclosporin increases overall systemic exposure (i.e., area under the curve, or AUC).

PHARMACOKINETICS Distribution: 84% protein bound. **Metabolism:** Non-hepatic degradation to inactive metabolites. **Elimination:** Fecal. **Half-Life:** 40–50 h.

CLINICAL IMPLICATIONS

Assessment & Drug Effects

- Prior to initiating therapy with anidulafungin, obtain specimen for fungal culture.
- Monitor for and report S&S of hypersensitivity (e.g., dyspnea, flushing, hypotension, swelling about the face, pruritus, rash, and urticaria) or liver dysfunction (e.g., jaundice, clay-colored stools).
- Discontinue infusion if signs of hypersensitivity appear.
- Monitor cardiac status especially with a preexisting history of dysrhythmias.
- Lab tests: Baseline and periodic liver function tests; periodic CBC with differential and platelet count; periodic serum electrolytes, amylase, and lipase.

Common adverse effects in *italic*, life-threatening effects <u>underlined</u>; generic names in **bold**; classifications in SMALL CAPS; ✦ Canadian drug name; ❷ Prototype drug

103

- Monitor for S&S hypokalemia and hepatic toxicity (see Appendix F).
- Monitor diabetics for loss of glycemic control.

Patient & Family Education

- Report any of the following immediately if experienced during or shortly after infusion: difficulty breathing, swelling about the face, itching, rash.
- Report S&S of jaundice to the physician: clay-colored stool, dark urine, yellow skin or sclera, unexplained abdominal pain, or fatigue.

APOMORPHINE HYDROCHLORIDE

(a-po-mor'feen)

Apokyn

Classifications: ANTIPARKINSON AGENT; DOPAMINE RECEPTOR AGONIST
Therapeutic: ANTIPARKINSON AGENT
Pregnancy Category: C

AVAILABILITY 10 mg/mL injection

ACTION & *THERAPEUTIC EFFECT*
Apomorphine has central dopamine receptor agonist properties. Its mechanism of action in treatment of Parkinson's is thought to be related to its stimulation of centrally located postsynaptic dopamine D_2-type receptors. *Diminishes hypomobility associated with "off" episodes ("end-of-dose wearing off" and unpredictable "on/off" episodes) in persons with advanced Parkinson's disease.*

USES Rescue of "off" episodes associated with advanced Parkinson's disease.

CONTRAINDICATIONS Concomitant use of drugs of the 5-HT$_3$ antagonist class (e.g., ondansetron, granisetron, dolasetron, palonosetron, and alosetron); hypersensitivity to the drug or its ingredients (i.e., sodium metabisulfite), benzyl alcohol hypersensitivity; renal failure; QT prolongation; heart failure, or shock; depression, suicidal ideation; decreased alertness, seizures, seizure disorder, unconscious state or coma, decreased alertness; pregnancy (category C); lactation.
CAUTIOUS USE Cardiovascular, cerebrovascular, respiratory, renal, or hepatic disease; CNS depression, history of (chronic) depression or suicidal ideation; hypotension; vomiting; bradycardia; hypokalemia and hypomagnesemia; older adult; hypersensitivity to sulfite.

ROUTE & DOSAGE

"Off" Episodes of Parkinson's Disease

Adult: **SC** Start with a test dose where BP can be closely monitored. Escalate test dose no sooner than 2 h after last dose until dose is not tolerated or patient has response. If test dose of 0.2 mL (2 mg) is tolerated and has positive response, continue with 0.2 mL (2 mg); if no response, use test dose of 0.4 mL (4 mg); if tolerated and has a positive response, continue with 0.3 mL (3 mg); if 0.4 mL test dose is not tolerated, try 0.3 mL (3 mg) test dose; if 0.3 mL is tolerated, continue with 0.2 mL (2 mg). May increase by 1 mg every few days, generally should not exceed 0.4 mL (4 mg) as an outpatient. Max dose: 0.6 mL as single injection and max 5 injections/d. If therapy is interrupted for 1 wk, restart with 2 mg dose.

ADMINISTRATION

Subcutaneous

- The dosing pen is marked in mL, not mg, increments; a 1 mg dose is equal to 0.1 mL.
- Aspirate to avoid intravascular injection and ensure the injection is SC and not intradermal.
- Rotate SC sites to reduce skin reactions.
- If the patient has not received apomorphine in more than 1 wk, reinstitute it by starting with the initial test dose and titrating to the desired dose.
- Apomorphine SC causes nausea and vomiting; thus the recommendation is to give 300 mg of trimethobenzamide PO t.i.d., starting 3 d before the first injection and continued for at least the first 2 mo of treatment.
- Store at 15°–30° C (59°–86° F).

ADVERSE EFFECTS (≥1%) Body as a Whole: Weakness, yawning, tiredness. CNS: CNS depression, dizziness, drowsiness, headache, lightheadedness, euphoria, restlessness, tremor, depression, *dyskinesias, hallucinations.* CV: <u>Acute circulatory failure</u>, bradycardia, hypertension, orthostatic hypotension, QT prolongation, vasovagal response, syncope. GI: *Nausea, vomiting,* hypersalivation, taste perversions. Metabolic: Peripheral edema. Respiratory: Respiratory depression, tachypnea, cough, pharyngitis, rhinitis. Skin: Contact dermatitis, *bruising,* granuloma, pruritus, sweating. Urogenital: *Frequent penile erections,* painful erections.

INTERACTIONS Drug: Alosetron, dolasetron, granisetron, ondansetron, palonosetron may cause severe hypotension and unconsciousness; alfuzosin, amoxapine, bepridil, chloroquine, clozapine, cyclobenzaprine, droperidol, flecainide, halofantrine, halothane, levomethadyl, LOCAL ANESTHETICS, MACROLIDES (clarithromycin, erythromycin, troleandomycin), maprotiline, mefloquine, methadone, pentamidine, PHENOTHIAZINES, probucol, gatifloxacin, gemifloxacin, grepafloxacin, levofloxacin, moxifloxacin, sparfloxacin, tacrolimus, TRICYCLIC ANTIDEPRESSANTS, amiodarone, clozapine, disopyramide, dofetilide, dolasetron, haloperidol, ibutilide, mesoridazine, palonosetron, pimozide, procainamide, quinidine, thioridazine, sotalol, ziprasidone may exacerbate QTc prolongation; may increase CNS depression with other CNS depressants, including TRICYCLIC ANTIDEPRESSANTS, ANXIOLYTICS, SEDATIVES, HYPNOTICS, dronabinol, GENERAL ANESTHETICS, mirtazapine, nefazodone, OPIATE AGONISTS, pramipexole, ropinirole, SKELETAL MUSCLE RELAXANTS, tramadol, trazodone. Herbal: Kava-kava may increase the symptoms of Parkinson's disease.

PHARMACOKINETICS Absorption: SC absorption dependent on site utilized—abdominal injection absorbed faster than thigh; lowering the temperature of the injection site slows absorption. Onset: 7–14 min. Peak: 40–60 min. Duration: Up to 2 h. Distribution: 85–90% protein bound. Metabolism: Metabolized by glucuronidation, sulfation, and N-demethylation. Elimination: Excreted by kidneys. Half-Life: 30–60 min.

CLINICAL IMPLICATIONS

Assessment & Drug Effects

- Periodic ECG, especially in those with known CV disease.
- Withhold drug & notify physician for S&S of torsades de pointes

---

Common adverse effects in *italic*, life-threatening effects <u>underlined</u>; generic names in **bold**; classifications in SMALL CAPS; ✚ Canadian drug name; ⊘ Prototype drug

105

(i.e., palpitations and syncope), especially in those with bradycardia or suspected hypokalemia or hypomagnesemia.

- Lab tests: Periodic serum electrolytes.
- Monitor closely for orthostatic hypotension, especially when doses are increased, and in patients taking antihypertensive medications and vasodilators (especially nitrates).

Patient & Family Education

- The dosing pen is marked in mL (not mg) increments; a 1 mg dose is equal to 0.1 mL.
- Avoid the use of alcohol while taking this drug.
- Report promptly any of the following: irregular or fast, pounding heartbeat, or palpitations; dizziness, lightheadedness, or fainting; unexplained weakness, tiredness, or sleepiness; confusion, hallucinations, or depression; unusual body movements; vomiting; or prolonged painful erections.
- Do not engage in potentially hazardous activities until reaction to drug is known.

APRACLONIDINE

(a-pra-clo'ni-deen)
Iopidine
Pregnancy Category: C
See Appendix A-1.

APREPITANT

(a-pre'pi-tant)
Emend
Classifications: ANTIEMETIC; SUBSTANCE P/NEUROKININ 1 (NK$_1$) RECEPTOR ANTAGONIST
Therapeutic: ANTIEMETIC
Pregnancy Category: B

AVAILABILITY 80 mg, 125 mg capsules

ACTION & *THERAPEUTIC EFFECT*
Aprepitant is a selective substance P/neurokinin 1 (NK$_1$) receptor antagonist. Substance P and the NK-1 receptors are present in areas in the brain that control the emetic reflex. Aprepitant crosses the blood–brain barrier and occupies brain NK$_1$ receptors. Peripheral blockade by NK$_1$ receptor antagonists at receptors located in the GI is an additional hypothesized mechanism of action. *Aprepitant augments the antiemetic activity of the 5-HT$_3$-receptor antagonist, ondansetron, and inhibits both the acute and delayed phases of emesis induced by chemotherapy agents.*

USES Prevention of acute and delayed nausea and vomiting associated with emetogenic chemotherapy.

CONTRAINDICATIONS Hypersensitivity to aprepitant; concurrent use of pimozide; children <18 y; lactation.
CAUTIOUS USE Chemotherapeutic agents metabolized through CYP3A4; severe hepatic impairment; severe renal impairment without dialysis; pregnancy (category B).

ROUTE & DOSAGE

Chemotherapy-Induced Nausea & Vomiting
Adult: **PO** 125 mg 1 h prior to chemotherapy, then 80 mg qam for the next 2 d in conjunction with other antiemetics

ADMINISTRATION
Oral
- Ensure that capsule is swallowed whole with a full glass of water.

Do not crush or sprinkle the contents of the capsule.
- Give 1 h before start of chemotherapy.
- Store at 20°–25° C (68°–77° F). Keep the desiccant in the original bottle.

ADVERSE EFFECTS (≥1%) **Body as a Whole:** *Fatigue,* asthenia, malaise, dehydration, fever. **CNS:** Dizziness, insomnia, headache, peripheral neuropathy, sensory neuropathy, anxiety, confusion, depression. **GI:** *Constipation, diarrhea, anorexia, nausea, hiccups,* abdominal pain, gastritis, gastroesophageal reflux, abnormal or impaired taste (dysgeusia), dyspepsia, dysphagia, flatulence, hypersalivation, increased taste disturbance, increased AST and ALT. **Hematologic:** Neutropenia, anemia. **Musculoskeletal:** Pain, myalgia. **Respiratory:** Cough, dyspnea, upper or lower respiratory infection, pneumonitis, respiratory insufficiency. **Special Senses:** Tinnitus.

INTERACTIONS Drug: Increased risk of cardiovascular toxicity with **dofetilide, pimozide;** may decrease **warfarin** concentrations and INR; may decrease levels and effectiveness of ORAL CONTRACEPTIVES; **carbamazepine, griseofulvin, modafinil, rifabutin, rifapentine, phenobarbital, primidone** may decrease antiemetic efficacy; may increase levels of **dexamethasone.** Because aprepitant is a substrate of CYP3A4, many additional drug interactions are theoretically possible. **Food: Grapefruit juice** may decrease effectiveness of aprepitant. **Herbal: St. John's wort** may decrease effectiveness of aprepitant.

PHARMACOKINETICS Absorption: 60–65% of oral dose reaches systemic circulation. **Peak:** 4 h. **Duration:** 95% protein bound; readily crosses the blood–brain barrier. **Metabolism:** In liver by CYP3A4. **Elimination:** Not renally excreted. **Half-Life:** 9–12 h.

CLINICAL IMPLICATIONS

Assessment & Drug Effects
- Monitor cardiac status especially with preexisting CV disease or concurrent use of any CYP3A4 substrate drug (e.g., ketoconazole, itraconazole, nefazodone, troleandomycin, clarithromycin).
- Lab tests: Monitor PT/INR 7–10 d after 3-d regimen with concurrent warfarin use; monitor phenytoin level with concurrent use; monitor serum electrolytes, UA, and CBC.

Patient & Family Education
- Report immediately to physician any of the following: skin rash; difficulty breathing or shortness of breath; rapid, slow, or irregular heartbeat; changes in BP; dizziness or confusion; unexplained sharp or severe pain in leg or stomach; rectal bleeding. Inform physician of all other drugs or herbal products you are using. Do not take new drugs (prescription, OTC, herbal) without first consulting physician.
- Use barrier contraception in addition to oral contraceptives while taking drug.

APROTININ

(a-pro′ti-nin)
Trasylol
Classifications: HEMOSTATIC; ANTIFIBRINOLYTIC; PROTEASE INHIBITOR
Therapeutic: HEMOSTATIC; ANTIFIBRINOLYTIC
Prototype: Aminocaproic acid
Pregnancy Category: B

Common adverse effects in *italic*, life-threatening effects underlined; generic names in **bold**; classifications in SMALL CAPS; ✦ Canadian drug name; ☻ Prototype drug

107

AVAILABILITY 10,000 KIU/mL injection (one KIU equals 0.14 mg)

ACTION & *THERAPEUTIC EFFECT*
A proteolytic enzyme inhibitor of bovine origin. It inhibits protease by interaction with certain proteases; aprotinin has antifibrinolytic effect, hemostatic stabilizing effect, and weak anticoagulant effect. *Aprotinin reduces postoperative bleeding in coronary bypass surgery patients by inhibiting fibrinolytic activity while preserving platelet adhesive function and prolonging postoperative bleeding time.*

USES Prophylactically to reduce perioperative blood loss and need for blood transfusions during cardiopulmonary bypass in the course of repeat coronary artery bypass surgery. May also be used in selected cases of primary coronary artery bypass graft surgery where the risk of bleeding is especially high (i.e., impaired hemostasis, coagulopathy).

CONTRAINDICATIONS Hypersensitivity to aprotinin and bovine products.

CAUTIOUS USE Patients with heparinized blood; patients previously treated with aprotinin; renal impairment, renal failure, pregnancy (category B). Safety and efficacy in children are not established.

ROUTE & DOSAGE

Cardiac Surgery
Adult: IV Test Dose 1 mL (10,000 kallikrein inactivator units [KIU]) given at least 10 min prior to loading dose (observe for signs of an allergic reaction) **Standard Regimen IV Loading Dose** 2 million KIU over 20–30 min; add 2 million KIU to the priming fluid of the cardiopulmonary priming pump; constant infusion of 500,000 KIU/h, continue until the patient leaves the OR **Alternate Regimen IV Loading Dose** 1 million KIU over 20–30 min; 1 million into pump prime volume; 250,000 KIU/h while in OR

ADMINISTRATION

Intravenous

PREPARE: **IV Test Dose/Loading Dose:** Use as supplied (1 mL = 1.4 mg or 10,000 KIU) without further dilution.
ADMINISTER: **IV Test Dose:** Give direct IV push over 1 min. **IV Loading Dose:** Give over 20–30 min. **Continuous:** Follow with infusion at 50 mL/h. Use central venous catheter exclusively for aprotinin.
INCOMPATIBILITIES Solution/additive: AMINO ACIDS, CORTICOSTEROIDS, fat emulsion, **heparin,** TETRACYCLINES.

▪ Store at controlled room temperature.

ADVERSE EFFECTS (≥1%) **Body as a Whole:** Hypersensitivity reactions (rash, urticaria, <u>anaphylaxis</u>). **CV:** Tachycardia, stroke, <u>MI</u>. **Hematologic:** Thromboembolism. **Skin:** Rash, urticaria. **Urogenital:** <u>Nephrotoxicity</u> (elevated serum creatinine). **Other:** <u>Bronchospasm</u>.

INTERACTIONS Drug: Heparin results in further prolongation of the whole blood activated clotting time (ACT).

PHARMACOKINETICS Distribution: Rapidly into extracellular fluid, then accumulates in proximal renal tubular epithelial cells; crosses placenta; distributed into breast milk. **Metabolism:** Primarily in kidneys to small peptides or amino acids. **Elimina-**

tion: By kidneys. **Half-Life:** Initial 0.7 h, terminal 7 h.

CLINICAL IMPLICATIONS

Assessment & Drug Effects

- Monitor carefully for S&S of hypersensitivity during administration (see Appendix F). If hypersensitivity occurs, immediately discontinue aprotinin and begin emergency treatment to prevent anaphylaxis.
- Monitor cardiac status and pulmonary function carefully during infusion. Patients with a history of hypersensitivity to any allergens or who have previously received aprotinin are at special risk for hypersensitivity.
- Lab tests: After surgery, monitor aPTT, ACT, and cardiac, pulmonary, renal, and liver functions.

ARGATROBAN

(ar-ga'tro-ban)
Acova, Novastan
Classifications: ANTICOAGULANT; THROMBIN INHIBITOR
Therapeutic: ANTICOAGULANT; THROMBIN INHIBITOR
Prototype: Lepirudin
Pregnancy Category: C

AVAILABILITY 250 mg/2.5 mL vials

ACTION & THERAPEUTIC EFFECT
Synthetic derivative of arginine that is a direct thrombin inhibitor. Capable of inhibiting the action of both free and clot-bound thrombin. *Reversibly binds to the thrombin active site, thereby blocking clot-forming activity of thrombin.*

USES Prophylaxis or treatment of thrombosis in patients with heparin-induced thrombocytopenia (HIT); prophylaxis or treatment of coronary artery thrombosis during percutaneous coronary interventions (PCI) in patients at risk for HIT.

UNLABELED USES Treatment of disseminated intravascular coagulation (DIC).

CONTRAINDICATIONS Hypersensitivity to argatroban; lactation. Any bleeding including intracranial bleeding, GI bleeding, retroperitoneal bleeding, pregnancy (category C); severe hepatic impairment.

CAUTIOUS USE Diseased states with increased risk of hemorrhaging; severe hypertension; GI ulcerations, hepatic impairment; spinal anesthesia, stroke, surgery, trauma. Safety and effectiveness in children <18 y are not established.

ROUTE & DOSAGE

Prevention & Treatment of Thrombosis
Adult: **IV** 2 mcg/kg/min, may be adjusted to maintain an aPTT of 1.5–3 times baseline (max: 10 mcg/kg/min)

Hepatic Impairment
Adult: **IV** 0.5 mcg/kg/min, may be adjusted to maintain an aPTT of 1.5–3 times baseline (max: 10 mcg/kg/min)

Prophylaxis or Treatment of Coronary Thrombosis during PCI
Adult: **IV** 350 mcg/kg administered via a large bore IV line over 3–5 min, then 25 mcg/kg/min by continuous infusion, maintain activated clotting time (ACT) 300–450 sec

Disseminated Intravascular Coagulation (DIC)
Adult: **IV** 0.7 mcg/kg/min continuous infusion

Common adverse effects in *italic*, life-threatening effects underlined; generic names in **bold**; classifications in SMALL CAPS; ♣ Canadian drug name; ☻ Prototype drug

109

Renal Impairment
No adjustment necessary
Hepatic Impairment
0.5 mcg/kg/min, may be adjusted to maintain an aPTT of 1.5–3 × baseline (max: 10 mcg/kg/min)

ADMINISTRATION

Intravenous

Note: Argatroban is supplied in 100 mg/mL vials which must be diluted 100-fold prior to infusion.

PREPARE: Continuous: Dilute each 2.5 mL vial by mixing with 250 mL of D5W, NS, or RL to yield 1 mg/mL. Mix by repeated inversion of the diluent bag for 1 min.

ADMINISTER: Heparin-Induced Thrombocytopenia (HIT/HITTS): Continuous: Before administration, discontinue heparin and obtain a baseline aPTT. Give at a rate of 2 mcg/kg/min, or as ordered. Lower initial doses are required with hepatic impairment. Check aPTT 2 h after initiation of therapy. After the initial dose, adjust dose (not to exceed 10 mcg/kg/min) until the steady-state aPTT is 1.5 to 3 times baseline (not to exceed 100 sec). Adjust dose to maintain aPTT at 1.5–3 times baseline, but not >100 sec. Check aPTT 2 h after initiation of therapy to confirm desired therapeutic range. **Percutaneous Coronary Intervention: Continuous:** Start an infusion at 25 mcg/kg/min and give a bolus of 350 mcg/kg, via a large bore IV line, over 3–5 min. Check ACT 5–10 min after the bolus dose. If the ACT is >450 sec, decrease infusion rate to 15 mcg/kg/min.

Check ACT q5–10min to maintain an ACT level 300–450 sec.
■ Diluted solutions are stable for 24 h at 25° C (77° F) in ambient indoor light. Protect from direct sunlight. Store solutions refrigerated at 2°–8° C (36°–46° F) in the dark.

ADVERSE EFFECTS (≥1%) **Body as a Whole:** Fever, sepsis, pain, allergic reactions (rare). **CV:** Hypotension, cardiac arrest, ventricular tachycardia. **GI:** Diarrhea, nausea, vomiting, coughing, abdominal pain. **Hematologic:** Major GI bleed, *minor GI bleeding, hematuria, decrease Hgb/Hct*, groin bleed, hemoptysis, brachial bleed. **Respiratory:** Dyspnea. **Urogenital:** UTI.

INTERACTIONS Drug: Heparin results in increased bleeding; may prolong PT with **warfarin;** may increase risk of bleeding with THROMBOLYTICS. **Herbal: Feverfew, garlic, ginger, ginkgo** may increase potential for bleeding.

PHARMACOKINETICS Peak: 1–3 h. **Distribution:** In extracellular fluid; 54% protein bound. **Metabolism:** In liver by CYP3A4/5. **Elimination:** Primarily in bile (78%). **Half-Life:** 39–51 min.

CLINICAL IMPLICATIONS

Assessment & Drug Effects

■ **Heparin-Induced Thrombocytopenia:** Monitor aPTT. Dose adjustment may be needed to reach the target aPTT. Check aPTT 2 h after initiation of therapy. After the initial dose, adjust dose (not to exceed 10 mcg/kg/min), until the steady-state aPTT is 1.5 to 3 times baseline (not to exceed 100 sec).
■ Monitor cardiovascular status carefully during therapy.

Common adverse effects in *italic*, life-threatening effects underlined; generic names in **bold**; classifications in SMALL CAPS; ✦ Canadian drug name; ⊙ Prototype drug

- Monitor for and report S&S of bleeding: Ecchymosis, epistaxis, GI bleeding, hematuria, hemoptysis.
- Note: Patients with history of GI ulceration, hypertension, recent trauma, or surgery are at increased risk for bleeding.
- Monitor neurologic status and report immediately focal or generalized deficits.
- Lab tests: Baseline and periodic ACT (activated clotting time), thrombin time (TT), platelet count, Hgb & Hct; daily INR when argatroban and warfarin are co-administered; periodic stool test for occult blood; urinalysis.

Patient & Family Education

- Report immediately any of the following to physician: Unexplained back or stomach pain; black, tarry stools; blood in urine, coughing up blood; difficulty breathing; dizziness or fainting spells; heavy menstrual bleeding; nosebleeds; unusual bruising or bleeding at any site.

ARIPIPRAZOLE

(a-rip′-i-pra-zole)
Abilify
Classifications: PSYCHOTHERAPEUTIC; ANTIPSYCHOTIC, ATYPICAL; DOPAMINE SYSTEM STABILIZER
Therapeutic: ATYPICAL ANTIPSYCHOTIC
Prototype: Clozapine
Pregnancy Category: C

AVAILABILITY 10 mg, 15 mg, 20 mg, 30 mg tablets; 1 mg/mL oral solution

ACTION & *THERAPEUTIC EFFECT*
Efficacy of aripiprazole may be mediated through a combination of partial agonist activity at D_2 and 5-HT$_{1A}$ receptors and antagonist activity at 5-HT$_{2A}$ receptors. *Partial dopaminergic agonist property of aripiprazole accounts for antipsychotic treatment of schizophrenic and bipolar individuals.*

USES Treatment of schizophrenia, bipolar mania, maintenance in bipolar 1 disorder.
UNLABELED USES Depression with psychotic features.

CONTRAINDICATIONS Hypersensitivity to aripiprazole; dementia in elderly; QT prolongation; lactation; pregnancy (category C).
CAUTIOUS USE History of seizures or conditions that lower seizure threshold (e.g., Alzheimer's dementia); suicidal ideation; brain tumor; dementia; diabetes mellitus; patients with known cardiovascular disease (history of MI or ischemic heart disease, heart failure, or conduction abnormalities), cerebrovascular disease, or conditions that predispose to hypotension (dehydration, hypovolemia, and treatment with antihypertensive medications); dysphagia; ethanol intoxication; hyperglycemia; hypothermia; obesity, elderly, children <18 y.

ROUTE & DOSAGE

Schizophrenia
Adult: **PO** 10–15 mg once daily, may increase at 2-wk intervals to max of 30 mg/d if needed

Bipolar Mania
Adult: **PO** 30 mg once daily, may reduce to 15 mg/d

ADMINISTRATION
Oral
- Note that dose should be reduced by 50% with concurrent treatment

Common adverse effects in *italic*, life-threatening effects underlined; generic names in **bold**; classifications in SMALL CAPS; ♣ Canadian drug name; ❷ Prototype drug

111

with ketoconazole, quinidine, fluoxetine, or paroxetine.
- Store at 15°–30° C (59°–86° F).

ADVERSE EFFECTS (≥1%) **Body as a Whole:** *Headache,* asthenia, fever, flu-like symptoms, peripheral edema, chest pain, neck pain, neck rigidity. **CNS:** *Anxiety, insomnia, lightheadedness, somnolence, akathisia,* tremor, extrapyramidal symptoms, depression, nervousness, increased salivation, hostility, suicidal thought, manic reaction, abnormal gait, confusion, cogwheel rigidity. **CV:** Hypertension, tachycardia, hypotension, bradycardia. Risk of stroke in elderly with dementia-related psychosis. **GI:** *Nausea, vomiting, constipation,* anorexia. **Hematologic:** Ecchymosis, anemia. **Metabolic:** Weight gain, weight loss, hyperglycemia, diabetes mellitus, increased creatine kinase. **Musculoskeletal:** Muscle cramp. **Respiratory:** Rhinitis, cough. **Skin:** Rash. **Special Senses:** Blurred vision.

INTERACTIONS Drug: Carbamazepine will decrease aripiprazole levels (may need to double aripiprazole dose); **ketoconazole, quinidine, fluoxetine, paroxetine** may increase aripiprazole levels (reduce dose by $1/2$); may enhance effects of ANTIHYPERTENSIVE AGENTS. **Herbal: St. John's wort** may decrease aripiprazole levels. **Food:** High fat meals may delay time to peak plasma levels.

PHARMACOKINETICS Absorption: 87% bioavailable. **Peak:** 3–5 h. **Metabolism:** In liver by CYP3A4 and 2D6. Major metabolite, has some activity. **Elimination:** 55% in feces, 25% in urine. **Half-Life:** 75 h (94 h for metabolite).

CLINICAL IMPLICATIONS

Assessment & Drug Effects
- Monitor diabetics for loss of glycemic control.
- Monitor cardiovascular status. Assess for and report orthostatic hypotension. Take BP supine then in sitting position. Report systolic drop of >15–20 mm Hg. Patients at increased risk are those who are dehydrated, hypovolemic, or receiving concurrent antihypertensive therapy.
- Monitor body temperature in situations likely to elevate core temperature (e.g., exercising strenuously, exposure to extreme heat, receiving drugs with anticholinergic activity, or being subject to dehydration).
- Monitor for and report signs of tardive dyskinesia.
- Monitor for and immediately report S&S of neuroleptic malignant syndrome (NMS) that include: hyperpyrexia, muscle rigidity, altered mental status, irregular pulse or blood pressure, tachycardia, diaphoresis, and cardiac dysrhythmia. Withhold drug if NMS is suspected.
- Lab tests: Monitor periodically Hct & Hgb. Monitor periodically blood glucose. Monitor for elevated CPK and myoglobinuria if NMS is suspected.

Patient & Family Education
- Carefully monitor blood glucose levels if diabetic.
- Do not drive or engage in other potentially hazardous activities until reaction to drug is known.
- Avoid situations where you are likely to become overheated or dehydrated.
- Notify physician if you become pregnant or intend to become pregnant while taking this drug.

ASCORBIC ACID (VITAMIN C)

Apo-C ♣, Ascorbicap, Cecon, Cetane, Cevalin, CeVi-Sol ♣, Flavorcee, Redoxon ♣, Schiff Effervescent Vitamin C, Vita-C

ASCORBATE, SODIUM

(a-skor′bate)
Cenolate
Classifications: VITAMIN
Therapeutic: VITAMIN SUPPLEMENT
Pregnancy Category: C

AVAILABILITY 25 mg, 50 mg, 100 mg, 250 mg, 500 mg, 1000 mg tablets; 500 mg/mL injection

ACTION & *THERAPEUTIC EFFECT*
Water-soluble vitamin essential for synthesis and maintenance of collagen and intercellular ground substance of body tissue cells, blood vessels, cartilage, bones, teeth, skin, and tendons. Unlike most mammals, humans are unable to synthesize ascorbic acid in the body; therefore it must be consumed daily. *Increases protective mechanism of the immune system, thus supporting wound healing. Necessary for wound healing and resistance to infection.*

USES Prophylaxis and treatment of scurvy and as a dietary supplement.
UNLABELED USES To acidify urine; to prevent and treat cancer; to treat idiopathic methemoglobinemia; as adjuvant during deferoxamine therapy for iron toxicity; in megadoses will possibly reduce severity and duration of common cold. Widely used as an antioxidant in formulations of parenteral tetracycline and other drugs.

CONTRAINDICATIONS Use of sodium ascorbate in patients on sodium restriction; use of calcium ascorbate in patients receiving digitalis; pregnancy (category C).
CAUTIOUS USE Excessive doses in patients with G6PD deficiency; hemochromatosis, thalassemia, sideroblastic anemia, sickle cell anemia; patients prone to gout or renal calculi.

ROUTE & DOSAGE

Therapeutic
Adult: **PO/IV/IM/SC** 150–500 mg/d in 1–2 doses
Child: **PO/IV/IM/SC** 100–300 mg/d in divided doses
Prophylactic
Adult: **PO/IV/IM/SC** 45–60 mg/d
Child: **PO/IV/IM/SC** 30–60 mg/d
Urinary Acidifier
Adult: **PO/IV/IM/SC** 4–12 g/d in divided doses
Child: **PO/IV/IM/SC** 500 mg q6–8h

ADMINISTRATION

Oral
- Give oral solutions mixed with food.
- Dissolve effervescent tablet in a glass of water immediately before ingestion.

Intramuscular, Subcutaneous
- Open ampules with caution. After prolonged storage, decomposition may occur with release of carbon dioxide and resulting increase in pressure within ampule.
- Be aware that ascorbic acid injection may gradually darken on exposure to light; slight coloration reportedly does not affect its therapeutic action.

Intravenous
Verify correct IV concentration and rate of infusion for children with physician.

Common adverse effects in *italic*, life-threatening effects underlined; generic names in **bold**; classifications in SMALL CAPS; ♣ Canadian drug name; ⊙ Prototype drug

113

PREPARE: Direct/Continuous/Intermittent: Give undiluted or diluted in solutions such as NS, D5W, D5/NS, RL. ▪ Be aware that parenteral vitamin C is incompatible with many drugs. ▪ Consult pharmacist for compatibility information.

ADMINISTER: Direct: Give undiluted at a rate of 100 mg or a fraction thereof over 1 min. **Continuous/Intermittent:** Give at ordered rate determined by volume of solution to be infused.

INCOMPATIBILITIES Solution/additive: Aminophylline, bleomycin, cephapirin, erythromycin, nafcillin, sodium bicarbonate, warfarin. **Y-site: Cefazolin, doxapram, sodium bicarbonate.**

▪ Store in airtight, light-resistant, nonmetallic containers, away from heat and sunlight, preferably at 15°–30° C (59°–86° F), unless otherwise specified by manufacturer.

ADVERSE EFFECTS (≥1%) **GI:** Nausea, vomiting, heartburn, diarrhea, or abdominal cramps (high doses). **Hematologic:** Acute hemolytic anemia (patients with deficiency of G6PD); sickle cell crisis. **CNS:** Headache or insomnia (high doses). **Urogenital:** Urethritis, dysuria, crystalluria, hyperoxaluria, or hyperuricemia (high doses). **Other:** Mild soreness at injection site; dizziness and temporary faintness with rapid IV administration.

DIAGNOSTIC TEST INTERFERENCE High doses of ascorbic acid can produce false-negative results for **urine glucose** with **glucose oxidase** methods (e.g., **Clinitest, Tes-Tape, Diastix**); false-positive results with **copper reduction methods** (e.g., Benedict's solution, Clinitest); and false increases in **serum uric acid** determinations (by **enzymatic methods**). Interferes with **urinary steroid** (17-OHCS) determinations (**by modified Reddy, Jenkins, Thorn procedure**), decreases in **serum bilirubin,** and may cause increases in **serum cholesterol, creatinine,** and **uric acid** (methodologic inferences). May produce false-negative tests for **occult blood** in stools if taken within 48–72 h of test.

INTERACTIONS Drug: Large doses may attenuate hypoprothrombinemic effects of ORAL ANTICOAGULANTS; SALICYLATES may inhibit ascorbic acid uptake by leukocytes and tissues, and ascorbic acid may decrease elimination of SALICYLATES; chronic high doses of ascorbic acid may diminish the effects of **disulfiram.**

PHARMACOKINETICS Absorption: Readily absorbed PO; however, absorption may be limited with large doses. **Distribution:** Widely distributed to body tissues; crosses placenta; distributed into breast milk. **Metabolism:** In liver. **Elimination:** Rapidly in urine when plasma level exceeds renal threshold of 1.4 mg/dL.

CLINICAL IMPLICATIONS

Assessment & Drug Effects
▪ Lab tests: Periodic Hct & Hgb, serum electrolytes.
▪ Monitor for S&S of acute hemolytic anemia, sickle cell crisis.

Patient & Family Education
▪ High doses of vitamin C are not recommended during pregnancy.
▪ Take large doses of vitamin C in divided amounts because the body uses only what is needed at a particular time and excretes the rest in urine.

- Megadoses can interfere with absorption of vitamin B_{12}.
- Note: Vitamin C increases the absorption of iron when taken at the same time as iron-rich foods.

ASPARAGINASE

(a-spar'a-gi-nase)
Colaspase, Elspar, Kidrolase A, L-asparaginase
Classifications: ANTINEOPLASTIC ENZYME; ANTIMETABOLITE
Therapeutic: ANTINEOPLASTIC; ANTIMETABOLITE
Pregnancy Category: C

AVAILABILITY 10,000 IU vial

ACTION & *THERAPEUTIC EFFECT*
A highly toxic drug with a low therapeutic index. Catalyzes asparagine to aspartic acid and ammonia, thus depleting extracellular supply of an amino acid essential to synthesis of DNA and other nucleoproteins. *Reduced availability of asparagine causes death of tumor cells, since unlike normal cells, tumor cells are unable to synthesize their own supply. Resistance to cytotoxic action develops rapidly, and it is not an effective treatment for solid tumors.*

USES Primarily in combination regimens with other antineoplastic agents to treat acute lymphocytic leukemia (ALL).
UNLABELED USES Other leukemias, lymphosarcoma, and (intraarterially) treatment of hypoglycemia due to pancreatic islet cell tumor.

CONTRAINDICATIONS Hypersensitivity to *Escherichia coli* protein; history of or existing pancreatitis; chickenpox (existing or recent illness or exposure), herpetic infection; pregnancy (category C), lactation.
CAUTIOUS USE Liver impairment; diabetes mellitus; anticoagulation therapy, coagulopathy; infections; history of urate calculi or gout; antineoplastic or radiation therapy.

ROUTE & DOSAGE

Induction Agent
Adult: **IV** 200 IU/kg/d for 28 d, inject over at least 30 min into running IV OR 5,000–10,000 U/m²/d q3wk OR 10,000–40,000 U q2–3wk
Child: **IV** 1000 U/kg/d ×10 d starting day 22 (along with prednisone and vincristine)

ADMINISTRATION

Intravenous
An intradermal skin test is usually performed prior to initial dose and when drug is readministered after an interval of a week or more; allergic reactions are unpredictable.

- Observe test site for at least 1 h for evidence of positive reaction (wheal, erythema). A negative skin test, however, does not preclude possibility of an allergic reaction.
- Administer test dose and IV infusion under constant supervision by clinician experienced in cancer chemotherapy.
- Use only clear solutions.

PREPARE: **Intermittent:** Reconstitute with sterile water or with 0.9% NaCl. ▪Each 10,000 IU vial is diluted with 5 mL of diluent to yield 2000 IU/mL. ▪ Shake vial well to promote dissolution of

Common adverse effects in *italic*, life-threatening effects <u>underlined</u>; generic names in **bold**; classifications in SMALL CAPS; ♣ Canadian drug name; ❶ Prototype drug

115

powder. Avoid vigorous shaking. Ordinary shaking does not inactivate the enzyme or cause foaming of content.

***ADMINISTER:* Intermittent:** Further dilute reconstituted solution with NS or D5W by administration into tubing of an already free flowing infusion of one of these solutions. ▪ Give over a period of not less than 30 min. ▪ Use a 5-mm filter to remove gelatinous fiber-like particles that can develop in solutions on standing.

▪ Store sealed vial of lyophilized powder below 8° C (46° F) unless otherwise directed by manufacturer. Store reconstituted solutions and solutions diluted for IV infusion at 2°–8° C (36°–46° F) for up to 8 h; then discard.

ADVERSE EFFECTS (≥1%) **Body as a Whole:** Hypersensitivity (*Skin rashes, urticaria*, respiratory distress, <u>anaphylaxis</u>), chills, fever, <u>fatal hyperthermia</u>, perspiration, weight loss. **CNS:** Depression, fatigue, lethargy, drowsiness, confusion, agitation, hallucinations, dizziness, Parkinson-like syndrome with tremor and progressive increase in muscle tone. **GI:** *Severe vomiting, nausea*, anorexia, abdominal cramps, diarrhea, acute pancreatitis, liver function abnormalities. **Urogenital:** Uric acid nephropathy, azotemia, proteinuria, <u>renal failure</u>. **Hematologic:** *Reduced clotting factors* (especially V, VII, VIII, IX), *decreased circulating platelets and fibrinogen,* leukopenia. **Metabolic:** Hyperglycemia, glycosuria, polyuria, hypoalbuminemia, hypocalcemia, hyperuricemia. **Other:** Flank pain, infections.

DIAGNOSTIC TEST INTERFERENCE Asparaginase may interfere with ***thyroid function*** tests: decreased

total ***serum thyroxine*** and increased ***thyroxine-binding globulin index;*** pretreatment values return within 4 wk after drug is discontinued.

INTERACTIONS Drug: Decreased hypoglycemic effects of SULFONYL-UREAS, **insulin;** increased potential for toxicity if asparaginase is given concurrently or immediately before CORTICOSTEROIDS, **vincristine; methotrexate's** antitumor effect blocked if asparaginase is given concurrently or immediately before it.

PHARMACOKINETICS Distribution: Into intravascular space (80%) and lymph; low levels in CSF, pleural and peritoneal fluids. **Elimination:** Small amounts found in urine. **Half-Life:** 8–30 h.

CLINICAL IMPLICATIONS

Assessment & Drug Effects

▪ Have immediately available: Personnel, drugs, and equipment for treating allergic reaction (which may range from urticaria to anaphylactic shock) whenever drug is administered, including skin testing.

▪ Monitor for S&S and be alert to evidence of hypersensitivity or anaphylactoid reaction (see Appendix F) during drug administration. Anaphylaxis usually occurs within 30–60 min after dose has been given and is more likely with intermittent administrations, particularly at intervals of ≥7 d.

▪ Monitor I&O and maintain adequate fluid intake.

▪ Evaluate CNS function (general behavior, emotional status, level of consciousness, thought content, motor function) before and during therapy.

▪ Note: Toxicity potential is increased when giving drug immediately before a course of pred-

Common adverse effects in *italic*, life-threatening effects <u>underlined</u>; generic names in **bold**; classifications in SMALL CAPS; ♣ Canadian drug name; ⊘ Prototype drug

nisone and vincristine; toxicity appears less when given after these drugs.

- Lab tests: Periodic serum amylase, serum calcium blood glucose, coagulation factors, ammonia and uric acid levels, hepatic and renal function tests, peripheral blood counts, and bone marrow function; liver function tests at least twice weekly during therapy.
- Monitor diabetics for loss of glycemic control.
- Monitor for and report S&S of hyperammonemia: anorexia, vomiting, lethargy, weak pulse, depressed temperature, irritability, asterixis, seizures, coma.
- Anticipate possible prolonged or exaggerated effects of concurrently given drugs or their toxicity because of potential serious hepatic dysfunction that reduces enzymatic detoxification of other drugs. Report incidence promptly.
- Watch for neurotoxic reaction (25% of patients) which usually appears within the first few days of therapy. It is manifested by tiredness and changing levels of consciousness (ranging from confusion to coma).
- Note: Protect from infection during first several days of treatment when circulating lymphoblasts decrease markedly and leukocyte counts may fall below normal. Report promptly S&S of infection: chill, fever, aches, sore throat.
- Report sudden severe abdominal pain with nausea and vomiting, particularly if these symptoms occur after medication is discontinued (may indicate pancreatitis).

Patient & Family Education

- Note: Therapeutic response will most likely be accompanied by some toxicity in all patients; toxicity is reportedly greater in adults than in children.
- Notify physician of continued loss of weight or onset of foot and ankle swelling.
- Notify physician without delay if nausea or vomiting makes it difficult to take all prescribed medication.
- Report onset of unusual bleeding, bruising, petechiae, melena, skin rash or itching, yellowed skin and sclera, joint pain, puffy face, or dyspnea.
- Do not drive or operate equipment that requires alertness and skill. Exercise caution with potentially hazardous activities. These effects can continue several weeks after last dose of the drug.

ASPIRIN (ACETYLSALICYLIC ACID) ℗

(as'pe-ren)

Alka-Seltzer, A.S.A., Aspergum, Astrin ◆, Bayer, Bayer Children's, Cosprin, Easprin, Ecotrin, Empirin, Entrophen ◆, Halfprin, Measurin, Novasen ◆, St. Joseph Children's, Supasa ◆, Triaphen-10 ◆, ZORprin

Classifications: ANALGESIC, SALICYLATE; ANTIPYRETIC; ANTIPLATELET
Therapeutic: NONNARCOTIC ANALGESIC, ANTIPYRETIC; ANTIPLATELET
Pregnancy Category: D

AVAILABILITY 81 mg chewable tablets; 325 mg, 500 mg tablets; 81 mg, 165 mg, 325 mg, 500 mg, 650 mg, 975 mg enteric-coated tablets; 650 mg, 800 mg sustained release tablets; 120 mg, 200 mg, 300 mg, 600 mg suppositories

ACTION & *THERAPEUTIC EFFECT*
Major action is primarily due to in-

Common adverse effects in *italic*, life-threatening effects underlined; generic names in **bold**; classifications in SMALL CAPS; ◆ Canadian drug name; ℗ Prototype drug

117

hibiting the formation of prostaglandins involved in the production of inflammation, pain, and fever. **Antiinflammatory action:** Inhibits prostaglandin synthesis. As an antiinflammatory agent, aspirin appears to be involved in enhancing antigen removal and in reducing the spread of inflammatory substances. **Analgesic action:** Principally peripheral with limited action in the CNS in the hypothalamus; results in relief of mild to moderate pain. **Antipyretic action:** Suppress the synthesis of prostaglandin in or near the hypothalamus. Aspirin also lowers body temperature in fever by indirectly causing centrally mediated peripheral vasodilation and sweating. **Antiplatelet action:** Aspirin (but not other salicylates) powerfully inhibits platelet aggregation. High serum salicylate concentrations can impair hepatic synthesis of blood coagulation factors VII, IX, and X. *Reduces inflammation, pain, and fever. Also inhibits platelet aggregation, reducing ability of blood to clot.*

USES To relieve pain of low to moderate intensity. Also for various inflammatory conditions, such as acute rheumatic fever, Systemic Lupus, rheumatoid arthritis, osteoarthritis, bursitis, and calcific tendonitis, and to reduce fever in selected febrile conditions. Used to reduce recurrence of TIA due to fibrin platelet emboli and risk of stroke in men; to prevent recurrence of MI; as prophylaxis against MI in men with unstable angina.

UNLABELED USES As prophylactic against thromboembolism; to prevent cataract and progression of diabetic retinopathy; and to control symptoms related to gluten sensitivity.

CONTRAINDICATIONS History of hypersensitivity to salicylates including methyl salicylate (oil of wintergreen); sensitivity to other NSAIDs; patients with "aspirin triad" (aspirin sensitivity, nasal polyps, asthma); chronic rhinitis; acute bronchospasm; agranulocytosis; head trauma; increased intracranial pressure; intracranial bleeding; chronic urticaria; history of GI ulceration, bleeding, or other problems; hypoprothrombinemia, vitamin K deficiency, hemophilia, or other bleeding disorders; CHF; pregnancy (category D), especially in third trimester; lactation; or in prematures, neonates, or children under 2 y, except under advice and supervision of physician; children or teenagers with chickenpox or influenza-like illnesses because of possible association with Reye's syndrome.

CAUTIOUS USE Otic diseases; gout; children with fever accompanied by dehydration; hyperthyroidism; immunosuppressed individuals; asthma; GI disease; history of gout; cardiac disease; renal or hepatic impairment; G6PD deficiency; vitamin K deficiency; anemia; preoperatively; Hodgkin's disease.

ROUTE & DOSAGE

Mild to Moderate Pain, Fever
Adult: **PO/PR** 350–650 mg q4h (max: 4 g/d)
Child: **PO/PR** 10–15 mg/kg in 4–6 h (max: 3.6 g/d)
Arthritic Conditions
Adult: **PO** 3.6–5.4 g/d in 4–6 divided doses
Child: **PO** 80–100 mg/kg/d in 4–6 divided doses; max 130 mg/kg/d

Thromboembolic Disorders
Adult: **PO** 81–325 mg qd

TIA Prophylaxis
Adult: **PO** 650 mg b.i.d.

MI Prophylaxis
Adult: **PO** 80–325 mg/d

ADMINISTRATION

Oral

- Give with a full glass of water (240 mL), milk, food, or antacid to minimize gastric irritation.
- Enteric-coated tablets dissolve too quickly if administered with milk and should not be crushed or chewed.
- Store at 15°–30° C (59°–86° F) in airtight container and dry environment unless otherwise directed by manufacturer. Store suppositories in a cool place or refrigerate but do not freeze.

ADVERSE EFFECTS (≥1%) **Body as a Whole:** Hypersensitivity (urticaria, bronchospasm, anaphylactic shock (laryngeal edema). **CNS:** Dizziness, confusion, drowsiness. **Special Senses:** Tinnitus, hearing loss. **GI:** *Nausea*, vomiting, diarrhea, anorexia, *heartburn, stomach pains,* ulceration, occult bleeding, GI bleeding. **Hematologic:** Thrombocytopenia, hemolytic anemia, prolonged bleeding time. **Skin:** Petechiae, easy bruising, rash. **Urogenital:** Impaired renal function. **Other:** Prolonged pregnancy and labor with increased bleeding.

DIAGNOSTIC TEST INTERFERENCE

Bleeding time is prolonged 3–8 d (life of exposed platelets) following a single 325-mg (5 grains) dose of aspirin. Large doses of salicylates equivalent to 5 g or more of aspirin per day may cause prolonged *prothrombin time* by decreasing prothrombin production; interference with *pregnancy tests* (using mouse or rabbit); decreases in *serum cholesterol, potassium, PBI, T_3 and T_4 concentrations,* and an increase in T_3 *resin uptake. Serum uric acid* may increase when plasma salicylate levels are below 10 and decrease when above 15 mg/dL using colorimetric methods. Urine 5-HIAA: Aspirin may interfere with tests using fluorescent methods. **Urine ketones:** Salicylates interfere with Gerhardt test (reaction with ferric chloride produces a reddish color that persists after boiling). **Urine glucose:** Moderate to large doses of salicylates equivalent to an aspirin dosage ≥2.4 g/d may produce false-negative results with glucose oxidase methods (e.g., Clinistix, Tes-Tape) and false-positive results with copper reduction methods (Benedict's solution, Clinitest). **Urinary PSP excretion** may be reduced by salicylates. Salicylates may cause **urine VMA** to be falsely elevated (by most tests), or reduced (by Pisano method). Salicylates may interfere with or cause false decreases in plasma theophylline levels using Schack and Waxler method. High plasma salicylate levels may cause abnormalities in *liver function tests.*

INTERACTIONS Drug: **Aminosalicylic acid** increases risk of SALICYLATE toxicity. **Ammonium chloride** and other ACIDIFYING AGENTS decrease renal elimination and increase risk of SALICYLATE toxicity. ANTICOAGULANTS increase risk of bleeding. ORAL HYPOGLYCEMIC AGENTS increase hypoglycemic activity with aspirin doses >2 g/d. CARBONIC ANHYDRASE INHIBITORS enhance SALICYLATE toxicity. CORTICOSTEROIDS add to ulcerogenic effects.

Common adverse effects in *italic*, life-threatening effects underlined; generic names in **bold**; classifications in SMALL CAPS; ♣ Canadian drug name; ⦿ Prototype drug

119

Methotrexate toxicity is increased. Low doses of SALICYLATES may antagonize uricosuric effects of **probenecid** and **sulfinpyrazone. Herbal: Feverfew, garlic, ginger, ginkgo** may increase bleeding potential.

PHARMACOKINETICS Absorption: 80–100% absorbed (depending on formulation), primarily in stomach and upper small intestine. **Peak levels:** 15 min to 2 h. **Distribution:** Widely distributed in most body tissues; crosses placenta. **Metabolism:** Aspirin is hydrolyzed to salicylate in GI mucosa, plasma, and erythrocytes; salicylate is metabolized in liver. **Elimination:** 50% of dose is eliminated in the urine in 2–4 h (low doses) or 15–30 h (high doses). Excreted into breast milk. **Half-Life:** Aspirin 15–20 min; salicylate 2–18 h (dose dependent).

CLINICAL IMPLICATIONS

Assessment & Drug Effects

- Monitor for loss of tolerance to aspirin. The reaction is nonimmunologic; symptoms usually occur 15 min to 3 h after ingestion: profuse rhinorrhea, erythema, nausea, vomiting, intestinal cramps, diarrhea.
- Lab tests: frequent PT and IRN with concurrent anticoagulant therapy; more frequent fasting blood glucose levels with diabetes.
- Monitor the diabetic child carefully for need to adjust insulin dose. Children on high doses of aspirin are particularly prone to hypoglycemia (see Appendix F).
- Monitor for salicylate toxicity. In adults, a sensation of fullness in the ears, tinnitus, and decreased or muffled hearing are the most frequent symptoms associated with chronic salicylate overdosage.

- Monitor children closely because salicylate toxicity is enhanced by the dehydration that frequently accompanies fever or illness. Children tend to manifest salicylate toxicity by hyperventilation, agitation, mental confusion, or other behavioral changes, drowsiness, lethargy, sweating, and constipation.
- Note: Potential for toxicity is high in older adults and patients with asthma, nasal polyps, perennial vasomotor rhinitis, hay fever, or chronic urticaria.

Patient & Family Education

- Do not give aspirin to children or teenagers with symptoms of varicella (chickenpox) or influenza-like illnesses because of association of aspirin usage with Reye's syndrome.
- Use enteric-coated tablets, extended release tablets, buffered aspirin, or aspirin administered with an antacid to reduce GI disturbances.
- Take aspirin 1–2 d before menses when prescribed for dysmenorrhea. When experiencing heavy menstrual blood loss, take another analgesic, such as acetaminophen, instead of aspirin.
- Discontinue aspirin therapy about 1 wk before surgery to reduce risk of bleeding. Do not use aspirin-containing gum or gargles or chew aspirin products for at least 1 wk following oral surgery.
- Note: Chronic use of high-dose aspirin during the last 3 mo of pregnancy can prolong pregnancy and labor, increase maternal bleeding before and after-delivery, and cause weight increase and hemorrhage in the neonate.
- Discontinue aspirin use with onset of ringing or buzzing in the ears, impaired hearing, dizziness,

Common adverse effects in *italic*, life-threatening effects <u>underlined</u>; generic names in **bold**; classifications in SMALL CAPS; ✦ Canadian drug name; ☯ Prototype drug

GI discomfort or bleeding, and report to physician.

- Do not use aspirin for self-medication of pain (adults) beyond 5 d without consulting a physician. Do not use aspirin longer than 3 d for fever (adults and children), never for fever over 38.9° C (102° F) in older adults or 39.5° C (103° F) in children and adults under 60 yrs or for recurrent fever without medical direction.
- Consult physician before using aspirin for any fever accompanied by rash, severe headache, stiff neck, marked irritability, or confusion (all possible symptoms of meningitis).
- Avoid alcohol when taking large doses of aspirin.
- Observe and report signs of bleeding (e.g., petechiae, ecchymoses, bleeding gums, bloody or black stools, cloudy or bloody urine).
- Maintain adequate fluid intake when taking repeated doses of aspirin.
- Avoid other medications containing aspirin unless directed by physician, because of danger of overdosing (there are more than 500 OTC aspirin-containing compounds).

ATAZANAVIR

(a-ta-zan′a-vir)
Reyataz
Classifications: ANTIVIRAL AGENT; ANTIRETROVIRAL AGENT; PROTEASE INHIBITOR
Therapeutic: ANTIRETROVIRAL; PROTEASE INHIBITOR
Prototype: Saquinavir
Pregnancy Category: B

AVAILABILITY 100 mg, 150 mg, 200 mg capsules

ACTION & *THERAPEUTIC EFFECT*

Atazanavir is an HIV-1 protease inhibitor that selectively inhibits the replication of HIV. Protease plays a major role in the virus-specific processing of gene products used in the replication enzymes of HIV-1 infected cells. Thus, protease is necessary for the production of mature viruses. Atazanavir reduces the viral load and increases CD4+ cell count. *Protease inhibition renders the virus noninfectious. Because HIV protease inhibitors inhibit the HIV replication cycle midway in the process, they are active in acutely and chronically infected cells.*

USES Treatment of HIV infection in combination with other antiretroviral agents.

CONTRAINDICATIONS Hypersensitivity to atazanavir; severe hepatic insufficiency; lactation; infants <3 mo old; lactation; lactase deficiency.

CAUTIOUS USE Moderate hepatic impairment, hepatitis B or C; pregnancy (category B); infants >3 mo old, children; elderly, females, diabetes mellitus, diabetic ketoacidosis; hemophilia, hepatic disease; hepatitis; jaundice, hypercholesterolemia, hypertriglyceridemia; lactic acidosis, obesity.

ROUTE & DOSAGE

HIV Infection (treatment-naïve)
Adult: **PO** 400 mg once/d with a light meal
HIV Infection (treatment-experienced)
Adult: **PO** 300 mg once/d plus 100 mg ritonavir with food
Hepatic Impairment
Reduce dose to 300 mg once/d in moderate hepatic insufficiency;

Common adverse effects in *italic*, life-threatening effects underlined; generic names in **bold**; classifications in SMALL CAPS; ♥ Canadian drug name; ☺ Prototype drug

121

not recommended for use in severe hepatic insufficiency

ADMINISTRATION

Oral

- Give with a light meal, not on an empty stomach.
- When coadministered with efavirenz, give atazanavir 300 mg and ritonavir 100 mg with efavirenz 600 mg (all as a single daily dose with food). Atazanavir without ritonavir should not be coadministered with efavirenz.
- When coadministered with didanosine buffered formulations, give atazanavir (with food) 2 h before or 1 h after didanosine.
- Give 2 h before/1 h after antacids or buffered drugs.
- Store at 15°–30° C (59°–86° F).

ADVERSE EFFECTS (≥1%) **Body as a Whole:** *Peripheral neuropathy,* fever, pain, fatigue, allergic reaction, angioedema, asthenia, burning sensation, chest pain, edema, facial atrophy, generalized edema, heat sensitivity, infection, malaise, pallor, peripheral edema, photosensitivity, substernal chest pain, sweating. **CNS:** *Headache,* depression, insomnia, dizziness, abnormal dream, abnormal gait, agitation, amnesia, anxiety, confusion, convulsion, decreased libido, emotional lability, hallucination, hostility, hyperkinesia, hypesthesia, increased reflexes, nervousness, psychosis, sleep disorder, somnolence, suicide attempt, twitch. **CV:** <u>Cardiac arrest</u>, heart block (PR prolongation), hypertension, myocarditis, palpitation, syncope, vasodilatation. **GI:** Hyperbilirubinemia, jaundice, *nausea, vomiting, diarrhea,* abdominal pain, anorexia, aphthous stomatitis, colitis, constipation, dental pain, dyspepsia, enlarged abdomen, esophageal ulcer, esophagitis, flatulence, gastritis, gastroenteritis, gastrointestinal disorder, hepatitis, hepatomegaly, hepatosplenomegaly, increased appetite, liver damage, liver fatty deposit, mouth ulcer, pancreatitis, peptic ulcer. **Endocrine:** Decreased male fertility. **Hematologic:** Ecchymosis, purpura. **Metabolic:** Lipodystrophy syndrome, hypercholesterolemia, hypertriglyceridemia. **Musculoskeletal:** Myalgia, arthralgia. **Respiratory:** Cough, dyspnea, hiccup. **Skin:** *Rash,* alopecia, cellulitis, dermatophytosis, dry skin, eczema, nail disorder, pruritus, seborrhea, urticaria, vesiculobullous rash. **Special Senses:** Otitis, taste perversion, tinnitus. **Urogenital:** Abnormal urine, amenorrhea, crystalluria, gynecomastia, hematuria, impotence, kidney calculus, kidney failure, kidney pain, menstrual disorder, oliguria, pelvic pain, polyuria, proteinuria, urinary frequency, urinary tract infection.

INTERACTIONS Drug: May increase levels and toxicity of **cyclosporine,** systemic **lidocaine, sirolimus, tacrolimus;** increase risk of myopathy and rhabdomyolysis with **atorvastatin, lovastatin, simvastatin;** may increase risk of heart block with **diltiazem;** ANTACIDS, H₂-RECEPTOR ANTAGONISTS, PROTON PUMP INHIBITORS may decrease absorption of atazanavir; **ritonavir** may increase atazanavir levels; may increase toxicity of **irinotecan;** increased risk of prolonged sedations with BENZODIAZEPINES; **indinavir** may increase risk of hyperbilirubinemia; **didanosine, efavirenz, rifampin** may decrease atazanavir levels; **ergotamine, ergonovine dihydroergotamine, bepridil, pimozide** may cause serious adverse reactions; may increase risk of hypotension, visual changes, and priapism with **sildena-**

Common adverse effects in *italic*, life-threatening effects <u>underlined</u>; generic names in **bold**; classifications in SMALL CAPS; ✦ Canadian drug name; ❶ Prototype drug

fil, tadalafil, vardenafil. **Herbal:** **St. John's wort** may decrease atazanavir levels.

PHARMACOKINETICS Absorption: 68% into systemic circulation; taking with food enhances bioavailability. **Peak:** 2–2.5 h. **Metabolism:** In liver by CYP3A4. **Elimination:** 70% in feces, 13% in urine. **Half-Life:** 7 h.

CLINICAL IMPLICATIONS

Assessment & Drug Effects

- Monitor CV status and ECG closely, especially with concurrent treatment with other drugs known to prolong the PR interval.
- Lab tests: Baseline and periodic LFTs; total bilirubin if jaundiced; periodic PT/INR with concurrent warfarin therapy; monitor blood glucose closely, especially if diabetic.

Patient & Family Education

- Do not alter the dose or discontinue therapy without consulting physician.
- Inform physician of all prescription, nonprescription, or herbal meds being used.
- Report promptly any of the following: dizziness or lightheadedness; muscle pain (especially with concurrent statin therapy); severe nausea, vomiting (especially if red or "coffee-ground" in appearance), stomach pain, black tarry stools; yellowing of skin or whites of eyes; skin rash or itchy skin; sore throat, fever, or other S&S of infection; unexplained tiredness or weakness.
- If taking both sildenafil and atazanavir, promptly report any of the following sildenafil-associated adverse effects: hypotension, visual changes, or prolonged penile erection.

ATENOLOL

(a-ten'oh-lole)
Apo-Atenolol ◆, Tenormin
Classifications: BETA-ADRENERGIC ANTAGONIST; ANTIHYPERTENSIVE AGENT
Therapeutic: ANTIHYPERTENSIVE
Prototype: Propranolol
Pregnancy Category: D

AVAILABILITY 25 mg, 50 mg, 100 mg tablets; 5 mg/10 mL vial

ACTION & *THERAPEUTIC EFFECT* Atenolol selectively blocks beta$_1$-adrenergic receptors located chiefly in cardiac muscle. Mechanisms for antihypertensive action include central effect leading to decreased sympathetic outflow to periphery, reduction in renin activity with consequent suppression of the renin-angiotensin-aldosterone system, and competitive inhibition of catecholamine binding at beta-adrenergic receptor sites. *Reduces rate and force of cardiac contractions (negative inotropic action); cardiac output is reduced, as well as systolic and diastolic BP. Atenolol decreases peripheral vascular resistance both at rest and with exercise.*

USES Management of hypertension as a single agent or concomitantly with other antihypertensive agents, especially a diuretic, and in treatment of stable angina pectoris, MI.
UNLABELED USES Antiarrhythmic, mitral valve prolapse, adjunct in treatment of pheochromocytoma and of thyrotoxicosis; and for vascular headache prophylaxis.

CONTRAINDICATIONS Sinus bradycardia, greater than first-degree AV heart block, uncompensated heart failure, cardiogenic shock, periph-

Common adverse effects in *italic*, life-threatening effects underlined; generic names in **bold**; classifications in SMALL CAPS; ◆ Canadian drug name; ❷ Prototype drug

123

eral vascular disease, Raynaud's disease, hypotension; abrupt discontinuation, pulmonary edema, acute bronchospasm; pregnancy (category D), lactation.

CAUTIOUS USE Hypertensive patients with CHF controlled by digitalis and diuretics, vasospastic angina (Prinzmetal's angina); asthma, bronchitis, emphysema, and COPD; major depression; diabetes mellitus; impaired renal function, dialysis; myasthenia gravis; pheochromocytoma, hyperthyroidism, thyrotoxicosis; older adults.

ROUTE & DOSAGE

Hypertension, Angina
Adult: **PO** 25–50 mg/d, may increase to 100 mg/d
Child: **PO** 0.8–1.5 mg/kg/d (max: 2 mg/kg/d)

MI
Adult: **PO** 10 min after second IV dose, start 50 mg/d **IV** 5 mg q5min times 2 doses, then switch to PO

Renal Impairment
Cl_{cr} <35 mL/min: lower dose

Hepatic Impairment
No adjustment needed

ADMINISTRATION

Oral
- Crush tablets, if necessary, before administration and give with fluid of patient's choice.

Intravenous

PREPARE: Direct: Use undiluted or diluted in 10–50 mL of NS, D5W, D5/NS, D5/0.45NS, or 0.45NS.
ADMINISTER: Direct: Give over 5 min.

- Store in tightly closed, light-resistant container at 15°–30° C (59°–86° F) unless otherwise directed.

ADVERSE EFFECTS (≥1%) **CNS:** Dizziness, vertigo, light-headedness, syncope, fatigue or weakness, lethargy, drowsiness, insomnia, mental changes, depression. **CV:** *Bradycardia, hypotension, CHF,* cold extremities, leg pains, dysrhythmias. **GI:** Nausea, vomiting, diarrhea. **Respiratory:** Pulmonary edema, dyspnea, bronchospasm. **Other:** May mask symptoms of hypoglycemia; decreased sexual ability.

INTERACTIONS Drug: Atropine and other ANTICHOLINERGICS may increase atenolol absorption from GI tract; NSAIDS may decrease hypotensive effects; may mask symptoms of a hypoglycemic reaction induced by **insulin,** SULFONYLUREAS; may increase **lidocaine** levels and toxicity; pharmacologic and toxic effects of both atenolol and **verapamil** are increased. **Prazosin, terazocin** may increase severe hypotensive response to first dose of atenolol.

PHARMACOKINETICS Absorption: 50% of PO dose absorbed. **Peak:** 2–4 h PO; 5 min IV. **Duration:** 24 h. **Distribution:** Does not readily cross blood–brain barrier. **Metabolism:** No hepatic metabolism. **Elimination:** 40–50% in urine; 50–60% in feces. **Half-Life:** 6–7 h.

CLINICAL IMPLICATIONS

Assessment & Drug Effects
- Neonates born to mothers who are receiving atenolol at parturition or breast–feeding may be at risk for hypoglycemia.
- Check apical pulse before giving oral drug, especially in patients receiving digitalis (both drugs slow AV conduction). If below 60

bpm (or other ordered parameter), withhold dose and consult physician.

- Monitor apical pulse, BP, respirations, and peripheral circulation throughout dosage adjustment period. Consult physician for acceptable parameters.

Patient & Family Education

- Adhere rigidly to dose regimen. Sudden discontinuation of drug can exacerbate angina and precipitate tachycardia or MI in patients with coronary artery disease, and thyroid storm in patients with hyperthyroidism.
- Make position changes slowly and in stages, particularly from recumbent to upright posture.

ATOMOXETINE

(a-to-mox'e-teen)

Strattera

Classifications: PSYCHOTHERAPEUTIC AGENT; SELECTIVE NOREPINEPHRINE REUPTAKE INHIBITOR (SNRI)
Therapeutic: ANTIPSYCHOTIC
Pregnancy Category: C

AVAILABILITY 10 mg, 18 mg, 25 mg, 40 mg, 60 mg capsules

ACTION & *THERAPEUTIC EFFECT*
Exact mechanism of action is unknown, but is thought to be related to selective inhibition of the presynaptic norepinephrine transporter, resulting in norepinephrine reuptake inhibition. *Improved attentiveness, ability to follow through on tasks with less distraction and forgetfulness, and diminished hyperactivity.*

USES Treatment of attention deficit/hyperactivity disorder (ADHD) in adults and children.

CONTRAINDICATIONS Hypersensitive to atomoxetine or any of its constituents; concomitant use or use within 2 wk of MAOIs; narrow angle glaucoma; jaundice; suicidal ideation; pregnancy (category C).

CAUTIOUS USE Severe liver injury may progress to liver failure or death in a small percentage of patients. Hypertension, tachycardia, cardiovascular or cerebrovascular disease; any condition that predisposes to hypotension; urinary retention or urinary hesitancy; concomitant use of CYP2D6 inhibitors (e.g., paroxetine, fluoxetine, quinidine), albuterol or other beta-2 agonists, vasopressor drugs; history of bipolar disorder. Safety and efficacy in children <6 y and the older adult have not been established; lactation.

ROUTE & DOSAGE

ADHD

Adult: **PO** Start with 40 mg in morning. May increase after 3 d to target dose of 80 mg/d given either once in the morning or divided morning and late afternoon/early evening. May increase to max of 100 mg/d if needed.

Child/Adolescent: **PO** <70 kg, start with 0.5 mg/kg/d. May increase after 3 d to target dose of 1.2 mg/kg/d. Administer once daily in morning or divide dose and give morning and late afternoon/early evening. Max dose is 1.4 mg/kg or 100 mg, whichever is less. >70 kg, the max total daily dose is 100 mg.

Hepatic Impairment

Child-Pugh Class B: Initial and target doses should be reduced to 50% of the normal dose.

Common adverse effects in *italic*, life-threatening effects underlined; generic names in **bold**; classifications in SMALL CAPS; ♦ Canadian drug name; ⊘ Prototype drug

125

Child-Pugh Class C: Initial dose and target doses should be reduced to 25% of normal.

ADMINISTRATION

Oral

- Note that total daily dose in children and adolescents is based on weight. Determine that ordered dose is appropriate for weight prior to administration of drug.
- Note manufacturer recommends dosage adjustments with concomitant administration of strong CYP2D6 inhibitors (e.g., paroxetine, fluoxetine, quinidine). Consult physician.
- Store at 15°–30° C (59°–86° F).

ADVERSE EFFECTS (≥1%) **Body as a Whole:** Flu-like syndrome, flushing, fatigue, fever, rigors. **CNS:** Dizziness, *headache*, somnolence, crying, tearfulness, irritability, mood swings, *insomnia*, depression, tremor, early morning awakenings, paresthesias, abnormal dreams, decreased libido, sleep disorder, <u>suicidal ideation</u>. **CV:** Increased blood pressure, sinus tachycardia, palpitations. **GI:** *Upper abdominal pain*, constipation, dyspepsia, *vomiting, decreased appetite*, anorexia, dry mouth, diarrhea, flatulence, <u>severe liver injury (rare)</u>. **Endocrine:** Hot flushes. **Metabolic:** Weight loss. **Hepatic:** Hepatotoxicity. **Musculoskeletal:** Arthralgia, myalgia. **Respiratory:** *Cough*, rhinorrhea, nasal congestion, sinusitis. **Skin:** Dermatitis, pruritus, increased sweating. **Special Senses:** Mydriasis. **Urogenital:** Urinary hesitation/retention, dysmenorrhea, ejaculation dysfunction, impotence, delayed onset of menses, irregular menstruation, prostatitis.

INTERACTIONS Drug: Albuterol may potentiate cardiovascular effects of atomoxetine; **fluoxetine, paroxetine, quinidine** may increase atomoxetine levels and toxicity; MAOIS may precipitate a hypertensive crisis; may attenuate effects of ANTIHYPERTENSIVE AGENTS.

PHARMACOKINETICS Absorption: Well absorbed from GI tract. **Peak:** 1–2 h. **Metabolism:** In liver by CYP2D6. **Elimination:** Primarily in urine. **Half-Life:** 5.2 h.

CLINICAL IMPLICATIONS

Assessment & Drug Effects

- Evaluate for continuing therapeutic effectiveness especially with long-term use.
- Monitor children and adolescents for behavior changes that may indicate suicidal ideation.
- Monitor cardiovascular status especially with preexisting hypertension.
- Monitor HR and BP at baseline, following a dose increase, and periodically while on therapy.
- Lab tests: Periodic LFTs.
- Report increased aggression and irritability as these may indicate a need to discontinue the drug.

Patient & Family Education

- Instruct patients on S&S of liver toxicity.
- Report any of the following to physician: chest pains or palpitations, urinary retention or difficulty initiating voiding urine, appetite loss and weight loss, or insomnia.
- Make position changes slowly if you experience dizziness with arising from a lying or sitting position.
- Do not drive or engage in potentially hazardous activities until reaction to the drug is known.

Common adverse effects in *italic*, life-threatening effects <u>underlined</u>; generic names in **bold**; classifications in SMALL CAPS; ♣ Canadian drug name; ⊙ Prototype drug

ATORVASTATIN CALCIUM

(a-tor-va'sta-tin)
Lipitor
Classifications: ANTILIPEMIC AGENT; HMG-CoA; REDUCTASE INHIBITOR (STATIN)
Therapeutic: ANTILIPEMIC; STATIN
Prototype: Lovastatin
Pregnancy Category: X

AVAILABILITY 10 mg, 20 mg, 40 mg tablets

ACTION & *THERAPEUTIC EFFECT*
Atorvastatin is an inhibitor of reductase 3-hydroxy-3-methyl-glutaryl coenzyme A (HMG-CoA), which is essential to hepatic production of cholesterol. Lipitor increases the number of hepatic low-density-lipid (LDL) receptors, thus increasing LDL uptake and catabolism of LDL. HDL cholesterol blood level increases with use of atorvastatin. *Atorvastatin reduces LDL and total triglyceride (TG) production as well as increases the plasma level of high-density lipids (HDL).*

USES Adjunct to diet for the reduction of LDL cholesterol and triglycerides in patients with primary hypercholesterolemia and mixed dyslipidemia, prevention of cardiovascular disease in patients with multiple risk factors.

CONTRAINDICATIONS Hypersensitivity to atorvastatin, myopathy, active liver disease, unexplained persistent transaminase elevations, renal failure, renal impairment, hepatic encephalopathy, hepatitis, hepatic disease; jaundice, rhabdomyolysis; uncontrolled seizure disorders; pregnancy (category X), lactation.
CAUTIOUS USE Hypersensitivity to other HMG-CoA reductase inhibitors, history of liver disease, patients who consume substantial quantities of alcohol. Safety and efficacy in children <10 y have not been established.

ROUTE & DOSAGE

Hypercholesterolemia/Prevention of Cardiovascular Disease
Adult: **PO** Start with 10–40 mg q.d., may increase up to 80 mg/d
Child/Adolescent: **PO** 10–17 y: Start with 10 mg q.d., may increase up to 20 mg/d

ADMINISTRATION

Oral
- May be given at any time of day.
- Store at 20°–25° C (68°–77° F).

ADVERSE EFFECTS (≥1%) **Body as a Whole:** Back pain, asthenia, hypersensitivity reaction, myalgia, rhabdomyolysis. **CNS:** Headache. **GI:** Abdominal pain, constipation, diarrhea, dyspepsia, flatulence, increased liver function tests. **Respiratory:** Sinusitis, pharyngitis. **Skin:** Rash.

INTERACTIONS Drug: May increase **digoxin** levels 20%, increases levels of **norethindrone** and **ethinyl estradiol** oral contraceptives; **erythromycin** may increase atorvastatin levels 40%; MACROLIDE ANTIBIOTICS, **cyclosporine, delaviradine, gemfibrozil, niacin, clofibrate,** AZOLE ANTIFUNGALS (**ketoconazole, itraconazole**) may increase risk of rhabdomyolysis; **nelfinavir** may increase atorvastatin levels. **Food: Grapefruit juice** (>1 qt/d) may increase risk of myopathy and rhabdomyolysis.

PHARMACOKINETICS Absorption: Rapidly from GI tract. 30% reaches the systemic circulation. **Onset:** Cholesterol reduction—2 wk. **Peak:** Plasma concentration, 1–2 h;

Common adverse effects in *italic*, life-threatening effects underlined; generic names in **bold**; classifications in SMALL CAPS; ♣ Canadian drug name; ☺ Prototype drug

127

effect 2–4 wk. **Distribution:** ≥98% protein bound. Crosses placenta, distributed into breast milk of animals. **Metabolism:** In the liver by CYP3A4 to active metabolites. **Elimination:** Primarily in bile; <2% in urine. **Half-Life:** 14 h; 20–30 h for active metabolites.

CLINICAL IMPLICATIONS

Assessment & Drug Effects

- Monitor for therapeutic effectiveness which is indicated by reduction in the level of LDL-C.
- Lab tests: Monitor lipid levels within 2–4 wk after initiation of therapy or upon change in dosage; monitor liver functions at 6 and 12 wk after initiation or elevation of dose, and periodically thereafter.
- Assess for muscle pain, tenderness, or weakness; and, if present, monitor CPK level (discontinue drug with marked elevations of CPK or if myopathy is suspected).
- Monitor carefully for digoxin toxicity with concurrent digoxin use.

Patient & Family Education

- Report promptly any of the following: Unexplained muscle pain, tenderness, or weakness, especially with fever or malaise; yellowing of skin or eyes; stomach pain with nausea, vomiting, or loss of appetite; skin rash or hives.
- Do not take drug during pregnancy because it may cause birth defects. Immediately inform physician of a suspected or known pregnancy.
- Inform physician regarding concurrent use of any of the following drugs: erythromycin, niacin, antifungals, or birth control pills.
- Minimize alcohol intake while taking this drug.

ATOVAQUONE

(a-to'va-quone)
Mepron
Classifications: ANTIPROTOZOAL
Therapeutic: ANTIPROTOZOAL
Prototype: Metronidazole
Pregnancy Category: C

AVAILABILITY 750 mg/5 mL suspension

ACTION & *THERAPEUTIC EFFECT*

Atovaquone is an antiprotozoal with antipneumocystic activity, including *Pneumocystis carinii* (PCP) and the *Plasmodium* species. The site of action in PCP is linked to inhibition of the electron transport system in the mitochondria. This results in the inhibition of nucleic acid and ATP synthesis. *Effective against* P. carinii *and the* Plasmodium *species, as well as other protozoans.*

USES Second-line oral therapy of mild to moderate *P. carinii* pneumonia (PCP) in immunocompromised patients intolerant of cotrimoxazole.

UNLABELED USES May be effective in the treatment of cerebral toxoplasmosis.

CONTRAINDICATIONS History of potential life-threatening allergies to atovaquone.
CAUTIOUS USE Severe PCP, concurrent pulmonary diseases, older adults, pregnancy (category C), or lactation; impaired hepatic function; neonates and infants.

ROUTE & DOSAGE

Mild to Moderate *Pneumocystis carinii* Pneumonia (PCP)

Adult: **PO** 750 mg (5 mL) suspension b.i.d. for 21 d

Common adverse effects in *italic*, life-threatening effects <u>underlined</u>; generic names in **bold**; classifications in SMALL CAPS; ◆ Canadian drug name; ☉ Prototype drug

ADMINISTRATION

Oral

- Give with meals, because food significantly enhances absorption.
- Store at room temperature 15°–30° C (59°–86° F) unless otherwise directed by the manufacturer.

ADVERSE EFFECTS (≥1%) **Body as a Whole:** *Fever.* **CV:** Hypotension. **CNS:** *Headache, insomnia, dizziness, strange or vivid dreams, anxiety, depression.* **Hematologic:** Anemia, neutropenia. **Metabolic:** Hyponatremia, hypoglycemia. **GI:** *Nausea, diarrhea, vomiting,* abdominal pain, anorexia, dyspepsia, oral candidiasis, oral ulcers. **Skin:** *Rash,* pruritus, erythema multiforme. **Respiratory:** Cough, sinusitis.

DIAGNOSTIC TEST INTERFERENCE May cause increase in **amylase** and other **liver function tests.**

INTERACTIONS Drug: Zidovudine may increase risk of bone marrow toxicity. **Food:** Oral absorption is increased 3- to 4-fold when administered with food, especially with fatty foods.

PHARMACOKINETICS Absorption: Poor, absorption improved when taken with a fatty meal. **Duration:** 6–23 wk after a 3-wk course of therapy. **Distribution:** Penetrates poorly into cerebrospinal fluid; >99.9% protein bound. **Metabolism:** Not metabolized. **Elimination:** >94% in feces over 21 d (enterohepatically cycled). **Half-Life:** 2–3 d.

CLINICAL IMPLICATIONS

Assessment & Drug Effects

- Assess for therapeutic failure in patients with GI disorders that may limit absorption of drug.
- Lab tests: Monitor CBC with differential, blood glucose, serum sodium, creatinine, BUN, and serum amylase periodically. Report abnormal elevations in these values; drug may need to be discontinued.

Patient & Family Education

- Note: It is necessary to take this drug exactly as prescribed because it is slowly eliminated from the body.

ATOVAQUONE/PROGUANIL HYDROCHLORIDE

(a-to′va-quone/pro′gua-nil)
Malarone, Malarone Pediatric
Classifications: ANTIMALARIAL
Therapeutic: ANTIMALARIAL
Prototype: Chloroquine HCl & Metronidazole
Pregnancy Category: C

AVAILABILITY Atovaquone 250 mg/proguanil HCl 100 mg, atovaquone 62.5 mg/proguanil HCl 25 mg tablets

ACTION & *THERAPEUTIC EFFECT* Combination of two antimalarial drugs. Atovaquone inhibits electron transport system in mitochondria of the malaria parasite, thus interfering with nucleic acid and ATP synthesis of the parasite. Proguanil interferes with DNA synthesis of the malaria parasite. *This drug combination has synergistic activity toward malarial treatment because each component has a different mode of action.*

USES Prevention and treatment of malaria due to *P. falciparum,* even in chloroquine-resistant areas.

CONTRAINDICATIONS Known hypersensitivity to atovaquone or

Common adverse effects in *italic*, life-threatening effects underlined; generic names in **bold**; classifications in SMALL CAPS; ♦ Canadian drug name; ⊙ Prototype drug

129

proguanil; pregnancy (category C); severe malaria.
CAUTIOUS USE Cerebral malaria, complicated malaria, pulmonary edema; renal failure, renal impairment; hepatic disease; lactation; older adults; African Americans, Chinese, Japanese; diarrhea, emesis, GI disease; hepatic disease, infection, sunlight (UV) exposure. Use in children weighing <9 kg is not established.

ROUTE & DOSAGE

Prevention of Malaria

Adult: **PO** 1 tablet q.d. with food starting 1–2 d before travel to malarial area and continuing for 7 d after return
Child: **PO** 11–20 kg, 1 pediatric tablet q.d.; 21–30 kg, 2 pediatric tablets q.d.; 31–40 kg, 3 pediatric tablets q.d.; >40 kg, 1 adult tablet q.d. with food starting 1–2 d before travel to malarial area and continuing for 7 d after return

Treatment of Malaria

Adult: **PO** 4 tablets as a single daily dose for 3 d
Child: **PO** 5–8 kg, 2 pediatric tablets; 9–10 kg, 3 pediatric tablets; 11–20 kg, 1 adult tablet; 21–30 kg, 2 adult tablets; 31–40 kg, 3 adult tablets; >40 kg, 4 adult tablets as a single daily dose for 3 d

ADMINISTRATION

Oral

- Give at the same time each day with food or a drink containing milk.
- Give a repeat dose if vomiting occurs within 1 h after dosing.

ADVERSE EFFECTS (≥1%) **Body as a Whole:** Fever, *myalgia*, back pain, asthenia, anorexia. **Digestive:** *Nausea, abdominal pain, diarrhea*, dyspepsia. **CNS:** *Headache.* **Respiratory:** Cough. **Skin:** Pruritus. **Other:** Anaphylactic reaction.

INTERACTIONS Drug: Rifampin, rifabutin, tetracycline may decrease serum levels; **metoclopramide** may decrease absorption.

PHARMACOKINETICS Absorption: Atovaquone (A), Poor, absorption improved when taken with a fatty meal; **Proguanil (P),** Extensively absorbed. **Duration:** A, 6–23 wk after a 3-wk course of therapy. **Distribution:** A, Penetrates poorly into cerebrospinal fluid; >99.9% protein bound; P, 75% protein bound. **Metabolism:** A, Not metabolized; P, Metabolized by CYP2C19 to cycloguanil. **Elimination:** A, >94% in feces over 21 d (enterohepatically cycled); P, Primarily in urine. **Half-Life:** A, 2–3 d; P, 12–21 h.

CLINICAL IMPLICATIONS

Assessment & Drug Effects

- Lab tests: Monitor AST and ALT periodically, especially with long-term therapy.
- Monitor for S&S of parasitemia in patients receiving tetracycline and in those experiencing diarrhea or vomiting.
- Note: Only use metoclopramide to control vomiting if other antiemetics are not available.

Patient & Family Education

- Take this drug at the same time each day for maximum effectiveness.
- Note: Absorption of this drug may be reduced with diarrhea and vomiting. Consult physician if either of these occurs.

ATRACURIUM BESYLATE ℗ᵣ

(a-tra-kyoor'ee-um)
Tracrium
Classifications: SKELETAL MUSCLE RELAXANT, NONDEPOLARIZING; NEUROMUSCULAR BLOCKER
Therapeutic: SKELETAL MUSCLE RELAXANT; NEUROMUSCULAR BLOCKER
Pregnancy Category: C

AVAILABILITY 10 mg/mL injection

ACTION & *THERAPEUTIC EFFECT*

Inhibits neuromuscular transmission by binding competitively with acetylcholine to muscle end plate receptors. Has no apparent effect on pain threshold, consciousness, or cerebration. Given in general anesthesia only after unconsciousness has been induced by other drugs. *Synthetic skeletal muscle relaxant that produces short duration of neuromuscular blockade, exhibits minimal direct effects on cardiovascular system, and has less histamine-releasing action.*

USES Adjunct for general anesthesia to produce skeletal muscle relaxation during surgery; to facilitate endotracheal intubation. Especially useful for patients with severe renal or hepatic disease, limited cardiac reserve, and in patients with low or atypical pseudocholinesterase levels.

CONTRAINDICATIONS Myasthenia gravis; pregnancy (category C). Safety during lactation is not established.

CAUTIOUS USE When appreciable histamine release would be hazardous (as in asthma or anaphylactoid reactions, significant cardiovascular disease), neuromuscular disease (e.g., Eaton-Lambert syndrome), carcinomatosis, electrolyte or acid–base imbalances, dehydration, impaired pulmonary function.

ROUTE & DOSAGE

Skeletal Muscle Relaxation
Adult/Child: **IV** ≥2 y, 0.4–0.5 mg/kg initial dose, then 0.08–0.1 mg/kg 20–45 min after the first dose if necessary, reduce doses if used with general anesthetics
Child: **IV** 1 mo–2 y, 0.3–0.4 mg/kg

Mechanical Ventilation
Adult: **IV** 5–9 mcg/kg/min by continuous infusion

ADMINISTRATION

▪ Verify correct concentration and rate of infusion for infants and children with physician.

Intravenous

PREPARE: **Direct:** Give initial bolus dose undiluted. **Continuous:** Maintenance dose must be diluted with NS, D5W or D5/NS. Do not mix in same syringe or administer through same needle as used for alkaline solutions [incompatible with alkaline solutions (e.g., barbiturates)].

ADMINISTER: **Direct:** Give as bolus dose. **Continuous:** Give infusion.

▪ Store at 2°–8° C (36°–46° F) to preserve potency unless otherwise directed. Avoid freezing.

ADVERSE EFFECTS (≥1%) **CV:** Bradycardia, tachycardia. **Respiratory:** <u>Respiratory depression</u>. **Other:** Increased salivation, <u>anaphylaxis</u>.

INTERACTIONS Drug: GENERAL ANESTHETICS increase magnitude and duration of neuromuscular blocking

Common adverse effects in *italic*, life-threatening effects <u>underlined</u>; generic names in **bold**; classifications in SMALL CAPS; ✚ Canadian drug name; ℗ Prototype drug

131

action; AMINOGLYCOSIDES, **bacitracin, polymyxin B, clindamycin, lidocaine, parenteral magnesium, quinidine, quinine, trimethaphan, verapamil** increase neuromuscular blockade; DIURETICS may increase or decrease neuromuscular blockade; **lithium** prolongs duration of neuromuscular blockade; NARCOTIC ANALGESICS present possibility of additive respiratory depression; **succinylcholine** increases onset and depth of neuromuscular blockade; **phenytoin** may cause resistance to or reversal of neuromuscular blockade.

PHARMACOKINETICS Onset: 2 min. **Peak:** 3–5 min. **Duration:** 60–70 min. **Distribution:** Well distributed to tissues and extracellular fluids; crosses placenta; distribution into breast milk unknown. **Metabolism:** Rapid nonenzymatic degradation in bloodstream. **Elimination:** 70–90% in urine in 5–7 h. **Half-Life:** 20 min.

CLINICAL IMPLICATIONS

Assessment & Drug Effects

- Lab tests: Baseline serum electrolytes, acid–base balance, and renal function as part of preanesthetic assessment.
- Note: Personnel and equipment required for endotracheal intubation, administration of oxygen under positive pressure, artificial respiration, and assisted or controlled ventilation must be immediately available.
- Evaluate degree of neuromuscular blockade and muscle paralysis to avoid risk of overdosage by qualified individual using peripheral nerve stimulator.
- Monitor BP, pulse, and respirations and evaluate patient's recovery from neuromuscular blocking (curare-like) effect as evidenced by ability to breathe

naturally or to take deep breaths and cough, keep eyes open, lift head keeping mouth closed, adequacy of hand-grip strength. Notify physician if recovery is delayed.

- Note: Recovery from neuromuscular blockade usually begins 35–45 min after drug administration and is almost complete in about 1 h. Recovery time may be delayed in patients with cardiovascular disease, edematous states, and in older adults.

ATROPINE SULFATE

(a′troe-peen)
Atropair ✦
Classifications: ANTICHOLINERGIC; ANTIMUSCARINIC
Therapeutic: ANTICHOLINERGIC; ANTIMUSCARINIC
Pregnancy Category: C

AVAILABILITY 0.4 mg tablets; 0.05 mg/mL, 0.1 mg/mL, 0.3 mg/mL, 0.4 mg/mL, 0.5 mg/mL, 0.8 mg/mL, 1 mg/mL injection

ACTION & *THERAPEUTIC EFFECT*

Acts by selectively blocking all muscarinic responses to acetylcholine (ACh), whether excitatory or inhibitory. Antisecretory action (vagolytic effect) suppresses sweating, lacrimation, salivation, and secretions from nose, mouth, pharynx, and bronchi. *Potent bronchodilator when bronchoconstriction has been induced by parasympathomimetics, and decreases bronchial secretions. Decreases GI spasm. Produces mydriasis and cycloplegia by blocking responses of iris sphincter muscle and ciliary muscle of lens to cholinergic stimulation. Blocks vagal impulses to heart with resulting decrease in AV con-*

duction time, increase in heart rate and cardiac output, and shortened PR interval.

USES Adjunct in symptomatic treatment of GI disorders (e.g., peptic ulcer, pylorospasm, GI hypermotility, irritable bowel syndrome) and spastic disorders of biliary tract. Relaxes upper GI tract and colon during hypotonic radiography. *Ophthalmic Use:* To produce mydriasis and cycloplegia before refraction and for treatment of anterior uveitis and iritis. *Preoperative Use:* To suppress salivation, perspiration, and respiratory tract secretions; to reduce incidence of laryngospasm, reflex bradycardia arrhythmia, and hypotension during general anesthesia. *Cardiac Uses:* For sinus bradycardia or asystole during CPR or that is induced by drugs or toxic substances (e.g., pilocarpine, beta-adrenergic blockers, organophosphate pesticides, and *Amanita* mushroom poisoning); for management of selected patients with symptomatic sinus bradycardia and associated hypotension and ventricular irritability; for diagnosis of sinus node dysfunction and in evaluation of coronary artery disease during atrial pacing; for management of chronic symptomatic sinus node dysfunction. *Other Uses:* Oral inhalation for short-term treatment and prevention of bronchospasms associated with asthma, bronchitis, and COPD and as drying agent in upper respiratory infection. Adjunctive therapy for hypermotility of GI tract.

CONTRAINDICATIONS Hypersensitivity to belladonna alkaloids; synechiae; angle-closure glaucoma; parotitis; obstructive uropathy, e.g., bladder neck obstruction caused by prostatic hypertrophy; intestinal atony, paralytic ileus, achalasia, pyloric stenosis, obstructive diseases of GI tract, severe ulcerative colitis, toxic megacolon; tachycardia secondary to cardiac insufficiency or thyrotoxicosis; acute hemorrhage; acute MI; myasthenia gravis; pregnancy (category C).

CAUTIOUS USE Myocardial infarction, hypertension, hypotension; coronary artery disease, CHF, tachyarrhythmias; gastric ulcer, GI infections, hiatal hernia with reflux esophagitis; hyperthyroidism; COPD; autonomic neuropathy; hepatic or renal disease; older adults; debilitated patients; children <6 y of age; Down syndrome; autonomic neuropathy, spastic paralysis, brain damage in children; patients exposed to high environmental temperatures; patients with fever.

ROUTE & DOSAGE

Preanesthesia

Adult: **IV/IM/SC** 0.4–0.6 mg 30–60 min before surgery
Child: **IV/IM/SC** <5 kg, 0.02 mg/kg; >5 kg, 0.01–0.02 mg/kg 30–60 min before surgery (max: 0.4 mg)

Arrhythmias

Adult: **IV/IM** 0.5–1 mg q1–2h prn (max: 3 mg)
Child: **IV/IM** 0.01–0.03 mg/kg for 1–2 doses

Organophosphate Antidote

Adult: **IV/IM** 1–2 mg q5–60min until muscarinic signs and symptoms subside (may need up to 50 mg)
Child: **IV/IM** 0.03–0.05 mg/kg q10–30 min until muscarinic signs and symptoms subside

---

Common adverse effects in *italic*, life-threatening effects <u>underlined</u>; generic names in **bold**; classifications in SMALL CAPS; ✢ Canadian drug name; ⊙ Prototype drug

COPD

Adult: **Inhalation** 0.025 mg/kg diluted with 3–5 mL saline, via nebulizer 3–4 times daily (max: 2.5 mg/d)
Child: **Inhalation** 0.03–0.05 mg/kg diluted with 3–5 mL saline, via nebulizer 3–4 times daily

Uveitis

Adult/Child: **Ophthalmic** 1–2 drops of solution or small amount of ointment in eye up to t.i.d.

Cycloplegia

Adult: **Ophthalmic** 1 drop of solution or small amount of ointment in eye 1 h before the procedure
Child: **Ophthalmic** 1–2 drops in eye b.i.d. for 1–3 d prior to procedure or a small amount of ointment in conjunctival sac t.i.d. for 1–3 d prior to procedure with last dose applied several hours before the procedure

ADMINISTRATION

Intravenous

PREPARE: Direct: Give undiluted or diluted in up to 10 mL of sterile water.
ADMINISTER: Direct: Give 1 mg or fraction thereof over 1 min directly into a Y-site.

▪ Store at room temperature 15°–30° C (59°–86° F) in protected airtight, light-resistant containers unless otherwise directed by manufacturer.

ADVERSE EFFECTS (≥1%) CNS:

Headache, ataxia, dizziness, excitement, irritability, convulsions, drowsiness, fatigue, weakness; mental depression, confusion, disorientation, hallucinations. **CV:** Hypertension or hypotension, ventricular tachycardia, palpitation, paradoxical bradycardia, AV dissociation, atrial or ventricular fibrillation. **GI:** Dry mouth with thirst, dysphagia, loss of taste; nausea, vomiting, constipation, delayed gastric emptying, antral stasis, paralytic ileus. **Urogenital:** Urinary hesitancy and retention, dysuria, impotence. **Skin:** Flushed, dry skin; anhidrosis, rash, urticaria, contact dermatitis, allergic conjunctivitis, fixed-drug eruption. **Special Senses:** Mydriasis, blurred vision, photophobia, increased intraocular pressure, cycloplegia, eye dryness, local redness.

DIAGNOSTIC TEST INTERFERENCE

Upper GI series: Findings may require qualification because of anticholinergic effects of atropine (reduced gastric motility and delayed gastric emptying). *PSP excretion test:* Atropine may decrease urinary excretion of PSP (phenolsulfonphthalein).

INTERACTIONS Drug: Amantadine,

ANTIHISTAMINES, TRICYCLIC ANTIDEPRESSANTS, **quinidine, disopyramide, procainamide** add to anticholinergic effects. **Levodopa** effects decreased. **Methotrimeprazine** may precipitate extrapyramidal effects. Antipsychotic effects of PHENOTHIAZINES are decreased due to decreased absorption.

PHARMACOKINETICS Absorption:

Well absorbed from all administration sites. Peak effect: 30 min IM, 2–4 min IV, 1–2 h SC, 1.5–4 h inhalation, 30–40 min topical. **Duration:** Inhibition of salivation 4 h; mydriasis 7–14 d. **Distribution:** In most body tissues; crosses blood–brain barrier and placenta. **Metabolism:** In liver. **Elimination:** 77–94% in urine in 24 h. **Half-Life:** 2–3 h.

CLINICAL IMPLICATIONS

Assessment & Drug Effects

▪ Monitor vital signs. HR is a sensitive indicator of patient's response

Common adverse effects in *italic*, life-threatening effects underlined; generic names in **bold**, classifications in SMALL CAPS; ♣ Canadian drug name; ⓟ Prototype drug

to atropine. Be alert to changes in quality, rate, and rhythm of HR and respiration and to changes in BP and temperature.

- Initial paradoxical bradycardia following IV atropine usually lasts only 1–2 min; it most likely occurs when IV is administered slowly (more than 1 min) or when small doses (less than 0.5 mg) are used. Postural hypotension occurs when patient ambulates too soon after parenteral administration.

- Note: Frequent and continued use of eye preparations, as well as overdosage, can have systemic effects. Some atropine deaths have resulted from systemic absorption following ocular administration in infants and children.

- Monitor I&O, especially in older adults and patients who have had surgery (drug may contribute to urinary retention). Palpate lower abdomen for distention. Have patient void before giving atropine.

- Monitor CNS status. Older adults and debilitated patients sometimes manifest drowsiness or CNS stimulation (excitement, agitation, confusion) with usual doses of drug or other belladonna alkaloids. In addition to dosage adjustment, side rails and supervision of ambulation may be indicated.

- Monitor infants, small children, and older adults for "atropine fever" (hyperpyrexia due to suppression of perspiration and heat loss), which increases the risk of heatstroke.

- Note: Intraocular tension and depth of anterior chamber should be determined before and during therapy with ophthalmic preparations to avoid glaucoma attacks (ophthalmic solutions and ointments are available in various strengths).

- Patients receiving atropine via inhalation sometimes manifest mild

CNS stimulation with doses in excess of 5 mg and mental depression and other mental disturbances with larger doses.

Patient & Family Education

- Follow measures to relieve dry mouth: adequate hydration; small, frequent mouth rinses with tepid water; meticulous mouth and dental hygiene; gum chewing or sucking sugarless sourballs.

- Note: Drug causes drowsiness, sensitivity to light, blurring of near vision, and temporarily impairs ability to judge distance. Avoid driving and other activities requiring visual acuity and mental alertness.

- Discontinue ophthalmic preparations and notify physician if eye pain, conjunctivitis, palpitation, rapid pulse, or dizziness occurs.

AURANOFIN ℗

(au-rane′eh-fin)
Ridaura
Classifications: GOLD COMPOUND; ANTIINFLAMMATORY; ANTIRHEUMATIC
Therapeutic: ANTIINFLAMMATORY; ANTIRHEUMATIC
Pregnancy Category: C

AVAILABILITY 3 mg capsules

ACTION & THERAPEUTIC EFFECT
Strongly lipophilic and almost neutral in solution, properties that may facilitate transport of agent across cell membranes. Action appears to be immunomodulatory: serum immunoglobulin concentrations and rheumatoid factor titers are decreased; and antiinflammatory: gold is taken up by macrophages with resulting inhibition of phagocytosis and lysosomal enzyme release. *Auranofin is immunomodulatory and antiinflammatory.*

Common adverse effects in *italic*, life-threatening effects underlined; generic names in **bold**; classifications in SMALL CAPS; ♦ Canadian drug name; ℗ Prototype drug

135

USES Management of active stage of classic or definite rheumatoid arthritis in adults who do not respond to or tolerate other antiarthritis agents (e.g., NSAIDs, other gold compounds).

UNLABELED USES Juvenile rheumatoid arthritis, active SLE, psoriatic arthritis.

CONTRAINDICATIONS History of gold-induced necrotizing enterocolitis, renal disease, exfoliative dermatitis or bone marrow aplasia; patient who has recently received radiation therapy, history of severe toxicity from previous exposure to gold or other heavy metals; uncontrolled CHF; marked hypertension; SLE; pregnancy (category C), lactation. **CAUTIOUS USE** Inflammatory bowel disease, rash, liver disease, renal disease; history of bone marrow depression; older adults; diabetes mellitus, CHF.

ROUTE & DOSAGE

Rheumatoid Arthritis

Adult: PO 6 mg/d in 1–2 divided doses, may increase to 6–9 mg/d in 3 divided doses after 6 mo (max: 9 mg/d)
Child: PO Initially 0.1 mg/kg/d, may increase to 0.15 mg/kg/d in 1–2 divided doses (max: 0.2 mg/kg/d)

ADMINISTRATION

Oral

- Give capsule with food or fluid of patient's choice.
- Store at 15°–30° C (59°–86° F); protect from light and moisture.
- Note: Expiration date is 4 y after date of manufacture.

ADVERSE EFFECTS (≥1%) **GI:** *Diarrhea, abdominal cramping* and pain; *nausea,* vomiting, anorexia, dysphagia; *stomatitis,* glossitis, metallic taste; flatulence, constipation, GI bleeding, melena. **Hematologic:** Thrombocytopenia, leukopenia, eosinophilia, agranulocytosis, aplastic anemia. **Urogenital:** Proteinuria, hematuria, renal failure. **Skin:** *Rash, pruritus,* dermatitis, urticaria.

DIAGNOSTIC TEST INTERFERENCE Auranofin may enhance response to a **tuberculin skin test.**

PHARMACOKINETICS Absorption: 20% from small intestine. **Peak:** 2 h. **Distribution:** Highest concentrations in kidneys, spleen, lungs, adrenals, and liver; unknown if crosses placenta; small amounts distributed into breast milk. **Elimination:** 60% of absorbed gold eliminated in urine, remainder in feces. **Half-Life:** 11–23 d.

CLINICAL IMPLICATIONS

Assessment & Drug Effects

- Monitor for therapeutic effectiveness which develops slowly and is not usually apparent for 3–4 mo.
- Report any of the following S&S promptly: unexplained bleeding or bruising, metallic taste, sore mouth; pruritus, rash; diarrhea and melena; yellow skin and sclera; unexplained cough or dyspnea.
- Lab tests: Test for signs of possible impending gold toxicity including decreased Hgb; leukocytes <4000/mm^3; granulocytes <1500/mm^3; platelets <150,000/mm^3; proteinuria <500 mg/d. Also urinary protein and hepatic function.
- Note: Drug-induced thrombocytopenia is usually spontaneously reversible several weeks after drug is withdrawn.
- Continue medical surveillance and supportive therapy after drug is dis-

continued because adverse effects (such as difficulty in breathing, diarrhea and abdominal pain, fatigue, weakness, unexplained bleeding and bruising, metallic taste) may persist for many months.

Patient & Family Education

- Report adverse effects of therapy, especially abdominal cramping and pain; discontinuance of therapy may be necessary.
- Report metallic taste and pruritus with or without rash. These are among earliest symptoms of impending gold toxicity.
- Do not change dosage (dose or dose interval) by omission, increase, or decrease without first consulting physician.
- Use antidiarrheal OTC drug and high-fiber diet for drug-induced diarrhea.
- Avoid exposure to sunlight (especially between 10 a.m. and 4 p.m.) or to artificial ultraviolet light to prevent photosensitivity reaction.
- Rinse mouth with water frequently for symptomatic treatment of mild stomatitis. Avoid commercial mouth rinses; clean teeth with soft tooth brush and gentle brushing to avoid gingival trauma. Floss at least once daily.

AZACITIDINE

(a-za-ci'ti-deen)
Vidaza
Classifications: ANTINEOPLASTIC AGENT; ANTIMETABOLITE (PYRIMIDINE)
Therapeutic: ANTINEOPLASTIC; ANTIMETABOLITE
Prototype: Fluorouracil
Pregnancy Category: D

AVAILABILITY 100 mg powder for injection

ACTION & *THERAPEUTIC EFFECT*

Causes changes in DNA in abnormal blood-forming cells in the bone marrow, resulting in restoration of normal function to tumor-suppressor genes that are responsible for regulating cell differentiation and growth. *Cytotoxic effects of azacitidine cause the death of rapidly dividing cancer cells that are no longer responsive to normal growth control mechanisms.*

USES Treatment of myelodysplastic syndrome, specifically refractory anemia.
UNLABELED USES Refractory acute lymphocytic and myelogenous leukemia

CONTRAINDICATIONS Hypersensitivity to azacitidine or mannitol; advanced malignant hepatic tumors, myelodysplastic syndrome with hepatic impairment; vaccination; active infection; dental work; intramuscular injections, if platelets <50,000 mm^3; pregnancy (category D), lactation. Safety and efficacy in children have not been established.
CAUTIOUS USE Hypoalbuminemia (<3 g/dL), hepatic disease; elderly; bone marrow depression; dental disease; history of varicella zoster or other herpes infections; renal impairment, renal failure; older adults.

ROUTE & DOSAGE

Myelodysplastic Syndrome

Adult: **SC** 75 mg/m^2 once daily for 7 d every 4 wk; may increase to 100 mg/m^2 if no beneficial response is seen after 2 treatment cycles and no toxicity other than nausea and vomiting has occurred

Renal Impairment

If unexplained elevations of BUN or creatinine occur, the next cycle

Common adverse effects in *italic*, life-threatening effects <u>underlined</u>; generic names in **bold**; classifications in SMALL CAPS; ♣ Canadian drug name; ◯ Prototype drug

137

should be delayed until the values return to normal or baseline, and the dose should be reduced by 50% in the next course

ADMINISTRATION

Subcutaneous

- Reconstitute by slowly injecting 4 mL of sterile water for injection into 100 mg vial to yield 25 mg/mL. Invert 2–3 times and gently rotate until a uniform suspension is achieved. The suspension will be cloudy. If not used immediately, see directions for storage.
- Doses greater than 4 mL should be divided equally into 2 syringes and injected into 2 separate sites. Rotate sites for each injection (thigh, abdomen, or upper arm). Give subsequent injections at least 1 in from an old site and never into areas where the site is tender, bruised, red, or hard.
- Storage: Reconstituted suspension may be kept in the vial or syringe. May refrigerate for up to 8 h. Before use, suspension may be kept at room temperature for up to 30 min. Resuspend by inverting the syringe 2–3 times and gently roll between the palms for 30 sec immediately before administration.

ADVERSE EFFECTS (≥1%) **Body as a Whole:** *Fever, fatigue, malaise, weakness, asthenia, limb pain, back pain,* lymphadenopathy, hematoma, night sweats, cellulitis, lethargy. **CNS:** *Dizziness, headache, depression,* syncope. **CV:** *Chest pain,* cardiac murmur, tachycardia, hypotension. **GI:** *Nausea, vomiting, diarrhea, constipation, anorexia, weight loss, abdominal pain,* stomatitis, dyspepsia. **Hematologic:** *Anemia, thrombocytopenia, leukopenia, neutropenia, ecchymosis, fe-*brile neutropenia. **Metabolic:** *Peripheral edema.* **Musculoskeletal:** *Myalgia, arthralgia,* muscle cramps. **Respiratory:** *Cough, dyspnea, pharyngitis, nasopharyngitis, pneumonia,* wheezing, pleural effusion, rhonchi. **Skin:** *Injection site erythema, injection site reactions, rash, pruritus, sweating,* urticaria. **Urogenital:** Dysuria, urinary tract infection.

INTERACTIONS Drug: ANTICOAGULANTS, NSAIDS, ANTIPLATELET AGENTS may increase risk of bleeding; **filgrastim, sargramostim** may interfere with the efficacy of azacitidine if given within 24 h of azacitidine dose.

PHARMACOKINETICS Peak: 30 min. **Metabolism:** In liver. **Elimination:** By kidneys. **Half-Life:** 4 h.

CLINICAL IMPLICATIONS

Assessment & Drug Effects

- Monitor for S&S of drug toxicity in those with renal insufficiency.
- Lab tests: Obtain LFTs and serum creatinine before initiation of therapy; monitor CBC with differential before each treatment cycle and prn.
- Withhold drug & notify physician for S&S of hepatic or renal insufficiency; lab values that indicate leukopenia, neutropenia, thrombocytopenia, or hepatic or renal insufficiency; or serum bicarbonate levels less than 20 mEq/L.

Patient & Family Education

- Promptly report S&S of infection or indication of unusual bleeding tendencies (e.g., dark, tarry stools and easy bruising).
- Women should avoid becoming pregnant and men should not father a child while taking this drug.

Common adverse effects in *italic*, life-threatening effects <u>underlined</u>; generic names in **bold**; classifications in SMALL CAPS; ♣ Canadian drug name; ◯ Prototype drug

AZATHIOPRINE

(ay-za-thye'oh-preen)

Azasan, Imuran

Classifications: IMMUNOSUPPRESSANT

Therapeutic: IMMUNOSUPPRESSANT

Prototype: Cyclosporine

Pregnancy Category: D

AVAILABILITY 25 mg, 50 mg, 75 mg, 100 mg tablets; 100 mg vial

ACTION & *THERAPEUTIC EFFECT*

Antagonizes purine metabolism and appears to inhibit DNA, RNA, and normal protein synthesis in rapidly growing cells. *Suppresses T cell effects before transplant rejection. Has immunosuppressant and antiinflammatory properties.*

USES Adjunctive agent to prevent rejection of kidney allografts, usually with other immunosuppressants. Also used in selective adult patients with severe, active rheumatoid arthritis; unresponsive to conventional therapy.

UNLABELED USES SLE, lupus nephritis, psoriatic arthritis; ulcerative colitis, pemphigus, nephrotic syndrome, and other inflammatory and immunologic diseases.

CONTRAINDICATIONS Hypersensitivity to azathioprine or mercaptopurine; clinically active infection, immunization of patient or close family members with live virus vaccines; anuria; pancreatitis; patients receiving alkylating agents (increased risk of neoplasms), concurrent radiation therapy; pregnancy (category D), lactation.

CAUTIOUS USE Impaired kidney and liver function; patients receiving cadaver kidney; myasthenia gravis.

ROUTE & DOSAGE

Renal Transplantation

Adult: **PO** 3–5 mg/kg/d initially, may be able to reduce to 1–3 mg/kg/d **IV** 3–5 mg/kg/d initially, may be able to reduce to 1–3 mg/kg/d

Rheumatoid Arthritis

Adult: **PO** 1 mg/kg/d initially, may be increased by 0.5 mg/kg/d at 4–6 wk intervals if needed up to 2.5 mg/kg/d

Obesity

Doses calculated on IBW

Renal Impairment

Cl_{cr} 10–50 mL/min: 75% of usual dose; <10 mL/min: 50% of usual dose

ADMINISTRATION

Oral

- Give oral drug in divided doses (as prescribed) with food or immediately after meals to minimize gastric disturbances.

Intravenous

PREPARE: Direct/Intermittent: Reconstitute by adding 10 mL sterile water for injection into vial; swirl until dissolved. May be further diluted with 50 mL NS, D5W, or D5/NS. Reconstituted solution may be stored at room temperature but must be used within 24 h after reconstitution (contains no preservatives).

ADMINISTER: Direct/Intermittent: May infuse over 5 min to 8 h. Typical infusion time is 30–60 min or longer. If longer infusion time is ordered, the final volume of the IV solution is increased appropriately. Check with physician.

Common adverse effects in *italic*, life-threatening effects underlined; generic names in **bold**; classifications in SMALL CAPS; ♣ Canadian drug name; ⊕ Prototype drug

139

▪ Store at 15°–30° C (59°–86° F) in tightly closed, light-resistant containers unless otherwise directed.

ADVERSE EFFECTS (≥1%) **Body as a Whole:** Hypersensitivity (skin eruptions, rash, arthralgia). **GI:** Nausea, vomiting, anorexia, esophagitis, diarrhea, steatorrhea, hepatitis with elevations in bilirubin, alkaline phosphatase, AST, ALT, biliary stasis, toxic hepatitis. **Hematologic:** <u>Bone marrow depression</u>, thrombocytopenia, leukopenia, anemia, <u>agranulocytosis</u>, pancytopenia. **Other:** *Secondary infection (immunosuppression);* dysarthria, alopecia; carcinogenic and teratogenic potential reported.

DIAGNOSTIC TEST INTERFERENCE Azathioprine may decrease plasma and urinary *uric acid* in patients with gout.

INTERACTIONS Drug: **Allopurinol** increases effects and toxicity of azathioprine by reducing metabolism of the active metabolite; **allopurinol** doses should be decreased by one third or one fourth; **tubocurarine** and other NONDEPOLARIZING SKELETAL MUSCLE RELAXANTS may reverse or inhibit neuromuscular blocking effects.

PHARMACOKINETICS Absorption: Readily from GI tract. **Distribution:** Crosses placenta. **Metabolism:** Extensively in liver to active metabolite mercaptopurine. **Elimination:** In urine. **Half-Life:** 3 h.

CLINICAL IMPLICATIONS
Assessment & Drug Effects
▪ Monitor therapeutic effectiveness which usually requires 6–8 wk of therapy for patients with rheumatoid arthritis (improvement in morning stiffness and grip strength). If no improvement has

occurred after 12-wk trial period, drug is generally discontinued.
▪ Lab tests: Perform CBC, including Hgb and platelet counts, prior to and at least weekly during first month of therapy, twice monthly during second and third months, and monthly, or more frequently thereafter, if indicated (e.g., by dosage or therapy changes).
▪ Monitor for toxicity. Drug has a high toxic potential. Because it may have delayed action, dosage should be reduced or drug withdrawn at the first indication of an abnormally large or persistent decrease in leukocyte or platelet count to avoid irreversible bone marrow depression.
▪ Monitor vital signs. Report signs of infection.
▪ Monitor kidney function (urine protein, urine electrolytes, creatinine clearance, serum creatinine, BUN) periodically.
▪ Monitor I&O ratio; note color, character, and specific gravity of urine. Report an abrupt decrease in urinary output or any change in I&O ratio.
▪ Monitor liver function (alkaline phosphatase, AST, ALT, serum bilirubin) and repeat at least every 3 mo or more frequently if indicated. If hepatic toxicity (see Appendix F) develops, therapy may have to be withdrawn.
▪ Monitor for signs of abnormal bleeding [easy bruising, bleeding gums, petechiae, purpura, melena, epistaxis, dark urine (hematuria), hemoptysis, hematemesis]. If thrombocytopenia occurs, invasive procedures should be withheld, if possible.
▪ Use protective isolation for the hospitalized patient to reduce risk of infections.

Common adverse effects in *italic*, life-threatening effects <u>underlined</u>; generic names in **bold**; classifications in SMALL CAPS; ♣ Canadian drug name; ◐ Prototype drug

Patient & Family Education

- Avoid contact with anyone who has a cold or other infection and report signs of impending infection. Exercise scrupulous personal hygiene because infection is a constant hazard of immunosuppressive therapy.
- Practice birth control during therapy and for 4 mo after drug is discontinued. This drug is associated with potential hazards in pregnancy.
- Do not receive/take vaccinations or other immunity-conferring agents during therapy because they may precipitate unusually severe reactions due to the immunosuppressive effects of the drug.

AZELAIC ACID

(a'ze-laic)

Azelex, Finacea

Classifications: ANTIACNE
Therapeutic: ANTIACNE
Prototype: Isotretinoin
Pregnancy Category: B

AVAILABILITY 20% cream; 15% gel

ACTION & *THERAPEUTIC EFFECT*
Azelaic acid is a naturally occurring dicarboxylic acid. Antimicrobial action is attributable to inhibition of the microbial cellular protein synthesis. A normalization of keratinization of the follicle occurs and it reduces the number of acne lesions. *Reduces the number of inflammatory pustules and papules.*

USES Mild to moderate inflammatory acne vulgaris, mild to moderate rosacea.

CONTRAINDICATIONS Hypersensitivity to any component in the drug.

CAUTIOUS USE Dark complexion, pregnancy (category B), lactation. Safety and efficacy in children <12 y are not established.

ROUTE & DOSAGE

Acne Vulgaris, Rosacea
Adult/Child: **Topical** >12 y, Apply thin film to clean and dry area b.i.d.

ADMINISTRATION

Topical

- Wash and dry skin thoroughly prior to application of drug.
- Apply by thoroughly massaging a thin film of the cream or gel into the affected area. Avoid occlusive dressing.
- Wash hands before and after application of cream or gel.
- Store at 15°–30° C (59°–86° F).

ADVERSE EFFECTS (≥1%) **Skin:** Pruritus, burning, stinging, tingling, erythema, dryness, rash, peeling, irritation, contact dermatitis, vitiligo depigmentation, hypertrichosis. **Other:** Worsening of asthma.

PHARMACOKINETICS Absorption: Approximately 4% absorbed through the skin. **Onset:** 4–8 wk. **Distribution:** Into all tissues. **Metabolism:** Partially by beta oxidation in liver. **Elimination:** Primarily in urine. **Half-Life:** 12 h.

CLINICAL IMPLICATIONS

Assessment & Drug Effects

- Assess for signs of hypopigmentation and report immediately.
- Monitor for sensitivity or severe irritation, which may warrant drug dosage reduction or discontinuation.

Patient & Family Education

- Learn proper application of cream or gel and avoid contact with eyes or mucous membranes.

Common adverse effects in *italic*, life-threatening effects <u>underlined</u>; generic names in **bold**; classifications in SMALL CAPS; ♦ Canadian drug name; ⊘ Prototype drug

141

- Wash eyes with copious amounts of water if contact with medication occurs.
- Note: Transient pruritus, burning, and stinging are common; however, severe skin irritation or hypopigmentation should be reported.

AZELASTINE HYDROCHLORIDE

(a-ze-las'teen)

Astelin, Optivar

Classifications: ANTIHISTAMINE; H_1-RECEPTOR ANTAGONIST; OCULAR ANTIHISTAMINE

Therapeutic: ANTIHISTAMINE
Prototype: Diphenhydramine
Pregnancy Category: C

AVAILABILITY 137 mcg/spray nasal spray; 0.05% ophthalmic solution

ACTION & THERAPEUTIC EFFECT
Potent histamine H_1 receptor antagonist and inhibitor of mast cell release of histamine. *Effective in the symptomatic treatment of seasonal allergic rhinitis and as a nasal decongestant.*

USES Seasonal allergic rhinitis, itching associated with allergic conjunctivitis.

CONTRAINDICATIONS Hypersensitivity to azelastine; concurrent use of CNS depressants; pregnancy (category C); lactation. Safety and efficacy in children <3 y for ophthalmic solution use, and <5 y for nasal spay use.

CAUTIOUS USE Hepatic or renal disease; asthmatics.

ROUTE & DOSAGE

Allergic Rhinitis
Adult: **Intranasal** 2 sprays per nostril b.i.d.

Child: **Intranasal** 5–11 y, 1 spray per nostril b.i.d.

Allergic Conjunctivitis
See Appendix A-1.

ADMINISTRATION

Intranasal
- Prime delivery unit before first use (see manufacturer's instructions).
- Instruct patient to clear nasal passages prior to drug installation; then tilt head forward slightly and sniff gently when drug is sprayed into each nostril.
- Store the bottle upright at room temperature, 15°–30° C (59°–86° F).

ADVERSE EFFECTS (≥1%) **Body as a Whole:** Fatigue, dizziness. **GI:** Dry mouth, nausea. **Metabolic:** Weight gain. **CNS:** *Headache, somnolence.* **Respiratory:** Pharyngitis, *rhinitis,* paroxysmal sneezing, *cough,* asthma. **Special Senses:** *Bitter taste,* nasal burning, epistaxis, conjunctivitis.

INTERACTIONS Drug: Alcohol and CNS DEPRESSANTS may cause reduced alertness.

PHARMACOKINETICS Absorption: 40% from nasal inhalation. **Peak:** 2–3 h. **Metabolism:** Active metabolites. **Elimination:** Primarily in feces. **Half-Life:** 22 h.

CLINICAL IMPLICATIONS

Assessment & Drug Effects
- Monitor level of alertness especially in older adults and with concurrent use of other CNS depressants.

Patient & Family Education
- Follow manufacturer's directions for priming the metered dose spray unit before first use and after storage of >3 d.

Common adverse effects in *italic*, life-threatening effects <u>underlined</u>; generic names in **bold**; classifications in SMALL CAPS; ◆ Canadian drug name; ⊚ Prototype drug

- Tilt head forward while instilling spray. Avoid getting spray in eyes.
- Do not drive or engage in potentially hazardous activities until response to drug is known.
- Avoid concurrent use of CNS depressants, such as alcohol, while taking this drug.
- Discard spray unit and dispensing package bottle after 3 mo.

AZITHROMYCIN

(a-zi-thro-mye'sin)
Zithromax, Zmax
Classifications: ANTIBIOTIC; MACROLIDE ANTIBIOTIC
Therapeutic: ANTIBIOTIC
Prototype: Erythromycin
Pregnancy Category: B

AVAILABILITY 250 mg, 500 mg, 600 mg tablets; 100 mg/5 mL, 200 mg/5 mL, 1 g/packet oral suspension; 500 mg injection; **Zmax** extended release: 176 mg/5 mL oral suspension

ACTION & *THERAPEUTIC EFFECT*

A macrolide antibiotic that reversibly binds to the 50S ribosomal subunit of susceptible organisms and consequently inhibits protein synthesis. *Effective for treatment of mild to moderate infections caused by pyogenic organisms.*

USES Pneumonia, lower respiratory tract infections, pharyngitis/tonsillitis, gonorrhea, nongonococcal urethritis, skin and skin structure infections due to susceptible organisms, otitis media, *Mycobacterium avium–intracellulare* complex infections, acute bacterial sinusitis. **Zmax:** acute bacterial sinusitis and community acquired pneumonia.

UNLABELED USES Bronchitis, *Helicobacter pylori* gastritis.

CONTRAINDICATIONS Hypersensitivity to azithromycin, erythromycin, or any of the macrolide antibiotics; viral infections.

CAUTIOUS USE Older adults or debilitated persons, hepatic or renal impairment; GI disease; ventricular arrhythmias, QT prolongation; UV exposure; pregnancy (category B), and lactation.

ROUTE & DOSAGE

Bacterial Infections

Adult: **PO** 500 mg on day 1, then 250 mg q24h for 4 more d **IV** 500 mg q.d. for at least 2 d, administer 1 mg/mL over 3 h or 2 mg/mL over 1 h
Child: **PO** ≥6 mo, 10 mg/kg on day 1, then 5 mg/kg for 4 more d (max: 250 mg/d)

Acute Bacterial Sinusitis

Adult: **PO** 500 mg once daily × 3 d. Zmax: single one-time dose of 2 g.
Child: **PO** ≥6 mo, 10 mg/kg once daily × 3 d

Otitis Media

Child: **PO** >6 mo, 30 mg/kg as a single dose or 10 mg/kg once daily (not to exceed 500 mg/d) for 3 d or 10 mg/kg as a single dose on day 1 followed by 5 mg/kg/d on days 2–5

Gonorrhea

Adult: **PO** 2 g as a single dose

Chancroid

Adult: **PO** 1 g as a single dose
Child: **PO** 20 mg/kg as single dose (max: 1 g)

Common adverse effects in *italic*, life-threatening effects underlined; generic names in **bold**; classifications in SMALL CAPS; ◆ Canadian drug name; ⊙ Prototype drug

143

Renal Impairment
Cl_{cr} <10 mL/min: Use with caution.

ADMINISTRATION

Oral
- Give capsule at least 1 h before or 2 h after a meal. Tablets may be taken without regard to food.
- Do not give within 2 h of an aluminum or magnesium-containing antacid.

Intravenous

PREPARE: Intermittent: Reconstitute 500-mg vial with 4.8 mL of sterile water for injection and shake until dissolved. Final concentration is 100 mg/mL. Solution must be further diluted to 1.0 or 2.0 mg/mL by adding 5 mL of the 100-mg/mL solution to 500 mL or 250 mL, respectively, of D5W, D5/NS, 0.45NS, or other compatible solution.

ADMINISTER: Intermittent: Administer diluted solution over at least 60 min. Do not give a bolus dose.

INCOMPATIBILITIES Y-site: Amikacin, aztreonam, cefotaxime, ceftazidime, ceftriaxone, cefuroxime, ciprofloxacin, clindamycin, famotidine, fentanyl, furosemide, gentamicin, imipenem/cilastatin, ketorolac, levofloxacin, morphine, piperacillin/tazobactam, ticarcillin/clavulanate, tobramycin.

- Store drug when diluted as directed for 24 h at or below 30° C (86° F) or for 7 d under 5° C (41° F).

ADVERSE EFFECTS (≥1%) CNS:
Headache, dizziness. **GI:** Nausea, vomiting, diarrhea, abdominal pain; hepatotoxicity, mild elevations in liver function tests.

DIAGNOSTIC TEST INTERFERENCE
Liver function tests: reversible, asymptomatic elevations in *liver enzymes (AST, ALT, gamma glutamyl transferase, alkaline phosphatase)* have been reported in some patients treated with azithromycin.

INTERACTIONS Drug: ANTACIDS may decrease peak level of azithromycin; may increase toxicity of **dihydroergotamine, ergotamine. Food:** Food will decrease the amount of azithromycin absorbed by 50%.

PHARMACOKINETICS Absorption: 37% of dose reaches the systemic circulation. **Onset:** 48 h. **Peak:** 2.5–4 h. **Distribution:** Extensively into tissues including sputum, blister, and vaginal secretions; tissue concentrations are often higher than serum concentrations. **Metabolism:** In liver. **Elimination:** 5–12% of dose in urine. **Half-Life:** 60–70 h.

CLINICAL IMPLICATIONS

Assessment & Drug Effects
- Monitor for and report loose stools or diarrhea, since pseudomembranous colitis (see Appendix F) must be ruled out.
- Monitor PT and INR closely with concurrent warfarin use.

Patient & Family Education
- Direct sunlight (UV) exposure should be minimized during therapy with drug.
- Take aluminum or magnesium antacids 2 h before or after drug.
- Report onset of loose stools or diarrhea.

Common adverse effects in *italic*, life-threatening effects underlined; generic names in **bold**, classifications in SMALL CAPS; ♣ Canadian drug name; ⊙ Prototype drug

AZTREONAM

(az-tree'oh-nam)

Azactam

Classifications: ANTIBIOTIC;
BETA-LACTAM ANTIBIOTIC
Therapeutic: ANTIBIOTIC
Prototype: Imipenem-Cilastatin
Pregnancy Category: B

AVAILABILITY 500 mg, 1 g, 2 g vials

ACTION & *THERAPEUTIC EFFECT*

Differs structurally from other beta-lactam antibiotics (penicillins and cephalosporins) in having a monocyclic rather than a bicyclic nucleus. Acts by inhibiting synthesis of bacterial cell wall by preferentially binding to specific penicillin-binding proteins (PBP) in the bacterial cell wall. *Highly resistant to beta-lactamases and does not readily induce their formation. Spectrum of activity limited to aerobic, gram-negative bacteria.*

USES Gram-negative infections of urinary tract, lower respiratory tract, skin and skin structures; and for intraabdominal and gynecologic infections, septicemia, and as adjunctive therapy for surgical infections. Often used in combination with other antibiotics active against gram-positive and anaerobic bacteria in mixed infections.

CONTRAINDICATIONS Lactation, viral infections.
CAUTIOUS USE History of hypersensitivity reaction to penicillin, cephalosporins, or to other drugs; impaired renal or hepatic function, elderly; pregnancy (category B).

ROUTE & DOSAGE

Urinary Tract Infection

Adult: **IV/IM** 0.5–1 g q8–12h

Moderate to Severe Infections

Adult: **IV/IM** 1–2 g q6–8h (max: 8 g/24 h)
Neonate: **IV/IM** ≤7 d, 60–90 mg/kg/d divided q8–12h; >7 d, 60–120 mg/kg/d divided q6–12h
Child: **IV/IM** >1 mo, 90–120 mg/kg/d divided q6–8h

Cystic Fibrosis

Child: **IV/IM** 50 mg/kg q6–8h (max: 8 g/d)

Renal Impairment

Cl_{cr} 10–30 mL/min: reduce dose 50%; <10mL/min: reduce dose 75%

ADMINISTRATION

Intramuscular

- Reconstitute with at least 3 mL of diluent per gram of drug for IM injection. Immediately and vigorously shake vial to dissolve. Suitable diluents include sterile water for injection; bacteriostatic water for injection (with benzyl alcohol and propyl parabens); NS 0.9% for injection.
- Give IM injections deeply into large muscle mass such as the upper outer quadrant of the gluteus maximus or lateral thigh. Rotate injection sites.

Intravenous

Verify correct IV concentration and rate of infusion/injection with physician before giving to neonates, infants, and children.

***PREPARE:* Direct:** Reconstitute a single dose with 6–10 mL of ster-

Common adverse effects in *italic*, life-threatening effects underlined; generic names in **bold**; classifications in SMALL CAPS; ♣ Canadian drug name; ⦿ Prototype drug

145

ile water for injection. ▪Immediately shake vial until solution is dissolved. ▪Reconstituted solutions are colorless to light straw yellow and turn slightly pink on standing. **Intermittent:** Each gram of reconstituted aztreonam must be further diluted in at least 50 mL of D5W, NS, or other solution approved by manufacturer to yield a concentration not to exceed 20 mg/mL.

ADMINISTER: **Direct:** Give over 3–5 min. **Intermittent:** Give over 20–60 min through Y-site.

INCOMPATIBILITIES **Solution/additive: Ampicillin, metronidazole, nafcillin. Y-site: Azithromycin.**

ADVERSE EFFECTS (≥1%) **Body as a Whole:** Hypersensitivity (urticaria, eosinophilia, <u>anaphylaxis</u>). **CNS:** Headache, dizziness, confusion, paresthesias, insomnia, seizures. **GI:** Nausea, *diarrhea,* vomiting, elevated liver function tests. **Hematologic:** Eosinophilia. **Special Senses:** Tinnitus, nasal congestion, sneezing, diplopia. **Skin:** Rash, purpura, erythema multiforme, exfoliative dermatitis, diaphoresis; petechiae, pruritus. **Other:** Local reactions (phlebitis, thrombophlebitis (following IV), pain at injection sites), superinfections (gram-positive cocci), vaginal candidiasis.

DIAGNOSTIC TEST INTERFERENCE
Aztreonam may cause transient elevations of *liver function tests,* increases in *PT* and *PTT,* minor changes in *Hgb,* and positive *Coombs' test.*

INTERACTIONS Drug: Imipenem-cilastatin, cefoxitin may be antagonistic, **probenecid** slows renal elimination of aztreonam.

PHARMACOKINETICS Peak: 1 h IM. **Distribution:** Widely distributed including synovial and blister fluid, bile, bronchial secretions, prostate, bone, and CSF; crosses placenta; distributed into breast milk in small amounts. **Metabolism:** Not extensively metabolized. **Elimination:** 60–70% in urine within 24 h. **Half-Life:** 1.6–2.1 h.

CLINICAL IMPLICATIONS

Assessment & Drug Effects

▪ Lab tests: Obtain baseline C&S test prior to initiation of therapy. Start drug pending results.

▪ Baseline and periodic renal function tests, particularly in older adults and in those with history of renal impairment.

▪ Inspect IV injection sites daily for signs of inflammation. Pain and phlebitis occur in a significant number of patients.

Patient & Family Education

▪ Determine previous hypersensitivity reactions to penicillins, cephalosporins, and other allergens prior to therapy.

▪ Monitor for S&S of opportunistic infections (diarrhea, rectal or vaginal itching or discharge, fever, cough) and promptly report onset to physician. Overgrowth of non-susceptible organisms, particularly *staphylococci, streptococci,* and fungi, is a threat, especially in patients receiving prolonged or repeated therapy.

▪ Note: IV therapy may cause a change in taste sensation. Report interference with eating.

BACITRACIN

(bass-i-tray'sin)

Baciim

Classifications: ANTIBIOTIC

Therapeutic: ANTIBIOTIC

Pregnancy Category: C

AVAILABILITY 50,000 unit vial; 500 units/g ophthalmic ointment

ACTION & *THERAPEUTIC EFFECT*

Polypeptide antibiotic derived from cultures of *Bacillus subtilis*. Interferes with the bacterial cell membrane by inhibiting cell wall synthesis. *Spectrum of antibacterial activity similar to that of penicillin. Active against many gram-positive organisms. Ineffective against most other gram-negative organisms.*

USES Parenteral therapy restricted to infants with *Staphylococcal* pneumonia and empyema where adequate laboratory facilities and constant supervision are available. Used topically in treatment of superficial infections of skin.

UNLABELED USES Orally for treatment of antibiotic-associated colitis.

CONTRAINDICATIONS Toxic reaction or renal dysfunction associated with bacitracin; pulmonary disease; atopic individuals; pregnancy (category C).

CAUTIOUS USE Myasthenia gravis or other neuromuscular disease; renal impairment, lactation. Patients allergic to neomycin may be sensitive to bacitracin.

ROUTE & DOSAGE

Systemic Infections

Child: **IM** <2.5 kg up to 900 U/kg/24 h divided q8–12h; >2.5 kg up to 1000 U/kg/24h divided q8–12h

Skin Infections

Adult: **Topical** Apply thin layer of ointment b.i.d., t.i.d., as solution of 250–1000 U/mL in wet dressing

ADMINISTRATION

Intramuscular

- Do not use parenteral bacitracin for longer than 12 d.
- Reconstitute with NS containing 2% procaine hydrochloride (prescribed). Do not reconstitute with diluents containing parabens because solution may precipitate or become cloudy.
- Alternate injection sites since injections are painful.
- Dry bacitracin vials should be stored in refrigerator at 2°–8° C (36°–46° F). Store solution for a maximum of 1 wk if refrigerated. Inactivation occurs at room temperature.

Topical

- Clean affected area prior to application. May be covered with a sterile bandage.
- Store ointments in tightly closed containers at 15°–30° C (59°–86° F) unless otherwise directed.

ADVERSE EFFECTS (≥1%) **GI:** Anorexia, nausea, vomiting, diarrhea, rectal itching and burning. **Hematologic:** Systemic use: Bone marrow depression, blood dyscrasias; eosinophilia. **Body as a Whole:** Hypersensitivity (erythema, anaphylaxis). **Urogenital:** Nephrotoxicity; dose related: Increased BUN, uremia, renal tubular and glomerular necrosis. **Special Senses:** Tinnitus. **Other:** Pain and inflammation at injection site, fever, superinfection, neuromuscular blockade with respiratory depression.

INTERACTIONS Drug: With AMINOGLYCOSIDES, possibility of additive

Common adverse effects in *italic*, life-threatening effects underlined; generic names in **bold**; classifications in SMALL CAPS; ✦ Canadian drug name; ⊘ Prototype drug

147

B

nephrotoxic and neuromuscular blocking effects; with **tubocurarine** and other NONDEPOLARIZING SKELETAL MUSCLE RELAXANTS, possibility of additive neuromuscular blocking effects.

PHARMACOKINETICS Absorption: Poorly absorbed from intact or denuded skin or mucous membranes. **Peak:** 1–2 h IM. **Duration:** 6–8 h. **Distribution:** Widely distributed including peritoneal and ascitic fluids. **Elimination:** Slow renal excretion (10–40% in 24 h).

CLINICAL IMPLICATIONS

Assessment & Drug Effects

- Lab tests: Baseline C&S tests prior to initiation of therapy; start drug pending results.
- Determine BUN and nonprotein nitrogen (NPN); examine urine for albumin, casts, and cellular elements, before systemic therapy is started. Monitor renal function daily throughout therapy.
- Watch for signs of local allergic reaction (itching, burning, redness) with topical skin applications. Local reactions have preceded life-threatening anaphylactic episodes.
- Monitor I&O during parenteral therapy. Adequate urinary output is important to reduce possibility of renal toxicity. If fluid intake is inadequate or urinary output decreases, report to physician.
- Inspect urine for turbidity and hematuria, and watch for other S&S of urinary tract dysfunction. Report any changes in urination pattern (e.g., oliguria, urinary frequency, nocturia).
- Note: Prolonged use may result in overgrowth of nonsusceptible organisms, especially *Candida albicans*.

Patient & Family Education

- Report local allergic reactions with topical applications (e.g., itching, burning, redness).

BACLOFEN

(bak'loe-fen)

Kemstro, Lioresal

Classifications: CENTRAL-ACTING SKELETAL MUSCLE RELAXANT; GABA AGONIST

Therapeutic: SKELETAL MUSCLE RELAXANT

Prototype: Cyclobenzaprine

Pregnancy Category: C

AVAILABILITY 10 mg, 20 mg tablets; 10 mg, 20 mg orally disintegrating tablets; 50 mcg/mL, 250 mcg/mL ampules

ACTION & *THERAPEUTIC EFFECT* Centrally acting skeletal muscle relaxant. Depresses monosynaptic and polysynaptic afferent reflex activity at spinal cord level. Baclofen stimulates the GABA receptors, which results in decreased excitatory input into alpha-motor neurons. *Reduces skeletal muscle spasm caused by upper motor neuron lesions.*

USES Symptomatic relief of painful spasms in multiple sclerosis and in the management of detrusor sphincter dyssynergia in spinal cord injury or disease.

UNLABELED USES Treatment of trigeminal neuralgia and of tardive dystonia associated with antipsychotic medications, chronic pain.

CONTRAINDICATIONS Pregnancy (category C), coagulopathy, bacteremia, intramuscular or intrathecal administration, subcutaneous administration.

Common adverse effects in *italic*, life-threatening effects underlined; generic names in **bold**; classifications in SMALL CAPS; ◆ Canadian drug name; ◎ Prototype drug

CAUTIOUS USE Impaired renal and hepatic function; bipolar disorder, psychosis, schizophrenia, seizure disorders, seizures, stroke, cerebral palsy, depression, diabetes mellitus, dialysis, head trauma, PKU, epilepsy; thrombocytopenia; psychiatric or brain disorders; older adults, children <2 y.

ROUTE & DOSAGE

Muscle Spasm

Adult: **PO** 5 mg t.i.d., may increase by 5 mg/dose q3d prn (max: 80 mg/d)
Child: **PO** 2–7 y, 10–15 mg/d divided q8h, may increase by 5–15 mg/d q3d (max: 40 mg/d); ≥8 y, 10–15 mg/d divided q8h, may increase by 5–15 mg/d q3d (max: 60 mg/d)
Adult: **Intrathecal** Prior to infusion pump implantation, initiate trial dose of 50 mcg/mL bolus administered in intrathecal space by barbotage over ≤1 min. Observe patient over next 4–8 h for significant decrease in muscle spasm. If response is less than desired, administer second bolus of 75 mcg/1.5 mL and observe 4–8 h. May repeat in 24 h with a 100 mcg/2-mL bolus if necessary.
Post-implant titration Use screening dose if response lasted >12 h or double screening dose if response lasted <12 h and administer over 24 h. After first 24 h, decrease dose by 10–30% q24h until desired response achieved. Maintenance doses range from 12–1500 mcg/d, with most patients maintained on 300–800 mcg/d.

ADMINISTRATION

Oral

- Give with food or milk to avoid GI distress.

Intrathecal

- Give by direct intrathecal injection (via lumbar puncture or catheter) over at least 1 min or longer.
- Dilute *only* with sterile, preservative free NS injection. Baclofen must be diluted to a concentration of 50 mcg/mL when preparing test doses.
- Intrathecal infusion pump: Do not abruptly discontinue as serious adverse effects may develop.
- Store at 15°–30° C (59°–86° F) in tightly closed container unless otherwise directed.

ADVERSE EFFECTS (≥1%) **CNS:** *Transient drowsiness,* vertigo, dizziness, weakness, fatigue, headache, confusion, insomnia; ataxia, loss of seizure control in epileptic patients; abrupt discontinuation of intrathecal administration may result in high fever, altered mental status, exaggerated rebound spasticity, and muscle rigidity, that in rare cases has advanced to rhabdomyolysis, multiple organ-system failure, and death. **CV:** Hypotension. **Special Senses:** Tinnitus, nasal congestion; blurred vision, mydriasis, nystagmus, diplopia, strabismus, miosis. **GI:** Nausea, constipation, vomiting; mild increases in AST, and alkaline phosphatase, jaundice. **Urogenital:** Urinary frequency.

DIAGNOSTIC TEST INTERFERENCE Possibility of increases in *blood-glucose,* serum *alkaline phosphatase,* and *AST* levels.

INTERACTIONS Drug: Alcohol, CNS DEPRESSANTS, MAO INHIBITORS, ANTIHISTAMINES compound CNS depression; baclofen may increase blood **glucose** levels, making it necessary to increase dosage of SULFONYLUREAS, **insulin.**

Common adverse effects in *italic*, life-threatening effects underlined; generic names in **bold**; classifications in SMALL CAPS; ✚ Canadian drug name; ❍ Prototype drug

149

PHARMACOKINETICS Absorption: Readily from GI tract. **Peak:** 2–3 h. **Duration:** 8 h. **Distribution:** Minimal amounts cross blood-brain barrier; crosses placenta; distribution into breast milk unknown. **Metabolism:** 15% in liver. **Elimination:** 70–85% in urine within 72 h; some elimination in feces. **Half-Life:** 3–4 h.

CLINICAL IMPLICATIONS
Assessment & Drug Effects
- Supervise ambulation. Initially, the loss of spasticity induced by baclofen may affect patient's ability to stand or walk.
- Lab tests: baseline and periodic BP, weight, blood sugar, hepatic function tests, and urine.
- Monitor for adverse neuropsychiatric or genitourinary symptoms that resemble those of the underlying disease. Assess them carefully and report to the physician.
- Observe carefully for side effects: mental confusion, depression, hallucinations. Older adults are especially sensitive to this drug.
- Monitor patients with epilepsy closely for possible loss of seizure control.

Patient & Family Education
- Note: CNS depressant effects will be additive to other CNS depressants, including alcohol.
- Monitor blood glucose for loss of glycemic control if diabetic.
- Do not drive or engage in other potentially hazardous activities until the response to drug is known.
- Report adverse reactions to physician. Most can be reduced by decreasing dosage. Incidence of CNS symptoms (drowsiness, dizziness, ataxia) are reportedly high in patients >40 y of age.
- Do not self-dose with OTC drugs without physician's approval.

- Do not stop this drug unless directed to do so by physician. Drug withdrawal needs to be accomplished gradually over a period of 2 wk or more. Abrupt withdrawal following prolonged administration may cause anxiety, agitated behavior, auditory and visual hallucinations, severe tachycardia, acute exacerbation of spasticity, and seizures.

BALSALAZIDE
(bal-sal′a-zide)
Colazal
Classifications: MUCOUS MEMBRANE AGENT; ANTIINFLAMMATORY AGENT
Therapeutic: ANTIINFLAMMATORY AGENT
Prototype: Mesalamine (5-ASA)
Pregnancy Category: B

AVAILABILITY 750 mg capsules

ACTION & *THERAPEUTIC EFFECT* A prodrug of mesalamine that remains intact until it reaches the lumen of the colon. Thought to decrease inflammation of the mucous lining of the colon by blocking cyclooxygenase and inhibiting prostaglandin synthesis in the lining of the colon. *An antiinflammatory agent and a prodrug of 5-ASA.*

USES Treatment of mild to moderate active ulcerative colitis.

CONTRAINDICATIONS Prior hypersensitivity to salicylates, balsalazide.
CAUTIOUS USE Hypersensitivity to mesalamine, sulfasalazine, olsalazine, salicylate. Allergic response to any medications; hepatic or renal impairment; pregnancy (category B), lactation; pyloric stenosis.

Safety and efficacy in children are not established.

ROUTE & DOSAGE

Ulcerative Colitis
Adult: **PO** 2250 mg (3 times 750 mg) t.i.d. for 8–12 wk

ADMINISTRATION

Oral
- Give in a consistent manner with respect to food intake (i.e., either always with or always without food).
- Store at room temperature, preferably between 15°–30° C (59°–86° F).

ADVERSE EFFECTS (≥1%) **Body as a Whole:** Arthralgia, fatigue, fever, pain, back pain. **CNS:** Headache, insomnia. **GI:** Abdominal pain, nausea, diarrhea, vomiting, rectal bleeding, flatulence, dyspepsia, coughing, anorexia. **Respiratory:** Rhinitis, pharyngitis.

INTERACTIONS No clinically significant interactions established.

PHARMACOKINETICS Absorption: Low and variable absorption from the colon. **Distribution:** >99% protein bound. **Metabolism:** Metabolized in colon by bacterial azoreductases to release 5-aminosalicylic acid and 4-aminobenzoyl-beta-alanine. **Elimination:** 25% of metabolites excreted in urine.

CLINICAL IMPLICATIONS

Assessment & Drug Effects
- Monitor for S&S of myelosuppression in patients also receiving azathioprine.
- Lab tests: Closely monitor CBS with concomitant azathioprine therapy; monitor renal and liver functions when used with other aminosalicylates.

Patient & Family Education
- Report worsening of S&S of colitis to physician (e.g., diarrhea, abdominal pain, fever, rectal bleeding).

BASILIXIMAB ℗
(bas-i-lix′i-mab)
Simulect
Classifications: IMMUNOSUPPRESSANT; MONOCLONAL ANTIBODY; INTERLEUKIN-2 RECEPTOR ANTIBODY
Therapeutic: IMMUNOSUPPRESSANT; MONOCLONAL ANTIBODY
Pregnancy Category: B

AVAILABILITY 20 mg vials

ACTION & THERAPEUTIC EFFECT
Immunosuppressant agent that is an interleukin-2 receptor monoclonal antibody produced by recombinant DNA technology. Binds to and blocks interleukin-2R-alpha chain (CD-25 antibodies) on surface of activated T lymphocytes. *Binding to CD-25 antibodies inhibits a critical pathway in the immune response of the lymphocytes involved in allograft rejection.*

USES Prophylaxis of acute renal transplant rejection.

CONTRAINDICATIONS Hypersensitivity to mannitol or murine protein; serious infection or exposure to viral infections (e.g., chickenpox, herpes zoster); lactation.
CAUTIOUS USE History of untoward reactions to dacliximab or other monoclonal antibodies; pregnancy (category B).

ROUTE & DOSAGE

Transplant Rejection Prophylaxis
Adult: **IV** 20 mg times 2 doses (1st dose 2 h before surgery, 2nd dose 4 d after transplant)

Common adverse effects in *italic*, life-threatening effects underlined; generic names in **bold**; classifications in SMALL CAPS; ♣ Canadian drug name; ℗ Prototype drug

151

Child: **IV** 2–15 y, 12 mg/m² (max: 20 mg/dose) times 2 doses (1st dose 2 h before surgery, 2nd dose 4 d after transplant)

ADMINISTRATION

Intravenous

***PREPARE:* IV infusion:** Add 5 mL sterile water for injection to a 20 mg vial, rock vial gently to dissolve then further dilute in an infusion bag to a volume of 50 mL of NS or D5W. The resulting solution has a concentration of 2.5 mg/mL. ▪ Invert IV bag to dissolve but do not shake. ▪ Discard if diluted solution is colored or has particulate matter. Use IV solution immediately.

ADMINISTER: Infuse the ordered dose of diluted drug over 20–30 min.

▪ If necessary the diluted solution may be stored at room temperature for 4 h or at 2°–8° C (36°–46° F) for 24 h. Discard after 24 h. ▪ Store undiluted drug at 2°–8° C (36°–46° F).

ADVERSE EFFECTS (≥1%) **Body as a Whole:** Pain, peripheral edema, edema, fever, viral infection, asthenia, arthralgia, acute hypersensitivity reactions with any dose. **CNS:** Headache, tremor, dizziness, insomnia, paresthesias, agitation, depression. **CV:** Hypertension, chest pain, hypotension, arrhythmias. **GI:** Constipation, nausea, diarrhea, abdominal pain, vomiting, dyspepsia, moniliasis, flatulence, GI hemorrhage, melena, esophagitis, erosive stomatitis. **Hematologic:** Anemia, thrombocytopenia, thrombosis, polycythemia. **Respiratory:** Dyspnea, URI, cough, rhinitis, pharyngitis, bronchospasm. **Skin:** Poor wound healing, acne. **Urogenital:** Dysuria, UTI, albuminuria, hematuria, oliguria, frequency, renal tubular necrosis, urinary retention. **Other:** Cataract, conjunctivitis. **Metabolic:** Hyperkalemia, hypokalemia, hyperglycemia, hyperuricemia, hypophosphatemia, hypocalcemia, increased weight, hypercholesterolemia, acidosis.

PHARMACOKINETICS Duration: 36 days. **Distribution:** Binds to interleukin-2R-alpha sites on lymphocytes. **Half-Life:** 7.2 ± 3.2 d in adults, 11.5 ± 6.3 d in children.

CLINICAL IMPLICATIONS

Assessment & Drug Effects

▪ Monitor carefully for and immediately report S&S of opportunistic infection or anaphylactoid reaction (see Appendix F).

Patient & Family Education

▪ Report any distressing adverse effects.
▪ Avoid vaccination for 2 wk following last dose of drug.

BCG (BACILLUS CALMETTE-GUÉRIN) VACCINE

(ba-cil′lus cal′met-te guer′in)
Tice, TheraCys
Classifications: VACCINE; ANTINEOPLASTIC; IMMUNOMODULATOR; BIOLOGIC RESPONSE MODIFIER
Therapeutic: ANTINEOPLASTIC; IMMUNOMODULATOR
Pregnancy Category: C

AVAILABILITY 50 mg, 81 mg, 120 mg powder for suspension

ACTION & *THERAPEUTIC EFFECT*

BCG vaccine is an immunization agent for tuberculosis (TB). This vaccine is also active immunotherapy. BCG vaccine stimulates the reticuloendothelial system (RES) to produce macrophages that do not

Common adverse effects in *italic*, life-threatening effects <u>underlined</u>; generic names in **bold**; classifications in SMALL CAPS; ◆ Canadian drug name; ⊙ Prototype drug

allow mycobacteria to multiply. BCG live is thought to cause a local, chronic inflammatory response involving macrophage and leukocyte infiltration of the bladder. This leads to destruction of superficial tumor cells. *BCG vaccine is an immunization agent for tuberculosis (TB). BCG is active immunotherapy that stimulates the immune mechanism to reject the tumor. It enhances the cytotoxicity of macrophages. BCG live is used intravesically as a biological response modifier for bladder cancer in situ.*

USES To protect tuberculin skin test-negative infants and children, and groups with an excessive rate of new TB infections; carcinoma in situ of the bladder.
UNLABELED USES Malignant melanoma.

CONTRAINDICATIONS Impaired immune responses, immunosuppressive corticosteroid therapy, active TB, concurrent infections; recent TURP, severe hematuria; asymptomatic carriers with positive HIV serology; fever; UTI; pregnancy (category C); lactation.
CAUTIOUS USE Hypersensitivity to BCG; high risk for HIV; aneurism or prothesis.

ROUTE & DOSAGE

> **Prevention of Tuberculosis (Tice only)**
>
> *Adult:* **Intradermal** 0.1 mL
> *Adult/Child:* **Percutaneous** >1 mo, After reconstitution, 0.2–0.3 mL of vaccine is dropped onto the cleansed surface of the skin and administered using a multiple-puncture disk applied through the vaccine
> *Child:* **Intradermal** <3 mo, 0.05 mL; >3 mo, 0.1 mL

> *Child:* **Percutaneous** <1 mo, reduce adult dose by 1/2 (reconstitute with 2 mL), may need to revaccinate with full dose at 1 y; same as adult
>
> **Carcinoma of the Bladder**
>
> *Adult:* **Intravesical** 3 vials of **TheraCys** at 27 mg each (81 mg total) of BCG reconstituted with accompanying diluent 7–14 d after biopsies/transurethral resections once/wk for 6 wk plus one treatment at 3, 6, 12, 18, and 24 mo; 1 vial of **Tice** per intravesical instillation once/wk for 6 wk plus one treatment/mo for 6–12 mo

ADMINISTRATION

WARNING: Do not inject intravenously, subcutaneously, or intradermally.

Percutaneous

- Prepare solution: Add 1 mL sterile water for injection to 1 ampul of vaccine. Draw into syringe and expel back into ampul 3 times to mix.
- Administer drug by dropping 0.2–0.3 mL onto clean surface of skin; then use a sterile multiple-puncture disk to create percutaneous skin punctures.
- Instruct to keep vaccination site dry for 24 h; no dressing is needed.
- Important: Avoid contact with BCG vaccine during preparation and administration.
- Store dry BCG powder, reconstituted vaccine, and diluent refrigerated at 2°–8° C (35°–46° F). Use reconstituted solution within 2 h.

Intravesical Instillation

- **TheraCys:** Dilute 3 vials of **TheraCys** in 50 mL of sterile preservative free NS and instill into bladder slowly by gravity flow via urethral catheter. Patient retains suspension for 2 h and then voids.

Common adverse effects in *italic*, life-threatening effects <u>underlined</u>; generic names in **bold**; classifications in SMALL CAPS; ♣ Canadian drug name; ☮ Prototype drug

153

- **Tice:** Instill 1 vial of **Tice** intravesically once/wk for 6 wk plus one per mo for 6–12 mo.
- Important: Exercise care when handling BCG vaccine to avoid contact with the product.

ADVERSE EFFECTS (≥1%) **CNS:** Intravesical administration: *malaise,* dizziness, headache, weakness. **Endocrine:** Hyperpyrexia. **GI:** Abdominal pain, anorexia, constipation, nausea, vomiting, diarrhea; hepatic dysfunction following intratumor injection, granulomatous hepatitis. **Urogenital:** Intravesical administration: bladder spasms, clot retention, decreased bladder capacity, decreased urine flow, *dysuria, hematuria,* incontinence, nocturia, UTI, cystitis, hemorrhagic cystitis, penile pain, prostatism. **Hematologic:** Thrombocytopenia, eosinophilia, *anemia,* leukopenia, <u>disseminated intravascular coagulation</u>. **Respiratory:** Cough (rare), pulmonary granulomas, pulmonary infection. **Skin:** Abscess with recurrent discharge, red papule that scales or ulcerates in about 5–6 wk, dermatomyositis, granulomas at injection site 4–6 wk after inoculation, keloid formation, lupus vulgaris. **Body as a Whole:** Systemic BCG infection, *chills, flu-like syndrome,* <u>anaphylaxis</u> (rare), allergic reactions, lymphadenitis.

DIAGNOSTIC TEST INTERFERENCE Prior BCG vaccination may result in false-positive *tuberculin skin test (PPD).* Following BCG vaccination, tuberculin sensitivity may persist for months to years.

INTERACTIONS Drug: Concurrent antimycobacterial therapy (**aminosalicylic acid, capreomycin, cycloserine, ethambutol, ethionamide, isoniazid, pyrazinamide, rifabutin, rifampin, streptomycin**) that inhibits multiplication of

BCG bacilli has the potential to antagonize or altogether negate the BCG vaccine-mediated immune response. **Cyclosporine** may reduce the immunologic response to BCG vaccine. *Cytomegalovirus immune globulin* and other live vaccines (measles/mumps/rubella, oral polio) may interfere with immune response to BCG. Previous vaccination with or other exposure to BCG may induce variable sensitivity to tuberculin. A greater booster effect following repeat tuberculin testing has been reported in individuals with prior BCG vaccination when compared with individuals without prior vaccination.

PHARMACOKINETICS Not studied.

CLINICAL IMPLICATIONS

Assessment & Drug Effects
- Monitor for S&S of systemic BCG infection: Fever, chills, severe malaise, or cough.
- Culture blood and urine, if systemic infection is suspected.
- Assess for regional lymph node enlargement and report fistula formation.

Patient & Family Education
- Review potential adverse effects.
- Keep vaccination site clean until local reaction has subsided.

BECAPLERMIN

(be-cap′ler-min)
Regranex
Classifications: GROWTH FACTOR
Therapeutic: GROWTH FACTOR
Pregnancy Category: C

AVAILABILITY 100 mcg/g gel

ACTION & THERAPEUTIC EFFECT
Recombinant human platelet-derived growth factor B in a topical gel. It induces fibroblast proliferation

in new granulation tissue. *Becaplermin enhances formation of new granulation tissue. It is effective against diabetic neuropathic ulcers that involve subcutaneous or deeper tissue and also have an adequate blood supply.*

USES Lower-extremity diabetic neuropathic ulcers.

CONTRAINDICATIONS Hypersensitivity to drug or any component in formulation; neoplasms at site of application; wounds that close by primary intention; pregnancy (category C), lactation.

CAUTIOUS USE Concurrent use of corticosteroids, cancer chemotherapy, or other immunosuppressive agents; ulcer wounds related to arterial or venous insufficiency; thermal, electrical, or radiation burns at wound site; malignancy.

ROUTE & DOSAGE

Diabetic Neuropathic Ulcers

Adult: **Topical** Calculate the length of gel based on ulcer size and apply once/d until healed

ADMINISTRATION

Topical

- Squeeze calculated length of gel onto clean, firm, nonabsorbable surface.
- Apply even layer to ulcer area with clean tongue depressor or cotton swab and cover with saline-moistened dressing. After 12 h, remove dressing, clean ulcer by rinsing with water or saline to remove residual gel, and apply new saline-moistened dressing without becaplermin for next 12 h. Repeat cycle.
- Apply only to ulcers with good blood supply.
- Dosage calculation: Measure greatest length (*L*) and greatest width

(*W*) of ulcer in inches or centimeters; using 15- or 7.5-g tube multiply (*L* × *W*) × 0.6 for dose in inches or (*L* × *W*)/4 for dose in cm; using 2-g tube multiply (*L* × *W*) × 1.3 for dose in inches or (*L* × *W*)/2 for dose in cm.
- Recalculate weekly/biweekly the amount of drug needed.
- Store at 2°–8° C (36°–46° F). Do not freeze and do not use beyond expiration date.

ADVERSE EFFECTS (≥1%) **Skin:** Erythematous rash.

PHARMACOKINETICS Absorption: <3% absorbed into systemic circulation.

CLINICAL IMPLICATIONS

Assessment & Drug Effects

- Therapeutic effectiveness: 30% decrease in ulcer size after 10 wk or complete healing after 20 wk.
- Monitor for and report appearance of erythematous rash.

Patient & Family Education

- Consult wound care provider who typically recalculates dosage weekly/biweekly.
- Follow directions for application carefully. Gel may be measured out on waxed paper.
- Wash hands prior to application and do not allow tip of tube to contact ulcer or any surface.
- Report worsening ulceration or development of skin rash.

BECLOMETHASONE DIPROPIONATE

(be-kloe-meth′a-sone)

Beconase AQ, QVAR, Vancenase AQ

Pregnancy Category: C

See Appendix A-3.

Common adverse effects in *italic*, life-threatening effects underlined; generic names in **bold**; classifications in SMALL CAPS; ♦ Canadian drug name; ⊕ Prototype drug

155

B

BELLADONNA TINCTURE

(bell-a-don'na)

Classifications: ANTICHOLINERGIC; ANTIMUSCARINIC, ANTISPASMODIC
Therapeutic: ANTICHOLINERGIC; ANTISPASMODIC
Prototype: Atropine
Pregnancy Category: C

AVAILABILITY 27–33 mg/100 mL tincture

ACTION & *THERAPEUTIC EFFECT*
Reversibly blocks action of acetylcholine at parasympathetic neuroeffector sites. *Belladonna inhibits smooth muscle contractions and suppresses secretions of secretory glands.*

USES Adjunct in treatment of peptic ulcer disease, irritable bowel syndrome, and neurogenic bowel disturbances. Also for dysmenorrhea, nocturnal enuresis, spasms of urinary tract, nausea and vomiting of pregnancy, vertigo, and for symptomatic relief of parkinsonism.

CONTRAINDICATIONS Hypersensitivity to anticholinergic drugs; obstructive uropathy, atony of urinary bladder; esophageal reflux, obstructive disease of GI tract, intestinal atony, paralytic ileus, severe ulcerative colitis, toxic megacolon; myasthenia gravis; narrow-angle glaucoma; unstable cardiovascular status in acute hemorrhages; pregnancy (category C), lactation.

CAUTIOUS USE Autonomic neuropathy; heart disease, hypertension; patients >40 y (higher incidence of glaucoma).

ROUTE & DOSAGE

Antispasmodic
Adult: PO 0.6–1 mL t.i.d. or q.i.d.
Child: PO 0.1 mL/kg/d in 3–4 divided doses (max: 3.5 mL/d)

ADMINISTRATION

Oral
- Administer 30–60 min before meals and at bedtime.
- Space administration of antacid and belladonna preparations at least 2 h apart.
- Store at 15°–30° C (59°–86° F) in tightly covered, light-resistant containers, unless otherwise directed.

ADVERSE EFFECTS (≥1%) **All:** Dose related. **CNS:** Excitement (young children and older adults), confusion, delirium. **CV:** Rapid heart beat, tachycardia, palpitation. **Special Senses:** Blurred vision, mydriasis, photophobia. **GI:** *Dry mouth, constipation.* **Urogenital:** Urinary retention, urgency.

INTERACTIONS Drug: **Amantadine,** ANTIHISTAMINES, TRICYCLIC ANTIDEPRESSANTS, **quinidine, disopyramide, procainamide** have additive anticholinergic effects; **levodopa** effects decreased; **methotrimeprazine** may precipitate extrapyramidal effects; antipsychotic effects of PHENOTHIAZINES decreased (decreased absorption).

PHARMACOKINETICS Absorption: Readily from GI tract. **Onset:** 1–2 h. **Distribution:** Well distributed in body; crosses blood brain barrier. **Elimination:** Unchanged in urine.

CLINICAL IMPLICATIONS

Assessment & Drug Effects
- Monitor ambulation of older adults or debilitated patients carefully, since drug may cause drowsiness and confusion.
- Monitor I&O and assess for urinary retention.

Patient & Family Education
- Note: Increase in fluid intake and bulk in diet may prevent or re-

Common adverse effects in *italic*, life-threatening effects <u>underlined</u>; generic names in **bold**; classifications in SMALL CAPS; ♣ Canadian drug name; ⦿ Prototype drug

lieve constipation. Notify physician if constipation persists.

- Avoid hot baths, saunas, and strenuous work or exercise during hot and humid weather.
- Do not drive or engage in potentially hazardous activities until response to drug is known.
- Practice meticulous oral hygiene. Sugarless gum, lemon drops, and frequent sips of water may help dry mouth.

BENAZEPRIL HYDROCHLORIDE
(ben-a′ze-pril)
Lotensin
Classifications: ANTIHYPERTENSIVE AGENT; ANGIOTENSIN-CONVERTING ENZYME (ACE) INHIBITOR
Therapeutic: ANTIHYPERTENSIVE AGENT; ACE INHIBITOR
Prototype: Enalapril
Pregnancy Category: D second and third trimester; C first trimester

AVAILABILITY 5 mg, 10 mg, 20 mg, 40 mg tablets

ACTION & *THERAPEUTIC EFFECT*
Lowers blood pressure by specific inhibition of the angiotensin-converting enzyme (ACE) and thus by decreasing angiotensin II (a potent vasoconstrictor) and aldosterone secretion. *Achieves an antihypertensive effect by suppression of the renin-angiotensin-aldosterone system.*

USES Treatment of mild to moderate hypertension.
UNLABELED USES CHF, reno-protective agent.

CONTRAINDICATIONS Hypersensitivity to benazepril or another ACE inhibitor; pregnancy (category C first trimester and category D second and third trimester), lactation,

or in children <6 y or with a GFR <30 mL/h.
CAUTIOUS USE Renal impairment, renal-artery stenosis; patients with hypovolemia, receiving diuretics, undergoing dialysis; patients in whom excessive hypotension would present a hazard (e.g., cerebrovascular insufficiency); CHF; hepatic impairment; diabetes mellitus.

ROUTE & DOSAGE

Hypertension
Adult: **PO** 10–40 mg/d in 1–2 divided doses

ADMINISTRATION
Oral
- Consult physician about initial dose if patient is also receiving diuretics. Typically an initial dose of 5 mg is used to minimize the risk of hypotension.
- Store at room temperature, but not above 30° C (86° F).

ADVERSE EFFECTS (≥1%) **CV:** Hypotension. **CNS:** *Headache,* dizziness, fatigue, weakness. **Endocrine:** Hyperkalemia (at higher doses). **GI:** Nausea, diarrhea or constipation, gastritis. **Urogenital:** Azotemia, oliguria, renal failure in patients with CHF. **Respiratory:** Cough, rhinitis, bronchitis. **Other:** Back pain.

DIAGNOSTIC TEST INTERFERENCE Elevations in *serum bilirubin* have been observed after benazepril administration. Benazepril inhibits *aldosterone* secretion, which causes an increase in *serum potassium.*

INTERACTIONS Drug: POTASSIUM-SPARING DIURETICS may increase the risk of hyperkalemia. Benazepril may increase **lithium** levels, resulting in **lithium** toxicity.

Common adverse effects in *italic*, life-threatening effects underlined; generic names in **bold**; classifications in SMALL CAPS; ♦ Canadian drug name; ◐ Prototype drug

157

B

PHARMACOKINETICS Absorption: Readily from GI tract; 37% reaches the systemic circulation. **Peak:** 2–6 h. **Duration:** 20–24 h. **Distribution:** Small amounts cross the blood-brain barrier; crosses placenta; small amount excreted in breast milk. **Metabolism:** In liver to active metabolite, benazeprilat. **Elimination:** Benazeprilat is primarily excreted in urine. **Half-Life:** Benazepril 0.6 h; benazeprilat 22 h.

CLINICAL IMPLICATIONS

Assessment & Drug Effects

- Assess for hypotension, especially in patients who may be volume depleted (e.g., prolonged diuretic therapy, recent vomiting or diarrhea, salt restriction) or who have CHF.
- Lab tests: Monitor serum potassium levels for hyperkalemia (see Appendix F).

Patient & Family Education

- Do not use salt substitutes unless recommended by physician.
- Report swelling of face, eyes, lips, or tongue or difficulty breathing immediately to physician.

BENZALKONIUM CHLORIDE

(benz-al-koe'nee-um)

Benza, Benzalchlor-50, Germicin, Pharmatex ◆, Sabol, Zephiran

Classifications: TOPICAL ANTIBIOTIC
Therapeutic: ANTIBIOTIC
Pregnancy Category: C

AVAILABILITY 17% concentrate, 1:750 solution, 1:750 tincture/tincture spray

ACTION & *THERAPEUTIC EFFECT*
Bacotericidal or bacteriostatic action (depending on concentration), probably due to inactivation of bacterial enzyme. *Effective against bacteria, some fungi (including yeasts) and certain protozoa. Generally not effective against spore-forming organisms.*

USES Antisepsis of intact skin, mucous membranes, superficial injuries, and infected wounds; also for irrigations of the eye and body cavities and for vaginal douching. A component of several contact lens wetting and cushioning solutions, and a preservative for ophthalmic solutions.

CONTRAINDICATIONS Casts, occlusive dressings, anal or vaginal packs, pregnancy (category C), lactation.
CAUTIOUS USE Irrigation of body cavities.

ROUTE & DOSAGE

Minor Wounds or Preoperative Disinfection
Adult: **Topical** 1:750 tincture or spray

Preoperative Disinfection of Denuded Skin and Mucous Membranes
Adult: **Topical** 1:10,000–1:2000 solution

Wet Dressings
Adult: **Topical** 1:5000 solution

Urinary Bladder Irrigation
Adult: **Topical** 1:20,000–1:5000 solution

Urinary Bladder Instillation
Adult: **Topical** 1:40,000–1:20,000 solution

Irrigation of Deep Infected Wounds
Adult: **Topical** 1:20,000–1:3000 solution

Common adverse effects in *italic*, life-threatening effects underlined; generic names in **bold**; classifications in SMALL CAPS; ◆ Canadian drug name; ☻ Prototype drug

Vaginal Irrigation
Adult: **Topical** 1:5000–1:2000 solution

Sterile Storage of Instruments, Thermometers, Ampules
Adult: **Topical** 1:750 solution

ADMINISTRATION

Topical
- Use sterile water for injection as diluent for aqueous solutions to be instilled in wounds or body cavities. For other uses, fresh sterile distilled water is used.
- Do not use tap water (especially hard water) because it may reduce antibacterial potency of benzalkonium chloride.
- Irrigate eyes immediately and repeatedly with water if medication solution stronger than 1:5000 enters eyes; see a physician promptly.
- Rinse first with water, then with 70% alcohol, before applying benzalkonium for preoperative skin preparation. Avoid pooling or prolonged contact of solution with skin.
- Note: Detergent action is antagonized by pus and other organic matter, and by soap substitutes. If these agents have been used, rinse skin thoroughly with water, dry, and then apply benzalkonium.
- Consult physician about proper dilution of solutions used on denuded skin or inflamed or irritated tissues.
- Store at room temperature, preferably between 15°–30° C (59°–86° F) in airtight container, protected from light.

ADVERSE EFFECTS (≥1%) **Body as a Whole:** Few or no toxic effects in recommended dilutions. **Skin:** Erythema, local burning, hypersensitivity reactions.

PHARMACOKINETICS Not studied.

CLINICAL IMPLICATIONS

Assessment & Drug Effects
- Monitor wounds carefully. Report increasing signs of infection or lack of healing.

BENZOCAINE

(ben'zoe-caine)
Americaine, Americaine Anesthetic Lubricant, Americaine-Otic, Anbesol Cold Sore Therapy, Chigger-Tox, Dermoplast, Foille, Hurricane, Orabase with Benzocaine, Orajel, Solarcaine, T-Caine
Classifications: LOCAL ANESTHETIC (ESTER TYPE); ANTIPRURITIC
Therapeutic: LOCAL ANESTHETIC; ANTIPRURITIC
Prototype: Procaine
Pregnancy Category: C

AVAILABILITY 5% spray, cream, ointment; 6% cream; 8% lotion, 20% spray, ointment, gel, liquid; 20% otic solution

ACTION & *THERAPEUTIC EFFECT*
Produces surface anesthesia by inhibiting conduction of nerve impulses from sensory nerve endings. Almost identical to procaine in chemical structure, but has prolonged duration of anesthetic action. *Temporary relief of pain and discomfort.*

USES Temporary relief of pain and discomfort in pruritic skin problems, minor burns and sunburn, minor wounds, and insect bites. Otic preparations are used to relieve pain and itching in acute congestive and serous otitis media, swimmer's ear, and otitis externa. Preparations are also available for

Common adverse effects in *italic*, life-threatening effects underlined; generic names in **bold**; classifications in SMALL CAPS; ♣ Canadian drug name; ⊘ Prototype drug

159

toothache, minor sore throat pain, canker sores, hemorrhoids, rectal fissures, pruritus ani or vulvae, as male genital desensitizer to slow onset of ejaculation, and for use as anesthetic-lubricant for passage of catheters and endoscopic tubes.

CONTRAINDICATIONS Hypersensitivity to benzocaine or other PABA derivatives (e.g., sunscreen preparations), or to any of the components in the formulation; use of ear preparation in patients with perforated eardrum or ear discharge; applications to large areas; use in children <2 y; pregnancy (category C). **CAUTIOUS USE** History of drug sensitivity; denuded skin or severely traumatized mucosa; children <6 y.

ROUTE & DOSAGE

Anesthetic
Adult: **Topical** Lowest effective dose
Child: **Topical** Lower strengths

ADMINISTRATION

Topical
▪ Avoid contact of all preparations with eyes and be careful not to inhale mist when spray form is used.
▪ Do not use spray near open flame or cautery and do not expose to high temperatures. Hold can at least 12 inches (30 cm) away from affected area when spraying.
▪ Wash and neutralize chemical burns before benzocaine is applied.
▪ Clean and dry rectal area before administration of hemorrhoidal preparation. Usually administered morning and evening and after each bowel movement.
▪ Store at 15°–30° C (59°–86° F) in tight, light-resistant containers unless otherwise specified.

ADVERSE EFFECTS (≥1%) **Body as a Whole:** Low toxicity; sensitization in susceptible individuals; allergic reactions, <u>anaphylaxis</u>. **Hematologic:** Methemoglobinemia reported in infants.

INTERACTIONS Drug: Benzocaine may antagonize antibacterial activity of SULFONAMIDES.

PHARMACOKINETICS Absorption: Poorly absorbed through intact skin; readily absorbed from mucous membranes. **Peak:** 1 min. **Duration:** 15–30 min. **Metabolism:** By plasma cholinesterases and to a lesser extent by hepatic cholinesterases. **Elimination:** In urine.

CLINICAL IMPLICATIONS

Assessment & Drug Effects
▪ Assess swallowing when used on oral mucosa, as benzocaine may interfere with second (pharyngeal) stage of swallowing; hold food and liquids accordingly.
▪ Assess for sensitivity. Local anesthetics are potentially sensitizing to susceptible individuals when applied repeatedly or over extensive areas.

Patient & Family Education
▪ Use specific benzocaine preparation ONLY as prescribed or recommended by manufacturer.
▪ Discontinue medication if the condition persists, worsens, or if signs of sensitivity, irritation, or infection occur.

BENZONATATE ⓟ

(ben-zoe′na-tate)
Tessalon
Classifications: ANTITUSSIVE
Therapeutic: ANTITUSSIVE; COUGH SUPPRESSANT
Pregnancy Category: C

AVAILABILITY 100 mg capsules

Common adverse effects in *italic*, life-threatening effects <u>underlined</u>; generic names in **bold**; classifications in SMALL CAPS; ♣ Canadian drug name; ⓟ Prototype drug

ACTION & *THERAPEUTIC EFFECT*

Nonnarcotic antitussive activity reported to be somewhat less effective than that of codeine. Does not inhibit respiratory center at recommended doses. *Decreases frequency and intensity of nonproductive cough.*

USES Decreases frequency and intensity of nonproductive cough in acute and chronic respiratory conditions. Also used in bronchoscopy, thoracentesis, and other procedures when coughing must be avoided.

CONTRAINDICATIONS Pregnancy (category C), children <10 y.
CAUTIOUS USE Lactation

ROUTE & DOSAGE

Antitussive

Adult/Child >10 y: **PO** 100 mg t.i.d. prn up to 600 mg/d

ADMINISTRATION

Oral

- Ensure that soft capsules called perles are swallowed whole.
- Store in airtight containers protected from light.

ADVERSE EFFECTS (≥1%) **Body as a Whole:** Low incidence. **CNS:** Drowsiness, sedation headache, mild dizziness. **GI:** Constipation, nausea. **Skin:** Rash, pruritus.

PHARMACOKINETICS Onset: 15–20 min. **Duration:** 3–8 h.

CLINICAL IMPLICATIONS

Assessment & Drug Effects

- Auscultate lungs anteriorly and posteriorly at scheduled intervals.
- Observe character and frequency of coughing and volume and quality of sputum. Keep physician informed.

Patient & Family Education

- Do not chew or allow perle to dissolve in mouth; swallow whole. If perle dissolves in mouth, the mouth, tongue, and pharynx will be anesthetized. Also it is unpleasant to taste.

BENZPHETAMINE HYDROCHLORIDE

(benz-fet'a-meen)
Didrex
Classifications: CEREBRAL STIMULANT; ANOREXIANT
Therapeutic: ANOREXIANT
Prototype: Amphetamine
Pregnancy Category: X
Controlled Substance: Schedule III

AVAILABILITY 50 mg tablets

ACTION & *THERAPEUTIC EFFECT*

Indirect acting sympathomimetic amine with amphetamine-like actions but with fewer side effects than amphetamine. Anorexiant effect thought to be secondary to stimulation of hypothalamus to release stored catecholamines in the CNS. *Effective as an appetite suppressant.*

USES Short-term adjunct in management of exogenous obesity.

CONTRAINDICATIONS Known hypersensitivity to sympathomimetic amines; angle-closure glaucoma; advanced arteriosclerosis, angina pectoris, severe cardiovascular disease, moderate to severe hypertension; hyperthyroidism, agitated states; history of drug abuse; children <12 y; lactation; pregnancy (category X).
CAUTIOUS USE Diabetes mellitus; older adults; psychosis.

Common adverse effects in *italic*, life-threatening effects underlined; generic names in **bold**; classifications in SMALL CAPS; ♣ Canadian drug name; ⊙ Prototype drug

161

ROUTE & DOSAGE

Obesity
Adult: PO 25–50 mg 1–3 times/d

ADMINISTRATION

Oral

- Give as a single daily dose, preferably midmorning or midafternoon, according to patient's eating habits.
- Schedule daily dose no later than 6 h before patient retires to avoid insomnia.
- Store in tight, light-resistant containers at 15°–30° C (59°–86° F) unless otherwise directed.

ADVERSE EFFECTS (≥1%) **CNS:** Euphoria, irritability, hyperactivity, nervousness, *restlessness, insomnia,* tremor, headache, light-headedness, dizziness, depression following stimulant effects. **CV:** *Palpitation,* tachycardia, elevated BP, irregular heart beat. **GI:** Xerostomia, nausea, vomiting, diarrhea or constipation, abdominal cramps. **Chronic Intoxication:** Marked insomnia, irritability, hyperactivity, personality changes, psychosis, severe dermatoses.

INTERACTIONS Drug: Acetazolamide, sodium bicarbonate decrease AMPHETAMINE elimination; **ammonium chloride, ascorbic acid** increase AMPHETAMINE elimination; BARBITURATES may antagonize the effects of both drugs; **furazolidone** may increase BP effects of AMPHETAMINES, and interaction may persist for several weeks after discontinuation of **furazolidone; guanethidine, guanadryl** antagonize antihypertensive effects; because MAO INHIBITORS, **selegiline** can cause hypertensive crisis (fatalities reported); do not administer AMPHETAMINES during or within 14 d of these drugs; PHENOTHIAZINES may inhibit mood-elevating effects of AMPHETAMINES; TRICYCLIC ANTIDEPRESSANTS enhance AMPHETAMINE effects because they increase **norepinephrine** release; BETA AGONISTS increase AMPHETAMINE'S adverse cardiovascular effects.

PHARMACOKINETICS Absorption: Readily absorbed from GI tract. **Duration:** 4 h. **Metabolism:** Via CYP3A4. **Elimination:** Renal elimination.

CLINICAL IMPLICATIONS

Assessment & Drug Effects

- Assess for signs of excessive CNS stimulation: insomnia, restlessness, tremor, palpitations. These may indicate need for dosage adjustment.
- Monitor vital signs; report elevated BP, tachycardia, and irregular heart rhythm.
- Monitor diabetics for loss of glycemic control.

Patient & Family Education

- Note: Anorexiant effects are temporary and tolerance may occur; long-term use is not indicated.
- Do not drive or engage in potentially hazardous activities until response to drug is known.
- Do not terminate high dosage therapy abruptly; GI distress, stomach cramps, trembling, unusual tiredness, weakness, and mental depression may result.

BENZTROPINE MESYLATE

(benz'troe-peen)
Apo-Benztropine ♣, Cogentin, PMS Benztropine ♣

Classifications: ANTICHOLINERGIC; ANTIPARKINSON AGENT
Therapeutic: ANTIPARKINSON AGENT
Prototype: Levodopa
Pregnancy Category: C

AVAILABILITY 0.5 mg, 1 mg, 2 mg tablets; 1 mg/mL ampules

ACTION & *THERAPEUTIC EFFECT*

Synthetic centrally acting anticholinergic (antimuscarinic) agent. Acts by diminishing excess cholinergic effect associated with dopamine deficiency. *Suppresses tremor and rigidity; does not alleviate tardive dyskinesia.*

USES Symptomatic treatment of all forms of parkinsonism (arteriosclerotic, idiopathic, postencephalitic) and to relieve extrapyramidal symptoms associated with neuroleptic drugs, e.g., haloperidol (Haldol), phenothiazines, thiothixene (Navane), acute dystonia. Commonly used as supplement with trihexyphenidyl, carbidopa, or levodopa therapy.

CONTRAINDICATIONS Narrow angle glaucoma; myasthenia gravis; obstructive diseases of GU and GI tracts; tendency to tachycardia; tardive dyskinesia, children <3 y; pregnancy (category C).
CAUTIOUS USE Older children, older adults or debilitated patients, patients with poor mental outlook, mental disorders; tachycardia; autonomic neuropathy; enlarged prostate; hypertension; history of renal or hepatic disease, lactation.

ROUTE & DOSAGE

Parkinsonism
Adult: **PO** 0.5–1 mg/d, may gradually increase as needed up to 6 mg/d
Extrapyramidal Reactions
Adult: **PO** 1–2 mg b.i.d. **IM/IV** 1–4 mg 1–2 times daily as needed
Child: **PO/IM/IV** >3 y, 0.02–0.05 mg/kg, 1–2 times/d
Acute Dystonia
Adult: **IV** 1–2 mg daily

ADMINISTRATION

Oral
- Give immediately after meals or with food to prevent gastric irritation. Tablet can be crushed and sprinkled on or mixed with food.
- Initiate and withdraw drug therapy gradually; effects are cumulative.
- Store in tightly covered, light-resistant container at 15°–30° C (59°–86° F) unless otherwise directed.

Intravenous

IV administration to infants and children: Verify correct IV concentration with physician.

PREPARE: **Direct:** Give undiluted.
ADMINISTER: **Direct:** Give 1 mg or a fraction thereof over 1 min.

ADVERSE EFFECTS (≥1%) **CNS:** *Sedation,* drowsiness, dizziness, paresthesias; agitation, irritability, restlessness, nervousness, insomnia, hallucinations, delirium, mental confusion, toxic psychosis, muscular weakness, ataxia, inability to move certain muscle groups. **CV:** Palpitation, tachycardia, flushing. **Special Senses:** Blurred vision, mydriasis, photophobia. **GI:** Nausea, vomiting, *constipation, dry mouth,* distention, paralytic ileus. **Urogenital:** Dysuria.

INTERACTIONS Drug: Alcohol, CNS DEPRESSANTS have additive sedation and depressant effects; **amantadine,** TRICYCLIC ANTIDEPRESSANTS, MAO INHIBITORS, PHENOTHIAZINES, **procainamide, quinidine** have additive anticholinergic effects and cause confusion, hallucinations, paralytic ileus.

PHARMACOKINETICS Onset: 15 min IM/IV; 1 h PO. **Duration:** 6–10 h.

CLINICAL IMPLICATIONS

Assessment & Drug Effects
- Assess therapeutic effectiveness. Clinical improvement may not be

Common adverse effects in *italic*, life-threatening effects underlined; generic names in **bold**; classifications in SMALL CAPS; ♣ Canadian drug name; ❷ Prototype drug

163

evident for 2–3 d after oral drug is started.

- Monitor I&O ratio and pattern. Advise patient to report difficulty in urination or infrequent voiding. Dosage reduction may be indicated.
- Closely monitor for appearance of S&S of onset of paralytic ileus including intermittent constipation, abdominal pain, diminution of bowel sounds on auscultation, and distention.
- Monitor for and report muscle weakness or inability to move certain muscle groups. Dosage reduction may be needed.
- Supervise ambulation and use bed side rails as necessary.
- Report immediately S&S of CNS depression or stimulation. These usually require interruption of drug therapy.

Patient & Family Education

- Do not drive or engage in potentially hazardous activities until response to drug is known. Seek help walking as necessary.
- Avoid alcohol and other CNS depressants because they may cause additive drowsiness. Do not take OTC cold, cough, or hay fever remedies unless approved by physician.
- Sugarless gum, hard candy, and rinsing mouth with tepid water will help dry mouth.
- Avoid doing manual labor or strenuous exercise in hot weather; diminished sweating may require dose adjustments because of possibility of heat stroke. This condition is most apt to occur in the older adults.

BERACTANT ℗

(ber-ac'tant)
Survanta

Classifications: LUNG SURFACTANT
Therapeutic: LUNG SURFACTANT
Pregnancy Category: Not applicable

AVAILABILITY 25 mg/mL suspension

ACTION & *THERAPEUTIC EFFECT*

Beractant is a sterile pulmonary surfactant. Endogenous pulmonary surfactant lowers surface tension on alveolar surfaces during respiration and stabilizes the alveoli against collapse at resting pressures. Deficiency of surfactant causes respiratory distress syndrome (RDS) in premature infants. *Beractant lowers minimum surface tension and restores pulmonary compliance and oxygenation in premature infants.*

USES Prevention and treatment of RDS in premature infants, especially those weighing <1250 g.
UNLABELED USES Infants weighing <600 g or >1750 g; treatment of RDS in adults.

CONTRAINDICATIONS Nosocomial infections; bovine protein hypersensitivity.
CAUTIOUS USE Lactation.

ROUTE & DOSAGE

Neonate: **Intratracheal** Instill 100 mg/kg (4 mL/kg) birth weight through endotracheal tube, may repeat no more frequently than q6h (max: 4 doses in the first 48 h of life)

ADMINISTRATION

Intratracheal
- Place refrigerated drug at room temperature for at least 20 min or warm in the hand for at least 8 min. Do not use artificial warming methods.

- Give to premature infants weighing less than 1250 g, or who have a surfactant deficiency, preferably within 15 min of birth.
- Give to infants requiring mechanical ventilation and with RDS confirmed by x-ray examination, within 8 h of birth.
- Suction infant before administration of beractant.
- Note: Drug color should be white to light brown. If drug has settled, swirl vial gently to suspend.
- Administer using a No. 5 French end-hole catheter inserted into the endotracheal tube.
- Follow specific dosing procedure recommended by the manufacturer. Carefully read and follow exactly accompanying drug administration literature.
- Do not suction for 1 h after drug is administered unless signs of significant airway obstruction occur.
- Unopened vials warmed to room temperature will not lose potency if refrigerated within 8 h of warming. Drug should not be warmed and returned to refrigerator more than once.
- Note: Vials are for single use only. Discard unused drug in opened vials.
- Store unopened vials inside carton to protect from light and refrigerated at 2°–8° C (36°–46° F) until ready to use.

ADVERSE EFFECTS (≥1%) **CV:** *Transient bradycardia.* **Respiratory:** *Oxygen desaturation.* **Other:** Increased probability of posttreatment nosocomial sepsis in surfactant-treated infants was observed in the controlled clinical trials but was not associated with increased mortality.

PHARMACOKINETICS Absorption: Absorbed from the alveolus into lung tissue, where it can be extensively catabolized and reutilized for further phospholipid synthesis and secretion. **Onset:** 0.5–4 h. **Peak:** 2 h. **Duration:** 48–72 h; may need multiple doses to sustain improvement. **Distribution:** Not distributed to the systemic circulation. **Metabolism:** Surfactant is recycled and metabolized exclusively in the lungs. **Elimination:** Recycling may be a dominant metabolic pathway by which surfactant is taken up by type II pneumocytes and reused. **Half-Life:** 20–30 h.

CLINICAL IMPLICATIONS

Assessment & Drug Effects

- Monitor heart rate, color, chest expansion, facial expressions, oximeter, and endotracheal tube patency and position, during administration. Most adverse effects occur during dosing.
- Monitor frequently with arterial or transcutaneous measurement of systemic oxygen and CO_2.
- Note: Rales and moist breath sounds may occur transiently following drug administration. These do not necessarily indicate a need for suctioning.

BETAMETHASONE

(bay-ta-meth′a-sone)
Betnelan ♣, Celestone

BETAMETHASONE ACETATE AND BETAMETHASONE SODIUM PHOSPHATE
Celestone Soluspan

BETAMETHASONE BENZOATE
Beben ♣

BETAMETHASONE DIPROPIONATE
Alphatrex, Diprolene

Common adverse effects in *italic*, life-threatening effects <u>underlined</u>; generic names in **bold**; classifications in SMALL CAPS; ♣ Canadian drug name; ❷ Prototype drug

165

B

BETAMETHASONE SODIUM PHOSPHATE (PH 8.5)

Betameth, Betnesol ✦, Celestone S

BETAMETHASONE VALERATE

Betaderm ✦, Beta-Val, Betnovate ✦, Celestoderm ✦, Ectosone Lotion ✦, Luxiq, Metaderm ✦, Novobetamet ✦, Valnac

Classifications: ANTIINFLAMMATORY; ADRENAL CORTICOSTEROID; GLUCOCORTICOID
Therapeutic: ANTIINFLAMMATORY; ADRENAL CORTICOSTEROID
Prototype: Hydrocortisone
Pregnancy Category: C

AVAILABILITY Betamethasone: 0.6 mg tablets; 0.6 mg/5 mL syrup; **Betamethasone Acetate and Betamethasone Sodium:** 3 mg acetate, 3 mg sodium phosphate/mL suspension; **Betamethasone Benzoate and Betamethasone Dipropionate:** 4 mg/mL injection; **Betamethasone Valerate:** 0.1% ointment; 0.01%, 0.05%, 0.1% cream; 0.1% lotion; 1.2 mg/g foam; **Betamethasone Sodium Phosphate:** 0.6 mg/5mL syrup

ACTION & *THERAPEUTIC EFFECT*

Synthetic, long-acting glucocorticoid with minor mineralocorticoid properties but strong immunosuppressive, antiinflammatory, and metabolic actions. *Relieves antiinflammatory manifestations and is an immunosuppressive agent.*

USES Reduces serum calcium in hypercalcemia, suppresses undesirable inflammatory or immune responses, produces temporary remission in nonadrenal disease, and blocks ACTH production in diagnostic tests. Topical use provides relief of inflammatory manifestations of corticosteroid-responsive dermatoses.

UNLABELED USES Prevention of neonatal respiratory distress syndrome (hyaline membrane disease).

CONTRAINDICATIONS In patients with systemic fungal infections. Pregnancy (category C), lactation; acne vulgaris; acne rosacea; Cushing's syndrome; periorbital dermatitis; vaccines.

CAUTIOUS USE Ocular herpes simplex; concomitant use of aspirin; osteoporosis; diverticulitis, nonspecific ulcerative colitis, abscess or other pyrogenic infection, peptic ulcer disease; asthmatics; diabetes mellitus; hypertension; renal insufficiency; myasthenia gravis.

ROUTE & DOSAGE

Antiinflammatory Agent

Adult: **PO** 0.6–7.2 mg/d **IM/IV** 0.5–9 mg/d as sodium phosphate

Topical (See Appendix A-4)

Child: **PO** 0.0175–0.25 mg/kg/d or 0.5–0.75 mg/m²/d divided q6–8h **IM** 0.0175–0.125 mg/kg/d or 0.5–0.75 mg/m²/d divided q6–8h

Respiratory Distress Syndrome

Adult: **IM** 2 mL of sodium phosphate to mother once daily 2–3 d before delivery

ADMINISTRATION

Oral
- Give with food or milk to lessen stomach irritation.

Intraarticular, Intramuscular, Intralesional
- Use Celestone Soluspan for intraarticular, IM, and intralesional injection. The preparation is not

intended for IV use. Do not mix with diluents containing preservatives (e.g., parabens, phenol).

- Use 1% or 2% lidocaine hydrochloride if prescribed. Withdraw betamethasone mixture first, then lidocaine; shake syringe briefly.

Intravenous

PREPARE: Direct: Give by direct IV undiluted or further diluted in D5W or NS.
ADMINISTER: Direct: Give at a rate of 1 dose/min.
INCOMPATIBILITIES Solution/additive: Amobarbital, ampicillin, bleomycin, colistimethate, dimenhydrinate, doxapram, doxorubicin, ephedrine, heparin, hydralazine, metaraminol, methicillin, nafcillin, pentobarbital, phenobarbital, prochlorperazine, promethazine, secobarbital, TETRACYCLINE. **Y-site:** Ergotamine, phenytoin.

ADVERSE EFFECTS (≥1%) **Body as a Whole:** Hypersensitivity or <u>anaphylactoid reactions; aggravation or masking of infections</u>; malaise, weight gain, obesity. Most adverse effects are dose and treatment duration dependent. **CNS:** Vertigo, headache, nystagmus, ataxia (rare), increased intracranial pressure with papilledema (usually after discontinuation of medication), mental disturbances, aggravation of preexisting psychiatric conditions, insomnia. **CV:** Hypertension; syncopal episodes, thrombophlebitis, thromboembolism or fat embolism, palpitation, tachycardia, necrotizing angiitis; CHF. **Endocrine:** Suppressed linear growth in children, decreased glucose tolerance; hyperglycemia, manifestations of latent diabetes mellitus; hypocorticism; amenorrhea and other menstrual difficulties. **Special Senses:** Posterior subcapsular cataracts (especially in children), glaucoma, exophthalmos, increased intraocular pressure with optic nerve damage, perforation of the globe, fungal infection of the cornea, decreased or blurred vision. **Metabolic:** Hypocalcemia; *sodium and fluid retention;* hypokalemia and hypokalemic alkalosis; negative nitrogen balance. **GI:** *Nausea,* increased appetite, ulcerative esophagitis, pancreatitis, abdominal distention, peptic ulcer with perforation and hemorrhage, melena; decreased serum concentration of vitamins A and C. **Hematologic:** Thrombocytopenia. **Musculoskeletal:** Osteoporosis, compression fractures, muscle wasting and weakness, tendon rupture, aseptic necrosis of femoral and humeral heads (all resulting from long-term use). **Skin:** Skin thinning and atrophy, *acne, impaired wound healing;* petechiae, ecchymosis, easy bruising; suppression of skin test reaction; hypopigmentation or hyperpigmentation, hirsutism, acneiform eruptions, subcutaneous fat atrophy; allergic dermatitis, urticaria, angioneurotic edema, increased sweating. **Urogenital:** Increased or decreased motility and number of sperm; urinary frequency and urgency, enuresis. **With parenteral therapy, IV site:** Pain, irritation, necrosis, atrophy, sterile abscess; Charcot-like arthropathy following intraarticular use; burning and tingling in perineal area (after IV injection).

DIAGNOSTIC TEST INTERFERENCE May increase serum *cholesterol, blood glucose,* serum *sodium, uric acid* (in acute leukemia) and *calcium* (in bone metastasis). It may decrease serum *calcium, potassium, PBI, thyroxin (T_4), triiodothyronine (T_3) and reduce*

Common adverse effects in *italic*, life-threatening effects <u>underlined</u>; generic names in **bold**; classifications in SMALL CAPS; ✤ Canadian drug name; ✪ Prototype drug

167

B

thyroid I 131 uptake. It increases *urine glucose* level and *calcium* excretion; decreases *urine 17-OHCS* and *17-KS* levels. May produce false-negative results with *nitroblue tetrazolium test* for systemic bacterial infection and may suppress reactions to skin tests.

INTERACTIONS Drug: BARBITURATES, **phenytoin, rifampin** may reduce pharmacologic effect of betamethasone by increasing its metabolism.

PHARMACOKINETICS Not studied.

CLINICAL IMPLICATIONS

Assessment & Drug Effects

- Assess therapeutic effectiveness. Response following intraarticular, intralesional, or intrasynovial administration occurs within a few hours and persists for 1–4 wk. Following IM administration response occurs in 2–3 h and persists for 3–7 d.

Patient & Family Education

- Monitor weight at least weekly.
- Discontinue slowly after systemic use of ≥1 wk. Abrupt withdrawal, especially following high doses or prolonged use, can cause dizziness, nausea, vomiting, fever, muscle and joint pain, weakness.

BETAXOLOL HYDROCHLORIDE

(be-tax′oh-lol)

Betoptic, Betoptic-S, Kerlone

Classifications: EYE PREPARATION; MIOTIC (ANTIGLAUCOMA AGENT); BETA-ADRENERGIC BLOCKER; ANTIHYPERTENSIVE AGENT

Therapeutic: ANTIGLAUCOMA AGENT (MIOTIC); ANTIHYPERTENSIVE AGENT

Prototype: Propranolol

Pregnancy Category: C

AVAILABILITY 10 mg, 20 mg tablets; 0.25%, 0.5% ophthalmic solution

ACTION & *THERAPEUTIC EFFECT*

Acts as a beta₁-selective adrenergic receptor blocking agent, especially in the cardioselective beta₁ receptors. Its antihypertensive effect is thought to be due to: (1) decreasing cardiac output, (2) reducing sympathetic nervous system outflow to the periphery resulting in vasodilatation, and (3) suppression of renin activity in the kidney. It reduces intraocular pressure within the eye by decreasing the production of aqueous humor. *All three mechanisms result in its antihypertensive effect.*

USES Hypertension. Ocular use for intraocular hypertension, chronic open angle glaucoma (**see Appendix A-1**).

CONTRAINDICATIONS Sinus bradycardia, AV block greater than first degree, cardiogenic shock, severe left ventricular heart failure; glaucoma, angle closure (unless with a miotic); pregnancy (category C); children <18 y.

CAUTIOUS USE Concomitant use of systemic beta-adrenergic blocking agents; history of heart failure; renal impairment, elderly; hyperthyroidism or thyrotoxicosis; diabetes mellitus; with evidence of airflow obstruction or reactive airway disease; depression; lactation.

ROUTE & DOSAGE

Hypertension

Adult: **PO** 5–10 mg q.d. (max: 20 mg/d in 1–2 divided doses)

Renal Impairment

Cl_{cr} <10mL/min: administer 50% of dose

Common adverse effects in *italic*, life-threatening effects underlined; generic names in **bold**; classifications in SMALL CAPS; ♣ Canadian drug name; ⊙ Prototype drug

ADMINISTRATION

Oral

- Check pulse before administering betaxolol, oral or ophthalmic. If there are extremes (rate or rhythm), withhold medication and call the physician.
- Be aware tablet may be crushed before administration and taken with fluid of patient's choice.

ADVERSE EFFECTS (≥1%) **CV:** Bradycardia, hypotension. **CNS:** Depression. **Respiratory:** Increased airway resistance. **Special Senses:** With ophthalmic solution, *mild ocular stinging* and discomfort, tearing.

INTERACTIONS Drug: Reserpine and other CATECHOLAMINE-DEPLETING AGENTS may cause additive hypotensive effects or bradycardia. **Verapamil** may cause additive heart block.

PHARMACOKINETICS Absorption: 90% of PO dose reaches systemic circulation. **Onset:** 0.5–1 h. **Peak:** 2 h. **Duration:** >12 h. **Metabolism:** In liver by CYP1A2 and 2D6. **Elimination:** 30–40% in urine, 50–60% in bile and feces. **Half-Life:** 3–4 h.

CLINICAL IMPLICATIONS

Assessment & Drug Effects

- Monitor pulse rate and BP at regular intervals in patients with severe heart disease.
- Monitor therapeutic effectiveness. Some patients develop tolerance during long-term therapy.

Patient & Family Education

- Report unusual pulse rate or significant changes to physician according to parameters provided.
- Adhere to regimen EXACTLY as prescribed. Do not stop drug abruptly; angina may be exacerbated; dosage is reduced over a period of 1–2 wk.
- Report difficulty in breathing promptly to physician. Drug withdrawal may be indicated.

BETHANECHOL CHLORIDE ⓟ

(be-than'e-kole)

Duvoid, Urecholine

Classifications: DIRECT-ACTING CHOLINERGIC AGENT

Therapeutic: CHOLINERGIC, PARASYMPATHOMIMETIC

Pregnancy Category: C

AVAILABILITY 5 mg, 10 mg, 25 mg, 50 mg tablets

ACTION & *THERAPEUTIC EFFECT*
Synthetic choline ester with effects similar to those of acetylcholine (ACh). Acts directly on postsynaptic receptors, and since it is not hydrolyzed by cholinesterase, its actions are more prolonged than those of ACh. Produces muscarinic effects primarily on GI tract and urinary bladder. Increases tone and peristaltic activity of esophagus, stomach, and intestine; contracts detrusor muscle of urinary bladder, usually enough to initiate micturition. *Bethanechol is a synthetic parasympathomimetic indicated for the treatment of urinary retention associated with neurogenic bladder.*

USES Acute postoperative and postpartum nonobstructive (functional) urinary retention, and for neurogenic atony of urinary bladder with retention.

UNLABELED USES In selected cases of adynamic ileus, gastric atony and retention, reflux esophagitis, congenital megacolon, familial dysautonomia; for prevention and treatment of bladder and salivary

Common adverse effects in *italic*, life-threatening effects underlined; generic names in **bold**; classifications in SMALL CAPS; ♣ Canadian drug name; ⓟ Prototype drug

169

gland inhibition induced by tricyclic antidepressants, and for prophylaxis and treatment of phenothiazine-induced bladder dysfunction.

CONTRAINDICATIONS COPD; history of or active bronchial asthma; hyperthyroidism; recent urinary bladder surgery, cystitis, bacteriuria, urinary bladder neck or intestinal obstruction, peptic ulcer, recent GI surgery, peritonitis; marked vagotonia, pronounced vasomotor instability, AV conduction defects, severe bradycardia, hypotension or hypertension, coronary artery disease, recent MI; epilepsy, parkinsonism; pregnancy (category C), lactation, children <8 y.
CAUTIOUS USE Urinary retention; bacteriemia; patients at risk for syncopy.

ROUTE & DOSAGE

Urinary Retention
Adult: **PO** 10–50 mg b.i.d. to q.i.d. (max: 120 mg/d)
Child: **PO** 0.2 mg/kg or 0.6 mg/m^2 t.i.d.

ADMINISTRATION

Oral
- Give on an empty stomach (1 h before or 2 h after meals) to lessen possibility of nausea and vomiting, unless otherwise advised by physician.
- Determine minimum effective dose: Give 5–10 mg initially and repeat this dose at 1–2 h (max: 50 mg), until a satisfactory response occurs. Alternatively, give 10 mg followed, at 6 h intervals, by 25 mg, then 50 mg, until desired response obtained.

ADVERSE EFFECTS (≥1%) **Body as a Whole:** Dose-related. Increased sweating, malaise, headache, substernal pain or pressure, hypothermia. **CV:** Hypotension with dizziness, faintness, flushing, orthostatic hypotension (large doses); mild reflex tachycardia, atrial fibrillation (hyperthyroid patients), transient complete heart block. **Special Senses:** Blurred vision, miosis, lacrimation. **GI:** Nausea, vomiting, abdominal cramps, diarrhea, borborygmi, belching, salivation, fecal incontinence (large doses), urge to defecate (or urinate). **Respiratory:** Acute asthmatic attack, dyspnea (large doses).

DIAGNOSTIC TEST INTERFERENCE Bethanechol may cause increases in *serum amylase* and *serum lipase,* by stimulating pancreatic secretions, and may increase *AST, serum bilirubin,* and *BSP retention* by causing spasms in sphincter of Oddi.

INTERACTIONS Drug: Ambenonium, neostigmine, other CHOLINESTERASE INHIBITORS compound cholinergic effects and toxicity; **mecamylamine** may cause abdominal symptoms and hypotension; **procainamide, quinidine, atropine, epinephrine** antagonize effects of bethanechol.

PHARMACOKINETICS Absorption: Well absorbed. **Onset:** 30 min. **Peak:** 60–90 min. **Duration:** 1–6 h. **Distribution:** Does not cross blood–brain barrier. **Metabolism:** Unknown. **Elimination:** Unknown.

CLINICAL IMPLICATIONS

Assessment & Drug Effects
- Monitor BP and pulse. Observe patient for at least 1 h following SC administration. Report early signs of overdosage: Salivation, sweating, flushing, abdominal cramps, nausea.

- Monitor I&O. Observe and record patient's response to bethanechol, and report any failure of the drug to relieve the particular condition for which it was prescribed.
- Monitor respiratory status. Promptly report dyspnea or any other indication of respiratory distress.
- Supervise ambulation as indicated by patient response to drug.

Patient & Family Education

- Make position changes slowly and in stages, particularly from lying down to standing.
- Do not stand still for prolonged periods; sit or lie down at first indication of faintness.
- Do not drive or engage in potentially hazardous activities until response to drug is known.
- Note: Drug may cause blurred vision; take appropriate precautions.

BEVACIZUMAB

(be-va-ci-zu'mab)
Avastin
Classifications: ANTINEOPLASTIC AGENT; BIOLOGIC RESPONSE MODIFIER; MONOCLONAL ANTIBODY
Therapeutic: ANTINEOPLASTIC; MONOCLONAL ANTIBODY
Pregnancy Category: C

AVAILABILITY 25 mg/mL injection

ACTION & THERAPEUTIC EFFECT
Binds to vascular endothelial growth factor (VEGF) and prevents the interaction of VEGF to its receptors on the surface of endothelial cells. This blocks endothelial cell proliferation and new blood vessel formation in tumor cells. *Believed to cause reduction of microvascularization in the tumor inhibiting the progression of metastatic disease.*

USES Metastatic colorectal cancer.
UNLABELED USES Metastatic renal cell cancer.

CONTRAINDICATIONS Pregnancy (category C), lactation, neonates; nephrotic syndrome; active bleeding, GI perforation; surgery within 28 d; dental work within 20 d. Safety and effectiveness in children and infants are not established.
CAUTIOUS USE Hypersensitivity to bevacizumab; renal disease; hypertension, history of arterial thromboembolic, cardiovascular, or cerebrovascular disease.

ROUTE & DOSAGE

Metastatic Colorectal Cancer
Adult: **IV** 5–10 mg/kg q14d until disease progression; in conjunction with 5-fluorouracil chemotherapy

ADMINISTRATION

Intravenous

PREPARE: IV Infusion: Withdraw the desired dose of 5 mg/kg and dilute in 100 mL of NS injection. Do not shake and do NOT mix or administer with dextrose solutions. Discard any unused portion.
ADMINISTER: IV Infusion: DO NOT administer IV push or bolus. Infuse first dose over 90 min; if well tolerated, infuse second dose over 60 min; if well tolerated, infuse all subsequent doses over 30 min.
INCOMPATIBILITIES Solution/additive: Dextrose-containing solutions. **Y-site: Dextrose**-containing solutions.

- Store diluted solution at 2°–8° C (36°–46° F) for up to 8 h. Store vials at 2°–8° C (36°–46° F) and protect from light.

Common adverse effects in *italic*, life-threatening effects underlined; generic names in **bold**; classifications in SMALL CAPS; ◆ Canadian drug name; ⊙ Prototype drug

171

ADVERSE EFFECTS (≥1%) **Body as a Whole:** *Asthenia,* pain, wound dehiscence. **CNS:** Syncope, headache, dizziness, confusion, abnormal gait, <u>leukoencephalopathy</u>. **CV:** DVT, *hypertension,* heart failure, intra-abdominal thrombosis, <u>cerebrovascular events</u>. **GI:** Abdominal pain, *diarrhea,* constipation, nausea, vomiting, anorexia, stomatitis, dyspepsia, weight loss, flatulence, dry mouth, colitis, <u>gastrointestinal perforation</u>. **Hematologic:** *Leukopenia, neutropenia,* thrombocytopenia, *thromboembolism.* **Metabolic:** Hypokalemia, hyperbilirubinemia. **Musculoskeletal:** Myalgia. **Respiratory:** Upper respiratory infection, epistaxis, dyspnea, <u>hemoptysis</u>. **Skin:** Exfoliative dermatitis, alopecia. **Special Senses:** Taste disorder, increased tearing. **Urogenital:** *Proteinuria,* urinary frequency/urgency.

INTERACTIONS Drug: None reported at this time.

PHARMACOKINETICS Half-Life: 20 d (11–50 d).

CLINICAL IMPLICATIONS

Assessment & Drug Effects

- Monitor for S&S of an infusion reaction (hypersensitivity); infusion should be interrupted in all patients with severe infusion reactions and appropriate therapy instituted.
- Monitor BP at least every 2–3 wk; if hypertension develops, monitor more frequently, even after discontinuation of bevacizumab.
- Withhold drug and promptly notify physician for S&S of CHF, hemorrhage (e.g., epistaxis, hemoptysis, or GI bleeding), or unexplained abdominal pain.
- Lab tests: Urinalysis for proteinuria and 24 h urine if protein 2+ or greater.

- Monitor for dizziness, lightheadedness, or loss of balance. Take appropriate safety measures.

Patient & Family Education

- Report any of the following to the physician: bloody or black, tarry stool; changes in patterns of urination; swelling of legs or ankles; increased shortness of breath; severe abdominal pain; change in mental awareness, inability to talk or move one side of the body.
- Women of childbearing age should use effective birth control while receiving bevacizumab.

BEXAROTENE

(bex-a-ro'teen)

Targretin

Classifications: ANTINEOPLASTIC AGENT; RETINOID

Therapeutic: ANTINEOPLASTIC; RETINOID

Prototype: Isotretinoin

Pregnancy Category: X

AVAILABILITY 75 mg capsules; 1% gel

ACTION & *THERAPEUTIC EFFECT*
Selectively binds to retinoid X receptors (RXR). Activation of the RXR pathway leads to cell death by interfering with cellular differentiation and proliferation of cells. *Inhibits the growth of tumor cells of squamous (skin) cell origin inducing tumor regression.*

USES Treatment of cutaneous manifestations of cutaneous T-cell lymphoma.

CONTRAINDICATIONS Hypersensitivity to bexarotene; pregnancy (X), lactation. Safety and efficacy in children are not established.

Common adverse effects in *italic*, life-threatening effects <u>underlined</u>; generic names in **bold**; classifications in SMALL CAPS; ♣ Canadian drug name; ⦿ Prototype drug

CAUTIOUS USE Hypersensitivity to retinoid agents; coronary artery disease; diabetes mellitus; alcoholism, history of pancreatitis, hepatitis; elevated triglycerides, hepatic impairment.

ROUTE & DOSAGE

T-Cell Lymphoma

Adult: **PO** 300 mg/m²/d as a single dose with a meal, if no response after 8 wk, may increase to 400 mg/m²/d. Adjust dose downward in 100 mg/m²/d increments if toxicity occurs **Topical** Apply once q.o.d. times 1 week, increase frequency at weekly intervals to once per day, b.i.d., t.i.d., and q.i.d.

ADMINISTRATION

Oral

- Give drug with or immediately following a meal.
- Do not give oral drug with grapefruit or grapefruit juice.
- Do not initiate therapy in a woman of childbearing age until the possibility of pregnancy has been completely ruled out.

Topical

- Apply a generous coating only to skin lesions; avoid normal skin.
- Do not cover with clothing until gel dries.
- Do not apply more frequently than prescribed.
- Store capsules and gel at 20°–25° C (36°–77° F). Protect from light and avoid high temperatures and humidity after bottle or tube is opened.

ADVERSE EFFECTS (≥1%) **Body as a Whole:** *Headache, asthenia, infection,* chills, fever, flu-like syndrome, back pain, bacterial infection. **CNS:** Insomnia. **CV:** *Peripheral edema.* **GI:** *Abdominal pain,* *nausea,* diarrhea, vomiting, anorexia. **Endocrine:** *Hyperthyroidism.* **Hematologic:** *Leukopenia,* anemia, hypochromic anemia. **Metabolic:** *Hyperlipidemia, hypercholesterolemia,* increased LDH. **Skin:** *Rash, dry skin,* exfoliative dermatitis, alopecia, photosensitivity.

INTERACTIONS No clinically significant interactions established.

PHARMACOKINETICS Absorption: Best with a fat-containing meal. **Peak:** 2 h. **Distribution:** >99% protein bound. **Metabolism:** Metabolized by CYP3A4. **Elimination:** Primarily in bile. **Half-Life:** 7 h.

CLINICAL IMPLICATIONS

Assessment & Drug Effects

- Monitor (with oral dose) for S&S of: hypothyroidism, hypertriglyceridemia, hypercholesterolemia, and pancreatitis.
- Lab tests (with oral dose): Baseline blood lipids, then weekly for 2–4 wks, and every 8 wks thereafter; baseline liver function tests, then repeat at 1, 2, 4 wks, and every 8 wks thereafter; baseline WBC and thyroid function tests, then repeat periodically thereafter; periodic serum calcium; for females, pregnancy test q mo throughout therapy.
- Withhold oral drug and notify physician if triglycerides >400 mg/dL or AST, ALT, or bilirubin >3 times upper limit of normal.

Patient & Family Education

- Use effective methods of contraception (both men and women) while taking/using this drug and for at least 1 mo after the last dose of the drug.
- Do not take this drug if you are or could be pregnant.
- Do not take this drug (oral form) if you are also taking gemfibrozil.

Common adverse effects in *italic*, life-threatening effects underlined; generic names in **bold**; classifications in SMALL CAPS; ♣ Canadian drug name; ☯ Prototype drug

173

- Report immediately any of the following: Swelling in the face, lips, or wheezing; persistent bloating, constipation, diarrhea, vomiting, or stomach pain; persistent headache, severe drowsiness or weakness.
- Limit vitamin A intake to ≤15,000 IU/d while taking this drug (oral form).
- Report changes in vision to the physician. An ophthalmologic evaluation may be needed.
- Limit exposure to sunlight or sun lamps and wear sunscreen.
- Do not use insect repellents that contain the chemical, DEET, while using bexarotene gel.
- Report significant skin irritation.

BICALUTAMIDE

(bi-ca-lu'ta-mide)
Casodex
Classifications: ANTINEOPLASTIC; ANTIANDROGEN
Therapeutic: ANTINEOPLASTIC; ANTIANDROGEN
Prototype: Flutamide
Pregnancy Category: X

AVAILABILITY 50 mg tablets

ACTION & *THERAPEUTIC EFFECT*
Bicalutamide is a nonsteroidal antiandrogen. It inhibits the pharmacologic effects of androgen by binding to the androgen receptors in the target tissue. *Prostatic carcinoma is androgen sensitive; it responds to removal of the source of androgen or treatment that counteracts the effects of androgen.*

USES In combination with a luteinizing hormone-releasing hormone (LHRH) analog for advanced prostate cancer.

CONTRAINDICATIONS Hypersensitivity to bicalutamide, pregnancy

(category X), hepatic failure; lactation.
CAUTIOUS USE Moderate to severe hepatic impairment. Safety and efficacy in children are not established.

ROUTE & DOSAGE

Advanced Prostate Cancer
Adult: **PO** 50 mg once/d

ADMINISTRATION

Oral
- Give drug at the same time each day.
- Start treatment with bicalutamide at the same time as treatment with a luteinizing hormone-releasing hormone (LHRH) analog.
- Store at 15°–30° C (59°–86° F).

ADVERSE EFFECTS (≥1%) **CNS:** Dizziness, paresthesia, insomnia, anxiety, decreased libido, confusion, neuropathy, somnolence, nervousness, headache. **CV:** *Hot flashes,* hypertension, chest pain, CHF. **GI:** *Constipation, nausea, diarrhea,* vomiting, increased liver function tests, abdominal pain, anorexia, dyspepsia, dry mouth, melena. **Urogenital:** Nocturia, hematuria, UTI, impotence, gynecomastia, incontinence, frequency, dysuria, urinary retention, urgency. **Metabolic:** Peripheral edema, hyperglycemia, weight loss, weight gain, gout. **Musculoskeletal:** Myasthenia, arthritis, myalgia, leg cramps, pathologic fractures. **Skin:** Rash, sweating, dry skin, pruritus, alopecia. **Body as a Whole:** Flu syndrome, bone pain, infection, anemia.

INTERACTIONS Drug: May increase effects of ORAL ANTICOAGULANTS.

PHARMACOKINETICS Absorption: Readily from GI tract. **Metabolism:** In liver. **Elimination:** In urine and feces. **Half-Life:** 5.8 d.

CLINICAL IMPLICATIONS

Assessment & Drug Effects
- Monitor for S&S of disease progression.
- Lab tests: Periodic PSA levels, CBC, liver functions, renal functions; with concurrent Coumadin therapy, closely monitor PT and INR.

Patient & Family Education
- Report jaundice or any other troubling adverse effects immediately.

BIMATOPROST

(bi-mat'o-prost)
Lumigan
Pregnancy Category: C
See Appendix A-1.

BIPERIDEN HYDROCHLORIDE

(bye-per'i-den)
Akineton

BIPERIDEN LACTATE

Akineton
Classifications: ANTICHOLINERGIC; ANTIPARKINSON AGENT
Therapeutic: ANTIPARKINSON AGENT
Prototype: Levodopa
Pregnancy Category: C

AVAILABILITY 2 mg tablets

ACTION & *THERAPEUTIC EFFECT*
Synthetic tertiary amine, antimuscarinic. In common with other antiparkinsonism drugs has atropine-like (anticholinergic) action. Antiparkinsonism activity is thought to be caused by reducing central excitatory action of acetylcholine on cholinergic receptors in the extrapyramidal system. *This action helps to establish some balance between cholinergic (excitatory) and dopaminergic (inhibitory) activity in the basal ganglia with the result of controlling the effect of extrapyramidal symptoms.*

USES Adjunct in all forms of parkinsonism, particularly postencephalitic and idiopathic parkinsonism (appears to be less effective in arteriosclerotic type). Also used to control drug-induced parkinsonism (extrapyramidal symptoms) associated with reserpine and phenothiazine therapy.

CONTRAINDICATIONS Narrow-angle glaucoma; GI or GU obstruction, megacolon; tardive dyskinesia; pregnancy (category C), lactation.
CAUTIOUS USE Older adults or debilitated patients; prostatic hypertrophy; glaucoma; cardiac arrhythmias; epilepsy.

ROUTE & DOSAGE

Parkinsonism
Adult: **PO** 2 mg 1–4 times/d
Geriatric: **PO** 2 mg 1–2 times/d

ADMINISTRATION

Oral
- Give with or after meals to relieve GI disturbances.
- Store in tightly closed, light-resistant containers at 15°–30° C (59°–86° F) unless otherwise directed.

ADVERSE EFFECTS (≥1%) **CNS:** Drowsiness, dizziness, muscle weakness, lack of coordination, disorientation, euphoria, agitation, confusion. **CV:** Mild, transient postural

---

Common adverse effects in *italic*, life-threatening effects underlined; generic names in **bold**; classifications in SMALL CAPS; ♦ Canadian drug name; ❷ Prototype drug

175

B

hypotension, tachycardia. **Special Senses:** *Blurred vision,* photophobia. **GI:** *Dry mouth,* nausea, vomiting, constipation.

INTERACTIONS Drug: Alcohol and other CNS DEPRESSANTS INCREASE SEDATION; **haloperidol,** PHENOTHIAZINES, OPIATES, TRICYCLIC ANTIDEPRESSANTS, **quinidine** increase risk of anticholinergic side effects.

PHARMACOKINETICS Unknown.

CLINICAL IMPLICATIONS

Assessment & Drug Effects

- Advise patient to make position changes slowly and in stages, particularly from recumbent to upright position.
- Monitor for and report immediately: Mental confusion, drowsiness, dizziness, agitation, hematuria, and decrease in urinary flow.
- Assess for and report blurred vision.
- Monitor I&O ratio and pattern.
- Note: Biperiden usually reduces muscle rigidity. In patients with severe parkinsonism, tremors may increase as spasticity is relieved.

Patient & Family Education

- Do not drive or engage in potentially hazardous activities until response to drug is known.
- Note: Patients on prolonged therapy can develop tolerance; an increase in dosage may be required.

BISACODYL ⦿

(bis-a-koe′dill)
Apo-Bisacodyl ♦, Bisacolax, Bisco-Lax ♦, Dacodyl, Deficol,
Doxidan, Dulcolax, Fleet Bisacodyl, Laxit ♦, Theralax
Classifications: STIMULANT LAXATIVE
Therapeutic: LAXATIVE
Pregnancy Category: C

AVAILABILITY 5 mg tablets, enteric coated; 5 mg tablet, delayed release; 10 mg suppository; 10 mg/30 mL enema

ACTION & *THERAPEUTIC EFFECT*
Expands intestinal fluid volume by increasing epithelial permeability. *Induces peristaltic contractions by direct stimulation of sensory nerve endings in the colonic wall.*

USES Temporary relief of acute constipation and for evacuation of colon before surgery, proctoscopic, sigmoidoscopic, and radiologic examinations. Also used to cleanse colon before delivery and to relieve constipation in patients with spinal cord damage.

CONTRAINDICATIONS Acute surgical abdomen, nausea, vomiting, abdominal cramps, intestinal obstruction, fecal impaction; use of rectal suppository in presence of anal or rectal fissures, ulcerated hemorrhoids, proctitis, bowel obstruction or perforation, ileus; pregnancy (category C), children <1 y.
CAUTIOUS USE Lactation.

ROUTE & DOSAGE

Laxative
Adult: **PO** 5–15 mg prn (max: 30 mg for special procedures) **PR** 10 mg prn
Child: **PO** ≥6 y, 5–10 mg prn **PR** ≥2 y, 10 mg; <2 y, 5 mg

Common adverse effects in *italic*, life-threatening effects underlined; generic names in **bold**; classifications in SMALL CAPS; ♦ Canadian drug name; ⦿ Prototype drug

ADMINISTRATION

Oral

- Give in the evening or before breakfast because of action time required.
- Give enteric coated tablets whole to avoid gastric irritation; do not cut or crush. Patient should not chew tablets. Preferably give with a full glass (240 mL) of water or other liquid.
- Do not give within 1 h of antacids or milk. These substances may cause premature dissolution of enteric coating; early release of drug in stomach may result in gastric irritation and loss of cathartic action.
- Store tablets in tightly closed containers at temperatures not exceeding 30° C (86° F).

Rectal

- Suppository may be inserted at time bowel movement is desired.
- Storage is same as tablets.

ADVERSE EFFECTS (≥1%) Systemic effects not reported. Mild cramping, nausea, diarrhea, fluid and electrolyte disturbances (especially potassium and calcium).

INTERACTIONS Drug: ANTACIDS will cause early dissolution of enteric coated tablets, resulting in abdominal cramping.

PHARMACOKINETICS Absorption: 5–15% from GI tract. **Onset:** 6–8 h PO; 15–60 min PR. **Metabolism:** In liver. **Elimination:** In urine, bile, and breast milk.

CLINICAL IMPLICATIONS

Assessment & Drug Effects

- Evaluate periodically patient's need for continued use of drug; bisacodyl usually produces 1 or 2 soft formed stools daily.

- Monitor patients receiving concomitant anticoagulants. Indiscriminate use of laxatives results in decreased absorption of vitamin K.

Patient & Family Education

- Add high-fiber foods slowly to regular diet to avoid gas and diarrhea. Adequate fluid intake includes at least 6–8 glasses/d.

BISMUTH SUBSALICYLATE ⊕

(bis'muth)
Pepto-Bismol
Classifications: ANTIDIARRHEAL; SALICYLATE
Therapeutic: ANTIDIARRHEAL
Pregnancy Category: C

AVAILABILITY 262 mg tablets/caplets; 130 mg/15 mL, 262 mg/15 mL, 524 mg/15 mL liquid

ACTION & *THERAPEUTIC EFFECT* Hydrolyzed in GI tract to salicylate, which is believed to inhibit synthesis of prostaglandins responsible for GI hypermotility and inflammation. It is also a direct mucosal protective agent. *Effectiveness as an antidiarrheal also appears to be due to direct antimicrobial action and to an antisecretory effect on intestinal secretions exposed to toxins.*

USES Prophylaxis and treatment of traveler's diarrhea (turista) and for temporary relief of indigestion.
UNLABELED USES *Helicobacter pylori* associated with peptic ulcer disease.

CONTRAINDICATIONS Hypersensitivity to aspirin or other salicylates; concurrent use with aspirin; coagulopathy, severe hepatic im-

---

Common adverse effects in *italic*, life-threatening effects <u>underlined</u>; generic names in **bold**; classifications in SMALL CAPS; ♣ Canadian drug name; ⊕ Prototype drug

177

pairment; use for more than 2 d in presence of high fever or in children <3 y unless prescribed by physician; chickenpox or flu; dysentery; pregnancy (category C).

CAUTIOUS USE Diabetes and gout; concurrent use with salicylates and anticoagulants; alcoholism; renal impairment; elderly; smoking; lactation.

ROUTE & DOSAGE

Diarrhea

Adult: **PO** 30 mL or 2 tab q30–60min prn (max: 8 doses/d)
Child: **PO** 3–6 y, 5 mL or 1/2 tab q30–60min prn (max: 8 doses/d); 6–9 y, 2/3 tab or 10 mL q30–60 min prn (max: 8 doses/d); 9–12 y, 15 mL or 1 tab q30–60min prn (max: 8 doses/d)

Traveler's Diarrhea

Adult: **PO** 2–4 tab or 15–30 mL q.i.d. for 3 wk

Peptic Ulcer Disease

Adult: **PO** 2 tablets q.i.d. with 2 additional antibiotics for 10–14 d
Child: **PO** <10 y, 15 mL q.i.d. times 6 wk

ADMINISTRATION

Oral

- Ensure chewable tablets are chewed or crushed before being swallowed and followed with at least 8 oz water or other liquid.
- Store at 15°–30° C (59°–86° F) unless otherwise directed.

ADVERSE EFFECTS (≥1%) **GI:** Temporary *darkening of stool* and tongue, metallic taste, bluish gum line; bleeding tendencies. With high doses: fecal impaction. **CNS:** Encephalopathy (disorientation, muscle twitching). **Hematologic:** Bleeding tendency. **Special Senses:** Tinnitus, hearing loss.

DIAGNOSTIC TEST INTERFERENCE Because bismuth subsalicylate is radiopaque, it may interfere with *radiographic studies* of GI tract.

INTERACTIONS Drug: Bismuth may decrease the absorption of TETRACYCLINES, QUINOLONES **(ciprofloxacin, norfloxacin, ofloxacin).** May increase level of **aspirin.**

PHARMACOKINETICS Absorption: Undergoes chemical dissociation in GI tract to bismuth subcarbonate and sodium salicylate; bismuth is minimally absorbed, but the salicylate is readily absorbed.

CLINICAL IMPLICATIONS

Assessment & Drug Effects

- Monitor bowel function; note that stools may darken and tongue may appear black. These are temporary effects and will disappear without treatment.
- Lab tests: *H. pylori* breath test when used for peptic ulcers.

Patient & Family Education

- Note: Bismuth contains salicylate. Use caution when taking aspirin and other salicylates. Many OTC medications for colds, fever, and pain contain salicylates.
- Consult physician if diarrhea is accompanied by fever or continues for more than 2 d.
- Note: Temporary grayish black discoloration of tongue and stool may occur.

BISOPROLOL FUMARATE

(bis-o-pro'lol fum'a-rate)
Zebeta
Classifications: BETA-ADRENERGIC ANTAGONIST; ANTIHYPERTENSIVE
Therapeutic: ANTIHYPERTENSIVE; BETA-ADRENERGIC ANTAGONIST
Prototype: Propranolol
Pregnancy Category: C

AVAILABILITY 5 mg, 10 mg tablets

ACTION & *THERAPEUTIC EFFECT*
Long-acting cardioselective (beta$_1$) adrenoreceptor blocking agent. To maintain beta$_1$ cardioselectivity, the lowest effective dose is necessary. Bisoprolol decreases heart rate, blood pressure, contractile force, and cardiac workload, which reduces myocardial oxygen consumption and increases blood flow to myocardium. *Bisoprolol has antianginal properties, especially improving exercise tolerance. It reduces both systolic and diastolic blood pressure at rest and with exercise.*

USES Hypertension.
UNLABELED USES Angina.

CONTRAINDICATIONS History of hypersensitivity to bisoprolol, severe sinus bradycardia, second- and third-degree AV block, overt cardiac failure, cardiogenic shock; pulmonary edema; pregnancy (category C).
CAUTIOUS USE Asthma or COPD, peripheral vascular disease, diabetes mellitus, Prinzmetal's angina; hyperthyroidism, renal or hepatic insufficiency, cerebrovascular disease, stroke; lactation; anesthetic use.

ROUTE & DOSAGE

Hypertension, Angina
Adult: **PO** 2.5–5 mg once daily, may increase to 20 mg/d if necessary

ADMINISTRATION

Oral
- Note: The half life of the drug is increased in those with significant liver dysfunction; usual initial dose is 2.5 mg and may be carefully titrated upward if necessary.
- Discontinue drug gradually over a period of 1–2 wk to avoid rebound, withdrawal angina, or hypertension.
- Store at room temperature, 15°–30° C (59°–86° F).

ADVERSE EFFECTS (≥1%) **CNS:** Dizziness, fatigue, tiredness, vertigo, anxiety, headache, sleep disturbances. **CV:** Bradycardia, orthostatic hypotension, rebound/withdrawal angina or hypertension following abrupt discontinuation, may exacerbate intermittent claudication. **Endocrine:** Increases serum levels of VLDL-C and decreases levels of HDL-C lipoproteins, may cause slight rise in serum potassium. **GI:** Abdominal pain, dyspepsia, nausea, vomiting, constipation, diarrhea. **Respiratory:** Asthma, bronchospasm, cough, dyspnea, pharyngitis, sinusitis. **Skin:** Rash, acne, pruritus, eczema. **Other:** Arthralgia.

INTERACTIONS Drug: Amiodarone may cause significant bradycardia; BETA BLOCKERS may reduce **glucose** tolerance, inhibit **insulin** secretion, alter rate of recovery from hypoglycemia, reduce peripheral circulation, and suppress hypoglycemic symptoms; **rifampin** decreases bisoprolol blood levels.

PHARMACOKINETICS Absorption: Readily from GI tract; 82–94% reaches systemic circulation. **Peak:** Therapeutic effect 2–4 wk. **Duration:** 24 h. **Distribution:** Some CNS penetration. **Metabolism:** 50% in liver by CYP3A4. **Elimination:** 50–60% unchanged in urine. **Half-Life:** 10–12.4 h.

CLINICAL IMPLICATIONS

Assessment & Drug Effects

- Monitor for therapeutic effectiveness. Time required to achieve optimum antihypertensive effect varies from a few days to several weeks.
- Monitor BP frequently during periods of dose adjustment or drug withdrawal.
- Monitor for activity-induced angina both during therapy and following discontinuation of drug.
- Monitor for and report severe hypotension and bradycardia. Dosage adjustment may be required.
- Monitor for bronchospasms in patients with a history of asthma or COPD.
- Monitor diabetics for loss of glycemic control.
- Lab tests: Periodic CBC, electrolytes, renal function, liver function, lipid profile.

Patient & Family Education

- Report orthostatic hypotension and dizziness to physician.
- Do not discontinue drug abruptly unless specifically instructed to do so.
- Note: Drug-induced nightmares and unpleasant dreams are possible when taking this drug.
- Monitor blood glucose for loss of glycemic control.
- Report cold extremities and development of symptoms of intermittent claudication to physician.

BIVALIRUDIN

(bi-val′i-ru-den)

Angiomax

Classifications: ANTICOAGULANT; THROMBIN INHIBITOR

Therapeutic: ANTICOAGULANT; THROMBIN INHIBITOR

Prototype: Lepirudin

Pregnancy Category: B

AVAILABILITY 250 mg vial

ACTION & *THERAPEUTIC EFFECT*

Direct inhibitor of thrombin similar to lepirudin. Capable of inhibiting the action of both free and clot-bound thrombin. *Reversibly binds to the thrombin active site, thereby blocking the thrombogenic activity of thrombin.*

USES Used with aspirin as an anticoagulant in patients undergoing PTCA.

UNLABELED USES Anticoagulant used in heparin-induced thrombocytopenia.

CONTRAINDICATIONS Hypersensitivity to bivalirudin; cerebral aneurysm, intracranial hemorrhage; patients with increased risk of bleeding (e.g., recent surgery, trauma, CVA, hepatic disease); coagulopathy; lactation. Safety and efficacy in children are not established.

CAUTIOUS USE Asthma or allergies; blood dyscrasia or thrombocytopenia; GI ulceration, serious hepatic disease; hypertension, renal impairment, pregnancy (category B).

ROUTE & DOSAGE

Anticoagulation

Adult: **IV** 0.75 mg/kg bolus followed by 1.75 mg/kg/h for the duration of the procedure, may continue at 0.2 mg/kg/h up to

20 h if needed; intended for use with aspirin 300–325 mg

ADMINISTRATION

Intravenous

PREPARE: **Direct/Continuous:** Push (bolus dose) and initial 4-h continuous infusion: Reconstitute each 250 mg vial with 5 mL of sterile water for injection; gently swirl until dissolved. Further dilute each reconstituted vial in 50 mL of D5W or NS to yield 5 mg/mL. **Continuous:** Subsequent infusions are low-rate continuous. Reconstitute each 250 mg vial as above. Further dilute each reconstituted vial in 500 mL of D5W or NS to yield 0.50 mg/mL.

ADMINISTER: **Direct:** Give bolus dose 0.75 mg/kg (see manufacturer's dosing table) IV push. **Continuous:** Give 1.75 mg/kg/h for the duration of the PTCA procedure. Subsequent doses, give 0.2 mg/kg/h for up to 20 h as ordered.

▪ Store reconstituted vials refrigerated at 2°–8° C (35.6°–46.4° F) for up to 24 h. Store diluted concentrations between 0.5 mg/mL and 5 mg/mL at room temperature, 15°–30° C (59°–86° F), for up to 24 h.

ADVERSE EFFECTS (≥1%) **Body as a Whole:** *Back pain,* pain, fever. **CV:** *Hypotension,* hypertension, bradycardia. **GI:** *Nausea,* vomiting, dyspepsia, abdominal pain. **Hematologic:** Bleeding. **CNS:** *Headache,* anxiety, nervousness. **Urogenital:** Urinary retention, pelvic pain. **Other:** Injection site pain.

INTERACTIONS No clinically significant interactions established.

PHARMACOKINETICS Duration: 1 h.

Distribution: No protein binding. **Metabolism:** Proteolytic cleavage and renal metabolism. **Elimination:** Renal. **Half-Life:** 25 min.

CLINICAL IMPLICATIONS

Assessment & Drug Effects

▪ Monitor cardiovascular status carefully during therapy.
▪ Monitor for and report S&S of bleeding: Ecchymosis, epistaxis, GI bleeding, hematuria, hemoptysis.
▪ Patients with history of GI ulceration, hypertension, recent trauma or surgery are at increased risk for bleeding.
▪ Monitor neurologic status and report immediately: focal or generalized deficits.
▪ Lab tests: Baseline and periodic ACT (activated clotting time), APTT, PT, INR, thrombin time (TT), plasma fibrinopeptide A (especially in unstable angina), platelet count, Hgb and Hct; periodic serum creatinine, stool for occult blood, urinalysis.

Patient & Family Education

▪ Report any of the following immediately: Unexplained back or stomach pain; black, tarry stools; blood in urine, coughing up blood; difficulty breathing; dizziness or fainting spells; heavy menstrual bleeding; nosebleeds; unusual bruising or bleeding at any site.

BLEOMYCIN SULFATE

(blee-oh-mye'sin)
Blenoxane
Classifications: ANTINEOPLASTIC; ANTIBIOTIC
Therapeutic: ANTINEOPLASTIC AGENT
Prototype: Doxorubicin
Pregnancy Category: D

Common adverse effects in *italic*, life-threatening effects underlined; generic names in **bold**; classifications in SMALL CAPS; ♣ Canadian drug name; ⊙ Prototype drug

181

B

AVAILABILITY 15 units, 30 units powder for injection

ACTION & *THERAPEUTIC EFFECT*

A toxic drug with low therapeutic index; intensely cytotoxic. By unclear mechanism, blocks DNA, RNA, and protein synthesis. A cell cycle-phase nonspecific agent. Widely used in combination with other chemotherapeutic agents because it lacks significant myelosuppressive activity. *This mixture of cytotoxic antibiotics from a strain of* Streptomyces verticillus *has strong affinity for skin and lung tumor cells, in contrast to its low affinity for cells in hematopoietic tissue.*

USES As single agent or in combination with other chemotherapeutic agents, as adjunct to surgery and radiation therapy. Squamous cell carcinomas of head, neck, penis, cervix, and vulva; lymphomas (including reticular cell sarcoma, lymphosarcoma, Hodgkin's); testicular carcinoma; malignant pleural effusions.

UNLABELED USES *Mycosis fungoides* and *Verruca vulgaris* (common warts).

CONTRAINDICATIONS History of hypersensitivity or idiosyncrasy to bleomycin; pulmonary infection; concurrent radiation therapy; women of childbearing age, pregnancy (category D), lactation.

CAUTIOUS USE Compromised hepatic, renal, or pulmonary function; peripheral vascular disease; history of tobacco use; previous cytotoxic drug or radiation therapy.

ROUTE & DOSAGE

Squamous Cell Carcinoma, Testicular Carcinoma
Adult/Child: **SC, IM, IV** 10–20 U/m^2 or 0.25–0.5 U/kg 1–2 times/wk (max: 300–400 U)

Lymphomas
Adult/Child: **SC, IM, IV** 10–20 U/m^2 1–2 times/wk after a 1–2 U test dose times 2 doses

Hodgkin's Disease, Maintenance
Adult/Child: **SC, IM, IV** 1 U IM or IV/d or 5 U/wk

Renal Impairment
Cl$_{cr}$ 10–50 mL/min: use 75% of dose; <10 mL/min: use 50% of dose

ADMINISTRATION

Note: Due to risk of anaphylactoid reaction, give lymphoma patients ≤2 U for first two doses. If no reaction, follow regular dosage schedule.

Subcutaneous/Intramuscular
- Reconstitute with sterile water, NS, or bacteriostatic water by adding 1–5 mL to the 15 U vial or 2–10 mL to the 30 U vial. Amount of diluent is determined by the total volume of solution that will be injected.
- Inject IM deeply into upper outer quadrant of buttock; change sites with each injection.

Intravenous
IV administration to infants and children: Verify correct IV concentration and rate of infusion with physician.

PREPARE: **Intermittent:** Dilute each 15 U with at least 5 mL of sterile water or NS. ▪May be further diluted in 50–100 mL of the chosen diluent. ▪Do not dilute with any solution containing D5W.

ADMINISTER: **Intermittent:** Give each 15 U or fraction thereof over 10 min through Y-tube of free-flowing IV.

INCOMPATIBILITIES **Solution/additive:** Aminophylline, ascorbic acid, carbenicillin, CEPHALOSPORINS, diazepam, hydrocortisone, methotrexate, mitomycin, nafcillin, penicillin G, terbutaline.

- Store unopened ampules at 15°–30° C (59°–86° F) unless otherwise specified by manufacturer.

ADVERSE EFFECTS (≥1%) **Body as a Whole:** Hypersensitivity (<u>anaphylactoid reaction</u>); *mild febrile reaction* **CNS:** Headache, mental confusion. **GI:** Stomatitis, ulcerations of tongue and lips, anorexia, nausea, vomiting, diarrhea, weight loss. **Hematologic:** Thrombocytopenia, leukopenia, (rare). **Respiratory:** <u>Pulmonary toxicity</u> (dose and age-related); interstitial pneumonitis, pneumonia, or fibrosis. **Skin:** Diffuse alopecia (reversible), *hyperpigmentation, pruritic erythema,* vesiculation, acne, thickening of skin and nail beds, *patchy hyperkeratosis,* striae, peeling, bleeding. **Other:** Pain at tumor site; phlebitis; necrosis at injection site.

INTERACTIONS Drug: Other ANTINEOPLASTIC AGENTS increase bone marrow toxicity; decreases effects of **digoxin, phenytoin.**

PHARMACOKINETICS Distribution: Concentrates mainly in skin, lungs, kidneys, lymphocytes, and peritoneum. **Metabolism:** Unknown. **Elimination:** 60–70% recovered in urine as parent compound. **Half-Life:** 2 h.

CLINICAL IMPLICATIONS

Assessment & Drug Effects

- Start with a test dose. Monitor patient closely for at least 24 h (vital signs, auscultation of chest, careful observations). If there is no acute reaction (hypotension, hyperpyrexia, chills, confusion, wheezing, cardiopulmonary collapse), start regular dosage schedule. Anaphylactoid reaction can be fatal (see Appendix F). It may occur immediately or several hours after first or second dose, especially in lymphoma patients (10%).

- Therapeutic effectiveness: Favorable response, if any, is expected within 2 wk for treatment of Hodgkin's or testicular tumor, and within 3 wk for squamous cell cancers.

- Monitor vital signs. Febrile reaction (mild chills and fever) is relatively common in patients receiving bleomycin therapy. It usually occurs within the first few hours after administration of a large single dose and lasts about 4–12 h. Reaction tends to become less frequent with continued drug administration, but can recur at any time.

- Monitor for and report any of the following: Unexplained bleeding or bruising; evidence of deterioration of renal function (changed I&O ratio and pattern, decreasing creatinine clearance, weight gain or edema); evidence of pulmonary toxicity (nonproductive cough, chest pain, dyspnea).

- Note: Stomatitis can be a dose-limiting factor because oral ulcerations may interfere with adequate nutrient intake, leading to severe debilitation. Consult physician if an oral local anesthetic is indicated. Apply 10 min before meals to take effect so that patient can eat with less pain.

- Check weight at regular intervals under standard conditions. Weight loss and anorexia may persist a long time after therapy has been discontinued.

- Report symptoms of skin toxicity (hypoesthesia, urticaria, tender swollen hands) promptly. May develop in second or third week of treatment and after 150–200 U of bleomycin have been administered. Therapy may be discontinued.

Common adverse effects in *italic*, life-threatening effects <u>underlined</u>; generic names in **bold**; classifications in SMALL CAPS; ✚ Canadian drug name; 🅿 Prototype drug

183

Patient & Family Education

- Avoid OTC drugs during antineoplastic treatment period unless approved by physician.
- Report skin irritation which may not develop for several weeks after therapy begins.
- Hyperpigmentation may occur in areas subject to friction and pressure, skin folds, nail cuticles, scars, and intramuscular sites.

BORTEZOMIB

(bor-te-zo'mib)
Velcade
Classifications: ANTINEOPLASTIC AGENT; BIOLOGIC RESPONSE MODIFIER; PROTEOSOME INHIBITOR
Therapeutic: ANTINEOPLASTIC AGENT; BIOLOGIC RESPONSE MODIFIER
Pregnancy Category: D

AVAILABILITY 3.5 mg powder for injection

ACTION & *THERAPEUTIC EFFECT*
Bortezomib is a reversible inhibitor of proteasome, which is responsible for regulation of protein expression and degradation of damaged or obsolete proteins within the cell; its activity is critical to activation or suppression of cellular functions including the cell cycle, oncogene expression, and apoptosis. Malignant cells are much more sensitive to the effects of proteasome inhibition than normal cells. *Proteasome inhibition may reverse some of the changes that allow proliferation of malignant cells and suppress apoptosis (programmed cell death) in malignant cells.*

USES Treatment of relapsed or refractory multiple myeloma in patients who have failed one prior therapy.

CONTRAINDICATIONS Hypersensitivity to bortezomib, boron, or mannitol; pregnancy (category D); lactation. Safety and effectiveness in children are not established.
CAUTIOUS USE Peripheral neuropathy; history of syncope, dehydration, hypotension; concurrent antihypertensive drugs; history of allergies, asthma; preexisting electrolyte or acid-base disturbances, especially hypokalemia or hyponatremia; liver disease; myelosuppression, renal impairment; history of peripheral neuropathy or other neurologic disorders; GI toxicities.

ROUTE & DOSAGE

Multiple Myeloma

Adult: **IV** 1.3 mg/m^2 twice weekly for 2 wk (days 1, 4, 8, and 11) followed by a 10-d rest period; at least 72 h should elapse between consecutive doses; 3 wk period is a treatment cycle

ADMINISTRATION

Intravenous
Wear protective gloves and prevent contact with skin.

***PREPARE:* Direct:** Reconstitute 3.6 mg vial with 3.5 mL of NS for injection to yield 1 mg/mL. Discard if not clear and colorless. Give within 8 h of reconstitution.
***ADMINISTER:* Direct:** Give as a bolus dose
- Store unopened vials at 15°–30° C (59°–86° F). Protect from light.
- Store reconstituted vials at 15°–30° C (59°–86° F). Give within 8 h of reconstitution. May store up to 3 h in a syringe; however, total storage time must not exceed 8 h when exposed to normal indoor lighting.

INCOMPATIBILITIES **Solution/additive:** No data available. Do not recommend mixing or injecting with any other drugs.

ADVERSE EFFECTS (≥1%) **Body as a Whole:** *Asthenia, weakness, fatigue, malaise, fever, dehydration, peripheral neuropathy, rigors, herpes zoster.* **CNS:** *Insomnia, headache, paresthesia, dizziness, anxiety.* **CV:** *Edema, hypotension, orthostatic hypotension.* **GI:** *Nausea, vomiting, diarrhea, anorexia, abdominal pain, constipation, dyspepsia, dysphagia.* **Hematologic:** *Thrombocytopenia, neutropenia, anemia.* **Musculoskeletal:** *Arthralgia, musculoskeletal pain, bone pain, myalgia, back pain, muscle cramps.* **Respiratory:** *Dyspnea, cough, upper respiratory infection.* **Skin:** *Rash, pruritus.* **Special Senses:** *Blurred vision, diplopia.*

INTERACTIONS Drug: Hypoglycemia and hyperglycemia have been reported with ANTIDIABETIC AGENTS; ANTIHYPERTENSIVE AGENTS may exacerbate hypotension; ANTICOAGULANTS, **antithymocyte globulin,** NSAIDS, PLATELET INHIBITORS, **aspirin,** THROMBOLYTIC AGENTS may increase risk of bleeding. **Food:** Grapefruit juice may increase drug levels.

PHARMACOKINETICS Metabolism: In the liver primarily by CYP3A4. **Half-Life:** 9–15 h

CLINICAL IMPLICATIONS
Assessment & Drug Effects
- Monitor for and report S&S of neuropathy (e.g., hyperesthesia, hypoesthesia, paresthesia, discomfort or neuropathic pain).
- Monitor postural vital signs for orthostatic hypotension.
- Monitor I&O and assess for S&S of dehydration or electrolyte imbalance if vomiting and/or diarrhea develop.
- Lab tests: Frequent CBC with platelet count; baseline and periodic LFTs; frequent blood glucose in diabetics.

Patient & Family Education
- Report promptly any of the following: dizziness, light-headedness or fainting spells; numbness, tingling, or other unusual sensations; signs of infection (e.g., fever, chills, cough, sore throat); bruising, pinpoint red spots on the skin; black, tarry stools, nosebleeds, or any other sign of bleeding.
- Do not drive or engage in other hazardous activities until reaction to drug is known.
- Females should use reliable methods of contraception to avoid pregnancy while on this drug.

BOTULINUM TOXIN TYPE A
(bo'tul-i-num)
Botox, BOTOX Cosmetic
Classifications: SKELETAL MUSCLE RELAXANT; ANTISPASMODIC
Therapeutic: MUSCLE RELAXANT
Pregnancy Category: C

AVAILABILITY 100 units powder for injection

ACTION & *THERAPEUTIC EFFECT*
Botulinum toxin type A blocks neuromuscular transmission by binding to receptor sites on motor nerve terminals, entering the nerve terminals, and inhibiting the release of acetylcholine. This inhibition occurs as the neurotoxin splits a protein molecule integral to the successful docking and releasing of acetylcholine from storage areas located within nerve endings. *When injected intramuscularly at thera-*

Common adverse effects in *italic*, life-threatening effects underlined; generic names in **bold**; classifications in SMALL CAPS; ♣ Canadian drug name; ⊕ Prototype drug

185

peutic doses, botulinum toxin type A produces partial chemical denervation of the muscle resulting in a localized reduction in muscle activity.

USES Treatment of blepharospasm, cervical dystonia, strabismus, glabellar frown wrinkles, severe axillary hyperhidrosis.
UNLABELED USES Treatment of other types of wrinkles, migraine headache, achalasia, focal spasticity associated with cerebral palsy with concurrent equinus gait, spasticity associated with stroke.

CONTRAINDICATIONS Presence of infection at the proposed injection site(s); hypersensitivity to Botox. Patients with dysphagia or respiratory compromise; pregnancy (category C).
CAUTIOUS USE Hypersensitivity to albumin; individuals with peripheral motor neuropathic diseases (e.g., amyotrophic lateral sclerosis, or motor neuropathy), or neuromuscular junctional disorders (e.g., myasthenia gravis or Lambert-Eaton syndrome); neuromuscular disorders; ocular disease; cardiovascular disease; elderly; inflammation at the proposed injection site; weakness in the target muscle(s), lactation.

ROUTE & DOSAGE

Blepharospasm
Adult/Child: **Intradermal** >12 y, 1.25–2.5 U injected at each site, may repeat in 3 mo if needed; cumulative dose should not exceed 200 U in a 30-d period

Cervical Dystonia
Adult/Adolescent: **IM** >16 y, 198–300 U divided among affected muscles

Frown Wrinkles
Adult: **IM** 25 U divided among affected muscles in 5 step doses, may repeat in 3–4 mo if needed

Other Wrinkles
Adult: **SC** 1–2 U per site

Spasticity
Adult: **IM** 20–50 U per affected site
Child: **IM** 2–18 y, 4 U/kg (max: 200 U per treatment) every 3 mo

Axillary Hyperhydrosis
Adult: **IM** 50 U per site, may repeat in 4 mo

ADMINISTRATION

Intramuscular, Intradermal, Subcutaneous
- Slowly inject required amount of nonpreserved NS (see dilution calculation) into vial. Discard vial if a vacuum does not pull diluent into vial. Gently rotate to mix. Discard if not clear, colorless, and free of particulate matter. Dilution calculation: add 1, 2, 4, or 6 mL of NS to yield, respectively, 10 U/0.1 mL, 5 U/0.1 mL, 2.5 U/0.1 mL, 1.25 U/0.1 mL.
- Note: Injection intervals of BOTOX® Cosmetic should be at least 3 mo apart.
- Store at 2°–8° C (refrigerated). Administer within 4 h of reconstitution.

INCOMPATIBILITIES Do not mix with other solutions/additives.

ADVERSE EFFECTS (≥1%) **Body as a Whole:** Injection site reactions (localized pain, tenderness, bruising), neck pain, flu-like symptoms, hypertonia, asthenia, fever. **CNS:** *Headache,* drowsiness. **GI:** *Dysphagia,* dry mouth, fever, nausea, vomiting. **Hematologic:** Ecchymosis. **Musculoskeletal:** Local muscle weakness, dysarthria. **Respiratory:** Cough, rhinitis, upper respiratory infection. **Special Senses:** *Ptosis, superficial punctate keratitis, dry eyes, ocular irritation, lacrimation,* photophobia, keratitis, diplopia.

INTERACTIONS Drug: AMINOGLYCO-SIDES, NEUROMUSCULAR BLOCKING AGENTS may potentiate neuromuscular blockade; **chloroquine** may antagonize blocking effects.

CLINICAL IMPLICATIONS

Assessment & Drug Effects

- Evaluate for therapeutic effectiveness, maximal at about 1–2 wk (lasting 3–4 mo).

Patient & Family Education

- Inform physician about all prescription, nonprescription, and herbal drugs being taken.
- Report immediately any of the following: difficulty breathing or swallowing, problem with speech; unusual bleeding, bruising, or swelling around injection site.
- Note: Effects of the injection generally last 3–4 mo and then repeat treatments may be given.

BRETYLIUM TOSYLATE

(bre-til′ee-um)

Classifications: ANTIARRHYTHMIC, CLASS III

Therapeutic: ANTIARRHYTHMIC, CLASS III

Prototype: Amiodarone

Pregnancy Category: C

AVAILABILITY 2 mg/mL, 4 mg/mL, 50 mg/mL injection

ACTION & *THERAPEUTIC EFFECT* Suppresses ventricular fibrillation by direct action on the myocardium and ventricular tachycardia by adre-

nergic blockade. Shortly after administration, norepinephrine is released from adrenergic postganglionic nerve terminals, resulting in a moderate increase in BP, heart rate, and ventricular irritability. Subsequently (1–2 h), drug-induced release and reuptake of norepinephrine are blocked, leading to a state resembling surgical sympathectomy. *Suppresses arrhythmias with a reentry mechanism and decreases dispersion of ectopic foci. PR, QT, and QRS intervals are unchanged. Because onset of desired action is delayed, bretylium is not a first-line antiarrhythmic agent.*

USES Short-term prophylaxis and treatment of ventricular fibrillation; life-threatening arrhythmias such as ventricular fibrillation not responsive to conventional therapy [e.g., lidocaine, procainamide, direct current (cardioversion)].

CONTRAINDICATIONS No contraindications for use in life-threatening refractory ventricular arrhythmias; digitalis toxicity; pregnancy (category C).

CAUTIOUS USE Digitalis-induced arrhythmias, patients with fixed cardiac output (e.g., severe aortic stenosis or severe pulmonary hypertension because profound hypotension may result), sinus bradycardia, patients on digitalis maintenance, angina pectoris, impaired renal function, renal disease; lactation.

ROUTE & DOSAGE

Ventricular Fibrillation

Adult: **IV** 5 mg/kg rapid IV injection, may increase to 10 mg/kg and repeat q15–30 min (max: 30 mg/kg/d); may also give by continuous infusion at 1–2 mg/min **IM** 5–10 mg/kg, may repeat in 1–

Common adverse effects in *italic*, life-threatening effects <u>underlined</u>; generic names in **bold**; classifications in SMALL CAPS; ♣ Canadian drug name; ⊕ Prototype drug

187

2 h if arrhythmia persists, then 5–10 mg/kg q6–8h for maintenance *Child:* **IV** 5 mg/kg, may repeat q10–20min (max: 30 mg/kg) **IM** 2–5 mg/kg as single dose

ADMINISTRATION

Limit use to patients in facilities adequately equipped and staffed for constant monitoring of ECG and BP and for cardiovascular/pulmonary resuscitation and cardioversion.

Intramuscular

- Administer no more than 5 mL in any one IM site.
- Keep a record of injection sites. Injection into same site can cause muscle atrophy, necrosis, and fibrosis.

Intravenous

IV administration to infants and children: Verify correct IV concentration and rate of infusion/injection with physician.

PREPARE: **Direct:** Give undiluted. **Intermittent:** Give diluted in 50 mL or more of NS or D5W.

ADMINISTER: **Direct:** Give undiluted at a rate of 1 dose/15 seconds. **Intermittent:** Give diluted at a rate of 1–2 mg/min.

INCOMPATIBILITIES **Solution/additive: Dobutamine, nitroglycerin, phenytoin. Y-site: Phenytoin.**

- Store at 15°–30° C (59°–86° F) unless otherwise directed.

ADVERSE EFFECTS (≥1%) **CV:** Both supine and postural *hypotension* with dizziness, vertigo, lightheadedness, faintness, syncope, transitory hypertension, bradycardia, increased frequency of PVCs, exacerbation of digitalis-induced arrhythmias. **GI:** *Nausea, vomiting* (particularly with rapid IV). **Respiratory:** Respiratory depression.

DIAGNOSTIC TEST INTERFERENCE

Urinary VMA, epinephrine, and *norepinephrine* levels may be decreased during bretylium therapy.

INTERACTIONS Drug: Lidocaine, procainamide, quinidine, propranolol may antagonize antiarrhythmic effects and compound hypotension; ANTIHYPERTENSIVE AGENTS will add to hypotensive effects; DIGITALIS GLYCOSIDES may worsen arrhythmias through **digitalis** toxicity.

PHARMACOKINETICS Onset: Minutes after IV; up to 6 h IM. **Peak:** 6–9 h. **Duration:** 6–24 h. **Distribution:** Does not cross blood–brain barrier; not known if crosses placenta or distributed into breast milk. **Metabolism:** Not metabolized. **Elimination:** 70–80% in urine in 24 h. **Half-Life:** 4–17 h.

CLINICAL IMPLICATIONS

Assessment & Drug Effects

- Anticipate vomiting. IV administration is associated with a high incidence of nausea and vomiting. These side effects can be minimized by slow administration of drug (≥10 min).
- Establish baseline readings and monitor BP and ECG when drug is administered. Observe for initial transient rise in BP, increased heart rate, PVCs and other arrhythmias, or worsening of existing arrhythmias, which may occur within a few minutes to 1 h after drug administration. Keep physician informed. Initial effect of hypertension is usually followed within 1 h by a fall in supine BP and by orthostatic hypotension.
- Use supine position until patient develops tolerance to hypotensive effect of bretylium (generally

in several days). Hypotension can occur in the supine position, particularly in patients with severely compromised cardiac function. It may not readily respond to therapy (e.g., vasopressors, fluids); early reporting is essential.

- Raise or lower head of bed slowly; advise patient to make position changes slowly in order to prevent orthostatic hypotension.
- Monitor I&O, particularly in patients with impaired renal function.

Patient & Family Education

- Make position changes slowly. If allowed to be out of bed, dangle legs for a few minutes before standing, but do not stand still for prolonged periods. Men should sit on toilet to urinate.

BRIMONIDINE TARTRATE

(bry-mon'i-deen)
Alphagan P
Pregnancy Category: B
See Appendix A-1.

BRINZOLAMIDE

(brin-zol'a-mide)
Azopt
Pregnancy Category: C
See Appendix A-1.

BROMFENAC

(brom'fen-ac)
Xibrom
Pregnancy Category: C
See Appendix A-1.

BROMOCRIPTINE MESYLATE

B

(broe-moe-krip'teen)
Parlodel
Classifications: ERGOT ALKALOID; ANTIPARKINSON AGENT
Therapeutic: ERGOT REPLACEMENT; ANTIDYSKINETIC
Prototype: Ergotamine
Pregnancy Category: C

AVAILABILITY 2.5 mg tablets; 5 mg capsules

ACTION & *THERAPEUTIC EFFECT*
Semisynthetic ergot alkaloid derivative, but devoid of oxytocic activity. Additionally, is a synthetic dopamine agonist. Reduces elevated serum prolactin levels in men and women by activating postsynaptic dopaminergic receptors in hypothalamus to stimulate release of prolactin-inhibiting factor and possibly luteinizing hormone release factor. Activates dopaminergic receptors in neostriatum of CNS, which may explain action in Parkinsonism. *Restores ovulation and ovarian function in amenorrheic women, thus correcting female infertility secondary to elevated prolactin levels. Activates dopaminergic receptors in CNS resulting in antiparkinsonism effect.*

USES Short-term management of amenorrhea/galactorrhea or female infertility associated with hyperprolactinemia (when there is no indication of pituitary tumor). Also used as adjunctive to levodopa or levodopa/carbidopa therapy to relieve symptoms of Parkinson's disease and to lower plasma growth hormone in patients with acromegaly.
UNLABELED USES To prevent postpartum lactation, to relieve premenstrual symptoms, to treat hypogonadism and galactorrhea in

Common adverse effects in *italic*, life-threatening effects <u>underlined</u>; generic names in **bold**; classifications in SMALL CAPS; ♣ Canadian drug name; ❷ Prototype drug

189

hyperprolactinemic men; for management of hepatic encephalopathy, Cushing's syndrome, drug-induced neuroleptic malignant syndrome, and cocaine withdrawal.

CONTRAINDICATIONS Hypersensitivity to ergot alkaloids; uncontrolled hypertension; severe ischemic heart disease or peripheral vascular disease; pituitary tumor; normal prolactin levels, lactation, pregnancy (category C); preeclampsia, eclampsia. Safe use in children <15 y is not established.

CAUTIOUS USE Hepatic and renal dysfunction; history of psychiatric disorder; history of GI bleeding or peptic ulcer; history of MI with residual arrhythmia.

ROUTE & DOSAGE

Amenorrhea or Galactorrhea, Female Infertility
Adult: PO 1.25–2.5 mg/d (max: 2.5 mg 2–3 times/d)

Suppression of Postpartum Lactation
Adult: PO 2.5 mg b.i.d. starting at least 4 h after delivery for 14–21 d

Parkinson's Disease
Adult: PO 1.25–2.5 mg/d (max: 100 mg/d in divided doses)

Acromegaly
Adult: PO 1.25–2.5 mg/d for 3 d, then increase by 1.25–2.5 mg q3–7d until desired effect is achieved, usually 30–60 mg/d in divided doses

ADMINISTRATION

Oral
- Do not begin therapy unless vital signs are stabilized.
- Give with meals, milk, or other food to reduce incidence of GI side effects.
- Have patient in supine position before receiving first dose because dizziness and fainting may occur. For this reason, initial dose is usually prescribed for evening administration.
- Note: Withhold therapy until 4 h after delivery and then begin only if vital signs have stabilized.
- Store in tightly closed, light-resistant containers, preferably at 15°–30° C (59°–86° F) unless otherwise directed.

ADVERSE EFFECTS (≥1%) **Body as a Whole:** Mostly dose related. **CNS:** Headache, dizziness, vertigo, light-headedness, fainting, sedation, nightmares, insomnia, dyskinesia, ataxia; mania, nervousness, anxiety, depression. **CV:** *Orthostatic hypotension*, underline{shock}, postpartum hypertension, palpitation, extrasystoles, Raynaud's phenomenon, red, tender, hot, edematous extremities (erythromelalgia), exacerbation of angina, arrhythmias, acute MI. **Special Senses:** Blurred vision, burning sensation in eyes, blepharospasm, diplopia. **GI:** *Nausea*, vomiting, abdominal cramps, epigastric pain, constipation (long-term use) or diarrhea; metallic taste, dry mouth, dysphagia, anorexia, peptic ulcers. **Skin:** Urticaria, rash, mottling, livedo reticularis. **Other:** Fatigue, nasal congestion, asthenia.

INTERACTIONS Drug: Possibility of decreased tolerance to **alcohol;** ANTIHYPERTENSIVE AGENTS add to hypotensive effects; ORAL CONTRACEPTIVES, **estrogen, progestins** may interfere with effect of bromocriptine by causing amenorrhea and galactorrhea; PHENOTHIAZINES, TRICYCLIC ANTIDEPRESSANTS, **methyldopa, re-**

serpine can cause an increase in **prolactin,** which may interfere with bromocriptine activity.

PHARMACOKINETICS Absorption: 28% from GI tract. **Peak:** 1–2 h. **Duration:** 4–8 h. **Metabolism:** In liver by CYP3A4. **Elimination:** 85% in feces in 5 d; 3–6% in urine. **Half-Life:** 50 h.

CLINICAL IMPLICATIONS

Assessment & Drug Effects

- Monitor vital signs closely during the first few days and periodically throughout therapy.
- Lab tests: Periodic CBC, liver functions and renal functions with prolonged therapy.
- Monitor for and report psychotic symptoms and other adverse reactions in Parkinson's patients because larger doses are used.
- Improvement in Parkinson's disease may be noted in 30–90 min following administration of bromocriptine, with maximum effect in 2 h.

Patient & Family Education

- Make position changes slowly and in stages, especially from lying down to standing, and to dangle legs over bed for a few minutes before walking. Lie down immediately if light-headedness or dizziness occurs.
- Do not drive or engage in other potentially hazardous activities until response to drug is known.
- Avoid exposure to cold and report the onset of pallor of fingers or toes.
- Note: Patients taking bromocriptine to suppress postpartum lactation may have temporary rebound breast enlargement and pain following drug withdrawal.
- Note: Restoration of regular menses usually occurs in 6–8 wk. Since fer-

tility may be restored during therapy, advise patients being treated for amenorrhea and galactorrhea to use barrier-type contraceptive measures until normal ovulating cycle is restored. Oral contraceptives are contraindicated.

- Inform physician immediately, if pregnancy occurs during therapy. Bromocriptine should be discontinued without delay.

BROMPHENIRAMINE MALEATE

(brome-fen-ir'a-meen)

Veltane

Classifications: ANTIHISTAMINE; H_1-RECEPTOR ANTAGONIST

Therapeutic: ANTIHISTAMINE; H_1-RECEPTOR ANTAGONIST

Prototype: Diphenhydramine

Pregnancy Category: C

AVAILABILITY 10 mg/mL injection; 2 mg/5 mL elixir; 4 mg tablet; ingredient in many oral combination products containing a decongestant, expectorant, and/or analgesic

ACTION & *THERAPEUTIC EFFECT*
Antihistamine that has less sedative effect than diphenhydramine. Competes with histamine for H_1-receptor sites on effector cells in the bronchi and bronchioles, thus blocking histamine-mediated responses. *Effective against upper respiratory symptoms and allergic manifestations.*

USES Symptomatic treatment of allergic manifestations. Also used in various cough mixtures and antihistamine-decongestant cold formulations.

CONTRAINDICATIONS Hypersensitivity to antihistamines; acute asthma; pregnancy (category C), newborns.

Common adverse effects in *italic*, life-threatening effects underlined; generic names in **bold**; classifications in SMALL CAPS; ◆ Canadian drug name; ⊚ Prototype drug

191

B

CAUTIOUS USE Older adults; prostatic hypertrophy; GI obstruction; asthma; narrow-angle glaucoma; COPD, cardiovascular or renal disease; seizure disorders; hyperthyroidism; lactation.

ROUTE & DOSAGE

Allergy

Adult: **PO** 4–8 mg t.i.d. or q.i.d. or 8–12 mg of sustained release b.i.d. or t.i.d. **SC/IM/IV** 5–20 mg q6–12h (max: 40 mg/24 h)
Geriatric: **PO** 4 mg 1–2 times/d
Child: **PO** >6 y, 2–4 mg t.i.d. or q.i.d. or 8–12 mg of sustained release b.i.d. (max: 12 mg/24 h); <6 y, 0.5 mg/kg in 3–4 divided doses

ADMINISTRATION

Oral
- Give with meals or a snack to prevent gastric irritation.

Subcutaneous, Intramuscular
- Give without further dilution or diluted to a 1:10 ratio with NS.

Intravenous

PREPARE: **Direct:** Give undiluted or diluted with 10 mL D5W or NS.
ADMINISTER: **Direct:** Give IV push slowly over 1 min to a recumbent patient.
INCOMPATIBILITIES **Solution/additive: Radio-contrast media (diatrizoate, iothalamate).**

- Store in tightly covered container at 15°–30° C (59°–86° F) unless otherwise directed. Elixir and parenteral form should be protected from light. Avoid freezing.

ADVERSE EFFECTS (≥1%) **Body as a Whole:** Hypersensitivity reaction (urticaria, increased sweating, <u>agranulocytosis</u>). **CNS:** *Sedation,* drowsiness, dizziness, headache, disturbed coordination. **GI:** Dry mouth, throat, and nose, stomach upset, constipation. **Special Senses:** Ringing or buzzing in ears. **Skin:** Rash, photosensitivity.

DIAGNOSTIC TEST INTERFERENCE
May cause false-negative **allergy skin tests.**

INTERACTIONS Drug: Alcohol and other CNS DEPRESSANTS add to sedation.

PHARMACOKINETICS Peak: 3–9 h. **Duration:** Up to 48 h. **Distribution:** Crosses placenta. **Elimination:** 40% in urine within 72 h; 2% in feces. **Half-Life:** 12–34 h.

CLINICAL IMPLICATIONS

Assessment & Drug Effects
- Drowsiness, sweating, transient hypotension, and syncope may follow IV administration; reaction to drug should be evaluated. Keep physician informed.
- Note: Older adults tend to be particularly susceptible to drug's sedative effect, dizziness, and hypotension. Most symptoms respond to reduction in dosage.
- Lab tests: Periodic CBC in patients receiving long-term therapy.

Patient & Family Education
- Acute hypersensitivity reaction can occur within minutes to hours after drug ingestion. Reaction is manifested by high fever, chills, and possible development of ulcerations of mouth and throat, pneumonia, and prostration. Patient should seek medical attention immediately.
- Follow diligent mouth care. Sugarless gum, lemon drops, or frequent rinses with warm water may relieve dry mouth.
- Do not drive a car or other potentially hazardous activities until response to drug is known.

Common adverse effects in *italic*, life-threatening effects <u>underlined</u>; generic names in **bold**; classifications in SMALL CAPS; ♣ Canadian drug name; ⊙ Prototype drug

- Do not take alcoholic beverages or other CNS depressants (e.g., tranquilizers, sedatives, pain or sleeping medicines) without consulting physician.

BUDESONIDE
(bu-des′o-nide)
Entocort EC, Pulmicort Turbuhaler, Rhinocort, Rhinocort Aqua, Rhinocort Turbuhaler
Classifications: ANTIINFLAMMATORY; ADRENAL CORTICOSTEROID; GLUCOCORTICOID; MINERALOCORTICOID
Therapeutic: ANTIINFLAMMATORY; ADRENAL CORTICOSTEROID
Prototype: Hydrocortisone
Pregnancy Category: B for inhaled; C for oral

AVAILABILITY 32 mcg/inhalation; 3 mg capsule

ACTION & *THERAPEUTIC EFFECT*
Has potent glucocorticoid activity. Its antiinflammatory action on nasal mucosa is thought to be a result of decreased IgE synthesis and decreased arachidonic acid metabolism. *Glucocorticoids have a wide range of inhibitory activities against multiple cell types (e.g., neutrophils, macrophages) and mediators (e.g., histamine, cytokines) involved in allergic and nonallergic/irritant-mediated inflammation.*

USES Treatment of allergic and perennial rhinitis, maintain remission in mild to moderate Crohn's disease; prophylaxis for asthma.

CONTRAINDICATIONS Hypersensitivity to budesonide, status asthmaticus, acute bronchospasms; peptic ulcer disease; pregnancy (category C for oral; category B for inhaled), lactation.

CAUTIOUS USE Concomitant administration of systemic oral steroids; active or quiescent tuberculosis; infections of respiratory tract; in sun-treated fungal, bacterial, or systemic viral infections or ocular herpes simplex; recent nasal septal ulcers; recurrent epistaxis; nasal surgery or trauma; psychosis; myasthenia gravis; diabetes mellitus; seizure disorders.

ROUTE & DOSAGE

> **Crohn's Disease**
> *Adult:* **PO** 9 mg once/d in a.m. for up to 8 wk, may taper to 6 mg q.d. for 2 wk prior to discontinuing. May repeat 8-wk course for recurring episodes of active Crohn's disease.
>
> **Asthma Prophylaxis, Rhinitis** See Appendix A-3.

ADMINISTRATION
Oral
- Ensure that capsules are swallowed whole and not chewed.
- Give only in the morning.
- Patients with moderate to severe liver disease should be monitored for increased signs and/or symptoms of hypercorticism. Reducing the dose of Entocort EC capsules should be considered in these patients
- Store at 25° C (77° F); excursions permitted to 15°–30° C (59°–86° F)

ADVERSE EFFECTS (≥1%) **Body as a Whole:** Arthralgia, fatigue, fever, hyperkinesis, myalgia, asthenia, paresthesia, tremor. **CNS:** Dizziness, emotional lability, facial edema, nervousness, *headache*, agitation, confusion, insomnia, drowsiness. **CV:** Chest pain, hypertension, palpitations, sinus tachycardia. **GI:** Abdom-

---

Common adverse effects in *italic*, life-threatening effects underlined; generic names in **bold**; classifications in SMALL CAPS; ♣ Canadian drug name; ⊘ Prototype drug

193

B

inal pain, dyspepsia, gastroenteritis, oral candidiasis, xerostomia, diarrhea, nausea, vomiting, cramps. **Hematologic:** Epistaxis. **Metabolic:** Hypokalemia, weight gain. **Respiratory:** Bronchospasms, *infections,* cough, rhinitis, sinusitis, dyspnea, hoarseness, wheezing. **Skin:** Eczema, pruritus, purpura, rash, alopecia. **Special Senses:** Contact dermatitis, reduced sense of smell, nasal pain. **Urogenital:** Intermenstrual bleeding, dysuria.

INTERACTIONS Drug: Ketoconazole may increase oral budesonide concentrations and toxicity; toxicity may also occur with **anastrozole** (high doses only)**, clarithromycin, cyclosporine, danazol, delavirdine, diltiazem, erythromycin, fluconazole, fluoxetine, fluvoxamine, indinavir, isoniazid, INH, itraconazole, mibefradil, nefazodone, nelfinavir, nicardipine, norfloxacin, oxiconazole, quinidine, quinine, ritonavir, saquinavir, troleandomycin, verapamil, and zafirlukast. Food:** Grapefruit juice will significantly increase bioavailability of oral budesonide.

PHARMACOKINETICS Absorption: 20% (nasal) dose, 6–13% of (orally inhaled) dose, 9% PO dose reaches systemic circulation; PO form is absorbed from duodenum at pH >5.5; oral bioavailability increases 2.5 times in hepatic cirrhosis. **Onset:** 8–12 h inhaled, 2 wk oral. **Peak:** 2 wk inhaled, 8 wk oral delayed by high-fat meal. **Distribution:** 90% protein bound. **Metabolism:** 85% of absorbed dose undergoes first pass metabolism by CYP3A4. **Elimination:** 60% in urine, 40% in feces. **Half-Life:** 2–3.6 h

CLINICAL IMPLICATIONS

Assessment & Drug Effects
- Monitor closely for S&S of hypercorticism if concomitant doses of ketoconazole or other CYP3A4 inhibitors (see Drug Interactions) are being given.
- Monitor patients with moderate to severe liver disease for increased S&S of hypercorticism.
- Lab tests: Periodic serum potassium.

Patient & Family Education
- Notify the physician immediately for any of the following: itching, skin rash, fever, swelling of face and neck, difficulty breathing, or if you develop S&S of infection.
- Do not drink grapefruit juice or eat grapefruit regularly.
- Avoid people with infections, especially those with chickenpox or measles if you have never had these conditions.

BUMETANIDE
(byoo-met′a-nide)
Bumex
Classifications: FLUID AND WATER BALANCE AGENT; LOOP DIURETIC
Therapeutic: LOOP DIURETIC; ANTIHYPERTENSIVE
Prototype: Furosemide
Pregnancy Category: C

AVAILABILITY 0.5 mg, 1 mg, 2 mg tablets; 0.25 mg/mL injection

ACTION & *THERAPEUTIC EFFECT*
Sulfonamide derivative structurally related to furosemide and with similar pharmacologic effects. Diuretic activity is 40 times greater, however, and duration of action is shorter than that of furosemide. Causes both potassium and magnesium wastage. Inhibits sodium and chloride reabsorption by direct action on proximal ascending limb of the loop of Henle. Also appears to

Common adverse effects in *italic*, life-threatening effects underlined; generic names in bold; classifications in SMALL CAPS; ♣ Canadian drug name; ⊕ Prototype drug

inhibit phosphate and bicarbonate reabsorption. *Produces only mild hypotensive effects at usual diuretic doses. Controls formation of edema.*

USES Edema associated with CHF; hepatic or renal disease, including nephrotic syndrome. Has been used in management of postoperative and premenstrual edema, edema accompanying disseminated carcinoma, and mild hypertension. May be used concomitantly with a potassium-sparing diuretic.

CONTRAINDICATIONS Hypersensitivity to bumetanide or to other sulfonamides; anuria, markedly elevated BUN; hepatic coma; acute MI, ventricular arrhythmias; severe electrolyte deficiency; severe renal disease; diabetes mellitus; lactation; pregnancy (category C).
CAUTIOUS USE Hepatic cirrhosis, as history of gout; history of hypersensitivity to furosemide; elderly.

ROUTE & DOSAGE

Edema
Adult: **PO** 0.5–2 mg once/d, may repeat at 4–5 h intervals if needed (max: 10 mg/d) **IV/IM** 0.5–1 mg over 1–2 min, repeated q2–3h prn (max: 10 mg/d)
Neonate: **PO/IM/IV** 0.01–0.05 mg/kg q24–48h
Infant/Child: **PO/IM/IV** 0.015–0.1 mg/kg q6–24h (max: 10 mg/d)

ADMINISTRATION
Oral
▪ Give with food or milk to reduce risk of gastrointestinal irritation.
▪ Administered in the morning as a single dose, either daily or by intermittent schedule. For some patients, diuresis is reportedly more effective when administered in two divided doses, morning and evening.
Intramuscular
▪ Use undiluted solution for injection.
Intravenous

PREPARE: **Direct/Continuous:** Give direct IV undiluted or diluted for infusion with D5W, NS, RL.
ADMINISTER: **Direct:** Give IV push at a rate of a single dose over 1–2 min. **Continuous:** Use diluted solution and give at prescribed rate.
INCOMPATIBILITIES **Solution/additive: Dobutamine.**
Diluted infusion should be used within 24 h after preparation.

▪ Store in tight, light-resistant container at 15°–30° C (59°–86° F) unless otherwise directed.

ADVERSE EFFECTS (≥1%) **Body as a Whole:** Sweating, hyperventilation, glycosuria. **CNS:** Dizziness, headache, weakness, fatigue. **CV:** Hypotension, ECG changes, chest pain, *hypovolemia.* **GI:** Nausea, vomiting, abdominal or stomach pain, GI distress, diarrhea, dry mouth. **Metabolic:** *Hypokalemia,* hyponatremia, hyperuricemia, hyperglycemia; *hypomagnesemia;* decreased calcium, chloride. **Musculoskeletal:** Muscle cramps, muscle pain, stiffness or tenderness; arthritic pain. **Special Senses:** Ear discomfort, ringing or buzzing in ears, impaired hearing.

INTERACTIONS Drug: AMINOGLYCOSIDES, **cisplatin** increase risk of ototoxicity; bumetanide increases risk of hypokalemia-induced **digoxin** toxicity; NONSTEROIDAL ANTIINFLAMMATORY DRUGS (NSAID) may attenuate diuretic and hypotensive response; **probenecid** may antagonize diuretic activity; bumetanide may decrease renal elimination of **lithium.**

Common adverse effects in *italic*, life-threatening effects underlined; generic names in **bold**; classifications in SMALL CAPS; ♣ Canadian drug name; ⊕ Prototype drug

195

PHARMACOKINETICS Absorption: Readily from GI tract. **Onset:** 30–60 min PO; 40 min IV. **Peak:** 0.5–2 h. **Duration:** 4–6 h. **Distribution:** Distributed into breast milk. **Metabolism:** In liver. **Elimination:** 80% in urine in 48 h, 10–20% in feces. **Half-Life:** 60–90 min.

CLINICAL IMPLICATIONS

Assessment & Drug Effects

- Monitor I&O and report onset of oliguria or other changes in I&O ratio and pattern promptly.
- Monitor weight, BP, and pulse rate. Assess for hypovolemia by taking BP and pulse rate while patient is lying, sitting, and standing. Older adults are particularly at risk for hypovolemia with resulting thrombi and emboli.
- Lab tests: Serum electrolytes, blood studies, liver and kidney function tests, uric acid (particularly patients with history of gout), and blood glucose. Determine values initially and at regular intervals; measurements are especially important in patients receiving prolonged treatment, high doses, or who are on sodium restriction.
- Monitor for S&S of hypomagnesemia and hypokalemia (see Appendix F) especially in those receiving digitalis or who have CHF, hepatic cirrhosis, ascites, diarrhea, or potassium-depleting nephropathy.
- Monitor patients with hepatic disease carefully for fluid and electrolyte imbalances which can precipitate encephalopathy (inappropriate behavior, altered mood, impaired judgment, confusion, drowsiness, coma).
- Question patient about hearing difficulty or ear discomfort. Patients at risk of ototoxic effects include those receiving the drug IV, especially at high doses, those with severely impaired renal function, and those receiving other potentially ototoxic or nephrotoxic drugs (see Appendix F).
- Monitor diabetics for loss of glycemic control.

Patient & Family Education

- Report symptoms of electrolyte imbalance to physician promptly (e.g., weakness, dizziness, fatigue, faintness, confusion, muscle cramps, headache, paresthesias).
- Eat potassium-rich foods such as fruit juices, potatoes, cereals, skim milk, and bananas while taking bumetanide.
- Report S&S of ototoxicity promptly to physician (see Appendix F).
- Monitor blood glucose for loss of glycemic control if diabetic.

BUPIVACAINE HYDROCHLORIDE

(byoo-piv′a-kane)

Marcaine, Sensorcaine

Classifications: LOCAL ANESTHETIC (AMIDE-TYPE)

Therapeutic: ANESTHETIC, LOCAL

Prototype: Procaine

Pregnancy Category: C

AVAILABILITY 0.25%, 0.5%, 0.75% injection

ACTION & *THERAPEUTIC EFFECT*

Anesthetic of the amide type that decreases sodium flux into nerve cell, inhibiting initial depolarization, and prevents propagation and conduction of the nerve impulse. Progression of anesthesia, related to diameter, myelination, and conduction velocity of affected fibers is manifested clinically as sequential loss of nerve function. *Primary depressant effect is in medulla and higher centers affecting patient's re-action to pain, temperature, and touch, as well as proprioception and skeletal muscle tone.*

USES Infiltration anesthesia; periph-eral, sympathetic nerve, and epidural (including caudal) block anesthesia; 0.75% bupivacaine solution in dex-trose is used for spinal anesthesia.

CONTRAINDICATIONS Known sen-sitivity to bupivacaine, local anes-thetics, other amide-type anesthet-ics. Parabens, or metabisulfites; acidosis; heart block; severe hemor-rhage, uncontrolled coagulopathy; hypotension and shock; hyperten-sion, cerebrospinal diseases; obstet-rical paracervical anesthesia or spi-nal anesthesia in septicemia; topical or IV regional anesthesia; intercur-rent use with chloroprocaine; his-tory of malignant hyperthermia; pregnancy (category C).
CAUTIOUS USE Older adults or de-bilitated patients, dehydration; he-patic or renal disease, neurologic diseases; known drug allergies and sensitivities; dysrhythmias; lactation; children >16 y; obstetrical delivery.

ROUTE & DOSAGE

Infiltration Anesthesia

Adult: **IM Local infiltration, sym-pathetic block** 0.25% solution; **Lumbar epidural** 0.25%, 0.5%, 0.75% solutions; **Caudal block, peripheral nerve block** 0.25%, 0.5% solutions; **Retrobulbar block** 0.75% solution
Child: **IM** 1–3.7 mg/kg

ADMINISTRATION

Intramuscular

■ Inject slowly with frequent aspira-tions to avoid intravascular injec-tion.

Intrathecal

■ Do not use preparations contain-ing preservatives for epidural or spinal anesthesia.
■ Do not use multiple-dose vial for lumbar or caudal epidural block.
■ Store ampules at 15°–30° C (59°–86° F); protect from freezing. Solu-tions with epinephrine should be protected from light.

***INCOMPATIBILITIES* Solution/addi-tive: Sodium bicarbonate**

ADVERSE EFFECTS (≥1%) **Body as a Whole:** Hypersensitivity [cuta-neous lesions, urticaria, sneezing, diaphoresis, syncope, hyperther-mia, angioneurotic edema (includ-ing laryngeal edema), anaphylaxis, anaphylactoid reaction]. **CNS:** Ner-vousness, unusual anxiety, excite-ment, dizziness, drowsiness, trem-ors, convulsions, unconsciousness, respiratory arrest. **Special Senses:** Pupillary constriction; blurred or double vision; tinnitus. **GI:** Nausea, vomiting. **Other:** Inflammation or sepsis at injection site, chills, pupil-lary constriction. **Associated with Epidural Anesthesia, Body as a Whole:** Total spinal block, persistent analgesia, paresthesia. **Urogenital:** Urinary retention, fecal incontinence, loss of perineal sensation and sex-ual function. **Other:** Slowing of la-bor, increased incidence of for-ceps delivery, cranial nerve palsies (with inadvertent intrathecal injec-tion).

INTERACTIONS Drug: CNS DEPRES-SANTS augment CNS depression; with **isoproterenol, ergonovine** there is persistent hypertension and a risk of CVA if bupivacaine used with **epi-nephrine.** MAO INHIBITORS, TRICYCLIC ANTIDEPRESSANTS, PHENOTHIAZINES cause severe or prolonged hypotension or hypertension if bupivacaine used with **epinephrine.**

Common adverse effects in *italic*, life-threatening effects underlined; generic names in **bold**; classifications in SMALL CAPS; ♣ Canadian drug name; ⊙ Prototype drug

197

PHARMACOKINETICS Onset: 4–17 min (epidural, caudal, peripheral, or sympathetic block); within 1 min (spinal block). **Duration:** 3–5 h (epidural, caudal, peripheral, or sympathetic block); 1.25–2.5 h (spinal block). **Distribution:** Crosses placenta. **Metabolism:** In liver. **Elimination:** 6% unchanged in urine. **Half-Life:** 1.5–5.5 h in adults, 8.1 h in neonates.

CLINICAL IMPLICATIONS

Assessment & Drug Effects

- Monitor for signs of inadvertent intravascular injection, which can produce a transient "epinephrine response" (increased heart rate or systolic BP or both, circumoral pallor, palpitations, nervousness) within 45 seconds in the unsedated patient and an increase by 20 bpm or more in heart rate for at least 15 seconds in sedated patient.
- Vasoconstrictor-containing solution should be administered cautiously, if at all, to areas with end arteries (e.g., digits, penis) or to areas that have a compromised blood supply; ischemia and gangrene can result. Inspect areas for evidence of reduced perfusion because of vasospasm: pale, cold, sensitive skin.
- Note: Systemic reactions (toxicity) are more apt to occur in children or older adults and may develop rapidly or be delayed for as long as 30 min after administration.
- Monitor for toxicity: CNS stimulation (unusual anxiety, excitement, restlessness) usually occurs first, followed by CNS depression (drowsiness, unconsciousness, respiratory arrest). However, because stimulation is apt to be transient or absent, drowsiness may be the first sign in some patients (especially children and older adults).
- Monitor BP and fetal heart rate continuously during labor because maternal hypotension may accompany regional anesthesia. Place mother on left side with legs elevated.
- Monitor cardiac and respiratory status continuously in patients receiving retrobulbar and dental blocks.

Patient & Family Education

- After spinal anesthesia, sensation to lower extremities may not return for 2.5–3.5 h.

BUPRENORPHINE HYDROCHLORIDE

(byoo-pre-nor′feen)

Buprenex, Subutex

Classifications: ANALGESIC; NARCOTIC (OPIATE) AGONIST-ANTAGONIST

Therapeutic: NARCOTIC ANALGESIC; OPIATE

Prototype: Pentazocine

Pregnancy Category: C

Controlled Substance: Schedule III

AVAILABILITY 0.3 mg (base)/mL injection; 2 mg, 8 mg sublingual tablets

ACTION & *THERAPEUTIC EFFECT*

Opiate agonist-antagonist with agonist activity approximately 30 times that of morphine and antagonist activity equal to or up to 3 times that of naloxone. Respiratory depression occurs infrequently, probably due to drug's opiate antagonist activity. Has a low level of physical dependence. *Dose-related analgesia results from a high affinity of buprenorphine for mu-opioid receptors and an antagonist at the kappa-opiate receptors in the CNS. Naloxone is an antagonist at the mu-opioid receptor.*

USES *Injectable* used principally for moderate to severe postoperative pain. Also for pain associated with cancer and trigeminal neuralgia, accidental trauma, ureteral calculi, MI. *Sublingual tablets* used for treatment of opioid dependence.
UNLABELED USES *Injectable* to reverse fentanyl-induced anesthesia. *Sublingual tablets* may be used to ease cocaine withdrawal.

CONTRAINDICATIONS Hypersensitivity to buprenorphine or hypersensitivity to naloxone; pregnancy (category C), lactation, children <2 y.
CAUTIOUS USE Patient with history of opiate use; compromised respiratory function [e.g., chronic obstructive pulmonary disease (COPD), cor pulmonale, decreased respiratory reserve, hypoxia, hypercapnia, or preexisting respiratory depression]; concomitant use of other respiratory depressants; hypothyroidism, myxedema, Addison's disease; severe renal or hepatic impairment; geriatric or debilitated patients; acute alcoholism, delirium tremens; prostatic hypertrophy, urethral stricture; comatose patient; patients with CNS depression, head injury, or intracranial lesion; biliary tract dysfunction.

ROUTE & DOSAGE

Postoperative Pain

Adult: **IV/IM** 0.3 mg q6h up to 0.6 mg q4h or 25–50 mcg/h by IV infusion
Geriatric: **IV/IM** 0.15 mg q6h
Child: **IV/IM** 2–12 y 2–6 mcg/kg q4–6h prn

Opioid Dependence/Cocaine Withdrawal

Adult: **SL** Initiate with 8 mg q.d. Subutex on day 1 at least 4 h after last opioid dose, 16 mg q.d. Subutex on day 2, then switch to Suboxone for maintenance therapy at the same buprenorphine dose as day 2 (e.g., 16 mg q.d.). Adjust dose daily until opiate withdrawal effects are suppressed. Maintenance dose range 4 mg–24 mg/ d buprenorphine.

ADMINISTRATION

Sublingual

- Place SUBONONE and SUBUTEX tablets under tongue until dissolved. For doses requiring more than two tablets, place all tablets at once under tongue, or if patient cannot accommodate all tablets, place two tablets at a time under tongue.
- Instruct to hold the tablets under tongue until dissolved; advise not to swallow.

Intramuscular

- Give undiluted, deep IM into a large muscle.

Intravenous

PREPARE: **Direct:** Give undiluted. Do not use if discolored or contains particulate matter.
ADMINISTER: **Direct:** Give slowly at a rate of 0.3 mg over 2 min to a patient in a recumbent position.

- Store at 15°–30° C (59°–86° F); avoid freezing.

ADVERSE EFFECTS (≥1%) **CNS:** *Sedation, drowsiness,* dizziness, vertigo, *headache,* amnesia, euphoria, asthenia, *insomnia, pain* (when used for withdrawal), *withdrawal symptoms.* **CV:** Hypotension, va-

Common adverse effects in *italic*, life-threatening effects <u>underlined</u>; generic names in **bold**; classifications in SMALL CAPS; ♣ Canadian drug name; ⊕ Prototype drug

199

sodilation. **Special Senses:** Miosis. **GI:** *Nausea,* vomiting, diarrhea, *constipation.* **Respiratory:** Respiratory depression, hyperventilation. **Skin:** Pruritus, injection site reactions, *sweating.*

INTERACTIONS Drug: Alcohol, OPIATES, other CNS DEPRESSANTS, BENZODIAZEPINES augment CNS depression; **diazepam** may cause respiratory or cardiovascular collapse; AZOLE ANTIFUNGALS (e.g., **fluconazole**), MACROLIDE ANTIBIOTICS (e.g., **erythromycin**), and PROTEASE INHIBITORS (e.g., **saquinavir**) may increase buprenorphine levels.

PHARMACOKINETICS Absorption: Widely variable sublingual absorption. **Onset:** 10–30 min IM/IV. **Peak:** 1 h IM/IV; 2–6 h SL. **Duration:** 6–10 h. **Metabolism:** Extensively in liver by CYP3A4 to active metabolite norbuprenorphine. **Elimination:** 70% in feces, 30% in urine in 7 d. **Half-Life:** 2.2 h IM/IV; 37 h SL.

CLINICAL IMPLICATIONS

Assessment & Drug Effects

- Monitor respiratory status during therapy. Buprenorphine-induced respiratory depression is about equal to that produced by 10 mg morphine, but onset is slower, and if it occurs, it lasts longer.
- Note: Respiratory depression in the healthy adult plateaus or may even decrease in severity with doses more than 1.2 mg because of antagonist activity of the drug.
- Use lower dosing of buprenorphine with a concurrent NSAID or other nonnarcotic analgesic due to additive analgesic effect.
- Monitor I&O ratio and pattern during buprenorphine therapy; urinary retention is a potential adverse effect.

- Lab tests: Baseline liver function, renal function, alkaline phosphatase, and PSA.
- Supervise ambulation; drowsiness occurs in 66% of patients taking this drug.

Patient & Family Education

- Do not drive or engage in other potentially hazardous activities until response to drug is known.
- Do not use alcohol or other CNS depressing drugs without consulting physician. An additive effect exists between buprenorphine hydrochloride and other CNS depressants including alcohol.

BUPROPION HYDROCHLORIDE

(byoo-pro′pi-on)

Wellbutrin, Wellbutrin SR, Wellbutrin XL, Zyban

Classifications: ANTIDEPRESSANT
Therapeutic: ANTIDEPRESSANT
Pregnancy Category: B

AVAILABILITY 75 mg, 100 mg tablets; 100 mg, 150 mg, 200 mg sustained-release tablets; 150 mg, 300 mg extended-release tablets

ACTION & *THERAPEUTIC EFFECT*

The neurochemical mechanism of bupropion is not fully understood. It selectively inhibits the neuronal reuptake of dopamine. *Its antidepressive effect is related to CNS stimulant effects.*

USES Indicated for mental depression; since it has been associated with increased risk of seizures, it is not the agent of first choice; adjunct for smoking cessation; seasonal affective disorder.

UNLABELED USES Schizoaffective disorders.

CONTRAINDICATIONS Hypersensitivity to bupropion; history of sei-

200

Common adverse effects in *italic*, life-threatening effects underlined; generic names in **bold**; classifications in SMALL CAPS; ♦ Canadian drug name; ⊘ Prototype drug

zure disorder; current or prior diagnosis of bulimia or anorexia nervosa; suicidal ideation; concurrent administration of an MAO inhibitor; head trauma; seizure disorder; CNS tumor; recent MI; abrupt discontinuation, anorexia nervosa, bulimia nervosa, children <18 y; lactation.

CAUTIOUS USE Renal or hepatic function impairment; drug abuse or dependence; pregnancy (category B); cardiac disease, MI, hepatic disease, biliary cirrhosis; hypertension, bipolar disorder, mania, psychosis, diabetes mellitus, older adults, ethanol intoxication, tics, Tourette's syndrome.

ROUTE & DOSAGE

Depression/Seasonal Affective Disorder

Adult: **PO** 75–100 mg t.i.d., start with 75 mg t.i.d., or 100 mg SR b.i.d., or 150 mg XL q.d., and increase dose q3d to 300 mg/d; doses >450 mg/d are associated with an increased risk of adverse reactions including seizures
Geriatric: **PO** 50–100 mg/d, may increase by 50–100 mg q3–4d (max: 150 mg/dose)

Smoking Cessation

Adult: **PO** Start with 150 mg once daily × 3 d, then increase to 150 mg b.i.d. (max: 300 mg/d) for 7–12 wk

ADMINISTRATION

Oral

- Give with meals to decrease incidence of nausea and vomiting.
- Ensure that sustained-release tablets are not chewed or crushed. They must be swallowed whole.
- Note: Increases in dosage should not exceed 100 mg/d over a 3-d period. Greater increments increase the seizure potential.

- Store away from heat, direct light, and moisture.

ADVERSE EFFECTS (≥1%) **Body as a Whole:** Weight loss, weight gain. **CNS:** Seizures. The risk of seizure appears to be strongly associated with dose (especially >450 mg/d) and may be increased by predisposing factors (e.g., head trauma, CNS tumor) or a history of prior seizure; *agitation, insomnia, dry mouth, blurred vision, headache, dizziness, tremor.* **GI:** *Nausea, vomiting, constipation.* **CV:** Tachycardia. **Skin:** Rash.

INTERACTIONS Drug: May increase metabolism of **carbamazepine, cimetidine, phenytoin, phenobarbital,** decreasing their effect; may increase incidence of adverse effects of **levodopa,** MAO INHIBITORS.

PHARMACOKINETICS Absorption: Readily from GI tract. **Onset:** 3–4 wk. **Peak:** 1–3 h. **Metabolism:** In liver (including first pass metabolism) to active metabolites by CYP2B6. **Elimination:** 80% in urine as inactive metabolites **Half-Life:** 8–24 h.

CLINICAL IMPLICATIONS

Assessment & Drug Effects

- Monitor for therapeutic effectiveness. The full antidepressant effect of drug may not be realized for 4 or more weeks.
- Close observation for worsening of depression or suicidal tendencies.
- Use extreme caution when administering drug to patient with history of seizures, cranial trauma, or other factors predisposing to seizures; during sudden and large increments in dose, seizure potential is increased.
- Report significant restlessness, agitation, anxiety, and insomnia. Symptoms may require treatment or discontinuation of drug.

Common adverse effects in *italic*, life-threatening effects underlined; generic names in **bold**; classifications in SMALL CAPS; ♣ Canadian drug name; ○ Prototype drug

201

- Monitor for and report delusions, hallucinations, psychotic episodes, confusion, and paranoia.
- Lab tests: Monitor hepatic and renal function tests while patient is taking this drug.

Patient & Family Education
- Take drug at the same times each day.
- Monitor your weight at least weekly. Report significant changes in weight (±5 lb) to physician.
- Minimize or avoid alcohol because it increases the risk of seizures.
- Do not drive or engage in potentially hazardous activities until response to drug is known because judgment or motor and cognitive skills may be impaired.
- Do not abruptly discontinue drug. Gradual dosage reduction may be necessary to prevent adverse effects.
- Do not take any OTC drugs without consulting physician.

BUSPIRONE HYDROCHLORIDE

(byoo-spye'rone)
BuSpar
Classifications: ANXIOLYTIC
Therapeutic: ANTIANXIETY
Prototype: Lorazepam
Pregnancy Category: B

AVAILABILITY 5 mg, 10 mg, 15 mg tablets

ACTION & *THERAPEUTIC EFFECT*
An anxiolytic that focuses mainly on the brain D_2-dopamine receptors. It has agonist effects on presynaptic dopamine receptors and also a high affinity for serotonin (5-HT_{1A}) receptors. *Antianxiety effect is due to serotonin reuptake inhibition and agonist effects on dopamine receptors of the brain.*

USES Management of anxiety disorders and for short-term treatment of generalized anxiety.
UNLABELED USES Adjuvant for nicotine withdrawal, premenstrual syndrome.

CONTRAINDICATIONS Concomitant use of alcohol and buspirone; concomitant use of MAOI therapy. Safety during labor and delivery, lactation, or in children <18 y is not established.
CAUTIOUS USE Moderate to severe renal or hepatic impairment, pregnancy (category B).

ROUTE & DOSAGE

Anxiety

Adult: **PO** 7.5–15 mg/d in divided doses, may increase by 5 mg/d q2–3d as needed (max: 60 mg/d)
Geriatric: **PO** 5 mg b.i.d., may increase to max 60 mg/d

ADMINISTRATION

Oral
- Give with food to decrease nausea.
- Give 8 h before or after drinking grapefruit juice.
- Store at 15°–30° C (59°–86° F) in tightly closed container unless otherwise directed.

ADVERSE EFFECTS (≥1%) **CNS:** Numbness, paresthesia, tremors, *dizziness, headache,* nervousness, *drowsiness,* light-headedness, dream disturbances, decreased concentration, excitement, mood changes. **CV:** Tachycardia, palpitation. **Special Senses:** Blurred vision. **GI:** *Nausea,* vomiting, dry mouth, abdominal/gastric distress, diarrhea, constipation. **Urogenital:** Urinary frequency, hesitancy. **Musculoskeletal:** Arthralgias. **Respiratory:** Hyperventilation, shortness of breath. **Skin:** Rash, edema, pruritus, flushing, easy bruising, hair loss, dry skin. **Other:** Fatigue, weakness.

DIAGNOSTIC TEST INTERFERENCE

Buspirone may increase serum concentrations of *hepatic aminotransferases (ALT, AST)*.

INTERACTIONS Drug: May cause

hypertension with MAO INHIBITORS, **trazodone,** possible increase in liver transaminases; increased **haloperidol** serum levels. **Food:** Grapefruit juice may increase drug levels. **Herb:** St. John's wort may increase drug levels.

PHARMACOKINETICS Absorption:

Readily from GI tract, undergoes first pass metabolism. **Onset:** 5–7 d. **Peak:** 1 h. **Metabolism:** In liver. **Elimination:** 30–63% in urine as metabolites within 24 h. **Half-Life:** 2–4 h.

CLINICAL IMPLICATIONS

Assessment & Drug Effects

- Monitor for therapeutic effectiveness. Desired response may begin within 7–10 d; however, optimal results take 3–4 wk. Reinforce the importance of continuing treatment to patient.
- Benzodiazepines or sedative-hypnotic drugs are withdrawn gradually before buspirone therapy is started. Observe patient for rebound symptoms, which may occur over varying time periods during first phase of treatment.
- Monitor for and report dystonia, motor restlessness, and involuntary repetitious movement of facial or cervical muscle.
- Observe for and report swollen ankles, decreased urinary output,

changes in voiding pattern, jaundice, itching, nausea, or vomiting.

Patient & Family Education

- Take exactly as prescribed: Specifically, do not omit, skip, increase or decrease doses without advice of the physician.
- Report any of the following immediately: Involuntary, repetitive movements of face or neck; weakness, nervousness, nightmares, headache, or blurred vision; depression or thoughts of suicide.
- Do not use OTC drugs without advice of the physician while taking buspirone.
- Note: Adverse effects subside during continued therapy with or without dosage adjustment. Do not discontinue therapy.
- Do not drive or engage in other potentially hazardous activities until response to drug is known.
- Alert physician if you become pregnant; buspirone must be discontinued during pregnancy.
- Discuss limits of alcohol intake with physician; cautious use is generally advised.
- Note: It is important to understand the planned schedule for changes in doses and intervals to ensure low incidence of withdrawal or rebound symptoms when therapy is discontinued.

BUSULFAN

(byoo-sul'fan)
Busulfex, Myleran
Classifications: ANTINEOPLASTIC; ALKYLATING AGENT
Therapeutic: ANTINEOPLASTIC
Prototype: Cyclophosphamide
Pregnancy Category: D

Common adverse effects in *italic*, life-threatening effects <u>underlined</u>; generic names in **bold**; classifications in SMALL CAPS; ♣ Canadian drug name; ⊘ Prototype drug

203

B

AVAILABILITY 2 mg tablets; 6 mg/mL injection

ACTION & *THERAPEUTIC EFFECT*

Potent cytotoxic alkylating agent that may be mutagenic or carcinogenic, and cell cycle nonspecific. Reduces total granulocyte mass but has little effect on lymphocytes and platelets except in large doses. May cause widespread epithelial cellular dysplasia severe enough to make it difficult to interpret exfoliative cytologic examinations. *Causes cell death by acting predominantly on slowly proliferating stem cells by inducing cross linkage in DNA, thus blocking replication.*

USES Palliative treatment of chronic myelogenous (myeloid, granulocytic, myelocytic) leukemia for patients no longer responsive to radiation therapy or to previously tried antineoplastics. Does not appreciably extend survival time. Stem cell transplant conditioning.

UNLABELED USES Polycythemia vera, severe thrombocytosis, as adjunct in treatment of myelofibrosis, allogeneic bone transplantation in patients with acute nonlymphocytic leukemia.

CONTRAINDICATIONS Therapy-resistant chronic lymphocytic leukemia; lymphoblastic crisis of chronic myelogenous leukemia; bone marrow depression, immunizations (patient and household members), chickenpox (including recent exposure), herpetic infections; pregnancy (category D), lactation.

CAUTIOUS USE Men and women in childbearing years; hepatic disease; history of gout or urate renal stones; prior irradiation or chemotherapy.

ROUTE & DOSAGE

Chronic Myelogenous Leukemia
Adult: **PO** 4–8 mg/d until maximal clinical and hematologic improvement, may use 1–4 mg/d if remission is shorter than 3 mo *Child:* **PO** 0.06–0.12 mg/kg/d or 1.8–4.6 mg/m²

Stem Cell Transplant Conditioning
Adult: **IV** (used with cyclophosphamide) 0.8mg/kg IBW or ABW (whichever is lower) q6h × 4 d

ADMINISTRATION

Oral
- Give at same time each day.
- Give on an empty stomach to minimize nausea and vomiting.
- Store in tightly capped, light-resistant container at 15°–30° C (59°–86° F), unless otherwise specified.

ADVERSE EFFECTS (≥1%) **Hematologic:** Major toxic effects are related to bone marrow failure; agranulocytosis (rare), pancytopenia, thrombocytopenia, leukopenia, *anemia*. **Urogenital:** Flank pain, renal calculi, uric acid nephropathy, acute renal failure, gynecomastia, testicular atrophy, azoospermia, impotence, sterility in males, ovarian suppression, menstrual changes, amenorrhea (potentially irreversible), menopausal symptoms. **Respiratory:** Irreversible pulmonary fibrosis ("busulfan lung"). **Skin:** Alopecia, hyperpigmentation. **Other:** Endocardial fibrosis, dizziness, cholestatic jaundice, infections.

DIAGNOSTIC TEST INTERFERENCE Busulfan may decrease *urinary 17-OHCS* excretion, and may increase *blood and urine uric acid* levels. Drug-induced cellular dys-

Common adverse effects in *italic*, life-threatening effects underlined; generic names in **bold**; classifications in SMALL CAPS; ♣ Canadian drug name; ⊘ Prototype drug

plasia may interfere with interpretation of *cytologic studies.*

INTERACTIONS Drug: Probenecid, **sulfinpyrazone** may increase **uric acid** levels.

PHARMACOKINETICS Absorption: Readily from GI tract. **Peak:** 4 h. **Duration:** 4 h. **Metabolism:** In liver by CYP3A4. **Elimination:** 10–50% in urine within 48 h.

CLINICAL IMPLICATIONS

Assessment & Drug Effects

- Monitor for therapeutic effectiveness: Normal leukocyte count is usually achieved in about 2 mo.
- Monitor the following: Vital signs, weight, I&O ratio and pattern. Urge patient to increase fluid intake to 10–12 (8 oz) glasses daily (if allowed) to assure adequate urinary output.
- Monitor for and report symptoms suggestive of superinfection (see Appendix F), particularly when patient develops leukopenia.
- Lab test: Baseline Hgb, Hct, WBC with differential, platelet count, liver function, kidney function, serum uric acid; repeat at least weekly.
- Avoid invasive procedures during periods of platelet count depression.

Patient & Family Education

- Report to physician any of the following: Easy bruising or bleeding, cloudy or pink urine, dark or black stools; sore mouth or throat, unusual fatigue, blurred vision, flank or joint pain, swelling of lower legs and feet; yellowing white of eye, dark urine, light-colored stools, abdominal discomfort, or itching (hepatotoxicity).
- Use contraceptive measures during busulfan therapy and for at least 3 mo after drug is withdrawn.

BUTABARBITAL SODIUM

B

(byoo-ta-bar'bi-tal)
Butisol Sodium
Classifications: BARBITURATE; ANXIOLYTIC; SEDATIVE-HYPNOTIC
Therapeutic: ANTIANXIETY; SEDATIVE-HYPNOTIC
Prototype: Phenobarbital
Pregnancy Category: C
Controlled Substance: Schedule III

AVAILABILITY 30 mg, 50 mg tablets; 30 mg/5 mL elixir

ACTION & *THERAPEUTIC EFFECT* Intermediate-acting barbiturate that appears to act at thalamus level, where it interferes with transmission of impulses to the cerebral cortex. *Preoperative sedative agent that also is an effective antianxiety agent.*

USES Hypnotic in short-term treatment of simple insomnia, as sedative for relief of anxiety, and to provide sedation preoperatively.

CONTRAINDICATIONS Porphyria; uncontrolled pain; severe respiratory disease; history of addiction; pregnancy (category C), lactation.
CAUTIOUS USE Severe renal or hepatic impairment; acute abdominal conditions; head trauma, history of seizures; history of herpes infection; older adults or debilitated patients.

ROUTE & DOSAGE

Daytime Sedation
Adult: **PO** 15–30 mg t.i.d. or q.i.d.

Preoperative Sedation
Adult: **PO** 50–100 mg 60–90 min before surgery

Common adverse effects in *italic*, life-threatening effects underlined; generic names in **bold**; classifications in SMALL CAPS; ♣ Canadian drug name; ⊕ Prototype drug

Child: **PO** 2–6 mg/kg/dose (max: 100 mg)
Hypnotic
Adult: **PO** 50–100 mg h.s.

ADMINISTRATION

Oral

- Schedule slow withdrawal following long-term use to avoid precipitating withdrawal symptoms.
- Store in tightly covered containers, preferably at 15°–30° C (59°–86° F), unless otherwise directed.

ADVERSE EFFECTS (≥1%) **CNS:** Drowsiness, *residual sedation* ("hangover"), headache. **GI:** Nausea, vomiting, constipation, diarrhea. **Skin:** Urticaria, skin rash. **Musculoskeletal:** Muscle or joint pain.

INTERACTIONS Drug: Alcohol and other CNS DEPRESSANTS add to CNS and respiratory depression; butabarbital increases the metabolism of ORAL ANTICOAGULANTS, BETA BLOCKERS, CORTICOSTEROIDS, **doxycycline, griseofulvin, quinidine,** THEOPHYLLINES, ORAL CONTRACEPTIVES, decreasing their effectiveness. **Herbal: Kava-kava, valerian** may potentiate sedation.

PHARMACOKINETICS Absorption: Readily from GI tract. **Onset:** 40–60 min. **Peak:** 3–4 h. **Duration:** 6–8 h. **Distribution:** Crosses placenta; distributed into breast milk. **Metabolism:** In liver. **Elimination:** In urine primarily as metabolites. **Half-Life:** Average 100 h.

CLINICAL IMPLICATIONS

Assessment & Drug Effects

- Assess for adverse effects. Older adults and debilitated patients sometimes manifest excitement, confusion, or depression. Children also may react with paradoxical excitement. Side rails may be advisable. Report these reactions to physician.

Patient & Family Education

- Do not drive or engage in other potentially hazardous activities until response to drug is known.
- Do not drink alcoholic beverages while taking this drug. Other CNS depressants may produce additive drowsiness; do not take without approval of physician.
- Note: Prolonged use is not recommended because tolerance to drug occurs in about 14 d.

BUTENAFINE HYDROCHLORIDE

(bu-ten′a-feen)
Lotrimin Ultra, Mentax
Classifications: ANTIFUNGAL ANTIBIOTIC
Therapeutic: ANTIBIOTIC, ANTIFUNGAL
Prototype: Terbinafine
Pregnancy Category: B

AVAILABILITY 1% cream

ACTION & *THERAPEUTIC EFFECT* Exerts antifungal action by inhibiting fungal sterol synthesis that is needed in formation of the fungal cell membrane. *Antifungal effectiveness against interdigital tinea pedis (athlete's foot), tinea corporis (ringworm), and tinea cruris (jock itch).*

USES Treatment of tinea pedis, tinea corporis, and tinea cruris due to *Epidermophyton floccosum, Trichophyton mentagrophytes, Trichophyton rubrum.*

CONTRAINDICATIONS Hypersensitivity to butenafine; ophthalmic or vaginal administration.

Common adverse effects in *italic*, life-threatening effects <u>underlined</u>; generic names in **bold**; classifications in SMALL CAPS; ♦ Canadian drug name; ☯ Prototype drug

CAUTIOUS USE Hypersensitivity to naftifine or tolnaftate; pregnancy (category B); lactation. Safety and efficacy in children <12 y are not established.

ROUTE & DOSAGE

Tinea Pedis

Adult/Child: **Topical** >12 y, apply to affected area and surrounding skin b.i.d. times 7 d or q.d. times 4 wk

Tinea Corporis, Tinea Cruris

Adult/Child: **Topical** >12 y, apply to affected area and surrounding skin once daily

ADMINISTRATION

Topical

▪ Apply sufficient cream to cover affected skin and surrounding areas.
▪ Do not use occlusive dressing unless specifically directed to do so.
▪ Store at 5°–30° C (41°–86° F).

ADVERSE EFFECTS (≥1%) **Skin:** Burning/stinging at application site, contact dermatitis, erythema, irritation, itching.

CLINICAL IMPLICATIONS

Assessment & Drug Effects

▪ Note: 2–4 wk of therapy are usually required for effective treatment.

Patient & Family Education

▪ Discontinue medication and notify physician if irritation or sensitivity develops.
▪ Avoid contact with mucous membranes.
▪ Wash hands thoroughly before and after application of cream.

BUTOCONAZOLE NITRATE

B

(byoo-toe-koe′na-zole)
Femstat 3, Gynazole 1
Classifications: ANTIFUNGAL ANTIBIOTIC
Therapeutic: ANTIFUNGAL; ANTIBIOTIC
Prototype: Fluconazole
Pregnancy Category: C

AVAILABILITY 2% cream

ACTION & *THERAPEUTIC EFFECT*
Imidazole derivative with antifungal activity. Alters fungal cell membrane permeability, permitting loss of phosphorous compounds, potassium, and other essential intracellular constituents with consequent loss of ability to replicate. Action takes place primarily on medicated infected surface tissues. *Has fungicidal effect as well as effectiveness against some gram-positive bacteria.*

USES Local treatment of vulvovaginal candidiasis.

CONTRAINDICATIONS Pregnancy (category C). Safety in children <12 y is not established.
CAUTIOUS USE Hypersensitivity to azole antifungals; HIV patients; diabetes mellitus; lactation.

ROUTE & DOSAGE

Vulvovaginal Candidiasis

Adult: **Topical** 1 applicator full intravaginally h.s. for 3 d, may be extended another 3 d if needed
Pregnant women: **Topical** 1 applicator full intravaginally h.s. for 6 d

ADMINISTRATION

Topical Intravaginal

▪ Continue treatment even during menstruation.

Common adverse effects in *italic*, life-threatening effects underlined; generic names in **bold**; classifications in SMALL CAPS; ♣ Canadian drug name; ☯ Prototype drug

207

- Store medication at 15°–30° C (59°–86° F); avoid extreme temperature and freezing.

ADVERSE EFFECTS (≥1%) **Urogenital:** Vulvar or vaginal burning, vulvar itching, discharge, soreness, swelling; urinary frequency and burning. **Skin:** Itching of fingers. **CNS:** Headache.

PHARMACOKINETICS Absorption: Small amount absorbed systemically from intravaginal administration. **Distribution:** Crosses placenta in animals. **Metabolism:** In liver. **Elimination:** In both urine and feces within 4–7 d. **Half-Life:** 21–24 h.

CLINICAL IMPLICATIONS

Assessment & Drug Effects
- Monitor for therapeutic effectiveness. Candidiasis in nonpregnant women is usually controlled in 3 d.

Patient & Family Education
- Take medication exactly as prescribed; do not increase or decrease dosage or discontinue or extend treatment period. Contact physician if symptoms (vaginal burning, discharge, or itching) persist; drug may be discontinued if acute irritation occurs.
- Patient's sexual partner should wear a condom during intercourse.

BUTORPHANOL TARTRATE

(byoo-tor'fa-nole)

Stadol, Stadol NS

Classifications: ANALGESIC; NARCOTIC (OPIATE) AGONIST-ANTAGONIST
Therapeutic: NARCOTIC ANALGESIC
Prototype: Pentazocine
Pregnancy Category: C
Controlled Substance: Schedule IV

AVAILABILITY 1 mg/mL, 2 mg/mL injection; 10 mg/mL spray

ACTION & *THERAPEUTIC EFFECT* Synthetic, centrally acting analgesic with mixed narcotic agonist and antagonist actions. Acts as agonist on one type of opioid receptor and as a competitive antagonist at others. Site of analgesic action believed to be subcortical, possibly in the limbic system. Respiratory depression does not increase appreciably with higher doses, as it does with morphine, but duration of action increases. *Narcotic analgesic that relieves moderate to severe pain with apparently low potential for physical dependence.*

USES Relief of moderate to severe pain, preoperative or preanesthetic sedation and analgesia, obstetrical analgesia during labor, cancer pain, renal colic, burns.
UNLABELED USES Musculoskeletal and post-episiotomy pain.

CONTRAINDICATIONS Narcotic-dependent patients; opiate agonist hypersensitivity; pregnancy and prior to labor (category C). Safety in children <18 y is not established.
CAUTIOUS USE History of drug abuse or dependence; emotionally unstable individuals; head injury, increased intracranial pressure; acute MI, ventricular dysfunction, coronary insufficiency, hypertension; patients undergoing biliary tract surgery; respiratory depression, bronchial asthma, obstructive respiratory disease; and renal or hepatic dysfunction.

ROUTE & DOSAGE

Pain Relief
Adult: **IM** 1–4 mg q3–4h as needed (max: 4 mg/dose)

Common adverse effects in *italic*, life-threatening effects underlined; generic names in bold; classifications in SMALL CAPS; ♣ Canadian drug name; ⊙ Prototype drug

IV 0.5–2 mg q3–4h as needed
Geriatric: **IM/IV** 0.25–1 mg q6–8h **Intranasal** 1 mg (1 spray) in one nostril, may repeat in 90 s, then may repeat these 2 doses q3–4h prn

Renal Impairment
For GFR <10 mL/min, use 50% of dose.

Hepatic Impairment
Use half normal dose and at least 6 h interval.

ADMINISTRATION

Intranasal
- Give 1 spray into one nostril only. One spray provides a 1 mg dose.

Intramuscular
- Do not give more than 4 mg in a single IM dose.
- Give preoperative IM injection 60–90 min before surgery.

Intravenous

PREPARE: **Direct:** Give undiluted.
ADMINISTER: **Direct:** Give at a rate of 2 mg over 3–5 min.
INCOMPATIBILITIES **Solution/additive: Dimenhydrinate, pentobarbital. Y-site: Pentobarbital.**

- Store at 15°–30° C (59°–86° F) unless otherwise directed. Protect from light.

ADVERSE EFFECTS (≥1%) **CNS:** Drowsiness, *sedation,* headache, vertigo, dizziness, floating feeling, weakness, lethargy, confusion, lightheadedness, insomnia, nervousness, respiratory depression. **CV:** Palpitation, bradycardia. **GI:** Nausea. **Skin:** Clammy skin, tingling sensation, flushing and warmth, cyanosis of extremities, diaphoresis, sensitivity to cold, urticaria, pruritus. **Genitourinary:** Difficulty in urinating, biliary spasm.

INTERACTIONS Drug: Alcohol and other CNS DEPRESSANTS augment CNS and respiratory depression.

PHARMACOKINETICS Onset: 10–30 min IM; 1 min IV. **Peak:** 0.5–1 h IM; 4–5 min IV. **Duration:** 3–4 h IM; 2–4 h IV. **Distribution:** Crosses placenta; distributed into breast milk. **Metabolism:** In liver in inactive metabolites. **Elimination:** Primarily in urine. **Half-Life:** 3–4 h.

CLINICAL IMPLICATIONS

Assessment & Drug Effects
- Monitor for respiratory depression. Do not administer drug if respiratory rate is <12 breaths/min.
- Monitor vital signs. Report marked changes in BP or bradycardia.
- Note: If used during labor or delivery, observe neonate for signs of respiratory depression.
- Note: Drug can induce acute withdrawal symptoms in opiate-dependent patients.
- Schedule gradual withdrawal following chronic administration. Abrupt withdrawal may produce vomiting, loss of appetite, restlessness, abdominal cramps, increase in BP and temperature, mydriasis, faintness. Withdrawal symptoms peak 48 h after discontinuation of drug.

Patient & Family Education
- Lie down to control drug-induced nausea.
- Do not take alcohol or other CNS depressants with this drug without consulting physician because of possible additive effects.
- Do not drive or engage in other potentially hazardous activities until response to drug is known.

Common adverse effects in *italic,* life-threatening effects underlined; generic names in **bold**; classifications in SMALL CAPS; ♣ Canadian drug name; ❹ Prototype drug

209

CABERGOLINE

(ka-ber'go-leen)
Dostinex
Classifications: ERGOT ALKALOID; DOPAMINE AGONIST
Therapeutic: ERGOT ALKALOID; ANTIPARKINSON AGENT
Prototype: Ergotamine
Pregnancy Category: B

AVAILABILITY 0.5 mg tablets

ACTION & *THERAPEUTIC EFFECT*

Cabergoline is a synthetic ergot derivative, long-acting dopamine receptor agonist with a high affinity for D_2 receptors in the anterior pituitary, suppresses prolactin secretion. *Cabergoline inhibits both puerperal lactation and pathologic hyperprolactinemia.*

USES Treatment of hyperprolactinemia (idiopathic or secondary to pituitary adenomas).
UNLABELED USES Treatment of Parkinson's disease.

CONTRAINDICATIONS Uncontrolled hypertension and hypersensitivity to ergot derivatives; pregnancy-induced hypertension, preeclampsia, eclampsia, lactation.
CAUTIOUS USE Hepatic function impairment; elderly, psychosis; pregnancy (category B). Safety and efficacy in pediatric patients are unknown.

ROUTE & DOSAGE

Hyperprolactinemia

Adult: **PO** Start with 0.25 mg 2 times/wk, may increase by 0.25 mg 2 times/wk to a max of 1 mg 2 times/wk

Parkinson's Disease

Adult: **PO** Start with 0.5 mg q.d., may increase up to 2.5 mg q.d. (max: 5 mg/d)

ADMINISTRATION

Oral

- Give on same days each week.

ADVERSE EFFECTS (≥1%) **Body as a Whole:** Asthenia, fatigue, hot flashes. **CV:** Postural hypotension. **GI:** *Nausea, constipation,* abdominal pain, dyspepsia, vomiting, dry mouth, diarrhea, flatulence. **Endocrine:** Breast pain, dysmenorrhea. **CNS:** *Headache, dizziness,* paresthesia, somnolence, depression, nervousness.

INTERACTIONS Drug: Concurrent use with PHENOTHIAZINES, BUTYROPHENONES, THIOXANTHINES, and **metoclopramide** decreases therapeutic effects of both drugs.

PHARMACOKINETICS Absorption: Rapidly absorbed GI tract, undergoes first-pass metabolism. **Peak:** 2–3 h. **Distribution:** 40–42% protein bound. Crosses placenta. **Metabolism:** Extensively metabolized. **Elimination:** Approximately 22% in urine, 60% in feces. **Half-Life:** 63–69 h.

CLINICAL IMPLICATIONS

Assessment & Drug Effects

- Lab tests: Monitor serum prolactin levels to assess response to each dosing level.
- Monitor for hypotension, especially when given with other drugs known to lower BP.

Patient & Family Education

- Discontinue this drug once physician advises that serum prolactin level has been maintained for 6 mo.

CAFFEINE ⓟ

(kaf-een')

Caffedrine, Dexitac, NoDoz, Quick Pep, S-250, Tirend, Vivarin

CAFFEINE AND SODIUM BENZOATE

CITRATED CAFFEINE

Cafcit

Classifications: RESPIRATORY AND CEREBRAL STIMULANT; XANTHINE
Therapeutic: RESPIRATORY AND CEREBRAL STIMULANT
Pregnancy Category: C

AVAILABILITY 100 mg, 150 mg, 200 mg tablets; 200 mg capsules; 10 mg/mL caffeine citrate oral solution; 10 mg/mL caffeine citrate injection

ACTION & *THERAPEUTIC EFFECT*
Chief action is thought to be related to inhibition of the enzyme phosphodiesterase, which results in higher concentrations of cyclic AMP. Releases epinephrine and norepinephrine from adrenal medulla, producing CNS stimulation. Small doses improve psychic and sensory awareness and reduce drowsiness and fatigue by stimulating cerebral cortex. Higher doses stimulate medullary, respiratory, vasomotor, and vagal centers. Produces smooth muscle relaxation by direct action on vascular musculature. Mild diuretic action may result from increase in renal blood flow and glomerular filtration rate and decrease in renal tubular reabsorption of sodium and water. *Effective in managing neonatal apnea, and as an adjuvant for pain control in headaches and following dural puncture. Relief of headache is perhaps due to mild cerebral vasoconstriction action and increased vascular tone. It acts as a bronchodilator in asthma.*

USES Orally as a mild CNS stimulant to aid in staying awake and restoring mental alertness, and as an adjunct in narcotic and nonnarcotic analgesia. Used parenterally as an emergency stimulant in acute circulatory failure, as a diuretic, and to relieve spinal puncture headache.
UNLABELED USES Topical treatment of atopic dermatitis; neonatal apnea.

CONTRAINDICATIONS Acute MI, symptomatic cardiac arrhythmias, palpitations; peptic ulcer; pulmonary disease; insomnia, panic attacks; pregnancy (category C). Safe use in children not established.
CAUTIOUS USE Diabetes mellitus; hiatal hernia; psychotic disorders; dementia; depressive disorders; hepatic disease; hypertension with heart disease.

ROUTE & DOSAGE

Mental Stimulant
Adult: **PO** 100–200 mg q3–4h prn

Circulatory Stimulant
Adult: **IM** 200–500 mg prn

Spinal Puncture Headaches
Adult: **IV** 500 mg over 1 h, may repeat times 1 dose

Neonatal Apnea
Neonate: **PO/IV** 20–30 mg/kg caffeine citrate as a loading dose, followed by a maintenance dose 5 mg/kg citrate 24 h later of once daily up to max 10–12 d

Common adverse effects in *italic*, life-threatening effects underlined; generic names in **bold**; classifications in SMALL CAPS; ♣ Canadian drug name; ⓟ Prototype drug

211

C

ADMINISTRATION

Oral

- Give sustained-release oral preparations not less than 6 h before bedtime.
- Ensure that timed-release form of drug is not chewed or crushed. It must be swallowed whole.

Intramuscular

- Give deep IM into a large muscle.

Intravenous

Note: IV route reserved for emergency situations only.

PREPARE: **Direct:** Give undiluted.
ADMINISTER: **Direct:** Emergency situations: IV push at a rate of 250 mg or fraction thereof over 1 min. With neonates use caffeine without sodium benzoate and check with physician regarding preferred rate.

ADVERSE EFFECTS (≥1%) **CV:** Tingling of face, flushing, palpitation, tachycardia, arrhythmia, angina, ventricular ectopic beats. **GI:** Nausea, vomiting; epigastric discomfort, gastric irritation (oral form), diarrhea, hematemesis, kernicterus (neonates). **CNS:** *Nervousness, insomnia,* restlessness, irritability, confusion, agitation, fasciculations, delirium, twitching, tremors, clonic convulsions. **Respiratory:** Tachypnea. **Special Senses:** Scintillating scotomas, tinnitus. **Urogenital:** Increased urination, diuresis.

DIAGNOSTIC TEST INTERFERENCE
Caffeine reportedly may interfere with diagnosis of pheochromocytoma or neuroblastoma by increasing urinary excretion of *catecholamines, VMA,* and *5-HIAA* and may cause false positive increases in *serum urate* (by *Bittner method*).

INTERACTIONS Drug: Increases effects of **cimetidine;** increases cardiovascular stimulating effects of BETA-ADRENERGIC AGONISTS; possibly increases **theophylline** toxicity.

PHARMACOKINETICS Absorption: Rapid. **Peak:** 15–45 min. **Distribution:** Widely throughout body; crosses blood-brain barrier and placenta. **Metabolism:** In liver. **Elimination:** In urine as metabolites; excreted in breast milk in small amounts. **Half-Life:** 3–5 h in adults, 36–144 h in neonates.

CLINICAL IMPLICATIONS

Assessment & Drug Effects

- Monitor vital signs closely as large doses may cause intensification rather than reversal of severe drug-induced depressions.
- Observe children closely following administration as they are more susceptible than adults to the CNS effects of caffeine.
- Lab tests: Monitor blood glucose and HbA_{1c} levels in diabetics.

Patient & Family Education

- Caffeine in large amounts may impair glucose tolerance in diabetics.
- Do not consume large amounts of caffeine as headache, dizziness, anxiety, irritability, nervousness, and muscle tension may result from excessive use, as well as from abrupt withdrawal of coffee (or oral caffeine). Withdrawal symptoms usually occur 12–18 h following last coffee intake.

CALCIPOTRIENE

(cal-ci′po-tri-een)
Dovonex
Classifications: VITAMIN D ANALOG
Therapeutic: VITAMIN D ANALOG
Prototype: Calcitriol
Pregnancy Category: C

AVAILABILITY 0.005% ointment and cream

ACTION & *THERAPEUTIC EFFECT*
Calcipotriene is a synthetic vitamin D₃ analog for the treatment of moderate plaque psoriasis. The scaly red patches of psoriasis are caused by abnormal growth and production of skin cells known as keratinocytes. *Calcipotriene controls psoriasis by inhibiting proliferation of psoiatic skin, reducing the number of polymorphonuclear leukocytes (PMNs) in the skin cells, and decreasing the number of epithelial cells.*

USES Treatment of moderate plaque psoriasis.

CONTRAINDICATIONS Hypersensitivity to calcipotriene, hypercalcemia or vitamin D toxicity; history of nephrolithiasis; pregnancy (category C), lactation.
CAUTIOUS USE Dermatoses other than psoriasis; patients >65 y. Safety and efficacy in children not established.

ROUTE & DOSAGE

Adult: **Topical** Apply a thin layer to affected area once or twice daily

ADMINISTRATION

Topical
- A thin layer should be applied to the affected skin and rubbed in gently and completely.
- Calcipotriene should not be applied to the face.
- Wash hands before and after application of medication.

ADVERSE EFFECTS (≥1%) **Skin:** Facial dermatitis, burning, stinging, erythema, folliculitis, mild transient itching.

INTERACTIONS No clinically significant interactions established.

PHARMACOKINETICS Absorption: 6% absorbed systemically. **Onset:** 1 wk. **Peak:** 8 wk. **Duration:** 4 wk. **Metabolism:** Recycled via liver. **Elimination:** In bile.

CLINICAL IMPLICATIONS

Assessment & Drug Effects
- Observe reductions in scaling, erythema, and lesion thickness indicating a positive therapeutic response.
- Significant reduction in psoriatic lesions usually occurs following 1 wk of treatment. Marked improvement is generally noted by the 8th wk of treatment.
- Lab tests: Monitor periodically serum calcium, phosphate, and calcitriol levels, during long-term therapy.

Patient & Family Education
- Treatment with calcipotriene may be indefinite, as reappearance of psoriatic lesions is common following discontinuation of the drug.
- Adverse effects may include burning and stinging with drug application; these are usually transient.
- Do not mix calcipotriene with any other topical medicine.
- Report appearance of facial dermatitis (erythema and scaling around mouth and nose).

CALCITONIN (SALMON)
Fortical, Miacalcin
Classifications: BISPHOSPHONATE; BONE METABOLISM REGULATOR
Therapeutic: BONE METABOLISM REGULATOR
Prototype: Etidronate
Pregnancy Category: C

Common adverse effects in *italic*, life-threatening effects underlined; generic names in **bold**; classifications in SMALL CAPS; ✚ Canadian drug name; ⊙ Prototype drug

213

AVAILABILITY 200 IU/mL injection; 200 IU/spray

ACTION & *THERAPEUTIC EFFECT*
Calcitonin salmon is a synthetic polypeptide. Calcitonin opposes the effects of parathyroid hormone on bone and kidneys, reduces serum calcium by binding to a specific receptor site on osteoclast cell membrane, and alters transmembrane passage of calcium and phosphorus. Promotes renal excretion of calcium and phosphorus. *Effective in osteoporosis due to inhibition of bone resorption. Effective in symptomatic hypercalcemia by rapidly lowering serum calcium.*

USES Symptomatic Paget's disease of bone (osteitis deformans), postmenopausal osteoporosis. Orphan drug approval (calcitonin human): short-term adjunctive treatment of severe hypercalcemic emergencies.
UNLABELED USES Diagnosis and management of medullary carcinoma of thyroid; treatment of osteogenesis imperfecta.

CONTRAINDICATIONS Hypersensitivity to fish proteins or to synthetic calcitonin; history of serious allergy; hypocalcemia; pregnancy (category C), lactation. Safe use in children not established.
CAUTIOUS USE Renal impairment; osteoporosis; pernicious anemia; Zollinger-Ellison syndrome.

ROUTE & DOSAGE

Paget's Disease
Adult: **SC/IM** 100 IU/d, may decrease to 50–100 IU/d or q.o.d.

Hypercalcemia
Adult: **SC/IM** 4 IU/kg q12h, may increase to 8 IU/kg q6h if needed

Postmenopausal Osteoporosis
Adult: **SC/IM** 100 IU/d **Intranasal** 1 spray (200 IU) daily, alternate nostrils

ADMINISTRATION

Allergy Test Dose
- An allergy skin test is usually done prior to initiation of therapy. The appearance of more than mild erythema or wheal 15 min after intracutaneous injection indicates that the drug should not be given.

Intranasal
- Activate the pump prior to first use; hold bottle upright and depress white side arms 6 times.
- The nasal spray is administered in one nostril daily; alternate nostrils.

Subcutaneous
- Calcitonin human is administered only by SC injection; calcitonin salmon may be administered by SC or IM injection.

Intramuscular
- Use IM route when the volume to be injected is >2 mL.
- Rotate injection sites.
- Store calcitonin (human) at 25° C (77° F) or less, protected from light, unless otherwise specified by manufacturer.
- Store calcitonin (salmon) in refrigerator, preferably at 2°–8° C (36°–46° F) unless otherwise directed.

ADVERSE EFFECTS (≥1%) **Body as a Whole:** Headache, eye pain, feverish sensation, hypersensitivity reactions, <u>anaphylaxis</u>. Reported for calcitonin human only: Urinary frequency, chills, chest pressure, weakness, paresthesias, tender palms and soles, dizziness, nasal congestion, shortness of breath. **GI:** *Transient nausea,* vomiting, anorexia, unusual taste sensation, abdominal pain, diarrhea. **Skin:** Inflammatory reactions at injection site, flushing of face or hands, pruritus of ear lobes, edema of feet, skin rashes. **Urogenital:** Nocturia, diuresis, abnormal urine sediment.

INTERACTIONS Drug: May decrease serum **lithium** levels.

PHARMACOKINETICS Onset: 15 min. **Peak:** 4 h. **Duration:** 8–24 h. **Distribution:** Does not cross placenta; distribution into breast milk unknown. **Metabolism:** In kidneys. **Elimination:** In urine. **Half-Life:** 1.25 h.

CLINICAL IMPLICATIONS

Assessment & Drug Effects

■ Have on hand epinephrine 1:1000, antihistamines, and oxygen in the event of a reaction. Also have readily available parenteral calcium, particularly during early therapy. Hypocalcemic tetany is a theoretical possibility.

■ Examine urine specimens periodically for sediment with long-term therapy.

■ Lab tests: Monitor for hypocalcemia (see Signs & Symptoms, Appendix F). Theoretically, calcitonin can lead to hypocalcemic tetany. Latent tetany may be demonstrated by Chvostek's or Trousseau's signs and by serum calcium values: 7–8 mg/dL (latent tetany); below 7 mg/dL (manifest tetany).

■ Examine nasal passages prior to treatment with the nasal spray and anytime nasal irritation occurs.

■ Nasal ulceration or heavy bleeding are indications for drug discontinuation.

Patient & Family Education

■ Use the SC route for self-administration.

■ Watch for redness, warmth, or swelling at injection site and re-

port to physician, as these may indicate an inflammatory reaction. The transient flushing that commonly occurs following injection of calcitonin, particularly during early therapy, may be minimized by administrating the drug at bedtime. Consult physician.

■ Maintain your drug regimen even though symptoms have been ameliorated to prevent early relapses.

■ Ensure that you feel comfortable using the nasal pump properly. Notify physician if significant nasal irritation occurs.

■ Consult physician before using OTC preparations. Some supervitamins, hematinics, and antacids contain calcium and vitamin D (vitamin may antagonize calcitonin effects).

CALCITRIOL ◐

(kal-si-trye'ole)
Calcijex, Rocaltrol
Classifications: VITAMIN D ANALOG
Therapeutic: VITAMIN D ANALOG
Pregnancy Category: C

AVAILABILITY 0.25 mcg, 0.5 mcg tablets; 1 mcg/mL oral solution; 1 mcg/mL, 2 mcg/mL injection

ACTION & *THERAPEUTIC EFFECT*

Synthetic form of an active metabolite of ergocalciferol (vitamin D_2). In the liver, cholecalciferol (vitamin D_3) and ergocalciferol (vitamin D_2) are enzymatically metabolized to calcifediol, an activated form of vitamin D_3. Calcifediol is biodegraded in the kidney to calcitriol, the most potent form of vitamin D_3. Patients with nonfunctioning kidneys are unable to synthesize sufficient calcitriol. *By promoting intestinal absorption and renal retention of calcium, calcitriol ele-*

Common adverse effects in *italic*, life-threatening effects underlined; generic names in **bold**; classifications in SMALL CAPS; ◆ Canadian drug name; ◐ Prototype drug

215

vates serum calcium levels, decreases elevated blood levels of phosphate and parathyroid hormone, and decreases subperiosteal bone resorption and mineralization defects.

USES Management of hypocalcemia in patients undergoing chronic renal dialysis and in patients with hypoparathyroidism or pseudohypoparathyroidism.

UNLABELED USES Selected patients with vitamin D–dependent rickets, familial hypophosphatemia (vitamin D–resistant rickets); management of hypocalcemia in premature infants.

CONTRAINDICATIONS Hypercalcemia or vitamin D toxicity; pregnancy (category C).

CAUTIOUS USE Hyperphosphatemia, renal failure; elderly; sarcoidosis; patients receiving digitalis glycosides.

ROUTE & DOSAGE

Hypocalcemia

Adult: **PO** 0.25 mcg/d, may be increased by 0.25 mcg/d q4–8wk for dialysis patients or q2–4wk for hypoparathyroid patients if necessary **IV** 0.5 mcg 3 times/wk at the end of dialysis, may need up to 3 mcg 3 times/wk
Child: **PO** On hemodialysis: 0.25–2 mcg/d. **IV** 0.01–0.05 mcg/kg 3 times/wk
Renal failure without dialysis: **PO** 0.014–0.041 mcg/kg/d

ADMINISTRATION

Oral

- Oral dose can be taken either with food or milk or on an empty stomach. Discuss with physician.
- When given for hypoparathyroidism, the dose is given in the morning.

- Capsules should be protected from heat, light, and moisture. Store in tightly closed container.

Intravenous

PREPARE: Direct: Give undiluted.
ADMINISTER: Direct: Give IV push over 30–60 s.

ADVERSE EFFECTS (≥1%) **Body as a Whole:** Muscle or bone pain. **CV:** Palpitation. **GI:** Anorexia, nausea, vomiting, dry mouth, thirst, constipation, abdominal cramps, metallic taste. **Metabolic:** Vitamin D intoxication, hypercalcemia, hypercalciuria, hyperphosphatemia. **CNS:** Headache, weakness. **Special Senses:** Blurred vision, photophobia. **Urogenital:** Increased urination.

INTERACTIONS Drug: THIAZIDE DIURETICS may cause hypercalcemia; calcifediol-induced hypercalcemia may precipitate digitalis arrhythmias in patients receiving DIGITALIS GLYCOSIDES.

PHARMACOKINETICS Absorption: Readily absorbed from GI tract. **Onset:** 2–6 h. **Peak:** 10–12 h. **Duration:** 3–5 d. **Metabolism:** In liver. **Elimination:** Mainly in feces. **Half-Life:** 3–6 h.

CLINICAL IMPLICATIONS

Assessment & Drug Effects

- Lab tests: Determine baseline and periodic levels of serum calcium, phosphorus, magnesium, alkaline phosphatase, creatinine; measure urinary calcium and phosphorus levels q24h.
- Effectiveness of therapy depends on an adequate daily intake of calcium and phosphate. The physician may prescribe a calcium supplement on an as-needed basis.
- Monitor for hypercalcemia (see Signs & Symptoms, Appendix F).

During dosage adjustment period, monitor serum calcium levels particularly twice weekly to avoid hypercalcemia.

- If hypercalcemia develops, withhold calcitriol and calcium supplements and notify physician. Drugs may be reinitiated when serum calcium returns to normal.

Patient & Family Education

- Discontinue the drug if experiencing any symptoms of hypercalcemia (see Appendix F) and contact physician.
- Do not use any other source of vitamin D during therapy, since calcitriol is the most potent form of vitamin D_3. This will avoid the possibility of hypercalcemia.
- Consult physician before taking an OTC medication. (Many products contain calcium, vitamin D, phosphates, or magnesium, which can increase adverse effects of calcitriol.)
- Maintain an adequate daily fluid intake unless you have kidney problems, in which case consult your physician about fluids.

CALCIUM CARBONATE

Apo-Cal ♣, BioCal, Calcite-500, Calsan ♣, Cal-Sup, Caltrate ♣, Chooz, Dicarbosil, Equilet, Mallamint, Mega-Cal, Nu-Cal, Os-Cal, Oystercal, Titralac, Tums

CALCIUM ACETATE

PhosLo

CALCIUM CITRATE

Citracal

CALCIUM PHOSPHATE TRIBASIC (TRICALCIUM PHOSPHATE)

Posture

CALCIUM LACTATE

Cal-Lac

Classifications: FLUID AND ELECTROLYTIC REPLACEMENT SOLUTION; ANTACID
Therapeutic: FLUID AND ELECTROLYTIC REPLACEMENT SOLUTION; ANTACID
Prototype: Calcium gluconate
Pregnancy Category: B for calcium acetate; other salts not rated

AVAILABILITY Calcium carbonate: 125 mg, 250 mg, 650 mg, 750 mg, 1.25 g, 1.5 g tablets; **Calcium acetate:** 667 mg tablets; **Calcium citrate:** 950 mg, 2376 mg tablets; **Calcium phosphate tribasic:** 1565.2 mg tablets

ACTION & *THERAPEUTIC EFFECT*
Calcium carbonate is a rapid-acting antacid with high neutralizing capacity and relatively prolonged duration of action. Decreases gastric acidity, thereby inhibiting proteolytic action of pepsin on gastric mucosa. All forms of calcium salts are used for calcium replacement therapy. *Effectively relieves symptoms of acid indigestion and useful as a calcium supplement.*

USES Relief of transient symptoms of hyperacidity as in acid indigestion, heartburn, peptic esophagitis, and hiatal hernia. Also used as calcium supplement when calcium intake may be inadequate and in treatment of mild calcium deficiency states. Control of hyperphosphatemia in chronic renal failure (calcium acetate).

UNLABELED USES For treatment of hyperphosphatemia in patients with chronic renal failure and to lower BP in selected patients with hypertension.

CONTRAINDICATIONS Hypercalcemia and hypercalciuria (e.g., hyper-

Common adverse effects in *italic*, life-threatening effects underlined; generic names in **bold**; classifications in SMALL CAPS; ♣ Canadian drug name; ⓟ Prototype drug

217

parathyroidism, vitamin D overdosage, decalcifying tumors, bone metastases), calcium loss due to immobilization, severe renal failure, renal calculi, GI hemorrhage or obstruction, dehydration, digitalis toxicity; hypochloremic alkalosis, ventricular fibrillation, cardiac disease, pregnancy (category B). **CAUTIOUS USE** Decreased bowel motility (e.g., with anticholinergics, antidiarrheals, antispasmodics), the older adult.

ROUTE & DOSAGE

All doses are in terms of *elemental calcium:* 1 g calcium carbonate = 400 mg (20 mEq, 40%) elemental calcium; 1 g calcium acetate = 250 mg (12.6 mEq, 25%) elemental calcium; 1 g calcium citrate = 210 mg (12 mEq, 21%) elemental calcium; 1 g tricalcium phosphate = 390 mg (19.3 mEq, 39%) elemental calcium; calcium lactate = 130 mg (6.5 mEq, 13%) elemental calcium

Supplement for Osteoporosis
Adult: **PO** 1–2 g b.i.d. or t.i.d.

Antacid
Adult: **PO** 0.5–2 g 4–6 times/d

Hyperphosphatemia
Adult: **PO** calcium acetate 2–4 tablets with each meal

Supplement for Mild Hypercalcemia
Child: **PO** 500 mg/kg/d in divided doses (lactate)

ADMINISTRATION

Oral

- When used as antacid, give 1 h after meals and at bedtime. When used as calcium supplement, give

1–1 $^1/_2$ h after meals, unless otherwise directed by physician.
- Chewable tablet should be chewed well before swallowing or allowed to dissolve completely in mouth, followed with water. Powder form may be mixed with water.
- Ensure that sustained-release form of drug is not chewed or crushed. It must be swallowed whole.

ADVERSE EFFECTS (≥1%) **GI:** *Constipation* or laxative effect, acid rebound, nausea, eructation, *flatulence,* vomiting, fecal concretions. **Metabolic:** Hypercalcemia with alkalosis, metastatic calcinosis, hypercalciuria, hypomagnesemia, hypophosphatemia (when phosphate intake is low). **CNS:** Mood and mental changes. **Urogenital:** Polyuria, renal calculi.

INTERACTIONS Drug: May enhance inotropic and toxic effects of **digoxin; magnesium** may compete for GI absorption; decreases absorption of TETRACYCLINES, QUINOLONES (**ciprofloxacin**).

PHARMACOKINETICS Absorption: Approximately $^1/_3$ of dose absorbed from small intestine. **Distribution:** Crosses placenta. **Elimination:** Primarily in feces; small amounts in urine, pancreatic juice, saliva, breast milk.

CLINICAL IMPLICATIONS

Assessment & Drug Effects

- Note number and consistency of stools. If constipation is a problem, physician may prescribe alternate or combination therapy with a magnesium antacid or advise patient to take a laxative or stool softener as necessary.
- Lab tests: Determine serum and urine calcium weekly in patients

receiving prolonged therapy and in patients with renal dysfunction.

- Record amelioration of symptoms of hypocalcemia (see Signs & Symptoms, Appendix F).
- Observe for S&S of hypercalcemia in patients receiving frequent or high doses, or who have impaired renal function (see Appendix F).

Patient & Family Education

- Do not continue this medication beyond 1–2 wk, since it may cause acid rebound, which generally occurs after repeated use for 1 or 2 wk and leads to chronic use. It is potentially dangerous to self-medicate. Do not take antacids longer than 2 wk without medical supervision.
- Avoid taking calcium carbonate with cereals or other foods high in oxalates. Oxalates combine with calcium carbonate to form insoluble, nonabsorbable compounds.
- Do not use calcium carbonate repeatedly with foods high in vitamin D (such as milk) or sodium bicarbonate, as it may cause milk-alkali syndrome: hypercalcemia, distaste for food, headache, confusion, nausea, vomiting, abdominal pain, metabolic alkalosis, hypercalciuria, polyuria, soft tissue calcification (calcinosis), hyperphosphatemia and renal insufficiency. Predisposing factors include renal dysfunction, dehydration, electrolyte imbalance, and hypertension.

CALCIUM CHLORIDE

Classifications: FLUID AND ELECTROLYTIC REPLACEMENT SOLUTION
Therapeutic: FLUID AND ELECTROLYTE REPLACEMENT
Prototype: Calcium gluconate
Pregnancy Category: C

AVAILABILITY 10% injection

ACTION & *THERAPEUTIC EFFECT*
Ionizes readily and provides excess chloride ions that promote acidosis and temporary (1–2 d) diuresis secondary to excretion of sodium. *Rapidly and effectively restores serum calcium levels in acute hypocalcemia of various origins and an effective cardiac stabilizer under conditions of hyperkalemia or resuscitation.*

USES Treatment of cardiac resuscitation when epinephrine fails to improve myocardial contractions; for treatment of acute hypocalcemia (as in tetany due to parathyroid deficiency, vitamin D deficiency, alkalosis, insect bites or stings, and during exchange transfusions), for treatment of hypermagnesemia, and for cardiac disturbances of hyperkalemia.

CONTRAINDICATIONS Ventricular fibrillation, hypercalcemia, digitalis toxicity, injection into myocardium or other tissue; pregnancy (category C).
CAUTIOUS USE Digitalized patients; sarcoidosis, renal insufficiency, history of renal stone formation; cardiac arrhythmias; dehydration; diarrhea; cor pulmonale, respiratory acidosis, respiratory failure; lactation.

ROUTE & DOSAGE

All doses are in terms of *elemental calcium*: 1 g calcium chloride = 272 mg (13.6 mEq) elemental calcium

Hypocalcemia

Adult: **IV** 0.5–1 g (7–14 mEq) at 1–3 d intervals as determined by patient response and serum calcium levels

Common adverse effects in *italic*, life-threatening effects underlined; generic names in **bold**; classifications in SMALL CAPS; ◆ Canadian drug name; ⊙ Prototype drug

219

C

Child: **IV** 2.7–5 mg/kg administered slowly
Neonate: **IV** <1 mEq/d

Hypocalcemic Tetany

Adult: **IV** 4.5–16 mEq prn
Child: **IV** 0.5–0.7 mEq/kg t.i.d.
or q.i.d.
Neonate: **IV** 2.4 mEq/kg/d in
divided doses

CPR

Adult: **IV** 2–4 mg/kg, may repeat
in 10 min
Child: **IV** 20 mg/kg, may repeat
in 10 min

ADMINISTRATION

Intravenous
IV administration to neonates, infants, and children: Verify correct
IV concentration and rate of infusion with physician.

PREPARE: **Direct:** May be given
undiluted or diluted (preferred)
with an equal volume of NS for
injection. Solution should be
warmed to body temperature before administration.
ADMINISTER: **Direct:** Give at 0.5–
1 mL/min or more slowly if irritation develops. Avoid rapid administration. Use a small-bore
needle and inject into a large
vein to minimize venous irritation and undesirable reactions
INCOMPATIBILITIES **Solution/ad-
ditive: Amphotericin B, chlo-
pheniramine, dobutamine,**
concentration-dependent incompatibility with other ELECTROLYTES.
**Y-site: Amphotericin B choles-
teryl complex, propofol, sodium bicarbonate**

ADVERSE EFFECTS (≥1%) **Body
as a Whole:** Tingling sensation.
With rapid IV, sensations of heat
waves (peripheral vasodilation),

fainting, **CV:** (With rapid infusion)
hypotension, bradycardia, cardiac
arrhythmias, cardiac arrest. **Skin:**
Pain and burning at IV site, severe
venous thrombosis, necrosis and
sloughing (with extravasation).

INTERACTIONS Drug: May enhance inotropic and toxic effects of
digoxin; antagonizes the effects of
verapamil and possibly other CAL-
CIUM CHANNEL BLOCKERS.

PHARMACOKINETICS Distribution:
Crosses placenta. **Elimination:** Primarily in feces; small amounts in
urine, pancreatic juice, saliva, and
breast milk.

CLINICAL IMPLICATIONS

Assessment & Drug Effects
■ Monitor ECG and BP and observe
patient closely during administration. IV injection may be accompanied by cutaneous burning
sensation and peripheral vasodilation, with moderate fall in BP.
■ Advise ambulatory patient to remain in bed for 15–30 min or
more depending on response following injection.
■ Observe digitalized patients closely
since an increase in serum calcium increases risk of digitalis
toxicity.
■ Lab tests: Determine serum pH,
calcium, and other electrolytes
frequently as guides to dosage
adjustments.

Patient & Family Education
■ Remain in bed for 15–30 min or
more following injection and depending on response.
■ Symptoms of mild hypercalcemia, such as loss of appetite, nausea, vomiting, or constipation
may occur. If hypercalcemia becomes severe, call health care
provider if feeling confused or
extremely excited.

- Do not use other calcium supplements or eat foods high in calcium, like milk, cheese, yogurt, eggs, meats, and some cereals, during therapy.

CALCIUM GLUCONATE ⓟ

(gloo'koe-nate)

Classifications: FLUID AND ELECTROLYTIC REPLACEMENT SOLUTION
Therapeutic: FLUID AND ELECTROLYTE REPLACEMENT
Pregnancy Category: B

AVAILABILITY 500 mg, 650 mg, 975 mg, 1 gm tablets; 10% injection

ACTION & *THERAPEUTIC EFFECT*
Calcium gluconate acts like digitalis on the heart, increasing cardiac muscle tone and force of systolic contractions (positive inotropic effect). *Rapidly and effectively restores serum calcium levels in acute hypocalcemia of various origins and effective as a cardiac stabilizer under conditions of hyperkalemia or resuscitation.*

USES Negative calcium balance (as in neonatal tetany, hypoparathyroidism, vitamin D deficiency, alkalosis). Also to overcome cardiac toxicity of hyperkalemia, for cardiopulmonary resuscitation, to prevent hypocalcemia during transfusion of citrated blood. Also as antidote for magnesium sulfate, for acute symptoms of lead colic, to decrease capillary permeability in sensitivity reactions, and to relieve muscle cramps from insect bites or stings. Oral calcium may be used to maintain normal calcium balance during pregnancy, lactation, and childhood growth and to prevent primary osteoporosis. Also in osteoporosis, osteomalacia,

chronic hypoparathyroidism, rickets, and as adjunct in treatment of myasthenia gravis and Eaton-Lambert syndrome.
UNLABELED USES To antagonize aminoglycoside-induced neuromuscular blockage, and as "calcium challenge" to diagnose Zollinger-Ellison syndrome and medullary thyroid carcinoma.

CONTRAINDICATIONS Ventricular fibrillation, metastatic bone disease, injection into myocardium; administration by SC or IM routes; renal calculi, hypercalcemia, predisposition to hypercalcemia (hyperparathyroidism, certain malignancies); digitalis toxicity.
CAUTIOUS USE Digitalized patients, renal or cardiac insufficiency, arrhythmias; dehydration; diarrhea; hyperphosphatemia; sarcoidosis, history of lithiasis, immobilized patients; pregnancy (category B).

ROUTE & DOSAGE

All doses are in terms of *elemental calcium*: 1 g calcium gluconate = 90 mg (4.5 mEq, 9.3%) elemental calcium

Supplement for Osteoporosis
Adult: **PO** 1–2 g b.i.d. to q.i.d. **IV** 7 mEq q1–3d
Child: **PO** 45–65 mg/kg/d in divided doses. **IV** 1–7 mEq q1–3d
Neonate: **PO** 50–130 mg/kg/d (max: 1 g) **IV** mEq q1–3d

Hypocalcemia
Adult: **IV** 2–15 g/d continuous or divided dose
Child: **IV** 200–500 mg/kg/d (max: 2–3 g/dose)
Neonate: **IV** 200–800 mg/kg/d (max: 1 g/dose)

Common adverse effects in *italic*, life-threatening effects underlined; generic names in **bold**; classifications in SMALL CAPS; ✚ Canadian drug name; ⓟ Prototype drug

221

Hypocalcemic Tetany

Adult: IV 1–3 g prn
Child: IV 100–200 mg/kg/dose, may repeat q6–8h
Neonate: IV 2.4 mEq/kg/d in divided doses

CPR

Adult: IV 2.3–3.7 mEq × 1

Hyperkalemia with Cardiac Toxicity

Adult: IV 2.25–14 mEq q 1–2 min

Exchange Transfusions with Citrated Blood

Adult: IV 500–1000 mg for each 500 mL of blood
Neonate: IV 98 mg for each 100 mL of blood

ADMINISTRATION

Oral

- Ensure that chewable tablets are chewed or crushed before being swallowed with a liquid.
- Give with meals to enhance absorption.

Intravenous

PREPARE: Direct: May be given undiluted **Intermittent/Continuous:** May be diluted in 1000 mL of NS.

ADMINISTER: Direct: Give direct IV at a rate of 0.5 mL or a fraction thereof over 1 min. Do not exceed 2 mL/min. **Intermittent/Continuous:** Give slowly, not to exceed 200 mg/min, through a small-bore needle into a large vein to avoid possibility of extravasation and resultant necrosis. With children, scalp veins should be avoided. Avoid rapid infusion. High concentrations of calcium suddenly reaching the heart can cause fatal cardiac arrest.

INCOMPATIBILITIES Solution/additive: Amphotericin B, cefamandole, dobutamine, methylprednisolone, metoclopramide, concentration-dependent incompatibility with other ELECTROLYTES. **Y-site: Amphotericin B cholesteryl complex, fluconazole, indomethacin.**

- Injection should be stopped if patient complains of any discomfort.
- Patient should be advised to remain in bed for 15–30 min or more following injection, depending on response.

ADVERSE EFFECTS (≥1%) **Body as a Whole:** Tingling sensation. With rapid IV, sensations of heat waves (peripheral vasodilation), fainting. **GI:** PO preparation: Constipation, increased gastric acid secretion. **CV:** (With rapid infusion) hypotension, bradycardia, cardiac arrhythmias, <u>cardiac arrest</u>, **Skin:** Pain and burning at IV site, severe venous thrombosis, necrosis and sloughing (with extravasation).

DIAGNOSTIC TEST INTERFERENCE IV calcium may cause false decreases in *serum and urine magnesium* (by *Titan yellow method*) and transient elevations of *plasma 11-OHCS* levels by *Glenn-Nelson technique.* Values usually return to control levels after 60 min; *urinary steroid values (17-OHCS)* may be decreased.

INTERACTIONS Drug: May enhance inotropic and toxic effects of **digoxin; magnesium** may compete for GI absorption; decreases absorption of TETRACYCLINES, QUINOLONES (**ciprofloxacin**); antagonizes the effects of **verapamil** and possibly other CALCIUM CHANNEL BLOCKERS (IV administration).

PHARMACOKINETICS Absorption: 30% from small intestine. **Onset:** Immediately after IV. **Distribution:** Crosses placenta. **Elimination:** Primarily in feces; small amounts in urine, pancreatic juice, saliva, and breast milk.

CLINICAL IMPLICATIONS

Assessment & Drug Effects

- Assess for cutaneous burning sensations and peripheral vasodilation, with moderate fall in BP, during direct IV injection.
- Monitor ECG during IV administration to detect evidence of hypercalcemia: decreased QT interval associated with inverted T wave.
- Observe IV site closely. Extravasation may result in tissue irritation and necrosis.
- Monitor for hypocalcemia and hypercalcemia (see Signs & Symptoms, Appendix F).
- Lab tests: Determine levels of calcium and phosphorus (tend to vary inversely) and magnesium frequently, during sustained therapy. Deficiencies in other ions, particularly magnesium, frequently coexist with calcium ion depletion.

Patient & Family Education

- Report S&S of hypercalcemia (see Appendix F) promptly to your care provider.
- Milk and milk products are the best sources of calcium (and phosphorus). Other good sources include dark green vegetables, soy beans, tofu, and canned fish with bones.
- Calcium absorption can be inhibited by zinc-rich foods: nuts, seeds, sprouts, legumes, soy products (tofu).
- Check with physician before self-medicating with a calcium supplement.

CALCIUM POLYCARBOPHIL

(pol-ee-kar'boe-fil)
FiberCon
Classifications: BULK LAXATIVE; ANTIDIARRHEAL
Therapeutic: BULK LAXATIVE; ANTIDIARRHEAL
Prototype: Psyllium hydrophilic mucilloid
Pregnancy Category: C

AVAILABILITY 500 mg, 625 mg, tablets

ACTION & THERAPEUTIC EFFECT
Hydrophilic, bulk-producing laxative that restores normal moisture level and bulk content of intestinal tract. In constipation, retains free water in intestinal lumen, thereby indirectly opposing dehydrating forces of the bowel; in diarrhea, when intestinal mucosa is incapable of absorbing fluid, drug absorbs fecal fluid to form a gel. In both conditions, peristalsis is encouraged and a well-formed stool is produced. *Relieves constipation or diarrhea associated with bowel disorders and acute nonspecific diarrhea.*

USES Constipation or diarrhea associated with diverticulitis or irritable bowel syndrome; acute nonspecific diarrhea.

CONTRAINDICATIONS GI obstruction; pregnancy (category C); children <6 y.
CAUTIOUS USE Lactation.

ROUTE & DOSAGE

Constipation or Diarrhea

Adult: **PO** 1 g q.i.d. as needed (max: 6 g/24 h)
Child: **PO** 6–12 y, 500 mg 1–3 times/d (max: 3 g/24 h); <6 y, 500 mg 1–2 times/d (max: 1.5 g/24 h)

Common adverse effects in *italic*, life-threatening effects <u>underlined</u>; generic names in **bold**; classifications in SMALL CAPS; ♣ Canadian drug name; ❂ Prototype drug

ADMINISTRATION

Oral

- Administer with at least 180–240 mL (6–8 oz) water or other fluid of patient's choice when used as a laxative and with at least 60–90 mL (2–3 oz) of fluid when used as an antidiarrheal. Chewed tablets should not be swallowed dry.
- If diarrhea is severe, dose can be repeated every half hour up to maximum daily dose.

ADVERSE EFFECTS (≥1%) **GI:** *Flatulence,* abdominal fullness, <u>intestinal obstruction</u>; laxative dependence (long-term use).

PHARMACOKINETICS Absorption: Not absorbed from the intestine. Bowel movement usually occurs within 12–72 h. **Elimination:** In feces.

CLINICAL IMPLICATIONS

Assessment & Drug Effects

- Evaluate effectiveness of medication. If it is ineffective as an antidiarrheal, report to physician.
- Report rectal bleeding, very dark stools, or abdominal pain promptly.

Patient & Family Education

- You will likely have a bowel movement within 12–72 h.
- This is an OTC product. Take this drug exactly as ordered. Do not increase the dose if response is inadequate. Consult physician. Do not use other laxatives while you are taking calcium polycarbophil.

CALFACTANT

(cal-fac'tant)

Infasurf

Classifications: LUNG SURFACTANT

Therapeutic: LUNG SURFACTANT
Prototype: Beractant
Pregnancy Category: Not applicable

AVAILABILITY 35 mg/mL suspension

ACTION & *THERAPEUTIC EFFECT*

Pulmonary surfactant. Lowers the surface tension on alveolar surfaces during respiration and stabilizes the alveoli against collapse at resting pressure. Deficiency of surfactant causes respiratory disease syndrome (RDS) in premature infants. *Effectively relieves and prevents RDS in neonates.*

USES Prevention and treatment of RDS in infants at high risk for RDS.

CONTRAINDICATIONS Bovine protein hypersensitivity; nosocomial infections.

CAUTIOUS USE Lactation.

ROUTE & DOSAGE

Prevention & Treatment of RDS

Infant: **Intratracheal** 3 mL/kg of birth weight administered through an endotracheal tube q12h times 3 doses

ADMINISTRATION

Intratracheal

- Swirl vial to disperse suspension; do not dilute and DO NOT SHAKE. Withdraw with 20-gauge or larger needle. Avoid excess foaming. Instill into the endotracheal tube, preferably within 30 min of birth.
- Stop administration of calfactant if reflux into endotracheal tube occurs as indicated by cyanosis, bradycardia, or other signs of airway obstruction.

ADVERSE EFFECTS (≥1%) **CV:** *Bradycardia.* **Respiratory:** *Cyanosis, airway obstruction, reflux of surfactant* into endotracheal tube.

INTERACTIONS Drug: No clinically significant interactions established.

PHARMACOKINETICS Absorption: Absorbs rapidly to air; liquid interface of lung surface.

CLINICAL IMPLICATIONS

Assessment & Drug Effects
- Monitor closely during and after administration; adjustments in oxygen therapy and ventilator pressures are usually needed.

Patient & Family Education
- This drug will help baby to breathe properly and support normal respiratory function.

CANDESARTAN CILEXETIL

(can-de-sar'tan ci-lex'e-til)
Atacand
Classifications: ANGIOTENSIN II RECEPTOR ANTAGONIST; ANTIHYPERTENSIVE AGENT
Therapeutic: ANTIHYPERTENSIVE AGENT; ANGIOTENSIN II RECEPTOR (ACE) INHIBITOR
Prototype: Losartan
Pregnancy Category: C first trimester; D second and third trimester

AVAILABILITY 4 mg, 8 mg, 16 mg, 32 mg tablets

ACTION & *THERAPEUTIC EFFECT*
Angiotensin II receptor (type AT_1) antagonist. Angiotensin II is a potent vasoconstrictor and primary vasoactive hormone of the renin–angiotensin–aldosterone system. Candesartan selectively blocks binding of angiotensin II to the AT_1 receptors found in many tissues (e.g., vascular smooth muscle, adrenal glands). *Results in blocking the vasoconstricting and aldosterone-secreting effects of angiotensin II, resulting in an antihypertensive effect. Effectively lowers BP from hypertensive to normotensive range.*

USES Hypertension, heart failure in conjunction with ACE inhibitor.

CONTRAINDICATIONS Known sensitivity to candesartan or any other angiotensin II (AT_1) receptor antagonist (e.g., losartan, valsartan); primary hyperaldosteronism; bilateral renal artery stenosis; pregnancy (category C, first trimester; category D, second and third trimesters); lactation. Safety and effectiveness in children not established.

CAUTIOUS USE Concurrent administration with high-dose diuretics, potassium-sparing diuretics, or potassium salt substitutes; unilateral renal artery stenosis; aortic or mitral valve stenosis; hypertrophic cardiomyopathy; CHF; diabetes; lactation; moderate heptic or renal impairment, significant renal failure.

ROUTE & DOSAGE

Hypertension
Adult: **PO** Start at 16 mg q.d. (range 8–32 mg divided once or twice daily)

Heart Failure
Adult: **PO** Start at 4 mcg once daily, double the dose at 2 wk intervals as tolerated by the patient until a dose of 32 mg is reached

Hepatic Impairment
For patients with moderate hepatic impairment, initiate therapy at lower dose.

Common adverse effects in *italic*, life-threatening effects underlined; generic names in **bold**; classifications in SMALL CAPS; ◆ Canadian drug name; ◎ Prototype drug

225

ADMINISTRATION

Oral

- Volume depletion should be corrected prior to initiation of therapy to prevent hypotension.
- Dose is individualized and may be given once or twice daily. The daily dose may be titrated up to 32 mg; larger doses are not likely to provide additional benefit.

ADVERSE EFFECTS (≥1%) **Body as a Whole:** Fatigue, peripheral edema, back pain, arthralgia. **CV:** Chest pain. **GI:** Nausea, abdominal pain, diarrhea, vomiting. **CNS:** Headache, dizziness. **Respiratory:** Cough, sinusitis, upper respiratory infection, pharyngitis, rhinitis. **Urogenital:** Albuminuria.

INTERACTIONS Drug: Use with **lithium** may increase risk of lithium toxicity.

PHARMACOKINETICS Absorption: Rapidly from GI tract; activated by ester hydrolysis; 15% reaches systemic circulation. **Peak:** Serum concentration, 3–4 h; therapeutic effect, 2–4 wk. **Duration:** 24 h. **Distribution:** >99% protein bound; crosses placenta; distributed into breast milk. **Metabolism:** Minimally in liver. **Elimination:** Primarily unchanged in bile (67%) and urine (33%). **Half-Life:** 9 h.

CLINICAL IMPLICATIONS

Assessment & Drug Effects

- Monitor BP as therapeutic effectiveness is indicated by decreases in systolic and diastolic BP within 2 wk with maximal effect at 4–6 wk.
- Monitor for transient hypotension in volume/salt-depleted patients; if hypotension occurs, place in supine position and notify physician.

- Monitor BP periodically; trough readings, just prior to the next scheduled dose, should be made when possible.
- Lab tests: Periodically monitor BUN and creatinine, serum potassium, liver enzymes, and CBC with differential.

Patient & Family Education

- Inform your physician immediately if you become pregnant.
- You may not notice maximum pressure-lowering effect for 6 wk.
- Report episodes of dizziness especially when making position changes.

CAPECITABINE

(cap-e-si′ta-been)
Xeloda
Classifications: ANTINEOPLASTIC; ANTIMETABOLITE, PYRIMIDINE
Therapeutic: ANTINEOPLASTIC; ANTIMETABOLITE
Prototype: Fluorouracil (5-FU)
Pregnancy Category: D

AVAILABILITY 150 mg, 500 mg tablets

ACTION & *THERAPEUTIC EFFECT*
Pyrimidine antagonist and cell cycle-specific antimetabolite. Prodrug of 5-FU. Blocks actions of enzymes essential to normal DNA and RNA synthesis. May become incorporated into RNA molecules of tumor cells, thereby interfering with RNA and protein synthesis. *Reduces or stabilizes tumor size in metastatic breast cancer.*

USES Metastatic breast cancer refractory to other treatments, colorectal cancer, single-agent adjuvant therapy for colon cancer after surgery.

CONTRAINDICATIONS Hypersensitivity to capecitabine, doxifluridine, 5-FU; myelosuppression; dihydropyrimidine dehydrogenase (DPD) deficiency; females of childbearing age; active infection; jaundice; severe renal failure or impairment; pregnancy (category D); lactation, children <18 y.

CAUTIOUS USE Mild to moderate renal or hepatic dysfunction; bacterial or viral infection; coronary artery disease, angina, cardiac arrhythmias; history of varicella zoster or other herpes infections; older adults.

ROUTE & DOSAGE

Breast Cancer, Colorectal Cancer
Adult: PO 2500 mg/m²/d in 2 divided doses times 2 wk, then 1 wk off. Repeat
Renal Impairment
Cl_{cr} 30–50 mL/min: reduce dose by 25%; <30 mL/min: do not use

ADMINISTRATION

Oral

- Morning and evening doses (about 12 h apart) should be given within 30 min of the end of a meal. Water is the preferred liquid for taking this drug.

ADVERSE EFFECTS (≥1%) **Body as a Whole:** *Fatigue,* pyrexia, pain, myalgia. **CV:** Edema. **GI:** *Severe diarrhea, nausea, vomiting, stomatitis,* abdominal pain, constipation, dyspepsia, *anorexia.* **Hematologic:** Neutropenia, thrombocytopenia, anemia, lymphopenia. **Metabolic:** Dehydration, hyperbilirubinemia. **CNS:** Paresthesias, headache, dizziness, insomnia. **Skin:** Hand-and-foot syndrome, dermatitis, nail disorder. **Special Senses:** Eye irritation.

INTERACTIONS Drug: Leucovorin increases concentration and toxicity of **5-FU,** altered coagulation and/or bleeding reported with **warfarin. Food:** Food decreases extent of absorption.

PHARMACOKINETICS Absorption: Absorption significantly reduced by food. **Peak:** 1.5–2 h. **Distribution:** Approx 35% protein bound. **Metabolism:** Extensively metabolized to 5-FU. **Elimination:** In urine. **Half-Life:** 45 min.

CLINICAL IMPLICATIONS

Assessment & Drug Effects

- Lab tests: Monitor periodically CBC with differential and liver functions including bilirubin, transaminases, alkaline phosphatase.
- Monitor carefully for S&S of grade 2 or greater toxicity: diarrhea >4 BMs/day or at night; vomiting >1 time/24 h; significant loss of appetite or anorexia; stomatitis; hand-and-foot syndrome (pain, swelling, erythema, desquamation, blistering); temperature = 100.5° F; and S&S of infection.
- Withhold drug and immediately report S&S of grade 2 or greater toxicity.
- Monitor for dehydration and replace fluids as needed.
- Monitor carefully patients with coronary artery disease for S&S of cardiotoxicity (e.g., increasing angina).

Patient & Family Education

- Report immediately significant nausea, loss of appetite, diarrhea, soreness of tongue, fever of 100.5° F or more, or signs of infection. Review patient drug package insert carefully for more detail.
- Inform physician immediately if you become pregnant.

Common adverse effects in *italic,* life-threatening effects underlined; generic names in **bold**; classifications in SMALL CAPS; ♣ Canadian drug name; ⊕ Prototype drug

227

CAPREOMYCIN SULFATE

(kap-ree-oh-mye'sin)
Capastat Sulfate
Classifications: ANTIBIOTIC; ANTI-TUBERCULOSIS AGENT
Therapeutic: ANTITUBERCULOSIS
Prototype: Isoniazid
Pregnancy Category: C

AVAILABILITY 1 g powder for injection

ACTION & THERAPEUTIC EFFECT

Polypeptide antibiotic. Action mechanism not clear, but it is bacteriostatic. *Bacteriostatic against human strains of* Mycobacterium tuberculosis *and other species of* Mycobacterium. *Effective second-line antimycobacterial in conjunction with other antitubercular drugs.*

USES Only in conjunction with other appropriate antitubercular drugs in treatment of pulmonary tuberculosis when bactericidal agents, e.g., isoniazid and rifampin, cannot be tolerated or when causative organism has become resistant.

CONTRAINDICATIONS Pregnancy (category C), in lactation. Safe use in infants and children not established.
CAUTIOUS USE Renal insufficiency (extreme caution); acoustic nerve impairment; history of allergies (especially to drugs); preexisting liver disease; myasthenia gravis; parkinsonism.

ROUTE & DOSAGE

Tuberculosis

Adult: **IM/IV** 1 g/d (not to exceed 20 mg/kg/d) for 60–120 d, then 1 g 2–3 times/wk. See prescribing information for dose adjustments for renal insufficiency.

ADMINISTRATION

Intramuscular
- Reconstitute by adding 2 mL of NS injection or sterile water for injection to each 1 g vial. Allow 2–3 min for drug to dissolve completely.
- Make IM injections deep into large muscle mass. Superficial injections are more painful and are associated with sterile abscess. Rotate injection sites.
- Solution may become pale straw color and darken with time, but this does not indicate loss of potency.
- After reconstitution, solution may be stored 48 h at room temperature and up to 14 d under refrigeration unless otherwise directed.

ADVERSE EFFECTS (≥1%) **Skin:** Urticaria, maculopapular rash, photosensitivity. **Hematologic:** Leukocytosis, leukopenia, *eosinophilia.* **CNS:** Neuromuscular blockage (large doses: skeletal muscle weakness, respiratory depression or arrest). **Urogenital:** Nephrotoxicity (long-term therapy), tubular necrosis. **Special Senses:** *Ototoxicity,* eighth nerve (auditory and vestibular) damage. **Metabolic:** Hypokalemia, and other electrolyte imbalances. **Other:** Impaired hepatic function (decreased BSP excretion); IM site reactions: pain, induration, excessive bleeding, sterile abscesses.

DIAGNOSTIC TEST INTERFERENCE
BSP and *PSP* excretion tests may be decreased.

INTERACTIONS Drug: Increased risk of nephrotoxicity and ototoxicity with AMINOGLYCOSIDES, **amphotericin B, colistin, polymyxin B, cisplatin, vancomycin.**

Common adverse effects in *italic*, life-threatening effects <u>underlined</u>; generic names in **bold**; classifications in SMALL CAPS; ♣ Canadian drug name; ⊕ Prototype drug

PHARMACOKINETICS Peak: 1–2 h. **Distribution:** Does not cross blood–brain barrier; crosses placenta. **Elimination:** 52% in urine unchanged in 12 h; small amount in bile. **Half-Life:** 4–6 h.

CLINICAL IMPLICATIONS

Assessment & Drug Effects

- Observe injection sites for signs of excessive bleeding and inflammation.
- Lab tests: Perform the following as guidelines for therapy before drug is started and at regular intervals during therapy: appropriate bacterial sensitivity tests; CBC; SMA-12 screening weekly; weekly renal function studies (BUN, NPN, creatinine clearance, sediment); liver function tests (periodically); serum potassium levels (monthly).
- Reduce dosage of capreomycin in patients with impaired renal function, as it is cumulative. Follow renal function tests closely.
- Monitor I&O rates and pattern: Report immediately any change in output or I&O ratio, any unusual appearance of urine, or elevation of BUN above 30 mg/dL. (Normal BUN: 10–20 mg/dL.)
- Evaluate hearing and balance by audiometric measurements (twice weekly or weekly) and tests of vestibular function (periodically).

Patient & Family Education

- Report any change in hearing or disturbance of balance. These effects are sometimes reversible if drug is withdrawn promptly when first symptoms appear.
- Ensure that you know about adverse reactions and what to do about them. Report immediately the appearance of any unusual symptom, regardless of how vague it may seem.

CAPSAICIN

(cap-say'i-sin)

Axsain, Capsaicin, Capsin, Capsacin-P, Dolorac, Zostrix, Zostrix-HP

Classifications: TOPICAL ANALGESIC

Therapeutic: TOPICAL ANALGESIC

AVAILABILITY 0.025%, 0.075% lotion; 0.025%, 0.075%, 0.25% cream; 0.025%, 0.05% gel

ACTION & *THERAPEUTIC EFFECT*
Capsaicin is an alkaloid derived from plants and used as a topical analgesic. Capsaicin depletes and prevents reaccumulation of Substance P, the primary chemical mediator of pain impulses from the periphery to the CNS. *Renders skin and joints insensitive to pain; therefore, it serves as an effective peripheral analgesic.*

USES Temporary relief of pain from arthritis, neuralgias, diabetic neuropathy, and herpes zoster.
UNLABELED USES Phantom limb pain, psoriasis, intractable pruritus.

CONTRAINDICATIONS Hypersensitivity to capsaicin or any ingredient in the cream.
CAUTIOUS USE Patients on ACE inhibitors. Safety and efficacy in children <2 y have not been established.

ROUTE & DOSAGE

Analgesia

Adult/Child >2 y: **Topical** Apply to affected area not more than 3–4 times/d

ADMINISTRATION

Topical

- Apply to affected areas only and avoid contact with eyes or broken or irritated skin.

Common adverse effects in *italic*, life-threatening effects underlined; generic names in **bold**; classifications in SMALL CAPS; ♣ Canadian drug name; ● Prototype drug

229

- If applied with bare hand, wash immediately following application. An applicator or gloved hand may be used to apply cream.
- Avoid tight bandages over areas of application of the cream.

ADVERSE EFFECTS (≥1%) **CNS:** Concentration >1%: neurotoxicity, hyperalgesia. **Skin:** *Burning, stinging, redness,* itching. **Other:** Cough.

INTERACTIONS Drug: May increase incidence of cough with ACE INHIBITORS.

PHARMACOKINETICS Onset: Postherpetic neuralgia: 2–6 wk.

CLINICAL IMPLICATIONS

Assessment & Drug Effects
- Monitor for significant pain relief, which may require 4–6 wk of application three or four times daily.
- Monitor for and report signs of skin breakdown as these generally indicate need for drug discontinuation.

Patient & Family Education
- Report local discomfort at site of application if discomfort is distressing or persists beyond the first 3–4 d of use.
- Use caution in handling contact lenses following application of cream. Wash hands thoroughly before touching lenses.
- Notify physician if symptoms do not improve or condition worsens within 14–28 d.
- Apply frequently three or four times daily to maximize therapeutic effectiveness.

CAPTOPRIL

(kap'toe-pril)
Capoten
Classifications: ANGIOTENSIN-CONVERTING ENZYME (ACE) INHIBITOR; ANTIHYPERTENSIVE AGENT

Therapeutic: ANTIHYPERTENSIVE AGENT; ACE INHIBITOR
Prototype: Enalapril
Pregnancy Category: C first trimester; D second and third trimester

AVAILABILITY 12.5 mg, 25 mg, 50 mg, 100 mg tablets

ACTION & THERAPEUTIC EFFECT
Lowers blood pressure by specific inhibition of the angiotensin-converting enzyme (ACE). This interrupts conversion sequences initiated by renin that lead to formation of angiotensin II, a potent vasoconstrictor. ACE inhibition alters hemodynamics without compensatory reflex tachycardia or changes in cardiac output (except in patients with CHF). Peripheral vascular resistance is lowered by vasodilation. Inhibition of ACE also leads to decreased circulating aldosterone. In heart failure, captopril administration is followed by a fall in CVP and pulmonary wedge pressure; hypotensive action appears to be unrelated to plasma renin levels. *Effective in stepped protocol management of hypertension to convert to normotensive range, and in congestive heart failure with resulting decreases in dyspnea and improved exercise tolerance.*

USES Hypertension; CHF (with digitalis and diuretics), diabetic nephropathy, left ventricular dysfunction post MI.
UNLABELED USES Idiopathic edema.

CONTRAINDICATIONS Angioedema, hypersensitivity to captopril or ACE inhibitors; hypotension; pregnancy (catetory C first trimester and category D second and third trimester), lactation.
CAUTIOUS USE Impaired renal function, patient with solitary kid-

ney; collagen-vascular diseases (scleroderma, SLE); patients receiving IMMUNOSUPPRESSANTS or other drugs that cause leukopenia or agranulocytosis; autoimmune disease, bone marrow suppression, coronary or cerebrovascular disease; cardiomyopathy, aortic stenosis; severe salt/volume depletion; heart failure, renal artery stenosis, renal disease, renal failure, renal impairment; hyperkalemia, elderly.

ROUTE & DOSAGE

Hypertension

Adult: **PO** 6.25–25 mg t.i.d., may increase to 50 mg t.i.d. (max: 450 mg/d)
Child: **PO** 0.3–12.5 mg/kg q12–24h, may titrate to max of 6 mg/kg/d in 2–4 divided doses
Infant: **PO** 0.15–0.3 mg/kg, may titrate up to 6 mg/kg/d in 1–4 divided doses
Neonate: **PO** 0.05–0.1 mg/kg q8–24 h, may titrate up to 0.5 mg/kg q6–24 h
Premature infant: **PO** 0.01 mg/kg q8–12h

Congestive Heart Failure

Adult: **PO** 6.25–12.5 mg t.i.d., may increase to 100 mg t.i.d. (max: 450 mg/d)

Renal Insufficiency

Cl_{cr} between 10–50 mL/min: 75% of dose; Cl_{cr} <10 mL/min: 50% of dose

ADMINISTRATION

Oral

- Give captopril 1 h before meals. Food reduces absorption by 30–40%.
- Store in light-resistant containers at no more than 30° C (86° F) unless otherwise directed.

ADVERSE EFFECTS (≥1%) **Body as a Whole:** Hypersensitivity reactions, serum sickness-like reaction, arthralgia, skin eruptions. **CV:** Slight increase in heart rate, first dose hypotension, dizziness, fainting. **GI:** Altered taste sensation (loss of taste perception, persistent salt or metallic taste); weight loss, intestinal angioedema. **Hematologic:** Hyperkalemia, neutropenia, <u>agranulocytosis</u> (rare). **Respiratory:** *Cough.* **Skin:** *Maculopapular rash,* urticaria, pruritus, <u>angioedema</u>, photosensitivity. **Urogenital:** Azotemia, impaired renal function, nephrotic syndrome, membranous glomerulonephritis. **Other:** Positive antinuclear antibody (ANA) titers.

DIAGNOSTIC TEST INTERFERENCE

Elevated ***urine protein levels*** may persist even after captopril has been discontinued. Possibility of transient elevations of ***BUN*** and ***serum creatinine,*** slight increase in ***serum potassium,*** and ***serum prolactin,*** increases in ***liver enzymes,*** and false-positive ***urine acetone*** (using ***sodium nitroprusside reagent***). Captopril may decrease ***fasting blood sugar*** in the nondiabetic and cause hypoglycemia in the diabetic patient controlled with antidiabetic drug therapy.

INTERACTIONS Drug:

NITRATES, DIURETICS, and ANTIHYPERTENSIVES enhance hypotensive effects. **Aspirin** and other NSAIDS may antagonize hypotensive effects. POTASSIUM-SPARING DIURETICS (**spironolactone, amiloride**) increase **potassium** levels. **Probenecid** decreases elimination and increases effects. **Food:** Food decreases absorption; take 30–60 min before meals.

PHARMACOKINETICS Absorption:

60–75% absorbed; food may de-

Common adverse effects in *italic*, life-threatening effects <u>underlined</u>; generic names in **bold**; classifications in SMALL CAPS; ♣ Canadian drug name; ⊙ Prototype drug

231

crease absorption 25–40%. **Onset:** 15 min. **Peak:** 1–2 h. **Duration:** 6–12 h. **Distribution:** To all tissues except CNS; crosses placenta. **Metabolism:** Some liver metabolism. **Elimination:** Primarily in urine; excreted in breast milk.

CLINICAL IMPLICATIONS

Assessment & Drug Effects

- Monitor BP closely following the first dose. A sudden exaggerated hypotensive response may occur within 1–3 h of first dose, especially in those with high BP or on a diuretic and restricted salt intake.
- Advise bed rest and BP monitoring for the first 3 h after the initial dose.
- Monitor therapeutic effectiveness. At least 2 wk of therapy may be required before full therapeutic effects are achieved.
- Lab tests: Establish baseline urinary protein levels before initiation of therapy and check at monthly intervals for the first 8 mo of treatment and then periodically thereafter. Perform WBC and differential counts before therapy is begun and at approximately 2-wk intervals for the first 3 mo of therapy and then periodically thereafter.

Patient & Family Education

- Report to physician without delay the onset of unexplained fever, unusual fatigue, sore mouth or throat, easy bruising or bleeding (pathognomonic of agranulocytosis).
- Mild skin eruptions are most likely to appear during the first 4 wk of therapy and may be accompanied by fever and eosinophilia.
- Consult physician promptly if vomiting or diarrhea occur.
- Report darkening or crumbling of nailbeds (reversible with dosage reduction).

- Taste impairment occurs in 5–10% of patients and generally reverses in 2–3 mo even with continued therapy.
- Use OTC medications only with approval of the physician. Inform surgeon or dentist that captopril is being taken. Alert diabetic patient that captopril may produce hypoglycemia. Monitor blood glucose and HbA_{1c} closely during first few weeks of therapy.

CARBACHOL INTRAOCULAR

(kar′ba-kole)
Miostat
Pregnancy Category: C
See Appendix A-1.

CARBAMAZEPINE ℗

(kar-ba-maz′e-peen)
Apo-Carbamazepine ♦, Carbatrol, Epitol, Equetro, Mazepine ♦, PMS-Carbamazepine ♦, Tegretol, Tegretol XR, Teril
Classifications: ANTICONVULSANT, TRICYCLIC
Therapeutic: ANTICONVULSANT
Pregnancy Category: D

AVAILABILITY 100 mg chewable tablets; 200 mg tablets; 100 mg, 200 mg, 400 mg sustained-release tablets; 100 mg, 200 mg, 300 mg sustained-release capsules; 100 mg/ 5 mL suspension

ACTION & *THERAPEUTIC EFFECT*
Structurally related to tricyclic antidepressants (TCAs) but lacks antidepressant properties. Anticonvulsant action appears to inhibit sustained repetitive impulses and reduces post-tetanic synaptic transmission in the spinal cord. It limits

the spread of seizure activity. Provides relief in trigeminal neuralgia by reducing synaptic transmission within trigeminal nucleus. Also has sedative, anticholinergic, antidepressant, and muscle relaxant (by inhibition of neuromuscular transmission) effects and slight analgesic actions. *Effective anticonvulsant for a range of seizure disorders and as an adjuvant reduces depressive signs and symptoms and stabilizes mood. It is effective for pain and other symptoms associated with neurologic disorders.*

USES Alone or with other anticonvulsants in treatment of grand mal and psychomotor or temporal lobe epilepsy and mixed seizures in patients who have not responded satisfactorily to other agents. Also used for symptomatic treatment of trigeminal (tic douloureux) and glossopharyngeal neuralgias and for pain and paroxysmal symptoms associated with multiple sclerosis and other neurologic disorders.

UNLABELED USES Certain psychiatric disorders including prophylaxis and treatment of manic-depressive illness, treatment of schizoaffective illness, resistant schizophrenia, dyscontrol syndrome; for management of alcohol withdrawal, rage outbursts, and for antidiuretic effect in diabetes insipidus.

CONTRAINDICATIONS Hypersensitivity to carbamazepine and to TCAs or MAOI therapy; history of myelosuppression or hematologic reaction to other drugs; increased IOP; SLE; cardiac, hepatic, or renal disease; coronary artery disease; hypertension; pregnancy (category D); children <6 y.

CAUTIOUS USE The older adult; history of cardiac disease, alcoholism; hepatic disease; cardiac arrhythmias.

ROUTE & DOSAGE

Epilepsy

Adult: **PO** 200 mg b.i.d., gradually increased to 800–1200 mg/d in 3–4 divided doses. Tegretol XR dosed b.i.d.
Child: **PO** <6 y: 10–20 mg/kg/d, may gradually increase weekly, recommended max 35 mg/kg/d in 3–4 divided doses; 6–12 y: 100 mg b.i.d., gradually increased to 400–800 mg/d in 3–4 divided doses (max: 1 g/d); <6 y: 20–30 mg/kg/d in 3–4 divided doses

Trigeminal Neuralgia

Adult: **PO** 100 mg b.i.d., gradually increased by 100 mg increments q12h until relief; usual dose 200–800 mg/d in 3–4 divided doses (max: 1.2 g/d). Tegretol XR dosed b.i.d.

ADMINISTRATION

Oral

- Do not administer within 14 d of patient receiving a MAO inhibitor.
- Give with a meal to increase absorption.
- Ensure that chewable tablets are chewed or crushed before being swallowed with a liquid.
- Ensure that sustained-release form of drug is not chewed or crushed. It must be swallowed whole.
- Do not administer carbamazepine suspension simultaneously with other liquid medications: a precipitate may form in the stomach.

ADVERSE EFFECTS (≥1%) **Body as a Whole:** Myalgia, arthralgia, leg cramps, carbamazepine-induced SLE. **CV:** Edema, syncope, arrhythmias, heart block. **GI:** Nausea, vomiting, anorexia, abdominal pain, di-

Common adverse effects in *italic*, life-threatening effects underlined; generic names in **bold**; classifications in SMALL CAPS; ♣ Canadian drug name; ⓟ Prototype drug

233

arrhea, constipation, dry mouth and pharynx, abnormal liver function tests, hepatitis, cholestatic and hepatocellular jaundice, pancreatitis. **Endocrine:** Hypothyroidism, SIADH. **Hematologic:** <u>Aplastic anemia</u>, *leukopenia* (transient), leukocytosis, <u>agranulocytosis</u>, eosinophilia, thrombocytopenia. **CNS:** Dizziness, vertigo, drowsiness, disturbances of coordination, ataxia, confusion, headache, fatigue, listlessness, speech difficulty, development of minor motor seizures, hyperreflexia, akathisia, involuntary movements, tremors, visual hallucinations, activation of latent psychosis, aggression; agitation, <u>respiratory depression</u>. **Skin:** Skin rashes, urticaria, petechiae, erythema multiforme, Stevens-Johnson syndrome, photosensitivity reactions, altered skin pigmentation, <u>exfoliative dermatitis</u>, alopecia. **Special Senses:** Abnormal hearing acuity, scotomas, conjunctivitis, blurred vision, transient diplopia, oculomotor disturbances, oscillopsia, nystagmus. **Urogenital:** Urinary frequency or retention, oliguria, impotence.

DIAGNOSTIC TEST INTERFERENCE
False-negative *pregnancy test* results with tests involving *human chorionic gonadotropin.*

INTERACTIONS Drug: Serum concentrations of other ANTICONVULSANTS may decrease because of increased metabolism; **verapamil, erythromycin, ketoconazole, nefazodone** may increase carbamazepine levels; decreases hypoprothrombinemic effects of ORAL ANTICOAGULANTS; increases metabolism of ESTROGENS, thus decreasing effectiveness of ORAL CONTRACEPTIVES. **Food:** Grapefruit juice may increase drug levels. **Herbal: Ginkgo** may decrease anticonvulsant effectiveness.

PHARMACOKINETICS Absorption: Slowly from GI tract. **Peak:** 2–8 h. **Distribution:** Widely distributed; high concentrations in CSF; crosses placenta; distributed into breast milk. **Metabolism:** In liver by CYP3A4; can induce liver microsomal enzymes. **Elimination:** In urine and feces. **Half-Life:** 14–16 h (decreases with long-term use).

CLINICAL IMPLICATIONS

Assessment & Drug Effects

- Lab tests: Baseline and periodic CBCs including platelets, reticulocytes, serum electrolytes and serum iron, liver function tests, BUN, and complete urinalysis.
- At least 3 mo into therapy, it is recommended that physician attempt dosage reduction or termination of drug therapy, if possible, in patients with trigeminal neuralgia. Some patients develop tolerance to the effects of carbamazepine.
- Monitor for the following reactions, which commonly occur during early therapy: drowsiness, dizziness, light-headedness, ataxia, gastric upset. If these symptoms do not subside within a few days, dosage adjustments may be indicated.
- Withhold drug and notify physician if any of the following signs of myelosuppression occur: RBC <4 million/mm^3, Hct <32%, Hgb <11 g/dL, WBC <4000/mm^3, platelet count <100,000/mm^3, reticulocyte count <20,000/mm^3, serum iron >150 mg/dL.
- Monitor for toxicity, which can develop when serum concentrations are even slightly above the therapeutic range.
- Monitor I&O ratio and vital signs during period of dosage adjustment. Report oliguria, signs of

Common adverse effects in *italic*, life-threatening effects <u>underlined</u>; generic names in **bold**; classifications in SMALL CAPS; ✦ Canadian drug name; ☻ Prototype drug

fluid retention, changes in I&O ratio, and changes in BP or pulse patterns.

- Cardiac syncope may resemble epileptic seizures. Therefore, it is recommended that patients who experience an apparent increase in frequency of seizures or a change in their character should be checked by continuous ECG monitoring for 24 h.
- Doses higher than 600 mg/d may precipitate arrhythmias in patients with heart disease.
- Confusion and agitation may be aggravated in the older adult; therefore, side rails and supervision of ambulation may be indicated.

Patient & Family Education

- Discontinue drug and notify physician immediately if early signs of toxicity or a possible hematologic problem appear, (e.g., anorexia, fever, sore throat or mouth, malaise, unusual fatigue, tendency to bruise or bleed, petechiae, ecchymoses, bleeding gums, nose bleeds).
- Avoid hazardous tasks requiring mental alertness and physical coordination until reaction to drug is known, since dizziness, drowsiness, and ataxia are common adverse effects.
- Remain under close medical supervision throughout therapy.
- Avoid excessive sunlight, as photosensitivity reactions have been reported. Apply a sunscreen (if allowed) with SPF of 12 or above.
- Carbamazepine may cause breakthrough bleeding and may also affect the reliability of oral contraceptives.
- Be aware that abrupt withdrawal of any anticonvulsant drug may precipitate seizures or even status epilepticus.

CARBENICILLIN INDANYL SODIUM

(kar-ben-i-sill′in)

Geocillin, Geopen Oral ♦

Classifications: ANTIBIOTIC; ANTI-PSEUDOMONAL PENICILLIN

Therapeutic: ANTIBIOTIC; PENICILLIN

Prototype: Piperacillin

Pregnancy Category: B

AVAILABILITY 382 mg tablets

ACTION & *THERAPEUTIC EFFECT*
Broad-spectrum, semisynthetic penicillin that rapidly hydrolyzes to carbenicillin in body. *Like carbenicillin disodium, it is bactericidal and penicillinase sensitive and has similar antimicrobial activity but achieves lower blood concentrations than parent compound.*

USES Mainly in the treatment of prostatitis and acute and chronic infections of upper and lower urinary tract.

CONTRAINDICATIONS Hypersensitivity to penicillins; coagulation disorders. Safe use in children not established.

CAUTIOUS USE History of or suspected atopy or allergies; history of allergy to cephalosporins or carbapenem; colitis; diabetes mellitus; lactation; impaired renal and hepatic function; patients on sodium restriction; pregnancy (category B).

ROUTE & DOSAGE

Urinary Tract Infections
Adult: **PO** 382–764 mg q6h for 10 d, continue for 2–4 wk for prostatitis

---

Common adverse effects in *italic*, life-threatening effects <u>underlined</u>; generic names in **bold**; classifications in SMALL CAPS; ♦ Canadian drug name; ☺ Prototype drug

235

ADMINISTRATION

Oral

- Give with a full glass (240 mL) of water on an empty stomach (either 1 h before or 2 h after meals) to attain maximum therapeutic drug levels in urine. Consult physician.
- Protect tablets from moisture.

ADVERSE EFFECTS (≥1%) **Body as a Whole:** Hypersensitivity (rash, fever, urticaria, eosinophilia, pruritus, anaphylaxis), superinfections, especially of vagina. **GI:** *Nausea,* vomiting, heartburn; *diarrhea,* abdominal cramps, flatulence, unpleasant aftertaste, dry mouth. **Hematologic:** Neutropenia, leukopenia, thrombocytopenia, hemolytic anemia, increased AST.

PHARMACOKINETICS Absorption: Incompletely from GI tract. **Peak:** 0.5–1 h. **Distribution:** Very low systemic concentrations; crosses placenta; distributed into breast milk. **Elimination:** 80–99% unchanged in urine within 24 h. **Half-Life:** 67 min.

CLINICAL IMPLICATIONS

Assessment & Drug Effects

- Lab tests: Perform culture and sensitivity tests prior to and at regular intervals throughout therapy. Therapy may be initiated pending test results. Evaluate renal, hepatic, and hematopoietic systems at regular intervals during prolonged therapy. Patients with creatinine clearance of less than 10 mL/min (normal: 105–130 mL/min) will not attain therapeutic urine levels.
- Inquire carefully concerning patient's previous exposure and sensitivity to penicillin and cephalosporins and other allergic reactions of any kind before treatment is initiated.

- Note that drug-induced nausea, unpleasant aftertaste and smell, dry mouth, and furry tongue may be so objectionable as to necessitate drug withdrawal. Report to physician if symptoms persist.
- Monitor I&O rates and pattern: Check with physician regarding optimum daily fluid intake. Report any change in quality or quantity of urine or in I&O ratio.
- Observe patient for signs of electrolyte imbalance. Each 1 g of drug contains approximately 1 mEq of sodium.

Patient & Family Education

- Take this medication with a full glass of water on an empty stomach.
- Take medication around the clock, do not miss any doses, and continue taking medication until it is all gone unless otherwise directed by physician.

CARBIDOPA-LEVODOPA

(kar-bi-doe´pa)
Sinemet, Sinemet-CR, Parcopa

CARBIDOPA

Lodosyn
Classifications: ANTICHOLINERGIC; ANTIPARKINSON AGENT
Therapeutic: ANTIPARKINSON AGENT
Pregnancy Category: C

AVAILABILITY Carbidopa: 25 mg tablet; **Carbidopa/Levodopa:** 10 mg/100 mg, 25 mg/100 mg, 25 mg/250 mg tablets; 25 mg/100 mg, 50 mg/200 mg sustained-release tablets and orally disintegrating tablets

ACTION & *THERAPEUTIC EFFECT*
When levodopa is given alone, large doses must be administered.

Carbidopa prevents peripheral metabolism (decarboxylation) of levodopa and thereby makes more levodopa available for transport to the brain. Carbidopa does not cross blood–brain barrier and therefore does not affect metabolism of levodopa within the brain. Carbidopa also prevents the inhibitory effect of pyridoxine (vitamin B_6) on levodopa. *Effective in management of symptoms of Parkinson's disease and parkinsonism of secondary origin and improving life expectancy and quality of life.*

USES Symptomatic treatment of idiopathic Parkinson's disease (paralysis agitans), postencephalitic parkinsonism, and parkinsonism following carbon dioxide and manganese intoxication. Carbidopa is available alone from manufacturer, on request by physician, for use with levodopa when separate titration of each agent is indicated, and for investigational purposes.

CONTRAINDICATIONS Hypersensitivity to carbidopa or levodopa; narrow-angle glaucoma; history of or suspected melanoma; pregnancy (category C), lactation. Safe use in women of childbearing potential and in children <18 y not established.

CAUTIOUS USE Cardiovascular, hepatic, pulmonary, or renal disorders; history of MI; urinary retention; history of peptic ulcer; psychiatric states; endocrine disease; chronic wide-angle glaucoma; seizure disorders.

ROUTE & DOSAGE

Parkinson's Disease in Patients Not Currently Receiving Levodopa
Adult: **PO** 1 tablet containing 10 mg carbidopa/100 mg levodopa *or* 25 mg carbidopa/100 mg

levodopa t.i.d., increased by 1 tablet q.d. or q.o.d. up to 6 tablets/d

Patients Receiving Levodopa
Adult: **PO** 1 tablet of the 25/250 mixture t.i.d. or q.i.d., adjusted by $1/2$–1 tablet as needed up to 8 tablets/d (start at 20–25% of initial dose of levodopa)

ADMINISTRATION

Oral

- Ensure that sustained-release form of drug (Sinemet CR) is not chewed or crushed. It may be broken in half but otherwise swallowed whole.
- Give consistently with respect to food. High protein meals may interfere with absorption of levodopa.
- When patient has been taking levodopa alone, carbidopa-levodopa is usually initiated with a morning dose after patient has been without levodopa for at least 8 h.
- Store in tight, light-resistant containers.

ADVERSE EFFECTS (≥1%) **Body as a Whole:** Hoarseness, unusual breathing patterns, neuroleptic malignant syndrome. **CV:** Orthostatic hypotension, irregular heartbeat, palpitation, arrhythmias, phlebitis, edema. **GI:** Nausea, anorexia, dry mouth, bruxism, vomiting, excess salivation. **Hematologic:** Hemolytic and nonhemolytic anemia, thrombocytopenia, agranulocytosis. **Metabolic:** Abnormal liver function tests, abnormal BUN. **CNS:** *Involuntary movements (dyskinetic, dystonic, choreiform),* ataxia, muscle twitching, increase in hand tremor, numbness, headache, dizziness, euphoria, fatigue, confusion, insomnia, nightmares, mental distur-

Common adverse effects in *italic*, life-threatening effects underlined; generic names in **bold**; classifications in SMALL CAPS; ♣ Canadian drug name; ☯ Prototype drug

237

bances, anxiety, <u>depression with suicidal tendencies</u>, delirium, seizures. **Skin:** Body odor, skin rash, dark sweat, loss of hair. **Special Senses:** Blepharospasm, mydriasis, miosis, blurred vision, diplopia, oculogyric crisis. **Urogenital:** Dark urine, priapism, urinary frequency, retention, incontinence.

DIAGNOSTIC TEST INTERFERENCE
Urine glucose: False-negative tests may result with use of *glucose oxidase methods* (e.g., *Clinistix, TesTape*) and false-positive results with *copper reduction methods* (e.g., *Benedict's, Clinitest*), especially in patients receiving large doses. It is reported that *Clinistix* and *TesTape* may be used if reading is taken at margin of wet and dry tape. There is also the possibility of false-positive tests for *urinary ketones* by *dipstick tests*, e.g., *Acetest* (equivocal), *Ketostix, Labstix;* false elevation of *serum* and *urinary uric acid* levels by *colorimetric methods* (*not* with *uricase*); and interference with *urine PKU test* results.

INTERACTIONS Drug:
MAO INHIBITORS may precipitate hypertensive crisis; TRICYCLIC ANTIDEPRESSANTS potentiate postural hypotension; ANTICHOLINERGIC AGENTS may enhance levodopa effects but can exacerbate involuntary movements; **methyldopa, guanethidine** increase hypotensive and CNS effects; PHENOTHIAZINES, haloperidol, **phenytoin, papaverine** may interfere with levodopa effects.

PHARMACOKINETICS Absorption:
40–70% of carbidopa absorbed after PO dose; carbidopa may enhance absorption of levodopa. **Distribution:** Widely distributed in most body tissues except CNS; crosses placenta; excreted in breast milk. **Elimination:** In urine. **Half-Life:** 2 h.

CLINICAL IMPLICATIONS
Assessment & Drug Effects
- Make accurate observations and report promptly adverse reactions and therapeutic effects. Rate of dosage increase is determined primarily by patient's tolerance and response to levodopa.
- Monitor vital signs, particularly during period of dosage adjustment. Report alterations in BP, pulse, and respiratory rate and rhythm.
- Monitor all patients closely for behavior changes. Patients in depression should be closely observed for suicidal tendencies.
- Monitor for changes in intraocular pressure in patients with chronic wide-angle glaucoma.
- Monitor patients with diabetes carefully for alterations in diabetes control. Frequent monitoring of blood sugar is advised.
- Lab tests: Periodic blood glucose, hepatic and renal function tests, CBC with differential, Hgb and Hct.
- Report promptly abnormal involuntary movement such as facial grimacing, exaggerated chewing, protrusion of tongue, rhythmic opening and closing of mouth, bobbing of head, jerky arm and leg movements, and exaggerated respiration.
- Assess for "on-off" phenomenon: sudden, unpredictable loss of drug effectiveness ("off" effect), which lasts 1 min–1 h. This is followed by an equally abrupt return of function ("on" effect). Sometimes symptoms can be controlled by increasing number of doses per day.
- Monitor therapeutic effects. Some patients manifest increase in bradykinesia ("leg freezing" or slow body movement). The patient is unable to start walking and fre-

quently falls. Reduction of dosage may be indicated in these patients.
- Patients who require more frequent drug administration are most likely to manifest gradual return of parkinsonian symptoms toward the end of a dose period.

Patient & Family Education
- Follow physician's directions regarding continuation or discontinuation of levodopa. Both adverse reactions and therapeutic effects occur more rapidly with carbidopa-levodopa combination than with levodopa alone.
- Make positional changes slowly and in stages, particularly from recumbent to upright position, dangle your legs a few minutes before standing, and walk in place before ambulating, as some patients experience weakness, dizziness, and faintness. Tolerance to this effect usually develops within a few months of therapy. Support stockings may help. Consult physician.
- Report muscle twitching and spasmodic winking promptly, as these may be early signs of overdosage.
- You may notice elevation of mood and sense of well-being before any objective improvement. Resume activities gradually and observe safety precautions to avoid injury.
- Maintain your prescribed drug regimen. Abrupt withdrawal can lead to parkinsonian crisis with return of marked muscle rigidity, akinesia, tremor, hyperpyrexia, mental changes.
- Avoid driving or other hazardous activities until reaction to drug is determined.
- Levodopa may cause urine to darken on standing and may also cause sweat to be dark-colored. This effect is not clinically significant.
- Wear medical identification. Inform all health care providers that you are taking carbidopa-levodopa.

CARBOPLATIN

(car-bo-pla'tin)
Paraplatin
Classifications: ANTINEOPLASTIC; ALKYLATING AGENT
Therapeutic: ANTINEOPLASTIC
Prototype: Cyclophosphamide
Pregnancy Category: D

AVAILABILITY 50 mg, 150 mg, 450 mg vials

ACTION & *THERAPEUTIC EFFECT*
Carboplatin is a platinum compound that is a chemotherapeutic agent. It produces interstrand DNA cross-linkages, thus interfering with DNA, RNA, and protein synthesis. Carboplatin is cell-cycle nonspecific, i.e., effective throughout the entire cell life cycle; it induces programmed cell death. *Full or partial activity against a variety of cancers resulting in reduction or stabilization of tumor size and useful in patients with impaired renal function, patients unable to accommodate high-volume hydration, or patients at high risk for neurotoxicity and/or ototoxicity.*

USES Monotherapy or combination therapy for ovarian cancer.
UNLABELED USES Combination therapy for breast, cervical, colon, endometrial, head and neck, and lung cancer; leukemia, lymphoma, and melanoma.

CONTRAINDICATIONS History of severe reactions to carboplatin or

Common adverse effects in *italic*, life-threatening effects underlined; generic names in **bold**; classifications in SMALL CAPS; ◆ Canadian drug name; ☯ Prototype drug

239

C

other platinum compounds, severe bone marrow depression; significant bleeding; impaired renal function; pregnancy (category D), and lactation.

CAUTIOUS USE Use with other nephrotoxic drugs; coagulapathy; previous radiation therapy; renal impairment.

ROUTE & DOSAGE

Ovarian Cancer
Adult: IV 360 mg/m² once q4wk. May be repeated when neutrophil count is at least 2000 mm³ and platelet count is at least 100,000 mm³. If neutrophil and platelet counts are lower, dose of carboplatin should be reduced by 50–75% of initial dose. Alternatively, 400 mg/m² as a 24-h infusion for 2 consecutive d can be used

Important Note
Aluminum reacts with carboplatin to form an inactive precipitate; therefore, intravenous infusion sets and needles containing aluminum should not be used.

ADMINISTRATION

Intravenous

PREPARE: **IV Infusion:** Do not use needles or IV sets containing aluminum. Immediately before use, reconstitute with either sterile water for injection or D5W or NS as follows: 50-mg vial plus 5 mL diluent; 150-mg vial plus 15 mL diluent; 450-mg vial plus 45 mL diluent. All dilutions yield 10 mg/mL. May be further diluted to 0.5 mg/mL with D5W or NS.

ADMINISTER: **IV Infusion:** Give IV solution over 15 min or longer, depending on total amount of solution and patient tolerance.

Lengthening duration of administration may decrease nausea and vomiting.

INCOMPATIBILITIES **Solution/additive: Sodium bicarbonate, flourouracil, mesna.** Y-site: **Amphotericin B cholesteryl complex.**

- Premedication with a parenteral antiemetic ¹/₂ h before and on a scheduled basis thereafter is normally used.

- Do not repeat doses until the neutrophil count is at least 2000/mm³ and platelet count at least 100,000/mm³.

- Protect from light. Reconstituted solutions are stable for 8 h at room temperature; discard solutions 8 h after dilution.

ADVERSE EFFECTS (≥1%) **Body as a Whole:** Hypersensitivity reactions. **GI:** *Mild to moderate nausea and vomiting,* anorexia, hypogeusia, dysgeusia, mucositis, diarrhea, constipation, elevated liver enzymes. **Hematologic:** <u>Thrombocytopenia, leukopenia, neutropenia, anemia.</u> **Metabolic:** *Mild hyponatremia, hypomagnesemia, hypocalcemia, and hypokalemia.* **CNS:** Peripheral neuropathy. **Skin:** Rash, alopecia. **Special Senses:** Tinnitus. **Urogenital:** Nephrotoxicity.

DIAGNOSTIC TEST INTERFERENCE Decreased ***calcium levels;*** mild increases in ***liver function tests;*** decreased levels of ***magnesium, potassium,*** and ***sodium.***

INTERACTIONS Drug: AMINOGLYCOSIDES may increase the risk of ototoxicity and nephrotoxicity. May decrease **phenytoin** levels.

PHARMACOKINETICS Onset: 8 wk (2 cycles). **Duration:** 2–16 mo. **Distribution:** Highest concentration in the liver, lung, kidney, skin, and tumors. Not bound to plasma proteins. **Metabolism:** Hydrolyzed in the serum. **Elimination:** Primarily by the kidneys; 60–80% excreted in urine within 24 h. **Half-Life:** 3 h.

CLINICAL IMPLICATIONS

Assessment & Drug Effects

- Monitor closely during first 15 min of infusion, since allergic reactions have occurred within minutes of carboplatin administration.
- Lab tests: Baseline and periodic CBC with differential, platelet count, Hgb and Hct. Monitor kidney function periodically with creatinine clearance tests and serum electrolytes.
- Monitor results of peripheral blood counts. Median nadir occurs at day 21. Leukopenia, neutropenia, and thrombocytopenia are dose related and may produce dose-limiting toxicity.
- Monitor for peripheral neuropathy (e.g., paresthesias), ototoxicity, and visual disturbances.
- Monitor serum electrolyte studies, because carboplatin has been associated with decreases in sodium, potassium, calcium, and magnesium. Special precautions may be warranted for patients on diuretic therapy.

Patient & Family Education

- Learn about the range of potential adverse effects. Strategies for nausea prevention should receive special attention.
- During therapy you are at risk for infection and hemorrhagic complications related to bone marrow suppression. Avoid unnecessary exposure to crowds or infected persons during the nadir period.
- Report paresthesias (numbness, tingling), visual disturbances, or

symptoms of ototoxicity (hearing loss and/or tinnitus).

CARBOPROST TROMETHAMINE

(kar'boe-prost)
Hemabate
Classifications: HORMONE; OXYTOCIC
Therapeutic: OXYTOCIC
Prototype: Oxytocin
Pregnancy Category: D

AVAILABILITY 250 mcg/mL injection

ACTION & *THERAPEUTIC EFFECT*
Synthetic analog of naturally occurring prostaglandin F_2 alpha with longer duration of biologic activity. Stimulates myometrial contractions of gravid uterus; contractions are qualitatively similar to those occurring at term labor. Mean time to abortion 16 h; mean dose required 2.6 mL. *Effectively stimulates uterine contraction and is used to induce abortion. Useful in treatment of postpartum hemorrhage due to uterine atony unresponsive to usual measures.*

USES To induce abortion between 13th and 20th week of pregnancy, as calculated from first day of last menstrual period. Also for refractory postpartum bleeding.
UNLABELED USES To reduce blood loss secondary to uterine atony; to induce labor in intrauterine fetal death and hydatidiform mole.

CONTRAINDICATIONS Acute pelvic inflammatory disease; active cardiac, pulmonary, renal, or hepatic disease; pregnancy (category D); lactation.
CAUTIOUS USE History of asthma; adrenal disease; anemia; hypotension; hypertension; diabetes melli-

Common adverse effects in *italic*, life-threatening effects underlined; generic names in **bold**; classifications in SMALL CAPS; ◆ Canadian drug name; ❷ Prototype drug

241

tus; epilepsy; history of uterine surgery; cervical stenosis; fibroids.

ROUTE & DOSAGE

Abortion, Postpartum Bleeding

Adult: **IM** Initial: 250 mcg (1 mL) repeated at 1.5–3.5-h intervals if indicated by uterine response. Dosage may be increased to 500 mcg (2 mL) if uterine contractility is inadequate after several doses of 250 mcg (1 mL), not to exceed total dose of 12 mg or continuous administration for more than 2 d.

ADMINISTRATION

- Because nausea and diarrhea occur in about 60% of patients, an antiemetic and an antidiarrheal agent may be prescribed before and during carboprost administration.
- Give deep IM into a large muscle. Aspirate carefully before injecting drug to avoid inadvertent entry into blood vessel which can result in bronchospasm, tetanic contractions, and shock. Do not use same site for subsequent doses.
- Store drug in refrigerator at 2°–4° C (36°–39° F) unless otherwise specified.

ADVERSE EFFECTS (≥1%) **Body as a Whole:** Fever, flushing, chills, cough, headache, pain (muscles, joints, lower abdomen, eyes), hiccups, breast tenderness. **GI:** *Nausea,* diarrhea, vomiting.

PHARMACOKINETICS Peak: 30–90 min. **Elimination:** Renal within 24 h.

CLINICAL IMPLICATIONS

Assessment & Drug Effects

- Monitor uterine contractions and observe and report excessive vaginal bleeding and cramping pain. Save all clots and tissue for physi-

cian inspection and laboratory analysis.
- Check vital signs at regular intervals. Carboprost-induced febrile reaction occurs in more than 10% of patients and must be differentiated from endometritis, which occurs around third day after abortion.

Patient & Family Education

- Report promptly onset of bleeding, foul-smelling discharge, abdominal pain, or fever.
- Since ovulation may reoccur as early as 2 wk post-abortion, you may wish to consider appropriate contraception.

CARISOPRODOL

(kar-eye-soe-proe′dole)
Soma
Classifications: SKELETAL MUSCLE RELAXANT, CENTRAL-ACTING
Therapeutic: SKELETAL MUSCLE RELAXANT, CENTRAL-ACTING
Prototype: Cyclobenzaprine
Pregnancy Category: C

AVAILABILITY 350 mg tablets

ACTION & *THERAPEUTIC EFFECT*

Skeletal muscle relaxant effect, unlike that of neuromuscular blocking agents, appears to be due to sedative action. Voluntary motor function is not lost, but there may be slight reduction in muscle tone leading to relief of pain and discomfort of muscle spasm. *Effective spasmolytic and reduces pain associated with acute musculoskeletal disorders.*

USES Skeletal muscle spasm, stiffness, and pain in a variety of musculoskeletal disorders and to relieve spasticity and rigidity in cerebral palsy.

CONTRAINDICATIONS Hypersensitivity to carisoprodol and related compounds (e.g., meprobamate, tybamate); acute intermittent porphyria; children <5 y; pregnancy (category C), lactation.

CAUTIOUS USE Impaired liver or kidney function, addiction-prone individuals; seizure disorder.

ROUTE & DOSAGE

Muscle Spasm
Adult: **PO** 350 mg t.i.d.
Child: **PO** >5 y, 25 mg/kg/d in 4 divided doses

ADMINISTRATION

Oral
- Give with food, as needed, to reduce GI symptoms. Last dose should be taken at bedtime.
- Store in tightly closed container.

ADVERSE EFFECTS (≥1%) **Body as a Whole:** Eosinophilia, asthma, fever, anaphylactic shock. **CV:** Tachycardia, postural hypotension, facial flushing. **GI:** Nausea, vomiting, hiccups. **CNS:** *Drowsiness, dizziness,* vertigo, ataxia, tremor, headache, irritability, depressive reactions, syncope, insomnia. **Skin:** Skin rash, erythema multiforme, pruritus.

INTERACTIONS Drug: Alcohol, CNS DEPRESSANTS potentiate CNS effects.

PHARMACOKINETICS Onset: 30 min. **Duration:** 4–6 h. **Distribution:** Crosses placenta. **Metabolism:** In liver by CYP2C19. **Elimination:** By kidneys; excreted in breast milk (2–4 times the plasma concentrations). **Half-Life:** 8 h.

CLINICAL IMPLICATIONS

Assessment & Drug Effects
- Monitor for allergic or idiosyncratic reactions that generally occur from the first to the fourth dose in patients taking the drug for the first time. Symptoms usually subside after several hours; they are treated by supportive and symptomatic measures.

Patient & Family Education
- Avoid driving and other potentially hazardous activities until response to the drug has been evaluated. Drowsiness is a common side effect and may require reduction in dosage.
- Report to physician if symptoms of dizziness and faintness persist. Symptoms may be controlled by making position changes slowly and in stages.
- Do not take alcohol or other CNS depressants (effects may be additive) unless otherwise directed by physician.
- Discontinue drug and notify physician if skin rash, diplopia, dizziness, or other unusual signs or symptoms appear.

CARMUSTINE

(kar-mus'teen)
BiCNU, Gliadel
Classifications: ANTINEOPLASTIC; ALKYLATING AGENT
Therapeutic: ANTINEOPLASTIC
Prototype: Cyclophosphamide
Pregnancy Category: D

AVAILABILITY 100 mg injection; 7.7 mg wafer

ACTION & *THERAPEUTIC EFFECT* Highly lipid-soluble nitrosourea derivative with cell-cycle-nonspecific activity against rapidly proliferating cells. Produces cross-linkage of DNA strands, thereby blocking DNA, RNA, and protein synthesis in

Common adverse effects in *italic*, life-threatening effects underlined; generic names in **bold**; classifications in SMALL CAPS; ♣ Canadian drug name; ⊘ Prototype drug

243

tumor cells. Major toxic effect is bone marrow suppression. *Drug metabolites thought to be responsible for antineoplastic activities. Full or partial activity against a variety of cancers resulting in reduction or stabilization of tumor size and increased survival rates.*

USES As single agent or with other antineoplastics in treatment of Hodgkin's disease and other lymphomas, melanoma, primary and metastatic tumors of brain, and GI tract malignancies.
UNLABELED USES Treatment of carcinomas of breast and lungs, Ewing's sarcoma, Burkitt's tumor, malignant melanoma, and topically for mycosis fungoides.

CONTRAINDICATIONS History of pulmonary function impairment; recent illness with or exposure to chickenpox or herpes zoster; infection; severe bone marrow depression, decreased circulating platelets, leukocytes, or erythrocytes; pregnancy (category D), lactation.
CAUTIOUS USE Hepatic and renal insufficiency; patient with previous cytotoxic medication, or radiation therapy; history of herpes infections.

ROUTE & DOSAGE

Previously Untreated Patients— Carcinoma
Adult: **IV** 150–200 mg/m² q6wk in one dose *or* given over 2 d
Child: **IV** 200–250 mg/m² q4– 6wk as single dose. Doses adjusted based on hematologic parameters.

Mycosis Fungoides
Adult: **Topical** 0.05–0.4% solution in 30% alcohol to paint entire body (60 mLs) or ointment 1–2 times/d for 6–8 wk (10 mg/d) (must be specially compounded)

ADMINISTRATION

Note: When administering IV to infants and children, verify correct IV concentration and rate of infusion with physician.

Intravenous

PREPARE: IV Infusion: Wear disposable gloves; contact of drug with skin can cause burning, dermatitis, and hyperpigmentation. Add supplied diluent to the 100 mg vial. Further dilute with 27 mL of sterile water for injection to yield a concentration of 3.3 mg/mL. Each dose is then added to 100–500 mL of D5W or NS. If possible avoid using PVC IV tubing and bags.
ADMINISTER: IV Infusion: Infuse a single dose over at least 1 h. Slow infusion over 1–2 h and adequate dilution will reduce pain of administration. Avoid starting infusion into dorsum of hand, wrist, or the antecubital veins; extravasation in these areas can damage underlying tendons and nerves leading to loss of mobility of entire limb.
INCOMPATIBILITIES Solution/additive: Sodium bicarbonate. Y-site: Allopurinol.
▪ Frequently check rate of flow and blood return; palpate injection site for extravasation. If there is any question about patency, line should be restarted.

▪ Reconstituted solutions of carmustine are clear and colorless and may be stored at 2°–8° C (36°–46° F) for 24 h protected from light. ▪ Store unopened vials at 2°–8° C (36°–46° F), protected from light, unless otherwise directed by manufacturer. ▪ Signs of decomposition of carmustine in unopened vial: liquefaction and appearance of oil film at bottom of vial. Discard drug in this condition.

ADVERSE EFFECTS (≥1%) **Hematologic:** Delayed myelosuppression (dose-related); thrombocytopenia. **CNS:** Dizziness, ataxia. **Respiratory:** Pulmonary infiltration or fibrosis. **Skin:** Skin flushing and burning pain at injection site, hyperpigmentation of skin (from contact). **Special Senses:** (with high doses) Eye infarctions, retinal hemorrhage, suffusion of conjunctiva. **GI:** Stomatitis, *nausea, vomiting*.

INTERACTIONS Drug: Cimetidine may potentiate neutropenia and thrombocytopenia.

PHARMACOKINETICS Distribution: Readily crosses blood–brain barrier; CSF concentrations 15–70% of plasma concentrations. **Metabolism:** Rapidly metabolized. **Elimination:** 60–70% in urine in 96 h; 6% via lungs, 1% in feces; excreted in breast milk.

CLINICAL IMPLICATIONS

Assessment & Drug Effects

- Monitor for nausea and vomiting (dose related), which may occur within 2 h after drug administration and persist for up to 6 h. Prior administration of an antiemetic may help to decrease or prevent these adverse effects.
- Lab tests: Baseline CBC with differential and platelet count, repeat blood studies following infusion at weekly intervals for at least 6 wk. Baseline and periodic tests of hepatic and renal function.
- Platelet nadir usually occurs within 4–5 wk, and leukocyte nadir within 5–6 wk after therapy is terminated. Thrombocytopenia may be more severe than leukopenia; anemia is less severe.

- Check temperature daily. Avoid use of rectal thermometer to prevent injury to mucosa. An elevation of 0.6° F or more above usual temperature warrants reporting.
- Report symptoms of lung toxicity (cough, shortness of breath, fever) to the physician immediately.
- Be alert to signs of hepatic toxicity (jaundice, dark urine, pruritus, light-colored stools) and renal insufficiency (dysuria, oliguria, hematuria, swelling of lower legs and feet).

Patient & Family Education

- Report burning sensation immediately, as carmustine can cause burning discomfort even in the absence of extravasation. Infusion will be discontinued and restarted in another site. Ice application over the area may decrease the discomfort.
- Intense flushing of skin may occur during IV infusion. This usually disappears in 2–4 h.
- You will be highly susceptible to infection and to hemorrhagic disorders. Be alert to hazardous periods that occur 4–6 wk after a dose of carmustine. If possible, avoid invasive procedures (e.g., IM injections, enemas, rectal temperatures) during this period.
- Report promptly the onset of sore throat, weakness, fever, chills, infection of any kind, or abnormal bleeding (ecchymosis, petechiae, epistaxis, bleeding gums, hematemesis, melena).

CARTEOLOL HYDROCHLORIDE

(car'tee-oh-lole)
Cartrol, Ocupress
Classifications: BETA-ADRENERGIC ANTAGONIST; ANTIHYPERTENSIVE

Common adverse effects in *italic*, life-threatening effects underlined; generic names in **bold**; classifications in SMALL CAPS; ◆ Canadian drug name; ⊘ Prototype drug

245

Therapeutic: ANTIHYPERTENSIVE;
BETA-ADRENERGIC BLOCKING AGENT
Prototype: Propranolol
Pregnancy Category: C

AVAILABILITY 2.5 mg, 5 mg tablets; 1% solution

ACTION & *THERAPEUTIC EFFECT*

Carteolol is a beta-adrenergic blocking agent (antagonist) that competes for available beta receptor sites. It inhibits both $beta_1$ receptors (chiefly in cardiac muscle) and $beta_2$ receptors (chiefly in the bronchial and vascular musculature). It decreases standing and supine hypertension. *Effective antihypertensive agent by reducing BP to normotensive range and useful in managing some angina, dysrhythmias, and CHF by decreasing myocardial oxygen demand and lowering cardiac work load.*

USES For hypertension, either alone or in combination with other drugs, particularly a thiazide diuretic (not indicated for hypertensive crisis); chronic open-angle glaucoma.
UNLABELED USES To reduce the frequency of anginal attacks.

CONTRAINDICATIONS Sinus bradycardia, severe CHF; greater than first-degree heart block, cardiogenic shock, CHF secondary to tachycardia treatable with beta-blockers, overt cardiac failure, hypersensitivity to beta-blocking agents, persistent severe bradycardia, bronchial asthma or bronchospasm, and severe COPD; pulmonary edema; pregnancy (category C).
CAUTIOUS USE CHF patients treated with digitalis and diuretics; peripheral vascular disease; diabetes, hypoglycemia, thyrotoxicosis; renal disease; CVA; lactation.

ROUTE & DOSAGE

Hypertension

Adult: **PO** 2.5 mg once/d, may increase to 5–10 mg if needed (max: 10 mg/d)

Open-Angle Glaucoma

Adult: **Ophthalmic** 1 drop in affected eye b.i.d.

ADMINISTRATION

Oral

- Consult physician if patient's creatinine clearance is below normal. Dosage adjustment may be needed.
- Administer capsule or tablet whole. Do not crush or break and instruct patient not to chew before swallowing.
- Store away from heat, light, or moisture.

ADVERSE EFFECTS (≥1%) **Body as a Whole:** Rash, muscle cramps, bronchospasm. **CV:** Increased angina, hypotension, CHF, bradycardia. **GI:** Abdominal pain, diarrhea, nausea. **Endocrine:** Hyperglycemia. **CNS:** *Headache, dizziness,* drowsiness, insomnia, anxiety, tremor, paresthesia, weakness.

INTERACTIONS Drug: DIURETICS and other HYPOTENSIVE AGENTS increase hypotensive effect; carteolol and **albuterol, metoproterenol, terbutaline, pirbuterol** are mutually antagonistic; NSAIDS may blunt hypotensive effect; decreases hypoglycemic effect of **glyburide**; may increase bradycardia and sinus arrest with **amiodarone.**

PHARMACOKINETICS Absorption: Readily from GI tract; 85% reaches systemic circulation. **Peak:** 1–3 h. **Duration:** 24–48 h. **Distribution:** Crosses placenta; distributed into

Common adverse effects in *italic*, life-threatening effects underlined; generic names in **bold**, classifications in SMALL CAPS; ♣ Canadian drug name; ⊘ Prototype drug

breast milk. **Metabolism:** In liver to active metabolite. **Elimination:** Primarily in urine. **Half-Life:** 4–6 h.

CLINICAL IMPLICATIONS

Assessment & Drug Effects

- Assess heart rate prior to administration. If pulse is less than 50 bpm, withhold drug and notify physician.
- Monitor BP and pulse frequently during period of adjustment and periodically throughout therapy.
- If hypotension (systolic BP <90 mm Hg) occurs, discontinue the drug and carefully assess the hemodynamic status of the patient.
- Monitor daily weight and assess for evidence of fluid overload since drug may precipitate CHF (see Signs & Symptoms, Appendix F).
- Monitor mental status. Mental depression may be increased by use of this drug.
- Assess respiratory status closely if the patient has history of bronchitis or emphysema, assess for respiratory difficulty.
- Monitor diabetic for loss of diabetic control. Drug may prevent the appearance of early S&S of acute hypoglycemia (see Appendix F).
- Drug may reduce tolerance to cold temperatures in older adults or in those who have circulatory problems.

Patient & Family Education

- Report the first sign or symptom of impending CHF (see Signs & Symptoms, Appendix F) or unexplained respiratory symptoms.
- Do not discontinue medication abruptly, since sudden withdrawal may precipitate or exacerbate angina.
- Do not use any OTC products such as nasal decongestants and cold preparations without consultation.
- Report slow pulse rate, confusion or depression, dizziness or light-headedness, skin rash, fever, sore throat, or unusual bleeding or bruising.
- Be cautious while driving or performing other hazardous activities until response to drug is known.
- Continue to take this medication as instructed by your physician no matter how well you feel.
- Take your BP at least twice a week and report significant changes.
- Take your pulse before and after taking the medication. If it is much slower than normal rate (or less than 50 bpm), check with your physician.

CARVEDILOL

(car-ve-di'lol)

Coreg, Kredex ♦

Classifications: ALPHA- AND BETA-ADRENERGIC ANTAGONIST; ANTIHYPERTENSIVE

Therapeutic: ANTIHYPERTENSIVE; ADRENERGIC BLOCKING AGENT

Prototype: Propanolol HCl

Pregnancy Category: C

AVAILABILITY 3.125 mg, 6.25 mg, 12.5 mg, 25 mg tablets

ACTION & *THERAPEUTIC EFFECT*

Adrenergic receptor blocking agent that combines selective alpha activity and nonselective beta-adrenergic blocking actions. Both activities contribute to blood pressure reduction. Peripheral vasodilatation and, therefore, decreased peripheral resistance results from alpha$_1$-blocking activity of Coreg. It is 3–5 times more potent than labetalol in lowering blood pressure. *An effective antihypertensive agent reducing BP to normotensive*

Common adverse effects in *italic*, life-threatening effects underlined; generic names in **bold**; classifications in SMALL CAPS; ♦ Canadian drug name; ⊙ Prototype drug

247

range and useful in managing some angina, dysrhythmias, and CHF by decreasing myocardial oxygen demand and lowering cardiac work load.

USES Management of essential hypertension, CHF, in conjunction with other heart failure medications, left ventricular dysfunction post MI.

CONTRAINDICATIONS Patients with class IV decompensated cardiac failure, bronchial asthma, or related bronchospastic conditions (e.g., chronic bronchitis and emphysema), pulmonary edema; second- and third-degree AV block, sick sinus syndome, cardiogenic shock or severe bradycardia; pregnancy (category C), lactation.

CAUTIOUS USE Patients on MAOI agents, diabetes, hypoglycemia; patients at high risk for anaphylactic reaction, peripheral vascular disease, cerebrovascular insufficiencies, major depression, hepatic or renal impairment. Safety and efficacy in patients <18 y of age have not been established.

ROUTE & DOSAGE

CHF
Adult: PO Start with 3.125 mg b.i.d. times 2 wk, may double dose q2wk as tolerated up to 25 mg b.i.d. if <85 kg or 50 mg b.i.d. if >85 kg

Hypertension
Adult: PO Start with 6.25 mg b.i.d., may increase by 6.25 mg b.i.d. to max of 50 mg/d

ADMINISTRATION

Oral
- Give with food to slow absorption and minimize risk of orthostatic hypotension.

- Dose increments should be made at 7- to 14-day intervals.

ADVERSE EFFECTS (≥1%) **Body as a Whole:** Increased sweating, fatigue, chest pain, pain, arthralgia. **CV:** Bradycardia, hypotension, syncope, hypertension, AV block, angina. **GI:** Diarrhea, nausea, abdominal pain, vomiting. **Respiratory:** Sinusitis, bronchitis. **Hematologic:** Thrombocytopenia, **Metabolic:** Hyperglycemia, weight increase, gout. **CNS:** *Dizziness,* headache, paresthesias.

INTERACTIONS Drug: Rifampin significantly decreases **carvedilol** levels; **cimetidine** may increase **carvedilol** levels; **clonidine, reserpine,** MAO INHIBITORS may cause hypotension or bradycardia; **carvedilol** may increase **digoxin** levels and may enhance hypoglycemic effects of **insulin** and oral HYPOGLYCEMIC AGENTS, may enhance the effects of ANTIHYPERTENSIVES.

PHARMACOKINETICS Absorption: Rapidly from GI tract, 25–35% reaches the systemic circulation. **Peak:** Antihypertensive effect 7–14 d. **Distribution:** >98% protein bound. **Metabolism:** In the liver by CYP2D6 and CYP2C9. **Elimination:** Primarily through feces. **Half-Life:** 7–10 h.

CLINICAL IMPLICATIONS

Assessment & Drug Effects
- Monitor for therapeutic effectiveness which is indicated by lessening of S&S of CHF and improved BP control.
- Lab tests: Monitor liver function tests periodically; at first sign of hepatic toxicity (see Appendix F) stop drug and notify physician.
- Monitor for worsening of symptoms in patients with PVD.

Common adverse effects in *italic*, life-threatening effects underlined; generic names in **bold**; classifications in SMALL CAPS; ♣ Canadian drug name; ◎ Prototype drug

- Monitor digoxin levels with concurrent use; plasma digoxin concentration may increase.

Patient & Family Education

- Do not abruptly discontinue taking this drug.
- You may experience dizziness or faintness, as a risk of orthostatic hypotension.
- Do not engage in hazardous activities while experiencing dizziness.
- If you have diabetes, the drug may increase effects of hypoglycemic drugs and mask S&S of hypoglycemia.

CASCARA SAGRADA

(kas-kar'a)

Classifications: GI STIMULANT, LAXATIVE
Therapeutic: LAXATIVE, GI STIMULANT
Prototype: Bisacodyl
Pregnancy Category: C

AVAILABILITY 325 mg tablets; liquid

ACTION & *THERAPEUTIC EFFECT*

Acts principally in large intestine by stimulating propulsive movements of colon through direct chemical irritation. Casanthrol, which is present in a variety of OTC mixtures, is a derivative of cascara sagrada. *Effective laxative with results in 6–12 h. Useful in conditions where straining at stool is to be avoided.*

USES Temporary relief of constipation and to prevent straining at stool in various disease conditions. Sometimes used with milk of magnesia.

CONTRAINDICATIONS Abdominal pain, fecal impaction; GI bleeding, ulcerations; appendicitis, gastroenteritis, intestinal obstruction, CHF; pregnancy (category C).
CAUTIOUS USE Lactation; renal impairment; diabetic patients; rectal bleeding; concomitant laxative use.

ROUTE & DOSAGE

Laxative

Adult: **PO** Tablet: 325–1000 mg/d; fluid extract: 0.5–1.5 mL/d; aromatic fluid extract: 2–6 mL/d
Child: **PO** 2–12 y, $^1/_2$ of adult dose; <2 y, $^1/_4$ of adult dose
Infant: **PO** Aromatic fluid extract: 1.25 mL/d as single dose

ADMINISTRATION

Oral

- Administer with a full glass of water on an empty stomach for best results. Results may be delayed somewhat by food.
- Store in tightly covered, light-resistant containers, unless otherwise directed by manufacturer.

ADVERSE EFFECTS (≥1%) **GI:** Anorexia, nausea, gripping, abnormally loose stools, constipation rebound, melanosis of colon. **Metabolic:** Hypokalemia, impaired glucose tolerance, calcium deficiency, **Urogenital:** Discoloration of urine.

DIAGNOSTIC TEST INTERFERENCE
Possibility of interference with *PSP excretion test* because of urine discoloration.

INTERACTIONS Drug: Decreased effect of ORAL ANTICOAGULANTS.

PHARMACOKINETICS Absorption: Minimal from GI tract. **Onset:** 6–12 h. **Metabolism:** In liver. **Elimination:** In feces and urine; excreted in breast milk.

Common adverse effects in *italic*, life-threatening effects underlined; generic names in **bold**; classifications in SMALL CAPS; ♣ Canadian drug name; ⊘ Prototype drug

249

CLINICAL IMPLICATIONS

Assessment & Drug Effects

- Monitor electrolyte balance if significant diarrhea occurs, especially with frail older adults.
- Monitor restoration of normal bowel function.

Patient & Family Education

- A single dose taken before retiring usually results in evacuation of soft stool 6–12 h later.
- Frequent or prolonged use of irritant cathartics disrupts normal reflex activity of colon and rectum and can lead to drug dependence for evacuation.
- See bisacodyl for additional information.

CASPOFUNGIN ℗

(cas-po-fun'gin)
Cancidas
Classifications: ANTIBIOTIC; ECHINOCANDIN ANTIFUNGAL
Therapeutic: ANTIFUNGAL ANTIBIOTIC
Pregnancy Category: C

AVAILABILITY 50 mg and 70 mg powder for injection

ACTION & THERAPEUTIC EFFECT

Caspofungin is an antifungal agent that inhibits the synthesis of an integral component of the fungal cell wall of susceptible species. *Interferes with reproduction and growth of susceptible fungi.*

USES Treatment of invasive aspergillosis in those refractory to or intolerant of other antifungal therapies; empirical therapy for presumed fungal infection with febrile neutropenia; treatment of candidemia and intra-abdominal abscesses, peritonitis, and pleural space infections due to *Candida*.

UNLABELED USES Treatment of esophageal candidiasis with or without oropharyngeal candidiasis (thrush).

CONTRAINDICATIONS Hypersensitivity to any component of this product; mannitol; pregnancy (category C); not studied in patients with ESRF, or children <18 y.

CAUTIOUS USE Patients with moderate hepatic insufficiency; cholestasis; concomitant use of cyclosporine; lactation.

ROUTE & DOSAGE

Invasive *Aspergillosis*, Empirical Therapy, *Candida*

Adult: **IV** 70 mg on day 1, then 50 mg qd thereafter

ADMINISTRATION

Intravenous _____
Allow vial to come to room temperature.

- A loading dose is usually administered on day 1 followed on subsequent days by a maintenance dose.

PREPARE: **IV Infusion:** Reconstitute a 50 mg or 70 mg vial with 10.5 mL of NS, sterile water for injection, or bacteriostatic water for injection to yield 5 mg/mL and 7 mg/mL, respectively. Mix gently until clear. Withdraw 10 mL of reconstituted solution and add to 250 mL of NS, 1/2NS, or 0.225% NS, or RL. **DO NOT** use diluents or IV solutions containing dextrose.

ADMINISTER: **IV Infusion:** Give slowly over at least 1 h. Do not coinfuse with any other medication.

INCOMPATIBILITIES **Solution/additive:** Any **dextrose**-containing solution. Do not mix or co-infuse with any other medications.

Common adverse effects in *italic*, life-threatening effects underlined; generic names in **bold**; classifications in SMALL CAPS; ♣ Canadian drug name; ℗ Prototype drug

- Store IV solution for up to 24 h at 25° C (77° F) or below or 48 h at 2°–8° C (36°–46° F). Reconstituted solution should be stored at ≤25° C (≤77° F) for 1 h prior to preparing the IV solution for infusion.

ADVERSE EFFECTS (≥1%) **Body as a Whole:** Anaphylaxis, chills, *injection site reaction,* sensation of warmth. **CNS:** Headache. **CV:** Sinus tachycardia. **GI:** *Nausea, vomiting,* diarrhea, abdominal pain. **Hematologic/Lymphatic:** *Phlebitis, thrombophlebitis,* vasculitis, anemia. **Hepatic:** Elevated liver enzymes. **Metabolic:** Anorexia, *hypokalemia.* **Musculoskeletal:** Pain, myalgia. **Respiratory:** <u>Acute respiratory distress syndrome,</u> dyspnea. **Skin:** Rash, facial swelling, pruritus.

INTERACTIONS Drug: C y c l o s p o r ine increases overall systematic exposure to caspofungin; inducers of drug clearance or mixed inducer/inhibitors (e.g., **carbamazepine, dexamethasone, efavirenz, nelfinavir, nevirapine, phenytoin, rifampin**) can decrease caspofungin levels; caspofungin decreases the overall systematic exposure to **tacrolimus**.

PHARMACOKINETICS Distribution: 97% protein bound. **Metabolism:** Liver and plasma to inactive metabolites. **Elimination:** Both in urine and feces. **Half-life:** 9–11 h.

CLINICAL IMPLICATIONS

Assessment & Drug Effects
- Monitor for S&S of hypersensitivity during IV infusion; frequently monitor IV site for thrombophlebitis.
- Monitor for and report S&S of fluid retention (e.g., weight gain, swelling, peripheral edema), especially with known cardiovascular disease.

- Lab tests: Baseline and periodic LFTs; periodic kidney function tests, serum electrolytes, and CBC with differential, platelet count.
- Monitor blood levels of tacrolimus with concurrent therapy.

Patient & Family Education
- Report immediately any of the following: facial swelling, wheezing, difficulty breathing or swallowing, tightness in chest, rash, hives, itching, or sensation of warmth.

CEFACLOR ℗

(sef'a-klor)
Ceclor, Ceclor CD
Classifications: ANTIBIOTIC; SECOND-GENERATION CEPHALOSPORIN
Therapeutic: ANTIBIOTIC; CEPHALOSPORIN
Pregnancy Category: B

AVAILABILITY 250 mg, 500 mg tablets; 375 mg, 500 mg sustained-release tablets; 125 mg/5 mL, 187 mg/5 mL, 250 mg/5 mL, 375 mg/5 mL suspension

ACTION & THERAPEUTIC EFFECT
Semisynthetic, second-generation oral cephalosporin antibiotic. Possibly more active than other oral cephalosporins against gram-negative bacilli, especially beta-lactamase-producing *Haemophilus influenzae,* including ampicillin-resistant strains and certain gram-positive strains. Preferentially binds to one or more of the penicillin-binding proteins (PBPs) located on cell walls of susceptible organisms. This inhibits third and final stage of bacterial cell wall synthesis, thus killing the bacterium. *Effective in treating acute otitis media and acute sinusitis*

Common adverse effects in *italic*, life-threatening effects <u>underlined</u>; generic names in **bold**; classifications in SMALL CAPS; ♣ Canadian drug name; ℗ Prototype drug

251

where the causative agent is resistant to other antibiotics. Useful in treating respiratory and urinary tract infections.

USES Treatment of otitis media and infections of upper and lower respiratory tract, urinary tract, and skin and skin structures caused by ampicillin-resistant *H. influenzae;* acute uncomplicated UTI.

CONTRAINDICATIONS Hypersensitivity to cephalosporins and related antibiotics; pregnancy (category B). Safe use in infants <1 mo not established.
CAUTIOUS USE History of sensitivity to penicillins or other drug allergies; GI disease, colitis; markedly impaired renal function; older adults; coagulopathy; lactation.

ROUTE & DOSAGE

Mild to Moderate Infections

Adult: **PO** 250–500 mg q8h, or Ceclor CD 250–500 mg/q12h
Child >1 mo: **PO** 20–40 mg/kg/d divided q8h (max: 2 g/d)

ADMINISTRATION

Oral

- Give sustained-release tablets with food to enhance absorption. Food does not affect absorption of capsules.
- Ensure that sustained-release tablets are not chewed or crushed. They must be swallowed whole.
- After stock oral suspension is prepared, it should be kept refrigerated. Expiration date should appear on label. Discard unused portion after 14 d. Shake well before pouring.
- Store pulvules in tightly closed container unless otherwise directed.

ADVERSE EFFECTS (≥1%) **Body as a Whole:** Serum sickness-like reaction, eosinophilia, joint pain or swelling, fever, superinfections. **GI:** *Diarrhea,* nausea, vomiting, anorexia, <u>pseudomembranous colitis</u> (rare). **Skin:** Urticaria, pruritus, morbilliform eruptions.

DIAGNOSTIC TEST INTERFERENCE Cefaclor may produce positive *direct Coombs' test,* which can complicate *cross-matching procedures* and *hematologic studies.* False-positive *urine glucose* determinations may result with use of *copper sulfate reduction methods,* e.g., *Clinitest* or *Benedict's reagent,* but not with *glucose oxidase* (enzymatic) *tests* such as *Clinistix, Diastix, TesTape.*

INTERACTIONS Drug: Probenecid decreases renal excretion of cefaclor.

PHARMACOKINETICS Absorption: Well absorbed; acid stable. **Peak:** 30–60 min. **Elimination:** 60% of dose eliminated renally in 8 h; crosses placenta; excreted in breast milk. **Half-Life:** 0.5–1 h.

CLINICAL IMPLICATIONS

Assessment & Drug Effects

- Determine previous hypersensitivity to cephalosporins, penicillins, and other drug allergies before therapy is initiated.
- Lab tests: Perform culture and sensitivity tests prior to and periodically during therapy.
- Diarrhea, the most frequent adverse effect, may be due to a pharmacologic effect or to associated change in intestinal flora. If it persists, interruption of therapy may be necessary.
- Monitor for manifestations of drug hypersensitivity (see Appendix F).

Common adverse effects in *italic*, life-threatening effects <u>underlined</u>; generic names in **bold**; classifications in SMALL CAPS; ♣ Canadian drug name; ⊙ Prototype drug

Discontinue drug and promptly report them if they appear.
- Monitor for manifestations of superinfection (see Appendix F). Promptly report their appearance.

Patient & Family Education
- Report promptly any signs or symptoms of superinfection (see Appendix F).
- Yogurt or buttermilk (if allowed) may serve as a prophylactic against intestinal superinfections by helping to maintain normal intestinal flora.
- Take your medication for the full course of therapy as directed by physician.

CEFADROXIL

(sef-a-drox'ill)
Duricef
Classifications: ANTIBIOTIC; FIRST-GENERATION CEPHALOSPORIN
Therapeutic: ANTIBIOTIC; CEPHALOSPORIN
Prototype: Cefazolin
Pregnancy Category: B

AVAILABILITY 500 mg capsules; 1 g tablets; 125 mg/5 mL, 250 mg/5 mL, 500 mg/5 mL suspension

ACTION & *THERAPEUTIC EFFECT*
Semisynthetic, first-generation cephalosporin antibiotic. Bactericidal action (similar to that of penicillins): drug penetrates bacterial cell wall, resists beta-lactamases, and inactivates enzymes essential to cell wall synthesis. *Active against organisms that liberate cephalosporinase and penicillinase (beta-lactamases). Effective in reducing signs and symptoms of urinary tract infections, bone and joint infections, skin and soft tissue infections, and pharyngitis.*

USES Primarily in treatment of urinary tract infections caused by *Escherichia coli, Proteus mirabilis,* and *Klebsiella* sp; infections of skin and skin structures caused by *Staphylococci* and *Streptococci;* and for treatment of group A beta-hemolytic streptococcal pharyngitis and tonsillitis.

CONTRAINDICATIONS Hypersensitivity to cephalosporins and penicillin.

CAUTIOUS USE Sensitivity to penicillins or other drug allergies; impaired renal function, elderly; GI disease, history of colitis, coagulopathy; pregnancy (category B).

ROUTE & DOSAGE

Uncomplicated Urinary Tract Infection
Adult: **PO** 1–2 g/d in 1–2 divided doses
Child: **PO** 30 mg/kg/d in 2 divided doses

Skin and Skin Structure Infections, Streptococcal Pharyngitis, or Tonsillitis
Adult: **PO** 1 g/d in 1–2 divided doses
Child: **PO** 30 mg/kg/d in 2 divided doses

Renal Impairment
Cl_{cr} <25 mL/min
Adult: **PO** 1 g q24h
Child: **PO** 15 mg/kg q24h

ADMINISTRATION

Oral
- Give with food or milk to reduce nausea. If nausea persists, termination of therapy may be necessary.
- Follow directions for mixing oral suspension found on drug label. Reconstituted suspension con-

Common adverse effects in *italic*, life-threatening effects underlined; generic names in **bold**; classifications in SMALL CAPS; ♦ Canadian drug name; ⊘ Prototype drug

253

tains 125 mg or 250 mg cefadroxil per 5 mL.

- Shake suspension well before use; discard after 14 d.
- Store in tight container unless otherwise directed. Oral suspensions are stable for 14 d under refrigeration at 2°–8° C (36°–46° F). Avoid freezing. Note expiration date on label.

ADVERSE EFFECTS (≥1%) **Body as a Whole:** Hypersensitivity [Rash, swollen eyelids (<u>angioedema</u>), pruritus, chills], superinfections. **GI:** Nausea, *diarrhea,* vomiting, heartburn, gastritis, bloating, abdominal cramps.

DIAGNOSTIC TEST INTERFERENCE False-positive *urine glucose* determinations using *copper sulfate reduction reagents,* such as *Clinitest* or *Benedict's reagent,* but not with *glucose oxidase tests,* e.g., *Clinistix, Diastix, TesTape. Cefadroxil-induced positive direct Coombs' test* may interfere with *cross-matching procedures* and *hematologic studies.*

INTERACTIONS Drug: Probenecid decreases renal excretion of cefadroxil.

PHARMACOKINETICS Absorption: Acid stable; rapidly absorbed from GI tract. **Peak:** 1 h. **Elimination:** 90% unchanged in urine within 8 h; bacterial inhibitory levels persist 20–22 h; crosses placenta; excreted in breast milk. **Half-Life:** 1–12 h.

CLINICAL IMPLICATIONS
Assessment & Drug Effects

- Determine previous hypersensitivity to cephalosporins, penicillins, and other drug allergies, before therapy is initiated.

- Lab tests: Perform culture and sensitivity testing prior to and periodically during therapy.
- Lab tests: Perform baseline and periodic renal function studies in patients with renal function impairment, and monitor I&O ratio and pattern.
- Monitor for manifestations of drug hypersensitivity (see Signs & Symptoms, Appendix F). Discontinue drug and promptly report them if they appear.
- Monitor for manifestations of superinfection (see Signs & Symptoms, Appendix F). Promptly report their appearance.

Patient & Family Education

- Report promptly the onset of rash, urticaria, pruritus, or fever, as the possibility of an allergic reaction is high, if you are allergic to penicillin.
- Take medication for the full course of therapy as directed by your physician.
- Report promptly S&S of superinfections (see Appendix F).

CEFAZOLIN SODIUM ℗

(sef-a′zoe-lin)
Ancef
Classifications: ANTIBIOTIC; FIRST-GENERATION CEPHALOSPORIN
Therapeutic: ANTIBIOTIC; CEPHALOSPORIN
Pregnancy Category: B

AVAILABILITY 250 mg, 500 mg, 1 g, injection

ACTION & *THERAPEUTIC EFFECT*
Semisynthetic, first-generation cephalosporin C with limited activity against gram-negative organisms. Bactericidal action: preferentially binds to one or more of the

penicillin-binding proteins (PBP) located on cell walls of susceptible organisms. This inhibits third and final stage of bacterial cell wall synthesis, thus killing the bacterium. *Effective treatment for bone and joint infections, biliary tract infections, endocarditis prophylaxis and treatment, respiratory tract and genital tract infections, septicemia and skin infections, and surgical prophylaxis.*

USES Severe infections of urinary and biliary tracts, skin, soft tissue, and bone, and for bacteremia and endocarditis caused by susceptible organisms; also perioperative prophylaxis in patients undergoing procedures associated with high risk of infection, e.g., open heart surgery.

CONTRAINDICATIONS Hypersensitivity to any cephalosporin and related antibiotics; pregnancy (category B).

CAUTIOUS USE History of penicillin sensitivity, impaired renal function, patients on sodium restriction; coagulopathy; GI disease, colitis.

ROUTE & DOSAGE

Moderate to Severe Infections

Adult: **IV/IM** 250 mg–2 g q8h, up to 2 g q4h (max: 12 g/d)
Child: **IV/IM** 25–100 mg/kg/d in 3–4 divided doses, up to 100 mg/kg/d (not to exceed adult doses)
Neonate: **IV** <7 d: 40 mg/kg/d divided q12h; ≥7 d: 40–60 mg/kg/d divided q8–12h

Surgical Prophylaxis

Adult: **IV/IM** 1–2 g 30–60 min before surgery, then 0.5–1 g q8h
Child: **IV/IM** 25–50 mg/kg 30–60 min before surgery, then q8h for 24 h

Renal Impairment

Cl_{cr} <35 mL/min: dose q12h; Cl_{cr} 10 mL/min: dose q24h

ADMINISTRATION

Intramuscular

- Preparation of IM solution: Reconstitute with sterile water for injection, bacteriostatic water for injection, or 0.9% sodium chloride injection. Reconstituted solutions are stable for 24 hr at room temperature and for 96 hr refrigerated.
- IM injections should be made deep into large muscle mass. Pain on injection is usually minimal. Rotate injection sites.

Intravenous

IV administration to neonates, infants, and children: Verify correct IV concentration and rate of infusion with physician.

PREPARE: Direct: Dilute each 1 g with 10 mL of sterile water for injection. **Intermittent:** Further dilute with 50–100 mL of NS or D5W.

ADMINISTER: Direct/Intermittent: Infuse 1 g over 5 min or longer as determined by the amount of solution. The risk of IV site reactions may be reduced by proper dilution of IV solution, use of small bore IV needle in a large vein, and by rotating injection sites.

INCOMPATIBILITIES Solution/additive: AMINOGLYCOSIDES, **ascorbic acid, atracurium, bleomycin, cimetidine, hydromorphone, lidocaine, ranitidine, vitamin B complex with C. Y-site:** **Amiodarone,** AMINOGLYCOSIDES, **amphotericin B cholesteryl complex, idarubicin, pentamidine, vinorelbine.**

Common adverse effects in *italic*, life-threatening effects underlined; generic names in **bold**; classifications in SMALL CAPS; ♣ Canadian drug name; ⊕ Prototype drug

255

ADVERSE EFFECTS (≥1%) **Body as a Whole:** Anaphylaxis, fever, eosinophilia, superinfections, seizure (high doses in patients with renal insufficiency). **GI:** *Diarrhea,* anorexia, abdominal cramps. **Skin:** Maculopapular rash, urticaria.

DIAGNOSTIC TEST INTERFERENCE Because of cefazolin effect on the *direct Coombs' test,* transfusion *cross-matching procedures* and *hematologic studies* may be complicated. False-positive *urine glucose* determinations are possible with use of *copper sulfate tests* (e.g., *Clinitest* or *Benedict's reagent*) but not with *glucose oxidase tests* such as *TesTape, Diastix,* or *Clinistix.*

INTERACTIONS Drug: Probenecid decreases renal elimination of cefazolin.

PHARMACOKINETICS Peak: 1–2 h after IM; 5 min after IV. **Distribution:** Poor CNS penetration even with inflamed meninges; high concentrations in bile and in diseased bone; crosses placenta. **Elimination:** 70% unchanged in urine in 6 h; small amount excreted in breast milk. **Half-Life:** 90–130 min.

CLINICAL IMPLICATIONS
Assessment & Drug Effects
- Determine history of hypersensitivity to cephalosporins, penicillins, and other drugs, before therapy is initiated.
- Lab tests: Perform culture and sensitivity testing prior to and during therapy. Therapy may be initiated pending results.
- Monitor I&O rates and pattern: Be alert to changes in BUN, serum creatinine.
- If patient has had a reaction to penicillin, be alert to signs of hy-

persensitivity with use of cefazolin. Cross-allergenicity between cephalosporins and penicillin has been reported. Prompt attention should be given to onset of signs of hypersensitivity (see Appendix F).
- Promptly report the onset of diarrhea, which may or may not be dose related. It is seen especially in patients with history of drug-related GI disturbances. Pseudomembranous colitis, a potentially life-threatening condition, starts with diarrhea.

Patient & Family Education
- Report promptly any signs or symptoms of superinfection (see Appendix F).
- Report signs of hemostatic defects: ecchymoses, petechiae, nosebleed.

CEFDINIR
(cef′di-nir)
Omnicef
Classifications: ANTIBIOTIC; THIRD-GENERATION CEPHALOSPORIN
Therapeutic: ANTIBIOTIC; CEPHALOSPORIN
Prototype: Cefotaxime sodium
Pregnancy Category: B

AVAILABILITY 300 mg capsules; 125 mg/5 mL suspension

ACTION & *THERAPEUTIC EFFECT*
Broad-spectrum semisynthetic third-generation beta-lactamase cephalosporin antibiotic. *Effective against a wide variety of gram-positive and gram-negative bacteria.*

USES Community-acquired pneumonia, acute exacerbations of chronic bronchitis, acute maxillary sinusitis, pharyngitis, tonsillitis, uncomplicated skin infections, bacterial otitis media.

CONTRAINDICATIONS Hypersensitivity to cefdinir and other cephalosporins.

CAUTIOUS USE Hypersensitivity to penicillins, penicillin derivatives; renal impairment; ulcerative colitis or antibiotic-induced colitis; bleeding disorders; GI disorders; liver or kidney disease; pregnancy (category B), lactation. Safety and efficacy in neonates and infants <6 mo old not established.

ROUTE & DOSAGE

Community-Acquired Pneumonia, Skin Infections
Adult: PO 300 mg q12h times 10 d
Child 6 mo–12 y: PO 7 mg/kg q12h times 10 d

Chronic Bronchitis, Maxillary Sinusitis, Pharyngitis, Tonsillitis
Adult: PO 600 mg q24h or 300 mg q12h times 10 d
Child 6 mo–12 y: PO 14 mg/kg q24h or 7 mg/kg q12h times 10 d

ADMINISTRATION

Oral
- Do not give within 2 h of aluminum- or magnesium-containing antacids or iron supplements.
- Reconstitute oral suspension to 125 mg/mL by adding water (38 mL to 60 mL bottle or 63 mL to 100 mL bottle). Shake well before each use.
- Consult physician for dosage adjustment if creatinine clearance <30 mL/min and for patients on hemodialysis.
- Store in tightly closed container. Discard after 10 days.

ADVERSE EFFECTS (≥1%) **GI:** *Diarrhea,* nausea, abdominal pain. **Metabolic:** Increased GGT, increased urine protein, hematuria. **CNS:** Headache. **Skin:** Rash, cutaneous moniliasis. **Urogenital:** Vaginal moniliasis, vaginitis.

DIAGNOSTIC TEST INTERFERENCE False positive for *ketones* or *glucose* in urine using *nitroprusside* or *Clinitest.*

INTERACTIONS Drug: ANTACIDS should be taken at least 2 h before or after cefdinir; **probenecid** prolongs cefdinir elimination; **iron** decreases absorption.

PHARMACOKINETICS Absorption: 16–25% bioavailability. **Peak:** 2–4 h. **Distribution:** 60–70% protein bound; penetrates sinus tissue, blister fluid, lung tissue, middle ear fluid. **Metabolism:** Hepatic. **Elimination:** In urine. **Half-Life:** 1.6 h.

CLINICAL IMPLICATIONS

Assessment & Drug Effects
- Determine previous hypersensitivity to cephalosporins, penicillins, and other drug allergies before therapy is initiated.
- Carefully monitor for and immediately report S&S of: hypersensitivity, superinfection, or pseudomembranous colitis (see Appendix F).
- Discontinue drug and notify physician if seizures associated with drug therapy occur.

Patient & Family Education
- Allow a minimum of 2 h between cefdinir and antacids containing aluminum or magnesium, or drugs containing iron.
- Immediately contact physician if a rash, diarrhea, or new infection (e.g., yeast infection) develops.
- Drug may cause false positive for urine ketones or glucose. Consult package insert.

Common adverse effects in *italic*, life-threatening effects underlined; generic names in **bold**; classifications in SMALL CAPS; ♣ Canadian drug name; ⊙ Prototype drug

257

CEFDITOREN PIVOXIL

(cef-ditor'en)
Spectracef
Classifications: ANTIBIOTIC;
THIRD-GENERATION CEPHALOSPORIN
Therapeutic: ANTIBIOTIC; CEPHALO-
SPORIN
Prototype: Cefotaxime sodium
Pregnancy Category: B

AVAILABILITY 200 mg tablets

ACTION & *THERAPEUTIC EFFECT*
Semisynthetic cephalosporin. Bactericidal activity results from the inhibition of cell wall synthesis
through an affinity for penicillin-
binding proteins (PBPs). Stable in
the presence of a variety of bacterial beta-lactamase enzymes, including penicillinases and some
cephalosporinases. *Antibacterial
activity is effective against both aerobic gram-positive and aerobic
gram-negative bacteria.*

USES Acute exacerbation of bacterial chronic bronchitis, pharyngitis,
tonsillitis, uncomplicated skin and
skin-structure infections.

CONTRAINDICATIONS Known allergy to cephalosporins or any of
the components of cefditoren; car-
nitine deficiency; milk protein hypersensitivity.
CAUTIOUS USE History of hypersensitivity to penicillin or other drugs;
renal or hepatic impairment; poor
nutritional status; coagulopathy; diabetes mellitus; colitis, GI disease;
older adults; concurrent anticoagulant therapy; pregnancy (category
B), lactation. Safety and efficacy in
children <12 y are not established.

ROUTE & DOSAGE

Chronic Bronchitis
Adult: **PO** 400 mg b.i.d. times 10 d

**Pharyngitis, Tonsillitis, Skin
Infections**
Adult: **PO** 200 mg b.i.d. times 10 d
Renal Impairment
Cl_{cr} 30–49 mL/min: 200 mg
b.i.d.; <30 mL/min: 200 mg q.d.

ADMINISTRATION

Oral
- Give with food to enhance absorption.
- Do not give within 2 h of an antacid or H_2-receptor antagonist
(such as cimetidine).
- Verify dose for patients with renal
insufficiency. Manufacturer recommends doses not to exceed 200
mg b.i.d. for patients with creatinine clearance of 30–49 mL/min
and doses not to exceed 200 mg
q.d. for patients with creatinine
clearance of <30 mL/min.
- Store at 15°–30° C (58°–86° F).
Protect from light and moisture.

ADVERSE EFFECTS (≥1%) **GI:** *Diarrhea,* nausea, abdominal pain,
dyspepsia, vomiting. **Hematologic:**
Anemia, leukocytosis. **CNS:** Headache. **Urogenital:** Vaginal moniliasis, hematuria.

INTERACTIONS Drug: ANTACIDS, H_2-
RECEPTOR ANTAGONISTS may decrease
absorption; **probenecid** will decrease elimination.

PHARMACOKINETICS Absorption:
14% reaches systemic circulation.
Distribution: 88% protein bound,
distributes into blister fluid, tonsils.
Metabolism: Hydrolyzed. **Elimination:** Primarily in urine. **Half-Life:**
1.6 h.

CLINICAL IMPLICATIONS

Assessment & Drug Effects
- Obtain history of hypersensitivity
to cephalosporins, penicillins, and
other drug allergies.

- Lab tests: Baseline C&S tests recommended prior to and periodically during therapy. Initiate drug pending results. Baseline and periodic studies of kidney function; frequent PT determinations in patients at risk for increased prothrombin time; as indicated, Hct & Hgb, CBC with differential, urinalysis, serum electrolytes, and liver enzymes.
- Monitor for manifestations of drug hypersensitivity (see Appendix F). Withhold drug and report promptly to physician if they appear.
- Monitor for and report promptly manifestations of superinfection (see Appendix F), especially diarrhea. Diarrhea may indicate a change in intestinal flora and development of enterocolitis. If it persists, interruption of therapy may be necessary.
- Monitor for and report immediately signs of seizure activity or loss of seizure control.

Patient & Family Education

- Do not take within 2 h of antacids or other drugs used to reduce stomach acids.
- Discontinue drug and report to physician signs of an allergic reaction (e.g., rash, urticaria, pruritus, fever).
- Report promptly S&S of superinfection (see Appendix F), especially unexplained diarrhea. Antibiotic-associated colitis is a superinfection that may occur in 4–9 d or as long as 6 wk after drug is discontinued.
- Use daily yogurt or buttermilk (if allowed) as a prophylactic against intestinal superinfections.

CEFEPIME HYDROCHLORIDE

(cef'e-peem)
Maxipime

Classifications: ANTIBIOTIC; FOURTH-GENERATION CEPHALOSPORIN
Therapeutic: ANTIBIOTIC; CEPHALOSPORIN
Prototype: Cefotaxime sodium
Pregnancy Category: B

AVAILABILITY 500 mg, 1 g, 2 g vials

ACTION & THERAPEUTIC EFFECT Cefepime, considered to be a fourth-generation cephalosporin antibiotic that preferentially binds to one or more of the penicillin-binding proteins (PBPs) located on cell walls of susceptible organisms. This inhibits the third and final stage of bacterial cell wall synthesis, thus killing the bacteria (bactericidal). *Cefepime is similar to third-generation cephalosporins with respect to broad gram-negative coverage; however, cefepime has broader gram-positive coverage than third-generation cephalosporins. It is highly resistant to hydrolysis by most beta-lactamase bacteria.*

USES Uncomplicated and complicated UTI, skin and soft tissue infections, pneumonia caused by susceptible organisms. Empiric monotherapy for febrile neutropenic patients.

CONTRAINDICATIONS Hypersensitivity to cefepime, other cephalosporins, severe reaction to penicillins, or other beta-lactam antibiotics.
CAUTIOUS USE Patients with history of GI disease, particularly colitis; renal insufficiency; pregnancy (category B), lactation. Safety and efficacy of cefepime in children <12 y not known.

ROUTE & DOSAGE

Mild to Moderate Infections
Adult: **IV/IM** 0.5–1g q12h for 7–10 d

Common adverse effects in *italic*, life-threatening effects underlined; generic names in **bold**; classifications in SMALL CAPS; ◆ Canadian drug name; ⊕ Prototype drug

259

C

Moderate to Severe Infections

Adult: **IV** 1–2g q12h for 10 d

Febrile Neutropenia

Adult: **IV** 2 g q8h for 7 d or until resolution of neutropenia
Child: **IV** 50 mg/kg q8h until resolution of neutropenia

UTI/Pneumonia

Child: **IV** 50 mg/kg q12h for 7–10 d

Renal Impairment

Cl_{cr} 30–60 mL/min: dose q24h; 11–29 mL/min: give 50% of normal dose q24h; <10 mL/min: 250–500 mg q24h
Hemodialysis: Administer dose after dialysis

ADMINISTRATION

Intramuscular

- Reconstitute 500-mg vial and 1-g vial, respectively, with 1.3 or 2.4 mL of one of the following: Sterile Water for Injection, 0.9% NaCl Injection, Bacteriostatic Water for Injection with Parabens or benzyl alcohol, or other compatible solution.

Intravenous

PREPARE: **Intermittent:** Dilute with 50–100 mL of one of the following: NS, D5W, D5/NS or other compatible solution.
ADMINISTER: **Intermittent:** Infuse over 30 min; with Y-type administration set, discontinue other compatible solutions while infusing cefepime.
INCOMPATIBILITIES Solution/additive: AMINOGLYCOSIDES, **ampicillin, aminophylline, metronidazole.** Y-site: **Acyclovir, amphotericin B, amphotericin B cholesteryl complex, chlordiazepoxide, chlorpromazine, cimetidine, ciprofloxacin, cis-**

platin, dacarbazine, daunorubicin, diazepam, diphenhydramine, dobutamine, dopamine, doxorubicin, droperidol, enalaprilat, etoposide, famotidine, filgrastim, floxuridine, ganciclovir, haloperidol, hydroxyzine, idarubicin, ifosfamide, magnesium sulfate, mannitol, mechlorethamine, meperidine, metoclopramide, mitomycin, mitoxantrone, morphine, nalbuphine, ofloxacin, ondansetron, plicamycin, prochlorperazine, promethazine, streptozocin, vancomycin, vinblastine, vincristine.

- Store reconstituted solution at 20°–25° C (68°–77° F) for 24 h or in refrigerator at 2°–8° C (36°–46° F) for 7 days. Protect from light.

ADVERSE EFFECTS (≥1%) **Body as a Whole:** Eosinophilia. **GI:** Antibiotic-associated colitis, diarrhea, nausea, oral moniliasis, vomiting, elevated liver function tests (ALT, AST). **CNS:** Headache, fever. **Skin:** Phlebitis, pain, inflammation, rash, pruritus, urticaria. **Urogenital:** Vaginitis.

DIAGNOSTIC TEST INTERFERENCE
Positive *Coombs' test* without hemolysis. May cause false-positive *urine glucose test* with *Clinitest.*

INTERACTIONS Drug: AMINOGLYCOSIDES may increase risk of nephrotoxicity and have additive/synergistic effects. May decrease efficacy of ORAL CONTRACEPTIVES. **Probenecid** may increase levels.

PHARMACOKINETICS Absorption: Well absorbed after IM administration; serum levels significantly lower than after equivalent IV dose. **Distribution:** Widely distributed, may cross inflamed meninges; crosses placenta, secreted into breast milk. **Metabolism:** In liver. **Elimination:** In urine. **Half-Life:** 2 h.

CLINICAL IMPLICATIONS

Assessment & Drug Effects

- Determine history of hypersensitivity reactions to cephalosporins, penicillins, or other drugs before therapy is initiated.
- Lab tests: Perform culture and sensitivity tests before initiation of therapy. Dosage may be started pending test results.
- Monitor for S&S of hypersensitivity (see Appendix F). Report their appearance promptly and discontinue drug.
- Monitor for S&S of superinfection or pseudomembranous colitis (see Appendix F); immediately report either to physician.
- With concurrent high-dose aminoglycoside therapy, closely monitor for nephrotoxicity and ototoxicity.

Patient & Family Education

- Promptly report any S&S of hypersensitivity, superinfection, and pseudomembranous colitis.

CEFIXIME

(ce-fix'ime)

Suprax

Classifications: ANTIBIOTIC, BETA-LACTAM; THIRD-GENERATION CEPHALOSPORIN
Therapeutic: ANTIBIOTIC; CEPHALOSPORIN
Prototype: Cefotaxime sodium
Pregnancy Category: B

AVAILABILITY 100 mg/5 mL suspension

ACTION & *THERAPEUTIC EFFECT*
Cefixime is a third-generation cephalosporin. As a beta-lactam antibiotic like the penicillins, it is mainly bactericidal. It inhibits the third and final stage of bacterial cell wall synthesis by preferentially binding to specific penicillin-binding proteins (PBPs) located inside the bacterial cell wall. *Cefixime is highly stable in the presence of beta-lactamases (penicillinases and cephalosporinases) and therefore has excellent activity against a wide range of gram-negative bacteria. It is bactericidal against susceptible bacteria.*

USES Effective against *Streptococcus pyogenes, Streptococcus pneumoniae,* and gram-negative bacilli, including *Haemophilus influenzae, Branhamella catarrhalis,* and *Neisseria gonorrhoeae.* Little activity against *Staphylococci,* and no activity against *Pseudomonas aeruginosa;* also uncomplicated UTI, otitis media, pharyngitis, tonsillitis, and bronchitis.

CONTRAINDICATIONS Patients with known allergy to the cephalosporin group of antibiotics, severe reaction to penicillin.
CAUTIOUS USE Allergy to penicillin, history of colitis, renal insufficiency, GI disease, coagulopathy, pregnancy (category B), lactation. Safety and effectiveness in infants <6 mo have not been established.

ROUTE & DOSAGE

Infection

Adult: **PO** 400 mg/d in 1–2 divided doses
Child: **PO** 8 mg/kg/d in 1–2 divided doses

ADMINISTRATION

Oral

- Do not substitute tablets for liquid in treatment of otitis media because of lack of bioequivalence.

Common adverse effects in *italic*, life-threatening effects <u>underlined</u>; generic names in **bold**; classifications in SMALL CAPS; ◆ Canadian drug name; ⊙ Prototype drug

261

C

- After reconstitution, suspension may be kept for 14 d at room temperature or refrigerated. Store away from heat and light. Keep tightly closed and shake well before using.

ADVERSE EFFECTS (≥1%) **GI:** *Diarrhea,* loose stools, nausea, vomiting, dyspepsia, flatulence. **CNS:** Drug fever, headache, dizziness. **Skin:** Rash, pruritus, **Urogenital:** Vaginitis, genital pruritus.

INTERACTIONS Drug: AMINOGLYCOSIDES may increase risk of nephrotoxicity and have additive/synergistic effects. May decrease efficacy of ORAL CONTRACEPTIVES. **Probenecid** may increase levels.

PHARMACOKINETICS Absorption: 40–50% from GI tract. **Peak:** 2–6 h. **Distribution:** Into breast milk. **Elimination:** 50% in urine, 50% in bile. **Half-Life:** 3–4 h.

CLINICAL IMPLICATIONS

Assessment & Drug Effects

- Determine previous hypersensitivity reactions to cephalosporins, penicillins, and history of other allergies, particularly to drugs prior to initiation of therapy.
- Lab tests: Perform culture and sensitivity tests prior to initiation of therapy and periodically during therapy. Therapy may be implemented pending test results.
- Discontinue if seizures associated with the drug therapy occur.
- Monitor for superinfections (see Appendix F) caused by overgrowth of nonsusceptible organisms, particularly during prolonged use.
- Monitor I&O rates and pattern: Nephrotoxicity occurs more frequently in patients >50 y, with impaired renal function, in the debilitated, and in patients receiving high doses or other nephrotoxic drugs.
- Carefully monitor anyone with a history of allergies, especially to drugs. Report manifestations of hypersensitivity (see Appendix F).
- Promptly report loose stools or diarrhea, which may indicate pseudomembranous colitis (see Appendix F). Discontinuation of drug may be necessary.

Patient & Family Education

- Report loose stools or diarrhea during drug therapy and for several weeks after. Older adult patients are especially susceptible to pseudomembranous colitis.
- Take this antibiotic for the full course of treatment.
- Do not miss any doses and take the doses at evenly spaced times, day and night.

CEFOPERAZONE SODIUM

(sef-oh-per′a-zone)
Cefobid
Classifications: ANTIBIOTIC; THIRD-GENERATION CEPHALOSPORIN
Therapeutic: ANTIBIOTIC; CEPHALOSPORIN
Prototype: Cefotaxime sodium
Pregnancy Category: B

AVAILABILITY 1 g, 2 g injection

ACTION & *THERAPEUTIC EFFECT*
Semisynthetic third-generation cephalosporin antibiotic. Preferentially binds to one or more of the penicillin-binding proteins (PBP) located on cell walls of susceptible organisms. This inhibits third and final stage of bacterial cell wall synthesis, thus killing the bacterium. Spectrum of activity is similar to that of cefotaxime. *Generally active against a wide variety of gram-*

negative bacteria, including some strains of Pseudomonas aeruginosa. Also active against some organisms resistant to first- and second-generation cephalosporins, some aminoglycoside antibiotics and penicillins.

USES Infections of skin and skin structures, urinary tract, respiratory tract; peritonitis and other intra-abdominal infections, pelvic inflammatory disease, endometritis and other infections of the female genital tract; bacterial septicemia. **UNLABELED USES** Children <12 y.

CONTRAINDICATIONS Hypersensitivity to cephalosporins and related beta-lactam antibiotics. **CAUTIOUS USE** History of hypersensitivity to penicillins, history of allergy, particularly to drugs; hepatic disease, history of colitis or other GI disease, history of bleeding disorders; pregnancy (category B), lactation.

ROUTE & DOSAGE

Moderate to Severe Infections
Adult: **IV/IM** 1–2 g q12h; up to 16 g/d in 2–4 divided doses

ADMINISTRATION

Intramuscular
- To prepare IM injections, appropriate diluents include sterile water for injection, bacteriostatic water for injection, and 0.5% lidocaine. See package insert for reconstitution procedure.
- Reconstitute for IM: Dilute each 1 g with 5 mL sterile water. Shake vigorously to dissolve. If concentrations of ≥250 mg/mL are needed for IM injection, 2% lidocaine should be added. See manufacturer's directions.

Intravenous
IV administration to infants and children: Verify correct IV concentration and rate of infusion with physician.
- Rapid, direct (bolus) IV injections are not recommended.

PREPARE: **Intermittent:** Dilute each 1 g with 5 mL sterile water. Shake vigorously to dissolve, then dilute in 50–100 mL of D5W or NS. **Continuous: Further** dilute in 500–1000 mL of the selected IV solution.

ADMINISTER: **Intermittent:** Give over 15–30 min. **Continuous:** Give 500–1000 mL over 6–24 h.

INCOMPATIBILITIES **Solution/additive:** AMINOGLYCOSIDES, **doxapram. Y-site:** AMINOGLYCOSIDES, **amifostine, amphotericin B cholesteryl complex, cisatracurium, diltiazem, doxorubicin liposome, filgrastim, gemcitabine, hetastarch, labetalol, meperidine, ondansetron, pentamidine, perphenazine, promethazine, sargramostim, vinorelbine.**

- Protect sterile powder and piggyback units from light and store at or below 25° C (77° F). Reconstituted solutions may be stored in original containers for 24 h at 15°–25° C (59°–77° F); for 5 d under refrigeration at 5° C (41° F) or less, or for at least 3 wk in freezer.

ADVERSE EFFECTS (≥1%) **Body as a Whole:** Fever, eosinophilia, phlebitis (IV site), transient pain (IM site), superinfections. **GI:** Abdominal cramps, bloating, loose stools or *diarrhea*, pseudomembranous colitis, elevated liver function tests (AST, ALT, alkaline phosphatase). **Hematologic:** Abnormal PT/INR and PTT; hypoprothrombinemia. **Skin:** Skin

Common adverse effects in *italic*, life-threatening effects underlined; generic names in **bold**; classifications in SMALL CAPS; ✤ Canadian drug name; ☉ Prototype drug

263

C

rash, urticaria, pruritus. **Urogenital:** Transient increases in serum creatinine and BUN, oliguria.

DIAGNOSTIC TEST INTERFERENCE

Cefoperazone can cause positive **direct Coombs' test,** which may result in interferences with **hematologic studies** and **cross-matching** procedures. False-positive results for **urine glucose** using **copper sulfate tests (Benedict's, Clinitest),** but not with **glucose enzymatic tests,** e.g., **Clinistix, TesTape, Diastix.** Also causes **prolonged prothrombin** twice during therapy.

INTERACTIONS Drug: Probenecid

decreases renal elimination of cefoperazone; **alcohol** produces disulfiram reaction.

PHARMACOKINETICS Peak: 1–2 h

after IM; 15–20 min after IV. **Distribution:** Low CNS penetration except with inflamed meninges; highest concentrations in bile; crosses placenta. **Elimination:** 70–75% excreted unchanged in bile in 6–12 h, small amount excreted in breast milk. **Half-Life:** 2 h.

CLINICAL IMPLICATIONS

Assessment & Drug Effects

- Determine hypersensitivity to cephalosporins, penicillins, and other drug allergies before therapy begins.
- Lab tests: Perform culture and sensitivity studies before initiation of therapy and during therapy, as indicated. Therapy may begin pending test results. Perform PTT and PT/INR before and during therapy.
- Observe for and question patient about signs of hemostatic defects: wound bleeding (e.g., surgical patient), nose bleeds, bleeding gums, bloody sputum, hema-

turia. Hypoprothrombinemia and vitamin K deficiency are possible complications of therapy and can result in significant blood loss in some patients. Patients at risk are those with poor nutritional states, malabsorption problems, patients on hyperalimentation regimens, and alcoholism. Vitamin K supplements may be prescribed for these patients, if indicated.

- Report the onset of loose stools or diarrhea. Most patients respond to replacement of fluids, electrolytes, and proteins. Discontinuation of drug may be required for some patients.
- Monitor cefoperazone serum levels (at steady state: 150 mg/mL) in patients with hepatic disease or biliary obstruction who are receiving over 4 g/d, patients with both hepatic and renal disease receiving over 1–2 g/d, and patients with renal impairment on high dose therapy.

Patient & Family Education

- Do not ingest alcohol within 72 h after drug administration as this will cause a disulfiram-like reaction (see Signs & Symptoms, Appendix F). Effects generally appear within 15–30 min after alcohol is taken and disappear spontaneously 1–2 h later.
- Report promptly any signs or symptoms of superinfection (see Appendix F).

CEFOTAXIME SODIUM ℗

(sef-oh-taks′eem)

Claforan

Classifications: BETA-LACTAM ANTIBIOTIC; THIRD-GENERATION CEPHALOSPORIN

Therapeutic: ANTIBIOTIC; CEPHALOSPORIN

Pregnancy Category: B

Common adverse effects in *italic*, life-threatening effects underlined; generic names in **bold**; classifications in SMALL CAPS; ✢ Canadian drug name; ℗ Prototype drug

AVAILABILITY 500 mg, 1 g, 2 g injection

ACTION & *THERAPEUTIC EFFECT*
Broad-spectrum semi-synthetic third-generation cephalosporin antibiotic. Preferentially binds to one or more of the penicillin-binding proteins (PBP) located on cell walls of susceptible organisms. This inhibits third and final stage of bacterial cell wall synthesis, thus killing the bacteria. *Generally active against a wide variety of gram-negative bacteria including most of the Enterobacteriaceae. Also active against some organisms resistant to first- and second-generation cephalosporins, and currently available aminoglycoside antibiotics and penicillins.*

USES Serious infections of lower respiratory tract, skin and skin structures, bones and joints, CNS (including meningitis and ventriculitis), gynecologic and GU tract infections, including uncomplicated gonococcal infections caused by penicillinase-producing *Neisseria gonorrhoeae* (PPNG). Also used to treat bacteremia or septicemia, intra-abdominal infections, and for perioperative prophylaxis.

UNLABELED USES Currently recommended by CDC for treatment of disseminated gonococcal infections (gonococcal arthritis-dermatitis syndrome) and as drug of choice for gonococcal ophthalmia caused by PPNG in adults, children, and neonates.

CONTRAINDICATIONS Hypersensitivity to cephalosporins and other beta-lactam antibiotics.
CAUTIOUS USE History of type I hypersensitivity reactions to penicillin; history of allergy to other beta-lactam; antibiotics; coagulopathy; renal impairment; history of colitis or other GI disease; pregnancy (category B).

ROUTE & DOSAGE

Moderate to Severe Infections
Adult: **IV/IM** 1–2 g q8–12h, up to 2 g q4h (max: 12 g/d)
Child: **IV/IM** ≤1wk: 50 mg/kg q12h; 1–4 wk: 50–200 mg/kg/24h divided q6–12h; 1 mo–12 y: 50–200 mg/kg/d divided q4–8h (max: 12 g/24h)
Disseminated Gonorrhea
Adult: **IV** 1 g q8h
Surgical Prophylaxis
Adult: **IV/IM** 1 g 30–90 min before surgery
Renal Impairment
Cl_{cr} 10–50 mL/min: dose q8–12h; <10 mL/min: dose q24h

ADMINISTRATION

Intramuscular
- Add 3 mL sterile water for injection or bacteriostatic water for injection to vial containing 1 g drug, providing a solution of approximately 300 mg cefotaxime/mL.
- Administer IM injection deeply into large muscle mass (e.g., upper outer quadrant of gluteus maximus). Aspirate to avoid inadvertent injection into blood vessel. If IM dose is 2 g, divide dose and administer into 2 different sites.
- Risk of phlebitis may be reduced by use of a small needle in a large vein.

Intravenous
IV administration to infants and children: Verify correct IV concentration and rate of infusion with physician.

Common adverse effects in *italic*, life-threatening effects underlined; generic names in **bold**; classifications in SMALL CAPS; ♣ Canadian drug name; Ⓟ Prototype drug

- Do not admix cefotaxime with sodium bicarbonate or any fluid with a pH >7.5.

PREPARE: **Direct:** Add 10 mL diluent to vial with 1 or 2 g drug providing a solution containing 95 or 180 mg/mL, respectively. **Intermittent:** To 1 or 2 g drug add 50 or 100 mL D5W, NS, D5/NS, D5/.45% NaCl, RL, or other compatible diluent. **Continuous:** Dilute in 500–1000 mL compatible IV solution. *ADMINISTER:* **Direct:** Give over 3–5 min. **Intermittent:** Give over 20–30 min, preferably via butterfly or scalp vein-type needles. **Continuous:** Infuse over 6–24 h. *INCOMPATIBILITIES* **Solution/additive:** AMINOGLYCOSIDES, **aminophylline, doxapram, sodium bicarbonate, vancomycin. Y-site:** Allopurinol, AMINOGLYCOSIDES, **aminophylline, azithromycin, doxapram, filgrastim, fluconazole, gemcitabine, hetastarch, sodium bicarbonate; pentamidine, vancomycin.**

- Protect from excessive light. Reconstituted solutions may be stored in original containers for 24 h at room temperature; for 10 days under refrigeration at 5° C (41° F) or less; or for at least 13 wk in frozen state.

ADVERSE EFFECTS (≥1%) **Body as a Whole:** Fever, nocturnal perspiration, inflammatory reaction at IV site, phlebitis, thrombophlebitis; pain, induration, and tenderness at IM site, superinfections. **GI:** Nausea, vomiting, *diarrhea,* abdominal pain, colitis, pseudomembranous colitis, anorexia. **Metabolic:** Transient increases in serum AST, ALT, LDH, bilirubin, alkaline phosphatase concentrations. **Skin:** Rash, pruritus.

DIAGNOSTIC TEST INTERFERENCE May cause falsely elevated *serum* or *urine creatinine* values *(Jaffe reaction).* False-positive reactions for *urine glucose* have not been reported using *copper sulfate reduction methods,* e.g., *Benedict's, Clinitest;* however, since it has occurred with other cephalosporins, it may be advisable to use *glucose oxidase tests (Clinistix, TesTape, Diastix).* Positive *direct antiglobulin (Coombs') test* results may interfere with *hematologic studies* and *cross-matching* procedures.

INTERACTIONS Drug: Probenecid decreases renal elimination; **alcohol** produces disulfiram reaction.

PHARMACOKINETICS Peak: 30 min after IM; 5 min after IV. **Distribution:** CNS penetration except with inflamed meninges; also penetrates aqueous humor, ascitic and prostatic fluids; crosses placenta. **Metabolism:** In liver to active metabolites. **Elimination:** 50–60% unchanged in urine in 24 h; small amount excreted in breast milk. **Half-Life:** 1 h.

CLINICAL IMPLICATIONS

Assessment & Drug Effects
- Determine previous hypersensitivity reactions to cephalosporins and penicillins, and history of other allergies, particularly to drugs, before therapy is initiated.
- Lab tests: Perform culture and sensitivity tests before initiation of therapy and periodically during therapy if indicated. Therapy may be instituted pending test results. Serum creatinine, creatinine clearance, BUN should be evaluated at regular intervals during therapy and for several months after drug has been discontinued. Perform periodic hematologic studies (including PT and PTT) and evalua-

tion of hepatic functions with high doses or prolonged therapy.

- Monitor I&O rates and patterns: Report change in I&O in patients with impaired renal function or with chronic UTI or who are receiving high dosages or an aminoglycoside concomitantly.

- Superinfection due to overgrowth of nonsusceptible organisms may occur, particularly with prolonged therapy.

- Report onset of diarrhea promptly. Check for fever. If diarrhea is mild, discontinuation of cefotaxime may be sufficient.

- If diarrhea is severe, suspect antibiotic-associated pseudomembranous colitis, a life-threatening superinfection (may occur in 4–9 d or as long as 6 wk after cephalosporin therapy is discontinued). Chronically ill or debilitated older adult patients undergoing abdominal surgery or those in an intensive care unit are most vulnerable.

Patient & Family Education

- Report any early signs or symptoms of superinfection promptly. Superinfections caused by overgrowth of nonsusceptible organisms may occur, particularly during prolonged use.

- Yogurt or buttermilk, 120 mL (4 oz) of either (if allowed), may serve as a prophylactic against intestinal superinfection by helping to maintain normal intestinal flora.

- Report loose stools or diarrhea.

CEFOTETAN DISODIUM

(sef'oh-tee-tan)
Cefotan
Classifications: ANTIBIOTIC; SECOND-GENERATION CEPHALOSPORIN
Therapeutic: ANTIBIOTIC; CEPHALOSPORIN

Prototype: Cefotaxime sodium
Pregnancy Category: B

AVAILABILITY 1 g, 2 g, 10 g injection

ACTION & *THERAPEUTIC EFFECT*
Semisynthetic beta-lactam antibiotic, classified as a second-generation cephalosporin. Preferentially binds to one or more of the penicillin-binding proteins (PBP) located on cell walls of susceptible organisms. This inhibits third and final stage of bacterial cell wall synthesis, thus killing the bacterium. *Generally less active against susceptible* Staphylococci *than first-generation cephalosporins but has broad spectrum of activity against gram-negative bacteria when compared to first- and second-generation cephalosporins.*

USES Infections caused by susceptible organisms in urinary tract, lower respiratory tract, skin and skin structures, bones and joints, gynecologic tract; also intra-abdominal infections, bacteremia, and perioperative prophylaxis.

CONTRAINDICATIONS Hypersensitivity to cephalosporins and related beta-lactam antibiotics.
CAUTIOUS USE Preexisting coagulopathy; colitis, GI disease; pregnancy (category B); renal impairment; lactation.

ROUTE & DOSAGE

Moderate to Severe Infections
Adult: **IV/IM** 1–2 g q12h
Child: **IV/IM** 40–80 mg/kg/d divided q12h (max: 6 g/d)
UTI
Adult: **IV** 500 mg q12h or 1–4 g/d
Surgical Prophylaxis
Adult: **IV/IM** 1–2 g 30–60 min before surgery

Common adverse effects in *italic*, life-threatening effects underlined; generic names in **bold**; classifications in SMALL CAPS; ♣ Canadian drug name; ❷ Prototype drug

C

Renal Impairment

Cl$_{cr}$ >30 mL/min: dose q12h; 10–30 mL/min: dose q24h; <10 mL/min: dose q48h. *Hemodialysis:* Give $^{1}/_{4}$ dose q24h on days between sessions, $^{1}/_{2}$ dose on day of dialysis.

ADMINISTRATION

Intramuscular

- For IM reconstitution (follow manufacturer's directions for selection of diluent), add 2 mL diluent to 1 g vial; yields approximately 2.4 mL (375 mg/mL).
- For IM administration, inject well into body of large muscle such as upper outer quadrant of buttock (gluteus maximus).

Intravenous

IV administration to infants and children: Verify correct IV concentration and rate of infusion with physician.

PREPARE: Direct: Dilute each 1 g with 10 mL of sterile water for injection. **Intermittent:** Following reconstitution, dilute each 1 g with 50–100 mL of D5W or NS.

ADMINISTER: Direct: Give over 3–5 min. **Intermittent:** Give a single dose over 30 min. For IV infusion, solution may be given for longer period of time through tubing system through which other IV solutions are being given.

INCOMPATIBILITIES Solution/additive: AMINOGLYCOSIDES, **doxapram,** HEPARIN, **promethazine,** TETRACYCLINES. **Y-site:** AMINOGLYCOSIDES, **promethazine, vancomycin, vinorelbine.**

- Protect sterile powder from light; store at 22° C (71.6° F) or less; remains stable 24 mo after date of manufacture. May darken with age, but potency is unaffected. Reconsti-

tuted solutions: stable for 24 h at 25° C (77° F); 96 h when refrigerated at 5° C (41° F); or at least 1 wk when frozen at –20° C (–4° F).

ADVERSE EFFECTS (≥1%) **Body as a Whole:** Fever, chills, injection site pain, inflammation, disulfiram-like reaction. **GI:** Nausea, vomiting, *diarrhea,* abdominal pain, antibiotic-associated colitis. **Hematologic:** Thrombocytopenia, prolongation of bleeding time or prothrombin time. **Skin:** Rash, pruritus.

DIAGNOSTIC TEST INTERFERENCE May cause falsely elevated **serum** or **urine creatinine** values **(Jaffe reaction).** False-positive reactions for **urine glucose** have not been reported using **copper sulfate reduction methods,** e.g., **Benedict's, Clinitest;** however, since it has occurred with other cephalosporins, it may be advisable to use **glucose oxidase tests (Clinistix, TesTape, Diastix).** Positive **direct antiglobulin (Coombs') test** results may interfere with **hematologic studies** and **cross-matching** procedures.

INTERACTIONS Drug: Probenecid decreases renal elimination of cefotetan; **alcohol** produces disulfiram reaction.

PHARMACOKINETICS Peak: 1.5–3 h after IM. **Distribution:** Poor CNS penetration; widely distributed to body tissues and fluids, including bile, sputum, prostatic and peritoneal fluids; crosses placenta. **Elimination:** 51–81% unchanged in urine; 20% in bile; small amount in breast milk. **Half-Life:** 180–270 min.

CLINICAL IMPLICATIONS

Assessment & Drug Effects

- Determine history of hypersensitivity to cephalosporins and peni-

C

cillins, and other drug allergies, before therapy begins.

▪ Lab tests: Perform culture and sensitivity studies before initiation of therapy and during therapy, as indicated. Therapy may begin pending test results. Perform periodic hematologic studies (including PT/INR and PTT) and evaluation of renal function, especially if cefotetan dose is high or if therapy is prolonged in order to recognize symptoms of nephrotoxicity and ototoxicity (see Appendix F).

▪ Report onset of loose stools or diarrhea. If diarrhea is severe, suspect pseudomembranous colitis (see Appendix F) caused by *Clostridium difficile*. Check temperature. Report fever and severe diarrhea to physician; drug should be discontinued.

Patient & Family Education

▪ Report promptly S&S of superinfection (see Appendix F).
▪ Report loose stools or diarrhea.

CEFOXITIN SODIUM

(se-fox'i-tin)
Mefoxin
Classifications: ANTIBIOTIC; SECOND-GENERATION CEPHALOSPORIN
Therapeutic: ANTIBIOTIC; CEPHALOSPORIN
Prototype: Cefaclor
Pregnancy Category: B

AVAILABILITY 1 g, 2 g injection

ACTION & *THERAPEUTIC EFFECT*
Semisynthetic, broad-spectrum beta-lactam antibiotic classified as second-generation cephalosporin; structurally and pharmacologically related to cephalosporins and penicillins. Preferentially binds to one or more of the penicillin-binding proteins (PBP) located on cell walls of susceptible organisms, thus making it bactericidal. *It shows enhanced activity against a wide variety of gram-negative organisms and is effective for mixed aerobic-anaerobic infections. Considerably less active than most cephalosporins against* Staphylococci.

USES Infections caused by susceptible organisms in the lower respiratory tract, urinary tract, skin and skin structures, bones and joints; also intra-abdominal endocarditis, gynecological infections, septicemia, uncomplicated gonorrhea, and perioperative prophylaxis in prosthetic arthroplasty or cardiovascular surgery. May be cephalosporin of choice for mixed aerobic-anaerobic infections (e.g., *Bacteroides fragilis*).

CONTRAINDICATIONS Hypersensitivity to cephalosporins and related antibiotics.
CAUTIOUS USE History of sensitivity to penicillin or other allergies, particularly to drugs; impaired renal function; coagulopathy; GI disease; colitis; pregnancy (category B).

ROUTE & DOSAGE

Moderate to Severe Infections
Adult: **IV/IM** 1–2 g q6–8h, up to 12 g/d
Child >3 mo: **IV/IM** 80–160 mg/kg/d in 4–6 divided doses (max: 12 g/d)
Neonate: **IV/IM** 90–100 mg/kg/d divided q8h

Surgical Prophylaxis
Adult: **IV/IM** 2 g 30–60 min before surgery, then 2 g q6h for 24 h
Child: **IV/IM** 30–40 mg/kg 30–60 min before surgery, then 30–40 mg q6h for 24 h

---

Common adverse effects in *italic*, life-threatening effects underlined; generic names in **bold**; classifications in SMALL CAPS; ♣ Canadian drug name; ⊘ Prototype drug

269

C

ADMINISTRATION

Intramuscular

- Reconstitute each 1 g with 2 mL sterile water for injection or 0.5 or 1% lidocaine hydrochloride (without epinephrine), used to reduce discomfort of IM injection. After reconstitution for IM use, shake vial and allow solution to stand until it becomes clear.
- Administer IM injections deep into large muscle mass such as upper outer quadrant of gluteus maximus. Aspirate before injecting drug. Rotate injection sites.

Intravenous

IV administration to neonates, infants and children: Verify correct IV concentration and rate of infusion/injection with physician.

PREPARE: **Direct:** Dilute each 1 g with 10 mL sterile water, D5W, or NS. **Intermittent:** Following reconstitution, dilute 1–2 g in 50–100 mL of D5W or NS.

ADMINISTER: **Direct:** Give over 3–5 min. **Intermittent:** Give over 15 min.

INCOMPATIBILITIES **Solution/additive:** AMINOGLYCOSIDES, **ranitidine. Y-site:** AMINOGLYCOSIDES, **filgrastim, hetastarch, pentamidine, vancomycin.**

- Reconstituted solution may become discolored (usually light yellow to amber) if exposed to high temperatures; however, potency is not affected. Solution may be cloudy immediately after reconstitution; let stand and it will clear.

- After reconstitution, solution is stable for 24 h at 25° C (77° F); 7 d when refrigerated at 4° C (39° F), or 30 wk when frozen at –20° C (–4° F).

ADVERSE EFFECTS (≥1%) **Body as a Whole:** Drug fever, eosinophilia, superinfections, local reactions: pain, tenderness, and induration (IM site), thrombophlebitis (IV site). **GI:** *Diarrhea,* pseudomembranous colitis. **Skin:** Rash, exfoliative dermatitis, pruritus, urticaria. **Urogenital:** Nephrotoxicity, interstitial nephritis.

DIAGNOSTIC TEST INTERFERENCE

Cefoxitin causes false-positive (black-brown or green-brown color) *urine glucose* reaction with *copper reduction reagents* such as *Benedict's* or *Clinitest,* but not with *enzymatic glucose oxidase reagents (Clinistix, TesTape).* With high doses, falsely elevated *serum and urine creatinine* (with *Jaffee reaction*) reported. False-positive *direct Coombs' test* (may interfere with *cross-matching procedures* and *hematologic studies*) has also been reported.

INTERACTIONS Drug: **Probenecid** decreases renal elimination of cefoxitin.

PHARMACOKINETICS Peak: 20–30 min after IM; 5 min after IV. **Distribution:** Poor CNS penetration even with inflamed meninges; widely distributed in body tissues including pleural, synovial, and ascitic fluid and bile; crosses placenta. **Elimination:** 85% unchanged in urine in 6 h, small amount in breast milk. **Half-Life:** 45–60 min.

CLINICAL IMPLICATIONS

Assessment & Drug Effects

- Determine previous hypersensitivity to cephalosporins, penicillins, and other drug allergies before therapy is initiated.
- Lab tests: Perform culture and sensitivity testing prior to and periodically during therapy. Periodic renal function tests.

Common adverse effects in *italic*, life-threatening effects underlined; generic names in **bold**; classifications in SMALL CAPS; ♣ Canadian drug name; ☻ Prototype drug

- Inspect injection sites regularly. Report evidence of inflammation and patient's complaint of pain.
- Monitor I&O rates and pattern: Nephrotoxicity occurs most frequently in patients >50 y, in patients with impaired renal function, the debilitated, and in patients receiving high doses or other nephrotoxic drugs.
- Be alert to S&S of superinfections (see Appendix F). This condition is most apt to occur in older adult patients, especially when drug has been used for prolonged period.
- Report onset of diarrhea (may be dose related). If severe, pseudomembranous colitis (see Signs & Symptoms, Appendix F) must be ruled out. Older adult patients are especially susceptible.

Patient & Family Education
- Report promptly S&S of superinfection (see Appendix F).
- Report watery or bloody loose stools or severe diarrhea.
- Report severe vomiting or stomach pain.
- Report infusion site swelling, pain, or redness.

CEFPODOXIME

(cef-po-dox'eem)
Vantin
Classifications: ANTIBIOTIC; THIRD-GENERATION CEPHALOSPORIN
Therapeutic: ANTIBIOTIC; CEPHALOSPORIN
Prototype: Cefotaxime sodium
Pregnancy Category: B

AVAILABILITY 100 mg, 200 mg tablets; 10 mg/mL, 20 mg/mL suspension

ACTION & THERAPEUTIC EFFECT
Semisynthetic beta-lactam cephalosporin antibiotic. It inhibits the third and final stage of bacterial cell wall synthesis by preferentially binding to specific penicillin-binding proteins (PBPs) within the bacterial cell wall. *Has antibacterial activity resembling that of other third-generation cephalosporins. Stable in the presence of beta-lactamases. Highly active against gram-negative bacteria.*

USES Gonorrhea, otitis media, lower and upper respiratory tract infections, urinary tract infections.
UNLABELED USES Skin and soft tissue infections.

CONTRAINDICATIONS Hypersensitivity to cephalosporins and other beta-lactam antibiotics.
CAUTIOUS USE Renal impairment, history of type I hypersensitivity reactions to penicillins; coagulopathy; history of colitis or other GI disease; lactation, pregnancy (category B).

ROUTE & DOSAGE

Respiratory Tract, Skin, and Soft Tissue Infections
Adult: **PO** 200 mg q12h for 10 d
Child: **PO** 10 mg/kg/d divided q12h

Urinary Tract Infections
Adult: **PO** 100 mg q12h

Gonorrhea
Adult: **PO** 200 mg as single dose

Otitis Media
Child 5 mo–12 y: **PO** 10 mg/kg/d divided q12–24h

ADMINISTRATION

Oral
- Give with food to enhance absorption.
- Give 1 h before or 2 h after an antacid.

Common adverse effects in *italic*, life-threatening effects underlined; generic names in **bold**; classifications in SMALL CAPS; ♣ Canadian drug name; ❶ Prototype drug

271

- Consult physician regarding patients with renal impairment (i.e., creatinine clearance less than 30 mL/min); dosage intervals should be every 12 h.
- Patients on hemodialysis should be given usual dose 3 times weekly after hemodialysis.
- Preparation of suspension: To either the 50 mg/5 mL strength or the 100 mg/5 mL strength, add 25 mL of distilled water, then shake vigorously for 15 seconds. Next, to the 50 mg/5 mL strength add 33 mL, or to the 100 mg/5 mL strength add 32 mL, of distilled water, and shake for at least 3 minutes.
- Store suspension for up to 14 d in a refrigerator (2°–8° C/36°–46° F). Shake well before using.

ADVERSE EFFECTS (≥1%) **Body as a Whole:** Eye itching, cough, epistaxis, fever, decreased appetite, malaise. **GI:** Diarrhea, nausea, vomiting, abdominal pain, soft stools, flatulance, <u>pseudomembranous colitis</u> (rare). **CNS:** rare: Headache, asthenia, dizziness, fatigue, anxiety, insomnia, flushing, nightmares, weakness. **Urogenital:** Vaginal candidiasis. **Skin:** Urticaria, rash, scaling, peeling.

INTERACTIONS Drug: ANTACIDS, **ranitidine** may decrease absorption. **Food:** Food may increase the absorption.

PHARMACOKINETICS Absorption: 40–50% absorbed from GI tract. **Onset:** Therapeutic effect in 3 d. **Distribution:** Distributes well into inflammatory, pulmonary, and pleural fluid, and tonsils. Some distribution into prostate. 40% bound to plasma proteins. Distributed into breast milk. **Elimination:** 80% in urine. **Half-Life:** 2–3 h.

CLINICAL IMPLICATIONS

Assessment & Drug Effects

- Determine history of hypersensitivity reactions to cephalosporins and penicillins, and history of allergies, particularly to drugs, before therapy is initiated.
- Lab tests: Perform culture and sensitivity tests before initiation of therapy and periodically during therapy, if indicated. Therapy may be instituted pending test results.
- Report onset of loose stools or diarrhea. Although pseudomembranous enterocolitis (see Appendix F) rarely occurs, this potentially life-threatening complication should be ruled out as the cause of diarrhea during and after antibiotic therapy.
- Monitor for manifestations of hypersensitivity (see Appendix F). Discontinue drug and report S&S of hypersensitivity promptly.
- Monitor I&O rates and pattern: Especially important with high doses; report any significant changes.

Patient & Family Education

- Report any signs or symptoms of hypersensitivity immediately.
- Report loose stools, or diarrhea, especially if containing blood, mucus, or pus.
- Complete the full course of drug therapy even if symptoms improve.

CEFPROZIL

(cef′pro-zil)

Cefzil

Classifications: ANTIBIOTIC; SECOND-GENERATION CEPHALOSPORIN
Therapeutic: ANTIBIOTIC; CEPHALOSPORIN
Prototype: Cefaclor
Pregnancy Category: B

AVAILABILITY 250 mg, 500 mg tablets; 125 mg/5 mL, 250 mg/5 mL suspension

ACTION & *THERAPEUTIC EFFECT*
Semisynthetic, second-generation cephalosporin antibiotic with drug structure characterized by a beta-lactam ring; generally resistant to hydrolysis by beta-lactamases. Preferentially binds to proteins in cell walls of susceptible organisms, thus killing the bacteria. *Third-generation cephalosporins are more active and have a broader spectrum against gram-negative bacteria than first- or second-generation of cephalosporins.*

USES Upper and lower respiratory tract infections, otitis media, skin infections.

CONTRAINDICATIONS Hypersensitivity to cephalosporin and related antibiotics; severely impaired renal or hepatic function; phenylketonuria (PKU); infants <6 mo.
CAUTIOUS USE Patients with delayed reaction to penicillin or other drugs; coagulopathy; renal impairment, renal disease; GI disease, especially colitis; pregnancy (category B).

ROUTE & DOSAGE

Mild to Moderate Infections
Adult: **PO** 250–500 mg q12–24h for 10–14 d
Child >6 mo: **PO** 15 mg/kg q12h

ADMINISTRATION
Oral
- Drug may be given without regard to meals.
- Consult physician for patients with impaired renal function. Dose is reduced by 50% when creatinine clearance is 0–30 mL/min.

- Administer after hemodialysis since drug is partially removed by dialysis.
- After reconstitution, oral suspension is refrigerated. Discard unused portion after 14 days.

ADVERSE EFFECTS (≥1%) **Body as a Whole:** Hypersensitivity reactions, superinfections. **GI:** Nausea, vomiting, diarrhea, abdominal pain. **Hematologic:** Eosinophilia. **CNS:** Headache. **Skin:** Rash, diaper rash. **Urogenital:** Genital pruritus, vaginal candidiasis.

DIAGNOSTIC TEST INTERFERENCE May cause a positive *direct Coombs' test;* false-negative results in the ferricyanide assay for *blood glucose;* false-positive reactions for *urine glucose* with *copper reduction tests* such as *Benedict's* or *Fehling's solution* or *Clinitest tablets;* increased *partial thromboplastin time,* indicating thrombocytosis, eosinophilia; minor elevations in *serum alanine aminotransferase (ALT), aspartate aminotransferase (AST),* and *bilirubin.*

INTERACTIONS Drug: Probenecid prolongs the elimination of cefprozil.

PHARMACOKINETICS Absorption: Readily from GI tract. **Peak:** 1–2 h. **Distribution:** Distributes into blister fluid at 50% of the serum level. **Elimination:** Primarily by kidneys. **Half-Life:** 1–2 h.

CLINICAL IMPLICATIONS
Assessment & Drug Effects
- Determine previous hypersensitivity to cephalosporins or penicillins before treatment.
- Withhold drug and notify physician if hypersensitivity occurs (e.g., rash, urticaria).

Common adverse effects in *italic,* life-threatening effects underlined; generic names in **bold**; classifications in SMALL CAPS; ♣ Canadian drug name; ⊙ Prototype drug

273

- Lab tests: Perform culture and sensitivity tests before and periodically during therapy. Therapy may be initiated while results are pending.
- Monitor for and report diarrhea, as pseudomembranous colitis is a potential adverse effect.
- Monitor for and report signs of superinfection (see Appendix F).
- When given concurrently with other cephalosporins or aminoglycosides, monitor for signs of nephrotoxicity.

Patient & Family Education

- Complete the prescribed course of therapy, even if symptom free.
- Report rash or other signs of hypersensitivity immediately.
- Report signs of superinfection (see Appendix F).
- Report loose stools and diarrhea even after completion of drug therapy.

CEFTAZIDIME

(sef′tay-zi-deem)
Fortaz, Tazicef
Classifications: ANTIBIOTIC; THIRD-GENERATION CEPHALOSPORIN
Therapeutic: ANTIBIOTIC; CEPHALO-SPORIN
Prototype: Cefotaxime sodium
Pregnancy Category: B

AVAILABILITY 500 mg, 1 g, 2 g injection

ACTION & *THERAPEUTIC EFFECT*
Semisynthetic, third-generation broad-spectrum cephalosporin antibiotic. Preferentially binds to one or more of the penicillin-binding proteins (PBP) located on cell walls of susceptible microbes; this inhibits third and final stage of bacterial cell wall synthesis, leading to cell death of the bacterium. *Third-generation cephalosporins are more active and have a broader spectrum against aerobic gram-negative bacteria than do either first- or second-generation agents.*

USES To treat infections of lower respiratory tract, skin and skin structures, urinary tract, bones, and joints; also used to treat bacteremia, gynecological, intra-abdominal, and CNS infections (including meningitis).
UNLABELED USES Surgical prophylaxis.

CONTRAINDICATIONS Hypersensitivity to cephalosporins and related beta-lactam antibiotics; viral disease.
CAUTIOUS USE Pregnancy (category B); elderly; coagulopathy, renal disease, renal impairment; GI disease; colitis.

ROUTE & DOSAGE

Moderate to Severe Infections
Adult: **IV/IM** 1–2 g q8–12h, up to 2 g q6h
Geriatric: **IV/IM** 1–2 g q12h
Child: **IV/IM** 30–50 mg/kg/d q8h (max: 6 g/d)
Neonate: **IV** 30 mg/kg q12h
Very Severe Infection
Adult: **IV** 2 g q8h
Renal Impairment
Cl$_{cr}$ 30–50 mL/min: dose q12h; 10–30 mL/min: dose q24h; <10 mL/min: dose q48–72h.
Hemodialysis: Removed by dialysis

ADMINISTRATION

Intramuscular
- Reconstitute by adding 3 mL sterile water or bacteriostatic water for in-

jection or 0.5% or 1% lidocaine HCl injection to 1 g vial to yield 280 mg/mL.

- Inject into large muscle mass (e.g., upper outer quadrant of gluteus maximus or lateral part of thigh).

Intravenous

PREPARE: **Direct:** Add 10 mL of sterile water for injection to 1 g to yield 280 mg/mL. **Intermittent:** Further dilute with 50–100 mL of D5W, NS, or RL.
ADMINISTER: **Direct:** Give over 3–5 min. **Intermittent:** Give over 30–60 min. If given through a Y-type set, discontinue other solutions during infusion of ceftazidime.
INCOMPATIBILITIES **Solution/additive:** AMINOGLYCOSIDES, **aminophylline, ranidine. Y-site: amiodarone,** AMINOGLYCOSIDES, **amphotericin B cholesteryl complex, amsacrine, azithromycin, doxorubicin liposome, fluconazole, idarubicin, midazolam, pentamidine, sargramostim, vancomycin, warfarin.**

- Protect sterile powder from light. Reconstituted solution is stable 7 d when refrigerated at 4°–5° C (39°–41° F); for 18–24 h when stored at 15°–30° C (59°–86° F).

ADVERSE EFFECTS (≥1%) **Body as a Whole:** Fever, phlebitis, pain or inflammation at injection site, superinfections. **GI:** Nausea, vomiting, *diarrhea,* abdominal pain, metallic taste, drug-associated <u>pseudomembranous colitis</u>. **Skin:** Pruritus, rash, urticaria. **Urogenital:** Vaginitis, candidiasis.

DIAGNOSTIC TEST INTERFERENCE

False-positive reactions for *urine glucose* have been reported using *copper sulfate* (e.g., *Benedict's solution, Clinitest*). *Glucose oxi-*

dase tests (Clinistix, TesTape) are unaffected. May cause positive *direct antiglobulin (Coombs') test* results, which can interfere with *hematologic studies* and *transfusion cross-matching procedures.*

INTERACTIONS Drug: Probenecid decreases renal elimination of ceftazidine.

PHARMACOKINETICS Peak: 1 h. **Distribution:** CNS penetration with inflamed meninges; also penetrates bone, gallbladder, bile, endometrium, heart, skin, and ascitic and pleural fluids; crosses placenta. **Metabolism:** Not metabolized. **Elimination:** 80–90% unchanged in urine in 24 h; small amount in breast milk. **Half-Life:** 25–60 min.

CLINICAL IMPLICATIONS

Assessment & Drug Effects

- Determine history of hypersensitivity to cephalosporins and penicillins, and other drug allergies, before therapy begins.
- Lab tests: Perform culture and sensitivity studies before initiation of therapy and during therapy as indicated. Therapy may begin pending test results.
- If administered concomitantly with another antibiotic, monitor renal function and report if symptoms of dysfunction appear (e.g., changes in I&O ratio and pattern, dysuria).
- Be alert to onset of rash, itching, and dyspnea. Check patient's temperature. If it is elevated, suspect onset of hypersensitivity reaction (see Appendix F).
- Monitor for superinfection. (See Appendix F.)
- If diarrhea occurs and is severe, suspect pseudomembranous colitis (caused by *Clostridium difficile*). Check temperature: Report fever

Common adverse effects in *italic*, life-threatening effects <u>underlined</u>; generic names in **bold**; classifications in SMALL CAPS; ✚ Canadian drug name; ⊘ Prototype drug

275

and severe diarrhea to physician; drug should be discontinued.

Patient & Family Education

- Report loose stools or diarrhea promptly.
- Report any signs or symptoms of superinfection promptly (see Appendix F).

CEFTIBUTEN

(sef-ti-bu′ten)

Cedax

Classifications: BETA-LACTAM ANTIBIOTIC; THIRD-GENERATION CEPHALOSPORIN

Therapeutic: ANTIBIOTIC; CEPHALOSPORIN

Prototype: Cefotaxime sodium

Pregnancy Category: B

AVAILABILITY 400 mg capsules; 90 mg/5 mL, 180 mg/5 mL suspension

ACTION & *THERAPEUTIC EFFECT*
Ceftibuten is a broad-spectrum, third-generation beta-lactam antibiotic. Preferentially binds to one or more of the penicillin-binding proteins located in the cell wall of susceptible organisms. This inhibits third and final stage of bacterial cell wall synthesis, thus killing the bacterium. It is highly resistant to hydrolysis by most beta-lactamase bacteria. *It has antibacterial activity against both gram-negative and gram-positive bacteria.*

USES Acute bacterial exacerbations of chronic bronchitis caused by *H. influenzae, Moraxella catarrhalis,* or *S. pneumoniae;* acute bacterial otitis media caused by *H. influenzae, M. catarrhalis,* or *S. pyogenes;* pharyngitis or tonsillitis caused by *S. pyogenes.*

CONTRAINDICATIONS Hypersensitivity to ceftibuten or cephalosporins.

CAUTIOUS USE Renal dysfunction, penicillin hypersensitivity, history of colitis or diabetes; GI disease; coagulopathy; pregnancy (category B), lactation. Safety and efficacy in infants <6 mo not established.

ROUTE & DOSAGE

Mild to Moderate Infections

Adult: **PO** 400 mg once daily for 10 d

Renal Impairment

Cl_{cr} 30–49: 200 mg q24h; Cl_{cr} <30: 100 mg q24h

Child (6 mo–12 y): **PO** 9 mg/kg once daily (max: 400 mg) for 10 d

Renal Impairment

Cl_{cr} 30–49 mL/min: 4.5 mg/kg q24h; <30 mL/min: 2.25 mg/kg q24h

ADMINISTRATION

Oral

- Give oral suspension 1 h before or 2 h after a meal.
- Children weighing more than 45 kg may receive maximum daily dose.
- Hemodialysis patients should receive drug at the end of dialysis.
- Store capsules at 2°–25° C (36°–77° F); keep container tightly closed. Reconstituted oral suspension is stable for 14 d under refrigeration at 2°–8° C (36°–46° F).

ADVERSE EFFECTS (≥1%) **Body as a Whole:** Dyspnea, dysuria, fatigue, vaginitis, moniliasis, urticaria, pruritus, rash, paresthesia, taste perversion. **GI:** Nausea, vomiting, diarrhea, dyspepsia, abdominal pain, anorexia, constipation, dry mouth, eructation, flatulence. **CNS:** Headache, dizziness, nasal congestion, somnolence.

INTERACTIONS Drug: AMINOGLYCOSIDES may increase risk of nephrotoxicity and have additive/synergistic effects. May decrease efficacy of ORAL CONTRACEPTIVES. **Probenecid** may increase levels.

PHARMACOKINETICS Absorption: Rapidly from GI tract. **Peak:** Approx. 2–3 h. **Distribution:** Bronchial mucosa levels are approx 37% of plasma levels, middle ear levels approx 50% of plasma levels. **Elimination:** Primarily in urine. **Half-Life:** 1.5–2.5 h.

CLINICAL IMPLICATIONS

Assessment & Drug Effects

- Determine history of hypersensitivity reactions to cephalosporins, penicillins, or other drugs, before therapy is initiated. Monitor for S&S of hypersensitivity (see Appendix F); report their appearance promptly and discontinue drug.
- Lab tests: Perform culture and sensitivity tests before initiation of therapy. Dosage may be started pending test results.
- Monitor for S&S of superinfection or pseudomembranous colitis (see Appendix F); immediately report either to physician.
- Closely monitor patients with renal impairment; if seizures develop, discontinue drug and notify physician.

Patient & Family Education

- If on dialysis treatment, take this drug after dialysis.
- Report any S&S of hypersensitivity, superinfection, and pseudomembranous colitis promptly.

CEFTIZOXIME SODIUM

(sef-ti-zox'eem)

Cefizox

Classifications: ANTIBIOTIC; THIRD-GENERATION CEPHALOSPORIN
Therapeutic: ANTIBIOTIC; CEPHALOSPORIN
Prototype: Cefotaxime sodium
Pregnancy Category: B

AVAILABILITY 1 g, 2 g injection

ACTION & *THERAPEUTIC EFFECT*
Semisynthetic third-generation cephalosporin antibiotic. Preferentially binds to one or more of the penicillin-binding proteins (PBP) located on cell walls of susceptible organisms. This inhibits third and final stage of bacterial cell wall synthesis, thus killing the bacterium. *Generally resistant to inactivation by beta-lactamases that act principally as cephalosporinases and penicillinases. Its spectrum includes some gram-positive organisms but has predominantly gram-negative coverage.*

USES Infections caused by susceptible organisms in lower respiratory tract, skin and skin structures, urinary tract, bones and joints; also used to treat intra-abdominal infections, pelvic inflammatory disease, uncomplicated gonorrhea, meningitis *(Haemophilus influenzae, Streptococcus pneumoniae),* and for surgical prophylaxis.
UNLABELED USES Meningitis caused by *Neisseria meningitidis* and *E. coli.*

CONTRAINDICATIONS Hypersensitivity to cephalosporins and other beta-lactam antibiotics; viral disease. Safe use in infants <6 mo not established.
CAUTIOUS USE Penicillin hypersensitivity; coagulopathy; GI disease,

Common adverse effects in *italic*, life-threatening effects underlined; generic names in **bold**; classifications in SMALL CAPS; ♣ Canadian drug name; ◍ Prototype drug

277

colitis; elderly; renal disease, renal impairment; lactation; pregnancy (category B).

ROUTE & DOSAGE

Moderate to Severe Infections

Adult: IV/IM 1–2 g q8–12h, up to 2 g q4h
Child: IV/IM ≥6 mo, 50 mg/kg q6–8h, up to 200 mg/kg/d

Renal Impairment

Use lower dose. Dialysis: administer dose after dialysis

ADMINISTRATION

Intramuscular

- Reconstitute as follows with sterile water for injection: add 1.5 mL to 500 mg to yield 280 mg/mL; add 3 mL to 1 g or 6 mL to 2 g to yield 270 mg/mL.
- Give deep IM into a large muscle. Give no more than 1 g into a single injection site.

Intravenous

PREPARE: Direct: Reconstitute each 1 g with 10 mL sterile water. Shake well. Intermittent: Further dilute in 50–100 mL D5W, NS, D5/NS, D5/.45% NaCl, RL, or other compatible IV solution.

ADMINISTER: Direct: Give over 3–5 min. Intermittent: Give over 30 min.

INCOMPATIBILITIES Solution/additive: AMINOGLYCOSIDES. Y-site: AMINOGLYCOSIDES, filgrastim.

- Protect from light. Consult manufacturer's directions concerning storage of reconstituted solutions.

ADVERSE EFFECTS (≥1%) Body as a Whole: Fever, phlebitis, vaginitis, pain and induration at injection site, paresthesia. GI: Nausea, vomiting, diarrhea, pseudomembranous colitis. Skin: Rash, pruritus.

DIAGNOSTIC TEST INTERFERENCE

Ceftizoxime causes false-positive direct Coombs' test (may interfere with cross-matching procedures and hematologic studies).

INTERACTIONS Drug: Probenecid decreases renal elimination of ceftizoxime.

PHARMACOKINETICS Peak: 1 h. Distribution: Crosses placenta. Metabolism: Not metabolized. Elimination: 80–90% unchanged in urine in 24 h; small amount in breast milk. Half-Life: 25–60 min.

CLINICAL IMPLICATIONS

Assessment & Drug Effects

- Determine history of hypersensitivity reactions to cephalosporins, penicillin, or other drugs before therapy is instituted. Report to physician history of allergy, particularly to drugs.
- Lab tests: Perform culture and sensitivity tests before initiation of therapy and periodically during therapy if indicated. Therapy may be instituted pending test results.
- Be alert to symptoms of hypersensitivity reaction (see Appendix F). Serious reactions may require emergency measures.

Patient & Family Education

- Report loose stools or diarrhea promptly.
- Report any signs or symptoms of hypersensitivity (see Appendix F) promptly.

CEFTRIAXONE SODIUM

(sef-try-ax'one)
Rocephin
Classifications: ANTIBIOTIC; THIRD-GENERATION CEPHALOSPORIN
Therapeutic: ANTIBIOTIC; CEPHALOSPORIN

Common adverse effects in *italic*, life-threatening effects underlined; generic names in **bold**; classifications in SMALL CAPS; ✦ Canadian drug name; ⊘ Prototype drug

Prototype: Cefotaxime sodium
Pregnancy Category: B

AVAILABILITY 250 mg, 500 mg, 1 g, 2 g injection

ACTION & *THERAPEUTIC EFFECT*
Semisynthetic third-generation cephalosporin antibiotic. Preferentially binds to one or more of the penicillin-binding proteins (PBP) located on cell walls of susceptible organisms. This inhibits third and final stage of bacterial cell wall synthesis, thus killing the bacterium. *Similar to other third-generation cephalosporins, ceftriaxone is effective against serious gram-negative organisms and also penetrates the CSF in concentrations useful in treatment of meningitis.*

USES Infections caused by susceptible organisms in lower respiratory tract, skin and skin structures, urinary tract, bones and joints; also intra-abdominal infections, pelvic inflammatory disease, uncomplicated gonorrhea, meningitis, and surgical prophylaxis.

CONTRAINDICATIONS Hypersensitivity to cephalosporins and related antibiotics; viral infections; neonates with hyperbilirubinemia, premature neonates.
CAUTIOUS USE Coagulopathy, GI disease, colitis; renal disease, renal impairment; pregnancy (category B).

ROUTE & DOSAGE

Moderate to Severe Infections
Adult: **IV/IM** 1–2 g q12–24h (max: 4 g/d)
Child: **IV/IM** 50–75 mg/kg/d in 2 divided doses (max: 2 g/d)

Meningitis
Adult: **IV/IM** 2 g q12h

Child: **IV/IM** 100 mg/kg/d in 2 divided doses (max: 4 g/d)

Surgical Prophylaxis
Adult: **IV/IM** 1 g 30–120 min before surgery

Uncomplicated Gonorrhea
Adult: **IM** 250 mg as single dose
Child: **IM** 125 mg as single dose

ADMINISTRATION

Intramuscular
▪ Reconstitute the 1 g or 2 g vial by adding 2.1 mL or 4.2 mL, respectively, of sterile water for injection. Yields 350 mg/mL. See manufacturer's directions for other dilutions.
▪ Give deep IM into a large muscle.

Intravenous
IV administration to infants and children: Verify correct IV concentration and rate of infusion with physician.

PREPARE: Intermittent: Reconstitute each 250 mg with 2.4 mL of sterile water, D5W, NS, or D5/NS to yield 100 mg/mL. Further dilute with 50–100 mL of the selected IV solution.
ADMINISTER: Intermittent: Give over 30 min.
INCOMPATIBILITIES Solution/additive: AMINOGLYCOSIDES, **aminophylline, clindamycin, lidocaine, metronidazole, theophylline.** Y-site: **amiodarone,** AMINOGLYCOSIDES, **amphotericin B cholesteryl complex, amsacrine, azithromycin, fluconazole, filgrastim, labetalol, pen- tamidine, vancomycin, vinorelbine.**
▪ Protect sterile powder from light. Store at 15°–25° C (59°–77° F). Reconstituted solutions: diluent, concentration of solutions are de-

C

terminants of stability. See manufacturer's instructions for storage.

ADVERSE EFFECTS (≥1%) **Body as a Whole:** Pruritus, fever, chills, pain, induration at IM injection site; phlebitis (IV site). **GI:** *Diarrhea*, abdominal cramps, <u>pseudomembranous colitis</u>, biliary sludge. **Urogenital:** Genital pruritus; moniliasis.

DIAGNOSTIC TEST INTERFERENCE Causes prolonged *PT/INR* during therapy.

INTERACTIONS Drug: Probenecid decreases renal elimination of ceftriaxone; **alcohol** produces disulfiram reaction.

PHARMACOKINETICS Peak: 1.5–4 h after IM; immediately after IV. **Distribution:** Widely distributed in body tissues and fluids; good CNS penetration; crosses placenta. **Metabolism:** Not metabolized. **Elimination:** 33–65% unchanged in urine; also in bile and breast milk. **Half-Life:** 5–10 h.

CLINICAL IMPLICATIONS

Assessment & Drug Effects

- Determine history of hypersensitivity reactions to cephalosporins and penicillins and history of other allergies, particularly to drugs, before therapy is initiated.
- Lab tests: Perform culture and sensitivity tests before initiation of therapy and periodically during therapy. Dosage may be started pending test results. Periodic coagulation studies (PT and INR) should be done.
- Inspect injection sites for induration and inflammation. Rotate sites. Note IV injection sites for signs of phlebitis (redness, swelling, pain).
- Monitor for manifestations of hypersensitivity (see Appendix F).

Report their appearance promptly and discontinue drug.

- Watch for and report signs: petechiae, ecchymotic areas, epistaxis, or any unexplained bleeding. Ceftriaxone appears to alter vitamin K–producing gut bacteria; therefore, hypoprothrombinemic bleeding may occur.
- Check for fever if diarrhea occurs: Report both promptly. The incidence of antibiotic-produced pseudomembranous colitis (see Appendix F) is higher than with most cephalosporins. Most vulnerable patients: chronically ill or debilitated older adult patients undergoing abdominal surgery.

Patient & Family Education

- Report any signs of bleeding.
- Report loose stools or diarrhea promptly.

CEFUROXIME SODIUM

(se-fyoor-ox′eem)

Zinacef

CEFUROXIME AXETIL

Ceftin

Classifications: ANTIBIOTIC; SECOND-GENERATION CEPHALOSPORIN
Therapeutic: ANTIBIOTIC; CEPHALOSPORIN
Prototype: Cefaclor
Pregnancy Category: B

AVAILABILITY 125 mg, 250 mg, 500 mg tablets; 125 mg/5 mL, 250 mg/5 mL suspension; 750 mg, 1.5 g injection

ACTION & *THERAPEUTIC EFFECT*
Semisynthetic second-generation cephalosporin beta-lactam antibiotic. Preferentially binds to one or more of the penicillin-binding proteins (PBP) located on cell walls of

susceptible organisms. This inhibits third and final stage of bacterial cell wall synthesis, thus killing the bacterium. *Resistance against beta-lactamase-producing strains exceeds that of first-generation cephalosporins. Similar to other second-generation cephalosporins, cefuroxime is more active against gram-negative bacteria than are the first-generation cephalosporins but not as active as the third-generation cephalosporins.*

USES Infections caused by susceptible organisms in the lower respiratory tract, urinary tract, skin, and skin structures; also used for treatment of meningitis, gonorrhea, and otitis media and for perioperative prophylaxis (e.g., open-heart surgery), early Lyme disease.

CONTRAINDICATIONS Hypersensitivity to cephalosporins and related antibiotics; viral infections.
CAUTIOUS USE History of allergy, particularly to drugs; penicillin sensitivity; renal insufficiency; history of colitis or other GI disease; potent diuretics; pregnancy (category B), lactation.

ROUTE & DOSAGE

Moderate to Severe Infections
Adult: **PO** 250–500 mg q12h **IV/IM** 750 mg–1.5 g q6–8h
Child (3 mo–12 y): **PO** 10–15 mg/kg (125–250 mg) q12h **IV/IM** 75–100 mg/kg/d divided q8h (max: 6 g/d)
Neonate: **IM/IV** 20–100 mg/kg/d divided q12h

Bacterial Meningitis
Adult: **IV/IM** 3 g q8h
Child: **IV/IM** 200–240 mg/kg/d divided q6–8h; reduced to 100 mg/kg/d upon improvement

Surgical Prophylaxis
Adult: **IV/IM** 1.5 g 30–60 min before surgery, then 750 mg q8h for 24 h
Child: **IV/IM** Same as for adult

Renal Impairment
Cl_{cr} 10–20 mL/min: give q12h; <10 mL/min: give q24h

ADMINISTRATION

Oral
- Cefuroxime tablets and oral suspension are not substitutable on a mg-for-mg basis.
- The oral suspension is for infants and children 3 mo to 12 y. Each teaspoon (5 mL) contains the equivalent of 125 mg cefuroxime. Shake oral suspension well before each use.

Intramuscular
- Shake IM suspension gently before administration. IM injections should be made deeply into large muscle mass. Rotate injection sites.

Intravenous
IV administration to neonates, infants and children: Verify correct IV concentration and rate of infusion/injection with physician.

PREPARE: **Direct:** Dilute each 750 mg with 9 mL sterile water, D5W, or NS. **Intermittent:** Further dilute in 50–100 mL of compatible solution. **Continuous:** May be added to 1000 mL of IV compatible solution.

ADMINISTER: **Direct:** Give slowly over 3–5 min. **Intermittent:** Give over 30 min. **Continuous:** Give over 6–24 h.

INCOMPATIBILITIES **Solution/additive:** AMINOGLYCOSIDES, **doxapram, ranitidine, sodium bicarbonate. Y-site:** amiodarone, AMINOGLYCOSIDES, **azithromycin, filgrastim, fluconazole, mid-**

Common adverse effects in *italic*, life-threatening effects underlined; generic names in **bold**, classifications in SMALL CAPS; ✤ Canadian drug name; ⦿ Prototype drug

281

azolam, sodium bicarbonate, vancomycin, vinorelbine.

Cefuroxime powder and solutions of the drug may range in color from light yellow to amber without adversely affecting product potency.

- Store powder protected from light unless otherwise directed. After reconstitution, store suspension at 2°–30° C (36°–86° F). Discard after 10 d.

ADVERSE EFFECTS (≥1%) **Body as a Whole:** Thrombophlebitis (IV site); pain, burning, cellulitis (IM site); superinfections, positive Coombs' test. **GI:** *Diarrhea,* nausea, antibiotic-associated colitis. **Skin:** Rash, pruritus, urticaria. **Urogenital:** Increased serum creatinine and BUN, decreased creatinine clearance.

DIAGNOSTIC TEST INTERFERENCE Cefuroxime causes false-positive (black-brown or green-brown color) *urine glucose* reaction with *copper reduction reagents,* e.g., *Benedict's* or *Clinitest,* but not with *enzymatic glucose oxidase reagents,* e.g., *Clinistix, TesTape.* False-positive *direct Coombs' test* (may interfere with *cross-matching procedures* and *hematologic studies*) has been reported.

INTERACTIONS Drug: Probenecid decreases renal elimination of cefuroxime, thus prolonging its action.

PHARMACOKINETICS Absorption: Well absorbed from GI tract; hydrolyzed to active drug in GI mucosa. **Peak:** PO 2 h; IM 30 min. **Distribution:** Widely distributed in body tissues and fluids; adequate CNS penetration with inflamed meninges; crosses placenta. **Elimination:** 66–100% in 24 h; in breast milk. **Half-Life:** 1–2 h.

CLINICAL IMPLICATIONS

Assessment & Drug Effects

- Determine history of hypersensitivity reactions to cephalosporins, penicillins, and history of allergies, particularly to drugs, before therapy is initiated.
- Lab tests: Perform culture and sensitivity tests before initiation of therapy and periodically during therapy if indicated. Therapy may be instituted pending test results. Monitor periodically BUN and creatinine clearance.
- Inspect IM and IV injection sites frequently for signs of phlebitis.
- Report onset of loose stools or diarrhea. Although pseudomembranous colitis (see Signs & Symptoms, Appendix F) rarely occurs, this potentially life-threatening complication should be ruled out as the cause of diarrhea during and after antibiotic therapy.
- Monitor for manifestations of hypersensitivity (see Appendix F). Discontinue drug and report their appearance promptly.
- Monitor I&O rates and pattern: Especially important in severely ill patients receiving high doses. Report any significant changes.

Patient & Family Education

- Report loose stools or diarrhea promptly.
- Report any signs or symptoms of hypersensitivity (see Appendix F).

CELECOXIB ℗

(cel-e-cox′ib)

Celebrex

Classifications: ANALGESIC, NSAID; CYCLOOXYGENASE-2 (COX-2) INHIBITOR; ANTIINFLAMMATORY

Therapeutic: ANALGESIC, NSAID; CYCLOOXYGENASE-2 (COX-2) INHIBITOR; ANTIINFLAMMATORY

Pregnancy Category: C first and second trimester; D third trimester

AVAILABILITY 100 mg, 200 mg, 400 mg capsules

ACTION & *THERAPEUTIC EFFECT*
Although an NSAID, unlike ibuprofen celecoxib inhibits prostaglandin synthesis by inhibiting cyclooxygenase-2 (COX-2), but does not inhibit cyclooxygenase-1 (COX-1). *Exhibits antiinflammatory, analgesic, and antipyretic activities. Reduces or eliminates the pain of rheumatoid and osteoarthritis.*

USES Relief of S&S of osteoarthritis and rheumatoid arthritis. Treatment of acute pain and primary dysmenorrhea. Reduction of polyp formation in familial adenomatous polyposis (FAP), ankylosing spondylitis

CONTRAINDICATIONS Severe hepatic impairment; hypersensitivity to celecoxib, salicylate, or sulfonamide; asthmatic patients with aspirin triad; advanced renal disease; concurrent use of diuretics and ACE inhibitors; anemia; pain from CABG surgery; pregnancy (category C in first and second trimesters and category D in third trimester); children <18 y; lactation.
CAUTIOUS USE Patients who are P450 2C9 poor metabolizers; patients who weigh <50 kg; mild or moderate hepatic impairment; renal insufficiency; aspirin use; prior history of GI bleeding or peptic ulcer disease; alcoholics; concurrent use of anticoagulants; asthmatics; bone marrow suppression; CVA; PVD; elevated liver function tests; heart failure; kidney disease; hypertension; fluid retention.

ROUTE & DOSAGE

Arthritis
Adult: **PO** 100–200 mg b.i.d. or 200 mg q.d.
Acute Pain, Dysmenorrhea
Adult: **PO** 400 mg 1st dose, then 200 mg same day if needed, then 200 mg b.i.d. prn
FAP
Adult: **PO** 400 mg b.i.d.

ADMINISTRATION

Oral
- Give 2 h before/after magnesium or aluminum-containing antacids.
- Store in tightly closed container and protect from light.

ADVERSE EFFECTS (≥1%) **Body as a Whole:** Back pain, peripheral edema. Increased risk of cardiovascular events. **GI:** Abdominal pain, diarrhea, dyspepsia, flatulence, nausea. **CNS:** Dizziness, headache, insomnia. **Respiratory:** Pharyngitis, rhinitis, sinusitis, URI. **Skin:** Rash.

INTERACTIONS Drug: May diminish effectiveness of ACE INHIBITORS; **fluconazole** increases celecoxib concentrations; may increase **lithium** concentrations; may increase INR in older patients on **warfarin.**

PHARMACOKINETICS Peak: 3 h. **Distribution:** 97% protein bound; crosses placenta. **Metabolism:** In liver by CYP2C9. **Elimination:** Primarily in feces (57%), 27% in urine. **Half-Life:** 11.2 h.

CLINICAL IMPLICATIONS

Assessment & Drug Effects
- Therapeutic effectiveness is indicated by relief of joint pain.
- Lab tests: Periodically monitor Hct and Hgb, liver functions,

---

Common adverse effects in *italic*, life-threatening effects <u>underlined</u>; generic names in **bold**; classifications in SMALL CAPS; ♣ Canadian drug name; ⊙ Prototype drug

283

C

BUN and creatinine, and serum electrolytes.
- Monitor closely lithium levels when the two drugs are given concurrently.
- Monitor closely PT/INR when used concurrently with warfarin.
- Monitor for fluid retention and edema especially in those with a history of hypertension or CHF.

Patient & Family Education
- Avoid using celecoxib during the third trimester of pregnancy.
- Promptly report any of the following: unexplained weight gain, edema, skin rash.
- Stop taking celecoxib and promptly report to physician if any of the following occurs: S&S of liver dysfunction including nausea, fatigue, lethargy, itching, jaundice, abdominal pain, and flulike symptoms; S&S of GI ulceration including black, tarry stools and upper GI distress.

CEPHALEXIN

(sef-a-lex′in)
Ceporex A, Keflex, Novolexin A
Classifications: BETA-LACTAM ANTIBIOTIC; FIRST-GENERATION CEPHALOSPORIN
Therapeutic: ANTIBIOTIC; CEPHALOSPORIN
Prototype: Cefazolin
Pregnancy Category: B

AVAILABILITY 250 mg, 500 mg capsules; 250 mg, 500 mg, 1 g tablets; 125 mg/5 mL, 250 mg/5 mL suspension

ACTION & *THERAPEUTIC EFFECT*
Semisynthetic beta-lactam cephalosporin. Preferentially binds to one or more of the penicillin-binding proteins (PBP) located on cell walls of susceptible organisms. This inhibits its third and final stage of bacterial cell wall synthesis, thus killing the bacterium. *Broad-spectrum, first-generation cephalosporin antibiotic active against many gram-positive aerobic cocci and much less active against gram-negative bacteria or anaerobic organisms.*

USES To treat infections caused by susceptible pathogens in respiratory and urinary tracts, middle ear, skin, soft tissue, and bone.

CONTRAINDICATIONS Hypersensitivity to cephalosporins and related antibiotics; viral infections. Safe use in infants <1 mo not established.

CAUTIOUS USE History of hypersensitivity to penicillin or other drug allergy; severely impaired renal function; GI disease, colitis; hepatic disease; coagulopathy; pregnancy (category B), lactation.

ROUTE & DOSAGE

Mild to Moderate Infection	
Adult: **PO** 250–500 mg q6h	
Child: **PO** 25–100 mg/kg/d in 4 divided doses	
Skin and Skin Structure Infections	
Adult: **PO** 500 mg q12h	
Otitis Media	
Child: **PO** 75–100 mg/kg/d in 4 divided doses	

ADMINISTRATION

Oral
- Cephalexin oral suspension should be refrigerated; discard unused portions 14 d after preparation. Label should indicate expiration date. Keep tightly covered.

Shake suspension well before pouring.

ADVERSE EFFECTS (≥1%) **Body as a Whole:** Angioedema, <u>anaphylaxis</u>, superinfections. **GI:** *Diarrhea* (generally mild), nausea, vomiting, anorexia, abdominal pain. **CNS:** Dizziness, headache, fatigue. **Skin:** Rash, urticaria.

DIAGNOSTIC TEST INTERFERENCE
False-positive *urine glucose* determinations using *copper sulfate reagents,* e.g., *Clinitest, Benedict's reagent,* but not with *glucose oxidase (enzymatic) tests,* e.g., *TesTape, Diastix, Clinistix.* Positive *direct Coombs' test* may complicate transfusion *crossmatching procedures* and *hematologic studies.*

INTERACTIONS Drug: Probenecid decreases renal elimination of cephalexin.

PHARMACOKINETICS Absorption: Rapidly from GI tract; stable in stomach acid. **Peak:** 1 h. **Distribution:** Widely distributed in body fluids with highest concentration in kidney; crosses placenta. **Elimination:** 80–100% unchanged in urine in 8 h; excreted in breast milk. **Half-Life:** 38–70 min.

CLINICAL IMPLICATIONS
Assessment & Drug Effects
- Determine history of hypersensitivity reactions to cephalosporins and penicillin and history of other drug allergies before therapy is initiated.
- Lab tests: Evaluate renal and hepatic function periodically in patients receiving prolonged therapy.
- Monitor for manifestations of hypersensitivity (see Signs & Symptoms, Appendix F). Discontinue

drug and report their appearance promptly.

Patient & Family Education
- Take medication for the full course of therapy as directed by physician.
- Keep physician informed if adverse reactions appear.
- Be alert to S&S of superinfections (see Appendix F). These symptoms should be reported promptly and appropriate therapy instituted.

CEPHRADINE
(sef′ra-deen)
Anspor, Velosef
Classifications: ANTIBIOTIC; FIRST-GENERATION CEPHALOSPORIN
Therapeutic: ANTIBIOTIC; CEPHALOSPORIN
Prototype: Cefazolin
Pregnancy Category: B

AVAILABILITY 250 mg, 500 mg capsules; 125 mg/5 mL, 250 mg/5 mL suspension

ACTION & *THERAPEUTIC EFFECT*
Semisynthetic acid-stable, first-generation cephalosporin. Preferentially binds to one or more of the penicillin-binding proteins (PBP) located on cell walls of susceptible organisms. This inhibits third and final stage of bacterial cell wall synthesis, thus killing the bacterium. *Broad-spectrum antibiotic that is active against many gram-positive aerobic cocci and much less active against gram-negative bacteria.*

USES Serious infections of respiratory and urinary tracts, skin and soft tissues, and for otitis media caused by susceptible pathogens;

Common adverse effects in *italic*, life-threatening effects <u>underlined</u>; generic names in **bold**; classifications in SMALL CAPS; ♣ Canadian drug name; ⊕ Prototype drug

285

for perioperative prophylaxis, in cesarean section (intraoperative and postoperative); in septicemia (due to *Streptococcus pneumoniae, Staphylococcus aureus, Proteus mirabilis,* and *Escherichia coli).* Also used to treat urinary tract infections due to *Klebsiella* sp and enterococci *(Streptococcus faecalis).*

CONTRAINDICATIONS Hypersensitivity to cephalosporins and related antibiotics; viral infections. Safe use in children <9 mo not established.

CAUTIOUS USE History of penicillin or other allergies, particularly to drugs; impaired renal function, sodium restriction (parenteral cephradine); coagulopathy, GI disease, colitis, pregnancy (category B), lactation.

ROUTE & DOSAGE

Mild to Moderate Infection

Adult: **PO** 250–500 mg q6h or 500 mg–1 g q12h up to 4 g/d
Child: **PO** 25–50 mg/kg/d in 2–4 divided doses up to 4 g/d

Perioperative Prophylaxis

Adult: **PO** 1 g 30–60 min before surgery; 1 g during surgery; then 1 g q4–6h for 24 h

ADMINISTRATION

Oral

▪ Oral cephradine may be given without regard to meals (acid stable); however, the presence of food may delay absorption.

ADVERSE EFFECTS (≥1%) **Body as a Whole:** Joint pains, eosinophilia, tightness in chest, pain, induration and tissue sloughing (IM injection site); thrombophlebitis (IV site); paresthesias, superinfections. **GI:** *Diarrhea* or loose stools, abdominal pain, heartburn. **CNS:** Dizziness. **Skin:** Urticaria, rash, pruritus.

DIAGNOSTIC TEST INTERFERENCE Cephradine causes false-positive (black-brown or green-brown color) **urine glucose** reaction with **copper reduction reagents,** (e.g., as **Benedict's** or **Clinitest),** but not with **enzymatic glucose oxidase reagents,** e.g., **Clinistix, TesTape.** False-positive **direct Coombs' test** (may interfere with **cross-matching procedures** and **hematologic studies)** has also been reported.

INTERACTIONS Drug: Probenecid decreases renal elimination of cephradine.

PHARMACOKINETICS Absorption: Well absorbed from GI tract. **Peak:** 1 h. **Distribution:** Widely distributed in body fluids, with highest concentration in kidney; crosses placenta. **Elimination:** 80–90% eliminated unchanged in urine in 6 h; excreted in breast milk. **Half-Life:** 1–2 h.

CLINICAL IMPLICATIONS

Assessment & Drug Effects

▪ Determine history of previous hypersensitivity to cephalosporins, penicillins, and other drug allergies before therapy is initiated.
▪ Inspect IV insertion site frequently for thrombophlebitis (see Signs & Symptoms, Appendix F).
▪ Lab tests: Perform culture and sensitivity tests and renal function studies before and periodically during drug therapy.

Common adverse effects in *italic,* life-threatening effects underlined; generic names in **bold**; classifications in SMALL CAPS; ✤ Canadian drug name; ⊙ Prototype drug

- Consult physician if patient's creatinine clearance is below normal. Recommended dosage schedule in patients with reduced renal function is lowered based on creatinine clearance determinations and severity of infection.
- Pseudomembranous enterocolitis, a potentially life-threatening superinfection caused by *Clostridium difficile*, may occur during or after cephalosporin therapy. If diarrhea occurs, check for fever. Report diarrhea and fever promptly.
- Monitor for signs of superinfection (see Appendix F). Report their appearance promptly.

Patient & Family Education
- Take this medication for the full course of therapy as directed by your physician. Therapy is usually continued for at least 48–72 h after you become asymptomatic.
- Superinfections caused by overgrowth of nonsusceptible organisms may occur. Report early S&S (see Appendix F) promptly.
- Report loose stools or diarrhea promptly.

CETIRIZINE
(ce-tir'i-zeen)
Reactine ♣, Zyrtec
Classifications: ANTIHISTAMINE; H₁-RECEPTOR ANTAGONIST; NON-SEDATING
Therapeutic: ANTIHISTAMINE, NON-SEDATING; H₁-RECEPTOR ANTAGONIST
Prototype: Loratidine
Pregnancy Category: B

AVAILABILITY 5 mg, 10 mg tablets; 5 mg, 10 mg chewable tablets; 5 mg/5 mL syrup

ACTION & *THERAPEUTIC EFFECT*
Cetirizine is a potent H₁-receptor antagonist and thus an antihistamine without significant anticholinergic or CNS activity. Low lipophilicity combined with its H₁-receptor selectivity probably accounts for its relative lack of anticholinergic and sedative properties. *Effectively treats allergic rhinitis and chronic urticaria by eliminating or reducing the local and systemic effects of histamine release.*

USES Seasonal and perennial allergic rhinitis and chronic idiopathic urticaria.

CONTRAINDICATIONS Hypersensitivity to H₁-receptor antihistamines or hydroxyzine; concurrent use of alcohol; hepatic or renal dysfunction; lactation, infants <6 mo.
CAUTIOUS USE Moderate to severe renal impairment, pregnancy (category B), children.

ROUTE & DOSAGE

Allergic Rhinitis
Adult: **PO** 5–10 mg once/d
Child: **PO** 2–5 y: 2.5 mg q.d. (max: 5 mg/d); ≥6 y: 5–10 mg q.d.

Chronic Urticaria
Adult: **PO** 10 mg q.d. or b.i.d.

ADMINISTRATION
Oral
- Consult physician about dosage if significant adverse effects appear. As elimination half-life is prolonged in the older adult, dosage adjustments may be warranted.

Common adverse effects in *italic*, life-threatening effects <u>underlined</u>; generic names in **bold**; classifications in SMALL CAPS; ♣ Canadian drug name; ⊘ Prototype drug

287

ADVERSE EFFECTS (≥1%) **GI:** Constipation, diarrhea, dry mouth. **CNS:** *Drowsiness, sedation, headache,* depression.

INTERACTIONS Drug: Theophylline may decrease cetirizine clearance leading to toxicity.

PHARMACOKINETICS Absorption: Readily from GI tract. **Peak:** 1 h. **Distribution:** 93% protein bound; minimal CNS concentrations. **Metabolism:** Minimal (by CYP3A4). **Elimination:** 60% unchanged in urine within 24 h, 5% in feces. **Half-Life:** 7.4 h.

CLINICAL IMPLICATIONS

Assessment & Drug Effects

- Monitor for drug interactions. As the drug is highly protein bound, the potential for interactions with other protein-bound drugs exists.
- Monitor for sedation, especially the older adult.

Patient & Family Education

- Do not use in combination with OTC antihistamines.
- Do not engage in driving or other hazardous activities, before experiencing your responses to the drug.

CETRORELIX

(ce-tro-re′lix)

Cetrotide

Classifications: HORMONE; GONADOTROPIN-RELEASING HORMONE ANTAGONIST

Therapeutic: GONADOTROPIN-RELEASING HORMONE

Pregnancy Category: X

AVAILABILITY 0.25 mg, 3 mg injection

ACTION & *THERAPEUTIC EFFECT*
Cetrotide is a luteinizing hormone-releasing hormone (LHRH) antagonist. *It prevents premature LH surges in patients undergoing controlled ovarian hyperstimulation for assisted reproduction.*

USES Treatment of infertility as part of an assisted reproduction program.

CONTRAINDICATIONS Hypersensitivity to cetrorelix, extrinsic peptide hormones, mannitol, gonadotropin-releasing hormone analogs; primary ovarian failure; renal failure; pregnancy (category X); known or suspected pregnancy; lactation.
CAUTIOUS USE Hepatic insufficiency; polycystic ovary syndrome.

ROUTE & DOSAGE

Infertility
Adult: **SC** 0.25 mg/d during early to mid follicular phase of the cycle (stimulation day 5 or 6) following the initiation of FSH or 3 mg as a single dose is administered when the serum estradiol level is indicative of an appropriate stimulation response, usually on FSH stimulation day 7 (range day 5–9). If HCG has not been administered within 4 d after the injection of 3 mg, then 0.25 mg should be administered once daily until HCG administration

ADMINISTRATION

Subcutaneous

- Reconstitute the 0.25 or 3 mL vial with 1 or 3 mL, respectively, of sterile water for injection.

- Inject into lower abdominal wall following reconstitution. Rotate injection sites.
- Store the 3 mg dose at room temperature, 15°–30° C (59°–86° F). Store the 0.25 mg dose in the refrigerator.

ADVERSE EFFECTS (≥1%) **CNS:** Headache. **GI:** Nausea, vomiting, abdominal pain. **Endocrine:** Hot flashes. **Skin:** Pruritus at injection site. **Urogenital:** Ovarian enlargement, ovarian hyperstimulation syndrome, pelvic pain.

INTERACTIONS Drug: Cimetidine, methyldopa, metoclopramide, reserpine, PHENOTHIAZINES may interfere with fertility efforts. **Herbal: Black cohosh, DHEA** may antagonize fertility efforts.

PHARMACOKINETICS Absorption: 85% absorbed from SC injection site. **Peak:** 1–2 h. **Metabolism:** Metabolized by peptidases. **Elimination:** 2–4% in urine, 5–10% in bile. **Half-Life:** 62 h after single dose, 20 h after multiple doses.

CLINICAL IMPLICATIONS

Assessment & Drug Effects
- Lab test: Monitor routine blood chemistries.
- Monitor weight and report development of edema and/or shortness of breath.

Patient & Family Education
- Contact physician immediately for any of the following: Abdominal or stomach pain, persistent or severe nausea, vomiting or diarrhea; decreased urination; pelvic pain; moderate to severe bloating, rapid weight gain; shortness of breath; swelling of lower legs.
- Understand that hot flashes are a common side effect of this drug.

CETUXIMAB

(ce-tux'i-mab)
Erbitux
Classifications: ANTINEOPLASTIC; MONOCLONAL ANTIBODY; EPIDERMAL GROWTH FACTOR RECEPTOR (EGFR) INHIBITOR
Therapeutic: ANTINEOPLASTIC; MONOCLONAL ANTIBODY; EGFR INHIBITOR
Prototype: Gefitinib
Pregnancy Category: C

AVAILABILITY 100 mg/50 mL injection

ACTION & THERAPEUTIC EFFECT
Cetuximab is a recombinant, monoclonal antibody that binds specifically to the epidermal growth factor receptor (EGFR, HER1, c-ErbB-1) on both normal and tumor cells. Binding to the EGFR results in inhibition of cell growth, induction of apoptosis, and decreased vascular endothelial growth factor production. *Overexpression of EGFR is detected in many human cancers, including those of the colon and rectum. Cetuximab inhibits the growth and survival of tumor cells that overexpress the EGFR.*

USES Treatment of EGFR-expressing metastatic colorectal cancer in combination with irinotecan in patients who are refractory to irinotecan-based chemotherapy or as monotherapy in patients who are intolerant to irinotecan-based chemotherapy. Used in combination with radiation for squamous cell cancer of head and neck.

CONTRAINDICATIONS Pregnancy (category C), lactation within 60 d of using cetuximab; worsening of preexisting pulmonary edema or interstitial lung disease. Safety and

Common adverse effects in *italic*, life-threatening effects underlined; generic names in **bold**; classifications in SMALL CAPS; ✦ Canadian drug name; ⊘ Prototype drug

289

C

efficacy in children have not been established.

CAUTIOUS USE Infusion reaction, especially with first time users; history of hypersensitivity to murine proteins or cetuximab; cardiac disease, coronary artery disease; pulmonary disease, pulmonary fibrosis; UV exposure, radiation therapy.

ROUTE & DOSAGE

Colorectal Cancer/Head and Neck Cancer

Adult: **IV** Start with 400 mg/m^2 over 2 h; continue with 250 mg/m^2 over 1 h weekly

ADMINISTRATION

Intravenous

Administer with full resuscitation equipment available and under the supervision of a physician experienced with chemotherapy.

- Premedication with an H$_1$-receptor antagonist (e.g., diphenhydramine 50 mg IV) is recommended.
- Monitor for an infusion reaction for at least 1 h following completion of infusion.

PREPARE: **IV Infusion:** Do not shake or further dilute vial. Do not mix with other medication. Inject cetuximab solution into a sterile, evacuated container or bag (i.e., glass, polyolefin, ethylene vinyl acetate, DEHP plasticized PVC, or PVC); repeat until needed dose has been added to container, using a new needle for each vial. Attach to infusion set with a low-protein-binding 0.22-micron filter and prime line with cetuximab. May also administer by syringe and syringe pump; use a new needle and filter for each vial.

ADMINISTER: **IV Infusion:** Do NOT administer a bolus dose. Give IV infusion via an infusion pump or syringe pump at ≤5 mL/min; piggyback into the patient's IV line.
- Flush line with NS after infusion. ▪Note: Slow infusion rate by 50% if a prior, mild infusion reaction occurred.

INCOMPATIBILITIES **Solution/additive:** Do not mix with other additives. **Y-site:** No data available.

- Store unopened vials at 2°–8° C (36°–46° F). Note: Vials may contain a small amount of easily visible, white particles.
- Cetuximab in IV bag is stable for up to 12 h refrigerated and up to 8 h at 20°–25° C (68°–77° F).

ADVERSE EFFECTS (≥1%) **Body as a Whole:** Infusion reactions (allergic reaction, anaphylactoid reaction, fever, chills, dyspnea, bronchospasm stridor, hoarseness, urticaria, hypotension), *fever, sepsis, asthenia, malaise,* pain, infection. **CNS:** *Headache,* insomnia, depression. **GI:** *Nausea, vomiting diarrhea, abdominal pain, constipation,* stomatitis, dyspepsia. **Hematologic:** Leukopenia, anemia. **Metabolic:** Weight loss, peripheral edema, dehydration, hypomagnesemia, hypokalemia. **Respiratory:** Pulmonary embolism, <u>pulmonary fibrosis (rare)</u>, *dyspnea,* cough. **Skin:** *Rash,* alopecia, pruritus. **Urogenital:** Kidney failure.

INTERACTIONS Drug: None reported to date.

PHARMACOKINETICS Half-Life: 114 h (75–188 h).

CLINICAL IMPLICATIONS

Assessment & Drug Effects

- Discontinue infusion and notify physician for S&S of a severe infusion reaction: chills, fever, bronchospasm, stridor, hoarseness, urticaria, and/or hypotension. Institute supportive measures immediately, including epinephrine, corticosteroids, IV antihistamines, bronchodilators, and oxygen. Carefully monitor until complete resolution of all S&S.

- Monitor pulmonary status and report onset of acute or worsening pulmonary symptoms.
- Lab tests: Periodic CBC with differential, Hct and Hgb.

Patient & Family Education
- Report immediately: especially difficulty breathing, wheezing, shortness of breath, hives, faintness and/or dizziness anytime during IV infusion.
- Report promptly any of the following: eye inflammation, mouth sores, skin rash, redness, or severe dry skin.
- Wear sunscreen and a hat and limit sun exposure while being treated with this drug.

CEVIMELINE HYDROCHLORIDE

(cev-i-may'leen)
Evoxac
Classifications: CHOLINERGIC AGONIST; CHOLINERGIC ENHANCER
Therapeutic: CHOLINERGIC ENHANCER
Pregnancy Category: C

AVAILABILITY 30 mg capsules

ACTION & *THERAPEUTIC EFFECT*
Cholinergic agent that binds to muscarinic receptors. *Increases secretion of exocrine glands, such as salivary and sweat glands. It relieves severe dry mouth.*

USES Treatment of dry mouth in patients with Sjögren's syndrome.

CONTRAINDICATIONS Hypersensitivity to cevimeline; uncontrolled asthma; acute iritis; narrow-angle glaucoma; lactation.
CAUTIOUS USE Controlled asthma; chronic bronchitis, COPD; cardiac disease, cardiac arrhythmias, myocardial infarction; history of nephrolithiasis or cholelithiasis; elderly; pregnancy (category C); older adults. Safety and effectiveness in children are not established.

ROUTE & DOSAGE

Dry Mouth
Adult: **PO** 30 mg t.i.d.

ADMINISTRATION

Oral
- Give without regard to food.
- Store refrigerated at 2°–8° C (35.6°–46.4° F) with occasional fluctuations between 15°–30° C (59°–86° F).

ADVERSE EFFECTS (≥1%) **Body as a Whole:** *Excessive sweating, headache,* back pain, dizziness, fatigue, pain, hot flushes, rigors, tremor, hypertonia, myalgia, fever, eye pain, ear ache, flu-like symptoms. **CNS:** Insomnia, anxiety, vertigo, depression, hyporeflexia. **CV:** Peripheral edema, chest pain. **GI:** *Nausea, diarrhea,* excessive salivation, dyspepsia, abdominal pain, coughing, vomiting, constipation, anorexia, dry mouth, hiccup. **Respiratory:** *Rhinitis, sinusitis, upper respiratory tract infection,* pharyngitis, bronchitis. **Skin:** Rash, conjunctivitis, pruritus. **Special Senses:** Abnormal vision. **Urogenital:** Urinary tract infection.

INTERACTIONS Drug: BETA-ADRENERGIC AGONISTS may cause conduction

Common adverse effects in *italic*, life-threatening effects underlined; generic names in **bold**; classifications in SMALL CAPS; ♦ Canadian drug name; ⊘ Prototype drug

291

disturbances; PARASYMPATHOMIMETIC DRUGS may have additive effects.

PHARMACOKINETICS Absorption: Rapidly absorbed. **Peak:** 1.5–2 h. **Distribution:** <20% protein bound. **Metabolism:** In liver by CYP2D6 and 3A3/4. **Elimination:** Primarily in urine. **Half-Life:** 5 h.

CLINICAL IMPLICATIONS

Assessment & Drug Effects

- Monitor for S&S of increased airway resistance, especially in patient with asthma, bronchitis, emphysema, or COPD.
- Monitor cardiac status, especially in those with known cardiac disease or dysfunction.
- Monitor fluid status, especially in those at risk for dehydration.
- Lab tests: Routine blood chemistry during long-term therapy.
- Report S&S of excess cholinergic activity (e.g., diaphoresis, frequent urge to urinate, nausea and/or diarrhea).

Patient & Family Education

- Do not drive or engage in potentially hazardous activities until response to drug is known.
- Consult physician if confusion, dizziness, or faintness occur.
- Report diminished night vision or depth perception.
- Drink fluids liberally (2000–3000 mL/d) in the event of excessive sweating when it occurs.

CHARCOAL, ACTIVATED (LIQUID ANTIDOTE)

Actidose, CharcoAid, Charcocaps, Charcodote, Insta-Char

Classifications: ANTIDOTE; ADSORBENT

Therapeutic: ANTIDOTE

Pregnancy Category: C

AVAILABILITY 208 mg/mL, 15 g, 30 g, 50 mg liquid/suspension

ACTION & *THERAPEUTIC EFFECT*
Activated charcoal (carbon) is a chemically inert, odorless, tasteless, fine black powder with wide spectrum of adsorptive activity. Acts by binding (adsorbing) toxic substances, thereby inhibiting their GI absorption, enterohepatic circulation, and thus bioavailability. *Action appears to result from drug diffusion from plasma into GI tract where it is adsorbed by activated charcoal. Effectively adsorbs toxins in the gut preventing their systemic absorption and impact.*

USES General purpose emergency antidote in the treatment of poisonings by most drugs and chemicals. Gastric dialysis (repetitive doses) in uremia to adsorb various waste products from GI tract; severe acute poisoning. Has been used to adsorb intestinal gases in treatment of dyspepsia, flatulence, and distension (value in these conditions not established). Sometimes used topically as a deodorant for foul-smelling wounds and ulcers.

CONTRAINDICATIONS Reportedly not effective for poisonings by cyanide, mineral acids, caustic alkalis, organic solvents, iron, ethanol, methanol; gag reflex depression, coma; GI obstruction; quinidine or quinine hypersensitivity; pregnancy (category C).

CAUTIOUS USE Lactation.

ROUTE & DOSAGE

Acute Poisonings
Adult: **PO** 30–100 g in at least 180–240 mL (6–8 oz) of water or 1 g/kg
Child 1–12 y: **PO** 1–2 g/kg or 15–30 g in at least 6–8 oz of water

Common adverse effects in *italic*, life-threatening effects underlined; generic names in **bold**; classifications in SMALL CAPS; ♣ Canadian drug name; ☻ Prototype drug

Infant <1 y: **PO** 1 g/kg

Gastric Dialysis

Adult: **PO** 20–40 g q6h for 1 or 2 d

GI Disturbances

Adult: **PO** 520–975 mg p.c. up to 5 g/d

ADMINISTRATION

Oral

- Activated charcoal tablets or capsules are less adsorptive and thus less effective than powder or liquid form; therefore, they are not recommended in treatment of acute poisoning.
- Drug is most effective when administered as soon as possible after acute poisoning (preferably within 30 min).
- In an emergency, dose may be approximated by stirring sufficient activated charcoal into tap water to make a slurry the consistency of soup (about 20–30 g in at least 240 mL of water).
- Activated charcoal can be swallowed or given through a nasogastric tube. If administered too rapidly, patient may vomit.
- If necessary, palatability may be improved by adding a small amount of concentrated fruit juice or chocolate powder to the slurry. Reportedly, these agents do not appreciably alter adsorptive activity.
- To prevent adsorption of gases from the air, store in tightly covered container.

ADVERSE EFFECTS (≥1%) **GI:** Vomiting (rapid ingestion of high doses), constipation, diarrhea (from sorbitol).

INTERACTIONS Drug: May decrease absorption of all other oral medications—administer at least 2 h apart.

PHARMACOKINETICS Absorption: Not absorbed. **Elimination:** In feces.

CLINICAL IMPLICATIONS

Assessment & Drug Effects

- Record appearance, color, consistency, frequency, and relative amount of stools. Inform patient that activated charcoal will color feces black.

CHLORAL HYDRATE

(klor'al hye'drate)

Aquachloral Supprettes, Noctec, Novochlorhydrate ◆

Classifications: ANXIOLYTIC, SEDATIVE-HYPNOTIC

Therapeutic: ANTIANXIETY; SEDATIVE-HYPNOTIC

Prototype: Secobarbital

Pregnancy Category: C

Controlled Substance: Schedule IV

AVAILABILITY 500 mg capsules; 250 mg/5 mL, 500 mg/5 mL syrup; 324 mg, 500 mg, 648 mg suppositories

ACTION & *THERAPEUTIC EFFECT*

Produces "physiologic sleep" by mild cerebral depression with little effect on respirations or BP and little or no hangover. *Chloral hydrate in low doses is a sedative-hypnotic which does not affect sleep physiology (e.g., REM sleep).*

USES Short-term management of insomnia, general sedation (especially in the young and the older adult), sedation before and after surgery, to reduce anxiety associated with drug withdrawal, and alone or with paraldehyde to prevent or suppress alcohol withdrawal symptoms.

Common adverse effects in *italic*, life-threatening effects underlined; generic names in **bold**; classifications in SMALL CAPS; ◆ Canadian drug name; ☉ Prototype drug

293

C

CONTRAINDICATIONS Known hypersensitivity to chloral hydrate or chloral derivatives; severe hepatic, renal, or cardiac disease; rectal dosage form in patients with proctitis; oral use in patients with esophagitis, gastritis, gastric or duodenal ulcers; pregnancy (category C).

CAUTIOUS USE History of intermittent porphyria, asthma, history of or proneness to drug dependence, depression, suicidal tendencies.

ROUTE & DOSAGE

Sedative
Adult: **PO/PR** 250 mg t.i.d. p.c.
Child: **PO/PR** 25–50 mg/kg/d divided q6–8h (max: 500 mg/dose)

Hypnotic
Adult: **PO/PR** 500 mg–1 g 15–30 min before h.s. or 30 min before surgery
Geriatric: **PO/PR** 250 mg h.s.
Child: **PO/PR** 50 mg/kg 15–30 min before h.s. or 30 min before surgery (max: 1 g)

EEG Premedication
Child: **PO/PR** 20–25 mg/kg 30–60 min prior to procedure

ADMINISTRATION

Oral
▪ Dilute liquid preparations in chilled fluids to minimize unpleasant taste.
▪ Watch to see that drug is not cheeked and hoarded.

Rectal
▪ Moisten suppository with a water-based lubricant, such as K-Y jelly, prior to insertion.
▪ Solutions are preserved in tightly covered, light-resistant containers.

ADVERSE EFFECTS (≥1%) **Body as a Whole:** Angioedema, eosino-philia, breath odor, leukopenia, ketonuria, renal and hepatic damage, sudden death. **CV:** Arrhythmias, cardiac arrest. **GI:** *Nausea, vomiting, diarrhea,* severe gastritis. **CNS:** Dizziness, motor incoordination, headache. **Skin:** Purpura, urticaria, erythematous rash, eczema, erythema multiforme, fixed drug eruptions. **Special Senses:** Conjunctivitis.

DIAGNOSTIC TEST INTERFERENCE False-positive results for *urine glucose* with *Benedict's solutions,* and possibly with *Clinitest* but not with *glucose oxidase methods* (e.g., *Clinistix, Diastix, Tes-Tape*). Possible interference with fluorometric test for *urine catecholamines* (if chloral hydrate is administered within 48 h of test) and *urinary 17-OHCS* determinations (by modification of *Reddy, Jenkins, Thorn procedure*).

INTERACTIONS Drug: Alcohol, BARBITURATES, **paraldehyde,** other CNS DEPRESSANTS potentiate CNS depression; tachycardia may also occur with **alcohol**; increases anticoagulant effect of ORAL ANTICOAGULANTS; **furosemide** IV can produce flushing, diaphoresis, BP changes.

PHARMACOKINETICS Absorption: Readily from oral or rectal administration. **Onset:** 30–60 min. **Peak:** 1–3 h. **Duration:** 4–8 h. **Distribution:** Well distributed to all tissues; 70–80% protein bound; crosses placenta. **Metabolism:** In liver to the active metabolite trichloroethanol. **Elimination:** Primarily by kidneys; small amount excreted in feces via bile. **Half-Life:** 8–11 h.

CLINICAL IMPLICATIONS

Assessment & Drug Effects
▪ Chloral hydrate is not intended for relief of pain. When used in

the presence of pain, it may cause excitement and delirium.

- Do not discontinue abruptly following prolonged use. Sudden withdrawal from dependent patients may produce delirium, mania, or convulsions.
- Monitor for S&S of allergic skin reactions, which may occur within several hours or as long as 10 d after drug administration.
- Evaluate patient's response to chloral hydrate and continued need for the drug.

Patient & Family Education
- Do not ambulate without assistance until response to drug is known.
- Avoid concomitant use of alcoholic beverages.
- Avoid driving and other potentially hazardous activities while under the influence of chloral hydrate.

CHLORAMBUCIL

(klor-am′byoo-sil)
Leukeran
Classifications: ANTINEOPLASTIC; ALKYLATING AGENT
Therapeutic: ANTINEOPLASTIC; NITROGEN MUSTARD
Prototype: Cyclophosphamide
Pregnancy Category: D

AVAILABILITY 2 mg tablets

ACTION & THERAPEUTIC EFFECT
Potent aromatic derivative of the alkylating agent nitrogen mustard which is slowest acting and least toxic of the nitrogen mustards. A cell-cycle nonspecific drug (kills both resting and dividing cells), it causes cytotoxic cross linkage in DNA, thus preventing synthesis of DNA, RNA, and proteins. Myelosuppression in therapeutic doses is moderate and rapidly reversible. *Lymphocytic effect is marked; thus it is effective in treatment of various lymphomas.*

USES As single agent or with other antineoplastics in treatment of chronic lymphocytic leukemia, malignant lymphomas including lymphosarcoma, Hodgkin's disease, and giant follicular lymphoma, and in treatment of carcinoma of the ovary, breast, and testes.

UNLABELED USES Nonneoplastic conditions: vasculitis complicating rheumatoid arthritis, autoimmune hemolytic anemias associated with cold agglutinins, lupus glomerulonephritis, idiopathic nephrotic syndrome, polycythemia vera, macroglobulinemia.

CONTRAINDICATIONS Hypersensitivity to chlorambucil or to other alkylating agents; administration within 4 wk of a full course of radiation or chemotherapy; full dosage if bone marrow is infiltrated with lymphomatous tissue or is hypoplastic; smallpox and other vaccines; pregnancy (category D), lactation.

CAUTIOUS USE Excessive or prolonged dosage, pneumococcus vaccination, history of seizures or head trauma.

ROUTE & DOSAGE

Malignant Diseases (Lymphomas, Hodgkin's Disease, etc.)
Adult: **PO** 0.1–0.2 mg/kg/d (usual dose 4–10 mg/d)
Child: **PO** 0.1–0.2 mg/kg/d in single or divided doses

ADMINISTRATION
Oral
- Control nausea and vomiting by giving entire daily dose at one

Common adverse effects in *italic*, life-threatening effects <u>underlined</u>; generic names in **bold**; classifications in SMALL CAPS; ♣ Canadian drug name; ⊘ Prototype drug

295

C

time, 1 h before breakfast or 2 h after evening meal, or at bedtime. Consult physician.

- With confirmation of bone marrow depression (low platelet and neutrophil counts or peripheral lymphocytosis), it is recommended that dosage not exceed 0.1 mg/kg.
- Store in tightly closed, light-resistant container.

ADVERSE EFFECTS (≥1%) **Body as a Whole:** Drug fever, skin rashes, papilledema, alopecia, peripheral neuropathy, sterile cystitis, pulmonary complications, seizures (high doses). **GI:** Low incidence of gastric discomfort, hepatotoxicity. **Hematologic:** Bone marrow depression: *leukopenia*, thrombocytopenia, anemia. **Metabolic:** Sterility, hyperuricemia.

INTERACTIONS Drug: May have to adjust dose of **allopurinol, colchicine** because of chlorambucil-associated hyperuricemia.

PHARMACOKINETICS Absorption: Rapidly and completely from GI tract. **Peak:** 1 h. **Distribution:** Extensively bound to plasma and tissue proteins; crosses placenta. **Metabolism:** In liver. **Elimination:** 60% in urine as metabolites within 24 h. **Half-Life:** 1.5–2.5 h.

CLINICAL IMPLICATIONS

Assessment & Drug Effects

- Lab tests: CBC, Hgb, total and differential leukocyte counts, and serum uric acid initially and at least once weekly during treatment.
- Leukopenia usually develops after the third week of treatment; it may continue for up to 10 d after last dose, then rapidly return to normal.
- Avoid or reduce to minimum injections and other invasive procedures (e.g., rectal temperatures,

enemas) when platelet count is low because of danger of bleeding.

- Monitor for S&S of skin rashes, which are rare, but appear to show a consistent pattern: pustular eruption on mouth, chin, cheeks; urticarial erythema on trunk that spreads to legs. The rash occurs early in treatment period and lasts about 10 d after last dose.

Patient & Family Education

- Keep appointments with physician. During treatment it is dangerous to go longer than 2 wk without a clinical examination and blood studies.
- Notify physician if the following symptoms occur: unusual bleeding or bruising, sores on lips or in mouth; flank, stomach, or joint pain; fever, chills, or other signs of infection, sore throat, cough, dyspnea.
- Report immediately the onset of cutaneous reaction.
- Drink at least 10–12 glasses (240 mL [8 oz] each) of fluid per day, if not contraindicated, and report to physician if urine output decreases below normal amounts.
- Report to physician immediately if pregnant, as there is a potential hazard to the fetus.

CHLORAMPHENICOL

(klor-am-fen′i-kole)
Chloromycetin, Novo-chloro-cap ◆

CHLORAMPHENICOL SODIUM SUCCINATE

Chloromycetin Sodium Succinate

Classifications: ANTIBIOTIC
Therapeutic: ANTIBIOTIC
Pregnancy Category: C

AVAILABILITY 250 mg capsules; 100 mg/mL injection; 5 mg/mL ophth solution; 10 mg/g ointment

ACTION & *THERAPEUTIC EFFECT*

Synthetic broad-spectrum antibiotic that is principally bacteriostatic but may be bactericidal in certain species (e.g., *Haemophilus influenzae*) or when given in higher concentrations. Believed to act by binding to the 50S ribosome of bacteria and thus interfering with protein synthesis. *Effective against a wide variety of gram-negative and gram-positive bacteria and most anaerobic microorganisms.*

USES Severe infections when other antibiotics are ineffective or are contraindicated. Particularly effective against *Salmonella typhi* and other *Salmonella* sp, *Streptococcus pneumoniae, Neisseria,* meningeal infections caused by *H. influenzae,* and infections involving *Bacteroides fragilis* and other anaerobic organisms, *Rickettsia rickettsii* (cause of Rocky Mountain spotted fever) and other rickettsiae, the lymphogranuloma-psittacosis group *(Chlamydia),* and *Mycoplasma.* Also used in cystic fibrosis antiinfective regimens and topically for infections of skin, eyes, and external auditory canal.

CONTRAINDICATIONS History of hypersensitivity or toxic reaction to chloramphenicol; treatment of minor infections, prophylactic use; typhoid carrier state, history or family history of drug-induced bone marrow depression, concomitant therapy with drugs that produce bone marrow depression; pregnancy (category C); lactation.

CAUTIOUS USE Impaired hepatic or renal function, premature and full-term infants, children; intermittent porphyria; patients with G6PD deficiency; patient or family history of drug-induced bone marrow depression.

ROUTE & DOSAGE

Serious Infections

Adult: **PO/IV** 50 mg/kg/d in 4 divided doses.
Neonate: **IV** 25–50 mg/kg/d divided q12–24h
Infant/Child: **PO/IV** 50–75 mg/kg/d divided q6h (max: 4 g/d)

Meningitis

Adult/Child: **IV** 75–100 mg/kg/d divided q6h

ADMINISTRATION

Oral

- Give preferably with a full glass of water on an empty stomach, at least 1 h before or 2 h after a meal, to achieve optimum blood levels.

Ophthalmic

- Apply light pressure to lacrimal duct after instillation for 1–2 min to prevent drainage into nasopharynx and systemic absorption. This is an extremely important step to decrease absorption. Several cases of aplastic anemia have been associated with use of ophthalmic preparations.

Intravenous

IV administration to neonates, infants, children: Verify correct IV concentration and rate of infusion with physician.

PREPARE: **Direct:** Dilute each 1 g with 10 mL of sterile water or D5W. **Intermittent:** Further dilute in 50–100 mL of D5W. **Continuous:** Dilute with additional D5W for a longer infusion time.

ADMINISTER: **Direct:** Give slowly over a period of at least 1 min. **Intermittent:** Give over 30–60 min. **Continuous:** Infuse over 4–6 h.

Common adverse effects in *italic,* life-threatening effects <u>underlined;</u> generic names in **bold;** classifications in SMALL CAPS; ♣ Canadian drug name; ⊕ Prototype drug

INCOMPATIBILITIES Solutions/additives: **Chlorpromazine, glycopyrrolate, metoclopramide, polymyxin B, prochlorperazine, promethazine,** TETRACYCLINES, **vancomycin.** Y-site: **Fluconazole.**

▪ Solution for infusion may form crystals or a second layer when stored at low temperatures. Solution can be clarified by shaking vial. Do not use cloudy solutions.

▪ Store topical ophthalmic, otic, and skin preparations, PO forms, and unopened ampuls at room temperature and protected from light unless otherwise directed by manufacturer.

ADVERSE EFFECTS (≥1%) **Body as a Whole:** Hypersensitivity, <u>angioedema,</u> dyspnea, fever, <u>anaphylaxis,</u> superinfections, Gray syndrome. **GI:** Nausea, vomiting, diarrhea, perianal irritation, enterocolitis, glossitis, stomatitis, unpleasant taste, xerostomia. **Hematologic:** <u>Bone marrow depression</u> (dose-related and reversible): reticulocytosis, leukopenia, granulocytopenia, thrombocytopenia, increased plasma iron, reduced Hgb, hypoplastic anemia, hypoprothrombinemia. Non-dose-related and irreversible <u>pancytopenia, agranulocytosis, aplastic anemia,</u> paroxysmal nocturnal hemoglobinuria, leukemia. **CNS:** Neurotoxicity: headache, mental depression, confusion, delirium, digital paresthesias, peripheral neuritis. **Skin:** Urticaria, contact dermatitis, maculopapular and vesicular rashes, fixed-drug eruptions. **Special Senses:** Visual disturbances, optic neuritis, optic nerve atrophy, contact conjunctivitis.

DIAGNOSTIC TEST INTERFERENCE
Possibility of false-positive results for **urine glucose** by **copper reduction methods** (e.g., *Benedict's solution, Clinitest*). Chloramphenicol may interfere with *17-OHCS* (urinary steroid) determinations (modification of *Reddy, Jenkins, Thorn procedure* not affected), with *urobilinogen excretion,* and with responses to *tetanus toxoid* and possibly other active immunizing agents.

INTERACTIONS Drug: The metabolism of **chlorpropamide, dicumarol, phenytoin, tolbutamide** may be decreased, prolonging their activity. **Phenobarbital** decreases chloramphenicol levels. The response to **iron** preparations, **folic acid,** and **vitamin B$_{12}$** may be delayed.

PHARMACOKINETICS Absorption: Rapidly from GI tract. **Peak:** PO: 1–3 h; IV: 1 h. **Distribution:** Widely distributed to most body tissues including saliva and ascitic, pleural and synovial fluid; concentrates in liver and kidneys; penetrates CNS; crosses placenta. **Metabolism:** Primarily inactivated in liver. **Elimination:** Much longer in neonates; metabolite and free drug excreted in urine; excreted in breast milk. **Half-Life:** 1.5–4.1 h.

CLINICAL IMPLICATIONS

Assessment & Drug Effects
▪ Lab tests: Perform bacterial culture and susceptibility tests prior to first dose and periodically thereafter. Baseline CBC, platelets, serum iron, and reticulocyte cell counts before initiation of therapy, at 48 h intervals during therapy, and periodically. Monitor chloramphenicol blood levels weekly or more frequently with hepatic dysfunction and in pa-

tients receiving therapy for longer than 2 wk. Desired concentrations: peak 10–20 mcg/mL; through 5–10 mcg/mL.

- Monitor blood studies. Chloramphenicol should be discontinued upon appearance of leukopenia, reticulocytopenia, thrombocytopenia, or anemia.
- Non-dose-related irreversible bone marrow depression may appear weeks or months after drug therapy is terminated. The potential for this side effect is greatest in patients with impaired hepatic or renal function, infants, children, and premenopausal women.
- Observe the patient closely, because blood studies are not always reliable predictors of irreversible bone marrow depression.
- Check temperature at least q4h. Usually chloramphenicol is discontinued if temperature remains normal for 48 h.
- Monitor I&O ratio or pattern: Report any appreciable change.
- More frequent determinations of serum glucose are recommended in patients receiving oral antidiabetic agents.
- Monitor for S&S of Gray syndrome, which has occurred 2–9 d after initiation of high dose chloramphenicol therapy in premature infants and neonates and in children ≤2 y. Report early signs: abdominal distention, failure to feed, pallor, changes in vital signs. Early detection and prompt termination of therapy can interrupt a potentially fatal course.

Patient & Family Education

- A bitter taste may occur 15–20 s after IV injection; it usually lasts only 2–3 min.
- Report immediately sore throat, fever, fatigue, petechiae, nose bleeds, bleeding gums, or other unusual bleeding or bruising, or any other suspicious sign of symptom. Drug therapy should be discontinued if abnormal bleeding occurs.
- Watch for S&S of superinfection (see Appendix F).
- Follow dosage and duration of therapy as prescribed by physician.
- Avoid prolonged or frequent intermittent use of topical preparations because systemic absorption and toxicity can occur.
- Withhold medication and check with physician immediately if signs of hypersensitivity reaction (see Appendix F), irritation, superinfection, or other adverse reactions appear.

CHLORDIAZEPOXIDE HYDROCHLORIDE

(klor-dye-az-e-pox′ide)
Librium, Solium ◆
Classifications: ANXIOLYTIC; SEDATIVE-HYPNOTIC; BENZODIAZEPINE
Therapeutic: ANTIANXIETY; SEDATIVE-HYPNOTIC
Prototype: Lorazepam
Pregnancy Category: D
Controlled Substance: Schedule IV

AVAILABILITY 5 mg, 10 mg, 25 mg capsules

ACTION & *THERAPEUTIC EFFECT*

Benzodiazepine derivative that acts on the limbic, thalamic, and hypothalamic areas of the CNS. Has long-acting hypnotic properties. Causes mild suppression of REM sleep and of deeper phases, particularly stage 4, while increasing total sleep time. *Produces mild anxiolytic (reduces anxiety), sedative,*

Common adverse effects in *italic*, life-threatening effects <u>underlined</u>; generic names in **bold**; classifications in SMALL CAPS; ◆ Canadian drug name; ⊘ Prototype drug

299

anticonvulsant, and skeletal muscle relaxant effects.

USES Relief of various anxiety and tension states, preoperative apprehension and anxiety, and for management of alcohol withdrawal.
UNLABELED USES Essential, familial, and senile action tremors.

CONTRAINDICATIONS Hypersensitivity to chlordiazepoxide and other benzodiazepines; narrow angle glaucoma, prostatic hypertrophy, shock, comatose states, primary depressive disorder or psychoses, pregnancy (category D), lactation, oral use in children <6 y, parenteral use in children <12 y, acute alcohol intoxication.
CAUTIOUS USE Anxiety states associated with impending depression, history of impaired hepatic or renal function; addiction-prone individuals, blood dyscrasias; in the older adult, debilitated patients, children; hyperkinesis, COPD.

ROUTE & DOSAGE

Mild Anxiety, Preoperative Anxiety
Adult: **PO** 5–10 mg t.i.d. or q.i.d.
Geriatric: **PO** 5 mg b.i.d. to q.i.d.
Child: **PO** 5 mg b.i.d. to q.i.d.; may be increased to 10 mg t.i.d.

Severe Anxiety and Tension
Adult: **PO** 20–25 mg t.i.d. or q.i.d.

Alcohol Withdrawal Syndrome
Adult: **PO** 50–100 mg prn up to 300 mg/d

ADMINISTRATION
Oral
- Give with or immediately after meals or with milk to reduce GI distress. If an antacid is prescribed, it should be taken at least 1 h before or after chlordiazepoxide to prevent delay in drug absorption.
- Supervise drug ingestion to prevent "cheeking" pills, a maneuver that leads to hoarding or omission of drug.
- Store in tight, light-resistant containers at room temperature unless otherwise specified by manufacturer.

ADVERSE EFFECTS (≥1%) **Body as a Whole:** Edema, pain in injection site, jaundice, hiccups, respiratory depression. **CV:** Orthostatic hypotension, tachycardia, changes in ECG patterns seen with rapid IV administration. **GI:** Nausea, dry mouth, vomiting, constipation, increased appetite. **CNS:** *Drowsiness, dizziness, lethargy,* changes in EEG pattern; vivid dreams, nightmares, headache, vertigo, syncope, tinnitus, confusion, hallucinations, parodoxic rage, depression, delirium, ataxia. **Skin:** Photosensitivity, skin rash. **Urogenital:** Urinary frequency.

DIAGNOSTIC TEST INTERFERENCE Chlordiazepoxide increases *serum bilirubin, AST* and *ALT;* decreases *radioactive iodine uptake;* and may falsely increase readings for *urinary 17-OHCS* (modified *Glenn-Nelson* technique).

INTERACTIONS Drug: Alcohol, CNS DEPRESSANTS, ANTICONVULSANTS potentiate CNS depression; **cimetidine** in-

---

creases **chlordiazepoxide** plasma levels, thus increasing toxicity; may decrease antiparkinson effects of **levodopa;** may increase **phenytoin** levels; smoking decreases sedative and antianxiety effects. **Herbal: Kava-kava, valerian** may potentiate sedation.

PHARMACOKINETICS Absorption: Well absorbed from GI tract. **Peak:** 1–4 h. **Distribution:** Widely distributed throughout body; crosses placenta. **Metabolism:** In liver via CYP3A4 to long-acting active metabolite. **Elimination:** Slowly excreted in urine (may last several days); excreted in breast milk. **Half-Life:** 5–30 h.

CLINICAL IMPLICATIONS

Assessment & Drug Effects

- Monitor for S&S of orthostatic hypotension and tachycardia, which occur more frequently with parenteral administration. Patient should stay recumbent 2–3 h after IM or IV injection; observe closely and monitor vital signs.
- Check BP and pulse before giving benzodiazepine in early part of therapy. If blood pressure falls 20 mm Hg or more or if pulse rate is above 120 bpm, delay medication and consult physician.
- Lab tests: Periodic blood cell counts and liver function tests are recommended during prolonged therapy.
- Monitor for S&S of agranulocytosis: sore throat or mouth, upper respiratory infection, fever, and malaise. Total and differential WBC counts should be ordered immediately, and protective isolation instituted.
- Monitor I&O until drug dosage is stabilized. Report changes in

I&O ratio and dysuria to physician. Cumulative (overdosage) effects can result in renal dysfunction. Older adults are especially vulnerable.

- Monitor for S&S of paradoxic reactions—excitement, stimulation, disturbed sleep patterns, acute rage—which may occur during first few weeks of therapy in psychiatric patients and in hyperactive and aggressive children receiving chlordiazepoxide. Withhold drug and report to physician.
- Assess patient's sleep pattern. If dreams or nightmares interfere with rest, notify physician. A change in the dosing schedule, dose, or an alternate drug may be prescribed.
- Supervision of ambulation especially with older adults & debilitated patients.
- Observe for signs of developing physical or psychologic dependency such as requests for change in drug regimen (dose and dose interval), diminishing favorable response (e.g., disturbed sleep pattern, increase in psychomotor activity), withdrawal symptoms. Investigate the symptoms of ataxia, vertigo, slurred speech; the patient may be taking more than the prescribed dose.
- Abrupt discontinuation of drug in patients receiving high doses for long periods (≥4 mo) has precipitated withdrawal symptoms, but not for at least 5–7 d because of slow elimination.

Patient & Family Education

- Take drug specifically as prescribed: do not skip, increase, or decrease doses, change intervals, or terminate therapy without

Common adverse effects in *italic*, life-threatening effects underlined; generic names in **bold**; classifications in SMALL CAPS; ✦ Canadian drug name; ⊙ Prototype drug

301

physician's advice and do not lend or offer any of drug to another person.

- Do not take OTC drugs unless prescribed.
- Long-term use of this drug may cause xerostomia. Good oral hygiene can alleviate the discomfort.
- Avoid activities requiring mental alertness until reaction to the drug has been evaluated.
- Avoid drinking alcoholic beverages. When combined with chlordiazepoxide, effects of both are potentiated.
- If pregnant during therapy or intending to become pregnant, communicate with physician about continuing therapy.
- Avoid excessive sunlight. Photosensitivity has been reported. Use sunscreen lotion (SPF 12 or above) if allowed.

CHLOROPROCAINE HYDROCHLORIDE

(klor-oh-proe'kane)

Nesacaine, Nesacaine-CE ♣

Classifications: LOCAL ANESTHETIC (ESTER-TYPE)

Therapeutic: LOCAL ANESTHETIC

Prototype: Procaine

Pregnancy Category: C

AVAILABILITY 1%, 2%, 3% injection

ACTION & *THERAPEUTIC EFFECT*
Short-acting ester-type local anesthetic similar to procaine. Decreases sodium influx into nerve cells, thus preventing initial depolarization, propagation, and conduction of the nerve impulse. *Pro-*

duces anesthetic effect, but not used for spinal, topical, or IV regional anesthesia.

USES Infiltration anesthesia and for peripheral, sympathetic, and epidural (including caudal) block anesthesia.

CONTRAINDICATIONS Known sensitivity to ester-type anesthetics, bisulfites, parabens (preservative) or PABA; intercurrent use of bupivacaine; coagulopathy; anticoagulant therapy; pregnancy (category C). Safe use children <12 y not established.

CAUTIOUS USE Cardiac function impairment; history of drug hypersensitivity; debilitated, older adult, or acutely ill patients; neurologic disease, myasthenia gravis; dysrhythmias; sepsis; lactation.

ROUTE & DOSAGE

Infiltration and Nerve Block

Adult: 1–2% solution: max of 800 mg without epinephrine, 1 g with epinephrine

Caudal and Epidural Block (Without Preservatives)

Adult: 2–3% solution: max of 800 mg without epinephrine, 1 g with epinephrine

ADMINISTRATION

Caudal/Epidural

- A test dose (3 mL of 3% solution or 5 mL of 2% solution) may be given before epidural use to check for intravascular or subarachnoid injection. Signs of intravascular injection: "epinephrine response" (tachycardia, circumoral pallor, palpitations, nervousness). Signs of subarachnoid injection: motor paralysis and extensive sensory anesthesia.

- If patient is moved with potential displacement of epidural catheter, test dose is repeated. At least 5 min should elapse between each test dose. Total dose for anesthesia is administered in fractional doses.

- Nesacaine formulation incorporates parabens (preservative) and sodium bisulfite; Nesacaine-CE is preservative-free but incorporates sodium bisulfite. Both parabens and bisulfites may initiate an allergic reaction in some individuals. Determine patient's sensitivity before administration of drug.

- Chloroprocaine is incompatible with alkali hydroxides and their carbonates: soaps, iodine, iodides, silver salts. Avoid use of any of these agents for skin or mucous membrane disinfection before chloroprocaine administration.

- Do not administer solution that is colored. Discard partially used solutions that are preservative-free.

- Store vials at 15°–30° C (59°–86° F); protect from freezing and from direct light.

ADVERSE EFFECTS (≥1%) **Body as a Whole: Sneezing**, <u>anaphylactoid reactions</u>. **CV:** Myocardial depression, hypotension, arrhythmias, bradycardia, <u>cardiac arrest</u>. **GI:** Nausea, vomiting. **CNS:** Anxiety, nervousness, tremors, sedation, circumoral paresthesia, convulsions followed by drowsiness, <u>respiratory arrest</u>. **Skin:** Cutaneous lesions of delayed onset; urti-

caria. **Special Senses:** Blurred or double vision, tinnitus. **Other:** With caudal or epidural anesthesia: urinary retention, fecal or urinary incontinence, slowing of labor and increased incidence of forceps delivery, headache, backache, edema, status asthmaticus.

INTERACTIONS Drug: May antagonize effects of SULFONAMIDES; increased risk of hypotension with MAO INHIBITORS, ANTIHYPERTENSIVE AGENTS.

PHARMACOKINETICS Onset: 6–12 min. **Duration:** 30–60 min without epinephrine; 60–90 min with epinephrine. **Metabolism:** Hydrolyzed by plasma pseudocholinesterases. **Elimination:** Excreted by kidneys.

CLINICAL IMPLICATIONS

Assessment & Drug Effects

- Monitor vital signs throughout period of drug use.
- Have immediately available resuscitation equipment, oxygen, resuscitative drugs, and vasopressors when chloroprocaine is in use.

Patient & Family Education

- Report urinary retention or urinary or fecal incontinence.

CHLOROQUINE PHOSPHATE ℗

(klor'oh-kwin)

Aralen

Classifications: ANTIMALARIAL
Therapeutic: ANTIMALARIAL
Pregnancy Category: C

Common adverse effects in *italic*, life-threatening effects <u>underlined</u>; generic names in **bold**; classifications in SMALL CAPS; ♣ Canadian drug name; ℗ Prototype drug

303

AVAILABILITY 150 mg (base), 300 mg (base) tablets

ACTION & *THERAPEUTIC EFFECT*
Antimalarial activity is believed to be based on its ability to form complexes with DNA of parasite, thereby inhibiting replication and transcription to RNA and nucleic acid synthesis. *Acts as a suppressive agent in patient with* P. vivax *or* P. malariae *malaria; terminates acute attacks and increases intervals between treatment and relapse of malaria. Abolishes the acute attack of* P. falciparum *malaria but does not prevent the infection. Chloroquine-resistant strains have been reported.*

USES Suppression and treatment of malaria caused by *P. malariae, P. ovale, P. vivax*, and susceptible forms of *P. falciparum*, and in the treatment of extraintestinal amebiasis. Concomitant therapy with primaquine is necessary for radical cure of *P. vivax* and *P. malariae* malarias.
UNLABELED USES Discoid and systemic lupus erythematosus, porphyria cutanea tarda, solar urticaria, polymorphous light eruptions, and in rheumatoid arthritis (as second-line therapy).

CONTRAINDICATIONS Hypersensitivity to 4-aminoquinolines, psoriasis; porphyria, renal disease, 4-aminoquinoline-induced retinal or visual field changes; long-term therapy in children; pregnancy (category C). Safe use in women of childbearing potential not established.
CAUTIOUS USE Impaired hepatic function, alcoholism, eczema, patients with G6PD deficiency, infants and children, hematologic, GI, and neurologic disorders.

ROUTE & DOSAGE

Doses are expressed in terms of chloroquine base.

Acute Malaria
Adult: **PO** 600 mg base followed by 300 mg base at 6, 24, and 48 h
Child: **PO** 10 mg base/kg, then 5 mg base/kg at 6, 24, and 48 h.

Malaria Suppression
Adult: **PO** 300 mg base the same day each week starting 2 wk before exposure and continuing for 4–6 wk after leaving the area of exposure (max: 300 mg base/wk)
Child: **PO** 5 mg base/kg the same day each week starting 2 wk before exposure and continuing for 4–6 wk after leaving the area of exposure (max: 300 mg base/wk)

Extraintestinal Amebiasis
Adult: **PO** 600 mg base/d for 2 d, then 300 mg base/d for 2–3 wk
Child: **PO** 10 mg base/kg/d for 2–3 wk

Rheumatoid Arthritis, SLE
Adult: **PO** 150 mg base/d with evening meal

ADMINISTRATION

Oral
- Give immediately before or after meals to minimize GI distress.

Common adverse effects in *italic*, life-threatening effects underlined; generic names in **bold**; classifications in SMALL CAPS; ♥ Canadian drug name; ⊕ Prototype drug

- Monitor child's dose closely. Children are extremely susceptible to overdosage.

ADVERSE EFFECTS (≥1%) **Body as a Whole:** Slight weight loss, myalgia, lymphedema of upper limbs. **CV:** Hypotension; ECG changes. **GI:** *Diarrhea,* abdominal cramps, *nausea,* vomiting, anorexia. **Hematologic:** Hemolytic anemia in patients with G6PD deficiency. **CNS:** Mild transient headache, fatigue, irritability, confusion, nightmares, skeletal muscle weakness, paresthesias, reduced reflexes, vertigo. **Skin:** Bleaching of scalp, eyebrows, body hair, and freckles, pruritus, patchy alopecia (reversible). **Special Senses:** (usually reversible): Blurred vision, disturbances of accommodation, night blindness, scotomas, visual field defects, photophobia, corneal edema, opacity or deposits, ototoxicity (rare).

INTERACTIONS Drug: Aluminum- and **magnesium**-containing ANTACIDS and LAXATIVES decrease chloroquine absorption, so separate administration by at least 4 h; chloroquine may interfere with response to **rabies vaccine.**

PHARMACOKINETICS Absorption: Rapidly and almost completely absorbed. **Peak:** 1–2 h. **Distribution:** Widely distributed; concentrates in lungs, liver, erythrocytes, eyes, skin, and kidneys; crosses placenta. **Metabolism:** Partially in liver to active metabolites. **Elimination:** In urine; excreted in breast milk. **Half-Life:** 70–120 h.

CLINICAL IMPLICATIONSß

Assessment & Drug Effects

- Lab tests: CBC and ECG are advised before initiation of therapy and periodically thereafter in patients on long-term therapy. A test for G6PD deficiency is recommended for American blacks and individuals of Mediterranean ancestry before therapy.
- Monitor for changes in vision. Retinopathy (generally irreversible) can be progressive even after termination of therapy. Patient may be asymptomatic or complain of night blindness, scotomas, visual field changes, blurred vision, or difficulty in focusing. Chloroquine should be discontinued immediately.
- Question patients on long-term therapy regularly about skeletal muscle weakness. Periodic tests should be made of muscle strength and deep tendon reflexes. Positive signs are indications to terminate therapy.

Patient & Family Education

- Report promptly visual or hearing disturbances, muscle weakness, or loss of balance, symptoms of blood dyscrasia (fever, sore mouth or throat, unexplained fatigue, easy bruising or bleeding).
- Use of dark glasses in sunlight or bright light may provide comfort (because of photophobia) and reduce risk of ocular damage.
- Avoid driving or other potentially hazardous activities until reaction to drug is known.
- May cause rusty yellow or brown discoloration of urine.

Common adverse effects in *italic*, life-threatening effects <u>underlined</u>; generic names in **bold**; classifications in SMALL CAPS; ♣ Canadian drug name; ⊚ Prototype drug

CHLOROTHIAZIDE
(klor-oh-thye′a-zide)

CHLOROTHIAZIDE SODIUM
Diuril

Classifications: ELECTROLYTE & WATER BALANCE AGENT; THIAZIDE DIURETIC; ANTIHYPERTENSIVE
Therapeutic: THIAZIDE DIURETIC; ANTIHYPERTENSIVE
Prototype: Hydrochlorothiazide
Pregnancy Category: C

AVAILABILITY 250 mg, 500 mg tablets; 500 mg injection

ACTION & *THERAPEUTIC EFFECT*
Thiazide diuretic chemically related to sulfonamides. Primary action is production of diuresis by direct action on the distal convoluted tubules. Inhibits reabsorption of sodium, potassium, and chloride ions. Promotes renal excretion of sodium (and water), bicarbonate, and potassium. *Antihypertensive mechanism is due to decreased peripheral resistance and reduced blood pressure.*

USES Adjunctively to manage edema associated with CHF, hepatic cirrhosis, renal dysfunction, corticosteroid, or estrogen therapy. Used alone as step 1 agent in stepped-care approach, or in combination with other agents for treatment of hypertension.
UNLABELED USES To reduce polyuria of central and nephrogenic diabetes insipidus, to prevent calcium-containing renal stones, and to treat renal tubular acidosis.

CONTRAINDICATIONS Hypersensitivity to thiazide or sulfonamides; anuria; hypokalemia; renal failure; jaundiced neonates; SLE; pregnancy (category C).

CAUTIOUS USE History of sulfa allergy; impaired renal or hepatic function or gout; hypercalcemia, diabetes mellitus, older adult or debilitated patients, pancreatitis, sympathectomy.

ROUTE & DOSAGE

Hypertension, Edema
Adult: **PO** 250 mg–1 g/d in 1–2 divided doses **IV** 500 mg–1 g/d in 1–2 divided doses
Geriatric: **PO** 500 mg qd or 1 g 3 times/wk

Edema
Child: **PO** <6 mo: 20–40 mg/kg/d in 1–2 divided doses; >6 mo: 20 mg/kg/d in 2 divided doses

ADMINISTRATION

Oral
- Give with or after food to prevent gastric irritation. Extent of absorption appears to be increased by taking it with food.
- Schedule daily doses to avoid nocturia and interrupted sleep.

Intravenous
Reserve for emergency or when patient unable to take oral medication. IV administration to infants and children: Verify correct IV concentration and rate of infusion with physician.

***PREPARE:* Intermittent:** Reconstitute the 500 mg vial with at least 18 mL sterile water for injection. May be further diluted with D5W or NS.
***ADMINISTER:* Intermittent:** Give at a rate of 0.5 gram over 5 min.
***INCOMPATIBILITIES* Solution/additive: Amikacin, chlorpromazine, hydralazine, insulin, levorphanol, morphine, norepinephrine, polymyxin B,**

Common adverse effects in *italic*, life-threatening effects <u>underlined</u>; generic names in **bold**; classifications in SMALL CAPS; ♥ Canadian drug name; ⊘ Prototype drug

procaine, prochlorperazine, promazine, promethazine, streptomycin, triflupromazine, vancomycin.

▪ Thiazide preparations are extremely irritating to the tissues, and great care must be taken to avoid extravasation. If infiltration occurs, stop medication, remove needle, and apply ice if area is small.

▪ Store tablets, PO solutions, and parenteral dosage forms at 15°–30° C (59°–86° F) unless otherwise directed by manufacturer. Unused reconstituted IV solutions may be stored at room temperature up to 24 h. Use only clear solutions.

ADVERSE EFFECTS (≥1%) **Body as a Whole:** Fever, respiratory distress, <u>anaphylactic reaction</u>. **CV:** Irregular heart beat, weak pulse, orthostatic hypotension. **GI:** Vomiting, acute pancreatitis, diarrhea. **Hematologic:** <u>Agranulocytosis</u> (rare), <u>aplastic anemia</u> (rare), asymptomatic hyperuricemia, hyperglycemia, glycosuria, SIADH secretion. **Metabolic:** *Hypokalemia,* hypercalcemia, hyponatremia, hypochloremic alkalosis, elevated cholesterol and triglyceride levels. **CNS:** Unusual fatigue, dizziness, mental changes, vertigo, headache. **Skin:** Urticaria, photosensitivity, skin rash.

DIAGNOSTIC TEST INTERFERENCE Chlorothiazide (thiazides) may cause: marked increases in *serum amylase* values, decrease in *PBI* determinations; increase in excretion of *PSP;* increase in *BSP retention;* false-negative *phentolamine* and *tyramine* tests; interference with *urine steroid* determinations, and possibly the *histamine test* for pheochromocytoma. Thiazides should be discontinued at least 3 d before *bentiro-*

mide test (thiazides can invalidate test) and before *parathyroid function tests* because they tend to decrease calcium excretion.

INTERACTIONS Drug: **Amphotericin B,** CORTICOSTEROIDS increase hypokalemic effects of chlorothiazide; the hypoglycemic effects of SULFONYLUREAS and **insulin** may be antagonized; **cholestyramine, colestipol** decrease thiazide absorption; intensifies hypoglycemic and hypotensive effects of **diazoxide;** increased potassium and magnesium loss may cause **digoxin** toxicity; decreases **lithium** excretion, increasing its toxicity; increases risk of NSAID-induced renal failure and may attenuate diuresis.

PHARMACOKINETICS Absorption: Incompletely absorbed PO. **Onset:** 2 h PO; 15 min IV. **Peak:** 3–6 h PO; 30 min IV. **Duration:** 6–12 h PO; 2 h IV. **Distribution:** Throughout extracellular tissue; concentrates in kidney; crosses placenta. **Metabolism:** Does not appear to be metabolized. **Elimination:** In urine and breast milk. **Half-Life:** 45–120 min.

CLINICAL IMPLICATIONS

Assessment & Drug Effects

▪ Monitor for therapeutic effect. Antihypertensive action of a thiazide diuretic requires several days before effects are observed; usually optimum therapeutic effect is not established for 3–4 wk.

▪ Lab tests: Baseline and periodic determinations are indicated for blood count, serum electrolytes, CO_2, BUN, creatinine, uric acid, and blood glucose.

▪ Monitor for hyperglycemia. Thiazide therapy can cause hyperglycemia (see Appendix F) and glycosuria in diabetic and diabetic-prone individuals. Dosage

Common adverse effects in *italic*, life-threatening effects <u>underlined</u>; generic names in **bold**; classifications in SMALL CAPS; ♣ Canadian drug name; ⊙ Prototype drug

307

adjustment of hypoglycemic drugs may be required.

- Monitor patients with gout. Asymptomatic hyperuricemia can be produced because of interference with uric acid excretion.
- Establish baseline weight before initiation of therapy. Weigh patient at the same time each a.m. under standard conditions. A gain of more than 1 kg (2.2) within 2 or 3 d and a gradual weight gain over the week's period is reportable. Tell patient to report signs of edema (hands, ankles, pretibial areas).
- Monitor BP closely during early drug therapy.
- Inspect skin and mucous membranes daily for evidence of petechiae in patients receiving large doses and those on prolonged therapy.
- Monitor I&O rates and patterns: Excessive diuresis or oliguria may cause electrolyte imbalance and necessitate prompt dosage adjustment.
- Monitor patients on digitalis therapy for S&S of hypokalemia (see Appendix G). Even moderate reduction in serum potassium can precipitate digitalis intoxication in these patients.

Patient & Family Education

- Urination will occur in greater amounts and with more frequency than usual, and there will be an unusual sense of tiredness. With continued therapy, diuretic action decreases; hypotensive effects usually are maintained, and sense of tiredness diminishes.
- If orthostatic hypotension is a troublesome symptom (and it may be, especially in the older adult), consult physician for measures that will help tolerate the effect and to prevent falling.

- Report to physician any illness accompanied by prolonged vomiting or diarrhea.
- Avoid drinking large quantities of coffee or other caffeine drinks. Caffeine is a CNS stimulant with diuretic effects.
- Report S&S of hypokalemia, hypercalcemia, or hyperglycemia (see Appendix F).
- Hypokalemia may be prevented if the daily diet contains potassium-rich foods. Eat a banana and drink at least 6 oz orange juice every day. Collaborate with dietitian and physician.
- Report photosensitivity reaction to physician if it occurs. Thiazide-related photosensitivity is considered a photoallergy (radiation changes drug structure and makes it allergenic for some individuals). It occurs $1^{1}/_{2}$–2 wk after initial sun exposure.

CHLORPHENIRAMINE MALEATE

(klor-fen-eer′a-meen)

Aller-Chlor, Chlo-Amine, Chlor-Trimeton, Chlor-Tripolon ◆, Novopheniram ◆, Phenetron, Telachlor, Teldrin, Trymegan

Classifications: ANTIHISTAMINE (H_1-RECEPTOR ANTAGONIST)

Therapeutic: ANTIHISTAMINE; H_1-RECEPTOR ANTAGONIST

Prototype: Diphenhydramine

Pregnancy Category: B first and second trimester; D third trimester

AVAILABILITY 2 mg, 4 mg tablets; 8 mg, 12 mg sustained-release tablets; 2 mg/5 mL syrup

ACTION & *THERAPEUTIC EFFECT*

Antihistamine that competes with

histamine for H_1-receptor sites on effector cells; thus it prevents histamine action that promotes capillary permeability and edema formation and constrictive action on respiratory, gastrointestinal, and vascular smooth muscles. Produces less drowsiness than other H_1-histamine antagonists. *Has effective antihistamine reaction resulting in decreasing allergic symptomatology.*

USES Symptomatic relief of various uncomplicated allergic conditions; to prevent transfusion and drug reactions in susceptible patients, and as adjunct to epinephrine and other standard measures in anaphylactic reactions.

CONTRAINDICATIONS Hypersensitivity to antihistamines of similar structure; lower respiratory tract symptoms, narrow-angle glaucoma, obstructive prostatic hypertrophy or other bladder neck obstruction, GI obstruction or stenosis; pregnancy (category B in first and second trimester and category D in third trimester), premature and newborn infants; during or within 14 d of MAO INHIBITOR therapy.

CAUTIOUS USE Convulsive disorders, increased intraocular pressure, hyperthyroidism, cardiovascular disease, hepatic disease; BPH; GI obstruction; hypertension, diabetes mellitus, history of bronchial asthma, COPD, older adult patients, patients with G6PD deficiency, lactation.

ROUTE & DOSAGE

Symptomatic Allergy Relief

Adult: **PO** 2–4 mg t.i.d. or q.i.d. *or* 8–12 mg b.i.d. or t.i.d., max: 24 mg/d
Geriatric: **PO** 4 mg q.d. or b.i.d. *or* 8 mg sustained-release h.s.

Child: **PO** 6–12 y: 2 mg q4–6h (max: 12 mg/d); 2–6 y: 1 mg q4–6h

ADMINISTRATION

Oral
- Give on an empty stomach for fastest response.
- Sustained-release tablets should be swallowed whole and not crushed or chewed.
- Ensure that chewable tablets are chewed or crushed before being swallowed with a liquid.

Subcutaneous, Intramuscular, Intravenous
- The 100 mg/mL preparation is intended for IM or SC use only. It should not be administered IV because it contains preservatives. The 10 mg/mL injection can be given IV, IM, or SC. It contains no preservatives.

Intravenous

PREPARE: **Direct:** Give undiluted.
ADMINISTER: **Direct:** Give 10 mg or fraction thereof over at least 1 min.

- If patient manifests any reaction after parenteral administration, drug should be discontinued. (Exception: Patient may experience transitory stinging sensation that rarely lasts longer than a few minutes.)

- Store preferably between 15° and 30° C (59° and 86° F) unless otherwise directed by manufacturer. Syrup and injection forms should be protected from light to prevent discoloration.

ADVERSE EFFECTS (≥1%) **Body as a Whole:** Sensation of chest tightness. **CV:** Palpitation, tachycardia, mild hypotension or hypertension. **GI:** Epigastric distress, anorexia, nausea, vomiting, constipation, or

Common adverse effects in *italic*, life-threatening effects underlined; generic names in **bold**; classifications in SMALL CAPS; ♣ Canadian drug name; ⊕ Prototype drug

309

diarrhea. **CNS:** *Drowsiness,* sedation, headache, dizziness, vertigo, fatigue, disturbed coordination, tremors, euphoria, nervousness, restlessness, insomnia. **Special Senses:** *Dryness of mouth,* nose, and throat, tinnitus, vertigo, acute labyrinthitis, thickened bronchial secretions, blurred vision, diplopia. **Urogenital:** Urinary frequency or retention, dysuria.

DIAGNOSTIC TEST INTERFERENCE
Antihistamines should be discontinued 4 d before *skin testing* procedures for allergy because they may obscure otherwise positive reactions.

INTERACTIONS Drug: Alcohol (ethanol) and other CNS DEPRESSANTS produce additive sedation and CNS depression.

PHARMACOKINETICS Absorption: Well absorbed from GI tract; about 45% of dose reaches systemic circulation intact. **Onset:** Within 6 h. **Peak:** 2–6 h. **Distribution:** Highest concentrations in lung, heart, kidney, brain, small intestine, and spleen. **Metabolism:** By CYP3A4. **Half-Life:** 12–43 h.

CLINICAL IMPLICATIONS
Assessment & Drug Effects
- Monitor for CNS depression and sedation, especially when chlorpheniramine is given in combination with other CNS depressants.
- Monitor BP in hypertensive patients since chlorpheniramine may elevate BP.

Patient & Family Education
- Avoid driving a car and other potentially hazardous activities until drug response has been determined.
- Avoid or minimize alcohol intake. Antihistamines have additive effects with alcohol.

- Report any of the following: tinnitus or palpitations.
- Consult physician before taking additional OTC drugs for allergy relief.

CHLORPROMAZINE (Pr)
(klor-proe′ma-zeen)

CHLORPROMAZINE HYDROCHLORIDE
Sonazine, Thorazine
Classifications: PSYCHOTHERAPEUTIC; ANTIPSYCHOTIC; PHENOTHIAZINE; ANTIEMETIC
Therapeutic: ANTIPSYCHOTIC; ANTIEMETIC
Pregnancy Category: C

AVAILABILITY 10 mg, 25 mg, 50 mg, 100 mg, 200 mg tablets; 30 mg, 75 mg, 150 mg, 200 mg sustained-release capsules; 10 mg/5 mL syrup; 30 mg/mL, 100 mg/mL oral concentrate; 25 mg/mL injection

ACTION & *THERAPEUTIC EFFECT*
Phenothiazine derivative with actions at all levels of CNS with a mechanism that produces strong antipsychotic effects. Actions on hypothalamus and reticular formation produce strong sedation, hypotension, and depressed temperature regulation. Has strong alpha-adrenergic blocking action. Exerts quinidine-like antiarrhythmic action. Antiemetic effect due to suppression of the chemoreceptor trigger zone (CTZ). Inhibitory effect on dopamine reuptake may be the basis for moderate extrapyramidal symptoms. Antipsychotic drugs are sometimes called neuroleptics because they tend to reduce initiative and interest in the environment, decrease displays of emotions or

affect, suppress spontaneous movements and complex behavior, as well as decrease psychotic symptoms. *Mechanism that produces strong antipsychotic effects is unclear, but thought to be related to blockade of postsynaptic dopamine receptors in the brain. Also has antiemetic effects due to its action on the CTZ.*

USES To control manic phase of manic-depressive illness, for symptomatic management of psychotic disorders, including schizophrenia, in management of severe nausea and vomiting, to control excessive anxiety and agitation before surgery, and for treatment of severe behavior problems in children, e.g., attention deficit disorder. Also used for treatment of acute intermittent porphyria, intractable hiccups, and as adjunct in treatment of tetanus.

CONTRAINDICATIONS Hypersensitivity to phenothiazine derivatives, sulfite, or benzyl alcohol; withdrawal states from alcohol; CNS depression; comatose states, brain damage, bone marrow depression, Reye's syndrome; children <6 mo; pregnancy (category C), lactation.
CAUTIOUS USE Agitated states accompanied by depression, seizure disorders, respiratory impairment due to infection or COPD; glaucoma, diabetes, hypertensive disease, peptic ulcer, prostatic hypertrophy; thyroid, cardiovascular, and hepatic disorders; patients exposed to extreme heat or organophosphate insecticides; previously detected breast cancer.

ROUTE & DOSAGE

Psychotic Disorders, Agitation
Adult: **PO** 25–100 mg t.i.d. or q.i.d., may need up to 1000 mg/d

IM/IV 25–50 mg up to 600 mg q4–6h
Child: **PO** >6 mo, 0.55 mg/kg q4–6h prn up to 500 mg/d **IM/IV** >6 mo, 0.5–1 mg/kg q6–8h

Nausea and Vomiting
Adult: **PO** 10–25 mg q4–6h prn
IM/IV 25–50 mg q4–6h prn
Child: **PO** >6 mo, 0.55 mg/kg q4–6h prn up to 500 mg/d **IM/IV** >6 mo, 0.55 mg/kg q6–8h

Dementia
Geriatric: **PO** Initial 10–25 mg 1–2 times/d, may increase q4–7d by 10–25 mg/d (max: 800 mg/d)

Intractable Hiccups
Adult: **PO/IM** 25–50 mg t.i.d. or q.i.d.

Tetanus
Adult: **IM/IV** 25–50 mg q6–8h
Child: **IM/IV** 0.5mg/kg q6–8h

ADMINISTRATION

Oral
- Give with food or a full glass of fluid to minimize GI distress.
- Ensure that oral drug is swallowed and not hoarded. Suicide attempt is a constant possibility in depressed patients, particularly when they are improving.
- Mix chlorpromazine concentrate just before administration in at least 1/2 glass juice, milk, water, coffee, tea, carbonated beverage, or with semisolid food.
- Ensure that sustained-release form of drug is not chewed or crushed. It must be swallowed whole.

Intramuscular, Intravenous
- Avoid parenteral drug contact with skin, eyes, and clothing because of its potential for causing contact dermatitis.
- Keep patient recumbent for at least 1/2 h after parenteral adminis-

Common adverse effects in *italic*, life-threatening effects underlined; generic names in **bold**; classifications in SMALL CAPS; ♣ Canadian drug name; ⓟ Prototype drug

311

tration. Observe closely. Report hypotensive reactions.

Intramuscular

- Inject IM preparations slowly and deep into upper outer quadrant of buttock. Avoid SC injection; it may cause tissue irritation and nodule formation. If irritation is a problem, consult physician about diluting medication with normal saline or 2% procaine. Rotate injection sites.

Intravenous

PREPARE: Direct: Dilute 25 mg with 24 mL of NS to yield 1 mg/mL. **Continuous:** May be further diluted in up to 1000 mL of NS.

ADMINISTER: Direct: Administer 1 mg or fraction thereof over 1 min for adults and over 2 min for children. **Continuous:** Give slowly at a rate not to exceed 1 mg/min.

INCOMPATIBILITIES Solution/additive: Aminophylline, amphotericin B, ampicillin, chloramphenicol, chlorothiazide, cimetidine, dimenhydrinate, furosemide, heparin, methohexital, penicillin G, pentobarbital, phenobarbital, thiopental. Y-site: Allopurinol, amifostine, aminophylline, amphotericin B; cholesteryl complex, aztreonam, cefepime, chloramphenicol, chlorothiazide, etoposide, fludarabine, melphalan, methotrexate, paclitaxel, piperacillin/tazobactam, remifentanil, sargramostim.

- Lemon yellow color of parenteral preparation does not alter potency; if otherwise colored or markedly discolored, solution should be discarded.

- All forms are stored preferably between 15°–30° C (59°–86° F) protected from light, unless otherwise specified by the manufacturer. Avoid freezing.

ADVERSE EFFECTS (≥1%) **Body as a Whole:** Idiopathic edema, muscle necrosis (following IM), SLE-like syndrome, <u>sudden unexplained death</u>. **CV:** Orthostatic hypotension, palpitation, tachycardia, ECG changes (usually reversible): prolonged QT and PR intervals, blunting of T waves, ST depression. **GI:** Dry mouth; constipation, <u>adynamic ileus</u>, cholestatic jaundice, aggravation of peptic ulcer, dyspepsia, increased appetite. **Hematologic:** <u>Agranulocytosis</u>, thrombocytopenic purpura, <u>pancytopenia</u> (rare). **Metabolic:** Weight gain, hypoglycemia, hyperglycemia, glycosuria (high doses), enlargement of parotid glands. **CNS:** *Sedation, drowsiness,* dizziness, restlessness, <u>neuroleptic malignant syndrome</u>, tardive dyskinesias, tumor, syncope, headache, weakness, insomnia, reduced REM sleep, bizarre dreams, cerebral edema, convulsive seizures, <u>hypothermia</u>, inability to sweat, depressed cough reflex, *extrapyramidal symptoms,* EEG changes. **Respiratory:** Laryngospasm. **Skin:** Fixed-drug eruption, urticaria, reduced perspiration, contact dermatitis, exfoliative dermatitis, photosensitivity, eczema, anaphylactoid reactions, hypersensitivity vasculitis; hirsutism (long-term therapy). **Special Senses:** Blurred vision, lenticular opacities, mydriasis, photophobia. **Urogenital:** Anovulation, infertility, pseudopregnancy, menstrual irregularity, gynecomastia, galactorrhea, priapism, inhibition of ejaculation, reduced libido, urinary retention and frequency.

DIAGNOSTIC TEST INTERFERENCE Chlorpromazine (phenothiazines) may increase ***cephalin floccula-***

C

tion,** and possibly other *liver function tests*; also may increase *PBI.* False-positive result may occur for *amylase, 5-hydroxyindole acetic acid, phenylketonuria, porphobilinogens, urobilinogen (Ehrlich's reagent),* and *urine bilirubin (Bili-Labstix).* False-positive or false-negative *pregnancy test* results possibly caused by a metabolite of phenothiazines, which discolors urine depending on test used.

INTERACTIONS Drug: Alcohol, CNS DEPRESSANTS increase CNS depression; ANTACIDS, ANTIDIARRHEALS decrease absorption—space administration 2 h before or after administration of chlorpromazine; **phenobarbital** increases metabolism of phenothiazine; GENERAL ANESTHETICS increase excitation and hypotension; antagonizes antihypertensive action of **guanethidine; phenylpropanolamine** poses possibility of sudden death; TRICYCLIC ANTIDEPRESSANTS intensify hypotensive and anticholinergic effects; ANTICONVULSANTS decrease seizure threshold—may need to increase anticonvulsant dose. **Herbal: Kava-kava** increased risk and severity of dystonic reaction.

PHARMACOKINETICS Absorption: Rapid absorption with considerable first pass metabolism in liver; rapid absorption after IM. **Onset:** 30–60 min. **Peak:** 2–4 h PO; 15–20 min IM. **Duration:** 4–6 h. **Distribution:** Widely distributed; accumulates in brain; crosses placenta. **Metabolism:** In liver by CYP2D6. **Elimination:** In urine as metabolites; excreted in breast milk. **Half-Life:** Biphasic 2 and 30 h.

CLINICAL IMPLICATIONS

Assessment & Drug Effects

- Establish baseline BP (in standing and recumbent positions), and pulse, before initiating treatment.

- Monitor BP frequently. Hypotensive reactions, dizziness, and sedation are common during early therapy, particularly in patients on high doses and in the older adult receiving parenteral doses. Patients usually develop tolerance to these adverse effects; however, lower doses or longer intervals between doses may be required.

- Lab tests: Periodic CBC with differential, liver function tests, urinalysis, and blood glucose.

- Monitor cardiac status with baseline ECG in patients with preexisting cardiovascular disease.

- Be alert for signs of neuroleptic malignant syndrome (see Appendix G). Report immediately.

- Observe and record smoking since it increases metabolism of phenothiazines, resulting in shortened half-life and more rapid clearance of drug. Higher dosage in smokers may be required. Advise patient to stop or at least reduce smoking, if possible.

- Monitor I&O ratio and pattern: Urinary retention due to mental depression and compromised renal function may occur. If serum creatinine becomes elevated, therapy should be discontinued.

- Monitor for antiemetic effect of chlorpromazine, which may obscure signs of overdosage of other drugs or other causes of nausea and vomiting.

- Be alert to complaints of diminished visual acuity, reduced night vision, photophobia, and a perceived brownish discoloration of objects. Patient may be more comfortable with dark glasses.

- Monitor diabetics or prediabetics on long-term, high-dose therapy for reduced glucose tolerance and loss of diabetes control.

Common adverse effects in *italic*, life-threatening effects underlined; generic names in **bold**; classifications in SMALL CAPS; ♣ Canadian drug name; ⊙ Prototype drug

313

- Ocular examinations, and EEG (in patients >50 y) are recommended before and periodically during prolonged therapy.

Patient & Family Education
- Take medication as prescribed and keep appointments for follow-up evaluation of dosage regimen. Improvement may not be experienced until 7 or 8 wk into therapy.
- Do not alter dosing regimen, and do not give the drug to another person.
- May cause pink to red-brown discoloration of urine.
- Wear protective clothing and sunscreen lotion with SPF above 12 when outdoors, even on dark days. Photosensitivity associated with chlorpromazine therapy is a phototoxic reaction. Severity of response depends on amount of exposure and drug dose. Exposed skin areas have appearance of an exaggerated sunburn. If reaction occurs, report to physician.
- Practice meticulous oral hygiene. Oral candidiasis occurs frequently in patients receiving phenothiazines.
- Report extrapyramidal symptoms that occur most often in patients on high dosage, the pediatric patient with severe dehydration and acute infection, the older adult, and women.
- Avoid driving a car or undertaking activities requiring precision and mental alertness until drug response is known.
- Do not abruptly stop this drug. Abrupt withdrawal of drug or deliberate dose skipping, especially after prolonged therapy with large doses, can cause onset of extrapyramidal symptoms (see Appendix F) and severe GI disturbances. When drug is to be discontinued, dosage must be tapered off gradually over a period of several weeks.

CHLORPROPAMIDE

(klor-proe′pa-mide)
Apo-Chlorpropamide ♣, Diabinese, Novopropamide ♣
Classifications: HORMONE; ANTIDIABETIC SULFONYLUREA
Therapeutic: ANTIDIABETIC; SULFONYLUREA
Prototype: Glyburide
Pregnancy Category: C

AVAILABILITY 100 mg, 250 mg tablets

ACTION & *THERAPEUTIC EFFECT*
Longest-acting first-generation sulfonylurea compound. Lowers blood glucose by stimulating beta cells in pancreas to synthesize and release endogenous insulin. May potentiate available antidiuretic hormone (ADH) secretion, a property not shared by other sulfonylureas. *Antidiabetic effect is due to the ability of the drug to stimulate the beta cells of the pancreas to manufacture and release insulin. Therapeutic effectiveness is indicated by HbA$_{1c}$ levels >7%.*

USES Stable non-insulin-dependent diabetes mellitus (type 2) in patients who cannot be controlled by diet alone and who do not have complications of diabetes.
UNLABELED USES Neurogenic diabetes insipidus.

CONTRAINDICATIONS Known hypersensitivity to sulfonylureas and to sulfonamides; diabetes complicated by severe infection; acidosis; severe renal, hepatic, or thyroid insufficiency; pregnancy (category

C), lactation. Safe use in children not established.

CAUTIOUS USE Older adult patients, Addison's disease, CHF, and hepatic porphyria.

ROUTE & DOSAGE

Antidiabetic

Adult: **PO** Initial: 100–250 mg/d with breakfast, adjust by 50–125 mg/d q3–5d until glycemic control is achieved, up to 750 mg/d

ADMINISTRATION

Oral

- Give as a single morning dose with breakfast. To reduce GI adverse effects, drug may be prescribed as 2 or 3 doses and taken with meals.
- Store below 40° C (104° F), preferably at 15°–30° C (59°–86° F) in a tightly closed container, unless otherwise directed.

ADVERSE EFFECTS (≥1%) **Body as a Whole:** Flushing, photosensitivity, alcohol intolerance. **GI:** GI distress, anorexia, nausea, diarrhea, constipation, cholestatic jaundice. **Hematologic:** Leukopenia, thrombocytopenia, agranulocytosis. **Metabolic:** Hypoglycemia, antidiuretic effect (SIADH), dilutional hyponatremia, water intoxication. **CNS:** Drowsiness, muscle cramps, weakness, paresthesias. **Skin:** Rash, pruritus.

INTERACTIONS Drug: Adverse effects of ORAL ANTICOAGULANTS, **phenytoin**, SALICYLATES, NSAIDS may be increased along with those of chlorpropamide; THIAZIDE DIURETICS may increase blood sugar; **alcohol** produces disulfiram reaction; **probenecid**, MAO INHIBITORS may increase hypoglycemic effects. **Herbal: Garlic, ginseng** may increase hypoglycemic effects.

PHARMACOKINETICS Absorption: Readily from GI tract. **Onset:** 1 h. **Peak:** 3–6 h. **Distribution:** Highly protein bound; distributed into breast milk. **Metabolism:** In liver. **Elimination:** 80–90% in urine in 96 h. **Half-Life:** 36 h.

CLINICAL IMPLICATIONS

Assessment & Drug Effects

- Monitor therapeutic effectiveness: Indicated by HbA_{1c} levels >7%.
- Monitor blood and urine glucose to determine effectiveness of glycemic control.
- Lab tests: Periodic fasting and postprandial blood glucose; HbA_{1c} every 3 mo; baseline and periodic hematologic and hepatic studies are advisable, particularly in patients receiving high doses. A CBC should be performed if symptoms of anemia appear.
- Report dizziness, shortness of breath, malaise, fatigue.
- Monitor for S&S of hypoglycemia (see Appendix F).
- Monitor I&O ratio and pattern: Infrequently, chlorpropamide produces an antidiuretic effect, with resulting severe hyponatremia, edema, and water intoxication. If fluid intake far exceeds output and edema develops (weight gain), report to the physician.

Patient & Family Education

- Report hypoglycemic episodes to physician. Because chlorpropamide has a long half-life, hypoglycemia can be severe, although onset is not as fast or as dramatic as with use of insulin.
- Report any of the following immediately to physician: skin eruptions, malaise, fever, or photosensitivity. Immediately report these symptoms to physician. A change to another hypoglycemic agent may be indicated.

Common adverse effects in *italic*, life-threatening effects <u>underlined</u>; generic names in **bold**; classifications in SMALL CAPS; ♣ Canadian drug name; ⊘ Prototype drug

- Do not self-dose with OTC drugs unless approved or prescribed by the physician.

CHLORTHALIDONE
(klor-thal'i-done)

Thalitone

Classifications: ELECTROLYTE & WATER BALANCE AGENT; DIURETIC; ANTIHYPERTENSIVE
Therapeutic: DIURETIC; ANTIHYPERTENSIVE
Prototype: Hydrochlorothiazide
Pregnancy Category: B first and second trimester; D third trimester

AVAILABILITY 15 mg, 25 mg, 50 mg, 100 mg tablets

ACTION & *THERAPEUTIC EFFECT*
Sulfonamide derivative that differs chemically from thiazides but shares similar actions. Increases excretion of sodium and chloride by inhibiting their reabsorption in the cortical diluting segment of the ascending loop of Henle. *Antihypertensive effect is correlated to the decrease in extracellular and intracellular volumes. Decreased volume results in reduced cardiac output with subsequent decrease in peripheral resistance.*

USES Edema associated with CHF, renal decompensation, hepatic cirrhosis, corticosteroid and estrogen therapy; as sole agent or with other antihypertensives to treat hypertension.

CONTRAINDICATIONS Hypersensitivity to sulfonamide or thiazide derivatives; anuria, hypokalemia; pregnancy (category B in first and second trimester, and category D in third trimester), neonates with jaundice.

CAUTIOUS USE History of renal and hepatic disease, gout, SLE, diabetes mellitus.

ROUTE & DOSAGE

Hypertension
Adult: **PO** 12.5–25 mg/d, may be increased to 100 mg/d if needed
Child: **PO** 2 mg/kg 3 times/wk
Edema
Adult: **PO** 50–100 mg/d, may be increased to 200 mg/d if needed

ADMINISTRATION

Oral
- Administer as single dose in a.m. to reduce potential for interrupted sleep because of diuresis.
- Consult physician when chlorthalidone is used as a diuretic; an intermittent dose schedule may reduce incidence of adverse reactions.
- Store tablets in tightly closed container at 15°–30° C (59°–86° F) unless otherwise advised.

ADVERSE EFFECTS (≥1%) **CV:** Orthostatic hypotension. **GI:** Anorexia, nausea, vomiting, diarrhea, constipation, cramping, jaundice. **Hematologic:** Agranulocytosis, thrombocytopenia, aplastic anemia. **CNS:** Dizziness, vertigo, paresthesias, headache. **Metabolic:** *Hypokalemia,* hyponatremia, hypochloremia, hypercalcemia, glycosuria, hyperglycemia, exacerbation of gout. **Skin:** Rash, urticaria, photosensitivity, vasculitis. **Urogenital:** Impotence.

INTERACTIONS Drug: Increased risk of **digoxin** toxicity because of hypokalemia; CORTICOSTEROIDS, **amphotericin B** increases hypokalemia; decreases **lithium** elimination; may antagonize the hypoglycemic effects of SULFONYLUREAS; NSAIDS may

Common adverse effects in *italic*, life-threatening effects underlined; generic names in **bold**; classifications in SMALL CAPS; ♣ Canadian drug name; ⊕ Prototype drug

attenuate diuretic effects; **cholestyramine** decreases thiazide absorption.

PHARMACOKINETICS Absorption: Readily from GI tract. **Onset:** 2 h. **Peak:** 3–6 h. **Duration:** 24–72 h. **Distribution:** Crosses placenta; appears in breast milk. **Elimination:** 30–60% in urine in 24 h. **Half-Life:** 54 h.

CLINICAL IMPLICATIONS

Assessment & Drug Effects

- Establish baseline BP measurements and check at regular intervals during period of dosage adjustment when chlorthalidone is used for hypertension.
- Be alert to signs of hypokalemia (see Appendix F). Older adult patients are more sensitive to adverse effects of drug-induced diuresis because of age-related changes in the cardiovascular and renal systems.
- Lab tests: Baseline and periodic: serum electrolytes (particularly K, Mg, Ca), serum uric acid, creatinine, BUN, and uric acid and blood glucose (especially in patients with diabetes).
- Monitor lithium and digoxin levels closely when either of these drugs is used concurrently.

Patient & Family Education

- Maintain adequate potassium intake, monitor weight, and make a daily estimate of I&O ratio.

CHLORZOXAZONE

(klor-zox′a-zone)
Classifications: CENTRALLY ACTING SKELETAL MUSCLE RELAXANT
Therapeutic: SKELETAL MUSCLE RELAXER; ANTISPASMODIC
Prototype: Cyclobenzaprine
Pregnancy Category: C

AVAILABILITY 250 mg, 500 mg tablets

ACTION & *THERAPEUTIC EFFECT* Centrally acting skeletal muscle relaxant. Acts indirectly by depressing nerve transmission through polysynaptic pathways in spinal cord, subcortical centers, and brainstem; also possibly has a sedative effect. *Effectively controls muscle spasms and pain associated with musculoskeletal conditions. Not effective for spastic or dyskinetic CNS disorders, e.g., cerebral palsy.*

USES Symptomatic treatment of muscle spasm and pain associated with various musculoskeletal conditions.

CONTRAINDICATIONS Impaired liver function; alcoholism; hepatic disease, jaundice; pregnancy (category C).
CAUTIOUS USE Patients with known allergies or history of drug allergies; renal impairment or failure; CNS depression; older adult patients, lactation.

ROUTE & DOSAGE

Skeletal Muscle Relaxant

Adult: **PO** 250–500 mg t.i.d. or q.i.d. (max: 3 g/d)
Child: **PO** 20 mg/kg/d in 3–4 divided doses

ADMINISTRATION

Oral

- Give with food or meals to prevent gastric distress. If necessary, tablet may be crushed and mixed with food or liquid, e.g., milk, fruit juice.
- Store in tight container at 15°–30° C (59°–86° F) unless otherwise directed.

ADVERSE EFFECTS (≥1%) **GI:** Anorexia, heartburn, nausea, vomit-

Common adverse effects in *italic*, life-threatening effects underlined; generic names in **bold**; classifications in SMALL CAPS; ♣ Canadian drug name; ⓟ Prototype drug

317

ing, constipation, diarrhea, abdominal pain, hepatotoxicity: jaundice, liver damage. **CNS:** *Drowsiness, dizziness,* light-headedness, headache, malaise, overstimulation. **Skin:** Erythema, rash, pruritus, urticaria, petechiae, ecchymoses.

INTERACTIONS Drug: Alcohol, CNS DEPRESSANTS add to CNS depression.

PHARMACOKINETICS Absorption: Readily absorbed from GI tract. **Onset:** 1 h. **Peak:** 1–4 h. **Duration:** 3–4 h. **Distribution:** Not known if crosses placenta or distributed into breast milk. **Metabolism:** In liver. **Elimination:** In urine. **Half-Life:** 66 min.

CLINICAL IMPLICATIONS

Assessment & Drug Effects

- Monitor ambulation during early drug therapy; some patients may require supervision.
- Lab tests: Periodic liver function tests are advised in patients receiving long-term therapy even if sporadic.
- Note: Since chlorzoxazone metabolite may discolor urine, dark urine cannot be a reliable sign of a hepatotoxic reaction.

Patient & Family Education

- Avoid activities requiring mental alertness, judgment, and physical coordination until reaction to drug is known, since sedation, drowsiness, and dizziness may occur.
- Drug may discolor urine orange to purplish red, but this is of no clinical significance.
- Discontinue drug and notify physician if signs of hypersensitivity (see Appendix F) or of liver dysfunction appear (abdominal discomfort, yellow sclerae or skin, pruritus, malaise, nausea, vomiting).
- Check with physician before taking an OTC depressant (e.g., antihistamine, sedative, alcohol) since effects may be additive.

CHOLESTYRAMINE RESIN ⓟ

(koe-less-tear′a-meen)

LoCHOLEST, Questran, Questran Light, Prevalite

Classifications: ANTILIPEMIC; BILE ACID SEQUESTRANT

Therapeutic: CHOLESTEROL-LOWERING AGENT; BILE ACID SEQUESTRANT

Pregnancy Category: C

AVAILABILITY 4 g powder for suspension; 1 g tablet

ACTION & *THERAPEUTIC EFFECT*
Anion-exchange resin used for its cholesterol-lowering effect. Adsorbs and combines with intestinal bile acids in exchange for chloride ions to form an insoluble, nonabsorbable complex that is excreted in the feces. As a result, bile salts are continually (but not entirely) prevented from reentry into the enterohepatic circulation, thus increasing fecal loss of bile acids. This leads to lowered serum total cholesterol by decreasing low-density lipoprotein (LDL) cholesterol. *The resin anion-exchange agent increases fecal loss of bile acids which leads to lowered serum total cholesterol by decreasing (LDL) cholesterol, and reducing bile acid deposit in dermal tissues (decreasing pruritus). Serum triglyceride levels may increase or remain unchanged.*

USES As adjunct to diet therapy in management of patients with primary hypercholesterolemia (type IIa hyperlipidemia) with a significant risk of atherosclerotic heart disease and MI; for relief of pruritus secondary to partial biliary stasis.

UNLABELED USES To control diarrhea caused by excess bile acids in colon; for hyperoxaluria.

CONTRAINDICATIONS Complete biliary obstruction or biliary cirrhosis, cholelithiasis; GI obstruction; hypersensitivity to bile acid sequestrants; coagulopathy; pregnancy (category C), lactation. Safe use in children ≤6 y not established.

CAUTIOUS USE Bleeding disorders; hemorrhoids; impaired GI function, decreased GI motility; peptic ulcer, malabsorption states (e.g., steatorrhea); phenylketonuria (Questran Light only); renal disease.

ROUTE & DOSAGE

Hypercholesterolemia
Adult: PO 4 g b.i.d. to q.i.d. a.c. and h.s., may need up to 24 g/d
Child: PO 240 mg/kg/d in 3 divided doses

Hyperlipoproteinemia
Adult: PO 4–8 g b.i.d. to q.i.d. a.c. and h.s. (≤32 g/d)

Pruritus
Adult: PO 4 g b.i.d. to q.i.d. a.c. and h.s. (≤16 g/d)

ADMINISTRATION

Oral
- Place contents of one packet or one level scoopful on surface of at least 120 to 180 mL (4–6 oz) of water or other preferred liquid. Permit drug to hydrate by standing without stirring 1–2 min, twirling glass occasionally, then stir until suspension is uniform. Rinse glass with small amount of liquid and have patient drink remainder to ensure entire dose is taken. Administer before meals.
- Always dissolve cholestyramine powder before administration; it is irritating to mucous membranes and may cause esophageal impaction if administered dry.
- Store in tightly closed container at 15°–30° C (59°–86° F) unless otherwise specified.

ADVERSE EFFECTS (≥1%) **GI:** *Constipation,* fecal impaction, hemorrhoids, abdominal pain and distension, flatulence, bloating sensation, belching, nausea, vomiting, heartburn, anorexia, diarrhea, steatorrhea. **Endocrine:** Increased libido. **Metabolic:** Weight loss or gain, iron, calcium, vitamin A, D, and K deficiencies (from poor absorption); hypoprothrombinemia, hyperchloremic acidosis, decreased erythrocyte folate levels. **Skin:** Rash, irritations of skin, tongue, and perianal areas. **Special Senses:** Arcus juvenilis, uveitis.

DIAGNOSTIC TEST INTERFERENCE Cholestyramine therapy may be accompanied by increased *serum AST, phosphorus, chloride,* and *alkaline phosphatase* levels; decreased *serum calcium, sodium,* and *potassium* levels.

INTERACTIONS Drug: Decreases the absorption of ORAL ANTICOAGULANTS, **digoxin,** TETRACYCLINES, **penicillins, phenobarbital,** THYROID HORMONES, THIAZIDE DIURETICS, IRON SALTS, FAT-SOLUBLE VITAMINS (A, D, E, K) from the GI tract—administer cholestyramine 4 h before or 2 h after these drugs. Can bind to and affect absorption of any drug.

PHARMACOKINETICS Absorption: Not absorbed from GI tract. **Elimination:** Excreted in feces as insoluble complex.

CLINICAL IMPLICATIONS

Assessment & Drug Effects
- Monitor therapeutic effect. Serum cholesterol levels are reduced

---

Common adverse effects in *italic*, life-threatening effects <u>underlined</u>; generic names in **bold**; classifications in SMALL CAPS; ✦ Canadian drug name; ⊘ Prototype drug

319

within 24–48 h after treatment starts and may continue to decline for a year. After withdrawal of cholestyramine, cholesterol levels usually return to baseline level in about 2 to 4 wk.

- Be alert to early symptoms of hypoprothrombinemia (petechiae, ecchymoses, abnormal bleeding from mucous membranes, tarry stools) and report their occurrence promptly. Long-term use of cholestyramine resin can increase bleeding tendency.
- Preexisting constipation may be worsened in the older adult, women, and in those taking >24 g/d.
- Consult physician regarding supplemental vitamins A and D and folic acid that may be required by patient on long-term therapy.
- Lab tests: Periodic CBC, platelet count, serum electrolytes, and lipid profile.

Patient & Family Education

- Report constipation immediately to physician. High-bulk diet with adequate fluid intake is an essential adjunct to cholestyramine treatment and generally resolves the problems of constipation and bloating sensation.
- Do not omit doses. Sudden withdrawal can promote uninhibited absorption of other drugs taken concomitantly, leading to toxicity or overdosage.
- GI adverse effects usually subside after the first month of drug therapy.
- The following symptoms may be drug-induced and should be reported promptly: severe gastric distress with nausea and vomiting, unusual weight loss, black stools, severe hemorrhoids (GI bleeding), sudden back pain.

CHOLINE MAGNESIUM TRISALICYLATE

(cho'leen mag-ne'si-um tri-sal'i-ci-late)

Trilisate

Classifications: ANALGESIC (SALICYLATE), NONSTEROIDAL ANTIINFLAMMATORY DRUG (NSAID); ANTIPYRETIC **Therapeutic:** NSAID, ANALGESIC (SALICYLATE)
Prototype: Aspirin
Pregnancy Category: C first and second trimester; D third trimester

AVAILABILITY 500 mg, 750 mg, 1000 mg tablets; 500 mg/5 mL liquid

ACTION & THERAPEUTIC EFFECT
Choline magnesium trisalicylate is a nonsteroidal, antiinflammatory preparation combining choline salicylate and magnesium salicylate. Mode of action is by inhibiting prostaglandin synthesis by reversibly inhibiting cyclooxygenase (both COX-1 and COX-2), resulting in its antiinflammatory properties as well as its analgesic property. *Has antiinflammatory, analgesic, and antipyretic action. Platelet aggregation is not affected.*

USES Osteoarthritis, rheumatoid arthritis, and other arthrides. Preferable to aspirin for patients with GI bleeding.

CONTRAINDICATIONS Hypersensitivity to nonacetylated salicylates; children <6 y; children and teenagers with chickenpox, influenza, or flu symptoms because of the potential for Reye's syndrome; coagulopathy, anticoagulant therapy, G6PD deficiency; pregnancy (category C first and second trimester and category D in third trimester); contraindicated in late

pregnancy, near term, or in labor and delivery.
CAUTIOUS USE Chronic renal and hepatic failure, history of GI disease, peptic ulcer; patients on coumadin or heparin, anemia; hypovolemic states; lactation; older adults.

ROUTE & DOSAGE

Arthritis
Adult: **PO** 1.5–2.5 g/d in 1–3 divided doses (max: 4.5 g/d)

Mild to Moderate Pain, Fever
Adult: **PO** 2–3 g/d in 2 divided doses
Child: **PO** 30–60 mg/kg/d in 3–4 divided doses

ADMINISTRATION

Oral
▪ Give with food to reduce gastric upset. Do not give with antacids.
▪ Store at 59°–86° F (15°–30° C).

ADVERSE EFFECTS (≥1%) **GI:** Vomiting, diarrhea. **CNS:** Headache, vertigo, confusion, drowsiness. **Special Senses:** Tinnitus.

INTERACTIONS Drug: Aminosalicylic acid increases risk of salicylate toxicity; **ammonium chloride** and other **acidifying agents** decrease its renal elimination, increasing risk of salicylate toxicity; ANTICOAGULANTS increase risk of bleeding; CARBONIC ANHYDRASE INHIBITORS enhance salicylate toxicity; CORTICOSTEROIDS compound ulcerogenic effects; increases **methotrexate** toxicity; low doses of salicylates may antagonize uricosuric effects of **probenecid, sulfinpyrazone.**

PHARMACOKINETICS Absorption: Readily absorbed from small intestine. **Onset:** 30 min. **Peak:** 1–3 h.

Metabolism: In liver. **Elimination:** In urine. **Half-Life:** 2–3 h.

CLINICAL IMPLICATIONS

Assessment & Drug Effects
▪ As with other NSAIDs, the antipyretic and antiinflammatory effects may mask usual S&S of infection or other diseases.
▪ Assess for GI discomfort; nausea, gastric irritation, indigestion, diarrhea, and constipation are frequent complaints.
▪ Monitor for S&S of bleeding. Closely monitor PT if used concurrently with warfarin.

Patient & Family Education
▪ Avoid taking aspirin, NSAIDs, or acetaminophen concurrently with drug.
▪ Avoid dangerous activities until reaction to drug is determined, due to possible CNS effects (e.g., vertigo, drowsiness).
▪ Report tinnitus or persistent gastric irritation and epigastric pain.
▪ Report any unexplained bruising or bleeding to physician.
▪ Hypoglycemic effects may be enhanced for those with type 2 diabetes taking an oral hypoglycemic agent (OHA).
▪ Do not give to children or teenagers with chickenpox, influenza, or flu symptoms because of association with Reye's syndrome.

CHORIONIC GONADOTROPIN
(go-nad'oh-troe-pin)
Pregnyl
Classifications: HORMONE; HUMAN CHORIONIC GONADOTROPIN (HCG)
Therapeutic: HCG HORMONE
Pregnancy Category: X

AVAILABILITY 10,000 unit vial

Common adverse effects in *italic*, life-threatening effects underlined; generic names in **bold**; classifications in SMALL CAPS; ♣ Canadian drug name; ❽ Prototype drug

321

C

ACTION & *THERAPEUTIC EFFECT*

Human chorionic gonadotropin (HCG) is a polypeptide hormone produced by the placenta and extracted from urine during first trimester of pregnancy. Actions nearly identical to those of pituitary luteinizing hormone (LH). Promotes production of gonadal steroid hormones by stimulating interstitial cells of the testes to produce androgen, and the corpus luteum of the ovary to produce progesterone. *Administration of HCG to women of childbearing age with normal functioning ovaries causes maturation of the ovarian follicle and triggers ovulation. When given during normal pregnancy, it maintains corpus luteum after LH decreases, supports continuing secretion of estrogen and progesterone, and prevents ovulation.*

USES Prepubertal cryptorchidism not due to anatomic obstruction and male hypogonadism secondary to pituitary deficiency. Also used in conjunction with menotropins to induce ovulation and pregnancy in infertile women in whom the cause of anovulation is secondary; ovulation usually occurs within 18 h. To stimulate spermatogenesis in males with hypogonadism.

UNLABELED USES Corpus luteum dysfunction.

CONTRAINDICATIONS Known hypersensitivity to HCG, hypogonadism of testicular origin, hamster protein hypersensitivity; hypertrophy or tumor of pituitary, prostatic carcinoma or other androgen-dependent neoplasms, precocious puberty; ovarian failure; dysfunctional uterine bleeding; adrenal insufficiency; uncontrolled thyroid disease; children <4 y; neonates; pregnancy (category X).

CAUTIOUS USE Epilepsy, migraine, asthma, cardiac or renal disease; endometriosis; thrombophlebitis; lactation.

ROUTE & DOSAGE

Prepubertal Cryptorchidism
Child: **IM** 4000 units 3 times/wk for 3 wk, *or* 5000 units q.o.d. for 4 doses, *or* 500–1000 units 3 times/wk for 4–6 wk

Hypogonadotropic Hypogonadism
Adult: **IM** 500–1000 units 3 times/wk for 3 wk, then 2 times/wk for 3 wk *or* 4000 units 3 times/wk for 6–9 mo followed by 2000 units 3 times/wk for 3 mo

Stimulation of Spermatogenesis
Adult: **IM** 5000 units 3 times/wk until normal testosterone levels are achieved (4–6 mo), then 2000 units 2 times/wk with menotropins for 4 mo

Induction of Ovulation
Adult: **IM** 500–1000 units 1 d following last dose of menotropins

ADMINISTRATION

- Reconstitute only with diluent supplied by manufacturer.
- Following reconstitution solution is stable for 30–90 d, depending on manufacturer, when refrigerated; thereafter potency decreases.
- Store powder for injection at 15°–30° C (59°–86° F) unless otherwise directed.

ADVERSE EFFECTS (≥1%) **Body as a Whole:** Edema, pain at injection site, arterial thromboembolism. **Endocrine:** Gynecomastia, precocious puberty, increased urinary steroid excretion, ectopic pregnancy (incidence low). When used with menotropins (human menopausal gonadotropin): Ovarian hyperstimulation (ascites with or without pain, pleural effusion, ruptured ovarian cysts with resultant hemoperitoneum, multiple births). **CNS:** Headache, irritability, restlessness, depression, fatigue.

DIAGNOSTIC TEST INTERFERENCE
Pregnancy tests: Possibility of false results.

INTERACTIONS Drug: No clinically significant drug interactions established. **Herbal: Black cohosh** may antagonize fertility effects.

PHARMACOKINETICS Onset: 2 h. **Peak:** 6 h. **Distribution:** Testes in males, ovaries in females. **Elimination:** 10–12% in urine within 24 h. **Half-Life:** 23 h.

CLINICAL IMPLICATIONS
Assessment & Drug Effects
- Assess prepubescent males for development of secondary sex characteristics.
- Assess females for and report excessive menstrual bleeding, irregular menstrual cycles, and abdominal/pelvic distention or pain.

Patient & Family Education
- Treatment for prepubertal cryptorchidism is usually started between 4 and 9 y. HCG can help predict whether orchidopexy will be needed in the future.
- When used for treatment of infertility, timing of coitus is important. Daily intercourse is encouraged from day before HCG is given until ovulation occurs.
- Report promptly onset of abdominal pain and distension (ovarian hyperstimulation syndrome).
- Report to physician if the following appear: axillary, facial, pubic hair; penile growth; acne; deepening of voice. Induction of androgen secretion by HCG may induce precocious puberty in patient treated for cryptorchidism.

- Observe for signs of fluid retention. A weight chart should be maintained for a biweekly record. Report to physician if weight gain is associated with edema.
- Report vaginal bleeding during treatment of corpus luteum deficiency; drug will be discontinued.

CICLESONIDE
(ci-cle-so′nide)
Omnaris
Pregnancy Category: C
See Appendix A-3.

CICLOPIROX OLAMINE
(sye-kloe-peer′ox)
Loprox, Penlac Nail Lacquer
Classifications: ANTIFUNGAL ANTIBIOTIC
Therapeutic: ANTIFUNGAL ANTIBIOTIC
Pregnancy Category: B

AVAILABILITY 1% cream, ointment; 8% nail lacquer; 1% shampoo

ACTION & *THERAPEUTIC EFFECT*
Synthetic broad-spectrum antifungal agent with activity against pathogenic fungi. Inhibits transport of amino acids within fungal cell, thereby interfering with synthesis of fungal protein, RNA, and DNA. *Effective against the following organisms: dermatophytes, yeasts, some species of* Mycoplasma *and* Trichomonas vaginalis, *and certain strains of gram-positive and gram-negative bacteria.*

USES Topically for treatment of tinea cruris and tinea corporis (ringworm) due to *Trichophyton rubrum, Trichophyton mentagrophytes, Epidermophyton floccosum,* and *Microsporum canis,* and for tinea (pityriasis) versicolor due to

Common adverse effects in *italic*, life-threatening effects underlined; generic names in **bold**; classifications in SMALL CAPS; ♣ Canadian drug name; ❸ Prototype drug

323

M. furfur; also cutaneous candidiasis (moniliasis) caused by *Candida albicans.* Nail lacquer indicated for onychomycosis of fingernails and toenails due to *T. rubrum;* seborrheic dermatitis of the scalp.

CONTRAINDICATIONS Hypersensitivity to ciclopirox olamine or to any component in the formulation; concurrent administration of corticosteroid therapy. Safe use in children <10 y not established.

CAUTIOUS USE Type 1 diabetic patient; history of seizure disorder; immunosuppression; pregnancy (category B); lactation.

ROUTE & DOSAGE

Tinea
Adult: **Topical** Massage cream into affected area and surrounding skin twice daily, morning and evening.

Onychomycosis
Adult: **Topical** Paint affected nail(s) under the surface of the nail and on the nail bed once daily at bedtime (at least 8 h before washing). After 7 d, remove lacquer with alcohol and remove or trim away unattached nail. Continue up to 48 wk.

Seborrheic Dermatitis
Adult: **Topical** Wet hair and apply approximately 1 tsp (5 mL) to the scalp (may use up to 10 mL for long hair), leave on scalp for 3 min, then rinse. Repeat treatment twice/wk × 4 wk, with a min 3 d between applications.

ADMINISTRATION

- Wash hands thoroughly before and after treatments.
- Consult with physician about specific procedure for cleansing the skin before medication is applied. Regardless of method used, dry skin thoroughly before drug application.
- Avoid occlusive dressing, wrapping, or clothing over site where cream is applied.
- Store at 15°–30° C (59°–86° F) unless otherwise directed.

ADVERSE EFFECTS (≥1%) **Skin:** Irritation, pruritus, burning, worsening of clinical condition.

INTERACTIONS Drug: No clinically significant interactions established.

PHARMACOKINETICS Absorption: 1.3% absorbed through intact skin. **Distribution:** Distributed to epidermis, corium (dermis), including hair and hair follicles and sebaceous glands; not known if crosses placenta or is distributed into breast milk. **Elimination:** Excreted primarily by kidneys. **Half-Life:** 1.7 h.

CLINICAL IMPLICATIONS

Assessment & Drug Effects
- Monitor for therapeutic effectiveness. Tinea versicolor generally responds to drug treatment in about 2 wk. Tinea pedis ("athlete's foot"), tinea corporis (ringworm), tinea cruris ("jock itch"), and candidiasis (moniliasis) require about 4 wk of therapy.

Patient & Family Education
- Use medication for the prescribed time even though symptoms improve.
- Report skin irritation or other possible signs of sensitization. A reaction suggestive of sensitization warrants drug discontinuation.
- Do not use occlusive dressings or wrappings.
- Avoid contact of drug in or near the eyes.
- Wear light clothing and footwear that will allow ventilation. Loose-fitting cotton underwear or socks are preferred.

Common adverse effects in *italic*, life-threatening effects underlined; generic names in **bold**; classifications in SMALL CAPS; ♣ Canadian drug name; ☯ Prototype drug

CIDOFOVIR

(cye-do'fo-ver)
Vistide
Classifications: ANTIVIRAL
Therapeutic: ANTIVIRAL
Prototype: Acyclovir
Pregnancy Category: C

AVAILABILITY 75 mg/mL injection

ACTION & *THERAPEUTIC EFFECT*
Cidofovir, a nucleotide analog, suppresses cytomegalovirus (CMV) replication by inhibiting CMV DNA polymerase. *Cidofovir reduces the rate of viral DNA synthesis of CMV. Cidofovir is limited for use in treating CMV retinitis in patients with AIDS.*

USES Treatment of CMV retinitis in patients with AIDS.

CONTRAINDICATIONS Hypersensitivity to cidofovir, history of severe hypersensitivity to probenecid or other sulfa-containing medications; childbearing women and men without barrier contraception; pregnancy (category C); lactation; severe renal dysfunction. Safety and effectiveness in children not established.

CAUTIOUS USE Renal function impairment, history of diabetes, myelosuppression, previous hypersensitivity to other nucleoside analogs; older adults.

ROUTE & DOSAGE

CMV Retinitis: Induction & Maintenance
Adult: IV 5 mg/kg once weekly for 2 wk. Also give 2 g probenecid 3 h prior to infusion and 1 g 8 h after infusion (4 g total). Continue every 2 wk.

Renal Impairment
If serum Cr increases by 0.3–0.4, lower dose to 3 mg/kg.

ADMINISTRATION
- Pretreatment: Prehydrate with IV of 1 L NS infused over 1–2 h immediately before cidofovir infusion. If able to tolerate fluid load, infuse second liter over 1–3 h starting at beginning (or end) of cidofovir infusion.

Intravenous

PREPARE: **IV Infusion:** Dilute the calculated dose in 100 mL of NS.
ADMINISTER: **IV Infusion:** Give over 1 h at constant rate.
- Do not coadminister with other agents with significant nephrotoxic potential.

- Store vials at 20°–25° C (68°–77° F); may store diluted IV solution at 2°–8° C (36°–46° F) for up to 24 h.

ADVERSE EFFECTS (≥1%) **Body as a Whole:** Infection, allergic reactions. **GI:** Nausea, vomiting, diarrhea. **Metabolic:** Metabolic acidosis. **Hematologic:** Neutropenia. **CNS:** *Fever, headache,* asthenia. **Respiratory:** Dyspnea, pneumonia. **Special Senses:** Ocular hypotony. **Urogenital:** *Nephrotoxicity, proteinuria.*

INTERACTIONS Drug: AMINOGLYCOSIDES, **amphotericin B, foscarnet, pentamidine** can increase risk of nephrotoxicity.

PHARMACOKINETICS Duration: Probenecid increases serum levels and area under concentration–time curve. **Elimination:** 80–100% in urine; probenecid delays urinary excretion.

CLINICAL IMPLICATIONS
Assessment & Drug Effects
- Evaluate concurrent medications. Nephrotoxic drugs are usually discontinued 7 d prior to starting cidofovir.

Common adverse effects in *italic*, life-threatening effects <u>underlined</u>; generic names in **bold**; classifications in SMALL CAPS; ♣ Canadian drug name; ☯ Prototype drug

325

C

- Lab tests: Baseline and periodic serum creatinine, urine protein; periodic and WBC count with differential prior to each dose. Dose adjustments or discontinuation may be required.
- In patients with proteinuria, administer IV hydration and repeat test.
- Periodically monitor visual acuity and intraocular pressure.
- Monitor for S&S of hypersensitivity (see Appendix F). Report their appearance promptly.

Patient & Family Education
- Those taking zidovudine should discontinue or decrease dose to 50% on days of cidofovir administration.
- Initiate or continue regular ophthalmologic exams.
- Be alert to potential adverse reactions caused by probenecid (e.g., headache, nausea, vomiting, hypersensitivity reactions) and cidofovir.
- Closely monitor renal function.
- Women: Use effective contraception during and 1 mo after treatment.
- Men: Use barrier contraception during and 3 mo after treatment.

CILOSTAZOL

(sil-os'tah-zol)
Pletal
Classifications: VASODILATOR; PHOSPHODIESTERASE INHIBITOR; ANTIPLATELET AGENT
Therapeutic: PERIPHERAL VASODILATOR
Pregnancy Category: C

AVAILABILITY 50 mg, 100 mg tablets

ACTION & THERAPEUTIC EFFECT
Inhibition of an isoenzyme which results in vasodilatation and inhibition of platelet aggregation induced by collagen or arachidonic acid. *Increases the skin temperature of the extremities and improves claudication. Effectiveness is indicated by increased ability to walk further without claudication.*

USES Intermittent claudication.

CONTRAINDICATIONS Congestive heart failure of any severity; hypersensitivity to cilostazol; acute MI; hemostatic disorders or pathologic bleeding; pregnancy (category C), lactation.

CAUTIOUS USE Cardiac arrhythmias, MI within 6 mo; valvular heart disease; peptic ulcer disease; renal failure. Safety and efficacy in children <18 y are not established.

ROUTE & DOSAGE

Intermittent Claudication
Adult: **PO** 100 mg b.i.d. 0.5 h before or 2 h after meals, may need to reduce to 50 mg b.i.d. with concomitant ketoconazole, itraconazole, erythromycin, diltiazem or omeprazole

ADMINISTRATION

Oral
- Give at least 1/2 h before or 2 h after a meal. Do not give with grapefruit juice.
- Store at 20°–25° C (68°–77° F).

ADVERSE EFFECTS (≥1%) **Body as a Whole:** Back pain, *headache*, infection, myalgia. **CNS:** Dizziness, vertigo. **CV:** Palpitations, tachycardia. **GI:** Abdominal pain, *abnormal stools, diarrhea,* dyspepsia, flatulence, nausea. **Respiratory:** Cough, pharyngitis, rhinitis.

INTERACTIONS Drug: Aspirin, clopidogrel, diltiazem, erythromycin, fluconazole, fluvoxamine, fluoxetine, ketoconazole, itraconazole, MACROLIDE ANTIBIOTICS, miconazole, nefazodone, omeprazole, sertraline may increase cilostazol levels. **Food:** High fat meals may increase peak concentrations. Grapefruit juice may increase concentration.

PHARMACOKINETICS Absorption: Well absorbed from GI tract. **Onset:** 2–4 wks. **Distribution:** 95–98% protein bound. Smoking may decrease serum levels. May be excreted in breast milk. **Metabolism:** Metabolized by CYP3A4 to active metabolites. **Elimination:** Metabolites primarily excreted in urine. **Half-Life:** 1–13 hr.

CLINICAL IMPLICATIONS

Assessment & Drug Effects
- Monitor therapeutic effectiveness indicated by ability to walk farther without leg pain.
- Monitor for S&S of CHF. Do not give cilostazol to patients with preexisting CHF.

Patient & Family Education
- Avoid grapefruit or grapefruit juice while taking cilostazol.
- Allow 2–12 wk for therapeutic response.

CIMETIDINE ⊙

(sye-met′i-deen)
Tagamet, Tagamet HB
Classifications: ANTISECRETORY (H₂-RECEPTOR ANTAGONIST)
Therapeutic: H₂-RECEPTOR ANTAGONIST; ANTISECRETORY
Pregnancy Category: B

AVAILABILITY 100 mg, 200 mg, 400 mg, 800 mg tablets; 300 mg/5 mL liquid; 150 mg/mL injection

ACTION & *THERAPEUTIC EFFECT*
Has high selectivity for histamine H₂-receptors on parietal cells of the stomach. By inhibition of histamine at the H₂-receptor sites, it suppresses all phases of daytime and nocturnal basal gastric acid secretion in the stomach. Indirectly reduces pepsin secretion. *Blocks the H₂-receptors on the parietal cells of the stomach, thus decreasing gastric acid secretion; raises the pH of the stomach and thereby reduces pepsin secretion.*

USES Short-term treatment of active duodenal ulcer and prevention of ulcer recurrence (at reduced dosage) after it is healed. Also used for short-term treatment of active benign gastric ulcer, pathologic hypersecretory conditions such as Zollinger-Ellison syndrome, and heartburn.
UNLABELED USES Prophylaxis of stress-induced ulcers, upper GI bleeding, and aspiration pneumonitis; gastroesophageal reflux; chronic urticaria; acetaminophen toxicity.

CONTRAINDICATIONS Known hypersensitivity to cimetidine or other H₂-receptor antagonists.
CAUTIOUS USE Older adults or critically ill patients; impaired renal or hepatic function; organic brain syndrome; gastric ulcers; immunocompromised patients, pregnancy (category B).

ROUTE & DOSAGE

Duodenal Ulcer
Adult: **PO** 300 mg q.i.d. *or* 400 mg b.i.d. *or* 800 mg h.s. **IM/IV** 300 mg q6–8h

Common adverse effects in *italic*, life-threatening effects underlined; generic names in **bold**; classifications in SMALL CAPS; ♣ Canadian drug name; ⊙ Prototype drug

327

C

Child: **PO/IM/IV:** 20–40 mg/kg/d in 4 divided doses
Neonate: **PO/IM/IV:** 5–10 mg/kg/d divided q8–12h
Infant: **PO/IM/IV:** 10–20 mg/kg/d divided q6–12h

Duodenal Ulcer, Maintenance Therapy
Adult: **PO** 400 mg h.s.

Gastric Ulcer
Adult: **PO** 300 mg q.i.d. with meals and h.s. **IM/IV** 300 mg q6–8h

Heartburn
Adult: **PO** 200 mg 2–4 times/d

Pathologic Hypersecretory Disease
Adult: **PO** 300 mg q.i.d. with meals and h.s., may increase up to 2400 mg/d **IM/IV** 300 mg q6–8h, may increase up to 2400 mg/d

Renal Impairment
Cl_{cr} 20–40 mL/min: dose q8h; Cl_{cr} <20 mL/min: dose q12h

ADMINISTRATION

Oral
• Give 1 h before or 2 h after an antacid.

Intravenous
IV administration to neonates, infants and children: Verify correct IV concentration and rate of infusion/injection with physician.

PREPARE: **Direct:** Dilute 300 mg in 18 mL D5W or NS to yield 300 mg/20 mL. **Intermittent:** Dilute 300 mg in 50 mL D5W or NS. **Continuous:** Further dilute in up to 1000 mL of selected IV solution.

ADMINISTER: **Direct:** Give 300 mg or fraction thereof over at least 5 min. **Intermittent:** Give over 15–20 min. **Continuous:** Give a loading dose of 150 mg at the intermittent infusion rate; then give continuous infusion equally spaced over 24 h.

INCOMPATIBILITIES **Solution/additive: Amphotericin B, atropine, cefamandole, cefazolin, chlorpromazine, pentobarbital, secobarbital. Y-site: Allopurinol, amphotericin B cholesteryl complex, amsacrine, cefepime, indomethacin, warfarin.**

• Parenteral solutions are stable for 48 h at room temperature when added to commonly used IV solutions for dilution. Follow manufacturer's directions. • Store all forms of cimetidine at 15°–30° C (59°–86° F) protected from light unless otherwise directed by manufacturer.

ADVERSE EFFECTS (≥1%) **Body as a Whole:** Fever. **CV (rare):** <u>Cardiac arrhythmias and cardiac arrest</u> after rapid IV bolus dose. **GI:** Mild transient diarrhea; severe diarrhea, constipation, abdominal discomfort. **Hematologic:** Increased prothrombin time; neutropenia (rare), thrombocytopenia (rare), <u>aplastic anemia</u>. **Metabolic:** Slight increase in serum uric acid, BUN, creatinine; transient pain at IM site; hypospermia. **Musculoskeletal:** Exacerbation of joint symptoms in patients with preexisting arthritis. **CNS:** Drowsiness, dizziness, light-headedness, depression, headache, reversible confusional states, paranoid psychosis. **Skin:** Rash, Stevens-Johnson syndrome, reversible alopecia. **Urogenital:** Gynecomastia and breast soreness, galactorrhea, reversible impotence.

DIAGNOSTIC TEST INTERFERENCE
Cimetidine may cause false-positive *Hemocult test for gastric*

bleeding if test is performed within 15 min of oral cimetidine administration.

INTERACTIONS Drug: Cimetidine decreases the hepatic metabolism of **warfarin, phenobarbital, phenytoin, diazepam, propranolol, lidocaine, theophylline,** thus increasing their activity and toxicity; ANTACIDS may decrease absorption of cimetidine.

PHARMACOKINETICS Absorption: 70% of PO dose absorbed from GI tract. **Peak:** 1–1.5 h. **Distribution:** Widely distributed; crosses blood–brain barrier and placenta. **Metabolism:** In liver by CYP1A2 and 3A4. **Elimination:** Most of drug excreted in urine in 24 h; excreted in breast milk. **Half-Life:** 2 h.

CLINICAL IMPLICATIONS

Assessment & Drug Effects

- Ulcer healing may occur within the first 2 wk of therapy but generally requires at least 4 wk in most patients. Short-term (i.e., 8 wk) therapy of active duodenal ulcer does not prevent ulcer recurrence when drug is discontinued.
- Monitor pulse of patient during first few days of drug regimen. Bradycardia after PO as well as IV administration should be reported. Pulse usually returns to normal within 24 h after drug discontinuation.
- Monitor I&O ratio and pattern: Particularly in the older adult, severely ill, and in patients with impaired renal function.
- Report loss of bowel sounds, absence of bowel movement or flatus, vomiting, crampy pain, abdominal distention. Adynamic ileus has been reported in patients receiving cimetidine to prevent and treat stress ulcers.

- Lab tests: Periodic evaluations of blood count and renal and hepatic function are advised during therapy.
- Be alert to onset of confusional states, particularly in the older adult or severely ill patient. Symptoms occur within 2–3 d after first dose. Report immediately: drug should be withdrawn. Symptoms usually resolve within 3–4 d after therapy is discontinued.
- Check BP and report an elevation to the physician, if patient complains of severe headache.
- Cimetidine impairs absorption of protein-bound vitamin B_{12}; therefore patient who takes cimetidine in divided doses to continuously suppress acid gastric secretion is at risk for vitamin B_{12} deficiency (no risk for patient who takes drug at bedtime to suppress nocturnal acid production).

Patient & Family Education

- Cimetidine must be taken exactly as prescribed. Sudden discontinuation of therapy reportedly has caused perforation of chronic peptic ulcer.
- Seek advice about self-medication with any OTC drug.
- Report breast tenderness or enlargement. Mild bilateral gynecomastia and breast soreness may occur after ≥1 mo of therapy. It may disappear spontaneously or remain throughout therapy.
- Report recurrence of gastric pain or bleeding (black, tarry stools or "coffee ground" vomitus) immediately, and notify physician if diarrhea continues more than 1 d.
- Avoid driving and other potentially hazardous activities until reaction to drug is known.
- Duodenal or gastric ulcer is a chronic, recurrent condition that

Common adverse effects in *italic*, life-threatening effects <u>underlined</u>; generic names in **bold**; classifications in SMALL CAPS; ♣ Canadian drug name; ● Prototype drug

329

requires long-term maintenance drug therapy.

- Maintenance therapy at reduced dosage after healing of active duodenal ulcer appears to limit recurrence, particularly if patient undertakes other antiulcer therapeutic measures: no smoking, life-style that promotes reduced stress.

CINACALCET HYDROCHLORIDE

(sin-a-kal'set)
Sensipar
Classifications: HORMONE; PARATHYROID HORMONE AGENT; CALCIUM RECEPTOR AGONIST
Therapeutic: PARATHYROID HORMONE AGENT
Pregnancy Category: C

AVAILABILITY 30 mg, 60 mg, 90 mg tablets

ACTION & *THERAPEUTIC EFFECT*
Directly lowers parathyroid hormone (PTH) levels by increasing the sensitivity of calcium-sensing receptors on the parathyroid gland to extracellular calcium. The reduction in PTH causes decreased calcium and phosphate adsorption from bone, and thus decreased serum calcium and phosphate levels. The drug is a calcium receptor agonist, also known as a calcimimetic agent. *Lowers PTH production; this also decreases rate of bone turnover and bone fibrosis in chronic renal failure disease (CRFD).*

USES Treatment of secondary hyperparathyroidism in patients with chronic kidney disease on dialysis; hypercalcemia in patients with parathyroid cancer.

CONTRAINDICATIONS Hypersensitivity to cinacalcet; pregnancy (category C), lactation, children <18 y.

CAUTIOUS USE Moderate and severe hepatic impairment, hypocalcemia, history of seizures.

ROUTE & DOSAGE

Secondary Hyperparathyroidism
Adult: **PO** Start with 30 mg once daily; may increase q2–4wk until target iPTH of 150–300 pg/mL (max: 300 mg/d)

Parathyroid Cancer
Adult: **PO** 30 mg twice daily; titrate q2–4wk as 60 mg b.i.d., 90 mg b.i.d., then 90 mg 3–4 times daily as needed to normalize calcium concentrations

ADMINISTRATION

Oral
- Give with food or shortly after a meal.
- Tablets should be swallowed whole and not divided, crushed, or chewed.
- Store at 15°–30° C (59°–86° F).

ADVERSE EFFECTS (≥1%) **Body as a Whole:** Dizziness, asthenia, noncardiac chest pain, dialysis access infection. **CV:** Hypertension. **GI:** *Nausea, vomiting, diarrhea,* anorexia. **Metabolic:** Hypocalcemia. **Musculoskeletal:** *Myalgia,* adynamic bone disease (renal osteodystrophy).

INTERACTIONS Drug: May increase **amoxapine, atomoxetine, carvedilol, metoprolol, propranolol, timolol, encainide, flecainide, mexiletine, propafenone, clozapine, codeine, cyclobenzaprine, fenfluramine, dexfenfluramine, dextromethorphan, donepezil, fluoxetine, haloperidol, hydrocodone, maprotiline, meperidine, methadone, methamphetamine, morphine, oxycodone,**

Common adverse effects in *italic*, life-threatening effects underlined; generic names in **bold**; classifications in SMALL CAPS; ◆ Canadian drug name; ● Prototype drug

paroxetine, perphenazine, risperidone, thioridazine (use may be contraindicated with cinacalcet), tramadol, trazodone, tricyclic antidepressants, venlafaxine, zolpidem levels; cinacalcet levels may be increased by strong CYP3A4 inhibitors such as fluconazole, itraconazole, ketoconazole, miconazole, voriconazole, clarithromycin, erythromycin, dalfopristin; quinupristin, troleandomycin, verapamil, diltiazem, amiodarone, aprepitant, fluvoxamine, nefazodone, zafirlukast, zileuton. Food: Grapefruit juice may increase cinacalcet levels.

PHARMACOKINETICS Peak: 2–6 h. Distribution: 93–97% protein bound. Metabolism: In liver by CYP3A4. Elimination: 80% by kidneys, 15% in feces. Half-Life: 30–40 h.

CLINICAL IMPLICATIONS

Assessment & Drug Effects

- Monitor for S&S of hypocalcemia (e.g., paresthesias, myalgias, cramping, tetany, convulsions).
- Withhold drug and notify physician for serum calcium <7.5 mg/dL or symptoms of hypocalcemia. Drug should not be resumed until serum calcium levels reach 8.0 mg/dL, and/or symptoms of hypocalcemia resolve.
- Lab tests: Serum calcium and phosphorus within 1 wk after and iPTH 1–4 wk after initiation of drug or dose adjustment; thereafter, monthly serum calcium and phosphorus (more often with a history of a seizure disorder), and iPTH every 1–3 mo.
- Closely monitor iPTH and serum calcium with concurrent administration of a strong CYP3A4 (e.g., ketoconazole, erythromycin, itraconazole).

Patient & Family Education

- Report promptly any of the following: seizure or convulsion; muscle spasms or cramping of the abdomen, back, legs, face; burning, numbness, pricking, tickling, or tingling of the face, lips, tongue, hands, or feet; changes in mental status.

CIPROFLOXACIN HYDROCHLORIDE ℗

(ci-pro-flox′a-cin)
Cipro, Cipro IV, Cipro XR, Proquin XR

CIPROFLOXACIN OPHTHALMIC

Ciloxan

Classifications: QUINOLONE ANTIBIOTIC

Therapeutic: QUINOLONE ANTIBIOTIC
Pregnancy Category: C

AVAILABILITY 100 mg, 250 mg, 500 mg, 750 mg tablets; 500 mg extended-release tablets; 50 mg/mL, 100 mg/mL suspension; 200 mg, 400 mg injection; 3.5 mg/mL ophth solution

ACTION & THERAPEUTIC EFFECT
Synthetic quinolone that is a broad-spectrum bactericidal agent. Inhibits DNA-gyrase, an enzyme necessary for bacterial DNA replication and some aspects of transcription, repair, recombination, and transposition. *Effective against many gram-positive and aerobic gram-negative organisms. Not active against anaerobes.*

USES UTIs, lower respiratory tract infections, skin and skin structure infections, bone and joint infections, GI infection or infectious diarrhea, chronic bacterial prostatitis, nosocomial pneumonia, acute sinusitis. Post-exposure prophylaxis

Common adverse effects in *italic*, life-threatening effects underlined; generic names in **bold**; classifications in SMALL CAPS; ♣ Canadian drug name; ℗ Prototype drug

331

for anthrax. **Ophthalmic:** Corneal ulcers, bacterial conjunctivitis caused by *Staphylococci, Streptococci,* and *Pseudomonas aeruginosa.*

CONTRAINDICATIONS Known hypersensitivity to ciprofloxacin or other quinolones, syphilis, viral infection; tendon inflammation or tendon pain; pregnant women (category C).

CAUTIOUS USE Known or suspected CNS disorders (i.e., severe cerebral arteriosclerosis or seizure disorders); myasthenia gravis; myocardial ischemia, atrial fibrillation, QT prolongation, CHF; GI disease, colitis; CVA; uncorrected hypokalemia; patients receiving theophylline derivatives or caffeine, severe renal impairment and crystalluria during ciprofloxacin therapy, and patients on coumarin therapy; children.

ROUTE & DOSAGE

Uncomplicated UTI
Adult: **PO** 250 mg q12h or 500 mg XR q.d. × 3 d **IV** 200 mg q12h

Complicated UTI
Adult: **PO** 1000 mg XR q.d. × 7–14 d **IV** 400 mg q12h

Acute Sinusitis
Adult: **PO** 500 mg b.i.d. × 10 d

Moderate to Severe Systemic Infection
Adult: **PO** 500–750 mg q12h **IV** 200–400 mg q12h

Renal Impairment
Cl_{cr} 30–50 mL/min: **PO** 250–500 mg q12h, **IV** no change in dose; <30 mL/min: **PO** 250–500 mg q18h, **IV** 200–400 mg q18–24h

Bacterial Conjunctivitis
Adult: **Ophthalmic** 1–2 drops in conjunctival sac q2h while awake for 2 d, then 1–2 drops q4h while awake for the next 5 d **Ointment** 1/2-inch ribbon into conjunctival sac t.i.d. times 2 d, then b.i.d. times 5 d

Corneal Ulcers
Adult: **Ophthalmic** 2 drops q15min for 6 h, 2 drops q30min for the next 18 h, then 2 drops q1h for 24 h, then 2 drops q4h for 14 d

ADMINISTRATION

- For patients with renal impairment, oral and IV doses are lowered according to creatinine clearance.

Oral

- Do not give an antacid within 4 h of the oral ciprofloxacin dose.

Intravenous

PREPARE: **Intermittent:** Dilute in NS or D5W to a final concentration of 0.5–2 mg/mL. Typical dilutions are 200 mg in 100–250 mL and 400 mg in 250–500 mL.

ADMINISTER: **Intermittent:** Give slowly over 60 min. Avoid rapid infusion and use of a small vein.

INCOMPATIBILITIES **Solution/additive: Aminophylline, clindamycin, heparin. Y-site: Aminophylline, ampicillin, ampicillin/sulbactam, azithromycin, cefepime, dexamethasone, furosemide, heparin, hydrocortisone, phenytoin, propofol, sodium bicarbonate, theophylline, warfarin.**

- Discontinue other IV infusion while infusing ciprofloxacin or infuse through another site. ■ Reconstituted IV solution is stable for 14 d refrigerated.

ADVERSE EFFECTS (≥1%) **GI:** Nausea, vomiting, diarrhea, cramps, gas, pseudomembranous colitis. **Metabolic:** Transient increases in liver transaminases, alkaline phosphatase, lactic dehydrogenase, and eosinophilia count. **Musculoskeletal:** Tendon rupture, cartilage erosion. **CNS:** Headache, vertigo, malaise, peripheral neuropathy, seizures (especially with rapid IV infusion). **Skin:** Rash, phlebitis, pain, burning, pruritus, and erythema at infusion site. **Special Senses:** *Local burning and discomfort, crystalline precipitate on superficial portion of cornea,* lid margin crusting, scales, foreign body sensation, itching, and conjunctival hyperemia.

DIAGNOSTIC TEST INTERFERENCE

Ciprofloxacin does not interfere with **urinary glucose** determinations using **cupric sulfate solution** or with **glucose oxidase tests;** may cause false positive on **opiate screening tests.**

INTERACTIONS Drug: May increase **theophylline** levels 15–30%; ANTACIDS, **sulcralfate, iron** decrease absorption of ciprofloxacin; may increase PT for patients on **warfarin.** **Food:** Calcium decreases the levels of ciprofloxacin.

PHARMACOKINETICS Absorption: 60–80% from GI tract. **Ophthalmic:** Minimal absorption through cornea or conjunctiva. **Onset:** Topical 0.5–2 h. **Duration:** Topical 12 h. **Peak:** Immediate release: 0.5–2h; Cipro XR: 1–2.5h; Proquin XR: 3.5–8.7h. **Distribution:** Widely distributed including prostate, lung, and bone; crosses placenta; distributed into breast milk. **Elimination:** Primarily in urine with some biliary excretion. **Half-Life:** 3.5–4 h.

CLINICAL IMPLICATIONS

Assessment & Drug Effects

- Report tendon inflammation or pain. Drug should be discontinued.

- Lab tests: Culture and sensitivity tests should be done prior to initial dose. Treatment may be implemented pending results.
- Monitor urine pH; it should be less than 6.8, especially in the older adult and patients receiving high dosages of ciprofloxacin, to reduce the risk of crystalluria.
- Monitor I&O ratio and patterns: Patients should be well hydrated; assess for S&S of crystalluria.
- Monitor plasma theophylline concentrations, since drug may interfere with half-life.
- Administration with theophylline derivatives or caffeine can cause CNS stimulation.
- Assess for S&S of GI irritation (e.g., nausea, diarrhea, vomiting, abdominal discomfort) in clients receiving high dosages and in older adults.
- Monitor PT and INR in patients receiving coumarin therapy.
- Assess for S&S of superinfections (see Appendix F).

Patient & Family Education

- Immediately report tendon inflammation or pain. Drug should be discontinued.
- Fluid intake of 2–3 L/d is advised, if not contraindicated.
- Report sudden, unexplained joint pain.
- Restrict caffeine due to the following effects (e.g., nervousness, insomnia, anxiety, tachycardia).
- Report possible toxicity. If taking theophylline derivatives, there is potential for adverse effects.
- Report nausea, diarrhea, vomiting, and abdominal pain or discomfort.
- Use caution with hazardous activities until reaction to drug is known. Drug may cause lightheadedness.

Common adverse effects in *italic*, life-threatening effects <u>underlined</u>; generic names in **bold**; classifications in SMALL CAPS; ♣ Canadian drug name; ☻ Prototype drug

C

CISATRACURIUM BESYLATE

(cis-a-tra-kyoo-ri′um)

Nimbex

Classifications: SKELETAL MUSCLE RELAXANT, NONDEPOLARIZING; NEUROMUSCULAR BLOCKER

Therapeutic: SKELETAL MUSCLE RELAXANT

Prototype: Atracurium

Pregnancy Category: B

AVAILABILITY 2 mg/mL, 10 mg/mL injection

ACTION & *THERAPEUTIC EFFECT*

Cisatracurium is a neuromuscular blocking agent with intermediate onset and duration of action compared with similar agents. It binds competitively to cholinergic receptors on the motor endplate of neurons, antagonizing the action of acetylcholine. *Antagonism of acetylcholine blocks neuromuscular transmission of nerve impulses. This action can be reversed or antagonized by acetylcholinesterase inhibitors (e.g., neostigmine).*

USES Adjunct to general anesthesia to facilitate tracheal intubation and provide skeletal muscle relaxation during surgery or mechanical ventilation.

CONTRAINDICATIONS Hypersensitivity to cisatracurium or other related agents; rapid-sequence endotracheal intubation. Not studied in infants <1 mo.

CAUTIOUS USE History of hemiparesis, electrolyte imbalances, burn patients, pulmonary disease, COPD; neuromuscular diseases (e.g., myasthenia gravis), older adults, renal function impairment, pregnancy (category B), lactation.

ROUTE & DOSAGE

Intubation

Adult: **IV** 0.15 or 0.20 mg/kg
Child ≥2 y: **IV** 0.1 mg/kg over 5–10 sec

Maintenance

Adult: **IV** 0.03 mg/kg q20min prn *or* 1–2 mcg/kg/min
Child ≥2 y: **IV** 1–2 mcg/kg/min

Mechanical Ventilation in ICU

Adult: **IV** 3 mcg/kg/min (can range from 0.5 to 10.2 mcg/kg/min)

ADMINISTRATION

- Administer carefully adjusted, individualized doses using a peripheral nerve stimulator to evaluate neuromuscular function.
- Give only by or under supervision of expert clinician familiar with the drug's actions and potential complications.
- Have immediately available personnel and facilities for resuscitation and life support and an antagonist of cisatracurium.
- Refer to manufacturer's guidelines for preparation and administration. Note that 10-mL multipledose vials contain benzyl alcohol and should not be used with neonates.

Intravenous

PREPARE: Direct: Give undiluted. **IV Infusion:** Dilute 10 mg in 95 mL or 40 mg in 80 mL of compatible IV fluid to prepare 0.1 mg/mL or 0.4 mg/mL, respectively, IV solution. Compatible IV fluids include D5W, NS, D5/NS, D5/RL. **ICU IV Infusion:** Dilute the contents of the 200 mg vial (i.e., 10 mg/mL) in 1000 mL or 500 mL of compatible IV fluid to prepare 0.2 mg/mL or 0.4 g/mL, respectively, IV solutions.

ADMINISTER: Direct: Give a single dose over 5–10 sec. **IV Infusion:** Adjust the rate based on patient's weight.

INCOMPATIBILITIES Solution/additive: **Ketorolac, propofol, sodium bicarbonate.** Y-site: **Amphotericin B, amphotericin B cholesteryl complex, cefoperazone, cefuroxime, diazepam, sodium bicarbonate.**

• Refrigerate vials at 2°–8° C (36°–46° F). Protect from light. Diluted solutions may be stored refrigerated or at room temperature for 24 h.

ADVERSE EFFECTS (≥1%) **CV:** Bradycardia, hypotension, flushing. **Respiratory:** Bronchospasm. **Skin:** Rash.

PHARMACOKINETICS Onset: Varies from 1.5 to 3.3 min (higher dose has faster onset). **Peak:** Varies from 1.5 to 3.3 min (higher dose has faster peak). **Duration:** Varies with dose from 46 to 121 min (higher dose, longer recovery time). **Metabolism:** Undergoes Hoffman elimination (pH- and temperature-dependent degradation) and hydrolysis by plasma esterases. **Elimination:** In urine. **Half-Life:** 22 min.

CLINICAL IMPLICATIONS

Assessment & Drug Effects

• Perform neuromuscular monitoring only on nonparetic limbs.
• Time-to-maximum neuromuscular block is ≈1 min slower in the older adult.
• Monitor for bradycardia, hypotension, and bronchospasms; monitor ICU patients for spontaneous seizures.
• Antagonists should not be given when complete neuromuscular block is present.

CISPLATIN (cis-DDP, cis-PLATINUM II)

(sis′pla-tin)
Abiplatin ♦, Platinol
Classifications: ANTINEOPLASTIC; ALKYLATING AGENT
Therapeutic: ANTINEOPLASTIC; ALKYLATING AGENT
Prototype: Cyclophosphamide
Pregnancy Category: D

AVAILABILITY 1 mg/mL injection

ACTION & THERAPEUTIC EFFECT
A heavy metal complex with platinum as central atom surrounded by 2 chloride atoms and 2 ammonia molecules in the cis chemical position. Biochemical properties similar to those of other alkylating agents. Produces interstrand and intrastrand cross linkage in DNA of rapidly dividing cells, thus preventing DNA, RNA, and protein synthesis. *Cell cycle-nonspecific, i.e., effective throughout the entire cell life cycle.*

USES Established combination therapy (cisplatin, vinblastine, bleomycin) in patient with metastatic testicular tumors and with doxorubicin for metastatic ovarian tumors following appropriate surgical or radiation therapy.
UNLABELED USES Carcinoma of endometrium, bladder, head, and neck.

CONTRAINDICATIONS History of hypersensitivity to cisplatin or other platinum-containing compounds; impaired renal function; severe myelosuppression; impaired hearing; active infection; history of gout and urate renal stones, renal failure; hypomagnesia; concurrent administration with loop diuretics; Raynaud syndrome; pregnancy (category D). Safe use in children not established, although

Common adverse effects in *italic*, life-threatening effects underlined; generic names in **bold**; classifications in SMALL CAPS; ♦ Canadian drug name; ❷ Prototype drug

335

experimental regimens have been used.

CAUTIOUS USE Previous cytotoxic drug or radiation therapy with other ototoxic and nephrotoxic drugs; peripheral neuropathy; hyperuricemia; electrolyte imbalances, moderate renal impairment; hepatic impairment; history of circulatory disorders.

ROUTE & DOSAGE

Testicular Neoplasms
Adult: **IV** 20 mg/m²/d for 5 d q3–4wk for 3 courses

Ovarian Neoplasms
Adult: **IV** *With cyclophosphamide:* 75–100 mg/m² once q4wk; *Single agent:* 100 mg/m² once q4wk

Advanced Bladder Cancer
Adult: **IV** 50–75 mg/m² q3–4 wk

ADMINISTRATION

▪ Administered only under supervision of a qualified physician experienced in the use of antineoplastics.
▪ Usually a parenteral antiemetic agent is administered ¹/₂ h before cisplatin therapy is instituted and given on a scheduled basis throughout day and night as long as necessary.
▪ Before the initial dose is given, hydration is started with 1–2 L IV infusion fluid to reduce risk of nephrotoxicity and ototoxicity.

Intravenous

PREPARE: **IV Infusion:** Use disposable gloves when preparing cisplatin solutions. If drug accidentally contacts skin or mucosa, wash immediately and thoroughly with soap and water. Do not use any equipment containing aluminum. Withdraw required dose and dilute in 2 L D5W 5% dextrose in ¹/₂ or ¹/₃ normal saline containing 37.5 g mannitol.
ADMINISTER: **IV Infusion:** Give 2 L over 6–8 h
INCOMPATIBILITIES **Solution/additive:** 5% dextrose, fluorouracil, mesna, metoclopramide, sodium bicarbonate, thiotepa. **Y-site:** Amifostine, amphotericin B, cholesteryl, cefepime, piperacillin/tazobactam, thiotepa, TPN.

▪ Hydration and forced diuresis are continued for at least 24 h after drug administration to ensure adequate urinary output.

▪ Store at 15°–30° C (59°–86° F). Do not refrigerate. Protect from light. Once vial is opened, solution is stable for 28 d protected from light or 7 d in fluorescent light.

ADVERSE EFFECTS (≥1%) **Body as a Whole:** <u>Anaphylactic-like reactions.</u> **CV:** Cardiac abnormalities. **GI:** *Marked nausea, vomiting,* anorexia, stomatitis, xerostomia, diarrhea, constipation. **Hematologic:** Myelosuppression (25–30% patients): leukopenia, thrombocytopenia; hemolytic anemia, hemolysis. **Metabolic:** Hypocalcemia, *hypomagnesemia,* hyperuricemia, elevated AST, SIADH. **CNS:** Seizures, headache; peripheral neuropathies (may be irreversible): paresthesia, unsteady gait, clumsiness of hands and feet, exacerbation of neuropathy with exercise, loss of taste. **Special Senses:** Ototoxicity (may be irreversible): tinnitus, hearing loss, deafness, vertigo, blurred vision, changes in ability to see colors (optic neuritis, papilledema). **Urogenital:** Nephrotoxicity.

INTERACTIONS Drug: AMINOGLYCO-SIDES, **amphotericin B, vancomy-**

cin, other **nephrotoxic drugs** increase nephrotoxicity and acute renal failure—try to separate by at least 1–2 wk; AMINOGLYCOSIDES, **furosemide** increase risk of ototoxicity.

PHARMACOKINETICS Peak: Immediately after infusion. **Distribution:** Widely distributed in body fluids and tissues; concentrated in kidneys, liver, and prostate; accumulated in tissues. **Metabolism:** Not known. **Elimination:** 15–50% in urine within 24–48 h. **Half-Life:** 73–290 h.

CLINICAL IMPLICATIONS

Assessment & Drug Effects

- Obtain baseline ECG and cardiac monitoring during induction therapy because of possible myocarditis or focal irritability.
- Lab tests: The following tests should be done *before* initiating every course of therapy and repeated each week during treatment period: serum uric acid, serum creatinine, BUN, urinary creatinine clearance. CBC and platelet counts are done weekly for 2 wk after each course of treatment. Monitor periodically serum electrolytes and liver function tests.
- A repeat course of therapy should not be given until (1) serum creatinine is below 1.5 mg/dL; (2) BUN is below 25 mg/dL; (3) platelets ≥100,000/mm³; (4) WBC ≥4000/mm³; (5) audiometric test is within normal limits.
- Monitor urine output and specific gravity for 4 consecutive hours before treatment and for 24 h after therapy. Report if output is less than 100 mL/h or if specific gravity is more than 1.030. A urine output of less than 75 mL/h necessitates medical intervention to avert a renal emergency.
- Audiometric testing should be performed before the first dose and before each subsequent dose. Ototoxicity (reported in 31% of patients) may occur after a single dose of 50 mg/m². Children who receive repeated doses are especially susceptible.
- Monitor for anaphylactoid reactions (particularly in patient previously exposed to cisplatin), which may occur within minutes of drug administration.
- Monitor closely for dose-related adverse reactions. Drug action is cumulative; therefore severity of most adverse effects increases with repeated doses.
- Nephrotoxicity (reported in 28–36% of patients receiving a single dose of 50 mg/m²) usually occurs within 2 wk after drug administration and becomes more severe and prolonged with repeated courses of cisplatin.
- Suspect ototoxicity if patient manifests tinnitus or difficulty hearing in the high frequency range.
- Intractable nausea and vomiting severe enough to warrant discontinuation of drug usually begin 1–4 h after treatment and may last 24 h or persist for up to 1 wk after treatment is ended.
- Monitor and report abnormal electrolyte levels: sodium >145 or <135 mEq/L, and potassium >5 or <3.5 mEq/L.
- Monitor results of blood studies. The nadirs in platelet and leukocyte counts occur between day 18 and 23 (range: 7.5–45) with most patients recovering in 13–62 d. A decrease in Hgb (more than 2 g/dL) occurs at approximately the same time and with the same frequency.
- Check BP, mental status, pupils, and fundi every hour during therapy. Hydration and mannitol may increase the danger of elevated intracranial pressure (ICP).

Common adverse effects in *italic*, life-threatening effects <u>underlined</u>; generic names in **bold**; classifications in SMALL CAPS; ✦ Canadian drug name; ❷ Prototype drug

337

- Neurologic examinations at regular intervals should include tests of muscle strength, Romberg, vibratory and position sense, tests of sensation.
- Monitor and report abnormal bowel elimination pattern. Constipation and the possibility of fecal impaction may be caused by neurotoxicity; diarrhea is a possible response to GI irritation.
- Inspect oral membranes for xerostomia (white patches and ulcerations) and tongue for signs of fungal overgrowth (black, furry appearance).
- Institute infection precautions promptly if a temperature increase of 0.6° F over the previous reading is noted.
- Weigh the patient under standard conditions every day. A gradual ascending weight profile occurring over a period of several days should be reported.

Patient & Family Education

- Continue maintenance of adequate hydration (at least 3000 mL/24 h oral fluid if physician agrees) and report promptly: reduced urinary output, flank pain, anorexia, nausea, vomiting, dry mucosae, itching skin, urine odor on breath, fluid retention, and weight gain.
- Avoid rapid changes in position to minimize risk of dizziness or falling.
- Tingling, numbness, and tremors of extremities, loss of position sense and taste, and constipation are early signs of neurotoxicity. Report their occurrence promptly to prevent irreversibility. Pain with heel walking and difficulty in getting out of bed or chair are late indicators of nerve damage.
- Report tinnitus or any hearing impairment.

- Report promptly evidence of unexplained bleeding and easy bruising.
- Report unusual fatigue, fever, sore mouth and throat, abnormal body discharges.

CITALOPRAM HYDROBROMIDE

(cit-a-lo′pram)
Celexa
Classifications: PSYCHOTHERAPEUTIC AGENT; SELECTIVE SEROTONIN-REUPTAKE INHIBITOR (SSRI)
Therapeutic: ANTIDEPRESSANT; SSRI
Prototype: Fluoxetine
Pregnancy Category: C

AVAILABILITY 20 mg, 40 mg tablets; 10 mg/5 mL oral solution

ACTION & *THERAPEUTIC EFFECT*
Selective serotonin reuptake inhibitor (SSRI) in the CNS. Antidepressant effect is presumed to be linked to its inhibition of CNS presynaptic neuronal uptake of serotonin which results in antidepressant activity. *Does not inhibit MAO. Selective serotonin reuptake inhibition mechanism results in the antidepressant activity of citalopram.*

USES Depression.

CONTRAINDICATIONS Hypersensitivity to citalopram; concurrent use of MAOIs or use within 14 d of discontinuing MAOIs; pregnancy (category C); mania; volume depleted; suicidal ideation; children <18 y.
CAUTIOUS USE Hypersensitivity to other SSRIs; renal or hepatic insufficiency; history of potential suicide; older adults; concurrent use of diuretics, dehydration, severe renal impairment or renal failure, cardiovascular disease (e.g., dysrhythmias, conduction defects, myocardial ischemia); history of seizure disorders

Common adverse effects in *italic*, life-threatening effects <u>underlined</u>; generic names in **bold**; classifications in SMALL CAPS; ♦ Canadian drug name; ● Prototype drug

or suicidal tendencies; bipolar disorder; ECT treatments; lactation.

ROUTE & DOSAGE

Depression
Adult: **PO** Start at 20 mg q.d., may increase to 40 mg q.d. if needed
Geriatric: **PO** 20 mg q.d.

ADMINISTRATION

Oral
- Do not begin this drug within 14 d of stopping an MAOI.
- Reduced doses are advised for the older adult and those with hepatic or renal impairment.
- Dose increments should be separated by at least 1 wk.
- Store at 15°–30° C (59°–86° F) in tightly closed container and protect from light.

ADVERSE EFFECTS (≥1%) **Body as a Whole:** Asthenia, fatigue, fever, arthralgia, myalgia. **CV:** Tachycardia, postural hypotension, hypotension. **GI:** *Nausea,* vomiting, diarrhea, dyspepsia, abdominal pain, *dry mouth,* anorexia, flatulence. **CNS:** Dizziness, *insomnia, somnolence,* agitation, tremor, anxiety, paresthesia, migraine. **Respiratory:** URI, rhinitis, sinusitis. **Skin:** Increased sweating. **Urogenital:** Dysmenorrhea, decreased libido, ejaculation disorder, impotence.

INTERACTIONS Drug: Combination with MAOIS could result in hypertensive crisis, hyperthermia, rigidity, myoclonus, autonomic instability; **cimetidine** may increase citalopram levels; **linezolid** may cause serotonin syndrome. **Herbal: St. John's wort** may cause serotonin syndrome.

PHARMACOKINETICS Absorption: Rapidly absorbed from GI tract; approximately 80% reaches systemic circulation. **Peak:** Steady-state serum concentrations in 1 wk; peak blood levels at 4 h. **Distribution:** 80% protein bound; crosses placenta; distributed into breast milk. **Metabolism:** In liver by cytochrome P450 3A4 and cytochrome P450 2C9 enzymes. **Elimination:** 20% in urine, 80% in bile. **Half-Life:** 35 h.

CLINICAL IMPLICATIONS

Assessment & Drug Effects
- Watch closely for worsening of depression or emergence of suicidal ideations.
- Monitor for therapeutic effectiveness: Indicated by elevation of mood; 1–4 wk may be needed before improvement is noted.
- Lab tests: Monitor periodically hepatic functions, CBC, serum sodium, and lithium levels when the two drugs are given concurrently.
- Monitor periodically HR and BP, and carefully monitor complete cardiac status in person with known or suspected cardiac disease.
- Monitor closely older adult patients for adverse effects especially with doses >20 mg/d.

Patient & Family Education
- Do not engage in hazardous activities until reaction to this drug is known.
- Avoid using alcohol while taking citalopram.
- Inform physician of commonly used OTC drugs as there is potential for drug interactions.
- Report distressing adverse effects including any changes in sexual functioning or response.
- Periodic ophthalmology exams are advised with long-term treatment.

Common adverse effects in *italic,* life-threatening effects underlined; generic names in **bold**; classifications in SMALL CAPS; ✦ Canadian drug name; ❻ Prototype drug

339

CLADRIBINE

(cla′dri-been)
Leustatin
Classifications: ANTINEOPLASTIC; ANTIMETABOLITE, PURINE ANTAGONIST
Therapeutic: ANTINEOPLASTIC; ANTIMETABOLITE
Prototype: 6-mercaptopurine
Pregnancy Category: D

AVAILABILITY 1 mg/mL injection

ACTION & *THERAPEUTIC EFFECT*

Cladribine is a synthetic antineoplastic agent with selective toxicity toward certain normal and malignant lymphocytes and monocytes. It accumulates intracellularly, preventing repair of single-stranded DNA breaks and ultimately interfering with cellular metabolism and DNA synthesis. *Cladribine is cytotoxic to both actively dividing and quiescent lymphocytes and monocytes, inhibiting both DNA synthesis and repair.*

USES Treatment of hairy cell leukemia.

UNLABELED USES Advanced cutaneous T-cell lymphomas, chronic lymphocytic leukemia, non-Hodgkin's lymphomas, acute myeloid leukemia, autoimmune hemolytic anemia, mycosis fungoides.

CONTRAINDICATIONS Hypersensitivity to cladribine; severe bone marrow suppression; pregnancy (category D).
CAUTIOUS USE Hepatic or renal impairment; previous radiation therapy or chemotherapy. Safety and efficacy in children not established.

ROUTE & DOSAGE

Hairy Cell Leukemia
Adult: **IV** 0.09 mg/kg/d by 7 d continuous infusion

Chronic Lymphocytic Leukemia
Adult: **IV** 0.1 mg/kg/d by 7 d continuous infusion or 0.028–0.14 mg/kg/d as 2 h infusion for 5 consecutive d

ADMINISTRATION

- Solutions for cladribine should not be mixed with any other IV drugs or additives, nor administered through an IV line used for other drugs or solutions.
- Use disposable gloves and protective clothing when handling the drug.
- Wash immediately if skin contact occurs.

Intravenous

PREPARE: **IV Infusion (single daily dose):** IV infusion (7-day dose): The calculated dose of cladribine is injected into an infusion reservoir using a 0.22 micron filter. An amount of bacteriostatic NS is added through a 0.22 micron filter to bring the total to 100 mL. (Note: Reservoir usually prepared by the pharmacist.)
ADMINISTER: **IV Infusion (single daily dose):** Distribute evenly over ordered time (i.e., 2 h or 24 h). **IV infusion (7-day dose):** Give through a central line and control by a pump device (e.g., Deltec pump) to deliver 100 mL evenly over 7 d.
INCOMPATIBILITIES **Solution/additive:** Do not mix with any other diluents or drugs.

- Diluted solutions of cladribine may be stored refrigerated for up to

8 h prior to administration. ▪ Store unopened vials in refrigerator (2°–8° C/36°–46° F), and protect from light.

ADVERSE EFFECTS (≥1%) **CNS:** Headache, dizziness. **GI:** Nausea, diarrhea. **Hematologic:** *Myelosuppression (neutropenia)*, *anemia*, thrombocytopenia. **Metabolic:** *Fever*. **CNS:** Headache, dizziness. **Urogenital:** Elevated serum creatinine.

INTERACTIONS Drug: Additive risk of bleeding with ANTICOAGULANTS, NSAIDS, PLATELET INHIBITORS, SALICYLATES.

PHARMACOKINETICS Onset: Therapeutic effect 10 d to 4 mo. **Duration:** 7–25+ mo. **Distribution:** Crosses placenta; distributed into breast milk. **Metabolism:** In malignant leukocytes, cladribine is phosphorylated to active forms, which are subsequently incorporated into cellular DNA. **Half-Life:** Initial 35 min, terminal 6.7 h.

CLINICAL IMPLICATIONS

Assessment & Drug Effects

▪ Monitor vital signs during and after drug infusion. Fever (>100° F) is common during the 5th to 7th day in patients with hairy cell leukemia, and severe fever (>104° F) may develop within the first month of therapy.
▪ Lab tests: Frequent hematologic studies; periodic serum creatinine and liver function tests.
▪ Closely monitor hematologic status; myelosuppression is common during the first month after starting therapy.
▪ Monitor for and report S&S of infection. Note that within the first month, fever may occur in the absence of infection.
▪ With high doses of cladribine, monitor for neurologic toxicity (paraparesis/quadriparesis) and acute nephrotoxicity.

Patient & Family Education

▪ Be fully informed regarding adverse responses to the drug.
▪ Understand the need for close follow-up during and after treatment with the drug.

CLARITHROMYCIN

(clar'i-thro-my-sin)
Biaxin Filmtabs, Biaxin XL
Classifications: MACROLIDE ANTIBIOTIC
Therapeutic: ANTIBIOTIC, MACROLIDE
Prototype: Erythromycin
Pregnancy Category: C

AVAILABILITY 250 mg, 500 mg tablets; 500 mg sustained-release tablets; 125 mg/5 mL, 250 mg/5 mL suspension

ACTION & *THERAPEUTIC EFFECT*
A semisynthetic macrolide antibiotic that binds to the 50S ribosomal subunit of susceptible bacterial organisms and, thereby, blocks RNA-mediated bacterial protein synthesis of the bacteria. *It is active against both aerobic and anaerobic gram-positive and gram-negative organisms.*

USES Treatment of upper respiratory, lower respiratory infections; acute maxillary sinusitis; otitis media; and skin and soft tissue infections caused by clinically significant aerobic and anaerobic gram-negative and gram-positive organisms, including *S. aureus, H. influenzae, S. pneumoniae, M. catarrhalis, S. pyogenes, M. pneumoniae.* Prevention and treatment of *Mycobacterium avium complex* (MAC) infections in patients with HIV. Used in combination for *Helicobacter pylori.*

CONTRAINDICATIONS Hypersensitivity to clarithromycin, erythro-

Common adverse effects in *italic*, life-threatening effects underlined; generic names in **bold**; classifications in SMALL CAPS; ♣ Canadian drug name; ✿ Prototype drug

341

mycin, or any other macrolide antibiotics; patients receiving pimozide; suspected or potential bacteremias; acute porphyria; severe hepatic or biliary disease; congenital QT prolongation, torsades de pointes; viral infections; pregnancy (category C). Safety and efficacy in infants <20 mo not established.

CAUTIOUS USE Renal impairment, older adults, GI disease, colitis; lactation.

ROUTE & DOSAGE

Mild to Moderate Infections
Adult: **PO** 250–500 mg b.i.d. or 500 mg XL q.d. for 10–14 d
Child: **PO** 7.5 mg/kg q12h

Mycobacterial Infections
Adult: **PO** 500 mg q12h
Child: **PO** 7.5 mg/kg q12h

H. pylori Infections
Adult: **PO** 500 mg b.i.d. to t.i.d.

Renal Impairment
Cl$_{cr}$ <30 mL/min: decrease dose by $^1/_2$ or double the dosing interval

ADMINISTRATION

Oral
- Ensure that sustained-release form of drug is not chewed or crushed. It must be swallowed whole.
- Shake suspension well before use.
- Store at 15°–30° C (59°–86° F).

ADVERSE EFFECTS (≥1%) **GI:** Diarrhea, abdominal discomfort, nausea, abnormal taste, dyspepsia. **Hematologic:** Eosinophilia. **CNS:** Headache. **Skin:** Rash, urticaria.

DIAGNOSTIC TEST INTERFERENCE May increase serum AST and ALT levels.

INTERACTIONS Drug: May increase **theophylline** levels; drugs known to interact with **erythromycin** (i.e., **digoxin, carbamazepine, triazolam, warfarin, ergotamine, dihydroergotamine**) should be monitored carefully for increased levels and toxicity; **pimozide** may increase risk of arrhythmias.

PHARMACOKINETICS Absorption: Readily absorbed from GI tract; 50% reaches the systemic circulation. **Peak:** 2–4 h. **Distribution:** Widely distributes into most body tissue (excluding CNS); high pulmonary tissue concentrations. **Metabolism:** Partially metabolized in the liver; active 14-OH metabolite acts synergistically with the parent compound against *H. influenzae*. **Elimination:** 20% excreted unchanged in urine; 10–15% of 14-OH metabolite excreted in urine. **Half-Life:** 3–5 h.

CLINICAL IMPLICATIONS

Assessment & Drug Effects
- Inquire about previous hypersensitivity to other macrolides (e.g., erythromycin) before treatment.
- Withhold drug and notify physician, if hypersensitivity occurs (e.g., rash, urticaria).
- Monitor for and report loose stools or diarrhea, since pseudomembranous colitis must be ruled out.
- When clarithromycin is given concurrently with anticoagulants, digoxin, or theophylline, blood levels of these drugs may be elevated. Monitor appropriate serum levels and assess for S&S of drug toxicity.

Patient & Family Education
- Complete prescribed course of therapy.
- Report rash or other signs of hypersensitivity immediately.
- Report loose stools or diarrhea even after completion of drug therapy.

Common adverse effects in *italic*, life-threatening effects <u>underlined</u>; generic names in **bold**; classifications in SMALL CAPS; ✚ Canadian drug name; ⊘ Prototype drug

CLEMASTINE FUMARATE

(klem'as-teen)
Tavist-1
Classifications: ANTIHISTAMINE (H$_1$-RECEPTOR ANTAGONIST)
Therapeutic: ANTIHISTAMINE; H$_1$-RECEPTOR ANTAGONIST
Prototype: Diphenhydramine
Pregnancy Category: B

AVAILABILITY 1.34 mg, 2.68 mg tablets; 0.67 mg/5 mL syrup

ACTION & *THERAPEUTIC EFFECT*
An antihistamine (H$_1$-receptor antagonist) that competes for H$_1$-receptor sites on effector cells, thus blocking histamine effectiveness. Has greater selectivity for peripheral H$_1$-receptors and, consequently, it produces little sedation. Has prominent antipruritic activity and low incidence of unpleasant adverse effects. *Effective in controlling various allergic reactions, e.g., nasal congestion, sneezing, itching.*

USES Symptomatic relief of allergic rhinitis (sneezing, rhinorrhea, pruritus) and mild uncomplicated allergic skin manifestations such as urticaria and angioedema.

CONTRAINDICATIONS Hypersensitivity to clemastine or to other antihistamines of similar chemical structure; lower respiratory tract symptoms, including acute asthma; concomitant MAO INHIBITOR therapy; closed angle glaucoma; children <6 y; lactation.
CAUTIOUS USE History of bronchial asthma, COPD; increased intraocular pressure; GI or GU obstruction; hyperthyroidism; hepatic disease; cardiovascular disease, hypertension, older adults; children, pregnancy (category B).

ROUTE & DOSAGE

Allergic Rhinitis
Adult: **PO** 1.34 mg b.i.d., may increase up to 8.04 mg/d
Child: **PO** >6 y: 0.67 mg b.i.d., may increase up to 4.02 mg/d; <6 y: 0.335–0.67 mg/kg/d in 2 divided doses (max: 1.34 mg/d)

Allergic Urticaria
Adult: **PO** 2.68 mg b.i.d. or t.i.d., may increase up to 8.04 mg/d
Child: **PO** 1.34 mg b.i.d., may increase up to 4.02 mg/d

ADMINISTRATION

Oral
- Drug may be administered with food, water, or milk to reduce possibility of gastric irritation.
- Older adult patients usually require less than average adult dose.
- Store at 15°–30° C (59°–86° F) unless otherwise directed.

ADVERSE EFFECTS (≥1%) **Body as a Whole:** <u>Anaphylaxis</u>, excess perspiration, chills. **CV:** Hypotension, palpitation, tachycardia, extrasystoles. **GI:** *Dry mouth,* epigastric distress, anorexia, nausea, vomiting, diarrhea, constipation. **Hematologic:** Hemolytic anemia, thrombocytopenia, <u>agranulocytosis</u>. **CNS:** Sedation, *transient drowsiness,* dry nose and throat, headache, dizziness, weakness, fatigue, disturbed coordination; confusion, restlessness, nervousness, hysteria, convulsions, tremors, irritability, euphoria, insomnia, paresthesias, neuritis. **Respiratory:** Dry nose and throat, thickening of bronchial secretions, tightness of chest, wheezing, nasal stuffiness. **Skin:** Urticaria, rash, photosensitivity. **Special Senses:** Vertigo, tinnitus, acute labyrinthitis, blurred

Common adverse effects in *italic*, life-threatening effects <u>underlined</u>; generic names in **bold**; classifications in SMALL CAPS; ♣ Canadian drug name; ❂ Prototype drug

343

vision, diplopia. **Urogenital:** Difficult urination, urinary retention, early menses.

INTERACTIONS Drug: Alcohol and other CNS DEPRESSANTS increase sedation; MAO INHIBITORS may prolong and intensify anticholinergic effects.

PHARMACOKINETICS Absorption: Readily from GI tract. **Peak:** 5–7 h. **Duration:** 10–12 h. **Distribution:** Into breast milk. **Metabolism:** In liver. **Elimination:** In urine.

CLINICAL IMPLICATIONS

Assessment & Drug Effects

- Monitor for drowsiness, poor coordination, or dizziness, especially in the older adult or debilitated. Supervision of ambulation may be warranted.
- Assess for symptomatic relief with use of the medication.
- Lab tests: Periodic hematological studies with long-term use.

Patient & Family Education

- Check with physician before taking alcohol or other CNS depressants, since effects may be additive.
- Clemastine may cause lethargy and drowsiness; therefore, necessary safety precautions should be taken.
- Older adults should make position changes slowly and in stages, particularly from recumbent to upright posture, as dizziness and hypotension occur more frequently than in younger patients.
- Avoid driving and other potentially hazardous activities until response to the drug has been established.
- Frequent sips of water or sugarless hard candy to relieve dry mouth.

CLINDAMYCIN HYDROCHLORIDE Ⓟ

(klin-da-mye′sin)
Cleocin, Dalacin C ♦

CLINDAMYCIN PALMITATE HYDROCHLORIDE
Cleocin Pediatric

CLINDAMYCIN PHOSPHATE
Cleocin Phosphate, Cleocin T, Dalacin C, Evoclin, Cleocin Vaginal Ovules or Cream

Classifications: ANTIBIOTIC
Therapeutic: ANTIBIOTIC
Pregnancy Category: B

AVAILABILITY 75 mg, 150 mg, 300 mg capsules; 75 mg/5 mL oral suspension; 150 mg/mL injection; 2% vaginal cream; 100 mg suppositories; 10 mg gel, lotion; 1% foam

ACTION & *THERAPEUTIC EFFECT*
Semisynthetic derivative of lincomycin with a greater degree of antibacterial activity in vitro, better absorption, and lower incidence of GI adverse effects than lincomycin. Suppresses protein synthesis by binding to 50 S subunits of bacterial ribosomes, and, therefore, inhibits other antibiotics (e.g., erythromycin) that act at this site. *Particularly effective against susceptible strains of anaerobic streptococci. Also effective against aerobic gram-positive cocci.*

USES Serious infections when less toxic alternatives are inappropriate. Topical applications are used in treatment of acne vulgaris. Vaginal applications are used in treatment of bacterial vaginosis in nonpregnant women.
UNLABELED USES In combination with pyrimethamine for toxoplasmosis in patients with AIDS.

CONTRAINDICATIONS History of hypersensitivity to clindamycin or lincomycin; history of regional enteritis, ulcerative colitis, or antibiotic-associated colitis; viral infection.

CAUTIOUS USE History of GI disease, renal or hepatic disease; atopic individuals (history of eczema, asthma, hay fever); older patients >60 y; pregnancy (category B).

ROUTE & DOSAGE

Moderate to Severe Infections

Adult: **PO** 150–450 mg q6h **IM/IV** 600–1200 mg/d in divided doses (max: 2700 mg/d)
Child: **PO** 10–30 mg/kg/d q6–8h **IM/IV** 20–40 mg/kg/d in divided doses
Neonate: **IM/IV** 15–20 mg/kg/d in divided doses

Acne Vulgaris

Adult: **Topical** Apply to affected areas b.i.d.; 1% foam qd application

Bacterial Vaginosis

Adult: **Topical** Insert 1 suppository intravaginally at bedtime times 3 d, or insert 1 applicator full of cream intravaginally at bedtime times 7 d

ADMINISTRATION

- Determine history of any previous sensitivities to drugs or other allergens prior to administration.

Oral

- Administer clindamycin capsules with a full [240 mL (8 oz)] glass of water to prevent esophagitis.
- Note expiration date of oral solution; retains potency for 14 d at room temperature. Do not refrigerate, as chilling causes thickening and thus makes pouring it difficult.

Intramuscular

- Deep IM injection is recommended. Rotate injection sites and observe daily for evidence of inflammatory reaction. Single IM doses should not exceed 600 mg.

Intravenous

IV administration to neonates, infants, and children: Verify correct IV concentration and rate of infusion with physician.

PREPARE: **Intermittent:** Each 18 mg must be diluted with at least 1 mL of D5W, NS, D5/.45% NaCl, or other compatible solution. Final concentration should never exceed 18 mg/mL.

ADMINISTER: **Intermittent:** Never give a bolus dose. Do not give >1200 mg in a single 1-h infusion. Infusion rate should not exceed 30 mg/min.

INCOMPATIBILITIES **Solution/additive: Aminophylline, ceftriaxone, ciprofloxacin, fluconazole, ranitidine, tobramycin. Y-site: Allopurinol, azithromycin, doxapram, filgrastim, fluconazole, idarubicin.**

- Store in tight containers at 15°–30° C (59°–86° F) unless otherwise directed.

ADVERSE EFFECTS (≥1%) **Body as a Whole:** Fever, serum sickness, sensitization, swelling of face (following topical use), generalized myalgia, superinfections, proctitis, vaginitis, pain, induration, sterile abscess (following IM injections); thrombophlebitis (IV infusion). **CV:** Hypotension (following IM), <u>cardiac arrest</u> (rapid IV). **GI:** *Diarrhea,* abdominal pain, flatulence, bloating, *nausea, vomiting,* <u>pseudomembranous colitis</u>; esophageal irritation, loss of taste, medicinal taste (high IV doses), jaundice, abnormal

---

Common adverse effects in *italic*, life-threatening effects <u>underlined</u>; generic names in **bold**; classifications in SMALL CAPS; ♣ Canadian drug name; ◉ Prototype drug

345

liver function tests. **Hematologic:** Leukopenia, eosinophilia, <u>agranulocytosis</u>, thrombocytopenia. **Skin:** *Skin rashes*, urticaria, pruritus, dryness, contact dermatitis, gram-negative folliculitis, irritation, oily skin.

DIAGNOSTIC TEST INTERFERENCE

Clindamycin may cause increases in *serum alkaline phosphatase, bilirubin, creatine phosphokinase (CPK)* from muscle irritation following IM injection; *AST, ALT.*

INTERACTIONS **Drug:** Chloramphenicol, erythromycin possibly are mutually antagonistic to clindamycin; neuromuscular blocking action enhanced by NEUROMUSCULAR BLOCKING AGENTS **(atracurium, tubocurarine, pancuronium).**

PHARMACOKINETICS **Absorption:** Approximately 90% absorbed from GI tract; 10% of topical application is absorbed through skin. **Peak:** 45–60 min PO; 3 h IM. **Duration:** 6 h PO; 8–12 h IM. **Distribution:** Widely distributed except for CNS; crosses placenta; distributed into breast milk. **Metabolism:** In liver. **Elimination:** In urine and feces. **Half-Life:** 2–3 h.

CLINICAL IMPLICATIONS

Assessment & Drug Effects

- Lab tests: Culture and susceptibility testing should be performed initially and periodically during therapy. Periodic CBC with differential and platelet count.
- Monitor BP and pulse in patients receiving drug parenterally. Hypotension has occurred following IM injection. Advise patient to remain recumbent following drug administration until BP has stabilized.
- Severe diarrhea and colitis, including pseudomembranous colitis, have been associated with oral (highest incidence), parenteral, and topical clindamycin. Report

immediately the onset of watery diarrhea, with or without fever; passage of tarry or bloody stools, pus, intestinal tissue, or mucus; abdominal cramps, or ileus. Symptoms may appear within a few days to 2 wk after therapy is begun or up to several weeks following cessation of therapy.

- Closely observe older adult and bedridden patients, as they are at a higher risk of developing severe colitis.
- Be alert to signs of superinfection (see Appendix F).
- Be alert for signs of anaphylactoid reactions (see Appendix F), that require immediate attention.

Patient & Family Education

- Take drug for the full course of therapy as prescribed.
- Report loose stools or diarrhea promptly.
- Stop drug therapy if significant diarrhea develops (more than 5 loose stools daily) and notify physician.
- Do not self-medicate with antidiarrheal preparations. Antiperistaltic agents may prolong and worsen diarrhea by delaying removal of toxins from colon.
- If using topical preparation for acne, discontinue other acne preparations unless otherwise directed by physician. Keep medication away from eyes.
- Since 10% absorption of topical medication is possible, report the onset of systemic reactions to physician.

CLIOQUINOL (IODOCHLORHYDROXYQUIN)

(klee-oh-kwee′nole)
Torofor, Vioform

Classifications: ANTIBIOTIC; ANTIFUNGAL

Common adverse effects in *italic*, life-threatening effects <u>underlined</u>; generic names in **bold**; classifications in SMALL CAPS; ◆ Canadian drug name; ☯ Prototype drug

Therapeutic: ANTIBIOTIC; ANTIFUNGAL
Pregnancy Category: C

AVAILABILITY 3% cream, ointment

ACTION & *THERAPEUTIC EFFECT*
Halogenated quinolone is a broad-spectrum topical antiinfective. *Antifungal and antibacterial in activity. Available OTC.*

USES Topically for treatment of inflamed cutaneous conditions such as eczema, athlete's foot, and other fungal conditions.

CONTRAINDICATIONS Hypersensitivity to chloroxine, iodine, or iodine-containing preparations; tuberculosis; vaccinia, varicella, or other viral skin conditions; severe renal disease; hepatic damage; thyroid disorder; children <2 y; pregnancy (category C), lactation.

ROUTE & DOSAGE

Inflamed Cutaneous Conditions
Adult: **Topical** Apply thin layer to affected area b.i.d. or t.i.d. for 1 wk only

ADMINISTRATION
Topical
- Wash area to be treated with soap and water and dry thoroughly before each application. Consult physician.
- Do not apply an occlusive dressing without a physician's order.
- Preserve in tightly covered, light-resistant containers at 15°–30° C (59°–86° F) unless otherwise directed.

ADVERSE EFFECTS (≥1%) **Body as a Whole:** Iodism, hypersensitivity reaction, slight enlargement of thyroid gland, hair loss, subacute myeloptic neuropathy. **Hematologic:** Agranulocytosis. **Skin:** Local burning, irritation, redness, swelling, itching, rash, staining of hair and skin.

DIAGNOSTIC TEST INTERFERENCE
Possibility of elevated *PBI*, decreased *iodine 131 thyroidal uptake,* and elevation of *butanol-extractable iodine (BEI).* False-positive *ferric chloride test* for *phenylketonuria (PKU)* may result if clioquinol is present on diaper or in urine.

PHARMACOKINETICS Absorption:
Minimally absorbed through intact skin. **Elimination:** Some is rapidly excreted in urine; the rest may persist in body 1 mo or more.

CLINICAL IMPLICATIONS
Assessment & Drug Effects
- Monitor for signs of skin irritation. Notify physician if they appear. Drug may be discontinued.
- Monitor for signs of systemic absorption such as thyroid enlargement and hair loss. Notify physician if they occur. Drug may be discontinued.

Patient & Family Education
- Avoid contact of drug in or around eyes. Drug may stain fabric, skin, or hair yellow on contact.
- Clioquinol should be discontinued if skin irritation, rash, or other signs of sensitivity or systemic absorption develop. Report to physician.
- Treatment is usually continued 4 wk for athlete's foot or ringworm and 2 wk for jock itch.
- Notify physician if there is no improvement within 1–2 wk. Apply the drug as directed and only for the period of time prescribed.

CLOBETASOL PROPIONATE

(cloe-bay'ta-sol)
Clobex, Temovate, Embeline gel; Olux Foam
Pregnancy Category: C
See Appendix A-4.

CLOCORTOLONE PIVALATE

(kloe-kor'toe-lone)
Cloderm
Pregnancy Category: C
See Appendix A-4.

CLOFARABINE

(clo-fa-ra'been)
Clolar

Classifications: ANTINEOPLASTIC; PURINE ANTIMETABOLITE
Therapeutic: ANTINEOPLASTIC; ANTIMETABOLITE
Prototype: 6-Mercaptopurine
Pregnancy Category: D

AVAILABILITY 1 mg/mL injection.

ACTION & *THERAPEUTIC EFFECT*
Clofarabine inhibits DNA repair within cancer cells, thus interfering with mitosis; it also disrupts the mitochondrial membrane, leading to cancer cell death. *Cytotoxic to rapidly proliferating and quiescent cancer cells.*

USES Treatment of persons 1–21 y of age with relapsed or refractory acute lymphocytic leukemia (ALL) after at least 2 prior regimens.

CONTRAINDICATIONS Severe bone marrow suppression; active infection; pregnancy (category D); lactation.

CAUTIOUS USE Renal or hepatic function impairment; thrombocytopenia; neutropenia; previous chemotherapy or radiation therapy; females of childbearing age; history of viral infections such as herpes; history of cardiac disease or hypotension.

ROUTE & DOSAGE

Acute Lymphocytic Leukemia
Adult/Adolescent/Child: **IV** 52 mg/m^2/d for 5 d

ADMINISTRATION

▪ Do not give drugs with known renal toxicity during the 5 d of clofarabine administration.

Intravenous

***PREPARE:* IV Infusion:** Withdraw required dose from vial using a 0.2 micron filter syringe. Further dilute with D5W or NS prior to infusion.
***ADMINISTER:* IV Infusion:** Give over 2 h. Note: It is recommended that IV fluids be given continuously throughout the 5 d of clofarabine administration.

▪ Store diluted solution at room temperature. Use within 24 h of mixing.

ADVERSE EFFECTS (≥1%) **CNS:** Anxiety, depression, dizziness, headache, irritability, somnolence. **CV:** *Tachycardia,* pericardial infusion, left ventricular systolic dysfunction (LSVT). **GI:** *Vomiting, nausea, and diarrhea,* abdominal pain, constipation. **Hematologic/Lymphatic:** *Anemia, leukopenia, thrombocytopenia, neutropenia, febrile neutropenia.* **Hepatic:** Jaundice, hepatomegaly. **Metabolic:** Anorexia, decreased appetite, edema,

Common adverse effects in *italic*, life-threatening effects <u>underlined</u>; generic names in **bold**; classifications in SMALL CAPS; ♦ Canadian drug name; ☻ Prototype drug

decreased weight. **Musculoskeletal:** Arthralgia, back pain, myalgia. **Respiratory:** Cough, dyspnea, epistaxis, pleural effusion, respiratory distress. **Skin:** Dermatitis, contusion, dry skin, erythema, palmar-plantar erythrodysesthesia syndrome, pruritus. **Body as a Whole:** Increase risk of infection.

PHARMACOKINETICS Distribution: 47% protein bound. **Metabolism:** Negligible. **Elimination:** Primarily unchanged in the urine. **Half-Life:** 5.2 h.

CLINICAL IMPLICATIONS

Assessment & Drug Effects

- Monitor vital signs frequently during infusion of clofarabine.
- Monitor closely for S&S of capillary leak syndrome or systemic inflammatory response syndrome (e.g., tachypnea, tachycardia, hypotension, pulmonary edema). If either is suspected, immediately DC IV, institute supportive measures and notify physician.
- Monitor I&O rates and pattern and watch for S&S of dehydration, including dizziness, lightheadedness, fainting spells, or decreased urine output.
- Withhold drug and notify physician if hypotension develops for any reason during 5-d period of drug administration.
- Lab tests: Baseline and periodic CBC and platelet counts (more frequent with cytopenias); frequent LFTs and kidney function test during the 5 d of clofarabine therapy.

Patient & Family Education

- Report any distressing adverse effect of therapy to physician.
- Use effective measures to avoid pregnancy while taking this drug.

CLOFIBRATE

(kloe-fy′brate)

Atromid-S, Claripex ♦, Novofibrate ♦

Classifications: ANTILIPEMIC; FIBRATE

Therapeutic: CHOLESTEROL-LOWERING AGENT; ANTIHYPERLIPIDEMIC

Prototype: Fenofibrate

Pregnancy Category: C

AVAILABILITY 500 mg capsules

ACTION & *THERAPEUTIC EFFECT*

Structurally related to gemfibrozil. Mechanism of action appears to inhibit cholesterol biosynthesis prior to transfer of triglycerides from liver to serum. Interferes with binding of free fatty acids to albumin and increases fecal excretion of neutral sterols. It affects the mobilization of cholesterol from tissue. *Clofibrate reduces very low density lipoproteins (VLDL) to a greater extent than it reduces low density lipoproteins (LDL). It also lowers serum triglycerides more dramatically than cholesterol.*

USES Adjunct for treatment of severe primary (type III) hyperlipidemia.

UNLABELED USES Management of diabetes insipidus.

CONTRAINDICATIONS Severely impaired renal function or significant hepatic dysfunction, primary biliary cirrhosis; hypothyroidism; peptic ulcer disease; pregnancy (category C), lactation. Safe use in children <14 y not established.

CAUTIOUS USE History of jaundice or mild to moderate hepatic disease; gallstones; peptic ulcer; hy-

---

Common adverse effects in *italic*, life-threatening effects underlined; generic names in **bold**; classifications in SMALL CAPS; ♦ Canadian drug name; ◐ Prototype drug

pothyroidism; cardiovascular disease.

ROUTE & DOSAGE

Hyperlipidemia
Adult: **PO** 2 g/d in 2–4 divided doses
Diabetes Insipidus
Adult: **PO** 1.5–2 g/d in 2–4 divided doses

ADMINISTRATION

Oral
- If gastric distress is a problem, administer drug with meals.
- Preserve in closed, light-resistant containers at 15°–30° C (59°–86° F) unless otherwise directed.

ADVERSE EFFECTS (≥1%) **CV:** Increase or decrease in angina, CHF, arrhythmias. **GI:** *Nausea,* vomiting, loose stools, diarrhea, flatulence, abdominal distress, gastritis, stomatitis, cholelithiasis. **Hematologic:** Neutropenia, leukopenia, anemia, eosinophilia, agranulocytosis, potentiation of anticoagulant effect. **Metabolic:** Elevated AST and ALT. **Musculoskeletal:** Flu-like symptoms. **CNS:** Drowsiness, dizziness, headache. **Skin:** Swelling and phlebitis at xanthoma sites, skin rash, allergy, urticaria, pruritus. **Urogenital:** Renal insufficiency, impotence, decreased libido.

DIAGNOSTIC TEST INTERFERENCE

Clofibrate therapy may lead to increased **BSP** retention, ***thymol*** turbidity; increased ***serum creatine phosphokinase (CPK); proteinuria,*** parodoxical increase in **LDL** or **cholesterol** levels (if there is a large decrease in VLDL level). Lower fasting ***blood glucose*** and ***serum insulin*** levels in patients with diabetes mellitus.

INTERACTIONS Drug: ORAL ANTICO-AGULANTS increase hypoprothrombinemia and increase risk of bleeding; **probenecid** increases effects of clofibrate; SULFONYLUREAS increase hypoglycemic effects.

PHARMACOKINETICS Absorption: Readily absorbed from GI tract. **Peak:** 4–6 h. **Distribution:** Distributed to extracellular space; crosses placenta; distribution into breast milk unknown. **Metabolism:** Hydrolyzed in plasma to clofibric acid, which is further metabolized in liver. **Elimination:** In urine. **Half-Life:** 12–35 h.

CLINICAL IMPLICATIONS

Assessment & Drug Effects
- Lab tests: Baseline and periodic lipid profile; periodic liver function tests, CBC, renal function tests, and determinations of plasma and urine steroid levels, serum electrolyte levels, and blood glucose.
- Therapeutic response generally occurs during the first or second month of therapy. Rebound may occur in second or third month, followed by a further decrease, and may also occur with sudden withdrawal of drug.
- Clofibrate therapy for increased serum cholesterol and triglycerides is generally withdrawn after 3 mo if the response is not adequate.

Patient & Family Education
- Report flu-like symptoms (malaise, muscle soreness, aching, weakness) promptly to physician. Other reportable conditions include leukopenia, pulmonary edema, and renal insufficiency (see Appendix F) and gastric pain, nausea, and vomiting.

- Women of childbearing years should be on birth control regimen. If pregnancy is desired, clofibrate therapy should be discontinued at least 2 mo before conception.
- Do not self-dose with OTC drugs without the approval of physician.

CLOMIPHENE CITRATE

(kloe'mi-feen)
Clomid, Milophene, Serophene
Classifications: HORMONE; OVULATION STIMULANT; ANTIESTROGENIC
Therapeutic: OVULATION STIMULANT
Pregnancy Category: X

AVAILABILITY 50 mg tablets

ACTION & *THERAPEUTIC EFFECT*
Oral nonsteroidal selective estrogen receptor modulator (SERM). Induces ovulation in selected infrequently ovulating or anovulatory women. Clomiphene blocks the normal negative feedback of circulating estradiol on the hypothalamus, preventing estrogen from lowering the output of gonadotropin releasing hormone (GnRH). It acts by binding to hypothalamic estrogen receptors, decreasing their numbers, and thereby inhibiting receptor replenishment. *Inhibition of receptor replenishment results in a false hypoestrogenic state which stimulates pituitary release of luteinizing hormone (LH), follicle-stimulating hormone (FSH), and gonadotropins, leading to ovarian stimulation.*

USES Infertility in appropriately selected women desiring pregnancy whose partners are fertile and potent.
UNLABELED USES Male infertility, menstrual abnormalities, gynecomastia, fibrocystic breast disease, regulation of cycles in patients using rhythm method of contraception, endometrial hyperplasia, persistent lactation.

CONTRAINDICATIONS Neoplastic lesions, ovarian cyst; hepatic disease or dysfunction; abnormal uterine bleeding; endometriosis; primary ovarian failure; men with testicular failure; untreated thyroid disease; visual abnormalities; major depression or psychosis; thrombophlebitis; pregnancy (category X); lactation.
CAUTIOUS USE Polycystic ovarian enlargement, pelvic discomfort, sensitivity to pituitary gonadotropins.

ROUTE & DOSAGE

Infertility
Adult: **PO First course:** 50 mg/d for 5 d; start on 5th day of cycle following start of spontaneous or induced bleeding (with progestin) or at any time in the patient who has had no recent uterine bleeding **Second course if ovulation:** Repeat first course until conception or for 3 cycles **Second course if no ovulation:** 100 mg/d for 5 d as above (max: 100 mg/d)

ADMINISTRATION

Oral
- Pretreatment with estrogen is indicated for the patient who has been hypoestrogenic for a long time. Estrogen therapy is stopped immediately before clomiphene therapy begins.
- Each course of therapy should start on or about the 5th cycle day once ovulation has been established.
- Store at 15°–30° C (59°–86° F) in tightly capped, light-resistant container.

Common adverse effects in *italic*, life-threatening effects <u>underlined</u>; generic names in **bold**; classifications in SMALL CAPS; ♣ Canadian drug name; ⊘ Prototype drug

351

ADVERSE EFFECTS (≥1%) **Body as a Whole:** *Vasomotor flushes,* breast discomfort, abdominal pain, heavy menses, exacerbation of endometriosis; mental depression, headache, fatigue, insomnia, dizziness, vertigo. **GI:** Nausea, vomiting, increased appetite with weight gain, constipation, bloating. **Endocrine:** Spontaneous abortion, multiple ovulations, ovarian failure, *ovarian hyperstimulation syndrome, enlarged ovaries with multiple follicular cysts.* **Special Senses:** Transient blurring, diplopia, scotomas, photophobia, floaters, prolonged after-images. **Urogenital:** Urinary frequency, polyuria.

DIAGNOSTIC TEST INTERFERENCE Clomiphene may increase BSP retention; **plasma transcortin, thyroxine** and **sex hormone binding globulin** levels. Also increases **follicle-stimulating** and **luteinizing hormone** secretion in most patients.

INTERACTIONS Drug: No clinically significant drug interactions established. **Herbal: Black cohosh** may antagonize infertility treatments.

PHARMACOKINETICS Absorption: Readily absorbed from GI tract. **Metabolism:** In liver. **Elimination:** Primarily in feces in 5 d; the remainder is excreted slowly from enterohepatic pool or is stored in body fat for later release. **Half-Life:** 5 d.

CLINICAL IMPLICATIONS

Assessment & Drug Effects

- Monitor for abnormal bleeding. If it occurs, full diagnostic measures are crucial. Report it immediately.
- Monitor for visual disturbances. Their occurrence indicates the need for a complete ophthalmologic evaluation. Drug will be stopped until symptoms subside.

- If clomiphene is continued more than 1 y, patient should have an ophthalmologic examination at regular intervals.
- Pelvic pain indicates the need for immediate pelvic examination for diagnostic purposes.

Patient & Family Education

- Take the medicine at same time every day to maintain drug levels and prevent forgetting a dose.
- Missed dose: Take drug as soon as possible. If not remembered until time for next dose, double the dose, then resume regular dosing schedule. If more than one dose is missed, check with physician.
- Incidence of multiple births during clomiphene use is reportedly increased to 6 times normal and appears to increase with dose increases.
- Patient who is going to respond usually ovulates 4–10 d after last day of treatment.
- Report these symptoms: hot flushes resembling those associated with menopause; nausea, vomiting, headache. Appropriate drug therapy may be prescribed. Symptoms disappear after clomiphene is discontinued.
- Reported promptly yellowing of eyes, light-colored stools, yellow, itchy skin, and fever symptomatic of jaundice.
- Stop taking clomiphene if pregnancy is suspected. Contact physician for a confirmatory examination.
- Because of the possibility of lightheadedness, dizziness, and visual disturbances, do not perform hazardous tasks requiring skill and coordination in an environment with variable lighting.
- Report promptly excessive weight gain, signs of edema, bloating, decreased urinary output.

CLOMIPRAMINE HYDROCHLORIDE

(clo-mi'pra-meen)

Anafranil

Classifications: PSYCHOTHERAPEUTIC; TRICYCLIC ANTIDEPRESSANT

Therapeutic: ANTIPSYCHOTIC; TRICYCLIC ANTIDEPRESSANT

Prototype: Imipramine

Pregnancy Category: C

AVAILABILITY 25 mg, 50 mg, 75 mg capsules

ACTION & *THERAPEUTIC EFFECT*
Inhibits the reuptake of norepinephrine and serotonin at the presynaptic neuron. Of the tricyclic antidepressants (TCAs), it is the most selective and potent inhibitor of serotonin (5-HT) reuptake. *The basis of its antidepressant effects is thought to be due to the elevated serum levels of norepinephrine and serotonin.*

USES Obsessive-compulsive disorder (OCD).

UNLABELED USES Panic disorder, anxiety, agoraphobia.

CONTRAINDICATIONS Hypersensitivity to other tricyclic compounds; acute recovery period after MI, QT elongation, cardiac arrhythmias (AV block, bundle-branch block); suicidal ideation; children <10 y, pregnancy (category C).

CAUTIOUS USE History of convulsive disorders, prostatic hypertrophy, urinary retention, cardiovascular, hepatic, GI, or blood disorders; history of seizure disorder; respiratory depression; older adults; diabetes mellitus; GERD; Parkinson's disease; closed angle glaucoma; asthma; bipolar disorder; history of suicidal ideation; lactation.

ROUTE & DOSAGE

Obsessive-Compulsive Disorder

Adult: **PO** 75–300 mg/d in divided doses

Child: **PO** 10–18 y: 100–200 mg/d in divided doses, start at 50 mg/d

Depression

Adult: **PO** 50–150 mg/d in single or divided doses

ADMINISTRATION

Oral

- Give in divided doses with meals to reduce GI adverse effects.
- Following titration to the full dose, drug may be given as a single dose at bedtime to reduce daytime sedation.
- Store at 15°–30° C (59°–86° F).

ADVERSE EFFECTS (≥1%) **Body as a Whole:** Diaphoresis. **CV:** Hypotension, tachycardia. **GI:** Constipation, *dry mouth*. **Endocrine:** Galactorrhea, hyperprolactinemia, amenorrhea, *weight gain*. **Hematologic:** Leukopenia, agranulocytosis, thrombocytopenia, anemia. **CNS:** Mania, *tremor*, dizziness, hyperthermia, neuroleptic malignant syndrome, seizures (especially with abrupt withdrawal). **Urogenital:** Delayed ejaculation, anorgasmia.

DIAGNOSTIC TEST INTERFERENCE
Clomipramine appears to elevate serum ***prolactin*** levels. ***Serum AST and ALT*** are elevated. Serum levels of ***triiodothyronine (T$_3$) and free triiodothyronine (FT$_3$)*** have been significantly reduced from baseline. ***Thyroxine-binding globulin (TBG)*** levels were increased from baseline, whereas ***thyroxine (T$_4$), free thyroxine (FT$_4$)***, and reverse T$_3$ were unchanged.

Common adverse effects in *italic*, life-threatening effects underlined; generic names in **bold**; classifications in SMALL CAPS; ♣ Canadian drug name; ⊕ Prototype drug

353

INTERACTIONS Drug: MAO INHIBITORS may precipitate hyperpyrexic crisis, tachycardia, or seizures; ANTIHYPERTENSIVE AGENTS potentiate orthostatic hypotension; CNS DEPRESSANTS, **alcohol** add to CNS depression; **norepinephrine** and other SYMPATHOMIMETICS may increase cardiac toxicity; **cimetidine** decreases hepatic metabolism, thus increasing imipramine levels; **methylphenidate** inhibits metabolism of **imipramine** and thus may increase its toxicity. **Herbal: Ginkgo** may decrease seizure threshold; **St. John's wort** may cause serotonin syndrome.

PHARMACOKINETICS Absorption: Rapidly absorbed from GI tract; 20–78% reaches systemic circulation. **Onset:** Depression: approx 2 wk; OCD: approx 4–10 wk. **Peak:** 2–6 h. **Distribution:** Widely distributed including the CSF; crosses placenta. **Metabolism:** Extensive first-pass metabolism in the liver; active metabolite is desmethylclomipramine. **Elimination:** 50–60% in urine, 24–32% in feces. **Half-Life:** 20–30 h.

CLINICAL IMPLICATIONS

Assessment & Drug Effects

- Monitor for seizures, especially in those with predisposing factors such as alcoholism, brain injury, or concurrent therapy with other drugs that lower seizure threshold.
- Lab tests: Periodic CBC with differential, platelet count, and Hct and Hgb. Monitor liver functions, especially with long-term therapy.
- Monitor for and report signs of neuroleptic malignant syndrome (see Appendix F).
- Monitor for sedation and vertigo, especially at the beginning of therapy and following dosage increases. Supervision of ambulation may be indicated.

- Notify physician of fever and complaints of sore throat since these may indicated need to rule out adverse hematologic changes.

Patient & Family Education

- Do not take nonprescribed drugs or discontinue therapy without consent of physician. Abrupt discontinuation may cause nausea, headache, malaise, or seizures.
- Men should understand that the drug may cause impotence or ejaculation failure. Advise them to report this problem to physician.
- Report promptly a sore throat accompanied by fever.
- Use caution with ambulation until response to drug is known.
- Moderate alcohol intake since it may potentiate adverse drug effects.

CLONAZEPAM

(kloe-na′zi-pam)
Klonopin, Klonopin Wafers, Rivotril ♦
Classifications: ANTICONVULSANT; BENZODIAZEPINE
Therapeutic: ANTICONVULSANT
Prototype: Diazepam
Pregnancy Category: D
Controlled Substance: Schedule IV

AVAILABILITY 0.5 mg, 1 mg, 2 mg tablets; 0.125 mg, 0.25 mg, 0.5 mg, 1 mg, and 2 mg orally disintegrating wafers

ACTION & *THERAPEUTIC EFFECT*

Benzodiazepine derivative with strong anticonvulsant activity and several other pharmacologic properties. It prevents seizures by potentiation of the effects of GABA, an inhibitory neurotransmitter. Suppresses the spread of seizure activity in the cortex, thalamus, and limbic regions of the brain. *Suppresses spike and wave discharge in absence seizures (petit mal) and decreases amplitude, frequency, duration, and spread of discharge in minor motor seizures.*

USES Alone or with other drugs in absence, myoclonic, and akinetic seizures, Lennox-Gastaut syndrome, absence seizures refractory to succinimides or valproic acid, and for infantile spasms and restless legs.
UNLABELED USES Panic disorder, complex partial seizure pattern, and generalized tonic-clonic convulsions.

CONTRAINDICATIONS Hypersensitivity to benzodiazepines; liver disease; acute narrow-angle glaucoma; pulmonary disease, COPD; coma or CNS depression; pregnancy (category D), lactation; children <10 y.
CAUTIOUS USE Renal or hepatic disease; COPD; drug-controlled open-angle glaucoma; bipolar disorder; preexisting depression; addiction-prone individuals; neuromuscular disease; children (because of unknown consequences of long-term use on growth and development); patient with mixed seizure disorders.

ROUTE & DOSAGE

Seizures
Adult: **PO** 1.5 mg/d in 3 divided doses, increased by 0.5–1 mg q3d until seizures are controlled or until intolerable adverse effects (max recommended dose: 20 mg/d)
Child: **PO** <10 y, 0.01–0.03 mg/kg/d (not to exceed 0.05 mg/kg/d) in 3 divided doses; may increase by 0.25–0.5 mg q3d until seizures are controlled or until intolerable adverse effects (max recommended dose: 0.2 mg/kg/d)

Panic Disorders
Adult: **PO** 1–2 mg/d in divided doses (max: 4 mg/d)

ADMINISTRATION

Oral
- Give largest dose at bedtime if daily dose cannot be equally divided.
- Place wafer form on tongue to dissolve.
- If clonazepam is to replace a different anticonvulsant, verify whether or not the prior drug should be gradually tapered.
- Store in tightly closed container protected from light at 15°–30° C (59°–86° F) unless otherwise specified.

ADVERSE EFFECTS (≥1%) **CV:** Palpitations. **GI:** Dry mouth, sore gums, anorexia, coated tongue, increased salivation, increased appetite, nausea, constipation, diarrhea. **Hematologic:** Anemia, leukopenia, thrombocytopenia, eosinophilia. **CNS:** *Drowsiness, sedation, ataxia,* insomnia, aphonia, choreiform movements, coma, dysarthria, "glassy-eyed" appearance, headache, hemiparesis, hypotonia, slurred speech, tremor, vertigo, confusion, depression, hallucinations, aggressive behavior problems, hysteria, suicide attempt. **Respiratory:** Chest congestion, respiratory depression, rhinorrhea, dyspnea, hypersecretion in upper respiratory passages. **Skin:** Hirsutism, hair loss, skin rash, ankle and facial edema. **Special Senses:** Diplopia, nystagmus, abnormal eye movements. **Urogenital:** Increased libido, dysuria, enuresis, nocturia, urinary retention.

DIAGNOSTIC TEST INTERFERENCE Clonazepam causes transient elevations of *serum transaminase* and *alkaline phosphatase.*

Common adverse effects in *italic*, life-threatening effects underlined; generic names in **bold**; classifications in SMALL CAPS; ♣ Canadian drug name; ⓟ Prototype drug

355

INTERACTIONS Drug: Alcohol and other CNS DEPRESSANTS increase sedation and CNS depression; may increase **phenytoin** levels. **Herbal: Kava-kava, valerian** may potentiate sedation.

PHARMACOKINETICS Absorption: Readily absorbed from GI tract. **Onset:** 60 min. **Peak:** 1–2 h. **Duration:** Up to 12 h in adults; 6–8 h in children. **Distribution:** Crosses placenta; distributed into breast milk. **Metabolism:** In liver. **Elimination:** In urine primarily as metabolites. **Half-Life:** 18–40 h.

CLINICAL IMPLICATIONS

Assessment & Drug Effects

- Monitor for signs of suicidal ideation in depressive individuals.
- Monitor I&O ratio and patterns: Excess accumulation of metabolites due to impaired excretion leads to toxicity.
- Assess carefully for signs of overdosage or drug interaction, i.e., increased depressant adverse effects, if multiple anticonvulsants are being given.
- Lab tests: Periodic liver function tests, platelet counts, blood counts, and renal function tests.
- Watch patient to see that he or she does not cheek the tablet. Both psychological and physical dependence may occur in the patient on long-term, high-dose therapy. Limit availability of large amounts of drug in the addiction-prone individual.
- Monitor for S&S of overdose, including somnolence, confusion, irritability, sweating, muscle and abdominal cramps, diminished reflexes, coma.

Patient & Family Education

- Report loss of seizure control promptly. Anticonvulsant activity is often lost after 3 mo of therapy; dosage adjustment may reestablish efficacy.
- Do not abruptly discontinue this drug. Abrupt withdrawal can precipitate seizures. Other withdrawal symptoms include convulsion, tremor, abdominal and muscle cramps, vomiting, sweating.
- Take drug as prescribed and do not alter dosing regimen without consulting physician.
- Do not self-medicate with OTC drugs before consulting the physician.
- Do not drive a car or engage in other activities requiring mental alertness and physical coordination until reaction to the drug is known. Drowsiness occurs in approximately 50% of patients.
- Carry identification (e.g., Medic Alert) bearing information about medication in use and the diagnosis.

CLONIDINE HYDROCHLORIDE

(kloe'ni-deen)

Catapres, Catapres-TTS, Dixaril ◆, Duraclon
Classifications: CENTRAL-ACTING ANTIHYPERTENSIVE; ANALGESIC
Therapeutic: ANTIHYPERTENSIVE, CENTRAL-ACTING; ANALGESIC
Prototype: Methyldopa
Pregnancy Category: C

AVAILABILITY 0.1 mg, 0.2 mg, 0.3 mg tablets; 0.1 mg/24 h, 0.2 mg/24 h, 0.3 mg/24 h transdermal patch; 100 mcg/mL, 500 mcg/mL injection

ACTION & *THERAPEUTIC EFFECT*
Centrally acting antiadrenergic derivative. Stimulates alpha$_2$-adrenergic receptors in CNS to inhibit sympathetic vasomotor centers. Central actions reduce plasma concentra-

tions of norepinephrine. It decreases systolic and diastolic BP and heart rate. Orthostatic effects tend to be mild and occur infrequently. *Decreases systolic and diastolic BP and heart rate. Reportedly minimizes or eliminates many of the common clinical S&S associated with withdrawal of heroin, methadone, or other opiates.*

USES Step 2 drug in stepped-care approach to treatment of hypertension, either alone or with diuretic or other antihypertensive agents. Epidural administration as adjunct therapy for severe pain.

UNLABELED USES Prophylaxis for migraine; treatment of dysmenorrhea, menopausal flushing, diarrhea, paroxysmal localized hyperhidroses; alcohol, smoking, opiate, and benzodiazepine withdrawal; in the clonidine suppression test for diagnosis of pheochromocytoma; Gilles de la Tourette syndrome; attention deficit disorder with hyperactivity (ADDH) in children.

CONTRAINDICATIONS Anticoagulant therapy, coagulopathy; use of clonidine patch in polyarteritis nodosa, scleroderma, SLE on affected areas; pregnancy (category C), lactation.

CAUTIOUS USE Severe coronary insufficiency, recent MI, sinus node dysfunction, cerebrovascular disease; diabetes mellitus; older adult; chronic renal failure; Raynaud's disease, thromboangiitis obliterans; history of major depression.

ROUTE & DOSAGE

Hypertension

Adult: **PO** 0.1 mg b.i.d. or t.i.d., may increase by 0.1–0.2 mg/d until desired response is achieved (max: 2.4 mg/d)

Transdermal 0.1 mg patch once q7d, may increase by 0.1 mg q1–2 wk
Geriatric: **PO** Start with 0.1 mg once daily
Child: **PO** 5–10 mcg/kg/d divided q8–12h, may increase to 5–25 mcg/kg/d divided q6h (max: 0.9 mg/d)

Severe Pain

Adult: **Epidural** Start infusion at 30 mcg/h and titrate to response. Use rates >40 mcg/h with caution
Child: **Epidural** Start infusion at 0.5 mcg/kg/h and titrate to response

ADDH

Child: **PO** 5 mcg/kg/d in 4 divided doses (average dose, 0.15–0.2 mg/d) **Transdermal** 0.2–0.3 mg/d q5–7d

ADMINISTRATION

- Give last PO dose immediately before patient retires to ensure overnight BP control and to minimize daytime drowsiness.
- Oral dosage is increased gradually over a period of weeks so as not to lower BP abruptly (especially important in the older adult). Follow-up visits should be scheduled every 2–4 wk until BP stabilizes, then every 2–4 mo.
- Apply transdermal patch to dry skin, free of hair and rash. Avoid irritated, abraded, or scarred skin. Recommended areas for applying transdermal patch are upper outer arm and anterior chest. Less drug is absorbed from thighs. Rotate application sites and keep a record.
- During change from PO clonidine to transdermal system, PO clonidine should be maintained for at least 24 h after patch is applied. Consult physician.

Common adverse effects in *italic*, life-threatening effects underlined; generic names in **bold**; classifications in SMALL CAPS; ♣ Canadian drug name; ⓟ Prototype drug

357

- Do not abruptly discontinue drug. It should be withdrawn over a period of 2–4 d. Abrupt withdrawal resembles sympathetic stimulation and may result in restlessness and headache 2–3 h after a missed dose and a hypertensive crisis within 8–18 h.
- Store in tightly closed container at 15°–30° C (59°–86° F) unless otherwise directed.

ADVERSE EFFECTS (≥1%) **CV:** *Hypotension (epidural),* postural hypotension (mild), peripheral edema, ECG changes, tachycardia, bradycardia, flushing, rapid increase in BP with abrupt withdrawal. **GI:** *Dry mouth, constipation,* abdominal pain, pseudo-obstruction of large bowel, altered taste, nausea, vomiting, hepatitis, hyperbilirubinemia, weight gain (sodium retention). **CNS:** *Drowsiness, sedation,* dizziness, headache, fatigue, weakness, sluggishness, dyspnea, vivid dreams, nightmares, insomnia, behavior changes, agitation, hallucination, nervousness, restlessness, anxiety, mental depression. **Skin:** Rash, pruritus, thinning of hair, exacerbation of psoriasis; with transdermal patch: hyperpigmentation, recurrent herpes simplex, skin irritation, contact dermatitis, mild erythema. **Special Senses:** Dry eyes. **Urogenital:** Impotence, loss of libido.

DIAGNOSTIC TEST INTERFERENCE Possibility of decreased urinary excretion of **aldosterone, catecholamines,** and **VMA** (however, sudden withdrawal of clonidine may cause increases in these values); transient increases in **blood glucose;** weakly positive **direct antiglobulin (Coombs') tests.**

INTERACTIONS Drug: Alcohol and other CNS DEPRESSANTS add to CNS depression; TRICYCLIC ANTIDEPRESSANTS may reduce antihypertensive effects. OPIATE ANALGESICS increase hypotension with epidural clonidine. Increased risk of bradycardia or AV block when epidural clonidine is used with **digoxin,** CALCIUM CHANNEL BLOCKERS, or BETA-BLOCKERS.

PHARMACOKINETICS Absorption: Readily absorbed from GI tract. **Onset:** 30–60 min PO; 1–3 d transdermal. **Peak:** 2–4 h PO; 2–3 d transdermal. **Duration:** 8 h PO; 7 d transdermal. **Distribution:** Widely distributed; crosses blood–brain barrier; not known if crosses placenta or distributed into breast milk. **Metabolism:** In liver. **Elimination:** 80% in urine, 20% in feces. **Half-Life:** 6–20 h.

CLINICAL IMPLICATIONS

Assessment & Drug Effects

- Monitor BR closely. Determine positional changes (supine, sitting, standing).
- With epidural administration, frequently monitor BP and HR. Hypotension is a common side effect that may require intervention.
- Monitor BP closely whenever a drug is added to or withdrawn from therapeutic regimen.
- Monitor I&O during period of dosage adjustment. Report change in I&O ratio or change in voiding pattern.
- Determine weight daily. Patients not receiving a concomitant diuretic agent may gain weight, particularly during first 3 or 4 d of therapy, because of marked sodium and water retention.
- Supervise closely patients with history of mental depression, as they may be subject to further depressive episodes.

Patient & Family Education

- Although postural hypotension occurs infrequently, make position

Common adverse effects in *italic*, life-threatening effects underlined; generic names in **bold**; classifications in SMALL CAPS; ✤ Canadian drug name; ⊙ Prototype drug

changes slowly, and in stages, particularly from recumbent to upright position, and dangle and move legs a few minutes before standing. Lie down immediately if faintness or dizziness occurs.

- Avoid potentially hazardous activities until reaction to drug has been determined due to possible sedative effects.
- Do not omit doses or stop the drug without consulting the physician.
- Do not take OTC medications, alcohol, or other CNS depressants without prior discussion with physician.
- Examine site when transdermal patch is removed and report to physician if erythema, rash, irritation, or hyperpigmentation occurs.
- If transdermal patch loosens, tape it in place with adhesive. The patch should never be cut or trimmed.

CLOPIDOGREL BISULFATE ℗

(clo-pi′do-grel)
Plavix
Classifications: ANTICOAGULANTS; ANTIPLATELET AGENT
Therapeutic: ANTICOAGULANTS; ANTI-PLATELET AGENT
Pregnancy Category: B

AVAILABILITY 75 mg tablets

ACTION & *THERAPEUTIC EFFECT*
Inhibits platelet aggregation by selectively preventing the binding of adenosine diphosphate to its platelet receptor. It is an analog of ticlopidine. The drug's effect on the adenosine diphosphate receptor of a platelet is irreversible. *Clopidogrel prolongs bleeding time, thereby reducing atherosclerotic events in high-risk patients.*

USES Secondary prevention of MI, stroke, and vascular death in patients with recent MI, stroke, unstable angina or established peripheral arterial disease.
UNLABELED USES Reduction of restenosis after stent placement.

CONTRAINDICATIONS Hypersensitivity to clopidogrel; intracranial hemorrhage, peptic ulcer, or any other active pathologic bleeding. Discontinue clopidogrel 7 d before surgery and during lactation. Safety and efficacy not established in children.
CAUTIOUS USE Concurrent use with drugs that might induce gastrointestinal bleeding; GI bleeding, peptic ulcer disease; hepatic impairment (moderate to severe); severe renal impairment; patients at risk for increased bleeding; pregnancy (category B).

ROUTE & DOSAGE

Secondary Prevention
Adult: **PO** 75 mg q.d.

ADMINISTRATION

Oral
- Do not administer to persons with active pathologic bleeding.
- Discontinue drug 7 d prior to surgery.
- Store at 15°–30° C (59°–86° F) in tightly closed container and protect from light.

ADVERSE EFFECTS (≥1%) **Body as a Whole:** Flu-like syndrome, fatigue, pain, arthralgia, back pain. **CV:** Chest pain, edema, hypertension, thrombocytopenic purpura. **GI:** Abdominal pain, dyspepsia, diarrhea, nausea, hypercholesterolemia. **Hematologic:** Thrombotic thrombocytopenic purpura, epistaxis. **CNS:** Headache, dizziness,

Common adverse effects in *italic*, life-threatening effects underlined; generic names in **bold**; classifications in SMALL CAPS; ♣ Canadian drug name; ℗ Prototype drug

359

C

depression. **Respiratory:** URI, dyspnea, rhinitis, bronchitis, cough. **Skin:** Rash, pruritus.

INTERACTIONS Drug: NSAIDS may increase risk of bleeding events. **Herbal: Feverfew, garlic, ginger, ginkgo** may increase risk of bleeding.

PHARMACOKINETICS Absorption: Rapidly absorbed from GI tract. **Onset:** 2 h; reaches steady state in 3–7 d. **Distribution:** 94–98% protein bound. **Metabolism:** Rapidly hydrolyzed in plasma to active metabolite. **Elimination:** 50% in urine and 50% in feces. **Half-Life:** 8 h.

CLINICAL IMPLICATIONS

Assessment & Drug Effects
- Carefully monitor for and immediately report S&S of GI bleeding, especially when coadministered with NSAIDS, aspirin, heparin, or warfarin.
- Lab tests: Periodic platelet count and lipid profile.
- Evaluate patients with unexplained fever or infection for myelotoxicity.

Patient & Family Education
- Report promptly any unusual bleeding (e.g., black, tarry stools).
- Avoid chronic aspirin or NSAID use unless approved by physician.

CLORAZEPATE DIPOTASSIUM

(klor-az′e-pate)

Novoclopate ♦, Tranxene, Tranxene-SD

Classifications: ANXIOLYTIC; SEDATIVE-HYPNOTIC; ANTICONVULSANT; BENZODIAZEPINE

Therapeutic: ANTIANXIETY AGENT; SEDATIVE-HYPNOTIC; ANTICONVULSANT

Prototype: Lorazepam

Pregnancy Category: D

Controlled Substance: Schedule IV

AVAILABILITY 3.75 mg, 7.5 mg, 15 mg capsules and tablets; 11.25 mg, 22.5 mg long acting tablets

ACTION & *THERAPEUTIC EFFECT*
Anxiolytic benzodiazepine with moderately rapid onset of action and a long half-life. Benzodiazepines exert their effects through enhancement of GABA-benzodiazepine receptor complex. GABA is an inhibitory neurotransmitter. Clorazepate has depressant effects on the CNS, thus controlling anxiety associated with stress and also resulting in sedative effects. *Effective in controlling anxiety and withdrawal symptoms of alcohol.*

USES Management of anxiety disorders, short-term relief of anxiety symptoms, as adjunct in management of partial seizures, and symptomatic relief of acute alcohol withdrawal.

CONTRAINDICATIONS Hypersensitivity to clorazepate and other benzodiazepines; acute narrow-angle glaucoma; depressive neuroses; pulmonary disease, COPD; psychotic reactions, drug abusers. Safe use during pregnancy (category D), lactation, and in children <9 y not established.

CAUTIOUS USE Older adults; debilitated patients; hepatic disease; kidney disease; Parkinson's disease; neuromuscular disease; seizure disorders; bipolar disorder, mania, history of suicidal ideation.

ROUTE & DOSAGE

Anxiety
Adult: **PO** 15 mg/d h.s., may increase to 15–60 mg/d in divided doses (max: 60 mg/d)

Common adverse effects in *italic*, life-threatening effects underlined; generic names in **bold**; classifications in SMALL CAPS; ♦ Canadian drug name; ⊕ Prototype drug

C

Acute Alcohol Withdrawal

Adult: **PO** 30 mg followed by 30–60 mg in divided doses (max: 90 mg/d), taper by 15 mg/d over 4 d to 7.5–15 mg/d until patient is stable

Partial Seizures

Adult: **PO** 7.5 mg t.i.d.
Child: **PO** 9–12 y: 3.75–7.5 mg b.i.d., may increase by no more than 3.75 mg/wk (max: 60 mg/d)

ADMINISTRATION

Oral

- Give with food to minimize gastric distress. Give antacid no less than 1 h before or 1 h after drug ingestion.
- Ensure that sustained-release form of drug is not chewed or crushed. It must be swallowed whole.
- Taper drug dose gradually over several days when drug is to be discontinued. Abrupt termination may lead to memory impairment, severe GI symptoms, muscle pain, restlessness, irritability, fatigue, insomnia.
- Store in light-resistant container at 15°–30° C (59°–86° F) unless otherwise specified.

ADVERSE EFFECTS (≥1%) **Body as a Whole:** Allergic reactions. **CV:** Hypotension. **GI:** GI disturbances, abnormal liver function tests, xerostomia. **Hematologic:** Decreased Hct, blood dyscrasias. **CNS:** *Drowsiness,* ataxia, dizziness, headache, paradoxical excitement, mental confusion, insomnia. **Special Senses:** diplopia, blurred vision.

INTERACTIONS Drug: **Alcohol** and other CNS DEPRESSANTS compound CNS depression; clorazepate increases effects of **cimetidine, disulfiram,** causing excessive sedation. **Herbal:** Ginkgo may decrease anticonvulsant effectiveness.

PHARMACOKINETICS Absorption: Decarboxylated in stomach; absorbed as active metabolite, desmethyldiazepam. **Peak:** 1 h. **Duration:** 24 h. **Distribution:** Crosses placenta; distributed into breast milk. **Metabolism:** In liver to oxazepam. **Elimination:** Primarily in urine. **Half-Life:** 30–200 h.

CLINICAL IMPLICATIONS

Assessment & Drug Effects

- Drowsiness, a common side effect, is more likely to occur at initiation of therapy and with dose increments on successive days.
- Lab tests: Periodic blood counts and tests of liver and kidney function should be performed throughout therapy.
- Monitor patient with history of cardiovascular disease in early therapy for drug-induced responses. If systolic BP drops more than 20 mm Hg or if there is a sudden increase in pulse rate, withhold drug and notify physician.

Patient & Family Education

- Take drug as prescribed and do not change dose or abruptly stop taking the drug without physician's approval.
- Do not self-dose with OTC drugs (cold remedies, sleep medications, antacids) without consulting physician.
- Avoid driving and other potentially hazardous activities until reaction to drug is known.
- Do not use alcohol and other CNS depressants while on clorazepate therapy.
- If a woman becomes pregnant during therapy or intends to become pregnant, communicate with physician about the desirability of discontinuing the drug.

Common adverse effects in *italic*, life-threatening effects <u>underlined</u>; generic names in **bold**; classifications in SMALL CAPS; ♣ Canadian drug name; ☻ Prototype drug

CLOTRIMAZOLE

(kloe-trim′a-zole)

Canesten ✦, Gyne-Lotrimin, Gyne-Lotrimin-3, Lotrimin, Mycelex, Mycelex-G

Classifications: ANTIBIOTIC; AZOLE ANTIFUNGAL

Therapeutic: ANTIBIOTIC; ANTIFUNGAL, AZOLE

Prototype: Fluconazole

Pregnancy Category: B (topical); C (oral)

AVAILABILITY 1% cream, solution, lotion; 10 mg troches; 100 mg, 200 mg, 500 mg vaginal tablets; 1% vaginal cream

ACTION & *THERAPEUTIC EFFECT*

Acts by altering fungal cell membrane permeability, permitting loss of phosphorous compounds, potassium, and other essential intracellular constituents with consequent loss of ability to replicate. *Has broad-spectrum fungicidal activity. Active against a wide variety of fungi, yeast, dermatophytes and certain gram-positive bacteria.*

USES Dermal infections including tinea pedis, tinea cruris, tinea corporis, tinea versicolor; also vulvovaginal and oropharyngeal candidiasis.

UNLABELED USES Trichomoniasis.

CONTRAINDICATIONS Ophthalmic uses; systemic mycoses. Safe use during pregnancy (category C for oral troches, category B for topical preparations), and in children <3 y not established.

CAUTIOUS USE Hyersensitivity to other azole antifungals; hepatic impairment, diabetes mellitus; HIV; lactation.

ROUTE & DOSAGE

Dermal Infections

Adult: **Topical** Apply small amount onto affected areas b.i.d. a.m. and p.m.

Vulvovaginal Infections

Adult: **Intravaginal** Insert 1 applicator full or one 100 mg vaginal tablet into vagina at bedtime for 7 d, or one 500 mg vaginal tablet at bedtime for 1 dose

Oropharyngeal Candidiasis

Adult/Child: **PO** 1 troche (lozenge) 5 times/d q3h for 14 d

ADMINISTRATION

- Instruct patient taking the oral lozenge to allow it to dissolve slowly in mouth over 15–30 min for maximum effectiveness.
- Apply skin cream and solution preparations sparingly. Protect hands with latex gloves when applying medication.
- Avoid contact of clotrimazole preparations with the eyes.
- Do not use occlusive dressings unless directed by physician to do so.
- Consult physician about skin cleansing procedure before applying medication. Regardless of procedure used, dry skin thoroughly.
- Store cream and solution formulations at 15°–30° C (59°–86° F); do not store troches or vaginal tablets above 35° C (95° F) unless otherwise directed.

ADVERSE EFFECTS (≥1%) **GI:** Abnormal liver function tests; occasional nausea and vomiting (with oral troche). **Skin:** Stinging, erythema, edema, vesication, desquamation, pruritus, urticaria, skin fissures. **Urogenital:** Mild burning sensation, lower abdominal cramps, bloating, cystitis, urethritis, mild urinary frequency, vulval erythema and itching, pain and vaginal soreness during intercourse.

INTERACTIONS Drug: Intravaginal preparations may inactivate SPERMICIDES.

PHARMACOKINETICS Absorption: Minimal systemic absorption; minimally absorbed topically. **Peak:** High saliva concentrations <3 h; high vaginal concentrations in 8–24 h. **Metabolism:** In liver. **Elimination:** Eliminated as metabolite in bile.

CLINICAL IMPLICATIONS

Assessment & Drug Effects

- Evaluate effectiveness of treatment. Report any signs of skin irritation with dermal preparations.
- Anticipate signs of clinical improvement within the first week of drug use.

Patient & Family Education

- Use clotrimazole as directed and for the length of time prescribed by physician.
- Generally, clinical improvement is apparent during first week of therapy. Report to physician if condition worsens or if signs of irritation or sensitivity develop, or if no improvement is noted after 4 wk of therapy.
- If receiving the drug vaginally, your sexual partner may experience burning and irritation of penis or urethritis; refrain from sexual intercourse during therapy or have sexual partner wear a condom.

CLOXACILLIN, SODIUM

(klox-a-sill'in)

Apo-Cloxi ◆, Cloxapen, Novo-cloxin ◆

Classifications: ANTIBIOTIC, PENICILLIN; BETA-LACTAM
Therapeutic: ANTIBIOTIC
Prototype: Penicillin G
Pregnancy Category: B

AVAILABILITY 250 mg, 500 mg capsules; 125 mg/5 mL oral suspension

ACTION & *THERAPEUTIC EFFECT*
Semisynthetic, penicillinase-resistant, beta-lactam penicillin. Cloxacillin inhibits third and final stage of bacterial cell wall synthesis by preferentially binding to specific penicillin-binding proteins (PBPs) that are located within the bacterial cell wall, which results in cell lysis and therefore cell death. *Effective against most gram-positive bacteria. Highly active against most penicillinase-producing staphylococci, and generally ineffective against gram-negative bacteria and methicillin-resistant staphylococci (MRSA).*

USES Primarily in infections caused by penicillinase-producing staphylococci and penicillin-resistant staphylococci. May be used to initiate therapy in suspected staphylococcal infections pending culture and susceptibility test results.

CONTRAINDICATIONS Sensitivity to penicillins; lactation. Safe use in neonates not established.

CAUTIOUS USE History of or suspected atopy or allergy (asthma, eczema, hives, hay fever), renal or hepatic function impairment, history of allergy to cephalosporins, pregnancy (category B).

ROUTE & DOSAGE

Mild to Moderate Infections
Adult: **PO** 250–500 mg q6h
Child: **PO** <20 kg: 12.5–25 mg/kg q6h (max: 4 g/d)

Common adverse effects in *italic*, life-threatening effects underlined; generic names in **bold**; classifications in SMALL CAPS; ◆ Canadian drug name; ◎ Prototype drug

363

C

ADMINISTRATION

Oral

- Give on an empty stomach (at least 1 h before or 2 h after meals) unless otherwise advised by physician. Food reduces rate and extent of drug absorption.
- After reconstitution PO solution retains potency for 14 d if refrigerated (shake well before pouring).
- Unless otherwise advised, store capsules at 15°–30° C (59°–86° F).

ADVERSE EFFECTS (≥1%) **Body as a Whole:** Wheezing, sneezing, chills, drug fever, <u>anaphylaxis</u>, superinfections. **GI:** *Nausea,* vomiting, flatulence, *diarrhea.* **Hematologic:** Eosinophilia, leukopenia, <u>agranulocytosis</u>. **Metabolic:** Elevated AST, ALT; jaundice (possibly of allergic etiology). **Skin:** Pruritus, urticaria, rash.

INTERACTIONS Drug: Probenecid decreases cloxacillin elimination.

PHARMACOKINETICS Absorption: 37–60% from GI tract. **Peak:** 0.5–2 h. **Duration:** 4–6 h. **Distribution:** Distributed throughout body with highest concentrations in liver, kidney, spleen, bone, bile, and pleural fluid; low CSF penetration; crosses placenta; distributed into breast milk. **Metabolism:** In liver. **Elimination:** Primarily in urine; some elimination via bile. **Half-Life:** 30–60 min.

CLINICAL IMPLICATIONS

Assessment & Drug Effects

- Determine previous exposure and sensitivity to penicillins and cephalosporins and other allergic reactions of any kind before treatment is initiated.
- Monitor for S&S of anaphylactoid reaction (see Appendix G) or other signs or symptoms of hypersensitivity reaction (see Appendix F) as with other penicillins.
- Lab tests: Periodic assessments of renal, hepatic, and hematopoietic function are advised in patients on long-term therapy.

Patient & Family Education

- Take medication around the clock, do not miss a dose, and continue taking the medication until it is finished.
- Report to physician the onset of hypersensitivity reaction (see Appendix F) and superinfections.
- Check with physician if GI adverse effects (nausea, vomiting, diarrhea) appear.

CLOZAPINE ℗

(clo´za-pin)

Clozaril, Fazaclo
Classifications: PSYCHOTHERAPEUTIC AGENT; ANTIPSYCHOTIC, ATYPICAL
Therapeutic: ATYPICAL ANTIPSYCHOTIC
Pregnancy Category: B

AVAILABILITY 25 mg, 100 mg tablets and orally disintegrating tablets

ACTION & *THERAPEUTIC EFFECT* Interferes with binding of dopamine to D_1 and D_2 receptors in the limbic region of brain. It binds primarily to nondopaminergic sites (e.g., alpha-adrenergic, serotonergic, and cholinergic receptors). *Limited to treatment of schizophrenia uncontrolled by other agents.*

USES Indicated only in the management of severely ill schizophrenic patients who have failed to respond to other neuroleptic agents.
UNLABELED USES Schizo-affective disorder, severe obsessive-compulsive disorder, bipolar disorder, dementia-related behavioral disorders.

CONTRAINDICATIONS Severe CNS depression, blood dyscrasia, history of bone marrow depression; patients with myeloproliferative disorders, uncontrolled epilepsy; clozapine-induced agranulocytosis, severe granulocytosis, chemotherapy, coma, leukemia, leukopenia, neutropenia, myocarditis, concurrent administration of benzodiazepines or other psychotropic drugs; renal failure, dialysis, hepatitis, jaundice; infants, lactation.

CAUTIOUS USE Arrhythmias, GI disorders, narrow-angle glaucoma, hepatic and renal impairment, prostatic hypertrophy, history of seizures; patients with cardiovascular and/or pulmonary disease; cerebrovascular disease, cardiac arrhythmias, tachycardia, dehydration, neurological disease, tardive dyskinesia, previous history of agranulocytosis; surgery, glaucoma, infection, pregnancy (category B); older adults. Safety and efficacy in children <9 y have not been established.

ROUTE & DOSAGE

Schizophrenia

Adult: **PO** *>16 y:* Initiate at 25–50 mg/d and titrate to a target dose of 350–450 mg/d in 3 divided doses at 2 wk intervals, further increases can be made if necessary, max of 900 mg/d

ADMINISTRATION

Oral

- Drug is usually withdrawn gradually over 1–2 wk if therapy must be discontinued.
- Store the drug away from heat or light.

ADVERSE EFFECTS (≥1%) **CV:** Orthostatic hypotension, *tachycardia,* ECG changes, increased risk of myocarditis especially during first month of therapy, pericarditis, pericardial effusion, cardiomyopathy, heart failure, MI, mitral insufficiency. **GI:** Nausea, dry mouth, constipation, hypersalivation. **Hematologic:** Agranulocytosis. **CNS:** Seizures, *transient fever,* sedation, neuroleptic malignant syndrome (rare), dystonic reactions (rare). **Metabolic:** Hyperglycemia, diabetes mellitus. **Urogenital:** Urinary retention. **Other:** Increased mortality from severe hematologic, cardiovascular, and respiratory adverse effects.

INTERACTIONS Drug: Alcohol and other CNS DEPRESSANTS compound depressant effects; ANTICHOLINERGIC AGENTS potentiate anticholinergic effects; ANTIHYPERTENSIVE AGENTS may potentiate hypotension. **Herbal: St. John's wort** and **kava-kava** may increase sedation.

PHARMACOKINETICS Absorption: Readily absorbed from GI tract. **Onset:** 2–4 wk. **Peak:** 2.5 h. **Distribution:** Possibly distributed into breast milk. **Metabolism:** In liver. **Elimination:** 50% in urine, 30% in feces. **Half-Life:** 8–12 h.

CLINICAL IMPLICATIONS

Assessment & Drug Effects

- Lab tests: Baseline WBC and absolute neutrophil count must be made before initial treatment, every week for first 6 mo, then every 2 wk for next 6 mo, then every 4 wk, and weekly for 4 wk after the drug is discontinued. Periodically monitor blood glucose.
- Monitor diabetics for loss of glycemic control.
- Monitor for seizure activity; seizure potential increases at the higher dose level.
- Closely monitor for recurrence of psychotic symptoms if the drug is being discontinued.

Common adverse effects in *italic*, life-threatening effects underlined; generic names in **bold**; classifications in SMALL CAPS; ✦ Canadian drug name; ⊘ Prototype drug

365

C

- Monitor cardiovascular and respiratory status, especially during the first month of therapy. Report promptly S&S of CHF and other potential cardiac problems.
- Monitor for development of tachycardia or hypotension, which may pose a serious risk for patients with compromised cardiovascular function.
- Monitor daily temperature and report fever. Transient elevation above 38° C (100.4° F), with peak incidence during first 3 wk of drug therapy, may occur.

Patient & Family Education

- Carefully monitor blood glucose levels if diabetic.
- Do not engage in any hazardous activity until response to the drug is known. Drowsiness and sedation are common adverse effects.
- Due to the risk of agranulocytosis (see Appendix F) it is important to comply with blood test regimen. Report flulike symptoms, fever, sore throat, lethargy, malaise, or other signs of infection.
- Rise slowly to avoid orthostatic hypotension.
- Report immediately any of the following: unexplained fatigue, especially with activity; shortness of breath, sudden weight gain or edema of the lower extremities.
- Take drug exactly as ordered.
- Do not use OTC drugs or alcohol without permission of physician.

COCAINE

(koe-kane´)

COCAINE HYDROCHLORIDE

Classifications: ANESTHETIC, LOCAL
Therapeutic: TOPICAL ANESTHETICS
Prototype: Procaine

Pregnancy Category: C
Controlled Substance: Schedule II

AVAILABILITY 4%, 10% topical solution

ACTION & *THERAPEUTIC EFFECT*
Alkaloid obtained from leaves of *Erythroxylon coca*. Topical application blocks nerve conduction and produces surface anesthesia accompanied by local vasoconstriction. Exerts adrenergic effect by potentiating action of endogenous (and injected) epinephrine and norepinephrine, possibly by inhibiting reuptake of catecholamines into sympathetic nerve terminals. Topical form of cocaine is a local anesthetic. *Systemic absorption produces descending CNS stimulation, with intense, short-lived euphoria accompanied by indifference to pain or hunger and with illusions of great strength, endurance, and mental capacity, all the basis for drug abuse.*

USES Surface anesthesia of ear, nose, throat, rectum, and vagina. Ophthalmic use largely abandoned because of its tendency to cause corneal sloughing. Sometimes used as ingredient in Brompton's cocktail.

CONTRAINDICATIONS Hypersensitivity to local anesthetics; sepsis in region of proposed application; acute MI, history of cardiac arrhythmias, cardiac disease; seizures or seizure disorders; thyrotoxicosis cerebrovascular disease; Tourette's syndrome; MAOI therapy; pregnancy (category C), lactation.
CAUTIOUS USE History of drug sensitivities, history of drug abuse.

ROUTE & DOSAGE

Surface Anesthesia
Adult: **Topical** 1–10% solution (use >4% solution with caution), max single dose of 1 mg/kg

Common adverse effects in *italic*, life-threatening effects underlined; generic names in **bold**; classifications in SMALL CAPS; ♣ Canadian drug name; ☺ Prototype drug

ADMINISTRATION

Topical
- Exercise caution to ensure that drug is taken as prescribed.
- Preserve in tightly closed, light-resistant containers.

ADVERSE EFFECTS (≥1%) **Body as a Whole:** Formication ("cocaine bugs"), hypersensitivity reactions. **CV:** Tachycardia, ventricular fibrillation, MI, angina pectoris. **GI:** Nausea, vomiting, anorexia, abdominal pain. **CNS:** *CNS stimulation* and CNS depression (respiratory and circulatory failure). **Respiratory:** pneumonia, lung damage (chronic cocaine smoking). **Special Senses:** Runny nose, perforated nasal septum; clouding, pitting, and ulceration of cornea.

INTERACTIONS Drug: Epinephrine entails risk of severe hypertension and arrhythmias; MAO INHIBITORS potentiate pharmacologic effects of cocaine.

PHARMACOKINETICS Absorption: Readily absorbed from mucous membranes; absorption limited by vasoconstriction. **Onset:** 1 min. **Peak:** 15–120 min. **Duration:** 30 min–2 h. **Distribution:** Crosses placenta; distributed into breast milk. **Metabolism:** Hydrolyzed in serum. **Elimination:** In urine; detectable for up to 30 h. **Half-Life:** 1–2.5 h.

CLINICAL IMPLICATIONS

Assessment & Drug Effects
- When used for anesthesia of throat, cocaine causes temporary paralysis of cilia of respiratory tract cells, reducing protection against aspiration. It also may interfere with pharyngeal stage of swallowing. Give nothing by mouth until sensation returns.

- Monitor cardiovascular status, especially in patients with known cardiac disease. Report promptly cardiac arrhythmias.

Patient & Family Education
- Promptly report angina or chest pain or respiratory distress.

CODEINE
(koe'deen)

CODEINE PHOSPHATE
Paveral ♦

CODEINE SULFATE

Classifications: NARCOTIC (OPIATE) AGONIST ANALGESIC; ANTITUSSIVE
Therapeutic: NARCOTIC ANALGESIC; ANTITUSSIVE
Prototype: Morphine
Pregnancy Category: C
Controlled Substance: Schedule II

AVAILABILITY 15 mg, 30 mg, 60 mg tablets; 15 mg/5 mL oral solution; 30 mg, 60 mg injection

ACTION & *THERAPEUTIC EFFECT*
Opium agonist in the CNS with actions similar to morphine. Parenteral codeine produces less analgesic and respiratory depression than morphine. Analgesia is mediated through changes in the perception of pain at the spinal cord and higher levels in the CNS. There is no ceiling effect of analgesia for opiates. The antitussive effects are mediated through direct action on receptors in the cough center of the medulla. Codeine also has a drying effect on the respiratory tract, thus increasing viscosity of bronchial secretions. *Analgesic potency is about one-sixth that of morphine; antitussive activity is also a little less than that of morphine.*

Common adverse effects in *italic*, life-threatening effects underlined; generic names in **bold**; classifications in SMALL CAPS; ♦ Canadian drug name; ⊕ Prototype drug

367

USES Symptomatic relief of mild to moderately severe pain when control cannot be obtained by nonnarcotic analgesics and to suppress hyperactive or nonproductive cough.

CONTRAINDICATIONS Hypersensitivity to codeine or other morphine derivatives; acute asthma, COPD; increased intracranial pressure, head injury, acute alcoholism, hepatic or renal dysfunction, hypothyroidism; pregnancy (category C). Safe use in neonates not established.

CAUTIOUS USE Prostatic hypertrophy, G6PD deficiency; GI disease; hepatic disease; hepatitis; immunosuppression; debilitated patients, very young and very old patients; history of drug abuse; lactation.

ROUTE & DOSAGE

Analgesic
Adult: **PO/IM/SC:** 15–60 mg q.i.d.
Child: **PO/IM/SC** 0.5–1 mg/kg q4–6h prn (max: 60 mg/dose)

Antitussive
Adult: **PO** 10–20 mg q4–6h prn (max: 120 mg/24 h)
Child: **PO** 6–12 y: 5–10 mg q4–6h (max: 60 mg/24 h); 2–6 y: 2.5–5 mg q4–6h (max: 30 mg/24 h)

ADMINISTRATION

Oral
- Administer PO codeine with milk or other food to reduce possibility of GI distress.

Subcutaneous/Intramuscular
- Give parenterally to achieve greatest effectiveness. An oral dose is about 60% as effective as an equal parenteral dose.
- Preserve in tight, light-resistant containers at 15°–30° C (59°–86° F) unless otherwise directed.

ADVERSE EFFECTS (≥1%) **Body as a Whole:** Shortness of breath, anaphylactoid reaction. **CV:** Palpitation, hypotension, orthostatic hypotension, bradycardia, tachycardia, circulatory collapse. **GI:** *Nausea,* vomiting, *constipation.* **CNS:** *Dizziness,* light-headedness, *drowsiness,* sedation, lethargy, euphoria, agitation; restlessness, exhilaration, convulsions, narcosis, respiratory depression. **Skin:** Diffuse erythema, rash, urticaria, *pruritus,* excessive perspiration, facial flushing, fixed-drug eruption. **Special Senses:** Miosis. **Urogenital:** Urinary retention.

INTERACTIONS Drug: Alcohol and other CNS DEPRESSANTS augment CNS depressant effects. **Herbal: St. John's wort** may cause increased sedation.

PHARMACOKINETICS Absorption: Readily from GI tract. **Onset:** 15–30 min. **Peak:** 1–1.5 h. **Duration:** 4–6 h. **Distribution:** Crosses placenta; distributed into breast milk. **Metabolism:** In liver. **Elimination:** In urine. **Half-Life:** 2.5–4 h.

CLINICAL IMPLICATIONS

Assessment & Drug Effects
- Record relief of pain and duration of analgesia.
- Evaluate effectiveness as cough suppressant. Treatment of cough is directed toward decreasing frequency and intensity of cough without abolishing cough reflex, need to remove bronchial secretions.
- Although codeine has less abuse liability than morphine, dependence is a major unwanted effect.
- Supervision of ambulation and use other safety precautions as warranted since drug may cause dizziness and light-headedness.
- Monitor for nausea, a common side effect. Report nausea accom-

panied by vomiting. Change to another analgesic may be warranted.

Patient & Family Education

- Make position changes slowly and in stages particularly from recumbent to upright posture. Lie down immediately if light-headedness or dizziness occurs.
- Lie down when feeling nauseated and to notify physician if this symptom persists. Nausea appears to be aggravated by ambulation.
- Avoid driving and other potentially hazardous activities until reaction to drug is known. Codeine may impair ability to perform tasks requiring mental alertness.
- Do not take alcohol or other CNS depressants unless approved by physician.
- Hyperactive cough may be lessened by avoiding irritants such as smoking, dust, fumes, and other air pollutants. Humidification of ambient air may provide some relief.

COLCHICINE

(kol′chi-seen)
Novocolchine ♦
Classifications: ANTIGOUT AGENT
Therapeutic: ANTIGOUT
Pregnancy Category: C

AVAILABILITY 0.5 mg, 0.6 mg tablets

ACTION & *THERAPEUTIC EFFECT*
Alkaloid of the plant *Colchicum* with antimitotic and indirect antiinflammatory properties. Colchicine inhibits the migration of neutrophils into the area of inflammation. Although it does not inhibit phagocytosis of uric acid crystals, it does appear to prevent the release of an inflammatory glycoprotein from phagocytes in the inflammatory process. *Inhibition of inflammation and reduction of pain and swelling, which occurs in gouty arthritis. Colchicine is nonanalgesic and nonuricosuric.*

USES Prophylactically for recurrent gouty arthritis and for acute gout, either as single agent or in combination with a uricosuric such as probenecid, allopurinol, or sulfinpyrazone.

UNLABELED USES Sarcoid arthritis, chondrocalcinosis (pseudogout), arthritis associated with erythema nodosum, leukemia, adenocarcinoma, acute calcific tendonitis, familial Mediterranean fever, multiple sclerosis, primary biliary cirrhosis, mycosis fungoides, and in experimental studies of normal and abnormal cell division.

CONTRAINDICATIONS Blood dyscrasias; severe GI, renal, hepatic, or cardiac disease; pregnancy (category C). Safe use in children not established.

CAUTIOUS USE Older adult and debilitated patients, early manifestations of GI, renal, hepatic, or cardiac disease.

ROUTE & DOSAGE

Acute Gouty Attack
Adult: **PO** 0.5–1.2 mg followed by 0.5–0.6 mg q1–2h until pain relief or intolerable GI symptoms (max: 4 mg/attack)

Prophylaxis
Adult: **PO** 0.5 or 0.6 mg every night or every other night as needed (up to 1.8 mg/d may be needed for severe cases)

Surgical Patients
Adult: **PO** 0.5 or 0.6 mg t.i.d. starting 3 d before surgery and continuing for 3 d after surgery

---

Common adverse effects in *italic*, life-threatening effects <u>underlined</u>; generic names in **bold**; classifications in SMALL CAPS; ♦ Canadian drug name; ❶ Prototype drug

C

Renal Impairment

Cl_{cr} 10–50 mL/min: prolonged use is not recommended. Cl_{cr} <10 mL/min: reduce recommended dose by 50%

ADMINISTRATION

Oral

- Administer oral drug with milk or food to reduce possibility of GI upset.

- Preserve in tight, light-resistant containers preferably between 15°–30° C (59°–86° F), unless otherwise directed by manufacturer.

ADVERSE EFFECTS (≥1%) **GI:** *Nausea, vomiting, diarrhea, abdominal pain,* anorexia, hemorrhagic gastroenteritis, steatorrhea, hepatotoxicity, pancreatitis. **Hematologic:** Neutropenia, <u>bone marrow depression</u>, thrombocytopenia, <u>agranulocytosis, aplastic anemia</u>. **CNS:** Mental confusion, peripheral neuritis, syndrome of muscle weakness (accompanied by elevated serum creatine kinase). **Skin:** Severe irritation and tissue damage if IV administration leaks around injection site. **Urogenital:** Azotemia, proteinuria, hematuria, oliguria.

DIAGNOSTIC TEST INTERFERENCE

Possible interference with ***urinary steroid (17-OHCS)*** determinations when done by modifications of ***Reddy, Jenkins, Thorn procedure.*** False-positive ***urine tests for RBCs and Hgb*** reported.

INTERACTIONS Drug: May decrease intestinal absorption of vitamin B_{12}.

PHARMACOKINETICS Absorption: Rapidly from GI tract. **Peak:** 0.5–2 h; may have multiple peaks because of enterohepatic cycling. **Distribution:** Widely distributed; concentrates in leukocytes, kidney, liver, spleen, and intestinal tract. **Metabolism:** Partially metabolized in liver. **Elimination:** Primarily in feces; 10–20% in urine in 24 h.

CLINICAL IMPLICATIONS

Assessment & Drug Effects

- Lab tests: Baseline and periodic determinations of serum uric acid and creatinine are advised, as well as CBC, including Hgb, platelet count, serum electrolytes, and urinalysis.

- Monitor for dose-related adverse effects; they are most likely to occur during the initial course of treatment.

- Monitor for early signs of colchicine toxicity including weakness, abdominal discomfort, anorexia, nausea, vomiting, and diarrhea, regardless of administration route. Report to physician. To avoid more serious toxicity, drug should be discontinued promptly until symptoms subside.

- Monitor I&O ratio and pattern (during acute gouty attack): High fluid intake promotes excretion and reduces danger of crystal formation in kidneys and ureters.

- Keep physician informed of patient's progress. Drug should be stopped when pain of acute gout is relieved. Therapeutic response: articular pain and swelling generally subside within 8–12 h and usually disappear in 24–72 h after PO therapy, and 6–12 h after IV administration.

Patient & Family Education

- If taking colchicine at home, withhold drug and report to the physi-

Common adverse effects in *italic*, life-threatening effects <u>underlined</u>; generic names in **bold**, classifications in SMALL CAPS; ♣ Canadian drug name; ⊕ Prototype drug

cian the onset of GI symptoms or signs of bone marrow depression (nausea, sore throat, bleeding gums, sore mouth, fever, fatigue, malaise, unusual bleeding or bruising).

- Keep colchicine on hand at all times to start therapy or increase dosage, as prescribed by physician, at the first suggestion of an acute attack.
- Physician may prescribe sodium bicarbonate, or sodium or potassium citrate, to maintain alkaline urine and thus prevent formation of urate stones.
- Avoid fermented beverages such as beer, ale, and wine as they may precipitate gouty attack. The physician may allow distilled alcoholic beverages in moderation.

COLESEVELAM HYDROCHLORIDE

(co-less'e-ve-lam)
Welchol
Classifications: ANTILIPEMIC; BILE ACID SEQUESTRANT
Therapeutic: CHOLESTEROL-LOWERING AGENT; BILE ACID SEQUESTRANT
Prototype: Cholestyramine resin
Pregnancy Category: B

AVAILABILITY 625 mg tablets

ACTION & *THERAPEUTIC EFFECT*
Anion exchange resin used for its cholesterol-lowering effect. Binds with bile salts in the intestinal tract to form an insoluble complex that is excreted in the feces, thus reducing circulating cholesterol and increasing serum LDL removal rate. Serum triglyceride levels may increase slightly. *Decreases serum LDL and total cho-*

lesterol level. Removes bile salts from the intestine.

USES Adjunctive therapy to diet and exercise for reduction of elevated LDL cholesterol alone or in combination with an HMG-CoA reductase inhibitor (statin).

CONTRAINDICATIONS Hypersensitivity to colesevelam; complete biliary obstruction; bowel obstruction; children <2 y of age.
CAUTIOUS USE Preexisting GI disorders or bowel disease, primary biliary cirrhosis, partial biliary obstruction, biliary atresia; hypertriglyceridemia; older adults, pregnancy (category B); malabsorption states; bleeding disorders.

ROUTE & DOSAGE

Hypercholesterolemia, Monotherapy
Adult: **PO** 3 tablets b.i.d. with meals or 6 tablets q.d. with a meal, may be increased to 7 tablets/d

Hypercholesterolemia, Combination Therapy
Adult: **PO** 4–6 tablets/d with meals or 6 tablets q.d. with a meal

ADMINISTRATION

Oral
- Give with meals (mandatory) and adequate liquid (e.g., 8 oz).
- Store at 15°–30° C (59°–86° F) with occasional fluctuations to 40° C (90° F); protect from moisture.

ADVERSE EFFECTS (≥1%) **Body as a Whole:** Infection, pain, flu-like syndrome, asthenia, myalgia. **CNS:** Headache. **GI:** Abdominal pain, *flatulence, constipation,* diarrhea, nau-

Common adverse effects in *italic*, life-threatening effects underlined; generic names in **bold**; classifications in SMALL CAPS; ◆ Canadian drug name; ❷ Prototype drug

371

sea, dyspepsia. **Respiratory:** Sinusitis, rhinitis, cough, pharyngitis.

INTERACTIONS Drug: May decrease absorption of **verapamil.** Can bind and affect absorption of any drug.

PHARMACOKINETICS Absorption: Not absorbed. **Metabolism:** Not metabolized. **Elimination:** In feces.

CLINICAL IMPLICATIONS

Assessment & Drug Effects

- Lab tests: Monitor total cholesterol, LDL-C, HDL-C, and triglycerides periodically.
- Withhold drug and notify physician for triglycerides >300 mg/dL.

Patient & Family Education

- Report S&S of GI distress (see Appendix F), especially constipation.

COLESTIPOL HYDROCHLORIDE

(koe-les′ti-pole)
Cholestabyl ✦, **Colestid, Lestid** ✦
Classifications: ANTILIPEMIC; BILE ACID SEQUESTRANT
Therapeutic: CHOLESTEROL-LOWERING AGENT; BILE ACID SEQUESTRANT
Prototype: Cholestyramine
Pregnancy Category: C

AVAILABILITY 1 g tablets; 5 g powder for suspension

ACTION & *THERAPEUTIC EFFECT*

Insoluble chloride salt of a basic anion exchange resin with high molecular weight, which adsorbs and combines with intestinal bile acids in exchange for chloride ions to form an insoluble, nonabsorbable complex that is excreted in the feces. *Reduces circulating cholesterol and increases se-rum LDL removal rate. Serum triglycerides are not affected or are minimally increased.*

USES Pruritus associated with partial biliary obstruction; biliary cirrhosis; also as adjunct to diet therapy of patient with primary hypercholesterolemia (type IIa hyperlipoproteinemia) or with coronary artery disease unresponsive to diet or other measures alone.

UNLABELED USES Digitoxin overdose and hyperoxaluria and to control postoperative diarrhea caused by excess bile acids in colon.

CONTRAINDICATIONS Complete biliary obstruction, biliary cirrhosis; hypersensitivity to bile acid sequestrants; renal disease; pregnancy (category C). Safe use in children not established.

CAUTIOUS USE Hemorrhoids; bleeding disorders; malabsorption states; GI motility disorders, dysphagia; older adult.

ROUTE & DOSAGE

Hypercholesterolemia
Adult: **PO** 15–30 g/d in 2–4 doses a.c. and h.s., or 1–2 tabs 1–2 times/d
Digitalis Toxicity
Adult: **PO** 10 g followed by 5 g q6–8h as needed

ADMINISTRATION

Oral

- Give 30 min before a meal when ordered a.c.
- Ensure that tablets are not chewed or crushed. They must be swallowed whole.
- Always mix granule form with liquids, juices, soups, cereals, or

Common adverse effects in *italic*, life-threatening effects underlined; generic names in **bold**; classifications in SMALL CAPS; ✦ Canadian drug name; ❷ Prototype drug

pulpy fruits. Add powder to at least 90 mL fluid. When carbonated drink is used, slowly stir in a large glass because excess foaming may occur. Rinse glass with small amount extra fluid to be sure all the drug is taken.

- Drugs given concomitantly should be scheduled at least 1 h before or 4 h after ingestion of colestipol to reduce interference with their absorption (see drug interactions).
- Store at 15°–30° C (59°–86° F) in tightly closed container unless otherwise instructed.

ADVERSE EFFECTS (≥1%) **Body as a Whole:** Joint and muscle pain, arthritis, shortness of breath. **GI:** *Constipation,* abdominal pain or distention, belching, flatulence, nausea, vomiting, diarrhea. **Metabolic:** Transient increases in liver enzyme tests, serum phosphorus and chloride; decreases in serum sodium and potassium. **Skin:** Dermatitis, urticaria.

INTERACTIONS Drug: Because it decreases the absorption from the GI tract of ORAL ANTICOAGULANTS, **digoxin,** TETRACYCLINES, PENICILLINS, **phenobarbital,** THYROID HORMONES, THIAZIDE DIURETICS, IRON SALTS, FAT-SOLUBLE VITAMINS (A, D, E, K), administer cholestyramine 4 h before or 2 h after these drugs. Can bind and affect absorption of any drug.

PHARMACOKINETICS Absorption: Not absorbed from GI tract. **Elimination:** In feces as insoluble complex.

CLINICAL IMPLICATIONS

Assessment & Drug Effects
- Watch for changes in bowel elimination pattern. Constipation should not be allowed to persist without medical attention.
- Lab test: Monitor serum sodium and potassium levels. Monitor

for and report S&S of hyponatremia and hypokalemia (see Appendix F).

Patient & Family Education
- Do not change the times for taking each drug, nor omit or increase doses. Any change in established regimens should be approved by the physician. It is important to keep to established regimens for colestipol and other drugs.
- If receiving prolonged therapy, report unusual bleeding (vitamin K deficiency). Colestipol prevents absorption of FAT-SOLUBLE VITAMINS (A, D, E, K).
- Do not use OTC drugs unless physician has given approval.
- Check with physician regarding permitted amount of alcohol intake.

COLFOSCERIL PALMITATE

(col-fos′ce-ril)
Exosurf Neonatal
Classifications: LUNG SURFACTANT
Therapeutic: LUNG SURFACTANT
Prototype: Beractant
Pregnancy Category: Not applicable

AVAILABILITY 108 mg powder for injection

ACTION & *THERAPEUTIC EFFECT*
Synthetic lung surfactant. Endogenous pulmonary surfactant lowers surface tension on alveolar surfaces during respiration and stabilizes the alveoli against collapse at resting pressures. Colfosceril lowers minimum surface tension on alveolar surfaces and restores pulmonary compliance and oxygenation in premature infants. *Helps to reverse the effects of the deficiency of surfactant that causes respiratory dis-*

Common adverse effects in *italic,* life-threatening effects <u>underlined</u>; generic names in **bold**; classifications in SMALL CAPS; ♣ Canadian drug name; ❷ Prototype drug

373

C

tress syndrome (RDS) in premature infants.

USES Prophylactic treatment of infants with birth weights <1350 g who are at risk of developing RDS. Prophylactic therapy of infants with birth weights >1350 g who show evidence of pulmonary immaturity. **UNLABELED USES** Rescue treatment of infants with established RDS; RDS in adults.

CONTRAINDICATIONS Infants who have major congenital abnormalities or who are suspected of having congenital infections.

ROUTE & DOSAGE

Prophylaxis

Infant: **Intratracheal** 3 doses of 5 mL/kg are recommended, with the first dose being given as soon as possible after birth and repeat doses 12 and 24 h later to infants who remain on mechanical ventilation

Rescue Therapy

Infant: **Intratracheal** 2 doses of 5 mL/kg are recommended, the first dose being initiated as soon as the diagnosis of RDS is confirmed and the second 12 h later in infants remaining on mechanical ventilation

ADMINISTRATION

Intratracheal

- Reconstitute immediately before use if possible. Use only supplied diluent for reconstitution.
- Reconstitute as follows: (1) withdraw diluent with 18–19-gauge needle attached to 10–12-mL syringe; (2) inject into vial by allowing vacuum to draw diluent in; (3) do not withdraw needle and aspirate as much of solution as possi-

ble back into syringe; (4) maintain vacuum and quickly release plunger. Repeat steps 3 and 4 three or four times to ensure adequate mixing.
- Reconstituted drug is a milky white suspension. Gently shake if needed to resuspend it.
- Withdraw entire ordered dose into syringe while maintaining vacuum in vial.
- Before administration of drug, ensure that endotracheal tube tip is in the trachea.
- Before administration of drug, the infant should be suctioned. If possible, avoid suctioning for 2 h after drug administration.
- Drug is administered without interrupting mechanical ventilation. Use side port on the endotracheal tube adaptor.
- Administer dose in halves, each half over 1–2 min. Give first half dose with head in midline position; then turn head and torso to the right. Wait 30 s; then return to midline position for second half dose. Give each dose in short bursts timed with inspiration. After second half dose, turn head and torso to left for 30 s; then return to midline.
- Slow or stop drug administration and adjust ventilator rate or FIO_2 if any of the following occur: heart rate decreases, infant becomes dusky or agitated, or O_2 saturation drops.
- Store at 15°–30° C (59°–86° F) in a dry place. Reconstituted solution is stable for 12 h.

INCOMPATIBILITIES Solution/additive: Do not mix any antibiotics with surfactant; this may inactivate surfactant.

ADVERSE EFFECTS (≥1%) **CV:** Bradycardia, tachycardia. **Respiratory:** Decreased oxygen saturation, mu-

Common adverse effects in *italic*, life-threatening effects <u>underlined</u>; generic names in **bold**, classifications in SMALL CAPS; ♣ Canadian drug name; ⊕ Prototype drug

cous plugging, apnea, pulmonary hemorrhage.

INTERACTIONS Drug: No clinically significant interactions established.

PHARMACOKINETICS Absorption: Absorbed from the alveolus into lung tissue, **Duration:** At least 7 d. **Distribution:** Distributes uniformly to all lobes of the lung, distal airways, and alveolar spaces; **Metabolism:** Recycled and metabolized exclusively in the lungs. **Half-Life:** 20–36 h.

CLINICAL IMPLICATIONS

Assessment & Drug Effects
- During administration of drug, continuous ECG and transcutaneous monitoring are required. Also monitor chest expansion and facial expression.
- Monitor pulmonary function during administration. Rapid changes may require immediate adjustment of peak inspiratory pressure, ventilator rate, or Fio$_2$.
- Monitor continuously for 30 min following administration. Frequent arterial blood gas sampling is required to prevent hyperoxia and hypocarbia.

COLISTIMETHATE SODIUM

(koe-lis-ti-meth'ate)
Coly-Mycin M
Classifications: URINARY TRACT ANTIINFECTIVE; ANTIBIOTIC
Therapeutic: ANTIBIOTIC
Prototype: Trimethoprim
Pregnancy Category: B

AVAILABILITY 150 mg injection

ACTION & *THERAPEUTIC EFFECT*
Similar to polymyxin B in structure and actions but about one-third to one-fifth as potent. Antibacterial activity and overall toxicity are less, but nephrotoxic potential is equivalent to polymyxin B. Believed to act by affecting phospholipid component in bacterial cytoplasmic membranes with resulting damage and leakage of essential intracellular components. *Bactericidal against most gram-negative organisms. Not effective against* Proteus *or* Neisseria *species.*

USES Particularly for severe, acute and chronic UTIs caused by susceptible strains of gram-negative organisms resistant to other antibiotics. Has been used with carbenicillin for *Pseudomonas* sepsis in children with acute leukopenia.

CONTRAINDICATIONS Hypersensitivity to polypeptide antibiotics; concomitant use of drugs that potentiate neuromuscular blocking effect (aminoglycoside antibiotics, other polymyxins, anticholinesterases, curariform muscle relaxants, ether, sodium citrate); nephrotoxic and ototoxic drugs; pregnancy (category B).
CAUTIOUS USE Impaired renal function; myasthenia gravis; older adult patients; infants; lactation.

ROUTE & DOSAGE

Urinary Tract Infections
Adult/Child: **IM/IV** 2.5–5 mg/kg/d divided in 2–4 doses, max of 5 mg/kg/d
Renal Impairment
S$_{cr}$ 1.3–1.5 mg/dL: 2.5–3.8 mg/kg/d in 2 divided doses; 1.6–2.5 mg/dL: 2.5 mg/kg/d in a single dose or 2 divided doses; 2.6–4 mg/dL: 1.5 mg/kg q36h

ADMINISTRATION

Intramuscular
- Reconstitute each 150-mg vial with 2 mL of sterile water for injection to

Common adverse effects in *italic*, life-threatening effects underlined; generic names in **bold**; classifications in SMALL CAPS; ♣ Canadian drug name; ⚙ Prototype drug

375

yield a concentration of 75 mg/mL. Swirl vial gently during reconstitution to avoid bubble formation. IM injection should be made deep into upper outer quadrant of buttock. Patients commonly experience pain at injection site. Rotate sites.

Intravenous

PREPARE: **Direct/Intermittent:** Prepare first half of total daily dose as directed for IM then further dilute with 20 mL sterile water for injection. Prepare second half of total daily dose by diluting further in 50 mL or more of D5W, NS, D5/NS, RL or other compatible solution. IV infusion solution should be freshly prepared and used within 24 h.

ADMINISTER: **Direct/Intermittent:** First half of total daily dose: Give slowly over 3–5 min. Second half of total daily dose: Starting 1–2 h after the first half dose has been given, infuse the second half dose over the next 22–23 h.

INCOMPATIBILITIES **Solution/additive: Carbenicillin, cephalothin, erythromycin, hydrocortisone, kanamycin.**

- Reconstituted solution may be stored in refrigerator at 2°–8° C (36°–46° F) or at controlled room temperature of 15°–30° C (59°–86° F). Use within 7 d. Store unopened vials at controlled room temperature.

ADVERSE EFFECTS (≥1%) **Body as a Whole:** Drug fever, pain at IM site. **GI:** GI disturbances. **CNS:** Circumoral, lingual, and peripheral paresthesias; visual and speech disturbances, neuromuscular blockade (generalized muscle weakness, dyspnea, respiratory depression or paralysis), seizures, psychosis. **Respiratory:** Respiratory arrest after IM injection. **Skin:** Pruritus, urticaria,

dermatoses. **Special Senses:** Ototoxicity. **Urogenital:** Nephrotoxicity.

INTERACTIONS Drug: Tubocurarine, pancuronium, atracurium, AMINOGLYCOSIDES may compound and prolong respiratory depression; AMINOGLYCOSIDES, **amphotericin B, vancomycin** augment nephrotoxicity.

PHARMACOKINETICS Peak: 1–2 h IM. **Duration:** 8–12 h. **Distribution:** Widely distributed in most tissues except CNS; crosses placenta; distributed into breast milk in low concentrations. **Metabolism:** In liver. **Elimination:** 66–75% in urine within 24h. **Half-Life:** 2–3 h.

CLINICAL IMPLICATIONS

Assessment & Drug Effects

- Lab tests: Culture and susceptibility tests should be performed initially and periodically during therapy to determine responsiveness of causative organisms. Baseline renal function tests should be performed prior to therapy; frequent monitoring of renal function and urine drug levels is advisable during therapy. Impaired renal function increases the possibility of nephrotoxicity, apnea, and neuromuscular blockade.
- Report restlessness or dyspnea promptly. Respiratory arrest has been reported after IM administration.
- Monitor I&O ratio and patterns: Decrease in urine output or change in I&O ratio and rising BUN, serum creatinine, and serum drug levels (without dosage increase) are indications of renal toxicity. If they occur, withhold drug and report to physician.
- Close monitoring of older adult patients and infants is essential. They are particularly prone to re-

---

Common adverse effects in *italic*, life-threatening effects underlined; generic names in **bold**; classifications in SMALL CAPS; ✦ Canadian drug name; ⦿ Prototype drug

nal toxicity because they tend to have inadequate renal reserves.

- Be alert to neurologic symptoms: changes in speech and hearing, visual changes, drowsiness, dizziness, ataxia, and transient paresthesias, and keep physician informed.

- Monitor closely postoperative patients who have received curariform muscle relaxants, ether, or sodium citrate for signs of neuromuscular blockade (delayed recovery, muscle weakness, depressed respiration).

Patient & Family Education

- Avoid operating a vehicle or other potentially hazardous activities while on drug therapy because of the possibility of transient neurologic disturbances.

CONIVAPTAN HYDROCHLORIDE

(con-i-vap'tin)
Vaprisol
Classifications: ELECTROLYTIC & WATER BALANCE AGENT; DIURETIC; VASOPRESSIN ANTAGONIST
Therapeutic: VASOPRESSIN ANTAGONIST; DIURETIC
Pregnancy Category: C

AVAILABILITY 5 mg/mL solution for injection

ACTION & THERAPEUTIC EFFECT
Conivaptan is an arginine vasopressin receptor (V2) antagonist that reduces the effect of arginine vasopressin in the kidney, thus increasing the excretion of free water into the renal collecting ducts. *Conivaptan increases urine output and decreases urine osmolality in patients with euvolemic hyponatremia, thus restoring serum sodium balance.*

USES Treatment of euvolemic hyponatremia (e.g., syndrome of inappropriate secretion of antidiuretic hormone, or SIADH) in hospitalized patients.

CONTRAINDICATIONS Hypersensitivity to conivaptan; CHF; hyponatremia associated with hypovolemia; hypotension, syncope; intravenous use only; concurrent administration of potent CYP3A4 inhibitors such as ketoconazole, itraconazole, ritonavir, etc.; pregnancy (category C), lactation. Safety and efficacy in children not established.

CAUTIOUS USE Renal or hepatic function impairment.

ROUTE & DOSAGE

Euvolemic Hyponatremia

Adult: **IV** 20 mg loading dose followed by 20 mg IV over 24 h. May repeat 20 mg/day dose for 1–3 d, or may titrate up to 40 mg/d based on response. Total duration of infusion should not exceed 4 d.

ADMINISTRATION

Intravenous

PREPARE: IV Infusion: Use a filter needle when withdrawing a drug from an ampule. *Loading dose infusion:* Withdraw 4 mL (20 mg) from one ampule and add to 100 mL of D5W. Gently invert the bag several times to mix. *Initial maintenance infusion:* Withdraw 4 mL (20 mg) from one ampule and add to 250 mL of D5W. Gently invert the bag several times to mix. *Maximum maintenance dose infusion:* Withdraw 8 mL (40 mg) from two ampules and add to 250 mL of D5W. Gently invert the bag several times to mix.

Common adverse effects in *italic*, life-threatening effects underlined; generic names in **bold**; classifications in SMALL CAPS; ✦ Canadian drug name; ❷ Prototype drug

377

ADMINISTER: **IV Infusion:** Give via a large vein and change infusion site every 24 h. *Loading dose:* Give over 30 min. *Maintenance dose:* Give over 24 h. Frequently monitor the serum sodium level. A reduction in dose or discontinuation of infusion may be required if the serum sodium rises too rapidly. Discontinue infusion immediately and notify physician of a rise in serum sodium >12 mEq/L/24 h. DO NOT resume infusion if serum sodium continues to rise. Infusion may be resumed ONLY if hyponatremia persists or reoccurs and patient demonstrates no indication of neurologic impairment. If the serum sodium rises too slowly, the dose may be titrated up to 40 mg over 24 h.

INCOMPATIBILITIES **Solution/additive:** Lactated Ringer's solution, sodium chloride 0.9%. **Y-site:** None listed.

▪ Store vials at 25° C (77° F). Ampules should be stored in the original container and protected from light until ready for use. After diluting with D5W, the solution should be used immediately, with infusion completed within 24 h of mixing.

ADVERSE EFFECTS (≥1%) **Body as a Whole:** Cannula-site reaction, *infusion-site reaction,* pain, peripheral edema, pyrexia, *thirst.* **CNS:** Confusional state, *headache,* insomnia. **CV:** Atrial fibrillation, hypertension, hypotension, orthostatic hypotension, phlebitis. **GI:** Constipation, diarrhea, dry mouth, nausea, vomiting. **Hematologic:** Anemia. **Metabolic:** Dehydration, hyperglycemia, hypoglycemia, *hypokalemia,* hypomagnesemia, hyponatremia. **Respiratory:** Pneumonia. **Skin:** Erythema. **Special Senses:** Oral candidiasis.

INTERACTIONS Drug: Compounds that inhibit CYP3A4 (e.g., **ketoconazole, itraconazole, clarithromycin, ritonavir, indinavir**) can increase conivaptan levels. Conivaptan can increase the levels of **digoxin** and drugs that require CYP3A4 for metabolism (e.g., **midazolam,** HMG COA REDUCTASE INHIBITORS, **amlodipine**). **Food:** Grapefruit juice may increase the level of conivaptan. **Herbal: St. John's wort** may decrease the level of conivaptan.

PHARMACOKINETICS Distribution: 99% protein bound. **Metabolism:** Extensive hepatic metabolism. **Elimination:** Primarily fecal elimination (83%) with minor renal elimination. **Half-Life:** 5 h.

CLINICAL IMPLICATIONS

Assessment & Drug Effects

▪ Monitor infusion site for erythema, phlebitis, or other site reaction.
▪ Monitor vital signs and neurologic status frequently; report immediately S&S of hypernatremia (see Appendix F).
▪ Lab tests: Baseline and frequent serum sodium, serum potassium, and urine osmolality.
▪ Monitor digoxin blood levels with concurrent therapy and assess for S&S of digoxin toxicity.
▪ Monitor I&O closely. Effective treatment is accompanied by increased urine output, whereas decreasing urine output and oliguria may indicate developing hypernatremia.

Patient & Family Education

▪ Report any of the following to a health care provider: pain at the infusion site, dizziness, confusion, palpitations, swelling of hands or feet.

CORTICOTROPIN REPOSITORY

(kor-ti-koe-troe'pin)

H.P. Acthar Gel

Classifications: HORMONE; ADRENAL CORTICOSTEROID
Therapeutic: HORMONE; ADRENAL CORTICOSTEROID
Prototype: Prednisone
Pregnancy Category: C

AVAILABILITY 40 units/mL, 80 units/mL

ACTION & *THERAPEUTIC EFFECT*

Adrenocorticotropic hormone (ACTH) extracted from pituitary of domestic animals (usually pigs). Stimulates functioning adrenal cortex to produce and secrete corticosterone, cortisol (hydrocortisone), several weak androgens, and limited amounts of aldosterone. *Therapeutic effects appear more rapidly than do those of prednisone. Suppresses further release of corticotropin by negative feedback mechanism. Chronic administration of exogenous corticosteroids decreases ACTH store and causes structural changes in pituitary.*

USES Diagnostic test of adrenocortical function and adjunctively to treat adrenal insufficiency secondary to inadequate corticotropin secretion. Effective in treatment of adrenocorticoid-responsive diseases, such as multiple sclerosis, but adrenocorticoid therapy is preferred.

CONTRAINDICATIONS Ocular herpes simplex; recent surgery; CHF; scleroderma; osteoporosis; systemic fungoid infections; hypertension; adrenal insufficiency; heart failure; herpes infection, active infection; scleroderma; sensitivity to porcine proteins; conditions accompanied by primary adrenocortical insufficiency or hyperfunction; long-term use in children, pregnancy (category C), lactation.

CAUTIOUS USE Patients with latent tuberculosis or those reacting to tuberculin; hypothyroiditis; diabetes mellitus; seizure disorders; renal disease; psychosis, emotional instability; thromboembolic disease; GI disease; impaired hepatic function.

ROUTE & DOSAGE

Therapeutic

Adult: **IM/SC** 40–80 U q24–72h
Child: **IM/IV/SC** 0.8 U/kg/d divided q12h

Acute Multiple Sclerosis

Adult: **IM/SC** 80–120 U/d for 2–3 wk

ADMINISTRATION

Subcutaneous, Intramuscular

- Dosage is individualized. Changes in dosage regimen are gradual and only after full drug effects have become apparent.
- Corticotropin repository is only for SC and IM use. Do not use IV.
- Shake corticotropin zinc hydroxide bottle well before injecting drug deep into gluteal muscle.
- Give deep IM into a large muscle.

Intravenous

IV administration to infants and children: Verify correct IV concentration and rate of infusion with physician.

PREPARE: **Continuous:** Use only the vial labeled for IV use. Dilute powder with 2 mL sterile water or NS for injection; desired dose is withdrawn from vial and further diluted with 500 mL of D5W. *ADMINISTER:* **Continuous:** Give over 8 h.

Common adverse effects in *italic*, life-threatening effects underlined; generic names in **bold**; classifications in SMALL CAPS; ♣ Canadian drug name; ⊙ Prototype drug

379

C

INCOMPATIBILITIES **Solution/additive: Aminophylline, sodium bicarbonate.**

▪ Administration of the hormone at high dosage levels is tapered rather than withdrawn suddenly. A 2–5 d period of adrenocortical hypofunction follows discontinuation of corticotropin.

▪ Storage: Corticotropin for injection (reconstituted solution) is stable for 24 h or 7 d, depending on product, when stored at 2°–8° C (36°–46° F). Store corticotropin repository at 2°–15° C (36°–59° F). Store corticotropin zinc hydroxide at 15°–30° C (59°–86° F).

ADVERSE EFFECTS (≥1%) **Body as a Whole:** Loss of muscle mass, hypersensitivity, activation of latent tuberculosis, vertebral compression fracture. **GI:** Nausea, vomiting, abdominal distention, peptic ulcer with perforation and hemorrhage. **Endocrine:** Hirsutism, amenorrhea, osteoporosis, cushingoid state, activation of latent diabetes mellitus. **Metabolic:** Sodium and water retention; potassium and calcium loss, negative nitrogen balance, hyperglycemia. **CNS:** Euphoria, insomnia, headache, convulsions, papilledema, mood swings, depression. **Skin:** Acne, impaired wound healing, fragile skin, petechiae, ecchymosis. **Special Senses:** Cataract, glaucoma.

INTERACTIONS **Drug: Aspirin,** NSAIDS increase potential for hypoprothrombinemia; BARBITURATES, **phenytoin, rifampin** decrease effects of corticotropin; ESTROGENS may increase corticotropin binding and effects; **amphotericin B,** THIAZIDE AND LOOP DIURETICS increase potassium loss.

PHARMACOKINETICS Onset: 6 h. **Duration:** 12–24 h repository. **Distri-**

bution: Concentrated in many tissues; not known if crosses placenta or distributed into breast milk. **Metabolism:** In liver. **Elimination:** In urine. **Half-Life:** <20 min.

CLINICAL IMPLICATIONS

Assessment & Drug Effects

▪ Before giving corticotropin to patient with suspected sensitivity to porcine proteins, hypersensitivity skin testing should be performed.

▪ Observe patient closely for 15 min for hypersensitivity reactions during IV administration or immediately after SC or IM injections (urticaria, pruritus, dizziness, nausea, vomiting, anaphylactic shock). Epinephrine 1:1000 should be readily available for emergency treatment.

▪ Prolonged use of corticotropin increases risk of hypersensitivity reaction (see Appendix F).

▪ Adrenal response to corticotropin is measured against a baseline plasma cortisol level 1 h before the 8 h test. Another plasma level is determined after at least 1 h of the infusion.

▪ Corticotropin may suppress S&S of chronic disease.

▪ New infections can appear during treatment. Because of decreased resistance and inability to localize the infection, it may be severe. Report immediately.

▪ Monitor carefully growth and development of a child receiving this drug.

Patient & Family Education

▪ Corticotropin administration increases requirements for insulin and oral antidiabetic agents. If you have diabetes mellitus, monitor blood glucose closely until response to the drug is stabilized.

▪ Monitor weight and report a steady gain, especially if accompanied by edema. Also promptly report headache, muscle weakness, abdominal pain.

- Do not self-medicate with OTC drugs without consulting physician.
- Eye examinations should be done before initiation of expected long-term therapy and periodically during treatment. Report to physician if blurred vision occurs.
- Dietary salt restriction and potassium supplementation may be necessary to minimize edema caused by overstimulation of the adrenal cortex by corticotropin.
- Do not receive live vaccine immunizations while receiving corticotropin.

CORTISONE ACETATE

(kor'ti-sone)
Cortistan, Cortone
Classifications: HORMONE; SYNTHETIC ADRENAL CORTICOSTEROID; GLUCOCORTICOID; ANTIINFLAMMATORY
Therapeutic: ANTIINFLAMMATORY; CORTICOSTEROID REPLACEMENT; IMMUNOSUPPRESSANT
Prototype: Prednisone
Pregnancy Category: D

AVAILABILITY 5 mg, 10 mg, 25 mg tablets; 50 mg/mL injection

ACTION & *THERAPEUTIC EFFECT*
Short-acting synthetic steroid with prominent glucocorticoid activity and minimal mineralocorticoid effects. Therapeutic activity of cortisone results from its conversion in body to cortisol, resulting in metabolic effects including promotion of protein, carbohydrate, and fat metabolism and interference with linear growth in children. *Has antiinflammatory and immunosuppressive actions. Glucocorticoids prevent or suppress inflammation caused by various events including radiant, mechanical, chemical, and infectious stimuli. Also suppress immune responses in diseases caused by undesirable immune reactions, such as in asthma, urticaria, or renal allograft.*

USES Replacement therapy for primary or secondary adrenocortical insufficiency and inflammatory and allergic disorders.

CONTRAINDICATIONS Hypersensitivity to glucocorticoids; psychoses; viral, fungal, or bacterial diseases of skin; Cushing's syndrome, immunologic procedures; pregnancy (category D), lactation.
CAUTIOUS USE Diabetes mellitus; hypertension, CHF; older adults; active or arrested tuberculosis; coagulopathy; hepatic disease; psychosis, emotional instability; renal disease, seizure disorders; active or latent peptic ulcer.

ROUTE & DOSAGE

Replacement or Inflammatory Disorders

Adult: **PO/IM** 20–300 mg/d in 1 or more divided doses, try to reduce periodically by 10–25 mg/d to lowest effective dose
Child: **PO** 2.5–10 mg/kg/d divided q6–8h; **IM** 1–5 mg/kg/d divided q12–24h

ADMINISTRATION

Oral
- Administer cortisone (usually in a.m.) with food or fluid of patient's choice to reduce gastric irritation.
- Sodium chloride and a mineralocorticoid are usually given with cortisone as part of replacement therapy.

Intramuscular
- Parenteral cortisone is a suspension (25 mg/mL) and therefore

Common adverse effects in *italic*, life-threatening effects <u>underlined</u>; generic names in **bold**; classifications in SMALL CAPS; ♣ Canadian drug name; ⊙ Prototype drug

381

C

should not be used IV. Shake bottle well before withdrawing dose.
- Give deep IM into a large muscle.
- Drug must be gradually tapered rather than withdrawn abruptly.
- Store at 15°–30° C (59°–86° F) in tightly closed container unless otherwise directed by manufacturer. Protect from heat and freezing.

ADVERSE EFFECTS (≥1%) **CV:** CHF, hypertension, *edema.* **GI:** *Nausea,* peptic ulcer, pancreatitis. **Endocrine:** Hyperglycemia. **Hematologic:** Thrombocytopenia. **Musculoskeletal:** *Compression fracture,* osteoporosis, muscle weakness. **CNS:** Euphoria, insomnia, vertigo, nystagmus. **Skin:** Impaired wound healing, petechiae, ecchymosis, acne. **Special Senses:** *Cataracts,* glaucoma, blurred vision.

INTERACTIONS Drug: BARBITURATES, **phenytoin, rifampin** decrease effects of cortisone.

PHARMACOKINETICS Absorption: Readily absorbed from GI tract. **Onset:** Rapid PO; 24–48 h IM. **Peak:** 2 h PO; 24–48 h IM. **Duration:** 1.25–1.5 d. **Distribution:** Concentrated in many tissues; crosses placenta; distributed into breast milk. **Metabolism:** In liver. **Elimination:** In urine. **Half-Life:** 0.5 h; HPA suppression: 8–12 h.

CLINICAL IMPLICATIONS

Assessment & Drug Effects
- Monitor for S&S of Cushing's syndrome (see Appendix F), especially in patients on long-term therapy.
- Lab tests: Periodic blood glucose and CBC with platelet count.
- Cortisone may mask some signs of infection, and new infections may appear.

- Be alert to clinical indications of infection: malaise, anorexia, depression, and evidence of delayed healing. (Classic signs of inflammation are suppressed by cortisone.)
- Report ecchymotic areas, unexplained bleeding, and easy bruising.

Patient & Family Education
- Take drug exactly as prescribed. Do not alter dose intervals or stop therapy abruptly.
- Monitor weight and report a steady gain especially if it is accompanied by signs of fluid retention (e.g., edema of ankles or hands).
- Report changes in visual acuity, including blurring, promptly.
- Inform physician or dentist that cortisone is being taken. Carry identification card or jewelry that states drug being taken and physician's name.

COSYNTROPIN

(koe-sin-troe'pin)
Cortrosyn
Classifications: DIAGNOSTIC AGENT
Therapeutic: DIAGNOSTIC AGENT
Prototype: Prednisone
Pregnancy Category: C

AVAILABILITY 0.25 mg injection

ACTION & *THERAPEUTIC EFFECT*
Synthetic polypeptide resembling corticotropin (ACTH) in relation to the first 24 of the 39 amino acids in naturally occurring ACTH. Has less immunologic activity and is associated with less risk of sensitivity than corticotropin. *In patient with normal adrenocortical function, stimulates adrenal cortex to secrete corticosterone, cortisol (hydrocortisone), several weak androgenic*

substances, and limited amounts of aldosterone.

USES Diagnostic tool to differentiate primary adrenal from secondary (pituitary) adrenocortical insufficiency.
UNLABELED USES In patients with normal adrenocortical function for the long-term treatment of chronic inflammatory or degenerative disorders responsive to glucocorticoids.

CONTRAINDICATIONS History of allergic disorders; scleroderma, osteoporosis; systemic fungal infections; ocular herpes simplex; recent surgery; history of or presence of peptic ulcer; CHF; hypertension; adrenocortical insufficiency and adrenocortical hyperfunction; immunizations; tuberculosis, infections; pregnancy (category C), lactation.
CAUTIOUS USE Multiple sclerosis, acute gouty arthritis, mental disturbances, diabetes, abscess, pyrogenic infections, diverticulitis, renal insufficiency, myasthenia gravis, children.

ROUTE & DOSAGE

Rapid Screening Test
Adult/Child >2 y: **IM/IV** 0.25 mg
Child <2 y: **IM** 0.125 mg; **IV** 0.125 mg
Neonate: **IM/IV** 0.015 mg/kg

ADMINISTRATION

Intramuscular
- Reconstitute cosyntropin powder by adding 1.1 mL NS (diluent provided by manufacturer) to vial labeled 0.25 mg to provide solution containing 0.25 mg/mL.
- Inject deep IM into a large muscle.

Intravenous
IV administration to neonates, infants and children: Verify correct IV concentration and rate of infusion/injection with physician.

PREPARE: Direct: Reconstitute as for IM. **IV Infusion:** Further dilute in 250–500 mL of D5W or NS.
ADMINISTER: Direct: Give over 2 min. **IV Infusion:** Give at an approximate rate of 40 mcg/h over 4–6 h.

- Reconstituted solutions remain stable 24 h at room temperature or 21 d at 2°–8° C. ▪ Cosyntropin should not be added to blood or to plasma infusions.

ADVERSE EFFECTS (≥1%) **Body as a Whole:** Mild fever. **GI:** Chronic pancreatitis. **Skin:** Pruritus.

DIAGNOSTIC TEST INTERFERENCE
Cortisone, hydrocortisone, estrogen, spironolactone elevated *bilirubin,* and presence of *free Hgb* in plasma may interfere with *plasma cortisol* determinations.

INTERACTIONS Drug: Cortisone, hydrocortisone can exhibit abnormally high baseline values of cortisol and a decreased response to cosyntropin test.

PHARMACOKINETICS Absorption: Plasma cortisol levels double in 15–30 min. **Peak:** 1 h. **Duration:** 2–4 h. **Distribution:** Unknown; does not cross placenta. **Metabolism:** Unknown.

CLINICAL IMPLICATIONS

Assessment & Drug Effects
- Normal 17-KS levels in men are 10–25 mg/24 h; in women <50 y, 5–15 mg/24 h; and in women >50 y, 4–8 mg/24 h.
- Normal 17-OHCS levels in men are 5–12 mg/24 h; in women, 3–10 mg/24 h; in children 8–12 y, <4.5 mg/24 h; in younger children, 1.5 mg/24 h. Levels may be slightly higher in obese or muscular individuals.

Common adverse effects in *italic*, life-threatening effects underlined; generic names in **bold**; classifications in SMALL CAPS; ♣ Canadian drug name; ⊕ Prototype drug

383

CROMOLYN SODIUM ℞

(kroe′moe-lin)

Disodium Cromoglycate, Crolom, DSCG, Fivent ♣, Intal, Nasalcrom, Opticrom, Rynacrom ♣, Vistacrom ♣, Gastrocrom

Classifications: MAST CELL STABILIZER; ANTIINFLAMMATORY; ANTIASTHMATIC
Therapeutic: ANTIASTHMATIC; ANTIINFLAMMATORY
Pregnancy Category: B

AVAILABILITY 20 mg/2 mL solution for nebulization; 800 mcg spray; 40 mg/mL nasal solution; 4% ophth solution; 100 mg/5 mL oral concentrate.

ACTION & *THERAPEUTIC EFFECT*

Synthetic asthma prophylactic agent with unique action. Inhibits release of bronchoconstrictors—histamine and SRS-A (slow-reacting substance of anaphylaxis) from sensitized pulmonary mast cells, thereby suppressing an allergic response. Additionally, cromolyn may also reduce the release of inflammatory leukotrienes. *Particularly effective for IgE-mediated or "extrinsic asthma" precipitated by exposure to specific allergen, e.g., pollens, dust, animal dander, by inhibiting the release of bronchoconstrictors.*

USES Primarily for prophylaxis of mild to moderate seasonal and perennial bronchial asthma and allergic rhinitis. Also used for prevention of exercise-related bronchospasm, prevention of acute bronchospasm induced by known pollutants or antigens, and for prevention and treatment of allergic rhinitis. Orally for systemic mastocytosis. **Ophthalmic use:** Allergic ocular disorders, conjunctivitis, vernal keratoconjunctivitis.

UNLABELED USES Orally for prophylaxis of GI and systemic reactions to food allergy.

CONTRAINDICATIONS Use of aerosol (because of fluorocarbon propellants) in patients with coronary artery disease or history of arrhythmias; dyspnea, acute asthma, status asthmaticus, or acute bronchospasm; patients unable to coordinate actions or follow instructions. Safe use in children <2 y not determined.

CAUTIOUS USE Renal or hepatic dysfunction; pregnancy (category B), lactation.

ROUTE & DOSAGE

Allergies

Adult: **Inhalation** Metered dose inhaler or capsule: 1 spray or 1 capsule inhaled q.i.d.; nasal solution: 1 spray in each nostril 3–6 times/d at regular intervals
Child: **Inhalation** >6 y: Metered dose inhaler or capsule: same as for adult; >6 y: nasal solution: same as for adult

Conjunctivitis

see Appendix A-1

Mastocytosis

Adult: **PO** 2 ampules q.i.d. 30 min a.c. and h.s.
Child: **PO** 2–12 y: 1 ampule q.i.d. 30 min a.c. and h.s.

ADMINISTRATION

- Patients should receive detailed instructions for loading and administering the spinhaler or nasalmatic device. See manufacturer's instructions. Therapeutic effect is dependent on proper inhalation technique.

- Advise patient to clear as much mucus as possible before inhalation treatments.
- Instruct patient to exhale as completely as possible before placing inhaler mouthpiece between lips, tilt head backward and inhale rapidly and deeply with steady, even breaths. Remove inhaler from mouth, hold breath for a few seconds, then exhale into the air. Repeat until entire dose is taken.
- Caution patient not to exhale into inhaler because moisture from breath will interfere with its proper operation. Also inform patient that capsule is intended for inhalation only and is ineffective if swallowed.
- Protect cromolyn from moisture and heat. Store in tightly closed, light-resistant container at 15°–30° C (59°–86° F) unless otherwise directed.

ADVERSE EFFECTS (≥1%) **Body as a Whole:** Peripheral eosinophilia, angioedema, bronchospasm, anaphylaxis (rare). **GI:** Swelling of parotid glands, dry mouth, slightly bitter after-taste, *nausea,* vomiting, esophagitis. **CNS:** Headache, dizziness, peripheral neuritis. **Skin:** Erythema, urticaria, rash, contact dermatitis. **Special Senses:** *Sneezing, nasal stinging and burning,* dryness and *irritation of throat and trachea; cough;* nasal congestion, itchy, puffy eyes, lacrimation, *transient ocular burning, stinging.*

INTERACTIONS Drug: No clinically significant interactions established.

PHARMACOKINETICS Absorption: Approximately 8% of dose absorbed from lungs. **Onset:** 1 wk with regular use. **Peak:** 15 min. **Duration:** 4–6 h; may last as long as 2–3 wk. **Elimination:** Excreted in bile and urine in equal amounts. **Half-Life:** 80 min.

CLINICAL IMPLICATIONS
Assessment & Drug Effects
- Withhold drug and notify physician if any of the following occur; angioedema or bronchospasm.
- Monitor for exacerbation of asthmatic symptoms including breathlessness and cough that may occur in patients receiving cromolyn during corticosteroid withdrawal.
- For patients with asthma, therapeutic effects may be noted within a few days but generally not until after 1–2 wk of therapy.

Patient & Family Education
- Throat irritation, cough, and hoarseness can be minimized by gargling with water, drinking a few swallows of water, or by sucking on a lozenge after each treatment.
- Talk to your physician about what to do in the event of an acute asthmatic attack. Cromolyn is of no value in acute asthma.
- Cromolyn does not eliminate the continued need for therapy with bronchodilators, expectorants, antibiotics, or corticosteroids, but the amount and frequency of use of these medications may be appreciably reduced.
- Report any unusual signs or symptoms. Hypersensitivity reactions (see Signs & Symptoms, Appendix F) can be severe and life-threatening. Drug should be discontinued if an allergic reaction occurs.
- Treatment with cromolyn 15 min before doing protracted exercises reportedly blunts the effects of vigorous exercise as well as cold air.
- Ophthalmic use: Do not wear soft contact lenses during therapy with ophthalmic drug. They may be worn within a few hours after therapy is discontinued.
- Learn the proper technique for instillation of ophthalmic drops.

Common adverse effects in *italic*, life-threatening effects underlined; generic names in **bold**; classifications in SMALL CAPS; ♣ Canadian drug name; ⊙ Prototype drug

CROTAMITON
(kroe-tam′i-tonn)
Eurax
Classifications: SCABICIDE; ANTI-PRURITIC
Therapeutic: SCABICIDE; ANTIPRURITIC
Prototype: Lindane
Pregnancy Category: C

AVAILABILITY 10% cream, lotion

ACTION & *THERAPEUTIC EFFECT*
By unknown mechanisms, drug eradicates *Sarcoptes scabiei* and effectively relieves itching. *Scabicidal and antipruritic agent.*

USES Treatment of scabies and for symptomatic treatment of pruritus.

CONTRAINDICATIONS Application to acutely inflamed skin, raw or weeping surfaces, eyes, or mouth; history of previous sensitivity to crotamiton; pregnancy (category C).

ROUTE & DOSAGE

Scabies

Adult/Child: **Topical** Apply a thin layer of cream from neck to toes; apply a second layer 24 h later. Bathe 48 h after last application to remove drug

ADMINISTRATION

Topical
- Shake container well before use of solution.
- The skin must be thoroughly dry before applying medication.
- If drug accidentally contacts eyes, thoroughly flush out medication with water.

- Pruritus treatment: massage medication gently into affected areas until it is completely absorbed. Repeat as needed (usually effective for 6–10 h).
- Store in tightly closed containers at 15°–30° C (59°–86° F). Do not freeze.

ADVERSE EFFECTS (≥1%) **Skin:** Skin irritation (particularly with prolonged use), rash, erythema, sensation of warmth, allergic sensitization.

INTERACTIONS Drug: No clinically significant interactions established.

CLINICAL IMPLICATIONS
Assessment & Drug Effects
- Monitor for and report significant skin irritation or allergic sensitization.

Patient & Family Education
- Review package insert before treatment begins.
- Discontinue medication and report to physician if irritation or sensitization develops.

CYANOCOBALAMIN
(sye-an-oh-koe-bal′a-min)
Anacobin ◆, Bedoz ◆, Nascobal, Rubion ◆
Classifications: VITAMIN B$_{12}$
Therapeutic: VITAMIN B$_{12}$
Pregnancy Category: A (PO or nasal spray); C (parenteral)

AVAILABILITY 25 mcg, 50 mcg, 100 mcg, 250 mcg tablets; 400 mcg/unit, 500 mcg/0.1 mL nasal gel; 500 mcg/0.1 mL nasal spray

ACTION & *THERAPEUTIC EFFECT*
Vitamin B$_{12}$ is a cobalt-containing B complex vitamin produced by *Streptomyces griseus*. Essential for normal growth, cell reproduction,

maturation of RBCs, nucleoprotein synthesis, maintenance of nervous system (myelin synthesis), and believed to be involved in protein and carbohydrate metabolism. Vitamin B$_{12}$ deficiency results in megaloblastic anemia, dysfunction of spinal cord with paralysis, GI lesions. *Therapeutically effective for treatment of vitamin B$_{12}$ deficiency and pernicious anemia.*

USES Vitamin B$_{12}$ deficiency due to malabsorption syndrome as in pernicious (Addison's) anemia, sprue; GI pathology, dysfunction, or surgery; fish tapeworm infestation, and gluten enteropathy. Also used in B$_{12}$ deficiency caused by increased physiologic requirements or inadequate dietary intake, and in vitamin B$_{12}$ absorption (Schilling) test.
UNLABELED USES To prevent and treat toxicity associated with sodium nitroprusside.

CONTRAINDICATIONS History of sensitivity to vitamin B$_{12}$, other cobalamins, or cobalt; early Leber's disease (hereditary optic nerve atrophy), indiscriminate use in folic acid deficiency; pregnancy [category A, category C (parenteral)].
CAUTIOUS USE Heart disease, anemia, pulmonary disease.

ROUTE & DOSAGE

Vitamin B$_{12}$ Deficiency
Adult: **IM/Deep SC** 30 mcg/d for 5–10 d, then 100–200 mcg/mo
Child: **IM/Deep SC** 100 mcg doses to a total of 1–5 mg over 2 wk, then 60 mcg/mo

Pernicious Anemia
Adult: **IM/Deep SC** 100–1000 mcg/d for 2–3 wk, then 100–1000 mcg q2–4wk **Intranasal** one pump in one nostril once weekly

Child: **IM** 30–50 mcg/d times 2 wk to total of 1000 mcg, then 100 mcg/mo
Infant: **IM** 1000 mcg/d times at least 2 wk, then 50 mcg/mo

Diagnosis of Megaloblastic Anemia
Adult: **IM/Deep SC** 1 mcg/d for 10 d while maintaining a low folate and vitamin B$_{12}$ diet

Schilling Test
Adult: **IM/Deep SC** 1000 mcg times 1 dose

Nutritional Supplement
Adult: **PO** 1–25 mcg/d
Child: **PO** <1 y: 0.3 mcg/d; ≥1 y: 1 mcg/d

ADMINISTRATION
Oral
- PO preparations may be mixed with fruit juices. However, administer promptly since ascorbic acid affects the stability of vitamin B$_{12}$.
- Administration of oral vitamin B$_{12}$ with meals increases its absorption.

Subcutaneous, Intramuscular
- Give deep SC by slightly tenting the skin at the injection site.
- IM may be given into any normal IM injection site.
- Preserved in light-resistant containers at room temperature preferably at 15°–30° C (59°–86° F) unless otherwise directed by manufacturer.

ADVERSE EFFECTS (≥1%) **Body as a Whole:** Feeling of swelling of body, anaphylactic shock, sudden death. **CV:** Peripheral vascular thrombosis, pulmonary edema, CHF. **GI:** Mild transient diarrhea. **Hematologic:** Unmasking of polycythemia vera (with correction of vitamin B$_{12}$ deficiency). **Metabolic:** Hy-

Common adverse effects in *italic*, life-threatening effects underlined; generic names in **bold**; classifications in SMALL CAPS; ♣ Canadian drug name; ⊘ Prototype drug

387

pokalemia. **Skin:** Itching, rash, flushing. **Special Senses:** Severe optic nerve atrophy (patients with Leber's disease).

DIAGNOSTIC TEST INTERFERENCE

Most antibiotics, methotrexate, and pyrimethamine may produce invalid diagnostic *blood assays for vitamin B_{12}.* Possibility of false-positive test for *intrinsic factor antibodies.*

INTERACTIONS Drug: **Alcohol, aminosalicylic acid, neomycin, colchicine** may decrease absorption of oral cyanocobalamin; **chloramphenicol** may interfere with therapeutic response to cyanocobalamin.

PHARMACOKINETICS Absorption:

Intestinal absorption requires presence of intrinsic factor in terminal ileum. **Distribution:** Widely distributed; principally stored in liver, kidneys, and adrenals; crosses placenta, excreted in breast milk. **Metabolism:** Converted in tissues to active co-enzymes; enterohepatically cycled. **Elimination:** 50–95% of doses ≥100 mcg are excreted in urine in 48 h. **Half-Life:** 6 d (400 d in liver).

CLINICAL IMPLICATIONS

Assessment & Drug Effects

- Lab tests: Before initiation of therapy, reticulocyte and erythrocyte counts, Hgb, Hct, vitamin B_{12}, and serum folate levels should be determined; then repeated between 5 and 7 d after start of therapy and at regular intervals during therapy. Monitor potassium levels during the first 48 h. Conversion to normal erythropoiesis increases erythrocyte potassium requirement and can result in severe hypokalemia and sudden death.
- Obtain a careful history of sensitivities. Sensitization to cyanocobalamin can take as long as 8 y to develop.

- Monitor vital signs in patients with cardiac disease and in those receiving parenteral cyanocobalamin, and be alert to symptoms of pulmonary edema, which generally occur early in therapy.
- Therapeutic response to drug therapy is usually dramatic, occurring within 48 h. Effectiveness is measured by laboratory values and improvement in manifestations of vitamin B_{12} deficiency.
- Characteristically, reticulocyte concentration rises in 3–4 d, peaks in 5–8 d, and then gradually declines as erythrocyte count and Hgb rise to normal levels (in 4–6 wk).
- Obtain a complete diet and drug history and inquire into alcohol drinking patterns for all patients receiving cyanocobalamin to identify and correct poor habits.

Patient & Family Education

- Notify physician of any intercurrent disease or infection. Increased dosage may be required.
- To prevent irreversible neurologic damage resulting from pernicious anemia, drug therapy must be continued throughout life.
- Rich food sources of B_{12} are nutrient-added breakfast cereals, vitamin B_{12}-fortified soy milk, organ meats, clams, oysters, egg yolk, crab, salmon, sardines, muscle meat, milk, and dairy products.

CYCLIZINE HYDROCHLORIDE

(sye′kli-zeen)
Marezine, Marzine ♦

CYCLIZINE LACTATE

Marezine Lactate, Marzine
Classifications: ANTIHISTAMINE (H_1-RECEPTOR ANTAGONIST); ANTIVERTIGO AGENT; ANTIEMETIC
Therapeutic: ANTIVERTIGO; ANTIEMETIC; ANTIHISTAMINE

Common adverse effects in *italic*, life-threatening effects underlined; generic names in **bold**; classifications in SMALL CAPS; ♦ Canadian drug name; ⊕ Prototype drug

Prototype: Meclizine
Pregnancy Category: B

AVAILABILITY 50 mg tablets; 50 mg/mL injection

ACTION & *THERAPEUTIC EFFECT*
Piperazine antihistamine (H_1-receptor antagonist) that exhibits CNS depression and anticholinergic, antispasmodic, local anesthetic, and antihistaminic activity. Has prominent depressant action on labyrinthine excitability and on conduction in vestibular-cerebellar pathways. *Produces marked antimotion and antiemetic effects.*

USES Chiefly for prevention and treatment of motion sickness and postoperative nausea and vomiting.

CONTRAINDICATIONS Increased intraocular pressure; asthma, closed-angle glaucoma; children <6 y.
CAUTIOUS USE Narrow-angle glaucoma; prostatic hypertrophy; elderly; obstructive disease of GU or GI tracts; postoperative patients; pregnancy (category B), lactation.

ROUTE & DOSAGE

Motion Sickness
Adult: **PO** 50 mg 30 min before travel, then q4–6h prn (max: 200 mg/d) **IM** 50 mg q4–6h prn
Child: **PO:** 6–12 y, 25 mg q4–6h prn (max: 75 mg/d): **IM:** 6–12 y, 1 mg/kg t.i.d. prn (max: 75 mg/d)

Postoperative Vomiting
Adult: **IM** 50 mg 15–30 min before end of operation, may repeat q4–6h (t.i.d.) prn during first few days after surgery

ADMINISTRATION

Oral
▪ Give dose 30 min prior to any activity likely to cause motion sickness.

Intramuscular
▪ Aspirate needle carefully before injecting IM. Anaphylactic reactions following inadvertent IV injection have been reported.
▪ For prophylaxis of postoperative nausea and vomiting, drug usually prescribed with preoperative medication or is administered 20–30 min before expected termination of surgery.
▪ Store tablets in tight, light-resistant container at 15°–30° C (59°–86° F) unless otherwise directed. Store parenteral form in a cold place at 5°–10° C (41°–50° F). When parenteral solution is stored at room temperature for prolonged periods, it may become slightly yellow, but this does not indicate loss of potency.

ADVERSE EFFECTS (≥1%) **CV:** Hypotension, palpitation, tachycardia. **GI:** Anorexia, nausea, vomiting, diarrhea, or constipation, cholestatic jaundice. **CNS:** *Drowsiness,* excitement, euphoria, auditory and visual hallucinations, hyperexcitability alternating with drowsiness, convulsions, respiratory paralysis (rare). **Skin:** Urticaria, rash. **Special Senses:** *Dry mouth,* nose, and throat; blurred vision, diplopia; tinnitus. **Other:** Pain at IM injection site.

DIAGNOSTIC TEST INTERFERENCE
Because cyclizine is an antihistamine, inform patient that ***skin testing*** procedures should not be scheduled for about 4 d after drug is discontinued or false-negative reactions may result.

Common adverse effects in *italic*, life-threatening effects underlined; generic names in **bold**; classifications in SMALL CAPS; ♣ Canadian drug name; ⊕ Prototype drug

389

INTERACTIONS Drug: Alcohol, BARBITURATES, CNS DEPRESSANTS (e.g., HYPNOTICS, SEDATIVES, and ANXIOLYTICS) may compound effects of cyclizine.

PHARMACOKINETICS Onset: Rapid. **Duration:** 4–6 h. **Metabolism:** Unknown.

CLINICAL IMPLICATIONS

Assessment & Drug Effects

▪ Monitor post-operative patient's vital signs closely, as cyclizine can cause hypotension.
▪ Monitor for and report signs of CNS stimulation (e.g., hyperexcitability, euphoria). Dose reduction or discontinuation of drug may be indicated.

Patient & Family Education

▪ Take cyclizine with food or a glass of milk or water to minimize GI irritation.
▪ Do not drive a car or engage in other potentially hazardous activities until reaction to the drug is known. Adverse effects include drowsiness and dizziness.
▪ Alcohol, barbiturates, narcotic analgesic, and other CNS depressants may compound sedative action.

CYCLOBENZAPRINE HYDROCHLORIDE ⓟ

(sye-kloe-ben′za-preen)
Cycoflex, Flexeril

Classifications: SKELETAL MUSCLE RELAXANT, CENTRAL ACTING
Therapeutic: SKELETAL MUSCLE RELAXANT; ANTISPASMODIC
Pregnancy Category: B

AVAILABILITY 5 mg, 10 mg tablets

ACTION & *THERAPEUTIC EFFECT*
Relieves skeletal muscle spasm of local origin without interfering with muscle function. Believed to act primarily within CNS at brain stem; some action at spinal cord level is also probable. It is not a peripheral neuromuscular blocker. Depresses tonic somatic motor activity, although both gamma and alpha motor neurons are affected. *Cyclobenzaprine is a skeletal muscle relaxant approved for the relief of muscle spasm associated with acute, painful musculoskeletal conditions.*

USES Short-term adjunct to rest and physical therapy for relief of muscle spasm associated with acute musculoskeletal conditions. Not effective in treatment of spasticity associated with cerebral palsy or cerebral or cord disease.

CONTRAINDICATIONS Acute recovery phase of MI, patients with cardiac arrhythmias, heart block or conduction disturbances, QT prolongation; CHF, hyperthyroidism; closed-angle glaucoma, increased intraocular pressure; moderate or severe hepatic impairment; MAOI therapy; cerebral palsy. Use for periods longer than 2 or 3 wk not recommended by manufacturer. Safe use in children <15 y not established.
CAUTIOUS USE Patients receiving anticholinergic medications; prostatic hypertrophy, history of urinary retention, seizures; cardiovascular disease; mild hepatic impairment; older adults, debilitated patients; history of psychiatric illness; pregnancy (category B), lactation.

ROUTE & DOSAGE

Muscle Spasm
Adult: **PO** 5–10 mg t.i.d. (max: 60 mg/d)
Geriatric: Start with 5 mg
Mild Hepatic Impairment
Start with 5 mg

Moderate to Severe Hepatic Impairment
Not recommended

ADMINISTRATION

Oral

- Do not administer drug if patient is receiving an MAO INHIBITOR (e.g., furazolidone, isocarboxazid, pargyline, tranylcypromine).
- Cyclobenzaprine is intended for short-term (2 or 3 wk) use.
- Store in tightly closed container, preferably at 15°–30° C (59°–86° F) unless otherwise directed by manufacturer.

ADVERSE EFFECTS (≥1%) **Body as a Whole:** Edema of tongue and face, sweating, myalgia, hepatitis, alopecia. Shares toxic potential of tricyclic antidepressants. **CV:** Tachycardia, syncope, palpitation, vasodilation, chest pain, orthostatic hypotension, dyspnea; with high doses, possibility of severe arrhythmias. **GI:** *Dry mouth,* indigestion, unpleasant taste, coated tongue, tongue discoloration, vomiting, anorexia, abdominal pain, flatulence, diarrhea, paralytic ileus. **CNS:** *Drowsiness, dizziness,* weakness, fatigue, asthenia, paresthesias, tremors, muscle twitching, insomnia, euphoria, disorientation, mania, ataxia. **Skin:** Pruritus, urticaria, skin rash. **Urogenital:** Increased or decreased libido, impotence.

INTERACTIONS Drug: **Alcohol,** BARBITURATES, other CNS DEPRESSANTS enhance CNS depression; potentiates anticholinergic effects of **phenothiazine** and other ANTICHOLINERGICS; MAO INHIBITORS may precipitate hypertensive crisis—use with extreme caution.

PHARMACOKINETICS Absorption: Well absorbed from GI tract with some first-pass elimination in liver.

Onset: 1 h. **Peak:** 3–8 h. **Duration:** 12–24 h. **Distribution:** Highly protein bound (93%). **Metabolism:** In liver to inactive metabolites. **Elimination:** Slowly excreted in urine with some elimination in feces; may be excreted in breast milk. **Half-Life:** 1–3 d.

CLINICAL IMPLICATIONS

Assessment & Drug Effects

- Supervision of ambulation may be indicated, especially in the older adult because of risk of drowsiness and dizziness.
- Withhold drug and notify physician if signs of hypersensitivity, e.g., pruritus, urticaria, rash, appear.

Patient & Family Education

- Avoid driving and other potentially hazardous activities until reaction to drug is known. Adverse effects include drowsiness and dizziness.
- Avoid alcohol and other CNS DEPRESSANTS (unless otherwise directed by physician) because cyclobenzaprine enhances their effects.
- Dry mouth may be relieved by increasing total fluid intake (if not contraindicated).
- Keep physician informed of therapeutic effectiveness. Spasmolytic effect usually begins within 1 or 2 d and may be manifested by lessening of pain and tenderness, increase in range of motion, and ability to perform ADL.

CYCLOPENTOLATE HYDROCHLORIDE ℗

(sye-kloe-pen′toe-late)
Ak-Pentolate, Cyclogyl, Pentalair
Classifications: EYE PREPARATION; CYCLOPLEGIC; MYDRIATIC
Therapeutic: EYE PREPARATION; MYDRIATIC
Pregnancy Category: C

Common adverse effects in *italic*, life-threatening effects underlined; generic names in **bold**; classifications in SMALL CAPS; ♣ Canadian drug name; ℗ Prototype drug

391

AVAILABILITY 0.5%, 1%, 2% ophth solution

ACTION & *THERAPEUTIC EFFECT*

Tertiary amine antimuscarinic compound with systemic side effects and CNS toxicity, similar to those of atropine. Acts by blocking response of iris sphincter muscle, and muscle of accommodation in the ciliary body to cholinergic stimulation. *Results in dilation and paralysis of accommodation of the eyes.*

USES Induction of cycloplegia or mydriasis for ophthalmic diagnostic procedures.

CONTRAINDICATIONS Narrow angle glaucoma, excessively increased intraocular pressure; pregnancy (category C), lactation; children with a history of epilepsy. **CAUTIOUS USE** Elderly patients, brain damage (in children), Down's syndrome, spastic paralysis in children, blue-eyed individuals; infants; seizure disorders.

ROUTE & DOSAGE

Cycloplegia or Mydriasis

Adult: **Topical:** 1 drop of 1% solution in eye 40–50 min before procedure, followed by 1 drop in 5 min; may need 2% solution in patients with darkly pigmented eyes.
Child: **Topical:** 1 drop of 0.5–1% solution in eye 40–50 min before procedure, followed by 1 drop in 5 min; may need 2% solution in patients with darkly pigmented eyes.

ADMINISTRATION

Topical
▪ Clarify with physician which strength (1% or 2%) should be used.

▪ Ask patient to remove soft contact lenses prior to installation of drops.

ADVERSE EFFECTS (≥1%) **Body as a Whole:** Flushing, fever. **CNS:** Drowsiness dysarthria, disorientation, ataxia, hallucinations, hyperkinesis, psychosis, seizures. **CV:** Sinus tachycardia, hypotension. **GI:** Dry mouth, abdominal distention in infants. **Skin:** Rash, contact urticaria. **Special Senses:** Burning, stinging, transient increases in intraocular pressure, irritation, punctate keratitis, blurred vision, hyperemia, synechiae, conjunctivitis, photophobia. **Urogenital:** Urinary retention.

INTERACTIONS Drug: May interfere with the ocular antihypertensive effects of **carbachol, pilocarpine, physostigmine.**

PHARMACOKINETICS Peak: 15–60 min. **Duration:** 24 h.

CLINICAL IMPLICATIONS

Assessment & Drug Effects
▪ Monitor cardiac status especially with preexisting heart disease.

Patient & Family Education
▪ Do not touch the dropper to any surface, including your skin or eyes.
▪ Exercise caution when driving or engaging in other potentially hazardous activities as cyclopentolate ophthalmic may cause blurred vision. If you experience blurred vision, avoid these activities.
▪ Protect your eyes when in bright light. Cyclopentolate ophthalmic may cause increased light sensitivity.
▪ Do not wear soft contact lenses when the eyedrops are being inserted.
▪ Report immediately any of the following: difficulty breathing,

swelling of your lips, tongue, face or hives; palpitations; and unusual behavior.

CYCLOPHOSPHAMIDE ℗

(sye-kloe-foss'fa-mide)

Cytoxan, Neosar, Procytox ✦

Classifications: ANTINEOPLASTIC; ALKYLATING AGENT

Therapeutic: ANTINEOPLASTIC; ALKYLATING AGENT

Pregnancy Category: C

AVAILABILITY 25 mg, 50 mg tablets; 100 mg, 200 mg, 500 mg, 1 g, 2 g vials

ACTION & *THERAPEUTIC EFFECT*

Cell-cycle-nonspecific alkylating agent chemically related to the nitrogen mustards. Action mechanism thought to be the result of cross-linkage of DNA strands, thereby blocking synthesis of DNA, RNA, and protein. Associated with increased risk of secondary malignancies that may be detected several years after cyclophosphamide has been discontinued. *Has pronounced immunosuppressive activity and is a highly toxic drug; thus therapeutic effects are usually accompanied by some evidence of toxicity.*

USES As single agent or in combination with other chemotherapeutic agents in treatment of malignant lymphoma, multiple myeloma, leukemias, mycosis fungoides (advanced disease), neuroblastoma, adenocarcinoma of ovary, carcinoma of breast, or malignant neoplasms of lung.

UNLABELED USES To prevent rejection in homotransplantation; to treat severe rheumatoid arthritis, multiple sclerosis, systemic lupus erythematosus, Wegener's granulomatosis, nephrotic syndrome.

CONTRAINDICATIONS Men and women in childbearing years; serious infections (including chickenpox, herpes zoster); live virus vaccines; myelosuppression; dehydration; pregnancy (category C), lactation.

CAUTIOUS USE History of radiation or cytotoxic drug therapy; hepatic and renal impairment, elderly; recent history of steroid therapy; bone marrow infiltration with tumor cells; history of urate calculi and gout; patients with leukopenia, thrombocytopenia.

ROUTE & DOSAGE

Neoplasm

Adult: **PO Initial:** 1–5 mg/kg/d; **Maintenance:** 1–5 mg/kg q7–10d. **IV Initial:** 40–50 mg/kg in divided doses over 2–5 d up to 100 mg/kg; **Maintenance:** 10–15 mg/kg q7–10d *or* 3–5 mg twice weekly

Child: **PO Initial:** 2–8 mg/kg or 60–250 mg/m²; **Maintenance:** 2–5 mg/kg *or* 50–150 mg/m² twice weekly. **IV Initial:** 2–8 mg/kg *or* 60–250 mg/m²

Renal Impairment

Cl$_{cr}$< 10mL/min: give 75% of dose; administer post-dialysis

ADMINISTRATION

Oral

- Administer PO drug on empty stomach. If nausea and vomiting are severe, however, it may be taken with food. An antiemetic medication may be prescribed to be given before the drug.
- Store cyclophosphamide PO solution in refrigerator at 2°–8° C (36°–46° F), and use within 14 d.

Common adverse effects in *italic*, life-threatening effects underlined; generic names in **bold**; classifications in SMALL CAPS; ✦ Canadian drug name; ℗ Prototype drug

393

Intravenous

PREPARE: Direct: Add 5 mL sterile water for injection or bacteriostatic water for injection (paraben-preserved only) to each 100 mg and shake gently to dissolve. **Intermittent:** May be further diluted with 100–250 mL D5W, NS, D5/NS, RL, or other compatible solution.
ADMINISTER: **Direct/Intermittent:** Give each 100 mg or fraction thereof over 10–15 min.
INCOMPATIBILITIES **Y-site: Amphotericin B, cholesteryl complex.**

▪ Store at temperature between 2° and 30° C (36° and 86° F) unless otherwise recommended by the manufacturer.

ADVERSE EFFECTS (≥1%) **Body as a Whole:** Transient dizziness, fatigue, facial flushing, diaphoresis, drug fever, <u>anaphylaxis</u>, secondary neoplasia. **GI:** *Nausea, vomiting,* mucositis, *anorexia,* hepatotoxicity, diarrhea. **Hematologic:** <u>Leukopenia</u>, *neutropenia,* acute myeloid leukemia, anemia, thrombophlebitis, interference with normal healing. **Metabolic:** Severe hyperkalemia, SIADH, hyponatremia, weight gain (but without edema) or weight loss, hyperuricemia. **Respiratory:** <u>Pulmonary emboli</u> and edema, pneumonitis, <u>interstitial pulmonary fibrosis</u>. **Skin:** *Alopecia* (reversible), transverse ridging of nails, pigmentation of nail beds and skin (reversible), nonspecific dermatitis, <u>toxic epidermal necrolysis, Stevens-Johnson syndrome</u>. **Urogenital:** <u>Sterile hemorrhagic and nonhemorrhagic cystitis</u>, bladder fibrosis, nephrotoxicity.

DIAGNOSTIC TEST INTERFERENCE
Cyclophosphamide suppresses positive reactions to ***Candida, mumps,*** ***trichophytons,*** and ***tuberculin PPD skin tests. Papanicolaou (PAP)*** smear may be falsely positive.

INTERACTIONS Drug: Succinylcholine, prolonged neuromuscular blocking activity; **doxorubicin** may increase cardiac toxicity.

PHARMACOKINETICS Absorption: Readily from GI tract. **Peak:** 1 h PO. **Distribution:** Widely distributed, including brain, breast milk; crosses placenta. **Metabolism:** In liver by CYP3A4. **Elimination:** In urine as active metabolites and unchanged drug. **Half-Life:** 4–6 h.

CLINICAL IMPLICATIONS
Assessment & Drug Effects
▪ Lab tests: Total and differential leukocyte count, platelet count, and Hct are determined initially and at least 2 times per week during maintenance period. Baseline and periodic determinations of liver and kidney function and serum electrolytes also should be made. Microscopic urine examinations are recommended after large IV doses.
▪ Thrombocytopenia is rare, but if it occurs (count of 100,000/mm^3 or lower), assess for signs of unexplained bleeding or easy bruising. If platelet count indicates thrombocytopenia (≤100,000/mm^3), drug will be discontinued.
▪ Marked leukopenia is the most serious side effect. It can be fatal. Nadir may occur in 2–8 d after first dose but may be as late as 1 mo after a series of several daily doses. Leukopenia usually reverses 7–10 d after therapy is discontinued.
▪ During severe leukopenic period, protect patient from infection and trauma and from visitors and medical personnel who have colds or other infections.

- Report onset of unexplained chills, sore throat, tachycardia. Monitor temperature carefully and report an elevation immediately. The development of fever in a neutropenic patient (granulocyte count <1000) is a medical emergency because sepsis can develop quickly in these patients.
- Observe and report character of wound drainage. During period of neutropenia, purulent drainage may become serosanguineous because there are not enough WBC to create pus. Because of suppressed immune mechanisms, wound healing may be prolonged or incomplete.
- Monitor I&O ratio and patterns: Since the drug is a chemical irritant, PO and IV fluid intake is generally increased to help prevent renal irritation and hemorrhagic cystitis. Have patient void frequently, especially after each dose and just before retiring to bed.
- Watch for symptoms of water intoxication or dilutional hyponatremia; patients are usually well hydrated as part of the therapy.
- Promptly report hematuria or dysuria. Drug schedule is usually interrupted and fluids are forced.
- Record body weight at least twice weekly (basis for dose determination). Alert physician to sudden change or slow, steady weight gain or loss over a period of time that appears inconsistent with caloric intake.
- Diarrhea may signal onset of hyperkalemia, particularly if accompanied by colicky pain, nausea, bradycardia, and skeletal muscle weakness. These symptoms warrant prompt reporting to physician.
- Monitor for hyperuricemia, which occurs commonly during early treatment period in patients with leukemias or lymphoma. Report

edema of lower legs and feet; joint, flank, or stomach pain.
- Protect patient from potential sources of infection. Cyclophosphamide makes the patient particularly susceptible to varicella-zoster infections (chickenpox, herpes zoster).
- Report any sign of overgrowth with opportunistic organisms, especially in patient receiving corticosteroids or who has recently been on steroid therapy.
- Report fever, dyspnea, and nonproductive cough. Pulmonary toxicity is not common, but the already debilitated patient is particularly susceptible.

Patient & Family Education

- Adhere to dosage regimen and do not omit, increase, decrease, or delay doses. If for any reason drug cannot be taken, notify physician.
- Alopecia occurs in about 33% of patients on cyclophosphamide therapy. Hair loss may be noted 3 wk after therapy begins; regrowth (often differs in texture and color) usually starts 5–6 wk after drug is withdrawn and may occur while on maintenance doses.
- Use adequate means of contraception during and for at least 4 mo after termination of drug treatment. Breast-feeding should be discontinued before cyclophosphamide therapy is initiated.
- Amenorrhea may last up to 1 y after cessation of therapy in 10–30% of women.

CYCLOSERINE

(sye-kloe-ser'een)
Seromycin
Classifications: ANTIBIOTIC; ANTITUBERCULOSIS AGENT
Therapeutic: ANTIBIOTIC; ANTITUBERCULOSIS AGENT
Pregnancy Category: C

Common adverse effects in *italic*, life-threatening effects underlined; generic names in **bold**; classifications in SMALL CAPS; ♦ Canadian drug name; ☺ Prototype drug

395

C

AVAILABILITY 250 mg capsules

ACTION & *THERAPEUTIC EFFECT*
Broad-spectrum antiinfective that inhibits cell wall synthesis in susceptible strains. Bacteriostatic or bactericidal depending on concentration and susceptibility of organism. It competitively interferes with the incorporation of D-alanine into the bacterial cell wall, resulting in cell death. *Effective against gram-positive and gram-negative bacteria and* Mycobacterium tuberculosis.

USES In conjunction with other tuberculostatic drugs in treatment of active pulmonary and extrapulmonary tuberculosis when primary agents isoniazid, rifampin, ethambutol, streptomycin have failed. Also used in treatment of acute UTI caused by *Enterobacter* sp. and *Escherichia coli* that are unresponsive to conventional treatment.
UNLABELED USES Treatment of tuberculosis meningitis and nocardiosis.

CONTRAINDICATIONS Epilepsy; depression, severe anxiety, history of psychoses; severe renal insufficiency; chronic alcoholism; pregnancy (category C). Safe use in children not established.
CAUTIOUS USE Renal impairment, lactation; anemia.

ROUTE & DOSAGE

Tuberculosis
Adult: **PO** 250 mg q12h for 2 wk, may increase to 500 mg q12h (max: 1 g/d)

Urinary Tract Infection
Adult: **PO:** 250 mg q12h for 2 wk

ADMINISTRATION
Oral
- Pyridoxine 200–300 mg/d may be ordered concurrently to prevent neurotoxic effects of cycloserine.
- Store in tightly closed container at 15°–30° C (59°–86° F) unless otherwise directed.

ADVERSE EFFECTS (≥1%) **CV:** Arrhythmias, CHF. **Hematologic:** Vitamin B_{12} and folic acid deficiency, megaloblastic or sideroblastic anemia. **CNS:** *Drowsiness,* anxiety, *headache,* tremors, myoclonic jerking, convulsions, vertigo, visual disturbances, speech difficulties (dysarthria), lethargy, depression, disorientation with loss of memory, confusion, nervousness, psychoses, tic episodes, character changes, hyperirritability, aggression, hyperreflexia, peripheral neuropathy, paresthesias, paresis, dyskinesias. **Skin:** Dermatitis, photosensitivity. **Special Senses:** Eye pain (optic neuritis), photophobia.

INTERACTIONS Drug: Alcohol increases risk of seizures; **ethionamide, isoniazid** potentiate neurotoxic effects; may inhibit **phenytoin** metabolism, increasing its toxicity.

PHARMACOKINETICS Absorption: 70–90% from GI tract. **Peak:** 3–4 h. **Distribution:** Distributed to lung, ascitic, pleural and synovial fluids, and CSF; crosses placenta; distributed into breast milk. **Metabolism:** Not metabolized. **Elimination:** 60–70% in urine within 72 h; small amount in feces. **Half-Life:** 10 h.

CLINICAL IMPLICATIONS
Assessment & Drug Effects
- Lab tests: Culture and susceptibility tests should be performed before initiation of therapy and

periodically thereafter to detect possible bacterial resistance. Monitor plasma drug levels weekly and hematologic, renal, and hepatic function at regular intervals.

- Maintenance of blood-drug level below 30 mg/mL considerably reduces incidence of neurotoxicity. Possibility of neurotoxicity increases when dose is 500 mg or more or when renal clearance is inadequate.
- Observe patient carefully for signs of hypersensitivity and neurologic effects. Neurotoxicity generally appears within first 2 wk of therapy and disappears after drug is discontinued.
- Drug should be withheld and physician notified or dosage reduced if symptoms of CNS toxicity or hypersensitivity reaction (see Appendix F) develop.

Patient & Family Education

- Take cycloserine after meals to prevent GI irritation.
- Notify physician immediately of the onset of skin rash and early signs of CNS toxicity (see Appendix F).
- Avoid potentially hazardous tasks such as driving until reaction to cycloserine has been determined.
- Take drug precisely as prescribed and to keep follow-up appointments. Continuous therapy may extend into months or years.

CYCLOSPORINE ℗

(sye'kloe-spor-een)
Gengraf, Neoral, Sandimmune, Restasis
Classifications: IMMUNOSUPPRESSANT
Therapeutic: IMMUNOSUPPRESSANT; ANTIRHEUMATIC; ANTIPSORIATIC
Pregnancy Category: C

AVAILABILITY Sandimmune: 25 mg, 50 mg, 100 mg capsules 100 mg/mL oral solution **Gengraf, Neoral:** (microemulsion) 25 mg, 100 mg capsules 100 mg/mL oral solution 50 mg/mL injection **Restasis:** 0.05% ophthalmic emulsion

ACTION & *THERAPEUTIC EFFECT*

Immunosuppressant agent derived from extract of a soil fungus. Action in reducing transplant rejection is due to selective and reversible inhibition of the first phase of T-cell activation with T-lymphocytes (which normally stimulate antibody production). *It is used to prevent allograft rejection in transplant patients.*

USES In conjunction with adrenal corticosteroids to prevent organ rejection after kidney, liver, and heart transplants (allografts). Has had limited use in pancreas, bone marrow, and heart/lung transplantations. Also used for treatment of chronic transplant rejection in patients previously treated with other immunosuppressants; rheumatoid arthritis, severe psoriasis. Ophthalmic emulsion for the treatment of keratoconjunctivitis sicca.
UNLABELED USES Sjögren's syndrome, to prevent rejection of heart-lung and pancreatic transplants, ulcerative colitis.

CONTRAINDICATIONS Hypersensitivity to cyclosporine or to ingredients in commercially available formulations, e.g., Cremophor (polyoxyl 35 castor oil); recent contact with or bout of chickenpox, herpes zoster; administration of live virus vaccines to patient or family members; RA patients with abnormal renal function, uncontrolled hypertension, or malignancies; ocular infection, pregnancy (category C), lactation.

Common adverse effects in *italic*, life-threatening effects underlined; generic names in **bold**; classifications in SMALL CAPS; ♣ Canadian drug name; ℗ Prototype drug

397

C

CAUTIOUS USE Renal, hepatic, pancreatic, or bowel dysfunction; biliary tract disease, jaundice, hyperkalemia; electrolyte imbalance, hyperuricemia, hypertension; infection; radiation therapy, older adults, encephalopathy, females of childbearing age, fungal or viral infection, gout, herpes infection, lymphoma, neoplastic disease, malabsorption problems (e.g., liver transplant patients).

ROUTE & DOSAGE

Prevention of Organ Rejection

Adult/Child: **PO** 14–18 mg/kg beginning 4–12 h before transplantation and continued for 1–2 wk after surgery, then gradual reduction by 5%/wk, max dose of microemulsion, 10 mg/kg/d; **Maintenance:** 5–10 mg/kg/d. **IV** 5–6 mg/kg beginning 4–12 h before transplantation and continued after surgery until patient can take oral

Rheumatoid Arthritis (Neoral)

Adult: **PO** 2.5 mg/kg/d divided into 2 doses. May increase by 0.5–0.75 mg/kg/d q4wk to a max of 4 mg/kg/d

Severe Psoriasis (Neoral)

Adult: **PO** 1.25 mg/kg b.i.d. If significant improvement has not occurred after 4 wk, may increase dose by 0.5 mg/kg/d every 2 wk to max of 4 mg/kg/d

Keratoconjunctivitis Sicca

Adult: **Ophthalmic** 1 drop in affected eye(s) twice daily approximately 12 h apart

ADMINISTRATION

Oral

- Do not dilute oral solution with grapefruit juice. Dilute with orange or apple juice, stir well, then administer immediately.
- Neoral (microemulsion) and Sandimmune are not bioequivalent and cannot be used interchangeably without physician supervision.

Intravenous

PREPARE: IV Infusion: Dilute each 1 mL immediately before administration in 20–100 mL of D5W or NS.

ADMINISTER: IV Infusion: Give by slow infusion over approximately 2–6 h. Rapid IV can result in nephrotoxicity.

INCOMPATIBILITIES Solution/additive: **Magnesium Sulfate.** Y-site: **Amphotericin B cholesteryl complex, TPN.**

- Store preferably at 15°–30° C (59°–86° F) in well-closed containers. Do not refrigerate. Protect ampules from light.

ADVERSE EFFECTS (≥1%) **Body as a Whole:** Lymphoma, gynecomastia, chest pain, leg cramps, edema, fever, chills, weight loss, increased risk of skin malignancies in psoriasis patients previously treated with methotrexate, psoralens, or UV light therapy. **CV:** *Hypertension,* MI (rare). **GI:** Gingival hyperplasia, diarrhea, nausea, *vomiting,* abdominal discomfort, anorexia, gastritis, constipation. **Hematologic:** Leukopenia, anemia, thrombocytopenia, *hypermagnesemia, hyperkalemia,* hyperuricemia, *decreased serum bicarbonate,* hyperglycemia. **CNS:** *Tremor,* convulsions, headache, paresthesias, hyperesthesia, flushing, night sweats, insomnia, visual hallucinations, confusion, anxiety, flat affect, depression, lethargy, weakness, paraparesis, ataxia, amnesia. **Skin:** *Hirsutism,* acne, oily skin, flushing. **Special Senses:** Sinusitis, tinnitus, hearing loss, sore throat. **Urogeni-**

Common adverse effects in *italic*, life-threatening effects underlined; generic names in **bold**; classifications in SMALL CAPS; ✦ Canadian drug name; ☻ Prototype drug

tal: Urinary retention, frequency, *nephrotoxicity (oliguria)*.

DIAGNOSTIC TEST INTERFERENCE
Hyperlipidemia and abnormalities in *electrophoresis* reported; believed to be due to polyoxyl 35 castor oil (Cremophor) in IV cyclosporine.

INTERACTIONS Drug: AMINOGLYCOSIDES, **danazol, diltiazem, doxycycline, erythromycin, ketoconazole, methylprednisolone, metoclopramide, nicardipine,** NSAIDS, **prednisolone, verapamil** may increase cyclosporine levels; **carbamazepine, isoniazid, octreotide, phenobarbital, phenytoin, rifampin** may decrease cyclosporine levels; **acyclovir,** AMINOGLYCOSIDES, **amphotericin B, cimetidine, erythromycin, ketoconazole, melphalan, ranitidine, cotrimoxazole, trimethoprim** may increase risk of nephrotoxicity; POTASSIUM-SPARING DIURETICS, ACE INHIBITORS **(captopril, enalapril)** may potentiate hyperkalemia. **Food:** Grapefruit juice may increase concentration. **Herbal:** **St. John's wort** may decrease cyclosporine levels.

PHARMACOKINETICS Absorption:
Variably and incompletely absorbed (30%). Microemulsion formulation (Neoral) has less variability in absorption and may produce significantly higher serum levels compared with the standard formulation. **Peak:** 3–4 h. **Distribution:** Widely distributed; 33–47% distributed to plasma; 41–50% to RBCs; crosses placenta; distributed into breast milk. **Metabolism:** In liver by CYP3A4, including significant first pass metabolism; considerable enterohepatic circulation. **Elimination:** Primarily in bile and feces; 6% in urine. **Half-Life:** 19–27 h.

CLINICAL IMPLICATIONS
Assessment & Drug Effects
- Observe patients receiving the drug parenterally for at least 30 min continuously after start of IV infusion, and at frequent intervals thereafter to detect allergic or other adverse reactions.
- Hypersensitivity reactions have been associated with Cremophor emulsifying agent in the parenteral formulation but not with the PO solution, which does not contain this ingredient.
- Monitor I&O ratio and pattern: Nephrotoxicity has been reported in about one third of transplant patients. It has occurred in mild forms as late as 2–3 mo after transplantation. In severe form, it can be irreversible, and therefore early recognition is critical.
- Monitor vital signs. Be alert to indicators of local or systemic infection that can be fungal, viral, or bacterial. Also report significant rise in BP.
- Lab tests: Baseline and periodic tests are advised for (1) renal function (BUN, serum creatinine), (2) liver function (AST, ALT, serum amylase, bilirubin, and alkaline phosphatase), and (3) serum potassium.
- Lab tests: In psoriasis patients, CBC, BUN, uric acid, potassium, lipids, and magnesium should be monitored biweekly during first 3 mo.
- Periodic tests should be made of neurologic function. Neurotoxic effects generally occur over 13–195 d after initiation of cyclosporine therapy. Signs and symptoms are reportedly fully reversible with dosage reduction or discontinuation of drug.
- Monitor blood or plasma drug concentrations at regular intervals, particularly in patients receiving

Common adverse effects in *italic*, life-threatening effects underlined; generic names in **bold**; classifications in SMALL CAPS; ✦ Canadian drug name; ⊘ Prototype drug

399

the drug orally for prolonged periods, as drug absorption is erratic.

Patient & Family Education

- Use the specially calibrated pipette provided to measure dose.
- Take medication with meals to reduce nausea or GI irritation.
- Enhance palatability of oral solution by mixing it with milk, chocolate milk, or orange juice, preferably at room temperature. Mix in a glass rather than a plastic container. Stir well, drink immediately, and rinse glass with small quantity of diluent to assure getting entire dose.
- Take medication at same time each day to maintain therapeutic blood levels.
- Keep scheduled follow-up appointments.
- If possible, see a dentist before start of cyclosporine treatment, and practice good oral hygiene. Inspect mouth daily for white patches, sores, swollen gums.
- Hirsutism is reversible with discontinuation of drug.

CYPROHEPTADINE HYDROCHLORIDE

(si-proe-hep'ta-deen)
Periactin, Vimicon ◆
Classifications: ANTIHISTAMINE (H$_1$-RECEPTOR ANTAGONIST); ANTIPRURITIC
Therapeutic: ANTIHISTAMINE; H$_1$-RECEPTOR ANTAGONIST
Prototype: Diphenhydramine
Pregnancy Category: B

AVAILABILITY 4 mg tablets

ACTION & *THERAPEUTIC EFFECT*
Potent piperidine antihistamine with pharmacologic actions that acts by competing with histamine for H$_1$-receptor sites on effector cells, thus preventing histamine-mediated responses. *Has significant antipruritic, local anesthetic, and antiserotonin activity. Produces mild central depression and moderate anticholinergic effects.*

USES Symptomatic relief of various allergic conditions, including hay fever, vasomotor rhinitis, allergic conjunctivitis, urticaria caused by cold sensitivity, and pruritus of allergic dermatoses. Effective in treatment of anaphylactoid reactions as adjunct to epinephrine and other standard measures after acute symptoms have been controlled.
UNLABELED USES Cushing's disease, carcinoid syndrome, vascular headaches, appetite stimulant.

CONTRAINDICATIONS Hypersensitivity to cyproheptadine or other H$_1$-receptor antagonist antihistamines; acute asthma attack; lactation. Safe use in children <2 y not established.
CAUTIOUS USE Older adult and debilitated patients; patients predisposed to urinary retention; glaucoma; asthma; COPD; hyperthyroidism; cardiovascular or hepatic disease, hypertension; GI or GU tract obstruction, children with a family history of SIDS; pregnancy (category B).

ROUTE & DOSAGE

Allergies

Adult: **PO** 4 mg t.i.d. or q.i.d. (4–20 mg/d), max 0.5 mg/kg/d
Geriatric: **PO** Start with 4 mg b.i.d.
Child: **PO** 0.25 mg/kg/d in 3–4 divided doses (max: 12 mg/d for 2–6 y, 16 mg/d for 6–12 y)

ADMINISTRATION

Oral

- GI adverse effects may be minimized by administering drug with food or milk.
- Store in tightly covered container at 15°–30° C (59°–86° F) unless otherwise directed.

ADVERSE EFFECTS (≥1%) **GI:** *Dry mouth,* nausea, vomiting, epigastric distress, appetite stimulation, weight gain, transient decrease in fasting blood sugar level, increased serum amylase level, cholestatic jaundice. **CNS:** *Drowsiness,* dizziness, faintness, headache, tremulousness, fatigue, disturbed coordination. **Respiratory:** Thickened bronchial secretions. **Skin:** Skin rash. **Special Senses:** Dry nose and throat. **Urogenital:** Urinary frequency, retention, and difficult urination.

DIAGNOSTIC TEST INTERFERENCE As a general rule, antihistamines are discontinued about 4 d before **skin testing procedures** are to be performed because they may produce false-negative results.

INTERACTIONS Drug: Alcohol and CNS DEPRESSANTS add to CNS depression; TRICYCLIC ANTIDEPRESSANTS and other ANTICHOLINERGICS have additive anticholinergic effects; may inhibit pressor effects of **epinephrine.**

PHARMACOKINETICS Absorption: Readily absorbed from GI tract. **Duration:** 6–9 h. **Distribution:** Distribution into breast milk not known. **Metabolism:** In liver. **Elimination:** In urine.

CLINICAL IMPLICATIONS

Assessment & Drug Effects

- Monitor level of alertness. In some patients, the sedative effect disappears spontaneously after 3–4 d of drug administration.

- Since drug may cause dizziness, supervision of ambulation and other safety precautions may be warranted.

Patient & Family Education

- Avoid activities requiring mental alertness and physical coordination, such as driving a car, until reaction to the drug is known.
- Drug causes sedation, dizziness, and hypotension in older adults. Report these symptoms. Children are more apt to manifest CNS stimulation, e.g., confusion, agitation, tremors, hallucinations. Reduction in dosage may be indicated.
- Cyproheptadine may increase and prolong the effects of alcohol, barbiturates, narcotic analgesics, anxiolytics, and other CNS depressants.
- Monitor weight and keep physician informed of any significant weight gain.
- Maintain sufficient fluid intake to help to relieve dry mouth and also reduce risk of cholestatic jaundice.

CYTARABINE

(sye-tare'a-been)

Cytosar-U, DepoCyt

Classifications: ANTINEOPLASTIC; ANTIMETABOLITE, PURINE ANTAGONIST

Therapeutic: ANTINEOPLASTIC; ANTIMETABOLITE

Prototype: 6-mercaptopurine

Pregnancy Category: D

AVAILABILITY 10 mg/mL liposomal, 20 mg/mL, 100 mg, 500 mg, 1g, 2 g injection

ACTION & *THERAPEUTIC EFFECT*

Pyrimidine analog with cell phase specificity affecting rapidly dividing cells in S phase (DNA synthesis). In certain conditions prevents development of cell from G_1 to S phase.

Common adverse effects in *italic,* life-threatening effects <u>underlined</u>; generic names in **bold**; classifications in SMALL CAPS; ♣ Canadian drug name; ☻ Prototype drug

401

Interferes with DNA and RNA synthesis in rapidly growing cells. *Antineoplastic agent which has strong myelosuppressant activity. Immunosuppressant properties are exhibited by obliterated cell-mediated immune responses, such as delayed hypersensitivity skin reactions.*

USES To induce and maintain remission in acute myelocytic leukemia, acute lymphocytic leukemia, and meningeal leukemia and for treatment of lymphomas. Used in combination with other antineoplastics in established chemotherapeutic protocols.

CONTRAINDICATIONS History of drug-induced myelosuppression; immunization procedures; pregnancy (category D) particularly during first trimester, lactation. Safe use in infants not established.

CAUTIOUS USE Impaired renal or hepatic function, elderly; neurologic disease; gout, drug-induced myelosuppression.

ROUTE & DOSAGE

Leukemias

Adult/Child: **IV** 100–200 mg/m^2 by continuous infusion over 24 h **SC** 1 mg/kg 1–2 times/wk **Intrathecal** 5–75 mg once q4d or once/d for 4 d

ADMINISTRATION

Intrathecal

- For intrathecal injection, reconstitute with an isotonic, buffered diluent without preservatives. Follow manufacturer's recommendations.

Intravenous

PREPARE: **Direct:** Reconstitute with bacteriostatic water for injection (without benzyl alcohol for neonates) as follows: add 5 mL to the 100-mg vial to yield 20 mg/mL; add 10 mL to the 500 mg vial to yield 50 mg/mL. **IV Infusion:** May be further diluted with 100 mL or more of D5W or NS.

ADMINISTER: **Direct:** Give at a rate of 100 mg or a fraction thereof over 3 min. **IV Infusion:** Give over 30 min or longer depending on the total volume of IV solution to be infused.

INCOMPATIBILITIES **Solution/additive: Fluorouracil, gentamicin, heparin, insulin, nafcillin, oxacillin, penicillin G. Y-site: Allopurinol, ganciclovir, TPN.**

- Store cytarabine in refrigerator until reconstituted. Reconstituted solutions may be stored at 15°–30° C (59°–86° F) for 48 h. Discard solutions with a slight haze.

ADVERSE EFFECTS (≥1%) **Body as a Whole:** Weight loss, sore throat, fever, thrombophlebitis and pain at injection site; pericarditis, bleeding (any site), pneumonia. Potentially carcinogenic and mutagenic. **GI:** *Nausea, vomiting,* diarrhea, stomatitis, oral or anal inflammation or ulceration, esophagitis, anorexia, hemorrhage, hepatotoxicity, jaundice. **Hematologic:** *Leukopenia, thrombocytopenia,* anemia, megaloblastosis, myelosuppression (reversible); transient hyperuricemia. **CNS:** Headache, neurotoxicity; peripheral neuropathy, brachial plexus neuropathy, personality change, neuritis, vertigo, lethargy, somnolence, confusion. **Skin:** Rash, erythema, freckling, cellulitis, skin ulcerations, pruritus, urticaria, bulla formation, desquamation. **Special Senses:** Conjunctivitis, keratitis, photophobia. **Urogenital:** Renal dysfunction, urinary retention.

Common adverse effects in *italic*, life-threatening effects underlined; generic names in **bold**; classifications in SMALL CAPS; ♣ Canadian drug name; ⊘ Prototype drug

INTERACTIONS Drug: GI toxicity may decrease **digoxin** absorption; decreases AMINOGLYCOSIDES activity against *Klebsiella pneumoniae.*

PHARMACOKINETICS Peak: 20–60 min SC. **Distribution:** Crosses blood-brain barrier and placenta. **Metabolism:** In liver. **Elimination:** 80% in urine in 24 h. **Half-Life:** 1–3 h.

CLINICAL IMPLICATIONS

Assessment & Drug Effects

- Inspect patient's mouth before the administration of each dose. Toxicity necessitating dosage alterations almost always occurs. Report adverse reactions immediately.
- Lab tests: Hct and platelet counts and total and differential leukocyte counts should be evaluated daily during initial therapy. Serum uric acid and hepatic function tests should be performed at regular intervals throughout treatment period.
- Hyperuricemia due to rapid destruction of neoplastic cells may accompany cytarabine therapy. A regimen that includes a uricosuric agent such as allopurinol, urine alkalinization, and adequate hydration may be started. To reduce potential for urate stone formation, fluids are forced in excess of 2 L, if tolerated. Consult physician.
- Monitor I&O ratio and pattern.
- Monitor body temperature. Be alert to the most subtle signs of infection, especially low-grade fever, and report promptly.
- When platelet count falls below 50,000/mm³ and polymorphonuclear leukocytes to below 1000/mm³, therapy may be suspended. WBC nadir is usually reached in 5–7 d after therapy has been stopped. Therapy is restarted with appearance of bone marrow recovery and when preceding cell counts are reached.

- Provide good oral hygiene to diminish adverse effects and chance of superinfection. Stomatitis and cheilosis usually appear 5–10 d into the therapy.

Patient & Family Education

- Report promptly protracted vomiting or signs of nephrotoxicity (see Appendix F).
- Flu-like syndrome occurs usually within 6–12 wk after drug administration and may recur with successive therapy. Report chills, fever, achy joints and muscles.
- Report any S&S of superinfection (see Appendix F).

CYTOMEGALOVIRUS IMMUNE GLOBULIN (CMVIG, CMV-IVIG)

(cy-to-meg′a-lo-vi-rus)

CytoGam

Classifications: BIOLOGIC RESPONSE MODIFIER; IMMUNOGLOBULIN
Therapeutic: IMMUNOGLOBULIN
Prototype: Interferon alfa-2a
Pregnancy Category: C

AVAILABILITY 50 mg/mL injection

ACTION & *THERAPEUTIC EFFECT*
Cytomegalovirus immune globulin (CMVIG) is a preparation of immunoglobulin G (IgG) antibodies derived from a large number of healthy donors with high concentrations of antibodies directed against cytomegalovirus (CMV). *The CMV antibodies attenuate or reduce the incidence of serious CMV disease, such as CMV-associated pneumonia, CMV-associated hepatitis, and concomitant fungi and parasitic superinfections.*

USES Attenuation of primary cytomegalovirus (CMV) disease associated with kidney transplantation.

Common adverse effects in *italic*, life-threatening effects <u>underlined</u>; generic names in **bold**; classifications in SMALL CAPS; ♣ Canadian drug name; ⊘ Prototype drug

403

UNLABELED USES Prevention of CMV disease in other organ transplants (especially heart) when the recipient is seronegative for CMV and the donor is seropositive.

CONTRAINDICATIONS History of previous severe reactions associated with CMVIG or other human immunoglobulin preparations, selective immunoglobulin A (IgA) deficiency; pregnancy (category C).
CAUTIOUS USE Myelosuppression, maltose or sucrose hypersensitivity; cardiac disease, lactation.

ROUTE & DOSAGE

Prevention of CMV Disease
Adult: **IV** 150 mg/kg within 72 h of transplantation, then 100 mg/kg 2, 4, 6, and 8 wk posttransplant, then 50 mg/kg 12 and 16 wk posttransplant

ADMINISTRATION

Intravenous
CMVIG should be administered through a separate IV line using an infusion pump. See manufacturer's directions if this is not possible.

PREPARE: **IV Infusion:** Use a double ended transfer needle or large syringe to reconstitute with 50 mL sterile water. Gently rotate vial to dissolve; do not shake. Allow 30 min to dissolve powder. Reconstituted solution contains 50 mg/mL. Must be completely infused within 12 h since solution contains no preservative.

ADMINISTER: **IV Infusion:** Use a constant infusion pump and give at rate of 15, 30, 60 mg/kg/h over first 30 min, second 30 min, third 30 min, respectively. Monitor closely during and after each rate change. If flushing, nausea, back pain, fever, or chills develops, slow or temporarily discontinue infusion. If BP begins to decrease, stop infusion and institute emergency measures. **Infusion of subsequent IV doses:** The intervals for increasing the dose from 15 to 30 to 60 mg may be shortened from 30 to 15 min. Never infuse more than 75 mL/h CMVIG.
▪ Reconstituted solution should be started within 6 h and completed within 12 h of preparation. Discard solution if cloudy.

ADVERSE EFFECTS (≥1%) **Body as a Whole:** Muscle aches, back pain, anaphylaxis (rare), fever and chills during infusion. **CV:** Hypotension, palpitations. **GI:** Nausea, vomiting, metallic taste. **CNS:** Headache, anxiety. **Respiratory:** Shortness of breath, wheezing. **Skin:** Flushing.

INTERACTIONS Drug: May interfere with the immune response to LIVE VIRUS VACCINES **(BCG, measles/mumps/rubella, live polio),** defer vaccination with live viral vaccines for approximately 3 mo after administration of CMVIG; revaccination may be necessary if these vaccines were given shortly after CMVIG.

CLINICAL IMPLICATIONS
Assessment & Drug Effects
▪ Monitor vital signs preinfusion, before increases in infusion rate, periodically during infusion, and postinfusion.
▪ Notify physician immediately if any of the following occur: flushing, nausea, back pain, fall in BP, other signs of anaphylaxis.
▪ Emergency drugs should be available for treatment of acute anaphylactic reactions.
▪ Monitor for CMV-associated syndromes (e.g., leukopenia, thrombo-

cytopenia, hepatitis, pneumonia) and for superinfections.

Patient & Family Education

- Familiarize yourself with potential adverse effects and know which to report to physician.
- Defer vaccination with live viral vaccines for 3 mo after administration of CMVIG.

DACARBAZINE

(da-kar'ba-zeen)
DTIC-Dome
Classifications: ANTINEOPLASTIC; ALKYLATING AGENT
Therapeutic: ANTINEOPLASTIC; ALKYLATING AGENT
Prototype: Cyclophosphamide
Pregnancy Category: C

AVAILABILITY 10 mg/mL injection

ACTION & *THERAPEUTIC EFFECT*
Cytotoxic agent with alkylating properties, which is cell-cycle nonspecific. Interferes with DNA replication, RNA transcription, and protein synthesis in rapidly proliferating cells. *Has carcinogenic, mutagenic, and teratogenic effects with minimal immunosuppressive activity.*

USES As single agent or in combination with other antineoplastics in treatment of metastatic malignant melanoma, refractory Hodgkin's disease, various sarcomas, and neuroblastoma.
UNLABELED USES Soft tissue metastatic sarcoma and malignant glucagonoma.

CONTRAINDICATIONS Hypersensitivity to dacarbazine; severe bone marrow suppression; active infection; lactation; pregnancy (category C).

CAUTIOUS USE Hepatic or renal impairment; previous radiation or chemotherapy.

ROUTE & DOSAGE

D

Neoplasms
Adult: **IV** 2–4.5 mg/kg/d for 10 d repeated at 4-wk intervals or 250 mg/m²/d for 5 d repeated at 3-wk intervals

Hodgkin's Disease
Adult: **IV** 150 mg/m²/d × 5 d; repeat at 4 wk intervals

ADMINISTRATION

Intravenous
IV administration to infants and children: Verify correct IV concentration and rate of infusion with physician.

- Wear gloves when handling this drug. If solution gets into the eyes, wash them with soap and water immediately, then irrigate with water or isotonic saline.

PREPARE: **Direct:** Reconstitute drug with sterile water for injection to make a solution containing 10 mg/mL dacarbazine (pH 3.0–4.0) by adding 9.9 mL to 100 mg or 19.8 mL to 200 mg. **IV Infusion:** Dilute further in 50 mL of D5W or NS.

ADMINISTER: **Direct:** Give by direct IV over 1 min. **IV Infusion:** Infuse IV over 30 min. If possible, avoid using antecubital vein or veins on dorsum of hand or wrist where extravasation could lead to loss of mobility of entire limb. Avoid veins in extremity with compromised venous or lymphatic drainage and veins near joint spaces.

INCOMPATIBILITIES **Solution/additive: Heparin.**

Common adverse effects in *italic*, life-threatening effects <u>underlined</u>; generic names in **bold**; classifications in SMALL CAPS; ♣ Canadian drug name; ⓓ Prototype drug

405

- Administer dacarbazine only to patients under close supervision because close observation and frequent laboratory studies are required during and after therapy. ■ IV extravasation: Monitor injection site frequently (instruct patient to do so, if able). Give prompt attention to patient's complaint of swelling, stinging, and burning sensation around injection site. Extravasation can occur painlessly and without visual signs. Danger areas for extravasation are dorsum of hand or ankle (especially if peripheral arteriosclerosis is present), joint spaces, and previously irradiated areas. If extravasation is suspected, infusion should be stopped immediately and restarted in another vein. Report to the physician. Prompt institution of local treatment is IMPERATIVE.

- Store reconstituted solution up to 72 h at 4° C (39° F) or at room temperature 15°–30° C (59°–86° F) for up to 8 h. Store diluted reconstituted solution for 24 h at 4° C (39° F) or at room temperature for up to 8 h. Protect from light.

ADVERSE EFFECTS (≥1%) **Body as a Whole:** Hypersensitivity (erythematosus, urticarial rashes, hepatotoxicity, photosensitivity); facial paresthesia and flushing, flu-like syndrome, myalgia, malaise, anaphylaxis. **CNS:** Confusion, headache, seizures, blurred vision. **GI:** *Anorexia, nausea, vomiting.* **Hematologic:** <u>Severe leukopenia and thrombocytopenia</u>, mild anemia. **Skin:** Alopecia. **Other:** *Pain along injected vein.*

PHARMACOKINETICS Distribution: Localizes primarily in liver. **Metabolism:** In liver by CYP1A2. **Elimination:** 35–50% in urine in 6 h. **Half-Life:** 5 h.

CLINICAL IMPLICATIONS

Assessment & Drug Effects

- Monitor IV site carefully for extravasation; if suspected, discontinue IV immediately and notify physician.
- Note: Skin damage by dacarbazine can lead to deep necrosis requiring surgical debridement, skin grafting, and even amputation. Older adults, the very young, comatose, and debilitated patients are especially at risk. Other risk factors include establishing an IV line in a vein previously punctured several times and the use of nonplastic catheters.
- Lab tests: Monitor for hematopoietic toxicity that usually appears about 4 wk after first dose. Generally, a leukocyte count of <3000/mm³ and a platelet count of <100,000/mm³ require suspension or cessation of therapy.
- Avoid, if possible, all tests and treatments during platelet nadir requiring needle punctures (e.g., IM). Observe carefully and report evidence of unexplained bleeding.
- Monitor for severe nausea and vomiting (>90% of patients) that begin within 1 h after drug administration and may last for as long as 12 h.
- Check patient's mouth for ulcerative stomatitis prior to the administration of each dose.
- Monitor I&O ratio and pattern and daily temperature. Renal impairment extends the half-life and increases danger of toxicity. Report symptoms of renal dysfunction and even a slight elevation of temperature.

Patient & Family Education

- Learn about all potential adverse drug effects.

Common adverse effects in *italic*, life-threatening effects <u>underlined</u>; generic names in **bold**; classifications in SMALL CAPS; ✦ Canadian drug name; ⊕ Prototype drug

- Report flu-like syndrome that may occur during or even a week after treatment is terminated and last 7–21 d. Symptoms frequently recur with successive treatments.
- Avoid prolonged exposure to sunlight or to ultraviolet light during treatment period and for at least 2 wk after last dose. Protect exposed skin with sunscreen lotion (SPF 15) and avoid exposure in midday.
- Report promptly the onset of blurred vision or paresthesia.

DACLIZUMAB

(dac'li-zu-mab)
Zenapax
Classifications: IMMUNOSUPPRESSANT; MONOCLONAL ANTIBODY; INTERLEUKIN-2 (IL-2) RECEPTOR ANTAGONIST
Therapeutic: IMMUNOSUPPRESSANT; IL-2 RECEPTOR ANTAGONIST
Pregnancy Category: C

AVAILABILITY 5 mg/mL injection

ACTION & *THERAPEUTIC EFFECT*
Immunosuppressant IgG-1 monoclonal antibody produced by recombinant DNA technology. Binds to interleukin-2 (IL-2) receptor complex of lymphocytes. *Daclizumab inhibits IL-2–mediated activation of lymphocytes which is the major pathway for cellular immune rejection of allografts.*

USES Prophylaxis of acute organ rejection in renal transplant.

CONTRAINDICATIONS Hypersensitivity to daclizumab; murine protein hypersensitivity, pregnancy (category C), lactation.
CAUTIOUS USE Moderate-to-severe renal impairment; allergies, asthma, or history of allergic responses to

medications; fungal or herpes infection, lymphoma, neoplastic disease, vaccination, varicella, viral infection.

ROUTE & DOSAGE

Renal Transplant
Adult/Child: **IV** >11 mo, 1 mg/kg. Start first dose no more than 24 h prior to transplant; repeat q14d for 4 more doses

ADMINISTRATION

Intravenous

PREPARE: **IV Infusion:** Add calculated amount of drug (based on patient's body weight) to 50 mL of NS. Invert infusion bag to dissolve, but do not shake. Discard if diluted solution is colored or has particulate matter.
ADMINISTER: **IV Infusion:** Infuse diluted drug over 15 min.

- Use diluted solution immediately or store at room temperature for 4 h or at 2°–8° C (36°–46° F) for 24 h. Discard after 24 h. ■ Store unopened vials at 2°–8° C (36°–46° F) and protect from light.

ADVERSE EFFECTS (≥1%) **Body as a Whole:** Edema (general and in extremities), pain, fever, fatigue, shivering, generalized weakness, arthralgia, myalgia, hypersensitivity reactions. **CNS:** Tremor, headache, dizziness, insomnia, anxiety, depression. **CV:** Chest pain, hypertension, hypotension, tachycardia, thrombosis, bleeding. **GI:** Constipation, nausea, diarrhea, vomiting, abdominal pain, dyspepsia, abdominal distention, epigastric pain, flatulence, gastritis, hemorrhoids. **Urogenital:** Oliguria, dysuria, renal tubular necrosis, hydronephrosis, urinary tract bleeding, renal insufficiency. **Respiratory:** Dyspnea, pulmonary edema, cough,

Common adverse effects in *italic*, life-threatening effects underlined; generic names in **bold**; classifications in SMALL CAPS; ♣ Canadian drug name; ⊘ Prototype drug

407

atelectasis, congestion, pharyngitis, rhinitis, hypoxia, rales, abnormal breath sounds, pleural effusion. **Skin:** Impaired wound healing, acne, pruritus, hirsutism, rash, night sweats. **Other:** Diabetes mellitus, dehydration, blurred vision.

INTERACTIONS Drug: Mycophenolate, cyclosporine may increase mortality.

PHARMACOKINETICS Duration: 120 d. **Half-Life:** 20 d (11–38 d).

CLINICAL IMPLICATIONS

Assessment & Drug Effects

- Monitor carefully for and immediately report S&S of opportunistic infection or anaphylactoid reaction (see Appendix F).

Patient & Family Education

- Use effective contraception before beginning daclizumab therapy, during therapy, and for 4 mo after completion of therapy.
- Avoid vaccinations during daclizumab therapy.

DACTINOMYCIN

(dak-ti-noe-mye′sin)
Cosmegen
Classifications: ANTINEOPLASTIC; ANTIBIOTIC
Therapeutic: ANTINEOPLASTIC
Prototype: Doxorubicin
Pregnancy Category: D

AVAILABILITY 0.5 mg injection

ACTION & *THERAPEUTIC EFFECT*
Potent cytotoxic cell cycle nonspecific antibiotic; toxic properties preclude its use as antibiotic. Complexes with DNA, thereby inhibiting DNA, RNA, and protein synthesis in actively proliferating cells. Causes delayed myelosuppression. Potenti-ates effects of x-ray therapy; the converse also appears likely. *Has antineoplastic properties that result from inhibiting DNA and RNA synthesis.*

USES As single agent or in combination with other antineoplastics or radiation to treat Wilms' tumor, rhabdomyosarcoma, carcinoma of testes and uterus, Ewing's sarcoma, and sarcoma botryoides.
UNLABELED USES Malignant melanoma, trophoblastic tumors, Kaposi's sarcoma, osteogenic sarcoma, among others.

CONTRAINDICATIONS Acute infection; pregnancy (category D), lactation, infants <6 mo.
CAUTIOUS USE Previous therapy with antineoplastics or radiation within 3–6 wk, bone marrow depression; infections; history of gout; impairment of kidney or liver function; obesity; chickenpox, herpes zoster, and other viral infections.

ROUTE & DOSAGE

Neoplasms
Adult: **IV** 500 mcg/d for 5 d max., may repeat at 2–4 wk intervals if tolerated (if patient is obese or edematous, give 400–600 mcg/m²/d to relate dosage to lean body mass); monitor for symptoms of toxicity from overdosage
Child: **IV** 15 mcg/kg/d (max: 500 mcg) for 5 d or 2.5 mg/m² over 7 d, may repeat at 2–4 wk intervals if tolerated

Wilm's Tumor, Childhood Rhabdomyosarcoma, Ewing's Sarcoma
Adult/Child: **IV** 15 mcg/kg/d × 5 d with other agents

Gestational Trophoblastic Neoplasia
Adult: **IV** 12 mcg/kg/d × 5 d

ADMINISTRATION

Intravenous

Use gloves and eye shield when preparing solution. If skin is contaminated, rinse with running water for 10 min; then rinse with buffered phosphate solution. If solution gets into the eyes, wash with water immediately; then irrigate with water or isotonic saline for 10 min.

PREPARE: Direct: Reconstitute 0.5 mg vial by adding 1.1 mL sterile water (without preservative) for injection; the resulting solution will contain approximately 0.5 mg/mL. **IV Infusion:** Further dilute in 50 mL of D5W or NS for infusion.

ADMINISTER: Direct: Use two-needle technique for direct IV: Withdraw calculated dose from vial with one needle, change to new needle to give directly into vein without using an infusion. Give over 2–3 min. Or give directly into an infusing solutions of D5W or NS, or into tubing or side arm of a running IV infusion. **IV Infusion:** Give diluted solution as a single dose over 15–30 min.

■ Store drug at 15°–30° C (59°–86° F) unless otherwise directed. Protect from heat and light.

ADVERSE EFFECTS (≥1%)

GI: *Nausea, vomiting,* anorexia, abdominal pain, diarrhea, proctitis, GI ulceration, *stomatitis,* cheilitis, glossitis, dysphagia, hepatitis. **Hematologic:** Anemia (including <u>aplastic anemia), agranulocytosis, leukopenia, thrombocytopenia,</u> pancytopenia, reticulopenia. **Skin:** Acne, desquamation, hyperpigmentation and reactivation of erythema especially over previously irradiated areas, *alopecia* (reversible). **Other:** Malaise, fatigue, lethargy, fever, myalgia, anaphylaxis, gonadal suppression, hypocalcemia, hyperuricemia, thrombophlebitis; *necrosis, sloughing, and contractures at site of extravasation;* hepatitis, hepatomegaly.

INTERACTIONS

Drug: Elevated **uric acid** level produced by dactinomycin may necessitate dose adjustment of ANTIGOUT AGENTS; effects of both dactinomycin and other MYELOSUPPRESSANTS are potentiated; effects of both **radiation** and dactinomycin are potentiated, and dactinomycin may reactivate erythema from previous radiation therapy; **vitamin K** effects (antihemorrhagic) decreased, leading to prolonged clotting time and potential hemorrhage.

PHARMACOKINETICS

Distribution: Concentrated in liver, spleen, kidneys, and bone marrow; does not cross blood–brain barrier; crosses placenta. **Elimination:** 50% unchanged in bile and 10% in urine; only 30% in urine over 9 d. **Half-Life:** 36 h.

CLINICAL IMPLICATIONS

Assessment & Drug Effects

■ Observe injection site frequently; if extravasation occurs, stop infusion immediately. Restart infusion in another vein. Report to physician. Institute prompt local treatment to prevent thrombophlebitis and necrosis.

■ Monitor for severe toxic effects that occur with high frequency. Effects usually appear 2–4 d after a course of therapy is stopped and may reach maximal severity 1–2 wk following discontinuation of therapy.

■ Use antiemetic drugs to control nausea and vomiting, which often occur a few hours after drug ad-

Common adverse effects in *italic*, life-threatening effects <u>underlined</u>; generic names in **bold**; classifications in SMALL CAPS; ♣ Canadian drug name; ⊘ Prototype drug

409

D

ministration. Vomiting may be severe enough to require intermittent therapy. Observe patient daily for signs of drug toxicity.

- Lab tests: Frequent renal, hepatic, and bone marrow function tests are advised. Perform WBC counts daily, and platelet counts every 3 d to detect hematopoietic depression.
- Monitor temperature and inspect oral membranes daily for stomatitis.
- Monitor for stomatitis, diarrhea, and severe hematopoietic depression. These may require prompt interruption of therapy until drug toxicity subsides.
- Report onset of unexplained bleeding, jaundice, and wheezing. Also, be alert to signs of agranulocytosis (see Appendix F). Report to physician. Antibiotic therapy, protective isolation, and discontinuation of the antineoplastic are indicated.
- Observe and report symptoms of hyperuricemia (see Appendix F). Urge patient to increase fluid intake up to 3000 mL/d if allowed.

Patient & Family Education

- Note: Infertility is a possible, irreversible adverse effect of this drug.
- Learn preventative measures to minimize nausea and vomiting.
- Note: Alopecia (hair loss) is an anticipated reversible adverse effect of this drug. Seek appropriate supportive guidance.

DALTEPARIN SODIUM

(dal-tep-a′rin)
Fragmin
Pregnancy Category: B
See Appendix A-2.

DANAZOL

(da′na-zole)
Cyclomen ◆
Classifications: ANDROGEN/ANABOLIC STEROID
Therapeutic: ANABOLIC STEROID
Prototype: Testosterone
Pregnancy Category: X

AVAILABILITY 50 mg, 100 mg, 200 mg capsules

ACTION & *THERAPEUTIC EFFECT* Synthetic androgen steroid; derivative of testosterone with dose-related mild androgenic effects but no estrogenic or progestational activity. Suppresses pituitary output of FSH and LH, resulting in anovulation and associated amenorrhea. *Interrupts progress and pain of endometriosis by causing atrophy and involution of both normal and ectopic endometrial tissue.*

USES Palliative treatment of endometriosis when alternative hormonal therapy is ineffective, contraindicated, or intolerable. Also used to treat fibrocystic breast disease and hereditary angioedema.
UNLABELED USES To treat precocious puberty, gynecomastia, menorrhagia, premenstrual syndrome (PMS), chronic immune thrombocytopenic purpura (ITP), autoimmune hemolytic anemia, hemophilia A and B.

CONTRAINDICATIONS Pregnancy (category X), lactation; children; undiagnosed abnormal genital bleeding; impaired renal, cardiac, or hepatic function; porphyria; vaginal bleeding.
CAUTIOUS USE Migraine headache, epilepsy; seizure disorders; elderly.

Common adverse effects in *italic*, life-threatening effects underlined; generic names in **bold**; classifications in SMALL CAPS; ◆ Canadian drug name; ❷ Prototype drug

ROUTE & DOSAGE

Endometriosis

Adult: **PO** 400 mg b.i.d. for 3–6 mo, start during menstruation or if pregnancy test is negative, may extended to 9 mo if necessary. Do not repeat regimen

Fibrocystic Breast Disease

Adult: **PO** 100–400 mg in 2 divided doses, start during menstruation or if pregnancy test is negative

Hereditary Angioedema

Adult: **PO** 200 mg b.i.d. or t.i.d., may decrease by 50% at intervals of 1–3 mo or longer, start during menstruation or if pregnancy test is negative

ADMINISTRATION

Oral

- Start therapy during menstruation, or after a negative pregnancy test.
- Store capsules at 15°–30° C (59°–86° F) in tightly closed container.

ADVERSE EFFECTS (≥1%) **Body as a Whole:** Hypersensitivity (skin rashes, nasal congestion). **Endocrine:** Androgenic effects (acne, mild hirsutism, deepening of voice, oily skin and hair, hair loss, edema, weight gain, pitch breaks, voice weakness, decrease in breast size); hypoestrogenic effects *(hot flashes;* sweating; emotional lability; nervousness; vaginitis with itching, drying, burning, or bleeding; *amenorrhea, irregular menstrual patterns);* impairment in glucose tolerance. **CNS:** Dizziness, sleep disorders, fatigue, tremor, irritability. **Special Senses:** Conjunctival edema. **CV:** Elevated BP. **GI:** Gastroenteritis, <u>hepatic damage</u> (rare), increased LDL, decreased HDL. **Urogenital:** Decreased libido. **Musculoskeletal:** Joint lock-up, joint swelling.

INTERACTIONS Herbal: Echinacea possibility of increased hepatotoxicity.

PHARMACOKINETICS Elimination: Other pharmacokinetic information is not known. **Half-Life:** 4.5 h.

CLINICAL IMPLICATIONS

Assessment & Drug Effects

- Routine breast examinations should be carried out during therapy. Carcinoma of the breast should be ruled out prior to start of therapy for fibrocystic breast disease. Advise patient to report to physician if any nodule enlarges or becomes tender or hard during therapy.
- Because danazol may cause fluid retention, patients with cardiac or renal dysfunction, epilepsy, or migraine should be observed closely during therapy, as these problems could worsen. Monitor weight.
- Drug-induced edema may compress the median nerve, producing symptoms of carpal tunnel syndrome. If patient complains of wrist pain that worsens at night, paresthesias in radial palmar aspect of the hand and fingers, consult physician.
- Lab tests: Baseline and periodic liver function tests should be performed in all patients. Patients with diabetes (or history of) should have blood glucose tests.

Patient & Family Education

- Note: Pain and discomfort are usually relieved in 2 or 3 mo; the nodularity in 4–6 mo. Menses may be regular or irregular in pattern during therapy.
- Note: Drug-induced amenorrhea is reversible. Ovulation and cyclic

Common adverse effects in *italic*, life-threatening effects <u>underlined</u>; generic names in **bold**; classifications in SMALL CAPS; ✦ Canadian drug name; ❶ Prototype drug

411

D

bleeding usually return within 60–90 d after therapeutic regimen is discontinued as well as the potential for conception.

- Use a nonhormonal contraceptive during treatment because ovulation may not be suppressed until 6–8 wk after therapy is begun. If pregnancy occurs while taking this drug, discontinue danzol. Continue discussing the question of continuing the pregnancy considered.

- Report voice changes promptly. Stop drug to avoid permanent damage to voice. Virilizing adverse effects may persist even after drug therapy is terminated.

DANTROLENE SODIUM

(dan'troe-leen)

Dantrium

Classifications: SKELETAL MUSCLE RELAXANT

Therapeutic: SKELETAL MUSCLE RELAXANT; ANTISPASMODIC

Prototype: Cyclobenzaprine

Pregnancy Category: C

AVAILABILITY 25 mg, 50 mg, 100 mg capsules; 20 mg vial

ACTION & THERAPEUTIC EFFECT

Hydantoin derivative with peripheral skeletal muscle relaxant action. Directly relaxes the spastic muscle by interfering with calcium ion release from sarcoplasmic reticulum within skeletal muscle. Clinical doses produce about a 50% decrease in contractility of skeletal muscles. *Relief of muscle spasticity, however, may be accompanied by muscle weakness sufficient to affect overall functional capacity of the patient.*

USES Orally for the symptomatic treatment of skeletal muscle spasms secondary to spinal cord injury, stroke, cerebral palsy, multiple sclerosis. Used intravenously for the management of malignant hyperthermia. Oral dantrolene can be used prophylactically for patients with a history of malignant hyperthermia or with a family history of the disorder.

UNLABELED USES Neuroleptic malignant syndrome, exercise-induced muscle pain, and flexor spasms.

CONTRAINDICATIONS Active hepatic disease; when spasticity is necessary to sustain upright posture and balance in locomotion or to maintain increased body function; spasticity due to rheumatic disorders; pregnancy (category C), lactation. Safe use in children <5 y is not established.

CAUTIOUS USE Impaired cardiac or pulmonary function, muscular sclerosis; neuromuscular disease; myopathy; patients >35 y, especially women.

ROUTE & DOSAGE

Relief of Spasticity

Adult: **PO** 25 mg once/d, increase to 25 mg b.i.d. to q.i.d., may increase q4–7d up to 100 mg b.i.d. to q.i.d.

Child: **PO** 0.5 mg/kg b.i.d., increase to 0.5 mg/kg t.i.d. or q.i.d., may increase by 0.5 mg/kg up to 3 mg/kg b.i.d. to q.i.d. (max: 100 mg q.i.d.)

Malignant Hyperthermia

Adult/Child: **IV** 1 mg/kg rapid direct IV push repeated prn up to a total of 10 mg/kg **PO** May be necessary to continue orally with 1–2 mg/kg q.i.d. for 1–3 d to prevent recurrence

ADMINISTRATION

Oral

- Prepare oral suspension for a single dose, when necessary, by emptying contents of capsule(s) into fruit juice or other liquid. Shake suspension well before pouring. Avoid contamination, keep refrigerated, and use within several days, since it will not contain a preservative.

Intravenous

PREPARE: **Direct:** Dilute each 20 mg with 60 mL sterile water without preservatives. Shake until clear.

ADMINISTER: **Direct:** Give by rapid direct IV push. Avoid extravasation; solution has a high pH and therefore is extremely irritating to tissue. Ensure IV patency prior to IV push.

- Store capsules in tightly closed, light-resistant container. Contents of vial (for IV use) must be protected from direct light and used within 6 h after reconstitution, since it does not contain a preservative. Store both PO and parenteral forms at 15°–30° C (59°–86° F) unless otherwise directed.

ADVERSE EFFECTS (≥1%) **Body as a Whole:** Hypersensitivity (pruritus, urticaria, eczematoid skin eruption, photosensitivity, eosinophilic pleural effusion). **CNS:** Drowsiness, *muscle weakness,* dizziness, lightheadedness, unusual fatigue, speech disturbances, headache, confusion, nervousness, mental depression, insomnia, euphoria, seizures. **CV:** Tachycardia, erratic BP. **Special Senses:** Blurred vision, diplopia, photophobia. **GI:** *Diarrhea,* constipation, nausea, vomiting, anorexia, swallowing difficulty, alterations of taste, gastric irritation, abdominal cramps, GI bleeding; hepatitis, jaundice, hepatomegaly, <u>hepatic necrosis</u> (all related to prolonged use of high doses). **Urogenital:** Crystalluria with pain or burning with urination, urinary frequency, urinary retention, nocturia, enuresis, difficult erection.

INTERACTIONS Drug: **Alcohol** and other CNS DEPRESSANTS compound CNS depression; **estrogens** increase risk of hepatotoxicity in women >35 y; **verapamil** and other CALCIUM CHANNEL BLOCKERS increase risk of ventricular fibrillation and cardiovascular collapse with IV dantrolene.

PHARMACOKINETICS Absorption: Incompletely absorbed from GI tract. **Peak:** 5 h. **Distribution:** Crosses placenta. **Metabolism:** In liver. **Elimination:** In urine chiefly as metabolites. **Half-Life:** 8.7 h.

CLINICAL IMPLICATIONS

Assessment & Drug Effects

- Monitor for therapeutic effectiveness. Improvement may not be apparent until 1 wk or more of drug therapy.
- Monitor vital signs during IV infusion. Also monitor ECG, CVP, and serum potassium.
- Supervise ambulation until patient's reaction to drug is known. Relief of spasticity may be accompanied by some loss of strength.
- Note: Most common adverse effects are generally transient, lasting up to 14 d after initiation of therapy. Keep physician informed.
- Monitor patients with impaired cardiac or pulmonary function closely for cardiovascular or respiratory symptoms such as tachycardia, BP changes, feeling of suffocation.
- Monitor for and report symptoms of allergy and allergic pleural ef-

Common adverse effects in *italic*, life-threatening effects <u>underlined</u>; generic names in **bold**; classifications in SMALL CAPS; ✦ Canadian drug name; ⊘ Prototype drug

413

fusion: Shortness of breath, pleuritic pain, dry cough.

- Alert physician if improvement is not evident within 45 d. Drug may be discontinued because of the possibility of hepatotoxicity (see Appendix F).
- Lab tests: Perform baseline and regularly scheduled hepatic function tests (alkaline phosphatase, AST, ALT, total bilirubin), blood cell counts, and renal function tests.
- Monitor bowel function. Persistent diarrhea may necessitate drug withdrawal. Severe constipation with abdominal distention and signs of intestinal obstruction have been reported.

Patient & Family Education

- Report promptly the onset of jaundice: yellow skin or sclerae; dark urine, clay-colored stools, itching, abdominal discomfort. Hepatotoxicity frequently occurs between 3rd and 12th mo of therapy.
- Do not drive or engage in other potentially hazardous activities until response to drug is known.
- Do not use OTC medications, alcoholic beverages, or other CNS depressants unless otherwise advised by physician. Liver toxicity occurs more commonly when other drugs are taken concurrently.

DAPSONE ⊘

(dap'sone)
Aczone, Avlosulfon ♦, DDS
Classifications: ANTILEPROSY
(SULFONE) AGENT
Therapeutic: ANTILEPROSY; SULFONE; IMMUNOSUPPRESSANT
Pregnancy Category: C

AVAILABILITY 25 mg, 100 mg tablets; 5% gel

ACTION & *THERAPEUTIC EFFECT*
Sulfone derivative chemically related to sulfonamides, with bacteriostatic and bactericidal activity similar to that group. Interferes with bacterial cell growth by competitive inhibition of folic acid synthesis by susceptible organisms. It also interferes with alternative pathways of complement system. *Drug is effective against dapsone-sensitive multibacillary (borderline, borderline lepromatous, or lepromatous) leprosy, and dapsone-sensitive paucibacillary (indeterminate, tuberculoid, or borderline tuberculoid) leprosy.*

USES Drug of choice for treatment of all forms of leprosy (unless organism is dapsone resistant). Used in dapsone-sensitive multibacillary leprosy (with clofazimine and rifampin) and in dapsone-sensitive paucibacillary leprosy (with rifampin, clofazimine, or ethionamide). Also used prophylactically in contacts of patients with all forms of leprosy except tuberculoid and indeterminate leprosy. Used for treatment of dermatitis herpetiformis. Gel used for acne vulgaris.
UNLABELED USES Chemoprophylaxis of malaria (with pyrimethamine), systemic and discoid lupus erythematosus, pemphigus vulgaris, dermatosis (especially those associated with bullous eruptions, mucocutaneous lesions, inflammation or pustules); rheumatoid arthritis, allergic vasculitis; treatment of initial episodes of *P. carinii* pneumonia (with trimethoprim) in limited number of adults with AIDS.

CONTRAINDICATIONS Hypersensitivity to sulfones or its derivatives; advanced renal amyloidosis, ane-

---

Common adverse effects in *italic*, life-threatening effects underlined; generic names in **bold**; classifications in SMALL CAPS; ♦ Canadian drug name; ⊘ Prototype drug

mia, methemoglobin reductase deficiency; pregnancy (category C).
CAUTIOUS USE Sulfonamide hypersensitivity; chronic renal, hepatic, pulmonary, or cardiovascular disease, refractory anemias, albuminuria, G6PD deficiency, lactation.

ROUTE & DOSAGE

Tuberculoid and Indeterminate-type Leprosy
Adult: **PO** 100 mg/d (with 6 mo of rifampin 600 mg/d) for a minimum of 3 y

Lepromatous and Borderline Lepromatous Leprosy
Adult: **PO** 100 mg/d for ≥10 y
Child: **PO** 1–2 mg/kg/d once daily in combination therapy (max: 100 mg/d)

Dermatitis Herpetiformis
Adult: **PO** 50 mg/d, may be increased to 300 mg/d if necessary (max: 500 mg/d)

Prophylaxis for Close Contacts of Patient with Multibacillary Leprosy
Adult: **PO** 50 mg/d
Child: **PO** <6 mo, 6 mg 3 times/wk; 6–23 mo, 12 mg 3 times/wk; 2–5 y, 25 mg 3 times/wk; 6–12 y, 25 mg/d

P. carinii Pneumonia Prophylaxis
Adult: **PO** 50 mg b.i.d. or 100 mg q.d.
Child: **PO** 2 mg/kg once daily (max: 100 mg/d)

Acne
Apply pea-sized amount of gel to affected area b.i.d.

ADMINISTRATION

Oral
- Give with food to reduce possibility of GI distress.

- Store in tightly covered, light-resistant containers at 15°–30° C (59°–86° F). Drug discoloration apparently does not indicate a chemical change.

Topical
- Clean skin with soap and water before application.

ADVERSE EFFECTS (≥1%) **Body as a Whole:** Hypersensitivity (cutaneous reactions); erythema multiforme, exfoliative dermatitis, <u>toxic epidermal necrolysis</u> (rare), allergic rhinitis, urticaria, fever, infectious mononucleosis-like syndrome. **CNS:** Headache, nervousness, insomnia, vertigo; paresthesia, *muscle weakness.* **CV:** Tachycardia. **GI:** Anorexia, nausea, vomiting, abdominal pain; <u>toxic hepatitis</u>, cholestatic jaundice (reversible with discontinuation of drug therapy); increased ALT, AST, LDH; hyperbilirubinemia. **Hematologic:** In patient with or without G6PD deficiency; *dose-related hemolysis,* Heinz body formation, *methemoglobinemia with cyanosis,* hemolytic anemia; <u>aplastic anemia</u> (rare), <u>agranulocytosis</u>. **Skin:** Drug-induced lupus erythematosus, phototoxicity. **Special Senses:** Blurred vision, tinnitus. **Other:** Male infertility; sulfone syndrome (fever, malaise, exfoliative dermatitis, hepatic necrosis with jaundice, lymphadenopathy, methemoglobinemia, anemia).

INTERACTIONS Drug: Activated charcoal decreases dapsone absorption and enterohepatic circulation; **pyrimethamine, trimethoprim** increase risk of adverse hematologic reactions; **rifampin** decreases dapsone levels 7–10 fold.

PHARMACOKINETICS Absorption: Rapidly and nearly completely absorbed from GI tract. **Peak:** 2–8 h. **Distribution:** Distributed to all body

Common adverse effects in *italic*, life-threatening effects <u>underlined</u>; generic names in **bold**; classifications in SMALL CAPS; ✦ Canadian drug name; ◯ Prototype drug

415

tissues; high concentrations in kidney, liver, muscle, and skin; crosses placenta; distributed into breast milk. **Metabolism:** In liver by CYP3A4. **Elimination:** 70–85% in urine; remainder in feces; traces of drug may be found in body for 3 wk after repeated doses. **Half-Life:** 20–30 h.

CLINICAL IMPLICATIONS

Assessment & Drug Effects

- Monitor for therapeutic effectiveness that may not appear for leprosy until after 3–6 mo of therapy. Skin lesions respond well; recovery from nerve involvement is usually limited.
- Lab tests: Perform baseline then weekly CBC during the first month of therapy, at monthly intervals for at least 6 mo, and semiannually thereafter.
- Determine periodic dapsone blood levels.
- Perform liver function tests in patients who complain of malaise, fever, chills, anorexia, nausea, vomiting, and have jaundice. Dapsone therapy is usually suspended until etiology is identified.
- Monitor severity of anemia. Nearly all patients demonstrate hemolysis. Manufacturer states that Hgb level is generally decreased by 1–2 g/dL; reticulocytes increase by 2–12%; RBC life span is shortened; and methemoglobinemia occurs in most patients receiving dapsone.
- Monitor temperature during first few weeks of therapy. If fever is frequent or severe, leprosy reactional state should be ruled out. Reduction of or interruption of therapy may be sufficient for improvement.
- Report cyanotic appearance or mucous membranes with brownish hue to physician as possible methemoglobinemia.

Patient & Family Education

- Report symptoms of leprosy that do not improve within 3 mo or get worse to physician.
- Report the appearance of a rash with bullous lesions around elbows and other joints promptly. Drug-induced or worsening skin lesions require withdrawal of dapsone.
- Report symptoms of peripheral neuropathy with motor loss (muscle weakness) promptly.

DAPTOMYCIN

(dap-to-my′sin)
Cubicin
Classifications: ANTIBIOTIC; LIPOPEPTIDE
Therapeutic: ANTIBIOTIC; LIPOPEPTIDE
Pregnancy Category: B

AVAILABILITY 500 mg vial

ACTION & *THERAPEUTIC EFFECT*
Daptomycin is cyclic lipopeptide antibiotic. It binds to bacterial membranes of gram-positive bacteria causing rapid depolarization of the membrane potential leading to inhibition of protein, DNA, and RNA synthesis and bacterial cell death. *Daptomycin is effective against a broad spectrum of gram-positive organisms, including both susceptible and resistant strains of S. aureus.*

USES Complicated skin and skin structure infections.

CONTRAINDICATIONS Pseudomembranous colitis. Safe use in infants or children <18 y is not known.
CAUTIOUS USE Severe renal or hepatic impairment, end-stage renal impairment; peripheral neuropa-

thy; GI disease; history of rhabdo-myolysis, myopathy; elderly; pregnancy (category B), lactation.

ROUTE & DOSAGE

Skin Infections
Adult: IV 4 mg/kg q24h × 7–14 d
Renal Impairment
Cl_{cr} <30 mL/min: dose q48h

ADMINISTRATION

Intravenous

PREPARE: IV Infusion: Reconstitute the 250 mg vial or the 500 mg vial with 5 mL or 10 mL, respectively, of NS to yield 50 mg/mL. Further dilute the 50 mg/mL solution in 50–100 mL of NS or RL.

ADMINISTER: IV Infusion: Infuse over 30 min; if same IV line is used for infusion of other drugs, flush line before/after with NS or RL.

INCOMPATIBILITIES Solution/additive: Little data available, thus additives or other medications should not be added or infused simultaneously through the same intravenous line.

▪ Store unopened vials in 2°–8° C (36°–46° F). Avoid excessive heat. May store reconstituted, single-use vials or IV solution for 12 h at room temperature or 48 h if refrigerated.

ADVERSE EFFECTS (≥1%) **Body as a Whole:** Injection site reactions, fever, fungal infections. **CNS:** Headache, insomnia, dizziness. **CV:** Hypotension, hypertension. **GI:** Constipation, nausea, vomiting, diarrhea, abnormal liver function tests. **Hematologic:** Anemia. **Metabolic:** Elevated CPK. **Musculoskeletal:** Limb pain, arthralgia. **Respiratory:** Dyspnea. **Skin:** Rash, pruritus. **Urogenital:** UTIs, renal failure.

INTERACTIONS Drug: Potential increased risk of myopathy with STATINS.

PHARMACOKINETICS Elimination: Primarily renal. **Half-Life:** 8 h.

D

CLINICAL IMPLICATIONS

Assessment & Drug Effects

▪ Monitor for and report: muscle pain or weakness, especially with concurrent therapy with HMG-CoA reductase inhibitors (statin drugs); S&S of peripheral neuropathy, superinfection such as candidiasis.

▪ Lab tests: Perform C&S before treatment is begun; baseline renal function tests; weekly CPK levels; PT/INR during first few days of daptomycin therapy with concurrent warfarin use; daily blood glucose monitoring in diabetics; serum electrolytes if S&S of hypokalemia or hypomagnesemia (see Appendix F) appear.

▪ Withhold drug and notify physician if S&S of myopathy develop with CPK elevation >1000 U/L (~5 × ULN), or if CPK level is ≥10 × ULN.

Patient & Family Education

▪ Report any of the following to the physician: muscle pain, weakness or unusual tiredness; numbness or tingling; difficulty breathing or shortness of breath; severe diarrhea or vomiting; skin rash or itching.

DARBEPOETIN ALFA

(dar-be-po-e′tin)
ARANESP
Classifications: BLOOD FORMER; HEMATOPOIETIC GROWTH FACTOR
Therapeutic: HUMAN ERYTHROPOIETIN; ANTIANEMIC
Prototype: Epoetin alfa
Pregnancy Category: C

Common adverse effects in *italic*, life-threatening effects underlined; generic names in **bold**; classifications in SMALL CAPS; ♣ Canadian drug name; ⊙ Prototype drug

D

AVAILABILITY 25 mcg/mL, 40 mcg/mL, 60 mcg/mL, 100 mcg/ mL, 150 mcg/mL, 200 mcg/mL, 300 mcg/mL, 500 mcg/mL vials; 40 mcg/0.4 mL, 60 mcg/0.3 mL, 100 mcg/0.5 mL, 150 mcg/0.3 mL, 200 mcg/0.4 mL, 300 mcg/ 0.6 mL, 500 mcg/mL syringe

ACTION & *THERAPEUTIC EFFECT*

An erythropoiesis-stimulating protein closely related to human erythropoietin. Erythropoietin is produced naturally in the kidney in response to hypoxia, and stimulates red blood cell production in the bone marrow. Production of endogenous erythropoietin is impaired in patients with chronic renal failure (CRF) resulting in anemia. *Darbepoetin stimulates release of reticulocytes from the bone marrow into the blood stream where they mature into RBCs.*

USES Treatment of anemia in patients with chronic renal failure or chemotherapy-associated anemia, treatment of chemotherapy-induced anemia in nonmyeloid malignancies.

CONTRAINDICATIONS Patients with uncontrolled hypertension; hypersensitivity to darbepoetin or human albumin; pregnancy (category C).

CAUTIOUS USE Controlled hypertension, elevated hemoglobin, folic acid or vitamin B_{12} deficiencies, infections, inflammatory or malignant processes, osteofibrosis, occult blood loss, hemolysis, severe aluminum toxicity, bone marrow fibrosis, chronic renal failure patients not on dialysis, lactation, hematologic diseases.

ROUTE & DOSAGE

Anemia

Adult: **IV/SC** Initially, 0.45 mcg/ kg once/wk. Reduce dose by 25% if there is a rapid increase (i.e., more than 1 g/dL in any 2-wk period) in Hgb or if the Hgb is approaching 12 g/dL. If the Hgb does not increase by 1 g/dL after 4 wk of therapy and iron stores are adequate, increase the dose by 25%. Maintenance dose is 0.26–0.65 mcg/kg once/wk

Converting Epoetin Alfa to Darbepoetin

Adults: **IV/SC** Estimate the starting dose of darbepoetin alfa based on the total weekly dose of epoetin alfa at the time of conversion. If the patient was receiving epoetin alfa 2–3 times/wk, administer darbepoetin alfa once per week; if the patient was receiving epoetin alfa once per week, administer darbepoetin alfa once every 2 wks. The route of administration (i.e., SC or IV) should be maintained. Note: The following darbepoetin alfa dosage recommendations are estimates based on total amount of epoetin alfa administered per week. Because of individual variability, titrate doses to maintain the target Hgb. **Epoetin alfa <2500 Units/wk:** Initial dose 6.25 mcg/wk **Epoetin alfa 2500–4999 Units/wk:** Initial dose 12.5 mcg/wk **Epoetin alfa 5000–10,999 Units/wk:** Initial dose 25 mcg/wk **Epoetin alfa 11,000–17,999 Units/wk:** Initial dose 40 mcg/wk **Epoetin alfa 18,000–33,999 Units/wk:** Initial dose 60 mcg/wk **Epoetin alfa 34,000–89,999 Units/wk:** Initial dose 100 mcg/wk

D

Epoetin alfa ≥90,000 Units/wk:
Initial dose 200 mcg/wk

ADMINISTRATION

All Routes
- Correct deficiencies of folic acid or vitamin B_{12} prior to initiation of therapy.

Subcutaneous
- Do not shake solution. Shaking may denature the darbepoetin, rendering it biologically inactive.
- Inspect solution for particulate matter prior to use. Do not use if solution is discolored or if it contains particulate matter.
- Use only one dose per vial, and do not reenter vial.
- Do not give with any other drug solution.

Intravenous

PREPARE: **Direct:** Withdraw the desired dose and give undiluted. Discard the unused portion.
ADMINISTER: **Direct:** Give direct IV as a bolus dose over 1 min.
- Discard any unused portion of the vial. It contains no preservatives.

- Store at 2°–8° C (36°–46° F). Do not freeze or shake. Protect from light.

ADVERSE EFFECTS (≥1%) **Body as a Whole:** Injection site pain, *peripheral edema,* fatigue, fever, <u>death</u>, chest pain, fluid overload, access infection, access hemorrhage, flu-like symptoms, asthenia, *infection.* **CNS:** *Headache,* dizziness. **CV:** *Hypertension, hypotension, arrhythmias,* <u>cardiac arrest</u>, angina, chest pain, vascular access thrombosis, CHF, red cell aplasia. **GI:** *Nausea, vomiting, diarrhea,* constipation. **Musculoskeletal:** *Myalgia, arthralgia,* limb pain, back pain. **Respira-**

tory: *Upper respiratory infection, dyspnea, cough,* bronchitis. **Skin:** Pruritus. **Other:** Increased risk of thrombotic events and mortality in cancer patients.

INTERACTIONS Drug: No clinically significant reactions reported.

PHARMACOKINETICS Absorption: 37% absorbed from SC site. **Peak:** 24–72 h SC. **Distribution:** Distribution confined primarily to intravascular space. **Elimination:** 10% in urine. **Half-Life:** 21 h IV, 49 h SC.

CLINICAL IMPLICATIONS

Assessment & Drug Effects
- Control BP adequately prior to initiation of therapy and closely monitor and control during therapy. Report immediately S&S of CHF, cardiac arrhythmias, or sepsis. Note that hypertension is an adverse effect that must be controlled.
- Notify physician of a rapid rise in Hgb as dosage will need to be reduced because of risk of serious hypertension. Note that BP may rise during early therapy as Hgb increases.
- Monitor for premonitory neurological symptoms (i.e., aura, and report their appearance promptly). The potential for seizures exists during periods of rapid Hgb increase (e.g., >1.0 g/dL in any 2-wk period).
- Monitor closely and report immediately S&S of thrombotic events (e.g., MI, CVA, TIA), especially for patients with CRF.
- Lab tests: At baseline and periodically thereafter, evaluate iron stores, including transferrin and serum ferritin; Hgb twice weekly until stabilized and maintenance dose is established, then weekly for at least 4 wk, and at regular intervals thereafter; CBC with differential and platelet count at regular inter-

Common adverse effects in *italic*, life-threatening effects <u>underlined</u>; generic names in **bold**; classifications in SMALL CAPS; ♣ Canadian drug name; ⊕ Prototype drug

419

val; periodic BUN, creatinine, serum phosphorus, and serum potassium.

Patient & Family Education

- Adhere closely to antihypertensive drug regimen and dietary restrictions.
- Monitor BP as directed by physician.
- Do not drive or engage in other potentially hazardous activity during the first 90 d of therapy because of possible seizure activity.
- Report any of the following to the physician: chest pain, difficulty breathing, shortness of breath, severe or persistent headache, fever, muscle aches and pains, or nausea.

DARIFENACIN HYDROBROMIDE

(dar-i-fen′a-sin)

Enablex

Classifications: ANTICHOLINERGIC; MUSCARINIC RECEPTOR ANTAGONIST; BLADDER ANTISPASMODIC
Therapeutic: BLADDER ANTISPASMODIC; MUSCARINIC RECEPTOR ANTAGONIST
Prototype: Ipratropium
Pregnancy Category: C

AVAILABILITY 7.5 mg and 15 mg extended release tablets

ACTION & *THERAPEUTIC EFFECT*
Darifenacin is a selective M3 muscarinic receptor antagonist. Muscarinic M3 receptors play an important role in contraction of the urinary bladder smooth muscle and stimulation of salivary secretion. *Control of urinary incontinence due to urgency and frequency.*

USES Treatment of overactive bladder with symptoms of urge urinary incontinence, urgency, and frequency.

CONTRAINDICATIONS Hypersensitivity to the drug; severe hepatic impairment (Child-Pugh C class); urinary retention; gastric obstruction; pyloric stenosis, ileus; urinary retention; uncontrolled narrow-angle glaucoma; pregnancy (category C).

CAUTIOUS USE Risk of urinary retention, clinically significant bladder outflow obstruction, renal disease; decreased GI motility, GERD, severe constipation, ulcerative colitis; myasthenia gravis; controlled narrow-angle glaucoma; lactation.

ROUTE & DOSAGE

Overactive Bladder
Adult: **PO** 7.5–15 mg qd

Moderate Hepatic Impairment (Child-Pugh B Class)
Max dose: ≤ 7.5 mg qd

ADMINISTRATION

Oral

- Ensure that the drug is not chewed or crushed. It must be swallowed whole.
- Note: Dosage should not exceed 7.5 mg daily with moderate hepatic impairment (i.e., Child-Pugh B class) or concurrent therapy with potent inhibitors of CYP3A4 (e.g., itraconazole, clarithromycin, nefazodone, nelfinavir, ritonavir).
- Store 15°–30° C (59°–86° F). Protect from light.

ADVERSE EFFECTS (≥1%) **Body as a Whole:** Flu-like symptoms, urinary tract infection. **CNS:** *Headache,* asthenia, dizziness. **GI:** *Constipation, dry mouth, dyspepsia, nausea,* abdominal pain, diarrhea.

INTERACTIONS Drug: Potent inhibitors of CYP3A4 (e.g., **clarithromycin, erythromycin, itraconazole, ketoconazole,**

Common adverse effects in *italic*, life-threatening effects underlined; generic names in **bold**; classifications in SMALL CAPS; ♣ Canadian drug name; ☻ Prototype drug

nefazodone, nelfinavir, and ritonavir) increase darifenacin levels. Darifenacin will cause additive anticholinergic effects with other ANTICHOLINERGIC drugs. Darifenacin can increase **digoxin** concentrations. **Food: Grapefruit juice** may increase darifenacin levels.

PHARMACOKINETICS Absorption: 15–19% bioavailability. **Peak:** 7 h. **Distribution:** 98% protein bound. **Metabolism:** Extensive hepatic metabolism. **Elimination:** Renal and fecal. **Half-Life:** 13–19 h.

CLINICAL IMPLICATIONS

Assessment & Drug Effects

- Monitor for adverse effects of concurrently used drugs that have a narrow therapeutic window and are metabolized by CYP26D (e.g., flecainide, thioridazine, or TRICYCLIC ANTIDEPRESSANTS).
- Lab tests: Monitor blood levels of digoxin with concurrent therapy and assess for S&S of digoxin toxicity.

Patient & Family Education

- Follow directions for taking the drug (see ADMINISTRATION).
- Do not drive or engage in potentially hazardous activities until response to drug is known.
- Use caution in hot environments to minimize the risk of heat prostration.
- Report any of the following to a health care provider: difficulty passing urine, unexplained nausea, or persistent constipation.

DARUNAVIR

(da-run'a-ver)
Prezista
Classifications: ANTIRETROVIRAL AGENT; HIV PROTEASE INHIBITOR

Therapeutic: ANTIRETROVIRAL; PROTEASE INHIBITOR
Prototype: Saquinavir
Pregnancy Category: B

AVAILABILITY 300 mg tablets

ACTION & *THERAPEUTIC EFFECT*
Darunavir is an inhibitor of HIV-1 protease that selectively inhibits the cleavage of HIV polyproteins in infected cells, thereby preventing the maturation of virus particles. *Darunavir reduces the viral load (decreases the number of RNA copies) and increases the number of T helper CD4 cells.*

USES Treatment of HIV infection, usually in combination with two nucleoside reverse transcriptase inhibitors, such as lamivudine and zidovudine.

CONTRAINDICATIONS Hypersensitivity to darunavir or protease inhibitors, ritonavir; pancreatitis; lactation. Safety and efficacy in children have not been established.
CAUTIOUS USE Hepatic function impairment, hepatitis; severe renal impairment, chronic renal failure; hemophilia A or B; diabetes mellitus; diabetes ketoacidosis; hyperglycemia; elderly; pregnancy (category B).

ROUTE & DOSAGE

HIV Infection
Adult: **PO** 600 mg b.i.d. with 100 mg ritonavir PO.

ADMINISTRATION

Oral

- Give with food and coadminister with 100 mg ritonavir.
- Tablets must be swallowed whole.
- Store at 15°–30° C (59°–86° F). Protect from light and moisture.

Common adverse effects in *italic*, life-threatening effects underlined; generic names in **bold**; classifications in SMALL CAPS; ♦ Canadian drug name; ❷ Prototype drug

421

D

ADVERSE EFFECTS (≥2%) **CNS:** *Headache*. **GI:** Abdominal pain, constipation, *diarrhea, vomiting*. **Skin:** Stevens-Johnson syndrome.

INTERACTIONS Drug: AZOLE ANTI-FUNGALS and **indinavir** increase the levels of darunavir. Coadministration of other inhibitors of CYP3A4 may also increase darunavir. ANTICONVULSANTS (e.g., **carbamazepine, phenobarbital, phenytoin**), CORTICOSTEROIDS (e.g., **dexamethasone**), **efavirenz**, RIFAMYCINS (e.g., **rifampin, rifabutin**), and **saquinavir** may decrease darunavir levels. Darunavir may increase the levels of AZOLE ANTIFUNGALS, CORTICOSTEROIDS, **efavirenz, indinavir**, RIFAMYCINS, **amiodarone, bepridil, lidocaine, quinidine**, CALCIUM CHANNEL BLOCKERS (e.g., **nifedipine, nicardipine, felodipine**), **clarithromycin**, IMMUNOSUPPRESSANTS (e.g., **cyclosporine, sirolimus, tacrolimus**), PHOSPHODIESTERASE TYPE 5 INHIBITORS (e.g., **sildenafil, tadalafil, vardenafil**), and trazodone, due in part to its ability to inhibit CYP3A4. Darunavir decreases the levels of the **lopinavir/ritonavir** combination, ORAL CONTRACEPTIVES (e.g., **ethinyl estradiol, norethindrone**), **methadone**, SELECTIVE SEROTONIN REUPTAKE INHIBITORS (SSRIs, e.g., **paroxetine, sertraline**), and **warfarin.** Coadministration of darunavir with BENZODIAZEPINES (e.g., **midazolam, triazolam**) increases the risk of prolonged or increased sedation or respiratory depression. Coadministration of darunavir with ERGOT ALKALOIDS may increase ergot toxicity. Coadministration of darunavir with HMG COA REDUCTASE INHIBITORS increases the risk of myopathy. Combination use of darunavir with **pimozide** increases the risk of cardiac arrhythmias. **Food:** Food enhances the bioavailability of darunavir. **Herbal: St. John's wort** decreases the level of darunavir.

PHARMACOKINETICS Absorption: 82% absorbed (in combination with ritonavir). **Peak:** 2.5–4 h. **Distribution:** 95% protein bound. **Metabolism:** In the liver. **Elimination:** Primarily fecal (80%) with minor elimination in urine. **Half-Life:** 15 h.

CLINICAL IMPLICATIONS

Assessment & Drug Effects

- Monitor for and report S&S of pancreatitis, as this may be an indication for discontinuation of darunavir.
- Monitor for S&S of skin rash. Notify physician immediately if a severe rash appears.
- Monitor diabetics for loss of glycemic control.
- Lab tests: Periodic CD4+ cell count, plasma HIV-RNA, lipid profile, LFTs; and plasma glucose.
- Increase monitoring of INR with concurrent warfarin therapy.
- Monitor for adverse effects or loss of efficacy of concurrent medications, as many drug interactions occur with darunavir.

Patient & Family Education

- Follow directions for taking the drug (see Administration). If a dose is missed by more than 6 h, wait until the next regularly scheduled dose. If a dose is missed by less than 6 h, take a dose and continue with the next regularly scheduled dose.
- Tell your health care professional about all medications you are taking, including non-prescription drugs, nutritional supplements, or herbal products.
- Ensure that you know which medicines should NOT be taken with darunavir, as serious consequences could occur.

- Report any of the following to a health care provider: blistering, redness, or peeling skin or mucus membranes; severe skin rash.
- Use or add a barrier contraceptive if using an estrogen-containing oral contraceptive in order to prevent pregnancy.

DASATINIB

(das-a′ti-nib)
Sprycel
Classifications: ANTINEOPLASTIC AGENT; TYROSINE KINASE INHIBITOR; BIOLOGIC RESPONSE MODIFIER
Therapeutic: ANTINEOPLASTIC; TYROSINE KINASE INHIBITOR
Prototype: Gefitinib
Pregnancy Category: D

AVAILABILITY 20 mg, 50 mg, and 70 mg tablets

ACTION & *THERAPEUTIC EFFECT*
Dasatinib is a BCR-ABL tyrosine kinase inhibitor. BCR-ABL tyrosine kinase is an enzyme produced by a chromosome translocation (Philadelphia chromosome, Ph) associated with chronic myeloid leukemia (CML) and certain types of acute lymphocytic leukemias (Ph+ ALL). *Dasatinib inhibits the growth of CML and ALL cell lines overexpressing BCR-ABL kinase.*

USES Treatment of chronic, accelerated, or myeloid or lymphoid blast phase chronic myelogenous leukemia (CML) in adults resistant or intolerant to prior therapy. Treatment of Philadelphia chromosome–positive (Ph+) acute lymphocytic leukemia (ALL) in adults resistant or intolerant to prior therapy.

CONTRAINDICATIONS Hypersensitivity to dasatinib; pregnancy (category D); lactation; active bleeding.

Concurrent use of anticoagulants or antiplatelet drugs; hypokalemia; hypomagnesemia. Safety and efficacy in children <18 y have not been established.
CAUTIOUS USE Hepatic impairment; bacterial or viral infection; history of GI bleeding; interstitial pneumonia; pleural effusion; QT prolongation; concurrent use of antiarrhythmic drugs.

ROUTE & DOSAGE

CML and Philadelphia Chromosome-Positive ALL
Adult: **PO** Starting dose 70 mg b.i.d. May increase/decrease dose by 20 mg based on response

Dosage Adjustments for Neutropenia and Thrombocytopenia
Chronic phase CML where absolute neutrophil count (ANC) <0.5 × 10^9/L and/or platelets <50 × 10^9/L
Step 1: DC dasatinib until the ANC ≥1 × 10^9/L and platelets ≥50 × 10^9/L
Step 2: Resume at 70 mg b.i.d.
Step 3: If platelets <25 ×10^9/L and/or recurrence of ANC <0.5 × 10^9/L for >7 d, repeat step 1 and resume at 50 mg b.i.d. (second episode) or 40 mg b.i.d. (third episode)
Accelerated phase CML, blast phase CML, and Ph+ ALL where ANC <0.5 × 10^9/L and/or platelets <10 × 10^9/L
Step 1: Assure that cytopenia is unrelated to the underlying leukemia. If so, DC until ANC ≥1 × 10^9/L and platelets ≥20 × 10^9/L
Step 2: Resume at 70 mg b.i.d.
Step 3: If cytopenia recurs, repeat step 1 and resume at 50 mg b.i.d. (second episode) or 40 mg b.i.d. (third episode)

Common adverse effects in *italic*, life-threatening effects <u>underlined</u>; generic names in **bold**; classifications in SMALL CAPS; ♣ Canadian drug name; ☺ Prototype drug

423

Step 4: If cytopenia is related to the underlying leukemia, may increase to 100 mg b.i.d.

ADMINISTRATION

Oral

- Do not crush or break tablets. They should be swallowed whole.
- Ensure that hypokalemia and hypomagnesemia are corrected prior to administering dasatinib.
- Store at 15°–30° C (59°–86° F).

ADVERSE EFFECTS (≥1%) **Body as a Whole:** Chills, contusion, febrile neutropenia, *hemorrhage, infection,* malaise, *pain, pyrexia,* tumor lysis syndrome, weight gain or weight loss. **CNS:** *Asthenia,* anxiety, confusional state, CNS bleeding, depression, dizziness, dysgeusia, *fatigue, headache,* insomnia, neuropathy, somnolence, syncope, tremor, vertigo. **CV:** Arrhythmia, chest pain, angina, congestive heart failure, pericardial effusion, cardiomegaly, hypertension, hypotension, myocardial infarction, palpitations. **GI:** *Abdominal distention and pain,* anal fissure, *anorexia,* ascites, colitis, constipation, *diarrhea,* dysphagia, gastritis, *GI bleeding, nausea,* oral soft tissue disorder, *vomiting, mucosal inflammation.* **Hematologic:** *Anemia, neutropenia,* pancytopenia, *thrombocytopenia, anemia,* elevated ALT and AST, hypocalcemia, hypophosphatemia. **Metabolic:** Appetite disturbances, *fluid retention, edema,* hyperuricemia. **Musculoskeletal:** *Arthralgia, musculoskeletal pain,* muscle inflammation, myalgia, musculoskeletal stiffness. **Respiratory:** Asthma, *cough, dyspnea,* lung infiltration, *plural effusion,* pneumonia, pulmonary edema, pulmonary hypertension, *upper respiratory tract infection.* **Skin:** Acne, alopecia, dermatitis, dry skin, hyperhidrosis, nail disorder, photosensitivity reaction, pigmentation disorder, pruritus, *skin rash.* **Special Senses:** Conjunctivitis, dry eye, tinnitus. **Urogenital:** Gynecomastia, renal failure, urinary frequency.

INTERACTIONS Drug: **Aluminum-** and **magnesium**-based ANTACIDS decrease dasatinib absorption. AZOLE ANTIFUNGAL AGENTS (e.g., **ketoconazole, itraconazole**), MACROLIDE ANTIBIOTICS (e.g., **clarithromycin, erythromycin, telithromycin**), HIV PROTEASE INHIBITORS (e.g., **indinavir, nelfinavir, ritonavir, saquinavir**), **nefazodone,** and other inhibitors of CYP3A4 may increase dasatinib levels. Compounds that induce CYP3A4 (e.g., **carbamazepine, dexamethasone, phenobarbital, phenytoin, rifampin**) may decrease dasatinib levels. PROTON PUMP INHIBITORS and H$_2$ ANTAGONISTS may reduce the absorption of dasatinib due to long-term suppression of gastric acid secretion. Dasatinib may alter the plasma concentrations of other drugs that require CYP3A4 and have a narrow therapeutic window (e.g., **cyclosporine,** ERGOT ALKALOIDS). Dasatinib increases the levels of **simvastatin. Food:** Food enhances the bioavailability of dasatinib. **Herbal: St. John's wort** may decrease the level of dasatinib.

PHARMACOKINETICS Peak: 0.5–6 h. **Distribution:** 93–96% protein bound. **Metabolism:** Extensive hepatic metabolism. **Elimination:** Fecal. **Half-Life:** 3–5 h.

CLINICAL IMPLICATIONS

Assessment & Drug Effects

- Monitor for and report S&S of fluid retention (e.g., pleural or pericardial effusion, peripheral or pulmonary edema, ascites).

- Monitor for S&S of cardiac dysfunction (e.g., heart failure, arrhythmias). ECG monitoring may be needed to evaluate potential QT interval prolongation.
- Monitor for numerous adverse side effects of dasatinib. Immediately report suspected bleeding or infection.
- Lab tests: Baseline and periodic serum potassium and magnesium; baseline CBC with differential (including ANC and platelet count), weekly for first 2 mo, then monthly; periodic LFTs.

Patient & Family Education

- Take antacids (if needed for GI distress) 2 h before or after dasatinib.
- Do not use over-the-counter medications for heartburn (other than antacids) without consulting physician.
- Inform your physician if you are pregnant or planning to become pregnant, as dasatinib may harm the fetus.
- Report immediately to your health care provider any of the following: bleeding (including wine- or coke-colored urine, or black tarry stools) or easy bruising, fever or other signs of an infection, severe lethargy or weakness.

DAUNORUBICIN HYDROCHLORIDE

(daw-noe-roo'bi-sin)
Cerubidine

DAUNORUBICIN CITRATED LIPOSOMAL

DaunoXome

Classifications: ANTINEOPLASTIC; ANTIBIOTIC; ANTHRACYCLINE

Therapeutic: ANTINEOPLASTIC; ANTHRACYCLINE; ANTIBIOTIC
Prototype: Doxorubicin HCl
Pregnancy Category: D

AVAILABILITY Daunorubicin HCl 10 mg, 20 mg, 50 mg, 100 mg lyophilized vials **Daunorubicin Citrated Liposomal** 2 mg/mL (equivalent to 50 mg daunorubicin base) injection

ACTION & *THERAPEUTIC EFFECT*
Cytotoxic and antimitotic anthracycline antibiotic; cell-cycle specific for S-phase of cell division. Toxic properties preclude its use as an antibiotic. Mechanism of action is due to rapid interaction with the DNA molecule changing its shape, thus resulting in inhibition of DNA, RNA, and protein synthesis. *Antineoplastic effects against acute leukemias with decreased incidence of cardiotoxicity than doxorubicin.*

USES To induce remission in acute nonlymphocytic leukemia (myelogenous, monocytic, erythroid) in adults.

UNLABELED USES Solid tumors of childhood and non-Hodgkin's lymphoma.

CONTRAINDICATIONS Severe myelosuppression; immunizations (patient, family), and preexisting cardiac disease unless risk-benefit is evaluated; uncontrolled systemic infection; pregnancy (category D), lactation.

CAUTIOUS USE History of gout, urate calculi, hepatic or renal function impairment; older adult patients with inadequate bone reserve due to age or previous cytotoxic drug therapy, tumor cell infiltration of bone marrow, patient who has received potentially cardiotoxic drugs or related antineoplastics.

Common adverse effects in *italic*, life-threatening effects <u>underlined</u>; generic names in **bold**; classifications in SMALL CAPS; ♣ Canadian drug name; ⊘ Prototype drug

425

D

ROUTE & DOSAGE

Neoplasms

Adult: **IV** As a single agent, 45 mg/m^2/d for 3–5 d q3–4wk (max: total cumulative dose 500–600 mg/m^2); as combination therapy, 30–45 mg/m^2/d on days 1, 2, 3 of first course and days 1 and 2 of subsequent courses

Child: **IV** As combination therapy, ≥2 y, 25–45 mg/m^2; <2 y, 1 mg/kg

Kaposi's Sarcoma (DaunoXome)

Adult: **IV** 40 mg/m^2 over 1 h, repeat q2wk (for serum bilirubin >3 mg/dL or S_{cr} >3 mg/dL, administer half the normal dose)

ADMINISTRATION

Intravenous

Use gloves during preparation for infusion to prevent skin contact with this drug. If contact occurs, decontaminate skin with copious amounts of water with soap.

PREPARE: Direct: Reconstitute 20 mg vial with 4 mL sterile water for injection. The concentration of the solution will be 5 mg/mL.
- Withdraw dose into syringe containing 10–15 mL normal saline. **IV Infusion:** Dilute further in 100 mL NS as required.
ADMINISTER: Direct: Inject over approximately 3 min into the tubing or side arm of a rapidly flowing IV infusion of D5W or NS. **Infusion:** Give a single dose over 30 min.

Specific to DaunoXome

PREPARE: IV Infusion: Each vial of DaunoXome contains the equivalent of 50 mg daunorubicin base. Dilute with enough D5W to produce a concentration of 1 mg/1 mL.
ADMINISTER: IV Infusion: Give DaunoXome over 60 min. Do not use a filter with DaunoXome.
INCOMPATIBILITIES Solution/additive: Dexamethasone, Heparin.
- Avoid extravasation because it can cause severe tissue necrosis.

- Store reconstituted solution at room temperature (15°–30° C; 59°–86° F) for 24 h and under refrigeration at 2°–8° C (36°–46° F) for 48 h. Protect from light.

ADVERSE EFFECTS (≥1%) **Body as a Whole:** Fever. **CNS:** Amnesia, anxiety, ataxia, confusion, hallucinations, emotional lability, tremors. **CV:** Pericarditis, myocarditis, arrhythmias, peripheral edema, CHF, hypertension, tachycardia. **GI:** *Acute nausea and vomiting* (mild), anorexia, *stomatitis,* mucositis, diarrhea (occasionally) hemorrhage. **Urogenital:** Dysuria, nocturia, polyuria, dry skin. **Hematologic:** <u>Bone marrow depression</u> thrombocytopenia, leukopenia, anemia, **Skin:** Generalized *alopecia* (reversible), transverse pigmentation of nails, severe cellulitis or tissue necrosis at site of drug extravasation. **Endocrine:** Hyperuricemia, gonadal suppression.

PHARMACOKINETICS Distribution: Highest concentrations in spleen, kidneys, liver, lungs, and heart; does not cross blood–brain barrier; crosses placenta. **Metabolism:** In liver to active metabolite. **Elimination:** 25% in urine, 40% in bile. **Half-Life:** 18.5–26.7 h.

CLINICAL IMPLICATIONS

Assessment & Drug Effects

- Monitor for therapeutic effectiveness. A profound suppression of bone marrow is required to induce a complete remission. Nadirs for thrombocytes and leukocytes are usually reached in 10–14 d.

- Monitor serum bilirubin; drug dose needs to be reduced when bilirubin is >1.2 mg/dL.
- Lab tests: Perform Hct, platelet count, total and differential leukocyte count, serum uric acid, chest x-ray, and cardiac, hepatic, and renal function tests prior to and periodically during therapy.
- Monitor BP, temperature, pulse, and respiratory function during treatment.
- Monitor for S&S of acute CHF. It can occur suddenly, especially when total dosage exceeds 550 mg/m^2, or in patients with compromised heart function because of previous radiation therapy to heart area.
- Report immediately: Breathlessness, orthopnea, change in pulse and BP parameters. Early clinical diagnosis of drug-induced CHF is essential for successful treatment.
- Report promptly S&S of superinfections including elevation of temperature, chills, upper respiratory tract infection, tachycardia, overgrowth with opportunistic organisms because myelosuppression imposes risk of superimposed infection (see Appendix F).
- Protect patient from contact with persons with infections. The most hazardous period is during nadirs of thrombocytes and leukocytes.
- Control nausea and vomiting (usually mild) by antiemetic therapy.
- Inspect oral membranes daily. Mucositis may occur 3–7 d after drug is administered.

Patient & Family Education

- Note: Loss of hair is probable; recovery is usual in 6–10 wk.
- Use barrier contraceptives during treatment because this drug is ter-

atogenic. Tell your physician immediately if you become pregnant during therapy.
- Note: A transient effect of the drug is to turn urine red on the day of infusion.

DECITABINE
(de-sit′a-bine)
Dacogen
Classifications: ANTINEOPLASTIC AGENT; ANTIMETABOLITE; PYRIMIDINE
Therapeutic: ANTINEOPLASTIC; ANTIMETABOLITE
Prototype: 5-Fluorouracil
Pregnancy Category: D

AVAILABILITY 50 mg lyophilized powder for injection

ACTION & THERAPEUTIC EFFECT
Decitabine is an antimetabolite that exerts antineoplastic effects after its direct incorporation into DNA and inhibition of DNA transferase, causing loss of cell differentiation and cell death. Nonproliferating cells are resistant to the effects of decitabine. *Decitabine-induced changes in neoplastic cells may restore normal function to genes that are critical for control of cellular differentiation and proliferation.*

USES Treatment of patients with myelodysplastic syndrome (MDS). This includes previously treated and untreated patients with de novo and secondary MDS of all French-American-British (FAB) subtypes (i.e., refractory anemia, refractory anemia with ringed sideroblasts, refractory anemia with excess blasts, refractory anemia with excess blasts in transformation, and chronic myelomonocytic leukemia) and intermediate-1, intermediate-2, and high-risk Interna-

Common adverse effects in *italic*, life-threatening effects underlined; generic names in **bold**; classifications in SMALL CAPS; ◆ Canadian drug name; ⊘ Prototype drug

427

D

tional Prognostic Scoring System (IPSS) groups.

UNLABELED USES Treatment of chronic myelogenous leukemia (CML).

CONTRAINDICATIONS Hypersensitivity to decitabine; conception within 2 mo of drug use; renal failure patients with Cl_{Cr} <2 mg/mL; liver dysfunction with transaminase >2 × upper limit of normal (ULN), or serum bilirubin >1.5 mg/dL; active infection; pregnancy (category D), lactation. Safety and efficacy in children not established.

CAUTIOUS USE Moderate to severe renal failure; hepatic impairment.

ROUTE & DOSAGE

Myelodysplastic Syndrome
Adult: **IV** 15 mg/m² q8h × 3 d. Patient should receive a minimum of 4 cycles of therapy repeated q6wk

ADMINISTRATION

Intravenous

PREPARE: IV infusion: Caution should be exercised when handling and preparing decitabine. Procedures for proper handling and disposal of antineoplastic drugs should be applied. Reconstitute each vial with 10 mL sterile water for injection to yield approximately 5 mg/mL at pH 6.7– 7.3. Immediately after reconstitution, further dilute with NS, D5W, or RL to a final drug concentration of 0.1–1 mg/mL. Use within 15 min of reconstitution (see Storage).

ADMINISTER: IV infusion: Premedicate with standard antiemetic therapy. Give decitabine over 3 h. NOTE: Withhold dose and notify physician of any of the following: absolute neutrophil count (ANC) <1000/mcL; platelet count <50,000/mcL; serum creatinine at 2 mg/dL or higher; ALT, total bilirubin ≥2 × ULN; or an active or uncontrolled infection.

- Store vials at 15°–30° C (59°– 86° F). Unless used within 15 min of reconstitution, the diluted solution must be prepared using cold (2°–8° C) infusion fluids and stored at 2°–8° C (36°–46° F) for up to a maximum of 7 h until administration.

ADVERSE EFFECTS (≥5%) **Body as a Whole:** *Fatigue, pyrexia, Mycobacterium avium* complex infection, peripheral edema, bacteremia, candidal infection, cellulitis, injection site reactions, rigors, tenderness, transfusion reaction, sinusitis, staphylococcal infection. **CNS:** <u>Intracranial hemorrhage</u>, anxiety, confusional state, dizziness, headache, hypesthesia, insomnia, pyrexia. **CV:** <u>Cardiorespiratory arrest</u>, cardiac murmur, hypotension. **GI:** *Nausea, vomiting, constipation, diarrhea,* abdominal distention and discomfort, anorexia, dyspepsia, gastroesophageal reflux disease, glossodynia, gingival bleeding, hemorrhoids, lip ulceration, stomatitis, tongue ulceration. **Hematologic:** *Anemia, neutropenia, thrombocytopenia,* hematoma, leukopenia, lymphadenopathy, thrombocythemia. **Metabolic:** *Hyperglycemia,* increased AST, decreased blood albumin, increased blood alkaline phosphatase, altered blood bicarbonate, decreased blood bilirubin, decreased blood chloride, increased blood lactate dehydrogenase, increased blood urea, decreased total protein, dehydration, hyperbilirubinemia, altered potassium levels, hypoalbuminemia, hypomagnese-

Common adverse effects in *italic*, life-threatening effects <u>underlined</u>; generic names in **bold**; classifications in SMALL CAPS; ✤ Canadian drug name; Ⓞ Prototype drug

mia, hyponatremia. **Musculoskeletal:** Arthralgia, back pain, chest wall pain, musculoskeletal discomfort, myalgia, pain in limb. **Respiratory:** *Cough,* lung crackles, hypoxia, pharyngitis, pneumonia, pulmonary edema, rales. **Skin:** Alopecia, ecchymosis, erythema, pallor, *petechiae,* pruritus, rash, skin lesion, swelling face, urticaria. **Special Senses:** Blurred vision. **Urogenital:** Dysuria, urinary frequency, urinary tract infection.

PHARMACOKINETICS Distribution: Negligible plasma protein binding. **Half-Life:** 0.2–0.8 h.

CLINICAL IMPLICATIONS

Assessment & Drug Effects

- Monitor for and report S&S of pulmonary or peripheral edema, cardiac arrhythmias, new-onset depression, or infection.
- Lab tests: CBC with differentials and platelet count prior to each chemotherapy cycle; baseline and periodic LFTs and serum creatinine.
- Avoid IM injections with platelet counts <50,000/mcL.
- Monitor diabetics for loss of glycemic control.

Patient & Family Education

- Do not accept vaccinations during treatment with decitabine.
- Avoid contact with anyone who recently received the oral poliovirus vaccine.
- Women of childbearing age should avoid becoming pregnant while receiving decitabine.
- Men should not father a child while receiving decitabine and for 2 mo after the end of therapy.
- Report any of the following to a health care provider: signs of infection such as fever, chills, sore throat; signs of bleeding such as easy bruising, black, tarry stools,

blood in the urine; irregular heart rate; significant tiredness or weakness.

DEFEROXAMINE MESYLATE

(de-fer-ox'a-meen)
Desferal
Classifications: CHELATING AGENT; ANTIDOTE
Therapeutic: ANTIDOTE
Pregnancy Category: C

AVAILABILITY 500 mg vials

ACTION & *THERAPEUTIC EFFECT*
Chelating agent isolated from *Streptomyces pilosus* with specific affinity for ferric ion and low affinity for calcium. Binds ferric ions to form a stable water soluble chelate readily excreted by kidneys. *Main effect is removal of iron from ferritin, hemosiderin, and transferrin of patient in iron toxicity.*

USES Adjunct in treatment of acute iron intoxication. Has been used in management of hemochromatosis and hemosiderosis secondary to increased iron storage as from multiple transfusions used in treatment of congenital anemias, e.g., thalassemia (Cooley's or Mediterranean anemia), sickle cell anemia, and other chronic anemias.
UNLABELED USES To promote aluminum excretion in aluminum-associated dialysis encephalopathy and aluminum accumulation in bones of patients in renal failure.

CONTRAINDICATIONS Severe renal disease, anuria, pyelonephritis; primary hemochromatosis; acute infection; pregnancy (category C).
CAUTIOUS USE History of pyelonephritis; infants and children <3 y; elderly, cardiac dysfunction; lactation.

Common adverse effects in *italic*, life-threatening effects <u>underlined</u>; generic names in **bold**; classifications in SMALL CAPS; ♣ Canadian drug name; ⦿ Prototype drug

429

ROUTE & DOSAGE

Acute Iron Intoxication
Adult: **IM/IV** 1 g followed by 500 mg at 4 h intervals for 2 doses, subsequent doses of 500 mg q4–12h may be given if necessary (max: 6 g/24 h), infuse at ≤15 mg/kg/h
Child: **IM/IV** 20 mg/kg followed by 10 mg/kg at 4 h intervals for 2 doses, subsequent doses of 10 mg/kg q4–12h may be given if necessary (max: 6 g/24 h), infuse at ≤15 mg/kg/h

Chronic Iron Overload
Adult/Child: **IM** 500 mg–1 g/d
SC 1–2 g/d (20–40 mg/kg/d) infused over 8–24 h (*Child,* max: 6 g/d or 2 g/dose)

ADMINISTRATION

Subcutaneous, Intramuscular
- Reconstitute by adding 2 mL sterile water for injection to 500 mg vial to yield 250 mg/mL. Dissolve drug completely before it is withdrawn from vial.
- Administer SC dose over 8–24 h using portable minipump devices.
- Use IM route for all patients not in shock; preferred route for acute intoxication.

Intravenous
For infants and children: Verify correct IV concentration and rate with physician.

PREPARE: **IV Infusion:** Reconstitute by adding 5 mL sterile water for injection to 500 mg vial to yield 100 mg/mL. ▪ After drug is completely dissolved, withdraw prescribed amount from vial and add to NS, D5W, or RL solution.
ADMINISTER: **IV Infusion:** Give initial 1000 mg dose at a rate not to exceed 15 mg/kg/h. ▪ Give subsequent 500 mg doses at a rate of 125 mg/h. ▪ Do not infuse IV rapidly; such infusion is associated with the occurrence of more adverse effects.

▪ Store at room temperature 15°–30° C (59°–86° F) for not longer than 1 wk. Protect from light.

ADVERSE EFFECTS (≥1%) **Body as a Whole:** Hypersensitivity (generalized itching, cutaneous wheal formation, rash, fever, <u>anaphylactoid reaction</u>). **CV:** Hypotension, tachycardia. **Special Senses:** Decreased hearing; blurred vision, decreased visual acuity and visual fields, color vision abnormalities, night blindness, retinal pigmentary degeneration. **GI:** Abdominal discomfort, diarrhea. **Urogenital:** Dysuria, exacerbation of pyelonephritis, orange-rose discoloration of urine. **Other:** *Pain and induration at injection site.*

PHARMACOKINETICS Distribution: Widely distributed in body tissues. **Metabolism:** Forms nontoxic complex with iron. **Elimination:** Primarily in urine; some in feces.

CLINICAL IMPLICATIONS
Assessment & Drug Effects
- Lab tests: Perform baseline kidney function tests prior to drug administration.
- Monitor injection site. If pain and induration occur, move infusion to another site.
- Monitor I&O ratio and pattern. Report any change. Observe stools for blood (iron intoxication frequently causes necrosis of GI tract).
- Note: Periodic ophthalmoscopic (slit lamp) examinations and audiometry are advised for patients on prolonged or high-dose therapy for chronic iron overload.

Patient & Family Education

- Deferoxamine chelate makes urine turn a reddish color.
- Report blurred vision or any other visual abnormality.

DELAVIRDINE MESYLATE

(del-a-vir′deen)
Rescriptor
Classifications: ANTIVIRAL; NON-NUCLEOSIDE REVERSE TRANSCRIPTASE INHIBITOR (NNRTI)
Therapeutic: ANTIVIRAL; NNRTI
Prototype: Efavirenz
Pregnancy Category: C

AVAILABILITY 100 mg tablets

ACTION & THERAPEUTIC EFFECT
Nonnucleoside reverse transcriptase inhibitor (NNRTI) of HIV-1 binds directly to reverse transcriptase (RT) and disrupts RNA- and DNA-dependent DNA polymerase activities. *It prevents replication of the HIV-1 virus. HIV-2 RT and human DNA polymerases such as polymerases alpha, gamma, and delta are NOT inhibited by delavirdine. Resistant strains appear rapidly.*

USES Treatment of HIV infection in combination with other antiretroviral agents.

CONTRAINDICATIONS Hypersensitivity to delavirdine; pregnancy (category C); lactation.
CAUTIOUS USE Impaired liver function; achlorhydria.

ROUTE & DOSAGE

HIV Infection
Adult: PO 400 mg t.i.d.
Child: PO ≤16 y, 400 mg t.i.d.

ADMINISTRATION

Oral

- Disperse in water by adding a single dose to at least 3 oz of water, let stand for a few minutes, then stir to create a uniform suspension just prior to administration.
- Give drug to patients with achlorhydria with an acid beverage such as orange or cranberry juice.
- Store at 20°–25° C (68°–77° F) and protect from high humidity in a tightly closed container.

ADVERSE EFFECTS (≥1%) **Body as a Whole:** Headache, fatigue, allergic reaction, chills, edema, arthralgia. **CNS:** Abnormal coordination, agitation, amnesia, anxiety, confusion, dizziness. **CV:** Chest pain, bradycardia, palpitations, postural hypotension, tachycardia. **GI:** Nausea, vomiting, diarrhea, increased LFTs, abdominal cramps, anorexia, aphthous stomatitis. **Hematologic:** Neutropenia. **Respiratory:** Bronchitis, cough, dyspnea. **Skin:** *Rash,* pruritus.

INTERACTIONS Drug: ANTACIDS, H₂-RECEPTOR ANTAGONISTS decrease absorption; **didanosine** and **delavirdine** should be taken 1 h apart to avoid decreased delavirdine levels; **clarithromycin, fluoxetine, ketoconazole** may increase delavirdine levels; **carbamazepine, phenobarbital, phenytoin, rifabutin, rifampin** may decrease delavirdine levels; delavirdine may increase levels of **clarithromycin, indinavir, saquinavir, dapsone, rifabutin, alprazolam, midazolam, triazolam,** DIHYDROPYRIDINE, CALCIUM CHANNEL BLOCKERS (e.g., **nifedipine, nicardipine,** etc.), **quinidine, warfarin.** Use with HMG-CoA REDUCTASE INHIBITORS may increase the risk of rhabdomyolysis. Use with **pimozide** may cause cardiac arrhythmias. Use with **trazodone** may in-

Common adverse effects in *italic*, life-threatening effects underlined; generic names in **bold**; classifications in SMALL CAPS; ◆ Canadian drug name; ⊘ Prototype drug

431

crease **trazodone** levels. Use with inhaled **fluticasone** may increase **fluticasone** levels. Use with HYPNOTICS, **alprazolam, midazolam, triazolam** can cause respiratory depression. **Herbal: St. John's wort** may decrease antiretroviral activity.

PHARMACOKINETICS Absorption: Rapidly from GI tract, 80% reaches systemic circulation. **Peak:** 1 h. **Distribution:** 98% protein bound. **Metabolism:** In the liver by CYP3A4. **Elimination:** Half in urine, 44% in feces. **Half-Life:** 2–11 h.

CLINICAL IMPLICATIONS

Assessment & Drug Effects
- Therapeutic effectiveness: Indicated by decreased viral load.
- Monitor for and immediately report appearance of a rash, generally within 1–3 wk of starting therapy; rash is usually diffuse, maculopapular, erythematous, and pruritic.

Patient & Family Education
- Take this drug exactly as prescribed. Missed doses increase risk of drug resistance.
- Do not take antacids and delavirdine at the same time; separate by at least 1 h.
- Report all prescription and nonprescription drugs used to physician because of multiple drug interactions.
- Discontinue medication and notify physician if rash is accompanied by any of the following: Fever, blistering, oral lesions, conjunctivitis, swelling, muscle or joint pain.

DEMECLOCYCLINE HYDROCHLORIDE

(dem-e-kloe-sye′kleen)
Declomycin
Classifications: ANTIBIOTIC; TETRACYCLINE

Therapeutic: TETRACYCLINE ANTIBIOTIC
Prototype: Tetracycline
Pregnancy Category: D

AVAILABILITY 150 mg capsules; 150 mg, 300 mg tablets

ACTION & *THERAPEUTIC EFFECT* Demeclocycline is a broad-spectrum, tetracycline antibiotic. It is pumped through the inner cytoplasmic membrane of bacteria. Demeclocycline blocks the binding of transfer RNA (tRNA) to the messenger RNA (mRNA) of the bacteria. Therefore, bacterial protein synthesis is inhibited and bacterial cells are destroyed. *Effective against both gram-positive and gram-negative bacteria.*

USES Similar to those of tetracycline.
UNLABELED USES Treatment of chronic SIADH (syndrome of inappropriate antidiuretic hormone) secretion.

CONTRAINDICATIONS Hypersensitivity to any of the tetracyclines; severe renal or hepatic disease; cirrhosis, common bile duct obstruction; period of tooth development in fetus; pregnancy (category D), lactation, children <8 y (causes permanent yellow discoloration of teeth, enamel hypoplasia, and retarded bone growth).
CAUTIOUS USE Mild or moderate impaired renal or hepatic function; nephrogenic diabetes insipidus; use of capsule or tablet formulations in patients with esophageal compression or obstruction.

ROUTE & DOSAGE

Antiinfective
Adult: **PO** 150 mg q6h or 300 mg q12h (max: 2.4 g/d)

Child: **PO** >*8 y,* 8–12 mg/kg/d divided q8–12h

Gonorrhea

Adult: **PO** 600 mg followed by 300 mg q12h for 4 d

SIADH

Adult: **PO** 600–1200 mg/d in 3–4 divided doses

ADMINISTRATION

Oral

- Give not less than 1 h before or 2 h after meals. Foods rich in iron (e.g., red meat or dark green vegetables) or calcium (e.g., milk products) impair absorption.
- Concomitant therapy: Do not give antacids with tetracyclines.
- Check expiration date before giving drug. Renal damage and death have resulted from use of outdated tetracyclines.
- Request physician order to give with light meal if gastric distress is a problem. Absorption may be reduced; keep meal dairy free.
- Store in tight, light-resistant containers, preferably at 15°–30° C (59°–86° F) unless otherwise directed. Tetracyclines form toxic products when outdated or exposed to light, heat, or humidity.

ADVERSE EFFECTS (≥1%) **Body as a Whole:** Hypersensitivity [*photosensitivity,* <u>pericarditis, anaphylaxis</u> (rare)]. **GI:** *Nausea,* vomiting, *diarrhea,* esophageal irritation or ulceration, enterocolitis, abdominal cramps, anorexia. **Urogenital:** Diabetes insipidus, azotemia, hyperphosphatemia. **Skin:** Pruritus, erythematous eruptions, exfoliative dermatitis.

DIAGNOSTIC TEST INTERFERENCE

Like other tetracyclines, demeclocycline may cause false increases in **urine catecholamines** (**fluoro-**metric methods); false decreases in **urine urobilinogen;** and false-negative **urine glucose** with **glucose oxidase** methods (e.g., **Clinistix, TesTape**).

INTERACTIONS Drug: ANTACIDS, IRON PREPARATION, **calcium, magnesium, zinc, kaolin-pectin, sodium bicarbonate** can significantly decrease demeclocycline absorption; effects of **desmopressin** and demeclocycline antagonized; increases **digoxin** absorption, increasing risk of **digoxin** toxicity; **methoxyflurane** increases risk of renal failure. **Food:** Dairy products significantly decrease demeclocycline absorption; food may decrease drug absorption also.

PHARMACOKINETICS Absorption:
60–80% absorbed from GI tract. **Peak:** 3–4 h. **Distribution:** Concentrated in liver; crosses placenta; distributed into breast milk. **Metabolism:** In liver; enterohepatic circulation. **Elimination:** 40–50% excreted in urine and 31% in feces in 48 h. **Half-Life:** 10–17 h.

CLINICAL IMPLICATIONS

Assessment & Drug Effects

- Lab tests: C&S prior to initial therapy and periodically during prolonged therapy. With prolonged therapy, add periodic evaluations of serum drug levels, electrolytes, and renal, hepatic, and hematopoietic systems.
- Monitor I&O ratio and pattern and record weights in patients with impaired kidney or liver function, or on prolonged or high dose therapy. Some patients develop diabetes insipidus-like syndrome (SIADH).

Patient & Family Education

- Do not use antacids while taking this drug.

Common adverse effects in *italic*, life-threatening effects <u>underlined</u>; generic names in **bold**; classifications in SMALL CAPS; ♣ Canadian drug name; ⊘ Prototype drug

433

- Take drug on an empty stomach to enhance absorption. Because esophageal irritation and ulceration have been reported, take each dose with a full glass (240 mL) of water; remain upright for at least 90 s after taking medication; and avoid taking drug within 1 h of lying down or bedtime.
- Notify physician if gastric distress is a problem; a snack or light meal free of dairy products may be added to the regimen.
- Report symptoms of superinfections; this is VERY important (see Appendix F).
- Demeclocycline-induced phototoxic reaction can be unusually severe. Avoid sunlight as much as possible and use sunscreen.

DENILEUKIN DIFTITOX

(den-i-leu'kin dif'ti-tox)
Ontak

Classifications: ANTINEOPLASTIC; CYTOTOXIC FUSION PROTEIN; INTERLEUKIN-2 (IL-2) RECEPTOR INHIBITOR
Therapeutic: ANTINEOPLASTIC; IL-2 RECEPTOR INHIBITOR; IMMUNOMODULATOR
Pregnancy Category: C

AVAILABILITY 150 mcg/mL vial

ACTION & *THERAPEUTIC EFFECT* A recombinant DNA cytotoxic protein that is an interleukin-2 (IL-2) receptor-specific protein that acts as an antineoplastic agent. It acts against malignant cells that express particular high-affinity IL-2 receptors on the cell surface, thus inhibiting cellular protein synthesis and causing cell death in malignant cells. *Effectiveness is indicated by reduced tumor burden. Interacts with high affinity to IL-2 receptors on the cell* surface *in particular leukemias and lymphomas.*

USES Persistent or recurrent T-cell lymphoma.

CONTRAINDICATIONS Hypersensitivity to denileukin, diphtheria toxin, or interleukin-2; serum albumin levels below 3 g/dL; pregnancy (category C), lactation.

CAUTIOUS USE Cardiovascular disease; peripheral vascular disease, coronary artery disease; hepatic and renal impairment, elderly; preexisting lowering of serum albumin levels. Safety and efficacy in children <18 y are unknown.

ROUTE & DOSAGE

T-Cell Lymphoma
Adult: IV 9 or 18 mcg/kg/d for 5 d every 21 d

ADMINISTRATION

Intravenous

PREPARE: **IV Infusion:** Bring vials to room temperature (solution will be clear when room temperature is reached). Swirl to mix, but do not shake. Use only plastic syringe and plastic IV bag. Withdraw the calculated dose and inject it into an empty IV bag. Add NO MORE THAN 9 mL sterile saline without preservative to IV bag for each 1 mL of drug. Use within 6 h of preparation.

ADMINISTER: **IV Infusion:** Infuse over at least 15 min without an in-line filter. Stop infusion and notify physician if S&S of hypersensitivity occur.

INCOMPATIBILITIES **Solution/additive:** Do not physically mix with any other drug.

ADVERSE EFFECTS (≥1%) **Body as a Whole:** *Chills, fever, asthenia, in-*

fection, pain, headache, chest pain, flu-like syndrome; injection site reaction; *acute hypersensitivity reaction (hypotension, back pain, dyspnea, vasodilation, rash, chest pain or tightness, tachycardia, dysphagia, syncope, anaphylaxis)*, myalgia, arthralgia. **CNS:** *Dizziness, paresthesia, nervousness,* confusion, insomnia. **CV:** *Vascular leak syndrome (hypotension, edema, hypoalbuminemia); hypotension, vasodilation, tachycardia,* thrombotic events, hypertension, arrhythmia. **GI:** *Nausea, vomiting, anorexia, diarrhea,* constipation, dyspepsia, dysphagia. **Hematologic:** *Anemia,* thrombocytopenia, leukopenia. **Metabolic:** *Hypoalbuminemia; transaminase increase; edema; hypocalcemia; weight loss;* dehydration; hypokalemia. **Respiratory:** *Dyspnea, cough, pharyngitis, rhinitis,* lung disorder. **Skin:** *Rash, pruritus, sweating.* **Urogenital:** *Hematuria, albuminuria, pyuria, increased creatinine.* **Special Senses:** Loss of visual acuity.

INTERACTIONS No clinically significant interactions established.

PHARMACOKINETICS Distribution: Primarily distributed to liver and kidneys. **Metabolism:** By proteolytic degradation. **Half-Life:** 70–80 min.

CLINICAL IMPLICATIONS

Assessment & Drug Effects

- Monitor and notify physician immediately for S&S of hypersensitivity or anaphylaxis that occur during/within 24 h of infusion.
- Monitor and notify physician immediately for S&S of flu-like syndrome that occur within several hours to days following infusion.
- Monitor outpatients for weight gain, developing edema, or declining blood pressure. Notify physician immediately for S&S of

vascular leak syndrome (e.g., edema PLUS hypotension or hypoalbuminemia) that may occur within 2 wk of infusion.

- Lab tests: Baseline and weekly CBC with differential, platelet count, blood chemistry panel (including serum electrolytes, serum albumin, renal and liver functions).

Patient & Family Education

- Report S&S of infection promptly to physician.
- Check weight daily and report rapid weight gain or swelling of extremities promptly.
- Report bothersome adverse effects or S&S of infection or flu-like symptoms (e.g., fever, nausea, vomiting, diarrhea, rash).

DESIPRAMINE HYDROCHLORIDE

(dess-ip′ra-meen)
Norpramin, Pertofrane
Classifications: PSYCHOTHERAPEUTIC; TRICYCLIC ANTIDEPRESSANT
Therapeutic: TRICYCLIC ANTIDEPRESSANT
Prototype: Imipramine
Pregnancy Category: C

AVAILABILITY 10 mg, 25 mg, 50 mg, 75 mg, 100 mg, 150 mg tablets

ACTION & *THERAPEUTIC EFFECT*
Desipramine is a tricyclic antidepressant (TCA) and the active metabolite of imipramine. Antidepressant activity appears to be related to blocking reuptake of norepinephrine and serotonin in the CNS, thus increasing their levels. A more recent theory of antidepressant action of the drug is thought to be a restoration of the balance of monoamine output. *In common with other TCAs, it has antidepressant activity.*

Common adverse effects in *italic*, life-threatening effects <u>underlined</u>; generic names in **bold**; classifications in SMALL CAPS; ♣ Canadian drug name; ⊘ Prototype drug

435

USES Endogenous depression and various depression syndromes.
UNLABELED USES Attention deficit disorder in children >6 y and adolescents; to prevent depression in cocaine withdrawal.

CONTRAINDICATIONS Hypersensitivity to tricyclic compounds; recent MI, QT prolongation, cardiac arrhythmias, AV block, bundle branch block; concurrent use of MAOI therapy; suicidal ideation; pregnancy (category C), lactation. Safe use in children <6 y is not established.
CAUTIOUS USE Urinary retention, prostatic hypertrophy; narrow-angle glaucoma; epilepsy; alcoholism; adolescents, older adults; bipolar disease; thyroid; cardiovascular, renal, and hepatic disease; suicidal tendency; ECT; elective surgery.

ROUTE & DOSAGE

Antidepressant

Adult: **PO** 75–100 mg/d at bedtime or in divided doses, may gradually increase to 150–300 mg/d (use lower doses in older adult patients)
Adolescent: **PO** 25–50 mg/d (max: 100 mg/d) in divided doses
Child: **PO** 6–12 y, 1–3 mg/kg/d in divided doses (max: 5 mg/kg/d)

ADMINISTRATION

Oral
- Give drug with or immediately after food to reduce possibility of gastric irritation.
- Give maintenance dose at bedtime to minimize daytime sedation.
- Store drug in tightly closed container at 15°–30° C (59°–86° F) unless otherwise specified.

ADVERSE EFFECTS (≥1%) **Body as a Whole:** Hypersensitivity (rash, urticaria, photosensitivity). **CNS:** *Drowsiness,* dizziness, weakness, fatigue, headache, insomnia, confusional states, depressive reaction, paresthesias, ataxia. **CV:** *Postural hypotension,* hypotension, palpitation, tachycardia, ECG changes, flushing, heart block. **Special Senses:** Tinnitus, parotid swelling; blurred vision, disturbances in accommodation, mydriasis, increased IOP. **GI:** *Dry mouth, constipation,* bad taste, diarrhea, nausea. **Urogenital:** *Urinary retention,* frequency, delayed micturition, nocturia; impaired sexual function, galactorrhea. **Hematologic:** Bone marrow depression and agranulocytosis (rare). **Other:** Sweating, craving for sweets, weight gain or loss, SIADH secretion, hyperpyrexia, eosinophilic pneumonia.

INTERACTIONS Drug: May somewhat decrease response TO ANTIHYPERTENSIVES; CNS DEPRESSANTS, **alcohol,** HYPNOTICS, BARBITURATES, SEDATIVES potentiate CNS depression; may increase hypoprothombinemic effect of ORAL ANTICOAGULANTS; **etchlorvynol** may cause transient delirium; **levodopa,** SYMPATHOMIMETICS (e.g., **epinephrine, norepinephrine**) pose possibility of sympathetic hyperactivity with hypertension and hyperpyrexia; MAO INHIBITORS pose possibility of severe reactions, toxic psychosis, cardiovascular instability; **methylphenidate** increases plasma TCA levels; THYROID AGENTS may increase possibility of arrhythmias; **cimetidine** may increase plasma TCA levels. **Herbal: Ginkgo** may decrease seizure threshold; **St. John's wort** may cause **serotonin** syndrome.

PHARMACOKINETICS Absorption: Rapidly absorbed from GI tract and injection sites. **Peak:** 4–6 h. **Distri-**

bution: Crosses placenta. **Metabolism:** In liver. **Elimination:** Primarily in urine. **Half-Life:** 7–60 h.

CLINICAL IMPLICATIONS

Assessment & Drug Effects

- Monitor children and adolescents for signs of suicidal ideation.
- Monitor for therapeutic effectiveness: Usually not realized until after at least 2 wk of therapy.
- Monitor BP and pulse rate during early phase of therapy, particularly in older adult, debilitated, or cardiovascular patients. If BP rises or falls more than 20 mm Hg or if there is a sudden increase in pulse rate or change in rhythm, withhold drug and inform physician.
- Note: Drowsiness, dizziness, and orthostatic hypotension are signs of impending toxicity in patient on long-term, high dosage therapy. Prolonged QT or QRS intervals indicate possible toxicity. Report to physician.
- Observe patient with history of glaucoma. Report symptoms that may signal acute attack: Severe headache, eye pain, dilated pupils, halos of light, nausea, vomiting.
- Monitor bowel elimination pattern and I&O ratio. Severe constipation and urinary retention are potential problems of TCA therapy.
- Note: Norpramin tablets may contain tartrazine, which can cause allergic-type reactions including bronchial asthma in susceptible individuals. Such individuals are frequently also sensitive to aspirin.

Patient & Family Education

- Make all position changes slowly and in stages, particularly from recumbent to standing position.
- Do not drive or engage in other potentially hazardous activities until reaction to drug is known.

- Take medication exactly as prescribed; do not change dose or dose intervals.
- Note: Patients who receive high doses for prolonged periods may experience withdrawal symptoms including headache, nausea, musculoskeletal pain, and weakness if drug is discontinued abruptly.
- Do not take OTC drugs unless physician has approved their use.
- Stop, or at least limit, smoking because it may increase the metabolism of desipramine, thereby diminishing its therapeutic action.

DESLORATADINE

(des-lor-a-ta′deen)

Clarinex, Clarinex Reditabs

Classifications: ANTIHISTAMINE, NONSEDATING; H$_1$-RECEPTOR ANTAGONIST

Therapeutic: ANTIHISTAMINE; H$_1$-RECEPTOR ANTAGONIST; ANTIALLERGIC

Prototype: Loratadine

Pregnancy Category: C

AVAILABILITY 5 mg tablets; 2.5 mg, 5 mg orally dissolving tablets; 0.5 mg/mL syrup

ACTION & *THERAPEUTIC EFFECT*

A long-acting, nonsedating antihistamine with selective H$_1$-receptor antagonist properties. The drug reduces human mast cell release of the inflammatory cytokines. Therefore, it also exhibits antiallergic effects. It is more potent than loratadine as an antagonist at H$_1$ receptors. *Desloratadine is effective in controlling allergic rhinitis and inhibiting histamine-induced wheals and flare (hives).*

Common adverse effects in *italic*, life-threatening effects underlined; generic names in **bold**; classifications in SMALL CAPS; ◆ Canadian drug name; ⊙ Prototype drug

437

USES Treatment of seasonal or perennial allergic rhinitis and idiopathic urticaria.

CONTRAINDICATIONS Hypersensitivity to desloratidine or loratadine; neonates; infants; pregnancy (category C); lactation.

CAUTIOUS USE Renal and hepatic insufficiencies; bladder neck obstruction or urinary retention; prostatic hypertrophy; asthma; glaucoma. Safety and efficacy in children <12 y not known.

ROUTE & DOSAGE

Allergic Rhinitis, Idiopathic Urticaria
Adult: **PO** 5 mg q.d.

Renal Impairment
Adult:: **PO** Cl$_{cr}$ <50 mL/min: 5 mg every other day

Hepatic Impairment
Adult: **PO** 5 mg every other day

ADMINISTRATION

Oral
- Note that drug should be given q.o.d. to patients with significant renal or hepatic impairment.
- Store between 2°–25° C (36°–77° F).

ADVERSE EFFECTS (≥1%) **Body as a Whole:** Pharyngitis, fatigue, flu-like symptoms, myalgia. **CNS:** Somnolence, dizziness. **GI:** Dry mouth, nausea, dry throat. **Urogenital:** Dysmenorrhea.

INTERACTIONS Drug: No clinically significant interactions established.

PHARMACOKINETICS Absorption: Well absorbed. **Peak:** 3 h. **Distribution:** 85–89% protein bound. **Metabolism:** Extensively metabolized in liver to 3-hydroxydesloratadine, an active metabolite. **Elimination:** Equally in urine and feces. **Half-Life:** 27 h.

CLINICAL IMPLICATIONS

Assessment & Drug Effects
- Assess carefully for and report distressing or dangerous S&S that occur after initiation of the drug. A variety of adverse effects, although not common, are possible. Some are an indication to discontinue the drug.
- Monitor cardiovascular status and report significant changes in BP and palpitations or tachycardia.
- Lab tests: Monitor periodically renal and liver function tests.
- Concurrent drugs: Monitor ECG when used in combination with any other drug that can increase blood level of desloratidine in patients with preexisting cardiac disease.

Patient & Family Education
- Drug may cause significant drowsiness in older adult patients and those with liver or kidney impairment.
- Note: Concurrent use of alcohol and other CNS depressants may have an additive effect.
- Do not take this drug more often than every other day if you have renal impairment.

DESMOPRESSIN ACETATE

(des-moe-pres′sin)
DDAVP, Stimate
Classifications: HORMONE; PITUITARY (ANTIDIURETIC) HORMONE
Therapeutic: ANTIDIURETIC HORMONE
Prototype: Vasopressin
Pregnancy Category: B

Common adverse effects in *italic*, life-threatening effects <u>underlined</u>; generic names in **bold**; classifications in SMALL CAPS; ◆ Canadian drug name; ⦿ Prototype drug

AVAILABILITY 0.1 mg, 0.2 mg tablets; 0.1% nasal solution; 0.15 mg/spray nasal spray; 4 mcg/mL, 15 mcg/mL injection

ACTION & *THERAPEUTIC EFFECT*

Synthetic analog of the natural human posterior pituitary (antidiuretic) hormone, arginine vasopressin. Has more specific and longer duration of action than antidiuretic hormone and lower incidence of allergic reactions. Reduces urine volume and osmolality in patients with central diabetes insipidus by increasing reabsorption of water by kidney collecting tubules. Produces a dose-related increase in factor VIII (antihemophilic factor) and von Willebrand's factor. *Desmopressin is an effective replacement for antidiuretic hormone. It also can shorten or normalize bleeding time, and correct platelet adhesion abnormalities in certain patients with bleeding disorders.*

USES To control and prevent symptoms and complications of central (neurohypophyseal) diabetes insipidus, and to relieve temporary polyuria and polydipsia associated with trauma or surgery in the pituitary region.

UNLABELED USES To increase factor VIII activity in selected patients with mild to moderate hemophilia A and in type I von Willebrand's disease or uremia, and to control enuresis in children.

CONTRAINDICATIONS Nephrogenic diabetes insipidus, type II B von Willebrand's disease; renal failure, renal impairment.

CAUTIOUS USE Coronary artery insufficiency, hypertensive cardiovascular disease; severe CHF; older adults; history of thromboembolic disease; pregnancy (category B).

ROUTE & DOSAGE

Diabetes Insipidus

Adult: **Intranasal** 0.1–0.4 mL (10–40 mcg) in 1–3 divided doses **IV/SC** 2–4 mcg in 2 divided doses **PO** 0.2–0.4 mg/d
Child: **Intranasal** 3 mo–12 y, 0.05–0.3 mL in 1–2 divided doses **IV/SC** 0.3 mcg/kg infused over 15–30 min **PO** 0.05 mg titrated to response

Enuresis

Adult/Child: **Intranasal** 5–40 mcg h.s.
Child: **PO** ≥6 y, 0.2 mg h.s., may titrate up to 0.6 mg h.s.

Von Willebrand's Disease

Adult/Child: **IV/SC** >3 mo, 0.3 mcg/kg 30 min preop, may repeat in 48 h if needed

Renal Impairment

Do not use if Cl$_{cr}$ is <50 mL/min.

ADMINISTRATION

Oral

- Note that 0.2 mg PO is equivalent to 10 mcg (0.1 mL) intranasal.

Intranasal

- Follow manufacturer's instructions for proper technique with nasal spray.
- Give initial dose in the evening, and observe antidiuretic effect. Dose is increased each evening until uninterrupted sleep is obtained. If daily urine volume is more than 2 L after nocturia is controlled, morning dose is started and adjusted daily until

Common adverse effects in *italic*, life-threatening effects <u>underlined</u>; generic names in **bold**; classifications in SMALL CAPS; ♣ Canadian drug name; ☺ Prototype drug

439

urine volume does not exceed 1.5–2 L/24 h.

Intravenous

PREPARE: **Direct:** Give undiluted for diabetes insipidus. **IV Infusion:** Dilute 0.3 mcg/kg in 10 mL of NS (children ≤10 kg) or 50 mL of NS (children >10 kg and adults) for von Willebrand's disease (type I).

ADMINISTER: **Direct:** Give direct IV over 30 s for diabetes insipidus. **IV Infusion:** Give over 15–30 min for von Willebrand's disease (type I).

▪ Store parenteral and nasal solution in refrigerator preferably at 4° C (39.2° F) unless otherwise directed. Avoid freezing. ▪ Nasal spray can be stored at room temperature. ▪ Discard solutions that are discolored or contain particulate matter.

ADVERSE EFFECTS (≥1%) **All:** Dose related. **CNS:** Transient headache, drowsiness, listlessness. **Special Senses:** Nasal congestion, rhinitis, nasal irritation. **GI:** Nausea, heartburn, mild abdominal cramps. **Other:** Vulval pain, shortness of breath, slight rise in BP, facial flushing, pain and swelling at injection site.

INTERACTIONS Drug: Demeclocycline, lithium, other VASOPRESSORS may decrease antidiuretic response; **carbamazepine, chlorpropamide, clofibrate** may prolong antidiuretic response.

PHARMACOKINETICS Absorption: 10–20% through nasal mucosa. **Onset:** 15–60 min. **Peak:** 1–5 h. **Duration:** 5–21 h. **Distribution:** Small amount crosses blood–brain barrier; distributed into breast milk. **Half-Life:** 76 min.

CLINICAL IMPLICATIONS

Assessment & Drug Effects

▪ Monitor I&O ratio and pattern (intervals). Fluid intake must be carefully controlled, particularly in older adults and the very young to avoid water retention and sodium depletion.

▪ Weigh patient daily and observe for edema. Severe water retention may require reduction in dosage and use of a diuretic.

▪ Monitor BP during dosage-regulating period and whenever drug is administered parenterally.

▪ Monitor urine and plasma osmolality. An increase in urine osmolality and a decrease in plasma osmolality indicate effectiveness of treatment in diabetes insipidus.

Patient & Family Education

▪ Report upper respiratory tract infection or nasal congestion.

▪ Follow manufacturer's instructions for insertion to ensure delivery of drug high into nasal cavity and not down throat. A flexible calibrated plastic tube is provided.

DESONIDE

(dess'oh-nide)
DesOwen, Tridesilon
Pregnancy Category: C
See Appendix A-4.

DESOXIMETASONE

(des-ox-i-met'a-sone)
Topicort, Topicort-LP
Pregnancy Category: C
See Appendix A-4.

DEXAMETHASONE

(dex-a-meth′a-sone)

Decadron, Deronil ♥, Dexamethasone Intensol, Maxidex, Mymethasone, Oradexon ♥

DEXAMETHASONE SODIUM PHOSPHATE

Decadron Phosphate, Maxidex Ophthalmic

Classifications: HORMONE; ADRENAL CORTICOSTEROID; GLUCOCORTICOID

Therapeutic: ADRENAL CORTICOSTEROID

Prototype: Prednisone

Pregnancy Category: C

AVAILABILITY **Dexamethasone** 0.25 mg, 0.5 mg, 0.75 mg, 1 mg, 1.5 mg, 2 mg, 4 mg, 6 mg tablets; 0.5 mg/5 mL, 0.5 mg/0.5 mg oral solution; 0.01%, 0.04% topical aerosol; **Dexamethasone sodium phosphate** 4 mg/mL, 10 mg/mL, 20 mg/mL, 24 mg/mL injection; 0.1% cream; 0.1% ophthalmic solution, suspension; 0.05% ophthalmic ointment

ACTION & *THERAPEUTIC EFFECT*

Long-acting synthetic adrenocorticoid with intense antiinflammatory (glucocorticoid) activity and minimal mineralocorticoid activity. *Antiinflammatory action:* Prevents accumulation of inflammatory cells at sites of infection; inhibits phagocytosis, lysosomal enzyme release, and synthesis of potent mediators of inflammation, prostaglandins, and leukotrienes; reduces capillary dilation and permeability. *Immunosuppression:* Not clearly understood, but may be due to prevention or suppression of delayed hypersensitivity immune reaction. *Has antiinflammatory and immunosuppression properties.*

USES Adrenal insufficiency concomitantly with a mineralocorticoid; inflammatory conditions, allergic states, collagen diseases, hematologic disorders, cerebral edema, and addisonian shock. Also palliative treatment of neoplastic disease, as adjunctive short-term therapy in acute rheumatic disorders and GI diseases, and as a diagnostic test for Cushing's syndrome and for differential diagnosis of adrenal hyperplasia and adrenal adenoma.

UNLABELED USES As an antiemetic in cancer chemotherapy; as a diagnostic test for endogenous depression; and to prevent hyaline membrane disease in premature infants.

CONTRAINDICATIONS Systemic fungal infection, acute infections, active or resting tuberculosis, vaccinia, varicella, administration of live virus vaccines (to patient, family members), latent or active amebiasis; Cushing's syndrome; neonates or infants <1300 g; pregnancy (category C), lactation. *Topical use:* Rosacea, perioral dermatitis; venous statis ulcers. *Ophthalmic use:* Primary open-angle glaucoma, eye infections, superficial ocular herpes simplex, keratitis, and tuberculosis of eye.

CAUTIOUS USE Stromal herpes simplex, keratitis, GI ulceration, renal disease, diabetes mellitus, hypothyroidism, myasthenia gravis, CHF, cirrhosis, psychic disorders, seizures; children; coagulopathy.

ROUTE & DOSAGE

Allergies, Inflammation, Neoplasias

Adult: **PO** 0.25–4 mg b.i.d. to q.i.d. **IM** 8–16 mg q1–3 wk or 0.8–1.6 mg intralesional q1–3 wk **IV** 0.75–0.9 mg/kg/d divided q6–12h

Common adverse effects in *italic*, life-threatening effects underlined; generic names in **bold**; classifications in SMALL CAPS; ♥ Canadian drug name; ⊙ Prototype drug

441

D

Child: **PO/IV/IM** 0.08–0.3 mg/kg/d divided q6–12h

Cerebral Edema

Adult: **IV** 10 mg followed by 4 mg q6h, reduce dose after 2–4 d then taper over 5–7 d
Child: **PO/IV/IM** 1–2 mg/kg loading dose, then 1–1.5 mg/kg/d divided q4–6h × 5 d (max: 16 mg/d)

Shock

Adult: **IV** 1–6 mg/kg as a single dose or 40 mg repeated q2–6h if needed

Dexamethasone Suppression Test

Adult: **PO** 0.5 mg q6h for 48 h

Inflammation

Adult/Child: **Ophthalmic/Topical/Inhalation/Intranasal** See Appendix A.

ADMINISTRATION

Oral
- Give the once-daily dose in the A.M. with food or liquid of patient's choice.
- Taper dosage over a period of time before discontinuing because adrenal suppression can occur with prolonged use.
- Do not store or expose aerosol to temperature above 48.9° C (120° F); do not puncture or discard into a fire or an incinerator.

Intramuscular
- Give IM injection deep into a large muscle mass (e.g., gluteus maximus). Avoid SC injection: Atrophy and sterile abscesses may occur.
- Use repository form, dexamethasone acetate, for IM or local injection only. The white suspension settles on standing; mild shaking will resuspend drug.

Intravenous

PREPARE: **Direct:** Give undiluted. **Intermittent:** Dilute in D5W or NS for infusion.

ADMINISTER: **Direct:** Give direct IV push over 30 sec or less. **Intermittent:** Set rate as prescribed or according to amount of solution to infuse.

INCOMPATIBILITIES Solution/additive: **Daunorubicin, doxorubicin, doxapram, glycopyrrolate, metaraminol, vancomycin.**

- Store at 15°–30° C (59°–86° F) unless otherwise directed.

ADVERSE EFFECTS (≥1%) **Aerosol Therapy:** *Nasal irritation,* dryness, epistaxis, rebound congestion, bronchial asthma, anosmia, perforation of nasal septum. **Systemic Absorption—CNS:** Euphoria, insomnia, convulsions, increased ICP, vertigo, headache, psychic disturbances. **CV:** CHF, hypertension, *edema.* **Endocrine:** Menstrual irregularities, *hyperglycemia;* cushingoid state; growth suppression in children; hirsutism. **Special Senses:** *Posterior subcapsular cataract,* increased IOP, glaucoma, exophthalmos. **GI:** Peptic ulcer with possible perforation, abdominal distension, nausea, increased appetite, heartburn, dyspepsia, pancreatitis, bowel perforation, *oral candidiasis.* **Musculoskeletal:** Muscle weakness, loss of muscle mass, vertebral compression fracture, pathologic fracture of long bones, tendon rupture. **Skin:** Acne, *impaired wound healing,* petechiae, ecchymoses, diaphoresis, allergic dermatitis, hypo- or hyperpigmentation, SC and cutaneous atrophy, burning and tingling in perineal area (following IV injection).

DIAGNOSTIC TEST INTERFERENCE
Dexamethasone suppression test for endogenous depression:

false-positive results may be caused by **alcohol, glutethimide, meprobamate;** false-negative results may be caused by high doses of benzodiazepines (e.g., **chlordiazepoxide** and **cyproheptadine**), long-term glucocorticoid treatment, **indomethacin, ephedrine,** estrogens or hepatic enzyme-inducing agents **(phenytoin)** may also cause false-positive results in *test for Cushing's syndrome*.

INTERACTIONS Drug: BARBITURATES, **phenytoin, rifampin** increase steroid metabolism—dosage of dexamethasone may need to be increased; **amphotericin B,** DIURETICS compound potassium loss; **ambenonium, neostigmine, pyridostigmine** may cause severe muscle weakness in patients with myasthenia gravis; may inhibit antibody response to VACCINES, TOXOIDS.

PHARMACOKINETICS Absorption: Readily from GI tract. **Onset:** Rapid. **Peak:** 1–2 h PO; 8 h IM. **Duration:** 2.75 d PO; 6 d IM; 1–3 wk intralesional, intraarticular. **Distribution:** Crosses placenta; distributed into breast milk. **Elimination:** Hypothalamus-pituitary axis suppression: 36–54 h. **Half-Life:** 3–4.5 h.

CLINICAL IMPLICATIONS

Assessment & Drug Effects

- Monitor and report S&S of Cushing's syndrome (see Appendix F) or other systemic adverse effects.
- Monitor neonates born to a mother who has been receiving a corticosteroid during pregnancy for symptoms of hypoadrenocorticism.
- Monitor for S&S of a hypersensitivity reaction (see Appendix F). The acetate and sodium phosphate formulations may contain bisulfites, parabens, or both; these inactive ingredients are allergenic to some individuals.

Patient & Family Education

- Take drug exactly as prescribed.
- Report lack of response to medication or malaise, orthostatic hypotension, muscular weakness and pain, nausea, vomiting, anorexia, hypoglycemic reactions (see Appendix F), or mental depression to physician. These symptoms may signal hypoadrenocorticism.
- Report changes in appearance and easy bruising to physician. These symptoms may signal hyperadrenocorticism.
- Note: Hiccups that occur for several hours following each dose may be a complication of high-dose oral dexamethasone.
- Keep appointments for checkups; make sure electrolytes and BP are evaluated during therapy at regular intervals.
- Add potassium-rich foods to diet; report signs of hypokalemia (see Appendix F). Concomitant potassium-depleting diuretic can enhance dexamethasone-induced potassium loss.
- Note: Dexamethasone dose regimen may need to be altered during stress (e.g., surgery, infections, emotional stress, illness, acute bronchial attacks, trauma). Consult physician if change in living or working environment is anticipated.
- Discontinue drug gradually under the guidance of the physician.
- Note: It is important to prevent exposure to infection, trauma, and sudden changes in environmental factors, as much as possible, because drug is an immunosuppressor.

Common adverse effects in *italic*, life-threatening effects <u>underlined</u>; generic names in **bold**; classifications in SMALL CAPS; ✚ Canadian drug name; ❷ Prototype drug

443

DEXCHLORPHENIRAMINE MALEATE

(dex-klor-fen-eer′a-meen)
Dexchlor, Mylaramine
Classifications: ANTIHISTAMINE;
H₁-RECEPTOR ANTAGONIST
Therapeutic: ANTIHISTAMINE; H₁-
RECEPTOR ANTAGONIST
Prototype: Diphenhydramine
Pregnancy Category: B

AVAILABILITY 2 mg tablets; 4 mg,
6 mg sustained release tablets; 2 mg/
5 mL syrup

ACTION & *THERAPEUTIC EFFECT*
H₁-receptor antagonist that competes for H₁-receptor sites on cells,
thus blocking histamine release.
*Has high antihistamine effects and
moderate anticholinergic effects.*

USES Perennial and seasonal allergic rhinitis, other manifestations of
allergy, and vasomotor rhinitis.
Also as adjunct to epinephrine in
treatment of anaphylactic reactions.

CONTRAINDICATIONS Hypersensitivity to antihistamines of similar
class; closed-angle glaucoma; acute
asthmatic attack, lower respiratory
tract symptoms, newborns, premature infants, children <2 y.

CAUTIOUS USE Increased intraocular pressure; prostatic hypertrophy;
hyperthyroidism; asthma, COPD;
renal, hepatic, and cardiovascular
disease; serious GI disorders; older
adults; pregnancy (category B), lactation.

ROUTE & DOSAGE

Allergic Rhinitis
Adult: **PO** 2 mg q4–6h or 4–6 mg
of repeat-action tablets h.s. or
q8–10h during the day

Child: **PO** 2–5 y, 0.5 mg q4–6h
(max: 3 mg/24 h); 6–11 y, 1 mg
q4–6h (max: 6 mg/24 h) or 4 mg
of repeat-action tablets h.s.

ADMINISTRATION

Oral
- Ensure that sustained release form
of drug is not chewed or crushed.
It must be swallowed whole.
- Give regular tablet whole or
crushed and taken with fluid or
mixed with food.
- Give medication with food, water,
or milk to lessen GI distress.
- Store at 15°–30° C (59°–86° F) unless otherwise directed.

ADVERSE EFFECTS (≥1%) **CNS:**
Drowsiness, dizziness, weakness,
headache, excitation, neuritis, disturbed coordination, insomnia, euphoria, paresthesias. **Special Senses:**
Vertigo, tinnitus, acute labyrinthitis;
blurred vision. **CV:** Palpitations,
tachycardia, hypotension, extrasystoles. **GI:** Nausea, vomiting,
anorexia, *dry mouth,* constipation,
diarrhea. **Urogenital:** Difficulty in
urinating, *urinary retention,* urinary
frequency, early menses. **Hematologic:** Agranulocytosis (rare),
hemolytic or hypoplastic anemia.
Skin: Skin eruptions, photosensitivity.

DIAGNOSTIC TEST INTERFERENCE
In common with other antihistamines, dexchlorpheniramine may
interfere with ***skin tests for al-
lergy;*** discontinue dexchlorpheniramine at least 72 h before tests.

INTERACTIONS Drug: Alcohol and
other CNS DEPRESSANTS, MAO INHIBITORS
compound CNS depression.

PHARMACOKINETICS Absorption:
Readily from GI tract. **Onset:** 15–30
min. **Peak:** 3 h. **Distribution:** Small
amounts into breast milk. **Metab-**

olism: In liver. **Elimination:** In urine within 24 h.

CLINICAL IMPLICATIONS

Assessment & Drug Effects

- Supervise ambulation and take safety precautions, especially with older adult patients.
- Monitor I&O and assess for difficulty voiding (e.g., frequency or retention).

Patient & Family Education

- Swallow timed or sustained release tablet whole. Do not break, crush, or chew.
- Do not drive or engage in other potentially hazardous activities until reaction to drug is known.
- Ask physician about the use of alcohol, tranquilizers, sedatives, or other CNS depressants because the effects of dexchlorpheniramine will be additive.
- Discontinue dexchlorpheniramine about 4 d before skin tests for allergies, since it can make test results inaccurate.

DEXMEDETOMIDINE HYDROCHLORIDE

(dex-med-e-to′mi-deen)

Precedex

Classifications: ALPHA₂-ADRENERGIC AGONIST; SEDATIVE-HYPNOTIC
Therapeutic: SEDATIVE-HYPNOTIC
Prototype: Methoxamine HCl
Pregnancy Category: C

AVAILABILITY 100 mcg/mL injection

ACTION & THERAPEUTIC EFFECT
Dexmedetomidine stimulates alpha₂-adrenergic receptors in the CNS (primarily in the medulla oblongata) causing inhibition of the sympathetic vasomotor center of the brain. Hemodynamic responses of the heart affected by alpha₂ receptors are better controlled with dexmedetomidine than with other related drugs (e.g., midazolam). *Sedative properties utilized in intubating patients and for initially maintaining them on a mechanical ventilator.*

USES Sedation of initially intubated or mechanically ventilated patients.

CONTRAINDICATIONS Hypersensitivity to dexmedetomidine; labor and delivery, including cesarean section, pregnancy (category C).
CAUTIOUS USE Patients with arrhythmias or cardiovascular disease, uncontrolled hypertension; hypotension; cerebrovascular disease; renal or hepatic insufficiency; signs of light anesthesia; lactation; older adults >65 y. Safety and efficacy in children <18 y are unknown.

ROUTE & DOSAGE

Sedation

Adult: **IV** Start with 1 mcg/kg infused over 10 min, then continue with infusion of 0.2–0.7 mcg/kg/hr for up to 24 h, may need to decrease dosage in patients with renal or hepatic impairment

ADMINISTRATION

Intravenous

PREPARE: **Continuous:** Withdraw 2 mL of dexmedetomidine and add to 48 mL of 0.9% NaCl injection. Shake gently to mix.
ADMINISTER: **Continuous:** Administer using a controlled infusion device. A loading dose of 1 mcg/kg is infused over 10 min followed by the ordered maintenance dose. Do **NOT** use administration set containing natural rubber. Do **NOT** infuse longer than 24 h.

- Store at 15°–30° C (59°–86° F).

Common adverse effects in *italic*, life-threatening effects underlined; generic names in **bold**; classifications in SMALL CAPS; ♣ Canadian drug name; ⊘ Prototype drug

445

D

ADVERSE EFFECTS (≥1%) **Body as a Whole:** Pain, infection. **CV:** *Hypotension,* bradycardia, atrial fibrillation. **GI:** *Nausea,* thirst. **Respiratory:** Hypoxia, pleural effusion, pulmonary edema. **Hematologic:** Anemia, leukocytosis. **Urogenital:** Oliguria.

INTERACTIONS Drug: BARBITURATES, BENZODIAZEPINES, GENERAL ANESTHETICS, OPIATE AGONISTS, ANXIOLYTICS, SEDATIVES/HYPNOTICS, TRICYCLIC ANTIDEPRESSANTS, **ethanol, tramadol,** PHENOTHIAZINES, SKELETAL MUSCLE RELAXANTS, **azatadine, brompheniramine, carbinoxamine, chlorpheniramine, clemastine, cyproheptadine, dexchlorpheniramine, dimenhydrinate, diphenhydramine, doxylamine, hydroxyzine, methdilazine, phenindamine, promethazine, tripelennamine** enhance CNS depression possibly prolong recovery from anesthesia.

PHARMACOKINETICS Metabolism: Extensively in liver (CYP2A6). **Elimination:** Primarily in urine. **Half-Life:** 2 h.

CLINICAL IMPLICATIONS
Assessment & Drug Effects

- Monitor for hypertension during loading dose; reduction of loading dose may be required.
- Monitor cardiovascular status continuously; notify physician immediately if hypotension or bradycardia occur.

DEXMETHYLPHENIDATE

(dex-meth-ill-fen'i-date)
Focalin, Focalin XR
Classifications: CEREBRAL STIMULANT
Therapeutic: CEREBRAL STIMULANT
Prototype: Amphetamine
Pregnancy Category: C
Controlled Substance: Schedule II

AVAILABILITY 2.5 mg, 5 mg, 10 mg tablets; 5 mg, 10 mg, 20 mg extended release capsules

ACTION & *THERAPEUTIC EFFECT* Thought to block the reuptake of norepinephrine and dopamine into the presynaptic neurons and, thereby, increases release of these substances into the synapse. The mode of action in controlling the symptoms of attention deficit hyperactivity disorder (ADHD) is not fully understood. *Is effective in controlling ADHD syndrome in conjunction with other measures (psychological, educational, and social).*

USES Attention deficit hyperactivity disorder (ADHD).

CONTRAINDICATIONS Hypersensitivity to dexmethylphenidate or methylphenidate; known structural cardiac abnormalities in children or adults, cardiomyopathy, congenital heart disease; coronary heart disease; severe agitation, anxiety, or tension; psychotic symptomatology; substance abuse; glaucoma; motor tics other than Tourette's syndrome; concurrent MAOI therapy; children <6 y; seizures; pregnancy (category C), lactation.

CAUTIOUS USE Moderate to severe hepatic insufficiency; Tourette's syndrome; depression; emotional instability; alcoholism or drug dependence; history of seizure disorders; hypertension, CHF, cardiac arrhythmias; hyperthyroidism.

ROUTE & DOSAGE

Attention Deficit Hyperactivity Disorder
Adult: **PO** 2.5 mg b.i.d., may increase by 2.5 mg–5 mg/d at weekly intervals to max of 20 mg/d. If converting from methylphenidate, start with ¹/₂ of methylphenidate dose.

Common adverse effects in *italic*, life-threatening effects underlined; generic names in **bold**; classifications in SMALL CAPS; ♦ Canadian drug name; ⊕ Prototype drug

Extended release: 10 mg daily, may increase by 5 mg at weekly intervals to max of 20 mg/d
Child: PO >6 y, 2.5 mg b.i.d., may increase by 2.5 mg–5 mg/d at weekly intervals to max of 20 mg/d. If converting from methylphenidate, start with $1/2$ of methylphenidate dose.
Extended release: 5 mg daily, may increase by 5 mg at weekly intervals to max of 20 mg/d.

ADMINISTRATION

Oral

- Do not administer with or within 14 d following discontinuation of an MAO inhibitor.
- Give sustained release capsules whole. They should not be crushed or chewed.
- Give b.i.d. doses at least 4 h apart.
- Store at 15°–30° C (59°–86° F).

ADVERSE EFFECTS (≥1%) **Body as a Whole:** Fever, allergic reactions. **CNS:** Dizziness, insomnia, nervousness, tics, abnormal thinking, hallucinations, emotional lability, CNS overstimulation or sympathomimetic effects [angina, anxiety, agitation, biting, blurred vision, delirium, diaphoresis, flushing or pallor, hallucinations, hyperthermia, labile blood pressure and heart rate (hypotension or hypertension), mydriasis, palpitations, paranoia, purposeless movements, psychosis, sinus tachycardia, tachypnea, or tremor]. **CV:** Hypertension, tachycardia. **GI:** *Abdominal pain,* decreased appetite, nausea, vomiting.

INTERACTIONS Drug: Additive stimulant effects with other STIMULANTS (including **amphetamine, caffeine**); increased vasopressor effects with **dopamine, epinephrine, norepinephrine, phenylpropanolamine, pseudoephedrine;** MAO INHIBITORS may cause hypertensive crisis; antagonizes hypotensive effects of **guanethidine, bretylium;** may inhibit metabolism and increase serum levels of **fosphenytoin, phenytoin, phenobarbital, and primidone, warfarin,** TRICYCLIC ANTIDEPRESSANTS.

PHARMACOKINETICS Absorption: Well absorbed. **Peak:** 1–1.5 h. **Metabolism:** De-esterified in liver. No interaction with CYP450 system. **Elimination:** Primarily in urine. **Half-Life:** 2.2 h.

CLINICAL IMPLICATIONS

Assessment & Drug Effects

- Withhold drug and notify physician if patient has a seizure. Monitor closely for loss of seizure control with a prior history of seizures.
- Monitor BP in all patients receiving this drug. Monitor cardiac status and report palpitations or other signs of arrhythmias.
- Monitor for potential abuse and dependence on this drug. Careful supervision is needed during drug withdrawal since severe depression may occur.
- Monitor for signs of aggression or psychotic behavior in adolescents and children.
- Lab tests: Periodic CBC, differential, platelet counts, and LFTs during prolonged therapy.
- Concurrent drugs: Monitor patients on BP-lowering drugs for loss of BP control. Monitor plasma levels of oral anticoagulants and anticonvulsants; doses of these drugs may need to be decreased.

Patient & Family Education

- Withhold drug and report immediately any of the following signs of overdose: vomiting, agitation, tremors, muscle twitching, convulsions, confusion, hallucinations,

Common adverse effects in *italic*, life-threatening effects <u>underlined</u>; generic names in **bold**; classifications in SMALL CAPS; ♣ Canadian drug name; ⊙ Prototype drug

447

D

delirium, sweating, flushing, headache, or headache, or high temperature.

- Note that drug is usually discontinued if improvement is not observed after appropriate dosage adjustment over 1 mo.

DEXRAZOXANE

(dex-ra-zox'ane)
Zinecard
Classifications: CHELATING AGENT; CHEMOPROTECTIVE AGENT; CARDIOPROTECTIVE FOR DOXORUBICIN
Therapeutic: CARDIOPROTECTIVE FOR DOXORUBICIN
Pregnancy Category: C

AVAILABILITY 250 mg, 500 mg vials for injection

ACTION & THERAPEUTIC EFFECT
A derivative of EDTA that readily penetrates cell membranes. Dexrazoxane is converted intracellularly to a chelating agent that interferes with iron-mediated free radical generation thought to be partially responsible for one form of cardiomyopathy. *Cardioprotective effect is related to its chelating activity.*

USES Reduction of the incidence and severity of cardiomyopathy associated with doxorubicin in women with metastatic breast cancer who have received a cumulative doxorubicin dose of 300 mg/m^2.

CONTRAINDICATIONS Chemotherapy regimens that do not contain anthracycline, pregnancy (category C), lactation.
CAUTIOUS USE Myelosuppression, elderly; prior radiation or chemotherapy; renal failure or impairment. Safety and efficacy in children have not been established.

ROUTE & DOSAGE

Cardiomyopathy
Adult: **IV** 10 parts dexrazoxane to 1 part doxorubicin or 500 mg/m^2 for every 50 mg/m^2 of doxorubicin

Renal Impairment
Cl_{cr} <40 mL/min: use a 5:1 ratio of dexrazoxane to doxorubicin

ADMINISTRATION

Intravenous
Wear gloves when handling dexrazoxane. Immediately wash with soap and water if drug contacts skin or mucosa.

- Doxorubicin dose MUST be started within 30 min of beginning dexrazoxane.

PREPARE: Direct: Reconstitute by adding 25 or 50 mL of 0.167 M sodium lactate injection (provided by manufacturer) to the 250- or 500-mg vial, respectively, to produce a 10-mg/mL solution. **IV Infusion:** Further dilute with NS or D5W in an IV bag to a concentration of 1.3–5.0 mg/mL for infusion.
ADMINISTER: Direct: Give slow IV push. **IV Infusion:** Give over 10 min.

- Store reconstituted solutions for 6 h at 15°–30° C (59°–86° F).

ADVERSE EFFECTS (≥1%) **All:** Adverse effects of dexrazoxane are difficult to distinguish from those of the chemotherapeutic agents. Pain at injection site, <u>leukopenia, granulocytopenia</u>, and <u>thrombocytopenia</u> appear to occur more frequently with the addition of dexrazoxane than with placebo.

PHARMACOKINETICS Distribution:
Not protein bound. **Metabolism:** In liver. **Elimination:** 42% in urine. **Half-Life:** 2–2.5 h.

CLINICAL IMPLICATIONS

Assessment & Drug Effects
- Monitor cardiac function. Drug does not eliminate risk of doxorubicin cardiotoxicity.
- Lab tests: Monitor hepatic, renal, and hematopoietic status throughout course of therapy.
- Note: Adverse effects are likely due to concurrent cytotoxic drugs rather than dexrazoxane.

Patient & Family Education
- Report any of the following to physician: Worsening shortness of breath, swelling extremities, or chest pains.

DEXTRAN 40

(dex'tran)
Gentran 40, 10% LMD, Rheomacrodex
Classifications: PLASMA VOLUME EXPANDER
Therapeutic: PLASMA VOLUME EXPANDER
Prototype: Albumin
Pregnancy Category: C

AVAILABILITY 10% solution in D5W or NS

ACTION & *THERAPEUTIC EFFECT*
Low-molecular-weight polysaccharide. As a hypertonic colloidal solution, produces immediate and short-lived expansion of plasma volume by increasing colloidal osmotic pressure and drawing fluid from interstitial to intravascular space. *Cardiovascular response to volume expansion includes increased BP, pulse pressure, CVP, cardiac output, venous return to heart, and urinary output.*

USES Adjunctively to expand plasma volume and provide fluid replacement in treatment of shock or impending shock caused by hemorrhage, burns, surgery, or other trauma. Also used in prophylaxis and therapy of venous thrombosis and pulmonary embolism. Used as priming fluid or as additive to other primers during extracorporeal circulation.

CONTRAINDICATIONS Hypersensitivity to dextrans, severe renal failure, hypervolemic conditions, severe CHF, significant anemia, hypofibrinogenemia or other marked hemostatic defects including those caused by drugs, (e.g., heparin, warfarin); pregnancy (category C), lactation.
CAUTIOUS USE Active hemorrhage; severe dehydration; chronic liver disease; impaired renal function; thrombocytopenia; patients susceptible to pulmonary edema or CHF.

ROUTE & DOSAGE

Shock
Adult: **IV** 500 mL administered rapidly (over 15–30 min), additional doses may be given more slowly up to 20 mL/kg in the first 24 h (doses up to 10 mL/kg/d may be given for an additional 4 d if needed)
Child: **IV** Total dose ≤20 mL/kg in first 24 h and ≤10 mL/kg/d (max: 5 d total)

Prophylaxis for Thromboembolic Complications
Adult: **IV** 500–1000 mL (10 mL/kg) on the day of operation followed by 500 mL/d for 2–3 d, may continue with 500 mL q2–3d for up to 2 wk if necessary

---

Common adverse effects in *italic*, life-threatening effects underlined; generic names in **bold**; classifications in SMALL CAPS; ◆ Canadian drug name; ● Prototype drug

449

Priming for Extracorporeal Circulation

Adult: **IV** 10–20 mL/kg added to perfusion circuit

ADMINISTRATION

Intravenous

If blood is to be administered, draw a cross-match specimen before dextran infusion.

PREPARE: **IV Infusion:** Use only if seal is intact, vacuum is detectable, and solution is absolutely clear.

ADMINISTER: **IV Infusion:** Specific flow rate should be prescribed by physician. For emergency treatment of shock in adults give first 500 mL rapidly (e.g., 20–40 mL/min); give remaining portion of the daily dose over 8–24 h or at the rate prescribed.

▪ Store at a constant temperature, preferably 25° C (77° F). Once opened, discard unused portion because dextran contains no preservative.

ADVERSE EFFECTS (≥1%) **Body as a Whole:** Hypersensitivity (mild to generalized urticaria, pruritus, ana-phylactic shock (rare), angioedema, dyspnea). **Other:** Renal tubular vacuolization (osmotic nephrosis), stasis, and blocking; oliguria, renal failure; increased AST and ALT, interference with platelet function, prolonged bleeding and coagulation times.

DIAGNOSTIC TEST INTERFERENCE

When blood samples are drawn for study, notify laboratory that patient has received dextran. *Blood glucose:* false increases (utilizing *ortho-toluidine methods* or *sulfuric* or *acetic acid* hydrolysis). *Urinary protein:* false increases (utilizing *Lowry method*). *Bilirubin assays:* false increases when alcohol is used. *Total protein assays:* false increases using *biuret reagent. Rh testing, blood typing* and *cross-matching* procedures: dextran may interfere with results (by inducing rouleaux formation) when *proteolytic enzyme techniques* are used (*saline agglutination* and *indirect antiglobulin methods* reportedly not affected).

PHARMACOKINETICS **Onset:** Volume expansion within minutes of infusion. **Duration:** 12 h. **Metabolism:** Degraded to glucose and metabolized to CO_2 and water over a period of a few weeks. **Elimination:** 75% excreted in urine within 24 h; small amount excreted in feces.

CLINICAL IMPLICATIONS

Assessment & Drug Effects

▪ Evaluate patient's state of hydration before dextran therapy begins. Administration to severely dehydrated patients can result in renal failure.

▪ Lab tests: Baseline Hct prior to and after initiation of dextran (dextran usually lowers Hct). Notify physician if Hct is depressed below 30% by volume.

▪ Monitor vital signs and observe patient closely for at least the first 30 min of infusion. Hypersensitivity reaction is most likely to occur during the first few minutes of administration. Terminate therapy at the first sign of a hypersensitivity reaction (see Appendix F).

▪ Monitor CVP as an estimate of blood volume status and a guide for determining dosage. Normal CVP: 5–10 cm H_2O.

▪ Observe for S&S of circulatory overload (see Appendix F).

▪ Note: When sodium restriction is indicated, know that 500 mL of dextran 40 in 0.9% normal saline contains 77 mEq of both sodium and chloride.

- Monitor I&O ratio and check urine specific gravity at regular intervals. Low urine specific gravity may signify failure of renal dextran clearance and is an indication to discontinue therapy.
- Report oliguria, anuria, or lack of improvement in urinary output (dextran usually causes an increase in urinary output). Discontinue dextran at first sign of renal dysfunction.
- High doses are associated with transient prolongation of bleeding time and interference with normal blood coagulation.

Patient & Family Education
- Report immediately S&S of bleeding: easy bruising, blood in urine or dark tarry stool.

DEXTRAN 70

(dex′tran)
Macrodex

DEXTRAN 75

Gentran 75
Classifications: PLASMA VOLUME EXPANDER
Therapeutic: PLASMA VOLUME EXPANDER
Prototype: Albumin
Pregnancy Category: C

AVAILABILITY 6% solution in D5W or NS

ACTION & *THERAPEUTIC EFFECT*
High-molecular-weight polysaccharide. The colloidal osmotic effect of dextran draws fluid into the vascular system from the interstitial spaces, resulting in increased circulating blood volume and decreasing blood viscosity. *Cardiovascular response to volume expansion includes in-creased BP, pulse pressure, CVP, cardiac output, venous return to heart, and urinary output.*

USES Primarily for emergency treatment of hypovolemic shock or impending shock caused by hemorrhage, burns, surgery, or other trauma. Intended for emergency treatment only when whole blood or blood products are not available or when haste precludes cross-matching of blood.
UNLABELED USES Nephrosis, toxemia of pregnancy, and prophylaxis of deep vein thrombosis.

CONTRAINDICATIONS Known hypersensitivity to dextrans; severe bleeding disorders; severe CHF; coagulopathy; severe renal failure; pregnancy (category C), lactation.
CAUTIOUS USE Impaired renal function, pulmonary edema, CHF, pathologic GI disorders; thrombocytopenia.

ROUTE & DOSAGE

Shock
Adult: **IV** 500 mL administered rapidly (over 15–30 min), additional doses may be given more slowly up to 20 mL/kg in the first 24 h (doses up to 10 mL/kg/d may be given for an additional 4 d if needed)

ADMINISTRATION
Intravenous

PREPARE: IV Infusion: Use only if seal is intact, vacuum is detectable, and solution is absolutely clear.
ADMINISTER: IV Infusion: Specific flow rate should be prescribed by physician. For emergency treatment of shock, rate of administration for first 500 mL may be 20–40

Common adverse effects in *italic*, life-threatening effects <u>underlined</u>; generic names in **bold**; classifications in SMALL CAPS; ♣ Canadian drug name; ⓓ Prototype drug

451

mL/min; thereafter, unless patient is hypovolemic, rate should not exceed 4 mL/min.

▪ Store at a constant temperature, preferably 25° C (77° F).

ADVERSE EFFECTS (≥1%) **All:** *Allergic reactions,* urticaria, wheezing, mild hypotension, nausea, vomiting, fever, arthralgia, <u>severe anaphylactoid</u> reaction.

PHARMACOKINETICS Onset: Volume expansion within minutes of infusion. **Duration:** 12 h. **Metabolism:** Degraded to glucose and metabolized to carbon dioxide and water over a period of a few weeks. **Elimination:** 75% in urine within 24 h; small amount in feces.

CLINICAL IMPLICATIONS
Assessment & Drug Effects
▪ Observe closely for S&S of anaphylaxis (see Appendix F) especially during first 30 min of infusion. Severe reactions have resulted in fatalities.
▪ Note: Bleeding time may be temporarily prolonged in patients receiving more than 1000 mL of dextran 70 or 75.
▪ Monitor I&O ratio and pattern. Monitor vital signs frequently as warranted by condition of patient.

Patient & Family Education
▪ Report immediately S&S of bleeding to physician: Easy bruising, blood in urine, or dark tarry stool.

DEXTROAMPHETAMINE SULFATE

(dex-troe-am-fet′a-meen)
Dexampex, Dexedrine, Oxydess II ◆, Spancap No. 1
Classifications: RESPIRATORY AND CEREBRAL STIMULANT; AMPHETAMINE; ANOREXIANT

Therapeutic: AMPHETAMINE; ANOREXIANT
Prototype: Amphetamine
Pregnancy Category: C
Controlled Substance: Schedule II

AVAILABILITY 5 mg, 10 mg tablets; 5 mg, 10 mg, 15 mg sustained release capsules

ACTION & *THERAPEUTIC EFFECT* An isomer of amphetamine, it has anorexigenic action; this is thought to result from CNS stimulation and possibly from loss of acuity of smell and taste. *Is a more potent appetite suppressant than amphetamine. CNS stimulating effect approximately twice that of racemic amphetamine. In hyperkinetic children, amphetamines reduce motor restlessness by an unknown mechanism.*

USES Adjunct in short-term treatment of exogenous obesity, narcolepsy, and attention deficit disorder with hyperactivity in children (also called minimal brain dysfunction or hyperkinetic syndrome).
UNLABELED USES Adjunct in epilepsy to control ataxia and drowsiness induced by barbiturates; to combat sedative effects of trimethadione in absence seizures.

CONTRAINDICATIONS Hypersensitivity to sympathomimetic amines, closed-angle glaucoma, agitated states, psychoses (especially in children), structural cardiac abnormalities, valvular heart disease; congenital heart disease, coronary heart disease, advanced arteriosclerosis, symptomatic heart disease, moderate to severe hypertension, hyperthyroidism, history of drug abuse, during or within 14 d of MAO INHIBITOR therapy, as anorexiant in children <12 y, for attention deficit disorder in children <3 y, pregnancy (category C); lactation.

Common adverse effects in *italic*, life-threatening effects <u>underlined</u>; generic names in **bold**; classifications in SMALL CAPS; ◆ Canadian drug name; ☻ Prototype drug

CAUTIOUS USE Bipolar disease; salicylate hypersensitivity; seizure disorders; suicidal ideation, depression; salicylate hypersensitivity. Safety and efficacy in children <3 y have not been established.

ROUTE & DOSAGE

Narcolepsy

Adult: PO 5–20 mg 1–3 times/d at 4–6 h intervals
Child: PO 6–12 y, 5 mg/d, may increase by 5 mg at weekly intervals; >12 y, 10 mg/d, may increase by 10 mg at weekly intervals

Attention Deficit Disorder

Child: PO 3–5 y, 2.5 mg 1–2 times/d, may increase by 2.5 mg at weekly intervals; ≥6 y, 5 mg 1–2 times/d, may increase by 5 mg at weekly intervals (max: 40 mg/d)

Obesity

Adult: PO 5–10 mg 1–3 times/d or 10–15 mg of sustained release once/d 30–60 min a.c.

ADMINISTRATION

Oral

- Ensure that sustained release capsule is not chewed or crushed. It MUST be swallowed whole.
- Give 30–60 min before meals for treatment of obesity. Give long-acting form in the morning.
- Give last dose no later than 6 h before patient retires (10–14 h before bedtime for sustained release form) to avoid insomnia.
- Store in tightly closed containers at 15°–30° C (59°–86° F) unless otherwise directed.

ADVERSE EFFECTS (≥1%) CNS:
Nervousness, *restlessness,* hyperactivity, *insomnia,* euphoria, dizziness, headache; *with prolonged use:* severe depression, psychotic reactions. **CV:** Palpitations, tachycardia, elevated BP. **GI:** Dry mouth, unpleasant taste, anorexia, weight loss, diarrhea, constipation, abdominal pain. **Other:** Impotence, changes in libido, unusual fatigue, increased intraocular pressure, marked dystonia of head, neck, and extremities; sweating.

DIAGNOSTIC TEST INTERFERENCE
Dextroamphetamine may cause significant elevations in **plasma corticosteroids** (evening levels are highest) and increases in **urinary epinephrine** excretion (during first 3 h after drug administration).

INTERACTIONS Drug: Acetazolamide, sodium bicarbonate decrease dextroamphetamine elimination; **ammonium chloride, ascorbic acid** increase dextroamphetamine elimination; effects of both BARBITURATES and dextroamphetamine may be antagonized; **furazolidone** may increase BP effects of AMPHETAMINES—interaction may persist for several weeks after discontinuing **furazolidone;** antagonizes antihypertensive effects of **guanethidine, guanadrel;** MAO INHIBITORS, **selegiline** can cause—hypertensive crisis (fatalities reported)—do not administer AMPHETAMINES during or within 14 d of these drugs; PHENOTHIAZINES may inhibit mood elevating effects of AMPHETAMINES; TRICYCLIC ANTIDEPRESSANTS enhance dextroamphetamine effects because of increased **norepinephrine** release; BETA-ADRENERGIC AGONISTS increase cardiovascular adverse effects.

PHARMACOKINETICS Absorption:
Rapid. **Peak:** 1–5 h. **Duration:** Up to 10 h. **Distribution:** All tissues especially the CNS. **Metabolism:** In liver. **Elimination:** Renal elimination;

Common adverse effects in *italic*, life-threatening effects underlined; generic names in **bold**; classifications in SMALL CAPS; ♥ Canadian drug name; ☺ Prototype drug

453

excreted in breast milk. **Half-Life:** 10–30 h.

CLINICAL IMPLICATIONS

Assessment & Drug Effects

- Monitor children, adolescents, and adults for signs and symptoms of adverse cardiac reactions (e.g., arrhythmias).
- Monitor growth rate closely in children.
- Interrupt therapy or reduce dosage periodically to assess effectiveness in behavior disorders.
- Monitor children and adolescents for development of aggressive or abnormal behaviors.
- Note: Tolerance to anorexiant effects may develop after a few weeks; however, tolerance does not appear to develop when dextroamphetamine is used to treat narcolepsy.

Patient & Family Education

- Swallow sustained release capsule whole with a liquid; do not chew or crush.
- Do not drive or engage in other potentially hazardous activities until response to drug is known.
- Taper drug gradually following long-term use to avoid extreme fatigue, mental depression, and prolonged sleep pattern.

DEXTROMETHORPHAN HYDROBROMIDE

(dex-troe-meth-or′fan)

Balminil DM ◆, Benylin DM, Cremacoat 1, Delsym, DM Cough, Hold, Koffex ◆, Mediquell, Neo-DM ◆, Ornex DM ◆, Pedia Care, Pertussin 8 Hour Cough Formula, Robidex ◆, Robitussin DM, Romilar CF, Romilar Children's Cough, Sedatuss ◆, Sucrets Cough Control

Classifications: ANTITUSSIVE
Therapeutic: ANTITUSSIVE
Prototype: Benzonatate
Pregnancy Category: C

AVAILABILITY 30 mg capsules; 2.5 mg, 5 mg, 7.5 mg, 15 mg lozenges; 10 mg/15 mL, 3.5 mg/5 mL, 7.5 mg/5 mL, 15 mg/5 mL liquid; 15 mg/15 mL, 10 mg/5 mL syrup

ACTION & *THERAPEUTIC EFFECT*

Nonnarcotic derivative of levorphanol. Chemically related to morphine but without central hypnotic or analgesic effect. Controls cough spasms by depressing the cough center in medulla. Antitussive activity comparable to that of codeine but is less likely than codeine to cause constipation, drowsiness, or GI disturbances. *Temporarily relieves coughing spasm.*

USES Temporary relief of cough spasms in nonproductive coughs due to colds, pertussis, and influenza.

CONTRAINDICATIONS Children <2 y, infants and neonates; asthma, COPD, productive cough, persistent or chronic cough; severe hepatic function impairment; concurrent MAOI therapy; pregnancy (category C).

CAUTIOUS USE Chronic pulmonary disease; enlarged prostate; patients on MAO INHIBITORS; mild or moderate hepatic impairment; lactation.

ROUTE & DOSAGE

Cough

Adult: **PO** 10–20 mg q4h or 30 mg q6–8h (max: 120 mg/d) or 60 mg of sustained action liquid b.i.d.

Common adverse effects in *italic*, life-threatening effects underlined; generic names in **bold**, classifications in SMALL CAPS; ◆ Canadian drug name; ⦿ Prototype drug

Child: **PO** 2–6 y, 2.5–5 mg q4h or 7.5 mg q6–8h (max: 30 mg/d) or 15 mg sustained action liquid b.i.d.; 6–12 y, 5–10 mg q4h or 15 mg q6–8h (max: 60 mg/d) or 30 mg sustained action liquid b.i.d.

ADMINISTRATION

Oral

- Do not give lozenges to children <6 y.
- Ensure that extended release form of drug is not chewed or crushed. It MUST be swallowed whole.
- Note: Although soothing local effect of the syrup may be enhanced if given undiluted, depression of cough center depends only on systemic absorption of drug.

ADVERSE EFFECTS (≥1%) **CNS:** Dizziness, drowsiness, CNS depression with very large doses; excitability, especially in children. **GI:** GI upset, constipation, abdominal discomfort.

INTERACTIONS Drug: High risk of excitation, hypotension, and hyperpyrexia with MAO INHIBITORS.

PHARMACOKINETICS Absorption: Readily from GI tract. **Onset:** 15–30 min. **Duration:** 3–6 h. **Metabolism:** In liver. **Elimination:** In urine.

CLINICAL IMPLICATIONS

Assessment & Drug Effects

- Monitor for dizziness and drowsiness, especially when concurrent therapy with CNS depressant is used.

Patient & Family Education

- Avoid irritants such as smoking, dust, fumes, and other air pollutants to lessen unnecessary cough. Humidify ambient air to provide some relief.

- Note: Treatment aims to decrease the frequency and intensity of cough without completely eliminating protective cough reflex.
- While dextromethorphan is available OTC, any cough persisting longer than 1 wk–10 d needs to be medically diagnosed.

D

DIAZEPAM ⊕

(dye-az′e-pam)

Apo-Diazepam ◆, Diastat, Diazemuls ◆, Novodipam ◆, **Valium**, Vivol ◆

Classifications: BENZODIAZEPINE ANTICONVULSANT; ANXIOLYTIC

Therapeutic: ANTICONVULSANT; ANTIANXIETY

Pregnancy Category: D

Controlled Substance: Schedule IV

AVAILABILITY 2 mg, 5 mg, 10 mg tablets; 1 mg/mL, 5 mg/mL, 5 mg/5 mL oral solution; 5 mg/mL injection; 2.5 mg, 5 mg, 10 mg, 15 mg, 20 mg rectal gel

ACTION & *THERAPEUTIC EFFECT*

Long-acting benzodiazepine psychotherapeutic agent. Benzodiazepines act at the the limbic, thalamic, and hypothalamic regions of the CNS and produce CNS depression resulting in sedation, hypnosis, skeletal muscle relaxation, and anticonvulsant activity dependent on the dosage. *Has antianxiety, anticonvulsant agent, and skeletal muscle relaxation properties.*

USES Drug of choice for status epilepticus. Management of anxiety disorders, for short-term relief of anxiety symptoms, to allay anxiety and tension prior to surgery, cardioversion and endoscopic procedures, as an amnesic, and treatment for restless legs. Also used to

Common adverse effects in *italic*, life-threatening effects underlined; generic names in **bold**; classifications in SMALL CAPS; ◆ Canadian drug name; ⊕ Prototype drug

455

alleviate acute withdrawal symptoms of alcoholism, voiding problems in older adults, and adjunctively for relief of skeletal muscle spasm associated with cerebral palsy, paraplegia, athetosis, stiff-man syndrome, tetanus.

CONTRAINDICATIONS Acute narrow-angle glaucoma, untreated open-angle glaucoma; during or within 14 d of MAOI therapy; pregnancy (category D), lactation. *Injectable form:* Shock, coma, acute alcohol intoxication, depressed vital signs, obstetric patients, infants <30 d of age. *Tablet form:* Infants <6 mo of age.

CAUTIOUS USE Epilepsy, psychoses, mental depression; myasthenia gravis; impaired hepatic or renal function; neuromuscular disease; bipolar disorder, dementia, Parkinson's disease; organic brain syndrome, psychosis, suicidal ideation; drug abuse, addiction-prone individuals. Use injectable diazepam used with extreme caution in older adults, the very ill, and patients with COPD, asthma.

ROUTE & DOSAGE

Status Epilepticus

Adult: **IV/IM** 5–10 mg, repeat if needed at 10–15 min intervals up to 30 mg, then repeat if needed q2–4h
Child: **IV/IM** <5 y, 0.2–0.5 mg slowly q2–5min up to 5 mg; >5 y, 1 mg slowly q2–5min up to 10 mg, repeat if needed q2–4 h

Anxiety, Muscle Spasm, Convulsions

Adult: **PO** 2–10 mg b.i.d. to q.i.d. or 15–30 mg/d sustained release **IV/IM** 2–10 mg, repeat if needed in 3–4 h

Geriatric: **PO** 1–2 mg 1–2 times/d (max: 10 mg/d)
Child: **PO** >6 mo, 1–2.5 mg b.i.d. or t.i.d.

Alcohol Withdrawal

Adult: **IV/IM** 10 mg, then 5–10 mg in 3–4 h

ADMINISTRATION

Oral
- Ensure that sustained release form is not chewed or crushed. It MUST be swallowed whole. Give other tablets crushed with fluid or mixed with food if necessary.
- Supervise oral ingestion to ensure drug is swallowed.
- Avoid abrupt discontinuation of diazepam. Taper doses to termination.

Intramuscular
- Give deep into large muscle mass. Inject slowly. Rotate injection sites.
- Do NOT give emulsion form (Dizac) as IM or SC. It is for IV use only.

Intravenous
PREPARE: **Direct:** Do not dilute or mix with any other drug.
ADMINISTER: **Direct:** Give direct IV by injecting drug slowly, taking at least 1 min for each 5 mg (1 mL) given to adults and taking at least 3 min to inject 0.25 mg/kg body weight of children.
- If injection cannot be made directly into vein, inject slowly through infusion tubing as close as possible to vein insertion. ▪The emulsion form is incompatible with PVC infusion sets. ▪ Avoid small veins and take extreme care to avoid intraarterial administration or extravasation.

INCOMPATIBILITIES Solution/additive: **Bleomycin, benzquinamide, dobutamine, doxapram, doxorubicin, fluorouracil, glycopyrrolate, heparin, nalbuphine, sufentanil.** Emulsion also incompatible with **morphine.** Y-site: **Furosemide, heparin, potassium chloride, tirofiban, vitamin B complex with C.** Emulsion also incompatible with **morphine.** Do not mix emulsion with any other drugs. Do not administer through **polyvinyl chloride (PVC)** infusion sets.

▪ Store in tight, light-resistant containers at 15°–30° C (59°–86° F), unless otherwise specified by manufacturer. Store Dizac emulsion at 2°–8° C (36°–46° F). Do not freeze.

ADVERSE EFFECTS (≥1%) **Body as a Whole:** Throat and chest pain. **CNS:** *Drowsiness,* fatigue, ataxia, confusion, paradoxic rage, dizziness, vertigo, amnesia, vivid dreams, headache, slurred speech, tremor; EEG changes, tardive dyskinesia. **CV:** Hypotension, tachycardia, edema, <u>cardiovascular collapse.</u> **Special Senses:** Blurred vision, diplopia, nystagmus. **GI:** Xerostomia, nausea, constipation, hepatic dysfunction. **Urogenital:** Incontinence, urinary retention, gynecomastia (prolonged use), menstrual irregularities, ovulation failure. **Respiratory:** Hiccups, coughing, <u>laryngospasm.</u> **Other:** Pain, venous thrombosis, phlebitis at injection site.

INTERACTIONS Drug: Alcohol, CNS DEPRESSANTS, ANTICONVULSANTS potentiate CNS depression; **cimetidine** increases diazepam plasma levels, increases toxicity; may decrease antiparkinson effects of **levodopa;** may increase **phenytoin** levels; smoking decreases sedative and anti-anxiety effects. **Herbal: Kava-kava, valerian** may potentiate sedation.

PHARMACOKINETICS Absorption: Readily from GI tract; erratic IM absorption. **Onset:** 30–60 min PO; 15–30 min IM; 1–5 min IV. **Peak:** 1–2 h PO. **Duration:** 15 min–1 h IV; up to 3 h PO. **Distribution:** Crosses blood-brain barrier and placenta; distributed into breast milk. **Metabolism:** In liver to active metabolites. **Elimination:** Primarily in urine. **Half-Life:** 20–50 h.

CLINICAL IMPLICATIONS
Assessment & Drug Effects

▪ Monitor for adverse reactions. Most are dose related. Physician will rely on accurate observation and reports of patient response to the drug to determine lowest effective maintenance dose.

▪ Monitor for therapeutic effectiveness. Maximum effect may require 1–2 wk; patient tolerance to therapeutic effects may develop after 4 wk of treatment.

▪ Observe necessary preventive precautions for suicidal tendencies that may be present in anxiety states accompanied by depression.

▪ Observe patient closely and monitor vital signs when diazepam is given parenterally; hypotension, muscular weakness, tachycardia, and respiratory depression may occur.

▪ Lab tests: Periodic CBC and liver function tests during prolonged therapy.

▪ Supervise ambulation. Adverse reactions such as drowsiness and ataxia are more likely to occur in older adults and debilitated or those receiving larger doses. Dosage adjustment may be necessary.

▪ Monitor I&O ratio, including urinary and bowel elimination.

Common adverse effects in *italic*, life-threatening effects <u>underlined</u>; generic names in **bold**; classifications in SMALL CAPS; ♣ Canadian drug name; ❷ Prototype drug

- Note: Smoking increases metabolism of diazepam; lowering clinical effectiveness. Heavy smokers may need a higher dose than the nonsmoker.
- Note: Psychic and physical dependence may occur in patients on long-term high dosage therapy, in those with histories of alcohol or drug addiction, or in those who self-medicate.

Patient & Family Education
- Avoid alcohol and other CNS depressants during therapy unless otherwise advised by physician. Concomitant use of these agents can cause severe drowsiness, respiratory depression, and apnea.
- Do not drive or engage in other potentially hazardous activities or those requiring mental precision until reaction to drug is known.
- Tell physician if you become or intend to become pregnant during therapy; drug may need to be discontinued.
- Take drug as prescribed; do not change dose or dose intervals.
- Check with physician before taking any OTC drugs.

DIAZOXIDE

(dye-az-ox′ide)
Hyperstat I.V., Proglycem
Classifications: ANTIHYPERTENSIVE; VASODILATOR; SULFONYLUREA; ANTIDIABETIC AGENT
Therapeutic: ANTIHYPERTENSIVE; ANTIDIABETIC AGENT
Prototype: Hydralazine
Pregnancy Category: C

AVAILABILITY 50 mg capsules; 50 mg/mL suspension; 15 mg/mL injection

ACTION & *THERAPEUTIC EFFECT*
Rapid-acting thiazide nondiuretic hypotensive and hyperglycemic agent. In contrast to thiazide diuretics, causes sodium and water retention and decreases urinary output, probably because it increases proximal tubular reabsorption of sodium and decreases glomerular filtration rate. Hypotensive effect may be accompanied by marked reflex increase in heart rate, cardiac output, and stroke volume; thus cerebral and coronary blood flow are usually maintained. *Reduces peripheral vascular resistance and BP by direct vasodilatory effect on peripheral arteriolar smooth muscles, perhaps by direct competition for calcium receptor sites.*

USES Intravenously for emergency lowering of BP in hospitalized patients with malignant hypertension, particularly when associated with renal impairment. Not effective in pheochromocytoma. Commonly used with a diuretic such as furosemide (Lasix) to counteract diazoxide-induced sodium and water retention. Orally in treatment of various diagnosed hypoglycemic states due to hyperinsulinism when other medical treatment or surgical management has been unsuccessful or is not feasible.

CONTRAINDICATIONS Hypersensitivity to diazoxide; cerebral bleeding, eclampsia; aortic coarctation; AV shunt, significant coronary artery disease; pheochromocytoma; pregnancy (category C), lactation. Use of oral diazoxide for functional hypoglycemia or in presence of increased bilirubin in newborns.
CAUTIOUS USE Diabetes mellitus; impaired cerebral or cardiac circulation; impaired renal function; patients taking corticosteroids or estrogen–progestogen combinations; hyperuricemia, history of gout, uremia; thiazide diuretic hypersensitivity.

ROUTE & DOSAGE

Severe Hypertension
Adult/Child: **IV** 1–3 mg/kg up to 150 mg, repeat at 5–15 min intervals if necessary

Hypoglycemia
Adult/Child: **PO** 3–8 mg/kg/d divided q8–12h
Neonate/Infant: **PO** 8–15 mg/kg/d divided q8–12h

ADMINISTRATION

Intravenous
Note: Give any prescribed diuretic 30–60 min prior to IV diazoxide. Keep patient recumbent 8–10 h because of possible additive hypotensive effect.

PREPARE: **Direct:** Give undiluted.
ADMINISTER: **Direct:** Give IV by rapid direct injection over 10–30 s. Keep patient recumbent while receiving IV and for at least 30 min following administration.

▪ Check IV injection site frequently. Solution is strongly alkaline. Extravasation of medication into tissues can cause severe inflammatory reaction. Administer drug by peripheral vein ONLY.
▪ Do not give darkened solutions. Store capsules, oral suspension, and injectables at 2°–30° C (36°–86° F) unless otherwise directed. Protect from light, heat, and freezing.

ADVERSE EFFECTS (≥1%) **CNS:** Headache, weakness, malaise, *dizziness,* polyneuritis, sleepiness, insomnia, euphoria, anxiety, extrapyramidal signs. **CV:** Palpitations, atrial and ventricular arrhythmias, flushing, shock; *orthostatic hypotension,* CHF, transient hypertension. **Special Senses:** Tinnitus, momentary hearing loss; blurred vision, transient cataracts, subconjunctival hemorrhage, ring scotoma, diplopia, lacrimation, papilledema. **GI:** *Nausea, vomiting,* abdominal discomfort, diarrhea, constipation, ileus, anorexia, transient loss of taste, impaired hepatic function. **Hematologic:** Transient neutropenia, eosinophilia, decreased Hgb/Hct, decreased IgG. **Body as a Whole:** Hypersensitivity (rash, fever, leukopenia); chest and back pain, muscle cramps. **Urogenital:** Decreased urinary output, nephrotic syndrome (reversible), hematuria, increased nocturia, proteinuria, azotemia; inhibition of labor. **Skin:** Pruritus, flushing, monilial dermatitis, herpes, hirsutism; loss of scalp hair, sweating, sensation of warmth, burning, or itching. **Endocrine:** Advance in bone age (children), *hyperglycemia, sodium and water retention, edema,* hyperuricemia, glycosuria, enlargement of breast lump, galactorrhea; decreased immunoglobulinemia, hirsutism.

DIAGNOSTIC TEST INTERFERENCE
Diazoxide can cause false-negative response to *glucagon.*

INTERACTIONS Drug: SULFONYLUREAS antagonize effects; THIAZIDE DIURETICS may intensify hyperglycemia and antihypertensive effects; **phenytoin** increases risk of hyperglycemia, and diazoxide may increase **phenytoin** metabolism, causing loss of seizure control.

PHARMACOKINETICS Onset: 30–60 s IV; 1 h PO. **Peak:** 5 min IV. **Duration:** 2–12 or more h IV; 8 h PO. **Distribution:** Crosses blood–brain barrier and placenta. **Metabolism:** Partially metabolized in the liver. **Elimination:** In urine. **Half-Life:** 21–45 h.

Common adverse effects in *italic,* life-threatening effects <u>underlined</u>; generic names in **bold**; classifications in SMALL CAPS; ♣ Canadian drug name; ⊘ Prototype drug

459

D

CLINICAL IMPLICATIONS

Assessment & Drug Effects

- Monitor for therapeutic effectiveness. Discontinue if not effective in 2 or 3 wk.
- Lab tests: Initial blood glucose, serum electrolytes, and CBC and at regular intervals in patients receiving multiple doses.
- Monitor BP q5min for the first 15–30 min or until stabilized, then hourly for balance of drug effect.
- Notify physician immediately if BP continues to fall 30 min or more after IV drug administration. Cause other than drug effect is probable.
- Monitor pulse: Tachycardia has occurred immediately following IV; palpitation and bradycardia have also been reported.
- Report promptly any change in I&O ratio.
- Observe patient closely for S&S of CHF (see Appendix F).
- Monitor diabetics carefully for loss of glycemic control.
- Evaluate serum electrolyte levels at regular intervals, particularly in patients with impaired renal function; hypokalemia potentiates hyperglycemic effect of diazoxide.
- Note: In contrast to IV diazoxide, oral administration usually does not produce marked effects on BP. However, do make periodic measurements of BP and vital signs.
- Monitor S&S for up to 7 d for both oral and parenteral forms; essential because of long half-life of diazoxide.

Patient & Family Education

- Note: Drug may cause hyperglycemia and glycosuria in diabetic and diabetic-prone individuals. Closely monitor blood and urine glucose; report any abnormalities to physician.

- Report palpitations, chest pain, dizziness, fainting, or severe headache.
- Note: Lanugo-type hirsutism occurs frequently, commonly in children and women. It is reversible with discontinuation of drug.

DIBUCAINE

(dye′byoo-kane)

Nupercainal

Classifications: ANESTHETIC, LOCAL (AMIDE-TYPE)
Therapeutic: LOCAL ANESTHETIC
Prototype: Procaine
Pregnancy Category: C

AVAILABILITY 1% ointment

ACTION & *THERAPEUTIC EFFECT*

Long-acting anesthetic of the amide type and reportedly one of the most potent and most toxic. Appears to inhibit initiation and conduction of nerve impulses by reducing permeability of nerve cell membrane to sodium ions. *Relief of pain and itching due to inhibiting conduction of nerve impulses.*

USES Fast, temporary relief of pain and itching due to hemorrhoids and other anorectal disorders, nonpoisonous insect bites, sunburn, minor burns, cuts, and scratches.

CONTRAINDICATIONS Hypersensitivity to amide-type anesthetics, pregnancy (category C), children <1 y.
CAUTIOUS USE Lactation, children <12 y.

ROUTE & DOSAGE

Itching Due to Insect Bites or Hemorrhoids

Adult: **Topical** Apply skin cream or ointment to affected area as needed [max: 1 oz (28 g)/24 h];

insert rectal ointment morning and evening and after each bowel movement
Child: **Topical** Apply skin cream or ointment to affected area as needed [max: $1/4$ oz (7 g)/ 24 h]

ADMINISTRATION

Topical
- Apply cream preparation after bathing or swimming (water soluble).
- Store at 15°–30° C (59°–86° F) in tight, light-resistant containers.

ADVERSE EFFECTS (≥1%) **Skin:** Irritation, contact dermatitis; rectal bleeding (suppository).

PHARMACOKINETICS Absorption: Poorly absorbed from intact skin; readily absorbed from mucous membranes or abraded skin. **Onset:** 15 min. **Duration:** 2–4 h.

CLINICAL IMPLICATIONS

Patient & Family Education
- Use OTC preparations as directed. Always review package instructions.
- Discontinue if irritation or rectal bleeding (following use of rectal preparations) develops and consult physician.
- Hemorrhoids can be caused or worsened by constipation, excessive straining at stool, excessive standing, sitting, and coughing.
- Physician may prescribe sitz baths 3–4 times/d to reduce the swelling and pain of hemorrhoids.
- Note: Medication is intended for temporary relief of mild to moderate itching or pain. Seek medical advice for continuing discomfort, pain, bleeding, or sensation of rectal pressure.

DICLOFENAC SODIUM
(di-klo'fen-ak)
Voltaren, Voltaren-XR, Solaraze

DICLOFENAC POTASSIUM
Cataflam

Classifications: ANALGESIC, NONSTEROIDAL ANTIINFLAMMATORY DRUG (NSAID); ANTIPYRETIC
Therapeutic: NSAID, ANALGESIC; ANTIPYRETIC
Prototype: Ibuprofen
Pregnancy Category: B

AVAILABILITY Diclofenac Sodium 25 mg, 50 mg, 75 mg tablets; 100 mg sustained release tablets; 0.1% ophthalmic solution; 3% gel **Diclofenac Potassium** 50 mg tablets

ACTION & *THERAPEUTIC EFFECT* Diclofenac competitively inhibits both cyclooxygenase (COX) isoenzymes, COX-1 and COX-2, by blocking arachidonic acid conversion to other chemicals, thus leading to its analgesic, antipyretic, and antiinflammatory pharmacologic effects. It appears to be a potent inhibitor of cyclooxygenase, thereby decreasing the synthesis of prostaglandins. *Nonsteroidal antiinflammatory drug (NSAID) with analgesic and antipyretic activity.*

USES Analgesic and antipyretic effects in symptomatic treatment of rheumatoid arthritis, osteoarthritis, and ankylosing spondylitis. Also acute gout; juvenile rheumatoid arthritis; various rheumatic conditions including bursitis, myalgia, sciatica, and tendinitis; acute soft tissue injuries including sprains and strains; dysmenorrhea; headache, migraine, and dental, minor surgical, and postpartum pain; and renal or biliary colic. **Ophthalmic:** Cataract surgery; photophobia associ-

Common adverse effects in *italic*, life-threatening effects <u>underlined</u>; generic names in **bold**; classifications in SMALL CAPS; ♣ Canadian drug name; ⊘ Prototype drug

461

ated with refractive surgery. **Topical:** Treatment of actinic keratosis.

CONTRAINDICATIONS Hypersensitivity to diclofenac, NSAIDS, or salicylate; patients in whom asthma, urticaria, angioedema, bronchospasm, severe rhinitis, history of GI bleeding; hepatic porphyria; shock, or other sensitivity reaction is precipitated by aspirin or other NSAIDS; postoperative CABG pain.

CAUTIOUS USE Geriatric patients and children; patients receiving anticoagulant therapy; diabetes mellitus; history of GI disease; hepatic disease; GU tract problems such as dysuria, cystitis, hematuria, nephritis, nephrotic syndrome, patients who must restrict their sodium intake; impaired hepatic function; SLE; heart failure, cardiac disease; hypertension; pregnancy (category B), lactation.

ROUTE & DOSAGE

Rheumatoid Arthritis

Adult: **PO** 150–200 mg/d in 3–4 divided doses
Child: **PO** 25 mg b.i.d. or t.i.d.

Osteoarthritis

Adult: **PO** 100–150 mg/d in 3–4 divided doses 100 mg sustained release q.d.

Ankylosing Spondylitis

Adult: **PO** 25 mg q.i.d. and 25 mg h.s.

Cataract Surgery

Adult: **Ophthalmic** 1 drop of 0.1% solution in affected eye q.i.d. beginning 24 h after surgery and continuing for 2 wk

Actinic Keratosis

Adult: **Topical** Apply to affected area b.i.d. for 60–90 d

ADMINISTRATION

Oral

- Ensure that sustained release or enteric coated forms of drug are not chewed or crushed. MUST be swallowed whole.
- Give on an empty stomach, 1 h before or after a meal; absorption is delayed markedly by food. Minimize gastric irritation by administering it with a full glass of milk or water.
- Schedule administration 30 min before physical therapy or planned exercise to keep discomfort at a minimum.
- Discontinue therapy about 1 wk before surgery to reduce risk of bleeding.
- Use with caution in anyone who must restrict sodium intake.
- Store at 15°–30° C (59°–86° F) away from heat and direct light.

ADVERSE EFFECTS (≥1%) **CNS:** Dizziness, headache, drowsiness. **Special Senses:** Tinnitus. **Skin:** Rash, pruritus. **GI:** *Dyspepsia,* nausea, vomiting, abdominal pain, cramps, constipation, diarrhea, indigestion, abdominal distension, flatulence, peptic ulcer; liver enzymes, transaminases increased, liver test abnormalities. **CV:** Fluid retention, hypertension, CHF. **Respiratory:** Asthma. **Body as a Whole:** Back, leg, or joint pain. **Endocrine:** Hyperglycemia. **Hematologic:** Prolonged bleeding time; inhibits platelet aggregation.

DIAGNOSTIC TEST INTERFERENCE Liver function test values may be increased. Liver function test abnormalities may return to normal despite continued use; however, if significant abnormalities occur, clinical signs and symptoms consistent with liver disease develop, or systemic manifestations such as eosinophilia or rash occur, the medication should be discontinued. Serum uric acid concentrations may be decreased because of increased renal clearance.

INTERACTIONS Drug: Increases **cyclosporine**-induced nephrotoxicity; increases **methotrexate** levels (increases toxicity); may decrease BP-lowering effects of DIURETICS; may increase levels and toxicity of **lithium;** may increase **digoxin** levels. **Herbal: Feverfew, garlic, ginger, ginkgo** may increase risk of bleeding.

PHARMACOKINETICS Absorption: Readily absorbed from GI tract; 50–60% reaches systemic circulation. **Peak:** 2–3 h. **Distribution:** Widely distributed including synovial fluid and into breast milk. **Metabolism:** Extensively metabolized in liver. **Elimination:** 50–70% in urine, 30–35% in feces. **Half-Life:** 1.2–2 h.

CLINICAL IMPLICATIONS

Assessment & Drug Effects

- Monitor for therapeutic effectiveness. Up to 3 wks may be needed for beneficial effects with rheumatoid arthritis or osteoarthritis.
- Lab tests: Periodic liver function, serum uric acid concentrations Hct, PT/INR, and blood glucose.
- Observe and report signs of bleeding (e.g., petechiae, ecchymoses, bleeding gums, bloody or black stools, cloudy or bloody urine).
- Monitor BP for hypertension and blood sugar for hyperglycemia.
- Monitor diabetics closely for loss of diabetic control.
- Monitor for increased serum sodium and potassium in patients receiving potassium-sparing diuretics.
- Monitor weight and report gains greater than 1 kg (2 lb)/24 h.

- Monitor for signs and symptoms of GI irritation and ulceration.

Patient & Family Education

Oral Form

- Do not lie down for 15–30 min after taking medicine to decrease esophageal irritation.
- Discontinue use with onset of ringing or buzzing in the ears, impaired hearing, dizziness, GI discomfort, or bleeding and notify physician.
- Do not take aspirin or other OTC analgesics without permission of the physician.
- Avoid alcohol or other CNS depressants.
- Do not drive or engage in other potentially hazardous activities until reaction to drug is known.
- Note: Diabetics need to monitor blood glucose carefully for loss of glycemic control.

DICLOXACILLIN SODIUM

(dye-klox-a-sill′in)

Dycill, Dynapen, Pathocil

Classifications: ANTIBIOTIC, PENICILLIN

Therapeutic: PENICILLIN ANTIBIOTIC

Prototype: Penicillin G potassium

Pregnancy Category: B

AVAILABILITY 125 mg, 250 mg, 500 mg capsules; 62.5 mg/5 mL suspension

ACTION & *THERAPEUTIC EFFECT*

Semisynthetic, acid-stable, penicillinase-resistant penicillin. It inhibits the final stage of bacterial cell wall synthesis by preferentially binding to specific penicillin-binding proteins (PBPs) that are located inside the bacterial cell wall; this leads to cell death. *Reportedly the most ac-*

Common adverse effects in *italic*, life-threatening effects <u>underlined</u>; generic names in **bold**; classifications in SMALL CAPS; ◆ Canadian drug name; ⊙ Prototype drug

463

D

tive of these penicillins (cloxacillin, oxacillin) against penicillinase-producing Staphylococci. *Generally ineffective against methicillin-resistant* Staphylococci *and gram-negative bacteria.*

USES Primarily in systemic infections caused by penicillinase-producing *Staphylococci* and penicillin-resistant *Staphylococci*.

CONTRAINDICATIONS Hypersensitivity to penicillins.

CAUTIOUS USE History of or suspected atopy or allergy (asthma, eczema, hives, hay fever); history of hypersensitivity to cephalosporins or carbapenem; GI disease, colitis; lactation; renal or hepatic impairment; pregnancy (category B).

ROUTE & DOSAGE

Mild to Moderate Infections

Adult: **PO** 125–500 mg q6h
Child: **PO** <40 kg, 12.5–25 mg/ kg q6h (max: 4 g/d)

ADMINISTRATION

Oral

- Give on an empty stomach at least 1 h before or 2 h after meals. Food reduces drug absorption.
- Reconstitute powder for oral suspension by shaking container to loosen powder. Add water according to label starting with half of the amount, then shake vigorously. Add remaining half and shake again vigorously. Shake well before each use.
- Store reconstituted oral suspensions for 7 d at room temperature (15°–30° C; 59°–86° F) or 14 d under refrigeration at 2°–8° C (36°–46° F). Date and label container. Store capsules at room tempera-

ture in tight containers unless otherwise directed.

ADVERSE EFFECTS (≥1%) **Body as a Whole:** Hypersensitivity (pruritus, urticaria, rash, wheezing, sneezing, anaphylaxis; eosinophilia). **GI:** Nausea, vomiting, flatulence, *diarrhea,* abdominal pain. **Other:** Transient elevations of ALT, superinfections.

INTERACTIONS Drug: Probenecid decreases dicloxacillin elimination.

PHARMACOKINETICS Absorption: 35–76% absorbed from GI tract. **Peak:** 0.5–2 h. **Duration:** 4–6 h. **Distribution:** Distributed throughout body with highest concentrations in liver and kidney; low CSF penetration; crosses placenta; distributed into breast milk. **Metabolism:** In liver. **Elimination:** Primarily in urine with some elimination through bile. **Half-Life:** 30–60 min.

CLINICAL IMPLICATIONS

Assessment & Drug Effects

- Note: Take care to establish previous exposure and sensitivity to penicillins and cephalosporins as well as other allergic reactions of any kind before initiating therapy.
- Obtain C&S prior to initiation of therapy to determine susceptibility of causative organism. Therapy may begin pending test results.
- Lab tests: Baseline blood cultures, WBC, and differential counts and at least weekly for patients on prolonged therapy. Periodic ALT and AST determinations, urinalysis, BUN, and creatinine are also advised for these patients.

Patient & Family Education

- Take medication around the clock. Do not miss a dose and continue taking medication until it is all gone, unless otherwise directed by physician.

- Check with physician if GI side effects appear.
- Watch for and report the signs of hypersensitivity reactions and superinfections (see Appendix F).

DICYCLOMINE HYDROCHLORIDE

(dye-sye′kloe-meen)

Bentyl, Bentylol ♦, Byclomine, Dibent, Dilomine, Formulex ♦, Lomine ♦, Nospaz, Protylol ♦, Spasmoject

Classifications: ANTICHOLINERGIC; ANTISPASMODIC
Therapeutic: ANTISPASMODIC
Prototype: Atropine
Pregnancy Category: B

AVAILABILITY 10 mg, 20 mg capsules; 20 mg tablets; 10 mg/5 mL syrup; 10 mg/mL injection

ACTION & *THERAPEUTIC EFFECT*
Synthetic tertiary amine with antispasmodic properties. Relieves smooth muscle spasm in GI and biliary tracts, uterus, and ureters by nonspecific direct relaxant action. *Exerts antispasmotic effect of the GI as well as the urinary tract.*

USES Adjunctively in treatment of functional bowel disorders/irritable bowel syndrome.
UNLABELED USES Acute enterocolitis, peptic ulcer, and infant colic, urinary incontinence.

CONTRAINDICATIONS Hypersensitivity to anticholinergic drugs; obstructive diseases of GU and GI tracts, paralytic ileus, intestinal atony, biliary tract disease; closed-angle glaucoma; unstable cardiovascular status; severe ulcerative colitis, toxic megacolon, esophagitis; myasthenia gravis; peripheral neuropathy; infants <6 mo; pregnancy (category B), lactation.

CAUTIOUS USE Prostatic hypertrophy; autonomic neuropathy; hyperthyroidism; coronary heart disease, CHF, arrhythmias, hypertension; hepatic or renal disease; GERD, hiatal hernia associated with esophageal reflux.

ROUTE & DOSAGE

Irritable Bowel Disorders
Adult: **PO** 20–40 mg q.i.d. **IM** 20 mg q.i.d.
Child: **PO** 10 mg t.i.d. or q.i.d. (max: 40 mg/d)
Infant >6 mo: **PO** 5 mg t.i.d. or q.i.d.

ADMINISTRATION

Oral
- Give 30 min before meals and at bedtime.

Intramuscular
- Give deep IM into a large muscle. Do NOT give IV.
- Store below 30° C (86° F) unless otherwise directed.

ADVERSE EFFECTS (≥1%) **All:** Dose related. **Body as a Whole:** Allergic reactions; curare-like effect (cyanosis, apnea, respiratory arrest); decreased sweating; suppression of lactation; urticaria. **CNS:** Lightheadedness, drowsiness, headache, insomnia, brief euphoria, fever, restlessness, irritability, coma, seizures. **CV:** Fluctuations in heart rate, palpitation, tachycardia. **GI:** *Dry mouth,* nausea, *constipation,* paralytic ileus, vomiting, diminished sense of taste, bloated feeling. **Urogenital:** Urinary hesitancy, *urinary retention,* impotence. **Special Senses:** Blurred vision.

PHARMACOKINETICS Absorption: Readily from GI tract. **Onset:** 1–2 h. **Duration:** 4 h. **Metabolism:** In liver. **Elimination:** 80% in urine, 10% in feces. **Half-Life:** 9–10 h.

Common adverse effects in *italic*, life-threatening effects underlined; generic names in **bold**; classifications in SMALL CAPS; ♦ Canadian drug name; ❷ Prototype drug

465

CLINICAL IMPLICATIONS

Assessment & Drug Effects

- Monitor for adverse effects especially in infants. Treatment of infant colic with dicyclomine includes some risk, especially in infants <2 mo of age. Doubling the usual dose of 5 mg can produce serious toxic effects. Infants <6 wk have developed respiratory symptoms as well as seizures, fluctuations in heart rate, weakness, and coma within minutes after taking syrup formulation. Symptoms generally last 20–30 min and are believed to be due to local irritation.
- Monitor I&O to assess for urinary retention.
- If drug produces drowsiness and light-headedness, supervision of ambulation and other safety precautions are warranted.

Patient & Family Education

- Exercise caution in hot weather. Dicyclomine may increase risk of heatstroke by decreasing sweating, especially in older adults.
- Do not drive or engage in other potentially hazardous activities until reaction to drug is known.
- Report changes in urine volume, voiding pattern.

DIDANOSINE (DDI)

(di-dan'o-sine)

Videx, Videx EC

Classifications: ANTIRETROVIRAL AGENT; NUCLEOSIDE REVERSE TRANSCRIPTASE INHIBITOR (NRTI)

Therapeutic: ANTIVIRAL; ANTIRETROVIRAL (NRTI)

Prototype: Lamivudine

Pregnancy Category: B

AVAILABILITY 25 mg, 50 mg, 100 mg, 150 mg, 200 mg tablets; 125 mg, 200 mg, 250 mg, 400 mg delayed release capsules; 100 mg, 167 mg, 250 mg, 2 g, 4 g powder for oral solution

ACTION & *THERAPEUTIC EFFECT*

DDI interferes with the HIV RNA-dependent DNA polymerase (reverse transcriptase), thus preventing replication of the virus. *Synthetic purine nucleotide that inhibits replication of HIV.*

USES Advanced HIV infection in patients who are intolerant to zidovudine (AZT) or who demonstrate significant clinical or immunological deterioration during zidovudine therapy.

CONTRAINDICATIONS Hypersensitivity to any of the components in the formulation; pancreatitis; PKU; lactation.

CAUTIOUS USE Individuals with peripheral vascular disease, history of neuropathy, chronic pancreatitis, renal impairment, or any liver impairment; patients on sodium restriction; renal failure, renal impairment; alcoholism; elderly; gout; pregnancy (category B).

ROUTE & DOSAGE

HIV Infection

Adult: **PO** <60 kg, tablets, 250 mg q.d. or 125 mg b.i.d. (take 2 tablets at each dose to ensure adequate buffering); <60 kg, powder, 167 mg b.i.d.; ≥60 kg, tablets, 400 mg q.d. or 200 mg b.i.d.; ≥60 kg, powder, 250 mg b.i.d. *Child:* **PO** 120 mg/m² b.i.d., <1 y, give a 1-tablet dose; >1 y, give a 2-tablet dose

ADMINISTRATION

Oral

- Give drug on an empty stomach. Food should not be consumed within 15–30 min of drug administration.

- Give with water. Do NOT give with fruit juice or any other acid-containing liquid.
- Chewable tablets must be thoroughly chewed or crushed and dispersed in at least 30 mL (1 oz) of water and immediately swallowed.
- Mix powder for oral solution (buffered) with at least 120 mL (4 oz) of water, stir until dissolved (requires 2–3 min), and immediately swallowed.
- Note: Powder for oral solution (pediatric) is prepared by pharmacist to yield a concentration of 10 mg/mL. Shake solution thoroughly before administration.
- Dosage reduction may be indicated in those with renal or hepatic impairment.
- Store reconstituted liquid in a tightly closed container in refrigerator for up to 30 d.

ADVERSE EFFECTS (≥1%) **CV:** Palpitations, thrombophlebitis, arrhythmias, *vasodilation.* **CNS:** *Headache, dizziness, nervousness, insomnia, peripheral neuropathy,* lethargy, poor coordination, seizures. **Special Senses:** Retinal depigmentation, photophobia, blurred vision, optic neuritis, diplopia, blindness. **GI:** *Abdominal pain, nausea, vomiting, diarrhea,* constipation, stomatitis, dry mouth, <u>pancreatitis</u>, increased liver enzymes. **Hematologic:** Increased WBC, neutrophil, lymphocyte, and platelet counts; increased Hgb, thrombocytopenia, ecchymosis, hemorrhage, petechiae. **Metabolic:** Hypocalcemia, hypokalemia, hypomagnesemia, hyperuricemia (asymptomatic), *hypertriglyceridemia.* **Musculoskeletal:** Muscle atrophy, myalgia, arthritis, decreased strength. **Respiratory:** *Asthma, cough, dyspnea, epistaxis, rhinitis, rhinorrhea,* hypoventilation, pharyngitis, rhonchi or rales, sinusitis, congestion. **Skin:** Rash, impetigo, eczema, *pruritus, sweating,* erythema.

INTERACTIONS Drug: ALUMINUM- and MAGNESIUM-CONTAINING ANTACIDS may increase the aluminum- and magnesium-associated adverse effects of tablets. The effectiveness of **dapsone** in prophylaxis of *Pneumocystis carinii* pneumonia may be reduced by concomitant didanosine. May cause additive neuropathy with **zalcitabine** (ddC). **Food:** Absorption is significantly decreased by food. Take on an empty stomach.

PHARMACOKINETICS Absorption: Rapidly absorbed from GI tract when administered to fasting patient with antacids; 23–40% reaches systemic circulation. **Peak:** 0.6–1 h. **Distribution:** Distributed primarily to body water; 21% reaches CSF; crosses placenta. **Elimination:** 36% in urine. **Half-Life:** 0.8–1.5 h.

CLINICAL IMPLICATIONS

Assessment & Drug Effects

- Monitor for S&S of pancreatitis (e.g., abdominal pain, nausea, vomiting, elevated serum amylase). Report immediately to physician and withhold drug until ruled out.
- Monitor for S&S of peripheral neuropathy (e.g., numbness, tingling, burning, pain in hands or feet). Report to physician; dose reduction may be indicated.
- Monitor patients with renal impairment for drug toxicity and hypermagnesemia manifested by muscle weakness and confusion.

Patient & Family Education

- Report immediately to physician any of the following: Abdominal pain, nausea, or vomiting.

Common adverse effects in *italic*, life-threatening effects <u>underlined</u>; generic names in **bold**; classifications in SMALL CAPS; ✢ Canadian drug name; ⊙ Prototype drug

467

D

DIETHYLPROPION HYDROCHLORIDE ℗

(dye-eth-il-proe′pee-on)

Nobesine ♣, Propion, Ten-Tab, Tenuate, Tenuate Dospan, Tepanil

Classifications: ANOREXIANT
Therapeutic: ANOREXIANT
Pregnancy Category: B
Controlled Substance: Schedule IV

AVAILABILITY 25 mg tablets; 75 mg sustained release tablets

ACTION & *THERAPEUTIC EFFECT*

Sympathomimetic amine chemically related to amphetamine. Has lower incidence of amphetamine-type adverse effects but reportedly is less effective as an appetite suppressant. Anorexigenic action probably secondary to direct (CNS) stimulation of appetite control center in hypothalamus and limbic regions. Also produces mild psychic stimulation and vasopressor effects. *Suppresses appetite as a result of drug action on CNS appetite control center.*

USES Used solely in management of exogenous obesity as short-term (a few weeks) adjunct in a regimen of weight reduction based on caloric restriction.

CONTRAINDICATIONS Known hypersensitivity or idiosyncrasy to sympathomimetic amines; severe hypertension, advanced arteriosclerosis, valvular heart disease; hyperthyroidism; glaucoma; history of drug abuse; anorexia nervosa; symptomatic cardiovascular disease, arrhythmias; MAOI therapy; pulmonary hypertension; children <6 y.

CAUTIOUS USE Hypertension, psychosis, mania, agitated states, epilepsy; diabetes mellitus; elderly, renal failure or impairment; seizure disorder; pregnancy (category B), lactation.

ROUTE & DOSAGE

Obesity

Adult: **PO** 25 mg t.i.d. 30–60 min a.c. or 75 mg sustained release q.d. midmorning

ADMINISTRATION

Oral

- Give on an empty stomach, $^1/_2$–1 h before meals.
- Note: Additional dose sometimes prescribed in midevening to control nighttime hunger. Rarely causes insomnia except in high doses.
- Titrate dosage carefully in patients with diabetes.
- Store between 15°–30° C (59°–86° F) in well-closed container unless otherwise specified.

ADVERSE EFFECTS (≥1%) **Body as a Whole:** Hypersensitivity (urticaria, rash, erythema); muscle pain, dyspnea, hair loss, blurred vision, severe dermatoses (chronic intoxication), increased sweating. **CNS:** Mild euphoria, restlessness, *nervousness,* dizziness, headache, irritability, hyperactivity, insomnia, drowsiness, mood changes, lethargy, increase in convulsive episodes in patients with epilepsy. **CV:** Palpitation, tachycardia, precordial pain, rise in BP. **GI:** Nausea, vomiting, diarrhea, constipation, dry mouth, unpleasant taste. **Urogenital:** Impotence, changes in libido, gynecomastia, menstrual irregularities; polyuria, dysuria.

INTERACTIONS Drug: Acetazolamide, sodium bicarbonate decrease diethylpropion elimination; **ammonium chloride, ascorbic acid** increase diethylpropion elimination; a BARBITURATE and diethylpropion taken together may antagonize the effects of both drugs; **furazolidone** may increase blood pressure effects of AMPHETAMINES, and interaction may persist for several weeks after discontinuation of **furazolidone; guanethidine, guanadryl** antagonize antihypertensive effects; MAO INHIBITORS, **selegiline** can cause hypertensive crisis (fatalities reported)—AMPHETAMINES should not be administered at the same time as or within 14 days of these drugs; PHENOTHIAZINES may inhibit mood elevating effects of AMPHETAMINES; TRICYCLIC ANTIDEPRESSANTS enhance AMPHETAMINES' effects by increasing **norepinephrine** release; BETA AGONISTS increase cardiovascular adverse effects.

PHARMACOKINETICS Absorption: Readily from GI tract. **Duration:** 4 h, regular tablets; 10–14 h, sustained release. **Elimination:** In urine. **Half-Life:** 4–6 h.

CLINICAL IMPLICATIONS

Assessment & Drug Effects

- Observe patients with epilepsy closely for reduction in seizure control.
- Anorexigenic effect seldom lasts more than a few weeks. Discontinue if tolerance develops.
- Note: Varying degrees of psychologic and rarely physical dependence can occur.

Patient & Family Education

- Swallow sustained release tablets whole; do NOT chew.
- Do not drive or engage in other potentially hazardous activities until reaction to drug is known.

DIFLORASONE DIACETATE

(dye-flor′a-sone)
Florone, Florone E, Maxiflor, Psorcon
Pregnancy Category: C
See Appendix A-4.

D

DIFLUNISAL

(dye-floo′ni-sal)
Dolobid
Classifications: ANALGESIC, NONSTEROIDAL ANTIINFLAMMATORY DRUG (NSAID); ANTIPYRETIC
Therapeutic: NSAID, ANALGESIC; ANTIPYRETIC
Prototype: Ibuprofen
Pregnancy Category: C

AVAILABILITY 250 mg, 500 mg tablets

ACTION & *THERAPEUTIC EFFECT* A long-acting nonsteroidal antiinflammatory drug (NSAID); unlike aspirin, inhibition of platelet function and effect on bleeding time are dose related and reversible, lasting only about 24 h after drug is discontinued. Is a non-narcotic analgesic agent. Exerts mild antipyretic effect; therefore it is not used clinically for this purpose. This NSAID has peripheral analgesic properties due to interfering with prostaglandin synthesis by inhibiting cyclooxygenase (COX) isoenzymes, COX-1 and COX-2. *Has analgesic and anti-inflammatory properties.*

USES Acute and long-term relief of mild to moderate pain and symptomatic treatment of osteoarthritis and rheumatoid arthritis.

CONTRAINDICATIONS Patients in whom aspirin or other NSAIDs precip-

Common adverse effects in *italic*, life-threatening effects underlined; generic names in **bold**; classifications in SMALL CAPS; ♣ Canadian drug name; ☻ Prototype drug

469

itate an acute asthmatic attack (bronchospasm), urticaria, angioedema, severe rhinitis, or shock; active peptic ulcer, GI bleeding; severe salicylate hypersensitivity. Safe use in children <12 y is not established. Pregnancy (category C); use during third trimester of pregnancy specifically contraindicated because NSAIDS are known to cause premature closure of ductus arteriosus in fetus.

CAUTIOUS USE History of upper GI disease; preexisting renal disease; impaired renal or hepatic function; alcoholics; compromised cardiac function, and other conditions associated with fluid retention; patients receiving diuretics; bone marrow suppression; geriatric patients; hypertension; patients who may be adversely affected by prolonged bleeding time; lactation.

ROUTE & DOSAGE

Pain Relief
Adult: **PO** 1000 mg followed by 500 mg q8–12h
Arthritis
Adult: **PO** 500–1000 mg/d in 2 divided doses (max: 1500 mg/d)

ADMINISTRATION

Oral
- Give with water, milk, or food to reduce GI irritation. Food causes slight reduction in absorption rate, but does not affect total amount absorbed.
- Store at 15°–30° C (59°–86° F) in tightly closed containers unless otherwise directed.

ADVERSE EFFECTS (≥1%) **Body as a Whole:** Hypersensitivity syndrome (fever, chills, rash, eosinophilia, changes in renal and hepatic function, <u>anaphylactic</u>

<u>reactions with bronchospasm</u>). **CNS:** Headache, drowsiness, insomnia, dizziness, vertigo, lightheadedness, fatigue, weakness, nervousness, confusion, disorientation. **CV:** Palpitation, tachycardia, *peripheral edema*. **Special Senses:** Tinnitus, hearing loss; blurred vision, reduced visual acuity, changes in color vision, scotomas, corneal deposits, retinal disturbances. **GI:** *Nausea,* GI pain, flatulence, GI bleeding, peptic ulcer, anorexia, eructation, cholestatic jaundice. **Urogenital:** Hematuria, proteinuria, interstitial nephritis, renal failure. **Hematologic:** Prolonged PT, anemia, decreased serum uric acid, transient elevations of liver function tests. **Skin:** Rash, toxic epidermal necrolysis, exfoliative dermatitis, urticaria. **Other:** Weight gain, hyperventilation, dyspnea, photosensitivity.

DIAGNOSTIC TEST INTERFERENCE Diflunisal can lower ***serum uric acid*** concentrations by as much as 1.4 mg/dL and increased renal clearance of uric acid.

INTERACTIONS Drug: ANTACIDS decrease diflunisal absorption; **aspirin** and other NSAIDS increase risk of GI bleeding; increases risk of **warfarin**-induced hypoprothrombinemia; increases **methotrexate** levels and toxicity.

PHARMACOKINETICS Absorption: Readily from GI tract. **Onset:** 1 h. **Peak:** 2–3 h. **Duration:** 12 h. **Distribution:** Probably crosses placenta; distributed into breast milk. **Metabolism:** In liver. **Elimination:** In urine. **Half-Life:** 8–12 h.

CLINICAL IMPLICATIONS

Assessment & Drug Effects
- Monitor for therapeutic effectiveness: Full antiinflammatory effect

for arthritis may not occur until 8 d to several weeks into therapy.

- Discontinue if patient presents signs of hepatic toxicity (see Appendix F).
- Note: Although the antipyretic effect is mild, chronic or high doses may mask fever in some patients.

Patient & Family Education

- Swallow tablet whole; do not crush or chew.
- Take drug as prescribed. Doubling the dosage can produce greater than doubling of drug accumulation, particularly in patients receiving repetitive doses.
- Report onset of visual or auditory problems immediately to physician.
- Be aware of I&O ratio and pattern and check for and report peripheral edema and unusual weight gain.
- Report promptly to physician the onset of melena, hematemesis, or severe stomach pain.
- Do not drive or engage in other potentially hazardous activities until reaction to drug is known.

DIGOXIN ℗

(di-jox′in)

Lanoxicaps, Lanoxin

Classifications: CARDIAC GLYCOSIDE; ANTIARRHYTHMIC
Therapeutic: CARDIAC GLYCOSIDE; ANTIARRHYTHMIC
Pregnancy Category: C

AVAILABILITY 0.05 mg, 0.1 mg, 0.2 mg capsules; 0.125 mg, 0.25 mg, 0.5 mg tablets; 0.05 mg/mL elixir; 0.25 mg/mL, 0.1 mg/mL injection

ACTION & THERAPEUTIC EFFECT
Widely used cardiac glycoside of *Digitalis lanata.* Acts by increasing the force and velocity of myocardial systolic contraction (positive inotropic effect). It also decreases conduction velocity through the atrioventricular node. Action is more prompt and less prolonged than that of digitalis and digitoxin. *Increases the contractility of the heart muscle (positive inotropic effect). Has antiarrhythmic properties that result from its effects on the AV node.*

USES Rapid digitalization and for maintenance therapy in CHF, atrial fibrillation, atrial flutter, paroxysmal atrial tachycardia.

CONTRAINDICATIONS Digitalis hypersensitivity, sick sinus syndrome, Wolff-Parkinson-White syndrome; ventricular fibrillation, ventricular tachycardia unless due to CHF. Full digitalizing dose not given if patient has received digoxin during previous week or if slowly excreted cardiotonic glycoside has been given during previous 2 wk.

CAUTIOUS USE Renal insufficiency, hypokalemia, advanced heart disease, cardiomyopathy, acute MI, incomplete AV block, cor pulmonale; hypothyroidism; lung disease; premature and immature infants, children, older adults, or debilitated patients; pregnancy (category C).

ROUTE & DOSAGE

Digitalizing Dose (Give ¹/₂ dose initially followed by ¹/₄ at 8–12 h intervals)
Adult: PO 0.75–1.5 mg IV 0.5–1 mg
Child: IV 2–10 y, 20–35 mcg/kg; >10 y, 8–12 mcg/kg PO 2–10 y, 30–40 mcg/kg; >10y, 10–15 mcg/kg
Infant: IV 30–50 mcg/kg PO 35–60 mcg/kg
Neonate: IV Preterm: 15–25 mcg/kg; Full-term: 20–30 mcg/kg

Common adverse effects in *italic*, life-threatening effects underlined; generic names in **bold**; classifications in SMALL CAPS; ♣ Canadian drug name; ℗ Prototype drug

471

D

Maintenance Dose

Adult: **PO/IV** 0.1–0.375 mg/d
Child: **PO/IV** <2 y, 7.5–9 mcg/kg/d; 2–10 y, 6–7.5 mcg/kg/d; >10 y, 0.125–0.25 mg/d
Neonate: **IV** 4–8 mcg/kg/d

ADMINISTRATION

Oral

- Give without regard to food. Administration after food may slightly delay rate of absorption, but total amount absorbed is not affected.
- Crush and mix with fluid or food if patient cannot swallow it whole.

Intravenous

PREPARE: Direct: Give undiluted or diluted in 4 mL of sterile water, D5W, or NS (less diluent may cause precipitation).

ADMINISTER: Direct: Give each dose over at least 5 min.

INCOMPATIBILITIES Solution/additive: Dobutamine, doxapram. Y-site: Amiodarone.

- Monitor IV site frequently. Infiltration of parenteral drug into subcutaneous tissue can cause local irritation and sloughing.

- Store tablets, elixir, and injection solution at 25° C (77° F) or at 15°–30° C (59°–86° F).

ADVERSE EFFECTS (≥1%) **CNS:** Fatigue, muscle weakness, headache, facial neuralgia, mental depression, paresthesias, hallucinations, confusion, drowsiness, agitation, dizziness. **CV:** Arrhythmias, hypotension, <u>AV block</u>. **Special Senses:** Visual disturbances. **GI:** Anorexia, *nausea*, vomiting, diarrhea. **Other:** Diaphoresis, recurrent malaise, dysphagia.

INTERACTIONS Drug: ANTACIDS, **cholestyramine, colestipol** decrease digoxin absorption; DIURETICS, CORTICOSTEROIDS, **amphotericin B**, LAXATIVES, **sodium polystyrene sulfonate** may cause hypokalemia, increasing the risk of digoxin toxicity; **calcium IV** may increase risk of arrhythmias if administered together with digoxin; **quinidine, verapamil, amiodarone, flecainide** significantly increase digoxin levels, and digoxin dose should be decreased by 50%; **erythromycin** may increase digoxin levels; **succinylcholine** may potentiate arrhythmogenic effects; **nefazodone** may increase digoxin levels. **Food:** High fiber intake may decrease absorption. **Herbal:** Ginseng increase digoxin toxicity; **ma huang, ephedra** may induce arrhythmias; **St. John's wort** decreases plasma concentration.

PHARMACOKINETICS Absorption: 70% PO tablets; 90% PO liquid and capsules. **Onset:** 1–2 h PO; 5–30 min IV. **Peak:** 6–8 h PO; 1–5 h IV. **Duration:** 3–4 d in fully digitalized patient. **Distribution:** Widely distributed; tissue levels significantly higher than plasma levels; crosses placenta. **Metabolism:** 14% in liver. **Elimination:** 80–90% by kidneys; may appear in breast milk. **Half-Life:** 34–44 h.

CLINICAL IMPLICATIONS

Assessment & Drug Effects

- Take apical pulse for 1 full min, noting rate, rhythm, and quality before administering drug.
- Withold medication and notify physician if apical pulse falls below ordered parameters (e.g., <50 or 60/min in adults and <60 or 70/min in children).
- Be familiar with patient's baseline data (e.g., quality of peripheral pulses, blood pressure, clinical symptoms, serum electrolytes, cre-

atinine clearance) as a foundation for making assessments.

- Lab tests: Baseline and periodic serum digoxin, potassium, magnesium, and calcium. Draw blood samples for determining plasma digoxin levels at least 6 h after daily dose and preferably just before next scheduled daily dose.
- Monitor for S&S of drug toxicity: In children, cardiac arrhythmias are usually reliable signs of early toxicity. Early indicators in adults (anorexia, nausea, vomiting, diarrhea, visual disturbances) are rarely initial signs in children.
- Monitor I&O ratio during digitalization, particularly in patients with impaired renal function. Also monitor for edema daily and auscultate chest for rales.
- Monitor serum digoxin levels closely during concurrent antibiotic–digoxin therapy, which can precipitate toxicity because of altered intestinal flora.
- Observe patients closely when being transferred from one preparation (tablet, elixir, or parenteral) to another; when tablet is replaced by elixir potential for toxicity increases since ≥30% of drug is absorbed.

Patient & Family Education

- Report to physician if pulse falls below 60 or rises above 110 or if you detect skipped beats or other changes in rhythm, when digoxin is prescribed for atrial fibrillation.
- Suspect toxicity and report to physician if any of the following occur: Anorexia, nausea, vomiting, diarrhea, or visual disturbances.
- Weigh each day under standard conditions. Report weight gain >1 kg (2 lb)/d.
- Take digoxin PRECISELY as prescribed. Do not skip or double a dose or change dose intervals, and take it at same time each day.
- Do not to take OTC medications, especially those for coughs, colds, allergy, GI upset, or obesity, without prior approval of physician.
- Continue with brand originally prescribed unless otherwise directed by physician.

DIGOXIN IMMUNE FAB (OVINE)

(di-jox′in)

Digibind, DigiFab

Classifications: ANTIDOTE
Therapeutic: ANTIDOTE
Pregnancy Category: C

AVAILABILITY 38 mg, 40 mg vial

ACTION & *THERAPEUTIC EFFECT*
Purified fragments of antibodies specific for digoxin (but also effective for digitoxin) produced in sheep. Use of fragments of anti-digoxin antibodies (Fab) instead of whole antibody molecules permits more extensive and faster distribution to serum and toxic cellular sites. Fab acts by selectively complexing with circulating digoxin or digitoxin, thereby preventing drug from binding at receptor sites; the complex is then eliminated in urine. *Digoxin immune Fab is a protein that consists of antibody fragments, which are used as an antidote for digitalis toxicity.*

USES Treatment of potentially life-threatening digoxin or digitoxin intoxication in carefully selected patients.

CONTRAINDICATIONS Hypersensitivity to sheep products; renal or cardiac failure; pregnancy (category C).
CAUTIOUS USE Prior treatment with sheep antibodies or ovine Fab frag-

Common adverse effects in *italic*, life-threatening effects underlined; generic names in **bold**; classifications in SMALL CAPS; ♣ Canadian drug name; ⊚ Prototype drug

473

ments; mannitol hypersensitivity; history of allergies; impaired renal function or renal failure; elderly; lactation.

ROUTE & DOSAGE

Serious Digoxin Toxicity Secondary to Overdose

Adult/Child: **IV** Dosages vary according to amount of digoxin to be neutralized; dosages are based on total body load or steady state serum digoxin concentrations (see package insert); some patients may require a second dose after several hours

ADMINISTRATION

Intravenous

***PREPARE:* Direct:** Reconstitute by dissolving 38 mg (1 vial) in 4 mL of sterile water for injection; mix gently (solution will contain 9.5 mg/mL). **IV Infusion:** Dilute further with any volume of NS compatible with cardiac status.
***ADMINISTER:* Direct:** Give undiluted bolus only if cardiac arrest is imminent. **IV Infusion:** Give IV infusion over 30 min, preferably through a 0.22-micron membrane filter.

• For administration to infants: Reconstitute for direct IV and administer with a tuberculin syringe. For small doses (e.g., 2 mg or less), dilute the reconstituted 40 mg vial with 36 mL of NS to yield 1 mg/mL. Closely monitor for fluid overload.

• Use reconstituted solutions promptly or refrigerated at 2°–8° C (36°–46° F) for up to 4 h.

ADVERSE EFFECTS (≥1%) Adverse reactions associated with use of digoxin immune Fab are related primarily to the effects of **digitalis** withdrawal on the heart (see Clinical Implications). Allergic reactions have been reported rarely. Hypokalemia.

DIAGNOSTIC TEST INTERFERENCE Digoxin immune Fab may interfere with *serum digoxin* determinations by immunoassay tests.

INTERACTIONS Drug: Not established.

PHARMACOKINETICS Onset: <1 min after IV administration. **Elimination:** Excreted in urine over 5–7 d. **Half-Life:** 14–20 h.

CLINICAL IMPLICATIONS

Assessment & Drug Effects

• Perform skin testing for allergy prior to administration of immune Fab, particularly in patients with history of allergy or who have had previous therapy with immune Fab.

• Keep emergency equipment and drugs immediately available before skin testing is done or first dose is given and until patient is out of danger.

• Monitor for therapeutic effectiveness: Reflected in improvement in cardiac rhythm abnormalities, mental orientation and other neurologic symptoms, and GI and visual disturbances. S&S of reversal of digitalis toxicity occurs in 15–60 min in adults and usually within minutes in children.

• Baseline and frequent vital signs and EGG during administration.

• Lab tests: Baseline and periodic serum potassium and serum digoxin; serum digoxin or digitoxin concentration (this measurement will not be accurate for at least 5–7 d after therapy begins because of test interference by immune Fab).

- Note: Serum potassium is particularly critical during first several hours following administration of immune Fab. Monitor closely.
- Monitor closely: Cardiac status may deteriorate as inotropic action of digitalis is withdrawn by action of immune Fab. CHF, arrhythmias, increase in heart rate, and hypokalemia can occur.
- Make sure serum digoxin levels and ECG readings are obtained for at least 2–3 wk.

Patient & Family Education

- Tell your prescriber or health care professional about all other medications you are taking, including non-prescription medications, nutritional supplements, or herbal products. Include information about whether you frequently consume drinks with caffeine or alcohol, if you smoke, or if you use illegal drugs. These may affect the way this medicine works.
- Check with your prescriber before stopping or starting any of your medicines.
- Inform the prescriber if you have any of the following conditions: kidney disease; an unusual or allergic reaction to sheep proteins, mannitol other medicines, foods, dyes, or preservatives.
- Report to a prescriber if you are pregnant.
- Report to prescriber if you are breast-feeding.

DIHYDROERGOTAMINE MESYLATE

(dye-hye-droe-er-got′a-meen)
D.H.E. 45, Migranal
Classifications: ALPHA-ADRENERGIC ANTAGONIST; ERGOT ALKALOID
Therapeutic: ANTIMIGRAINE; ERGOT ALKALOID

Prototype: Ergotamine
Pregnancy Category: X

AVAILABILITY 4 mg/mL nasal spray; 1 mg/mL injection

ACTION & THERAPEUTIC EFFECT Alpha-adrenergic blocking agent and dihydrogenated ergot alkaloid with direct constricting effect on smooth muscle of peripheral and cranial blood vessels. Additionally, its ergot properties act as selective serotonin agonists at the 5-HT-1 receptors located on intracranial blood vessels, which may also cause vasoconstriction of large intracranial conductance arteries; this correlates with relief of migraine headaches. *Reduces rate of serotonin-induced platelet aggregation. Has somewhat weaker vasoconstrictor action than ergotamine but greater adrenergic blocking activity, resulting in relief from migraine headaches.*

USES To prevent or abort vascular headache (e.g., migraine or histaminic cephalalgia) when rapid control is desired or other routes are not feasible. With low-dose heparin therapy to prevent postoperative deep-vein thrombosis and pulmonary embolism.

UNLABELED USES To treat postural hypotension.

CONTRAINDICATIONS History of hypersensitivity to ergot preparations; peripheral vascular disease, coronary heart disease, MI, hypertension; peptic ulcer; severely impaired hepatic or renal function; sepsis; within 48 h of surgery; pregnancy (category X), lactation. Safe use in children <6 y is not established.

CAUTIOUS USE Moderate or mild renal or hepatic impairment; obesity; diabetes mellitus; postmenopausal women; males >40 y; pulmonary heart disease; valvular heart disease; smokers.

Common adverse effects in *italic*, life-threatening effects <u>underlined</u>; generic names in **bold**; classifications in SMALL CAPS; ♦ Canadian drug name; ☺ Prototype drug

475

D

ROUTE & DOSAGE

Migraine Headache
Adult: **IV/IM/SC** 1 mg, may be repeated at 1 h intervals to a total of 3 mg IM or 2 mg IV/SC (max: 6 mg/wk) **Intranasal** 1 spray (0.5 mg) in each nostril, may repeat with additional spray in 15 min if no relief (max: 4 sprays per attack); wait 6–8 h before treating another attack (max: 8 sprays per 24 h, 24 sprays/wk)

ADMINISTRATION

Intranasal
- Give at first warning of migraine headache.
- Optimum results: Titrate the doses required to bring relief for several headaches to determine the minimal effective dose. Use the established dose for subsequent attacks.

Intramuscular/Subcutaneous
- Withdraw IM or SC dose directly from ampule. Do not dilute.
- Note: Onset of action is about 20 min; when rapid relief is required, the IV route is prescribed.

Intravenous

PREPARE: **Direct:** Give undiluted.
ADMINISTER: **Direct:** Give at a rate of 1 mg/60 sec.

- Store at 15°–30° C (59°–86° F) unless otherwise directed. ▪ Protect ampules from heat and light; do not freeze. ▪ Discard ampule if solution appears discolored.

ADVERSE EFFECTS (≥1%) **CV:**
Vasospasm: coldness, numbness and tingling in fingers and toes, muscle pains and weakness of legs, precordial distress and pain, transient tachycardia or bradycardia, hypertension (large doses). **GI:** *Nausea, vomiting.* **Body as a Whole:** Dizziness, dysphoria, *localized edema and itching;* ergotism (excessive doses).

INTERACTIONS Drug: BETA BLOCKERS, **erythromycin** increase peripheral vasoconstriction with risk of ischemia; increased **ergotamine** toxicity with drugs that inhibit CYP3A4 (e.g., PROTEASE INHIBITORS, **amprenavir, ritonavir, nelfinavir, indinavir, saquinavir**), MACROLIDE ANTIBIOTICS (**erythromycin, azithromycin, clarithromycin**), AZOLE ANTIFUNGALS (**ketoconazole, itraconazole, fluconazole, clotrimazole), nefazodone, fluoxetine, fluvoxamine. Food:** Grapefruit juice may increase toxicity.

PHARMACOKINETICS Onset: 15–30 min IM; <5 min IV. **Duration:** 3–4 h. **Distribution:** Probably distributed into breast milk. **Metabolism:** In liver by CYP3A4. **Elimination:** Primarily in urine; some in feces. **Half-Life:** 21–32 h.

CLINICAL IMPLICATIONS

Assessment & Drug Effects
- Monitor cardiac status, especially when large doses are given.
- Monitor for and report numbness and tingling of fingers and toes, extremity weakness, muscle pain, or intermittent claudication.

Patient & Family Education
- Take at first warning of migraine headache.
- Lie down in a quiet, darkened room for several hours after drug administration for best results.
- Report immediately if any of the following S&S develop: Chest pain, nausea, vomiting, change in heartbeat, numbness, tingling, pain or weakness of extremities, edema, or itching.

DIHYDROTACHYSTEROL

(dye-hye-droe-tak-iss′ter-ole)
DHT, DHT Intensol
Classifications: VITAMIN D; SERUM CALCIUM REGULATOR
Therapeutic: VITAMIN D
Pregnancy Category: C

AVAILABILITY 0.125 mg, 0.2 mg, 0.4 mg tablets; 0.2 mg/mL oral solution

ACTION & *THERAPEUTIC EFFECT*

Oil-soluble reduction product of ergocalciferol (vitamin D_2) with pharmacologic actions similar to those of both ergocalciferol and parathyroid hormone. In comparison with ergocalciferol, dihydrotachysterol promotes less intestinal absorption of calcium but almost equal phosphate diuresis. *Acts like parathyroid hormone in ability to raise serum calcium concentrations rapidly; also reported to increase intestinal absorption of sodium, potassium, and magnesium.*

USES Hypocalcemia associated with hypoparathyroidism, both postoperative and idiopathic, and in pseudohypoparathyroidism. Also for prophylaxis of hypocalcemic tetany following thyroid surgery.

UNLABELED USES Vitamin D-resistant rickets (familial hypophosphatemia), osteoporosis, and renal osteodystrophy.

CONTRAINDICATIONS Sensitivity to vitamin D; hypercalcemia and hypocalcemia associated with renal insufficiency and hyperphosphatemia; renal stones, hypervitaminosis D; pregnancy (category C). Safe use in children in amounts exceeding RDA is not established.

CAUTIOUS USE Cardiac disease, arteriosclerosis; hyperphosphatemia; renal disease; sarcoidosis; lactation.

ROUTE & DOSAGE

Hypoparathyroidism, Pseudohypoparathyroidism
Adult: **PO** 0.75–2.5 mg/d for several days, then 0.2–1 mg/d (may need 1.5 mg/d)
Child: **PO** 1–5 mg/d for 4 d, then 0.5–1.5 mg/d
Neonate: **PO** 0.05–0.1 mg/d

Thyroidectomy-induced Hypocalcemia
Adult: **PO** 0.25 mg/d

Renal Osteodystrophy
Adult: **PO** 0.1–0.6 mg/d
Child: **PO** 0.1–0.5 mg/d

ADMINISTRATION

Oral

- Withhold drug if signs and symptoms of hypercalcemia appear (see Appendix F) and report to physician.
- Store in tightly closed, light-resistant containers at 15°–30° C (59°–86° F) unless otherwise directed.

ADVERSE EFFECTS (≥1%) **CNS:** Drowsiness, headache, weakness, vertigo, ataxia, atonia, mental depression. **Endocrine:** Hypercalcemia. **GI:** Anorexia, nausea, vomiting, metallic taste, dry mouth, thirst, diarrhea, constipation, abdominal pain. **Urogenital:** Nocturia, polyuria, renal calculi. **Special Senses:** Tinnitus.

INTERACTIONS Drug: Not established.

PHARMACOKINETICS Absorption: Readily from small intestines. **Peak:** 2 wk. **Duration:** 2 wk. **Distribution:** Distributed in breast milk. **Metabolism:** In liver to active metabolite. **Elimination:** Primarily in bile and feces.

Common adverse effects in *italic*, life-threatening effects underlined; generic names in **bold**; classifications in SMALL CAPS; ✦ Canadian drug name; ⦿ Prototype drug

477

CLINICAL IMPLICATIONS

Assessment & Drug Effects

- Lab tests: serum and urinary calcium levels at least weekly during first month of therapy until they are stabilized, then monthly thereafter.
- Supplement with 10–15 g of oral calcium lactate or gluconate daily; adequate calcium intake is necessary for clinical response to therapy.
- Restrict dietary phosphate or administer calcium carbonate supplements with meals, or both, to bind intestinal phosphates and improve calcium balance in patients with hyperphosphatemia.
- Monitor hypoparathyroid patients receiving thiazide diuretics closely; they are prone to develop hypercalcemia.

Patient & Family Education

- Learn S&S of hypercalcemia (see Appendix F).

DILTIAZEM

(dil-tye′a-zem)

Cardizem, Cardizem CD, Cardizem LA, Cartia XT, Dilacor XR, Tiazac, Taztia XT

DILTIAZEM IV

Cardizem IV

Classifications: CALCIUM CHANNEL BLOCKING AGENT; ANTIHYPERTENSIVE
Therapeutic: ANTIHYPERTENSIVE; ANTIARRHYTHMIC
Prototype: Verapamil
Pregnancy Category: C

AVAILABILITY 30 mg, 60 mg, 90 mg, 120 mg tablets; 120 mg, 180 mg, 240 mg sustained release tablets; 60 mg, 90 mg, 120 mg, 180 mg, 240 mg, 300 mg, 360 mg sustained release capsules; 120 mg, 180 mg, 240 mg, 300 mg, 360 mg, 420 mg extended release tablets; 25 mg, 50 mg vials

ACTION & *THERAPEUTIC EFFECT*
Inhibits calcium ion influx through slow channels into cell of myocardial and arterial smooth muscle (both coronary and peripheral blood vessels). Improves myocardial perfusion, and reduces left ventricular workload. *Slows SA and AV node conduction (antiarrhythmic effect). Dilates coronary arteries and arterioles and inhibits coronary artery spasm; thus myocardial oxygen delivery is increased (antianginal effect). By vasodilation of peripheral arterioles, drug decreases total peripheral vascular resistance and reduces arterial BP at rest (antihypertensive effect).*

USES Vasospastic angina (Prinzmetal's variant or at rest angina), chronic stable (classic effort-associated) angina, essential hypertension. *IV form:* Atrial fibrillation, atrial flutter, supraventricular tachycardia.
UNLABELED USES Prevention of reinfarction in non-Q-wave MI.

CONTRAINDICATIONS Known hypersensitivity to drug; sick sinus syndrome (unless pacemaker is in place and functioning); acute MI; CHF; left ventricular dysfunction; second- or third-degree AV block, Wolff-Parkinson-White syndrome, Lown-Ganong-Levine syndrome; severe hypotension (systolic <90 mm Hg or diastolic <60 mm Hg); patients undergoing intracranial surgery; bleeding aneurysms; pregnancy (category C). Safe use in children is not established.
CAUTIOUS USE Sinoatrial nodal dysfunction, sick sinus syndrome; right ventricular dysfunction, severe bradycardia; conduction ab-

normalities; renal or hepatic impairment; older adults.

ROUTE & DOSAGE

Angina
Adult: **PO** 30 mg q.i.d., may increase q1–2d as required (usual range: 180–360 mg/d in divided doses)

Hypertension
Adult: **PO** 60–120 mg sustained release b.i.d. (usual range: 240–360 mg/d) or 120–540 mg of CD or LA once daily

Atrial Fibrillation
Adult: **IV** 0.25 mg/kg IV bolus over 2 min, if inadequate response, may repeat in 15 min with 0.35 mg/kg, followed by a continuous infusion of 5–10 mg/h (max: 15 mg/h for 24 h)

ADMINISTRATION

Oral
- Do not crush sustained release capsules or tablets. They must be swallowed whole.
- Withhold if systolic BP is <90 mm Hg or diastolic is <60 mm Hg.
- Give before meals and at bedtime.
- Store at 15°–30° C (59°–86° F).

Intravenous

PREPARE: **Direct:** Give undiluted. **Continuous:** For IV infusion, add to a volume of D5W, NS, or D5/0.45% NaCl that can be administered in 24 h or less.
ADMINISTER: **Direct:** Give as a bolus dose over 2 min. A second bolus may be given after 15 min. **Continuous:** Give at a rate 5–15 mg/h. Infusion duration longer than 24 h and infusion rate >15 mg/h are not recommended.

D

INCOMPATIBILITIES **Solution/additive: Furosemide. Y-site: Furosemide.**

ADVERSE EFFECTS (≥1%) **CNS:** *Headache,* fatigue, dizziness, asthenia, drowsiness, nervousness, insomnia, confusion, tremor, gait abnormality. **CV:** Edema, arrhythmias, angina, second- or third-degree AV block, bradycardia, CHF, flushing, hypotension, syncope, palpitations. **GI:** Nausea, constipation, anorexia, vomiting, diarrhea, impaired taste, weight increase. **Skin:** Rash.

INTERACTIONS Drug: BETA BLOCKERS, **digoxin** may have additive effects on av node conduction prolongation; may increase **digoxin** or **quinidine** levels; **cimetidine** may increase diltiazem levels, thus increasing effects; may increase **cyclosporine** levels.

PHARMACOKINETICS Absorption: Approximately 80% absorbed from GI tract, with 40% reaching systemic circulation. **Peak:** 2–3 h; 6–11 h sustained release; 11–18 h Cardizem LA. **Distribution:** Into breast milk. **Metabolism:** In liver (CYP3A4). **Elimination:** Primarily in urine with some elimination in feces. **Half-Life:** Oral 3.5–9 h, IV 2 h.

CLINICAL IMPLICATIONS

Assessment & Drug Effects
- Check BP and ECG before initiation of therapy and monitor particularly during dosage adjustment period.
- Lab tests: Do baseline and periodic liver and renal function tests.
- Monitor for and report S&S of CHF.
- Monitor for headache. An analgesic may be required.
- Supervise ambulation as indicated.

Common adverse effects in *italic*, life-threatening effects underlined; generic names in **bold**; classifications in SMALL CAPS; ♣ Canadian drug name; ⊘ Prototype drug

479

D

Patient & Family Education
- Make position changes slowly and in stages; light-headedness and dizziness (hypotension) are possible.
- Do not drive or engage in other potentially hazardous activities until reaction to drug is known.
- Keep follow-up appointments and physician informed.

DIMENHYDRINATE

(dye-men-hye′dri-nate)

Calm-X, Dimenhydrinate Injection

Classifications: ANTIHISTAMINE (H₁-RECEPTOR ANTAGONIST); ANTIEMETIC; ANTIVERTIGO AGENT
Therapeutic: ANTIHISTAMINE; ANTIEMETIC; ANTIVERTIGO AGENT
Prototype: Diphenhydramine
Pregnancy Category: B

AVAILABILITY 50 mg tablets; 50 mg/mL injection; 15.62 mg/5 mL, 12.5 mg/4 mL, 12.5 mg/5 mL liquid

ACTION & *THERAPEUTIC EFFECT*
H₁-receptor antagonist and salt of diphenhydramine, with which it shares similar properties. Precise mode of antiemetic action is thought to involve ability to inhibit cholinergic stimulation in vestibular and associated neural pathways. It has been reported to inhibit labyrinthine stimulation for up to 3 h. *Has antihistamine, antiemetic, and antivertigo activity.*

USES Chiefly in prevention and treatment of motion sickness. Also has been used in management of vertigo, nausea, and vomiting associated with radiation sickness, labyrinthitis, Ménière's syndrome, stapedectomy, anesthesia, and various medications.

CONTRAINDICATIONS Narrow-angle glaucoma, BPH; GI obstruction; urinary tract obstruction; CNS depression; lactation, neonates. Safe use in children <2 y is not established.
CAUTIOUS USE Convulsive disorders; asthma, COPD; severe hepatic disease; PKU; history of porphyria; closed-angle glaucoma; elderly; pregnancy (category B).

ROUTE & DOSAGE

Motion Sickness
Adult: **PO** 50–100 mg q4–6h (max: 400 mg/24 h) **IV/IM** 50 mg as needed *Child:* **PO** 2–6 y, up to 25 mg q6–8h (max: 75 mg/24 h); 6–12 y, 25–50 mg q6–8h (max:150 mg/24 h) **IM** 1.25 mg/kg q.i.d. up to 300 mg/d

ADMINISTRATION
- Note: Give 30–60 min before treatment, then repeat 90 min after treatment, and again in 3 h to prevent radiation sickness.

Intramuscular
- Give undiluted and inject deep IM into a large muscle.

Intravenous
PREPARE: Direct: Dilute each 50 mg in 10 mL of NS.
ADMINISTER: Direct: Give each 50 mg or fraction thereof over 2 min.
INCOMPATIBILITIES Solution/additive: Aminophylline, amobarbital, butorphanol, chlorpromazine, glycopyrrolate, hydroxyzine, midazolam, pentobarbital, prochlorperazine, promazine, promethazine, thiopental.

- Store preferably at 15°–30° C (59°–86° F), unless otherwise directed by manufacturer. ▪Examine parenteral preparation for particulate matter and discoloration. Do not use unless absolutely clear.

ADVERSE EFFECTS (≥1%) **CNS:** *Drowsiness,* headache, incoordination, dizziness, blurred vision, nervousness, restlessness, *insomnia (especially children).* **CV:** Hypotension, palpitation. **GI:** Dry mouth, nose, throat; anorexia, constipation or diarrhea. **Urogenital:** Urinary frequency, dysuria.

DIAGNOSTIC TEST INTERFERENCE *Skin testing* procedures should not be performed within 72 h after use of an antihistamine.

INTERACTIONS Drug: Alcohol and other CNS DEPRESSANTS enhance CNS depression, drowsiness; TRICYCLIC ANTIDEPRESSANTS compound anticholinergic effects.

PHARMACOKINETICS Absorption: Readily absorbed from GI tract. **Onset:** 15–30 min PO; immediate IV; 20–30 min IM. **Duration:** 3–6 h. **Distribution:** Distributed into breast milk. **Elimination:** In urine.

CLINICAL IMPLICATIONS

Assessment & Drug Effects

▪Use side rails and supervise ambulation; drug produces high incidence of drowsiness.
▪Note: Tolerance to CNS depressant effects usually occurs after a few days of drug therapy; some decrease in antiemetic action may result with prolonged use.
▪Monitor for dizziness, nausea, and vomiting; these may indicate drug toxicity.

Patient & Family Education

▪Do not drive or engage in other potentially hazardous activities until response to drug is known.

▪Take 30 min before departure to prevent motion sickness; repeat before meals and upon retiring.

D

DIMERCAPROL

(dye-mer-kap′role)
BAL in Oil, British Anti-Lewisite
Classifications: CHELATING AGENT; ANTIDOTE
Therapeutic: ANTIDOTE
Pregnancy Category: C

AVAILABILITY 100 mg/mL injection

ACTION & *THERAPEUTIC EFFECT* Dithiol compound that combines with ions of various heavy metals to form relatively stable, nontoxic, soluble complexes called chelates, which can be excreted; inhibition of enzymes by toxic metals is thus prevented. *Neutralizes the effects of various heavy metals.*

USES Acute poisoning by arsenic, gold, and mercury; as adjunct to edetate calcium disodium (EDTA) in treatment of lead encephalopathy.
UNLABELED USES Chromium dermatitis; ocular and dermatologic manifestations of arsenic poisoning, as adjunct to penicillamine to increase rate of copper excretion in Wilson's disease, and for poisoning with antimony, bismuth, chromium, copper, nickel, tungsten, zinc.

CONTRAINDICATIONS Hepatic insufficiency (with exception of postarsenical jaundice); history of peanut oil hypersensitivity; severe renal insufficiency; poisoning due to cadmium, iron, selenium, or uranium; pregnancy (category C), lactation.
CAUTIOUS USE Hypertension; oliguria; patients with G6PD deficiency; preexisting renal disease; rheumatoid arthritis.

Common adverse effects in *italic*, life-threatening effects <u>underlined</u>; generic names in **bold**; classifications in SMALL CAPS; ♣ Canadian drug name; ☻ Prototype drug

481

ROUTE & DOSAGE

Arsenic or Gold Poisoning
Adult/Child: **IM** 2.5–3 mg/kg q4h for first 2 d, then q.i.d. on third day, then b.i.d. for 10 d

Mercury Poisoning
Adult/Child: **IM** 5 mg/kg initially, followed by 2.5 mg/kg 1–2 times/d for 10 d

Acute Lead Encephalopathy
Adult/Child: **IM** 4 mg/kg initially, then 3–4 mg/kg q4h with EDTA for 2–7 d depending on response

ADMINISTRATION

Intramuscular

- Initiate therapy ASAP (within 1–2 h) after ingestion of the poison because irreversible tissue damage occurs quickly, particularly in mercury poisoning.
- Give by deep IM injection only. Local pain, gluteal abscess, and skin sensitization possible. Rotate injection sites and observe daily.
- Determine if a local anesthetic may be given with the injection to decrease injection site pain.
- Handle with caution; contact of drug with skin may produce erythema, edema, dermatitis.
- Note: Presence of sediment in ampule reportedly does not indicate drug deterioration.

ADVERSE EFFECTS (≥1%) **CNS:** Headache, anxiety, muscle pain or weakness, restlessness, paresthesias, tremors, *convulsions,* shock. **CV:** *Elevated BP,* tachycardia. **Special Senses:** Rhinorrhea; burning sensation, feeling of pain and constriction in throat. **GI:** Nausea, *vomiting;* burning sensation in lips and mouth, halitosis, salivation; abdominal pain, metabolic acidosis. **Urogenital:** Burning sensation in penis, renal damage. **Other:** Pains in chest or hands, pain and sterile abscess at injection site, sweating, reduction in polymorphonuclear leukocytes, dental pain.

DIAGNOSTIC TEST INTERFERENCE I^{131} *thyroid uptake* values may be decreased if test is done during or immediately following dimercaprol therapy.

INTERACTIONS Drug: **Iron, cadmium, selenium, uranium** form toxic complexes with dimercaprol.

PHARMACOKINETICS Peak: 30–60 min. **Distribution:** Distributed mainly in intracellular spaces, including brain; highest concentrations in liver and kidneys. **Elimination:** Completely excreted in urine and bile within 4 h. **Half-Life:** Short.

CLINICAL IMPLICATIONS

Assessment & Drug Effects

- Monitor vital signs. Elevations of systolic and diastolic BPs accompanied by tachycardia frequently occur within a few minutes following injection and may remain elevated up to 2 h.
- Note: Fever occurs in approximately 30% of children receiving treatment and may persist throughout therapy.
- Monitor I&O. Drug is potentially nephrotoxic. Report oliguria or change in I&O ratio to physician.
- Keep urine alkaline to reduce possibility of renal damage during elimination of dimercaprol chelate.
- Check urine daily for albumin, blood, casts, and pH. Blood and urinary levels of the metal serve as guides for dosage adjustments.
- Minor adverse reactions generally reach maximum 15–20 min after drug administration and subside in 30–90 min. Ephedrine or

an antihistamine is sometimes administered to prevent symptoms.

Patient & Family Education
- Drink as much fluid as the physician will permit.

DIMETHYL SULFOXIDE

(dye-meth'il sul-fox'ide)
DMSO, Rimso-50
Classifications: ANTIINFLAMMATORY, LOCAL
Therapeutic: TOPICAL ANTIINFLAMMATORY
Pregnancy Category: C

AVAILABILITY 50% solution

ACTION & *THERAPEUTIC EFFECT*
Reported effects include antiinflammatory effects, membrane penetration, collagen dissolution, vasodilation, muscle relaxation, diuresis, initiation of histamine release at administration site, cholinesterase inhibition. *Has symptomatic relief of interstitial cystitis with local antiinflammatory properties.*

USES Symptomatic treatment of interstitial cystitis.
UNLABELED USES Topical treatment of a variety of musculoskeletal disorders, arthritis, scleroderma, tendinitis, breast and prostate malignancies, retinitis pigmentosa, herpesvirus infections, head and spinal cord injuries, shock, and as a carrier to enhance penetration and absorption of other drugs. Also used to protect living cells and tissues during cold storage (cryo-protection). Widely used as an industrial solvent and in veterinary medicine for treatment of musculoskeletal injuries.

CONTRAINDICATIONS Urinary tract malignancy; pregnancy (category C), lactation. Safe use in children is not established.

CAUTIOUS USE Hepatic or renal dysfunction.

ROUTE & DOSAGE

Interstitial Cystitis
Adult: **Instillation** 50 mL of 50% solution instilled slowly into urinary bladder and retained for 15 min; may repeat q2wk until maximum relief obtained, then increase intervals between treatments

ADMINISTRATION

Instillation
- Apply analgesic lubricant such as lidocaine jelly to urethra to facilitate insertion of catheter.
- Instruct patient to retain instillation for 15 min and then expel it by spontaneous voiding.
- Note: Discomfort associated with instillation usually lessens with repeated administration. Physician may prescribe an oral analgesic or suppository containing belladonna and an opiate prior to instillation to reduce bladder spasm.
- Store at 15°–30° C (59°–86° F) unless otherwise directed. Protect from strong light. Avoid contact with plastics.

ADVERSE EFFECTS (≥1%) **Special Senses:** Transient disturbances in color vision, photophobia. **GI:** Nausea, diarrhea. Hypersensitivity: Local or generalized rash, erythema, pruritus, urticaria, swelling of face, dyspnea (<u>anaphylactoid reaction</u>). **Other:** Nasal congestion, headache, sedation, drowsiness. **Following instillation:** *Garlic-like odor on breath and skin; garlic-like taste;* discomfort during administration; transient cystitis. **Following topical application:** Vesicle formation.

INTERACTIONS Drug: Decreases effectiveness of **sulindac,** possibly

Common adverse effects in *italic*, life-threatening effects <u>underlined</u>; generic names in **bold**; classifications in SMALL CAPS; ♦ Canadian drug name; ❷ Prototype drug

483

causing severe peripheral neuropathy.

PHARMACOKINETICS Absorption: Readily absorbed systemically. **Peak:** 4–8 h. **Distribution:** Widely distributed in tissues and body fluids; penetrates blood–brain barrier; distributed into breast milk. **Metabolism:** Metabolized to dimethyl sulfide (garlic breath) and dimethyl sulfone. **Elimination:** Dimethyl sulfide excreted through lungs and skin; dimethyl sulfone may remain in serum >2 wk and is excreted in urine and feces.

CLINICAL IMPLICATIONS

Assessment & Drug Effects

- Lab tests: Do CBC and liver and renal function tests initially and at 6-mo intervals.
- Do complete eye evaluation including slit-lamp examination prior to and at regular intervals during therapy.

Patient & Family Education

- Note: Garlic-like taste may be experienced within minutes after drug instillation and may last for several hours. Garlic-like odor on breath and skin may last as long as 72 h.
- Do not use OTC topical medications without consulting physician.

DINOPROSTONE (PGE₂, PROSTAGLANDIN E₂)

(dye-noe-prost′one)

Cervidil, Prostin E₂, Prepidil

Classifications: OXYTOCIC

Therapeutic: OXYTOCIC; PROSTAGLANDIN

Prototype: Oxytocin

Pregnancy Category: C

AVAILABILITY 20 mg suppository; **Prepidil** 0.5 mg gel; **Cervidil** 10 mg vaginal insert

ACTION & *THERAPEUTIC EFFECT*

Synthetically prepared member of the prostaglandin E₂ series that appears to act directly on myometrium and on gastrointestinal, bronchial, and vascular smooth muscle. Stimulation of gravid uterus in early weeks of gestation is more potent than that of oxytocin. *Contractions are qualitatively similar to those that occur during term labor. Has high success rate when used as abortifacient before twentieth week and for stimulation of labor in cases of intrauterine fetal death.*

USES To terminate pregnancy from twelfth week through second trimester as calculated from first day of last regular menstrual period; to evacuate uterine contents in management of missed abortion or intrauterine fetal death up to 28 wk gestational age; to manage benign hydatidiform mole; cervical ripening prior to labor induction.

CONTRAINDICATIONS Acute pelvic inflammatory disease; abnormal fetal position; history of pelvic surgery, uterine fibroids, cervical stenosis, active cardiac, pulmonary, renal, or hepatic disease, pregnancy (category C).

CAUTIOUS USE History of hypertension, hypotension, asthma, epilepsy, anemia, diabetes mellitus; jaundice, history of hepatic, renal, or cardiovascular disease; cervicitis, acute vaginitis, infected endocervical lesion; previous history of caesarean section.

ROUTE & DOSAGE

Induction of Labor

Adult: **Endocervical** Place *Prepidil* 0.5 mg endocervically, may repeat q6h (max: of 1.5 mg);

Place *Cervidil* insert 10 mg transversely in the posterior fornix of the vagina, remove on onset of active labor or 12 h after insertion

Evacuation of Uterus

Adult: **Intravaginal** Insert suppository high in vagina, repeat q2–5h until abortion occurs or membranes rupture (max: total dose 240 mg)

ADMINISTRATION

Endocervical & Intravaginal

- Antiemetic and antidiarrheal medication may be prescribed to be given before dinoprostone to minimize GI side effects.
- Place vaginal insert in the vagina immediately after removal from the foil package. DO NOT use without retrieval system.
- Keep patient in supine position for 10 min after administration of suppository to prevent expulsion and enhance absorption.
- Store suppositories in freezer at temperature not exceeding –20° C (–4° F) unless otherwise specified.

ADVERSE EFFECTS (≥1%) **CNS:** Headache, tremor, tension. **CV:** Transient hypotension, flushing, cardiac arrhythmias. **GI:** *Nausea, vomiting, diarrhea.* **Urogenital:** Vaginal pain, endometritis, <u>uterine rupture</u>. **Respiratory:** Dyspnea, cough, hiccups. **Body as a Whole:** Chills, *fever,* dehydration, diaphoresis, rash.

INTERACTIONS Drug: OXYTOCICS used with extreme caution.

PHARMACOKINETICS Absorption: Slowly absorbed from vagina; Cervidil insert releases approximately 0.3 mg/h. **Onset:** 10 min. **Duration:** 2–3 h. **Distribution:** Widely distributed in body. **Metabolism:** Rapidly metabo-lized in lungs, kidneys, spleen, and other tissues. **Elimination:** Mainly in urine; some in feces.

CLINICAL IMPLICATIONS

Assessment & Drug Effects

- Observe patient carefully, after insertion of the drug. Rupture of the membranes is not a contraindication to drug, but be aware that profuse bleeding may result in expulsion of the suppository. Report wheezing, chest pain, dyspnea, and significant changes in BP and pulse to the physician.
- Monitor uterine contractions and observe for and report excessive vaginal bleeding and cramping pain. Keep pad count. Save all clots and tissues for physician inspection and laboratory analysis.
- Abortion usually occurs within 30 h. When used in conjunction with oxytocin, time may be shortened to 12–14 h.
- Monitor vital signs. Fever is a physiologic response of the hypothalamus to use of dinoprostone and occurs within 15–45 min after insertion of suppository. Temperature returns to normal within 2–6 h after discontinuation of medication.

Patient & Family Education

- Continue taking your temperature (late afternoon) for a few days after discharge. Contact physician with onset of fever, bleeding, abdominal cramps, abnormal or foul-smelling vaginal discharge.
- Avoid douches, tampons, intercourse, and tub baths for at least 2 wk. Clarify with physician.
- Note: Dinoprostone may exacerbate joint pain and limitation due to its effect on the inflammatory process.

Common adverse effects in *italic*, life-threatening effects <u>underlined</u>; generic names in **bold**; classifications in SMALL CAPS; ✤ Canadian drug name; ⊘ Prototype drug

485

DIPHENHYDRAMINE HYDROCHLORIDE ℗

(dye-fen-hye′dra-meen)
Allerdryl ✦, Benadryl, Benadryl Dye-Free, Sleep-Eze 3, Sominex Formula 2, Tusstat, Twilite, Valdrene

Classifications: ANTIHISTAMINE; H_1-RECEPTOR ANTAGONIST
Therapeutic: ANTIHISTAMINE; H_1-RECEPTOR ANTAGONIST
Pregnancy Category: C

AVAILABILITY 25 mg, 50 mg capsules, tablets; 6.25 mg/5 mL, 12.5 mg/5 mL syrup; 50 mg/mL injection

ACTION & *THERAPEUTIC EFFECT*
H_1-receptor antagonist and antihistamine with significant anticholinergic activity. Competes for H_1-receptor sites on effector cells, thus blocking histamine release. High incidence of drowsiness, but GI side effects are minor. Effects in parkinsonism and drug-induced extrapyramidal symptoms are apparently related to its ability to suppress central cholinergic activity and to prolong action of dopamine by inhibiting its reuptake and storage. *Has antihistamine, antivertigo, antiemetic, antianaphylactic, antitussive, antidyskinetic, and sedative-hypnotic effects.*

USES Temporary symptomatic relief of various allergic conditions and to treat or prevent motion sickness, vertigo, and reactions to blood or plasma in susceptible patients. Also used in anaphylaxis as adjunct to epinephrine and other standard measures after acute symptoms have been controlled; in treatment of parkinsonism and drug-induced extrapyramidal reactions; as a nonnarcotic cough suppressant; as a sedative-hypnotic; and for treatment of intractable insomnia.

CONTRAINDICATIONS Hypersensitivity to antihistamines of similar structure; lower respiratory tract symptoms (including acute asthma); narrow-angle glaucoma; prostatic hypertrophy, bladder neck obstruction; GI obstruction or stenosis; pregnancy (category C), lactation, premature neonates, and neonates; use as nighttime sleep aid in children <2 y.

CAUTIOUS USE History of asthma; COPD; convulsive disorders; increased IOP; hyperthyroidism; hypertension, cardiovascular disease; hepatic disease; diabetes mellitus; older adults, infants, and young children.

ROUTE & DOSAGE

Allergy Symptoms, Antiparkinsonism, Motion Sickness, Nighttime Sedation
Adult: **PO** 25–50 mg t.i.d. or q.i.d. (max: 300 mg/d) **IV/IM** 10–50 mg q4–6h (max: 400 mg/d)
Child: **PO** 2–6 y, 6.25 mg q4–6h (max: 300 mg/24 h); 6–12 y, 12.5–25 mg q4–6h (max: 300 mg/24 h) **IV/IM** 5 mg/kg/d divided into 4 doses (max: 300 mg/d)

Nonproductive Cough
Adult: **PO** 25 mg q4–6h (max: 100 mg/d)
Child: **PO** 2–6 y, 6.25 mg q4–6h (max: 25 mg/24 h); 6–12 y, 12.5 mg q4–6h (max: 50 mg/24 h)

ADMINISTRATION

Oral
- Give with food or milk to lessen GI adverse effects.
- For motion sickness: Give the first dose 30 min before exposure to

motion; give remaining doses before meals and at bedtime.

Intramuscular

- Give IM injection deep into large muscle mass; alternate injection sites. Avoid perivascular or SC injections because of its irritating effects.
- Note: Hypersensitivity reactions (including anaphylactic shock) are more likely to occur with parenteral than PO administration.

Intravenous

PREPARE: **Direct:** Give undiluted.
ADMINISTER: **Direct:** Give at a rate of 25 mg or a fraction thereof over 1 min.
INCOMPATIBILITIES **Y-site: Furosemide.**

- Store in tightly covered containers at 15°–30° C (59°–86° F) unless otherwise directed by manufacturer. Keep injection and elixir formulations in light-resistant containers.

ADVERSE EFFECTS (≥1%) **CNS:** *Drowsiness,* dizziness, headache, fatigue, disturbed coordination, tingling, heaviness and weakness of hands, tremors, euphoria, nervousness, restlessness, insomnia; confusion; (especially in children): excitement, fever. **CV:** Palpitation, *tachycardia,* mild hypotension or hypertension, cardiovascular collapse. **Special Senses:** Tinnitus, vertigo, dry nose, throat, nasal stuffiness; blurred vision, diplopia, photosensitivity, dry eyes. **GI:** *Dry mouth,* nausea, epigastric distress, anorexia, vomiting, constipation, or diarrhea. **Urogenital:** Urinary frequency or retention, dysuria. **Body as a Whole:** Hypersensitivity (skin rash, urticaria, photosensitivity, anaphylactic shock). **Respiratory:** Thickened bronchial secretions, wheezing, sensation of chest tightness.

DIAGNOSTIC TEST INTERFERENCE
Diphenhydramine should be discontinued 4 d prior to *skin testing* procedures for allergy because it may obscure otherwise positive reactions.

INTERACTIONS Drug: Alcohol and other CNS DEPRESSANTS, MAO INHIBITORS compound CNS depression.

PHARMACOKINETICS Absorption: Readily absorbed from GI tract but only 40–60% reaches systemic circulation. **Onset:** 15–30 min. **Peak:** 1–4 h. **Duration:** 4–7 h. **Distribution:** Crosses placenta; distributed into breast milk. **Metabolism:** In liver; some degradation in lung and kidney. **Elimination:** Mostly in urine within 24 h.

CLINICAL IMPLICATIONS
Assessment & Drug Effects
- Monitor cardiovascular status especially with preexisting cardiovascular disease.
- Monitor for adverse effects especially in children and the older adult.
- Supervise ambulation and use side-rails as necessary. Drowsiness is most prominent during the first few days of therapy and often disappears with continued therapy. Older adults are especially likely to manifest dizziness, sedation, and hypotension.

Patient & Family Education
- Do not use alcohol and other CNS depressants because of the possible additive CNS depressant effects with concurrent use.
- Do not drive or engage in other potentially hazardous activities until the response to drug is known.
- Increase fluid intake, if not contraindicated; drug has an atropine-like drying effect (thickens bronchial secretions) that may make expectoration difficult.

Common adverse effects in *italic*, life-threatening effects underlined; generic names in **bold**; classifications in SMALL CAPS; ♣ Canadian drug name; ❷ Prototype drug

487

D

DIPHENOXYLATE HYDROCHLORIDE WITH ATROPINE SULFATE

(dye-fen-ox′i-late)

Diphenatol, Lofene, Lomanate, Lomotil, Lonox, Lo-Trol, Low-Quel, Nor-Mil

Classifications: ANTIDIARRHEAL

Therapeutic: ANTIDIARRHEAL

Pregnancy Category: C

Controlled Substance: Schedule V

AVAILABILITY 2.5 mg tablets; 2.5 mg/5 mL liquid

ACTION & *THERAPEUTIC EFFECT*

Diphenoxylate is a synthetic narcotic opiate agonist. Commercially available only with atropine sulfate, added in subtherapeutic doses to discourage deliberate overdosage. Inhibits mucosal receptors responsible for peristaltic reflex, thereby reducing GI motility. *Reduces GI motility. Has little or no analgesic activity or risk of dependence, except in high doses.*

USES Adjunct in symptomatic management of diarrhea.

CONTRAINDICATIONS Hypersensitivity to diphenoxylate or atropine; severe dehydration or electrolyte imbalance, advanced liver disease, obstructive jaundice, diarrhea caused by pseudomembranous enterocolitis associated with use of broad-spectrum antibiotics; diarrhea associated with organisms that penetrate intestinal mucosa; diarrhea induced by poisons until toxic material is eliminated from GI tract; glaucoma; children <2 y of age; pregnancy (category C); lactation.

CAUTIOUS USE Advanced hepatic disease, abnormal liver function tests; renal function impairment;

MAOI therapy; patients receiving addicting drugs, addiction-prone individuals, or those whose history suggests drug abuse; ulcerative colitis; young children (particularly patients with Down syndrome).

ROUTE & DOSAGE

Diarrhea

Adult: **PO** 1–2 tablets or 1–2 teaspoons full (5 mL) 3–4 times/d (each tablet or 5 mL contains 2.5 mg diphenoxylate HCl and 0.025 mg atropine sulfate)
Child: **PO** 2–12 y, 0.3–0.4 mg/kg/d of liquid in divided doses

ADMINISTRATION

Oral

- Crush tablet if necessary and give with fluid of patient's choice.
- Reduce dosage as soon as initial control of symptoms occurs.
- Withhold drug in presence of severe dehydration or electrolyte imbalance until appropriate corrective therapy has been initiated.
- Note: Treatment is generally continued for 24–36 h before it is considered ineffective.
- Store in tightly covered, light-resistant container, preferably 15°–30° C (59°–86° F), unless otherwise directed by manufacturer.

ADVERSE EFFECTS (≥1%) **Body as a Whole:** Hypersensitivity (pruritus, angioneurotic edema, giant urticaria, rash). **CNS:** Headache, sedation, drowsiness, dizziness, lethargy, numbness of extremities; restlessness, euphoria, mental depression, weakness, general malaise. **CV:** Flushing, palpitation, tachycardia. **Special Senses:** Nystagmus, mydriasis, blurred vision, miosis (toxicity). **GI:** Nausea, vomiting, anorexia, dry mouth, abdominal discomfort or distension, paralytic ileus, toxic megacolon. **Other:** Urinary retention, swelling of gums.

INTERACTIONS Drug: MAO INHIBITORS may precipitate hypertensive crisis; **alcohol** and other CNS DEPRESSANTS may enhance CNS effects; also see **atropine.**

PHARMACOKINETICS Absorption: Readily absorbed from GI tract. **Onset:** 45–60 min. **Peak:** 2 h. **Duration:** 3–4 h. **Distribution:** Distributed into breast milk. **Metabolism:** Rapidly metabolized to active and inactive metabolites in liver. **Elimination:** Slowly through bile into feces; small amount in urine. **Half-Life:** 4.4 h.

CLINICAL IMPLICATIONS

Assessment & Drug Effects
- Assess GI function; report abdominal distention and signs of decreased peristalsis.
- Monitor for S&S of dehydration (see Appendix F). It is essential to monitor young children closely; dehydration occurs more rapidly in this age group and may influence variability of response to diphenoxylate and predispose patient to delayed toxic effects.
- Monitor frequency and consistency of stools.

Patient & Family Education
- Take medication only as directed by physician.
- Notify physician if diarrhea persists or if fever, bloody stools, palpitation, or other adverse reactions occur.
- Do not drive or engage in other potentially hazardous activities until response to drug is known.

DIPIVEFRIN HYDROCHLORIDE
(dye-pi′ve-frin)
Propine
Pregnancy Category: B
See Appendix A-1.

D

DIPYRIDAMOLE
(dye-peer-id′a-mole)
Apo-Dipyridamole ♦, Persantine
Classifications: ANTIPLATELET AGENT; PLATELET AGGREGATE INHIBITOR; CORONARY VASODILATOR
Therapeutic: PLATELET AGGREGATE INHIBITOR
Pregnancy Category: B

AVAILABILITY 25 mg, 50 mg, 75 mg tablets; 10 mg injection

ACTION & *THERAPEUTIC EFFECT*
Nonnitrate coronary vasodilator that increases coronary blood flow by selectively dilating coronary arteries, thereby increasing myocardial oxygen supply. Exhibits mild inotropic action. Also has antiplatelet aggregation activity. *Has antiplatelet, coronary vasodilator activities.*

USES To prevent postoperative thromboembolic complications associated with prosthetic heart valves and as adjunct for thallium stress testing.
UNLABELED USES To reduce rate of reinfarction following MI; to prevent TIAs (transient ischemic attacks) and coronary bypass graft occlusion.

CONTRAINDICATIONS Safety and efficacy in children <12 y are not established.
CAUTIOUS USE Hypotension, anticoagulant therapy; aspirin sensitivity; elderly; severe hepatic dysfunc-

Common adverse effects in *italic*, life-threatening effects underlined; generic names in **bold**; classifications in SMALL CAPS; ♦ Canadian drug name; 🅿 Prototype drug

489

tion; syncopy; pregnancy (category B), lactation.

ROUTE & DOSAGE

Prevention of Thromboembolism in Cardiac Valve Replacement
Adult: **PO** 75–100 mg q.i.d.
Child: **PO** 1–2 mg t.i.d.

Thromboembolic Disorders
Adult: **PO** 150–400 mg/d in divided doses

Thallium Stress Test
Adult: **IV** 0.142 mg/kg/min for 4 min

ADMINISTRATION

Oral
- Give on an empty stomach at least 1 h before or 2 h after meals, with a full glass of water. Physician may prescribe with food if gastric distress persists.

Intravenous

PREPARE: Direct: Dilute to at least a 1:2 ratio with 0.45% NaCl, NS, or D5W to yield a final volume of 20–50 mL.
ADMINISTER: Direct: Give a single dose over 4 min (0.142 mg kg/min).

- Store in tightly closed container at 15°–30° C (59°–86° F) unless otherwise directed. Protect injection from direct light.

ADVERSE EFFECTS (≥1%) Usually dose related, minimal, and transient. **CNS:** Headache, dizziness, faintness, syncope, weakness. **CV:** Peripheral vasodilation, flushing. **GI:** Nausea, vomiting, diarrhea, abdominal distress. **Skin:** Skin rash, pruritus.

PHARMACOKINETICS Absorption: Readily absorbed from GI tract. **Peak:** 45–150 min. **Distribution:** Small amount crosses placenta. **Me-**

tabolism: In liver. **Elimination:** Mainly in feces. **Half-Life:** 10–12 h.

CLINICAL IMPLICATIONS

Assessment & Drug Effects
- Monitor therapeutic effectiveness. Clinical response may not be evident before second or third month of continuous therapy. Effects include reduced frequency or elimination of anginal episodes, improved exercise tolerance, reduced requirement for nitrates.

Patient & Family Education
- Notify physician of any adverse effects.
- Make all position changes slowly and in stages, especially from recumbent to upright posture, if postural hypotension or dizziness is a problem.

DIRITHROMYCIN

(dir-ith-roe-my′sin)
Dynabac
Classifications: MACROLIDE ANTIBIOTIC
Therapeutic: ANTIBIOTIC
Prototype: Erythromycin
Pregnancy Category: C

AVAILABILITY 250 mg enteric tablets

ACTION & THERAPEUTIC EFFECT
Dirithromycin is an analog of erythromycin. It binds reversibly to the 50-S ribosomal subunit of the bacteria, thus inhibiting RNA-dependent protein synthesis in bacterial cells. It has no apparent effect on the cytochrome P-450 hepatic enzyme system as erythromycin does. *It is more active against gram-positive organisms than gram-negative organisms.*

USES Acute bacterial exacerbations of chronic bronchitis, community-acquired pneumonia, pharyngitis/

tonsillitis, uncomplicated skin/skin structure infections due to susceptible bacteria.

CONTRAINDICATIONS Known hypersensitivity to dirithromycin, erythromycin, or any other macrolide antibiotic; known or suspected bacteremias; viral infections; pregnancy (category C).

CAUTIOUS USE Severe hepatic impairment, GI disease; lactation. Safety and effectiveness in children <12 y are not established.

ROUTE & DOSAGE

Bacterial Infections
Adult/Child: **PO** 500 mg once/d

ADMINISTRATION

Oral
- Give with food or within 1 h of eating.
- Do not cut, crush, or chew tablets.
- Store at 15°–30° C (59°–86° F).

ADVERSE EFFECTS (≥1%) **CNS:** Headache, dizziness, asthenia. **CV:** Chest pain. **GI:** *Abdominal pain, nausea, diarrhea, vomiting, dyspepsia, flatulence;* elevated liver function tests (ALT, AST, GGT). **Skin:** Rash, urticaria. **Respiratory:** Dyspnea, asthma-like symptoms, rhinitis, pharyngitis, increased coughing.

INTERACTIONS Drug: May increase **theophylline** levels.

PHARMACOKINETICS Absorption: Readily absorbed from GI tract; 60–90% hydrolyzed to active metabolite, erythromycylamine, within 35 min. **Peak:** 1.5 h. **Distribution:** High tissue concentrations of active metabolite; slowly released back into the circulation. **Metabolism:** Rapidly converted to active metabolite, erythromycylamine, in absorption

and distribution phases. **Elimination:** 81–97% in bile and feces. **Half-Life:** 20–50 h.

CLINICAL IMPLICATIONS

Assessment & Drug Effects
- Take history of previous hypersensitivity to other macrolides (e.g., erythromycin) prior to initiation of therapy.
- Withhold drug and notify physician if signs and symptoms of hypersensitivity occur (see Appendix F).
- Monitor liver and renal function in patients with mild liver or renal impairment.
- Monitor for S&S of superinfection (see Appendix F).
- Monitor theophylline levels if given concurrently with dirithromycin.
- Note: Dirithromycin may increase the blood level of theophylline, necessitating theophylline dosage adjustment.

Patient & Family Education
- Take tablets whole and within 1 h of meals.
- Monitor for and report S&S of superinfection or pseudomembranous enterocolitis (see Appendix F).
- Report any worsening of signs and symptoms of infection.

DISOPYRAMIDE PHOSPHATE

(dye-soe-peer′a-mide)
Napamide, Norpace, Norpace CR, Rythmodan ◆, Rythmodan-LA ◆

Classifications: ANTIARRHYTHMIC, CLASS IA
Therapeutic: ANTIARRHYTHMIC, CLASS IA
Prototype: Procainamide
Pregnancy Category: C

Common adverse effects in *italic*, life-threatening effects underlined; generic names in **bold**; classifications in SMALL CAPS; ◆ Canadian drug name; ⊙ Prototype drug

491

D

AVAILABILITY 100 mg, 150 mg regular and sustained release capsules

ACTION & *THERAPEUTIC EFFECT*

Class IA antiarrhythmic agent that decreases myocardial conduction velocity and excitability in the atria, ventricles, and accessory pathways. It prolongs the QRS and QT intervals in normal sinus rhythm and artial arrhythmias. *Acts as myocardial depressant by reducing rate of spontaneous diastolic depolarization in pacemaker cells, thereby suppressing ectopic focal activity.*

USES To suppress and prevent recurrence of premature ventricular contractions (unifocal, multifocal, paired) and ventricular tachycardia not severe enough to require cardioversion.

UNLABELED USES In combination with other antiarrhythmic drugs to treat or prevent serious refractory arrhythmias. To convert atrial fibrillation, atrial flutter, and paroxysmal atrial tachycardia to normal sinus rhythm.

CONTRAINDICATIONS Cardiogenic shock, preexisting 2nd or 3rd degree AV block (if no pacemaker is present); sick sinus syndrome (bradycardia-tachycardia); Wolff-Parkinson-White (WPW) syndrome or bundle branch block, history of torsade de pointes; cardiogenic shock; QT prolongation; uncompensated or inadequately compensated CHF, hypotension (unless secondary to cardiac arrhythmia), hypokalemia; pregnancy (category C).

CAUTIOUS USE Myocarditis or other cardiomyopathy, underlying cardiac conduction abnormalities; hepatic or renal impairment; urinary tract disease (especially prostatic hypertrophy); diabetes mellitus; myasthenia gravis; elderly; narrow-angle glaucoma; family history of glaucoma; lactation.

ROUTE & DOSAGE

> ### Arrhythmias
> *Adult:* **PO** *<50 kg,* 100 mg q6h or 200 mg sustained release q12h; *>50 kg,* 100–200 mg q6h or 300 mg sustained release capsule q12h
> *Child:* **PO** *<1 y,* 10–30 mg/kg/d in divided doses q6h; *1–4 y,* 10–20 mg/kg/d in divided doses q6h; *4–12 y,* 10–15 mg/kg/d in divided doses q6h; *12–18 y,* 6–15 mg/kg/d in divided doses q6h

ADMINISTRATION

Oral

- Start drug 6–12 h after last quinidine dose and 3–6 h after last procainamide dose for patients who have been receiving either quinidine or procainamide.
- Give sustained release capsules whole.
- Do not use sustained release capsules in loading doses when rapid control is required or in patients with creatinine clearance of ≤40 mL/min.
- Start sustained release capsules 6 h after last dose of conventional capsule if change in drug form is made.
- Store at 15°–30° C (59°–86° F) unless otherwise directed.

ADVERSE EFFECTS (≥1%) **Body as a Whole:** Hypersensitivity (pruritus, urticaria, rash, photosensitivity, <u>laryngospasm</u>). **CNS:** Dizziness, headache, fatigue, muscle weakness, convulsions, paresthesias, nervousness, acute psychosis, peripheral neuropathy. **CV:** *Hypotension,* chest pain, edema, dyspnea, syncope, bradycardia, tachycardia; worsening of CHF or cardiac arrhythmia; cardiogenic shock, heart block; edema with weight gain. **Special Senses:** *Blurred vision,* dry eyes, increased IOP, precipitation of acute angle-closure glaucoma. **GI:** *Dry mouth, constipation,* epigastric or abdominal pain, cholestatic jaundice. **Urogenital:** *Hesitancy* and *retention,* urinary frequency, urgency, renal insufficiency. **Other:** Dry nose and throat, drying of bronchial secretions, initiation of uterine contractions (pregnant patient); muscle aches, precipitation of myasthenia gravis, agranulocytosis (rare), thrombocytopenia.

INTERACTIONS Drug: ANTICHOLINERGIC DRUGS (e.g., TRICYCLIC ANTIDEPRESSANTS, ANTIHISTAMINES) compound anticholinergic effects; other ANTIARRHYTHMICS compound toxicities; **phenytoin, rifampin** may increase disopyramide metabolism and decrease levels; may increase **warfarin**-induced hypoprothrombinemia.

PHARMACOKINETICS Absorption: Readily from GI tract; 60–83% reaches systemic circulation. **Onset:** 30 min–3.5 h. **Peak:** 1–2 h. **Duration:** 1.5–8.5 h. **Distribution:** Distributed in extracellular fluid; crosses placenta; distributed into breast milk. **Metabolism:** In liver. **Elimination:** 80% in urine, 10% in feces. **Half-Life:** 4–10 h.

CLINICAL IMPLICATIONS

Assessment & Drug Effects

- Check apical pulse before administering drug. Withhold drug and notify physician if pulse rate is slower than 60 bpm, faster than 120 bpm, or if there is any unusual change in rate, rhythm, or quality.

- Monitor ECG closely. The following signs are indications for drug withdrawal: Prolongation of QT interval and worsening of arrhythmia interval, QRS widening (>25%).

- Monitor for rapid weight gain or other signs of fluid retention.

- Lab tests: Baseline and periodic hepatic and renal function tests, blood glucose, and serum potassium. Correct hypokalemia or other imbalances before initiation of therapy.

- Monitor BP closely in all patients during periods of dosage adjustment and in those receiving high dosages.

- Monitor I&O, particularly in older adults and patients with impaired renal function or prostatic hypertrophy. Persistent urinary hesitancy or retention may necessitate lower dosage or discontinuation of drug.

- Report S&S of hyperkalemia (see Appendix F); it enhances drug's toxic effects.

- Measure IOP before treatment begins in patients with a family history of glaucoma.

- Monitor for S&S of CHF.

- Discontinue promptly if S&S of agranulocytosis, peripheral neuritis, or jaundice appear (see Appendix F).

Patient & Family Education

- Take drug precisely as prescribed to maintain regularity of heartbeat. Do not skip or stop medication or change dose without consulting physician.

- Weigh daily under standard conditions and check ankles for edema. Report to physician a weekly weight gain of ≥1–2 kg (2–4 lb).

- Make position changes slowly, particularly when getting up from lying down because of the possibility of hypotension; dangle legs for a few minutes before walking,

Common adverse effects in *italic,* life-threatening effects underlined; generic names in **bold;** classifications in SMALL CAPS; ✦ Canadian drug name; ⓟ Prototype drug

493

D

and do not stand still for pro-longed periods. If you feel light-headed, lie down or sit down.

- Do not take OTC medications un-less approved by physician.
- Avoid exposure to sunlight or ul-traviolet light; drug may cause photosensitivity.
- Do not drive or engage in other potentially hazardous activities until response to drug is known.
- Do not drink alcoholic beverages while taking disopyramide.

DISULFIRAM

(dye-sul′fi-ram)
Antabuse, Cronetal, Ro-sulfiram
Classifications: ENZYME INHIBITOR; ANTIALCOHOL AGENT
Therapeutic: ALCOHOL ABUSE DE-TERRANT
Pregnancy Category: B

AVAILABILITY 250 mg, 500 mg tab-lets

ACTION & *THERAPEUTIC EFFECT*
Acts as a deterrent to alcohol inges-tion by inhibiting the enzyme acetal-dehyde dehydrogenase, which nor-mally metabolizes alcohol in the body. *When a small amount of al-cohol is ingested, a complex of highly unpleasant symptoms known as the disulfiram reaction occurs, which serves as a deterrent to fur-ther drinking.*

USES Adjunct in treatment of the pa-tient with chronic alcoholism who sincerely wants to maintain sobriety.

CONTRAINDICATIONS Severe myo-cardial disease; cardiac disease; psychosis; patients who have re-cently ingested alcohol, metronida-zole, paraldehyde; multiple drug dependence.

CAUTIOUS USE Diabetes mellitus; epilepsy; seizure disorders; hy-pothyroidism; coronary artery dis-ease, cerebral damage; chronic and acute nephritis; renal disease; he-patic cirrhosis or insufficiency; ab-normal EEG; pregnancy (category B), lactation.

ROUTE & DOSAGE

Alcoholism
Adult: **PO** 500 mg/d for 1–2 wk, then 125–500 mg/d (max: 500 mg/d)

ADMINISTRATION

Oral
- Give daily dose in the morning when the resolve not to drink may be strongest.
- Give at bedtime to minimize sed-ative effect of the drug. Decrease in dose may also reduce sedative effect.
- Make sure patient has abstained from alcohol and alcohol-contain-ing preparations for at least 12 h and preferably 48 h before initiat-ing therapy.
- Determine compliance periodi-cally. Maintenance therapy may be required for months or even years.
- Store at 15°–30° C (59°–86° F) un-less otherwise directed. Protect tablets from light.

ADVERSE EFFECTS (≥1%) **Reac-tion with alcohol ingestion:** Flush-ing of face, chest, arms, pulsating headache, nausea, violent vomiting, thirst, sweating, marked uneasiness, confusion, weakness, vertigo, blurred vision, pruritic skin rash, hy-perventilation, abnormal gait, slurred speech, disorientation, con-fusion, personality changes, bizarre behavior, psychoses, tachycardia, palpitation, chest pain, <u>hypotension</u>

to shock level arrhythmias, acute congestive failure. **Severe reactions:** Marked respiratory depression, unconsciousness, convulsions, sudden death. **Body as a Whole:** Hypersensitivity (allergic or acneiform dermatitis; urticaria, fixed-drug eruption). **CNS:** Drowsiness, fatigue, restlessness, headache, tremor, psychoses (usually with high doses), polyneuritis, peripheral neuropathy, optic neuritis. **GI:** Mild GI disturbances, garlic-like or metallic taste, hepatotoxicity, hypersensitivity hepatitis.

DIAGNOSTIC TEST INTERFERENCE

Disulfiram can reduce *uptake of I^{131};* or decreases *PBI* test results (rare).

INTERACTIONS

Drug: Alcohol (including in liquid OTC drugs, **IV nitroglycerin, IV cotrimoxazole**), **metronidazole, paraldehyde** will produce disulfiram reaction; **isoniazid** can produce neurological symptoms; may increase blood levels and toxicity of **warfarin, paraldehyde,** BARBITURATES, **phenytoin.**

PHARMACOKINETICS

Absorption: Readily absorbed from GI tract. **Onset:** Up to 12 h. **Duration:** Up to 2 wk. **Distribution:** Initially deposited in fat. **Metabolism:** Metabolized slowly in liver. **Elimination:** 5–20% excreted in feces; 20% remains in body for 1–2 wk; some may be excreted in breath as carbon disulfide.

CLINICAL IMPLICATIONS

Assessment & Drug Effects

- Do a complete physical examination and careful drug history prior to initiation of therapy.
- Lab tests: Baseline and follow-up transaminase studies every 10–14 d to detect hepatic dysfunction, and perform CBC and sequential multiple analysis (SMA-12) tests every 6 mo.
- Note: Disulfiram reaction occurs within 5–10 min following ingestion of alcohol and may last 30 min to several hours. Intensity of reaction varies with each individual, but is generally proportional to the amount of alcohol ingested.
- Treat patient with severe disulfiram reaction as though in shock. Monitor potassium levels, especially if patient has diabetes mellitus.

Patient & Family Education

- Understand fully the possible dangers if alcohol is ingested during disulfiram treatment before consenting to therapy.
- Report promptly to physician the onset of nausea with right upper quadrant pain or discomfort, itching, jaundiced sclerae or skin, dark urine, clay-colored stools. Withhold drug pending liver function tests.
- Note: Ingestion of even small amounts of alcohol or use of external applications that contain alcohol may be sufficient to produce a reaction. Read all labels and avoid use of anything containing alcohol.
- Prolonged administration of disulfiram does not produce tolerance; the longer the therapy, the higher the sensitivity to alcohol.
- Alcohol sensitivity may last as long as 2 wk after disulfiram has been discontinued.
- Note: Adverse effects of drug are often experienced during first 2 wk of therapy; symptoms usually disappear with continued therapy or with dose reduction.
- Carry an identification card stating you are on disulfiram therapy and describing the symptoms of disulfiram reaction. Also provide the name of the physician or institution to contact in an emergency.

Common adverse effects in *italic*, life-threatening effects underlined; generic names in **bold**; classifications in SMALL CAPS; ✦ Canadian drug name; ◎ Prototype drug

495

- Do not drive or engage in other potentially hazardous activities until response to drug is known.

D

DOBUTAMINE HYDROCHLORIDE

(doe-byoo′ta-meen)
Dobutrex
Classifications: BETA-ADRENER-GIC AGONIST; CATECHOLAMINE
Therapeutic: CARDIAC STIMULANT
Prototype: Isoproterenol
Pregnancy Category: C

AVAILABILITY 12.5 mg/mL injection

ACTION & *THERAPEUTIC EFFECT*
Produces inotropic effect by acting on beta receptors and primarily on myocardial alpha-adrenergic receptors. Increases cardiac output and decreases pulmonary wedge pressure and total systemic vascular resistance with comparatively little or no effect on BP. Also increases conduction through AV node, and has lower potential for precipitating arrhythmias than dopamine. *In CHF or cardiogenic shock, increase in cardiac output enhances renal perfusion and increases renal output and renal sodium excretion.*

USES Inotropic support in short-term treatment of adults with cardiac decompensation due to depressed myocardial contractility (cardiogenic shock) resulting from either organic heart disease or from cardiac surgery.
UNLABELED USES To augment cardiovascular function in children undergoing cardiac catheterization, stress thallium testing.

CONTRAINDICATIONS History of hypersensitivity to other sympathomimetic amines or sulfites, ventricular tachycardia, idiopathic hypertrophic

subaortic stenosis; hypovolemia; pregnancy (category C).
CAUTIOUS USE Preexisting hypertension, hypotension; atrial fibrillation; acute MI; unstable angina, severe coronary artery disease.

ROUTE & DOSAGE

Cardiac Decompensation
Adult/Child: IV 2.5–15 mcg/kg/min (max: 40 mcg/kg/min)

ADMINISTRATION

Intravenous ———

***PREPARE:* Continuous:** Reconstitute by adding 10 mL sterile water for injection or D5W to 250-mg vial; if not completely dissolved, add an additional 10 mL of diluent. ▪ Further dilute to a volume of at least 50 mL with D5W, NS, LR, D5/LR, or sodium lactate injection. ▪ Use IV solutions within 24 h.
***ADMINISTER:* Continuous:** Rate of infusion is determined by body weight and controlled by an infusion pump (preferred) or a microdrip IV infusion set. ▪ IV infusion rate and duration of therapy are determined by heart rate, blood pressure, ectopic activity, urine output, and whenever possible, by measurements of cardiac output and central venous or pulmonary wedge pressures.
***INCOMPATIBILITIES* Solution/additive: Sodium bicarbonate, aminophylline, bretylium, bumetanide, calcium chloride, calcium gluconate, diazepam, doxapram, digoxin, epinephrine, furosemide, heparin, insulin, magnesium sulfate, nitroprusside sodium, phenytoin, potassium chloride,**

potassium phosphate. Y-site: Acyclovir, aminophylline, sodium bicarbonate.

- Refrigerate reconstituted solution at 2°–15° C (36°–59° F) for 48 h or store for 6 h at room temperature.

ADVERSE EFFECTS (≥1%) **All:** Generally dose related. **CNS:** Headache, tremors, paresthesias, mild leg cramps, nervousness, fatigue (with overdosage). **CV:** *Increased heart rate and BP,* premature ventricular beats, palpitation, *anginal pain.* **GI:** Nausea, vomiting. **Other:** Nonspecific chest pain, shortness of breath.

INTERACTIONS Drug: GENERAL ANESTHETICS (especially **cyclopropane** and **halothane**) may sensitize myocardium to effects of CATECHOLAMINES such as dobutamine and lead to serious arrhythmias—used with extreme caution; BETA-ADRENERGIC BLOCKING AGENTS, e.g., **metoprolol, propranolol,** may make dobutamine ineffective in increasing cardiac output, but total peripheral resistance may increase—concomitant use generally avoided; MAO INHIBITORS, TRICYCLIC ANTIDEPRESSANTS potentiate pressor effects—use with extreme caution.

PHARMACOKINETICS Onset: 2–10 min. **Peak:** 10–20 min. **Metabolism:** Metabolized in liver and other tissues by COMT. **Elimination:** In urine. **Half-Life:** 2 min.

CLINICAL IMPLICATIONS

Assessment & Drug Effects

- Correct hypovolemia by administration of appropriate volume expanders prior to initiation of therapy.
- Monitor therapeutic effectiveness. At any given dosage level, drug takes 10–20 min to produce peak effects.
- Monitor ECG and BP continuously during administration.
- Note: Marked increases in blood pressure (systolic pressure is the most likely to be affected) and heart rate, or the appearance of arrhythmias or other adverse cardiac effects are usually reversed promptly by reduction in dosage.
- Observe patients with preexisting hypertension closely for exaggerated pressor response.
- Note: Tolerance has been observed with continuous or prolonged infusions; adverse reactions are no different than those seen with shorter infusions.
- Monitor I&O ratio and pattern. Urine output and sodium excretion generally increase because of improved cardiac output and renal perfusion.

Patient & Family Education

- Report anginal pain to physician promptly.

DOCETAXEL

(doc-e-tax′el)
Taxotere
Classifications: ANTINEOPLASTIC AGENT; TAXANE AGENT
Therapeutic: ANTINEOPLASTIC
Prototype: Paclitaxel
Pregnancy Category: D

AVAILABILITY 20 mg, 80 mg injection

ACTION & *THERAPEUTIC EFFECT*

Docetaxel is a semisynthetic analog of paclitaxel. Potential advantages over paclitaxel are greater antitumor activity and lower toxicity potential. Docetaxel, like paclitaxel, binds to the microtubule network essential for interphase and mitosis of the cell cycle. *Docetaxel stabilizes the mi-*

Common adverse effects in *italic*, life-threatening effects underlined; generic names in **bold**; classifications in SMALL CAPS; ◆ Canadian drug name; ◎ Prototype drug

497

crotubules involved in cell division and prevents their normal functioning, which results in inhibiting mitosis in cancer cells.

USES Metastatic breast cancer, metastatic prostate cancer, non-small cell lung cancer.

CONTRAINDICATIONS Hypersensitivity to docetaxel or other drugs formulated with polysorbate 80, paclitaxel, neutrophil count <1500 cells/mm^3, biliary tract disease, hepatic disease, jaundice, neutropenia, intramuscular injections, thrombocytopenia, lactation, pregnancy (category D), acute infection.

CAUTIOUS USE Bone marrow suppression, bone marrow transplant patients; CHF, ascites, peripheral edema, pleural effusion; radiation therapy; pulmonary disorders, acute bronchospasm; cardiac tamponade; dental disease, dental work, herpes infection; hypotension, elderly; infection. Safety and effectiveness in children <16 y are not established.

ROUTE & DOSAGE

Breast Cancer
Adult: **IV** 60–100 mg/m^2 every 3 wk (premedicate patients with dexamethasone 8 mg b.i.d. × 5 d, starting 1 d prior to docetaxel)

Prostate Cancer
Adult: **IV** 75 mg/m^2 every 21 d plus prednisone (5 mg PO twice daily) for 10 cycles (premedicate patients with dexamethasone 8 mg q12h, 3h, and 1h prior to starting docetaxel infusion)

Non-Small Cell Lung Cancer
Adult: **IV** 75 mg/m^2 every 3 wk

ADMINISTRATION

▪ Note: If drug contacts skin during preparation, wash immediately with soap and water.

Intravenous

***PREPARE:* IV Infusion:** Bring vials to room temperature for 5 min; add provided diluent, gently rotate for 15 s; let stand until surface foam dissipates. ▪ Inject required amount of diluted solution into a 250-mL, or larger, bag of NS or D5W; the final concentration should not exceed 0.9 mg/mL. ▪Use glass or polypropylene bottles or polypropylene or polyolefin plastic bags and administer through polyethylene-lined administration sets. Do not use PVC administration sets or containers. ▪ Mix completely by manual rotation. ▪Use within 4 h (including the 1 h infusion time).

***ADMINISTER:* IV Infusion:** Give at a constant rate over 1 h. Administer ONLY after premedication with corticosteroids to prevent hypersensitivity. ▪ Reduce dose by 25% following severe neutropenia (<500 cells/mm^3) for 7 d or longer for febrile neutropenia, severe cutaneous reactions, or severe peripheral neuropathy.

▪ Refrigerate vials at 2°–8° C (36°–46° F). Protect from light. Do not store in PVC solutions. Store diluted solutions in refrigerator or at room temperature for 8 h.

ADVERSE EFFECTS (≥1%) **CNS:** Paresthesia, pain, burning sensation, weakness, confusion. **CV:** Hypotension, *fluid retention (peripheral edema, weight gain),* pleural effusion. **GI:** *Nausea, vomiting, diarrhea, stomatitis,* abdominal pain; increased liver function tests (AST or ALT). **Hematologic:** <u>Neutropenia, leukopenia, thrombocytopenia, anemia</u>, febrile neutropenia. **Skin:** Rash, localized eruptions, desquamation, *alopecia,* nail changes (hyper/hypopigmentation, onycholysis). **Body as**

a Whole: *Hypersensitivity reactions,* infusion site reactions (hyperpigmentation, inflammation, redness, dryness, phlebitis, extravasation).

INTERACTIONS Drug: Possibility of interacting with other drugs metabolized by CYP3A4.

PHARMACOKINETICS Distribution: 97% protein bound. **Metabolism:** In liver by CYP3A4. **Elimination:** 80% in feces, 20% renally. **Half-Life:** 11.1 h.

CLINICAL IMPLICATIONS

Assessment & Drug Effects

- Lab tests: Monitor bilirubin, AST or ALT, and alkaline phosphatase prior to each drug cycle. Generally, do not give to patients with elevations of bilirubin or with significant elevations of transaminases concurrent with elevations of alkaline phosphatase. Monitor frequently CBCs with differential. Withhold drug if platelets <100,000 or neutrophils <1500 cells/mm^3.
- Monitor for S&S of hypersensitivity (see Appendix F), which may develop within a few minutes of initiation of infusion. It is usually not necessary to discontinue infusion for minor reactions (i.e., flushing or local skin reaction).
- Assess throughout therapy and report cardiovascular dysfunction, respiratory distress; fluid retention; development of neurosensory symptoms; severe, cutaneous eruptions on feet, hands, arms, face, or thorax; and S&S of infection.

Patient & Family Education

- Learn common adverse effects and measures to control or minimize them when possible. Report immediately any distressing adverse effects.
- Note: It is extremely important to comply with corticosteroid therapy and monitoring of lab values.
- Avoid pregnancy during therapy.

DOCOSANOL
(doc'os-a-nol)
Abreva
Classifications: ANTIVIRAL-LIKE
Therapeutic: ANTIVIRAL-LIKE
Pregnancy Category: C

AVAILABILITY 10% cream

ACTION & *THERAPEUTIC EFFECT*
Docosanol inhibits viral replication by interfering with the early intracellular events surrounding viral entry into target cells. It exhibits preferential activity against lipid-enveloped viruses that use fusion mechanisms for entry into target cells. This renders such target cells less susceptible to viral fusion or entry. *Believed to exert its antiviral effect by inhibiting fusion of the HSV (herpesvirus) envelope with the human cell plasma membrane, therefore making it difficult for the virus to enter the cell and replicate.*

USES Treatment of herpes simplex infections of the face and lips (i.e., cold sores).

CONTRAINDICATIONS Hypersensitivity to docosanol or any of the inactive ingredients in the ointment; immunosuppressant patients; pregnancy (category C); lactation.
CAUTIOUS USE Safety and efficacy in children are not established.

ROUTE & DOSAGE

Herpes Simplex Infections

Adult: **Topical** Apply to lesions 5 times/day for up to 10 d, starting at onset of symptoms

---

Common adverse effects in *italic*, life-threatening effects <u>underlined</u>; generic names in **bold**; classifications in SMALL CAPS; ♣ Canadian drug name; ☻ Prototype drug

499

ADMINISTRATION

Topical
- Apply cream only to the affected areas using a gloved finger. Rub in gently but completely.
- Do not apply near or in the eyes.
- Avoid application to the mucous membranes inside of the mouth.
- Store at 20°–25° C (68°–77° F).

ADVERSE EFFECTS (≥1%) **CNS:** Headache. **Skin:** Skin irritation, burning.

INTERACTIONS Drug: No clinically significant interactions established.

CLINICAL IMPLICATIONS

Assessment & Drug Effects
- Monitor severity and extent of infection.
- Notify physician if improvement is not seen within 10 days of initiating treatment

Patient & Family Education
- Wash hands before and after applying cream.
- Do not share this cream with any other individual as this may spread the herpes virus.
- Report to physician if your condition worsens or does not improve within 10 days of beginning treatment.
- Report to the emergency room or contact a poison control center immediately if a significant amount of cream is swallowed.

DOCUSATE CALCIUM (DIOCTYL CALCIUM SULFOSUCCINATE) ⓟ

(dok′yoo-sate)
DCS, PMS-Docusate Calcium, Pro-Cal-Sof, Surfak

DOCUSATE POTASSIUM
Dialose, Diocto-K, Kasof

DOCUSATE SODIUM
Colace, Colace Enema, Dio-Sul, Disonate, DGSS, D-S-S, Duosol, Lax-gel, Laxinate 100, Modane Soft, Pro-Sof, Regulax ♦, Regutol, Therevac-Plus, Therevac-SB

Classifications: STOOL SOFTENER
Therapeutic: STOOL SOFTENER
Pregnancy Category: C

AVAILABILITY Docusate Calcium 50 mg, 240 mg capsules **Docusate Potassium** 100 mg tablets; 240 mg capsules **Docusate Sodium** 100 mg tablets; 50 mg, 100 mg, 240 mg, 250 mg capsules; 50 mg/15 mL 60 mg/15 mL, 150 mg/15 mL syrup

ACTION & *THERAPEUTIC EFFECT* Anionic surface-active agent with emulsifying and wetting properties. *Detergent action lowers surface tension, permitting water and fats to penetrate and soften stools for easier passage.*

USES Prophylactically in patients who should avoid straining during defecation and for treatment of constipation associated with hard, dry stools (e.g., following anorectal surgery, MI).

CONTRAINDICATIONS Atonic constipation, nausea, vomiting, abdominal pain, fecal impaction, structural anomalies of colon and rectum, intestinal obstruction or perforation; use of docusate sodium in patients on sodium restriction; use of docusate potassium in patients with renal dysfunction; concomitant use of mineral oil; pregnancy (category C).
CAUTIOUS USE History of CHF, edema, diabetes melitus.

Common adverse effects in *italic*, life-threatening effects <u>underlined</u>; generic names in **bold**; classifications in SMALL CAPS; ♦ Canadian drug name; ⓟ Prototype drug

ROUTE & DOSAGE

Stool Softener
Adult: PO 50–500 mg/d PR 50–100 mg added to enema fluid
Child: PO <3 y, 10–40 mg/d; 3–6 y, 20–60 mg/d; 6–12 y, 40–120 mg/d

ADMINISTRATION

Oral
- Give with a full glass of water if allowed.
- Store syrup formulations in tight, light-resistant containers at 15°–30° C (59°–86° F) unless directed otherwise.

Rectal
- Microenema: Insert full length of nozzle (half length for children) into the rectum. Squeeze entire contents of tube and remove completely before releasing grip on tube.
- Store in tightly covered containers.

ADVERSE EFFECTS (≥1%) **GI:** Occasional mild abdominal cramps, *diarrhea,* nausea, bitter taste. **Other:** Throat irritation (liquid preparation), rash.

INTERACTIONS Drug: Docusate will increase systemic absorption of **mineral oil.**

PHARMACOKINETICS Not studied.

CLINICAL IMPLICATIONS

Assessment & Drug Effects
- Withhold drug if diarrhea develops and notify physician.
- Therapeutic effectiveness: Usually apparent 1–3 d after first dose.

Patient & Family Education
- Take sufficient liquid with each dose and increase fluid intake during the day, if allowed. Oral liquid (NOT syrup) may be administered in milk, fruit juice, or infant formula to mask bitter taste.
- Do not take concomitantly with mineral oil.
- Do not take for prolonged periods in lieu of proper dietary management or treatment of underlying causes of constipation.

DOFETILIDE
(do-fe-ti'lyde)
Tikosyn
Classifications: ANTIARRHYTHMIC, CLASS III; POTASSIUM CHANNEL BLOCKER
Therapeutic: ANTIARRHYTHMIC, CLASS III
Prototype: Amiodarone HCl
Pregnancy Category: C

AVAILABILITY 125 mcg, 250 mcg, 500 mcg capsules

ACTION & *THERAPEUTIC EFFECT* Class III antiarrhythmic agent that prolongs the cardiac action potential by blocking the potassium channels and thus one or more of the potassium currents. Action results in suppression of arrhythmias dependent upon reentry of potassium ions. It also prolongs the atrial and ventricular refractory period. *Effectiveness indicated by correction of cardiac arrhythmias.*

USES Symptomatic atrial fibrillation and flutter.

CONTRAINDICATIONS QT prolongation; ventricular arrhythmias; history of torsades de points; hypersensitivity to dofetilide; electrolyte imbalances (e.g., hypokalemia, hypomagnesemia, etc.); renal failure; pregnancy (category C); lactation.

Common adverse effects in *italic,* life-threatening effects underlined; generic names in **bold**; classifications in SMALL CAPS; ♦ Canadian drug name; ⊙ Prototype drug

501

CAUTIOUS USE Atrioventricular block, bradycardia, CHF, concurrent administration of potassium depleting diuretics, hepatic or renal impairment; history of moderate QT_C interval prolongation; moderate to severe hypertension; recent MI or unstable angina; vascular heart disease; older adults. Safety and efficacy in children <18 y are unknown.

ROUTE & DOSAGE

Atrial Fibrillation/Flutter

Adult: **PO** Based on creatinine clearance (Cl_{cr}) and QT_c interval, if QT_c increases by >15% from baseline or is >500 msec 2–3 h after initial dose. Decrease subsequent doses by 50%

Renal Impairment

Cl_{cr} >60 mL/min: 500 mcg b.i.d.; 40–60 mL/min: 250 mcg b.i.d.; 20–39 mL/min: 125 mcg b.i.d.

ADMINISTRATION

Oral

- Do not give dofetilide if QT/QT_c interval >420 milliseconds (or >500 milliseconds with ventricular conduction abnormalities).
- Individualize doses on creatinine clearance; QT_c interval is used if HR <60 bpm.
- Administer only with continuous ECG monitoring.
- Do not initiate therapy until 3 mo after withdrawal of previous antiarrhythmic therapy.
- Do not initiate therapy until 3 mo after amiodarone has been withdrawn or plasma level is <0.3 mcg/mL.
- Store at 15°–30° C (59°–86° F); protect from moisture and humidity.

ADVERSE EFFECTS (≥1%) **Body as a Whole:** Flu-like syndrome, back

pain. **CNS:** *Headache,* dizziness, insomnia. **CV:** <u>Torsades de pointes arrhythmia, *ventricular arrhythmias,*</u> AV block, *chest pain.* **GI:** Nausea, diarrhea, abdominal pain. **Respiratory:** Respiratory infection, dyspnea. **Skin:** Rash.

INTERACTIONS Drug: Dofetilide levels increased by **verapamil, cimetidine, trimethoprim, ketoconazole, prochlorperazine, megestrol;** do not give with drugs known to increase the QT_c interval such as **bepridil,** PHENOTHIAZINE, TRICYCLIC ANTIDEPRESSANTS, ORAL MACROLIDES, other ANTIARRHYTHMICS.

PHARMACOKINETICS Absorption: >90% bioavailable. **Peak:** 2–3 h. **Distribution:** 60–70% protein bound. **Metabolism:** In liver. **Elimination:** Primarily excreted unchanged in urine. **Half-Life:** 10 h.

CLINICAL IMPLICATIONS

Assessment & Drug Effects

- Monitor ECG continuously during first 3 mo of therapy; then periodically.
- Do not discharge patient until 12 h after conversion to normal sinus rhythm.
- Lab tests: Baseline and periodic serum electrolytes (including magnesium), periodic CBC, and routine blood chemistry. Serum potassium must be within normal limits prior to and throughout therapy with dofetilide.
- Notify physician immediately of electrolyte imbalances, especially hypokalemia and hypomagnesemia.

Patient & Family Education

- Report immediately conditions that cause potassium loss (e.g., prolonged vomiting, diarrhea, excessive sweating).

- Do **NOT** take concurrently cimetidine, verapamil, ketoconazole, trimethoprim.

DOLASETRON MESYLATE

(dol-a-se'tron)
Anzemet

Classifications: ANTIEMETIC; SELECTIVE SEROTONIN (5-HT$_3$) RECEPTOR ANTAGONIST
Therapeutic: ANTIEMETIC
Prototype: Ondansetron
Pregnancy Category: B

AVAILABILITY 50 mg, 100 mg tablets; 20 mg/mL injection

ACTION & *THERAPEUTIC EFFECT*
Dolasetron is a selective serotonin (5-HT$_3$) receptor antagonist used for control of nausea and vomiting associated with cancer chemotherapy. Serotonin receptors affected by dolasetron are located in the chemoreceptor trigger zone (CTZ) of the brain and peripherally on the vagal nerve terminal. Serotonin, released from the cells of the small intestine, activate 5-HT$_3$ receptors located on vagal efferent neurons, thus initiating the vomiting reflex. Dolasetron causes ECG changes lasting from 6 to 24 h. *Has antiemetic properties that help patients on chemotherapy.*

USES Prevention of nausea and vomiting from emetogenic chemotherapy, prevention and treatment of postoperative nausea and vomiting.

CONTRAINDICATIONS Hypersensitivity to dolasetron. Safety and efficacy in children <2 y are not established.
CAUTIOUS USE Patients who have or may develop prolongation of cardiac conduction intervals, particularly QT$_c$ (i.e., patients with hypokalemia, hypomagnesemia, diuretics, congenital QT syndrome; patients taking antiarrhythmic drugs and high-dose anthracycline therapy, etc.), pregnancy (category B), and lactation.

ROUTE & DOSAGE

Prevention of Chemotherapy-induced Nausea and Vomiting
Adult/Child (>2 y): **IV** 1.8 mg/kg or 100 mg administered 30 min prior to chemotherapy **PO** 100 mg 1 h prior to chemotherapy

Pre-/Postoperative Nausea and Vomiting
Adult: **IV** 12.5 mg 15 min before cessation of anesthesia or when post-op nausea and vomiting occurs **PO** 100 mg within 2 h prior to surgery
Child (>2 y): **IV** 0.35 mg/kg up to 12.5 mg 15 min before cessation of anesthesia or when post-op nausea and vomiting occurs **PO** 1.2 mg/kg up to 100 mg starting 2 h prior to surgery (may also mix IV formulation in apple or apple-grape juice and administer orally)

ADMINISTRATION

Oral
- Give dissolved in apple or apple-grape juice 1 h before chemotherapy.
- Give within 2 h before surgery, when used for post-op nausea.

Intravenous

PREPARE: Direct: Give undiluted. **IV Infusion:** Dilute in 50 mL of any of the following: NS, D5W, D5/0.45% NaCl, LR.
ADMINISTER: Direct: Inject undiluted drug over 30 s. **IV Infusion:** Infuse diluted drug over 15 min.

Common adverse effects in *italic*, life-threatening effects underlined; generic names in **bold**; classifications in SMALL CAPS; ♣ Canadian drug name; ⊙ Prototype drug

503

▪ Store at 20°–25° C (66°–77° F) and protect from light. ▪ Diluted IV solution may be stored refrigerated up to 48 h.

ADVERSE EFFECTS (≥1%) **Body as a Whole:** Fever, fatigue, pain, chills or shivering. **CNS:** *Headache*, dizziness, drowsiness. **CV:** Hypertension. **GI:** *Diarrhea*, increased LFTs, abdominal pain. **Genitourinary:** Urinary retention.

PHARMACOKINETICS Absorption: Rapidly absorbed from GI tract. **Peak:** 0.6 h IV, 1 h PO. **Distribution:** Crosses placenta, distributed into breast milk. **Metabolism:** Metabolized to hydrodolasetron by carbonyl reductase. Hydrodolasetron is metabolized in the liver by CYP2D6. **Elimination:** Primarily in urine as hydrodolasetron. **Half-Life:** 10 min dolasetron, 7.3 h hydrodolasetron.

CLINICAL IMPLICATIONS

Assessment & Drug Effects

▪ Therapeutic effectiveness: Prevention of nausea and vomiting.
▪ Determine serum electrolytes before initiating drug. Hypokalemia and hypomagnesemia should be correct before initiating therapy.
▪ Monitor closely cardiac status especially with vomiting, excess diuresis, or other conditions that may result in electrolyte imbalances.
▪ Monitor ECG, especially in those taking concurrent antiarrhythmic or other drugs that may cause QT prolongation.
▪ Monitor for and report signs of bleeding (e.g., hematuria, epistaxis, purpura, hematoma).
▪ Lab tests: With prolonged therapy, periodically monitor liver functions, PTT, CBC with platelet count, and alkaline phosphatase.

Patient & Family Education

▪ Headache requiring analgesic for relief is a common adverse effect.

DONEPEZIL HYDROCHLORIDE ℗ℛ

(don-e′pe-zil)
Aricept, Aricept ODT
Classifications: CHOLINERGIC, CENTRAL ACTING; CHOLINESTERASE INHIBITOR
Therapeutic: ANTIDEMENTIA
Pregnancy Category: C

AVAILABILITY 5 mg, 10 mg tablets and orally disintegrating tablets

ACTION & *THERAPEUTIC EFFECT*
In early stages of Alzheimer's disease, pathologic changes in neurons result in deficiency of acetylcholine. Aricept, a cholinesterase inhibitor, presumably elevates acetylcholine concentration in the cerebral cortex by slowing degrading acetylcholine released by remaining intact neurons. *Improves global function, cognition, and behavior of patients with mild to moderate Alzheimer's.*

USES Mild to moderate dementia of Alzheimer's type.

CONTRAINDICATIONS Hypersensitivity to donepezil or tracine; pregnancy (category C), lactation; children; GI bleeding, jaundice.
CAUTIOUS USE Anesthesia, sick sinus rhythm, AV block, bradycardia, cardiac arrhythmias, cardiac disease, hypotension; hyperthyroidism, history of ulcers, abnormal liver function; patients with asthma or obstructive pulmonary disease, history of seizures, seizures, urinary tract obstruction, intestinal obstruction;

---

diarrhea, emesis, GI disease, renal failure, renal impairment, surgery.

ROUTE & DOSAGE

Alzheimer's Disease
Adult: **PO** 5–10 mg h.s.

ADMINISTRATION

Oral
- Give at h.s. just prior to going to bed.
- Increase dosage to 10 mg ONLY after 4–6 wk of therapy with the 5-mg dose.
- Store at 15°–30° C (59°–86° F).

ADVERSE EFFECTS (≥1%) **Body as a Whole:** *Headache,* fatigue. **CNS:** *Insomnia,* dizziness, depression, tremor, irritability, vertigo, ataxia. **CV:** Syncope, hypertension, atrial fibrillation, hot flashes, hypotension. **GI:** *Nausea, diarrhea, vomiting, muscle cramps, anorexia,* GI bleeding, bloating, fecal incontinence, epigastric pain. **Respiratory:** Dyspnea. **Skin:** Pruritus, sweating, urticaria. **Other:** Ecchymoses, muscle cramps, dehydration, blurred vision, urinary incontinence, nocturia.

INTERACTIONS Drug: Ketoconazole, quinidine may inhibit donepezil metabolism; **carbamazepine, dexamethasone, phenobarbital, phenytoin, rifampin** may increase donepezil elimination; donepezil may interfere with the action of ANTICHOLINERGIC AGENTS.

PHARMACOKINETICS Absorption: Rapidly absorbed from GI tract. **Peak:** 3–4 h. **Distribution:** 96% protein bound. **Metabolism:** Metabolized in the liver by CYP2D6 and CYP3A4 to at least 2 active metabolites. **Elimination:** Primarily in urine. **Half-Life:** 70 h.

CLINICAL IMPLICATIONS

Assessment & Drug Effects
- Monitor therapeutic effectiveness: Improvement as noted on the Alzheimer's Disease Assessment Scale.
- Monitor closely for S&S of GI ulceration and bleeding, especially with concurrent use of NSAIDS.
- Monitor carefully patients with a history of asthma or obstructive pulmonary disease.
- Monitor cardiovascular status; drug may have vagotonic effect on the heart, causing bradycardia, especially in presence of conduction abnormalities.

Patient & Family Education
- Exercise caution. Fainting episodes related to slowing the heart rate may occur.
- Report immediately to physician any S&S of GI ulceration or bleeding (e.g., "coffee-grounds" emesis, tarry stools, epigastric pain).

DOPAMINE HYDROCHLORIDE
(doe′pa-meen)
Classifications: ALPHA- AND BETA-ADRENERGIC AGONIST
Therapeutic: CARDIAC STIMULANT; ADRENERGIC AGONIST
Prototype: Epinephrine
Pregnancy Category: C

AVAILABILITY 40 mg/mL, 80 mg/mL, 160 mg/mL injection

ACTION & *THERAPEUTIC EFFECT*
Major cardiovascular effects produced by direct action on alpha- and beta-adrenergic receptors and on specific dopaminergic receptors in mesenteric and renal vascular beds. Positive inotropic effect on myocardium increases cardiac output with increase in systolic and

Common adverse effects in *italic*, life-threatening effects <u>underlined</u>; generic names in **bold**, classifications in SMALL CAPS; ♣ Canadian drug name; ☻ Prototype drug

505

D

pulse pressure and little or no effect on diastolic pressure. Improves circulation to renal vascular bed by decreasing renal vascular resistance with resulting increase in glomerular filtration rate and urinary output. *Hemodynamic effects of dopamine are dose-dependent. Due to its potential for inotropic, chronotropic, and vasopressor effects, dopamine has several clinical uses, including decreased cardiac output, as well as correction of hypotension associated with cardiogenic and septic shock.*

USES To correct hemodynamic imbalance in shock syndrome due to MI (cardiogenic shock), trauma, endotoxic septicemia (septic shock), open heart surgery, and CHF.

UNLABELED USES Acute renal failure; cirrhosis; hepatorenal syndrome; barbiturate intoxication.

CONTRAINDICATIONS Pheochromocytoma; tachyarrhythmias or ventricular fibrillation; pregnancy (category C).

CAUTIOUS USE Patients with history of occlusive vascular disease (e.g., Buerger's or Raynaud's disease); CAD; cold injury; acute MI; diabetic endarteritis, arterial embolism; neonates, lactation.

ROUTE & DOSAGE

Shock

Adult/Child: **IV** 2–5 mcg/kg/min increased gradually up to 20–50 mcg/kg/min if necessary

ADMINISTRATION

Intravenous ⎯⎯⎯⎯⎯⎯⎯

PREPARE: **Continuous:** Dilute just prior to administration. ▪ Dilute each ampule in one of the following: D5W, D5/NS, D5/LR,

D5/0.45% NaCl, NS. ▪ Dilute 200 mg ampule in 250 mL, 500 mL, or 1000 mL IV solution to yield 800 mcg/mL, 400 mcg/mL, or 200 mcg/mL, respectively. Dilute 400 mg ampule in 250 mL, 500 mL, or 1000 mL IV solution to yield 1600 mcg/mL, 800 mcg/mL or 400 mcg/mL, respectively. ▪ Dilute 800 mg ampule in 250 mL, 500 mL, or 1000 mL IV solution to yield 3200 mcg/mL, 1600 mcg/mL or 800 mcg/mL, respectively. ▪ Consult package information for other dilutions.

ADMINISTER: **Continuous:** Infusion rate is based on body weight. ▪ Infusion rate and guidelines for adjusting rate relative changes in blood pressure are prescribed by physician. ▪ Microdrip and other reliable metering device should be used for accuracy of flow rate.

INCOMPATIBILITIES **Solution/additive: Sodium bicarbonate, aminophylline, amphotericin B, ampicillin, cephalothin, penicillin G. Y-site: Acyclovir, aminophylline, amphotericin B, sodium bicarbonate.**

▪ Correct hypovolemia, if possible, with either whole blood or plasma before initiation of dopamine therapy. ▪ Monitor infusion continuously for free flow, and take care to avoid extravasation, which can result in tissue sloughing and gangrene. Use a large vein of the antecubital fossa. ▪ Antidote for extravasation: Stop infusion promptly and remove needle. Immediately infiltrate the ischemic area with 5–10 mg phentolamine mesylate in 10–15 mL of NS, using syringe and fine needle. ▪ Protect dopamine from light. Discolored solutions should not be used.

Common adverse effects in *italic*, life-threatening effects underlined; generic names in **bold**; classifications in SMALL CAPS; ✤ Canadian drug name; ⓟ Prototype drug

• Store reconstituted solution for 24 h at 2°–15° C (36°–59° F) or 6 h at room temperature 15°–30° C.

ADVERSE EFFECTS (≥1%) **CV:** *Hypotension,* ectopic beats, *tachycardia,* anginal pain, palpitation, vasoconstriction (indicated by disproportionate rise in diastolic pressure), cold extremities; less frequent: aberrant conduction, bradycardia, widening of QRS complex, elevated blood pressure. **GI:** Nausea, vomiting. **CNS:** Headache. **Skin:** Necrosis, tissue sloughing with extravasation, gangrene, piloerection. **Other:** Azotemia, dyspnea, dilated pupils (high doses).

DIAGNOSTIC TEST INTERFERENCE Dopamine may modify test response when histamine is used as a control for *intradermal skin tests.*

INTERACTIONS Drug: MAO INHIBITORS, ERGOT ALKALOIDS, increase alpha-adrenergic effects (headache, hyperpyrexia, hypertension); **guanethidine, phenytoin** may decrease dopamine action; BETA BLOCKERS antagonize cardiac effects; ALPHA BLOCKERS antagonize peripheral vasoconstriction; **halothane, cyclopropane** increase risk of hypertension and ventricular arrhythmias.

PHARMACOKINETICS Onset: <5 min. **Duration:** <10 min. **Distribution:** Widely distributed; does not cross blood–brain barrier. **Metabolism:** Inactive in the liver, kidney, and plasma by monoamine oxidase and COMT. **Elimination:** In urine. **Half-Life:** 2 min.

CLINICAL IMPLICATIONS
Assessment & Drug Effects
• Monitor blood pressure, pulse, peripheral pulses, and urinary output at intervals prescribed by physician. Precise measurements are essential for accurate titration of dosage.

• Report the following indicators promptly to physician for use in decreasing or temporarily suspending dose: Reduced urine flow rate in absence of hypotension; ascending tachycardia; dysrhythmias; disproportionate rise in diastolic pressure (marked decrease in pulse pressure); signs of peripheral ischemia (pallor, cyanosis, mottling, coldness, complaints of tenderness, pain, numbness, or burning sensation).

• Monitor therapeutic effectiveness. In addition to improvement in vital signs and urine flow, other indices of adequate dosage and perfusion of vital organs include loss of pallor, increase in toe temperature, adequacy of nail bed capillary filling, and reversal of confusion or comatose state.

DORNASE ALFA
(dor′naze)
Pulmozyme
Classifications: MUCOLYTIC
Therapeutic: MUCOLYTIC
Pregnancy Category: B

AVAILABILITY 1 mg/mL solution for inhalation

ACTION & THERAPEUTIC EFFECT
Dornase is a solution of recombinant human deoxyribonuclease (DNAse), an enzyme that selectively cleaves DNA. In cystic fibrosis (CF) patients, viscous, purulent secretions in the airway reduce pulmonary function and lead to exacerbations of infection. Purulent pulmonary secretions contain very high concentrations of DNA released by degenerating leukocytes

Common adverse effects in *italic*, life-threatening effects underlined; generic names in **bold**; classifications in SMALL CAPS; ◆ Canadian drug name; ⦿ Prototype drug

507

D

that are present in response to infection. *Dornase hydrolyzes the DNA in sputum of CF patients and reduces sputum viscosity. Use of dornase significantly reduces number of upper respiratory infections acquired by patients with CF.*

USES In combination with standard therapies to reduce the frequency of respiratory infections in patients with CF and to improve pulmonary function.

UNLABELED USES Chronic bronchitis.

CONTRAINDICATIONS Hypersensitivity to dornase or hamster protein; infants <3 mo.

CAUTIOUS USE Pregnancy (category B), lactation.

ROUTE & DOSAGE

Cystic Fibrosis
Adult/Child: **Inhalation** *>3 mo,* 2.5 mg (1 ampule) inhaled once daily using a recommended nebulizer, may increase to twice daily (do not mix with other agents in nebulizer)

ADMINISTRATION

Inhalation
- Do not dilute or mix with any other drugs or solutions in the nebulizer.
- Use only with nebulizer systems recommended by the drug manufacturer.
- Do not shake ampuls; do not use ampuls that have been at room temperature longer than 24 h or have become cloudy or discolored.
- Store refrigerated at 2°–8° C (36°–46° F) in protective foil pouch.

ADVERSE EFFECTS (≥1%) **Respiratory:** Hoarseness, sore throat, voice alterations, pharyngitis, laryngitis, cough, rhinitis. **Other:** Conjunctivitis, chest pain, rash.

PHARMACOKINETICS Absorption: Minimal systemic absorption. **Onset:** 3–8 d. **Duration:** Benefit lasts up to 4 d after discontinuing treatment.

CLINICAL IMPLICATIONS

Assessment & Drug Effects
- Monitor for improvement in dyspnea and sputum clearance.
- Monitor for S&S of hypersensitivity (see Appendix F). Patients with a history of hypersensitivity to bovine pancreatic dornase are at high risk.
- Monitor for adverse effects; rarely, dosage adjustments may be required.

Patient & Family Education
- Report rash, hives, itching, or other S&S of hypersensitivity to physician immediately.
- Know potential adverse effects and report those that are bothersome or do not disappear.
- Take a missed dose as soon as possible; if it is almost time for the next dose, skip the missed dose.

DORZOLAMIDE HYDROCHLORIDE
(dor-zol′a-mide)
Trusopt
Classifications: EYE PREPARATION; CARBONIC ANHYDRASE INHIBITOR
Therapeutic: CARBONIC ANHYDRASE INHIBITOR
Prototype: Acetazolamide
Pregnancy Category: C

AVAILABILITY 2% ophthalmic solution

ACTION & *THERAPEUTIC EFFECT*
Dorzolamide is a sulfonamide and

inhibits carbonic anhydrase in the eye, thus reducing the rate of aqueous humor formation with subsequent lowering of IOP. Elevated IOP is a major risk factor in the pathogenesis of optic nerve damage and visual field loss due to glaucoma. *Lowers IOP in glaucoma or ocular hypertension.*

USES Elevated intraocular pressure in patients with ocular hypertension or open-angle glaucoma.

CONTRAINDICATIONS Previous hypersensitivity to dorzolamide; pregnancy (category C).
CAUTIOUS USE History of hypersensitivity to other carbonic anhydrase inhibitors, sulfonamides, or thiazide diuretics; ocular infection or inflammation; recent ocular surgery; moderate-to-severe renal or hepatic insufficiency; angle-closure glaucoma; concomitant use of oral carbonic anhydrase inhibitors; older adults, corneal abrasion.

ROUTE & DOSAGE

Glaucoma, Ocular Hypertension
Adult/Child: **Ophthalmic** 1 drop in affected eye t.i.d.

ADMINISTRATION

Instillation
- Apply gentle pressure to lacrimal sac during and immediately following drug instillation for about 1 min to lessen degree of systemic absorption.
- Administer at least 10 min apart, if another ophthalmic drug is being used concurrently.
- Store at 15°–30° C (59°–86° F).

ADVERSE EFFECTS (≥1%) **CNS:** Headache. **GI:** Bitter taste, nausea. **Special Senses:** *Transient burning or stinging, transient blurred vision,*

superficial punctate keratitis, tearing, dryness, photophobia, ocular allergic reaction. **Skin:** Rash.

PHARMACOKINETICS Absorption: Some systemic absorption from topical instillation. **Onset:** 2 h. **Duration:** 8–12 h. **Distribution:** Distributes into red blood cells. **Elimination:** In urine. **Half-Life:** RBC elimination about 4 mo.

CLINICAL IMPLICATIONS

Assessment & Drug Effects
- Inquire about previous hypersensitivity to sulfonamides prior to therapy.
- Withhold drug and notify physician if S&S of local or systemic hypersensitivity occur (see Appendix F).
- Withhold the drug and notify the physician if ocular irritation occurs.
- Lab tests: Monitor CBC, serum electrolytes, and renal and liver function tests periodically with long-term therapy.

Patient & Family Education
- Learn proper technique for applying eyedrops.
- Do not allow tip of drug dispenser to come in contact with the eye.
- Discontinue drug and report to physician: ocular irritation, infection, or S&S of systemic hypersensitivity occur (see Appendix F).

DOXAPRAM HYDROCHLORIDE

(dox′a-pram)
Dopram
Classifications: CEREBRAL STIMULANT
Therapeutic: CEREBRAL STIMULANT
Prototype: Caffeine
Pregnancy Category: B

AVAILABILITY 20 mg/mL injection

Common adverse effects in *italic*, life-threatening effects underlined; generic names in **bold**; classifications in SMALL CAPS; ♣ Canadian drug name; ☺ Prototype drug

509

D

ACTION & *THERAPEUTIC EFFECT*

Short-acting analeptic capable of stimulating all levels of the cerebrospinal axis. Respiratory stimulation by direct medullary action or possibly by indirect activation of peripheral chemoreceptors increases tidal volume and slightly increases respiratory rate. *Decreases Pco_2 and increases Po_2 by increasing alveolar ventilation; may elevate BP and pulse rate by stimulation of brainstem vasomotor area. It is used to stimulate respiration postanesthesia, for drug-induced CNS depression, and for chronic pulmonary disease associated with acute hypercapnia.*

USES Short-term adjunctive therapy to alleviate postanesthesia and drug-induced respiratory depression and to hasten arousal and return of pharyngeal and laryngeal reflexes. Also as a temporary measure (approximately 2 h) in hospitalized patients with COPD associated with acute respiratory insufficiency as an aid to prevent elevation of $Paco_2$ during administration of oxygen. (Not used with mechanical ventilation.)

UNLABELED USES Neonatal apnea refractory to xanthine therapy.

CONTRAINDICATIONS Epilepsy and other convulsive disorders; of ventilatory mechanism due to muscle paresis, pulmonary fibrosis, flail chest, pneumothorax, airway obstruction, extreme dyspnea, or acute bronchial asthma; severe hypertension, coronary artery disease, uncompensated heart failure, CVA; MAOI; lactation; children <12 y.

CAUTIOUS USE History of bronchial asthma, COPD; cardiac disease, severe tachycardia, arrhythmias, hypertension; hyperthyroidism; pheochromocytoma; head injury,

cerebral edema, increased intracranial pressure; peptic ulcer, patients undergoing gastric surgery; acute agitation; pregnancy (category B).

ROUTE & DOSAGE

Postanesthesia
Adult: **IV** 0.5–1 mg/kg single injection not to exceed 1.5 mg/kg or 2 mg/kg total dose when repeated at 5 min intervals or 1–3 mg/min infusion (max: 4 mg/kg or 300 mg, not to exceed 3 g/d)

Drug-Induced CNS Depression
Adult: **IV** 1–2 mg/kg repeat in 5 min, then q1–2h until patient awakens [if relapse occurs, resume q1–2h injections (max: total dose 3 g), if no response after priming dose, may give 1–3 mg/min for up to 2 h until patient awakens]

Chronic Obstructive Pulmonary Disease
Adult: **IV** 1–2 mg/min for a max of 2 h (max: rate 3 mg/min)

Neonatal Apnea
Neonate: **IV** 2.5–3 mg/kg followed by 1 mg/kg/h (titrate to max: 2.5 mg/kg/h)

ADMINISTRATION

- IV administration to neonates: Verify correct IV concentration and rate of infusion with physician. Generally do not use in newborns because doxapram contains benzyl alcohol.
- Ensure adequacy of airway and oxygenation before initiation of doxapram therapy.

Intravenous

PREPARE: Direct: Give undiluted. **IV Infusion:** Dilute 250 mg (12.5 mL) in 250 mL of D5W or NS.

Common adverse effects in *italic*, life-threatening effects underlined; generic names in **bold**; classifications in SMALL CAPS; ♣ Canadian drug name; ⊘ Prototype drug

- Report to the physician episodes of dizziness or palpitations. These will require a dosage adjustment.

DOXEPIN HYDROCHLORIDE

(dox'e-pin)

Adapin, Sinequan, Triadapin ◆, Zonalon

Classifications: PSYCHOTHERAPEUTIC; TRICYCLIC ANTIDEPRESSANT; ANXIOLYTIC
Therapeutic: TRICYCLIC ANTIDEPRESSANT; ANTIANXIETY AGENT
Prototype: Imipramine
Pregnancy Category: C

AVAILABILITY 10 mg, 25 mg, 50 mg, 75 mg, 100 mg, 150 mg capsules; 10 mg/mL oral concentrate

ACTION & *THERAPEUTIC EFFECT*

Dibenzoxepin is one of the most sedating tricyclic antidepressants (TCAs). Inhibits serotonin reuptake from the synaptic gap; also inhibits norepinephrine reuptake to a moderate degree. Recent evidence suggests that the upset of monoamine oxidase output seen in depressed patients may be regulated by long-term treatment with antidepressants due to their action on beta-adrenergic receptors. This action on beta-receptors may be a better explanation than the reuptake theory for TCAs' antidepressant effects. *Effective for treatment of both depression and anxiety.*

USES Psychoneurotic anxiety or depressive reactions; mixed symptoms of anxiety and depression; anxiety or depression associated with alcoholism; organic disease; psychotic depressive disorders; topical for treatment of pruritus.

UNLABELED USES Peptic ulcer disease, neuralgia.

CONTRAINDICATIONS Prior sensitivity to any TCA; during acute recovery phase following MI; bundle-branch block, cardiac arrhythmias, QT prolongation; ileus; glaucoma; increased intraocular pressure; prostatic hypertrophy; tendency for urinary retention; concurrent use of MAO inhibitors; pregnancy (category C), lactation. Safe use in children <12 y is not established.
CAUTIOUS USE Patients receiving electroconvulsive therapy, patients with suicidal tendency, bipolar disorder, schizophrenia, psychosis; diabetes mellitus; GI disease; GERD; Parkinson's disease; seizure disorders; renal, cardiovascular, or hepatic dysfunction.

ROUTE & DOSAGE

Antidepressant

Adult: **PO** 30–150 mg/d h.s. or in divided doses, may gradually increase to 300 mg/d (use lower doses in older adult patients)
Geriatric: **PO** 10–25 mg h.s., may gradually increase to 75 mg/d
Child: **PO** 1–3 mg/kg/d in single or divided doses

Pruritus

Adult: **Topical** Apply a thin film q.i.d. with at least 3–4 h between applications, may use up to 8 d

ADMINISTRATION

Oral

- Give oral concentrate diluted with approximately 120 mL water, milk, or fruit juice.
- Empty capsule and swallow contents with fluid or mix with food as necessary if it cannot be swallowed whole.

Common adverse effects in *italic*, life-threatening effects underlined; generic names in **bold**; classifications in SMALL CAPS; ◆ Canadian drug name; ☻ Prototype drug

513

D

- Inform physician if daytime sedation is pronounced. Entire daily dose (up to 150 mg) may be prescribed for bedtime administration.

Topical

- Apply a thin film to affected areas; allow 3–4 h between applications.
- Store all forms at 15°–30° C (59°–86° F) in tightly closed, light-resistant container.

ADVERSE EFFECTS (≥1%) **All:** Anticholinergic. **CNS:** *Drowsiness,* dizziness, weakness, fatigue, headache, hypomania, confusion, tremors, paresthesias. **CV:** *Orthostatic hypotension,* palpitation, hypertension, tachycardia, ECG changes. **Special Senses:** Mydriasis, blurred vision, photophobia. **GI:** *Dry-mouth,* sour or metallic taste, epigastric distress, constipation. **Urogenital:** Urinary retention, delayed micturition, urinary frequency. **Other:** Increased perspiration, tinnitus, weight gain, photosensitivity reaction, skin rash, agranulocytosis, *burning or stinging at application site,* edema.

INTERACTIONS Drug: May decrease some antihypertensive response to ANTIHYPERTENSIVES; CNS DEPRESSANTS, **alcohol,** HYPNOTICS, BARBITURATES, SEDATIVES potentiate CNS depression; may increase hypoprothrombinemic effect of ORAL ANTICOAGULANTS; **ethchlorvynol** may cause transient delirium; **levodopa,** SYMPATHOMIMETICS (e.g., **epinephrine, norepinephrine**) introduce possibility of sympathetic hyperactivity with hypertension and hyperpyrexia; MAO INHIBITORS introduce possibility of severe reactions, toxic psychosis, cardiovascular instability; **methylphenidate** increases plasma TCA levels; THYROID AGENTS may increase possibility of arrhythmias; **cimetidine** may increase plasma TCA levels. **Herbal:** Ginkgo may decrease seizure threshold; **St. John's wort** may cause **serotonin** syndrome.

PHARMACOKINETICS Absorption: Rapidly absorbed from GI sites through intact skin. **Peak:** 2 h. **Distribution:** Crosses placenta; distributed into breast milk. **Metabolism:** In liver. **Elimination:** Primarily in urine. **Half-Life:** 6–8 h.

CLINICAL IMPLICATIONS

Assessment & Drug Effects

- Monitor use of other CNS depressants, including alcohol. Danger of overdosage or suicide attempt is increased when patient uses excessive amounts of alcohol.
- Be alert to changes in voiding and evaluate patient for constipation and abdominal distention; drug has moderate to strong anticholinergic effects.

Patient & Family Education

- Maintain established dosage regimen and avoid change of intervals, doubling, reducing, or skipping doses.
- Consult physician about safe amount of alcohol, if any, that can be taken. The actions of both alcohol and doxepin are potentiated when used together and for up to 2 wk after doxepin is discontinued.
- Do not drive or engage in other potentially hazardous activities until response to drug is known.

DOXERCALCIFEROL

(dox-er-kal′si-fe-rol)

Hectorol

Classifications: VITAMIN D ANALOG
Therapeutic: ANTIHYPERPARATHYROID AGENT; VITAMIN D ANALOG
Prototype: Calcitriol
Pregnancy Category: B

Common adverse effects in *italic*, life-threatening effects <u>underlined</u>; generic names in **bold**; classifications in SMALL CAPS; ◆ Canadian drug name; ⊚ Prototype drug

AVAILABILITY 0.5 mcg, 2.5 mcg capsule; 2 mcg/mL injection

ACTION & *THERAPEUTIC EFFECT*
Vitamin D$_2$ analog that is activated by the liver. Activated vitamin D is needed for absorption of dietary calcium in the intestine, and the parathyroid hormone (PTH), which mobilizes calcium from the bone tissue. *Regulates the blood calcium level.*

USES Reduction of elevated iPTH in secondary hyperparathyroidism in patients undergoing chronic renal dialysis; secondary hyperparathyroidism in chronic kidney disease not on dialysis.

CONTRAINDICATIONS Hypersensitivity to doxercalciferol or other vitamin D analogs; recent hypercalcemia, recent hyperphosphatemia, hypervitaminosis D.
CAUTIOUS USE Renal or hepatic insufficiency; renal osteodystrophy with hyperphosphatemia, prolonged hypercalcemia; pregnancy (category B), lactation. Safety and efficacy in children are not established.

ROUTE & DOSAGE

Secondary Hyperparathyroidism
Adult: **PO** 10 mcg 3 times per wk at dialysis, adjust dose as needed to lower iPTH into the range of 150–300 pg/mL by increasing the dose in 2.5 mcg increments every 8 wks (max: 60 mcg/wk) **IV** 4 mcg 3 times/wk at end of dialysis (max: 18 mcg/wk)

ADMINISTRATION

Oral
- Give at time of dialysis.
- Withhold drug and notify physician if any of the following occurs: iPTH <100 pg/mL, hypercalcemia,

hyperphosphatemia, or product of serum calcium times serum phosphorus >70.
- Use beyond 16 wk is not recommended.
- Store at 20°–25° C (66°–77° F); excursions to 15°–30° C (59°–86° F) are permitted.

Intravenous

***PREPARE:* Direct:** No dilution is needed. ▪ Withdraw appropriate dose from ampule using a filter needle. ▪ Change needles before injecting as an IV bolus. Discard any unused portion.
***ADMINISTER:* Direct:** Give a bolus injection at the end of dialysis sessions.

- Store at 15°–20° C (59°–77° F).

ADVERSE EFFECTS (≥1%) **Body as a Whole:** Abscess, *headache, malaise,* arthralgia. **CNS:** *Dizziness,* sleep disorder. **CV:** Bradycardia, *edema.* **GI:** Anorexia, constipation, dyspepsia, *nausea, vomiting.* **Respiratory:** *Dyspnea.* **Skin:** Pruritus. **Other:** Weight gain.

INTERACTIONS Drug: Cholesty-ramine, mineral oil may decrease absorption; MAGNESIUM-CONTAINING ANTACIDS may cause hypermagnesemia; other VIT D ANALOGS may increase toxicity and hypercalcemia.

PHARMACOKINETICS Absorption: Absorbed from GI tract and is activated in the liver. **Peak:** 11–12 h. **Metabolism:** Activated by CYP 27 to form 1alpha, 25-(OH)$_2$D$_2$ (major metabolite) and 1alpha, 24-dihy-droxyvitamin D$_2$ (minor metabolite). **Half-Life:** 32–37 h.

CLINICAL IMPLICATIONS

Assessment & Drug Effects
- Lab tests: Baseline and periodic iPTH, serum calcium, serum phos-

Common adverse effects in *italic*, life-threatening effects underlined; generic names in **bold**; classifications in SMALL CAPS; ✚ Canadian drug name; ◔ Prototype drug

515

phorus. Monitor levels weekly during dose titration.

- Monitor for S&S of hypercalcemia (see Appendix F).

Patient & Family Education

- Do not take antacids without consulting the physician.
- Notify the physician if you become pregnant while taking this drug.
- Do not use mineral oil on the days doxercalciferol is taken. Mineral oil may decrease absorption of drug.
- Do not take nonprescription drugs containing magnesium while taking doxercalciferol.
- Report S&S of hypercalcemia immediately: Bone or muscle pain, dry mouth with metallic taste, rhinorrhea, itching, photophobia, conjunctivitis, frequent urination, anorexia and weight loss.

DOXORUBICIN HYDROCHLORIDE ℞

(dox-oh-roo'bi-sin)
Adriamycin, Rubex

DOXORUBICIN LIPOSOME

Doxil
Classifications: ANTINEOPLASTIC; ANTIBIOTIC
Therapeutic: ANTINEOPLASTIC; ANTIBIOTIC
Pregnancy Category: D

AVAILABILITY 10 mg, 20 mg, 50 mg, 100 mg, 150 mg powder for injection; 2 mg/mL injection; 20 mg liposomal injection

ACTION & *THERAPEUTIC EFFECT*
Cytotoxic antibiotic with wide spectrum of antitumor activity and strong immunosuppressive properties. Intercalates with preformed DNA residues, blocking effective DNA and RNA transcription. A potent radiosensitizer capable of enhancing radiation reactions. *Highly destructive to rapidly proliferating cells and slowly developing carcinomas; selectively toxic to cardiac tissue.*

USES To produce regression in neoplastic conditions, including acute lymphoblastic and myeloblastic leukemias, Wilms' tumor, neuroblastoma, soft tissue and bone sarcomas, breast and ovary carcinomas, lymphomas, bronchogenic carcinoma, ovarian cancer relapse. Generally used in combined modalities with surgery, radiation, and immunotherapy. Effective pretreatment to sensitize superficial tumors to local radiation therapy. Kaposi's sarcoma (Doxil).
UNLABELED USES Multiple myeloma.

CONTRAINDICATIONS Myelosuppression, thrombocytopenia; impaired cardiac function, obstructive jaundice, previous treatment with complete cumulative doses of doxorubicin or daunorubicin; lactation; pregnancy (category D).
CAUTIOUS USE Impaired hepatic or renal function; patients who have received cyclophosphamide or pelvic irradiation or radiotherapy to areas surrounding heart; history of atopic dermatitis.

ROUTE & DOSAGE

Neoplasm
Adult: **IV** 60–75 mg/m^2 as single dose at 21 d intervals or 30 mg/m^2 on each of 3 consecutive days repeated every 4 wk (max: total cumulative dose 500–550 mg/m^2)

Common adverse effects in *italic*, life-threatening effects underlined; generic names in **bold**; classifications in SMALL CAPS; ✦ Canadian drug name; ℗ Prototype drug

Child: **IV** 35–75 mg/m² as single dose, repeat at 21-d interval, or 20–30 mg/m² once weekly

Kaposi's Sarcoma

Adult: **IV Doxil** 20 mg/m² every 3 wk. Infuse over 30 min (do not use in-line filters)

ADMINISTRATION

Intravenous

- IV administration to infants and children: Verify correct IV concentration and rate of infusion with physician. ▪ Wear gloves and use caution when preparing drug solution. If powder or solution contacts skin or mucosa, wash copiously with soap and water. ▪ Exposure to doxorubicin during the first trimester of pregnancy can result in losing the fetus.

PREPARE: **Direct:** Dilute the powder with NS to yield a final concentration of 2 mg/mL. Bacteriostatic diluents are not recommended.

ADMINISTER: **Direct:** Administer slowly into y-site of freely running IV infusion of NS or D5W. Tubing should be attached to a butterfly needle inserted into a large vein. Usually infused over 3–5 min. Rate will be specifically ordered.

INCOMPATIBILITIES **Solution/additive: Aminophylline, cephalothin, dexamethasone, diazepam, fluorouracil, furosemide, hydrocortisone, heparin, vinblastine. Y-site: Furosemide, heparin,** TPN.

- Facial flushing and local red streaking along the vein may occur if drug is administered too rapidly. ▪ Avoid using antecubital vein or veins on dorsum of hand or wrist, if possible, where extravasation could damage underlying tendons and nerves. Also avoid veins in extremity with compromised venous or lymphatic drainage.

- Store reconstituted solution for 24 h at room temperature; refrigerated at 4°–10° C (39°–50° F) for 48 h. Protect from sunlight; discard unused solution.

ADVERSE EFFECTS (≥1%) **Body as a Whole:** Hypersensitivity (red flare around injection site, erythema, skin rash, pruritus, angioedema, urticaria, eosinophilia, fever, chills, <u>anaphylactoid reaction</u>). **CV:** <u>Serious, irreversible myocardial toxicity with delayed CHF, ventricular arrhythmias, acute left ventricular failure,</u> hypertension, hypotension, cardiomyopathy. **GI:** *Stomatitis,* esophagitis with ulcerations; nausea, vomiting, anorexia, inanition, diarrhea. **Hematologic:** *Severe myelosuppression* (60–85% of patients); <u>*leukopenia (principally granulocytes)*,</u> thrombocytopenia, anemia. **Skin:** Hyperpigmentation of nail beds, tongue, and buccal mucosa (especially in blacks); *complete alopecia* (reversible), hyperpigmentation of dermal creases (especially in children), rash, *recall phenomenon (skin reaction due to prior radiotherapy).* **Other:** Lacrimation, drowsiness, fever, facial flush with too rapid IV infusion rate, microscopic hematuria, hyperuricemia, *hand-foot syndrome. With extravasation: severe cellulitis, vesication, tissue necrosis,* lymphangitis, phlebosclerosis.

INTERACTIONS Drug: BARBITURATES may decrease pharmacologic effects of doxorubicin by increasing its hepatic metabolism—increase in doxorubicin dosage may be needed; **streptozocin** (Zanosar)

Common adverse effects in *italic*, life-threatening effects underlined; generic names in **bold**; classifications in SMALL CAPS; ♥ Canadian drug name; ☺ Prototype drug

517

D

may prolong doxorubicin half-life—dosage reduction of doxorubicin may be indicated.

PHARMACOKINETICS Distribution: Widely distributed; does not cross blood–brain barrier; crosses placenta. **Metabolism:** In liver to active metabolite. **Elimination:** Primarily in bile. **Half-Life:** 16.7–31.7 h.

CLINICAL IMPLICATIONS

Assessment & Drug Effects

- Stop infusion, remove IV needle, and notify physician promptly if patient complains of stinging or burning sensation at the injection site.
- Monitor any area of extravasation closely for 3–4 wk. If ulceration begins (usually 1–4 wk after extravasation), a plastic surgeon should be consulted.
- Begin a flow chart to establish baseline data. Include temperature, pulse, respiration, BP, body weight, laboratory values, and I&O ratio and pattern.
- Lab tests: Baseline and periodic hepatic function, renal function, CBC with differential throughout therapy.
- Note: The nadir of leukopenia (an expected 1000/mm^3) typically occurs 10–14 d after single dose, with recovery occurring within 21 d.
- Evaluate cardiac function (ECG) prior to initiation of therapy, at regular intervals, and at end of therapy.
- Be alert to and report early signs of cardiotoxicity (see Appendix F). Acute life-threatening arrhythmias may occur within a few hours of drug administration.
- Report promptly objective signs of hepatic dysfunction (jaundice, dark urine, pruritus) or kidney dysfunction (altered I&O ratio and pattern, local discomfort with voiding).

- Promote fastidious oral hygiene, especially before and after meals. Stomatitis, generally maximal in second week of therapy, frequently begins with a burning sensation accompanied by erythema of oral mucosa that may progress to ulceration and dysphagia in 2 or 3 d.
- Report signs of superinfection (see Appendix F) promptly; these may result from antibiotic therapy during leukopenic period.
- Avoid rectal medications and use of rectal thermometer; rectal trauma is associated with bloody diarrhea resulting from an antiblastic effect on rapidly growing intestinal mucosal cells.

Patient & Family Education

- Note: Complete loss of hair (reversible) is an expected adverse effect. It may also involve eyelashes and eyebrows, beard and mustache, pubic and axillary hair. Regrowth of hair usually begins 2–3 mo after drug is discontinued.
- Drug turns urine red for 1–2 d after administration.
- Keep hands away from eyes to prevent conjunctivitis. Increased tearing for 5–10 d after a single dose is possible.

DOXYCYCLINE HYCLATE

(dox-i-sye′kleen)

Apo-Doxy ✦, Doryx, Doxy, Doxycin ✦, Monodox, Novodoxylin ✦, Vibramycin, Vibra-Tabs

Classifications: ANTIBIOTIC; TETRACYCLINE
Therapeutic: ANTIBIOTIC
Prototype: Tetracycline
Pregnancy Category: D

AVAILABILITY 50 mg, 75 mg, 100 mg capsules, tablets; 200 mg injection

Common adverse effects in *italic*, life-threatening effects underlined; generic names in **bold**; classifications in SMALL CAPS; ✦ Canadian drug name; ● Prototype drug

ACTION & *THERAPEUTIC EFFECT*

Semisynthetic broad-spectrum long-acting tetracycline antibiotic derived from oxytetracycline. Doxycycline is more lipophilic than the other tetracyclines, which allows it to pass easily through the lipid layer of bacteria where reversible binding to the 30 S ribosomal subunits of bacteria occurs. This blocks the binding of transfer RNA (tRNA) to the messenger RNA (mRNA) of the bacteria, resulting in inhibition of bacterial protein synthesis. *Primarily bacteriostatic against both gram-positive and gram-negative bacteria. Similar in use to tetracycline.*

USES Similar to those of tetracycline, e.g., chlamydial and mycoplasmal infections; gonorrhea, syphilis in penicillin-allergic patients; rickettsial diseases; acute exacerbations of chronic bronchitis.

UNLABELED USES Treatment of acute PID, leptospirosis, prophylaxis for rape victims, suppression and chemoprophylaxis of chloroquine-resistant *Plasmodium falciparum* malaria, short-term prophylaxis and treatment of travelers' diarrhea caused by enterotoxigenic strains of *Escherichia coli.* Intrapleural administration for malignant pleural effusions.

CONTRAINDICATIONS Sensitivity to any of the tetracyclines; use during period of tooth development including last half of pregnancy; pregnancy (category D), lactation, infants, and children <8 y (causes permanent yellow discoloration of teeth, enamel hypoplasia, and retardation of bone growth).

CAUTIOUS USE Alcoholism; hepatic disease; GI disease; sulfite hypersensitivity; sunlight (UV) exposure.

ROUTE & DOSAGE

Antiinfective

Adult: **PO/IV** 100 mg q12h on day 1, then 100 mg/d as single dose (max: 100 mg q12h)
Child: **PO/IV** *>8 y,* 4.4 mg/kg in 1–2 doses on day 1, then 2.2–4.4 mg/kg/d in 1–2 divided doses

Gonorrhea

Adult: **PO** 200 mg immediately, followed by 100 mg h.s., then 100 mg b.i.d. for 3 d

Primary and Secondary Syphilis

Adult: **PO** 300 mg/d in divided doses for at least 10 d

Travelers' Diarrhea

Adult: **PO** 100 mg/d during risk period (up to 2 wk) beginning day 1 of travel

Acute Pelvic Inflammatory Disease

Adult: **IV** 100 mg q12h until improved, then 100 mg PO bid to complete 14 d

Acne

Adult: **PO** 100 mg q12h on day 1, then 100 mg q.d.
Child: **PO** *>8 y and >45 kg,* 100 mg q12h on day 1, then 100 mg q.d.; *>8 y and <45 kg,* 2.2 mg/kg q12h day 1 then 2.2 mg/kg/q.d.

ADMINISTRATION

Oral

- Check expiration date. Degradation products of tetracycline are toxic to the kidneys.
- Give with food or a full glass of milk to minimize nausea without significantly affecting bioavailability of drug (UNLIKE MOST TETRACYCLINES).

Common adverse effects in *italic*, life-threatening effects underlined; generic names in **bold**; classifications in SMALL CAPS; ♣ Canadian drug name; ⊙ Prototype drug

D

- Consult physician about ordering the oral suspension for patients who are bedridden or have difficulty swallowing.

Intravenous

PREPARE: **Intermittent/Continuous:** Reconstitute by adding 10 mL sterile water for injection, or D5W, NS, LR, D5/LR, or other diluent recommended by manufacturer, to each 100 mg of drug. ▪Further dilute with 100–1000 mL (per 100 mg of drug) of compatible infusion solution to produce concentrations ranging from 0.1 to 1 mg/mL.

ADMINISTER: **Intermittent/Continuous:** IV infusion rate will usually be prescribed by physician. ▪Duration of infusion varies with dose but is usually 1–4 h. ▪Recommended minimum infusion time for 100 mg of 0.5 mg/mL solution is 1 h. Infusion should be completed within 12 h of dilution. ▪When diluted with LR or D5/LR, infusion must be completed within 6 h to ensure adequate stability. ▪Protect all solutions from direct sunlight during infusion.

- Store oral and parenteral forms (prior to reconstitution) in tightly covered, light-resistant containers at 15°–30° C (59°–86° F) unless otherwise directed. ▪Refrigerate reconstituted solutions for up to 72 h. After this time, infusion must be completed within 12 h.

ADVERSE EFFECTS (≥1%) **Special Senses:** Interference with color vision. **GI:** Anorexia, *nausea,* vomiting, diarrhea, enterocolitis; esophageal irritation (oral capsule and tablet). **Skin:** Rashes, photosensitivity reaction. **Other:** Thrombophlebitis (IV use), superinfections.

DIAGNOSTIC TEST INTERFERENCE Like other *tetracyclines,* doxycycline may cause false increases in **urinary catecholamines** (fluorometric methods); false decreases in **urinary urobilinogen;** false-negative **urine glucose** with **glucose oxidase methods** (e.g., **Clinistix, TesTape**); parenteral doxycycline (containing ascorbic acid) may cause false-positive determinations using **Benedict's reagent** or **Clinitest.**

INTERACTIONS Drug: ANTACIDS, **iron** preparation, **calcium, magnesium, zinc, kaolin-pectin, sodium bicarbonate** can significantly decrease absorption; effects of both doxycycline and **desmopressin** antagonized; increases **digoxin** absorption, thus increasing risk of **digoxin** toxicity; **methoxyflurane** increases risk of renal failure.

PHARMACOKINETICS Absorption: Completely absorbed from GI tract. **Peak:** 1.5–4 h. **Distribution:** Penetrates eye, prostate, and CSF; crosses placenta; distributed into breast milk. **Metabolism:** In GI tract. **Elimination:** 20–30% in urine and 20–40% in feces in 48 h. **Half-Life:** 14–24 h.

CLINICAL IMPLICATIONS

Assessment & Drug Effects

- Report sudden onset of painful or difficult swallowing promptly to physician. Doxycycline (capsule and tablet forms) is associated with a comparatively high incidence of esophagitis, especially in patients >40 y.
- Report evidence of superinfections (see Appendix F).

Patient & Family Education

- Take capsule or tablet forms with a full glass (240 mL) of water to ensure passage into stomach and prevent esophageal ulceration. Avoid

Common adverse effects in *italic*, life-threatening effects underlined; generic names in **bold**; classifications in SMALL CAPS; ✚ Canadian drug name; Ⓟ Prototype drug

taking capsule or tablet within 1 h of lying down or retiring.

- Avoid exposure to direct sunlight and ultraviolet light during and for 4 or 5 d after therapy is terminated to reduce risk of phototoxic reaction. Phototoxic reaction appears like an exaggerated sunburn. Sunscreens provide little protection.

DRONABINOL

(droe-nab'i-nol)
Marinol, THC
Classifications: ANTIEMETIC; CANNABINOID
Therapeutic: ANTIEMETIC; APPETITE STIMULANT
Pregnancy Category: C
Controlled Substance: Schedule III

AVAILABILITY 2.5 mg, 5 mg, 10 mg capsules

ACTION & *THERAPEUTIC EFFECT*
Synthetic derivative of tetrahydrocannabinol (THC), the principal psychoactive constituent of marijuana *(Cannabis sativa)*. Mechanism unclear: Inhibits vomiting through the control mechanism in the medulla oblongata, producing potent antiemetic effect. Has complex CNS effect that necessitates close supervision of the patient during drug use. Decreases REM sleep; effect on BP is unpredictable; oral temperature may be decreased, and heart rate may be increased. Risk of drug abuse is high. *Produces potent antiemetic effect and is used to treat chemotherapy-induced nausea and vomiting.*

USES To treat chemotherapy-induced nausea and vomiting in cancer patients who fail to respond to conventional antiemetic therapy. Appetite stimulant for AIDS patients.

UNLABELED USES Glaucoma.

CONTRAINDICATIONS Nausea and vomiting caused by other than chemotherapeutic agents; hypersensitivity to dronabinol or sesame oil; pregnancy (category C); lactation.
CAUTIOUS USE First exposure, especially in the older adult or cardiac patient; hypertension, cardiovascular disorders; epilepsy; psychiatric illness, patient receiving other psychoactive drugs; severe hepatic dysfunction.

ROUTE & DOSAGE

Chemotherapy-Induced Nausea
Adult/Child: **PO** 5 mg/m^2 1–3 h before administration of chemotherapy, then q2–4h after chemotherapy for a total of 4–6 doses, dose may be increased by 2.5 mg/m^2 (max: of 15 mg/m^2 if necessary)

Appetite Stimulant
Adult: **PO** 2.5 mg b.i.d., before lunch and dinner

ADMINISTRATION

Oral
- Do not repeat dose following a reaction until patient's mental state has returned to normal and the circumstances have been evaluated.
- Store at 8°–15° C (46°–59° F).

ADVERSE EFFECTS (≥1%) **CNS:** *Drowsiness,* psychologic high, dizziness, anxiety, confusion, euphoria, sensory or perceptual difficulties, impaired coordination, depression, irritability, headache, ataxia, memory lapse, paresthesias, paranoia, depersonalization, disorientation, tinnitus, nightmares, speech difficulty, facial flush, diaphoresis. **CV:** Tachycardia, orthostatic hypotension, hyperten-

Common adverse effects in *italic*, life-threatening effects underlined; generic names in **bold**; classifications in SMALL CAPS; ◆ Canadian drug name; ☯ Prototype drug

521

sion, syncope. **GI:** Dry mouth, diarrhea, fecal incontinence. **Other:** Muscular pains.

INTERACTIONS Drug: Alcohol and other CNS DEPRESSANTS may exaggerate psychoactive effects of dronabinol; TRICYCLIC ANTIDEPRESSANTS, **atropine** may cause tachycardia.

PHARMACOKINETICS Absorption: Rapidly absorbed from GI tract, with bioavailability of 10–20%. **Peak:** 2–3 h. **Distribution:** Fat soluble; distributed to many organs; distributed into breast milk. **Metabolism:** In liver; extensive first-pass metabolism. **Elimination:** Principally in bile; 50% in feces within 72 h; 10–15% in urine. **Half-Life:** 25–36 h.

CLINICAL IMPLICATIONS

Assessment & Drug Effects

- Monitor patients with hypertension or heart disease for BP and cardiac status.
- Response to dronabinol is varied, and previous uneventful use does not guarantee that adverse reactions will not occur. Effects of drug may persist an unpredictably long time (days). Extended use at therapeutic dosage may cause accumulation of toxic amounts of dronabinol and its metabolites.
- Watch for disturbing psychiatric symptoms if dose is increased: Altered mental state, loss of coordination, evidence of a psychologic high (easy laughing, elation and heightened awareness), or depression.
- Note: Abrupt withdrawal is associated with symptoms (within 12 h) of irritability, insomnia, restlessness. Peak intensity occurs at about 24 h: Hot flashes, diaphoresis, rhinorrhea, watery diarrhea, hiccups, anorexia. Usually, syndrome is over in 96 h.

Patient & Family Education

- Do not drive or engage in other potentially hazardous activities that require alertness and judgment because of high incidence of dizziness and drowsiness.
- Understand potential (reversible) for drug-induced mood or behavior changes that may occur during dronabinol use.
- Do not ingest alcohol during period of systemic dronabinol effect. Effect on blood ethanol levels is complex and unpredictable.

DROPERIDOL

(droe-per'i-dole)

Inapsine

Classifications: BUTYROPHENONE; ANTIEMETIC

Therapeutic: ANTIEMETIC

Prototype: Haloperidol

Pregnancy Category: C

AVAILABILITY 2.5 mg/mL injection

ACTION & *THERAPEUTIC EFFECT*

Butyrophenone derivative structurally and pharmacologically related to haloperidol. Antagonizes emetic effects of morphine-like analgesics and other drugs that act on chemoreceptor trigger zone. *Sedative property reduces anxiety and motor activity without necessarily inducing sleep; patient remains responsive. Potentiates other CNS depressants. Also has antiemetic properties.*

USES To produce tranquilizing effect and to reduce nausea and vomiting during surgical and diagnostic procedures. Also for premedication, during induction, and as adjunct in maintenance of general or regional anesthesia. Principally used in fixed combination with the potent narcotic analgesic fentanyl (Innovar) to produce neuroleptanalgesia (quiescence, reduced motor activity, and indifference to pain and environmental stimuli) to permit carrying out a variety of diagnostic and minor surgical procedures.

UNLABELED USES IV antiemetic in cancer chemotherapy.

CONTRAINDICATIONS Known or suspected QT elongation; history of torsades de pointes; known intolerance to droperidol; pregnancy (category C), lactation. Safe use in children <2 y is not established.

CAUTIOUS USE Older adult, debilitated, and other poor-risk patients; Parkinson's disease; cardiac disease; cardiac bradyarrhythmias, cardiac arrhythmias, CHF, hypotension; liver, kidney.

ROUTE & DOSAGE

Nausea Prevention

Adult: **IV/IM** 2.5 mg; additional doses of 1.25 mg may be given
Child: **IV/IM** 0.1 mg/kg (max: 2.5 mg)

ADMINISTRATION

Intramuscular
- Give deep IM into a large muscle.

Intravenous
IV administration to infants and children: Verify correct rate of IV injection with physician.

PREPARE: **Direct:** Give undiluted.

ADMINISTER: **Direct:** Give at a rate of 10 mg or fraction thereof over 30–60 s.

INCOMPATIBILITIES **Solution/additive: Fluorouracil, furosemide, heparin, leucovorin, methotrexate, pentobarbital. Y-site: Fluorouracil, furosemide, heparin, leucovorin, methotrexate, nafcillin.**

- Store at 15°–30° C (59°–86° F), unless otherwise directed by manufacturer. Protect from light.

ADVERSE EFFECTS (≥1%) **CNS:** *Postoperative drowsiness, extrapyramidal symptoms:* dystonia, akathisia, oculogyric crisis; dizziness, restlessness, anxiety, hallucinations, mental depression. **CV:** *Hypotension, tachycardia,* irregular heartbeats *(prolonged QTc interval even at low doses).* **Other:** Chills, shivering, laryngospasm, bronchospasm.

PHARMACOKINETICS Onset: 3–10 min. **Peak:** 30 min. **Duration:** 2–4 h; may persist up to 12 h. **Distribution:** Crosses placenta. **Metabolism:** In liver. **Elimination:** In urine and feces.

CLINICAL IMPLICATIONS

Assessment & Drug Effects
- Monitor ECG throughout therapy. Report immediately prolongation of QTc interval.
- Monitor vital signs closely. Hypotension and tachycardia are common adverse effects.
- Exercise care in moving medicated patients because of possibility of severe orthostatic hypotension. Avoid abrupt changes in position.
- Observe patients for signs of impending respiratory depression carefully when receiving a concurrent narcotic analgesic carefully.
- Note: EEG patterns are slow to return to normal during the postoperative period.
- Observe carefully and report promptly to physician early signs of acute dystonia: Facial grimacing, restlessness, tremors, torticollis, oculogyric crisis. Extrapyramidal symptoms may occur within 24–48 h postoperatively.
- Note: Droperidol may aggravate symptoms of acute depression.

Common adverse effects in *italic*, life-threatening effects underlined; generic names in **bold**; classifications in SMALL CAPS; ♣ Canadian drug name; ⊘ Prototype drug

523

DROTRECOGIN ALFA (ACTIVATED)

(dro-tree'co-gin)

Xigris

Classifications: IMMUNOMODU-LATOR; RECOMBINANT HUMAN ACTI-VATED PROTEIN C

Therapeutic: ANTIINFLAMMATORY; ANTITHROMBOLYTIC

Pregnancy Category: C

AVAILABILITY 5 mg, 20 mg vials

ACTION & *THERAPEUTIC EFFECT*

Drotrecogin alfa is a recombinant form of human activated protein C (APC). Protein C deficiencies are found in most septic patients and result in a higher mortality rate. Activated protein C exerts antithrombotic and anticoagulant effects by inhibiting clotting factor Va and VIIIa. Activated protein C may exert an antiinflammatory effect by inhibiting human tumor necrosis factor (TNF) produced by monocytes, and by limiting the thrombin-induced inflammatory responses of the endothelial lining of the vasculature. *Drotrecogin alfa possesses profibrinolytic and antiinflammatory properties.*

USES Reduction in mortality in patients with severe sepsis and evidence of organ dysfunction.

CONTRAINDICATIONS Prior hypersensitivity to drotrecogin alfa; chronic severe hepatic disease; active internal bleeding or trauma; recent hemorrhagic stroke (within 3 months); invasive surgery or invasive procedures; recent intracranial or intraspinal surgery, or severe head trauma (within 2 mo); intracranial neoplasm, lesion, aneurysm, or herniation; presence of an epidural catheter; pregnancy (category C), lactation.

CAUTIOUS USE Immunosuppression; increased risk of bleeding, hypercoagulability; concurrent use of anticoagulants, or aspirin; thrombocytopenia; children <18; recent ischemic stroke, or intracranial aneurysm.

ROUTE & DOSAGE

Sepsis

Adult: **IV** 24 mcg/kg/h continuous infusion for 96 h

ADMINISTRATION

Intravenous

PREPARE: **Continuous:** Prepare immediately prior to use. Reconstitute 5 mg or 20 mg vials with 2.5 mL or 10 mL, respectively, of sterile water for injection to yield approximate concentration of 2 mg/mL. Slowly add sterile water to vial, avoid inverting or shaking vial, gently swirl until powder is completely dissolved. Slowly withdraw calculated dose from vial, add to infusion bag of NS by directing stream to side of bag to minimize agitation, then gently invert to mix. Final concentration should be 100–200 mcg/mL. Do not transport infusion bag between locations attached to mechanical pump. Note: When using a syringe pump, solution is typically diluted to a final concentration of 100–1000 mcg/mL.

ADMINISTER: **Continuous:** Give over 96 h. Dose adjustment based on clinical or laboratory parameters is not recommended. IV must be completed within 12 h after solution is prepared.

INCOMPATIBILITIES **Solution/additive:** Do not mix with any other drugs. **Y-site:** Do not infuse with any other drugs.

Common adverse effects in *italic*, life-threatening effects underlined; generic names in **bold**; classifications in SMALL CAPS; ✦ Canadian drug name; ⊙ Prototype drug

■ Storage: Reconstituted vial may be held at 15°–30° C (59°–86° F), but must be used within 3 h of preparation.

ADVERSE EFFECTS (≥1%) **Hematologic:** *Bleeding* (including intracranial).

DIAGNOSTIC TEST INTERFERENCE May affect the **APTT assay.** This interference may result in an apparent factor concentration that is lower than the true concentration.

INTERACTIONS Drug: ANTICOAGULANTS, NSAIDS, ANTIPLATELET AGENTS may increase risk of bleeding.

PHARMACOKINETICS Absorption: Steady state reached in 2 h. **Duration:** Serum levels undetectable 2 h after end of infusion. **Half-Life:** 1.6 h.

CLINICAL IMPLICATIONS
Assessment & Drug Effects
■ Monitor closely for S&S of hemorrhage. Stop infusion immediately should clinically important bleeding occur. There is no antidote for drotrecogin alfa.
■ Discontinue drotrecogin alfa 2 h prior to invasive procedures with an inherent risk of bleeding. Reinitiation may be reconsidered 12 h after major invasive procedure or immediately after uncomplicated less invasive procedures.
■ Lab tests: Monitor closely PT; APTT is not a reliable indication of coagulation.

DULOXETINE HYDROCHLORIDE

(du-lox′e-teen)

Cymbalta

Classifications: PSYCHOTHERAPEUTIC AGENT; ANTIDEPRESSANT; SEROTONIN NOREPINEPHRINE REUPTAKE INHIBITOR (SNRI)

Therapeutic: ANTIDEPRESSANT; SNRI; NEUROPATHIC PAIN RELIEVER
Prototype: Venlafaxine
Pregnancy Category: C

AVAILABILITY 20 mg, 30 mg, 60 mg capsules

ACTION & THERAPEUTIC EFFECT
As a selective serotonin and norepinephrine reuptake inhibitor (SSNRI), duloxetine causes potentiation of serotonergic and noradrenergic activity in the CNS. *Antidepressant effect is presumed to be due to its dual inhibition of CNS presynaptic neuronal uptake of serotonin and norepinephrine, thus increasing the serum levels of both substances.*

USES Treatment of major depression, diabetic peripheral neuropathy.
UNLABELED USES Chronic pain syndromes.

CONTRAINDICATIONS Concurrent administration of MAOI therapy; uncontrolled narrow-angle glaucoma; alcoholism; chronic hepatic disease; hepatitis; jaundice; abrupt discontinuation; pregnancy (category C), third trimester of pregnancy, lactation. Safety and efficacy in children <18 y not established.
CAUTIOUS USE Anorexia nervosa, bipolar disease; history of mania, history of suicidal ideation; cardiac disease; renal impairment or renal failure; hypertension.

ROUTE & DOSAGE

Depression
Adult: **PO** 40–60 mg/d in one or two divided doses
Diabetic Neuropathy or Chronic Pain
Adult: **PO** 60 mg/d in one or two divided doses

Common adverse effects in *italic*, life-threatening effects underlined; generic names in **bold**; classifications in SMALL CAPS; ◆ Canadian drug name; ⊚ Prototype drug

525

ADMINISTRATION

Oral

- Do not initiate therapy within 14 d of the last dose of an MAOI.
- Must be swallowed whole. Do not cut, chew, or crush. Do not sprinkle on food or mix with liquids.
- Store at 15°–30° C (59°–86° F).

ADVERSE EFFECTS (≥1%) **Body as a Whole:** Fatigue, hot flashes. **CNS:** Dizziness, somnolence, tremor, *insomnia.* **GI:** *Nausea, dry mouth, constipation,* diarrhea, vomiting. **Metabolic:** Decreased appetite, weight loss. **Skin:** Increased sweating. **Special Senses:** Blurred vision. **Urogenital:** Decreased libido, abnormal orgasm, erectile dysfunction, ejaculatory dysfunction. Cholestatic jaundice and hepatitis.

INTERACTIONS Drug: Alcohol may result in increased liver function tests; MAOIS may result in hyperthermia, rigidity, mental status changes, myoclonus, autonomic instability, features resembling neuroleptic malignant syndrome; **cimetidine, fluoxetine, fluvoxamine, paroxetine, quinidine,** QUINOLONES may increase levels and half-life of duloxetine; may increase levels and toxicity of **thioridazine,** TRICYCLIC ANTIDEPRESSANTS. **Amphetamine, dextroamphetamine, buspirone, cocaine, dexfenfluramine, fenfluramine, lithium, phentermine, sibutramine, nefazodone,** SSRIS, TRIPTANS, **tramadol, trazodone** may cause serotonin syndrome. **Herbal: St. John's wort, tryptophan** may cause serotonin syndrome.

PHARMACOKINETICS Peak: 6 h. **Metabolism:** In the liver by CYP2D6 and CYP1A2. **Elimination:** 70% in urine, 20% in feces. **Half-Life:** 12 h (8–17 h).

CLINICAL IMPLICATIONS

Assessment & Drug Effects

- Ensure that a complete list of all concurrent medications is obtained.
- Monitor for S&S of numerous drug-drug interactions (see Interaction section).
- Lab test: LFTs for unexplained abdominal pain or enlarged liver.
- Monitor closely for and report suicide ideation, especially when drug is initiated or dosage changed.
- Report emergence of any of the following: anxiety, agitation, panic attacks, insomnia, irritability, hostility, psychomotor restlessness, hypomania, and mania.
- Monitor BP, especially in those being treated for hypertension.

Patient & Family Education

- The beneficial effects of this drug may not be felt for approximately 4 wk.
- Report any of the following: suicidal ideation (especially early in treatment or when dosage is changed), palpitations, anxiety, hyperactivity, agitation, panic attacks, insomnia, irritability, hostility, restlessness.
- Do not abruptly discontinue taking this drug. Notify physician if side effects are bothersome.
- Avoid or minimize use of alcohol while taking this drug.
- Do not self-treat for coughs, colds, or allergies. Consult physician.

DUTASTERIDE

(du-tas′ter-ide)
Avodart

Common adverse effects in *italic*, life-threatening effects underlined; generic names in **bold**; classifications in SMALL CAPS; ◆ Canadian drug name; ◉ Prototype drug

Classifications: ANTIANDROGEN; 5-ALPHA REDUCTASE INHIBITOR; BENIGN PROSTATIC HYPERPLASIA (BPH) AGENT
Therapeutic: BPH AGENT
Prototype: Finasteride
Pregnancy Category: X

AVAILABILITY 0.5 mg capsules

ACTION & *THERAPEUTIC EFFECT*

Specific inhibitor of the steroid 5-alpha-reductase, an enzyme necessary to convert testosterone into the potent androgen 5-alpha-dihydrotestosterone (DHT) in the prostate gland. *Decreases the production of testosterone in the prostate gland.*

USES Treatment of benign prostatic hypertrophy (BPH).
UNLABELED USES Treatment of male pattern baldness.

CONTRAINDICATIONS Hypersensitivity to dutasteride or finasteride; pregnancy (category X), lactation, and children <18 y.
CAUTIOUS USE Hepatic impairment, obstructive uropathy.

ROUTE & DOSAGE

BPH
Adult: **PO** 0.5 mg once daily
Male Pattern Baldness
Adult: **PO** 0.25–0.5 mg once daily

ADMINISTRATION

Oral
- Do not handle capsules if you are or may become pregnant because of the potential for absorption of dutasteride and the subsequent risk to a developing male fetus.
- Do not open or crush capsules. They must be swallowed whole.
- Store at 15°–30° C (59°–86° F).

ADVERSE EFFECTS (≥1%) **Endocrine:** Gynecomastia. **Urogenital:** Ejaculation dysfunction, impotence, decreased libido.

INTERACTIONS Drug: Diltiazem, verapamil may decrease clearance of dutasteride. **Herbal:** May see exaggerated effects with **saw palmetto.**

PHARMACOKINETICS Absorption: Rapidly absorbed. 60% bioavailability. **Peak:** 2–3 h. **Distribution:** 99% protein bound. **Metabolism:** Metabolized in liver by CYP3A4 to one active and 2 inactive metabolites. **Elimination:** Primarily in feces. **Half-Life:** 5 wk.

CLINICAL IMPLICATIONS

Assessment & Drug Effects
- Monitor voiding patterns, assessing for ease of starting a stream, frequency, and urgency.
- Lab tests: Monitor baseline PSA and again at 3–6 mo to establish new baseline to use to assess potentially cancer-related changes in PSA. After 6 mo of treatment, obtained PSA values should be doubled for comparison with normal values in untreated men.

Patient & Family Education
- Do not donate blood until at least 6 mo following last dose to prevent administration of dutasteride to a pregnant female transfusion recipient.
- Ejaculate volume might be decreased during treatment but this does not seem to interfere with normal sexual function.
- Note that the incidence of most drug-related sexual adverse events (impotence, decreased libido, and ejaculation disorder) typically decrease with duration of treatment.

Common adverse effects in *italic*, life-threatening effects underlined; generic names in **bold**; classifications in SMALL CAPS; ♣ Canadian drug name; ⊕ Prototype drug

527

DYPHYLLINE
(dye'fi-lin)

Dilor, Lufyllin, Protophylline ♦
Classifications: BRONCHODILATOR; RESPIRATORY SMOOTH MUSCLE RELAXANT; XANTHINE
Therapeutic: BRONCHODILATOR
Prototype: Theophylline
Pregnancy Category: C

AVAILABILITY 200 mg, 400 mg tablets

ACTION & *THERAPEUTIC EFFECT*
Xanthine and derivative of theophylline that results in bronchodilation, myocardial stimulation, and smooth muscle relaxation. Unlike other xanthines, dyphylline is not metabolized to theophylline in body; therefore serum theophylline levels are not useful. *Drug has bronchodilator effects.*

USES Acute bronchial asthma and reversible bronchospasm associated with chronic bronchitis and emphysema.

CONTRAINDICATIONS Hypersensitivity to xanthine compounds; apnea in newborns; pregnancy (category C).
CAUTIOUS USE Severe cardiac disease, hypertension, acute myocardial injury; renal or hepatic dysfunction; glaucoma; seizure disorders; hyperthyroidism; peptic ulcer; in the older adults or children; concomitant administration of other xanthine formulations or other CNS-stimulating drugs; lactation.

ROUTE & DOSAGE

Asthma

Adult: **PO** 200–800 mg q6h up to 15 mg/kg q.i.d.

Child: **PO** ≥6 y, 4.4–6.6 mg/kg/d in divided doses

ADMINISTRATION

Oral
- Give oral preparation with a full glass of water on an empty stomach (e.g., 1 h before or 2 h after meals) to enhance absorption. However, administration after meals may help to relieve gastric discomfort.
- Exercise care in the amount of elixir given to children because it has a high alcohol content (18–20%).

ADVERSE EFFECTS (≥1%) **CNS:** Headache, irritability, restlessness, dizziness, insomnia, light-headedness, muscle twitching, <u>convulsions</u>. **CV:** Palpitation, *tachycardia*, extrasystoles, flushing, hypotension. **GI:** *Nausea*, vomiting, diarrhea, anorexia, epigastric distress. **Respiratory:** Tachypnea. **Other:** Albuminuria, fever, dehydration.

INTERACTIONS Drug: BETA BLOCKERS may antagonize bronchodilating effects of dyphylline; **halothane** increases risk of cardiac arrhythmias; **probenecid** may decrease dyphylline elimination.

PHARMACOKINETICS Absorption: Readily absorbed from GI tract. **Peak:** 1 h. **Metabolism:** In liver (but not to theophylline). **Elimination:** In urine. **Half-Life:** 2 h.

CLINICAL IMPLICATIONS

Assessment & Drug Effects
- Lab tests; baseline and periodic pulmonary function tests to assess therapeutic effectiveness.
- Monitor therapeutic effectiveness; usually occurs at a blood level of at least 12 mcg/mL.

Common adverse effects in *italic*, life-threatening effects underlined; generic names in **bold**; classifications in SMALL CAPS; ♦ Canadian drug name; ☉ Prototype drug

- Note: Toxic dyphylline plasma levels, although near normal dosage, are a risk in patients with a diminished capacity for dyphylline clearance, e.g., those with CHF or hepatic impairment or who are >55 y or <1 y of age.

Patient & Family Education
- Take medication consistently with or without food at the same time each day.
- Notify physician of adverse effects: Nausea, vomiting, insomnia, jitteriness, headache, rash, severe GI pain, restlessness, convulsions, or irregular heartbeat.
- Avoid alcohol and also large amounts of coffee and other xanthine-containing beverages (e.g., tea, cocoa, cola) during therapy.
- Consult physician before taking OTC preparations. Many OTC drugs for coughs, colds, and allergies contain ephedrine or other sympathomimetics and xanthines (e.g., caffeine, theophylline, aminophylline).

ECHOTHIOPHATE IODIDE

(ek-oh-thye'oh-fate)
Phospholine Iodide
Pregnancy Category: C
See Appendix A-1.

ECONAZOLE NITRATE

(e-kone'a-zole)
Ecostatin ♦, Spectazole
Classifications: ANTIBIOTIC; AZOLE ANTIFUNGAL
Therapeutic: AZOLE ANTIFUNGAL
Prototype: Fluconazole
Pregnancy Category: C

AVAILABILITY 1% cream

ACTION & *THERAPEUTIC EFFECT*
Azole antifungal antibiotic with broad spectrum of activity similar to that of miconazole. It disrupts normal fungal cell membrane permeability. *Active against dermatophytes, yeasts, and many other fungi. Also appears to be active against some gram-positive bacteria.*

USES Topically for treatment of tinea pedis (athlete's foot or ringworm of foot), tinea cruris ("jock itch" or ringworm of groin), tinea corporis (ringworm of body), tinea versicolor, and cutaneous candidiasis (moniliasis).
UNLABELED USES Has been used for topical treatment of erythrasma and with corticosteroids for fungal or bacterial dermatoses associated with inflammation.

CONTRAINDICATIONS Pregnancy (category C), infants <3 mo old.
CAUTIOUS USE Lactation

ROUTE & DOSAGE

Tinea Cruris, Tinea Corporis, Tinea Pedis, Cutaneous Candidiasis
Adult/Child: **Topical** Apply sufficient amount to affected areas twice daily, morning and evening

Tinea Versicolor
Adult: **Topical** Apply sufficient amount to affected areas once daily

ADMINISTRATION

Topical
- Cleanse skin with soap and water and dry thoroughly before applying medication (unless otherwise directed by physician). Wash hands thoroughly before and after treatments.

Common adverse effects in *italic*, life-threatening effects underlined; generic names in **bold**; classifications in SMALL CAPS; ♦ Canadian drug name; ⊘ Prototype drug

529

- Do not use occlusive dressings unless prescribed by physician.
- Store at less than 30° C (86° F) unless otherwise directed.

ADVERSE EFFECTS (≥1%) **Skin:** Burning, stinging sensation, pruritus, erythema.

INTERACTIONS Drug: No clinically significant interactions established.

PHARMACOKINETICS Absorption: Minimal percutaneous absorption through intact skin; increased absorption from denuded skin. **Peak:** 0.5–5 h. **Elimination:** <1% of applied dose is eliminated in urine and feces.

CLINICAL IMPLICATIONS

Patient & Family Education

- Use medication for the prescribed time even if symptoms improve and report to physician skin reactions suggestive of irritation or sensitization.
- Notify physician if full course of therapy does not result in improvement. Diagnosis should be reevaluated.
- Do not to apply the topical cream in or near the eyes or intravaginally.

EDETATE CALCIUM DISODIUM

(ed′e-tate)
Calcium Disodium Versenate
Classifications: CHELATING AGENT
Therapeutic: CHELATING AGENT;
ANTIPOISON AGENT
Pregnancy Category: B

AVAILABILITY 200 mg/mL injection

ACTION & *THERAPEUTIC EFFECT*
Chelating agent that combines with divalent and trivalent metals to form stable, nonionizing soluble complexes that can be readily excreted by kidneys. Action is dependent on ability of heavy metal to displace the less strongly bound calcium in the drug molecules. *Chelating agent that binds with heavy metals such as lead to form a soluble complex that can be excreted through the kidney, thereby ridding the body of the poisonous substance.*

USES As adjunct in treatment of acute and chronic lead poisoning (plumbism). Generally used in combination with dimercaprol (BAL) in treatment of lead encephalopathy or when blood lead level exceeds 100 mcg/dL. Also used to diagnose suspected lead poisoning.
UNLABELED USES Treatment of poisoning from other heavy metals such as chromium, manganese, nickel, zinc, and possibly vanadium; removal of radioactive and nuclear fission products such as plutonium, yttrium, uranium. Not effective in poisoning from arsenic, gold, or mercury.

CONTRAINDICATIONS Severe kidney disease, active renal disease, anuria, oliguria; hepatitis; IV use in patients with lead encephalopathy not generally recommended (because of possible increase in intracranial pressure).
CAUTIOUS USE Kidney dysfunction; active tubercular lesions; history of gout; pregnancy (category C); lactation.

ROUTE & DOSAGE

Diagnosis of Lead Poisoning
Adult: **IV/IM** 500 mg/m² (max: 1 g) over 1 h, then collect urine for 24 h (if mcg lead:mg EDTA ratio in urine is >1, the test is positive)

Child: IM 50 mg/kg (max: 1 g), then collect urine for 6–8 h, (if mcg lead:mg EDTA ratio in urine is >0.5, the test is positive)

Treatment of Lead Poisoning

Adult/Child: IV 1–1.5 g/m²/d infused over 8–24 h for up to 5 d
IM 1–1.5 g/m²/d divided q8–12 h

Lead Nephropathy/Renal Impairment

Adult: IV Based on serum creatinine <2 mg/dL 1 g/m²/d, 2–3 mg/dL 500 mg/m²/d, 3.1–4 mg/dL 500 mg/m² q48h, >4 mg/dL 500 mg/m² once/wk. Infuse over 8–24 h for 5 d, may repeat monthly

ADMINISTRATION

▪ Note: Calcium disodium edetate can produce potentially fatal effects when higher than recommended doses are used or when it is continued after toxic effects appear.

Intramuscular

▪ IM route preferred for symptomatic children and recommended for patients with incipient or overt lead-induced encephalopathy.

▪ Add Procaine HCl to minimize pain at injection site (usually 1 mL of procaine 1% to each 1 mL of concentrated drug). Consult physician.

▪ Use separate injection sites when dimercaprol (BAL) and Calcium EDTA are given concurrently.

Intravenous

PREPARE: **IV Infusion:** Dilute the 5 mL ampule with 250–500 mL of NS or D5W.

ADMINISTER: **IV Infusion:** Warning: Rapid IV infusion may be LE-THAL by suddenly increasing intracranial pressure in patients who already have cerebral edema. Manufacturer recommends total daily dose over 8–12 h. Some clinicians recommend infusing over 1–2 h. Consult physician for specific rate.

INCOMPATIBILITIES Solution/additive: **Amphotericin B, hydralazine, Ringer's lactate.**

E

ADVERSE EFFECTS (≥1%) **CV:** Hypotension, thrombophlebitis. **GI:** Anorexia, nausea, vomiting, diarrhea, abdominal cramps, cheilosis. **Hematologic:** Transient bone marrow depression, depletion of blood metals. **Urogenital:** Nephrotoxicity (renal tubular necrosis), proteinuria, hematuria. **Body as a Whole:** *Febrile reaction* (excessive thirst, fever, chills, severe myalgia, arthralgia, GI distress), *histamine-like reactions* (flushing, throbbing headache, sweating, sneezing, nasal congestion, lacrimation, postural hypotension, tachycardia).

DIAGNOSTIC TEST INTERFERENCE

Edetate calcium disodium may decrease *serum cholesterol, plasma lipid* levels (if elevated), and *serum potassium* values. *Glycosuria* may occur with toxic doses.

INTERACTIONS Drug: No clinically significant interactions established.

PHARMACOKINETICS Absorption:
Well absorbed IM. **Onset:** 1 h. **Peak:** Peak chelation 24–48 h. **Distribution:** Distributed to extracellular fluid; does not enter CSF. **Metabolism:** Not metabolized. **Elimination:** Chelated lead excreted in urine; 50% excreted in 1 h. **Half-Life:** 20–60 min IV, 90 min IM.

CLINICAL IMPLICATIONS

Assessment & Drug Effects

▪ Determine adequacy of urinary output prior to therapy. This may

---

Common adverse effects in *italic*, life-threatening effects underlined; generic names in **bold**; classifications in SMALL CAPS; ✚ Canadian drug name; ⊘ Prototype drug

531

be done by administering IV fluids before giving first dose.

- Increase fluid intake to enhance urinary excretion of chelates. Avoid excess fluid intake, however, in patients with lead encephalopathy because of the danger of further increasing intracranial pressure. Consult physician regarding allowable intake.
- Monitor I&O. Since drug is excreted almost exclusively via kidneys, toxicity may develop if output is inadequate. Stop therapy if urine flow is markedly diminished or absent. Report any change in output or I&O ratio to physician.
- Lab tests: Obtain serum creatinine, calcium, and phosphorus before and during each course of therapy. Monitor baseline and frequent BUN levels and ECG during therapy. With prolonged therapy determine periodic determinations of blood trace element metals (e.g., copper, zinc, magnesium).
- Be alert for occurrence of febrile reaction that may appear 4–8 h after drug infusion (see ADVERSE EFFECTS).

EDROPHONIUM CHLORIDE

(ed-roe-foe'nee-um)
Enlon, Tensilon
Classifications: CHOLINERGIC AGENT; CHOLINESTERASE INHIBITOR
Therapeutic: CHOLINESTERASE INHIBITOR
Prototype: Neostigmine
Pregnancy Category: C

AVAILABILITY 10 mg/mL injection

ACTION & *THERAPEUTIC EFFECT*
Indirect-acting cholinesterase inhibitor that acts as antidote to curariform drugs by displacing them from muscle cell receptor sites, thus permitting resumption of normal transmission of neuromuscular impulses. *Acts as antidote to curariform drugs by displacing them from muscle cell receptor sites, thus permitting resumption of normal transmission of neuromuscular impulses.*

USES Differential diagnosis and as adjunct in evaluation of treatment requirements of myasthenia gravis, for differentiating myasthenic from cholinergic crisis, and to reverse neuromuscular blockade produced by overdosage of nondepolarizing skeletal muscle relaxants, e.g., tubocurarine, gallamine. Not recommended for maintenance therapy in myasthenia gravis because of its short duration of action.

UNLABELED USES To terminate paroxysmal atrial tachycardia, as an aid in diagnosing supraventricular tachyarrhythmias, and to evaluate function of demand pacemakers.

CONTRAINDICATIONS Hypersensitivity to anticholinesterase agents; cholinesterase inhibitor toxicity; intestinal and urinary obstruction; pregnancy (category C), lactation.
CAUTIOUS USE Sulfite hypersensitivity; bronchial asthma; cardiac arrhythmias; bradycardia; peptic ulcer disease; hypotension; patients receiving digitalis.

ROUTE & DOSAGE

Myasthenia Gravis Diagnosis

Adult: **IV** Prepare 10 mg in a syringe; inject 2 mg over 15–30 sec, if no reaction after 45 sec, inject the remaining 8 mg, may repeat test after 30 min **IM** Inject 10 mg, if cholinergic reaction occurs, retest after 30 min with 2 mg to rule out false-negative reaction

Child: **IV** ≤*34 kg,* 1 mg, if no response after 45 sec, dose may be titrated up to 5 mg **IM** 2 mg **IV** >*34 kg,* 2 mg, if no response after 45 sec, dose may be titrated up to 10 mg **IM** 5 mg
Infant: **IM** 0.5–1 mg

Evaluation of Myasthenia Treatment

Adult: **IV** 1–2 mg administered 1 h after last PO dose of anticholinesterase medication

ADMINISTRATION

• Note: Have antidote (atropine sulfate) immediately available and facilities for endotracheal intubation, tracheostomy, suction, assisted respiration, and cardiac monitoring for treatment of cholinergic reaction.

Intravenous

PREPARE: **Direct:** May be given undiluted.

ADMINISTER: **Direct:** USE for diagnosis of MG—Inject 2 mg (adult & child >34 kg) or 1 mg (child ≤34 kg) over 15–30 sec; if no reaction after 45 sec, inject additional 8 mg (adult) or titrate up to a total of 8 mg additional (child >34 kg) or titrate in 1 mg increments up to a total of 4 mg additional (child ≤34 kg), may repeat test after 30 min. If cholinergic reaction (increased muscle weakness) is obtained after initial 1 or 2 mg, discontinue test and give atropine IV (as ordered).

• Note: Some clinicians recommend giving a 1–2 mg test dose of edrophonium to older adult patients, to those with history of heart disease or who take digitalis, and possibly to all patients.

ADVERSE EFFECTS (≥1%) **Body as a Whole:** Severe adverse effects un-

common with usual doses. **CNS:** Weakness, muscle cramps, dysphoria, fasciculations, incoordination, dysarthria, dysphagia, convulsions, respiratory paralysis. **CV:** Bradycardia, irregular pulse, hypotension, pulmonary edema. **Special Senses:** Miosis, blurred vision, diplopia, lacrimation. **GI:** Diarrhea, abdominal cramps, nausea, vomiting, excessive salivation. **Respiratory:** Increased bronchial secretions, bronchospasm, laryngospasm, pulmonary edema. **Other:** Excessive sweating, urinary frequency, incontinence.

INTERACTIONS Drug: **Procainamide, quinidine** may antagonize the effects of edrophonium; DIGITALIS GLYCOSIDES increase the sensitivity of the heart to edrophonium; **succinylcholine, decamethonium** may prolong neuromuscular blockade.

PHARMACOKINETICS Onset: 30–60 sec IV; 2–10 min IM. **Duration:** 5–10 min IV; 5–30 min IM.

CLINICAL IMPLICATIONS

Assessment & Drug Effects

• Monitor vital signs. Observe for signs of respiratory distress. Patients >50 y are particularly likely to develop bradycardia, hypotension, and cardiac arrest.

• Edrophonium test for myasthenia gravis: All cholinesterase inhibitors (anticholinesterases) should be discontinued for at least 8 h before test. Positive response to edrophonium test consists of brief improvement in muscle strength unaccompanied by lingual or skeletal muscle fasciculations.

• Evaluation of myasthenic treatment: *Myasthenic response* (immediate subjective improvement with increased muscle strength, absence of fasciculations; generally indicates that patient requires larger

Common adverse effects in *italic*, life-threatening effects underlined; generic names in **bold**; classifications in SMALL CAPS; ✦ Canadian drug name; ❷ Prototype drug

533

E

dose of anticholinesterase agent or longer-acting drug); *Cholinergic response* [muscarinic adverse effects (lacrimation, diaphoresis, salivation, abdominal cramps, diarrhea, nausea, vomiting; accompanied by decrease in muscle strength; usually indicates overtreatment with cholinesterase inhibitor)]; *Adequate response* [no change in muscle strength; fasciculations may be present or absent; minimal cholinergic adverse effects (observed in patients at or near optimal dosage level)].

EFALIZUMAB

(e-fal-i-zoo′-mab)
Raptiva
Classifications: BIOLOGIC RESPONSE MODIFIER; MONOCLONAL ANTIBODY; IMMUNOSUPPRESSANT
Therapeutic: IMMUNOSUPPRESSANT
Pregnancy Category: C

AVAILABILITY 125 mg vial

ACTION & *THERAPEUTIC EFFECT*
An anti-CD11a antibody that targets the antigen-1 subunit on the surface of T-leukocytes; inhibits binding of T-cells to endothelial cells, prevents migration of T-cells out of the bloodstream into the skin, and prevents activation of T-cells. Lymphocyte activation and movement to skin play a key role in the pathophysiology of chronic plaque psoriasis. *Prevents activation of T-cells and their migration out of the circulatory system to sites of inflammation, thus slowing processes that result in plaque psoriasis.*

USES Treatment of moderate to severe plaque psoriasis.

CONTRAINDICATIONS Hypersensitivity to efalizumab; hamster protein hypersensitivity; severe infection or exposure to viral infections (e.g., chicken pox, herpes zoster), live vaccines; children <18 y; pregnancy (category C).
CAUTIOUS USE History of untoward reactions to other monoclonal antibodies; lactation.

ROUTE & DOSAGE

Plaque Psoriasis
Adult: **SC** 0.7 mg/kg first dose, then 1 mg/kg (max: 200 mg) once weekly

ADMINISTRATION

Subcutaneous
- Note: A reduced initial dose is used to prevent first dose reaction including headache, fever, nausea, and vomiting.
- Reconstitute immediately before use. Inject 1.3 mL of the supplied diluent (using prefilled syringe with sterile water for injection) slowly into vial. Swirl gently to dissolve but DO NOT SHAKE; dissolves in >5 min. Should be clear to pale yellow and free of particulates.
- Replace needle on syringe used for reconstitution with a new needle. Insert needle into vial keeping needle below the level of the liquid; withdraw the required dose.
- Inject SC into thigh, abdomen, buttocks, or upper arm. Rotate sites.
- If reconstituted vial is not used immediately, store at room temperature but use within 8 h.
- Store powder vials at 2°–8° C (36°–46° F). Protect from light.

ADVERSE EFFECTS (≥1%) **Body as a Whole:** First dose reaction (headache, fever, nausea, vomiting, myalgia), increased risk of *infection* or reactivation of latent infection, *chills,* pain, myalgia, flu syndrome,

Common adverse effects in *italic,* life-threatening effects underlined; generic names in **bold**; classifications in SMALL CAPS; ◆ Canadian drug name; ⦿ Prototype drug

asthenia, hypersensitivity reactions, peripheral edema, serious infection. **CNS:** *Headache.* **GI:** *Nausea.* **Hematologic:** Thrombocytopenia, hemolytic anemia. **Musculoskeletal:** Arthralgia. **Skin:** Worsening of psoriasis, acne, urticaria.

INTERACTIONS Drug: Do not administer live or live-attenuated VACCINES; increased risk of immunosuppression with other IMMUNOSUPPRESSANTS.

PHARMACOKINETICS Absorption: 50% absorbed from SC site. **Peak:** Steady-state levels reached in 4 wk. **Elimination:** Drug eliminated approximately 25 d after last steady-state dose.

CLINICAL IMPLICATIONS

Assessment & Drug Effects
- Monitor for S&S of infection. Withhold drug and notify physician if infection is suspected.
- Lab tests: Periodic Hgb & Hct and platelet counts.

Patient & Family Education
- Seek immediate medical attention for bleeding from gums, bruising, petechiae (numerous small red spots on skin), or S&S of an infection (fever, abscess, sore throat with breathing difficulty, etc.), or worsening of psoriasis.
- Do not accept a live virus vaccine without consulting physician.
- Notify physician immediately if you become pregnant while taking this drug, or within 6 wk of last dose of drug.

EFAVIRENZ ⓟ

(e-fa'vi-renz)
Sustiva
Classifications: ANTIRETROVIRAL AGENT; NONNUCLEOSIDE REVERSE TRANSCRIPTASE INHIBITOR (NNRTI)

Therapeutic: ANTIRETROVIRAL; NNRTI
Pregnancy Category: D

AVAILABILITY 50 mg, 100 mg, 200 mg capsules; 300 mg, 600 mg tablets

ACTION & *THERAPEUTIC EFFECT*
Nonnucleoside reverse transcriptase inhibitor (NNRTI) of HIV-1. Binds directly to reverse transcriptase and blocks RNA polymerase activities of the HIV-1 virus, thus preventing replication of the virus. *Prevents replication of the HIV-1 virus. HIV-2 reverse transcriptase and DNA polymerases alpha, beta, gamma, and delta are not inhibited by efavirenz. Resistant strains appear rapidly. Effectiveness is indicated by reduction in viral load (plasma level HIV RNA).*

USES HIV-1 infection in combination with other antiretroviral agents.

CONTRAINDICATIONS Hypersensitivity to efavirenz; pregnancy (category D), lactation.
CAUTIOUS USE Liver disease, alcoholism, hepatitis, hypertriglyceridemia, hypercholesterolemia, substance abuse, antimicrobial resistance, bipolar disorder, depression, suicidal ideation, exfoliative dermatitis; females of childbearing age, CNS disorders; history of seizures. Safety and efficacy in children <3 y old or who weigh <13 kg (29 lb) are not known.

ROUTE & DOSAGE

HIV Infection
Adult: **PO** 600 mg q.d.
Child: **PO** ≥3 y, 10–15 kg, 200 mg q.d.; 15–20 kg, 250 mg q.d.; 20–25 kg, 300 mg q.d.; 25–32.5 kg, 350 mg q.d.; 32.5–40 kg, 400 mg q.d.; >40 kg, 600 mg q.d.

Common adverse effects in *italic*, life-threatening effects underlined; generic names in **bold**; classifications in SMALL CAPS; ◆ Canadian drug name; ⓟ Prototype drug

535

ADMINISTRATION

Oral

- Use bedtime dosing to increase tolerability of CNS adverse effects.
- Give exactly as ordered. Do not skip a dose or discontinue therapy without consulting the physician.
- Do not give efavirenz following a high fat meal.
- Store at 15°–30° C (59°–86° F) in a tightly closed container and protect from light.

ADVERSE EFFECTS (≥1%) **Body as a Whole:** Fatigue, fever. **CNS:** Dizziness, headache, hypoesthesia, impaired concentration, insomnia, abnormal dreams, somnolence, depression, nervousness, adverse psychiatric experiences. **CV:** Hypercholesterolemia. **GI:** *Nausea,* vomiting, *diarrhea,* dyspepsia, abdominal pain, flatulence, anorexia, increased liver function tests (ALT, AST). **Respiratory:** Cough. **Skin:** *Rash* (erythematous rash, pruritus, *maculopapular rash,* erythema multiforme, Stevens-Johnson syndrome, toxic epidermal necrolysis), increased sweating. **Urogenital:** Renal calculus, hematuria.

DIAGNOSTIC TEST INTERFERENCE False-positive urine tests for **marijuana.**

INTERACTIONS Drug: Decreased concentrations of **clarithromycin, indinavir, nelfinavir, saquinavir, voriconazole;** increased concentrations of **ritonavir, azithromycin, ethinyl estradiol.** Efavirenz levels are increased by **ritonavir, fluconazole** and decreased by **saquinavir, rifampin.** Additional drugs not recommended for administration with efavirenz include **midazolam, triazolam,** ERGOT DERIVATIVES, **warfarin. Herbal:** St. John's wort may decrease antiretroviral activity.

PHARMACOKINETICS Peak: 5 h; steady-state 6–10 d. **Distribution:** 99% protein bound. **Metabolism:** In liver by cytochrome P450 3A4 and 2B6; can induce (increase) its own metabolism. **Elimination:** 14–34% in urine, 16–61% in feces. **Half-Life:** 52–76 h after single dose, 40–55 h after multiple doses.

CLINICAL IMPLICATIONS

Assessment & Drug Effects

- Monitor for suicidal ideation in patients who are depressed, or who have a history of depression.
- Monitor GI status and evaluate ability to maintain a normal diet.
- Lab tests: Periodic liver functions and lipid profile.

Patient & Family Education

- Contact physician promptly if any of the following occurs: skin rash, delusions, inappropriate behavior, thoughts of suicide.
- Use or add barrier contraception if using hormonal contraceptive.
- Notify physician immediately if you become pregnant.
- Do not drive or engage in potentially hazardous activities until response to the drug is known. Dizziness, impaired concentration, and drowsiness usually improve with continued therapy.

EFLORNITHINE HYDROCHLORIDE

(e-flor′ni-theen)

Vaniqa

Classifications: DERMATOLOGIC AGENT

Therapeutic: DERMATOLOGIC AGENT

Pregnancy Category: C

AVAILABILITY 13.9% cream

Common adverse effects in *italic*, life-threatening effects underlined; generic names in **bold**; classifications in SMALL CAPS; ♣ Canadian drug name; ⊕ Prototype drug

ACTION & *THERAPEUTIC EFFECT*
Inhibits enzyme activity in the skin that is required for hair growth. *Results in retarding the rate of hair growth.*

USES Reduction of unwanted facial hair in women.

CONTRAINDICATIONS Hypersensitivity to eflornithine or its components; pregnancy (category C); children <12 y.
CAUTIOUS USE Bone marrow suppression; HIV; lactation.

ROUTE & DOSAGE

Hair Removal
Adult: **Topical** Apply thin layer to affected areas of the face and adjacent involved areas under the chin and rub in thoroughly b.i.d. at least 8 h apart

ADMINISTRATION

Topical
- Apply thin layer to affected skin areas on face and under chin and rub in thoroughly.
- Do not wash treated areas for at least 4 h after application.
- Store at 15°–30° C (59°–86° F).

ADVERSE EFFECTS (≥1%) **Body as a Whole:** Facial edema. **CNS:** Dizziness. **GI:** Dyspepsia, anorexia. **Skin:** *Acne, pseudofolliculitis barbae,* stinging, burning, pruritus, erythema, tingling, irritation, rash, alopecia, folliculitis, ingrown hair.

INTERACTIONS : No clinically significant interactions established.

PHARMACOKINETICS Absorption: <1% absorbed through intact skin. **Metabolism:** Not metabolized. **Elimination:** Primarily in urine. **Half-Life:** 8 h.

CLINICAL IMPLICATIONS
Assessment & Drug Effects
- Monitor for and report skin irritation.
- Note: Drug slows growth of facial hair, but is not a depilatory.

Patient & Family Education
- Note: Effect of drug is usually not apparent for 4–8 wk.
- Reduce frequency of drug application to once daily if skin irritation occurs. If irritation continues, contact physician.

E

ELETRIPTAN HYDROBROMIDE
(e-le-trip'tan)
Relpax
Classifications: 5-HT$_1$ SEROTONIN AGONIST
Therapeutic: ANTIMIGRAINE
Prototype: Sumatriptan
Pregnancy Category: C

AVAILABILITY 20 mg, 40 mg tablets

ACTION & *THERAPEUTIC EFFECT*
Eletriptan is a potent agonist at central serotonin 5-HT$_{1B}$, 5-HT$_{1D}$, and 5-HT$_{1F}$ receptors. Eletriptan stimulates presynaptic 5-HT$_{1D}$ receptors inhibiting dural vasodilation and agonizes vascular 5-HT$_{1B}$ receptors causing vasoconstriction of intracranial extracerebral vessels. *Inhibits dural vasodilation and inflammation, and causes vasoconstriction of painfully dilated intracranial extracerebral vessels, thus relieving the migraine headache. Also relieves photophobia, phonophobia, and nausea and vomiting associated with migraine attacks.*

USES Treatment of acute migraine attacks with or without aura.

CONTRAINDICATIONS Hypersensitivity to eletriptan; history of coro-

---

Common adverse effects in *italic*, life-threatening effects underlined; generic names in **bold**; classifications in SMALL CAPS; ◆ Canadian drug name; ⊘ Prototype drug

537

nary artery disease; ischemic or vasospastic coronary artery disease, arteriosclerosis, history of MI; ischemic colititis, Raynaud's disease uncontrolled hypertension; CVA or TIA; within 24 h of administering of another ergotamine; pregnancy (category C), lactation within 24 h after dose; children <18 y; severe hepatic insufficiency; hemiplegic or basilar migraine; peripheral vascular disease; concurrent MAOI therapy.

CAUTIOUS USE Hypotension in the elderly; older adults >65 y; mild to moderate hepatic impairment; diabetes, obesity, smoking, high cholesterol; men >40 y; postmenopausal women. Use within 72 h of potent CYP3A4 metabolizing drugs; lactation.

ROUTE & DOSAGE

Acute Migraine

Adult: **PO** 20 mg or 40 mg at onset of migraine (max: 40 mg/dose and 80 mg/d), may repeat dose in 2 h if partial response
Geriatric: Use not recommended

Hepatic Impairment

Use not recommended in severe hepatic impairment

ADMINISTRATION

Oral

- Give one tablet as soon as the migraine begins.
- May give 2nd tablet if headache improves but returns after 2 h.
- If 1st tablet is ineffective, do not give a 2nd without consulting physician.
- Do not give within 72 h of potent CYP3A4 inhibitors (see INTERACTIONS).

- Store at 15°–30° C (59°–86° F). Protect from light and moisture.

ADVERSE EFFECTS (≥1%) **Body as a Whole:** *Asthenia,* paresthesia, flushing, back pain, chills. **CNS:** Dizziness, drowsiness, headache, somnolence, hypertonia, hypesthesia. **CV:** Chest tightness/pressure, palpitation, hypertension. The following are rare, usually seen in patients with cardiovascular disease risk factors: Coronary vasospasm, transient myocardial ischemia, <u>MI</u>, ventricular tachycardia, atrial fibrillation, ventricular fibrillation. **GI:** Abdominal pain, dyspepsia, dysphagia, nausea, vomiting, dry mouth. **Respiratory:** Pharyngitis. **Skin:** Sweating.

INTERACTIONS Drug: Drugs that inhibit CYP3A4 may increase eletriptan levels and toxicity, do not administer eletriptan within 72 h of AZOLE ANTIFUNGALS (especially **itraconazole, ketoconazole, voriconazole**), **amiodarone, cimetidine, dalfopristin, quinupristin, diltiazem, metronidazole, nicardipine, norfloxacin, quinine, verapamil, zafirlukast, zileuton,** MACROLIDE ANTIBIOTICS, NONNUCLEOTIDE REVERSE TRANSCRIPTASE INHIBITORS, PROTEASE INHIBITORS, SELECTIVE SEROTONIN REUPTAKE INHIBITORS, **sibutramine;** ERGOT ALKALOIDS may prolong vasospastic adverse reactions (do not use within 24 h of ergot-containing drugs); do not administer within 24 h of other 5-HT$_1$ AGONISTS (may cause increased adverse effects). **Food:** Grapefruit juice may increase eletriptan levels and toxicity. **Herbal: Gingko, ginseng, echinacea, St. John's wort** may increase triptan toxicity.

PHARMACOKINETICS Absorption: Rapidly absorbed, 50% reaches systemic circulation. **Onset:** 1–2 h. **Peak:** 1.5 h. **Distribution:** 85% protein bound. **Metabolism:** In liver by CYP3A4. **Elimination:** 90% cleared by nonrenal routes, 9% eliminated in urine. **Half-Life:** 4–5 h.

CLINICAL IMPLICATIONS

Assessment & Drug Effects

- Monitor CV status carefully following first dose in patients at risk for coronary artery disease (e.g., history of hypertension, postmenopausal women, men >40 y, persons with known CAD risk factors) or who have coronary artery vasospasms.
- Report immediately chest pain, tightness in chest or throat that is severe or does not quickly resolve following a dose of eletriptan.
- Monitor therapeutic effectiveness. Pain relief is usually achieved within 1 h.

Patient & Family Education

- Note: If first dose is ineffective, do not take a second dose as it will not work for the same attack.
- Inform physician of all prescription, nonprescription, and herbal drugs you are taking. Do not add additional drugs without informing physician as many drugs interact with eletriptan.
- Report promptly any of the following: headache more severe than usual, migraine; dizziness, faintness, blurred vision; chest, neck, or throat pain; irregular heart beat, palpitations; shortness of breath, wheezing, difficulty breathing; tingling, pain, or numbness in the face, hands, or feet; seizures; severe stomach pain, cramping, or bloody diarrhea.
- Do not drive or engage in any potentially hazardous task until reaction to drug is known.

EMEDASTINE DIFUMARATE

(em-e-das′teen di-foom′a-rate)

Emadine

Classifications: EYE PREPARATION; ANTIHISTAMINE, OCULAR; H₁-RECEPTOR ANTAGONIST

Therapeutic: OCULAR ANTIHISTAMINE

Pregnancy Category: B

AVAILABILITY 0.05% ophthalmic solution

ACTION & *THERAPEUTIC EFFECT*

Emedastine is a selective antagonist at H₁-receptors. It blocks H₁-receptors and inhibits histamine-stimulated vascular permeability in the conjunctiva. As a result, emedastine relieves the ocular pruritus associated with allergic conjunctivitis. *Relieves ocular pruritus related to allergic response to histamine.*

USES Temporary relief of seasonal allergic conjunctivitis.

CONTRAINDICATIONS Hypersensitivity to emedastine.

CAUTIOUS USE Hypersensitivity to other antihistamines, soft contact lenses; pregnancy (category B), lactation. Safety and efficacy in children <3 y are not established.

ROUTE & DOSAGE

Allergic Conjunctivitis

Adult: **Ophthalmic** 1 drop in affected eye q.i.d.

ADMINISTRATION

Instillation

- Wash hands before and after use.
- Shake well before using. Apply drops in the center of the lower conjunctival sac. Do not touch eyelids with dropper. ▪ Gently close eyes for 1–2 min after installa-

Common adverse effects in *italic*, life-threatening effects underlined; generic names in **bold**; classifications in SMALL CAPS; ◆ Canadian drug name; ◑ Prototype drug

539

tion of drops. ▪ Wait 10 min after installation of drug before inserting soft lenses into eyes ▪ Store in a tightly closed bottle. Protect the solution from light. ▪ Do not use if discolored.

ADVERSE EFFECTS (≥1%) **CNS:** Headache. **Special Senses:** *Ocular irritation, mild transient stinging and burning,* conjunctival congestion, eyelid edema, eye pain, photophobia, abnormal lacrimation.

INTERACTIONS Drug: No clinically significant interactions established.

PHARMACOKINETICS Absorption: Minimal. **Half-Life:** 3–4 h.

CLINICAL IMPLICATIONS

Assessment & Drug Effects

▪ Monitor for S&S of hypersensitivity to the drug (see Appendix F).

▪ Evaluate safety of engaging in hazardous activities since drowsiness is a potential adverse effect.

Patient & Family Education

▪ Learn potential adverse responses to emedastine.

▪ Eye drops contain benzalkonium chloride, which may damage soft contact lenses. After instillation of drops, wait 10 min before inserting these contact lens into the eye.

▪ Contact your physician if symptoms do not start to improve in 2 or 3 d.

EMLA (EUTECTIC MIXTURE OF LIDOCAINE AND PRILOCAINE)

EMLA Cream

Classifications: LOCAL ANESTHETIC

Therapeutic: LOCAL ANESTHETIC
Prototype: Procaine
Pregnancy Category: B

AVAILABILITY 2.5% lidocaine/2.5% prilocaine cream

ACTION & *THERAPEUTIC EFFECT*
EMLA cream is a mixture of lidocaine and prilocaine. The mixture forms a liquid at room temperature. Concentration of anesthetic in liquid versus an emulsifier is 80% versus 20%. *EMLA is a topical analgesic.*

USES Topical anesthetic on normal intact skin for local anesthesia.
UNLABELED USES Topical anesthetic prior to leg ulcer debridement; treatment of postherpetic neuralgia.

CONTRAINDICATIONS Patients with known sensitivity to local anesthetics; patients with congenital or idiopathy methemoglobinemia; tympanic membrane perforation; children <1 mo of age.
CAUTIOUS USE Acutely ill, debilitated, or older adult patients; severe liver disease; pregnancy (category B), lactation.

ROUTE & DOSAGE

Topical Anesthetic

Adult/Child: **Topical** >1 mo, Apply 2.5 g of cream ($^1/_2$ of 5 g tube) over 20–25 cm^2 of skin, cover with occlusive dressing and wait at least 1 h, then remove dressing and wipe off cream, cleanse area with an antiseptic solution and prepare patient for the procedure

---

Common adverse effects in *italic*, life-threatening effects underlined; generic names in **bold**; classifications in SMALL CAPS; ◆ Canadian drug name; ⊘ Prototype drug

ADMINISTRATION

Topical

▪ Apply a thick layer to skin (approximately $1/2$ of 5-g tube per 20–25 cm^2 or 2 × 2 in) at site of procedure. Apply an occlusive dressing. Do not spread out cream. Seal edges of dressing well to avoid leakage.

▪ Apply EMLA cream 1 h before routine procedure and 2 h before painful procedure.

▪ Remove EMLA cream prior to skin puncture and clean area with an aseptic solution.

▪ Store at room temperature 15°–30° C (59°–86° F).

ADVERSE EFFECTS (≥1%) **Hematologic:** Methemoglobinemia, especially in infants, small children, and patients with G6PD deficiency. **Skin:** *Blanching and redness,* itching, heat sensation. **Body as a Whole:** Edema, soreness, aching, numbness, heaviness. **Other:** The adverse effects of lidocaine could occur with large doses or if there is significant systemic absorption.

INTERACTIONS Drug: May cause additive toxicity with CLASS I ANTIARRHYTHMICS; may increase risk of developing methemoglobin when used with **acetaminophen, chloroquine, dapsone, fosphenytoin,** NITRATES and NITRITES, **nitric oxide, nitrofurantoin, nitroprusside, pamaquine, phenobarbital, phenytoin, primaquine, quinine,** or SULFONAMIDES.

PHARMACOKINETICS Absorption: Penetrates intact skin. **Onset:** 15–60 min. **Peak:** 2–3 h. **Duration:** 1–2 h after removal of cream. **Distribution:** Crosses blood–brain barrier and placenta, distributed into breast milk. **Metabolism:** In liver. **Elimination:** 98% of absorbed dose is ex-

creted in urine. **Half-Life:** 60–150 min.

CLINICAL IMPLICATIONS

Assessment & Drug Effects

▪ Monitor for local skin reactions including erythema, edema, itching, abnormal temperature sensations, and rash. These reactions are very common and usually disappear in 1–2 h.

▪ Note: Patients taking Class 1 antiarrhythmic drugs may experience toxic effects on the cardiovascular system. EMLA should be used with caution in these patients.

▪ Wash immediately with water or saline if contact with the eye occurs; protect the eye until sensation returns.

Patient & Family Education

▪ Skin analgesia lasts for 1 h following removal of the occlusive dressing. Analgesia may be accompanied by temporary loss of all sensation in the treated skin. Advise caution until sensation returns.

EMTRICITABINE

(em-tri'ci-ta-been)

Emtriva

Classifications: ANTIRETROVIRAL; NUCLEOSIDE REVERSE TRANSCRIPTASE INHIBITOR (NRTI)

Therapeutic: ANTIVIRAL; ANTIRETROVIRAL, NRTI

Prototype: Zidovudine

Pregnancy Category: D

AVAILABILITY 200 mg capsules; 10 mg/mL oral solution

ACTION & *THERAPEUTIC EFFECT*

Emtricitabine is a synthetic nucleoside reverse transcriptase analogue with inhibitory activity against HIV.

Common adverse effects in *italic*, life-threatening effects underlined; generic names in **bold**; classifications in SMALL CAPS; ♣ Canadian drug name; ☻ Prototype drug

541

It inhibits HIV-1 reverse transcriptase (RT), both by competing with the natural DNA nucleoside and by incorporation into viral DNA, which terminates the formation of the viral DNA chain. *The viral load is decreased as measured by an increase in CD4 leukocyte count and suppression of viral RNA.*

USES Treatment of HIV in combination with other antiretroviral agents. **UNLABELED USES** Treatment of chronic hepatitis B in HIV-positive patients.

CONTRAINDICATIONS Children <3 mo; suicidal ideation; HBV infection; pregnancy (category D); lactation.
CAUTIOUS USE Renal impairment, and with end-stage renal disease; hepatic impairment; history of mental illness including bipolar disorder, psychosis; alcoholism; substance abuse; seizure disorders; hypercholesterolemia, hypertriglyceridemia.

ROUTE & DOSAGE

HIV

Adult: **PO** 200 mg once/d
Children (3 mo–17 yrs): **PO** 6 mg/kg d (max 240mg/d) OR if >33 kg 200 mg qd

Renal Impairment

Cl$_{cr}$ 30–49 mL/min: 200 mg q48h; 15–29 mL/min: 200 mg q72h; <15 mL/min: 200 mg q96h

ADMINISTRATION

Oral
- Give at the same time daily.
- Store between 15°–30° C (59°–86° F) in a tightly closed container.

ADVERSE EFFECTS (≥1%) **Body as a Whole:** Asthenia, neuropathy, peripheral neuritis. **CNS:** *Headache,* depression, dizziness, insomnia. **GI:** *Diarrhea, nausea,* dyspepsia, abdominal pain, hepatomegaly. **Metabolic:** Lactic acidosis. **Musculoskeletal:** Arthralgia, myalgia, paresthesias. **Respiratory:** Cough, rhinitis. **Skin:** *Rash,* hyperpigmentation of palms and soles of feet.

INTERACTIONS None yet reported.

PHARMACOKINETICS Absorption: 93% reaches systemic circulation. **Peak:** 1–2 h. **Distribution:** 4% protein bound. **Metabolism:** In liver. **Elimination:** Urine. **Half-Life:** 10 h (active metabolite has intracellular half-life of 39 h).

CLINICAL IMPLICATIONS

Assessment & Drug Effects
- Note: Persons with a detectable viral load to be switched from lamivudine to emtricitabine should have genotypic testing to determine whether the M184 mutation is present.
- Monitor individuals with a history of depression for signs and symptoms of suicidal ideation.
- Monitor closely for S&S of lactic acidosis, especially in persons with known risk factors such as female gender, obesity, alcoholism, or hepatic disease.
- Withhold drug and notify physician if S&S suggestive of lactic acidosis or hepatotoxicity occur.
- Lab tests: Baseline renal function tests; frequent LFTs and serum electrolytes during the last trimester of pregnancy; complete blood chemistry if lactic acidosis is suspected; and periodic lipid profile; serum cholesterol and triglycerides; bone density monitoring for history of osteoporosis.
- Monitor closely for severe exacerbation of hepatitis B in coinfected patients if this drug is discontinued.

Patient & Family Education

- Inform physician, prior to taking this drug, if you have used lamivudine and developed resistance to it.
- May cause serious CNS effects. Avoid driving or operating machinery until individual reaction to the drug is known.
- Report any of the following to the physician: difficulty breathing, shortness of breath, fast or irregular heartbeat; weight gain with fullness around waist and/or face; vomiting or diarrhea; unexplained muscle aches, pains, weakness, or fatigue; yellow eyes or skin.
- Avoid alcoholic drinks while taking this drug.
- Do not self-treat nausea, vomiting, or stomach pain. Contact physician for guidance.

ENALAPRIL MALEATE ℗ᵣ

(e-nal'a-pril)
Vasotec

ENALAPRILAT

Vasotec I.V.

Classifications: ANGIOTENSIN-CONVERTING ENZYME (ACE) INHIBITOR; ANTIHYPERTENSIVE
Therapeutic: ANTIHYPERTENSIVE; ACE INHIBITOR
Pregnancy Category: C first trimester; D second and third trimester

AVAILABILITY 2.5 mg, 5 mg, 10 mg, 20 mg tablets; 1.25 mg/mL injection; 1 mg/mL suspension

ACTION & *THERAPEUTIC EFFECT*

Angiotensin-converting enzyme (ACE) inhibitor that catalyzes the conversion of angiotensin I to angiotensin II, a vasoconstrictor substance. Therefore, inhibition of ACE decreases angiotensin II levels, thus decreasing vasopressor activity and aldosterone secretion. Both actions achieve an antihypertensive effect by suppression of the renin–angiotensin–aldosterone system. ACE inhibitors also reduce peripheral arterial resistance (afterload), pulmonary capillary wedge pressure (PCWP), a measure of preload, pulmonary vascular resistance, and improve cardiac output as well as exercise tolerance. *Antihypertensive effect related to suppression of the renin-angiotensin-aldosterone system causes vasodilation and, therefore, lower blood pressure. Improvement in cardiac output results in increased exercise tolerance.*

USES Management of mild to moderate hypertension as monotherapy or with a diuretic. Malignant, refractory, accelerated, and renovascular hypertension (except in bilateral renal artery stenosis or renal artery stenosis in a solitary kidney), CHF.
UNLABELED USES Hypertension or renal crisis in scleroderma.

CONTRAINDICATIONS Hypersensitivity to enalapril or captopril; hypotension. There has been evidence of fetotoxicity and kidney damage in newborns exposed to ACE inhibitors during pregnancy (category C in first trimester, and category D in second and third trimester); infants and children with $Cl_{cr} < 30$ mL/min/1.73 m^2.
CAUTIOUS USE Renal impairment, renal artery stenosis; patients with hypovolemia, receiving diuretics; undergoing dialysis; hepatic disease; bone marrow suppression; patients in whom excessive hypotension would present a hazard (e.g., cerebrovascular insufficiency); CHF; aortic stenosis, cardiomyopathy hepatic impairment; diabetes mellitus, lactation.

Common adverse effects in *italic*, life-threatening effects <u>underlined</u>; generic names in **bold**; classifications in SMALL CAPS; ♣ Canadian drug name; ℗ Prototype drug

543

E

ROUTE & DOSAGE

Hypertension

Adult: **PO** 5 mg/d, may increase to 10–40 mg/d in 1–2 divided doses **IV** 1.25 mg q6h, may give up to 5 mg q6h in hypertensive emergencies
Neonate: **PO** 0.1 mg/kg q24h
Child: **PO** 0.08 mg/kg/d in 1–2 divided doses, may increase (max: 5 mg/kg/d)

Congestive Heart Failure

Adult: **PO** 2.5 mg 1–2 times/d, may increase up to 5–20 mg/d in 1–2 divided doses (max: 40 mg/d)

Renal Impairment

Enalapril: Cl_{cr} <30 mL/min, start with 2.5 mg dose then titrate.
Enalaprilat: Cl_{cr} <30 mL/min, start with dose of 0.625 mg q6h then titrate.
Hemodialysis: Administer post-dialysis or give 20–25% supplemental dose.

ADMINISTRATION

Oral

- Discontinue diuretics, if possible, for 2–3 d prior to initial oral dose to reduce incidence of hypotension. If the diuretic cannot be discontinued, give an initial dose of 2.5 mg. Keep patient under medical supervision for at least 2 h and until BP has stabilized for at least an additional hour.
- Give with food or drink of patient's choice.
- Protect from heat and light. Expiration date: 30 mo following date of manufacture if stored at <30° C.
- Conversion from IV to oral therapy: Recommended initial dose is 5 mg once a day with a creatinine clearance (Cl_{cr}) >30 mL/min, and 2.5 mg once daily with a Cl_{cr} <30 mL/min.

- Store tablets at 30° C (86° F); protect from heat and light.

Intravenous

Note: Verify correct IV concentration and rate of infusion/injection with physician for neonates, infants, children.

PREPARE: **Direct:** Give undiluted. **Intermittent:** Dilute in 50 mL of D5W, NS, D5/NS, D5/LR.
ADMINISTER: **Direct/Intermittent:** Give direct IV slowly over at least 5 min through a port of a free flowing infusion of D5W or NS or as an infusion over 5 min.
INCOMPATIBILITIES Y-site: **Amphotericin B, amphotericin B cholesteryl, cefepime, phenytoin.**

ADVERSE EFFECTS (≥1%) **CNS:** *Headache, dizziness,* fatigue, nervousness, paresthesias, asthenia, insomnia, somnolence. **CV:** *Hypotension including postural hypotension;* syncope, palpitations, chest pain. **GI:** Diarrhea, nausea, abdominal pain, loss of *taste,* dyspepsia. **Hematologic:** Decreased Hgb and Hct. **Urogenital:** <u>Acute kidney failure</u>, deterioration in kidney function. **Skin:** Pruritus with and without *rash,* angioedema, erythema. **Metabolic:** Hyperkalemia. **Respiratory:** Cough.

INTERACTIONS Drug: Indomethacin and other NSAIDs may decrease antihypertensive activity; POTASSIUM SUPPLEMENTS, POTASSIUM-SPARING DIURETICS may cause hyperkalemia; may increase **lithium** levels and toxicity.

PHARMACOKINETICS Absorption: 70% absorbed from GI tract. **Onset:** 1 h PO; 15 min IV. **Peak:** 4–8 h PO; 4 h IV. **Duration:** 12–24 h PO; 6 h IV. **Distribution:** Limited amount crosses blood–brain barrier; crosses placenta. **Metabolism:** PO dose undergoes first-pass metabolism in liver to active form, enalaprilat. **Elimination:** 60% in urine, 33% in feces within 24 h. **Half-Life:** 2 h.

CLINICAL IMPLICATIONS

Assessment & Drug Effects

- Monitor for therapeutic effectiveness. Peak effects after the first IV dose may not occur for up to 4 h; peak effects of subsequent doses may exceed those of the first.
- Maintain bedrest and monitor BP for the first 3 h after the initial IV dose. First-dose phenomenon (i.e., a sudden exaggerated hypotensive response) may occur within 1–3 h of first IV dose, especially in the patient with very high blood pressure or one on a diuretic and controlled salt intake regimen. An IV infusion of normal saline for volume expansion may be ordered to counteract the hypotensive response. This initial response is not an indicator to stop therapy.
- Monitor BP for first several days of therapy. If antihypertensive effect is diminished before 24 h, the total dose may be given as 2 divided doses.
- Report transient hypotension with lightheadedness. Older adults are particularly sensitive to drug-induced hypotension. Supervise ambulation until BP has stabilized.
- Lab tests: Monitor serum potassium and be alert to symptoms of hyperkalemia (K^+ >5.7 mEq/L). Patients who have diabetes, impaired kidney function, or CHF are at risk of developing hyperkalemia during enalapril treatment. Monitor kidney function closely during first few weeks of therapy.

Patient & Family Education

- Full antihypertensive effect may not be experienced until several weeks after enalapril therapy starts.

- When drug is discontinued due to severe hypotension, the hypotensive effect may persist a week or longer after termination because of long duration of drug action.
- Do not follow a low-sodium diet (e.g., low-sodium foods or low-sodium milk) without approval from physician.
- Avoid use of salt substitute (principal ingredient: potassium salt) and potassium supplements because of the potential for hyperkalemia.
- Notify physician of a persistent nonproductive cough, especially at night, accompanied by nasal congestion.
- Report to physician promptly if swelling of face, eyelids, tongue, lips, or extremities occurs. Angioedema is a rare adverse effect and, if accompanied by laryngeal edema, may be fatal.
- Do not drive or engage in other potentially hazardous activities until response to drug is known.

ENFUVIRTIDE

(en-fu-vir'tide)
Fuzeon
Classifications: ANTIVIRAL; ANTIRETROVIRAL; FUSION INHIBITOR
Therapeutic: ANTIRETROVIRAL; FUSION INHIBITOR
Pregnancy Category: B

AVAILABILITY 90 mg/mL injection

ACTION & *THERAPEUTIC EFFECT*

Enfuvirtide interferes with entry of HIV-1 into host cells by inhibiting fusion of the virus with the host cell membranes. In order for HIV-1 to enter and infect a human cell, the viral surface glycoprotein (gp41) must bind to the host CD4+ cells. Then, the viral glycoprotein undergoes a change in shape facil-

---

Common adverse effects in *italic*, life-threatening effects underlined; generic names in **bold**; classifications in SMALL CAPS; ◆ Canadian drug name; ◑ Prototype drug

545

itating the fusion of viral membranes with the host cell membrane. Enfuvirtide binds to viral envelope glycoprotein (gp41) and prevents the change in shape required for membrane fusion and viral entry into target cells. *Prevents entry of the HIV-1 virus into host cells.*

USES Treatment of advanced HIV disease with evidence of resistance to other therapies.

CONTRAINDICATIONS Hypersensitivity to enfuvirtide or any of its components; lactation.
CAUTIOUS USE Renal and hepatic impairment; renal clearance of <35 mL/min; bacterial pneumonia, low initial CD4 count, past history of lung disease, high initial viral load, IV drug use; mannitol hypersensitivity; history of pulmonary disease; pregnancy (category B).

ROUTE & DOSAGE

Advanced HIV Disease

Adult/Adolescent: **SC** ≥16 y or ≥42.6 kg, 90 mg b.i.d.
Child/Adolescent: **SC** 6–16 y or <42.6 kg, 2 mg/kg (up to 90 mg) b.i.d.

ADMINISTRATION

Subcutaneous

- Reconstitute by adding 1.1 mL sterile water for injection into vial. Mix by gently tapping vial for 10 sec, then gently rolling in palms of hands. Ensure that no drug is remaining on vial wall. Allow vial to stand until powder completely dissolves (up to 45 min). Solution should be clear, colorless, and without bubbles or particulate matter.
- Bring refrigerated reconstituted solution to room temperature before injection. Ensure that powder is

fully dissolved and solution is clear, colorless, and without bubbles or particulate matter.
- Inject into upper arm, abdomen, or anterior thigh.
- Rotate injection sites and inject in an area with no current injection site reaction.
- Store unreconstituted vials at 15°–30° C (59°–86° F) or refrigerated at 2°–6° C (3°–46° F); do not freeze.

ADVERSE EFFECTS (≥1%) **Body as a Whole:** *Injection site reactions (pain, induration, erythema, nodules, cysts, pruritus, ecchymoses),* infection at injection site, *fatigue,* systemic hypersensitivity reactions, Guillain-Barré syndrome, asthenia, herpes simplex infections, influenza, lymphadenopathy, myalgia, peripheral neuropathy. **CNS:** Anxiety, depression, *insomnia.* **GI:** *Diarrhea, nausea,* abdominal pain, anorexia, constipation, dysgeusia, pancreatitis, weight loss. **Hematologic:** Eosinophilia, anemia. **Metabolic:** Increased amylase, increased lipase, increased ALT and AST, hypertriglyceridemia. **Respiratory:** Bacterial pneumonia, acute respiratory distress syndrome, cough, sinusitis. **Skin:** Pruritus, skin papilloma. **Special Senses:** Conjunctivitis. **Urogenital:** Glomerulonephritis.

INTERACTIONS : None yet reported.

PHARMACOKINETICS Absorption: 84.3% absorbed from SC site. **Peak:** Average 4–8 h. **Distribution:** 92% protein bound. **Metabolism:** Catabolized into constituent amino acids. **Half-Life:** 4 h.

CLINICAL IMPLICATIONS

Assessment & Drug Effects

- Inspect SC sites for S&S of site reactions (e.g., itching, swelling, redness, pain, tenderness, or

hardened skin) that usually last for <7 d postinjection.
- Monitor closely for S&S of pneumonia, especially with low initial CD4 count, high initial viral load, IV drug use, smoking, or prior history of lung disease.
- Lab tests: Periodic LFTs, serum lipase and amylase, lipid profile, and CBC with differential.

Patient & Family Education
- Report promptly S&S of infection at SC injection sites: increased heat, redness, pain, or oozing.
- Report promptly S&S of pneumonia: cough with fever, rapid breathing, shortness of breath.

ENOXAPARIN ◉

(e-nox'a-pa-rin)
Lovenox
Classifications: ANTICOAGULANT; LOW MOLECULAR WEIGHT HEPARIN
Therapeutic: ANTITHROMBOTIC; LOW MOLECULAR WEIGHT HEPARIN
Pregnancy Category: B

AVAILABILITY 30 mg/0.3 mL, 40 mg/0.4 mL, 60 mg/0.6 mL, 80 mg/ 0.8 mL, 100 mg/1 mL injection

ACTION & *THERAPEUTIC EFFECT*
Low molecular weight heparin with antithrombotic properties. Does not affect PT. Does affect thrombin time (TT) and activated thromboplastin time (aPTT) up to 1.8 times the control value. Antithrombotic properties are due to its antifactor Xa and antithrombin (antifactor IIa) in the coagulation activities. *An effective anticoagulation agent, it is used for prophylactic treatment as an antithrombotic agent following certain types of surgery.*

USES Prevention of deep vein thrombosis (DVT) after hip, knee, or ab-dominal surgery, treatment of DVT and pulmonary embolism, management of acute coronary syndrome.

CONTRAINDICATIONS Patients with active major bleeding, GI bleeding, hemophilia, heparin hypersensitivity, heparin-induced thrombocytopenia (HIT), thrombocytopenia associated with an antiplatelet antibody in the presence of enoxaparin, bleeding disorders, idiopathic thrombocytopenia purpura (ITP), hypersensitivity to enoxaparin; porcine protein hypersensitivity, neonates, infants and children.
CAUTIOUS USE Uncontrolled arterial hypertension, recent history of GI disease, conditions or surgery with increased risk of bleeding, hepatic disease, hypertension, coagulopathy, thrombocytopenia, dental disease, diabetic retinopathy, dialysis, diverticulitis, inflammatory bowel disease, peptic ulcer disease, older adults, endocarditis, renal disease, renal impairment, stroke, surgery, pregnancy (category B), lactation.

ROUTE & DOSAGE

Prevention of DVT after Hip or Knee Surgery
Adult: **SC** 30 mg b.i.d. for 10–14 d starting 12–24 h post-surgery

Prevention of DVT after Abdominal Surgery
Adult: **SC** 40 mg q.d. starting 2 h before surgery and continuing for 7–10 d (max: 12 d)

Treatment of DVT and Pulmonary Embolus
Adult: **SC** 1 mg/kg q12h or 1.5 mg/kg/d; monitor anti-Xa activity to determine appropriate dose

Acute Coronary Syndrome
Adult: **SC** 1 mg/kg q12h for 2–8 d, give concurrently with aspirin 100–325 mg/d

Common adverse effects in *italic*, life-threatening effects underlined; generic names in **bold**; classifications in SMALL CAPS; ♣ Canadian drug name; ◉ Prototype drug

547

Renal Impairment

Cl_{cr} <30 mL/min: 30 mg or 1 mg/kg q24h

ADMINISTRATION

Subcutaneous

- Use a TB syringe or prefilled syringe to ensure accurate dosage.
- Do not expel the air bubble from the 30 or 40 mg prefilled syringe before injection.
- Place patient in a supine position for injection of the drug.
- Alternate injections between left and right anterolateral and posterolateral abdominal wall.
- Hold the skin fold between the thumb and forefinger and insert the whole length of the needle into the skin fold. Hold skin fold throughout the injection. Do not rub site post injection.
- Store at 15°–30° C (59°–86° F).

ADVERSE EFFECTS (≥1%) **Body as a Whole:** Allergic reactions (rash, urticaria), fever, angioedema arthralgia, pain and inflammation at injection site, peripheral edema, arthralgia, fever. **Digestive:** Abnormal liver function tests. **Hematologic:** _Hemorrhage,_ thrombocytopenia, ecchymoses, anemia. **Respiratory:** Dyspnea. **Skin:** Rash, pruritus.

INTERACTIONS Drug: Aspirin, NSAIDS, **warfarin** can increase risk of hemorrhage. **Herbal: Garlic, ginger, ginkgo, feverfew, horse chestnut** may increase risk of bleeding.

PHARMACOKINETICS Absorption: 91% absorbed from SC injection site. **Peak:** 3 h. **Duration:** 4.6 h. **Distribution:** Appears to accumulate in liver, kidneys, and spleen. Does not cross placenta. **Elimination:** Primarily in urine. **Half-Life:** 4.6 h.

CLINICAL IMPLICATIONS

Assessment & Drug Effects

- Lab tests: Baseline coagulation studies; periodic CBC, platelet count, urine and stool for occult blood.
- Monitor platelet count closely. Withhold drug and notify physician if platelet count less than 100,000/mm^3.
- Monitor closely patients with renal insufficiency and older adults who are at higher risk for thrombocytopenia.
- Monitor for and report immediately any sign or symptom of unexplained bleeding.

Patient & Family Education

- Report to physician promptly signs of unexplained bleeding such as: pink, red, or dark brown urine; red or dark brown vomitus; bleeding gums or bloody sputum; dark, tarry stools.
- Do not take any OTC drugs without first consulting physician.

ENTACAPONE

(en-ta′ca-pone)

Comtan

Classifications: CATECHOLAMINE O-METHYLTRANSFERASE (COMT) INHIBITOR; ANTIPARKINSON AGENT

Therapeutic: ANTIPARKINSON AGENT

Prototype: Tolcapone

Pregnancy Category: C

AVAILABILITY 200 mg tablets

ACTION & THERAPEUTIC EFFECT

Selective inhibitor of catecholamine O-methyltransferase (COMT). COMT is responsible for metabolizing levodopa to an intermediate compound 3-O-methyldopa, a chemical which interferes with the availability of levodopa to the brain. Therefore, it increases availability of levodopa in CNS. *Taken with levodopa, it decreases the formation of 3-O-methyldopa, thus increasing the duration of the motor response of the brain to levodopa in Parkinson's disease. Effectiveness is indicated by diminished Parkinson's manifestations.*

USES Adjunct to levodopa/carbidopa to treat Parkinson's disease.

CONTRAINDICATIONS Hypersensitivity to entacapone; concurrent MAO inhibitors; children; pregnancy (category D).
CAUTIOUS USE Hepatic impairment; biliary obstruction; concomitant administration with CNS depressants; drugs metabolized by COMT (e.g., isoproterenol, epinephrine, etc.); history of hypotension or syncope; lactation.

ROUTE & DOSAGE

Parkinson's Disease
Adult: **PO** 200 mg administered with each dose of levodopa/carbidopa up to 8 times/d

ADMINISTRATION

Oral
- Give simultaneously with each levodopa/carbidopa dose.
- Must be tapered if discontinued. Never discontinue abruptly.
- Do not administer to patients receiving nonselective MAO inhibitors.
- Store at 15°–30° C (59°–86° F).

ADVERSE EFFECTS (≥1%) **Body as a Whole:** Back pain, fatigue, asthenia. **CNS:** *Dyskinesia, hyperkinesia,* hypokinesia, dizziness, anxiety, somnolence, agitation. **GI:** Taste perversion, *nausea, diarrhea,* abdominal pain, constipation, vomiting, dry mouth, dyspepsia, flatulence, gastritis. **Respiratory:** Dyspnea. **Skin:** Increased sweating. **Other:** *Urine discoloration,* purpura.

INTERACTIONS Drug: Extreme caution must be used if administered with a nonselective MAOI; **bitolterol, dobutamine, dopamine, epinephrine, isoetharine, isoproterenol, methyldopa, norepinephrine** may increase heart rates, possibly cause arrhythmias, excessive changes in BP.

PHARMACOKINETICS Absorption: Rapidly absorbed, 35% bioavailable. **Peak:** 1 h. **Distribution:** Highly protein bound. **Metabolism:** Extensively metabolized in plasma and erythrocytes. **Elimination:** Primarily in feces. **Half-Life:** 2.4 h (terminal).

CLINICAL IMPLICATIONS

Assessment & Drug Effects
- Monitor carefully for hyperpyrexia, confusion, or emergence of Parkinson's S&S during drug withdrawal.
- Monitor for orthostatic hypotension & worsening of dyskinesia or hyperkinesia.
- Lab tests: Hgb and serum ferritin levels with prolonged therapy.

Patient & Family Education
- Take with levodopa/carbidopa; not effective alone.
- Do not discontinue abruptly; gradually reduce dosage.
- Exercise caution when rising from a sitting or lying position because faintness/dizziness can occur.
- Exercise caution with hazardous activities until reaction to the drug is known.
- Harmless brownish-orange discoloration of urine is possible.
- Report unusual adverse effects (e.g., hallucinations/unexplained diarrhea).

Common adverse effects in *italic*, life-threatening effects underlined; generic names in **bold**, classifications in SMALL CAPS; ♣ Canadian drug name; ☯ Prototype drug

549

ENTECAVIR

(en-te'ca-vir)
Baraclude
Classifications: ANTIVIRAL AGENT; ANTIRETROVIRAL; NUCLEOSIDE REVERSE TRANSCRIPTASE INHIBITOR (NRTI)
Therapeutic: ANTIRETROVIRAL; NRTI
Prototype: Lamivudine
Pregnancy Category: C

AVAILABILITY 0.5 and 1 mg tablets; 0.05 mg/mL oral solution

ACTION & *THERAPEUTIC EFFECT*
Inhibits hepatitis B viral (HBV) DNA polymerase by inhibiting viral reverse transcriptase of messenger RNA that ultimately results in inhibiting the synthesis of HBV DNA. *The antiviral activity of entecavir inhibits HBV DNA synthesis.*

USES Treatment of chronic hepatitis B infection in patients who have shown resistance to lamivudine or in nucleoside-treatment-naïve patients.

CONTRAINDICATIONS Hypersensitivity to entecavir; pregnancy (category C), lactation; safety and effectiveness in children <16 y have not been established.
CAUTIOUS USE Liver transplant patients; concurrent use of cyclosporine; renal impairment, ESRF, dialysis; labor and delivery.

ROUTE & DOSAGE

Chronic Hepatitis B (nucleoside-treatment–naïve patients)
Adult/Adolescent ≥16 y: **PO** 0.5 mg qd

Chronic Hepatitis B (lamivudine-resistant patients)
Adult/Adolescent ≥16 y: **PO** 1 mg qd

Renal Impairment
Cl_{cr} 30–49 mL/min: decrease dose by 50%; 10–29 mL/min: decrease dose by 70%; <10 mL/min: decrease dose by 90%

ADMINISTRATION

Oral
- Give on an empty stomach (at least 2 h before/after a meal).
- Administer after hemodialysis.
- Dosage adjustment is recommended with Cl_{cr} <50 mL/min.
- Store in a tightly closed container at 15°–30° C (59°–86° F)

ADVERSE EFFECTS (≥1%) **CNS:** Dizziness, fatigue, headache, insomnia, somnolence. **GI:** Diarrhea, dyspepsia, nausea, vomiting. **Metabolic:** Elevated liver enzymes (ALT, AST), hyperamylasemia, elevated lipase concentration, hyperbilirubinemia, fasting hyperglycemia, glycosuria, hematuria, <u>lactic acidosis</u>.

INTERACTIONS Drug: Use of entecavir with drugs that reduce renal function or compete for active tubular secretion may increase serum concentrations of either drug. **Food:** High-fat meal reduces oral absorption.

PHARMACOKINETICS Peak: 0.5–1 h. **Distribution:** 13% protein bound. **Metabolism:** Minimal. **Elimination:** Primarily in the urine. **Half-Life:** 128–149 h.

CLINICAL IMPLICATIONS

Assessment & Drug Effects
- Monitor closely for adverse reactions when drugs that are known to affect renal function are taken concurrently.

- Lab tests: Periodic LFTs; monitor hepatic function for several months after drug is D/C; periodic fasting plasma glucose.
- Monitor for S&S of lactic acidosis, including respiratory distress, tachycardia, and irregular HR.

Patient & Family Education

- Follow directions for taking the drug (see ADMINISTRATION).
- Do not discontinue medication without consent of physician.
- Do not drive or engage in potentially hazardous activities until response to drug is known.
- Inform physician if you are or plan to become pregnant.
- Report any of the following to a health care provider: unexplained tiredness or weakness, unusual muscle pain, difficulty breathing, cold extremities, dizziness or light-headedness, irregular heartbeat, loss of appetite, stomach pain, nausea, vomiting, clay-colored stool, dark urine, or jaundice.

EPHEDRINE HYDROCHLORIDE

(e-fed′rin)
Efedron

EPHEDRINE SULFATE

Ectasule, Ephedsol, Vatronol
Classifications: ALPHA- AND BETA-ADRENERGIC AGONIST; BRONCHODILATOR
Therapeutic: BRONCHODILATOR
Prototype: Epinephrine HCl
Pregnancy Category: C

AVAILABILITY 25 mg capsules; 50 mg/mL injection; 0.25% nasal spray; 1% nasal gel

ACTION & THERAPEUTIC EFFECT
Both indirect- and direct-acting sympathomimetic amine. Thought to act indirectly by releasing tissue stores of norepinephrine and directly by stimulation of alpha-, beta$_1$-, and beta$_2$-adrenergic receptors. Like epinephrine, contracts dilated arterioles of nasal mucosa, thus reducing engorgement and edema and facilitating ventilation and drainage. *Ephedrine relaxes bronchial smooth muscle by the stimulation of beta$_2$-receptors, relieving mild bronchospasm, improving air exchange and increasing vital capacity.*

USES Temporary relief of congestion of hay fever, allergic rhinitis, and sinusitis; and in treatment and prophylaxis of mild cases of acute asthma and in patients with chronic asthma requiring continuing treatment. Also has been used for its CNS stimulant actions in treatment of narcolepsy, to improve respiration in narcotic and barbiturate poisoning, to combat hypotensive states, especially those associated with spinal anesthesia; in management of enuresis or impaired bladder control; as adjunct in treatment of myasthenia gravis; as mydriatic; to relieve dysmenorrhea; and for temporary support of ventricular rate in Adams-Stokes syndrome; for peripheral edema secondary to type I diabetic neuropathy.

CONTRAINDICATIONS History of hypersensitivity to ephedrine or other sympathomimetics; narrow-angle glaucoma; angina pectoris, coronary insufficiency, chronic heart disease, uncontrolled hypertension, cardiac arrhythmias, cardiomyopathy; hypovolemia; concurrent MAOI therapy; pregnancy (category C), lactation.
CAUTIOUS USE Hypertension, arteriosclerosis, closed-angle glaucoma; diabetes mellitus; hyperthyroidism; prostatic hypertrophy.

Common adverse effects in *italic*, life-threatening effects underlined; generic names in **bold**; classifications in SMALL CAPS; ♣ Canadian drug name; ⊘ Prototype drug

551

E

ROUTE & DOSAGE

Bronchodilator, Nasal Decongestant

Adult: **PO** 25–50 mg q3–4h prn (max: 150 mg/24 h) **IM/IV/SC** 12.5–25 mg
Child: **PO** >2 y, 2–3 mg/kg/d in 4–6 divided doses; 6–12 y, 6.25–12.5 mg q4h (max: 75 mg/24 h)

Hypotension

Adult: **PO** 25 mg 1–4 times/d (max: 150 mg/24 h) **IM/SC/IV** 10–50 mg IM/SC or 10–25 mg slow IV, may repeat in 5–10 min if necessary (max: 150 mg/24 h)
Child: **PO/IM/SC/IV** 3 mg/kg/d in 4–6 divided doses (max: 75 mg/24 h)

Myasthenia Gravis

Adult: **PO** 25 mg t.i.d. or q.i.d.

Enuresis

Adult: **PO** 25 mg h.s.

Urinary Incontinence

Geriatric: **PO** 25–50 mg q6h.

Nasal Decongestant

Adult: **Intranasal** 2–4 drops or a small amount of jelly in each nostril no more than q.i.d. for 3–4 consecutive days

ADMINISTRATION

Oral

- Administer last dose a few hours before bedtime, if possible, to minimize insomnia.
- Store at 15°–30° C (59°–86° F) in tightly closed, light-resistant containers unless otherwise directed by the manufacturer.

Intranasal

- Have patient clear nose before instilling drops. Instruct patient to blow gently with both nostrils open. Generally, nose drops are instilled with head in lateral, head-low position to avoid entry of drug into throat. Check with physician.

Intravenous

PREPARE: Direct: Give undiluted.
ADMINISTER: Direct: Direct IV at a rate of 10 mg or fraction thereof over 30–60 sec.
INCOMPATIBILITIES Solution/additive: Hydrocortisone, pentobarbital, phenobarbital, secobarbital, thiopental. Y-site: Thiopental.

- Store in tightly closed, light-resistant containers. Do not use liquid formulation unless it is absolutely clear.

ADVERSE EFFECTS (≥1%) **CNS:** Headache, insomnia, *nervousness,* anxiety, tremulousness, giddiness. **CV:** Palpitation, tachycardia, precordial pain, cardiac arrhythmias. **GU:** Difficult or painful urination, acute urinary retention (especially older men with prostatism). **GI:** Nausea, vomiting, anorexia. **Body as a Whole:** Sweating, thirst, overdosage: euphoria, confusion, delirium, convulsions, pyrexia, hypertension, rebound hypotension, respiratory difficulty. **Skin:** Fixed-drug eruption. Topical use: *Burning, stinging,* dryness of nasal mucosa, sneezing, rebound congestion.

DIAGNOSTIC TEST INTERFERENCE Ephedrine is generally withdrawn at least 12 h before *sensitivity tests* are made to prevent false-positive reactions.

INTERACTIONS Drug: MAO INHIBITORS, TRICYCLIC ANTIDEPRESSANTS, **furazolidone, guanethidine** may increase alpha-adrenergic effects (headache, hyperpyrexia, hypertension); **sodium bicarbonate** decreases renal elimination of ephe-

Common adverse effects in *italic*, life-threatening effects underlined; generic names in **bold**; classifications in SMALL CAPS; ♣ Canadian drug name; ⨀ Prototype drug

drine, increasing its CNS effects; **epinephrine, norepinephrine** compound sympathomimetic effects; effects of ALPHA AND BETA BLOCKERS and ephedrine antagonized.

PHARMACOKINETICS Absorption: Readily absorbed from GI tract. **Peak:** 15 min–1 h. **Duration:** Bronchodilation 2–4 h; cardiac & pressor effects up to 4 h PO and 1 h IV. **Distribution:** Widely distributed; crosses blood–brain barrier and placenta; distributed into breast milk. **Metabolism:** Small amounts metabolized in liver. **Elimination:** In urine. **Half-Life:** 3–6 h.

CLINICAL IMPLICATIONS

Assessment & Drug Effects

- Supervise continuously patients receiving ephedrine IV. Take baseline BP and other vital signs. Check BP repeatedly during first 5 min, then q3–5min until stabilized.
- Monitor I&O ratio and pattern, especially in older male patients. Encourage patient to void before taking medication (see ADVERSE EFFECTS).
- Monitor for systemic effects of nose drops that can occur because of excessive dosage from rapid absorption of drug solution through nasal mucosa. This is most likely to occur in older adults.

Patient & Family Education

- Note: Ephedrine is a commonly abused drug. Learn adverse effects and dangers; take medication ONLY as prescribed.
- Do not take OTC medications for coughs, colds, allergies, or asthma unless approved by physician. Ephedrine is a common ingredient in these preparations.

EPINASTINE HYDROCHLORIDE

(e-pi-nas′teen)
Elestat
Pregnancy Category: C
See Appendix A-1.

E

EPINEPHRINE 🅟

(ep-i-ne′frin)
Epinephrine Pediatric, EpiPen Auto-Injector, Primatene Mist Suspension

EPINEPHRINE BITARTRATE

AsthmaHaler, Bronkaid Mist Suspension, Bronitin Mist Suspension, Epitrate, Primatene Mist Suspension

EPINEPHRINE HYDROCHLORIDE

Adrenalin Chloride, Bronkaid Mistometer, Dysne-Inhal, Sus-Phrine ◆

EPINEPHRINE, RACEMIC

Vaponefrin ◆

Classifications: ALPHA- AND BETA-ADRENERGIC AGONIST; CARDIAC STIMULANT; VASOPRESSOR
Therapeutic: ANTI-ANAPHYLACTIC; CARDIAC STIMULANT; VASOPRESSOR
Pregnancy Category: C

AVAILABILITY 1:100, 1:1000, 2.25% solution for inhalation; 0.35 mg, 0.2 mg spray; 1:1000, 1:2000, 1:10,000, 1:100,000 injection; 1:200 suspension; 0.1%, 0.5%, 1%, 2% ophthalmic solution; 0.1% nasal solution

ACTION & *THERAPEUTIC EFFECT* Naturally occurring catecholamine obtained from animal adrenal

Common adverse effects in *italic*, life-threatening effects underlined; generic names in **bold**; classifications in SMALL CAPS; ◆ Canadian drug name; 🅟 Prototype drug

553

glands; it is also prepared synthetically. Acts directly on both alpha and beta receptors; the most potent activator of alpha receptors. Strengthens myocardial contraction; increases systolic but may decrease diastolic blood pressure; increases cardiac rate and cardiac output. Constricts bronchial arterioles and inhibits histamine release, thus reducing congestion and edema and increasing tidal volume and vital capacity. Relaxes uterine smooth musculature and inhibits uterine contractions. *Imitates all actions of sympathetic nervous system except those on arteries of the face and sweat glands.*

USES Temporary relief of bronchospasm, acute asthmatic attack, mucosal congestion, hypersensitivity and anaphylactic reactions, syncope due to heart block or carotid sinus hypersensitivity, and to restore cardiac rhythm in cardiac arrest. Ophthalmic preparation is used in management of simple (open-angle) glaucoma, generally as an adjunct to topical miotics and oral carbonic anhydrase inhibitors; also used as ophthalmic decongestant. Relaxes myometrium and inhibits uterine contractions; prolongs action and delays systemic absorption of local and intraspinal anesthetics. Used topically to control superficial bleeding.

CONTRAINDICATIONS Hypersensitivity to sympathomimetic amines; narrow-angle glaucoma; hemorrhagic, traumatic, or cardiogenic shock; cardiac dilatation, cerebral arteriosclerosis, coronary insufficiency, arrhythmias, organic heart or brain disease; during second stage of labor; for local anesthesia of fingers, toes, ears, nose, genitalia; pregnancy (category C).

CAUTIOUS USE Older adults or debilitated patients; prostatic hypertrophy; hypertension; diabetes mellitus; hyperthyroidism; Parkinson's disease; tuberculosis; psychoneurosis; in patients with long-standing bronchial asthma and emphysema with degenerative heart disease; lactation.

ROUTE & DOSAGE

Anaphylaxis

Adult: **SC** 0.1–0.5 mL of 1:1000 q10–15min prn **IV** 0.1–0.25 mL of 1:1000 q10–15min
Child: **SC** 0.01 mL/kg of, 1:1000 q10–15min prn **IV** 0.01 mL/kg of 1:1000 q10–15min
Neonate: **IV Intratracheal** 0.01–0.05 mg/kg q3–5min prn

Cardiac Arrest

Adult: **IV** 1 mg q3–5min as needed **Intracardiac** 0.1–1 mg
Child: **IV** 0.01 mg/kg q3–5min as needed **Intracardiac** 0.05–0.1 mg/kg

Asthma

Adult: **SC** 0.1–0.5 mL of 1:1000 q20min–4h **Inhalation** 1 inhalation q4h prn
Child: **SC** 0.01 mL/kg of 1:1000 q20min–4h **Inhalation** 1 inhalation q4h prn

Glaucoma

Adult/Child: **Instillation** 1–2 drops 0.25–2% solution 1/d or b.i.d.

Ocular Mydriasis

See Appendix A-1

Nasal Hemostasis

Adult/Child: **Instillation** 1–2 drops 0.1% ophthalmic or 0.1% nasal solution

Topical Hemostatic

Adult/Child: **Topical** 1:50,000–1:1000 applied topically or 1:500,000–1:50,000 mixed with a local anesthetic

ADMINISTRATION

Inhalation

- Have patient in an upright position when aerosol preparation is used. The reclining position can result in overdosage by producing large droplets instead of fine spray.
- Instruct patient to rinse mouth and throat with water immediately after inhalation to avoid swallowing residual drug (may cause epigastric pain and systemic effects from the propellant in the aerosol preparation) and to prevent dryness of oropharyngeal membranes.
- Do not give isoproterenol concurrently with epinephrine. Allow 4-h interval to elapse before a change is made from one drug to the other.

Instillation

- Instill nose drops with head in lateral, head-low position to prevent entry of drug into throat.
- Instruct patient to rinse nose dropper or spray tip with hot water after each use to prevent contamination of solution with nasal secretions.

Ophthalmic

- Remove soft contact lenses before instilling eye drops.
- Instruct patient to apply gentle finger pressure against nasolacrimal duct immediately after drug is instilled for at least 1 or 2 min following instillation to prevent excessive systemic absorption.
- When separate solutions of epinephrine and a topical miotic are used, the miotic should be instilled 2–10 min prior to epinephrine because of the conjunctival sac's limited capacity.

Subcutaneous

- Use tuberculin syringe to ensure greater accuracy in measurement of parenteral doses.
- Protect epinephrine injection from exposure to light at all times. Do not remove ampule or vial from carton until ready to use.
- Shake vial or ampule thoroughly to disperse particles before withdrawing epinephrine suspension into syringe; then inject promptly.
- Aspirate carefully before injecting epinephrine. Inadvertent IV injection of usual SC doses can result in sudden hypertension and possibly cerebral hemorrhage.
- Rotate injection sites and observe for signs of blanching. Vascular constriction from repeated injections may cause tissue necrosis.

Intravenous

Note: Verify correct rate of IV injection to neonates, infants, children with physician.

- Note: 1:1000 solution contains 1 mg/1 mL. 1:10,000 solution contains 0.1 mg/1 mL.

PREPARE: Direct: Dilute each 1 mg of 1:1000 solution with 10 mL of NS to yield 1:10,000 solution. **IV Infusion:** Further dilute in 250–500 mL of D5W.

ADMINISTER: Direct: Give each 1 mg over 1 min or longer; may give more rapidly in cardiac arrest. **IV Infusion:** 1–10 mcg/min titrated according to patient's condition.

INCOMPATIBILITIES Solution/additive: Aminophylline, cephapirin, hyaluronidase, mephentermine, sodium bicarbonate, warfarin. Y-site: Ampicillin, thiopental, sodium bicarbonate.

ADVERSE EFFECTS (≥1%) Special

Senses: *Nasal burning or stinging,* dryness of nasal mucosa, sneezing, rebound congestion. *Transient stinging or burning of eyes,* lacrimation, browache, headache, rebound conjunctival hyperemia, allergy, iritis; with prolonged use: melanin-like

E

deposits on lids, conjunctiva, and cornea; corneal edema; loss of lashes (reversible); maculopathy with central scotoma in aphakic patients (reversible). **Body as a Whole:** *Nervousness,* restlessness, sleeplessness, fear, anxiety, *tremors,* severe headache, cerebrovascular accident, weakness, dizziness, syncope, pallor, sweating, dyspnea. **GI:** Nausea, vomiting. **CV:** Precordial pain, *palpitations,* hypertension, MI, tachyarrhythmias including ventricular fibrillation. **Respiratory:** Bronchial and pulmonary edema. **Urogenital:** Urinary retention. **Skin:** Tissue necrosis with repeated injections. **Metabolic:** Metabolic acidoses, elevated serum lactic acid, transient elevations of blood glucose. **CNS:** Altered state of perception and thought, psychosis.

INTERACTIONS Drug: May increase hypotension in circulatory collapse or hypotension caused by PHENOTHIAZINES, **oxytocin, entacapone.** Additive toxicities with other SYMPATHOMIMETICS **(albuterol, dobutamine, dopamine, isoproterenol, metaproterenol, norepinephrine, phenylephrine, phenylpropanolamine, pseudoephedrine, ritodrine, salmeterol, terbutaline),** MAO INHIBITORS, TRICYCLIC ANTIDEPRESSANTS. ALPHA- AND BETA-ADRENERGIC BLOCKING AGENTS (e.g., **ergotamine, propranolol)** antagonize effects of epinephrine. GENERAL ANESTHETICS increase cardiac irritability.

PHARMACOKINETICS Absorption: Inactivated in GI tract. **Onset:** 3–5 min, 1 h on conjunctiva. **Peak:** 20 min, 4–8 h on conjunctiva. **Duration:** 12–24 h topically. **Distribution:** Widely distributed; does not cross blood–brain barrier; crosses placenta. **Metabolism:** Metabolized in tissue and liver by monoamine oxidase (MAO) and catecholamine-methyltransferase (COMT). **Elimination:** Small amount excreted unchanged in urine; excreted in breast milk.

CLINICAL IMPLICATIONS

Assessment & Drug Effects

- Monitor BP, pulse, respirations, and urinary output and observe patient closely following IV administration. Epinephrine may widen pulse pressure. If disturbances in cardiac rhythm occur, withhold epinephrine and notify physician immediately.
- Keep physician informed of any changes in intake-output ratio.
- Use cardiac monitor with patients receiving epinephrine IV. Have full crash cart immediately available.
- Check BP repeatedly when epinephrine is administered IV during first 5 min, then q3–5min until stabilized.
- Advise patient to report to physician if symptoms are not relieved in 20 min or if they become worse following inhalation.
- Advise patient to report bronchial irritation, nervousness, or sleeplessness. Dosage should be reduced.
- Monitor blood glucose & HbA$_{1c}$ for loss of glycemic control if diabetic.

Patient & Family Education

- Be aware intranasal application may sting slightly.
- Administer ophthalmic drug at bedtime or following prescribed miotic to minimize mydriasis, with blurred vision and sensitivity to light (possible in some patients being treated for glaucoma).
- Transitory stinging may follow initial ophthalmic administration and that headache and browache occur frequently at first but usually

Common adverse effects in *italic,* life-threatening effects underlined; generic names in **bold**; classifications in SMALL CAPS; ♣ Canadian drug name; ☺ Prototype drug

subside with continued use. Notify physician if symptoms persist.

- Discontinue epinephrine eye drops and consult a physician if signs of hypersensitivity develop (edema of lids, itching, discharge, crusting eyelids).
- Learn how to administer epinephrine subcutaneously. Keep medication and equipment available for home emergency. Confer with physician.
- Note: Inhalation epinephrine reduces bronchial secretions and thus may make mucous plugs more difficult to dislodge.
- Report tolerance to physician; may occur with repeated or prolonged use. Continued use of epinephrine in the presence of tolerance can be dangerous.
- Take medication only as prescribed and immediately notify physician of onset of systemic effects of epinephrine.
- Discard discolored or precipitated solutions.

EPIRUBICIN HYDROCHLORIDE

(e-pi-roo'bi-sin)
Ellence
Classifications: ANTINEOPLASTIC;
ANTIBIOTIC
Therapeutic: ANTINEOPLASTIC
Prototype: Doxorubicin HCl
Pregnancy Category: D

AVAILABILITY 2 mg/mL

ACTION & *THERAPEUTIC EFFECT*
Cytotoxic antibiotic with wide spectrum of antitumor activity and strong immunosuppressive properties. Less myelotoxic than doxorubicin. Complexes with DNA causing the DNA helix to change shape, thus blocking effective DNA and RNA transcription. *Highly destructive to rapidly proliferating cells. Effectiveness indicated by tumor regression.*

USES Adjunctive therapy for axillary node-positive breast cancer.

CONTRAINDICATIONS Hypersensitivity to epirubicin and other related drugs; marked myelosuppression, severely impaired cardiac function, severe cardiac arrhythmias, recent MI; severe hepatic disease, jaundice; previous treatment with maximum doses of epirubicin, doxorubicin, or daunorubicin; pregnancy (category D), lactation.
CAUTIOUS USE Arrhythmias; mild or moderate liver dysfunction; severe renal insufficiency or renal failure.

ROUTE & DOSAGE

Breast Cancer
Adult: **IV** 100–120 mg/m² infused on day 1 of a 3–4 wk cycle or 50–60 mg/m² on day 1 and 8 of a 3–4 wk cycle
Hepatic Impairment
Bilirubin 1.2–3 mg/dL: give 50% of dose; bilirubin over 3 mg/dL: give 25% of dose

ADMINISTRATION
Intravenous
Note: Pregnant women should **NOT** prepare or administer this drug. Wear protective goggles, gowns and disposable gloves and masks when handling this drug. Discard **ALL** equipment used in preparation of this drug in high-risk, waste-disposal bags for incineration. Treat accidental contact with skin or eyes by rinsing with copious amounts of water followed by prompt medical attention.

- Note: Reduce dosages when serum creatinine >5 mg/dL or

Common adverse effects in *italic*, life-threatening effects underlined; generic names in **bold**; classifications in SMALL CAPS; ♣ Canadian drug name; ☯ Prototype drug

557

E

AST 2–4 times the upper limit of normal.

PREPARE: **IV Infusion:** Epirubicin is manufactured as a preservative-free ready-to-use solution. The contents of a vial must be used within 25 h of first penetrating the rubber stopper. Discard unused solution.

ADMINISTER: **IV Infusion:**
Measure ordered dose and inject into a port of a freely flowing IV solution of D5W or NS over 3–5 min. **DO NOT** give by direct IV push into a vein. Avoid IV sites that enter small veins or repeated injections into the same vein. Monitor IV site closely for S&S of extravasation and if suspected, notify physician immediately.

INCOMPATIBILITIES **Solution/additive:** ALKALINE SOLUTIONS (including **sodium bicarbonate**), **fluorouracil, ifosfamide, heparin, fluorouracil.**

▪ Store between 2°–8° C (36°–46° F). Protect from light.

ADVERSE EFFECTS (≥1%) **Body as a Whole:** *Lethargy,* fever. **CV:** Asymptomatic decrease in LVEF, CHF. **GI:** *Nausea, vomiting, mucositis, diarrhea,* anorexia. **Hematologic:** <u>Leukopenia, neutropenia, anemia, thrombocytopenia, AML</u>. **Skin:** *Alopecia, injection site reaction,* rash, itching, skin changes. **Other:** *Amenorrhea, hot flashes, infection, conjunctivitis/keratitis,* <u>secondary acute myelogenous leukemia</u> (related to cumulative dose).

INTERACTIONS Drug: Cimetidine increases epirubicin levels; concomitant use with cardioactive drugs (e.g., CALCIUM CHANNEL BLOCKERS) may affect cardiac function.

PHARMACOKINETICS Distribution: Widely distributed, 77% protein bound, concentrated in red blood cells. **Metabolism:** Extensively metabolized in liver, blood and other organs. Clearance is reduced in patients with hepatic impairment. **Elimination:** Primarily excreted in bile, some urinary excretion; clearance decreases in older adult female patients. **Half-Life:** 33 h.

CLINICAL IMPLICATIONS

Assessment & Drug Effects

▪ Withhold drug and notify physician of any of the following: neutrophil count <1500 cells/mm^3, recent MI, suspicion of severe myocardial insufficiency.

▪ Obtain baseline and periodic (before each cycle of therapy) cardiac evaluation: left ventricular ejection fraction, ECG and ECHO (tests are recommended especially in the presence of risk factors of cardiac toxicity).

▪ Monitor cardiac status closely throughout therapy as the risk of developing severe CHF increases rapidly when cumulative doses approach 900 mg/m^2. Report significant ECG changes immediately. Report immediately S&S of the following: tachycardia, gallop rhythm, pleural effusion, pulmonary edema, dependent edema, ascites, or hepatomegaly.

▪ Lab tests: Baseline and periodic (before each cycle of therapy) CBC with differential, platelet count, serum total bilirubin, AST, serum creatinine.

Patient & Family Education

▪ Review all literature regarding the adverse effects of epirubicin therapy carefully.

▪ Report any of the following to physician immediately: Pain at the site of IV infusion, chest pain, palpitations, shortness of breath or difficulty breathing, sudden weight

gain, swelling of hands, feet or legs, or any unexplained bleeding.
- Be aware that your urine may turn red for 1–2 d after receiving this drug. This change is expected and harmless.
- Do not take OTC cimetidine or any other OTC drug without consulting physician.
- Use effective means of contraception (both men and women) while on epirubicin therapy.

EPLERENONE

(e-ple're-none)
Inspra
Classifications: ELECTROLYE & WATER BALANCE AGENT; SELECTIVE ALDOSTERONE RECEPTOR ANTAGONIST (SARA); ANTIHYPERTENSIVE
Therapeutic: ANTIHYPERTENSIVE; DIURETIC; SARA
Prototype: Spironolactone
Pregnancy Category: B

AVAILABILITY 25 mg, 50 mg, 100 mg tablets

ACTION & *THERAPEUTIC EFFECT*
Binds to mineralocorticoid receptors and blocks the binding of aldosterone, a component of the renin-angiotensin-aldosterone system (RAAS). Thus eplerenone blocks the primary effect of aldosterone which is sodium reabsorption. *Lowers blood pressure by inhibiting sodium and water retention, thus reducing total plasma volume.*

USES Treatment of hypertension, alone or with other antihypertensive agents. Adjunctive therapy for post MI heart failure.

CONTRAINDICATIONS Serum potassium >5.5 mEq/L; type 2 diabetes with microalbuminuria; serum creatinine >2.0 mg/dL in males or >1.8 mg/dL in females; creatinine clearance <50 mL/min; concomitant treatment with potassium supplements or potassium-sparing diuretics (amiloride, spironolactone, or triamterene), or strong inhibitors of CYP450 3A4 (e.g., ketoconazole, itraconazole); lactation.

CAUTIOUS USE Hepatic impairment; concomitant use of another mineralocorticoid receptor blocker and ACE inhibitors or angiotensin II antagonists; severe hepatic disease; concomitant treatment with moderate inhibitors of CYP450 3A4 (e.g., fluconazole, erythromycin, verapamil, saquinavir); pregnancy (category B); safety and efficacy in children, infants, or neonates are not established.

ROUTE & DOSAGE

Hypertension
Adult: **PO** 50 mg once daily, may be increased to 50 mg b.i.d. or 100 mg q.d., if inadequate response after 4 wk
Renal Impairment
Do not administer if Cl$_{cr}$ <50 mL/min due to risk of hyperkalemia.

ADMINISTRATION
Oral
- Do not administer in combination with potassium supplements or potassium-sparing diuretics.
- Manufacturer recommends dosage reduction to 25 mg once daily with concurrent administration of erythromycin, saquinavir, verapamil, or fluconazole.
- Store at 15°–30° C (59°–86° F).

ADVERSE EFFECTS (≥1%) **Body as a Whole:** Fatigue, flu-like syndrome. **CNS:** Headache, dizziness. **CV:** Angina, MI. **GI:** Diarrhea, ab-

Common adverse effects in *italic*, life-threatening effects underlined; generic names in **bold**; classifications in SMALL CAPS; ♥ Canadian drug name; ❷ Prototype drug

559

dominal pain. **Endocrine:** Gynecomastia. **Metabolic:** *Hyperkalemia,* increased GGT, hypercholesterolemia, hypertriglyceridemia, decreased sodium levels. **Respiratory:** Cough. **Urogenital:** Albuminuria, abnormal vaginal bleeding.

INTERACTIONS Drug: ACE INHIBITORS, ANGIOTENSIN II RECEPTOR BLOCKERS, AZOLE ANTIFUNGALS (e.g., **fluconazole, itraconazole, ketoconazole**), **erythromycin, saquinavir, verapamil** may increase risk of hyperkalemia. **Food: Potassium**-containing SALT SUBSTITUTES may increase risk of hyperkalemia.

PHARMACOKINETICS Absorption: Rapidly absorbed. **Peak:** 1.5 h. **Distribution:** 50% protein bound, primarily to alpha1-acid glycoproteins. **Metabolism:** In liver by CYP3A4. **Elimination:** 32% in feces, 67% in urine. **Half-Life:** 4–6 h.

CLINICAL IMPLICATIONS

Assessment & Drug Effects

- Monitor cardiovascular status with frequent BP determinations. Note that BP lowering usually occurs within 2 wk with maximal antihypertensive effects achieved within 4 wk.
- Lab tests: Monitor baseline and periodic serum potassium, serum sodium, renal function tests, lipid profile, and LFTs. Monitor type 2 diabetics for microalbuminuria.
- Concurrent drugs: Monitor serum potassium levels more frequently when patient also receiving an ACE inhibitor or an angiontensin II receptor antagonist. Monitor frequently for lithium toxicity with concurrent use.
- Withhold drug and notify physician for any of the following: serum potassium >5.5 mEq/L, serum creatinine >2.0 mg/dL in males or

>1.8 mg/dL in females, creatinine clearance <50 mL/min, microalbuminuria in type 2 diabetics.

Patient & Family Education

- Do not use potassium supplements, salt substitutes containing potassium, or contraindicated drugs (e.g., ketoconazole, itraconazole) without consulting physician.
- Do not use OTC nonsteroidal anti-inflammatory drugs without consulting physician.
- Do not drive or operate machinery until reaction to drug is known. It may cause dizziness.

EPOETIN ALFA (HUMAN RECOMBINANT ERYTHROPOIETIN) Ⓟ

(e-po-e-tin)

Epogen, Eprex ♦, Procrit

Classifications: BLOOD FORMER; HEMATOPOIETIC GROWTH FACTOR

Therapeutic: ANTIANEMIC; HUMAN ERYTHROPOIETIN

Pregnancy Category: C

AVAILABILITY 2000 units/mL, 3000 units/mL, 4000 units/mL, 10,000 units/mL, 20,000 units/mL

ACTION & *THERAPEUTIC EFFECT*

Human erythropoietin is produced in the kidney and stimulates bone marrow production of RBCs (erythropoiesis). Hypoxia and anemia generally increase the production of erythropoietin. Epoetin alpha is a glycoprotein that stimulates RBC production. *Stimulates the production of RBCs in the bone marrow of severely anemic patients.*

USES Elevates the hematocrit of patients with anemia secondary to chronic kidney failure (CRF); patients may or may not be on dialysis;

other anemias related to malignancies and AIDS. Autologous blood donations for anticipated transfusions. Reduces need for blood in anemic surgical patients.

CONTRAINDICATIONS Uncontrolled hypertension and known hypersensitivity to mammalian cell–derived products and albumin (human); hamster protein hypersensitivity; iron-deficiency anemia, pregnancy (category C); lactation; neonates.

CAUTIOUS USE Leukemia, sickle cell disease; coagulopathy; seizure disorders.

ROUTE & DOSAGE

Anemia

Adult: **SC/IV** Start with 50–100 U/kg/dose until target Hct range of 30–33% (max: 36%) is reached, Hct should not increase by more than 4 points in any 2-wk period, rapid increase in Hct increases the risk of serious adverse reactions (hypertension, seizures), may increase dose if Hct has not increased 5–6 points after 8 wk of therapy, reduce dose after target range is reached or the Hct increases by >4 points in any 2-wk period, dose usually increased or decreased by 25 U/kg increments *Child:* **SC/IV** 50 U/kg/dose 3 times/wk initially, when Hct increased to 35%, decrease dose by 25 U/kg/dose until Hct reaches 40%

ADMINISTRATION

Subcutaneous

- Do not shake solution. Shaking may denature the glycoprotein, rendering it biologically inactive.
- Inspect solution for particulate matter prior to use. Do not use if

solution is discolored or if it contains particulate matter.

- Use only one dose per vial, and do not reenter vial.
- Do not give with any other drug solution.

Intravenous

PREPARE: **Direct:** Give undiluted.
ADMINISTER: **Direct:** Give direct IV as a bolus dose over 1 min.

- Discard any unused portion of the vial. It contains no preservatives. ■ Store at 2°–8° C (36°–46° F). Do not freeze or shake.

ADVERSE EFFECTS (≥1%) **CNS:** Seizures, *headache.* **CV:** *Hypertension.* **GI:** Nausea, diarrhea. **Hematologic:** *Iron deficiency,* thrombocytosis, pure red cell aplasia, *clotting of AV fistula.* **Other:** Sweating, bone pain, arthralgias.

INTERACTIONS Drug: No clinically significant interactions established.

PHARMACOKINETICS Onset: 7–14 d. **Metabolism:** In serum. **Elimination:** Minimal recovery in urine. **Half-Life:** 4–13 h.

CLINICAL IMPLICATIONS

Assessment & Drug Effects

- Control BP adequately prior to initiation of therapy and closely monitor and control during therapy. Hypertension is an adverse effect that must be controlled.
- Be aware that BP may rise during early therapy as the Hct increases. Notify physician of a rapid rise in Hct (>4 points in 2 wk). Dosage will need to be reduced because of risk of serious hypertension.
- Monitor for hypertensive encephalopathy in patients with CRF during period of increasing Hct.
- Monitor for premonitory neurological symptoms (i.e., aura, and report their appearance promptly).

Common adverse effects in *italic*, life-threatening effects underlined; generic names in **bold**; classifications in SMALL CAPS; ♣ Canadian drug name; ⊚ Prototype drug

561

The potential for seizures exists during periods of rapid Hct increase (>4 points in 2 wk).

- Monitor closely for thrombotic events (e.g., MI, CVA, TIA), especially for patients with CRF.
- Lab tests: Baseline transferrin and serum ferritin. Monitor aPTT & INR closely. Patients may require additional heparin during dialysis to prevent clotting of the vascular access or artificial kidney. Determine Hct twice weekly until it is stabilized in the target range (30–33%) and the maintenance dose of epoetin alfa has been determined; then monitor at regular intervals. Perform CBC with differential and platelet count regularly. Monitor BUN, creatinine, phosphorus, and potassium regularly.

Patient & Family Education

- Important to comply with antihypertensive medication and dietary restrictions.
- Do not drive or engage in other potentially hazardous activity during the first 90 d of therapy because of possible seizure activity.
- Note: As Hct increases, there is an improved sense of well-being and quality of life. It is important to continue compliance with dietary and dialysis prescriptions.
- Understand that headache is a common adverse effect. Report if severe or persistent, may indicate developing hypertension.
- Keep all follow-up appointments.

EPOPROSTENOL SODIUM ℗

(e-po-pros′te-nol)
Flolan
Classifications: PROSTAGLANDIN; ANTIHYPERTENSIVE
Therapeutic: PULMONARY ANTIHYPERTENSIVE
Pregnancy Category: B

AVAILABILITY 0.5 mg, 1.5 mg powder for injection

ACTION & *THERAPEUTIC EFFECT*
Naturally occurring prostaglandin that reduces right and left ventricular afterload, increases cardiac output, and increases stroke volume through its vasodilation effect. May also decrease pulmonary vascular resistance and mean systemic arterial pressure, depending on the dose. Potent pulmonary vasodilator that reduces pulmonary hypertension. *Potent vasodilator of pulmonary and systemic arterial vascular beds and an inhibitor of platelet aggregation.*

USES Long-term treatment of primary pulmonary hypertension in NYHA Class III and IV patients.

CONTRAINDICATIONS Chronic use with left ventricular systolic dysfunction in CHF patients, hypersensitivity to epoprostenol or related compounds.

CAUTIOUS USE Older adults, pregnancy (category B), concurrent use of hypotensive drugs. Safety and efficacy in children are not established.

ROUTE & DOSAGE

Primary Pulmonary Hypertension
Adult: **IV** *Acute dose,* Initiate with 2 ng/kg/min, increase by 2 ng/kg/min q15 min until dose-limiting effects occur (e.g., nausea, vomiting, headache, hypotension, flushing); *Chronic administration,* Start infusion at 4 ng/kg/min less than the maximum tolerated infusion; if maximum tolerated infusion is ≤5 ng/kg/min, start maintenance infusion at 50% of maximum tolerated dose

ADMINISTRATION

▪ Note: Anticoagulation therapy is generally initiated along with epoprostenol to reduce the risk of developing thromboembolic disease.

Intravenous

PREPARE: **Continuous:** Must be reconstituted using sterile diluent for epoprostenol; must not be mixed with any other medications or solution prior to or during administration. To make 100 mL of 3000 ng/mL, add 5 mL of diluent to one 0.5 mg vial; withdraw 3 mL and add to enough diluent to make a total of 100 mL. To make 100 mL of 5000 ng/mL, add 5 mL of diluent to one 0.5 mg vial; withdraw contents of vial and add to enough diluent to make a total of 100 mL. To make 100 mL of 10,000 ng/mL, add 5 mL of diluent to each of two 0.5 mg vials; withdraw contents of each vial and add to enough diluent to make a total of 100 mL. To make 100 mL of 15,000 ng/mL, add 5 mL of diluent to a 1.5 mg vial; withdraw contents of vial and add to enough diluent to make a total of 100 mL.

ADMINISTER: **Continuous:** Give at ordered rate using an infusion control device. Avoid abrupt infusion interruption or large dosage reduction.

INCOMPATIBILITIES **Solution/additive:** Do not mix or infuse with any other drugs.

▪ Store unopened vials at 15°–25° C (59°–77° F). Protect from light. See manufacturer's directions for stability or storage of reconstituted solutions.

ADVERSE EFFECTS (≥1%) CNS:

Chills, fever, flu-like syndrome, dizziness, syncope, *headache, anxiety/ nervousness,* hyperesthesia, paresthesia, dizziness. **CV:** *Tachycardia, hypotension, flushing, chest pain,* bradycardia. **GI:** *Diarrhea, nausea, vomiting,* abdominal pain. **Musculoskeletal:** *Jaw pain, myalgia, nonspecific musculoskeletal pain.* **Respiratory:** Dyspnea. **Other:** Dose-limiting effects.

INTERACTIONS Drug: Hypotension

if administered with other VASODILATORS or ANTIHYPERTENSIVES.

PHARMACOKINETICS Peak: Ap-

proximately 15 min. **Metabolism:** Rapidly hydrolyzed at neutral pH in blood; also subject to enzyme degradation. **Elimination:** 82% in urine. **Half-Life:** Approximately 6 min.

CLINICAL IMPLICATIONS

Assessment & Drug Effects

▪ Assess carefully for development of pulmonary edema during dose ranging.
▪ Monitor respiratory and cardiovascular status frequently during entire period of chronic use of epoprostenol.
▪ Monitor for and report recurrence or worsening of symptoms associated with primary pulmonary hypertension (e.g., dyspnea, dizziness, exercise intolerance) or adverse effects of drug; dosage adjustments may be needed.

Patient & Family Education

▪ Learn correct techniques for storage, reconstitution, and administration of drug, and maintenance of catheter site (see ADMINISTRATION).
▪ Notify physician immediately of S&S of worsening primary pulmonary hypertension, adverse drug reactions, and S&S of infection at catheter site or sepsis.

Common adverse effects in *italic*, life-threatening effects underlined; generic names in **bold**; classifications in SMALL CAPS; ♣ Canadian drug name; ❷ Prototype drug

563

EPROSARTAN MESYLATE

(e-pro-sar'tan)

Teveten

Classifications: ANGIOTENSIN II RE-
CEPTOR (ACE) ANTAGONIST; ANTIHY-
PERTENSIVE

Therapeutic: ANTIHYPERTENSIVE; ACE
INHIBITOR

Prototype: Losartan potassium

Pregnancy Category: C first trimester; D second and third trimester

AVAILABILITY 400 mg, 600 mg
tablets

ACTION & *THERAPEUTIC EFFECT*

Selectively blocks the binding of
angiotensin II to the AT_1 receptors
found in many tissues. This blocks
the vasoconstricting and aldosterone-secreting effects of angiotensin
II, thus resulting in an antihypertensive effect. *It decreases both the
systolic and diastolic BP.*

USES Treatment of hypertension.

CONTRAINDICATIONS Hypersensitivity to eprosartan, losartan, or
other angiotensin II receptor antagonists; pregnancy (category C first
trimester, and category D second
and third trimesters), lactation; children <18 y.

CAUTIOUS USE Angioedema, aortic
or mitral value stenosis, coronary
artery disease, cardiomyopathy, hypotension, CHF; biliary obstruction;
older adults; severe hepatic dysfunction, renal artery stenosis, renal
disease, renal impairment.

ROUTE & DOSAGE

Hypertension

Adult: **PO** 600 mg q.d. or 400 mg
q.d. to b.i.d. (max: 800 mg/d)

ADMINISTRATION

Oral

- Correct volume depletion prior to
therapy to prevent hypotension.
- Store at 15°–30° C (59°–86° F); protect from moisture and direct light.

ADVERSE EFFECTS (≥1%) **Body as
a Whole:** Viral infection, fatigue, arthralgia. **CNS:** Depression. **GI:** Abdominal pain, hypertriglyceridemia.
Respiratory: Upper respiratory infection, rhinitis, pharyngitis, cough.

PHARMACOKINETICS Absorption:
Only 13% of oral dose reaches
systemic circulation. **Peak:** 1–2 h.
Metabolism: Minimal metabolism.
Elimination: 61% in feces and 37% in
urine. **Half-Life:** 5–9 h.

CLINICAL IMPLICATIONS

Assessment & Drug Effects

- Monitor BP periodically; do trough
readings just before scheduled
dose when possible.
- Monitor for S&S of angioedema
(may occur within 30 min or as
long as 30 d after initial dose).
- Lab tests: Monitor liver function,
BUN & creatinine, serum potassium, CBC with differential periodically.

Patient & Family Education

- Inform physician immediately of
pregnancy.
- Report episodes of dizziness especially associated with position
changes.
- Report swelling of lips, tongue,
face, or feeling of obstruction in
neck immediately.

EPTIFIBATIDE

(ep-ti-fib'a-tide)

Integrilin

Common adverse effects in *italic*, life-threatening effects <u>underlined</u>; generic names
in **bold**; classifications in SMALL CAPS; ♣ Canadian drug name; ⑩ Prototype drug

Classifications: ANTITHROMBOTIC AGENT; ANTIPLATELET ANTIBODY; PLATELET GLYCOPROTEIN (GP IIB/IIIA) INHIBITOR; (GP IIB/IIIA) INHIBITOR
Therapeutic: ANTIPLATELET; PLATELET (GP IIB/IIIA) INHIBITOR
Prototype: Abciximab
Pregnancy Category: B

AVAILABILITY 0.75 mg/mL, 2 mg/mL injection

ACTION & *THERAPEUTIC EFFECT*
Binds to the glycoprotein IIb/IIIa (GPIIb/IIIa) receptor sites of platelets. *Inhibits platelet aggregation by preventing fibrinogen, von Willebrand's factor, and other molecules from adhering to GPIIb/IIIa receptor sites on platelets.*

USES Treatment of acute coronary syndromes (unstable angina, non-Q-wave MI) and patients undergoing percutaneous coronary interventions (PCIs).

CONTRAINDICATIONS Hypersensitivity to eptifibatide; active bleeding; GI or GU bleeding within 6 weeks; thrombocytopenia; renal failure requiring dialysis; coagulopathy; recent major surgery or trauma; intracranial neoplasm, intracranial bleeding within 6 mo; concurrent administration of another GPIIb/IIIa receptor inhibitor (e.g., abciximab); renal dialysis; severe hypertension (systolic blood pressure >200 mm Hg or diastolic blood pressure >110 mm Hg), aneurysm.
CAUTIOUS USE Hypersensitivity to related compounds (e.g., abciximab, tirofiban, lamifiban); concurrent administration of other anticoagulants; pregnancy (category B), lactation. Safety and effectiveness in children are not established.

ROUTE & DOSAGE

Acute Coronary Syndromes (ACS)
Adult: **IV** 180 mcg/kg initial bolus followed by 2 mcg/kg/min until hospital discharge or up to 72 h

Percutaneous Coronary Interventions (PCI)
Adult: **IV** 180 mcg/kg initial bolus followed by 2 mcg/kg/min; after 10 min, a second 180 mcg/kg bolus should be given; the infusion should continue up to 24 h after the end of the procedure

Renal Impairment
If Cl_{cr} < 50 mL/min, then give 1 mcg/kg/min continuous infusion

ADMINISTRATION

▪ Note: Review contraindications to administration prior to giving this drug.

Intravenous

PREPARE: **Direct:** Give undiluted.
ADMINISTER: **Direct:** Give bolus doses IV push over 1–2. **Continuous:** Start continuous infusion immediately following bolus dose. Give undiluted directly from the 100-mL vial (at a rate based on patient's weight) using a vented infusion set. May be given in the same IV line with NS or D5/NS (either solution may contain up to 60 mEq KCl).

▪ Store unopened vials at 2°–8° C (36°–46° F) and protect from light. Discard any unused portion in opened vial.

ADVERSE EFFECTS (≥1%) **CNS:** Intracranial bleed (rare). **GI:** GI bleeding. **Hematologic:** *Bleeding* (major bleeding 4.4–11%), anemia, thrombocytopenia.

INTERACTIONS Drug: ORAL ANTICOAGULANTS, NSAIDS, **dipyridamole,**

Common adverse effects in *italic*, life-threatening effects underlined; generic names in **bold**; classifications in SMALL CAPS; ♣ Canadian drug name; ⊕ Prototype drug

565

E

ticlopidine, dextran may increase risk of bleeding.

PHARMACOKINETICS Duration: 6–8 h after stopping infusion. **Metabolism:** Minimally metabolized. **Elimination:** 50% in urine. **Half-Life:** 2.5 h.

CLINICAL IMPLICATIONS

Assessment & Drug Effects

- Lab tests: Prior to infusion determine PT/aPTT & INR, ACT for those undergoing percutaneous coronary intervention (PCI); Hct or Hgb; platelet count; and serum creatinine.
- Lab tests: Monitor aPTT & INR (target aPPT, 50–70 s); during PCI (target ACT, 300–350 s).
- Minimize all vascular and other trauma during treatment. When obtaining IV access, avoid using a noncompressible site such as the subclavian vein.
- Monitor carefully for and immediately report S&S of bleeding (e.g., femoral artery access site bleeding, intracerebral hemorrhage, GI bleeding).
- Immediately stop infusion of eptifibatide and heparin if bleeding at the arterial access site cannot be controlled by pressure.
- Achieve hemostasis at the arterial access site by standard compression for a minimum of 4 h prior to hospital discharge following discontinuation of eptifibatide and heparin.

ERGOCALCIFEROL

(er-goe-kal-si′fe-role)

Activated Ergosterol, Drisdol, D-ViSol, Ostoforte ♦, Radiostol ♦, Radiostol Forte ♦, Vitamin D₂

Classifications: VITAMIN D ANALOG
Therapeutic: VITAMIN D ANALOG
Prototype: Calcitriol
Pregnancy Category: C

AVAILABILITY 8000 IU/mL oral liquid; 50,000 units capsules, tablets; 500,000 IU/mL injection

ACTION & *THERAPEUTIC EFFECT*

The name vitamin D encompasses two related fat-soluble substances (sterols) that occur in nature or are synthetically prepared. Vitamin D acts like a hormone in that it is distributed through the circulation and plays a major regulatory role. Reponsible for regulation of serum calcium level. *Maintains normal blood calcium and phosphate ion levels by enhancing their intestinal absorption and by promoting mobilization of calcium from bone and renal tubular resorption of phosphate.*

USES Familial hypophosphatemia (vitamin D–resistant rickets), osteomalacia (adult rickets), anticonvulsant-induced rickets and osteomalacia, osteoporosis, renal osteodystrophy, hypocalcemia associated with hypoparathyroidism; prophylaxis and treatment of nutritional rickets. Also hypophosphatemia in Fanconi's syndrome.

UNLABELED USES With varying clinical results in lupus vulgaris, psoriasis, and rheumatoid arthritis.

CONTRAINDICATIONS Hypersensitivity to vitamin D, hypervitaminosis D, hypercalcemia, hyperphosphatemia, renal osteodystrophy with hyperphosphatemia, malabsorption syndrome, decreased kidney function. Safe use of amounts in excess of 400 IU (10 mcg) daily during pregnancy (category C) is not established.

CAUTIOUS USE Coronary disease; arteriosclerosis (especially in older adults); history of kidney stones; biliary tract disease; lactation.

ROUTE & DOSAGE

Nutritional Rickets, Osteomalacia
Adult: **PO/IM** 25–125 mcg/d for 6–12 wk, may need up to 7.5 mg/d in patients with malabsorption
Child: **PO/IM** 50–125 mcg/d, may need up to 250–625 mcg/d in patients with malabsorption

Vitamin D–Dependent Rickets
Adult: **PO/IM** 250 mcg–1.5 mg/d, may need up to 12.5 mg/d (prolonged therapy with >2.5 mg/d increases risk of toxicity)
Child: **PO/IM** 75–125 mcg/d, may need up to 1.5 mg/d

Hypoparathyroidism, Pseudo-hypoparathyroidism
Adult: **PO/IM** 625 mcg–5 mg/d, may need up to 10 mg/d (prolonged therapy with >2.5 mg/d increases risk of toxicity)
Child: **PO/IM** 1.25–5 mg/d, (prolonged therapy with >2.5 mg/d increases risk of toxicity)

ADMINISTRATION

- Note: 40 U = 1 mcg. Reduce dosage, once symptoms of vitamin D deficiency are relieved, to prevent hypercalcemia.

Intramuscular

- Give injection deeply, preferably into gluteus maximus and inject slowly. Aspirate carefully. Rotate injection sites.
- Preserve in tightly covered, light-resistant containers. Drug decomposes when exposed to light and air.

ADVERSE EFFECTS (≥1%) **Body as a Whole:** Fatigue, weakness, vertigo, tinnitus, ataxia, muscle and joint pain, hypotonia (infants), exanthema, rhinorrhea; pruritus; mild acidosis. **CNS:** Headache, drowsiness, convulsions. **GI:** Metallic taste, dry mouth, anorexia, nausea, vomiting, diarrhea, constipation, abdominal cramps. **Hematologic:** Anemia. **Musculoskeletal:** Calcification of soft tissues (kidneys, blood vessels, myocardium, lungs, skin). **Urogenital:** Nephrotoxicity (polyuria, hyposthenuria, polydipsia, nocturia, casts, albuminuria, hematuria), kidney failure. **CV:** Hypertension, cardiac arrhythmias. **Special Senses:** Conjunctivitis (calcific); photophobia. **Metabolic:** Osteoporosis (adults); weight loss, chronic hypervitaminosis D in children (<u>mental and physical retardation</u>, suppression of linear growth).

DIAGNOSTIC TEST INTERFERENCE
Vitamin D may cause false increase in ***serum cholesterol*** measurements ***(Zlatkis-Zak reaction).***

INTERACTIONS Drug: **Cholestyramine, colestipol, mineral oil** may decrease absorption of vitamin D.

PHARMACOKINETICS Absorption:
Readily from GI tract. **Peak:** After 4 wk. **Duration:** 2 mo or more. **Distribution:** Most of drug first appears in lymph, stored chiefly in liver and in skin, brain, spleen, and bones. **Metabolism:** In liver and kidney to active metabolites. **Elimination:** About 50% of PO dose in bile; may be stored in tissues for months. **Half-Life:** 12–24 h.

CLINICAL IMPLICATIONS

Assessment & Drug Effects

- Monitor closely patients receiving therapeutic doses of vitamin D; must remain under close medical supervision.
- Lab tests: When high therapeutic doses are used, progress is followed by frequent determinations

Common adverse effects in *italic*, life-threatening effects <u>underlined</u>; generic names in **bold**; classifications in SMALL CAPS; ♣ Canadian drug name; ⊙ Prototype drug

567

(q2wk or more often) of serum calcium, phosphorus, magnesium, alkaline phosphatase, BUN, and determinations of urine calcium, casts, albumin, and RBC. Blood calcium concentration is generally kept between 9 and 10 mg/dL.

- Monitor for hypercalcemia; in patients with osteomalacia a decrease in serum alkaline phosphatase may signal the onset of hypercalcemia.

Patient & Family Education

- Avoid magnesium-containing antacids and laxatives with chronic kidney failure when receiving vitamin D preparations since vitamin D increases the risk of magnesium intoxication than other patients.
- Do not use OTC medications unless approved by physician.

ERGOLOID MESYLATE

(er'goe-loid mess'i-late)
Gerimal, Hydergine
Classifications: ALPHA-ADREN-ERGIC ANTAGONIST; ERGOT ALKALOID
Therapeutic: ANTIDEMENTIA
Prototype: Ergotamine tartrate
Pregnancy Category: X

AVAILABILITY 0.5 mg, 1 mg sublingual tablets; 1 mg tablets; 1 mg/mL oral liquid

ACTION & THERAPEUTIC EFFECT
Produces peripheral vasodilation primarily by central action and may cause slight reduction in BP and heart rate. Relieves symptoms of cerebral arteriosclerosis. *Some improvements in Alzheimer's dementia symptoms, possibly by increasing cerebral metabolism with consequent increase in blood flow. Improvement may not be apparent until after 3–4 wk of therapy.*

USES Senile dementia of Alzheimer type.

CONTRAINDICATIONS Acute or chronic psychosis; hypersensitivity to ergoloid; pregnancy (category X), lactation.

CAUTIOUS USE Acute intermittent porphyria; elderly; hepatic disease; hypotension; bradycardia.

ROUTE & DOSAGE

Senile Dementia of Alzheimer Type
Adult: **PO** 1 mg t.i.d.; doses up to 4.5–12 mg/d have been used

ADMINISTRATION

Sublingual

- Instruct patient to allow sublingual (SL) tablet to dissolve under tongue and not to drink, eat, or smoke while tablet is in place. Do not crush SL tablets.
- Store in tightly closed container.

ADVERSE EFFECTS (≥1%) **Body as a Whole:** Mostly dose related. **CV:** Orthostatic hypotension, dizziness or light-headedness, flushing, sinus bradycardia. **Special Senses:** Blurred vision, nasal stuffiness, increased nasopharyngeal secretions. **GI:** Sublingual irritation, anorexia, stomach cramps, transient nausea and vomiting, heartburn. **Skin:** Skin rash. **CNS:** Drowsiness, headache. **Other:** Precipitation of acute intermittent porphyria.

INTERACTIONS Drug: No clinically significant interactions established.

PHARMACOKINETICS Absorption: Incompletely from GI tract; 50% reaches systemic circulation. **Peak:** 1.5–3 h. **Metabolism:** Undergoes rapid first-pass metabolism in liver. **Elimination:** Primarily in feces. **Half-Life:** 2–12 h.

CLINICAL IMPLICATIONS

Assessment & Drug Effects

- Establish baseline values of BP and pulse; check at regular intervals throughout therapy.
- Report to physician sinus bradycardia (40 bpm); has been reported in patients receiving 1.5 mg doses. Pulse rate usually returns to normal within 2 d after drug is discontinued.
- Withdraw drug permanently if marked bradycardia or hypotension occurs.

Patient & Family Education

- Make position changes slowly, particularly from recumbent to upright posture, and move ankles and feet for a few minutes before walking.

ERGOTAMINE TARTRATE ℗

(er-got′a-meen)

Ergomar, Ergostat

Classifications: ALPHA-ADRENERGIC ANTAGONIST; ERGOT ALKALOID
Therapeutic: ANTIMIGRAINE
Pregnancy Category: X

AVAILABILITY 2 mg sublingual tablets

ACTION & *THERAPEUTIC EFFECT*

Natural amino acid alkaloid of ergot. Alpha-adrenergic blocking agent with direct stimulating action on cranial and peripheral vascular smooth muscles and depressant effect on central vasomotor centers. Ergotamine activity can damage vascular endothelium with subsequent occlusion, thrombosis, and gangrene. *In vascular headache, exerts vasoconstrictive action on previously dilated cerebral vessels, reduces amplitude of arterial pulsations, and antagonizes effects of serotonin.*

USES As single agent or in combination with caffeine to prevent or abort migraine, cluster headache (histamine cephalalgia), and other vascular headaches. Not recommended for migraine prophylaxis because of the possibility of adverse effects.

CONTRAINDICATIONS Hypersensitivity to ergotamine; sepsis, obliterative vascular disease, thromboembolic disease, prolonged use of excessive dosage, liver and kidney disease, severe pruritus, diabetes mellitus; marked arteriosclerosis, history of MI, peripheral vascular disease; coronary artery disease, angina; basilar/hemiplegic migraine; hepatic disease; biliary tract disease; cholestasis; hypertension; infectious states, anemia, malnutrition; pregnancy (category X), use in children.

CAUTIOUS USE Lactation, older adult patients.

ROUTE & DOSAGE

Vascular Headaches

Adult: **SL** 1–2 mg followed by 1–2 mg q30min until headache abates or until max of 6 mg/24h or 10 mg/wk

ADMINISTRATION

Sublingual

- Instruct patient to allow sublingual (SL) tablet to dissolve under tongue and not to drink, eat, or smoke while tablet is in place. Do not crush SL tablets.

ADVERSE EFFECTS (≥1%) **Body as a Whole:** Paresthesias; pain (spasms) of facial muscles, tongue, limbs, and lumbar region with difficulty in walking; muscle pains, *weakness, numbness, coldness and cyanosis of*

Common adverse effects in *italic*, life-threatening effects underlined; generic names in **bold**, classifications in SMALL CAPS; ♣ Canadian drug name; ℗ Prototype drug

569

digits (Raynaud's phenomenon). **CNS:** Delirium; convulsive seizures; confusion; depression; drowsiness. **GI:** *Nausea; vomiting;* diarrhea; abdominal pain; unquenchable thirst; partial necrosis of tongue, disagreeable aftertaste. **CV:** Rapid, weak, or irregular pulse; intermittent claudication, complete absence of medium- and large-vessel pulsations in extremities; precordial distress and pain; angina pectoris, transient bradycardia or tachycardia; elevated or lowered BP. **Skin:** Itching and cold skin; gangrene of nose, digits, ears. **Urogenital:** Kidney failure. **Other:** Symptoms of ergotism.

INTERACTIONS Drug: With high doses of BETA-ADRENERGIC BLOCKERS, SYMPATHOMIMETICS, possibility of additive vasoconstrictor effects; **erythromycin, troleandomycin** may cause severe peripheral vasospasm. **Eletriptan, naratriptan, rizatriptan, sumatriptan, or zolmitriptan** may increase risk of coronary ischemia, separate drugs by 24 h; AZOLE ANTIFUNGALS **(ketoconazole, itraconazole, fluconazole, clotrimazole), nefazodone, fluoxetine, fluvoxamine,** amprenavir, **delavirdine, efavirenz, indinavir, nelfinavir, ritonavir, and saquinavir,** may inhibit ergot metabolism and increase toxicity; **sibutramine, dexfenfluramine, nefazodone, fluvoxamine** may increase risk of serotonin syndrome. **Food:** Grapefruit juice may increase toxicity.

PHARMACOKINETICS Absorption: Variable absorption orally. **Peak:** 0.5–3 h. **Distribution:** Crosses blood-brain barrier. **Metabolism:** Extensive first-pass metabolism in liver. **Elimination:** 96% eliminated in feces; excreted in breast milk. **Half-Life:** 2.7 h initial phase, 21 h terminal phase.

CLINICAL IMPLICATIONS

Assessment & Drug Effects

- Monitor adverse GI effects. Nausea and vomiting are adverse reactions that occur in about 10% of patients after they take ergotamine. Patient may need an antiemetic. Consult with physician.
- Monitor patients with PVD carefully for development of peripheral ischemia.
- Monitor long-term effectiveness. Patients receiving high ergotamine doses for prolonged periods may experience increased frequency of headaches, fatigue, and depression. Discontinuation of the drug in these patients results in severe withdrawal headache that may last a few days.
- Overdose symptoms: Nausea, vomiting, weakness, and pain in legs, numbness and tingling in fingers and toes, tachycardia or bradycardia, hypertension or hypotension, and localized edema.

Patient & Family Education

- Begin drug therapy as soon after onset of migraine attack as possible, preferably during migraine prodrome (scintillating scotomas, visual field defects, nausea, paresthesias usually on side opposite to that of the migraine).
- Notify physician if migraine attacks occur more frequently or are not relieved.
- Lie down in a quiet, dark room for 2–3 h after drug administration.
- Report claudication, muscle pain or weakness of extremities, cold or numb digits, irregular heartbeat, nausea, or vomiting. Carefully protect extremities from exposure to cold temperatures; provide warmth, but not heat, to ischemic areas.
- Do NOT increase dosage without consulting physician; overdosage

Common adverse effects in *italic*, life-threatening effects underlined; generic names in **bold**; classifications in SMALL CAPS; ✦ Canadian drug name; ❶ Prototype drug

is the chief cause of adverse effects from the drug.

ERLOTINIB

(er-lo'ti-nib)
Tarceva
Classifications: ANTINEOPLASTIC AGENT; TYROSINE KINASE INHIBITOR; EPIDERMAL GROWTH FACTOR RECEPTOR (EGFR) INHIBITOR
Therapeutic: ANTINEOPLASTIC; EGFR INHIBITOR
Prototype: Gefitinib
Pregnancy Category: D

AVAILABILITY 25 mg, 100 mg, 150 mg tablets

ACTION & *THERAPEUTIC EFFECT*
Erlotinib is a human epidermal growth factor receptor type 1 (HER1/EGFR) inhibitor. Antitumor action of erlotinib is believed to be due to inhibition of EGFR present on the cell surface of both normal and cancer cells. *Inhibition of EGFR in cancer cells diminishes their capacity for cell proliferation, cell survival, and decreases metastases.*

USES Treatment of patients with locally advanced or metastatic non–small cell lung cancer (NSCLC) after failure of at least one prior chemotherapy regimen.
UNLABELED USES Pancreatic cancer.

CONTRAINDICATIONS Hypersensitivity to erlotinib; pregnancy (category D); lactation.
CAUTIOUS USE Hepatic dysfunction, interstitial pulmonary disease (interstitial pneumonia, pneumonitis, alveolitis); myelosuppression; ocular toxicities (corneal ulcer, eye pain).

ROUTE & DOSAGE

Metastatic Non–Small Cell Lung Cancer
Adult: **PO** 150 mg once daily at least 1 h before or 2 h after meals

ADMINISTRATION
Oral
- Give at least 1 h before or 2 h after eating.
- Store at 15–30° C (59–86° F). Keep container tightly closed. Protect from light.

ADVERSE EFFECTS (≥1%) **Body as a Whole:** Infection. **GI:** *Diarrhea,* anorexia, *fatigue,* nausea, vomiting, stomatitis, abdominal pain. **Metabolic:** Increased LFTs. **Respiratory:** *Dyspnea,* cough, interstitial lung disease (sometimes fatal). **Skin:** *Acneiform rash,* pruritus, dry skin. **Special Senses:** Conjunctivitis, dry eyes.

INTERACTIONS Drug: **Atazanavir, clarithromycin, indinavir, itraconazole, ketoconazole, nefazodone, nelfinavir, ritonavir, saquinavir, telithromycin, troleandomycin, voriconazole** may increase erlotinib levels and toxicity; **rifampin, rifabutin, rifapentine, phenytoin, carbamazepine, phenobarbital** may decrease erlotinib levels. **Herbal: St. John's wort** may decrease erlotinib levels.

PHARMACOKINETICS Absorption: 60% absorbed orally; food can increase to 100%. **Peak:** 4 h. **Metabolism:** In liver by CYP3A4. **Elimination:** Primarily in feces (83%). **Half-Life:** 36.2 h.

CLINICAL IMPLICATIONS
Assessment & Drug Effects
- Monitor closely changes in pulmonary function.

Common adverse effects in *italic*, life-threatening effects underlined; generic names in **bold**; classifications in SMALL CAPS; ♦ Canadian drug name; ❷ Prototype drug

571

E

- Withhold drug and notify physician for acute onset of new or progressive pulmonary symptoms (e.g., dyspnea, cough, or fever) or significant changes in liver functions as indicated by elevated transaminases, bilirubin, and alkaline phosphatase.
- Lab tests: periodic LFTs.

Patient & Family Education

- Report promptly any of the following: severe or persistent diarrhea, nausea, anorexia, or vomiting; onset or worsening of unexplained shortness of breath or cough; eye irritation.
- Monitor closely PT/INR values with concurrent warfarin therapy.
- Women should use effective means to avoid pregnancy while taking this drug.

ERTAPENEM SODIUM

(er-ta-pen'em)

Invanz

Classifications: BETA-LACTAM ANTIBIOTIC

Therapeutic: ANTIBIOTIC

Prototype: Imipenem-Cilastatin

Pregnancy Category: B

AVAILABILITY 1 g vial

ACTION & *THERAPEUTIC EFFECT*

Broad-spectrum carbapenem antibiotic that inhibits the cell wall synthesis of gram-positive and gram-negative bacteria by its strong affinity for penicillin-binding proteins (PBPs) of the bacterial cell wall. *Effective against both gram-positive and gram-negative bacteria. Highly resistant to most bacterial beta-lactamases.*

USES Complicated intraabdominal infections, complicated skin and skin structure infections, community-acquired pneumonia, complicated UTI (including pyelonephritis), and acute pelvic infections due to susceptible bacteria.

CONTRAINDICATIONS Hypersensitivity to ertapenem; hypersensitivity to penicillins; hypersensitivity to amide-type local anesthetics such as lidocaine; hypersensitivity to meropenem or imipenem; previous anaphylactic reaction to beta-lactams.

CAUTIOUS USE Renal impairment; history of CNS disorders; history of seizures; hypersensitivity to other beta-lactam antibiotics (penicillins, cephalosporins); hypersensitivity to other allergens; meningitis; pregnancy (category B); lactation (bottle feed during and for 5 d after therapy ends).

ROUTE & DOSAGE

Community-Acquired Pneumonia; Complicated UTI

Adult: **IV/IM** 1 g q.d. × 10–14 d May switch to appropriate PO antibiotic after 3 d if responding
Child: **IV/IM** 15 mg/kg q12h × 10–14 d

Intraabdominal Infection

Adult: **IV/IM** 1 g q.d. × 5–14 d

Skin and Skin Structure Infections

Adult: **IV/IM** 1 g q.d. × 7–14 d

Acute Pelvic Infections

Adult: **IV/IM** 1 g q.d. × 3–10 d

Renal Impairment

Cl_{cr} <30 mL/min: reduce dose to 500 mg q.d.

ADMINISTRATION

Intramuscular

- Reconstitute 1 g vial with 3.2 mL of 1.0% lidocaine HCl injection (without epinephrine). Shake vial thoroughly to form solution. Use immediately.

- Inject deep IM into a large muscle mass (such as the gluteal muscles or lateral part of the thigh).
- The reconstituted IM solution should be used within 1 h after preparation. Note: DO NOT use this solution for IV administration.

Intravenous

PREPARE: **Intermittent:** Reconstitute 1 g vial with 10 mL of sterile water for injection, NS, or bacteriostatic water for injection. Shake well to dissolve and immediately transfer contents to 50 mL of NS injection solution.

ADMINISTER: **Intermittent:** Infuse over 30 min. Note: Infusion should be completed within 6 h of reconstitution.

INCOMPATIBILITIES **Solution/additive: Dextrose. Y-site:** Do not mix or infuse with any other drugs.

- Store lyophilized powder above 25° C (77° F). May store reconstituted solution for 6 h at room temperature (not greater than 25° C/ 77° F) or for 24 h under refrigeration. Use within 4 h of removal from refrigeration. Do not freeze.

ADVERSE EFFECTS (≥1%) **Body as a Whole:** Phlebitis or thrombosis at injection site, asthenia, fatigue, death, fever, leg pain. **CNS:** Anxiety, altered mental status, dizziness, headache, insomnia. **CV:** Chest pain, hypertension, hypotension, tachycardia, edema. **GI:** Abdominal pain, *diarrhea*, acid regurgitation, constipation, dyspepsia, nausea, vomiting, increased AST and ALT. **Respiratory:** Cough, dyspnea, pharyngitis, rales/rhonchi, and respiratory distress. **Skin:** Erythema, pruritus, rash. **Urogenital:** Vaginitis.

INTERACTIONS Drug: Probenecid decreases renal excretion.

PHARMACOKINETICS Absorption: 90% absorbed from IM site. **Peak:** 2.3 h. **Distribution:** 95% protein bound, distributes into breast milk, may cross placenta. **Metabolism:** Hydrolysis of beta-lactam ring. **Elimination:** 80% in urine, 10% in feces. **Half-Life:** 4.5 h.

CLINICAL IMPLICATIONS
Assessment & Drug Effects
- Lab tests: Perform C&S tests prior to therapy. Monitor periodically liver and kidney function.
- Determine history of hypersensitivity reactions to other beta-lactams, cephalosporins, penicillins, or other drugs.
- Discontinue drug and immediately report S&S of hypersensitivity (see Appendix F).
- Report S&S of superinfection or pseudomembranous colitis (see Appendix F).
- Monitor for seizures especially in older adults and those with renal insufficiency.
- Lab tests: Monitor AST, ALT, alkaline phosphatase, CBC, platelet count, and routine blood chemistry during prolonged therapy.

Patient & Family Education
- Learn S&S of hypersensitivity, superinfection, and pseudomembranous colitis (see Appendix F); report any of these to physician promptly.

ERYTHROMYCIN

(er-ith-roe-mye'sin)

Apo-Erythro Base ◆, A/T/S, E-Mycin, Eryc, EryDerm, EryTab, Erythrocin, Erythromid ◆, Erythromycin Base, Novory-thro ◆, PCE, Ro-Mycin ◆

Common adverse effects in *italic*, life-threatening effects underlined; generic names in **bold**; classifications in SMALL CAPS; ◆ Canadian drug name; ⊙ Prototype drug

573

E

ERYTHROMYCIN ESTOLATE
Nororythro ✦

ERYTHROMYCIN STEARATE
Apo-Erythro-S ✦, Erythrocin Stearate, SK-Erythromycin

Classifications: MACROLIDE ANTIBIOTIC
Therapeutic: ANTIBIOTIC
Pregnancy Category: B

AVAILABILITY Erythromycin 250 mg, 333 mg, 500 mg tablets, capsules; 2% topical solution; 2% gel; 2% ointment; 2% pledgets; 5% ophthalmic ointment; **Erythromycin Estolate** 125 mg, 250 mg capsules; 125 mg/mL, 250 mg/mL suspension; **Erythromycin Stearate** 250 mg, 500 mg tablets

ACTION & *THERAPEUTIC EFFECT*
Macrolide antibiotic produced by a strain of *Streptomyces erythreus.* Erythromycin binds to the 50S ribosomal subunit, inhibiting bacterial protein synthesis. *More active against gram-positive organisms than against gram-negative organisms due to its superior penetration into gram-positive organisms.*

USES Pneumococcal pneumonia, *Mycoplasma pneumoniae* (primary atypical pneumonia), acute pelvic inflammatory disease caused by *Neisseria gonorrhoeae* in females sensitive to penicillin, infections caused by susceptible strains of staphylococci, streptococci, and certain strains of *Haemophilus influenzae.* Also used in intestinal amebiasis, Legionnaires' disease, uncomplicated urethral, endocervical, and rectal infections caused by *Chlamydia trachomatis,* for prophylaxis of ophthalmia neonatorum caused by *N. gonorrhoeae, C. trachomatis,* and for chlamydial conjunctivitis in neonates. Considered an acceptable alternative to penicillin for treatment of streptococcal pharyngitis, for prophylaxis of rheumatic fever and bacterial endocarditis, for treatment of diphtheria as adjunct to antitoxin and for carrier state, and as alternate choice in treatment of primary syphilis in patients allergic to penicillins. **Topical applications:** Pyodermas, acne vulgaris, and external ocular infections, including neonatal chlamydial conjunctivitis and gonococcal ophthalmia.

CONTRAINDICATIONS Hypersensitivity to erythromycins or other macrolide antibiotics; congenital QT prolongation; electrolyte imbalances. **Estolate:** History of hepatotoxicity in patients with hepatic disease.
CAUTIOUS USE Impaired liver function; seizure disorders; history of GI disorders; pregnancy (category B).

ROUTE & DOSAGE

Moderate to Severe Infections
Adult: **PO** 250–500 mg q6h; 333 mg q8h
Child: **PO** 30–50 mg/kg/d divided q6h **Topical** Apply ointment to infected eye 1 or more times/d
Neonate: **PO** ≤7 d, 10 mg/kg q12h; >7 d, 10 mg/kg q8–12h **Topical** 0.5–1 cm in conjunctival sac once

Chlamydia trachomatis Infections
Adult: **PO** 500 mg q.i.d. or 666 mg q8h
Child: **Topical** Apply 0.5–1 cm ribbon in lower conjunctival sacs shortly after birth

ADMINISTRATION
Oral
▪ Give on an empty stomach 1 h before or 3 h after meals. Do not give

with, or immediately before or after, fruit juices, and advise patient not to crush or chew tablets.

- Give enteric-coated tablets without regard to meals.
- Ensure that enteric-coated tablets are not chewed or crushed. They must be swallowed whole.
- Note: When switching from tablet to a PO liquid preparation, dosing may require adjustment.

Topical
- Prophylaxis for neonatal eye infection: Ribbon of ointment approximately 0.5–1 cm long is placed into lower conjunctival sac of neonate shortly after birth. Use a new tube of erythromycin for each neonate.
- Use only preparations labeled for ophthalmic use for treatment of eye infections.
- Store all forms at 15°–30° C (59°–86° F) in tightly capped containers unless otherwise directed by manufacturer.

ADVERSE EFFECTS (≥1%) **GI:** *Nausea, vomiting, abdominal cramping,* diarrhea, heartburn, anorexia. **Body as a Whole:** Fever, eosinophilia, urticaria, skin eruptions, fixed drug eruption, anaphylaxis. Superinfections by nonsusceptible bacteria, yeasts, or fungi. **Special Senses:** Ototoxicity: reversible bilateral hearing loss, tinnitus, vertigo. **Digestive:** (Estolate) Cholestatic hepatitis syndrome. **Skin:** (topical use) Erythema, desquamation, burning, tenderness, dryness or oiliness, pruritus.

DIAGNOSTIC TEST INTERFERENCE
False elevations of *urinary catecholamines, urinary steroids,* and *AST, ALT* (by *colorimetric methods*).

INTERACTIONS Drug: Serum levels and toxicities of **alfentanil, bexar-**

otene, carbamazepine, cevimeline, cilostazol, clozapine, cyclosporine, disopyramide, estazolam, fentanyl, midazolam, methadone, modafinil, quinidine, sirolimus, digoxin, theophylline, triazolam, warfarin are increased. **Ergotamine, dihydroergotamine** may increase peripheral vasospasm.

PHARMACOKINETICS Absorption: Erythromycin base is acid labile; most erythromycins are absorbed in small intestine. **Peak:** 1–4 h PO. **Distribution:** Widely distributed to most body tissues; low concentrations in CSF; concentrates in liver and bile; crosses placenta. **Metabolism:** Partially metabolized in liver. **Elimination:** Primarily in bile; excreted in breast milk. **Half-Life:** 1.5–2 h.

CLINICAL IMPLICATIONS
Assessment & Drug Effects
- Report onset of GI symptoms after PO administration to physician. These are dose related; if symptoms persist after dosage reduction, physician may prescribe drug to be given with meals in spite of impaired absorption.
- Monitor for adverse GI effects. Pseudomembranous enterocolitis (see Appendix F), a potentially life-threatening condition, may occur during or after antibiotic therapy.
- Observe for S&S of superinfection by overgrowth of nonsusceptible bacteria or fungi. Emergence of resistant staphylococcal strains is highly predictable during prolonged therapy.
- Lab tests: Periodic liver function tests during prolonged therapy.
- Monitor for S&S of hepatotoxicity. Premonitory S&S include: Abdominal pain, nausea, vomiting,

Common adverse effects in *italic*, life-threatening effects underlined; generic names in **bold**; classifications in SMALL CAPS; ✦ Canadian drug name; ◎ Prototype drug

575

E

fever, leukocytosis, and eosin-ophilia; jaundice may or may not be present. Symptoms may appear a few days after initiation of drug but usually occur after 1–2 wk of continuous therapy. Symptoms are reversible with prompt discontinuation of erythromycin.

▪ Monitor for ototoxicity that appears to develop most frequently in patients receiving 4 g/d or more, older adults, female patients, and patients with kidney or liver dysfunction. It is reversible with prompt discontinuation of drug.

Patient & Family Education

▪ Notify physician for S&S of superinfection (see Appendix F).

▪ Notify physician immediately for S&S of pseudomembranous enterocolitis (see Appendix F), which may occur even after the drug is discontinued.

▪ Report any ototoxic effects including dizziness, vertigo, nausea, tinnitus, roaring noises, hearing impairment (see Appendix F).

ERYTHROMYCIN ETHYLSUCCINATE

(er-ith-roe-mye'sin)
Apo-Erythro-ES ♦, E.E.S., E.E.S.-200, E.E.S.-400, EryPed, Pediamycin

Classifications: MACROLIDE ANTI-BIOTIC
Therapeutic: ANTIBIOTIC
Prototype: Erythromycin
Pregnancy Category: B

AVAILABILITY 200 mg chewable tablet, 400 mg tablets; 100 mg/2.5 mL, 200 mg/5 mL, 400 mg/5 mL suspension

ACTION & *THERAPEUTIC EFFECT*
Macrolide antibiotic that binds to

the 50 S ribosomal subunit of bacteria, thus inhibiting bacterial protein synthesis. *More active against gram-positive than gram-negative bacteria.*

USES See erythromycin.

CONTRAINDICATIONS Hypersensitivity to erythromycins or any macrolide antibiotic; history of erythromycin-associated hepatitis; preexisting liver disease; congenital QT prolongation; electrolyte imbalances.

CAUTIOUS USE Myasthenia gravis; history of GI disease; seizure disorders; pregnancy (category B), lactation.

ROUTE & DOSAGE

Infection
Adult: **PO** 400 mg q6h up to 4 g/d according to severity of infection
Child: **PO** 30–50 mg/kg/d in 4 divided doses (max: 100 mg/kg/d) for severe infections

ADMINISTRATION

▪ Note: 400 mg erythromycin ethylsuccinate is approximately equal to 250 mg erythromycin base.

Oral

▪ Chewable tablets should be chewed and not swallowed whole.

▪ Suspensions are stable for 14 d at room temperature unless otherwise stated by manufacturer. Note expiration date.

▪ Store tablets in tight containers unless otherwise directed.

ADVERSE EFFECTS (≥1%) **GI:** Diarrhea, *nausea,* vomiting, stomatitis, *abdominal cramps,* anorexia, hepatotoxicity. **Skin:** Skin eruptions. **Spe-**

cial Senses: Ototoxicity. **Body as a Whole:** Potential for superinfections.

INTERACTIONS Drug: Serum levels and toxicities of **alfentanil, bexarotene, carbamazepine, cevimeline, cilostazol, clozapine, cyclosporine, disopyramide, estazolam, fentanyl, midazolam, methadone, modafinil, quinidine, sirolimus, digoxin, theophylline, triazolam, warfarin** are increased. **Ergotamine** may increase peripheral vasospasm. May increase risk of arrhythmias.

PHARMACOKINETICS Absorption: Readily absorbed from GI tract. **Peak:** 2 h. **Distribution:** Concentrates in liver; crosses placenta; distributed into breast milk. **Metabolism:** In liver. **Elimination:** Primarily in bile and feces. **Half-Life:** 2–5 h.

CLINICAL IMPLICATIONS

Assessment & Drug Effects

- Lab tests: Determine C&S prior to treatment. Periodic liver function tests and blood cell counts if therapy is prolonged 10 d.
- Cholestatic hepatitis syndrome is most likely to occur in adults who have received erythromycin estolate for >10 d or who have had repeated courses of therapy. The condition generally clears within 3–5 d after cessation of therapy.

Patient & Family Education

- Advise patient to report immediately the onset of adverse reactions and to be on the alert for signs and symptoms associated with jaundice (see Appendix F).
- Ototoxicity is most likely to occur in patients receiving high dosage or who have impaired kidney function. Report immediately the onset of tinnitus, vertigo, or hearing impairment.

ERYTHROMYCIN GLUCEPTATE

(er-ith-roe-mye′sin)
Ilotycin Gluceptate

ERYTHROMYCIN LACTOBIONATE

Erythrocin Lactobionate-I.V.

Classifications: MACROLIDE ANTIBIOTIC
Therapeutic: ANTIBIOTIC
Prototype: Erythromycin
Pregnancy Category: B

E

AVAILABILITY 500 mg, 1 g injection

ACTION & *THERAPEUTIC EFFECT*
Soluble salt of erythromycin. It binds to the 50S ribosome subunits of susceptible bacteria, resulting in the suppression of protein synthesis of bacteria. *More active against gram-positive than gram-negative bacteria.*

USES When oral administration is not possible or the severity of infection requires immediate high serum levels. See erythromycin.

CONTRAINDICATIONS Hypersensitivity to erythromycin or macrolide antibiotics; congenital QT prolongation; electrolyte imbalances.
CAUTIOUS USE Impaired liver function; seizure disorders; pregnancy (category B), lactation.

ROUTE & DOSAGE

Infections
Adult/Child: IV 15–20 mg/kg/d in 4 divided doses
Legionnaires' Disease
Adult: IV 1–4 g in divided dose
Pelvic Inflammatory Disease
Adult: IV 500 mg q6h × 3d, then convert to PO

Common adverse effects in *italic*, life-threatening effects underlined; generic names in **bold**, classifications in SMALL CAPS; ◆ Canadian drug name; ● Prototype drug

577

E

ADMINISTRATION

Intravenous

PREPARE: **Intermittent/Continuous:** Initial solution is prepared by adding 10 mL sterile water for injection without preservatives to each 500 mg or fraction thereof. Shake vial until drug is completely dissolved. **Intermittent:** Further dilute each 1 gm dose in 100–250 mL of D5W or NS. **Continuous:** Further dilute each 1 gm in 1000 mL D5W or NS. Give within 4 h.

ADMINISTER: **Intermittent:** Give 1 gm or fraction thereof over 20–60 min. Slow rate if pain develops along course of vein. **Continuous:** Continuous infusion is administered slowly, usually over 6 h.

INCOMPATIBILITIES **Solution/additive:** **Dextrose**-containing solutions, **aminophylline, ampicillin,** TETRACYCLINES, **pentobarbital, secobarbital, streptomycin, heparin, cephalothin, colistimethate, floxacillin, furosemide, metaraminol, metoclopramide, vitamin B complex with C, ampicillin, amikacin.** **Y-site:** **Aminophylline, fluconazole, heparin,** TETRACYCLINES.

- Store: **Gluceptate,** reconstituted solution is stable up to 7 d if refrigerated at 2°–8° C (36°–46° F); use solution diluted for infusion within 4 h. **Lactobionate,** reconstituted solution is stable up to 14 d if refrigerated at 2°–8° C (36°–46° F); use solution diluted for infusion within 8 h.

ADVERSE EFFECTS (≥1%) **Body as a Whole:** *Pain and venous irritation after IV injection;* allergic reactions, <u>anaphylaxis</u> (rare); superinfec-

tions. **GI:** *Nausea,* vomiting, diarrhea, *abdominal cramps,* variations in liver function tests following prolonged or repeated therapy. (See also **erythromycin.**)

INTERACTIONS Drug: Serum levels and toxicities of **alfentanil, bexarotene, carbamazepine, cevimeline, cilostazol, clozapine, cyclosporine, disopyramide, estazolam, fentanyl, midazolam, methadone, modafinil, quinidine, sirolimus, digoxin, theophylline, triazolam, warfarin** are increased. **Ergotamine** may increase peripheral vasospasm. May increase risk of arrhythmias.

PHARMACOKINETICS Peak: 1 h. **Distribution:** Concentrates in liver; crosses placenta; distributed into breast milk. **Metabolism:** In liver. **Elimination:** Primarily in bile and feces; 12–15% in urine. **Half-Life:** 3–5 h.

CLINICAL IMPLICATIONS

Assessment & Drug Effects

- Lab tests: Determine C&S prior to initiation of therapy. Periodic liver function tests with daily high doses or prolonged or repeated therapy.
- Monitor hearing impairment may occur with large doses of this drug. It may occur as early as the second day and as late as the third week of therapy.
- Monitor for S&S of thrombophlebitis (see Appendix F). IV infusion of large doses is reported to increase risk.

Patient & Family Education

- Notify physician immediately of tinnitus, dizziness, or hearing impairment.

Common adverse effects in *italic*, life-threatening effects <u>underlined</u>; generic names in **bold**; classifications in SMALL CAPS; ✦ Canadian drug name; ⊘ Prototype drug

ESCITALOPRAM OXALATE

(es-ci-tal'o-pram)

Lexapro

Classifications: PSYCHOTHERAPEUTIC AGENT; ANTIDEPRESSANT; SELECTIVE SEROTONIN REUPTAKE INHIBITOR (SSRI)

Therapeutic: ANTIDEPRESSANT; SSRI
Prototype: Fluoxetine
Pregnancy Category: C

AVAILABILITY 5 mg, 10 mg, 20 mg tablets; 5 mg/5 mL liquid

ACTION & *THERAPEUTIC EFFECT*

Selective serotonin reuptake inhibitor (SSRI) in the CNS. Antidepressant effect is presumed to be linked to its inhibition of CNS presynaptic neuronal uptake of serotonin. *Selective serotonin reuptake inhibition mechanism results in the antidepressant activity with or without anxiety symptoms.*

USES Depression, generalized anxiety disorder.
UNLABELED USES Treatment of panic disorders.

CONTRAINDICATIONS Hypersensitivity to citalopram; concurrent use of MAOIS or use within 14 d of discontinuing MAOIS; pregnancy (category C); volume depleted; suicidal ideation.
CAUTIOUS USE Hypersensitivity to other SSRIs; suicidal ideations, depression, mania, hyponatremia, ethanol intoxication, ECT, dehydration, renal or hepatic insufficiency; older adults; concurrent use of diuretics, cardiovascular disease (e.g., dysrhythmias, conduction defects, myocardial ischemia); history of seizure disorders or suicidal tendencies; lactation. Safety and efficacy in children <18 y are unknown.

ROUTE & DOSAGE

Depression, Generalized Anxiety
Adult: **PO** 10 q.d., may increase to 20 mg q.d. if needed after 1 wk
Geriatric: **PO** 10 mg q.d.

Panic Disorder
Adult: **PO** 5 q.d., may increase to 20 mg q.d. if needed after 1 wk

Hepatic Impairment
Adult: **PO** 10 q.d.

ADMINISTRATION

Oral
- Do not begin this drug within 14 d of stopping an MAOI.
- Reduced doses are advised for the older adult and those with hepatic or renal impairment.
- Dose increments should be separated by at least 1 wk.
- Store at 15°–30° C (59°–86° F) in tightly closed container and protect from light.

ADVERSE EFFECTS (≥1%) **Body as a Whole:** Fatigue, fever, arthralgia, myalgia. **CV:** Palpitation, hypertension. **GI:** *Nausea,* diarrhea, dyspepsia, abdominal pain, dry mouth, vomiting, flatulence, reflux. **CNS:** Dizziness, *insomnia, somnolence,* paresthesia, migraine, tremor, vertigo. **Metabolic:** Increased or decreased weight. **Respiratory:** URI, rhinitis, sinusitis. **Skin:** Increased sweating. **Urogenital:** Dysmenorrhea, decreased libido, ejaculation disorder, impotence, menstrual cramps.

INTERACTIONS Drug: Combination with MAOI could result in hypertensive crisis, hyperthermia, rigidity, myoclonus, autonomic instability; **cimetidine** may increase escitalopram levels; **linezolid** may cause serotonin syndrome. **Herbal: St. John's**

Common adverse effects in *italic*, life-threatening effects underlined; generic names in **bold**; classifications in SMALL CAPS; ♣ Canadian drug name; ⊘ Prototype drug

579

wort may cause serotonin syndrome.

PHARMACOKINETICS Absorption: Rapidly absorbed from GI tract. **Onset:** Approximately 1 wk. **Peak:** 3 h. **Distribution:** 80% protein bound; crosses placenta; distributed into breast milk. **Metabolism:** In liver by CYP3A4, 2C19, and 2D6 enzymes. **Elimination:** 20% in urine, 80% in bile. **Half-Life:** 25 h.

CLINICAL IMPLICATIONS

Assessment & Drug Effects

- Monitor for therapeutic effectiveness: Indicated by elevation of mood; 1–4 wk may be needed before improvement is noted.
- Closely observe for worsening of depression or emergence of suicidality especially in adolescents or children.
- Lab tests: Monitor periodically hepatic functions, CBC, serum sodium, and lithium levels when the two drugs are given concurrently.
- Monitor periodically HR and BP, and carefully monitor complete cardiac status in person with known or suspected cardiac disease.
- Monitor closely older adult patients for adverse effects, especially with doses >20 mg/d.

Patient & Family Education

- Do not engage in hazardous activities until reaction to this drug is known.
- Avoid using alcohol while taking escitalopram.
- Inform physician of commonly used OTC drugs as there is potential for drug interactions.
- Report distressing adverse effects including any changes in sexual functioning or response.
- Periodic ophthalmology exams are advised with long-term treatment.

ESMOLOL HYDROCHLORIDE

(ess'moe-lol)
Brevibloc
Classifications: BETA-ADRENERGIC ANTAGONIST; ANTIARRHYTHMIC
Therapeutic: ANTIARRHYTHMIC
Prototype: Propranolol
Pregnancy Category: C

AVAILABILITY 10 mg/mL, 250 mg/mL injection

ACTION & *THERAPEUTIC EFFECT*
Ultrashort-acting beta$_1$-adrenergic blocking agent with cardioselective properties. Hemodynamic effects are mild, with potency as a beta blocker about $1/100$ that of propranolol. Inhibits the agonist effect of catecholamines by competitive binding at beta-adrenergic receptors. Antiarrhythmic properties occur at the AV node. *Effective as an antiarrhythmic agent on the AV-nodal conduction system. Blocks sympathetically mediated increases in cardiac rate and BP since it binds predominantly to beta$_1$-receptors in cardiac tissue.*

USES Supraventricular tachyarrhythmias (SVT) in perioperative and postoperative periods or in other critical situations. Also short-term treatment of noncompensating sinus tachycardia and in the control of heart rate for patients with MI.
UNLABELED USES Moderate postoperative hypertension; treatment of intense transient adrenergic response to surgical stress in cardiac as well as noncardiac surgery.

CONTRAINDICATIONS Hypersensitivity to esmolol; cardiac failure, heart block greater than first degree, sinus bradycardia, cardiogenic shock; decompensated CHF; pulmonary disease such as bron-

chial asthma, acute bronchospasm, COPD, pulmonary edema; pregnancy (category C). Safety in children is not established.
CAUTIOUS USE History of allergy; CHF; diabetes mellitus; kidney function impairment; lactation.

ROUTE & DOSAGE

Supraventricular Tachyarrhythmias

Adult: **IV** 500 mcg/kg loading dose followed by 50 mcg/kg/min, may increase dose q5–10min prn (max: 200 mcg/kg/min)

Intraoperative/Postoperative Tachycardia

Adult: **IV** 80 mg bolus followed by 150 mcg/kg/min

ADMINISTRATION

▪ Note: Do not use the 2500 mg ampule for direct IV injection.

Intravenous

PREPARE: **Direct:** Use the 10 mg/mL vial undiluted for the loading dose. **IV Infusion:** Prepare maintenance infusion by adding 250 mL of diluent to each 2500 mg ampul to yield 10 mg/mL. Compatible diluents include D5W, D5/RL, D5/NS, D5/.45NS, RL.

ADMINISTER: **Direct:** Give loading dose over 1 min. **IV Infusion:** Give maintenance infusion over 4 min. If adequate response is noted, continue maintenance infusion with periodic adjustments as needed. If an adequate response has not occurred, repeat loading dose and follow with an increased maintenance infusion of 100 mcg/kg/min. May continue titration cycle with same loading dose while increasing maintenance infusion by 50 mcg/kg/min

until desired end point is near. Then omit loading dose and titrate maintenance dose up or down by 25 to 50 mcg/kg/min until desired heart rate is reached. *INCOMPATIBILITIES* **Solution/Additive: Procainamide.** Y-site: **Amphotericin B cholesteryl, furosemide, warfarin.**

▪ Diluted infusion solution is stable for at least 24 h at room temperature.

ADVERSE EFFECTS (≥1%) **CNS:** Headache, *dizziness,* somnolence, confusion, agitation. **CV:** *Hypotension* (dose related), cold hands and feet, bradyarrhythmias, flushing, myocardial depression. **GI:** Nausea, vomiting. **Respiratory:** Dyspnea, chest pain, rhonchi, <u>bronchospasm</u>. **Skin:** *Infusion site inflammation* (redness, swelling, induration).

INTERACTIONS Drug: May increase **digoxin** IV levels 10–20%; **morphine** IV may increase esmolol levels by 45%; **succinylcholine** may prolong neuromuscular blockade.

PHARMACOKINETICS Onset: <5 min. **Peak:** 10–20 min. **Duration:** 10–30 min. **Metabolism:** Hydrolyzed by RBC esterases. **Elimination:** In urine. **Half-Life:** 9 min.

CLINICAL IMPLICATIONS

Assessment & Drug Effects

▪ Monitor BP, pulse, ECG, during esmolol infusion. Hypotension may have its onset during the initial titration phase; thereafter the risk increases with increasing doses. Usually the hypotension experienced during esmolol infusion is resolved within 30 min after infusion is reduced or discontinued.

▪ Change injection site if local reaction occurs. IV site reactions (burning, erythema) or diaphoresis may develop during infusion. Both

Common adverse effects in *italic*, life-threatening effects <u>underlined</u>; generic names in **bold**; classifications in SMALL CAPS; ♦ Canadian drug name; ✪ Prototype drug

581

reactions are temporary. Blood chemistry abnormalities have not been reported.

- Overdose symptoms: Discontinue administration if the following symptoms occur: bradycardia, severe dizziness or drowsiness, dyspnea, bluish-colored fingernails or palms of hands, seizures.

ESOMEPRAZOLE MAGNESIUM

(e-so-me′pra-zole)
Nexium
Classifications: PROTON PUMP INHIBITOR
Therapeutic: ANTIULCER
Prototype: Omeprazole
Pregnancy Category: B

AVAILABILITY 20 mg, 40 mg capsules; 20 mg, 40 mg powder for injection

ACTION & *THERAPEUTIC EFFECT*
Isomer of omeprazole. A weak base that is converted to the active form in the highly acidic environment of the gastric parietal cells. Inhibits the enzyme H^+K^+-ATPase (the acid pump), thus suppressing gastric acid secretion. *Due to inhibition of the H^+K^+-ATPase, esomeprazole substantially decreases both basal and stimulated acid secretion through inhibition of the acid pump in parietal cells.*

USES Erosive esophagitis, gastrointestinal reflux disease (GERD), duodenal ulcer associated with *H. pylori* in combination with antibiotics.

CONTRAINDICATIONS Hypersensitivity to esomeprazole magnesium, omeprazole, or other proton pump inhibitors; gastric malignancy; lactation.

CAUTIOUS USE Severe renal insufficiency; severe hepatic impairment; treatment for more than a year; gastric ulcers; pregnancy (category B). Safety and efficacy in children are not established.

ROUTE & DOSAGE

Healing of Erosive Esophagitis
Adult: **PO or IV** 20–40 mg q.d. at least 1 h before meals times 4–8 wks
GERD, Erosive Esophagitis Maintenance
Adult: **PO** 20 mg q.d.
Duodenal Ulcer
Adult: **PO** 40 mg q.d. times 10 d

ADMINISTRATION

Oral
- Give at least 1 h before eating.
- Do not crush or chew capsule. Must be swallowed whole.
- Open capsule and mix pellets with applesauce (cold or room temperature) if patient cannot swallow capsules. DO NOT crush pellets. Applesauce should be swallowed immediately after mixing without chewing.
- May take with antacids.
- Store in the original blister package 15°–30° C (59°–86° F).

Intravenous

PREPARE: Direct: Reconstitute powder with 5 mL of NS. **IV Infusion:** Further dilute reconstituted solution in 50 mL of NS, LR, or D5W.

ADMINISTER: Direct: Withdraw 5 mL of reconstituted solution and give over no less than 3 min. **IV Infusion:** Give IV solution over 10–30 min.

INCOMPATIBILITIES Do not give simultaneously with any other

Common adverse effects in *italic*, life-threatening effects underlined; generic names in **bold**; classifications in SMALL CAPS; ♥ Canadian drug name; ❷ Prototype drug

medication through the same IV site or line. Flush IV line with NS, LR, or D5W before/after infusion.

- Store reconstituted solution at room temperature up to 30° C (86° F); give within 12 h of reconstitution with NS or LR and within 6 h of reconstitution with D5W.

ADVERSE EFFECTS (≥1%) **CNS:** Headache. **GI:** Nausea, vomiting, diarrhea, constipation, abdominal pain, flatulence, dry mouth.

INTERACTIONS Drug: May increase **diazepam, phenytoin, warfarin** levels. **Food:** Food decreases absorption by up to 35%.

PHARMACOKINETICS Absorption: Destroyed in acidic environment, therefore capsules are designed for delayed absorption in the small intestine. 70% reaches systemic circulation. **Metabolism:** In liver by CYP2C19. **Elimination:** Inactive metabolites excreted in both urine and feces. **Half-Life:** 1.5 h.

CLINICAL IMPLICATIONS

Assessment & Drug Effects
- Monitor for S&S of adverse CNS effects (vertigo, agitation, depression) especially in severely ill patients.
- Monitor phenytoin levels with concurrent use.
- Monitor INR/PT with concurrent warfarin use.
- Lab tests: Periodic liver function tests, CBC, Hct & Hbg, urinalysis for hematuria and proteinuria.

Patient & Family Education
- Report any changes in urinary elimination such as pain or discomfort associated with urination to physician.
- Report severe diarrhea. Drug may need to be discontinued.

ESTAZOLAM

(es-ta-zo'lam)
Prosom
Classifications: ANXIOLYTIC; SEDATIVE-HYPNOTIC; BENZODIAZEPINE
Therapeutic: ANTIANXIETY; SEDATIVE-HYPNOTIC
Prototype: Lorazepam
Pregnancy Category: X
Controlled Substance: Schedule IV

AVAILABILITY 1 mg, 2 mg tablets

ACTION & *THERAPEUTIC EFFECT*
Benzodiazepine whose effects (anxiolytic, sedative, hypnotic, skeletal muscle relaxant) are mediated by the inhibitory neurotransmitter gamma-aminobutyric acid (GABA). GABA acts at the thalamic, hypothalamic, and limbic levels of CNS. *Benzodiazepines generally decrease the number of awakenings from sleep. Stage 2 sleep is increased with all benzodiazepines. Estazolam shortens stages 3 and 4 (slow-wave sleep), and REM sleep is shortened. The total sleep time, however, is increased.*

USES Short-term management of insomnia.

CONTRAINDICATIONS Known sensitivity to benzodiazepines; acute closed-angle glaucoma, primary depressive disorders or psychosis; abrupt discontinuation; children <18 y; coma, shock, acute alcohol intoxication; pregnancy (category X), lactation.
CAUTIOUS USE Renal and hepatic impairment, renal failure; organic brain syndrome, alcoholism, benzodiazepine dependence, suicidal ideations, CNS depression, seizure disorder, status epilepticus; substance abuse; shock, coma; dementia, mania, psychosis; myasthenia gravis, Parkinson's disease; sleep

Common adverse effects in *italic*, life-threatening effects underlined; generic names in **bold**; classifications in SMALL CAPS; ♣ Canadian drug name; ⊘ Prototype drug

583

E

apnea; open-angle glaucoma, GI disorders, older adult and debilitated patients; limited pulmonary reserve, pulmonary disease, COPD.

ROUTE & DOSAGE

Insomnia
Adult: **PO** 1 mg h.s. may increase up to 2 mg if necessary (some debilitated older adult patients should start with 0.5 mg h.s.)

ADMINISTRATION

Oral
- For older adult patients in good health, a 1-mg dose is indicated; reduce initial dose to 0.5 mg for debilitated or small older adult patients.
- Dosage reduction also may be needed in the presence of hepatic impairment.

ADVERSE EFFECTS (≥1%) **CNS:** Headache, dizziness, impaired coordination, hypokinesia, *somnolence,* hangover, weakness. **CV:** Palpitations, arrhythmias, syncope (all rare). **Hematologic:** Leukopenia, agranulocytosis. **GI:** Constipation, xerostomia, anorexia, flatulence, vomiting. **Musculoskeletal:** Arthritis, arthralgia, myalgia, muscle spasm.

INTERACTIONS Drug: Cimetidine may decrease metabolism of estazolam and increase its effects; **alcohol** and other CNS DEPRESSANTS may increase drowsiness; CYP3A4 inhibitors **(ketoconazole, itraconazole, nefazodone, diltiazem, fluvoxamine, cimetidine, isoniazid, erythromycin)** can increase concentrations and toxicity of estazolam; **carbamazepine, phenytoin, rifampin,** BARBITURATES may decrease estazolam concentrations. **Food:** Grapefruit juice >1 quart may increase toxicity. **Herbal: Kava-kava, valerian** may potentiate sedation.

PHARMACOKINETICS Absorption: Rapidly absorbed from GI tract. **Onset:** 20–30 min. **Peak:** 2 h. **Distribution:** Crosses rapidly into brain; crosses placenta; distributed into breast milk. **Metabolism:** Extensively in liver. **Elimination:** In urine. **Half-Life:** 10–24 h.

CLINICAL IMPLICATIONS

Assessment & Drug Effects
- Monitor for improvement in S&S of insomnia.
- Assess for excess CNS depression or daytime sedation.
- Assess for safety, especially with older adult or debilitated patients, as dizziness and impaired coordination are known adverse effects.

Patient & Family Education
- Learn adverse effects and report those experienced to the physician.
- Avoid using this drug in combination with other CNS depressant drugs or alcohol.
- Do not drive or engage in other potentially hazardous activities until response to drug is known.

ESTRADIOL ℗

(ess-tra-dye′ole)
Alora, Climara, Esclim, Estrace, Estraderm, Estrasorb, EstroGel, FemPatch, Menorest, Menostar, Vivelle, Vivelle DOT, Estring, Vagifem

ESTRADIOL ACETATE
Femring, Femtrace

ESTRADIOL CYPIONATE
Depo-Estradiol Cypionate, Estro-Cyp

ESTRADIOL VALERATE
Delestrogen, Femogex ✦

Classifications: HORMONE; ESTROGEN
Therapeutic: ESTROGEN REPLACEMENT
Pregnancy Category: X

AVAILABILITY Estradiol 0.025 mg, 0.0375 mg, 0.05 mg, 0.06 mg, 0.075 mg, 0.1 mg patch; 14 mcg/24 h transdermal patch; 0.5 mg, 1 mg, 2 mg tablets; 25 mcg vaginal tablets, 2 mg vaginal ring, 0.1 mg vaginal cream; 2.5 mg/g topical emulsion; 0.06% topical gel; **Cypionate** 5 mg/mL injection; **Valerate** 10 mg/mL, 20 mg/mL, 40 mg/mL injection; **Acetate** 0.45 mg, 0.9 mg, 1.8 mg tablets; 0.05 mg/d, 0.1 mg/d vaginal insert

ACTION & *THERAPEUTIC EFFECT*
Natural or synthetic steroid hormone secreted principally by the ovarian follicles, and also by the adrenals, corpus luteum, placenta, and testes. Estrogen binds to a specific intracellular receptor, forming a complex that stimulates synthesis of proteins responsible for estrogenic effects. Promotes endometrial lining development, but long-time use leads to abnormal endometrial hyperplasia, and abnormal bleeding. Conversely, estrogen-stimulated endometrium suddenly deprived of estrogen may bleed within 48–72 h. *Estradiol (estrogens) effects simulate those produced by the endogenous hormone. May mask onset of climacteric.*

USES Natural or surgical menopausal symptoms, kraurosis vulvae, atrophic vaginitis, primary ovarian failure, female hypogonadism, castration. Used adjunctively with diet, calcium, and physical therapy to prevent and treat postmenopausal osteoporosis; also for palliation in advanced prostatic carcinoma and inoperable metastatic breast cancer in women at least 5 y after menopause. Combined with progestins in many oral contraceptive formulations.

CONTRAINDICATIONS Known or suspected pregnancy (category X); estrogenic-dependent neoplasms, breast cancer (except in selected patients being treated for metastatic disease). History of thromboembolic disorders; active arterial thrombosis or thrombophlebitis; undiagnosed abnormal genital bleeding; uterine fibroids; endometriosis; history of cholestatic disease; hepatic disease; thyroid dysfunction; blood dyscrasias; hypercalcemia; lupus (SLE).
CAUTIOUS USE Adolescents with incomplete bone growth; endometriosis; hypertension, cardiac insufficiency; diseases of calcium and phosphate metabolism (metabolic bone disease); cerebrovascular disease; mental depression; benign breast disease, family history of breast or genital tract neoplasm; diabetes mellitus; gall bladder disease; preexisting leiomyoma, abnormal mammogram, history of idiopathic jaundice of pregnancy; varicosities; asthma; epilepsy; migraine headaches; liver or kidney dysfunction; jaundice, acute intermittent porphyria, pyridoxine deficiency.

ROUTE & DOSAGE

Menopause, Atrophic Vaginitis, Kraurosis Vulvae, Female Hypogonadism, Female Castration, Primary Ovarian Failure
Adult: **PO** 0.45–2 mg/d in a cyclic regimen **Topical** 2–4 g vaginal cream intravaginally once/d for 1–2 wk, then 1–2 g/d for 1–2 wk, then 1 g 1–3 times/wk; **Transdermal patch Estraderm** twice weekly;

Common adverse effects in *italic*, life-threatening effects underlined; generic names in **bold**, classifications in SMALL CAPS; ✦ Canadian drug name; ⊘ Prototype drug

585

Climara, FemPatch, Menostar qwk in a cyclic regimen; **Estrasorb** Apply 1 packet to the left thigh and calf and 1 packet to the right thigh and calf once daily in the morning; **EstroGel** Apply 1.25 g (one-half applicatorful) to one arm every day (usually in the morning). **IM Cypionate** 1–5 mg once q3–4wk; **Valerate** 10–25 mg once q4wk; **Acetate** Insert 1 vaginal ring into the upper third of the vaginal vault. Keep in place continuously for 3 mo, then remove.

Metastatic Breast Cancer

Adult: **PO** 10 mg t.i.d.

Prostatic Cancer

Adult: **PO** 1–2 mg t.i.d. **IM Valerate** 30 mg once q1–2wk

Postpartum Breast Engorgement

Adult: **IM Valerate** 10–25 mg at end of first stage of labor

ADMINISTRATION

Oral

- Give with or immediately after solid food to reduce nausea.
- Protect tablets from light and moisture in well-closed container. Protect from freezing, unless otherwise directed by manufacturer.

Intravaginal

- Insert calibrated dosage applicator approximately 5 cm (2 in.) into vagina, directing it slightly back toward sacrum. Instill medication by pushing plunger. Patient should remain in recumbent position about 30 min to prevent losing the medication. Observe perineal area before each administration: if mucosa is red, swollen, or excoriated or if there is a change in vaginal discharge, report to physician.

Topical

- Cleanse and dry selected skin area. Apply as directed under Route & Dosage.

Transdermal

- Cleanse and dry selected skin area on trunk of body, preferably the abdomen. Avoid application to the breasts, to an irritated, abraded, oily area, or to the waistline. If system falls off, it may be reapplied, or if necessary, a new one can be applied. Return to original treatment schedule. Rotate application site with an interval of at least 1 wk between applications to a particular site.

Intramuscular

- Give deep into a large muscle.
- Store at 15°–30° C (59°–86° F); protect from light and freezing.

ADVERSE EFFECTS (≥1%) **CNS:** Headache, migraine, dizziness, mental depression, chorea, convulsions, increased risk of dementia. **CV:** Thromboembolic disorders, stroke, CAD, hypertension. **Special Senses:** Intolerance to contact lenses, worsening of myopia or astigmatism, scotomas. **GI:** *Nausea,* vomiting, anorexia, increased appetite, diarrhea, abdominal cramps or pain, constipation, bloating, colitis, acute pancreatitis, cholestatic jaundice, benign hepatoadenoma. **Urogenital:** Mastodynia, breast secretion, spotting, changes in menstrual flow, dysmenorrhea, amenorrhea, cervical erosion, altered cervical secretions, premenstrual-like syndrome, vaginal candidiasis, endometrial cystic hyperplasia, reactivation of endometriosis, increased size of preexisting fibromyomas, cystitis-like syndrome, hemolytic uremic syndrome, change in libido; in men: gynecomastia, testicular atrophy, feminization, impotence (reversible). **Metabolic:** Reduced carbohydrate tolerance, hyperglycemia, hypercalcemia, folic acid deficiency, fluid retention. **Skin:** Dermatitis, pruritus, seborrhea, oily skin, acne; photosensitivity, chloasma, loss of scalp hair, hirsutism. **Body as a Whole:** Pain and postinjection flare at injection site; sterile abscess; leg cramps, weight changes. **Hematologic:** Acute intermittent porphyria.

DIAGNOSTIC TEST INTERFERENCE
Estradiol reduces response of *metyrapone* test and excretion of *pregnanediol. Increases: BSP* retention, norepinephrine-induced *platelet aggregability, hydrocortisone, PBI, T_4, sodium, thyroxine-binding globulin (TBG), prothrombin and factors VII, VIII, IX,* and *X; serum triglyceride,* and *phospholipid* concentrations, *renin* substrate. *Decreases: antithrombin III, pyridoxine* and *serum folate* concentrations, serum *cholesterol,* values for the *T_3 resin uptake* test, *glucose tolerance.* May cause false-positive test for *LE cells* or *antinuclear antibodies (ANA).*

INTERACTIONS Drug: BARBITURATES, **phenytoin, rifampin** decrease estrogen effect by increasing its metabolism; ORAL ANTICOAGULANTS may decrease hypoprothrombinemic effects; interfere with effects of **bromocriptine;** may increase levels and toxicity of **cyclosporine,** TRICYCLIC ANTIDEPRESSANTS, **theophylline;** decrease effectiveness of **clofibrate.**

PHARMACOKINETICS Absorption: Rapid from GI tract; readily through skin and mucous membranes; slow from IM injections. **Distribution:** Throughout body tissues, especially in adipose tissue; crosses placenta. **Metabolism:** Primarily in liver. **Elimi-**

nation: Excreted in urine; excreted in breast milk.

CLINICAL IMPLICATIONS

Assessment & Drug Effects
- Monitor adverse GI effects. Nausea, frequently at breakfast time, usually disappears after 1 or 2 wk of drug use.
- Check BP on a regular basis in patients with cardiac or kidney dysfunction or hypertension; monitored carefully.
- Note: Severe hypercalcemia (>15 mg/dL) may be caused by estradiol therapy in patients with breast cancer and bone metastasis.
- Interrupt estrogen treatment at least 4 wk before surgery associated with a prolonged period of immobilization or vascular complications.

Patient & Family Education
- Comply with established dosage schedule. Do not alter unless physician prescribes a change.
- Read patient package insert (PPI) carefully.
- Notify physician of intermittent breakthrough bleeding, spotting, bleeding, or unexplained and sudden pain.
- Determine weight under standard conditions 1 or 2 times/wk; report sudden weight gain or other signs of fluid retention.
- Notify physician of positive Homans' sign (calf pain upon flexing foot) and the following symptoms of thromboembolic disorders immediately: Tenderness, swelling, and redness in extremity; sudden, severe headache or chest pain; slurring of speech; change in vision; tenderness, pain, sudden shortness of breath.
- Monitor urine or blood glucose & HbA1c for glycemic control if diabetic.

Common adverse effects in *italic*, life-threatening effects underlined; generic names in **bold**; classifications in SMALL CAPS; ✦ Canadian drug name; ☉ Prototype drug

587

- Decrease caffeine intake, since estrogen depresses caffeine metabolism.
- Learn self-examination of breasts and follow a monthly schedule.
- Reduce or terminate long-term or high-dosage therapy with estrogens gradually.
- Estrogen-induced feminization and impotence in male patients are reversible with termination of therapy.
- Estrogen-primed or -stimulated endometrium may bleed 48–72 h after dose is discontinued. In cyclic therapy, estradiol is resumed on schedule before drug-induced vaginal bleeding stops.
- Withdrawal bleeding may occur even after oophorectomy and after menopause.

ESTRAMUSTINE PHOSPHATE SODIUM

(ess-tra-muss'teen)

Emcyt

Classifications: ANTINEOPLASTIC; ALKYLATING AGENT; NITROGEN MUSTARD
Therapeutic: ANTINEOPLASTIC NITROGEN MUSTARD
Prototype: Cyclophosphamide
Pregnancy Category: D

AVAILABILITY 140 mg capsules

ACTION & *THERAPEUTIC EFFECT*
Conjugate of estradiol and the carbamate of nitrogen mustard. Incorporation of estramustine in tumor tissues is probably due to the presence of estramustine-binding protein (EMBP), which is found in prostate carcinoma, glioma, melanoma, and breast carcinoma. Binds to proteins and microtubulin resulting in microtubule changes in the cell division cycle, thus arresting cell division in the G2/M phase of the cell cycle. *Major effectiveness reported to be in patients who have been refractory to estrogen therapy alone.*

USES Palliative treatment of metabolic or progressive carcinoma of prostate.

CONTRAINDICATIONS Hypersensitivity to either estradiol or nitrogen mustard; active thrombophlebitis or thromboembolic disorders; pregnancy (category D), lactation.
CAUTIOUS USE History of thrombophlebitis, thromboses, or thromboembolic disorders; cerebrovascular or coronary artery disease; gallstones or peptic ulcer; impaired liver function; metabolic bone diseases associated with hypercalcemia; diabetes mellitus; hypertension, conditions that might be aggravated by fluid retention (e.g., epilepsy, migraine, kidney dysfunction); older adult patients.

ROUTE & DOSAGE

Neoplasm
Adult: **PO** 14 mg/kg/d in 3–4 divided doses

ADMINISTRATION

Oral

- Give with meals to reduce incidence of GI adverse effects. Some patients require drug withdrawal because of intolerable GI effects.
- Store at 2°–8° C (38°–46° F) in tight, light-resistant containers, unless otherwise directed by manufacturer.

ADVERSE EFFECTS (≥1%) **CNS:** Lethargy, emotional lability, insomnia, headache, anxiety. **CV:** CVA, MI, *thrombophlebitis,* CHF, *periph-*

eral edema. **GI:** *Nausea,* diarrhea, anorexia, flatulence, vomiting, thirst, GI bleeding. **Hematologic:** Leukopenia, thrombocytopenia, *abnormalities in liver function tests,* hypercalcemia, <u>bone marrow depression</u> (rare). **Respiratory:** Hoarseness, burning sensation in throat, dyspnea, upper respiratory discharge, <u>pulmonary emboli.</u> **Skin:** Rash, pruritus, urticaria, dry skin, easy bruising, flushing, peeling skin and fingertips, thinning hair. **Special Senses:** Tearing of eyes. **Urogenital:** Gynecomastia, breast tenderness, impotence. **Endocrine:** Decrease in glucose tolerance. **Musculoskeletal:** Leg cramps.

INTERACTIONS Food: Milk, dairy products, calcium supplements may decrease estramustine absorption.

PHARMACOKINETICS Absorption: Readily absorbed from GI tract. **Peak:** 2–3 h. **Metabolism:** Dephosphorylated in intestines to estramustine, estradiol, estrone, and nitrogen mustard; further metabolized in liver. **Elimination:** In feces via bile. **Half-Life:** 20 h.

CLINICAL IMPLICATIONS

Assessment & Drug Effects

- Monitor weight and examine for peripheral edema. Be mindful that drug can cause CHF.
- Monitor I&O ratio and pattern to prevent dehydration and electrolyte imbalance, especially with vomiting or diarrhea.
- Observe diabetics closely because of possibility of estramustine-induced reduction in glucose tolerance. Monitor baseline and periodic glucose tolerance tests.
- Lab tests: Perform baseline and periodic liver enzymes and bilirubin tests; repeat after drug has been discontinued for 2 mo.

Patient & Family Education

- Eat small meals at frequent intervals to reduce drug-induced nausea, eat slowly, and try cold food if food odors are offensive.
- Drink liquids 1 h before or 1 h after rather than with meals; clear liquids may be more palatable.

E

ESTROGEN-PROGESTIN COMBINATIONS (CONTRACEPTIVES)

Oral

Monophasic: Apri, Alesse, Aviane, Balziva, Brevicon, Cryselle, Demulen, Desogen, Gencept, Junel, Lessina, Levlite, Levora, Loestrin, Lo/Ovral, Low-Ogestrel, Microgestin, Modicon, Nordette, Norethin, Norinyl, Nortrel, Ogestrel, Ortho-Cept, Ortho-Cyclen, Ortho-Novum, Ovcon, Portia, Previfem, Seasonale, Sprintec, Yasmin, Yaz, Zovia
Biphasic: Kariva, Mircette, Ortho-Novum 10/11
Triphasic: Aranelle, Cyclessa, Enpresse, Estrostep, Estrostep Fe, Ortho-Novum 7/7/7, Ortho Tri-Cyclen, Ortho Tri-Cyclen Lo, Tri-Norinyl, Tri-Previfem, Tri-Sprintec, Triphasil, Trivora, Velivet
Postcoital Contraceptives: Plan B, Preven
Transdermal
Ortho Evra
Intravaginal
NuvaRing

Classifications: HORMONE; ESTROGEN-PROGESTIN COMBINATIONS
Therapeutic: CONTRACEPTIVE
Prototype: Estradiol, Norgestrel
Pregnancy Category: X

AVAILABILITY Combination oral contraceptives contain one of the following estrogens and one of the following progestins. **Estrogen:**

Common adverse effects in *italic*, life-threatening effects <u>underlined</u>; generic names in **bold**; classifications in SMALL CAPS; ✦ Canadian drug name; ◯ Prototype drug

589

Ethinyl estradiol 10 mcg, 20 mcg, 25 mcg, 30 mcg, 35 mcg, 40 mcg, 50 mcg; mestranol 50 mcg; **Progestin:** Desogestrel 0.15 mg; drospirenone 3 mg; ethynodiol diacetate 1 mg; levonorgestrel 0.05 mg, 0.075 mg, 0.1 mg, 0.125 mg, 0.15 mg, 0.25 mg, 0.75 mg; norethindrone 0.4 mg, 0.5 mg, 0.75 mg, 1 mg; norethindrone acetate 1 mg, 1.5 mg; norgestimate 0.18 mg, 0.215 mg, 0.25 mg; norgestrel 0.3 mg, 0.5 mg; **Transdermal:** Norelgestromin 6 mg/0.75 mg ethinyl estradiol patch; **Vaginal:** Etonogestrel 11.7 mg/2.7 mg ethinyl estradiol vaginal insert

ACTION & *THERAPEUTIC EFFECT*

Three types of estrogen-progestin combinations are available: (1) monophasic, fixed dosage of estrogen-progestin throughout the cycle; (2) biphasic, amount of estrogen remains the same throughout cycle, less progestin in first half of cycle and increased progestin in second half; (3) triphasic, estrogen amount is the same or varies throughout cycle, progestin amount varies. *Fixed combination of estrogen and progestin produces contraception by preventing ovulation and rendering reproductive tract structures hostile to sperm penetration and zygote implantation.*

USES To prevent conception and to treat hypermenorrhea and endometriosis; postcoital contraceptive or "morning after pill"; moderate acne in females ≥15 y (Tri-Cyclen).

CONTRAINDICATIONS Familial or personal history of or existence of breast or other estrogen-dependent neoplasm, recurrent chronic cystic mastitis, history of or existence of thrombophlebitis or thromboembolic disorders, cerebral vascular or coronary artery disease, MI, serious hepatic dysfunction, hepatic neoplasm, family history of hepatic porphyria, undiagnosed abnormal vaginal bleeding, women age 40 and over, adolescents with incomplete epiphyseal closure; pregnancy (category X), lactation, missed abortion.

CAUTIOUS USE History of depression, preexisting hypertension, or cardiac or renal disease; impaired liver function, history of migraine, convulsive disorders, or asthma; multiparous women with grossly irregular menses, diabetes, or familial history of diabetes; gallbladder disease, lupus erythematosus, rheumatic disease, varicosities, smokers.

ROUTE & DOSAGE

Contraception

Adult: **PO** 1 active tablet daily for 21 d, then placebo tablet or no tablets for 7 d, repeat cycle **Continuous regimen** (Seasonale) 1 tablet daily × 84 consecutive days. Wait 7 d for withdrawal bleeding before starting next cycle **Topical** Apply one patch once weekly for 3 wk, then have 1 wk patch-free before repeating the cycle **Intravaginal** Insert 1 ring on or before day 5 of the cycle. Remove ring after 3 wk, followed by a 1/wk rest. Then insert new ring.

Postcoital Contraception (Plan B, Preven, Ovral)

Adult: **PO** Ovral, 2 tablets within 72 h of intercourse, then 2 tablets 12 h later; 1 (Plan B) or 2 (Preven) tablets within 72 h of unprotected intercourse, take second dose of 1 (Plan B) or 2 (Preven) tablets 12 h later

ADMINISTRATION

- Give without regard to meals.

Common adverse effects in *italic*, life-threatening effects underlined; generic names in **bold**, classifications in SMALL CAPS; ♣ Canadian drug name; ⊙ Prototype drug

• Do not exceed 24-h intervals between the daily doses; taking with a meal or at bedtime is a helpful reminder.

ADVERSE EFFECTS (≥1%) **Body as a Whole:** Paresthesias. **CV:** Malignant hypertension, thrombotic and thromboembolic disorders, *mild to moderate increase in BP,* increase in size of varicosities, edema. **Endocrine:** Estrogen excess (*nausea, bloating, menstrual tension, cervical mucorrhea, polyposis, chloasma, hypertension,* migraine headache, breast fullness or tenderness, edema); estrogen deficiency (hypomenorrhea, *early or mid-cycle breakthrough bleeding,* increased spotting); progestin excess (hypomenorrhea, breast regression, *vaginal candidiasis,* depression, fatigue, weight gain, increased appetite, acne, oily scalp, hair loss); progestin deficiency (late-cycle breakthrough bleeding, amenorrhea). **GI:** *Nausea,* cholelithiasis, gallbladder disease, cholestatic jaundice, benign hepatic adenomas; diarrhea, constipation, abdominal cramps. **Metabolic:** *Decreased glucose tolerance,* pyridoxine deficiency (see also diagnostic test interferences), acute intermittent porphyria. **Skin:** Rash (allergic), photosensitivity (photoallergy or phototoxicity), irritation from patch. **Special Senses:** Unexplained loss of vision, optic neuritis, proptosis, diplopia, change in corneal curvature (steepening), intolerance to contact lenses, retinal thrombosis, papilledema. **Urogenital:** Ureteral dilation, increased incidence of urinary tract infection, hemolytic uremia syndrome, renal failure, increased risk of congenital anomalies, decreased quality and quantity of breast milk, dysmenorrhea, increased size of preexisting uterine fibroids, *menstrual disorders.* Foreign body sensation, coital problems, device expulsion, vaginal discomfort, vaginitis, leukorrhea from ring.

DIAGNOSTIC TEST INTERFERENCE
ORAL CONTRACEPTIVES (OCS) increase *BSP* retention, *prothrombin* and *coagulation factors II, VII, VIII, IX, X; platelet agregability, thyroid-binding globulin, PBI, T_4; transcortin; corticosteroid, triglyceride* and *phospholipid* levels; *ceruloplasmin, aldosterone, amylase, transferrin; renin* activity, *vitamin A.* OCS decrease *antithrombin III, T_3 resin uptake, serum folate, glucose tolerance, albumin, vitamin B_{12}* and reduce the *metyrapone* test response.

INTERACTIONS Drug: **Aminocaproic acid** may increase clotting factors, leading to hypercoagulable state; BARBITURATES, ANTICONVULSANTS, ANTIBIOTICS, **rifampin,** ANTIFUNGALS reduce efficacy of OCS and increase incidence of breakthrough bleeding and risk of pregnancy. May decrease efficacy of **lamotrigine. Herbal: St. John's wort** may decrease efficacy of OCs.

PHARMACOKINETICS Absorption: Oral: Readily from GI tract; or from transdermal patch placed on abdomen, buttock, upper outer arm and upper torso (excluding breast). Vaginal insert: norgestrel 100% absorbed, ethinyl estradiol 56% absorbed. **Peak:** Patch: 48 h. **Duration:** Patch: 1 wk. **Distribution:** Widely distributed; crosses placenta; small amount distributed into breast milk. **Metabolism:** In liver. **Elimination:** In urine and feces. **Half-Life:** 6–45 h oral. Following removal of the patch: norelgestromin 28 h, ethinyl estradiol 17 h; vaginal ring: norgestrel 29 h; ethinyl estradiol 45 h.

Common adverse effects in *italic,* life-threatening effects underlined; generic names in **bold**; classifications in SMALL CAPS; ♣ Canadian drug name; ⊕ Prototype drug

591

CLINICAL IMPLICATIONS

Assessment & Drug Effects

- Take complete medical and family history prior to initiation of OC therapy. Physical exam: Baseline and periodic BP, breasts, abdomen, pelvis, Pap smear, and other relevant tests.
- Rule out pregnancy before OC therapy is begun.
- Check BP periodically. In some women, changes in BP occur within each cycle; in others, slow increase of pressure, particularly diastolic, over several months is significant. Drug-induced BP elevation is usually reversible with cessation of OC.
- Nausea with or without vomiting occurs in approximately 10% of patients during the first cycle and is reportedly one of the major reasons for voluntary discontinuation of therapy. Most adverse effects tend to disappear in third or fourth cycle of use. Instruct patient to report symptoms that persist after fourth cycle. Dose adjustment or a different product may be indicated.
- Hirsutism and loss of hair are reversible with discontinuation of OC or by change of selected combination.
- Acne may improve, worsen, or develop for first time. In women on OC for at least 1 y, postcontraceptive acne sometimes occurs 3–4 mo after stopping drug and may continue for 6–12 mo.
- Anovulation or amenorrhea following termination of OC regimen may persist more than 6 mo. The user with pretreatment oligomenorrhea or secondary amenorrhea is most apt to have oversuppression syndrome.

Patient & Family Education

- Use an additional method of birth control during the first week of the initial cycle.
- Missed dose: Take tablet as soon as remembered or take 2 tablets the next day. If 2 consecutive tablets are omitted, take 2 tablets daily for the next 2 d, then resume the regular schedule. If 3 consecutive tablets are missed, begin a new compact of tablets, starting 7 d after last tablet was taken.
- Use an additional form of birth control for 7 d after 2 missed doses; 14 d after 3 missed doses.
- Ovulation is unlikely with omission of 1 daily dose; however, the possibility of escaped ovulation, spotting, or breakthrough bleeding increases with each missed dose.
- Discontinue medication if intra-cycle bleeding resembling menstruation occurs. Begin taking tablets from a new compact on day 5. If bleeding persists, see physician.
- Transdermal patches: Apply only one patch at a time and never cut or otherwise alter a patch prior to application.
- See physician to rule out pregnancy if 2 consecutive periods are missed, before continuing on OC.
- Do not skip scheduled visits for physical checkups while on OC therapy. Learn breast self-examination and do every month.
- Record frequent weight checks to permit early recognition of fluid retention.
- Understand the increased risk of thromboembolic and cardiovascular problems and increased incidence of gallbladder disease with OC use. Be alert to manifestations of thrombotic or thromboembolic disorders: severe headache (especially if persistent and recurrent), dizziness, blurred vision, leg or chest pain, respiratory distress, un-

Common adverse effects in *italic*, life-threatening effects underlined; generic names in **bold**; classifications in SMALL CAPS; ✚ Canadian drug name; ⊘ Prototype drug

explained cough. Discontinue drug if any of these symptoms appear and report them promptly to physician.

- Report sudden abdominal pain immediately to physician in order to rule out ectopic pregnancy.
- Be aware that ophthalmic sequelae can occur as soon as 24 h after initiation of OC. Stop drug and contact physician if unexplained partial or complete, sudden or gradual loss of vision, protrusion of eyeballs (proptosis), or diplopia occurs.
- Leukorrhea (increased clear discharge) is an expected physical reaction to the OC; however, if OC use is accompanied by vaginal itching and irritation, report to physician promptly to rule out candidiasis.
- Monitor urine and blood glucose closely if diabetic. Adjustment of antidiabetic medication may be necessary.
- Be aware that smokers using OC have a fivefold greater risk of fatal MI than nonsmoker OC users and a tenfold greater risk than non-OC users who are nonsmokers. The risk increases with age (marked in women >35 y) and with heavy smoking (15 or more cigarettes/d).
- Oral contraception can be started immediately after delivery in the nonlactating mother.
- Use alternate method of birth control when breast feeding until infant is weaned.

ESTROGENS, CONJUGATED

(ess′tro-jenz)

C.E.S. ✦, Cenestin, Enjuvia, Premarin, Progens

Classifications: HORMONE; ESTROGENS

Therapeutic: FEMALE HORMONE REPLACEMENT THERAPY (HRT)
Prototype: Estradiol
Pregnancy Category: X

AVAILABILITY 0.3 mg, 0.45 mg, 0.625 mg, 0.9 mg, 1.25 mg, 2.5 mg tablets; 25 mg injection; 0.625 mg vaginal cream

ACTION & *THERAPEUTIC EFFECT*

Circulating estrogens modulate the pituitary secretion of the gonadotropins luteinizing hormone (LH) and follicle stimulating hormone (FSH) through a negative feedback mechanism. Estrogens act to reduce the elevated levels of these gonadotropins seen in postmenopausal women. *Binds to intracellular receptors that stimulate DNA and RNA to synthesize proteins responsible for effects of estrogen.*

USES Atrophic vaginitis, kraurosis vulvae, and abnormal bleeding (hormonal imbalance); also female hypogonadism, primary ovarian failure, vasomotor symptoms associated with menopause; to retard progression of osteoporosis and as palliative therapy of breast and prostatic carcinomas.
UNLABELED USES Postcoital contraceptive.

CONTRAINDICATIONS Breast cancer, except for palliative therapy; vaginal and cervical cancers; endometrial cancer; endometrial hyperplasia; abnormal vaginal bleeding; hepatic disease or cancer; hypercalcemia; ovarian cancer; history of thromboembolic disease; known or suspected pregnancy (category X).
CAUTIOUS USE Hypertension; gallbladder disease; diabetes mellitus; heart failure; kidney dysfunction.

Common adverse effects in *italic*, life-threatening effects underlined; generic names in **bold**; classifications in SMALL CAPS; ✦ Canadian drug name; ☢ Prototype drug

593

ROUTE & DOSAGE

Menopause, Osteoporosis, Atrophic Vaginitis, Kraurosis Vulvae

Adult: **PO** 0.3–1.25 mg/d for 21 d each month, adjust to lowest level that gives symptom control (≤0.625 mg/d) **IV/IM** 25 mg, repeated in 6–12 h if needed **Topical** 2–4 g of cream/d

Female Hypogonadism

Adult: **PO** 2.5–7.5 mg/d in 1–3 divided doses for 20 d, followed by a 10 d rest period

Postcoital Contraception

Adult: **PO** 30 mg/d in divided doses for 5 consecutive days beginning within 72 h of coitus

Breast Cancer

Adult: **PO** 10 mg t.i.d. for at least 3 mo

Prostatic Cancer Palliation

Adult: **PO** 1.25–2.5 mg t.i.d.

ADMINISTRATION

Oral
- Give cyclically except when used for treatment of postpartum breast engorgement and for palliation of cancer. Cyclic regimen is to dose for 3 wk followed by 1 wk off.

Topical
- Use calibrated dosage applicator dispensed with the cream.

Intramuscular
- Reconstitute by first removing approximately 5 mL of air from the dry-powder vial, then slowly inject the supplied diluent to the vial by aiming it at the side of the vial. Gently agitate to dissolve but DO NOT SHAKE.
- Use within a few hours of reconstitution.

Intravenous

PREPARE: **Direct:** Reconstitute as for IM injection.
ADMINISTER: **Direct:** Give slowly at a rate of 5 mg/min. Estrogen solution is compatible with D5W and NS and may be added to IV tubing just distal to the needle if necessary.

- Store ampule and reconstituted solution at 2°–8° C (38°–46° F) and protected from light; stable for 60 d. Discard precipitated or discolored solution.

ADVERSE EFFECTS (≥1%) **CNS:** Headache, dizziness, depression, *libido changes*. **CV:** <u>Thromboembolic disorders</u>, hypertension. **GI:** *Nausea,* vomiting, diarrhea, bloating, cholestatic jaundice. **Urogenital:** Mastodynia, spotting, changes in menstrual flow, dysmenorrhea, amenorrhea. **Metabolic:** Reduced carbohydrate tolerance, fluid retention. **Other:** Leg cramps, intolerance to contact lenses.

INTERACTIONS Drug: BARBITURATES, **carbamazepine, phenytoin, rifampin** decrease estrogen effect by increasing its metabolism; ORAL ANTICOAGULANTS may decrease hypoprothrombinemic effects; interfere with effects of **bromocriptine;** may increase levels and toxicity of **cyclosporine,** TRICYCLIC ANTIDEPRESSANTS, **theophylline;** decrease effectiveness of **clofibrate.**

PHARMACOKINETICS Absorption: Rapid absorption from GI tract; readily absorbed through skin and mucous membranes (including vaginal mucosa); slow absorption from IM injections. **Distribution:** Distributed throughout body tissues, especially in adipose tissue; crosses placenta, excreted in breast milk. Conjugated estrogens are bound primarily to albumin. **Metabolism:** Me-

Common adverse effects in *italic*, life-threatening effects <u>underlined</u>; generic names in **bold**; classifications in SMALL CAPS; ♣ Canadian drug name; ⊕ Prototype drug

tabolized primarily in liver to glucuronide and sulfate conjugates of estradiol, estrone, and estriol. **Elimination:** In urine. **Half-Life:** 4–18 h.

CLINICAL IMPLICATIONS

Assessment & Drug Effects

- See additional implications under estradiol.
- Monitor for and report breakthrough vaginal bleeding.
- Assess for relief of menopausal symptoms.
- If depression develops, discontinue the drug.
- Lab tests: Monitor serum phosphatase levels with prostate cancer.
- Monitor bone density annually when used for osteoporosis prophylaxis.

Patient & Family Education

- Be aware of importance of taking drug exactly as prescribed: Specifically, do not omit, increase, or decrease doses without advice of physician.
- Intravaginal administration: For self-administration, wash hands well before and after application, and avoid contact of denuded areas with the cream. Do not use tampons while on vaginal cream therapy.
- Notify physician promptly of adverse symptoms.
- Risk of blood clot formation is high with morning after pill. Know signs of thrombophlebitis (see Appendix F).
- Review package insert to ensure understanding of estrogen therapy.

ESTROGENS, ESTERIFIED

(ess'tro-jenz)

Estratab, Menest, Menrium, Neo-Estrone ♦

Classifications: HORMONE; ESTROGEN
Therapeutic: ESTROGEN; FEMALE HORMONE REPLACEMENT THERAPY (HRT)
Prototype: Estradiol
Pregnancy Category: X

AVAILABILITY 0.3 mg, 0.625 mg, 1.25 mg, 2.5 mg tablets

ACTION & *THERAPEUTIC EFFECT*

At the cellular level, estrogens increase cervical secretions, result in proliferation of the endometrium, and increase uterine tone. Estrogens also can affect bone calcium deposition and accelerate epiphyseal closure. Estrogens appear to prevent osteoporosis associated with the onset of menopause; they generally do not reverse bone density loss that has already developed. *Binds to intracellular receptors that stimulate DNA and RNA to synthesize proteins responsible for effects of estrogen.*

USES Atrophic vaginitis, kraurosis vulvae and abnormal bleeding (hormonal imbalance), female hypogonadism, castration, primary ovarian failure, vasomotor symptoms associated with menopause, palliative therapy of breast and prostatic carcinomas; prevention of osteoporosis.

CONTRAINDICATIONS Breast cancer; cervical cancer; endometrial cancer; endometrial hyperplasia; prostate cancer; hepatic disease or cancer; hypercalcemia; lupus (SLE); history of thromboembolic disease; known or suspected pregnancy (category X); lactation.

CAUTIOUS USE Hypertension; gallbladder disease; diabetes mellitus; heart failure; kidney dysfunction; migraine headaches; seizure disorders.

Common adverse effects in *italic*, life-threatening effects underlined; generic names in **bold**; classifications in SMALL CAPS; ♦ Canadian drug name; ⊘ Prototype drug

595

ROUTE & DOSAGE

Menopause
Adult: **PO** 0.3–1.25 mg/d for 21 d each month, adjust to lowest level that gives symptom control (≤0.625 mg/d)

Female Hypogonadism, Primary Ovarian Failure, Female Castration
Adult: **PO** 2.5–7.5 mg/d in 1–3 divided doses for 20 d followed by a 10-d rest period, during last 5 d of estrogen, give a PO progestin

Breast Cancer
Adult: **PO** 10 mg t.i.d. for 2–3 mo

Prostatic Cancer (palliation)
Adult: **PO** 1.25–2.5 mg t.i.d. for several weeks

Prevention of Osteoporosis
Adult: **PO** 0.3 mg q.d.

ADMINISTRATION

Oral
- Give with food or fluid of patient's choice.
- Give cyclically, except when used for palliation of cancer.
- Store tablets at 15°–30° C (59°–86° F) in a tightly closed container.

ADVERSE EFFECTS (≥1%) **CNS:** Headache, dizziness, depression, *libido changes.* **CV:** <u>Thromboembolic disorders</u>, hypertension. **GI:** *Nausea,* vomiting, diarrhea, bloating, cholestatic jaundice. **Urogenital:** Mastodynia, spotting, changes in menstrual flow, dysmenorrhea, amenorrhea. **Metabolic:** Reduced carbohydrate tolerance, fluid retention. **Other:** Leg cramps, intolerance to contact lenses.

INTERACTIONS Drug: BARBITURATES, **phenytoin, rifampin** decrease estrogen effect by increasing its metabolism; ORAL ANTICOAGULANTS may decrease hypoprothrombinemic effects; interfere with effects of **bromocriptine;** may increase levels and toxicity of **cyclosporine,** TCAS, **theophylline;** decrease effectiveness of **clofibrate.**

PHARMACOKINETICS Absorption: Well absorbed with first pass metabolism. **Metabolism:** Metabolized in GI mucosa and liver to estrone, further metabolized to inactive metabolites. **Elimination:** In urine and bile. **Half-Life:** 4–18.5 h.

CLINICAL IMPLICATIONS

Assessment & Drug Effects
- See clinical implications under estradiol.
- Monitor for and report breakthrough vaginal bleeding.
- Assess for relief of menopausal symptoms.
- Lab tests: Monitor serum phosphatase levels with prostate cancer.
- Monitor bone density annually when used for osteoporosis prophylaxis.

Patient & Family Education
- Be aware of importance of taking drug exactly as prescribed: Specifically, do not omit, increase, or decrease doses without advice of physician. Know what to do when a dose is missed.
- Review package insert to ensure understanding of estrogen therapy.

ESTRONE
(ess'trone)

Classifications: HORMONE; ESTROGEN
Therapeutic: ESTROGEN; FEMALE HORMONE REPLACEMENT THERAPY (HRT)
Prototype: Estradiol
Pregnancy Category: X

Common adverse effects in *italic*, life-threatening effects <u>underlined</u>; generic names in **bold**; classifications in SMALL CAPS; ♦ Canadian drug name; ❶ Prototype drug

AVAILABILITY 5 mg/mL injection

ACTION & *THERAPEUTIC EFFECT*

Estrone is one-third less active at the cellular level than estradiol, the principal premenopausal estrogen. Due to increased risk of serious complications from extended use, estrogen HRT or estrogen-progestin HRT should be prescribed for the shortest duration possible consistent with the treatment goals of post menopausal symptoms. *Replaces estrogen in postmenopausal women, relieving symptoms of menopause.*

USES Atrophic vaginitis, kraurosis vulvae, and abnormal bleeding (hormonal imbalance); also female hypogonadism, primary ovarian failure, vasomotor symptoms associated with menopause, and as palliative therapy of prostatic carcinoma.

CONTRAINDICATIONS Breast cancer; liver dysfunction; history of thromboembolic disease; known or suspected pregnancy (category X), lactation.

CAUTIOUS USE Hypertension; gallbladder disease; diabetes mellitus; heart failure; kidney dysfunction; seizure disorders.

ROUTE & DOSAGE

Menopause
Adult: **IM** 0.1–0.5 mg 2–3 times/wk

Female Hypogonadism, Primary Ovarian Failure
Adult: **IM** 0.1–1 mg/wk in single or divided doses

Inoperable Prostatic Cancer Palliation
Adult: **IM** 2–4 mg/d 2–3 times/wk

ADMINISTRATION

Intramuscular
- Shake vial and syringe well to suspend medication before withdrawing and injecting medication.
- Give deep into a large muscle.
- Store at 15°–30° C (59°–86° F); protect from light and do not freeze.

ADVERSE EFFECTS (≥1%) **CNS:** Headache, dizziness, depression, *libido changes.* **CV:** Thromboembolic disorders, hypertension. **GI:** *Nausea,* vomiting, diarrhea, bloating, cholestatic jaundice. **Urogenital:** Mastodynia, spotting, changes in menstrual flow, dysmenorrhea, amenorrhea. **Metabolic:** Reduced carbohydrate tolerance, fluid retention. **Other:** Leg cramps, intolerance to contact lenses.

INTERACTIONS Drug: Carbamazepine, phenytoin, rifampin decrease estrogen levels because they increase metabolism; may enhance steroid effects of CORTICOSTEROIDS; may decrease anticoagulant effects of ORAL ANTICOAGULANTS.

PHARMACOKINETICS Absorption: Occurs over several days. **Metabolism:** Converts to estradiol in GI mucosa. **Half-Life:** 4–18.5 h.

CLINICAL IMPLICATIONS

Assessment & Drug Effects
- See clinical implications under estradiol.
- Monitor for and report breakthrough vaginal bleeding.
- Assess for relief of menopausal symptoms.
- Lab tests: Monitor serum phosphatase levels with prostate cancer.
- Monitor patients with conditions that may be influenced by fluid retention carefully (e.g., migraine, cardiac or kidney dysfunction, asthma, epilepsy, hypertension). Check BP on a regular basis.

Common adverse effects in *italic*, life-threatening effects underlined; generic names in **bold**; classifications in SMALL CAPS; ♣ Canadian drug name; ⊘ Prototype drug

597

E

■ Note: Spotting or breakthrough bleeding occurring when other drugs and estrone are taken concurrently indicates reduced availability of the estrogen.

Patient & Family Education

■ Review package insert to assure understanding of estrogen therapy.
■ Determine weight under standard conditions 1 or 2 times/wk and report sudden weight gain or other signs of fluid retention.
■ Notify physician of positive Homans' sign (calf pain upon flexing foot) and the following symptoms of thromboembolic disorders immediately: Tenderness, swelling, and redness in extremity; sudden, severe headache or chest pain; slurring of speech; change in vision; sudden shortness of breath.
■ Report symptoms of vaginal candidiasis (thick, white, curd-like secretions and inflamed, congested introitus) to permit appropriate treatment.
■ Notify physician of severe abdominal pain and tenderness or abdominal mass.

ESTROPIPATE

(es-troe-pi′pate)
Ogen, Ortho-Est
Classifications: HORMONE; ESTROGEN
Therapeutic: ESTROGEN; FEMALE HORMONE REPLACEMENT THERAPY (HRT)
Prototype: Estradiol
Pregnancy Category: X

AVAILABILITY 0.625 mg, 1.25 mg, 2.5 mg, 5 mg tablets; 1.5 mg/g cream

ACTION & *THERAPEUTIC EFFECT*
Water-soluble preparation of pure crystalline estrone. Estrone is one-third less active at the cellular level than estradiol, the principal pre-

menopausal estrogen. Due to increased risk of serious complications from extended use, estrogen HRT or estrogen-progestin HRT should be prescribed for the shortest duration possible consistent with the treatment goals of postmenopausal symptoms. *Replaces estrogen in postmenopausal women relieving symptoms of menopause.*

USES Atrophic vaginitis, kraurosis vulvae, and abnormal ▮▮eding (hormonal imbalance); also female hypogonadism, primary ovarian failure, vasomotor symptoms associated with menopause, and as palliative therapy of prostatic carcinoma.

CONTRAINDICATIONS Estrogen hypersensitivity; breast cancer; vaginal cancer; endometrial hyperplasia; history of thromboembolic disease; known or suspected pregnancy (category X); lactation.
CAUTIOUS USE Hypertension; gallbladder disease; diabetes mellitus; heart failure; kidney dysfunction; seizure disorders.

ROUTE & DOSAGE

Menopause, Atrophic Vaginitis, Kraurosis Vulvae
Adult: **PO** 0.75–6 mg/d for 21 d each month; adjust to lowest level that gives symptom control **Intravaginal** 2–4 g of cream once/d in a cyclic regimen

Female Hypogonadism, Primary Ovarian Failure, Female Castration
Adult: **PO** 1.5–9 mg/d in 1–3 divided doses for 21 d, followed by an 8–10-d drug-free period

ADMINISTRATION

Oral
■ Give with food or fluid of patient's choice.

Intravaginal
- Apply vaginal cream using calibrated dosage applicator dispensed with drug. Squeeze tube of cream to force sufficient amount into applicator so that number on plunger indicating prescribed dose is level with top of barrel.
- Store at 15°–30° C (59°–86° F) in tightly closed containers unless otherwise directed.

ADVERSE EFFECTS (≥1%) **CNS:** Headache, dizziness, depression, *libido changes.* **CV:** <u>Thromboembolic disorders</u>, edema, hypertension. **GI:** *Nausea,* vomiting, diarrhea, bloating, cholestatic jaundice. **Urogenital:** Mastodynia, spotting, changes in menstrual flow, dysmenorrhea, amenorrhea. **Metabolic:** Reduced carbohydrate tolerance, fluid retention. **Other:** Leg cramps, intolerance to contact lenses.

INTERACTIONS Drug: Carbamazepine, phenytoin, rifampin decrease estrogen levels because they increase its metabolism; may enhance steroid effects of CORTICOSTEROIDS; may decrease anticoagulant effects of ORAL ANTICOAGULANTS. **Herbal: St. John's wort** may decrease blood levels. **Dong quai, red clover, black cohosh,** and **saw palmetto** may have additive hormonal effects.

PHARMACOKINETICS Absorption: Absorbed with some metabolism occuring in GI tract. Some systemic absorption from vaginal administration. **Metabolism:** In GI tract and liver. **Half-Life:** 4–18.5 h.

CLINICAL IMPLICATIONS
Assessment & Drug Effects
- See clinical implications under estradiol.
- Monitor for and report breakthrough vaginal bleeding.

- Assess for relief of menopausal symptoms.
- Lab tests: Monitor serum phosphatase levels with prostate cancer.

Patient & Family Education
- Do not use tampons while on vaginal cream therapy.
- Intravaginal administration: For self-administration, wash hands well before and after application, and avoid contact of denuded areas with the cream.
- Do not use tampons while on vaginal cream therapy. Pull plunger out of barrel and wash applicator in warm soapy water after use. Do not place plunger in hot or boiling water.
- Note: Sudden discontinuation of vaginal cream after high dosage or prolonged use may evoke withdrawal bleeding.
- Review patient package insert (PPI).

ESZOPICLONE
(es-zo′pi-clone)
Lunesta
Classifications: SEDATIVE-HYPNOTIC; ANXIOLYTIC
Therapeutic: SEDATIVE-HYPNOTIC
Pregnancy Category: C
Controlled Substance: Schedule IV

AVAILABILITY 1 mg, 2 mg, 3 mg tablets

ACTION & *THERAPEUTIC EFFECT*
Eszopiclone is a nonbenzodiazepine sedative-hypnotic agent. The precise mechanism of action is unknown but believed to result from its interaction with GABA-receptor complexes at binding sites close to or coupled to benzodiazepine receptors in the brain. *Improves sleep maintenance in transient insomnia.*

Common adverse effects in *italic*, life-threatening effects <u>underlined</u>; generic names in **bold**; classifications in SMALL CAPS; ♣ Canadian drug name; ❷ Prototype drug

E

E

USES Treatment of insomnia.

CONTRAINDICATIONS Hypersensitivity to eszopiclone; concurrent administration with CYP3A4 inhibitor drugs; alcohol intoxication; alcoholism; children <18 y; suicidal tendencies or ideation; pregnancy (category C).

CAUTIOUS USE Hepatic impairment; elderly or debilitated patients; concurrent administration of CNS DEPRESSANTS; signs and symptoms of depression; COPD; lactation.

ROUTE & DOSAGE

Insomnia
Adult: **PO** 2–3 mg h.s.
Geriatric: **PO** 1–2 mg h.s.
Severe Hepatic Impairment
PO ≤2 mg

ADMINISTRATION

Oral
- Give immediately prior to bedtime.
- Store at 15°–30° C (59°– 86° F).

ADVERSE EFFECTS (≥1%) **CNS:** Anxiety, confusion, depression, dizziness, hallucinations, *headache,* irritability, decreased libido, nervousness, *somnolence.* **CV:** *Tachycardia,* pericardial infusion, left ventricular systolic dysfunction (LVSD). **GI:** Dry mouth, dyspepsia, nausea, vomiting. **GU:** Dysmenorrhea, gynecomastia. **Respiratory:** Infection. **Skin:** Rash, pruritus. **Special Senses:** *Unpleasant taste.*

INTERACTIONS Drug: Inhibitors of CYP3A4, including (but not limited to) **amiodarone,** ANTIRETROVIRAL PROTEASE INHIBITORS, **aprepitant, clarithromycin, dalfopristin/ quinupristin, delavirdine, diltiazem, efavirenz** (inducer or inhibitor), **erythromycin, fluconazole, fluoxetine, fluvoxamine, itraconazole, ketoconazole, mifepristone, nefazodone, norfloxacin,** other systemic AZOLE ANTIFUNGALS (**miconazole** and **voriconazole**), **troleandomycin,** and **zafirlukast** increase eszopiclone levels. **Ethanol** and other CNS DEPRESSANT agents can produce additive effects in combination with eszopiclone. **Herbal: St. John's wort** can increase eszopiclone levels.

PHARMACOKINETICS Absorption: Rapidly absorbed from GI tract. **Distribution:** 52–59% protein bound. **Peak:** 1 h. **Metabolism:** Extensive hepatic metabolism. **Elimination:** Primarily in the urine. **Half-Life:** 5– 6 h.

CLINICAL IMPLICATIONS

Assessment & Drug Effects
- Monitor for and report worsening insomnia and cognitive or behavioral changes.
- Monitor for suicidal ideation in depressive patients.
- Monitor for S&S of CNS depression when other CNS DEPRESSANTS are used concurrently.
- Supervise ambulation if patient is out of bed after taking eszopiclone.

Patient & Family Education
- Follow directions for taking the drug (see Administration).
- Do not take this drug unless you can get at least 8 h of sleep.
- Do not consume alcohol while taking this drug.
- Do not take with or immediately after a high fat meal.
- Do not drive or engage in potentially hazardous activities until response to drug is known.
- Report any of the following to a health care provider: worsening insomnia, cognitive or behavioral changes, problem with reproductive function.

ETANERCEPT ⊘

(e-tan'er-cept)
Enbrel

Classifications: BIOLOGIC RE-
SPONSE MODIFIER; TUMOR NECROSIS
FACTOR MODIFIER
Therapeutic: DISEASE-MODIFYING
ANTIRHEUMATIC DRUG (DMARD)
Pregnancy Category: B

AVAILABILITY 25 mg, 50 mg injection; 50 mg/mL prefilled syringe

ACTION & *THERAPEUTIC EFFECT*
Produced by recombinant DNA
technology. Binds specifically to tumor necrosis factor (TNF) and
blocks it from attaching to cell surface TNF receptors. This naturally
occurring cytokine (e.g., TNF) is
part of the normal immune and inflammatory response. TNF mediates inflammation and modulates
cellular immune responses. Elevated levels of TNF are found in
the synovial fluids of rheumatoid
arthritis (RA) patients. *Effectiveness is indicated by improved RA
symptomatology and/or decreased
inflammation in other inflammatory disorders.*

USES Reduction of the signs and
symptoms of RA and psoriatic RA in
adults, and polyarticular juvenile RA
(JRA) in children with inadequate
response to other disease-modifying
antirheumatic drugs. Treatment of
ankylosing spondylitis.

CONTRAINDICATIONS Patients with
sepsis or other active infection;
agranulocytosis; hypersensitivity to
etanercept; malignancy; benzyl alcohol hypersensitivity; bleeding, hematologic disease, fever, infection;
intramuscular administration, intravenous administration; latex hypersensitivity; sepsis; varicella; lactation.

CAUTIOUS USE Immunosuppression;
autoimmune disease, bone marrow
suppression; diabetes mellitus; hamster protein hypersensitivity; heart
failure; multiple sclerosis, neoplastic
disease, neurological disease, seizure
disorder, seizures; pregnancy (category B). Safety and efficacy in children <4 y of age are not established.

ROUTE & DOSAGE

Rheumatoid Arthritis, Psoriatic Arthritis, Ankylosing Spondylitis
Adult: **SC** 25 mg twice weekly; or 0.08 mg/kg or 50 mg once weekly *Child:* **SC** >4 y, 0.4 mg/kg (max: 25 mg/dose) twice weekly

ADMINISTRATION

Subcutaneous

- Do not administer to a patient who
  has known or suspected sepsis.
- Reconstitute by slowly injecting
  the supplied diluent into the vial.
  Swirl gently to dissolve and do
  not shake. Reconstituted solution
  should be clear and colorless. Use
  within 6 h.
- Inject into thigh, abdomen, upper
  arm; rotate injection sites and
  never inject into an old injection
  site or where skin is tender,
  bruised, red, or hard.
- Store reconstituted solution up to 6
  h refrigerated at 2°–8° C (36°–46°
  F). Store unopened dose tray refrigerated at 2°–8° C (36°–46° F).

ADVERSE EFFECTS (≥1%) **Body as
a Whole:** Asthenia, serious *infections*, sepsis, monitor for reactivation of tuberculosis. **CNS:** Headache, dizziness, cerebral ischemia,
depression, demyelinating disorders (multiple sclerosis, myelitis, optic neuritis). **CV:** Heart failure, <u>MI</u>,
myocardial ischemia, hypertension,
hypotension. **GI:** Abdominal pain,

Common adverse effects in *italic*, life-threatening effects <u>underlined</u>; generic names
in **bold**; classifications in SMALL CAPS; ✚ Canadian drug name; ⊘ Prototype drug

601

dyspepsia, cholecystitis, pancreatitis, GI hemorrhage. **Respiratory:** Rhinitis, URI, pharyngitis, cough, respiratory disorder, sinusitis, dyspnea may reactivate latent tuberculosis (TB). **Skin:** Rash; injection site reactions (*erythema, itching, pain, swelling*). **Musculoskeletal:** Bursitis. **Hematologic:** <u>Pancytopenia</u>.

INTERACTIONS Drug: Concurrent or recent use with **azathioprine, cyclophosphamide, leflunomide, methotrexate** has been associated with pancytopenia.

PHARMACOKINETICS Onset: 1–2 wk. **Peak:** 72 h. **Half-Life:** 115 h.

CLINICAL IMPLICATIONS

Assessment & Drug Effects
- Monitor carefully for and immediately report S&S of infection.

Patient & Family Education
- A PPD test is recommended before starting therapy to check for TB.
- Discard all needles and syringes after use; do not reuse.
- Withhold etanercept and notify physician before resuming drug if you develop an infection or are exposed to varicella virus.
- Avoid vaccinations, in general, and live vaccines, in particular, while on etanercept.
- Note: Injection site reactions (e.g., redness, pain, swelling) are common in the first month of therapy but generally decrease over time.

ETHACRYNIC ACID

(eth-a-krin′ik)
Edecrin

ETHACRYNATE SODIUM

Sodium Edecrin

Classifications: ELECTROLYTIC AND WATER BALANCE AGENT; LOOP DIURETIC; ANTIHYPERTENSIVE
Therapeutic: LOOP DIURETIC; ANTIHYPERTENSIVE
Prototype: Furosemide
Pregnancy Category: B

AVAILABILITY 25 mg, 50 mg tablet; 50 mg injection

ACTION & *THERAPEUTIC EFFECT*
Inhibits sodium and chloride reabsorption in proximal tubule and most segments of loop of Henle, promotes potassium and hydrogen ion excretion, and decreases urinary ammonium ion concentration as well as pH of the blood. Promotes calcium elimination in hypercalcemia and nephrogenic diabetes insipidus. Hypotensive effect may be due to hypovolemia secondary to diuresis and in part to decreased vascular resistance. *Rapid and potent diuretic effect resulting in hypotensive effect. Fluid and electrolyte loss may exceed that caused by thiazides.*

USES Severe edema associated with CHF, hepatic cirrhosis, ascites of malignancy, kidney disease, nephrotic syndrome, lymphedema.
UNLABELED USES Treatment of nephrogenic diabetes insipidus, hypercalcemia, mild to moderate hypertension, and as adjunct in therapy of hypertensive crisis complicated by pulmonary edema.

CONTRAINDICATIONS History of hypersensitivity to ethacrynic acid; increasing azotemia, anuria; hepatic coma; severe diarrhea, dehydration, electrolyte imbalance, hypotension; lactation, infants, and neonates; parenteral use in pediatric patients.
CAUTIOUS USE Hepatic cirrhosis; older adult cardiac patients; diabetes mellitus; history of gout; pulmo-

Common adverse effects in *italic*, life-threatening effects <u>underlined</u>; generic names in **bold**; classifications in SMALL CAPS; ◆ Canadian drug name; ◯ Prototype drug

nary edema associated with acute MI; hyperaldosteronism; nephrotic syndrome; history of pancreatitis; pregnancy (category B).

ROUTE & DOSAGE

Edema

Adult: **PO** 50–100 mg 1–2 times/d, may increase by 25–50 mg prn up to 400 mg/d **IV** 0.5–1 mg/kg or 50 mg up to 100 mg, may repeat if necessary
Child: **PO** 1 mg/kg q.d., may increase to 3 mg/kg/d

ADMINISTRATION

Oral

- Give after a meal or food to prevent gastric irritation.
- Schedule doses to avoid nocturia and thus sleep interference. Avoid administration within at least 4 h of bedtime, if possible. This recommendation may not apply to the patient who accumulates fluid and develops respiratory symptoms during sleep.

Intravenous

PREPARE: **Direct/Intermittent:** Reconstitute by adding 50 mL of D5W or NS to vial. Use solution within 24 h. Vials reconstituted with D5W may turn cloudy; if so, discard the vial.
ADMINISTER: **Direct:** Give at a rate of 10 mg/min. **Intermittent:** Give over 15–30 min. If a second IV dose is required, a new site should be selected to prevent thrombophlebitis.
INCOMPATIBILITIES **Solution/additive: Hydralazine, procainamide, ranitidine, tolazoline, triflupromazine.**

- Store oral and parenteral form at 15°–30° C (59°–86° F) unless otherwise directed.

ADVERSE EFFECTS (≥1%) **CNS:** Headache, fatigue, apprehension, confusion. **CV:** *Postural hypotension* (dizziness, light-headedness). **Metabolic:** Hyponatremia, *hypokalemia,* hypochloremic alkalosis, hypomagnesemia, hypocalcemia, hypercalciuria, hyperuricemia, hypovolemia, hematuria, glycosuria, hyperglycemia, gynecomastia, elevated BUN, creatinine, and urate levels. **Special Senses:** Vertigo, tinnitus, sense of fullness in ears, temporary or permanent deafness. **GI:** Anorexia, diarrhea, nausea, vomiting, dysphagia, abdominal discomfort or pain, GI bleeding (IV use), abnormal liver function tests. **Hematologic:** Thrombocytopenia, agranulocytosis (rare), severe neutropenia (rare). **Skin:** Skin rash, pruritus. **Body as a Whole:** Fever, chills, acute gout; local irritation and thrombophlebitis with IV injection.

INTERACTIONS Drug: THIAZIDE DIURETICS increase potassium loss; increased risk of **digoxin** toxicity from hypokalemia; CORTICOSTEROIDS, **amphotericin B** increase risk of hypokalemia; decreased **lithium** clearance, so increased risk of lithium toxicity; SULFONYLUREA effect may be blunted, causing hyperglycemia; ANTIHYPERTENSIVE AGENTS increase risk of orthostatic hypotension; AMINOGLYCOSIDES may increase risk of ototoxicity; **warfarin** potentiates hypoprothrombinemia.

PHARMACOKINETICS Absorption: Rapidly absorbed from GI tract. **Onset:** 30 min PO; 5 min IV. **Peak:** 2 h PO; 15–30 min IV. **Duration:** 6–8 h PO; 2 h IV. **Distribution:** Does not cross CSF. **Metabolism:** Metabolized to cysteine conjugate. **Elimination:** 30–65% in urine; 35–40% in bile. **Half-Life:** 30–70 min.

Common adverse effects in *italic*, life-threatening effects underlined; generic names in **bold**; classifications in SMALL CAPS; ♣ Canadian drug name; ⊘ Prototype drug

603

CLINICAL IMPLICATIONS

Assessment & Drug Effects

- Observe closely when receiving the drug by IV infusion. Rapid, copious diuresis following IV administration can produce hypotension.
- Monitor IV site closely. Extravasation of IV drug causes local pain and tissue irritation from dehydration and blood volume depletion.
- Monitor BP during initial therapy. Because orthostatic hypotension can occur, supervise ambulation.
- Monitor BP and pulse throughout therapy in patients with impaired cardiac function. Diuretic-induced hypovolemia may reduce cardiac output, and electrolyte loss promotes cardiotoxicity in those receiving digitalis (cardiac) glycosides.
- Establish baseline weight prior to start of therapy; weigh patient under standard conditions. Keep physician informed of weight loss or gain in excess of 1 kg (2 lb)/d.
- Monitor I&O ratio. Drug should be discontinued if excessive diuresis, oliguria, hematuria, or sudden profuse diarrhea occurs. Report signs to physician.
- Lab tests: Determine baseline and periodic blood count, serum electrolytes, CO_2, BUN, creatinine, blood glucose, uric acid, and liver function.
- Observe for and report S&S of electrolyte imbalance: Anorexia, nausea, vomiting, thirst, dry mouth, polyuria, oliguria, weakness, fatigue, dizziness, faintness, headache, muscle cramps, paresthesias, drowsiness, mental confusion. Instruct patient to report these symptoms promptly to physician.
- Report immediately possible signs of thromboembolic complications (see Appendix F).

- Impaired glucose tolerance with hyperglycemia and glycosuria has occurred in patients receiving doses in excess of 200 mg/d.

Patient & Family Education

- Learn S&S of hypokalemia and hyponatremia (see Appendix F), and report any of these promptly to physician.
- Make position changes slowly, particularly from lying to upright posture.
- Report GI adverse effects to physician; they occur most frequently after 1–3 mo of PO therapy or in patients on high dosage. The onset of loose stools or other GI symptoms at any time during therapy indicates possible need for dosage adjustment or discontinuation of drug.
- Notify physician immediately of any evidence of impaired hearing. Hearing loss may be preceded by vertigo, tinnitus, or fullness in ears; it may be transient, lasting 1–24 h, or it may be permanent.

ETHAMBUTOL HYDROCHLORIDE

(e-tham′byoo-tole)

Etibi ◆, Myambutol

Classifications: ANTITUBERCULOSIS AGENT
Therapeutic: ANTITUBERCULAR
Prototype: Isoniazid
Pregnancy Category: B

AVAILABILITY 100 mg, 400 mg tablets

ACTION & THERAPEUTIC EFFECT

Mode of action not completely understood, but it appears to inhibit RNA synthesis and thus arrests multiplication of tubercle bacilli. The emergence of resistant strains is delayed by administering ethambutol in combination with other antituberculosis drugs. *Synthetic antituberculosis agent with bacteriostatic effect. Also effective against atypical mycobacterial infections.*

USES In conjunction with other antituberculosis agents in treatment of pulmonary tuberculosis.

UNLABELED USES Atypical mycobacterial infections.

CONTRAINDICATIONS Optic neuritis; hypersensitivity to ethambutol; optic neuritis, patients unable to report changes in vision (young children, or unconscious patients); children <6 y.

CAUTIOUS USE Renal impairment, hepatic disease; gout; ocular defects (e.g., cataract, recurrent ocular inflammatory conditions, diabetic retinopathy); pregnancy (category B).

ROUTE & DOSAGE

Tuberculosis

Adult: **PO** 15 mg/kg q24h; for retreatment start with 25 mg/kg/d for 60 d, then decrease to 15 mg/kg/d
Child: **PO** 6–12 y, 10–15 mg/kg/d

ADMINISTRATION

Oral

- Give with food if GI irritation occurs.
- Protect ethambutol from light, moisture, and excessive heat. Store at 15°–30° C (59°–86° F) in tightly closed container unless otherwise directed.

ADVERSE EFFECTS (≥1%) **CNS:** Headache, dizziness, confusion, hallucinations, paresthesias, joint pains. **Special Senses:** Ocular toxicity: *retrobulbar optic neuritis;* possibility of anterior optic neuritis with decrease in visual acuity, temporary loss of vision, constriction of visual fields, red–green color blindness, central and peripheral scotomas, eye pain, photophobia; retinal hemorrhage and edema. **GI:** Anorexia, nausea, vomiting, abdominal pain. **Body as a Whole:** Hypersensitivity (pruritus, dermatitis, <u>anaphylaxis</u>).

INTERACTIONS Drug: Aluminum-containing antacids can decrease absorption.

PHARMACOKINETICS Absorption: 70–80% from GI tract. **Peak:** 2–4 h. **Distribution:** Distributes to most body tissues; highest concentrations in erythrocytes, kidney, lungs, saliva; crosses placenta; distributed into breast milk. **Metabolism:** In liver. **Elimination:** 50% in urine within 24 h; 20–22% in feces. **Half-Life:** 3–4 h.

CLINICAL IMPLICATIONS

Assessment & Drug Effects

- Perform C&S prior to and periodically throughout therapy.
- Perform ophthalmoscopic examination prior to and at monthly intervals during therapy. Test eyes separately as well as together.
- Note: Ocular toxicity generally appears within 1–7 mo after start of therapy. Symptoms usually disappear within several weeks to months after drug is discontinued, depending on degree of ocular damage.
- Monitor I&O ratio in patients with renal impairment. Report oliguria or any significant changes in ratio or in laboratory reports of kidney function. Systemic accumulation with toxicity can result from delayed drug excretion.
- Lab tests: Perform liver and kidney function tests, CBC, and se-

Common adverse effects in *italic*, life-threatening effects <u>underlined</u>; generic names in **bold**; classifications in SMALL CAPS; ♣ Canadian drug name; ✪ Prototype drug

605

rum uric acid levels at regular intervals throughout therapy.

Patient & Family Education
- Adhere to drug regimen exactly and keep follow-up appointments.
- Notify physician promptly of the onset of blurred vision, changes in color perception, constriction of visual fields, or any other visual symptoms. Have eyes checked periodically. Ethambutol can cause irreversible blindness due to optic neuritis.

ETHINYL ESTRADIOL

(eth'in-il ess-tra-dye'ole)
Estinyl, Feminone
Classifications: HORMONE; ESTROGEN
Therapeutic: ESTROGEN; FEMALE HORMONE REPLACEMENT THERAPY (HRT)
Prototype: Estradiol
Pregnancy Category: X

AVAILABILITY 0.02 mg, 0.05 mg, 0.5 mg tablets

ACTION & *THERAPEUTIC EFFECT*
Potent oral estrogen with actions similar to those of estradiol. Given cyclically for short-term use. Ethinyl estradiol is not commonly used as a single agent, but most commonly found in combination oral contraceptives. *May be used to prevent osteoporosis and relieve symptoms associated with menopause.*

USES Moderate to severe vasomotor symptoms associated with menopause; also postmenopausal osteoporosis, female hypogonadism, and as palliation for inoperable, metastatic cancer of female breast (at least 5 y postmenopause) and of the prostate.
UNLABELED USES Postcoital contraceptive.

CONTRAINDICATIONS Breast, ovarian, cervical, or endometrial cancer; endometrial hyperplasia; uterine or vaginal cancer; abnormal vaginal bleeding; hepatic disease or cancer; jaundice; MI; history of thromboembolic disease; heart failure; coagulopathies; lupus; known or suspected pregnancy (category X), lactation.
CAUTIOUS USE Hypertension; gallbladder disease; diabetes mellitus; kidney dysfunction.

ROUTE & DOSAGE

Menopause, Postmenopausal Osteoporosis
Adult: **PO** 0.02–0.05 mg/d for 21 d each month, adjust to lowest level that gives symptom control

Female Hypogonadism
Adult: **PO** 0.05 mg 1–3 times/d for 2 wk, followed by 2 wk of progestin, continue this regimen for 3–6 mo

Breast Cancer
Adult: **PO** 1 mg t.i.d. for 2–3 mo

Prostatic Cancer Palliation
Adult: **PO** 0.15–2 mg/d

Postcoital Contraceptive
Adult: **PO** 5 mg/d for 5 consecutive days beginning within 72 h of coitus

ADMINISTRATION

Oral
- Morning-after pill: Start drug within 24 h and not later than 72 h after sexual exposure when used as an emergency postcoital contraceptive. Perform a pregnancy test prior to dosing.
- Store at 15°–30° C (59°–86° F) in tight, light-resistant container.

ADVERSE EFFECTS (≥1%) **CNS:** Headache, dizziness, depression, *libido changes*. **CV:** Thromboembolic disorders, hypertension. **GI:** *Nausea, vomiting, diarrhea, anorexia, weight changes, bloating,* cholestatic jaundice. **Urogenital:** Mastodynia, breakthrough bleeding, changes in menstrual flow, dysmenorrhea, amenorrhea; in men: impotence, gynecomastia, testicular atrophy. **Metabolic:** Reduced carbohydrate tolerance, fluid retention. **Body as a Whole:** Leg cramps, edema, intolerance to contact lenses.

INTERACTIONS Drug: Carbamazepine, phenytoin, rifampin decrease estrogen levels because they increase its metabolism; may enhance steroid effects of CORTICOSTEROIDS; may decrease anticoagulant effects of ORAL ANTICOAGULANTS.

PHARMACOKINETICS Absorption: 83% absorbed. **Metabolism:** Extensively metabolized in liver. **Elimination:** In urine and feces. **Half-Life:** 3–27 h.

CLINICAL IMPLICATIONS

Assessment & Drug Effects

- Check BP on a regular basis in patients with conditions that may be influenced by fluid retention (migraine, cardiac or kidney dysfunction, asthma, epilepsy, hypertension).
- Supplement pyridoxine (vitamin B_6) in patients on long-term therapy, especially if undernourished; levels are lowered by estrogens.

Patient & Family Education

- Be aware that risk of blood clot formation is high. Notify physician immediately of positive Homans' sign (calf pain upon foot flexion) and the following symptoms of thromboembolic disorders: Tenderness, pain, swelling, and redness in extremity; sudden, severe headache or chest pain, slurring of speech; change in vision; sudden shortness of breath. If physician is not available, go to the nearest emergency room.
- Report severe abdominal pain and tenderness, or abdominal mass.
- Determine weight under standard conditions 1 or 2 times/wk and report sudden weight gain or other signs of fluid retention.
- Notify physician of yellow skin and sclera, pruritus, dark urine, and light-colored stools; history of jaundice in pregnancy increases the possibility of estrogen-induced jaundice. Estrogen therapy is usually interrupted pending clinical investigation.
- Abrupt withdrawal of vitamin C may lead to breakthrough bleeding; high vitamin C intake (e.g., 1 g/d) may increase ethinyl estradiol levels.
- Report symptoms of vaginal candidiasis (thick, white, curd-like secretions and inflamed congested introitus) to permit appropriate treatment.
- Note: Estrogen-induced feminization and impotence in male patients are reversible with termination of therapy.
- Decrease caffeine intake from sources such as tea, coffee, and cola; estrogenic depression of caffeine metabolism may cause caffeinism.

ETHIONAMIDE

(e-thye-on-am'ide)
Trecator
Classifications: ANTITUBERCULOSIS AGENT; ANTILEPROSY (SULFONE) AGENT

E

Therapeutic: ANTITUBERCULAR; ANTI-LEPROSY
Prototype: Isoniazid
Pregnancy Category: D

AVAILABILITY 250 mg tablets

ACTION & *THERAPEUTIC EFFECT*

Ethionamide appears to inhibit mycolic acid synthesis, which disrupts the formation of the mycobacterial cell wall. Bacteriostatic or bactericidal depending on concentration used and susceptibility of organism. Emergence of resistant strains may be delayed or prevented when administered concurrently with other antituberculosis drugs. *Effective against human and bovine strains of* Mycobacterium tuberculosis *and* M. kansasii *and some strains of* Mycobacterium avium-*intracellulare complex. Also active against* M. leprae.

USES Any form of active tuberculosis when treatment with primary antituberculosis drugs (e.g., isoniazid, streptomycin, ethambutol, rifampin) has failed. Must be given with at least one other effective antituberculosis agent.
UNLABELED USES Atypical mycobacterial infections and tuberculous meningitis.

CONTRAINDICATIONS Hypersensitivity to ethionamide and chemically related drugs [e.g., isoniazid, niacin (nicotinamide)]; severe liver damage; hepatic encephalopathy; pregnancy (category C), in children <12 y.
CAUTIOUS USE Diabetes mellitus, liver dysfunction, history of psychiatric illnesses including depression; history of thyroid disease; lactation.

ROUTE & DOSAGE

Tuberculosis

Adult: **PO** 0.5–1 g/d divided q8–12h
Child: **PO** 15–20 mg/kg/d in 2–3 equally divided doses (max: 1 g/d)

ADMINISTRATION

Oral

- Give with or after meals to minimize GI adverse effects. Some patients tolerate ethionamide best when it is taken as a single dose after the evening meal or as a single dose at bedtime. GI symptoms appear to increase with divided doses, although serum concentrations may be higher.
- About 50% of patients cannot tolerate a single dose larger than 500 mg because of GI adverse effects. An antiemetic may be prescribed, but if symptoms persist, drug should be discontinued.
- Physician may prescribe pyridoxine (vitamin B$_6$) concurrently to prevent or relieve peripheral neuritis and other neurotoxic effects.
- Store in a cool, dry place at 8°–15° C (46°–59° F) in a tightly closed container unless otherwise directed.

ADVERSE EFFECTS (≥1%) **CNS:** Headache, restlessness, mental depression, drowsiness, dizziness, ataxia, hallucinations, paresthesias, convulsions. **GI:** Dose related and frequent; symptoms may be due to CNS stimulation rather than to GI irritation: anorexia, *epigastric distress, nausea, vomiting,* metallic taste, *diarrhea,* stomatitis, sialorrhea. **Metabolic:** Elevated ALT, AST; hepatitis

Common adverse effects in *italic*, life-threatening effects underlined; generic names in **bold**; classifications in SMALL CAPS; ♣ Canadian drug name; ☺ Prototype drug

(with jaundice), hypothyroidism. **Urogenital:** Menorrhagia, impotence. **Body as a Whole:** Postural hypotension.

INTERACTIONS Drug: Cycloserine, isoniazid may increase neurotoxic effects.

PHARMACOKINETICS Absorption: 80% absorbed from GI tract. **Peak:** 3 h. **Duration:** 9 h. **Distribution:** Widely distributed including CSF; crosses placenta; distribution into breast milk unknown. **Metabolism:** In liver. **Elimination:** In urine. **Half-Life:** 3 h.

CLINICAL IMPLICATIONS

Assessment & Drug Effects
- Lab tests: Perform C&S prior to start of therapy. Baseline liver function tests (AST and ALT), CBC, and kidney function tests including urinalysis and every 2–4 wk during therapy.
- Report onset of skin rash. Progression to exfoliative dermatitis can occur if drug is not promptly discontinued.
- Monitor blood glucose & HbA1c closely in the diabetic until response to drug is established. These patients appear to be especially prone to hepatotoxicity (see Appendix F).

Patient & Family Education
- Avoid alcohol or use in moderation because ethionamide may increase potential for liver dysfunction.
- Notify physician of S&S of hepatotoxicity (see Appendix F); generally reversible if drug is promptly withdrawn.
- Make position changes slowly and in stages, particularly from lying to upright posture if experiencing hypotension.

ETHOSUXIMIDE ℞

(eth-oh-sux'i-mide)
Zarontin
Classifications: SUCCINIMIDE ANTICONVULSANT
Therapeutic: ANTICONVULSANT
Pregnancy Category: C

E

AVAILABILITY 250 mg capsules; 250 mg/5 mL syrup

ACTION & *THERAPEUTIC EFFECT*
Succinimide anticonvulsant that reduces the current in T-type calcium channel found on primary afferent neurons. Activation of the T channel causes low-threshold calcium spikes in neurons, believed to play a role in the spike-and-wave pattern observed during petit mal seizures. *Reduces frequency of epileptiform attacks, apparently by depressing motor cortex and elevating CNS threshold to stimuli.*

USES Management of absence (petit mal) seizures, myoclonic seizures, and akinetic epilepsy. May be administered with other anticonvulsants when other forms of epilepsy coexist with petit mal.

CONTRAINDICATIONS Hypersensitivity to succinimides; severe liver or kidney disease; bone marrow suppression; use alone in mixed types of epilepsy (may increase frequency of grand mal seizures); pregnancy (category C), children <3 y.
CAUTIOUS USE Hematologic disease; preexisting hepatic disease; intermittent porphyria; renal disease.

ROUTE & DOSAGE

Absence Seizures
Adult/Child: **PO** *6–12 y,* 250 mg b.i.d., may increase q4–7d prn (max: 1.5 g/d)

Common adverse effects in *italic*, life-threatening effects underlined; generic names in **bold**; classifications in SMALL CAPS; ♣ Canadian drug name; ℗ Prototype drug

Child: PO 3–6 y, 250 mg/d, may increase q4–7d prn (max: 1.5 g/d)

ADMINISTRATION

Oral

- Give with food if GI distress occurs.
- Store all forms at 15°–30° C (59°–86° F); capsules in tight containers, and syrup in light-resistant containers; avoid freezing.

ADVERSE EFFECTS (≥1%) **CNS:** Drowsiness, hiccups, ataxia, dizziness, headache, euphoria, restlessness, irritability, anxiety, hyperactivity, aggressiveness, inability to concentrate, lethargy, confusion, sleep disturbances, night terrors, hypochondriacal behavior, muscle weakness, fatigue. **Special Senses:** Myopia. **GI:** Nausea, vomiting, *anorexia, epigastric distress,* abdominal pain, *weight loss,* diarrhea, constipation, gingival hyperplasia. **Urogenital:** Vaginal bleeding. **Hematologic:** Eosinophilia, leukopenia, thrombocytopenia, agranulocytosis, pancytopenia, aplastic anemia, positive direct Coombs' test. **Skin:** Hirsutism, pruritic erythematous skin eruptions, urticaria, alopecia, erythema multiforme, exfoliative dermatitis.

INTERACTIONS Drug: **Carbamazepine** decreases ethosuximide levels; **isoniazid** significantly increases ethosuximide levels; levels of both **phenobarbital** and ethosuximide may be altered with increased seizure frequency. **Herbal:** **Ginkgo** may decrease anticonvulsant effectiveness.

PHARMACOKINETICS Absorption: Readily from GI tract. **Peak:** 4 h; steady state: 4–7 d. **Metabolism:** In liver. **Elimination:** In urine; small amounts in bile and feces. **Half-Life:** 30 h (child), 60 h (adult).

CLINICAL IMPLICATIONS

Assessment & Drug Effects

- Lab tests: Perform baseline and periodic hematologic studies, liver and kidney function.
- Monitor adverse drug effects. GI symptoms, drowsiness, ataxia, dizziness, and other neurologic adverse effects occur frequently and indicate the need for dosage adjustment.
- Observe closely during period of dosage adjustment and whenever other medications are added or eliminated from the drug regimen. Therapeutic serum levels: 40–80 mcg/mL.
- Observe patients with prior history of psychiatric disturbances for behavioral changes. Close supervision is indicated. Drug should be withdrawn slowly if these symptoms appear.

Patient & Family Education

- Discontinue drug only under physician supervision; abrupt withdrawal of ethosuximide (whether used alone or in combination therapy) may precipitate seizures or petit mal status.
- Do not drive or engage in other potentially hazardous activities until response to drug is known.
- Monitor weight on a weekly basis. Report anorexia and weight loss to physician; may indicate need to reduce dosage.

ETIDRONATE DISODIUM ℗

(e-ti-droe'nate)
Didronel, EHDP

Classifications: BISPHOSPHONATE; REGULATOR, BONE METABOLISM
Therapeutic: BONE METABOLISM REGULATOR
Pregnancy Category: C

Common adverse effects in *italic*, life-threatening effects underlined; generic names in **bold**; classifications in SMALL CAPS; ♣ Canadian drug name; ℗ Prototype drug

AVAILABILITY 200 mg, 400 mg tablets

ACTION & *THERAPEUTIC EFFECT*
Diphosphate preparation with primary action on bone. Reduces elevated cardiac output associated with Paget's disease by decreasing vascularity of bone. Induces reversible hyperphosphemia without adverse effects. *Slows rate of bone resorption and new bone formation in pagetic bone lesions and in normal remodeling process. Lowers serum alkaline phosphatase. Response of Paget's disease may be slow (1–3 mo) and may continue for months after treatment is discontinued.*

USES Symptomatic Paget's disease and heterotopic ossification due to spinal cord injury or after total hip replacement.
UNLABELED USES Prevention and treatment of corticosteroid-induced osteoporosis.

CONTRAINDICATIONS Enterocolitis; children; pathologic fractures; renal failure; pregnancy (category C); lactation. Safety and effectiveness in children are not established.
CAUTIOUS USE Renal impairment; asthma; colitis; dysphagia; esophagitis; gastritis; patients on restricted calcium and vitamin D intake.

ROUTE & DOSAGE

Paget's Disease
Adult: **PO** 5–10 mg/kg/d for up to 6 mo or 11–20 mg/kg/d for up to 3 mo, may repeat after 3–6 mo off the drug if necessary

Heterotopic Ossification Due to Spinal Cord Injury
Adult: **PO** 20 mg/kg/d for 2 wk, then 10 mg/kg/d for an additional 10 wk

Heterotopic Ossification Due to Total Hip Arthroplasty
Adult: **PO** 20 mg/kg/d starting 1 mo before the procedure and continuing for 3 mo after

ADMINISTRATION
Oral
- Give as single dose on empty stomach 2 h before meals with full glass of water or juice to reduce gastric irritation.
- Relieve GI adverse effects by dividing total oral daily dose.

ADVERSE EFFECTS (≥1%) **GI:** Nausea, diarrhea, *loose bowel movements,* metallic or altered taste. **Musculoskeletal:** Increased or recurrent bone pain in pagetic sites, onset of bone pain in previously asymptomatic sites, increased risk of fractures in patient with Paget's disease. **Metabolic:** Hypocalcemia, hyperphosphatemia, elevated serum phosphatase, suppressed mineralization of uninvolved skeleton (focal osteomalacia). **Urogenital:** Renal insufficiency (high doses).

INTERACTIONS Drug: CALCIUM SUPPLEMENTS, ANTACIDS, IRON AND OTHER MINERAL SUPPLEMENTS may decrease absorption of etidronate (give etidronate 2 h before other drugs). **Food:** Food, especially milk and dairy products, will decrease absorption of etidronate (give 2 h before meals).

PHARMACOKINETICS Absorption: Variably from GI tract. **Distribution:** 50% distributed to bone. **Metabolism:** Not metabolized. **Elimination:** 50% in urine. **Half-Life:** 6 h.

CLINICAL IMPLICATIONS
Assessment & Drug Effects
- Report persistent nausea or diarrhea; GI adverse effects may inter-

Common adverse effects in *italic,* life-threatening effects underlined; generic names in **bold;** classifications in SMALL CAPS; ♣ Canadian drug name; ☻ Prototype drug

611

E

fere with adequate nutritional status and need to be treated promptly.

- Monitor I&O ratio, serum creatinine, or BUN of patient with impaired kidney function.
- Lab tests: Periodic serum calcium and phosphate.
- Monitor for signs of hypocalcemia. Latent tetany (hypocalcemia) may be detected by Chvostek's and Trousseau's signs and a serum calcium value of 7–8 mg/dL.
- Note: Serum phosphate levels generally return to normal 2–4 wk after medication is discontinued.

Patient & Family Education

- Avoid eating 2 h before or after taking etidronate. Drug absorption is decreased by food, especially milk, milk products, and other foods high in calcium, mineral supplements, and antacids.
- Notify physician promptly of sudden onset of unexplained pain. Risk of pathological fractures increases when daily dose of 20 mg/kg is taken longer than 3 mo.
- Report promptly if bone pain, restricted mobility, heat over involved bone site occur.

ETODOLAC

(e-to'do-lac)
Classifications: ANALGESIC, NONSTEROIDAL ANTIINFLAMMATORY AGENT (NSAID); ANTIPYRETIC
Therapeutic: NSAID, ANALGESIC; ANTIPYRETIC
Prototype: Ibuprofen
Pregnancy Category: C

AVAILABILITY 400, 500 mg tablets; 200 mg, 300 mg capsules; 400, 500 mg, 600 mg sustained release tablets

ACTION & THERAPEUTIC EFFECT
Inhibits cyclooxygenase (COX-1

and COX-2) enzyme activity and prostaglandin synthesis. NSAIDs may also suppress production of rheumatoid factor. *Produces analgesic and antiinflammatory effects of an NSAID.*

USES Osteoarthritis and acute pain, rheumatoid arthritis.
UNLABELED USES Temporal arteritis.

CONTRAINDICATIONS Hypersensitivity to NSAIDs, salicylates; ulceration or inflammation; perioperative CABG pain; pregnancy (category C), lactation. Safety and efficacy in children <6 y are not established.
CAUTIOUS USE Renal impairment, liver function impairment, GI disorders; cardiac disorders; dehydration; diabetes mellitus; patients over 65 y, and lactation.

ROUTE & DOSAGE

Acute Pain
Adult: **PO** 200–400 mg q6–8h prn
Osteoarthritis
Adult: **PO** 600–1200 mg/d in 2–4 divided doses, (max: 1200 mg/d or 20 mg/kg for patients ≤60 kg; Lodine XL 400–1000 mg once daily)
Rheumatoid Arthritis
Adult: **PO** 500 mg b.i.d.

ADMINISTRATION

Oral

- Give with food or antacid to reduce risk of GI ulceration.
- Ensure that sustained release form of drug is not chewed or crushed. It must be swallowed whole.
- Store at 15°–25° C (59°–77° F); tablets and capsules in bottles; sustained release capsules in unit-dose packages. Protect all forms from moisture.

Common adverse effects in *italic*, life-threatening effects <u>underlined</u>; generic names in **bold**; classifications in SMALL CAPS; ♣ Canadian drug name; ❸ Prototype drug

ADVERSE EFFECTS (≥1%) **CV:** Fluid retention, edema. **CNS:** Dizziness, headache, drowsiness, insomnia. **GI:** *Dyspepsia, nausea, vomiting, diarrhea,* indigestion, heartburn, abdominal pain, constipation, flatulence, gastritis, melena, peptic ulcer, GI bleeding. **Hematologic:** Thrombocytopenia, increased bleeding time. **Skin:** Rash, pruritus. **Urogenital:** Urinary frequency. **Metabolic:** Hepatotoxicity. **Special Senses:** Blurred vision; tinnitus. **Respiratory:** Asthma.

DIAGNOSTIC TEST INTERFERENCE May cause a false-positive *urinary bilirubin* test and a false-positive *ketone* test done with the dipstick method. May cause a small decrease (1 to 2 mg/dL) in *serum uric acid* levels.

INTERACTIONS Drug: May reduce effects of **diuretics** and antihypertensive effects of **beta blockers** and other ANTIHYPERTENSIVE MEDICATIONS. May increase **digoxin** and **lithium** levels and nephrotoxicity due to **cyclosporine. Herbal: Feverfew, garlic, ginger, ginkgo** may increase bleeding.

PHARMACOKINETICS Absorption: Readily from GI tract. **Onset:** 30 min. **Peak:** 1–2 h. **Duration:** 4–12 h. **Distribution:** Widely distributed; 99% protein bound; not known if crosses placenta or if distributed into breast milk. **Metabolism:** Extensively in liver. **Elimination:** 72% in urine, 16% in feces. **Half-Life:** 6–7 h.

CLINICAL IMPLICATIONS
Assessment & Drug Effects
- Assess for signs of GI ulceration and bleeding. Risk factors include high doses of etodolac, history of peptic ulcer disease, alcohol use, smoking, and concomitant use of aspirin.
- Assess carefully for fluid retention by monitoring weight and observing for edema in patients with a history of CHF.
- Monitor for decreased BP control in hypertensive patients.
- Lab tests: Periodic CBC and kidney and liver function.
- Monitor for drug toxicity when used concurrently with either digoxin or lithium.
- Monitor for rhinitis, urticaria, or other signs of allergic reactions. Discontinue drug and notify physician when present.
- Monitor carefully increases in etodolac dosage with older adult patients; adverse effects are more pronounced.
- Monitor for headaches, especially at high doses. Discontinuation of therapy may be indicated.

Patient & Family Education
- Learn S&S of GI ulceration. Stop medication in presence of bleeding and contact the physician immediately.
- Do not take aspirin, which may potentiate ulcerogenic effects.

ETOPOSIDE

(e-toe-po'side)
Etopophos, VePesid
Classifications: ANTINEOPLASTIC; MITOTIC INHIBITOR
Therapeutic: ANTINEOPLASTIC, CELL-CYCLE SPECIFIC
Prototype: Vincristine
Pregnancy Category: D

AVAILABILITY 50 mg capsules; 20 mg/mL injection; 100 mg lyophilized powder for injection

ACTION & THERAPEUTIC EFFECT
Semisynthetic derivative of May apple plant. Produces cytotoxic action

Common adverse effects in *italic*, life-threatening effects underlined; generic names in **bold**; classifications in SMALL CAPS; ◆ Canadian drug name; ⊙ Prototype drug

613

by arresting G_2 (resting or premitotic) phase of cell cycle; also acts on S phase of DNA synthesis. High doses cause lysis of cells entering mitotic phase, and lower doses inhibit cells from entering prophase. *Antineoplastic effect is due to its ability to arrest mitosis (cell division).*

USES Treatment of refractory testicular neoplasms, in patients who have already received appropriate surgical, chemotherapeutic, and radiation therapy; for treatment of choriocarcinoma in women and small cell carcinoma of the lung.

UNLABELED USES Hodgkin's and non-Hodgkin's lymphomas, acute myelogenous (nonlymphocytic) leukemia.

CONTRAINDICATIONS Severe bone marrow depression; severe hepatic or renal impairment; existing or recent viral infection, bacterial infection; intraperitoneal, intrapleural, or intrathecal administration; pregnancy (category D), lactation. Safe use in children is not established.
CAUTIOUS USE Impaired kidney or liver function; gout; radiation therapy.

ROUTE & DOSAGE

Testicular Carcinoma
Adult: **IV** 50–100 mg/m²/d for 5 consecutive days or 100 mg/m² on days 1, 3, and 5 q3–4wk for 3–4 courses **PO** Twice the IV dose rounded to the nearest 50 mg

Small Cell Lung Carcinoma
Adult: **IV** 35 mg/m²/d for 4 consecutive days to 50 mg/m²/d for 5 consecutive days q3–4wk **PO** Twice the IV dose rounded to the nearest 50 mg

ADMINISTRATION

Oral
- Oral dose is usually in the range of 70–100 mg/m² daily, rounded to nearest 50 mg.
- Refrigerate capsules at 2°–8° C (36°–46° F) unless otherwise directed. Do not freeze.

Intravenous
Note: Wear disposable surgical gloves when preparing or disposing of etoposide. Wash immediately with soap and water if skin comes in contact with drug.

PREPARE: **IV Infusion:** Each 100 mg must be diluted with 250–500 mL of D5W or NS to produce final concentrations of 0.2–0.4 mg/mL.

ADMINISTER: **IV Infusion:** Give by slow IV infusion over 30–60 min to reduce risk of hypotension and bronchospasm. Before administration, inspect solution for particulate matter and discoloration. Solution should be clear and yellow. If crystals are present, discard.

INCOMPATIBILITIES **Y-site: Amphotericin B, cefepime, chlorpromazine, filgrastim, idarubicin, imipenem-cilastatin, methylprednisolone, mitomycin, prochlorperazine.**

- Diluted solutions with concentration of 0.2 mg/mL are stable for 96 h, and the 0.4 mg/mL solutions are stable for 48 h under normal room fluorescent light in glass or plastic (PVC) containers.

ADVERSE EFFECTS (≥1%) **Body as a Whole:** Hypersensitivity (sweating, chills, fever, coryza, tachycardia; throat, back and general body pain; abdominal cramps, flushing, substernal chest pain, dyspnea, bronchospasm, pulmonary edema, anaphylactoid reaction). **CNS:** Peripheral neuropathy, paresthesias, weakness, somnolence, unusual tiredness, transient confusion. **CV:** Transient hypotension; thrombophlebitis with extravasation. **GI:** *Nausea, vomiting, dyspepsia*, anorexia, diarrhea, constipation, stomatitis. **Hematologic:** *Leukopenia (principally granulocytopenia), thrombocytopenia, severe myelosuppression, anemia, pancytopenia, neutropenia.* **Respiratory:** Pleural effusion, bronchospasm. **Skin:** *Reversible alopecia* (can progress to total baldness); radiation recall dermatitis; necrosis, *pain at IV site.*

INTERACTIONS Drug: ANTICOAGULANTS, ANTIPLATELET AGENTS, NSAIDS, **aspirin** may increase risk of bleeding.

PHARMACOKINETICS Absorption: Approximately 50% from GI tract. **Peak:** 1–1.5 h. **Distribution:** Variable penetration into CSF. **Metabolism:** In liver. **Elimination:** 44–60% in urine, 2–16% in feces over 3 d. **Half-Life:** 5–10 h.

CLINICAL IMPLICATIONS

Assessment & Drug Effects

- Check IV site during and after infusion. Extravasation can cause thrombophlebitis and necrosis.
- Be prepared to treat an anaphylactoid reaction (see Appendix F). Stop infusion immediately if the reaction occurs.
- Monitor vital signs during and after infusion. Stop infusion immediately if hypotension occurs.
- Lab tests: Perform baseline all prior to and at regular intervals during therapy, and before each subsequent treatment course. Tests include: CBC with differential; liver and kidney function tests (AST, ALT, serum bilirubin, LDH, BUN, serum creatinine).

- Withhold therapy when an absolute neutrophil count is below 500/mm^3 or a platelet count below 50,000/mm^3.
- Be alert to evidence of patient complaints that might suggest development of leukopenia (see Appendix F), infection (immunosuppression), and bleeding.
- Protect patient from any trauma that might precipitate bleeding during period of platelet nadir particularly. Withhold invasive procedures if possible.

Patient & Family Education

- Learn possible adverse effects of etoposide, such as blood dyscrasias, alopecia, carcinogenesis, before treatment begins.
- Make position changes slowly, particularly from lying to upright position because transient hypotension after therapy is possible.
- Inspect mouth daily for ulcerations and bleeding. Avoid obvious irritants such as hot or spicy foods, smoking, alcohol.

EXEMESTANE

(ex-e-mes'tain)

Aromasin

Classifications: ANTINEOPLASTIC; AROMATASE INHIBITOR, STEROIDAL; ANTIESTROGEN
Therapeutic: ANTINEOPLASTIC; STEROIDAL AROMATASE INHIBITOR
Prototype: Anastrozole
Pregnancy Category: D

AVAILABILITY 25 mg tablet

ACTION & *THERAPEUTIC EFFECT*
Steroidal aromatase inhibitor that suppresses plasma estrogens estradiol and estrone without affecting cortisol or aldosterone synthesis in the adrenal glands. The enzyme,

Common adverse effects in *italic*, life-threatening effects underlined; generic names in **bold**; classifications in SMALL CAPS; ♣ Canadian drug name; ⊙ Prototype drug

615

aromatase converts estrone to estradiol. *Breast tumor regression is possible in postmenopausal women. Effectiveness is indicated by evidence of tumor regression.*

USES Estrogen-receptor positive early breast cancer following treatment with tamoxifen, treatment of advanced breast cancer in postmenopausal women whose disease has progressed following tamoxifen therapy.

CONTRAINDICATIONS Hypersensitivity to exemestane; pregnancy (category D), lactation. Safety and efficay in children not established.
CAUTIOUS USE Hepatic or renal insufficiency; GI disorders; cardiovascular disease; hyperlipidemia.

ROUTE & DOSAGE

> **Early and Advanced Breast Cancer**
> *Adult:* **PO** 25 mg q.d. after a meal

ADMINISTRATION

Oral
- Give following a meal.
- Store at 15°–30° C (59°–86° F).

ADVERSE EFFECTS (≥1%) **Body as a Whole:** *Fatigue, hot flashes, pain,* flu-like symptoms; edema; fever; paresthesia. **CNS:** *Depression, insomnia, anxiety;* dizziness; headache. **CV:** Hypertension. **GI:** *Nausea,* vomiting, abdominal pain, anorexia, constipation, diarrhea, increased appetite. **Respiratory:** Dyspnea, cough, bronchitis, sinusitis. **Skin:** Increased sweating, rash, itching. **Other:** U T I ; lymphedema.

PHARMACOKINETICS Absorption: Rapidly, approximately 42% reaches systemic circulation. **Distribution:** Extensive tissue distribution, 90% protein bound. **Metabolism:** Extensively in liver (CYP3A4). **Elimination:** Equally in urine and feces. **Half-Life:** 24 h.

CLINICAL IMPLICATIONS
Assessment & Drug Effects
- Lab tests: Baseline liver function, BUN and creatinine; periodic WBC with differential, lipid profile, routine blood chemistry.

Patient & Family Education
- Review manufacturer's patient literature thoroughly to reinforce understanding of likely adverse effects.
- Report bothersome adverse effects to physician.

EXENATIDE
(e-xe′na-tide)
Byetta
Classifications: ANTIDIABETIC AGENT, INCRETIN MIMETIC
Therapeutic: ANTIDIABETIC; INCRETIN MIMETIC
Pregnancy Category: C

AVAILABILITY 250 mcg/mL injection

ACTION & *THERAPEUTIC EFFECT*
Improves glycemic control in people with type 2 diabetes mellitus by mimicking the functions of incretin, a glucagon-like peptide-1 (GLP-1). Exenatide enhances glucose-dependent insulin secretion by pancreatic beta-cells, suppresses inappropriately elevated glucagon secretion, and slows gastric emptying. These actions decrease glucagon stimulation of hepatic glucose output and decrease insulin demand. *Improves glycemic control by reducing fasting and postprandial glucose concentrations in patients with type 2 diabetes.*

USES Adjunct treatment of type 2 diabetes mellitus in those inadequately managed by metformin, a sulfonylurea, or a combination of these agents.

CONTRAINDICATIONS Hypersensitivity to exenatide, or cresol; severe GI disease (i.e., ulcerative colitis; Crohn's disease, diabetic ketoacidosis; gastroparesis; end-stage renal disease, renal failure or severe renal impairment (Cl_{cr} <30 mL/ min); pregnancy (category C).
CAUTIOUS USE Elderly; renal impairment; renal disease; thyroid disease; lactation.

ROUTE & DOSAGE

Type 2 Diabetes Mellitus

Adult: **SC** Initial dose of 5 mcg b.i.d., within 60 min prior to the morning and evening meal. After one month, may increase to 10 mcg b.i.d., within 60 min prior to the morning and evening meal.

ADMINISTRATION

- Give SC into thigh, abdomen, or upper arm within 60 min before the morning and evening meals. Do not administer after a meal.
- Do not give within 1 h of oral antibiotics, an oral contraceptive, or acetaminophen.
- Store at 36°–46° F (2°–8° C) and protect from light. Discard pen 30 d after first use. Do not use if pen has been frozen.

ADVERSE EFFECTS (≥1%) **CNS:** Asthenia, dizziness, restlessness, jittery feeling. **GI:** Nausea, vomiting, diarrhea, dyspepsia, anorexia, gastroesophageal reflux. **Metabolic:** Hypoglycemia, excessive sweating (hyperhidrosis or diaphoresis).

INTERACTIONS Drug: Due to its ability to slow gastric emptying, exenatide can decrease the rate and/or serum levels of oral medications that require GI absorption.

PHARMACOKINETICS Peak: 2 h. **Elimination:** Primarily in urine. **Half-Life:** 2.4 h.

CLINICAL IMPLICATIONS

Assessment & Drug Effects
- Monitor for and report S&S of significant GI distress, including NV&D.
- Monitor for S&S of hypoglycemia when used in combination with a sulfonylurea drug.
- Lab tests: Periodic fasting and postprandial plasma glucose and periodic HbA1c; baseline and periodic renal function tests.

Patient & Family Education
- Follow directions for taking this drug (see Administration).
- If a dose is missed, wait for the next scheduled dose.
- Discard any pen that has been in use for greater than 30 d.
- Exenatide may cause decreased appetite and some weight loss.
- Report significant GI distress to physician.

EZETIMIBE

(e-ze-ti′mibe)
Zetia, Ezetrol ♦
Classifications: ANTILIPEMIC
Therapeutic: CHOLESTEROL LOWERING AGENT
Pregnancy Category: C

AVAILABILITY 10 mg tablets

ACTION & *THERAPEUTIC EFFECT*
Works at the lining of the small intestine inhibiting the absorption of

Common adverse effects in *italic*, life-threatening effects underlined; generic names in **bold**; classifications in SMALL CAPS; ♦ Canadian drug name; ☻ Prototype drug

617

E

cholesterol, but does not inhibit cholesterol synthesis in the liver or increases bile acid excretion. Thus it decreases the amount of intestinal cholesterol available to the liver. *Lowers both total cholesterol and low-density lipid (LDL) cholesterol; its mechanism of action is complimentary to statins.*

USES Treatment of primary hypercholesterolemia alone or with an HMG-CoA reductase inhibitor (statin); treatment of homozygous sitosterolemia as an adjunct to diet.

CONTRAINDICATIONS Hypersensitivity to ezetimibe; concurrent use with HMG-CoA reductase inhibitor in patients with active liver disease or elevated serum transaminases; moderate to severe hepatic disease; concurrent administration with fibrates; lactation; pregnancy (category C); children <10 y.
CAUTIOUS USE Mild hepatic insufficiency.

ROUTE & DOSAGE

Hypercholesterolemia
Adult: **PO** 10 mg q.d.

ADMINISTRATION

Oral
- Give no sooner than 2 h before or 4 h after administration of a bile acid sequestrant such as cholestyramine.
- Store at 15°–30° C (59°–86° F). Protect from moisture.

ADVERSE EFFECTS (≥1%) **Body as a Whole:** Fatigue, arthralgia, back pain, myalgia, angioedema, myopathy. **CNS:** Dizziness, headache. **GI:** Abdominal pain, diarrhea. **Respiratory:** Pharyngitis, sinusitis,

cough. **Hematologic:** Thrombocytopenia. **Skin:** Rash. **Other:** Hepatitis, pancreatitis, rhabdomyolysis.

INTERACTIONS Drug: BILE ACID SEQUESTRANTS (e.g., **cholestyramine**) may decrease absorption (give ezetimibe 2 h before or 4 h after these drugs); **cyclosporine** or FIBRIC ACID DERIVATIVES can significantly increase ezetimibe levels.

PHARMACOKINETICS Absorption: Well absorbed from the small intestine. **Peak:** 4–12 h. **Distribution:** Ezetimibe-glucuronide is 99% protein bound. **Metabolism:** Extensively conjugated to an active glucuronide compound (ezetimibe-glucuronide). Metabolized in small intestine and liver. **Elimination:** Primarily in feces. **Half-Life:** 22 h.

CLINICAL IMPLICATIONS

Assessment & Drug Effects
- Lab tests: Monitor baseline and periodic lipid profile; periodic Hgb & Hct and platelet count. Monitor baseline LFTs and when used with a statin, monitor periodic LFTs in accordance with the monitoring schedule for that statin.
- Assess for and report unexplained muscle pain, especially when used in combination with a statin drug.
- Monitor closely patients who take both ezetimibe and cyclosporine.

Patient & Family Education
- Report unexplained muscle pain, tenderness, or weakness.
- Females should use effective methods of contraception to prevent pregnancy while taking this drug.

FAMCICLOVIR

(fam-ci'clo-vir)

Famvir

Classifications: ANTIVIRAL
Therapeutic: ANTIVIRAL
Prototype: Acyclovir
Pregnancy Category: B

AVAILABILITY 125 mg, 250 mg, 500 mg tablets

ACTION & *THERAPEUTIC EFFECT*

Prodrug of the antiviral agent penciclovir; may have an advantage over acyclovir because of its greater stability intracellularly in infected cells. Prevents viral replication by inhibition of DNA synthesis in herpes virus–infected cells. *Effectiveness is indicated by decreasing pain and crusting of lesions followed by loss of vesicles, ulcers, and crusts. Interferes with DNA synthesis of herpes simplex virus type 1 and 2 (HSV-1 and HSV-2) infections, varicella-zoster virus, and cytomegalovirus.*

USES Management of acute herpes zoster, genital herpes, recurrent episodes of genital herpes in immunocompromised adults. Suppression of recurrent episodes of genital herpes in immunocompetent adults.

CONTRAINDICATIONS Hypersensitivity to famciclovir, lactation.
CAUTIOUS USE Renal or hepatic impairment, carcinoma, older adults, pregnancy (category B). Safety in children <18 y is not established.

ROUTE & DOSAGE

Herpes Zoster, Treatment

Adult: PO 500 mg q8h for 7 d, start within 48–72 h of onset of rash

Renal Impairment

Cl$_{cr}$ 40–59 mL/min: 500 mg q12h; 20–39 mL/min: 500 mg q24h

Treatment of Recurrent Genital Herpes

Adult: PO 125 mg b.i.d. times 5 d

Suppression of Recurrent Genital Herpes

Adult: PO 250 mg b.i.d. for up to 1 y

ADMINISTRATION

Oral

- Reduce dosage in patients with reduced kidney function.
- Store at room temperature, 15°–30° C (59°–86° F).

ADVERSE EFFECTS (≥1%) **CNS:** *Headache,* somnolence, dizziness, paresthesias, fatigue, fever, rigors. **Hematologic:** Purpura. **GI:** Nausea, diarrhea, vomiting, constipation, anorexia, abdominal pain. **Body as a Whole:** Pharyngitis, sinusitis, pruritus.

INTERACTIONS Drug: Probenecid may decrease elimination; famciclovir may increase **digoxin** levels.

PHARMACOKINETICS Absorption: Readily absorbed from GI tract and rapidly converted to penciclovir in intestinal and liver tissue. **Onset:** Median times to full crusting of lesions, loss of vesicles, loss of ulcers, and loss of crusts were 6, 5, 7, and 19 d, respectively; median time to loss of acute pain was 21 d. **Peak:** 1 h. **Distribution:** Distributes into breast milk of animals. **Metabolism:** Metabolized in liver and intestinal tissue to penciclovir, which is the active antiviral agent. **Elimination:** Approximately 60% recovered in urine as penciclovir. **Half-Life:** Penciclovir 2–3 h.

Common adverse effects in *italic*, life-threatening effects <u>underlined</u>; generic names in **bold**; classifications in SMALL CAPS; ✚ Canadian drug name; ⊘ Prototype drug

619

F

CLINICAL IMPLICATIONS

Assessment & Drug Effects

- Lab tests: Baseline CBC and routine blood chemistry studies prior to and after short courses of therapy; periodically during prolonged treatment.
- Monitor digoxin level and assess for S&S of digoxin toxicity when digoxin is used concurrently with famciclovir.

Patient & Family Education

- Learn potential adverse effects and report those that are bothersome to physician.
- Be aware that a full therapeutic response may take several weeks.
- Report S&S of hypersensitivity immediately to physician.

FAMOTIDINE

(fa-moe′ti-deen)
Pepcid, Pepcid AC
Classifications: ANTISECRETORY AGENT (H$_2$-RECEPTOR ANTAGONIST)
Therapeutic: ANTIULCER; H$_2$-RECEPTOR ANTAGONIST
Prototype: Cimetidine
Pregnancy Category: B

AVAILABILITY 10 mg, 20 mg, 40 mg tablets; 40 mg/5 mL suspension; 10 mg/mL, 20 mg/50 mL injection

ACTION & *THERAPEUTIC EFFECT*

A potent competitive inhibitor of histamine at histamine (H$_2$) receptor sites in gastric parietal cells. Inhibits basal, nocturnal, meal-stimulated, and pentagastrin-stimulated gastric secretion; also inhibits pepsin secretion. *Reduces parietal cell output of hydrochloric acid; thus, detrimental effects of acid on gastric mucosa are diminished.*

USES Short-term treatment of active duodenal ulcer. Maintenance therapy for duodenal ulcer patients on reduced dosage after healing of an active ulcer. Treatment of pathologic hypersecretory conditions (e.g., Zollinger-Ellison syndrome), benign gastric ulcer, gastroesophageal reflux disease (GERD), gastritis.

UNLABELED USES Stress ulcer prophylaxis.

CONTRAINDICATIONS Hypersensitivity to famotidine or other H$_2$-receptor antagonists; sudden GI bleeding; lactation.

CAUTIOUS USE Renal insufficiency; renal failure; PKU; hepatic disease; elderly; pregnancy (category B).

ROUTE & DOSAGE

Duodenal Ulcer
Adult: **PO** 40 mg h.s. or 20 mg b.i.d. **PO Maintenance Therapy** 20 mg h.s. **IV** 20 mg q12h
Child: **PO/IV** 0.25 mg/kg q12h (max: 40 mg/d)

Pathological Hypersecretory Conditions
Adult: **PO** 20–160 mg q6h

GERD, Gastritis
Adult: **PO** 10 mg b.i.d.
Child: **PO** 1 mg/kg/d in 2 divided doses (max: 40 mg b.i.d.)

Renal Impairment
Cl$_{cr}$ <50 mL/min: 50% of usual dose or usual dose q36–48h

ADMINISTRATION

Oral

- Give with liquid or food of patient's choice; an antacid may also be given if patient is also on antacid therapy.
- Store at 15°–30° C (59°–86° F). Protect from moisture and strong light; do not freeze.

Common adverse effects in *italic*, life-threatening effects underlined; generic names in **bold**; classifications in SMALL CAPS; ♣ Canadian drug name; ⓓ Prototype drug

620

Intravenous

Note: Verify correct IV concentration and rate of infusion/injection with physician before administration to infants or children.

PREPARE: **Direct:** Dilute 20 mg (2 mL) famotidine IV solution (containing 10 mg/mL) with D5W, NS, or other compatible IV diluent (see manufacturer's directions) to a total volume of 5 or 10 mL. **IV Infusion:** Dilute 2 mL famotidine IV with 100 mL compatible IV solution.

ADMINISTER: **Direct:** Give over not less than 2 min. **IV Infusion:** Infuse over 15–30 min.

INCOMPATIBILITIES **Y-site: Amphotericin B, azithromycin, cholesteryl complex, cefepime.**

▪ Store IV solution at 2°–8° C (36°–46° F); reconstituted IV solution is stable for 48 h at room temperature 15°–30° C (59°–86° F).

ADVERSE EFFECTS (≥1%) **CNS:** Dizziness, headache, confusion, depression. **GI:** Constipation, diarrhea. **Skin:** Rash, acne, pruritus, dry skin, flushing. **Hematologic:** Thrombocytopenia. **Urogenital:** Increases in BUN and serum creatinine.

INTERACTIONS Drug: No clinically significant interactions established.

PHARMACOKINETICS Absorption: Incompletely from GI tract (40–50% reaches systemic circulation). **Onset:** 1 h. **Peak:** 1–3 h PO; 0.5–3 h IV. **Duration:** 10–12 h. **Metabolism:** In liver. **Elimination:** In urine. **Half-Life:** 2.5–4 h.

CLINICAL IMPLICATIONS

Assessment & Drug Effects

▪ Monitor for improvement in GI distress.
▪ Monitor for signs of GI bleeding.

Patient & Family Education

▪ Be aware that pain relief may not be experienced for several days after starting therapy.

FAT EMULSION, INTRAVENOUS

(fat e-mul'sion)

Intralipid, Liposyn II, Soyacal
Classifications: CALORIC AGENT; LIPID EMULSION
Therapeutic: NUTRITIONAL SUPPLEMENT; LIPID EMULSION
Pregnancy Category: B for Soyacal 10%; C for all others

AVAILABILITY 10%, 20%, 30% emulsion

ACTION & *THERAPEUTIC EFFECT*
Soybean oil in water emulsion containing egg yolk phospholipids and glycerin. Liposyn 10% is a safflower oil in water emulsion containing egg phosphatides and glycerin. *Used as a nutritional supplement. Fat emulsions contain a mixture of neutral triglycerides, and mostly unsaturated fatty acids.*

USES Fatty acid deficiency. Also to supply fatty acids and calories in high-density form to patients receiving prolonged TPN therapy who cannot tolerate high dextrose concentrations or when fluid intake must be restricted as in renal failure, CHF, ascites.

CONTRAINDICATIONS Hyperlipemia; bone marrow dyscrasias; impaired fat metabolism as in pathological hyperlipemia, lipoid nephrosis, acute pancreatitis accompanied by hyperlipemia; pregnancy (category C).
CAUTIOUS USE Severe hepatic or pulmonary disease; coagulation disorders; anemia; newborns, premature neonates, infants with hyperbil-

Common adverse effects in *italic*, life-threatening effects underlined; generic names in **bold**; classifications in SMALL CAPS; ♣ Canadian drug name; ⓟ Prototype drug

621

irubinemia; when danger of fat embolism exists; diabetes mellitus; thrombocytopenia; history of gastric ulcer.

ROUTE & DOSAGE

Prevention of Essential Fatty Acid Deficiency
Adult: IV 500 mL of 10% or 250 mL of 20% solution twice/wk (max: rate of 100 mL/h)
Child: IV 5–10 mL/kg/d twice/wk (max: 3–4 g/kg/d; max: rate of 100 mL/h)

Calorie Source in Fluid-restricted Patients
Adult: IV Up to 2.5 g/kg or 60% of nonprotein calories daily (max: rate of 100 mL/h)
Child: IV Up to 4 g/kg or 60% of nonprotein calories daily (max: rate of 100 mL/h)
Premature neonate: IV 0.25–0.5 g/kg/d, increase by 0.25–0.5 g/kg/d (max: 3–4 g/kg/d; max: infusion 0.15 g/kg/h)

ADMINISTRATION

Intravenous
Do not use if oil appears to be separating out of the emulsion.

PREPARE: **IV Infusion:** Allow preparations that have been refrigerated to stand at room temperature for about 30 min before using whenever possible. Check with a pharmacist before mixing fat emulsions with electrolytes, vitamins, drugs, or other nutrient solutions.

ADMINISTER: **IV Infusion:** Give fat emulsions via a separate peripheral site or by piggyback into same vein receiving amino acid injection and dextrose mixtures or give by piggyback through a Y-connector near infusion site so that the two solutions mix only in a short piece of tubing proximal to needle. ▪ Must hang fat emulsion higher than hyperalimentation solution bottle to prevent backup of fat emulsion into primary line. ▪ Do not use an inline filter because size of fat particles is larger than pore size. Control flow rate of each solution by separate infusion pumps. Use a constant rate over 20–24 h to reduce risk of hyperlipemia in neonates and prematures because they tend to metabolize fat slowly.

INCOMPATIBILITIES **Solution/additive: Aminophylline, amphotericin B, ampicillin, calcium chloride, calcium gluconate, gentamicin, hetastarch, magnesium chloride methicillin, penicillin G, phenytoin, ranitidine, tetracycline, vitamin B complex. Y-site: Acyclovir, amphotericin B, cyclosporine, doxorubicin, doxycycline, droperidol, ganciclovir, haloperidol, heparin, hetastarch, hydromorphone, levorphanol, lorazepam, midazolam, minocycline, nalbuphine, ondansetron, pentobarbital, phenobarbital, phenytoin, potassium phosphate, sodium phosphate, tetracycline.**

▪ Discard contents of partly used containers. ▪ Store, unless otherwise directed by manufacturer, Intralipid 10% and Liposyn 10% at room temperature [25° C (77° F) or below]; refrigerate Intralipid 20%. Do not freeze.

ADVERSE EFFECTS (≥1%) **Body as a Whole:** Hypersensitivity reactions (to egg protein), irritation at infusion site. **Hematologic:** Hypercoagulability, thrombocytopenia in neonates. **GI:** *Transient increases in liver function tests, hyperlipemia.* **[Long-Term Administration]** Sepsis, jaundice (cholestasis), hepatomegaly, kernicterus (infants with hyperbilirubinemia), shock (rare).

DIAGNOSTIC TEST INTERFERENCE
Blood samples drawn during or shortly after fat emulsion infusion may produce abnormally high **hemoglobin MCH and MCHC** values. Fat emulsions may cause transient abnormalities in **liver function tests** and may interfere with estimations of **serum bilirubin** (especially in infants).

INTERACTIONS Drug: No clinically significant interactions established.

CLINICAL IMPLICATIONS
Assessment & Drug Effects
- Observe patient closely. Acute reactions tend to occur within the first $2^1/_2$ h of therapy.
- Lab tests: Determine baseline values for hemoglobin, platelet count, blood coagulation, liver function, plasma lipid profile (especially serum triglycerides and cholesterol, free fatty acids in plasma). Repeat 1 or 2 times weekly during therapy in adults; more frequently in children. Report significant deviations promptly.
- Lab tests: Obtain daily platelet counts in neonates during first week of therapy, then every other day during second week, and 3 times a week thereafter because newborns are prone to develop thrombocytopenia.
- Note: Lipemia must clear after each daily infusion. Degree of lipemia is measured by serum

triglycerides and cholesterol levels 4–6 h after infusion has ceased.

Patient & Family Education
- Report difficulty breathing, nausea, vomiting, or headache to physician.

FELBAMATE
(fel′ba-mate)
Felbatol
Classifications: ANTICONVULSANT
Therapeutic: ANTICONVULSANT
Prototype: Phenytoin
Pregnancy Category: C

AVAILABILITY 400 mg, 600 mg tablets; 600 mg/5 mL suspension

ACTION & THERAPEUTIC EFFECT
Anticonvulsant mechanism has not been identified. Blocks repetitive firing of neurons and increases seizure threshold; prevents seizure spread. *Increases seizure threshold and prevents seizure spread.*

USES Treatment of Lennox–Gastaut syndrome and partial seizures.
UNLABELED USES Monotherapy or in combination with other anticonvulsants for the treatment of generalized tonic/clonic seizures.

CONTRAINDICATIONS Hypersensitivity to felbamate, history of blood dyscrasia or hepatic dysfunction; pregnancy (category C).
CAUTIOUS USE Renal impairment, renal failure; older adults; hypersensitivity to other carbamates; thrombocytopenia; iron-deficiency anemia; lactation. Safety and effectiveness in children other than those with Lennox–Gastaut syndrome are not established.

Common adverse effects in *italic*, life-threatening effects underlined; generic names in **bold**; classifications in SMALL CAPS; ♣ Canadian drug name; ❷ Prototype drug

623

ROUTE & DOSAGE

Partial Seizures

Adult: PO Initiate with 1200 mg/d in 3–4 divided doses, may increase by 600 mg/d q2wk (max: 3600 mg/d); when converting to monotherapy, reduce dose of concomitant anticonvulsants by $^1/_3$ when initiating felbamate, then continue to decrease other anticonvulsants by $^1/_3$ with each increase in felbamate q2wk; when using as adjunctive therapy, decrease other anticonvulsants by 20% when initiating felbamate and note that further reductions in other anticonvulsants may be required to minimize side effects and drug interactions

Lennox–Gastaut Syndrome

Child: PO Start at 15 mg/kg/d in 3 or 4 divided doses, reduce concurrent antiepileptic drugs by 20%, further reductions may be required to minimize side effects due to drug interactions, may increase felbamate by 15 mg/kg/d at weekly intervals (max: 45 mg/kg/d)

ADMINISTRATION

Oral

- Do not give this drug to anyone with a history of blood dyscrasia or hepatic dysfunction.
- Titrate dose under close clinical supervision.
- Shake suspension well before giving a dose.
- Store in airtight container at room temperature, 15°–30° C (59°–86° F).

ADVERSE EFFECTS (≥1%) **CNS:** Mild tremors, headache, dizziness, ataxia, diplopia, blurred vision; agitation, aggression, hallucinations, fatigue, psychological disturbances. **Endocrine:** Slight elevation of serum cholesterol, hyponatremia, hypokalemia, weight gain and loss. **GI:** *Nausea and vomiting,* anorexia, constipation, hiccup, taste disturbance, indigestion, esophagitis, increased appetite, <u>acute liver failure</u>. **Hematologic:** <u>*Aplastic anemia*</u>.

INTERACTIONS Drug: Felbamate reduces serum **carbamazepine** levels by a mean of 25%, but increases levels of its active metabolite, increases serum **phenytoin** levels approximately 20%, and increases **valproic acid** levels. **Herbal: Gingko** may decrease anticonvulsant effectiveness.

PHARMACOKINETICS Absorption: 90% from GI tract. Absorption of tablet not affected by food. **Onset:** Therapeutic effect approximately 14 d. **Peak:** Peak plasma levels at 1–6 h. **Distribution:** 20–25% protein bound, readily crosses the blood–brain barrier. **Metabolism:** In the liver via the cytochrome P-450 system. **Elimination:** 40–50% excreted unchanged in urine, rest excreted in urine as metabolites. **Half-Life:** 20–23 h.

CLINICAL IMPLICATIONS

Assessment & Drug Effects

- Lab tests: Obtain baseline values for liver function and complete hematologic studies before initiating therapy, repeat frequently during therapy, and for a lengthy period after discontinuation of felbamate. Monitor serum sodium and potassium levels periodically because hyponatremia and hypokalemia have been reported.
- Report immediately any hematologic abnormalities.
- Monitor results of hepatic function tests throughout therapy.

■Note: When used concomitantly with either phenytoin or carbamazepine, carefully monitor serum levels of these drugs when felbamate is added, when adjustments in felbamate dosing are made, or when felbamate is discontinued.

■Note: A reduction in phenytoin of 10–40% is usually needed when felbamate is added to the regimen.

■Monitor weight, because both weight gain and loss have been reported.

■Monitor for S&S of drug toxicity including GI distress and CNS toxicity.

Patient & Family Education

■Note: It is highly recommended that patients and physicians review the indication for treatment, risks associated with the drug, and the importance of undergoing regular blood monitoring.

■Report unusual changes (e.g., blurred vision, dysplopia) to physician.

■Report S&S of hypersensitivity including pruritus, urticaria, and (rarely) photosensitivity allergic reaction to physician.

■Learn adverse effects and report these to physician immediately.

FELODIPINE

(fel-o'di-peen)
Plendil
Classifications: CALCIUM CHANNEL BLOCKER; ANTIHYPERTENSIVE
Therapeutic: ANTIHYPERTENSIVE
Prototype: Nifedipine
Pregnancy Category: C

AVAILABILITY 2.5 mg, 5 mg, 10 mg sustained release tablets

ACTION & *THERAPEUTIC EFFECT*
Calcium antagonist with high vascular selectivity that reduces systolic, diastolic, and mean arterial pressure at rest and during exercise. Felodipine inhibits influx of extracellular calcium across myocardial and vascular smooth muscle cell membranes. Resultant decrease in intracellular calcium inhibits contractility of smooth muscle, resulting in dilation of coronary and systemic arteries. *BP reduction is due to reduction in peripheral vascular resistance (afterload) against which the heart works. This reduces oxygen demand by the heart and may account for its effectiveness in chronic stable angina.*

USES Mild to moderate hypertension.
UNLABELED USES Severe hypertension, angina, CHF, pulmonary hypertension.

CONTRAINDICATIONS Hypersensitivity to felodipine; sick sinus rhythm or second- or third-degree heart block except with the use of a pacemaker; abnormal aortic stenosis; hypotension; bradycardia; cardiogenic shock; acute MI; left ventricular dysfunction; pregnancy (category C). Safety and efficacy in children are not established.
CAUTIOUS USE Hypotension, CHF, angina; aortic stenosis, cardiomyopathy; older adults; GERD; hiatal hernia; hepatic impairment; lactation.

ROUTE & DOSAGE

Hypertension
Adult: **PO** 5–10 mg once/d (max: 20 mg/d)

Hepatic Impairment
Start older adults and patients with impaired liver function at 2.5 mg q.d.

Common adverse effects in *italic*, life-threatening effects underlined; generic names in **bold**; classifications in SMALL CAPS; ♣ Canadian drug name; ⊙ Prototype drug

625

ADMINISTRATION

Oral
- Give tablet whole. Do not crush or chew tablets.
- Store at or below 30° C (86° F) in a tightly closed, light-resistant container.

ADVERSE EFFECTS (≥1%) **Body as a Whole:** Most adverse effects appear to be dose dependent. **CV:** Tachycardia, *palpitations, flushing, peripheral edema.* **CNS:** *Dizziness, fatigue,* headache. **GI:** Nausea, flatulence, diarrhea, dyspepsia. **Hematologic:** Small but significant decreases in Hct, Hgb, and RBC count.

DIAGNOSTIC TEST INTERFERENCE Serum *alkaline phosphatase* may be slightly but significantly increased. Plasma total and ionized *calcium* levels rise significantly. Serum *gamma-glutamyl transferase* may increase.

INTERACTIONS Drug: Adenosine may cause prolonged bradycardia if it is used to treat patients with toxic concentrations of CALCIUM CHANNEL BLOCKERS. **Carbamazepine, phenobarbital, phenytoin** may decrease felodipine bioavailability and serum concentrations. **Cimetidine** may increase felodipine bioavailability (competes for hepatic metabolism). Concomitant felodipine and **digoxin** administration produces only transient increases in plasma **digoxin** concentrations (35–40% increase), which are not sustained with continued administration. This interaction may be of clinical relevance in patients whose plasma **digoxin** concentration is in the upper portion of the therapeutic range or in patients with preexisting renal insufficiency.

PHARMACOKINETICS Absorption: Completely absorbed from GI tract; it undergoes extensive first-pass metabolism with only about 15% of dose reaching systemic circulation. **Onset:** <1 h. **Peak:** 2–4 h. **Duration:** 20–24 h (sustained release formulation). **Distribution:** >99% bound to plasma proteins. **Metabolism:** Metabolized via hepatic cytochrome P-450 mixed function oxidase system. **Elimination:** 60–70% of metabolites are excreted in urine within 72 h. **Half-Life:** 10 h.

CLINICAL IMPLICATIONS

Assessment & Drug Effects
- Monitor BP carefully, especially at initiation of drug therapy, in patients >64 y, and in those with impaired liver function.
- Anticipate BP reduction with possible reflex heart rate increase (5–10 bpm) 2–5 h after dosing.
- Report sustained hypotension promptly; more common with concurrent beta-blocker therapy.
- Assess for and report reflex tachycardia; may precipitate angina.
- Monitor patients for possible digoxin toxicity when taking concurrent digoxin.

Patient Education
- Report peripheral edema, headache, or flushing to physician. These may necessitate discontinuation of drug.
- Get up from lying down slowly and in stages; there is potential for dizziness and hypotension.

FENOFIBRATE ℗

(fen-o-fi′brate)
Tricor, Triglide, Lofibra, Antara
Classifications: ANTILIPEMIC
Therapeutic: CHOLESTEROL-LOWERING AGENT
Pregnancy Category: C

AVAILABILITY 48 mg, 50 mg, 154 mg, 160 mg tablets; 43 mg, 67 mg, 87 mg, 134 mg, 200 mg capsules or 50 mg, 100 mg, 150 mg, 160 mg capsules

ACTION & *THERAPEUTIC EFFECT*

Fibric acid derivative with lipid-regulating properties. Lowers plasma triglycerides apparently by inhibiting triglyceride synthesis and, as a result, lowers VLDL production as well as stimulates the catabolism of triglyceride-rich lipoprotein (e.g., VLDL). Produces a moderate increase in HDL cholesterol levels in most patients. *Effectiveness indicated by reduction in the level of serum triglycerides and VLDL production; interferes with synthesis of serum triglycerides.*

USES Adjunctive therapy to diet for patients with high triglycerides.

CONTRAINDICATIONS Hypersensitivity to fenofibrate or other fibric acid derivatives (e.g., clofibrate, benzofibrate); liver or severe kidney dysfunction; unexplained liver function abnormality; preexisting hepatic disease; primary biliary cirrhosis; preexisting gallbladder disease; pregnancy (category C); lactation; thrombocytopenia. Safety and efficacy in children <10 y (capsules), <18 y (Tricor tablets) are not established.

CAUTIOUS USE Concomitant therapy with HMG-CoA reductase inhibitors (e.g., lovastatin, pravastatin, simvastatin), oral anticoagulant medications; renal impairment; older adults; history of bleeding disorders; myelosuppression.

ROUTE & DOSAGE

Hypertriglyceridemia
Adult: **PO** 54 mg q.d. (max: 160 mg/d)

ADMINISTRATION

Oral

- Limit dose to 54 mg/d in older adults or those with impaired kidney function.
- Give at least 1 h before or 4–6 h after cholestyramine.
- Store at 15°–30° C (59°–86° F) in a tightly closed container and protect from light.

ADVERSE EFFECTS (≥1%) **Body as a Whole:** Asthenia, fatigue, infections, flu-like syndrome, localized pain, arthralgia. **CNS:** Headache, paresthesia, dizziness, insomnia. **CV:** Arrhythmia. **GI:** Dyspepsia, eructation, flatulence, nausea, vomiting, abdominal pain, constipation, diarrhea, increased appetite. **Respiratory:** Cough, rhinitis, sinusitis. **Skin:** Pruritus, rash. **Special Senses:** Earache, eye floaters, blurred vision, conjunctivitis, eye irritation, **Urogenital:** Decreased libido, polyuria, vaginitis.

INTERACTIONS Drug: May potentiate anticoagulant effects of **warfarin;** combination with an HMG-COA REDUCTASE INHIBITOR (STATIN) may result in rhabdomyolysis or acute renal failure; **cholestyramine, colestipol** may decrease absorption (give fenofibrate 1 h before or 4–6 h after BILE ACID SEQUESTRANTS); may increase risk of nephrotoxicity of **cyclosporine.**

PHARMACOKINETICS Absorption: Well absorbed from the GI tract; increased with food. **Peak:** 6–8 h. **Distribution:** 99% protein bound; excreted in breast milk. **Metabolism:** Rapidly hydrolyzed by esterases to active metabolite, fenofibric acid. **Elimination:** 60% in urine, 25% in feces. **Half-Life:** 20 h.

Common adverse effects in *italic*, life-threatening effects underlined; generic names in **bold**; classifications in SMALL CAPS; ✤ Canadian drug name; ⦿ Prototype drug

CLINICAL IMPLICATIONS

Assessment & Drug Effects

- Lab tests: Periodically monitor lipid levels, liver functions, and CBC with differential.
- Discontinue therapy after 2 mo if adequate lipid reduction is not achieved with the maximum dose of 201 mg/d.
- Assess for muscle pain, tenderness, or weakness and, if present, monitor CPK level. Withdraw drug with marked elevations of CPK or if myopathy is suspected.
- Monitor patients on coumarin-type drugs closely for prolongation of PT/INR.

Patient & Family Education

- Contact physician immediately if any of the following develops: Unexplained muscle pain, tenderness, or weakness, especially with fever or malaise; yellowing of skin or eyes; nausea or loss of appetite; skin rash or hives.
- Inform physician regarding concurrent use of cholestyramine, oral anticoagulants, or cyclosporine.

FENOLDOPAM MESYLATE

(fen-ol'do-pam mes'y-late)

Corlopam

Classifications: NON-NITRATE VASODILATOR; DOPAMINE AGONIST AGENT; ANTIHYPERTENSIVE

Therapeutic: NON-NITRATE VASODILATOR; ANTIHYPERTENSIVE

Pregnancy Category: B

AVAILABILITY 10 mg/mL injection

ACTION & *THERAPEUTIC EFFECT*

Rapid-acting vasodilator that is a dopamine D_1-like receptor agonist. Exerts hypotensive effects by decreasing peripheral vascular resistance while increasing renal blood flow, diuresis, and natriuresis. *Indicated by rapid reduction in BP. Decreases both systolic and diastolic pressures.*

USES Short-term (up to 48 h) management of severe hypertension.

CONTRAINDICATIONS Hypersensitivity to fenoldopam. Avoid concomitant use with beta blockers.

CAUTIOUS USE Asthmatic patients; hepatic cirrhosis, portal hypertension, or variceal bleeding; arrhythmias, tachycardia, or angina, particularly unstable angina; elevated IOP; angular-closure glaucoma; hypotension; hypokalemia; acute cerebral infarct or hemorrhage; pregnancy (category B), lactation.

ROUTE & DOSAGE

Severe Hypertension

Adult: **IV** 0.1–0.3 mcg/kg/min by continuous infusion for up to 48 h, may increase by 0.05–0.1 mcg/kg/min q15min (dosage range: 0.01–1.6 mcg/kg/min)
Child: **IV** 0.2 mcg/kg/min, may increase to 0.3–0.5 mcg/kg/min

ADMINISTRATION

Intravenous

PREPARE: **Continuous:** Dilute to a final concentration of 40 mcg/mL by adding 1 mL (10 mg), 2 mL (20 mg), or 3 mL (30 mg) of fenoldopam to 250, 500, or 1000 mL, respectively, of NS or D5W.

ADMINISTER: **Continuous:** Give only by continuous infusion; never give a direct or bolus dose. Titrate initial dose up or down no more frequently than q15min.
- Note: Diluted solution is stable under normal room temperature and light for 24 h. Discard any unused solution after 24 h.

■ Store at 15°–30° C (59°–86° F) in a tightly closed container and protect from light.

INCOMPATIBILITIES **Y-site: Aminophylline, ampicillin, amphotericin B, bumetanide, cefoxitin, dexamethasone, diazepam, fosphenytoin, furosemide, ketorolac, methohexital, methylprednisolone, pentobarbital, phenytoin, prochlorperazine, sodium bicarbonate, thiopental.**

ADVERSE EFFECTS (≥1%) **Body as a Whole:** Injection site reaction, pyrexia, nonspecific chest pain. **CNS:** Headache, nervousness, anxiety, insomnia, dizziness. **CV:** *Hypotension, tachycardia,* T-wave inversion, flushing, postural hypotension, extrasystoles, palpitations, bradycardia, heart failure, ischemic heart disease, <u>MI</u>, angina. **GI:** Nausea, vomiting, abdominal pain or fullness, constipation, diarrhea. **Metabolic:** Increased creatinine, BUN, glucose, transaminases, LDH; hypokalemia. **Respiratory:** Nasal congestion, dyspnea, upper respiratory disorder. **Skin:** Sweating. **Other:** UTI, leukocytosis, bleeding.

INTERACTIONS : No clinically significant interactions established.

PHARMACOKINETICS Onset: 5 min. **Peak:** 15 min. **Duration:** 15–30 min. **Distribution:** Crosses placenta. **Metabolism:** Conjugated in liver. **Elimination:** 90% in urine, 10% in feces. **Half-Life:** 5 min.

CLINICAL IMPLICATIONS
Assessment & Drug Effects
■ Monitor BP and HR carefully at least q15min or more often as warranted; expect dose-related tachycardia.
■ Lab tests: Carefully monitor serum electrolytes (especially serum potassium), BUN and creatinine, liver enzymes, and blood glucose and HbA_{1c}.

FENOPROFEN CALCIUM
(fen-oh-proe′fen)
Nalfon
Classifications: ANALGESIC, NONSTEROIDAL ANTIINFLAMMATORY DRUG (NSAID); ANTIPYRETIC
Therapeutic: NSAID, ANALGESIC; ANTIPYRETIC
Prototype: Ibuprofen
Pregnancy Category: B first and second trimester; D third trimester

AVAILABILITY 200 mg, 300 mg capsules; 600 mg tablets

ACTION & *THERAPEUTIC EFFECT*
Exhibits antiinflammatory, analgesic, and antipyretic properties of an NSAID. Fenoprofen competitively inhibits both cyclooxygenase COX-1 and COX-2 enzymes by blocking arachidonate binding to prostaglandin G_2 resulting in its pharmacologic effects. *Has nonsteroidal, antiinflammatory, antipyretic, antiarthritic properties that provide relief from mild to severe pain.*

USES Antiinflammatory and analgesic effects in the symptomatic treatment of acute and chronic rheumatoid arthritis and osteoarthritis; relief of mild to moderate pain.
UNLABELED USES Juvenile rheumatoid arthritis, acute gouty arthritis, ankylosing spondylitis; fever associated with pulmonary tuberculosis, type A influenza, colds; neoplasms.

CONTRAINDICATIONS Hypersensitivity to fenoprofen or other NSAIDS; history of nephrotic syndrome associated with aspirin or other NSAIDS; patient in whom urti-

Common adverse effects in *italic*, life-threatening effects <u>underlined</u>; generic names in **bold**; classifications in SMALL CAPS; ♣ Canadian drug name; ⊚ Prototype drug

629

caria, severe rhinitis, bronchospasm, angioedema, nasal polyps are precipitated by aspirin or other NSAIDS; severe renal or hepatic dysfunction; perioperative pain associated in CABG; pregnancy (category B first and second trimester, and category D in third trimester). Safety in lactation or children is not established.

CAUTIOUS USE History of upper GI tract disorders; lupus; older adults; renal failure; renal impairment; hemophilia or other bleeding tendencies; compromised cardiac function, hypertension; impaired hearing; lactation.

ROUTE & DOSAGE

Inflammatory Disease
Adult: **PO** 300–600 mg t.i.d. or q.i.d. (max: 3200 mg/d)
Child: **PO** 900 mg/m^2 in divided doses, may increase over 4 wk to 1.8 g/m^2
Mild to Moderate Pain
Adult: **PO** 200 mg q4–6h prn

ADMINISTRATION

Oral

- Give on an empty stomach 30–60 min before or 2 h after meals. Give with meals, milk, or antacid (prescribed) if patient experiences GI disturbances.
- May crush tablets or empty capsule and mix with fluid or mix with food.
- Store capsules and tablets in tightly closed containers at 15°–30° C (59°–86° F); avoid freezing.

ADVERSE EFFECTS (≥1%) **CNS:** *Headache, drowsiness,* dizziness, fatigue, lassitude, tremor, confusion, insomnia, nervousness, depression. **Special Senses:** Tinnitus, decreased hearing, deafness; blurred vision.

GI: *Indigestion, nausea, vomiting,* anorexia, *constipation,* diarrhea, flatulence, abdominal pain, dry mouth; infrequent: gastritis, peptic ulcer, GI bleeding. **Urogenital:** Dysuria, cystitis, hematuria, oliguria, azotemia, anuria, allergic nephritis, papillary necrosis, nephrotoxicity (rare). **Hematologic:** (infrequent) Thrombocytopenia, hemolytic anemia, agranulocytosis, pancytopenia. **Skin:** (may or may not be hypersensitivity reaction) Pruritus, rash, purpura, increased sweating, urticaria. **Body as a Whole:** Dyspnea, malaise, anaphylaxis, edema.

INTERACTIONS Drug: Fenoprofen may prolong bleeding time; should not be given with ORAL ANTICOAGULANTS, **heparin;** action and side effects of **phenytoin,** SULFONYLUREAS, SULFONAMIDES, and fenoprofen may be potentiated. **Herbal: Feverfew, garlic, ginger, gingko** may increase bleeding potential.

PHARMACOKINETICS Absorption: 80% from GI tract. **Onset:** 2 h. **Peak:** 2 h. **Duration:** 4–6 h. **Distribution:** Small amounts distributed into breast milk. **Metabolism:** In liver. **Elimination:** Primarily in urine; some biliary excretion. **Half-Life:** 3 h.

CLINICAL IMPLICATIONS

Assessment & Drug Effects

- Lab tests: Baseline evaluations of Hct and Hgb, kidney and liver function.
- Baseline and periodic auditory and ophthalmic examinations are recommended in patients receiving prolonged or high-dose therapy.
- Monitor for S&S of GI bleeding.
- Note: Dosage adjustment of fenoprofen may be required when phenobarbital is added to or withdrawn from patient's drug regimen.

Patient & Family Education

- Do not drive or engage in potentially hazardous activities until response to drug is known; fenoprofen may cause dizziness and drowsiness.
- Report immediately the onset of unexplained fever, rash, arthralgia, oliguria, edema, weight gain to physician. Possible symptoms of nephrotic syndrome are rapidly reversible if drug is promptly withdrawn.
- Understand that alcohol and aspirin may increase risk of GI ulceration and bleeding tendencies; avoid both unless otherwise advised by physician.
- Inform dentist or surgeon that you are taking fenoprofen because it may prolong bleeding time.

FENTANYL CITRATE

(fen′ta-nil)

Duragesic, Actiq Oralet, Sublimaze, Ionsys

Classifications: ANALGESIC; NARCOTIC (OPIATE) AGONIST
Therapeutic: NARCOTIC ANALGESIC; OPIATE AGONIST
Prototype: Morphine
Pregnancy Category: C (B for fentanyl injection)
Controlled Substance: Schedule II

AVAILABILITY 0.05 mg/mL injection; 100 mcg, 200 mcg, 300 mcg, 400 mcg lozenges; 200 mcg, 400 mcg, 600 mcg, 800 mcg, 1200 mcg, 1600 mcg lozenges on a stick; 12 mcg/h, 25 mcg/h, 50 mcg/h, 75 mcg/h, 100 mcg/h transdermal patch

ACTION & THERAPEUTIC EFFECT
Synthetic, potent narcotic agonist analgesic with pharmacologic actions qualitatively similar to those of morphine, but action is more prompt and less prolonged. Principal actions: analgesia and sedation. Drug-induced alterations in respiratory rate and alveolar ventilation may persist beyond the analgesic effect. *Provides analgesia for moderate to severe pain as well as sedation.*

USES Short-acting analgesic during operative and perioperative periods, as a narcotic analgesic supplement in general and regional anesthesia, and with droperidol or with diazepam to produce neuroleptanalgesia. Also given with oxygen and a skeletal muscle relaxant (neuroleptoanesthesia) to selected high-risk patients (e.g., those undergoing open heart surgery) when attenuation of the response to surgical stress without use of additional anesthesia agents is important.

CONTRAINDICATIONS Patients who have received MAO INHIBITORS within 14 d; substance abuse; myasthenia gravis; labor and delivery; pregnancy (category C, and category B for fentanyl injection).
CAUTIOUS USE Head injuries, increased intracranial pressure; older adults, debilitated, poor-risk patients; cardiac diseases, angina, hypotension, or cardiac arrhythmias; COPD, other respiratory problems; liver and kidney dysfunction; bradyarrhythmias; children.

ROUTE & DOSAGE

Premedication

Adult: IM 50–100 mcg 30–60 min before surgery **PO** Suck on 400-mcg lozenge until sedated
Child: **PO** Suck on lozenge until sedated, *10–25 kg,* 200-mcg lozenge; *25–35 kg,* 300-mcg lozenge; *35–40 kg,* 400-mcg lozenge

Common adverse effects in *italic*, life-threatening effects <u>underlined</u>; generic names in **bold**; classifications in SMALL CAPS; ♣ Canadian drug name; ⊘ Prototype drug

631

F

Adjunct for Regional Anesthesia
Adult: **IM/IV** 50–100 mcg

General Anesthesia
Adult: **IV** 2–20 mcg/kg, additional doses of 25–100 mcg as required
Child: **IV** 2–3 mcg/kg as needed

Postoperative Pain
Adult: **IM** 50–100 mcg q1–2h prn
Child: **IM** 1.7–3.3 mcg/kg q1–2h prn

Chronic Pain
Adult: **Transdermal** Individualize and regularly reassess doses of transdermal fentanyl; for patient not already receiving an opioid, the initial dose is 25 mcg/h patch q3d; for patients already on opioids, see package insert for conversions **Stick lozenge (Actiq)** Place in mouth between cheek and lower gum and suck on lozenge; should be consumed over 15-min period

ADMINISTRATION

Intravascular

PREPARE: Direct: Give parenteral doses undiluted or diluted in 5 mL sterile water or NS.
ADMINISTER: Direct: Infuse over 1–2 min.
INCOMPATIBILITIES Solution/additive: Fluorouracil, pentobarbital, thiopental. Y-site: Azithromycin.

- Store at 15°–30° C (59°–86° F) unless otherwise directed. Protect drug from light.

ADVERSE EFFECTS (≥1%) CNS:
Sedation, euphoria, dizziness, diaphoresis, delirium, convulsions with high doses. **CV:** Hypotension, brady-cardia, circulatory depression, cardiac arrest. **Special Senses:** Miosis, blurred vision. **GI:** *Nausea,* vomiting, constipation, ileus. **Respiratory:** Laryngospasm, bronchoconstriction, respiratory depression or arrest. **Body as a Whole:** Muscle rigidity, especially muscles of respiration after rapid IV infusion, urinary retention. **Skin:** Rash, contact dermatitis from patch.

INTERACTIONS Drug: Alcohol and other CNS DEPRESSANTS potentiate effects; MAO INHIBITORS may precipitate hypertensive crisis.

PHARMACOKINETICS Absorption: Absorbed through the skin, leveling off between 12–24 h. **Onset:** Immediate IV; 7–15 min IM; 12–24 h transdermal. **Peak:** 3–5 min IV; 24–72 h transdermal. **Duration:** 30–60 min IV; 1–2 h IM; 72 h transdermal. **Metabolism:** In liver by CYP3A4. **Elimination:** In urine. **Half-Life:** 17 h transdermal.

CLINICAL IMPLICATIONS

Assessment & Drug Effects
- Monitor vital signs and observe patient for signs of skeletal and thoracic muscle (depressed respirations) rigidity and weakness.
- Watch carefully for respiratory depression and for movements of various groups of skeletal muscle in extremities, external eye, and neck during postoperative period. These movements may present patient management problems; report promptly.
- Note: Duration of respiratory depressant effect may be considerably longer than narcotic analgesic effect. Have immediately available oxygen, resuscitative and intubation equipment, and an opioid antagonist such as naloxone.

FERROUS SULFATE ⊕

(fer'rous sul'fate)

Feosol, Fer-In-Sol, Fer-Iron, Fero-Gradumet, Ferospace, Ferralyn, Ferra-TD, Fesofor, Hematinic, Mol-Iron, Novoferrosulfa ♣, Slow-Fe

FERROUS FUMARATE

(fer'rous foo'ma-rate)

Feco-T, Femiron, Feostat, Fersamal, Fumasorb, Fumerin, Hemocyte, Ircon-FA, Neo-Fer-50 ♣, Novofumar ♣, Palafer ♣, Palmiron

FERROUS GLUCONATE

(fer'rous gloo'koe-nate)

Fergon, Fertinic ♣, Novoferrogluc ♣, Simron

Classifications: BLOOD FORMER; IRON PREPARATION
Therapeutic: ANTIANEMIC; IRON SUPPLEMENT
Pregnancy Category: A

AVAILABILITY Ferrous Sulfate 167 mg, 200 mg, 324 mg, 325 mg tablets; 160 mg sustained release tablets, capsules; 90 mg/5 mL syrup; 220 mg/5 mL elixir; 75 mg/0.6 mL drops **Ferrous Fumarate** 63 mg, 100 mg, 200 mg, 324 mg, 325 mg, 350 mg tablets; 100 mg/5 mL suspension; 45 mg/0.6 mL drops **Ferrous Gluconate** 240 mg, 325 mg tablets

ACTION & THERAPEUTIC EFFECT
Ferrous sulfate: Standard iron preparation that corrects erythropoietic abnormalities induced by iron deficiency but does not stimulate erythropoiesis. *Ferrous gluconate:* Claimed to cause less gastric irritation and be better tolerated than ferrous sulfate. *Effectiveness is experienced within 48 h as a sense of well-being, increased vigor, improved appetite, and decreased irritability (in children). Reticulocyte response begins in about 4 d; it usually peaks in 7–10 d and returns to normal after 2 or 3 wk. Hemoglobin generally increases by 2 g/dL and hematocrit by 6% in 3 wk.*

USES To correct simple iron deficiency and to treat iron deficiency (microcytic, hypochromic) anemias. Also may be used prophylactically during periods of increased iron needs, as in infancy, childhood, and pregnancy.

CONTRAINDICATIONS Peptic ulcer, regional enteritis, ulcerative colitis; hemolytic anemias (in absence of iron deficiency), hemochromatosis, hemosiderosis, patients receiving repeated transfusions, pyridoxine-responsive anemia; cirrhosis of liver. **CAUTIOUS USE** Hepatic disease; GI diseases; sulfite hypersensitivity; pregnancy (category A).

ROUTE & DOSAGE

Iron Deficiency

Adult: PO Sulfate (30% elemental iron) 750–1500 mg/d in 1–3 divided doses; Fumarate (33% elemental iron) 200 mg t.i.d. or q.i.d.; Gluconate (12% elemental iron) 325–600 mg q.i.d., may be gradually increased to 650 mg q.i.d. as needed and tolerated
Child: PO Sulfate (30% elemental iron) <6 y, 75–225 mg/d in divided doses; 6–12 y, 600 mg/d in divided doses; Fumarate (33% elemental iron) 3 mg/kg t.i.d.; Gluconate (12% elemental iron) <6 y, 100–300 mg/d in divided doses; 6–12 y, 100–300 mg t.i.d.

Iron Supplement

Adult: PO Sulfate *Pregnancy,* 300–600 mg/d in divided doses; Fumarate 200 mg once/d; Gluconate 325–600 mg once/d

---

Common adverse effects in *italic*, life-threatening effects underlined; generic names in **bold**; classifications in SMALL CAPS; ♣ Canadian drug name; ⊕ Prototype drug

F

Child: **PO Fumarate** 3 mg/kg once/d; **Gluconate** <*6 y,* 100–300 mg/d in divided doses; *6–12 y,* 100–300 mg once/d
Infant: **PO Fumarate** *Low birth weight,* 2 mg/kg/d up to 15 mg/d; ≤*3 y,* 1 mg/kg/d (max: 15 mg/d)

ADMINISTRATION

Oral

- Give on an empty stomach if possible because oral iron preparations are best absorbed then (i.e., between meals). Minimize gastric distress if needed by giving with or immediately after meals with adequate liquid.
- Do not crush tablet or empty contents of capsule when administering.
- Do not give tablets or capsules within 1 h of bedtime.
- Consult physician about prescribing a liquid formulation or a less corrosive form, such as ferrous gluconate, if the patient experiences difficulty in swallowing tablet or capsule.
- Dilute liquid preparations well and give through a straw or placed on the back of tongue with a dropper to prevent staining of teeth and to mask taste. Instruct the patient to rinse mouth with clear water immediately after ingestion.
- Mix ferosol elixir with water; not compatible with milk or fruit juice. Fer-In-Sol (drops) may be given in water or in fruit or vegetable juice, according to manufacturer.
- Do not use discolored tablets.
- Store in tightly closed containers and protect from moisture. Store at 15°–30° C (59°–86° F).

ADVERSE EFFECTS (≥1%) **GI:** *Nausea, heartburn,* anorexia, *constipation,* diarrhea, epigastric pain, abdominal distress, *black stools.* **Spe-cial Senses:** Yellow-brown discoloration of eyes and teeth (liquid forms.) **Large Chronic Doses in Infants** Rickets (due to interference with phosphorus absorption). **Massive Overdosage** Lethargy, drowsiness, nausea, vomiting, abdominal pain, diarrhea, local corrosion of stomach and small intestines, pallor or cyanosis, metabolic acidosis, <u>shock, cardiovascular collapse</u>, convulsions, <u>liver necrosis</u>, coma, renal failure, <u>death</u>.

DIAGNOSTIC TEST INTERFERENCE

By coloring feces black, large iron doses may cause false-positive tests for **occult blood with orthotoluidine (Hematest, Occultist, Labstix); guaiac reagent benzidine test** is reportedly not affected.

INTERACTIONS Drug: ANTACIDS decrease iron absorption; iron decreases absorption of TETRACYCLINES, **ciprofloxacin, ofloxacin; chloramphenicol** may delay iron's effects; iron may decrease absorption of **penicillamine. Food:** Food decreases absorption of iron; **ascorbic acid (vitamin C)** may increase iron absorption.

PHARMACOKINETICS Absorption: 5–10% absorbed in healthy individuals; 10–30% absorbed in iron-deficiency; food decreases amount absorbed. **Distribution:** Transported by transferrin to bone marrow, where it is incorporated into hemoglobin; crosses placenta. **Elimination:** Most of iron released from hemoglobin is reused in body; small amounts are lost in desquamation of skin, GI mucosa, nails, and hair; 12–30 mg/mo lost through menstruation.

CLINICAL IMPLICATIONS

Assessment & Drug Effects

- Lab tests: Monitor Hgb and reticulocyte values during therapy. Investigate the absence of satisfactory response after 3 wk of drug treatment.

- Continue iron therapy for 2–3 mo after the hemoglobin level has returned to normal (roughly twice the period required to normalize hemoglobin concentration).
- Monitor bowel movements as constipation is a common adverse effect.

Patient & Family Education

- Note: Ascorbic acid increases absorption of iron. Consuming citrus fruit or tomato juice with iron preparation (except the elixir) may increase its absorption.
- Be aware that milk, eggs, or caffeine beverages when taken with the iron preparation may inhibit absorption.
- Be aware that iron preparations cause dark green or black stools.
- Report constipation or diarrhea to physician; symptoms may be relieved by adjustments in dosage or diet or by change to another iron preparation.

FEXOFENADINE

(fex-o-fen'a-deen)
Allegra

Classifications: ANTIHISTAMINE; H$_1$-RECEPTOR ANTAGONIST, NON-SEDATING
Therapeutic: ANTIHISTAMINE; NON-SEDATING H$_1$-RECEPTOR ANTAGONIST
Prototype: Loratadine
Pregnancy Category: C

AVAILABILITY 30 mg, 60 mg, 180 mg tablets; 60 mg capsules

ACTION & *THERAPEUTIC EFFECT*
Competes with free histamine for binding at the H$_1$-receptor. This competitive antagonism blocks effects of histamine on H$_1$-receptors in bronchial smooth muscle. This also results in decreased formation of edema, flare, and pruritus that result from histaminic activity. *Inhibits antigen-induced bronchospasm and histamine release from mast cells. Efficacy is indicated by reduction of the following: nasal congestion and sneezing; watery or red eyes; itching nose, palate, or eyes.*

USES Relief of symptoms associated with seasonal allergic rhinitis, and chronic urticaria.

CONTRAINDICATIONS Hypersensitivity to fexofenadine or terfenadine; neonates; pregnancy (category C).
CAUTIOUS USE Mild to severe renal and hepatic insufficiency, hypertension, diabetes mellitus, ischemic heart disease, increased ocular pressure, hyperthyroidism, renal impairment, or prostatic hypertrophy; young children.

ROUTE & DOSAGE

Allergic Rhinitis
Adult/Child: >12 y, **PO** 60 mg b.i.d.
Child: **PO** 6–11, 30 mg b.i.d.
Chronic Urticaria
Adult: **PO** 60 mg b.i.d.
Child: **PO** >6 y, 30 mg b.i.d.
Renal Impairment
Cl$_{cr}$ <80 mL/min
Adult: **PO** 60 mg q.d.
Child: **PO** 30 mg q.d.

ADMINISTRATION

Oral

- Reduce starting dose for those with decreased kidney function.
- Do not give within 15 min of an aluminum- or magnesium-containing antacid.

Common adverse effects in *italic*, life-threatening effects underlined; generic names in **bold**; classifications in SMALL CAPS; ♣ Canadian drug name; ⊘ Prototype drug

635

■ Store at 20°–25° C (68°–77° F). Protect from excess moisture.

ADVERSE EFFECTS (≥1%) **CNS:** *Headache,* drowsiness, fatigue. **GI:** Nausea, dyspepsia, throat irritation.

INTERACTIONS Drug: ANTACIDS will decrease serum level of fexofenadine. **Herbal: St. John's wort** will decrease serum level of fexofenadine.

PHARMACOKINETICS Absorption: Rapidly from GI tract, 33% reaches systemic circulation. **Onset:** 1 h. **Peak:** 2–3 h. **Duration:** At least 12 h. **Distribution:** 60–70% bound to plasma proteins. **Metabolism:** Only 5% of dose metabolized in liver. **Elimination:** 80% in urine, 11% in feces. **Half-Life:** 14.4 h.

CLINICAL IMPLICATIONS

Assessment & Drug Effects

■ Monitor therapeutic effectiveness, which is indicated by decreased nasal congestion, sneezing, watery or red eyes, and itching nose, palate, or eyes.

Patient & Family Education

■ Note: Drug is well tolerated and causes minimal adverse effects.

FILGRASTIM

(fil-gras'tim)
Neupogen
Classifications: BLOOD FORMER; HEMATOPOIETIC GROWTH FACTOR
Therapeutic: ANTINEUTROPENIC; GRANULOCYTE COLONY-STIMULATING FACTOR (G-CSF)
Prototype: Epoetin alfa
Pregnancy Category: C

AVAILABILITY 300 mcg/mL injection

ACTION & *THERAPEUTIC EFFECT*
Human granulocyte colony-stimulating factor (G-CSF) produced by recombinant DNA technology. Endogenous G-CSF regulates the production of neutrophils within the bone marrow; primarily affects neutrophil proliferation, differentiation, and selected end-cell functional activity (including enhanced phagocytic activity and antibody-dependent killing). *Increases neutrophil proliferation and differentiation within the bone marrow.*

USES To decrease the incidence of infection, as manifested by febrile neutropenia, in patients with non-myeloid malignancies receiving myelosuppressive anticancer drugs associated with a significant incidence of severe neutropenia with fever; to decrease neutropenia associated with bone marrow transplant; to treat chronic neutropenia; to mobilize peripheral blood stem cells (PBSCs) for autologous transplantation.

CONTRAINDICATIONS Hypersensitivity to *Escherichia coli*–derived proteins, simultaneous administration with chemotherapy, radiation, or myeloid cancers; ARDS; pregnancy (category C).
CAUTIOUS USE Sickle cell disease; lactation.

ROUTE & DOSAGE

Neutropenia

Adult/Child: **IV** 5 mcg/kg/d by 30 min infusion, may increase by 5 mcg/kg/d (max: 30 mcg/kg/d) **SC** 5 mcg/kg/d as single dose, may increase by 5 mcg/kg/d (max: 20 mcg/kg/d)

ADMINISTRATION

Subcutaneous & Intravenous
- Do not administer filgrastim 24 h before or after cytotoxic chemotherapy. ▪ Use only one dose per vial; do not reenter the vial.
- Prior to injection, filgrastim may be allowed to reach room temperature for a maximum of 6 h. Discard any vial left at room temperature for >6 h.

PREPARE: Intermittent/Continuous: May dilute with 10–50 mL D5W to yield 15 mcg/mL or greater. If more diluent is used to yield concentrations of 5–15 mcg/mL, 2 mL of 5% human albumin must be added for each 50 mL D5W (prior to adding filgrastim) to prevent adsorption to plastic IV infusion materials.

ADMINISTER: Intermittent: Give a single dose over 15–30 min. **Continuous:** Give a single dose over 4–24 h.

INCOMPATIBILITIES Y-site: Amphotericin B, cefepime, cefoperazone, cefotaxime, cefoxitin, ceftizoxime, ceftriaxone, cefuroxime, clindamycin, dactinomycin, etoposide, fluorouracil, furosemide, gentamicin, heparin, imipenem, mannitol, methylprednisolone, metronidazole, mitomycin, piperacillin, prochlorperazine, thiotepa.

- Store refrigerated at 2°–8° C (36°–46° F). Do not freeze. Avoid shaking.

ADVERSE EFFECTS (≥1%) **CV:** Abnormal ST segment depression. **Hematologic:** Anemia. **GI:** Nausea, anorexia. **Body as a Whole:** *Bone pain,* hyperuricemia, *fever.*

DIAGNOSTIC TEST INTERFERENCE
Elevations in **leukocyte alkaline phosphatase, serum alkaline phosphatase, lactate dehydrogenase,** and **uric acid** have been reported. These elevations appear to be related to increased bone marrow activity.

INTERACTIONS Drug: Can interfere with activity of CYTOTOXIC AGENTS, do not use 24 h before or after CYTOTOXIC AGENTS

PHARMACOKINETICS Absorption: Readily from SC site. **Onset:** 4 h. **Peak:** 1 h. **Elimination:** Probably in urine. **Half-Life:** 1.4–7.2 h.

CLINICAL IMPLICATIONS

Assessment & Drug Effects
- Lab tests: Obtain a baseline CBC with differential and platelet count prior to administering drug. Obtain CBC twice weekly during therapy to monitor neutrophil count and leukocytosis. Monitor Hct and platelet count regularly.
- Discontinue filgrastim if absolute neutrophil count exceeds 10,000/mm^3 after the chemotherapy-induced nadir. Neutrophil counts should then return to normal.
- Monitor patients with preexisting cardiac conditions closely. MI and arrhythmias have been associated with a small percent of patients receiving filgrastim.
- Monitor temperature q4h. Incidence of infection should be reduced after administration of filgrastim.
- Assess degree of bone pain if present. Consult physician if non-narcotic analgesics do not provide relief.

Patient & Family Education
- Report bone pain and, if necessary, to request analgesics to control pain.

Common adverse effects in *italic*, life-threatening effects underlined; generic names in **bold**; classifications in SMALL CAPS; ✦ Canadian drug name; ☯ Prototype drug

637

■Note: Proper drug administration and disposal are important. A puncture-resistant container for the disposal of used syringes and needles should be available to the patient.

F

FINASTERIDE ℗

(fin-as'te-ride)
Propecia, Proscar
Classifications: HORMONE; ANTI-ANDROGEN; 5-ALPHA REDUCTASE INHIBITOR
Therapeutic: ANTIANDROGEN
Pregnancy Category: X

AVAILABILITY 1 mg, 5 mg tablets

ACTION & *THERAPEUTIC EFFECT*
Specific inhibitor of the steroid 5-alpha-reductase, an enzyme necessary to convert testosterone into the potent androgen 5-alpha-dihydrotestosterone (DHT) in the prostate gland. *Decreases the production of testosterone in the prostate gland.*

USES Benign prostatic hypertrophy, male pattern hair loss (androgenetic alopecia).

CONTRAINDICATIONS Hypersensitivity to finasteride; pregnancy (category X), lactation, females, and children.
CAUTIOUS USE Hepatic impairment, obstructive uropathy.

ROUTE & DOSAGE

Benign Prostatic Hypertrophy
Adult: **PO** 5 mg/d

Male Pattern Hair Loss
Adult: **PO** 1 mg q.d.

ADMINISTRATION
Oral
■Crush tablets if necessary. Pregnant women should not handle the crushed drug; if absorbed through the skin it may be harmful to a male fetus.
■Store at 15°–30° C (59°–86° F) unless otherwise directed.

ADVERSE EFFECTS (≥1%) **Urogenital:** Impotence, decreased libido, decreased volume of ejaculate.

DIAGNOSTIC TEST INTERFERENCE Depresses levels of **DHT** and **prostate-specific antigen (PSA)**. **Testosterone** levels usually are increased.

INTERACTIONS Drug: No clinically significant interactions established. **Herbal: Saw palmetto** may potentiate effects of finasteride.

PHARMACOKINETICS Absorption: Readily from GI tract. **Onset:** 3–6 mo. **Duration:** 5–7 d. **Elimination:** 39% in urine, 57% in feces. **Half-Life:** 5–7 h.

CLINICAL IMPLICATIONS
Assessment & Drug Effects
■Evaluate carefully any sustained increase in serum PSA levels while patient is taking finasteride. It may indicate the presence of prostate cancer or noncompliance with the therapy.
■Monitor patients with a large residual urinary volume or decreased urinary flow. These patients may not be candidates for this therapy.

Patient & Family Education
■Use a barrier contraceptive to prevent pregnancy in a sexual partner.
■Be aware that impotence and decreased libido may occur with treatment.

Common adverse effects in *italic*, life-threatening effects underlined; generic names in **bold**; classifications in SMALL CAPS; ♣ Canadian drug name; ℗ Prototype drug

FLAVOXATE HYDROCHLORIDE

(fla-vox'ate)

Urispas

Classifications: ANTICHOLINERGIC; ANTISPASMODIC

Therapeutic: URINARY TRACT ANTISPASMODIC

Prototype: Atropine

Pregnancy Category: C

AVAILABILITY 100 mg tablets

ACTION & *THERAPEUTIC EFFECT*

Exerts spasmolytic (papaverine-like) action on smooth muscle. Reported to produce an increase in urinary bladder capacity in patients with spastic bladder, possibly by direct action on detrusor muscle. Also demonstrates local anesthetic and analgesic action. *Has antispasmodic action on the urinary bladder.*

USES Symptomatic relief of dysuria, frequency, urgency, nocturia, incontinence, and suprapubic pain associated with various urologic disorders.

CONTRAINDICATIONS Pyloric or duodenal obstruction, obstructive intestinal lesions, ileus, achalasia, GI hemorrhage; obstructive uropathies of lower urinary tract; pregnancy (category C). Safety in children <12 y is not established.

CAUTIOUS USE Elderly; suspected or closed-angle glaucoma; myasthenia gravis; autonomic neuropathy; dehydration.

ROUTE & DOSAGE

Dysuria, Nocturia, Incontinence
Adult: **PO** 100–200 mg t.i.d. or q.i.d.

ADMINISTRATION

Oral
- Give without regard to meals.
- Store at 15°–30° C (59°–86° F) unless otherwise directed.

ADVERSE EFFECTS (≥1%) **CNS:** Headache, vertigo, drowsiness, mental confusion (especially in older adults). **CV:** Palpitation, tachycardia. **Special Senses:** Blurred vision, increased intraocular tension, disturbances of eye accommodation. **GI:** Nausea, vomiting, dry mouth (and throat), constipation (with high doses). **Skin:** Dermatosis, urticaria. **Other:** Dysuria, hyperpyrexia, eosinophilia, leukopenia (rare).

INTERACTIONS Drug: May antagonize the GI motility effects of **metoclopramide.**

PHARMACOKINETICS Elimination: 10–30% in urine within 6 h.

CLINICAL IMPLICATIONS

Assessment & Drug Effects
- Monitor heart rate. Take apical pulse for 1 full minute. Report tachycardia.
- Lab tests: Obtain periodic evaluation of blood counts during therapy.

Patient & Family Education
- Do not drive or engage in potentially hazardous activities until response to drug is known.
- Report adverse reactions to physician as well as clinical improvement or the lack of a favorable response.

FLECAINIDE ⊕

(fle-kay'nide)

Tambocor

Common adverse effects in *italic*, life-threatening effects underlined; generic names in **bold**; classifications in SMALL CAPS; ♣ Canadian drug name; ⊙ Prototype drug

639

Classifications: ANTIARRHYTHMIC, CLASS IC
Therapeutic: ANTIARRHYTHMIC, CLASS IC
Pregnancy Category: C

AVAILABILITY 50 mg, 100 mg, 150 mg tablets

ACTION & *THERAPEUTIC EFFECT*
Local (membrane) anesthetic and antiarrhythmic with electrophysiologic properties similar to other class IC antiarrhythmic drugs. Slows conduction velocity throughout myocardial conduction system, increases ventricular refractoriness. *Is an effective suppressant of PVCs and a variety of atrial and ventricular arrhythmias.*

USES Life-threatening ventricular arrhythmias.
UNLABELED USES Atrial tachycardia and other arrhythmias unresponsive to standard agents (e.g., quinidine), Wolff-Parkinson-White syndrome, and recurrent ventricular tachycardias.

CONTRAINDICATIONS Hypersensitivity to flecainide; preexisting second- or third-degree AV block, right bundle branch block when associated with a left hemiblock unless a pacemaker is present; cardiogenic shock, significant hepatic impairment; CHF, acute MI; QT prolongation syndromes; electrolyte imbalances; pregnancy (category C).
CAUTIOUS USE Atrial fibrillation; cardiac disease; elderly; sick sinus syndrome, renal impairment; children and infants.

ROUTE & DOSAGE

Life-threatening Ventricular Arrhythmias
Adult: **PO** 100 mg q12h, may increase by 50 mg b.i.d. q4d (max: 400 mg/d)

Child: **PO** 1–3 mg/kg/d in 3 divided doses (max: 8 mg/kg/d)

ADMINISTRATION
Oral
- Do not increase dosage more frequently than every 4 d.
- Store in tightly covered, light-resistant containers at 15°–30° C (59°–86° F) unless otherwise directed.

ADVERSE EFFECTS (≥1%) **CNS:** *Dizziness,* headache, light-headedness, unsteadiness, paresthesias, fatigue. **CV:** Arrhythmias, chest pain, worsening of CHF. **Special Senses:** *Blurred vision, difficulty in focusing,* spots before eyes. **GI:** *Nausea,* constipation, change in taste perception. **Body as a Whole:** Dyspnea, fever, edema.

INTERACTIONS Drug: Cimetidine may increase flecainide levels; may increase **digoxin** levels 15–25%; BETA BLOCKERS may have additive negative inotropic effects.

PHARMACOKINETICS Absorption: Readily from GI tract. **Peak:** 2–3 h. **Distribution:** Crosses placenta; distributed into breast milk. **Metabolism:** In liver. **Elimination:** Mainly in urine. **Half-Life:** 7–22 h.

CLINICAL IMPLICATIONS
Assessment & Drug Effects
- Correct preexisting hypokalemia or hyperkalemia before treatment is initiated.
- Note: ECG monitoring, including Holter monitor for ambulating patients, is essential because of the possibility of drug-induced arrhythmias.
- Determine pacing threshold for patients with pacemakers before initiation of therapy, after 1 wk of therapy, and at regular intervals thereafter.

Common adverse effects in *italic,* life-threatening effects underlined; generic names in **bold**; classifications in SMALL CAPS; ♣ Canadian drug name; ☯ Prototype drug

- Monitor plasma level recommended, especially in patients with severe CHF or renal failure because drug elimination may be delayed in these patients.
- Note: Effective trough plasma levels are between 0.7–1 mcg/mL. The probability of adverse reactions increases when trough levels exceed 1 mcg/mL.
- Attempt dosage reduction with caution after arrhythmia is controlled.

Patient & Family Education
- Note: It is VERY important to take this drug at the prescribed times.
- Report visual disturbances to physician.

FLOXURIDINE

(flox-yoor′i-deen)
FUDR

Classifications: ANTINEOPLASTIC; ANTIMETABOLITE, PYRIMIDINE
Therapeutic: ANITNEOPLASTIC; ANTI-METABOLITE
Prototype: Fluorouracil
Pregnancy Category: D

AVAILABILITY 500 mg powder for injection

ACTION & *THERAPEUTIC EFFECT*
Pyrimidine antagonist and cell-cycle specific. Catabolized to fluorouracil in the body; highly toxic because it blocks an enzyme essential to normal DNA and RNA synthesis. *Proliferative cells of neoplasms are affected more than healthy tissue cells.*

USES Palliative agent in management of selected patients with GI metastasis to liver.
UNLABELED USES Carcinoma of breast, ovary, cervix, urinary bladder, and prostate not responsive to other antimetabolites.

CONTRAINDICATIONS Existing or recent viral infections; pregnancy (category D); lactation.
CAUTIOUS USE Poor nutritional status, bone marrow depression, serious infections; high-risk patients: prior high-dose pelvic irradiation, use of alkylating agents; impaired kidney or liver function.

ROUTE & DOSAGE

Carcinoma
Adult: **Intraarterial** 0.1–0.6 mg/kg/d by continuous intraarterial infusion

ADMINISTRATION

Intraarterial Infusion

PREPARE: **Direct:** Reconstitute with 5 mL sterile distilled water for injection; further dilute with D5W or NS injection to a volume appropriate for the infusion apparatus to be used.
ADMINISTER: **Direct:** It is administered by pump to overcome pressure in large arteries and to ensure a uniform rate. Examine infusion site frequently for signs of extravasation. If this occurs, stop infusion and restart in another vessel.
INCOMPATIBILITIES **Y-site: Allopurinol, cefepime.**

- Keep reconstituted solutions, which are stable at 2°–8° C (36°–46° F), for no more than 2 wk. ▪ Store at 15°–30° C (59°–86° F) unless otherwise directed.

ADVERSE EFFECTS (≥1%) **CNS:** Vertigo, convulsions, depression, hemiplegia. **CV:** Myocardial ischemia, angina. **GI:** *Nausea, vomit-*

Common adverse effects in *italic*, life-threatening effects underlined; generic names in **bold**; classifications in SMALL CAPS; ✦ Canadian drug name; ✿ Prototype drug

641

ing, stomatitis, diarrhea, cramps, anorexia, enteritis, gastritis, esophagopharyngitis. **Hematologic:** Leuko<u>penia</u>, *thrombocytopenia.* **Skin:** Dermatitis, alopecia (usually reversible), *erythema* or increased skin pigmentation (photosensitivity), dry skin, pruritic ulcerations, rash. **Body as a Whole:** Hiccups, fever, epistaxis, decreased resistance to disease. **Urogenital:** Renal insufficiency.

INTERACTIONS Drug: Metronidazole may increase general floxuridine toxicity; may increase or decrease serum levels of **phenytoin, fosphenytoin; hydroxyurea** can decrease conversion to active metabolite.

PHARMACOKINETICS Distribution: Distributed to tumor, intestinal mucosa, bone marrow, liver, and CSF; probably crosses placenta. **Metabolism:** Rapidly metabolized in liver to fluorouracil. **Elimination:** 15% excreted in urine, 60–80% excreted through lungs as carbon dioxide. **Half-Life:** 16 min.

CLINICAL IMPLICATIONS

Assessment & Drug Effects
- Discontinue therapy promptly with onset of any of the following: Stomatitis, esophagopharyngitis, intractable vomiting, diarrhea, leukopenia (WBC <3500/mm^3), or rapidly falling WBC count, thrombocytopenia (platelets 100,000/mm^3), GI bleeding, hemorrhage from any site.
- Lab tests: Obtain baseline and periodic total and differential leukocyte counts, Hct, platelet count, serum uric acid creatinine, and liver function tests.

Patient & Family Education
- Be aware that floxuridine sometimes causes temporary thinning of hair.

FLUCONAZOLE ℗

(flu-con'a-zole)
Diflucan
Classifications: ANTIBIOTIC; AZOLE ANTIFUNGAL
Therapeutic: AZOLE ANTIFUNGAL ANTIBIOTIC
Pregnancy Category: C

AVAILABILITY 50 mg, 100 mg, 150 mg, 200 mg tablets; 10 mg/mL, 40 mg/mL suspension; 2 mg/mL injection

ACTION & *THERAPEUTIC EFFECT* Fungistatic, but may also be fungicidal depending on concentration. Interferes with formation of ergosterol, the principal sterol in the fungal cell membrane leading to cell death. *Antifungal properties are related to the drug effect on the functioning of fungal cell membrane.*

USES Cryptococcal meningitis and oropharyngeal and systemic candidiasis, both commonly found in AIDS and other immunocompromised patients; vaginal candidiasis.

CONTRAINDICATIONS Hypersensitivity to fluconazole or other azole antifungals; pregnancy (category C). **CAUTIOUS USE** AIDS or malignancy; hepatic impairment; structural cardiac disease; history of torsades de pointes; renal impairment or failure; lactation.

ROUTE & DOSAGE

Oropharyngeal Candidiasis
Adult: **PO/IV** 200 mg day 1, then 100 mg/d × 14 d
Child: **PO/IV** 3–6 mg/kg/d × 14 d

Esophageal Candidiasis
Adult: **PO/IV** 200 mg day 1, then 100 mg q.d. × 3 wk
Child: **PO/IV** 3–6 mg/kg/d × 21 d

Systemic Candidiasis

Adult: **PO/IV** 400 mg day 1, then 200 mg q.d. × 4 wk
Child: **PO/IV** 6 mg/kg q12h × 28 d

Vaginal Candidiasis

Adult: **PO** 150 mg × 1 dose

Cryptococcal Meningitis

Adult: **PO/IV** 400 mg day 1, then 200 mg q.d. × 10–12 wk
Child: **PO/IV** 12 mg/kg day 1 then, 6–12 mg/kg/d × 10–12 wk

ADMINISTRATION

Oral

- Take this medication for the full course of therapy, which may take weeks or months.
- Take next dose as soon as possible if you miss a dose; however, do not take a dose if it is almost time for next dose. Do not double dose.

Intravenous

PREPARE: **Continuous:** Packaged ready for use as a 2 mg/mL solution. Remove wrapper just prior to use.

ADMINISTER: **Continuous:** Give at a maximum rate of approximately 200 mg/h. Give after hemodialysis is completed.

- Do not use IV admixtures of fluconazole and other medications.

INCOMPATIBILITIES **Solution/additive:** Trimethoprim-sulfamethoxazole. **Y-site:** Amphotericin B, amphotericin B cholesteryl, ampicillin, calcium gluconate, ceftazidime, ceftriaxone, cefuroxime, chloramphenicol, clindamycin, diazepam, digoxin, erythromycin, furosemide, haloperidol, hydroxyzine, imipenem-cilastatin, pentamidine, piperacillin, ticarcillin, trimethoprim-sulfamethoxazole.

ADVERSE EFFECTS (≥1%) **CNS:** Headache. **GI:** Nausea, vomiting, abdominal pain, diarrhea, increase in AST in patients with cryptococcal meningitis and AIDS. **Skin:** Rash.

INTERACTIONS Drug: Increased PT in patients on **warfarin;** may increase **alosetron, bexarotene, phenytoin, cevimeline, cilostazol, cyclosporine, dihydroergotamine, ergotamine, dofetilide, haloperidol, levobupivicaine, modafinil, zonisamide** levels and toxicity; hypoglycemic reactions with ORAL SULFONYLUREAS; decreased fluconazole levels with **rifampin, cimetidine;** may prolong the effects of **fentanyl, alfentanil, methadone.**

PHARMACOKINETICS Absorption: 90% from GI tract. **Peak:** 1–2 h. **Distribution:** Widely distributed, including CSF. **Metabolism:** 11% of dose metabolized in liver. **Elimination:** In urine. **Half-Life:** 20–50 h.

CLINICAL IMPLICATIONS

Assessment & Drug Effects

- Monitor for allergic response. Patients allergic to other azole antifungals may be allergic to fluconazole.
- Lab tests: Monitor BUN, serum creatinine, and liver function.
- Note: Drug may cause elevations of the following laboratory serum values: ALT, AST, alkaline phosphatase, bilirubin.
- Monitor for S&S of hepatotoxicity.

Patient & Family Education

- Monitor carefully for loss of glycemic control if diabetic.
- Inform physician of all medications being taken.

Common adverse effects in *italic*, life-threatening effects underlined; generic names in **bold**; classifications in SMALL CAPS; ♣ Canadian drug name; ⦿ Prototype drug

643

FLUCYTOSINE

(floo-sye'toe-seen)
Ancobon, Ancotil ✦

Classifications: ANTIBIOTIC; ANTI-FUNGAL
Therapeutic: ANTIBIOTIC; ANTIFUNGAL
Prototype: Fluconazole
Pregnancy Category: C

AVAILABILITY 250 mg, 500 mg capsules

ACTION & *THERAPEUTIC EFFECT*
Ineffective for cancerous tumors possibly because it does not enter mammalian cells. Selectively penetrates fungal cell and is converted to fluorouracil, an antimetabolite believed to be responsible for antifungal activity. *Has antifungal activity against* Cryptococcus *and* Candida *as well as* Chromomycosis.

USES Alone or in combination with amphotericin B for serious systemic infections caused by susceptible strains of *Cryptococcus* and *Candida* species.
UNLABELED USES *Chromomycosis.*

CONTRAINDICATIONS Pregnancy (category C), lactation.
CAUTIOUS USE Extreme caution in impaired kidney function; hepatic disease; electrolyte imbalance; bone marrow depression, hematologic disorders, patients being treated with or having received radiation or bone marrow depressant drugs.

ROUTE & DOSAGE

Fungal Infection
Adult: PO 50–150 mg/kg/d divided q6h
Child: PO <50 kg, 1.5–4.5 g/m²/d divided q6h; >50 kg, 50–150 mg/kg/d divided q6h

Neonate: PO 50–100 mg/kg/d in 1–2 divided doses

ADMINISTRATION

Oral
- Give lower dosages with longer dosage intervals in patients with serum creatinine of 1.7 mg/dL or higher. Check with physician.
- Give capsules a few at a time over 15 min to decrease incidence and severity of nausea and vomiting.
- Store in light-resistant containers at 15°–30° C (59°–86° F).

ADVERSE EFFECTS (≥1%) **CNS:** Confusion, hallucinations, headache, sedation, vertigo. **GI:** Nausea, vomiting, diarrhea, abdominal bloating, enterocolitis. **Hematologic:** Hypoplasia of bone marrow: anemia, leukopenia, thrombocytopenia, <u>agranulocytosis</u>, eosinophilia. **Skin:** Rash. **Metabolic:** Elevated levels of serum alkaline phosphatase, AST, ALT, BUN, serum creatinine. **GI:** Hepatomegaly, hepatitis.

DIAGNOSTIC TEST INTERFERENCE False elevations of *serum creatinine* can occur with *Ektachem analyzer.*

INTERACTIONS Drug: Amphotericin B produces additive or synergistic effects and can increase flucytosine toxicity by inhibiting its renal clearance.

PHARMACOKINETICS Absorption: Readily from GI tract. **Peak:** 2 h. **Distribution:** Widely distributed in body tissues including aqueous humor and CSF; crosses placenta. **Metabolism:** Minimal. **Elimination:** 75–90% in urine unchanged. **Half-Life:** 3–6 h.

CLINICAL IMPLICATIONS

Assessment & Drug Effects
- C&S tests should be performed before initiation of therapy and at

weekly intervals during therapy. Organism resistance has been reported.

- Lab tests: Obtain baseline hematology, kidney and liver function on all patients before and at frequent intervals during therapy. Twice weekly leukocyte and differential counts with WBC with differential and platelet counts are recommended.
- Do frequent assays of blood drug level, especially in patients with impaired kidney function to determine adequacy of drug excretion (therapeutic range: 25–120 mg/mL).
- Monitor I&O. Report change in I&O ratio or pattern. Because most of drug is eliminated unchanged by kidneys, compromised function can lead to drug accumulation.

Patient & Family Education

- Report fever, sore mouth or throat, and unusual bleeding or bruising tendency to physician.
- Be aware that the general duration of therapy is 4–6 wk, but it may continue for several months.

FLUDARABINE

(flu-dar′a-bine)
Fludara

Classifications: ANTINEOPLASTIC; ANTIMETABOLITE, PURINE ANTAGONIST; IMMUNOSUPPRESSANT
Therapeutic: ANTINEOPLASTIC; ANTIMETABOLITE; IMMUNOSUPPRESSANT
Prototype: Mercaptopurine
Pregnancy Category: D

AVAILABILITY 50 mg powder for injection; 25 mg/mL solution for injection

ACTION & *THERAPEUTIC EFFECT*
Believed to act by inhibiting DNA polymerase alpha, ribonucleotide reductase, and DNA primase, thus inhibiting DNA synthesis in tumor-sensitive cells. *Fludarabine has cytotoxic effects on lymphocytic leukemia and lymphoma as well as immunosuppressant properties.*

USES Treatment of B-cell chronic lymphocytic leukemia (CLL) in patients who fail to respond to a regimen containing at least one standard alkylating agent.
UNLABELED USES Non-Hodgkin's lymphoma; in combination therapy for the treatment of primary resistant or relapsing acute myelogenous leukemia (AML), acute lymphoblastic leukemia (ALL), and secondary AML; cutaneous T-cell lymphoma; macroglobulinemia; myelodysplastic syndrome; prolymphocytic leukemia (PLL); stem-cell transplant preparation.

CONTRAINDICATIONS Hypersensitivity to fludarabine; concomitant administration of pentostatin; pregnancy (category D); lactation. Safety and efficacy in children have not been established.
CAUTIOUS USE Renal impairment; patients at risk for tumor lysis syndrome; history of herpes or viral infection.

ROUTE & DOSAGE

Treatment of Unresponsive B-cell Chronic Lymphocytic Leukemia
Adult: **IV** 25 mg/m^2 q.d. × 5 d; repeat q28d
Renal Impairment
Cl$_{cr}$ 30–70 mL/min/1.73 m^2: 20% dose reduction
Cl$_{cr}$ <30 mL/min/1.73 m^2: should not receive fludarabine

---

Common adverse effects in *italic*, life-threatening effects underlined; generic names in **bold**; classifications in SMALL CAPS; ♣ Canadian drug name; ☻ Prototype drug

ADMINISTRATION

Intravenous

***PREPARE:* IV Infusion:** Exercise caution in the preparation and handling of fludarabine. Avoid exposure by inhalation or direct contact with skin or mucous membranes. Reconstitute each 50 mg vial by adding 2 mL of sterile water for injection to yield 25 mg/mL. The solution should dissolve within 15 s and have a pH of 7.2-8.2. Further dilute in 100–125 mL of D5W or NS. Administer within 8 h of reconstitution.

***ADMINISTER:* IV Infusion:** Give over 30 min.

***INCOMPATIBILITIES* Y-site:** Acyclovir, amphotericin B, chlorpromazine, daunorubicin, ganciclovir, hydroxyzine, miconazole, prochlorperazine.

- Store unreconstituted vials at 2°–8° C (36°–46° F). Discard any unused reconstituted product.

ADVERSE EFFECTS (≥1%) **Body as a Whole:** *Fever, chills, fatigue, infection, pain,* malaise, diaphoresis, anaphylaxis, hyperglycemia, dehydration. **CNS:** *Weakness,* paresthesia. **CV:** *Edema.* **GI:** *Nausea, vomiting, diarrhea, anorexia, stomatitis,* GI bleeding, esophagitis, mucositis. **Hematologic:** *Neutropenia, thrombocytopenia,* <u>hemolytic anemia</u>. **Musculoskeletal:** Myalgia. **Respiratory:** *Cough, pneumonia, dyspnea,* sinusitis, pharyngitis, upper respiratory tract infection. **Skin:** *Rash,* pruritus. **Special Senses:** Visual disturbance, hearing loss. **Urogenital:** Dysuria, urinary infection, hematuria.

INTERACTIONS Drug: Combined use with **pentostatin** increases the risk of severe pulmonary toxicity.

PHARMACOKINETICS Metabolism: Rapid conversion to active metabolite (2-fluoro-ara-A). **Elimination:** Renal. **Half-Life:** 7–12 h.

CLINICAL IMPLICATIONS

Assessment & Drug Effects

- Review creatinine clearance values prior to drug administration. A 20% dose reduction is recommended for Cl_{cr} 30–70 mL/min. Withhold drug and notify physician if Cl_{cr} <30 mL/min.
- Monitor for and report S&S of hemolysis, infection, tumor lysis syndrome (e.g., flank pain, hematuria), peripheral neuropathy, or respiratory distress.
- Lab tests: Baseline CBC with differential and platelet count, repeat prior to each treatment cycle, and more often as indicated; periodic serum electrolytes, serum uric acid, and renal function tests.

Patient & Family Education

- Report any of the following to a health care provider: fever, chills, cough, sore throat, or other signs of infection; pain or difficulty passing urine; signs of bleeding such as easy bruising, black, tarry stools, nosebleeds; signs of anemia such as excessive weakness, lightheadedness, or confusion; difficulty breathing or shortness of breath; decreased vision; mouth sores or skin rash.
- Avoid activities that could cause physical injury and predispose to severe bleeding.
- Women of childbearing age should avoid becoming pregnant while receiving decitabine.

FLUDROCORTISONE ACETATE ℗

(floo-droe-kor′ti-sone)

Florinef Acetate

Classifications: ADRENAL CORTI-COSTEROID; MINERALOCORTICOID; ANTIINFLAMMATORY AGENT

Therapeutic: ANTIINFLAMMATORY; CORTICOSTEROID

Pregnancy Category: C

AVAILABILITY 0.1 mg tablets

ACTION & *THERAPEUTIC EFFECT*
Long-acting synthetic steroid with potent mineralocorticoid activity. Small doses produce marked sodium retention, increased urinary potassium excretion, and elevated BP. *Synthetic corticosteroid replacement product for adrenocortical insufficiency.*

USES Partial replacement therapy for adrenocortical insufficiency and for treatment of salt-losing forms of congenital adrenogenital syndrome.

UNLABELED USES To increase systolic and diastolic blood pressure in patients with severe hypotension secondary to diabetes mellitus or to levodopa therapy.

CONTRAINDICATIONS Hypersensitivity to glucocorticoids, idiopathic thrombocytopenic purpura, psychoses, acute glomerulonephritis, viral or bacterial diseases of skin, infections not controlled by antibiotics, active or latent amebiasis, hypercorticism (Cushing's syndrome), smallpox vaccination or other immunologic procedures; pregnancy (category C). Topical steroids are contraindicated in presence of varicella, vaccinia, on surfaces with compromised circulation, and in children <2 y.

CAUTIOUS USE Children; diabetes mellitus; chronic, active hepatitis positive for hepatitis B surface antigen; hyperlipidemia; cirrhosis; stromal herpes simplex; glaucoma, tuberculosis of eye; osteoporosis; convulsive disorders; hypothyroidism; diverticulitis; nonspecific ulcerative colitis; fresh intestinal anastomoses; active or latent peptic ulcer; gastritis; esophagitis; thromboembolic disorders; CHF; metastatic carcinoma; hypertension; renal insufficiency; history of allergies; active or arrested tuberculosis; systemic fungal infection; myasthenia gravis; lactation.

ROUTE & DOSAGE

Adrenocortical Insufficiency
Adult: **PO** 0.1 mg/d, may range from 0.1 mg 3 times/wk to 0.2 mg/d
Child: **PO** 0.05–0.1 mg/d

Salt-Losing Adrenogenital Syndrome
Adult: **PO** 0.1–0.2 mg/d
Child: **PO** 0.05–0.1 mg/d

ADMINISTRATION

Oral
- Note: Concomitant oral cortisone or hydrocortisone therapy may be advisable to provide substitute therapy approximating normal adrenal activity.
- Store in airtight containers at 15°–30° C (59°–86° F). Protect from light.

ADVERSE EFFECTS (≥1%) **CNS:** Vertigo, headache, nystagmus, increased intracranial pressure with papilledema (usually after discontinuation of medication), mental disturbances, aggravation of preexisting psychiatric conditions, insomnia, ataxia (rare). **CV:** CHF, hypertension, thromboembolism (rare), tachycardia. **Endocrine:** Suppressed linear growth in children, decreased glucose tolerance; hyperglycemia, manifestations of latent diabetes mellitus; hypocorticism; amenorrhea and other menstrual

Common adverse effects in *italic*, life-threatening effects underlined; generic names in **bold**; classifications in SMALL CAPS; ✚ Canadian drug name; ◉ Prototype drug

647

difficulties. **Special Senses:** Posterior subcapsular cataracts (especially in children), glaucoma, exophthalmos, increased intraocular pressure with optic nerve damage, perforation of the globe. **Metabolic:** Hypocalcemia; *sodium and fluid retention;* hypokalemia and hypokalemic alkalosis, negative nitrogen balance, decreased serum concentration of vitamins A and C. **GI:** *Nausea,* increased appetite, ulcerative esophagitis, pancreatitis, abdominal distension, peptic ulcer with perforation and hemorrhage, melena. **Hematologic:** Thrombocytopenia. **Musculoskeletal:** (long-term use) Osteoporosis, compression fractures, muscle wasting and weakness, tendon rupture, aseptic necrosis of femoral and humeral heads. **Skin:** Skin thinning and atrophy, *acne, impaired wound healing;* petechiae, ecchymosis, easy bruising; suppression of skin test reaction; hypopigmentation or hyperpigmentation, hirsutism, acneiform eruptions, subcutaneous fat atrophy; allergic dermatitis, urticaria, angioneurotic edema, increased sweating. **Body as a Whole:** <u>Anaphylactoid reactions</u> (rare), <u>aggravation or masking of infections</u>; malaise, weight gain, obesity. **Urogenital:** Increased or decreased motility and number of sperm.

INTERACTIONS Drug: The antidiabetic effects of **insulin** and SULFONYLUREAS may be diminished; **amphotericin B,** DIURETICS may increase **potassium** loss; **warfarin** may decrease prothrombin time; **indomethacin, ibuprofen** can potentiate the pressor effect of fludrocortisone; ANABOLIC STEROIDS increase risk of edema and acne; **rifampin** may increase the hepatic metabolism of fludrocortisone.

PHARMACOKINETICS Absorption: Readily from GI tract. **Peak:** 1.7 h. **Metabolism:** In liver. **Half-Life:** 3.5 h.

CLINICAL IMPLICATIONS

Assessment & Drug Effects

- Monitor weight and I&O ratio to observe onset of fluid accumulation, especially if patient is on unrestricted salt intake and without potassium supplement. Report weight gain of 2 kg (5 lb)/wk.
- Monitor and record BP daily. If hypertension develops as a consequence of therapy, report to physician. Usually, the dose will be reduced to 0.05 mg/d.
- Check BP q4–6h and weight at least every other day during periods of dosage adjustment.
- Lab tests: Periodic serum electrolytes and ABGs during prolonged therapy.
- Monitor for S&S of hypokalemia and hyperkalemic metabolic alkalosis (see Appendix F).
- Monitor for signs of overdosage (hypercorticism): psychosis, excess weight gain, edema, congestive heart failure, ravenous appetite, severe insomnia, and increase in BP.
- Note: Signs of insufficient dosage (hypocorticism) are loss of weight and appetite, nausea, vomiting, diarrhea, muscular weakness, increased fatigue, and hypotension.

Patient & Family Education

- Report signs of hypokalemia (see Appendix F).
- Be aware of signs of potassium depletion associated with high sodium intake: Muscle weakness, paresthesias, circumoral numbness; fatigue, anorexia, nausea, mental depression, polyuria, delirium, diminished reflexes, arrhythmias, cardiac failure, ileus, ECG changes.

Common adverse effects in *italic*, life-threatening effects <u>underlined</u>; generic names in **bold**, classifications in SMALL CAPS; ♣ Canadian drug name; ● Prototype drug

- Advise patient to eat foods with high potassium content.
- Signs of edema should be reported immediately. Sodium intake may or may not require regulation, depending on individual needs and clinical situation.
- Weigh daily under standard conditions and report steady weight gain.
- Report intercurrent infection, trauma, or unexpected stress of any kind promptly when taking maintenance therapy.
- Carry medical identification at all times. It needs to indicate medical diagnosis, medication(s), physician's name, address, and telephone number.

FLUMAZENIL ℗

(flu-ma′ze-nil)

Mazicon ♦, Romazicon

Classifications: BENZODIAZEPINE ANTAGONIST

Therapeutic: BENZODIAZEPINE ANTIDOTE

Pregnancy Category: C

AVAILABILITY 0.1 mg/mL injection

ACTION & *THERAPEUTIC EFFECT*
Antagonizes the effects of benzodiazepine on the CNS, including sedation, impairment of recall, and psychomotor impairment. Does not reverse the effects of opioids. *Reverses the action of a benzodiazepine.*

USES Reversal of sedation induced by benzodiazepine for anesthesia or diagnostic or therapeutic procedures and through overdose.

UNLABELED USES Seizure disorders, alcohol intoxication, hepatic encephalopathy, facilitation of weaning from mechanical ventilation.

CONTRAINDICATIONS Hypersensitivity to flumazenil or to benzodiazepines; patients given a benzodiazepine for control of a life-threatening condition; patients showing signs of cyclic antidepressant overdose; seizure-prone individuals; during labor and delivery; pregnancy (category C).

CAUTIOUS USE Hepatic function impairment, older adults, lactation, intensive care patients, head injury, anxiety or pain disorder; drug- and alcohol-dependent patients, and physical dependence upon benzodiazepines.

ROUTE & DOSAGE

Reversal of Sedation

Adult: **IV** 0.2 mg over 15 sec, may repeat 0.2 mg each min for 4 additional doses or a cumulative dose of 1 mg
Child: **IV** 0.01 mg/kg may repeat each min (max dose: 1 mg)

Benzodiazepine Overdose

Adult: **IV** 0.2 mg over 30 sec, if no response after 30 sec, then 0.3 mg over 30 sec, may repeat with 0.5 mg each min (max: cumulative dose of 3 mg)

ADMINISTRATION

Intravenous

PREPARE: Direct: May give undiluted or diluted. If diluted use D5W, Lactated Ringer's, NS.

***ADMINISTER:* Direct (for reversal of anesthesia):** ■ Ensure patency of IV before administration of flumazenil, since extravasation will cause local irritation. ■ Do not give as bolus dose. Give through an IV that is freely flowing into a large vein. Give each dose slowly over 15 sec. Repeat at 60 sec intervals (see Route & Dosage). In high-risk patients,

Common adverse effects in *italic*, life-threatening effects underlined; generic names in **bold**; classifications in SMALL CAPS; ♦ Canadian drug name; ℗ Prototype drug

649

slow the rate to provide the smallest effective dose. ■ Use all diluted solutions within 24 h of dilution.

ADVERSE EFFECTS (≥1%) **CNS:** Emotional lability, headache, *dizziness*, agitation, *resedation*, seizures, blurred vision. **GI:** *Nausea, vomiting,* hiccups. **Other:** Shivering, pain at injection site, hypoventilation.

INTERACTIONS Drug: May antagonize effects of **zaleplon, zolpidem;** may cause convulsions or arrhythmias with TRICYCLIC ANTIDEPRESSANTS.

PHARMACOKINETICS Onset: 1–5 min. **Peak:** 6–10 min. **Duration:** 2–4 h. **Metabolism:** In the liver to inactive metabolites. **Elimination:** 90–95% in urine, 5–10% in feces within 72 h. **Half-Life:** 54 min.

CLINICAL IMPLICATIONS

Assessment & Drug Effects

■ Monitor respiratory status carefully until risk of resedation is unlikely (up to 120 min). Drug may not fully reverse benzodiazepine-induced ventilatory insufficiency.

■ Monitor carefully for seizures and take appropriate precautions.

Patient & Family Education

■ Do not drive or engage in potentially hazardous activities until at least 18–24 h after discharge following a procedure.

■ Do not ingest alcohol or nonprescription drugs for 18–24 h after flumazenil is administered or if the effects of the benzodiazepine persist.

FLUNISOLIDE

(floo-niss'oh-lide)
AeroBid, Nasalide, Nasarel
Pregnancy Category: C
See Appendix A-3.

FLUOCINOLONE ACETONIDE

(floo-oh-sin'oh-lone)
Fluoderm ◆, Synalar
Prototype: Hydrocortisone
Pregnancy Category: C
See Appendix A-4.

FLUOCINONIDE

(floo-oh-sin'oh-nide)
Lidemol, Lidex, Lidex-E, Lyderm, Topsyn, Vanos
Pregnancy Category: C
See Appendix A-4.

FLUORESCEIN SODIUM

(flure'e-seen)
Fluorescite
Classification: OPHTHALMIC DIAGNOSTIC AGENT
Therapeutic: OPHTHALMIC DIAGNOSTIC AGENT
Pregnancy Category: X

AVAILABILITY 100 mg/mL injection

ACTION & *THERAPEUTIC EFFECT* Mildly antiseptic fluorescent dye related chemically to phenolphthalein that demonstrates defects of the corneal epithelium. *Any break in the epithelial tissue allows the dye to enter the tissue. Epithelial damage will appear as a bright green area.*

USES Used IV as a diagnostic aid in retinal angiography. Also used as an antidote for aniline dye.

CONTRAINDICATIONS Intraarterial administration; intrathecal administration; pregnancy (category X).
CAUTIOUS USE History of hypersensitivity, allergies, bronchial asthma.

Common adverse effects in *italic*, life-threatening effects underlined; generic names in **bold**; classifications in SMALL CAPS; ◆ Canadian drug name; ⦿ Prototype drug

ROUTE & DOSAGE

Retinal Angiography

Adult: **IV** 5 mL of 10% solution or 3 mL of 25% solution injected rapidly in antecubital vein

Child: **IV** 7.5 mg/kg injected rapidly in antecubital vein

ADMINISTRATION

Intravenous

ADMINISTER: **Adult IV Direct:** 5 mL of 10% solution or 3 mL of 25% solution injected rapidly in antecubital vein. **Child IV Direct:** 7.5 mg/kg injected rapidly in antecubital vein.

ADVERSE EFFECTS (≥1%) **CNS:** Headache, paresthesias, pyrexia, convulsions. **CV:** Hypotension, transient dyspnea, acute pulmonary edema, basilar artery ischemia, syncope, <u>severe shock, cardiac arrest</u>. **GI:** Nausea, vomiting, strong metallic taste following high dosage. **Body as a Whole:** Hypersensitivity (urticaria, pruritus, angioneurotic edema, <u>anaphylactic reaction</u>). **Skin:** Thrombophlebitis at injection site, temporary discoloration of skin and urine.

CLINICAL IMPLICATIONS

Assessment & Drug Effects

- Have facilities for treatment of anaphylactic reaction immediately available (e.g., epinephrine 1:1000 for IV or IM use, an antihistamine, and oxygen).
- Discontinue fluorescein immediately if S&S of sensitivity develop.

Patient & Family Education

- Note: IV administration may impart a yellowish orange discoloration to skin and to urine. Skin discoloration usually fades in 6–12 h; urine clears in 24–36 h.

FLUOROMETHOLONE

(flure-oh-meth'oh-lone)

Fluor-Op, FML Forte, FML Liquifilm Ophthalmic

Pregnancy Category: C

See Appendix A-1.

FLUOROURACIL [5-FLUOROURACIL (5-FU)] Ⓟ

(flure-oh-yoor'a-sil)

Carac, Efudex, Fluoroplex

Classifications: ANTINEOPLASTIC AGENT; ANTIMETABOLITE, PYRIMIDINE

Therapeutic: ANTINEOPLASTIC

Pregnancy Category: D

AVAILABILITY 50 mg/mL injection; 1%, 2%, 5% topical solution; 0.5%, 1%, 5% topical cream

ACTION & *THERAPEUTIC EFFECT*

Pyrimidine antagonist and cell-cycle specific. Blocks action of enzymes essential to normal DNA and RNA synthesis and may become incorporated in RNA to form a fraudulent molecule; unbalanced growth and death of cell follow. Exhibits higher affinity for tumor tissue than healthy tissue. *Highly toxic, especially to proliferative cells in neoplasms, bone marrow, and intestinal mucosa. Low therapeutic index with high potential for severe hematologic toxicity.*

USES Systemically as single agent and in combination with other antineoplastics for palliative treatment of carefully selected patients with inoperable neoplasms of breast, colon or rectum, stomach, pancreas, urinary bladder, ovary, cervix, liver. Also topically for solar or actinic keratoses and superficial basal cell carcinoma.

UNLABELED USES To induce repigmentation in vitiligo; actinic cheili-

Common adverse effects in *italic*, life-threatening effects <u>underlined</u>; generic names in **bold**; classifications in SMALL CAPS; ◆ Canadian drug name; Ⓟ Prototype drug

651

tis; malignant effusions; mucosal leukoplakia.

CONTRAINDICATIONS Poor nutritional status; myelosuppression; pregnancy (category D), lactation.
CAUTIOUS USE Major surgery during previous month; history of high-dose pelvic irradiation, metastatic cell infiltration of bone marrow, previous use of alkylating agents; cardiac disease, CAD, angina; men and women in childbearing ages; hepatic or renal impairment.

ROUTE & DOSAGE

Carcinoma
Adult: **IV** 12 mg/kg/d for 4 consecutive days up to 800 mg or until toxicity develops or 12 d therapy, may repeat at 1 mo intervals; if toxicity develops, 15 mg/kg once weekly can be given until toxicity subsides

Actinic and Solar Keratosis
Adult: **Topical** Apply cream or solution b.i.d. for 2–4 wk; apply Carac once daily

Superficial Basal Cell Carcinoma
Adult: **Topical** Apply 5% cream b.i.d. for 3–6 wk

ADMINISTRATION

Topical
- Use gloved fingers to apply topical drug.
- Do not use occlusive dressings with topical drug. Use a porous gauze dressing for cosmetic purposes; does not cause inflammation.
- Note: Second-degree burns resulting from contact between plastic eyeglass frames and treated skin have been reported. Reduce risk of burns or irritation by treating skin that contacts frames only at night when glasses are not worn,

and using the lowest effective strength of topical preparation.
- Store at 15°–30° C (59°–86° F) unless otherwise directed. Protect from light and freezing.

Intravenous
Note: Parenteral dose is determined by actual weight unless patient is obese, in which case ideal weight is used.

- Safe Handling: Double-glove with latex gloves, and change the double set after every 30 min of exposure. If a drug spill occurs, change gloves immediately after it is cleaned up.

PREPARE: Direct: This drug may be given without dilution.
ADMINISTER: Direct: Give by direct IV injection over 1–2 min. Inspect injection site frequently; avoid extravasation. If it occurs, stop infusion and restart in another vein. Ice compresses may reduce danger of local tissue damage from infiltrated solution.
INCOMPATIBILITIES Solution/additive: Carboplatin, cisplatin, cytarabine, diazepam, doxorubicin, droperidol, epirubicin, fentanyl, leucovorin calcium, metoclopramide, morphine. Y-site: Amphotericin B cholesteryl, droperidol, filgrastim, ondansetron, TPN, **vinorelbine.**

- Fluorouracil solution is normally colorless to faint yellow. Slight discoloration during storage does not appear to affect potency or safety. Discard dark yellow solution. If a precipitate forms, redissolve drug by heating to 60° C (140° F) and shake vigorously. Allow to cool to body temperature before administration.

ADVERSE EFFECTS (≥1%) **CNS:** Euphoria, acute cerebellar syndrome (dysmetria, nystagmus, ataxia, severe mental deterioration); pustular contact hypersensitivity. **CV:** Cardiotoxicity (rare), angina. **GI:** Anorexia, *nausea, vomiting, stomatitis,* esophagopharyngitis, medicinal taste, *diarrhea,* proctitis. **Hematologic:** Anemia, leukopenia, thrombocytopenia, eosinophilia. **Body as a Whole:** Hypersensitivity: Pustular contact eruption, edema of face, eyes, tongue, legs. **Skin:** SLE-like dermatitis, *alopecia,* photosensitivity, erythema, increased pigmentation, skin dryness and fissuring, pruritic maculopapular rash. **[Topical]** Local pain, pruritus, hyperpigmentation, burning at site of application, dermatitis, suppuration, swelling, scarring, toxic granulation.

DIAGNOSTIC TEST INTERFERENCE
Fluorouracil may increase excretion of *5-hydroxyindoleacetic acid (5-HIAA)* and decrease *plasma albumin* (because of drug-induced protein malabsorption).

INTERACTIONS Drug: **Metronidazole** may increase general floxuridine toxicity; may increase or decrease serum levels of **phenytoin, fosphenytoin; hydroxyurea** can decrease conversion to active metabolite.

PHARMACOKINETICS Distribution: Distributed to tumor, intestinal mucosa, bone marrow, liver, and CSF; probably crosses placenta. **Metabolism:** In liver. **Elimination:** 15% in urine, 60–80% through lungs as carbon dioxide. **Half-Life:** 16 min.

CLINICAL IMPLICATIONS
Assessment & Drug Effects
▪ Lab tests: Obtain total and differential leukocyte counts before each dose is administered. Discontinue drug if leukopenia occurs (WBC <3500/mm³) or if patient develops thrombocytopenia (platelet count

<100,000/mm³). Baseline and periodic checks of Hct and liver and kidney function are also advised.
▪ Use protective isolation of patient during leukopenic period (WBC <3500/mm³).
▪ Watch for and report signs of abnormal bleeding from any source during thrombocytopenic period (day 7–17); inspect skin for ecchymotic and petechial areas. Protect patient from trauma.
▪ Report disorientation or confusion; drug should be withdrawn immediately.
▪ Establish a reference data base for body weight, I&O ratio and pattern, food preferences and dietary habits, bowel habits, and condition of mouth.
▪ Report intractable vomiting to physician.
▪ Indications to discontinue drug: Severe stomatitis, leukopenia (WBC <3500/mm³ or rapidly decreasing count), intractable vomiting, diarrhea, thrombocytopenia (platelets <100,000/mm³), and hemorrhage from any site.
▪ Inspect patient's mouth daily. Promptly report cracked lips, xerostomia, white patches, and erythema of buccal membranes.
▪ Report development of maculopapular rash; it usually responds to symptomatic treatment and is reversible.
▪ Be aware of expected response of lesion to topical 5-FU: Erythema followed in sequence by vesiculation, erosion, ulceration, necrosis, epithelialization. Applications of drug are continued until ulcerative stage is reached (2–6 wk after initial applications) and then discontinued.
▪ Note: Systemic toxicity may follow use of topical drug on large ulcerated area. Report symptoms promptly.

Patient & Family Education

- Understand that it is very important to report the first signs of toxicity: Anorexia, vomiting, nausea, stomatitis, diarrhea, GI bleeding.
- Schedule and make sure to complete periodic checks on liver and kidney function.
- Do not change dosage regimen (i.e., do not increase or omit doses or change dosage intervals).
- Avoid exposure to sunlight or ultraviolet lamp treatments. Protect exposed skin. Photosensitivity usually subsides 2–3 mo after last dose.
- Report promptly to physician any difficulty in maintaining balance while ambulating.
- Be aware that your hair may fall out; new hair growth usually begins within 6–8 wk.
- Use contraception during 5-FU treatment. If you suspect you are pregnant, tell your physician.

FLUOXETINE HYDROCHLORIDE ℗ᵣ

(flu'ox-e-tine)

Prozac, Prozac Weekly, Sarafem
Classifications: PSYCHOTHERAPEUTIC AGENT; SELECTIVE SEROTONIN REUPTAKE INHIBITOR (SSRI); ANTIDEPRESSANT
Therapeutic: ANTIDEPRESSANT; SSRI
Pregnancy Category: C

AVAILABILITY 10 mg tablets; 10 mg, 20 mg capsules; 20 mg/5 mL solution; 90 mg sustained-release capsules (Prozac Weekly)

ACTION & THERAPEUTIC EFFECT

A selective serotonin reuptake inhibitor (SSRI). Antidepressant effect is presumed to be linked to its inhibition of CNS neuronal uptake of serotonin, a neurotransmitter. *Effectiveness may take from several days to 5 wk to develop fully. Drug has antidepressant, antiobsessive-compulsive, and antibulimic actions.*

USES Depression, geriatric depression, obsessive-compulsive disorder (OCD), bulimia nervosa, premenstrual dysphoric disorder.
UNLABELED USES Obesity.

CONTRAINDICATIONS Hypersensitivity to fluoxetine or other SSRI drugs; concurrent administration with MAOIS, or thioridazine; pregnancy (category C), children <7 y for OCD, children <8 y for depression; suicidal ideation.
CAUTIOUS USE Hepatic and renal impairment, renal failure, abrupt discontinuation, anorexia nervosa, mania, bleeding; hyponatremia, cardiac disease, dehydration, diabetes mellitus, patients with history of suicidal ideations; seizure disorders, ECT, hepatic disease. Older adults may require dose adjustments; lactation.

ROUTE & DOSAGE

Depression, Obsessive-Compulsive Disorder

Adult: **PO** 20 mg/d in a.m., may increase by 20 mg/d at weekly intervals (max: 80 mg/d); 20 mg/d in a.m.; when stable may switch to 90 mg sustained-release capsule qwk (max: 90 mg/wk)
Child: **PO** > 7 y 10–20 mg/d in a.m. (max: 60 mg/d for OCD)
Geriatric: **PO** Start with 10 mg/d

Premenstrual Dysphoric Disorder

Adult: **PO** 10–20 mg q.d. (max: 60 mg/d)

Bulimia Nervosa

Adult: **PO** 60 mg q.d.

ADMINISTRATION

Oral

- Give as a single dose in morning. Give in two divided doses; one in

654

Common adverse effects in *italic*, life-threatening effects underlined; generic names in **bold**; classifications in SMALL CAPS; ◆ Canadian drug name; ℗ Prototype drug

a.m. and one at noon to prevent insomnia, when more than 20 mg/d prescribed.

- Provide suicidal or potentially suicidal patient with small quantities of prescription medication.
- Monitor for worsening of depression or expression of suicidal ideations.
- Store at 15°–25° C (59°–77° F).

ADVERSE EFFECTS (≥1%) **CNS:** *Headache, nervousness, anxiety, insomnia,* drowsiness, fatigue, tremor, dizziness. **CV:** Palpitations, hot flushes, chest pain. **GI:** *Nausea, diarrhea,* anorexia, dyspepsia, increased appetite, dry mouth. **Skin:** Rash, pruritus, sweating, hypersensitivity reactions. **Special Senses:** Blurred vision. **Body as a Whole:** Myalgias, arthralgias, flu-like syndrome, hyponatremia. **Urogenital:** Sexual dysfunction, menstrual irregularities.

INTERACTIONS Drug: Concurrent use of **tryptophan** may cause agitation, restlessness, and GI distress; MAO INHIBITORS, **selegiline** may increase risk of severe hypertensive reaction and death; increases half-life of **diazepam;** may increase toxicity of TRICYCLIC ANTIDEPRESSANTS; AMPHETAMINES, **cilostazol, nefazodone, pentazocine, propafenone, sibutramine, tramadol, venlafaxine** may increase risk of serotonin syndrome; may inhibit metabolism of **carbamazepine, phenytoin, ritonavir;** increased ergotamine toxicity with **dihydroergotamine, ergotamine.** ANTIPSYCHOTICS like **pimozide** can cause QT prolongation. **Herbal: St. John's wort** may cause serotonin syndrome.

PHARMACOKINETICS Absorption: 60–80% from GI tract. **Onset:** 1–3 wk. **Peak:** 4–8 h. **Distribution:** Widely distributed, including CNS.

Metabolism: In liver to active metabolite, norfluoxetine. **Elimination:** >80% in urine; 12% in feces. **Half-Life:** Fluoxetine 2–3 d, norfluoxetine 7–9 d.

CLINICAL IMPLICATIONS

Assessment & Drug Effects

- Monitor children and adolescents for changes in behavior and suicidal ideation.
- Use with caution in the older adult patient or patient with impaired renal or hepatic function (may need lower dose).
- Use with caution in anorexic patient, since weight loss is a possible side effect.
- Monitor for S&S of anaphylactoid reaction (see Appendix F).
- Lab tests: Periodic serum electrolytes; monitor closely plasma glucose in diabetes.
- Monitor serum sodium level for development of hyponatremia, especially in patients who are taking diuretics or are otherwise hypovolemic.
- Monitor diabetics for loss of glycemic control; hypoglycemia has occurred during initiation of therapy, and hyperglycemia during drug withdrawal.
- Monitor for S&S of improved affect. Requires approximately 2–3 wk for therapeutic effects to be felt.
- Weigh weekly to monitor weight loss, particularly in the older adult or nutritionally compromised patient. Report significant weight loss to physician.
- Observe for and promptly report rash or urticaria and S&S of fever, leukocytosis, arthralgias, carpal tunnel syndrome, edema, respiratory distress, and proteinuria. Drug may have to be discontinued or adjunctive therapy instituted with steroids or antihistamines.

Common adverse effects in *italic*, life-threatening effects underlined; generic names in **bold**; classifications in SMALL CAPS; ✦ Canadian drug name; ⊕ Prototype drug

- Observe for dizziness and drowsiness and employ safety measures (up with assistance, side rails, etc.) as indicated.
- Monitor for and report increased anxiety, nervousness, or insomnia; may need modification of drug dose.
- Monitor for seizures in patients with a history of seizures. Use appropriate safety precautions.
- Supervise patients closely who are high suicide risks; especially during initial therapy.
- Monitor patients with hepatic or renal impairment carefully for S&S of toxicity (e.g., agitation, restlessness, nausea, vomiting, seizures).

Patient & Family Education
- Notify physician of intent to become pregnant.
- Notify physician of any rash; possible sign of a serious group of adverse effects.
- Do not drive or engage in potentially hazardous activities until response to drug is known; especially if dizziness noted.
- Monitor blood glucose for loss of glycemic control if diabetic.
- Note: Drug may increase seizure activity in those with history of seizure.

FLUOXYMESTERONE

(floo-ox-ee-mess'te-rone)
Halotestin, Ora Testryl ♦

Classifications: HORMONE; ANDROGEN/ANABOLIC STEROID
Therapeutic: ANABOLIC STEROID; MALE HORMONE REPLACEMENT
Prototype: Testosterone
Pregnancy Category: X
Controlled Substance: Schedule III

AVAILABILITY 2 mg, 5 mg, 10 mg tablets

ACTION & *THERAPEUTIC EFFECT* Short-acting, orally effective derivative of testosterone with hypercholesterolemic effect. Retention of sodium is minimal; thus, hypertension and edema rarely complicate therapy. *Replacement therapy for endogenous testosterone. Promotes recalcification of osseous metastases and regression of soft tissue lesions.*

USES In men as replacement therapy in conditions associated with testicular hormone deficiency; in women to antagonize effects of estrogen in androgen-responsive inoperable breast cancer. Also in combination with estrogens for management of severe postmenopausal vasomotor symptoms.

CONTRAINDICATIONS Breast cancer in men, prostatic cancer, benign obstructive prostatic hypertrophy; hypercalcemia; diabetes mellitus; severe cardiorenal disease or liver damage; nephrosis or nephrotic phase of nephritis; history of MI; athletes; infants; women with inoperable mammary cancer <1 y or >5 y after menopause; pregnancy (category X), lactation.
CAUTIOUS USE Children, older males, history of MI, or coronary disease, hepatic, renal or congestive heart failure, women.

ROUTE & DOSAGE

Male Hypogonadism
Adult: **PO** 2.5–20 mg/d

Metastatic Carcinoma of Female Breast
Adult: **PO** 10–40 mg/d in divided doses

Postpartum Breast Engorgement
Adult: **PO** 2.5 mg shortly after delivery, then 5–10 mg/d in divided doses for 4–5 d

Common adverse effects in *italic*, life-threatening effects underlined; generic names in **bold**; classifications in SMALL CAPS; ♣ Canadian drug name; ☯ Prototype drug

ADMINISTRATION
Oral
- Give immediately before or with meals to diminish GI distress.

ADVERSE EFFECTS (≥1%) **Endocrine:** Virilization (women), gynecomastia (men). **Urogenital:** Priapism, impotence. **Metabolic:** Jaundice (reversible), hypoglycemia, hypercalcemia. **GI:** <u>Hepatocellular carcinoma</u>, peliosis hepatitis, nausea, vomiting, diarrhea, symptoms resembling peptic ulcer. **Body as a Whole:** <u>Anaphylactic reactions</u> (rare), *edema, acne.*

INTERACTIONS Drug: ORAL ANTICOAGULANTS increase risk of bleeding. Possibly increases risk of **cyclosporine** toxicity. **Insulin** and ORAL HYPOGLYCEMIC AGENTS may decrease **glucose** level; dose will need to be adjusted. **Herbal: Echinacea** may increase hepatotoxicity.

PHARMACOKINETICS Absorption: Readily from GI tract. **Metabolism:** In liver. **Half-Life:** 9.5 h.

CLINICAL IMPLICATIONS
Assessment & Drug Effects
- Lab test: Obtain baseline and periodic liver function and serum electrolytes, Hgb, Hct, and serum and urine calcium; also serial serum cholesterol in patients with history of MI or coronary artery disease.
- Monitor I&O ratio and pattern and weight, and check for edema; report significant changes.
- Monitor for S&S of hypercalcemia (see Appendix F); particularly likely in patients with metastatic breast carcinoma. Stop anabolic therapy if it develops.
- Be alert for voice change in female patient, an early sign of virilism. Virilism may be irreversible even after prompt discontinuation of therapy.

- Note: When used in pediatric patients, therapy is preceded by x-ray of wrist bones to establish level of bone maturation. During treatment, bone maturation may proceed more rapidly than linear growth; therefore, intermittent dosage schedule and periodic x-rays are usual.
- Observe children <7 y closely for precocious development of male sexual characteristics or masculinization because they are particularly sensitive to androgenic effects.
- Watch for symptoms of hypoglycemia (see Appendix F) and report to physician. Anabolic treatment may reduce blood glucose in diabetic patients.
- Observe patient on concomitant anticoagulant therapy for ecchymotic areas, petechiae, or abnormal bleeding from any site. Close monitoring of PT & INR is essential.
- Note: When used for palliation of mammary cancer, subjective effects of therapy may not be experienced for 1 mo; objective symptoms may be delayed for as long as 3 mo.
- Be aware that anabolic response may be evidenced by euphoria and gain in weight and appetite, especially in emaciated and debilitated patient.

Patient & Family Education
- Adhere to scheduled appointments for laboratory tests.
- Good personal hygiene, including meticulous skin care is very important (females and prepubertal males are especially likely to develop acne).
- Note and report symptoms of jaundice (see Appendix F) to physician. Dose adjustment may reverse the condition.
- Report menstrual irregularities.
- Keep child's appointments for bone maturation studies (usually

every 3–6 mo) to prevent compromised adult height.

- Report priapism (prolonged erection) to physician promptly, it is a symptom of overdosage. A temporary interruption of regimen may be indicated. Also report persistent GI distress, diarrhea, or the onset of jaundice.
- Be aware that virilization usually occurs. Report to physician any voice change (hoarseness or deepening), increased libido (associated with clitoral enlargement), hirsutism immediately. Usually, stopping therapy will end further development of symptoms but will not reverse hirsutism or voice change.

FLUPHENAZINE DECANOATE

(floo-fen′a-zeen)

Prolixin Decanoate, Modecate Decanoate ♦

FLUPHENAZINE ENANTHATE

Moditen Enanthate ♦, Prolixin Enanthate

FLUPHENAZINE HYDROCHLORIDE

Moditen HCl ♦, Permitil, Prolixin

Classifications: PSYCHOTHERAPEUTIC; ANTIPSYCHOTIC; PHENOTHIAZINE
Therapeutic: ANTIPSYCHOTIC
Prototype: Chlorpromazine
Pregnancy Category: C

AVAILABILITY 1 mg, 2.5 mg, 5 mg, 10 mg tablets; 2.5 mg/5 mL elixir; 5 mg/mL oral concentrate; 2.5 mg/mL, 25 mg/mL injection

ACTION & *THERAPEUTIC EFFECT*
Potent phenothiazine, antipsychotic agent. Blocks postsynaptic dopamine receptors in the brain. Similar to other phenothiazines with the following exceptions: more potent per weight, higher incidence of extrapyramidal complications, and lower frequency of sedative, hypotensive, and antiemetic effects. *Effective for treatment of antipsychotic symptoms including schizophrenia.*

USES Management of manifestations of psychotic disorders.
UNLABELED USES As antineuralgia adjunct.

CONTRAINDICATIONS Known hypersensitivity to phenothiazines; subcortical brain damage, comatose or severely depressed states, blood dyscrasias, renal or hepatic disease; pregnancy (category C), lactation. Parenteral form not recommended for children <12 y.
CAUTIOUS USE With anticholinergic agents, other CNS depressants; older adults, previously diagnosed breast cancer; closed-angle glaucoma; GI disorders; significant pulmonary disease; renal failure; seizure disorders; history of suicidal ideation or high risk for suicide attempt; cardiovascular diseases; pheochromocytoma; history of convulsive disorders; patients exposed to extreme heat or phosphorous insecticides; peptic ulcer; respiratory impairment.

ROUTE & DOSAGE

Psychosis

Adult: **PO** 0.5–10 mg/d in 1–4 divided doses (max: of 20 mg/d) **IM/SC HCl** 2.5–10 mg/d divided q6–8h (max: 10 mg/d); **Decanoate** 12.5–25 mg q1–4wk; **Enanthate** 25 mg q2wk

Dementia Behavior

Geriatric: **PO** 1–2.5 mg/d, may increase every 4–7 d by 1–2.5 mg/d (max: 20 mg/d in 2–3 divided doses)

ADMINISTRATION

▪ Note: Fluphenazine hydrochloride (HCl) is given PO and IM. Fluphenazine enanthate and decanoate are given IM or SC.

Oral

▪ Give sustained release tablets whole (need to be swallowed whole; not recommended for children).

▪ Dilute oral concentrate in fruit juice, water, carbonated beverage, milk, soup. Avoid caffeine-containing beverages (cola, coffee) as a diluent, also tannic acid (tea) or pectinates (apple juice).

▪ Be careful not to contact skin or clothing with drug when preparing oral concentrate or liquid preparations for injection. Warn patient to avoid spilling drug. If drug contacts skin, rinse/flush skin promptly with warm water.

▪ Give oral preparations at least 1 h before or 2 h after the antacid. Antacids diminish absorption.

▪ Protect all preparations from light and freezing. Solutions may safely vary in color from almost colorless to light amber. Discard dark or otherwise discolored solutions.

▪ Store in tightly closed container at 15°–30° C (59°–86° F) unless otherwise specified by manufacturer. Protect all forms from light.

ADVERSE EFFECTS (≥1%) CNS: *Extrapyramidal symptoms* (resembling Parkinson's disease), <u>tardive dyskinesia</u>, sedation, drowsiness, dizziness, headache, mental depression, catatonic-like state, <u>impaired thermoregulation</u>, grand mal seizures. **CV:** Tachycardia, hypertension, hypotension. **GI:** Dry mouth, nausea, epigastric pain, constipation, fecal impaction, cholecystic jaundice. **Urogenital:** Urinary retention, polyuria, inhibition of ejaculation. **Hematologic:** Transient leukopenia, <u>agranulocytosis</u>. **Skin:** Contact dermatitis. **Body as a Whole:** Peripheral edema. **Special Senses:** Nasal congestion, blurred vision, increased intraocular pressure, *photosensitivity*. **Endocrine:** Hyperprolactinemia.

INTERACTIONS Drug: Alcohol and other CNS DEPRESSANTS may potentiate depressive effects; decreases seizure threshold, may need to adjust dosage of ANTICONVULSANTS. **Herbal: Kava-kava** may increase risk and severity of dystonic reactions.

PHARMACOKINETICS Absorption: HCl is readily absorbed PO and IM; decanoate, enanthate have delayed IM absorption. **Onset:** 1 h HCl; 24–72 h decanoate, enanthate. **Peak:** 0.5 h PO; 1.5–2 h IM HCl. **Duration:** 6–8 h HCl; 1–6 wk decanoate; 2–4 wk enanthate. **Distribution:** Crosses blood–brain barrier and placenta. **Metabolism:** In liver. **Half-Life:** 15 h HCl; 3.6 d enanthate; 7–10 d decanoate.

CLINICAL IMPLICATIONS

Assessment & Drug Effects

▪ Report immediately onset of mental depression and extrapyramidal symptoms. Both occur frequently, particularly with long-acting forms (decanoate and enanthate).

▪ Be alert for appearance of acute dystonia (see Appendix F). Symptoms can be controlled by reducing dosage or by adding an antiparkinsonism drug such as benztropine.

▪ Be alert for red, dry, hot skin; full, bounding pulse, dilated pupils, dyspnea, mental confusion, elevated BP, temperature over 40.6° C (105° F). Inform physician and institute measures to reduce body temperature rapidly. Extended exposure to high environmental temperature, to sun's rays, or to a high

---

Common adverse effects in *italic*, life-threatening effects <u>underlined</u>; generic names in **bold**; classifications in SMALL CAPS; ♣ Canadian drug name; ⊘ Prototype drug

fever places the patient taking this drug at risk for heat stroke.

- Lab tests: Monitor kidney function in patients on long-term treatment. Withhold drug and notify physician if BUN is elevated (normal BUN: 10–20 mg/dL). Also perform WBC with differential, liver function tests, periodically.
- Monitor BP during early therapy. If systolic drop is more than 20 mm Hg, inform physician.
- Monitor I&O ratio and bowel elimination pattern. Check for abdominal distension and pain. Monitor for xerostomia and constipation.
- Monitor children with routine cardiac studies for signs and symptoms of cardiac adverse effects.
- Note: Patients on large doses who undergo surgery and those with cerebrovascular, cardiac, or renal insufficiency are especially prone to hypotensive effects.

Patient & Family Education

- Do not drive or engage in potentially hazardous activities until response to drug is known.
- Do not alter dosage regimen or stop taking drug abruptly. Do not give drug to any one else.
- Seek and obtain physician approval before taking any OTC drugs.
- Be alert for adverse effects, early detection is critical because both decanoate and enanthate have a long duration of action. Inform physician promptly if following symptoms appear: Light-colored stools, changes in vision, sore throat, fever, cellulitis, rash, any interference with your willful (volitional) movements.
- Make sure to eat and drink adequately in order to prevent constipation and dry mouth.
- Be aware that it may be difficult for you to adjust to extremes in

temperature. Use caution because of this possible impaired thermoregulation.

- Avoid exposure to sun; wear protective clothing and cover exposed skin surfaces with sun screen lotion (SPF above 12).
- Avoid alcohol while on fluphenazine therapy.
- Note: Fluphenazine may discolor urine pink to red or reddish brown.
- Periodic ophthalmologic exams are recommended.

FLURANDRENOLIDE

(flure-an-dren'oh-lide)
Cordran, Cordran SP, Drenison ◆
Pregnancy Category: C
See Appendix A-4.

FLURAZEPAM HYDROCHLORIDE

(flure-az'e-pam)
Apo-Flurazepam ◆, Dalmane, Novoflupam ◆
Classifications: ANXIOLYTIC; SEDATIVE-HYPNOTIC; BENZODIAZEPINE
Therapeutic: SEDATIVE-HYPNOTIC; ANTIANXIETY
Prototype: Lorazepam
Pregnancy Category: X
Controlled Substance: Schedule IV

AVAILABILITY 15 mg, 30 mg capsules

ACTION & *THERAPEUTIC EFFECT*
Benzodiazepine derivative, with hypnotic activity equal to or greater than that produced by barbiturates. Benzodiazepines enhance the GABA-benzodiazepine receptor complex. GABA is an inhibitory neurotransmitter involved in anxiolytic and sedative effects. Flurazepam appears to act at limbic

and subcortical levels of CNS to produce sedation, skeletal muscle relaxation, and anticonvulsant effects. *Reduces sleep induction time; produces marked reduction of stage 4 sleep (deepest sleep stage) while at the same time increasing duration of total sleep time.*

USES Hypnotic in management of all kinds of insomnia (e.g., difficulty in falling asleep, frequent nocturnal awakening or early morning awakening or both). Also for treatment of poor sleeping habits.

CONTRAINDICATIONS Prolonged administration; sleep apnea; benzodiazepine hypersensitivity; ethanol intoxication; COPD, sleep apnea; major depression or psychosis; intermittent porphyria; acute narrow-angle glaucoma; children <15 y; pregnancy (category X), lactation. **CAUTIOUS USE** Impaired renal or hepatic function; mental depression, psychoses, history of suicidal tendencies; bipolar disorder; addiction-prone individuals; older adult or debilitated patients; COPD.

ROUTE & DOSAGE

Sedative, Hypnotic
Adult: **PO** ≥15 y, 15–30 mg h.s.
Geriatric: **PO** 15 mg h.s.

ADMINISTRATION

Oral
- Give once patient is in bed and ready to fall asleep.
- Store in light-resistant container with childproof cap at 15°–30° C (59°–86° F) unless otherwise specified.

ADVERSE EFFECTS (≥1%) **CNS:** *Residual sedation, drowsiness,* lightheadedness, dizziness, ataxia, headache, nervousness, apprehen-

sion, talkativeness, irritability, depression, hallucinations, nightmares, confusion, paradoxic reactions: excitement, euphoria, hyperactivity, disorientation, coma (overdosage). **Special Senses:** Blurred vision, burning eyes. **GI:** Heartburn, nausea, vomiting, diarrhea, abdominal pain. **Body as a Whole:** Immediate allergic reaction, hypotension, granulo–cytopenia (rare), jaundice (rare).

DIAGNOSTIC TEST INTERFERENCE Flurazepam may increase serum levels of *total and direct bilirubin, alkaline phosphatase, AST,* and *ALT.* False-negative *urine glucose* reactions may occur with *Clinistix* and *Diastix;* no effect with *TesTape.*

INTERACTIONS Drug: Alcohol, CNS DEPRESSANTS, ANTICONVULSANTS potentiate CNS depression; **cimetidine, disulfiram** may increase flurazepam levels, thus increasing its toxicity. **Herbal: Kava-kava, valerian** may potentiate sedation.

PHARMACOKINETICS Absorption: Readily from GI tract. **Onset:** 15–45 min. **Duration:** 7–8 h. **Distribution:** Crosses blood–brain barrier and placenta; distributed into breast milk. **Metabolism:** In liver to active metabolites. **Elimination:** Primarily in urine. **Half-Life:** 47–100 h.

CLINICAL IMPLICATIONS

Assessment & Drug Effects
- Monitor effectiveness. Hypnotic effect is apparent on second or third night of consecutive use and continues 1–2 nights after drug is stopped (drug has a long half-life).
- Supervise ambulation. Residual sedation and drowsiness are relatively common. Excessive drowsiness, ataxia, vertigo, and falling occur more frequently in older adults or debilitated patients.

- Monitor drug ingestion if patient has a history of drug abuse. Prolonged use of large doses can result in psychic and physical dependence.
- Lab tests: Obtain blood counts and liver and kidney function with repeated use.
- Be aware that withdrawal symptoms have occurred 3 d after abrupt discontinuation after prolonged use and include worsening of insomnia, dizziness, blurred vision, anorexia, GI upset, nasal congestion, paresthesias.

Patient & Family Education
- Avoid potentially hazardous activities until response to drug is known.
- Avoid alcohol. Concurrent ingestion with flurazepam intensifies CNS depressant effects; symptoms may occur even when alcohol is ingested as long as 10 h after last flurazepam dose.
- Be aware of the possible additive depressant effects when drug is combined with barbiturates, tranquilizers, or other CNS depressants.
- Do not change dose intervals or dosage. Do not take for a self-diagnosed problem.
- Ask physician about the desirability of discontinuing the drug if you become or intend to become pregnant during therapy.
- Note: Prolonged use of this hypnotic is inadvisable because insomnia is usually transient.

FLURBIPROFEN SODIUM

(flure-bi′proe-fen)
Ansaid, Ocufen
Classifications: ANALGESIC, NONSTEROIDAL ANTIINFLAMMATORY DRUG (NSAID); COX-1 AND COX-2 INHIBITOR; ANTIPYRETIC
Therapeutic: NSAID, ANALGESIC; ANTIPYRETIC
Prototype: Ibuprofen
Pregnancy Category: B first or second trimester; D third trimester

AVAILABILITY 50 mg, 100 mg tablets; 0.03% ophthalmic solution

ACTION & *THERAPEUTIC EFFECT*
Inhibits prostaglandin synthesis including in the conjunctiva and uvea by inhibiting the COX-1 or COX-2 enzymes; structurally and pharmacologically related to ibuprofen. When administered prophylactically, ocular flurbiprofen reduces miosis, permitting maintenance of drug-induced mydriasis during surgical procedures. *An antiinflammatory, nonsteroidal analgesic. Also inhibits migration of leukocytes into inflamed tissues, depresses monocyte function, and may inhibit platelet aggregation.*

USES Inhibition of intraoperative miosis; arthritis and other inflammatory diseases; mild to moderate pain.
UNLABELED USES Management of postoperative ocular inflammation, prevention of postcystoid macular edema.

CONTRAINDICATIONS Epithelial herpes simplex; keratitis; perioperative pain from CABG; pregnancy (category B in first and second trimester, and D in third trimester), lactation. Safety in children is not established. For additional contraindications to oral use, see ibuprofen.
CAUTIOUS USE Concomitant use with other NSAIDs; patient who may be adversely affected by prolonged bleeding time; patient in whom asthma, rhinitis, or urticaria is precipitated by aspirin or other NSAIDs.

ROUTE & DOSAGE

Inflammatory Disease
Adult: **PO** 200–300 mg/d in 2–4 divided doses (max: 300 mg/d)

Mild to Moderate Pain
Adult: **PO** 50–100 mg q6–8h

Inhibition of Intraoperative Miosis
Adult: **Topical** 1 drop in eye approximately q30min beginning 2 h before surgery for a total of 4 drops per affected eye

ADMINISTRATION

Topical
- Instill ophthalmic preparation with great care to avoid contamination of solution. Do not touch eye surface with dropper.

Oral
- Use the 300 mg dose for initiation of therapy or for acute exacerbations of disease.
- Store at 15°–30° C (59°–86° F) in tight, light-resistant container.

ADVERSE EFFECTS (≥1%) **Special Senses:** *Mild ocular stinging,* burning, itching, or foreign body sensation (transient). **Other:** Slowed corneal healing; increased bleeding time. **For adverse effects to oral preparations, see ibuprofen.**

INTERACTIONS Drug: ORAL ANTICOAGULANTS, **heparin** may prolong bleeding time; actions and side effects of both flurbiprofen and **phenytoin,** SULFONYLUREAS, or SULFONAMIDES may be potentiated. **Herbal: Feverfew, garlic, ginger, gingko** may increase bleeding potential.

PHARMACOKINETICS Absorption: 80% absorbed from GI tract. **Onset:** 2 h. **Peak:** 2 h. **Duration:** 6–8 h. **Distribution:** Small amounts distributed into breast milk. **Metabolism:** In liver. **Elimination:** Primarily in urine; some biliary excretion. **Half-Life:** 5 h.

CLINICAL IMPLICATIONS

Assessment & Drug Effects
- Observe patients with history of cardiac decompensation closely for evidence of fluid retention and edema.
- Lab tests: Baseline and periodic evaluations of Hgb, renal and hepatic function, and auditory and ophthalmologic examinations are recommended in patients receiving prolonged or high-dose therapy.
- Monitor for GI distress and S&S of GI bleeding.
- Note: Symptoms of acute toxicity in children include apnea, cyanosis, response only to painful stimuli, dizziness, and nystagmus.

Patient & Family Education
- Report ocular irritation that persists after flurbiprofen use during surgery (tearing, dry eye sensation, dull eye pain, photophobia) to physician.
- Be alert for bleeding tendency and report unexplained bleeding, prolongation of bleeding time, or bruises. Minor systemic absorption may temporarily increase bleeding time.
- Notify physician immediately of passage of dark tarry stools, "coffee ground" emesis, frankly bloody emesis, or other GI distress, as well as blood or protein in urine, and onset of skin rash, pruritus, jaundice.
- Do not drive or engage in potentially hazardous activities until response to the drug is known.
- Do not self-medicate with OTC drugs without consulting physician.
- Avoid alcohol and NSAIDs unless otherwise advised by physician. Concurrent use may increase risk

Common adverse effects in *italic*, life-threatening effects underlined; generic names in **bold**; classifications in SMALL CAPS; ♣ Canadian drug name; ⊘ Prototype drug

663

of GI ulceration and bleeding tendencies.

FLUTAMIDE ℗

(flu'ta-mide)
Eulexin
Classifications: ANTINEOPLASTIC; ANTIANDROGEN
Therapeutic: ANTINEOPLASTIC
Pregnancy Category: D

AVAILABILITY 125 mg capsules

ACTION & *THERAPEUTIC EFFECT*
Nonsteroidal, nonhormonal, antiandrogenic drug that inhibits androgen uptake or binding of androgen to target tissues (i.e., prostatic cancer cells). *Interferes with the binding of both testosterone and dihydrotestosterone to target tissue (i.e., prostate cancer cells).*

USES In combination with luteinizing hormone-releasing hormone agonists (i.e., leuprolide) or castration for early stage and metastatic prostate cancer.

CONTRAINDICATIONS Hypersensitivity to flutamide; severe liver impairment if ALT is equal to twice the normal value; females; pregnancy (category D), lactation.
CAUTIOUS USE Lactase deficiency.

ROUTE & DOSAGE

Prostate Cancer
Adult: **PO** 250 mg (2 caps) q8h

ADMINISTRATION

Oral
- Use with caution in patients with severe hepatic impairment.
- Store at 2°–30° C (36°–86° F) in a tightly closed, light-resistant container.

ADVERSE EFFECTS (≥1%) **CNS:** Drowsiness, confusion, depression, anxiety, nervousness. **GI:** Diarrhea, nausea, vomiting, anorexia, hepatitis, cholestatic jaundice, encephalopathy, hepatic necrosis, acute hepatic failure, may increase ALT, AST, bilirubin. **Urogenital:** *Hot flashes, loss of libido, impotence.* **Hematologic:** Anemia, leukopenia, thrombocytopenia. **Skin:** Rash. **Body as a Whole:** Edema. **Endocrine:** Gynecomastia, galactorrhea.

INTERACTIONS Drug: may increase INR in patients on **warfarin.**

PHARMACOKINETICS Absorption: Readily absorbed from GI tract. **Onset:** Antiandrogenic activity 2.2 h; symptomatic relief 2–4 wk. **Duration:** 3 mo–2.5 y, with an average of 10.5 mo. **Metabolism:** Metabolized in liver to at least 10 different metabolites; the major metabolite, 2-hydroxyflutamide (SCH-16423), is an alpha-hydroxylated derivative that is biologically active. **Elimination:** 98% in urine. **Half-Life:** 5–6 h.

CLINICAL IMPLICATIONS

Assessment & Drug Effects
- Monitor therapeutic response with acid and alkaline phosphatase tests, bone and liver scans, chest x-ray, and physical exam.
- Monitor for symptomatic relief of bone pain.
- Assess for development of gynecomastia and galactorrhea; if these become bothersome, dosage reduction may be warranted.
- Lab tests: Monitor liver function and serum bilirubin periodically.
- Monitor for and report development of a lupus-like syndrome.

Patient & Family Education
- Be aware of potential adverse effects of therapy.

- Notify physician immediately of the following: Pain in upper abdomen, yellowing of skin and eyes, dark urine, respiratory problems, rashes on face, difficulty urinating, sore throat, fever, chills.

FLUTICASONE

(flu-ti-ca′sone)
Flonase, Flovent, Flovent HFA, Cutivate
Pregnancy Category: C
See Appendixes A-3, A-4.

FLUVASTATIN

(flu-vah-stat′in)
Lescol, Lescol XL
Classifications: HMG-COA REDUCTASE INHIBITOR (STATIN); ANTILIPEMIC AGENT
Therapeutic: CHOLESTEROL-LOWERING AGENT (STATIN)
Prototype: Lovastatin
Pregnancy Category: X

AVAILABILITY 20 mg, 40 mg capsules; 80 mg extended release tablet

ACTION & *THERAPEUTIC EFFECT*
Inhibits reductase 3-hydroxy-3-methylglutaryl coenzyme A (HMG-CoA) that is essential to hepatic production of cholesterol. Cholesterol-lowering effect triggers induction of LDL receptors, which promotes removal of LDL and VLDL remnants (precursors of LDL) from plasma. *Results in an increase in plasma HDL concentration. HDLs collect excess cholesterol from body cells and transport it to the liver for excretion.*

USES Adjunct to diet for the reduction of elevated total LDL cholesterol in patients with primary hypercholesterolemia (Types IIa and IIb).
UNLABELED USES Other types of hyperlipidemias.

CONTRAINDICATIONS Hypersensitivity to fluvastatin, lovastatin, pravastatin, or simvastatin; active liver disease or unexplained persistent elevated liver function tests; pregnancy (category X), lactation; children ≤10 y.
CAUTIOUS USE Patients who consume substantial quantities of alcohol; history of liver disease; renal impairment.

ROUTE & DOSAGE

Hypercholesterolemia
Adult: **PO** 20 mg h.s., may increase up to 80 mg/d in 1–2 doses

ADMINISTRATION

Oral
- Give at bedtime.
- Ensure the extended release tablet is not chewed or crushed. It must be swallowed whole.
- Separate doses of this drug and bile-acid resin (e.g., cholestyramine) by at least 2 h when given concomitantly.
- Note: Dosage adjustments may be required in patients with significant renal or hepatic impairment.
- Store at room temperature, 15°–30° C (59°–86° F).

ADVERSE EFFECTS (≥1%) **CNS:** Headache, fatigue. **Body as a Whole:** Myalgia. **GI:** Dyspepsia, diarrhea, abdominal pain. **Skin:** Rash.

INTERACTIONS Drug: May increase risk of bleeding with **warfarin; cholestyramine** decreases fluvastatin absorption; **rifampin** increases metabolism of fluvastatin;

Common adverse effects in *italic*, life-threatening effects underlined; generic names in **bold**; classifications in SMALL CAPS; ✦ Canadian drug name; ⊘ Prototype drug

665

may increase risk of myopathy and rhabdomyolysis with **gemfibrozil, fenofibrate, clofibrate.**

PHARMACOKINETICS Absorption:
Readily from GI tract; about 24% reaches systemic circulation after first-pass metabolism. **Onset:** 3–6 wk. **Peak:** Serum level 0.5–1 h. **Distribution:** 98% protein bound; distributed into breast milk. **Metabolism:** In liver. **Elimination:** 95% in bile; 5% in urine. **Half-Life:** 0.5–1 h.

CLINICAL IMPLICATIONS
Assessment & Drug Effects
- Lab tests: Monitor lipoprotein levels; maximal lipid-lowering effect occurs in 4–6 wk. Monitor serum transaminase and CPK levels every 3–4 mo for the first year and periodically thereafter.
- Monitor PT & INR in patients on concurrent warfarin therapy; PT & INR may be prolonged.

Patient & Family Education
- Take fluvastatin at bedtime.
- Be alert & report signs of bleeding immediately when also taking warfarin.
- Notify physician immediately of the following: Fever; rash; muscle pain, weakness, tenderness, or cramping.
- Reduce or eliminate alcohol consumption while taking fluvastatin.

FLUVOXAMINE

(flu-vox′a-meen)

Luvox

Classifications: PSYCHOTHERAPEUTIC AGENT; SELECTIVE SEROTONIN REUPTAKE INHIBITOR (SSRI); ANTIDEPRESSANT
Therapeutic: ANTIDEPRESSANT; SSRI
Prototype: Fluoxetine
Pregnancy Category: C

AVAILABILITY 25 mg, 50 mg, 100 mg tablets

ACTION & *THERAPEUTIC EFFECT*
Antidepressant with potent, selective, inhibitory activity on neuronal (5-HT) serotonin reuptake (SSRI). Compared with TCAs, shows fewer anticholinergic effects and no severe cardiovascular effects. *Effective as an antidepressant and for control of obsessive-compulsive disorders.*

USES Treatment of depression and obsessive-compulsive disorders.
UNLABELED USES Chronic tension-type headaches, panic attacks.

CONTRAINDICATIONS Hypersensitivity to fluvoxamine or fluoxetine; suicidal ideation; concurrent MAOI therapy; bipolar disorder; pregnancy (category C), children ≤6 y, and ≤8 y for use with obsessive-compulsive disorder.
CAUTIOUS USE Liver disease, renal impairment, abrupt discontinuation; cardiac disease, dehydration, hyponatremia, older adults, ECT, seizure disorders, history of suicidal ideation, tobacco smoking; lactation.

ROUTE & DOSAGE

Depression, Obsessive-Compulsive Disorder
Adult: **PO** Start with 50 mg q.d., may increase slowly up to 300 mg/d given q.h.s. or divided b.i.d.
Child: **PO** 8–11 y, Start with 25 mg q.h.s., may increase by 25 mg q4–7d (max: 200 mg/d in divided doses)

ADMINISTRATION
Oral
- Give starting doses at bedtime to improve tolerance to nausea and vomiting; both are common early in therapy.

Common adverse effects in *italic*, life-threatening effects underlined; generic names in **bold**; classifications in SMALL CAPS; ◆ Canadian drug name; ⓟ Prototype drug

■ Store at room temperature, 15°–30° C (59°–86° F), away from moisture and light.

ADVERSE EFFECTS (≥1%) **CNS:** *Somnolence, headache, agitation, insomnia, dizziness,* seizures. **CV:** Orthostatic hypotension, slight bradycardia. **GI:** *Nausea, vomiting, dry mouth, constipation, anorexia.* **Urogenital:** Sexual dysfunction. **Skin:** Stevens-Johnson syndrome, toxic epidermal necrolysis (rare).

DIAGNOSTIC TEST INTERFERENCE *Gamma-glutamyl transferase* increased by more than 3-fold following 3 wk of therapy.

INTERACTIONS Drug: Fluvoxamine has been shown to significantly increase plasma levels of **amitriptyline, clomipramine,** and other TRICYCLIC ANTIDEPRESSANTS to mildly increase levels of their metabolites. May antagonize the blood pressure-lowering effects of **atenolol** and other BETA BLOCKERS. May increase levels and toxicity of **carbamazepine, mexiletine.** May increase **lithium** levels causing neurotoxicity, **serotonin** syndrome, somnolence, and mania. One report of increased **theophylline** levels with toxicity. Increases prothrombin time in patients on **warfarin;** increased ergotamine toxicity with **dihydroergotamine, ergotamine.** Use with CYP 1A2 INHIBITORS **(thioridazine, pimozide, alosetron, tizanidine)** increases **fluvoxamine** levels and toxicity. **Herbal:** Melatonin may increase and prolong drowsiness; **St. John's wort** may cause **serotonin** syndrome.

PHARMACOKINETICS Absorption: Almost completely absorbed from GI tract. **Onset:** 4–7 d. **Distribution:** Approximately 77% bound to plasma proteins; excreted in human breast milk but in an amount that poses little risk to the nursing infant. **Metabolism:** In liver. **Elimination:** Completely in urine. **Half-Life:** 16–24 h.

CLINICAL IMPLICATIONS

Assessment & Drug Effects
■ Monitor for significant nausea and vomiting, especially during initial therapy.
■ Monitor for worsening of depression or emergence of suicidal ideations.
■ Assess safety; drowsiness and dizziness are common adverse effects.
■ Monitor PT and INR carefully with concurrent warfarin therapy; adjust warfarin as needed.

Patient & Family Education
■ Note: Nausea and vomiting are common in early therapy. Notify physician if these adverse effects last more than a few days.
■ Exercise caution with hazardous activity until response to the drug is known.

FOLIC ACID (VITAMIN B₉, PTEROYLGLUTAMIC ACID)
(fol′ic)
Apo-Folic ✦, Folacin, Novofolacid ✦

FOLATE SODIUM
Folvite Sodium

Classifications: VITAMIN B₉
Therapeutic: VITAMIN SUPPLEMENT
Pregnancy Category: A

AVAILABILITY 0.4 mg, 0.8 mg, 1 mg tablets; 5 mg/mL injection

ACTION & THERAPEUTIC EFFECT Vitamin B₉ essential for nucleoprotein synthesis and maintenance of normal erythropoiesis. Acts against

Common adverse effects in *italic*, life-threatening effects underlined; generic names in **bold**; classifications in SMALL CAPS; ✦ Canadian drug name; ⦿ Prototype drug

667

folic acid deficiency that results in production of defective DNA that leads to megaloblast formation and arrest of bone marrow maturation. *Stimulates production of RBCs, WBCs, and platelets in patients with megaloblastic anemias.*

USES Folate deficiency, macrocytic anemia, and megaloblastic anemias associated with malabsorption syndromes, alcoholism, primary liver disease, inadequate dietary intake, pregnancy, infancy, and childhood.

CONTRAINDICATIONS Folic acid alone for pernicious anemia or other vitamin B₁₂ deficiency states; normocytic, refractory, aplastic, or undiagnosed anemia; neonates. **CAUTIOUS USE** Pregnancy (category A).

ROUTE & DOSAGE

Therapeutic
Adult: **PO/IM/SC/IV** ≤1 mg/d
Child: **PO/IM/SC/IV** ≤1 mg/d

Maintenance
Adult: **PO/IM/SC/IV** ≤0.4 mg/d
Child: **PO/IM/SC/IV** <4 y, ≤0.3 mg/d; >4 y, ≤0.1 mg/d
Infant: **PO/IM/SC/IV** 0.1 mg/d

ADMINISTRATION

Intravenous

PREPARE: **Direct/Continuous:** Given undiluted.
ADMINISTER: **Direct/Continuous:** Give over 30–60 sec. May also add to a continuous infusion.
INCOMPATIBILITIES **Solution/additive: Doxapram.**

- Store at 15°–30° C (59°–86° F) in tightly closed containers protected from light, unless otherwise directed.

ADVERSE EFFECTS (≥1%) Reportedly nontoxic. Slight flushing and feeling of warmth following IV administration.

DIAGNOSTIC TEST INTERFERENCE Falsely low serum *folate levels* may occur with **Lactobacillus casei** *assay* in patients receiving antibiotics such as TETRACYCLINES.

INTERACTIONS Drug: Chloramphenicol may antagonize effects of **folate** therapy; **phenytoin** metabolism may be increased, thus decreasing its levels.

PHARMACOKINETICS Absorption: Readily from proximal small intestine. **Peak:** 30–60 min PO. **Distribution:** Distributed to all body tissues; high concentrations in CSF; crosses placenta; distributed into breast milk. **Metabolism:** In liver to active metabolites. **Elimination:** Small amounts in urine in folate-deficient patients; large amounts excreted in urine with high doses.

CLINICAL IMPLICATIONS

Assessment & Drug Effects

- Obtain a careful history of dietary intake and drug and alcohol usage prior to start of therapy. Drugs reported to cause folate deficiency include oral contraceptives, alcohol, barbiturates, methotrexate, phenytoin, primidone, and trimethoprim. Folate deficiency may also result from renal dialysis.
- Keep physician informed of patient's response to therapy.
- Monitor patients on phenytoin for subtherapeutic plasma levels.

Patient & Family Education

- Remain under close medical supervision while taking folic acid therapy. Adjustment of maintenance dose should be made if there is threat of relapse.

FONDAPARINUX SODIUM

(fon-da-par′i-nux)

Arixtra

Classifications: ANTICOAGULANT; ANTITHROMBOTIC; LOW MOLECULAR WEIGHT HEPARIN
Therapeutic: ANTICOAGULANT; ANTITHROMBOTIC; LOW MOLECULAR WEIGHT HEPARIN
Prototype: Enoxaparin
Pregnancy Category: B

AVAILABILITY 2.5 mg/0.5 mL, 5 mg/0.4 mL, 7.5 mg/0.6 mL, 10 mg/0.8 mL syringe

ACTION & *THERAPEUTIC EFFECT*

Fondaparinux sodium causes antithrombin III (ATIII)-mediated selective inhibition of Factor Xa. Fondaparinux selectively binds to ATIII, potentiating the innate neutralization of Factor Xa by ATIII. Neutralization of Factor Xa by fondaparinux interrupts the blood coagulation cascade, inhibiting thrombin formation and, thus, thrombus development. Fondaparinux sodium does not inactivate thrombin (activated Factor II) and has no known effect on platelet function; therefore, it rarely causes thrombocytopenia. *Effective in the prevention and treatment of deep-vein thrombosis measured by the laboratory value of the amount of anti-Xa assay expressed in mg.*

USES Prophylaxis for DVT or pulmonary embolism (PE) in patients undergoing hip or knee replacement surgery or abdominal surgery; treatment of acute DVT without PE with warfarin, treatment of PE with warfarin.

CONTRAINDICATIONS Hypersensitivity to fondaparinux; active bleeding; GI bleeding; severe renal impairment with a creatinine clearance of <30 mL/min; weight <50 kg; active major bleeding; bacterial endocarditis; intramuscular administration; thrombocytopenia associated with fondaparinux. Safety and effectiveness in children have not been established.

CAUTIOUS USE Renal impairment or disease; older adult; indwelling epidural catheter; dental disease, dental work; diabetic retinopathy; diverticulitis; endocarditis, epidural anesthesia; hemophilia, heparin-induced thrombocytopenia (HIT), hepatic disease, hypertension, idiopathic thrombocytopenia purpura (ITP); inflammatory bowel disease, lumbar puncture, spinal anesthesia; stroke, surgery; thrombocytopenia, thrombolytic therapy; vaginal bleeding, menstruation; peptic ulcer disease; pregnancy (category B); bleeding disorders including a history of GI ulceration, etc., history of heparin-induced thrombocytopenia; lactation.

ROUTE & DOSAGE

DVT, Pulmonary Embolism Prophylaxis

Adult: **SC** >50 kg 2.5 mg q.d. starting at least 6 h postsurgery times 5–9 d; *for hip fracture patients,* up to 24 d additional use

Treatment of DVT, Pulmonary Embolism

Adult: **SC** <50 kg, 5 mg; 50–100 kg, 7.5 mg; >100 kg, 10 mg once daily × 5–9 d

Renal Impairment

Cl$_{cr}$ 30–50 mL/min: use with caution; <30 mL/min: use is contraindicated

ADMINISTRATION

Subcutaneous

- Consult physician about discontinuing other agents that may en-

---

Common adverse effects in *italic*, life-threatening effects <u>underlined</u>; generic names in **bold**; classifications in SMALL CAPS; ♣ Canadian drug name; ☯ Prototype drug

669

hance the risk of hemorrhage prior to initiation of fondaparinux.

- Give no sooner than 6 h after surgery.
- Adjust doses in older adults based on renal function.
- Inspect visually for particulate matter and discoloration prior to administration.
- Do not expel the air bubble from the syringe before the injection.
- Use prefilled syringe to inject into fatty tissue, alternating injection sites (e.g., between L and R abdominal wall).
- Store at 25° C (77° F); excursions permitted to 15°–30° C (59°–86° F).

ADVERSE EFFECTS (≥1%) **Body as a Whole:** Fever, edema. **CNS:** Insomnia, dizziness, confusion, headache. **CV:** Hypotension. **GI:** Nausea, constipation, vomiting, diarrhea, dyspepsia, elevated LFTs. **Endocrine:** Hypokalemia. **Hematologic:** Hemorrhage, *anemia,* hematoma. **Skin:** Irritation at injection site, rash, purpura, bullous eruption. **Urogenital:** UTI, urinary retention.

INTERACTIONS Drug: ANTICOAGULANTS, ANTIPLATELETS, NSAIDS, **aspirin** may increase risk of bleeding. **Herbal: Feverfew, ginkgo, ginger** may potentiate bleeding.

PHARMACOKINETICS Absorption: Rapidly and completely absorbed from SC injection site. **Peak:** 2–3 h. **Distribution:** Primarily in blood. **Metabolism:** Negligible metabolism. **Elimination:** In urine. **Half-Life:** 18 h.

CLINICAL IMPLICATIONS

Assessment & Drug Effects

- Monitor for S&S of bleeding or hemorrhage. If noted, withhold fondaparinux and notify physician immediately.

- Monitor closely patients with epidural catheters for signs of paralysis below catheter level.
- Withhold fondaparinux and notify physician if platelet count falls below 100,000/mm^3.
- Lab tests: Monitor baseline and periodic renal function rests; periodic CBC including platelet count, serum creatinine level, and stool occult blood tests. Lab test for measuring drug effectiveness is amount of anti-Xa assay expressed in mg. (Note: PT and aPTT are relatively insensitive measures of fondaparinux activity and unsuitable for monitoring.)

Patient & Family Education

- Report any of the following to a health care provider: signs of unexplained bleeding such as: pink, red, or dark brown urine; red or dark brown vomitus; bleeding gums or bloody sputum; dark, tarry stools.
- Learn proper injection technique if you are to self-administer this drug.
- Do not take any OTC drugs without first consulting physician.

FORMOTEROL FUMARATE

(for-mo-ter′ol)
Foradil Aerolizer
Classifications: BETA-ADRENERGIC AGONIST; BRONCHODILATOR
Therapeutic: BRONCHODILATOR
Prototype: Albuterol
Pregnancy Category: C

AVAILABILITY 12 mcg inhalation capsules

ACTION & *THERAPEUTIC EFFECT*
Long-acting selective beta$_2$-adrenergic receptor agonist. Stimulates production of intracellular

Common adverse effects in *italic*, life-threatening effects <u>underlined</u>; generic names in **bold**; classifications in SMALL CAPS; ♦ Canadian drug name; ⊙ Prototype drug

cyclic AMP, which causes relaxation of bronchial smooth muscle. Also inhibits release of mediators of immediate hypersensitivity (e.g., histamine and leukotrienes) from mast cells in the lung. *Acts locally in lung as a bronchodilator; prevents bronchoconstriction that occurs during an asthma attack.*

USES Treatment of asthma, prevention of exercise induced asthma, prevention of bronchospasm in COPD.
UNLABELED USES Bronchitis.

CONTRAINDICATIONS Hypersensitivity to formoterol; significantly worsening or acutely deteriorating asthma; severe asthmatic attacks; paradoxical bronchospasm; pregnancy (category C); lactation; children ≤5 y.
CAUTIOUS USE Cardiovascular disorders (especially coronary insufficiency, cardiac arrhythmias, and hypertension), QT prolongation; convulsive disorders; thyrotoxicosis; heightened responsiveness to sympathomimetic amines; diabetes mellitus.

ROUTE & DOSAGE

Treatment of Asthma, COPD
Adult/Child: **Inhaled** ≥5 y, Inhale contents of 1 capsule q12h

Prevention of Exercise-Induced Asthma
Adult/Child: **Inhaled** ≥12 y, Inhale contents of 1 capsule at least 15 min before exercise, do not repeat for at least 12 h

ADMINISTRATION
Oral Inhalation
▪ Remove capsule from blister IMMEDIATELY before use.

▪ Avoid exposing capsules to moisture.
▪ Give capsules only by the oral inhalation route and only by using the Aerolizer Inhaler™. Review use of the Aerolizer Inhaler in *Patient Instructions for Use* provided by manufacturer. Do not use a spacer with the Aerolizer.
▪ Instruct patient not to swallow capsule and not to exhale into the Aerolizer.
▪ Patients who have been taking the inhaled form, short-acting beta$_2$-agonists regularly (e.g., 3–4 times a day) are usually instructed to use these drugs ONLY for symptomatic relief of acute asthma symptoms. Check with physician.
▪ Store capsules in the blister at 20°–25° C (86°–77° F).

ADVERSE EFFECTS (≥1%) **Body as a Whole:** *Viral infections,* chest infection, chest pain, fatigue. **CNS:** Headache, tremor, dizziness, insomnia. **GI:** Abdominal pain, dyspepsia, nausea. **Respiratory:** Pharyngitis, bronchitis, dyspnea, tonsillitis, dysphonia, fatal exacerbation of asthma. **Skin:** Rash.

INTERACTIONS Drug: Effects may be antagonized by NON-SELECTIVE BETA BLOCKERS; XANTHINES, STEROIDS; DIURETICS may potentiate hypokalemia.

PHARMACOKINETICS Absorption: Rapidly absorbed into plasma after oral inhalation. **Onset:** 1–3 min. **Peak:** 1–3 h. **Metabolism:** Metabolized by glucuronidation in the liver. **Elimination:** 60% in urine, 33% in feces. **Half-Life:** 10 h.

CLINICAL IMPLICATIONS
Assessment & Drug Effects
▪ Monitor cardiovascular status with periodic ECG, BP, and HR determinations.

Common adverse effects in *italic*, life-threatening effects underlined; generic names in **bold**; classifications in SMALL CAPS; ♣ Canadian drug name; ⊘ Prototype drug

671

- Withhold drug and notify physician immediately of S&S of bronchospasm.
- Lab tests: Monitor serum potassium and blood glucose periodically.
- Monitor diabetics closely for loss of glycemic control.

Patient & Family Education
- Do not take this drug more frequently than every 12 h.
- Use a short-acting inhaler if symptoms develop between doses of formoterol.
- Seek medical care immediately if a previously effective dosage regimen fails to provide the usual response, or if swelling about the face and neck and difficulty breathing develop.
- Report any of the following immediately to the physician: Rash, hives, palpitations, chest pain, rapid heart rate, tremor or nervousness.
- Note to diabetics: Monitor blood glucose levels carefully since hyperglycemia is a possible adverse reaction.

FOSAMPRENAVIR CALCIUM

(fos-am-pre'na-vir)
Lexiva
Classifications: ANTIRETROVIRAL AGENT; PROTEASE INHIBITOR
Therapeutic: ANTIRETROVIRAL; PROTEASE INHIBITOR
Prototype: Saquinavir
Pregnancy Category: C

AVAILABILITY 700 mg tablet

ACTION & *THERAPEUTIC EFFECT*
Fosamprenavir is a prodrug rapidly converted to amprenavir. Amprenavir is an HIV-1 protease inhibitor that binds to the active site of HIV-1 protease. Binding prevents processing of viral Gag and Gag-Pol polyprotein precursors, resulting in formation of immature noninfectious viral particles. *Inhibits normal replication of the HIV virus rending the virus noninfectious.*

USES Treatment of HIV infection in combination with other antiretroviral agents.

CONTRAINDICATIONS Hypersensitivity to amprenavir; ergot derivatives, pimozide, midazolam, triazolam; coadministration of ritonavir, flecainide, and propafenone; severe hepatic impairment; pregnancy (category C), lactation. Safety and efficacy in children <18 y have not been established.
CAUTIOUS USE Sulfonamide allergy; mild to moderate hepatic impairment; elderly; hemophilia.

ROUTE & DOSAGE

HIV Infection
Adult: **PO** 700 mg b.i.d. in combination with 100 mg ritonavir b.i.d. (preferred if previously on a protease inhibitor); or 1400 mg b.i.d.; or 1400 mg q.d. in combination with 200 mg ritonavir q.d.

Hepatic Impairment
Mild to Moderate Impairment Reduce dose to 700 mg b.i.d. without ritonavir; not recommended in severe hepatic impairment

ADMINISTRATION

Oral
- Ensure that patient is not receiving drugs contraindicated with fosamprenavir.
- Store at 15°–30° C (59°–86° F) in a tightly closed container.

ADVERSE EFFECTS (≥1%) **Body as a Whole:** Fatigue. **CNS:** *Oral/perioral paresthesia,* peripheral paresthesia, depression, mood disorders. **GI:** *Nausea, vomiting, diarrhea,* abdominal pain, taste disorders, increased triglycerides, and hyperglycemia. **Skin:** *Rash,* pruritus, Stevens-Johnson syndrome.

INTERACTIONS Note: Interaction profile can be significantly affected by coadministration with **ritonavir. Drug:** Administration with **amiodarone, bepridil, dihydroergotamine, ergotamine, flecainide, itraconazole, ketoconazole, lidocaine, midazolam, pimozide, propafenone, quinidine, triazolam,** and TRICYCLIC ANTIDEPRESSANTS may cause life-threatening reactions; **rifampin, rifabutin,** ORAL CONTRACEPTIVES, **phenobarbital, phenytoin, carbamazepine** decrease **amprenavir** concentrations; **amprenavir** may increase **dihydroergotamine, ergotamine, sildenafil** concentrations and toxicity; **amprenavir** may decrease **methadone** levels; monitor INR with **warfarin;** increased risk of myopathy and rhabdomyolysis with **lovastatin, simvastatin;** may decrease antiviral effectiveness of **delavirdine or lopinavir/ritonavir. Herbal:** St. **John's wort** may decrease antiretroviral activity.

PHARMACOKINETICS Absorption: Prodrug is rapidly hydrolyzed to amprenavir (active component) by gut enzymes during absorption. **Peak:** 2.5 h. **Metabolism:** In liver by CYP3A4. **Elimination:** 14% in urine, 75% in feces. **Half-Life:** 7.7 h.

CLINICAL IMPLICATIONS
Assessment & Drug Effects
- Ensure that patient has provided a complete list of all prescription, nonprescription, or herbal drugs being used.
- Monitor closely diabetics for loss of glycemic control.

- Monitor males taking PDE5 inhibitors for erectile dysfunction for adverse events including hypotension, visual changes, and priapism. Report promptly.
- Lab test: Baseline and periodic LFTs; periodic lipid profile; periodic blood glucose.

Patient & Family Education
- If you miss a dose by >4 h, wait and take the next dose at the regular time.
- Do not take other prescription, nonprescription, or herbal drugs without consulting physician.
- Monitor blood glucose more often than usual if diabetic.
- To prevent pregnancy, use a barrier contraceptive in addition to hormonal contraception.

FOSCARNET
(fos'car-net)
Foscavir
Classifications: ANTIVIRAL
Therapeutic: ANTIVIRAL
Pregnancy Category: C

AVAILABILITY 24 mg/mL injection

ACTION & *THERAPEUTIC EFFECT*
Inhibits the replication of all known herpes viruses in vitro. *Acts against cytomegalovirus (CMV), herpes simplex virus types 1 and 2 (HSV-1, HSV-2), human herpesvirus 6 (HHV-6), Epstein-Barr virus (EBV), and varicella-zoster virus (VZV).*

USES CMV retinitis, mucocutaneous HSV, acyclovir-resistant HSV in immunocompromised patients.
UNLABELED USES Other CMV infections, herpes zoster infections in AIDS patients.

CONTRAINDICATIONS Hypersensitivity to foscarnet; pregnancy (category C), lactation.

Common adverse effects in *italic,* life-threatening effects underlined; generic names in **bold;** classifications in SMALL CAPS; ♣ Canadian drug name; ⊙ Prototype drug

673

CAUTIOUS USE Kidney function impairment, cardiac disease; mineral and electrolyte imbalances, seizures, older adults. Safety and efficacy in children are not established.

ROUTE & DOSAGE

CMV Retinitis
Adult: **IV Induction** 60 mg/kg infused over 1 h q8h for 2–3 wk OR 90 mg/kg q12h for 2–3 wk; induction may be repeated if relapse occurs during maintenance therapy **Maintenance Dose** 90–120 mg/kg/d infused over 2 h

Acyclovir-Resistant HSV in Immunocompromised Patients
Adult: **IV** 40 mg/kg q8–12h for up to 3 wk or until lesions heal

Renal Impairment
See package insert

ADMINISTRATION

▪ Note: Dose must be adjusted for renal insufficiency. See package insert for specific dosing adjustment.

Intravenous

PREPARE: Direct: Given undiluted (24 mg/mL) through a central line. For peripheral infusion, dilute to 12 mg/mL with D5W or NS. Do not give other IV solution or drug through the same catheter with foscarnet.

ADMINISTER: Direct: Give at a constant rate not to exceed 1 mg/kg/min over the specified period of infusion with an infusion pump. Do not increase the rate of infusion or shorten the specified interval between doses. ▪ Use prepared IV solutions within 24 h.

INCOMPATIBILITIES Solution/additive: **Ringer's lactate, acyclovir, amphotericin B, calcium, co-trimoxazole, diazepam, digoxin, diphenhydramine, dobutamine, droperidol, ganciclovir, haloperidol, leucovorin, lorazepam, midazolam, pentamidine, phenytoin, prochlorperazine, promethazine, trimetrexate, vancomycin.** Y-site: **Acyclovir, amphotericin B, calcium, co-trimoxazole, diazepam, digoxin, diphenhydramine, dobutamine, droperidol, ganciclovir, haloperidol, leucovorin, lorazepam, midazolam, pentamidine, phenytoin, prochlorperazine, promethazine, trimetrexate, vancomycin.**

▪ Prehydrate and continue daily hydration with 2.5 L of NS to reduce nephrotoxicity.

▪ Store according to manufacturer's directions.

ADVERSE EFFECTS (≥1%) **CV:** Thrombophlebitis if infused through a peripheral vein. **CNS:** Tremor, muscle twitching, headache, weakness, fatigue, confusion, anxiety. **Endocrine:** *Hyperphosphatemia,* hypophosphatemia, hypocalcemia. **GI:** Nausea, vomiting, diarrhea. **Urogenital:** Penile ulceration. **Hematologic:** *Anemia,* leukopenia, thrombocytopenia. **Renal:** <u>Nephrotoxicity</u> (acute renal failure, tubular necrosis). **Skin:** Fixed drug eruption, rash.

DIAGNOSTIC TEST INTERFERENCE May cause increase or decrease in serum *calcium, phosphorus,* and *magnesium.* Decreases *Hct* and *Hgb.* Increased serum *creatinine.*

INTERACTIONS Drug: AMINOGLYCOSIDES, **amphotericin B, vancomy-**

cin may increase risk of nephrotoxicity. **Etidronate, pamidronate, pentamidine (IV)** may exacerbate hypocalcemia.

PHARMACOKINETICS Onset: 3–7 d. **Duration:** Relapse usually occurs 3–4 wk after end of therapy. **Distribution:** 3–28% of dose may be deposited in bone; variable penetration into CSF; crosses placenta; distributed into breast milk. **Metabolism:** Not metabolized. **Elimination:** 73–94% in urine. **Half-Life:** 3–4 h.

CLINICAL IMPLICATIONS

Assessment & Drug Effects

- Monitor for cardiac arrhythmias, especially in presence of known cardiac abnormalities.
- Lab tests: Periodic CBC, serum electrolytes, serum creatinine, and creatinine clearance throughout therapy.
- Monitor serum creatinine and creatinine clearance values. Drug dose will be decreased in response to decreased clearance.
- Monitor for electrolyte imbalances.
- Monitor for seizures and take appropriate precautions.
- Question patients regarding local irritation of the penile or vulvovaginal epithelium. If either occurs, increase hydration and better personal hygiene.

Patient & Family Education

- Report perioral tingling, numbness, and paresthesia to physician immediately.
- Understand that drug is not a cure for CMV retinitis; regular ophthalmologic exams are necessary.
- Note: Good hydration is important to maintain adequate output of urine.

FOSFOMYCIN TROMETHAMINE

(fos-fo-my′sin)
Monurol
Classifications: ANTIBIOTIC
Therapeutic: ANTIBIOTIC; URINARY TRACT ANTIINFECTIVE
Prototype: Nitrofurantoin
Pregnancy Category: B

AVAILABILITY 3 g packets

ACTION & *THERAPEUTIC EFFECT*

Synthetic, broad-spectrum, bactericidal antibiotic active against gram-negative and gram-positive aerobic organisms that blocks the first steps in bacterial cell wall synthesis. *Acts as a bactericidal agent against* Enterococcus faecalis, E. faecium, *and* Escherichia coli. *In addition, it is effective against* Klebsiella, Proteus, *and* Serratia. *Indicated by improvement in cystitis symptoms within 2–3 d.*

USES Treatment of uncomplicated UTIs in women due to susceptible strains of *E. coli* and *E. faecalis.*

CONTRAINDICATIONS Hypersensitivity to fosfomycin.
CAUTIOUS USE Pregnancy (category B); lactation. Safety and efficiency in children <12 y are not established.

ROUTE & DOSAGE

UTI

Adult: **PO** 3 g sachet dissolved in 3–4 oz of water as a single dose given once

ADMINISTRATION

Oral

- Pour entire contents of a single dose into 3–4 oz water (not hot), stir to dissolve completely, and

Common adverse effects in *italic*, life-threatening effects underlined; generic names in **bold**; classifications in SMALL CAPS; ♣ Canadian drug name; ⊘ Prototype drug

675

give immediately. Drug must not be taken in the dry form.
- Store at 15°–30° C (59°–86° F).

ADVERSE EFFECTS (≥1%) **Body as a Whole:** Pain. **CNS:** *Headache,* dizziness. **GI:** *Diarrhea,* nausea, abdominal pain, dyspepsia. **Respiratory:** Rhinitis, pharyngitis. **Urogenital:** Vaginitis, dysmenorrhea.

INTERACTIONS Drug: Metoclopramide may decrease urinary excretion of fosfomycin.

PHARMACOKINETICS Absorption: Rapidly from GI tract, 37% of dose reaches systemic circulation as free acid. **Peak Urine Concentration:** 2–4 h. **Distribution:** Not protein bound, distributed to kidneys, bladder wall, prostate, and seminal vesicles. **Elimination:** Primarily in urine. **Half-Life:** 5.7 h.

CLINICAL IMPLICATIONS
Assessment & Drug Effects
- Lab tests: Obtain urine C&S before and after therapy.

Patient & Family Education
- Notify physician if symptoms do not improve in 2–3 d.

FOSINOPRIL

(fos-in′o-pril)
Monopril
Classifications: ANGIOTENSIN-CONVERTING ENZYME (ACE) INHIBITOR; ANTIHYPERTENSIVE AGENT
Therapeutic: ANTIHYPERTENSIVE; ACE INHIBITOR
Prototype: Enalapril
Pregnancy Category: C first trimester; D second and third trimester

AVAILABILITY 10 mg, 20 mg, 40 mg tablets

ACTION & *THERAPEUTIC EFFECT*
Lowers BP by interrupting conversion sequences initiated by renin that lead to formation of angiotensin II, a potent vasoconstrictor. Inhibition of ACE also leads to decreased circulating aldosterone, a secretory response to angiotensin II stimulation. *Lowers blood pressure and reduces peripheral arterial resistance (afterload) and improves cardiac output as well as activity tolerance.*

USES Mild to moderate hypertension, CHF.

CONTRAINDICATIONS Hypersensitivity to fosinopril or any other ACE inhibitor; history of angioedema; renal artery stenosis; pregnancy [category C (first trimester), category D (second or third trimester)], lactation. **CAUTIOUS USE** Impaired kidney function, hepatic disease; hyperkalemia, or surgery and anesthesia; aortic stenosis or cardiomyopathy; elderly. Safety in children is not established.

ROUTE & DOSAGE

Hypertension, CHF
Adult: **PO** 5–40 mg once/d (max: 80 mg/d)

ADMINISTRATION
Oral
- Discontinue diuretics 2–3 d before initiation of therapy if possible. If diuretics cannot be discontinued, start initial dose ≤10 mg.
- Store at 15°–30° C (59°–86° F) and protect from moisture.

ADVERSE EFFECTS (≥1%) **CV:** Hypotension. **CNS:** Headache, fatigue, dizziness. **Endocrine:** Hyperkalemia. **GI:** Nausea, vomiting, diarrhea. **Urogenital:** Proteinuria. **Respiratory:** Cough. **Skin:** Rash.

INTERACTIONS Drug: NSAIDS may decrease antihypertensive effects of fosinopril. POTASSIUM SUPPLEMENTS, POTASSIUM-SPARING DIURETICS increase risk of hyperkalemia. ACE inhibitors may increase **lithium** levels and toxicity.

PHARMACOKINETICS Absorption: Readily absorbed from GI tract; converted to its active form, fosinoprilat, in the liver. **Peak:** 3 h. **Duration:** 24 h. **Distribution:** Approximately 90% protein bound; crosses placenta. **Metabolism:** Hydrolyzed by intestinal and hepatic esterases to its active form, fosinoprilat. **Elimination:** 44% in urine, 46% in feces. **Half-Life:** 3–4 h (fosinoprilat).

CLINICAL IMPLICATIONS

Assessment & Drug Effects

- Monitor BP at the time of peak effectiveness, 2–6 h after dosing and at the end of the dosing interval just before next dose.
- Report diminished antihypertensive effect toward the end of the dosing interval. An inadequate trough response may be an indication for dividing the daily dose.
- Monitor for first-dose hypotension, especially in salt- or volume-depleted patients.
- Lab tests: Obtain BUN and serum creatinine periodically. Increases may necessitate dose reduction or discontinuation of the drug. Monitor serum potassium.
- Observe for S&S of hyperkalemia (see Appendix F).

Patient & Family Education

- Discontinue fosinopril and report to physician any of the following: S&S of angioedema (e.g., swelling of face or extremities, difficulty breathing or swallowing); syncope; chronic, nonproductive cough.
- Maintain adequate fluid intake and avoid potassium supplements or salt substitutes unless specifically prescribed by the physician.
- Report vomiting or diarrhea to physician immediately.

FOSPHENYTOIN SODIUM

(fos-phen′i-toin)
Cerebyx
Classifications: HYDANTOIN ANTI-CONVULSANT AGENT
Therapeutic: ANTICONVULSANT
Prototype: Phenytoin
Pregnancy Category: D

AVAILABILITY 150 mg, 750 mg vials

ACTION & *THERAPEUTIC EFFECT*
Prodrug of phenytoin that converts to the anticonvulsant phenytoin after parenteral administration. Thought to modulate the sodium channels of neurons, calcium flux across neuronal membranes, and enhance the sodium–potassium ATPase activity of neurons and glial cells. *The cellular mechanism of phenytoin is thought to be responsible for the anticonvulsant activity of fosphenytoin.*

USES Control of generalized convulsive status epilepticus and the prevention and treatment of seizures during neurosurgery, or as a parenteral short-term substitute for oral phenytoin.
UNLABELED USES Antiarrhythmic agent especially in treatment of digitalis-induced arrhythmia; treatment of trigeminal neuralgia (tic douloureux).

CONTRAINDICATIONS Hypersensitivity to hydantoin products, rash, seizures due to hypoglycemia, sinus bradycardia, complete or incomplete heart block; Adams–Stokes syndrome; pregnancy (category D).

Common adverse effects in *italic*, life-threatening effects underlined; generic names in **bold**; classifications in SMALL CAPS; ♦ Canadian drug name; ⊕ Prototype drug

677

CAUTIOUS USE Impaired liver or kidney function, alcoholism, hypotension, heart block, bradycardia, severe CAD, diabetes mellitus, hyperglycemia, respiratory depression, acute intermittent porphyria; lactation.

ROUTE & DOSAGE

Status Epilepticus

Adult: **IV Loading Dose** 15–20 mg PE/kg (PE = phenytoin sodium equivalents) administered at 100–150 mg PE/min **IV Maintenance Dose** 4–6 mg PE/kg/d

Substitution for Oral Phenytoin Therapy

Adult: **IV/IM** Substitute fosphenytoin at the same total daily dose in mg PE as the oral dose at a rate of infusion not greater than 150 mg PE/min

ADMINISTRATION

- Note: All dosing is expressed in phenytoin sodium equivalents (PE) to avoid the need to calculate molecular weight adjustments between fosphenytoin and phenytoin sodium doses. **ALWAYS** prescribe and fill fosphenytoin in PE units.

Intramuscular

- Follow institutional policy regarding maximum volume to inject into one IM site.

Intravenous

PREPARE: Direct: Dilute in DSW or NS to a concentration of 1.5–25 mg PE/mL.

ADMINISTER: Direct: Do not administer at a rate >150 mg PE/min.

- Store at 2°–8° C (36°–46° F); may store at room temperature not to exceed 48 h.

ADVERSE EFFECTS (≥1%) **CNS:** Usually dose related. Paresthesia, tinnitus, *nystagmus, dizziness, somnolence, drowsiness,* ataxia, mental confusion, tremors, insomnia, headache, seizures, increased reflexes, dysarthria, intracranial hypertension. **CV:** Bradycardia, tachycardia, asystole, hypotension, hypertension, cardiovascular collapse, cardiac arrest, heart block, ventricular fibrillation, phlebitis. **Special Senses:** Photophobia, conjunctivitis, diplopia, blurred vision. **GI:** *Gingival hyperplasia,* nausea, vomiting, constipation, epigastric pain, dysphagia, loss of taste, weight loss, hepatitis, liver necrosis. **Hematologic:** Thrombocytopenia, leukopenia, leukocytosis, agranulocytosis, pancytopenia, eosinophilia; megaloblastic, hemolytic, or aplastic anemias. **Metabolic:** Fever, hyperglycemia, glycosuria, weight gain, edema, transient increase in serum thyrotropic (TSH) level, hyperkalemia, osteomalacia or rickets associated with hypocalcemia and elevated alkaline phosphatase activity. **Skin:** Alopecia, hirsutism (especially in young female); rash: scarlatiniform, maculopapular, urticarial, morbilliform (may be fatal); bullous, exfoliative, or purpuric dermatitis; Stevens–Johnson syndrome, toxic epidermal necrolysis, keratosis, neonatal hemorrhage, *pruritus.* **Urogenital:** Acute renal failure, Peyronie's disease. **Respiratory:** Acute pneumonitis, pulmonary fibrosis. **Musculoskeletal:** Periarteritis nodosum, acute systemic lupus erythematosus, craniofacial abnormalities (with enlargement of lips). **Other:** Lymphadenopathy, injection site pain, chills.

DIAGNOSTIC TEST INTERFERENCE

Fosphenytoin may produce lower than normal values for *dexa-*

methasone or *metyrapone* tests; may increase serum levels of *glucose, BSP,* and *alkaline phosphatase* and may decrease *PBI* and *urinary steroid* levels.

INTERACTIONS Drug: Alcohol decreases fosphenytoin effects; OTHER ANTICONVULSANTS may increase or decrease fosphenytoin levels; fosphenytoin may decrease absorption and increase metabolism of ORAL ANTICOAGULANTS; fosphenytoin increases metabolism of CORTICOSTEROIDS and ORAL CONTRACEPTIVES, thus decreasing their effectiveness; **amiodarone, chloramphenicol, omeprazole** increase fosphenytoin levels; ANTITUBERCULOSIS AGENTS decrease fosphenytoin levels. **Food: Folic acid, calcium, vitamin D** absorption may be decreased by fosphenytoin; fosphenytoin absorption may be decreased by enteral nutrition supplements. **Herbal: Ginkgo** may decrease anticonvulsant effectiveness.

PHARMACOKINETICS Absorption: Completely absorbed after IM administration. **Peak:** 30 min IM. **Distribution:** 95–99% bound to plasma proteins, displaces phenytoin from protein binding sites; crosses placenta, small amount in breast milk. **Metabolism:** Converted to phenytoin by phosphatases; phenytoin is oxidized in liver to inactive metabolites. **Elimination:** Half-life 15 min to convert fosphenytoin to phenytoin, 22 h phenytoin; phenytoin metabolites excreted in urine.

CLINICAL IMPLICATIONS

Note: See **phenytoin** for additional clinical implications.

Assessment & Drug Effects

- Monitor ECG, BP, and respiratory function continuously during and for 10–20 min after infusion.

- Discontinue infusion and notify physician if rash appears. Be prepared to substitute alternative therapy rapidly to prevent withdrawal-precipitated seizures.
- Lab tests: Monitor CBC with differential, platelet count, serum electrolytes, and blood glucose.
- Allow at least 2 h after IV infusion and 4 h after IM injection before monitoring total plasma phenytoin concentration.
- Monitor diabetics for loss of glycemic control.
- Monitor carefully for adverse effects, especially in patients with renal or hepatic disease or hypoalbuminemia.

Patient & Family Education

- Be aware of potential adverse effects. Itching, burning, tingling, or paresthesia are common during and for some time following IV infusion.

FROVATRIPTAN

(fro-va-trip'tan)
Frova
Classifications: ADRENERGIC AGONIST; SEROTONIN 5-HT$_1$-RECEPTOR AGONIST
Therapeutic: ANTIMIGRAINE; 5-HT$_1$-RECEPTOR AGONIST
Prototype: Sumatriptan
Pregnancy Category: C

AVAILABILITY 2.5 mg tablets

ACTION & *THERAPEUTIC EFFECT*
Selective agonist that binds with high affinity to 5-HT$_{1D}$, 5-HT$_{1B}$, 5-HT$_{1F}$ serotonin receptors which are found on extracerebral and intracranial blood vessels, and on other structures in the central nervous system. This results in vasoconstriction and agonist effects on nerve

F

Common adverse effects in *italic*, life-threatening effects underlined; generic names in **bold**; classifications in SMALL CAPS; ♣ Canadian drug name; ⊕ Prototype drug

679

F

terminals in trigeminal system. *Activation of 5-HT₁ receptors results in constriction of cranial vessels which become dilated during a migraine attack, inhibition of neuropeptide release, and reduced signal transmission in the pain pathways.*

USES Treatment of migraine headache with or without aura.

CONTRAINDICATIONS Hypersensitivity to frovatriptan; significant cardiovascular disease such as ischemic heart disease, coronary artery vasospasms, peripheral vascular disease, history of cerebrovascular events, or uncontrolled hypertension; within 24 h of receiving another 5-HT₁ agonist or an ergotamine-containing or ergot-type drug; basilar or hemiplegic migraine, pregnancy (category C). Safety and efficacy in children <18 y are not established.

CAUTIOUS USE Significant risk factors for coronary artery disease unless a cardiac evaluation has been done; hypertension; risk factors for cerebrovascular accident; impaired liver or kidney function; lactation.

ROUTE & DOSAGE

Migraine Headache
Adult: **PO** 2.5 mg. If headache returns, may repeat after at least 2 h (max: 7.5 mg/24 h)

ADMINISTRATION

Oral
- Do not give within 24 h of an ergot-containing drug.
- Administer any time after symptoms of migraine appear.
- Do not administer a second dose without consulting the physician for any attack during which the FIRST dose did NOT work.

- Give a second dose if headache was relieved by first dose but symptoms return; however, wait at least 2 h after the first dose before giving a second dose.
- Do not give more than two doses in 24 h.
- Store at 15°–30° C (59°–86° F).

ADVERSE EFFECTS (≥1%) **Body as a Whole:** Fatigue, hot or cold sensation, flushing. **CNS:** Dizziness, headache, paresthesia, somnolence, insomnia, anxiety. **CV:** Chest pain, palpitation. **GI:** Dyspepsia, nausea, vomiting, diarrhea, dry mouth. **Musculoskeletal:** Skeletal pain. **Special Senses:** Abnormal vision. **Skin:** Sweating.

INTERACTIONS Drug: Dihydroergotamine, methysergide, other 5-HT₁ AGONISTS may cause prolonged vasospastic reactions; SSRIS, **sibutramine** have rarely caused weakness, hyperreflexia, and incoordination; MAOIS should not be used with 5-HT₁ AGONISTS. **Herbal: Gingko, ginseng, echinacea, St. John's wort** may increase triptan toxicity.

PHARMACOKINETICS Absorption: 20–30% bioavailability. **Peak:** 2–4 h. **Distribution:** 15% protein bound. **Metabolism:** In liver by CYP1A2. **Elimination:** 30% renally, 60% in feces. **Half-Life:** 26 h.

CLINICAL IMPLICATIONS

Assessment & Drug Effects
- Monitor cardiovascular status carefully following first dose in patients at relatively high risk for coronary artery disease (e.g., postmenopausal women, men over 40 years old, persons with known CAD risk factors), or who have coronary artery vasospasms.
- Report to physician immediately chest pain or tightness in chest or

throat that is severe, or does not quickly resolve following a dose of frovatriptan.

- Pain relief usually begins within 10 min of ingestion, with complete relief in approximately 65% of all patients within 2 h.
- Monitor BP, especially in those being treated for hypertension.

Patient & Family Education

- Review patient information leaflet provided by the manufacturer carefully.
- Notify physician immediately if symptoms of severe angina (e.g., severe or persistent pain or tightness in chest, back, neck, or throat) or hypersensitivity (e.g., wheezing, facial swelling, skin rash, itching, or hives) occur.
- Do not take any other serotonin receptor agonist (e.g., Imitrex, Maxalt, Zomig, Amerge) within 24 h of taking frovatriptan.
- Advise physician of any drugs taken within 1 wk of beginning frovatriptan.
- Check with physician regarding drug interactions before taking any new OTC or prescription drugs.
- Report any other adverse effects (e.g., tingling, flushing, dizziness) at next physician visit.

FULVESTRANT

(ful-ves'trant)

Faslodex

Classifications: ANTINEOPLASTIC; HORMONE, ANTIESTROGEN

Therapeutic: ANTINEOPLASTIC; ANTI-ESTROGEN

Prototype: Tamoxifen citrate

Pregnancy Category: D

AVAILABILITY 50 mg/mL

ACTION & *THERAPEUTIC EFFECT*

Fulvestrant is an estrogen receptor antagonist that selectively binds to the estrogen receptors (ER) of breast cancer cells. It competes well with estradiol (estrogen) in binding to these receptor sites. Estrogen stimulates the tumor growth of estrogen-sensitive breast tissue cancer cells in postmenopausal women. *In postmenopausal women, many breast cancers have estrogen receptors (ERs), and the growth of these tumors is stimulated by estrogen. Therefore, fulvestrant decreases estrogen-sensitive breast tissue tumor growth.*

USES Treatment of hormone receptor-positive metastatic breast cancer in postmenopausal women with disease progression following antiestrogen therapy.

CONTRAINDICATIONS Hypersensitivity to fulvestrant; pregnancy (category D); lactation.

CAUTIOUS USE Moderate to severe liver impairment; biliary disease; coagulopathy; anticoagulant therapy. Safety and effectiveness in children not established.

ROUTE & DOSAGE

Metastatic Breast Cancer
Adult: **IM** 250 mg once/mo

ADMINISTRATION

Intramuscular

- Do not administer unless the possibility of pregnancy has been ruled out.
- Break the seal of the white plastic cover on the syringe luer connector to remove the cover with the attached rubber tip cap. Twist to lock the needle to the luer connec-

---

Common adverse effects in *italic*, life-threatening effects <u>underlined</u>; generic names in **bold**; classifications in SMALL CAPS; ♣ Canadian drug name; ⊙ Prototype drug

681

F

tor. Remove excess gas from the syringe (a small gas bubble may remain).

- Administer slowly in the buttock.
- Immediately activate needle protection device upon withdrawal from patient by pushing lever arm completely forward until needle tip is fully covered.
- Store in a refrigerator, 2°–8° C (36°–46° F) in original container.

ADVERSE EFFECTS (≥1%) **Body as a Whole:** *Asthenia, pain, injection site pain,* flu-like syndrome, fever, peripheral edema. **CNS:** Dizziness, insomnia, paresthesia, depression, anxiety. **CV:** *Vasodilation.* **GI:** *Nausea, vomiting, constipation, diarrhea,* anorexia. **Hematologic:** Anemia. **Musculoskeletal:** *Bone pain,* arthritis. **Respiratory:** *Pharyngitis, dyspnea, cough.* **Skin:** Rash, sweating.

PHARMACOKINETICS Peak: 7 d. **Duration:** 1 mo. **Distribution:** 99% protein bound. **Metabolism:** In liver via CYP3A4. **Elimination:** 90% in feces. **Half-Life:** 40 d.

CLINICAL IMPLICATIONS

Assessment & Drug Effects
- Monitor for S&S of tumor progression.
- Lab tests: Monitor periodic CBC with differential.

Patient & Family Education
- Use two methods of contraception while taking this drug. Immediately notify physician if you think you are pregnant.
- Report vaginal bleeding to physician. Understand the possibility of drug-induced menstrual irregularities before starting treatment.

FURAZOLIDONE

(fur-a-zoe'li-done)
Furoxone
Classifications: NITROFURAN ANTIBIOTIC
Therapeutic: ANTIBIOTIC
Pregnancy Category: C

AVAILABILITY 100 mg tablets; 50 mg/15 mL liquid

ACTION & *THERAPEUTIC EFFECT*
Synthetic nitrofuran with antibacterial and antiprotozoal properties. Acts by interfering with several bacterial enzyme systems including cell wall synthesis of bacteria. *Bactericidal against majority of GI pathogens, gram-positive and gram-negative bacteria, as well as protozoa.*

USES Bacterial or protozoal diarrhea and enteritis caused by susceptible organisms.

CONTRAINDICATIONS Hypersensitivity to furazolidone, concurrent use with alcohol, MAO INHIBITOR, tyramine-containing foods, indirect-acting sympathomimetic amines; infants <1 mo; neonates; pregnancy (category C), lactation.

CAUTIOUS USE If at all, patients with glucose-6-phosphate dehydrogenase (G6PD) deficiency due to possible development of reversible hemolysis.

ROUTE & DOSAGE

Diarrhea and Enteritis
Adult: **PO** 100 mg q.i.d.
Child: **PO** 1 mo–1 y, 8–17 mg q.i.d.; 1–4 y, 17–25 mg q.i.d.; ≥5 y, 25–50 mg q.i.d. (max: 8.8 mg/kg/d)

ADMINISTRATION

Oral

▪ Store in tight, light-resistant containers (drug darkens on exposure to light). Protect from excessive heat.

ADVERSE EFFECTS (≥1%) **GI:** *Nausea, vomiting,* abdominal pain, diarrhea. **Hypersensitivity:** Fever, arthralgia, hypotension, urticaria, angioedema, vesicular or morbilliform rash. **Body as a Whole:** Headache, malaise, dizziness, hypoglycemia. **Hematologic:** Intravascular hemolysis in patients with G6PD deficiency, <u>agranulocytosis (rare)</u>. **Special Senses:** Partial deafness.

DIAGNOSTIC TEST INTERFERENCE Furazolidone metabolite reportedly may cause false-positive reactions for ***urine glucose*** with ***copper sulfate reduction methods,*** e.g., ***Benedict's reagent, Clinitest,*** and ***Fehling's solution.***

INTERACTIONS Drug: Alcohol may elicit disulfiram-type reaction up to 4 d after the drug is stopped; MAO INHIBITORS, NARCOTICS, SYMPATHOMIMETIC AMINES, **ephedrine**, **phenylpropanolamine** may cause a hypertensive reaction; TRICYCLIC ANTIDEPRESSANTS may cause toxic psychosis. **Food:** may interact with tyramine-containing foods, resulting in flushing, tachycardia, and hypertensive crisis. See **phenelzine** (MAO INHIBITOR prototype). **Herbal: Ginseng** may cause hypertension, manic symptoms, headaches, nervousness; **ma-huang, ephedra, St. John's wort** may lead to hypertensive crisis.

PHARMACOKINETICS Absorption: Poorly absorbed from GI tract. **Metabolism:** In intestines. **Elimination:** In urine.

CLINICAL IMPLICATIONS

Assessment & Drug Effects

▪ Monitor for nausea and vomiting. Dosage reduction may be needed.
▪ Note: Bed rest, fluid and electrolyte replacement (as indicated) are important adjuncts to therapy. Consult physician regarding dietary allowances.
▪ Keep physician informed of S&S of dehydration (see Appendix F) and electrolyte imbalance.
▪ Monitor patients for lost glycemic control because drug may cause hypoglycemia (see Appendix F). Use glucose oxidase methods for urine testing (e.g., Clinistix, Diastix, TesTape).

Patient & Family Education

▪ Report the following to physician: Faintness, weakness, and lightheadedness. These may be symptoms of hypersensitivity reaction or hypoglycemia.
▪ Be aware of and avoid foods high in tyramine (e.g., aged and fermented food and drinks) that may produce hypertensive reaction. Hypertensive crisis is most likely to occur when drug is continued beyond 5 d or when large doses are given.
▪ Do not drink alcohol during furazolidone therapy and for at least 4 d after drug is stopped. Ingestion of alcohol may cause disulfiram-type reaction (see Appendix F); symptoms may last up to 24 h.
▪ Note: Drug may impart a harmless brown color to urine.
▪ Monitor blood glucose for loss of glucemic control if diabetic.

FUROSEMIDE ⊙

(fur-oh′se-mide)
Fumide ✦, Furomide ✦, Lasix, Luramide ✦

Common adverse effects in *italic*, life-threatening effects <u>underlined</u>; generic names in **bold**; classifications in SMALL CAPS; ✦ Canadian drug name; ⊙ Prototype drug

683

Classifications: ELECTROLYTIC AND WATER BALANCE AGENT; LOOP DIURETIC; ANTIHYPERTENSIVE
Therapeutic: LOOP DIURETIC; ANTI-HYPERTENSIVE
Pregnancy Category: C

AVAILABILITY 20 mg, 40 mg, 80 mg tablets; 10 mg/mL, 40 mg/5 mL oral solution; 10 mg/mL injection

ACTION & *THERAPEUTIC EFFECT*
Rapid-acting potent sulfonamide "loop" diuretic and antihypertensive. Inhibits reabsorption of sodium and chloride primarily in loop of Henle and also in proximal and distal renal tubules; decreases renal vascular resistance and may increase renal blood flow. *An antihypertensive that decreases edema and intravascular volume. Reportedly less ototoxic than ethacrynic acid.*

USES Treatment of edema associated with CHF, cirrhosis of liver, and kidney disease, including nephrotic syndrome. May be used for management of hypertension, alone or in combination with other antihypertensive agents, and for treatment of hypercalcemia. Has been used concomitantly with mannitol for treatment of severe cerebral edema, particularly in meningitis.

CONTRAINDICATIONS History of hypersensitivity to furosemide or sulfonamides; increasing oliguria, anuria, fluid and electrolyte depletion states; hepatic coma; peclampsia, eclampsia; pregnancy (category C).

CAUTIOUS USE Infants, older adults; hepatic disease; hepatic cirrhosis; renal disease, nephrotic syndrome; cardiogenic shock associated with acute MI; ventricular arrhythmias,

CHF, diarrhea; history of SLE, history of gout; diabetes mellitus; patients receiving digitalis glycosides or potassium-depleting steroids, lactation.

ROUTE & DOSAGE

Edema

Adult: **PO** 20–80 mg in 1 or more divided doses up to 600 mg/d if needed **IV/IM** 20–40 mg in 1 or more divided doses up to 600 mg/d
Child: **PO** 2 mg/kg, may be increased by 1–2 mg/kg q6–8h (max: 6 mg/kg/dose) **IV/IM** 1 mg/kg, may be increased by 1 mg/kg q2h if needed (max: 6 mg/kg/dose)
Neonate: **PO** 1–4 mg/kg q12–24h **IV/IM** 1–2 mg/kg q12–24h

Hypertension

Adult: **PO** 10–40 mg b.i.d. (max: 480 mg/d)

ADMINISTRATION

Oral
- Give with food or milk to reduce possibility of gastric irritation.
- Schedule doses to avoid sleep disturbance (e.g., a single dose is generally given in the morning; twice-a-day doses at 8 a.m. and 2 p.m.).
- Note: Slight discoloration of tablets reportedly does not alter potency.
- Store tablets at controlled room temperature, preferably at 15°–30° C (59°–86° F) unless otherwise directed. Protect from light.
- Store oral solution in refrigerator, preferably at 2°–8° C (36°–46° F). Protect from light and freezing.

Intramuscular
- Protect syringes from light once they are removed from package.
- Discard yellow or otherwise discolored injection solutions.

F

Intravenous

Note: Verify correct IV concentration and rate of infusion/injection with physician before administration to infants or children.

PREPARE: **Direct:** Give undiluted.

ADMINISTER: **Direct:** Give undiluted at a rate of 20 mg or a fraction thereof over 1 min. With high doses a rate of 4 mg/min is recommended to decrease risk of ototoxicity.

INCOMPATIBILITIES Solution/additive: **Buprenorphine, chlorpromazine, ciprofloxacin, diazepam, diphenhydramine, dobutamine, doxapram, doxorubicin, droperidol, erythromycin, gentamicin, isoproterenol, labetalol, meperidine, metoclopramide, milrinone, netilmicin, pancuronium, prochlorperazine, promethazine, quinidine, thiamine vinblastine, vincristine.** Y-site: **Amrinone, amsacrine, azithromycin, ciprofloxacin, diazepam, diltiazem, dobutamine, diphenhydramine, dopamine, doxorubicin, droperidol, esmolol, filgrastim, fluconazole, gemcitabine, gentamicin, hydralazine, idarubicin, methocarbamol, metoclopramide, midazolam, milrinone, morphine, netilmicin, nicardipine, ondansetron, quinidine, thiopental, tobramycin, vecuronium, vinblastine, vincristine, vinorelbine,** TPN.

▪ Use infusion solutions within 24 h. ▪ Store parenteral solution at controlled room temperature, preferably at 15°–30° C (59°–86° F) unless otherwise directed. Protect from light.

ADVERSE EFFECTS (≥1%) **CV:** Postural hypotension, dizziness with excessive diuresis, acute hypotensive episodes, <u>circulatory collapse</u>. **Metabolic:** Hypovolemia, dehydration, hyponatremia *hypokalemia,* hypochloremia metabolic alkalosis, hypomagnesemia, hypocalcemia (tetany), hyperglycemia, glycosuria, elevated BUN, hyperuricemia. **GI:** Nausea, vomiting, oral and gastric burning, anorexia, diarrhea, constipation, abdominal cramping, acute pancreatitis, jaundice. **Urogenital:** Allergic interstitial nephritis, irreversible renal failure, urinary frequency. **Hematologic:** Anemia, leukopenia, thrombocytopenic purpura; <u>aplastic anemia, agranulocytosis</u> (rare). **Special Senses:** Tinnitus, vertigo, feeling of fullness in ears, hearing loss (rarely permanent), blurred vision. **Skin:** Pruritus, urticaria, exfoliative dermatitis, purpura, photosensitivity, porphyria cutanea tarda, necrotizing angiitis (vasculitis). **Body as a Whole:** Increased perspiration; paresthesias; activation of SLE, muscle spasms, weakness; thrombophlebitis, pain at IM injection site.

DIAGNOSTIC TEST INTERFERENCE
Furosemide may cause elevations in *BUN, serum amylase, cholesterol, triglycerides, uric acid* and *blood glucose* levels, and may decrease *serum calcium, magnesium, potassium,* and *sodium* levels.

INTERACTIONS Drug: OTHER DIURETICS enhance diuretic effects; with **digoxin** increased risk of toxicity because of hypokalemia; NONDEPOLARIZING NEUROMUSCULAR BLOCKING AGENTS (e.g., **tubocurarine**) prolong neuromuscular blockage; CORTICOSTEROIDS, **amphotericin B** potentiate hypokalemia; decreased **lithium** elimination and increased toxicity; SULFONYLUREAS, **insulin**

Common adverse effects in *italic*, life-threatening effects <u>underlined</u>; generic names in **bold**; classifications in SMALL CAPS; ✦ Canadian drug name; ⊚ Prototype drug

685

blunt hypoglycemic effects; NSAIDs may attenuate diuretic effects.

PHARMACOKINETICS Absorption: 60% PO dose from GI tract. **Peak:** 60–70 min PO; 20–60 min IV. **Onset:** 30–60 min PO; 5 min IV. **Duration:** 2 h. **Distribution:** Crosses placenta. **Metabolism:** Small amount in liver. **Elimination:** Rapidly in urine; 50% of oral dose and 80% of IV dose excreted within 24 h; excreted in breast milk. **Half-Life:** 30 min.

CLINICAL IMPLICATIONS

Assessment & Drug Effects
- Observe patients receiving parenteral drug carefully; closely monitor BP and vital signs. Sudden death from cardiac arrest has been reported.
- Monitor for S&S of hypokalemia (see Appendix F).
- Monitor BP during periods of diuresis and through period of dosage adjustment.
- Observe older adults closely during period of brisk diuresis. Sudden alteration in fluid and electrolyte balance may precipitate significant adverse reactions. Report symptoms to physician.
- Lab tests: Obtain frequent blood count, serum and urine electrolytes, CO_2, BUN, blood sugar, and uric acid values during first few months of therapy and periodically thereafter.
- Monitor I&O ratio and pattern. Report decrease or unusual increase in output. Excessive diuresis can result in dehydration and hypovolemia, circulatory collapse, and hypotension. Weigh patient daily under standard conditions.
- Monitor urine and blood glucose & HbA_{1C} closely in diabetics and patients with decompensated he-

patic cirrhosis. Drug may cause hyperglycemia.
- Note: Excessive dehydration is most likely to occur in older adults, those with chronic cardiac disease on prolonged salt restriction, or those receiving sympatholytic agents.

Patient & Family Education
- Consult physician regarding allowable salt and fluid intake.
- Ingest potassium-rich foods daily (e.g., bananas, oranges, peaches, dried dates) to reduce or prevent potassium depletion.
- Learn S&S of hypokalemia (see Appendix F). Report muscle cramps or weakness to physician.
- Make position changes slowly because high doses of antihypertensive drugs taken concurrently may produce episodes of dizziness or imbalance.
- Avoid replacing fluid losses with large amounts of water.
- Avoid prolonged exposure to direct sun.

GABAPENTIN ℗

(gab-a-pen'tin)
Neurontin, Gabarone
Classifications: ANTICONVULSANT; GABA ANALOG
Therapeutic: ANTICONVULSANT
Pregnancy Category: C

AVAILABILITY 100 mg, 300 mg, 400 mg capsules; 100 mg, 300 mg, 400 mg, 600 mg, 800 mg tablets; 250 mg/5 mL solution

ACTION & *THERAPEUTIC EFFECT*
Gabapentin is a GABA neurotransmitter analog; however, it does not interact with GABA receptors, and it does not inhibit GABA uptake or

degradation. Mechanism of action is unknown. *Used in conjunction with other anticonvulsants to control certain types of seizures in patients with epilepsy. Effective in controlling painful neuropathies.*

USES Adjunctive therapy for partial seizures with or without secondary generalization in adults, post-herpetic neuralgia.
UNLABELED USES Add-on therapy for generalized seizures, peripheral neuropathy, migraine prophylaxis.

CONTRAINDICATIONS Hypersensitivity to gabapentin; pregnancy (category C), lactation. Safety and efficacy in infants and children <3 y are not established.
CAUTIOUS USE Status epilepticus, renal impairment, older adults.

ROUTE & DOSAGE

Adjunctive Therapy for Seizure Disorder
Adult/Child: PO >12 y, Start 300 mg on day 1, 300 mg b.i.d. on day 2, 300 mg t.i.d. on day 3, and continue to increase over a week to an initial total dose of 400 mg/d. (1200 mg/d); may increase to 1800–2400 mg/d depending on response (most patients receive 900–1800 mg/d in 3 divided doses) 400 mg t.i.d. (1200 mg/d)
Child: PO 3–12 y, Start 10–15 mg/kg/d in 3 divided doses, titrate q3d to target dose of 40 mg/kg/d in pts 3–4 y or 25–35 mg/kg/d in pts ≥5 y in 3 divided doses

Post-Herpetic Neuralgia
Adult: PO Start 300 mg day 1, 300 mg b.i.d. day 2, and 300 mg t.i.d. day 3; may increase up to 600 mg t.i.d. if needed

Renal Impairment
Cl_{cr} >60 mL/min: 400 mg t.i.d.; 30–60 mL/min: 300 mg b.i.d.; 15–30 mL/min: 300 mg q.d.; <15 mL/min: 300 mg q.o.d. *Hemodialysis:* 200–300 mg following dialysis

ADMINISTRATION

Oral
- Adjust dosage for patients with creatinine clearance of 60 mL/min or less. See manufacturer's recommendations.
- Separate doses of gabapentin and antacids by 2 h.
- Withdraw drug gradually over 1 wk; abrupt discontinuation may cause status epilepticus.
- Store at 15°–30° C (59°–86° F); protect from heat, moisture, and direct light.

ADVERSE EFFECTS (≥1%) **CNS:** *Drowsiness, fatigue,* dizziness, tremor, slurred speech, impaired concentration, headache, increased frequency of partial seizures. **Endocrine:** Weight gain. **GI:** Nausea, gastric upset, vomiting. **Special Senses:** Blurred vision, nystagmus. **Skin:** Rash, eczema.

INTERACTIONS Drug: Increase in **phenytoin** levels at higher doses (300–600 mg/d gabapentin). Does not affect serum levels of other ANTICONVULSANTS. ANTACIDS reduce absorption of gabapentin. **Herbal:** **Ginkgo** may decrease effectiveness.

PHARMACOKINETICS Absorption: 50–60% from GI tract. **Peak:** Peak level 1–3 h; peak effect 2–4 wk. **Distribution:** Crosses the blood–brain barrier; readily passes into cerebrospinal fluid; not bound to plasma proteins; highest concentrations found in pancreas and kid-

Common adverse effects in *italic*, life-threatening effects underlined; generic names in **bold**; classifications in SMALL CAPS; ♣ Canadian drug name; ⊘ Prototype drug

687

neys. **Metabolism:** Does not appear to be metabolized. **Elimination:** 76–81% unchanged in 96 h; 10–23% recovered in feces. **Half-Life:** 5–6 h.

CLINICAL IMPLICATIONS

Assessment & Drug Effects
- Monitor for therapeutic effectiveness; may not occur until several weeks following initiation of therapy.
- Assess frequency of seizures: In rare cases, the drug has increased the frequency of partial seizures.
- Assess safety: Vision, concentration, and coordination may be impaired by gabapentin.

Patient & Family Education
- Learn potential adverse effects of drug.
- Notify physician immediately if any of the following occur: increased seizure frequency, visual changes, unusual bruising or bleeding.
- Do not drive or engage in other potentially hazardous activities until response to drug is known.
- Do not abruptly discontinue use of drug; do not take drug within 2 h of an antacid.

GALANTAMINE HYDROBROMIDE

(ga-lan'ta-meen)
Razadyne, Razadyne ER
Classifications: CHOLINESTERASE INHIBITOR; CENTRAL ACTING; ANTIDEMENTIA AGENT
Therapeutic: ANTIALZHEIMER; ANTIDEMENTIA; CHOLINESTERASE INHIBITOR
Prototype: Donezepril HCl
Pregnancy Category: B

AVAILABILITY 4 mg, 8 mg, 12 mg tablets; 8 mg, 16 mg, 24 mg extended release capsules; 4 mg/mL oral solution

ACTION & *THERAPEUTIC EFFECT*
Competitive and reversible inhibitor of acetylcholinesterase which is the enzyme responsible for the hydrolysis (breakdown) of the neurotransmitter, acetylcholine. The cholinergic system is known to be important in the processing needed for attention, memory, and modulation of excitatory neurotransmission. *In Alzheimer's disease cholinesterase inhibitors are designed to offset loss of presynaptic cholinergic function, slowing decline of memory and maintaining ability to perform functions of daily living.*

USES Treatment of mild to moderate dementia of Alzheimer's type.

UNLABELED USES Vascular dementia.

CONTRAINDICATIONS Hypersensitivity to galantamine. Not recommended with severe renal or hepatic impairment; lactation, or in children.

CAUTIOUS USE Bradycardia, heart block or other cardiac conduction disorders; asthma; COPD; potential bladder outflow obstruction; a history of seizures or GI bleeding; concurrent use of drugs which slow the heart rate, drugs which may cause syncope, NSAIDS, or neuromuscular blocking agents during anesthesia, pregnancy (category B).

ROUTE & DOSAGE

Alzheimer's Disease
Adult: **PO** Initiate with 4 mg b.i.d. times at least 4 wks, if tolerated may increase by 4 mg b.i.d. q4wk to target dose of 12 mg b.i.d. (8–16 mg b.i.d.)

Common adverse effects in *italic*, life-threatening effects <u>underlined</u>; generic names in **bold**; classifications in SMALL CAPS; ♣ Canadian drug name; ⊙ Prototype drug

Hepatic Impairment
Not recommended with severe hepatic impairment
Renal Impairment
Cl_{cr} <9 mL/min: Not recommended

ADMINISTRATION

Oral
- Give with meals (breakfast and dinner) to reduce the risk of nausea.
- Extended release capsules should be swallowed whole and not crushed or chewed.
- Make increases in dosage increments at 4-wk intervals.
- If drug is interrupted for several days or more, restart at the lowest dose and gradually increase to the current dose.
- Store at 15°–30° C (59°–86° F).

ADVERSE EFFECTS (≥1%) **Body as a Whole:** Weight loss, fatigue, rhinitis, syncope, malaise, asthenia, fever. **CNS:** Dizziness, headache, depression, insomnia, somnolence, tremor. **CV:** Bradycardia, chest pain. **GI:** *Nausea, vomiting,* diarrhea, anorexia, abdominal pain, dyspepsia, flatulence. **Hematologic:** Anemia. **Urogenital:** UTI, hematuria, incontinence. **Nervous System:** Tinnitus, leg cramps. **Other:** Increased mortality in patients with mild cognitive impairment.

INTERACTIONS Drug: Additive effects with other CHOLINESTERASE INHIBITORS (e.g., **succinylcholine, bethanecol**); **cimetidine, erythromycin, ketoconazole, paroxetine** may increase levels and toxicity.

PHARMACOKINETICS Absorption: Rapidly and completely. **Peak:** 1 h. **Distribution:** Mainly distributes to red blood cells. **Metabolism:** In liver by CYP2D6 and CYP3A4. **Elimi-**

nation: 95% in urine. **Half-Life:** 7 h (4.4–10 h).

CLINICAL IMPLICATIONS
Assessment & Drug Effects
- Monitor cardiovascular status including baseline and periodic EKG and BP readings. Assess for postural hypotension.
- Monitor respiratory status; report worsening of preexisting asthma or COPD.
- Monitor I&O rates and pattern for urinary incontinence or urinary retention.
- Monitor appetite and food intake. Weigh weekly and report significant weight loss.
- Lab tests: Baseline ALT/AST, BUN and creatinine; periodic blood glucose, alkaline phosphatase, urinalysis, stool for occult blood.

Patient & Family Education
- Report any of the following to a health care provider immediately: loss of weight, urinary retention, chest pain, palpitations, difficulty breathing, fainting, dark stools, blood in the urine.

GALLIUM NITRATE
(gal'li-um)
Ganite
Classifications: BONE RESORPTION INHIBITOR
Therapeutic: BONE RESORPTION INHIBITOR; CALCIUM, REGULATOR
Pregnancy Category: C

AVAILABILITY 25 mg/mL injection

ACTION & *THERAPEUTIC EFFECT*
The precise mechanism is not known. *Induces hypocalcemia by inhibiting calcium resorption from bone.*

USES Hypercalcemia of malignancy.

Common adverse effects in *italic*, life-threatening effects underlined; generic names in **bold**; classifications in SMALL CAPS; ♦ Canadian drug name; ⊘ Prototype drug

UNLABELED USES Paget's disease, painful bone metastases, adjuvant therapy for bladder cancer and lymphomas.

CONTRAINDICATIONS Severe renal impairment (serum creatinine >2.5 mg/dL), lactation.
CAUTIOUS USE Renal function impairment, pregnancy (category C). Safety and efficacy in children are not established.

ROUTE & DOSAGE

Hypercalcemia
Adult: **IV** 100–200 mg/m^2/d × 5 d

Bone Metastases
Adult: **IV** 200 mg/m^2/d × 7 d

ADMINISTRATION

Intravenous

Hydrate patient with oral or IV NS to produce a urine output of 2 L/d; maintain adequate hydration throughout treatment.

PREPARE: **Continuous:** Dilute each daily dose with 1000 mL NS (preferred if not contraindicated) or D5W.

ADMINISTER: **Continuous:** Infuse over 24 h taking care to avoid rapid infusion. Control rate with infusion pump or micro-drip device.
- Do not administer concurrently with potentially nephrotoxic drugs.
- Store IV solutions at 15°–30° C (59°–86° F) for 48 h or refrigerated at 2°–8° C (36°–46° F) for 7 d. Discard unused portions.

ADVERSE EFFECTS (≥1%) **CNS:** *Fatigue,* paresthesia, hyperthermia. **CV:** Hypotension. **GI:** *Nausea, vomiting, diarrhea,* anorexia, stomatitis, dysgeusia, mucositis, metallic taste. **Hematologic:** Anemia, granulocyto-

penia, thrombocytopenia. **Metabolic:** Hypocalcemia, hypophosphatemia, hypomagnesemia. **Urogenital:** Nephrotoxicity, acute renal failure. **Other:** Optic neuritis, maculopapular rash.

INTERACTIONS Drug: AMINOGLYCOSIDES, **amphotericin B, vancomycin** increase the risk of nephrotoxicity.

PHARMACOKINETICS Onset: 48 h. **Duration:** 4–14 d after discontinuation of therapy. **Distribution:** Concentrates in tumors; distributed to lung, skin, muscle, and heart with high concentrations in liver and kidney; not known if crosses placenta or is distributed into breast milk. **Metabolism:** Not metabolized. **Elimination:** 35–71% via kidneys within first 24 h. **Half-Life:** 25–111 h.

CLINICAL IMPLICATIONS

Assessment & Drug Effects
- Lab tests: Monitor BUN and serum creatinine throughout therapy. Notify physician if serum creatinine exceeds 2–5 mg/dL; discontinue drug if this occurs. Also, check baseline serum calcium and serum phosphorus; follow with assessments daily and twice weekly, respectively.
- Note: If hypocalcemia occurs, withhold gallium nitrate and notify physician.

Patient & Family Education
- Learn S&S of hypocalcemia (see Appendix F). Notify physician immediately if any occur.

GANCICLOVIR

(gan-ci′clo-vir)
Cytovene
Classifications: ANTIVIRAL AGENT

Common adverse effects in *italic,* life-threatening effects underlined; generic names in **bold;** classifications in SMALL CAPS; ✦ Canadian drug name; ⊙ Prototype drug

Therapeutic: ANTIVIRAL
Prototype: Acyclovir
Pregnancy Category: C

AVAILABILITY 250 mg, 500 mg capsules; 500 mg powder for injection

ACTION & *THERAPEUTIC EFFECT*

Ganciclovir is a synthetic purine nucleoside analog that is an antiviral drug active against cytomegalovirus (CMV). It inhibits the replication of CMV DNA. *Sensitive human viruses include CMV, herpes simplex virus-1 and -2 (HSV-1, HSV-2), Epstein-Barr virus, and varicella-zoster virus.*

USES CMV retinitis, prophylaxis and treatment of systemic CMV infections in immunocompromised patients including HIV-positive and transplant patients.

CONTRAINDICATIONS Hypersensitivity to ganciclovir or acyclovir; infection; severe thrombocytopenia; pregnancy (category C), lactation.
CAUTIOUS USE Renal impairment, older adults, bone marrow suppression; chemotherapy; radiation therapy.

ROUTE & DOSAGE

Induction Therapy
Adult/Child: **IV** >3 mo, 5 mg/kg q12h for 14–21 d (doses may range from 2.5–5 mg/kg q8–12h for 10–35 d)

Maintenance Therapy
Adult/Child: **IV** 5 mg/kg qd 7 d/wk or 6 mg/kg qd 5 d/wk **PO** 1000 mg t.i.d. or 500 mg 6 times/d q3h while awake

Prevention of CMV Disease in Transplant Recipients
Adult/Child: **IV** 5 mg/kg q12h 7–14 d, then 5 mg/kg q.d. or 6 mg/kg/d 5 d/wk

Renal Impairment
Cl_{cr} 50–70 mL/min: use 50% of dose; 25–50 mL/min: use 50% of dose and q24h interval; 10–25 mL/min: use 25% of dose and q24h interval
Hemodialysis: Give dose postdialysis

ADMINISTRATION

- Note: Do not administer if neutrophil count falls below 500/mm^3 or platelet count falls below 25,000/mm^3.
- Avoid direct contact of powder in capsules or solution with skin and mucous membranes. Wash thoroughly with soap and water if contact occurs.

Oral
- Give with food.

Intravenous
IV administration to infants and children: Verify correct IV concentration and rate of infusion with physician.

PREPARE: **Intermittent:** Reconstitute the 500-mg vial using only 10 mL of sterile water (supplied) for injection immediately before use to yield 50 mg/mL. ▪ Shake well to dissolve. ▪ Withdraw the ordered amount and add to 100 mL of NS, D5W, or RL (volume less than 100 mL may be used, but the final concentration should be <10 mg/mL).

ADMINISTER: **Intermittent:** Give at a constant rate over 1 h. Avoid rapid infusion or bolus injection.

INCOMPATIBILITIES **Solution/additive:** Amino acid solutions (TPN), bacteriostatic water for injection, **fludarabine, foscarnet, ondansetron.** Y-site: **Total parenteral nutrition.**

Common adverse effects in *italic*, life-threatening effects <u>underlined</u>; generic names in **bold**; classifications in SMALL CAPS; ♣ Canadian drug name; ❷ Prototype drug

691

G

▪Store reconstituted solutions refrigerated at 4° C; use within 12 h.
▪Store infusion solution refrigerated up to 24 h of preparation.

ADVERSE EFFECTS (≥1%) **CNS:** *Fever,* headache, disorientation, mental status changes, ataxia, coma, confusion, dizziness, paresthesia, nervousness, somnolence, tremor. **CV:** Edema, phlebitis. **GI:** *Nausea, diarrhea,* anorexia, elevated liver enzymes. **Hematologic:** *Bone marrow suppression, thrombocytopenia, granulocytopenia, eosinophilia, leukopenia,* hyperbilirubinemia. **Metabolic:** Hyperthermia, hypoglycemia. **Urogenital:** Infertility. **Skin:** Rash.

INTERACTIONS Drug: ANTINEOPLASTIC AGENTS, **amphotericin B, didanosine, trimethoprim-sulfamethoxazole (TMP-SMZ), dapsone, pentamidine, probenecid, zidovudine** may increase bone marrow suppression and other toxic effects of ganciclovir; may increase risk of nephrotoxicity from **cyclosporine;** may increase risk of seizures due to **imipenem-cilastatin.**

PHARMACOKINETICS Onset: 3–8 d. **Duration:** Clinical relapse can occur 14 d to 3.5 mo after stopping therapy; positive blood and urine cultures recur 12–60 d after therapy. **Distribution:** Distributes throughout body including CSF, eye, lungs, liver, and kidneys; crosses placenta in animals; not known if distributed into breast milk. **Metabolism:** Not metabolized. **Elimination:** Unchanged in urine. **Half-Life:** 2.5–4.2 h.

CLINICAL IMPLICATIONS
Assessment & Drug Effects
▪Lab tests: Neutrophil and platelet counts at least every other day during twice-daily dosing and weekly thereafter; more frequent monitoring may be indicated in certain patients. Monitor serum creatinine or creatinine clearance at least q2wk. Closely monitor renal function in the older adult.
▪Inspect IV insertion site throughout infusion for signs and symptoms of phlebitis.

Patient & Family Education
▪Note: Drug is not a cure for CMV retinitis; follow regular ophthalmologic examination schedule.
▪Drink lots of fluids during therapy.
▪Use barrier contraception throughout therapy and for at least 90 d afterwards.
▪Maintain frequent hematologic monitoring.

GANIRELIX ACETATE ℗

(gan-i-rel′ix)
Antagon
Classifications: HORMONE; GONADOTROPIN-RELEASING HORMONE (GNRH) ANTAGONIST
Therapeutic: GNRH ANTAGONIST
Prototype: Ganirelix
Pregnancy Category: X

AVAILABILITY 250 mcg/0.5 mL syringe

ACTION & *THERAPEUTIC EFFECT*
Ganirelix is a gonadotropin-releasing hormone (GnRH) antagonist that suppresses pituitary gonadotropins and sex hormones. *It prevents LH surges in reproductive protocols, and causes shrinkage of uterine fibroids.*

USES Infertility treatment.

CONTRAINDICATIONS Prior hypersensitivity to ganirelix, LHRH, or other LHRH analogs, mannitol hypersensitivity; ovarian cyst; primary ovarian failure; pregnancy (category X), lactation.

CAUTIOUS USE History of current allergic disorders (e.g., asthma, hay fever, urticaria, eczema) or a history of allergic reactions to medications; renal/hepatic dysfunction; endocrine disorders; alcohol consumption.

ROUTE & DOSAGE

Infertility
Adult: **SC** After initiating follicle-stimulating hormone (FSH) therapy on day 2 or 3 of the cycle, give 250 mcg once daily during the early-to-mid-follicular phase

ADMINISTRATION
▪ Note: The packaging of the product, Antagon, contains natural rubber latex which may cause allergic reactions.

Subcutaneous
▪ Inject SC into the abdomen around the umbilicus or into the upper thigh.
▪ Rotate injection sites.
▪ Store at 5°–30° C (59°–86° F) and protect from light.

ADVERSE EFFECTS (≥1%) **CNS:** Headache. **GI:** Abdominal pain, nausea. **Endocrine:** Ovarian hyperstimulation syndrome. **Skin:** Injection site reaction. **Urogenital:** Vaginal bleeding.

INTERACTIONS Drug: No clinically significant interactions established.

PHARMACOKINETICS Absorption: 91% from SC site. **Peak:** 1 h. **Distribution:** 81% protein bound. **Elimination:** 75% in feces; 22% in urine. **Half-Life:** 13–16 h.

CLINICAL IMPLICATIONS
Assessment & Drug Effects
▪ Exercise caution with patients with hypersensitivity to GnRH or with known allergic disorders

(e.g., asthma, hay fever). These patients should be carefully monitored after the first injection for S&S of an anaphylactic reaction.
▪ Lab tests: Monitor baseline and periodic CBC with differential, and periodic total bilirubin.

Patient & Family Education
▪ Report menstrual disorders (e.g., spotting, frank vaginal bleeding) to physician.
▪ Notify physician immediately if you think you are pregnant.

G

GATIFLOXACIN
(gat-i-flox′a-sin)
Zymer
Classifications: ANTIBIOTIC; QUINOLONE
Therapeutic: ANTIBIOTIC
Prototype: Ciprofloxacin
Pregnancy Category: C

AVAILABILITY 200 mg, 400 mg tablets; 0.3% ophthalmic solution

ACTION & *THERAPEUTIC EFFECT* Synthetic quinolone that is a broad-spectrum bactericidal agent. Inhibits DNA-gyrase, topoisomerase II, an enzyme necessary for bacterial replication, transcription, repair, and recombination. *Effective against gram-positive and gram-negative bacteria.*

USES Acute bacterial exacerbation of chronic bronchitis; acute sinusitis; community-acquired pneumonia; uncomplicated or complicated UTI; pyelonephritis; gonorrhea due to susceptible organisms.

CONTRAINDICATIONS Hypersensitivity to gatifloxacin or other quinolone antibiotics; diabetes mellitus; viral infections; pregnancy (category C); lactation. Safety and efficacy in

Common adverse effects in *italic*, life-threatening effects underlined; generic names in **bold**; classifications in SMALL CAPS; ♣ Canadian drug name; ☻ Prototype drug

693

children <18 y are unknown. Ophthalmic use in infants <1 mo.

CAUTIOUS USE Patients with CNS disorders including seizures or epilepsy; myasthenia gravis; GI disorders, renal dysfunction; hypersensitivity to other medications; concurrent administration of aluminum-containing antacids.

ROUTE & DOSAGE

Acute Bacterial Exacerbation of Chronic Bronchitis, Complicated
Adult: **PO** 400 mg q.d. times 5 d

Complicated UTI, Acute Pyelonephritis
Adult: **PO** 400 mg q.d. times 7–10 d

Acute Sinusitis
Adult: **PO** 400 mg q.d. times 10 d

Community-Acquired Pneumonia
Adult: **PO** 400 mg q.d. times 7–14 d

Uncomplicated UTI
Adult: **PO** 400 mg as a single dose or 200 mg q.d. times 3 d

Uncomplicated Gonorrhea
Adult: **PO** 400 mg as a single dose

Renal Impairment
Cl_{cr} <40 mL/min or on dialysis: 400 mg times 1 d, then 200 mg q.d.

ADMINISTRATION

Oral
- Give at least 4 h before or after an aluminum- or magnesium-containing antacid, or iron-containing products.
- Store at 15°–30° C (59°–86° F).

ADVERSE EFFECTS (≥1%) **Body as a Whole:** Headache, allergic reactions, chills, fever; back pain, chest pain. **CNS:** Dizziness, abnormal dreams, insomnia, paresthesia, tremor, vasodilatation, vertigo. **CV:** Palpitation; peripheral edema. **GI:** Nausea, diarrhea, abdominal pain, constipation, dyspepsia, glossitis, oral moniliasis, stomatitis, vomiting. **Respiratory:** Dyspnea, pharyngitis. **Skin:** Rash, sweating. **Urogenital:** Vaginitis, dysuria, hematuria. **Special Senses:** Abnormal vision, taste perversion, tinnitus. **Metabolic:** Hyperglycemia, hypoglycemia. **Other:** Cartilage erosion.

DIAGNOSTIC TEST INTERFERENCE May cause false positive on *opiate screening tests*.

INTERACTIONS Drug: Probenecid decreases elimination of **gatifloxacin; ferrous sulfate,** ALUMINUM- or MAGNESIUM-CONTAINING ANTACIDS reduce absorption of **gatifloxacin; gatifloxacin** may cause slight increase in **digoxin** levels.

PHARMACOKINETICS Absorption: 96% from GI tract. **Peak:** 1–2 h PO. **Distribution:** 20% protein bound. **Metabolism:** Minimal metabolism (<1%). **Elimination:** Primarily in urine. **Half-Life:** 7–14 h (up to 35–40 h in severe renal failure).

CLINICAL IMPLICATIONS

Assessment & Drug Effects
- Monitor for S&S of CNS disturbance especially with history of cerebrovascular disease or seizures.
- Lab tests: C&S prior to initiation of therapy; WBC with differential.
- Monitor diabetics for loss of glycemic control.
- Monitor for changes in digoxin blood levels with coadministered drugs.

Patient & Family Education
- Be aware that increased risk of seizures are associated with drug

use in patient with history of seizures.

- Report unexplained dizziness or problems with balance, tendon pain, severe diarrhea, skin rash, mental status changes.

GEFITINIB ⊕
(ge-fi'ti-nib)
Iressa
Classifications: ANTINEOPLASTIC AGENT; EPIDERMAL GROWTH FACTOR RECEPTOR (EGFR); TYROSINE KINASE INHIBITOR (TKI)
Therapeutic: ANTINEOPLASTIC; EGFR-TKI
Pregnancy Category: D

AVAILABILITY 250 mg tablets

ACTION & *THERAPEUTIC EFFECT*
Gefitinib is a selective epidermal growth factor receptor (EGFR) tyrosine kinase inhibitor (EGFR-TKI). EGFR is expressed or overexpressed in many cancers. EGFR expression is associated with poor prognosis for cancer, development of metastasis, and resistance to chemotherapy, hormonal therapy, and radiation therapy. *Inhibits up-regulation or overexpression of EGRF in cancer cells, thus diminishing their capacity for cell proliferation, cell survival, and decreasing their invasive capacity and metastases.*

USES Treatment of locally advanced or metastatic non-small cell lung cancer after failure of both platinum and docetaxel therapy in patients who have previously used gefitinib.
UNLABELED USES Treatment of head and neck and other solid tumors.

CONTRAINDICATIONS Hypersensitivity to gefitinib; pregnancy (category D), lactation; children <18 y.

CAUTIOUS USE Severe renal impairment; hepatic impairment; bacterial/viral infection; dermatologic toxicities; GI disorders; hepatic insufficiency; interstitial lung disease (interstitial pneumonia, pneumonitis, and alveolitis), pulmonary fibrosis, respiratory insufficiency; myelosuppression; females of childbearing age; prior chemotherapy, radiation therapy; ocular toxicities (corneal ulcer, eye pain).

ROUTE & DOSAGE

Non-Small Cell Lung Cancer
Adult: **PO** 250 mg q.d., may increase to 500 mg q.d. if on enzyme-inducing drugs
Head and Neck Cancers
Adult: **PO** 500 mg/d

ADMINISTRATION
Oral
- Give without regard to meals.
- Store tablets at 15°–30° C (59°–86° F).

ADVERSE EFFECTS (≥1%) **Body as a Whole:** Asthenia, peripheral edema. **GI:** *Diarrhea, nausea, vomiting,* anorexia, weight loss, stomatitis. **Respiratory:** Dyspnea, interstitial lung disease. **Skin:** *Acne/acneiform rash, dry skin,* pruritus, vesicular/bullous rash. **Special Senses:** Amblyopia, conjunctivitis, aberrant eyelash growth.

INTERACTIONS Drug: BARBITURATES, **bosentan, carbamazepine, dexamethasone, nevirapine, oxcarbazepine, phenytoin or fosphenytoin, rifampin, rifabutin, rifapentine** may increase metabolism and decrease levels of **gefitinib; amiodarone,** PROTEASE INHIBITORS, **cimetidine, clarithromycin, dalfopristin; quinupristin, del-**

Common adverse effects in *italic*, life-threatening effects underlined; generic names in **bold**; classifications in SMALL CAPS; ♣ Canadian drug name; ⊕ Prototype drug

695

avirdine, efavirenz, **erythromycin, fluconazole, fluvoxamine, fluoxetine, imatinib, itraconazole, ketoconazole, mifepristone, nefazodone** and **voriconazole** may increase levels and toxicity of gefitinib; may increase INR with **warfarin;** H₂-RECEPTOR ANTAGONISTS, PROTON PUMP INHIBITORS may decrease absorption of gefitinib. **Food:** Grapefruit juice may increase levels and toxicity of gefitinib. **Herbal: St. John's wort** may decrease levels of **gefitinib.**

PHARMACOKINETICS Absorption: Slowly absorbed, 60% reaches systemic circulation. **Peak:** 3–7 h. **Metabolism:** In liver primarily by CYP3A4. **Elimination:** 86% in feces. **Half-Life:** 48 h.

CLINICAL IMPLICATIONS

Assessment & Drug Effects
- Monitor pulmonary status and report promptly dyspnea, cough, and fever.
- Withhold drug and notify physician for significant elevations of transaminases, bilirubin, or alkaline phosphatase.
- Monitor for adverse effects, especially with concurrent use of drugs that may inhibit CYP3A4 (e.g., amiodarone, cimetidine, erythromycin, fluconazole, grapefruit juice, etc.). See INTERACTIONS.
- Lab tests: Periodic LFTs; frequent PT/INR with concurrent warfarin.

Patient & Family Education
- Report promptly any of the following: eye pain or irritation; fever; breathing difficulty or shortness of breath; mouth sores.
- Inform physician of all prescription, nonprescription, or herbal drugs you are taking.
- Females should use reliable contraceptives while taking this drug.

- Minimize or avoid intake of grapefruit juice while taking this drug.

GEMCITABINE HYDROCHLORIDE

(gem-ci′ta-been)
Gemzar
Classifications: ANTINEOPLASTIC AGENT; ANTIMETABOLITE, PYRIMIDINE
Therapeutic: ANTINEOPLASTIC; ANTIMETABOLITE
Prototype: Fluorouracil
Pregnancy Category: D

AVAILABILITY 20 mg/mL injection

ACTION & *THERAPEUTIC EFFECT*
Pyrimidine analog with cell phase specificity by affecting rapidly dividing cells in S phase (DNA synthesis). It also blocks the progression of cells from G₁ phase to S phase of cell cycle. Gemcitabine interferes with DNA synthesis by inhibiting ribonucleotide reductase, which results in a reduction in the concentration of deoxynucleotides. In addition, if gemcitabine is incorporated into the DNA strand, it inhibits further growth of the DNA strand. *Gemcitabine induces DNA fragmentation in dividing cells, resulting in the cell death of tumor cells.*

USES Locally advanced or metastatic adenocarcinoma of the pancreas, non-small cell lung cancer, breast cancer.

CONTRAINDICATIONS Hypersensitivity to gemcitabine, severe thrombocytopenia, acute infection, pregnancy (category D), lactation.
CAUTIOUS USE Myelosuppression, renal or hepatic dysfunction, older adults; neutropenia; history of bleeding disorders, infection, previous cytotoxic or radiation treatment. Safety and effectiveness in children are not established.

ROUTE & DOSAGE

Pancreatic Cancer

Adult: **IV** 1000 mg/m² once weekly for up to 7 wk, followed by 1 wk rest from treatment; may repeat once weekly for 3 of every 4 wk

Non-Small Cell Lung Cancer

Adult: **IV** 1000 mg/m² on days 1, 8, 15 of 28-d cycle OR 1250 mg/m² on days 1 and 8 of 21 d cycle. Given with cisplatin.

Breast Cancer

Adult: **IV** 1250 mg/m² on days 1 and 8 of 21 d cycle. Given with paclitaxel.

ADMINISTRATION

Intravenous

PREPARE: **IV Infusion:** Dilute with NS without preservatives by adding 5 mL or 25 mL to the 200 mg or 1 g vial, respectively, to yield 40 mg/mL. ▪ Shake to dissolve. ▪ Dilute further if necessary with NS to concentrations as low as 0.1 mg/mL.

ADMINISTER: **IV Infusion:** Infuse over 30 min. Infusion time >60 min is associated with increased toxicity.

▪ Store reconstituted solutions unrefrigerated at 20°–25° C (68°–77° F). Use within 24 h of reconstitution.

ADVERSE EFFECTS (≥1%) **CNS:** *Fever, flu-like syndrome (anorexia, headache, cough, chills, myalgia),* paresthesias. **GI:** *Nausea, vomiting, diarrhea,* stomatitis, *transient elevations of liver transaminases.* **Hematologic:** <u>Myelosuppression (anemia, leukopenia, neutropenia, thrombocytopenia)</u>. **Skin:** Bullous skin eruption, desquamation. **Urogenital:** Mild

proteinuria and hematuria. **Other:** *Dyspnea, edema, peripheral edema, infection,* elevated liver function tests.

PHARMACOKINETICS Peak: Peak concentrations reached 30 min after infusion; lower clearance in women and older adult results in higher concentrations at any given dose. **Distribution:** Crosses placenta, distributed into breast milk. **Metabolism:** Intracellularly by nucleoside kinases to active diphosphate and triphosphate nucleosides. **Elimination:** 92–98% recovered in urine within 1 wk. **Half-Life:** 32–94 min.

CLINICAL IMPLICATIONS

Assessment & Drug Effects

▪ Lab tests: Monitor CBC with differential and platelet count prior to each dose. Monitor baseline and periodic renal and hepatic function.

Patient & Family Education

▪ Learn about common adverse effects and measures to control or minimize when possible. Notify physician immediately of any distressing adverse effects.

▪ Note: Fever with flu-like symptoms, rash, and GI distress are very common.

GEMFIBROZIL

(gem-fi′broe-zil)

Lopid

Classifications: ANTILIPEMIC; FIBRATE

Therapeutic: CHOLESTEROL-LOWERING AGENT; FIBRATE

Prototype: Fenofibrate

Pregnancy Category: C

AVAILABILITY 600 mg tablets

ACTION & *THERAPEUTIC EFFECT*
Fibric acid derivative with lipid regu-

Common adverse effects in *italic*, life-threatening effects <u>underlined</u>; generic names in **bold**; classifications in SMALL CAPS; ◆ Canadian drug name; ⊙ Prototype drug

lating properties. Blocks lipolysis of stored triglycerides in adipose tissue and inhibits hepatic uptake of fatty acids. *Decreases VLDL and therefore triglyceride synthesis. Produces a moderate increase in HDL cholesterol levels and reduces levels of total and LDL cholesterol and triglycerides.*

USES Patients with very high serum triglyceride levels (above 750 mg/dL) (type IV and V hyperlipidemia) who have not responded to intensive diet restriction and are at risk of pancreatitis and abdominal pain. Also severe familial hypercholesterolemia (type IIa or IIb) that developed in childhood and has failed to respond to dietary control or to other cholesterol-lowering drugs.

CONTRAINDICATIONS Gallbladder disease, biliary cirrhosis, hepatic or severe renal dysfunction; pregnancy (category C), lactation. Safety and efficacy in children <18 y are not established.

CAUTIOUS USE Diabetes mellitus, hypothyroidism; renal impairment, cholelithiasis.

ROUTE & DOSAGE

Hypertriglyceridemia
Adult: **PO** 600 mg b.i.d. 30 min before morning and evening meal, may increase up to 1500 mg/d

ADMINISTRATION

Oral
- Give 30 min before breakfast and evening meal.
- Store at 15°–30° C (59°–86° F) unless otherwise directed.

ADVERSE EFFECTS (≥1%) **CNS:** Headache, dizziness, blurred vision. **GI:** *Abdominal* or *epigastric pain,* diarrhea, nausea, vomiting, flatulence. **Hematologic:** Eosinophilia, mild decreases in Hct, Hgb. **Musculoskeletal:** Painful extremities, back pain, muscle cramps, myalgia, arthralgia, swollen joints. **Skin:** Rash, dermatitis, pruritus, urticaria. **Endocrine:** Hypokalemia, moderate hyperglycemia.

INTERACTIONS Drug: May potentiate hypoprothrombinemic effects of ORAL ANTICOAGULANTS; **lovastatin** increases risk of myopathy and rhabdomyolysis; may increase hypoglycemic effects of ANTIDIABETIC MEDICATIONS.

PHARMACOKINETICS Absorption: Readily from GI tract. **Peak:** 1–2 h. **Metabolism:** Undergoes enterohepatic circulation. **Elimination:** In urine; 6% in feces. **Half-Life:** 1.3–1.5 h.

CLINICAL IMPLICATIONS

Assessment & Drug Effects
- Lab tests: Monitor baseline and at regular intervals during first year of therapy for serum LDL and VLDL, triglycerides, total cholesterol, CBC, blood glucose, liver function tests.
- Note: Mild decreases in WBC, Hgb, Hct may occur during early stage of treatment but generally stabilize with continued therapy.
- Notify physician if the lipid response is not adequate after 3 mo of therapy.
- Notify physician if patient presents S&S suggestive of cholelithiasis or cholecystitis; gallbladder studies may be indicated. Symptoms often occur during the night or early morning; jaundice may or may not be present.

Patient & Family Education
- Notify physician promptly if unexplained bleeding occurs (e.g., easy bruising, epistaxis, hematuria).

- Do not drive or engage in other potentially hazardous activities until response to drug is known.
- Note: Patients with high serum triglyceride levels are generally advised to lose excess weight and to restrict carbohydrate and alcohol intake (alcohol increases serum triglyceride levels).

GEMIFLOXACIN

(gem-i-flox′a-cin)
Factive
Classifications: ANTIBIOTIC; QUINOLONE
Therapeutic: ANTIBIOTIC
Prototype: Ciprofloxacin HCl
Pregnancy Category: C

AVAILABILITY 320 mg tablet

ACTION & *THERAPEUTIC EFFECT*
Gemifloxacin inhibits bacterial DNA gyrases (topoisomerase II), enzymes essential in replication, transcription, and repair of bacterial DNA. *Gemifloxacin is active against a wide range of gram-positive and gram-negative bacteria. Gemifloxacin has greater activity against gram-positive cocci and against penicillin- and ciprofloxacin-resistant Streptococcus pneumoniae than other fluoroquinolones.*

USES Treatment of acute exacerbations of chronic bronchitis, mild to moderate community-acquired pneumonia.
UNLABELED USES Acute sinusitis, UTI, acute pyelonephritis.

CONTRAINDICATIONS Hypersensitivity to gemifloxacin or other fluoroquinolone antibiotics; known QT prolongation; tendon pain; viral disease; pregnancy (category C), lactation. Safety and effectiveness

in children <18 y have not been established.
CAUTIOUS USE Hypokalemia, hypomagnesemia, or concurrent use of Class IA or III antiarrhythmic agents; bradycardia, acute myocardial ischemia; concurrent use of other medications that may prolong the QT interval; renal disease or impairment; hepatic disease; central nervous system disorders such as epilepsy; glucose 6-phosphate dehydrogenase deficiency; tendonitis, elderly, concurrent use of corticosteroids.

ROUTE & DOSAGE

Acute Exacerbation of Chronic Bronchitis
Adult: **PO** 320 mg q.d. × 5 d
Community-Acquired Pneumonia
Adult: **PO** 320 mg q.d. × 7 d
Sinusitis
Adult: **PO** 320 mg q.d. × 10 d
UTI
Adult: **PO** 320 mg q.d. × 3 d
Renal Impairment
Cl_{cr} ≤40 mL/min: 160 mg q.d.

ADMINISTRATION

Oral

- Give 2 h before/3 h after drugs containing aluminum, magnesium, iron, zinc, or buffered tablets of any type.
- Give at least 2 h before sucralfate.
- Store at 15°–30° C (59°–86° F) and protect from light.

ADVERSE EFFECTS (≥1%) **CNS:** Headache. **GI:** Nausea, vomiting, diarrhea, elevated liver enzymes. **Skin:** Rash.

INTERACTIONS Drug: ANTACIDS, **didanosine (tablets and powder),**

Common adverse effects in *italic*, life-threatening effects underlined; generic names in **bold**; classifications in SMALL CAPS; ✦ Canadian drug name; ⊙ Prototype drug

699

iron, sevelamer, sulcralfate decrease absorption; may prolong the QT interval with **amiodarone, bretylium, disopyramide, dofetilide, ibutilide, quinidine, procainamide, sotalol** leading to arrhythmias; may augment phototoxicity of RETINOIDS.

PHARMACOKINETICS Absorption: 71% absorbed. **Peak:** 0.5–2 h. **Metabolism:** Minimally in liver. **Elimination:** Primarily renal. **Half-Life:** 7 h.

CLINICAL IMPLICATIONS

Assessment & Drug Effects

- Monitor cardiac status, especially with concurrent use of drugs that may prolong the QT interval. Report immediately bradycardia or S&S of heart failure.
- Withhold drug and report to physician any of the following: tremors, restlessness, lightheadedness, confusion, hallucinations, paranoia, depression, nightmares, and insomnia.
- Lab tests: C&S prior to initiation of therapy; baseline and periodic serum electrolytes; frequent blood glucose levels in diabetics; CBC with differential and platelet count with prolonged treatment.

Patient & Family Education

- Use sunscreen and protective clothing outdoors. Avoid sun lamps.
- Stop gemifloxacin and notify physician for pain or swelling of a tendon or around a joint.
- Drink fluid liberally (unless contraindicated) while taking this drug.
- Do not drive or engage in other hazardous activities until reaction to drug is known.

GEMTUZUMAB OZOGAMICIN

(gem-tu′zu-mab)

Mylotarg

Classifications: ANTINEOPLASTIC AGENT; IMMUNOSUPPRESSANT; MONOCLONAL ANTIBODY

Therapeutic: ANTINEOPLASTIC AGENT; IMMUNOSUPPRESSANT; MONOCLONAL (I_GG_4) ANTIBODY

Pregnancy Category: D

AVAILABILITY 5 mg vial

ACTION & *THERAPEUTIC EFFECT*

Chemotherapeutic agent composed of recombinant I_GG_4 antibodies which bind specifically to CD33 antigens that are expressed on the surface of leukemic myeloblasts and immature normal cells of myelomonocytic origin. *Cytotoxic to the CD33 positive human leukemia cells in the bone marrow. CD33 antigens are found on the surface of leukemic cells.*

USES Treatment of CD33 positive acute myeloid leukemia (AML) in first relapse in patients ≥60 y.

CONTRAINDICATIONS Hypersensitivity to gemtuzumab or anti-CD33 antibody therapy, murine protein hypersensitivity; systemic infections; pregnancy (category D), lactation. **CAUTIOUS USE** Hepatic impairment including jaundice; renal dysfunction; pulmonary disease; moderate or severe thrombocytopenia or neutropenia. History of asthma or allergies; concurrent administration with antiplatelet agents or anticoagulants.

ROUTE & DOSAGE

Acute Myeloid Leukemia (AML)
Adult: **IV** 9 mg/m^2 infused over 2 h, repeat in 14 d

Common adverse effects in *italic*, life-threatening effects underlined; generic names in **bold**; classifications in SMALL CAPS; ♣ Canadian drug name; ⦿ Prototype drug

ADMINISTRATION

Intravenous

Protect gemtuzumab from sunlight and unshielded fluorescent light during preparation and administration.

- Allow vials to come to room temperature before reconstitution.
- Acetaminophen 650 mg orally and diphenhydramine 25–50 mg IV are normally given prior to infusion to control adverse effects.

PREPARE: **Continuous:** Reconstitute each vial with 5 mL of sterile water for injection to yield 1 mg/mL. Gently swirl to dissolve. Dilute the reconstituted drug further just prior to administration by withdrawing the required amount of drug and adding it to 100 mL of NS. Cover the IV bag with a UV protectant cover.

ADMINISTER: **Continuous:** Infuse over 2 h through a separate IV line with a nonpyrogenic low-protein-binding 1.2 micron filter. Do not give push as a bolus dose.

INCOMPATIBILITIES **Solution/additive &: Y-site:** Do not mix with other drugs.

- Store unopened vials refrigerated at 2°–8° C (36°–46° F). Store reconstituted drug refrigerated at 2°–8° C (36°–46° F) and protected for light for ≤8 h.

ADVERSE EFFECTS (≥1%) Body as a Whole: Severe hypersensitivity *anaphylaxis, chills, fever, asthenia, infection, sepsis.* **CV:** *Hypotension,* hypertension, tachycardia. **GI:** *Nausea, vomiting, mucositis, abdominal pain, anorexia, constipation, diarrhea, stomatitis.* **Hematologic:** <u>*Neutropenia, thrombocytopenia, anemia,*</u> *bleeding,* epistaxis, cerebral hemorrhage, hematuria, ecchymosis. **Metabolic:** Hyperglycemia, *hyperbilirubinemia,* abnormal AST, ALT, hypokalemia, hypomagnesemia, increased lactic dehydrogenase. **Musculoskeletal:** Arthralgia. **CNS:** *Headache,* depression, dizziness, *insomnia.* **Respiratory:** Hypoxia, *dyspnea, cough,* pharyngitis, rhinitis, pneumonia, *fatal pulmonary events.* **Skin:** *Rash, herpes simplex, local reactions from infusion, peripheral edema, petechiae.*

INTERACTIONS : No clinically significant interactions established.

PHARMACOKINETICS Metabolism: Hydrolyzed in liver to calicheamicin. **Half-Life:** 45–100 h.

CLINICAL IMPLICATIONS

Assessment & Drug Effects

- Monitor for S&S of postinfusion syndrome: fever, chills, and rigors which occur 2–4 h after initiation of infusion; hypotension and dyspnea which may occur during first 24 h after infusion.
- Monitor vital signs during and for at least 2 h after infusion.
- Lab tests: Monitor CBC with differential, platelet count, lymphoblast smears at least weekly. Periodically monitor liver functions and routine blood chemistry.

Patient & Family Education

- Report S&S of infection immediately to physician (e.g., chills, fever, sore throat, lower back or side pain).
- Report unusual bleeding or bruising, black tarry stools, or pinpoint red spots on skin to physician immediately.
- Avoid exposure to infections.
- Avoid immunizations unless approved by physician; avoid contact with anyone who has received oral polio virus vaccine.

Common adverse effects in *italic*, life-threatening effects <u>underlined</u>; generic names in **bold**; classifications in SMALL CAPS; ✚ Canadian drug name; ⊘ Prototype drug

701

- Avoid situations that could result in injury during periods of bone marrow suppression.

GENTAMICIN SULFATE ℞

(jen-ta-mye′sin)
Garamycin Ophthalmic, Genoptic
Classifications: AMINOGLYCOSIDE ANTIBIOTIC
Therapeutic: ANTIBIOTIC
Pregnancy Category: C

AVAILABILITY 10 mg/mL, 40 mg/mL; 0.1% ointment, cream; 3 mg/mL ophthalmic solution; 3 mg/g ophthalmic ointment

ACTION & THERAPEUTIC EFFECT
Broad-spectrum aminoglycoside antibiotic derived from *Micromonospora purpurea. Active against a wide variety of aerobic gram-negative but not anaerobic gram-negative bacteria. Also effective against certain gram-positive organisms, particularly penicillin-sensitive and some methicillin-resistant strains of* Staphylococcus aureus *(MRSA).*

USES Parenteral use restricted to treatment of serious infections of GI, respiratory, and urinary tracts, CNS, bone, skin, and soft tissue (including burns) when other less toxic antimicrobial agents are ineffective or are contraindicated. Has been used in combination with other antibiotics. Also used topically for primary and secondary skin infections and for superficial infections of external eye and its adnexa.
UNLABELED USES Prophylaxis of bacterial endocarditis in patients undergoing operative procedures or instrumentation.

CONTRAINDICATIONS History of hypersensitivity to or toxic reaction with any aminoglycoside antibiotic; pregnancy (category C).
CAUTIOUS USE Impaired renal function; history of eighth cranial (acoustic) nerve impairment; preexisting vertigo or dizziness or tinnitus; dehydration, fever; renal impairment, dehydration; Fabry disease; use in older adults, premature infants, neonates, and infants; obesity, neuromuscular disorders: myasthenia gravis, parkinsonian syndrome; hypocalcemia, heart failure, topical applications to widespread areas.

ROUTE & DOSAGE

Moderate to Severe Infection
Adult: **IV/IM** 1–2 mg/kg loading dose followed by 3–5 mg/kg/d in 3 divided doses **Intrathecal** 4–8 mg preservative free q.d. **Topical** 1–2 drops of solution in eye q4h up to 2 drops q1h or small amount of ointment b.i.d. or t.i.d.
Child: **IV/IM** 6–7.5 mg/kg/d in 3 divided doses **Intrathecal** >3 *mo,* 1–2 mg preservative free q.d.
Neonate: **IV/IM** 2.5 mg/kg/d

Prophylaxis of Bacterial Endocarditis
Adult: **IV/IM** 1.5 mg/kg 30 min before procedure, may repeat in 8 h
Child: **IV/IM** < *27 kg,* 2 mg/kg 30 min before procedure, may repeat in 8 h

Obesity
Dose based on IBW, in morbid obesity use IBW +0.4.

Renal Impairment
Reduce dose or extend dosing interval.

ADMINISTRATION

Ophthalmic

- Apply pressure to inner canthus for 1 min immediately after instillation of drops.
- Have patient keep eyes closed for 1–2 min after administration of ophthalmic ointment. Caution patient that vision will be blurred for a few minutes.

Topical

- Wash affected area with mild soap and water, rinse, and dry thoroughly. Gently apply small amount of medication to lesions; cover with sterile gauze.
- Do not apply topical preparations, particularly cream, to large denuded body surfaces because systemic absorption and toxicity are possible.

Intramuscular

- Give deep into a large muscle.
- Do not use solutions that are discolored or that contain particulate matter; drug for IV or IM is clear and colorless or slightly yellow.

Intrathecal

- Note: Intrathecal formulation is a clear and colorless solution.
- Use promptly after opening; contains no preservatives and any unused portion should be discarded.

Intravenous

PREPARE: **Intermittent:** Dilute a single dose with 50–200 mL of D5W or NS. For pediatric patients, amount of infusion fluid may be proportionately smaller depending on patient's needs but should be sufficient to be infused over the same time period as for adults. *ADMINISTER:* **Intermittent:** Give over 30 min–2 h.

INCOMPATIBILITIES **Solution/additive:** Fat emulsion, TPN, **amphotericin B, ampicillin, carbenicillin,** CEPHALOSPORINS, **cytarabine, heparin. Y-site: Azithromycin, furosemide, iodipamide.**

- Store all gentamicin solutions between 2°–30° C (36°–86° F) unless otherwise directed by manufacturer.

ADVERSE EFFECTS (≥1%) **Special Senses:** Ototoxicity (vestibular disturbances, impaired hearing), optic neuritis. **CNS:** Neuromuscular blockade: skeletal muscle weakness, apnea, respiratory paralysis (high doses); arachnoiditis (intrathecal use). **CV:** hypotension or hypertension. **GI:** Nausea, vomiting, transient increase in AST, ALT, and serum LDH and bilirubin; hepatomegaly, splenomegaly. **Hematologic:** Increased or decreased reticulocyte counts; granulocytopenia, thrombocytopenia (fever, bleeding tendency), thrombocytopenic purpura, anemia. **Body as a Whole:** Hypersensitivity (rash, pruritus, urticaria, exfoliative dermatitis, eosinophilia, burning sensation of skin, drug fever, joint pains, laryngeal edema, anaphylaxis). **Urogenital:** <u>Nephrotoxicity</u>: proteinuria, tubular necrosis, cells or casts in urine, hematuria, rising BUN, nonprotein nitrogen, serum creatinine; *decreased creatinine clearance.* **Other:** Local irritation and pain following IM use; thrombophlebitis, abscess, superinfections, syndrome of hypocalcemia (tetany, weakness, hypokalemia, hypomagnesemia). **Topical and Ophthalmic:** Photosensitivity, sensitization, erythema, pruritus; burning, stinging, and lacrimation (ophthalmic formulation).

INTERACTIONS Drug: **Amphotericin B, capreomycin, cisplatin, methoxyflurane, polymyxin B, vancomycin, ethacrynic acid,** and **furosemide** increase risk of

Common adverse effects in *italic*, life-threatening effects <u>underlined</u>; generic names in **bold**; classifications in SMALL CAPS; ♣ Canadian drug name; ❷ Prototype drug

703

nephrotoxicity. GENERAL ANESTHETICS and NEUROMUSCULAR BLOCKING AGENTS (e.g., **succinylcholine**) potentiate neuromuscular blockade. **Indomethacin** may increase gentamicin levels in neonates.

PHARMACOKINETICS Absorption: Well absorbed from IM site. **Peak:** 30–90 min IM. **Distribution:** Widely distributed in body fluids, including ascitic, peritoneal, pleural, synovial, and abscess fluids; poor CNS penetration; concentrates in kidney and inner ear; crosses placenta. **Metabolism:** Not metabolized. **Elimination:** Excreted unchanged in urine; small amounts accumulate in kidney and are eliminated over 10–20 d; small amount excreted in breast milk. **Half-Life:** 2–4 h.

CLINICAL IMPLICATIONS
Assessment & Drug Effects
- Lab tests: Perform C&S and renal function prior to first dose and periodically during therapy; therapy may begin pending test results. Determine creatinine clearance and serum drug concentrations at frequent intervals, particularly for patients with impaired renal function, infants (renal immaturity), older adults, patients receiving high doses or therapy beyond 10 d, patients with fever or extensive burns, edema, obesity.
- Repeat C&S if improvement does not occur in 3–5 d; reevaluate therapy.
- Note: Dosages are generally adjusted to maintain peak serum gentamicin concentrations of 4–10 mcg/mL, and trough concentrations of 1–2 mcg/mL. Prolonged peak concentrations above 12 mcg/mL and trough concentrations above 2 mcg/mL are associated with toxicity.

- Draw blood specimens for peak serum gentamicin concentration 30 min–1h after IM administration, and 30 min after completion of a 30–60 min IV infusion. Draw blood specimens for trough levels just before the next IM or IV dose. Use nonheparinized tubes to collect blood.
- Check baseline weight and vital signs; determine vestibular and auditory function before therapy and at regular intervals. Check vestibular and auditory function again 3–4 wk after drug is discontinued (the time that deafness is most likely to occur).
- Monitor I&O. Keep patient well hydrated to prevent chemical irritation of renal tubules. Report oliguria, unusual appearance of urine, change in I&O ratio or pattern, and presence of edema (prolongs elimination time).
- Note: Ototoxic effect (see Appendix F) is greatest on the vestibular branch of eighth cranial (acoustic) nerve (symptoms: headache, dizziness or vertigo, nausea and vomiting with motion, ataxia, nystagmus). However, damage to the auditory branch (tinnitus, roaring noises, sensation of fullness in ears, hearing impairment) may also occur. Report promptly to prevent permanent damage.
- Watch for S&S of bacterial overgrowth (opportunistic infections) with resistant or nonsusceptible organisms (diarrhea, anogenital itching, vaginal discharge, stomatitis, glossitis).

Patient & Family Education
- Note: When using topical applications: Avoid excessive exposure to sunlight because of danger of photosensitivity; withhold medication and notify physician if condition fails to improve within 1 wk, wors-

ens, or signs of irritation or sensitivity occur; and apply medication as directed and only for length of time prescribed (overuse can result in superinfections).

GLATIRAMER ACETATE

(gla-tir′a-mer)
Copaxone, Copolymer-1
Classifications: IMMUNOMODULATOR
Therapeutic: IMMUNOMODULATOR
Pregnancy Category: B

AVAILABILITY 20 mg injection

ACTION & *THERAPEUTIC EFFECT*
Glatiramer is a random synthetic copolymer of L-alanine, L-glutamic acid, L-lysine, and L-tyrosine. It modifies immune processes that are responsible for the pathogenesis of multiple sclerosis. *Its function is to reduce the relapse rate of multiple sclerosis (MS), a demyelinating disease of the CNS of unknown origin. During an autoimmune response, glatiramer is thought to divert immune cells away from their myelin target as occurs in multiple sclerosis.*

USES Reduction of the frequency of relapses in patients with relapsing–remitting multiple sclerosis.

CONTRAINDICATIONS Hypersensitivity to glatiramer acetate or mannitol. Safety and effectiveness in children <18 y of age have not been established.
CAUTIOUS USE Immunosuppression, history of asthma or other respiratory disorders; pregnancy (category B), lactation.

ROUTE & DOSAGE

Multiple Sclerosis
Adult: **SC** 20 mg q.d.

ADMINISTRATION

Subcutaneous
- Use recommended SC injection sites: Arms, abdomen, hips, and thighs.
- Reconstitute with supplied diluent, swirl gently, let stand at room temperature until completely dissolved, then use immediately.
- Do not store reconstituted drug. Before reconstitution, store vials at −20° to −10° C (−4° to −14° F).

ADVERSE EFFECTS (≥1%) **Body as a Whole:** *Asthenia, back pain,* chills, facial edema, fever, *flu-like syndrome, infection, pain, arthralgia.* **CNS:** Migraine, agitation, *anxiety, hypotonia.* **CV:** *Chest pain, palpitations,* syncope, tachycardia, *vasodilation.* **GI:** *Diarrhea, nausea,* anorexia, gastroenteritis, vomiting. **Respiratory:** *Dyspnea, rhinitis,* bronchitis. **Skin:** *Rash, pruritus, sweating.* **Other:** *Postinjection reaction (flushing, chest pain, palpitations, anxiety, dyspnea, constriction of throat, urticaria), injection site reactions (erythema, hemorrhage, pain, pruritus, urticaria, swelling),* ecchymoses, *lymphadenopathy,* ear pain, dysmenorrhea, urinary urgency.

CLINICAL IMPLICATIONS

Assessment & Drug Effects
- Monitor for therapeutic effectiveness: Indicated by longer remission periods and reduced frequency of attacks.
- Assess for systemic postinjection reactions (see PATIENT & FAMILY EDUCATION). Assure patient that reaction is self-limiting. Assess for local reactions at injection sites including erythema, itching, induration, and soreness.

Common adverse effects in *italic*, life-threatening effects underlined; generic names in **bold**; classifications in SMALL CAPS; ♣ Canadian drug name; ● Prototype drug

705

G

- Monitor for S&S of compromised immune response (e.g., increasing frequency of infections).

Patient & Family Education

- Note: Systemic postinjection reaction with chest pain, palpitations, flushing, urticaria, anxiety, dyspnea, and laryngeal constriction may occur immediately after injection. These symptoms are transient (lasting from 30 sec–30 min), require no treatment, and resolve spontaneously.
- Notify physician of a planned or suspected pregnancy.
- Report any distressing adverse drug effects.

GLIMEPIRIDE

(gli-me′pi-ride)
Amaryl
Classifications: HORMONE; ANTI-DIABETIC; SULFONYLUREA
Therapeutic: ANTIDIABETIC; SULFO-NYLUREA
Prototype: Glyburide
Pregnancy Category: C

AVAILABILITY 1 mg, 2 mg, 4 mg tablets

ACTION & *THERAPEUTIC EFFECT*
Second-generation sulfonylurea hypoglycemic agent used for once-a-day dosing. Directly stimulates functioning pancreatic beta cells to secrete insulin, leading to a direct drop in blood glucose. Indirect action leads to increased sensitivity of peripheral insulin receptors, resulting in increased insulin binding in peripheral tissues. *Lowers blood sugar by increasing secretion of insulin from pancreatic beta cells. Glimepiride improves postprandial glycemic control.*

USES Adjunct to diet and exercise in patients with type 2 diabetes, may also be used in combination with insulin in type 2 diabetes.

CONTRAINDICATIONS Hypersensitivity to glimepiride, diabetic ketoacidosis, pregnancy (category C), lactation, nondiabetic patients with renal glycosuria.
CAUTIOUS USE Previous hypersensitivity to other sulfonylureas, sulfonamides, or thiazide diuretics; hypoglycemia or conditions predisposing to hypoglycemia (e.g., prolonged nausea and vomiting, alcohol ingestion, renal or hepatic function impairment, severe infections, surgery). Safe use in children is not established.

ROUTE & DOSAGE

Type 2 Diabetes Mellitus
Adult: **PO** Start with 1–2 mg once daily with breakfast or first main meal, may increase to usual maintenance dose of 1–4 mg once daily (max: 8 mg/d)

ADMINISTRATION

Oral

- Give with breakfast or first main meal.
- Note: Maximum starting dose is ≤2 mg. With renal or hepatic insufficiency, initial recommended dose is 1 mg. Increase by ≤2 mg at 1- to 2-wk intervals maximum of 8 mg/d.
- Store in tightly closed container at 15°–30° C (59°–86° F).

ADVERSE EFFECTS (≥1%) **CNS:** Dizziness, asthenia, headache, blurred vision, changes in accommodation. **GI:** Nausea, vomiting, diarrhea, abdominal pain. **Hematologic:** Leukopenia, agranulocytosis (rare), thrombocytopenia. **Meta-**

Common adverse effects in *italic*, life-threatening effects underlined; generic names in **bold**; classifications in SMALL CAPS; ♣ Canadian drug name; ☯ Prototype drug

bolic: Hypoglycemia. **Skin:** Rash, pruritus, erythema, urticaria, maculopapular eruptions.

INTERACTIONS Drug: Hypoglycemic effects may be potentiated by other highly protein-bound drugs (e.g., ADRENERGIC ANTAGONISTS, **chloramphenicol**, MAO INHIBITORS, NSAIDS, **probenecid**, SALICYLATES, SULFONAMIDES, **warfarin**). CORTICOSTEROIDS, **phenytoin, isoniazid, nicotinic acid**, SYMPATHOMIMETIC AMINES, THIAZIDE DIURETICS may attenuate effects of glimepiride. **Herbal:** **Ginseng, garlic** may increase hypoglycemic effects.

PHARMACOKINETICS Absorption: Completely absorbed from GI tract. **Onset:** 1 h. **Peak:** 2–3 h. **Distribution:** >99.5% protein bound; probably secreted into breast milk. **Metabolism:** In liver by cytochrome P4502C9 (CYP2C9). **Elimination:** 60% in urine, 40% in feces. **Half-Life:** 5–9 h.

CLINICAL IMPLICATIONS

Assessment & Drug Effects
- Lab tests: monitor fasting and postprandial blood glucose and urinary glucose frequently. Monitor glycosylated hemoglobin every 3–6 mo. Monitor periodically during long-term therapy: Liver function tests, serum osmolarity, serum sodium, and CBC with differential.
- Monitor for hypoglycemia especially with concurrent drugs which enhance hypoglycemic effects.

Patient & Family Education
- Take a missed dose as soon as possible unless it is almost time for next dose; NEVER take two doses at the same time.
- Avoid drinking alcohol or using OTC drugs without informing physician.
- Use sunscreen and avoid sunlamps.

- Learn about adverse reactions and drug interactions.

GLIPIZIDE

(glip′i-zide)
Glucotrol, Glucotrol XL
Classifications: HORMONE; ANTIDIABETIC AGENT; SULFONYLUREA
Therapeutic: ANTIDIABETIC; SULFONYLUREA
Prototype: Glyburide
Pregnancy Category: C

AVAILABILITY 5 mg, 10 mg tablets; 5 mg, 10 mg sustained release tablets

ACTION & *THERAPEUTIC EFFECT*
Second-generation sulfonylurea hypoglycemic agent. Potency is enhanced by as much as 200-fold over first-generation agents. Directly stimulates functioning pancreatic beta cells to secrete insulin, leading to an acute drop in blood glucose. Indirect action leads to altered numbers and sensitivity of peripheral insulin receptors, resulting in increased insulin binding. It also causes inhibition of hepatic glucose production and reduction in serum glucagon levels. *It lowers blood glucose level by stimulating pancreatic beta cells.*

USES Adjunct to diet for control of hyperglycemia in patient with type 2 diabetes mellitus after dietary control alone has failed; also used to treat transient loss of control in patient usually controlled well on diet.

CONTRAINDICATIONS Hypersensitivity to sulfonylureas; diabetic ketoacidosis; pregnancy (category C), lactation. Safe use in children is not established.
CAUTIOUS USE Impaired renal and hepatic function; thyroid disease; older adults; debilitated, malnour-

Common adverse effects in *italic*, life-threatening effects <u>underlined</u>; generic names in **bold**; classifications in SMALL CAPS; ♣ Canadian drug name; ⦿ Prototype drug

707

G

ished patients; patients with adrenal or pituitary insufficiency.

ROUTE & DOSAGE

Control of Hyperglycemia

Adult: **PO** 2.5–5 mg/d 30 min before breakfast, may increase by 2.5–5 mg q1–2wk; >15 mg/d in divided doses 30 min before morning and evening meal (max: 40 mg/d); 5–10 mg sustained release tablets once/d

ADMINISTRATION

Oral

- Give once-daily dosing 30 min before the first meal of the day.
- Ensure that sustained release form of drug is not chewed or crushed. It must be swallowed whole.
- Store in tightly closed, light-resistant container at 15°–30° C (59°–86° F).

ADVERSE EFFECTS (≥1%) **GI:** Nausea, diarrhea, constipation, gastralgia, cholestatic jaundice (rare). **Metabolic:** Hepatic porphyria, <u>hypoglycemia</u>. **Skin:** Erythema, morbilliform or maculopapular rash, pruritus, urticaria, eczema (transient). **Body as a Whole:** Hypersensitivity (fatigue, drowsiness, hunger, GI distress with heartburn, abdominal pain, anorexia). **CNS:** Transient drowsiness, headache, anxiety, ataxia, confusion; seizures, <u>coma</u>. **CV:** Tachycardia. **Special Senses:** Visual disturbances.

INTERACTIONS Drug: Alcohol produces **disulfiram**-like reaction in some patients; ORAL ANTICOAGULANTS, **chloramphenicol, clofibrate, phenylbutazone,** MAO INHIBITORS, SALICYLATES, **probenecid,** SULFONAMIDES may potentiate hypoglycemic actions; THIAZIDES may antagonize hypoglycemic effects; **cimetidine** may increase glipizide levels, causing hypoglycemia. **Herbal: Ginseng, garlic** may increase hypoglycemic effects.

PHARMACOKINETICS Absorption: Readily from GI tract. **Onset:** 15–30 min. **Peak:** 1–2 h. **Duration:** Up to 24 h. **Metabolism:** Metabolized extensively in liver. **Elimination:** Mainly in urine with some excretion via bile in feces. **Half-Life:** 3–5 h.

CLINICAL IMPLICATIONS

Assessment & Drug Effects

- Observe response to the initial dose and establish maintenance regimen cautiously in older adult or debilitated patients; early signs of hypoglycemia are easily overlooked.
- Lab tests: monitor periodically during long-term therapy: Liver function tests, serum electrolytes, and serum osmolarity.
- Note: Severe drug-induced skin rashes and pruritus may necessitate discontinuation of drug use. Symptoms usually subside rapidly when drug is withdrawn.
- Check urine for sugar and ketone bodies at least 3 times daily during insulin withdrawal and transfer to glipizide. Contact physician if tests are abnormal.
- Note: Patients transferred from a sulfonylurea with a long half-life (e.g., chlorpropamide, half-life: 30–40 h) must be observed for hypoglycemic responses (see Appendix F) for 1–2 wk because of potential overlapping of drug effect.
- Note: The first signs of hypoglycemia may be hard to detect in patients receiving concurrent beta blockers or older adults.

Patient & Family Education

- Overdose treatment: Treat mild hypoglycemia (reaction without loss of consciousness or neurologic symptoms) with PO glucose and adjustment of dosage and meal pattern; monitor closely for at least 5–7 d to assure reestablishment of safe control. Severe hypoglycemia requires emergency hospitalization to permit treatment to maintain a blood glucose level above 100 mg/dL.
- Note: Glipizide therapy accompanies (does NOT substitute for) continued control of diet and (if patient is obese) a weight-loss program.
- Test fasting and postprandial blood glucose frequently.
- Exercise is an important part of the total control program.
- When a drug that affects the hypoglycemic action of sulfonylureas (see DRUG INTERACTIONS) is withdrawn or added to the glipizide regimen, be alert to the added danger of loss of control. Urine and blood glucose tests and test for ketone bodies should be carefully monitored.

GLUCAGON

(gloo'ka-gon)
GlucaGen
Classifications: HORMONE; ANTIHYPOGLYCEMIC AGENT
Therapeutic: HORMONE; ANTIHYPOGLYCEMIC; DIAGNOSTIC TEST AID
Pregnancy Category: B

AVAILABILITY 1 mg powder for injection

ACTION & *THERAPEUTIC EFFECT*
Recombinant glucagon identical to glucagon produced by alpha cells of islets of Langerhans. Stimulates uptake of amino acids and their conversion to glucose precursors. Promotes lipolysis in liver and adipose tissue with release of free fatty acid and glycerol, which further stimulates ketogenesis and hepatic gluconeogenesis. *Increases blood glucose secondary to gluconeogenesis. Action in hypoglycemia relies on presence of adequate liver glycogen stores.*

USES Emergency treatment of severe hypoglycemic reactions in diabetic patients who are unconscious or unable to swallow food or liquids and in psychiatric patients receiving insulin shock therapy. Also radiologic studies of GI tract to relax smooth muscle and thereby allow finer detail of mucosa; to diagnose insulinoma.

UNLABELED USES GI disturbances associated with spasm, cardiovascular emergencies, and to overcome cardiotoxic effects of beta blockers, quinidine, tricyclic antidepressants; as an aid in abdominal imaging.

CONTRAINDICATIONS Hypersensitivity to glucagon or protein compounds; depleted glycogen stores in liver; insulinoma; pheochromocytoma.
CAUTIOUS USE Cardiac disease, CAD; pregnancy (category B), lactation.

ROUTE & DOSAGE

Hypoglycemia
Adult: **IM/IV/SC** 1 mg, may repeat q5–20min if no response for 1–2 more doses
Child: **IM/IV/SC** (Over 20 kg) 1 mg (under 20 kg) 20–30 mcg/kg (max: 1 mg/dose), may repeat q5–20min if no response for 1–2 more doses

Common adverse effects in *italic*, life-threatening effects underlined; generic names in **bold**; classifications in SMALL CAPS; ♣ Canadian drug name; ☻ Prototype drug

709

G

Insulin Shock Therapy

Adult: **IM/IV/SC** 1 mg usually 1 h after coma develops, may repeat in 25 min if no response

Diagnostic Aid to Relax Stomach or Upper GI Tract

Adult: **IM/IV** 0.25–2 mg 10 min before procedure

Diagnostic Aid for Colon Exam

Adult: **IM/IV** 2 mg 10 min before procedure

ADMINISTRATION

Note: 1 mg = 1 unit

Subcutaneous
Intramuscular

- Dilute 1 unit (1 mg) of glucagon with 1 mL of diluent supplied by manufacturer.
- Use immediately after reconstitution of dry powder. Discard any unused portion.
- Note: Glucagon is incompatible in syringe with any other drug.

Intravenous

PREPARE: **Direct:** Prepare as noted above. Do not use a concentration >1 unit/mL.

ADMINISTER: **Direct:** Give 1 unit or fraction thereof over 1 min. May be given through a Y-site D5W (not NS) infusing.

INCOMPATIBILITIES **Solution/additive:** Sodium chloride.

- Store unreconstituted vials and diluent at 20°–25° C (68°–77° F).

ADVERSE EFFECTS (≥1%) **GI:** Nausea and vomiting. **Body as a Whole:** Hypersensitivity reactions. **Skin:** Stevens-Johnson syndrome (erythema multiforme). **Metabolic:** Hyperglycemia, hypokalemia.

PHARMACOKINETICS Onset: 5–20 min. **Peak:** 30 min. **Duration:** 1–1.5 h. **Metabolism:** In liver, plasma, and kidneys. **Half-Life:** 3–10 min.

CLINICAL IMPLICATIONS

Assessment & Drug Effects

- Be prepared to give IV glucose if patient fails to respond to glucagon. Notify physician immediately.
- Note: Patient usually awakens from (diabetic) hypoglycemic coma 5–20 min after glucagon injection. Give PO carbohydrate as soon as possible after patient regains consciousness.
- Note: After recovery from hypoglycemic reaction, symptoms such as headache, nausea, and weakness may persist.

Patient & Family Education

- Note: Physician may request that a responsible family member be taught how to administer glucagon SC or IM for patients with frequent or severe hypoglycemic reactions. Notify physician promptly whenever a hypoglycemic reaction occurs so the reason for the reaction can be determined.
- Review package insert and directions (see ADMINISTRATION).

GLYBURIDE ⊕

(glye′byoor-ide)

DiaBeta, Euglucon ◆, Glynase, Micronase

Classifications: HORMONE; ANTIDIABETIC AGENT; SULFONYLUREA
Therapeutic: ANTIDIABETIC; SULFONYLUREA
Pregnancy Category: C

AVAILABILITY 1.25 mg, 2.5 mg, 5 mg tablets; 1.5 mg, 3 mg, 4.5 mg, 6 mg micronized tablets

ACTION & *THERAPEUTIC EFFECT*

One of the most potent of the second-generation sulfonylurea hypoglycemic agents. Potency is enhanced by as much as 200-fold over first-generation agents. Appears to lower blood sugar concentration in both diabetic and nondiabetic individuals by sensitizing functioning pancreatic beta cells to release insulin in the presence of elevated serum glucose levels. *Blood glucose-lowering effect persists during long-term glyburide treatment, but there is a gradual decline in meal-stimulated secretion of endogenous insulin toward pretreatment levels.*

USES Adjunct to diet to lower blood glucose in patients with type 2 diabetes mellitus; after dietary control alone has failed.

CONTRAINDICATIONS Hypersensitivity to glyburide or sulfonylureas; diabetic ketoacidosis; as sole therapy for type 2 diabetes mellitus; moderate or severe renal impairment (Cl_{cr} <50 mL/min) or renal failure; pregnancy (category C); withhold 14 d before labor and delivery; lactation. Safe use in children is not established.

CAUTIOUS USE Limit use in patients with cardiovascular disease; thyroid disease; mild renal impairment or hepatic disease; older adults, debilitated, or malnourished patients; adrenal or pituitary insufficiency.

ROUTE & DOSAGE

Control of Hyperglycemia
Adult: **PO** 1.25–5 mg/d with breakfast, may increase by 2.5–5 mg q1–2wk; >15 mg/d should be given in divided doses with morning and evening meal (max: 20 mg/d); Micronized 1.5–3 mg/d (max: 12 mg/d)

ADMINISTRATION

Oral
- Give once daily in the morning with breakfast or with first main meal.
- Store in tightly closed, light-resistant container at 15°–30° C (59°–86° F).

ADVERSE EFFECTS (≥1%) **Metabolic:** <u>Hypoglycemia</u>. **GI:** Epigastric fullness, heartburn, nausea, vomiting. **Skin:** Pruritus, erythema, urticarial or cholestatic jaundice (rare) morbilliform eruptions. **Special Senses:** Blurred vision.

INTERACTIONS Drug: Alcohol causes disulfiram-like reaction in some patients; ORAL ANTICOAGULANTS, **chloramphenicol, clofibrate, phenylbutazone,** MAO INHIBITORS, SALICYLATES, **probenecid,** SULFONAMIDES may potentiate hypoglycemic actions; THIAZIDES may antagonize hypoglycemic effects; **cimetidine** may increase glyburide levels, causing hypoglycemia. **Herbal: Ginseng, garlic** may increase hypoglycemic effects.

PHARMACOKINETICS Absorption: Readily absorbed from GI tract. **Onset:** 15–60 min. **Peak:** 1–2 h. **Duration:** Up to 24 h. **Distribution:** Distributed in highest concentrations in liver, kidneys, and intestines; crosses placenta. **Metabolism:** Extensively in liver. **Elimination:** Equally in urine and feces. **Half-Life:** 10 h.

CLINICAL IMPLICATIONS

Assessment & Drug Effects
- Monitor blood glucose levels carefully during the dangerous early treatment period when dosage is being individualized. Older adults are especially vulnerable to glyburide-induced hypoglycemia (see

Common adverse effects in *italic*, life-threatening effects <u>underlined</u>; generic names in **bold**; classifications in SMALL CAPS; ✚ Canadian drug name; ⊙ Prototype drug

711

Appendix F) because the antidiabetic agent is long-acting.

- Note: The first signs of hypoglycemia may be hard to detect when the patient is also receiving a beta blocker or is an older adult.
- Lab tests: Monitor at regular intervals: Blood and urine glucose, HbA$_{1c}$, urine ketones, and liver function tests.

Patient & Family Education

- Eat or drink some form of sugar (e.g., corn syrup, orange juice with 2 or 3 tsp of table sugar) when symptoms of hypoglycemia occur. Report reaction to physician promptly.
- Remember that loss of control of diabetes may result from stress such as fever, surgery, trauma, or infection. Check blood glucose and urine for ketones more frequently during stress periods; transfer from the sulfonylurea to insulin may be necessary.
- Keep all follow-up medical appointments and adhere to dietary instructions, regular exercise program, and scheduled urine and blood testing.
- Report blurred vision to physician.

GLYCERIN

(gli′ser-in)
Fleet Babylax, Glycerol, Osmoglyn

GLYCERIN ANHYDROUS

Ophthalgan
Classifications: FLUID AND ELECTROLYTE AGENT; HYPEROSMOTIC LAXATIVE; ANTIGLAUCOMA
Therapeutic: HYPEROSMOTIC LAXATIVE; ANTIGLAUCOMA
Pregnancy Category: C

AVAILABILITY 50% oral solution; suppositories; 4 mL/applicator, ophthalmic solution

ACTION & *THERAPEUTIC EFFECT*
When administered orally, glycerin raises plasma osmotic pressure by withdrawing fluid from extravascular spaces; lowers ocular tension by decreasing volume of intraocular fluid. May also reduce CSF pressure. Topical application to eye reduces edema by hydroscopic effect. Glycerin suppositories apparently work by causing dehydration of exposed tissue, which produces an irritant effect, and by absorbing water from tissues, thus creating more bowel mass. Both actions stimulate peristalsis in the large bowel. *Reduces intraocular pressure by lowering intraocular fluid. Relieves constipation by absorption of water and stimulation of peristalsis.*

USES Orally to reduce elevated intraocular pressure (IOP) before or after surgery in patients with acute narrow-angle glaucoma, retinal detachment, or cataract and to reduce elevated CSF pressure. Sterile glycerin (anhydrous) is used topically to reduce superficial corneal edema resulting from trauma, surgery, or disease and to facilitate ophthalmoscopic examination. Used rectally (suppository or enema) to relieve constipation.
UNLABELED USES To reduce mortality due to strokes in older adults.

CONTRAINDICATIONS Diabetic ketoacidosis; moderate or severe renal impairment (Cl$_{cr}$ <50 mL/min), renal failure; pregnancy (category C); lactation.
CAUTIOUS USE Cardiac disease, mild renal impairment; hepatic disease; diabetes mellitus; thyroid disease; dehydrated or older adult patients.

ROUTE & DOSAGE

Decrease IOP
Adult/Child: **PO** 1–1.8 g/kg 1–1.5 h before ocular surgery, may repeat q5h

Constipation
Adult/Child: **PR** ≥6 y, Insert 1 suppository or 5–15 mL of enema high into rectum and retain for 15 min
Child: **PR** <6 y, Insert 1 infant suppository or 2–5 mL of enema high into rectum and retain for 15 min
Neonate: **PR** 0.5 mL of rectal solution (enema)

Reduction of Corneal Edema
Adult: **Topical** 1–2 drops instilled into eye q3–4h

ADMINISTRATION

Oral
- Pour commercially available flavored solution over crushed ice, then sip through a straw. Lemon or lime juice and NS (if allowed) may be added to unflavored solution for palatability.
- Prevent or relieve headache (from cerebral dehydration) by having patient lie down during and after administration of drug.

Rectal
- Ensure that suppository is inserted beyond rectal sphincter.

ADVERSE EFFECTS (≥1%) **CNS:**
Headache, dizziness, disorientation. **CV:** Irregular heartbeat. **GI:** Nausea, vomiting, thirst, diarrhea, abdominal cramps, rectal discomfort, hyperemia of rectal mucosa. **Metabolic:** Hyperglycemia, glycosuria, dehydration, hyperosmolar nonketotic coma.

PHARMACOKINETICS Absorption:
Readily absorbed from GI tract after oral administration; rectal preparations are poorly absorbed. **Onset:** 10 min PO. **Peak:** 30 min–2 h. **Duration:** 4–8 h. **Metabolism:** 80% metabolized in liver; 10–20% metabolized in kidneys to CO_2 and water or utilized in glucose or glycogen synthesis. **Elimination:** 7–14% excreted unchanged in urine. **Half-Life:** 30–40 min.

CLINICAL IMPLICATIONS
Assessment & Drug Effects
- Consult physician regarding fluid intake in patients receiving drug for elevated IOP. Although hypotonic fluids will relieve thirst and headache caused by the dehydrating action of glycerin, these fluids may nullify its osmotic effect.
- Monitor glycemic control in diabetics. Drug may cause hyperglycemia (see Appendix F).

Patient & Family Education
- Evacuation usually comes 15–30 min after administration of glycerin rectal suppository or enema.
- Note: Slight hyperglycemia and glycosuria may occur with PO use; adjustment in antidiabetic medication dosage may be required.

GLYCOPYRROLATE
(glye-koe-pye′roe-late)
Robinul, Robinul Forte
Classifications: ANTICHOLINERGIC; ANTIMUSCARINIC; ANTISPASMODIC
Therapeutic: GI ANTISPASMODIC
Prototype: Atropine
Pregnancy Category: B

AVAILABILITY 1 mg, 2 mg tablets; 0.2 mg/mL injection

ACTION & *THERAPEUTIC EFFECT*
Synthetic anticholinergic (antimuscarinic) compound with pharmaco-

logic effects similar to those of atropine. Inhibits muscarinic action of acetylcholine on autonomic neuro-effector sites innervated by postganglionic cholinergic nerves. *Inhibits motility of GI tract and genitourinary tract and decreases volume of gastric and pancreatic secretions, saliva, and perspiration.*

USES Adjunctive management of peptic ulcer and other GI disorders associated with hyperacidity, hypermotility, and spasm. Also used parenterally as preanesthetic medication and to reverse neuromuscular blockade.

CONTRAINDICATIONS Glaucoma; asthma; prostatic hypertrophy, obstructive uropathy; obstructive lesions or atony of GI tract; achalasia; severe ulcerative colitis; myasthenia gravis; BPH; urinary tract obstruction; during cyclopropane anesthesia; neonates <1 mo.

CAUTIOUS USE Autonomic neuropathy, hepatic or renal disease; cardiac arrhythmias; pregnancy (category B), lactation.

ROUTE & DOSAGE

Peptic Ulcer
Adult: **PO** 1 mg t.i.d or 2 mg b.i.d. or t.i.d. in equally divided intervals (max: 8 mg/d), then decrease to 1 mg b.i.d. **IM/IV** 0.1–0.2 mg 3–4 times per day

Reversal of Neuromuscular Blockade
Adult/Child: **IV** 0.2 mg administered with 1 mg of neostigmine or 5 mg pyridostigmine

Preanesthetic
Child: **PO** 40–100 mcg/kg t.i.d.– q.i.d. **IM** 4–10 mcg/kg q3–4h
Adult: **IM** 4 mcg/kg 30–60 min before procedure

ADMINISTRATION

Oral
▪ Give without regard to meals.
Intramuscular
▪ Give undiluted, deep into a large muscle.

Intravenous

PREPARE: **Direct:** Give undiluted. ▪ Inspect for cloudiness and discoloration. Discard if present.
ADMINISTER: **Direct:** Give 0.2 mg or fraction thereof over 1–2 min.
INCOMPATIBILITIES **Solution/additive: Methylprednisolone, chloramphenicol, dexamethasone, diazepam, dimenhydrinate, methohexital, pentazocine, phenobarbital, secobarbital, sodium bicarbonate, thiopental. Y-site: Diazepam, dimenhydrinate, methohexital, pentazocine, phenobarbital, secobarbital, thiopental.**

▪ Store at 20°–25° C (68°–77° F).

ADVERSE EFFECTS (≥1%) **Body as a Whole:** *Decreased sweating,* weakness. **CNS:** Dizziness, drowsiness, overdosage (<u>neuromuscular blockade</u> with curare-like action leading to muscle weakness and <u>paralysis</u> is possible). **CV:** Palpitation, tachycardia. **GI:** *Xerostomia,* constipation. **GU:** *Urinary hesitancy or retention.* **Special Senses:** Blurred vision, mydriasis.

INTERACTIONS Drug: **Amantadine,** ANTIHISTAMINES, TRICYCLIC ANTIDEPRESSANTS, **quinidine, disopyramide, procainamide** compound anticholinergic effects; decreases **levodopa** effects; **methotrimeprazine** may precipitate extrapyramidal effects; decreases antipsychotic effects (decreased absorption) of PHENOTHIAZINES.

PHARMACOKINETICS Absorption: Poorly and incompletely absorbed from GI tract. **Onset:** 1 min IV; 15–30 min IM/SC; 1 h PO. **Peak:** 30–45 min IM/SC; 1 h PO. **Duration:** 2–7 h IM/SC; 8–12 h PO. **Distribution:** Crosses placenta. **Metabolism:** Minimally in liver. **Elimination:** 85% in urine. **Half-Life:** 30–70 min (adult), 20–99 min (child), 20–120 min (infant).

CLINICAL IMPLICATIONS

Assessment & Drug Effects

- Incidence and severity of adverse effects are generally dose related.
- Monitor I&O ratio and pattern particularly in older adults. Watch for urinary hesitancy and retention.
- Monitor vital signs, especially when drug is given parenterally. Report any changes in heart rate or rhythm.

Patient & Family Education

- Avoid high environmental temperatures (heat prostration can occur because of decreased sweating).
- Do not drive or engage in other potentially hazardous activities requiring mental alertness until response to drug is known.
- Use good oral hygiene, rinse mouth with water frequently and use a saliva substitute to lessen effects of dry mouth.

GOLD SODIUM THIOMALATE

(thye-oh-mah´late)
Myochrysine ✦
Classifications: GOLD COMPOUND; ANTIMUSCARINIC; IMMUNOMODULATOR; DISEASE-MODIFYING ANTIRHEUMATIC DRUG (DMARD)
Therapeutic: DMARD; GOLD COMPOUND
Prototype: Auranofin
Pregnancy Category: C

AVAILABILITY 50 mg/mL injection

ACTION & *THERAPEUTIC EFFECT*

Water-soluble gold compound. Drug appears to act by suppression of phagocytosis, altered immune responses, and possibly by inhibition of prostaglandin synthesis. *Has immunomodulatory and antiinflammatory effects.*

USES Selected patients (adults and juveniles) with acute rheumatoid arthritis.

UNLABELED USES Psoriatic arthritis, Felty's syndrome.

CONTRAINDICATIONS History of severe toxicity from previous exposure to gold or other heavy metals; severe debilitation; SLE, Sjögren's syndrome in rheumatoid arthritis; renal disease; hepatic dysfunction, history of infectious hepatitis or hematologic disorders; uncontrolled diabetes or CHF; pregnancy (category C).

CAUTIOUS USE History of drug allergies or hypersensitivity, hypertension.

ROUTE & DOSAGE

Rheumatoid Arthritis

Adult: **IM** 10 mg wk 1, 25 mg wk 2, then 25–50 mg/wk to a cumulative dose of 1 g (if improvement occurs, continue at 25–50 mg q2 wk for 2–20 wk, then q3–4 wk indefinitely or until adverse effects occur)
Child: **IM** 10 mg test dose, then 1 mg/kg/wk or 2.5–5 mg for wk 1 and 2, followed by 1 mg/kg q1–4 wk (max: single dose 50 mg)

ADMINISTRATION

Intramuscular

- Agitate vial before withdrawing dose to ensure uniform suspension.
- Give deep into upper outer quadrant of gluteus maximus with patient lying down. Patient should remain recumbent for at least 30

Common adverse effects in *italic*, life-threatening effects <u>underlined</u>; generic names in **bold**; classifications in SMALL CAPS; ✦ Canadian drug name; ⊘ Prototype drug

715

min after injection because of the danger of "nitritoid reaction" (transient giddiness, vertigo, facial flushing, fainting).

- Observe for allergic reactions.
- Store in tight, light-resistant containers at 15°–30° C (59°–86° F). Do not use if any darker than pale yellow.

ADVERSE EFFECTS (≥1%) **CNS:** Dizziness, syncope, sweating, flushing. **CV:** Bradycardia. **GI:** Hepatitis, metallic taste, *stomatitis,* nausea, vomiting. **Hematologic:** Agranulocytosis, aplastic anemia, eosinophilia (all rare). **Urogenital:** Nephrotic syndrome, glomerulitis with hematuria, *proteinuria.* **Skin:** Transient pruritus, *erythema, dermatitis,* fixed drug eruption, alopecia, shedding of nails, gray to blue pigmentation of skin (chrysiasis). **Special Senses:** Gold deposits in ocular tissues, *photosensitivity.* **Body as a Whole:** Peripheral neuritis, angioneurotic edema, interstitial pneumonitis, anaphylaxis (rare). **Respiratory:** Pulmonary fibrosis.

INTERACTIONS Drug: ANTIMALARIALS, IMMUNOSUPPRESSANTS, **penicillamine, phenylbutazone** increase risk of blood dyscrasias.

PHARMACOKINETICS Absorption: Slowly and irregularly absorbed from IM site. **Peak:** 3–6 h. **Distribution:** Widely distributed, especially to synovial fluid, kidney, liver, and spleen; does not cross blood–brain barrier; crosses placenta. **Metabolism:** Not studied. **Elimination:** 60–90% of dose ultimately excreted in urine; also eliminated in feces; traces may be found in urine for 6 mo. **Half-Life:** 3–168 d.

CLINICAL IMPLICATIONS

Assessment & Drug Effects

- Lab tests: Prior to each injection, urinalysis for protein, blood, and sediment. Withhold drug and notify physician promptly if proteinuria or hematuria develops. Also do baseline Hgb and RBC, WBC count, differential count, platelet count before initiation of therapy and at regular intervals.
- Note: Rapid reduction in hemoglobin level, WBC count below 4000/mm³, eosinophil count above 5%, and platelet count below 100,000/mm³ signify possible toxicity.
- Interview and examine patient before each injection to detect occurrence of transient pruritus or dermatitis (both are common early indications of toxicity), stomatitis (sore tongue, palate, or throat), metallic taste, indigestion, or other signs and symptoms of possible toxicity. Interrupt treatment immediately and notify physician if any of these reactions occurs.
- Observe for allergic reaction, which may occur almost immediately after injection, 10 min after injection, or at any time during therapy. Withhold drug and notify physician if observed. Keep antidote dimercaprol (BAL) on hand during time of injection.

Patient & Family Education

- Therapeutic effects may not appear until after 2 mo of therapy.
- Notify physician of rapid improvement in joint swelling; this is indicative that you are closely approaching drug tolerance level.
- Use protective measures in sunlight. Exposure to sunlight may aggravate gold dermatitis.
- Notify physician at the appearance of purpura or ecchymoses; this is always an indication for doing a platelet count.
- Know possible adverse reactions and report any symptom suggestive of toxicity immediately to physician.

Common adverse effects in *italic,* life-threatening effects underlined; generic names in **bold**; classifications in SMALL CAPS; ✦ Canadian drug name; ⓖ Prototype drug

GOSERELIN ACETATE

(gos-er'e-lin)
Zoladex
Classifications: HORMONE; GO-NADOTROPIN-RELEASING HORMONE (GNRH) ANALOG
Therapeutic: GNRH ANALOG
Prototype: Leuprolide
Pregnancy Category: X

AVAILABILITY 3.6 mg, 10.8 mg SC implant

ACTION & *THERAPEUTIC EFFECT*
A synthetic form of luteinizing hormone-releasing hormone (LHRH or GnRH) that inhibits pituitary gonadotropin secretion. *With chronic administration, serum testosterone levels fall into the range normally seen with surgically castrated men.*

USES Prostate cancer, breast cancer. Endometrial thinning agent prior to endometrial ablation for dysfunctional uterine bleeding.
UNLABELED USES Endometriosis, uterine leiomyomas.

CONTRAINDICATIONS Known hypersensitivity to an LHRH; vaginal bleeding; endometriosis or endometrial thinning; hypercalcemia; pregnancy (category X); lactation.
CAUTIOUS USE Urinary tract obstruction and children; family history of osteoporosis; concurrent use with anticonvulsants or corticosteroids; osteoporosis; patients at risk for spinal cord compression or urinary tract obstruction. Safety and efficacy in children are not established.

ROUTE & DOSAGE

Prostate Cancer, Breast Cancer, Endometriosis, Uterine Leiomyomas
Adult: SC 3.6 mg once q28d. 10.8 mg depot q12 wk

Endometrial Thinning Prior to Endometrial Ablation
Adult: SC 3.6 mg once q28d

ADMINISTRATION

Subcutaneous
- Follow manufacturer's directions exactly for implanting the drug SC in the upper abdominal wall.
- Store at room temperature not to exceed 25° C (77° F).

ADVERSE EFFECTS (≥1%) **CNS:** Headache, tumor flare. **Endocrine:** Gynecomastia, breast swelling and tenderness, *postmenopausal symptoms* (*hot flashes*, vaginal dryness). **GI:** Nausea. **Urogenital:** Vaginal spotting, breakthrough bleeding, decreased libido, *impotence.* **Musculoskeletal:** Bone pain, bone loss.

DIAGNOSTIC TEST INTERFERENCE Increased levels of ***alkaline phosphatase*** and ***estradiol*** in the first 1–8 d; initial increase then decrease in ***FSH, LH,*** and ***testosterone.***

INTERACTIONS Drug: No clinically significant interactions established.

PHARMACOKINETICS Absorption: Rapidly absorbed following SC administration. **Duration:** 29 d. **Elimination:** Excreted by kidneys. **Half-Life:** 4.9 h.

CLINICAL IMPLICATIONS

Assessment & Drug Effects
- Monitor carefully during the first month of therapy for S&S of spinal cord compression or ureteral obstruction in patients with prostate cancer. Report immediately to physician.
- Anticipate a transient worsening of symptoms (e.g., bone pain) during the first weeks of therapy in patients with prostate cancer.

Common adverse effects in *italic*, life-threatening effects underlined; generic names in **bold**; classifications in SMALL CAPS; ♣ Canadian drug name; ✪ Prototype drug

717

Patient & Family Education
- Note: Sexual dysfunction in men and hot flashes may accompany drug use.
- Notify physician immediately of symptoms of spinal cord compression or urinary obstruction.

GRANISETRON

(gran'i-se-tron)
Kytril
Classifications: ANTIEMETIC; 5-HT$_3$ ANTAGONIST
Therapeutic: ANTIEMETIC; 5-HT$_3$ ANTAGONIST
Prototype: Ondansetron
Pregnancy Category: B

AVAILABILITY 1 mg tablets; 1 mg/mL injection

ACTION & *THERAPEUTIC EFFECT*
Granisetron is a selective serotonin (5-HT$_3$) receptor antagonist. Serotonin receptors of the 5-HT$_3$ type are located centrally in the chemoreceptor trigger zone, and peripherally on the vagal nerve terminals. Serotonin released from the wall of the small intestine stimulates the vagal afferent neurons through the serotonin (5-HT$_3$) receptors, and initiates the vomiting reflex. *This selective serotonin (5-HT$_3$) receptor antagonist is used for the prevention of nausea and vomiting associated with cancer chemotherapy.*

USES Prevention of nausea and vomiting associated with initial and repeat courses of emetogenic cancer therapy, including high-dose cisplatin, postoperative nausea and vomiting.

CONTRAINDICATIONS Hypersensitivity to granisetron, or benzyl alcohol; GI obstruction; neonates; children less than 2 y.
CAUTIOUS USE Hypersensitivity to ondansetron or similar drugs; liver disease, pregnancy (category B), lactation.

ROUTE & DOSAGE

Chemotherapy-Related Nausea and Vomiting
Adult/Child: **IV** >2 y, 10 mcg/kg, beginning at least 30 min before initiation of chemotherapy (up to 40 mcg/kg per dose has been used) **PO** 1 mg b.i.d., start 1 mg up to 1 h prior to chemotherapy, then second tab 12 h later OR 2 mg q.d.

Postoperative Nausea and Vomiting
Adult: **IV** 1 mg before anesthesia induction or before reversal of anesthesia

ADMINISTRATION

Oral
- Give only on the day of chemotherapy.

Intravenous

PREPARE: Direct: Give undiluted. **IV Infusion:** Dilute in NS or D5W to a total volume of 20–50 mL. Prepare infusion at time of administration; do not mix in solution with other drugs.
ADMINISTER: Direct: Give a single dose over 30 sec. **IV Infusion:** Infuse diluted drug over 5 min or longer; complete infusion 20–30 min prior to initiation of chemotherapy.

- Store at 15°–30° C (59°–86° F) for 24 h after dilution under normal lighting conditions.

ADVERSE EFFECTS (≥1%) **CNS:** *Headache,* dizziness, somnolence,

---

Common adverse effects in *italic*, life-threatening effects underlined; generic names in **bold**; classifications in SMALL CAPS; ♦ Canadian drug name; ⊘ Prototype drug

insomnia, labile mood, anxiety, fatigue. **GI:** Constipation, diarrhea, elevated liver function tests.

PHARMACOKINETICS Onset: Several minutes. **Duration:** Approximately 24 h. **Distribution:** Widely distributed in body tissues. **Metabolism:** Appears to be metabolized in liver. **Elimination:** Excreted in urine as metabolites. **Half-Life:** 10–11 h in cancer patients, 4–5 h in healthy volunteers.

CLINICAL IMPLICATIONS

Assessment & Drug Effects
- Monitor the frequency and severity of nausea and vomiting.
- Lab tests: Monitor liver function; elevated AST and ALT values usually normalize within 2 wk of last dose.
- Assess for headache, which usually responds to nonnarcotic analgesics.

Patient & Family Education
- Note: Headache requiring an analgesic for relief is a common adverse effect.
- Learn ways to manage constipation.

GRISEOFULVIN MICRO-SIZE

(gri-see-oh-ful′vin)
Fulvicin-U/F, Grifulvin V, Grisactin, Grisovin-FP ♦

GRISEOFULVIN ULTRAMICROSIZE

Fulvicin P/G, Grisactin Ultra, Gris-PEG
Classifications: ANTIBIOTIC; ANTIFUNGAL
Therapeutic: ANTIFUNGAL ANTIBIOTIC
Pregnancy Category: C

AVAILABILITY Griseofulvin Micro-Size 250 mg, 500 mg tablets, 250 mg capsules; 125 mg/5 mL Suspension **Griseofulvin Ultramicrosize** 125 mg, 165 mg, 250 mg, 330 mg tablets.

ACTION & *THERAPEUTIC EFFECT*
Fungistatic antibiotic derived from species of *Penicillium*. Arrests metaphase of cell division by disrupting mitotic spindle structure in fungal cells. Deposits in keratin precursor cells and has special affinity for diseased tissue. It is tightly bound to new keratin of skin, hair, and nails, that becomes highly resistant to fungal invasion. *Effective against various species of* Epidermophyton, Microsporum, *and* Trichophyton *(has no effect on other fungi, including* Candida, *bacteria, and yeasts).*

USES Mycotic disease of skin, hair, and nails not amenable to conventional topical measures. Concomitant use of appropriate topical agent may be required, particularly for tinea pedis.
UNLABELED USES Raynaud's disease, angina pectoris, and gout.

CONTRAINDICATIONS SLE; pregnancy (category C), lactation, children ≤2 y, prophylaxis against fungal infections.
CAUTIOUS USE Penicillin-sensitive patients (possibility if cross-sensitivity with penicillin exists; however, reportedly penicillin-sensitive patients have been treated without difficulty); porphyria; hepatic disease.

ROUTE & DOSAGE

Tinea Corporis, Tinea Cruris, Tinea Capitis
Adult: PO 500 mg micro-size or 330–375 mg ultramicrosize daily in single or divided doses

Common adverse effects in *italic*, life-threatening effects underlined; generic names in **bold**; classifications in SMALL CAPS; ♦ Canadian drug name; ☻ Prototype drug

719

G

Child: **PO** 10–20 mg/kg/d micro-size or 5–10 mg/kg/d ultramicrosize in single or divided doses

Tinea Pedis, Tinea Unguium

Adult: **PO** 0.75–1 g micro-size or 660–750 mg ultramicrosize daily in single or divided doses (decrease micro-size dose to 500 mg/d after response is noted)
Child: **PO** 10–20 mg/kg/d micro-size or 5–10 mg/kg/d ultramicrosize in single or divided doses

ADMINISTRATION

Oral
- Give with or after meals to allay GI disturbances.
- Give the micro-size formulations with a high fat content meal (increases drug absorption rate) to enhance serum levels. Consult physician.
- Store at 15°–30° C (59°–86° F) in tightly covered containers unless otherwise directed.

ADVERSE EFFECTS (≥1%) **Body as a Whole:** Hypersensitivity (urticaria, photosensitivity, skin rashes, pruritus, fixed drug eruption, serum sickness syndromes, severe angioedema). **CNS:** *Severe headache,* insomnia, fatigue, mental confusion, impaired performance of routine functions, psychotic symptoms, vertigo. **GI:** Heartburn, nausea, vomiting, diarrhea, flatulence, dry mouth, thirst, decreased taste acuity, anorexia, unpleasant taste, furred tongue, oral thrush. **Hematologic:** Leukopenia, neutropenia, granulocytopenia, punctate basophilia, monocytosis. **Urogenital:** Nephrotoxicity (proteinuria); hepatotoxicity; estrogen-like effects (in children);

aggravation of SLE. **Other:** Overgrowth of nonsusceptible organisms; candidal intertrigo.

INTERACTIONS Drug: Alcohol may cause flushing and tachycardia; BARBITURATES may decrease activity of griseofulvin; may decrease hypoprothrombinemic effects of ORAL ANTICOAGULANTS; may increase **estrogen** metabolism, resulting in break through bleeding, and decrease contraceptive efficacy of ORAL CONTRACEPTIVES.

PHARMACOKINETICS Absorption: Absorbed primarily from duodenum; micro-size is variably and unpredictably absorbed; ultramicrosize is almost completely absorbed. **Peak:** 4–8 h. **Distribution:** Concentrates in skin, hair, nails, fat, and skeletal muscle; crosses placenta. **Metabolism:** In liver. **Elimination:** Mainly in urine; some excretion in perspiration. **Half-Life:** 9–24 h.

CLINICAL IMPLICATIONS

Assessment & Drug Effects
- Inquire about history of sensitivity to griseofulvin, penicillins, or other allergies prior to initiating treatment.
- Monitor food intake. Drug may alter taste sensations, and this may cause appetite suppression and inadequate nutrient intake.
- Lab tests: WBC with differential at least once weekly during first month of therapy or longer; periodic renal and hepatic function tests are also advised.
- Continue treatment until there is clinical improvement or until 2 or 3 consecutive weekly cultures are negative.

Patient & Family Education
- Continuing treatment as prescribed to prevent relapse, even if you

Common adverse effects in *italic*, life-threatening effects underlined; generic names in **bold**; classifications in SMALL CAPS; ♣ Canadian drug name; ⊙ Prototype drug

experience symptomatic relief after 48–96 h of therapy.

- Note: Duration of treatment depends on time required to replace infected skin, hair, or nails, and thus varies with infection site. Average duration of treatment for tinea capitis (scalp ringworm), 4–6 wk; tinea corporis (body ringworm), 2–4 wk; tinea pedis (athlete's foot), 4–8 wk; tinea unguium (nail fungus), at least 4 mo for fingernails, depending on rate of growth, and 6 mo or more for toenails.
- Avoid exposure to intense natural or artificial sunlight, because photosensitivity-type reactions may occur.
- Note: Headaches often occur during early therapy but frequently disappear with continued drug administration.
- Disulfiram-type reaction (see Appendix F) are possible with ingestion of alcohol during therapy.
- Pharmacologic effects of oral contraceptives may be reduced. Breakthrough bleeding and pregnancy may occur. Alternative forms of birth control should be used during therapy.

GUAIFENESIN ⓟ

(gwye-fen′e-sin)
Amonidrin, Anti-Tuss, Breonesin, Gee-Gee, GG-Cen, Glyceryl Guaiacolate, Glycotuss, Glytuss, Guaituss, Hytuss, Malotuss, Mytussin, Mucinex, Nortussin, Resyl ♦, Robitussin
Classifications: EXPECTORANT
Therapeutic: EXPECTORANT
Pregnancy Category: C

AVAILABILITY 100 mg/5 mL syrup; 100 mg/5 mL, 200 mg/5 mL liquid; 200 mg capsules; 300 mg sustained release capsules; 100 mg, 200 mg, 1200 mg tablets; 600 mg sustained release tablets

ACTION & *THERAPEUTIC EFFECT*
Enhances reflex outflow of respiratory tract fluids by irritation of gastric mucosa. *Aids in expectoration by reducing adhesiveness and surface tension of secretions.*

USES To combat dry, nonproductive cough associated with colds and bronchitis. A common ingredient in cough mixtures.

CONTRAINDICATIONS Hypersensitivity to guaifenesin; pregnancy (category C), lactation. Cough due to CHF, ACE inhibitor therapy, or tobacco smoking.
CAUTIOUS USE Chronic cough; asthma; lactation.

ROUTE & DOSAGE

Cough
Adult: **PO** 200–400 mg q4h up to 2.4 g/d
Child: **PO:** <2 y, 12 mg/kg/d in 6 divided doses; 2–5 y, 50–100 mg q4h up to 600 mg/d; 6–11 y, 100–200 mg q4h up to 1.2 g/d

ADMINISTRATION
Oral
- Ensure that sustained release form of drug is not chewed or crushed. It must be swallowed whole.
- Follow dose with a full glass of water if not contraindicated.
- Carefully observe maximum daily doses for adults and children.

ADVERSE EFFECTS (≥1%) **GI:** Low incidence of nausea. **CNS:** Drowsiness.

DIAGNOSTIC TEST INTERFERENCE Guaifenesin may produce color interference with certain laboratory

Common adverse effects in *italic*, life-threatening effects underlined; generic names in **bold**; classifications in SMALL CAPS; ♦ Canadian drug name; ⓟ Prototype drug

721

determinations of **urinary 5-hydroxyindoleacetic acid (5-HIAA)** and **vanillylmandelic acid (VMA).**

INTERACTIONS Drug: By inhibiting platelet function, guaifenesin may increase risk of hemorrhage in patients receiving **heparin** therapy.

CLINICAL IMPLICATIONS

Assessment & Drug Effects

- Monitor for therapeutic effectiveness. Persistent cough may indicate a serious condition requiring further diagnostic work.
- Notify physician if high fever, rash, or headaches develop.

Patient & Family Education

- Increase fluid intake to help loosen mucus; drink at least 8 glasses of fluid daily.
- Contact physician if cough persists beyond 1 wk.
- Contact physician if high fever, rash, or headache develops.

GUANABENZ ACETATE

(gwan'a-benz)

Wytensin

Classifications: ALPHA-ADRENERGIC AGONIST; CENTRAL-ACTING ANTIHYPERTENSIVE

Therapeutic: ANTIHYPERTENSIVE

Prototype: Methyldopa

Pregnancy Category: C

AVAILABILITY 4 mg, 8 mg tablets

ACTION & THERAPEUTIC EFFECT
Centrally acting alpha₂-adrenergic agonist. Pharmacologic actions closely resemble those of clonidine. Lowers BP, primarily by stimulating central alpha-adrenergic receptors that lead to inhibition of sympathetic outflow from brain. Has no effect on exercise tolerance or on potassium levels. *Reduces both supine and standing BP, usually without producing postural hypotension, and slightly lowers pulse rate. Given the fact that central adrenergic hyperactivity causes symptoms of narcotic withdrawal, guanabenz appears to help control abstinence symptoms by reducing norepinephrine output.*

USES Used alone in treatment of hypertension or in combination with a thiazide diuretic.

UNLABELED USES Opiate detoxification, analgesic for chronic pain.

CONTRAINDICATIONS Pregnancy (category C), lactation. Safe use in children is not established.

CAUTIOUS USE Severe coronary insufficiency, recent MI, cerebrovascular disease, severe hepatic or renal failure; older adults; concurrent use of MAOI therapy.

ROUTE & DOSAGE

Hypertension
Adult: **PO** 4 mg b.i.d., may increase by 4–8 mg/d q 1–2 wk up to 32 mg b.i.d.
Geriatric: **PO** 4 mg once daily, may increase every 1–2 wk
Opiate Withdrawal
Adult: **PO** 4 mg b.i.d. to q.i.d.

ADMINISTRATION

Oral

- Give one dose at bedtime to ensure overnight control and reduce possibility of daytime drowsiness or sedation.
- Store at 15°–30° C (59°–86° F) in tightly closed containers unless otherwise directed.

Common adverse effects in *italic*, life-threatening effects underlined; generic names in **bold**; classifications in SMALL CAPS; ♣ Canadian drug name; ⊙ Prototype drug

ADVERSE EFFECTS (≥1%) **CNS:** *Drowsiness* or *sedation,* dizziness, weakness, headache, anxiety, ataxia, depression, sleep disturbances, somnolence. **CV:** Chest pain, edema, arrhythmias, palpitation, hypotension, bradycardia, nervousness. **GI:** *Dry mouth,* nausea, epigastric pain, diarrhea, vomiting, constipation, abdominal discomfort, taste disorders. **Urogenital:** Increased urination, urinary frequency, sexual dysfunction. **Special Senses:** Blurred vision, miosis, nasal congestion. **Body as a Whole:** Dyspnea, muscle aches, aches in extremities, lethargy, irritability, unusual fatigue or weakness. **Skin:** Rash, pruritus.

INTERACTIONS Drug: Alcohol and other CNS DEPRESSANTS compound CNS depression; TRICYCLIC ANTIDEPRESSANTS may reduce antihypertensive effects of guanabenz.

PHARMACOKINETICS Absorption: 75% absorbed from GI tract. **Onset:** 60 min. **Peak:** 2–5 h. **Duration:** 6–12 h. **Distribution:** Widely distributed; crosses blood–brain barrier; not known if crosses placenta or distributed into breast milk. **Metabolism:** Extensively metabolized. **Elimination:** 80% in urine; 20% in feces. **Half-Life:** 4–14 h.

CLINICAL IMPLICATIONS

Assessment & Drug Effects
- Monitor BP and HR. Report palpitations or hypotension to physician.
- Evaluate mental status and alertness.
- Lab tests: Baseline and periodic blood chemistry (serum potassium, CBC, creatinine, uric acid, cholesterol, glucose), urinalysis for protein and sugar, and ECG.
- Give early attention and specific treatment to dry mouth. It can interfere with patient's food and fluid intake; deprivation of normal salivary flow is a potential dental hazard since it favors demineralization of teeth; and it can be a factor in noncompliance.

Patient & Family Education
- Make all position changes slowly and in stages in the event that you experience orthostatic hypotension. This is important in older adults, who tend to be more sensitive to normal adult doses of antihypertensive drugs because of deficient baroreceptor reflexes.
- Do not omit a dose or stop drug therapy without consulting physician. Do not discontinue therapy abruptly; can cause sympathetic overactivity (anxiety, nervousness, palpitation, chest pain, fast or irregular heartbeat, trembling, flushing, headache, increased sweating and salivation, elevation of BP, usually above basal level).
- Do not drive or engage in potentially hazardous activities until response to drug is known. Also, guanabenz may reduce tolerance to alcohol and other CNS depressants.

GUANFACINE HYDROCHLORIDE

(gwahn'fa-seen)
Tenex
Classifications: ALPHA-ADRENERGIC AGONIST; CENTRAL-ACTING ANTIHYPERTENSIVE
Therapeutic: ANTIHYPERTENSIVE
Prototype: Methyldopa
Pregnancy Category: B

AVAILABILITY 1 mg, 2 mg tablets

ACTION & *THERAPEUTIC EFFECT*
Central-acting antihypertensive with alpha$_2$-adrenergic agonist properties. In cerebral cortex, stimulation

of alpha$_2$-adrenoreceptors triggers inhibitory neurons to reduce central sympathetic outflow (i.e., impulses from vasomotor center to heart and blood vessels). *Results in decreased peripheral vascular resistance, thus lowering blood pressure, and a slightly reduced (5 bpm) heart rate.*

USES Management of mild to moderate hypertension.
UNLABELED USES Adjunct in heroin withdrawal.

CONTRAINDICATIONS Treatment of acute hypertension associated with toxemia of pregnancy; children <12 y; lactation.
CAUTIOUS USE Severe coronary insufficiency, recent MI, cerebrovascular disease; chronic renal or hepatic failure; older adult; pregnancy (category B).

ROUTE & DOSAGE

Hypertension
Adult: **PO** 1 mg/d h.s., may be gradually increased to 3 mg/d if needed

ADMINISTRATION

Oral
- Take single dose at bedtime to reduce effect of somnolence.
- Discontinue treatment gradually with planned tapering of schedule.
- Store tablets at 15°–30° C (59°–86° F) in tightly closed container; protect from light.

ADVERSE EFFECTS (≥1%) **CNS:** Confusion, amnesia, mental depression, drowsiness, *dizziness, sedation,* headache, asthenia, *fatigue,* insomnia. **CV:** Bradycardia, palpitation, substernal pain. **Special Senses:** Rhinitis, tinnitus, taste change; vision disturbances, conjunctivitis, iritis. **GI:** *Dry mouth, constipation,* abdominal pain, diarrhea, dysphagia, nausea. **Urogenital:** *Impotence,* testicular disorder, urinary incontinence. **Musculoskeletal:** Leg cramps, hypokinesia. **Skin:** Dermatitis, pruritus, purpura, sweating. **Other:** Dyspnea.

INTERACTIONS Drug: Alcohol and other CNS DEPRESSANTS compound sedation and CNS depression.

PHARMACOKINETICS Absorption: Readily absorbed from GI tract. **Onset:** 2 h. **Peak:** 6 h. **Duration:** Up to 24 h. **Distribution:** Crosses placenta. **Metabolism:** In liver. **Elimination:** 80% in the urine in 24 h. **Half-Life:** 17 h.

CLINICAL IMPLICATIONS

Assessment & Drug Effects
- Do not discontinue abruptly; may cause plasma and urinary catecholamine increases leading symptoms of tachycardia, insomnia, anxiety, nervousness. Rebound hypertension (i.e., increases in BP to levels significantly greater than those before therapy) may occur 2–7 d after abrupt drug withdrawal, but serious effects rarely develop.
- Monitor BP until it is stabilized. Report a rise in pressure that occurs toward end of dose interval; a divided dose schedule may be ordered.
- Assess mental status and alertness. Adverse effects tend to be dose-dependent, increasing significantly with doses above 3 mg/d.

Patient & Family Education
- Continue drug even after you feel well. This is a maintenance dosage regimen (dose and dose intervals). If 2 or more doses are missed, consult physician about how to reestablish dosage regimen.
- Employ measures to keep mouth moist; saliva substitutes (e.g., Moi-

Common adverse effects in *italic*, life-threatening effects underlined; generic names in **bold**; classifications in SMALL CAPS; ♣ Canadian drug name; ◎ Prototype drug

Stir, Xero-Lube) are available OTC. If dry mouth persists >2 wk, patient should check with dentist.

- Do not drive or engage in other potentially hazardous tasks requiring alertness until response to drug is known.
- Avoid alcohol and do not self-medicate with OTC drugs such as sleeping medications, or cough medications without consulting physician.

HAEMOPHILUS b CONJUGATE VACCINE (HiB)

(hee-mof'il-us)

HibTITER, PedvaxHIB, ProHIBiT

Classifications: VACCINE
Therapeutic: VACCINE
Prototype: Hepatitis B vaccine
Pregnancy Category: C

AVAILABILITY 7.5 mcg, 10 mcg, 15 mcg, 25 mcg injection

ACTION & *THERAPEUTIC EFFECT*

A highly purified capsular polysaccharide extracted from *Haemophilus influenzae* type b (Hib). Hib, principal antigen in the vaccine, promotes production of Hib anticapsular antibodies. It mediates complement-dependent bacteriolyses of *H. influenzae* type b organism. *The vaccine produces antibodies effective against* H. influenza *type b.*

USES To provide active immunity to *H. influenzae* type b (Hib) infection in children 2 mo–5 y.

UNLABELED USES Adults at risk of Hib infection who have Hodgkin's disease, before immunosuppressive chemotherapy.

CONTRAINDICATIONS Hypersensitivity to any component of vaccine (e.g., thiomersal); febrile illness (other than upper respiratory tract infection); active infection;. immunosuppression; infants <2 mo; pregnancy (category C).

CAUTIOUS USE Latex hypersensitivity.

ROUTE & DOSAGE

Immunoprophylaxis for *H. influenzae* type b Infection

Child: **IM** 2–6 mo, **HibTITER** 0.5 mL, 3 doses 2 mo apart with booster at 15 mo; **PedvaxHIB** 0.5 mL, 2 doses 2 mo apart with booster at 12 mo; 7–11 mo, **HibTITER** 0.5 mL, 2 doses 2 mo apart with booster at 15 mo; **PedvaxHIB** 0.5 mL, 2 doses 2 mo apart with booster at 15 mo; 12–14 mo, **HibTITER** 0.5 mL, 1 dose with booster at 15 mo; **PedvaxHIB** 0.5 mL, 1 dose with booster at 15 mo; 15 mo–5 y, all vaccines 0.5 mL as 1 dose

ADMINISTRATION

Intramuscular
- Reconstitute lyophilized powder with supplied diluent.
- Note: Use different sites when giving Hib polysaccharide vaccine and DPT (diphtheria, pertussis, tetanus) at the same time.
- Store at 2°–8° C (36°–46° F); may be frozen without loss of potency. Do not freeze the diluent.

ADVERSE EFFECTS (≥1%) **Skin:** Irritation at injection site (4–9%). **Other:** Acute febrile reactions (13%), irritability, anorexia, anaphylactoid reaction (rare).

DIAGNOSTIC TEST INTERFERENCE

Hib polysaccharide vaccine may interfere with interpretation of *antigen detection tests* (e.g., latex agglutination) used in diagnosis of systemic Hib disease.

Common adverse effects in *italic*, life-threatening effects underlined; generic names in **bold**; classifications in SMALL CAPS; ♦ Canadian drug name; ☯ Prototype drug

725

INTERACTIONS Drug: IMMUNOSUP-PRESSANT DRUGS, STEROIDS may decrease antibody response.

PHARMACOKINETICS Onset: Antibody levels detected within 2 wk. **Peak:** 3 wk. **Duration:** 1.5–3.5 y. **Distribution:** Crosses placenta; distributed into breast milk.

CLINICAL IMPLICATIONS

Assessment & Drug Effects
- Be prepared for anaphylactoid reaction (see Appendix F) by having epinephrine 1:1000 available.

Patient & Family Education
- Note: Local reactions to the vaccine at the injection site (erythema, tenderness, induration, swelling, pain) may appear within 6 h after administration; usually symptoms are mild and disappear in 24 h.
- Monitor temperature after injection. An acute febrile reaction with temperature above 38.3° C (101° F) may follow vaccination (less than 1% of recipients). Notify physician.

HALCINONIDE

(hal-sin′oh-nide)
Halog
Classifications: ANTIINFLAMMATORY; FLUORINATED STEROID
Therapeutic: ANTIINFLAMMATORY; STEROID
Prototype: Hydrocortisone
Pregnancy Category: C

AVAILABILITY 0.1% ointment, cream, solution

ACTION & *THERAPEUTIC EFFECT*
Fluorinated steroid with substituted 17-hydroxyl group. Crosses cell membranes, complexes with nuclear DNA and stimulates synthesis of enzymes thought to be responsible for antiinflammatory effects. *Exhibits antiinflammatory, antipyretic, and vasocontrictive properties.*

USES Relief of pruritic and inflammatory manifestations of corticosteroid-responsive dermatoses.

CONTRAINDICATIONS Use on large body surface area; long-term use; infection; acne vulgaris, acne rosacea, perioral dermatitis; pregnancy (category C), lactation.
CAUTIOUS USE Diabetes mellitus; older adults.

ROUTE & DOSAGE

Inflammation

Adult: **Topical** Apply thin layer b.i.d. or t.i.d.
Child: **Topical** Apply thin layer once/d

ADMINISTRATION

Topical
- Wash skin gently and dry thoroughly before each application.
- Note: Ointment is preferred for dry scaly lesions. Moist lesions are best treated with solution.
- Do not apply in or around the eyes.
- Do not apply occlusive dressings over areas covered with halcinonide unless specifically prescribed.
- Store at 15°–30° C (59°–86° F).

ADVERSE EFFECTS (≥1%) **Endocrine:** Reversible HPA axis suppression, hyperglycemia, glycosuria. **Skin:** Burning, itching, irritation, erythema, dryness, folliculitis, hypertrichosis, pruritus, acneiform eruptions, hypopigmentation, perioral dermatitis, allergic contact dermatitis, stinging cracking/tightness of skin, secondary infection, skin atrophy, striae, miliaria, telangiectasia.

PHARMACOKINETICS Absorption: Minimum through intact skin; increased from axilla, eyelid, face, scalp, scrotum, or with occlusive dressing.

CLINICAL IMPLICATIONS

Assessment & Drug Effects

- Discontinue if signs of infection or irritation occur.
- Monitor for systemic corticosteroid effects that may occur with occlusive dressings or topical applications over large areas of skin.

Patient & Family Education

- Do not use an occlusive dressing with this drug unless specifically directed to do so by physician.
- Wash your hands before and after applying this topical medicine.
- Do not get any of the medication in your eyes. If you do, rinse it out with plenty of cool tap water.

HALOPERIDOL ℗

(ha-loe-per'i-dole)
Haldol, Peridol ♦

HALOPERIDOL DECANOATE

Haldol LA
Classifications: PSYCHOTHERAPEUTIC; ANTIPSYCHOTIC; BUTYROPHENONE
Therapeutic: ANTIPSYCHOTIC
Pregnancy Category: C

AVAILABILITY 0.5 mg, 1 mg, 2 mg, 5 mg, 10 mg, 20 mg tablets; 2 mg/mL oral solution; 5 mg/mL, 50 mg/mL, 100 mg/mL injection

ACTION & *THERAPEUTIC EFFECT*
Blocks postsynaptic dopamine (D2) receptors in the limbic system of the brain. Decrease in dopamine neurotransmission has been correlated with its antipsychotic effects, and its higher instance of extrapyramidal effects. *Decreases psychotic manifestations and exerts strong antiemetic effect.*

USES Management of manifestations of psychotic disorders and for control of tics and vocal utterances of Gilles de la Tourette's syndrome; for treatment of agitated states in acute and chronic psychoses. Used for short-term treatment of hyperactive children and for severe behavior problems in children of combative, explosive hyperexcitability.

UNLABELED USES Cancer chemotherapy as an antiemetic in doses smaller than those required for antipsychotic effects; treatment of autism; alcohol dependence; chorea.

CONTRAINDICATIONS Parkinson's disease, parkinsonism, seizure disorders, coma; alcoholism; severe mental depression, CNS depression; pregnancy (category C), lactation. Safe use in children <3 y is not established.

CAUTIOUS USE Older adult or debilitated patients, urinary retention, glaucoma, severe cardiovascular disorders; thyrotoxicosis; patients receiving anticonvulsant, anticoagulant, or lithium therapy.

ROUTE & DOSAGE

Psychosis

Adult: **PO** 0.2–5 mg b.i.d. or t.i.d. **IM** 2–5 mg repeated q4h prn; Decanoate: 50–100 mg q4wk
Child: **PO** 0.5 mg/d in 2–3 divided doses, may be increased by 0.5 mg q5–7d to 0.05–0.15 mg/kg/d

---

Common adverse effects in *italic*, life-threatening effects underlined; generic names in **bold**; classifications in SMALL CAPS; ♦ Canadian drug name; ℗ Prototype drug

727

Severe Psychosis

Adult: **PO** 3–5 mg b.i.d. or t.i.d., may need up to 100 mg/d **IM** 2–5 mg, may repeat q.h. prn; Decanoate: 50–100 mg q4wk
Child: **PO** 0.05–0.15 mg/kg/d in 2–3 divided doses

Dementia

Geriatric: **PO** 0.25–0.5 mg 1–2 times daily, may increase every 4–7 d (max: 4 mg/d in 2–3 divided doses)

Tourette's Disorder

Adult: **PO** 0.2–5 mg b.i.d. or t.i.d.
Child: **PO** 0.05–0.075 mg/kg/d in 2–3 divided doses

ADMINISTRATION

Oral

- Give with a full glass (240 mL) of water or with food or milk.
- Taper dosing regimen when discontinuing therapy. Abrupt termination can initiate extrapyramidal symptoms.

Intramuscular

- Give by deep injection into a large muscle. Do not exceed 3 mL per injection site.
- Have patient recumbent at time of parenteral administration and for about 1 h after injection. Assess for orthostatic hypotension.
- Store in light-resistant container at 15°–30° C (59°–86° F), unless otherwise specified by manufacturer. Discard darkened solutions.

ADVERSE EFFECTS (≥1%) CNS:

Extrapyramidal reactions: Parkinsonian symptoms, dystonia, akathisia, tardive dyskinesia (after long-term use); insomnia, restlessness, anxiety, euphoria, agitation, drowsiness, mental depression, lethargy, fatigue, weakness, tremor, ataxia, headache, confusion, vertigo; neuroleptic malignant syndrome, hyperthermia, grand mal seizures, exacerbation of psychotic symptoms. **CV:** Tachycardia, ECG changes, hypotension, hypertension (with overdosage). **Endocrine:** Menstrual irregularities, galactorrhea, lactation, gynecomastia, impotence, increased libido, hyponatremia, hyperglycemia, hypoglycemia. **Special Senses:** Blurred vision. **Hematologic:** Mild transient leukopenia, agranulocytosis (rare). **GI:** Dry mouth, anorexia, nausea, vomiting, constipation, diarrhea, hypersalivation. **Urogenital:** Urinary retention, priapism. **Respiratory:** Laryngospasm, bronchospasm, increased depth of respiration, bronchopneumonia, respiratory depression. **Skin:** Diaphoresis, maculopapular and acneiform rash, photosensitivity. **Other:** Cholestatic jaundice, variations in liver function tests, decreased serum cholesterol.

INTERACTIONS Drug:

CNS DEPRESSANTS, OPIATES, **alcohol** increase CNS depression; may antagonize activity of ORAL ANTICOAGULANTS; ANTICHOLINERGICS may increase intraocular pressure; **methyldopa** may precipitate dementia.

PHARMACOKINETICS Absorption:

Well absorbed from GI tract; 60% reaches systemic circulation. **Onset:** 30–45 min IM. **Peak:** 2–6 h PO; 10–20 min IM; 6–7 d decanoate. **Distribution:** distributes mainly to liver with lower concentration in brain, lung, kidney, spleen, heart. **Metabolism:** In liver. **Elimination:** 40% excreted in urine within 5 d; 15% eliminated in feces; excreted in breast milk. **Half-Life:** 13–35 h.

CLINICAL IMPLICATIONS

Assessment & Drug Effects

- Monitor for therapeutic effectiveness. Because of long half-life, therapeutic effects are slow to develop in early therapy or when established dosing regimen is changed. "Therapeutic window" effect (point at which increased dose or concentration actually decreases therapeutic response) may occur after long period of high doses. Close observation is imperative when doses are changed.

- Target symptoms expected to decrease with successful haloperidol treatment include hallucinations, insomnia, hostility, agitation, and delusions.
- Monitor patient's mental status daily.
- Monitor for neuroleptic malignant syndrome (NMS) (see Appendix F), especially in those with hypertension or taking lithium. Symptoms of NMS can appear suddenly after initiation of therapy or after months or years of taking neuroleptic (antipsychotic) medication. Immediately discontinue drug if NMS suspected.
- Monitor for parkinsonism and tardive dyskinesia (see Appendix F). Risk of tardive dyskinesia appears to be greater in women receiving high doses and in older adults. It can occur after long-term therapy and even after therapy is discontinued.
- Monitor for extrapyramidal (neuromuscular) reactions that occur frequently during first few days of treatment. Symptoms are usually dose related and are controlled by dosage reduction or concomitant administration of antiparkinson drugs.
- Be alert for behavioral changes in patients who are concurrently receiving antiparkinson drugs.
- Monitor for exacerbation of seizure activity.
- Observe patients closely for rapid mood shift to depression when ha-

loperidol is used to control mania or cyclic disorders. Depression may represent a drug adverse effect or reversion from a manic state.

- Lab tests: Monitor WBC count with differential and liver function in patients on prolonged therapy.

Patient & Family Education

- Avoid use of alcohol during therapy.
- Do not drive or engage in other potentially hazardous activities until response to drug is known.
- Discuss oral hygiene with health care provider; dry mouth may promote dental problems. Drink adequate fluids.
- Avoid overexposure to sun or sunlamp and use a sunscreen; drug can cause a photosensitivity reaction.

HEMIN

(hee′min)
Panhematin
Classifications: BLOOD DERIVATIVE; ENZYME INHIBITOR
Therapeutic: ENZYME INHIBITOR
Pregnancy Category: C

AVAILABILITY 7 mg/mL injection

ACTION & *THERAPEUTIC EFFECT*
Derived from processed red blood cells. Represses synthesis of porphyrin in liver or bone marrow by blocking production of delta-aminolevulinic acid (ALA) synthetase, an essential enzyme in the porphyrin-heme biosynthetic pathway. *Effective in ameliorating recurrent attacks of acute intermittent porphyria (AIP).*

USES Recurrent attacks of acute intermittent porphyria (AIP) only after an appropriate period of alter-

Common adverse effects in *italic*, life-threatening effects underlined; generic names in **bold**; classifications in SMALL CAPS; ✦ Canadian drug name; ❷ Prototype drug

729

nate therapy has been tried (i.e., glucose 400 g/d for 1–2 d).

CONTRAINDICATIONS History of hypersensitivity to hemin; anticoagulation therapy; porphyria cutanea tarda; pregnancy (category C).
CAUTIOUS USE Lactation. Safe use in children less than 16 y is not established.

ROUTE & DOSAGE

Acute Intermittent Porphyria
Adult: **IV** 1–4 mg/kg/d administered over 10–15 min for 3–14 d, do not repeat dose earlier than q12h (max: 6 mg/kg in 24 h)

ADMINISTRATION

Intravenous
Administer via a large arm vein or central venous catheter to reduce risk of phlebitis. Terminal filtration through a sterile 0.45 micron or smaller filter is recommended.

PREPARE: **IV Infusion:** Reconstitute immediately before use by aseptically adding 43 mL sterile water for injection to vial to yield 7 mg/mL. ▪ Shake well for 2–3 min to dissolve all particles. ▪ Discard unused portions.
ADMINISTER: **IV Infusion:** Give a single dose over 10–15 min.

▪ Freeze and store lyophilized powder until time of use.

ADVERSE EFFECTS (≥1%) **Body as a Whole:** *Phlebitis* (when administered into small veins). **Hematologic:** Decreased Hct, anticoagulant effect (prolonged PT, thromboplastin time, thrombocytopenia, hypofibrinogenemia). **Urogenital:** Reversible renal shutdown (with excessive doses).

INTERACTIONS Drug: Potentiates anticoagulant effects of ANTICOAGULANTS; BARBITURATES, ESTROGENS, CORTICOSTEROIDS may antagonize hemin effect.

PHARMACOKINETICS Duration: Can be detected in plasma up to 5 d. **Elimination:** Excess amounts eliminated in bile and urine.

CLINICAL IMPLICATIONS
Assessment & Drug Effects
▪ Monitor IV site for signs and symptoms of thrombophlebitis (see Appendix F).
▪ Monitor throughout therapy (decrease in these values indicates favorable clinical response): ALA, UPG (uroporphyrinogen), PBG (porphobilinogen or coproporphyrin).
▪ Monitor clinical effect of drug therapy by checking patient's symptoms and complaints associated with acute porphyria, which may include depression, insomnia, anxiety, disorientation, hallucinations, psychoses; dark urine, nausea, vomiting, abdominal pain, low back and leg pain, pareses (neuropathy), seizures.
▪ Monitor I&O and promptly report the onset of oliguria or anuria.

Patient & Family Education
▪ Notify physician of bruising, hematuria, tarry black stools, and nosebleeds.

HEPARIN SODIUM ⊙
(hep'a-rin)
Hepalean ◆, Heparin Sodium Lock Flush Solution, Hep-Lock
Classifications: ANTICOAGULANT
Therapeutic: ANTICOAGULANT
Pregnancy Category: C

AVAILABILITY 10 units/mL, 100 units/mL, 1000 units/mL 2000 units/mL, 5000 units/mL, 10,000 units/mL, 20,000 units/mL, 40,000 units/mL injection

ACTION & *THERAPEUTIC EFFECT*
Exerts direct effect on the cascade of blood coagulation (clotting) by enhancing the inhibitory actions of antithrombin III (heparin cofactor) on several factors essential to normal blood clotting, thereby blocking the conversion of prothrombin to thrombin and fibrinogen to fibrin. *Inhibits formation of new clots. High molecular weight mucopolysaccharide with rapid anticoagulant effect. Does not lyse already existing thrombi but may prevent their extension and propagation.*

USES Prophylaxis and treatment of venous thrombosis and pulmonary embolism and to prevent thromboembolic complications arising from cardiac and vascular surgery, frostbite, and during acute stage of MI. Also used in treatment of disseminated intravascular coagulation (DIC), atrial fibrillation with embolization, and as anticoagulant in blood transfusions, extracorporeal circulation, and dialysis procedures.
UNLABELED USES Prophylaxis in hip and knee surgery. Heparin Sodium Lock Flush Solution is used to maintain potency of indwelling IV catheters in intermittent IV therapy or blood sampling. It is not intended for anticoagulant therapy.

CONTRAINDICATIONS History of hypersensitivity to heparin (white clot syndrome); active bleeding, bleeding tendencies (hemophilia, purpura, thrombocytopenia); jaundice; ascorbic acid deficiency; inaccessible ulcerative lesions; visceral carcinoma; open wounds, extensive denudation of skin, suppurative thrombophlebitis; advanced kidney, liver, or biliary disease; active tuberculosis; bacterial endocarditis; continuous tube drainage of stomach or small intestines; threatened abortion; suspected intracranial hemorrhage, severe hypertension; recent surgery of eye, brain, or spinal cord; spinal tap; shock; pregnancy (category C), especially the last trimester.
CAUTIOUS USE Alcoholism; history of allergy (asthma, hives, hay fever, eczema); during menstruation; immediate postpartum period; patients with indwelling catheters; older adults; use of acid-citrate-dextrose (ACD)-converted blood (may contain heparin); patients in hazardous occupations; cerebral embolism.

H

ROUTE & DOSAGE

Treatment of Thromboembolism
Adult: **IV** 5000-unit bolus dose, then 20,000–40,000 units infused over 24 h, dose adjusted to maintain desired APTT or 5000–10,000 unit IV piggyback q4–6h **SC** 10,000–20,000 unit followed by 8000–20,000 units q8–12h
Child: **IV** 50 unit/kg bolus, then 20,000 unit/m^2/24 h or 50–100 unit/kg q4h

Open Heart Surgery
Adult: **IV** 150–400 units/kg

Prophylaxis of Embolism
Adult: **SC** 5000 units q8–12h until patient is ambulatory

ADMINISTRATION

■ Note: Before administration, check coagulation test values; if results are not within therapeutic range, notify physician for dosage adjustment. Do not use solutions of heparin or heparin lock-flush that contain benzyl alcohol preservative in neonates.

Common adverse effects in *italic*, life-threatening effects underlined; generic names in **bold**; classifications in SMALL CAPS; ♣ Canadian drug name; ⊘ Prototype drug

H

Subcutaneous

- Use more concentrated heparin solutions for SC injection.
- Make injections into the fatty layer of the abdomen or just above the iliac crest. Avoid injecting within 5 cm (2 in.) of umbilicus or in a bruised area. Insert needle into tissue roll perpendicular to skin surface. Do not withdraw plunger to check entry into blood vessel. Systematically rotate injection sites and keep record.
- Exercise caution to avoid IM injection.

Intravenous

PREPARE: Direct: Give undiluted. **Intermittent/Continuous:** May add to any amount of NS, D5W, or Ringer's for injection. ▪ Invert IV solution container at least 6 times to ensure adequate mixing.

ADMINISTER: Direct: Give a single dose over 60 sec. **Intermittent/Continuous:** Use infusion pump and give over 4–24 h.

INCOMPATIBILITIES Solution/additive: Amikacin, codeine, chlorpromazine, cytarabine, diazepam, dobutamine, doxorubicin, droperidol, erythromycin, gentamicin, haloperidol, hyaluronidase, hydrocortisone, kanamycin, levorphanol, meperidine, methadone, methicillin, methotrimeprazine, morphine, netilmicin, nitroglycerin, pentazocine, polymyxin B, promethazine, streptomycin, tetracycline, tobramycin, triflupromazine, vancomycin. Y-site: Amikacin, dacarbazine, diazepam, diphenhydramine, doxycycline, doxorubicin, droperidol, ergotamine, erythromycin, gentamicin, haloperidol, kanamycin, methotrimeprazine, netilmicin, nitroglycerin, phenytoin, polymyxin B, streptomycin, tobramycin, triflupromazine, vancomycin.

- Store at 15°–30° C (59°–86° F). Protect from freezing.

ADVERSE EFFECTS (≥1%) **Hematologic:** <u>Spontaneous bleeding,</u> *transient thrombocytopenia,* hypofibrinogenemia, "white clot syndrome." **Body as a Whole:** Fever, chills, urticaria, pruritus, skin rashes, itching and burning sensations of feet, numbness and tingling of hands and feet, elevated BP, headache, nasal congestion, lacrimation, conjunctivitis, chest pains, arthralgia, <u>bronchospasm, anaphylactoid reactions.</u> **Endocrine:** Osteoporosis, hypoaldosteronism, suppressed renal function, hyperkalemia; rebound hyperlipidemia (following termination of heparin therapy). **GI:** increased AST, ALT. **Urogenital:** Priapism (rare). **Skin:** Injection site reactions: pain, itching, ecchymoses, tissue irritation and sloughing; cyanosis and pains in arms or legs (vasospasm), reversible transient alopecia (usually around temporal area).

DIAGNOSTIC TEST INTERFERENCE Notify laboratory that patient is receiving heparin, when a test is to be performed. Possibility of false-positive rise in *BSP* test and in *serum thyroxine;* and increases in *resin T₃* uptake; false-negative ¹²⁵*I fibrinogen uptake.* Heparin prolongs *PT.* Valid readings may be obtained by drawing blood samples at least 4–6 h after an IV dose (but at any time during heparin infusion) and 12–24 h after an SC heparin dose.

INTERACTIONS Drug: May prolong PT, which is used to monitor therapy with ORAL ANTICOAGULANTS; **aspi-**

rin, NSAIDs increase risk of bleeding; **nitroglycerin** IV may decrease anticoagulant activity; **protamine** antagonizes effects of heparin. **Herbal: Feverfew, ginkgo, ginger** may potentiate bleeding.

PHARMACOKINETICS Onset: 20–60 min SC. **Peak:** Within minutes. **Duration:** 2–6 h IV; 8–12 h SC. **Distribution:** Does not cross placenta; not distributed into breast milk. **Metabolism:** In liver and by reticuloendothelial system. **Elimination:** In urine. **Half-Life:** 90 min.

CLINICAL IMPLICATIONS

Assessment & Drug Effects

- Lab tests: Baseline blood coagulation tests, Hct, Hgb, RBC, and platelet counts prior to initiation of therapy and at regular intervals throughout therapy.
- Monitor APTT levels closely.
- Note: In general, dosage is adjusted to keep APTT between 1.5–2.5 times normal control level.
- Draw blood for coagulation test 30 min before each scheduled SC or intermittent IV dose and approximately q4h for patients receiving continuous IV heparin during dosage adjustment period. After dosage is established, tests may be done once daily.
- Patients vary widely in their reaction to heparin; risk of hemorrhage appears greatest in women, all patients >60 y, and patients with liver disease or renal insufficiency.
- Monitor vital signs. Report fever, drop in BP, rapid pulse, and other S&S of hemorrhage.
- Observe all needle sites daily for hematoma and signs of inflammation (swelling, heat, redness, pain).
- Antidote: Have on hand protamine sulfate (1% solution), specific heparin antagonist.

Patient & Family Education

- Protect from injury and notify physician of pink, red, dark brown, or cloudy urine; red or dark brown vomitus; red or black stools; bleeding gums or oral mucosa; ecchymoses, hematoma, epistaxis, bloody sputum; chest pain; abdominal or lumbar pain or swelling; unusual increase in menstrual flow; pelvic pain; severe or continuous headache, faintness, or dizziness.
- Note: Menstruation may be somewhat increased and prolonged; usually, this is not a contraindication to continued therapy if bleeding is not excessive.
- Learn correct technique for SC administration if discharged from hospital on heparin.
- Engage in normal activities such as shaving with a safety razor in the absence of a low platelet (thrombocyte) count. Usually, heparin does not affect bleeding time.
- Caution: Smoking and alcohol consumption may alter response to heparin and are not advised.
- Do not take aspirin or any other OTC medication without physician's approval.

HEPATITIS A VACCINE

(hep′a-ti-tis)
Havrix, Vaqta
Classifications: VACCINE
Therapeutic: VACCINE
Prototype: Hepatitis B vaccine
Pregnancy Category: C

AVAILABILITY 720 EIU/0.5 mL, 1440 EIU/1 mL (Havrix); 25 U/0.5 mL, 50 U/1 mL (Vaqta)

ACTION & *THERAPEUTIC EFFECT*
Anti-hepatitis A virus antibody titers following administration of hepati-

Common adverse effects in *italic*, life-threatening effects underlined; generic names in **bold**; classifications in SMALL CAPS; ♣ Canadian drug name; ⊘ Prototype drug

733

transmission of hepatitis infection or AIDS from H-BIG is remote. *Preparation contains a high antibody titer specific to hepatitis B surface antigen (anti-HBs); plasma does not show serologic evidence of hepatitis B surface antigen (HBsAg).*

USES Prophylactically to provide passive immunity to hepatitis B infection in individuals exposed to HBV or HBsAg-positive materials (blood plasma, serum). Also as postexposure prophylaxis after bite or percutaneous exposure, ingestion, direct mucous membrane contact, sexual or intimate contact, and in neonates born to HBsAg-positive women.

CONTRAINDICATIONS Pregnancy (category C).
CAUTIOUS USE History of systemic allergic reactions to immune globulin, concurrent administration of immunosuppression drugs; thrombocytopenia or bleeding disorders, HBsAg-positive individuals, patients with specific immunoglobulin A (IgA) deficiency; lactation.

ROUTE & DOSAGE

Hepatitis B Prophylaxis
Adult/Child: **IM** 0.06 mL/kg as soon as possible after exposure, preferably within 24 h, but no later than 7 d, repeat 28–30 d after exposure

Newborn Exposure
Child: **IM** 0.5 mL as soon as possible after birth, but no later than 24 h, repeat dose 3 and 6 mo later

ADMINISTRATION
Intramuscular
- Give hepatitis B immune globulin at the same time or up to 1 mo

preceding hepatitis B vaccination (hepatitis B vaccine) does not impair the active immune response from the vaccination.
- Give preferably into deltoid muscle or anterolateral aspect of thigh.
- Note: For neonates and small children the preferred injection site is the anterolateral aspect of the thigh.
- Do NOT administer by IV; inadvertent IV or intravascular administration can cause a precipitous fall in BP and an anaphylactic reaction.
- Store at 2°–8° C (36°–46° F) unless otherwise directed. Avoid freezing.

ADVERSE EFFECTS (≥1%) **Body as a Whole:** Muscle stiffness; pain, tenderness, swelling, erythema of injection site, nausea, faintness, fever, dizziness, malaise, lassitude, body and joint pain, leg cramps. **Skin:** Urticaria, rash, angioedema, pruritus, erythema, sensitization (following large or repeated doses), anaphylaxis (rare).

INTERACTIONS Drug: May interfere with immune response to LIVE-VIRUS VACCINES (measles/mumps/rubella/poliovirus).

PHARMACOKINETICS Absorption: Slowly absorbed from IM site. **Onset:** 1–6 d. **Peak:** 3–11 d. **Duration:** 2–6 mo. **Elimination:** Half-life 21 d.

CLINICAL IMPLICATIONS
Assessment & Drug Effects
- Have epinephrine 1:1000 readily available; hypersensitivity reactions are most likely to occur in patients receiving large doses or repeated injections.

Patient & Family Education
- Learn potential adverse reactions.

Common adverse effects in *italic*, life-threatening effects <u>underlined</u>; generic names in **bold**; classifications in SMALL CAPS; ♣ Canadian drug name; ⊘ Prototype drug

735

HEPATITIS B VACCINE (RECOMBINANT) 🅟

(hep′a-ti-tis)

Engerix-B, Recombivax HB
Classifications: VACCINE
Therapeutic: VACCINE
Pregnancy Category: C

AVAILABILITY 10 mcg/mL, 5 mcg/0.5 mL, 40 mcg/mL (Recombivax); 20 mcg/mL, 10 mcg/0.5 mL (Engerix-B)

ACTION & *THERAPEUTIC EFFECT*
Suspension of inactivated and purified hepatitis B surface antigen (HBsAg) derived from human plasma of screened asymptomatic HBsAg-positive carriers of hepatitis B virus. Hepatitis B vaccine recombinant is the first vaccine produced by gene splicing. No human plasma is used in its production. *The recommended 3-dose regimen produces active immunity against hepatitis B infection by inducing protective antibody (anti-HBs) formation.*

USES To promote active immunity in individuals at high risk of potential exposure to hepatitis B virus or HBsAg-positive materials. Has been used simultaneously (into different sites) with hepatitis B immune globulin (H-BIG) for post-exposure prophylaxis in selected patients and in infants born to HBsAg-positive mothers.

CONTRAINDICATIONS History of allergic reaction to hepatitis B vaccine or to any ingredient in the formulation; HBsAg carriers; pregnancy (category C).
CAUTIOUS USE Compromised cardiopulmonary status, serious active infection or fever; renal disease, renal failure; thrombocytopenia or other bleeding disorders; lactation.

ROUTE & DOSAGE

Hepatitis B Prophylaxis

Adult: **IM** Recombivax 1 mL (10 mcg) at 0, 1, and 6 mo; Engerix-B 1 mL (20 mcg) at 0, 1, and 6 mo or 0, 1, 2, and 12 mo
Child: **IM** Recombivax 0.5 mL (5 mcg) at 0, 1, and 6 mo; Engerix-B 0.5 mL (10 mcg) at 0, 1, and 6 mo or 0, 1, 2, and 12 mo

Dialysis and Immunodeficient Patients

Adult: **IM** Recombivax 2 mL (20 mcg) at 0, 1, and 6 mo Engerix-B 2 mL (40 mcg) at 0, 1, and 6 mo or 0, 1, 2, and 12 mo

ADMINISTRATION

Intramuscular

- Give preferably into the deltoid and in neonates into the anterolateral thigh, avoiding blood vessels and nerves. Carefully aspirate to prevent inadvertent intravascular injection.
- Have epinephrine immediately available to treat anaphylaxis.
- Shake vial well before withdrawing dose to assure uniform suspension.
- Store unopened and opened vials at 2°–8° C (36°–46° F) unless otherwise directed. Avoid freezing (freezing destroys potency).

ADVERSE EFFECTS (≥1%) **Body as a Whole:** *Mild local tenderness at injection site, local inflammatory reaction* (swelling, heat, redness, induration, pain); *fever, malaise, fatigue,* headache, dizziness, faintness, leg cramps, myalgia, arthralgia. **GI:** Nausea, vomiting, diarrhea. **Skin:** Rash, urticaria, pruritus.

INTERACTIONS Drug: No clinically significant interactions established.

PHARMACOKINETICS Absorption: Slowly absorbed from IM site. **Onset:** 2 wk. **Peak:** 6 mo. **Duration:** At least 3 y.

CLINICAL IMPLICATIONS

Assessment & Drug Effects
- Note: The ACIP recommends serologic confirmation of postvaccination immunity in patients undergoing dialysis and in immunodeficient patients.
- Monitor temperature. Some patients develop a temperature elevation of 38.3° C (101° F) following vaccination that may last 1 or 2 d.

Patient & Family Education
- Learn potential adverse reaction.

HETASTARCH

(het′a-starch)
HES, Hespan, Hydroxyethyl Starch, Hextend
Classifications: PLASMA VOLUME EXPANDER
Therapeutic: PLASMA VOLUME EXPANDER
Prototype: Albumin
Pregnancy Category: C

AVAILABILITY 6 g/100 mL injection

ACTION & *THERAPEUTIC EFFECT*

Synthetic starch closely resembling human glycogen. Acts much like albumin and dextran but is claimed to be less likely to produce anaphylaxis or to interfere with cross matching or blood typing procedures. Causes no significant alterations in fibrinogen or clotting time but may prolong the PTT and PT. Not a substitute for blood or plasma. In hypovolemic patients, it increases arterial and venous pressures, heart rate, cardiac output, urine output, and colloidal osmotic pressure. *Colloidal osmotic properties are approximately equal to those of human serum albumin.*

USES Early fluid replacement and plasma volume expansion when whole blood is not available or when there is no time for necessary cross matching. Used to expand plasma volume during cardiopulmonary bypass and in adjunctive treatment of shock caused by hemorrhage, burns, surgery, sepsis, or other trauma. Also used as sedimenting agent in preparation of granulocytes by leukapheresis.

UNLABELED USES As a priming fluid in pump oxygenators for perfusion during extracorporeal circulation and as a cryoprotective agent for long-term storage of whole blood.

CONTRAINDICATIONS Severe bleeding disorders, CHF, renal failure with oliguria and anuria, treatment of shock not accompanied by hypovolemia, intracranial bleeding; pregnancy (category C). Safe use in children is not established.
CAUTIOUS USE Hepatic or renal insufficiency, pulmonary edema in the very young or older adults, patients on sodium restriction.

ROUTE & DOSAGE

Plasma Volume Expansion
Adult: **IV** 500–1000 mL or 20 mL/kg/d (max: 1500 mL/d)
Leukapheresis
Adult: **IV** 250–750 mL infused at a constant fixed ratio of 1:8 to venous whole blood
Renal Impairment
Cl_cr < 10 mL/min: use original initial dose, then reduce doses by 25–50%

Common adverse effects in *italic*, life-threatening effects <u>underlined</u>; generic names in **bold**; classifications in SMALL CAPS; ♣ Canadian drug name; ☻ Prototype drug

737

ADMINISTRATION

Intravenous

PREPARE: **IV Infusion:** Use undiluted as prepared by manufacturer.

ADMINISTER: **IV Infusion:** Specific flow rate is prescribed by physician. Rate may be as high as 20 mL/kg/h in acute hemorrhagic shock. Rate is usually reduced in patients with burns or septic shock.

▪ Store at room temperature; avoid extremes of heat or cold. ▪ Discard partially used bags.

ADVERSE EFFECTS (≥1%) **CV:** Peripheral edema, <u>circulatory overload, heart failure</u>. **Hematologic:** With large volumes, prolongation of PT, PTT, clotting time, and bleeding time; decreased Hct, Hgb, platelets, calcium, and fibrinogen; dilution of plasma proteins, hyperbilirubinemia, increased sedimentation rate. **Body as a Whole:** Pruritus, <u>anaphylactoid reactions</u> (periorbital edema, urticaria, wheezing), vomiting, mild fever, chills, influenza-like symptoms, headache, muscle pains, submaxillary and parotid glandular swelling.

INTERACTIONS Drug: No clinically significant interactions established.

PHARMACOKINETICS Duration: 24–36 h. **Distribution:** Remains in intravascular space. **Metabolism:** In reticuloendothelial system. **Elimination:** In urine with some biliary excretion.

CLINICAL IMPLICATIONS

Assessment & Drug Effects

▪ Monitor for S&S of hypersensitivity reaction (see Appendix F).
▪ Measure and record I&O. Report oliguria or significant changes in I&O ratio.

▪ Monitor BP and vital signs and observe patient for unusual bruising or bleeding.
▪ Lab tests: Monitor WBC count with differential, platelet count, and PT & PTT during leukapheresis.
▪ Observe for signs of circulatory overload (see Appendix F).
▪ Check laboratory reports of Hct values. Notify physician if there is an appreciable drop in Hct or if value approaches 30% by volume. Hct should not be allowed to drop below 30%.

Patient & Family Education

▪ Notify physician for any of the following: Difficulty breathing, nausea, chills, headache, itching.

HOMATROPINE HYDROBROMIDE 📦

(hoe-ma′troe-peen)
AK-Homatropine, Homatropine, Isopto Homatropine
Pregnancy Category: C
See Appendix A-1.

HYALURONIDASE, OVINE

(hi-a-lu-ron′i-dase)
Amphadase, Vitrase
Classifications: ENZYME; ABSORPTION AND DISPERSING ENHANCER
Therapeutic: ABSORPTION AND DISPERSING ENHANCER
Pregnancy Category: C

AVAILABILITY 150 units/mL and 200 units/mL for injection; lyophilized powder, 6200 units

ACTION & *THERAPEUTIC EFFECT*
Hyaluronidase is a diffusing substance that modifies the permeability of connective tissue through the

hydrolysis of hyaluronic acid found in the intercellular substance of connective tissue. It temporarily decreases the viscosity of cellular cement and promotes diffusion of injected fluids or exudates, adding to their absorption. *It increases the absorption and dispersion of solutions in the intercellular spaces.*

USES Adjuvant to increase the absorption and dispersion of other injected drugs; hypodermoclysis; adjunct in subcutaneous urography for improving resorption of radiopaque agents.

UNLABELED USES Adjunct for ophthalmic anesthesia, treatment of vitreous hemorrhage and diabetic retinopathy.

CONTRAINDICATIONS Hypersensitivity to hyaluronidase or any other ingredient in formulation; concurrent use with dopamine or alpha-agonist drugs; injection into infected or acutely inflamed area, area of swelling due to bites or stings; corneal injection; injection by IV; pregnancy (category C).

CAUTIOUS USE Lactation.

ROUTE & DOSAGE

Adjuvant to Increase the Absorption and Dispersion of Other Drugs

Adult: 150 units (range: 50–300) added to solution
Child: 150 units (range: 50–300) added to solution

Hypodermoclysis

Adult: 15 units added to each 100 mL of fluid
Child ≥3 y: 15 units added to each 100 mL of fluid

Subcutaneous Urography

Adult: **SC** 75 units prior to contrast medium

Child: **SC 75 units prior to contrast medium**

ADMINISTRATION

Subcutaneous or Solution Additive

- Reconstitute vial with 6.2 mL NS for injection to yield 1000 U/mL. Apply the 5-micron filter needle to the 1 mL syringe in injection kit and further dilute: To produce 50 U/mL, withdraw 0.05 mL reconstituted solution and add 0.95 mL NS. To produce 75 U/mL, withdraw 0.075 mL reconstituted solution and add 0.925 mL NS. To produce 150 U/mL, withdraw 0.15 mL reconstituted solution and add 0.85 mL NS. To produce 300 U/mL, withdraw 0.3 mL reconstituted solution and add 0.7 mL NS. Use immediately after preparation.
- Give SC prior to contrast media. Do not inject near an infected or acutely inflamed area.
- Store unopened vial at 2°–8° C (35°–46° F). After reconstitution, store at 20°–25° C (59°–77° F), and use within 6 h. Protect from light.

ADVERSE EFFECTS (≥1%) **CV:** Edema. **Other:** Injection site reaction (e.g., erythema, irritation); enhanced adverse events associated with coadministered drugs.

INTERACTIONS Drug: SALICYLATES, CORTICOSTEROIDS, ESTROGENS, or H₁-BLOCKERS may confer partial resistant to the action of hyaluronidase in some tissues.

CLINICAL IMPLICATIONS

Assessment & Drug Effects

- Monitor for S&S of hypersensitivity: urticaria, erythema, chills, nausea, vomiting, dizziness, tachycardia, and hypotension. Withhold and notify physician if hypersensitivity occurs.

Common adverse effects in *italic*, life-threatening effects <u>underlined</u>; generic names in **bold**; classifications in SMALL CAPS; ♣ Canadian drug name; ⊘ Prototype drug

739

- Note: Those receiving large doses of salicylates, cortisone, ACTH, estrogens, or antihistamines may require larger amounts of hyaluronidase for equivalent dispersing effect.

Patient & Family Education
- Report immediately any of the following: rash, itching, chills, nausea, vomiting, dizziness, or palpitations.

HYDRALAZINE HYDROCHLORIDE ℞

(hye-dral′a-zeen)
Classifications: NONNITRATE VASODILATOR; ANTIHYPERTENSIVE
Therapeutic: ANTIHYPERTENSIVE
Pregnancy Category: C

AVAILABILITY 10 mg, 25 mg, 50 mg, 100 mg tablets; 20 mg/mL vial

ACTION & *THERAPEUTIC EFFECT*
Reduces BP mainly by direct effect on vascular smooth muscles of arterial-resistance vessels, resulting in vasodilation. Has little effect on venous-capacitance vessels. Hypotensive effect may be limited by sympathetic reflexes that increase heart rate, stroke volume, and cardiac output. *Diastolic response is often greater than systolic response. Vasodilation reduces peripheral resistance and substantially improves cardiac output, and renal and cerebral blood flow.*

USES Most commonly in stepped-care approach to treat moderate to severe hypertension. Also in early malignant hypertension and resistant hypertension that persists after sympathectomy.
UNLABELED USES Conjunctively with cardiac glycosides and other vasodilators in short-term treatment

of acute CHF; unexplained pulmonary hypertension; eclampsia.

CONTRAINDICATIONS Coronary artery disease, mitral valvular rheumatic heart disease, MI, tachycardia, SLE; pregnancy (category C).
CAUTIOUS USE Cerebrovascular accident, advanced renal impairment, coronary heart disease, renal disease; renal failure; use with MAO INHIBITORS.

ROUTE & DOSAGE

Hypertension
Adult: **PO** 10–50 mg q.i.d. **IM** 10–50 mg q4–6h **IV** 10–20 mg q4–6h, may increase to 40 mg
Geriatric: **PO** Start with 10 mg 2–3 times/d
Child: **PO** 3–7.5 mg/kg/d in 4 divided doses **IV/IM** 0.1–0.2 mg/kg in divided doses (max 20 mg)
Renal Impairment
Cl_{cr} 10–50 mL/min dose q8h

ADMINISTRATION

Oral
- Give with food; bioavailability is increased by taking it with food.
- Discontinue gradually to avoid sudden rise in BP and acute heart failure.
- Inform patients of the dangers of abrupt withdrawal.

Intramuscular
- Give deep into a large muscle.

Intravenous ———
***PREPARE:* Direct:** Give undiluted. Use immediately after being drawn into syringe. Do not add to IV solutions.
***ADMINISTER:* Direct:** Give each 10 mg or fraction thereof over 1 min.
***INCOMPATIBILITIES* Solution/additive: Aminophylline, ampicillin, chlorothiazide, edetate**

calcium disodium, hydrocortisone, mephentermine, methohexital, nitroglycerin, phenobarbital, verapamil.

▪ Store at 15°–30° C (59°–86° F) in tight, light-resistant containers unless otherwise directed. Avoid freezing.

ADVERSE EFFECTS (≥1%) **Body as a Whole:** Hypersensitivity (rash, urticaria, pruritus, fever, chills, arthralgia, eosinophilia, cholangitis, hepatitis, obstructive jaundice). **CNS:** *Headache,* dizziness, tremors. **CV:** *Palpitation,* angina, *tachycardia,* flushing, paradoxical pressor response. Overdose: arrhythmia, shock. **Special Senses:** Lacrimation, conjunctivitis. **GI:** Anorexia, nausea, vomiting, diarrhea, constipation, abdominal pain, paralytic ileus. **Urogenital:** Difficulty in urination, glomerulonephritis. **Hematologic:** Decreased hematocrit and hemoglobin, anemia, agranulocytosis (rare). **Other:** Nasal congestion, muscle cramps, SLE-like syndrome, fixed drug eruption, edema.

DIAGNOSTIC TEST INTERFERENCE
Positive *direct Coombs' tests* in patients with hydralazine-induced SLE. Hydralazine interferes with urinary *17-OHCS* determinations *(modified Glenn-Nelson technique).*

INTERACTIONS Drug: BETA BLOCKERS and other ANTIHYPERTENSIVE AGENTS compound hypotensive effects.

PHARMACOKINETICS Absorption: Readily absorbed from GI tract. **Onset:** 20–30 min. **Peak:** 2 h. **Duration:** 2–6 h. **Distribution:** Crosses placenta; distributed into breast milk. **Metabolism:** In liver. **Elimination:** 90% in urine; 10% in feces. **Half-Life:** 2–8 h.

CLINICAL IMPLICATIONS

Assessment & Drug Effects
▪ Lab tests: Determine antinuclear antibody titer before initiation of therapy and periodically during prolonged therapy.
▪ Make baseline and periodic determinations of BUN, creatinine clearance, uric acid, serum potassium, blood glucose, and ECG.
▪ Monitor for S&S of SLE, especially with prolonged therapy.
▪ Monitor BP and HR closely. Check every 5 min until it is stabilized at desired level, then every 15 min thereafter throughout hypertensive crisis.
▪ Monitor I&O when drug is given parenterally and in those with renal dysfunction.

Patient & Family Education
▪ Monitor weight, check for edema, and report weight gain to physician.
▪ Note: Some patients experience headache and palpitations within 2–4 h after first PO dose; symptoms usually subside spontaneously.
▪ Make position changes slowly and avoid standing still, hot baths/showers, strenuous exercise, and excessive alcohol intake.
▪ Do not drive or engage in other potentially hazardous activities until response to drug is known.

HYDROCHLOROTHIAZIDE ℗

(hye-droe-klor-oh-thye′a-zide)
Apo-Hydro ♦, Esidrix, Oretic, HCTZ, Urozide ♦
Classifications: ELECTROLYTIC AND WATER BALANCE AGENT; DIURETIC; THIAZIDE
Therapeutic: DIURETIC
Pregnancy Category: B

Common adverse effects in *italic*, life-threatening effects underlined; generic names in **bold**; classifications in SMALL CAPS; ♦ Canadian drug name; ℗ Prototype drug

741

AVAILABILITY 12.5 mg capsules; 25 mg, 50 mg, 100 mg tablets; 50 mg/5 mL oral solution

ACTION & *THERAPEUTIC EFFECT*
Diuretic action is associated with drug interference with absorption of sodium ions across the distal renal tubular segment of the nephron. This enhances excretion of sodium, chloride, potassium, bicarbonates, and water. *It has hypotensive action, elevates plasma renin activity.*

USES Adjunct in treatment of edema associated with CHF, hepatic cirrhosis, renal failure, and in the management of hypertension.
UNLABELED USES Nephrogenic diabetes insipidus, hypercalciuria, and treatment of electrolyte disturbances associated with renal tubular acidosis.

CONTRAINDICATIONS Hypersensitivity to thiazides or other sulfonamides; anuria.
CAUTIOUS USE Bronchial asthma, allergy; hepatic cirrhosis; renal dysfunction; CHF; stroke, CVA; history of gout, SLE; diabetes mellitus; older adults; pregnancy (category B).

ROUTE & DOSAGE

Edema
Adult: **PO** 25–200 mg/d in 1–3 divided doses

Hypertension
Adult: **PO** 12.5–100 mg/d in 1–2 divided doses
Child: **PO** 2.2 mg/kg/d in 2 divided doses
Neonate: **PO** <6 mo, 2–4 mg/kg/d in 2 divided doses

ADMINISTRATION
Oral
- Give with food or milk to reduce GI upset.
- Schedule doses to avoid nocturia and interrupted sleep. If given in 2 doses, schedule second dose no later than 3 p.m.
- Store tablets in tightly closed container at 15°–30° C (59°–86° F) unless otherwise directed.

ADVERSE EFFECTS (≥1%) **CNS:** Mood changes, unusual tiredness or weakness, dizziness, light-headedness, paresthesias. **CV:** Irregular heartbeat, weak pulse, orthostatic hypotension. **GI:** Dry mouth, increased thirst, nausea, vomiting, anorexia, diarrhea, pancreatitis, jaundice. **Hematologic:** Agranulocytosis, thrombocytopenia, aplastic anemia, leukopenia. **Metabolic:** *Hyperglycemia,* glycosuria, *hyperuricemia, hypokalemia.* **Other:** Hypersensitivity reactions, photosensitivity, blurred vision, yellow vision (xanthopsia), muscle spasm.

DIAGNOSTIC TEST INTERFERENCE Falsely decreased value in *total urinary estrogen* by *spectrophotometric assay.* See *chlorothiazide.*

INTERACTIONS Drug: Amphotericin B, CORTICOSTEROIDS increase hypokalemic effects; SULFONYLUREAS, **insulin** may antagonize hypoglycemic effects; **cholestyramine, colestipol** decrease THIAZIDE absorption; **diazoxide** intensifies hypoglycemic and hypotensive effects; increased **potassium** and **magnesium** loss may cause **digoxin** toxicity; decreases **lithium** excretion and increases toxicity; increases risk of NSAID-induced renal failure and may attenuate diuresis.

PHARMACOKINETICS Absorption: Incompletely absorbed. **Onset:** 2 h. **Peak:** 4 h. **Duration:** 6–12 h. **Distribution:** Distributed throughout extracellular tissue; concentrates in kidney; crosses placenta; distributed in breast milk. **Metabolism:** Does not appear to be metabolized. **Elimination:** In urine. **Half-Life:** 45–120 min.

CLINICAL IMPLICATIONS

Assessment & Drug Effects

- Monitor for therapeutic effectiveness. Antihypertensive effects may be noted in 3–4 d; maximal effects may require 3–4 wk.
- Lab tests: Baseline and periodic determinations of serum electrolytes, blood counts, BUN, blood glucose, uric acid, CO_2, are recommended.
- Check BP before initiation of therapy and at regular intervals.
- Monitor closely for hypokalemia; it increases the risk of digoxin toxicity.
- Monitor I&O and check for edema.
- Note: Drug may cause hyperglycemia and loss of glycemic control in diabetics.
- Note: Drug may cause orthostatic hypotension, dizziness.

Patient & Family Education

- Consult physician before using OTC drugs. Many contain large amounts of sodium as well as potassium.
- Monitor weight daily.
- Note: Diabetic patients need to monitor blood glucose closely. This drug causes impaired glucose tolerance.
- Report signs of hypokalemia (see Appendix F) to physician.
- Change positions slowly; avoid hot baths or showers, extended exposure to sunlight, and sitting or standing still for long periods.
- Note: Photosensitivity reaction may occur 10–14 d after initial sun exposure.

HYDROCODONE BITARTRATE

(hye-droe-koe'done)
Dihydrocodeinone Bitartrate, Hycodan, Robidone A, Vicodin (with acetaminophen)
Classifications: NARCOTIC (OPIATE) AGONIST ANALGESIC; ANTITUSSIVE
Therapeutic: NARCOTIC ANALGESIC
Prototype: Morphine
Pregnancy Category: C
Controlled Substance: Schedule III

AVAILABILITY 5 mg hydrocodone usually with 500 mg or more acetaminophen

ACTION & *THERAPEUTIC EFFECT*
Morphine derivative similar to codeine but more addicting and with slightly greater antitussive activity, and analgesic effect. CNS depressant with moderate to severe relief of pain. Available in the United States only in combination with other drugs. *Suppresses cough reflex by direct action on cough center in medulla. CNS depressant with moderate to severe relief of pain.*

USES Symptomatic relief of hyperactive or nonproductive cough and for relief of moderate to moderately severe pain. A common ingredient in a variety of proprietary mixtures.

CONTRAINDICATIONS Hypersensitivity to hydrocodone; children <2 y; pregnancy (category C); acute or severe asthymatic bronchitis; COPD; upper airway obstruction; lactation.

CAUTIOUS USE Respiratory depression, asthma, emphysema; history of drug abuse or dependence; postoperative patients; hepatic or renal disease; renal impairment or failure; older adults, debilitated patients; children <1 y; patients; children weighing <50 kg; G6PD defi-

Common adverse effects in *italic*, life-threatening effects underlined; generic names in **bold**; classifications in SMALL CAPS; ◆ Canadian drug name; ⊕ Prototype drug

743

ciency; GI disease; patients with preexisting increased intracranial pressure.

ROUTE & DOSAGE

Mild to Moderate Pain, Cough
Adult: **PO** 5–10 mg q4–6h prn (max: 15 mg/dose)
Child: **PO** 2–12 y, 1.25–5 mg q4–6h (max: 10 mg/dose)

ADMINISTRATION
Oral
- Give with food or milk to prevent GI irritation.
- Preserve in tight, light-resistant containers.

ADVERSE EFFECTS (≥1%) **GI:** Dry mouth, *constipation, nausea, vomiting.* **CNS:** Light-headedness, sedation, dizziness, *drowsiness,* euphoria, dysphoria. **Respiratory:** *Respiratory depression.* **Skin:** Urticaria, rash, pruritus.

INTERACTIONS Drug: Alcohol and other CNS DEPRESSANTS compound sedation and CNS depression. **Herbal: St. John's wort** increases sedation.

PHARMACOKINETICS Onset: 10–20 min. **Duration:** 3–6 h. **Distribution:** Crosses placenta; distributed into breast milk. **Metabolism:** In liver. **Elimination:** In urine. **Half-Life:** 3.8 h.

CLINICAL IMPLICATIONS
Assessment & Drug Effects
- Monitor for effectiveness of drug for pain relief.
- Monitor for nausea and vomiting, especially in ambulatory patients.
- Monitor respiratory status and bowel elimination.

Patient & Family Education
- Avoid hazardous activities until response to drug is determined.
- Do not use alcohol or other CNS depressants; may cause additive CNS depression.
- Drink plenty of liquids for adequate hydration.
- Do not take larger doses than prescribed since abuse potential is high.

HYDROCORTISONE ⓟ
(hye-droe-kor′ti-sone)
Aeroseb-HC, Cetacort, Cortaid, Cortenema, Dermolate, Hytone, Rectocort ♣, Synacort

HYDROCORTISONE ACETATE
Anusol HC, Carmol HC, Cortaid, Cort-Dome, Corticaine, Cortifoam, Cortiment ♣, Epifoam

HYDROCORTISONE CYPIONATE
Cortef

HYDROCORTISONE SODIUM SUCCINATE
A-Hydrocort, Solu-Cortef

HYDROCORTISONE VALERATE
Westcort

Classifications: ANTIINFLAMMATORY; SYNTHETIC HORMONE; ADRENAL CORTICOSTEROIDS; GLUCOCORTICOID; MINERALOCORTICOID
Therapeutic: ADRENAL CORTICOSTEROID; ANTIINFLAMMATORY; IMMUNOSUPPRESSANT
Pregnancy Category: C

AVAILABILITY Hydrocortisone 5 mg, 10 mg, 20 mg tablets; 0.5%, 1%, 2.5% cream, lotion, ointment, spray **Hydrocortisone Acetate** 25 mg/mL, 50 mg/mL suspension; 0.5%, 1% cream, ointment; **Hydrocortisone Cypionate** 5 mg, 20 mg tablet; **Hydrocortisone Sodium Succinate** 100 mg/2 mL, 250 mg/2 mL, 500 mg/4 mL, 1000 mg/8 mL vials; **Hydrocortisone Valerate** 0.2% cream, ointment

ACTION & *THERAPEUTIC EFFECT*

Short-acting synthetic steroid with both glucocorticoid and mineralocorticoid properties that affect nearly all systems of the body. **Antiinflammatory (glucocorticoid) action:** Stabilizes leukocyte lysosomal membranes; inhibits phagocytosis and release of allergic substances; suppresses fibroblast formation and collagen deposition; reduces capillary dilation and permeability; and increases responsiveness of cardiovascular system to circulating catecholamines. **Immunosuppressive action:** Modifies immune response to various stimuli; reduces antibody titers; and suppresses cell-mediated hypersensitivity reactions. **Mineralocorticoid action:** Promotes sodium retention, but under certain circumstances (e.g., sodium loading), enhances sodium excretion; promotes potassium excretion; and increases glomerular filtration rate (GFR). **Metabolic action:** Promotes hepatic gluconeogenesis, protein catabolism, redistribution of body fat, and lipolysis. *Has antiinflammatory, immunosuppressive, and metabolic functions in the body.*

USES Replacement therapy in adrenocortical insufficiency; to reduce serum calcium in hypercalcemia, to suppress undesirable inflammatory or immune responses, to produce temporary remission in nonadrenal disease, and to block ACTH production in diagnostic tests. Use as antiinflammatory or immunosuppressive agent largely replaced by synthetic glucocorticoids that have minimal mineralocorticoid activity.

CONTRAINDICATIONS Hypersensitivity to glucocorticoids, idiopathic thrombocytopenic purpura, psychoses, acute glomerulonephritis, viral or bacterial diseases of skin, infections not controlled by antibiotics, active or latent amebiasis, hypercorticism (Cushing's syndrome), smallpox vaccination or other immunologic procedures; acne. Topical steroids contraindicated in presence of varicella, vaccinia, on surfaces with compromised circulation, and in children <2 y; pregnancy (category C).

CAUTIOUS USE Children; diabetes mellitus; chronic, active hepatitis positive for hepatitis B surface antigen; hyperlipidemia; cirrhosis; stromal herpes simplex; glaucoma, tuberculosis of eye; osteoporosis; convulsive disorders; hypothyroidism; diverticulitis; nonspecific ulcerative colitis; fresh intestinal anastomoses; active or latent peptic ulcer; gastritis; esophagitis; thromboembolic disorders; CHF; metastatic carcinoma; hypertension; renal insufficiency; history of allergies; active or arrested tuberculosis; systemic fungal infection; myasthenia gravis; lactation.

ROUTE & DOSAGE

Adrenal Insufficiency, Antiinflammatory
Adult: **PO** 10–320 mg/d in 3–4 divided doses **IV/IM** 15–800 mg/d in 3–4 divided doses (max: 2 g/d) **SC** Sodium phosphate only, 15–240 mg/d
Child: **PO** 2.5–10 mg/kg/d in 3–4 divided doses **IV/IM** 1–5 mg/kg/d divided q12–24 h

Intraarticular, Intralesional (Acetate Salt)
Adult: **IM** 5–50 mg q3–5d for bursae; 5–50 mg once q1–4 wk for joints

Common adverse effects in *italic*, life-threatening effects underlined; generic names in **bold**; classifications in SMALL CAPS; ♣ Canadian drug name; ⊘ Prototype drug

745

> **Antiinflammatory Agent**
>
> *Adult:* **Topical** Apply a small amount to the affected area 1–4 times/d **PR** Insert 1% cream, 10% foam, 10–25 mg suppository, or 100 mg enema nightly

ADMINISTRATION

Note: Hydrocortisone phosphate may be given SC, IM, or IV. Hydrocortisone succinate may be given IM or IV.

Oral
▪ Give oral drug with food.

Rectal
▪ Administer retention enema preferably after a bowel movement; retain at least 1 h or all night if possible.

Topical
▪ Apply medication sparingly, rub until it disappears, and then reapply, leaving a thin coat over lesion. Completely cover area with transparent plastic or other occlusive device or vehicle when so ordered.
▪ Avoid covering a weeping or exudative lesion.
▪ Note: Occlusive dressings usually are not applied to face, scalp, scrotum, axilla, and groin.
▪ Inspect skin carefully between applications for ecchymotic, petechial, and purpuric signs, maceration, secondary infection, skin atrophy, striae or miliaria; if present, stop medication and notify physician.
▪ Store medication at 15°–30° C (59°–86° F) unless otherwise directed by manufacturer; protect from light and freezing.

Intramuscular
▪ Inject deep into gluteal muscle.

Intravenous
▪ IV administration to infants, children: Verify correct IV concentration and rate of infusion/injection with physician.

PREPARE: **Direct:** Give undiluted (preferred). **Intermittent:** Dilute in 50–100 mL of D5W, NS, or D5/NS.

ADMINISTER: **Direct:** Give each dose at a rate of 500 mg or fraction thereof (succinate) over 1 min. **Intermittent:** Give over 10 min.

INCOMPATIBILITIES **Solution/additive: Amobarbital, ampicillin, bleomycin, colistimethate, dimenhydrinate, doxapram, doxorubicin, ephedrine, heparin, hydralazine, metaraminol, methicillin, nafcillin, pentobarbital, phenobarbital, prochlorperazine, promethazine, secobarbital, tetracycline. Y-site: Ergotamine, phenytoin.**
▪ Administer solutions that have been diluted for IV infusion within 24 h.

ADVERSE EFFECTS (≥1%) **Body as a Whole:** Hypersensitivity or <u>anaphylactoid reactions; aggravation or masking of infections</u>; malaise, weight gain, obesity; urogenital urinary frequency and urgency, enuresis increased or decreased motility and number of sperm. **CNS:** Vertigo, headache, nystagmus, ataxia (rare), increased intracranial pressure with papilledema (usually after discontinuation of medication), mental disturbances, aggravation of preexisting psychiatric conditions, insomnia, anxiety, mental confusion, depression. **CV:** Syncopal episodes, thrombophlebitis, thromboembolism or fat embolism, palpitation, tachycardia, necrotizing angiitis, CHF, hypertension edema. **Endocrine:** Suppressed linear growth in children, decreased glucose tolerance; hyperglycemia, manifestations of latent diabetes mellitus; hypocorticism; amenorrhea and other menstrual difficulties; moon facies. **Special Senses:** Posterior subcapsular cataracts (especially in children), glaucoma, exophthalmos, increased intraocular pressure with optic nerve damage, perforation of the globe, fungal infection of the cornea, decreased or blurred vision. **Metabolic:** Hypocalcemia; *sodium* and *fluid retention;* hypokalemia and hypokalemic alkalosis decreased serum concentration of vitamins A and C; hyperglycemia, hypernatremia. **GI:** Cramping, bleeding, *nausea,* increased appetite, ulcerative esophagitis, pancreatitis, abdominal distention, peptic ulcer with perforation and hemorrhage, melena. **Hematologic:** Thrombocytopenia, polycythemia, ecchymoses. **Musculoskeletal:** Osteoporosis, compression fractures, muscle wasting and weakness, tendon rupture, aseptic necrosis of femoral and humeral heads. **Skin:** Skin thinning and atrophy, *acne, impaired wound healing;* petechiae, ecchymosis, easy bruising; suppression of skin test reaction; hypopigmentation or hyperpigmentation, hirsutism, acneiform eruptions, subcutaneous fat atrophy; allergic dermatitis, urticaria, angioneurotic edema, increased sweating. With parenteral therapy at IV site–pain, irritation, necrosis, atrophy, sterile abscess; Charcot-like arthropathy following intraarticular use; burning and tingling in perineal area (after IV injection).

DIAGNOSTIC TEST INTERFERENCE

Hydrocortisone (corticosteroids) may increase serum *cholesterol, blood glucose,* serum *sodium, uric acid* (in acute leukemia) and *calcium* (in bone metastasis). It may decrease serum *calcium, potassium, PBI, thyroxin (T₄), triiodothyronine (T₃) and reduce thyroid I 131* uptake. It increases *urine glucose* level and *calcium* excretion; decreases *urine 17-OHCS* and *17-KS* levels. May produce false-negative results with **nitroblue tetrazolium test** for systemic bacterial infection and may suppress reactions to skin tests.

INTERACTIONS Drug:
BARBITURATES, **phenytoin, rifampin** may increase hepatic metabolism, thus decreasing cortisone levels; ESTROGENS potentiate the effects of hydrocortisone; NSAIDS compound ulcerogenic effects; **cholestyramine, colestipol** decrease hydrocortisone absorption; DIURETICS, **amphotericin B** exacerbate hypokalemia; ANTICHOLINESTERASE AGENTS (e.g., **neostigmine**) may produce severe weakness; immune response to VACCINES and TOXOIDS may be decreased.

PHARMACOKINETICS Absorption:
Readily from GI tract and IM injection site. **Onset:** 1–2 h PO; immediately IV; 3–5 d PR. **Peak:** 1 h PO; 4–8 h IM. **Duration:** 1–1.5 d PO/IM; 0.5–4 wk intraarticular. **Distribution:** Distributed primarily to muscles, liver, skin, intestines, kidneys; crosses placenta. **Metabolism:** In liver. **Elimination:** HPA suppression 8–12 h; metabolites excreted in urine; excreted in breast milk. **Half-Life:** 1.5–2 h.

CLINICAL IMPLICATIONS

Assessment & Drug Effects

- Establish baseline and continuing data on BP, weight, fluid and electrolyte balance, and blood glucose.
- Lab tests: Periodic serum electrolytes blood glucose, Hct and Hgb, platelet count, and WBC with differential.

Common adverse effects in *italic*, life-threatening effects underlined; generic names in **bold**; classifications in SMALL CAPS; ♣ Canadian drug name; ⊘ Prototype drug

747

H

- Monitor for adverse effects. Older adults and patients with low serum albumin are especially susceptible to adverse effects.
- Be alert to signs of hypocalcemia (see Appendix F).
- Ophthalmoscopic examinations are recommended every 2–3 mo, especially if patient is receiving ophthalmic steroid therapy.
- Monitor for persistent backache or chest pain; compression and spontaneous fractures of long bones and vertebrae present hazards.
- Monitor for and report changes in mood and behavior, emotional instability, or psychomotor activity, especially with long-term therapy.
- Be alert to possibility of masked infection and delayed healing (antiinflammatory and immunosuppressive actions).
- Note: Dose adjustment may be required if patient is subjected to severe stress (serious infection, surgery, or injury).
- Note: Single doses of corticosteroids or use for a short period (<1 wk) do not produce withdrawal symptoms when discontinued, even with moderately large doses.

Patient & Family Education

- Expect a slight weight gain with improved appetite. After dosage is stabilized, notify physician of a sudden slow but steady weight increase [2 kg (5 lb)/wk].
- Avoid alcohol and caffeine; may contribute to steroid-ulcer development in long-term therapy.
- Do not ignore dyspepsia with hyperacidity. Report symptoms to physician and do NOT self-medicate to find relief.
- Do NOT use aspirin or other OTC drugs unless prescribed specifically by the physician.
- Note: A high protein, calcium, and vitamin D diet is advisable to

reduce risk of corticosteroid-induced osteoporosis.

- Notify physician of slow healing, any vague feeling of being sick, or return to pretreatment symptoms.
- Do not abruptly discontinue drug; doses are gradually reduced to prevent withdrawal symptoms.
- Report exacerbation of disease during drug withdrawal.
- Carry medical identification at all times. It needs to indicate medical diagnosis, drug therapy, and name of physician.
- Apply topical preparations sparingly in small children. The hazard of systemic toxicity is higher because of the greater ratio of skin surface area to body weight.
- Check shelf-life date on topical corticosterone during long-term use.

HYDROMORPHONE HYDROCHLORIDE

(hye-droe-mor′fone)
Dilaudid, Dilaudid-HP
Classifications: NARCOTIC (OPIATE) AGONIST; ANALGESIC
Therapeutic: NARCOTIC ANALGESIC
Prototype: Morphine
Pregnancy Category: C
Controlled Substance: Schedule II

AVAILABILITY 2 mg, 4 mg, 8 mg tablets; 5 mg/5 mL oral liquid; 1 mg/mL, 10 mg/mL injection

ACTION & *THERAPEUTIC EFFECT*
Semisynthetic derivative structurally similar to morphine but with 8–10 times more potent analgesic effect. Has more rapid onset and shorter duration of action than morphine, and is reported to have less hypnotic action and less tendency to produce nausea and vomiting. *Is a narcotic analgesic which controls*

mild to moderate pain. Has antitussive properties.

USES Relief of moderate to severe pain and control of persistent nonproductive cough.

CONTRAINDICATIONS Intolerance to opiate agonists; opiate-naïve patients; acute bronchial asthma, COPD, upper airway obstruction, decreased respiratory reserve, severe respiratory depression; pregnancy (category C); lactation.

CAUTIOUS USE Abrupt discontinuation, alcoholism; angina; biliary tract disease; older adults; epidural administration; GI disease, GI obstruction; head trauma; heart failure; hepatic disease; hypotension, hypovolemia, oliguria, prostatic hypertrophy; pulmonary disease; renal disease, renal impairment; paralytic ileus; increased intracranial pressure; inflammatory bowel disease; labor; latex hypersensitivity; obstetric delivery; bladder obstruction; cardiac arrhythmias, cardiac disease; respiratory depression; seizure disorder, seizures; substance abuse; surgery; ulcerative colitis; urethral stricture, urinary retention; neonates, and infants <6 mo.

ROUTE & DOSAGE

Moderate to Severe Pain

Adult: **PO** 2–4 mg q4–6h prn in naïve patients. **SC/IM/IV** 0.75–2 mg q4–6h depending on patient response
Child: **PO** 0.03–0.08 mg/kg q4–6h (max: 5 mg/dose) **IV** 0.015 mg/kg q4–6h prn

Antitussive

Adult: **PO** 1 mg q3–4h prn
Child: **PO** 6–12 y, 0.5 mg q3–4h prn

ADMINISTRATION

■Note: A fixed schedule when narcotic therapy is initiated provides more effective management than a prn schedule.

Intravenous
IV administration to infants, children: Verify correct IV concentration and rate of infusion with physician.

PREPARE: **Direct:** Dilute each dose in at least 5 mL of sterile water or NS. **IV Infusion:** Using Dilaudid-HP, reconstitute 250 mg dry powder vial immediately prior to use with 25 mL sterile water for injection to yield 10 mg/mL. Final dilution of Dilaudid-HP 250 and HP 500 (supplied 500 mg/50 mL) must be ordered by physician.

ADMINISTER: **Direct:** Give 2 mg or fraction thereof over 3–5 min. **IV Infusion:** Both final volume and rate of infusion must be ordered by physician.

INCOMPATIBILITIES **Solution/additive: Prochlorperazine, sodium bicarbonate, thiopental. Y-site: Minocycline, prochlorperazine, tetracycline.**

■A slight discoloration in ampules or multidose vials causes no loss of potency. ■Store in tight, light–resistant containers at 15°–30° C (59°–86° F).

ADVERSE EFFECTS (≥1%) **GI:** Nausea, vomiting, constipation. **CNS:** Euphoria, dizziness, sedation, *drowsiness.* **CV:** Hypotension, bradycardia or tachycardia. **Respiratory:** <u>Respiratory depression.</u> **Special Senses:** Blurred vision.

INTERACTIONS Drug: Alcohol and other CNS DEPRESSANTS compound sedation and CNS depression. **Herbal: St. John's wort, kava-kava** may increase sedation.

Common adverse effects in *italic*, life-threatening effects <u>underlined</u>; generic names in **bold**; classifications in SMALL CAPS; ♣ Canadian drug name; ⊙ Prototype drug

749

PHARMACOKINETICS Absorption: 60% absorbed from GI tract. **Onset:** 15 min IV, 30 min PO. **Peak:** 30–90 min. **Duration:** 3–4 h. **Distribution:** Crosses placenta; distributed into breast milk. **Metabolism:** In liver. **Elimination:** In urine. **Half-life:** 2–3 h.

CLINICAL IMPLICATIONS

Assessment & Drug Effects

- Note baseline respiratory rate, rhythm, and depth and size of pupils before administration. Respirations of 12/min or less and mitosis are signs of toxicity. Withhold drug and promptly notify physician.
- Monitor vital signs at regular intervals. Drug-induced respiratory depression may occur even with small doses and increases progressively with higher doses.
- Assess effectiveness of pain relief 30 min after medication administration.
- Monitor drug effects carefully in older adult or debilitated patients and those with impaired renal and hepatic function.
- Assess effectiveness of cough. Drug depresses cough and sigh reflexes and may induce atelectasis, especially in postoperative patients and those with pulmonary disease.
- Note: Nausea and orthostatic hypotension most often occur in ambulatory patients or when a supine patient assumes the head-up position.
- Monitor I&O ratio and pattern. Assess lower abdomen for bladder distension. Report oliguria or urinary retention.
- Monitor bowel pattern; drug-induced constipation may require treatment.

Patient & Family Education

- Request medication at the onset of pain and do not wait until pain is severe.

- Use caution with activities requiring alertness; drug may cause drowsiness, dizziness, and blurred vision.
- Avoid alcohol and other CNS depressants while taking this drug.

HYDROQUINONE

(hye′droe-kwin-one)

Eldopaque, Eldoquin, Esoterica Regular, Melanex, Porcelana, Solaquin

Classifications: DEPIGMENTOR
Therapeutic: DEPIGMENTOR
Pregnancy Category: C

AVAILABILITY 1.5%, 2%, 3%, 4% cream, gel, solution

ACTION & *THERAPEUTIC EFFECT* Topical agent that causes reversible bleaching of hyperpigmented skin due to increased melanin. Interferes with formation of new melanin but does not destroy existing pigment. Depresses melanin synthesis and melanocytic growth, possibly by increasing excretion of melanin from melanocytes. *Interferes with formation of new melanin but does not destroy existing pigment.*

USES Gradual bleaching of hyperpigmented skin conditions such as chloasma or melasma, severe freckling, senile lentigines (age spots or liver spots). Also as an antioxidant in topical preparations. Some formulations include a sunscreening agent (e.g., Porcelana with Sunscreen, Mercolized Cocrema, Pabaquinone, and Solaquin).

CONTRAINDICATIONS Hyersensitivity to hydroquinone, PABA, paraben, or sulfite; prickly heat, sunburn, irritated skin, depilatory usage; pregnancy (category C), lactation.

CAUTIOUS USE Safe use in children <12 y not established.

ROUTE & DOSAGE

Bleaching of Hyperpigmented Skin

Adult: **Topical** Apply thin layer and rub into hyperpigmented skin b.i.d., a.m. and p.m.

ADMINISTRATION

Topical

- Test skin for sensitivity before treatment is initiated. Apply small amount of drug (about 25 mm in diameter) to an unbroken patch of skin and check in 24 h. Do not use drug if vesicle formation, itching, or excessive inflammation occur. Minor redness is not a contraindication.
- Limit applications to an area no larger than that of face and neck.

ADVERSE EFFECTS (≥1%) **Skin:** Dryness and fissuring of paranasal and infraorbital areas, inflammatory reaction, erythema; stinging, tingling, burning sensations; irritation, sensitization, and contact dermatitis.

INTERACTIONS Drug: No clinically significant interactions established.

CLINICAL IMPLICATIONS

Assessment & Drug Effects

- Monitor for therapeutic effectiveness: In general, complete depigmentation occurs in 1–4 mo and lasts 2–6 mo after hydroquinone is discontinued. Once desired results are obtained, reduce amount and frequency of applications to the least that will maintain depigmentation.
- Discontinue if bleaching or skin lightening does not occur after 2 or 3 mo of therapy.

Patient & Family Education

- Use a sunscreen agent or a hydroquinone formulation containing a sunscreen for daytime applications.
- Wash drug off if rash or irritation develops and consult physician.
- Avoid contact with the eyes and not to use on open lesions, sunburned, irritated, or otherwise damaged skin.
- Continue use of protective clothing and sunscreening agent after treatment is terminated to reduce possibility of repigmentation.

HYDROXOCOBALAMIN (VITAMIN B₁₂ ALPHA)

(hye-drox-oh-koe-bal′a-min)

Hydrobexan, Hydroxo-12, LA-12

Classifications: VITAMIN B₁₂ ANTIDOTE

Therapeutic: VITAMIN SUPPLEMENT; ANTIDOTE

Prototype: Cyanocobalamin

Pregnancy Category: A (C if >RDA)

AVAILABILITY 1000 mcg/mL injection

ACTION & *THERAPEUTIC EFFECT*

Cobalamin derivative similar to cyanocobalamin (vitamin B₁₂). More slowly absorbed from injection site than cyanocobalamin and may be taken up by liver in larger quantities. Essential for normal cell growth, cell reproduction maturation of RBCs, myelin synthesis, and believed to be involved in protein synthesis. *Effective in vitamin B₁₂ deficiency that results in megaloblastic anemia.*

USES Treatment of vitamin B₁₂ deficiency.

UNLABELED USES Cyanide poisoning and tobacco amblyopia.

Common adverse effects in *italic*, life-threatening effects underlined; generic names in **bold**; classifications in SMALL CAPS; ♣ Canadian drug name; ☻ Prototype drug

751

CONTRAINDICATIONS History of sensitivity to vitamin B$_{12}$, other cobalamins, or cobalt; indiscriminate use in folic acid deficiency.

CAUTIOUS USE Pregnancy [category A, category C (parenteral)], lactation, children.

ROUTE & DOSAGE

Vitamin B$_{12}$ Deficiency
Adult: IM 30 mcg/d for 5–10 d and then 100–200 mcg/mo or 1000 mcg qod until remission and then 1000 mcg/mo
Child: IM 100 mcg doses to a total of 1–5 mg over 2 wk and then 30–50 mcg/mo

ADMINISTRATION

Intramuscular
- Give deep into a large muscle.

INTERACTIONS Drug: Chloramphenicol may interfere with therapeutic response to hydroxocobalamin.

PHARMACOKINETICS Distribution: Widely distributed; principally stored in liver, kidneys, and adrenals; crosses placenta. **Metabolism:** Converted in tissues to active coenzymes; enterohepatically cycled. **Elimination:** 50–95% of doses ≥100 mcg are excreted in urine in 48 h; excreted in breast milk.

CLINICAL IMPLICATIONS

Assessment & Drug Effects

- Monitor for therapeutic effectiveness: Response to drug therapy is usually dramatic, occurring within 48 h. Effectiveness is measured by laboratory values and improvement in manifestations of vitamin B$_{12}$ deficiency. Characteristically, reticulocyte concentration rises in 3–4 d, peaks in 5–8 d, and then gradually declines as erythrocyte count and hemoglobin rise to normal levels (in 4–6 wk).
- Lab tests: Prior to therapy determine reticulocyte and erythrocyte counts, Hgb, Hct, vitamin B$_{12}$, and serum folate levels; repeated 5–7 d after start of therapy and at regular intervals during therapy.
- Obtain a careful history of sensitivities. Sensitization can take as long as 8 y to develop.
- Monitor potassium levels during the first 48 h, particularly in patients with Addisonian pernicious anemia or megaloblastic anemia. Conversion to normal erythropoiesis increases erythrocyte potassium requirement and can result in severe hypokalemia and sudden death.
- Monitor vital signs in patients with cardiac disease and in those receiving parenteral cyanocobalamin, and be alert to symptoms of pulmonary edema; generally occur early in therapy.
- Note: Some patients experience mild pain at injection site after administration.
- Monitor bowel function. Bowel regularity is essential for consistent absorption of oral preparations.
- Note: Smokers appear to have increased requirements for vitamin B$_{12}$.

Patient & Family Education

- Notify physician of any intercurrent disease or infection. Increased dosage may be required.
- Note: It is imperative to understand that drug therapy must be continued throughout life for pernicious anemia to prevent irreversible neurologic damage.
- Neurologic damage is considered irreversible if there is no improvement after 1–1$^{1}/_{2}$ y of adequate therapy.

▪ Dietary deficiency of vitamin B₁₂ has been observed in strict vegetarians (vegans) and their breast-fed infants as well as in the elderly.

HYDROXYCHLOROQUINE

(hye-drox-ee-klor'oh-kwin)
Plaquenil Sulfate
Classifications: ANTIMALARIAL
Therapeutic: ANTIMALARIAL
Prototype: Chloroquine
Pregnancy Category: C

AVAILABILITY 200 mg tablets

ACTION & *THERAPEUTIC EFFECT*

Derivative closely related to chloroquine. Antimalarial activity is believed to be based on ability to form complexes with DNA of parasite, thereby inhibiting replication and transcription to RNA and DNA synthesis of the parasite. *Effective against* Plasmodium vivax *and* Plasmodium malariae.

USES Suppressive prophylaxis and treatment of acute malarial attacks due to all forms of susceptible malaria. Used adjunctively with primaquine for eradication of *Plasmodium vivax* and *Plasmodium malariae*. More commonly prescribed than chloroquine for treatment of rheumatoid arthritis and lupus erythematosus (usually in conjunction with salicylate or corticosteroid therapy).

UNLABELED USES Porphyria cutanea tarda.

CONTRAINDICATIONS Known hypersensitivity to, retinal or visual field changes associated with quinoline compounds; psoriasis, porphyria, G6PD deficiency; long-term therapy in children; pregnancy

(category C). Safe use in juvenile arthritis is not established.

CAUTIOUS USE Hepatic disease; alcoholism, use with hepatotoxic drugs; impaired renal function, porphoria; metabolic acidosis; patients with tendency to dermatitis.

ROUTE & DOSAGE

Note: Doses are expressed in terms of hydroxychloroquine base: 400-mg tablet = 310-mg base; 800-mg tablet = 620-mg base

Acute Malaria

Adult: **PO** 620-mg base followed by 310-mg base at 6, 18, and 24 h
Child: **PO** 10-mg base/kg, then 5-mg base/kg at 6, 18, and 24 h

Malaria Suppression

Adult: **PO** 310-mg base the same day each week starting 2 wk before exposure and continuing for 4–6 wk after leaving the area of exposure
Child: **PO** 5-mg base/kg the same day each week starting 2 wk before exposure and continuing for 4–8 wk after leaving the area of exposure

Lupus Erythematosus

Adult: **PO** 310-mg base 1–2 times/d
Child: **PO** 3–5 mg/kg/d in 1–2 divided doses (max: 400 mg/d or 7 mg/kg/d)

Rheumatoid Arthritis

Adult: **PO** 400–600 mg/d until response, then decrease to lowest maintenance levels possible
Child: **PO** 3–5 mg/kg/d in 1–2 divided doses (max: 400 mg/d or 7 mg/kg/d)

Common adverse effects in *italic*, life-threatening effects <u>underlined</u>; generic names in **bold**; classifications in SMALL CAPS; ♣ Canadian drug name; ⊘ Prototype drug

753

ADMINISTRATION

Oral

- Give drug with meals or milk to reduce incidence of GI distress.
- Give antacids and laxatives at least 4 h before or after hydroxychloroquine.
- Store at 15°–30° C (59°–86° F) unless otherwise directed.

ADVERSE EFFECTS (≥1%) **CNS:** Fatigue, vertigo, headache, mood or mental changes, anxiety, *retinopathy,* blurred vision, difficulty focusing. **GI:** Anorexia, nausea, vomiting, diarrhea, abdominal cramps, weight loss. **Hematologic:** Hemolysis in patients with G6PD deficiency, <u>agranulocytosis</u> (rare), <u>aplastic anemia</u> (rare), thrombocytopenia. **Skin:** Bleaching or loss of hair, unusual pigmentation (blue-black) of skin or inside mouth, skin rash, itching.

INTERACTIONS Drug: Aluminum- and **magnesium-**containing ANTACIDS and LAXATIVES decrease hydroxychloroquine absorption; separate administrations by at least 4 h; hydroxychloroquine may interfere with response to **rabies vaccine.**

PHARMACOKINETICS Absorption: Rapidly and almost completely absorbed. **Peak:** 1–2 h. **Distribution:** Widely distributed; concentrates in lungs, liver, erythrocytes, eyes, skin, and kidneys; crosses placenta. **Metabolism:** Partially in liver to active metabolite. **Elimination:** In urine; excreted in breast milk. **Half-Life:** 70–120 h.

CLINICAL IMPLICATIONS

Assessment & Drug Effects

- Monitor for therapeutic effectiveness; may not appear for several weeks, and maximal benefit may not occur for 6 mo.

- Do baseline and periodic ophthalmoscopic examinations and blood cell counts on all patients on long-term therapy.
- Discontinue drug if weakness, visual symptoms, hearing loss, unusual bleeding, bruising, or skin eruptions occur.

Patient & Family Education

- Learn about adverse effects and their symptoms when taking prolonged therapy.
- Follow drug regimen exactly as prescribed by the physician.
- Make sure to keep this drug out of reach of children.

HYDROXYUREA

(hye-drox′ee-yoo-ree-ah)

Hydrea, Droxia

Classifications: ANTINEOPLASTIC; ANTIMETABOLITE

Therapeutic: ANTINEOPLASTIC; ANTIMETABOLITE

Pregnancy Category: D

AVAILABILITY 500 mg capsules

ACTION & *THERAPEUTIC EFFECT*

A cell-cycle-phase antineoplastic agent; hydroxyurea causes an immediate inhibition of DNA synthesis by acting as an RNA reductase inhibitor, necessary for DNA synthesis but without interfering with the synthesis of RNA or protein. *Cytotoxic effect limited to tissues with high rates of cell proliferation. No cross resistance with other antineoplastics has been demonstrated.*

USES Palliative treatment of metastatic melanoma, chronic myelocytic leukemia; recurrent metastatic, or inoperable ovarian cancer. Also used as adjunct to x-ray therapy for treatment of advanced primary squamous cell (epidermoid) carcinoma of head (excluding lip), neck, lungs.

UNLABELED USES Psoriasis; combination therapy with radiation of lung carcinoma; sickle cell anemia.

CONTRAINDICATIONS Pregnancy (category D), lactation, children, myelosuppression.

CAUTIOUS USE Recent use of other cytotoxic drugs or irradiation; bone marrow depression; renal dysfunction; older adults; history of gout.

ROUTE & DOSAGE

Palliative Therapy

Adult: **PO** 80 mg/kg q3d or 20–30 mg/kg/d

Sickle Cell Anemia

Adult: **PO** 15 mg/kg/d, may increase by 5 mg/kg/d (max: of 35 mg/kg/d or until toxicity develops)

Renal Impairment

Cl_{cr} 10–50 mL/min: administer 50% of dose; <10 mL/min: administer 20% of dose
Hemodialysis: Administer dose after hemodialysis; no supplemental dose needed

ADMINISTRATION

Oral

- Open, mix with water, and give immediately when patient has difficulty swallowing capsule.
- Store in tightly covered container at 15°–30° C (59°–86° F) unless otherwise directed.

ADVERSE EFFECTS (≥1%) **CNS:** Rare: Headache, dizziness, hallucinations, convulsions. **GI:** Stomatitis, anorexia, nausea, vomiting, diarrhea, constipation. **Hematologic:** Bone marrow suppression (*leukope-*

nia, anemia, thrombocytopenia), megaloblastic erythropoiesis. **Skin:** Maculopapular rash, facial erythema, postirradiation erythema. **Urogenital:** Renal tubular dysfunction, elevated BUN, serum, creatinine levels, hyperuricemia. **Body as a Whole:** Fever, chills, malaise.

INTERACTIONS Drug: No clinically significant interactions established.

PHARMACOKINETICS Absorption: Readily absorbed from GI tract. **Peak:** 2 h. **Distribution:** Crosses blood–brain barrier. **Metabolism:** In liver. **Elimination:** As respiratory CO_2 and as urea in urine.

CLINICAL IMPLICATIONS

Assessment & Drug Effects

- Lab tests: Determine status of kidney, liver, and bone marrow function before and periodically during therapy; monitor hemoglobin, WBC, platelet counts at least once weekly.
- Interrupt therapy if WBC drops to 2500/mm^3 or platelets to 100,000/mm^3.
- Monitor I&O. Advise patients with high serum uric acid levels to drink at least 10–12 240 mL (8 oz) glasses of fluid daily to prevent uric acid nephropathy.
- Note: Patients with marked renal dysfunction may rapidly develop visual and auditory hallucinations and hematologic toxicity.

Patient & Family Education

- Note: Incidence of toxicity is as high as 66% with doses of 40 mg/kg body weight.
- Notify physician of fever, chills, sore throat, nausea, vomiting, diarrhea, loss of appetite, and unusual bruising or bleeding.
- Use barrier contraceptive during therapy. Drug is teratogenic.

H

Common adverse effects in *italic*, life-threatening effects underlined; generic names in **bold**; classifications in SMALL CAPS; ✦ Canadian drug name; ⊙ Prototype drug

755

H

HYDROXYZINE HYDROCHLORIDE 🅟ᵣ

(hye-drox′i-zeen)

Atarax Syrup, Hyzine-50, Vistaril Intramuscular, Vistacon, Vistaject-25 & -50

HYDROXYZINE PAMOATE

Vistaril Oral

Classifications: ANTIHISTAMINE; H₁-RECEPTOR ANTAGONIST; ANTIPRURITIC

Therapeutic: ANTIHISTAMINE; ANTIPRURITIC; ANTIANXIETY; ANTIEMETIC

Pregnancy Category: C

AVAILABILITY Hydroxyzine HCl 10 mg, 25 mg, 50 mg tablets; 10 mg/ 5 mL syrup; 25 mg/5 mL oral suspension; 25 mg/mL, 50 mg/mL injection **Hydroxyzine Pamoate** 25 mg, 50 mg, 100 mg capsules; 25 mg/ 5 ml suspension

ACTION & *THERAPEUTIC EFFECT*

H₁-receptor antagonist; effective in treatment of histamine-mediated pruritus or other allergic reactions. Its tranquilizing effect is produced primarily by depression of hypothalamus and brain-stem reticular formation, rather than cortical areas. *Effective as an antianxiety agent and sedative. Additionally, it is an effective agent for pruritus.*

USES Emotional or psychoneurotic states characterized by anxiety, tension, or psychomotor agitation; to relieve anxiety, control nausea and emesis, and reduce narcotic requirements before or after surgery or delivery. Also used in management of pruritus due to allergic conditions, e.g., chronic urticaria, atopic and contact dermatoses, and in treatment of acute and chronic alcoholism with withdrawal symptoms or delirium tremens.

CONTRAINDICATIONS Known hypersensitivity to hydroxyzine; use as sole treatment in psychoses or depression; pregnancy (category C); lactation.

CAUTIOUS USE History of allergies; GI disorders; cardiac disease; COPD; older adults.

ROUTE & DOSAGE

Anxiety

Adult: **PO** 25–100 mg t.i.d. or q.i.d. **IM** 25–100 mg q4–6h
Child: **PO** <6 y, 50 mg/d in divided doses; >6 y, 50 mg/d in divided doses **IM** 1.1 mg/kg q4–6h

Pruritus

Adult: **PO** 25 mg t.i.d. or q.i.d. **IM** 25 mg q4–6h
Geriatric: **PO** 10 mg 3–4 times daily
Child: **PO** >6 y, 50–100 mg/d in divided doses; <6 y, 50 mg/d in divided doses **IM** 1.1 mg/kg q4–6h

Nausea

Adult: **IM** 25–100 mg q4–6h
Child: **IM** 1.1 mg/kg q4–6h

ADMINISTRATION

Oral

- Note: Tablets may be crushed and taken with fluid of patient's choice. Capsule may be emptied and contents swallowed with water or mixed with food. Liquid formulations are available.

Intramuscular

- Give deep into body of a relatively large muscle. The Z-track technique of injection is recommended to prevent SC infiltration.
- Recommended site: In adult, the gluteus maximus or vastus lateralis; in children, the vastus lateralis.

- Protect all forms from light. Store at 15°–30° C (59°–86° F) unless otherwise specified.

***INCOMPATIBILITIES* Solution/additive: Aminophylline, amobarbital, chloramphenicol, dimenhydrinate, penicillin G, pentobarbital, phenobarbital.**

ADVERSE EFFECTS (≥1%) **CNS:** *Drowsiness* (usually transitory), sedation, dizziness, headache. **CV:** Hypotension. **GI:** *Dry mouth.* **Body as a Whole:** Urticaria, dyspnea, chest tightness, wheezing, involuntary motor activity (rare). **Hematologic:** Phlebitis, hemolysis, thrombosis. **Skin:** Erythematous macular eruptions, erythema multiforme, digital gangrene from inadvertent IV or intraarterial injection, injection site reactions.

DIAGNOSTIC TEST INTERFERENCE Possibility of false-positive ***urinary 17-hydroxycorticosteroid*** determinations (modified ***Glenn-Nelson technique***).

INTERACTIONS Drug: Alcohol and CNS DEPRESSANTS add to CNS depression; TRICYCLIC ANTIDEPRESSANTS and other ANTICHOLINERGICS have additive anticholinergic effects; may inhibit pressor effects of **epinephrine.**

PHARMACOKINETICS Absorption: Readily from GI tract. **Onset:** 15–30 min PO. **Duration:** 4–6 h. **Distribution:** Not known if it crosses placenta or is distributed into breast milk. **Metabolism:** In liver. **Elimination:** In bile.

CLINICAL IMPLICATIONS
Assessment & Drug Effects
- Evaluate alertness. Drowsiness may occur and usually disappears with continued therapy or following reduction of dosage.

- Monitor condition of oral membranes daily when patient is on high dosage of hydroxyzine.
- Reevaluate usefulness of drug periodically.
- Reduce dosage of the depressant up to 50% when CNS depressants are prescribed concomitantly.

Patient & Family Education
- Do not drive or engage in other potentially hazardous activities until response to drug is known.
- Do NOT take alcohol and hydroxyzine at the same time.
- Notify physician immediately if you become pregnant.
- Relieve dry mouth by frequent warm water rinses, increasing fluid intake, and use of a salivary substitute (e.g., Moi-Stir, Xero-Lube).
- Give teeth scrupulous care. Avoid irritation or abrasion of gums and other oral tissues.
- Consult physician before self-dosing with OTC medications.

HYOSCYAMINE SULFATE

(hye-oh-sye′a-meen)
Anaspaz, Cystospaz, Levsin, Levsinex, NuLev
Classifications: ANTICHOLINERGIC; ANTIMUSCARINIC; ANTISPASMODIC
Therapeutic: ANTISPASMODIC; ANTICHOLINERGIC
Prototype: Atropine
Pregnancy Category: C

AVAILABILITY 0.125 mg, 0.150 mg tablets; 0.125 mg sublingual tablets; 0.375 sustained release capsules; 0.125 mg orally disintegrating tablet 0.125 mg/mL oral solution; 0.125 mg/5 mL elixir; 0.5 mg/mL injection

ACTION & *THERAPEUTIC EFFECT*
Competitive inhibitor at autonomic

Common adverse effects in *italic*, life-threatening effects underlined; generic names in **bold**; classifications in SMALL CAPS; ♣ Canadian drug name; ⊘ Prototype drug

757

postganglionic cholinergic receptors. It does not block acetycholine at the neuromuscular junction. Extremely potent belladonna alkaloid with anticholinergic and antispasmodic activity. *Anticholinergic and antispasmodic action is produced by competitive inhibition of acetylcholine at the parasympathetic neuroeffector junctions.*

USES GI tract disorders caused by spasm and hypermotility, as conjunct therapy with diet and antacids for peptic ulcer management, and as an aid in the control of gastric hypersecretion and intestinal hypermotility. Also symptomatic relief of biliary and renal colic, as a "drying agent" to relieve symptoms of acute rhinitis, to control preanesthesia salivation and respiratory tract secretions, to treat symptoms of parkinsonism, and to reduce pain and hypersecretion in pancreatitis.

CONTRAINDICATIONS Hypersensitivity to belladonna alkaloids, prostatic hypertrophy, obstructive diseases of GI or GU tract, ulcerative colitis, paralytic ileus or intestinal atony; myasthenia gravis; children <2 y; pregnancy (category C), lactation.

CAUTIOUS USE Diabetes mellitus, cardiac disease, cardiac arrhythmias; autonomic neuropathy; closed-angle glaucoma; GERD, hiatal hernia; pulmonary disease; renal or hepatic disease.

ROUTE & DOSAGE

> **GI Spasms**
>
> *Adult:* **IV/IM/SC** 0.25–0.5 mg q4h **PO/SL** 0.125–0.25 mg t.i.d. or q.i.d. prn
> *Child:* **PO** 2–12 y, 0.0625–0.125 mg q4h prn (max: 0.75 mg/d)

ADMINISTRATION

- Note: Dose for older adults may need to be less than the standard adult dose. Observe patient carefully for signs of paradoxic reactions.

Oral
- Give preparations about 1 h before meals and at bedtime (at least 2 h after last meal).
- Ensure that sustained release form of drug is not chewed or crushed. It must be swallowed whole.

Intravenous

PREPARE: Direct: Give undiluted.
ADMINISTER: Direct: Give a single dose over 60 sec.
- Store 15°–30° C (59°–86° F).

ADVERSE EFFECTS (≥1%) **CNS:** Headache, unusual tiredness or weakness, confusion, *drowsiness,* excitement in older adult patients. **CV:** Palpitations, tachycardia. **Special Senses:** *Blurred vision,* increased intraocular tension, cycloplegia, mydriasis. **GI:** *Dry mouth, constipation,* paralytic ileus. **Other:** *Urinary retention,* anhidrosis, suppression of lactation.

INTERACTIONS Drug: Amantadine, ANTIHISTAMINES, TRICYCLIC ANTIDEPRESSANTS, **quinidine, disopyramide, procainamide** add anticholinergic effects; decreases **levodopa** effects; **methotrimeprazine** may precipitate extrapyramidal effects; decreases antipsychotic effects of PHENOTHIAZINES (decreased absorption).

PHARMACOKINETICS Absorption: Well absorbed from all administration sites. **Onset:** 2–3 min IV; 20–30 min PO. **Peak:** 15–30 min IV; 30–60 min PO. **Duration:** 4–6 h (up to 12 h with sustained release form). **Distribution:** Distributed in most body tissues; crosses blood–brain barrier and placenta; distributed in breast milk. **Metabolism:** In liver. **Elimination:** In urine. **Half-Life:** 3.5–13 h.

CLINICAL IMPLICATIONS

Assessment & Drug Effects

- Monitor bowel elimination; may cause constipation.
- Monitor urinary output.
- Lessen risk of urinary retention by having patient void prior to each dose.
- Assess for dry mouth and recommend good practices of oral hygiene.

Patient & Family Education

- Avoid excessive exposure to high temperatures; drug-induced heatstroke can develop.
- Do not drive or engage in other potentially hazardous activities until response to drug is known.
- Use dark glasses if experiencing blurred vision, but if this adverse effect persists, notify physician for dose adjustment or possible drug change.

IBANDRONATE SODIUM

Boniva

Classifications: BISPHOSPHONATE; REGULATOR, BONE METABOLISM
Therapeutic: BONE METABOLISM REGULATOR
Prototype: Etidronate
Pregnancy Category: C

AVAILABILITY 2.5 mg and 150 mg tablets

ACTION & *THERAPEUTIC EFFECT*

Ibandronate is a potent third-generation bisphosphonate. It inhibits activity of osteoclasts and reduces bone resorption and turnover in the matrix of the bone. *In postmenopausal women, it reduces the rate of bone turnover, resulting in a net gain in bone mass.*

USES Prevention and treatment of osteoporosis in postmenopausal women.

UNLABELED USES Treatment of metastatic bone disease in breast cancer.

CONTRAINDICATIONS Hypersensitivity to ibandronate; severe renal impairment; hypocalcemia, vitamin D deficiency; inability to stand or sit up straight for 60 min; achalasia, esophageal stricture, dysphagia; concurrent administration with antacids, supplements, or vitamins; children <18 y; pregnancy (category C).

CAUTIOUS USE Mild or moderate renal impairment; history of GI bleeding or disease, esophagitis, esophageal, or gastric ulcers; older adults; lactation.

ROUTE & DOSAGE

Postmenopausal Osteoporosis
Adult: **PO** 2.5 mg qd or 150 mg once monthly on the same day each month

Renal Impairment
Cl_{cr} <30 mL/min: Use not recommended.

ADMINISTRATION

- Correct hypocalcemia before administering ibandronate.
- Give at least 60 min before food, beverage, or other medications (including vitamins).
- Instruct to swallowed whole with a full glass of plain water (180–240 mL; 6–8 oz) while standing or sitting in an upright position.
- Keep patient sitting up or ambulating for 60 min after taking drug.

Common adverse effects in *italic*, life-threatening effects underlined; generic names in **bold**; classifications in SMALL CAPS; ◆ Canadian drug name; ⓟ Prototype drug

759

- Store between 15° and 30° C (59° and 86° F).

ADVERSE EFFECTS (≥1%) **CNS:** Dizziness, headache, nerve root lesion, vertigo. **GI:** Dyspepsia, constipation, diarrhea, esophagitis, gastritis, pharyngitis, nausea, vomiting. **Respiratory:** Upper respiratory infection, pharyngitis. **Skin:** Rash. **Body as a Whole:** Back pain. **Other:** Tooth disorder.

DIAGNOSTIC TEST INTERFERENCE Interferes with the use of bone-imaging agents.

INTERACTIONS Drug: Concurrent administration of **calcium, magnesium,** or **iron** reduces ibandronate adsorption. **Food:** Food reduces ibandronate absorption (ibandronate should be taken in a fasting state).

PHARMACOKINETICS Absorption: Bioavailability poor (0.6%). **Peak:** 0.5–2 h. **Distribution:** 86–99% protein bound. **Metabolism:** None. **Elimination:** Renal. **Half-Life:** 10–60 h.

CLINICAL IMPLICATIONS

Assessment & Drug Effects

- Lab tests: Monitor albumin-adjusted serum calcium, serum phosphate, serum alkaline phosphatase, fasting and 24 h urinary calcium, and serum electrolytes; baseline and periodic renal function.
- Withhold drug and notify physician if the Cl_{cr} <30 mL/min.
- Diagnostic test: Bone density scan every 12–18 mo.
- Monitor for S&S of upper GI distress, especially with concurrent use of NSAIDS or aspirin.

Patient & Family Education

- Take the monthly dose (150 mg) on the same day each month. Carefully follow directions for taking the drug (see Administration).

- If a monthly dose is missed, and the next scheduled dose is more than 7 d away, take one 150 mg tablet the next morning then resume the original monthly schedule. Do not take two 150 mg tablets in the same week.
- Report to physician any of the following: severe bone, joint, or muscle pain; heartburn, pain behind the sternum, difficulty or pain with swallowing.

IBUPROFEN 🅿️

(eye-byoo′proe-fen)

Advil, Amersol ♦, Children's Motrin, Ibuprin, Junior Strength Motrin Caplets, Motrin, Nuprin, Pediaprofen, Pamprin-IB, Rufen, Trendar

Classifications: ANALGESIC, NONSTEROIDAL ANTIINFLAMMATORY DRUG (NSAID) (COX-1 AND COX-2 INHIBITOR); ANTIPYRETIC
Therapeutic: NSAID, ANALGESIC; ANTIPYRETIC
Pregnancy Category: B

AVAILABILITY 100 mg, 200 mg, 400 mg, 600 mg, 800 mg tablets; 50 mg, 100 mg chewable tablets; 100 mg/5 mL, 100 mg/2.5 mL suspension; 40 mg/mL drops

ACTION & THERAPEUTIC EFFECT Prototype of the propionic acid NSAIDs (COX-1 and COX-2) inhibitor with nonsteroidal antiinflammatory activity and significant antipyretic and analgesic properties. It blocks prostaglandin synthesis. Ibuprofen activity also includes modulation of T-cell function, inhibition of inflammatory cell chemotaxis, decreased release of superoxide radicals, or increased scavenging of these compounds at inflammatory sites. *Has nonsteroidal antiinflammatory, analgesic, and antipyretic* *effects. Inhibits platelet aggregation and prolongs bleeding time but does not affect prothrombin or whole blood clotting times.*

USES Chronic, symptomatic rheumatoid arthritis and osteoarthritis; relief of mild to moderate pain; primary dysmenorrhea; reduction of fever.
UNLABELED USES Gout, juvenile rheumatoid arthritis, psoriatic arthritis, ankylosing spondylitis, vascular headache.

CONTRAINDICATIONS Patient in whom urticaria, severe rhinitis, bronchospasm, angioedema, nasal polyps are precipitated by aspirin or other NSAIDs; active peptic ulcer, bleeding abnormalities; perioperative pain related to CABG. Safe use in children <6 mo is not established. **CAUTIOUS USE** Hypertension, history of GI ulceration; diabetes mellitus, impaired hepatic or renal function, history of coronary artery disease, angina, MI cardiac decompensation; chronic renal failure, patients with SLE; pregnancy (category B).

ROUTE & DOSAGE

Inflammatory Disease
Adult: **PO** 400–800 mg t.i.d. or q.i.d. (max: 3200 mg/d)
Child: **PO** *<20 kg,* up to 400 mg/d in divided doses; *20–30 kg,* up to 600 mg/d in divided doses; *30–40 kg,* up to 800 mg/d in divided doses

Mild to Moderate Pain, Dysmenorrhea
Adult: **PO** 400 mg q4–6h up to 1200 mg/d

Fever
Adult: **PO** 200–400 mg t.i.d. or q.i.d. (max: 1200 mg/d)
Child: **PO** *6 mo–12 y,* 5–10 mg/kg q4–6h up to 40 mg/kg/d

ADMINISTRATION
Oral
- Give on an empty stomach, 1 h before or 2 h after meals. May be taken with meals or milk if GI intolerance occurs.
- Ensure that chewable tablets are chewed or crushed before being swallowed.
- Note: Tablet may be crushed if patient is unable to swallow it whole and mixed with food or liquid before swallowing.
- Store in tightly closed, light-resistant container unless otherwise directed by manufacturer.

ADVERSE EFFECTS (≥1%) **CNS:** Headache, dizziness, light-headedness, anxiety, emotional lability, fatigue, malaise, drowsiness, anxiety, confusion, depression, aseptic meningitis. **CV:** Hypertension, palpitation, congestive heart failure (patient with marginal cardiac function); peripheral edema. **Special Senses:** Amblyopia (blurred vision, decreased visual acuity, scotomas, changes in color vision); nystagmus, visual-field defects; tinnitus, impaired hearing. **GI:** Dry mouth, gingival ulcerations, dyspepsia, *heartburn, nausea,* vomiting, anorexia, diarrhea, constipation, bloating, flatulence, epigastric or abdominal discomfort or pain, GI ulceration, *occult blood loss.* **Hematologic:** Thrombocytopenia, neutropenia, hemolytic or aplastic anemia, leukopenia; decreased Hgb, Hct; transitory rise in AST, ALT, serum alkaline phosphatase; rise in (Ivy) bleeding time. **GU:** Acute renal failure, polyuria, azotemia, cystitis, hematuria, nephrotoxicity, decreased creatinine clearance. **Skin:** Maculopapular and vesicobullous skin eruptions, erythema multiforme, pruritus, rectal itching, acne. **Body as a Whole:** Fluid retention with

Common adverse effects in *italic*, life-threatening effects underlined; generic names in **bold**; classifications in SMALL CAPS; ♣ Canadian drug name; ⊕ Prototype drug

761

edema, Stevens-Johnson syndrome, <u>toxic hepatitis</u>, hypersensitivity reactions, <u>anaphylaxis</u>, bronchospasm, serum sickness, SLE, angioedema.

INTERACTIONS Drug: ORAL ANTICOAGULANTS, **heparin** may prolong bleeding time; may increase **lithium** and **methotrexate** toxicity. **Herbal:** Feverfew, garlic, ginger, ginkgo may increase bleeding potential.

PHARMACOKINETICS Absorption: 80% from GI tract. **Onset:** 1 h (antipyretic). **Peak:** 1–2 h. **Duration:** 6–8 h. **Metabolism:** In liver. **Elimination:** Primarily in urine; some biliary excretion. **Half-Life:** 2–4 h.

CLINICAL IMPLICATIONS

Assessment & Drug Effects

- Monitor for therapeutic effectiveness. Optimum response generally occurs within 2 wk (e.g., relief of pain, stiffness, or swelling; or improved joint flexion and strength).
- Observe patients with history of cardiac decompensation closely for evidence of fluid retention and edema.
- Lab tests: Baseline and periodic evaluations of Hgb, renal and hepatic function, and auditory and ophthalmologic examinations are recommended in patients receiving prolonged or high-dose therapy.
- Monitor for GI distress and S&S of GI bleeding.
- Note: Symptoms of acute toxicity in children include apnea, cyanosis, response only to painful stimuli, dizziness, and nystagmus.

Patient & Family Education

- Notify physician immediately of passage of dark tarry stools, "coffee ground" emesis, frankly bloody emesis, or other GI distress, as well as blood or protein in urine, and onset of skin rash, pruritus, jaundice.
- Do not drive or engage in other potentially hazardous activities until response to the drug is known.
- Do not self-medicate with ibuprofen if taking prescribed drugs or being treated for a serious condition without consulting physician.
- Do not give to children <3 mo or for longer than 2 d without consulting physician.
- Do not take aspirin concurrently with ibuprofen.
- Avoid alcohol and NSAIDs unless otherwise advised by physician. Concurrent use may increase risk of GI ulceration and bleeding tendencies.

IBUTILIDE FUMARATE

(i-bu′ti-lide)
Corvert
Classifications: ANTIARRHYTHMIC AGENT, CLASS III
Therapeutic: ANTIARRHYTHMIC AGENT, CLASS III
Prototype: Amiodarone HCl
Pregnancy Category: C

AVAILABILITY 0.1 mg/mL injection

ACTION & THERAPEUTIC EFFECT
Ibutilide is a Class III antiarrhythmic agent. It prolongs the cardiac action potential and increases both atrial and ventricular refractoriness without affecting conduction (i.e., Class III antiarrhythmic electrophysiologic effects). *It is used to treat recently occurring atrial arrhythmias. Like other Class III antiarrhythmic drugs it may produce proarrhythmic effects that can be life threatening.*

USES Rapid conversion of atrial fibrillation or atrial flutter of recent onset.

CONTRAINDICATIONS Hypersensitivity to ibutilide, hypokalemia, hypomagnesemia; pregnancy (category C). Safety and effectiveness in children <18 y are not established.

CAUTIOUS USE History of CHF, cardiac ejection fraction of 35% or less, recent MI, prolonged QT intervals, ventricular arrhythmias; renal or liver disease, cardiovascular disorder other than atrial arrhythmias, other drugs that prolong QT interval, lactation.

ROUTE & DOSAGE

Atrial Fibrillation or Flutter
Adult: IV <60 kg, 0.01 mg/kg, may repeat in 10 min if inadequate response; ≥60 kg, 1 mg, may repeat in 10 min if inadequate response

ADMINISTRATION

- Hypokalemia and hypomagnesemia should be corrected prior to treatment with ibutilide.
- Class Ia and other class III antiarrhythmic drugs should not be given concurrently or within 4 h of ibutilide.

Intravenous

PREPARE: Direct: Give undiluted. **IV Infusion:** Contents of 1 mg vial may be diluted in 50 mL of D5W or NS to yield 0.017 mg/mL.

ADMINISTER: Direct/IV Infusion: Give a single dose by direct injection or infusion over 10 min.
- Stop injection/infusion as soon as presenting arrhythmia is terminated or with appearance

of ventricular tachycardia or marked prolongation of QT or QT_c.

- Store diluted solution up to 24 h at 15°–30° C (59°–86° F) or 48 h refrigerated at 2°–8° C (36°–46° F).

ADVERSE EFFECTS (≥1%) **CNS:** Headache. **CV:** Proarrhythmic effects (sustained and nonsustained polymorphic ventricular tachycardia), AV block, bundle branch block, ventricular extrasystoles, hypotension, postural hypotension, bradycardia, tachycardia, palpitations, prolonged QT segment. **GI:** Nausea.

INTERACTIONS Drug: Increased potential for proarrhythmic effects when administered with PHENOTHIAZINES, TRICYCLIC ANTIDEPRESSANTS, **amiodarone, disopyramide, quinidine, procainamide, sotalol** may cause prolonged refractoriness if given within 4 h of ibutilide.

PHARMACOKINETICS Onset: 30 min. **Metabolism:** In liver. **Elimination:** 82% in urine, 19% in feces. **Half-Life:** 6 h (range 2–21 h).

CLINICAL IMPLICATIONS

Assessment & Drug Effects
- Monitor for therapeutic effectiveness. Conversion to normal sinus rhythm normally occurs within 30 min of initiation of infusion.
- Observe with continuous ECG, BP, and HR monitoring during and for at least 4 h after infusion or until QT_c has returned to baseline. Monitor for longer periods with liver dysfunction or if proarrhythmic activity is observed.

Patient & Family Education
- Consult physician and understand the potential risks of ibutilide therapy.

Common adverse effects in *italic*, life-threatening effects <u>underlined</u>; generic names in **bold**; classifications in SMALL CAPS; ♣ Canadian drug name; ⊕ Prototype drug

763

IDARUBICIN

(i-da-a-roo'bi-cin)

Idamycin PFS

Classifications: ANTINEOPLASTIC; ANTIBIOTIC

Therapeutic: ANTINEOPLASTIC; ANTIBIOTIC

Prototype: Doxorubicin

Pregnancy Category: D

AVAILABILITY 5 mg, 10 mg, 20 mg vials; 1 mg/mL injection

ACTION & *THERAPEUTIC EFFECT*

Cytotoxic anthracycline antibiotic. Potency of idarubicin is greater than that of daunorubicin or doxorubicin. It may be less cardiotoxic than other anthracyclines. Idarubicin exhibits inhibitory effects on DNA topoisomerase II, an enzyme responsible for repairing faulty sections of DNA. It results in breaks in the helix of the DNA, and thus affects RNA and protein synthesis in rapidly dividing cells. *Idarubicin exhibits inhibitory effects on DNA and RNA polymerase and, therefore, on nucleic acid synthesis.*

USES In combination with other antineoplastic drugs for treatment of AML.

UNLABELED USES Breast cancer, other solid tumors.

CONTRAINDICATIONS Myelosuppression, hypersensitivity to idarubicin or doxorubicin, children <2 y, pregnancy (category D), lactation.

CAUTIOUS USE Impaired renal or hepatic function; patients who have received irradiation or radiotherapy to areas surrounding heart; cardiac disease.

ROUTE & DOSAGE

Acute Myelogenous Leukemia (AML)

Adult: **IV** 12 mg/m^2 daily for 3 d injected slowly over 10–15 min

Acute Nonlymphocytic Leukemia, Acute Lymphocytic Leukemia

Child: **IV** 10–12 mg/m^2/d for 3 d

Renal Impairment

Creatinine >2 mg/dL: give 75% of dose

Hepatic Impairment

Bilirubin 1.5–5 mg/dL: give 50% of dose; if >5 mg/dL: do not use drug

ADMINISTRATION

Intravenous

IV administration to infants, children: Verify correct IV concentration and rate of infusion with physician.

PREPARE: **IV Infusion:** Reconstitute 5- and 10-mg vials with 5 and 10 mL, respectively, of nonbacteriostatic NS to yield 1 mg/mL. ▪ Vials are under negative pressure, therefore, carefully insert needle into vial to reconstitute. ▪ Wash skin accidentally exposed with soap and water.

ADMINISTER: **IV Infusion:** Give slowly over 10–15 min into tubing of free flowing IV of NS or D5W.

▪ If extravasation is suspected, immediately stop infusion, elevate the arm, and apply ice pack for $^1/_2$ h then q.i.d. for $^1/_2$ h × 3 d.

INCOMPATIBILITIES **Solution/additive:** Acyclovir, ALKALINE SOLUTIONS (i.e., **sodium bicarbonate**), **ampicillin/sulbactam,** cefazolin, ceftazidime, clinda-mycin, dexamethasone, eto-poside, furosemide, gentami-cin, heparin, hydrocortisone, imipenem/cilastatin, meperi-dine, methotrexate, mezlocil-lin, sargramostim, sodium bicarbonate, vancomycin, vincristine. **Y-site:** Same as above.

- Store reconstituted solutions up to 7 d refrigerated at 2°–8° C (36°–46° F) and 72 h at room temperature 15°–30° C (59°–86° F).

ADVERSE EFFECTS (≥1%) **CV:** CHF, atrial fibrillation, chest pain, <u>MI</u>. **GI:** *Nausea, vomiting, diarrhea, abdominal pain,* mucositis. **Hematologic:** *Anemia, leukopenia,* thrombocytopenia. **Other:** Nephrotoxicity, hepatotoxicity, *alopecia,* rash.

INTERACTIONS Drug: IMMUNOSUP-PRESSANTS cause additive bone marrow suppression; ANTICOAGULANTS, NSAIDS, SALICYLATES, **aspirin,** THROM-BOLYTIC AGENTS increase risk of bleeding; idarubicin may blunt the effects of **filgrastim, sargramostim.**

PHARMACOKINETICS Onset: Median time to remission 28 d. **Peak:** Serum level 4 h. **Duration:** Serum levels 120 h. **Distribution:** Concentrates in nucleated blood and bone marrow cells. **Metabolism:** In liver to idarubicinol, which may be as active as idarubicin. **Elimination:** 16% in urine; 17% in bile. **Half-Life:** Idarubicin 15–45 h, idarubicinol 45 h.

CLINICAL IMPLICATIONS

Assessment & Drug Effects

- Monitor infusion site closely, as extravasation can cause severe local tissue necrosis. Notify physician if pain, erythema, or edema develops at insertion site.

- Lab tests: Monitor hepatic and renal function, CBC with differential and coagulation studies periodically.
- Monitor cardiac status closely, especially in older adult patients or those with preexisting cardiac disease.
- Monitor hematologic status carefully; during the period of myelosuppression, patients are at high risk for bleeding and infection.
- Monitor for development of hyperuricemia secondary to lysis of leukemic cells.

Patient & Family Education

- Learn all potential adverse reactions to idarubicin.
- Anticipate possible hair loss.
- Discuss interventions to minimize nausea, vomiting, diarrhea, and stomatitis with health care providers.

IDOXURIDINE (IDU)

(eye-dox-yoor'i-deen)
Dendrid, Herplex Liquifilm
Classifications: ANTIVIRAL
Therapeutic: ANTIVIRAL
Prototype: Acyclovir
Pregnancy Category: C

AVAILABILITY 0.1% ophthalmic solution

ACTION & *THERAPEUTIC EFFECT*
Topical antiviral agent. Pyrimidine nucleoside structurally related to thymidine, a nucleic acid essential for synthesis of viral DNA. Antiviral activity is primarily due to inhibition of viral replication. *Inhibits growth of* herpes simplex types I *and II, varicella-zoster, vaccinia, cytomegalovirus, and small animal viruses containing DNA.*

USES Herpes simplex keratitis as single agent or conjunctively with a corticosteroid.
UNLABELED USES Cutaneous herpes simplex.

CONTRAINDICATIONS Hypersensitivity to idoxuridine, iodine or iodine-containing preparations, or any components in the formulation, pregnancy (category C), lactation.
CAUTIOUS USE Corticosteroid therapy.

ROUTE & DOSAGE

Herpes Simplex Keratitis
Adult/Child: **Topical** 1 drop in conjunctival sac hourly during the day and q2h at night until improvement occurs, then decrease to q2h during the day and q4h at night

ADMINISTRATION

Topical
- Prevent the possibility of systemic absorption by applying light finger pressure to head of lacrimal duct for 1 min when eyedrop is instilled.
- Follow manufacturer's directions regarding storage. Decomposed idoxuridine not only has reduced antiviral activity but also may be toxic.
- Store ophthalmic solution refrigerated at 2°–8° C (36°–46° F) in a tight, light-resistant container unless otherwise directed.

ADVERSE EFFECTS (≥1%) **Body as a Whole:** Sensitization, systemic absorption (stomatitis, anorexia, nausea, vomiting, alopecia, leukopenia, thrombocytopenia, iodism, hepatotoxicity). **Special Senses:** Local irritation, pain, burning, lacrimation, pruritus, inflammation, or edema of eyes, lids, and surrounding face; follicular conjunctivitis, photophobia; corneal ulceration and swelling; delayed healing, small defects in corneal epithelium (local overdosage).

INTERACTIONS Drug: Boric acid-containing solutions may cause precipitation.

PHARMACOKINETICS Absorption: Poorly absorbed from eye tissues. **Distribution:** Crosses placenta. **Metabolism:** In liver.

CLINICAL IMPLICATIONS

Assessment & Drug Effects
- Monitor for therapeutic effectiveness. Epithelial infections usually improve within 7–8 d. If patient continues to improve, therapy is generally continued ≤21 d.
- Supervise patients closely by ophthalmologist.

Patient & Family Education
- Learn proper technique for eye drop instillation.
- Do not exceed the recommended frequency and duration of therapy.
- Wear sunglasses if photosensitivity is troublesome.

IFOSFAMIDE
(i-fos'fa-mide)
Classifications: ANTINEOPLASTIC; ALKYLATING AGENT
Therapeutic: ANTINEOPLASTIC
Prototype: Cyclophosphamide
Pregnancy Category: D

AVAILABILITY 1 g, 3 g vials

ACTION & *THERAPEUTIC EFFECT*
Ifosfamide is a chemotherapeutic agent chemically related to nitrogen mustards. The alkylated metabolites of ifosfamide interact with DNA. It is a cell cycle nonspecific

agent. Antineoplastic or cytotoxic action is primarily due to cross-linking of strands of DNA and RNA, as well as inhibition of protein synthesis. *It has antineoplastic and cytotoxic action on cancer cells that results in cell death.*

USES In combination with other agents in various regimens for germ cell testicular cancer, soft tissue sarcomas, Ewing's sarcoma, and non-Hodgkin's lymphoma. Also for lung and pancreatic sarcoma.

CONTRAINDICATIONS Patients with severe bone marrow depression or who have demonstrated previous hypersensitivity to ifosfamide; dehydration; pregnancy (category D), lactation.
CAUTIOUS USE Impaired renal function, renal failure; hepatic disease; prior radiation or prior therapy with other cytotoxic agents.

ROUTE & DOSAGE

Antineoplastic
Adult: **IV** 1.2 g/m^2/d for 5 consecutive d; administer over at least 30 min, repeat q3wk or after recovery from hematologic toxicity (platelets ≥100,000/mm^3; WBC ≥4,000/mm^3)

ADMINISTRATION
Intravenous

PREPARE: **IV Infusion:** Dilute each 1 g in 20 mL of sterile water or bacteriostatic water to yield 50 mg/mL. ▪ Shake well to dissolve. ▪ May be further diluted with D5W, NS, or RL to achieve concentrations of 0.6–20 mg/mL. ▪ Use solution prepared with sterile water within 6 h.
ADMINISTER: **IV Infusion:** Give slowly over 30 min.

▪ Note: Mesna is always given concurrently with ifosfamide; never give ifosfamide alone.

▪ Store reconstituted solution prepared with bacteriostatic solution up to a week at 30° C (86° F) or 6 wk at 5° C (41° F).

ADVERSE EFFECTS (≥1%) **CNS:** *Somnolence, confusion, hallucinations,* coma, dizziness, seizures, cranial nerve dysfunction. **GI:** *Nausea, vomiting,* anorexia, diarrhea, metabolic acidosis, hepatic dysfunction. **Hematologic:** Neutropenia, thrombocytopenia. **Urogenital:** Hemorrhagic cystitis, nephrotoxicity. **Skin:** *Alopecia,* skin necrosis with extravasation.

INTERACTIONS Drug: HEPATIC ENZYME INDUCERS (BARBITURATES, **phenytoin, chloral hydrate**) may increase hepatic conversion of ifosfamide to active metabolite; CORTICOSTEROIDS may inhibit conversion to active metabolites.

PHARMACOKINETICS Distribution: Distributed into breast milk. **Metabolism:** In liver via CYP3A4. **Elimination:** 70–86% in urine. **Half-Life:** 7–15 h.

CLINICAL IMPLICATIONS
Assessment & Drug Effects
▪ Lab tests: Monitor CBC with differential prior to each dose and at regular intervals; urinalysis prior to each dose for microscopic hematuria.
▪ Hold drug and notify physician if WBC count is below 2000/mm^3 or platelet count is below 50,000/mm^3.
▪ Reduce risk of hemorrhagic cystitis by hydrating with 3000 mL of fluid daily prior to therapy and for at least 72 h following treatment to ensure ample urine output.

Common adverse effects in *italic*, life-threatening effects underlined; generic names in **bold**; classifications in SMALL CAPS; ✦ Canadian drug name; ❷ Prototype drug

767

- Discontinue therapy if any of the following CNS symptoms occur: Somnolence, confusion, depressive psychosis, and hallucinations.

Patient & Family Education

- Void frequently to lessen contact of irritating chemical with bladder mucosa by keeping well hydrated.
- Note: Susceptibility to infection may increase. Avoid people with infection. Notify physician of any infection, fever or chills, cough or hoarseness, lower back or side pain, painful or difficult urination.
- Check with physician immediately if there is any unusual bleeding or bruising, black tarry stools, or blood in urine or if pinpoint red spots develop on skin.
- Discuss possible adverse effects (e.g., alopecia, nausea, and vomiting) and measures that can minimize them with health care provider.

ILOPROST

(i'lo-prost)
Classifications: PROSTAGLANDIN; ANTIHYPERTENSIVE, PULMONARY
Therapeutic: PULMONARY ANTIHYPERTENSIVE
Prototype: Epoprostenol
Pregnancy Category: C

AVAILABILITY 2 mcg/2 mL ampule

ACTION & *THERAPEUTIC EFFECT*
Iloprost is a synthetic analog of prostaglandin. It dilates systemic and pulmonary arterial vascular beds. *Dilation of the pulmonary arterial vessels reduces pulmonary hypertension.*

USES Treatment of pulmonary arterial hypertension in patients with New York Heart Association (NYHA) class III or IV symptoms.

UNLABELED USES Treatment of severe Raynaud phenomenon associated with systemic sclerosis.

CONTRAINDICATIONS Systolic blood pressure <85 mm Hg; pregnancy (category C), lactation; children.
CAUTIOUS USE Impaired hepatic function, elderly, renal impairment with inhaled iloprost; asthma, acute respiratory infection, COPD; elderly; dialysis, concurrent use of vasodilators and/or antihypertensive drugs.

ROUTE & DOSAGE

Pulmonary Hypertension
Adult: **Inhaled** 2.5–5 mcg 6–9 times daily, but no more than q2h during waking hours

ADMINISTRATION

Inhalation

- Transfer the contents of one ampule to the drug delivery system medication chamber immediately before use. Follow instructions provided by manufacturer for the delivery system. Do not allow contact with skin or eyes.
- Do not administer if systolic BP is <85 mg Hg.
- Do not administer any sooner than 2 h after the previous dose.
- Discard any solution remaining in the medication chamber after the inhalation session.
- Store at 20°–25° C (68°–77° F).

ADVERSE EFFECTS (≥1%) **CNS:** *Headache*, insomnia. **CV:** *Hypotension*, *vasodilation (flushing)*, palpitations, syncope, chest pain, tachycardia, congestive heart failure. **GI:** *Nausea, vomiting.* **Hepatic:** Increased alkaline phosphatase, increased gamma-glutamyltransferase (GGT). **Musculoskeletal:** Back pain, muscle cramps, *trismus*. **Renal:** Kid-

Common adverse effects in *italic*, life-threatening effects underlined; generic names in **bold**; classifications in SMALL CAPS; ♣ Canadian drug name; ⊘ Prototype drug

ney failure. **Respiratory:** *Cough*, dyspnea, hemoptysis, pneumonia, peripheral edema. **Body as a Whole:** *Flu-like syndrome*, tongue pain.

INTERACTIONS Drug: Enhanced hypotension when given with other VASODILATORS or ANTIHYPERTENSIVE agents; increased risk of bleeding when given with other ANTICOAGULANTS or ANTITHROMBOTIC agents.

PHARMACOKINETICS Distribution: 60% protein bound. **Metabolism:** Completely metabolized to inactive products. **Elimination:** Urine (major) and feces. **Half-Life:** 20–30 min.

CLINICAL IMPLICATIONS

Assessment & Drug Effects

- Supervise ambulation, especially with concurrent use of other drugs known to cause dizziness or syncope.
- Monitor vital signs closely during initiation of drug therapy.
- Monitor for and report S&S of heart failure.
- Withhold drug and notify physician if S&S of pulmonary edema appear.
- Lab tests: Monitor blood levels of anticoagulants when used concurrently.

Patient & Family Education

- Follow directions for taking the drug (see Administration). Iloprost inhalation should be used with the Prodose AAD system. Do not use it with other types of nebulizers.
- Make position changes slowly, especially when arising from a chair or bed.
- Do not drive or engage in potentially hazardous activities until response to drug is known.
- Report any of the following to a health care provider: dizziness or fainting, especially upon exertion, or increased difficulty breathing.

IMATINIB MESYLATE

(i-ma'ti-nib)
Gleevec
Classifications: ANTINEOPLASTIC; MONOCLONAL ANTIBODY; TYROSINE KINASE INHIBITOR (TKI); SIGNAL TRANSDUCTOR INHIBITOR (STI)
Therapeutic: ANTINEOPLASTIC; MONOCLONAL ANTIBODY; TKI
Prototype: Gefitinib
Pregnancy Category: D

AVAILABILITY 100 mg capsule

ACTION & *THERAPEUTIC EFFECT*
Tyrosine kinase inhibitor and signal transductor inhibitor (STI); STIs interfere with intracellular signaling pathways that are involved in the development of malignancies. Imatinib inhibits abnormal Bcr-Abl tyrosine kinase created by the Philadelphia chromosome abnormality in chronic myeloid leukemia (CLM). Tyrosine kinase is required for activation of a wide variety of intracellular activities vital to cell functioning and intracellular metabolic pathways. *Inhibits WBC cell proliferation and induces cell death in Bcr-Abl tyrosine kinase positive cells as well as in newly formed leukemic cells. Thus, it interferes with progression of chronic myeloid leukemia (CML).*

USES Treatment of CML in blast crisis, or in chronic phase after failure of interferon-alpha therapy; unresectable and/or metastatic malignant gastrointestinal stromal tumors (GISTs).
UNLABELED USES Acute lymphocytic leukemia (ALL), soft tissue sarcoma.

CONTRAINDICATIONS Hypersensitivity to imatinib or any of its components; viral infections, including herpes and chickenpox; intramus-

---

Common adverse effects in *italic*, life-threatening effects underlined; generic names in **bold**; classifications in SMALL CAPS; ♣ Canadian drug name; ❷ Prototype drug

769

cular injections with concurrent thrombocytopenia; pregnancy (category D), lactation; children <3 y.

CAUTIOUS USE History of hypersensitivity to other monoclonal antibodies; hepatic or renal impairment; bleeding, bone marrow suppression; cardiac disease; dental disease, dental work; older adults, females of childbearing age; fungal infections; GI bleeding; heart failure; hepatic disease; herpes infection, immunosuppression, infection; jaundice; neutropenia; peripheral edema, renal disease; thrombocytopenia, vaccination, varicella, viral infection; concurrent administration of drugs which are CYP3A4 inhibitors (i.e., ketoconazole, itraconazole, erythromycin, clarithromycin).

ROUTE & DOSAGE

CML Chronic Phase

Adult: **PO** 400–800 mg q.d. with a meal and large glass of water
Child: **PO** >3 y, 260 mg/m²/d in 1 or 2 divided dose(s) (max: 340 mg/m²/d)

CML Accelerated Phase or Blast Crisis

Adult: **PO** 600 mg q.d. with a meal and large glass of water

GISTs

Adult: **PO** 400–600 mg q.d. times up to 24 mo

Hepatic Impairment

Reduce dose to 300 mg q.d. (chronic) or 400 mg q.d. (accelerated, blast crisis)

ADMINISTRATION

Oral

- Give with meal and large glass of water (at least 8 oz).
- Store at 15°–30° C (59°–86° F).

ADVERSE EFFECTS (≥1%) **Body as a Whole:** *Fluid retention, edema, fatigue,* weight gain, *fever,* night sweats, weakness. **CNS:** <u>CNS hemorrhage</u>, *headache.* **GI:** *Nausea, vomiting, diarrhea,* <u>GI hemorrhage</u>, dyspepsia, *abdominal pain, constipation, anorexia,* increased AST, ALT, and bilirubin. **Hematologic:** <u>Hemorrhage,</u> *neutropenia, thrombocytopenia,* petechiae, epistaxis, <u>pancytopenia</u> (rare), <u>thrombocytopenia</u> (rare). **Metabolic:** Hypokalemia. **Musculoskeletal:** *Muscle cramps, pain, arthralgia,* myalgia. **Respiratory:** *Cough, dyspnea,* pharyngitis, pneumonia. **Skin:** *Rash,* pruritus.

INTERACTIONS Drug: Clarithromycin, erythromycin, ketoconazole, itraconazole may increase imatinib levels and toxicity; **carbamazepine, dexamethasone, phenobarbital, phenytoin, rifampin** may decrease imatinib levels; may increase levels of BENZODIAZEPINES, DIHYDROPYRIDINE, CALCIUM CHANNEL BLOCKERS (e.g., **nifedipine**), **warfarin. Herbal: St. John's wort** may decrease imatinib levels.

PHARMACOKINETICS Absorption: Well absorbed, 98% reaches systemic circulation. **Peak:** 2–4 h. **Metabolism:** Primarily by CYP3A4 in liver. **Elimination:** Primarily in feces. **Half-Life:** 18 h imatinib, 40 h active metabolite.

CLINICAL IMPLICATIONS

Assessment & Drug Effects

- Monitor for S&S of fluid retention. Weigh daily and report rapid weight gain immediately.
- Lab tests: CBC with platelet count and differential weekly times 1 mo, biweekly for the 2nd mo, periodically thereafter as clinically indicated; baseline and monthly

AST, ALT, alkaline phosphatase, bilirubin; periodic serum creatinine and electrolytes.

- Withhold drug and notify physician for any of the following: bilirubin >3 times ULN, AST/ALT >5 times ULN; treatment may be reinstituted when bilirubin <1.5 times ULN and AST/ALT <2.5 times ULN.
- Review concurrent medications. Consult physician about switching patients taking warfarin to low-molecular weight or standard heparin. Patients taking ketoconazole and other CYP3A4 inhibitors may experience increased adverse drug reactions.

Patient & Family Education

- Do not take any OTC drugs (e.g., acetaminophen, St. John's wort) without consulting physician.
- Report any S&S of bleeding immediately to physician (e.g., black tarry stool, bright red or coke colored urine, bleeding from gums).
- Report immediately to physician any unexplained change in mental status.
- Use effective means of contraception while taking this drug. Women of childbearing age should avoid becoming pregnant.

IMIPENEM-CILASTATIN SODIUM ⓟ

(i-mi-pen'em sye-la-stat'in)
Primaxin
Classifications: BETA-LACTAM ANTIBIOTIC
Therapeutic: ANTIBIOTIC
Pregnancy Category: C

AVAILABILITY 250 mg, 500 mg vials

ACTION & *THERAPEUTIC EFFECT*
Fixed combination of imipenem, a beta-lactam antibiotic, and cilasta-

tin. Action of imipenem: inhibition of mucopeptide synthesis in bacterial cell walls leading to cell death. Cilastatin increases the serum half-life of imipenem. *Effectively used for severe or resistant infections. Acts synergistically with aminoglycoside antibiotics against some isolates of Pseudomonas aeruginosa. Infections resistant to cephalosporins, penicillins, and aminoglycosides have responded to treatment with this combination.*

USES Treatment of serious infections caused by susceptible organisms in the urinary tract, lower respiratory tract, bones and joints, skin and skin structures; also intraabdominal, gynecologic, and mixed infections; bacterial septicemia and endocarditis.

CONTRAINDICATIONS Hypersensitivity to any component of product, multiple allergens; carbapenem hypersensitivity; penicillin hypersensitivity; pregnancy (category C). **CAUTIOUS USE** Patients with CNS disorders (e.g., seizures, brain lesions, history of recent head injury); seizures; renal failure, renal impairment, renal disease; patients with history of cephalosporin allergies; lactation.

ROUTE & DOSAGE

Serious Infections
Adult: **IV** 250–500 mg infused over 20–30 min q6–8h **IM** 500 or 750 mg q12h
Child: **IV** >3 mo, 60–100 mg/kg/d in divided doses; 1–3 mo, 100 mg/kg/d in divided doses **IM** 15–25 mg/kg q12h
Neonate: **IV** <1 wk, 40–50 mg/kg/d in divided doses; >1 wk, 60–75 mg/kg/d in divided doses

---

Common adverse effects in *italic*, life-threatening effects underlined; generic names in **bold**; classifications in SMALL CAPS; ♣ Canadian drug name; ⓞ Prototype drug

771

Renal Impairment

Cl_{cr} 20–30 mL/min: dose q8–12h; <20 mL/min: dose q12h

ADMINISTRATION

Caution: IM and IV solutions are NOT interchangeable; do NOT give IM solution by IV, and do NOT give IV solution as IM.

Intramuscular

- Reconstitute powder for IM injection as follows: Add 2 mL or 3 mL of 1% lidocaine HCl solution without epinephrine, respectively, to the 500 mg vial or the 750 mg vial. Agitate to form a suspension then withdraw and inject entire contents of the vial IM.
- Give IM suspension by deep injection into the gluteal muscle or lateral thigh.
- Use reconstituted IM injection within 1 h after preparation.

Intravenous

PREPARE: **Intermittent:** Dilute each dose with 10 mL of D5W, NS, or other compatible infusion solution. ▪ Agitate the solution until clear. Color should range from colorless to yellow. ▪ Further dilute with 100 mL of same solution used for initial dilution.

ADMINISTER: **Intermittent:** Give each 500 mg or fraction thereof over 20–30 min. DO NOT give as a bolus dose. Nausea appears to be related to infusion rate, and if it presents during infusion, slow the rate (occurs most frequently with 1-g doses).

INCOMPATIBILITIES **Solution/additive: Ringer's lactate,** stable in **dextrose**-containing solutions for only 4 h. **Y-site: Azithromycin, milrinone.**

- Store according to manufacturer's recommendations; stability of IV solutions depends on diluent used for reconstitution. ▪ Most IV solutions retain potency for 4 h at 15°–30° C (59°–86° F) or for 24 h if refrigerated at 4° C (39° F). Avoid freezing.

ADVERSE EFFECTS (≥1%) **Body as a Whole:** Hypersensitivity (rash, fever, chills, dyspnea, pruritus), weakness, oliguria/anuria, polyuria, polyarthralgia; *phlebitis and pain at injection site,* superinfections. **CNS:** Seizures, dizziness, confusion, somnolence, encephalopathy, myoclonus, tremors, paresthesia, headache. **GI:** *Nausea, vomiting,* diarrhea, pseudomembranous colitis, hemorrhagic colitis, gastroenteritis, abdominal pain, glossitis, heartburn. **Respiratory:** Chest discomfort, hyperventilation, dyspnea. **Skin:** Rash, pruritus, urticaria, candidiasis, flushing, increased sweating, skin texture change, facial edema. **Metabolic:** Hyponatremia, hyperkalemia. **Special Senses:** Transient hearing loss; increased WBC, AST, ALT, alkaline phosphatase, BUN, LDH, creatinine; decreased Hgb, Hct, eosinophilia.

INTERACTIONS Drug: Aztreonam, cephalosporins, penicillins may antagonize the antibacterial effects.

PHARMACOKINETICS Distribution: Widely distributed; limited concentrations in CSF; crosses placenta; in breast milk. **Elimination:** 70% in urine within 10 h. **Half-Life:** 1 h.

CLINICAL IMPLICATIONS

Assessment & Drug Effects

- Determine previous hypersensitivity reaction to beta-lactam antibiotics (penicillins and cephalosporins) or to other allergens.
- Monitor for S&S of hypersensitivity (see Appendix F). Discontinue drug and notify physician if S&S occur.

- Monitor closely patients vulnerable to CNS adverse effects.
- Notify physician if focal tremors, myoclonus, or seizures occur; dosage adjustment may be needed.
- Monitor for S&S of superinfection (see Appendix F).
- Notify physician promptly to rule out pseudomembranous enterocolitis if severe diarrhea accompanied by abdominal pain and fever occurs (see Appendix F).
- Note: Sodium content derived from drug is high; consider in patient on restricted sodium intake.
- Monitor renal, hematologic, and liver function periodically.

Patient & Family Education
- Notify physician immediately to report pruritus or symptoms of respiratory distress.
- Report pain or discomfort at IV infusion site.
- Report loose stools or diarrhea promptly.

IMIPRAMINE HYDROCHLORIDE ℗

(im-ip'ra-meen)
Impril ♦, Novopramine ♦, Tofranil

IMIPRAMINE PAMOATE
Tofranil-PM

Classifications: PSYCHOTHERAPEUTIC; TRICYCLIC ANTIDEPRESSANT
Therapeutic: TRICYCLIC ANTIDEPRESSANT
Pregnancy Category: C

AVAILABILITY 10 mg, 25 mg, 50 mg tablets; 75 mg, 100 mg, 125 mg, 150 mg capsules; **Imipramine pamoate:** 75 mg, 100 mg, 125 mg, 150 mg capsules

ACTION & *THERAPEUTIC EFFECT*
Tricyclic antidepressant (TCA) and tertiary amine, structurally related to the phenothiazines. In contrast with phenothiazines that act on dopamine receptors, TCAs potentiate both norepinephrine and serotonin in the CNS by blocking their reuptake by presynaptic neurons. Imipramine decreases number of awakenings from sleep, markedly reduces time in REM sleep, and increases stage 4 sleep. *As a TCA antidepressant, imipramine potentiates the effects of both norepinephrine and serotonin in the CNS by blocking their reuptake by the neurons. Relief of nocturnal enuresis is due to anticholinergic activity and to nervous system stimulation, resulting in earlier arousal to sensation of full bladder.*

USES Endogenous depression and occasionally for reactive depression. Imipramine is the only TCA used as temporary adjuvant treatment of enuresis in children >6 y.
UNLABELED USES Certain syndromes that mimic or overlap diagnostically with depression: alcoholism, cocaine withdrawal; attention deficit disorder with or without hyperactivity (children >6 y and adolescents); with amphetamines or methylphenidate for narcolepsy; phobic anxiety syndromes such as panic disorders and agoraphobia; obsessive-compulsive neurosis; chronic intractable pain.

CONTRAINDICATIONS Hypersensitivity to tricyclic drugs; concomitant use of MAOIs; acute recovery period after MI, defects in bundle-branch conduction, QT prolongation; severe renal or hepatic impairment; use of imipramine HCl in children <12 y except to treat enuresis; use of pamoate in children of any age; pregnancy (category D), lactation.

Common adverse effects in *italic*, life-threatening effects underlined; generic names in **bold**; classifications in SMALL CAPS; ♦ Canadian drug name; ℗ Prototype drug

773

CAUTIOUS USE Children, adolescents, older adults; respiratory difficulties; cardiovascular, hepatic, or GI diseases; blood disorders; increased intraocular pressure, narrow-angle glaucoma; schizophrenia, hypomania or manic episodes, patient with suicidal tendency, seizure disorders; prostatic hypertrophy, urinary retention; alcoholism, hyperthyroidism; electroshock therapy.

ROUTE & DOSAGE

Depression

Adult: **PO** 75–100 mg/d (max: 300 mg/d) in 1 or more divided doses **IM** 50–100 mg/d in divided doses
Child: **PO** 1.5 mg/kg/d, may increase by 1 mg/kg/d q3–4d (max: 5 mg/kg/d)

Enuresis in Childhood

Child: **PO** 25 mg 1 h before bedtime; <12 y, may increase to 50 mg nightly (max: 2.5 mg/kg); >12 y, may increase to 75 mg nightly (max: 2.5 mg/kg)

ADMINISTRATION

Oral

- Do NOT make dosage adjustments more frequently than q4d.
- Give with or immediately after food.
- Note: Single doses can be given h.s. or q.a.m., respectively, if drowsiness or insomnia results.

Intramuscular

- Use IM form only for those unable/unwilling to take oral form.
- Dissolve crystals by immersing intact ampule in warm water for about 1 min.

ADVERSE EFFECTS (≥1%) **Body as a Whole:** Hypersensitivity (skin rash, erythema, petechiae, urticaria, pruritus, photosensitivity, <u>angioedema</u> of face, tongue, or generalized; drug fever). **CNS:** *Sedation, drowsiness,* dizziness, headache, fatigue, numbness, tingling (paresthesias) of extremities; incoordination, ataxia, tremors, peripheral neuropathy, extrapyramidal symptoms (including parkinsonism effects and tardive dyskinesia); lowered seizure threshold, altered EEG patterns, delirium, disturbed concentration, confusion, hallucinations, anxiety, nervousness, insomnia, vivid dreams, restlessness, agitation, shift to hypomania, mania; exacerbation of psychoses; hyperpyrexia. **CV:** *Orthostatic hypotension,* mild sinus tachycardia; *arrhythmias,* hypertension or hypotension, palpitation, <u>MI</u>, CHF, *heart block,* ECG changes, stroke, flushing, cold cyanotic hands and feet (peripheral vasospasm). **Endocrine:** Testicular swelling, gynecomastia (men), galactorrhea and breast enlargement (women), increased or decreased libido, ejaculatory and erectile disturbances, delayed or absent orgasm (male and female); elevation or depression of blood glucose levels. **Special Senses:** Nasal congestion, tinnitus; *blurred vision,* disturbances of accommodation, *slight mydriasis,* nystagmus. **GI:** *Dry mouth,* constipation, heartburn, excessive appetite, weight gain, nausea, vomiting, diarrhea, slowed gastric emptying time, flatulence, abdominal cramps, esophageal reflux, anorexia, stomatitis, increased salivation, black tongue, peculiar taste, paralytic ileus. **Urogenital:** *Urinary retention,* delayed micturition, nocturia, paradoxic urinary frequency. **Hematologic:** Bone marrow depression; <u>agranulocytosis</u>, eosinophilia, thrombocytopenia. **Other:** Excessive perspiration, cholestatic jaundice, precipitation of acute intermittent porphyria; dyspnea, changes in heat and cold tolerance, hair loss, syndrome of inappropriate antidiuretic hormone secretion (SIADH).

DIAGNOSTIC TEST INTERFERENCE

Imipramine elevates *serum bilirubin, alkaline phosphatase* and may increase or decrease *blood glucose.* It decreases *urinary 5-HIAA* and *VMA* excretion and may falsely increase excretion of *urinary catecholamines.*

INTERACTIONS Drug: MAO INHIBITORS

may precipitate hyperpyrexic crisis, tachycardia, or seizures; ANTIHYPERTENSIVE AGENTS potentiate orthostatic hypotension; CNS DEPRESSANTS, **alcohol** add to CNS depression; **norepinephrine** and other SYMPATHOMIMETICS may increase cardiac toxicity; **cimetidine** decreases hepatic metabolism, thus increasing imipramine levels; **methylphenidate** inhibits metabolism of imipramine and thus may increase its toxicity. **Herbal: Ginkgo** may decrease seizure threshold; **St. John's wort** may cause **serotonin** syndrome.

PHARMACOKINETICS Absorption:

Completely absorbed from GI tract. **Peak:** 1–2 h PO; 30 min IM. **Metabolism:** Metabolized to the active metabolite desipramine in liver. **Elimination:** Primarily in urine, small amount in feces; crosses placenta; may be secreted in breast milk. **Half-Life:** 8–16 h.

CLINICAL IMPLICATIONS

Assessment & Drug Effects

- Monitor for therapeutic effectiveness: May not occur for 2 wk or more.
- Monitor children and adolescents for increase in suicidality.
- Prevent serious adverse effects by accurate early reporting to physi-

cian about patient's response to drug.

- Note: Dose sensitivity and adverse effects are most likely to occur in adolescents and older adults; use a lower initial dose in these patients.
- Lab tests: Monitor hepatic and renal function, CBC with differential, and fluid and electrolyte balance periodically.
- Monitor HR and BP frequently. Orthostatic hypotension may be marked in pretreatment hypertensive or cardiac patients.
- Monitor for potential signs of toxicity: QRS prolongation (to 100 millisecond or greater), arrhythmias, hypotension, respiratory depression, altered level of consciousness, seizures. Overdose onset may be sudden.
- Note: During the first 2 wk of therapy, older adults may develop confusion, restlessness, disturbed sleep, forgetfulness. Symptoms last 3–20 d. Report to physician.
- Weigh patient under standard conditions biweekly: report a gain of 0.5–1.0 kg (1^1/$_2$–2 lb) within 2–3 d and frank edema.
- Monitor urinary and bowel elimination, at least until maintenance dosage is stabilized, to detect urinary retention or frequency, constipation, or paralytic ileus.
- Report promptly early signs of agranulocytosis (see Appendix F).
- Report signs of cholestatic jaundice: flu-like symptoms, yellow skin or sclerae, dark urine, light-colored stools, pruritus.
- Notify physician of extrapyramidal symptoms (tremors, twitching, ataxia, incoordination, hyperreflexia, drooling) in patients receiving large doses and especially in older adults.
- Monitor diabetic patients for loss of glycemic control. Hyperglyce-

Common adverse effects in *italic*, life-threatening effects <u>underlined</u>; generic names in **bold**; classifications in SMALL CAPS; ✦ Canadian drug name; ⊘ Prototype drug

775

mia or hypoglycemia (see Appendix F) occur in some patients.

- Inspect oral mucosa frequently, especially gingival surfaces under dentures.

Patient & Family Education

- Change position slowly and in stages, especially from lying down to upright posture and dangle legs over bed for a few minutes before walking.
- Note: Effectiveness can decrease with continued drug administration in some patients. Inform physician if this occurs.
- Do NOT use OTC drugs while on a TCA without physician approval.
- Do not drive or engage in other potentially hazardous activities until response to drug is known.
- Avoid exposure to strong sunlight because of potential photosensitivity. Use sunscreen with at least SPF of 12–15 if allowed.

IMIQUIMOD

(i-mi'qui-mod)
Aldara
Classifications: KERATOLYTIC AGENT; IMMUNE RESPONSE MODIFIER
Therapeutic: IMMUNE RESPONSE MODIFIER; KERATOLYTIC
Pregnancy Category: C

AVAILABILITY 5% cream in 250 mg single use packets

ACTION & *THERAPEUTIC EFFECT*
An immune response modifier; exact mechanism of action is unknown. Induces cytokine production, including interferon-alfa, which may interfere with viral replication. *Does not totally eradicate HPV. Despite destruction of HPV warts, latent or subclinical HPV in-*

fection can persist, and recurrence of visible warts is common.

USES Treatment of external genital and perianal warts *(Condylomata acuminata),* actinic keratosis on the face and scalp of immunocompetent adults, and superficial basal cell carcinoma.
UNLABELED USES Treatment of common warts.

CONTRAINDICATIONS Occlusive dressing; ocular exposure; excessive sun exposure or sunburn; UV exposure; surgery or drug treatment on affected area; pregnancy (category C); children <12 y.
CAUTIOUS USE Hypersensitivity to benzyl alcohol or paraben; HIV infection; lactation

ROUTE & DOSAGE

Genital and Perianal Warts
Adult/Adolescent: **Topical** >12 y Apply a thin layer to the affected areas once daily 3 times per week just before bedtime. Wash off cream after 6–10 h (max: 16 wk therapy).

Actinic Keratosis
Adult: **Topical** Apply a thin layer to the affected areas once daily 2 times per week just before sleep for 16 wks. Wash off cream after 8 h.

Superficial Basal Cell Carcinoma
Adult: **Topical** Apply a thin layer to the affected areas once daily 5 times per week just before sleep for 6 wk. Wash off cream after 8 h.

ADMINISTRATION

Topical
- Hand washing before and after application is recommended.

- Wash treatment area with soap and water and allow to dry thoroughly (at least 10 min).
- Single-use packets contain sufficient cream to cover an area of up to 20 cm^2 (approx. 8 in. by 8 in.).
- Instruct patient to apply a thin layer of cream (avoid using excessive cream), and work into area until no longer visible. Do not occlude the application site.
- After each treatment period, remove the cream by washing the treated area with soap and water.
- Store below 25° C (77° F).

ADVERSE EFFECTS (≥1%) **Body as a Whole:** Fungal infections, flu-like symptoms, myalgia. **CNS:** Headache. **Skin:** *Application site reactions, pruritus,* burning, bleeding, stinging, redness, tenderness, irritation, *erythema,* edema, weeping/exudates, dry skin, scabbing/crusting, hyperkeratosis.

PHARMACOKINETICS Absorption: Minimal absorption through intact skin.

CLINICAL IMPLICATIONS
Patient & Family Education
- Uncircumcised males with warts under the foreskin: Pull back the foreskin and clean the area daily to help avoid penile skin reactions.
- Females should not apply cream directly into the vagina. Application to the labia may cause pain or swelling and may cause difficulty in passing urine.
- Avoid or minimize UV light exposure (artificial and sunlight) during treatment of actinic keratosis. Wear protective clothing. If sunburn develops, avoid using imiquimod cream until fully recovered.

IMMUNE GLOBULIN INTRAMUSCULAR [IGIM, GAMMA GLOBULIN, IMMUNE SERUM GLOBULIN (ISG)] 🅿️

(im'mune glob'u-lin)
BayGam

IMMUNE GLOBULIN INTRAVENOUS (IGIV)

Flebogamma, Gammagard, Gammar-P IV, Gamunex, IGIV, Iveegam, Octagam, Sandoglobulin

Classifications: BIOLOGIC RESPONSE MODIFIER; IMMUNOGLOBULIN
Therapeutic: IMMUNOGLOBULIN
Pregnancy Category: C

AVAILABILITY IGIM 2 mL, 10 mL vials **IGIV** 5%, 10% solution; 50 mg/mL powder for injection

ACTION & *THERAPEUTIC EFFECT*
Sterile concentrated solution containing globulin (primarily IgG) prepared from large pools of normal human plasma of either venous or placental origin and processed by a special fractionating technique. *Like hepatitis B immune globulin (H-BIG), contains antibodies specific to hepatitis B surface antigen but in lower concentrations. Therefore, not considered treatment of first choice for postexposure prophylaxis against hepatitis B but usually an acceptable alternative when H-BIG is not available.*

USES IGIM: In susceptible persons to provide passive immunity or to modify severity of certain infectious diseases, e.g., rubeola (measles), rubella (German measles), varicella-zoster (chickenpox), type A (infectious) hepatitis, and as replacement therapy in congenital agammaglobulinemia or IgG defi-

Common adverse effects in *italic*, life-threatening effects underlined; generic names in **bold**; classifications in SMALL CAPS; ♣ Canadian drug name; 🅿️ Prototype drug

777

ciency diseases. May be used as an alternative to H-BIG to provide passive immunity in hepatitis B infection. Also for postexposure prophylaxis of hepatitis non-A, non-B, and nonspecific hepatitis. **IGIV:** Principally as maintenance therapy in patients unable to manufacture sufficient quantities of IgG antibodies, in patients requiring an immediate increase in immunoglobulin levels, and when IM injections are contraindicated as in patients with bleeding disorders or who have small muscle mass. Also in chronic autoimmune thrombocytopenia and idiopathic thrombocytopenic purpura (ITP). Treatment of primary immunodeficiency disorders associated with defects in humoral immunity.

UNLABELED USES Kawasaki syndrome, chronic lymphocytic leukemia, AIDS, premature and low-birth-weight neonates, autoimmune neutropenia, or hemolytic anemia.

CONTRAINDICATIONS History of anaphylaxis or severe reaction to human immune serum globulin (IG) or to any ingredient in the formulation such as thimerosal (mercury derivative) preservative in IM formulations and maltose (stabilizing agent) in IV formulations; persons with clinical hepatitis A; IGIV for patients with class-specific anti-IgA deficiencies; IGIM in severe thrombocytopenia or other bleeding disorders; intramuscular injection, pregnancy (category C).

CAUTIOUS USE Dehydration, diabetes mellitus, children, older adults, hypovolemia, IgA deficiency, infection; renal disease, renal failure, renal impairment; sepsis; sucrose hypersensitivity; vaccination, viral infection; lactation.

ROUTE & DOSAGE

Hepatitis A Exposure
Adult/Child: **IM** 0.02 mL/kg as soon as possible after exposure; if period of exposure will be ≥3 mo, give 0.05–0.06 mL/kg once q4–6mo

Hepatitis B Exposure
Adult/Child: **IM** 0.02–0.06 mL/kg as soon as possible after exposure if H-BIG is unavailable

Rubella Exposure
Adult: **IM** 20 mL as single dose in susceptible pregnant women

Rubeola Exposure
Adult/Child: **IM** 0.25 mL/kg within 6 d of exposure

Varicella-Zoster Exposure
Adult/Child: **IM** 0.6–1.2 mL/kg promptly

Immunoglobulin Deficiency
*Dosages may vary between brands
Adult/Child: **IV** 200–400 mg/kg monthly **IM** 1.2 mL/kg followed by 0.6 mL/kg q2–4wk

Idiopathic Thrombocytopenia Purpura
Adult/Child: **IV** 400 mg/kg/d for 5 consecutive d or 1 g/kg × 1–2 d

Obesity
Dose based on IBW or adjusted IBW

ADMINISTRATION

■ Note: In hepatitis A (infectious hepatitis), immune globulin is most effective when given before or as soon as possible after exposure but not more than 2 wk after (incubation period for hepatitis A is 15–50 d).

Do not give immune globulin to those presenting clinical manifestations of hepatitis A. For hepatitis B (serum hepatitis), give immune globulin within 24 h and not more than 7 d after exposure. IGIM and IGIV formulations are NOT interchangeable.

Intramuscular

- Give adults and older children injections into deltoid or anterolateral aspect of thigh; neonates and small children, into anterolateral aspect of thigh.
- Avoid gluteal injections; however, when large volumes of immune globulin are prescribed or when large doses must be divided into several injections, the upper outer quadrant of the gluteus has been used in adults.

Intravenous

PREPARE: **IV Infusion:** Refer to manufacturer's directions for information on reconstitution and dilution of the specific product.

ADMINISTER: **IV Infusion:** Flow rates vary with product being infused. Refer to manufacturer's directions for the specific product.

- Store as directed by manufacturer for specific product. Avoid freezing. Do not use if turbidity has occurred or if product has been frozen. • Do not mix with other drugs. • Discard partially used vial.

ADVERSE EFFECTS (≥1%) **Body as a Whole:** *Pain, tenderness, muscle stiffness at IM site;* local inflammatory reaction, erythema, urticaria, angioedema, headache, malaise, fever, arthralgia, nephrotic syndrome, hypersensitivity (fever, chills, anaphylactic shock), infusion reactions (*nausea, flushing, chills,* headache, chest tightness, wheezing, skeletal pain, back pain, abdominal cramps, anaphylaxis), renal dysfunction, renal failure.

INTERACTIONS Drug: May interfere with antibody response to LIVE VIRUS VACCINES (measles/mumps/rubella); give VACCINES 14 d before or 3 mo after IMMUNE GLOBULINS.

PHARMACOKINETICS Peak: 2 d. **Distribution:** Rapidly and evenly distributed to intravascular and extravascular fluid compartments. **Half-Life:** 21–23 d.

CLINICAL IMPLICATIONS

Assessment & Drug Effects

- Make sure emergency drugs and appropriate emergency facilities are immediately available for treatment of anaphylaxis or sensitization.
- Note: Hypersensitivity reactions (see Appendix F) are most likely in patients receiving large IM doses, repeated injections, or rapid IV infusion.
- Monitor vital signs and infusion rate closely when patient is receiving IGIV.
- Note: IGIV has a mild diuretic effect in some patients due to presence of maltose.

Patient & Family Education

- Report immediately S&S of hypersensitivity (see Appendix F).
- Report immediately infusion symptoms of nausea, chills, headache, and chest tightness; these are indications to slow rate of infusion.
- Note: Passive immunity to measles (rubeola) lasts about 3–4 wk after immune globulin. In general, children ≤15 mo need active immunization with measles virus vaccine 3 mo after IGIM.

Common adverse effects in *italic*, life-threatening effects <u>underlined</u>; generic names in **bold**; classifications in SMALL CAPS; ✦ Canadian drug name; ⊘ Prototype drug

779

INAMRINONE LACTATE ℞

(in-am′ri-none)

Amrinone

Classifications: CARDIAC INOTROPIC AGENT; VASODILATOR

Therapeutic: CARDIAC INOTROPIC AGENT

Pregnancy Category: C

AVAILABILITY 5 mg/mL injection

ACTION & *THERAPEUTIC EFFECT*

A new chemical class of cardiac inotropic agents with vasodilator activity. Mode of action appears to differ from that of the digitalis glycosides and beta-adrenergic stimulants. In patients with depressed myocardial function, it enhances myocardial contractility, increases cardiac output and stroke volume, and reduces right and left ventricular filling pressure, pulmonary capillary wedge pressure (PCWP), and systemic vascular resistance. *It reduces afterload and preload by its direct relaxant effect on vascular smooth muscle. Inamrinone produces hemodynamic improvements and symptomatic relief in patients in CHF due to ischemic heart disease.*

USES Short-term management of CHF in patients not adequately controlled by traditional therapy, such as digitalis, diuretics, and vasodilators, and may be used in conjunction with these agents.

CONTRAINDICATIONS Hypersensitivity to inamrinone or to bisulfites; severe aortic or pulmonic valvular disease in lieu of appropriate surgery, acute MI; uncorrected hypokalemia or dehydration; pregnancy (category C). Safe use in children is not established.

CAUTIOUS USE Compromised renal or hepatic function, arrhythmias, hypertrophic subaortic stenosis; decreased platelets. Concomitant cardiac glycoside therapy recommended in patients with atrial flutter or fibrillation, lactation.

ROUTE & DOSAGE

Congestive Heart Failure

Adult: **IV** 0.75 mg/kg bolus given slowly over 2–3 min, then start infusion at 5–10 mcg/kg/min, may repeat bolus in 30 min (max: 10 mg/kg/d)

Renal Impairment

Cl_{cr} <10 mL/min: give 50–75% of dose

ADMINISTRATION

Intravenous

PREPARE: Direct: Give loading dose undiluted or diluted by adding 1 mL of NS or 0.45% NS to each 5 mg (1 mL). **IV Infusion:** Dilute 300 mg (60 mL) in 60 mL of NS or 0.45% NS to yield 2.5 mg/mL. ▪ Natural color is clear yellow. Discard discolored solutions and those with precipitate.

ADMINISTER: Direct: Give loading dose over 2–3 min. May inject into a running D5W infusion through Y-connector or directly. **IV Infusion:** Give diluted solution at a rate of 5–10 mg/kg/min. ▪ Use infusion pump to regulate rate.

INCOMPATIBILITIES Solution/additive: Sodium bicarbonate, dextrose-containing solutions. **Y-site: Furosemide.**

▪ Use all diluted solutions within 24 h. ▪ Protect ampules from light.

ADVERSE EFFECTS (≥1%) **Body as a Whole:** Hypersensitivity (pericarditis, pleuritis; myositis with interstitial shadows on chest x-ray and elevated sedimentation rate; vasculitis with nodular pulmonary densities, hypoxemia, ascites, jaundice). **CV:** Hypotension, arrhythmias. **Endocrine:** Nephrogenic diabetes insipidus. **GI:** Nausea, vomiting, anorexia, abdominal cramps, hepatotoxicity. **Hematologic:** Asymptomatic thrombocytopenia.

INTERACTIONS Drug: Possibility of excessive hypotension with disopyramide.

PHARMACOKINETICS Onset: 2–5 min. **Peak:** 10 min. **Duration:** About 2 h. **Distribution:** Unknown if it crosses placenta or into breast milk. **Metabolism:** In liver. **Elimination:** Primarily in urine. **Half-Life:** 3.6–7.5 h.

CLINICAL IMPLICATIONS

Assessment & Drug Effects

- Monitor for therapeutic effectiveness: Increased cardiac output, decreased PCWP, relief of symptoms of CHF. Central venous pressure may be used to assess hypotension and blood volume.
- Monitor BP, heart rate, and respirations and keep physician informed. Rate of administration and duration of therapy are prescribed according to clinical response and adverse effects.
- Consult physician for guidelines. In general, rate of infusion should be slowed or stopped with excessive drop in BP or arrhythmias.
- Monitor infusion site to prevent extravasation.
- Monitor I&O ratio and pattern and daily weights. Improvement in cardiac output enhances diuresis with consequent danger of hypokalemia and arrhythmias, particularly in digitalized patients.
- Lab tests: Monitor closely platelet counts, liver enzymes, fluid and

electrolyte balances, renal function.
- Correct hypokalemia before and during therapy.
- Note: If platelet count falls below 150,000/mm^3, report immediately to physician; may indicate thrombocytopenia.
- Allergy alert: IV preparation contains sodium metabisulfite, a reducing agent to which certain susceptible individuals are allergic. Discontinue immediately if patient shows hypersensitivity reactions.
- Observe patient closely when drug is withdrawn after prolonged therapy; clinical deterioration may occur within hours.

INDAPAMIDE

(in-dap'a-mide)
Lozide ◆, Lozol
Classifications: ELECTROLYTIC AND WATER BALANCE AGENT; THIAZIDE DIURETIC
Therapeutic: THIAZIDE DIURETIC
Prototype: Hydrochlorothiazide
Pregnancy Category: B

AVAILABILITY 1.25, 2.5 mg tablets

ACTION & *THERAPEUTIC EFFECT*
Sulfonamide derivative which has both diuretic and direct vascular effects. Action mechanism is similar to that of the thiazide diuretics. Principal site of action is on the proximal portion of the distal renal tubules. Enhances excretion of sodium, potassium, and water by interfering with sodium transfer across renal epithelium of the tubules. *Hypotensive activity appears to result from a decrease in plasma and extracellular fluid volume, decreased peripheral vascular resistance, direct arteriolar dilation, and calcium channel blockade.*

Common adverse effects in *italic*, life-threatening effects underlined; generic names in **bold**; classifications in SMALL CAPS; ◆ Canadian drug name; ⊙ Prototype drug

781

USES Alone or with other antihypertensives in the management of hypertension in patients who have failed to respond to diet, exercise, or weight reduction.

UNLABELED USES Edema associated with CHF.

CONTRAINDICATIONS Hypersensitivity to indapamide or other sulfonamide derivatives, anuria, renal failure.

CAUTIOUS USE Electrolyte imbalance, hypokalemia, severe renal disease; impaired hepatic function or progressive liver disease; prediabetic and type II diabetic patient, hyperparathyroidism, thyroid disorders; SLE; sympathectomized patient; history of gout; pregnancy (category B), lactation. Safe use in children is not established.

ROUTE & DOSAGE

Hypertension, Edema
Adult: **PO** 2.5 mg once/d, may increase to 5 mg/d if needed

ADMINISTRATION

Oral

- Give with food or milk to reduce GI irritation.
- Administer in a.m. to prevent nocturia. Urge patient to take at least 240 mL (8 oz) of fluid (if allowed) with the medication.
- Store in tight, light-resistant container unless otherwise directed.

ADVERSE EFFECTS (≥1%) **CNS:** Headache, dizziness, fatigue, weakness, muscle cramps or spasm, paresthesia, tension, anxiety, nervousness, agitation, vertigo, insomnia, mental depression, blurred vision, drowsiness. **CV:** Orthostatic hypotension, PVCs, dysrhythmias, flush-

ing, palpitation. **GI:** Dry mouth, anorexia, nausea, vomiting, diarrhea, constipation, abdominal cramps or pain. **Urogenital:** Urinary frequency, nocturia, polyuria, glycosuria, impotence or reduced libido. **Skin:** Rash, hives, pruritus, vasculitis, photosensitivity. **Metabolic:** Dilutional hyponatremia, *hyperuricemia,* exacerbation of gout; *hypokalemia,* hyperglycemia, hypochloremia, hypercalcemia, increased BUN or creatinine, weight loss, exacerbation of SLE; increased cholesterol.

DIAGNOSTIC TEST INTERFERENCE Since indapamide may cause hypercalcemia (and hypophosphatemia), it is generally withheld before tests for *parathyroid function* are performed.

INTERACTIONS Drug: Effects of **diazoxide** and indapamide intensified; increased risk of **digoxin** toxicity with hypokalemia; decreased renal **lithium** clearance may increase risk of **lithium** toxicity.

PHARMACOKINETICS Absorption: Readily from GI tract. **Peak:** 2–2.5 h. **Duration:** Up to 36 h. **Metabolism:** In liver. **Elimination:** 60% in urine; 16–23% in feces. **Half-Life:** 14–18 h.

CLINICAL IMPLICATIONS

Assessment & Drug Effects

- Monitor BP periodically throughout therapy.
- Lab tests: Obtain baseline and periodic BUN, serum creatinine, uric acid, blood glucose, serum electrolytes, and fluid balance.
- Monitor for digitalis toxicity with concurrent therapy.
- Note: Electrolyte imbalances may be clinically serious with protracted vomiting and diarrhea, ex-

cessive sweating, GI drainage, and paracentesis.
- Report promptly signs of hyponatremia or hypokalemia (see Appendix F).
- Monitor diabetics for loss of glycemic control.

Patient & Family Education
- Notify physician of decreased urine output, dizziness, weakness or muscle cramps, nausea, jaundice, or blurred vision.
- Take precautions from sun exposure because of risk of photosensitivity.
- Record weight at least every other day; inspect ankles and legs for edema. Report unexplained, progressive weight gain [e.g., 1–1.5 kg (2–3 lb) in 2–3 d].

INDINAVIR SULFATE

(in-din'a-vir)
Crixivan
Classifications: ANTIVIRAL AGENT; PROTEASE INHIBITOR
Therapeutic: ANTIVIRAL; PROTEASE INHIBITOR
Prototype: Saquinavir
Pregnancy Category: C

AVAILABILITY 100 mg, 200 mg, 333 mg, 400 mg capsules

ACTION & *THERAPEUTIC EFFECT*
Indinavir is an HIV protease inhibitor. HIV protease is an enzyme required to produce the polyprotein precursors of the functional proteins in infectious HIV. Indinavir binds to the protease active site and thus inhibits activity of the enzyme. *Protease inhibitors prevent cleavage of the HIV viral polyproteins, resulting in formation of immature noninfectious virus particles.*

USES Treatment of HIV infection, usually in combination with other antiretroviral agents or protease inhibitors.

CONTRAINDICATIONS Hypersensitivity to indinavir; pregnancy (category C), lactation.
CAUTIOUS USE Hepatic dysfunction, renal impairment, history of nephrolithiasis, diabetes mellitus; history of adverse responses to other protease inhibitors. Safety and efficacy in children are not established.

ROUTE & DOSAGE

HIV
Adult: **PO** 800 mg (2 × 400 mg) q8h 1 h before or 2 h after meal
With ritonavir: 800 mg b.i.d. plus 100–200 mg ritonavir b.i.d.

ADMINISTRATION

Oral
- Give with water on an empty stomach 1 h before or 2 h after meal; if needed, may be given with a very light meal or beverage.
- Note: When didanosine and indinavir are ordered concurrently, give each on empty stomach at least 1 h apart.
- Do not administer concurrently with midazolam or triazolam.
- Store tightly closed with desiccant in original bottle.

ADVERSE EFFECTS (≥1%) **CNS:** Fatigue, headache, insomnia, dizziness, somnolence, nervousness, agitation, anxiety, paresthesia, peripheral neuropathy, tremor, vertigo. **CV:** Palpitations. **Hematologic:** Anemia, splenomegaly, lymphadenopathy. **GI:** *Nausea,* diarrhea, abdominal discomfort, dyspepsia, stomatitis, anorexia, dry mouth, cholecystitis,

Common adverse effects in *italic*, life-threatening effects underlined; generic names in **bold**; classifications in SMALL CAPS; ♦ Canadian drug name; ⊘ Prototype drug

783

cholestasis, constipation, flatulence. **Skin:** Body odor, rash, pruritus, seborrhea, skin ulceration, dry skin, sweating, urticaria. **Other:** Myalgia, allergic reaction, bronchitis, cough, rhinitis, taste alterations, visual disturbances, hyperglycemia, diabetes, kidney stones.

INTERACTIONS Drug: Rifabutin, rifampin significantly decrease indinavir levels. **Ketoconazole** significantly increases indinavir levels. Indinavir could inhibit the metabolism and increase the toxicity of **midazolam, sildenafil, tadalafil, trazodone, triazolam, vardenafil.** Indinavir and **didanosine** should be administered at least 1 h apart on empty stomach to permit full absorption of each; increased **ergotamine** toxicity with indinavir. **Herbal: St. John's wort,** garlic decreases ANTIRETROVIRAL activity of indinavir.

PHARMACOKINETICS Absorption: Rapidly absorbed from GI tract; a meal high in calories, fat, and protein significantly reduces absorption. **Distribution:** 60% protein bound. **Metabolism:** In liver by cytochrome P4503A4 (CYP3A4). **Elimination:** Primarily in feces (>80%), 20% in urine.

CLINICAL IMPLICATIONS

Assessment & Drug Effects
- Lab tests: Monitor CBC with differential and platelet count, liver function tests, CPK, urinalysis, and serum amylase periodically.
- Assess for S&S of renal dysfunction, respiratory dysfunction, GI distress, and other common adverse effects.

Patient & Family Education
- Learn drug interactions and potential adverse reactions. Drink plenty of liquids to minimize risk of renal stones.
- Notify physician of flank pain, hematuria, S&S of jaundice, or other distressing adverse effects.

INDOMETHACIN

(in-doe-meth′a-sin)
Indocid ♦, **Indocin, Indocin SR**
Classifications: ANALGESIC, NONSTEROIDAL ANTIINFLAMMATORY (NSAID); ANTIPYRETIC
Therapeutic: NSAID, ANALGESIC; ANTIPYRETIC
Prototype: Ibuprofen
Pregnancy Category: B first and second trimester; D third trimester

AVAILABILITY 25 mg, 50 mg capsules; 75 mg sustained release capsules; 25 mg/5 mL oral suspension; 50 mg suppositories; 1 mg injection

ACTION & THERAPEUTIC EFFECT
Potent nonsteroidal compound with antiinflammatory, analgesic, and antipyretic effects. It competes with COX-1 and COX-2 enzymes, thus interfering with formation of prostaglandin. Appears to reduce motility of polymorphonuclear leukocytes, development of cellular exudates, and vascular permeability in injured tissue resulting in its antiinflammatory effects. *Antipyretic and antiinflammatory actions may be related to its ability to inhibit prostaglandin biosynthesis. It is a potent analgesic.*

USES Palliative treatment in active stages of moderate to severe rheumatoid arthritis, ankylosing rheumatoid spondylitis, acute gouty arthritis, and osteoarthritis of hip in patients intolerant to or unresponsive to adequate trials with salicylates and other therapy. Also used

IV to close patent ductus arteriosus in the premature infant.

UNLABELED USES To relieve biliary pain and dysmenorrhea, Paget's disease, athletic injuries, juvenile arthritis, idiopathic pericarditis.

CONTRAINDICATIONS Allergy to indomethacin, aspirin, or other NSAID; nasal polyps associated with angioedema; history of GI lesions; perioperative pain with CABG; pregnancy (category B; D in third trimester).

CAUTIOUS USE History of psychiatric illness, epilepsy, parkinsonism; impaired renal or hepatic function; uncontrolled infections; coagulation defects, CHF; older adults, persons in hazardous occupations.

ROUTE & DOSAGE

Rheumatoid Arthritis
Adult: **PO** 25–50 mg b.i.d or t.i.d. (max: 200 mg/d) or 75 mg sustained release 1–2 times/d

Pediatric Arthritis
Child: **PO** 1–2 mg/kg/d in 2–4 divided doses (max: 4 mg/kg/d) or 150–200 mg/d

Acute Gouty Arthritis
Adult: **PO/PR** 50 mg t.i.d. until pain is tolerable, then rapidly taper

Bursitis
Adult: **PO** 25–50 mg t.i.d. or q.i.d. (max: 200 mg/d) or 75 mg sustained release 1–2 times/d

Close Patent Ductus Arteriosus
Premature neonate: **IV** *<48 h,* 0.2 mg/kg followed by 2 doses of 0.1 mg/kg q12–24h; *2–7 d,* 0.2 mg/kg followed by 2 doses of 0.2 mg/kg q12–24h; *<7 d,* 0.2 mg/kg followed by 2 doses of 0.25 mg/kg q12–24h

ADMINISTRATION

Oral
- Give immediately after meals, or with food, milk, or antacid (if prescribed) to minimize GI side effects.

Rectal
- Indomethacin rectal suppository use is contraindicated with history of proctitis or recent bleeding.

Intravenous

PREPARE: **Direct:** Dilute 1 mg with 1 mL of NS or sterile water for injection without preservatives. Resulting concentration (1 mg/mL) may be further diluted with an additional 1 mL for each 1 mg to yield 0.5 mg/mL.

ADMINISTER: **Direct:** Give by direct IV with a single dose given over 5–10 s.
- Avoid extravasation or leakage; drug can be irritating to tissue. • Discard any unused drug, since it contains no preservative.

- Store oral and rectal forms in tight, light-resistant containers unless otherwise directed. Do not freeze.

ADVERSE EFFECTS (≥1%) **Body as a Whole:** Hypersensitivity (rash, purpura, pruritus, urticaria, angioedema, angiitis, rapid fall in blood pressure, dyspnea, asthma syndrome in aspirin-sensitive patients), edema, weight gain, flushing, sweating. **CNS:** Headache, *dizziness,* vertigo, light-headedness, syncope, fatigue, muscle weakness, ataxia, insomnia, nightmares, drowsiness, confusion, coma, convulsions, peripheral neuropathy, psychic disturbances (hallucinations, depersonalization, depression), aggravation of epilepsy, parkinsonism. **CV:** Elevated BP, palpita-

Common adverse effects in *italic*, life-threatening effects underlined; generic names in **bold**; classifications in SMALL CAPS; ♦ Canadian drug name; ⊕ Prototype drug

785

I

tion, chest pains, tachycardia, brady-cardia, CHF. **Special Senses:** Blurred vision, lacrimation, eye pain, visual field changes, corneal deposits, reti-nal disturbances including macula, *tinnitus,* hearing disturbances, epistaxis. **GI:** *Nausea, vomiting,* di-arrhea, anorexia, bloating, abdom-inal distention, ulcerative stomati-tis, proctitis, rectal bleeding, <u>GI ulceration, hemorrhage, perfora-tion, toxic hepatitis</u>. **Hematologic:** Hemolytic anemia, <u>aplastic anemia</u> (sometimes fatal), <u>agranulocytosis</u>, leukopenia, thrombocytopenic pur-pura, inhibited platelet aggregation. **Urogenital:** Renal function impair-ment, hematuria, urinary frequency; vaginal bleeding, breast changes. **Skin:** Hair loss, exfoliative dermati-tis, erythema nodosum, tissue irrita-tion with extravasation. **Metabolic:** Hyponatremia, hypokalemia, hy-perkalemia, hypoglycemia or hy-perglycemia, glycosuria (rare).

DIAGNOSTIC TEST INTERFERENCE
Increased *AST, ALT, bilirubin, BUN;* positive direct *Coombs' test.*

INTERACTIONS Drug: ORAL ANTICO-AGULANTS, **heparin, alcohol** may prolong bleeding time; may increase **lithium** toxicity; effects of ORAL AN-TICOAGULANTS, **phenytoin,** SALICYL-ATES, SULFONAMIDES, SULFONYLUREAS in-creased because of protein-binding displacement; increased toxicity in-cluding GI bleeding with SALICYLATES, NSAIDS; may blunt effects of ANTIHY-PERTENSIVES and DIURETICS. **Herbal: Feverfew, garlic, ginger, ginkgo** may increase bleeding potential.

PHARMACOKINETICS Absorption:
Completely absorbed from GI tract. **Onset:** 1–2 h. **Peak:** 3 h. **Duration:** 4–6 h. **Metabolism:** In liver. **Elimina-tion:** Primarily in urine. **Half-Life:** 2.5–124 h.

CLINICAL IMPLICATIONS
Assessment & Drug Effects
- Monitor for therapeutic effective-ness: In acute gouty attack, relief of joint tenderness and pain is usually apparent in 24–36 h; swelling generally disappears in 3–5 d. In rheumatoid arthritis: Re-duced fever, increased strength, reduced stiffness, and relief of pain, swelling, and tenderness.
- Question patient carefully regard-ing aspirin sensitivity before initi-ation of therapy.
- Observe patients carefully; in-struct to report adverse reactions promptly to prevent serious and sometimes irreversible or fatal ef-fects.
- Lab tests: Monitor renal function, hepatic function, CBC with differ-ential, BP and HR, visual and hearing acuity periodically.
- Monitor weight and observe de-pendent areas for signs of edema in patients with underlying car-diovascular disease.
- Monitor I&O closely and keep physician informed during IV ad-ministration for patent ductus ar-teriosus. Significant impairment of renal function is possible; urine output may decrease by 50% or more. Also monitor BUN, serum creatinine, glomerular filtration rate, creatinine clearance, and se-rum electrolytes.

Patient & Family Education
- Notify physician of S&S of GI bleeding, visual disturbance, tin-nitus, weight gain, or edema.
- Do not take aspirin or other NSAIDS; they increase possibility of ulcers.
- Note: Frontal headache is the most frequent CNS adverse effect; if it persists, dosage reduction or drug withdrawal may be indi-cated. Take drug at bedtime with

Common adverse effects in *italic*, life-threatening effects <u>underlined</u>; generic names in **bold**; classifications in SMALL CAPS; ♣ Canadian drug name; ☺ Prototype drug

milk to reduce the incidence of morning headache.

- Do not drive or engage in other potentially hazardous activities until response to drug is known.

INFLIXIMAB

(in-flix′i-mab)
Remicade
Classifications: BIOLOGIC RESPONSE MODIFIER; TUMOR NECROSIS FACTOR MODIFIER
Therapeutic: ANTIINFLAMMATORY; MONOCLONAL ANTIBODY (IgG)
Pregnancy Category: B

AVAILABILITY 100 mg powder for injection

ACTION & *THERAPEUTIC EFFECT*
IgG$_1$-K monoclonal antibody that binds specifically to tumor necrosis factor-alpha (TNF-alpha), a cytokine, preventing TNF-alpha from binding to its receptors. TNF-alpha induces proinflammatory cytokines. Infliximab reduces infiltration of inflammatory cells and TNF-alpha production in inflamed areas of the intestine, as seen in Crohn's disease. *Infliximab reduces concentrations of TNF-alpha production.*

USES Moderately to severely active Crohn's disease, including fistulizing Crohn's disease, rheumatoid arthritis, ankylosing spondylitis, ulcerative colitis.

CONTRAINDICATIONS Hypersensitivity to infliximab; CHF; infection, sepsis; murine protein hypersensitivity; lactation.
CAUTIOUS USE History of allergic phenomena or untoward responses to monoclonal antibody preparation; renal or hepatic impairment; multiple sclerosis (potential exacer-

bation); fungal infection; heart failure, human antichimeric antibody (HACA); leukopenia, thrombocytopenia; immunosuppressed patients; neoplastic disease; tuberculosis; vaccination; vasculitis; neurological disease; neutropenia; seizure disorder, seizures; older adults; pregnancy (category B).

ROUTE & DOSAGE

Crohn's Disease
Adult: **IV** 5 mg/kg infused over at least 2 h, repeat at 2 and 6 wk for fistulizing disease, then q8wk
Child: **IV** 5 mg/kg at weeks 0, 2, and 6, then 5 mg/kg q8wk

Rheumatoid Arthritis
Adult: **IV** 3 mg/kg at weeks 0, 2, and 6, then q8wk

Ulcerative Colitis
Adult: **IV** 5 mg/kg at weeks 0, 2, and 6, then 5 mg/kg q8wk

Ankylosing Spondylitis
Adult: **IV** 5 mg/kg at weeks 0, 2, and 6, then 5 mg/kg q6wk

ADMINISTRATION

- Note: Do not administer to a patient who has known or suspected sepsis.

Intravenous

PREPARE: **IV Infusion:** Reconstitute each vial with 10 mL of sterile water for injection using a 21-gauge or smaller syringe. Inject sterile water against wall of vial, then gently swirl to dissolve but do not shake. ▪ Let stand for 5 min. ▪ Solution should be colorless to light yellow with a few translucent particles. Discard if particles are opaque. ▪ Further dilute by first removing from a 250-mL IV bag of NS a volume of

Common adverse effects in *italic*, life-threatening effects underlined; generic names in **bold**; classifications in SMALL CAPS; ✦ Canadian drug name; ❷ Prototype drug

787

NS equal to the volume of reconstituted infliximab to be added to the IV bag. Slowly add the total volume of reconstituted infliximab solution to the 250-mL infusion bag and gently mix. ▪ Infusion concentration should be 0.4 to 4 mg/mL. ▪ Begin infusion within 3 h of preparation.

ADMINISTER: **IV Infusion:** Give over at least 2 h using a polyethylene-lined infusion set with an in-line, low-protein-binding filter (pore size 1.2 micron or less).

▪ Infliximab is INCOMPATIBLE with PVC equipment or devices.
▪ Discard unused infusion solution.

INCOMPATIBILITIES **Solution/additive:** Incompatible with PVC bags and tubing. **Y-site:** Do not infuse with any other drugs.

▪ Store unopened vials at 2°–8° C (36°–46° F).

ADVERSE EFFECTS (≥1%) **Body as a Whole:** Fatigue, fever, pain, myalgia, back pain, chills, hot flashes, arthralgia; infusion-related reactions (fever, chills, pruritus, urticaria, chest pain, hypotension, hypertension, dyspnea). Increased risk of opportunistic infections, including tuberculosis. **CNS:** Headache, dizziness, involuntary muscle contractions, paresthesias, vertigo, anxiety, depression, insomnia. **CV:** Chest pain, peripheral edema, hypotension, hypertension, tachycardia, anemia, CHF, pericardial effusion, systemic and cutaneous vasculitis. **GI:** Nausea, diarrhea, abdominal pain, vomiting, constipation, dyspepsia, flatulence, intestinal obstruction, ulcerative stomatitis, increased hepatic enzymes. **Hematologic:** Leukopenia, neutropenia, thrombocytopenia, pancytopenia. **Respiratory:** URI, pharyngitis, bronchitis, rhinitis, coughing, sinusitis, dyspnea. **Skin:** Rash, pruritus, acne, alopecia, fungal dermatitis, eczema, dry skin, increased sweating, urticaria. **Other:** Infections, development of autoantibodies, lupus-like syndrome, conjunctivitis, dysuria, urinary frequency.

INTERACTIONS Drug: May blunt effectiveness of VACCINES given concurrently.

PHARMACOKINETICS Distribution: Distributed primarily to the vascular compartment. **Half-Life:** 9.5 d.

CLINICAL IMPLICATIONS

Assessment & Drug Effects

▪ Discontinue IV infusion and notify physician for fever, chills, pruritus, urticaria, chest pain, dyspnea, hypo/hypertension.
▪ Monitor for and immediately report S&S of local IV site or more generalized infection.

Patient & Family Education

▪ Report any infection to your physician promptly.

INSULIN ASPART

(in′su-lyn)
NovoLog
Classifications: HORMONE; ANTIDIABETIC AGENT; INSULIN, RAPID-ACTING
Therapeutic: ANTIDIABETIC; INSULIN RAPID-ACTING
Prototype: Insulin injection
Pregnancy Category: C

AVAILABILITY 100 U/mL injection

ACTION & *THERAPEUTIC EFFECT*
A recombinant insulin analog that is more rapidly absorbed than human insulin, with a more rapid on-

set and shorter duration than regular human insulin. *Provides better blood glucose control than regular human insulin when given before a meal.*

USES Treatment of diabetes mellitus.

CONTRAINDICATIONS Systemic allergic reactions; history of allergic reactions to insulin; hypoglycemia; pregnancy (category C).

CAUTIOUS USE Fever, hyperthyroidism, surgery or trauma; decreased insulin requirements due to diarrhea, nausea, or vomiting, malabsorption; renal or hepatic impairment, hypokalemia.

ROUTE & DOSAGE

Diabetes
Adult: SC 0.25–0.7 units/kg/d injected 5–10 min before each meal

ADMINISTRATION

Subcutaneous

- Note: Must give 5–10 min before a meal.
- Draw up insulin aspart first when mixing with NPH insulin. Give injection immediately after it is mixed. Do not give NPH mixture by IV.
- Store refrigerated at 2°–8° C (36°–46° F); may be stored at room temperature, 15°–30° C (59°–86° F) for up to 28 d. Do not expose to excessive heat or sunlight, and do not freeze.

ADVERSE EFFECTS (≥1%) **Body as a Whole:** Allergic reactions. **Endocrine:** Hypoglycemia, hypokalemia. **Skin:** Injection site reaction, lipodystrophy, pruritus, rash.

INTERACTIONS Drug: ORAL ANTIDIABETIC AGENTS, ACE INHIBITORS, **disopyr-amide, fluoxetine,** MAO INHIBITORS, **propoxyphene,** SALICYLATES, SULFON-AMIDE ANTIBIOTICS, **octreotide** may enhance hypoglycemia; CORTICOSTER-OIDS, **niacin, danazol,** DIURETICS, SYMPATHOMIMETIC AGENTS, PHENOTHIA-ZINES, THYROID HORMONES, ESTROGENS, PROGESTOGENS, **isoniazid, somatropin** my decrease hypoglycemic effects; BETA-BLOCKERS, **clonidine, lithium, alcohol** may either potentiate or weaken effects of insulin; **pentamidine** may cause hypoglycemia followed by hyperglycemia. **Herbal: Garlic, ginseng** may potentiate hypoglycemic effects.

PHARMACOKINETICS Absorption: Rapidly absorbed from SC injection site. **Onset:** 15 min. **Peak:** 1–3 h. **Duration:** 3–5 h. **Distribution:** Low protein binding. **Metabolism:** In liver with some metabolism in the kidneys. **Half-Life:** 81 min.

CLINICAL IMPLICATIONS

Assessment & Drug Effects

- Monitor for S&S of hypoglycemia (see Appendix F). Initial hypoglycemic response begins within 15 min and peaks 45–90 min after injection.
- Lab tests: Periodically monitor fasting blood glucose and HbA$_{1C}$.
- Withhold drug and notify physician if patient is hypokalemic.

Patient & Family Education

- Do not inject into areas with redness, swelling, itching, or dimpling.
- Ingest some form of sugar (e.g., orange juice, dissolved table sugar, honey) if symptoms of hypoglycemia develop, and seek medical assistance.
- Check blood sugar as prescribed, especially postprandial values; notify physician of fasting blood glucose <80 and >120 mg/dL.
- Notify the physician of any of the following: Fever, infection,

---

Common adverse effects in *italic*, life-threatening effects underlined; generic names in **bold**; classifications in SMALL CAPS; ✦ Canadian drug name; ● Prototype drug

789

trauma, diarrhea, nausea or vomiting. Dosage adjustment may be needed.

- Do not take any other medication unless approved by the physician.

INSULIN DETEMIR

in'su-lyn det'e-mir
Levemir

Classifications: HORMONE; ANTIDIABETIC AGENT; INSULIN, LONG-ACTING
Therapeutic: ANTIDIABETIC; INSULIN
Prototype: Insulin injection
Pregnancy Category: C

AVAILABILITY 100 units/mL available in 10 mL multidose vials and 3 mL prefilled syringes

ACTION & *THERAPEUTIC EFFECT*
Insulin detemir, a long-acting insulin, exerts its action by binding to insulin receptors. Receptor-bound insulin lowers blood glucose by facilitating cellular uptake of glucose into skeletal muscle and fat, and inhibiting the output of glucose from the liver. *Insulin detemir is effective as a glucose-lowering agent, with glycemic control equivalent to that of NPH insulin.*

USES Treatment of type 1 and type 2 diabetes mellitus.

CONTRAINDICATIONS Hypersensitivity to insulin detemir, or cresol; use in insulin infusion pumps; diabetic ketoacidosis, coma, hyperosmolar hyperglycemic state, hypoglycemia; pregnancy C. Safe and effective use in children with type 2 diabetes has not been established.
CAUTIOUS USE Renal and hepatic impairment; older adults; cardiac disease, CHF, concurrent use of beta-blocking agent(s); lactation.

ROUTE & DOSAGE

Diabetes
Adult/Child: **SC** Insulin-naïve patients: 0.1–0.2 units/kg q.d. in evening or 10 units q.d. or b.i.d. in evenly spaced doses. For those taking a basal insulin product (i.e., NPH insulin, insulin glargine), a unit-to-unit dose conversion can be used.

ADMINISTRATION
Subcutaneous
- Once-daily injections should be given with the evening meal or at bedtime. With twice-daily dosing, the evening dose may be given with the evening meal, at bedtime, or 12 h after the morning dose.
- Do not administer IV or IM. With thin patients, inject at a 45-degree angle into a pinched fold of skin to avoid IM injection.
- Do not mix with any other type of insulin. Do not use with an insulin infusion pump.
- Store unopened vials under refrigeration at 2°–8° C (36°–46° F). Once removed from refrigeration, pens, cartridges, and other delivery devices must be kept at room temperature (not to exceed 30° C or 85° F) and either used within 42 d or discarded.

***INCOMPATIBILITIES* Solution/additive:** Insulin detemir should not be mixed with any other insulin preparations.

ADVERSE EFFECTS (≥1%) [See INSULIN (REGULAR)] **Body as a Whole:** Allergic reactions. **Metabolic:** Hypoglycemia, weight gain. **Skin:** Lipodystrophy, pruritus, rash.

DIAGNOSTIC TEST INTERFERENCE
See INSULIN INJECTION (REGULAR).

INTERACTIONS Drug: See INSULIN INJECTION (REGULAR). **Herbal: Garlic** and **green tea** may potentiate hypoglycemic effects.

PHARMACOKINETICS Absorption: Slow, prolonged absorption over 24 h. **Peak:** 6–8 h. **Distribution:** 98–99% protein bound. **Half-Life:** 5–7 h.

CLINICAL IMPLICATIONS

Assessment & Drug Effects

- Monitor for S&S of hypoglycemia (see Appendix F), especially after changes in insulin dose or type.
- Lab tests: Periodic fasting blood glucose and HbA$_{1C}$; periodic serum potassium with concurrent potassium-lowering drugs.
- Monitor weight periodically.

Patient & Family Education

- Follow directions for taking the drug (see Administration). Rotate injection sites and never inject into an area with redness, swelling, itching, or dimpling.
- Know parameters for withholding drug. Check blood sugar as prescribed; notify physician of fasting blood glucose below 80 or above 120 mg/dL.
- Ingest some form of sugar (e.g., orange juice, dissolved table sugar, honey) if symptoms of hypoglycemia develop; and seek medical assistance.
- Notify the physician of any of the following: fever, infection, trauma, diarrhea, nausea, or vomiting.
- Do not take any other medication unless approved by physician.

INSULIN GLARGINE

(in'su-lin glar'geen)
Lantus
Classifications: HORMONE; ANTI-DIABETIC AGENT; INSULIN LONG-ACTING

Therapeutic: ANTIDIABETIC; INSULIN LONG-ACTING
Prototype: Insulin injection
Pregnancy Category: C

AVAILABILITY 100 U/mL injection; 3 mL cartridge

ACTION & *THERAPEUTIC EFFECT*
A recombinant human insulin analog with a long duration of action. Lowers blood glucose levels over an extended period of time by stimulating peripheral glucose uptake especially in muscle and fat tissue. In addition, insulin inhibits hepatic glucose production. *Lowers blood glucose levels over an extended period of time. It also prevents the conversion of glucagon to glucose in the liver.*

USES Bedtime dosing of adults and children with type 1 diabetes, or adults with type 2 diabetes.

CONTRAINDICATIONS Prior hypersensitivity to insulin glargine; hypoglycemia; pregnancy (category C). Safety and efficacy in children with type 2 diabetes are unknown.
CAUTIOUS USE Renal and hepatic impairment; lactation. Safety and efficacy in children <6 y of age in type 1 diabetes.

ROUTE & DOSAGE

Type 1 Diabetes
Adult/Child: **SC** If not taking insulin, give 10 U at same time each day (usually at bedtime) once daily; if taking NPH or ultralente insulin once daily, give same dose at same time each day (usually at bedtime); if taking NPH insulin twice daily, give 80% of total daily dose at same time each day (usually at bedtime)

Common adverse effects in *italic*, life-threatening effects <u>underlined</u>; generic names in **bold**; classifications in SMALL CAPS; ♣ Canadian drug name; ✪ Prototype drug

791

Type 2 Diabetes

Adult: SC If already taking oral hypoglycemic drugs, start with 10 U at same time each day (usually at bedtime) once daily and adjust according to patient's needs

ADMINISTRATION

Subcutaneous

- Do not give this product IV.
- Give at same time each day (usually at bedtime) and do not mix with any other insulin product.
- Store in refrigerator at 2°–8° C (36°–46° F), may store at room temperature, 15°–30° C (59°–86° F). Discard opened refrigerated vials after 28 d and unrefrigerated vials after 14 d. Do not expose to excessive heat or sunlight, and do not freeze.

ADVERSE EFFECTS (≥1%) **Body as a Whole:** Allergic reactions. **Endocrine:** Hypoglycemia, hypokalemia. **Skin:** Injection site reaction, lipodystrophy, pruritus, rash.

INTERACTIONS Drug: ORAL ANTIDIABETIC AGENTS, ACE INHIBITORS, **disopyramide, fluoxetine,** MAO INHIBITORS, **propoxyphene,** SALICYLATES, SULFONAMIDE ANTIBIOTICS, **octreotide** may enhance hypoglycemia; CORTICOSTEROIDS, **niacin, danazol,** DIURETICS, SYMPATHOMIMETIC AGENTS, PHENOTHIAZINES, THYROID HORMONES, ESTROGENS, PROGESTOGENS, **isoniazid, somatropin** may decrease hypoglycemic effects; BETA-BLOCKERS, **clonidine, lithium, alcohol** may either potentiate or weaken effects of insulin; **pentamidine** may cause hypoglycemia followed by hyperglycemia. **Herbal: Garlic, ginseng** may potentiate hypoglycemic effects.

PHARMACOKINETICS Absorption: Slowly absorbed from SC injection site. **Onset:** 3–4 h. **Duration:** 10.4– 24 h. **Metabolism:** In liver to active metabolites.

CLINICAL IMPLICATIONS

Assessment & Drug Effects

- Monitor for S&S of hypoglycemia (see Appendix F), especially after changes in insulin dose or type.
- Lab tests: Monitor fasting blood glucose and HbA$_{1C}$ periodically.
- Withhold drug and notify physician if patient is hypokalemic.

Patient & Family Education

- Do not inject into areas with redness, swelling, itching, or dimpling.
- Absorption patterns for this drug are not dependent on the injection site.
- Ingest some form of sugar (e.g., orange juice, dissolved table sugar, honey) if symptoms of hypoglycemia develop; and seek medical assistance.
- Check blood sugar as prescribed; notify physician of fasting blood glucose <80 and >120 mg/dL.
- Notify the physician of any of the following: fever, infection, trauma, diarrhea, nausea, or vomiting. Dosage adjustment may be needed.
- Do not take any other medication unless approved by physician.

INSULIN GLULISINE

(in'su-lin glu-li'seen)

Apidra

Classifications: HORMONE; ANTIDIABETIC AGENT; INSULIN RAPID-ACTING

Therapeutic: ANTIDIABETIC; INSULIN RAPID-ACTING

Prototype: Insulin injection (Regular)

Pregnancy Category: C

AVAILABILITY 100 units/mL multi-dose (10 mL) vials

ACTION & *THERAPEUTIC EFFECT*
Insulin glulisine, formed by recombinant DNA, is a rapid-acting insulin. Insulin lowers blood glucose by stimulating peripheral glucose uptake by skeletal muscle and fat and by inhibiting hepatic glucose production. Insulin causes lipolysis in the adipocytes, inhibits proteolysis, and enhances protein synthesis. *Insulin glulisine has a more rapid onset of action and a shorter duration of action than regular human insulin; thus, it provides good postprandial blood glucose control.*

USES Treatment of diabetes mellitus.

CONTRAINDICATIONS Hypoglycemia; systemic allergy to insulin; pregnancy (category C).

CAUTIOUS USE Renal impairment, hepatic dysfunction; thyroid disease; fever; older adults; children; lactation.

ROUTE & DOSAGE

Diabetes
Adult: **SC** 5–10 units within 15 min before starting a meal or within 20 min after starting a meal. Dose should be individualized.

ADMINISTRATION

Subcutaneous
- Give within 15 min before or up to 20 min after a meal.
- Store refrigerated at 36° F to 46° F (2° C to 8° C). Discard vial if frozen. Protect from light.

ADVERSE EFFECTS (≥1%) **[see INSULIN (REGULAR)] Body as a Whole:** Allergic reactions. **Metabolic:** Hy-poglycemia. **Skin:** Injection site reactions, lipodystrophy, pruritus, rash.

DIAGNOSTIC TEST INTERFERENCE
See INSULIN INJECTION (REGULAR).

PHARMACOKINETICS Absorption: 70% bioavailable from injection sites. **Onset:** 15–30 min. **Peak:** 55 min. **Duration:** 3–4 h. **Metabolism:** In liver with some metabolism in the kidney. **Half-Life:** 42 min SC.

CLINICAL IMPLICATIONS

Assessment & Drug Effects
- Monitor for S&S of hypoglycemia (see Appendix F). Initial hypoglycemic response begins within 15 min and peaks, on average, 40–60 min after injection.
- Lab tests: Periodically monitor fasting and postprandial blood glucose and HbA$_{1C}$.

Patient & Family Education
- Do not inject into areas with redness, swelling, itching, or dimpling.
- If mixing with NPH human insulin, draw up insulin glulisine first. Inject immediately after mixing.
- Ingest some form of sugar (e.g., orange juice, dissolved table sugar, honey) if symptoms of hypoglycemia develop, and seek medical assistance.
- Check blood sugar as prescribed, especially postprandial values; notify physician of fasting blood glucose <80 and >140 mg/dL.
- Notify the physician of any of the following: fever, infection, trauma, diarrhea, nausea, or vomiting. Dosage adjustment may be needed.
- Do not take any other medication unless approved by the physician.

Common adverse effects in *italic*, life-threatening effects underlined; generic names in **bold**; classifications in SMALL CAPS; ♣ Canadian drug name; ❖ Prototype drug

793

INSULIN HUMAN INHALED

(in'su-lin)

Exubera

Classifications: HORMONE; ANTI-DIABETIC AGENT; INSULIN

Therapeutic: HORMONE; ANTIDIABETIC; INSULIN

Prototype: Insulin injection

Pregnancy Category: C

AVAILABILITY 1 mg and 3 mg blister packs with powder for inhalation; 1 mg is equivalent to 3 units of regular SC insulin; 3 mg is equivalent to 8 units of regular SC insulin

ACTION & *THERAPEUTIC EFFECT*
Inhaled insulin hormone regulates carbohydrate, fat, and protein metabolism. Insulin lowers plasma glucose concentration by facilitating uptake of glucose into muscle and adipose tissue, as well as by inhibiting hepatic glucose production by both glycogenolysis and gluconeogenesis. *Inhaled insulin lowers plasma glucose level and improves glycemic control as indicated by a lowering of postprandial plasma glucose and HbA$_{1c}$ levels.*

USES Treatment of type 1 and type 2 diabetes mellitus.

CONTRAINDICATIONS Hypersensitivity to inhaled human insulin; diabetic ketoacidosis; coma; hyperosmolar hyperglycemic state; tobacco smoking; poorly controlled pulmonary disease; moderate to severe COPD; cystic fibrosis; asthma; upper respiratory infection; pregnancy (category C). Safety and efficacy in children have not been established.

CAUTIOUS USE Hepatic disease, renal impairment; renal failure; thyroid disease; infection; surgery, trauma; emesis, diarrhea.

ROUTE & DOSAGE

Diabetes

Adult: **Inhaled** 2–3 times daily no more than 10 min a.c. Initial doses: 30–39.9 kg, 1 mg; 40–59.9 kg, 2 mg; 60–79.9 kg, 3 mg; 80–99.9 kg, 4 mg; 100–119.9 kg, 5 mg; 120–139.9 kg, 6 mg. Initial premeal dose calculation: body weight (kg) × 0.05 mg/kg = premeal dose (mg) rounded down to the nearest whole milligram

ADMINISTRATION

Inhaled

- Give no sooner than 10 min a.c.
- Supplied in 1 mg and 3 mg blisters. The **least number** of blisters per dose should be used. To give a 4 mg dose, use one 1 mg and one 3 mg blister rather than four 1 mg blisters. To give a 5 mg dose, use two 1 mg blisters and one 3 mg blister. To give a 6 mg dose, use two 3 mg blisters.
- **Do not** substitute three 1 mg blisters for one 3 mg blister because consecutive inhalation of three 1 mg blisters provides much greater insulin exposure than one 3 mg blister. If 3 mg blisters are temporarily unavailable, use two 1 mg blisters for a 3 mg dose and monitor blood glucose closely.
- Store at 15°–30° C (59°–86° F).

ADVERSE EFFECTS (≥1%) **[see INSULIN (REGULAR)] Body as a Whole:** Chest pain. **GI:** Dry mouth. **Respiratory:** Asthma, bronchitis, *cough*, dyspnea, epistaxis, laryngitis, *pharyngitis, respiratory disorder, respiratory tract infection, rhinitis, sinusitis,* sputum increase. **Special Senses:** Otis media.

DIAGNOSTIC TEST INTERFERENCE

See INSULIN INJECTION (REGULAR).

INTERACTIONS Drug: See INSULIN INJECTION (REGULAR). **Herbal: Garlic** and **green tea** may potentiate hypoglycemic effects.

PHARMACOKINETICS Absorption: Rapid pulmonary absorption. **Onset:** 10–20 min. **Peak:** 30–90 min. **Distribution:** Throughout extracellular fluids. **Metabolism:** Primarily in liver with some metabolism in kidneys. **Elimination:** <2% in urine. **Half-Life:** Biologic, up to 13 h.

CLINICAL IMPLICATIONS

Assessment & Drug Effects

- Monitor for hypoglycemia (see Appendix F) at time of peak action of insulin. Onset of hypoglycemia (blood sugar: 50–40 mg/dL) may be rapid and sudden.
- Lab tests: Periodic postprandial blood glucose and HbA₁C. Test urine for ketones in new, unstable, and type 1 diabetes; if patient has lost weight, exercises vigorously, or has an illness; whenever blood glucose is substantially elevated.
- Notify physician promptly for presence of acetone with sugar in the urine; may indicate onset of ketoacidosis. Acetone without sugar in the urine usually signifies insufficient carbohydrate intake.

Patient & Family Education

- Follow directions for taking the drug (see Administration).
- Read the Medication Guide provided with the medication. Ensure that you have the correct dosage forms from the pharmacy (i.e., correct number of 1 mg and 3 mg

blister packets to provide the right dose as outlined in the Medication Guide).

- Change the release unit of the inhaler every 2 wk and change the inhaler 1 y after first use.
- Do not use inhaled insulin if you currently smoke or have smoked within the last 6 mo. Failure to follow this guideline may result in serious hypoglycemia.
- Note: Hypoglycemia can result from excess insulin, insufficient food intake, vomiting, diarrhea, unaccustomed exercise, infection, illness, nervous or emotional tension, or overindulgence in alcohol.
- Respond promptly to beginning symptoms of hypoglycemia. Take 4 oz (120 mL) of any fruit juice or regular carbonated beverage [1.5–3 oz (45–90 mL) for child] followed by a meal of longer-acting carbohydrate or protein food. Failure to show signs of recovery within 30 min indicates need for emergency treatment.
- Carry some form of fast-acting carbohydrate (e.g., lump sugar, Life-Savers, or other candy) at all times to treat hypoglycemia.
- Avoid OTC medications unless approved by physician.

INSULIN (REGULAR) ℗

(in'su-lin)
Humulin R, Novolin R, Regular Insulin, Velosulin BR

Classifications: HORMONE; ANTI-DIABETIC AGENT; INSULIN SHORT-ACTING
Therapeutic: ANTIDIABETIC; INSULIN SHORT-ACTING
Pregnancy Category: B

AVAILABILITY 100 units/mL

Common adverse effects in *italic*, life-threatening effects underlined; generic names in **bold**; classifications in SMALL CAPS; ♣ Canadian drug name; ℗ Prototype drug

795

I

ACTION & *THERAPEUTIC EFFECT*

Short-acting, clear, colorless solution of exogenous unmodified insulin extracted from beta cells in pork pancreas or synthesized by recombinant DNA technology (human). Enhances transmembrane passage of glucose across cell membranes in muscle and adipose tissue. Promotes conversion of glucose to glycogen in the liver. *It lowers blood glucose levels by increasing peripheral glucose uptake and by inhibiting the liver from changing glycogen to glucose.*

USES Emergency treatment of diabetic ketoacidosis or coma, to initiate therapy in patient with insulin-dependent diabetes mellitus, and in combination with intermediate-acting or long-acting insulin to provide better control of blood glucose concentrations in the diabetic patient. Used IV to stimulate growth hormone secretion (glucose counter regulatory hormone) to evaluate pituitary growth hormone reserve in patient with known or suspected growth hormone deficiency. Other uses include promotion of intracellular shift of potassium in treatment of hyperkalemia (IV) and induction of hypoglycemic shock as therapy in psychiatry.

CONTRAINDICATIONS Hypersensitivity to insulin animal protein.
CAUTIOUS USE Pregnancy (category B), renal impairment, renal failure; hepatic impairment, fever, thyroid disease; older adults; children and infants.

ROUTE & DOSAGE

Diabetes Mellitus
Adult: **SC** 5–10 U 15–30 min a.c. and h.s. (dose adjustments based on blood glucose determinations)
Child: **SC** 2–4 U 15–30 min a.c. and h.s. (dose adjustments based on blood glucose determinations)

Ketoacidosis
Adult: **IV** 2.4–7.2 U loading dose, followed by 2.4–7.2 U/h continuous infusion
Child: **IV** 0.1 U/kg loading dose, followed by 0.1 U/h continuous infusion

ADMINISTRATION

Note: Insulins should not be mixed unless prescribed by physician. In general, regular insulin is drawn up into syringe first. Any change in the strength (e.g., U-40, U-100), brand (manufacturer), purity, type (regular, etc.), species (pork, human), or sequence of mixing two kinds of insulin is made by the physician only, since a simultaneous change in dosage may be necessary.

Subcutaneous
- Use an insulin syringe.
- Give regular insulin 30 min before a meal.
- Avoid injection of cold insulin; it can lead to lipodystrophy, reduced rate of absorption, and local reactions.
- Common injection sites: Upper arms, thighs, abdomen [avoid area over urinary bladder and 2 in. (5 cm) around navel], buttocks, and upper back (if fat is loose enough to pick up). Rotate sites.

Intravenous
PREPARE: **Direct:** Give undiluted. **Continuous:** Typically diluted in NS or 0.45% NaCl. 100 U added to 1000 mL yields 0.1 U/mL.
ADMINISTER: **Direct:** Give 50 U or a fraction thereof over 1 min. **Continuous:** Rate must be ordered by physician.

Common adverse effects in *italic*, life-threatening effects <u>underlined</u>; generic names in **bold**; classifications in SMALL CAPS; ✦ Canadian drug name; ⊙ Prototype drug

INCOMPATIBILITIES Solution/additive: **Aminophylline, amobarbital, chlorothiazide, cytarabine, dobutamine, pentobarbital, phenobarbital, phenytoin, secobarbital, sodium bicarbonate, thiopental.** Y-site: **Dobutamine.**

- Regular insulin may be adsorbed into the container or tubing when added to an IV infusion solution. Amount lost is variable and depends on concentration of insulin, infusion system, contact duration, and flow rate. - Monitor patient response closely.

- Insulin is stable at room temperature up to 1 mo. Avoid exposure to direct sunlight or to temperature extremes [safe range is wide: 5°–38° C (40°–100° F)]. Refrigerate but do not freeze stock supply. Insulin tolerates temperatures above 38° C with less harm than freezing.

ADVERSE EFFECTS (≥1%) **Body as a Whole:** Most adverse effects are related to hypoglycemia; <u>anaphylaxis</u> (rare), hyperinsulinemia (*profuse sweating,* hunger, headache, *nausea, tremulousness,* tremors, *palpitation,* tachycardia, weakness, fatigue, nystagmus, circumoral pallor); numb mouth, tongue, and other paresthesias; visual disturbances (diplopia, blurred vision, mydriasis), staring expression, confusion, personality changes, ataxia, incoherent speech, apprehension, irritability, inability to concentrate, personality changes, uncontrolled yawning, loss of consciousness, delirium, hypothermia, convulsions, Babinski reflex, <u>coma</u>. (Urine glucose tests will be negatives.) **CNS:** With overdose, psychic disturbances (i.e., aphasia, personality changes, maniacal behavior). **Metabolic:** Posthypoglyce-mia or rebound hyperglycemia (Somogyi effect), lipoatrophy and lipohypertrophy of injection sites; insulin resistance. **Skin:** Localized allergic reactions at injection site; generalized urticaria or bullae, lymphadenopathy.

DIAGNOSTIC TEST INTERFERENCE
Large doses of insulin may increase urinary excretion of *VMA.* Insulin can cause alterations in *thyroid function tests* and *liver function test* and may decrease *serum potassium* and *serum calcium.*

INTERACTIONS Drug: Alcohol, ANABOLIC STEROIDS, MAO INHIBITORS, **guanethidine,** SALICYLATES may potentiate hypoglycemic effects; **dextrothyroxine,** CORTICOSTEROIDS, **epinephrine** may antagonize hypoglycemic effects; **furosemide,** THIAZIDE DIURETICS increase **serum glucose** levels; **propranolol** and other BETA BLOCKERS may mask symptoms of hypoglycemic reaction. **Herbal:** Garlic, ginseng may potentiate hypoglycemic effects.

PHARMACOKINETICS Absorption: Rapidly absorbed from IM and SC injections. **Onset:** 0.5–1 h. **Peak:** 2–4 h. **Duration:** 5–7 h. **Distribution:** Throughout extracellular fluids. **Metabolism:** In liver with some metabolism in kidneys. **Elimination:** <2% excreted in urine. **Half-Life:** Biological, up to 13 h.

CLINICAL IMPLICATIONS
Assessment & Drug Effects
- Note: Frequency of blood glucose monitoring is determined by the type of insulin regimen and health status of the patient.
- Lab tests: Periodic postprandial blood glucose, and HbA$_{1C}$. Test urine for ketones in new, unstable, and type 1 diabetes; if patient has

---

Common adverse effects in *italic*, life-threatening effects <u>underlined</u>; generic names in **bold**; classifications in SMALL CAPS; ✚ Canadian drug name; ➋ Prototype drug

797

lost weight, exercises vigorously, or has an illness; whenever blood glucose is substantially elevated.

- Notify physician promptly for presence of acetone with sugar in the urine; may indicate onset of ketoacidosis. Acetone without sugar in the urine usually signifies insufficient carbohydrate intake.
- Monitor for hypoglycemia (see Appendix F) at time of peak action of insulin. Onset of hypoglycemia (blood sugar: 50–40 mg/dL) may be rapid and sudden.
- Check BP, I&O ratio, and blood glucose and ketones every hour during treatment for ketoacidosis with IV insulin.
- Give patients with severe hypoglycemia glucagon, epinephrine, or IV glucose 10–50%. As soon as patient is fully conscious, give oral carbohydrate (e.g., dilute corn syrup or orange juice with sugar, Gatorade, or Pedialyte) to prevent secondary hypoglycemia.

Patient & Family Education

- Learn correct injection technique.
- Inject insulin into the abdomen rather than a near muscle that will be heavily taxed, if engaged in active sports.
- Notify physician of local reactions at injection site; may develop 1–3 wk after therapy starts and last several hours to days, usually disappear with continued use.
- Do not change prescription lenses during early period of dosage regulation; vision stabilizes, usually 3–6 wk.
- Note: Hypoglycemia can result from excess insulin, insufficient food intake, vomiting, diarrhea, unaccustomed exercise, infection, illness, nervous or emotional tension, or overindulgence in alcohol.
- Respond promptly to beginning symptoms of hypoglycemia. Severe

hypoglycemia is an emergency situation. Take 4 oz (120 mL) of any fruit juice or regular carbonated beverage [1.5–3 oz (45–90 mL) for child] followed by a meal of longer-acting carbohydrate or protein food. Failure to show signs of recovery within 30 min indicates need for emergency treatment.

- Carry some form of fast-acting carbohydrate (e.g., lump sugar, Life-Savers, or other candy) at all times to treat hypoglycemia.
- Check blood glucose regularly during menstrual period; loss of diabetes control (hyperglycemia or hypoglycemia) is common; adjust insulin dosage accordingly, as prescribed by physician.
- Notify physician of S&S of diabetic ketoacidosis.
- Continue taking insulin during an illness, go to bed, and drink noncaloric liquids liberally (every hour if possible). Consult physician for insulin regulation if unable to eat prescribed diet.
- Avoid OTC medications unless approved by physician.

INSULIN, ISOPHANE (NPH)

(in'su-lin)
Humulin N, Novolin 70/30, Novolin N

Classifications: HORMONE; ANTIDIABETIC AGENT; INTERMEDIATE ACTING INSULIN
Therapeutic: ANTIDIABETIC; INSULIN INTERMEDIATE ACTING
Prototype: Insulin
Pregnancy Category: B

AVAILABILITY 100 units/mL

ACTION & *THERAPEUTIC EFFECT*
Intermediate-acting, cloudy suspension of zinc insulin crystals modified by protamine in a neutral buffer.

NPH Iletin II (pork), and Insulatard NPH are "purified" or "single component" insulins that have been purified and are less likely to cause allergic reactions than nonpurified preparations. Lowers blood glucose levels by increasing peripheral glucose uptake, especially by skeletal muscle and fat tissue, and by inhibiting the liver from changing glycogen to glucose. *Controls postprandial hyperglycemia, usually without supplemental doses of insulin injection.*

USES Used to control hyperglycemia in the diabetic patient. Mixtard and Novolin 70/30 are fixed combinations of purified regular insulin 30% and NPH 70%.

CONTRAINDICATIONS During episodes of hypoglycemia or in patients sensitive to any ingredient in the formulation; intravenous route; diabetic ketoacidosis; hyperosmolar hyperglycemic state.

CAUTIOUS USE In insulin-resistant patients, hyperthyroidism or hypothyroidism; fever; older adults, pregnancy (category B), renal or hepatic impairment; children.

ROUTE & DOSAGE

Diabetes Mellitus
Adult: **SC** Individualized doses (see INSULIN, REGULAR)

ADMINISTRATION

Subcutaneous
- Give isophane insulin 30 min before first meal of the day. If necessary, a second smaller dose may be prescribed 30 min before supper or at bedtime.
- Ensure complete dispersion by mixing thoroughly by gently rotating vial between palms and inverting it end to end several times. Do not shake.
- Do NOT mix insulins unless prescribed by physician. In general, when insulin injection (regular insulin) is to be combined, it is drawn first.
- Note: Isophane insulin may be mixed with insulin injection without altering either solution. Do NOT mix with Lente forms.
- Store unopened vial at 2°–8° C (36°–46° F). Avoid freezing and exposure to extremes in temperature or to direct sunlight.

ADVERSE EFFECTS (≥1%) (see INSULIN, REGULAR).

INTERACTIONS (see INSULIN, REGULAR).

PHARMACOKINETICS Onset: 1–2 h. **Peak:** 4–12 h NPH. **Duration:** 18–24 h NPH. **Metabolism:** In liver and kidney. **Elimination:** <2% excreted unchanged in urine. **Half-Life:** up to 13 h.

CLINICAL IMPLICATIONS
(see INSULIN, REGULAR)

Assessment & Drug Effects
- Suspect hypoglycemia if fatigue, weakness, sweating, tremor, or nervousness occur.

Patient & Family Education
- If insulin was given before breakfast, a hypoglycemic episode is most likely to occur between mid-afternoon and dinnertime, when insulin effect is peaking. Advise to eat a snack in mid-afternoon and to carry sugar or candy to treat a reaction. A snack at bedtime will prevent insulin reaction during the night.
- Learn the S&S of hypoglycemia and hyperglycemia (see Appendix F).

Common adverse effects in *italic*, life-threatening effects underlined; generic names in **bold**; classifications in SMALL CAPS; ✦ Canadian drug name; ⊘ Prototype drug

799

INSULIN LISPRO

(in'su-lin lis'pro)

Humalog

Classifications: HORMONE AND SYNTHETIC SUBSTITUTE; ANTIDIA-BETIC AGENT; INSULIN RAPID-ACTING

Therapeutic: ANTIDIABETIC; INSULIN RAPID-ACTING

Prototype: Insulin injection

Pregnancy Category: B

AVAILABILITY 100 units/mL

ACTION & *THERAPEUTIC EFFECT*
Insulin lispro of recombinant DNA origin is a human insulin that is a rapid-acting, glucose-lowering agent of shorter duration than human regular insulin. It lowers blood glucose levels by increasing peripheral glucose uptake, especially by skeletal muscle and fat tissue, and by inhibiting the liver from changing glycogen to glucose. *It lowers blood glucose levels and inhibits liver from changing glycogen to glucose.*

USES Treatment of diabetes mellitus.

CONTRAINDICATIONS During episodes of hypoglycemia or in patients sensitive to any ingredient in the formulation; intravenous administration.

CAUTIOUS USE In insulin-resistant patients, hyperthyroidism or hypothyroidism; older adults, renal or hepatic impairment; children, pregnancy (category B), lactation.

ROUTE & DOSAGE

Diabetes Mellitus (type 1)
Adult: **SC** 5–10 U 0–15 min a.c. (dose adjustments based on blood glucose determinations)

ADMINISTRATION

Subcutaneous
- Give 0–15 min before meals.
- Note: May be given in same syringe with longer-acting insulins but absorption may be delayed.

ADVERSE EFFECTS (≥1%) (see IN-SULIN INJECTIONS, REGULAR).

INTERACTIONS : (see INSULIN INJECTION, REGULAR).

PHARMACOKINETICS Absorption: Rapidly absorbed from IM and SC injection sites. **Onset:** <15 min. **Peak:** 0.5–1 h. **Duration:** 3–4 h. **Distribution:** Throughout extracellular fluids. **Metabolism:** Metabolized in liver with some metabolism in kidneys. **Elimination:** <2% excreted in urine. **Half-Life:** Biologic, up to 13 h.

CLINICAL IMPLICATIONS

(see INSULIN INJECTION, REGULAR)

Assessment & Drug Effects
- Assess for hypoglycemia from 1 to 3 h after injection.
- Assess highly insulin-dependent patients for need for increases in intermediate/long-acting insulins.

Patient & Family Education
- Note: Risk of hypoglycemia is greatest 1–3 h after injection.

INSULIN ZINC SUSPENSION (LENTE)

(in'su-lin)

Humulin L, Novolin L

Classifications: HORMONE; ANTI-DIABETIC AGENT; INSULIN INTERMEDI-ATE-ACTING

Therapeutic: ANTIDIABETIC; INSULIN INTERMEDIATE-ACTING

Prototype: Insulin injection

Pregnancy Category: B

AVAILABILITY 100 units/mL

ACTION & *THERAPEUTIC EFFECT*
Intermediate-acting human insulin created by adding zinc ions to human regular insulin. It lowers blood glucose levels by increasing peripheral glucose uptake, especially by skeletal muscle and fat tissue, and by inhibiting the liver from changing glycogen to glucose. It is not the ideal basal insulin since its absorption is variable. *It lowers glucose level over a longer period of time than regular human insulin.*

USES Hyperglycemia in diabetic patients allergic to other preparations of insulin. Also for patients with evidence of thrombotic phenomena in which protamine may be a factor.

CONTRAINDICATIONS During episodes of hypoglycemia or in patients sensitive to any ingredient in the formulation; insulin pump; intravenous administration; hyperosmolar hyperglycemic state; diabetic ketoacidosis.

CAUTIOUS USE In insulin resistant patients, hyperthyroidism or hypothyroidism; lactation, older adults, pregnancy (category B), renal or hepatic impairment; children.

ROUTE & DOSAGE

Diabetes Mellitus
Adult: **IM/SC** Individualized doses (see INSULIN INJECTION, REGULAR)

ADMINISTRATION

Subcutaneous, Intramuscular
- Give insulin zinc suspensions 30 min before breakfast. Some patients require another injection 30 min before supper time or at bedtime.

- Note: Zinc insulin preparation (Lente) is compatible with regular insulin.
- Ensure complete dispersion by mixing thoroughly by gently rotating the vial between the palms and by inverting it end-to-end several times. Do not shake.
- Note: Time of action of insulin zinc (Lente) approximates that of isophane insulin suspension (NPH) allowing patients usually to be transferred directly to the latter on a unit-for-unit basis.
- Store unopened vial at 2°–8° C (36°–46° F). Avoid freezing and exposure to extremes in temperature or to direct sunlight.

ADVERSE EFFECTS (≥1%) (see INSULIN INJECTION, REGULAR).

INTERACTIONS (see INSULIN INJECTION).

PHARMACOKINETICS Onset: 1–2 h. **Peak:** 8–12 h. **Duration:** 18–24 h. **Metabolism:** In liver and kidney. **Elimination:** <2% excreted unchanged in urine. **Half-Life:** Up to 13 h.

CLINICAL IMPLICATIONS
(see INSULIN INJECTION, REGULAR)

Patient & Family Education
- Be alert for S&S of hypoglycemia (see Appendix F); most apt to occur between mid-afternoon and dinner time (an early symptom may be a sense of extreme fatigue). Immediately take soluble carbohydrate (e.g., orange juice, honey). If the time between the midday and evening meal is prolonged, an afternoon snack may be needed.
- Do not overlook possibility of nocturnal hypoglycemia, especially during dose adjustment. Signs include restlessness or profuse sweating during sleep.

Common adverse effects in *italic*, life-threatening effects underlined; generic names in **bold**; classifications in SMALL CAPS; ✚ Canadian drug name; ⓟ Prototype drug

801

INTERFERON ALFA-2α ℗

(in-ter-feer′on)
Roferon-A Injection
Classifications: ANTINEOPLASTIC;
IMMUNOMODULATOR; INTERFERON
Therapeutic: ANTINEOPLASTIC; IMMU-
NOMODULATOR
Pregnancy Category: C

AVAILABILITY 3 million IU/mL, 6
million IU/mL, 9 million IU/mL.

ACTION & *THERAPEUTIC EFFECT*
Interferon (IFN) alfa-2a, one of 4
types of alpha interferons, is a
highly purified protein and natural
product of human leukocytes
within 4–6 h after viral stimulation.
Also produced by recombinant
DNA technology (rIFN-A). **Antiviral action:** Reprograms virus-infected cells to inhibit various stages
of virus replication. **Antitumor action:** Suppresses cell proliferation.
Immunomodulating action: Enhances phagocytic activity of macrophages and augments specific cytotoxicity of lymphocytes for target
cells. IFN is species specific but not
virus specific; it partially inhibits viral replication and is immediately
produced at site of viral entry by
any cell; thus, the immune system
and the interferon system of defense are complementary. *Has a
broad spectrum of antiviral, cytotoxic, and immunomodulating activity (i.e., favorably adjusts immune system to better combat
foreign invasion of antigens, cancers, and viruses).*

USES To induce hairy cell leukemia
remission in splenectomized and
non-splenectomized patients; treatment of hepatitis C, adjunct to surgery for malignant melanoma.
UNLABELED USES Chronic hepatitis B virus infection, solid tumors,
human papillomavirus (HPV)-
associated diseases, AIDS associated Kaposi's sarcoma.

CONTRAINDICATIONS Hypersensitivity to alpha interferons or any
component of product and to
mouse immunoglobulin; *E. coli*
protein hypersensitivity; history of
autoimmune disease; infants and
neonates; pregnancy (category C),
lactation.
CAUTIOUS USE Cardiac disease or
history of cardiac illness, severe
cardiac, renal, or hepatic disease;
depression or severe psychiatric
disorder, bipolar disorder; alcoholism; substance abuse; seizure disorders, compromised CNS function;
myelosuppression; chickenpox
(existing or recent, including recent
exposure), herpes zoster.

ROUTE & DOSAGE

Hairy Cell Leukemia
Adult: **SC/IM** 3 million U/d for
16–24 wk, may be reduced to 3
times/wk for maintenance therapy

AIDS-Related Kaposi's Sarcoma
Adult: **SC/IM** 36 million U/d for
10–12 wk, may then be reduced
to 3 times/wk

Genital and Anal Warts
Adult: **Intralesional** 1 million U
injected in each lesion 3 times/wk
on alternate days for 3 wk

Chronic Viral Hepatitis
Adult: **SC/IM** 1–3 million U/d for
1 wk, then 3 times/wk for 48–52
wk

ADMINISTRATION

Note: IFN should be administered
under the guidance of a qualified
physician.

Subcutaneous, Intramuscular

- Reconstitute by adding supplied diluent to the sterile powder vial.
- Use reconstituted solutions within 30 d. Inspect solution for particulate matter and discoloration before administration.
- Note: SC administration is recommended especially for patient who is at risk for bleeding (platelet count less than 50,000).
- Store sterile powder and its accompanying diluent, reconstituted solution, and injectable solution in refrigerator at 2°–8° C (36°–46° F). Do not freeze or shake solution.

ADVERSE EFFECTS (≥1%) **Body as a Whole:** *Flu-like syndrome (fever, chills, myalgia, headache).* **CNS:** *Fatigue, dizziness,* confusion, paresthesias, neutropenia, lethargy, psychosis, depression, nervousness, forgetfulness. **CV:** Dyspnea, edema, hypertension, palpitations. **GI:** *Nausea,* vomiting, *diarrhea, anorexia,* abdominal pain, change in taste, mild to moderate hepatotoxicity. **Hematologic:** Leukopenia, neutropenia, thrombocytopenia, <u>myelosuppression</u>. **Skin:** *Rash,* dry skin, pruritus, partial alopecia (eyelash growth increases), urticaria, reactivation of herpes labialis. **Respiratory:** Dryness or inflammation of oropharynx, *coughing.* **Other:** Transient impotence, arthralgia.

DIAGNOSTIC TEST INTERFERENCE
Decreased Hgb, Hct; elevated fasting blood sugar, serum phosphorus, serum creatinine, AST, ALT, alkaline phosphatase, LDH; hypocalcemia.

INTERACTIONS Drug: May increase **theophylline** levels; additive myelosuppression with ANTINEOPLASTICS, **zidovudine** may increase hematologic toxicity, increase **doxorubicin** toxicity, increase neurotoxicity with **vinblastine. Al-**

desleukin (IL-2) may potentiate the risk of renal failure.

PHARMACOKINETICS Absorption: Well absorbed after IM or SC injection. **Peak:** 15–60 min IV; 1–8 h IM. **Distribution:** Concentrating in spleen, kidney, liver, and lung. **Metabolism:** Principally in kidney. **Half-Life:** 5.1 h.

CLINICAL IMPLICATIONS

Assessment & Drug Effects

- Lab tests: Establish baseline data for CBC and platelet count, peripheral and bone marrow hairy cells, liver and renal function. Monitor monthly during treatment.
- Monitor I&O ratio and pattern. Patient should be well hydrated during early stages of treatment. Encourage increased intake to at least 2500 mL if tolerated.
- Be aware of potential side effects. If detected early, most are reversible.
- Note: Flu-like syndrome (fever, chills) occurs in most patients 2–6 h after a dose of IFN. Anorexia may persist after such an episode. Symptoms tend to lessen with continued therapy.
- Monitor for ecchymoses, petechiae, unexplained bleeding.
- Monitor BP, vital signs, and cardiac function. Older adults are particularly susceptible to cardiotoxicity.
- Monitor for gait difficulty, dizziness, and hypotension. Advise against hazardous activity until response to drug is known.
- Monitor for oral superinfection with *Candida albicans.* Alert physician if stomatitis (sore mouth with ulceration), gingivitis, or white patches on oropharyngeal membrane surfaces are evidenced.

Common adverse effects in *italic*, life-threatening effects <u>underlined</u>; generic names in **bold**; classifications in SMALL CAPS; ✤ Canadian drug name; ⊚ Prototype drug

803

Patient & Family Education

- Understand the risks of severe and even fatal adverse reactions as well as the benefits from IFN therapy.
- Learn to self-administer after therapy is well established. Read and keep handy patient information sheet about IFN.
- Avoid exposure to infection during nadir period.
- Follow up with careful periodic neuropsychiatric monitoring.
- Notify physician promptly if symptoms of infection develop (sore throat, fever, vomiting, diarrhea).
- Note: Fertile, nonpregnant women need to use effective contraception.
- Do not change brands of interferon alfa without first consulting the physician (because of risk of dosage change).

INTERFERON ALFA-2b

(in-ter-feer'on)

Intron A

Classifications: IMMUNOMODULATOR; INTERFERON; ANTINEOPLASTIC
Therapeutic: IMMUNOMODULATOR; INTERFERON; ANTINEOPLASTIC
Prototype: Interferon alfa-2a
Pregnancy Category: C

AVAILABILITY 5 million IU, 10 million IU, 18 million IU, 25 million IU, 50 million IU vials

ACTION & *THERAPEUTIC EFFECT*
Interferon (IFN) alfa-2b, one of 4 types of alpha interferons, is a highly purified protein and natural product of human leukocytes within 4–6 h after viral stimulation. Produced by recombinant DNA technology (rIFN-A). **Antiviral action:** Reprograms virus-infected cells to inhibit various stages of virus replication. **Antitumor action:** Suppresses cell proliferation. **Immunomodulating action:** Enhances phagocytic activity of macrophages and augments specific cytotoxicity of lymphocytes for target cells. The immune system and the interferon system of defense are complementary. *Has a broad spectrum of antiviral, cytotoxic, and immunomodulating activity (i.e., favorably adjusts immune system to better combat foreign invasion of antigens, cancers, and viruses).*

USES Hairy cell leukemia in splenectomized and non-splenectomized patients ≥18 y, chronic hepatitis B or C, malignant melanoma, condylomata acuminata, AIDS-related Kaposi's sarcoma.
UNLABELED USES Multiple sclerosis, condylomata acuminata.

CONTRAINDICATIONS Hypersensitivity to interferon alfa-2b or to any components of the product; colitis; pancreatitis; neonates, pregnancy (category C), lactation.
CAUTIOUS USE Severe, preexisting cardiac, renal, or hepatic disease; pulmonary disease (e.g., COPD); diabetes mellitus patients prone to ketoacidosis; coagulation disorders; severe myelosuppression; recent MI; previous dysrhythmias.

ROUTE & DOSAGE

Hairy Cell Leukemia
Adult: **IM/SC** 2 million U/m² 3 times/wk

Kaposi's Sarcoma
Adult: **IM/SC** 30 million U/m² 3 times/wk

Condylomata Acuminata
Adult: **IM/SC** 1 million U/m² 3 times/wk

Chronic Hepatitis B or C

Adult: **SC** 3 million U 3 times/wk x 18–24 mo

Malignant Melanoma

Adult: **IV** 20 million IU/m² daily for 5 d per wk x 4 wk; maintenance dose is 10 million IU/m² given SC weekly x 48 wk

Renal Impairment

Not removed by dialysis.

ADMINISTRATION

Note: Interferon alfa-2b should be administered under the guidance of a qualified physician.

Subcutaneous, Intramuscular

- Reconstitution: The final concentration with the amount of required diluent is determined by the condition being treated (see manufacturer's directions). Inject diluent (bacteriostatic water for injection) into interferon alfa-2b vial; gently agitate solution before withdrawing dose with a sterile syringe.
- Make sure reconstituted solution is clear and colorless to light yellow and free of particulate material; discard if there are particles or solution is discolored.
- Store vials and reconstituted solutions at 2°–8° C (36°–46° F); remains stable for 1 mo.

ADVERSE EFFECTS (≥1%) **Body as a Whole:** *Flu-like syndrome (fever, chills) associated with myalgia and arthralgia,* leg cramps. **CNS:** Depression, nervousness, anxiety, confusion, *dizziness, fatigue,* somnolence, insomnia, altered mental states, ataxia, tremor, paresthesias, *headache.* **CV:** Hypertension, dyspnea, *hot flushes.* **Special Senses:** Epistaxis, pharyngitis, sneezing; abnormal vision. **GI:** Taste alteration, *anorexia,* weight loss, *nausea,* vomiting, stomatitis, *diarrhea,* flatulence. **Hematologic:** Mild thrombocytopenia, transient granulocytopenia, anemia, *neutropenia,* leukemia. **Skin:** Mild pruritus, mild alopecia, rash, dry skin, herpetic eruptions, nonherpetic cold sores, urticaria.

INTERACTIONS Drug: May increase **theophylline** levels; additive myelosuppression with ANTINEOPLASTICS, **zidovudine** may increase hematologic toxicity, increase **doxorubicin** toxicity, increase neurotoxicity with **vinblastine.** Use with **ribavirin** increases risk of hemolytic anemia; do not use in combination with **ribavirin** if Cl$_{cr}$ <50 mL/min.

PHARMACOKINETICS Peak: 6–8 h. **Metabolism:** In kidneys. **Half-Life:** 6–7 h.

CLINICAL IMPLICATIONS
(see INTERFERON ALFA-2A)

Assessment & Drug Effects

- Assess hydration status; patient should be well hydrated, especially during initial stage of treatment and if vomiting or diarrhea occurs.
- Lab tests: Closely monitor CBC with differential and platelet counts.
- Monitor for ecchymoses, petechiae, and bruising.
- Assess for flu-like symptoms, which may be relieved by acetaminophen (if prescribed).
- Monitor level of GI distress and ability to consume fluids and food.
- Monitor mental status and alertness; implement safety precautions if needed.

Patient & Family Education

- Learn techniques for reconstitution and administration of drug.

Common adverse effects in *italic*, life-threatening effects <u>underlined</u>; generic names in **bold**; classifications in SMALL CAPS; ♣ Canadian drug name; ⊘ Prototype drug

805

- Do NOT change brands of interferon without first consulting the physician.
- Note: If flu-like symptoms develop, take acetaminophen as advised by physician and take interferon at bedtime.
- Note: Fertile, nonpregnant women need to use effective contraception.
- Use caution with hazardous activities until response to drug is known.
- Learn about adverse effects and notify physician about those that cause significant discomfort.

INTERFERON ALFACON-1

(in-ter-fer'on al'fa-con)
Infergen
Classifications: IMMUNOMODULATOR; ANTIVIRAL; INTERFERON
Therapeutic: ANTIVIRAL; INTERFERON
Prototype: Interferon alfa-2a
Pregnancy Category: C

AVAILABILITY 9 mcg, 15 mcg injection

ACTION & *THERAPEUTIC EFFECT*
DNA recombinant Type 1 interferon. Its antiviral, antiproliferative, and natural killer (NK) cell activity is five times greater than interferon alpha-2a or interferon alpha-2b. *Effectiveness is measured by normalization of ALT level and serum HCV RNA <100 copies/mL. Type 1 interferons bind to the cell surface receptors inducing biologic responses including antiviral, antiproliferative, and immunomodulatory activities.*

USES Treatment of chronic hepatitis C.

CONTRAINDICATIONS Hypersensitivity to alpha interferons or *E. coli* products; patients with decompensated liver disease such as jaundice, ascites, etc.; pregnancy (category C), lactation, children <18 y.

CAUTIOUS USE History of severe psychiatric disorder, depression, or suicidal ideation; preexisting cardiac disease, myelosuppression, previous hypersensitivity to interferon therapy; history of endocrine disorders; ophthalmic disorders or autoimmune disorders.

ROUTE & DOSAGE

Chronic Hepatitis C
Adult: **SC** 9 mcg 3 times/wk times 24 wk

ADMINISTRATION

Subcutaneous
- Allow at least 24 h to elapse between doses of interferon alfacon-1.
- Give only one dose per vial or per prefilled syringe. Enter each vial only once. Discard unused portion of a vial or prefilled syringe immediately.
- Initiate treatment only if acceptable baseline lab values are obtained: Platelet count $\geq 75 \times 10^9$/L, Hgb ≥ 100 g/L, ANC $\geq 1500 \times 10^6$/L, serum creatinine <2.0 mg/dL, serum albumin ≥ 25 g/L, bilirubin WNL, TSH, and T_4 WNL.
- Store vials and syringes at 2°–8° C (36°–46° F). Avoid direct sunlight and vigorous shaking.

ADVERSE EFFECTS (≥1%) **Body as a Whole:** *Asthenia, headache, fatigue, fever, chills, injection site reaction (pain, edema, hemorrhage, inflammation), pain, myalgia, arthralgia,* increased sweating. **CNS:** *Insomnia, depression, dizziness, paresthesia nervousness, depression, anxiety,* agitation. **CV:** Hypertension, palpitation. **GI:** *Nausea, diarrhea, abdominal pain, anorexia, vomiting, dyspepsia,* constipation, flatulence, toothache, hemorrhoids, weight loss, hepatotoxicity. **Hematologic:** *Granulocytopenia, thrombocytopenia, leukopenia,* ecchymosis, lymphadenopathy, lymphocytosis. **Respiratory:** *Cough, bronchitis, dyspnea, pneumonia, rhinitis,* pharyngitis. **Skin:** *Alopecia, rash,* dry skin, *pruritus,* erythema. **Urogenital:** Dysmenorrhea, vaginitis, menstrual disorder.

INTERACTIONS No clinically significant interactions established.

PHARMACOKINETICS Peak: 24–36 h.

CLINICAL IMPLICATIONS

Assessment & Drug Effects
- Monitor for and report any of the following S&S immediately: Depression, suicidal ideation, suicide attempt, or other indications of psychiatric disturbance.
- Withhold drug and notify physician if symptoms of hepatic decompensation such as jaundice or ascites develop. Withhold drug and notify physician if any other severe adverse reaction occurs.
- Lab tests: Baseline, 2 wk after initiation of therapy, and periodically thereafter: platelet count, Hgb and Hct, WBC and ANC, serum creatinine, serum albumin, bilirubin, thyroid function, and triglyceride; periodic ALT to determine liver functions.

Patient & Family Education
- Report immediately any signs of psychiatric disturbance including depression, thoughts of suicide, nervousness, anxiety, agitation, apathy, or significant mood swings to physician.

INTERFERON BETA-1a

(in-ter-fer′on)

Avonex, Rebif

Classifications: IMMUNOMODULATOR; INTERFERON

Therapeutic: IMMUNOMODULATOR; INTERFERON

Prototype: Interferon alfa-2a

Pregnancy Category: C

AVAILABILITY Avonex 33 mcg vial; 30 mcg/5 mL prefilled syringe; **Rebif** 22 mcg, 44 mcg vial

ACTION & *THERAPEUTIC EFFECT*
Interferon beta-1a is produced by recombinant DNA technology. Interferon beta-1a inhibits expression of pro-inflammatory cytokines including INF-G, thought to be a major factor in triggering the autoimmune reaction that leads to multiple sclerosis. It is believed that INF-G stimulates cytotoxic T-cells and causes degradation by macrophages' enzymes on the myelin sheath of neurons in the spinal cord. *The mechanisms by which interferon beta-1a exerts its effect on multiple sclerosis is not fully defined; however, time of onset of progression in disability was significantly longer in patients treated with interferon beta-1a.*

USES Relapsing-remitting multiple sclerosis.

CONTRAINDICATIONS Previous hypersensitivity to interferon beta or human albumin, albumin hypersensitivity, hamster protein hypersensitivity; pregnancy (category C) but may cause a spontaneous abortion, lactation.

CAUTIOUS USE Suicidal tendencies, depression, preexisting psychiatric disorders; bone marrow depression; cardiac disease; seizure

Common adverse effects in *italic*, life-threatening effects underlined; generic names in **bold**; classifications in SMALL CAPS; ♣ Canadian drug name; ⊙ Prototype drug

807

disorders; thyroid disease; hepatic impairment. Safety and efficacy in children <18 y are not established.

ROUTE & DOSAGE

Multiple Sclerosis

Adult: **IM Avonex** 30 mcg qwk
SC Rebif 44 mcg 3 times/wk

ADMINISTRATION

Intramuscular

- Avonex: Reconstitute single use Avonex vial (33 mcg of lyophilized powder) with 1.1 mL of supplied diluent and swirl gently to dissolve. Withdraw 1.0 mL for administration. Discard any residual drug as the product contains no preservatives.
- Use within 6 h of reconstitution.

Subcutaneous

- Rebif: Give at the same time each day (preferably in the late afternoon or evening) on the same three days of the week at least 48 h apart each week. Dose is usually titrated up from 8.8 mcg to 44 mcg three times a week over a 4-wk period.
- Inject SC using either a 22 or 44 mcg prefilled syringe. Discard any residual drug as the product contains no preservatives.
- Store unreconstituted vials or prefilled syringes at 2°–8° C (36°–46° F). May store for ≤30 d at room temperature up to 25° C (77° F). Do not use beyond expiration date.

ADVERSE EFFECTS (≥1%) **Body as a Whole:** Alopecia, myalgias, *flu-like syndrome,* anaphylaxis. **CNS:** Headache, *fever,* fatigue, lethargy, depression, somnolence, weakness, agitation, malaise, confusion or reduced ability to concentrate, anxiety, dementia, emotional lability, depersonalization, suicide attempts,

worsening of psychiatric disorders. **CV:** Tachycardia, CHF (rare). **GI:** Nausea, vomiting, *diarrhea, hepatic injury.* **Hematologic:** *Leukopenia, thrombocytopenia,* anemia, pancytopenia (rare), thrombocytopenia (rare). **Metabolic:** Hypocalcemia, elevated serum creatinine, elevated liver transaminases. **Skin:** Local skin necrosis at injection site, *pain at injection site.*

PHARMACOKINETICS Peak: Avonex 7.8–9.8 h; **Rebif** 16 h. **Metabolism:** Rapidly inactivated in body fluids and tissue. **Half-Life:** Avonex 8.6–10 h; **Rebif** 69 h.

CLINICAL IMPLICATIONS

Assessment & Drug Effects

- Withhold drug and notify physician if depression or suicidal ideation develops or if there is a worsening of psychiatric symptoms.
- Monitor patients with cardiac disease carefully for worsening cardiac function.
- Lab tests: Monitor periodically liver function tests, renal function tests, routine blood chemistry, and CBC with differential, and platelet count. Monitor thyroid function tests q6mo with preexisting thyroid dysfunction or when clinically indicated.

Patient & Family Education

- Take a missed dose as soon as possible but not within 48 h of next scheduled dose.
- Learn about common adverse effects, especially flu-like syndrome (headache, fatigue, fever, rigors, chest pain, back pain, myalgia).
- Withhold drug and notify physician of depression or suicidal ideation or exacerbation of a preexisting seizure disorder.
- Note: Women who wish to become pregnant must discontinue therapy.

INTERFERON BETA-1b

(in-ter-fer'on)
Betaseron
Classifications: IMMUNOMODULA-
TOR; INTERFERON; ANTINEOPLASTIC
Therapeutic: IMMUNOMODULATOR;
INTERFERON
Prototype: Interferon alfa-2a
Pregnancy Category: C

AVAILABILITY 0.3 mg vial

ACTION & *THERAPEUTIC EFFECT*
Interferon beta-1b is a glycoprotein
produced by recombinant DNA
techniques using a strain of *E. coli.*
Both natural and recombinant DNA
interferon beta-1b possess antiviral,
antiproliferative, antitumor, and im-
munomodulatory activity. The effec-
tiveness of interferon beta-1b for
multiple sclerosis (MS) is based on
the assumption that MS is an immu-
nologically mediated illness.

USES Relapsing and relapsing-
remitting multiple sclerosis.
UNLABELED USES AIDS, AIDS-
related Kaposi's sarcoma, metastatic renal cell carcinoma, malignant melanoma, cutaneous T-cell
lymphoma, acute hepatitis C.

CONTRAINDICATIONS Previous hypersensitivity to interferon beta-1b
or human albumin, mannitol hypersensitivity; pregnancy (category
C) but may cause a spontaneous
abortion, lactation.
CAUTIOUS USE Suicidal/mental disorders especially chronic depression; seizures; cardiac disease.
Safety and efficacy in children <18
y are not established.

ROUTE & DOSAGE

Multiple Sclerosis
Adult: SC 0.25 mg (8 million IU)
q.o.d.

ADMINISTRATION

Subcutaneous
- Reconstitute by adding 1.2 mL of
  the supplied diluent (0.54%
  NaCl) to vial and gently swirl. Do
  NOT shake. The resultant solution
  contains 0.25 mg (8 million
  units)/mL.
- Discard reconstituted solution if it
  contains particulate matter or is
  discolored. Also discard unused
  solution.
- Rotate injection sites; use 27-gauge
  needle to administer drug.
- Store vials under refrigeration, 2°–
  8° C (36°–46° F) or at room temperature.

ADVERSE EFFECTS (≥1%) **CNS:**
Headache, *fever,* fatigue, dizziness,
lethargy, depression, somnolence,
weakness, agitation, malaise, confusion or reduced ability to concentrate, anxiety, dementia, emotional
lability, depersonalization, suicide
attempts. **CV:** Tachycardia, peripheral
edema, CHF (rare). **GI:** Nausea,
vomiting, *diarrhea.* **Hematologic:**
Leukopenia, thrombocytopenia,
anemia. **Metabolic:** Hypocalcemia,
elevated serum creatinine, elevated liver transaminases, autoimmune hepatitis, hepatic failure.
Skin: Local skin necrosis at injection
site, rash, *pain at injection site.*
Body as a Whole: Alopecia, myalgias, *flu-like syndrome.*

INTERACTIONS Drug: Zidovudine
(AZT) levels are increased, resulting
in toxicity.

PHARMACOKINETICS Absorption:
About 50% absorbed from SC
sites. **Distribution:** Penetrates intact blood–brain barrier poorly;
crosses placenta; distributed into
breast milk. **Metabolism:** Rapidly
inactivated in body fluids and tissue.

Common adverse effects in *italic*, life-threatening effects underlined; generic names
in **bold**; classifications in SMALL CAPS; ♣ Canadian drug name; ☻ Prototype drug

809

CLINICAL IMPLICATIONS

Assessment & Drug Effects

- Monitor vital signs, neurologic status, and neuropsychiatric status frequently during therapy.
- Lab tests: Monitor liver function at 1, 3, and 6 mo after initiation of therapy and as clinically warranted thereafter; monitor renal function, complete blood counts, and serum electrolytes periodically.
- Assess for and promptly treat flu-like symptom complex (fever, chills, myalgia, etc.).
- Assess injection sites; pain and redness are common reactions. Report tissue ulceration promptly.

Patient & Family Education

- Learn and understand potential adverse drug reactions.
- Learn proper technique for solution preparation and injection.
- Self-medicate with acetaminophen (if not contraindicated) if flu-like symptom complex develops.
- Avoid prolonged exposure to sunlight.
- Use caution when performing hazardous activities until response to drug is known.

INTERFERON GAMMA-1b

(in-ter-feer'on)

Actimmune

Classifications: IMMUNOMODULATOR; INTERFERON; ANTINEOPLASTIC
Therapeutic: IMMUNOMODULATOR; INTERFERON; ANTINEOPLASTIC
Prototype: Interferon alfa-2a
Pregnancy Category: C

AVAILABILITY 100 mcg (2 million IU)/0.5 mL vial

ACTION & *THERAPEUTIC EFFECT*
Antiviral: Has potent phagocyte-activating effects that include stimulating macrophages and generation of toxic oxygen metabolites (i.e., free radicals) capable of destroying virally infected cells. **Antineoplastic:** It also exerts antitumor effects by increasing expression of tumor suppressor genes and activating macrophages to lyse tumor cells. **Immunomodulatory:** Interferon gamma is produced by T-cells and natural killer (NK) cells after activation with immune or inflammatory stimuli. Interferon gamma stimulates macrophages to increase IL-12 and TNF-alpha production, which enhances interferon gamma synthesis. Interleukin-10 down-regulates interferon gamma production by NK and T-cells by preventing macrophage secretion of IL-12 and TNF-alpha. *Is a naturally occurring cytokine with antiviral, immunomodulatory, and antiproliferative activity. It enhances phagocyte function in chronic granulomatous disease and improves killing of viruses; also enhances osteoclast function in malignant osteopetrosis.*

USES Chronic granulomatous disease, severe malignant osteopetrosis
UNLABELED USES Idiopathic pulmonary fibrosis, refractory mycobacterium infection, ovarian cancer.

CONTRAINDICATIONS Hypersensitivity to interferon gamma or products derived from *E. coli;* pregnancy (category C); lactation.
CAUTIOUS USE Preexisting cardiac disease, CHF, cardiac arrhythmias; seizure disorders and compromised CNS function; myelosuppression. Safety and efficacy in infants <1 y are not established.

Common adverse effects in *italic*, life-threatening effects <u>underlined</u>; generic names in **bold**; classifications in SMALL CAPS; ♣ Canadian drug name; ⊙ Prototype drug

ROUTE & DOSAGE

Chronic Granulomatous Disease, Osteopetrosis
Adult/Child: SC BSA ≥0.5 m^2 50 mcg/m^2 3 times weekly
Adult/Child: SC BSA ≤0.5 m^2 1.5 mcg/kg 3 times weekly

Idiopathic Pulmonary Fibrosis
Adult: SC 180–200 mcg 3 times weekly

ADMINISTRATION

▪ Note: Pretreatment (4 h before) with acetaminophen is recommended to reduce headache, myalgia, and fever. Treatment should be continued 24 h postinjection.

Subcutaneous
▪ Do not shake vial. Inject SC undiluted into right or left deltoid area or anterior thigh area
▪ Avoid intradermal or IV injection. Rotate injection sites.
▪ Store 2°–8° C (36°–46° F); do not freeze. Discard any unused portions or any vial left at room temperature for >12 h.

ADVERSE EFFECTS (≥1%) **Body as a Whole:** *Fever, fatigue, chills,* myalgia, arthralgia, night sweats. **CNS:** *Headache,* altered mental status, ataxia, confusion, dizziness, Parkinsonian symptoms, disorientation, seizures, hallucinations. **CV:** Heart block, heart failure, DVT, hypotension, MI, syncope, tachyarrhythmia. **GI:** *Nausea, vomiting, diarrhea.* **Hematologic:** *Leukopenia, thrombocytopenia.* **Respiratory:** Bronchospasm, interstitial pneumonitis, pulmonary embolism, tachypnea. **Skin:** Local skin necrosis at injection site, *pain at injection site, rash.* **Urogenital:** Reversible renal insufficiency.

INTERACTIONS Drug: Use cautiously with **amiophylline, fosphenytoin, phenytoin, theophylline, warfarin.**

PHARMACOKINETICS Absorption: 90% absorbed from SC site. **Peak:** 7 h. **Half-Life:** 5.9 h.

CLINICAL IMPLICATIONS

Assessment & Drug Effects
▪ Monitor CV status frequently. Report promptly severe hypotension and/or syncope.
▪ Monitor for and report S&S of infection.
▪ Lab tests: Baseline and at 3 mo CBC with differential and platelet counts; complete blood chemistry (including renal and liver function tests), and urinalysis.

Patient & Family Education
▪ Report promptly: skin rash, itching, unusual weakness or tiredness, chest pain or palpitations, or signs of an infection.
▪ Do not accept vaccination with a live vaccine during or for 3 mo following the end of therapy.

IODOQUINOL
(eye-oh-do-kwin′ole)
Diiodohydroxyquin, Yodoxin
Classifications: AMEBICIDE; ANTIPROTOZOAL
Therapeutic: ANTIPROTOZOAL; AMEBICIDE
Prototype: Emetine
Pregnancy Category: C

AVAILABILITY 210 mg, 650 mg tablets

ACTION & *THERAPEUTIC EFFECT*
Direct-acting (contact) amebicide. *Effective against both trophozoites and cyst forms of* Entamoeba his-

---

Common adverse effects in *italic*, life-threatening effects <u>underlined</u>; generic names in **bold**; classifications in SMALL CAPS; ♣ Canadian drug name; ⊙ Prototype drug

811

tolytica *in intestinal lumen. Not useful for extraintestinal amebiasis.*

USES Intestinal amebiasis and for asymptomatic passers of cysts. Commonly used either concurrently or in alternating courses with another intestinal amebicide.

UNLABELED USES *Balantidiasis* and *Acrodermatitis enteropathica;* traveler's diarrhea; shampoo preparation (Sebaquin) used for control of seborrheic dermatitis of scalp.

CONTRAINDICATIONS Hypersensitivity to any 8-hydroxyquinoline or to iodine-containing preparations or foods; hepatic or renal damage; pregnancy (category C).

CAUTIOUS USE Severe thyroid disease; minor self-limiting problems; prolonged high-dosage therapy; pre-existing optic neuropathy; lactation.

ROUTE & DOSAGE

Intestinal Amebiasis

Adult: **PO** 650 mg t.i.d. for 20 d (max: 2 g/d); may repeat after a 2–3 wk drug-free interval
Child: **PO** 30–40 mg/kg/d in 2–3 divided doses for 20 d (max: 1.95 g/d); may repeat after a 2–3 wk drug-free interval

ADMINISTRATION

Oral
- Give drug after meals. If patient has difficulty swallowing tablet, crush and mix with applesauce.

ADVERSE EFFECTS (≥1%) **Body as a Whole:** Hypersensitivity (urticaria, pruritus). **CNS:** Headache, agitation, retrograde amnesia, vertigo, ataxia, peripheral neuropathy (especially in children); muscle pain, weakness usually below T_{12} vertebrae, dysesthesias especially of lower limbs, paresthesias, increased sense of warmth. **Special Senses:** Blurred vision, <u>optic atrophy</u>, optic neuritis, <u>permanent loss of vision</u>. **GI:** Nausea, vomiting, anorexia, abdominal cramps, diarrhea, constipation, rectal irritation and itching. **Skin:** Discoloration of hair and nails, acne, hair loss, urticaria, various forms of skin eruptions. **Hematologic:** <u>Agranulocytosis</u> (rare). **Endocrine:** Thyroid hypertrophy, iodism [generalized furunculosis (iodine toxiderma), skin eruptions, fever, chills, weakness].

DIAGNOSTIC TEST INTERFERENCE Iodoquinol can cause elevations of **PBI** and decrease of **I-131 uptake** (effects may last for several weeks to 6 mo even after discontinuation of therapy). **Ferric chloride test for PKU** (phenylketonuria) may yield false-positive results if iodoquinol is present in urine.

PHARMACOKINETICS Absorption: Small amount from GI tract. **Elimination:** In feces.

CLINICAL IMPLICATIONS

Assessment & Drug Effects
- Monitor I&O ratio. Record characteristics of stools: color, consistency, frequency, presence of blood, mucus, or other material.
- Note: ophthalmologic examinations are recommended at regular intervals during prolonged therapy.
- Monitor and report immediately the onset of blurred or decreased vision or eye pain. Also report symptoms of peripheral neuropathy: pain, numbness, tingling, or weakness of extremities.

Patient & Family Education
- Report skin rash and symptoms of agranulocytosis (see Appendix F).
- Complete full course of treatment. Stool needs be examined again 1,

3, and 6 mo after termination of treatment.

- Note: Intestinal amebiasis is spread mainly by contaminated water, raw fruits or vegetables, flies, roaches, and hand-to-mouth transfer of infected feces. It is very important to wash hands after defecation and before eating.

IPECAC SYRUP

(ip′e-kak)

Ipecac Syrup

Classifications: EMETIC
Therapeutic: EMETIC
Pregnancy Category: C

AVAILABILITY 15 mL, 30 mL doses

ACTION & *THERAPEUTIC EFFECT*
Derived from dried roots of *Cephaelis ipecacuanha*. Contains cephaeline (produces emesis) and emetine, a toxic alkaloid that is excreted slowly from the body. Emetine can cause potentially fatal cumulative toxicity with repeated use. It appears to inhibit protein synthesis and energy production in muscle tissue with resultant skeletal and cardiac muscle toxicity. *Acts locally on gastric mucosa and centrally on chemoreceptor trigger zone (CTZ) in the medulla to induce vomiting.*

USES Emergency emetic to remove unabsorbed ingested poisons.

CONTRAINDICATIONS Comatose, semicomatose, inebriated, deeply sedated patients; patients in shock; patients with depressed gag reflex; seizures, active or impending; treatment of ingested strong alkali, acids, or other corrosives; strychnine, petroleum distillates, volatile oils, or rapid-acting CNS depressants; pregnancy (category C), lactation, infants <6 mo

CAUTIOUS USE Impaired cardiac function; elderly; arteriosclerosis; cerebovascular disease; head trauma.

ROUTE & DOSAGE

Emergency Emesis

Adult: **PO** 30 mL followed by 1–2 240 mL (8 oz) glasses of water, may repeat once in 20 min if necessary
Child: **PO** >1 y, 15 mL followed by 1–2 240 mL (8 oz) glasses of water, may repeat once in 20 min if necessary; <1 y, 5–10 mL followed by 120–240 mL (4–8 oz) of water, may repeat once in 20 min if necessary

ADMINISTRATION

Oral

- Do not confuse with ipecac fluid extract, which is 14 times stronger and has caused deaths when mistakenly given at the same dosage as ipecac syrup.
- Do not induce vomiting if victim is unconscious, semiconscious, or convulsing.
- Store in tight containers at temperature not exceeding 25° C (77° F).

ADVERSE EFFECTS (≥1%) **Body as a Whole:** Achy, stiff muscles, severe myopathy, convulsions, <u>coma</u>. **CV:** <u>Cardiomyopathy, cardiotoxicity</u>, cardiac arrhythmias, atrial fibrillation, tachycardia, chest pain, dyspnea, hypotension, <u>fatal myocarditis</u>. **GI:** Diarrhea, mild GI upset. If drug is not vomited but absorbed or if ipecac overdosage: *persistent vomiting*, gastroenteritis, bloody diarrhea, sensory disturbances, stomach cramps, tremor.

Common adverse effects in *italic*, life-threatening effects <u>underlined</u>; generic names in **bold**; classifications in SMALL CAPS; ♣ Canadian drug name; ⊘ Prototype drug

813

PHARMACOKINETICS Onset: 15–30 min. **Duration:** 25 min. **Elimination:** Metabolite can be detected in urine up to 60 d after excessive doses.

CLINICAL IMPLICATIONS

Assessment & Drug Effects

- Note: Emetic effect occurs in 15–30 min and continues for 20–25 min. If vomiting does not occur in 20–30 min, repeat dose once.
- Contact physician immediately if vomiting does not occur within 15–20 min after a second dose. Dosage should be recovered by gastric lavage and activated charcoal if necessary.
- Note: Ipecac syrup can be cardiotoxic if not vomited and allowed to be absorbed.
- Report immediately to physician if vomiting persists longer than 2–3 h after ipecac syrup is given.

Patient & Family Education

- Call an emergency room, poison control center, or physician before using ipecac syrup.

IPRATROPIUM BROMIDE ℗

(i-pra-troe′pee-um)
Atrovent, Atrovent HFA
Classifications: ANTICHOLINERGIC; ANTIMUSCARINIC; BRONCHODILATOR
Therapeutic: BRONCHODILATOR
Pregnancy Category: B

AVAILABILITY 0.02% solution for inhalation; 18 mcg inhaler; 0.03%, 0.06% nasal spray

ACTION & *THERAPEUTIC EFFECT*

Results in bronchodilation by inhibiting acetylcholine at its receptor sites, thereby blocking cholinergic bronchomotor tone (bronchoconstriction); also abolishes vagally mediated reflex bronchospasm triggered by such nonspecific agents as cigarette smoke, inert dusts, cold air, and a range of inflammatory mediators (e.g., histamine). *Produces local, site-specific effects on the larger central airways including bronchodilation and prevention of bronchospasms.*

USES Maintenance therapy in COPD including chronic bronchitis and emphysema; nasal spray for perennial rhinitis and symptomatic relief of rhinorrhea associated with the common cold.
UNLABELED USES Perennial nonallergic rhinitis.

CONTRAINDICATIONS Use as primary treatment for acute episodes; hypersensitivity to atropine, bromides, peanut oils, soy lecithin. Safe use in children ≤3 y (inhalation) or ≤5 y (intranasal) is not established.
CAUTIOUS USE Pregnancy (category B), narrow-angle glaucoma; prostatic hypertrophy, bladder neck obstruction.

ROUTE & DOSAGE

COPD

Adult: **Inhalation** 2 inhalations of MDI q.i.d. at no less than 4 h intervals (max: 12 inhalations in 24 h) **Nebulizer** 500 mcg (1 unit dose vial) q6–8h
Child: **Inhalation** 3–12 y, 1–2 inhalations t.i.d. (max: 6/d) **Nebulizer** 125–250 mcg t.i.d.

Rhinitis

Adult: **Intranasal** ≥5 y, 2 sprays of 0.03% each nostril b.i.d. or t.i.d.

Common Cold

Adult: **Intranasal** 2 sprays of 0.06% each nostril t.i.d. or q.i.d. up to 4 d

ADMINISTRATION

Intranasal, Inhalation, Nebulizer

- Demonstrate aerosol use and check return demonstration.
- Wait 3 min between inhalations if more than one inhalation per dose is ordered.
- Avoid contact with eyes.

ADVERSE EFFECTS (≥1%) **Special Senses:** Blurred vision (especially if sprayed into eye), difficulty in accommodation, acute eye pain, worsening of narrow-angle glaucoma. **GI:** Bitter taste, dry oropharyngeal membranes. With higher doses: nausea, constipation. **Respiratory:** *Cough,* hoarseness, exacerbation of symptoms, drying of bronchial secretions, mucosal ulcers, epistaxis, nasal dryness. **Skin:** Rash, hives. **Urogenital:** Urinary retention. **CNS:** Headache.

PHARMACOKINETICS Absorption: 10% of inhaled dose reaches lower airway; approximately 0.5% of dose is systemically absorbed. **Peak:** 1.5–2 h. **Duration:** 4–6 h. **Elimination:** 48% of dose excreted in feces; <5% excreted in urine. **Half-Life:** 1.5–2 h.

CLINICAL IMPLICATIONS

Assessment & Drug Effects

- Monitor respiratory status; auscultate lungs before and after inhalation.
- Report treatment failure (exacerbation of respiratory symptoms) to physician.

Patient & Family Education

- Note: This medication is not an emergency agent because of its delayed onset and the time required to reach peak bronchodilation.
- Review patient information sheet on proper use of nasal spray.
- Allow 30–60 sec between puffs for optimum results. Do not let medication contact your eyes.

- Wait 5 min between this and other inhaled medications. Check with physician about sequence of administration.
- Take medication only as directed, noting some leniency in number of puffs within 24 h. Supervise child's administration until certain all of dose is being administered.
- Rinse mouth after medication puffs to reduce bitter taste.
- Discuss changes in normal urinary pattern with the physician (more common in older adults).
- Call physician if you note changes in sputum color or amount, ankle edema, or significant weight gain.

IRBESARTAN

(ir-be-sar′tan)

Avapro

Classifications: ANGIOTENSIN II RECEPTOR ANTAGONIST; ANTIHYPERTENSIVE

Therapeutic: ANTIHYPERTENSIVE; ANGIOTENSIN II RECEPTOR ANTAGONIST

Prototype: Losartan

Pregnancy Category: C first trimester; D second and third trimester

AVAILABILITY 75 mg, 150 mg, 300 mg tablets

ACTION & *THERAPEUTIC EFFECT*

Irbesartan is an angiotensin II receptor (type AT_1) antagonist. Angiotensin II is a hormone of the renin–angiotensin–aldosterone system. Irbesartan selectively blocks the binding of angiotensin II to the AT_1 receptors found in many tissues (e.g., vascular smooth muscle, adrenal glands), resulting in vasodilation of vascular smooth muscle. *Binding to the angiotensin receptors results in blocking the vasoconstricting and aldosterone-secreting effects of*

Common adverse effects in *italic*, life-threatening effects <u>underlined</u>; generic names in **bold**; classifications in SMALL CAPS; ♦ Canadian drug name; ⊘ Prototype drug

815

angiotensin II, thus resulting in an antihypertensive effect.

USES Hypertension, treatment of diabetic nephropathy in patients with hypertension and type 2 diabetes.
UNLABELED USES CHF.

CONTRAINDICATIONS Hypersensitivity to irbesartan, losartan, or valsartan; hypovolemia; pregnancy (category C first trimester, category D second and third trimester), lactation, children.
CAUTIOUS USE Patients on diuretics, arterial stenosis of the renal artery, hepatic disease; severe CHF, African American patients.

ROUTE & DOSAGE

Hypertension
Adult: **PO** Start with 150 mg once daily, may increase to 300 mg/d

ADMINISTRATION

Oral
- Correct volume depletion prior to initiation of therapy to prevent hypotension. Titrate daily dose up to 300 mg; larger doses, however, are not likely to provide additional benefit.

ADVERSE EFFECTS (≥1%) **Body as a Whole:** Edema, fatigue, pain. **CNS:** Dizziness, headache, anxiety, nervousness. **CV:** Tachycardia, chest pain. **GI:** Diarrhea, dyspepsia, nausea, vomiting, abdominal pain. **Respiratory:** Upper respiratory infection, cough, sinus disorder, pharyngitis, rhinitis. **Skin:** Rash. **Other:** UTI, hepatitis.

PHARMACOKINETICS Absorption: Rapidly absorbed from GI tract, 60–80% bioavailability. **Distribution:** 90% protein bound. **Metabolism:** In the liver primarily by CYP2C9. **Elimination:** Primarily in feces. **Half-Life:** 11–15 h.

CLINICAL IMPLICATIONS

Assessment & Drug Effects
- Monitor for therapeutic effectiveness: Maximum pressure lowering effect may not be evident for 6–12 wk; indicated by decreases in systolic and diastolic BP.
- Monitor BP periodically; trough readings, just prior to the next scheduled dose, should be made when possible.
- Lab tests: Monitor periodically BUN and creatinine, serum potassium, and CBC with differential.

Patient & Family Education
- Inform physician immediately if you become pregnant.
- Notify physician of episodes of dizziness, especially when making position changes.

IRINOTECAN HYDROCHLORIDE

(eye-ri-no'te-can)
Camptosar
Classifications: ANTINEOPLASTIC; CAMPTOTHECIN
Therapeutic: ANTINEOPLASTIC
Prototype: Topotecan
Pregnancy Category: D

AVAILABILITY 20 mg/mL injection

ACTION & *THERAPEUTIC EFFECT*
Irinotecan is a camptothecin analog that displays antitumor activity by inhibiting the intranuclear enzyme topoisomerase I. Thus, it is a strong inhibitor of DNA and RNA synthesis. Topoisomerase I is an essential intranuclear enzyme that relaxes the supercoiled DNA, thus enabling replication and transcription to take place. By inhibiting topoisomerase I, irinotecan and its active metabo-

lite SN-38 cause double-stranded DNA damage during the synthesis (S) phase of DNA synthesis. *Irinotecan inhibits both DNA and RNA synthesis.*

USES Metastatic carcinoma of colon or rectum.

CONTRAINDICATIONS Previous hypersensitivity to irinotecan, topotecan, or other camptothecin analogs; acute infection, diarrhea, pregnancy (category D), lactation. Safety and effectiveness in children are not established.

CAUTIOUS USE Gastrointestinal disorders, myelosuppression, renal or hepatic function impairment, history of bleeding disorders, previous cytotoxic or radiation therapy.

ROUTE & DOSAGE

Metastatic Carcinoma

Adult: **IV** 125 mg/m² once weekly for 4 wk, then a 2-wk rest period (future courses may be adjusted to range from 50 to 150 mg/m² depending on tolerance; see complete prescribing information for specific dosage adjustment recommendations based on toxic effects)

ADMINISTRATION

Intravenous

Administer only after premedication (at least 30 min prior) with an antiemetic.

- Wash immediately with soap and water if skin contacts drug during preparation.

PREPARE: **IV Infusion:** Dilute the ordered dose in enough D5W (preferred) or NS to yield a concentration of 0.12–1.1 mg/mL. Typical amount of diluent used is 500 mL.

ADMINISTER: **IV Infusion:** Infuse over 90 min. Closely monitor IV site; if extravasation occurs, immediately flush with sterile water and apply ice.

- Store undiluted at 15°–30° C (59°–86° F) and protect from light. Use reconstituted solutions within 24 h.

ADVERSE EFFECTS (≥1%) **Body as a Whole:** *Asthenia, fever, pain,* chills, edema, abdominal enlargement, back pain. **CNS:** Headache, *insomnia, dizziness.* **CV:** Vasodilation/flushing. **GI:** *Diarrhea (early and late onset), dehydration, nausea, vomiting, anorexia, weight loss, constipation, abdominal cramping and pain,* flatulence, stomatitis, dyspepsia, increased alkaline phosphatase and AST. **Hematologic:** <u>Leukopenia, neutropenia</u>, anemia. **Respiratory:** *Dyspnea,* cough, rhinitis. **Skin:** *Alopecia,* sweating, rash.

INTERACTIONS Drug: ANTICOAGULANTS, ANTIPLATELET AGENTS, NSAIDS may increase risk of bleeding; **carbamazepine, phenytoin, phenobarbital** may decrease irinotecan levels. **Herbal:** **St. John's wort** may decrease irinotecan levels.

PHARMACOKINETICS Peak: 1 h. **Distribution:** Irinotecan is 30% protein bound; active metabolite SN-38 is 95% protein bound. **Metabolism:** In liver by carboxylesterase enzyme to active metabolite SN-38. **Elimination:** 10 h for SN-38; 20% excreted in urine. **Half-Life:** 10–20 h.

CLINICAL IMPLICATIONS

Assessment & Drug Effects

- Lab tests: Monitor WBC with differential, Hgb, and platelet count before each dose; monitor closely coagulation parameters especially with concurrent use of other drugs which affect these parameters.

Common adverse effects in *italic*, life-threatening effects <u>underlined</u>; generic names in **bold**; classifications in SMALL CAPS; ♣ Canadian drug name; ⊘ Prototype drug

817

- Lab tests: Monitor fluid and electrolyte balance closely during and after periods of diarrhea. Monitor liver and renal function tests and blood glucose periodically.
- Monitor for acute GI distress, especially early diarrhea (within 24 h of infusion), which may be preceded by diaphoresis and cramping, and late diarrhea (>24 h after infusion).

Patient & Family Education
- Learn about common adverse effects and measures to control or minimize when possible.
- Notify physician immediately when you experience diarrhea, vomiting, and S&S of infection. Diarrhea requires prompt treatment to prevent serious fluid and electrolyte imbalances.

IRON DEXTRAN

(i'ern dek'stran)

Dexferrum, Imfed, Proferdex

Classifications: BLOOD FORMER; IRON PREPARATION; ANTIANEMIC

Therapeutic: ANTIANEMIC

Prototype: Ferrous sulfate

Pregnancy Category: C

AVAILABILITY 50 mg elemental iron/mL

ACTION & *THERAPEUTIC EFFECT*

A dark brown, slightly viscous liquid complex of ferric hydroxide with dextran in 0.9% NaCl solution for injection. Reticuloendothelial cells of liver, spleen, and bone marrow dissociate iron from iron dextran complex. The released ferric ion combines with transferrin and is transported to bone marrow, where it is incorporated into hemoglobin. *Effective in replacement of iron needed in iron deficiency anemia, thus replenishing hemoglobin and depleted iron stores.*

USES Only in patients with clearly established iron deficiency anemia when oral administration of iron is unsatisfactory or impossible.

CONTRAINDICATIONS Hypersensitivity to the product; all anemias except iron-deficiency anemia; acute phase of infectious renal disease; pregnancy (category C); infants less than 5 kg, and neonates.

CAUTIOUS USE Rheumatoid arthritis, ankylosing spondylitis; renal disease; SLE; impaired hepatic function; cardiac disease; history of allergies or asthma.

ROUTE & DOSAGE

Iron Deficiency

Adult: **IM/IV** Dose is individualized and determined based on patient's weight and hemoglobin (see package insert); do not administer more than 100 mg (2 mL) of iron dextran within 24 h
Child: **IM/IV** <5 kg, no more than 0.5 mL (25 mg)/d; 5–10 kg, no more than 1 mL (50 mg)/d; >10 kg, no more than 2 mL (100 mg)/d

ADMINISTRATION

Note: The multiple-dose vial is used ONLY for IM injections. It is not suitable for IV use because it contains a preservative (phenol).

Test Dose
- Give a test dose of 0.5 mL over a 5 min period before the first IM or IV therapeutic dose to observe patient's response to the drug. Have epinephrine (0.5 mL of a 1:1000 solution) immediately available for hypersensitivity emergency.
- Note: Although anaphylactic reactions (see Appendix F) usually oc-

cur within a few minutes after injection, it is recommended that 1 h or more elapse before remainder of initial dose is given following test dose.

Intramuscular

- Use the multiple-dose vial ONLY for IM injections. It is not suitable for IV use because it contains a preservative (phenol).

- Give injection only into the muscle mass in upper outer quadrant of buttock (never in the upper arm). In small child, use the lateral thigh. Use a 2- or 3-inch, 19- or 20-gauge needle. The Z-track technique is recommended. Use one needle to withdraw drug from container and another needle for injection.

- Note: If patient is receiving IM in standing position, patient should be bearing weight on the leg opposite the injection site; if in bed, patient should be in the lateral position with injection site uppermost.

Intravenous

Ensure that ONLY the vial for IV use is selected.

PREPARE: **Direct:** If the IV injection does not exceed 100 mg, it is administered undiluted. **IV Infusion:** Dilute in 250–1000 mL of NS.

ADMINISTER: **Direct:** Give 50 mg (1 mL) or fraction thereof over 60 sec. **IV Infusion:** Give test dose of 25 mg (0.5 mL) over 5 min. If no adverse reactions occur, infuse remainder over 1–8 h.

- After infusion is completed, flush vein with 10 mL of NS.

- Have patient remain in bed for at least 30 min after IV administration to prevent orthostatic hypotension. • Monitor BP and pulse.

- Store below 30° C (86° F) unless otherwise directed.

ADVERSE EFFECTS (≥1%) **Body as a Whole:** Hypersensitivity (urticaria, skin rash, allergic purpura, pruritus, fever, chills, dyspnea, arthralgia, myalgia; anaphylaxis). **CNS:** Headache, shivering, transient paresthesias, syncope, dizziness, coma, seizures. **CV:** *Peripheral vascular flushing (rapid IV), hypotension,* precordial pain or pressure sensation, tachycardia, fatal cardiac arrhythmias, circulatory collapse. **GI:** Nausea, vomiting, transient loss of taste perception, metallic taste, diarrhea, melena, abdominal pain, hemorrhagic gastritis, intestinal necrosis, hepatic damage. **Skin:** Sterile abscess and brown skin discoloration (IM site), local phlebitis (IV site), lymphadenopathy, *pain at IM injection site.* **Metabolic:** Hemosiderosis, metabolic acidosis, hyperglycemia, reactivation of quiescent rheumatoid arthritis, exogenous hemosiderosis. **Hematologic:** Bleeding disorder with severe toxicity.

DIAGNOSTIC TEST INTERFERENCE Falsely elevated *serum bilirubin* and falsely decreased *serum calcium* values may occur. Large doses of iron dextran may impart a brown color to serum drawn 4 h after iron administration. *Bone scans* involving Tc-99m diphosphonate have shown dense areas of activity along contour of iliac crest 1–6 d after IM injections of iron dextran.

INTERACTIONS May decrease absorption of oral **iron, chloramphenicol** may decrease effectiveness of iron, a toxic complex may form with **dimercaprol.**

PHARMACOKINETICS Absorption: 60% from IM site by 3 d; 90% absorbed by 1–3 wk. **Distribution:** Crosses placenta; distributed into breast milk. **Metabolism:** In reticuloendothelial system. **Half-Life:** 6 h.

Common adverse effects in *italic*, life-threatening effects <u>underlined</u>; generic names in **bold**; classifications in SMALL CAPS; ✦ Canadian drug name; ⊙ Prototype drug

819

CLINICAL IMPLICATIONS

Assessment & Drug Effects

- Monitor for therapeutic effectiveness: Anticipated response to parenteral iron therapy is an average weekly hemoglobin rise of about 1 g/d. Peak levels are generally reached in about 4–8 wk.
- Note: Systemic reactions may occur over 24 h after parenteral iron has been administered. Large IV doses are associated with increased frequency of adverse effects.
- Lab tests: Periodic determinations of Hgb and Hct, and reticulocyte count should be made.

Patient & Family Education

- Do not take oral iron preparations when receiving iron injections.
- Eat foods high in iron and vitamin C.
- Notify physician of any of the following: backache or muscle ache, chills, dizziness, fever, headache, nausea or vomiting, paresthesias, pain or redness at injection site, skin rash or hives, or difficulty breathing.

IRON SUCROSE INJECTION

(i′ron su′crose)

Venofer

Classifications: BLOOD FORMER; IRON PREPARATION; ANTIANEMIC
Therapeutic: ANTIANEMIC
Prototype: Ferrous sulfate
Pregnancy Category: B

AVAILABILITY 20 mg elemental iron/mL

ACTION & *THERAPEUTIC EFFECT*

A complex of polynuclear iron (III) hydroxide in sucrose. It is dissociated by the reticuloendothelial system (RES) into iron (ferric ion) and sucrose. Normal erythropoiesis depends on the concentration of iron (ferric ion) and erythropoietin available in the plasma; both are decreased in renal failure. Exogenous administration of erythropoietin increases red blood cell production and iron utilization, contributing to iron deficiency in hemodialized patients. Therefore, intravenous iron sucrose injection has been used to treat anemia associated with hemodialysis and may reduce need for erythropoietin dosage by about 40%. *Increases serum iron (ferric ion) level in chronic renal failure patients, and results in increased hemoglobin level.*

USES Treatment of iron deficiency anemia in patients with chronic renal failure (with or without concurrent administration of erythropoietin).

CONTRAINDICATIONS Patients with iron overload, hypersensitivity to Venofer, or for anemia not caused by iron deficiency; hemochromatosis; concomitant use with an oral iron preparation.

CAUTIOUS USE Patients with a history of hypotension; pregnancy (category B), lactation; older adults, decreased renal, hepatic, or cardiac function. Safety and effectiveness in infants or children are not established.

ROUTE & DOSAGE

Iron Deficiency Anemia
Adult: IV 100 mg given 1–3 times/wk up to total of 10 doses

ADMINISTRATION

Intravenous

PREPARE: Direct: Give undiluted. **IV Infusion:** Dilute one vial (100 mg) in a maximum of 100 mL NS immediately prior to infusion. **ADMINISTER: Direct:** Give undiluted by IV push at a rate of 1 mL (20 mg) per min during dialysis. Do not exceed one vial (100 mg) per injection. Avoid rapid injection. **IV Infusion:** Infusion diluted solution into dialysis line at a rate of 100 mg over at least 15 min. Avoid rapid infusion.

***INCOMPATIBILITIES* Solution/additive:** Do not mix with other medications or parenteral nutrition solutions.

▪ Store unopened vials preferably at 25° C (77° F), but room temperature permitted. Discard unused portion in opened vial.

ADVERSE EFFECTS (≥1%) **Body as a Whole:** Fever, pain, asthenia, malaise, <u>anaphylactoid reactions</u>. **Cardiovascular:** *Hypotension,* chest pain, hypertension, hypervolemia. **Digestive:** Nausea, vomiting, diarrhea, abdominal pain, elevated liver function tests. **Musculoskeletal:** *Leg cramps,* muscle pain. **CNS:** Headache, dizziness. **Respiratory:** Dyspnea, pneumonia, cough. **Skin:** Pruritus, injection site reaction.

INTERACTIONS Drug: May reduce absorption of ORAL IRON PREPARATIONS.

PHARMACOKINETICS Peak: 4 wk. **Distribution:** Primarily to blood with some distribution to liver, spleen, bone marrow. **Metabolism:** Dissociated to iron and sucrose in reticuloendothelial system. **Elimination:** Sucrose is eliminated in urine, 5% of iron excreted in urine. **Half-Life:** 6 h.

CLINICAL IMPLICATIONS

Assessment & Drug Effects

▪ Withhold drug and notify physician when serum ferritin level equals or exceeds established guidelines.
▪ Stop infusion and notify physician for S&S overdosage or infusing too rapidly: hypotension, edema; headache, dizziness, nausea,

vomiting, abdominal pain, joint or muscle pain, and paresthesia.
▪ Lab tests: Periodic serum ferritin, transferrin saturation, Hct, and Hgb.
▪ Monitor patient carefully during the first 30 min after initiation of IV therapy for signs of hypersensitivity and anaphylactoid reaction (see Appendix F).

Patient & Family Education
▪ Report any of the following promptly: Itching, rash, chest pain, headache, dizziness, nausea, vomiting, abdominal pain, joint or muscle pain, and numbness and tingling.

ISOCARBOXAZID

(eye-soe-kar-box′a-zid)
Marplan
Classifications: PSYCHOTHERAPEUTIC; ANTIDEPRESSANT; MONOAMINE OXIDASE INHIBITOR (MAOI)
Therapeutic: ANTIDEPRESSANT; MAOI
Prototype: Phenelzine
Pregnancy Category: C

AVAILABILITY 10 mg tablets

ACTION & *THERAPEUTIC EFFECT*
MAO INHIBITOR of the hydrazine group. Inhibits monoamine oxidase, the enzyme involved in the catabolism of catecholamine neurotransmitters and serotonin. *Effectiveness as an antidepressant is due to its inhibition of MAO.*

USES Symptomatic treatment of depressed patients refractory to or intolerant of TCAs or electroconvulsive therapy.

CONTRAINDICATIONS Hypersensitivity to MAO INHIBITORS; pheochromocytoma; children (<16 y); older adults (>60 y) or debilitated patients; cardiac arrhythmias, hypertension,

Common adverse effects in *italic*, life-threatening effects <u>underlined</u>; generic names in **bold**; classifications in SMALL CAPS; ◆ Canadian drug name; ☻ Prototype drug

821

CHF, MI; severe renal or hepatic impairment; increased intracranial pressure, stroke, head trauma; pregnancy (category C), lactation.

CAUTIOUS USE Hyperthyroidism, parkinsonism, epilepsy, schizophrenia; psychosis; suicidal risks or ideation.

ROUTE & DOSAGE

Refractory Depression
Adult: **PO** 10–30 mg/d in 1–3 divided doses (max: 30 mg/d)

ADMINISTRATION

Oral
- Note: Dosage is individualized on the basis of patient response. Lowest effective dosage should be used.
- Store in a tight, light-resistant container.

ADVERSE EFFECTS (≥1%) **CNS:** Dizziness, light-headedness, tiredness, weakness, *drowsiness,* vertigo, headache, *overactivity,* hyperreflexia, muscle twitching, tremors, mania hypomania, *insomnia,* confusion, memory impairment. **CV:** *Orthostatic hypotension,* paradoxical hypertension, palpitation, tachycardia, other arrhythmias. **Special Senses:** *Blurred vision,* nystagmus, glaucoma. **GI:** Increased appetite, weight gain, *nausea,* diarrhea, *constipation, anorexia,* black tongue, *dry mouth,* abdominal pain. **Urogenital:** Dysuria, *urinary retention,* incontinence, sexual disturbances. **Body as a Whole:** Peripheral edema, excessive sweating, chills, skin rash, hepatitis, jaundice.

INTERACTIONS Drug: TRICYCLIC ANTIDEPRESSANTS, **fluoxetine,** AMPHETAMINES, **ephedrine, phenylpropanolamine, reserpine, guane-**
thidine, buspirone, methyldopa, dopamine, levodopa, tryptophan may precipitate hypertensive crisis, headache, or hyperexcitability; **alcohol** and other CNS DEPRESSANTS compound CNS depressant effects; **meperidine** can cause fatal cardiovascular collapse; ANESTHETICS exaggerate hypotensive and CNS depressant effects; **metrizamide** increases risk of seizures; compounds hypotensive effects of DIURETICS and other ANTIHYPERTENSIVE AGENTS. **Food:** All **tyramine**-containing foods (aged cheeses, processed cheeses, sour cream, wine, champagne, beer, pickled herring, anchovies, caviar, shrimp, liver, dry sausage, figs, raisins, overripe bananas or avocados, chocolate, soy sauce, bean curd, yeast extracts, yogurt, papaya products, meat tenderizers, broad beans) may precipitate hypertensive crisis. **Herbal: Ginseng, ephedra, ma huang, St. John's wort** may precipitate hypertensive crisis.

PHARMACOKINETICS Duration: Up to 2 wk. **Metabolism:** In liver.

CLINICAL IMPLICATIONS

Assessment & Drug Effects
- Monitor for therapeutic effectiveness: May be apparent within 1 wk or less, but in some patients there may be a time lag of 3–4 wk before improvement occurs.
- Monitor BP. Monitor for orthostatic hypotension by evaluating BP with patient recumbent and standing.
- Check for peripheral edema daily and monitor weight several times weekly.
- Note: Toxic symptoms from overdosage or from ingestion of contraindicated substances (e.g., foods high in tyramine) may occur within hours.

- Monitor I&O and bowel elimination patterns.

Patient & Family Education
- Make position changes slowly and in stages; lie down or sit down if faintness occurs.
- Use caution when performing potentially hazardous activities.
- Consult physician before self-medicating with OTC agents (e.g., cough, cold, hay fever, or diet medications).
- Avoid alcohol and excessive caffeine-containing beverages and tryptophan and tyramine-containing foods including cheeses, yeast, meat extracts, smoked or pickled meat, poultry, or fish, fermented sausages, and overripe fruit.

ISOETHARINE HYDROCHLORIDE

(eye-soe-eth′a-reen)
Beta-2
Classifications: BETA-ADRENERGIC AGONIST; BRONCHODILATOR
Therapeutic: BRONCHODILATOR; BETA-ADRENERGIC AGONIST
Prototype: Albuterol
Pregnancy Category: C

AVAILABILITY 1% solution

ACTION & *THERAPEUTIC EFFECT*
Synthetic sympathomimetic stimulant with relatively rapid onset and long duration of action. Has selective affinity for beta$_2$ adreno-receptors on bronchial and selected arteriolar musculature. Relieves reversible bronchospasm and by bronchodilation facilitates expectoration of pulmonary secretions. Increases vital capacity and decreases airway resistance. *Effective in relieving brochospasms as well as facilitating expectoration of respiratory secretions.*

USES Bronchial asthma and reversible bronchospasm occurring with bronchitis and emphysema.

CONTRAINDICATIONS Known hypersensitivity to sympathomimetic amines and to bisulfites; concomitant use with epinephrine or other sympathomimetic amines; patients with preexisting cardiac arrhythmias associated with tachycardia; pregnancy (category C).

CAUTIOUS USE Older adults; hypertension; acute coronary artery disease; CHF; cardiac diseases; asthma; hyperthyroidism, diabetes mellitus; tuberculosis; history of seizures.

ROUTE & DOSAGE

Bronchospasm

Adult: **Inhalation** 0.5–1 mL 0.5% or 0.5 mL 1% solution diluted 1:3 with normal saline or 2–4 mL 0.125% solution undiluted or 2–5 mL 0.2% solution undiluted or 2 mL 0.25% solution undiluted per nebulizer q4h (max: 5 times/d); 1–2 inhalations from an MDI q4h up to 5 times/d
Child: **Inhalation** 0.01 mL/kg of 1% solution (max: 0.5 mL) diluted in 2–3 mL normal saline

ADMINISTRATION

Inhalation
- Give on arising in morning and before meals to reduce fatigue from activity by improving lung ventilation.
- Wait 1 full min after initial 1 or 2 inhalations (Bronkometer) to be sure of necessity for another dose. Action should begin immediately and peak within 5–15 min.
- Alternate therapy with concurrent epinephrine administration but do not administer simultaneously because of danger of excessively rapid heartbeat.

Common adverse effects in *italic*, life-threatening effects <u>underlined</u>; generic names in **bold**; classifications in SMALL CAPS; ✦ Canadian drug name; ❂ Prototype drug

823

- Do not use discolored or precipitated solutions.
- Protect solutions from light, freezing, and heat.

ADVERSE EFFECTS (≥1%) **CV:** *Tachycardia, palpitations,* changes in BP, <u>cardiac arrest</u>. **GI:** Nausea, vomiting. **CNS:** Headache, *anxiety,* tension, restlessness, insomnia, *tremor,* weakness, dizziness, excitement. **Respiratory:** Cough, bronchial irritation and edema; tachyphylaxis.

INTERACTIONS Drug: Epinephrine, other SYMPATHOMIMETIC BRONCHODILATORS possibly have additive effects; MAO INHIBITORS, TRICYCLIC ANTIDEPRESSANTS potentiate action on vascular system; effects of both BETA-ADRENERGIC BLOCKERS and isoetharine antagonized when given together.

PHARMACOKINETICS Onset: Immediate. **Peak:** 5–15 min. **Duration:** 1–4 h. **Metabolism:** In lungs, liver, GI tract, and other tissues. **Elimination:** Excreted by kidneys.

CLINICAL IMPLICATIONS

Assessment & Drug Effects

- Do not use this product if patient has a history of allergy to sulfite agents. The preservative sodium bisulfite is in the hydrochloride formulation.
- Monitor cardiac status and report tachycardia and palpitations. Older adults may be especially sensitive to adrenergic drug effects.

Patient & Family Education

- Close eyes when actuating the nebulizer.
- Use inhalation therapy according to prescribed regimen. Overuse may decrease desired effect and cause symptoms including tachycardia, palpitations, headache, nausea, dizziness.

- Read information and instructions furnished with the aerosol form of isoetharine.
- Increase daily fluid intake to aid in liquefaction of bronchial secretions.
- Discontinue drug and notify physician if a sudden increase in dyspnea occurs.
- Do not discard drug applicator. Refill units are available.

ISOMETHEPTENE/ DICHLORALPHENAZONE/ ACETAMINOPHEN

(i-so-meth′ep-tene/di-chlor-al-phen′a-zone/a-cet′a-min-o-phen)
Isopap, Duradrin, Midrin, Migratine

Classifications: SYMPATHOMIMETIC; ANALGESIC, NONNARCOTIC
Therapeutic: ANTIMIGRAINE; ANALGESIC, NON-NARCOTIC
Prototype: Isometheptene/dichloralphenazone/acetaminophen
Pregnancy Category: C
Controlled Substance: Schedule C-IV

AVAILABILITY 65 mg; **isometheptene mucate,** 100 mg **dichloralphenazone,** 325 mg **APAP** capsules

ACTION & *THERAPEUTIC EFFECT*
Isometheptene is a sympathomimetic amine that acts by constricting cranial and cerebral arterioles. Isometheptene relieves vascular headaches. Dichloralphenazone is a mild sedative that helps reduce headache pain. Acetaminophen is a mild analgesic. *Effective as a mild sedative, reduces headache pain as well as being a mild analgesic.*

USES Relief for tension, vascular, and migraine headaches.

CONTRAINDICATIONS Patients with glaucoma; severe renal disease, organic heart disease; hepatic disease; concurrent MAO inhibitors; pregnancy (category C), lactation.
CAUTIOUS USE Hypertension; peripheral vascular disease, and recent cardiovascular attacks; older adults; pulmonary disease.

ROUTE & DOSAGE

Tension Headache
Adult: **PO** 1–2 capsules q4h up to 8 capsules/24 h

Migraine Headache
Adult: **PO** 2 capsules at onset, then 1 capsule qh until relief (max: 5 capsules/12 h)

ADMINISTRATION

Oral
- Do not give this drug to anyone who is concurrently using an MAOI. Allow 14 d to elapse between discontinuation of the MAOI and administration of this drug.
- Do not give more than 8 capsules in a 24 h period.
- Store at 15°–30° C (59°–86° F) in a dry place.

ADVERSE EFFECTS (≥1%) **CNS:** Transient dizziness. **GI:** Acetaminophen hepatotoxicity. **Skin:** Rash.

INTERACTIONS Drug: MAOIS may cause hypertensive crisis; other **acetaminophen**-containing drugs (including OTC) may increase risk of hepatotoxicity.

PHARMACOKINETICS Absorption: Rapidly absorbed. **Metabolism:** Dichloralphenazone is metabolized to chloral hydrate and antipyrine. See ACETAMINOPHEN and CHLORAL HYDRATE for more detail. **Elimination:** Renal and hepatic. **Half-Life:** 12 h.

CLINICAL IMPLICATIONS

Assessment & Drug Effects
- Monitor BP closely with preexisting hypertension.
- Monitor lower extremity perfusion with a history of PVD.

Patient & Family Education
- Avoid, or moderate, alcohol use while taking this drug.
- Do not drive or engage in other potentially hazardous activities until response to drug is known.
- Report any decrease in tolerance to walking if you have a history of PVD.

ISONIAZID (ISONICOTINIC ACID HYDRAZIDE) ℗

(eye-soe-nye′a-zid)
INH, Isotamine ♦, Laniazid, Nydrazid, PMS Isoniazid ♦
Classifications: ANTIBIOTIC; ANTI-TUBERCULOSIS AGENT
Therapeutic: ANTIBIOTIC; ANTITUBERCULOSIS
Pregnancy Category: C

AVAILABILITY 50 mg, 100 mg, 300 mg tablets; 50 mg/5 mL syrup; 100 mg/mL injection

ACTION & *THERAPEUTIC EFFECT* Hydrazide of isonicotinic acid with highly specific action against *Mycobacterium tuberculosis*. Postulated to act by interfering with biosynthesis of bacterial proteins, nucleic acid, and lipids. *Exerts bacteriostatic action against actively growing tubercle bacilli; may be bactericidal in higher concentrations.*

USES Treatment of all forms of active tuberculosis caused by susceptible organisms and as preventive in high-risk persons (e.g., household members, persons with posi-

Common adverse effects in *italic*, life-threatening effects underlined; generic names in **bold**; classifications in SMALL CAPS; ♦ Canadian drug name; ℗ Prototype drug

825

tive tuberculin skin test reactions). May be used alone or with other tuberculostatic agents.

UNLABELED USES Treatment of atypical mycobacterial infections; tuberculous meningitis; action tremor in multiple sclerosis.

CONTRAINDICATIONS History of isoniazid-associated hypersensitivity reactions, including hepatic injury; acute liver damage of any etiology; pregnancy (category C) unless risk is warranted.

CAUTIOUS USE Chronic liver disease; HIV infection; hepatitis; severe renal dysfunction; history of convulsive disorders; chronic alcoholism; persons over 50 y.

ROUTE & DOSAGE

Treatment of Active Tuberculosis
Adult: **PO/IM** 5 mg/kg (max: 300 mg/d)
Child: **PO/IM** 10–20 mg/kg (max: 300–500 mg/d)

Preventive Therapy
Adult: **PO** 300 mg/d
Child: **PO** 10 mg/kg up to 300 mg/d or 15 mg/kg 3 times/wk

ADMINISTRATION

Oral
- Give on an empty stomach at least 1 h before or 2 h after meals. If GI irritation occurs, drug may be taken with meals.

Intramuscular
- Note: Isoniazid solution for IM injection tends to crystallize at low temperatures; if this occurs, solution should be allowed to warm to room temperature to redissolve crystals before use.
- Give deep into a large muscle and rotate injection sites; local transient pain may follow IM injections.

- Store in tightly closed, light-resistant containers.

ADVERSE EFFECTS (≥1%) **Body as a Whole:** Drug-related fever, rheumatic and lupus erythematosus-like syndromes, irritation at injection site; hypersensitivity (fever, chills, skin eruption, vasculitis). **CNS:** *Paresthesias, peripheral neuropathy,* headache, unusual tiredness or weakness, tinnitus, dizziness, hallucinations. **Special Senses:** Blurred vision, visual disturbances, optic neuritis, atrophy. **GI:** Nausea, vomiting, epigastric distress, dry mouth, constipation; hepatotoxicity (*elevated AST, ALT;* bilirubinemia, jaundice, <u>hepatitis</u>). **Hematologic:** <u>Agranulocytosis</u>, hemolytic or <u>aplastic anemia</u>, thrombocytopenia, eosinophilia, methemoglobinemia. **Metabolic:** Decreased vitamin B_{12} absorption, pyridoxine (vitamin B_6) deficiency, pellagra, gynecomastia, hyperglycemia, glycosuria, hyperkalemia, hypophosphatemia, hypocalcemia, acetonuria, metabolic acidosis, proteinuria. **Other:** Dyspnea, urinary retention (males).

DIAGNOSTIC TEST INTERFERENCE Isoniazid may produce false-positive results using *copper sulfate tests* (e.g., *Benedict's solution, Clinitest*) but not with **glucose oxidase methods** (e.g., **Clinistix, Dextrostix, TesTape**).

INTERACTIONS Drug: Cycloserine, ethionamide enhance CNS toxicity; may increase **phenytoin** levels, resulting in toxicity; ALUMINUM-CONTAINING ANTACIDS decrease GI absorption; **disulfiram** may cause coordination difficulties or psychotic reactions; **alcohol** increases risk of hepatotoxicity. **Food:** Food decreases rate and extent of isoniazid absorption; should be taken 1 h before meals.

PHARMACOKINETICS Absorption: Readily from GI tract; food may reduce rate and extent of absorption. **Peak:** 1–2 h. **Distribution:** Distributed to all body tissues and fluids including the CNS; crosses placenta. **Metabolism:** Inactivated by acetylation in liver. **Elimination:** 75–96% in urine in 24 h; excreted in breast milk. **Half-Life:** 1–4 h.

CLINICAL IMPLICATIONS

Assessment & Drug Effects

- Monitor for therapeutic effectiveness: Evident within the first 2–3 wk of therapy. Over 90% of patients receiving optimal therapy have negative sputum by the sixth month.
- Perform appropriate susceptibility tests before initiation of therapy and periodically thereafter to detect possible bacterial resistance.
- Lab tests: Monitor hepatic function periodically. Isoniazid hepatitis (sometimes fatal) usually develops during the first 3–6 mo of treatment, but may occur at any time during therapy; much more frequent in patients 35 y or older, especially in those who ingest alcohol daily.
- Monitor for visual disturbance. An eye examination may be warranted.
- Note: Inactivation of the drug is genetically determined. Slow inactivation leads to high plasma drug levels and increased risk of toxicity.
- Isoniazid-induced pyridoxine (vitamin B_6) depletion causes neurotoxic effects. B_6 supplementation (10–50 mg) usually accompanies isoniazid use.
- Peripheral neuritis, the most common toxic effect, is usually preceded by paresthesias of feet and hands (numbness, tingling, burning). Patients particularly susceptible include alcoholics and patients

with liver disease, malnourished patients, diabetics, slow inactivators, pregnant women, and older adults.

- Monitor BP during period of dosage adjustment. Some experience orthostatic hypotension; therefore, caution against rapid positional changes.
- Monitor diabetics for loss of glycemic control.
- Check weight at least twice weekly under standard conditions.

Patient & Family Education

- Note: Eating tyramine-containing foods (e.g., aged cheeses, smoked fish) may cause palpitation, flushing, and blood pressure elevation. Histamine-containing foods (e.g., skipjack, tuna, sauerkraut juice, yeast extracts) may cause exaggerated drug response (headache, hypotension, palpitation, sweating, itching, flushing, diarrhea).
- Withhold medication and notify physician if S&S of hepatotoxicity develop (e.g., dark urine, jaundice, clay-colored stools).
- Avoid or at least reduce alcohol intake while on isoniazid therapy because of increased risk of hepatotoxicity.
- Withhold all drugs and notify physician of hypersensitivity reaction immediately; generally occurs within 3–7 wk after initiation of therapy.

ISOPROTERENOL HYDROCHLORIDE 🅟

(eye-soe-proe-ter′e-nole)

Isuprel

Classifications: BETA-ADRENERGIC AGONIST; BRONCHODILATOR

Therapeutic: BRONCHODILATOR; BETA-ADRENERGIC AGONIST

Pregnancy Category: C

Common adverse effects in *italic*, life-threatening effects underlined; generic names in **bold**; classifications in SMALL CAPS; ◆ Canadian drug name; 🅟 Prototype drug

827

AVAILABILITY Isoproterenol HCl 0.2 mg/mL, 0.02 mg/mL injection

ACTION & *THERAPEUTIC EFFECT*
Synthetic sympathomimetic amine. Acts directly on $beta_1$-adrenergic receptors with little or no effect on alpha-adrenoceptors. Stimulation of $beta_2$-adrenoreceptors relaxes bronchospasm and, by increasing ciliary motion, facilitates expectoration of pulmonary secretions. Induces stimulation of $beta_1$-adrenergic receptors and results in increased cardiac output and cardiac workload by increasing strength of contraction and, to a slight degree, rate of contraction of the heart. *Effectiveness in bronchodilation reverses bronchospasm as well as facilitates removal of bronchial secretion. Increases cardiac output and cardiac workload.*

USES Reversible bronchospasm induced by anesthesia. As cardiac stimulant in cardiac arrest, carotid sinus hypersensitivity, cardiogenic and bacteremic shock, Adams-Stokes syndrome, or ventricular arrhythmias. Used in treatment of shock that persists after replacement of blood volume.

UNLABELED USES Treatment of status asthmaticus in children.

CONTRAINDICATIONS Preexisting cardiac arrhythmias associated with tachycardia; tachycardia caused by digitalis intoxication, central hyperexcitability, cardiogenic shock secondary to coronary artery occlusion and MI; simultaneous administration with epinephrine, ventricular fibrillation; pregnancy (category C).
CAUTIOUS USE Sensitivity to sympathomimetic amines; older adult and debilitated patients, hypertension, coronary insufficiency and other cardiovascular disorders, angina; renal dysfunction, hyperthyroidism, diabetes, prostatic hypertrophy, glaucoma, tuberculosis, during anesthesia by cyclopropane; lactation.

ROUTE & DOSAGE

Bronchospasm
Adult: **IV** 0.01–0.02 mg prn
Cardiac Arrhythmias/Cardiac Resuscitation
Adult: **IV** 0.02–0.06 mg bolus, followed by 5 mcg/min infusion
Child: **IV** 0.1 mcg/kg/min by continuous infusion
Shock/Hypoperfusion
Adult: **IV** 0.5–5 mcg/min

ADMINISTRATION

Intravenous

PREPARE: Direct: Dilute 1 mL of 1:5000 solution with 9 mL NS or D5W to produce a 1:50,000 (0.02 mg/mL) solution. **IV Infusion:** Dilute 10 mL of 1:5000 solution in 500 mL D5W to produce a 1:250,000 (4 mcg/mL) solution.
ADMINISTER: Direct: Give each 1 mL of 1:50,000 solution over 1 min. Flush with 15–20 mL NS. **IV Infusion:** Infusion rate is generally decreased or infusion may be temporarily discontinued if heart rate exceeds 110 bpm, because of the danger of precipitating arrhythmias. Microdrip or constant-infusion pump is recommended to prevent sudden influx of large amounts of drug. IV administration is regulated by continuous ECG monitoring. Patient must be observed and response to therapy must be monitored continuously.
***INCOMPATIBILITIES* Solution/additive:** Sodium bicarbonate, **aminophylline.**

- Isoproterenol solutions lose potency with standing. Discard if precipitate or discoloration is present.

ADVERSE EFFECTS (≥1%) **CNS:** Headache, mild tremors, nervousness, anxiety, insomnia, excitement, fatigue. **CV:** Flushing, palpitations, tachycardia, unstable BP, anginal pain, ventricular arrhythmias. **GI:** Swelling of parotids (prolonged use), bad taste, buccal ulcerations (sublingual administration), nausea. **Other:** Severe prolonged asthma attack, sweating, bronchial irritation and edema. **Acute Poisoning:** Overdosage, especially after excessive use of aerosols (*tachycardia,* palpitations, nervousness, nausea, vomiting).

INTERACTIONS Drug: Epinephrine and other SYMPATHOMIMETIC AMINES increase effects and cause cardiac toxicity. HALOGENATED GENERAL ANESTHETICS exacerbate arrhythmias; while BETA BLOCKERS antagonize effects.

PHARMACOKINETICS Absorption: Rapidly from parenteral administration. **Onset:** Immediate. **Metabolism:** Metabolized by COMT in liver, lungs, and other tissues. **Elimination:** 40–50% unchanged in urine.

CLINICAL IMPLICATIONS
Assessment & Drug Effects
- Check pulse before and during IV administration. Rate >110 usually indicates need to slow infusion rate or discontinue infusion. Consult physician for guidelines. Incidence of arrhythmias is high, particularly when drug is administered IV to patients with cardiogenic shock or ischemic heart disease, digitalized patients, or to those with electrolyte imbalance.
- Note: Tolerance to bronchodilating effect and cardiac stimulant

effect may develop with prolonged use.
- Note: Once tolerance has developed, continued use can result in serious adverse effects including rebound bronchospasm.

Patient & Family Education
- Before IV isoproterenol is administered, tell the physician if you have any of the following diseases: asthma, diabetes mellitus, overactive thyroid, phenocytoma, allergic reaction to this drug, if you are pregnant or trying to become pregnant, or if you are breastfeeding.
- Before the IV is initiated, tell the physician all of the medications that you are currently taking, including nutritional supplements and OTC medicines.
- If you are frequent user of caffeinated beverages, alcohol, or illegal drugs, tell your physician before the IV is started. All of these chemicals may interfere with the effectiveness of this drug.

ISOSORBIDE DINITRATE

(eye-soe-sor′bide)
Coronex ♦, Dilatrate-SR, Iso-Bid, Isordil, Novosorbide ♦
Classifications: NITRATE VASODILATOR
Therapeutic: VASODILATOR; NITRATE
Prototype: Nitroglycerin
Pregnancy Category: C

AVAILABILITY 2.5 mg, 5 mg, 10 mg sublingual tablets; 5 mg, 10 mg chewable tablets; 5 mg, 10 mg, 20 mg, 30 mg, 40 mg tablets; 40 mg sustained release tablets, capsules

ACTION & *THERAPEUTIC EFFECT*
Relaxes vascular smooth muscle with resulting vasodilation. Dilation of peripheral blood vessels tends to cause peripheral pooling of

Common adverse effects in *italic*, life-threatening effects underlined; generic names in **bold**; classifications in SMALL CAPS; ♦ Canadian drug name; ⊘ Prototype drug

829

blood, decreased venous return to heart, and decreased left ventricular end-diastolic pressure, with consequent reduction in myocardial oxygen consumption. *Has an antianginal effect as a result of vasodilation of the coronary arteries.*

USES Relief of acute anginal attacks and for management of long-term angina pectoris.

UNLABELED USES Alone or in combination with a cardiac glycoside or with other vasodilators (e.g., hydralazine, prazosin, for refractory CHF; diffuse esophageal spasm without gastroesophageal reflux and heart failure).

CONTRAINDICATIONS Hypersensitivity to nitrates or nitrites; severe anemia; head trauma; increased intracranial pressure; recent MI; GI disease; pregnancy (category C).

CAUTIOUS USE Glaucoma, hypotension, hypovolemia; hyperthyroidism; hepatic disease; elderly; lactation.

ROUTE & DOSAGE

Angina Prophylaxis
Adult: **PO** Regular tablets 2.5–30 mg q.i.d. a.c. and h.s.; Sublingual tablet 2.5–10 mg q4–6h; Chewable tablet 5–30 mg chewed q2–3h; Sustained release tablets 40 mg q6–12h

Acute Anginal Attack
Adult: **PO** Sublingual tablet 2.5–10 mg q2–3h prn; Chewable tablet 5–30 mg chewed prn for relief

ADMINISTRATION

Oral
- Do not confuse with isosorbide, an oral osmotic diuretic.
- Give regular oral forms on an empty stomach (1 h a.c. or 2 h

p.c.). If patient complains of vascular headache, however, it may be taken with meals.
- Advise patient not to eat, drink, talk, or smoke while sublingual tablet is under tongue.
- Instruct patient to place sublingual tablet under tongue at first sign of an anginal attack. If pain is not relieved, repeat dose at 5–10 min intervals to a maximum of 3 doses. If pain continues, notify physician or go to nearest hospital emergency room.
- Chewable tablet must be thoroughly chewed before swallowing.
- Do not crush sustained release form. It must be swallowed whole.
- Have patient sit when taking rapid-acting forms of isosorbide dinitrate (sublingual and chewable tablets) because of the possibility of faintness.
- Store in tightly closed container in a cool, dry place. Do not expose to extremes of temperature.

ADVERSE EFFECTS (≥1%) **Body as a Whole:** Hypersensitivity reaction, paradoxical increase in anginal pain, methemoglobinemia (overdose). **CNS:** Headache, dizziness, weakness, *lightheadedness,* restlessness. **CV:** Palpitation, postural hypotension, tachycardia. **GI:** Nausea, vomiting. **Skin:** *Flushing,* pallor, perspiration, rash, exfoliative dermatitis.

INTERACTIONS Drug: Alcohol may enhance hypotensive effects and lead to cardiovascular collapse; ANTI-HYPERTENSIVE AGENTS, PHENOTHIAZINES add to hypotensive effects.

PHARMACOKINETICS Absorption: Significant first pass metabolism with PO absorption, with 10–90% reaching systemic circulation. **Onset:** 2–5 min SL; within 1 h regular tabs; within 3 min chewable tabs; 30 min sustained release tabs. **Duration:** 1–

2 h SL; 4–6 h regular tabs; 0.5–2 h chewable tabs; 6–8 h sustained release tabs. **Metabolism:** In liver. **Elimination:** 80–100% in urine within 24 h.

CLINICAL IMPLICATIONS

Assessment & Drug Effects

- Monitor effectiveness of drug in relieving angina.
- Note: Headaches tend to decrease in intensity and frequency with continued therapy but may require administration of analgesic and reduction in dosage.
- Note: Chronic administration of large doses may produce tolerance and thus decrease effectiveness of nitrate preparations.

Patient & Family Education

- Make position changes slowly, particularly from recumbent to upright posture, and dangle feet and ankles before walking.
- Lie down at the first indication of light-headedness or faintness.
- Keep a record of anginal attacks and the number of sublingual tablets required to provide relief.
- Do not drink alcohol because it may increase possibility of light-headedness and faintness.

ISOSORBIDE MONONITRATE

(eye-soe-sor′bide)
Ismo, Imdur, Monoket
Classifications: NITRATE VASODILATOR
Therapeutic: VASODILATOR; NITRATE
Prototype: Nitroglycerin
Pregnancy Category: C

AVAILABILITY 10 mg, 20 mg tablets; 30 mg, 60 mg, 120 mg sustained release tablets

ACTION & *THERAPEUTIC EFFECT*

Isosorbide mononitrate is a long-acting metabolite of the coronary vasodilator isosorbide dinitrate. It decreases preload as measured by pulmonary capillary wedge pressure (PCWP), and left ventricular end volume and diastolic pressure (LVEDV), with a consequent reduction in myocardial oxygen consumption. *It is equally or more effective than isosorbide dinitrate in the treatment of chronic, stable angina. It is a potent vasodilator with antianginal and antiischemic effects.*

USES Prevention of angina. Not indicated for acute attacks.

CONTRAINDICATIONS Hypersensitivity to nitrates; severe anemia; closed-angle glaucoma; recent MI; postural hypotension, head trauma, cerebral hemorrhage (increases intracranial pressure); pregnancy (category C). Extended form should not be used in patients with GI disease.
CAUTIOUS USE Older adults, hypotension; lactation.

ROUTE & DOSAGE

Prevention of Angina

Adult: **PO** Regular release (ISMO, Monoket) 20 mg b.i.d. 7 h apart; Sustained release (Imdur) 30–60 mg every morning, may increase up to 120 mg once daily after several days if needed (max: dose 240 mg)

ADMINISTRATION

Oral

- Give first dose in morning on arising and second dose 7 h later with twice daily dosing regimen. Give in morning on arising with once daily dosing.
- Store sustained release tablets in a tight container.

ADVERSE EFFECTS (≥1%) **CNS:** Headache, agitation, anxiety, confu-

Common adverse effects in *italic*, life-threatening effects underlined; generic names in **bold**; classifications in SMALL CAPS; ♣ Canadian drug name; ☻ Prototype drug

831

sion, loss of coordination, hypoes-thesia, hypokinesia, insomnia or somnolence, nervousness, migraine headache, paresthesia, vertigo, ptosis, tremor. **CV:** Aggravation of angina, abnormal heart sounds, murmurs, <u>MI</u>, transient hypotension, palpitations. **Hematologic:** Hypochromic anemia, purpura, thrombocytopenia, methemoglobinemia (high doses). **GI:** Nausea, vomiting, dry mouth, abdominal pain, constipation, diarrhea, dyspepsia, flatulence, tenesmus, gastric ulcer, hemorrhoids, gastritis, glossitis. **Metabolic:** Hyperuricemia, hypokalemia. **GU:** Renal calculus, UTI, atrophic vaginitis, dysuria, polyuria, urinary frequency, decreased libido, impotence. **Respiratory:** Bronchitis, pneumonia, upper respiratory tract infection, nasal congestion, bronchospasm, coughing, dyspnea, rales, rhinitis. **Skin:** Rash, pruritus, hot flashes, acne, abnormal texture. **Special Senses:** Diplopia, blurred vision, photophobia, conjunctivitis.

INTERACTIONS Drug: Alcohol may cause severe hypotension and cardiovascular collapse. **Aspirin** may increase nitrate serum levels. CALCIUM CHANNEL BLOCKERS may cause orthostatic hypotension.

PHARMACOKINETICS Absorption: Completely and rapidly absorbed from GI tract; 93% reaches systemic circulation. **Onset:** 1 h. **Peak:** Regular release 30–60 min; sustained release 3–4 h. **Duration:** Regular release 5–12 h; sustained release 12 h. **Metabolism:** In liver by denitration and conjugation to inactive metabolites. **Elimination:** Primarily by kidneys. **Half-Life:** 4–5 h.

CLINICAL IMPLICATIONS

Assessment & Drug Effects

▪ Monitor cardiac status, frequency and severity of angina, and BP.

▪ Assess for and report possible S&S of toxicity, including orthostatic hypotension, syncope, dizziness, palpitations, light-headedness, severe headache, blurred vision, and difficulty breathing.
▪ Lab tests: Monitor serum electrolytes periodically.

Patient & Family Education

▪ Do not crush or chew sustained release tablets. May break tablets in two and take with adequate fluid (4–8 oz).
▪ Do not withdraw drug abruptly; doing so may precipitate acute angina.
▪ Maintain correct dosing interval with twice daily dosing.
▪ Note: Geriatric patients are more susceptible to the possibility of developing postural hypotension.
▪ Avoid alcohol ingestion and aspirin unless specifically permitted by physician.

ISOTRETINOIN (13-*cis*-RETINOIC ACID) ℗

(eye-soe-tret′i-noyn)
Accutane, Claravis

Classifications: ANTIACNE (RETINOID)
Therapeutic: ANTIACNE; ANTINEOPLASTIC
Pregnancy Category: X

AVAILABILITY 10 mg, 20 mg, 40 mg capsules

ACTION & *THERAPEUTIC EFFECT* Highly toxic metabolite of retinol (vitamin A). Principal actions: regulation of cell (e.g., epithelial) differentiation and proliferation and of altered lipid composition on skin surface. Decreases sebum secretion by reducing sebaceous gland size; inhibits gland cell differentiation; blocks follicular keratinization. *Has antiacne properties and may be used as a chemotherapeutic agent for epithelial carcinomas.*

USES Treatment of severe recalcitrant cystic or conglobate acne in patient unresponsive to conventional treatment, including systemic antibiotics.
UNLABELED USES Lamellar ichthyosis, oral leukoplakia, hyperkeratosis, acne rosacea, scarring gram-negative folliculitis; adjuvant therapy of basal cell carcinoma of lung and cutaneous T-cell lymphoma (mycosis fungoides); psoriasis; chemoprevention for prostate cancer.

CONTRAINDICATIONS Tinnitus; hypersensitivity to parabens (preservatives in the formulation), retinoid hypersensitivity, leukopenia, neutropenia; UV exposure; pregnancy (category X), females of childbearing age, lactation.
CAUTIOUS USE Coronary artery disease; major depression, psychosis, history of suicides, alcoholism; hepatitis, hepatic disease; visual disturbance; rheumatologic disorders, osteoporosis; history of pancreatitis, inflammatory bowel disease; diabetes mellitus; obesity; retinal disease; elevated triglycerides, hyperlipidemia.

ROUTE & DOSAGE

Cystic Acne
Adult: **PO** 0.5–1 mg/kg/d in 2 divided doses (max: recommended dose 2 mg/kg/d)
Disorders of Keratinization
Adult: **PO** up to 4 mg/kg/d in divided doses

ADMINISTRATION

Oral
- Give with or shortly after meals.

- Reassess regimen after 2 wk of treatment and dose adjusted as warranted.
- Note: A single course of therapy provides adequate control in many patients. If a second course is necessary, it is delayed at least 8 wk because improvement may continue without the drug.
- Store in tight, light-resistant container. Capsules remain stable for 2 y.

ADVERSE EFFECTS (≥1%) **Body as a Whole:** Most are dose-related (i.e., occurring at doses >1 mg/kg/d), reversible with termination of therapy. **CNS:** Lethargy, headache, fatigue, visual disturbances, pseudotumor cerebri, paresthesias, dizziness, depression, psychosis, suicide (rare). **Special Senses:** Reduced night vision, dry eyes, papilledema, eye irritation, *conjunctivitis,* corneal opacities. **GI:** *Dry mouth,* anorexia, nausea, vomiting, abdominal pain, nonspecific GI symptoms, <u>acute hepatotoxic reactions</u> (rare), inflammation and bleeding of gums, increased AST, ALT, acute pancreatitis. **Hematologic:** Decreased Hct, Hgb, elevated sedimentation rate. **Musculoskeletal:** Arthralgia; bone, joint, and muscle pain and stiffness; chest pain, skeletal hyperostosis (especially in athletic people and with prolonged therapy), mild bruising. **Skin:** *Cheilitis,* skin fragility, dry skin, pruritus, peeling of face, palms, and soles; photosensitivity (photoallergic and phototoxic), erythema, skin infections, petechiae, rash, urticaria, exaggerated healing response (painful exuberant granulation tissue with crusting), brittle nails, thinning hair. **Respiratory:** Epistaxis, *dry nose.* **Metabolic:** Hyperuricemia, *increased serum concentrations of triglycerides by 50–70%,* serum cholesterol by 15–20%,

Common adverse effects in *italic*, life-threatening effects <u>underlined</u>; generic names in **bold**; classifications in SMALL CAPS; ♣ Canadian drug name; ❷ Prototype drug

833

VLDL cholesterol by 50–60%, LDL cholesterol by 15–20%.

INTERACTIONS Drug: VITAMIN A SUPPLEMENTS increase toxicity; decreases effectiveness of ESTROGEN hormonal contraceptives in oral form as well as topical/injectable/implantable/insertable ESTROGEN hormonal birth control.

PHARMACOKINETICS Absorption: Rapid absorption after slow dissolution in GI tract; 25% of administered drug reaches systemic circulation. **Peak:** 3.2 h. **Distribution:** Not fully understood; appears in liver, ureters, adrenals, ovaries and lacrimal glands. **Metabolism:** In liver; enterohepatically cycled. **Elimination:** In urine and feces in equal amounts. **Half-Life:** 10–20 h.

CLINICAL IMPLICATIONS

Assessment & Drug Effects

- Lab tests: Determine baseline blood lipids at outset of treatment, then at 2 wk, 1 mo, and every month thereafter throughout course of therapy; liver function tests at 2- or 3-wk intervals for 6 mo and once a month thereafter during treatment.
- Report signs of liver dysfunction (jaundice, pruritus, dark urine) promptly.
- Monitor closely for loss of glycemic control in diabetic and diabetic-prone patients.
- Monitor for development of depression and suicidal ideation.
- Note: Persistence of hypertriglyceridemia (levels above 500–800 mg/dL) despite a reduced dose indicates necessity to stop drug to prevent onset of acute pancreatitis.

Patient & Family Education

- Maintain drug regimen even if during the first few weeks transient exacerbations of acne occur.

Recurring symptoms may signify response of deep unseen lesions.

- Discontinue medication at once and notify physician if visual disturbances occur along with nausea, vomiting, and headache.
- Rule out pregnancy within 2 wk of starting treatment. Use a reliable contraceptive 1 mo before, throughout, and 1 mo after therapy is discontinued.
- Do not self-medicate with multivitamins, which usually contain vitamin A. Toxicity of isotretinoin is enhanced by vitamin A supplements.
- Avoid or minimize exposure of the treated skin to sun or sunlamps. Photosensitivity (photoallergic and phototoxic) potential is high; risk of skin cancer may be increased by this drug.
- Notify physician immediately of abdominal pain, rectal bleeding, or severe diarrhea, which are possible symptoms of drug-induced inflammatory bowel disease.
- Keep lips moist and softened (use thin layer of lubricant such as petroleum jelly); dry mouth and cheilitis (inflamed, chapped lips), frequent adverse effects of isotretinoin.
- Notify physician of joint pain, such as pain in the great toe (symptom of gout and hyperuricemia).

ISOXSUPRINE HYDROCHLORIDE

(eye-sox′syoo-preen)

Vasodilan, Voxsuprine

Classifications: BETA-ADRENERGIC AGONIST; VASODILATOR

Therapeutic: VASODILATOR; BETA-ADRENERGIC AGONIST; ALPHA-ADRENERGIC INHIBITOR

Prototype: Albuterol

Pregnancy Category: C

AVAILABILITY 10 mg, 20 mg tablets

ACTION & *THERAPEUTIC EFFECT*
Sympathomimetic with beta-adrenergic stimulant activity and with an inhibitory effect on alpha receptors. Vasodilating action on arteries within skeletal muscles is greater than on cutaneous vessels. *Has both cerebral and peripheral vasodilatory properties.*

USES Adjunctive therapy in treatment of cerebral vascular insufficiency and peripheral vascular disease, such as arteriosclerosis obliterans, thromboangiitis obliterans (Buerger's disease), and Raynaud's disease.

CONTRAINDICATIONS Immediately postpartum; presence of arterial bleeding; parenteral use in presence of hypotension, fetal distress; intrauterine fetal death; vaginal bleeding; tachycardia; pregnancy (category C).

CAUTIOUS USE Bleeding disorders; severe cerebrovascular disease, severe obliterative coronary artery disease, recent MI; lactation.

ROUTE & DOSAGE

Cerebral Vascular Insufficiency, Peripheral Vascular Disease
Adult: **PO** 10–20 mg t.i.d. or q.i.d.

ADMINISTRATION

Oral
- When used with premature labor: Do not give immediately after delivery because it causes uterine relaxation, or in the presence of arterial bleeding.

ADVERSE EFFECTS (≥1%) **CV:** Flushing, orthostatic hypotension with light-headedness, faintness; palpitation, tachycardia. **CNS:** Dizzi-

ness, nervousness, trembling, weakness. **GI:** Nausea, vomiting, abdominal distress, abdominal distention.

PHARMACOKINETICS Absorption: Readily from GI tract. **Peak:** 1 h. **Duration:** 3 h. **Distribution:** Crosses placenta. **Metabolism:** In blood. **Elimination:** In urine. **Half-Life:** 1.25 h.

CLINICAL IMPLICATIONS

Assessment & Drug Effects
- Monitor for therapeutic effectiveness: Response to treatment of peripheral vascular disorders may take several weeks. Evaluate clinical manifestations of arterial insufficiency.
- Monitor BP and pulse; may cause hypotension and tachycardia. Supervise ambulation.
- Observe both mother and baby for hypotension and irregular and rapid heartbeat if isoxsuprine is used to delay premature labor. Hypocalcemia, hypoglycemia, and ileus have been observed in babies born of mothers taking isoxsuprine.

Patient & Family Education
- Notify physician of adverse reactions (skin rash, palpitation, flushing) promptly; symptoms are usually effectively controlled by dosage reduction or discontinuation of drug.
- Prevent orthostatic hypotension by making position changes slowly and in stages, particularly from lying down to sitting upright and avoid standing still.
- Note: For treatment of menstrual cramps, isoxsuprine is usually started 1–3 d before onset of menstruation and continued until pain is relieved or menstrual flow stops.

Common adverse effects in *italic*, life-threatening effects underlined; generic names in **bold**; classifications in SMALL CAPS; ✦ Canadian drug name; ⊘ Prototype drug

835

ISRADIPINE

(is-ra'di-peen)
DynaCirc, DynaCirc CR
Classifications: CALCIUM CHANNEL
BLOCKER; ANTIHYPERTENSIVE
Therapeutic: ANTIHYPERTENSIVE; CAL-
CIUM CHANNEL BLOCKER
Prototype: Nifedipine
Pregnancy Category: C

AVAILABILITY 2.5 mg, 5 mg capsules; 5 mg, 10 mg sustained release tablets

ACTION & *THERAPEUTIC EFFECT*

Inhibits calcium ion influx into cardiac muscle and smooth muscle without changing calcium concentrations, thus affecting contractility. Isradipine relaxes coronary vascular smooth muscle with little or no negative inotropic effect. It significantly decreases systemic vascular resistance and reduces BP at rest and during isometric and dynamic exercise. *Reduces BP and has an antianginal effect.*

USES Mild to moderate hypertension.
UNLABELED USES Angina, CHF.

CONTRAINDICATIONS Hypersensitivity to isradipine; pregnancy (category C), lactation.
CAUTIOUS USE CHF, acute MI, severe bradycardia, cardiogenic shock, ventricular dysfunction; older adult; mild renal impairment; hepatic impairment; GERD, hiatal hernia with esophageal reflux. Safety and effectiveness in children are not established.

ROUTE & DOSAGE

Hypertension
Adult: **PO** 1.25–10 mg b.i.d. (max: 20 mg/d); DynaCirc CR dosed q.d.

Angina
Adult: **PO** 2.5–7.5 mg t.i.d. (max: 15 mg/d)

ADMINISTRATION

Oral
- Do not crush sustained release form. It must be swallowed whole.
- Note: After the first 2–4 wk of therapy, dose may be increased for improved BP control in increments of 5 mg/d at 2–4 wk intervals up to a maximum dose of 20 mg/d.
- Store in tight, light-resistant container.

ADVERSE EFFECTS (≥1%) **CNS:** Headache, dizziness, fainting, fatigue, sleep disturbances, vertigo. **CV:** Flushing, ankle edema, palpitations, tachycardia, hypotension, chest pain, CHF. **GI:** Nausea, vomiting, abdominal discomfort, constipation, increased liver enzymes. **Respiratory:** Dyspnea. **Skin:** Rash, decreased skin sensation.

INTERACTIONS Drug: Adenosine may prolong bradycardia. May increase **cyclosporine** levels and toxicity.

PHARMACOKINETICS Absorption: Rapidly and completely absorbed from GI tract, but only 15–24% reaches systemic circulation because of first-pass metabolism. **Onset:** 1 h. **Peak:** 2–3 h. **Duration:** 12 h. **Distribution:** Not known if crosses placenta or is distributed into breast milk. **Metabolism:** Extensive first-pass metabolism in liver. **Elimination:** 70% in urine as inactive metabolites; 30% in feces. **Half-Life:** 5–11 h.

CLINICAL IMPLICATIONS

Assessment & Drug Effects
- Monitor BP throughout course of therapy.

- Monitor patients with a history of CHF carefully, especially with concurrent beta blocker use. Promptly report S&S of worsening heart failure.
- Monitor ambulation, especially with older adult patients, until response to drug is known.

Patient & Family Education

- Notify physician promptly of shortness of breath, palpitations, or other signs of adverse cardiovascular effects.
- Do not drive or engage in other potentially hazardous activities until response to drug is known.

ITRACONAZOLE

(i-tra-con′a-zole)
Sporanox
Classifications: ANTIBIOTIC; ANTIFUNGAL
Therapeutic: ANTIFUNGAL, ANTIBIOTIC
Prototype: Fluconazole
Pregnancy Category: C

AVAILABILITY 100 mg capsules; 10 mg/mL oral solution; 10 mg/mL injection

ACTION & *THERAPEUTIC EFFECT*
Interferes with formation of ergosterol, the principal sterol in the fungal cell membrane that, when depleted, interrupts fungal membrane functioning. *Antifungal properties affect the fungal cell membrane functioning. Fungistatic; may also be fungicidal depending on the concentration of drug.*

USES Treatment of systemic fungal infections caused by blastomycosis, histoplasmosis, aspergillosis, onychomycosis due to dermatophytes of the toenail with or without fingernail involvement; oropharyngeal and esophageal candidiasis; orally to treat superficial mycoses (*Candida,* pityriasis versicolor). IV for treatment of blastomycosis, histoplasmosis, and aspergillosis.
UNLABELED USES Systemic and vaginal candidiasis.

CONTRAINDICATIONS Hypersensitivity to itraconazole; renal failure; systolic BP <90 mm of Hg (hypotension); pregnancy (category C), lactation.
CAUTIOUS USE Hypersensitivity to other azole antifungal agents, achlorhydria; GERD; COPD, cystic fibrosis; dialysis; older adults, females of childbearing age; hepatic disease, hepatitis, HIV infection; hypochlorhydria; pulmonary disease; renal disease, renal impairment; valvular heart disease, ventricular dysfunction, angina, cardiac disease; children.

ROUTE & DOSAGE

Blastomycosis, Nonmeningeal Histoplasmosis, Aspergillosis
Adult: **PO** 200 mg once daily (increase to max: 200 mg b.i.d. if no apparent improvement). Continue for at least 3 mo; for life-threatening infections, start with 200 mg t.i.d. for 3 d, then 200–400 mg/d. **IV** 200 mg b.i.d. infused over 1 h for 4 doses, then 200 mg daily
Child: **PO** 3–5 mg/kg/d for 3–6 mo

Oropharyngeal Candidiasis
Adult: **PO** 200 mg daily for 1–2 wk

Esophageal Candidiasis
Adult: **PO** 100 mg daily for at least 3 wk (max: 200 mg/d)

Vaginal Candidiasis
Adult: **PO** 200 mg daily for 3 d

Common adverse effects in *italic*, life-threatening effects underlined; generic names in **bold**; classifications in SMALL CAPS; ♣ Canadian drug name; ● Prototype drug

837

Life-Threatening Infections
Adult: **IV** 200 mg b.i.d. × 4 d, then 200 mg daily **PO** 200 mg t.i.d. × 3 d

Onychomycosis
Adult: **PO** 200 mg daily × 3 mo

ADMINISTRATION

Oral
- Give capsules with a full meal.
- Give oral solution without food. Liquid should be vigorously swished for several seconds and swallowed.
- Do not interchange oral solution and capsules.
- Divide dosages greater than 200 mg/d into two doses.
- Store liquid at or below 25° C (77° F).

Intravenous

PREPARE: Intermittent: Withdraw 25 mL from the ampule and add to infusion bag provided (contains 50 mL of NS). Mix gently to disperse evenly. IV solution contains 3.33 mg/mL.

ADMINISTER: Intermittent: Use a flow control device and the infusion set provided to infuse 60 mL (200 mg) of the diluted solution over 60 min. Stop the infusion and flush set with 15–20 mL NS over 1–15 min via the 2-way stopcock. Then discard the entire infusion set.

INCOMPATIBILITIES Solution/additive or Y-site: Do not mix with any other drugs or infuse other drugs concomitantly through the same line.

ADVERSE EFFECTS (≥1%) **CV:** Hypertension with higher doses. **CNS:** Headache, dizziness, fatigue, somnolence (euphoria, drowsiness <1%). **Endocrine:** Gynecomastia, hypokalemia (especially with higher doses), hypertriglyceridemia. **GI:** *Nausea, vomiting, dyspepsia, abdominal pain, diarrhea, anorexia, flatulence, gastritis;* elevations of serum transaminases, alkaline phosphatase, and bilirubin. **Urogenital:** Decreased libido, impotence. **Skin:** Rash, pruritus. **Acute Poisoning:** Severe toxicity (doses exceeding 400 mg daily have been associated with higher risk of hypokalemia, hypertension, adrenal insufficiency).

INTERACTIONS Drug: Itraconazole may increase levels and toxicity of **ergotamine, dihydroergotamine,** ORAL HYPOGLYCEMIC AGENTS **warfarin, ritonavir, indinavir, vinca alkaloids, busulfan, ergonovine, methylergonovine, midazolam, triazolam, diazepam, nifedipine, nicardipine, amlodipine, felodipine, lovastatin, simvastatin, cyclosporine, tacrolimus, methylprednisolone, digoxin.** Combination with **dofetilide, levomethadyl, oral midazolam, pimozide, quinidine, triazolam** may cause severe cardiac events including cardiac arrest or sudden death. Itraconazole levels are decreased by **carbamazepine, phenytoin, phenobarbital, isoniazid, rifabutin, rifampin.** Herbal: **St. John's wort** and **garlic** may decrease itraconazole levels.

PHARMACOKINETICS Absorption: Well absorbed from GI tract when taken with food. **Onset:** 2 wk–3 mo. **Peak:** Peak levels at 1.5–5 h. Steady-state concentrations reached in 10–14 d. **Distribution:** Highly protein bound, minimal concentrations in CSF. Higher concentrations in tissues than in plasma. **Metabolism:** Extensively in liver by CYP3A4, may undergo enterohepatic recirculation. **Elimination:** 35% in urine, 55% in feces. **Half-Life:** 34–42 h.

CLINICAL IMPLICATIONS

Assessment & Drug Effects

- Lab tests: C&S tests should be done before initiation of therapy. Drug may be started pending results. Monitor hepatic functions especially in those with preexisting hepatic abnormalities.
- Monitor for digoxin toxicity when given concurrently with digoxin.
- Monitor PT and INR carefully when given concurrently with warfarin.
- Monitor for S&S of hypersensitivity (see Appendix F); discontinue drug and notify physician if noted.

Patient & Family Education

- Take capsules, but NOT oral solution, with food.
- Notify physician promptly for S&S of liver dysfunction, including anorexia, nausea, and vomiting; weakness and fatigue; dark urine and clay-colored stool.
- Note: Risk of hypoglycemia may increase in diabetics on oral hypoglycemic agents.

IVERMECTIN

(i-ver-mec′tin)

Stromectol

Classifications: ANTHELMINTIC
Therapeutic: ANTHELMINTIC; ANTI-PARASITIC
Prototype: Mebendazole
Pregnancy Category: C

AVAILABILITY 3 mg tablets

ACTION & *THERAPEUTIC EFFECT*

A semisynthetic anthelmintic agent which is a broad-spectrum antiparasitic agent with a unique mode of action. It leads to an increase in permeability to chloride ions of the cell membrane of the parasites, resulting in hyperpolarization of nerve or muscle cells of parasites. Hyperpolarization of nerve and muscle cells of parasites results in their paralysis and cell death. *Causes cell death of parasites.*

USES Treatment of strongyloidiasis of the intestinal tract, onchocerciasis.

CONTRAINDICATIONS Hypersensitivity to ivermectin; pregnancy (category C). Safety and efficacy in children weighing ≤15 kg are not established.

CAUTIOUS USE Asthma; older adults; moderate or severe hepatic disease.

ROUTE & DOSAGE

Strongyloides
Adult/Child: **PO** ≥15 kg, 200 mcg/kg times 1 dose
Onchocerciasis
Adult/Child: **PO** ≥15 kg, 150 mcg/kg times 1 dose, may repeat q3–12 mo prn

ADMINISTRATION

Oral

- Give tablets with water rather than any other type of liquid.
- Store below 30° C (86° F).

ADVERSE EFFECTS (≥1%) **Body as a Whole:** *Fever,* peripheral edema. **CNS:** Dizziness. **CV:** Tachycardia. **GI:** Diarrhea, nausea. **Skin:** *Pruritus, rash.* **Other:** Arthralgia/synovitis, lymphadenopathy.

PHARMACOKINETICS Peak: 4 h. **Distribution:** Distributed into breast milk. **Metabolism:** In the liver. **Elimination:** In feces over 12 d. **Half-Life:** 16 h.

CLINICAL IMPLICATIONS

Assessment & Drug Effects

- Monitor for therapeutic effectiveness: Indicated by negative stool samples.

Common adverse effects in *italic*, life-threatening effects underlined; generic names in **bold**; classifications in SMALL CAPS; ♣ Canadian drug name; ☻ Prototype drug

839

- Monitor for cardiovascular effects such as orthostatic hypotension and tachycardia.
- Monitor for and report inflammatory conditions of the eyes.

Patient & Family Education

- Get a follow-up stool examination to determine effectiveness of treatment. Treatment for worms does not kill adult parasites; repeated follow-up and retreatment are usually needed.
- Notify physician if eye discomfort develops.

KANAMYCIN

(kan-a-mye′sin)
Kantrex
Classifications: ANTIBIOTIC; AMINOGLYCOSIDE
Therapeutic: ANTIBIOTIC; AMINOGLYCOSIDE
Prototype: Gentamicin
Pregnancy Category: D

AVAILABILITY 75 mg, 500 mg; 1 g vials

ACTION & *THERAPEUTIC EFFECT*
Broad-spectrum, aminoglycoside antibiotic derived from *Streptomyces kanamyceticus*. It is known that aminoglycosides bind irreversibly to aminoglycoside-binding sites on 30 S ribosomal subunit of bacteria, subsequently inhibiting bacterial protein synthesis. To be bacteriocidal, an aminoglycoside needs to achieve intracellular concentrations in excess of extracellular ones. *Usually bacteriocidal in action. Active against many aerobic gram-negative micro-organisms, as well as some gram positive bacteria. It is not effective against anaerobic gram-negative bacteria.*

USES Orally to reduce ammonia-producing bacteria in intestinal tract, as adjunctive treatment of hepatic coma, and for preoperative bowel antisepsis; parenterally for short-term treatment of serious infections; intraperitoneally after fecal spill during surgery; as irrigation solution; and as aerosol treatment. In conjunction with other drugs to treat tuberculosis in patients resistant to conventional therapy.

CONTRAINDICATIONS History of hypersensitivity to kanamycin or other aminoglycosides; history of drug-induced ototoxicity, preexisting hearing loss, vertigo, or tinnitus; long-term therapy; PO use in intestinal obstruction or ulcerative bowel lesions; intraperitoneally to patients under effects of inhalation anesthetics or skeletal muscle relaxants; pregnancy (category D).
CAUTIOUS USE Impaired renal function; older adults, neonates, and infants (immature renal systems); myasthenia gravis; parkinsonian syndrome.

ROUTE & DOSAGE

Preoperative Intestinal Antisepsis
Adult: **PO** 1 g q1h for 4 doses, then q6h for 36–72 h

Hepatic Coma
Adult: **PO** 8–12 g/d in divided doses

Serious Infection
Adult/Child: **IV/IM** 15 mg/kg/d in equally divided doses q8–12h
Adult: **Intraperitoneal** 500 mg diluted in 20 mL sterile water instilled through wound catheter **Inhalation** 250 mg diluted in 3 mL NS administered per nebulizer q6–12h **Irrigation** 0.25% solution prn

Renal Impairment

Cl_{cr} 50–80 mL/min: give 60–90% of dose; 10–50 mL/min: give 30–70% of dose or q12h; less than 10 mL/min: give 20–30% of dose or q24–48h

ADMINISTRATION

Oral

- Give on a full or empty stomach.
- Store capsules at 15°–30° C (59°–86° F) unless otherwise directed.

Intramuscular

- Administer IM injection deep into upper outer quadrant of gluteal muscle (often painful).
- Observe sites daily for signs of irritation; rotate injection sites.

Intravenous

PREPARE: **Intermittent:** Dilute each 500 mg with at least 100 mL NS, D5W, D5/NS.
ADMINISTER: **Intermittent:** Over 30–60 min.
INCOMPATIBILITIES **Solution/additive: Amphotericin B, cefazolin, cefoxitin, ceftazidime, cefuroxime, Cephalothin, cephapirin, chlorpheniramine, colistimethate, heparin, hyaluronidase, hydrocortisone, lincomycin, methicillin, methohexital, nitrofurantoin, pentobarbital, phenobarbital, prochlorperazine, sodium bicarbonate, thiopental, warfarin.**

- Store vials at 15°–30° C (59°–86° F) unless otherwise directed. Some vials may darken with time, but this does not affect potency. Discard partially used vials within 48 h.

ADVERSE EFFECTS (≥1%) **All:**
Dose related. **Body as a Whole:** Eosinophilia, maculopapular rash, pruritus, urticaria, drug fever, <u>anaphylaxis</u>. **CNS:** Dizziness, circumoral and other paresthesias, optic neuritis, peripheral neuritis, headache, restlessness, tremors, lethargy, convulsions; <u>neuromuscular paralysis, respiratory depression</u> (rarely). **Special Senses:** Deafness (can be irreversible), *tinnitus, vertigo* or *dizziness,* ataxia, nystagmus. **GI:** Nausea, vomiting, diarrhea, appetite changes, abdominal discomfort, stomatitis, proctitis, malabsorption syndrome (with prolonged oral administration). **Hematologic:** Anemia, increased or decreased reticulocytes, granulocytopenia, <u>agranulocytosis</u>, thrombocytopenia, purpura. **Urogenital:** <u>Nephrotoxicity</u>; hematuria, urine casts and cells, proteinuria; elevated serum creatinine and BUN. **Other:** Superinfections; local pain; nodular formation at injection site.

INTERACTIONS Drug: Amphotericin B, cisplatin, methoxyflurane, vancomycin add to nephrotoxicity; GENERAL ANESTHETICS, SKELETAL MUSCLE RELAXANTS add to neuromuscular blocking effects; **capreomycin** compounds ototoxicity and nephrotoxicity; LOOP AND THIAZIDE DIURETICS, carboplatin may increase risk of ototoxicity.

PHARMACOKINETICS Absorption: Poorly absorbed from GI tract; readily absorbed from peritoneal cavity, bronchial tree, and wounds. **Peak:** 1–2 h. **Distribution:** Crosses placenta; distributed into breast milk. **Elimination:** 80–90% in urine within 24 h. **Half-Life:** 2–4 h.

CLINICAL IMPLICATIONS

Assessment & Drug Effects

- Lab tests: Monitor baseline C&S, urinalysis, and kidney function prior to initiation of therapy and periodically thereafter. Monitor serum sodium, potassium, calcium, and magnesium.
- Notify physician immediately of signs of renal irritation: albumin-

Common adverse effects in *italic*, life-threatening effects <u>underlined</u>; generic names in **bold**; classifications in SMALL CAPS; ✦ Canadian drug name; ● Prototype drug

841

uria, casts, red and white cells in urine, increasing BUN, and serum creatinine, decreasing creatinine clearance, oliguria, and edema.

- Monitor peak and trough serum kanamycin concentrations: Assess peak specimen 30–60 min after IM administration; 30 min after completion of a 30–60 min IV infusion. Assess trough levels just before the next IM or IV dose.
- Keep patient well hydrated to prevent chemical irritation of renal tubules.
- Monitor I&O. Report decrease in urine output or change in I&O ratio.
- Determine baseline weight and vital signs and monitor at regular intervals during therapy.
- Report signs of superinfection (see Appendix F).
- Monitor for hearing and balance problems; stop drug if ototoxicity occurs. Tinnitus is not a reliable index of ototoxicity in the very elderly. Risk of ototoxicity is high in patients with impaired renal function, older adults, poorly hydrated patients, and with therapy ≥5 d.
- Note: Deafness has occurred 2–7 d or more after termination of therapy in patients with impaired renal function.

Patient & Family Education
- Report ototoxic symptoms such as dizziness, hearing loss, weakness, or loss of balance; drug may need to be discontinued.

KAOLIN AND PECTIN

(kay'oh-lin and pek'tin)
Kaolin w/Pectin
Classifications: ANTIDIARRHEAL
Therapeutic: ANTIDIARRHEAL
Prototype: Loperamide
Pregnancy Category: C

AVAILABILITY 5.2 g Kaolin/260 mg pectin/30 mL, 90 g Kaolin/2 g pectin/30 mL

ACTION & *THERAPEUTIC EFFECT*
Kaolin is hydrated aluminum silicate adsorpant. Kaolin is reported to have adsorbent, protectant, and demulcent properties. Mechanism of action of pectin may help consolidate stool. *Effective as an antidiarrheal agent.*

USES Adjunct in symptomatic treatment of mild to moderately severe acute diarrhea. Commonly used in antidiarrheal combination products.

CONTRAINDICATIONS Suspected obstructive bowel lesion, pseudomembranous colitis, diarrhea associated with bacterial toxins; presence of fever; use for more than 48 h without medical direction; pregnancy (category C), lactation.
CAUTIOUS USE Infants or children ≤3 y, older adults.

ROUTE & DOSAGE

Diarrhea

Adult: **PO** 60–120 mL of regular suspension or 45–90 mL of concentrated suspension after each loose bowel movement
Child: **PO** 3–5 y, 15–30 mL regular suspension or 15 mL concentrated suspension after each loose bowel movement; 6–11 y, 30–60 mL regular suspension or 30 mL concentrated suspension after each loose bowel movement; ≥12 y, 60 mL regular suspension or 45 mL concentrated suspension after each loose bowel movement

ADMINISTRATION

Oral

- Administer at least 2–4 h before other oral medications.
- Shake suspension well before pouring.
- Store in tightly closed container at 15°–30° C (59°–86° F) unless otherwise directed. Protect from freezing.

ADVERSE EFFECTS (≥1%) **GI:** Constipation usually mild and transient.

INTERACTIONS Drug: Chloroquine, digoxin, penicillamine, tetracycline, ciprofloxacin, and most other drugs.

PHARMACOKINETICS Absorption: Not absorbed from GI tract.

CLINICAL IMPLICATIONS

Assessment & Drug Effects

- Assess for abdominal distension and number of stools per day.
- Note: Fecal impaction may result from taking kaolin and pectin, especially in older adults.
- Note: Drug may decrease absorption of any orally administered medication.

Patient & Family Education

- Do not to exceed prescribed dosage.
- Notify physician if diarrhea is not controlled within 48 h or if fever develops.

KETOCONAZOLE

(ke-to-con′a-zol)

Nizoral, Nizoral A–D

Classifications: ANTIBIOTIC; AZOLE ANTIFUNGAL

Therapeutic: AZOLE ANTIFUNGAL ANTIBIOTIC

Prototype: Fluconazole

Pregnancy Category: C

AVAILABILITY 200 mg tablets; 2% cream; 2% shampoo

ACTION & *THERAPEUTIC EFFECT*
Fungistatic; may also be fungicidal depending on concentration. Interferes with formation of ergosterol, the principal sterol in the fungal cell membrane that, when depleted, interrupts membrane function by increasing its permeability. *Antifungal properties are related to the drug effect on the fungal cell membrane functioning.*

USES Oral—Severe systemic fungal infections including candidiasis (e.g., oral thrush, candiduria), chronic mucocutaneous candidiasis, pulmonary and disseminated coccidioidomycosis, histoplasmosis, paracoccidioidomycosis, blastomycosis, and chromomycosis. **Topical**—Tinea corporis and tinea cruris (caused by *Epidermophyton floccosum, Trichophyton mentagrophytes,* and *Trichophyton rubrum*) and in treatment of tinea versicolor (pityriasis) caused by *Malassezia furfur (Pityrosporum obiculare),* seborrheic dermatitis.

UNLABELED USES Oral—Onychomycosis, vaginal candidiasis, Cushing's syndrome associated with adrenal or pituitary adenoma; precocious puberty, dysfunctional hirsutism, and as swish and swallow preparation for prophylaxis against fungal infections in patients with neutropenia induced by cancer chemotherapy and in patients with AIDS.

CONTRAINDICATIONS Hypersensitivity to ketoconazole or any component in the formulation; chronic alcoholism, fungal meningitis; onychomycosis; ocular exposure, ophthalmic administration; pregnancy (category C).
CAUTIOUS USE Azole antifungal hypersensitivity; achlorhydria, hypo-

Common adverse effects in *italic*, life-threatening effects underlined; generic names in **bold**; classifications in SMALL CAPS; ♣ Canadian drug name; ☉ Prototype drug

843

chlorhydria; history of hepatic disease, HIV infection; alcoholism; azole antifungal hypersensitivity. Safe use in children <2 y is not established.

ROUTE & DOSAGE

Fungal Infections

Adult: **PO** 200–400 mg once/d
Topical Apply 1–2 times/d to affected area and surrounding skin
Child: **PO** >2 y, 3.3–6.6 mg/kg/d as single dose

Dandruff

Adult/Child: **Topical** Shampoo twice a week for 4 wk with at least 3 d between shampoos

ADMINISTRATION

Oral

- Give with water, fruit juice, coffee, or tea; drug requires an acid medium for dissolution and absorption.
- Relieve nausea and vomiting during early therapy by taking drug with food and dividing into 2 daily doses.
- Do not give with antacids.
- Store in tightly covered container at 15°–30° C (59°–86° F) unless otherwise directed.

Topical

- Apply sufficient shampoo to produce lather to wash scalp and hair and gently massage over entire scalp area for 1 min, rinse hair thoroughly and repeat, leaving shampoo on scalp for 3 min. Rinse thoroughly.

ADVERSE EFFECTS (≥1%) **Oral— Body as a Whole:** Skin rash, erythema, urticaria, pruritus, angioedema, <u>anaphylaxis</u>. **GI:** *Nausea, vomiting,* anorexia, epigastric or abdominal pain, constipation, diarrhea, transient elevation in serum liver enzymes, <u>fatal hepatic necrosis</u> (rare). **Hematologic:** With high doses, lowers serum testosterone and ACTH-induced corticosteroid serum levels, transient decreases in serum cholesterol and triglycerides; hyponatremia (rare). **Urogenital:** Gynecomastia (males), breast pain; uterine bleeding, loss of libido, impotence, oligospermia, hair loss. **Other:** <u>Acute hypoadrenalism (reduction of adrenal stress syndrome), renal hypofunction.</u> **Topical—Skin:** Mild transient erythema, severe irritation, pruritus, stinging.

INTERACTIONS Drug: **Alcohol** may cause sunburnlike reaction; ANTACIDS, ANTICHOLINERGICS, H₂-RECEPTOR ANTAGONISTS decrease ketoconazole absorption; **isoniazid, rifampin** increase ketoconazole metabolism, thus decreasing its activity; levels of **phenytoin** and ketoconazole decreased; may increase levels of **cyclosporine** or **carbamazepine,** increasing the risk of toxicity; **warfarin** may potentiate hypoprothrombinemia; may increase ergotamine toxicity of **dihydroergotamine, ergotamine;** may increase concentration and toxicity of **trazodone. Herbal: Echinacea** may increase risk of hepatotoxicity.

PHARMACOKINETICS Absorption: Erratically from GI tract (needs an acid pH); minimal absorption topically. **Peak:** 1–2 h. **Distribution:** Distributed to saliva, urine, sebum, and cerumen; CSF levels unpredictable; distributed into breast milk. **Metabolism:** In liver (CYP3A4). **Elimination:** Primarily in feces, 13% in urine. **Half-Life:** 8 h.

CLINICAL IMPLICATIONS

Assessment & Drug Effects

- Lab tests: Monitor baseline liver function tests (AST, ALT, alkaline phosphatase, and bilirubin) and repeat at least monthly throughout therapy.

- Monitor for S&S of hepatotoxicity (see Appendix F). Discontinue drug immediately to prevent irreversible liver damage and report to physician.

Patient & Family Education
- Report S&S of hepatotoxicity promptly to physician (see Appendix F).
- Note: Drowsiness and dizziness are early and time-limited adverse effects.
- Do not drive or engage in potentially hazardous activities until response to drug is known.
- Avoid OTC drugs for gastric distress, such as Rolaids, Tums, Alka-Seltzer and check with physician before taking any other nonprescription medicines.
- Do not alter dose or dose interval and do not stop taking ketoconazole before consulting the physician.
- Notify physician if skin condition fails to respond to topical therapy or worsens or if signs of irritation or sensitivity occur.

KETOPROFEN

(kee-toe-proe'fen)
Oruvail
Classifications: ANALGESIC, NONSTEROIDAL ANTIINFLAMMATORY DRUG (NSAID); ANTIPYRETIC
Therapeutic: NSAID, ANALGESIC; ANTIPYRETIC
Prototype: Ibuprofen
Pregnancy Category: B

AVAILABILITY 25 mg, 50 mg, 75 mg capsules; 100 mg, 150 mg, 200 mg sustained release capsules

ACTION & *THERAPEUTIC EFFECT*
Nonsteroidal antiinflammatory drug (NSAID) that inhibits both COX-1 and COX-2 enzymes; thus it also inhibits prostaglandin synthesis, and therefore interferes with the inflammatory process. It inhibits platelet aggregation and prolongs bleeding time. *Has analgesic, antiinflammatory, and antiplatelet properties.*

USES Acute or long-term treatment of rheumatoid arthritis and osteoarthritis; primary dysmenorrhea; headache; symptomatic relief of postoperative, dental, and postpartum pain; visceral pain associated with cancer. **UNLABELED USES** Reiter's syndrome, juvenile arthritis, acute gouty arthritis, biliary pain, renal colic.

CONTRAINDICATIONS Patient in whom aspirin or another NSAID induces asthma, urticaria, bronchospasm, severe rhinitis, shock. Safety during pregnancy (category B), lactation, or in children <12 y is not established.
CAUTIOUS USE History of GI disease, GI bleeding, active ulcer; renal or hepatic impairment, patient who may be adversely affected by prolongation of bleeding time; heart failure, hypertension; patient receiving diuretics; geriatric patient; myasthenia gravis.

ROUTE & DOSAGE

Inflammatory Disease
Adult: **PO** 75 mg t.i.d. or 50 mg q.i.d. (max: 300 mg/d) or 200 mg sustained release q.d.
Geriatric: **PO** Start with 25 mg q.i.d., may also start with 50 mg t.i.d.

Mild to Moderate Pain, Dysmenorrhea
Adult: **PO** 12.5–50 mg q6–8h

Common adverse effects in *italic*, life-threatening effects underlined; generic names in **bold**; classifications in SMALL CAPS; ♣ Canadian drug name; ⊘ Prototype drug

845

ADMINISTRATION

Oral

- Do not crush.
- Give with food, milk, or prescribed antacid to reduce GI irritation.
- Store drug at 15°–30° C (59°–86° F) in tightly closed, light-resistant container unless otherwise directed.

ADVERSE EFFECTS (≥1%) **CNS:** Trouble in sleeping, nervousness, *headache,* dizziness; depression, drowsiness, confusion, migraine, vertigo. **CV:** Peripheral edema, palpitations, hypertension, tachycardia. **Special Senses:** Visual disturbances, conjunctivitis, eye pain, retinal hemorrhage, pigmentation changes; Dry nose or throat, tinnitus, hearing impairment. **GI:** *Dyspepsia,* <u>drug-induced peptic ulcer, GI bleeding,</u> nausea, vomiting, diarrhea, constipation, flatulence, stomach pain, anorexia, dry mouth, gingivitis, rectal burning and hemorrhage, melena, jaundice, elevated ALT, AST. **Hematologic:** Prolonged bleeding time, anemia, purpura, <u>agranulocytosis,</u> thrombocytosis. **Urogenital:** Gynecomastia, changes in libido, urinary tract irritation (dysuria, frequency/urgency), renal impairment. **Respiratory:** <u>Laryngospasm, bronchospasm, laryngeal edema,</u> pharyngitis. **Skin:** Rash, pruritus, urticaria, erythema, photosensitivity. **Endocrine:** Aggravation of diabetes mellitus.

INTERACTIONS Drug: ORAL ANTICOAGULANTS, **heparin** may prolong bleeding time; may increase **lithium** toxicity; may increase **methotrexate** toxicity. **Herbal: Feverfew, garlic, ginger, ginkgo** increases bleeding potential.

PHARMACOKINETICS Absorption: Readily from GI tract. **Onset:** 1–2 h. **Peak:** 1–2 h. **Duration:** 4–6 h. **Metabolism:** In liver. **Elimination:** Primarily in urine, some biliary excretion. **Half-Life:** 1.1–4 h.

CLINICAL IMPLICATIONS

Assessment & Drug Effects

- Lab tests: Monitor baseline and periodic evaluations of hemoglobin, renal and hepatic function.
- Monitor for and report tinnitus, hearing impairment, and visual disturbance, especially during prolonged or high-dose therapy.
- Monitor for S&S of GI ulceration (e.g., stool for occult blood, persistent indigestion).

Patient & Family Education

- Report promptly signs of jaundice (see Appendix F) as well as the following: blurred vision, tinnitus, urinary urgency or frequency, unexplained bleeding, weight gain with edema.
- Note: Possible CNS adverse effects (e.g., light-headedness, dizziness, drowsiness).
- Do not drive or engage in potentially hazardous activities until response to drug is known.
- Note: Alcohol, aspirin, or other NSAIDS may increase risk of GI ulceration and bleeding tendencies and therefore should be avoided.
- Tell dentist or surgeon that you are taking ketoprofen.

KETOROLAC TROMETHAMINE

(ke-tor′o-lac)

Toradol, Acular, Acular LS

Classifications: ANALGESIC, NONSTEROIDAL ANTIINFLAMMATORY DRUG (NSAID); ANTIPYRETIC

Therapeutic: NSAID, ANALGESIC; ANTIPYRETIC

Prototype: Ibuprofen

Pregnancy Category: B

AVAILABILITY 10 mg tablets; 15 mg/mL, 30 mg/mL injection; 0.4%, 0.5% ophthalmic solution

ACTION & *THERAPEUTIC EFFECT* It inhibits synthesis of prostaglandins by inhibiting both COX-1 and COX-2 enzymes. Is a peripherally acting analgesic. *Exhibits analgesic, antiinflammatory, and antipyretic activity. Effective in controlling acute post-operative pain.*

USES *Short-term* management of pain; ocular itching due to seasonal allergic conjunctivitis, reduction of post-operative pain and photophobia after refractive surgery.

CONTRAINDICATIONS Hypersensitivity to ketorolac; individuals with complete or partial syndrome of nasal polyps, angioedema, and bronchospastic reaction to aspirin or other NSAIDS; during labor and delivery; patients with severe renal impairment or at risk for renal failure due to volume depletion; patients with risk of bleeding; active peptic ulcer disease; pre- or intraoperatively; intrathecal or epidural administration; in combination with other NSAIDS.

CAUTIOUS USE History of peptic ulcers; impaired renal or hepatic function; older adults; debilitated patients; diabetes mellitus; SLE; CHF; pregnancy (category B); children under 2 years; children under 3 years with ophthalmic solution.

ROUTE & DOSAGE

Pain
Adult: **IV Loading Dose** 30 mg (15 mg <50 kg) **IM** 30–60 mg loading dose, then 15–30 mg q6h [max: 150 mg/d on first day, then 120 mg subsequent days (30 mg load, then 15 mg q6h if <50 kg)]

PO 10 mg q6h prn (max: 40 mg/d) max duration all routes 5 d
Geriatric: **IV Loading Dose** 15 mg **IM** 30 mg loading dose, then 15 mg q6h **PO** 5–10 mg q6h prn (max: 40 mg/d) max duration all routes 5 d

Pain after Refractive Surgery
Adult: **Ophthalmic** *Acular LS only* 1 drop in operative eye q.i.d. up to 4 d

Allergic Conjunctivitis
Adult: **Ophthalmic** 1 drop 0.5% solution q.i.d.

ADMINISTRATION

WARNING: DO NOT ADMINISTER IV, IM, OR PO KETOROLAC LONGER THAN 5 D.

Oral
- Give with food to reduce GI effects.

Instillation
- Do not touch container to the eye when applying ophthalmic drops.

Intramuscular
- Inject IM drug slowly and deeply into a large muscle.
- Rotate injection sites to avoid injection site pain in patients receiving multiple doses.

Intravenous

PREPARE: **Direct:** Give undiluted.
ADMINISTER: **Direct:** Give IV bolus dose over at least 15 s. Preferred method is to give through a Y-tube in a free-flowing IV.
INCOMPATIBILITIES **Solution/additive:** Haloperidol, hydroxyzine, meperidine, morphine, prochlorperazine, promethazine **Y-site: Azithromycin, fenoldopam.**

- Store all forms at 15°–30° C (59°–86° F).

ADVERSE EFFECTS (≥1%) **CNS:** *Drowsiness,* dizziness, headache. **GI:** *Nausea,* dyspepsia, GI pain,

Common adverse effects in *italic*, life-threatening effects underlined; generic names in **bold**; classifications in SMALL CAPS; ♣ Canadian drug name; ☻ Prototype drug

847

hemorrhage. **Other:** Edema, sweating, pain at injection site.

INTERACTIONS Drug: May increase **methotrexate** levels and toxicity; may increase **lithium** levels and toxicity. **Herbal: Feverfew, garlic, ginger, ginkgo** increased bleeding potential.

PHARMACOKINETICS Peak: 45–60 min. **Distribution:** Into breast milk. **Metabolism:** In liver. **Elimination:** In urine. **Half-Life:** 4–6 h.

CLINICAL IMPLICATIONS

Assessment & Drug Effects

- Correct hypovolemia prior to administration of ketorolac.
- Lab tests: Periodic serum electrolytes and liver functions; urinalysis (for hematuria and proteinuria) with long-term use.
- Monitor urine output in older adults and patients with a history of cardiac decompensation, renal impairment, heart failure, or liver dysfunction as well as those taking diuretics. Discontinuation of drug will return urine output to pretreatment level.
- Monitor for S&S of GI distress or bleeding including nausea, GI pain, diarrhea, melena, or hematemesis. GI ulceration with perforation can occur anytime during treatment. Drug decreases platelet aggregation and thus may prolong bleeding time.
- Monitor for fluid retention and edema in patients with a history of CHF.

Patient & Family Education

- Watch for S&S of GI ulceration and bleeding (e.g., bloody emesis, black tarry stools) during long-term therapy.
- Note: Possible CNS adverse effects (e.g., light-headedness, dizziness, drowsiness).
- Do not drive or engage in potentially hazardous activities until response to drug is known.
- Do not use other NSAIDs while taking this drug.

KETOTIFEN FUMARATE

(kee-toe-tye'fen)
Zaditor
Pregnancy Category: C
See Appendix A-1.

LABETALOL HYDROCHLORIDE

(la-bet'a-lole)
Trandate
Classifications: ALPHA- & BETA-ADRENERGIC ANTAGONIST; ANTIHYPERTENSIVE AGENT
Therapeutic: ANTIHYPERTENSIVE; ALPHA- & BETA-ADRENERGIC ANTAGONIST
Prototype: Propranolol
Pregnancy Category: B first and second trimester; D third trimester

AVAILABILITY 100 mg, 200 mg, 300 mg tablet; 5 mg/mL injection

ACTION & *THERAPEUTIC EFFECT*
Acts as an adrenergic receptor blocking agent that combines selective alpha activity and nonselective beta-adrenergic blocking actions. The alpha blockade results in vasodilation, decreased peripheral resistance, and orthostatic hypotension and only slightly affects cardiac output and coronary artery blood flow. It has beta-blocking effects on the sinus node, AV node, and ventricular muscle, which lead to bradycardia, delay in AV conduction, and depression of cardiac contractility. *Effective in reducing blood pressure by vasodilation as well as depression of cardiac contractility.*

USES Mild, moderate, and severe hypertension. May be used alone or in combination with other antihypertensive agents, especially thiazide diuretics.

CONTRAINDICATIONS NSAID or salicylate hypersensitivity; bronchial asthma; uncontrolled cardiac failure, heart block (greater than first degree), cardiogenic shock, severe bradycardia; perioperative CABG pain; pregnancy (category B in first and second trimester and category D in third trimester). Safe use in children is not established.

CAUTIOUS USE Nonallergic bronchospastic disease (COPD); renal disease, renal failure, hepatic disease; well-compensated patients with history of heart failure; acute MI; coronary artery disease; pheochromocytoma; impaired liver function, jaundice; diabetes mellitus; SLE; peripheral vascular disease.

ROUTE & DOSAGE

Hypertension

Adult: **PO** 100 mg b.i.d., may gradually increase to 200–400 mg b.i.d. (max: 1200–2400 mg/d). **IV** 20 mg slowly over 2 min, with 40–80 mg q10min if needed up to 300 mg total or 2 mg/min continuous infusion (max: 300 mg total dose)
Geriatric: **PO** Start with 100 mg daily **IV** 20 mg slowly over 2 min, with 40–80 mg q10min if needed up to 300 mg total or 2 mg/min continuous infusion (max: 300 mg total dose)

ADMINISTRATION

Oral
- Give with or immediately after food consistently. Food increases drug bioavailability.

Intravenous
Note: Amount of IV solution may be changed depending on patient status.

PREPARE: **Direct:** Give undiluted. **Continuous:** Dilute 300 mg in 240 of D5W, NS, D5/NS, RL, or other compatible IV solution to yield 1 mg/mL.

ADMINISTER: **Direct:** Give a 20-mg dose slowly over 2 min. Maximum hypotensive effect occurs 5–15 min after each administration. **Continuous:** Normal rate is 2 mg/min. Keep patient supine when receiving labetalol IV. Take BP immediately before administration. Rate is adjusted according to BP response. Discontinue drug once the desired BP is attained.

INCOMPATIBILITIES **Solution/additive: Sodium bicarbonate, ceftriaxone, tenecteplase. Y-site: Amphotericin B cholesteryl, cefoperazone, furosemide, heparin, nafcillin, thiopental, warfarin.**

- Controlled infusion pump device is recommended for maintaining accurate flow rate during IV infusion. Usually administered at rate of 2 mg/min.

- Store at 2°–30° C (36°–86° F) unless otherwise advised. Do not freeze. Protect tablets from moisture.

ADVERSE EFFECTS (≥1%) **CNS:** Dizziness, fatigue/malaise, headache, tremors, transient paresthesias (especially scalp tingling), hypoesthesia (numbness) following IV, mental depression, drowsiness, sleep disturbances, nightmares. **CV:** *Postural hypotension,* angina pectoris, palpitation, bradycardia, syncope, pedal or peripheral edema, pulmonary edema, CHF, flushing, cold extremities, arrhythmias (following IV), paradoxical hyperten-

L

Common adverse effects in *italic*, life-threatening effects underlined; generic names in **bold**; classifications in SMALL CAPS; ✦ Canadian drug name; ◎ Prototype drug

849

sion (patients with pheochromocytoma). **Special Senses:** Dry eyes, vision disturbances, nasal stuffiness, rhinorrhea. **GI:** Nausea, vomiting, dyspepsia, constipation, diarrhea, taste disturbances, cholestasis with or without jaundice, increases in serum transaminases, dry mouth. **Urogenital:** Acute urinary retention, difficult micturition, impotence, ejaculation failure, loss of libido, Peyronie's disease. **Respiratory:** Dyspnea, <u>bronchospasm</u>. **Skin:** Rashes of various types, increased sweating, pruritus. **Body as a Whole:** Myalgia, muscle cramps, toxic myopathy, antimitochondrial antibodies, positive antinuclear antibodies (ANA), SLE syndrome, pain at IV injection site.

DIAGNOSTIC TEST INTERFERENCE
False increases in *urinary catecholamines* when measured by *nonspecific trihydroxyindole (THI) reaction* (due to labetalol metabolites) but not with specific *radioenzymatic* or *high-performance liquid chromatography assay techniques.*

INTERACTIONS Drug: Cimetidine may increase effects of labetalol; **glutethimide** decreases effects of labetalol; **halothane** adds to hypotensive effects; may mask symptoms of hypoglycemia caused by ORAL SULFONYLUREAS, **insulin;** BETA AGONISTS antagonize effects of labetalol.

PHARMACOKINETICS Absorption: Readily from GI tract, only 25% reaches systemic circulation due to first pass metabolism. **Onset:** 20 min–2 h PO; 2–5 min IV. **Peak:** 1–4 h PO; 5–15 min IV. **Duration:** 8–24 h PO; 2–4 h IV. **Distribution:** Crosses placenta; distributed into breast milk. **Metabolism:** In liver (CYP2D6). **Elimination:** 60% in urine, 40% in bile. **Half-Life:** 3–8 h.

CLINICAL IMPLICATIONS
Assessment & Drug Effects
- Monitor BP and pulse during dosage adjustment period. Use standing BP as indicator for making dosage adjustments for oral drugs and assessing patient's tolerance of dosage increases. Take after patient stands for 10 min. Clarify with physician.
- Monitor BP at 5 min intervals for 30 min after IV administration; then at 30 min intervals for 2 h; then hourly for about 6 h; and as indicated thereafter.
- Monitor diabetic patients closely; drug may mask usual cardiovascular response to acute hypoglycemia (e.g., tachycardia).
- Convert from IV to PO therapy only when supine diastolic pressure rises about 10 mm Hg.
- Maintain patient in supine position for at least 3 h after IV administration. Then determine patient's ability to tolerate elevated and upright positions before allowing ambulation. Manage this slowly.

Patient & Family Education
- Note: Postural hypotension is most likely to occur during peak plasma levels (i.e., 2–4 h after drug administration).
- Make all position changes slowly and in stages, particularly from lying to upright position. Older adult patients are especially sensitive to hypotensive effects.
- Do not drive or engage in other potentially hazardous activities until response to drug is known.
- Note: Most adverse effects (e.g., scalp tingling) are mild, transient, and dose related and occur early in therapy.
- Be sure to keep follow-up appointments. Get liver and kidney

Common adverse effects in *italic*, life-threatening effects <u>underlined</u>; generic names in **bold**; classifications in SMALL CAPS; ✦ Canadian drug name; ⊙ Prototype drug

function tests periodically during therapy.

- Discontinue drug gradually over 1–2 wk period after chronic administration. Close monitoring during this time is very important.

LACTULOSE

(lak'tyoo-lose)
Cephulac, Chronulac
Classifications: HYPEROSMOTIC LAXATIVE
Therapeutic: LAXATIVE, HYPEROSMOTIC
Pregnancy Category: B

AVAILABILITY 10 g/15 mL solution, syrup

ACTION & *THERAPEUTIC EFFECT*
Reduces blood ammonia; appears to involve metabolism of lactose to organic acids by resident intestinal bacteria. Acidifies colon contents, which retards diffusion of nonionic ammonia (NH_3) from colon to blood while promoting its migration from blood to colon. In the acidic colon, NH_3 is converted to nonabsorbable ammonium ions (NH_{4+}) and is then expelled in feces by laxative action. *Osmotic effect of organic acids causes laxative action, which moves water from plasma to intestines, softening stools, and stimulates peristalsis by pressure from water content of stool. Decreased blood ammonia in a patient with hepatic encephalopathy is marked by improved EEG patterns and mental state (clearing of confusion, apathy, and irritation).*

USES Prevention and treatment of portal-systemic encephalopathy (PSE), including stages of hepatic precoma and coma, and by prescription for relief of chronic constipation.

UNLABELED USES to restore regular bowel habit posthemorrhoidectomy; to evacuate bowel in older adult patients with severe constipation after barium studies; and for treatment of chronic constipation in children.

CONTRAINDICATIONS Low galactose diet.

CAUTIOUS USE Diabetes mellitus; concomitant use with electrocautery procedures (proctoscopy, colonoscopy); older adult and debilitated patients; pediatric use; pregnancy (category C); lactation.

ROUTE & DOSAGE

Prevention and Treatment of Portal-Systemic Encephalopathy
Adult: **PO** 30–45 mL t.i.d. or q.i.d. adjusted to produce 2–3 soft stools/d
Adolescent/Child: **PO** 40–90 mL/d in divided doses adjusted to produce 2–3 soft stools/d
Infant: **PO** 2.5–10 mL/d in 3–4 divided doses adjusted to produce 2–3 soft stools/d

Management of Acute Portal-Systemic Encephalopathy
Adult: **PO** 30–45 mL q1–2 h until laxation is achieved, then adjusted to produce 2–3 soft stools/d. **Rectal** 300 mL diluted with 700 mL water given via rectal balloon catheter, and retained for 30–60 min, may repeat in 4–6 h if necessary or until patient can take PO

Chronic Constipation
Adult: **PO** 30–60 mL/d prn

Common adverse effects in *italic*, life-threatening effects <u>underlined</u>; generic names in **bold**; classifications in SMALL CAPS; ♣ Canadian drug name; ☼ Prototype drug

851

Child: **PO** 7.5 mL/d after breakfast

ADMINISTRATION

Oral

- Give with fruit juice, water, or milk (if not contraindicated) to increase palatability. Laxative effect is enhanced by taking with ample liquids. Avoid meal times.

Rectal

- Administer as a retention enema via a rectal balloon catheter. If solution is evacuated too soon, instillation may be promptly repeated.
- Do not freeze. Avoid prolonged exposure to temperatures above 30° C (86° F) or to direct light. Normal darkening does not affect action, but discard solution that is very dark or cloudy.

ADVERSE EFFECTS (≥1%) **GI:** Flatulence, borborygmi, belching, abdominal cramps, pain, and distention (initial dose); *diarrhea* (excessive dose); nausea, vomiting, colon accumulation of hydrogen gas; hypernatremia.

INTERACTIONS Drug: LAXATIVES may incorrectly suggest therapeutic action of lactulose.

PHARMACOKINETICS Absorption: Poorly absorbed from GI tract. **Metabolism:** In gut by intestinal bacteria.

CLINICAL IMPLICATIONS

Assessment & Drug Effects

- In children if the initial dose causes diarrhea, dosage is reduced immediately. Discontinue if diarrhea persists.
- Promote fluid intake (≥1500–2000 mL/d) during drug therapy for constipation; older adults often self-limit liquids. Lactulose-induced osmotic changes in the bowel support intestinal water loss and potential hypernatremia. Discuss strategy with physician.

Patient & Family Education

- Laxative action is not instituted until drug reaches the colon; therefore, about 24–48 h is needed.
- Do not self-medicate with another laxative due to slow onset of drug action.
- Notify physician if diarrhea (i.e., more than 2 or 3 soft stools/d) persists more than 24–48 h. Diarrhea is a sign of overdosage. Dose adjustment may be indicated.

LAMIVUDINE ⓟ

(lam-i-vu′deen)
Epivir, Epivir-HBV, Heptovir ♦
Classifications: ANTIRETROVIRAL AGENT; NUCLEOSIDE REVERSE TRANSCRIPTASE INHIBITOR (NRTI)
Therapeutic: ANTIRETROVIRAL; NRTI
Pregnancy Category: C

AVAILABILITY 100 mg, 150 tablets; 5 mg/mL, 10 mg/mL oral solution

ACTION & *THERAPEUTIC EFFECT*

Lamivudine is a synthetic nucleoside analog reverse transcriptase inhibitor. It inhibits the transcription of the HIV viral RNA chain, as well as the hepatitis B viral RNA chain. *Antiviral action is effective against HIV viruses and hepatitis B (HBV) viral infections.*

USES HIV infection in combination with zidovudine; treatment of chronic hepatitis B.

CONTRAINDICATIONS Hypersensitivity to lamivudine, pregnancy (category C), lactation.

CAUTIOUS USE Renal impairment, renal failure; diabetes mellitus, diabetes mellitus; obesity; children.

ROUTE & DOSAGE

HIV Infection

Adult: Epivir **PO** 150 mg b.i.d.
Child: Epivir **PO** 3 mo–16 y, 4 mg/kg b.i.d. (max: of 150 mg b.i.d.)

Renal Impairment

Cl_{cr} 30–49 mL/min: 150 mg q.d.; 15–29 mL/min: 150 mg first dose, then 100 mg q.d.; 5–14 mL/min: 150 mg first dose, then 50 mg q.d.; <5 mL/min: 50 mg first dose, then 25 mg q.d.

Chronic Hepatitis B

Adult: Epivir-HBV: **PO** 100 mg q.d.

Renal Impairment

Cl_{cr} 30–49 mL/min: 100 mg first dose, then 50 mg q.d.; 15–29 mL/min: 100 mg first dose, then 25 mg q.d.; 5–14 mL/min: 35 mg first dose, then 15 mg q.d.; <5 mL/min: 35 mg first dose, then 10 mg q.d.

ADMINISTRATION

Oral

- Give Epivir b.i.d. in combination with AZT. The recommended dose for adults who weigh <50 kg (110 lb) is 2 mg/kg. Give Epivir-HBV qd; do NOT give in combination with AZT.
- Store solution at 2°–25° C (36°–77° F) tightly closed.

ADVERSE EFFECTS (≥1%) **CNS:** *Neuropathy, insomnia,* sleep disorders, *dizziness,* depression, *headache,* fatigue, *fever, chills.* **GI:** *Nausea, diarrhea,* vomiting, anorexia, abdominal pain, cramps, dyspepsia, increased LFTs (ALT, amylase), <u>hepatomegaly with steatosis</u>. **Hematologic:** Neutropenia, anemia, thrombocytopenia. **Musculoskeletal:** Myalgia, arthralgia, malaise, pain. **Skin:** Rash. **Respiratory:** Nasal symptoms, cough. **Metabolic:** <u>Lactic acidosis</u>.

INTERACTIONS Drug: Increases the C_{max} of **zidovudine. Trimethoprim-sulfamethoxazole** increases serum levels of lamivudine. Increased risk of lactic acidosis in combination with other REVERSE TRANSCRIPTASE INHIBITORS and ANTIRETROVIRAL AGENTS.

PHARMACOKINETICS Absorption: Rapidly absorbed from GI tract (86% reaches systemic circulation). **Distribution:** Low binding to plasma proteins. **Metabolism:** Minimal. **Elimination:** Excreted primarily unchanged in urine. **Half-Life:** 2–4 h.

CLINICAL IMPLICATIONS

Assessment & Drug Effects

- Monitor children closely for S&S of pancreatitis; if they occur, immediately stop drug and notify physician.
- Lab tests: Monitor CBC with differential, kidney & liver function, and serum amylase throughout therapy.
- Monitor for and report all significant adverse reactions.

Patient & Family Education

- Report any of the following immediately: nausea, vomiting, anorexia, abdominal pain, jaundice.
- Note: The long-term effects of lamivudine are unknown.

L

Common adverse effects in *italic*, life-threatening effects <u>underlined</u>; generic names in **bold**; classifications in SMALL CAPS; ✦ Canadian drug name; ☯ Prototype drug

853

LAMOTRIGINE

(la-mo'tri-geen)

Lamictal

Classifications: ANTICONVULSANT
Therapeutic: ANTICONVULSANT
Prototype: Phenytoin
Pregnancy Category: C

AVAILABILITY 25 mg, 100 mg, 150 mg, 200 mg tablets; 2 mg, 5 mg, 25 mg chewable tablets

ACTION & *THERAPEUTIC EFFECT*

Exact mechanism of anticonvulsant activity is not known; thought to act by inhibiting the release of glutamate, an excitatory neurotransmitter at voltage-sensitive sodium channels, resulting in decreased seizure activity. *Anticonvulsant action results because it stabilizes neuronal membranes and inhibits neurotransmitter release (i.e., glutamate) in brain tissue, decreasing seizure activity.*

USES Adjunctive therapy for partial seizures in adults and children (>2 y). Generalized tonic–clonic, absence, or myoclonic seizures in adults, treatment of bipolar disorder.

CONTRAINDICATIONS Hypersensitivity to lamotrigine, suicidal ideation; pregnancy (category C), lactation. Safety and efficacy in children ≤2 y are not established.

CAUTIOUS USE Renal insufficiency, concomitant administration of other anticonvulsants, bipolar disorder, history of suicidal tendencies; elderly; CHF, cardiac or liver function impairment. Note: Fatal rash has been reported in children <16 y.

ROUTE & DOSAGE

Partial Seizures, Patients Receiving Anticonvulsants Other Than Valproic Acid

Adult: **PO** Start with 50 mg q.d. for 2 wk, then 50 mg b.i.d. for 2 wk, may titrate up to 300–500 mg/d in 2 divided doses (max: 700 mg/d)

Child: **PO** 2–16 y, 1 mg/kg b.i.d. times 2 wk, then 2.5 mg/kg b.i.d. times 2 wk, then 5 mg/kg b.i.d. (max: 15 mg/kg/d or 400 mg/d)

Partial Seizures, Patients Receiving Valproic Acid

Adult: **PO** Start with 25 mg q.o.d. for 2 wk, then 25 mg q.d. for 2 wk, may titrate up to 150 mg/d in 2 divided doses (max: 200 mg/d)

Child: **PO** 2–16 y, 0.2 mg/kg/d × 2 wk, then 0.5 mg/kg/d × 2 wk, then 1 mg/kg/d (max: 5 mg/kg/d or 250 mg/d)

Bipolar Disorder, Patients Not Receiving Valproate or Carbamazepine

Adult: **PO** Start with 25 mg q.d. for 2 wk, then 50 mg q.d. for 2 wk, then 100 mg/d for 1 wk, then 200 mg q.d.

Bipolar Disorder, Patients Receiving Valproic Acid

Adult: **PO** Start with 25 mg q.o.d. for 2 wk, then 25 mg q.d. for 2 wk, then 50 mg q.d. for 1 wk, then 100 mg q.d.

Bipolar Disorder, Patients Receiving Carbamazepine

Adult: **PO** Start with 50 mg q.d. for 2 wk, then 50 mg b.i.d. for 2 wk, then 100 b.i.d for 1 wk, then 150 mg b.i.d. for 1 wk, then 200 mg b.i.d.

Common adverse effects in *italic*, life-threatening effects underlined; generic names in **bold**; classifications in SMALL CAPS; ♣ Canadian drug name; ☯ Prototype drug

ADMINISTRATION

Oral

- Note: Reduced dose may be warranted with renal and hepatic impairment.
- Ensure that chewable tablets are chewed or crushed before being swallowed with a liquid.
- When discontinued, drug should be tapered off gradually over a 2-wk period, unless patient safety is at risk.

ADVERSE EFFECTS (≥1%) **CNS:** *Dizziness, ataxia, somnolence, headache,* aphasia, vertigo, confusion, slurred speech, irritability, depression, incoordination, hostility. **GI:** *Nausea,* vomiting, anorexia, abdominal pain, diarrhea, dyspepsia, constipation. **Urogenital:** Hematuria, dysmenorrhea, vaginitis. **Special Senses:** *Diplopia, blurred vision.* **Musculoskeletal:** Peripheral neuropathy, chills, tremor, arthralgia. **Skin:** Rash (including <u>Stevens-Johnson syndrome, toxic epidermal necrolysis</u>), urticaria, pruritus, alopecia, acne. **Respiratory:** *Rhinitis,* pharyngitis, cough.

INTERACTIONS Drug: Carbamazepine, phenobarbital, primidone, phenytoin, fosphenytoin, ORAL CONTRACEPTIVES may decrease lamotrigine levels. **Valproic acid** may increase lamotrigine levels. Lamotrigine may decrease serum levels of **valproic acid.** May affect efficacy of ORAL CONTRACEPTIVES. Chronic **acetaminophen** use may affect serum concentrations of lamotrigine. **Herbal: Ginkgo** may decrease anticonvulsant effectiveness. **Evening primrose** oil may affect seizure threshold.

PHARMACOKINETICS Absorption: Readily absorbed from GI tract; 98% reaches systemic circula-

tion. **Onset:** 12 wk. **Peak:** 1–4 h. **Distribution:** 55% protein bound; crosses placenta; distributed into breast milk. **Metabolism:** In liver to inactive metabolite. **Elimination:** Can induce own metabolism; excreted in urine. **Half-Life:** 25–30 h.

CLINICAL IMPLICATIONS

Assessment & Drug Effects

- Withhold drug if rash develops and immediately report to physician.
- Monitor the plasma levels of lamotrigine and other anticonvulsants when given concomitantly.
- Monitor patients with bipolar disorder for worsening of their symptoms and suicidal ideation. Withhold the drug and immediately report to physician.
- Monitor for adverse reactions when lamotrigine is used with other anticonvulsants, especially valproic acid.
- Be aware of drug interactions and closely monitor when interacting drugs are added or discontinued.

Patient & Family Education

- Do not take drug if a skin rash develops. Contact your physician immediately.
- Notify physician for any of the following: Worsening seizure control, skin rash, ataxia, blurred vision or diplopia, fever or flu-like symptoms.
- Do not drive or engage in other potentially hazardous activities until response to the drug is known.
- Use protection from sunlight or ultraviolet light until tolerance is known; drug increases photosensitivity.
- Women using oral contraceptives to avoid pregnancy should add a barrier contraceptive.
- Schedule periodic ophthalmologic exams with long-term use.
- Do not discontinue lamotrigine abruptly.

Common adverse effects in *italic*, life-threatening effects <u>underlined</u>; generic names in **bold**; classifications in SMALL CAPS; ✦ Canadian drug name; ⊘ Prototype drug

855

LANSOPRAZOLE

(lan'so-pra-zole)

Prevacid, Prevacid IV

Classifications: ANTISECRETORY; PROTON PUMP INHIBITOR

Therapeutic: ANTIULCER; ANTISECRETORY; PROTON PUMP INHIBITOR

Prototype: Omeprazole

Pregnancy Category: B

AVAILABILITY 15 mg, 30 mg sustained release capsules; 15 mg, 30 mg orally disintegrating tablets; 15 mg, 30 mg packets for suspension; 30 mg powder for injection

ACTION & *THERAPEUTIC EFFECT*
Belongs to a class of antisecretory compounds that are gastric acid pump inhibitors. Specifically, it suppresses gastric acid secretion by inhibiting the H^+, K^+-ATPase enzyme [the acid (proton H^+) pump] in the parietal cells. *Suppresses gastric acid formation in the stomach.*

USES Short-term treatment of duodenal ulcer (up to 4 wk) and erosive esophagitis (up to 8 wk), pathologic hypersecretory disorders, gastric ulcers; in combination with clarithromycin and amoxicillin for *Helicobacter pylori*. Gastroesophageal reflux disease (GERD).

CONTRAINDICATIONS Hypersensitivity to lansoprazole, severe hepatic impairment, proton pump inhibitors (PPIs) hypersensitivity, lactation, infants.

CAUTIOUS USE Hepatic disease, pregnancy (category B).

ROUTE & DOSAGE

Duodenal Ulcer
Adult: **PO** 15 mg once daily times 4 wk

Erosive Esophagitis
Adult: **PO** 30 mg once daily times 8 wk, then decrease to 15 mg once daily **IV** 30 mg once daily for up to 7 d

GERD
Adult: **PO** 15 mg once daily for up to 8 wk
Child: **PO** 1–11 y, 1.5 mg/kg/d (max: 30 mg/d)

Hypersecretory Disorder
Adult: **PO** 60 mg once daily (max: 120 mg/d in divided doses), may need to be adjusted for hepatic impairment

H. pylori
Adult: **PO** 30 mg b.i.d. times 2 wk, in combination with 2 antibiotics

Hepatic Impairment
Dose reduction required in severe hepatic disease

ADMINISTRATION

Oral
- *All forms:* Administer dosage 30 min a.c. Give once daily dose before breakfast.
- Give at least 30 min prior to any concurrent sucralfate therapy.
- Do not crush or chew capsules. Capsules can be opened and granules sprinkled on food or mixed with 40 mL of apple juice and administered through an NG tube. Do not crush or chew granules.
- Note: Disintegrating tablets contain phenylalanine and should not be used for patients with PKU. Capsule and syrup formulations do not contain phenylalanine.

Intravenous

PREPARE: IV Infusion: Add 5 mL of sterile water for injection to each 30 mg vial to yield 6 mg/mL.

Swirl gently to mix. Further dilute in 50 mL of NS, RL, or D5W. If reconstituted with NS or LR, administer within 24 h. If reconstituted with D5W, administer within 12 h. *ADMINISTER:* **IV Infusion:** Infuse over 30 min through the in-line filter provided. Use a dedicated line or a Y-site; flush Y-site with NS before and after administration. Do NOT give IV push. Immediately stop infusion if precipitation or discoloration occurs.

INCOMPATIBILITIES **Solution/additive, Y-site:** Do not administer with other drugs or diluents.

▪ Reconstituted solution can be held for 1 h at 25° C (77° F) before further dilution.

ADVERSE EFFECTS (≥1%) **CNS:** Fatigue, dizziness, headache. **GI:** Nausea, *diarrhea,* constipation, anorexia, increased appetite, thirst, elevated serum transaminases (AST, ALT). **Skin:** Rash.

INTERACTIONS Drug: May decrease **theophylline** levels. **Sucralfate** decreases lansoprazole bioavailability. May interfere with absorption of **ketoconazole, digoxin, ampicillin,** or IRON SALTS. Use with **warfarin** may increase INR. May alter **tacrolimus** concentration. **Food:** Food reduces peak lansoprazole levels by 50%.

PHARMACOKINETICS Absorption: Rapidly from GI tract after leaving stomach; unstable in acidic media. **Onset:** Acid reduction within 2 h; ulcer relief within 1 wk. **Peak:** 1.5–3 h. **Duration:** 24 h. **Distribution:** 97% bound to plasma proteins. **Metabolism:** In liver via CYP2C19 and 3A4. **Elimination:** 14–25% in urine as metabolites; part of dose eliminated in bile and feces. **Half-Life:** 1.5 h.

CLINICAL IMPLICATIONS

Assessment & Drug Effects

▪ Lab tests: Monitor CBC, kidney & liver function tests, and serum gastric levels periodically.

▪ Monitor for therapeutic effectiveness of concurrently used drugs that require an acid medium for absorption (e.g., digoxin, ampicillin, ketoconazole).

Patient & Family Education

▪ Inform physician of significant diarrhea.

LANTHANUM CARBONATE

(lan-tha′num)
Fosrenol
Classifications: ELECTROLYTE AND WATER BALANCE AGENT; PHOSPHATE BINDER
Therapeutic: PHOSPHATE BINDER
Prototype: Sevelamer Hydrochloride
Pregnancy Category: C

AVAILABILITY 250 mg, 500 mg, 750 mg, 1g chewable tablets

ACTION & *THERAPEUTIC EFFECT*
Lanthanum is used for the management of hyperphosphatemia in end-stage renal disease; it is a calcium/aluminum-free phosphate binding agent. Has a higher affinity for binding to phosphate than calcium or aluminum. Low systemic absorption minimizes the risk of aluminum intoxication and hypercalcemia. Lanthanum decreases phosphate absorption from the diet. Dietary phosphate bound to lanthanum carbonate is excreted in the feces. *Lowers serum phosphate.*

USES Reduce serum phosphate levels in patients with end-stage renal disease.

Common adverse effects in *italic*, life-threatening effects underlined; generic names in **bold**; classifications in SMALL CAPS; ✦ Canadian drug name; ⑩ Prototype drug

857

CONTRAINDICATIONS Prior hypersensitivity to lanthanum carbonate; pregnancy (category C); children <18 y.
CAUTIOUS USE Bowel obstruction, Crohn's disease, acute peptic ulcer, ulcerative colitis; lactation.

ROUTE & DOSAGE

Hyperphosphatemia
Adult: **PO** 250–500 mg t.i.d. with or immediately after meals; may titrate up every 2–3 wk in increments of 750 mg/d to achieve acceptable serum phosphate levels (max: 3750 mg/d)

ADMINISTRATION
Oral
- Give with or immediately after a meal.
- Tablets must be chewed completely before swallowing. Whole tablets should not be swallowed.
- Store at 15°–30° C (59°–86° F).

ADVERSE EFFECTS (≥1%) **CNS:** Headache. **CV:** Hypotension. **GI:** *Nausea, vomiting, diarrhea,* abdominal pain, constipation. **Respiratory:** Bronchitis, rhinitis. **Other:** Dialysis graft occlusion.

PHARMACOKINETICS Absorption: Minimal from GI tract. **Metabolism:** Not metabolized. **Elimination:** In feces. **Half-Life:** 53 h.

CLINICAL IMPLICATIONS
Assessment & Drug Effects
- Monitor for dialysis graft occlusion, as lanthanum therapy may increase occlusion risk.
- Lab tests: serum phosphate levels during dosage titration and regularly throughout treatment; periodic serum calcium, bicarbonate, and chloride.

Patient & Family Education
- Chew chewable tablets completely, then swallow.
- Report promptly any of the following: headache, drowsiness, dizziness, fainting, confusion, irritability, nausea, vomiting, or loss of appetite.

LARONIDASE

(la-ron'i-dase)
Aldurazyme
Classifications: ENZYME REPLACEMENT THERAPY
Therapeutic: ENZYME REPLACEMENT THERAPY
Prototype: Pancrelipase
Pregnancy Category: B

AVAILABILITY 2.9 mg/5 mL injection

ACTION & THERAPEUTIC EFFECT
Laronidase is a recombinant form of human alpha-L-iduronidase used for enzyme replacement therapy in individuals with mucopolysaccharidosis I (MPSI). This is an inherited lysosomal storage disease caused by deficiency of the enzyme alpha-L-iduronidase. *Replacement therapy for individuals lacking the enzyme alpha-L-iduronidase in mucopolysaccharidosis.*

USES Treatment of Hurler and Hurler-Scheie forms of mucopolysaccharidosis I (MPS I); treatment of moderate to severe Scheie form of MPS I.

CONTRAINDICATIONS Hypersensitivity to laronidase; children <5 y.
CAUTIOUS USE Renal or hepatic dysfunction; history of allergies, asthma; hypersensitivity to drugs, especially recombinant forms; pregnancy (category B), lactation.

ROUTE & DOSAGE

Mucopolysaccharidosis
Adult/Child: **IV** *>5 y,* 0.58 mg/kg infused over 3–4 h once/wk

ADMINISTRATION

Intravenous
▪ Pretreatment with antipyretics and/or antihistamines 60 min prior to infusion is recommended.

PREPARE: **IV Infusion:** Determine volume of infusion based on the patient's body weight (100 mL if ≤20 kg or 250 mL if >20 kg). Prepare IV infusion of 0.1% albumin (human) in NS injection as follows: 1) remove and discard a volume of NS injection equal to the volume of albumin (human) to be added to the IV bag (for 100 mL infusion use 2 mL of 5% albumin of 0.4 mL or 25% albumin, for 250 mL infusion use 5 mL of 5% albumin or 1 mL of 25% albumin); 2) add the appropriate volume of albumin to the IV bag and gently rotate; 3) add the albumin to IV bag and gently rotate to mix; 4) withdraw and discard a volume of the 0.1% albumin in NS injection from the IV bag equal to the volume of laronidase concentrate to be added; 5) slowly withdraw the required amount of laronidase from vials (avoid excessive agitation), then slowly add laronidase to the IV solution. Use immediately.

ADMINISTER: **IV Infusion:** Infuse initially at 10 mcg/kg/h; may increase q15min during first h, as tolerated, to a max rate of 200 mcg/kg/hr. Maintain max for remainder of the infusion (2–3 h).
▪ Store at 2°–8° C (36°–46° F). Do not freeze or shake. Discard any unused drug.

INCOMPATIBILITIES **Solution/additive:** No compatibility data available. Do not recommend mixing or infusing with other drugs.

ADVERSE EFFECTS (≥1%) **Body as a Whole:** Infusion reactions (flushing, fever, headache, rash), injection site pain, hypersensitivity reactions. **CNS:** Hyperreflexia, paresthesias. **CV:** Chest pain, hypotension, edema. **Hematologic:** Thrombocytopenia. **Respiratory:** Upper respiratory tract infection. **Skin:** Rash.

PHARMACOKINETICS Half-Life: 1.5–3.6 h.

CLINICAL IMPLICATIONS

Assessment & Drug Effects
▪ Monitor for infusion-related reactions. Slow or stop infusion and notify physician for any of the following: cough, bronchospasm, dyspnea, urticaria, angioedema, pruritus, or other signs of hypersensitivity.
▪ Lab tests: Periodic platelet count.

Patient & Family Education
▪ Report promptly difficulty breathing, rash, or itching.

LATANOPROST ℗

(la-tan′o-prost)
Xalatan
Classifications: EYE PREPARATION; PROSTAGLANDIN
Therapeutic: PROSTAGLANDIN
Pregnancy Category: C

AVAILABILITY 0.005% solution

ACTION & *THERAPEUTIC EFFECT*
Prostaglandin analog that is thought to reduce intraocular pressure (IOP) by increasing the outflow of aqueous humor. *Reduces elevated in-*

Common adverse effects in *italic*, life-threatening effects <u>underlined</u>; generic names in **bold**; classifications in SMALL CAPS; ♣ Canadian drug name; ℗ Prototype drug

859

traocular pressure in patients with open-angle glaucoma.

USES Treatment of open-angle glaucoma, ocular hypertension and elevated intraocular pressure (IOP).

CONTRAINDICATIONS Hypersensitivity to latanoprost or another component in the solution; pregnancy (category C); lactation; intraocular infection; conjunctivitis.

CAUTIOUS USE Lactation; active intraocular inflammation such as: iritis or uveitis; patients at risk for macular edema; hepatic or renal impairment. Safety and effectiveness in children are not established.

ROUTE & DOSAGE

Glaucoma
Adult: **Ophthalmic** 1 drop in affected eye(s) q.d. in evening

ADMINISTRATION

Installation

- Ensure that contact lenses are removed prior to installation and not reinserted for 15 min after installation.
- Apply only to affected eye(s). Ensure that only one drop is instilled.
- Do not allow tip of dropper to touch eye.
- Wait at least 5 min before/after instillation of other eye drops.
- Refrigerate at 2°–8° C (36°–46° F). Protect from light.

ADVERSE EFFECTS (≥1%) **Body as a Whole:** Headaches, asthenia, flu-like symptoms. **GI:** Abnormal liver function tests. **Skin:** Rash. **Special Senses:** *Conjunctival hyperemia, growth of eyelashes, ocular pruritus,* ocular dryness, visual disturbance, ocular burning, foreign body sensation, eye pain, pigmenta-

tion of the periocular skin, blepharitis, cataract, superficial punctate keratitis, eyelid erythema, ocular irritation, and eyelash darkening, eye discharge, tearing, photophobia, allergic conjunctivitis, increases in iris pigmentation (brown pigment), conjunctival edema.

INTERACTIONS Drug: Precipitation may occur if mixed with eye drops containing **thimerosal;** space other EYE PREPARATIONS at least 5 min apart.

PHARMACOKINETICS Absorption: Absorbed through the cornea. **Onset:** 3–4 h. **Peak IOP reduction:** 8–12 h. **Distribution:** Minimal systemic distribution. **Metabolism:** Hydrolyzed in aqueous humor to active form. **Elimination:** Renally excreted. **Half-Life:** 17 min.

CLINICAL IMPLICATIONS

Assessment & Drug Effects

- Withhold eye drops and notify physician if acute intraocular inflammation (iritis or uveitis) or external eye inflammation are noted.
- Note that increased pigmentation of the iris and eyelid, and additional growth of eyelashes on the treated eye are adverse effects that may develop gradually over months to years.

Patient & Family Education

- Contact physician immediately if any ocular reaction occurs, especially conjunctivitis and lid reactions.
- Note: Increased pigmentation of the iris and eyelid, and additional growth of eyelashes on the treated eye, are possible adverse effects of this drug. Persons with light colored eyes receiving treatment to one eye may develop a darker eye.

LEFLUNOMIDE

(le-flu′no-mide)
Arava
Classifications: BIOLOGIC RE-
SPONSE MODIFIER; IMMUNOMODU-
LATOR; ANTIINFLAMMATORY
Therapeutic: DISEASE-MODIFYING
ANTIRHEUMATIC DRUG (DMARD)
Pregnancy Category: X

AVAILABILITY 10 mg, 20 mg, 100
mg tablets

ACTION & *THERAPEUTIC EFFECT*

An immunomodulator that demonstrates antiinflammatory effects. Suppression of pyrimidine
synthesis in T and B lymphocytes
interferes with RNA and protein
synthesis in cells that are involved
in the inflammatory process
within affected joints. Reduction
in activity of these lymphocytes
leads to reduced cytokine and an-
tibody-mediated destruction of
the synovial joints as well as attenuation of the inflammatory
process. *Reduces the S&S of rheumatoid arthritis (RA), retards structural joint damage, and improves
physical function.*

USES Active RA.

CONTRAINDICATIONS Hepatic disease; jaundice; lactase deficiency;
hypersensitivity to leflunomide;
patients with positive hepatitis B
or C serology; malignancy, particularly lymphoproliferative disorders; severe immunosuppression;
vaccination, infants; uncontrolled
infection; pregnancy (category X),
lactation.

CAUTIOUS USE Renal insufficiency;
renal failure; alcoholism; immunosuppression; lactase deficiency; infection. Use in patients <18 y has
not been fully studied.

ROUTE & DOSAGE

Rheumatoid Arthritis

Adult: **PO** Initiate with a loading
dose of 100 mg/d times 3 d, then
maintenance dose of 20 mg q.d.,
may decrease to 10 mg/d if
higher dose is not tolerated

ADMINISTRATION

Oral
- Initiate with a 3-d loading dose followed by a lower maintenance
dose.

ADVERSE EFFECTS (≥1%) **Body
as a Whole:** Allergic reaction, asthenia, flu-like syndrome, infection,
pain, back pain, arthralgia, leg
cramps, synovitis, tenosynovitis.
CNS: Dizziness, headache, paresthesias, peripheral neuropathy. **CV:**
Hypertension, chest pain. **GI:** *Diarrhea,* increased LFTs (ALT and AST),
abdominal pain, anorexia, dyspepsia, gastroenteritis, nausea, mouth
ulcer, vomiting, weight loss, hepatotoxicity. **Metabolic:** Hypokalemia.
Respiratory: Bronchitis, cough, respiratory infection, pharyngitis, pneumonia, rhinitis, sinusitis. **Skin:** Rash,
alopecia, eczema, pruritus, dry skin,
Stevens-Johnson syndrome, toxic
epidermal necrolysis (rare). **Urogenital:** UTI.

INTERACTIONS Drug: Rifampin
may significantly increase leflunomide levels; **cholestyramine,
charcoal** decrease absorption; caution should be used with other
hepatotoxic drugs.

PHARMACOKINETICS Absorption:
Approximately 80% reaches systemic circulation. **Peak:** 6–12 h for
active metabolite. **Distribution:** >99%
protein bound. **Metabolism:** Metabolized primarily to M1 (active me-

Common adverse effects in *italic*, life-threatening effects underlined; generic names
in **bold**; classifications in SMALL CAPS; ♣ Canadian drug name; ☉ Prototype drug

861

tabolite). **Elimination:** 43% in urine, 48% in feces. **Half-Life:** 19 d for active metabolite.

CLINICAL IMPLICATIONS
Assessment & Drug Effects

- Lab tests: Baseline screening to rule out hepatitis B or C; baseline and monthly liver enzymes × 12 mo, then every 6 mo thereafter.
- Monitor carefully for and report immediately S&S of infection; withhold leflunomide if infection is suspected.
- Monitor BP and weight periodically. Doses greater than 25 mg/d are associated with a greater incidence of side effects such as alopecia, weight loss, and elevated liver enzymes.

Patient & Family Education

- Use reliable contraception while taking leflunomide.
- Note: Both women and men need to discontinue leflunomide and undergo a drug elimination procedure prescribed by the physician BEFORE conception.
- Withhold drug if you develop an infection and notify the physician before resuming the drug.
- Notify physician about any of the following: hair loss, weight loss, GI distress, rash, or itching.

LEPIRUDIN ⊕

(le-pir'u-din)
Refludan
Classifications: ANTICOAGULANT; DIRECT THROMBIN INHIBITOR
Therapeutic: ANTICOAGULANT; ANTI-THROMBOTIC
Pregnancy Category: B

AVAILABILITY 50 mg powder for injection

ACTION & *THERAPEUTIC EFFECT*
Highly specific direct inhibitor of thrombin, including thrombin entrapped within established clots. One molecule of lepirudin binds to one molecule of thrombin and thereby blocks the thrombogenic activity of thrombin. Increases PT/INR and aPTT values in relation to the dose given. *Has antithrombotic activity; effectiveness is indicated by aPTT ratio in target range of 1.5 to 2.5.*

USES Anticoagulation in patients with heparin-induced thrombocytopenia (HIT).

CONTRAINDICATIONS Hypersensitivity to lepirudin; intracranial bleeding; patients with increased risk of bleeding (e.g., recent surgery, CVA, advanced kidney impairment); lactation. Safety and efficacy in children not established.

CAUTIOUS USE Serious liver injury (e.g., cirrhosis); concomitant administration with streptokinase; renal impairment; pregnancy (category B).

ROUTE & DOSAGE

Anticoagulation

Adult: **IV** 0.4 mg/kg initial bolus (max: 44 mg) followed by 0.15 mg/kg/h (max: 16.5 mg/h) for 2–10 d, adjust rate to maintain aPTT of 1.5–2.5

Renal Impairment

Cl_{cr} 45–60 mL/min: initial dose 0.2 mg/kg, then 0.075 mg/kg/h; 30–44 mL/min: initial dose 0.2 mg/kg then 0.045 mg/kg/h; 15–29 mL/min: initial dose 0.2 mg/kg, then 0.0225 mg/kg/h; <15 mL/min: do not use

ADMINISTRATION

Intravenous

PREPARE: Direct: Reconstitute by adding 1 mL of sterile water for injection or NS to the 50-mg vial. To prepare bolus dose, withdraw reconstituted solution into a 10-cc syringe and dilute to 10 mL with sterile water for injection, NS or D5W to yield 5 mg/mL. **Continuous:** Transfer the contents of two reconstituted vials into 250 or 500 mL of D5W or NS to yield of 0.4 or 0.2 mg/mL, respectively. ***ADMINISTER: Direct:*** Give over 15–20 sec. **Continuous:** Give at a rate determined by body weight.

- Diluted solution is stable for 24 h during infusion. Store unopened vials at 2°–25° C (36°–77° F).

ADVERSE EFFECTS (≥1%) **CNS:** Intracranial bleeding. **CV:** Heart failure, ventricular fibrillation, pericardial effusion, MI. **GI:** Abnormal LFTs. **Hematologic:** Bleeding from injection site, anemia, hematoma, bleeding, hematuria, GI and rectal bleeding, epistaxis, hemothorax, vaginal bleeding. **Respiratory:** Pneumonia, cough, bronchospasm, stridor, dyspnea. **Skin:** Allergic skin reactions. **Body as a Whole:** Sepsis, abnormal kidney function, multiorgan failure.

INTERACTIONS Drug: Warfarin, NSAIDS, SALICYLATES, ANTIPLATELET AGENTS increases risk of bleeding. **Herbal: Feverfew, ginkgo, ginger, valerian** may potentiate bleeding.

PHARMACOKINETICS Distribution: Distributed primarily to extracellular compartment. **Metabolism:** By catabolic hydrolysis in serum. **Elimination:** 48% in urine. **Half-Life:** 1.3 h.

CLINICAL IMPLICATIONS

Assessment & Drug Effects

- Lab tests: Baseline PT/INR and aPTT prior to initiation of therapy (withhold therapy and notify physician if baseline aPTT ratio ≥2.5); aPTT 4 h after start of therapy and at least once daily (more often with renal or hepatic impairment) thereafter.
- Give with extreme caution to those at increased risk for bleeding.
- Monitor carefully for bleeding events (e.g., from puncture wounds, hematoma, hematuria); and report immediately.
- Do not give oral anticoagulants until lepirudin dose has been reduced and aPTT ratio lowered to just above 1.5.

LETROZOLE

(le′tro-zole)

Femara

Classifications: ANTINEOPLASTIC; AROMATASE INHIBITOR

Therapeutic: ANTINEOPLASTIC; AROMATASE INHIBITOR

Prototype: Anastrozole

Pregnancy Category: D

AVAILABILITY 2.5 mg tablets

ACTION & *THERAPEUTIC EFFECT* Nonsteroid competitive inhibitor of aromatase, the enzyme that converts androgens to estrogens. It does not inhibit adrenal steroid synthesis. *Results in the regression of estrogen-dependent tumors.*

USES Advanced breast cancer in postmenopausal women following antiestrogen therapy, first-line treatment of locally advanced or metastasized breast cancer in postmenopausal women.

CONTRAINDICATIONS Hypersensitivity to letrozole; pregnancy (cate-

Common adverse effects in *italic*, life-threatening effects underlined; generic names in **bold**; classifications in SMALL CAPS; ✦ Canadian drug name; ⊙ Prototype drug

863

gory D), pregnant women, women of childbearing age, premenopausal females, hormone replacement therapy (HRT).

CAUTIOUS USE Moderate to severe hepatic impairment; lactation. Safety and efficacy in children are not established.

ROUTE & DOSAGE

Breast Cancer
Adult: **PO** 2.5 mg q.d.

Hepatic Impairment
Reduce the dose in severe hepatic impairment (Child-Pugh C class) by 50%.

ADMINISTRATION

Oral
- Give without regard to food.

ADVERSE EFFECTS (≥1%) **Body as a Whole:** Fatigue, peripheral edema, asthenia, weight increase, *musculoskeletal pain,* arthralgia. **CNS:** Headache, somnolence, dizziness. **CV:** Chest pain, hypertension, hypercholesterolemia. **GI:** Nausea, vomiting, constipation, diarrhea, abdominal pain, anorexia, dyspepsia. **Respiratory:** Dyspnea, cough. **Skin:** Hot flushes, rash, pruritus.

INTERACTIONS Drug: ESTROGENS, ORAL CONTRACEPTIVES could interfere with the pharmacologic action of letrozole.

PHARMACOKINETICS Absorption: Rapidly absorbed from GI tract. **Metabolism:** In liver by cytochromes P450 3A4 and 2A6. **Elimination:** 90% in urine. **Half-Life:** 2 d.

CLINICAL IMPLICATIONS

Assessment & Drug Effects
- Lab tests: Periodically monitor serum calcium and CBC with differential.

- Monitor carefully for S&S of thrombophlebitis or thromboembolism; report immediately.

Patient & Family Education
- Notify physician immediately if S&S of thrombophlebitis develop (see Appendix F).

LEUCOVORIN CALCIUM

(loo-koe-vor'in)
Classifications: BLOOD FORMER; ANTIANEMIC AGENT; ANTIDOTE
Therapeutic: ANTIANEMIC; ANTIDOTE
Pregnancy Category: C

AVAILABILITY 5 mg, 10 mg, 15 mg, 25 mg tablets; 50 mg, 100 mg, 350 mg vials

ACTION & *THERAPEUTIC EFFECT*

A reduced form of folic acid; unlike folic acid, it does not require enzymatic reduction and therefore is readily available to participate in reactions. Functions as an essential cell growth factor. When given during antineoplastic therapy, it prevents serious toxicity by protecting cells from the action of folic acid antagonists such as methotrexate. *Antidote against folic acid antagonists such as methotrexate.*

USES Folate-deficient megaloblastic anemias due to sprue, pregnancy, and nutritional deficiency when oral therapy is not feasible. Also to prevent or diminish toxicity of antineoplastic folic acid antagonists, particularly methotrexate. Also to treat advanced colorectal cancer when given concurrently with 5-fluorouracil (5-FU).

CONTRAINDICATIONS Undiagnosed anemia, pernicious anemia, or other megaloblastic anemias secondary to vitamin B_{12} deficiency; intrathecal

administration; oral form with stomatitis; pregnancy (category C).
CAUTIOUS USE Renal dysfunction, elderly; seizure disorders; lactation.

ROUTE & DOSAGE

Megaloblastic Anemia
Adult/Child: **IV/IM** Up to 1 mg/d

Leucovorin Rescue for Methotrexate Toxicity
Adult/Child: **PO/IM/IV** 10 mg/m^2 q6h until serum methotrexate levels are reduced

Leucovorin Rescue for Other Folate Antagonist Toxicity
Adult/Child: **PO/IM/IV** 5–15 mg/d

Advanced Colorectal Cancer
Adult: **IV** 200 mg/m^2 followed by fluorouracil 370 mg/m^2

ADMINISTRATION

- Note: Oral route is NOT recommended for doses higher than 25 mg or if patient is likely to vomit.

Intramuscular
- Use 3 mg ampules for IM injection.
- Give deep into a large muscle.

Intravenous

PREPARE: **Direct:** Give 1 mL (3 mg) ampules, which contain benzyl alcohol, undiluted. **IV Infusion:** For doses <10 mg/m^2, reconstitute each 50 mg in 5 mL (10 mg per 1 mL in 10 mL) of bacteriostatic water for injection with benzyl alcohol. For doses >10 mg/m^2 reconstitute, as above, but with sterile water for injection without a preservative. Final concentration is 10 mg/mL. Further dilute in 100–500 mL of IV solutions (e.g., D5W, NS, RL) to yield a concentration of 10–20 mg/mL of IV solution.

ADMINISTER: **Direct:** Give 160 mg or fraction thereof over 1 min. **IV Infusion:** Do not exceed direct IV rate. Give more slowly if the volume of IV solution to be infused is large; over 15–60 min, depending on the volume of solution.

INCOMPATIBILITIES **Solution/additive: Fluorouracil. Y-site: Amphotericin B cholesteryl complex, droperidol, foscarnet, sodium bicarbonate.**

- Use solution reconstituted with bacteriostatic water within 7 d. Use solution reconstituted with sterile water for injection immediately.
- Protect from light.

ADVERSE EFFECTS (≥1%) **Body as a Whole:** Allergic sensitization (urticaria, pruritus, rash, wheezing). **Hematologic:** Thrombocytosis.

INTERACTIONS Drug: May enhance adverse effects of **fluorouracil;** may reverse therapeutic effects of **trimethoprim-sulfamethoxazole.**

PHARMACOKINETICS Onset: Within 30 min. **Duration:** 3–6 h. **Distribution:** Crosses placenta; distributed into breast milk. **Metabolism:** In liver and intestinal mucosa to tetrahydrofolic acid derivatives. **Elimination:** 80–90% in urine, 5–8% in feces.

CLINICAL IMPLICATIONS

Assessment & Drug Effects
- Monitor neurologic status. Use of leucovorin alone in treatment of pernicious anemia or other megaloblastic anemias associated with vitamin B_{12} deficiency can result in an apparent hematological remission while allowing already present neurologic damage to progress.
- Lab tests: Do Cl_{cr} determinations prior to initiation of leucovorin, urine pH prior to and about every

Common adverse effects in *italic*, life-threatening effects underlined; generic names in **bold**; classifications in SMALL CAPS; ♣ Canadian drug name; ⊘ Prototype drug

865

6 h throughout therapy; daily serum creatinine levels are recommended to detect onset of kidney function impairment.

Patient & Family Education
- Notify physician of S&S of a hypersensitivity reaction immediately (see Appendix F).

LEUPROLIDE ACETATE ℗℟

(loo-proe'lide)

Eligard, Lupron, Lupron Depot, Lupron Depot-Ped, Viadur

Classifications: GONADOTROPIN-RELEASING HORMONE (GNRH) ANALOG

Therapeutic: GNRH ANALOG
Pregnancy Category: X

AVAILABILITY 5 mg/mL injection; 3.75 mg, 7.5 mg, 11.25 mg, 15 mg, 22.5 mg, 30 mg microspheres for injection (depot formulations); 65 mg implant

ACTION & *THERAPEUTIC EFFECT*
Occupies and desensitizes pituitary GnRH receptors, resulting initially in release of gonadotropins LH and FSH and stimulation of ovarian and testicular steroidogenesis. *Long-term administration suppresses both gonadotropin secretion and steroidogenesis and leads to prostatic and testicular atrophy. **Antitumor effect:** May inhibit growth of hormone-dependent tumors as indicated by reduction in concentrations of PSA and serum testosterone to levels equal to or less than pretreatment levels. **Contraceptive effect:** By inhibiting gonadotropin release, ovulation or spermatogenesis is suppressed. Has antitumor effect in males, and contraceptive effects in both males and females.*

USES Palliative treatment of advanced prostatic carcinoma as alternative to orchiectomy or estrogen administration; endometriosis; anemia caused by leiomyomata.

UNLABELED USES Breast cancer; male contraceptive; delayed puberty.

CONTRAINDICATIONS Known hypersensitivity to benzyl alcohol, GnRH analog hypersensitivity; following orchiectomy or estrogen therapy; metastatic cerebral lesions; menstruation, abnormal vaginal bleeding, pregnancy (category X), lactation.

CAUTIOUS USE Life-threatening carcinoma in which rapid symptomatic relief is necessary; osteoporosis; elderly.

ROUTE & DOSAGE

Palliative Treatment for Prostate Cancer

Adult: **SC** 1 mg/d **IM** 7.5 mg/mo or 22.5 mg q3mo or 30 mg q4mo (depot preparation) **Implant** one implant q12mo

Endometriosis, Anemia

Adult: **IM** 3.75 mg qmo or 11.25 mg q3mo

Precocious Puberty

Child: **IM** Depot-Ped, 0.15–0.3 mg/kg q28d (min: 7.5 mg), titrate by 3.75-mg increments q4wk

ADMINISTRATION

Subcutaneous
- Do not use Depot-Ped form for SC injection.
- Rotate injection sites.

Intramuscular
- Prepare solution for Depot-Ped injection using a 22-gauge needle (or syringe provided by manufacturer), withdraw 1.5 mL of diluent

from the supplied ampul and inject it into the vial. Shake well to form a uniform suspension. Withdraw entire contents and administer immediately.

- Do not administer parenteral drug formulation if particulate matter or discoloration is present.
- Refrigerate unopened vials. Store vial in use at room temperature for several months with minimal loss of potency. Protect from light and freezing.

ADVERSE EFFECTS (≥1%) **Body as a Whole:** *Disease flare (worsening of S&S of carcinoma),* injection site irritation, asthenia, fatigue, fever, facial swelling. **CNS:** Dizziness, pain, headache, paresthesia. **CV:** *Peripheral edema,* cardiac arrhythmias, <u>MI</u>. **Endocrine:** *Hot flushes, impotence, decreased libido,* gynecomastia, breast tenderness, amenorrhea, vaginal bleeding, thyroid enlargement, hypoglycemia. **GI:** Nausea, vomiting, constipation, anorexia, sour taste, GI bleeding, diarrhea. **Musculoskeletal:** Increased bone pain, myalgia. **Renal:** Increased hematuria, dysuria, flank pain. **Respiratory:** Pleural rub, pulmonary fibrosis flare. **Hematologic:** Decreased Hct, Hgb. **Skin:** Pruritus, rash, hair loss.

INTERACTIONS Drug: ANDROGENS, ESTROGENS would counteract therapeutic effects.

PHARMACOKINETICS Absorption: Readily absorbed from SC or IM sites. **Metabolism:** By enzymes in hypothalamus and anterior pituitary. **Half-Life:** 3 h.

CLINICAL IMPLICATIONS

Assessment & Drug Effects

- Monitor PSA and testosterone levels in males with prostate cancer.

A gradual rise in values after their decrease may signify treatment failure.

- Inspect injection site. If local hypersensitivity reactions occur (erythema, induration), suspect sensitivity to benzyl alcohol. Report to physician.
- Monitor I&O ratio and pattern. Report hematuria and decreased output. Carefully monitor voiding problems.

Patient & Family Education

- When used for prostate cancer, bone pain and voiding problems (i.e., symptoms of tumor obstruction) usually increase during first several weeks of continuous treatment but are transient. Hot flushes also may be experienced.
- Notify physician of neurologic S&S (paresthesia and weakness in lower limbs). Exercise caution when walking without assistance.
- When used for endometriosis. Continuous treatment may cause amenorrhea and other menstrual irregularities.

LEVALBUTEROL HYDROCHLORIDE

(lev-al-bu′ter-ole)

Xopenex, Xopenex HFA

Classifications: BETA-ADRENERGIC AGONIST; BRONCHODILATOR

Therapeutic: BRONCHODILATOR; BETA-ADRENERGIC AGONIST

Prototype: Albuterol

Pregnancy Category: C

AVAILABILITY 0.63 mg/3 mL, 1.25 mg/3 mL inhalation solution

ACTION & *THERAPEUTIC EFFECT*

An isomer of albuterol with beta$_2$-adrenergic agonist properties, drug acts on the beta$_2$ receptors of the

Common adverse effects in *italic*, life-threatening effects <u>underlined</u>; generic names in **bold**; classifications in SMALL CAPS; ♣ Canadian drug name; ☯ Prototype drug

867

smooth muscles of the bronchial tree, thus resulting in bronchodilation. *Effective bronchodilator that decreases airway resistance, facilitates mucous drainage, and increases vital capacity.*

USES Treatment or prevention of bronchospasm in patients with reversible obstructive airway disease.

CONTRAINDICATIONS Hypersensitivity to levalbuterol or albuterol; angioedema; pregnancy (category C); children <6 y; lactation.

CAUTIOUS USE Cardiovascular disorders especially coronary insufficiency, cardiac arrhythmias, hypertension, QT elongation, convulsive disorders; diabetes mellitus, diabetic ketoacidosis; older adults; seizures, status asthmaticus, tachycardia; hypersensitivity to sympathetic amines; hyperthyroidism, thyrotoxicosis.

ROUTE & DOSAGE

Bronchospasm

Adult: **Inhalation** 0.63 mg by nebulization t.i.d. every 6–8 h, may increase to 1.25 mg t.i.d. if needed
Child: **Inhalation** 6–11 y, 0.31 mg by nebulization t.i.d. every 6–8 h (max: 0.63 mg t.i.d.)

ADMINISTRATION

Inhalation

- Use vials within 2 wk of opening pouch. Protect vial from light and use within one wk after removal from pouch. Use only if solution in vial is colorless.

INCOMPATIBILITIES **Solution/additive:** Compatibility when mixed with other drugs in a nebulizer has not been established.

- Store at 15°–25° C (59°–77° F) in protective foil pouch.

ADVERSE EFFECTS (≥1%) **Body as a Whole:** Allergic reactions, flu syndrome, pain. **CNS:** Migraine, dizziness, nervousness, tremor, anxiety. **CV:** Tachycardia. **GI:** Dyspepsia. **Respiratory:** Increased cough, viral infection, rhinitis, sinusitis, turbinate edema, paradoxical bronchospasm. **Endocrine:** Increase in serum glucose.

INTERACTIONS Drug: BETA-ADRENERGIC BLOCKERS may antagonize **levalbuterol** effects; MAOI, TRICYCLIC ANTIDEPRESSANTS may potentiate **levalbuterol** effects on vascular system; ECG changes or hypokalemia may be exacerbated by LOOP or THIAZIDE DIURETICS.

PHARMACOKINETICS Onset: 5–15 min. **Duration:** 3–6 h. **Half-Life:** 3.3 h.

CLINICAL IMPLICATIONS

Assessment & Drug Effects

- Monitor for S&S of CNS or cardiovascular stimulation (e.g., BP, HR, respiratory status).
- Lab tests: Periodic serum potassium levels especially with coadministered loop or thiazide diuretics.
- Monitor diabetics for loss of glycemic control.

Patient & Family Education

- Seek medical advice immediately if a previously effective dose becomes ineffective.
- Report immediately to physician: chest pains or palpitations, swelling of the eyelids, tongue, lips or face; increased wheezing or difficulty breathing.
- Do not use drug more frequently than prescribed.
- Exercise caution with hazardous activities; dizziness and vertigo are possible side effects.
- Check with physician before taking OTC cold medication.

LEVETIRACETAM

(lev-e-tir′a-ce-tam)
Keppra
Classifications: ANTICONVULSANT
Therapeutic: ANTICONVULSANT
Pregnancy Category: C

AVAILABILITY 250 mg, 500 mg, 750 mg tablets; 100 mg/mL oral solution

ACTION & *THERAPEUTIC EFFECT*

The precise mechanism of antiepileptic effects is unknown. It is a broad spectrum antiepileptic agent, which does not involve GABA inhibition. It prevents epileptiform burst firing and propagation of seizure activity. *Inhibits complex partial seizures and prevents epileptic and seizure activity.*

USES Adjunctive therapy for partial onset seizures in adults and children >4 y of age.

CONTRAINDICATIONS Hypersensitivity to levetiracetam; labor; pregnancy (category C), lactation; children <4 y; suicidal ideation.

CAUTIOUS USE Renal impairment; renal disease; renal failure; older adults; history of psychosis or depression, suicidal tendencies.

ROUTE & DOSAGE

Partial Onset Seizures

Adult: PO 500 mg b.i.d., may increase by 500 mg b.i.d. q2wk (max: 3000 mg/d)
Child (4–16 y): PO 20 mg/kg/d in 2 divided doses; may increase by 20 mg/kg q2wk up to 60 mg/kg/d

Renal Impairment

Cl_{cr} 50–80 mL/min: 500–1000 mg q12h; 30–50 mL/min: 250–750 mg q12h; <30 mL/min: 250–500 mg q12h; hemodialysis: 500–1000 mg q24h

ADMINISTRATION

Oral

- Reduced doses are indicated when creatinine clearance is <80 mL/min.
- Make dosage increment changes at 2-wk intervals.
- Taper dose if discontinued.
- Give supplemental doses to dialysis patients after dialysis.
- Store at 15°–30° C (59°–86° F).

ADVERSE EFFECTS (≥1%) **Body as a Whole:** *Asthenia, headache, infection,* pain. **CNS:** *Somnolence,* amnesia, anxiety, ataxia, depression, dizziness, emotional lability, hostility, nervousness, vertigo, paradoxical increase in seizures (as add-on therapy). **GI:** Anorexia. **Respiratory:** Cough, pharyngitis, rhinitis, sinusitis. **Special Senses:** Diplopia. **Other:** Increased symptoms of depression; suicidal ideation.

INTERACTIONS Drug: Levetiracetam does not decrease **estrogen, warfarin,** or **digoxin** levels or affect levels of other antiepileptic drugs.

PHARMACOKINETICS Absorption: Rapidly and almost completely absorbed. **Peak:** 1 h; steady-state 2 d. **Distribution:** <10% protein bound. **Metabolism:** Minimal hepatic metabolism. **Elimination:** Renally eliminated. **Half-Life:** 7.1 h (9.6 h in older adults).

CLINICAL IMPLICATIONS

Assessment & Drug Effects

- Monitor individuals with a history of psychosis or depression for signs and symptoms of suicidal tendencies, suicidal ideation, and suicidality. Report any of these symptoms to the physician.
- Monitor & notify physician of difficulty with gait or coordination.

L

Common adverse effects in *italic*, life-threatening effects underlined; generic names in **bold**; classifications in SMALL CAPS; ✦ Canadian drug name; ✪ Prototype drug

869

- Lab tests: Periodic CBC with differential, Hct & Hgb, LFTs.
- Monitor for changes in phenytoin blood levels with coadministered drugs.

Patient & Family Education
- Monitor for signs and symptoms of suicidality, especially in children with a history of depression or psychosis.
- Do not drive or engage in potentially hazardous activities until response to drug is known.
- Do not abruptly discontinue drug. MUST use gradual dose reduction/taper.
- Notify physician of intention to become pregnant.

LEVOBETAXOLOL HYDROCHLORIDE

(le-vo-be-tax'oh-lol)
Betaxon
Pregnancy Category: C
See Appendix A-1.

LEVOBUNOLOL

(lee-voe-byoo'noe-lole)
Betagan
Pregnancy Category: C
See Appendix A-1.

LEVODOPA (L-DOPA) ⊙

(lee-voe-doe'pa)
Classifications: ANTICHOLINERGIC; ANTIPARKINSON AGENT
Therapeutic: ANTIPARKINSON AGENT
Pregnancy Category: C

AVAILABILITY 100 mg, 250 mg, 500 mg tablets and capsules

ACTION & *THERAPEUTIC EFFECT*
Drug is a metabolic precursor of dopamine, a catecholamine neurotransmitter. Unlike dopamine, levodopa readily crosses the blood–brain barrier. Precise mechanism of action unknown. *Levodopa restores dopamine levels in extrapyramidal centers (believed to be depleted in parkinsonism).*

USES Idiopathic Parkinson's disease, postencephalitic and arteriosclerotic parkinsonism, and parkinsonism symptoms associated with manganese and carbon monoxide poisoning.
UNLABELED USES To relieve pain of herpes zoster (shingles), liver coma (caused by cirrhosis or fulminating hepatitis), bone pain in metastatic breast carcinoma, adjunctive therapy in CHF.

CONTRAINDICATIONS Known hypersensitivity to levodopa; narrow-angle glaucoma patients with suspicious pigmented lesion or history of melanoma; acute psychoses, severe psychoneurosis, within 2 wk of use of MAO INHIBITORS; pregnancy (category C), lactation. Safe use in children <2 y is not established.
CAUTIOUS USE Cardiovascular, kidney, liver, or endocrine disease, history of MI with residual arrhythmias; peptic ulcer; convulsions; psychiatric disorders; chronic wide-angle glaucoma; diabetes; pulmonary diseases, bronchial asthma; patients receiving antihypertensive drugs.

ROUTE & DOSAGE

Parkinson's Disease
Adult: **PO** 500 mg to 1 g daily in 2 or more equally divided doses, may be increased by 100–750 mg q3–7d (max: 8 g/d); used in combination with carbidopa, decrease levodopa dose by 75–80%

Common adverse effects in *italic*, life-threatening effects underlined; generic names in **bold**; classifications in SMALL CAPS; ✦ Canadian drug name; ⊙ Prototype drug

ADMINISTRATION

Oral

- Give with food to reduce nausea. Absorption is decreased with high-protein meals.
- Crush tablets or empty capsule content into fruit juice as needed.
- Store in tight, light-resistant containers.

ADVERSE EFFECTS (≥1%) CNS: *Choreiform and involuntary movements,* increased hand tremor, bradykinetic episodes (on–off phenomena), trismus, grinding of teeth (bruxism), ataxia, muscle twitching, numbness, weakness, fatigue, headache, opisthotonos, confusion, agitation, anxiety, euphoria, insomnia, nightmares; psychotic episodes with paranoid delusions or hallucinations, severe depression, including suicidal tendencies, hypomania. **CV:** *Orthostatic hypotension;* palpitations, tachycardia, hypertension. **Special Senses:** *Blepharospasm,* diplopia, blurred vision, dilated pupils. **GI:** *Anorexia, nausea, vomiting,* abdominal distress, flatulence, dry mouth, dysphagia, sialorrhea; burning sensation of tongue, bitter taste, diarrhea or constipation; GI bleeding, hepatotoxicity. **Body as a Whole:** Flushing, increased sweating, weight gain or loss, edema, dark sweat or urine. **Urogenital:** Urinary retention or incontinence, increased sexual drive, priapism, postmenopausal bleeding. **Skin:** Skin rashes, loss of hair. **Respiratory:** Rhinorrhea, bizarre breathing patterns.

DIAGNOSTIC TEST INTERFERENCE

Altered laboratory values: Elevated *BUN, AST, ALT, alkaline phosphatase, LDH, bilirubin, protein-bound iodine,* serum level of *growth hormone;* decreased *glucose tolerance; hypokalemia,* decreased *WBC, Hgb, Hct. Urine glucose:* False-negative tests may result with use of *glucose oxidase methods* (e.g., *Clinistix, Tes-Tape*) and false-positive results with the *copper reduction method* (e.g., *Clinitest*), especially in patients receiving large doses. It is reported that *Clinistix* and *TesTape* may be used if reading is taken at margin of wet and dry tape. *Urinary ketones:* There is possibility of false-positive tests by dipsticks, e.g., *Acetest* (equivocal), *Ketostix, Labstix; Serum and urinary uric acid:* False elevations by *colorimetric methods,* but not with *uricase; Urinary protein:* False increases by *Lowry method; Urinary VMA:* False decreases by *Pisano method; Urinary catecholamine:* False increases by *Hingerty method. PKU urine test:* Interference.

INTERACTIONS Drug: MAO INHIBITORS may precipitate hypertensive crisis; TRICYCLIC ANTIDEPRESSANTS augment postural hypotension; PHENOTHIAZINES, **haloperidol** may antagonize the therapeutic effects of levodopa; **pyridoxine** can reverse effects of levodopa; ANTICHOLINERGICS may exacerbate abnormal involuntary movements; **methyldopa** may increase toxic CNS effects; HALOGENATED GENERAL ANESTHETICS increase risk of arrhythmias. **Food:** food decreases the rate and extent of levodopa absorption. **Herbal: Kava-kava** may worsen parkinsonian symptoms.

PHARMACOKINETICS Absorption: Rapidly and well absorbed from GI tract; lower absorption if taken with food. **Peak:** 1–3 h. **Distribution:** Widely distributed in body. **Metabolism:** Most of drug is decarboxylated to dopamine in lumen of GI tract, liver, and serum. **Elimination:** 80–85% of dose excreted in urine in 24 h. **Half-Life:** 1 h.

L

Common adverse effects in *italic*, life-threatening effects underlined; generic names in **bold**; classifications in SMALL CAPS; ✚ Canadian drug name; ⊘ Prototype drug

871

CLINICAL IMPLICATIONS

Assessment & Drug Effects

- Monitor vital signs, particularly during period of dosage adjustment. Report alterations in BP, pulse, and respiratory rate and rhythm.
- Supervise ambulation as indicated. Orthostatic hypotension is usually asymptomatic, but some patients experience dizziness and syncope. Tolerance to this effect usually develops within a few months of therapy.
- Make accurate observations and report adverse reactions and therapeutic effects promptly. Rate of dosage increase is determined primarily by patient's tolerance and response to drug.
- Monitor all patients closely for behavior changes.
- Monitor patients with chronic wide-angle glaucoma for changes in intraocular pressure.
- Monitor diabetics for loss of glycemic control.
- Lab tests: Monitor blood glucose & HbA$_{1c}$, CBC, Hgb and Hct, serum potassium, and liver & kidney function periodically.
- Report promptly muscle twitching and spasmodic winking (blepharospasm); these are early signs of overdosage. Patients on full therapeutic doses for >1 y may develop such abnormal involuntary movements as well as jerky arm and leg movements. Symptoms tend to increase if dosage is not reduced.
- Report to physician any S&S of the on–off phenomenon sometimes associated with chronic management: Rapid unpredictable swings in intensity of motor symptoms of parkinsonism evidenced by increase in bradykinesia (attacks of "leg freezing" or slow body movement).
- Monitor mental status for S&S of drug-induced neuropsychiatric adverse reactions.

Patient & Family Education

- Do not take with high-protein foods. Also avoid high consumption of food sources of pyridoxine, including wheat germ, green vegetables, banana, whole-grain cereals, muscular and glandular meats (especially liver), legumes. Learn good dietary practices.
- Do not take OTC preparations or fortified cereals unless approved by physician. Multivitamins, antinauseants, and fortified cereals usually contain vitamin B$_6$.
- Make positional changes slowly, particularly from lying to upright position, and dangle legs a few minutes before standing.
- Resume activities gradually, observing safety precautions to avoid injury. Elevation of mood and sense of well-being may precede objective improvement. Significant improvement usually occurs during second or third wk of therapy, but may not occur for 6 mo or more in some patients.
- Follow prescribed drug regimen. Sudden withdrawal of medication can lead to parkinsonism crisis (with return of marked rigidity, akinesia, tremor, hyperpyrexia) or neuroleptic malignant syndrome (NMS).
- A metabolite of levodopa may cause urine to darken and sweat to be dark-colored.

LEVOFLOXACIN

(lev-o-flox′a-sin)

Levaquin, Iquix, Quixin

Classifications: ANTIBIOTIC; QUINOLONE

Therapeutic: ANTIBIOTIC, QUINO-LONE
Prototype: Ciprofloxacin
Pregnancy Category: C

AVAILABILITY 250 mg, 500 mg, 750 mg tablets; 25 mg/mL solution; 25 mg/mL injection; 0.5%, 1.5% ophthalmic solution

ACTION & *THERAPEUTIC EFFECT*
A broad-spectrum fluoroquinolone antibiotic that inhibits DNA-gyrase, an enzyme necessary for bacterial replication, transcription, repair, and recombination. *Effective against many gram-positive and gram-negative organisms.*

USES Treatment of maxillary sinusitis, acute exacerbations of bacterial bronchitis, community-acquired pneumonia, uncomplicated skin/skin structure infections, UTI, acute pyelonephritis caused by susceptible bacteria; acute bacterial sinusitis; chronic bacterial prostatitis; bacterial conjunctivitis.

CONTRAINDICATIONS Hypersensitivity to levofloxacin and quinolone antibiotics; hypokalemia, tendon pain, pregnancy (category C); syphilis; viral infections; phototoxicity; lactation. Safety and efficacy in children <18 y are not established.
CAUTIOUS USE Known or suspected CNS disorders predisposed to seizure activity (e.g., severe cerebral atherosclerosis), risk factors associated with potential seizures (e.g., some drug therapy, renal insufficiency), dehydration, colitis; QT prolongation, cardiac arrhythmias; renal impairment; diabetes; patients receiving theophylline or caffeine; older adults.

ROUTE & DOSAGE

Infections
Adult: **PO** 500 mg q24h × 10 d
IV 500 mg infused over 60 min q24h × 7–14 d

Community-Acquired Pneumonia
Adult: **PO/IV** 750 mg q24h × 5 d

Uncomplicated UTI
Adult: **PO/IV** 250 mg q24h × 14 d

Complicated UTI, Pyelonephritis
Adult: **PO/IV** 250 mg q24h × 10 d

Acute Bacterial Sinusitis
Adult: **PO/IV** 750 mg q.d. × 5 d

Chronic Bacterial Prostatitis
Adult: **PO/IV** 500 mg q24h × 28 d

Skin & Skin Structure Infections
Adult: **PO** 750 mg q24h × 14 d

Renal Impairment
For initial dose of 500 mg, adjust as follows: Cl_{cr} 20–50 mL/min: 250 mg q24h; <20 mL/min: 250 mg q48h
For initial dose of 750 mg, adjust as follows: Cl_{cr} 20–50 mL/min: 750 mg q48h; 10–19 mL/min: 500 mg q48h; <20 mL/min: 250 mg q48h

Bacterial Conjunctivitis
Adult: **Ophthalmic** Days 1–2, 1–2 drops in affected eye(s) q2h while awake (max: 8 times/d), days 3–7, 1–2 drops in affected eye(s) q4h while awake (max: 4 times/d)

ADMINISTRATION

Oral
- Do not give oral drug within 2 h of drugs containing aluminum or magnesium (antacids), iron, zinc, or sucralfate.

Common adverse effects in *italic*, life-threatening effects underlined; generic names in **bold**; classifications in SMALL CAPS; ♣ Canadian drug name; ⊘ Prototype drug

873

Intravenous

PREPARE: Intermittent: Withdraw the desired dose from 500 mg (25 mg/mL) single-use vial. Add to enough D5W, NS, D5/NS, D5/RL, or other compatible solutions to produce a concentration of 5 mg/mL [e.g., 500 mg (or 20 mL) added to 80 mL]. Discard any unused drug remaining in the vial.

ADMINISTER: Intermittent: Give over ≥60 min. Do NOT give a bolus dose or infuse too rapidly.

INCOMPATIBILITIES Y-site: Do not add any drugs to levofloxacin solution or infuse simultaneously through the same line (manufacturer recommendation). **Azithromycin, furosemide, heparin, indomethacin, insulin, nitroglycerin, nitroprusside, propofol.**

- Store tablets in a tightly closed container. IV solution is stable for 72 h at 25° C (77° F).

ADVERSE EFFECTS (≥1%) **CNS:** Headache, insomnia, dizziness. **GI:** Nausea, diarrhea, constipation, vomiting, abdominal pain, dyspepsia. **Skin:** Rash, pruritus. **Special Senses:** Decreased vision, foreign body sensation, transient ocular burning, ocular pain, photophobia. **Urogenital:** Vaginitis. **Body as a Whole:** Injection site pain or inflammation, chest or back pain, fever, pharyngitis. **Other:** Cartilage erosion.

DIAGNOSTIC TEST INTERFERENCE May cause false positive on **opiate screening tests.**

INTERACTIONS Drug: Magnesium or **aluminum**-containing antacids, **sucralfate, iron, zinc** may decrease levofloxacin absorption; NSAIDS may increase risk of CNS reactions, including seizures; may cause hyper- or hypoglycemia in patients on ORAL HYPOGLYCEMIC AGENTS.

PHARMACOKINETICS Absorption: Rapidly from GI tract. **Peak:** PO 1–2 h. **Distribution:** Penetrates lung tissue, 24–38% protein bound. **Metabolism:** Minimally in the liver. **Elimination:** Primarily unchanged in urine. **Half-Life:** 6–8 h.

CLINICAL IMPLICATIONS

Assessment & Drug Effects

- Lab tests: Do C&S test prior to beginning therapy and periodically.
- Withhold therapy and report to physician immediately any of the following: Skin rash or other signs of a hypersensitivity reaction (see Appendix F); CNS symptoms such as seizures, restlessness, confusion, hallucinations, depression; skin eruption following sun exposure; symptoms of colitis such as persistent diarrhea; joint pain, inflammation, or rupture of a tendon; hypoglycemic reaction in diabetic on an oral hypoglycemic agent.

Patient & Family Education

- Learn important indications for discontinuing drug and immediately notifying physician.
- If tendon pain occurs, discontinue the drug and notify the physician.
- Consume fluids liberally while taking levofloxacin.
- Allow a minimum of 2 h between drug dosage and taking any of the following: Aluminum or magnesium antacids, iron supplements, multivitamins with zinc, or sucralfate.
- Avoid exposure to excess sunlight or artificial UV light.
- Avoid NSAIDS while taking levofloxacin, if possible.

LEVONORGESTREL-RELEASING INTRAUTERINE SYSTEM

(lee′vo-nor-jes-trel)

Mirena

Classifications: HORMONE; PRO-GESTIN

Therapeutic: PROGESTIN; HORMONE

Prototype: Norgestrel

Pregnancy Category: X

AVAILABILITY 52 mg unit

ACTION & *THERAPEUTIC EFFECT*

A progestogen that induces morphological changes in the endometrium including glandular atrophy, leukocytic infiltration, and decrease in glandular and stromal mitoses. Contraceptive effect may result by preventing follicular maturation and ovulation, thickening of the cervical mucus of the uterus, thus preventing passage of sperm into the uterus, or decreasing ability of sperm to survive in an environment of altered endometrium. *Effective contraceptive.*

USES Hormonal contraception.

CONTRAINDICATIONS Hypersensitivity to any component of the product; previously inserted IUD which has not been removed; pregnancy (category X), suspicion of pregnancy, within 6 wk of giving birth or prior to complete involution of the uterus; history of ectopic pregnancy or any condition which predisposes to ectopic pregnancy; history of uterine anomalies which distort the uterine cavity; acute PID or history of PID unless there has been a subsequent intrauterine pregnancy; cervicitis or vaginitis or other lower genital tract infection; genital actinomycosis; woman or partner has multiple sex partners; vaginal bleeding of un-known etiology; postpartum endometriosis or septic abortion in past 3 mo; abnormal Pap or suspected/known cervical neoplasm; known or suspected carcinoma of the breast; acute liver disease or liver tumor; immune deficiency states.

CAUTIOUS USE Women at risk for venereal disease; anemia; diabetes mellitus; history of psychic depression; persons susceptible to acute intermittent porphyria; fluid retention; history of migraines; impaired liver function; presence or history of salpingitis; venereal disease; genital bleeding of unknown etiology; anticoagulant therapy or coagulopathy; previous pelvic surgery.

ROUTE & DOSAGE

Contraception

Adult: **Intrauterine** Insert device on 7th day of menstrual cycle; may leave in place up to 5 y

ADMINISTRATION

Intrauterine

- Inserted only by physician or other person qualified by special training in the intrauterine system.

ADVERSE EFFECTS (≥1%) **CV:** Hypertension. **GI:** Abdominal pain, nausea. **Endocrine:** Breast tenderness/pain. **Hematologic:** Anemia. **Metabolic:** Weight gain. **CNS:** Depression, emotional lability, headache (including migraine), nervousness. **Skin:** Acne, alopecia, eczema. **Urogenital:** Amenorrhea, dysmenorrhea, leukorrhea, decreased libido, vaginal moniliasis, vulvo-vaginal disorders, cervicitis, dyspareunia.

INTERACTIONS Drug: No clinically significant interactions established.

L

Common adverse effects in *italic*, life-threatening effects underlined; generic names in **bold**; classifications in SMALL CAPS; ✦ Canadian drug name; ✿ Prototype drug

875

PHARMACOKINETICS Peak: Few weeks. **Duration:** 5 y. **Distribution:** 86% protein bound. **Metabolism:** In liver. **Elimination:** In both urine and feces. **Half-Life:** 37 h.

CLINICAL IMPLICATIONS

Assessment & Drug Effects

- Monitor for decreased pulse, perspiration, or pallor during insertion. Keep patient supine until these signs have disappeared.
- Monitor BP especially with preexisting hypertension.
- Monitor diabetics for loss of glycemic control.

Patient & Family Education

- Report S&S of PID immediately: (e.g., prolonged or heavy bleeding, unusual vaginal discharge, abdominal or pelvic pain or tenderness, painful sexual intercourse, chills, fever, and flu-like symptoms).
- Report any of the following to physician immediately: Migraine (if not experienced before) or exceptionally severe headache, or jaundice.
- Note: Diabetics should monitor blood glucose closely for indications of loss of control.

LEVORPHANOL TARTRATE

(lee-vor'fa-nole)

Levo-Dromoran

Classifications: ANALGESIC; NARCOTIC (OPIATE) AGONIST
Therapeutic: NARCOTIC ANALGESIC
Prototype: Morphine Sulfate
Pregnancy Category: B; D with long-time use or high doses
Controlled Substance: Schedule II

AVAILABILITY 2 mg tablets

ACTION & *THERAPEUTIC EFFECT*
A potent synthetic morphine derivative with agonist activity only. Reported to cause less nausea, vomiting, and constipation than equivalent doses of morphine but may produce more sedation, smooth-muscle stimulation, and respiratory depression. *More potent as an analgesic and has somewhat longer duration of action than morphine.*

USES To relieve moderate to severe pain. Also preoperatively to allay apprehension.

CONTRAINDICATIONS Hypersensitivity to levorphanol; labor and delivery, pregnancy (category B, and D with long time use or high doses); lactation.

CAUTIOUS USE Patients with impaired respiratory reserve, or depressed respirations from another cause (e.g., severe infection, obstructive respiratory conditions, chronic bronchial asthma). Patients with head injury or increased intracranial pressure; acute MI, cardiac dysfunction; liver disease, biliary surgery, alcohol or delirium tremens; liver or kidney dysfunction, hypothyroidism, Addison's disease, toxic psychosis, prostatic hypertrophy, or urethral stricture; concurrent use with CNS depressant drugs; older adults, other vulnerable populations; renal impairment.

ROUTE & DOSAGE

Moderate to Severe Pain
Adult: **PO** 2–3 mg q6–8h prn

ADMINISTRATION

Oral

- Give in the smallest effective dose to minimize the possibility of tolerance and physical dependence.

- Store tablets at 15°–30° C (59°–86° F) unless otherwise directed. Store in tightly covered, light-resistant containers.

ADVERSE EFFECTS (≥1%) **CNS:** Euphoria, *sedation, drowsiness,* nervousness, confusion. **CV:** Hypotension, fast, slow, or pounding heartbeat. **GI:** *Nausea,* vomiting, dry mouth, cramps, *constipation.* **Urogenital:** Urinary frequency, urinary retention, sedation. **Special Senses:** Blurred vision. **Respiratory:** Respiratory depression. **Body as a Whole:** Physical dependence.

INTERACTIONS Drug: Alcohol and other CNS DEPRESSANTS compound sedation and CNS depression. **Herbal: St. John's wort** may increase sedation.

PHARMACOKINETICS Peak: 60–90 min. **Duration:** 6–8 h. **Distribution:** Crosses placenta; distributed into breast milk. **Metabolism:** In liver. **Elimination:** In urine. **Half-Life:** 1.2 h.

CLINICAL IMPLICATIONS

Assessment & Drug Effects
- Assess degree of pain relief. Drug is most effective when peaks and valleys of pain relief are avoided.
- Monitor bowel function.
- Monitor ambulation, especially in older adult patients.

Patient & Family Education
- Do not drive or engage in other potentially hazardous activities.
- Avoid alcohol and other CNS depressants unless approved by physician.
- Note: Ambulation may increase frequency of nausea and vomiting.
- Increase fluid and fiber intake to offset constipating effects of the drug.

LEVOTHYROXINE SODIUM (T₄) ℞

(lee-voe-thye-rox′een)

Eltroxin ✦, Levothroid, Levoxyl, Levo-T, Levolet, Novothyrox, Synthroid, Unithroid
Classifications: HORMONE; THYROID HORMONE REPLACEMENT
Therapeutic: THYROID HORMONE REPLACEMENT
Pregnancy Category: A

AVAILABILITY 25 mcg, 50 mcg, 75 mcg, 88 mcg, 100 mcg, 112 mcg, 125 mcg, 137 mcg, 150 mcg 175 mcg, 200 mcg, 300 mcg tablets

ACTION & *THERAPEUTIC EFFECT*
Synthetically prepared levo-isomer of thyroxine (T₄), with similar actions and uses (thyroxine, principal component of thyroid gland secretions, determines normal thyroid function). Principal effects include diuresis, loss of weight and puffiness, increased sense of well-being and activity tolerance, and rise of T₃ and T₄ serum levels toward normal *By replacing decreased or absent thyroid hormone, it restores metabolic rate of a hypothyroid individual.*

USES Specific replacement therapy for diminished or absent thyroid function resulting from primary or secondary atrophy of gland, surgery, excessive radiation or antithyroid drugs, congenital defect. Administered orally for hypothyroid state; administered IV for myxedematous coma or other thyroid dysfunctions demanding rapid replacement, as well as in failure to respond to oral therapy.

CONTRAINDICATIONS Hypersensitivity to levothyroxine; thyrotoxicosis; severe cardiovascular condi-

Common adverse effects in *italic,* life-threatening effects underlined; generic names in **bold**; classifications in SMALL CAPS; ✦ Canadian drug name; ℗ Prototype drug

877

tions, acute MI; obesity treatment; adrenal insufficiency.

CAUTIOUS USE Cardiac disease, angina pectoris, cardiac arrhythmias, hypertension; diabetes mellitus; older adult, impaired kidney function, pregnancy (category A).

ROUTE & DOSAGE

Thyroid Replacement

Adult: **PO** 25–50 mcg/d, gradually increased by 50–100 mcg q1–4wk to usual dose of 100–400 mcg/d
Child: **PO** 0–6 mo, 8–10 mcg/kg/d or 25–50 mcg/d; 6–12 mo, 6–8 mcg/kg/d or 50–75 mcg/d; 1–5 y, 5–6 mcg/kg/d or 75–100 mcg/d; 6–12 y, 4–5 mcg/kd/d or 100–150 mcg/d; >12 y, 2–3 mcg/kg/d or >150 mcg/d

ADMINISTRATION

Oral

- Give as a single dose, preferably 1 h before or 2 h after breakfast, to prevent insomnia. Give consistently with respect to meals.
- Maintenance dosage for older adults may be 25% lower than for heavier and younger adults.
- Store in tight, light-resistant container.

ADVERSE EFFECTS (≥1%) **CNS:** Irritability, nervousness, *insomnia,* headache (pseudotumor cerebri in children), tremors, craniosynostosis (excessive doses in children). **CV:** Palpitations, tachycardia, arrhythmias, angina pectoris, hypertension. **GI:** Nausea, diarrhea, change in appetite. **Urogenital:** Menstrual irregularities. **Body as a Whole:** Weight loss, heat intolerance, sweating, fever, leg cramps, temporary hair loss (children).

INTERACTIONS Drug: **Cholestyramine, colestipol** decrease absorption of levothyroxine; **epinephrine, norepinephrine** increase risk of cardiac insufficiency; ORAL ANTICOAGULANTS may potentiate hypoprothrombinemia.

PHARMACOKINETICS Absorption: Variable and incompletely absorbed from GI tract (50–80%). **Peak:** 3–4 wk. **Duration:** 1–3 wk. **Distribution:** Gradually released into tissue cells. **Half-Life:** 6–7 d.

CLINICAL IMPLICATIONS

Assessment & Drug Effects

- Monitor pulse before each dose during dose adjustment. If rate is >100, consult physician.
- Monitor for adverse effects during early adjustment. If metabolism increases too rapidly, especially in older adults and heart disease patients, symptoms of angina or cardiac failure may appear.
- Note: Levothyroxine may aggravate severity of previously obscured symptoms of diabetes mellitus, Addison's disease, or diabetes insipidus. Therapy for these disorders may require adjustment.
- Lab tests: Baseline and periodic tests of thyroid function. Closely monitor PT/INR and assess for evidence of bleeding if patient is receiving concurrent anticoagulant therapy. A decrease in anticoagulant dosage may be needed 1–4 wk after concurrent levothyroxine is started.
- Monitor bone age, growth, and psychomotor function in children.
- Some children have partial hair loss after a few months; it returns even with continued therapy.
- Synthroid 100 and 300 mcg tablets contain tartrazine, which may cause an allergic-type reaction in

certain patients; particularly those who are hypersensitive to aspirin.

Patient & Family Education

- Thyroid replacement therapy is usually lifelong.
- Learn how to self-monitor pulse rate. Notify physician if rate begins to increase above 100 or if rhythm changes are noted.
- Notify physician immediately of signs of toxicity (e.g., chest pain, palpitations, nervousness).
- Avoid OTC medications unless approved by physician.

LIDOCAINE HYDROCHLORIDE ℗ℝ

(lye′doe-kane)

Anestacon, Dilocaine, L-Caine, Lidoderm, Lida-Mantle, Lido-ject-1, LidoPen Auto Injector, Nervocaine, Octocaine, Xylocaine, Xylocard ♦

Classifications: ANTIARRHYTHMIC, CLASS IB; LOCAL ANESTHETIC (AMIDE TYPE)
Therapeutic: ANTIARRHYTHMIC, CLASS IB; LOCAL ANESTHETIC (AMIDE TYPE)
Pregnancy Category: B

AVAILABILITY Antidysrhythmic 300 mg/3 mL auto-injector; 0.2%, 0.4%, 0.8%, 1%, 2%, 4%, 10%, 20% injections **Local Anesthetic** 0.5%, 1%, 1.5%, 2%, 4% injection **Topical** 2%, 2.5%, 4%, 5% solution; 2.5%, 5% ointment; 0.5%, 4% cream; 0.5%, 2.5% gel; 0.5%, 10% spray; 2% jelly; 0.5% patch

ACTION & *THERAPEUTIC EFFECT*
Similar to those of procainamide and quinidine, but has little effect on myocardial contractility, AV and intraventricular conduction, cardiac output, and systolic arterial pressure in equivalent doses. Exerts antiarrhythmic action (Class IB) by suppressing automaticity in His-Purkinje system and by elevating electrical stimulation threshold of ventricle during diastole. Action as local anesthetic is more prompt, more intense, and longer lasting than that of procaine. *Suppresses automaticity in His-Purkinje system and elevates electrical stimulation threshold of ventricle during diastole. Prompt, intense, and long-lasting local anesthetic. It decreases pain through a reversible nerve conduction blockade.*

USES Rapid control of ventricular arrhythmias occurring during acute MI, cardiac surgery, and cardiac catheterization and those caused by digitalis intoxication. Also as surface and infiltration anesthesia and for nerve block, including caudal and spinal block anesthesia and to relieve local discomfort of skin and mucous membranes. Patch for relief of pain associated with post-herpetic neuralgia.

UNLABELED USES Refractory status epilepticus.

CONTRAINDICATIONS History of hypersensitivity to amide-type local anesthetics; application or injection of lidocaine anesthetic in presence of severe trauma or sepsis, blood dyscrasias, supraventricular arrhythmias, Stokes-Adams syndrome, untreated sinus bradycardia, severe degrees of sinoatrial, atrioventricular, and intraventricular heart block.

CAUTIOUS USE Liver or kidney disease, CHF, marked hypoxia, respiratory depression, hypovolemia, shock; myasthenia gravis; debilitated patients, older adults; family history of malignant hyperthermia (fulminant hypermetabolism); pregnancy (category B). Topical use in eyes,

Common adverse effects in *italic*, life-threatening effects underlined; generic names in **bold**; classifications in SMALL CAPS; ♦ Canadian drug name; ℗ Prototype drug

879

over large body areas, over prolonged periods, in severe or extensive trauma or skin disorders.

ROUTE & DOSAGE

Ventricular Arrhythmias

Adult: **IV** 50–100 mg bolus at a rate of 20–50 mg/min, may repeat in 5 min, then start infusion of 1–4 mg/min immediately after first bolus, not more than 300 mg/h **IM/SC** 200–300 mg IM, may repeat once after 60–90 min
Child: **IV** 1 mg/kg bolus dose, then 20–50 mcg/kg/min infusion

Anesthetic Uses

Adult: **Infiltration** 0.5–1% solution **Nerve Block** 1–2% solution **Epidural** 1–2% solution **Caudal** 1–1.5% solution **Spinal** 5% with glucose **Saddle Block** 1.5% with dextrose **Topical** 2.5–5% jelly, ointment, cream, or solution

Post-Herpetic Neuralgia

Adult: **Topical** Apply up to 3 patches over intact skin in most painful areas once for up to 12 h per 24 h period

ADMINISTRATION

Intramuscular

- Give in deltoid muscle as preferred site.

Topical

- Do not apply topical lidocaine to large areas of skin or to broken or abraded surfaces. Consult physician about covering area with a dressing.
- Avoid topical preparation contact with eyes.

Intravenous

- Note: Do not use lidocaine solutions containing preservatives for spinal or epidural (including caudal) block. Use ONLY lidocaine HCl injection without preservatives or epinephrine that is specifically labeled for IV injection or infusion.

PREPARE: Direct: Give undiluted. **IV Infusion:** Use D5W for infusion. For adults, add 1 g to 250 or 500 mL to yield 2 or 4 mg/mL, respectively; for children, add 120 mg to 100 m to yield 1.2 mg/mL. ▪ Do not use solutions with particulate matter or discoloration.
ADMINISTER: Direct: Give at a rate of 50 mg or fraction thereof over 1 min. **IV Infusion:** Use microdrip and infusion pump. Rate of flow is usually ≤4 mg/min.
INCOMPATIBILITIES Solution/additive: Ampicillin, cefazolin, methohexital, phenytoin. Y-site: Amphotericin B cholesteryl complex, phenytoin, thiopental.

- Discard partially used solutions of lidocaine without preservatives.

ADVERSE EFFECTS (≥1%) **CNS:** Drowsiness, dizziness, light-headedness, restlessness, confusion, disorientation, irritability, apprehension, euphoria, wild excitement, numbness of lips or tongue and other paresthesias including sensations of heat and cold, chest heaviness, difficulty in speaking, <u>difficulty in breathing or swallowing</u>, muscular twitching, tremors, psychosis. With high doses: <u>convulsions, respiratory depression and arrest</u>. **CV:** With high doses, hypotension, bradycardia, conduction disorders including heart block, <u>cardiovascular collapse, cardiac arrest</u>. **Special Senses:** Tinnitus, decreased hearing; blurred or double vision, impaired color perception. **Skin:** Site of topical application may develop erythema, edema. **GI:** Anorexia, nausea, vomiting. **Body as a Whole:** Excessive perspiration, soreness at IM site, local thrombophlebitis (with prolonged IV infusion), hypersensitivity reactions (urticaria, rash, edema, <u>anaphylactoid reactions</u>).

DIAGNOSTIC TEST INTERFERENCE
Increases in *creatine phosphokinase (CPK)* level may occur for 48 h after IM dose and may interfere with test for presence of MI.

INTERACTIONS Drug: Lidocaine patch may increase toxic effects of **tocainide, mexiletine;** BARBITURATES decrease lidocaine activity; **cimetidine,** BETA BLOCKERS, **quinidine** increase pharmacologic effects of lidocaine; **phenytoin** increases cardiac depressant effects; **procainamide** compounds neurologic and cardiac effects.

PHARMACOKINETICS Absorption: Topical application is 3% absorbed through intact skin. **Onset:** 45–90 sec IV; 5–15 min IM; 2–5 min topical. **Duration:** 10–20 min IV; 60–90 min IM; 30–60 min topical; >100 min injected for anesthesia. **Distribution:** Crosses blood–brain barrier and placenta; distributed into breast milk. **Metabolism:** In liver via CYP3A4 and 2D6. **Elimination:** In urine. **Half-Life:** 1.5–2 h.

CLINICAL IMPLICATIONS
Assessment & Drug Effects
- Stop infusion immediately if ECG indicates excessive cardiac depression (e.g., prolongation of PR interval or QRS complex and the appearance or aggravation of arrhythmias).
- Monitor BP and ECG constantly; assess respiratory and neurologic status frequently to avoid potential overdosage and toxicity.
- Auscultate lungs for basilar rales, especially in patients who tend to

metabolize the drug slowly (e.g., CHF, cardiogenic shock, hepatic dysfunction).
- Watch for neurotoxic effects (e.g., drowsiness, dizziness, confusion, paresthesias, visual disturbances, excitement, behavioral changes) in patients receiving IV infusions or with high lidocaine blood levels.
- Note: Lidocaine blood levels of 1.5–6 mcg/mL are reported to provide "usually effective" antiarrhythmic activity. Blood levels greater than 7 mcg/mL are potentially toxic.

Patient & Family Education
- Swish and spit out when using lidocaine solution for relief of mouth discomfort; gargle for use in pharynx, may be swallowed (as prescribed).
- Oral topical anesthetics (e.g., Xylocaine Viscous) may interfere with swallowing reflex. Do NOT ingest food within 60 min after drug application; especially pediatric, geriatric, or debilitated patients. Do not chew gum while buccal and throat membranes are anesthetized to prevent biting trauma.

LINCOMYCIN HYDROCHLORIDE

(lin-koe-mye′sin)
Lincocin
Classification: LINCOSAMIDE ANTIBIOTIC
Therapeutic: ANTIBIOTIC
Prototype: Clindamycin
Pregnancy Category: B

AVAILABILITY 300 mg injection

ACTION & *THERAPEUTIC EFFECT*
Derived from *Streptomyces lincolnensis.* Similar to clindamycin in antibacterial activity. Binds to the 50 S ribosomal subunits of the

Common adverse effects in *italic*, life-threatening effects <u>underlined</u>; generic names in **bold**; classifications in SMALL CAPS; ✦ Canadian drug name; ⊘ Prototype drug

881

bacteria and inhibits protein synthesis, eventually resulting in inhibition of bacterial cell growth or bacterial death. Antibacterial activity primarily results from inhibition of peptide bond formation. *Bacteriostatic or bactericidal depending on concentration used and sensitivity of organism. Effective against most of the common gram-positive pathogens, particularly streptococci, pneumococci, and staphylococci. Also effective against Bacteriodes and other anaerobes.*

USES Reserved for treatment of serious infections caused by susceptible bacteria in penicillin-allergic patients or patients for whom penicillin is inappropriate.

CONTRAINDICATIONS Previous hypersensitivity to lincomycin and clindamycin; impaired liver function, known monilial infections (unless treated concurrently); use in newborns, lactation.

CAUTIOUS USE Impaired kidney function; history of GI disease, particularly colitis; history of liver, endocrine, or metabolic diseases; history of asthma, hay fever, eczema, drug or other allergies; older adult patients, pregnancy (category B).

ROUTE & DOSAGE

Infections

Adult: **IM** 600 mg q12–24 h **IV** 600 mg–1 g q8–12h (max: 8 g/d)
Child: **IM** 10 mg/kg q12–24h **IV** 10–20 mg/kg/d q8–12h

ADMINISTRATION

Intramuscular

▪ Give injection deep into large muscle mass; inject slowly to minimize pain. Rotate injection sites.

Intravenous

PREPARE: Intermittent: Dilute 1 g of lincomycin in at least 100 mL of D5W, NS, or other compatible solution.
ADMINISTER: Intermittent: Give at a rate ≤1 g/h.
INCOMPATIBILITIES Solution/additive: Carbenicillin, kanamycin, methicillin penicillin G, phenytoin.

▪ Follow manufacturer's directions for further information on reconstitution, storage time, compatible IV fluids, and IV administration rates.

ADVERSE EFFECTS (≥1%) **Body as a Whole:** Hypersensitivity (pruritus, urticaria, skin rashes, exfoliative and vesiculobullous dermatitis, erythema multiforme [rare], angioedema, photosensitivity, anaphylactoid reaction, serum sickness); superinfections (proctitis, pruritus ani, vaginitis); vertigo, dizziness, headache, generalized myalgia, thrombophlebitis following IV use; pain at IM injection site. **CV:** Hypotension, syncope, cardiopulmonary arrest (particularly after rapid IV). **GI:** Glossitis, stomatitis, *nausea, vomiting,* anorexia, decreased taste acuity, unpleasant or altered taste, abdominal cramps, *diarrhea,* acute enterocolitis, pseudomembranous colitis (potentially fatal). **Hematologic:** Neutropenia, leukopenia, agranulocytosis, thrombocytopenic purpura, aplastic anemia. **Special Senses:** Tinnitus.

INTERACTIONS Drug: Kaolin and pectin decrease lincomycin absorption; **tubocurarine, pancuro-**

nium may enhance neuromuscular blockade.

PHARMACOKINETICS Peak: 30 min IM. **Duration:** 12–14 h IM; 14 h IV. **Distribution:** High concentrations in bone, aqueous humor, bile, and peritoneal, pleural, and synovial fluids; crosses placenta; distributed into breast milk. **Metabolism:** Partially in liver. **Elimination:** In urine and feces. **Half-Life:** 5 h.

CLINICAL IMPLICATIONS

Assessment & Drug Effects
- Lab tests: Perform C&S initially and during therapy to determine continued microbial susceptibility. Periodic liver & kidney function tests and CBC are indicated during prolonged drug therapy.
- Take a careful history of previous sensitivities to drugs or other allergens.
- Monitor BP and pulse. Have patient remain recumbent following drug administration until BP stabilizes.
- Monitor closely and report changes in bowel frequency. Discontinue drug if significant diarrhea occurs.
- Diarrhea, acute colitis, or pseudomembranous colitis (see Appendix F) may occur up to several weeks after cessation of therapy.
- Examine IM/IV injection sites daily for signs of inflammation.
- Monitor serum drug levels closely in patients with severe impairment of kidney function (levels tend to be higher).
- Superinfections by nonsusceptible organisms are most likely to occur when duration of therapy exceeds 10 d (see Appendix F).

Patient & Family Education
- Notify physician immediately of symptoms of hypersensitivity (see Appendix F). Drug should be discontinued.
- Notify physician promptly of the onset of perianal irritation, diarrhea, or blood and mucus in stools. Do not self-medicate for diarrhea—anti-diarrheal agents may prolong and worsen diarrhea by delaying removal of toxins from colon.
- Take drug as prescribed for full course of therapy.

LINDANE ⓟ

(lin'dane)
Gamma Benzene, Kwell, Scabene
Classifications: SCABICIDE; PEDICULICIDE
Therapeutic: ANTIPARASITIC; PEDICULICIDE
Pregnancy Category: C

AVAILABILITY 1% lotion, shampoo

ACTION & *THERAPEUTIC EFFECT*
Related to its direct absorption by parasites and ova (nits). Drug absorption through the parasite exoskeleton results in death of parasites and their ova. *Has ectoparasitic and ovicidal activity against the two variants of* Pediculus humanus, Pediculus capitis *(head louse) and* Pediculus pubis *(crab louse), and the arthropod* Sarcoptes scabiei *(scabies).*

USES To treat head and crab lice and scabies infestations and to eradicate their ova.

CONTRAINDICATIONS Premature neonates, patient with known seizure disorders; application to eyes, face, mucous membranes, urethral meatus, open cuts or raw, weeping surfaces; prolonged or excessive

Common adverse effects in *italic*, life-threatening effects underlined; generic names in **bold**; classifications in SMALL CAPS; ♦ Canadian drug name; ⓟ Prototype drug

883

applications or simultaneous application of creams, ointments, oils; extensive dermatitis; uncontrolled seizures; pregnancy (category C), lactation, infants, neonates, children <10 y, individuals <110 lb.

CAUTIOUS USE History of seizures; HIV infection; alcoholism.

ROUTE & DOSAGE

Lice and Scabies Infestation

Adult/Child: **Topical** Apply to all body areas except the face, leave lotion on 8–12 h, then rinse off; leave shampoo on 5 min, then rinse thoroughly; do NOT repeat in <1 wk

ADMINISTRATION

Note: Caregiver needs to wear plastic disposable or rubber gloves when applying lindane, especially if pregnant or applying medication to more than one patient, to avoid prolonged skin contact.

Topical

- Remove all skin lotions, creams, and oil-based hair dressings completely and allow skin to dry and cool before applying lindane; this will reduce percutaneous absorption.
- Shake cream or lotion container well. *Scabies:* Apply thin film from neck down over entire body surface including soles of feet. Avoid face and urethral meatus. Pay particular attention to intertriginous areas (finger webs and other body creases and folds), wrists, elbows, and belt line. Rub drug in; allow skin to dry and cool after application. After 8–12 h, remove medication by bath or shower. *Crab lice:* Apply thin film of drug to hair and skin of pubic area and, if infected, to thighs, trunk, axillary areas. Leave in place 8–12 h and follow with bath or shower. Observation

of living lice after 7 d indicates the need for reapplication.

- Shampoo *(head lice):* Apply sufficient quantity to wet hair and skin. Work drug thoroughly onto hair shafts and scalp and allow to remain in place 4 min. Add small amounts of water sufficient to make a thick lather; then rinse well with water. Pay particular attention to areas above and behind ears and occipital region. Use fine-tooth comb or tweezers to remove remaining nit shells. If necessary, treatment may be repeated after 7 d but not more than twice in 1 wk. *Crab lice:* See above. Repeat treatment after 7 d only if live lice can be demonstrated.
- Store in tight container away from direct light and heat. Protect from freezing.

ADVERSE EFFECTS (≥1%) **CNS:** CNS stimulation (usually after accidental ingestion or misuse of product): restlessness, dizziness, tremors, convulsions; seizures; <u>death</u>. **Body as a Whole:** Inhalation (headache, nausea, vomiting, irritation of ENT). **Skin:** Eczematous eruptions.

INTERACTIONS Drug: No clinically significant interactions established.

PHARMACOKINETICS Absorption: Slowly and incompletely absorbed through intact skin; maximum absorption from face, scalp, axillae. **Distribution:** Stored in body fat. **Metabolism:** In liver. **Elimination:** In urine and feces.

CLINICAL IMPLICATIONS

Assessment & Drug Effects

- Monitor for seizure activity in individuals with a history of seizures. Withhold drug and report to physician immediately.
- Suspect scabies if a person complains of nocturnal itching (classic

Common adverse effects in *italic*, life-threatening effects <u>underlined</u>; generic names in **bold**; classifications in SMALL CAPS; ✦ Canadian drug name; ⊘ Prototype drug

symptom). Infestation sources: sex partner, other family members, people and animals in close contact.

- Identify and treat the sex partner simultaneously because both scabies and *P. pubis* infestation are sexually transmitted diseases.
- Burrows made by scabies mites (may or may not be visible) appear as grayish black straight or S-shaped lines with a papule containing the mite at one end and surrounded by a mild erythematous area.

Patient & Family Education

- Lindane is highly toxic drug if topical applications are excessive or if swallowed or inhaled. Keep out of reach of children.
- Note: Lindane shampoo is an effective disinfectant for personal items such as combs, brushes.
- Skin penetration with scabies mites causes an intolerable itching that may persist 2–3 wk after they have been killed.
- Discontinue medication and notify physician if skin eruptions appear.
- Do not apply medication to face, mouth, open skin lesions, or to eyelashes; avoid contact with eyes. If accidental eye contact occurs, flush with water.
- Recurring limited infestations of scabies may indicate a domestic animal source (e.g., cat, dog, cattle, poultry).

LINEZOLID

(lin-e-zo'lid)

Zyvox, Zyvoxam ♣

Classifications: ANTIBIOTIC, OXAZOLIDINONE

Therapeutic: ANTIBIOTIC, OXAZOLIDINONE

Pregnancy Category: C

AVAILABILITY 400 mg, 600 mg tablets; 100 mg/5 mL suspension; 200 mg, 400 mg, 600 mg injection

ACTION & *THERAPEUTIC EFFECT*
Synthetic antibiotic of a new class, the oxazolidinone group, that is bacteriocidal against gram-positive, gram-negative, and anaerobic bacteria. It binds to a site on the bacterial 23S ribosomal RNA of the bacteria which prevents the bacterial RNA translation process. *Bacteriostatic against enterococci and staphylococci, and bactericidal against streptococci.*

USES Treatment of vancomycin-resistant (VREF) *Enterococcus faecium,* nosocomial pneumonia, complicated and uncomplicated skin and skin structure infections, community-acquired pneumonia due to susceptible gram-positive organisms.

CONTRAINDICATIONS Hypersensitivity to linezolid, pregnancy (category C), lactation.

CAUTIOUS USE Lactation, history of thrombocytopenia, thrombocytopenia; patients on MAOI, or serotonin reuptake inhibitors, or adrenergic agents, active alcoholism, anemia, bleeding, bone marrow suppression, cardiac arrhythmias, cardiac disease, cerebrovascular disease, chemotherapy, coagulopathy, colitis, diarrhea, hypertension, hyperthyroidism, leukopenia, MI, radiographic contrast administration, spinal anesthesia, surgery, hypertension; phenylketonuria; carcinoid syndrome.

ROUTE & DOSAGE

Vancomycin-Resistant *Enterococcus faecium*
Adult/Adolescent: **PO/IV** >12 y, 600 mg q12h × 14–28 d
Child: **PO/IV** 2–11 y, 10 mg/kg q8h × 14–28 d

Common adverse effects in *italic*, life-threatening effects underlined; generic names in **bold**; classifications in SMALL CAPS; ♣ Canadian drug name; ⊘ Prototype drug

885

Nosocomial or Community-Acquired Pneumonia, Complicated Skin Infections

Adult/Adolescent: **PO/IV** *>12 y,* 600 mg q12h × 10–14 d
Child: **PO/IV** *5–11 y,* 10 mg/kg q8h × 10–14 d

Uncomplicated Skin Infections

Adult: **PO** 400 mg q12h × 10–14 d
Adolescent: **PO** 600 mg q12h × 10–14 d
Child: **PO** *< 5 y,* 10 mg/kg q8h × 10–14 d *5–11 y,* 10 mg/kg q12h × 10–14 d

ADMINISTRATION

Note: No dosage adjustment is necessary when switching from IV to oral administration.

Oral

- Reconstitute suspension by adding 123 mL distilled water in two portions; after adding first half, shake to wet all of the powder, then add second half of water and shake vigorously to produce a uniform suspension with a concentration of 100 mg/5 mL.
- Before each use, mix suspension by inverting bottle 3–5 times, but DO NOT SHAKE. Discard unused suspension after 21 d.

Intravenous

PREPARE: Intermittent: IV solution is supplied in a single-use, ready-to-use infusion bag. Remove from protective wrap immediately prior to use. Check for minute leaks by firmly squeezing bag. Discard if leaks are detected.
ADMINISTER: Intermittent: Do not use infusion bag in a series connection. Give over 30–120 min. If IV line is used to infuse other drugs, flush before and after with D5W, NS, or LR.

INCOMPATIBILITIES Solution/additive: **Ceftriaxone, erythromycin, trimethoprim-sulfamethoxazole.** Y-site: **Amphotericin B, ceftriaxone, chlorpromazine, diazepam, pentamidine, phenytoin.**

- Store at 25° C (77° F) preferred; 15°–30° C (59°–86° F) permitted. Protect from light and keep bottles tightly closed.

ADVERSE EFFECTS (≥1%) **Body as a Whole:** Fever. **GI:** Diarrhea, nausea, vomiting, constipation, taste alteration, abnormal LFTs, tongue discoloration. **Hematologic:** Thrombocytopenia, leukopenia. **CNS:** Headache, insomnia, dizziness. **Skin:** Rash. **Urogenital:** Vaginal moniliasis.

INTERACTIONS Drug: MAO INHIBITORS may cause hypertensive crisis; **pseudoephedrine** may cause elevated BP; may cause **serotonin** syndrome with SELECTIVE SEROTONIN REUPTAKE INHIBITORS. **Food:** Tyramine-containing food may cause elevated BP. **Herbal:** Ginseng, ephedra, ma huang may lead to elevated BP, headache, nervousness.

PHARMACOKINETICS Absorption: Rapidly or extensively absorbed, 100% bioavailable. **Peak:** 1–2 h PO. **Distribution:** 31% protein bound. **Metabolism:** By oxidation. **Elimination:** Primarily in urine. **Half-Life:** 6–7 h.

CLINICAL IMPLICATIONS

Assessment & Drug Effects

- Monitor for signs and symptoms in individuals with a history of seizure activity or conditions that make them prone to seizures. If a seizure occurs, discontinue the drug and report to the physician immediately.

- Monitor for S&S of: Bleeding; hypertension; or pseudomembranous colitis that begins with diarrhea.
- Lab tests: C&S before initiating therapy and during therapy as indicated; drug may be started pending results. Monitor complete blood count, including platelet count and Hgb & Hct, in those at risk for bleeding or with >2 wk of linezolid therapy.

Patient & Family Education

- Report any of the following to physician promptly: Onset of diarrhea; easy bruising or bleeding of any type; or S&S of superinfection (see Appendix F), S&S of seizure activity.
- Avoid foods and beverages high in tyramine (e.g., aged, fermented, pickled, or smoked foods, and beverages). Limit tyramine intake to >100 mg per meal (see *Information for Patients* provided by the manufacturer).
- Do not take OTC cold remedies or decongestants without consulting physician.
- Note for phenylketonurics: Each 5 mL oral suspension contains 20 mg phenylalanine.

LIOTHYRONINE SODIUM (T₃)

(lye-oh-thye'roe-neen)
Cytomel, Triostat
Classifications: HORMONE; THYROID HORMONE REPLACEMENT
Therapeutic: THYROID HORMONE REPLACEMENT
Prototype: Levothyroxine Sodium
Pregnancy Category: A

AVAILABILITY 5 mcg, 25 mcg, 50 mcg tablets; 10 mcg/mL injection

ACTION & *THERAPEUTIC EFFECT*
Synthetic form of natural thyroid hormone (T₃). Shares actions and uses of thyroid but has more rapid action and more rapid disappearance of effect, permitting quick dosage adjustment if necessary. Replacement therapy for absent or decreased thyroid hormone. *Replacement therapy for insufficient thyroid hormone. Principal effect: increase in the metabolic rate of all body tissues.*

USES Replacement or supplemental therapy for cretinism, myxedema, goiter, secondary (pituitary) or tertiary (hypothalamic) hypothyroidism, and T₃ suppression test.

CONTRAINDICATIONS Hypersensitivity to liothyronine; thyrotoxicosis; obesity treatment; severe cardiovascular conditions, acute MI, uncontrolled hypertension; adrenal insufficiency.
CAUTIOUS USE Angina pectoris, hypertension; diabetes mellitus; impaired kidney function, renal failure; older adult; pregnancy (category A), lactation.

ROUTE & DOSAGE

Thyroid Replacement
Adult: **PO** 25–75 mcg/d
Geriatric: **PO** 5 mcg/d, increase by 5 mcg/d every 1–2 wk
Child: **PO** 5 mcg/d gradually increased by 5 mcg/d q3–4d until desired response

Myxedema
Adult: **PO** 5–100 mcg/d **IV** 25–50 mcg, may repeat between 4 and 12 h after previous dose. Target dose >65 mcg/d (max: 100 mcg/d).
Geriatric: **PO** Start at 5 mcg/d

Goiter
Adult: **PO** 5–75 mcg/d

L

Common adverse effects in *italic*, life-threatening effects <u>underlined</u>; generic names in **bold**; classifications in SMALL CAPS; ♦ Canadian drug name; ◐ Prototype drug

887

> Geriatric: **PO** Start at 5 mcg/d
> Child: **PO** 5 mcg/d, increase by
> 5 mcg q1–2 wk (usual mainte-
> nance dose 15–20 mcg/d)
> **T₃ Suppression Test**
> Adult: **PO** 75–100 mcg/d times 7 d

ADMINISTRATION

Oral
- Give daily before breakfast.
- Discontinue other thyroid drug when changing to liothyronine; initiate liothyronine at low dosage with gradual increases according to patient's response.

Intravenous

PREPARE: Direct: Give undiluted.
ADMINISTER: Direct: Give each 10 mcg or fraction thereof over 1 min.

- Store tablets in heat-, light-, and moisture-proof container.

ADVERSE EFFECTS (≥1%) **Endocrine:** Result from overdosage evidenced as S&S of hyperthyroidism (see Appendix F). **Musculoskeletal:** Accelerated rate of bone maturation in children.

INTERACTIONS Drug: Cholestyramine, colestipol decrease absorption; **epinephrine, norepinephrine** increase risk of cardiac insufficiency; ORAL ANTICOAGULANTS may potentiate hypoprothrombinemia.

PHARMACOKINETICS Absorption: Completely absorbed from GI tract. **Peak:** 24–72 h. **Duration:** Up to 72 h. **Distribution:** Gradually released into tissue cells. **Half-Life:** 6–7 d.

CLINICAL IMPLICATIONS

Assessment & Drug Effects
- Watch for possible additive effects during the early period of liothyronine substitution for another preparation, particularly in older adults, children, and patients with cardiovascular disease. Residual actions of other thyroid preparations may persist for weeks.
- Metabolic effects of liothyronine persist a few days after drug withdrawal.
- Withhold drug for 1–2 d at onset of overdosage symptoms (hyperthyroidism, see Appendix F); usually therapy can be resumed with lower dosage.

Patient & Family Education
- Take medication exactly as ordered.
- Learn S&S of hyperthyroidism (see Appendix F); notify physician promptly if they appear.

LIOTRIX (T₃-T₄)

(lye'oh-trix)
Thyrolar
Classifications: HORMONE; THYROID HORMONE REPLACEMENT
Therapeutic: THYROID HORMONE REPLACEMENT
Prototype: Levothyroxine Sodium
Pregnancy Category: A

AVAILABILITY 0.0125 mcg, 3.1 mcg, 6.25 mcg, 12.5 mcg, 25 mcg, 37.5 mcg

ACTION & *THERAPEUTIC EFFECT*
Synthetic levothyroxine (T₄) and liothyronine (T₃) combined in a constant 4:1 ratio by weight. Thyroid hormones influence growth and maturation of tissues, increase energy expenditure, and affect turnover of essentially all substrates. Thyroid hormones play an integral role in metabolic processes, and are important to development of

the CNS in newborns. *Increases metabolic rate of all body tissues.*

USES Replacement or supplemental therapy for cretinism, myxedema, goiter, and secondary (pituitary) or tertiary (hypothalamic) hypothyroidism. Also with antithyroid agents in thyrotoxicosis and to prevent goitrogenesis and hypothyroidism.

CONTRAINDICATIONS Untreated thyrotoxicosis, acute MI, morphologic hypogonadism, nephrosis, adrenal deficiency due to hypopituitarism; tartrazine dye hypersensitivity, obesity treatment.
CAUTIOUS USE Concomitant anticoagulant therapy; myxedema; hypertension, angina, cardiac arrhythmias, cardiac disease, coronary artery disease; older adults; hypertension; neonates, infants, children; arteriosclerosis; kidney dysfunction, pregnancy (category A), lactation.

ROUTE & DOSAGE

> **Thyroid Replacement**
> *Adult/Child:* **PO** 12.5–30 mcg/d, gradually increase to desired response

ADMINISTRATION

Oral
- Give as a single daily dose, preferably before breakfast.
- Make dose increases at 1- to 2-wk intervals.
- Store in heat-, light-, and moisture-proof container. Shelf-life: 2 y.

ADVERSE EFFECTS (≥1%) **CNS:** Nervousness, headache, tremors, insomnia. **CV:** Palpitation, tachycardia, angina pectoris, cardiac arrhythmias, hypertension, CHF. **GI:** Nausea, abdominal cramps, diarrhea. **Body as a Whole:** Weight loss, heat intolerance, fever, sweating, menstrual irregularities. **Musculoskeletal:** Accelerated rate of bone maturation in infants and children.

INTERACTIONS Drug: Cholestyramine, colestipol decrease absorption; **epinephrine, norepinephrine** increase risk of cardiac insufficiency; ORAL ANTICOAGULANTS may potentiate hypoprothrombinemia.

PHARMACOKINETICS Not studied.

CLINICAL IMPLICATIONS

Assessment & Drug Effects
- Watch for possible additive effects during the early period of liothyronine substitution for another preparation, particularly in older adults, children, and patients with cardiovascular disease. Residual actions of other thyroid preparations may persist for weeks.
- Note: Metabolic effects of liotrix persist a few days after drug withdrawal.
- Withhold drug for 1–2 d at onset of overdosage symptoms (hyperthyroidism, see Appendix F); usually therapy can be resumed with lower dosage.
- Monitor diabetics for glycemic control; an increase in insulin or oral hypoglycemic may be required.

Patient & Family Education
- Follow directions for taking this drug (see ADMINISTRATION).
- Notify physician of headache (euthyroid patients); may indicate need for dosage adjustment or change to another thyroid preparation.
- Take medication exactly as ordered.
- Learn S&S of hyperthyroidism (see Appendix F); notify physician if they appear.

Common adverse effects in *italic*, life-threatening effects underlined; generic names in **bold**; classifications in SMALL CAPS; ✦ Canadian drug name; ⊘ Prototype drug

889

LISINOPRIL

(ly-sin'o-pril)
Prinivil, Zestril
Classifications: ANGIOTENSIN-CONVERTING ENZYME (ACE) INHIBITOR; ANTIHYPERTENSIVE AGENT
Therapeutic: ANTIHYPERTENSIVE AGENT; ACE INHIBITOR
Prototype: Enalapril
Pregnancy Category: C first trimester; D second and third trimester

AVAILABILITY 2.5 mg, 5 mg, 10 mg, 20 mg, 30 mg, 40 mg tablets

ACTION & *THERAPEUTIC EFFECT*
Lowers BP by specific inhibition of the angiotensin-converting enzyme (ACE). This interrupts conversion sequences initiated by renin that form angiotensin II, a potent vasoconstrictor. ACE inhibition alters hemodynamics without compensatory reflex tachycardia or changes in cardiac output (except in patients with CHF). *Improved cardiac output and exercise tolerance due to inhibition of ACE also decreases circulating aldosterone, which is normally released in response to angiotensin II stimulation. Reduced aldosterone is associated with a potassium-sparing effect. Also decreases peripheral resistance (afterload) and pulmonary vascular resistance.*

USES Hypertension, alone or concomitantly with other classes of antihypertensive agents; CHF; to improve MI survival.

CONTRAINDICATIONS Patients with a history of angioedema related to treatment with an ACE inhibitor, ACE inhibitor hypersensitivity; pregnancy (C first trimester, category D second and third trimester), children <6 y; lactation.

CAUTIOUS USE Impaired kidney function, renal artery stenosis, renal disease, renal failure, hyperkalemia, patients on diuretic therapy; aortic stenosis, cardiomyopathy; cerebrovascular disease; collagen vascular disease; coronary artery disease, dialysis; older adults; heart failure, hyperkalemia, hypotension, hypovolemia; African Americans; autoimmune diseases, especially systemic lupus erythematosus (SLE).

ROUTE & DOSAGE

Hypertension
Adult: **PO** 10 mg once/d, may increase up to 20–40 mg 1–2 times/d (max: 80 mg/d)
Child: **PO** 6–16 y, Start at 0.07 mg/kg (max 5 mg) once/d (max: 40 mg/d)
Geriatric: **PO** Initial 2.5–5 mg/d, may increase by 2.5–5 mg/d every 1–2 wk (max: 40 mg/d).

Heart Failure
Adult: **PO** 5–40 mg/d

ADMINISTRATION

Oral
- Give an initial dose of 5 mg for diuretic-treated patients. Monitor drug effect for 2 h or until the BP is stabilized for at least 1 additional hour. Concurrent administration with a diuretic may compound hypotensive effect.
- Give before dialysis; lisinopril is removed from blood by hemodialysis.
- Store away from both moisture and heat.

ADVERSE EFFECTS (≥1%) **CNS:** Headache, dizziness, fatigue. **CV:** Hypotension, chest pain. **GI:** Nausea, vomiting, diarrhea, anorexia, constipation, intestinal angioedema. **Hematologic:** Neutropenia. **Respiratory:** Dyspnea, cough. **Skin:** Rash. **Metabolic:** Azotemia, hyperkalemia, increased BUN, and creatinine levels.

INTERACTIONS Drug: Indomethacin and other NSAIDS may decrease antihypertensive activity; POTASSIUM SUPPLEMENTS, POTASSIUM-SPARING DIURETICS may cause hyperkalemia; may increase **lithium** levels and toxicity.

PHARMACOKINETICS Absorption: 25% absorbed from GI tract. **Onset:** 1 h. **Peak:** 6–8 h. **Duration:** 24 h. **Distribution:** Limited amount crosses blood–brain barrier; crosses placenta; small amount distributed in breast milk. **Metabolism:** Is not metabolized. **Elimination:** Primarily in urine. **Half-Life:** 12 h.

CLINICAL IMPLICATIONS

Assessment & Drug Effects

- Place patient in supine position and notify physician if sudden and severe hypotension occurs within the first 1–5 h after initial drug dose; possible particularly in patients who are sodium- or volume-depleted because of diuretic therapy.
- Measure BP just prior to dosing to determine whether satisfactory control is being maintained for 24 h. If the antihypertensive effect is diminished in less than 24 h, an increase in dosage may be necessary.
- Monitor closely for angioedema of extremities, face, lips, tongue, glottis, and larynx. Discontinue drug promptly and notify physician if such symptoms appear; carefully monitor for airway obstruction until swelling is relieved.
- Monitor serum sodium and serum potassium levels for hyponatremia and hyperkalemia.

- Lab tests: Determine WBC count prior to initiation of treatment, every month for the first 3–6 mo of therapy, and at periodic intervals for 1 y. Withhold therapy and notify physician if neutropenia (neutrophil count <1000/mm^3) develops; kidney function tests at periodic intervals, especially in patients with severe volume or sodium replacement or those with severe CHF.

Patient & Family Education

- Discontinue drug and contact physician immediately for severe hypersensitivity reaction (e.g., hoarseness, swelling of the face, mouth, hands, or feet, or sudden trouble breathing).
- Be aware of importance of proper diet, including sodium and potassium restrictions. Do NOT use salt substitute containing potassium.
- Continued compliance with high BP medication is very important. If a dose is missed, take it as soon as possible but not too close to next dose.
- Do not drive or engage in other potentially hazardous activities until response to the drug is known.
- With concomitant therapy, lisinopril increases the risk of lithium toxicity.
- Notify physician promptly of any indication of infection (e.g., sore throat, fever).
- Do not store drug in a moist area. Heat and moisture may cause the medicine to break down.

LITHIUM CARBONATE ⊕

(li'thee-um)

Eskalith, Eskalith CR, Lithane, Lithobid, Lithonate, Lithotabs

L

LITHIUM CITRATE
Cibalith-S

Classifications: PSYCHOTHERAPEU-TIC AGENT; MOOD STABILIZER
Therapeutic: MOOD STABILIZER; AN-TIMANIC AND ANTIDEPRESSANT
Pregnancy Category: C first trimester; D second and third trimester

AVAILABILITY Lithium Carbonate 150 mg, 300 mg, 600 mg capsules; 300 mg, 450 mg sustained release tablets **Lithium Citrate** 300 mg/5 mL syrup

ACTION & *THERAPEUTIC EFFECT*
The lithium ion behaves in the body much like the sodium ion; but its exact mechanism of action is unclear. Competes with various physiologically important cations: Na^+, K^+, Ca^{++}, Mg^{++}; therefore, it affects cell membranes, body water, and neurotransmitters. At the synapse, it accelerates catecholamine destruction, inhibits the release of neurotransmitters and decreases sensitivity of postsynaptic receptors. *Inhibits neurotransmitters; decreases over-activity of receptors involved in stimulating manic states. Response evidenced by changed facial affect, improved posture, assumption of self-care, improved ability to concentrate, improved sleep pattern.*

USES Control and prophylaxis of acute mania and the acute manic phase of mixed bipolar disorder.
UNLABELED USES Acute and recurrent depression (unipolar affective disorder), schizophrenic disorders, disorders of impulse control, alcohol dependence, antineoplastic drug-induced neutropenia, aplastic anemia, SIADH, cyclic neutropenia.

CONTRAINDICATIONS History of ACE inhibitor induced angioedema; significant cardiovascular or kidney disease, brain damage, severe debilitation, dehydration or sodium depletion; patients on low-salt diet or receiving diuretics; pregnancy (category C in first trimester, category D in second and third trimester), lactation, children <12 y.
CAUTIOUS USE Older adults; thyroid disease; epilepsy; concomitant use with haloperidol and other antipsychotics; cardiac disease, cardiac arrhythmias, dehydration, diarrhea; older adults; fever, hyponatremia, hypothyroidism, concurrent infection; leukemia; mental status changes, organic brain syndrome, parkinsonism; psoriasis; renal disease, renal impairment; seizure disorder, sick sinus syndrome, sodium restriction, suicidal ideation, thyroid disease, urinary retention; diabetes mellitus; severe infections; urinary retention.

ROUTE & DOSAGE

Mania
Adult: **PO Loading Dose** 600 mg t.i.d. or 900 mg sustained-release b.i.d. or 30 mL (48 mEq) of solution t.i.d. **PO Maintenance Dose** 300 mg t.i.d. or q.i.d. or 15–20 mL (24–32 mEq) solution in 2–4 divided doses (max: 2.4 g/d)
Child: **PO** 15–60 mg/kg/d in divided doses

ADMINISTRATION
Oral
- Give with meals.
- Ensure that sustained release tablets are not chewed or crushed; must be swallowed whole.
- Protect from light and moisture.

ADVERSE EFFECTS (≥1%) **CNS:** Dizziness, *headache, lethargy,* drowsiness, *fatigue,* slurred speech,

Common adverse effects in *italic*, life-threatening effects <u>underlined</u>; generic names in **bold**; classifications in SMALL CAPS; ✦ Canadian drug name; ☯ Prototype drug

psychomotor retardation, giddiness, incontinence, restlessness, seizures, confusion, blackout spells, disorientation, *recent memory loss,* stupor, coma, EEG changes. **CV:** Arrhythmias, hypotension, vasculitis, <u>peripheral circulatory collapse</u>, ECG changes. **Special Senses:** Impaired vision, transient scotomas, tinnitus. **Endocrine:** Diffuse thyroid enlargement, hypothyroidism, *nephrogenic diabetes insipidus,* transient hyperglycemia, glycosuria, hyponatremia. **GI:** *Nausea, vomiting, anorexia, abdominal pain, diarrhea, dry mouth,* metallic taste. **Musculoskeletal:** *Fine hand tremors,* coarse tremors, choreoathetotic movements; fasciculations, clonic movements, incoordination including ataxia, *muscle weakness,* hyperreflexia, encephalopathic syndrome (weakness, lethargy, fever, tremors, confusion, extrapyramidal symptoms). **Skin:** Thought to be toxicity rather than allergy: Pruritus, maculopapular rash, hyperkeratosis, chronic folliculitis, transient acneiform papules (face, neck, intertriginous areas), anesthesia of skin, cutaneous ulcers, drying and thinning of hair, allergic vasculitis. **Hematologic:** *Reversible leukocytosis* (14,000 to 18,000/mm^3). **Urogenital:** Albuminuria, oliguria, urinary incontinence, polyuria, polydipsia, increased uric acid excretion. **Body as a Whole:** Edema, weight gain (common) or loss, exacerbation of psoriasis; flu-like symptoms.

INTERACTIONS Drug: **Carbamazepine, haloperidol,** PHENOTHIAZINES increase risk of neurotoxicity, extrapyramidal effects, and tardive dyskinesias; DIURETICS, NSAIDS, **methyldopa, probenecid,** TETRACYCLINES decrease renal clearance of lithium, increasing pharmacologic and toxic effects; THEOPHYLLINES, **urea, sodium bicarbonate, sodium or potassium citrate** increase renal clearance of lithium, decreasing its pharmacologic effects.

PHARMACOKINETICS Absorption: Readily absorbed from GI tract. **Peak:** 0.5–3 h carbonate; 15–60 min citrate. **Distribution:** Crosses blood–brain barrier and placenta; distributed into breast milk. **Metabolism:** Not metabolized. **Elimination:** 95% in urine, 1% in feces, 4–5% in sweat. **Half-Life:** 20–27 h.

CLINICAL IMPLICATIONS

Assessment & Drug Effects

- Monitor response to drug. Usual lag of 1–2 wk precedes response to lithium therapy. Keep physician informed of progress.
- Lab test: Periodic lithium levels (draw blood sample prior to next dose or 8–12 h after last dose); periodic thyroid function tests.
- Monitor for S&S of lithium toxicity (e.g., vomiting, diarrhea, lack of coordination, drowsiness, muscular weakness, slurred speech when level is 1.5–2.0 mEq/L; ataxia, blurred vision, giddiness, tinnitus, muscle twitching, coarse tremors, polyuria when >2.0 mEq/L). Withhold one dose and call physician. Drug should not be stopped abruptly.
- Monitor older adults carefully to prevent toxicity, which may occur at serum levels ordinarily tolerated by other patients.
- Be alert to and report symptoms of hypothyroidism (see Appendix F).
- Weigh patient daily; check ankles, tibiae, and wrists for edema. Report changes in I&O ratio, sudden weight gain, or edema.
- Report early signs of extrapyramidal reactions promptly to physician.

L

Common adverse effects in *italic,* life-threatening effects <u>underlined</u>; generic names in **bold**; classifications in SMALL CAPS; ♣ Canadian drug name; ⊕ Prototype drug

893

Patient & Family Education

- Be alert to increased output of dilute urine and persistent thirst. Dose reduction may be indicated.
- Contact physician if diarrhea or fever develops. Avoid practices that may encourage dehydration: hot environment, excessive caffeine beverages (diuresis).
- Drink plenty of liquids (2–3 L/d) during stabilization period and at least 1–1$^1/_2$ L/d during ongoing therapy.
- Avoid self-prescribed low-salt regimen, self-dosing with antacids containing sodium, and high-sodium foods (e.g., prepared meats and diet soda).
- Do not drive or engage in other potentially hazardous activities until response to drug is known. Lithium may impair both physical and mental ability.
- Use effective contraceptive measures during lithium therapy. If therapy is continued during pregnancy, serum lithium levels must be closely monitored to prevent toxicity.

LODOXAMIDE

(lo-dox'a-mide)
Alomide
Pregnancy Category: B
See Appendix A-1

LOMEFLOXACIN

(lo-me-flox'a-cin)
Maxaquin
Classifications: QUINOLONE ANTIBIOTIC
Therapeutic: ANTIBIOTIC
Prototype: Ciprofloxacin
Pregnancy Category: C

AVAILABILITY 400 mg tablets

ACTION & *THERAPEUTIC EFFECT*
An oral fluoroquinolone broad spectrum bactericidal agent that inhibits DNA gyrase, an enzyme necessary for bacterial DNA replication and some aspects of its transcription, repair, recombination, and transposition. *Inhibits replication of susceptible gram-negative and gram-positive bacteria. Antibiotic spectrum of activity is similar to that of other fluoroquinolones.*

USES Urinary tract infections, transurethral surgery prophylaxis.
UNLABELED USES Lower respiratory tract infections.

CONTRAINDICATIONS Known hypersensitivity to lomefloxacin or any other quinolone; tendon pain; QT prolongation; renal failure or Cl_{cr} <10 mL/min; pregnancy (category C), lactation.
CAUTIOUS USE Kidney disease; acute MI, atrial fibrillation, bradycardia; cerebrovascular disease; myasthenia gravis; patients with a history of epilepsy, psychosis, or increased intracranial pressure; children and adolescents.

ROUTE & DOSAGE

Urinary Tract & Lower Respiratory Tract Infections
Adult: **PO** 400 mg q.d. × 10 d
Transurethral Surgery Prophylaxis
Adult: **PO** 400 mg 2–6 h before surgery

ADMINISTRATION

Oral
- Avoid giving mineral supplements or vitamins with iron or zinc within 2 h of lomefloxacin.
- Do not give antacids with magnesium, aluminum, or sucralfate within 4 h before or 2 h after drug.

▪ Give hemodialysis patients an initial 400 mg loading dose followed by a 200 mg/d maintenance dose.

ADVERSE EFFECTS (≥1%) **CNS:** *Headache, peripheral neuropathy.* **GI:** Nausea, abdominal discomfort. **Skin:** Photosensitivity. **Musculoskeletal:** Risk of tendon rupture (rare).

DIAGNOSTIC TEST INTERFERENCE May cause false positive on *opiate screening tests.*

INTERACTIONS Drug: ALUMINUM- and MAGNESIUM-CONTAINING ANTACIDS decrease systemic bioavailability of lomefloxacin. Concurrent CORTICOSTEROID use may increase the risk of tendon rupture.

PHARMACOKINETICS Absorption: Readily from GI tract. **Peak:** 1–2 h. **Distribution:** Crosses placenta; distributed into breast milk. **Elimination:** 76% in urine within 48 h. **Half-Life:** 6.35–7.77 h.

CLINICAL IMPLICATIONS

Assessment & Drug Effects

▪ Lab tests: Draw C&S prior to first dose; drug may be started pending results of C&S.
▪ Take thorough history of hypersensitivity reactions to quinolones or other drugs prior to therapy.
▪ Discontinue lomefloxacin and notify physician at the first sign of a skin rash or other allergic reaction.
▪ Monitor for tendon pain. If it occurs, hold the drug and report to physician.
▪ Monitor for seizures, especially in patients with known or suspected CNS disorders. Discontinue lomefloxacin and notify physician immediately if a seizure occurs.
▪ Assess for S&S of superinfection (see Appendix F).

Patient & Family Education

▪ Notify physician of loose stools or diarrhea promptly.
▪ Drink fluids liberally, if not contraindicated.
▪ Take appropriate cautions, dizziness or light-headedness may occur.
▪ Be aware of the possibility of phototoxicity; avoid excessive sunlight or artificial ultraviolet light.

LOMUSTINE

(loe-mus′teen)
CeeNU, CCNU
Classifications: ANTINEOPLASTIC; ALKYLATING AGENT
Therapeutic: ANTINEOPLASTIC
Prototype: Cyclophosphamide
Pregnancy Category: D

AVAILABILITY 10 mg, 40 mg, 100 mg capsules

ACTION & *THERAPEUTIC EFFECT* Lipid-soluble alkylating nitrosourea with actions like those of carmustine (e.g., cell-cycle-nonspecific activity against rapidly proliferating cell populations). Inhibits synthesis of both DNA and RNA. *Has antineoplastic and myelosuppressive effect.*

USES Palliative therapy in addition to other modalities or with other chemotherapeutic agents in primary and metastatic brain tumors and as secondary therapy in Hodgkin's disease.
UNLABELED USES GI, lung, and renal carcinomas, non-Hodgkin's lymphomas, malignant melanoma, and multiple myelomas.

CONTRAINDICATIONS Immunization with live virus vaccines, viral infections; severe bone marrow

Common adverse effects in *italic*, life-threatening effects underlined; generic names in **bold**; classifications in SMALL CAPS; ◆ Canadian drug name; ☻ Prototype drug

895

suppression; active infection; pregnancy (category D), lactation.

CAUTIOUS USE Patients with decreased circulating platelets, leukocytes, or erythrocytes; kidney or liver function impairment; previous cytotoxic or radiation therapy; pulmonary disease.

ROUTE & DOSAGE

Palliative Therapy
Adult: **PO** 130 mg/m² as single dose, repeated in 6 wk; subsequent doses based on hematologic response (WBC >4000/mm³, platelets >100,000/mm³)
Child: **PO** 75–150 mg/m² q6wk

ADMINISTRATION
Oral

- Give on an empty stomach to reduce possibility of nausea, may also give an antiemetic before drug to prevent nausea.
- Store capsules away from excessive heat (over 40° C).

ADVERSE EFFECTS (≥1%) **CNS:** Lethargy, ataxia, disorientation. **GI:** Anorexia, *nausea, vomiting,* stomatitis, transient elevations of LFTs. **Hematologic:** Delayed (cumulative) myelosuppression: (thrombocytopenia, leukopenia); anemia. **Skin:** Alopecia, skin rash, itching. **Urogenital:** Nephrotoxicity. **Respiratory:** Pulmonary toxicity (rare).

INTERACTIONS Drug: Cimetidine can increase bone marrow toxicity; ANTICOAGULANTS, NSAIDS, SALICYLATES increase risk of bleeding.

PHARMACOKINETICS Absorption: Readily absorbed from GI tract. **Peak:** 1–6 h. **Distribution:** Readily crosses blood–brain barrier; crosses placenta; distributed into breast milk. **Metabolism:** In liver to several active metabolites. **Elimination:** In urine. **Half-Life:** 16–48 h.

CLINICAL IMPLICATIONS
Assessment & Drug Effects

- Lab tests: Monitor blood counts weekly for at least 6 wk after last dose. Liver and kidney function tests should be performed periodically.
- A repeat course is not given until platelets have returned to above 100,000/mm³ and leukocytes to above 4000/mm³.
- Avoid invasive procedures during nadir of platelets.
- Thrombocytopenia occurs about 4 wk and leukopenia about 6 wk after a dose, persisting 1–2 wk.
- Inspect oral cavity daily for S&S of superinfections (see Appendix F) and stomatitis or xerostomia.

Patient & Family Education

- Nausea and vomiting may occur 3–5 h after drug administration, usually lasting less than 24 h.
- Anorexia may persist for 2 or 3 d after a dose.
- Notify physician of signs of sore throat, cough, fever. Also report unexplained bleeding or easy bruising.
- Use reliable contraceptive measures during therapy.
- Be aware of the possibility of hair loss while taking this drug.
- A given dose may include capsules of different colors; the pharmacist prepares prescribed dose by combining various capsule strengths.

LOPERAMIDE ℗

(loe-per′a-mide)
Imodium, Imodium AD, Kaopectate III, Maalox Anti-diarrheal, Pepto Diarrhea Control
Classifications: ANTIDIARRHEAL

Therapeutic: ANTIDIARRHEAL
Pregnancy Category: C

AVAILABILITY 2 mg tablets, capsules; 1 mg/mL, 1 mg/5 mL liquid

ACTION & *THERAPEUTIC EFFECT*
Effective antidiarrheal; synthetic piperidine derivative chemically related to diphenoxylate and to meperidine. Inhibits GI peristaltic activity by direct action on circular and longitudinal intestinal muscles. Prolongs transit time of intestinal contents, increases consistency of stools, and reduces fluid and electrolyte loss. *Effective as an antidiarrheal agent by prolonging transit time in the colon.*

USES Acute nonspecific diarrhea, chronic diarrhea associated with inflammatory bowel disease, and to reduce fecal volume from ileostomies.

CONTRAINDICATIONS Conditions in which constipation should be avoided, ileus, severe colitis, bacterial gastroenteritis; acute diarrhea caused by broad-spectrum antibiotics (pseudomembranous colitis) or associated with microorganisms that penetrate intestinal mucosa (e.g., toxigenic *Escherichia coli, Salmonella,* or *Shigella*); GI bleeding. Safe use in children <2 y is not established.
CAUTIOUS USE Dehydration; diarrhea caused by invasive bacteria; ulcerative colitis; impaired liver function; prostatic hypertrophy; history of narcotic dependence.

ROUTE & DOSAGE

Acute Diarrhea
Adult: **PO** 4 mg followed by 2 mg after each unformed stool (max: 16 mg/d)
Child: **PO** 2–6 y, 1 mg t.i.d.; 6–8 y, 2 mg b.i.d.; 8–12 y, 2 mg t.i.d.

Chronic Diarrhea
Adult: **PO** 4 mg followed by 2 mg after each unformed stool until diarrhea is controlled (max: 16 mg/d)
Child: **PO** 0.1 mg/kg after each unformed stool (usually 1 mg)

ADMINISTRATION
Oral
▪ Do not give prn doses to a child with acute diarrhea.

ADVERSE EFFECTS (≥1%) **Body as a Whole:** Hypersensitivity (skin rash); fever. **CNS:** Drowsiness, fatigue, dizziness, CNS depression (overdosage). **GI:** Abdominal discomfort or pain, abdominal distention, bloating, constipation, nausea, vomiting, anorexia, dry mouth; <u>toxic megacolon</u> (patients with ulcerative colitis).

INTERACTIONS Drug: No clinically significant interactions established.

PHARMACOKINETICS Absorption: Poorly absorbed from GI tract. **Onset:** 30–60 min. **Peak:** 2.5 h solution; 4–5 h capsules. **Duration:** 4–5 h. **Metabolism:** In liver. **Elimination:** Primarily in feces, <2% in urine. **Half-Life:** 11 h.

CLINICAL IMPLICATIONS
Assessment & Drug Effects
▪ Monitor therapeutic effectiveness. Chronic diarrhea usually responds within 10 d. If improvement does not occur within this time, it is unlikely that symptoms will be controlled by further administration.
▪ Discontinue if there is no improvement after 48 h of therapy for acute diarrhea.
▪ Monitor fluid and electrolyte balance.
▪ Notify physician promptly if the patient with ulcerative colitis devel-

Common adverse effects in *italic*, life-threatening effects <u>underlined</u>; generic names in **bold**; classifications in SMALL CAPS; ♣ Canadian drug name; ✪ Prototype drug

897

ops abdominal distention or other GI symptoms (possible signs of potentially fatal toxic megacolon).

Patient & Family Education
- Notify physician if diarrhea does not stop in a few days or if abdominal pain, distension, or fever develops.
- Record number and consistency of stools.
- Do not drive or engage in other potentially hazardous activities until response to drug is known.
- Do not take alcohol and other CNS depressants concomitantly unless otherwise advised by physician; may enhance drowsiness.
- Learn measures to relieve dry mouth; rinse mouth frequently with water, suck hard candy.

LOPINAVIR/RITONAVIR
(lop-i-na′ver/rit-o-na′ver)
Kaletra
Classifications: ANTIRETROVIRAL AGENT; PROTEASE INHIBITOR
Therapeutic: ANTIRETROVIRAL AGENT; PROTEASE INHIBITOR
Prototype: Saquinavir mesylate
Pregnancy Category: C

AVAILABILITY 200 mg lopinavir/50 mg ritonavir tablets; 400 mg lopinavir/100 mg ritonavir/5 mL suspension

ACTION & *THERAPEUTIC EFFECT*
Lopinavir, an HIV protease inhibitor that inhibits the activity of HIV protease and prevents the cleavage of viral polyproteins essential for the maturation of HIV. Ritonavir inhibits the CYP3A metabolism of lopinavir, thereby, increasing the blood level of lopinavir. *Decreases plasma HIV RNA level; reduces viral load as a result of the combined*

therapy of the two drugs in HIV infected patients.

USES Treatment of HIV infection in combination with other antiretroviral agents.

CONTRAINDICATIONS Hypersensitivity to lopinavir or ritonavir; concurrent administration with drugs that utilize CYP3A or CYP2D6 for metabolism (e.g., ergotamine, pimozide); pregnancy (category C), lactation. Safety and efficacy in children <6 mo are not established. **CAUTIOUS USE** Hepatic impairment, patients with hepatitis B or C, older adults; diabetes mellitus.

ROUTE & DOSAGE

HIV Infection—Treatment Naïve
Adult: **PO** 800/200 mg q.d.
HIV Infection—Treatment Experienced
Adult: **PO** 400/100 mg (3 capsules or 5 mL suspension) b.i.d., increase dose to 533/133 mg (4 capsules or 6.5 mL) b.i.d., with concurrent efavirenz or nevirapine
Child: **PO** 6 mo–12 y, 7–15 kg, 12/3 mg/kg; 15–40 kg, 10/2.5 mg/kg; >40 kg, 400/100 mg b.i.d., increase dose 7–15 kg, 13/3.25 mg/kg; 15–40 kg, 11/2.75 mg/kg; >40 kg, 533/133 mg b.i.d., with concurrent efavirenz or nevirapine

ADMINISTRATION

Note: Take with food.
Oral
- Give with a meal or light snack.
- Note: If didanosine is concurrently ordered, give didanosine 1 h before or 2 h after lopinavir/ritonavir.
- Store refrigerated at 2°–8° C (36°–46° F). If stored at room tempera-

ture ≤25° C (77° F), discard after 2 mo.

ADVERSE EFFECTS (≥1%) **Body as a Whole:** Asthenia, pain. **GI:** Abdominal pain, abnormal stools, *diarrhea, nausea,* vomiting. **CNS:** Headache, insomnia. **Skin:** Rash.

INTERACTIONS Drug: Flecainide, propafenone, pimozide may lead to life-threatening arrhythmias; **rifampin** may decrease antiretroviral response; **dihydroergotamine, ergonovine, ergotamine, methylergonovine** may lead to acute ergot toxicity; HMG-COA REDUCTASE INHIBITORS may increase risk of myopathy and rhabdomyolysis; BENZODIAZEPINES may have prolonged sedation or respiratory depression; **efavirenz, nevirapine,** ANTICONVULSANTS, STEROIDS may decrease lopinavir levels; **delavirdine, ritonavir** may increase lopinavir levels; may increase levels of **amprenavir, indinavir, saquinavir, ketoconazole, itraconazole, midazolam, triazolam, rifabutin, sildenafil, atorvastatin, cerivastatin,** IMMUNOSUPPRESSANTS; may decrease levels of **atovaquone, methadone, ethinyl estradiol.** Also see INTERACTIONS in **ritonavir** monograph. **Herbal: St. John's wort,** garlic may decrease ANTIRETROVIRAL activity.

PHARMACOKINETICS Absorption: Increased absorption when taken with food. **Peak:** 4 h. **Distribution:** 98–99% protein bound. **Metabolism:** Extensively metabolized by CYP3A. **Elimination:** Primarily in feces. **Half-Life:** 5–6 h lopinavir.

CLINICAL IMPLICATIONS

Assessment & Drug Effects
▪Monitor for S&S of: Pancreatitis, especially with marked triglyceride elevations; new onset diabetes or loss of glycemic control; hypothyroidism or Cushing's syndrome.
▪Lab test: Periodically monitor fasting blood glucose, AST & ALT, total cholesterol & triglycerides, serum amylase, inorganic phosphorus, CBC with differential, and thyroid functions.

Patient & Family
▪Report all prescription and nonprescription drugs being taken. Do not use herbal products, especially St. John's wort, without first consulting the physician.
▪Become familiar with the potential adverse effects of this drug; report those that are bothersome to physician.
▪Concurrent use of sildenafil (Viagra) increases risk for adverse effects such as hypotension, changes in vision, and sustained erection; promptly report any of these to the physician.
▪Use additional or alternative contraceptive measures if estrogen-based hormonal contraceptives are being used.

LORACARBEF
(lor-a-car'bef)
Lorabid
Classifications: ANTIBIOTIC; BETA-LACTAM; SECOND-GENERATION CEPHALOSPORIN
Therapeutic: ANTIBIOTIC; CEPHALOSPORIN
Prototype: Cefonicid
Pregnancy Category: B

AVAILABILITY 200 mg, 400 mg capsules; 100 mg/5 mL, 200 mg/5 mL suspension

ACTION & *THERAPEUTIC EFFECT*
Second-generation cephalosporin antibiotic with drug structure characterized by a beta-lactam ring (like the

Common adverse effects in *italic*, life-threatening effects underlined; generic names in **bold**; classifications in SMALL CAPS; ◆ Canadian drug name; ⊘ Prototype drug

899

penicillin structure), and inhibits cell wall synthesis of bacteria. By preferentially binding to penicillin-binding proteins (PBPs) located inside the bacterial cell wall, loracarbef inhibits the third and final stage of bacterial cell wall synthesis. Penicillin-binding proteins (PBPs) are responsible for several steps in the synthesis of the bacterial cell wall. This interference results in cell death of these bacteria. *Effective against gram-positive and gram-negative bacteria.*

USES Upper and lower respiratory tract infections, skin and skin structure infections, urinary tract infections.

CONTRAINDICATIONS Hypersensitivity to cephalosporins and related antibiotics.
CAUTIOUS USE Renal impairment, renal failure or Cl_{cr} <49 mL/min; seizures; history of GI disease, colitis, diarrhea; older adults; PKU; pregnancy (category B).

ROUTE & DOSAGE

Upper & Lower Respiratory Tract Infections
Adult: **PO** 200–400 mg q12h taken 1 h a.c. or 2 h p.c.
Child: **PO** 15–30 mg/kg/d divided q12h taken 1 h a.c. or 2 h p.c.

Skin & Skin Structure Infections
Adult: **PO** 200 mg q12h taken 1 h a.c. or 2 h p.c.
Child: **PO** 15 mg/kg/d divided q12h taken 1 h a.c. or 2 h p.c.

Urinary Tract Infections
Adult: **PO** 200 mg q24h or 400 mg q12h taken 1 h a.c. or 2 h p.c.

Otitis Media
Child: **PO** 30 mg/kg/d divided q12h taken 1 h a.c. or 2 h p.c.

Renal Impairment
Cl_{cr} 10–49 mL/min: reduce recommended dose by 50% or give standard dose q24h; <10 mL/min: extend dosing interval to every 3–5 d

ADMINISTRATION

Oral
- Reconstitute suspension by adding 30 or 60 mL of water to the 50- or 100-mL bottles, respectively, of dry mixture. Add the water in 2 portions and shake bottle after each portion.
- Give at least 1 h before or 2 h after meals.
- Give half of the normal dose if Cl_{cr} lies between 10 and 49 mL/min.
- Store suspension in a tightly closed container. Discard after 14 d.

ADVERSE EFFECTS (≥1%) **CNS:** Headache. **GI:** Nausea, vomiting, diarrhea, diaper rash, abdominal pain. **Other:** Rash, candidiasis.

INTERACTIONS Drug: May have prolonged bleeding time with **warfarin.**

PHARMACOKINETICS Absorption: Readily absorbed from GI tract. **Peak:** 45–60 min. **Distribution:** Distributes into middle ear fluid. **Elimination:** In urine. **Half-Life:** 0.78–0.85 h.

CLINICAL IMPLICATIONS

Assessment & Drug Effects
- Take a careful history to determine previous hypersensitivity reaction to beta-lactam antibiotics (penicillins and cephalosporins) or to other allergens.
- Discontinue drug and notify the physician immediately if allergic reaction occurs (e.g., hives, wheezing, rash, pruritus).

- Inspect patient's mouth on a regular basis to detect superinfection (see Appendix F).
- Rule out pseudomembranous enterocolitis (see Appendix F) if severe diarrhea accompanied by abdominal pain and fever occurs. Notify physician immediately.
- Monitor kidney function throughout therapy with concurrent diuretic use.

Patient & Family Education
- Notify physician immediately of rash or any other allergic reaction.
- Report loose stools or diarrhea promptly.

LORATADINE ⊙

(lor'a-ta-deen)
Alavert, Claritin, Claritin Reditabs
Classifications: ANTIHISTAMINE; H₁-RECEPTOR ANTAGONIST; NON-SEDATING
Therapeutic: ANTIHISTAMINE; H₁-RECEPTOR ANTAGONIST
Pregnancy Category: B

AVAILABILITY 10 mg tablets; 1 mg/mL syrup

ACTION & *THERAPEUTIC EFFECT*
Long-acting nonsedating antihistamine with selective peripheral H₁-receptor sites, thus blocking histamine release. It has poor affinity to CNS H₁ receptors. Loratadine is a long-acting H₁-receptor antagonist of histamine that disrupts capillary permeability, edema formation, and constriction of respiratory, GI, and vascular smooth muscle. *Effective in relieving allergic reactions related to histamine release.*

USES Relief of symptoms of seasonal allergic rhinitis; idiopathic chronic urticaria.

CONTRAINDICATIONS Hypersensitivity to loratadine.
CAUTIOUS USE Hepatic and renal impairment, renal disease, renal failure; asthma; pregnancy (category B).

ROUTE & DOSAGE

Allergic Rhinitis
Adult: **PO** 10 mg once/d on an empty stomach; start patients with liver disease with 10 mg every other day
Child: **PO** <30 kg, 5 mg q.d.; >30 kg, 10 mg q.d.

ADMINISTRATION

Oral
- Give on an empty stomach, 1 h before or 2 h after a meal.
- Store in a tightly closed container.

ADVERSE EFFECTS (≥1%) **CNS:** Dizziness, dry mouth, fatigue, headache, somnolence, altered salivation and lacrimation, thirst, flushing, anxiety, depression, impaired concentration. **CV:** Hypotension, hypertension, palpitations, syncope, tachycardia. **GI:** Nausea, vomiting, flatulence, abdominal distress, constipation, diarrhea, weight gain, dyspepsia. **Body as a Whole:** Arthralgia, myalgia. **Special Senses:** Blurred vision, earache, eye pain, tinnitus. **Skin:** Rash, pruritus, photosensitivity.

PHARMACOKINETICS Absorption: Readily from GI tract. **Onset:** 1–3 h. **Peak:** 8–12 h; reaches steady state levels in 3–5 d. **Duration:** 24 h. **Distribution:** Distributed into breast milk. **Metabolism:** In liver to active metabolite, descarboethoxyloratidine. **Elimination:** In urine and feces. **Half-Life:** 12–15 h.

Common adverse effects in *italic*, life-threatening effects underlined; generic names in **bold**; classifications in SMALL CAPS; ♣ Canadian drug name; ⊙ Prototype drug

901

CLINICAL IMPLICATIONS

Assessment & Drug Effects

- Assess carefully for and report distressing or dangerous S&S that occur after initiation of the drug. A variety of adverse effects, although not common, are possible. Some are an indication to discontinue the drug.
- Monitor cardiovascular status and report significant changes in BP and palpitations or tachycardia.

Patient & Family Education

- Drug may cause significant drowsiness in older adult patients and those with liver or kidney impairment.
- Note: Concurrent use of alcohol and other CNS depressants may have an additive effect.

LORAZEPAM ⏺

(lor-a′ze-pam)
Ativan
Classifications: ANXIOLYTIC; SEDATIVE-HYPNOTIC; BENZODIAZEPINE
Therapeutic: ANTIANXIETY; SEDATIVE-HYPNOTIC
Pregnancy Category: D
Controlled Substance: Schedule IV

AVAILABILITY 0.5 mg, 1 mg, 2 mg tablets; 2 mg/mL oral solution; 2 mg/mL, 4 mg/mL injection

ACTION & *THERAPEUTIC EFFECT*

Most potent of the available benzodiazepines. Effects (anxiolytic, sedative, hypnotic, and skeletal muscle relaxant) are mediated by the inhibitory neurotransmitter GABA. Action sites: are thalamic, hypothalamic, and limbic levels of CNS. *Antianxiety agent that also causes mild suppression of REM sleep, while increasing total sleep time.*

USES Management of anxiety disorders and for short-term relief of symptoms of anxiety. Also used for preanesthetic medication to produce sedation and to reduce anxiety and recall of events related to day of surgery; for management of status epilepticus.

UNLABELED USES Chemotherapy-induced nausea and vomiting.

CONTRAINDICATIONS Known sensitivity to benzodiazepines; acute narrow-angle glaucoma; primary depressive disorders or psychosis; COPD; children <12 y (PO preparation); coma, shock, sleep apnea; acute alcohol intoxication; dementia; pregnancy (category D), and lactation.

CAUTIOUS USE Renal or hepatic impairment; renal failure; organic brain syndrome; myasthenia gravis; narrow-angle glaucoma; pulmonary disease; mania; psychosis; suicidal tendency; history of seizure disorders; GI disorders; older adult and debilitated patients; limited pulmonary reserve.

ROUTE & DOSAGE

Antianxiety

Adult: **PO** 2–6 mg/d in divided doses (max: 10 mg/d)
Geriatric: **PO** 0.5–1 mg/d (max: 2 mg/d)
Child: **PO/IV** 0.05 mg/kg q4–8h (max: 2 mg/dose)

Insomnia

Adult: **PO** 2–4 mg at bedtime
Geriatric: **PO** 0.5–1 mg h.s.

Premedication

Adult: **IM** 2–4 mg (0.05 mg/kg) at least 2 h before surgery **IV** 0.044 mg/kg up to 2 mg 15–20 min before surgery

Child: **PO/IV/IM** 0.05 mg/kg (range: 0.02–0.09 mg/kg)

Status Epilepticus

Adult: **IV** 4 mg injected slowly at 2 mg/min, may repeat dose once if inadequate response after 10 min

ADMINISTRATION

Oral

▪ Increase the evening dose when higher oral dosage is required, before increasing daytime doses.

Intramuscular

▪ Injected undiluted, deep into a large muscle mass.

Intravenous

▪ IV administration to neonates, infants, children: Verify correct IV concentration and rate of infusion with physician. ▪ Patients >50 y may have more profound and prolonged sedation with IV lorazepam (usual max: initial dose of 2 mg).

PREPARE: **Direct:** Prepare lorazepam immediately before use. Dilute with an equal volume of sterile water, D5W, or NS.

ADMINISTER: **Direct:** Inject directly into vein or into IV infusion tubing at rate not to exceed 2 mg/min and with repeated aspiration to confirm IV entry. Take extreme precautions to PREVENT intraarterial injection and perivascular extravasation.

INCOMPATIBILITIES **Solution/additive: Dexamethasone. Y-site: Aldesleukin, aztreonam, fluconazole, foscarnet, gallium, idarubicin, imipenem/cilastin, omeprazole, ondansetron, sargramostim, sufentanil, thiopental, TPN with albumin.**

▪ Keep parenteral preparation in refrigerator; do not freeze. ▪ Do not use a discolored solution or one with a precipitate.

ADVERSE EFFECTS (≥1%) **Body as a Whole:** Usually disappear with continued medication or with reduced dosage. **CNS:** Anterograde amnesia, *drowsiness, sedation,* dizziness, weakness, unsteadiness, disorientation, depression, sleep disturbance, restlessness, confusion, hallucinations. **CV:** Hypertension or hypotension. **Special Senses:** Blurred vision, diplopia; depressed hearing. **GI:** Nausea, vomiting, abdominal discomfort, anorexia.

INTERACTIONS Drug: Alcohol, CNS DEPRESSANTS, ANTICONVULSANTS potentiate CNS depression; **cimetidine** increases lorazepam plasma levels, increases toxicity; lorazepam may decrease antiparkinsonism effects of **levodopa;** may increase **phenytoin** levels; smoking decreases sedative and antianxiety effects. **Herbal: Kava-kava, valerian** may potentiate sedation.

PHARMACOKINETICS Absorption: Readily absorbed from GI tract. **Onset:** 1–5 min IV; 15–30 min IM. **Peak:** 60–90 min IM; 2 h PO. **Duration:** 12–24 h. **Distribution:** Crosses placenta; distributed into breast milk. **Metabolism:** Not metabolized in liver. **Elimination:** In urine. **Half-Life:** 10–20 h.

CLINICAL IMPLICATIONS

Assessment & Drug Effects

▪ Have equipment for maintaining patent airway immediately available before starting IV administration.

▪ IM or IV lorazepam injection of 2–4 mg is usually followed by a depth of drowsiness or sleepiness that permits patient to respond to simple instructions whether patient appears to be asleep or awake.

▪ Supervise ambulation of older adult patients for at least 8 h after lorazepam injection to prevent falling and injury.

Common adverse effects in *italic*, life-threatening effects <u>underlined</u>; generic names in **bold**; classifications in SMALL CAPS; ♣ Canadian drug name; ⊙ Prototype drug

903

- Lab tests: Assess CBC and liver function tests periodically for patients on long-term therapy.
- Supervise patient who exhibits depression with anxiety closely; the possibility of suicide exists, particularly when there is apparent improvement in mood.

Patient & Family Education

- Do not drive or engage in other hazardous activities for a least 24–48 h after receiving IM injection of lorazepam.
- Do not drink large volumes of coffee. Anxiolytic effects of lorazepam can be significantly altered by caffeine.
- Do not consume alcoholic beverages for at least 24–48 h after an injection and avoid when taking an oral regimen.
- Notify physician if daytime psychomotor function is impaired; a change in regimen or drug may be needed.
- Terminate regimen gradually over a period of several days. Do not stop long-term therapy abruptly; withdrawal may be induced with feelings of panic, tonic–clonic seizures, tremors, abdominal and muscle cramps, sweating, vomiting.
- Do not self-medicate with OTC drugs; seek physician guidance.
- Discuss discontinuation of drug with physician if you wish to become pregnant.

LOSARTAN POTASSIUM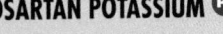

(lo-sar′tan)
Cozaar
Classifications: ANGIOTENSIN II RE-CEPTOR ANTAGONIST; ANTIHYPERTEN-SIVE

Therapeutic: ANTIHYPERTENSIVE; AN-GIOTENSIN II RECEPTOR ANTAGONIST
Pregnancy Category: C first trimester; D second and third trimester

AVAILABILITY 25 mg, 50 mg tablet

ACTION & *THERAPEUTIC EFFECT*
Angiotensin II receptor (type AT_1) antagonist acts as a potent vasoconstrictor and primary vasoactive hormone of the renin–angiotensin–aldosterone system. Selectively blocks the binding of angiotensin II to the AT_1 receptors found in many tissues (e.g., vascular smooth muscle, adrenal glands). Antihypertensive effect results from blocking vasoconstricting and aldosterone-secreting effects of angiotensin II. *Antihypertensive effect is due to vasodilation and inhibition of aldosterone effects on sodium and water retention.*

USES Hypertension.

CONTRAINDICATIONS Hypersensitivity to losartan, children <6 y or children with Cl_{cr} <30 mL/min/ 1.73 m^2; pregnancy [category C (first trimester), category D (second and third trimesters)], lactation.
CAUTIOUS USE Patients on diuretics, heart failure; hyperkalemia; hypovolemia; renal or hepatic impairment.

ROUTE & DOSAGE

Hypertension
Adult: **PO** 25–50 mg in 1–2 divided doses (max: 100 mg/d); start with 25 mg/d if volume depleted (i.e., on diuretics)

ADMINISTRATION

Oral
- Note: Starting dose is reduced 50% in patients with possible

volume depletion or a history of liver disease.

ADVERSE EFFECTS (≥1%) **CNS:** Dizziness, insomnia, headache. **GI:** Diarrhea, dyspepsia. **Musculoskeletal:** Muscle cramps, myalgia, back or leg pain. **Respiratory:** Nasal congestion, cough, upper respiratory infection, sinusitis.

INTERACTIONS Drug: Phenobarbital decreases serum levels of losartan and its metabolite.

PHARMACOKINETICS Absorption: Rapidly absorbed from GI tract; approximately 25–33% reaches systemic circulation. **Peak:** 6 h. **Duration:** 24 h. **Distribution:** Highly bound to plasma proteins; does not appear to cross blood–brain barrier. **Metabolism:** Extensively metabolized in liver by cytochrome P450 enzymes to an active metabolite. **Elimination:** 35% in urine, 60% in feces. **Half-Life:** Losartan 1.5–2 h; metabolite 6–9 h.

CLINICAL IMPLICATIONS

Assessment & Drug Effects

- Monitor BP at drug trough (prior to a scheduled dose).
- Monitor drug effectiveness, especially in African-Americans when losartan is used as monotherapy.
- Inadequate response may be improved by splitting the daily dose into twice-daily dose.
- Lab tests: Monitor CBC, electrolytes, liver & kidney function with long-term therapy.

Patient & Family Education

- Notify physician of symptoms of hypotension (e.g., dizziness, fainting).
- Notify physician immediately of pregnancy.

LOTEPREDNOL ETABONATE

(lo-te′pred-nol e-ta-bo′nate)
Alrex, Lotemax
Pregnancy Category: C
See Appendix A-1.

LOVASTATIN ⊕

(loe-vah-stat′in)
Altoprev, Mevacor
Classifications: ANTILIPEMIC; LIPID-LOWERING AGENT; HMG-COA REDUCTASE INHIBITOR (STATIN) **Therapeutic:** LIPID-LOWERING AGENT; STATIN
Pregnancy Category: X

AVAILABILITY 10 mg, 20 mg, 40 mg tablets; 10 mg, 20 mg, 40 mg, 60 mg extended-release tablets

ACTION & *THERAPEUTIC EFFECT* Reduces plasma cholesterol levels by interfering with body's ability to produce its own cholesterol. This cholesterol-lowering effect triggers induction of LDL receptors, which promote removal of LDL and VLDL remnants (precursors of LDL) from plasma. Also results in an increase in plasma HDL concentrations (HDL collects excess cholesterol from body cells and transports it to liver for excretion). *Reduces plasma cholesterol levels by interfering with body's ability to produce its own cholesterol, and it also lowers LDL and VLDL cholesterol.*

USES Adjunct to diet for treatment of primary moderate hypercholesterolemia (types IIa and IIb) when diet and other nonpharmacologic measures have failed to reduce elevated total LDL cholesterol levels. Lovastatin is less effective in treatment of homozygous familial hy-

Common adverse effects in *italic*, life-threatening effects underlined; generic names in **bold**; classifications in SMALL CAPS; ✚ Canadian drug name; ⊕ Prototype drug

905

percholesterolemia than primary hypercholesterolemia, possibly because in these persons LDL receptors are not functional.

CONTRAINDICATIONS Active liver disease, unexplained elevations of serum transaminases; cholestasis, hepatic encephalopathy, hepatic disease, hepatitis, jaundice; rhabdomyolysis; surgery, trauma; hypotension, renal failure; pregnancy (category X), lactation, children <10 y.

CAUTIOUS USE Patient who consumes substantial quantities of alcohol; history of liver disease; electrolyte imbalance, endocrine disease, females of childbearing age, infection, myopathy, renal disease, renal impairment, seizure disorder. Patient with risk factor predisposing to development of kidney failure secondary to rhabdomyolysis.

ROUTE & DOSAGE

Hypercholesterolemia
Adult: **PO** 20–40 mg 1–2 times/d

ADMINISTRATION

Oral

- Give with the evening meal if q.d. Give the first of 2 daily doses with breakfast.
- Store tablets at 5°–30° C (41°–86° F) in light-resistant, tightly closed container.
- Ensure that extended-release tablets are not crushed or chewed. They must be swallowed whole.

ADVERSE EFFECTS (≥1%) **Body as a Whole:** Generally well tolerated. **CNS:** Dizziness, mild transient headache, insomnia, fatigue. **Special Senses:** Blurred vision. **GI:** Dyspepsia, dysgeusia, heartburn, nausea, constipation, diarrhea, flatus, ab-

dominal pain, and cramps. **Metabolic:** Increases in serum transaminases, elevated creatine phosphokinase (CPK). **Skin:** Rash, pruritus.

INTERACTIONS Drug: Clarithromycin, clofibrate, cyclosporine, danazol, erythromycin, fenofibrate, fluconazole, gemfibrozil, itraconazole, ketoconazole, miconazole, niacin, and PROTEASE INHIBITORS increase risk of myopathy and rhabdomyolysis; potentiate hypoprothrombinemia with warfarin. **Food:** Grapefruit juice (>1 qt/d) may increase risk of myopathy and rhabdomyolysis.

PHARMACOKINETICS Absorption: 30% from GI tract; extensive first-pass metabolism. **Onset:** 2 wk. **Peak:** 4–6 wk. **Distribution:** Crosses blood–brain barrier and placenta; distributed into breast milk. **Metabolism:** In liver to active metabolites. **Elimination:** 83% in feces; 10% in urine. **Half-Life:** 1.1–1.7 h.

CLINICAL IMPLICATIONS

Assessment & Drug Effects

- Lab tests: Perform liver function tests q4–6wk during first 15 mo of therapy. Monitor blood cholesterol levels and lipid profile periodically.
- Drug-induced increases in serum transaminases, usually not associated with jaundice or other clinical S&S, return to normal when drug is discontinued. If these values rise and remain at 3 times upper level of normal, drug will be discontinued and liver biopsy considered.

Patient & Family Education

- Do not interrupt, increase, decrease, or omit dosage without advice of physician.
- Notify physician promptly of muscle tenderness or pain, especially if accompanied by fever or malaise. If CPK is elevated or if myo-

sitis is diagnosed, drug will be discontinued.

- Avoid or at least reduce alcohol consumption.
- Understand that lovastatin is not a substitute for, but an addition to, diet therapy.

LOXAPINE HYDROCHLORIDE

(lox'a-peen)
Loxitane C, Loxitane IM

LOXAPINE SUCCINATE

Loxitane, Loxapac ✦
Classifications: PSYCHOTHERAPEUTIC; ANTIPSYCHOTIC
Therapeutic: ANTIPSYCHOTIC
Prototype: Chlorpromazine
Pregnancy Category: C

AVAILABILITY 5 mg, 10 mg, 25 mg, 50 mg capsules; 25 mg/mL oral solution; 50 mg/mL injection

ACTION & *THERAPEUTIC EFFECT*

This dibenzoxazepine antipsychotic blocks postsynaptic dopamine receptors in limbic system and increases dopamine turnover by blockade of D_2-receptors in that region. After approximately 12 wk of chronic therapy, depolarization blockade of dopamine occurs, decreasing dopamine neurotransmission. This correlates with its antipsychotic effects. D_2-receptor blockade is also responsible for the potent extrapyramidal effects observed with this drug. Dopamine blockade in the chemoreceptor trigger zone is responsible for antiemetic effects of the drug. *Stabilizes emotional component of schizophrenia by acting on subcortical level of CNS.*

USES Manifestations of psychotic disorders.

UNLABELED USES Anxiety associated with mental depression.

CONTRAINDICATIONS Severe drug-induced CNS depression; Parkinson's disease; comatose states, children <16 y; pregnancy (category C), lactation.

CAUTIOUS USE Glaucoma, prostatic hypertrophy, urinary retention, history of convulsive disorders, cardiovascular disease; alcoholism; brain tumor; older adults; hematologic disease; hepatic disease; peptic ulcer disease; renal impairment; thyroid disease.

ROUTE & DOSAGE

Psychosis
Adult: **PO** Start with 10 mg b.i.d. and rapidly increase to maintenance levels of 60–100 mg/d in 2–4 divided doses (max: 250 mg/d) **IM** 12.5–50 mg q4–6h
Dementia Behavior
Geriatric: **PO** 5–10 mg 1–2 times/d, may increase q4–7d (max: 125 mg/d)

ADMINISTRATION

Oral

- Give with food, milk, or water to reduce possibility of stomach irritation.
- Dilute oral concentrate in about 2–3 oz (60–90 mL) water or orange or grapefruit juice shortly before administration. Measure concentrate with calibrated dropper dispensed with drug. Do not store diluted solution.

Intramuscular

- Use only with acute psychosis or when oral route not feasible.
- Reduce dosage gradually over period of several days when therapy is to be terminated.

Common adverse effects in *italic*, life-threatening effects <u>underlined</u>; generic names in **bold**; classifications in SMALL CAPS; ✦ Canadian drug name; ◗ Prototype drug

907

- Protect from light and freezing. Intensification of straw color to light amber is acceptable. Discard if solution is noticeably discolored.

ADVERSE EFFECTS (≥1%) **CNS:** *Drowsiness,* sedation, dizziness, syncope, EEG changes, paresthesias, staggering gait, muscle weakness, *extrapyramidal effects,* akathisia, tardive dyskinesia, neuroleptic malignant syndrome. **CV:** *Orthostatic hypotension,* hypertension, tachycardia. **Special Senses:** Nasal congestion, tinnitus; blurred vision, ptosis. **GI:** Constipation, dry mouth. **Skin:** Dermatitis, facial edema, pruritus, photosensitivity. **Urogenital:** Urinary retention, menstrual irregularities. **Body as a Whole:** Polydipsia, weight gain or loss, hyperpyrexia, transient leukopenia.

INTERACTIONS Drug: Alcohol and other CNS DEPRESSANTS potentiate CNS depression; will inhibit vasopressor effects of **epinephrine.**

PHARMACOKINETICS Absorption: Readily absorbed from GI tract. **Onset:** 20–30 min. **Peak:** 1.5–3 h. **Duration:** 12 h. **Distribution:** Widely distributed; crosses placenta; distributed into breast milk. **Metabolism:** In liver. **Elimination:** 50% in urine, 50% in feces. **Half-Life:** 19 h.

CLINICAL IMPLICATIONS

Assessment & Drug Effects

- Monitor baseline BP pattern prior and during therapy; both hypotension and hypertension have been reported as adverse reactions.
- Observe carefully for extrapyramidal effects such as acute dystonia (see Appendix F) during early therapy. Most symptoms disappear with dose adjustment or with antiparkinsonism drug therapy.
- Discontinue therapy and report promptly to physician the first signs of impending tardive dyskinesia (fine vermicular movements of the tongue) when patient is on long-term treatment.
- Monitor I&O and bowel elimination patterns and check for bladder distention. Depressed patients often fails to report urinary retention or constipation.
- Risk of seizures is increased in those with history of convulsive disorders.

Patient & Family Education

- Do NOT change dosage regimen in any way without physician approval.
- Avoid self-dosing with OTC drugs unless approved by the physician.
- Drowsiness usually decreases with continued therapy. If it persists and interferes with daily activities, consult physician. A change in time of administration or dose may help.
- Avoid potentially hazardous activity until response to drug is known.
- Learn measures to relieve dry mouth; rinse mouth frequently with water, suck hard candy. Avoid commercial products that may contain alcohol and enhance drying and irritation.
- Notify physician of blurred or colored vision.
- Do not take drug dose and notify physician of following: Light-colored stools, bruising, unexplained bleeding, prolonged constipation, tremor, restlessness and excitement, sore throat and fever, rash.
- Stay out of bright sun; cover exposed skin with sunscreen.

Common adverse effects in *italic*, life-threatening effects <u>underlined</u>; generic names in **bold**; classifications in SMALL CAPS; ♣ Canadian drug name; ⦿ Prototype drug

LUBIPROSTONE

(lu-bi-pros'tone)

Amitiza

Classifications: LAXATIVE AND STOOL SOFTENER; PROSTAGLANDIN; CHLORIDE CHANNEL ACTIVATOR

Therapeutic: LAXATIVE AND STOOL SOFTENER; PROSTAGLANDIN

Prototype: Misoprostol

Pregnancy Category: C

AVAILABILITY 24 mcg capsule

ACTION & *THERAPEUTIC EFFECT*
Lubiprostone activates chloride channels in the intestine that enhance chloride-rich intestinal fluid secretion without changing serum sodium and potassium concentrations. *The increase in intestinal fluid secretion enhances intestinal motility, thereby increasing the passage of stool and alleviating symptoms associated with chronic idiopathic constipation.*

USES Treatment of chronic idiopathic constipation.

CONTRAINDICATIONS Hypersensitivity to lubiprostone or misoprostol; history of mechanical GI obstruction: Crohn's disease, volvulus, diverticulitis, etc.; severe diarrhea; pregnancy (category C), lactation. Safe use in children is unknown.

CAUTIOUS USE GI disease.

ROUTE & DOSAGE

Chronic Idiopathic Constipation
Adult: **PO** 24 mcg b.i.d.

ADMINISTRATION

Oral
- Administer with food to minimize nausea.

- Do not administer to a patient with severe diarrhea or suspected bowel obstruction.
- Store at 15°–30° C (59°–86° F).

ADVERSE EFFECTS (≥1%) **Body as a Whole:** Chest pain, peripheral edema, pyrexia. **CNS:** Anxiety, depression, dizziness, fatigue, *headache,* insomnia. **CV:** Hypertension. **GI:** *Abdominal pain and discomfort,* constipation, *diarrhea,* dry mouth, dyspepsia, *flatulence,* viral gastroenteritis, gastroesophageal reflux disease, loose stools, *nausea,* vomiting. **Musculoskeletal:** Arthralgia, back pain, pain in extremities. **Respiratory:** Bronchitis, cough, dyspnea, nasopharyngitis, sinusitis, upper respiratory infection. **Urogenital:** Urinary tract infection.

PHARMACOKINETICS Absorption: Very low. **Peak:** 1.1 h (M3). **Distribution:** 94% protein bound. **Metabolism:** Extensive non-hepatic metabolism. **Elimination:** Urine (major) and feces. **Half-Life:** 0.9–1.4 h.

CLINICAL IMPLICATIONS

Assessment & Drug Effects
- Monitor for and report S&S of bowel obstruction.
- Lab tests: Baseline LFTs.

Patient & Family Education
- Follow directions for taking the drug (see Administration).
- Report to physician if you experience severe or prolonged diarrhea, or new or worsening abdominal pain.
- Do not drive or engage in potentially hazardous activities until response to drug is known.

LYMPHOCYTE IMMUNE GLOBULIN

(lymph'o-site)

Common adverse effects in *italic*, life-threatening effects <u>underlined</u>; generic names in **bold**; classifications in SMALL CAPS; ♣ Canadian drug name; ⊙ Prototype drug

Antithymocyte Globulin, ATG, Atgam

Classifications: BIOLOGIC RE-
SPONSE MODIFIER; IMMUNOGLOBULIN
Therapeutic: IMMUNOGLOBULIN;
IMMUNOSUPPRESSANT
Prototype: Immune globulin
Pregnancy Category: C

AVAILABILITY 50 mg/mL injection

ACTION & *THERAPEUTIC EFFECT*
An immunoglobulin (IgG) and lym-
phocyte-selective immunosuppressant derived from serum of healthy
horses that have been immunized
with human thymus lymphocytes.
During rejection of allografts, human leukocyte antigens (HLAs)
bind to peptides and form complexes. Helper T-lymphocytes activate these complexes and produce
interleukins, cytotoxic T-cells, and
natural killer cells, resulting in destruction of transplanted tissue. Antithymocyte globulin (ATG) reduces
the number of circulating T-lymphocytes, altering T-cell activation
and cytotoxic function. *Alters the
formation of T lymphocytes (killer
cells) and reduces their number,
thus reversing acute allograft rejection. As with other immunosuppressant agents, carcinogenicity of this
drug may be expressed.*

USES Primarily to prevent or delay
onset or to reverse acute renal allograft rejection.
UNLABELED USES Moderate and severe aplastic anemia in patients unsuitable for bone marrow transplantation, T-cell malignancy, acute
and chronic graft-vs-host disease,
and to prevent rejection of skin allografts.

CONTRAINDICATIONS Hypersensitivity to thimerosal (preservative) or
to other equine gamma globulin
preparations; history of previous

systemic reaction to ATG, hemorrhagic diatheses; leporine protein
hypersensitivity; use in kidney
transplant patient not receiving a
concomitant immunosuppressant;
fungal or viral infections; pregnancy (category C), lactation.
CAUTIOUS USE Children (experience limited); hypotension, infection, leukopenia, lymphoma, neoplastic disease, thrombocytopenia,
vaccination, varicella.

ROUTE & DOSAGE

Renal Allotransplantation
Adult: **IV** 10–30 mg/kg/d by
slow **IV** infusion
Child: **IV** 5–25 mg/kg/d by slow
IV infusion

Prevention of Allograft Rejection
Adult: **IV** 15 mg/kg/d for 14 d
followed by 15 mg/kg every
other day for 14 d

Treatment of Allograft Rejection
Adult: **IV** 10–15 mg/kg/d for 14
d followed by 15 mg/kg every
other day for 14 d if needed

Aplastic Anemia
Adult/Child: **IV** 10–20 mg/kg/d
× 8–14 d followed by 10–20 mg/
kg every other day for 7 doses

ADMINISTRATION

Intravenous
Administer lymphocyte immune
globulin (ATG) ONLY if experienced with immunosuppressant
therapy and management of kidney transplant patients.

- Do an intradermal skin test to
  rule out allergy to the drug before first dose. Inject 0.1 mL of
  a 1:1000 dilution (5 mcg equine
  IgG in normal saline) and a saline control. If local reaction

Common adverse effects in *italic*, life-threatening effects <u>underlined</u>; generic names
in **bold**; classifications in SMALL CAPS; ✦ Canadian drug name; ◐ Prototype drug

occurs (wheal or erythema more than 10 mm) or if there is pseudopod formation, itching, or local swelling, use caution during infusion. Discontinue infusion if systemic reaction develops (generalized rash, tachycardia, dyspnea, hypotension, anaphylaxis).

PREPARE: **IV Infusion:** Withdraw required dose of ATG concentrate and inject into IV solution container of 0.45% NaCl or NS. Invert IV container during injection of ATG to prevent its contact with air inside container. Use enough IV solution to create a concentration ≤4 mg/mL. ▪ Inspect concentrate and diluted solution for particulate matter (may develop during storage) and discoloration; discard if present.

ADMINISTER: **IV Infusion:** Give through an in-line 0.2–1.0 mcg filter into a high-flow vein to decrease potential for phlebitis and thrombosis. Give over ≥4 h (usually 4–8 h). Must finish infusion within 12 h of preparation.

▪ Total storage time for diluted solutions: NO MORE than 12 h (including storage time and actual infusion time). Refrigerate ampules and diluted solutions (if prepared before time of infusion) at 2°–8° C (35°–46° F). Do not freeze.

ADVERSE EFFECTS (≥1%) **CNS:** Headache, paresthesia, seizures. **CV:** Peripheral thrombophlebitis, hypotension, underline. **GI:** Nausea, vomiting, diarrhea, stomatitis, hiccups, epigastric pain, abdominal distension. **Hematologic:** *Leukopenia, thrombocytopenia.* **Musculoskeletal:** Arthralgia, myalgias, chest or back pain. **Respiratory:** Dyspnea, laryngospasm, pulmonary edema. **Skin:** *Rash, pruritus,* urticaria, wheal

and flare. **Body as a Whole:** *Chills, fever,* night sweats, pain at infusion site, hyperglycemia, systemic infection, wound dehiscence; anaphylaxis, *serum sickness,* herpes simplex virus reactivation.

INTERACTIONS Drug: Azathioprine, CORTICOSTEROIDS, other IMMUNOSUPPRESSANTS increase degree of immunosuppression.

PHARMACOKINETICS Distribution: Poorly distributed into lymphoid tissues (spleen, lymph nodes); probably crosses placenta and into breast milk. **Elimination:** About 1% of dose is excreted in urine. **Half-Life:** Approximately 6 d.

CLINICAL IMPLICATIONS

Assessment & Drug Effects

▪ Discontinue infusion and initiate appropriate therapy promptly with onset of anaphylactic response (respiratory distress; pain in chest, flank, back; hypotension, anxiety).

▪ Monitor BP, vital signs, and patient's complaints during entire administration period carefully. Prompt treatment is indicated for observed and reported symptoms of anaphylaxis (incidence: 1%), serum sickness, or allergic response. Always have equipment for assisted respiration, epinephrine, antihistamines, corticosteroid, and vasopressor available at bedside.

▪ Predictive value of skin test is not proven. Observe patient carefully; allergic reaction can occur even when test is negative.

▪ Watch closely for S&S of serum sickness: fever, malaise, arthralgia, nausea, vomiting, lymphadenopathy and morbilliform eruptions on trunk and extremities. Rash begins as asymptomatic pale pink macules in periumbilical region, axilla, and groin, then rapidly be-

Common adverse effects in *italic*, life-threatening effects underline; generic names in **bold**; classifications in SMALL CAPS; ✦ Canadian drug name; ⦾ Prototype drug

911

comes generalized, erythematous, and confluent. Bands of progressive erythema along the sides of hands, fingers, feet, toes, and at margins of palm or plantar skin are characteristic. In ATG-induced serum sickness, when platelet count is low, petechiae and purpura rapidly replace rash distribution over the body. Petechial areas are especially noticeable on legs but also on palms and soles. Serum sickness usually occurs 6–18 d after initiation of therapy; may occur during drug administration or when treatment is stopped.

- Monitor carefully for S&S of thrombocytopenia, concurrent infection, and leukopenia; patient usually receives concomitant corticosteroids and antimetabolites.
- Monitor patient's temperature and attend to complaints of sore throat or rhinorrhea. Report to physician; ATG treatment may be stopped.

Patient & Family Education
- Notify physician immediately of pain in chest, flank, or back; chills; pruritus; night sweats; sore throat.

MAFENIDE ACETATE

(ma'fe-nide)
Sulfamylon
Classifications: ANTIBIOTIC; SULFONAMIDE DERIVATIVE
Therapeutic: ANTIBIOTIC
Prototype: Sulfisoxazole
Pregnancy Category: C

AVAILABILITY 5% solution; cream

ACTION & THERAPEUTIC EFFECT
Topical sulfonamide derivative effective against both gram-positive and gram-negative drugs. Topical applications produce marked reduction of bacterial growth in vascular tissue. Active in presence of purulent matter and serum and not affected by changes in pH of tissue environment. *Bacteriostatic against many gram-positive and gram-negative organisms, including* Pseudomonas aeruginosa, *and certain strains of anaerobes.*

USES Adjunctive therapy in second- and third-degree burns to prevent sepsis.

CONTRAINDICATIONS History of hypersensitivity to mafenide; respiratory (inhalation) injury, pulmonary infection; pregnancy (category C), lactation, children <3 mo.
CAUTIOUS USE Impaired kidney or pulmonary function, burn patients with acute kidney failure.

ROUTE & DOSAGE

Burns
Adult: Topical Apply aseptically to burn areas to a thickness of approximately 15 mm (¹/₁₆ in) once or twice daily

ADMINISTRATION

Topical
- Apply cream or solution aseptically to cleansed, debrided burn areas with sterile gloved hand.
- Cover burn areas with cream at all times. Make reapplications to areas from which cream has been removed as necessary.
- Store in tight, light-resistant containers. Avoid extremes of temperature.

ADVERSE EFFECTS (≥1%) **Hypersensitivity:** Pruritus, rash, urticaria, blisters, facial edema, eosinophilia. **Skin:** *Intense pain, burning, or stinging at application sites,* bleeding of skin, excessive body water loss, delayed eschar separation, excoriation of new skin, superinfections. **Hematologic:** <u>Hemolytic anemia, bone marrow suppression</u> (rare). **Other:** Metabolic acidosis.

INTERACTIONS Drug: No clinically significant interactions established.

PHARMACOKINETICS Absorption: Rapidly from burn surface. **Peak:** 2–4 h. **Metabolism:** Rapidly inactivated in blood to a weak carbonic anhydrase inhibitor. **Elimination:** Via kidneys.

CLINICAL IMPLICATIONS
Assessment & Drug Effects
- Monitor vital signs. Report immediately changes in BP, pulse, and respiratory rate and volume.
- Monitor I&O. Report oliguria or changes in I&O ratio and pattern.
- Lab tests: Monitor fluid and electrolyte status throughout therapy; acid–base balance should be monitored in patients with extensive burns and in those with pulmonary or kidney dysfunction.
- Be alert to S&S of metabolic acidosis (see Appendix F).
- Be alert to evidence of superinfections (see Appendix F), particularly in and below burn eschar.
- Observe carefully; accuracy is critical. It is frequently difficult to distinguish between adverse reactions to mafenide and the effects of severe burns.
- Note: Allergic reactions have reportedly occurred 10–14 d after initiation of mafenide therapy. Temporary discontinuation of drug may be necessary.
- Report intense local pain to physician; pain caused by drug may require administration of analgesic.

Patient & Family Education
- Apply only a thin dressing over burns unless otherwise directed.

- Therapy is usually continued until healing is progressing well (usually 60 d) or site is ready for grafting (after about 35–40 d). It is not withdrawn while there is a possibility of infection unless adverse reactions intervene.
- Report any of the following to the physician immediately: Foul-smelling drainage from wounds, bleeding at wound site, unexplained fever.

MAGALDRATE
(mag′al-drate)
Riopan
Classifications: ANTACID
Therapeutic: ANTACID
Prototype: Aluminum hydroxide
Pregnancy Category: B with occasional use

AVAILABILITY 540 mg/5 mL suspension

ACTION & *THERAPEUTIC EFFECT* By reducing gastric acidity, stomach pH increases and proteolytic activity of pepsin is inhibited. Reportedly does not produce alkalosis or acid rebound and is not as likely to produce alterations of bowel function that occur with either aluminum or magnesium hydroxide alone. *Nonsystemic antacid with true buffering action and high acid-neutralizing capacity.*

USES Symptomatic relief of hyperacidity associated with peptic ulcer, gastritis, peptic esophagitis, and hiatal hernia, particularly in patients who need to restrict sodium.

CONTRAINDICATIONS Sensitivity to components; hypermagnesia; appendicitis, colostomy, diverticulitis,

ileostomy, ulcerative colitis; pregnancy (category B) with occasional use; children <2 y.
CAUTIOUS USE Impaired kidney function, dialysis patients; CHF; biliary cirrhosis, GI obstruction, constipation.

ROUTE & DOSAGE

Antacid
Adult: **PO** 480–1080 mg (5–10 mL suspension or 1–2 tablets) q.i.d. (max: 20 tablets or 100 mL/d)

ADMINISTRATION

Oral
- Shake suspension vigorously before pouring. Preferably give between meals and at bedtime.
- Give suspension with sufficient water to ensure passage of drug into stomach.
- Make sure chewable tablets are chewed thoroughly before being swallowed. Give tablet to be swallowed whole with enough water to ensure prompt swallowing without chewing.

ADVERSE EFFECTS (≥1%) **GI:** Infrequent constipation or diarrhea (with prolonged use). **Urogenital:** Hypermagnesemia (in patients with impaired kidney function).

INTERACTIONS Drug: Will decrease absorption of TETRACYCLINES.

PHARMACOKINETICS Absorption: Minimally from GI tract. **Duration:** Buffering action up to 60 min.

CLINICAL IMPLICATIONS
Assessment & Drug Effects
- Question patient about effectiveness of medication in relieving GI distress.
- Lab tests: Check patients on prolonged therapy periodically for

electrolyte imbalance (i.e., hypermagnesemia).

Patient & Family Education
- Be aware that, in common with other antacids, magaldrate may cause premature dissolution and absorption of enteric-coated tablets and interfere with the absorption of oral tetracyclines and other oral medications.
- Do not take other oral drugs, generally, within 1–2 h of an antacid.

MAGNESIUM CITRATE

(mag-nes′i-um)
Citrate of Magnesia, Citroma, Citro-Nesia
Classifications: SALINE CATHARTIC
Therapeutic: LAXATIVE
Prototype: Magnesium hydroxide
Pregnancy Category: B

AVAILABILITY 1.75 g/30 mL solution

ACTION & *THERAPEUTIC EFFECT* Hyperosmotic laxative. Promotes bowel evacuation by causing osmotic retention of fluid, which distends colon and stimulates peristaltic activity. *Evacuates bowels.*

USES To evacuate bowel prior to certain surgical and diagnostic procedures and to help eliminate parasites and toxic materials after treatment with a vermifuge.

CONTRAINDICATIONS Severe renal impairment, renal failure; nausea, vomiting, diarrhea, abdominal pain, acute surgical abdomen; intestinal impaction, obstruction or perforation; rectal bleeding; use of solutions containing sodium bicarbonate in patients on sodium-restricted diets; children <2 y.

CAUTIOUS USE Mild or moderate renal impairment; cardiac disease; older adults; pregnancy (category B).

ROUTE & DOSAGE

Bowel Evacuation
Adult: **PO** 240 mL once
Child: **PO** *2–6 y,* 4–12 mL; *6–12 y,* 50–100 mL

ADMINISTRATION

Oral

- Give on an empty stomach with a full (240 mL) glass of water. Time dosing so that it does not interfere with sleep. Drug produces a watery or semifluid evacuation in 2–6 h.
- Chill solution by pouring it over ice or refrigerate it until ready to use to increase palatability.
- Be aware that once container is opened, effervescence will decrease. This does not effect the quality of preparation.
- Store at 2°–30° C (36°–86° F) in tightly covered containers.

ADVERSE EFFECTS (≥1%) **GI:** Abdominal cramps, nausea, fluid and electrolyte imbalance, hypermagnesemia (prolonged use).

INTERACTIONS Drug: May decrease effectiveness of **digoxin**, ORAL ANTICOAGULANTS, PHENOTHIAZINES; will decrease absorption of **ciprofloxacin**, TETRACYCLINES; **sodium polystyrene sulfonate** will bind magnesium, decreasing its effectiveness.

PHARMACOKINETICS Onset: 0.5–2 h.

CLINICAL IMPLICATIONS

Assessment & Drug Effects

- Monitor for dehydration, hypokalemia, and hyponatremia (see Appendix F) since drug may cause intense bowel evacuation.

Patient & Family Education

- Do not use for routine treatment of constipation (especially in older adult).
- Expect some degree of abdominal cramping.

MAGNESIUM HYDROXIDE ⓟ

(mag-nes´i-um)
Magnesia, Magnesia Magma, Milk of Magnesia, M.O.M.
Classifications: SALINE CATHARTIC; ANTACID
Therapeutic: LAXATIVE; ANTACID
Pregnancy Category: B

AVAILABILITY 311 mg tablets; 400 mg/5 mL, 800 mg/5 mL suspension

ACTION & *THERAPEUTIC EFFECT*

Aqueous suspension of magnesium hydroxide with rapid and long-acting neutralizing action. May cause slight acid rebound. Causes osmotic retention of fluid, which distends colon, resulting in mechanical stimulation of peristaltic activity. *Acts as antacid in low doses and as mild saline laxative at higher doses.*

USES Short-term treatment of occasional constipation, for relief of GI symptoms associated with hyperacidity, and as adjunct in treatment of peptic ulcer. Also has been used in treatment of poisoning by mineral acids and arsenic, and as mouthwash to neutralize acidity.

CONTRAINDICATIONS Abdominal pain, nausea, vomiting, chronic diarrhea, severe kidney dysfunction, fecal impaction, intestinal obstruction or perforation, rectal bleeding, colostomy, ileostomy, children <2 y is not established.

M

Common adverse effects in *italic*, life-threatening effects <u>underlined</u>; generic names in **bold**; classifications in SMALL CAPS; ♦ Canadian drug name; ⓟ Prototype drug

CAUTIOUS USE Older adults, renal impairment, renal disease; pregnancy category B, lactation.

ROUTE & DOSAGE

Laxative

Adult: **PO** 2.4–4.8 g (30–60 mL)/d in 1 or more divided doses
Child: **PO** 2–5 y, 0.4–1.2 g (5–15 mL)/d in 1 or more divided doses; 6–11 y, 1.2–2.4 g (15–30 mL)/d in 1 or more divided doses

ADMINISTRATION

Oral

- Shake bottle well before pouring to assure mixing of suspension.
- Follow drug with at least a full glass of water to enhance drug action for laxative effect. Administer in the morning or at bedtime. Most effective when taken on an empty stomach.
- Store at 15°–30° C (59°–86° F) in tightly covered container. Slowly absorbs carbon dioxide on exposure to air. Avoid freezing.

ADVERSE EFFECTS (≥1%) **GI:** Nausea, vomiting, abdominal cramps, *diarrhea*. **Urogenital:** Alkalinization of urine. **Body as a Whole:** Weakness, lethargy, mental depression, hyporeflexia, dehydration, coma. **Metabolic:** Electrolyte imbalance with prolonged use. **CV:** Hypotension, bradycardia, complete heart block and other ECG abnormalities. **Respiratory:** Respiratory depression.

INTERACTIONS Drug: Milk of Magnesia decreases absorption of **chlordiazepoxide, dicumarol, digoxin, isoniazid,** QUINOLONES, TETRACYCLINES.

PHARMACOKINETICS Absorption: 15–30% of magnesium is absorbed. **Onset:** 3–6 h. **Distribution:** Small amounts distributed in saliva and breast milk. **Elimination:** In feces; some renal excretion.

CLINICAL IMPLICATIONS

Assessment & Drug Effects

- Evaluate the patient's continued need for drug. Prolonged and frequent use of laxative doses may lead to dependence. Additionally, even therapeutic doses can raise urinary pH and thereby predispose susceptible patients to urinary infection and urolithiasis.
- Lab tests: Monitor serum magnesium with signs of hypermagnesemia such as bradycardia (see Appendix F), especially with frequent use or any degree of renal impairment.

Patient & Family Education

- Investigate the cause of persistent or recurrent constipation or gastric distress with physician.

MAGNESIUM OXIDE

(mag-nes'i-um)

Mag-Ox, Maox, Par-Mag, Uro-Mag
Classifications: ANTACID; SALINE CATHARTIC
Therapeutic: ANTACID; MAGNESIUM SUPPLEMENT; LAXATIVE
Prototype: Magnesium hydroxide
Pregnancy Category: A

AVAILABILITY 400 mg, 420 mg, 500 mg tablets; 140 mg capsules

ACTION & THERAPEUTIC EFFECT
Nonsystemic antacid with high neutralizing capacity and relatively long duration of action. *Acts as an antacid in low doses and a mild saline laxative at higher doses. Also effective as a magnesium supplement.*

USES Essentially the same as magnesium hydroxide. May also be used as magnesium supplement.

CONTRAINDICATIONS Abdominal pain, nausea, vomiting, diarrhea, severe kidney dysfunction, fecal impaction, intestinal obstruction or perforation, ileus; rectal bleeding, colostomy, ileostomy; AV block; hypermagnesia; children <2 y.

CAUTIOUS USE Cardiac disease, renal disease, renal impairment; electrolyte imbalance; pregnancy (category A), lactation.

ROUTE & DOSAGE

Antacid
Adult: **PO** 280–1500 mg with water or milk q.i.d., p.c. and h.s.

Laxative
Adult: **PO** 2–4 g with water or milk h.s.

Magnesium Supplement
Adult: **PO** 400–1200 mg/d in divided doses

ADMINISTRATION

Oral
■ Separate administration of this drug from other oral drugs by 1–2 h.
■ Store at 15°–30° C (59°–86° F) in airtight containers. On exposure to air, magnesium oxide rapidly absorbs moisture and carbon dioxide.

ADVERSE EFFECTS (≥1%) **GI:** *Diarrhea,* abdominal cramps, nausea; hypermagnesemia, kidney stones (chronic use).

INTERACTIONS Drug: See magnesium hydroxide.

PHARMACOKINETICS Absorption: 30–50% from GI tract. **Elimination:** In urine.

CLINICAL IMPLICATIONS

Assessment & Drug Effects
■ Monitor for dehydration, hypokalemia, and hyponatremia (see Appendix F) since drug may cause intense bowel evacuation.
■ Lab tests: Check patients on prolonged therapy periodically for electrolyte imbalance (i.e., hypermagnesemia).

Patient & Family Education
■ Liquid preparation is reportedly more effective than the tablet form, as with other antacids.

MAGNESIUM SALICYLATE

(mag-nes'i-um)
Doan's Pills, Magan, Mobidin
Classifications: ANALGESIC (SALICYLATE), NONSTEROIDAL ANTIINFLAMMATORY DRUG (NSAID); ANTIPYRETIC
Therapeutic: NSAID, ANALGESIC; ANTIPYRETIC
Prototype: Aspirin
Pregnancy Category: C first and second trimester; D third trimester

AVAILABILITY 467 mg, 500 mg, 580 mg caplets; 545 mg, 600 mg tablets

ACTION & *THERAPEUTIC EFFECT*
Sodium-free salicylate derivative that is a nonsteroidal antiinflammatory drug (NSAID) with low incidence of GI irritation. It inhibits prostaglandin synthesis. Unlike aspirin, not associated with asthmatic reactions and does not inhibit platelet aggregation or increase bleeding time. *In equal doses, less potent than aspirin as an analgesic and antipyretic. Has antiinflammatory effects.*

USES Relief of pain and inflammation in rheumatoid arthritis, osteoarthritis, bursitis, and other musculoskeletal disorders.

Common adverse effects in *italic*, life-threatening effects underlined; generic names in **bold**; classifications in SMALL CAPS; ◆ Canadian drug name; ❷ Prototype drug

917

CONTRAINDICATIONS Hypersensitivity to salicylates; erosive gastritis, peptic ulcer; advanced renal insufficiency, liver damage; thrombolytic therapy; bleeding disorders; before surgery; pregnancy (category C first and second trimester, category D third trimester); children <12 y.

CAUTIOUS USE Serious acid base imbalances; renal disease, history of GI bleeding, or peptic ulcers; SLE; history of acute bronchospasm; lactation.

ROUTE & DOSAGE

> **Analgesic/Antipyretic**
> *Adult:* **PO** 650 mg t.i.d. or q.i.d.
>
> **Arthritic Conditions**
> *Adult:* **PO** Up to 9.6 g/d in divided doses

ADMINISTRATION

Oral
- Give with a full glass of water, food, or milk to minimize gastric irritation.

ADVERSE EFFECTS (≥1%) **Body as a Whole:** Salicylism [dizziness, drowsiness, tinnitus, hearing loss, nausea, vomiting, hypermagnesemia (with high doses in patients with renal insufficiency)].

INTERACTIONS Drug: A m i n o s a l i cylic acid increases risk of SALICYLATE toxicity; **ammonium chloride** and other ACIDIFYING AGENTS decrease renal elimination and increase risk of SALICYLATE toxicity; anticoagulants— added risk of bleeding with ANTICOAGULANTS; CARBONIC ANHYDRASE INHIBITORS enhance SALICYLATE toxicity; CORTICOSTEROIDS compound ulcerogenic effects; increases **methotrexate** toxicity; low doses of SALICYLATES may antagonize uricosuric effects of **probenecid, sulfinpyrazone.**

PHARMACOKINETICS Absorption: Well absorbed from the GI tract. **Peak:** 20 min. **Distribution:** W i d e l y distributed with high levels of salicylic acid in liver and kidney, crosses placenta, excreted in breast milk. **Metabolism:** Salicylic acid is metabolized in liver. **Elimination:** In kidneys. **Half-Life:** 2–3 h with single dose, 15–30 h with chronic dosing.

CLINICAL IMPLICATIONS

Assessment & Drug Effects
- Lab tests: Monitor serum magnesium levels hypermagnesemia if used in high dosages or patients with any degree of renal impairment.
- Do not use salicylates in children or teenagers with influenza or chickenpox because of association with development of Reye's syndrome.

Patient & Family Education
- Report to physician promptly tinnitus, hearing loss, or dizziness.
- Do not to take aspirin-containing drugs without consent of physician.
- Check ingredients. Doan's pills may contain acetaminophen plus salicylamide.

MAGNESIUM SULFATE

(mag-nes′i-um)
Epsom Salt
Classifications: SALINE CATHARTIC; REPLACEMENT AGENT; ANTICONVULSANT
Therapeutic: LAXATIVE; ELECTROLYTE REPLACEMENT; ANTICONVULSANT
Prototype: Magnesium hydroxide
Pregnancy Category: A

AVAILABILITY 0.8 mEq/mL, 1 mEq/mL, 4 mEq/mL injection

ACTION & *THERAPEUTIC EFFECT*
Orally: Acts as a laxative by osmotic

L

retention of fluid, which distends colon, increases water content of feces, and causes mechanical stimulation of bowel activity. *Parenterally:* Acts as a CNS depressant and also as a depressant of smooth, skeletal, and cardiac muscle function. Anticonvulsant properties thought to be produced by CNS depression, principally by decreasing the amount of acetylcholine liberated from motor nerve terminals, thus producing peripheral neuromuscular blockade. *Effective parenterally as a CNS depressant, smooth muscle relaxant and anticonvulsant in labor and delivery, and cardiac disorders. It is a laxative when taken orally.*

USES Orally to relieve acute constipation and to evacuate bowel in preparation for x-ray of intestines. Parenterally to control seizures in toxemia of pregnancy, epilepsy, and acute nephritis and for prophylaxis and treatment of hypomagnesemia. Topically to reduce edema, inflammation, and itching.
UNLABELED USES To inhibit premature labor (tocolytic action) and as adjunct in hyperalimentation, to alleviate bronchospasm of acute asthma, to reduce mortality post-MI.

CONTRAINDICATIONS Myocardial damage; AV heart block; cardiac arrest except for certain arrhythmias; hypermagnesemia; GI obstruction; IV administration during the 2 h preceding delivery; PO use in patients with abdominal pain, nausea, vomiting, fecal impaction, or intestinal irritation, obstruction, or perforation.
CAUTIOUS USE Renal disease; renal failure; renal impairment; acute MI; digitalized patients; concomitant use of other CNS depressants; neuromuscular blocking agents, or cardiac glycosides; children.

ROUTE & DOSAGE

Laxative
Adult: **PO** 10–15 g once/d
Seizures
Adult: **IV** 1 g, may need to repeat dose
Preeclampsia, Eclampsia
Adult: **IM/IV** 4–5 g in 250 mL D5W infused slowly; simultaneously, 5 g **IM** in alternate buttocks q4h
Hypomagnesemia
Adult: **IM/IV** *Mild,* 1 g q6h for 4 doses; *Severe,* 5 g infused over 3 h
Child: **IV** 25–50 mg/kg q4–6h prn (max single dose: 2000 mg)
Total Parenteral Nutrition
Adult: **IV** 0.5–3 g/d

ADMINISTRATION

Oral
- Give in the morning or mid-afternoon in a glass of water for laxative action. Disguise bitter, salty taste by chilling or flavoring with lemon or orange juice.

Intramuscular
- Give deep using the 50% concentration for adults and the 20% concentration for children.

Intravenous
Note: Verify correct IV concentration and rate of infusion for administration to infants, children with physician.

PREPARE: **Direct/IV Infusion:** Give solutions with concentrations of ≤20% undiluted.
ADMINISTER: **Direct:** Give at a rate of 150 mg over at least 1 min. Note: 20% solution contains 200 mg/mL, 10% solution contains 100 mg/mL. **IV Infusion:** Give required dose over 4 h. Do not exceed the direct rate.

Common adverse effects in *italic*, life-threatening effects <u>underlined</u>; generic names in **bold**; classifications in SMALL CAPS; ✦ Canadian drug name; ◉ Prototype drug

919

M

***INCOMPATIBILITIES* Solution/additive:** 10% fat emulsion; amphotericin B, calcium, chlorpromazine, clindamycin, cyclosporine, dobutamine, hydralazine, polymyxin B sulfate, potassium, procaine, prochlorperazine, sodium bicarbonate. **Y-site:** Amiodarone, amphotericin B, cholesteryl, cefepime, ciprofloxacin, haloperidol.

ADVERSE EFFECTS (≥1%) **Body as a Whole:** Flushing, sweating, extreme thirst, sedation, confusion, depressed reflexes or no reflexes, muscle weakness, <u>flaccid paralysis,</u> hypothermia. **CV:** Hypotension, depressed cardiac function, <u>complete heart block, circulatory collapse</u>. **Respiratory:** <u>Respiratory paralysis</u>. **Metabolic:** Hypermagnesemia, hypocalcemia, dehydration, electrolyte imbalance including hypocalcemia with repeated laxative use.

INTERACTIONS Drug: NEUROMUSCULAR BLOCKING AGENTS add to respiratory depression and apnea.

PHARMACOKINETICS Onset: 1–2 h PO; 1 h IM. **Duration:** 30 min IV; 3–4 h PO. **Distribution:** Crosses placenta; distributed into breast milk. **Elimination:** In kidneys.

CLINICAL IMPLICATIONS
Assessment & Drug Effects

- Observe constantly when given IV. Check BP and pulse q10–15 min or more often if indicated.
- Lab tests: Monitor plasma magnesium levels in patients receiving drug parenterally (normal: 1.8–3.0 mEq/L). Plasma levels in excess of 4 mEq/L are reflected in depressed deep tendon reflexes and other symptoms of magnesium intoxication (see ADVERSE EFFECTS). Cardiac arrest occurs at levels in excess of 25 mEq/L. Monitor calcium and phosphorus levels also.
- Early indicators of magnesium toxicity (hypermagnesemia) include cathartic effect, profound thirst, feeling of warmth, sedation, confusion, depressed deep tendon reflexes, and muscle weakness.
- Monitor respiratory rate closely. Report immediately if rate falls below 12.
- Test patellar reflex before each repeated parenteral dose. Depression or absence of reflexes is a useful index of early magnesium intoxication.
- Check urinary output, especially in patients with impaired kidney function. Therapy is generally not continued if urinary output is less than 100 mL during the 4 h preceding each dose.
- Observe newborns of mothers who received parenteral magnesium sulfate within a few hours of delivery for signs of toxicity, including respiratory and neuromuscular depression.
- Observe patients receiving drug for hypomagnesemia for improvement in these signs of deficiency: Irritability, choreiform movements, tremors, tetany, twitching, muscle cramps, tachycardia, hypertension, psychotic behavior.
- Have calcium gluconate readily available in case of magnesium sulfate toxicity.

Patient & Family Education
- Drink sufficient water during the day when drug is administered orally to prevent net loss of body water.
- Recommended daily allowances of magnesium are obtained in a normal diet. Rich sources are whole-grain cereals, legumes, nuts, meats, seafood, milk, most green leafy vegetables, and bananas.

MANNITOL ⊕

(man'i-tole)

Osmitrol

Classifications: ELECTROLYTIC AND WATER BALANCE AGENT; OSMOTIC DIURETIC

Therapeutic: OSMOTIC DIURETIC

Pregnancy Category: C

AVAILABILITY 5%, 10%, 15%, 20%, 25% injection

ACTION & *THERAPEUTIC EFFECT*

In large doses, increases rate of electrolyte excretion by the kidney, particularly sodium, chloride, and potassium. Induces diuresis by raising osmotic pressure of glomerular filtrate, thereby inhibiting tubular reabsorption of water and solutes. Reduces elevated intraocular and cerebrospinal pressures by increasing plasma osmolality, thus inducing diffusion of water from these fluids back into plasma and extravascular space. *Parenteral osmotic diuretic that reduces intracranial pressure, cerebral edema, intraocular pressure, and promotes diuresis, thus preventing or treating oliguria.*

USES To promote diuresis in prevention and treatment of oliguric phase of acute kidney failure following cardiovascular surgery, severe traumatic injury, surgery in presence of severe jaundice, hemolytic transfusion reaction. Also used to reduce elevated intraocular (IOP) and intracranial pressure (ICP), to measure glomerular filtration rate (GFR), to promote excretion of toxic substances, to relieve symptoms of pulmonary edema, and as irrigating solution in transurethral prostatic reaction to minimize hemolytic effects of water.

Commercially available in combination with sorbitol for urogenital irrigation.

CONTRAINDICATIONS Anuria; severe renal failure with azotemia or increasing oliguria; marked pulmonary congestion or edema; severe CHF; metabolic edema; hypovolemia; organic CNS disease, intracranial bleeding; shock, severe dehydration, history of allergy; pregnancy (category C), lactation; concomitantly with blood.

CAUTIOUS USE Older adult; electrolyte imbalance.

ROUTE & DOSAGE

Acute Kidney Failure

Adult: **IV Test Dose** 0.2 g/kg over 3–5 min **Positive Response** 30–50 mL of urine over next 2–3 h, may repeat test dose 1 time. If still negative, do not use. **Treatment** 50–100 g as 15–20% solution over 90 min to several hours

Child: **IV Test Dose** 200 mg/kg (max: 12.5 g) over 3–5 min **Positive Response** Urine flow of 1 mL/kg/h for 1–2 h **Maintenance** 0.25–0.5 g/kg q4–6 h

Edema, Ascites

Adult: **IV** 100 g as a 10–20% solution over 2–6 h

Elevated IOP or ICP

Adult: **IV** 1.5–2 mg/kg as a 15–25% solution over 30–60 min

Acute Chemical Toxicity

Adult: **IV** 100–200 g depending on urine output

Measurement of GFR

Adult: **IV** 100 mL of 20% solution diluted with 180 mL NaCl injection infused at a rate of 20 mL/min

Common adverse effects in *italic*, life-threatening effects underlined; generic names in **bold**; classifications in SMALL CAPS; ♣ Canadian drug name; ⊕ Prototype drug

921

ADMINISTRATION

Intravenous

Note: Verify correct IV concentration and rate of infusion for administration to infants, children with physician.

PREPARE: **IV Infusion:** Give undiluted.

ADMINISTER: **IV Infusion:** Give a single dose over 30–90 min. Oliguria: A test dose is given to patients with marked oliguria to check adequacy of kidney function. Response is considered satisfactory if urine flow of at least 30–50 mL/h is produced over 2–3 h after drug administration; then rate is adjusted to maintain urine flow at 30–50 mL/h with a single dose usually being infused over ≥90 min. Concentrations higher than 15% have a greater tendency to crystallize. Use an administration set with an in-line IV filter when infusing concentrations of 15% or above.

INCOMPATIBILITIES **Solution/additive: Furosemide, imipenem-cilastatin, meropenem, potassium chloride, sodium chloride, whole blood.** Y-site: **Cefepime, doxorubicin liposome, filgrastim.**

• Store at 15°–30° C (59°–86° F) unless otherwise directed. Avoid freezing.

ADVERSE EFFECTS (≥1%) **CNS:**
Headache, tremor, convulsions, dizziness, transient muscle rigidity. **CV:** Edema, CHF, angina-like pain, hypotension, hypertension, thrombophlebitis. **Eye:** Blurred vision. **GI:** Dry mouth, nausea, vomiting. **Urogenital:** Marked diuresis, urinary retention, nephrosis, uricosuria. **Metabolic:** *Fluid and electrolyte imbalance,* especially <u>hyponatremia</u>; de-

hydration, acidosis. **Other:** With extravasation (local edema, skin necrosis; chills, fever, allergic reactions).

INTERACTIONS **Drug:** Increases urinary excretion of **lithium,** SALICYLATES, BARBITURATES, **imipramine, potassium.**

PHARMACOKINETICS **Onset:** 1–3 h diuresis; 30–60 min IOP; 15 min ICP. **Duration:** 4–6 h IOP; 3–8 h ICP. **Distribution:** Confined to extracellular space; does not cross blood-brain barrier except with very high plasma levels in the presence of acidosis. **Metabolism:** Small quantity metabolized to glycogen in liver. **Elimination:** Rapidly excreted by kidneys. **Half-Life:** 100 min.

CLINICAL IMPLICATIONS

Assessment & Drug Effects

• Take care to avoid extravasation. Observe injection site for signs of inflammation or edema.

• Lab tests: Monitor closely serum and urine electrolytes and kidney function during therapy.

• Measure I&O accurately and record to achieve proper fluid balance.

• Monitor vital signs closely. Report significant changes in BP and signs of CHF.

• Monitor for possible indications of fluid and electrolyte imbalance (e.g., thirst, muscle cramps or weakness, paresthesias, and signs of CHF).

• Be alert to the possibility that a rebound increase in ICP sometimes occurs about 12 h after drug administration. Patient may complain of headache or confusion.

• Take accurate daily weight.

Patient & Family Education

• Report any of the following: Thirst, muscle cramps or weak-

ness, paresthesia, dyspnea, or headache.
- Family members should immediately report any evidence of confusion.

MAPROTILINE HYDROCHLORIDE

(ma-proe'ti-leen)
Maprotiline HCl
Classifications: PSYCHOTHERAPEUTIC; TETRACYCLIC ANTIDEPRESSANT
Therapeutic: ANTIDEPRESSANT
Prototype: Mirtazapine
Pregnancy Category: B

AVAILABILITY 25 mg, 50 mg, 75 mg tablets

ACTION & THERAPEUTIC EFFECT It selectively inhibits reuptake of norepinephrine at the neuronal membrane. More recent evidence suggests that a better explanation than norepinephrine reuptake may be that the upset of monoamine output (MAO) present in depressed individuals may be regulated by the action of beta-adrenergic receptors following long-term use of these drugs. *Useful in depression associated with anxiety and sleep disturbances.*

USES Treatment of depressive neurosis (dysthymic disorder) and manic-depressive illness, depressed type (major depressive disorder).
UNLABELED USES Bulimia, pain, panic attack.

CONTRAINDICATIONS Acute MI, AV block, cardiac arrhythmias, QT prolongation; MAOI therapy; tricyclic antidepressant therapy; patients <18 y; history of alcoholism; suicidal ideation; lactation.
CAUTIOUS USE History of seizure activity; psychotic disorders; diabetes mellitus; hepatic disease; GI disease; GERD; BPH; respiratory depression; pregnancy (category B).

ROUTE & DOSAGE

Mild to Moderate Depression

Adult: **PO** Start at 75 mg/d and gradually increase q2wk up to 150 mg/d in single or divided doses
Geriatric: **PO** Start with 25 mg h.s. and gradually increase to 50–75 mg/d

Severe Depression

Adult: **PO** Start at 100–150 mg/d and gradually increase up to 300 mg/d in single or divided doses if needed

ADMINISTRATION

Oral

- Give as single dose or in divided doses. Initiate therapy with low dosages to reduce risk of seizures.
- Store at 15°–30° C (59°–86° F) unless otherwise specified.

ADVERSE EFFECTS (≥1%) **CNS:** Seizures, exacerbation of psychosis, hallucinations, tremors, excitement, confusion, dizziness, *drowsiness.* **CV:** *Orthostatic hypotension,* hypertension, tachycardia. **Special Senses:** Accommodation disturbances, blurred vision, mydriasis. **GI:** Nausea, vomiting, epigastric distress, *constipation, dry mouth.* **Urogenital:** *Urinary retention,* frequency. **Skin:** Hypersensitivity reactions (skin rash, urticaria, photosensitivity).

INTERACTIONS Drug: May decrease some response to ANTIHYPERTENSIVES; CNS DEPRESSANTS, **alcohol,** HYPNOTICS, BARBITURATES, SEDATIVES potentiate CNS depression; may increase hypoprothrombinemic effect of ORAL ANTICOAGULANTS; transient delirium with

Common adverse effects in *italic*, life-threatening effects <u>underlined</u>; generic names in **bold**; classifications in SMALL CAPS; ◆ Canadian drug name; ⊘ Prototype drug

923

ethchlorvynol; with **levodopa,** SYMPATHOMIMETICS (e.g., **epinephrine, norepinephrine**) there is possibility of sympathetic hyperactivity with hypertension and **hyperpyrexia;** with MAO INHIBITORS or **linezolid** there is possibility of severe reactions, toxic psychosis, cardiovascular instability; **methylphenidate** increases plasma TCA levels; THYROID DRUGS increase possibility of arrhythmias; **cimetidine** may increase plasma TCA levels.

PHARMACOKINETICS Absorption: Slowly absorbed from GI tract. **Peak:** 12 h. **Distribution:** Distributed chiefly to brain, lungs, liver, and kidneys. **Metabolism:** In liver. **Elimination:** 70% in urine, 30% in feces. **Half-Life:** 51 h.

CLINICAL IMPLICATIONS

Assessment & Drug Effects

- Monitor for therapeutic effectiveness; 2–3 wk are usually necessary for full effect.
- Monitor for increased suicidality, unusual changes in behavior, or suicide attempt. Inform the physician immediately.
- Assess level of sedative effect. If recovering patient becomes too lethargic to care for personal hygiene or to maintain food intake and interactions with others, report to physician.
- Monitor bowel elimination pattern and I&O ratio. Severe constipation and urinary retention are potential problems, especially in the older adult. Advise increased fluid intake (at least 1500 mL/d).
- Observe seizure precautions; risk of seizures appears to be high in heavy drinkers.
- Bear in mind that if patient uses excessive amounts of alcohol, potentiated effects of maprotiline

may increase the danger of overdosage or suicide attempt.

Patient & Family Education

- Report symptoms of stomatitis and dry mouth when taking high doses. Sore or dry mouth can lead to lack of compliance.
- Use caution with tasks that require alertness and skill; ability may be impaired during early therapy.
- Do not change dose or dose schedule without consulting physician.
- Do not use OTC drugs unless approved by physician.
- Avoid alcohol; the effects of maprotiline are potentiated when both are used together and for 2 wk after maprotiline is discontinued.

MASOPROCOL CREAM

(mas-o-pro'col)

Actinex

Classifications: SKIN AND MUCOUS MEMBRANE AGENT; ANTIPROLIFERATIVE **Therapeutic:** ANTIPROLIFERATIVE; ACTINIC KERATOSIS AGENT

Pregnancy Category: B

AVAILABILITY 10% cream

ACTION & *THERAPEUTIC EFFECT* Mechanism of action of masoprocol in the treatment of actinic keratoses is unknown. *Antiproliferative activity against keratinocytes.*

USES Treatment of actinic keratosis. **UNLABELED USES** Malignant melanoma.

CONTRAINDICATIONS Hypersensitivity to masoprocol. **CAUTIOUS USE** Pregnancy (category B); lactation. Safety and efficacy in children are not established.

ROUTE & DOSAGE

Actinic Keratosis
Adult: **Topical** Apply to lesions b.i.d. for 14–28 d

ADMINISTRATION

Topical

- Use externally only. Do not apply on mucous membranes. In case of eye contact, wash eye with water immediately.
- Wash and dry affected areas before application. Gently massage into area until it is evenly distributed.
- Wash hand immediately if cream is applied without a glove.
- Do not apply occlusive dressings over cream.
- Store at 15°–30° C (59°–86° F) unless otherwise directed.

ADVERSE EFFECTS (≥1%) **Skin:** *Inflammation, erythema, dryness, flaking,* itching, burning, tightness, bleeding, edema.

INTERACTIONS Drug: No clinically significant interactions established.

PHARMACOKINETICS Absorption: <2% absorbed through intact skin. **Onset:** 2–4 wk.

CLINICAL IMPLICATIONS

Assessment & Drug Effects

- Assess for allergic contact dermatitis, which is an indication to discontinue.
- Report severe skin reactions of any kind to physician.

Patient & Family Education

- Learn proper technique for application of the cream.
- Be prepared for a transient local burning sensation immediately following application.
- Local skin reactions are common but usually disappear within 2 wk of discontinuing cream application.
- Be aware that this product contains sulfites.
- Masoprocol may stain clothing.

MEBENDAZOLE ⊘

(me-ben′da-zole)
Classifications: ANTHELMINTIC
Therapeutic: ANTHELMINTIC
Pregnancy Category: C

AVAILABILITY 100 mg tablets

ACTION & *THERAPEUTIC EFFECT* Carbamate with unusually broad spectrum of anthelmintic activity. Inhibits formation of worm's microtubules and inhibits glucose and other nutrient uptake by susceptible helminths. *Effective against susceptible helminths (nematodes) by interfering with their survival.*

USES Treatment of *Trichuris trichiura* (whipworm), *Enterobius vermicularis* (pinworm), *Ascaris lumbricoides* (roundworm), *Ancylostoma duodenale* (common hookworm), *Necator americanus* (American hookworm) in single or mixed infections.
UNLABELED USES Beef, dwarf, and pork tapeworm and threadworm infections.

CONTRAINDICATIONS Safety during pregnancy (category C), or in children <2 y is not established.
CAUTIOUS USE Inflammatory bowel disease, ulcerative colitis, Crohn's disease; hepatic disease; lactation.

ROUTE & DOSAGE

Enterobiasis
Adult: **PO** 100 mg as single dose
Child: **PO** 100 mg as single dose

M

Common adverse effects in *italic*, life-threatening effects underlined; generic names in **bold**; classifications in SMALL CAPS; ♣ Canadian drug name; ⊘ Prototype drug

925

Other Infestations
Adult: **PO** 100 mg b.i.d. times 3 d
Child: **PO** 100 mg b.i.d. times 3 d

ADMINISTRATION

Oral
- Allow tablets to be chewed and swallowed, or crushed and mixed with food if needed.

ADVERSE EFFECTS (≥1%) **GI:** Transient abdominal pain, diarrhea. **Body as a Whole:** Dizziness, fever (possibly due to tissue necrosis in cysts).

INTERACTIONS Drug: Carbamazepine, phenytoin can increase metabolism of mebendazole.

PHARMACOKINETICS Absorption: Minimal from GI tract (2–10% of dose). **Metabolism:** Metabolized to inactive metabolite. **Elimination:** Primarily in feces. **Half-Life:** 3–9 h.

CLINICAL IMPLICATIONS

Assessment & Drug Effects
- Initiate second course of treatment if cure does not occur within 3 wk.
- Examine and treat all family members simultaneously because pinworms are readily transmitted from person to person.

Patient & Family Education
- Practice thorough hand washing after touching any potentially contaminated item.
- Change underclothing, bedclothes, towels, and facecloths daily; bathe frequently, preferably by showering. Infected person should sleep alone.

MECAMYLAMINE HYDROCHLORIDE

(mek-a-mill'a-meen)

Inversine
Classifications: CENTRAL ACTING ANTIHYPERTENSIVE
Therapeutic: ANTIHYPERTENSIVE
Prototype: Methyldopa
Pregnancy Category: C

AVAILABILITY 2.5 mg tablets

ACTION & *THERAPEUTIC EFFECT*
Potent, long-acting nondepolarizing ganglionic blocking agent. Blocks neurotransmission at both sympathetic and parasympathetic ganglia by competing with acetylcholine (Ach) for cholinergic receptor sites on postsynaptic membranes. Reduces BP generally with greater decrease in standing or sitting BP than in supine BPs. *Reduces BP in both normotensive and hypertensive individuals.*

USES Moderately severe to severe hypertension and uncomplicated malignant hypertension.

CONTRAINDICATIONS Coronary insufficiency, pyloric stenosis; glaucoma; uremia, chronic pyelonephritis; recent MI; mild labile hypertension; unreliable uncooperative patients; pregnancy (category C), lactation.
CAUTIOUS USE Rising or elevated BUN; renal, cerebral, or coronary vascular pathology; recent CVA; prostatic hypertrophy, bladder neck obstruction, urethral stricture.

ROUTE & DOSAGE

Moderately Severe to Severe Hypertension
Adult: **PO** 2.5 mg b.i.d. p.c. for 2 d, increased by increments of 2.5 mg at intervals of ≥2 d until desired BP response is attained (2.5–25 mg/d in 2–4 divided doses)

ADMINISTRATION

Oral

- Give after meals for more gradual absorption and smoother control of BP. Schedule consistently relative to meals.
- Note: Because of diurnal variations in BP, physician may prescribe a relatively small dose in the morning or omission of morning dose (morning BP usually lower) and larger doses for afternoon or evening.
- Do not suddenly discontinue drug; may result in severe hypertensive rebound with CVA and acute CHF. Usually, other antihypertensive therapy must be substituted gradually, and patient must be supervised daily during period of dosage adjustment.
- Store at 15°–30° C (59°–86° F) unless otherwise directed.

ADVERSE EFFECTS (≥1%) **CNS:** Weakness, fatigue, sedation, headache, paresthesias, confusion, depression, choreiform movements, tremor. **CV:** *Orthostatic hypotension,* changes in heart rate, dizziness, syncope, precipitation of angina. **Special Senses:** Mydriasis, *blurred vision,* cycloplegia, nasal congestion, *dry mouth* with dysphagia, glossitis. **GI:** *Anorexia, nausea, vomiting, constipation, diarrhea,* adynamic ileus. **Urogenital:** Decreased libido, impotence, *urinary retention.*

INTERACTIONS Drug: Alcohol, other ANTIHYPERTENSIVE AGENTS, **bethanechol,** THIAZIDE DIURETICS potentiate hypotensive effects; **acetazolamide, sodium bicarbonate** increase mecamylamine toxicity because they decrease its elimination.

PHARMACOKINETICS Absorption: Almost completely from GI tract. **Onset:** 30 min–2 h. **Peak:** 3–5 h.

Duration: 6–12 h. **Distribution:** Crosses blood–brain barrier and placenta; distributed into breast milk. **Metabolism:** In liver. **Elimination:** Primarily in urine.

CLINICAL IMPLICATIONS

Assessment & Drug Effects

- Monitor therapeutic effectiveness by taking BP readings in standing position at time of maximal drug effect. Assess for symptoms of orthostatic hypotension (faintness, dizziness, light-headedness). Also note any changes in pulse rate.
- Monitor BP closely. Partial tolerance may develop in some patients, necessitating dosage adjustment.
- Report promptly constipation, frequent loose stools with abdominal distension, or decreased bowel sounds; may be the first signs of paralytic ileus (relatively frequent). Paralytic ileus is sometimes preceded by small, frequent stools.

Patient & Family Education

- Make position changes slowly and in stages, particularly from recumbent to upright posture; sit on edge of bed and move ankles and feet before walking.
- Lie down immediately if feeling light-headed or dizzy. Report adverse reactions immediately because drug effects may last hours to days after drug is discontinued.
- Seasonal variations may alter the hypotensive effect (e.g., usually smaller doses are required in summer than in winter).
- Do not drive or engage in potentially hazardous activities until response to drug is known.
- Learn measures to relieve dry mouth; rinse mouth frequently with water, suck hard candy.

Common adverse effects in *italic*, life-threatening effects <u>underlined</u>; generic names in **bold**; classifications in SMALL CAPS; ✣ Canadian drug name; ⊕ Prototype drug

927

MECHLORETHAMINE HYDROCHLORIDE

(me-klor-eth′a-meen)

Mustargen

Classifications: ANTINEOPLASTIC; ALKYLATING AGENT; NITROGEN MUSTARD

Therapeutic: ANTINEOPLASTIC; NITROGEN MUSTARD

Prototype: Cyclophosphamide

Pregnancy Category: D

AVAILABILITY 10 mg powder for injection

ACTION & *THERAPEUTIC EFFECT*
Analog of mustard gas and standard of reference for nitrogen mustards. Forms highly reactive carbonium ion, which causes cross-linking and abnormal base-pairing in DNA, thereby interfering with DNA replication and RNA and protein synthesis. Cell-cycle nonspecific inhibitor of DNA and RNA synthesis. *Antineoplastic agent that simulates actions of x-ray therapy, but nitrogen mustards produce more acute tissue damage and more rapid recovery.*

USES Generally confined to nonterminal stages of neoplastic disease. Employed as single agent or in combination with other agents in palliative treatment of Hodgkin's disease (stages III and IV), lymphosarcoma, mycosis fungoides, polycythemia vera, bronchogenic carcinoma, chronic myelocytic or chronic lymphocytic leukemia. Also for intrapleural, intrapericardial, and intraperitoneal palliative treatment of metastatic carcinoma resulting in effusion.

CONTRAINDICATIONS Myelosuppression; infectious granuloma; known infectious diseases, acute herpes zoster; intracavitary use with other systemic bone marrow suppressants; pregnancy (category D), lactation.

CAUTIOUS USE Bone marrow infiltration with malignant cells, chronic lymphocytic leukemia; men or women in childbearing age; use with x-ray treatment or other chemotherapy in alternating courses.

ROUTE & DOSAGE

Advanced Hodgkin's Disease
Adult: IV 6 mg/m^2 on day 1 and 8 of a 28 d cycle

Other Neoplasms
Adult: IV 0.4 mg/kg given as a single dose or in divided doses of 0.1–0.2 mg/kg/d, may repeat course in 3–6 wk

ADMINISTRATION

Intravenous
Wear surgical gloves during preparation and administration of solution.

- Avoid inhalation of vapors and dust and contact of drug with eyes and skin.
- Flush contaminated area immediately if drug contacts the skin. Use copious amounts of water for at least 15 min, followed by 2% sodium thiosulfate solution. Irritation may appear after a latent period.
- Irrigate immediately if eye contact occurs. Use copious amounts of NS followed by ophthalmologic examination as soon as possible.

***PREPARE*: IV Infusion:** Reconstitute immediately before use by adding 10 mL sterile water for injection or NS injection to vial to yield 1 mg/mL. With needle still in stopper, shake vial several times to dissolve. Discard colored solution or contents of any vial which has drops of moisture. **ADMINISTER: IV Infusion:** To reduce risk of severe infections from extravasation or high concentration of the drug, inject into tubing or sidearm of freely flowing IV infusion. Flush vein with running IV solution for 2–5 min to clear tubing of any remaining drug. **INCOMPATIBILITIES Solution/additive:** D5W, methohexital. **Y-site:** Allopurinol, cefepime.

▪ Be alert for extravasation. Treat promptly with subcutaneous or intradermal injection with isotonic sodium thiosulfate solution (1/6 molar) and application of ice compresses intermittently for a 6–12 h period to reduce local tissue damage and discomfort. Tissue induration and tenderness may persist 4–6 wk, and tissue may slough.

ADVERSE EFFECTS (≥1%) **CNS:** Neurotoxicity: vertigo, tinnitus, headache, drowsiness, peripheral neuropathy, light-headedness, paresthesias, cerebral deterioration, coma. **GI:** Stomatitis, xerostomia, anorexia, *nausea, vomiting,* diarrhea. **Hematologic:** Leukopenia, *thrombocytopenia,* lymphocytopenia, <u>agranulocytosis,</u> *anemia,* hyperheparinemia. **Skin:** Pruritus, hyperpigmentation, herpes zoster, alopecia. **Urogenital:** Amenorrhea, azoospermia, chromosomal abnormalities, hyperuricemia. **Body as a Whole:** Weakness, hypersensitivity reactions. *With extravasation: painful inflammatory reaction, tissue sloughing, thrombosis, thrombophlebitis.*

INTERACTIONS Drug: Mechlorethamine (NITROGEN MUSTARDS) may reduce effectiveness of ANTIGOUT AGENTS by raising serum **uric acid** levels; dosage adjustments may be necessary; may prolong neuromuscular blocking effects of **succinylcholine;** may potentiate bleeding effects of ANTICOAGULANTS, SALICYLATES, NSAIDS, PLATELET INHIBITORS.

PHARMACOKINETICS Metabolism: Rapid hydrolysis and demethylation. **Elimination:** In urine. **Half-life:** <1 min.

CLINICAL IMPLICATIONS

Assessment & Drug Effects

▪ Establish baseline data for body weight, I&O ratio and pattern, and blood labs as reference for design of drug and care regimens.
▪ Lab tests: Monitor CBC with differential and platelet count. Periodic serum uric acid levels.
▪ Record daily weight. Alert physician to sudden or slow, steady weight gain.
▪ Monitor and record patient's fluid losses carefully. Prolonged vomiting and diarrhea can produce volume depletion.
▪ Report immediately petechiae, ecchymoses, or abnormal bleeding from intestinal and buccal membranes. Keep injections and other invasive procedures to a minimum during period of thrombocytopenia.
▪ Report symptoms of agranulocytosis (e.g., unexplained fever, chills, sore throat, tachycardia, and mucosal ulceration).
▪ Prevent exposure to people with infection, especially upper respiratory tract infections.
▪ Note and record state of hydration of oral mucosa, condition of gingiva, teeth, tongue, mucosa, and lips.

Patient & Family Education

▪ Report any signs of bleeding immediately.

- Use caution to prevent falls or other traumatic injuries, especially during periods of low platelet counts.
- Increase fluid intake up to 3000 mL/d if allowed to minimize risk of kidney stones. Report promptly all symptoms, including flank or joint pain, swelling of lower legs and feet, changes in voiding pattern.

MECLIZINE HYDROCHLORIDE ℗

(mek'li-zeen)

Antivert, Antrizine, Bonamine ◆, Bonine, Dizmiss, RuVert-M
Classifications: ANTIHISTAMINE; H₁-RECEPTOR ANTAGONIST; ANTI-VERTIGO AGENT
Therapeutic: ANTIHISTAMINE, H₁-RECEPTOR ANTAGONIST, ANTIVERTIGO
Pregnancy Category: B

AVAILABILITY 12.5 mg, 25 mg, 50 mg tablets; 25 mg, 30 mg capsules

ACTION & *THERAPEUTIC EFFECT*
Long-acting antihistamine, with marked effect in blocking histamine-induced vasopressive response but only slight anticholinergic action. Marked depressant action on labyrinthine excitability and on conduction in vestibular-cerebellar pathways. *Exhibits antivertigo, and antiemetic effects.*

USES Management of nausea, vomiting, and dizziness associated with motion sickness and in vertigo associated with diseases affecting vestibular system.

CONTRAINDICATIONS Hypersensitivity to meclizine; GI obstruction, ileus.
CAUTIOUS USE Angle-closure glaucoma, older adults, asthma, prostatic hypertrophy, pregnancy (category B), lactation. Safety in children less than 12 y is not established.

ROUTE & DOSAGE

Motion Sickness
Adult: **PO** 25–50 mg 1 h before travel, may repeat q24h if necessary for duration of journey

Vertigo
Adult: **PO** 25–100 mg/d in divided doses

ADMINISTRATION

Oral
- Give without regard to meals.
- Ensure that chewable tablets are chewed or crushed before being swallowed with a liquid.

ADVERSE EFFECTS (≥1%) **CNS:** *Drowsiness.* **GI:** Dry mouth. **Special Senses:** Blurred vision. **Body as a Whole:** Fatigue.

INTERACTIONS Drug: alcohol, CNS DEPRESSANTS may potentiate sedative effects of meclizine.

PHARMACOKINETICS Absorption: Readily absorbed from GI tract. **Onset:** 1 h. **Duration:** 8–24 h. **Distribution:** Crosses placenta. **Elimination:** Primarily in feces. **Half-Life:** 6 h.

CLINICAL IMPLICATIONS

Assessment & Drug Effects
- Supervision of ambulation, particularly with the older adult, since drug may cause drowsiness.
- Assess effectiveness of drug and inform physician when prescribed for vertigo; dosage adjustment may be required.

Patient & Family Education
- Do not drive or engage in potentially hazardous activities until response to drug is known.

M

- Be aware that sedative action may add to that of alcohol, barbiturates, narcotic analgesics, or other CNS depressants.
- Take 1 h before departure when prescribed for motion sickness.

MECLOFENAMATE SODIUM

(me-kloe-fen-am′ate)

Classifications: ANALGESIC, NONSTEROIDAL ANTIINFLAMMATORY DRUG (NSAID); ANTIPYRETIC
Therapeutic: NSAID, ANALGESIC; ANTIPYRETIC
Prototype: Ibuprofen
Pregnancy Category: C first and second trimester; D third trimester

AVAILABILITY 50 mg, 100 mg capsules

ACTION & *THERAPEUTIC EFFECT*
Inhibits prostaglandin synthesis by inhibiting both the COX-1 and COX-2 enzymes necessary for its synthesis and competes for binding at prostaglandin receptor sites. Does not appear to alter course of arthritis. *Palliative antiinflammatory, analgesic, and antipyretic activity.*

USES Symptomatic treatment of acute or chronic rheumatoid arthritis and osteoarthritis. Also in combination with gold salts or corticosteroids in treatment of rheumatoid arthritis.
UNLABELED USES Management of psoriatic arthritis, mild to moderate postoperative pain, dysmenorrhea.

CONTRAINDICATIONS Patient in whom bronchospasm, urticaria, and allergic rhinitis are induced by aspirin or other NSAIDs; active peptic ulcer, ulcerative colitis; perioperative pain related to CABG surgery; renal disease; pregnancy (category C first and second trimester, category D third trimester), lactation, children <14 y, patient designated as functional class IV rheumatoid arthritis (incapacitated, bedridden, or confined to wheelchair, little or no self-care).
CAUTIOUS USE History of upper GI tract disease; coronary artery disease; acute MI, cardiac arrhythmias; CVA; diabetes mellitus; SLE; compromised cardiac and kidney function, or other conditions predisposing to fluid retention.

ROUTE & DOSAGE

Inflammatory Disease
Adult: **PO** 200–400 mg/d in 3–4 divided doses (max: 400 mg/d)

ADMINISTRATION

Oral
- Give with food or milk if patient complains of GI distress. An aluminum and magnesium hydroxide antacid (Maalox) also may be prescribed. Consult physician if symptoms persist.
- Withhold dose and report to physician if significant diarrhea occurs.
- Store at 15°–30° C (59°–86° F) in airtight, light-resistant container.

ADVERSE EFFECTS (≥1%) **CNS:** *Dizziness,* vertigo, lack of concentration, confusion, *headache,* tinnitus. **CV:** Edema. **GI:** *Severe diarrhea (dose-related),* peptic ulceration, <u>GI bleeding</u>, dyspepsia, abdominal pain, *nausea,* vomiting (may be severe), flatulence, eructation, pyrosis, anorexia, constipation. **GI:** *Abnormal liver function tests,* cholestatic jaundice. **Special Senses:** Blurred vision. **Urogenital:** Elevated BUN and creatinine, kidney failure. **Skin:** Rash, pruritus, urticaria.

Common adverse effects in *italic*, life-threatening effects <u>underlined</u>; generic names in **bold**; classifications in SMALL CAPS; ✦ Canadian drug name; ⊙ Prototype drug

931

INTERACTIONS Drug: ORAL ANTICO-AGULANTS, **heparin** may prolong bleeding time; may increase **lithium** toxicity; increases pharmacologic and toxic activity of **phenytoin**, SULFONYLUREAS, SULFONAMIDES, **warfarin** through protein-binding displacement. **Herbal: Feverfew, garlic, ginger, ginkgo** increase bleeding potential.

PHARMACOKINETICS Absorption: Rapidly and completely from GI tract. **Peak:** 1–2 h. **Duration:** 2–4 h. **Distribution:** Crosses placenta. **Metabolism:** In liver. **Elimination:** 60% in urine, 30% in feces. **Half-Life:** 2–3.3 h.

CLINICAL IMPLICATIONS

Assessment & Drug Effects

- Expect clinical improvement in the rheumatoid patient within 2–3 wk with reduction in number of tender joints, severity of tenderness, and duration of morning stiffness.
- Observe improvement in the osteoarthritic patient as reflected by reduced night pain, pain on walking, starting pain, and pain with passive motion and improved joint function.
- Report diarrhea promptly. It is the most frequent adverse effect and usually dose related.
- Lab tests: Monitor kidney function where incidence of adverse reactions is potentially high because drug is excreted primarily by the kidneys. Monitor PT, PTT, and INR frequently with concurrent anticoagulant therapy.
- Monitor I&O ratio. Encourage fluid intake of at least 8 glasses of liquid a day.
- Consider sodium content of meclofenamate tablets if patient is on restricted sodium intake.

Patient & Family Education

- Stop taking drug and promptly notify the physician if nausea, vomiting, severe diarrhea, and abdominal pain occur. Generally dose reduction or temporary withdrawal will control symptoms.
- Report to physician without delay: Blurred vision, tinnitus, or taste disturbances.
- Schedule ophthalmic examinations before and periodically during treatment and whenever you experience visual disturbances.
- Notify physician if you become pregnant.
- Weigh under standard conditions (similar clothing, same time of day) twice weekly. Report weight gain of more than 2.5 to 3.5 kg (3–4 lb)/wk as well as signs of edema: Swollen ankles, tibiae, hands, feet.
- Do not use OTC drugs without approval of physician.
- Dizziness, a troublesome early side effect, frequently disappears in time. Avoid driving a car or potentially hazardous activities until response to drug is known.
- Report immediately to physician any sign of bleeding (e.g., melena, epistaxis, ecchymosis) when taking concomitant oral anticoagulant.

MEDROXYPROGESTERONE ACETATE

(me-drox'ee-proe-jess'te-rone)
Depo-Provera, Depo-subQ Provera 104, Provera
Classifications: HORMONE; PRO-GESTIN
Therapeutic: PROGESTIN
Prototype: Progesterone
Pregnancy Category: X

AVAILABILITY 2.5 mg, 5 mg, 10 mg tablets; 104 mg/0.65 mL, 150 mg/mL, 400 mg/mL injection

ACTION & *THERAPEUTIC EFFECT* Induces and maintains endometrium, preventing uterine bleeding; inhibits production of pituitary gonadotropin, thus preventing ovulation and producing thick cervical mucus resistant to passage of sperm. *Slows release of luteinizing hormone (LH) preventing follicular maturation and ovulation. Has prolonged, variable duration of action and androgenic and antiestrogenic activity.*

USES Dysfunctional uterine bleeding; secondary amenorrhea; parenteral form (Depo-Provera) used in adjunctive, palliative treatment of inoperable, recurrent, and metastatic endometrial or renal carcinoma; contraception; endometriosis-associated pain.
UNLABELED USES Obstructive sleep apnea.

CONTRAINDICATIONS History of thromboembolic disorders; breast cancer, cervical cancer, uterine cancer, vaginal cancer; hepatic disease; abnormal vaginal bleeding, incomplete abortion; pregnancy (category X).
CAUTIOUS USE Asthma, seizure disorders, CVA; migraine, cardiac or kidney dysfunction, liver disease.

ROUTE & DOSAGE

Secondary Amenorrhea
Adult: **PO** 5–10 mg/d for 5–10 d beginning any time if endometrium is adequately estrogen primed (withdrawal bleeding occurs in 3–7 d after discontinuing therapy)

Abnormal Bleeding Due to Hormonal Imbalance
Adult: **PO** 5–10 mg/d for 5–10 d beginning on the assumed or calculated 16th or 21st day of menstrual cycle; if bleeding is controlled, administer 2 subsequent cycles

Carcinoma
Adult: **IM** 400–1000 mg/wk; continue at 400 mg/mo if improvement occurs and disease stabilizes

Contraceptive
Adult: **IM** 100 mg q3mo

Sleep Apnea
Adult: **PO** 20 mg t.i.d.

ADMINISTRATION
Oral
▪ Oral drug may be given with food to minimize GI distress.
Intramuscular
▪ Administer IM deep into a large muscle.
▪ Store both formulations at 15°–30° C (59°–86° F); protect from freezing.

ADVERSE EFFECTS (≥1%) **CNS:** Cerebral thrombosis or hemorrhage, depression. **CV:** Hypertension, pulmonary embolism, edema. **GI:** Vomiting, nausea, cholestatic jaundice, abdominal cramps. **Urogenital:** *Breakthrough bleeding,* changes in menstrual flow, dysmenorrhea, vaginal candidiasis. **Skin:** Angioneurotic edema. **Body as a Whole:** Weight changes; *breast tenderness,* enlargement or secretion. **Musculoskeletal:** Loss of bone mineral density.

INTERACTIONS Drug: A m i n o g l u - **tethimide** decreases serum concentrations of medroxyprogesterone; BARBITURATES, **carbamazepine, ox-**

M

carbazepine, phenytoin, primidone, rifampin, modafinil, rifabutin, topiramate can increase metabolism and decrease serum levels of medroxyprogesterone. **Herbal:** Intermenstrual bleeding and loss of contraceptive efficacy may occur with **St. John's wort.**

PHARMACOKINETICS Peak: 2–4 h PO, 3 wk IM. **Distribution:** >90% protein bound. **Metabolism:** In liver. **Elimination:** Primarily in feces. **Half-Life:** 30 d PO, 50 d IM.

CLINICAL IMPLICATIONS

Assessment & Drug Effects
- See progesterone for numerous additional clinical implications.
- Be aware that IM injection may be painful. Monitor sites for evidence of sterile abscess. A residual lump and discoloration of tissue may develop.
- Monitor for S&S of thrombophlebitis (see Appendix F).
- Note: Planned menstrual cycling with medroxyprogesterone may benefit the patient with a history of recurrent episodes of abnormal uterine bleeding.

Patient & Family Education
- Be aware that after repeated IM injections, infertility and amenorrhea may persist as long as 18 mo.
- Learn breast self-examination.
- Review package insert to ensure complete understanding of progestin therapy.

MEFENAMIC ACID

(me-fe-nam'ik)
Ponstel
Classifications: ANALGESIC, NONSTEROIDAL ANTIINFLAMMATORY DRUG (NSAID); ANTIPYRETIC

Therapeutic: NSAID, ANALGESIC; ANTIPYRETIC
Prototype: Ibuprofen
Pregnancy Category: C

AVAILABILITY 250 mg tablets

ACTION & *THERAPEUTIC EFFECT*
NSAID that inhibits COX-1 and COX-2 enzymes necessary for prostaglandin synthesis. It affects platelet function. *Analgesic, antiinflammatory, and antipyretic actions.*

USES Short-term relief of mild to moderate pain including primary dysmenorrhea.

CONTRAINDICATIONS Hypersensitivity to drug; GI inflammation, or ulceration. Safety in children <14 y, during pregnancy (category C) is not established.
CAUTIOUS USE History of kidney or liver disease; blood dyscrasias; asthma; cardiac arrhythmias; CHF; edema; diabetes mellitus; SLE; hypersensitivity to aspirin. Long term use increases risk of serious adverse events (see DRUG INTERACTIONS).

ROUTE & DOSAGE

Mild to Moderate Pain
Adult: **PO Loading Dose** 500 mg
PO Maintenance Dose 250 mg
q6h prn

ADMINISTRATION

Oral
- Give with meals, food, or milk to minimize GI adverse effects.
- Do not use drug for a period exceeding 1 wk (manufacturer's warning).

ADVERSE EFFECTS (≥1%) **CNS:** Drowsiness, insomnia, dizziness, nervousness, confusion, headache. **GI:** *Severe diarrhea,* ulceration, and bleeding; *nausea, vomiting,* abdominal cramps, flatus, constipation, hepatic toxicity. **Hematologic:** Prolonged prothrombin time, severe autoimmune hemolytic anemia (long-term use), leukopenia, eosinophilia, <u>agranulocytosis</u>, thrombocytopenic purpura, megaloblastic anemia, pancytopenia, bone marrow hypoplasia. **Urogenital:** Nephrotoxicity, dysuria, albuminuria, hematuria, elevation of BUN. **Skin:** Urticaria, rash, facial edema. **Special Senses:** Eye irritation, loss of color vision (reversible), blurred vision, ear pain. **Body as a Whole:** Perspiration. **CV:** Palpitation. **Respiratory:** Dyspnea; acute exacerbation of asthma; bronchoconstriction (in patients sensitive to aspirin).

DIAGNOSTIC TEST INTERFERENCE False-positive reactions for *urinary bilirubin* (using *diazo tablet test*).

INTERACTIONS Drug: Mefenamic acid may prolong bleeding time with ORAL ANTICOAGULANTS, **heparin;** may increase **lithium** toxicity; increases pharmacologic and toxic activity of **phenytoin,** SULFONYLUREAS, SULFONAMIDES, **warfarin** because of protein binding displacement. **Herbal: Feverfew, garlic, ginger, ginkgo** increase bleeding potential.

PHARMACOKINETICS Absorption: Rapidly and completely from GI tract. **Peak:** 2–4 h. **Duration:** 6 h. **Distribution:** Distributed in breast milk. **Metabolism:** Partially in liver. **Elimination:** 50% in urine, 50% in feces. **Half-Life:** 2 h.

CLINICAL IMPLICATIONS
Assessment & Drug Effects
- Assess patients who develop severe diarrhea and vomiting for dehydration and electrolyte imbalance.

- Lab tests: With long-term therapy (not recommended) obtain periodic complete blood counts, Hct and Hgb, and kidney function tests.

Patient & Family Education
- Discontinue drug promptly if diarrhea, dark stools, hematemesis, ecchymoses, epistaxis, or rash occur and do not use again. Contact physician.
- Notify physician if persistent GI discomfort, sore throat, fever, or malaise occur.
- Do not drive or engage in potentially hazardous activities until response to drug is known. It may cause dizziness and drowsiness.
- Monitor blood glucose for loss of glycemic control if diabetic.

M

MEFLOQUINE HYDROCHLORIDE
(me-flo'quine)
Lariam
Classifications: ANTIMALARIAL
Therapeutic: ANTIMALARIAL
Prototype: Chloroquine
Pregnancy Category: C

AVAILABILITY 250 mg tablets

ACTION & *THERAPEUTIC EFFECT*
Antimalarial agent, structurally related to quinine. *Effective against all types of malaria, including chloroquine-resistant malaria.*

USES Treatment of mild to moderate acute malarial infections, prevention of chloroquine-resistant malaria caused by *Plasmodium falciparum* and *P. vivax.*

CONTRAINDICATIONS Hypersensitivity to mefloquine or a related compound; with a calcium channel blocking agent, severe heart arrhythmias, history of QTc prolonga-

Common adverse effects in *italic*, life-threatening effects <u>underlined</u>; generic names in **bold**; classifications in SMALL CAPS; ♣ Canadian drug name; ⊕ Prototype drug

935

tion; aggressive behavior; active depression, or history of depression, suicidal ideation; generalized anxiety disorder, psychosis, schizophrenia, or other major psychiatric disorders; seizure disorders; pregnancy (category C); lactation.

CAUTIOUS USE Persons piloting aircraft or operating heavy machinery.

ROUTE & DOSAGE

Note: FDA has NOT approved use of mefloquine in children, and the U.S. Public Health Service does NOT recommend its use in children <15 kg or in pregnant women

Treatment of Malaria

Adult: **PO** 1250 mg (5 tablets) as single oral dose taken with at least 8 oz of water
Child: **PO** 20–30 mg/kg as single dose

Prophylaxis for Malaria

Adult: **PO** 250 mg once/wk × 4 wk (beginning 1 wk before travel), then 250 mg every other wk for duration of exposure and for 2 doses after leaving endemic area
Child: **PO** 15–19 kg, $^1/_4$ tablet; 20–30 kg, $^1/_2$ tablet; 31–45 kg, $^3/_4$ tablet

ADMINISTRATION

Oral

- Give with food and at least 8 oz water.
- Do not give concurrently with quinine or quinidine; wait at least 12 h beyond last dose of either drug before administering mefloquine.
- Store at 15°–30° C (59°–86° F).

ADVERSE EFFECTS (≥1%) **Body as a Whole:** Arthralgia, chills, fatigue, fever. **CNS:** Dizziness, nightmares, visual disturbances, headache, syncope, confusion, psychosis, aggres-

sion, suicide ideation (rare). **CV:** Bradycardia, ECG changes (including QTc prolongation), first-degree AV block. **GI:** Nausea, vomiting, abdominal pain, anorexia, diarrhea. **Skin:** Rash, itching.

DIAGNOSTIC TEST INTERFERENCE Transient increase in liver transaminases.

INTERACTIONS Drug: Mefloquine can prolong cardiac conduction in patients taking BETA BLOCKERS, CALCIUM CHANNEL BLOCKERS, and possibly **digoxin. Quinine** may decrease plasma mefloquine concentrations. Mefloquine may decrease **valproic acid** serum concentrations by increasing its hepatic metabolism. Administration with **chloroquine** may increase risk of seizures. Increased risk of cardiac arrest and seizures with **quinidine**.

PHARMACOKINETICS Absorption: 85% absorbed, concentrates in red blood cells. **Onset:** 59 and 28 h for parasite and fever clearance times in patients with *P. vivax* infections, respectively; 166 and 93 h in patients with *P. malariae* infections. **Distribution:** Concentrated in red blood cells due to high-affinity binding to red blood cell membranes; 98% protein bound; distributed minimally into breast milk. **Metabolism:** In liver. **Elimination:** Primarily in bile and feces. **Half-Life:** 10–21 d (shorter in patients with acute malaria).

CLINICAL IMPLICATIONS

Assessment & Drug Effects

- Monitor carefully during prophylactic use for development of unexplained anxiety, depression, restlessness, or confusion; such manifestations may indicate a need to discontinue the drug.
- Evaluate cardiac and liver functions periodically with prolonged use.

Common adverse effects in *italic*, life-threatening effects <u>underlined</u>; generic names in **bold**; classifications in SMALL CAPS; ✦ Canadian drug name; ⊙ Prototype drug

- Lab tests: Monitor periodically CBC with differential during prolonged use.
- Monitor blood levels of anticonvulsants with concomitant therapy closely.

Patient & Family Education
- Take drug on the same day each week when used for malaria prophylaxis.
- Do not perform potentially hazardous activities until response to drug is known.
- Report any of the following immediately: Fever, sore throat, muscle aches, visual problems, anxiety, confusion, mental depression, hallucinations.

MEGESTROL ACETATE

(me-jess'trole)
Megace, Megace ES
Classifications: ANTINEOPLASTIC; HORMONE; PROGESTIN
Therapeutic: ANTINEOPLASTIC; PROGESTIN
Prototype: Progesterone
Pregnancy Category: X (oral suspension) and D (tablets)

AVAILABILITY 40 mg/mL, 125 mg/mL suspension; 20 mg, 40 mg tablets

ACTION & *THERAPEUTIC EFFECT*
Progestational hormone with antineoplastic properties. Mechanism of action unclear; however, an antiluteinizing effect mediated via the pituitary has been postulated. *Antineoplastic agent effective for treating breast, renal cell, or endometrial carcinoma. Also effective as an appetite enhancer. Has a local effect when instilled directly into the endometrial cavity.*

USES Palliative agent for treatment of advanced carcinoma of breast or endometrium. AIDS-related wasting or cachexia.

CONTRAINDICATIONS Diagnostic test for pregnancy; pregnancy category X (oral suspension) and category D (tablet); lactation.
CAUTIOUS USE Older adults; severe hepatic disease; diabetes mellitus; renal impairment; thromboembolic disease.

ROUTE & DOSAGE

Palliative Treatment for Advanced Breast Cancer
Adult: **PO** 40 mg q.i.d.

Palliative Treatment for Advanced Endometrial Cancer
Adult: **PO** 40–320 mg/d in divided doses

Appetite Stimulation
Adult: **PO** 200 mg q6h

HIV-Related Cachexia
Adult: **PO (suspension)** 800 mg q.d. or 625 mg of **Megace ES**

ADMINISTRATION

Oral
- Give with meals or food if GI distress occurs.
- Shake oral suspension well before use.
- Store at 15°–30° C (59°–86° F) in tightly closed container.

ADVERSE EFFECTS (≥1%) **Urogenital:** Vaginal bleeding. **Body as a Whole:** Breast tenderness, headache, increased appetite, weight gain, allergic-type reactions (including bronchial asthma). **GI:** Abdominal pain, nausea, vomiting. **Hematologic:** DVT.

INTERACTIONS Drug: May increase levels of **warfarin;** may decrease renal clearance of **dofetilide.**

Common adverse effects in *italic*, life-threatening effects underlined; generic names in **bold**; classifications in SMALL CAPS; ♣ Canadian drug name; ⊘ Prototype drug

937

PHARMACOKINETICS Absorption:
Appears to be well absorbed from GI tract. **Onset:** Onset of objective response in breast cancer in 6–8 wk. **Peak:** 1–3 h. **Duration:** 3–12 mo. **Metabolism:** Completely metabolized in liver. **Elimination:** 57–78% of dose excreted in urine within 10 d.

CLINICAL IMPLICATIONS

Assessment & Drug Effects
- Monitor weight periodically.
- Notify physician if abdominal pain, headache, nausea, vomiting, or breast tenderness become pronounced.
- Monitor for allergic reactions, including breathing distress characteristic of asthma, rash, urticaria, anaphylaxis, tachypnea, anxiety. Stop medication if they appear and notify physician.

Patient & Family Education
- Use contraception measures during therapy for carcinoma.
- Learn breast self-examination.
- Learn S&S of thrombophlebitis (see Appendix F).
- Review package insert to ensure understanding of megestrol therapy.

MELOXICAM

(mel-ox′-i-cam)
Mobic
Classifications: ANALGESIC, NONSTEROIDAL ANTIINFLAMMATORY DRUG (NSAID); ANTIPYRETIC
Therapeutic: NSAID, ANALGESIC; ANTIPYRETIC
Prototype: Ibuprofen
Pregnancy Category: C

AVAILABILITY 7.5 mg tablets

ACTION & *THERAPEUTIC EFFECT*
Is a nonsteroidal antiinflammatory drug (NSAID) that is less selective in inhibiting only COX-2 enzyme than celecoxib; meloxicam inhibits both COX-1 and COX-2 enzymes that are necessary for synthesis. *Exhibits antiinflammatory, analgesic, and antipyretic actions.*

USES Relief of the signs and symptoms of osteoarthritis, rheumatoid arthritis.

CONTRAINDICATIONS Hypersensitivity to meloxicam; rhinitis, urticaria/angioedema, asthma; allergic reactions to aspirin or other antiinflammatory agents; NSAID hypersensitivity; GI bleeding; peptic ulcer disease; severe renal or hepatic disease; salicylate hypersensitivity; perioperative pain with CABG surgery; pregnancy (category C), lactation; bleeding.

CAUTIOUS USE *Helicobacter pylori* infections; history of coagulation defects, liver dysfunction, gastrointestinal disease or ulceration, anemia, anticoagulant therapy; asthma; bone marrow suppression; corticosteroid therapy, dehydration, edema, older adults; females of childbearing age; GI bleeding, GI diseases, GI perforation; heart failure; hepatic disease, renal impairment; hypertension, hypovolemia, immunosuppression; jaundice, lactase deficiency, advanced renal dysfunction; hypertension or cardiac conditions aggravated by fluid retention and edema.

ROUTE & DOSAGE

Osteoarthritis
Adult: **PO** 7.5–15 mg once daily
Rheumatoid Arthritis
Adult: **PO** 15 mg once daily

ADMINISTRATION

Oral
- Do not exceed the maximum recommended daily dose of 15 mg.

- Use the lowest effective dose for the shortest duration to minimize risk of serious adverse effects.
- Store at 15°–30° C (59°–86° F).

ADVERSE EFFECTS (≥1%) **Body as a Whole:** Edema, fall, flu-like syndrome, pain. **GI:** Abdominal pain, diarrhea, dyspepsia, flatulence, nausea, constipation, <u>ulceration, GI bleed</u>. **Hematologic:** Anemia. **Musculoskeletal:** Arthralgia. **CNS:** Dizziness, headache, insomnia. **Respiratory:** Pharyngitis, upper respiratory tract infection, cough. **Skin:** Rash, pruritus. **Urogenital:** Micturition frequency, urinary tract infection.

INTERACTIONS Drug: May decrease effectiveness of ACE INHIBITORS, DIURETICS; **aspirin, warfarin** may increase risk of bleed; may increase **lithium** levels and toxicity. **Herbal: Feverfew, garlic, ginger, ginkgo** may increase bleeding potential.

PHARMACOKINETICS Absorption: 89% bioavailable. **Peak:** 4–5 h. **Distribution:** >99% protein bound, distributes into synovial fluid. **Metabolism:** In liver (CYP2C9). **Elimination:** Equally in urine and feces. **Half-Life:** 15–20 h.

CLINICAL IMPLICATIONS
Assessment & Drug Effects
- Monitor for and immediately report S&S of GI ulceration or bleeding, including black, tarry stool, abdominal or stomach pain; hepatotoxicity, including fatigue, lethargy, pruritus, jaundice, flu-like symptoms; skin rash; weight gain and edema.
- Withhold drug and notify physician if hepatotoxicity or GI bleeding is suspected.
- Monitor carefully patients with a history of CHF, HTN, or edema for fluid retention.

- Monitor diabetics using sulfonylureas for hypoglycemia.
- Lab tests: Hgb & Hct, CBC with differential, liver function tests, serum electrolytes, BUN, and creatinine within 3 mo of initiating therapy and every 6–12 mo thereafter; with high-risk patients (e.g., >60 y, history of peptic ulcer disease, prolonged or high-dose NSAID therapy, concurrent use of corticosteroids or anticoagulants) monitor within first 3–4 wk and every 3–6 mo thereafter.
- Coadministered drugs: With warfarin, closely monitor INR when meloxicam is initiated or dose changed; monitor for lithium toxicity, especially during addition, withdrawal, or change in dose of meloxicam.

Patient & Family Education
- Report any of the following to the physician immediately: nausea, black tarry stool, abdominal or stomach pain, unexplained fatigue or lethargy, itching, jaundice, flu-like symptoms, skin rash, weight gain, or edema.
- Minimize alcohol intake and use of tobacco. Discontinue drug if hepatotoxicity or GI bleeding is suspected. Note that GI bleeding may occur without forewarning and is more likely in older adults, in those with a history of ulcers or GI bleeding, and with alcohol consumption and cigarette smoking.
- Do not take aspirin or other NSAIDs while on this medication.

M

MELPHALAN

(mel′fa-lan)
Alkeran
Classifications: ANTINEOPLASTIC; ALKYLATING AGENT

Common adverse effects in *italic*, life-threatening effects <u>underlined</u>; generic names in **bold**; classifications in SMALL CAPS; ✦ Canadian drug name; ⓟ Prototype drug

939

Therapeutic: ANTINEOPLASTIC;
ALKYLATING AGENT
Prototype: Cyclophosphamide
Pregnancy Category: D

AVAILABILITY 2 mg tablets; 50 mg/
vial injection

ACTION & *THERAPEUTIC EFFECT*
Forms a highly reactive carbonium
ion which causes cross-linking and
abnormal base-pairing in DNA,
thereby interfering with DNA as
well as RNA replication and protein
synthesis. *Strong immunosuppressive and myelosuppressive effects.*

USES Chiefly for palliative treatment of multiple myeloma. Also
many other neoplasms, including
Hodgkin's disease and carcinomas of breast and ovary.
UNLABELED USES Polycythemia
vera.

CONTRAINDICATIONS Severe bone
marrow suppression; hepatic disease; renal impairment, renal failure;
severe electrolyte imbalance; lactation; pregnancy (category D); men
and women of childbearing age.
CAUTIOUS USE Recent treatment
with other chemotherapeutic agents;
concurrent administration with radiation therapy; severe anemia, neutropenia, or thrombocytopenia.

ROUTE & DOSAGE

Multiple Myeloma
Adult: **PO** 6 mg/d for 2–3 wk, drug
then withdrawn for 4–5 wk, restart
at 2 mg/d when WBC and platelet
counts start to rise **IV** 16 mg/m²
over 15 min q2wk for 4 doses

Epithelial Ovarian Cancer
Adult: **PO** 0.2 mg/kg/d for 5 d
as single course, may repeat
course q4–5 wk

ADMINISTRATION

Oral
- Give with meals to reduce nausea
and vomiting. An antiemetic may
be ordered.

Intravenous

***PREPARE:* IV Infusion:** Reconsti-
tute melphalan powder by **RAP-
IDLY** injecting 10 mL of the provided diluent into the vial to
yield 5 mg/mL. Shake vigorously
until clear. Immediately dilute
further with NS to a concentration of 0.45 mg/mL or less. Note:
45 mg in 100 mL yields 0.45 mg/
mL. Do not refrigerate reconstituted solution prior to infusion.
***ADMINISTER:* IV Infusion:** Give
over ≥15 min. Administration
MUST be completed within 60
min of reconstitution of drug because both reconstituted and diluted solutions are unstable.
***INCOMPATIBILITIES* Solution/Ad-
ditive: D5W, Ringer's lactate Y-
site: Amphotericin B, chlorpromazine.**
- Store at 15°–30° C (59°–86° F) in
light-resistant, airtight containers.

ADVERSE EFFECTS (≥1%) **Hematologic:** Leukopenia, agranulocytosis, thrombocytopenia, anemia,
acute nonlymphatic leukemia. **Body
as a Whole:** Uremia, angioneurotic
peripheral edema. **GI:** Nausea, vomiting, stomatitis. **Skin:** Temporary
alopecia. **Respiratory:** Pulmonary
fibrosis.

INTERACTIONS Drug: Increases risk
of nephrotoxicity with **cyclosporine, cimetidine** may decrease efficacy. **Food:** Food decreases absorption.

PHARMACOKINETICS Absorption:
Incompletely and variably absorbed
from GI tract. **Peak:** 2 h. **Distribu-**

tion: Widely distributed to all tissues. **Metabolism:** By spontaneous hydrolysis in plasma. **Elimination:** 25–50% in feces; 25–30% in urine. **Half-Life:** 1.5 h.

CLINICAL IMPLICATIONS

Assessment & Drug Effects

- Lab tests: Monitor WBC and platelet counts 2–3 times/wk during dosage adjustment period; determine WBC each week for 6–8 wk during maintenance therapy. Monitor serum uric acid levels.
- Monitor laboratory reports to anticipate leukopenic and thrombocytopenic periods.
- A degree of myelosuppression is maintained during therapy so as to keep leukocyte count in range of 3000–3500/mm³.
- Assess for flank and joint pains that may signal onset of hyperuricemia.

Patient & Family Education

- Be alert to onset of fever, profound weakness, chills, tachycardia, cough, sore throat, changes in kidney function, or prolonged infections and report to physician.
- Understand that reversible hair loss is an expected adverse effect.

MEMANTINE

(me-man′teen)

Namenda

Classifications: N-METHYL-D-ASPARTATE (NMDA) RECEPTOR ANTAGONIST; ANTIDEMENTIA AGENT

Therapeutic: ANTIDEMENTIA AGENT; NMDA RECEPTOR ANTAGONIST

Pregnancy Category: B

AVAILABILITY 5 mg, 10 mg tablets; 2 mg/mL solution

ACTION & *THERAPEUTIC EFFECT*

Glutamate activation at the (N-methyl-D-aspartate) NMDA receptor is needed for memory and learning processes in the brain. Excess glutamate may play a role in Alzheimer's disease by over-stimulating NMDA receptors, thus causing increased Ca^{2+} movement into neurons leading to neuronal damage. Memantine is a low-affinity, uncompetitive antagonist at NMDA receptors in the brain. Blockade of NMDA receptors may slow intracellular calcium accumulation, preventing nerve damage without interfering with actions of glutamate that are required for memory and learning. *Improves cognitive functioning in moderate-to-severe Alzheimer's disease (AD) and in mild-to-moderate vascular dementia.*

USES Treatment of symptoms of moderate to severe Alzheimer's disease

UNLABELED USES Treatment of moderate to severe vascular dementia

CONTRAINDICATIONS Renal failure. Safety and efficacy in children are unknown.

CAUTIOUS USE Moderate to severe renal impairment; history of seizure disorder; older adults; concurrent use with carbonic anhydrase inhibitors, or sodium bicarbonate, pregnancy (category B), lactation.

ROUTE & DOSAGE

Alzheimer's Disease

Adult: **PO** Initiate with 5 mg once daily, increase dose by 5 mg/wk over a 3-wk period to target dose of 10 mg b.i.d.

Severe Renal Impairment

Decrease to 5 mg b.i.d.

Common adverse effects in *italic*, life-threatening effects underlined; generic names in **bold**; classifications in SMALL CAPS; ♣ Canadian drug name; ⊙ Prototype drug

941

ADMINISTRATION

Oral

- Note: The recommended interval between dose increases is 1 wk.
- Dose reductions should be considered with moderate renal impairment.
- Store between 15°–30° C (59°–86° F).

ADVERSE EFFECTS (≥1%) **Body as a Whole:** Fatigue, pain, flu-like symptoms, peripheral edema. **CNS:** Dizziness, headache, confusion, somnolence, hallucinations, agitation, insomnia, abnormal gait, depression, anxiety, syncope, TIA, vertigo, ataxia, hypokinesia, aggressive reaction. **CV:** Hypertension, cardiac failure. **GI:** Constipation, vomiting, diarrhea, nausea, anorexia. **Hematologic:** Anemia. **Metabolic:** Weight loss, increased alkaline phosphatase. **Musculoskeletal:** Back pain, arthralgia. **Respiratory:** Coughing, dyspnea, bronchitis, upper respiratory infections, pneumonia. **Skin:** Rash. **Special Senses:** Conjunctivitis. **Urogenital:** Urinary incontinence, UTI, frequent micturition.

INTERACTIONS Drug: Drugs that increase the pH of the urine (CARBONIC ANHYDRASE INIBITORS, **sodium bicarbonate**) may increase levels of memantine; may enhance the effects of **amantadine, dextromethorphan, ketamine, bromocriptine, pergolide, pramipexole,** and **ropinirole;** may enhance the adverse effects of **levodopa**-containing drugs.

PHARMACOKINETICS Absorption: 100% from GI tract. **Duration:** 4–6 h. **Distribution:** Easily crosses the blood–brain barrier. **Metabolism:** Minimal. **Elimination:** Primarily excreted unchanged in urine. Increases in urinary pH can decrease elimination of drug. **Half-Life:** 60–80 h.

CLINICAL IMPLICATIONS

Assessment & Drug Effects

- Monitor respiratory and CV status, especially with preexisting heart disease.
- Assess for and report S&S of focal neurologic deficits (e.g., TIA, ataxia, vertigo).
- Lab tests: Periodic Hct & Hgb, serum sodium, alkaline phosphatase, and blood glucose.
- Monitor diabetics for loss of glycemic control.

Patient & Family Education

- Report any of the following to the physician: problems with vision, skin rash, shortness of breath, swelling in throat or tongue, agitation or restlessness, confusion, dizziness, or incontinence.
- Do not drive or engage in other hazardous activities until reaction to drug is known.

MEPERIDINE HYDROCHLORIDE

(me-per′i-deen)
Demerol, Pethadol ✦, Pethidine Hydrochloride ✦
Classifications: NARCOTIC (OPIATE) AGONIST ANALGESIC
Therapeutic: NARCOTIC ANALGESIC
Prototype: Morphine
Pregnancy Category: B (D at term)
Controlled Substance: Schedule II

AVAILABILITY 50 mg, 100 mg tablets; 50 mg/5 mL syrup; 10 mg/mL, 25 mg/mL, 50 mg/mL, 75 mg/mL, 100 mg/mL injection

ACTION & *THERAPEUTIC EFFECT*

Synthetic morphine-like compound. Opiates do not alter the pain threshold of afferent nerve endings, nor do they affect the con-

Common adverse effects in *italic*, life-threatening effects <u>underlined</u>; generic names in **bold**; classifications in SMALL CAPS; ✦ Canadian drug name; ⊙ Prototype drug

ductance of impulses along peripheral nerves. Analgesia is mediated through changes in the perception of pain at the spinal cord (mu$_2$, delta, kappa receptors) and higher levels in the CNS (mu$_1$ and kappa$_3$ receptors). *Control of moderate to severe pain.*

USES Relief of moderate to severe pain, for preoperative medication, for support of anesthesia, and for obstetric analgesia.

CONTRAINDICATIONS Hypersensitivity to meperidine; convulsive disorders; acute abdominal conditions prior to diagnosis; MAOI therapy; pregnancy prior to labor [(category C), at term (category D)].

CAUTIOUS USE Head injuries, increased intracranial pressure; asthma and other respiratory conditions; supraventricular tachycardias; prostatic hypertrophy; urethral stricture; glaucoma; older adult or debilitated patients; impaired kidney or liver function, hypothyroidism, Addison's disease.

ROUTE & DOSAGE

Moderate to Severe Pain
Adult: **PO/SC/IM/IV** 50–150 mg q3–4h prn
Child: **PO/SC/IM/IV** 1–1.5 mg/kg q3–4h (max: ≤100 mg q4h) prn

Preoperative
Adult: **IM/SC** 50–150 mg 30–90 min before surgery
Child: **IM/SC** 1.1–2.2 mg/kg 30–90 min before surgery

Obstetric Analgesia
Adult: **IM/SC** 50–100 mg when pains become regular, may be repeated q1–3h

ADMINISTRATION

Oral
- Give syrup formulation in half a glass of water. Undiluted syrup may cause topical anesthesia of mucous membranes.

Subcutaneous and Intramuscular Injections
- Be aware that SC route is painful and can cause local irritation. IM route is generally preferred when repeated doses are required.
- Aspirate carefully before giving IM injection to avoid inadvertent IV administration. IV injection of undiluted drug can cause a marked increase in heart rate and syncope.

Intravenous
Note: Verify correct IV concentration and rate of infusion/injection for administration to infants or children with physician.

PREPARE: Direct: Dilute 50 mg in at least 5 mL of NS or sterile water to yield 10 mg/mL. **IV Infusion:** Dilute to a concentration of 1–10 mg/mL in NS, D5W, or other compatible solution.

ADMINISTER: Direct: Give at a rate not to exceed 25 mg/min. Slower injection preferred. **IV Infusion:** Usually given through a controlled infusion device at a rate not to exceed 25 mg/min.

***INCOMPATIBILITIES* Solution/additive: Aminophylline,** BARBITURATES, **furosemide, heparin, methicillin, morphine, phenytoin, sodium bicarbonate. Y-site: Allopurinol, amphotericin B cholesteryl complex, cefepime, cefoperazone, doxorubicin liposome, furosemide, idarubicin, imipenem/cilastatin, mezlocillin, minocycline, tetracycline.**

- Store at 15°–30° C (59°–86° F) in tightly closed, light-resistant con-

M

Common adverse effects in *italic*, life-threatening effects underlined; generic names in **bold**; classifications in SMALL CAPS; ♣ Canadian drug name; ☺ Prototype drug

943

tainers unless otherwise directed by manufacturer.

ADVERSE EFFECTS (≥1%) **Body as a Whole:** Allergic (*Pruritus,* urticaria, skin rashes, wheal and flare over IV site), profuse perspiration. **CNS:** *Dizziness,* weakness, euphoria, dysphoria, *sedation,* headache, uncoordinated muscle movements, disorientation, decreased cough reflex, miosis, corneal anesthesia, <u>respiratory depression</u>. Toxic doses: muscle twitching, tremors, hyperactive reflexes, excitement, hypersensitivity to external stimuli, agitation, confusion, hallucinations, dilated pupils, <u>convulsions</u>. **CV:** Facial flushing, light-headedness, hypotension, syncope, palpitation, bradycardia, tachycardia, <u>cardiovascular collapse, cardiac arrest (toxic doses)</u>. **GI:** Dry mouth, *nausea,* vomiting, *constipation,* biliary tract spasm. **Urogenital:** Oliguria, urinary retention. **Respiratory:** <u>Respiratory depression in newborn,</u> bronchoconstriction (large doses). **Skin:** Phlebitis (following IV use), pain, tissue irritation and induration, particularly following subcutaneous injection. **Metabolic:** Increased levels of serum amylase, BSP retention, bilirubin, AST, ALT.

DIAGNOSTIC TEST INTERFERENCE High doses of meperidine may interfere with *gastric emptying studies* by causing delay in gastric emptying.

INTERACTIONS Drug: **Alcohol** and other CNS DEPRESSANTS, **cimetidine** cause additive sedation and CNS depression; AMPHETAMINES may potentiate CNS stimulation; MAO INHIBITORS, **selegiline, furazolidone** may cause excessive and prolonged CNS depression, convulsions, cardiovascular collapse; **phenytoin** may increase toxic meperidine metabolites. **Herbal:** **St. John's wort** may increase sedation.

PHARMACOKINETICS Absorption: 50–60% from GI tract. **Onset:** 15 min PO; 10 min IM, SC; 5 min IV. **Peak:** 1 h PO, IM, SC. **Duration:** 2–4 h PO, IM, SC; 2 h IV. **Distribution:** Crosses placenta; distributed into breast milk. **Metabolism:** In liver. **Elimination:** In urine. **Half-Life:** 3–5 h.

CLINICAL IMPLICATIONS

Assessment & Drug Effects

- Give narcotic analgesics in the smallest effective dose and for the least period of time compatible with patient's needs.
- Assess patient's need for prn medication. Record time of onset, duration, and quality of pain.
- Note respiratory rate, depth, and rhythm and size of pupils in patients receiving repeated doses. If respirations are 12/min or below and pupils are constricted or dilated (see ACTIONS AND USES) or breathing is shallow, or if signs of CNS hyperactivity are present, consult physician before administering drug.
- Monitor vital signs closely. Heart rate may increase markedly, and hypotension may occur. Meperidine may cause severe hypotension in postoperative patients and those with depleted blood volume.
- Schedule deep breathing, coughing (unless contraindicated), and changes in position at intervals to help to overcome respiratory depressant effects.
- Chart patient's response to drug and evaluate continued need.
- Repeated use can lead to tolerance as well as psychic and physical dependence of the morphine type.
- Be aware that abrupt discontinuation following repeated use results in morphine-like withdrawal symptoms. Symptoms develop more rapidly (within 3 h, peaking

in 8–12 h) and are of shorter duration than with morphine. Nausea, vomiting, diarrhea, and pupillary dilatation are less prominent, but muscle twitching, restlessness, and nervousness are greater than produced by morphine.

Patient & Family Education

- Do not smoke and walk without assistance after receiving the drug. Bed side rails may be advisable.
- Be aware nausea, vomiting, dizziness, and faintness associated with fall in BP are more pronounced when walking than when lying down (these symptoms may also occur in patients without pain who are given meperidine). Symptoms are aggravated by the head-up position.
- Do not drive or engage in potentially hazardous activities until any drowsiness and dizziness have passed.
- Do not take other CNS depressants or drink alcohol because of their additive effects.

MEPHOBARBITAL

(me-foe-bar′bi-tal)
Mebaral, Methylphenobarbital
Classifications: ANTICONVULSANT; BARBITURATE; SEDATIVE-HYPNOTIC
Therapeutic: ANTICONVULSANT; SEDATIVE-HYPNOTIC
Prototype: Phenobarbital
Pregnancy Category: D
Controlled Substance: Schedule IV

AVAILABILITY 32 mg, 50 mg, 100 mg tablets

ACTION & *THERAPEUTIC EFFECT*
Long-acting barbiturate that limits the spread of seizure activity by increasing the threshold for motor cortex stimuli. Exerts strong seda-

tive effect, but relatively mild hypnotic effect. *Reduces seizure activity by decreasing excitability in nerve cells. Depresses CNS producing drowsiness, hypnosis, and sedation.*

USES To control grand mal and petit mal epilepsy, alone or in combination with other anticonvulsant agents, and for sedative effect in management of delirium tremens and other acute agitation and anxiety states.

CONTRAINDICATIONS Hypersensitivity to barbiturates; coma; ethanol intoxication hepatic encephalopathy; porphyria; status epilepticus; pregnancy (category D).
CAUTIOUS USE Fever, hyperthyroidism, alcoholism; respiratory disorders, COPD, sleep apnea; mental status changes, major depression; suicidal ideation; liver, kidney, or cardiac dysfunction; lactation.

ROUTE & DOSAGE

Anticonvulsant
Adult: **PO** 400–600 mg/d in divided doses
Child: **PO** ≤5 y, 16–32 mg t.i.d. or q.i.d.; ≥5 y, 32–64 mg t.i.d. or q.i.d.
Sedative
Adult: **PO** 32–100 mg t.i.d. or q.i.d.
Child: **PO** ≤5 y, 16–32 mg t.i.d. or q.i.d.; ≥5 y, 32–64 mg t.i.d. or q.i.d.
Delirium Tremens
Adult: **PO** 200 mg t.i.d. or q.i.d.

ADMINISTRATION

Oral
- Change from other anticonvulsant by gradually tapering off the former as mephobarbital doses

M

Common adverse effects in *italic*, life-threatening effects <u>underlined</u>; generic names in **bold**; classifications in SMALL CAPS; ♣ Canadian drug name; ⊘ Prototype drug

945

M

are increased to maintain seizure control.
- When prescribed concurrently with phenobarbital, dose should be about one-half the amount of each used alone. When prescribed concurrently with phenytoin, the dose of phenytoin is usually reduced.
- Reduce discontinued drug dosage gradually over 4 or 5 days to avoid precipitating seizures of status epilepticus.

ADVERSE EFFECTS (≥1%) **CNS:** *Drowsiness,* dizziness, unsteadiness, hangover, paradoxical excitement. **GI:** Nausea, vomiting, constipation. **Body as a Whole:** Hypersensitivity reactions, respiratory depression.

INTERACTIONS Drug: Alcohol, CNS DEPRESSANTS compound CNS depression; may decrease absorption and increase metabolism of ORAL ANTICOAGULANTS; increases metabolism of CORTICOSTEROIDS, ORAL CONTRACEPTIVES, ANTICONVULSANTS, **digitoxin,** possibly decreasing their effects; ANTIDEPRESSANTS potentiate adverse effects; **griseofulvin** decreases absorption of mephobarbitol. **Herbal: Kava-kava, valerian** may potentiate sedation.

PHARMACOKINETICS Absorption: 50% from GI tract. **Onset:** 60 min. **Duration:** 10–12 h. **Metabolism:** In liver to phenobarbital. **Elimination:** In urine. Alkalinization of urine or increase of urinary flow significantly increases the rate of phenobarbital excretion. **Half-Life:** 34 h.

CLINICAL IMPLICATIONS
Assessment & Drug Effects
- Monitor respiratory status, especially with concurrent CNS therapy with other drugs.
- Be prepared for paradoxical response to barbiturate therapy (i.e.,

irritability, marked excitement, aggression in children, depression, confusion) in older adults, debilitated patients, or children.

Patient & Family Education
- Be aware that abrupt cessation after prolonged therapy may result in withdrawal symptoms (tremulousness, weakness, insomnia, delirium, convulsions).
- Avoid driving and potentially hazardous activities until response to drug has stabilized.
- Do not take alcohol in any amount with a barbiturate.

MEPROBAMATE 🅿️

(me-proe-ba′mate)
Classifications: PSYCHOTHERAPEUTIC; CARBAMATE; ANXIOLYTIC; SEDATIVE-HYPNOTIC
Therapeutic: ANTIANXIETY; SEDATIVE-HYPNOTIC
Pregnancy Category: D
Controlled Substance: Schedule IV

AVAILABILITY 200 mg, 400 mg tablets

ACTION & *THERAPEUTIC EFFECT* Carbamate derivative. CNS depressant actions similar to those of barbiturates. Acts on multiple sites in CNS and appears to block corticothalamic impulses. *Antianxiety agent. Hypnotic doses suppress REM sleep.*

USES To relieve anxiety and tension of psychoneurotic states and as adjunct in disease states associated with anxiety and tension. Also used to promote sleep in anxious, tense patients.

CONTRAINDICATIONS History of hypersensitivity to meprobamate or related carbamates; ethanol intoxication; history of acute intermittent porphyria; pregnancy (category D), lactation, children <6 y.

CAUTIOUS USE Impaired kidney or liver function; convulsive disorders; history of alcoholism or drug abuse; patients with suicidal tendencies.

ROUTE & DOSAGE

Sedative
Adult: **PO** 1.2–1.6 g/d in 3–4 divided doses (max: 2.4 g/d) *Child:* **PO** 100–200 mg b.i.d. or t.i.d.

Hypnotic
Adult: **PO** 400–800 mg *Geriatric:* **PO** 200 mg 2–3 times/d *Child:* **PO** 200 mg

ADMINISTRATION

Oral

- Give with food to minimize gastric distress.
- Treatment physical dependence by gradual drug withdrawal over 1–2 wk to prevent onset of withdrawal symptoms.
- Store at 15°–30° C (59°–86° F) unless otherwise specified by manufacturer.

ADVERSE EFFECTS (≥1%) **Body as a Whole:** Allergy or idiosyncratic reactions (itchy, urticarial, or erythematous maculopapular rash; exfoliative dermatitis, petechiae, purpura, ecchymoses, eosinophilia, peripheral edema, angioneurotic edema, adenopathy, fever, chills, proctitis, bronchospasm, oliguria, anuria, Stevens-Johnson syndrome); anaphylaxis. **CNS:** *Drowsiness* and *ataxia,* dizziness, vertigo, slurred speech, headache, weakness, paresthesias, impaired visual accommodation, paradoxic euphoria and rage reactions, seizures in epileptics, panic reaction, rapid EEG activity. **CV:** Hypotensive crisis, syncope, palpitation, tachycardia, arrhythmias, transient ECG changes, circulatory collapse (toxic doses). **GI:** Anorexia, nausea, vomiting, diarrhea. **Hematologic:** Aplastic anemia (rare): leukopenia, agranulocytosis, thrombocytopenia, exacerbation of acute intermittent porphyria. **Respiratory:** Respiratory depression.

DIAGNOSTIC TEST INTERFERENCE

Meprobamate may cause falsely high *urinary steroid* determinations. *Phentolamine* tests may be falsely positive; meprobamate should be withdrawn at least 24 h and preferably 48–72 h before the test.

INTERACTIONS Drug: Alcohol entacapone, TRICYCLIC ANTIDEPRESSANTS, ANTIPSYCHOTICS, OPIATES, SEDATING ANTIHISTAMINES, **pentazocine, tramadol,** MAOIS, SEDATIVE-HYPNOTICS, ANXIOLYTICS may potentiate CNS depression. **Herbal: Kava-kava, valerian** may potentiate sedation.

PHARMACOKINETICS Absorption: Well absorbed from GI tract. **Peak:** 1–3 h. **Onset:** 1 h. **Distribution:** Uniformly throughout body; crosses placenta. **Metabolism:** Rapidly in liver. **Elimination:** Renally excreted; excreted in breast milk. **Half-Life:** 10–11 h.

CLINICAL IMPLICATIONS

Assessment & Drug Effects

- Supervise ambulation, if necessary. Older adults and debilitated patients are prone to oversedation and to the hypotensive effects, especially during early therapy.
- Utilize safety precautions for hospitalized patients. Hypnotic doses may cause increased motor activity during sleep.
- Consult physician if daytime psychomotor function is impaired. A

M

Common adverse effects in *italic*, life-threatening effects underlined; generic names in **bold**; classifications in SMALL CAPS; ✦ Canadian drug name; ⊘ Prototype drug

947

change in regimen or drug may be indicated.

- Withdraw gradually in physically dependent patients to prevent pre-existing symptoms or withdrawal reactions within 12–48 h: Vomiting, ataxia, muscle twitching, mental confusion, hallucinations, convulsions, trembling, sleep disturbances, increased dreaming, nightmares, insomnia. Symptoms usually subside within 12–48 h.

Patient & Family Education
- Take drug as prescribed. Psychic or physical dependence may occur with long-term use of high doses.
- Be aware that tolerance to alcohol will be lowered.
- Make position changes slowly, especially from lying down to upright; dangle legs for a few minutes before standing.
- Avoid driving or engaging in hazardous activities until response to drug is known.
- Report immediately onset of skin rash, sore throat, fever, bruising, unexplained bleeding.

MEQUINOL/TRETINOIN
(me-qui′nol/tre-ti′noyn)
Solagé
Classifications: RETINOID
Therapeutic: DEPIGMENTING AGENT;
RETINOID
Prototype: Isotretinoin
Pregnancy Category: X

AVAILABILITY 2%/0.01% solution

ACTION & *THERAPEUTIC EFFECT*
Mequinol is a depigmenting agent and tretinoin is a retinoid used to improve dermatologic changes (e.g., fine wrinkling, mottled hyperpigmentation, roughness) associated with photo-damage and aging. Mequinol's mechanism of depigmentation is probably due to oxidation by tyrosine to cytotoxic products in melanocytes, and/or inhibition of melanin formation. Tretinoin, a retinoid, is used to improve photo-damage to the skin by acting via retinoic acid receptors (RARs). *Mequinol has depigmenting properties; tretinoin improves sun damaged skin.*

USES Treatment of solar lentigines.

CONTRAINDICATIONS Pregnancy (category X), lactation, children, hypersensitivity to mequinol, tretinoin. **CAUTIOUS USE** History of hypersensitivity to acitretin, isotretinoin, etretinate, or other vitamin A derivatives, or hydroquinone; patients with eczema, moderate to severe skin pigmentation, vitiligo; concurrent use of photosensitive medications (e.g., thiazide diuretics, fluoroquinolones, phenothiazines, sulfonamides), concurrent use of astringents; cold weather; eczema; vitiligo.

ROUTE & DOSAGE

Solar Lentigines
Adult: **Topical** Apply to solar lentigines b.i.d. at least 8 h apart

ADMINISTRATION

Topical
- Apply doses at least 8 h apart; avoid application to unaffected areas.
- Avoid contact with eyes, lips, mucus membranes, or paranasal creases.
- Protect from light.

ADVERSE EFFECTS (≥1%) **Skin:** *Erythema, burning, stinging, tingling, desquamation, pruritus,* skin irritation, temporary hypopigmen-

Common adverse effects in *italic*, life-threatening effects <u>underlined</u>; generic names in **bold**; classifications in SMALL CAPS; ♣ Canadian drug name; Ⓟ Prototype drug

tation, rash, dry skin, crusting, application site reaction.

INTERACTIONS Drug: THIAZIDE DIURETICS, TETRACYCLINES, FLUOROQUINOLONES, PHENOTHIAZINES, SULFONAMIDES may augment phototoxicity.

PHARMACOKINETICS Absorption: 4.4% through skin. **Peak:** 1–2 h.

CLINICAL IMPLICATIONS

Assessment & Drug Effects
- Monitor for and report peeling, erythema, or hypopigmentation.
- Monitor for signs of tretinoin toxicity: headache, fever, weakness, and fatigue.

Patient & Family Education
- Do not apply larger than recommended amounts.
- Do not wash affected area for at least 6 h after drug application; do not apply cosmetics to affected area for at least 30 min after drug application.
- Minimize exposure to sunlight or sunlamps. Use extra caution if also taking concurrently other drugs that are photosensitizing (e.g., thiazide diuretics, phenothiazines).
- Notify physician if vitiligo (hypopigmentation of skin) or S&S of tretinoin toxicity develop (see ASSESSMENT & DRUG EFFECTS).

MERCAPTOPURINE (6-MP, 6-MERCAPTOPURINE) ℗

(mer-kap-toe-pyoor'een)
Purinethol
Classifications: ANTINEOPLASTIC; ANTIMETABOLITE, PURINE ANTAGONIST; IMMUNOSUPPRESSANT
Therapeutic: ANTINEOPLASTIC; IMMUNOSUPPRESSANT
Pregnancy Category: D

AVAILABILITY 50 mg tablets

ACTION & *THERAPEUTIC EFFECT*
Antimetabolite and purine antagonist. Inhibits purine metabolism. Blocks conversion of inosinic acid to adenine and xanthine ribotides within sensitive tumor cells. Also inhibits adenine-containing coenzymes, suggesting an influence over multiple cellular reactions. *Delayed immunosuppressive properties and carcinogenic potential.*

USES Primarily for acute lymphocytic and myelogenous leukemia. Response in adults is less than in children, but mercaptopurine is initial drug of choice. In chronic granulocytic leukemia, produces temporary remission.
UNLABELED USES Prevention of transplant graft rejection; SLE; rheumatoid arthritis; Crohn's disease.

CONTRAINDICATIONS Prior resistance to mercaptopurine; first trimester of pregnancy (category D); lactation; infections.
CAUTIOUS USE Impaired kidney or liver function; concomitant use with allopurinol.

ROUTE & DOSAGE

Leukemias

Adult/Child: **PO Loading Dose** 2.5 mg/kg/d, may increase up to 5 mg/kg/d after 4 wk if needed **PO Maintenance Dose** 1.25–2.5 mg/kg/d

ADMINISTRATION

Oral
- Give total daily dose at one time.
- Reduce dose of mercaptopurine usually by $1/3$–$1/4$ when given concurrently with allopurinol.
- Store tablets in light- and air-resistant container.

M

Common adverse effects in *italic*, life-threatening effects underlined; generic names in **bold**; classifications in SMALL CAPS; ◆ Canadian drug name; ℗ Prototype drug

949

ADVERSE EFFECTS (≥1%) **GI:** Stomatitis, esophagitis, anorexia, nausea, vomiting, diarrhea, intestinal ulcerations, impaired liver function, <u>hepatic necrosis</u>. **Hematologic:** <u>Leukopenia</u>, anemia, eosinophilia, pancytopenia, <u>thrombocytopenia</u>, abnormal bleeding, bone marrow hypoplasia. **Urogenital:** Hyperuricemia, oliguria, renal impairment. **Skin:** Rash. **Body as a Whole:** Drug fever.

INTERACTIONS Drug: Allopurinol may inhibit metabolism and thus increase toxicity of mercaptopurine; may potentiate or antagonize anticoagulant effects of **warfarin.**

PHARMACOKINETICS Absorption: Approximately 50% absorbed from GI tract. **Peak:** 2 h. **Distribution:** Distributes into total body water. **Metabolism:** Rapidly by xanthine oxidase in liver. **Elimination:** 11% in urine within 6 h. **Half-Life:** 20–50 min.

CLINICAL IMPLICATIONS

Assessment & Drug Effects

- Lab tests: Monitor CBC with differential, platelet count, Hgb, Hct, and liver functions closely.
- Monitor for S&S of liver damage. Hepatic toxicity occurs most often when dose exceeds 2.5 mg/kg/d. Jaundice signals onset of hepatic toxicity and may necessitate terminating use.
- Withhold drug and notify physician at the first sign of an abnormally large or rapid fall in platelet and leukocyte counts.
- Record baseline data related to I&O ratio and pattern and body weight.
- Check vital signs daily. Report febrile states promptly.
- Protect patient from exposure to trauma, infections, or other stresses (restrict visitors and personnel who have colds) during periods of leukopenia.
- Report nausea, vomiting, or diarrhea. These may signal excessive dosage, especially in adults.
- Watch for signs of abnormal bleeding (ecchymoses, petechiae, melena, bleeding gums) if thrombocytopenia develops; report immediately.

Patient & Family Education

- Report any signs of bleeding (e.g., hematuria, bruising, bleeding gums).
- Report signs of hepatic toxicity (see Appendix F).
- Increase hydration (10–12 glasses of fluid daily) to reduce risk of hyperuricemia. Consult physician about desirable volume.
- Notify physician of onset of chills, nausea, vomiting, flank or joint pain, swelling of legs or feet, or symptoms of anemia.

MEROPENEM

(mer-o'pe-nem)
Merrem
Classifications: CARBAPENEM ANTIBIOTIC
Therapeutic: CARBAPENEM ANTIBIOTIC
Prototype: Imipenem
Pregnancy Category: B

AVAILABILITY 500 mg, 1 g injection

ACTION & *THERAPEUTIC EFFECT* Broad-spectrum carbapenem antibiotic that inhibits the cell wall synthesis of gram-positive and gram-negative bacteria by its strong affinity for penicillin-binding proteins of bacterial cell wall. *Effective against both gram-positive and gram-negative bacteria. High resistance to most bacterial beta-lactamases.*

USES Complicated appendicitis and peritonitis, bacterial meningitis caused by susceptible bacteria, complicated skin infections, intraabdominal infections, skin/soft tissue infections.

UNLABELED USES Febrile neutropenia.

CONTRAINDICATIONS Hypersensitivity to meropenem, other carbapenem antibiotics including imipenem, penicillins, cephalosporins, or other beta-lactams;. Safety and effectiveness in infants <3 mo not established.

CAUTIOUS USE History of asthma or allergies, renal impairment, renal disease; epileptics, history of neurologic disorders, older adult, pregnancy (category B). Safety and effectiveness in infants <3 mo not established.

ROUTE & DOSAGE

Intraabdominal Infections
Adult/Child >50 kg: **IV** 1 g q8h
Child ≥3 mo under 50 kg: **IV** 20 mg/kg q8h (max: 1 g q8h)

Bacterial Meningitis
Adult/Child >50 kg: **IV** 2 g q8h
Child ≥3 mo under 50 kg: **IV** 40 mg/kg q8h (max: 2 g q8h)

Complicated Skin Infection
Adult/Child >50 kg: **IV** 500 mg q8h
Child >3 mo under 50 kg: **IV** 10 mg/kg q8h (max: 500 mg q8h)

Renal Impairment
Cl_{cr} 26–50 mL/min: q12h; 10–25 mL/min: $^1/_2$ dose q12h; <10 mL/min: $^1/_2$ dose q24h

ADMINISTRATION

Intravenous
Note: Dosage reduction is recommended for older adults.

PREPARE: Direct: Reconstitute the 500-mg or 1-g vial, respectively, by adding 10 or 20 mL sterile water for injection to yield approximately 50 mg/mL. Shake to dissolve and let stand until clear. **IV Infusion:** Further dilute in 50–100 mL of D5W, NS, or D5/NS.

ADMINISTER: Direct: Give over 3–5 min. **IV Infusion:** Give over 15–30 min.

INCOMPATIBILITIES Solution/additive: D5W, Ringer's lactate, mannitol, amphotericin B, metronidazole, multivitamins, sodium bicarbonate. Y-site: Amphotericin B, diazepam, doxycycline, metronidazole, ondansetron, zidovudine.

■ Store undiluted at 15°–30° C (59°–86° F), diluted IV solutions should generally be used within 1 h of preparation.

ADVERSE EFFECTS (≥1%) **GI:** Diarrhea, nausea, vomiting, constipation. **Other:** Inflammation at injection site, phlebitis, thrombophlebitis. **CNS:** Headache. **Skin:** Rash, pruritus, diaper rash. **Body as a Whole:** Apnea, oral moniliasis, sepsis, shock. **Hematologic:** Anemia.

INTERACTIONS Drug: Probenecid delays meropenem excretion; may decrease **valproic acid** serum levels.

PHARMACOKINETICS Distribution: Attains high concentrations in bile, bronchial secretions, cerebrospinal fluid. **Metabolism:** Renal and extrarenal metabolism via dipeptidases or nonspecific degradation. **Elimination:** In urine. **Half-Life:** 0.8–1 h.

CLINICAL IMPLICATIONS

Assessment & Drug Effects
■ Lab tests: Perform C&S tests prior to therapy. Monitor periodically liver and kidney function.

M

Common adverse effects in *italic*, life-threatening effects <u>underlined</u>; generic names in **bold**; classifications in SMALL CAPS; ♣ Canadian drug name; ✪ Prototype drug

951

- Determine history of hypersensitivity reactions to other beta-lactams, cephalosporins, penicillins, or other drugs.
- Discontinue drug and immediately report S&S of hypersensitivity (see Appendix F).
- Report S&S of superinfection or pseudomembranous colitis (see Appendix F).
- Monitor for seizures especially in older adults and those with renal insufficiency.

Patient & Family Education
- Learn S&S of hypersensitivity, superinfection, and pseudomembranous colitis; report any of these to physician promptly.

MESALAMINE ⊕

(me-sal′a-meen)
Asacol, Canasa, Rowasa, Salofalk ◆, Pentasa
Classifications: ANTIINFLAMMATORY; PROSTAGLANDIN INHIBITOR
Therapeutic: ANTIINFLAMMATORY; PROSTAGLANDIN INHIBITOR
Pregnancy Category: B

AVAILABILITY 250 mg controlled release capsule (Pentasa); 400 mg delayed release tablet (Asacol); 500 mg suppository, 4 g/60 mL rectal suspension (Rowasa); 500 mg suppositories (Canasa)

ACTION & *THERAPEUTIC EFFECT*
Thought to diminish inflammation by blocking cyclooxygenase and inhibiting prostaglandin synthesis in the colon. *Provides topical antiinflammatory action in the colon of patients with ulcerative colitis.*

USES Indicated in active mild to moderate distal ulcerative colitis, proctosigmoiditis, or proctitis; maintenance of remission of ulcerative colitis.
UNLABELED USES Crohn's disease.

CONTRAINDICATIONS Hypersensitivity to mesalamine, aminosalicylates, or salicylates.
CAUTIOUS USE Renal impairment, renal disease, renal failure, pregnancy (category B), lactation; older adults; sulfite hypersensitivity; sensitivity to sulfasalazine.

ROUTE & DOSAGE

Ulcerative Colitis
Adult: **Rectal** (Rowasa) 4 g once/d h.s., enema should be retained for about 8 h if possible or 1 suppository (500 mg) b.i.d.; (Canasa) 500 mg b.i.d., may increase up to 500 mg t.i.d. **PO** (Asacol) 800 mg t.i.d. times 6 wk; (Pentasa) 500 mg t.i.d. times 6 wk. **Maintenance Dose** (Asacol) 800 mg b.i.d. or 400 mg q.i.d.
Child: **PO** 50 mg/kg/d divided q6–12h

ADMINISTRATION

Oral
- Ensure that controlled-release and enteric forms of the drug are not crushed or chewed.
- Shake the bottle well to make sure the suspension is mixed.

Rectal
- Use rectal suspension at bedtime with the objective of retaining it all night.
- Store at 15°–30° C (59°–86° F) away from heat and light.

ADVERSE EFFECTS (≥1%) **CNS:** *Headache,* fatigue, asthenia, malaise, weakness, dizziness. **GI:** *Abdominal pain, cramps,* or *discomfort,* flatulence, nausea, diarrhea, constipation, hemorrhoids, rectal pain, hepatitis (rare). **Skin:** Sensitiv-

Common adverse effects in *italic*, life-threatening effects <u>underlined</u>; generic names in **bold**; classifications in SMALL CAPS; ◆ Canadian drug name; ⊕ Prototype drug

ity reactions, rash, pruritus, alopecia. **Body as a Whole:** Fever. **Hematologic:** Thrombocytopenia (rare), eosinophilia. **Urogenital:** Interstitial nephritis.

PHARMACOKINETICS Absorption: PR 5–35% absorbed from colon depending on retention time of enema or suppository. PO Asacol, approximately 28% absorbed; 80% of drug is released in colon 12 h after ingestion. PO Pentasa, 50% of drug is released in colon at a pH <6. **Peak:** 3–6 h. **Distribution:** Rectal administration may reach as high as the ascending colon. Asacol is released in the ileum and colon; Pentasa is released in the jejunum, ileum, and colon. Low concentrations of mesalamine and higher concentrations of its metabolites are excreted in breast milk. **Metabolism:** Rapidly acetylated in the liver and colon wall. **Elimination:** Primarily in feces; absorbed drug excreted in urine. **Half-Life:** 2–15 h (depending on formulation).

CLINICAL IMPLICATIONS

Assessment & Drug Effects
- Lab tests: Monitor carefully urinalysis, BUN, and creatinine, especially in patients with preexisting kidney disease. The kidney is the major target organ for toxicity.
- Assess for S&S of allergic-type reactions (e.g., hives, itching, wheezing, anaphylaxis). Suspension contains a sulfite that may cause reactions in asthmatics and some nonasthmatic persons.
- Expect response to therapy within 3–21 d; however, the usual course of therapy is from 3–6 wk depending on symptoms and sigmoidoscopic examinations.

Patient & Family Education
- Report to physician promptly: Cramping, abdominal pain, or bloody diarrhea, which are indications for immediate drug withdrawal.
- Check with doctor if rectal irritation (e.g., bleeding, blistering, pain, burning, itching) occurs while using this drug.
- Check with physician before using any new medicine (prescription or OTC).
- Continue medication for full time of treatment even if you are feeling better.

MESNA

(mes'na)
Mesnex
Classifications: CHEMOPROTECTANT; DETOXIFYING AGENT
Therapeutic: DETOXIFYING AGENT
Pregnancy Category: B

AVAILABILITY 100 mg/mL injection; 400 mg tablet

ACTION & *THERAPEUTIC EFFECT* Detoxifying agent used to inhibit the hemorrhagic cystitis induced by ifosfamide. *Reacts chemically with urotoxic ifosfamide metabolites, resulting in their detoxification, and thus significantly decreases the incidence of hematuria.*

USES Prophylaxis for ifosfamide-induced hemorrhagic cystitis. Not effective in preventing hematuria due to other pathologic conditions such as thrombocytopenia.

UNLABELED USES Reduces the incidence of cyclophosphamide-induced hemorrhagic cystitis.

CONTRAINDICATIONS Hypersensitivity to mesna or other thiol compounds; neonates; lactation.

M

CAUTIOUS USE Autoimmune diseases; infants (injection) pregnancy (category B).

ROUTE & DOSAGE

Ifosfamide-Induced Hemorrhagic Cystitis

Adult: **IV** Dose = 20% of ifosfamide dose and is given at time of ifosfamide administration and 4 and 8 h after ifosfamide dose **PO** 40% of ifosfamide dose 2 and 6 h after each ifofsamide dose

ADMINISTRATION

▪ Note: To be effective, mesna must be administered with each dose of ifosfamide.

Intravenous

PREPARE: **Direct:** Add 4 mL of D5W, NS, or RL for each 100 mg of mesna to yield 20 mg/mL.
ADMINISTER: **Direct:** Give a single dose by direct IV over 60 sec.
INCOMPATIBILITIES **Solution/additive: Carboplatin, cisplatin, ifosfamide with epirubicin. Y-site: Amphotericin B cholesteryl complex.**
Inspect parenteral drug products visually for particulate matter and discoloration prior to administration.

▪ Discard any unused portion of the ampul because drug oxidizes on contact with air.

▪ Refrigerate diluted solutions or use within 6 h of mixing even though diluted solutions are chemically and physically stable for 24 h at 25° C (77° F). ▪ Store unopened ampul at 15°–30° C (59°–86° F) unless otherwise specified.

ADVERSE EFFECTS (≥1%) **GI:** *Bad taste in mouth, soft stools,* nausea, vomiting.

DIAGNOSTIC TEST INTERFERENCE May produce a false-positive result in test for **urinary ketones.**

INTERACTIONS : May decrease the effect of **warfarin**.

PHARMACOKINETICS Bioavailability: 45%–79% **Metabolism:** Rapidly oxidized in liver to active metabolite dimesna; dimesna is further metabolized in kidney. **Elimination:** 65% in urine within 24 h. **Half-Life:** Mesna 0.36 h, dimesna 1.17 h.

CLINICAL IMPLICATIONS

Assessment & Drug Effects
▪ Monitor urine for hematuria.
▪ Be aware that a false-positive test for urinary ketones may arise in patients treated with mesna. In this test, a red-violet color develops that, with the addition of glacial acetic acid, will turn to violet.
▪ About 6% of patients treated with mesna along with ifosfamide still develop hematuria.

Patient & Family Education
▪ Mesna prevents ifosfamide-induced hemorrhagic cystitis; it will not prevent or alleviate other adverse reactions or toxicities associated with ifosfamide therapy.
▪ Report any unusual or allergic reactions to physician.
▪ Check with physician before using any new prescription or OTC medicine.

METAPROTERENOL SULFATE

(met-a-proe-ter'e-nole)
Alupent, Metaprel
Classifications: BETA-ADRENERGIC AGONIST; BRONCHODILATOR;
Therapeutic: BRONCHODILATOR
Prototype: Albuterol
Pregnancy Category: C

Common adverse effects in *italic*, life-threatening effects <u>underlined</u>; generic names in **bold**; classifications in SMALL CAPS; ♣ Canadian drug name; ⊙ Prototype drug

AVAILABILITY 10 mg, 20 mg tablet; 10 mg/5 mL syrup; 75 mg, 150 mg metered dose inhaler; 0.4%, 0.6%, 5% solution for inhalation

ACTION & *THERAPEUTIC EFFECT*
Potent synthetic beta-adrenergic agonist that acts selectively on beta₂-adrenergic receptors to relax smooth muscle of bronchi, uterus, and blood vessels supplying skeletal muscles. *Bronchodilator; controls bronchospasm in asthmatics.*

USES Bronchodilator in symptomatic relief of asthma and reversible bronchospasm associated with bronchitis and emphysema.
UNLABELED USES Treatment and prophylaxis of heart block and to avert progress of premature labor (tocolytic action).

CONTRAINDICATIONS Sensitivity to other sympathomimetic agents; seizure disorders, seizures; diabetes mellitus; hyperthyroidism; pregnancy (category C). Safety in children <12 y (for aerosol use) and children <6 y (tablets) is not established.
CAUTIOUS USE Older adults; hypertension, cardiovascular disorders including coronary artery disease, cardiac arrhythmias, QT prolongation; MAOI therapy; lactation.

ROUTE & DOSAGE

Bronchospasm
Adult: **PO** 20 mg q6–8h **Metered Dose Inhaler** 2–3 inhalations q3–4h (max: 12 inhalations/d) **Nebulizer** 5–10 inhalations of undiluted 5% solution **IPPB** 2.5 mL of 0.4–0.6% solution q4–6h
Geriatric: **PO** 10 mg 3–4 times/d, may increase to 20 mg 3–4 times/d

Child: **PO** <2 y, 0.4 mg/kg t.i.d.–q.i.d.; 2–6 y, 1.2–2.6 mg/kg/d in 3–4 divided doses; 6–9 y, 10 mg q6–8h; >9 y, 20 mg q6–8h

ADMINISTRATION
▪ Note: Patient may use tablets and aerosol concomitantly.
Oral
▪ Give with food to reduce GI distress.
Inhalation
▪ Instruct patient to shake metered dose aerosol container, exhale through nose as completely as possible, administer aerosol while inhaling deeply through mouth, and to hold breath about 10 sec before exhaling slowly. Administer second inhalation 10 min after first.
▪ Store all forms at 15°–30° C (59°–86° F); protect from light and heat.

ADVERSE EFFECTS (≥1%) **CNS:** Nervousness, weakness, drowsiness, *tremor (particularly after PO administration),* headache, fatigue. **CV:** *Tachycardia,* hypertension, <u>cardiac arrest</u>, palpitation. **GI:** Nausea, vomiting, bad taste. **Urogenital:** Occasional difficulty in micturition and muscle cramps. **Respiratory:** Throat irritation, cough, exacerbation of asthma.

INTERACTIONS Drug: Epinephrine, other SYMPATHOMIMETIC BRONCHODILATORS may compound effects of metaproterenol; MAO INHIBITORS, TRICYCLIC ANTIDEPRESSANTS potentiate action of metaproterenol on vascular system; the effects of both metaproterenol and BETA-ADRENERGIC BLOCKERS are antagonized.

PHARMACOKINETICS Absorption: 40% of PO doses reach systemic circulation. **Onset:** Inhaled: 1 min; PO

M

Common adverse effects in *italic*, life-threatening effects <u>underlined</u>; generic names in **bold**; classifications in SMALL CAPS; ♣ Canadian drug name; ☻ Prototype drug

955

15 min. **Peak:** 1 h all routes. **Duration:** Inhaled: 1–5 h; PO 4 h. **Metabolism:** In liver. **Elimination:** In urine.

CLINICAL IMPLICATIONS
Assessment & Drug Effects
- Monitor respiratory status. Auscultate lungs before and after inhalation to determine efficacy of drug in decreasing airway resistance.
- Monitor cardiac status. Report tachycardia and hypotension.

Patient & Family Education
- Report failure to respond to usual dose. Drug may have shorter duration of action after long-term use.
- Do not increase dose or frequency unless ordered by physician; there is the possibility of serious adverse effects.
- Anticipate tremor as a possible adverse effect.

M

METFORMIN ℗

(met-for′min)
Fortamet, Glucophage, Glucophage XR, Glumetza, Riomet
Classifications: HORMONE & ANTIDIABETIC AGENT; BIGUANIDES
Therapeutic: ANTIDIABETIC; BIGUANIDE
Pregnancy Category: B

AVAILABILITY 500 mg, 850 mg, 1000 mg tablets; 500 mg, 750 mg, 1000 mg sustained-release tablets; 100 mg/mL oral solution

ACTION & *THERAPEUTIC EFFECT*
Biguanide oral hypoglycemic agent with a mechanism of action thought to be due to both increasing the binding of insulin to its receptors and potentiating insulin action. Improves tissue sensitivity to insulin, increases glucose transport into skeletal muscles and fat, and suppresses gluconeogenesis and hepatic production of glucose, thus lowering blood glucose levels. *Effective in suppressing hepatic production of glucose as well as increasing the binding of insulin to its receptors in muscle tissue.*

USES Treatment of type 2 diabetes mellitus in patients not controlled with diet alone. May be used with an oral sulfonylurea.

CONTRAINDICATIONS Hypersensitivity to metformin; hepatic or cardiopulmonary insufficiency; alcoholism; concurrent infection; acute MI, cardiogenic shock; diabetic ketoacidosis; hypoxemia, lactic acidosis; radiographic contrast administration; renal disease, renal failure, renal impairment; sepsis; surgery; children <10 y.

CAUTIOUS USE Previous hypersensitivity to phenformin or buformin; anemia; coma; dehydration, diarrhea; older adults; ethanol intoxication; fever; gastroparesis, GI obstruction; heart failure; hyperthyroidism, pituitary insufficiency; polycystic ovary syndrome; trauma, emesis; pregnancy (category B), lactation.

ROUTE & DOSAGE

Type 2 Diabetes Mellitus
Adult: **PO** Start with 500 mg q.d. to t.i.d. or 850 mg q.d. to b.i.d. with meals, may increase by 500–850 mg/d every 1–3 wk (max: 2550 mg/d); or start with 500 mg sustained-release with p.m. meal, may increase by 500 mg/d at p.m. meal qwk (max: 2000 mg/d)

ADMINISTRATION
Oral
- Ensure that extend-release tablets are not crushed or chewed. They must be swallowed whole.

Common adverse effects in *italic*, life-threatening effects <u>underlined</u>; generic names in **bold**; classifications in SMALL CAPS; ♦ Canadian drug name; ℗ Prototype drug

- Use a calibrated oral syringe or container to measure the oral solution for accurate dosing.
- Give with or shortly after main meals.
- Withhold metformin 48 h before and 48 h after receiving IV contrast dye.
- Make dose increment, if needed, at 2- to 3-wk intervals.
- Store at 15°–30° C (59°–86° F).

ADVERSE EFFECTS (≥1%) **CNS:** Headache, dizziness, agitation, fatigue. **Metabolic:** Lactic acidosis. **GI:** *Nausea, vomiting, abdominal pain, bitter or metallic taste, diarrhea, bloatedness, anorexia;* malabsorption of amino acids, vitamin B$_{12}$, and folic acid possible.

INTERACTIONS Drug: Captopril, furosemide, nifedipine may increase risk of hypoglycemia. **Cimetidine** reduces clearance of metformin. Concomitant therapy with AZOLE ANTIFUNGAL AGENTS **(fluconazole, ketoconazole, itraconazole)** and ORAL HYPOGLYCEMIC DRUGS has been reported in severe hypoglycemia. IODINATED RADIOCONTRAST DYES can cause lactic acidosis and acute kidney failure. **Amiloride, cimetidine digoxin, dofetilide, midodrine, morphine, procainamide, quinidine, quinine, ranitidine, triamterene, trimethoprim, or vancomycin** may decrease metformin elimination by competing for common renal tubular transport systems. **Acarbose** may decrease metformin levels. **Iodinated contrast dyes** may cause lactic acidosis or acute kidney failure. **Herbal:** Garlic, ginseng, glucomannan may increase hypoglycemic effects. Guar gum decreases absorption.

PHARMACOKINETICS Absorption: 50–60% of dose reaches systemic circulation. **Peak:** 1–3 h. **Distribution:** Not bound to plasma proteins. **Metabolism:** Not metabolized. **Elimination:** In urine. **Half-Life:** 6.2–17.6 h.

CLINICAL IMPLICATIONS

Assessment & Drug Effects

- Lab tests: Obtain baseline and periodic kidney and liver function tests; drug contraindicated in the presence of renal or hepatic insufficiency. Monitor blood glucose and HbA$_{1C}$, and lipid profile periodically.
- Monitor known or suspected alcoholics carefully for decreased liver function.
- Monitor cardiopulmonary status throughout course of therapy; cardiopulmonary insufficiency may predispose to lactic acidosis.

Patient & Family Education

- Be aware that hypoglycemia is not a risk when drug is taken in recommended therapeutic doses unless combined with other drugs which lower blood glucose.
- Report to physician immediately S&S of infection, which increase the risk of lactic acidosis (e.g., abdominal pains, nausea, and vomiting, anorexia).

M

METHADONE HYDROCHLORIDE

(meth′a-done)

Dolophine, Methadose

Classifications: NARCOTIC (OPIATE) AGONIST; ANALGESIC

Therapeutic: NARCOTIC (OPIATE) ANALGESIC

Prototype: Morphine

Pregnancy Category: C

Controlled Substance: Schedule II

AVAILABILITY 5 mg, 10 mg, 40 mg tablets; 1 mg/mL, 2 mg/mL, 10 mg/mL oral solution; 10 mg/mL injection

ACTION & *THERAPEUTIC EFFECT*

Synthetic derivative similar to morphine but is orally effective and has longer duration of action. A single oral dose produces less sedation and euphoria than does morphine, but repeated doses produce marked sedation. Causes less constipation than morphine, but respiratory depressant effect and antitussive actions are comparable. Highly addictive, with abuse potential that matches that of morphine; abstinence syndrome develops more slowly; withdrawal symptoms are less intense but more prolonged. *Relieves severe pain and manages withdrawal therapy from narcotics.*

USES To relieve severe pain; for detoxification and temporary maintenance treatment in hospital and in federally controlled maintenance programs for ambulatory patients with narcotic abstinence syndrome.

CONTRAINDICATIONS Severe pulmonary disease; COPD; obstetric analgesia; pregnancy (category C). **CAUTIOUS USE** History of QT prolongation; liver, kidney, or cardiac dysfunction.

ROUTE & DOSAGE

Pain
Adult: **PO/SC/IM** 2.5–10 mg q3–4h prn **IV** 2.5-10 mg q8–12h prn (opiate naïve patient)
Child: **PO/IV/SC/IM** 0.1–0.2 mg/kg times 2–3 doses, then q6–12h prn (max: 5–10 mg/dose)

Detoxification Treatment
Adult: **PO/SC/IM** 15–40 mg once/d, usually maintained at 20–120 mg/d

Renal Impairment
Cl_{cr} <10 mL/min use 50–75% of dose

ADMINISTRATION

Oral
- Give for analgesic effect in the smallest effective dose to minimize the possible tolerance and physical and psychic dependence.
- Dilute dispersible tablets in 120 mL of water or fruit juice and allow at least 1 min for dispersion.

Subcutaneous, Intramuscular
- Note: IM route is preferred over SC when repeated parenteral administration is required (SC injections may cause local irritation and induration). Rotate injection sites.

Intravenous
Verify correct IV concentration and rate of infusion for administration to neonates, infants, children with physician.

- IV route is used rarely. Get specific orders from physician.
INCOMPATIBILITIES Y-site: **Phenytoin**.

- Store at 15°–30° C (59°–86° F) in tight, light-resistant containers.

ADVERSE EFFECTS (≥1%) **CNS:** *Drowsiness,* light-headedness, dizziness, hallucinations. **GI:** Nausea, vomiting, dry mouth, *constipation.* **Body as a Whole:** Transient fall in BP, bone and muscle pain. **Urogenital:** Impotence. **Respiratory:** Respiratory depression.

INTERACTIONS Drug: Alcohol and other CNS DEPRESSANTS, **cimetidine** add to sedation and CNS depression; AMPHETAMINES may potentiate CNS stimulation; with MAO INHIBITORS, **selegiline, furazolidone** causes excessive and prolonged CNS depression, convulsions, cardiovascular collapse. **Food:** Grapefruit juice may increase serum levels and adverse effects. **Herbal: St. John's wort** decreases plasma levels.

PHARMACOKINETICS Absorption: Well absorbed from GI tract, variable IM absorption. **Onset:** 30–60 min PO; 10–20 min IM/SC. **Peak:** 1–2 h. **Duration:** 6–8 h PO, IM, SC; may last 22–48 h with chronic dosing. **Distribution:** Crosses placenta; distributed into breast milk. **Metabolism:** In liver (CYP3A4). **Elimination:** In urine. **Half-Life:** 15–25 h.

CLINICAL IMPLICATIONS

Assessment & Drug Effects
- Evaluate patient's continued need for methadone for pain. Adjustment of dosage and lengthening of between-dose intervals may be possible.
- Monitor respiratory status. Principal danger of overdosage, as with morphine, is extreme respiratory depression.
- Be aware that because of the cumulative effects of methadone, abstinence symptoms may not appear for 36–72 h after last dose and may last 10–14 d. Symptoms are usually of mild intensity (e.g., anorexia, insomnia, anxiety, abdominal discomfort, weakness, headache, sweating, hot and cold flashes).
- Observe closely for recurrence of respiratory depression during use of narcotic antagonists such as naloxone, naltrexone, and levallorphan to terminate methadone intoxication. Since antagonist action is shorter (1–3 h) than that of methadone (36–48 h or more), repeated doses for 8–24 h may be required.

Patient & Family Education
- Be aware that orthostatic hypotension, sweating, constipation, drowsiness, GI symptoms, and other transient adverse effects of therapeutic doses appear to be more prominent in ambulatory patients. Most adverse effects disappear over a period of several weeks.
- Make position changes slowly, particularly from lying down to upright position; sit or lie down if you feel dizzy or faint.
- Do not drive or engage in potentially hazardous activities until response to drug is known.

METHAMPHETAMINE HYDROCHLORIDE

(meth-am-fet′a-meen)
Desoxyephedrine, Desoxyn
Classifications: CEREBRAL STIMULANT; ANOREXIANT; AMPHETAMINE
Therapeutic: CEREBRAL STIMULANT; ANOREXIANT
Prototype: Amphetamine sulfate
Pregnancy Category: C
Controlled Substance: Schedule II

AVAILABILITY 5 mg tablets; 5 mg, 10 mg, 15 mg long-acting tablets

ACTION & *THERAPEUTIC EFFECT*
Sympathomimetic amine chemically related to amphetamine. CNS stimulant actions approximately equal to those of amphetamine, but accompanied by less peripheral activity. However, larger doses produce increased cardiac output, possibly reflex slowing of heart rate, and sustained increase in BP, chiefly by cardiac stimulation. *CNS stimulant actions approximately equal to those of amphetamine, but accompanied by less peripheral activity.*

USES Short-term adjunct in management of exogenous obesity, as adjunctive therapy in attention deficit disorder (ADD), narcolepsy, epilepsy, and postencephalitic parkinsonism, and in treatment of certain depressive reactions, especially when characterized by apathy and psychomotor retardation.

M

Common adverse effects in *italic*, life-threatening effects underlined; generic names in **bold**; classifications in SMALL CAPS; ♦ Canadian drug name; ❷ Prototype drug

959

CONTRAINDICATIONS During pregnancy, especially first trimester (category C), lactation; as anorexiant in children <12 y; patients receiving MAO INIBITORS; arteriosclerotic parkinsonism.

CAUTIOUS USE Mild hypertension; psychopathic personalities; hyperexcitability states; history of suicide attempts; older adult or debilitated patients.

ROUTE & DOSAGE

Attention Deficit Disorder
Child: **PO** ≥6 y, 2.5–5 mg 1–2 times/d, may increase by 5 mg at weekly intervals up to 20–25 mg/d

Obesity
Adult: **PO** 2.5–5 mg 1–3 times/d 30 min before meals or 5–15 mg of long-acting form once/d

ADMINISTRATION

Oral
- Give early in the day to avoid insomnia, if possible.
- Ensure that long-acting tablets are not chewed or crushed; these need to be swallowed whole.
- Give 30 min before each meal when used for treatment of obesity. If insomnia results, advise patient to inform physician.
- Preserve in tight, light-resistant containers.

ADVERSE EFFECTS (≥1%) **CNS:** Restlessness, tremor, hyperreflexia, insomnia, headache, nervousness, anxiety, dizziness, euphoria or dysphoria. **CV:** Palpitation, arrhythmias, hypertension, hypotension, circulatory collapse. **GI:** Dry mouth, unpleasant taste, nausea, vomiting, diarrhea, constipation. **Special Senses:** Increased intraocular pressure.

INTERACTIONS Drug: Acetazolamide, sodium bicarbonate decreases methamphetamine elimination; **ammonium chloride, ascorbic acid** increases methamphetamine elimination; effects of both methamphetamine and BARBITURATES may be antagonized; **furazolidone** may increase BP effects of AMPHETAMINES—interaction may persist for several weeks after discontinuing **furazolidone**; antagonizes antihypertensive effects of **guanethidine, guanadrel;** MAO INHIBITORS, **selegiline** can cause hypertensive crisis (fatalities reported)—do not administer AMPHETAMINES during or within 14 d of administration of these drugs; PHENOTHIAZINES may inhibit mood elevating effects of AMPHETAMINES; TRICYCLIC ANTIDEPRESSANTS enhance methamphetamine effects because they increase norepinephrine release; BETA-ADRENERGIC AGONISTS increase adverse cardiovascular effects of AMPHETAMINES.

PHARMACOKINETICS Absorption: Readily absorbed from the GI tract. **Duration:** 6–12 h. **Distribution:** All tissues especially the CNS; excreted in breast milk. **Metabolism:** In liver. **Elimination:** Renal elimination.

CLINICAL IMPLICATIONS

Assessment & Drug Effects
- Monitor weight throughout period of therapy.
- Be alert for paradoxic increase in depression or agitation in depressed patients. Report immediately; drug should be withdrawn.
- Do not exceed duration of a few weeks for treatment of obesity.

Patient & Family Education
- Be alert for development of tolerance; happens readily, and prolonged use may lead to drug dependence. Abuse potential is

high. Methamphetamine is commonly known as "speed" or "crystal" among drug abusers.

- Withdrawal after prolonged use is frequently followed by lethargy that may persist for several weeks.
- Weigh every other day under standard conditions and maintain a record of weight loss.

METHAZOLAMIDE

(meth-a-zoe'la-mide)

Classifications: EYE PREPARATION; CARBONIC ANHYDRASE INHIBITOR; SULFONAMIDE DERIVATIVE; ANTI-GLAUCOMA

Therapeutic: ANTI-GLAUCOMA; CARBONIC ANHYDRASE INHIBITOR

Prototype: Acetazolamide

Pregnancy Category: C

AVAILABILITY 25 mg, 50 mg tablets

ACTION & THERAPEUTIC EFFECT
Inhibits carbonic anhydrase activity in eye by reducing rate of aqueous humor formation with consequent lowering of intraocular pressure. *Effective in lowering intraocular pressure in glaucoma patients.*

USES Adjunctive treatment in chronic simple (open-angle) glaucoma and secondary glaucoma and preoperatively in acute angle-closure glaucoma when delay of surgery is desired in order to lower intraocular pressure. May be used concomitantly with miotic and osmotic agents.

CONTRAINDICATIONS Glaucoma due to severe peripheral anterior synechiae, severe or absolute glaucoma, hemorrhagic glaucoma; hypokalemia, hyponatremia; dialysis; hepatic disease; renal disease, anuria, renal failure; pregnancy (category C).

CAUTIOUS USE Pulmonary disease, COPD; diabetes mellitus; renal impairment; lactation.

ROUTE & DOSAGE

Glaucoma
Adult: PO 50–100 mg b.i.d. or t.i.d.

ADMINISTRATION

Oral
- Give with meals to minimize GI distress.

ADVERSE EFFECTS (≥1%) **Body as a Whole:** Malaise, drowsiness, fatigue, lethargy. **GI:** Mild GI disturbance, anorexia. **CNS:** Headache, vertigo, paresthesias, mental confusion, depression.

INTERACTIONS Drug: Renal excretion of AMPHETAMINES, **ephedrine, flecainide, quinidine, procainamide,** TRICYCLIC ANTIDEPRESSANTS may be decreased, thereby enhancing or prolonging their effects; increases renal excretion of **lithium;** excretion of **phenobarbital** may be increased; **amphotericin B,** CORTICOSTEROIDS may add to potassium loss; hypokalemia caused by methazolamide may predispose patients on DIGITALIS GLYCOSIDES to **digitalis** toxicity; patients on high doses of SALICYLATES are at higher risk for SALICYLATE toxicity.

PHARMACOKINETICS Absorption: Slowly from GI tract. **Onset:** 2–4 h. **Peak:** 6–8 h. **Duration:** 10–18 h. **Distribution:** throughout body, concentrating in RBCs, plasma, and kidneys; crosses placenta. **Metabolism:** Partially in liver. **Elimination:** Primarily in urine.

CLINICAL IMPLICATIONS

Assessment & Drug Effects
- Supervise ambulation in older adult, since drug may cause vertigo.

M

Common adverse effects in *italic*, life-threatening effects underlined; generic names in **bold**, classifications in SMALL CAPS; ♣ Canadian drug name; ⊕ Prototype drug

961

- Assess patient's ability to perform ADL since drug may cause fatigue and lethargy.
- Lab tests: Obtain periodic serum electrolytes, especially in older adults. Monitor lithium levels with concurrent administration of lithium and methazolamide.

Patient & Family Education
- Be aware that drug may cause drowsiness. Advise caution with hazardous activities until response to drug is known.

METHENAMINE HIPPURATE

(meth-en'a-meen hip'yoo-rate)
Hiprex, Urex

METHENAMINE MANDELATE

Mandelamine
Classifications: URINARY TRACT ANTIINFECTIVE
Therapeutic: URINARY TRACT ANTIINFECTIVE
Prototype: Trimethoprim
Pregnancy Category: C

AVAILABILITY Methenamine Hippurate 1 g tablets **Methenamine Mandelate** 0.5 g, 1 g tablets; 0.5 g/5 mL suspension

ACTION & THERAPEUTIC EFFECT Tertiary amine liberates formaldehyde in an acid medium. Nonspecific antibiotic agent with bactericidal activity. *Most bacteria and fungi are susceptible to formaldehyde; however, bacteria that are urease-positive (e.g., Proteus sp) convert urea to ammonium hydroxide, which prevents the generation of formaldehyde from methenamine.*

USES Prophylactic treatment of recurrent urinary tract infections (UTIs). Also long-term prophylaxis when residual urine is present (e.g., neurogenic bladder).

CONTRAINDICATIONS Renal insufficiency; liver disease; gout; severe dehydration; combined therapy with sulfonamides; pregnancy (category C). Safety during lactation is not established.
CAUTIOUS USE Oral suspension for patients susceptible to lipoid pneumonia (e.g., older adults, debilitated patients); gout.

ROUTE & DOSAGE

UTI Prophylaxis
Adult: **PO** (Hippurate) 1 g b.i.d.; (Mandelate) 1 g q.i.d.
Child: **PO** ≤6 y, (Mandelate) 18.4 mg/kg q.i.d.; 6–12 y, (Hippurate) 0.5–1 g b.i.d.; (Mandelate) 500 mg q.i.d. or 50 mg/kg/d in 3 divided doses

ADMINISTRATION

Oral
- Give after meals and at bedtime to minimize gastric distress.
- Give oral suspension with caution to older adult or debilitated patients because of the possibility of lipid (aspiration) pneumonia; it contains a vegetable oil base.
- Store at 15°–30° C (59°–86° F) in tightly closed container; protect from excessive heat.

ADVERSE EFFECTS (≥1%) **GI:** Nausea, vomiting, diarrhea, abdominal cramps, anorexia. **Renal:** Bladder irritation, dysuria, frequency, albuminuria, hematuria, crystalluria.

DIAGNOSTIC TEST INTERFERENCE Methenamine (formaldehyde) may produce falsely elevated values for ***urinary catecholamines*** and ***urinary steroids (17-hydroxycorti-***

costeroids) (by *Reddy method*). Possibility of false *urine glucose determinations* with *Benedict's* test. Methenamine interferes with *urobilinogen* and possibly *urinary VMA* determinations.

INTERACTIONS Drug: Sulfamethoxazole forms insoluble precipitate in acid urine; **acetazolamide, sodium bicarbonate** may prevent hydrolysis to formaldehyde.

PHARMACOKINETICS Absorption: Readily from GI tract, although 10–30% of dose is hydrolyzed to formaldehyde in stomach. **Peak:** 2 h. **Duration:** Up to 6 h or until patient voids. **Distribution:** Crosses placenta; distributed into breast milk. **Metabolism:** Hydrolyzed in acid pH to formaldehyde. **Elimination:** In urine. **Half-Life:** 4 h.

CLINICAL IMPLICATIONS

Assessment & Drug Effects
- Monitor urine pH; value of 5.5 or less is required for optimum drug action.
- Monitor I&O ratio and pattern; drug most effective when fluid intake is maintained at 1500 or 2000 mL/d.
- Do not force fluids with this drug; copious amounts may increase diuresis, elevate urine pH, and dilute formaldehyde concentration to subinhibitory levels.
- Consult physician about changing to enteric-coated tablet if patient complains of gastric distress.
- Supplemental acidification to maintain pH of 5.5 or below required for drug action may be necessary. Accomplish by drugs (ascorbic acid, ammonium chloride) or by foods.

Patient & Family Education
- Do not self-medicate with OTC antacids containing sodium bicarbonate or sodium carbonate (to prevent raising urine pH).
- Achieve supplementary acidification by limiting intake of foods that can increase urine pH [e.g., vegetables, fruits, and fruit juice (except cranberry, plum, prune)] and increasing intake of foods that can decrease urine pH (e.g., proteins, cranberry juice, plums, prunes).

METHIMAZOLE

(meth-im'a-zole)
Tapazole
Classifications: HORMONE; ANTITHYROID AGENT
Therapeutic: ANTITHYROID
Prototype: Propylthiouracil
Pregnancy Category: D

AVAILABILITY 5 mg, 10 mg, 15 mg, 20 mg tablets

ACTION & *THERAPEUTIC EFFECT*
Actions are less consistent, but effects appear more promptly than with propylthiouracil. Inhibits synthesis of thyroid hormones as the drug accumulates in the thyroid gland. Does not affect existing T_3 or T_4 levels. *Corrects hyperthyroidism by inhibiting synthesis of the thyroid hormone.*

USES Hyperthyroidism and prior to surgery or radiotherapy of the thyroid; may be used cautiously to treat hyperthyroidism in pregnancy.

CONTRAINDICATIONS Pregnancy (category D).
CAUTIOUS USE Other drugs known to cause agranulocytosis; bone marrow suppression; older adults; hepatic disease.

ROUTE & DOSAGE

Hyperthyroidism
Adult: **PO** 5–15 mg q8h

M

Common adverse effects in *italic*, life-threatening effects underlined; generic names in **bold**; classifications in SMALL CAPS; ♦ Canadian drug name; ◎ Prototype drug

963

Child: **PO** 0.2–0.4 mg/kg/d divided q8h

ADMINISTRATION

Oral

- Give at same time each day relative to meals.
- Store at 15°–30° C (59°–86° F) in light-resistant container.

ADVERSE EFFECTS (≥1%) **GI:** <u>hepatotoxicity (rare)</u>. **Endocrine:** Hypothyroidism. **Hematologic:** *Leukopenia,* agranulocytosis, granulocytopenia, thrombocytopenia, pancytopenia, and aplastic anemia. **Musculoskeletal:** Arthralgia. **CNS:** Peripheral neuropathy, drowsiness, neuritis, paresthesias, vertigo. **Skin:** Rash, alopecia, skin hyperpigmentation, urticaria, and pruritus. **Urogenital:** Nephrotic syndrome.

INTERACTIONS Drug: Can reduce anticoagulant effects of **warfarin;** may increase serum levels of **digoxin;** may alter **theophylline** levels; may need to decrease dose of BETA-BLOCKERS.

PHARMACOKINETICS Absorption: Readily absorbed from GI tract. **Onset:** 30–40 min. **Peak:** 1 h. **Duration:** 2–4 h. **Distribution:** Crosses placenta; distributed into breast milk. **Elimination:** 12% in urine within 24 h. **Half-Life:** 5–13 h.

CLINICAL IMPLICATIONS

Assessment & Drug Effects

- Lab tests: Periodic blood work, since agranulocytosis is a rare, but possible adverse effect.
- Closely monitor PT and INR in patients on oral anticoagulants. Anticoagulant activity may be potentiated.

Patient & Family Education

- Adhere to established dosage regimen (i.e., not to double, decrease, or omit doses and not to alter the interval between doses).
- Be aware that skin rash or swelling of cervical lymph nodes may indicate need to discontinue drug and change to another antithyroid agent. Consult physician.
- Notify physician promptly if the following symptoms appear: Bruising, unexplained bleeding, sore throat, fever, jaundice.
- Drug-induced jaundice may persist up to 10 wk after withdrawal of drug.
- Methimazole does not induce hypothyroiditis.

METHOCARBAMOL

(meth-oh-kar′ba-mole)
Robaxin
Classifications: SKELETAL MUSCLE RELAXANT; CENTRAL-ACTING
Therapeutic: SKELETAL MUSCLE RELAXANT, CENTRAL ACTING
Prototype: Cyclobenzaprine
Pregnancy Category: C

AVAILABILITY 500 mg, 750 mg tablet; 100 mg/mL injection

ACTION & *THERAPEUTIC EFFECT*

Exerts skeletal muscle relaxant action by depressing multisynaptic pathways in the spinal cord and possibly by sedative effect. *No direct action on skeletal muscles; just on multisynaptic pathways in spinal cord that control muscular spasm.*

USES Adjunct to physical therapy and other measures in management of discomfort associated with acute musculoskeletal disorders. Also used intravenously as adjunct in management of neuromuscular manifestations of tetanus.

CONTRAINDICATIONS Comatose states; CNS depression; acidosis, older adults; kidney dysfunction (injectable methocarbamol contains polyethylene glycol 300 in vehicle, which may cause urea retention and acidotic problems); pregnancy (category C).

CAUTIOUS USE Epilepsy; females of childbearing age; renal disease, renal failure, renal impairment, seizure disorder; lactation, children less than 16 y.

ROUTE & DOSAGE

Acute Musculoskeletal Disorders

Adult: **PO** 1.5 g q.i.d. for 2–3 d, then 4–4.5 g/d in 3–6 divided doses **IV/IM** 1 g q8h

Tetanus

Adult: **IV** 1–3 g may be repeated q6h
Child: **PO** 15 mg/kg repeated q6h as needed up to 1.8 g/m²/d for 3 consecutive d if necessary

ADMINISTRATION

Intramuscular

▪ Do not exceed IM dose of 5 mL (0.5 g) into each gluteal region. Insert needle deep and carefully aspirate. Inject drug slowly. Rotate injection sites and observe daily for evidence of irritation.

Intravenous

PREPARE: Direct: May be given undiluted or diluted in up to 250 mL of NS or D5W.

ADMINISTER: Direct: Give at a rate of 300 mg or fraction thereof over 1 min or longer.

▪ Keep patient recumbent during and for at least 15 min after IV injection in order to reduce possibility of orthostatic hypotension and other adverse reactions. ▪ Monitor vital signs and IV flow rate. ▪ Take care to avoid extravasation of IV solution, which may result in thrombophlebitis and sloughing.

INCOMPATIBILITIES Y-site: Furosemide.

▪ Store at 15°–30° C (59°–86° F).

ADVERSE EFFECTS (≥1%) **Body as a Whole:** Fever, <u>anaphylactic reaction</u>, flushing, syncope, convulsions. **Skin:** Urticaria, pruritus, rash, thrombophlebitis, pain, sloughing (with extravasation). **Special Senses:** Conjunctivitis, blurred vision, nasal congestion. **CNS:** *Drowsiness, dizziness, light-headedness,* headache. **CV:** Hypotension, bradycardia. **GI:** Nausea, metallic taste. **Hematologic:** Slight reduction of white cell count with prolonged therapy. **Renal:** Polyethylene glycol in the injection may increase preexisting acidosis and urea retention in patients with renal impairment.

DIAGNOSTIC TEST INTERFERENCE Methocarbamol may cause false increases in *urinary 5-HIAA* (with *nitrosonaphthol reagent*) and *VMA (Gitlow method).*

INTERACTIONS Drug: Alcohol and other CNS DEPRESSANTS enhance CNS depression.

PHARMACOKINETICS Absorption: Readily absorbed from GI tract. **Onset:** 30 min. **Peak:** 1–2 h. **Metabolism:** In liver. **Elimination:** In urine. **Half-Life:** 1–2 h.

CLINICAL IMPLICATIONS

Assessment & Drug Effects

▪ Lab tests: Obtain periodic WBC counts during prolonged therapy.
▪ Monitor vital signs closely during IV infusion.
▪ Supervise ambulation following parenteral administration.

Common adverse effects in *italic*, life-threatening effects <u>underlined</u>; generic names in **bold**; classifications in SMALL CAPS; ✤ Canadian drug name; ☺ Prototype drug

965

Patient & Family Education

- Make position changes slowly, particularly from lying down to upright position; dangle legs before standing.
- Be aware that adverse reactions after oral administration are usually mild and transient and subside with dosage reduction. Use caution regarding drowsiness and dizziness. Avoid activities requiring mental alertness and physical coordination until response to drug is known.
- Urine may darken to brown, black, or green on standing.

METHOHEXITAL SODIUM

(meth-oh-hex′i-tal)
Brevital Sodium
Classifications: GENERAL ANESTHETIC; BARBITURATE
Therapeutic: GENERAL ANESTHETIC; BARBITUATE
Prototype: Thiopental
Pregnancy Category: B
Controlled Substance: Schedule IV

AVAILABILITY 500 mg, 2.5 g, 5 g powder for injection

ACTION & *THERAPEUTIC EFFECT*
Rapid, ultra-short-acting barbiturate anesthetic agent. More potent than thiopental but has less cumulative effect and shorter duration of action, and recovery is more rapid. *Induces brief general anesthesia without analgesia by depression of the CNS.*

USES Induction of anesthesia, as supplement for other anesthetics, and as general anesthetic for brief operative procedures.

CONTRAINDICATIONS Hypersensitivity to methohexital sodium; agranulocytosis; barbiturate hypersensitivity; hepatic encephalopathy; intraarterial administration; shock, heart failure, PVD, severe hypo- and hypertension, respiratory depression, infants <1 mo; neonates.

CAUTIOUS USE Pregnancy (category B), labor; adrenal insufficiency, anemia, carbamazepine hypersensitivity; cardiac disease, COPD; uncontrolled asthma, status asthmaticus, sleep apnea, respiratory insufficiency, CNS depression; depression, ethanol intoxication; exfoliative dermatitis; hepatic disease; hydantoin hypersensitivity, older adult; neuromuscular disease; obesity; porphyria; pulmonary disease, renal disease, uremia, renal impairment; seizure disorders, status epilepticus, seizures; shock.

ROUTE & DOSAGE

Induction of Anesthesia
Adult: **IV** 50–120 mg at a rate of 5 mg q5min, then 20–40 mg q4–7min prn
Child: **IV** 1–2 mg/kg **PR** 20–35 mg/kg (max: 500 mg/dose)
Infant >1 mo: **IM** 6.6–10 mg/kg of 5% solution **PR** 25 mg/kg of 1% solution

ADMINISTRATION

Intravenous

- Give to recumbent patient. Fall in BP may occur in susceptible patients receiving drug in upright position.
- Note: Verify with physician correct IV or IM concentration for infants or children as well as rate of IV infusion for administration to children.

PREPARE: **Direct:** Prepare a 1% solution (10 mg/mL) by diluting with sterile water for injection, D5W, or NS. Use only clear, colorless solutions. Do not allow contact with rubber stoppers or parts of syringes treated with silicone because solution is incompatible with acid solutions (see IMCOMPATIBILITIES).

ADMINISTER: Direct: Give 5 mg over 5–10 sec.

INCOMPATIBILITIES Solution/additive: Atropine, chlorpromazine, glycopyrrolate, hydralazine, kanamycin, lidocaine, mechlorethamine, methyldopa, prochlorperazine, promazine, promethazine, streptomycin. Y-site: Fenoldopam.

▪ Store drug in sterile water for injection at room temperature for at least 6 wk. Solutions prepared with isotonic NaCl injection or 5% dextrose injection are stable for **ONLY** about 24 h.

ADVERSE EFFECTS (≥1%) **CV:** Hypotension, cardiac arrhythmias, cardiac arrest. **Musculoskeletal:** Muscle spasm. **CNS:** Postoperative psychomotor impairment that persists for 24 hours, anxiety, drowsiness, emergence delirium, restlessness, and seizures. **Respiratory:** Bronchospasm, cough, hiccups, respiratory depression, apnea, dyspnea, <u>respiratory arrest</u>. **Skin:** Phlebitis and nerve injury adjacent to the injection site, local irritation, edema, ulceration, necrosis.

INTERACTIONS Drug: Alcohol and other CNS DEPRESSANTS enhance CNS depression.

PHARMACOKINETICS Absorption: 17% absorbed PR. **Distribution:** Crosses CNS, placenta and excreted in breast milk. **Metabolism:** Oxidized in liver. **Elimination:** Primarily excreted in urine.

CLINICAL IMPLICATIONS

Assessment & Drug Effects
▪ Hiccups are common, particularly with rapid injection; they sometimes persist after anesthesia.

▪ Keep facilities for assisting respiration and administration of oxygen readily available in the event of respiratory distress.

METHOTREXATE SODIUM ℗

(meth-oh-trex′ate)

MTX

Classifications: ANTINEOPLASTIC AGENT; ANTIMETABOLITE, ANTIFOLATE; IMMUNOSUPPRESSANT

Therapeutic: ANTINEOPLASTIC; IMMUNOSUPPRESSANT; ANTIFOLATE

Pregnancy Category: X

AVAILABILITY 2.5 mg tablets; 2.5 mg/mL, 25 mg/mL injection

ACTION & *THERAPEUTIC EFFECT*
Antimetabolite and folic acid antagonist. Blocks folic acid participation in nucleic acid synthesis, thereby interfering with mitotic process. Rapidly proliferating tissues (malignant cells, bone marrow) are sensitive to interference of the mitotic process by this drug. *In psoriasis, reproductive rate of epithelial cells is higher than in normal cells. Induces remission slowly; use often preceded by other antineoplastic therapies. Also has immunosuppressant effects.*

USES Principally in combination regimens to maintain induced remissions in neoplastic diseases. Effective in treatment of gestational choriocarcinoma and hydatidiform mole and as immunosuppressant in kidney transplantation, for acute and subacute leukemias and leukemic meningitis, especially in children. Used in lymphosarcoma, in certain inoperable tumors of head, neck, and pelvis, and in mycosis fungoides. Also used to treat severe psoriasis nonresponsive to other forms of therapy, rheumatoid arthritis.

Common adverse effects in *italic*, life-threatening effects <u>underlined</u>; generic names in **bold**; classifications in SMALL CAPS; ✦ Canadian drug name; ℗ Prototype drug

967

UNLABELED USES Psoriatic arthritis, SLE, polymyositis.

CONTRAINDICATIONS Pregnancy (category X), men and women in childbearing age; lactation; hepatic and renal insufficiency; concomitant administration of hepatotoxic drugs and hematopoietic depressants; alcohol; ultraviolet exposure to psoriatic lesions; pre-existing blood dyscrasias.

CAUTIOUS USE Infections; peptic ulcer, ulcerative colitis; very young or old patients; cancer patients with preexisting bone marrow impairment; poor nutritional status.

ROUTE & DOSAGE

Trophoblastic Neoplasm
Adult: **PO/IM** 15–30 mg/d for 5 d, repeat for 3–5 courses

Leukemia
Adult: **IM/IV Loading Dose** 3.3 mg/m^2/d **PO/IM/IV Maintenance Dose** 30 mg/m^2 weekly in 2 doses

Meningeal Leukemia
Child: **Intrathecal** 10–15 mg/m^2

Lymphoma
Adult: **PO** 10–25 mg/kg for 4–8 d

Osteosarcoma
Adult: **IV** 12 g/m^2, dose repeated at weeks 4, 5, 6, 7, 11, 12, 15, 16, 29, 39, 44, 45

Psoriasis/Rheumatoid Arthritis
Adult: **PO** 2.5 mg q12h for 3 doses each wk or 7.5 mg once/wk
Child: **PO/IM** 5–15 mg/m^2/wk as single dose or in 3 divided doses 12 h apart

Mycosis Fungoides
Adult: **PO/IM** 5–50 mg weekly

ADMINISTRATION

Oral
- Give 1 h before or 2 h after meals.
- Use a test dose (5–10 mg parenterally) 1 wk before therapy for treatment of psoriasis.
- Avoid skin exposure and inhalation of drug particles.

Intravenous
Note: Verify correct IV concentration and rate of infusion for administration to children with physician.

PREPARE: **Direct:** Reconstitute powder vial by adding 2 mL of NS or D5W without preservatives to each 5 mg to yield 2.5 mg/mL. Reconstitute 1 g high-dose vial with 19.4 mL D5W or NS to yield 50 mg/mL. **IV Infusion:** Further dilute contents of high-dose vial in D5W or NS.

ADMINISTER: **Direct:** Give at rate of 10 mg or fraction thereof over 60 s. **IV Infusion:** Give over 1–4 h or as prescribed.

INCOMPATIBILITIES **Solution/additive: Bleomycin, metoclopramide, prednisolone, ranitidine. Y-site: Chlorpromazine, droperidol, gemcitabine, idarubicin, ifosfamide, midazolam, nalbuphine, promethazine, propofol.**

- Preserve drug in tight, light-resistant container.

ADVERSE EFFECTS (≥1%) **CNS:** *Headache,* drowsiness, blurred vision, dizziness, aphasia, hemiparesis; arachnoiditis, convulsions (after intrathecal administration); mental confusion, tremors, ataxia, coma. **GI:** <u>Hepatotoxicity</u>, GI ulcerations and hemorrhage, *ulcerative stomatitis, glossitis, gingivitis,* pharyngitis, nausea, vomiting, diarrhea, <u>hepatic cirrhosis</u>. **Urogenital:** Defective oogenesis or spermatogenesis, nephropathy, hematuria, menstrual dysfunction, infertility, abortion, fetal defects. **Hematologic:** *Leukopenia, thrombocytopenia,* anemia, <u>marked myelosuppression, aplastic bone marrow,</u> telangiectasis, thrombophlebitis at intraarterial catheter site, hypogammaglobulinemia, and hyperuricemia. **Skin:** Erythematous rashes, pruritus, urticaria, folliculitis, vasculitis, photosensitivity, depigmentation, hyperpigmentation, alopecia. **Body as a Whole:** Malaise, undue fatigue, systemic toxicity (after intrathecal and intraarterial administration), chills, fever, decreased resistance to infection, septicemia, osteoporosis, metabolic changes precipitating diabetes and <u>sudden death, pneumonitis, pulmonary fibrosis.</u>

DIAGNOSTIC TEST INTERFERENCE
Severe reactions may occur when *live vaccines* are administered because of immunosuppressive activity of methotrexate.

INTERACTIONS Drug: Acitretin, alcohol, azathioprine, sulfasalazine increase risk of hepatotoxicity; **chloramphenicol, etretinate,** SALICYLATES, NSAIDS, SULFONAMIDES, SULFONYLUREAS, **phenylbutazone, phenytoin,** TETRACYCLINES, **PABA, penicillin, probenecid** may increase methotrexate levels with increased toxicity; **folic acid** may alter response to methotrexate. May increase **theophylline** levels; **cholestyramine** enhances methotrexate clearance. **Herbal: Echinacea** may increase risk of hepatotoxicity. **Food: Caffeine** >180 mg/d (3–4 cups) may decrease effectiveness for rheumatoid arthritis.

PHARMACOKINETICS Absorption:
Readily absorbed from GI tract. **Peak:** 0.5–2 h IM/IV; 1–4 h PO. **Distribution:** Widely distributed with highest concentrations in kidneys, gallbladder, spleen, liver, and skin; minimal passage across blood–brain barrier; crosses placenta; distributed into breast milk. **Metabolism:** In liver. **Elimination:** Primarily in urine. **Half-Life:** 2–4 h.

CLINICAL IMPLICATIONS
Assessment & Drug Effects
- Lab tests: Obtain baseline liver and kidney function, CBC with differential, platelet count, and chest x-rays. Repeat weekly during therapy. Monitor blood glucose and HbA_{1c} periodically in diabetics.
- Prolonged treatment with small frequent doses may lead to hepatotoxicity, which is best diagnosed by liver biopsy.
- Monitor for and report ulcerative stomatitis with glossitis and gingivitis, often the first signs of toxicity. Inspect mouth daily; report patchy necrotic areas, bleeding and discomfort, or overgrowth (black, furry tongue).
- Monitor I&O ratio and pattern. Keep patient well hydrated (about 2000 mL/24 h).
- Prevent exposure to infections or colds during periods of leukopenia. Be alert to onset of agranulocytosis (cough, extreme fatigue, sore throat, chills, fever) and report symptoms promptly.
- Be alert for and report symptoms of thrombocytopenia (e.g., ecchymoses, petechiae, epistaxis, melena, hematuria, vaginal bleeding, slow and protracted oozing following trauma).

Patient & Family Education
- Report promptly any abnormal symptoms to physician.
- Avoid or moderate alcohol ingestion, which increases the incidence and severity of methotrexate hepatotoxicity.

M

Common adverse effects in *italic*, life-threatening effects <u>underlined</u>; generic names in **bold**; classifications in SMALL CAPS; ✢ Canadian drug name; ◑ Prototype drug

969

- Practice fastidious mouth care to prevent infection, provide comfort, and maintain adequate nutritional status.
- Do not self-medicate with vitamins. Some OTC compounds may include folic acid (or its derivatives), which alters methotrexate response.
- Use contraceptive measures during and for at least 8 wk following therapy.
- Avoid exposure to sunlight and ultraviolet light. Wear sunglasses and sunscreen.

METHOXSALEN ℗

(meth-ox'a-len)

8-MOP, Oxsoralen, Uvadex

Classifications: PSORALEN; PIGMENTING AGENT

Therapeutic: PIGMENTING AGENT

Pregnancy Category: C

AVAILABILITY 10 mg capsules, 20 mcg/mL solution; 1% lotion

ACTION & *THERAPEUTIC EFFECT*

Plant derivative with strong photosensitizing effects: used with ultraviolet-A light (UVA) in therapeutic regimens called PUVA (P-psoralen). After photoactivation by long wavelength, UVA, methoxsalen combines with epidermal cell DNA causing photodamage (cytotoxic action). *Photodamage inhibits rapid and uncontrolled epidermal cell turnover characteristic of psoriasis. Results in an inflammatory reaction with erythema. Strongly melanogenic.*

USES With controlled exposure to UVA to repigment vitiliginous skin and for symptomatic treatment of severe disabling psoriasis that is refractory to other forms of therapy.

UNLABELED USES (PUVA therapy) mycosis fungoides.

CONTRAINDICATIONS Sunburn, sensitivity (or its history) to psoralens, diseases associated with photosensitivity (e.g., SLE, albinism, melanoma or its history); invasive squamous cell cancer; cataract; aphakia; previous exposure to arsenic or ionizing radiation; pregnancy (category C), lactation. Safety (oral) in children is not established.

CAUTIOUS USE Hepatic insufficiency; GI disease; chronic infection; treatment with known photosensitizing agents; immunosuppressed patient; cardiovascular disease; lactation. Safety (lotion) in children <12 y is not established.

ROUTE & DOSAGE

Idiopathic Vitiligo

Adult: **Topical** Apply lotion 1–2 h before exposure to UV light once/wk

Psoriasis

Adult: **PO** Give 1.5–2 h before exposure to UV light 2–3 times/wk: *<30 kg,* 10 mg; *30–50 kg,* 20 mg; *51–65 kg,* 30 mg; *66–80 kg,* 40 mg; *81–90 kg,* 50 mg; *91–115 kg,* 60 mg; *>115 kg,* 70 mg

ADMINISTRATION

- Note: Methoxsalen therapy with UV light (PUVA therapy) should be done under the complete control of a physician with special competence and experience in photochemotherapy.

Oral

- Give with milk or food to prevent GI distress.
- Maintain consistent time relationship between food–drug ingestion.

Food digestion and absorption appear to affect drug serum levels.

Topical

- Only small (<10 cm^2), well-defined areas are treated with lotion. Systemic treatment is used for large areas.
- Apply lotion with cotton swabs, allow to dry 1–2 min, then reapply. Protect borders of the lesion with petrolatum and sunscreen lotion to prevent hyperpigmentation.
- Use finger cots or gloves to apply lotion and prevent photosensitization and burned skin.
- Apply sunscreen lotion to the skin for about one third of the initial exposure time during PUVA therapy until there is sufficient tanning. Do not apply to psoriatic areas before treatment.
- Store lotion and capsules at 15°–30° C (59°–86° F) in light-resistant containers unless otherwise directed by manufacturer.

ADVERSE EFFECTS (≥1%) **CNS:** Nervousness, dizziness, headache, mental depression or excitation, vertigo, insomnia. **Special Senses:** Cataract formation, ocular damage. **GI:** Cheilitis, *nausea* and other GI disturbances, toxic hepatitis. **Skin:** Phototoxic effects: <u>severe edema and erythema</u>, *pruritus,* painful blisters; <u>burning</u>, peeling, thinning, freckling, and accelerated aging of skin; hyper- or hypopigmentation; severe skin pain (lasting 1–2 mo), photoallergic contact dermatitis (with topical use), exacerbation of latent photosensitive dermatoses, <u>malignant melanoma</u> (rare). **Body as a Whole:** Transient loss of muscular coordination, edema, leg cramps, systemic immune effects, drug fever.

INTERACTIONS Drug: Anthralin, coal tar, griseofulvin, PHENOTHIAZINES, **nalidixic acid,** SULFONAMIDES, BACTERIOSTATIC SOAPS, TETRACYCLINES, THIAZIDES compound photosensitizing effects. **Food:** Food will increase peak and extent of absorption.

PHARMACOKINETICS Absorption: Variably from GI tract. **Peak:** 2 h. **Duration:** 8–10 h. **Distribution:** Preferentially taken up by epidermal cells; distributes into lens of eye. **Elimination:** 80–90% in urine within 8 h. **Half-Life:** 0.75–2.4 h.

CLINICAL IMPLICATIONS

Assessment & Drug Effects

- Schedule a pretreatment ophthalmologic exam to rule out cataracts; repeat periodically during treatment and at yearly intervals thereafter.
- Lab tests: Monitor CBC, kidney and liver function, and antinuclear antibody tests during oral therapy.
- Fair-skinned patients appear to be at greatest risk for phototoxicity from PUVA therapy (see ADVERSE EFFECTS).
- Be aware that repigmentation is more rapid on fleshy areas (i.e., face, abdomen, buttocks) than on hands or feet.

Patient & Family Education

- Expect that effective repigmentation may require 6–9 mo of treatment; periodic treatment usually is necessary to retain pigmentation. If, after 3 mo of treatment, there is no apparent response, drug is discontinued.
- Avoid additional exposure to UV light (direct or indirect) for at least 8 h after oral drug ingestion and UVA exposure.
- Understand intended treatment schedule: After topical application, the initial sunlight exposure is limited to 1 min, with subsequent gradual and incremental exposures by prescription.

M

Common adverse effects in *italic*, life-threatening effects <u>underlined</u>; generic names in **bold**; classifications in SMALL CAPS; ✤ Canadian drug name; ⊘ Prototype drug

971

- Avoid additional UV light for 24–48 h after topical application and UVA exposure.
- Wear sunscreen lotion (with SPF 15 or higher) and protective clothing (hat, gloves) to cover all exposed areas including lips, to prevent burning or blistering if sunlight cannot be avoided after the treatment.
- Do not sunbathe for at least 48 h after PUVA treatment. Sunburn and photochemotherapy are additive in the production of burning and erythema.
- Wear wraparound sunglasses with UVA-absorbing properties both indoors and outdoors during daylight hours for 24 h. Do not substitute prescription sunglasses or photosensitive darkening glasses; they may actually increase danger of cataract formation.
- Alert physician to appearance of new psoriatic areas, flares, or regressed cleared skin areas during treatment and maintenance periods.

METHSCOPOLAMINE BROMIDE

(meth-skoe-pol′a-meen)
Pamine
Classifications: ANTICHOLINERGIC; ANTIMUSCARINIC; ANTISPASMODIC
Therapeutic: ANTISPASMODIC; ANTICHOLINERGIC
Prototype: Atropine
Pregnancy Category: C

AVAILABILITY 2.5 mg tablets

ACTION & *THERAPEUTIC EFFECT*
Methscopolamine decreases GI tone and decreases amplitude and frequency of peristaltic contractions of the esophagus, stomach, duodenum, jejunum, ileum, and colon. Greater selectivity in blocking vagal impulses from GI tract than either scopolamine or atropine. *Its spasmolytic and antisecretory actions are quantitatively similar to those of atropine but they last longer.*

USES Adjunct in treatment of peptic ulcer, irritable bowel syndrome, and a variety of other GI conditions. Also may be used to control excessive sweating and salivation, migraine headaches, and premenstrual cramps.

CONTRAINDICATIONS Hypersensitivity to any of the drug's constituents; prostatic hypertrophy; pyloric obstruction; intestinal atony; tachycardia, cardiac disease; MS; pyloric stenosis; pregnancy (category C), lactation.

CAUTIOUS USE Older adult and debilitated patients; chronic pulmonary diseases (COPD).

ROUTE & DOSAGE

Irritable Bowel Syndrome
Adult: **PO** 2.5–5 mg 30 min a.c. and h.s.

ADMINISTRATION

Oral
- Give 30 min before meals and at bedtime.
- Preserve in tight, light-resistant containers.

ADVERSE EFFECTS (≥1%) **GI:** Dry mouth, constipation. **Special Senses:** Blurred vision. **CNS:** Dizziness, drowsiness, flushing of skin. **Urogenital:** Urinary hesitancy or retention.

INTERACTIONS Drug: Amantadine, TRICYCLIC ANTIDEPRESSANTS increase anticholinergic effects; may increase effects of **atenolol, digoxin;** may decrease effectiveness of PHENOTHIAZINES.

Common adverse effects in *italic*, life-threatening effects <u>underlined</u>; generic names in **bold**; classifications in SMALL CAPS; ♣ Canadian drug name; ⊙ Prototype drug

PHARMACOKINETICS Absorption: Erratic after PO administration. **Onset:** Approximately 1 h. **Duration:** 4–6 h. **Elimination:** Primarily in urine and bile; some unchanged drug excreted in feces.

CLINICAL IMPLICATIONS

Assessment & Drug Effects
- Incidence and severity of adverse effects are generally dose-related. Dosage is usually maintained at a level that produces slight dryness of mouth.
- Report urinary retention promptly; may indicate discontinuation.

Patient & Family Education
- Do not drive or engage in potentially hazardous activities until response to drug is known.
- Make position changes slowly and in stages.
- Learn measures to relieve dry mouth; rinse mouth frequently with water, suck hard candy.

METHYCLOTHIAZIDE

(meth-i-kloe-thye′a-zide)
Duretic ♦, Enduron
Classifications: THIAZIDE DIURETIC; ANTIHYPERTENSIVE AGENT
Therapeutic: ANTIHYPERTENSIVE; THIAZIDE DIURETIC
Prototype: Hydrochlorothiazide
Pregnancy Category: D first trimester; C second and third trimester

AVAILABILITY 2.5 mg, 5 mg tablets

ACTION & *THERAPEUTIC EFFECT*
Thiazide diuretic similar to hydrochlorothiazide. Diuretic effect results from a drug-induced inhibition of the renal tubular reabsorption of electrolytes. The excretion of sodium and chloride is enhanced.

There is also a loss of potassium ions via the kidney. BP is lowered, probably by the loss of sodium, chloride and water, and, consequently, blood volume. Edema is also decreased in CHF patients by the same mechanism. *Antihypertensive effect as well as enhanced excretion of sodium and water.*

USES Antihypertensive treatment and adjunctively in the management of edema associated with CHF, renal pathology, and hepatic cirrhosis.

CONTRAINDICATIONS Hypersensitivity to thiazides, and sulfonamide derivatives; anuria, hypokalemia, pregnancy (category D) in first trimester and pregnancy (category C second and third trimester), lactation. **CAUTIOUS USE** Renal disease; impaired kidney or liver function; older adults; gout; SLE; hypercalcemia; diabetes mellitus, children.

ROUTE & DOSAGE

Edema
Adult: **PO** 2.5–10 mg once/d or 3–5 times/wk
Hypertension
Adult: **PO** 2.5–10 mg/d
Child: **PO** 0.05–0.2 mg/kg/d

ADMINISTRATION

Oral
- Give early in a.m. after eating (reduces gastric irritation) to prevent sleep interruption because of diuresis. If 2 doses are ordered, administer second dose no later than 3 p.m.
- Store at 15°–30° C (59°–86° F) unless otherwise instructed.

ADVERSE EFFECTS (≥1%) **Body as a Whole:** Postural hypotension,

M

Common adverse effects in *italic*, life-threatening effects underlined; generic names in **bold**; classifications in SMALL CAPS; ♦ Canadian drug name; ⓟ Prototype drug

973

sialadenitis, unusual fatigue, dizziness, paresthesias. **Skin:** Photosensitivity. **Special Senses:** Yellow vision. **Metabolic:** *Hypokalemia*. **Hematologic:** Agranulocytosis.

INTERACTIONS Drug: Amphotericin B, CORTICOSTEROIDS increase hypokalemic effects; may antagonize hypoglycemic effects of **insulin**, SULFONYLUREAS; **cholestyramine, colestipol** decrease thiazide absorption; intensifies hypoglycemic and hypotensive effects of **diazoxide;** increased potassium and magnesium loss may cause **digoxin** toxicity; decreases **lithium** excretion, increasing its toxicity; NSAIDS may attenuate diuresis, and risk of NSAID-induced kidney failure increased.

PHARMACOKINETICS Absorption: Incompletely absorbed. **Onset:** 2 h. **Peak:** 6 h. **Duration:** >24 h. **Distribution:** Distributed throughout extracellular tissue; concentrates in kidney; crosses placenta; distributed in breast milk. **Metabolism:** Does not appear to be metabolized. **Elimination:** In urine.

CLINICAL IMPLICATIONS

Assessment & Drug Effects

- Expect antihypertensive effects in 3–4 d; maximal effects may require 3–4 wk.
- Monitor BP and I&O ratio during first phase of antihypertensive therapy. Report a sudden fall in BP, which may initiate severe postural hypotension and potentially dangerous perfusion problems, especially in the extremities.
- Lab tests: Periodic serum electrolytes and CBC with differential.
- Monitor patient for S&S of hypokalemia (see Appendix F). Report promptly. Physician may change dose and institute replacement therapy.

Patient & Family Education

- Eat a balanced diet to protect against hypokalemia; generally not severe even with long-term therapy. Prevent onset by eating potassium-rich foods including a banana (about 370 mg potassium) and at least 180 mL (6 oz) orange juice (about 330 mg potassium) every day.
- Watch carefully for loss of glycemic control (diabetics) and early signs of hyperglycemia (see Appendix F). Symptoms are slow to develop.
- Avoid OTC drugs unless the physician approves them. Many preparations contain both potassium and sodium, and may induce electrolyte imbalance adverse effects.
- Older adults are more responsive to excessive diuresis; orthostatic hypotension may be a problem.
- Change positions slowly and in stages from lying down to upright positions; avoid hot baths or showers, extended exposure to sunlight, and standing still. Accept assistance as necessary to prevent falling.
- Do not drive or engage in potentially hazardous activities until adjustment to the hypotensive effects of drug has been made.

METHYLDOPA 🅟

(meth-ill-doe′pa)
Apo-Methyldopa ♣, **Novomedopa** ♣

METHYLDOPATE HYDROCHLORIDE

(meth-ill-doe′pate)
Classifications: CENTRAL-ACTING ANTIHYPERTENSIVE; ALPHA-ADRENERGIC AGONIST
Therapeutic: ANTIHYPERTENSIVE, CENTRAL-ACTING
Pregnancy Category: B

M

Common adverse effects in *italic*, life-threatening effects underlined; generic names in **bold**; classifications in SMALL CAPS; ♣ Canadian drug name; 🅟 Prototype drug

AVAILABILITY 125 mg, 250 mg, 500 mg tablets; 50 mg/mL injection

ACTION & *THERAPEUTIC EFFECT* Structurally related to catecholamines and their precursors. Has weak neurotransmitter properties; inhibits decarboxylation of dopa, thereby reducing concentration of dopamine, a precursor of norepinephrine. It also inhibits the precursor of serotonin. Reduces renal vascular resistance; maintains cardiac output without acceleration, but may slow heart rate; tends to support sodium and water retention. *Lowers standing and supine BP, and unlike adrenergic blockers, is not so prone to produce orthostatic hypotension, diurnal BP variations, or exercise hypertension.*

USES Treatment of sustained moderate to severe hypertension, particularly in patients with kidney dysfunction. Also used in selected patients with carcinoid disease. Parenteral form has been used for treatment of hypertensive crises but is not preferred because of its slow onset of action.

CONTRAINDICATIONS Active liver disease (hepatitis, cirrhosis); pheochromocytoma; blood dyscrasias. Safety during pregnancy (category B) is not established.

CAUTIOUS USE History of impaired liver or kidney function or disease; renal failure; autoimmune disease; cardiac disease; angina pectoris; history of mental depression; Parkinson's disease; young or older adult patients.

ROUTE & DOSAGE

Hypertension
Adult: **PO** 250 mg b.i.d. or t.i.d., may be increased up to 3 g/d in divided doses, Usual range 250–1000 mg total per day

IV 250–500 mg q6h, may be increased up to 1 g q6h
Geriatric: **PO** 125 mg b.i.d. or t.i.d., may increase gradually (max: 3 g/d)
Child: **PO** 10 mg/kg/d in 2–4 divided doses (max: 3 g/d) **IV** 2–4 mg/kg/d in divided doses (max: 3 g/d)

Renal Impairment Dosage
Cl_{cr} >50 mL/min: dose q8h; Cl_{cr} 10–50 mL/min: dose q8–12h; Cl_{cr} <10 mL/min: dose q12–24h

ADMINISTRATION

Oral
▪ Make dosage increases in evening to minimize daytime sedation. Some patients maintain adequate BP control with a single evening dose.

Intravenous

***PREPARE:* Intermittent:** Dilute in 100–200 mL of D5W, as needed, to yield 10 mg/mL.
***ADMINISTER:* Intermittent:** Give over 30–60 min.
***INCOMPATIBILITIES* Solution/additive: Amphotericin B, hydrocortisone, methohexital, tetracycline. Y-site: Fat emulsion.**

ADVERSE EFFECTS (≥1%) **Body as a Whole:** Hypersensitivity (*fever, skin eruptions, ulcerations of soles of feet, flu-like symptoms, lymphadenopathy, eosinophilia*). **CNS:** *Sedation, drowsiness,* sluggishness, headache, weakness, fatigue, dizziness, vertigo, *decrease in mental acuity,* inability to concentrate, amnesia-like syndrome, parkinsonism, mild psychoses, depression, nightmares. **CV:** Orthostatic hypotension, syncope, bradycardia, myocarditis, edema, weight gain *(sodium and water retention),* paradoxic hypertensive reaction (especially with IV

M

Common adverse effects in *italic*, life-threatening effects <u>underlined</u>; generic names in **bold**, classifications in SMALL CAPS; ✚ Canadian drug name; ⊘ Prototype drug

975

administration). **GI:** Diarrhea, constipation, abdominal distension, malabsorption syndrome, nausea, vomiting, dry mouth, sore or black tongue, sialadenitis, abnormal liver function tests, jaundice, hepatitis, <u>hepatic necrosis</u> (rare). **Hematologic:** *Positive direct Coombs' test* (common especially in African-Americans), <u>granulocytopenia</u>. **Special Senses:** *Nasal stuffiness.* **Endocrine:** Gynecomastia, lactation, *decreased libido, impotence,* hypothermia (large doses), positive tests for lupus and rheumatoid factors. **Skin:** Granulomatous skin lesions.

DIAGNOSTIC TEST INTERFERENCE
Methyldopa may interfere with *serum creatinine* measurements using *alkaline picrate method, AST* by *colorimetric methods,* and *uric acid* measurements by *phosphotungstate method* (with high methyldopa blood levels); it may produce false elevations of *urinary catecholamines* and increase in *serum amylase* in methyldopa-induced sialadenitis.

INTERACTIONS Drug: AMPHETAMINES, TRICYCLIC ANTIDEPRESSANTS, PHENOTHIAZINES, BARBITUATES may attenuate antihypertensive response; methyldopa may inhibit effectiveness of **ephedrine; haloperidol** may exacerbate psychiatric symptoms; with **levodopa** additive hypotension, increased CNS toxicity, especially psychosis; increases risk of **lithium** toxicity; **methotrimeprazine** causes excessive hypotension; MAO INHIBITORS may cause hallucinations; **phenoxybenzamine** may cause urinary incontinence. **Herbal:** Licorice may affect electrolyte levels; ephedra, yohimbe, ginseng may decrease efficacy.

PHARMACOKINETICS Absorption: About 50% absorbed from GI tract. **Peak:** 4–6 h. **Duration:** 24 h PO; 10–16 h IV. **Distribution:** Crosses placenta, distributed into breast milk. **Metabolism:** In liver and GI tract. **Elimination:** Primarily in urine. **Half-Life:** 1.7 h.

CLINICAL IMPLICATIONS
Assessment & Drug Effects
- Check BP and pulse at least q30min until stabilized during IV infusion and observe for adequacy of urinary output.
- Take BP taken at regular intervals in lying, sitting, and standing positions during period of dosage adjustment if physician requests.
- Be aware that transient sedation, drowsiness, mental depression, weakness, and headache commonly occur during first 24–72 h of therapy or whenever dosage is increased. Symptoms tend to disappear with continuation of therapy or dosage reduction.
- Supervision of ambulation in older adults and patients with impaired kidney function; both are particularly likely to manifest orthostatic hypotension with dizziness and light-headedness during period of dosage adjustment.
- Monitor fluid and electrolyte balance and I&O. Report oliguria and changes in I&O ratio. Weigh patient daily, and check for edema because methyldopa favors sodium and water retention.
- Lab tests: Schedule baseline and periodic blood counts and liver function tests especially during first 6–12 wk of therapy or if patient develops unexplained fever; periodic serum electrolytes.
- Be alert to and report symptoms of mental depression (e.g., anorexia, insomnia, inattention to

Common adverse effects in *italic*, life-threatening effects <u>underlined</u>; generic names in **bold**; classifications in SMALL CAPS; ♣ Canadian drug name; Ⓟ Prototype drug

personal hygiene, withdrawal). Drug-induced depression may persist after drug is withdrawn.

- Be alert that rising BP indicating tolerance to drug effect may occur during week 2 or 3 of therapy.

Patient & Family Education

- Exercise caution with hot baths and showers, prolonged standing in one position, and strenuous exercise that may enhance orthostatic hypotension. Make position changes slowly, particularly from lying down to upright posture; dangle legs a few minutes before standing.
- Avoid potentially hazardous tasks such as driving until response to drug is known; drug may affect ability to perform activities requiring concentrated mental effort, especially during first few days of therapy or whenever dosage is increased.
- Do not to take OTC medications unless approved by physician.

METHYLERGONOVINE MALEATE

(meth-ill-er-goe-noe′veen)
Methergine
Classifications: ADRENERGIC ANTAGONIST; ERGOT ALKALOID; OXYTOCIC
Therapeutic: ERGOT ALKALOID; OXYTOCIC
Prototype: Ergotamine
Pregnancy Category: C

AVAILABILITY 0.2 mg tablet; 0.2 mg/mL injections

ACTION & *THERAPEUTIC EFFECT*

Ergot alkaloid that induces rapid, sustained tetanic uterine contraction that shortens third stage of labor and reduces blood loss. *Administered after delivery of the pla-*centa. *It minimizes the risk of post-partal hemorrhage.*

USES Routine management after delivery of placenta and for postpartum atony, subinvolution, and hemorrhage. With full obstetric supervision, may be used during second stage of labor.

CONTRAINDICATIONS Hypersensitivity to ergot preparations; induction of labor; use prior to delivery of placenta; threatened spontaneous abortion; prolonged use; uterine sepsis; hypertension; toxemia; angina; arteriosclerosis; CAD; dysfunctional uterine bleeding; eclampsia; hypertension; MI; neonates; PVD; preeclampsia; Raynaud's disease; sepsis; stroke; thromboangiitis obliterans; thrombophlebitis; pregnancy (category C).
CAUTIOUS USE Diabetes mellitus; hepatic disease; migraine headaches; renal failure, renal impairment; pulmonary disease; lactation.

ROUTE & DOSAGE

Postpartum Hemorrhage
Adult: **PO** 0.2 q6–8h × 2–7 d **IM/IV** 0.2 mg q2–4h (max: 5 doses)

ADMINISTRATION

- Use parenteral routes only in emergencies.

Oral

- Note: Dosing should not exceed 1 wk.

Intravenous

PREPARE: Direct: Give undiluted or diluted in 5 mL of NS.
ADMINISTER: Direct: Give 0.2 mg or fraction thereof over 60 sec.

- Do not use ampuls containing discolored solution or visible particles.

Common adverse effects in *italic*, life-threatening effects <u>underlined</u>; generic names in **bold**; classifications in SMALL CAPS; ◆ Canadian drug name; ⊙ Prototype drug

977

- Store at 15°–30° C (59°–86° F) unless otherwise directed. Protect from light.

ADVERSE EFFECTS (≥1%) **GI:** *Nausea, vomiting* (especially with IV doses). **CV:** Severe hypertensive episodes, bradycardia. **Body as a Whole:** Allergic phenomena including <u>shock</u>, ergotism.

INTERACTIONS Drug: PARENTERAL SYMPATHOMIMETICS, other ERGOT ALKALOIDS, TRIPTANS add to pressor effects and carry risk of hypertension; PROTEASE INHIBITORS, itraconazole may increase the risk of toxicity.

PHARMACOKINETICS Absorption: Readily from GI tract. **Onset:** 5–15 min PO; 2–5 min IM; immediate IV. **Duration:** 3 or more h PO; 3 h IM; 45 min IV. **Distribution:** Distributed into breast milk. **Metabolism:** Slowly in liver. **Elimination:** Mainly in feces, small amount in urine. **Half-Life:** 0.5–2 h.

CLINICAL IMPLICATIONS
Assessment & Drug Effects
- Monitor vital signs (particularly BP) and uterine response during and after parenteral administration of methylergonovine until partum period is stabilized (about 1–2 h).
- Notify physician if BP suddenly increases or if there are frequent periods of uterine relaxation.

Patient & Family Education
- Report severe cramping for increased bleeding.
- Report any of the following: Cold or numb fingers or toes, nausea or vomiting, chest or muscle pain.

METHYLPHENIDATE HYDROCHLORIDE
(meth-ill-fen'i-date)

Concerta, Daytrana, Metadate CD, Metadate ER, Methylin, Methylin ER, Ritalin, Ritalin LA, Ritalin SR
Classifications: CEREBRAL STIMULANT
Therapeutic: CEREBRAL STIMULANT
Prototype: Amphetamine
Pregnancy Category: C
Controlled Substance: Schedule II

AVAILABILITY 5 mg, 10 mg, 20 mg tablets; 2.5 mg, 5 mg, 10 mg chewable tablets; 5 mg/5 mL, 10 mg/5 mL oral solution; 10 mg, 20 mg, 30 mg, 40 mg sustained release capsules; 10 mg, 18 mg, 20 mg, 27 mg, 36 mg, 54 mg sustained release tablet; 10 mg, 15 mg, 20 mg, 30 mg transdermal patch

ACTION & *THERAPEUTIC EFFECT*
Piperidine derivative with actions and abuse potential qualitatively similar to those of amphetamine. Acts mainly on cerebral cortex exerting a stimulant effect. Results in mild CNS and respiratory stimulation with potency intermediate between amphetamine and caffeine. *Effects are more prominent on mental rather than on motor activities. Also believed to have an anorexiant effect.*

USES Adjunctive therapy in hyperkinetic syndromes characterized by attention deficit disorder, narcolepsy, mild depression, and apathetic or withdrawn senile behavior.

CONTRAINDICATIONS Hypersensitivity to drug; history of marked anxiety, agitation; aortic stenosis; serious cardic disorders including arrhythmias; valvular heart disease; ventricular dysfunction; motor tics or Tourette's disease; substance abuse; severe anxiety, psychosis, major depression, suicidal ideation; glaucoma; pregnancy (category C), lactation, children <6 y of age.

CAUTIOUS USE Alcoholic; emotionally unstable patient; abrupt discontinuation; recent MI, anxiety, cardiac arrhythmias, cardiac disease, dysphagia, older adults; esophageal stricture, GI obstruction, heart failure, hepatic disease, hyperthyroidism, history of paralytic ileus, cystic fibrosis, mania, radiographic contrast administration, seizure disorder, hypertension; history of seizures.

ROUTE & DOSAGE

Narcolepsy

Adult: **PO** 10 mg b.i.d. or t.i.d. 30–45 min p.c. (range: 20–40 mg/d)

Attention Deficit Disorder

Child: **PO** 5–10 mg before breakfast and lunch, with a gradual increase of 5–10 mg/wk as needed (max: 60 mg/d) or 20–40 mg sustained release q.d. before breakfast (max dose: 72 mg q.d.) **Transdermal patch** 10 mg patch worn for 9 hours × 1 wk then taper as needed. Increase no more than once weekly. Apply 2 hr before desired effect.

Depression

Geriatric: **PO** 2.5 mg in morning before 9 a.m., may increase by 2.5–5 mg q2–3d (max: 20 mg/d) divided 7 a.m. and noon

ADMINISTRATION

Oral

- Give 30–45 min before meals. To avoid insomnia, give last dose before 6 p.m.
- Ensure that sustained-release form is not chewed or crushed. It must be swallowed whole.
- Can open Metadate CD capsules and sprinkle on food
- Store at 15°–30° C (59°–86° F).

ADVERSE EFFECTS (≥1%) **CNS:** Dizziness, drowsiness, *nervousness, insomnia.* **CV:** Palpitations, changes in BP and pulse rate, angina, cardiac arrhythmias, exacerbation of underlying CV conditions. **Special Senses:** Difficulty with accommodation, blurred vision. **GI:** Dry throat, anorexia, nausea; HEPATOTOXICITY; abdominal pain. **Body as a Whole:** Hypersensitivity reactions (rash, fever, arthralgia, urticaria, <u>exfoliative dermatitis</u>, erythema multiforme); long-term growth suppression.

INTERACTIONS Drug: MAO INHIBITORS may cause hypertensive crisis; antagonizes hypotensive effects of **guanethidine, bretylium;** potentiates action of CNS STIMULANTS (e.g. **amphetamine, caffeine**); may inhibit metabolism and increase serum levels of **fosphenytoin, phenytoin, phenobarbital, and primidone, warfarin,** TRICYCLIC ANTIDEPRESSANTS.

PHARMACOKINETICS Absorption: Readily from GI tract. Transdermal absorption increased with heat or inflamed skin. **Peak:** 1.9 h; 4–7 h sustained release, 2 h transdermal. **Duration:** 3–6 h; 8 h sustained release. **Elimination:** In urine.

CLINICAL IMPLICATIONS

Assessment & Drug Effects

- Monitor BP and pulse at appropriate intervals.
- Lab tests: Obtain periodic CBC with differential and platelet counts during prolonged therapy.
- Chronic abusive use can lead to tolerance, psychic dependence, and psychoses.
- Assess patient's condition with periodic drug-free periods during prolonged therapy.
- Supervise drug withdrawal carefully following prolonged use.

M

Common adverse effects in *italic*, life-threatening effects <u>underlined</u>; generic names in **bold**; classifications in SMALL CAPS; ✦ Canadian drug name; ⊚ Prototype drug

979

Abrupt withdrawal may result in severe depression and psychotic behavior.

Patient & Family Education

- Report adverse effects to physician, particularly nervousness and insomnia. These effects may diminish with time or require reduction of dosage or omission of afternoon or evening dose.
- Check weight at least 2 or 3 times weekly and report weight loss. Check height and weight in children; failure to gain in either should be reported to physician.

METHYLPREDNISOLONE

(meth-ill-pred-niss′oh-lone)
Medrol

METHYLPREDNISOLONE ACETATE

Depo-Medrol

METHYLPREDNISOLONE SODIUM SUCCINATE

A-Methapred, Solu-Medrol

Classifications: HORMONE; ADRENAL CORTICOSTEROID; ANTIINFLAMMATORY

Therapeutic: ADRENAL CORTICOSTEROID; ANTIINFLAMMATORY
Prototype: Prednisone
Pregnancy Category: C

AVAILABILITY Methylprednisolone 2 mg, 4 mg, 8 mg, 16 mg, 24 mg, 32 mg tablets; **Methylprednisolone Acetate** 20 mg/mL, 40 mg/mL, 80 mg/mL injection; **Methylprednisolone Sodium Succinate** 40 mg, 125 mg, 500 mg, 1 g, 2 g powder for injection

ACTION & *THERAPEUTIC EFFECT*
Intermediate-acting synthetic adrenal corticosteroid with similar glucocorticoid activity; has considerably fewer sodium and water retention effects than hydrocortisone. Acetate has longer duration of action and more rapid onset of activity than parent compound. Sodium succinate form is characterized by rapid onset of action and is used for emergency therapy of short duration. It inhibits phagocytosis, and release of allergic substances. Also modifies the immune response of the body to various stimuli. *Has antiinflammatory and immunosuppressive properties.*

USES An antiinflammatory agent in the management of acute and chronic inflammatory diseases, for palliative management of neoplastic diseases, and for control of severe acute and chronic allergic processes. High-dose, short-term therapy: management of acute bronchial asthma, prevention of fat embolism in patient with long-bone fracture. Short term management of rheumatic disorders.
UNLABELED USES Acetate form used as a long-acting contraceptive and for spinal cord injury, lupus nephritis, multiple sclerosis.

CONTRAINDICATIONS Systemic fungal infections; pregnacy (category C), lactation.
CAUTIOUS USE Cushing's syndrome; GI disease, GI ulceration; hepatic disease; renal disease; hypertension; varicella, vaccinia; CHF; diabetes mellitus; glaucoma; coagulopathy; emotional instability or psychotic tendencies.

ROUTE & DOSAGE

Inflammation
Adult: **PO** 2–60 mg/d in 1 or more divided doses **IM** (Acetate) 10–80 mg/wk weekly or every other week; (Succinate) 10–80 mg daily

IV 10–40 mg prn or 30 mg/kg q4–6h × 48 h
Child: **PO/IM/IV** 0.5–1.7 mg/kg/d divided q6–12h

Status Asthmaticus

Adult/Child: **IV** 2 mg/kg then 1–5 mg/kg qh

Acute Spinal Cord Injury

Adult/Child: **IV** 30 mg/kg over 15 min, followed in 45 min by 5.4 mg/kg/h times 23 h

Obesity

Dose on IBW or ABW, whichever is lower

ADMINISTRATION

Oral

- Crush tablet before and give with fluid of patient's choice.
- Note: Preparation less irritating if given with food.
- Use alternate day therapy when given over long period.

Intramuscular

- Give injection deep into large muscle (not deltoid).

Intravenous

Note: Do NOT use methylprednisolone acetate for IV.

PREPARE: Direct/Intermittent: Available in ACT-O-Vial from which the desired dose may be withdrawn after initial dilution with supplied diluent. May be further diluted according to physician's orders.

ADMINISTER: Direct/Intermittent: Give each 500 mg or fraction thereof over 2–3 min.

INCOMPATIBILITIES Solution/additive: Dextrose 5%/sodium chloride 0.45%, aminophylline, calcium gluconate, glycopyrrolate, metaraminol, nafcillin, penicillin G sodium, Y-site: Allopurinol, amsacrine, ciprofloxacin, cisatracurium (≥2 mg/mL concentration), **diltiazem, docetaxel, etoposide, filgrastim, fenoldopam, gemcitabine, ondansetron, paclitaxel, potassium chloride, propofol, sargramostim, vinorelbine.**

- Store at 15°–30° C (59°–86° F). Do not freeze.

ADVERSE EFFECTS (≥1%) **CNS:** Euphoria, headache, insomnia, confusion, psychosis. **CV:** CHF, edema. **GI:** Nausea, vomiting, peptic ulcer. **Musculoskeletal:** Muscle weakness, delayed wound healing, muscle wasting, osteoporosis, aseptic necrosis of bone, spontaneous fractures. **Endocrine:** Cushingoid features, growth suppression in children, carbohydrate intolerance, hyperglycemia. **Special Senses:** Cataracts. **Hematologic:** Leukocytosis. **Metabolic:** Hypokalemia.

INTERACTIONS Drug: Amphotericin B, furosemide, THIAZIDE DIURETICS increase potassium loss; with ATTENUATED VIRUS VACCINES, may enhance virus replication or increase vaccine adverse effects; **isoniazid, phenytoin, phenobarbital, rifampin** decrease effectiveness of methylprednisolone because they increase metabolism of STEROIDS.

PHARMACOKINETICS Absorption: Readily absorbed from GI tract. **Peak:** 1–2 h PO; 4–8 d IM. **Duration:** 1.25–1.5 d PO; 1–5 wk IM. **Metabolism:** In liver. **Half-Life:** >3.5 h; HPA suppression: 18–36 h.

CLINICAL IMPLICATIONS

Assessment & Drug Effects

- Lab tests: Monitor periodically kidney and liver function, thyroid function, CBC, serum electrolytes, weight, and total cholesterol.

Common adverse effects in *italic*, life-threatening effects <u>underlined</u>; generic names in **bold**; classifications in SMALL CAPS; ◆ Canadian drug name; ❷ Prototype drug

981

- Monitor diabetics for loss of glycemic control.
- Monitor serum potassium and report S&S of hypokalemia (see Appendix F).
- Monitor for and report S&S of Cushing's syndrome (see Appendix F).

Patient & Family Education

- Consult physician for any of the following: slow wound healing, significant insomnia or confusion, or unexplained bone pain.
- Do not alter established dosage regimen (i.e., not to increase, decrease, or omit doses or change dose intervals). Withdrawal symptoms (rebound inflammation, fever) can be induced with sudden discontinuation of therapy.
- Report onset of signs of hypocorticism adrenal insufficiency immediately: Fatigue, nausea, anorexia, joint pain, muscular weakness, dizziness, fever.

METHYLTESTOSTERONE

(meth-ill-tess-toss′te-rone)
Android, Metandren ◆, Testred, Virilon
Classifications: HORMONE; ANDROGEN/ANABOLIC STEROID
Therapeutic: ANABOLIC STEROID
Prototype: Testosterone
Pregnancy Category: X
Controlled Substance: Schedule III

AVAILABILITY 10 mg, 25 mg tablets

ACTION & *THERAPEUTIC EFFECT*
Short-acting steroid with androgen/anabolic activity ratio (1:1) similar to that of testosterone but less effective than its esters. Fails to produce full sexual maturation when administered to preadolescent male with complete testicular failure unless preceded by testosterone therapy. *Androgen activity is similar to testosterone; used in replacement therapy, and palliative treatment of postmenopausal female breast cancer.*

USES Androgen replacement therapy, delayed puberty (male), palliation of female mammary cancer (1–5 y postmenopausal), postpartum breast engorgement.

CONTRAINDICATIONS Liver dysfunction; prostate cancer; severe cardiac, renal, or hepatic disease; pregnancy (category X), lactation.
CAUTIOUS USE Mild or moderate liver, kidney, or cardiac dysfunction; heart failure, diabetes mellitus; prostatic hypertrophy.

ROUTE & DOSAGE

Replacement
Adult: **PO** 10–50 mg/d in divided doses

Breast Cancer
Adult: **PO** 50–200 mg/d in divided doses for duration of therapeutic response or no longer than 3 mo if no remission

Postpartum Breast Engorgement
Adult: **PO** 80 mg/d for 3–5 d

ADMINISTRATION

Oral
- Place buccal tablets between cheek and gum. Ensure that tablet is absorbed, not chewed or swallowed; and eating or drinking avoided until absorption is complete.
- Store at 15°–30° C (59°–86° F). Avoid freezing.

ADVERSE EFFECTS (≥1%) **GI:** <u>Cholestatic hepatitis with jaundice</u>, irritation of oral mucosa with buccal administration. **Urogenital:** Renal calculi (especially in immobilized patient), priapism. **Endocrine:** *Acne, gynecomastia, edema,* oligospermia, menstrual irregularities.

INTERACTIONS Drug: Increases risk of bleeding associated with ORAL ANTICOAGULANTS; possibly increases risk of **cyclosporine** toxicity; may decrease glucose level, making adjustment of doses of **insulin,** SULFONYLUREAS necessary. **Herbal:** Echinacea may increase risk of hepatotoxicity.

PHARMACOKINETICS Absorption: Readily from GI tract. **Metabolism:** In liver. **Elimination:** In urine.

CLINICAL IMPLICATIONS

Assessment & Drug Effects

- Lab tests: Monitor liver function periodically; report signs of hepatic toxicity (see Appendix F).
- Monitor for flank pain, abdominal pain radiating to groin, or other symptoms of renal calculi.

Patient & Family Education

- Be prepared for distressing and undesirable adverse effects of virilization (women) since dosage sufficient to produce remission in breast cancer is quantitatively similar to that used for androgen replacement in the male.
- Report signs of virilism promptly. Voice change and hirsutism may be irreversible, even after drug is withdrawn.
- Report priapism (men) or other signs of excess sexual stimulation. The physician will terminate therapy.
- Report symptoms of jaundice with or without pruritus to physician; appears to be dose related. If liver function tests are altered at the same time, this drug will be withdrawn.

METIPRANOLOL HYDROCHLORIDE

(me-ti-pran'ol-ol)
OptiPranolol
Pregnancy Category: C
See Appendix A-1.

METOCLOPRAMIDE HYDROCHLORIDE Ⓟᵣ

(met-oh-kloe-pra'mide)
Emex ♦, Maxeran ♦, Reglan
Classifications: PROKINETIC AGENT (GI STIMULANT)
Therapeutic: GI STIMULANT
Pregnancy Category: B

AVAILABILITY 5 mg, 10 mg tablets; 5 mg/5 mL solution; 5 mg/mL injection

ACTION & *THERAPEUTIC EFFECT*
Potent central dopamine receptor antagonist. Increases resting tone of esophageal sphincter, and tone and amplitude of upper GI contractions. As a result, gastric emptying and intestinal transit are accelerated with little effect, if any, on gastric, biliary, or pancreatic secretions. Antiemetic action results from drug-induced elevation of CTZ threshold and enhanced gastric emptying. *Enhances GI motility and is an effective antinauseant. In diabetic gastroparesis, indicated by relief of anorexia, nausea, vomiting, persistent fullness after meals.*

USES Management of diabetic gastric stasis (gastroparesis); to prevent nausea and vomiting associated with emetogenic cancer chemotherapy (e.g., cisplatin, da-

M

Common adverse effects in *italic*, life-threatening effects <u>underlined</u>; generic names in **bold**; classifications in SMALL CAPS; ♦ Canadian drug name; Ⓟ Prototype drug

983

carbazine) or surgery; to facilitate intubation of small bowel; symptomatic treatment of gastroesophageal reflux.

CONTRAINDICATIONS Sensitivity or intolerance to metoclopramide; allergy to sulfiting agents; history of seizure disorders; concurrent use of drugs that can cause extrapyramidal symptoms; pheochromocytoma; mechanical GI obstruction or perforation; ileus; history of breast cancer; pregnancy (category B), children <6 y, infants, and neonates.

CAUTIOUS USE CHF, cardiac disease; sulfite hypersensitivity, asthma, hypokalemia, hypertension; depression; hepatic disease, infertility, methemoglobin reductase deficiency, Parkinson's disease, kidney dysfunction; GI hemorrhage; G6PD deficiency, procainamide hypersensitivity, seizure disorder, seizures, tardive dyskinesia; history of intermittent porphyria; lactation.

ROUTE & DOSAGE

Gastroesophageal Reflux

Adult: **PO** 10–15 mg q.i.d. a.c. and h.s.
Child: **PO** 0.4–0.8 mg/kg/d in 4 divided doses

Diabetic Gastroparesis

Adult: **PO/IV/IM** 10 mg q.i.d. a.c. and h.s. for 2–8 wk
Geriatric: **PO** 5 mg a.c and h.s.

Small-bowel Intubation, Radiologic Examination

Adult: **IM/IV** 10 mg administered over 1–2 min
Child: **IM/IV** <6 y, 0.1 mg/kg over 1–2 min; 6–14 y, 2.5–5 mg over 1–2 min

Chemotherapy-induced Emesis

Adult: **PO** 20–40 mg q4–6h, may repeat **IM/IV** 2 mg/kg 30 min before antineoplastic administration, may repeat q2h for 2 doses, then q3h for 3 doses if needed

Postoperative Nausea/Vomiting

Adult: **IM/IV** 10–20 mg near end of surgery

ADMINISTRATION

Oral
- Give 30 min before meals and at bedtime.

Intravenous
Note: Verify correct IV concentration and rate of infusion for administration to infants or children with physician.

PREPARE: Direct: Doses of 10 mg or less may be given undiluted. **IV Infusion:** Doses >10 mg IV should be diluted in at least 50 mL of D5W, NS, D5/.45% NaCl, RL or other compatible solution.

ADMINISTER: Direct: Give over 1–2 min. **IV Infusion:** Give over 15 min. Note: Bags of metoclopramide should be protected from light during IV infusion (use of aluminum foil or a thick cotton cover).

INCOMPATIBILITIES Solution/additive: **Calcium gluconate, chloramphenicol, cisplatin, dexamethasone, erythromycin, floxacillin, fluorouracil, furosemide, lorazepam, methotrexate, penicillin G potassium, sodium bicarbonate,** TETRACYCLINES. **Y-site: Allopurinol, amphotericin B cholesteryl complex, amsacrine, cefepime, doxorubicin liposome, furosemide, propofol, TPN.**

- Discard open ampules; do not store for future use.

- Store at 15°–30° C (59°–86° F) in light-resistant bottle. Tablets are stable for 3 y; solutions and injections, for 5 y.

ADVERSE EFFECTS (≥1%) **CNS:** *Mild sedation, fatigue, restlessness,* agitation, headache, insomnia, disorientation, *extrapyramidal symptoms* (acute dystonic type), neurologic malignant syndrome with injection. **GI:** Nausea, constipation, *diarrhea,* dry mouth, altered drug absorption. **Skin:** Urticarial or maculopapular rash. **Body as a Whole:** Glossal or periorbital edema. **Hematologic:** Methemoglobinemia. **Endocrine:** Galactorrhea, gynecomastia, amenorrhea, impotence. **CV:** <u>Hypertensive crisis</u> (rare).

DIAGNOSTIC TEST INTERFERENCE Metoclopramide may interfere with gonadorelin test by increasing *serum prolactin* levels.

INTERACTIONS Drug: Alcohol and other CNS DEPRESSANTS add to sedation; ANTICHOLINERGICS, OPIATE ANALGESICS may antagonize effect on GI motility; PHENOTHIAZINES may potentiate extrapyramidal symptoms; may decrease absorption of **acetaminophen, aspirin, atovaquone, diazepam, digoxin, lithium, tetracycline;** may antagonize the effects of **amantadine, bromocriptine, levodopa, pergolide, ropinirole, pramipexole;** may cause increase in extrapyramidal and dystonic reactions with PHENOTHIAZINES, THIOXANTHENES, **droperidol, haloperidol, loxapine, metyrosine;** may prolong neuromuscular blocking effects of **succinylcholine.**

PHARMACOKINETICS Absorption: Readily from GI tract. **Onset:** 30–60 min PO; 10–15 min IM; 1–3 min IV.

Peak: 1–2 h. **Duration:** 1–3 h. **Distribution:** to most body tissues including CNS; crosses placenta; distributed into breast milk. **Metabolism:** Minimally in liver. **Elimination:** 95% in urine, 5% in feces. **Half-Life:** 2.5–6 h.

CLINICAL IMPLICATIONS

Assessment & Drug Effects

- Report immediately the onset of restlessness, involuntary movements, facial grimacing, rigidity, or tremors. Extrapyramidal symptoms are most likely to occur in children, young adults, and the older adult and with high-dose treatment of vomiting associated with cancer chemotherapy. Symptoms can take months to regress.

- Be aware that during early treatment period, serum aldosterone may be elevated; after prolonged administration periods, it returns to pretreatment level.

- Lab tests: Periodic serum electrolyte.

- Monitor for possible hypernatremia and hypokalemia (see Appendix F), especially if patient has CHF or cirrhosis.

- Adverse reactions associated with increased serum prolactin concentration (galactorrhea, menstrual disorders, gynecomastia) usually disappear within a few weeks or months after drug treatment is stopped.

Patient & Family Education

- Avoid driving and other potentially hazardous activities for a few hours after drug administration.

- Avoid alcohol and other CNS depressants.

- Report S&S of acute dystonia, such as trembling hands and facial grimacing (see Appendix F), immediately.

Common adverse effects in *italic*, life-threatening effects <u>underlined</u>; generic names in **bold**; classifications in SMALL CAPS; ✦ Canadian drug name; ⊚ Prototype drug

985

METOLAZONE

(me-tole'a-zone)

Zaroxolyn ✦

Classifications: THIAZIDE-LIKE DIURETIC; ANTIHYPERTENSIVE

Therapeutic: ANTIHYPERTENSIVE; THIAZIDE-LIKE DIURETIC

Prototype: Hydrochlorothiazide

Pregnancy Category: D

AVAILABILITY 2.5 mg, 5 mg, 10 mg tablets

ACTION & *THERAPEUTIC EFFECT*
Diuretic structurally and pharmacologically similar to hydrochlorothiazide. Diuretic action is associated with interference with transport of sodium ions across renal tubular epithelium. This enhances excretion of sodium, chloride, potassium, bicarbonate, and water. *Produces a decrease in the systolic and diastolic BPs, and reduces edema in CHF and kidney failure patients.*

USES Management of hypertension as sole agent or to enhance effectiveness of other antihypertensives in severe form of hypertension; also edema associated with CHF and kidney disease.

CONTRAINDICATIONS Anuria, hypokalemia; hepatic coma or precoma; hypersensitivity to metolazone and sulfonamides; SLE; pregnancy (category D), lactation.
CAUTIOUS USE History of gout; elderly; allergies; concomitant use of digitalis glycosides; kidney and liver dysfunction.

ROUTE & DOSAGE

Edema
Adult: **PO** 5–20 mg/d
Child: **PO** 0.2–0.4 mg/kg/d divided q12–24h

Hypertension
Adult: **PO** 2.5–5 mg/d

ADMINISTRATION

Oral
- Do not interchange slow availability tablets and rapid availability tablets. They are not equivalent.
- Schedule doses to avoid nocturia and interrupted sleep. Give early in a.m. after eating to prevent gastric irritation (if given in 2 doses, schedule second dose no later than 3 p.m.).
- Store at 15°–30° C (59°–86° F) in tightly closed container.

ADVERSE EFFECTS (≥1%) **GI:** Cholestatic jaundice. **Body as a Whole:** Vertigo, orthostatic hypotension. **Hematologic:** Venous thrombosis, leukopenia. **Metabolic:** Dehydration, *hypokalemia, hyperuricemia, hyperglycemia.*

INTERACTIONS Drug: Amphotericin B, CORTICOSTEROIDS increase hypokalemic effects; may antagonize hypoglycemic effects of SULFONYLUREAS, **insulin; cholestyramine, colestipol** decrease thiazide absorption; intensifies hypoglycemic and hypotensive effects of **diazoxide;** because of increased potassium and magnesium loss, may cause **digoxin** toxicity; decreases **lithium** excretion, increasing its toxicity; NSAIDS may attenuate diuresis—increased risk of NSAID-induced kidney failure.

PHARMACOKINETICS Absorption: Incomplete; Mykrox has greater absorption. **Onset:** 1 h. **Peak:** 2–8 h. **Duration:** 12–24 h. **Distribution:** Distributed throughout extracellular tissue; concentrates in kidney; crosses placenta; distributed in breast milk. **Metabolism:** Does not appear to be metabolized. **Elimination:** In urine. **Half-Life:** 14 h.

CLINICAL IMPLICATIONS

Assessment & Drug Effects

- Anticipate overdosage and adverse reactions in geriatric patients; may be more sensitive to effects of usual adult dose.
- Terminate therapy when adverse reactions are moderate to severe.
- Expect possible antihypertensive effects in 3 or 4 d, but 3–4 wk are required for maximum effect.
- Lab tests: Determine serum potassium at regular intervals. Prolonged treatment and inadequate potassium intake increase potential for hypokalemia (see Appendix F). Periodic plasma glucose and urinalysis determinations.

Patient & Family Education

- Do not drink alcohol; it potentiates orthostatic hypotension.
- Antihypertensive therapy may require as adjunct a high-potassium, low-sodium, and low-calorie diet.
- Include potassium-rich foods in the diet.
- Be aware that if hypokalemia develops, dietary potassium supplement of 1000–2000 mg (25–50 mEq) is usually adequate treatment.

METOPROLOL TARTRATE

(me-toe'proe-lole)
Apo-Metoprolol ♦, Betaloc ♦, Lopressor, Toprol XL
Classifications: BETA-ADRENERGIC ANTAGONIST; ANTIHYPERTENSIVE; ANTIANGINAL
Therapeutic: ANTIHYPERTENSIVE; ANTIANGINAL
Prototype: Propranolol
Pregnancy Category: C

AVAILABILITY 25 mg, 50 mg, 100 mg tablets; 25 mg, 50 mg, 100 mg, 200 mg sustained release tablets; 1 mg/mL injection

ACTION & *THERAPEUTIC EFFECT* Beta-adrenergic blocking agent with preferential effect on $beta_1$ receptors located primarily on cardiac muscle. At higher doses, metoprolol also inhibits $beta_2$ receptors located chiefly on bronchial and vascular musculature. Antihypertensive action may be due to competitive antagonism of catecholamines at cardiac adrenergic neuron sites, drug-induced reduction of sympathetic outflow to the periphery, and to suppression of renin activity. *Reduces heart rate and cardiac output at rest and during exercise; lowers both supine and standing BP, slows sinus rate and decreases myocardial automaticity. Antianginal effect is like that of propranolol.*

USES Management of mild to severe hypertension (monotherapy or in combination with a thiazide or vasodilator or both); long-term treatment of angina pectoris and prophylactic management of stable angina pectoris reduce the risk of mortality after an MI.
UNLABELED USES CHF.

CONTRAINDICATIONS Cardiogenic shock, sinus bradycardia, heart block greater than first degree, overt cardiac failure, right ventricular failure secondary to pulmonary hypertension. Safety during pregnancy (category C) or in children is not established.
CAUTIOUS USE Impaired liver or kidney function; cardiomegaly, CHF controlled by digitalis and diuretics; AV conduction defects; bronchial asthma and other bronchospastic diseases; history of al-

M

---

lergy; thyrotoxicosis; diabetes mellitus; peripheral vascular disease.

ROUTE & DOSAGE

Hypertension
Adult: **PO** 50–100 mg/d in 1–2 divided doses, may increase weekly up to 100–450 mg/d
Geriatric: **PO** 25 mg/d (range: 25–300 mg/d)

Angina Pectoris
Adult: **PO** 100 mg/d in 2 divided doses, may increase weekly up to 100–400 mg/d

Myocardial Infarction
Adult: **IV** 5 mg q2min for 3 doses, followed by PO therapy **PO** 50 mg q6h for 48 h, then 100 mg b.i.d.

ADMINISTRATION

Oral
- Ensure that sustained-release form is not chewed or crushed. It must be swallowed whole.
- Give with food to slightly enhance absorption; however, administration with food not essential. It is important to give with or without food consistently to minimize possible variations in bioavailability.

Intravenous

PREPARE: Direct: Give undiluted.
ADMINISTER: Direct: Give at a rate of 5 mg over 60 sec. Note conditions which are contraindications to drug administration.
INCOMPATIBILITIES Y-site: Amphotericin B cholesteryl complex

- Store at 15°–30° C (59°–86° F). Protect from heat, light, and moisture.

ADVERSE EFFECTS (≥1%) **Body as a Whole:** Hypersensitivity (erythe-matous rash, fever, headache, muscle aches, sore throat, laryngospasm, respiratory distress). **CNS:** *Dizziness, fatigue, insomnia,* increased dreaming, mental depression. **CV:** *Bradycardia,* palpitation, cold extremities, Raynaud's phenomenon, intermittent claudication, angina pectoris, CHF, intensification of AV block, AV dissociation, complete heart block, cardiac arrest. **GI:** Nausea, *heartburn,* gastric pain, diarrhea or constipation, flatulence. **Hematologic:** Eosinophilia, thrombocytopenic and nonthrombocytopenic purpura, agranulocytosis (rare). **Skin:** Dry skin, pruritus, skin eruptions. **Special Senses:** Dry mouth and mucous membranes. **Metabolic:** Hypoglycemia. **Respiratory:** Bronchospasm (with high doses), *shortness of breath.*

DIAGNOSTIC TEST INTERFERENCE In common with other beta blockers, metoprolol may cause elevated *BUN* and **serum creatinine levels** (patients with severe heart disease), elevated **serum transaminase, alkaline phosphatase, lactate dehydrogenase,** and **serum uric acid.**

INTERACTIONS Drug: BARBITURATES, **rifampin** may decrease effects of metoprolol; **cimetidine, methimazole, propylthiouracil,** ORAL CONTRACEPTIVES may increase effects of metoprolol; additive bradycardia with **digoxin;** effects of both metoprolol and **hydralazine** may be increased; **indomethacin** may attenuate hypotensive response; BETA AGONISTS and metoprolol mutually antagonistic; **verapamil** may increase risk of heart block and bradycardia; increases **terbutaline** serum levels.

PHARMACOKINETICS Absorption: Readily from GI tract; 50% of dose reaches systemic circulation. **Onset:** 15 min. **Peak:** 1.5 h; IV form: 20 min. **Duration:** 13–19 h. **Distribution:** Crosses blood–brain barrier and placenta; distributed into breast milk. **Metabolism:** Extensively in liver (CYP2D6). **Elimination:** In urine. **Half-Life:** 3–4 h.

CLINICAL IMPLICATIONS
Assessment & Drug Effects

- Take apical pulse and BP before administering drug. Report to physician significant changes in rate, rhythm, or quality of pulse or variations in BP prior to administration.
- Monitor BP, HR, and ECG carefully during IV administration.
- Expect maximal effect on BP after 1 wk of therapy.
- Take several BP readings close to the end of a 12 h dosing interval to evaluate adequacy of dosage for patients with hypertension, particularly in patients on twice daily doses. Some patients require doses 3 times a day to maintain satisfactory control.
- Observe hypertensive patients with CHF closely for impending heart failure: Dyspnea on exertion, orthopnea, night cough, edema, distended neck veins.
- Lab tests: Obtain baseline and periodic evaluations of blood cell counts, blood glucose, liver and kidney function.
- Monitor I&O, daily weight; auscultate daily for pulmonary rales.
- Withdraw drug if patient presents symptoms of mental depression because it can progress to catatonia. Possible symptoms of depression: disinterest in people, surroundings, food, personal hygiene; withdrawal, apathy, sadness, difficulty in concentrating, insomnia.
- Monitor patients with thyrotoxicosis closely since drug masks signs

of hyperthyroidism (see Appendix F). Abrupt withdrawal may precipitate thyroid storm.

Patient & Family Education

- Learn how to take radial pulse before each dose. Report to physician if pulse is slower than base rate (e.g., 60 bpm) or becomes irregular. Consult physician for parameters.
- Reduce insomnia or increased dreaming by avoiding late evening doses.
- Monitor blood glucose (diabetics) for loss of glycemic control. Drug may mask some symptoms of hypoglycemia (e.g., BP and HR changes) and prolong hypoglycemia. Be alert to other possible signs of hypoglycemia not affected by metoprolol and report to physician if present: Sweating, fatigue, hunger, inability to concentrate.
- Protect extremities from cold and do not smoke. Report cold, painful, or tender feet or hands or other symptoms of Raynaud's disease (intermittent pallor, cyanosis or redness, paresthesias). Physician may prescribe a vasodilator.
- Report immediately to physician the onset of problems with vision.
- Learn measures to relieve dry mouth; rinse mouth frequently with water, increase noncalorie liquid intake if inadequate, suck sugarless gum or hard candy.
- Relieve eye dryness by using sterile artificial tears available OTC.
- Do not drive or engage in potentially hazardous activities until response to drug is known.
- Do not alter established dosage regimen; compliance is very important.
- Reduce dosage reduced gradually over a period of 1–2 wk when drug is discontinued. Sudden withdrawal can result in increase in anginal at-

M

Common adverse effects in *italic*, life-threatening effects underlined; generic names in **bold**; classifications in SMALL CAPS; ✦ Canadian drug name; ☺ Prototype drug

989

tacks and MI in patients with angina pectoris and thyroid storm in patients with hyperthyroidism.

METRONIDAZOLE ⓟ

(me-troe-ni′da-zole)
Flagyl, Flagyl ER, Flagyl IV, MetroCream, MetroGel, Metro-Gel Vaginal, MetroLotion, Noritate, Vandazole
Classifications: ANTITRICHOMONAL; AMEBICIDE; AZOLE ANTIBIOTIC
Therapeutic: AMEBICIDE; AZOLE ANTIBIOTIC
Pregnancy Category: B

AVAILABILITY 250 mg, 500 mg tablets; 375 mg capsules; 750 mg sustained release tablets; 500 mg vials; 0.75% lotion, emulsion; 0.75%, 1% cream; 0.75%, 1% gel

ACTION & *THERAPEUTIC EFFECT* Synthetic compound with trichomonacidal and amebicidal activity as well as antibacterial activity against anaerobic bacteria and some gram-negative bacteria. *Has direct trichomonacidal and amebicidal activity; exhibits antibacterial activity against obligate anaerobic bacteria, gram-negative anaerobic bacilli, and* Clostridia.

USES Asymptomatic and symptomatic trichomoniasis in females and males; acute intestinal amebiasis and amebic liver abscess; preoperative prophylaxis in colorectal surgery, elective hysterectomy or vaginal repair, and emergency appendectomy. IV metronidazole is used for the treatment of serious infections caused by susceptible anaerobic bacteria in intraabdominal infections, skin infections, gynecologic infections, septicemia, and for both pre- and postoperative prophylaxis, bacterial vaginosis. *Topical:* Rosacea.

UNLABELED USES Treatment of pseudomembranous colitis, Crohn's disease, *H. pylori* eradication.

CONTRAINDICATIONS Blood dyscrasias; active CNS disease; lactation.
CAUTIOUS USE Coexistent candidiasis; seizure disorders; heart failure; older adults; severe hepatic disease; renal impairment/failure; pregnancy (category B); alcoholism; liver disease.

ROUTE & DOSAGE

Trichomoniasis
Adult: **PO** 2 g once or 250 mg t.i.d.; × 7 d
Child/Infant: **PO** 15–30 mg/kg/d q8h × 7 d

Giardiasis, *Gardnerella*
Adult: **PO** 500 mg b.i.d. × 7 d OR 750 ER tablet q.d. × 7 d
Vaginal Once or twice daily × 5 d

Amebiasis
Adult: **PO** 500–750 mg t.i.d. × 5–10 d
Child: **PO** 35–50 mg/kg/d in 3 divided doses × 10 d

Anaerobic Infections
Adult: **PO** 7.5 mg/kg q6h (max: 4 g/d) **IV Loading Dose** 15 mg/kg **IV Maintenance Dose** 7.5 mg/kg q6h (max: 4 g/d)
Child: **PO** 15–35 mg/kg/d divided q8h (max: 4 g/d) **IV** 30 mg/kg/d divided q6h
Neonate: **IV** *Weight* <1.2 kg, 7.5 mg q48h; <7 d/between 1.2 kg and 2 kg, 7.5 mg q24h; <7 d/>2 kg, 15 mg/kg q12h; >7 d/between 1.2 kg and 2 kg, 15 mg/kg q12h; >7 d/>2 kg, 30 mg/kg q12h

M

Common adverse effects in *italic*, life-threatening effects <u>underlined</u>; generic names in **bold**; classifications in SMALL CAPS; ♦ Canadian drug name; ⓟ Prototype drug

Pseudomembranous Colitis
Adult: **PO** 250–500 mg 3–4 times daily × 10 d

Rosacea
Adult: **Topical** Apply 0.75% gel as a thin film to affected area b.i.d.; apply 1% gel as a thin film to affected area q.d.

ADMINISTRATION

Oral

- Crush tablets before ingestion if patient cannot swallow whole.
- Ensure that Flagyl ER (extend-release form) is not chewed or crushed. It must be swallowed whole. Give on an empty stomach, 1 h before or 2 h after meals.
- Give immediately before, with, or immediately after meals or with food or milk to reduce GI distress.
- Give lower than normal doses in presence of liver disease.

Topical

- Apply a thin film to affected area only.

Intravenous

Note: Verify correct IV concentration and rate of infusion for administration to neonates, infants, or children with physician.

PREPARE: **Intermittent:** Sequence for preparing solution (important) consists of (1) reconstitution with 4.4 mL sterile water or NS, (2) dilution in IV solution to yield 8 mg/mL in NS, D5W, or RL, (3) pH neutralization with approximately 5 mEq sodium bicarbonate injection for each 500 mg of Flagyl IV used. Avoid use of aluminum-containing equipment when manipulating IV product (including syringes equipped with aluminum needles or hubs). Note: Flagyl IV RTU does not require mixing, diluting, or neutral-izing. Each container contains 14 mEq of sodium.

ADMINISTER: **Intermittent:** Give IV solution slowly at a rate of one dose per hour.

INCOMPATIBILITIES **Solution/additive:** TPN, **amoxicillin/clavulanate, aztreonam, dopamine. Y-site: Amphotericin B cholesteryl complex, aztreonam, filgrastim, meropenem, warfarin.**

- Note: Precipitation occurs if neutralized solution is refrigerated. Use diluted and neutralized solution within 24 h of preparation.

- Store at 15°–30° C (59°–86° F); protect from light. Reconstituted Flagyl I.V. is chemically stable for 96 h when stored below 30° C (86° F) in room light. Diluted and neutralized IV solutions containing Flagyl I.V. should be used within 24 h of mixing.

ADVERSE EFFECTS (≥1%) **Body as a Whole:** Hypersensitivity (rash, urticaria, pruritus, flushing), fever, fleeting joint pains, overgrowth of *Candida.* **CNS:** Vertigo, headache, ataxia, confusion, irritability, depression, restlessness, weakness, fatigue, drowsiness, insomnia, paresthesias, sensory neuropathy (rare). **GI:** *Nausea,* vomiting, anorexia, epigastric distress, abdominal cramps, diarrhea, constipation, dry mouth, metallic or bitter taste, proctitis. **Urogenital:** Polyuria, dysuria, pyuria, incontinence, cystitis, decreased libido, dyspareunia, dryness of vagina and vulva, sense of pelvic pressure. **Special Senses:** Nasal congestion. **CV:** ECG changes (flattening of T wave).

DIAGNOSTIC TEST INTERFERENCE
Metronidazole may interfere with certain chemical analyses for *AST,* resulting in decreased values.

M

Common adverse effects in *italic*, life-threatening effects <u>underlined</u>; generic names in **bold**; classifications in SMALL CAPS; ♦ Canadian drug name; ⊘ Prototype drug

991

INTERACTIONS Drug: ORAL ANTICO-AGULANTS potentiate hypoprothrombinemia; **alcohol** may elicit disulfiram reaction; oral solutions of **citalopram, ritonavir; lopinavir/ritonavir,** and IV formulations of **sulfamethoxazole; trimethoprim, SMX-TMP, nitroglycerin** may elicit disulfiram reaction due to the alcohol content of the dosage form; **disulfiram** causes acute psychosis; **phenobarbital** increases metronidazole metabolism; may increase **lithium** levels; **fluorouracil, azathioprine** may cause transient neutropenia.

PHARMACOKINETICS Absorption: 80% absorbed from GI tract. **Peak:** 1–3 h. **Distribution:** Widely distributed to most body tissues, including CSF, bone, cerebral and hepatic abscesses; crosses placenta; distributed in breast milk. **Metabolism:** 30–60% in liver. **Elimination:** 77% in urine; 14% in feces within 24 h. **Half-Life:** 6–8 h.

CLINICAL IMPLICATIONS

Assessment & Drug Effects
- Discontinue therapy immediately if symptoms of CNS toxicity (see Appendix F) develop. Monitor especially for seizures and peripheral neuropathy (e.g., numbness and paresthesia of extremities).
- Lab tests: Obtain total and differential WBC counts before, during, and after therapy, especially if a second course is necessary.
- Monitor for S&S of sodium retention, especially in patients on corticosteroid therapy or with a history of CHF.
- Monitor patients on lithium for elevated lithium levels.
- Report appearance of candidiasis or its becoming more prominent with therapy to physician promptly.

- Repeat feces examinations, usually up to 3 mo, to ensure that amebae have been eliminated.

Patient & Family Education
- Adhere closely to the established regimen without schedule interruption or changing the dose.
- Refrain from intercourse during therapy for trichomoniasis unless male partner wears a condom to prevent reinfection.
- Have sexual partners receive concurrent treatment. Asymptomatic trichomoniasis in the male is a frequent source of reinfection of the female.
- Do not drink alcohol during therapy; may induce a disulfiram-type reaction (see Appendix F). Avoid alcohol or alcohol-containing medications for at least 48 h after treatment is completed.
- Urine may appear dark or reddish brown (especially with higher than recommended doses). This appears to have no clinical significance.
- Report symptoms of candidal overgrowth: Furry tongue, color changes of tongue, glossitis, stomatitis; vaginitis, curd-like, milky vaginal discharge; proctitis. Treatment with a candidacidal agent may be indicated.

METYROSINE

(me-tye′roe-seen)
Demser
Classifications: HORMONE; ENZYME INHIBITOR
Therapeutic: ENZYME INHIBITOR
Pregnancy Category: C

AVAILABILITY 250 mg capsules

ACTION & *THERAPEUTIC EFFECT*
Blocks the enzyme tyrosine hydroxylase inhibiting the conver-

992

Common adverse effects in *italic,* life-threatening effects <u>underlined</u>; generic names in **bold**; classifications in SMALL CAPS; ♣ Canadian drug name; ⊙ Prototype drug

sion of tyrosine to DOPA, which is the initial and rate-setting step in synthesis of catecholamines (dopamine, epinephrine, norepinephrine). *In patients with pheochromocytoma, reduces catecholamine synthesis as much as 80%, ameliorating hypertensive attacks and associated symptoms.*

USES Short-term management of pheochromocytoma until surgery is performed, in long-term control when surgery is contraindicated, and in patients with malignant pheochromocytoma.

UNLABELED USES Has been used in selected patients with schizophrenia to potentiate antipsychotic effects of phenothiazines.

CONTRAINDICATIONS Control of essential hypertension; dehydration; pregnancy (category C). Safe use in children <12 y is not established.

CAUTIOUS USE Impaired liver or kidney function; Parkinson's disease; lactation.

ROUTE & DOSAGE

Pheochromocytoma

Adult: **PO** 250 mg q.i.d., may increase to 2–3 g/d in divided doses (max: 4 g/d)

ADMINISTRATION

Oral

- Give each dose with a full glass of water and be consistent about time medication is to be taken.
- Store at 15°–30° C (59°–86° F).

ADVERSE EFFECTS (≥1%) **CNS:** *Sedation,* fatigue; *extrapyramidal signs: drooling, difficulty in speaking (dysarthria), tremors,* jaw stiffness (trismus); frank parkinsonism, psychic disturbances (anxiety, de-

pression, hallucinations, disorientation, confusion), headache, muscle spasms. **GI:** *Diarrhea,* nausea, vomiting, abdominal pain, dry mouth. **Skin:** Rash, urticaria. **Urogenital:** Transient dysuria, crystalluria, hematuria, impotence, failure of ejaculation. **Endocrine:** Breast swelling, galactorrhea. **Body as a Whole:** Peripheral edema, nasal stuffiness, shortness of breath. **Hematologic:** Eosinophilia.

DIAGNOSTIC TEST INTERFERENCE False increases in *urinary catecholamines* may occur because of catechol metabolites of metyrosine.

INTERACTIONS Drug: Alcohol and other CNS DEPRESSANTS add to sedation and CNS depression; **droperidol, haloperidol,** PHENOTHIAZINES potentiate extrapyramidal effects.

PHARMACOKINETICS Absorption: Readily absorbed from GI tract. **Peak:** 2–3 d. **Duration:** 3–4 d. **Distribution:** Crosses blood–brain barrier. **Elimination:** In urine. **Half-Life:** 3.4–7.2 h.

CLINICAL IMPLICATIONS

Assessment & Drug Effects

- Monitor therapeutic effectiveness with frequent assessment of vital signs.
- Monitor I&O ratio and pattern. Fluid intake must be enough (e.g., 10–12 glasses or more) to maintain urinary output of 2000 mL or more to minimize risk of crystalluria.
- Perform routine urinalysis; if crystals occur, increase fluid intake further. If crystalluria persists, decrease drug dosage or discontinued.
- Lab tests: Obtain baseline and periodic measurements of urinary catecholamines and their metabolites (metanephrines and VMA). Metabolite excretion should de-

Common adverse effects in *italic*, life-threatening effects <u>underlined</u>; generic names in **bold**; classifications in SMALL CAPS; ♣ Canadian drug name; ⊘ Prototype drug

993

crease in patients with pheochromocytoma. Other baseline and regular determinations include kidney and liver function tests (in patients with dysfunction), and blood and urine glucose tests.
- Supervise ambulation. Sedative effects occur commonly within the first 24 h after drug is started. Maximal sedative effects in 2 or 3 d.

Patient & Family Education
- Notify physician if following adverse effects occur: Diarrhea, particularly if it is severe or persists, painful urination, jaw stiffness, drooling, difficult speech, tremors, disorientation. Dosage reduction or discontinuation of drug may be indicated.
- Avoid driving and potentially hazardous activities until response to drug is known.
- Be aware that abrupt withdrawal of metyrosine may result in psychic stimulation, feeling of increased energy, temporary changes in sleep pattern (usually insomnia). Symptoms may last for 2 or 3 d.
- Carry medical identification at all times if on prolonged therapy and notify all physicians and dentists involved in care about drug regimen.

MEXILETINE

(mex-il'e-teen)
Mexitil
Classifications: ANTIARRHYTHMIC, CLASS IB
Therapeutic: ANTIARRHYTHMIC, CLASS IB
Prototype: Lidocaine
Pregnancy Category: C

AVAILABILITY 150 mg, 200 mg, 250 mg capsules

ACTION & *THERAPEUTIC EFFECT*
Analog of lidocaine with class IB electrophysiologic properties similar to those of procainamide. Shortens action potential refractory period duration and improves resting potential. Has little or no effect on atrial tissue and produces modest suppression of sinus node automatically and AV nodal conduction. Prolongs the His-to-ventricular interval (HQ) only if patient has preexisting conduction disturbance. *Has antiarrhythmic properties for ventricular disturbances.*

USES Acute and chronic ventricular arrhythmias; prevention of recurrent cardiac arrests; suppression of PVCs due to ventricular tachyarrhythmias.
UNLABELED USES Wolff-Parkinson-White syndrome and supraventricular arrhythmias.

CONTRAINDICATIONS Severe left ventricular failure, cardiogenic shock, severe bradyarrhythmias. Preexisting second- or third-degree heart block; cardiogenic shock; pregnancy (category C); concurrent administration of drugs which alter urinary pH.
CAUTIOUS USE Patients with sinus node conduction irregularities, intraventricular conduction abnormalities; hypotension; severe congestive heart failure; renal failure; liver dysfunction.

ROUTE & DOSAGE

Ventricular Arrhythmias
Adult: **PO** 200–300 mg q8h (max: 1200 mg/d)
Child: **PO** 1.4–5 mg/kg q8h

ADMINISTRATION
Oral
- Give with food or milk to reduce gastric distress.

Common adverse effects in *italic*, life-threatening effects underlined; generic names in **bold**, classifications in SMALL CAPS; ♦ Canadian drug name; ⊘ Prototype drug

ADVERSE EFFECTS (≥1%) **CNS:** *Dizziness, tremor, nervousness, incoordination,* headache, blurred vision, paresthesias, numbness. **CV:** Exacerbated arrhythmias, palpitations, chest pain, syncope, hypotension. **GI:** *Nausea, vomiting, heartburn,* diarrhea, constipation, dry mouth, abdominal pain. **Skin:** Rash. **Body as a Whole:** Dyspnea, edema, arthralgia, fever, malaise, hiccups. **Urogenital:** Impotence, urinary retention.

INTERACTIONS Drug: Phenytoin, phenobarbital, rifampin may decrease mexiletine levels; **cimetidine, fluvoxamine** may increase mexiletine levels; may increase **theophylline** levels; may increase proarrhythmic effects of **dofetilide** (separate administration by at least 1 wk).

PHARMACOKINETICS Absorption: Readily from GI tract. **Peak:** 2–3 h. **Distribution:** Distributed into breast milk. **Metabolism:** In liver. **Elimination:** In urine; renal elimination increases with urinary acidification. **Half-Life:** 10–12 h.

CLINICAL IMPLICATIONS

Assessment & Drug Effects
- Check pulse and BP before administration; make sure both are stabilized.
- Effective serum concentration range is 0.5–2 mcg/mL.
- Lab tests: Baseline and periodic liver function tests.
- Supervise ambulation in the weak, debilitated patient or the older adult during drug stabilization period. CNS adverse reactions predominate (e.g., intention tremors, nystagmus, blurred vision, dizziness, ataxia, confusion, nausea).
- Encourage drug compliance; affected particularly by the distressing adverse effects of tremor, ataxia, and eye symptoms.
- Check frequently with patient about adherence to drug regimen. If adverse effects are increasing, consult physician. Dose adjustment or discontinuation may be needed.

Patient & Family Education
- Learn about pulse parameters to be reported: Changes in rhythm and rate (bradycardia = pulse below 60); symptomatic bradycardia (light-headedness, syncope, dizziness), and postural hypotension.

MICAFUNGIN

(my-ca-fun′gin)
Mycamine
Classifications: ANTIBIOTIC; ECHINOCANDIN, ANTIFUNGAL
Therapeutic: ANTIFUNGAL, ECHINOCANDIN
Prototype: Caspofungin
Pregnancy Category: C

AVAILABILITY 50 mg vial

ACTION & THERAPEUTIC EFFECT
Micafungin is an antifungal agent that inhibits the synthesis of glucan, an essential component of fungal cell walls. Micafungin does not allow Candida fungi to replicate. *Has antifungal effects against various species of* Candida.

USES Treatment of patients with esophageal candidiasis, and for prophylaxis of *Candida* infections in patients undergoing hematopoietic stem cell transplantation. Susceptible organisms include *C. albicans, C. glabrata, C. krusei, C. parapsilosis,* and *C. tropicalis.*
UNLABELED USES Treatment of pulmonary *Aspergillus* infection.

CONTRAINDICATIONS Hypersensitivity to any component in micafungin; pregnancy (category C). Safety and efficacy in children <18 y are unknown.

CAUTIOUS USE Hepatic and renal dysfunction; lactation; older adult.

ROUTE & DOSAGE

Esophageal Candidiasis

Adult: **IV** 150 mg/d over 1 h × 14 d

Candidiasis Prophylaxis in Hematopoietic Stem Cell Transplantation Patients

Adult: **IV** 50 mg/d over 1 h × 18 d

ADMINISTRATION

Intravenous

PREPARE: **IV Infusion:** Reconstitute the 50 mg vial with 5 mL NS (without a bacteriostatic agent) to yield 10 mg/mL. Gently swirl, but do not shake, to dissolve. Solution should be clear. For *Candida* prophylaxis, add contents of one reconstituted vial to 100 mL NS. For esophageal candidiasis, add contents of three reconstituted vials to 100 mL NS.

ADMINISTER: **IV Infusion:** Give slowly over 1 h. Flush existing IV line with NS before/after infusion. Protect IV solution from light.

INCOMPATIBILITIES Do not mix or infuse with any other medications.

• Store reconstituted vial and IV solution for up to 24 h at 25° C (77° F). Protect from light.

ADVERSE EFFECTS (≥1%) **CNS:** *Headache,* dizziness, somnolence. **CV:** Flushing, hypertension, phlebitis. **GI:** *Nausea, vomiting, diarrhea,* abdominal pain. **Hematologic/Lymphatic:** Anemia, hemolytic anemia, leukemia, neutropenia, thrombocy-

topenia. **Hepatic:** Elevated liver enzymes, jaundice. **Metabolic:** Hypocalcemia, hypokalemia, hypomagnesemia. **Skin:** Pruritus, rash. **Body as a Whole:** Injection site pain, pyrexia, rigors.

INTERACTIONS Drug: Micafungin increases levels of **sirolimus** and **nifedipine**.

PHARMACOKINETICS Distribution: 99% protein bound. **Metabolism:** Biotransformation primarily in the liver. **Elimination:** Fecal (major) and renal. **Half-Life:** 14–17 h.

CLINICAL IMPLICATIONS

Assessment & Drug Effects

• Monitor for S&S of hypersensitivity during IV infusion; frequently monitor IV site for thrombophlebitis.
• Monitor for S&S of hemolytic anemia (i.e., jaundice).
• Lab tests: Periodic LFTs, kidney function tests, serum electrolytes, and CBC.
• Monitor blood levels of sirolimus or nifedipine with concurrent therapy. If sirolimus or nifedipine toxicity occurs, dosages of these drugs should be reduced.

Patient & Family Education

• Report immediately any of the following: facial swelling, wheezing, difficulty breathing or swallowing, tightness in chest, rash, hives, itching, or sensation of warmth.

MICONAZOLE NITRATE

(mi-kon′a-zole)

Monistat-Derm, Monistat 3, Monistat 7, Femizol-M, M-Zole, Micatin, Tetterine, Fungoid, Lotrimin AF, Desenex

Classifications: ANTIBIOTIC; AZOLE ANTIFUNGAL

Therapeutic: ANTIBIOTIC; AZOLE ANTIFUNGAL

Prototype: Fluconazole
Pregnancy Category: B

AVAILABILITY 100 mg, 200 mg vaginal suppositories; 2% cream; 2% ointment; 2% powder; 2% spray; 2% solution

ACTION & *THERAPEUTIC EFFECT*
Broad-spectrum agent with fungicidal activity. Mode of action appears to inhibit uptake of components essential for cell reproduction and growth as well as cell wall structure, thus promoting cell death of fungi. *Effective against* Candida albicans *and other species of this genus. Inhibits growth of common dermatophytes, and the organism responsible for* tinea versicolor *(*Malassezia furfur*).*

USES Vulvovaginal candidiasis, tinea pedis (athlete's foot), tinea cruris, tinea corporis, and tinea versicolor caused by dermatophytes.

CONTRAINDICATIONS Hypersensitivity to miconazole; azole antifungal agents; children <2 y.
CAUTIOUS USE Pregnancy (category B), lactation.

ROUTE & DOSAGE

Fungal Infection

Adult: **Topical** Apply cream sparingly to affected areas twice a day, and once daily for tinea versicolor, for 2 wk (improvement expected in 2–3 d, tinea pedis is treated for 1 mo to prevent recurrence) **Intravaginal** Insert suppository or vaginal cream q h.s. times 7 d (100 mg) or 3 d (200 mg)

ADMINISTRATION

Topical
- Apply cream sparingly to intertriginous areas (between skin folds) to avoid maceration of skin.
- Massage affected area gently until cream disappears.
- Store at 15°–30° C (59°–86° F) unless otherwise directed.

ADVERSE EFFECTS (≥1%) **Urogenital:** Vulvovaginal burning, itching, or irritation; maceration, allergic contact dermatitis.

INTERACTIONS Drug: may increase INR with **warfarin;** may inactivate **nonoxynol-9** spermicides.

PHARMACOKINETICS Absorption: Small amount absorbed from vagina. **Metabolism:** Rapidly metabolized in liver. **Elimination:** In urine and feces. **Half-Life:** 2.1–24 h.

CLINICAL IMPLICATIONS

Assessment & Drug Effects
- Expect clinical improvement from topical application in 1 or 2 wk. If no improvement in 4 wk, diagnosis is reevaluated. Treat tinea pedis infection for 1 mo to assure permanent recovery.

Patient & Family Education
- Complete full course of treatment to ensure recovery.
- Do not interrupt vaginal application during menstrual period.
- Avoid contact of drug with eyes.

MIDAZOLAM HYDROCHLORIDE
(mid'az-zoe-lam)
Classifications: BENZODIAZEPINE ANXIOLYTIC; SEDATIVE-HYPNOTIC
Therapeutic: ANTIANXIETY; SEDATIVE-HYPNOTIC
Prototype: Lorazepam
Pregnancy Category: D
Controlled Substance: Schedule IV

AVAILABILITY 2 mg/mL syrup; 1 mg/mL, 5 mg/mL injection

Common adverse effects in *italic*, life-threatening effects <u>underlined</u>; generic names in **bold**, classifications in SMALL CAPS; ♣ Canadian drug name; ⓜ Prototype drug

997

ACTION & THERAPEUTIC EFFECT
Short-acting parenteral benzodiazepine that intensifies activity of
gamma-aminobenzoic acid (GABA),
a major inhibitory neurotransmitter
of the brain, by interfering with its
reuptake and promoting its accumulation at neuronal synapses.
This calms the patient, relaxes skeletal muscles, and in high doses
produces sleep. *Has CNS depressant with muscle relaxant, sedative-
hypnotic, anticonvulsant, and amnestic properties.*

USES Sedation before general anesthesia, induction of general anesthesia; to impair memory of perioperative events (anterograde
amnesia); for conscious sedation
prior to short diagnostic and endoscopic procedures; and as the
hypnotic supplement to nitrous
oxide and oxygen (balanced anesthesia) for short surgical procedures.

CONTRAINDICATIONS Intolerance
to benzodiazepines; acute narrow-
angle glaucoma; shock, coma;
acute alcohol intoxication; intraarterial injection; status asthmaticus;
pregnancy (category D), obstetric
delivery, lactation.

CAUTIOUS USE Patient with COPD;
chronic kidney failure; cardiac disease; pulmonary insufficiency; dementia; electrolyte imbalance; neuromuscular disease; Parkinson's
disease; psychosis; CHF; older
adults; bipolar disorder.

ROUTE & DOSAGE

Conscious Sedation

Adult: **IM** 0.07–0.08 mg/kg 30–
60 min before procedure **IV** 1–
2.5 mg, may repeat in 2 min prn;
Intubated Patients, 0.05–0.2 mg/
kg/h by continuous infusion

Child: **IM** 0.08 mg/kg times 1
dose **PR** 0.3 mg/kg times 1 dose;
Intubated Patients, 2 mcg/kg/min
by continuous infusion, may
increase by 1 mcg/kg/min q30
min until light sleep is induced
Neonate: **IV** 0.5–1 mcg/kg/min

IV Induction for General Anesthesia

Adult: **IV** *Premedicated,* 0.15–
0.25 mg/kg over 20–30 s, allow
2 min for effect **IV** *Non premedicated,* 0.3–0.35 mg/kg over 20–
30 s, allow 2 min for effect
Child: **IV** 0.15 mg/kg followed
by 0.05 mg/kg q2 min times 1–3
doses

Status Epilepticus

Child: **IV Loading Dose** >2 mo,
0.15 mg/kg **IV Maintenance
Dose** 1 mcg/kg/min infusion, may
titrate upward as needed q5min

Preoperative Sedation

Child: **PO** <5 y, 0.5 mg/kg; >5 y,
0.4–0.5 mg/kg

ADMINISTRATION

Intramuscular
- Inject IM drug deep into a large
  muscle mass.

Intravenous

PREPARE: Direct: Dilute in D5W
or NS to a concentration of 0.25
mg/mL (e.g., 1 mg in 4 mL or 5
mg in 20 mL). **IV Infusion:** Add 5
mL of the 5 mg/mL concentration to 45 mL of D5W or NS to
yield 0.5 mg/mL.
ADMINISTER: Direct: *Sedation,*
Give over ≥2 min; *Induction of
Anesthesia,* Give over 20–30 sec.
IV Infusion: Give at a rate based
on weight.
**INCOMPATIBILITIES Solution/ad-
ditive: Lactated Ringer's, pentobarbital, perphenazine, pro-**

Common adverse effects in *italic*, life-threatening effects underlined; generic names
in **bold**; classifications in SMALL CAPS; ♣ Canadian drug name; ⊕ Prototype drug

chlorperazine. **Y-site: Albumin, amoxicillin, amoxicillin/clavulanate, amphotericin B cholesteryl complex, ampicillin, bumetanide, butorphanol, ceftazidime, cefuroxime, clonidine, dexamethasone, foscarnet, fosphenytoin, furosemide, hydrocortisone, imipenem/cilastatin, methotrexate, nafcillin, omeprazole, sodium bicarbonate, thiopental, TPN, trimethoprim/sulfamethoxazole.**

▪ Store at 15°–30° C (59°–86° F), therapeutic activity is retained for 2 y from date of manufacture.

ADVERSE EFFECTS (≥1%) **CNS:** *Retrograde amnesia,* headache, euphoria, drowsiness, excessive sedation, confusion. **CV:** Hypotension. **Special Senses:** Blurred vision, diplopia, nystagmus, pinpoint pupils. **GI:** Nausea, vomiting. **Respiratory:** Coughing, laryngospasm (rare), respiratory arrest. **Skin:** Hives, swelling, burning, pain, induration at injection site, tachypnea. **Body as a Whole:** Hiccups, chills, weakness.

INTERACTIONS Drug: Alcohol, CNS DEPRESSANTS, ANTICONVULSANTS potentiate CNS depression; **cimetidine** increases midazolam plasma levels, increasing its toxicity; may decrease antiparkinsonism effects of **levodopa;** may increase **phenytoin** levels; **smoking** decreases sedative and antianxiety effects. **Food:** Grapefruit juice (>1 qt/d) may increase risk of myopathy and rhabdomyolysis. **Herbal: Kava-kava, valerian** may potentiate sedation. **Echinacea, St. John's wort** may reduce efficacy.

PHARMACOKINETICS Onset: 1–5 min IV; 5–15 min IM, 20–30 min PO. **Peak:** 20–60 min. **Duration:** <2 h IV; 1–6 h IM. **Distribution:** Crosses blood–brain barrier and placenta.

Metabolism: In liver (CYP3A4). **Elimination:** In urine. **Half-Life:** 1–4 h.

CLINICAL IMPLICATIONS

Assessment & Drug Effects

▪ Inspect insertion site for redness, pain, swelling, and other signs of extravasation during IV infusion.

▪ Monitor for hypotension, especially if the patient is premedicated with a narcotic agonist analgesic.

▪ Monitor vital signs for entire recovery period. In obese patient, half-life is prolonged during IV infusion; therefore, duration of effects is prolonged (i.e., amnesia, postoperative recovery).

▪ Be aware that overdose symptoms include somnolence, confusion, sedation, diminished reflexes, coma, and untoward effects on vital signs.

Patient & Family Education

▪ Do not drive or engage in potentially hazardous activities until response to drug is known. You may feel drowsy, weak, or tired for 1–2 d after drug has been given.

▪ Be prepared for amnesia to prevent an upsetting postoperative period.

▪ Review written instructions to assure future understanding and compliance. Patient teaching during amnestic period may not be remembered. Even if dose is small and depth of amnesia is unclear, relearn information.

MIDODRINE HYDROCHLORIDE

(mid′o-dreen)

Orvaten, ProAmatine

Classifications: ALPHA₁ AGONIST; VASOPRESSOR

Therapeutic: ANTIHYPOTENSIVE; VASOPRESSOR

Common adverse effects in *italic,* life-threatening effects underlined; generic names in **bold**; classifications in SMALL CAPS; ◆ Canadian drug name; ⊘ Prototype drug

999

MIDODRINE HYDROCHLORIDE

Prototype: Methoxamine
Pregnancy Category: C

AVAILABILITY 2.5 mg, 5 mg, 10 mg tablets

ACTION & *THERAPEUTIC EFFECT*
Vasopressor and alpha$_1$ agonist. Activates the alpha-adrenergic receptors of the arteries and veins, resulting in increased vascular tone and elevation in blood pressure. *Affects standing, sitting, and supine systolic and diastolic blood pressures. Indicated by an increase in 1-min standing systolic BP and subjective feelings of clinical improvement.*

USES Treatment of symptomatic orthostatic hypotension.

CONTRAINDICATIONS Severe organic heart disease; heart failure; acute kidney disease; urinary retention; pheochromocytoma; thyrotoxicosis; MAOI therapy; persistent and excessive supine hypertension; pregnancy (category C).
CAUTIOUS USE Renal impairment, hepatic impairment; history of visual problems; diabetes with hypotension or visual disorders; lactation. Safety and efficacy in children are not established.

ROUTE & DOSAGE

Orthostatic Hypotension

Adult: **PO** 10 mg t.i.d. during the daytime hours, dosed not less that 3 h apart with last dose at least 4 h before bedtime (max: 20 mg/dose)

ADMINISTRATION

Oral
- Do not give at bedtime or before napping (within 4 h of lying supine for any length of time)

- Give with caution in persons with pretreatment, supine systolic BP ≥170 mm Hg.
- Store at 15°–30° C (59°–86° F).

ADVERSE EFFECTS (≥1%) **Body as a Whole:** *Paresthesia,* chills, pain, facial flushing. **CNS:** Confusion, nervousness, anxiety. **CV:** *Hypertension.* **GI:** Dry mouth. **Skin:** *Pruritus, piloerection,* rash. **Urogenital:** *Dysuria, urinary retention, urinary frequency.*

INTERACTIONS Drug: may antagonize effects of **doxazosin, prazosin, terazosin;** may potentiate vasoconstrictive effects of **ephedrine, phenylephrine, pseudoephedrine;** may cause hypertensive crisis with MAOIS.

PHARMACOKINETICS Absorption: Rapidly from GI tract. **Peak:** Midodrine 0.5 h; desglymidodrine 1–2 h. **Metabolism:** Rapidly metabolized to desglymidodrine, the active metabolite. **Elimination:** In urine. **Half-Life:** Midodrine 25 min, desglymidodrine 3–4 h.

CLINICAL IMPLICATIONS

Assessment & Drug Effects
- Lab tests: Evaluate kidney and liver function prior to initiating therapy.
- Monitor supine and standing BP regularly. Stop drug if supine BP increases excessively; determine acceptable parameters.
- Monitor carefully effect of the drug in diabetics with orthostatic hypotension and those taking fludrocortisone acetate, which may increase intraocular pressure.

Patient & Family Education
- Take last daily dose 4 h before bedtime.
- Report immediately to physician sensations associated with supine hypertension (e.g., pounding in

ears, headache, blurred vision, awareness of heart beating).
- Discontinue drug and report to physician if S&S of bradycardia develop (e.g., dizziness, pulse slowing, fainting).
- Do not take allergy drugs, cold preparations, or diet pills without consulting physician.

MIGLITOL

(mig'li-tol)
Glyset
Classifications: HORMONE; ANTI-DIABETIC AGENT; ALPHA-GLUCOSI-DASE INHIBITOR
Therapeutic: ANTIDIABETIC; ALPHA-GLUCOSIDASE INHIBITOR
Prototype: Acarbose
Pregnancy Category: B

AVAILABILITY 25 mg, 50 mg, 100 mg tablets

ACTION & *THERAPEUTIC EFFECT*
Enzyme inhibition of intestinal glucosidases that delays the formation of glucose from saccharides in the small intestine. Miglitol does not enhance insulin secretion. *It delays the digestion of carbohydrates, lowers the postprandial hyperglycemia, and reduces the levels of glysylated hemoglobin (HbA$_{1C}$) in type 2 diabetics.*

USES Adjunct to diet for control of type 2 diabetes; may be used alone or with a sulfonylurea.

CONTRAINDICATIONS Diabetic ketoacidosis; digestive or absorptive disorders; history of or partial intestinal obstruction, inflammatory bowel disease; hypersensitivity to miglitol; lactation.
CAUTIOUS USE Hypersensitivity to acarbose; creatinine clearance above

2 mg/dL; concomitant use with sulfonylurea; high stress conditions (i.e., surgery, trauma, etc.); pregnancy (category B). Safety and efficacy in children <18 y unknown.

ROUTE & DOSAGE

Type 2 Diabetes Mellitis
Adult: **PO** 25 mg t.i.d. at the start of each meal, may increase after 4–8 wk to 50 mg t.i.d. (max: 100 mg t.i.d.)

ADMINISTRATION

Oral
- Give drug with first bite of each of the three main meals.
- Store at 15°–30° C (59°–86° F).

ADVERSE EFFECTS (≥1%) **GI:** *Abdominal pain, diarrhea, flatulence.* **Skin:** Rash. **Metabolic:** Hypoglycemia.

INTERACTIONS Drug: Miglitol may reduce bioavailability of **propranolol, ranitidine; charcoal, pancreatin, amylase, pancrelipase** may decrease effectiveness of **miglitol. Herbal: Garlic, ginseng** may potentiate hypoglycemic effects.

PHARMACOKINETICS Absorption: 25 mg dose is completely absorbed, amount absorbed decreases with increasing dose to where 100 mg dose is 50–70% absorbed. **Peak:** 2–3 h. **Distribution:** Minimal protein binding (<4%). **Metabolism:** Not metabolized. **Elimination:** Half-life 2 h; 95% excreted unchanged in urine, lower doses should be used in patients with renal impairment.

CLINICAL IMPLICATIONS
Assessment & Drug Effects
- Monitor for therapeutic effectiveness: Indicated by improved blood

M

Common adverse effects in *italic*, life-threatening effects <u>underlined</u>; generic names in **bold**; classifications in SMALL CAPS; ♣ Canadian drug name; ⊕ Prototype drug

1001

glucose levels and decreased HbA$_{1C}$.

- Monitor for S&S of hypoglycemia when used in combination with sulfonylureas, insulin, other hypoglycemia agents.
- Lab tests: Monitor HbA$_{1C}$ q3mo.
- Treat hypolgycemia with oral glucose (dextrose); miglitol interferes with the breakdown of sucrose (table sugar).

Patient & Family Education

- Keep a source of oral glucose available to treat low blood sugar; miglitol prevents digestive breakdown of table sugar.
- Abdominal discomfort, flatulence, and diarrhea tend to diminish with continued therapy.

MILRINONE LACTATE

(mil'ri-none)
Primacor
Classifications: INOTROPIC AGENT; VASODILATOR
Therapeutic: VASODILATOR; INOTROPIC AGENT
Prototype: Inamrinone
Pregnancy Category: C

AVAILABILITY 1 mg/mL, 200 mcg/mL injection

ACTION & *THERAPEUTIC EFFECT*

Member of a class of inotropic/vasodilator agents. Positive inotropic action and vasodilator, with little chronotropic activity; mode of action and structure are different from digitalis and catecholamines as well as beta-adrenergic agonists. Inhibitory action against cyclic-AMP phosphodiesterase in cardiac and smooth vascular muscle. Increases cardiac contractility. *Increases myocardial contractility. Therefore, increases cardiac output and decreases pulmonary wedge pressure and vascular resistance, without increasing myocardial oxygen demand or significantly increasing heart rate.*

USES Short-term management of CHF.
UNLABELED USES Short-term use to increase the cardiac index in patients with low cardiac output after surgery. To increase cardiac function prior to heart transplantation.

CONTRAINDICATIONS Hypersensitivity to milrinone; valvular heart disease; acute MI; pregnancy (category C).
CAUTIOUS USE Older adult; atrial fibrillation, atrial flutter; renal disease; renal impairment, renal failure; lactation. Safety and efficacy in children are not established.

ROUTE & DOSAGE

Heart Failure
Adult: **IV Loading Dose** 50 mcg/kg IV over 10 min **IV Maintenance Dose** 0.375–0.75 mcg/kg/min

ADMINISTRATION

Intravenous
Note: Correct preexisting hypokalemia before administering milrinone. See manufacturer's information for dosage reduction in the presence of renal impairment.

PREPARE: Loading Dose: Give undiluted or dilute each 1 mg in 1 mL NS or 0.45% NaCl. **IV Infusion:** Dilute 20 mg of milrinone in D5W, NS, or 0.45% NaCl to yield: 100 mcg/mL with 180 mL diluent; 150 mcg/mL with 113 mL diluent; 200 mcg/mL with 80 mL diluent.

ADMINISTER: Loading Dose: Give 50 mcg/kg over 10 min. **IV Infusion:** Give at a rate based on weight. Use a microdrip set and infusion pump.
INCOMPATIBILITIES Solution/additive: Furosemide, procainamide. Y-site: Furosemide, imipenem/cilastatin, procainamide.

▪ Store according to manufacturer's directions.

ADVERSE EFFECTS (≥1%) **CV:** Increased ectopic activity, PVCs, ventricular tachycardia, ventricular fibrillation, supraventricular arrhythmias; possible increase in angina symptoms, hypotension.

INTERACTIONS Drug: Disopyramide may cause excessive hypotension.

PHARMACOKINETICS Peak: 2 min. **Duration:** 2 h. **Distribution:** 70% protein bound. **Elimination:** 80–85% excreted unchanged in urine within 24 h. Active renal tubular secretion is primary elimination pathway. **Half-Life:** 1.7–2.7 h.

CLINICAL IMPLICATIONS
Assessment & Drug Effects
▪ Monitor cardiac status closely during and for several hours following infusion. Supraventricular and ventricular arrhythmias have occurred.
▪ Monitor BP and promptly slow or stop infusion in presence of significant hypotension. Closely monitor those with recent aggressive diuretic therapy for decreasing blood pressure.
▪ Monitor fluid and electrolyte status. Hypokalemia should be corrected whenever it occurs during administration.

Patient & Family Education
▪ Report immediately angina that occurs during infusion to physician.
▪ Be aware that drug may cause a headache, which can be treated with analgesics.

MINOCYCLINE HYDROCHLORIDE
(mi-noe-sye′kleen)
Arestin, Dynacin, Minocin
Classifications: TETRACYCLINE ANTIBIOTIC
Therapeutic: ANTIBIOTIC; TETRACYCLINE
Prototype: Tetracycline
Pregnancy Category: D

AVAILABILITY 50 mg, 75 mg, 100 mg capsules; 50 mg, 75 mg, 100 mg tablets; 50 mg/5 mL suspension; 1 mg sustained release microspheres

ACTION & THERAPEUTIC EFFECT
Semisynthetic tetracycline derivative which appears to be active against strains of *Staphylococci* resistant to other tetracyclines; photosensitivity occurs only rarely. Bacteriostatic action appears to be a result of reversible binding to ribosomal units of susceptible bacteria and inhibition of bacterial protein synthesis. *Effective against gram-positive and gram-negative bacteria, but usually use against gram-negative bacteria. Effective against* Mycobacterium marinum *infections,* U. urealyticum, N. gonorrhoeae.

USES Treatment of mucopurulent cervicitis, granuloma inguinale, lymphogranuloma venereum, proctitis, bronchitis, lower respiratory tract infections caused by *Mycoplasma pneumoniae*, Rickettsial infections, chlamydial in-

M

fections, non-gonococcal urethritis, chlamydial conjunctivitis, plague, brucellosis, bartonellosis, tularemia, UTI, and prostatitis; *acne vulgaris,* gonorrhea, cholera, meningococcal carrier state.

CONTRAINDICATIONS Hypersensitivity to tetracyclines; oral administration in meningococcal infections; sunlight (UV) exposure; pregnancy (category D), lactation, children <8 y.

CAUTIOUS USE Renal and hepatic impairment; older adults.

ROUTE & DOSAGE

Antiinfective

Adult: **PO** 200 mg followed by 100 mg q12h
Child: **PO** >8 y, 4.4 mg/kg followed by 2 mg/kg q12h

Acne

Adult: **PO** 50 mg 1–3 times/d

Meningococcal Carrier State

Adult: **PO** 100 mg q12h times 5 d
Child: **PO** >8 y, 4 mg/kg followed by 2 mg/kg q12h times 5 d (max: 100 mg/dose)

ADMINISTRATION

Oral

- Shake suspension well before administration.
- Oral therapy is the preferred route; institute as soon as possible.
- Check expiration date. Outdated tetracycline can cause severe adverse effects.

ADVERSE EFFECTS (≥1%) **CNS:** *Weakness, light-headedness, ataxia, dizziness, or vertigo.* **GI:** Nausea,

cramps, diarrhea, flatulence. **Hepatic:** Hepatitis, liver enzyme increases, <u>hepatotoxicity.</u>

INTERACTIONS Drug: ANTACIDS, **iron, calcium, magnesium, zinc, kaolin and pectin, sodium bicarbonate, bismuth subsalicylate** can significantly decrease minocycline absorption; effects of both **desmopressin** and minocycline antagonized; increases **digoxin** absorption, increasing risk of **digoxin** toxicity; **methoxyflurane** increases risk of kidney failure. **Food:** Dairy products significantly decrease minocycline absorption; food may also decrease its absorption.

PHARMACOKINETICS Absorption: 90–100% from GI tract. **Peak:** 2–3 h. **Distribution:** Tends to accumulate in adipose tissue; crosses placenta; distributed into breast milk. **Metabolism:** Partially metabolized. **Elimination:** 20–30% in feces; ~12% in urine. **Half-Life:** 11–26 h.

CLINICAL IMPLICATIONS

Assessment & Drug Effects

- Obtain history of hypersensitivity reactions prior to administration; drug is contraindicated with known tetracycline hypersensitivity.
- Lab: C&S should be drawn prior to initiation of therapy.
- Monitor carefully for signs of hypersensitivity response (see Appendix F), particularly in patients with history of allergies, especially to drugs.
- Monitor at-risk patients for S&S of superinfection (see Appendix F).
- Assess risk of toxic effects carefully; increases with renal and hepatic impairment.

- Supervise ambulation, since lightheadedness, dizziness, and vertigo occur frequently.

Patient & Family Education
- Avoid hazardous activities or those requiring alertness while taking minocycline.
- Use sunscreen when outdoors and otherwise protect yourself from direct sunlight since photosensitivity reaction may occur.
- Report vestibular adverse effects (e.g., dizziness), which usually occur during first week of therapy. Effects are reversible if drug is withdrawn.
- Report loose stools or diarrhea or other signs of superinfection promptly to physician.
- Use or add barrier contraceptive while taking this drug if using hormonal contraceptive.

MINOXIDIL

(mi-nox'i-dill)
Rogaine
Classifications: NONNITRATE VASODILATOR; ANTIHYPERTENSIVE
Therapeutic: ANTIHYPERTENSIVE; NONNITRATE VASODILATOR
Prototype: Hydralazine
Pregnancy Category: C

AVAILABILITY 2.5 mg, 10 mg tablets; 2% solution

ACTION & *THERAPEUTIC EFFECT*
Direct-acting vasodilator similar to other drugs of this class, but hypotensive effect is more pronounced. Appears to act by blocking calcium uptake through cell membrane. Reduces elevated systolic and diastolic blood pressures in supine and standing positions, by decreasing peripheral vascular resistance. *Effective as an antihypertensive agent. It increases heart rate and cardiac output. Topical minoxidil reverses balding to some degree.*

USES Treat severe hypertension that is symptomatic or associated with damage to target organs and is not manageable with maximum therapeutic doses of a diuretic plus two other antihypertensive drugs. Used with a diuretic to prevent fluid retention and a beta adrenergic blocking agent (e.g., propranolol) or an alpha-adrenergic agonist (e.g., clonidine or methyldopa) to prevent tachycardia. *(Topical)* to treat alopecia areata and male pattern alopecia.

CONTRAINDICATIONS Pheochromocytoma; acute MI, dissecting aortic aneurysm, valvular dysfunction, heart failure; CVA; pulmonary hypertension. Severe renal failure Cl_{cr} <10 mL/min, pregnancy (category C), children.
CAUTIOUS USE Severe renal impairment; recent MI (within preceding month); coronary artery disease, chronic CHF.

ROUTE & DOSAGE

Hypertension

Adult: **PO** 5 mg/d, increased q3–5d up to 40 mg/d in single or divided doses as needed (max: 100 mg/d)
Child: **PO** 0.2 mg/kg/d (max: 5 mg/d) initially, gradually increased to 0.25–1 mg/kg/d in divided doses (max: 50 mg/d)

Common adverse effects in *italic*, life-threatening effects underlined; generic names in **bold**; classifications in SMALL CAPS; ♣ Canadian drug name; ⊕ Prototype drug

1005

M

Alopecia

Adult: **Topical** Apply 1 mL of 2% solution to affected area b.i.d.

ADMINISTRATION

Oral

- Dose increments are usually made at 3–5 d intervals. If more rapid adjustment is necessary, adjustments can be made q6h with careful monitoring.

Topical

- Do not apply topical product to an irritated scalp (e.g., sunburn, psoriasis).
- Store at 15°–30° C (59°–86° F) in tightly covered container unless otherwise directed.

ADVERSE EFFECTS (≥1%) **CV:** *Tachycardia,* angina pectoris, *ECG changes,* pericardial effusion and tamponade, rebound hypertension (following drug withdrawal); *edema,* including pulmonary edema; *CHF (salt and water retention).* **Skin:** *Hypertrichosis,* transient pruritus, darkening of skin, hypersensitivity rash, <u>Stevens-Johnson syndrome</u>. With topical use: itching, flushing, scaling, dermatitis, folliculitis. **Body as a Whole:** Fatigue.

DIAGNOSTIC TEST INTERFERENCE *Hct, Hgb,* and **erythrocyte count** usually decrease (about 7%) during early therapy; ***serum alkaline phosphatase, BUN,*** and ***creatinine*** may increase during early therapy.

INTERACTIONS Drug: Epinephrine, norepinephrine cause excessive cardiac stimulation; **guanethidine** causes profound orthostatic hypotension.

PHARMACOKINETICS Absorption: Readily absorbed from GI tract. **Onset:** 30 min PO; at least 4 mo topical. **Peak:** 2–8 h PO. **Duration:** 2–5 d PO; new hair growth will remain 3–4 mo after withdrawal of topical. **Distribution:** Widely distributed including into breast milk. **Metabolism:** In liver. **Elimination:** 97% in urine and feces. **Half-Life:** 4.2 h.

CLINICAL IMPLICATIONS

Assessment & Drug Effects

- Take BP and apical pulse before administering medication and report significant changes. Consult physician for parameters.
- Lab tests: Periodic serum electrolytes.
- Do not stop drug abruptly. Abrupt reduction in BP can result in CVA and MI. Keep physician informed.
- Monitor fluid and electrolyte balance closely throughout therapy. Sodium and water retention commonly occur. Consult physician regarding sodium restriction. Monitor potassium intake and serum potassium levels in patient on diuretic therapy.
- Monitor I&O and daily weight. Report unusual changes in I&O ratio or daily weight gain, greater than 1 kg (2 lb).
- Observe patient daily for edema and auscultate lungs for rales. Be alert to signs and symptoms of CHF (see Appendix F).
- Observe for symptoms of pericardial effusion or tamponade. Symptoms are similar to those of CHF, but additionally patient may have paradoxical pulse (normal inspiratory reduction in systolic BP may fall as much as 10–20 mm Hg).

Patient & Family Education

- Learn about usual pulse rate and count radial pulse for one full minute before taking drug. Report an increase of 20 or more bpm.
- Notify physician promptly if the following S&S appear: Increase of

20 or more bpm in resting pulse; breathing difficulty; dizziness; light-headedness; fainting; edema (tight shoes or rings, puffiness, pitting); weight gain, chest pain, arm or shoulder pain; easy bruising or bleeding.

- Be aware of possibility of hypertrichosis: Elongation, thickening, and increased pigmentation of fine body hair, especially of face, arms, and back. Develops 3–9 wk after start of therapy and occurs in approximately 80% of patients; reversible within 1–6 mo after drug withdrawal.
- Report any dermatologic adverse effects or any other adverse effect promptly to physician.
- Schedule follow-up examinations for q4–6 mo.
- Comply strictly with regular regimen; maximizes chance of at least some hair regrowth.

MIRTAZAPINE ⓟ

(mir-taz´a-peen)
Remeron, Remeron SolTab
Classifications: PSYCHOTHERAPEUTIC AGENT; ANTIDEPRESSANT, TETRACYCLIC; ANXIOLYTIC AGENT
Therapeutic: ANTIDEPRESSANT, TETRACYCLIC; ANTIANXIETY
Pregnancy Category: C

AVAILABILITY 15 mg, 30 mg, 45 mg tablets and orally disintegrating tablets

ACTION & *THERAPEUTIC EFFECT*
Tetracyclic antidepressant pharmacologically and therapeutically similar to tricyclic antidepressants. Tetracyclics enhance central nonadrenergic and serotonergic activity; thought to be due to normalizing of neurotransmission efficacy. Mirtazapine is a potent antagonist of 5-HT$_2$ and 5-HT$_3$ serotonin receptors. *Acts as antidepressant. Effectiveness is indicated by mood elevation.*

USES Treatment of depression.

CONTRAINDICATIONS Hypersensitivity to mirtazapine or mianserin; hypersensitivity to other antidepressants (e.g., tricyclic antidepressants and MAOI depressants), acute MI; fever, infection; agranulocytosis, neutropenia, hematologic disease; suicidal ideation; jaundice, ethanol intoxication; pregnancy (category C), lactation.

CAUTIOUS USE History of cardiovascular or GI disorders; BPH, urinary retention; narrow-angle glaucoma, increased intraocular pressure; hepatic or renal impairment, renal failure; hypercholesterolemia, hypertriglyceridemia, thrombocytopenia; older adults; angina, cardiac arrhythmias, anticholinergic medications; bipolar disorder, mania, bone marrow suppression, PKU, history of MI; cerebrovascular disease, seizure disorder, seizures, stroke; depression; hypovolemia, surgery; closed-angle glaucoma; ileus, GI obstruction, dehydration; diabetes mellitus, diabetic ketoacidosis. Safety and effectiveness in children are not established.

ROUTE & DOSAGE

Depression
Adult: **PO** 15 mg/d in single dose h.s., may increase q1–2wk (max: 45 mg/d)
Geriatric: **PO** Use lower doses
Renal or Hepatic Impairment
Use lower doses

ADMINISTRATION

Oral
- Give preferably prior to sleep to minimize injury potential.

Common adverse effects in *italic*, life-threatening effects <u>underlined</u>; generic names in **bold**; classifications in SMALL CAPS; ◆ Canadian drug name; ⓟ Prototype drug

1007

- Begin drug no sooner than 14 d after discontinuation of an MAO inhibitor.
- Reduce dosage as warranted with severe renal or hepatic impairment and in older adults.
- Store at 20°–25° C (68°–77° F) in tight, light-resistant container.

ADVERSE EFFECTS (≥1%) **Body as a Whole:** Asthenia, flu syndrome, back pain, general and peripheral edema, malaise. **CNS:** *Somnolence,* dizziness, abnormal dreams, abnormal thinking, tremor, confusion, depression, agitation, vertigo, twitching. **CV:** Hypertension, vasodilation. **GI:** Nausea, vomiting, abdominal pain, *increased appetite*/weight gain, *dry mouth, constipation,* anorexia, cholecystitis, stomatitis, colitis, abnormal liver function tests. **Respiratory:** Dyspnea, cough, sinusitis. **Skin:** Pruritus, rash. **Urogenital:** Urinary frequency.

INTERACTIONS Drug: Additive cognitive and motor impairment with **alcohol** or BENZODIAZEPINES; increase risk of hypertensive crisis with MAOIS. **Herbal: Kava-kava, valerian** may potentiate sedative effects.

PHARMACOKINETICS Absorption: Rapidly absorbed from GI tract, 50% reaches systemic circulation. **Peak:** 2 h. **Distribution:** 85% protein bound. **Metabolism:** In liver by cytochrome P450 system (CYP2D6, CYP1A2, CYP3A). **Elimination:** 75% in urine, 15% in feces. **Half-Life:** 20–40 h.

CLINICAL IMPLICATIONS

Assessment & Drug Effects

- Lab tests: Monitor WBC count with differential, lipid profile, and ALT/AST periodically.
- Patients should be monitored for worsening of depression or emergence of suicidality.
- Assess for weight gain and excessive somnolence or dizziness.
- Monitor for orthostatic hypotension with a history of cardiovascular or cerebrovascular disease. Periodically monitor ECG especially in those with known cardiovascular disease.
- Monitor those with a history of increased intraocular pressure or urinary retention carefully for worsening or recurrence.
- Monitor those with history of seizures for lowering of the seizure threshold.

Patient & Family Education

- Do not drive or engage in potentially hazardous activities until response to drug is known.
- Do not use alcohol while taking drug.
- Report immediately unexplained fever or S&S of infection, especially flu-like symptoms, to physician.
- Do not take other prescription or OTC drugs without consulting physician.
- Make position changes slowly especially from lying or sitting to standing. Report dizziness, palpitations, and fainting.
- Notify (women) physician immediately if you become pregnant.
- Monitor weight periodically and report significant weight gains.

MISOPROSTOL

(my-so-prost'ole)

Cytotec

Classifications: PROSTAGLANDIN
Therapeutic: PROSTAGLANDIN
Pregnancy Category: X

AVAILABILITY 100 mcg, 200 mcg tablets

Common adverse effects in *italic*, life-threatening effects underlined; generic names in **bold**; classifications in SMALL CAPS; ♣ Canadian drug name; ⊘ Prototype drug

ACTION & *THERAPEUTIC EFFECT*

Synthetic prostaglandin E_1 analog, with both antisecretory (inhibiting gastric acid secretion) and mucosal protective properties. Increases bicarbonate and mucosal protective properties. Inhibits basal and nocturnal gastric acid secretion and acid secretion in response to a variety of stimuli, including meals, histamine, pentagastrin, and coffee. Produces uterine contractions that may endanger pregnancy and cause a miscarriage. *Inhibits basal and nocturnal gastric acid secretion.*

USES Prevention of NSAID (including aspirin-induced) gastric ulcers in patients at high risk of complications from a gastric ulcer (e.g., the older adult and patients with a concomitant debilitating disease or a history of ulcers). Drug is taken for the duration of NSAID therapy and does not interfere with the efficacy of the NSAID.

UNLABELED USES Short-term treatment of duodenal ulcers; cervical ripening and induction of labor.

CONTRAINDICATIONS History of allergies to prostaglandins; *Topical Use:* abnormal fetal position, caesarean section, ectopic pregnancy; fetal disease, incomplete abortion multiparity, placenta previa, vaginal bleeding; pregnancy (category X), lactation.

CAUTIOUS USE Renal impairment; inflammatory bowel disease. Safety in children <18 y is not established.

ROUTE & DOSAGE

Prevention of NSAID-Induced Ulcers

Adult: **PO** 100–200 mcg q.i.d. p.c. and h.s. or 200 mcg b.i.d. or t.i.d.

ADMINISTRATION

Oral

- Give with food to minimize GI adverse effects (manufacturer recommendation).
- Store away from heat, light, and moisture.

ADVERSE EFFECTS (≥1%) **CNS:** Headache. **GI:** *Diarrhea, abdominal pain,* nausea, flatulence, dyspepsia, vomiting, constipation. **Urogenital:** Spotting, cramps, dysmenorrhea, uterine contractions.

INTERACTIONS Drug: MAGNESIUM-CONTAINING ANTACIDS may increase diarrhea.

PHARMACOKINETICS Absorption: Readily from GI tract; extensive first pass metabolism. **Onset:** 30 min. **Peak:** 60–90 min. **Duration:** At least 3 h. **Metabolism:** In liver. **Elimination:** Primarily in urine; small amount in feces. **Half-Life:** 20–40 min.

CLINICAL IMPLICATIONS

Assessment & Drug Effects

- Monitor for diarrhea; may be minimized by giving drug after meals and at bedtime. Diarrhea is a common adverse effect that is dose related and usually self-limiting (often resolving in 8 d).

Patient & Family Education

- Avoid using concurrent magnesium-containing antacids because of increased incidence of diarrhea.
- Report postmenopausal bleeding to physician; it may be drug related.
- Avoid pregnancy during misoprostol therapy; use an effective contraception method while taking drug.
- Drug has abortifacient property. Contact physician and immediately discontinue drug if you become pregnant.

Common adverse effects in *italic*, life-threatening effects underlined; generic names in **bold**; classifications in SMALL CAPS; ✚ Canadian drug name; ⊚ Prototype drug

M

MITOMYCIN

(mye-toe-mye'sin)
Mutamycin, Mytozytrex
Classifications: ANTINEOPLASTIC;
ANTIBIOTIC
Therapeutic: ANTINEOPLASTIC; AN-
TIBIOTIC
Prototype: Doxorubicin
Pregnancy Category: X

AVAILABILITY 5 mg, 20 mg, 40 mg
injection

ACTION & *THERAPEUTIC EFFECT*
Potent antibiotic antineoplastic
compound. Effective in certain tumors unresponsive to surgery, radiation, or other chemotherapeutic agents. Action mechanism
unclear but reportedly combines
with DNA, thereby interfering
with cellular and enzymatic RNA
and protein synthesis. *Highly destructive to rapidly proliferating
cells and slowly developing carcinomas.*

USES In combination with other
chemotherapeutic agents in palliative, adjunctive treatment of
disseminated adenocarcinoma of
breast, pancreas, or stomach,
squamous cell carcinoma of head,
neck, lung, and cervix. Not recommended to replace surgery or
radiotherapy or as a single primary therapeutic agent.

CONTRAINDICATIONS Hypersensitivity or idiosyncrasy reaction;
severe bone marrow suppression;
thrombocytopenia; coagulation
disorders or bleeding tendencies; pregnancy (category X), lactation.
CAUTIOUS USE Renal impairment;
myelosuppression; pulmonary disease or respiratory insufficiency.

ROUTE & DOSAGE

Cancer
Adult/Child: **IV** 10–20 mg/m^2/d
as a single dose q6–8wk, additional doses based on hematologic response
Renal Impairment
Cl$_{cr}$ <10 mL/min: use 75% of
dose

ADMINISTRATION

Intravenous
Note: Verify correct IV concentration and rate of infusion/injec-
tion for administration to
children with physician.

PREPARE: IV Infusion: Dilute each
5 mg with 10 mL sterile water for
injection. Shake to dissolve. If
product does not clear immediately, allow to stand at room
temperature until solution is obtained. Reconstituted solution is
purple.
ADMINISTER: IV Infusion: Give reconstituted solution over 5–10
min or longer as determined by
total volume of solution. Monitor
IV site closely. Avoid extravasation to prevent extreme tissue reaction (cellulitis) to the toxic
drug.
**INCOMPATIBILITIES Solution/ad-
ditive:** DEXTROSE-CONTAINING SOLU-
TIONS, **bleomycin. Y-site: Aztreonam, cefepime, etoposide,
filgrastim, gemcitabine,** piper-
acillin/tazobactam, **sargramostim,** topotecan, **vinorelbine.**

■ Store drug reconstituted with sterile water for injection (0.5 mg/mL)
for 14 d refrigerated or 7 d at room
temperature. Drug diluted in D5W
(20–40 mcg/mL) is stable at room
temperature for 3 h.

ADVERSE EFFECTS (≥1%) **CNS:** Paresthesias. **GI:** Stomatitis, *nausea, vomiting*, anorexia, hematemesis, diarrhea. **Hematologic:** <u>Bone marrow toxicity</u> (*thrombocytopenia, leukopenia* occurring 4–8 wk after treatment onset), anemia. **Respiratory:** <u>Acute bronchospasm</u>, hemoptysis, dyspnea, nonproductive cough, pneumonia, <u>interstitial pneumonitis</u>. **Skin:** Desquamation; induration, pain, necrosis, cellulitis at injection site; reversible alopecia, purple discoloration of nail beds. **Body as a Whole:** Pain, headache, fatigue, edema. **Urogenital:** <u>Hemolytic uremic syndrome</u>, renal toxicity.

PHARMACOKINETICS Metabolism: Metabolized rapidly in liver. **Elimination:** In urine. **Half-Life:** 23–78 min.

CLINICAL IMPLICATIONS

Assessment & Drug Effects

- Lab tests: Perform WBC with differential, platelet count, PT, INR, aPTT, Hgb, Hct, and serum creatinine frequently during and for at least 7 wk after treatment.
- Do not administer if serum creatinine is >1.7 mg/dL or if platelet count falls below 150,000/mm^3 and WBC is down to 4000/mm^3 or if prothrombin or bleeding times are prolonged.
- Monitor I&O ratio and pattern. Report any sign of impaired kidney function: Change in ratio, dysuria, hematuria, oliguria, frequency, urgency. Keep patient well hydrated (at least 2000–2500 mL orally daily if tolerated). Drug is nephrotoxic.
- Observe closely for signs of infection. Monitor body temperature frequently.
- Inspect oral cavity daily for signs of stomatitis or superinfection (see Appendix F).

Patient & Family Education

- Report respiratory distress to physician immediately.
- Report signs of common cold to physician immediately.
- Understand that hair loss is reversible after cessation of treatment.

MITOTANE

(mye´toe-tane)

Lysodren

Classifications: ANTINEOPLASTIC
Therapeutic: ANTINEOPLASTIC
Pregnancy Category: C

AVAILABILITY 500 mg tablets

ACTION & *THERAPEUTIC EFFECT*
Cytotoxic agent with suppressant action on the adrenal cortex. Modifies peripheral metabolism of steroids and reduces production of adrenal steroids. Extra-adrenal metabolism of cortisol is altered, leading to reduction in 17-hydroxycorticosteroids (17-OHCS); however, plasma levels of corticosteroids do not fall. *Cytotoxic agent with suppressant action on the adrenal cortex.*

USES Inoperable adrenal cortical carcinoma (functional and nonfunctional).

UNLABELED USES Cushing's syndrome secondary to pituitary disorders.

CONTRAINDICATIONS Pregnancy (category C), lactation; children.
CAUTIOUS USE Liver disease.

ROUTE & DOSAGE

Adrenocortical Carcinoma
Adult: **PO** 9–10 g/d in divided doses t.i.d. or q.i.d. (tolerated doses range: 2–16 g/d)

M

ADMINISTRATION

Oral
- Withhold temporarily and consult physician if emergency occurs, since adrenal suppression is its prime action. Exogenous steroids may be required until the already depressed adrenal starts secreting steroids.
- Store at 15°–30° C (59°–86° F) in tight, light-resistant containers.

ADVERSE EFFECTS (≥1%) **CNS:** Vertigo, dizziness, drowsiness, tiredness, depression, *lethargy, sedation,* headache, confusion, tremors. **CV:** Hypertension, hypotension, flushing. **GI:** *Anorexia, nausea, vomiting, diarrhea.* **Urogenital:** Hematuria, hemorrhagic cystitis, albuminuria. **Endocrine:** Adrenocortical insufficiency. **Special Senses:** Blurred vision, diplopia, lens opacity, toxic retinopathy. **Body as a Whole:** Generalized aching, fever, muscle twitching, hypersensitivity reactions, hyperpyrexia. **Skin:** *Rash,* cutaneous eruptions and pigmentation. **Metabolic:** *Hypouricemia, hypercholesterolemia.*

DIAGNOSTIC TEST INTERFERENCE
Mitotane decreases **protein-bound iodine (PBI)** and **urinary 17-OHCS levels**.

INTERACTIONS Drug: Potentiates sedative effects of **alcohol** and other CNS DEPRESSANTS; may increase the metabolism of **phenytoin, phenobarbital, warfarin,** decreasing their effectiveness.

PHARMACOKINETICS Absorption: Approximately 40% absorbed from GI tract. **Onset:** 2–4 wk. **Peak:** 3–5 h. **Distribution:** Deposits in most body tissues, especially adipose tissue. **Metabolism:** In liver. **Elimination:** Small amount excreted in bile. **Half-Life:** 18–159 d.

CLINICAL IMPLICATIONS

Assessment & Drug Effects
- Monitor pulse and BP for early signs of shock (adrenal insufficiency).
- Observe for symptoms of hepatotoxicity (see Appendix F). Report them promptly, since reduced hepatic capacity can increase toxicity of mitotane and because dose may have to be decreased.
- Notify physician if following persist and become more severe: Aching muscles, fever, flushing, and muscle twitching.
- Monitor obese patient for symptoms of adrenal hypofunction. Because a large portion of the drug deposits in fatty tissue, the obese are particularly susceptible to prolonged adverse effects.
- Make neurologic and behavioral assessments at regular intervals throughout therapy.

Patient & Family Education
- Be aware that mitotane does not cure but does reduce tumor mass, pain, weakness, anorexia, and steroid symptoms.
- Report symptoms of adrenal insufficiency (weakness, fatigue, orthostatic hypotension, pigmentation, weight loss, dehydration, anorexia, nausea, vomiting, and diarrhea) to physician.
- Exercise caution when driving or performing potentially hazardous tasks requiring alertness because of drug-induced drowsiness, tiredness, dizziness. Symptoms tend to recede with continuation in therapy.
- Use contraceptive measures during therapy because of teratogenic properties of drug. Notify physician if you suspect you are pregnant.

M

Common adverse effects in *italic,* life-threatening effects <u>underlined</u>; generic names in **bold**; classifications in SMALL CAPS; ✤ Canadian drug name; ☯ Prototype drug

MITOXANTRONE HYDROCHLORIDE

(mi-tox′an-trone)

Novantrone

Classifications: ANTINEOPLASTIC; ANTIBIOTIC; IMMUNOSUPPRESSANT

Therapeutic: ANTINEOPLASTIC; IMMUNOSUPPRESSANT

Prototype: Doxorubicin

Pregnancy Category: D

AVAILABILITY 2 mg/mL injection

ACTION & *THERAPEUTIC EFFECT*
Non-cell-cycle specific antitumor agent with less cardiotoxicity than doxorubicin. Interferes with DNA synthesis by intercalating with the DNA double helix, blocking effective DNA and RNA transcription. *Highly destructive to rapidly proliferating cells in all stages of cell division.*

USES In combination with other drugs for the treatment of acute nonlymphocytic leukemia (ANLL) in adults, bone pain in advanced prostate cancer. Reducing neurologic disability and/or the frequency of clinical relapses in patients with multiple sclerosis.

UNLABELED USES Breast cancer, non-Hodgkin's lymphomas.

CONTRAINDICATIONS Hypersensitivity to mitoxantrone; myelosuppression; multiple sclerosis; baseline LVEF less than 50%; pregnancy (category D), lactation.

CAUTIOUS USE Impaired cardiac function; impaired liver and kidney function; systemic infections.

ROUTE & DOSAGE

Combination Therapy for ANLL

Adult: **IV Induction Therapy:** 12 mg/m²/d on days 1–3, may need to repeat induction course

IV Consolidation Therapy: 12 mg/m² on days 1 and 2 (max: lifetime dose 80–120 mg/m²)

Prostate Cancer

Adult: **IV** 12–14 mg/m² q21d

Multiple Sclerosis

Adult: **IV** 12 mg/m² over 5–15 min q3mo (max: lifetime dose 140 mg/m²)

ADMINISTRATION

Intravenous

If mitoxantrone touches skin, wash immediately with copious amounts of warm water.

***PREPARE:* IV Infusion:** Withdraw contents of vial and add to at least 50 mL of D5W or NS. Use of goggles, gloves, and protective gown during drug preparation and administration.

***ADMINISTER:* IV Infusion:** Give into the tubing as a freely running IV of D5W or NS and infused over at least 3 min or longer (i.e., 30–60 min) depending on the total volume of IV solution. If extravasation occurs, stop infusion and immediately restart in another vein.

***INCOMPATIBILITIES* Solution/additive:** Heparin, hydrocortisone, paclitaxel. **Y-site:** Amphotericin B cholesteryl complex, aztreonam, cefepime, doxorubicin liposome, paclitaxel, piperacillin/tazobactam, propofol, TPN.

■ Discard unused portions of diluted solution. ■ Once opened, multiple-use vials may be stored refrigerated at 2°–8° C (35°–46° F) for 14 d.

ADVERSE EFFECTS (≥1%) **CV:** Arrhythmias, decreased left ventricular function, *CHF*, tachycardia, ECG

Common adverse effects in *italic*, life-threatening effects underlined; generic names in **bold**; classifications in SMALL CAPS; ♣ Canadian drug name; ⊙ Prototype drug

1013

changes, <u>MI</u> (occurs with cumulative doses of >80–100 mg/m²), edema, <u>increased risk of cardiotoxicity</u>. **GI:** *Nausea, vomiting,* diarrhea, <u>hepatotoxicity</u>. **Hematologic:** <u>*Leukopenia, thrombocytopenia*</u>. **Other:** Discolors urine and sclera a blue-green color. **Skin:** Mild phlebitis, blue skin discoloration, alopecia.

INTERACTIONS Drug: May impair immune response to VACCINES such as influenza and pneumococcal infections. May have increased risk of infection with **yellow fever vaccine.**

PHARMACOKINETICS Distribution: Rapidly taken up by tissues and slowly released into plasma, 95% protein bound. **Metabolism:** In liver. **Elimination:** Primarily in bile. **Half-Life:** 37 h.

CLINICAL IMPLICATIONS

Assessment & Drug Effects
- Monitor IV insertion site. Transient blue skin discoloration may occur at site if extravasation has occurred.
- Monitor cardiac functioning throughout course of therapy; report signs and symptoms of CHF or cardiac arrhythmias.
- Lab tests: Perform liver function tests prior to and during course of treatment. Monitor serum uric acid levels and initiate hypouricemic therapy before antileukemic therapy. Monitor carefully CBC with differential prior to and during therapy.

Patient & Family Education
- Understand potential adverse effects of mitoxantrone therapy.
- Expect urine to turn blue-green for 24 h after drug administration; sclera may also take on a bluish color.

- Be aware that stomatitis/mucositis may occur within 1 wk of therapy.
- Do not to risk exposure to those with known infections during the periods of myelosuppression.

MIVACURIUM CHLORIDE

(miv-a-cur′i-um)

Mivacron

Classifications: SKELETAL MUSCLE RELAXANT, NONDEPOLARIZING

Therpeutic: SKELETAL MUSCLE RELAXANT, NONDEPOLARIZING

Prototype: Atracurium

Pregnancy Category: C

AVAILABILITY 2 mg/mL injection

ACTION & *THERAPEUTIC EFFECT* Short-acting, skeletal muscle relaxant that combines competitively to cholinergic receptors on the motor neuron end-plate. Antagonizes action of acetylcholine, and blocks neuromuscular transmission. Neuromuscular blocking action is readily reversible with an anticholinesterase agent. *Blocks nerve impulse transmission, which results in skeletal muscle relaxation and paralysis.*

USES Adjunct to general anesthesia, to facilitate tracheal intubation, and to provide skeletal muscle relaxation during surgery or mechanical ventilation.

CONTRAINDICATIONS Allergic reactions to mivacurium or its ingredients; neonates; pregancy (category C).

CAUTIOUS USE Kidney function impairment, liver function impairment; older adult patients; pulmonary disease, COPD; lactation.

ROUTE & DOSAGE

Tracheal Intubation and Mechanical Ventilation

Adult: **IV Loading Dose** 0.15–0.25 mg/kg given over 5–15 sec (over 60 sec in patients with cardiovascular disease) **IV Maintenance Dose** 0.1 mg/kg generally q15min **IV Continuous Infusion** Initial infusion of 9–10 mcg/kg/min, then 6–7 mcg/kg/min
Child: **IV Loading Dose** 2–12 y, 0.2 mg/kg given over 5–15 sec (range: 0.09–0.2 mg/kg) then 14 mcg/kg/min

Obesity
Use IBW

Renal Impairment
Decrease infusion rates by up to 50%

Hepatic Impairment
May decrease infusing rate up to 50%

ADMINISTRATION

Intravenous

PREPARE: **Direct:** Add 3 mL of D5W, NS, D5/NS, RL, or D5/RL to each 1 mL mivacurium to yield 0.5 mg/mL. **IV Infusion:** Available premixed (50 mL of 0.5 mg/mL). *ADMINISTER:* **Direct:** Give over 15–60 sec. **IV Infusion:** Refer to manufacturer's infusion rate tables. The use of a peripheral nerve stimulator permits optimal dosing and minimizes risks of overdose or underdose.

- Store diluted solution at 5°–25° C (41°–77° F) for up to 24 h.

ADVERSE EFFECTS (≥1%) **CV:** Transient decrease in arterial BP, hypotension, increases and decreases in heart rate. **Skin:** *Transient flushing about the face, neck, and/or chest* (especially with rapid administration).

INTERACTIONS Drug: GENERAL ANESTHETICS may enhance the degree of neuromuscular blockade produced by mivacurium. AMINOGLYCOSIDES, TETRACYCLINES, **bacitracin,** POLYMYXINS, **lincomycin, clindamycin, colistin, magnesium salts, lithium,** LOCAL ANESTHETICS, **procainamide,** and **quinidine** may enhance the neuromuscular blockade.

PHARMACOKINETICS Peak: 2–6 min. **Duration:** 25–30 min in adults, 8–16 min in children. **Distribution:** Limited tissue distribution. **Metabolism:** Rapidly hydrolyzed by plasma cholinesterase.

CLINICAL IMPLICATIONS

Assessment & Drug Effects

- Assess patients with neuromuscular disease carefully and adjust drug dosage using a peripheral nerve stimulator when they experience prolonged neuromuscular blocks.
- Monitor hemodynamic status carefully in patients with significant cardiovascular disease or those with potentially greater sensitivity to release of histamine-type mediators (e.g., asthma).
- Monitor for significant drop in BP because overdose may increase the risk of hemodynamic adverse effects.

MODAFINIL

(mod-a′fi-nil)
Provigil, Alertec ♦
Classifications: CEREBRAL STIMULANT; MISCELLANEOUS
Therapeutic: CEREBRAL STIMULANT; MISCELLANEOUS
Pregnancy Category: C
Controlled Substance: Schedule IV

Common adverse effects in *italic*, life-threatening effects underlined; generic names in **bold**; classifications in SMALL CAPS; ♦ Canadian drug name; ⊘ Prototype drug

1015

AVAILABILITY 100 mg, 200 mg capsules

ACTION & *THERAPEUTIC EFFECT*
Primary sites of CNS stimulant activity of modafinil appear to be in the hippocampus, the centrolateral nucleus of the thalamus, and the central nucleus of the amygdala. Limited animal studies demonstrate that modafinil may increase excitatory glutaminergic transmission in the thalamus and hippocampus. *Modafinil causes wakefulness, increased locomotor activity, and psychoactive and euphoric effects.*

USES Improve wakefulness in patients with narcolepsy or excessive sleepiness associated with shift work sleep disorder, obstructive sleep apnea/hypnea syndrome.
UNLABELED USES Fatigue related to organic brain syndrome or multiple sclerosis.

CONTRAINDICATIONS Hypersensitivity to modafinil; acute MI, valvular heart disease; pregnancy (category C); lactation. Safety and efficacy in children <16 y are unknown.
CAUTIOUS USE Cardiovascular disease including left ventricular hypertrophy; cardiac disease, ischemic ECG changes, chest pain, arrhythmias, mitral valve prolapse, recent MI, unstable angina; older adults; history of drug or alcohol abuse; psychosis or emotional instability; leukopenia, MI, neurological disease, hypertension, severe hepatic disease, severe renal impairment, renal failure, seizure disorder, sleep apnea.

ROUTE & DOSAGE

> **Narcolepsy, Fatigue**
> *Adult:* **PO** 200 mg/d as single dose in the morning

> *Hepatic Impairment*
> Reduce dose by 50%

ADMINISTRATION
Oral
- Give in the morning shortly after awakening.
- Store at 15°–30° C (59°–86° F).

ADVERSE EFFECTS (≥1%) **Body as a Whole:** Chest pain, neck pain, chills, eosinophilia. **CNS:** *Headache,* nervousness, dizziness, depression, anxiety, cataplexy, insomnia, paresthesia, dyskinesia, hypertonia. **CV:** Hypotension, hypertension, vasodilation, arrhythmia, syncope. **GI:** *Nausea,* diarrhea, dry mouth, anorexia, abnormal LFTs, vomiting, mouth ulcer, gingivitis, thirst. **Respiratory:** Rhinitis, pharyngitis, lung disorder, dyspnea. **Skin:** Dry skin. **Special Senses:** Amblyopia, abnormal vision.

INTERACTIONS Drug: Methylphenidate may delay absorption of **modafinil; modafinil** may decrease levels of **cyclosporine,** ORAL CONTRACEPTIVES; **modafinil** may increase levels of **clomipramine, phenytoin, warfarin,** TRICYCLIC ANTIDEPRESSANTS.

PHARMACOKINETICS Absorption: Rapidly absorbed. **Peak:** 2–4 h. **Distribution:** Approximately 60% protein bound. **Metabolism:** In liver to inactive metabolites. **Elimination:** In urine. **Half-Life:** 15 h.

CLINICAL IMPLICATIONS
Assessment & Drug Effects
- Therapeutic effectiveness: Indicated by improved daytime wakefulness.
- Monitor BP and cardiovascular status, especially with preexisting hypertension and mitral valve prolapse or other CV condition.

M

Common adverse effects in *italic*, life-threatening effects <u>underlined</u>; generic names in **bold**; classifications in SMALL CAPS; ✚ Canadian drug name; ⊘ Prototype drug

- Monitor for S&S of psychosis, especially when history of psychotic episodes exists.
- Lab tests: Periodic liver function tests.
- Coadministered drugs: Monitor INR with warfarin for first several months and when dosage is changed; monitor for toxicity with phenytoin.

Patient & Family Education
- Use barrier contraceptive instead of/in addition to hormonal contraceptive.
- Inform physician of all prescription or OTC drugs in/added to your regimen.
- Notify physician if any S&S of an allergic reaction appear.

MOEXIPRIL HYDROCHLORIDE

(mo-ex'i-pril)

Univasc

Classifications: ANGIOTENSIN-CONVERTING ENZYME (ACE) INHIBITOR; ANTIHYPERTENSIVE

Therapeutic: ANTIHYPERTENSIVE, ACE INHIBITOR

Prototype: Enalapril

Pregnancy Category: C first trimester; D second and third trimester

AVAILABILITY 7.5 mg, 15 mg tablets

ACTION & THERAPEUTIC EFFECT
ACE inhibitor that results in decreased conversion of angiotensin I to angiotensin II. Results in decreased vasopressor activity and aldosterone secretion. Lowering angiotensin II plasma levels results in blood pressure decreases and plasma renin activity increases. *ACE inhibition and decreased aldosterone secretion are responsible for its antihypertensive effect.*

USES Hypertension.
UNLABELED USES CHF, left ventricular dysfunction.

CONTRAINDICATIONS Hypersensitivity to moexipril; history of angioedema related to an ACE inhibitor; pregnancy [(category C) first trimester; (category D) second and third trimesters], lactation.

CAUTIOUS USE Hypersensitivity to any other ACE inhibitor; renal impairment, renal artery stenosis, volume-depleted patients; hypertensive patient with CHF; history of autoimmune disease; severe liver dysfunction; immunosuppressed patients; hyperkalemia; patients undergoing surgery/anesthesia; preexisting neutropenia; concurrent lithium therapy. Safety and efficacy in children are not established.

ROUTE & DOSAGE

Hypertension
Adult: **PO** 7.5 mg once/d, may increase up to 30 mg/d in divided doses
Renal Impairment
Cl_cr ≤40 mL/min: Start with 3.75 mg q.d. (also if patient is volume depleted or on diuretics)

$Cl_{cr} \leq 40$ mL/min

ADMINISTRATION

Oral
- Give 1 h before or 2 h after meals. Food greatly reduces absorption of moexipril.
- May need to reduce starting dose 50% in patients with possible volume depletion or a history of renal insufficiency.
- Store at 15°–30° C (59°–86° F).

ADVERSE EFFECTS (≥1%) **CNS:** Headache, *dizziness,* drowsiness, sleep disturbances, nervousness, anxiety, mood changes. **CV:** Hypo-

---

Common adverse effects in *italic*, life-threatening effects underlined; generic names in **bold**; classifications in SMALL CAPS; ♣ Canadian drug name; ⦾ Prototype drug

1017

tension, chest pain, angina, peripheral edema, MI, palpitations, arrhythmias. **Endocrine:** Hyperkalemia. **GI:** Diarrhea, nausea, dyspepsia, abdominal pain, taste disturbances, constipation, vomiting, dry mouth, pancreatitis. **Urogenital:** Urinary frequency, increased BUN and serum creatinine. **Hematologic:** Neutropenia, hemolytic anemia. **Respiratory:** Cough, pharyngitis, rhinitis, flu-like symptoms. **Skin:** <u>Angioedema</u> (rare), rash, flushing.

INTERACTIONS Drug: Capsaicin may exacerbate cough. NSAIDS may reduce antihypertensive effects. May increase **lithium** levels and toxicity. POTASSIUM SUPPLEMENTS and POTASSIUM-SPARING DIURETICS may increase risk of hyperkalemia. **Food:** Food greatly reduces absorption of moexipril.

PHARMACOKINETICS Absorption: Readily absorbed from GI tract; approximately 13% of active metabolite reaches systemic circulation; absorption greatly reduced by food. **Onset:** 1 h. **Duration:** 24 h. **Distribution:** Approximately 50% protein bound. **Metabolism:** In liver to moexiprilat (active metabolite). **Elimination:** 13% in urine, 53% in feces. **Half-Life:** 2–9 h.

CLINICAL IMPLICATIONS

Assessment & Drug Effects
- Monitor closely for systematic hypotension that may occur within 1–3 h of first dose, especially in those with high blood pressure, on a diuretic or restricted salt intake, or otherwise volume depleted.
- Monitor BP and HR frequently during initiation of therapy, whenever a diuretic is added, and periodically throughout therapy.
- Determine trough BP (just before next dose) before dose adjustments are made.

- Lab tests: Monitor serum electrolytes, WBC with differential, Hct and Hgb, UA, and kidney and liver function tests periodically throughout therapy.
- Supervise therapeutic response closely in patients with CHF.

Patient & Family Education
- Report to physician immediately swelling around face or neck or in extremities.
- Report S&S of hypotension (e.g., dizziness, weakness, syncope); nonproductive cough; skin rash; flu-like symptoms; jaundice; irregular heartbeat or chest pains; and dehydration from vomiting, diarrhea, or diaphoresis.
- Consult physician before using potassium-containing salt substitutes.

MOLINDONE HYDROCHLORIDE
(moe-lin′done)
Moban
Classifications: PSYCHOTHERAPEUTIC; ANTIPSYCHOTIC, PHENOTHIAZINE
Therapeutic: ANTIPSYCHOTIC
Prototype: Chlorpromazine
Pregnancy Category: C

AVAILABILITY 5 mg, 10 mg, 25 mg, 50 mg, 100 mg tablets; 20 mg/mL liquid

ACTION & *THERAPEUTIC EFFECT*
Phenothiazine antipsychotic thought to block postsynaptic dopamine receptors in the brain. Has less sedative but greater incidence of extrapyramidal adverse effects than chlorpromazine. EEG studies suggest ascending reticular system is chief site of action. *Reportedly lowers convulsive threshold and produces tranquilization without compromising alertness. Antipsychotic effect includes reduction in*

bizarre behavior, and control of aggressiveness.

USES Management of manifestations of psychotic disorders.

CONTRAINDICATIONS Known hypersensitivity to molindone or to phenothiazines, or sulfites; severe CNS depression; severe cardiovascular disease; comatose states; children less than 12 y, pregnancy (category C), lactation.

CAUTIOUS USE Those harmed by increase in physical activity; prostatic hypertrophy; cardiovascular disease; previously detected cancer of breast.

ROUTE & DOSAGE

Psychotic Disorders
Adult: **PO** 50–75 mg/d in 3–4 divided doses, may be increased to 100 mg/d in 3–4 d or may be able to decrease to 15–60 mg/d in divided doses (max: 225 mg/d)

ADMINISTRATION

Oral
- Be certain patient swallows the medication.
- Store medication in tightly capped, light-resistant bottles. Protect from heat and moisture.

ADVERSE EFFECTS (≥1%) **CNS:** *Transient drowsiness,* insomnia, *extrapyramidal symptoms* (dose related), euphoria, neuroleptic malignant syndrome. **GI:** Dry mouth, constipation, hepatotoxicity. **Special Senses:** Tinnitus, blurred vision, nasal congestion. **Urogenital:** Urinary retention. **Skin:** Mild photosensitivity. **CV:** Tachycardia. **Body as a Whole:** Change in weight. **Endocrine:** SLE-like syndrome, heavy menses, amenorrhea, galactorrhea, gynecomastia, increased libido, premature ejaculation.

INTERACTIONS Drug: May potentiate CNS depression with CNS DEPRESSANTS, **alcohol. Herbal: Kava-kava** may increase risk and severity of dystonic reactions.

PHARMACOKINETICS Absorption: Readily from GI tract. **Peak:** 1 h. **Duration:** 24–36 h. **Distribution:** Into breast milk. **Metabolism:** In liver. **Elimination:** In urine and feces. **Half-Life:** 1.5 h.

CLINICAL IMPLICATIONS

Assessment & Drug Effects
- Withhold dose and consult with physician if the following symptoms occur: Tremor, involuntary twitching, exaggerated restlessness, changes in vision, light-colored stools, sore throat, fever, rash.
- Monitor bowel pattern and urinary output. The depressed patient may not report constipation or urinary retention, both adverse effects of this medicine.
- Supervise ambulation and other ADL in the older adult or debilitated or patient with impaired vision to prevent injury or falling because drug increases motor activity.
- Be alert early during treatment to onset of parkinsonism (extrapyramidal) symptoms: Rigidity, immobility, reduction of voluntary movements, tremors, fine vermicular tongue movements. Withhold dose and report promptly to physician.

Patient & Family Education
- Take drug as prescribed: do not alter dose regimen or stop medication without consulting physician.
- Dizziness during early therapy usually disappears as treatment continues.

M

Common adverse effects in *italic*, life-threatening effects underlined; generic names in **bold**; classifications in SMALL CAPS; ✦ Canadian drug name; ⊚ Prototype drug

1019

- Do not drive or engage in potentially hazardous activities requiring mental or physical coordination until response to drug is known.
- Avoid alcohol and self-medication with other depressants during therapy. Get physician approval before using any OTC drug.
- Relieve dry mouth by rinsing frequently with warm water, increasing noncaloric fluid intake, sucking hard candy.
- Avoid overexertion (patient with angina) and report increase in frequency of precordial pain.
- Schedule periodic ophthalmic examinations when treatment is long-term.

MOMETASONE FUROATE

(mo-met′a-sone)
Asmanex Twisthaler, Elocon, Nasonex
Pregnancy Category: C
See Appendix A-3.

MONTELUKAST

(mon-te-lu′cast)
Singulair
Classifications: BRONCHODILATOR (RESPIRATORY SMOOTH MUSCLE RELAXANT); LEUKOTRIENE RECEPTOR ANTAGONIST
Therapeutic: BRONCHODILATOR; LEUKOTRIENE RECEPTOR ANTAGONIST
Prototype: Zafirlukast
Pregnancy Category: B

AVAILABILITY 5 mg, 10 mg tablets; 4 mg chewable tablets; 4 mg oral granules

ACTION & *THERAPEUTIC EFFECT*
Selective receptor antagonist of leukotriene D$_4$, thus inhibiting bronchoconstriction. Leukotrienes are considered more important than prostaglandins as inflammatory agents; they induce bronchoconstriction and mucus production. Elevated sputum and blood levels of leukotrienes have been documented during acute asthma attacks. *Controls asthmatic attacks by inhibiting leukotriene release as well as inflammatory action associated with the attack. Indicated by improved pulmonary functions and better controlled asthmatic symptoms.*

USES Prophylaxis and chronic treatment of asthma or allergic rhinitis.

CONTRAINDICATIONS Hypersensitivity to montelukast; acute asthma attacks; bronchoconstriction due to asthma or NSAIDs; status asthmaticus; children <6 mo; lactation.
CAUTIOUS USE Hypersensitivity to other leukotriene receptor antagonists (e.g., zafirlukast, zileuton); severe liver disease; jaundice, PKU; severe asthma; pregnancy (category B).

ROUTE & DOSAGE

Asthma
Adult: **PO** 10 mg q.d. in evening
Child: **PO** 12 mo–5 y, 4 mg q.d. in evening; 6–14 y, 5 mg chewable tablet q.d. in evening

ADMINISTRATION

Oral
- Give in the evening for maximum effectiveness.
- Ensure chewable tablets for children are not swallowed whole.
- Store at 15°–30° C (59°–86° F) in a tightly closed container and protect from light.

Common adverse effects in *italic*, life-threatening effects <u>underlined</u>; generic names in **bold**; classifications in SMALL CAPS; ♣ Canadian drug name; ⊘ Prototype drug

ADVERSE EFFECTS (≥1%) **Body as a Whole:** Asthenia, fever, trauma. **CNS:** Dizziness, *headache.* **GI:** Abdominal pain, dyspepsia, gastroenteritis, dental pain, abnormal liver function tests (ALT, AST), diarrhea, nausea. **Respiratory:** Nasal congestion, cough, influenza, laryngitis, pharyngitis, sinusitis. **Skin:** Rash. **Urogenital:** Pyuria.

PHARMACOKINETICS Absorption: Rapidly absorbed from GI tract, bioavailability 64%. **Peak:** 3–4 h for oral tablet, 2–2.5 h for chewable tablet. **Distribution:** >99% protein bound. **Metabolism:** Extensively metabolized by cytochromes P450 3A4 and 2C9. **Elimination:** In feces. **Half-Life:** 2.7–5.5 h.

CLINICAL IMPLICATIONS
Assessment & Drug Effects
- Monitor effectiveness carefully when used in combination with phenobarbital or other potent cytochrome P450 enzyme inducers.
- Lab test: Periodic liver function tests.

Patient & Family Education
- Do not use for reversal of an acute asthmatic attack.
- Inform physician if short-acting inhaled bronchodilators are needed more often than usual with montelukast.
- Use chewable tablets (contain phenylalanine) with caution with PKU.

MORICIZINE

(mor-i′ci-zeen)
Ethmozine
Classifications: ANTIARRHYTHMIC AGENT, CLASS IC
Therapeutic: ANTIARRHYTHMIC, CLASS IC
Prototype: Flecainide
Pregnancy Category: B

AVAILABILITY 200 mg, 250 mg, 300 mg tablets

ACTION & *THERAPEUTIC EFFECT*
Class IC antiarrhythmic agent with potent local anesthetic effect and myocardial membrane stabilizing effects. Shortens phase II and phase III repolarization, resulting in a decreased action potential duration and effective refractory period of the cardiac muscle. Decrease in the maximum rate of phase 0 depolarization (V_{max}) occurs. Sinus node and atrial tissue are not affected. *Prolongs atrioventricular conduction in patients with ventricular tachycardia. In patients with impaired left ventricular functioning, has minimal effects on cardiac index, pulmonary wedge pressure, and ejection fraction, either at rest or during exercise.*

USES Treatment of ventricular tachycardia and ventricular premature depolarizations.
UNLABELED USES Supraventricular arrhythmias.

CONTRAINDICATIONS Preexisting second- and third-degree AV block, right bundle branch block unless a pacemaker is used; cardiogenic shock; hypersensitivity to moricizine; lactation.
CAUTIOUS USE Non-life-threatening arrhythmia; coronary artery disease; hypokalemia, hyperkalemia, hypomagnesia; sick sinus syndrome; hepatic impairment, renal impairment; pregnancy (category B). Safety and efficacy in children <18 y are not established.

ROUTE & DOSAGE

Ventricular and Supraventricular Arrhythmias
Adult: **PO** 200–300 mg q8h

M

Common adverse effects in *italic*, life-threatening effects <u>underlined</u>; generic names in **bold**; classifications in SMALL CAPS; ♦ Canadian drug name; ⊚ Prototype drug

1021

Renal or Hepatic Impairment
Start with 600 mg/d or less

ADMINISTRATION
Oral
- Withdraw previous drug for 1–2 half-lives before transferring to moricizine.
- Dose increments are usually limited to 150 mg/d at 3-d intervals.
- Store at 15°–30° C (59°–86° F) unless otherwise directed by manufacturer.

ADVERSE EFFECTS (≥1%) CV: <u>Arrhythmias, including PVCs and ventricular tachycardia.</u> CNS: *Dizziness, light-headedness, anxiety, headache, euphoria, perioral numbness.* GI: Nausea, diarrhea, dry mouth, abdominal discomfort. **Body as a Whole:** Hyperthermia (rare).

INTERACTIONS Drug: May decrease **theophylline** concentrations. May increase the hypoprothrombinemic effects of **warfarin.**

PHARMACOKINETICS Absorption: Readily absorbed from GI tract. 30–40% reaches systemic circulation due to extensive first-pass metabolism. **Onset:** 2 h. **Peak:** 10–14 h. **Duration:** 10 h. **Distribution:** 92–95% bound to plasma proteins. Distributed into breast milk. **Metabolism:** Extensively metabolized in the liver. **Elimination:** 39% in urine over 2 d, 56% in feces over 4–5 d. **Half-Life:** elimination 10 h.

CLINICAL IMPLICATIONS
Assessment & Drug Effects
- Lab tests: Baseline serum electrolytes, liver and kidney function tests.
- Correct electrolyte imbalances, especially hypo/hyperkalemia and hypomagnesemia prior to beginning drug.

- Monitor cardiac status at beginning and throughout therapy closely because drug may cause serious new arrhythmias or worsening of preexisting arrhythmias.
- Monitor patients with liver or kidney dysfunction closely for adverse effects.
- Monitor patients with sick sinus syndrome or conduction abnormalities carefully. Drug may interfere with sinus activity or cause AV block, both of which may necessitate prompt withdrawal of drug.
- Use precautions for dizziness; it occurs ≥15% of those taking drug.

Patient & Family Education
- Understand seriousness of taking moricizine exactly as prescribed.
- Take drug consistently with respect to meals.
- Keep regular follow-up appointments while taking this drug.
- Report immediately palpitations, irregular heartbeat, chest pains, or fever to physician.

MORPHINE SULFATE ℗

(mor'feen)

Astramorph PF, Avinza, Depo-Dur, Duramorph, Epimorph ✦, Kadian, MSIR, MS Contin, Oramorph SR, Roxanol, RMS, Statex ✦

Classifications: ANALGESIC; NARCOTIC (OPIATE) AGONIST
Therapeutic: NARCOTIC (OPIATE) ANALGESIC
Pregnancy Category: C (D in long-term use or high dose, or close to term)
Controlled Substance: Schedule II

AVAILABILITY 10 mg, 15 mg, 30 mg tablets/capsules; 15 mg, 20 mg, 30 mg, 50 mg, 60 mg, 90 mg, 100 mg, 120 mg, 200 mg controlled release tablets/capsules; 10 mg/2.5 mL, 10 mg/5 mL, 20 mg/mL, 20 mg/5 mL, 30 mg/1.5 mL, 100 mg/5 mL oral solution; 0.5 mg/mL, 1 mg/mL, 2 mg/mL, 4 mg/mL, 5 mg/mL, 8 mg/mL, 10 mg/mL, 15 mg/mL, 25 mg/mL, 50 mg/mL injection; 10 mg/mL extended release lysosomal injection; 5 mg, 10 mg, 20 mg, 30 mg suppositories

ACTION & *THERAPEUTIC EFFECT*
Natural opium alkaloid with agonist activity by binding with the same receptors as endogenous opioid peptides. Narcotic agonist effects are identified with 3 locations of receptors: analgesia at supraspinal level, euphoria, respiratory depression and physical dependence; analgesia at spinal level, sedation and miosis; and dysphoric, hallucinogenic, and cardiac stimulant effects. *Controls severe pain; also used as an adjunct to anesthesia.*

USES Symptomatic relief of severe acute and chronic pain after nonnarcotic analgesics have failed and as preanesthetic medication; also used to relieve dyspnea of acute left ventricular failure and pulmonary edema and pain of MI.

CONTRAINDICATIONS Hypersensitivity to opiates; increased intracranial pressure; convulsive disorders; acute alcoholism; acute bronchial asthma, chronic pulmonary diseases, severe respiratory depression; chemical-irritant induced pulmonary edema; prostatic hypertrophy; diarrhea caused by poisoning until the toxic material has been eliminated; undiagnosed acute abdominal conditions; following biliary tract surgery and surgical anastomosis; pancreatitis; acute ulcerative colitis; severe liver or renal insufficiency; Addison's disease; hypothyroidism; during labor for delivery of a premature infant, in premature infants; pregnancy (category C; D in longterm use or when high dose is used, or close to term).

CAUTIOUS USE Toxic psychosis; cardiac arrhythmias, cardiovascular disease; emphysema; kyphoscoliosis; cor pulmonale; severe obesity; reduced blood volume; very old, very young, or debilitated patients; labor.

ROUTE & DOSAGE

Pain Relief
Adult: **PO** 10–30 mg q4h prn or 15–30 mg sustained release q8–12h; **(Kadian)** dose q12–24h, increase dose prn for pain relief; **(Avinza)** dose q24h **IV** 2.5–15 mg/70 kg q2–4h or 0.8–10 mg/h by continuous infusion, may increase prn to control pain or 5–10 mg given epidurally q24h **Epidural (DepoDur** only) 10–15 mg as single dose 30 min before surgery (max: 20 mg) **IM/SC** 5–20 mg q4h **PR** 10–20 mg q4h prn
Child: **IV** 0.05–0.1 mg/kg q4h or 0.025–2.6 mg/kg/h by continuous infusion (max: 10 mg/dose) **IM/SC** 0.1–0.2 mg/kg q4h (max: 15 mg/dose) **PO** 0.2–0.5 mg/kg q4–6h; 0.3–0.6 mg/kg sustained release q12h
Neonate: **IV/IM/SC** 0.05 mg/kg q4–8h (max: 0.1 mg/kg/dose) or 0.01–0.02 mg/kg/h

Renal Impairment
Cl_{cr} 10–50 mL/min: use 75% of dose, if lower use 50% of dose

ADMINISTRATION
Oral
- Use a fixed, individualized schedule when narcotic analgesic therapy is started to provide effective management; blood levels can be

maintained and peaks of pain can be prevented (usually a 4-h interval is adequate).

- Use lower dosage for older adult or debilitated patients than for adults.
- Do not break in half, crush, or allow sustained release tablet to be chewed.
- Do not give patient sustained release tablet within 24 h of surgery.
- Dilute oral solution in approximately 30 mL or more of fluid or semisolid food. A calibrated dropper comes with the bottle. Read labels carefully when using liquid preparation; available solutions: 20 mg/mL; 100 mg/mL.

Intravenous

Note: Verify correct IV concentration and rate of infusion/injection for administration to neonates, infants, or children with physician.

PREPARE: Direct: Dilute 2–10 mg in at least 5 mL of sterile water for injection.

ADMINISTER: Direct: Give a single dose over 4–5 min. Avoid rapid administration.

INCOMPATIBILITIES Solution/additive: Alteplase, Aminophylline, amobarbital, chlorothiazide, floxacillin, fluorouracil, haloperidol, heparin, meperidine, nitrofurantoin, pentobarbital, phenobarbital, perphenazine, phenytoin, sodium bicarbonate, thiopental. Y-site: Amphotericin B cholesteryl complex, azithromycin, cefepime, doxorubicin liposome, gallium, minocycline, phenytoin, sargramostim, tetracycline.

- Store at 15°–30° C (59°–86° F). Avoid freezing. Refrigerate suppositories. Protect all formulations from light.

ADVERSE EFFECTS (≥1%) **Body as a Whole:** Hypersensitivity [*Pruritus*, rash, urticaria, edema, hemorrhagic urticaria (rare), <u>anaphylactoid reaction</u> (rare)], sweating, skeletal muscle flaccidity; cold, clammy skin, hypothermia. **CNS:** Euphoria, insomnia, disorientation, visual disturbances, dysphoria, paradoxic CNS stimulation (restlessness, tremor, delirium, insomnia), convulsions (infants and children); decreased cough reflex, drowsiness, dizziness, deep sleep, coma, continuous intrathecal infusion may cause granulomas leading to paralysis. **Special Senses:** Miosis. **CV:** Bradycardia, palpitations, syncope; flushing of face, neck, and upper thorax; orthostatic hypotension, <u>cardiac arrest</u>. **GI:** *Constipation*, anorexia, dry mouth, biliary colic, *nausea*, vomiting, elevated transaminase levels. **Urogenital:** Urinary retention or urgency, dysuria, oliguria, reduced libido or potency (prolonged use). **Other:** Prolonged labor and respiratory depression of newborn. **Hematologic:** Precipitation of porphyria. **Respiratory:** <u>Severe respiratory depression</u> (as low as 2–4/min) or <u>arrest</u>; pulmonary edema.

DIAGNOSTIC TEST INTERFERENCE
False-positive *urine glucose* determinations may occur using *Benedict's solution*. *Plasma amylase* and *lipase* determinations may be falsely positive for 24 h after use of morphine; *transaminase levels* may be elevated.

INTERACTIONS Drug: CNS DEPRESSANTS, SEDATIVES, BARBITURATES, BENZODIAZEPINES, and TRICYCLIC ANTIDEPRESSANTS potentiate CNS depressant effects. Use MAO INHIBITORS cautiously; they may precipitate hypertensive crisis. PHENOTHIAZINES may antagonize analgesia. Use with **al-**

Common adverse effects in *italic*, life-threatening effects <u>underlined</u>; generic names in **bold**; classifications in SMALL CAPS; ♣ Canadian drug name; ● Prototype drug

cohol may lead to potentially fatal overdoses. **Herbal: Kava-kava, valerian, St. John's wort** may increase sedation.

PHARMACOKINETICS Absorption: Variably from GI tract. **Peak:** 60 min PO; 20–60 min PR; 50–90 min SC; 30–60 min IM; 20 min IV. **Duration:** Up to 7 h. **Distribution:** Crosses blood–brain barrier and placenta; distributed in breast milk. **Metabolism:** In liver. **Elimination:** 90% in urine in 24 h; 7–10% in bile.

CLINICAL IMPLICATIONS

Assessment & Drug Effects

- Obtain baseline respiratory rate, depth, and rhythm and size of pupils before administering the drug. Respirations of 12/min or below and miosis are signs of toxicity. Withhold drug and report to physician.
- Observe patient closely to be certain pain relief is achieved. Record relief of pain and duration of analgesia.
- Be alert to elevated pulse or respiratory rate, restlessness, anorexia, or drawn facial expression that may indicate need for analgesia.
- Differentiate among restlessness as a sign of pain and the need for medication, restlessness associated with hypoxia, and restlessness caused by morphine-induced CNS stimulation (a paradoxic reaction that is particularly common in women and older adult patients).
- Monitor for respiratory depression; it can be severe for as long as 24 h after epidural or intrathecal administration.
- Monitor carefully those at risk for severe respiratory depression after epidural or intrathecal injection: Older adult or debilitated patients or those with decreased respira-

tory reserve (e.g., emphysema, severe obesity, kyphoscoliosis).

- Continue monitoring for respiratory depression for at least 24 h after each epidural or intrathecal dose.
- Assess vital signs at regular intervals. Morphine-induced respiratory depression may occur even with small doses, and it increases progressively with higher doses (generally max: 90 min after SC, 30 min after IM, and 7 min after IV).
- Encourage changes in position, deep breathing, and coughing (unless contraindicated) at regularly scheduled intervals. Narcotic analgesics also depress cough and sigh reflexes and thus may induce atelectasis, especially in postoperative patients.
- Be alert for nausea and orthostatic hypotension (with light-headedness and dizziness) in ambulatory patients or when a supine patient assumes the head-up position or in patients not experiencing severe pain.
- Monitor I&O ratio and pattern. Report oliguria or urinary retention. Morphine may dull perception of bladder stimuli; therefore, encourage the patient to void at least q4h. Palpate lower abdomen to detect bladder distention.

Patient & Family Education

- Avoid alcohol and other CNS depressants while receiving morphine.
- Do not use of any OTC drug unless approved by physician.
- Do not smoke or ambulate without assistance after receiving drug. Bedside rails are advised.
- Use caution or avoid tasks requiring alertness (e.g., driving a car) until response to drug is known since morphine may cause drowsiness, dizziness, or blurred vision.

Common adverse effects in *italic*, life-threatening effects underlined; generic names in **bold**; classifications in SMALL CAPS; ♣ Canadian drug name; ⊙ Prototype drug

1025

MOXIFLOXACIN HYDROCHLORIDE

(mox-i-flox'a-sin)
Avelox, Vigamox
Classifications: ANTIBIOTIC;
QUINOLONE
Therapeutic: ANTIBIOTIC; QUINOLONE
Prototype: Ciprofloxacin
Pregnancy Category: C

AVAILABILITY 400 mg tablets;
0.5% ophthalmic solution; 160 mg/
100 mL infusion

ACTION & *THERAPEUTIC EFFECT*
Moxifloxacin is a synthetic broad-
spectrum antibiotic belonging to
the fluoroquinolone class of drugs.
It inhibits DNA gyrase, an enzyme
required for DNA replication, transcription, repair, and recombination
of bacterial DNA. *Broad spectrum
antibiotic that is bactericidal
against gram-positive and gram-
negative organisms.*

USES Treatment of acute bacterial
sinusitis, acute bacterial exacerbation of chronic bronchitis, community-acquired pneumonia, skin and
skin structure infections, bacterial
conjunctivitis, complicated skin infections.

CONTRAINDICATIONS Hypersensitivity to moxifloxacin or other quinolones; moderate to severe hepatic
insufficiency; syphilis; patients with
history of prolonged QTc interval
on ECG, history of ventricular arrhythmias, atrial fibrillation, hypokalemia, bradycardia, acute myocardial ischemia, acute MI, patients
receiving Class IA or Class III antiarrhythmic drugs; tendon pain; viral infection; torsades de pointes;
pregnancy (category C); lactation;
ocular preparation use in children
<1 y.

CAUTIOUS USE CNS disorders;
cerebrovascular disease, colitis, diarrhea, GI disease; diabetes mellitus; mild or moderate heart insufficiency; myasthenia gravis; seizure
disorder; sunlight (UV) exposure.

ROUTE & DOSAGE

**Acute Bacterial Sinusitis, Acute
Bacterial Exacerbation of Chronic
Bronchitis, Community-Acquired
Pneumonia, Skin Infections**
Adult: **PO/IV** 400 mg q.d. × 5–
14 d

Complicated Skin Infection
Adult: **PO/IV** 400 mg q.d. × 7–
21 d

Bacterial Conjunctivitis
Adult/Child: **Ophthalmic** >1 y, 1
drop in affected eye(s) t.i.d. × 7 d

ADMINISTRATION

▪ Note: Do not administer to persons with QTc prolongation, hypokalemia, or those receiving Class IA
or Class III antiarrhythmic drugs.

Intravenous

PREPARE: **IV Infusion:** Avelox
(400 mg) is supplied in ready-
to-use 250 mL IV bags. No further dilution is necessary.
ADMINISTER: **IV Infusion:** Give
over 60 min. AVOID RAPID OR
BOLUS DOSE.

Oral

▪ Administer at least 4 h before or 8
h after multivitamins containing
iron or zinc, or antacids containing
magnesium, calcium, aluminum,
or sucralfate.
▪ Store at 15°–30° C (59°–86° F);
protect from high humidity.

ADVERSE EFFECTS (≥1%) CNS:
Dizziness, headache, peripheral
neuropathy. **GI:** Nausea, diarrhea,

abdominal pain, vomiting, taste perversion, abnormal liver function tests, dyspepsia. **Musculoskeletal:** Tendon rupture, cartilage erosion.

DIAGNOSTIC TEST INTERFERENCE May cause false positive on *opiate screening tests.*

INTERACTIONS Drug: Iron, zinc, ANTACIDS, **aluminum, magnesium, calcium, sucralfate** decrease absorption; **atenolol, erythromycin,** ANTIPSYCHOTICS, TRICYCLIC ANTIDEPRESSANTS, **quinidine, procainamide, amiodarone, sotalol** may cause prolonged QT$_C$ interval.

PHARMACOKINETICS Absorption: 90% bioavailable. **Steady State:** 3 d. **Distribution:** 50% protein bound. **Metabolism:** In liver. **Elimination:** Unchanged drug: 20% in urine, 25% in feces; metabolites: 38% in feces, 14% in urine. **Half-Life:** 12 h.

CLINICAL IMPLICATIONS

Assessment & Drug Effects

▪ Monitor therapeutic effectiveness indicated by clinical improvement of infection.
▪ Monitor for and notify physician immediately of adverse CNS effects.
▪ Notify physician immediately for S&S of hypersensitivity (see Appendix F).
▪ Lab tests: C&S before initiation of therapy and baseline serum potassium with history of hypokalemia.

Patient & Family Education

▪ Exercise care in timing of consumption of vitamins and antacids (see ADMINISTRATION).
▪ Drink fluids liberally, unless directed otherwise.
▪ Increased seizure potential is possible, especially when history of seizure exists.

▪ Stop taking drug and notify physician if experiencing palpitations, fainting, skin rash, severe diarrhea, ankle/foot pain, agitation, insomnia.
▪ Avoid engaging in hazardous activities until reaction to drug is known.

MUPIROCIN

(mu-pi-ro′sin)
Bactroban, Bactroban Nasal
Classifications: PSEUDOMONIC ACID ANTIBIOTIC
Therapeutic: ANTIBIOTIC
Pregnancy Category: B

AVAILABILITY 2% ointment; cream

ACTION & THERAPEUTIC EFFECT Topical antibacterial produced by fermentation of *Pseudomonas fluorescens.* Inhibits bacterial protein synthesis by binding with the bacterial transfer RNA. *Susceptible bacteria are* Staphylococcus aureus *[including methicillin-resistant (MRSA) and beta-lactamase-producing strains] and other* Staphylococcus *and* Streptococcus pyogenes.

USES Impetigo due to *Staphylococcus aureus*, beta-hemolytic *Streptococci*, and *Streptococcus pyogenes;* nasal carriage of *S. aureus*.
UNLABELED USES Superficial skin infections; burns.

CONTRAINDICATIONS Hypersensitivity to any of its components and for ophthalmic use; lactation (do not apply to breast); children <12 y (intranasal form); moderate to severe renal impairment.
CAUTIOUS USE Pregnancy (category B), lactation.

Common adverse effects in *italic*, life-threatening effects underlined; generic names in **bold**; classifications in SMALL CAPS; ♦ Canadian drug name; ⊘ Prototype drug

1027

ROUTE & DOSAGE

Impetigo

Adult/Child: **Topical** Apply to affected area t.i.d., if no response in 3–5 d, reevaluate (usually continue for 1–2 wk)

Elimination of Staphylococcal Nasal Carriage

Child: **Intranasal** Apply intranasally b.i.d. to q.i.d. for 5–14 d

ADMINISTRATION

Topical

- Apply thin layer of medication to affected area.
- Cover area being treated with a gauze dressing if desired.

ADVERSE EFFECTS (≥1%) **Skin:** Burning, stinging, pain, pruritus, rash, erythema, dry skin, tenderness, swelling. **Special Senses:** Intranasal, local stinging, soreness, dry skin, pruritus.

INTERACTIONS Drug: Incompatible with **salicylic acid 2%**; do not mix in HYDROPHILIC VEHICLES (e.g., **Aquaphor**) or COAL TAR SOLUTIONS; **chloramphenicol** may interfere with bactericidal action of mupirocin.

PHARMACOKINETICS Absorption: Not systemically absorbed.

CLINICAL IMPLICATIONS

Assessment & Drug Effects

- Watch for signs and symptoms of superinfection (see Appendix F). Prolonged or repeated therapy may result in superinfection by nonsusceptible organisms.
- Reevaluate drug use if patient does not show clinical response within 3–5 d.
- Discontinue the drug and notify physician if signs of contact dermatitis develop or if exudate production increases.

Patient & Family Education

- Discontinue drug and contact physician if a sensitivity reaction or chemical irritation occurs (e.g., increased redness, itching, burning).

MUROMONAB-CD3

(myoo-roe-moe′nab)
Orthoclone OKT3
Classifications: IMMUNOSUPPRESSANT; MONOCLONAL ANTIBODY
Therapeutic: IMMUNOSUPPRESSANT
Prototype: Cyclosporine
Pregnancy Category: C

AVAILABILITY 1 mg/mL injection

ACTION & *THERAPEUTIC EFFECT*
Murine monoclonal antibody (purified IgG$_2$). Specifically targets the T$_3$ (CD$_3$) molecule in the antigenic recognition site of the human T-cell membrane. Following this antigenic challenge, CD$_3$-positive T-cells are rapidly removed from circulation, and T-lymphocyte action leading to renal inflammation and destruction is blocked, thus reversing graft rejection. *CD$_3$-positive T-lymphocyte immunosuppression results in reversing graft rejection of a transplanted kidney.*

USES Acute allograft rejection in kidney transplant patients.
UNLABELED USES Acute allograft rejection in heart and liver transplant patients.

CONTRAINDICATIONS Intolerance to any product of murine origin; patient with fluid overload; weight gain of more than 3% within week prior to treatment; infection: chickenpox (existing, recent, including

M

recent exposure), seizure disorders; herpes zoster; pregnancy (category C), lactation.

CAUTIOUS USE Recent MI; ischemic cardiac disease, CAD; pulmonary edema; repeated courses.

ROUTE & DOSAGE

Transplant Rejection

Adult: **IV** 5 mg/d for 10–14 d
Child: **IV** ≤30 kg, 2.5 mg q.d.; >30 kg, 5 mg q.d.

ADMINISTRATION

Note: Only persons experienced with immunosuppressive therapy and management of kidney transplant patients should administer muromonab-CD3 and only in an area equipped with staff and facilities to deal with cardiac resuscitation.

Intravenous

Note: Verify correct rate of IV injection for administration to infants or children with physician.

- Administer IV methylprednisolone sodium succinate before and IV hydrocortisone sodium succinate 30 min after muromonab-CD3 to decrease incidence of first dose reaction.
- Be aware that concomitant maintenance immunosuppressive therapy is reduced or discontinued during drug therapy with muromonab-CD3 and resumed about 3 d prior to end of therapy.

PREPARE: Direct: Give undiluted. Do not shake ampule. Draw sterile solution into syringe through a low protein-binding 0.2- or 0.22-micron filter. Discard filter; attach syringe to an appropriate needle for IV bolus injection.

ADMINISTER: Direct: Give by rapid (bolus) injection. Do not give by IV infusion or in conjunction with other drug solutions.

- Store at 2°–8° C (36°–46° F) unless otherwise stipulated. Avoid freezing.

ADVERSE EFFECTS (≥1%) **All:** Especially during first 2 d of therapy. **GI:** *Nausea, vomiting, diarrhea.* **Respiratory:** <u>Severe pulmonary edema</u>, *dyspnea, chest pain, wheezing.* **Body as a Whole:** *Fever, chills,* malaise, *tremor, increased susceptibility to cytomegalovirus, herpes simplex, Pneumocystis carinii, Legionella, Cryptococcus, Serratia* organisms, and gram-negative bacteria. **CV:** Tachycardia.

PHARMACOKINETICS Onset: The number of circulating CD3-positive T-cells decreases within minutes. **Peak:** 2–7 d. **Duration:** 7 d.

CLINICAL IMPLICATIONS

Assessment & Drug Effects

- Assess and monitor vital signs. If temperature rises above 37.8° C (100° F), suspect infection (commonly observed in first 45 d of therapy). Take temperature before treatment and several hours after drug administration to detect first signs of infection.
- Consult physician if patient has a fever exceeding 37.8° C (100° F) before treatment. Make immediate attempts to lower temperature to at least 37.8° C (100° F) with antipyretics before muromonab-CD3 is administered.
- Be alert to susceptibility of patient with pretreatment fluid over-load to acute pulmonary edema (may be fatal). Be prepared for prompt intubation, oxygenation, and cor-

M

Common adverse effects in *italic*, life-threatening effects <u>underlined</u>; generic names in **bold**; classifications in SMALL CAPS; ♣ Canadian drug name; ⊘ Prototype drug

1029

ticosteroid drug administration should it occur.

■ Monitor patient's response closely for 48 h for first dose reaction (occurs within 45–60 min after first dose and lasts several hours). It may occur (less severe) after second dose; then usually does not occur with subsequent doses. Symptoms: Chills, dyspnea, malaise, high fever.

Patient & Family Education

■ Report any of the following to physician: Chest pain, difficulty breathing, wheezing, nausea and vomiting, significant weight gain, an infection, or fever.

■ Use an effective method of birth control for 12 wk following the end of therapy.

MYCOPHENOLATE MOFETIL

(my-co-phen'o-late mo'fe-till)
CellCept

MYCOPHENOLATE ACID

Myfortic

Classifications: BIOLOGIC RESPONSE MODIFIER; IMMUNOSUPPRESSANT
Therapeutic: IMMUNOSUPPRESSANT
Prototype: Cyclosporine
Pregnancy Category: C

AVAILABILITY 250 mg capsules; 500 mg tablets; 180 mg, 360 mg delayed-release tablets; 500 mg injection; 200 mg/mL oral solution

ACTION & THERAPEUTIC EFFECT
Prodrug with immunosuppressant properties; inhibits T- and B-lymphocyte proliferation responses; inhibits antibody formation, and blocks the generation of cytotoxic T-cells. *Antirejection effects attributed to decreased number of activated lymphocytes in the graft site. Synergistic with cyclosporine.*

USES Prophylaxis of organ rejection in patients receiving allogenic kidney, liver, or heart transplants.
UNLABELED USES Treatment of rheumatoid arthritis and psoriasis.

CONTRAINDICATIONS Hypersensitivity to mycophenolate mofetil; vaccination, varicella; pregnancy (category C), lactation; children <5 y.
CAUTIOUS USE Viral or bacterial infections; presence or history of carcinoma; bone marrow suppression; active peptic ulcer disease; cholestasis; gallbladder disease; GI disease, severe diarrhea; malabsorption syndromes; hepatic encephalopathy, hepatic or renal impairment; renal failure, uremia; herpes infection, infection; hypoalbuminemia; PKU; lactase deficiency.

ROUTE & DOSAGE

Note: CellCept and Myfortic are not interchangeable.

Prophylaxis for Kidney Transplant Rejection

Adult: **PO/IV** Start within 24 h of transplant, 1 g (mofetil) or 720 mg (sodium) b.i.d. in combination with corticosteroids and cyclosporine
Child: **PO** 600 mg/m² (mofetil) or 400 mg/m² (sodium) b.i.d. (max: 2 g/d mofetil, 720 mg/d sodium)

Prophylaxis for Heart/Liver Transplant Rejection

Adult: **PO/IV** 1.5 g (mofetil) b.i.d. started within 24 h of transplant

ADMINISTRATION

Oral

- Give oral drug on an empty stomach.
- Adjust dosage with severe chronic kidney failure.
- Do not open or crush capsules; avoid contact with powder in capsules, and wash thoroughly with soap and water if contact occurs.

Intravenous

PREPARE: **IV Infusion:** Reconstitute each vial with 14 mL D5W. Further dilute vial used in an additional 70 mL with D5W to yield 6 mg/mL.

ADMINISTER: **IV Infusion:** Slowly infuse over ≥2 h. Avoid rapid injection.

INCOMPATIBILITIES **Solution/additive & Y-site:** Do not mix or infuse with other medications.

- Begin IV mycophenolate mofetil within 24 h of transplant and continued for up to 14 d.
- Switch patient to oral drug as soon as possible.
- Store at 15°–30° C (59°–86° F).

ADVERSE EFFECTS (≥1%) CNS:
Headache, tremor, insomnia, dizziness, weakness. **CV:** *Hypertension.* **Endocrine:** Hyperglycemia, hypercholesterolemia, hypophosphatemia, hypokalemia, hyperkalemia, *peripheral edema.* **GI:** *Diarrhea, constipation, nausea,* anorexia, vomiting, *abdominal pain, dyspepsia.* **Urogenital:** *UTI, hematuria,* renal tubular necrosis, burning, frequency, vaginal burning or itching, vaginal bleeding, kidney stones. **Hematologic:** *Leukopenia, anemia, thrombocytopenia,* hypochromic anemia, leukocytosis. **Respiratory:** *Respiratory infection, dyspnea,* increased cough, pharyngitis. **Skin:** Rash. **Body as a Whole:** Leg or hand cramps, bone pain, myalgias, *sepsis (bacterial, fungal, viral).*

INTERACTIONS Drug: Acyclovir, ganciclovir may increase mycophenolate serum levels. ANTACIDS, **cholestyramine** decreases mycophenolate absorption. **Mycophenolate** may decrease protein binding of **phenytoin** or **theophylline,** causing increased serum levels.

PHARMACOKINETICS Absorption:
Rapidly from GI tract; 94% reaches systemic circulation; absorption decreased by food. **Onset:** 4 wk. **Metabolism:** In liver to active form, mycophenolic acid. **Elimination:** 87% in urine. **Half-Life:** 11 h.

CLINICAL IMPLICATIONS

Assessment & Drug Effects

- Lab tests: Monitor CBC weekly for first month, biweekly for second and third months, then once per month for first year. If neutropenia develops (ANC <1.3 × 10³/mcL), withhold dose and notify physician. Periodically monitor and report abnormalities for any of the following: Kidney and liver function, serum electrolytes, lipase, and amylase; blood glucose; routine urinalysis.
- Monitor for and report any S&S of sepsis or infection.

Patient & Family Education

- Comply exactly with dosing regimen and scheduled laboratory tests.
- Report to physician immediately S&S of infection, such as UTI or respiratory infection.
- Report all troubling adverse reactions (e.g., blood in urine and swelling in arms and legs) to physician as soon as possible.
- Avoid taking OTC antacids simultaneously with mycophenolate mofetil. Separate the two drugs by 2 h.

M

NABILONE

(nab'i-lone)
Cesamet
Classifications: SYNTHETIC CAN-
NABINOID; ANTIEMETIC
Therapeutic: ANTIEMETIC; CANNAB-
INOID
Pregnancy Category: C
Controlled Substance: Schedule II

AVAILABILITY 1 mg capsules

ACTION & *THERAPEUTIC EFFECT*
Nabilone is a synthetic cannabinoid with multiple effects on the
CNS. It is thought that the antiemetic effect results from its interaction with the cannabinoid receptor system (CB 1 receptor) in
neural tissues. In therapeutic
doses, it produces relaxation,
drowsiness, and euphoria. *It effectively controls emesis in patients receiving chemotherapy when other
drugs have failed.*

USES Prevention and treatment of
nausea and vomiting in adult patients induced by cancer chemotherapy refractory to standard antiemetic therapy.

CONTRAINDICATIONS Hypersensitivity to any cannabinoid; hypovolemia; pregnancy (category C); lactation.
CAUTIOUS USE Children; older
adults; history of psychosis.

ROUTE & DOSAGE

Nausea and Vomiting
Adult: **PO:** Initial dose of 1 or 2
mg b.i.d. 1–3 h before chemotherapy. May increase to max
of 2 mg t.i.d. May continue for
48 h after last dose of chemotherapy

ADMINISTRATION
Oral
- Give 1–3 h before chemotherapy
is begun. A dose of 1–2 mg the
night before chemotherapy may
be helpful in relieving nausea.
- Store at 15°–30° C (59°–86° F).

ADVERSE EFFECTS (≥1%) **CNS:**
Asthenia, *ataxia, confusion difficulties,* depersonalization, *depression,*
disorientation, *drowsiness, dysphoria, euphoria,* headache, sedation,
sleep disturbance, vertigo. **CV:** Hypotension. **GI:** Anorexia, *dry mouth,*
increased appetite, nausea. **Special
Senses:** *Visual disturbances.*

INTERACTIONS Drug: SEDATIVES, HYP-
NOTICS, and other psychoactive substances can potentiate the CNS effects of nabilone. Coadministration
of cannabinoids with **amphetamine, cocaine,** TRICYCLIC ANTIDEPRES-
SANTS, and/or SYMPATHOMIMETIC
AGENTS can produce additive hypertension and tachycardia. Coadministration of cannabinoids with ANTIHIS-
TAMINES or ANTICHOLINERGIC AGENTS
can produce additive tachycardia
and drowsiness. Coadministration of
cannabinoids with BARBITURATES, BEN-
ZODIAZEPINES, **buspirone, ethanol,
lithium,** MUSCLE RELAXANTS, OPIOIDS,
and other CNS DEPRESSANTS can produce additive drowsiness and CNS-
depressant effects. **Food: Alcohol**
can potentiate the CNS effects of
nabilone.

PHARMACOKINETICS Absorption:
Complete absorption from GI tract.
Peak: 2 h. **Metabolism:** Extensive
hepatic metabolism. **Elimination:** Fecal (major) and urine. **Half-Life:** 2 h.

CLINICAL IMPLICATIONS
Assessment & Drug Effects
- Monitor for and report S&S of adverse psychiatric reactions (e.g.,

disorientation, hallucinations, psychosis) for 48–72 h after last dose of nabilone.

- Monitor for S&S of tachycardia and postural hypotension, especially in the older adult and those with a history of heart disease or hypertension.
- Lab tests: Periodic CBC with Hgb & Hct.

Patient & Family Education

- Do not use alcohol or other CNS depressants while using this medication.
- Do not drive or engage in potentially hazardous activities until response to drug is known.
- Report any of the following to a health care provider: confusion, disorientation, hallucinations, or other bizarre behavior.

NABUMETONE

(na-bu-me'tone)

Relafen

Classifications: ANALGESIC, NONSTEROIDAL ANTIINFLAMMATORY DRUG (NSAID); ANTIPYRETIC
Therapeutic: NSAID, ANALGESIC; ANTIPYRETIC
Prototype: Ibuprofen
Pregnancy Category: C

AVAILABILITY 500 mg, 750 mg tablets

ACTION & *THERAPEUTIC EFFECT*
Blocks prostaglandin synthesis by inhibiting cyclooxygenase, an enzyme that converts arachidonic acid to precursors of prostaglandins. *Antiinflammatory, analgesic, and antipyretic effects. Inhibits platelet aggregation and prolongs bleeding time but does not affect prothrombin or whole blood clotting times.*

USES Rheumatoid arthritis and osteoarthritis.

CONTRAINDICATIONS Patients in whom urticaria, severe rhinitis, bronchospasm, angioedema, or nasal polyps are precipitated by aspirin or other NSAIDs; salicylate hypersensitivity; active peptic ulcer; bleeding abnormalities; CABG perioperative pain; pregnancy (category C), lactation. Safe use in children <6 mo is not established.
CAUTIOUS USE Hypertension, history of GI ulceration, impaired liver or kidney function, chronic kidney failure, cardiac decompensation, bone marrow suppression; patients with SLE.

ROUTE & DOSAGE

Rheumatoid & Osteoarthritis
Adult: **PO** 1000 mg/d as a single dose, may increase (max: of 2000 mg/d in 1–2 divided doses)

ADMINISTRATION

Oral

- Give with food, milk, or antacid (if prescribed) to reduce the possibility of GI upset.
- Store at 15°–30° C (59°–86° F).

ADVERSE EFFECTS (≥1%) **GI:** Diarrhea, abdominal pain, nausea, dyspepsia, flatulence, melena, ulcers, constipation, dry mouth, gastritis. **CNS:** Tinnitus, dizziness, headache, insomnia, vertigo, fatigue, diaphoresis, nervousness, somnolence. **Skin:** Rash, pruritus.

INTERACTIONS Drug: May attenuate the antihypertensive response to DIURETICS. NSAIDs increase the risk of **methotrexate** toxicity. **Food:** Food may increase the peak but not the overall absorption of nabumetone. **Herbal: Feverfew, garlic, ginger,**

Common adverse effects in *italic*, life-threatening effects <u>underlined</u>; generic names in **bold**; classifications in SMALL CAPS; ♣ Canadian drug name; ☺ Prototype drug

1033

ginkgo may increase bleeding potential.

PHARMACOKINETICS Absorption: Readily absorbed from GI tract; approximately 35% is converted to its active metabolite on first pass through the liver. **Onset:** 1–3 wk for antirheumatic action. **Peak:** 3–6 h. **Distribution:** 99% protein bound; distributes into synovial fluid. **Metabolism:** In liver to its active metabolite, 6-methoxy-2-naphthylacetic acid (6MNA). **Elimination:** 80% of dose is excreted in urine as 6MNA; 10% excreted in feces. **Half-Life:** 24 h (6MNA).

CLINICAL IMPLICATIONS

Assessment & Drug Effects

▪ Lab tests: Obtain baseline and periodic evaluation of Hgb and Hct levels with prolonged or high-dose therapy.

▪ Monitor for signs and symptoms of GI bleeding.

Patient & Family Education

▪ Use caution with hazardous activities since nabumetone may cause dizziness, drowsiness, and blurred vision.

▪ Report abdominal pain, nausea, dyspepsia, or black tarry stools.

▪ Be aware that alcohol and aspirin will increase the risk of GI ulceration and bleeding.

▪ Notify your physician if any of the following occur: persistent headache, skin rash or itching, visual disturbances, weight gain, or edema.

NADOLOL

(nay-doe'lole)
Corgard
Classifications: BETA-ADRENERGIC ANTAGONIST (ADRENERGIC BLOCKING AGENT); ANTIHYPERTENSIVE

Therapeutic: ANTIHYPERTENSIVE; BETA-ADRENERGIC ANTAGONIST
Prototype: Propranolol
Pregnancy Category: C

AVAILABILITY 20 mg, 40 mg, 80 mg, 120 mg, 160 mg tablets

ACTION & *THERAPEUTIC EFFECT*
Nonselective beta-adrenergic blocking agent pharmacologically and chemically similar to propranolol. Inhibits response to adrenergic stimuli by competitively blocking beta-adrenergic receptors within the heart. Reduces heart rate and cardiac output at rest and during exercise, and also decreases conduction velocity through AV node and myocardial automaticity. *Decreases both systolic and diastolic BP at rest and during exercise. Suppression of $beta_2$-adrenergic receptors in bronchial and vascular smooth muscle may cause bronchospasm and a Raynaud's-like phenomenon.*

USES Hypertension, either alone or in combination with a diuretic. Also long-term prophylactic management of angina pectoris.

CONTRAINDICATIONS Bronchial asthma, severe COPD, inadequate myocardial function, sinus bradycardia, greater than first-degree conduction block, overt cardiac failure, cardiogenic shock; pregnancy (category C). Safe use in children <18 y is not established.
CAUTIOUS USE CHF; diabetes mellitus; hyperthyroidism; renal failure, renal impairment.

ROUTE & DOSAGE

Hypertension, Angina
Adult: **PO** 40 mg once/d, may increase up to 240–320 mg/d in 1–2 divided doses

ADMINISTRATION

Note: Dose is usually titrated up in 40–80 mg increments until optimum dose is achieved.

Oral

- Do not discontinue abruptly; reduce dosage over a 1–2-wk period. Abrupt withdrawal can precipitate MI or thyroid storm in susceptible patients.
- Store at 15°–30° C (59°–86° F); protect drug from light.

ADVERSE EFFECTS (≥1%) **Body as a Whole:** Hypersensitivity (rash, pruritus, <u>laryngospasm, respiratory disturbances</u>). **CV:** *Bradycardia, peripheral vascular insufficiency (Raynaud's type),* palpitation, postural hypotension, conduction or rhythm disturbances, CHF. **GI:** Dry mouth. **CNS:** *Dizziness, fatigue,* sedation, headache, paresthesias, behavioral changes. **Special Senses:** Blurred vision, dry eyes. **Skin:** Dry skin. **Urogenital:** Impotence.

INTERACTIONS Drug: NSAIDS may decrease hypotensive effects; may mask symptoms of a hypoglycemic reaction to **insulin,** SULFONYLUREAS; **prazosin, terazosin** may increase severe hypotensive response to first dose.

PHARMACOKINETICS Absorption: 30–40% of PO dose absorbed. **Peak:** 2–4 h. **Duration:** 17–24 h. **Distribution:** Widely distributed; crosses placenta; distributed in breast milk. **Elimination:** 70% in urine; also in feces. **Half-Life:** 10–24 h.

CLINICAL IMPLICATIONS

Assessment & Drug Effects

- Assess heart rate and BP before administration of each dose. Withhold drug and notify physician if apical pulse drops below 60 bpm or systolic BP below 90 mm Hg.
- Monitor weight. Advise patient to report weight gain of 1–1.5 kg (2–3 lb) in a day and any other possible signs of CHF (e.g., cough, fatigue, dyspnea, rapid pulse, edema).
- Evaluate effectiveness for patients with angina by reduction in frequency of anginal attacks and improved exercise tolerance. Improvement should coincide with steady state serum concentration reached within 6–9 d. Keep physician informed of drug effect.
- Monitor patients with diabetes mellitus closely. Beta-adrenergic blockade produced by nadolol may prevent important clinical manifestations of hypoglycemia (e.g., tachycardia, BP changes).
- Monitor I&O ratio and creatinine clearance in patients with impaired kidney function or with cardiac problems. Dosage intervals will be lengthened with decreases in creatinine clearance.

Patient & Family Education

- Check pulse before taking each dose. Do not take your medication if pulse rate drops below 60 (or other parameter set by physician) or becomes irregular. Consult your physician right away.
- Do not stop taking your medication or alter dosage without consulting your physician.
- Do not drive or engage in potentially hazardous activities until response to drug is known.

NAFARELIN ACETATE

(na-fa′re-lin)
Synarel
Classifications: HORMONE; GONADOTROPIN-RELEASING HORMONE ANALOG

N

Common adverse effects in *italic*, life-threatening effects <u>underlined</u>; generic names in **bold**; classifications in SMALL CAPS; ♣ Canadian drug name; ⊘ Prototype drug

1035

Therapeutic: GONADOTROPIN-RELEAS-
ING HORMONE ANALOG
Prototype: Leuprolide
Pregnancy Category: X

AVAILABILITY 0.2 mg/spray solution

ACTION & *THERAPEUTIC EFFECT*
Potent agonist analog of gonadotropin-releasing hormone (GnRH).
Inhibits pituitary gonadotropin secretion of LH and FSH. *Decrease
in serum estradiol or testosterone
concentrations results in the quiescence of tissues and functions that
depend on LH and FSH.*

USES Endometriosis and precocious puberty.
UNLABELED USES Uterine leiomyomas, benign prostatic hypertrophy.

CONTRAINDICATIONS Hypersensitivity to GnRH or GnRH agonist analog; undiagnosed abnormal vaginal bleeding; pregnancy (category
X), lactation.
CAUTIOUS USE Polycystic ovarian
disease; osteoporosis.

ROUTE & DOSAGE

Endometriosis
Adult: **Inhalation** 2 inhalations/d
(200 mcg/inhalation), one in each
nostril, begin between days 2 and
4 of menstrual cycle; in patients
with persistent regular menstruation
after 2 mo of therapy, may increase
to 800 mcg/d as 2 inhalations (one
in each nostril) b.i.d.; do not
exceed 6 mo of treatment

Precocious Puberty
Child: **Inhalation** 800–1200
mcg/d divided q8–12h

ADMINISTRATION
Inhalation
- Withhold any topical nasal decongestant, if being used, until at
least 30 min after nafarelin administration.
- Store at 15°–30° C (59°–86° F);
protect from light.

ADVERSE EFFECTS (≥1%)   **GI:**
Bloating, abdominal cramps,
weight gain, nausea. **Endocrine:**
*Hot flashes, anovulation, amenor-
rhea, vaginal dryness,* galactorrhea.
Metabolic: Decreased bone mineral
content (reversible). **CNS:** Transient
headache, inertia, mild depression,
moodiness, fatigue. **Respiratory:** Nasal irritation. **Urogenital:** *Impotence,
decreased libido,* dyspareunia.

DIAGNOSTIC TEST INTERFERENCE
Increased *alkaline phosphatase;*
marked increase in *estradiol* in first
2 wk, then decrease to below baseline; decreased *FSH* and *LH* levels;
decreased *testosterone* levels.

INTERACTIONS Drug: No clinically
significant interactions established.

PHARMACOKINETICS Absorption:
21% absorbed from nasal mucosa.
Onset: 4 wk. **Peak:** 12 wk. **Duration:** 30–50 d after discontinuing
drug. **Distribution:** 78–84% bound to
plasma proteins; crosses placenta.
Metabolism: Hydrolyzed in kidney.
Elimination: 44–55% in urine over 7
d, 19–44% in feces. **Half-Life:** 2.7 h.

CLINICAL IMPLICATIONS
Assessment & Drug Effects
- Make appropriate inquiries about
breakthrough bleeding, which
may indicate that patient has
missed successive drug doses.

Patient & Family Education
- Read the information pamphlet
provided with nafarelin.
- Inform physician if breakthrough
bleeding occurs or menstruation
persists.
- Use or add barrier contraceptive
during treatment.

NAFCILLIN SODIUM

(naf-sill'in)

Classifications: BETA-LACTAM ANTIBIOTIC; PENICILLIN; ANTISTAPHYLOCOCCAL PENICILLIN
Therapeutic: BETA-LACTAM ANTIBIOTIC
Prototype: Penicillin G potassium
Pregnancy Category: B

AVAILABILITY 1 g, 2 g injection

ACTION & *THERAPEUTIC EFFECT*

Semisynthetic, acid-stable, penicillinase-resistant penicillin. Mechanism of bactericidal action is by interfering with synthesis of mucopeptides essential to formation and integrity of bacterial cell wall leading to bacterial cell lysis. *Effective against both penicillin-sensitive and penicillin-resistant strains of* Staphylococcus aureus. *Also active against pneumococci and group A beta-hemolytic streptococci.*

USES Primarily, infections caused by penicillinase-producing staphylococci. May also be used to initiate treatment in suspected staphylococcal infections pending culture and sensitivity test results. Serum concentrations are considerably enhanced by concurrent use of probenecid.

CONTRAINDICATIONS Hypersensitivity to penicillins, cephalosporins, and other allergens; use of oral drug in severe infections, gastric dilatation, cardiospasm, or intestinal hypermotility.
CAUTIOUS USE History of or suspected atopy or allergy (eczema, hives, hay fever, asthma); GI disease; hepatic disease; pregnancy (category B); lactation.

ROUTE & DOSAGE

Staphylococcal Infections

Adult: **IM/IV** 500 mg–1 g q4h up to 12 g/d
Child: **IM/IV** 100–200 mg/kg/d divided q4–6h
Neonate: **IM/IV** 50–100 mg/kg/d divided q6–12h

ADMINISTRATION

Intramuscular

- Reconstitute each 500 mg with 1.7 mL of sterile water for injection or NaCl injection to yield 250 mg/mL. Shake vigorously to dissolve.
- In adults: Make certain solution is clear. Select site carefully. Inject deeply into gluteal muscle. Rotate injection sites.
- In children: The preferred IM site in children <3 y is the midlateral or anterolateral thigh. Check agency policy.
- Label and date vials of reconstituted solution. Remains stable for 7 d under refrigeration and for 3 d at 15°–30° C (59°–86° F).

Intravenous

Note: Verify correct IV concentration and rate of infusion in neonates, infants, children with physician.

PREPARE: Direct: Reconstitute as for IM injection. Further dilute with 15–30 mL of D5W, NS, or 0.45% NaCl. **Intermittent:** Dilute reconstituted solution in 100–150 mL of compatible IV solution. **Continuous:** Add desired dose to a volume of IV solution that maintains concentration of drug between 2–40 mg/mL.

ADMINISTER: Direct: Give over at least 10 min. **Intermittent:** Give over 30–90 min. **Continuous:** Give at ordered rate.

Common adverse effects in *italic*, life-threatening effects underlined; generic names in **bold**; classifications in SMALL CAPS; ✚ Canadian drug name; ⊘ Prototype drug

1037

INCOMPATIBILITIES Solution/additive: **Aminophylline, ascorbic acid, aztreonam, bleomycin, cytarabine, gentamicin, hydrocortisone, methylprednisolone, promazine.** Y-site: **Droperidol, insulin regular, labetalol, midazolam, nalbuphine, pentazocine, vancomycin, verapamil.**

- Note: Usually, limit IV therapy to 24–48 h because of the possibility of thrombophlebitis (see Appendix F), particularly in older adults.
- Discard unused portions 24 h after reconstitution.

ADVERSE EFFECTS (≥1%) **Body as a Whole:** Drug fever, <u>anaphylaxis</u> (particularly following parenteral therapy). **GI:** Nausea, vomiting, *diarrhea,* increase in serum transaminase activity (following IM). **Hematologic:** Eosinophilia, thrombophlebitis following IV; neutropenia (long-term therapy). **Metabolic:** Hypokalemia (with high IV doses). **Skin:** Urticaria, pruritus, rash, pain and tissue irritation. **Urogenital:** Allergic interstitial nephritis.

DIAGNOSTIC TEST INTERFERENCE Nafcillin in large doses can cause false-positive ***urine protein*** tests using *sulfosalicylic acid method* or serum protein tests.

INTERACTIONS Drug: May antagonize hypoprothrombinemic effects of **warfarin.**

PHARMACOKINETICS Peak: 30–120 min IM; 15 min IV. **Duration:** 4–6 h IM. **Distribution:** Distributes into CNS with inflamed meninges; crosses placenta; distributed into breast milk, 90% protein bound. **Metabolism:** Enters enterohepatic circulation. **Elimination:** Primarily in bile; 10–30% in urine. **Half-Life:** 1 h.

CLINICAL IMPLICATIONS

Assessment & Drug Effects

- Lab tests: Perform C&S prior to initiation of therapy and periodically thereafter. Obtain twice weekly differential WBC counts in patients receiving IV nafcillin therapy for longer than 2 wk.
- Obtain a careful history before therapy to determine any prior allergic reactions to penicillins, cephalosporins, and other allergens.
- Inspect IV site for inflammatory reaction. Also check IV site for leakage; in the older adult patient especially, loss of tissue elasticity with aging may promote extravasation around the needle.
- Note: Allergic reactions, principally rash, occur most commonly.
- Monitor neutrophil count. Nafcillin-induced neutropenia (agranulocytosis) occurs commonly during third week of therapy. It may be associated with malaise, fever, sore mouth, or throat. Perform periodic assessments of liver and kidney functions during prolonged therapy.
- Be alert for signs of bacterial or fungal superinfections (see Appendix F) in patients on prolonged therapy.
- Determine IV sodium intake for patients with sodium restriction. Nafcillin sodium contains approximately 3 mEq of sodium per gram.

Patient & Family Education

- Report promptly S&S of neutropenia (see Assessment & Drug Effects), superinfection, or hypokalemia (see Appendix F).

NAFTIFINE

(naf'ti-feen)
Naftin
Classifications: ANTIBIOTIC; AN-TIFUNGAL
Therapeutic: ANTIFUNGAL ANTIBIOTIC
Prototype: Terbinafine
Pregnancy Category: B

AVAILABILITY 1% cream, gel

ACTION & *THERAPEUTIC EFFECT*
Synthetic broad-spectrum antifungal agent that may be fungicidal depending on the organism. Interferes in the synthesis of ergosterol, the principal sterol in the fungus cell membrane. Ergosterol becomes depleted and membrane function is affected. *Effective against topical infections caused by fungal organisms.*

USES Tinea pedis, tinea cruris, and tinea corporis.

CONTRAINDICATIONS Hypersensitivity to naftifine; occlusive dressing.
CAUTIOUS USE Pregnancy (category B), lactation. Safety and efficacy in children are not established.

ROUTE & DOSAGE

Tinea Infections
Adult: **Topical** Apply cream daily, or apply gel twice daily, up to 4 wk

ADMINISTRATION
Topical
▪ Gently massage into affected area and surrounding skin. Wash hands before and after application.
▪ Do not apply occlusive dressing unless specifically directed to do so.
▪ Store at 15°–30° C (59°–86° F).

ADVERSE EFFECTS (≥1%) **Skin:** Burning or stinging, dryness, erythema, itching, local irritation.

INTERACTIONS No clinically significant interactions established.

PHARMACOKINETICS Absorption: 2.5–6% absorbed through intact skin. **Onset:** 7 d. **Metabolism:** In liver. **Elimination:** In urine and feces. **Half-Life:** 2–3 d.

CLINICAL IMPLICATIONS
Assessment & Drug Effects
▪ Assess for irritation or sensitivity to cream; these are indications to discontinue use.
▪ Reevaluate use of drug if no improvement is noted after 4 wk.

Patient & Family Education
▪ Learn correct application technique.
▪ Avoid contact with eyes or mucous membranes.

NALBUPHINE HYDROCHLORIDE

(nal'byoo-feen)
Nubain
Classifications: ANALGESIC; NAR-COTIC (OPIATE) AGONIST-ANTAGONIST
Therapeutic: NARCOTIC ANALGESIC
Prototype: Pentazocine
Pregnancy Category: C

AVAILABILITY 10 mg/mL, 20 mg/mL injection

ACTION & *THERAPEUTIC EFFECT*
Synthetic narcotic analgesic with agonist and weak antagonist properties. Analgesic potency is approximately equal to that produced by equivalent doses of morphine. On a weight basis, produces respiratory depression about equal to that of morphine; however, in contrast

Common adverse effects in *italic*, life-threatening effects underlined; generic names in **bold**; classifications in SMALL CAPS; ✤ Canadian drug name; ❷ Prototype drug

1039

to morphine, doses greater than 30 mg produce no further respiratory depression. Antagonistic potency is approximately one-fourth that of naloxone. *Analgesic action that relieves moderate to severe pain with apparently low potential for dependence.*

USES Symptomatic relief of moderate to severe pain. Also preoperative sedation analgesia and as a supplement to surgical anesthesia.

CONTRAINDICATIONS History of hypersensitivity to nalbuphine, opiate agonists; pregnancy (category C). Prolonged use during pregnancy could result in neonatal withdrawal.

CAUTIOUS USE History of emotional instability or drug abuse; head injury, increased intracranial pressure; cardiac disease; impaired respirations, COPD; GI disorders; impaired kidney or liver function; MI; biliary tract surgery; lactation.

ROUTE & DOSAGE

Moderate to Severe Pain
Adult: **IV/IM/SC** 10 mg/70 kg q3–6h prn (max: 160 mg/d)

Surgery Anesthesia Supplement
Adult: **IV** Induction: 0.3–3 mg/kg then 0.25–0.5 mg/kg as required

ADMINISTRATION

Intramuscular, Subcutaneous
▪ Inject undiluted.

Intravenous

PREPARE: **Direct:** Give undiluted.
ADMINISTER: **Direct:** Give at a rate of 10 mg or fraction thereof over 3–5 min.

INCOMPATIBILITIES **Solution/additive: Diazepam, dimenhydrinate, ketorolac, pentobarbital, promethazine, thiethylperazine. Y-site: Allopurinol, amphotericin B cholesteryl, cefepime, docetaxel, methotrexate, nafcillin, piperacillin/tazobactam, sargramostim, sodium bicarbonate.**

▪ Store at 15°–30°C (59°–86°F), avoid freezing.

ADVERSE EFFECTS (≥1%) **CV:** Hypertension, hypotension, bradycardia, tachycardia, flushing. **GI:** Abdominal cramps, bitter taste, *nausea, vomiting,* dry mouth. **CNS:** *Sedation, dizziness,* nervousness, depression, restlessness, crying, euphoria, dysphoria, distortion of body image, unusual dreams, confusion, hallucinations; numbness and tingling sensations, headache, vertigo. **Respiratory:** Dyspnea, asthma, <u>respiratory depression</u>. **Skin:** Pruritus, urticaria, burning sensation, *sweaty, clammy skin.* **Special Senses:** Miosis, blurred vision, speech difficulty. **Urogenital:** Urinary urgency.

INTERACTIONS Drug: Alcohol and other CNS DEPRESSANTS add to CNS depression.

PHARMACOKINETICS Onset: 2–3 min IV; 15 min IM. **Peak:** 30 min IV. **Duration:** 3–6 h. **Distribution:** Crosses placenta. **Metabolism:** In liver. **Elimination:** In urine. **Half-Life:** 5 h.

CLINICAL IMPLICATIONS

Assessment & Drug Effects
▪ Assess respiratory rate before drug administration. Withhold drug and notify physician if respiratory rate falls below 12.
▪ Watch for allergic response in persons with sulfite sensitivity.

Common adverse effects in *italic*, life-threatening effects <u>underlined</u>; generic names in **bold**; classifications in SMALL CAPS; ✦ Canadian drug name; ⊘ Prototype drug

- Administer with caution to patients with hepatic or renal impairment.
- Monitor ambulatory patients; nalbuphine may produce drowsiness.
- Watch for respiratory depression of newborn if drug is used during labor and delivery.
- Avoid abrupt termination of nalbuphine following prolonged use, which may result in symptoms similar to narcotic withdrawal: nausea, vomiting, abdominal cramps, lacrimation, nasal congestion, piloerection, fever, restlessness, anxiety.

Patient & Family Education
- Do not drive or engage in potentially hazardous activities until response to drug is known.
- Avoid alcohol and other CNS depressants.

NALIDIXIC ACID

(nal-i-dix'ik)
NegGram
Classifications: URINARY TRACT ANTIINFECTIVE; ANTIBIOTIC, QUINOLONE
Therapeutic: URINARY TRACT ANTIINFECTIVE; QUINOLONE ANTIBIOTIC
Prototype: Ciprofloxacin
Pregnancy Category: B second and third trimester

AVAILABILITY 250 mg, 500 mg, 1 g tablets

ACTION & THERAPEUTIC EFFECT Synthetic quinolone. Intracellular action inhibits microbial DNA replication and RNA synthesis. *Marked bactericidal activity against most gram-negative urinary tract pathogens with the exception of strains of* Pseudomonas.

USES Urinary tract infections caused by susceptible gram-negative organisms including most *Proteus*

strains, *Klebsiella, Enterobacter,* and *Escherichia coli.*
UNLABELED USES GI tract infections caused by susceptible strains of *Shigella sonnei;* prophylaxis of bacteriuria and in bladder irrigation for low-grade cystitis.

CONTRAINDICATIONS History of convulsive disorders; first trimester of pregnancy; infants <3 mo.
CAUTIOUS USE Prepubertal child; second and third trimesters of pregnancy (category B); kidney or liver disease; epilepsy; cerebral arteriosclerosis; respiratory insufficiency; patients and breast-feeding infants with G6PD deficiency.

ROUTE & DOSAGE

Urinary Tract Infections
Adult: **PO** Acute therapy: 1 g q.i.d. Chronic therapy: 500 mg q.i.d.
Child: **PO** >3 mo, Acute therapy: 55 mg/kg/d in 4 divided doses; Chronic therapy: 33 mg/kg/d in 4 divided doses

ADMINISTRATION

Oral
- Give with food or milk if drug causes GI distress. Otherwise, give on an empty stomach 1 h before or 2 h after meals.
- Store at 15°–30° C (59°–86° F) in tight container and avoid freezing.

ADVERSE EFFECTS (≥1%) **Body as a Whole:** Angioedema, fever, chills, arthralgia, hypersensitivity pneumonitis, anaphylaxis (rare). **CNS:** Drowsiness, headache, malaise, dizziness, vertigo, syncope, weakness, myalgia, peripheral neuritis, confusion, excitement, mental depression, seizures, insomnia. **GI:** Abdominal pain, *nausea, vomiting,* diarrhea,

Common adverse effects in *italic*, life-threatening effects underlined; generic names in **bold**; classifications in SMALL CAPS; ♦ Canadian drug name; ● Prototype drug

1041

cholestasis, transient increase in AST. **Hematologic:** Eosinophilia, hemolytic anemia (especially in G6PD deficiency). **Skin:** Photosensitivity, pruritus, urticaria, rash. **Other:** Cartilage erosion.

DIAGNOSTIC TEST INTERFERENCE
False-positive urine tests for *glucose* with *cupric sulfate reagent* (e.g., *Benedict's* or *Clinitest*) but not with *glucose oxidase methods* (e.g., *Clinistix, TesTape*). May cause elevation of *urinary 17-ketosteroids (Zimmerman method)* and *urine vanillylmandelic acid (VMA).*

INTERACTIONS Drug: ANTACIDS, **sucralfate, calcium, magnesium, didanosine,** MULTIVITAMINS (containing **iron** or **zinc**) may decrease absorption of nalidixic acid; may increase hypoprothrombinemic effects of **warfarin.**

PHARMACOKINETICS Absorption: Readily from GI tract. **Peak:** Urine: 3–4 h. **Distribution:** Crosses placenta; distributed into breast milk. **Metabolism:** Partially in liver; some in kidneys. **Elimination:** In urine. **Half-Life:** 1.1–2.5 h.

CLINICAL IMPLICATIONS
Assessment & Drug Effects
- Lab tests: Perform C&S tests prior to initiation of treatment and periodically thereafter. Obtain blood counts and kidney or liver function tests if therapy is continued longer than 2 wk.
- Watch for CNS reactions, which tend to occur 30 min after initiation of treatment or after second or third dose. Infants, children, and older adults are especially susceptible. Report immediately the onset of marked irritability, vomiting, bulging of anterior fontanelle, headache, excitement or drowsiness, papilledema, vertigo.

Patient & Family Education
- Use drug exactly as prescribed and do not change dosage. Omitted doses, especially in early days of therapy, may promote development of bacterial resistance. Take full amount of medication.
- Contact physician immediately for unexplained behavior changes or severe headaches.
- Maintain adequate hydration (2000–3000 mL/d if tolerated) during treatment period. Consult physician if you notice a change in your urination pattern.
- Avoid exposure to direct sunlight or ultraviolet light while receiving drug. Contact physician if photosensitivity occurs. You may be photosensitive up to 3 mo after termination of drug.
- Contact your physician if you notice visual disturbances during first few days of therapy. Symptoms usually disappear promptly with reduction of dosage or discontinuation of therapy.

NALMEFENE HYDROCHLORIDE
(nal'me-feen)
Revex
Classifications: NARCOTIC (OPIATE) ANTAGONIST
Therapeutic: NARCOTIC ANTAGONIST
Prototype: Naloxone
Pregnancy Category: B

AVAILABILITY 100 mcg/mL, 1 mg/mL injection

ACTION & THERAPEUTIC EFFECT
Opiate antagonist that has no opioid agonist activity; also has no pharmacologic activity when given in the absence of an opioid ago-

nist. *Prevents or reverses the effects of opiates, including respiratory depression, sedation, and hypotension; these effects are dose related.*

USES Complete or partial reversal of opioid drug effects, management of opioid overdose.

CONTRAINDICATIONS Hypersensitivity to nalmefene.

CAUTIOUS USE Patients at high cardiovascular risk or who have received potential cardiotoxic drugs; patients with known physical dependence on opioids; renal or hepatic impairment; pregnancy (category B), lactation. Safety and efficacy in children are not established.

ROUTE & DOSAGE

Reversal of Postoperative Opioid Depression (use 100 mcg/mL)

Adult: **IV/IM/SC** 0.25 mcg/kg followed by 0.25 mcg/kg incremental doses q2–5min until desired degree of reversal or 1 mcg/kg cumulative dose is reached

Known/Suspected Opioid Overdose (use 1 mg/mL)

Adult: **IV/IM/SC** For nonopioid-dependent patients: 0.5 mg/70 kg, may repeat with 1 mg/70 kg 2–5 min later; for opioid-dependent patients: 0.1 mg/70 kg, if no evidence of withdrawal in 2 min, continue with 0.5 mg/70 kg, may repeat with 1 mg/70 kg 2–5 min later (doses >1.5 mg/70 kg not likely to be more effective)

ADMINISTRATION

- Note: When using the 100 mcg/mL concentration, calculate the volume of a dose equal to 0.25 mcg/kg by multiplying the weight in kilograms by 0.0025. When using the 1 mg/mL concentration, calculate the volume of a dose equal to 0.1, 0.5, or 1 mg/70 kg by dividing the weight in kilograms by 70, then multiplying that result by the number of milligrams ordered per 70 kg.

Intramuscular, Subcutaneous

- Note: If IV access is lost, a single 1-mg dose may be given IM or SC. Allow 5–15 min for effect to occur.

Intravenous

PREPARE: **Direct:** Give undiluted.
ADMINISTER: **Direct:** Give over 15–30 sec. In patients with kidney failure give over 60 sec.

ADVERSE EFFECTS (≥1%) **Body as a Whole:** Fever, chills. **CV:** Tachycardia, hypotension, hypertension, pulmonary edema, ventricular arrhythmias (especially in patients with preexisting cardiovascular disease). **GI:** *Nausea, vomiting,* diarrhea, dry mouth, dyspepsia, elevation of liver function tests. **CNS:** Dizziness, headache, irritability, tremor, paresthesias, confusion, paranoia, drowsiness, fatigue, vertigo, agitation, nervousness. **Special Senses:** Blurred vision.

INTERACTIONS Drug: Potential risk of seizures when combined with **flumazenil.**

PHARMACOKINETICS Absorption: Well absorbed from IM and SC sites. **Onset:** 2–5 min IV; 15 min IM/SC. **Peak:** 5 min IV; 2 h IM/SC. **Duration:** 4–8 h. **Distribution:** Blocks >80% of brain opioid receptors within 5 min; distributed into breast milk of rats. **Metabolism:** In liver by glucuronidation. **Elimination:** Metabolites primarily in urine, 17% in feces. **Half-Life:** 8.5–10.8 h.

CLINICAL IMPLICATIONS

Assessment & Drug Effects

- Monitor carefully for reversal of opioid depression within 2–5 min of an IV dose or 5–15 min of an IM/SC dose.

- Note: If recurrent respiratory depression following the reversal, titrate the dose again to avoid over-reversal.
- Monitor cardiovascular status closely, assessing for changes in blood pressure and heart rate and development of arrhythmias.

Patient & Family Education

- Tell your physician all of the other drugs that you are taking including over-the-counter drugs, herbals, and nutritional products.

NALOXONE HYDROCHLORIDE Ⓟ

(nal-ox′one)

Narcan

Classifications: NARCOTIC (OPIATE) ANTAGONIST

Therapeutic: NARCOTIC ANTAGONIST

Pregnancy Category: C

AVAILABILITY 0.02 mg/mL, 0.4 mg/mL, 1 mg/mL injection

ACTION & THERAPEUTIC EFFECT
Analog of oxymorphone. A "pure" narcotic antagonist, essentially free of agonistic (morphine-like) properties. Thus, it produces no significant analgesia, respiratory depression, psychotomimetic effects, or miosis when administered in the absence of narcotics and possesses more potent narcotic antagonist action. *Reverses the effects of opiates, including respiratory depression, sedation, and hypotension.*

USES Narcotic overdosage; complete or partial reversal of narcotic depression including respiratory depression induced by natural and synthetic narcotics and by pentazocine and propoxyphene. Drug of choice when nature of depressant drug is not known and for diagnosis of suspected acute opioid overdosage.

UNLABELED USES Shock and to reverse alcohol-induced or clonidine-induced coma or respiratory depression.

CONTRAINDICATIONS Hypersensitivity to naloxone, naltrexone, nalmefene; respiratory depression due to nonopioid drugs; substance abuse; pregnancy (category C).

CAUTIOUS USE Neonates and children; known or suspected narcotic dependence; brain tumor, head trauma, increased ICP; history of substance abuse; cardiac irritability; seizure disorders; lactation.

ROUTE & DOSAGE

Opiate Overdose
Adult: **IV** 0.4–2 mg, may repeat q2–3min up to 10 mg if necessary
Child: **IV** 0.01–0.1 mg/kg, may repeat q2–3min up to 10 mg if necessary
Neonate: **IV/SC/IM** 0.01 mg/kg, may repeat q2–3min

Postoperative Opiate Depression
Adult: **IV** 0.1–0.2 mg, may repeat q2–3min for up to 3 doses if necessary
Child: **IV** 0.005–0.01 mg/kg, may repeat q2–3min up to 3 doses if necessary

ADMINISTRATION

Intravenous

PREPARE: Direct: May be given undiluted. **IV Infusion:** Dilute 2 mg in 500 mL of D5W or NS to yield 4 mcg/mL (0.004 mg/mL).
ADMINISTER: Direct: Give 0.4 mg or fraction thereof over 10–15

sec. **IV Infusion:** Adjust rate according to patient response.
***INCOMPATIBILITIES* Y-site: Amphotericin B cholesteryl complex.**

▪ Use IV solutions within 24 h.
▪ Store at 15°–30° C (59°–86° F), protect from excessive light.

ADVERSE EFFECTS (≥1%) **Body as a Whole:** Reversal of analgesia, tremors, hyperventilation, slight drowsiness, sweating. **CV:** Increased BP, tachycardia. **GI:** Nausea, vomiting. **Hematologic:** Elevated partial thromboplastin time.

INTERACTIONS Drug: Reverses analgesic effects of NARCOTIC (OPIATE) AGONISTS and NARCOTIC (OPIATE) AGONIST-ANTAGONISTS.

PHARMACOKINETICS Onset: 2 min. **Duration:** 45 min. **Distribution:** Crosses placenta. **Metabolism:** In liver. **Elimination:** In urine. **Half-Life:** 60–90 min.

CLINICAL IMPLICATIONS

Assessment & Drug Effects

▪ Observe patient closely; duration of action of some narcotics may exceed that of naloxone. Keep physician informed; repeat naloxone dose may be necessary.
▪ May precipitate opiate withdrawal if administered to a patient who is opiate dependent.
▪ Note: Narcotic abstinence symptoms induced by naloxone generally start to diminish 20–40 min after administration and usually disappear within 90 min.
▪ Monitor respirations and other vital signs.
▪ Monitor surgical and obstetric patients closely for bleeding. Naloxone has been associated with abnormal coagulation test results. Also observe for reversal of analgesia, which may be manifested by nausea, vomiting, sweating, tachycardia.

Patient & Family Education

▪ Report postoperative pain that emerges after administration of this drug to physician.

NALTREXONE HYDROCHLORIDE

(nal-trex′one)
ReVia, Vivitrol
Classifications: NARCOTIC (OPIATE) ANTAGONIST
Therapeutic: NARCOTIC ANTAGONIST
Prototype: Naloxone HCl
Pregnancy Category: C

AVAILABILITY 25 mg, 50 mg, 100 mg tablets; 380 mg injection

ACTION & *THERAPEUTIC EFFECT* Pure opioid antagonist with prolonged pharmacologic effect, structurally and pharmacologically similar to naloxone. Mechanism of action not clearly delineated, but it appears that its competitive binding at opioid receptor sites reduces euphoria and drug craving without supporting the addiction. *Weakens or completely and reversibly blocks the subjective effects (the "high") of IV opioids and analgesics possessing both agonist and antagonist activity.*

USES Adjunct to the maintenance of an opioid-free state in detoxified addicts who are and desire to remain narcotic free. Management of alcohol dependence as an adjunct to social and psychotherapeutic methods.
UNLABELED USES Obesity.

CONTRAINDICATIONS Patients receiving opioid analgesics or in acute opioid withdrawal; opioid-

Common adverse effects in *italic*, life-threatening effects <u>underlined</u>; generic names in **bold**; classifications in SMALL CAPS; ♣ Canadian drug name; ⊘ Prototype drug

1045

dependent patient; acute hepatitis, liver failure. Also contraindicated in any individual who (1) fails naloxone challenge, (2) has a positive urine screen for opioids, or (3) has a history of sensitivity to naltrexone; pregnancy (category C), lactation. Safe use in children <18 y is not established.

ROUTE & DOSAGE

Treatment of Opiate Cessation

Adult: **PO** 25 mg followed by another 25 mg in 1 h if no withdrawal response; maintenance regimen is individualized (max: 800 mg/d)

Alcohol Dependence

Adult: **PO** 50 mg once/d **IM** 380 mg q month

ADMINISTRATION

Challenge Test

Give the naloxone challenge test (administered IV of SC) before starting the abstinence program with naltrexone.

- SC dose: The SC dose is followed by an observation period of 45 min for symptoms of withdrawal (see below).
- IV dose: A portion of the IV dose is injected and, with the needle left in place, the patient is observed for 30 sec for withdrawal symptoms. If none are observed, remainder of dose is injected and patient is observed for the next 20 min.
- Withdrawal symptoms: Stuffiness or runny nose; tearing; yawning; sweating; tremors; vomiting; gooseflesh; feeling of temperature change; bone, joint, and muscle pains; abdominal cramps.
- Interpretation: Evidence of withdrawal symptoms indicates that the patient is a potential risk and

should not enter a naltrexone program.
- Do not give naltrexone until patient is opiate free for at least 7–10 d.

Oral

- Give without regard to food.

ADVERSE EFFECTS (≥1%) **GI:** Dry mouth, anorexia, *nausea, vomiting,* constipation, *abdominal cramps/ pain,* <u>hepatotoxicity</u>. **Musculoskeletal:** *Muscle and joint pains.* **CNS:** *Difficulty sleeping, anxiety, headache, nervousness,* reduced or increased energy, irritability, dizziness, depression. **Skin:** Skin rash. **Body as a Whole:** Chills.

INTERACTIONS Drug: Increased somnolence and lethargy with PHENOTHIAZINES; reverses analgesic effects of NARCOTIC (OPIATE) AGONISTS and NARCOTIC (OPIATE) AGONIST-ANTAGONISTS.

PHARMACOKINETICS Absorption: Rapidly from GI tract; 20% reaches systemic circulation (first pass effect). **Onset:** 15–30 min. **Peak:** 1 h. **Duration:** 24–72 h PO; 4 wk IM. **Metabolism:** In liver to active metabolite. **Elimination:** In urine. **Half-Life:** 10–13 h PO, 5–10 d IM.

CLINICAL IMPLICATIONS

Assessment & Drug Effects

- Lab tests: Check liver function before the treatment is started, at monthly intervals for 6 mo, and then periodically as indicated.

Patient & Family Education

- Note: Naltrexone therapy may put you in danger of overdosing if you use opiates. Small doses even at frequent intervals will give no desired effects; however, a dose large enough to produce a high is dangerous and may be fatal.

- It may be possible to transfer from methadone to naltrexone. This can be done after gradual withdrawal and final discontinuation of methadone.
- Report promptly onset of signs of hepatic toxicity (see Appendix F) to physician. The drug will be discontinued.
- Do not self-dose with OTC drugs for treatment of cough, colds, diarrhea, or analgesia. Many available preparations contain small doses of an opioid. Consult physician for safe drugs if they are needed.
- Tell a doctor or dentist before treatment that you are using naltrexone.
- Wear identification jewelry indicating naltrexone use.

NANDROLONE DECANOATE

(nan′droe-lone)
Classifications: HORMONE; ANABOLIC/ANDROGEN STEROID
Therapeutic: ANABOLIC STEROID
Prototype: Testosterone
Pregnancy Category: X
Controlled Substance: Schedule III

AVAILABILITY 100 mg/mL, 200 mg/mL injection

ACTION & THERAPEUTIC EFFECT
Synthetic steroid with high ratio of anabolic activity to androgenic activity. Actions last 3–4 wk. *Increases hemoglobin and red cell mass and increases lean body mass in patients with cachexia (muscle wasting).*

USES Control of metastatic breast cancer, management of anemia of renal insufficiency.

CONTRAINDICATIONS Males with prostate or breast cancer; severe cardiac disease; liver dysfunction; severe renal disease; nephrotic syndrome, hypercalcemia; pregnancy (category X), lactation.
CAUTIOUS USE Benign prostatic hypertrophy, history of MI; CAD; diabetes mellitus; heart failure; BPH; children.

ROUTE & DOSAGE

Anemia (Decanoate)
Adult: **IM** 50–200 mg/wk
Child: **IM** 2–13 y, 25–50 mg q3–4wk

Metastatic Breast Cancer
Adult: **IM** 50–100 mg/wk

ADMINISTRATION

Intramuscular
- Inject drug deep IM, preferably into gluteal muscle in adult. Follow agency policy regarding IM site in small child.
- Intermittent therapy is usually recommended (4-mo course of treatment followed by 6–8-wk rest period).

ADVERSE EFFECTS (≥1%) **Body as a Whole:** Muscle cramps. **GI:** *Nausea, vomiting,* diarrhea, anorexia, abdominal fullness, cholestatic jaundice, hepatic necrosis, hepatocellular neoplasms. **Hematologic:** Leukopenia. **Metabolic:** Sodium, chloride, water, potassium, phosphate, and calcium retention, ankle edema, glucose intolerance, increased cholesterol. **CNS:** Excitation, insomnia, chills, toxic confusion. **Endocrine:** *Acne, virilization.*

INTERACTIONS Drug: May increase hypoprothrombinemic effects of **warfarin;** may decrease **insulin** and SULFONYLUREA requirements; CORTICOSTEROIDS may increase edema. **Herbal: Echinacea** may increase risk of hepatotoxicity.

Common adverse effects in *italic*, life-threatening effects underlined; generic names in **bold**; classifications in SMALL CAPS; ♦ Canadian drug name; ☉ Prototype drug

1047

PHARMACOKINETICS Absorption: Slowly absorbed from IM injection site over 4 d. **Peak:** 3–6 d. **Metabolism:** In liver to active metabolite. **Half-Life:** 6–8 d.

CLINICAL IMPLICATIONS

Assessment & Drug Effects

- Lab tests: Obtain baseline and periodic liver function evaluations and electrolyte levels.
- Monitor for S&S of hepatic toxicity (see Appendix F) and electrolyte imbalance, especially hyperkalemia and hypercalcemia (see Appendix F).
- Monitor diabetics for loss of glycemic control.

Patient & Family Education

- Note: In women, the drug may cause virilization (e.g., increased facial and body hair, deepening of voice).

NAPHAZOLINE HYDROCHLORIDE ℗

(naf-az′oh-leen)

Ak-Con, Albalon, Allerest, Clear Eyes, Comfort, Degest-2, Nafazair, Naphcon, Privine, Vaso-Clear, Vasocon

Classifications: EYE, EAR, NOSE AND THROAT (EENT) PREPARATION; VASOCONSTRICTOR; ALPHA-ADRENERGIC AGONIST; DECONGESTANT
Therapeutic: TOPICAL VASOCONSTRICTOR; DECONGESTANT
Pregnancy Category: C

AVAILABILITY 0.012%, 0.02%, 0.03%, 0.1% ophthalmic solution; 0.05% nasal solution

ACTION & *THERAPEUTIC EFFECT*
Direct-acting imidazoline derivative with marked alpha-adrenergic activity. Differs from other sympathomimetic amines in that systemic absorption may cause CNS depression rather than stimulation. *Produces rapid and prolonged vasoconstriction of arterioles, thereby decreasing fluid exudation and mucosal engorgement.*

USES Nasal decongestant and ocular vasoconstrictor.

CONTRAINDICATIONS Narrow-angle glaucoma; concomitant use with MAO inhibitors or tricyclic antidepressants; pregnancy (category C), lactation. Safe use in children <6y has not been established.
CAUTIOUS USE Hypertension, cardiac irregularities, advanced arteriosclerosis; diabetes; hyperthyroidism; older adult patients.

ROUTE & DOSAGE

Congestion

Adult: **Intranasal** 2 drops or sprays of 0.05% solution in each nostril q3–6h for no more than 3–5 d. **Ophthalmic** See Appendix A
Child: **Intranasal** 1–2 drops or sprays of 0.025% solution q3–6h for no more than 3–5 d

ADMINISTRATION

Instillation

- Instill nasal spray with patient in upright position. If administered in reclining position, a stream rather than a spray may be ejected, with possibility of systemic reaction.
- Minimize amount of drug swallowed by taking care not to direct the flow toward nasopharynx and by positioning patient properly with the head tilted slightly downward.
- Store at 15°–30° C (59°–86° F), protect from freezing.

ADVERSE EFFECTS (≥1%) **Body as a Whole:** Hypersensitivity reactions, headache, nausea, weakness, sweating, drowsiness, hypothermia, <u>coma</u>. **CV:** Hypertension, bradycardia, <u>shock-like hypotension</u>. **Special Senses:** Transient nasal stinging or burning, dryness of nasal mucosa, pupillary dilation, increased intraocular pressure, rebound redness of the eye.

INTERACTIONS Drug: TRICYCLIC ANTIDEPRESSANTS, **maprotiline** may potentiate pressor effects.

PHARMACOKINETICS Onset: Within 10 min. **Duration:** 2–6 h.

CLINICAL IMPLICATIONS

Assessment & Drug Effects

- Watch for rebound congestion and chemical rhinitis with frequent and continued use.
- Monitor BP periodically for development or worsening of hypertension, especially with ophthalmic route.
- Overdose: Bradycardia and hypotension can result. Report promptly.

Patient & Family Education

- Do not exceed prescribed regimen. Systemic effects can result from swallowing excessive medication.
- Discontinue medication and contact physician if nasal congestion is not relieved after 5 d.
- Prevent contamination of eye solution by taking care not to touch eyelid or surrounding area with dropper tip.

NAPROXEN

(na-prox'en)
Apo-Naproxen ♦, EC-Naprosyn, Naprelan, Naprosyn, Naxen ♦, Novonaprox ♦

NAPROXEN SODIUM

Aleve, Anaprox, Anaprox DS
Classifications: ANALGESIC, NONSTEROIDAL ANTIINFLAMMATORY DRUG (NSAID); ANTIPYRETIC
Therapeutic: NSAID, ANALGESIC; ANTIPYRETIC
Prototype: Ibuprofen
Pregnancy Category: B

AVAILABILITY 200 mg, 250 mg, 375 mg, 500 mg tablets; 375 mg, 500 mg sustained release tablets

ACTION & *THERAPEUTIC EFFECT*
Propionic acid derivative. An NSAID with properties similar to those of other propionic acid derivatives, e.g., ibuprofen, fenoprofen, ketoprofen. Mechanism of action thought to be related to inhibition of prostaglandin synthesis by inhibiting COX-1 and COX-2 isoenzymes. *Analgesic, antiinflammatory and antipyretic effects; also inhibits platelet aggregation and prolongs bleeding time but does not alter whole blood clotting, prothrombin time, or platelet count.*

USES Antiinflammatory and analgesic effects in symptomatic treatment of acute and chronic rheumatoid arthritis, juvenile arthritis (naproxen only), and for treatment of primary dysmenorrhea. Also management of ankylosing spondylitis, osteoarthritis, and gout.
UNLABELED USES Paget's disease of bone, Bartter's syndrome.

CONTRAINDICATIONS Active peptic ulcer; patients in whom asthma, rhinitis, urticaria, bronchospasm, or shock is precipitated by aspirin or other NSAIDs; perioperative pain associated with CABG; hypersensitivity to any NSAID; cardiac disease. Safety during pregnancy (category B) or in children <2 y is not established.

N

Common adverse effects in *italic*, life-threatening effects <u>underlined</u>; generic names in **bold**; classifications in SMALL CAPS; ♦ Canadian drug name; ⊘ Prototype drug

1049

CAUTIOUS USE History of upper GI tract disorders; impaired kidney, liver, or cardiac function; patients on sodium restriction (naproxen sodium); low pretreatment Hgb concentration; fluid retention, hypertension, heart failure; older adults; coagulopathy; SLE.

ROUTE & DOSAGE

Note: 275 mg naproxen sodium = 250 mg naproxen

Inflammatory Disease

Adult: **PO** 250–500 mg b.i.d. (max: 1000 mg/d naproxen, 1100 mg/d naproxen sodium); Naprelan is dosed q.d.
Child: **PO** >2 y, 10–15 mg/kg/d in 2 divided doses (max: 1000 mg/d)

Mild to Moderate Pain, Dysmenorrhea

Adult: **PO** 500 mg followed by 200–250 mg q6–8h prn up to 1250 mg/d
Child: **PO** >2 y, 5–7 mg/kg q8–12h

ADMINISTRATION

Oral

- Ensure that extended release or enteric-coated form is not chewed or crushed. It must be swallowed whole.
- Give with food or an antacid (if prescribed) to reduce incidence of GI upset.
- Store at 15°–30° C (59°–86° F) in tightly closed container; protect from freezing.

ADVERSE EFFECTS (≥1%) **CNS:** *Headache, drowsiness, dizziness,* lightheadedness, depression. **CV:** Palpitation, dyspnea, peripheral edema, CHF, tachycardia. **Special Senses:** Blurred vision, tinnitus, hearing loss. **GI:** *Anorexia, heartburn,* indigestion, *nausea,* vomiting, thirst, GI bleeding, elevated serum ALT, AST. **Hematologic:** Thrombocytopenia, leukopenia, eosinophilia, inhibited platelet aggregation, agranulocytosis (rare). **Skin:** Pruritus, rash, ecchymosis. **Urogenital:** Nephrotoxicity. **Respiratory:** Pulmonary edema.

DIAGNOSTIC TEST INTERFERENCE Transient elevations in *BUN* and serum *alkaline phosphatase* may occur. Naproxen may interfere with some urinary assays of *5-HIAA* and may cause falsely high *urinary 17-KGS* levels (using *m-dinitrobenzene reagent*). Naproxen should be withdrawn 72 h before adrenal function tests.

INTERACTIONS Drug: Bleeding time effects of ORAL ANTICOAGULANTS, **heparin** may be prolonged; may increase **lithium** toxicity. **Herbal:** **Feverfew, garlic, ginger, ginkgo** may increase bleeding potential.

PHARMACOKINETICS Absorption: Almost completely from GI tract when taken on empty stomach. **Peak:** 2 h naproxen; 1 h naproxen sodium. **Duration:** 7 h. **Metabolism:** In liver. **Elimination:** Primarily in urine; some biliary excretion (<1%). **Half-Life:** 12–15 h.

CLINICAL IMPLICATIONS

Assessment & Drug Effects

- Take detailed drug history prior to initiation of therapy. Observe for signs of allergic response in those with aspirin or other NSAID sensitivity.
- Lab tests: Obtain baseline and periodic evaluations of Hgb and kidney and liver function in patients receiving prolonged or high dose therapy.

N

- Schedule baseline and periodic auditory and ophthalmic examinations in patients receiving prolonged or high dose therapy.
- Monitor therapeutic effectiveness. Patients with arthritis may experience symptomatic relief (reduction in joint pain, swelling, stiffness) within 24–48 h with naproxen sodium therapy and in 2–4 wk with naproxen.

Patient & Family Education
- Be aware that the therapeutic effect of naproxen may not be experienced for 3–4 wk.
- Do not drive or engage in potentially hazardous activities until response to drug is known.
- Avoid alcohol and aspirin (as well as other NSAIDs) unless otherwise advised by a physician. Potential to increase risk of GI ulceration and bleeding.
- Tell your dentist or surgeon if you are taking naproxen before any treatment; it may prolong bleeding time.

NARATRIPTAN

(nar-a-trip'tan)
Amerge
Classifications: ADRENERGIC ANTAGONIST; 5-HT$_1$ SEROTONIN AGONIST
Therapeutic: ANTIMIGRAINE; 5-HT$_1$ SEROTONIN AGONIST
Prototype: Sumatriptan
Pregnancy Category: C

AVAILABILITY 1 mg, 2.5 mg tablets

ACTION & *THERAPEUTIC EFFECT*
Binds to the serotonin receptors (5-HT$_{1D}$ and 5-HT$_{1B}$) on intracranial blood vessels, resulting in selective vasoconstriction of dilated vessels in the carotid circulation. It also inhibits the release of proinflammatory neuropeptides associated with a migraine attack. *Inhibits vasoconstriction of dilated vessels selectively. This results in the relief of acute migraine headache attacks.*

USES Acute migraine headaches with or without aura.

CONTRAINDICATIONS Severe renal impairment (creatinine clearance <15 mL/min); severe hepatic impairment; history of ischemic heart disease (i.e., angina pectoris, MI), arteriosclerosis, cardiac arrhythmias; cardiac disease, CAD, older adults, peripheral vascular disease; cerebrovascular syndromes (i.e., strokes or TIA); uncontrolled hypertension; patients with hemiplegic or basilar migraine; hypersensitivity to naratriptan; older adults, pregnancy (category C).
CAUTIOUS USE Cardiovascular disease; renal or hepatic insufficiency; lactation. Safety and efficacy in children <18 y are not established.

ROUTE & DOSAGE

Acute Migraine
Adult: **PO** 1–2.5 mg; may repeat in 4 h if necessary (max: 5 mg/ 24 h); patients with mild or moderate renal or hepatic impairment should not exceed 2.5 mg/24 h

ADMINISTRATION
Oral
- Give any time after symptoms of migraine appear. If the first tablet was effective but symptoms return, a second tablet may be given, but no sooner than 4 h after the first. Do not exceed 5 mg in 24 h.
- If there is no response to the first tablet, contact physician before administering a second tablet.

N

- Do not give within 24 h of an ergot-containing drug or other 5-HT₁ agonist.
- Store at 2°–25° C (36°–77° F); protect from light.

ADVERSE EFFECTS (≥1%) **Body as a Whole:** Asthenia, fatigue, malaise, pain, pressure sensation, paresthesias, throat pressure, warm/cold sensations, hot flushes. **CNS:** Somnolence, dizziness, drowsiness, headache, hypesthesia, decreased mental acuity, euphoria, tremor. **CV:** Coronary artery vasospasm, transient myocardial ischemia, MI, ventricular tachycardia, ventricular fibrillation, chest pain/tightness/heaviness, palpitations. **GI:** Dry mouth, nausea, vomiting, diarrhea. **Respiratory:** Dyspnea. **Skin:** Flushing.

INTERACTIONS Drug: Dihydroergotamine, methysergide, and other 5-HT₁ AGONISTS may cause prolonged vasospastic reactions; SSRIs have rarely caused weakness, hyperreflexia, and incoordination; MAOIS should not be used with 5-HT₁ agonists. **Herbal: Gingko, ginseng, echinacea, St. John's wort** may increase triptan toxicity.

PHARMACOKINETICS Absorption: Rapidly absorbed, 70% bioavailability. **Peak:** 2–4 h. **Distribution:** 28–31% protein bound. **Metabolism:** In liver. **Elimination:** Primarily in urine. **Half-Life:** 6 h.

CLINICAL IMPLICATIONS
Assessment & Drug Effects
- Monitor carefully cardiovascular status following first dose in patients at risk for CAD (e.g., postmenopausal women, men over 40 y, persons with known CAD risk factors) or coronary artery vasospasms.
- Be aware that ECG is recommended following first administration of naratriptan to someone with known CAD risk factors and periodically with long-term use.
- Report immediately to the physician: chest pain, nausea, or tightness in chest or throat that is severe or does not quickly resolve.
- Obtain periodic cardiovascular evaluation with continued use.

Patient & Family Education
- Carefully review patient information leaflet and guidelines for administration.
- Contact physician immediately for any of the following: symptoms of angina (e.g., severe and/or persistent pain or tightness in chest or throat, severe nausea); hypersensitivity (e.g., wheezing, facial swelling, skin rash, or hives); or abdominal pain.
- Report any other adverse effects (e.g., tingling, flushing, dizziness) at next physician visit.

NATALIZUMAB

(na-tal'-i-zu-mab)
Tysabri
Classifications: BIOLOGIC RESPONSE MODIFIER; MONOCLONAL ANTIBODY; INTEGRIN INHIBITOR
Therapeutic: IMMUNOMODULATOR; MONOCLONAL ANTIBODY
Prototype: Basiliximab
Pregnancy Category: C

AVAILABILITY 300 mg/15 mL injection

ACTION & *THERAPEUTIC EFFECT*
Natalizumab is a recombinant immunoglobulin-G4 (IgG4) monoclonal antibody thought to interfere with the migration of lymphocytes and monocytes into the CNS endothelium of patients with multiple sclerosis, thereby reducing inflam-

mation and demyelination of CNS white matter. *Inhibition of T-cell infiltration into the brain is thought to impede the demyelinating process of multiple sclerosis. It reduces relapses and occurrence of brain lesions. Natalizumab is also thought to attenuate T-lymphocyte–mediated intestinal inflammation in Crohn's disease and possibly ulcerative colitis.*

USES Treatment of relapsing forms of multiple sclerosis.
UNLABELED USES Treatment of Crohn's disease.

CONTRAINDICATIONS Safety and efficacy of the drug have not been established for chronic progressive multiple sclerosis. Prior hypersensitivity to natalizumab; murine protein hypersensitivity; progressive multifocal leukoencephalopathy; active infection; females of childbearing age; pregnancy (category C); lactation; children <18 y.
CAUTIOUS USE Coadministration with other immunosuppressive medication; diabetes mellitus, immunocompromised patients; exposure to infection or tuberculosis.

ROUTE & DOSAGE

Multiple Sclerosis
Adult: **IV** 300 mg infused over 1 h every 4 wk

ADMINISTRATION

Intravenous

***PREPARE:* IV Infusion:** Before and after dilution, solution should be colorless and clear to slightly opaque. Do not use if the solution has visible particles, flakes, color, or is cloudy. Withdraw 15 mL from the vial and add to an IV bag with 100 mL of NS. Do not use with any other diluent.

Gently invert the bag to mix; do not shake. The IV solution must be used within 8 h.
***ADMINISTER:* IV Infusion:** Flush IV line before/after with NS. Infuse over 1 h. Do not give a bolus dose. Stop infusion immediately if S&S of hypersensitivity appear.
***INCOMPATIBILITIES* Solution/additive/Y-site:** Do not mix or infuse with other drugs.

■ Store IV solution for up to 8 h at 2°–8° C (36°–46° F). Allow solution to warm to room temperature before administration

ADVERSE EFFECTS (≥1%) **Body as a Whole:** <u>Anaphylaxis</u> (rare, usually within 2 h of infusion), infections, fatigue, rigors. **CNS:** Depression, headache, syncope, tremor. **CV:** Chest discomfort. **GI:** Abdominal discomfort, abnormal liver function tests. **Hematologic:** Local bleeding from infusion site. **Musculoskeletal:** Arthralgia. **Respiratory:** Pneumonia. **Skin:** Acute urticaria. **Urogenital:** Urinary frequency, irregular menstruation, amenorrhea, dysmenorrhea. **Other:** Infusion-related reactions (headache, dizziness, fatigue, hypersensitivity reactions, urticaria, pruritus, and rigors).

INTERACTIONS Drug: May reduce the effectiveness of VACCINES and TOXOIDS; may increase risk of infection with IMMUNOSUPPRESSANTS.

PHARMACOKINETICS Half-Life: 11 d.

CLINICAL IMPLICATIONS

Assessment & Drug Effects
■ During IV infusion and for 1–2 h after, monitor closely for S&S of hypersensitivity (e.g., urticaria, dizziness, fever, rash, chills, pruritus, nausea, flushing, hypotension, dyspnea, and chest pain).

N

Common adverse effects in *italic*, life-threatening effects <u>underlined</u>; generic names in **bold**; classifications in SMALL CAPS; ◆ Canadian drug name; ⊙ Prototype drug

1053

Patient & Family Education

- Report immediately any of the following during/after IV infusion: difficulty breathing, wheezing or shortness of breath, swelling or tightness about the neck and throat, chest pain, skin rash or hives.
- Report promptly S&S of infection (e.g., cough, fever, chills, or sore throat).

NATAMYCIN

(na-ta-mye′sin)
Natacyn
Classifications: ANTIFUNGAL AGENT
Therapeutic: ANTIFUNGAL
Prototype: Amphotericin B
Pregnancy Category: C

AVAILABILITY 5% suspension

ACTION & *THERAPEUTIC EFFECT*

Mechanism of action simulates that of amphotericin B and nystatin by binding to sterols in the fungal cell membrane resulting in cell death of fungi. *Effective against many yeasts and filamentous fungi including* Candida, Aspergillus, Cephalosporium, Fusarium, *and* Penicillium. *Limited activity in vivo against* Trichomonas vaginalis.

USES Blepharitis, conjunctivitis, and keratitis caused by susceptible fungi. Drug of choice for *Fusarium solani* keratitis.

UNLABELED USES Oral, cutaneous, and vaginal candidiasis; intranasal treatment of pulmonary aspergillosis.

CONTRAINDICATIONS Concomitant administration of a corticosteroid.
CAUTIOUS USE Pregnancy (category C) or lactation. Safety and efficacy in children are not established.

ROUTE & DOSAGE

Fungal Keratitis

Adult: **Ophthalmic** 1 drop in conjunctival sac of infected eye q1–2h for 3–4 d, then decrease to 1 drop q6–8h, then gradually decrease to 1 drop q4–7d

ADMINISTRATION

Instillation

- Wash hands thoroughly before and after treatment. Infection is easily transferred from infected to noninfected eye and to other individuals.
- Shake well before using.
- Store at 2°–24° C (36°–75° F).

ADVERSE EFFECTS (≥1%) **Special Senses:** Blurred vision, photophobia, eye pain. Uneven adherence of suspension to epithelial ulcerations or in fornices.

INTERACTIONS Drug: No clinically significant interactions established.

PHARMACOKINETICS Absorption: Drug adheres to ulcerated surface of the cornea and is retained in conjunctival fornices. Does not appear to be systemically absorbed.

CLINICAL IMPLICATIONS

Assessment & Drug Effects

- Inspect eye for response and tolerance at least twice weekly.
- Note: Lack of improvement in keratitis within 7–10 d suggests that causative organisms may not be susceptible to natamycin. Reevaluation is indicated and possibly a change in therapy.

Patient & Family Education

- Learn appropriate technique for application of eye drops.
- Expect temporary light sensitivity. Be prepared to wear sunglasses

outdoors after drug administration and perhaps for a few hours indoors.
- Return to ophthalmologist for re-evaluation of eye problem if you experience symptoms of conjunctivitis: pain, discharge, itching, scratching "foreign body sensation," changes in vision.
- Do not share facecloths and hand towels; this will help prevent transmission of the fungal infection.

NATEGLINIDE

(nat-e′gli-nide)
Starlix
Classifications: HORMONE; ANTIDIABETIC; MEGLITINIDE
Therapeutic: ANTIDIABETIC; MEGLITINIDE
Prototype: Repaglinide
Pregnancy Category: C

AVAILABILITY 60 mg, 120 mg tablets

ACTION & *THERAPEUTIC EFFECT*
Lowers blood glucose levels by stimulating the release of insulin from the pancreatic cells of a type 2 diabetic. Significantly reduces postprandial blood glucose in type 2 diabetics and improves glycemic control when given before meals. There is minimal risk of hypoglycemia. *Effectiveness is indicated by preprandial blood glucose between 80 and 120 mg/dL and HbA$_{1c}$ ≤6.5%.*

USES Alone or in combination with metformin for the treatment of non-insulin-dependent diabetes mellitus.

CONTRAINDICATIONS Prior hypersensitivity to nateglinide. Type 1 (insulin-dependent) diabetes mellitus, diabetic ketoacidosis; hypoglycemia; pregnancy (category C).
CAUTIOUS USE Renal impairment; liver dysfunction; adrenal or pituitary insufficiency; malnutrition; infection, trauma, surgery or unusual stress; concurrent therapy of drugs which inhibit cytochrome P450-3A4 (e.g., erythromycin, ketoconazole); concurrent therapy with drugs which are inducers of cytochrome P450-3A4 (e.g., rifampin); other medications, especially beta-adrenergic blocking agents; surgery; trauma; lactation.

ROUTE & DOSAGE

Diabetes Mellitus
Adult: **PO** 60–120 mg t.i.d. 1–30 min prior to meals

ADMINISTRATION

Oral
- Give, preferably, 10 min before meals. Omit the dose if the meal is skipped. Add a dose if an extra meal is eaten. Never double the dose.
- Store at 15°–30° C (59°–86° F).

ADVERSE EFFECTS (≥1%) **Body as a Whole:** Back pain, flu-like symptoms. **CV:** Dizziness. **GI:** *Diarrhea.* **Metabolic:** Hypoglycemia. **Musculoskeletal:** Arthropathy. **Respiratory:** Upper respiratory infection, bronchitis, cough.

INTERACTIONS Drug: NSAIDS, SALICYLATES, MAO INHIBITORS, BETA-ADRENERGIC BLOCKERS, may potentiate hypoglycemic effects; THIAZIDE DIURETICS, CORTICOSTEROIDS, THYROID PREPARATIONS, SYMPATHOMIMETIC AGENTS may attenuate hypoglycemic effects. **Herbal: Garlic, ginseng** may potentiate hypoglycemic effects.

PHARMACOKINETICS Absorption: Rapidly absorbed, 73% bioavailability. **Peak:** 1 h. **Distribution:** 98% protein bound. **Metabolism:** In liver by CYP2C9 (70%) and

N

Common adverse effects in *italic*, life-threatening effects <u>underlined</u>; generic names in **bold**; classifications in SMALL CAPS; ◆ Canadian drug name; ⊘ Prototype drug

1055

CYP3A4 (30%). **Elimination:** Primarily in urine. **Half-Life:** 1.5 h.

CLINICAL IMPLICATIONS

Assessment & Drug Effects
- Lab tests: Frequent FBS monitoring and HbA$_{1C}$ q3mo to determine effective dose.
- Monitor carefully for S&S of hypoglycemia especially during the one-week period following transfer from a longer acting sulfonylurea such as chlorpropamide.

Patient & Family Education
- Take only before a meal to lessen the chance of hypoglycemia.
- When transferred to nateglinide from another oral hypoglycemia drug, start nateglinide the morning after the other agent is stopped, unless directed otherwise by physician.
- Watch for S&S of hyperglycemia or hypoglycemia (see Appendix F); report poor blood glucose control to physician.
- Report gastric upset or other bothersome GI symptoms to physician.

NEDOCROMIL SODIUM

(ned'o-cro-mil)
Tilade, Alocril
Classifications: ANTIINFLAMMATORY; MAST CELL STABILIZER; ANTIASTHMATIC
Therapeutic: ANTIASTHMATIC; MAST CELL STABILIZER
Prototype: Cromolyn sodium
Pregnancy Category: B

AVAILABILITY 1.75 mg aerosol; 2% ophthalmic solution

ACTION & *THERAPEUTIC EFFECT*
Inhibits activation of and mediators released from inflammatory cell types associated with asthma (e.g., neutrophils, mast cells, monocytes). *Inhibits release of inflammatory mediators including histamine and prostaglandin D$_2$.*

USES Maintenance therapy for patients with mild to moderate asthma. Ocular use for allergic conjunctivitis (see Appendix A-1).

CONTRAINDICATIONS Hypersensitivity to nedocromil; acute bronchospasm, particularly status asthmaticus; children <6 y.
CAUTIOUS USE Pregnancy (category B), lactation.

ROUTE & DOSAGE

Asthma
Adult: **Inhalation** 2 inhalations q.i.d. at regular intervals, NOT for acute asthma attacks
Child: **Inhalation** ≥6 y, 2 inhalations q.i.d.

ADMINISTRATION

Inhalation
- Use correct administration technique to ensure maximum drug efficacy. Review instruction leaflet supplied by manufacturer.
- Reduce dosage in stages, with each lower dose maintained for several weeks of good control prior to further decreasing dose.

ADVERSE EFFECTS (≥1%) **GI:** *Abnormal bitter taste,* nausea, vomiting. **CNS:** Headache, dizziness. **Respiratory:** Sore throat irritation, cough.

INTERACTIONS Drug: No clinically significant interactions established.

PHARMACOKINETICS Absorption: 90% of dose is deposited in throat and swallowed. Less than 7% is absorbed systemically in patients with asthma. **Onset:** 1 wk for therapeutic effect. **Peak:** 10–20 min. **Metabolism:** Does not appear to be metabolized. **Elimination:** 6% in urine in 72 h. **Half-Life:** 2.3 h.

CLINICAL IMPLICATIONS

Assessment & Drug Effects

- Assess for coughing and bronchospasms induced by nedocromil. These are indications for discontinuation of drug and should be promptly reported.
- Monitor patients for whom systemic or inhaled steroid therapy has been reduced, as nedocromil may not fully substitute for the decrease in dose of steroid.

Patient & Family Education

- Learn to administer the drug properly. Review patient instruction leaflet.
- Do not use it to treat acute bronchospasms because nedocromil is not a bronchodilator.
- Continue regular nedocromil therapy even during symptom-free periods.

NEFAZODONE

(nef-a-zo'done)
Classifications: PSYCHOTHERAPEUTIC AGENT; ANTIDEPRESSANT; SELECTIVE SEROTONIN REUPTAKE INHIBITOR (SSRI)
Therapeutic: ANTIDEPRESSANT; SSRI
Prototype: Fluoxetine HCl
Pregnancy Category: C

AVAILABILITY 50 mg, 100 mg, 150 mg, 200 mg, 250 mg tablets

ACTION & _THERAPEUTIC EFFECT_
Antidepressant with a dual mechanism of action. Inhibits neuronal serotonin (5-HT$_1$) reuptake and also possesses 5-HT$_2$ antagonist properties. _Antidepressant effects with minimal cardiovascular effects, fewer anticholinergic effects, less sedation, and less sexual dysfunction than other antidepressants._

USES Treatment of depression.

CONTRAINDICATIONS Hypersensitivity to nefazodone or alcohol; hepatic disease, hepatitis, jaundice; MAOI therapy; mania; severe restlessness, suicidal ideation; surgery; neonates; pregnancy (category C), lactation.

CAUTIOUS USE Older adults, women of childbearing age; history of seizure disorders, seizures; renal or hepatic impairment; recent MI, unstable cardiac disease; hypotension; angina, stroke, hypovolemia, dehydration, bipolar disorder; history of mania; ECT therapy. Safety and efficacy in children <18 y are not established.

ROUTE & DOSAGE

Depression
Adult: **PO** 50–100 mg b.i.d., may need to increase up to 300–600 mg/d in 2–3 divided doses
Geriatric: **PO** Start with 50 mg b.i.d.

ADMINISTRATION

Oral

- Do not give within 14 d of discontinuation of an MAO INHIBITOR.
- Store at 15°–30° C (59°–86° F).

ADVERSE EFFECTS (≥1%) **Body as a Whole:** Anaphylactic reactions, angioedema. **CNS:** _Headache, dizziness, drowsiness,_ asthenia, tremor, insomnia, agitation, anxiety. **GI:** Dry mouth, constipation, nausea, liver toxicity. **Special Senses:** Visual disturbances, blurred vision, scotomata. **Endocrine:** Galactorrheas, gynecomastia, serotonin syndrome.

Common adverse effects in _italic_, life-threatening effects underlined; generic names in **bold**; classifications in SMALL CAPS; ♣ Canadian drug name; ⊘ Prototype drug

1057

Skin: <u>Stevens-Johnson syndrome, liver failure.</u>

INTERACTIONS Drug: May cause serotonin syndrome (see Appendix F) with maois or ssris; may increase plasma levels of some benzodiazepines, including **alprazolam** and **triazolam.** May decrease plasma levels and effects of **propranolol.** May increase levels and toxicity of **buspirone, carbamazepine, cilostazol, digoxin;** reports of QTc prolongation and ventricular arrhythmias with **pimozide;** increased risk of rhabdomyolysis with **lovastatin, simvastatin;** increased risk of **ergotamine** toxicity with **dihydroergotamine, ergotamine. Herbal: St. John's wort** may cause **serotonin** syndrome.

PHARMACOKINETICS Onset: 1 wk. **Peak:** 3–5 wk. **Metabolism:** In liver to at least two active metabolites. **Half-Life:** Nefazodone 3.5 h, metabolites 2–33 h.

CLINICAL IMPLICATIONS

Assessment & Drug Effects
- Monitor for worsening of depression or emergence of suicidal ideation.
- Evaluate concurrent drugs for possible interactions.
- Monitor patients with a history of seizures for increased activity.
- Assess safety, as dizziness and drowsiness are common adverse effects.
- Lab tests: Monitor periodically liver function and CBC during long-term therapy.

Patient & Family Education
- Be aware that significant improvement in mood may not occur for several weeks following initiation of therapy.

- Do not drive or engage in potentially hazardous activities until response to the drug is known.
- Report changes in visual acuity.

NELARABINE

Arranon
Classifications: ANTINEOPLASTIC; PYRIMIDINE, ANTIMETABOLITE
Therapeutic: ANTINEOPLASTIC; ANTIMETABOLITE
Prototype: 5-Fluorouracil
Pregnancy Category: D

AVAILABILITY 5 mg/mL solution

ACTION & *THERAPEUTIC EFFECT*
Nelarabine inhibits DNA synthesis in lymphoblastic T-cells of acute leukemia and lymphoma. *The incorporation of a nelarabine metabolite in the leukemic blast cells halts DNA synthesis and causes cell death.*

USES Treatment of patients with T-cell acute lymphoblastic leukemia and T-cell lymphoblastic lymphoma.

CONTRAINDICATIONS Severe bone marrow suppression; older adults; pregnancy (category D); lactation.

CAUTIOUS USE Severe renal impairment, renal failure; hepatic impairment.

ROUTE & DOSAGE

Adult T-Cell Leukemia/Lymphoma
Adult: **IV** 1500 mg/m² over 2 h on days 1, 3, and 5, repeated every 21 d
Child: **IV** 650 mg/m² over 1 h for 5 d, repeated every 21 d

ADMINISTRATION

- Standard IV hydration, urine alkalinization, and prophylaxis with

allopurinol are advised to manage hyperuricemia in those at risk for tumor lysis syndrome.
- Use gloves and protective clothing to prevent skin contact.

Intravenous

PREPARE: **IV Infusion:** Do not dilute. Transfer the required dose to a PVC or glass container for infusion.

ADMINISTER: **IV Infusion:** *Adult:* Give over 2 h. *Child:* Give over 1 h.
- Discontinue IV and notify physician for neurologic adverse events of NCI Common Toxicity Criteria grade 2 or greater.
- Store vials at 15°–30° C (59°–86° F). Nelarabine is stable in PVC bags or glass infusion containers for 8 h up to 30° C.

ADVERSE EFFECTS (≥1%) **Body as a Whole:** Abnormal gait, *fatigue, pyrexia,* rigors. **CNS:** *Asthenia,* ataxia, *dizziness, headache, hypoesthesia, neuropathy, paresthesia, somnolence,* tremor. **CV:** Chest pain, *edema,* hypotension, *petechiae,* sinus tachycardia. **GI:** Abdominal pain, *constipation, diarrhea, nausea, vomiting,* stomatitis. **Hematologic/Lymphatic:** *Anemia, neutropenia, thrombocytopenia,* increased risk of infection. **Hepatic:** AST levels increased. **Metabolic:** Anorexia, dehydration, hyperglycemia. **Musculoskeletal:** Arthralgia, back pain, muscular weakness, *myalgia,* pain in extremities. **Respiratory:** *Cough, dyspnea, pleural effusion,* epistaxis, wheezing.

PHARMACOKINETICS Distribution: Extensive. **Metabolism:** Bioactivation to ara-GTP, oxidized to uric acid. **Elimination:** Renal. **Half-Life:** 3 h (active metabolite).

CLINICAL IMPLICATIONS

Assessment & Drug Effects
- Monitor for and report immediately S&S of adverse CNS effects, including altered mental status (e.g., confusion, severe somnolence), seizures, and peripheral neuropathy (e.g., numbness, paresthesias, motor weakness, ataxia, paralysis).
- Monitor diabetics for loss of glycemic control.
- Note: Previous or concurrent treatment with intrathecal chemotherapy or previous craniospinal irradiation may increase risk of CNS toxicity.

Patient & Family Education
- Do not drive or engage in potentially hazardous activities until response to drug is known.
- Report any of the following to a health care provider: seizures; tingling or numbness in hands and feet; problems with fine motor coordination; unsteady gait and increased weakness with ambulating; fever or other signs of infections.
- Use effective contraceptive measures to avoid pregnancy while taking this drug.

N

NELFINAVIR MESYLATE

(nel-fin'a-vir)
Viracept
Classifications: ANTIRETROVIRAL AGENT; PROTEASE INHIBITOR
Therapeutic: ANTIRETROVIRAL; PROTEASE INHIBITOR
Prototype: Saquinavir
Pregnancy Category: B

AVAILABILITY 250 mg, 625 mg tablets; 50 mg/g powder

ACTION & THERAPEUTIC EFFECT Inhibits HIV-1 protease, which is responsible for the production of

Common adverse effects in *italic*, life-threatening effects <u>underlined</u>; generic names in **bold**; classifications in SMALL CAPS; ◆ Canadian drug name; ☻ Prototype drug

1059

HIV-1 viral particles in an infected individual. Inhibition of the viral protease prevents the cleavage of the viral polypeptide, resulting in the production of an immature, noninfectious virus. *Effectiveness is indicated by decreased viral load.*

USES Treatment of HIV infection in combination with a nucleoside analog.

CONTRAINDICATIONS Hypersensitivity to nelfinavir; concurrent administration with amiodarone, quinidine, rifampin, triazolam, or midazolam; lactation. Safety and effectiveness in children <2 y are not established.
CAUTIOUS USE Liver function impairment, hemophilia; pregnancy (category B).

ROUTE & DOSAGE

HIV Infection
Adult: **PO** 750 mg t.i.d. or 1250 mg (2 × 625 mg) b.i.d. with food
Child: **PO** 2–13 y, 20–30 mg/kg t.i.d. with food (max: 750 mg/dose)

ADMINISTRATION

Oral
- Give with a meal or light snack.
- Oral powder may be mixed with a small amount of water, milk, soy milk, or dietary supplements; liquid should be consumed immediately. Do not mix oral powder in original container nor with acid food or juice (e.g., orange or apple juice, or applesauce).
- Store at 15°–30° C (59°–86° F).

ADVERSE EFFECTS (≥1%) **Body as a Whole:** Allergic reactions, back pain, fever, malaise, pain, asthenia, myalgia, arthralgia. **CNS:** Head-ache, anxiety, depression, dizziness, insomnia, seizures. **GI:** Abdominal pain, *diarrhea*, nausea, flatulence, anorexia, dyspepsia, <u>GI bleeding</u>, hepatitis, vomiting, pancreatitis, increased liver function tests. **Hematologic:** Anemia, leukopenia, thrombocytopenia. **Respiratory:** Dyspnea, pharyngitis, rhinitis. **Skin:** Rash, pruritus, sweating, urticaria.

INTERACTIONS Drug: Other PRO-TEASE INHIBITORS, **ketoconazole** may increase nelfinavir levels; **rifabutin, rifampin** may decrease nelfinavir levels; nelfinavir will decrease ORAL CONTRACEPTIVE levels; may increase levels of **atorvastatin, simvastatin;** increase risk of **ergotamine** toxicity with **dihydroergotamine, ergotamine. Herbal:** St. John's wort, **garlic** may decrease antiretroviral activity.

PHARMACOKINETICS Absorption: Food increases the amount of drug absorbed. **Distribution:** >98% protein bound. **Metabolism:** In the liver (CYP3A). **Elimination:** Primarily in feces. **Half-Life:** 3.5–5 h.

CLINICAL IMPLICATIONS

Assessment & Drug Effects
- Monitor hemophiliacs (type A or B) closely for spontaneous bleeding.
- Monitor carefully patients with hepatic impairment for toxic drug effects.

Patient & Family Education
- Drug must be taken exactly as prescribed. Do not alter dose or discontinue drug without consulting physician.
- Use a barrier contraceptive even if using hormonal contraceptives.
- Be aware that diarrhea is a common adverse effect that can usually be controlled by OTC medications.

NEOMYCIN SULFATE

(nee-oh-mye′sin)
Mycifradin, Myciguent, Neo-Tabs, Neo-fradin
Classifications: AMINOGLYCOSIDE ANTIBIOTIC
Therapeutic: ANTIBIOTIC; AMINO-GLYCOSIDE
Prototype: Gentamicin
Pregnancy Category: C

AVAILABILITY 500 mg tablet; 125 mg/5 mL oral solution; 3.5 mg/g ointment, cream

ACTION & *THERAPEUTIC EFFECT*
Aminoglycoside antibiotic obtained from *Streptomyces fradiae*. It inhibits bacterial protein synthesis through irreversible binding to the 30S ribosomal subunit within susceptible bacteria. Causes bacteria not to replicate. *Active against a wide variety of gram-negative bacteria. Effective against certain gram-positive organisms, particularly penicillin-sensitive and some methicillin-resistant strains of* Staphylococcus aureus *(MRSA).*

USES Severe diarrhea caused by enteropathogenic *Escherichia coli;* preoperative intestinal antisepsis; to inhibit nitrogen-forming bacteria of GI tract in patients with cirrhosis or hepatic coma and for urinary tract infections caused by susceptible organisms. Also topically for short-term treatment of eye, ear, and skin infections.

CONTRAINDICATIONS Use of oral drug in patients with intestinal obstruction; ulcerative bowel lesions; topical applications over large skin areas; hypersensitivity to aminoglycosides; parkinsonism; myasthenia gravis; pregnancy (category C), lactation.

CAUTIOUS USE Topical otic applications in patients with perforated eardrum, children; dehydration; renal disease, renal impairment.

ROUTE & DOSAGE

Intestinal Antisepsis
Adult: **PO** 1 g q1h times 4 doses, then 1 g q4h times 5 doses
Child: **PO** 10.3 mg/kg q4–6h for 3 d

Hepatic Coma
Adult: **PO** 4–12 g/d in 4 divided doses for 5–6 d
Child: **PO** 437.5–1225 mg/m² q6h for 5–6 d

Diarrhea
Adult: **PO** 50 mg/kg in 4 divided doses for 2–3 d **IM** 1.3–2.6 mg/kg q6h
Child: **PO** 8.75 mg/kg q6h for 2–3 d

Cutaneous Infections
Adult: **Topical** Apply 1–3 times/d

ADMINISTRATION

Oral
- Preoperative bowel preparation: Saline laxative is generally given immediately before neomycin therapy is initiated.

Topical
- Consult physician about what to use for cleansing skin before each application.
- Make sure ear canal is clean and dry prior to instillation for topical therapy of external ear.

ADVERSE EFFECTS (≥1%) **Body as a Whole:** <u>Neuromuscular blockade</u> with muscular and <u>respiratory paralysis</u>; hypersensitivity reactions. **GI:** Mild laxative effect, diarrhea, nausea, vomiting; prolonged ther-

---

apy: malabsorption-like syndrome including cyanocobalamin (vitamin B_{12}) deficiency, low serum cholesterol. **Urogenital:** Nephrotoxicity. **Special Senses:** Ototoxicity. **Skin:** *Redness,* scaling, pruritus, dermatitis.

INTERACTIONS Drug: May decrease absorption of **cyanocobalamin.**

PHARMACOKINETICS Absorption: 3% absorbed from GI tract in adults; up to 10% absorbed in neonates. **Peak:** 1–4 h. **Elimination:** 97% excreted unchanged in feces. **Half-Life:** 3 h.

CLINICAL IMPLICATIONS

Assessment & Drug Effects

- Perform audiometric studies twice weekly in patients with kidney or liver dysfunction receiving extended oral therapy.
- Lab tests: Obtain baseline and daily urinalysis for albumin, casts, and cells; and BUN every other day. Also, serum drug levels (toxic levels reportedly range from 8 to 30 mcg/mL, although individual variations exist).
- Monitor I&O in patients receiving oral or parenteral therapy. Report oliguria or changes in I&O ratio. Inadequate neomycin excretion results in high serum drug levels and risk of nephrotoxicity and ototoxicity.

Patient & Family Education

- Stop treatment and consult your physician if irritation occurs when you are using topical neomycin. Allergic dermatitis is common.
- Report any unusual symptom related to ears or hearing (e.g., tinnitus, roaring sounds, loss of hearing acuity, dizziness).
- Do not exceed prescribed dosage or duration of therapy.

NEOSTIGMINE METHYLSULFATE ℗

(nee-oh-stig'meen)

Prostigmin

Classifications: CHOLINERGIC AGENT; CHOLINESTERASE INHIBITOR
Therapeutic: CHOLINESTERASE INHIBITOR

Pregnancy Category: C

AVAILABILITY 1:1000, 1:2000, 1:4000 injection

ACTION & *THERAPEUTIC EFFECT*

Produces reversible cholinesterase inhibition or inactivation. Has direct stimulant action on voluntary muscle fibers and possibly on autonomic ganglia and CNS neurons. Allows intensified and prolonged effect of acetylcholine at cholinergic synapses (basis for use in myasthenia gravis). *Produces generalized cholinergic response including miosis, increased tonus of intestinal and skeletal muscles, constriction of bronchi and ureters, slower pulse rate, and stimulation of salivary and sweat glands.*

USES To prevent and treat postoperative abdominal distension and urinary retention; for symptomatic control of and sometimes for differential diagnosis of myasthenia gravis; and to reverse the effects of nondepolarizing muscle relaxants (e.g., tubocurarine).

CONTRAINDICATIONS Hypersensitivity to neostigmine, cholinergics; cholinesterase inhibitor toxicity; GI obstruction; ileus; bradycardia, hypotension; mechanical obstruction of intestinal or urinary tract; peritonitis; administration with other cholinergic drugs; pregnancy (category C), lactation.

CAUTIOUS USE Recent ileorectal anastamoses; epilepsy; bronchial asthma; hepatic disease; bradycardia, recent coronary occlusion; vagotonia; hyperthyroidism; cardiac arrhythmias; renal failure; renal impairment; renal disease; peptic ulcer; seizure disorder.

ROUTE & DOSAGE

Diagnosis of Myasthenia Gravis
Adult: **IM** 0.02 mg/kg
Child: **IM** 0.04 mg/kg

Treatment of Myasthenia Gravis
Adult: **IM/SC** 0.5–2.5 mg q1–3h (max 10 mg/day)
Child: **IM/SC** 0.01–0.04 mg/kg q2–4h

Reversal of Nondepolarizing Neuromuscular Blockade
Adult: **IV** 0.5–2.5 mg slowly (max dose 5 mg)
Child: **IV** 0.025–0.08 mg/kg
Infant: **IV** 0.025–0.1 mg/kg

Postoperative Distention and Urinary Retention
Adult: **IM/SC** 0.25 mg q4–6h for 2–3 d

Renal Impairment
Cl_{cr} 10–50 mL/min: use 50% of dose; <10 mL/min: use 25% of dose

ADMINISTRATION

Intramuscular, Subcutaneous
▪ Note: 1 mg = 1 mL of the 1:1000 solution; 0.5 mg = 1 mL of the 1:2000 solution; 0.25 mg = 1 mL of the 1:4000 solution.
▪ Give undiluted.

Intravenous
PREPARE: **Direct:** Give undiluted.

ADMINISTER: **Direct:** Give at a rate of 0.5 mg or a fraction thereof over 1 min.

ADVERSE EFFECTS (≥1%) **Body as a Whole:** Muscle cramps, *fasciculations,* twitching, pallor, fatigability, generalized weakness, paralysis, agitation, fear, <u>death</u>. **CV:** Tightness in chest, bradycardia, hypotension, elevated BP. **GI:** *Nausea,* vomiting, eructation, epigastric discomfort, abdominal cramps, diarrhea, involuntary or difficult defecation. **CNS:** CNS stimulation. **Respiratory:** *Increased salivation* and bronchial secretions, sneezing, cough, dyspnea, diaphoresis, respiratory depression. **Special Senses:** Lacrimation, miosis, blurred vision. **Urogenital:** Difficult micturition.

INTERACTIONS Drug: Succinylcholine decamethonium may prolong phase I block or reverse phase II block; neostigmine antagonizes effects of **tubocurarine; atracurium, vecuronium, pancuronium; procainamide, quinidine, atropine** antagonize effects of neostigmine.

PHARMACOKINETICS Onset: 10–30 min IM or IV. **Peak:** 20–30 min IM or IV. **Distribution:** Not reported to cross placenta or appear in breast milk. **Metabolism:** In liver. **Elimination:** 80% of drug and metabolites excreted in urine within 24 h. **Half-Life:** 50–90 min.

CLINICAL IMPLICATIONS

Assessment & Drug Effects
▪ Check pulse before giving drug to bradycardic patients. If below 60/min or other established parameter, consult physician. Atropine will be ordered to restore heart rate.

Common adverse effects in *italic*, life-threatening effects <u>underlined</u>; generic names in **bold**; classifications in SMALL CAPS; ♣ Canadian drug name; ⓟ Prototype drug

1063

- Monitor pulse, respiration, and BP during period of dosage adjustment in treatment of myasthenia gravis.
- Report promptly and record accurately the onset of myasthenic symptoms and drug adverse effects in relation to last dose in order to assist physician in determining lowest effective dosage schedule.
- Note time of muscular weakness onset carefully in myasthenic patients. It may indicate whether patient is in cholinergic or myasthenic crisis: Weakness that appears approximately 1 h after drug administration suggests cholinergic crisis (overdose) and is treated by prompt withdrawal of neostigmine and immediate administration of atropine. Weakness that occurs 3 h or more after drug administration is more likely due to myasthenic crisis (underdose or drug resistance) and is treated by more intensive anticholinesterase therapy.
- Record drug effect and duration of action. S&S of myasthenia gravis relieved by neostigmine include lid ptosis; diplopia; drooping facies; difficulty in chewing, swallowing, breathing, or coughing; and weakness of neck, limbs, and trunk muscles.
- Manifestations of neostigmine overdosage often appear first in muscles of neck and those involved in chewing and swallowing, with muscles of shoulder girdle and upper extremities affected next.
- Monitor respiration, maintain airway or assisted ventilation, and give oxygen as indicated, when used as antidote for tubocurarine or other nondepolarizing neuromuscular blocking agents (usually preceded by atropine). Respiratory assistance is continued until recovery of respiration and neuromuscular transmission is assured.
- Report to physician if patient does not urinate within 1 h after first dose when used to relieve urinary retention.

Patient & Family Education
- Be aware that regulation of dosage interval is extremely difficult; dosage must be adjusted for each patient to deal with unpredictable exacerbations and remissions.
- Keep a diary of "peaks and valleys" of muscle strength.
- Keep an accurate record for physician of your response to drug. Learn how to recognize adverse effects, how to modify dosage regimen according to your changing needs, or how to administer atropine if necessary.
- Be aware that certain factors may require an increase in size or frequency of dose (e.g., physical or emotional stress, infection, menstruation, surgery), whereas remission requires a decrease in dosage.
- Some patients become refractory to neostigmine after prolonged use and require change in dosage or medication.

NEPAFENAC

(nep'a-fe-nac)

Nevanac
Pregnancy Category: C
See Appendix A-1.

NESIRITIDE

(nes-ir'i-tide)

Natrecor

Classifications: ATRIAL NATRIURETIC PEPTIDE HORMONE

Therapeutic: CARDIOVASCULAR; ATRIAL NATRIURETIC HORMONE (ANH)

Pregnancy Category: C

AVAILABILITY 1.5 mg vial

ACTION & *THERAPEUTIC EFFECT*
Nesiritide is a human B-type natriuretic peptide (hBNP), produced by recombinant DNA, which mimics the actions of human atrial natriuretic hormone (ANH). ANH is secreted by the right atrium when atrial blood pressure increases. Nesiritide, like ANH, inhibits antidiuretic hormone (ADH) by increasing urine sodium loss by the kidney and triggering the formation of a large volume of dilute urine. Nesiritide binds to a cyclic nucleic acid, which results in smooth muscle cell relaxation. *Effective in causing smooth muscle relaxation. Nesiritide binds to a cyclic nucleic acid, which results in smooth muscle cell relaxation. The drug also causes dilation of veins and arteries. It is effective in managing dyspnea at rest in patients with acute congestive heart failure (CHF).*

USES Acute treatment of decompensated CHF in patients who have dyspnea at rest or with minimal activity.

CONTRAINDICATIONS Hypersensitivity to nesiritide, patients with a systolic blood pressure <90 mm Hg, cardiogenic shock, patients with low cardiac filling pressures, patients who should not receive vasodilators, such as those with significant valvular stenosis, restrictive or obstructive cardiomyopathy, pericardial perfusion; constrictive pericarditis, pericardial tamponade; pregnancy (category C).

CAUTIOUS USE Lactation, concurrent administration of ACE inhibitors or vasodilators. Safety and efficacy in pediatric patients have not been established.

ROUTE & DOSAGE

Acute Decompensated CHF

Adult: **IV** 2 mcg/kg bolus administered over 60 s, followed by a continuous infusion of 0.01 mcg/kg/min (0.1 mL/kg/h) (max: 0.03 mcg/kg/min). Monitor blood pressure. If hypotension occurs, the dose should be reduced or discontinued. The infusion can subsequently be restarted at a dose that is reduced by 30% (with no bolus administration) after stabilization of hemodynamics.

ADMINISTRATION

Intravenous

PREPARE: **Direct and IV Infusion:** Reconstitute one 1.5 mg vial by adding 5 mL of IV solution removed from a 250 mL bag of selected diluent (i.e., D5W, NS, D5/0.45% NaCl, D5/0.2% NaCl). Rock the vial gently so that all surfaces, including the stopper, contact the diluent ensuring complete reconstitution. Do not shake the vial. Add the entire contents of the vial to the 250 mL IV bag to yield approximately 6 mcg/mL. Invert the bag several times to mix completely. Use within 24 h. Prime the IV tubing with 25 mL prior to connecting to the vascular access port.

N

Common adverse effects in *italic*, life-threatening effects <u>underlined</u>; generic names in **bold**; classifications in SMALL CAPS; ♣ Canadian drug name; ⊘ Prototype drug

1065

ADMINISTER: Direct: Withdraw the bolus dose from the prepared infusion bag. Determine dose as follows: bolus volume (mL) = (0.33) × (patient weight in kg). Give the bolus dose over 60 sec through an IV port in the tubing. **IV Infusion:** Infuse remainder of IV infusion immediately following the bolus dose. Determine the infusion rate as follows: flow rate (mL/h) = (0.1) × (patient weight in kg).

INCOMPATIBILITIES **Solution/additive and Y-site: Bumetanide, enalaprilat, ethacrynic acid, furosemide, heparin, hydralazine, insulin.**

- Store at controlled room temperature at 20°–25° C (68°–77° F) or refrigerated.

ADVERSE EFFECTS (≥1%) **Body as a Whole:** Headache, back pain, catheter pain, fever, injection site pain, leg cramps. **CNS:** Insomnia, dizziness, anxiety, confusion, paresthesia, somnolence, tremor. **CV:** *Hypotension,* ventricular tachycardia, ventricular extrasystoles, angina, bradycardia, tachycardia, atrial fibrillation, AV node conduction abnormalities. **GI:** Abdominal pain, nausea, vomiting. **Respiratory:** Cough, hemoptysis, apnea. **Skin:** Sweating, pruritus, rash. **Special Senses:** Amblyopia. **Renal:** Renal failure in acutely decompensated heart failure patients.

INTERACTIONS Drug: Additive effects with ANTIHYPERTENSIVES.

PHARMACOKINETICS Onset: 15 min. **Duration:** >60 min depending on dose. **Metabolism:** Proteolytic cleavage, proteolysis. **Half-Life:** 18 min.

CLINICAL IMPLICATIONS
Assessment & Drug Effects
- Monitor hemodynamic parameters (e.g., BP, PCWP, HR, ECG)

throughout therapy. Notify physician immediately if systolic BP <90 mm Hg.
- Establish hypotension parameters prior to initiating therapy.
- Reduce the dose or withhold the drug if hypotension occurs during administration. Reinitiate therapy infusion only after hypotension is corrected. Subsequent doses following a hypotensive episode are usually reduced by 30% and given without a prior bolus dose.
- Lab tests: Baseline and periodic serum creatinine.

NEVIRAPINE

(ne-vir′a-peen)
Viramune
Classifications: ANTIRETROVIRAL AGENT; NONNUCLEOSIDE REVERSE TRANSCRIPTASE INHIBITOR (NNRTI)
Therapeutic: ANTIRETROVIRAL; NNRTI
Prototype: Efavirenz
Pregnancy Category: C

AVAILABILITY 200 mg tablets; 10 mg/mL suspension

ACTION & *THERAPEUTIC EFFECT*
Nonnucleoside reverse transcriptase inhibitor (NNRI) of HIV-1. Binds directly to reverse transcriptase and blocks RNA- and DNA-dependent polymerase activities, thus preventing replication of the virus. *Prevents replication of the HIV-1 virus. Does not inhibit HIV-2 reverse transcriptase and DNA polymerases such as alpha, beta, gamma, and delta polymerases. Resistant strains appear rapidly.*

USES In combination with nucleoside analogs for treatment of HIV.

CONTRAINDICATIONS Hypersensitivity to nevirapine; hormonal contraceptives; pregnancy (category C), neonates; lactation.

CAUTIOUS USE Liver or renal disease, hemodialysis; hepatitis B or C; CNS disorders.

ROUTE & DOSAGE

HIV
Adult: **PO** 200 mg once daily for first 14 d, then increase to 200 mg b.i.d. *Child:* **PO** 120 mg/m² q.d. × 14 d, then increase q12h, if tolerated, to 120–200 mg/m² q12h (max: 200 mg/dose)

ADMINISTRATION

Oral
- Reinitiate with 200 mg/d for 14 d, then increase to b.i.d. dosing, when dosing is interrupted for >7 d.
- Store at 15°–30° C (59°–86° F) in a tightly closed container.

ADVERSE EFFECTS (≥1%) **Body as a Whole:** Fever, paresthesia, myalgia. **CNS:** Headache. **GI:** Nausea, diarrhea, abdominal pain, hepatitis, increased liver function tests, <u>hepatotoxicity</u> (including <u>fulminant and cholestatic hepatitis, hepatic necrosis, and hepatic failure</u>, especially with long-term use). **Hematologic:** Anemia, neutropenia. **Skin:** *Rash,* <u>Stevens-Johnson syndrome</u>.

INTERACTIONS Drug: May decrease plasma concentrations of PROTEASE INHIBITORS, ORAL CONTRACEPTIVES; may decrease **methadone** levels inducing opiate withdrawal. **Herbal: St. John's wort, garlic** may decrease antiretroviral activity.

PHARMACOKINETICS Absorption: Rapidly from GI tract. **Peak:** 4h. **Distribution:** 60% protein bound,

crosses placenta, distributed into breast milk. **Metabolism:** In liver (CYP3A). **Elimination:** Primarily in urine. **Half-Life:** 25–40 h.

CLINICAL IMPLICATIONS

Assessment & Drug Effects
- Lab tests: Obtain baseline and periodic liver and kidney function tests, routine blood chemistry, and CBC.
- Monitor weight, temperature, respiratory status with chest x-ray throughout therapy.
- Monitor carefully, especially during first 6 wk of therapy, for severe rash (with or without fever, blistering, oral lesions, conjunctivitis, swelling, joint aches, or general malaise).
- Withhold drug and notify physician if rash develops or liver function tests are abnormal.

Patient & Family Education
- Learn about common adverse effects.
- Withhold drug and notify physician if severe rash appears.
- Do not drive or engage in potentially hazardous activities until response to drug is known. There is a high potential for drowsiness and fatigue.
- Use or add barrier contraceptive if using hormonal contraceptive.

NIACIN (VITAMIN B₃, NICOTINIC ACID)

(nye′a-sin)

Niacor, Niaspan, Nicobid, Nico-400, Nicotinex, Novoniacin ◆, Slo-Niacin, Tri-B3 ◆

NIACINAMIDE (NICOTINAMIDE)

Classifications: VITAMIN B₃; ANTI-LIPEMIC; LIPID-LOWERING AGENT

Common adverse effects in *italic*, life-threatening effects <u>underlined</u>; generic names in **bold**; classifications in SMALL CAPS; ◆ Canadian drug name; ⊚ Prototype drug

1067

Therapeutic: VITAMIN B₃; LIPID-LOW-ERING AGENT
Pregnancy Category: C

AVAILABILITY 50 mg, 100 mg, 250 mg, 500 mg tablets; 125 mg, 250 mg, 400 mg, 500 mg, 750 mg, 1000 mg sustained release tablets, capsules

ACTION & *THERAPEUTIC EFFECT*
Water-soluble, heat-stable, B-complex vitamin (B₃) that functions with riboflavin as a control agent in coenzyme system that converts protein, carbohydrate, and fat to energy through oxidation-reduction. Niacinamide, an amide of niacin, is used as an alternative in the prevention and treatment of pellagra. *Produces vasodilation by direct action on vascular smooth muscles. Inhibits hepatic synthesis of VLDL, cholesterol, and triglyceride, and, indirectly, LDL. Large doses effectively reduce elevated serum cholesterol and total lipid levels in hypercholesterolemia and hyperlipidemic states.*

USES In prophylaxis and treatment of pellagra, usually in combination with other B-complex vitamins, and in deficiency states accompanying carcinoid syndrome, isoniazid therapy, Hartnup's disease, and chronic alcoholism. Also in adjuvant treatment of hyperlipidemia (elevated cholesterol or triglycerides) in patients who do not respond adequately to diet or weight loss. Also as vasodilator in peripheral vascular disorders, Ménière's disease, and labyrinthine syndrome, as well as to counteract LSD toxicity and to distinguish between psychoses of dietary and nondietary origin.

CONTRAINDICATIONS Hypersensitivity to niacin; hepatic impairment; severe hypotension; hemorrhaging or arterial bleeding; active peptic ulcer; pregnancy (category C), lactation, and children <16 y.

CAUTIOUS USE History of gallbladder disease, liver disease, and peptic ulcer; severe renal impairment; glaucoma; angina; coronary artery disease; diabetes mellitus; predisposition to gout; allergy; thrombocytopenia.

ROUTE & DOSAGE

Niacin Deficiency
Adult: **PO** 10–20 mg/d

Pellagra
Adult: **PO** 50–100 mg 3–4 times/day
Child: **PO** 50–100 mg t.i.d.

Hyperlipidemia
Adult: **PO** 1.5–3 g/d in divided doses, may increase up to 6 g/d if necessary
Child: **PO** 100–250 mg/d in 3 divided doses, may increase by 250 mg/d q2–3wk as tolerated

ADMINISTRATION

Oral
- Give oral drug with meals to decrease GI distress. Give with cold water (not hot beverage) to facilitate swallowing.
- Ensure that sustained release form is not chewed or crushed. It must be swallowed whole.
- Store at 15°–30° C (59°–86° F) in a light and moisture proof container.

ADVERSE EFFECTS (≥1%) **CNS:** *Transient headache, tingling of extremities,* syncope. With chronic use: nervousness, panic, toxic amblyopia, proptosis, blurred vision, loss of central vision. **CV:** *Generalized flushing with sensation of warmth,* postural hypotension, vasovagal attacks, arrhythmias (rare). **GI:** *Abnormalities of liver function tests; jaundice, bloating, flatulence, nausea,* vomiting, GI disorders, activation of peptic ulcer, xerostomia. **Skin:** *Increased sebaceous gland activity,* dry skin, skin rash, *pruritus,* keratitis nigricans. **Metabolic:** Hyperuricemia, hyperglycemia, glycosuria, hypoprothrombinemia, hypoalbuminemia.

DIAGNOSTIC TEST INTERFERENCE
Niacin causes elevated serum *bilirubin, uric acid, alkaline phosphatase, AST, ALT, LDH* levels and may cause *glucose intolerance.* Decreases *serum cholesterol* 15–30% and may cause false elevations with certain *fluorometric methods* of determining *urinary catecholamines.* Niacin may cause false-positive *urine glucose* tests using *copper sulfate reagents,* e.g., *Benedict's* solution.

INTERACTIONS Drug: Potentiates hypotensive effects of ANTIHYPERTENSIVE AGENTS.

PHARMACOKINETICS Absorption: Readily from GI tract. **Peak:** 20–70 min. **Distribution:** Into breast milk. **Metabolism:** In liver. **Elimination:** Primarily in urine. **Half-Life:** 45 min.

CLINICAL IMPLICATIONS
Assessment & Drug Effects
- Monitor therapeutic effectiveness and record effect of therapy on clinical manifestations of deficiency (fiery red tongue, excessive saliva secretion and infection of oral membranes, nausea, vomiting, diarrhea, confusion). Therapeutic response usually begins within 24 h.

- Lab tests: Obtain baseline and periodic tests of blood glucose and liver function in patients receiving prolonged high dose therapy.
- Monitor diabetics and patients on high doses closely. Hyperglycemia, glycosuria, ketonuria, and increased insulin requirements have been reported.
- Observe patients closely for evidence of liver dysfunction (jaundice, dark urine, light-colored stools, pruritus) and hyperuricemia in patients predisposed to gout (flank, joint, or stomach pain; altered urine excretion pattern).

Patient & Family Education
- Be aware that you may feel warm and flushed in face, neck, and ears within first 2 h after oral ingestion and immediately after parenteral administration and may last several hours. Effects are usually transient and subside as therapy continues.
- Sit or lie down and avoid sudden posture changes if you feel weak or dizzy. Report these symptoms and persistent flushing to your physician. Relief may be obtained by reduction of dosage, increasing subsequent doses in small increments, or by changing to sustained release formulation.
- Be aware that alcohol and large doses of niacin cause increased flushing and sensation of warmth.
- Avoid exposure to direct sunlight until lesions have entirely cleared if you have skin manifestations.

N

NICARDIPINE HYDROCHLORIDE

(ni-car'di-peen)
Cardene, Cardene SR
Classifications: CALCIUM CHANNEL BLOCKER; ANTIHYPERTENSIVE AGENT

Common adverse effects in *italic*, life-threatening effects underlined; generic names in **bold**; classifications in SMALL CAPS; ✦ Canadian drug name; ☯ Prototype drug

1069

Therapeutic: ANTIHYPERTENSIVE; CALCIUM CHANNEL BLOCKER
Prototype: Nifedipine
Pregnancy Category: C

AVAILABILITY 20 mg, 30 mg capsules; 30 mg, 45 mg, 60 mg sustained release capsules; 2.5 mg/mL injection

ACTION & *THERAPEUTIC EFFECT*
Calcium channel entry blocker that inhibits the transmembrane influx of calcium ions into cardiac muscle and smooth muscle, thus affecting contractility. More selectively affects vascular smooth muscle than cardiac muscle; relaxes coronary vascular smooth muscle with little or no negative inotropic effect. *Significantly decreases systemic vascular resistance. It reduces BP at rest and during isometric and dynamic exercise.*

USES Either alone or with beta blockers for chronic, stable (effort-associated) angina; either alone or with other antihypertensives for essential hypertension.
UNLABELED USES CHF, cerebral ischemia, migraine.

CONTRAINDICATIONS Hypersensitivity to nicardipine; advanced aortic stenosis; cardiogenic shock; hypotension; pregnancy (category C); lactation.
CAUTIOUS USE CHF; renal and hepatic impairment; severe bradycardia; older adult; GERD; hiatal hernia; renal disease; renal impairment; acute stroke; acute myocardial infarction.

ROUTE & DOSAGE

Hypertension, Angina
Adult: PO 20–40 mg t.i.d. or 30–60 mg SR b.i.d. IV Initiation of therapy in a drug-free patient: 5 mg/h initially, increase dose by 2.5 mg/h q15min (or faster) (max: 15 mg/h); for severe hypertension: 4–7.5 mg/h; for postop hypertension: 10–15 mg/h initially, then 1–3 mg/h

Substitute for Oral Nicardipine
Adult: IV 20 mg q8h PO = 0.5 mg/h; 30 mg q8h PO = 1.2 mg/h; 40 mg q8h PO = 2.2 mg/h

ADMINISTRATION

Note: To prevent symptoms of withdrawal, do not abruptly discontinue drug.
Oral
- Give on empty stomach. High-fat meals may decrease blood levels.
- Ensure that sustained release form is not chewed or crushed. It must be swallowed whole.
- When converting from IV to oral dose, give first dose of t.i.d. regimen 1 h before discontinuing infusion.

Intravenous

PREPARE: IV Infusion: Dilute each 25 mg ampul with 240 mL of D5W or NS to yield 0.1 mg/mL.
ADMINISTER: IV Infusion: For adults, usually initiated at 50 mL/h (5 mg/h) with rate increases of 25 mL/h (2.5 mg/h) q5–15 min up to a maximum of 150 mL/h. Infusion is usually slowed to 30 mL/h once the target BP is reached.
INCOMPATIBILITIES Solution/additive: Sodium bicarbonate. **Y-site:** Ampicillin, ampicillin/sulbactam, cefoperazone, **furosemide, heparin, thiopental.**

ADVERSE EFFECTS (≥1%) **CNS:** Dizziness or headache, fatigue, anxiety, depression, paresthesias, insomnia, somnolence, nervousness.

CV: Pedal edema, hypotension, flushing, palpitations, tachycardia, increased angina. **GI:** Anorexia, nausea, vomiting, dry mouth, constipation, dyspepsia. **Skin:** Rash, pruritus. **Body as a Whole:** Arthralgia or arthritis.

INTERACTIONS Drug: Adenosine prolongs bradycardia. **Amiodarone** may cause sinus arrest and AV block. **Benazepril** blunts increase in heart rate and increase in plasma **norepinephrine** and **aldosterone** seen with nicardipine. BETA BLOCKERS cause hypotension and bradycardia. **Cimetidine** increases levels of nicardipine, resulting in hypotension. Concomitant nicardipine and **cyclosporine** result in significant increase in **cyclosporine** serum concentrations 1–30 d after initiation of nicardipine therapy; following withdrawal of nicardipine, **cyclosporine** levels decrease. **Magnesium**, when used to retard premature labor, may cause severe hypotension and neuromuscular blockade. **Food:** Grapefruit juice (>1 qt/day) may increase plasma concentrations and adverse effects.

PHARMACOKINETICS Absorption: Immediately 35% of oral dose reaches systemic circulation. **Onset:** 1 min IV; 20 min PO. **Peak:** 0.5–2 h. **Duration:** 3 h IV. **Distribution:** 95% protein bound; distributed in breast milk. **Metabolism:** Rapidly and extensively in liver (CYP3A4); active metabolite has <1% activity of parent compound. **Elimination:** 35% in feces, 60% in urine; not affected by hemodialysis. **Half-Life:** 8.6 h.

CLINICAL IMPLICATIONS

Assessment & Drug Effects
- Establish baseline data before treatment is started including BP, pulse, and lab values of liver and kidney function.
- Monitor BP during initiation and titration of dosage carefully. Hypotension with or without an increase in heart rate may occur, especially in patients who are hypertensive or who are already taking antihypertensive medication.
- Avoid too rapid reduction in either systolic or diastolic pressure during parenteral administration.
- Discontinue IV infusion if hypotension or tachycardia develop.
- Observe for large peak and trough differences in BP. Initially, measure BP at peak effect (1–2 h after dosing) and at trough effect (8 h after dosing).

Patient & Family Education
- Record and report any increase in frequency, duration, and severity of angina when initiating or increasing dosage. Keep a record of nitroglycerin use and promptly report any changes in previous anginal pattern. Increased incidence and severity of angina has occurred in some patients using nicardipine.
- Do not change dosage regimen without consulting physician.
- Be aware that abrupt withdrawal may cause an increased frequency and duration of chest pain. This drug must be gradually tapered under medical supervision.
- Rise slowly from a recumbent position; avoid driving or operating potentially dangerous equipment until response to nicardipine is known.
- Notify physician if any of the following occur: Irregular heart beat, shortness of breath, swelling of the feet, pronounced dizziness, nausea, or drop in BP.

Common adverse effects in *italic*, life-threatening effects underlined; generic names in **bold**; classifications in SMALL CAPS; ♦ Canadian drug name; ❂ Prototype drug

1071

NICOTINE ℗

(nik'o-teen)

Nicotrol NS, Nicotrol Inhaler, Commit

NICOTINE POLACRILEX

Nicorette Gum, Nicorette DS

NICOTINE TRANSDERMAL SYSTEM

Habitrol, Nicoderm, Nicotrol, ProStep

Classifications: SMOKING DETERRENT; CHOLINERGIC

Therapeutic: SMOKING DETERRENT

Pregnancy Category: D (nasal spray, transdermal system); C (gum)

AVAILABILITY 2 mg, 4 mg gum; 2 mg, 4 mg lozenges; 0.5 mg spray; 4 mg inhaler; 7 mg/d, 14 mg/d, 21 mg/d, 5 mg/d, 10 mg/d, 15 mg/d, 11 mg/d, 22 mg/d transdermal patch.

ACTION & *THERAPEUTIC EFFECT*
Ganglionic cholinergic receptor antagonist that has both adrenergic and cholinergic effects. Include stimulant and depressant effects on the peripheral nervous system and CNS; respiratory stimulation; peripheral vasoconstriction; increased heart rate, contractile force cardiac output, and stroke volume; increased tone and motor activity of GI smooth muscles; increased bronchial secretions (initially); antidiuretic activity. Heavy smokers are tolerant of these effects. *Rationale for use of nicotine is to reduce withdrawal symptoms accompanying cessation of smoking. Success rate appears to be greatest in smokers with high "physical" type of nicotine dependence.*

USES In conjunction with a medically supervised behavior modification program, as a temporary and alternate source of nicotine by the nicotine-dependent smoker who is withdrawing from cigarette smoking.

CONTRAINDICATIONS Nonsmokers, immediate post-MI period; life-threatening arrhythmias; active temporomandibular joint disease; severe angina pectoris; women with childbearing potential (unless effective contraception is used). *Nicotine Gum:* pregnancy (category C); *Nicotine Transdermal, Inhaler System:* pregnancy (category D). Safety in children and adolescents is not established.

CAUTIOUS USE Vasospastic disease (e.g., Buerger's disease, Prinzmetal's variant angina), cardiac arrhythmias, hyperthyroidism, type 1 diabetes, pheochromocytoma, esophagitis, oral and pharyngeal inflammation; patient with dentures, denture caps, or partial bridges; hypertension and peptic ulcer disease (active or inactive); GERD. During lactation, only if benefit of a smoking cessation program outweighs risks.

ROUTE & DOSAGE

Smoking Cessation

Adult: **PO** Chew 1 piece of gum whenever have urge to smoke, may be repeated as needed (max: 30 pieces of gum/d) **Intranasal** 1 dose = 2 sprays, 1 in each nostril, start with 1–2 doses (2–4 sprays) each hour (max: 5 doses/h, 40 doses/d), may continue for 3 mo **Topical** Apply 1 transdermal patch q24h by the following schedule: *Habitrol, Nicoderm:* 21 mg/d × 6 wk, 14 mg/d × 2 wk, 7 mg/d × 2 wk; *weight <45 kg (100 lb), smoke <1/2 pack/d, or have cardiovascular disease,* 14 mg/d × 6 wk, 7 mg/d × 2–4 wk.

ProStep: 22 mg/d × 4–8 wk, 11 mg/d × 2–4 wk; *weight <45 kg (100 lb), smoke <1/2 pack/d, or have cardiovascular disease,* 11 mg/d × 4–8 wk. *Nicotrol:* Apply 1 transdermal patch 16 h/d by the following schedule: 15 mg/d × 4–12 wk, 10 mg/d × 2–4 wk, 5 mg/d × 2–4 wk

ADMINISTRATION

Oral
- Note: Most adverse local effects (irritation of tongue, mouth, and throat, jaw-muscle aches, dislike of taste) are transient and subside in a few days. Modification of the chewing technique may help.

Transdermal
- Remove the old patch before applying the next new patch.
- Apply patch to nonhairy, clean, dry skin site; immediately remove from protective container.
- Store at or below 30° C (86° F); patches are sensitive to heat.

ADVERSE EFFECTS (≥1%) CNS:
Headache, dizziness, light-headedness, insomnia, irritability, dependence on nicotine. **CV:** Arrhythmias, tachycardia, palpitations, hypertension. **GI:** Air swallowing, *jaw ache, nausea,* belching, salivation, anorexia, dry mouth, laxative effects, constipation, *indigestion,* diarrhea, dyspepsia, vomiting, sialorrhea, abdominal pain, diarrhea. **Respiratory:** *Sore mouth or throat, cough, hiccups,* hoarseness; injury to mouth, teeth, temporomandibular joint pain, *irritation/tingling of tongue.* **Skin:** *Erythema, pruritus, local edema, rash;* skin reactions may be delayed, occurring after 3 wk of patch use. **Special Senses:** *Runny nose, nasal irritation, throat irritation, watering eyes,* minor epistaxis, nasal ulceration. **Body as a Whole:** Acute over-dose/nicotine intoxication (perspiration; severe headache; dizziness; disturbed hearing and vision; mental confusion; severe weakness; fainting; hypotension; dyspnea; weak, rapid, irregular pulse; seizures); death (from respiratory failure secondary to drug-induced respiratory muscle paralysis).

INTERACTIONS Drug: May increase metabolism of **caffeine, theophylline, acetaminophen, insulin, oxazepam, pentazocine propranolol. Food:** Coffee, cola may decrease nicotine absorption from nicotine gum.

PHARMACOKINETICS Absorption: Approximately 90% of the nicotine in a piece of gum is released slowly over 15–30 min; rate of release is controlled by vigor and duration of chewing; readily absorbed from buccal mucosa; transdermal 75–90% absorbed through skin; 53–58% of nasal spray is absorbed. **Peak:** Transdermal 8–9 h; nasal spray 4–15 min. **Distribution:** Crosses placenta; distributed into breast milk. **Metabolism:** In liver, primarily to cotinine. **Elimination:** In urine. **Half-Life:** 30–120 min.

CLINICAL IMPLICATIONS
Assessment & Drug Effects
- Be aware that transient erythema, pruritus, or burning is common with transdermal patch and usually disappears 24 h after patch removal.
- Differentiate cutaneous hypersensitivity (contact sensitization) that does not resolve in 24 h from a transient local reaction. The former is an indication to discontinue the transdermal patch.

Patient & Family Education
- Review carefully specific written instructions packaged with the chewing gum.

N

Common adverse effects in *italic,* life-threatening effects underlined; generic names in **bold;** classifications in SMALL CAPS; ♣ Canadian drug name; ⊚ Prototype drug

- Chew a piece of gum for approximately 30 min to get the full dose of nicotine.
- Chew only one piece of gum at a time. Chewing gum too rapidly can cause excessive buccal absorption and lead to adverse effects: nausea, hiccups, throat irritation.
- Gradually decrease number of pieces of gum chewed in 24 h. Usually, a period of 3 mo is allowed before tapering use of gum.
- Promptly discontinue use of transdermal patch and notify physician if a severe or persistent local or generalized skin reaction occurs.
- Be aware that smoking while using the transdermal nicotine patch increases the risk of adverse reactions.

NIFEDIPINE ⦿

(nye-fed'i-peen)
Adalat CC, Procardia, Procardia XL

Classifications: CALCIUM CHANNEL BLOCKER; ANTIARRHYTHMIC (CLASS IV); NONNITRATE VASODILATOR; ANTIANGINAL
Therapeutic: ANTIARRHYTHMIC (CLASS IV); ANTIANGINAL
Pregnancy Category: C

AVAILABILITY 10 mg, 20 mg capsules; 30 mg, 60 mg, 90 mg sustained release tablets

ACTION & *THERAPEUTIC EFFECT*
Calcium channel blocking agent that selectively blocks calcium ion influx across cell membranes of cardiac muscle and vascular smooth muscle without changing serum calcium concentrations. Reduces myocardial oxygen utilization and supply and relaxes and prevents coronary artery spasm; has little or no effect on SA and AV nodal conduction with therapeutic dosing. Decreases peripheral vascular resistance and increases cardiac output. *Class IV antiarrhythmic. Decreased peripheral vascular resistance, leading to a rise in peripheral blood flow, the basis for use of this drug in treatment of Raynaud's phenomenon.*

USES Vasospastic "variant" or Prinzmetal's angina and chronic stable angina without vasospasm. Mild to moderate hypertension alone or in combination with a diuretic.
UNLABELED USES Esophageal disorders; vascular headaches; Raynaud's phenomenon; asthma; cardiomyopathy; primary pulmonary hypertension.

CONTRAINDICATIONS Known hypersensitivity to nifedipine; unstable angina; acute MI; cardiogenic shock; aortic stenosis; GI obstruction. Safety during pregnancy (category C) or in children is not established.
CAUTIOUS USE Concomitant use with hypotensives; GERD; CHF; lactation.

ROUTE & DOSAGE

Angina
Adult: **PO** 10–20 mg t.i.d. up to 180 mg/d

Hypertension
Adult: **PO** 10–20 mg t.i.d. up to 180 mg/d or 30–90 mg sustained release once/d

ADMINISTRATION

Oral
- Do not give within the first 1–2 wk following an MI.
- Use only the sustained release form to treat chronic hypertension. Ensure that sustained release form

is not chewed or crushed. It must be swallowed whole.

- Discontinue drug gradually, with close medical supervision to prevent severe hypertension and other adverse effects.
- Store at 15°–25° C (59°–77° F); protect from light and moisture.

ADVERSE EFFECTS (≥1%) **Body as a Whole:** Sore throat, weakness, fever, sweating, chills, febrile reaction. **CNS:** *Dizziness, light-headedness,* nervousness, mood changes, weakness, jitteriness, sleep disturbances, blurred vision, retinal ischemia, difficulty in balance, *headache.* **CV:** Hypotension, *facial flushing, heat sensation,* palpitations, *peripheral edema,* MI (rare), prolonged systemic hypotension with overdose. **GI:** Nausea, heartburn, *diarrhea,* constipation, cramps, flatulence, gingival hyperplasia, hepatotoxicity. **Musculoskeletal:** Inflammation, joint stiffness, muscle cramps. **Respiratory:** Nasal congestion, dyspnea, cough, wheezing. **Skin:** Dermatitis, pruritus, urticaria. **Urogenital:** Sexual difficulties, possible male infertility.

DIAGNOSTIC TEST INTERFERENCE
Nifedipine may cause mild to moderate increases of **alkaline phosphatase, CPK, LDH, AST, ALT.**

INTERACTIONS Drug: BETA BLOCKERS may increase likelihood of CHF; may increase risk of **phenytoin** toxicity. **Herbal: Melatonin** may increase blood pressure and heart rate. **Ginkgo, ginseng** may increase plasma concentrations. **St. John's wort** may decrease plasma concentrations. **Food:** Grapefruit juice (>1 qt/d) may increase plasma concentrations and adverse effects.

PHARMACOKINETICS Absorption:
Readily absorbed from GI tract; 45–75% reaches systemic circulation (first pass metabolism). **Onset:** 10–30 min. **Peak:** 30 min. **Distribution:** Distributed into breast milk. **Metabolism:** In liver. **Elimination:** 75–80% in urine, 15% in feces. **Half-Life:** 2–5 h.

CLINICAL IMPLICATIONS

Assessment & Drug Effects

- Monitor BP carefully during titration period. Patient may become severely hypotensive, especially if also taking other drugs known to lower BP. Withhold drug and notify physician if systolic BP <90.
- Monitor blood sugar in diabetic patients. Nifedipine has diabetogenic properties.
- Monitor for gingival hyperplasia and report promptly. This is a rare but serious adverse effect (similar to phenytoin-induced hyperplasia).

Patient & Family Education

- Keep a record of nitroglycerin use and promptly report any changes in previous pattern. Occasionally, people develop increased frequency, duration, and severity of angina when they start treatment with this drug or when dosage is increased.
- Be aware that withdrawal symptoms may occur with abrupt discontinuation of the drug (chest pain, increase in anginal episodes, MI, dysrhythmias).
- Inspect gums visually every day. Changes in gingivae may be gradual, and bleeding may be exhibited only with probing.
- Seek prompt treatment for symptoms of gingival hyperplasia (easy bleeding of gingivae and gradual enlarging of gingival mass, especially on buccal side of lower anterior teeth). Drug will be discontinued if gingival hyperplasia occurs.

N

Common adverse effects in *italic*, life-threatening effects <u>underlined</u>; generic names in **bold**; classifications in SMALL CAPS; ♦ Canadian drug name; ❷ Prototype drug

1075

- Research shows that smoking decreases the efficacy of nifedipine and has direct and adverse effects on the heart in the patient on nifedipine treatment.

NILUTAMIDE

(ni-lu'ta-mide)
Nilandron
Classifications: ANTINEOPLASTIC AGENT; ANTIANDROGEN
Therapeutic: ANTINEOPLASTIC; ANTIANDROGEN
Prototype: Flutamide
Pregnancy Category: C

AVAILABILITY 150 mg tablets

ACTION & *THERAPEUTIC EFFECT* Nonsteroidal with antiandrogen activity. Blocks the effects of testosterone at the androgen receptor sites, thus preventing the normal androgenic response. *Effective in blocking testosterone in treatment of metastatic prostate carcinoma.*

USES Use with surgical castration for metastatic prostate cancer.

CONTRAINDICATIONS Severe hepatic impairment; severe respiratory insufficiency; hypersensitivity to nilutamide; pregnancy (category C), lactation.
CAUTIOUS USE Asian patients relative to causing interstitial pneumonitis; alcoholics. Safety and effectiveness in children are not established.

ROUTE & DOSAGE

Metastatic Prostate Cancer
Adult: **PO** 300 mg q.d. × 30 d, then 150 mg q.d.

ADMINISTRATION

Oral
- Give first dose on the day of or day after surgical castration.
- Store below 15°–30° C (59°–86° F) and protect from light.

ADVERSE EFFECTS (≥1%) **Body as a Whole:** *Hot flushes, impotence, decreased libido, malaise,* edema, weight loss, arthritis. **CNS:** Nervousness, paresthesias. **CV:** Angina, heart failure, syncope. **GI:** Diarrhea, GI hemorrhage, melena, dry mouth. **Respiratory:** Cough, interstitial lung disease, rhinitis. **Skin:** Pruritus. **Other:** Alcohol intolerance. **Special Senses:** Cataracts, photophobia.

INTERACTIONS Drug: Carbamazepine, rifampin, phenytoin may decrease level; fluconazole, gemfibrozil, omeprazole may increase levels. **Herbal: St. John's wort** may decrease levels.

PHARMACOKINETICS Absorption: Rapidly from GI tract. **Metabolism:** In the liver (CYP2C19). **Elimination:** In urine. **Half-Life:** 38–50 h.

CLINICAL IMPLICATIONS

Assessment & Drug Effects
- Obtain baseline chest x-ray before treatment and periodically thereafter.
- Closely monitor for S&S of pneumonitis; at the first sign of adverse pulmonary effects, withhold drug and notify physician. Abnormal ABGs may indicate need to discontinue drug.
- Lab tests: Monitor liver function before beginning treatment and at 3-mo intervals; if serum transaminases increase >2–3 times upper limit of normal, discontinue treatment.
- Monitor patients taking phenytoin, theophylline, or warfarin

closely for toxic levels of these drugs.

Patient & Family Education

- Report following S&S of adverse effects on lungs to physician immediately: Development of chest pain, dyspnea, and cough with fever.
- Report S&S of liver injury to physician: Jaundice, dark urine, fatigue, or signs of GI distress including nausea, vomiting, abdominal pain.
- Use caution when moving from lighted to dark areas because the drug may slow visual adaptation to darkness. Tinted glasses may partially alleviate the problem.

NIMODIPINE

(ni-mo′di-peen)
Nimotop
Classifications: CALCIUM CHANNEL BLOCKER; CEREBRAL ANTISPASMODIC AGENT
Therapeutic: CEREBRAL ANTISPAS-MODIC; CALCIUM CHANNEL BLOCKER
Prototype: Nifedipine
Pregnancy Category: C

AVAILABILITY 30 mg capsule

ACTION & THERAPEUTIC EFFECT
Calcium channel blocking agent that is relatively selective for cerebral arteries compared with arteries elsewhere in the body. This may be attributed to the drug's high lipid solubility and specific binding to cerebral tissue. *Reduces vascular spasms in cerebral arteries during a stroke.*

USES To improve neurologic deficits due to spasm following subarachnoid hemorrhage from ruptured congenital intracranial aneurysms in patients who are in good neurologic condition posticus (e.g., Hunt and Hess Grades I–III).

UNLABELED USES Migraine headaches, ischemic seizures.

CONTRAINDICATIONS Near-fatal reaction to intravenous administration; hypotension; intraarterial administration; cardiogenic shock; pregnancy (category C), lactation.
CAUTIOUS USE Hepatic impairment; acute MI; heart failure, ventricular dysfunction; and lactation. Safety and effectiveness in children are not established.

ROUTE & DOSAGE

Subarachnoid Hemorrhage
Adult: **PO** 60 mg q4h for 21 d, start therapy within 96 h of subarachnoid hemorrhage
Hepatic Impairment
Decrease dose to 30 mg q4h

ADMINISTRATION

Oral

- Make a hole in both ends of the capsule with an 18-gauge needle and extract the contents into a syringe if patient is unable to swallow. Empty the contents into an enteral (if in use) tube and wash down with 30 mL of NS.
- Do not administer nimodipine intravascularly. It causes a fatal reaction.
- Store below 40° C (104° F); protect from light.

ADVERSE EFFECTS (≥1%) **CNS:** Headache. **CV:** *Hypotension.* **GI:** Hemorrhage, mild, transient increase in liver function tests.

INTERACTIONS Drug: Hypotensive effects increased when combined with other CALCIUM CHANNEL BLOCK-ERS. **Food:** Grapefruit juice (>1 qt/d) may increase plasma concentrations and adverse effects.

Common adverse effects in *italic*, life-threatening effects underlined; generic names in **bold**; classifications in SMALL CAPS; ◆ Canadian drug name; ⊙ Prototype drug

1077

PHARMACOKINETICS Absorption: Readily from GI tract; approximately 13% reaches systemic circulation (first pass metabolism). **Peak:** 1 h. **Distribution:** Crosses blood–brain barrier; possibly crosses placenta; distributed into breast milk. **Metabolism:** 85% in liver; 15% in kidneys. **Elimination:** >50% in urine, 32% in feces. **Half-Life:** 8–9 h.

CLINICAL IMPLICATIONS

Assessment & Drug Effects

- Take apical pulse prior to administering drug and hold it if pulse is below 60. Notify the physician.
- Establish baseline data before treatment is started: BP, pulse, and laboratory evaluations of liver and kidney function.
- Monitor frequently for adverse drug effects, including hypotension, peripheral edema, tachycardia, or skin rash.
- Monitor frequently for dizziness or lightheadedness in older adult patients; risk of hypotension is increased.

Patient & Family Education

- Report gradual weight gain and evidence of edema (e.g., tight rings on fingers, ankle swelling).
- Keep follow-up appointments for monitoring of progress during therapy.

NISOLDIPINE

(ni-sol′di-peen)

Sular

Classifications: CALCIUM CHANNEL BLOCKER; ANTIHYPERTENSIVE; ANTIANGINAL

Therapeutic: ANTIHYPERTENSIVE; ANTIANGINAL

Prototype: Nifedipine

Pregnancy Category: C

AVAILABILITY 10 mg, 20 mg, 30 mg, 40 mg sustained release tablets

ACTION & *THERAPEUTIC EFFECT* Inhibits calcium ion influx across cell membranes of cardiac muscle and vascular smooth muscle, which results in vasodilation, inotropism, and negative chronotropism. *Inhibits vasoconstriction in the peripheral vasculature (10 times as potent as nifedipine). Significantly reduces total peripheral resistance, decreases blood pressure, and increases cardiac output. It is also a potent coronary vasodilator.*

USES Hypertension, angina.
UNLABELED USES CHF.

CONTRAINDICATIONS Hypersensitivity to nisoldipine or other calcium blockers; systolic BP <90 mm Hg, advanced aortic stenosis, advanced heart failure, cardiogenic shock, severe hypotension, acute MI, sick sinus syndrome; pregnancy (category C); lactation.
CAUTIOUS USE Liver dysfunction; older adult; paroxysmal atrial fibrillation; GERD; CHF; digital ischemia, ulceration, or gangrene; nonobstructive hypertrophic cardiomyopathy; Duchenne muscular dystrophy.

ROUTE & DOSAGE

Hypertension, Angina
Adult: **PO** 10–40 mg/d (max: 60 mg/d), may need to reduce dose in patients with liver disease (cirrhosis, chronic hepatitis)

ADMINISTRATION

Oral
- Give drug with food to decrease GI distress, but do not give with grapefruit juice or a high-fat meal.

Common adverse effects in *italic*, life-threatening effects <u>underlined</u>; generic names in **bold**; classifications in SMALL CAPS; ◆ Canadian drug name; Ⓟ Prototype drug

- Ensure that sustained release form is not chewed or crushed. It must be swallowed whole.
- Discontinue drug gradually to prevent adverse effects.
- Consider dosage reductions in older adults; initiate therapy at lower doses and follow with gradual increases.
- Store at 15°–30° C (59°–86° F).

ADVERSE EFFECTS (≥1%) **CNS:** Dizziness, anxiety, tremor, weakness, fatigue, *headache.* **CV:** Hypotension, peripheral edema, palpitations, orthostatic hypotension. **GI:** Abdominal pain, cramps, constipation, dry mouth, diarrhea, nausea. **Skin:** *Flushing,* rash, erythema, urticaria. **Urogenital:** Urinary frequency. **Respiratory:** Pulmonary edema (patients with CHF), wheezing, dyspnea. **Body as a Whole:** Myalgia.

INTERACTIONS Drug: May cause significant increase in **digoxin** level in patients with CHF. BETA BLOCKERS may cause hypotension and bradycardia. **Phenytoin, carbamazepine, phenobarbital** may significantly decrease levels. Azole antifungals may affect metabolism; avoid combination. **Food:** High-fat food increases availability.

PHARMACOKINETICS Absorption: Rapidly from GI tract; 4–8% reaches systemic circulation. **Peak Effect:** 1–3 h. **Duration:** 8–12 h for hypertension, 7–8 h for angina. **Distribution:** 99% protein bound. **Metabolism:** Extensively in liver. **Elimination:** 70–75% in urine as metabolites. **Half-Life:** 2–14 h.

CLINICAL IMPLICATIONS
Assessment & Drug Effects
- Monitor blood pressure carefully during period of drug initiation and with dosage increments.
- Monitor cardiovascular status especially heart rate, frequency of angina attacks, or worsening heart failure.
- Assess for and report edematous weight gain.
- Monitor digoxin levels closely with concurrent use and watch for S&S of digoxin toxicity (see Appendix F).

Patient & Family Education
- Do not discontinue the drug abruptly.
- Report symptoms of orthostatic hypotension or other bothersome adverse effects to physician.
- Do not drive or engage in potentially hazardous activities until response to drug is known.

NITAZOXANIDE
(nit-a-zox′-a-nide)
Alinia
Classifications: ANTIPROTOZOAL
Therapeutic: ANTIPROTOZOAL
Prototype: Metronidazole
Pregnancy Category: B

AVAILABILITY 100 mg/5 mL oral suspension; 500 mg tablets

ACTION & *THERAPEUTIC EFFECT* Antiprotozoal activity believed to be due to interference with an essential enzyme needed for anaerobic energy metabolism in protozoa. Interference with the enzyme may not be the only pathway by which nitazoxanide exhibits antiprotozoal activity. *Inhibits growth of sporozoites and oocysts of* Cryptosporidium parvum *and trophozoites of* Giardia lamblia.

USES Treatment of diarrhea caused by *Cryptosporidium parvum* and *Giardia lamblia.*

Common adverse effects in *italic*, life-threatening effects underlined; generic names in **bold**; classifications in SMALL CAPS; ♣ Canadian drug name; ☺ Prototype drug

1079

CONTRAINDICATIONS Prior hypersensitivity to nitazoxanide.

CAUTIOUS USE Hepatic and biliary disease, renal disease, renal impairment, renal failure, and combined renal and hepatic disease; pregnancy (category B); lactation. Safety and efficacy in children <1 y or >11 y have not been studied.

ROUTE & DOSAGE

Diarrhea
Adult: **PO** 500 mg q12h × 3 d
Child: **PO** *12–47 mo,* 100 mg q12h × 3 d; *4–11 y,* 200 mg q12h × 3 d

ADMINISTRATION

Oral
- Prepare suspension as follows: Tap bottle until powder loosens. Draw up 48 mL of water, add half to bottle, shake to suspend powder, then add remaining 24 mL of water and shake vigorously.
- Give required dose (5 or 10 mL) with food.
- Keep container tightly closed, and shake well before each administration.
- Suspension may be stored for 7 d at 15°–30° C (59°–86° F), after which any unused portion must be discarded.

ADVERSE EFFECTS (≥1%) **CNS:** Headache. **GI:** Abdominal pain, diarrhea, vomiting.

INTERACTIONS Food: Increases levels.

PHARMACOKINETICS Peak: 1–4 h. **Distribution:** 99% protein bound. **Metabolism:** Rapidly hydrolyzed in liver to an active metabolite, tizoxanide (desacetyl-nitazoxanide). **Elimination:** In urine, bile, and feces.

CLINICAL IMPLICATIONS

Assessment & Drug Effects
- Monitor for therapeutic effectiveness: No watery stools and ≤2 soft stools with no hematochezia within the past 24 h or no symptoms and no unformed stools within the past 48 h.
- Monitor closely patients with pre-existing hepatic or biliary disease for adverse reactions.
- Assess appetite, level of abdominal discomfort and extent of bloating.
- Assess frequency and quantity of diarrhea and monitor total hydration status.
- Weigh daily to aid in assessment of possible fluid loss from diarrhea.

Patient & Family Education
- Note that 5 mL of the oral suspension contains approximately 1.5 g of sucrose.
- Report either no improvement in or worsening of diarrhea and abdominal discomfort.

NITROFURANTOIN

(nye-troe-fyoor'an-toyn)
Novo-Furan ♦

NITROFURANTOIN MACROCRYSTALS

Macrobid, Macrodantin
Classifications: URINARY TRACT ANTIBIOTIC
Therapeutic: URINARY TRACT ANTIBIOTIC
Pregnancy Category: B

AVAILABILITY 25 mg/mL suspension; 25 mg, 50 mg, 100 mg capsules

ACTION & *THERAPEUTIC EFFECT*
Synthetic nitrofuran derivative presumed to act by interfering with several bacterial enzyme systems.

Highly soluble in urine and reportedly most active in acid urine. Antimicrobial concentrations in urine exceed those in blood. *Active against wide variety of gram-negative and gram-positive microorganisms.*

USES Pyelonephritis, pyelitis, and cystitis caused by susceptible organisms.

CONTRAINDICATIONS Anuria, oliguria, significant impairment of kidney function (Cl$_{cr}$ <60 mL/min); G6PD deficiency; infants <1 mo; pregnancy at term (38–42 wk), labor, or obstetric delivery.

CAUTIOUS USE History of asthma, anemia, diabetes, vitamin B deficiency, hepatic disease; pulmonary disease; mild to moderate renal disease; electrolyte imbalance, debilitating disease; B$_{12}$ deficiency; pregnancy (category B).

ROUTE & DOSAGE

Pyelonephritis, Cystitis
Adult: **PO** 50–100 mg q.i.d. × 7d or Macrobid 100 mg b.i.d. × 7d
Child: **PO** 1 mo–12 y, 5–7 mg/kg/d in 4 divided doses (max: 400 mg/d)

Chronic Suppressive Therapy
Adult: **PO** 50–100 mg h.s.
Child: **PO** 1 mo–12 y, 1 mg/kg/d in 1–2 divided doses (max: 100 mg/d)

Renal Impairment
Avoid if Cl$_{cr}$ <60 mL/min

ADMINISTRATION

Oral
- Give with food or milk to minimize gastric irritation.
- Avoid crushing tablets because of the possibility of tooth staining; rather dilute oral suspension in milk, water, or fruit juice, and rinse mouth thoroughly after taking drug.

ADVERSE EFFECTS (≥1%) **CNS:** Peripheral neuropathy, headache, nystagmus, drowsiness, vertigo. **GI:** *Anorexia, nausea, vomiting,* abdominal pain, diarrhea, cholestatic jaundice, hepatic necrosis. **Hematologic (rare):** Hemolytic or megaloblastic anemia (especially in patients with G6PD deficiency), granulocytosis, eosinophilia. **Body as a Whole:** Angioedema, anaphylaxis, drug fever, arthralgia. **Respiratory:** Allergic pneumonitis, asthmatic attack (patients with history of asthma), pulmonary sensitivity reactions (interstitial pneumonitis or fibrosis). **Skin:** Skin eruptions, pruritus, urticaria, exfoliative dermatitis, transient alopecia. **Urogenital:** Genitourinary superinfections (especially with *Pseudomonas*), crystalluria (older adult patients), dark yellow or brown urine. **Other:** Tooth staining from direct contact with oral suspension and crushed tablets (infants).

DIAGNOSTIC TEST INTERFERENCE Nitrofurantoin metabolite may produce false-positive *urine glucose* test results with Benedict's reagent.

INTERACTIONS Drug: ANTACIDS may decrease absorption of nitrofurantoin; **nalidixic acid,** other QUINOLONES may antagonize antimicrobial effects; **probenecid, sulfinpyrazone** increase risk of nitrofurantoin toxicity.

PHARMACOKINETICS Absorption: Readily from GI tract. **Peak:** Urine: 30 min. **Distribution:** Crosses placenta; distributed into breast milk. **Metabolism:** Partially in liver. **Elimination:** Primarily in urine. **Half-Life:** 20 min.

Common adverse effects in *italic*, life-threatening effects underlined; generic names in **bold**; classifications in SMALL CAPS; ✦ Canadian drug name; ⓟ Prototype drug

1081

CLINICAL IMPLICATIONS
Assessment & Drug Effects

- Lab tests: Perform C&S prior to therapy; recommended in patients with recurrent infections.
- Monitor I&O. Report oliguria and any change in I&O ratio. Drug should be discontinued if oliguria or anuria develops or creatinine clearance falls below 40 mL/min.
- Be alert to signs of urinary tract superinfections (e.g., milky urine, foul-smelling urine, perineal irritation, dysuria).
- Assess for nausea (which occurs fairly frequently). May be relieved by using macrocrystalline preparation (Macrodantin) or by reducing dosage.
- Watch for acute pulmonary sensitivity reaction, usually within first week of therapy and apparently more common in older adults. May be manifested by mild to severe flu-like syndrome. Eosinophilia generally develops in a few days. Recovery usually occurs rapidly after drug is discontinued.
- With prolonged therapy, monitor for subacute or chronic pulmonary sensitivity reaction, commonly manifested by insidious onset of malaise, cough, dyspnea on exertion, altered ABGs.
- Be alert for and advise the patient to report onset of muscle weakness, tingling, numbness, or other sensations. Peripheral neuropathy can be severe and irreversible. Drug should be withdrawn immediately.

Patient & Family Education

- Be aware that IM injection of nitrofurantoin may be painful (pain may be severe enough to warrant discontinuation of drug by this route).
- Nitrofurantoin may impart a harmless brown color to urine.
- Consult physician regarding fluid intake. Generally, fluids are not forced; however, intake should be adequate.

NITROFURAZONE
(nye-troe-fyoor′a-zone)
Classifications: ANTIBIOTIC
Therapeutic: ANTIBIOTIC
Pregnancy Category: C

AVAILABILITY 0.2% ointment

ACTION & *THERAPEUTIC EFFECT*
Synthetic nitrofuran related to nitrofurantoin. Acts by inhibiting aerobic and anaerobic cycles in bacterial carbohydrate metabolism. *Bactericidal against most microorganisms causing surface infections, including many that have developed antibiotic resistance. Effective against gram-positive and gram-negative bacteria.*

USES As adjunctive therapy to combat bacterial infection in second- and third-degree burns; to prevent infection of skin grafts and donor sites. Has been used orally in other countries for treatment of late stage of African trypanosomiasis.

CONTRAINDICATIONS Hypersensitivity to nitrofurazone; renal impairment; pregnancy (category C).
CAUTIOUS USE Known or suspected renal impairment; G6PD deficiency; lactation.

ROUTE & DOSAGE

Bacterial Infections Associated with Burns or Skin Grafts
Adult: **Topical** Apply directly to lesion or dressings; reapply daily for second- or third-degree burns or q4–5d for second-degree burn with minimum exudation

Common adverse effects in *italic*, life-threatening effects <u>underlined</u>; generic names in **bold**; classifications in SMALL CAPS; ♣ Canadian drug name; ⦿ Prototype drug

ADMINISTRATION

Topical

- Confine applications to the part of body being treated. With wet dressings: Protect normal skin surrounding the wound with an agent such as sterile petrolatum, petrolatum gauze, or zinc oxide. Consult physician.
- Facilitate dressing removal by flushing the gauze with sterile isotonic saline solution.
- Consult physician regarding procedure for cleaning wound following each dressing removal.
- Preserve in tight, light-resistant container, away from heat.

ADVERSE EFFECTS (≥1%) **Skin:** *Allergic contact dermatitis,* irritation, sensitization, superinfections.

CLINICAL IMPLICATIONS

Assessment & Drug Effects

- Withhold drug and notify physician at onset of symptoms of sensitization or allergy (e.g., redness, itching, burning, swelling, rash, failure to heal), and superinfections (e.g., black furry tongue, thrush, malodorous vaginal discharge, anogenital itching, diarrhea).

Patient & Family Education

- Learn appropriate technique for applying medication to skin lesions.

NITROGLYCERIN ℗⃝

(nye-troe-gli′ser-in)

Minitran, Nitrocap, Nitrodisc, Nitro-Dur, Nitrogard, Nitrogard-SR, Nitrong SR, Nitrospan, Nitrostat, Nitrostat I.V.

Classifications: NITRATE VASODILATOR

Therapeutic: ANTIANGINAL; NITRATE VASODILATOR
Pregnancy Category: C

AVAILABILITY 5 mg/mL injection; 0.3 mg, 0.4 mg, 0.6 mg sublingual tablets; 2.5 mg, 6.5 mg, 9 mg sustained release tablets, capsules; 0.1 mg/h, 0.2 mg/h, 0.3 mg/h, 0.4 mg/h, 0.6 mg/h, 0.8 mg/h transdermal patch; 2% ointment

ACTION & *THERAPEUTIC EFFECT*
Organic nitrate and potent vasodilator that relaxes vascular smooth muscle after conversion to nitric oxide that leads to dose-related dilation of both venous and arterial blood vessels. Promotes peripheral pooling of blood, reduction of peripheral resistance, and decreased venous return to the heart. Both left ventricular preload and afterload are reduced and myocardial oxygen consumption or demand is decreased. *Therapeutic doses may reduce systolic, diastolic, and mean BP; heart rate is usually slightly increased. Produces antianginal, antiischemic, and antihypertensive effects.*

USES Prophylaxis, treatment, and management of angina pectoris. IV nitroglycerin is used to control BP in perioperative hypertension, CHF associated with acute MI; to produce controlled hypotension during surgical procedures, and to treat angina pectoris in patients who have not responded to nitrate or beta-blocker therapy.

UNLABELED USES Sublingual and topical to reduce cardiac workload in patients with acute MI and in CHF. Ointment for adjunctive treatment of Raynaud's disease.

CONTRAINDICATIONS Hypersensitivity, idiosyncrasy, or tolerance to nitrates; severe anemia; head

Common adverse effects in *italic*, life-threatening effects underlined; generic names in **bold**; classifications in SMALL CAPS; ♣ Canadian drug name; ℗⃝ Prototype drug

1083

trauma, increased ICP; glaucoma (sustained release forms). Also (IV nitroglycerin): hypotension, uncorrected hypovolemia, constrictive pericarditis, pericardial tamponade; pregnancy (category C).

CAUTIOUS USE Severe liver or kidney disease, conditions that cause dry mouth, early MI; lactation.

ROUTE & DOSAGE

Angina

Adult: **Sublingual** 1–2 sprays (0.4–0.8 mg) or a 0.3–0.6-mg tablet q3–5min as needed (max: 3 doses in 15 min) **PO** 1.3–9 mg q8–12h **IV** Start with 5 mcg/min and titrate q3–5min until desired response (up to 200 mcg/min) **Transdermal Unit** Apply once q24h or leave on for 10–12 h, then remove and have a 10–12 h nitrate free interval **Topical** Apply 1.5–5 cm ($^1/_2$–2 in) of ointment q4–6h

Child: **IV** 0.25–0.5 mcg/kg/min, titrate by 0.5–1 mcg/kg/min q3–5 min (max 5 mg/kg/min)

ADMINISTRATION

Note: Drug forms appropriate for angina prophylaxis include ointment, transdermal unit, translingual spray, transmucosal tablet, and oral sustained release forms. Drug forms appropriate for acute angina include sublingual tablet, translingual spray, or transmucosal tablet.

Sublingual Tablet

- Give 1 tablet and if pain is not relieved, give additional tablets at 5-min intervals, but not more than 3 tablets in a 15-min period.
- Typically available for self-administration in their original container. Instruct in correct use. Request patient to report all attacks. Count tablets daily.

- Instruct to sit or lie down upon first indication of oncoming anginal pain and to place tablet under tongue or in buccal pouch (hypotensive effect of drug is intensified in the upright position).

Sustained Release Tablet or Capsule

- Give on an empty stomach (1 h before or 2 h after meals), with a full glass of water. Ensure it is swallowed whole.
- Be aware that sustained release form helps to prevent anginal attacks; it is not intended for immediate relief of angina.
- Ensure that tablet is not crushed or chewed.

Transdermal Ointment

- Using dose-determining applicator (paper application patch) supplied with package, squeeze prescribed dose onto this applicator. Using applicator, spread ointment in a thin, uniform layer to premarked 5.5 by 9 cm (2 $^1/_4$ by 3 $^1/_2$ in.) square. Place patch with ointment side down onto nonhairy skin surface (areas commonly used: chest, abdomen, anterior thigh, forearm). Cover with transparent wrap and secure with tape. Avoid getting ointment on fingers.
- Rotate application sites to prevent dermal inflammation and sensitization. Remove ointment from previously used sites before reapplication.
- Keep ointment container tightly closed and store in cool place.

Transdermal Unit

- Apply transdermal unit (transdermal patch) at the same time each day, preferably to skin site free of hair and not subject to excessive movement. Avoid abraded, irritated, or scarred skin. Clip hair if necessary.

- Change application site each time to prevent skin irritation and sensitization.

Intravenous

Note: Verify correct IV concentration and rate of infusion in infants and children with physician.

- Check to see if patient has transdermal patch or ointment in place before starting IV infusion. The patch (or ointment) is usually removed to prevent overdosage.
- Be aware that when switching from IV to transdermal nitroglycerin, the IV infusion rate is reduced by 50% with simultaneous application of 5 or 10 mg/24 h transdermal patch.

PREPARE: **IV Infusion:** IV nitroglycerin is available in differing concentrations. Be attentive to the dilution, dosage, and directions for administration on each vial or ampul. Note that a number of nitroglycerin preparations are available prediluted. Other forms must be diluted in D5W or NS, usually to concentrations between 25–500 mcg/mL. Use only glass bottles and manufacturer-supplied IV tubing. Withdraw medication into syringe and inject immediately into the IV solution to minimize contact with plastic. Regular IV tubing can absorb 40–80% of nitroglycerin.

ADMINISTER: **IV Infusion:** Give by continuous infusion regulated exactly by an infusion pump. IV dosage titration requires careful and continuous hemodynamic monitoring.

INCOMPATIBILITIES **Solution/additive: Caffeine, hydralazine, phenytoin. Y-site: Alteplase, levofloxacin.**

- Use only glass containers for storage of reconstituted IV solution. Polyvinyl chloride (PVC) plastic can absorb nitroglycerin and therefore should not be used. Non-polyvinyl-chloride (non-PVC) sets are recommended or provided by manufacturer.

ADVERSE EFFECTS (≥1%) **CNS:** *Headache,* apprehension, blurred vision, weakness, vertigo, dizziness, faintness. **CV:** *Postural hypotension,* palpitations, tachycardia (sometimes with paradoxical bradycardia), increase in angina, syncope, and <u>circulatory collapse</u>. **GI:** Nausea, vomiting, involuntary passing of urine and feces, abdominal pain, dry mouth. **Hematologic:** Methemoglobinemia (high doses). **Skin:** Cutaneous vasodilation with flushing, rash, exfoliative dermatitis, contact dermatitis with transdermal patch; topical allergic reactions with ointment: pruritic eczematous eruptions, <u>anaphylactoid reaction</u> characterized by oral mucosal and conjunctival edema. **Body as a Whole:** Muscle twitching, pallor, perspiration, cold sweat; local sensation in oral cavity at point of dissolution of sublingual forms.

DIAGNOSTIC TEST INTERFERENCE

Nitroglycerin may cause increases in determinations of ***urinary catecholamines*** and ***VMA;*** may interfere with the ***Zlatkis-Zak color reaction,*** causing a false report of decreased ***serum cholesterol.***

INTERACTIONS Drug: Alcohol, ANTIHYPERTENSIVE AGENTS compound hypotensive effects; IV nitroglycerin may antagonize **heparin** anticoagulation. Vasodilating effects may be enhanced by **sildenafil, vardenafil,** or **tadalafil,** so this combination should be avoided.

PHARMACOKINETICS Absorption: Significant loss to first pass metabo-

N

Common adverse effects in *italic*, life-threatening effects <u>underlined</u>; generic names in **bold**; classifications in SMALL CAPS; ✦ Canadian drug name; ⊘ Prototype drug

1085

lism after oral dosing. **Onset:** 2 min SL; 3 min PO; 30 min ointment. **Duration:** 30 min SL; 3–5 h PO; 3–6 h ointment. **Distribution:** Widely distributed; not known if distributes to breast milk. **Metabolism:** Extensively in liver. **Elimination:** Inactive metabolites in urine. **Half-Life:** 1–4 min.

CLINICAL IMPLICATIONS

Assessment & Drug Effects

- Administer IV nitroglycerin with extreme caution to patients with hypotension or hypovolemia since the IV drug may precipitate a severe hypotensive state.
- Monitor patient closely for change in levels of consciousness and for dysrhythmias. IV nitroglycerin solution contains a substantial amount of ethanol as diluent. Ethanol intoxication can develop with high doses of IV nitroglycerin (vomiting, lethargy, coma, breath smells of alcohol). If intoxication occurs, infusion should be stopped promptly; patient recovers immediately with discontinuation of drug administration.
- Be aware that moisture on sublingual tissue is required for dissolution of sublingual tablet. However, because chest pain typically leads to dry mouth, a patient may be unresponsive to sublingual nitroglycerin.
- Assess for headaches. Approximately 50% of all patients experience mild to severe headaches following nitroglycerin. Transient headache usually lasts about 5 min after sublingual administration and seldom longer than 20 min. Assess degree of severity and consult as needed with physician about analgesics and dosage adjustment.
- Supervise ambulation as needed, especially with older adult or debilitated patients. Postural hypotension may occur even with small doses of nitroglycerin. Patients may complain of dizziness or weakness due to postural hypotension.
- Take baseline BP and heart rate with patient in sitting position before initiation of treatment with transdermal preparations.
- One hour after transdermal (ointment or unit) medication has been applied, check BP and pulse again with patient in sitting position. Report measurements to physician.
- Assess for and report blurred vision or dry mouth.
- Assess for and report the following topical reactions. Contact dermatitis from the transdermal patch; pruritus and erythema from the ointment.
- Be aware that local burning or tingling from the sublingual form has no clinical significance.
- Be alert for overdose symptoms: Hypotension, tachycardia; warm, flushed skin becoming cold and cyanotic; headache, palpitations, confusion, nausea, vomiting, moderate fever, and paralysis. Tissue hypoxia leads to coma, convulsions, cardiovascular collapse. Death can occur from asphyxia.

Patient & Family Education

- Store tablet form in its original container.
- Sit or lie down upon first indication of oncoming anginal pain.
- Spit out the rest of your sublingual tablet as soon as pain is completely relieved, especially if you are experiencing unpleasant adverse effects such as headache. Relax for 15–20 min after taking tablet to prevent dizziness or faintness.

- Be aware that pain not relieved by 3 sublingual tablets over a 15-min period may indicate acute MI or severe coronary insufficiency. Contact physician immediately or go directly to emergency room.
- Note: Sublingual tablets may be taken prophylactically 5–10 min prior to exercise or other stimulus known to trigger angina (drug effect lasts 30–60 min).
- Keep record for physician of number of angina attacks, amount of medication required for relief of each attack, and possible precipitating factors.
- Be aware that contact with water (swimming, bathing) does not affect your transdermal unit.
- Remove transdermal unit or ointment immediately from skin and notify physician if faintness, dizziness, or flushing occurs following application.
- You can use a sublingual formulation while transdermal unit or ointment is in place.
- Report blurred vision or dry mouth. Both warrant withdrawal of drug.
- Change position slowly and avoid prolonged standing. Dizziness, light-headedness, and syncope (due to postural hypotension) occur most frequently in older adults.
- Do not drink alcohol too soon after taking nitroglycerin. It may cause severe postural hypotension (sharp drop in BP), vertigo, flushing, or pallor if you drink alcohol too soon after taking nitroglycerin.
- Report any increase in frequency, duration, or severity of anginal attack.
- Withdraw gradually after prolonged use to prevent precipitating anginal attack.

NITROPRUSSIDE SODIUM

(nye-troe-pruss′ide)

Nitropress

Classifications: NONNITRATE VASODILATOR; ANTIHYPERTENSIVE

Therapeutic: ANTIHYPERTENSIVE; NONNITRATE VASODILATOR

Prototype: Hydralazine

Pregnancy Category: C

AVAILABILITY 50 mg injection

ACTION & *THERAPEUTIC EFFECT*
Potent, rapid-acting hypotensive agent with effects similar to those of nitrates. Acts directly on vascular smooth muscle to produce peripheral vasodilation, with consequent marked lowering of arterial BP, associated with slight increase in heart rate, mild decrease in cardiac output, and moderate lowering of peripheral vascular resistance. *Effective antihypertensive agent used for rapid reduction of high blood pressure.*

USES Short-term, rapid reduction of BP in hypertensive crises and for producing controlled hypotension during anesthesia to reduce bleeding.

UNLABELED USES Refractory CHF or acute MI.

CONTRAINDICATIONS Compensatory hypertension, as in atriovenous shunt or coarctation of aorta, and for control of hypotension in patients with inadequate cerebral circulation; pregnancy (category C), lactation.

CAUTIOUS USE Hepatic insufficiency, hypothyroidism, severe renal impairment, hyponatremia, older adult patients with low vitamin B_{12} plasma levels or with Leber's optic atrophy.

Common adverse effects in *italic*, life-threatening effects underlined; generic names in **bold**; classifications in SMALL CAPS; ✦ Canadian drug name; ⊘ Prototype drug

1087

ROUTE & DOSAGE

Hypertensive Crisis
Adult: **IV** 0.3–0.5 mcg/kg/min (average 3 mcg/kg/min)
Child: **IV** 1 mcg/kg/min (average 3 mcg/kg/min) (max 5 mcg/kg/min)

ADMINISTRATION

Intravenous

Note: Solutions must be freshly prepared with D5W and used no later than 4 h after reconstitution.

PREPARE: **Continuous:** Dissolve each 50 mg in 2–3 mL of D5W. Further dilute in 250 mL D5W to yield 200 mcg/mL or 500 mL D5W to yield 100 mcg/mL. Following reconstitution, solutions usually have faint brownish tint; if solution is highly colored, do not use it. Promptly wrap container with aluminum foil or other opaque material to protect drug from light.

ADMINISTER: **Continuous:** Administer by infusion pump or similar device that will allow precise measurement of flow rate required to lower BP. Give at the rate required to lower BP but do not exceed the maximum dose of 10 mcg/kg/min.

INCOMPATIBILITIES **Solution/additive: Amiodarone, propafenone. Y-site: Cisatracurium, haloperidol, levofloxacin.**

- Store reconstituted solutions protected from light; stable for 24 h.

ADVERSE EFFECTS (≥1%) **Body as a Whole:** Diaphoresis, apprehension, restlessness, muscle twitching, retrosternal discomfort. <u>Thiocyanate toxicity</u> (profound hypotension, tinnitus, blurred vision, fatigue, meta-bolic acidosis, pink skin color, absence of reflexes, faint heart sounds, loss of consciousness). **CV:** Profound hypotension, palpitation, increase or transient lowering of pulse rate, bradycardia, tachycardia, ECG changes. **GI:** Nausea, retching, abdominal pain. **Metabolic:** Increase in serum creatinine, fall or rise in total plasma cobalamins. **CNS:** Headache, dizziness. **Special Senses:** Nasal stuffiness. **Other:** Irritation at infusion site.

INTERACTIONS No clinically significant interactions established.

PHARMACOKINETICS Onset: Within 2 min. **Duration:** 1–10 min after infusion is terminated. **Metabolism:** Rapidly converted to cyanogen in erythrocytes and tissue, which is metabolized to thiocyanate in liver. **Elimination:** Excreted in urine primarily as thiocyanate. **Half-Life:** (thiocyanate): 2.7–7 d.

CLINICAL IMPLICATIONS

Assessment & Drug Effects

- Monitor constantly to titrate IV infusion rate to BP response.
- Relieve adverse effects by slowing IV rate or by stopping drug; minimize them by keeping patient supine.
- Notify physician immediately if BP begins to rise after drug infusion rate is decreased or infusion is discontinued.
- Monitor I&O.
- Lab tests: Monitor blood thiocyanate level in patients receiving prolonged treatment or in patients with severe kidney dysfunction (levels usually are not allowed to exceed 10 mg/dL). Determine plasma cyanogen level following 1 or 2 d of therapy in patients with impaired liver function.

NIZATIDINE

(ni-za'ti-deen)
Axid, Axid AR
Classifications: H_2-RECEPTOR ANTAGONIST; ANTISECRETORY
Therapeutic: ANTIULCER; H_2-RECEPTOR ANTAGONIST
Prototype: Cimetidine
Pregnancy Category: B

AVAILABILITY 75 mg tablets; 150 mg, 300 mg capsules; 15 mg/mL oral solution

ACTION & *THERAPEUTIC EFFECT*
Inhibits secretion of gastric acid by reversible, competitive blockage of histamine at the H_2 receptor, particularly those in the gastric parietal cells. *Significantly reduces nocturnal gastric acid secretion for up to 12 h.*

USES Active duodenal ulcers; maintenance therapy for duodenal ulcers.

CONTRAINDICATIONS Hypersensitivity to nizatidine; lactation; children ≤12 y.
CAUTIOUS USE Hypersensitivity to other H_2-receptor antagonists; renal impairment or renal failure; older adults; pregnancy (category B).

ROUTE & DOSAGE

Active Duodenal Ulcer
Adult: **PO** 150 mg b.i.d. or 300 mg h.s.

Maintenance Therapy
Adult: **PO** 150 mg h.s.

ADMINISTRATION

Oral
- Give drug usually once daily at bedtime. Dose may be divided and given twice daily.
- Administer oral liquid drug using a calibrated measuring device.

- Be aware that antacids consisting of aluminum and magnesium hydroxides with simethicone decrease nizatidine absorption by about 10%. Administer the antacid 2 h after nizatidine.

ADVERSE EFFECTS (≥1%) **CNS:** Somnolence, fatigue. **Skin:** Pruritus, sweating. **Metabolic:** Hyperuricemia.

INTERACTIONS Drug: May decrease absorption of **delavirdine, didanosine, itraconazole, ketoconazole;** ANTACIDS may decrease absorption of nizatidine. May increase **alcohol** levels.

PHARMACOKINETICS Absorption: >90% from GI tract. **Peak:** 0.5–3 h. **Metabolism:** In liver. **Elimination:** 60% in urine unchanged. **Half-Life:** 1–2 h.

CLINICAL IMPLICATIONS

Assessment & Drug Effects
- Monitor patient for alleviation of symptoms. Most ulcers should heal within 4 wk.
- Monitor cardiac patient's apical pulse because asymptomatic ventricular tachycardia is an adverse effect of the drug.
- Monitor for persistence of ulcer symptoms in patients who continue to smoke during therapy.
- Lab tests: Monitor liver enzyme studies (AST, ALT) and alkaline phosphatase. Nizatidine may cause hepatocellular injury.

Patient & Family Education
- Take medications for the full course of therapy even though symptoms may be relieved.
- Do not take other prescription or OTC medications without consulting physician.
- Stop smoking; smoking adversely affects healing of ulcers and effectiveness of the drug.

N

Common adverse effects in *italic*, life-threatening effects underlined; generic names in **bold**; classifications in SMALL CAPS; ♣ Canadian drug name; ☯ Prototype drug

1089

NONOXYNOL-9

(noe-nox′ee-nole)

Conceptrol, Delfen, Emko, Gynol II, Koromex

Classifications: SPERMICIDE CONTRACEPTIVE

Therapeutic: SPERMICIDE CONTRACEPTIVE

Pregnancy Category: C

AVAILABILITY 1%, 2%, 2.2%, 3.5%, 4%, 5% gel; 8%, 12.5% foam; 2.27%, 100 mg, 150 mg suppositories

ACTION & *THERAPEUTIC EFFECT*

Nonionic surfactant spermicidal incorporated into foams, gels, jelly, or suppositories. Immobilizes sperm by cell membrane disruption. *Applied over the cervix, blocks entrance to uterus by sperm, traps and absorbs seminal fluid, then releases the immediately available spermicide.*

USES As barrier contraceptive alone or in conjunction with a vaginal diaphragm or with a condom.

CONTRAINDICATIONS Cystocele, prolapsed uterus, sensitivity or allergy to polyurethane or to nonoxynol-9; vaginitis; history of TSS; pregnancy (category C); immediately after delivery or abortion; during menstruation.

ROUTE & DOSAGE

Contraceptive

Adult: **Topical** Apply or insert 30–60 min before intercourse. Repeat before each intercourse

ADMINISTRATION

Topical

- Apply foams, gels, jelly, cream: Fully load intravaginal applicator and insert about $^2/_3$ of its length [7.5–10 cm (3–4 in.)] into vagina.

- Use with diaphragm: Place 1–3 tsp spermicide formulation in dome prior to insertion. After diaphragm is in place, additional spermicide is recommended. Leave spermicide and diaphragm in place 6 h after intercourse.

ADVERSE EFFECTS (≥1%) **Urogenital:** *Candidiasis;* vaginal irritation and dryness; increase in vaginal infections; menstrual and nonmenstrual <u>toxic shock syndrome (TSS)</u>.

INTERACTIONS Drug: Intravaginal AZOLE ANTIFUNGALS may inactivate the spermicides.

PHARMACOKINETICS Onset: Spermicidal action is prompt upon contact with sperm; minimal systemic absorption.

CLINICAL IMPLICATIONS

Patient & Family Education

- Stop using nonoxynol-9 if pregnancy is suspected.
- Report symptoms of vaginal infection to physician: Burning, inflammation, intense vaginal and vulvar itching, cheesy, curd-like discharge, painful intercourse, dysuria. Nonoxynol-9 antifungal properties are weaker than its antibacterial potency, thus vulvovaginal candidiasis frequently occurs.
- Use spermicide before the first and every subsequent act of intercourse.

NOREPINEPHRINE BITARTRATE

(nor-ep-i-nef′rin)

Levarterenol, Levophed, Noradrenaline

Classifications: ALPHA- AND BETA-ADRENERGIC AGONIST; VASOCONSTRICTOR

Therapeutic: VASOCONSTRICTOR; INOTROPIC
Prototype: Epinephrine
Pregnancy Category: C

AVAILABILITY 1 mg/mL injection

ACTION & *THERAPEUTIC EFFECT*
Direct-acting sympathomimetic amine identical to body catecholamine norepinephrine. Acts directly and predominantly on alpha-adrenergic receptors; little action on beta receptors except in heart (beta$_1$ receptors). Vasoconstriction and cardiac stimulation; also powerful constrictor action on resistance and capacitance blood vessels. *Peripheral vasoconstriction and moderate inotropic stimulation of heart result in increased systolic and diastolic blood pressure, myocardial oxygenation, coronary artery blood flow, and work of heart.*

USES To restore BP in certain acute hypotensive states such as shock, sympathectomy, pheochromocytomectomy, spinal anesthesia, poliomyelitis, MI, septicemia, blood transfusion, and drug reactions. Also as adjunct in treatment of cardiac arrest.

CONTRAINDICATIONS Use as sole therapy in hypovolemic states, except as temporary emergency measure; mesenteric or peripheral vascular thrombosis; profound hypoxia or hypercarbia; use during cyclopropane or halothane anesthesia; hypertension; hyperthyroidism; MAOI therapy; pregnancy (category C).
CAUTIOUS USE Severe heart disease; older adult patients; within 14 d of MAOI therapy; patients receiving tricyclic antidepressants; lactation.

ROUTE & DOSAGE

Hypotension
Adult: **IV** Initial 0.5–1 mcg/min, titrate to response; usual range 8–30 mcg/min
Child: **IV** 0.05–0.1 mcg/kg/min; titrate to response (max: 1–2 mcg/kg/min)

ADMINISTRATION

Intravenous

PREPARE: **IV Infusion:** Dilute a 4 mL ampule in 1000 mL of D5W or D5/NS. Do not use solution if discoloration or precipitate is present. Protect from light.
ADMINISTER: **IV Infusion:** Initial rate of infusion is 2–3 mL/min (8–12 mcg/min), then titrated to maintain BP, usually 0.5–1 mL/min (2–4 mcg/min). An infusion pump is used. Usually give at the slowest rate possible required to maintain BP. Constantly monitor flow rate. Check infusion site frequently and immediately report any evidence of extravasation: blanching along course of infused vein (may occur without obvious extravasation), cold, hard swelling around injection site. Antidote for extravasation ischemia: Phentolamine, 5–10 mg in 10–15 mL NS injection, is infiltrated throughout affected area (using syringe with fine hypodermic needle) as soon as possible. If therapy is to be prolonged, change infusion sites at intervals to allow effect of local vasoconstriction to subside. Avoid abrupt withdrawal; when therapy is discontinued, infusion rate is slowed gradually.
INCOMPATIBILITIES **Solution/additive: Aminophylline, amobarbital, ampicillin, whole blood, cephapirin, chlorothi-**

N

Common adverse effects in *italic*, life-threatening effects underlined; generic names in **bold**; classifications in SMALL CAPS; ✦ Canadian drug name; ⊙ Prototype drug

1091

azide, chlorpheniramine, diazepam, pentobarbital, phenobarbital, phenytoin, secobarbital, sodium bicarbonate,
sodium iodide, streptomycin,
thiopental, warfarin. Y-site: Insulin, thiopental.

ADVERSE EFFECTS (≥1%) **Body as
a Whole:** Restlessness, anxiety,
tremors, dizziness, weakness, insomnia, pallor, plasma volume depletion, edema, hemorrhage, intes-
tinal, <u>hepatic</u>, or renal <u>necrosis</u>,
retrosternal and pharyngeal pain,
profuse sweating. **CV:** Palpitation,
hypertension, reflex bradycardia, <u>fa-
tal arrhythmias</u> (large doses), severe
hypertension. **GI:** Vomiting. **Metabolic:** Hyperglycemia. **CNS:** Headache, violent headache, <u>cerebral
hemorrhage</u>, convulsions. **Respiratory:** Respiratory difficulty. **Skin:**
Tissue necrosis at injection site (with
extravasation). **Special Senses:**
Blurred vision, photophobia.

INTERACTIONS Drug: ALPHA AND
BETA BLOCKERS antagonize pressor effects; ERGOT ALKALOIDS, **furazolidone, guanethidine, methyldopa,** TRICYCLIC ANTIDEPRESSANTS may
potentiate pressor effects; **halothane, cyclopropane** increase
risk of arrhythmias.

PHARMACOKINETICS Onset: Very
rapid. **Duration:** 1–2 min after infusion. **Distribution:** Localizes in sympathetic nerve endings; crosses placenta. **Metabolism:** In liver and
other tissues by catecholamine o-
methyl transferase and monoamine
oxidase. **Elimination:** In urine.

CLINICAL IMPLICATIONS

Assessment & Drug Effects

- Monitor constantly while patient
is receiving norepinephrine. Take
baseline BP and pulse before start
of therapy, then q2min from initi-

ation of drug until stabilization
occurs at desired level, then every
5 min during drug administration.

- Adjust flow rate to maintain BP at
low normal (usually 80–100 mm
Hg systolic) in normotensive patients. In previously hypertensive
patients, systolic is generally maintained no higher than 40 mm Hg
below preexisting systolic level.

- Observe carefully and record
mental status (index of cerebral
circulation), skin temperature of
extremities, and color (especially
of earlobes, lips, nail beds) in addition to vital signs.

- Monitor I&O. Urinary retention
and kidney shutdown are possi-
bilities, especially in hypovolemic patients. Urinary output is a
sensitive indicator of the degree
of renal perfusion. Report decrease in urinary output or
change in I&O ratio.

- Be alert to patient's complaints of
headache, vomiting, palpitation,
arrhythmias, chest pain, photophobia, and blurred vision as
possible symptoms of overdosage. Reflex bradycardia may occur as a result of rise in BP.

- Continue to monitor vital signs
and observe patient closely after
cessation of therapy for clinical
sign of circulatory inadequacy.

NORETHINDRONE

(nor-eth-in′drone)
Micronor, Norlutin, Nor-Q.D.

NORETHINDRONE ACETATE

Aygestin ◆, Norlutate ◆

Classifications: HORMONE; PRO-
GESTIN
Therapeutic: HORMONE; PROGESTIN
Prototype: Norgestrel
Pregnancy Category: X

AVAILABILITY 0.35 mg, 5 mg tablets

ACTION & *THERAPEUTIC EFFECT*
Synthetic progestational hormone with androgenic, anabolic, and estrogenic properties. Progestin-only contraceptives alter cervical mucus, exert progestational effect on endometrium, interfere with implantation, and, in some cases, suppress ovulation. May produce excess estrogenic effect. *Contraceptive that suppresses the midcycle surge of leutinizing hormone (LH).*

USES Amenorrhea, abnormal uterine bleeding due to hormonal imbalance in absence of organic pathology; endometriosis. Also alone or in combination with an estrogen for birth control.

CONTRAINDICATIONS Thromboembolic disorders, cerebral vascular or coronary vascular disease; carcinoma of breast, endometrium, or liver; abnormal vaginal bleeding; known or suspected pregnancy (category X); children <16 y.

CAUTIOUS USE Cardiac disease; history of depression, seizure disorders, migraine; diabetes mellitus; CHF; history of thrombophlebitis or thromboembolic disease.

ROUTE & DOSAGE

Amenorrhea
Adult: **PO Norethindrone** 5–20 mg on day 5 through day 25 of menstrual cycle; **Acetate** 2.5–10 mg on day 5 through day 25 of menstrual cycle

Endometriosis
Adult: **PO Norethindrone** 10 mg/d for 2 wk; increase by 5 mg/d q2wk up to 30 mg/d, dose may remain at this level for 6–9 mo or until breakthrough bleeding;

Acetate 5 mg/d for 2 wk, increase by 2.5 mg/d q2wk up to 15 mg/d, dose may remain at this level for 6–9 mo or until breakthrough bleeding

Progestin-Only Contraception
Adult: **PO Norethindrone** 0.35 mg/d starting on day 1 of menstrual flow, then continuing indefinitely

ADMINISTRATION

Oral
- Note: Dosing schedule is based on a 28-d menstrual cycle.
- Use or add a barrier contraceptive when starting the minipill regimen (progestin-only contraception) for the first cycle or for 3 wk to ensure full protection.
- Protect drug from light and from freezing.

ADVERSE EFFECTS (≥1%) **CNS:** Cerebral thrombosis or hemorrhage, depression. **CV:** Hypertension, pulmonary embolism, edema. **GI:** Nausea, vomiting, cholestatic jaundice, abdominal cramps. **Urogenital:** *Breakthrough bleeding,* cervical erosion, changes in menstrual flow, dysmenorrhea, vaginal candidiasis. **Other:** *Weight changes; breast tenderness,* enlargement or secretion.

INTERACTIONS Drug: BARBITURATES, **carbamazepine, fosphenytoin, modafinil, phenytoin, primidone, pioglitazone, rifampin rifabutin, rifapentine, topiramate, troglitazone** can decrease contraceptive effectiveness.

PHARMACOKINETICS Absorption: Readily absorbed from GI tract. **Metabolism:** In liver. **Elimination:** In urine and feces as metabolites.

Common adverse effects in *italic*, life-threatening effects underlined; generic names in **bold**; classifications in SMALL CAPS; ♥ Canadian drug name; ◐ Prototype drug

1093

CLINICAL IMPLICATIONS

Assessment & Drug Effects

- Monitor for S&S of thrombophlebitis (see Appendix F).
- Withhold drug and notify physician if any of the following occur: Sudden, complete, or partial loss of vision, proptosis, diplopia, or migraine headache.

Patient & Family Education

- Wait at least 3 mo before becoming pregnant after stopping the minipill to prevent birth defects. Use a barrier or nonhormonal method of contraception until pregnancy is desired.
- If you have not taken all your pills and you miss a period, consider the possibility of pregnancy after 45 d from the last menstrual period; stop using progestin-only contraceptive until pregnancy is ruled out.
- If you have taken all your pills and you miss 2 consecutive periods, rule out pregnancy and use a barrier or nonhormonal method of contraception before continuing the regimen.
- Review package insert to ensure you understand how to use norethindrone.
- Promptly report prolonged vaginal bleeding or amenorrhea.
- Learn and do breast self-examination.
- Keep appointments for physical checkups (q6–12mo) while you are taking hormonal birth control.

NORFLOXACIN

(nor-flox'a-sin)
Noroxin
Classifications: QUINOLONE ANTIBIOTIC

Therapeutic: ANTIBIOTIC; QUINOLONE
Prototype: Ciprofloxacin
Pregnancy Category: C

AVAILABILITY 400 mg tablets

ACTION & THERAPEUTIC EFFECT
Potent broad-spectrum antibiotic activity. Alters structure of bacterial DNA gyrase, thus promoting double-stranded DNA breakage, thus interfering with synthesis of bacterial protein and blocking bacterial survival. *Active against many bacterial pathogens of the urinary tract.*

USES Complicated and uncomplicated urinary tract infection (UTI) caused by susceptible organisms. Conjunctivitis.
UNLABELED USES Gonorrhea, gastroenteritis, and prevention of travelers' diarrhea.

CONTRAINDICATIONS Use in individual with known factors that predispose to seizures; history of hypersensitivity to norfloxacin and other quinolone antibiotics; history of QT prolongation; tendon pain; pregnancy (category C), lactation; children <18 y.
CAUTIOUS USE Impaired kidney function, adolescents if skeletal growth is complete; G6PD deficiency; GI disease; myasthenia gravis.

ROUTE & DOSAGE

Urinary Tract Infection
Adult: PO 400 mg b.i.d.

Gonorrhea or Gonococcal Urethritis
Adult: PO 800 mg once/d

Bacterial Gastroenteritis
Adult: PO 400 mg q8–12h

ADMINISTRATION

Oral

- Give 1 h before or 2 h after meals with a full glass of water.
- Administer concomitant antacid at least 2 h after norfloxacin to prevent interference with absorption. Aluminum or magnesium ions in the antacid may bind to and form insoluble complexes with the quinolone in GI tract.
- Store at 40° C (104° F) or less in tightly closed container. Do not freeze.

ADVERSE EFFECTS (≥1%) **Musculoskeletal:** Joint swelling, cartilage erosion in weight-bearing joints, tendonitis. In immunosuppressed adult: acute ankle and hip pain followed by acute pain, tenderness, and swelling of tendon sheath of middle finger of both hands after 4 wk of therapy. **CNS:** *Headache, dizziness, lightheadedness, fatigue,* drowsiness, somnolence, depression, insomnia, seizures, peripheral neuropathy. **GI:** *Nausea,* abdominal pain, diarrhea, vomiting, anorexia, dyspepsia, dysphagia, dry mouth, bitter taste, heartburn, flatulence, pruritus ani, increased serum AST, ALT, alkaline phosphatase. **Hematologic:** Leukopenia, neutropenia. **Urogenital:** With high doses: Crystalluria (not associated with renal toxicity), vulvar irritation.

DIAGNOSTIC TEST INTERFERENCE May cause false positive on *opiate screening tests.*

INTERACTIONS Drug: ANTACIDS, **iron, sucralfate,** zinc decrease absorption; **nitrofurantoin** may antagonize antibacterial effects; may increase hypoprothrombinemic effects of **warfarin;** may cause slight increase in **theophylline** levels; concurrent administration with CLASS IA and CLASS III ANTIARRHYTHMICS may result in development of QT prolongation as well as torsades de points.

PHARMACOKINETICS Absorption: 30–40% from GI tract. **Peak:** 1–2 h. **Distribution:** Renal parenchyma, gallbladder, liver, prostate; crosses placenta; distributed into breast milk. **Metabolism:** In liver. **Elimination:** In urine and feces. **Half-Life:** 3–4 h.

CLINICAL IMPLICATIONS

Assessment & Drug Effects

- Collect urine specimens for testing before initiating antibiotic.
- Monitor patient for tendon pain. Norfloxacin should be discontinued and physician informed.
- Lab tests: Periodic WBC with differential, liver enzymes, and alkaline phosphatase, especially with prolonged use.
- Report to the physician if patient is adequately hydrated, yet I&O ratio and pattern changes are noted, or if condition does not improve within a few days. Dosage may need to be modified.

Patient & Family Education

- Take drug at same times each day.
- Take drug exactly as prescribed. Erratic dosing can encourage emergence of resistant bacteria; underdosing or premature discontinuation of treatment can cause return of UTI symptoms.
- Keep fluid intake high (at least 2500–3000 mL/d if tolerated) to provide adequate urine output and hydration, important in the prevention of crystalluria (rare side effect).

N

Common adverse effects in *italic*, life-threatening effects underlined; generic names in **bold**; classifications in SMALL CAPS; ✚ Canadian drug name; ⊘ Prototype drug

1095

NORGESTREL ⊕

(nor-jess'trel)
Classifications: HORMONE; PRO-
GESTIN
Therapeutic: HORMONE; PROGESTIN
Pregnancy Category: X

AVAILABILITY 0.075 mg tablets

ACTION & *THERAPEUTIC EFFECT*
Potent progestational hormone with
androgenic, antiestrogenic, and anabolic properties. Induces and maintains endometrium, preventing uterine bleeding; inhibits production of
pituitary gonadotropin, preventing
ovulation; produces thick cervical
mucus resistant to passage of
sperm. *Effective progestin contraceptive that prevents ovulation.*

USES A progestin-only contraceptive
(minipill).

CONTRAINDICATIONS Thromboembolic disorders; cerebral vascular or
coronary vascular disease; carcinoma of breast, endometrium, or
liver; abnormal vaginal bleeding;
known or suspected pregnancy
(category X); children <16 y.
CAUTIOUS USE Cardiac disease;
cerebrovascular disease; depression, migraine, seizure disorders.

ROUTE & DOSAGE

Progestin-Only Contraception
Adult: **PO** 0.075 mg/d starting
on day 1 of menstrual flow, then
continuing indefinitely

ADMINISTRATION
Oral
▪ Use a barrier method of contraception, when starting the minipill
regimen, for the first cycle or for 3
wk to insure full protection.

▪ The minipill can be started right after delivery in the nonlactation
mother; however, she should be
aware of an increased risk of
thromboembolic disease during
the postpartum period.
▪ Take the minipill at same time
each day, even if menstruating.
▪ Store at 15°–30° C (59°–86° F) in a
tightly closed container.

ADVERSE EFFECTS (≥1%) **CNS:**
Cerebral thrombosis or hemorrhage,
depression. **CV:** Hypertension, pulmonary embolism, edema. **GI:** Nausea, vomiting, cholestatic jaundice,
abdominal cramps. **Urogenital:**
Breakthrough bleeding, cervical erosion, changes in menstrual flow,
dysmenorrhea, vaginal candidiasis.
Endocrine: *Weight changes; breast
tenderness,* enlargement, or secretion.

INTERACTIONS No clinically significant interactions established.

PHARMACOKINETICS Absorption:
Readily absorbed from GI tract.
Metabolism: In liver. **Elimination:** In
urine and feces as metabolites.

CLINICAL IMPLICATIONS
Assessment & Drug Effects
▪ Monitor for S&S of thrombophlebitis (see Appendix F).
▪ Withhold drug and notify physician if any of the following occur:
Sudden complete or partial loss of
vision, proptosis, diplopia, or migraine headache.

Patient & Family Education
▪ Be aware that amount and duration
of flow, cycle length, breakthrough
bleeding, spotting, and amenorrhea
vary greatly with use of the progestin-only contraceptive.
▪ Wait at least 3 mo before becoming pregnant after stopping the
minipill to prevent birth defects.

Common adverse effects in *italic*, life-threatening effects <u>underlined</u>; generic names
in **bold**; classifications in SMALL CAPS; ✦ Canadian drug name; ⊕ Prototype drug

Use a barrier method of contraception until pregnancy is desired.

- If you have not taken all your pills and you miss a period, consider the possibility of pregnancy after 45 d from the last menstrual period; stop using progestin-only contraceptive until pregnancy is ruled out.
- If you have taken all your pills and you miss 2 consecutive periods, rule out pregnancy and use a barrier or nonhormonal method of contraception before continuing the regimen.
- Review package insert to ensure you understand how to use norgestrel.
- Learn and do breast self-examination.

NORMAL SERUM ALBUMIN, HUMAN ℗

(al-byoo′min)
Albuminar, Albutein, Buminate, Plasbumin

Classifications: BLOOD DERIVATIVE; PLASMA VOLUME EXPANDER
Therapeutic: PLASMA VOLUME EXPANDER
Pregnancy Category: C

AVAILABILITY 5%, 20%, 25% injection

ACTION & *THERAPEUTIC EFFECT*
Obtained by fractionating pooled venous and placental human plasma, which is then sterilized by filtration and heat to minimize possibility of transmitting hepatitis B virus or HIV. Risk of sensitization is reduced because it lacks cellular elements and contains no coagulation factors, Rh factor, or blood group antibodies. Plasma volume expander that increases the osmotic pressure of plasma. *Expands volume of circulating blood by osmotically shifting tissue fluid into general circulation.*

USES To restore plasma volume and maintain cardiac output in hypovolemic shock; for prevention and treatment of cerebral edema; as adjunct in exchange transfusion for hyperbilirubinemia and erythroblastosis fetalis; to increase plasma protein level in treatment of hypoproteinemia; and to promote diuresis in refractory edema. Also used for blood dilution prior to or during cardiopulmonary bypass procedures. Has been used as adjunct in treatment of adult respiratory distress syndrome (ARDS).

CONTRAINDICATIONS Hypersensivity to albumin; severe anemia; cardiac failure; within 24 h of severe burns; heart failure; patients with normal or increased intravascular volume; pregnancy (category C).
CAUTIOUS USE Low cardiac reserve, pulmonary disease, absence of albumin deficiency; liver or kidney failure, dehydration, hypertension, hypernatremia; restricted sodium intake.

ROUTE & DOSAGE

Emergency Volume Replacement
Adult: **IV** 25 g, may repeat in 15–30 min if necessary (max: 250 g)

Colloidal Volume Replacement (Nonemergency)
Child: **IV** 12.5 g, may repeat in 15–30 min if necessary

Hypoproteinemia
Adult: **IV** 50–75 g (max: 2 mL/min)
Child: **IV** 25 g (max: 2 mL/min)

N

Common adverse effects in *italic*, life-threatening effects underlined; generic names in **bold**; classifications in SMALL CAPS; ♦ Canadian drug name; ℗ Prototype drug

1097

ADMINISTRATION

Intravenous

Note: 5% solution = 5 g/100 mL; 25% solution = 25 g/mL.

PREPARE: **IV Infusion:** Normal serum albumin, 5%, is infused without further dilution. Normal serum albumin, 25%, may be infused undiluted in NS or D5W (with sodium restriction).

ADMINISTER: **IV Infusion: Hypovolemic Shock:** Give initially as rapidly as necessary to restore blood volume. As blood volume approaches normal, rate should be reduced to avoid circulatory overload and pulmonary edema. Give 5% albumin at rate not exceeding 2–4 mL/min. Give 25% albumin at a rate not to exceed 1 mL/min. **With Normal Blood Volume:** Give 5% albumin human at a rate not to exceed 5–10 mL/min; give 25% albumin at a rate not to exceed 2 or 3 mL/min. **Children:** Usual rate is $^1/_4$–$^1/_2$ the adult rate.

INCOMPATIBILITIES **Solution/additive: Amino acids, verapamil. Y-site: Fat emulsion, midazolam, vancomycin, verapamil.**

■ Store at temperature not to exceed 37° C (98.6° F). ■ Use solution within 4 h, once container is opened, because it contains no preservatives or antimicrobials. Discard unused portion.

ADVERSE EFFECTS (≥1%) **Body as a Whole:** Fever, chills, flushing, increased salivation, headache, back pain. **Skin:** Urticaria, rash. **CV:** Circulatory overload, pulmonary edema (with rapid infusion); hypotension, hypertension, dyspnea, tachycardia. **GI:** Nausea, vomiting.

DIAGNOSTIC TEST INTERFERENCE False rise in *alkaline phosphatase* when albumin is obtained partially from pooled placental plasma (levels reportedly decline over period of weeks).

CLINICAL IMPLICATIONS

Assessment & Drug Effects

■ Monitor BP, pulse and respiration, and IV albumin flow rate. Adjust flow rate as needed to avoid too rapid a rise in BP.

■ Lab tests: Monitor dosage of albumin using plasma albumin (normal): 3.5–5 g/dL; total serum protein (normal): 6–8.4 g/dL; Hgb; Hct; and serum electrolytes.

■ Observe closely for S&S of circulatory overload and pulmonary edema (see Appendix F). If S&S appear, slow infusion rate just sufficiently to keep vein open, and report immediately to physician.

■ Observe for bleeding points that did not bleed at lower BP with injuries or surgery and as BP rises.

■ Monitor I&O ratio and pattern. Report changes in urinary output. Increase in colloidal osmotic pressure usually causes diuresis, which may persist 3–20 h.

■ Withhold fluids completely during succeeding 8 h, when albumin is given to patients with cerebral edema.

Patient & Family Education

■ Report chills, nausea, headache, or back pain to physician immediately.

NORTRIPTYLINE HYDROCHLORIDE

(nor-trip′ti-leen)

Aventyl, Pamelor

Classifications: PSYCHOTHERAPEUTIC; TRICYCLIC ANTIDEPRESSANT

Therapeutic: TRICYCLIC ANTIDEPRESSANT
Prototype: Imipramine
Pregnancy Category: D

AVAILABILITY 10 mg, 25 mg, 50 mg, 75 mg capsules; 10 mg/5 mL solution

ACTION & *THERAPEUTIC EFFECT*
Secondary amine derivative of amitriptyline that enhances action of norepinephrine and serotonin by blocking their reuptake at the neuronal membrane. Nortriptyline is more likely to inhibit the reuptake of serotonin than norepinephrine. *Mood elevation may be due to its inhibition of reuptake of serotonin at the presynaptic membrane.*

USES Endogenous depression. Similar in actions, uses, limitations, and interactions to imipramine.

UNLABELED USES Nocturnal enuresis in children.

CONTRAINDICATIONS Hypersensitivity to tricyclic antidepressants; acute recovery period after MI; AV block; history of QT prolongation; suicidal ideation; during or within 14 d of MAO inhibitor therapy. Children <12 y, pregnancy (category D), lactation.

CAUTIOUS USE Narrow-angle glaucoma, cardiac disease; hyperthyroidism, concurrent administration of thyroid medications, concurrent use with electroshock therapy; history of suicides; Parkinson's disease; asthma; bipolar disorder.

ROUTE & DOSAGE

Antidepressant
Adult: **PO** 25 mg t.i.d. or q.i.d., gradually increased to 100–150 mg/d

Geriatric: **PO** Start with 10–25 mg h.s., increase by 25 mg q3d to 75 mg h.s. (max: 150 mg/d)
Adolescent: **PO** 30–50 mg/d in divided doses
Child 6–12 y: **PO** 10–20 mg/d in 3–4 divided doses

Nocturnal Enuresis
Child: **PO** 6–7 y, 10 mg/d; 8–11 y, 10–20 mg/d; >11 y, 25–35 mg/d given 30 min before h.s.

ADMINISTRATION

Oral
- Give with food to decrease gastric distress.
- In older adults, total daily dose may be given once a day h.s. (preferred).
- Be aware that Aventyl is a 4% alcohol solution.
- Supervise drug ingestion to be sure patient swallows medication.
- Store at 15°–30° C (59°–86° F) in tightly closed container.

ADVERSE EFFECTS (≥1%) **Body as a Whole:** Tremors, hyperhydrosis. **CV:** *Orthostatic hypotension.* **GI:** Paralytic ileus, *dry mouth.* **Hematologic:** <u>Agranulocytosis</u> (rare). **CNS:** Drowsiness, confusional state (especially in older adults and with high dosage). **Skin:** Photosensitivity reaction. **Special Senses:** Blurred vision. **Urogenital:** *Urinary retention.*

INTERACTIONS Drug: May decrease response to ANTIHYPERTENSIVES; CNS DEPRESSANTS, **alcohol,** HYPNOTICS, BARBITURATES, SEDATIVES potentiate CNS depression; may increase hypoprothrombinemic effect of ORAL ANTICOAGULANTS; SYMPATHOMIMETICS (e.g., **epinephrine, norepinephrine**) pose possibility of sympathetic hyperactivity with hypertension and hyperpyrexia; MAO INHIBITORS pose possibility of severe

N

Common adverse effects in *italic*, life-threatening effects <u>underlined</u>; generic names in **bold**; classifications in SMALL CAPS; ✦ Canadian drug name; ⊘ Prototype drug

1099

reactions: toxic psychosis, cardiovascular instability; **methylphenidate** increases plasma TCA levels; THYROID DRUGS may increase possibility of arrhythmias; **cimetidine** may increase plasma TCA levels. **Herbal: Ginkgo** may decrease seizure threshold. **St. John's wort** may cause **serotonin** syndrome (see Appendix F).

PHARMACOKINETICS Absorption: Rapidly from GI tract. **Peak:** 7–8.5 h. **Duration:** Crosses placenta; distributed in breast milk. **Metabolism:** In liver (CYP2D6). **Elimination:** Primarily in urine. **Half-Life:** 16–90 h.

CLINICAL IMPLICATIONS

Assessment & Drug Effects

- Be aware that nortriptyline has a narrow therapeutic plasma level range, or "therapeutic window." Drug levels above or below the therapeutic window are associated with decreased rate of response.
- Therapeutic response may not occur for 2 wk or more.
- Monitor carefully for signs and symptoms of suicidality in children and adults.
- Monitor BP and pulse rate during adjustment period of TCA therapy. If systolic BP falls more than 20 mm Hg or if there is a sudden increase in pulse rate, withhold medication and notify the physician.
- Notify physician if psychotic signs increase. Because of the small therapeutic window, a substitute TCA may be prescribed rather than an increase in dosage.
- Inspect oral membranes daily if patient is on high doses of TCA. Urge outpatient to report stomatitis or dry mouth. Sore mouth can be a major cause of poor nutrition and noncompliance. Consult physician about use of a saliva substitute (e.g., VA-Oralube, Moi-Stir).

- Monitor bowel elimination pattern and I&O ratio. Urinary retention and severe constipation are potential problems, especially in older adults. Advise increased fluid intake; consult physician about stool softener.
- Observe patient with history of glaucoma. Symptoms that may signal acute attack (severe headache, eye pain, dilated pupils, halos of light, nausea, vomiting) should be reported promptly.
- Report reduction or alleviation of fine tremors.
- Be aware that alcohol potentiation may increase the danger of overdosage or suicide attempt.

Patient & Family Education

- Be aware that your ability to perform tasks requiring alertness and skill may be impaired.
- Do not use OTC drugs unless physician approves.
- Consult physician about safe amount of alcohol, if any, that can be ingested. Alcohol and nortriptyline both have increased effects when used together and for up to 2 wk after the TCA is discontinued.
- Nortriptyline enhances the effects of barbiturates and other CNS depressants are enhanced.

NYSTATIN

(nye-stat'in)
Mycostatin, Nadostine ♦, Nilstat, Nyaderm ♦, Nystex, O-V Statin
Classifications: ANTIFUNGAL ANTIBIOTIC
Therapeutic: ANTIFUNGAL ANTIBIOTIC
Prototype: Amphotericin B
Pregnancy Category: C

AVAILABILITY 500,000 unit tablets; 100,000 units/mL oral suspension; 200,000 troches; 100,000 units vaginal tablets; 100,000 units/g cream, ointment, powder.

ACTION & *THERAPEUTIC EFFECT*
Nontoxic, nonsensitizing antifungal antibiotic produced by *Streptomyces noursei*. Binds to sterols in fungal cell membrane, thereby changing membrane potential and allowing leakage of intracellular components that leads to fungi cell death. *Fungistatic and fungicidal activity against a variety of yeasts and fungi; not appreciably active against bacteria, viruses, or protozoa.*

USES Local infections of skin and mucous membranes caused by *Candida* sp. including *Candida albicans* (e.g., paronychia; cutaneous, oropharyngeal, vulvovaginal, and intestinal candidiasis).

CONTRAINDICATIONS Use of vaginal tablets during pregnancy (category C); vaginal infections caused by *Gardnerella vaginalis* or *Trichomonas* sp.
CAUTIOUS USE Lactation (PO form); diabetes mellitus.

ROUTE & DOSAGE

Candida Infections
Adult: **PO** 500,000–1,000,000 U t.i.d.; 1–4 troches 4–5 times/d; Suspension: 400,000–600,000 U q.i.d. **Intravaginal** 1–2 tablets daily for 2 wk
Child: **PO** Suspension: 400,000–600,000 U q.i.d.
Infant: **PO** 100,000–200,000 U q.i.d.

ADMINISTRATION
Oral
▪ Give reconstituted powder for oral suspension immediately after mixing.

▪ Rinse mouth with 1–2 tsp using oral suspension. Keep in mouth (swish) as long as possible (at least 2 min), then spit it out. (If you cannot keep the liquid in your mouth or cannot spit, or if you have been told to "swish and swallow," you may swallow the drug.) For children, infants: Apply drug with swab to each side of mouth. Avoid food or drink for 30 min after treatment.
Topical
▪ Store vaginal tablets in refrigerator below 15° C (59° F).

ADVERSE EFFECTS (≥1%) **GI:** Nausea, vomiting, epigastric distress, diarrhea (especially with high oral doses).

PHARMACOKINETICS Absorption: Poorly absorbed from GI tract. **Elimination:** In feces.

CLINICAL IMPLICATIONS
Assessment & Drug Effects
▪ Monitor oral cavity, especially the tongue, for signs of improvement.
▪ Avoid occlusive dressings or applications of ointment preparation to moist, dark areas of body because they favor growth of yeast.

Patient & Family Education
▪ This drug may cause contact dermatitis. Stop using the drug and report to physician if redness, swelling, or irritation develops.
▪ Take for oral candidiasis (thrush) treatment after meals and at bedtime.
▪ Dissolve troche in mouth (about 30 min). Do not chew or swallow. Avoid food and drink during period of dissolving and for 30 min after treatment.
▪ Care of dentures: Remove dentures before each rinse with oral suspension and before use of tro-

Common adverse effects in *italic*, life-threatening effects underlined; generic names in **bold**; classifications in SMALL CAPS; ♣ Canadian drug name; ⊘ Prototype drug

1101

che. Remove dentures at night (infection occurs more frequently in person who wears dentures 24 h a day).

- Dust shoes and stockings, as well as feet, with nystatin dusting powder.
- Gently clean infected areas with tepid water before each application of topical preparation.
- Continue medication for vulvovaginal candidiasis during menstruation.
- Use vaginal tablets up to 6 wk before term to prevent thrush in the newborn.

OCTREOTIDE ACETATE

(oc-tre'o-tide)
Sandostatin, Sandostatin LAR depot
Classifications: HORMONE; SOMATOSTATIN; ANTIDIARRHEAL
Therapeutic: ANTIDIARRHEAL
Pregnancy Category: B

AVAILABILITY 0.05 mg/mL, 0.1 mg/mL, 0.2 mg/mL, 0.5 mg/mL, 1 mg/mL injection; 10 mg/5 mL, 20 mg/5 mL, 30 mg/5 mL depot injection

ACTION & THERAPEUTIC EFFECT A long-acting peptide that mimics the natural hormone somatostatin. Suppresses secretion of serotonin, pancreatic peptides, gastrin, vasoactive intestinal peptide, insulin, glucagon, secretin, and motilin. *Stimulates fluid and electrolyte absorption from the GI tract, prolongs intestinal transit time, and also inhibits the growth hormone.*

USES Symptomatic treatment of severe diarrhea and flushing episodes associated with metastatic carcinoid tumors. Also watery diarrhea associated with vasoactive intestinal peptide (VIP) tumors.
UNLABELED USES Acromegaly associated with pituitary tumors, fistula drainage, variceal bleeding.

CONTRAINDICATIONS Hypersensitivity to octreotide.
CAUTIOUS USE Cholelithiasis, renal impairment; dialysis; hepatic disease; cardiac disease; diabetes, hypothyroidism; pregnancy (category B); lactation.

ROUTE & DOSAGE

Carcinoid Syndrome
Adult: **SC/IV** 100–600 mcg/d in 2–4 divided doses, titrate to response **IM** May switch to depot injection after 2 wk at 20 mg q4wk times 3 mo

VIPoma
Adult: **SC/IV** 200–300 mcg/d in 2–4 divided doses, titrate to response **IM** May switch to depot injection after 2 wk at 20 mg q4wk times 2 mo

Acromegaly
Adult: **SC** 50 mcg t.i.d., titrate up to 100 mcg–500 mcg t.i.d. **IM** May switch to depot injection after 2 wk at 20 mg q4wk times at least 3 mo, then reassess

ADMINISTRATION

Subcutaneous, Intramuscular
- Note: Subcutaneous is the preferred route.
- Minimize GI side effects by giving injections between meals and at bedtime.
- Avoid multiple injections into the same site. Rotate SC sites on abdomen, hip, and thigh.
- Give deep IM into a large muscle. To reduce local irritation, allow

solution to reach room temperature before injection and administer slowly.

Intravenous

PREPARE: Direct: Give undiluted. **Intermittent:** Dilute in 50–200 mL D5W.
ADMINISTER: Direct: Give a single dose over 3 min. In carcinoid give rapid IV bolus over 60 sec. **Intermittent:** Give over 15–30 min.
INCOMPATIBILITIES Solution/additive: Fat emulsion, regular insulin.

ADVERSE EFFECTS (≥1%) **CNS:** Headache, fatigue, dizziness. **GI:** *Nausea, diarrhea,* abdominal pain and discomfort. **Metabolic:** Hypoglycemia, hyperglycemia, increased liver transaminases, hypothyroidism (after long-term use). **Body as a Whole:** Flushing, edema, injection site pain.

INTERACTIONS Drug: May decrease **cyclosporine** levels; may alter other drug and nutrient absorption because of alterations in GI motility.

PHARMACOKINETICS Absorption: Rapidly from SC injection. **Peak:** 0.4 h. **Duration:** Up to 12 h. **Metabolism:** In liver. **Elimination:** In urine. **Half-Life:** 1.5 h.

CLINICAL IMPLICATIONS

Assessment & Drug Effects

- Lab tests: Periodic blood glucose, liver function tests, and serum electrolytes.
- Monitor for hypoglycemia and hyperglycemia (see Appendix F), because octreotide may alter the balance between insulin, glucagon, and growth hormone.
- Monitor fluid and electrolyte balance, as octreotide stimulates fluid and electrolyte absorption from GI tract.

- Dietary fat absorption may be altered in some clients. Monitor fecal fat and serum carotene to aid in the assessment of possible drug-induced aggravation of fat malabsorption.

Patient & Family Education

- Learn proper technique for SC injection if self-medication is required.
- Note: Preferred sites for SC injections of octreotide are the hip, thigh, and abdomen. Multiple injections at the same SC injection site within short periods of time are not recommended. This is to avoid irritating the area.

OFLOXACIN

(o-flox'a-cin)
Floxin, Floxin Otic, Ocuflox
Classifications: ANTIBIOTIC, QUINOLONE
Therapeutic: ANTIBIOTIC, QUINOLONE
Prototype: Ciprofloxacin
Pregnancy Category: C

0

AVAILABILITY 200 mg, 300 mg, 400 mg tablets; 40 mg/mL injection; 0.3% ophthalmic solution; 0.3% otic solution

ACTION & *THERAPEUTIC EFFECT*

A fluoroquinolone antibiotic that inhibits DNA gyrase, an enzyme necessary for bacterial DNA replication and some aspects of its transcription, repair, recombination, and transposition. *Has a broad spectrum of activity against gram-positive and gram-negative bacteria. Most effective against gram-negative organisms including aerobic and anaerobic bacteria.*

USES *Chlamydia trachomatis* infection, uncomplicated gonorrhea,

Common adverse effects in *italic*, life-threatening effects underlined; generic names in **bold**; classifications in SMALL CAPS; ♦ Canadian drug name; ⊘ Prototype drug

1103

prostatitis, respiratory tract infections, skin and skin structure infections, urinary tract infections due to susceptible bacteria, superficial ocular infections, pelvic inflammatory disease. Otic: otitis externa, otitis media with perforated tympanic membranes.

UNLABELED USES EENT infections, *Helicobacter pylori* infections, *Salmonella* gastroenteritis.

CONTRAINDICATIONS Hypersensitivity to ofloxacin or other quinolone antibacterial agents; tendon pain; sunlight (UV) exposure; QT prolongation; viral infection; pregnancy (category C).

CAUTIOUS USE Renal disease; patients with a history of epilepsy, psychosis, or increased intracranial pressure, cerebrovascular disease, CNS disorders such as seizures, epilepsy, myasthenia gravis; GI disease, colitis, dehydration; syphilis; atrial fibrillation; acute MI; CVA; children and adolescents <18 y (except for otic preparation).

ROUTE & DOSAGE

Uncomplicated Gonorrhea
Adult: **PO** 400 mg for 1 dose

Urinary Tract, Respiratory Tract, and Skin and Skin Structure Infections
Adult: **PO** 200–400 mg q12h times 7–10 d **IV** 400 mg q12h times 7 d

Prostatitis
Adult: **PO** 300 mg b.i.d. times 6 wk

Superficial Ocular Infections
Adult: **Ophthalmic** Instill 1–2 drops q2–4h for first 2 d, then q.i.d. for up to 5 additional d

Otitis Media with Perforation
Adult: **Otic** 10 drops (0.5 mL) q12h for 14 d
Child: **Otic** ≥1 y, 5 drops (0.25 mL) q12h for 14 d

Otitis Externa
Adult: **Otic** 10 drops (0.5 mL) q12h for 7 d
Child: **Otic** 6 mo–13 y, 5 drops (0.25 mL) q12h for 7 d

Renal Impairment
Cl_{cr} 20–50mL/min: dose should be given q24h; <20 mL/min: $^1/_2$ the dose q24h

Hepatic Impairment
Severe impairment: 400 mg qd

ADMINISTRATION

Oral
- Do not give with meals.
- Avoid administering mineral supplements or vitamins with iron or zinc within 2 h of drug.
- Do not give antacids with magnesium, aluminum, or sucralfate within 4 h before or 2 h after drug.

Instillation
- Do NOT allow tip of dropper for ocular preparation to contact any surface.

Intravenous

PREPARE: Intermittent: Withdraw the required dose from a 10 mL (40 mg/mL) or 20 mL (20 mg/mL) vial and add to 100 mL D5W, NS, D5/NS or other compatible solution. Final concentration may range from 0.4 mg/mL to 4 mg/mL.

ADMINISTER: Intermittent: Give a single dose over at least 60 min. Avoid rapid infusion.

INCOMPATIBILITIES Y-site: **Amphotericin B cholesteryl sulfate complex, cefepime, doxorubicin liposome.**

ADVERSE EFFECTS (≥1%) **CNS:** *Headache, dizziness, insomnia,* hallucinations. **GI:** Nausea, vomiting, diarrhea, GI discomfort. **Urogenital:** Pruritus, pain, irritation, burning, vaginitis, vaginal discharge, dysmenorrhea, menorrhagia, dysuria, urinary frequency. **Skin:** Pruritus, rash. **Other:** Cartilage erosion.

DIAGNOSTIC TEST INTERFERENCE May cause false positive on *opiate screening tests.*

INTERACTIONS Drug: Ofloxacin absorption decreased when it is administered with MAGNESIUM- or ALUMINUM-CONTAINING ANTACIDS. Other CATIONS, including **calcium, iron,** and **zinc,** also appear to interfere with ofloxacin absorption. May have additive effect with ANTIDIABETICS.

PHARMACOKINETICS Absorption: 90–98% from GI tract. **Peak:** 1–2 h. **Distribution:** Distributes to most tissues; 50% crosses into CSF with inflamed meninges; 20–32% protein bound; crosses placenta; distributed into breast milk. **Metabolism:** Slightly in liver. **Elimination:** 72–98% in urine within 48 h. **Half-Life:** 5–7.5 h.

CLINICAL IMPLICATIONS
Assessment & Drug Effects
- Lab tests: Do C&S tests prior to initial dose. Treatment may be implemented pending results.
- Determine history of hypersensitivity reactions to quinolones or other drugs before therapy is started.
- Withhold ofloxacin and notify physician at first sign of tendon pain, a skin rash, or other allergic reaction.
- Monitor for seizures, especially in patients with known or suspected CNS disorders. Discontinue ofloxacin and notify physician immediately if seizure occurs.
- Assess for signs and symptoms of superinfection (see Appendix F).

Patient & Family Education
- Drink fluids liberally unless contraindicated.
- Be aware that dizziness or lightheadedness may occur; use appropriate caution.
- Avoid excessive sunlight or artificial ultraviolet light because of the possibility of phototoxicity.

OLANZAPINE

(o-lan′za-peen)
Zyprexa, Zyprexa Zydis
Classifications: PSYCHOTHERAPEUTIC AGENT; ANTIPSYCHOTIC AGENT; ATYPICAL; SELECTIVE SEROTONIN REUPTAKE INHIBITOR; DOPAMINE-REUPTAKE INHIBITOR
Therapeutic: ANTIPSYCHOTIC, ATYPICAL
Prototype: Clozapine
Pregnancy Category: C

AVAILABILITY 2.5 mg, 5 mg, 7.5 mg, 10 mg, 15 mg tablets; 10 mg, 15 mg, 20 mg orally disintegrating tablets; 10 mg powder for injection

ACTION & *THERAPEUTIC EFFECT*
Antipsychotic activity is thought to be due to antagonism for both serotonin $5HT_{2A/2C}$ and dopamine D_{1-4} receptors. May inhibit the CNS presynaptic neuronal reuptake of serotonin and dopamine. Antagonism of alpha-adrenergic receptors results in the adverse effect of orthostatic hypotension. *Effective antipsychotic activity.*

USES Management of psychotic disorders, treatment of bipolar disorder, acute agitation (IM).
UNLABELED USES Alzheimer's dementia.

CONTRAINDICATIONS Hypersensitivity to olanzapine; abrupt discontinuation, coma, severe CNS depression, subcutaneous or intramuscular injection of olanzapine; tardive dyskinesia; infants, pregnancy (category C), lactation.

CAUTIOUS USE Known cardiovascular disease, neurological disease, stroke, cerebrovascular disease, Parkinson disease, dementia; history of seizures, conditions that predispose to hypotension (i.e., dehydration, hypovolemia); history of syncope; history of breast cancer; Japanese; diabetes mellitus; prostatic hypertrophy; closed-angle glaucoma; paralytic ileus; urinary retention; hepatic or renal impairment, concurrent use of hepatotoxic drugs, jaundice; predisposition to aspiration pneumonia; may increase risk of stroke in elderly patients with dementia; history of or high risk for suicide. Safety and effectiveness in children and adolescents are not established.

ROUTE & DOSAGE

Psychotic Disorders

Adult: **PO** Start with 5–10 mg once/d, may increase by 2.5–5 mg q wk until desired response (usual range 10–15 mg/d, max: 20 mg/d)
Geriatric: **PO** Start with 5 mg once/d

Bipolar Mania

Adult: **PO** Start with 10–15 mg once/d, may increase by 5 mg q24h if needed

Acute Agitation

Adult: **IM** 10 mg, do not repeat more frequently than q2h (max: 30 mg/24h)
Geriatric: **IM** 2.5–5 mg once

ADMINISTRATION

Oral

- Do not push orally disintegrating tablet through blister foil. Peel foil back and remove tablet. Tablet will disintegrate with/without liquid.

ADVERSE EFFECTS (≥1%) **Body as a Whole:** *Weight gain,* fever, back and chest pain, peripheral and lower extremity edema, joint pain, twitching, premenstrual syndrome. **CNS:** *Somnolence, dizziness, headache, agitation, insomnia, nervousness, hostility,* anxiety, personality disorder, akathisia, hypertonia, tremor amnesia, euphoria, stuttering, extrapyramidal symptoms (dystonic events, *parkinsonism, akathisia*), tardive dyskinesia. **CV:** Postural hypotension, hypotension, tachycardia. **Special Senses:** Amblyopia, blepharitis. **GI:** Abdominal pain, constipation, dry mouth, increased appetite, increased salivation, nausea, vomiting, elevated liver function tests. **Metabolic:** Hyperglycemia, diabetes mellitus. **Urogenital:** Premenstrual syndrome, hematuria, urinary incontinence, metrorrhagia. **Respiratory:** Rhinitis, cough, pharyngitis, dyspnea. **Skin:** Rash.

INTERACTIONS Drug: May enhance hypotensive effects of ANTIHYPERTENSIVES. May enhance effects of other CNS ACTIVE DRUGS, **alcohol. Carbamazepine, omeprazole, rifampin** may increase metabolism and clearance of olanzapine. **Fluvoxamine** may inhibit metabolism and clearance of olanzapine.

PHARMACOKINETICS Absorption: Rapidly from GI tract; 60% reaches systemic circulation. **Onset:** 15 min IM. **Peak:** 6 h. **Distribution:** 93% protein bound, secreted into breast milk of animals (human secretion unknown). **Metabolism:** In liver (CYP1A2). **Elimination:** Approximately 57% in urine, 30% in feces. **Half-Life:** 21–54 h.

CLINICAL IMPLICATIONS

Assessment & Drug Effects

- Monitor diabetics for loss of glycemic control.
- Withdraw drug and immediately report S&S of neuroleptic malignant syndrome (see Appendix F); assess for and report S&S of tardive dyskinesia (see Appendix F).
- Lab tests: Periodically monitor ALT, especially in those with hepatic dysfunction or being treated with other potentially hepatotoxic drugs. Periodic blood glucose monitoring.
- Monitor BP and HR periodically. Monitor temperature, especially under conditions such as strenuous exercise, extreme heat, or treatment with other anticholinergic drugs.
- Monitor for seizures, especially in older adults and cognitively impaired persons.

Patient & Family Education

- Carefully monitor blood glucose levels if diabetic.
- Do not drive or engage in potentially hazardous activities until response to drug is known; drug increases risk of orthostatic hypotension and cognitive impairment.
- Learn common adverse effects and possible drug interactions.
- Avoid alcohol and do not take additional medications without informing physician.
- Do not become overheated; avoid conditions leading to dehydration.

OLMESARTAN MEDOXOMIL

(ol-me-sar'tan)

Benicar

Classifications: ANGIOTENSIN II RECEPTOR (ACE) ANTAGONIST; ANTIHYPERTENSIVE

Therapeutic: ANTIHYPERTENSIVE; ACE INHIBITOR

Prototype: Losartan
Pregnancy Category: C first trimester; D second and third trimester

AVAILABILITY 5 mg, 20 mg, 40 mg tablets

ACTION & *THERAPEUTIC EFFECT*

Angiotensin II receptor (type AT_1) antagonist acts as a potent vasodilator and primary vasoactive hormone of the renin-angiotensin-aldosterone system. Selectively blocks the binding of angiotensin II to the AT_1 receptors found in many tissues (e.g., vascular smooth muscle, adrenal glands). Antihypertensive effect results from blocking the vasoconstricting and aldosterone-secreting effects of angiotensin II. *Antihypertensive effect is due to its potent vasodilation effect.*

USES Treatment of hypertension.

CONTRAINDICATIONS Hypersensitivity to pimecrolimus or components in the cream; Netherton's syndrome; application to active cutaneous viral infection; pregnancy (category C first trimester, and category D in second and third trimester); lactation, children.

CAUTIOUS USE Renal artery stenosis; heart failure; severe renal impairment; hypovolemia.

ROUTE & DOSAGE

Hypertension

Adult: **PO** 20 mg q.d., may increase to 40 mg q.d. Start with 5–10 mg q.d. if volume depleted

ADMINISTRATION

Oral

- Determine if patient is volume depleted (e.g., patients treated with

Common adverse effects in *italic*, life-threatening effects <u>underlined</u>; generic names in **bold**; classifications in SMALL CAPS; ◆ Canadian drug name; ◉ Prototype drug

1107

diuretics) prior to first administration of drug. If volume depletion is suspected, a lower starting dose is recommended.

▪ Store at 20°–25° C (68°–77° F).

ADVERSE EFFECTS (≥1%) **Body as a Whole:** Back pain, flu-like symptoms. **CNS:** Headache. **CV:** Hypotension (especially if dehydrated). **GI:** Diarrhea. **Metabolic:** Increased CPK, hyperglycemia, hypertriglyceridemia. **Respiratory:** Bronchitis, pharyngitis, rhinitis, sinusitis, upper respiratory infection. **Urogenital:** Hematuria.

INTERACTIONS Drug: May increase hypotensive effect of other ANTIHYPERTENSIVES; may cause hyperkalemia with POTASSIUM-SPARING DIURETICS, POTASSIUM SUPPLEMENTS; increase risk of **lithium** toxicity. **Herbal: Ephedra, ma-huang** may antagonize antihypertensive effects.

PHARMACOKINETICS Absorption: Rapidly absorbed, 26% reaches systemic circulation. **Peak:** 1–2 h. **Distribution:** 99% protein bound. **Metabolism:** Not metabolized by CYP 450 system. **Elimination:** 50% in urine, 50% in feces. **Half-Life:** 13 h.

CLINICAL IMPLICATIONS
Assessment & Drug Effects
▪ Monitor closely any volume-depleted patient following initial drug doses. If serious hypotension occurs, place patient in supine position and notify physician immediately.
▪ Monitor BP and HR at drug trough (prior to a scheduled dose). Report hypotension or bradycardia.
▪ Monitor drug effectiveness, especially in African-Americans, when olmesartan is used as monotherapy.

▪ Lab tests: Monitor baseline and periodic renal functions; monitor CBC, electrolytes, and liver function with long-term therapy.

Patient & Family Education
▪ Discontinue drug and notify physician if you experience swelling of the face, tongue, or throat, or if you believe you are pregnant.
▪ Notify physician of symptoms of hypotension (e.g., dizziness, fainting).

OLOPATADINE HYDROCHLORIDE

(o-lo-pa'ta-deen)
Patanol
Pregnancy Category: C
See Appendix A-1.

OLSALAZINE SODIUM

(ol-sal'a-zeen)
Dipentum
Classifications: MUCOUS MEMBRANE; ANTIINFLAMMATORY AGENT
Therapeutic: ANTIINFLAMMATORY; GI
Prototype: Mesalamine
Pregnancy Category: C

AVAILABILITY 250 mg capsules

ACTION & *THERAPEUTIC EFFECT*
Converted to 5-aminosalicylic acid (5-ASA) by colonic bacteria. The 5-ASA is absorbed slowly, resulting in a very high local concentration in the colon. 5-ASA inhibits prostaglandin production in the colon, thus leading to anti-inflammatory properties of the drug. *5-ASA has antiinflammatory activity in ulcerative colitis.*

USES Maintenance therapy in patients with ulcerative colitis.
UNLABELED USES Acute flare-up of ulcerative colitis.

CONTRAINDICATIONS Hypersensitivity to salicylates or 5-ASA; pregnancy (category C).
CAUTIOUS USE Patients with preexisting kidney disease; lactation. Safety and effectiveness in children are not established.

ROUTE & DOSAGE

Ulcerative Colitis
Adult: **PO** 500 mg b.i.d., may increase up to 1.5–3 g/d in 2–4 divided doses

ADMINISTRATION

Oral
- Give with food in two evenly divided doses.

ADVERSE EFFECTS (≥1%) **CNS:** Headache. **GI:** *Diarrhea,* nausea, abdominal pain, indigestion, vomiting, bloating. **Skin:** Rash. **Body as a Whole:** Arthralgia.

PHARMACOKINETICS Absorption: 1–3% from GI tract; high colonic concentrations are associated with efficacy. **Metabolism:** Olsalazine, a prodrug, is composed of 2 molecules of 5-ASA; colonic bacterial azo-reductases break the azo bond, releasing 2 active molecules of 5-ASA. **Elimination:** Primarily in feces as 5-ASA. **Half-Life:** At least 6 h.

CLINICAL IMPLICATIONS

Assessment & Drug Effects
- Monitor kidney function in patients with preexisting renal disease.
- Monitor for S&S of a hypersensitivity reaction (see Appendix F). Withhold olsalazine and notify physician at first sign of an allergic response.

Patient & Family Education
- Report diarrhea, a possible adverse effect, to the physician.

OMALIZUMAB

(o-mal-i-zoo′mab)
Xolair
Classifications: BIOLOGIC RESPONSE MODIFIER; MONOCLONAL ANTIBODY; RESPIRATORY ANTIINFLAMMATORY AGENT
Therapeutic: ANTIALLERGIC; ANTIASTHMATIC; ANTIINFLAMMATORY
Pregnancy Category: B

AVAILABILITY 75 mg, 150 mg vial

ACTION & *THERAPEUTIC EFFECT*
DNA recombinant monoclonal antibody that selectively binds to human IgE. It inhibits binding of IgE to high-affinity IgE receptors on the surface of mast cells and basophils, limiting the release of inflammatory mediators. *Inhibits release of mediators of the allergic response and has an anti-inflammatory action on the respiratory system.*

USES Control of moderate to severe allergic asthma.
UNLABELED USES Seasonal allergic rhinitis, food allergies.

CONTRAINDICATIONS Hypersensitivity to omalizumab; severe infections, including chicken pox and other viral infections; acute bronchospasm, status asthmaticus; malignancies; children <12 y.
CAUTIOUS USE Pregnancy (category B), lactation.

ROUTE & DOSAGE

Allergic Asthma
Adult/Adolescent: **SC** 150–375 mg q2–4wk. Dose is based on baseline IgE serum levels.

Common adverse effects in *italic*, life-threatening effects <u>underlined</u>; generic names in **bold**; classifications in SMALL CAPS; ♦ Canadian drug name; ⊘ Prototype drug

ADMINISTRATION

Subcutaneous

- Reconstitute as follows: 1) Draw 1.4 mL of sterile water for injection into a 3-cc syringe with a 1-inch, 18-gauge needle. 2) Place vial upright on flat surface and inject sterile water. Keep vial upright and gently swirl for about 1 min to wet powder. Do not shake. 3) Gently swirl vial for 5–10 sec q5min to dissolve remaining solids. Some vials may take >20 min to dissolve. Do not use if not completely dissolved by 40 min. 4) Once dissolved, invert vial for 15 sec to allow solution to drain toward stopper. 5) Using a new 3-cc syringe with a 1-inch, 18-gauge needle, insert needle into inverted vial with tip at the very bottom of solution, then withdraw solution. Before removing needle from vial, pull the plunger to end of syringe barrel to remove all solution from inverted vial. 6) Replace 18-gauge needle with a 25-gauge needle for SC injection. 7) Expel air, large bubbles, and any excess solution to obtain the required 1.2 mL dose. A thin layer of small bubbles may remain at top of the solution in syringe.
- Give SC and rotate injection sites. Solution is viscous and takes 5–10 sec to inject.
- Use within 8 h of reconstitution when stored in the vial at 2°–8° C (36°–46° F), or within 4 h of reconstitution when stored at room temperature.

ADVERSE EFFECTS (≥1%) **Body as a Whole:** Anaphylaxis/anaphylactoid reactions, *injection site reactions (bruising, erythema, warmth, burning, stinging, pruritus, hive formation, pain, induration, inflammation)*, fatigue, generalized pain. **CNS:** Headache, dizziness. **GI:** *Nausea, vomiting, diarrhea, abdominal pain.* **Hematologic:** Epistaxis, menorrhagia, hematoma, anemia. **Musculoskeletal:** Arthralgia. **Respiratory:** Upper respiratory tract infections, sinusitis, pharyngitis. **Skin:** Rash, pruritus, urticaria, dermatitis. **Special Senses:** Earache.

PHARMACOKINETICS Absorption: Slowly absorbed from SC site; 53–71% reaches systemic circulation. **Peak:** 7–8 d. **Half-Life:** 22 d.

CLINICAL IMPLICATIONS

Assessment & Drug Effects

- Monitor for injection site reactions including bruising, redness, warmth, burning, stinging, itching, hive formation, pain, indurations, mass, and inflammation.
- Lab test: Platelet counts if signs of increased tendency to bleed appear.

Patient & Family Education

- Do not use this drug for relief of acute bronchospasm or status asthmaticus.
- Promptly report any of the following: bleeding or unusual bruising, difficulty breathing or shortness of breath, skin rash or hives.
- Do not accept a live virus vaccine without consulting physician.

OMEGA-3 FATTY ACIDS (EICOSAPENTAENOIC ACID AND DOCOSAHEXAENOIC ACID) EPA & DHA

(o-me′ga-3)

Dr. Sears OmegaRx, Eskimo-3, Fish Oil, Omega-3 Fatty Acids, ICAR Prenatal Essential Omega-3, Mega Twin EPA, Natrol DHA Neuromins, Natrol Omega-3, Natural Fish Oil, Oleomed Heart, Omacor, Omega-3 Fish Oil Concentrate, Sea Omega, ZonePerfect Omega 3

Classifications: NUTRITIONAL SUPPLEMENT; OMEGA-3 FATTY ACIDS
Therapeutic: OMEGA-3 FATTY ACIDS
Pregnancy Category: C

AVAILABILITY 100 mg, 200 mg, 300 mg, 360 mg, 375 mg, 500 mg, 517 mg, 840 mg, 1000 mg, 1760 mg capsules; 900 mg/5 mL and 1800 mg/5 mL oil for oral ingestion.

ACTION & *THERAPEUTIC EFFECT* The mechanism of action of omega-3-acid ethyl esters is not completely understood. Potential mechanisms of action include inhibition of acetyl-CoA and increased peroxisomal beta-oxidation in the liver. *Triglyceride lowering is the most consistent effect observed.*

USES Adjunct to diet to reduce hypertriglyceridemia.
UNLABELED USES Adjunct nutritional supplementation for hypertriglyceridemia, rheumatoid arthritis, or for the general purpose of maintaining a healthy heart.

CONTRAINDICATIONS Hypersensitivity to any component of the medication; pregnancy (category C); infants.
CAUTIOUS USE Known sensitivity or allergy to fish; concurrent use of anticoagulants or thrombolytics; lactation.

ROUTE & DOSAGE

Hypertriglyceridemia
Adult: **PO** 4 g b.i.d. or qd

ADMINISTRATION
Oral
▪ The daily dose may be given as one dose or divided b.i.d.
▪ Store 15°–30° C (59°–86° F).

ADVERSE EFFECTS (≥1%) **Body as a Whole:** Back pain, flu syndrome, unspecified pain. **GI:** Diarrhea, dyspepsia, eructation, nausea, vomiting. **Metabolic/Nutritional:** Increased total cholesterol and/or LDL levels, weight gain. **Skin:** Rash. **Special Senses:** Halitosis, taste disturbances.

INTERACTIONS Drug: ANTICOAGULANTS and THROMBOLYTICS are affected by inhibition of platelet aggregation with omega-3 fatty acids.

PHARMACOKINETICS Metabolism: Extensive liver metabolism.

CLINICAL IMPLICATIONS
Assessment & Drug Effects
▪ Monitor for S&S of hypersensitivity in those with known allergy to fish.
▪ Monitor diabetics for loss of glycemic control.
▪ Lab tests: Baseline and periodic lipid profile.
▪ Note: Poor therapeutic response after 2 mo is an indication to discontinue drug.
▪ Monitor blood levels of anticoagulants with concurrent therapy.

Patient & Family Education
▪ Do not take omega-3 fatty acids without consulting physician if you have a chronic medical disorder.

OMEPRAZOLE ℞

(o-me′pra-zole)
Losec ♦, Prilosec, Prilosec OTC, Zegerid
Classifications: PROTON PUMP INHIBITOR
Therapeutic: ANTIULCER; PROTON PUMP INHIBITOR
Pregnancy Category: C

AVAILABILITY 10 mg, 20 mg, 40 mg capsules; 20 mg powder for oral suspension

Common adverse effects in *italic*, life-threatening effects <u>underlined</u>; generic names in **bold**; classifications in SMALL CAPS; ♦ Canadian drug name; ℗ Prototype drug

1111

ACTION & *THERAPEUTIC EFFECT*
An antisecretory compound that is a gastric acid pump inhibitor. Suppresses gastric acid secretion by inhibiting the H^+, K^+-ATPase enzyme system [the acid (proton H^+) pump] in the parietal cells. *Suppresses gastric acid secretion relieving gastrointestinal distress and promoting ulcer healing.*

USES Duodenal and gastric ulcer. Gastroesophageal reflux disease including severe erosive esophagitis (4 to 8 wk treatment). Long-term treatment of pathologic hypersecretory conditions such as Zollinger-Ellison syndrome, multiple endocrine adenomas, and systemic mastocytosis. In combination with clarithromycin to treat duodenal ulcers associated with *Helicobacter pylori*.
UNLABELED USES Healing or prevention of NSAID-related ulcers.

CONTRAINDICATIONS Long-term use for gastroesophageal reflux disease (GERD), duodenal ulcers; proton pump inhibitors (PPIs), hypersensitivity; children <2 y; use of OTC formulation in children <18 y or GI bleeding; use of Zegerid in metabolic alkalosis, hypocalcemia, vomiting, GI bleeding; pregnancy (category C); lactation.
CAUTIOUS USE Dysphagia; metabolic or respiratory alkalosis; hepatic disease.

ROUTE & DOSAGE

> **Gastroesophageal Reflux, Erosive Esophagitis, Duodenal Ulcer**
> *Adult:* **PO** 20 mg once/d for 4–8 wk
>
> **Gastric Ulcer**
> *Adult:* **PO** 20 mg b.i.d. for 4–8 wk

> **Hypersecretory Disease**
> *Adult:* **PO** 60 mg once/d up to 120 mg t.i.d.
>
> **Duodenal Ulcer Associated with *H. pylori***
> *Adult:* **PO** 40 mg once/d for 14 d, then 20 mg/d for 14 d, in combination with clarithromycin 500 mg t.i.d. for 14 d

ADMINISTRATION
Oral
- Give before food, preferably breakfast; capsules must be swallowed whole (do not open, chew, or crush).
- Note: Antacids may be administered with omeprazole.

ADVERSE EFFECTS (≥1%) **CNS:** Headache, dizziness, fatigue. **GI:** Diarrhea, abdominal pain, nausea, mild transient increases in liver function tests. **Urogenital:** Hematuria, proteinuria. **Skin:** Rash.

DIAGNOSTIC TEST INTERFERENCE Omeprazole has been reported to significantly impair peak **cortisol** response to exogenous ACTH. This finding is undergoing further investigation.

INTERACTIONS Drug: Concomitant administration of **diazepam** and omeprazole may increase diazepam concentrations. Concomitant administration of **phenytoin** and omeprazole may increase **phenytoin** levels. Concomitant administration of **warfarin** and omeprazole may increase **warfarin** levels. **Herbal: Ginkgo, St. John's wort** may decrease plasma concentrations.

PHARMACOKINETICS Absorption: Poorly from GI tract; 30–40% reaches systemic circulation. **Onset:** 0.5–3.5 h. **Peak:** Peak inhibition of gastric acid secretion: 5 d. **Metabolism:** In liver. **Elimination:** 80% in urine, 20% in feces. **Half-Life:** 0.5–1.5 h.

CLINICAL IMPLICATIONS

Assessment & Drug Effects

- Lab tests: Monitor urinalysis for hematuria and proteinuria. Periodic liver function tests with prolonged use.

Patient & Family Education

- Report any changes in urinary elimination such as pain or discomfort associated with urination, or blood in urine.
- Report severe diarrhea; drug may need to be discontinued.

ONDANSETRON HYDROCHLORIDE ⊕

(on-dan'si-tron)
Zofran, Zofran ODT
Classifications: ANTIEMETIC; 5-HT₃ ANTAGONIST
Therapeutic: ANTIEMETIC; SEROTONIN (HT₃) ANTAGONIST
Pregnancy Category: B

AVAILABILITY 4 mg, 8 mg, 16 mg, 24 mg tablets; 4 mg, 8 mg orally disintegrating tablets; 4 mg/5 mL oral solution; 2 mg/mL, 8 mg/50 mL, 32 mg/50 mL injection

ACTION & *THERAPEUTIC EFFECT*

Selective serotonin (5-HT₃) receptor antagonist. Serotonin receptors are located centrally in the chemoreceptor trigger zone (CTZ) and peripherally on the vagal nerve terminals. Serotonin is released from the wall of the small intestine and stimulates the vagal efferent nerves through the serotonin receptors and initiates the vomiting reflex. *Prevents nausea and vomiting associated with cancer chemotherapy and anesthesia.*

USES Prevention of nausea and vomiting associated with initial and repeated courses of cancer chemotherapy, including high-dose cisplatin; postoperative nausea and vomiting.

UNLABELED USES Treatment of hyperemesis gravidarum

CONTRAINDICATIONS Hypersensitivity to ondansetron; children <4 y (PO route).

CAUTIOUS USE Hepatic disease; QT prolongation; PKU; pregnancy (category B), lactation.

ROUTE & DOSAGE

Prevention of Chemotherapy-Induced Nausea and Vomiting

Adult: **PO** 8–24 mg 30 min before chemotherapy, then q8h times 2 more doses **IV** 32 mg or three 0.15 mg/kg doses starting 30 min before chemotherapy, then 4 and 8 h after
Adult/Child: **IV** 6 mo–18 y, 0.15 mg/kg infused over 15 min beginning 30 min before start of chemotherapy, then 4 and 8 h after first dose of ondansetron
Child: **PO** >4 y, 4 mg 30 min before chemotherapy, then q8h times 2 more doses

Nausea & Vomiting with Highly Emetogenic Chemotherapy

Adult: **PO** Single 24 mg dose 30 min before administration of single-day highly emetogenic chemotherapy

Postoperative Nausea and Vomiting

Adult: **PO** 8–16 mg 1 h preoperatively **IM/IV** 4 mg injected immediately prior to anesthesia induction or once postoperatively if patient experiences nausea/vomiting shortly after surgery

---

Common adverse effects in *italic*, life-threatening effects <u>underlined</u>; generic names in **bold**; classifications in SMALL CAPS; ♣ Canadian drug name; ⊕ Prototype drug

1113

Child: **IV** 1 mo–12 y, <40 kg, 0.1 mg/kg 1 mo–12 y, >40 kg, 4 mg dose

Hepatic Impairment

Child-Pugh class C: Maximum dose 8 mg/d

ADMINISTRATION

Oral

- Give tablets 30 min prior to chemotherapy and 1–2 h prior to radiation therapy.
- Do NOT push orally disintegrating tablet through blister foil. Peel foil back and remove tablet. Tablets will disintegrate with/without liquid.

Intravenous

PREPARE: Direct: May be given undiluted. **IV Infusion:** Dilute a single does in 50 mL of D5W or NS. May be further diluted in selected IV solution.

ADMINISTER: Direct: Give over at least 30 sec, 2–5 min preferred. **IV Infusion:** Give over 15 min. When three separate doses are administered, infuse each over 15 min.

INCOMPATIBILITIES Solution/additive: Meropenem. Y-site: Acyclovir, allopurinol, aminophylline, amphotericin B, amphotericin B cholesteryl, ampicillin, ampicillin/sulbactam, amsacrine, cefepime, cefoperazone, fluorouracil, furosemide, ganciclovir, lorazepam, meropenem, methylprednisolone, piperacillin, sargramostim, sodium bicarbonate, TPN.

ADVERSE EFFECTS (≥1%) **CNS:** Dizziness and light-headedness, _headache, sedation_. **GI:** _Diarrhea_, constipation, dry mouth, transient in-creases in liver aminotransferases and bilirubin. **Body as a Whole:** Hypersensitivity reactions.

INTERACTIONS Drug: Rifampin may decrease ondansetron levels.

PHARMACOKINETICS Peak: 1–1.5 h. **Metabolism:** In liver (CYP3A4). **Elimination:** 44–60% in urine within 24 h; ~25% in feces. **Half-Life:** 3 h.

CLINICAL IMPLICATIONS

Assessment & Drug Effects

- Monitor fluid and electrolyte status. Diarrhea, which may cause fluid and electrolyte imbalance, is a potential adverse effect of the drug.
- Monitor cardiovascular status, especially in patients with a history of coronary artery disease. Rare cases of tachycardia and angina have been reported.

Patient & Family Education

- Be aware that headache requiring an analgesic for relief is a common adverse effect.

OPIUM, POWDERED OPIUM TINCTURE (LAUDANUM)

(oh'pee-um)

Deodorized Opium Tincture

Classifications: NARCOTIC (OPIATE) AGONIST; NARCOTIC ANALGESIC; ANTIDIARRHEAL

Therapeutic: NARCOTIC ANALGESIC; ANTIDIARRHEAL

Prototype: Morphine

Pregnancy Category: C

Controlled Substance: Schedule II

AVAILABILITY 10%, 2 mg/5 mL liquid

ACTION & THERAPEUTIC EFFECT Is obtained from the unripe capsules of _Papaver somniferum_ or _Papaver_

album and contains several natural alkaloids including morphine, codeine, papaverine. Antidiarrheal due to inhibition of GI motility and propulsion; leads to prolonged transit of intestinal contents, desiccation of feces, and constipation. *Antidiarrheal activity due to inhibition of GI motility.*

USES Symptomatic treatment of acute diarrhea and to treat severe withdrawal symptoms in neonates born to women addicted to opiates.

CONTRAINDICATIONS Diarrhea caused by poisoning (until poison is completely eliminated); pregnancy (category C).
CAUTIOUS USE History of opiate agonist dependence; asthma; severe prostatic hypertrophy; hepatic disease; lactation.

ROUTE & DOSAGE

Acute Diarrhea
Adult: **PO** 0.6 mL q.i.d. up to 1 mL q.i.d. (max: 6 mL/d)
Child: **PO** 0.005–0.01 mL/kg q3–4h (max: 6 doses/24 h)

Neonatal Withdrawal
Child: **PO** make a 1:25 aqueous dilution, then give 3–6 drops q3–6h as needed or 0.2 mL q3h, may increase by 0.05 mL q3h until withdrawal symptoms are controlled, then gradually decrease dose after withdrawal symptoms have stabilized

ADMINISTRATION

Oral
- Do not confuse this preparation with camphorated opium tincture (paregoric), which contains only 2 mg anhydrous morphine/5 mL, thus requiring a higher dose volume than that required for therapeutic dose of Deodorized Opium Tincture.
- Give drug diluted with about one third glass of water to ensure passage of entire dose into stomach.
- Store in tight, light-resistant containers.

ADVERSE EFFECTS (≥1%) **GI:** Nausea and other GI disturbances. **CNS:** Depression of CNS.

INTERACTIONS Drug: Alcohol and other CNS DEPRESSANTS add to CNS effects.

PHARMACOKINETICS Absorption: Variable absorption from GI tract. **Distribution:** Crosses placenta; distributed into breast milk. **Metabolism:** In liver. **Elimination:** In urine.

CLINICAL IMPLICATIONS

Assessment & Drug Effects
- Withhold medication and report to physician if respirations are 12/min or below or have changed in character and rate.
- Discontinue as soon as diarrhea is controlled; note character and frequency of stools.
- Offer small amounts of fluid frequently but attempt to maintain 3000–4000 mL fluid total in 24 h.
- Monitor body weight, I&O ratio and pattern, and temperature. If patient develops fever of 38.8° C (102° F) or above, electrolyte and hydration levels may need to be evaluated. Consult physician.

Patient & Family Education
- Be aware that constipation may be a consequence of antidiarrheal therapy but that normal habit pattern usually is reestablished with resumption of normal dietary intake.
- Note: Addiction is possible with prolonged use or with drug abuse.

Common adverse effects in *italic*, life-threatening effects <u>underlined</u>; generic names in **bold**; classifications in SMALL CAPS; ♣ Canadian drug name; ⊙ Prototype drug

1115

OPRELVEKIN

(o-prel′ve-kin)
Neumega
Classifications: BLOOD FORMER;
HEMATOPOIETIC GROWTH FACTOR
Therapeutic: HEMATOPOIETIC
GROWTH FACTOR
Prototype: Epoetin alfa
Pregnancy Category: C

AVAILABILITY 5 mg injection

ACTION & *THERAPEUTIC EFFECT*

Hematopoietic growth factor (interleukin-11) that is produced by recombinant DNA. *Indicated by return of postnadir platelet count toward normal (≥50,000). Increases platelet count in a dose-dependent manner.*

USES Prevention of severe thrombocytopenia following myelosuppressive chemotherapy (not effective after myeloablative chemotherapy).

CONTRAINDICATIONS Hypersensitivity to oprelvekin; myeloablative chemotherapy; myeloid malignancies; pregnancy (category C).
CAUTIOUS USE Patients with left ventricular dysfunction, cardiac disease, CHF, history of atrial arrhythmias, or other arrhythmias; electrolyte imbalance, hypokalemia; respiratory disease; papilledema; thromboembolic disorders; older adults; cerebrovascular disease, stroke, TIAs; pleural effusion, pericardial effusion, ascites; increased intracranial pressure, brain tumor, visual disturbances; hepatic or renal dysfunction; lactation.

ROUTE & DOSAGE

Thrombocytopenia
Adult: **SC** 50 mcg/kg once daily starting 6–24 h after completing chemotherapy and continuing until platelet count is ≥50,000 cells/mcL or up to 21 d

Child: **SC** 8 mo–17 y, 75–100 mcg/kg once daily starting 6–24 h after completing chemotherapy and continuing until platelet count is ≥50,000 cells/mcL or up to 21 d

ADMINISTRATION

- Note: Do not use if solution is discolored or if it contains particulate matter.

Subcutaneous

- Reconstitute solution by gently injecting 1 mL of sterile water for injection (without preservative) toward the sides of the vial. Keep needle in vial and gently swirl to dissolve but do not shake solution. Without removing needle, withdraw specified amount of oprelvekin for injection.
- Give as single dose into the abdomen, thigh, hip, or upper arm.
- Discard any unused portion of the vial. It contains no preservatives.
- Use reconstituted solution within 3 h; store at 2°–8° C (36°–46° F) until used.
- Store unopened vials at 2°–8° C (36°–46° F). Do not freeze.

ADVERSE EFFECTS (≥1%) **Body as a Whole:** *Edema, neutropenic fever, fever,* asthenia, pain, chills, myalgia, bone pain, dehydration. **CNS:** *Headache, dizziness, insomnia,* nervousness. **CV:** *Tachycardia,* vasodilation, palpitations, syncope, atrial fibrillation/flutter, peripheral edema, capillary leak syndrome. **GI:** *Nausea, vomiting, mucositis, diarrhea,* oral moniliasis, anorexia, constipation, dyspepsia. **Hematologic:** Ecchymosis. **Respiratory:** *Dyspnea, rhinitis, cough, pharyngitis,* pleural effusion, pulmonary edema, exacerbation of preexisting pleural effusion. **Skin:** Alopecia, *rash,* skin discoloration, exfoliative dermatitis. **Special Senses:** Conjunctival injection, amblyopia.

Common adverse effects in *italic*, life-threatening effects <u>underlined</u>; generic names in **bold**; classifications in SMALL CAPS; ♣ Canadian drug name; ✪ Prototype drug

INTERACTIONS Drug: No clinically significant interactions established.

PHARMACOKINETICS Absorption: 80% from SC injection site. **Onset:** Days 5–9. **Duration:** 7 d after last dose. **Distribution:** Distributes to highly perfused organs. **Elimination:** In urine. **Half-Life:** 6.9 h.

CLINICAL IMPLICATIONS

Assessment & Drug Effects

▪ Lab tests: Monitor platelet counts until adequate recovery; periodically monitor CBC with differential and serum electrolytes.

▪ Monitor carefully for and immediately report S&S of fluid overload, hypokalemia, and cardiac arrhythmias.

▪ Monitor persons with preexisting fluid retention carefully (e.g., CHF, pleural effusion, ascites) for worsening of symptoms.

Patient & Family Education

▪ Review patient information leaflet with special attention to administration directions.

▪ Report any of the following to the physician: Shortness of breath, edema of arms and/or legs, chest pain, unusual fatigue or weakness, irregular heartbeat, blurred vision.

ORLISTAT

(or'li-stat)
Alli, Xenical
Classifications: ANORECTANT; NONSYSTEMIC LIPASE INHIBITOR
Therapeutic: NONSYSTEMIC LIPASE INHIBITOR
Prototype: Diethylpropion
Pregnancy Category: B

AVAILABILITY 60 mg, 120 mg capsules

ACTION & *THERAPEUTIC EFFECT*

Nonsystemic inhibitor of gastrointestinal lipase. Reduces intestinal absorption of dietary fat by forming inactive enzymes with pancreatic and gastric lipase in the GI tract. *Indicated by weight loss/decreased body mass index (BMI). Reduces the intestinal absorption of dietary fat because at least 95% of orlistat is eliminated in the feces; reduces caloric intake in obese individuals.*

USES Weight loss and weight maintenance in patients with BMI ≥30 kg/m^2 or ≥27 kg/m^2 in patients with other risk factors. Reduce risk for weight regain after prior weight loss.

CONTRAINDICATIONS Hypersensitivity to orlistat; malabsorption syndrome; cholestasis; gallbladder disease; hypothyroidism; organic causes of obesity; anorexia nervosa, bulimia nervosa; organic causes of obesity, lactation. Safety and efficacy in children <12 y are not established.

CAUTIOUS USE Gastrointestinal diseases including frequent diarrhea; known dietary deficiencies in fat soluble vitamins (i.e., A, D, E); history of calcium oxalate nephrolithiasis or hyperoxaluria; older adults; pregnancy (category B).

ROUTE & DOSAGE

Weight Loss
Adult/Adolescent: **PO** >16 y, 60–120 mg t.i.d. with each main meal containing fat

ADMINISTRATION

Oral

▪ Give during or up to 1 h after a meal containing fat.
▪ Omit dose with nonfat-containing meal or if meal is skipped.
▪ Store at 15°–30° C (59°–86° F). Keep bottle tightly closed; do **NOT**

Common adverse effects in *italic*, life-threatening effects <u>underlined</u>; generic names in **bold**; classifications in SMALL CAPS; ♣ Canadian drug name; ◎ Prototype drug

1117

use after the printed expiration date.

ADVERSE EFFECTS (≥1%) **Body as a Whole:** Fatigue. **CNS:** *Headache, dizziness,* anxiety. **CV:** Hypertension, stroke. **GI:** *Oily spotting, flatus with discharge, fecal urgency, fatty/oily stool, oily evacuation, increased defecation,* fecal incontinence, *abdominal pain/discomfort,* nausea, infectious diarrhea, rectal pain/discomfort, tooth disorder, gingival disorder, vomiting. **Skin:** Rash. **Urogenital:** Menstrual irregularity.

DIAGNOSTIC TEST INTERFERENCE Monitor PT/INR in patients on chronic stable doses of **warfarin**.

INTERACTIONS Drug: Orlistat may increase absorption of **pravastatin;** may decrease absorption of fat soluble VITAMINS (A, D, E, K).

PHARMACOKINETICS Absorption: Minimal. **Metabolism:** In gastrointestinal wall. **Elimination:** In feces. **Half-Life:** 1–2 h.

CLINICAL IMPLICATIONS

Assessment & Drug Effects
- Monitor weight & BMI; closely monitor diabetics for hypoglycemia.
- Coadministered drugs: Monitor PT/INR with warfarin.
- Monitor BP frequently, especially with preexisting hypertension.

Patient & Family Education
- Take a daily multivitamin containing fat-soluble vitamins at least 2 h before/after orlistat.
- Remember common GI adverse effects typically resolve after 4 wk therapy.
- Avoid high fat meals to minimize adverse GI effects. Distribute fat calories over three main meals daily.

- Monitor weight several times weekly. Diabetics: Monitor blood glucose carefully following any weight loss.

ORPHENADRINE CITRATE

(or-fen'a-dreen)

Norflex

Classifications: SKELETAL MUSCLE RELAXANT, CENTRAL ACTING
Therapeutic: SKELETAL MUSCLE RELAXANT, CENTRAL ACTING
Prototype: Cyclobenzaprine
Pregnancy Category: C

AVAILABILITY 100 mg sustained release tablets; 30 mg/mL injection

ACTION & THERAPEUTIC EFFECT Tertiary amine anticholinergic agent and central-acting skeletal muscle relaxant. Relaxes tense skeletal muscles indirectly, possibly by analgesic action or by atropinelike central action. *Relieves skeletal muscle spasm.*

USES To relieve muscle spasm discomfort associated with acute musculoskeletal conditions.

CONTRAINDICATIONS Narrow-angle glaucoma; pyloric or duodenal obstruction, stenosing peptic ulcers; prostatic hypertrophy or bladder neck obstruction; myasthenia gravis; cardiospasm (megaloesophagus); tachycardia; pregnancy (category C). Safe use in the pediatric age group is not established.
CAUTIOUS USE History of cardiac disease, arrhythmias, coronary insufficiency; renal disease; renal impairment; lactation.

ROUTE & DOSAGE

Muscle Spasm
Adult: **PO** 100 mg b.i.d. **IM/IV** 60 mg, may repeat in 12 h if needed

Common adverse effects in *italic*, life-threatening effects <u>underlined</u>; generic names in **bold**; classifications in SMALL CAPS; ♣ Canadian drug name; ⑫ Prototype drug

ADMINISTRATION

Oral

* Ensure that sustained release form is not chewed or crushed. It must be swallowed whole.

Intravenous

PREPARE: Direct: Give undiluted. Protect from light.
ADMINISTER: Direct: Give at a rate of 60 mg (2 mL) over 5 min.

ADVERSE EFFECTS (≥1%) **CNS:** *Drowsiness,* weakness, headache, dizziness; mild CNS stimulation (high doses: restlessness, anxiety, tremors, confusion, hallucinations, agitation, tachycardia, palpitation, syncope). **Special Senses:** Increased ocular tension, dilated pupils, blurred vision. **GI:** *Dry mouth,* nausea, vomiting, abdominal cramps, constipation. **Urogenital:** *Urinary hesitancy* or *retention.* **Body as a Whole:** Hypersensitivity [pruritus, urticaria, rash, <u>anaphylactic reaction</u> (rare)].

INTERACTIONS Drug: Propoxyphene may cause increased confusion, anxiety, and tremors; may worsen schizophrenic symptoms, or increase risk of tardive dyskinesia with **haloperidol;** additive CNS depressant with ANXIOLYTICS, SEDATIVES, HYPNOTICS, **butorphanol, nalbuphine,** OPIATE AGONISTS, **pentazocine, tramadol. Herbal: Valerian, kava** potentiate sedation.

PHARMACOKINETICS Absorption: Readily from GI tract. **Peak:** 2 h. **Duration:** 4–6 h. **Distribution:** Rapidly distributed in tissues; crosses placenta. **Metabolism:** In liver. **Elimination:** In urine. **Half-Life:** 14 h.

CLINICAL IMPLICATIONS

Assessment & Drug Effects

* Lab tests: Periodic blood, urine, and liver function studies with prolonged therapy.
* Report complaints of mouth dryness, urinary hesitancy or retention, headache, tremors, GI problems, palpitation, or rapid pulse to physician. Dosage reduction or drug withdrawal is indicated.
* Monitor elimination patterns. Older adults are particularly sensitive to anticholinergic effects (urinary hesitancy, constipation); closely observe.
* Monitor therapeutic drug effect. In the patient with parkinsonism, orphenadrine reduces muscular rigidity but has little effect on tremors. Some reduction in excessive salivation and perspiration may occur, and patient may appear mildly euphoric.

Patient & Family Education

* Relieve mouth dryness by frequent rinsing with clear tepid water, increasing noncaloric fluid intake, sugarless gum, or lemon drops. If these measures fail, a saliva substitute may help.
* Do not drive or engage in potentially hazardous activities until response to drug is known.
* Avoid concomitant use of alcohol and other CNS depressants; these may potentiate depressant effects.

OSELTAMIVIR PHOSPHATE

(o-sel′tam-i-vir)
Tamiflu
Classifications: ANTIVIRAL AGENT
Therapeutic: ANTIVIRAL
Pregnancy Category: C

AVAILABILITY 75 mg capsule; 12 mg/mL suspension

Common adverse effects in *italic*, life-threatening effects <u>underlined</u>; generic names in **bold**; classifications in SMALL CAPS; ♣ Canadian drug name; ⊕ Prototype drug

1119

ACTION & *THERAPEUTIC EFFECT*

Inhibits influenza A and B viral neuraminidase enzyme, preventing the release of newly formed virus from the surface of the infected cells. Inhibits replication of the influenza A and B virus. *Effectiveness indicated by relief of flu symptoms. Prevents viral spread across the mucous lining of the respiratory tract.*

USES Treatment of uncomplicated acute influenza in adults symptomatic for no more than 2 d.

CONTRAINDICATIONS Hypersensitivity to oseltamivir; pregnancy (category C); infants less than 1 y or neonates. Safety in hepatic disease has not been established.

CAUTIOUS USE Renal impairment; lactation. Safety and efficacy in chronic cardiac/respiratory disease are not established.

ROUTE & DOSAGE

Influenza Treatment

Adult: **PO** 75 mg b.i.d. times 5 d
Child: **PO** 1–12 y, 15 kg, 30 mg b.i.d.; >15–23 kg, 45 mg b.i.d.; >23–40 kg, 60 mg b.i.d.; >40 kg, 75 mg b.i.d. × 5 d

Influenza Prevention

Adult/Child: **PO** >13 y, 75 mg qd × 7 d; begin within 2 d of contact with infected person

Renal Impairment

Cl_{cr} <30 mL/min: 75 mg q.d. times 5 d

ADMINISTRATION

Oral

- Give with food to decrease the risk of GI upset.
- Start within 48 h of onset of flu symptoms.

- Take missed dose as soon as possible unless next dose is due within 2 h.
- Store at 15°–30° C (59°–86° F); protect from moisture, keep dry.

ADVERSE EFFECTS (≥1%) **Body as a Whole:** Fatigue. **CNS:** Dizziness, headache, insomnia, vertigo. **GI:** Nausea, vomiting, diarrhea, abdominal pain. **Respiratory:** Bronchitis, cough.

PHARMACOKINETICS Absorption: Readily absorbed, 75% bioavailable. **Distribution:** 42% protein bound. **Metabolism:** Extensively metabolized to active metabolite oseltamivir carboxylate by liver esterases. **Elimination:** Primarily in urine. **Half-Life:** 1–2 h; oseltamivir carboxylate 6–10 h.

CLINICAL IMPLICATIONS

Assessment & Drug Effects

- Monitor ambulation in frail and older adult patients due to potential for dizziness and vertigo.
- Monitor children for abnormal behavior such as delirium or self-injury.

Patient & Family Education

- Contact your physician regarding the use of this drug in children.

OXACILLIN SODIUM

(ox-a-sill'in)

Bactocill

Classifications: ANTIBIOTIC, PENICILLIN; ANTISTAPHYLOCOCCAL PENICILLIN

Therapeutic: PENICILLIN ANTIBIOTIC
Prototype: Penicillin G
Pregnancy Category: B

AVAILABILITY 250 mg, 500 mg capsules; 250 mg/5 mL suspension; 250 mg, 500 mg, 1 g, 2 g, 4 g injection

ACTION & *THERAPEUTIC EFFECT*

Semisynthetic, acid-stable, penicillinase-resistant isoxazolyl penicillin. Oxacillin inhibits final stage of bacterial cell wall synthesis by preferentially binding to specific penicillin-binding proteins (PBPs) located within the bacterial cell wall. This leads to destruction of the cell wall of the organism. *It is highly active against most penicillinase-producing staphylococci, and is generally ineffective against gram-negative bacteria and methicillin-resistant staphylococci (MRSA).*

USES Primarily, infections caused by penicillinase-producing staphylococci and penicillin-resistant staphylococci. As with other penicillins, serum concentrations are enhanced by concurrent use of probenecid.

CONTRAINDICATIONS Hypersensitivity to penicillins or cephalosporins.

CAUTIOUS USE History of or suspected atopy or allergy (hives, eczema, hay fever, asthma); history of GI disease; hepatic disease; renal disease; premature infants, neonates, lactation (may cause infant diarrhea), pregnancy (category B).

ROUTE & DOSAGE

Staphylococcal Infections

Adult: **PO** 500 mg–1 g q4–6h
IM/IV 250 mg–1 g q4–6h (max: 12 g/d)
Child: **PO** 50–100 mg/kg/d divided q4–6h **IM/IV** 100–200 mg/kg/d divided q4–6h (max: 12 g/d)
Neonate: **IV** 50–100 mg/kg/d divided q6–12h

ADMINISTRATION

Note: The total sodium content (including that contributed by buffer) in each gram of oxacillin is approximately 3.1 mEq or 71 mg.

Oral
- Give with a full glass of water on an empty stomach (either 1 h before meals or 2 h after meals). Food reduces absorption.

Intramuscular
- Reconstitute each 250 mg with 1.4 mL sterile water for injection to yield 250 mg/1.5 mL. Shake vial vigorously until drug is completely dissolved. Discard unused portions after 3 d at room temperature or 7 d under refrigeration.
- Administer deep IM to adults by deep intragluteal injection. Follow agency policy for IM site in young children and infants. Rotate injection sites.

Intravascular
Note: Verify correct IV concentration and rate of infusion/injection with physician before IV administration to neonates, infants, children.

PREPARE: **Direct:** Reconstitute each 500 mg or fraction thereof with 5 mL with sterile water for injection or NS to yield 250 mg/1.5 mL. **Intermittent:** Further dilute in 50–100 mL of D5W, NS, D5/NS, or RL. **Continuous:** Further dilute in up to 1000 mL of compatible IV solutions.

ADMINISTER: **Direct:** Give at a rate of 1 g or fraction thereof over 10 min. **Intermittent:** Give over 15–30 min. **Continuous:** Give over 6 h.

INCOMPATIBILITIES Solution: **additive: Caffeine citrate, cephalothin, cytarabine, erythromycin, hyaluronidase, hydrocortisone, nitrofurantoin, pentobarbital, phenobarbital,** TETRACYCLINES, **warfarin. Y-site: Sodium bicarbonate, verapamil.**

Common adverse effects in *italic*, life-threatening effects <u>underlined</u>; generic names in **bold**; classifications in SMALL CAPS; ♣ Canadian drug name; ⊙ Prototype drug

1121

ADVERSE EFFECTS (≥1%) **Body as a Whole:** Thrombophlebitis (IV therapy), superinfections, wheezing, sneezing, fever, anaphylaxis. **GI:** Nausea, vomiting, flatulence, *diarrhea,* hepatocellular dysfunction (elevated AST, ALT, hepatitis). **Hematologic:** Eosinophilia, leukopenia, thrombocytopenia, granulocytopenia, agranulocytosis; neutropenia (reported in children). **Skin:** Pruritus, rash, urticaria. **Urogenital:** Interstitial nephritis, transient hematuria, albuminuria, azotemia (newborns and infants on high doses).

DIAGNOSTIC TEST INTERFERENCE Oxacillin in large doses can cause false-positive *urine protein tests* using sulfosalicylic acid methods.

PHARMACOKINETICS Absorption: Incompletely and erratically absorbed orally. **Peak:** 30–120 min IM; 15 min IV. **Duration:** 4 h PO; 4–6 h IM. **Distribution:** Distributes into CNS with inflamed meninges; crosses placenta; distributed into breast milk, 90% protein bound. **Metabolism:** Enters enterohepatic circulation. **Elimination:** Primarily in urine, some in bile. **Half-Life:** 0.5–1 h.

CLINICAL IMPLICATIONS

Assessment & Drug Effects

▪ Ask patient prior to first dose about hypersensitivity reactions to penicillins, cephalosporins, and other allergens.

▪ Lab tests: periodic liver functions, CBC with differential, platelet count, and urinalysis.

▪ Hepatic dysfunction (possibly a hypersensitivity reaction) has been associated with IV oxacillin; it is reversible with discontinuation of drug. Symptoms may resemble viral hepatitis or general signs of hypersensitivity and should be reported promptly: hives, rash, fever, nausea, vomiting, abdominal discomfort, anorexia, malaise, jaundice (with dark yellow to brown urine, light-colored or clay-colored stools, pruritus).

▪ Withhold next drug dose and report the onset of hypersensitivity reactions and superinfections (see Appendix F).

Patient & Family Education

▪ Take oral medication around the clock; do not miss a dose. Take all of the medication prescribed even if you feel better, unless otherwise directed by physician.

OXALIPLATIN

(ox-a-li-pla′tin)
Eloxatin
Classifications: ANTINEOPLASTIC; ALKYLATING AGENT
Therapeutic: ANTINEOPLASTIC
Prototype: Cyclophosphamide
Pregnancy Category: D

AVAILABILITY 5 mg/mL injection

ACTION & *THERAPEUTIC EFFECT* Oxaliplatin forms inter- and intrastrand DNA cross-links. These cross-links inhibit DNA replication and transcription. The cytotoxicity of oxaliplatin is cell-cycle nonspecific. *Antitumor activity of oxaliplatin in combination with 5-fluorouracil (5-FU) has antiproliferative activity against colon carcinoma that is greater than either compound alone.*

USES Metastatic cancer of colon and rectum.
UNLABELED USES Non-small cell lung cancer, non-Hodgkin's lymphoma, ovarian cancer.

CONTRAINDICATIONS History of known allergy to oxaliplatin or other platinum compounds; myelosuppression; pregnancy (category D); lactation. Safety and effectiveness in children are not established.

CAUTIOUS USE Renal impairment, because clearance of ultrafilterable platinum is decreased in mild, moderate, and severe renal impairment; older adults; hepatic impairment.

ROUTE & DOSAGE

Metastatic Colon or Rectal Cancer
Adult: **IV** 85 mg/m^2 infused over 120 min once every 2 wk

Renal Impairment
Cl_{cr} <19 mL/min: omit dose or change therapy

ADMINISTRATION

Intravenous

Premedication with an antiemetic is recommended.

PREPARE: **IV Infusion:** NEVER reconstitute with NS or any solution containing chloride. Reconstitute the 50 mg vial or the 100 mg vial by adding 10 mL or 20 mL, respectively, of sterile water for injection or D5W. MUST further dilute in 250–500 mL of D5W for infusion.

ADMINISTER: **IV Infusion:** Do NOT use needles or infusion sets containing aluminum parts. Flush infusion line with D5W before and after administration of any other concomitant medication. Give over 120 min with frequent monitoring of the IV insertion site. Discontinue at the first sign of extravasation and restart IV in a different site.

INCOMPATIBILITIES **Solution/additive:** CHLORIDE-CONTAINING SOLUTIONS, ALKALINE SOLUTIONS, including **sodium bicarbonate, 5-fluorouracil (5-FU)** **Y-site:** ALKALINE SOLUTIONS, including **sodium bicarbonate, 5-fluorouracil (5-FU).**

▪ Store reconstituted solution up to 24 h under refrigeration at 2°–8° C (36°–46° F). After final dilution, the IV solution may be stored for 6 h at room temperature [20°–25° C (68°–77° F)] or up to 24 h under refrigeration.

ADVERSE EFFECTS (≥1%) **Body as a Whole:** *Fever, edema, pain,* allergic reaction, arthralgia, rigors. **CNS:** *Fatigue, neuropathy, headache,* dizziness, insomnia. **CV:** Chest pain. **GI:** *Diarrhea, nausea, vomiting, anorexia, stomatitis, constipation, abdominal pain,* reflux, dyspepsia, taste perversion, mucositis, flatulence. **Hematologic:** *Anemia, leukopenia, thrombocytopenia,* neutropenia, thromboembolism. **Metabolic:** Hypokalemia, dehydration. **Respiratory:** *Dyspnea, cough,* rhinitis, pharyngitis, epistaxis, hiccup. **Skin:** Flushing, rash, alopecia, injection site reaction. **Urogenital:** Dysuria.

INTERACTIONS Drug: AMINOGLYCOSIDES, **amphotericin B, vancomycin,** and other **nephrotoxic drugs** may increase risk of renal failure.

PHARMACOKINETICS Distribution: >90% protein bound. **Metabolism:** Rapid and extensive non-enzymatic biotransformation. **Elimination:** Primarily in urine. **Half-Life:** 391 h.

CLINICAL IMPLICATIONS

Assessment & Drug Effects

▪ Monitor for S&S of hypersensitivity (e.g., rash, urticaria, erythema, pruritis; rarely, bronchospasm and hypotension). Discontinue drug and notify physician if any of these occur.

▪ Monitor insertion site. Extravasation may cause local pain and in-

Common adverse effects in *italic*, life-threatening effects underlined; generic names in **bold**; classifications in SMALL CAPS; ♣ Canadian drug name; ⦿ Prototype drug

1123

flammation that may be severe and lead to complications, including necrosis.

- Monitor for S&S of coagulation disorders including GI bleeding, hematuria, and epistaxis.
- Monitor for S&S of peripheral neuropathy (e.g., paresthesia, dysesthesia, hypoesthesia in the hands, feet, perioral area, or throat, jaw spasm, abnormal tongue sensation, dysarthria, eye pain, and chest pressure). Symptoms may be precipitated or exacerbated by exposure to cold temperature or cold objects.
- Lab tests: Before each administration cycle, monitor WBC count with differential, hemoglobin, platelet count, and blood chemistries (including ALT, AST, bilirubin, and creatinine). Monitor baseline and periodic renal functions.
- Do not apply ice to oral mucous membranes (e.g., mucositis prophylaxis) during the infusion of oxaliplatin as cold temperature can exacerbate acute neurological symptoms.

Patient & Family Education
- Use effective methods of contraception while receiving this drug.
- Avoid cold drinks, use of ice, and cover exposed skin prior to exposure to cold temperature or cold objects.
- Do not drive or engage in potentially hazardous activities until response to drug is known.
- Report any of the following to a health care provider: difficulty writing, buttoning, swallowing, walking; numbness, tingling or other unusual sensations in extremities; non-productive cough or shortness of breath; fever, particularly if associated with persistent diarrhea or other evidence of infection.
- Report promptly S&S of a bleeding disorder such as black tarry stool, coke-colored or frankly bloody urine, bleeding from the nose or mucous membranes.

OXANDROLONE

(ox-an'dro-lone)

Oxandrin

Classifications: HORMONE; ANDRO-GEN/ANABOLIC STEROID

Therapeutic: ANABOLIC STEROID

Prototype: Testosterone

Pregnancy Category: X

Controlled Substance: Schedule III

AVAILABILITY 2.5 mg tablets

ACTION & THERAPEUTIC EFFECT
Synthetic steroid with anabolic and androgenic activity. *Androgenic activity: Responsible for the growth spurt of the adolescent and for growth termination by epiphyseal closure. Increases erythropoiesis, possibly by stimulating production of erythropoietin, and promotes vascularization and darkening of skin. Antagonizes effects of estrogen excess on female breast and endometrium. Anabolic activity: Increases protein metabolism and decreases its catabolism. Large doses suppress spermatogenesis, thereby causing testicular atrophy. Controls development and maintenance of secondary sexual characteristics.*

USES Adjunctive therapy to promote weight gain, offset protein catabolism associated with prolonged administration of corticosteroids, relieve bone pain accompanying osteoporosis.

CONTRAINDICATIONS Hypersensitivity or toxic reactions to androgens; severe cardiac, hepatic, or renal disease; pregnancy (category X), lactation; possibility of virilization of external genitalia of female fetus; polycythemia; hypercalcemia; known or suspected prostatic or breast cancer in males; benign prostatic hypertrophy with obstruction; patients easily stimulated sexually; asthenic males who may react adversely to androgenic overstimulation; conditions aggravated by fluid retention; hypertension.

CAUTIOUS USE Cardiac, hepatic, and mild to moderate renal disease, hypercholesterolemia, heart failure, peripheral edema, arteriosclerosis, coronary artery disease, MI; cholestasis; diabetes mellitus; prostatic hypertrophy; prepubertal males, geriatric patients, acute intermittent porphyria; older adults.

ROUTE & DOSAGE

Weight Gain
Adult: **PO** 2.5 mg b.i.d. to q.i.d. (max: 20 mg/d) for 2–4 wk
Child: **PO** 0.1 mg/kg/d

ADMINISTRATION

Oral
- Individualize doses; great variations in response exist.
- Store at 15°–30° C (59°–86° F).

ADVERSE EFFECTS (≥1%) **CNS:** Habituation, excitation, insomnia, depression, changes in libido. **Urogenital:** *Males:* Phallic enlargement, increased frequency or persistence of erections, inhibition of testicular function, testicular atrophy, oligospermia, impotence, chronic priapism, epididymitis, bladder irritability; *Females:* Clitoral enlargement, menstrual irregularities. **Hepatic:** Cholestatic jaundice with or without hepatic necrosis and death, hepatocellular neoplasms, peliosis hepatitis (long-term use). **Skin:** Hirsutism and male pattern baldness in females,

acne. **Endocrine:** Gynecomastia, deepening of voice in females, premature closure of epiphyses in children, edema, decreased glucose tolerance.

DIAGNOSTIC TEST INTERFERENCE
May decrease levels of thyroxine-binding globulin (decreased total T_4 and increased T_3 RU and free T_4).

INTERACTIONS Drug: May increase INR with **warfarin.** May inhibit metabolism of ORAL HYPOGLYCEMIC AGENTS. Concomitant STEROIDS may increase edema. **Herbal: Echinacea** may increase risk of hepatotoxicity.

PHARMACOKINETICS Half-Life: 10–13 h (increased in elderly patients).

CLINICAL IMPLICATIONS

Assessment & Drug Effects
- Monitor weight closely throughout therapy.
- Assess for and report development of edema or S&S of jaundice (see Appendix F).
- Lab tests: Monitor periodically liver function, lipid profile, Hct and Hgb, PT and INR, serum electrolytes, and CPK.
- Withhold and notify physician if hypercalcemia develops in breast cancer patient.
- Monitor growth in children closely.

Patient & Family Education
- Women: Report signs of virilization, including acne and changes in menstrual periods.
- Men: Report too frequent or prolonged erections or appearance/worsening of acne.
- Report S&S of jaundice (see Appendix F) or edema.
- Monitor blood glucose for loss of glycemic control if diabetic.

Common adverse effects in *italic*, life-threatening effects underlined; generic names in **bold**; classifications in SMALL CAPS; ♣ Canadian drug name; Ⓟ Prototype drug

1125

OXAPROZIN

(ox-a-pro'zin)
Daypro
Classifications: ANALGESIC, NON-STEROIDAL ANTIINFLAMMATORY DRUG (NSAID); ANTIPYRETIC
Therapeutic: NSAID, ANALGESIC; ANTI-RHEUMATIC; ANTIPYRETIC
Prototype: Ibuprofen
Pregnancy Category: C

AVAILABILITY 600 mg tablet

ACTION & *THERAPEUTIC EFFECT*
Long-acting NSAID agent, which is an effective prostaglandin synthetase inhibitor. It inhibits COX-1 and COX-2 enzymes needed for prostaglandin synthesis at the site of inflammation. *Has antiinflammatory, antipyretic, and analgesic properties.*

USES Treatment of osteoarthritis and rheumatoid arthritis.
UNLABELED USES Ankylosing spondylitis, chronic pain, gout, oral surgery pain, temporal arteritis, tendinitis.

CONTRAINDICATIONS Hypersensitivity to oxaprozin or any other NSAID; complete or partial syndrome of nasal polyps; angioedema; CABG perioperative pain; pregnancy (category C) in first and second trimesters, and pregnancy (category D) in third trimester; lactation.
CAUTIOUS USE History of GI bleeding, alcoholism, smoking; history of severe hepatic dysfunction, renal insufficiency; cardiac disease; coagulopathy; photosensitivity; older adults. Safety and effectiveness in children <6 y are not established.

ROUTE & DOSAGE

Osteoarthritis, Rheumatoid Arthritis
Adult: **PO** 600–1200 mg q.d. (max: 1800 mg/d or 25 mg/kg, whichever is lower)

ADMINISTRATION

Oral
- Give with meals or milk to decrease GI distress.
- Divide doses in those unable to tolerate once-daily dosing.
- Use lower starting doses for those with renal or hepatic dysfunction, advanced age, low body weight, or a predisposition to GI ulceration.

ADVERSE EFFECTS (≥1%) **CNS:** Tinnitus, headache, insomnia, somnolence. **GI:** Diarrhea, abdominal pain, nausea, dyspepsia, flatulence, melena, ulcers, constipation, dry mouth, gastritis. **Skin:** Rash, pruritus. **Urogenital:** Dysuria, urinary frequency.

DIAGNOSTIC TEST INTERFERENCE May cause false-positive reactions for BENZODIAZEPINES with *urine drug-screening* tests.

INTERACTIONS Drug: May attenuate the antihypertensive response to DIURETICS. NSAIDs increase the risk of **methotrexate** or **lithium** toxicity. May increase **aspirin** toxicity. **Herbal: Feverfew, garlic, ginger, ginkgo** may increase risk of bleeding.

PHARMACOKINETICS Absorption: Readily from GI tract. **Peak:** 125 min. **Onset:** 1–6 wk for maximum therapeutic effect. **Distribution:** 99% protein bound. Distributes into synovial fluid, crosses placenta. Distributed into breast milk. **Metabolism:** in the liver. **Elimination:** 60% in urine, 30–35% in feces. **Half-Life:** 40 h.

CLINICAL IMPLICATIONS

Assessment & Drug Effects

- Monitor for S&S of GI bleeding, especially in patients with a history of inflammation or ulceration of upper GI tract, or those treated chronically with NSAIDS.
- Monitor patients with CHF for increased fluid retention and edema. Report rapid weight increases accompanied by edema.
- Lab tests: Perform baseline and periodic evaluation of Hgb, kidney and liver function. Auditory and ophthalmologic exams are recommended with prolonged or high-dose therapy.

Patient & Family Education

- Be aware that alcoholism and smoking increase risk of GI ulceration.
- Report immediately dark tarry stools, "coffee ground" or bloody emesis, or other GI distress.
- Avoid aspirin or other NSAIDS without explicit permission of physician.
- Be aware of the possibility of photosensitivity, which results in a rash on sun-exposed skin.
- Report immediately to physician ringing in ears, decreased hearing, or blurred vision.
- Do not exceed ordered dose. The goal of therapy is lowest effective dose.

OXAZEPAM

(ox-a'ze-pam)
Ox-Pam ♦, Serax, Zapex ♦
Classifications: ANXIOLYTIC; SEDATIVE-HYPNOTIC; BENZODIAZEPINE
Therapeutic: ANTIANXIETY; SEDATIVE-HYPNOTIC

Prototype: Lorazepam
Pregnancy Category: D
Controlled Substance: Schedule IV

AVAILABILITY 10 mg, 15 mg, 30 mg capsules; 15 mg tablets

ACTION & *THERAPEUTIC EFFECT*
Benzodiazepine derivative related to lorazepam. Effects are mediated by the inhibitory neurotransmitter GABA. Acts on the thalamic, hypothalamic, and limbic levels of CNS. *Has anxiolytic, sedative, hypnotic, and skeletal muscle relaxant effects.*

USES Management of anxiety and tension associated with a wide range of emotional disturbances. Also to control acute withdrawal symptoms in chronic alcoholism.

CONTRAINDICATIONS Hypersensitivity to oxazepam and other benzodiazepines; respiratory depression; psychoses, suicidal ideation; acute alcohol intoxication; acute-angle glaucoma; pregnancy (category D), lactation, children <6 y.
CAUTIOUS USE Older adult and debilitated patients; impaired kidney and liver function; addiction-prone patients; COPD; history of seizures; history of suicide; mental depression; bipolar disorder.

ROUTE & DOSAGE

Anxiety
Adult: **PO** 10–30 mg t.i.d. or q.i.d.
Acute Alcohol Withdrawal
Adult: **PO** 15–30 mg t.i.d. or q.i.d.

ADMINISTRATION

Oral

- Give with food if GI upset occurs.
- Store in tightly closed container at 15°–30° C (59°–86° F) unless otherwise specified.

Common adverse effects in *italic*, life-threatening effects underlined; generic names in **bold**; classifications in SMALL CAPS; ♦ Canadian drug name; ❷ Prototype drug

1127

ADVERSE EFFECTS (≥1%) **CNS:** *Drowsiness,* dizziness, mental confusion, vertigo, ataxia, headache, lethargy, syncope, tremor, slurred speech, paradoxic reaction (euphoria, excitement). **GI:** Nausea, xerostomia, jaundice. **Skin:** Skin rash, edema. **CV:** Hypotension, edema. **Hematologic:** Leukopenia. **Urogenital:** Altered libido.

INTERACTIONS Drug: Alcohol, CNS DEPRESSANTS, ANTICONVULSANTS potentiate CNS depression; **cimetidine** increases oxazepam plasma levels, increasing its toxicity; may decrease antiparkinsonism effects of **levodopa;** may increase **phenytoin** levels; smoking decreases sedative and antianxiety effects. **Herbal: Kava-kava, valerian** may potentiate sedation.

PHARMACOKINETICS Absorption: Readily absorbed from GI tract. **Peak:** 2–3 h. **Distribution:** Crosses placenta; distributed into breast milk. **Metabolism:** In liver. **Elimination:** Primarily in urine, some in feces. **Half-Life:** 2–8 h.

CLINICAL IMPLICATIONS

Assessment & Drug Effects

- Observe older adult patients closely for signs of overdosage. Report to physician if daytime psychomotor function is depressed.
- Monitor for increased signs and symptoms of suicidality.
- Lab tests: Perform liver function and white blood cell counts on a regular planned basis.
- Note: Excessive and prolonged use may cause physical dependence.

Patient & Family Education

- Report promptly any mild paradoxic stimulation of affect and excitement with sleep disturbances that may occur within the first 2 wk of therapy. Dosage reduction is indicated.
- Do not change dose or dose schedule and refrain from using drug to treat a self-diagnosed condition.
- Consult physician before self-medicating with OTC drugs.
- Do not drive or engage in potentially hazardous activities until response to drug is known.
- Do not drink alcoholic beverages while taking oxazepam. The CNS depressant effects of each agent may be intensified.
- Contact physician if you intend to or do become pregnant during therapy about discontinuing the drug.
- Withdraw drug slowly following prolonged therapy to avoid precipitating withdrawal symptoms (seizures, mental confusion, nausea, vomiting, muscle and abdominal cramps, tremulousness, sleep disturbances, unusual irritability, hyperhidrosis).

OXCARBAZEPINE

(ox-car′ba-ze-peen)
Trileptal
Classifications: ANTICONVULSANT
Therapeutic: ANTICONVULSANT
Prototype: Carbamazepine
Pregnancy Category: C

AVAILABILITY 150 mg, 300 mg, 600 mg tablets; 300 mg/5 mL suspension

ACTION & *THERAPEUTIC EFFECT*
Anticonvulsant properties may result from blockage of voltage-sensitive sodium channels, which results in stabilization of hyperexcited neural membranes. *Inhibits repetitive neuronal firing, and decreased propagation of neuronal impulses.*

USES Monotherapy or adjunctive therapy in the treatment of partial seizures in adults and children age 4–16.

CONTRAINDICATIONS Hypersensitivity to oxcarbazepine; pregnancy (category C); children <3 y.

CAUTIOUS USE Older adults; renal impairment; renal failure; children <8 y; infertility, hyponatremia, SIADH, and drugs associated with SIADH as an adverse effect; lactation.

ROUTE & DOSAGE

Partial Seizures

Adult: **PO** Start with 300 mg b.i.d. and increase by 600 mg/d q wk to 2400 mg/d in 2 divided doses for monotherapy or 1200 mg/d as adjunctive therapy
Child: **PO** *4–16 y,* Initiate with 8–10 mg/kg/d divided b.i.d. (max: 600 mg/d), gradually increase weekly to target dose (divided b.i.d.) based on weight: *20–29 kg,* 900 mg/d; *29.1–39 kg,* 1200 mg/d; *>39 kg,* 1800 mg/d

Renal Impairment

Cl_{cr} <30 mL/min: Initiate at $^1/_2$ usual starting dose (300 mg b.i.d.)

ADMINISTRATION

Oral

- Initiate therapy at one-half the usual starting dose (300 mg/d) if creatinine clearance <30 mL/min.
- Do not abruptly stop this medication; withdraw drug gradually when discontinued to minimize seizure potential.
- Store preferably at 25° C (77° F), but room temperature permitted. Keep container tightly closed.

ADVERSE EFFECTS (≥1%) **Body as a Whole:** *Fatigue,* asthenia, peripheral edema, generalized edema, chest pain, weight gain. **CV:** Hypotension. **GI:** *Nausea, vomiting, abdominal pain,* diarrhea, dyspepsia, constipation, gastritis, anorexia, dry mouth. **Hematologic:** Lymphadenopathy. **Metabolic:** Hyponatremia. **Musculoskeletal:** Muscle weakness. **CNS:** *Headache, dizziness, somnolence, ataxia, nystagmus, abnormal gait,* insomnia, tremor, nervousness, agitation, abnormal coordination, speech disorder, confusion, abnormal thinking, aggravate convulsions, emotional lability. **Respiratory:** Rhinitis, cough, bronchitis, pharyngitis. **Skin:** Acne, hot flushes, purpura, <u>Stevens-Johnson syndrome, toxic epidermal necrolysis</u>. **Special Senses:** *Diplopia, vertigo, abnormal vision,* abnormal accommodation, taste perversion, ear ache. **Urogenital:** Urinary tract infection, micturition frequency, vaginitis.

INTERACTIONS Drug: **Carbamazepine, phenobarbital, phenytoin, valproic acid, verapamil,** CALCIUM CHANNEL BLOCKERS may decrease oxcarbazepine levels; may increase levels of **phenobarbital, phenytoin;** may decrease levels of **felodipine,** ORAL CONTRACEPTIVES. **Herbal: Ginkgo** may decrease anticonvulsant effectiveness. **Evening primrose oil** may decrease the seizure threshold.

PHARMACOKINETICS Absorption: Rapidly and completely from GI tract. **Peak:** Steady-state levels reached in 2–3 d. **Distribution:** 40% protein bound. **Metabolism:** Extensively metabolized in liver to active 10-monohydroxy metabolite (MHD). **Elimination:** 95% in kidneys. **Half-Life:** 2 h, MHD 9 h.

Common adverse effects in *italic*, life-threatening effects <u>underlined</u>; generic names in **bold**; classifications in SMALL CAPS; ♣ Canadian drug name; ⊕ Prototype drug

1129

CLINICAL IMPLICATIONS

Assessment & Drug Effects

- Monitor for and report S&S of: Hyponatremia (e.g., nausea, malaise, headache, lethargy, confusion); CNS impairment (e.g., somnolence, excessive fatigue, cognitive deficits, speech or language problems, incoordination, gait disturbances).
- Monitor phenytoin levels when administered concurrently.
- Lab tests: Periodic serum sodium, T_4 level; when oxcarbazepine is used as adjunctive therapy, closely monitor plasma level of the concomitant antiepileptic drug during titration of the oxcarbazepine dose.

Patient & Family Education

- Notify physician of the following: Dizziness, excess drowsiness, frequent headaches, malaise, double vision, lack of coordination, or persistent nausea.
- Exercise special caution with concurrent use of alcohol or CNS depressants.
- Use caution with potentially hazardous activities and driving until response to drug is known.
- Use or add barrier contraceptive since drug may render hormonal methods ineffective.

OXICONAZOLE NITRATE

(ox-i-con′a-zole)

Oxistat

Classifications: AZOLE ANTIFUNGAL
Therapeutic: ANTIFUNGAL
Prototype: Fluconazole
Pregnancy Category: B

AVAILABILITY 1% cream, lotion

ACTION & *THERAPEUTIC EFFECT*

Topical synthetic antifungal agent that presumably works by altering the cellular membrane of the fungi, resulting in increased membrane permeability, secondary metabolic effects, and growth inhibition. *Effective against fungi.*

USES Topical treatment of tinea pedis, tinea cruris, and tinea corporis due to *Trichophyton rubrum* and *Trichophyton mentagrophytes;* also used for cutaneous candidiasis caused by *Candida albicans* and *Candida tropicalis.*

CONTRAINDICATIONS Hypersensitivity to oxiconazole.

CAUTIOUS USE Hypersensitivity to other azole antifungals; pregnancy (category B), lactation.

ROUTE & DOSAGE

Tinea and Other Dermal Infections
Adult: **Topical** Apply to affected area once daily in the evening

ADMINISTRATION

Topical

- Apply cream to cover the affected areas once daily (in the evening).
- Treat tinea corporis and tinea cruris for 2 wk; tinea pedis for 1 mo to reduce the possibility of recurrence.
- Store at 15°–30° C (59°–86° F).

ADVERSE EFFECTS (≥1%) **Skin:** Transient burning and stinging, dryness, erythema, pruritus, and local irritation.

INTERACTIONS Drug: No clinically significant interactions established.

PHARMACOKINETICS Absorption: <0.3% is absorbed systemically.

CLINICAL IMPLICATIONS

Patient & Family Education

- Use only externally. Do not use intravaginally.

- Discontinue drug and contact physician if irritation or sensitivity develops.
- Avoid contact with eyes.
- Contact physician if no improvement is noted after the prescribed treatment period.

OXTRIPHYLLINE

(ox-trye'fi-lin)
Choledyl SA

Classifications: BRONCHODILATOR (RESPIRATORY SMOOTH MUSCLE RELAXANT); XANTHINE
Therapeutic: BRONCHODILATOR
Prototype: Theophylline
Pregnancy Category: C

AVAILABILITY 400 mg, 600 mg sustained release tablets

ACTION & *THERAPEUTIC EFFECT* Choline salt of theophylline. Relaxes smooth muscle by direct action, particularly of bronchi and pulmonary vessels, and stimulates medullary respiratory center with resulting increase in vital capacity. *Relaxes bronchi smooth muscle and stimulates respiratory center in the medulla of the brain.*

USES As bronchodilator to control asthma or COPD.

CONTRAINDICATIONS Hypersensitivity to xanthines; coronary artery disease; renal or hepatic impairment. Safe use during pregnancy (category C), lactation, or in children <1 y is not established.
CAUTIOUS USE Peptic ulcer; prostatic hypertrophy; diabetes mellitus; glaucoma.

ROUTE & DOSAGE

Asthma, COPD
Adult: **PO** 4.7 mg/kg (usual dose 200 mg) q8h

Child: **PO** 1–9 y, 6.2 mg/kg q6h; 9–16 y and adult smoker, 4.7 mg/kg (usual dose 200 mg) q6h

ADMINISTRATION

Oral
- Give on an empty stomach (30 min to 1 h before or 2 h after meals); may be taken after meals and at bedtime to reduce GI distress. Sustained-release tablet permits dosing q12h.
- Ensure that sustained-release form is not chewed or crushed. It must be swallowed whole.
- Protect elixir from light.

ADVERSE EFFECTS (≥1%) **CNS:** Restlessness, dizziness, insomnia, <u>convulsions</u>, *muscle twitching.* **CV:** Palpitation, tachycardia, flushing, hypotension. **GI:** *Nausea,* vomiting, anorexia, epigastric pain, diarrhea, activation of peptic ulcer. **Urogenital:** Transient urinary frequency, kidney irritation. **Body as a Whole:** Urticaria, fever, dehydration.

INTERACTIONS Drug: Lowers lithium levels; **cimetidine,** high dose **allopurinol** (600 mg/d), **ciprofloxacin, erythromycin, troleandomycin** can significantly increase levels. **Herbal: St. John's wort** may decrease plasma levels.

PHARMACOKINETICS Absorption: Well absorbed from GI tract. **Duration:** 4–8 h; varies with age, smoking, and liver function. **Distribution:** Crosses placenta; distributed into breast milk. **Metabolism:** Extensively in liver. **Elimination:** Parent drug and metabolites excreted by kidneys. **Half-Life:** 4 h in adults.

CLINICAL IMPLICATIONS

Note: See theophylline for numerous additional clinical implications.

Common adverse effects in *italic,* life-threatening effects <u>underlined</u>; generic names in **bold**; classifications in SMALL CAPS; ♣ Canadian drug name; ☺ Prototype drug

1131

Assessment & Drug Effects

- Determine patient's tobacco use. Cigarette smoking may alter hepatic microsomal enzyme activity and indicate increase in dosage.
- Use safety precautions with older adults during early therapy; dizziness is a relatively common adverse effect.
- Monitor vital signs and I&O. Improvement in quality of pulse and respiration and diuresis are expected clinical effects.
- Observe and report early signs of possible toxicity: anorexia, nausea, vomiting, dizziness, shakiness, restlessness, abdominal discomfort, irritability, palpitation, tachycardia, marked hypotension, cardiac arrhythmias, seizures.

Patient & Family Education

- Report gastric distress, palpitation, and CNS stimulation (irritability, restlessness, nervousness, insomnia) to physician. Reduction in dosage may be indicated.
- Limit caffeine intake; it may increase incidence of adverse effects.
- Do not take OTC medications, especially cough suppressants, which may cause retention of secretions and CNS depression, without consulting physician.
- Drink adequate fluids (at least 2000 mL/d) to decrease viscosity of airway secretions.

OXYBUTYNIN CHLORIDE

(ox-i-byoo′ti-nin)

Ditropan, Ditropan XL, Oxytrol

Classifications: ANTICHOLINERGIC; ANTIMUSCARINIC; ANTISPASMODIC
Therapeutic: ANTISPASMODIC; ANTICHOLINERGIC
Prototype: Atropine
Pregnancy Category: B

AVAILABILITY 5 mg tablets; 5 mg, 10 mg sustained release tablets; 5 mg/5 mL syrup; 3.9 mg/d transdermal patch

ACTION & THERAPEUTIC EFFECT
Synthetic tertiary amine that exerts direct antispasmodic action and inhibits muscarinic effects of acetylcholine on smooth muscle of the urinary muscle. *Prominent antispasmodic activity of the urinary muscle.*

USES To relieve symptoms associated with voiding in patients with uninhibited neurogenic bladder and reflex neurogenic bladder. Also has been used to relieve pain of bladder spasm following transurethral surgical procedures.

CONTRAINDICATIONS Hypersensitivity of oxybutynin; narrow angle glaucoma, myasthenia gravis, partial or complete GI obstruction, gastric retention, paralytic ileus, intestinal atony (especially older adult or debilitated patients), megacolon, severe colitis, GU obstruction, urinary retention, unstable cardiovascular status; extended release form with renal impairment; lactation, infants.

CAUTIOUS USE Older adults; autonomic neuropathy, hiatus hernia with reflex esophagitis; hepatic or renal dysfunction; urinary infection; hyperthyroidism; CHF, coronary artery disease, hypertension; prostatic hypertrophy; pregnancy (category B).

ROUTE & DOSAGE

Neurogenic Bladder
Adult: **PO** 5 mg b.i.d. or t.i.d. (max: 20 mg/d) or 5 mg sustained release q.d., may increase up to 30 mg/d **Topical** Apply 1 patch twice weekly

Geriatric: **PO** 2.5–5 mg b.i.d. (max: 15 mg/d) or 5 mg sustained release q.d., may increase up to 30 mg/d **Topical** Apply 1 patch twice weekly
Child: **PO** *1–5 y,* 0.2 mg/kg b.i.d.–q.i.d.; *>5 y,* 5 mg b.i.d. (max: 15 mg/d)

ADMINISTRATION

Oral
- Ensure that sustained release form is not chewed or crushed. It must be swallowed whole.

Topical
- Ensure that old patch is removed prior to application of new patch.

ADVERSE EFFECTS (≥1%) **Body as a Whole:** Severe allergic reactions including urticaria, skin rashes, suppression of lactation, decreased sweating, fever. **CNS:** *Drowsiness,* dizziness, weakness, insomnia, restlessness, psychotic behavior (overdosage). **CV:** Palpitations, tachycardia, flushing. **Special Senses:** Mydriasis, *blurred vision,* cycloplegia, increased ocular tension. **GI:** *Dry mouth,* nausea, vomiting, *constipation,* bloated feeling. **Skin:** *Pruritus at application site,* rash, application site vesicles, erythema. **Urogenital:** Urinary hesitancy or retention, impotence.

PHARMACOKINETICS **Absorption:** Diffuses across intact skin. **Onset:** 0.5–1 h. **Peak:** 3–6 h. **Duration:** 6–10 h. **PO:** 96 h Transdermal. **Metabolism:** In liver. **Elimination:** Primarily in urine. **Half-Life:** 2–5 h

CLINICAL IMPLICATIONS

Assessment & Drug Effects
- Periodic interruptions of therapy are recommended to determine patient's need for continued treatment. Tolerance has occurred in some patients.
- Keep physician informed of expected responses to drug therapy (e.g., effect on urinary frequency, urgency, urge incontinence, nocturia, completeness of bladder emptying).
- Monitor patients with colostomy or ileostomy closely; abdominal distension and the onset of diarrhea in these patients may be early signs of intestinal obstruction or of toxic megacolon.

Patient & Family Education
- Do not drive or engage in potentially hazardous activities until response to drug is known.
- Exercise caution in hot environments. By suppressing sweating, oxybutynin can cause fever and heat stroke.

OXYCODONE HYDROCHLORIDE

(ox-i-koe′done)

OxyContin, Percolone, Endocodone, OxyFAST, Roxicodone
Classifications: NARCOTIC (OPIATE) AGONIST; ANALGESIC
Therapeutic: NARCOTIC ANALGESIC
Prototype: Morphine
Pregnancy Category: B (D for prolonged use or use of high doses at term)
Controlled Substance: Schedule II

AVAILABILITY 5 mg, 15 mg, 30 mg tablets; **OxyContin** 10 mg, 20 mg, 40 mg, 80 mg, 160 mg sustained release tablets; 5 mg/5 mL, 20 mg/mL oral solution

ACTION & *THERAPEUTIC EFFECT*
Semisynthetic derivative of an opium alkaloid with actions qualitatively similar to those of morphine. Binds with stereo-specific

Common adverse effects in *italic*, life-threatening effects <u>underlined</u>; generic names in **bold**; classifications in SMALL CAPS; ◆ Canadian drug name; ⊙ Prototype drug

1133

receptors in various sites of CNS to alter both perception of pain and emotional response to pain, but precise mechanism of action not clear. *Active against moderate to moderately severe pain. Appears to be more effective in relief of acute than long-standing pain.*

USES Relief of moderate to moderately severe pain such as may occur with bursitis, dislocations, simple fractures and other injuries, and neuralgia. Relieves postoperative, postextractional, postpartum pain.

CONTRAINDICATIONS Hypersensitivity to oxycodone and principal drugs with which it is combined; bronchial asthma; pregnancy (category B); for prolonged use or high doses at term (category D); lactation, children <6 y.

CAUTIOUS USE Alcoholism; renal or hepatic disease; viral infections; Addison's disease; cardiac arrhythmias; chronic ulcerative colitis; history of drug abuse or dependency; gallbladder disease, acute abdominal conditions; head injury, intracranial lesions; hypothyroidism; prostatic hypertrophy; respiratory disease; urethral stricture; older adult or debilitated patients; peptic ulcer or coagulation abnormalities (combination products containing aspirin).

ROUTE & DOSAGE

Moderate to Severe Pain

Adult: **PO** 5–10 mg q6h prn; OxyContin can be dosed q8h
Child: **PO** 6–12 y, 1.25 mg q6h prn; ≥12 y, 2.5 mg q6h

ADMINISTRATION

Oral

- Ensure that sustained release form is not chewed or crushed. It must be swallowed whole.

- Store this **DANGEROUS** medication in a place inaccessible to children at 15°–30° C (59°–86° F). Protect from light.

ADVERSE EFFECTS (≥1%) **CNS:** Euphoria, dysphoria, light-headedness, dizziness, *sedation.* **GI:** Anorexia, nausea, vomiting, *constipation,* jaundice, hepatotoxicity (combinations containing acetaminophen). **Respiratory:** Shortness of breath, respiratory depression. **Skin:** Pruritus, skin rash. **CV:** Bradycardia. **Body as a Whole:** Unusual bleeding or bruising. **Urogenital:** Dysuria, frequency of urination, urinary retention.

DIAGNOSTIC TEST INTERFERENCE *Serum amylase* levels may be elevated because oxycodone causes spasm of sphincter of Oddi. *Blood glucose determinations:* false decrease (measured by *glucose oxidase-peroxidase method*). *5-HIAA determination:* false positive with use of *nitrosonaphthol reagent* (quantitative test is unaffected).

INTERACTIONS Drug: Alcohol and other CNS DEPRESSANTS add to CNS depressant activity. **Herbal: St. John's wort** may increase sedation.

PHARMACOKINETICS Absorption: Readily from GI tract. **Onset:** 10–15 min. **Peak:** 30–60 min. **Duration:** 4–5 h. **Distribution:** Crosses placenta; distributed into breast milk. **Metabolism:** In liver. **Elimination:** Primarily in urine. **Half-Life:** 3–5 h.

CLINICAL IMPLICATIONS

Assessment & Drug Effects

- Monitor patient's response closely, especially to sustained-release preparations.
- Consult physician if nausea continues after first few days of therapy.

Common adverse effects in *italic*, life-threatening effects underlined; generic names in **bold**; classifications in SMALL CAPS; ✦ Canadian drug name; ❂ Prototype drug

- Note: Light-headedness, dizziness, sedation, or fainting appear to be more prominent in ambulatory than in nonambulatory patients and may be alleviated if patient lies down.
- Evaluate patient's continued need for oxycodone preparations. Psychic and physical dependence and tolerance may develop with repeated use. The potential for drug abuse is high.
- Lab tests: Check hepatic function and hematologic status periodically in patients on high dosage.
- Be aware that serious overdosage of any oxycodone preparation presents problems associated with a narcotic overdose (respiratory depression, circulatory collapse, extreme somnolence progressing to stupor or coma).

Patient & Family Education
- Do not alter dosage regimen by increasing, decreasing, or shortening intervals between doses. Habit formation and liver damage may result.
- Avoid potentially hazardous activities such as driving a car or operating machinery while using oxycodone preparation.
- Do not drink large amounts of alcoholic beverages while using oxycodone preparations; risk of liver damage is increased.
- Check with physician before taking OTC drugs for colds, stomach distress, allergies, insomnia, or pain.
- Inform surgeon or dentist that you are taking an oxycodone preparation before any surgical procedure is undertaken.

OXYMETAZOLINE HYDROCHLORIDE

(ox-i-met-az′oh-leen)

Afrin, Dristan Long Lasting, Duramist Plus, Duration, Nafrine ✦, Neo-Synephrine 12 Hour, Nostrilla, Sinex Long Lasting
Classifications: NASAL PREPARATION; DECONGESTANT
Therapeutic: DECONGESTANT
Prototype: Naphazoline
Pregnancy Category: C

AVAILABILITY 0.025%, 0.05% solution

ACTION & *THERAPEUTIC EFFECT*
Sympathomimetic agent that acts directly on alpha receptors of sympathetic nervous system resulting in relief of nasal congestion. *Constricts smaller arterioles in nasal passages and has prolonged decongestant effect.*

USES Relief of nasal congestion in a variety of allergic and infectious disorders of the upper respiratory tract; used as nasal tampon to facilitate intranasal examination or before nasal surgery. Also used as adjunct in treatment and prevention of middle ear infection by decreasing congestion of eustachian ostia.

CONTRAINDICATIONS Use in children <2 y; closed-angle glaucoma; pregnancy (category C); lactation.
CAUTIOUS USE Within 14 d of MAO inhibitors, coronary artery disease, hypertension, hyperthyroidism, diabetes mellitus.

ROUTE & DOSAGE

Nasal Congestion
Adult: **Intranasal** 2–3 drops or 2–3 sprays of 0.05% solution into each nostril b.i.d. for up to 3–5 d

Common adverse effects in *italic*, life-threatening effects underlined; generic names in **bold**; classifications in SMALL CAPS; ✦ Canadian drug name; ⊘ Prototype drug

1135

Child: **Intranasal** 2–5 y, 2–3 drops or 2–3 sprays of 0.025% solution into each nostril b.i.d. for up to 3–5 d; >6 y, same as for adult

ADMINISTRATION

Instillation

- Place spray nozzle in nostril without occluding it and tilt head slightly forward prior to instillation of spray; sniff briskly during administration.
- Rinse dropper or spray tip in hot water after each use to prevent contamination of solution by nasal secretions.
- Usually given in the morning and at bedtime. Effects appear within 30 min and last about 6–7 h.

ADVERSE EFFECTS (≥1%) **Special Senses:** *Burning,* stinging, dryness of nasal mucosa, *sneezing.* **Body as a Whole:** Headache, light-headedness, drowsiness, insomnia, palpitations, *rebound congestion.*

INTERACTIONS Drug: No clinically significant interactions established.

PHARMACOKINETICS Onset: 5–10 min. **Duration:** 6–10 h.

CLINICAL IMPLICATIONS

Assessment & Drug Effects

- Monitor for S&S of excess use. If noted, discuss possibility of rebound congestion.

Patient & Family Education

- Wash hands carefully after handling oxymetazoline. Anisocoria (inequality of pupil size, blurred vision) can develop if eyes are rubbed with contaminated fingers.
- Do not to exceed recommended dosage. Rebound congestion (chemical rhinitis) may occur with prolonged or excessive use.
- Systemic effects can result from swallowing excessive medication.

OXYMETHOLONE

(ox-i-meth'oh-lone)

Anadrol-50

Classifications: HORMONE; ANDROGEN/ANABOLIC STEROID
Therapeutic: ANABOLIC STEROID
Prototype: Testosterone
Pregnancy Category: X
Controlled Substance: Schedule III

AVAILABILITY 50 mg tablets

ACTION & *THERAPEUTIC EFFECT*
Potent steroid with anabolic activity. Mechanism of action in refractory anemias is unclear but may be due to direct stimulation of bone marrow, protein anabolic activity, or to androgenic stimulation of erythropoiesis. *Stimulates formation of red blood cells in the bone marrow. Stimulates bone growth, aids in bone matrix reconstitution.*

USES Aplastic anemia.
UNLABELED USES Osteoporosis, catabolic conditions.

CONTRAINDICATIONS Prostatic hypertrophy with obstruction; pregnancy (category X); prostatic or male breast cancer; cardiac, renal, hepatic decompensation; nephrosis; premature infant; use during lactation is not established.
CAUTIOUS USE Prepubertal males; geriatric male patients; diabetes mellitus; coronary disease; patient taking ACTH, corticosteroids, anticoagulants.

ROUTE & DOSAGE

Aplastic Anemia
Adult/Child: **PO** 1–5 mg/kg/d

ADMINISTRATION

Oral
- A course of therapy for treatment of osteoporosis is 7–21 d.
- For treatment of anemias, a minimum trial period of 3–6 mo is recommended, since response tends to be slow.
- Store at 15°–30° C (59°–86° F). Protect from heat and light.

ADVERSE EFFECTS (≥1%) Endocrine: Androgenic in women: Suppression of ovulation, lactation, or menstruation; *hoarseness or deepening of voice* (often irreversible); *hirsutism; oily skin; acne;* clitoral enlargement; regression of breasts; male-pattern baldness (in disseminated breast cancer). Hypoestrogenic effects in women: Flushing, sweating; vaginitis with pruritus, drying, bleeding; menstrual irregularities. Men: prepubertal: premature epiphyseal closure, phallic enlargement, priapism. Postpubertal: testicular atrophy, decreased ejaculatory volume, azoospermia, oligospermia (after prolonged administration or excessive dosage), impotence, epididymitis, gynecomastia. **CV:** *Edema,* skin flush. **GI:** *Nausea, vomiting, anorexia,* diarrhea, jaundice, hepatotoxicity. **Urogenital:** Bladder irritability. **Metabolic:** Hypercalcemia.

INTERACTIONS Drug: May enhance hypoprothrombinemic effects of **warfarin. Herbal: Echinacea** may increase risk of hepatotoxicity.

PHARMACOKINETICS Absorption: Readily from GI tract. **Metabolism:** In liver. **Elimination:** In urine. **Half-Life:** 9 h.

CLINICAL IMPLICATIONS

Assessment & Drug Effects
- Monitor patient with a history of seizures closely because an increase in their frequency may be noted.
- Monitor periodically for edema that may develop with or without CHF.
- Monitor for hypercalcemia (see Appendix F), especially in women with breast cancer.
- Lab tests: Periodic serum calcium; periodic liver function tests are especially important for the older adult patient. Drug should be stopped with first sign of liver toxicity (jaundice).

Patient & Family Education
- Monitor blood glucose for loss of glycemic control if diabetic.
- Women: Notify physician of signs of virilization.

OXYMORPHONE HYDROCHLORIDE

(ox-i-mor'fone)

Numorphan, Opana, Opana ER
Classifications: NARCOTIC (OPIATE) AGONIST; ANALGESIC
Therapeutic: NARCOTIC ANALGESIC
Prototype: Morphine
Pregnancy Category: C
Controlled Substance: Schedule II

AVAILABILITY 1 mg/mL, 1.5 mg/mL injection; 5 mg suppositories; 10 mg extended release tablets; 10 mg tablets

ACTION & THERAPEUTIC EFFECT
Structurally and pharmacologically related to morphine. Analgesic action for moderate to severe pain. Produces mild sedation and, unlike morphine, has little antitussive action. *Effective in relief of moderate to severe pain.*

USES Relief of moderate to severe pain, preoperative medication, obstetric analgesia, support of anesthesia, and relief of anxiety in patients with dyspnea associated with acute ventricular failure and pulmonary edema.

CONTRAINDICATIONS Pulmonary edema resulting from chemical respiratory irritants; ileus; status asthmaticus; pregnancy (category C), children <12 y.

CAUTIOUS USE Alcoholism; biliary tract disease; bladder obstruction; severe pulmonary disease, respiratory insufficiency, COPD; depression; older adults; lactation.

ROUTE & DOSAGE

Moderate to Severe Pain
Adult: **PO** 10–20 mg q4–6h prn; extended release 5–10 mg q12h **SC/IM** 1–1.5 mg q4–6h prn **IV** 0.5 mg q4–6h **PR** 5 mg q4–6h prn

Analgesia during Labor
Adult: **IM** 0.5–1 mg

ADMINISTRATION

Subcutaneous, Intramuscular
- Give undiluted.

Intravenous

PREPARE: Direct: Dilute in 5 mL of sterile water or NS.
ADMINISTER: Direct: Give at a rate of 0.5 mg over 2–5 min.

- Protect drug from light. Store suppositories in refrigerator 2°–15° C (36°–59° F).

ADVERSE EFFECTS (≥1%) **GI:** *Nausea, vomiting, euphoria.* **CNS:** *Dizziness,* lightheadedness, sedation. **Respiratory:** Respiratory depression (see morphine), apnea, respiratory arrest. **Body as a Whole:** Sweating, coma, shock. **CV:** Cardiac arrest, circulatory depression.

INTERACTIONS Drug: Alcohol and other CNS DEPRESSANTS add to CNS depression; **propofol** increases risk of bradycardia.

PHARMACOKINETICS Onset: 5–10 min IV; 10–15 min IM; 15–30 min PR. **Peak:** 1–1.5 h. **Duration:** 3–6 h. **Distribution:** Crosses placenta. **Metabolism:** In liver. **Elimination:** In urine. **Half-Life:** PO 7–9 h; extended release 9–11 h

CLINICAL IMPLICATIONS

Assessment & Drug Effects
- Monitor respiratory rate. Withhold drug and notify physician if rate falls below 12 breaths per minute.
- Supervise ambulation and advise patient of possible light-headedness. Older adult and debilitated patients are most susceptible to CNS depressant effects of drug.
- Evaluate patient's continued need for narcotic analgesic. Prolonged use can lead to dependence of morphine type.
- Medication contains sulfite and may precipitate a hypersensitivity reaction in susceptible patient.

Patient & Family Education
- Use caution when walking because of potential for injury from dizziness.
- Do not consume alcohol while taking oxymorphone.

OXYTETRACYCLINE

(ox-i-tet-ra-sye′kleen)
Terramycin
Classifications: ANTIBIOTIC; TETRACYCLINE
Therapeutic: ANTIBIOTIC; TETRACYCLINE
Prototype: Tetracycline
Pregnancy Category: D

AVAILABILITY 250 mg capsules; 50 mg/mL, 125 mg/mL injection

ACTION & *THERAPEUTIC EFFECT*
Broad-spectrum antibiotic with actions similar to tetracycline. *Effective against a variety of gram-positive and gram-negative bacteria and against most Chlamydiae, Mycoplasmas, Rickettsiae, and certain protozoa (e.g., amebae).*

USES Treatment of gonorrhea, Lyme disease, upper and lower respiratory tract infections, Q fever, Rocky Mountain spotted fever, skin and skin structure infections, traveler's diarrhea, and UTIs.

CONTRAINDICATIONS Hypersensitivity to tetracyclines; during tooth development [last half of pregnancy (category D)], lactation, infancy, childhood to age 8 y.
CAUTIOUS USE Impaired kidney function.

ROUTE & DOSAGE

Antiinfective
Adult: **PO** 250–500 mg q6–12h **IM** 100 mg q8–12h or 250 mg q24h **IV** 250–500 mg q12h (max: 500 mg q6h)
Child: **PO** >8 y, 25–50 mg/kg/d in 4 divided doses

ADMINISTRATION

Oral
- Check expiration date. Degradation products of outdated tetracyclines can be highly nephrotoxic.
- Give at least 1 h before or 2 h following meals. Food may interfere with rate and extent of absorption of oral drug. Do **NOT** give with antacids, milk, milk products, or other calcium-containing foods.

Intramuscular
- Note: Commercially available solution contains only 2% lidocaine. Administer by deep IM.
- Do not use IM solution for IV administration.

Intravenous

PREPARE: Intermittent: Use only oxytetracycline HCl for IV. Prepare by adding 10 mL of sterile water for injection or D5W to the 250 or 500 mg vial. Further dilute with a minimum of 100 mL D5W, NS, or RL.

ADMINISTER: Intermittent: Give slowly over 15–30 min. A slower rate of infusion and a large amount of diluent will reduce vein irritation.

- Store reconstituted solutions in refrigerator at 2°–8° C (36°–46.4° F) for up to 48h.

INCOMPATIBILITIES Solution/additive: Acetylcysteine, amikacin, aminophylline, amphotericin B, ampicillin, calcium gluconate, cephazolin, cephalothin, erythromycin gluceptate, iron dextran, magnesium sulfate, nafcillin, oxacillin, penicillin G, pentobarbital, phenobarbital, phenytoin, prochlorperazine, sodium bicarbonate.

ADVERSE EFFECTS (≥1%) **GI:** Nausea, vomiting, diarrhea, stomatitis, anorexia, epigastric distress, esophageal ulcers, fatty liver, hepatotoxicity, elevated hepatic enzymes. **Skin:** Skin rash, photosensitivity. **Body as a Whole:** Lightheadedness, dizziness, pseudotumor cerebri, superinfections. **Urogenital:** Renal toxicity. **Hematologic:** Hemolytic anemia, thrombocytopenia. (Also see TETRACYCLINE.)

INTERACTIONS Drug: ANTACIDS, **iron, calcium, magnesium, zinc,**

0

Common adverse effects in *italic*, life-threatening effects underlined; generic names in **bold**; classifications in SMALL CAPS; ✦ Canadian drug name; ⊘ Prototype drug

1139

kaolin and pectin, sodium bicarbonate, bismuth subsalicylate can significantly decrease oxytetracycline absorption; effects of both **desmopressin** and oxytetracycline antagonized; increases **digoxin** absorption, increasing risk of **digoxin** toxicity; **methoxyflurane** increases risk of renal failure. **Food: Dairy products** significantly decrease absorption.

PHARMACOKINETICS Absorption: About 60% from GI tract and IM site. **Peak:** 2–4 h. **Distribution:** Appears to concentrate in hepatic system; crosses placenta; distributed into breast milk. **Metabolism:** Partially metabolized. **Elimination:** In feces and urine. **Half-Life:** 6–10 h.

CLINICAL IMPLICATIONS
Assessment & Drug Effects
- Monitor for S&S of superinfection (see Appendix F).
- Lab test: Baseline renal function tests. Dosage may need to be reduced in the presence of renal impairment.
- Discontinue drug and notify physician at the first sign of a hypersensitivity response (see Appendix F).

Patient & Family Education
- Discard unused drug when course of therapy has ended.
- Avoid excessive exposure to sunlight because of the possibility of photosensitivity.

OXYTOCIN INJECTION ℞

(ox-i-toe′sin)
Pitocin
Classifications: HORMONE; OXYTOCIC
Therapeutic: OXYTOCIC
Pregnancy Category: X

AVAILABILITY 10 units/mL injection

ACTION & *THERAPEUTIC EFFECT*
Synthetic, water-soluble polypeptide consisting of eight amino acids, identical pharmacologically to the oxytocin released by posterior pituitary. By direct action on myofibrils, produces phasic contractions characteristic of normal delivery. Uterine sensitivity to oxytocin increases during gestation period and peaks sharply before parturition. *Effective in initiating or improving uterine contractions at term.*

USES To initiate or improve uterine contraction at term, management of inevitable, incomplete, or missed abortion; stimulation of uterine contractions during third stage of labor; stimulation to overcome uterine inertia; control of postpartum hemorrhage and promotion of postpartum uterine involution. Also used to induce labor in cases of maternal diabetes, preeclampsia, eclampsia, and erythroblastosis fetalis.

CONTRAINDICATIONS Hypersensitivity to oxytocin; significant cephalopelvic disproportion, unfavorable fetal position or presentations that are undeliverable without conversion before delivery, obstetric emergencies in which benefit-to-risk ratio for mother or fetus favors surgical intervention, fetal distress in which delivery is not imminent, prematurity, placenta previa, prolonged use in severe toxemia or uterine inertia, hypertonic uterine patterns, previous surgery of uterus or cervix including cesarean section, conditions predisposing to thromboplastin or amniotic fluid embolism (dead fetus, abruptio placentae), grand multiparity, invasive cervical carcinoma, primipara greater than 35 y of age, past history of uterine sepsis or of traumatic delivery, intranasal route during labor, simultaneous administration of drug by two routes.

Common adverse effects in *italic*, life-threatening effects underlined; generic names in **bold**; classifications in SMALL CAPS; ◆ Canadian drug name; ℞ Prototype drug

CAUTIOUS USE Concomitant use with cyclopropane anesthesia or vasoconstrictive drugs.

ROUTE & DOSAGE

Labor Induction
Adult: **IV** Start at 0.5–1 mU/min, may increase by 1 mU/min q15min (max: 20 mU/min)

Postpartum Bleeding
Adult: **IM** 10 U total dose **IV** Infuse a total of 10–40 U at a rate of 20–40 mU/min after delivery

Incomplete Abortion
Adult: **IV** 10–20 mU/min

ADMINISTRATION

Intravenous

PREPARE: **IV Infusion:** When diluting oxytocin for IV infusion, rotate bottle gently to distribute medicine throughout solution. **For inducing labor:** Add 10 U (1 mL) of oxytocin to 1 L of D5W or NS to yield 10 mU/mL. **For postpartum bleeding:** Add 10–40 U (1–4 mL) of oxytocin to 1 L of D5W or NS to yield 10–40 mU/mL.

ADMINISTER: **IV Infusion:** See ROUTE & DOSAGE for recommended rates (mU/min).

INCOMPATIBILITIES **Solution/additive: Fibrinolysin, norepinephrine, prochlorperazine, warfarin.**

ADVERSE EFFECTS (≥1%) **Body as a Whole:** Fetal trauma from too rapid propulsion through pelvis, fetal <u>death</u>, anaphylactic reactions, postpartum hemorrhage, precordial pain, edema, cyanosis or redness of skin. **CV:** Fetal bradycardia and arrhythmias, maternal cardiac arrhythmias, hypertensive episodes, <u>subarachnoid hemorrhage</u>, increased blood flow, <u>fatal afibrinogenemia</u>, ECG changes, PVCs, <u>cardiovascular spasm and collapse.</u> **GI:** Neonatal jaundice, maternal nausea, vomiting. **Endocrine:** ADH effects leading to severe water intoxication and hyponatremia, hypotension. **CNS:** Fetal <u>intracranial hemorrhage</u>, anxiety. **Respiratory:** Fetal hypoxia, maternal dyspnea. **Urogenital:** Uterine hypertonicity, tetanic contractions, <u>uterine rupture</u>, pelvic hematoma.

INTERACTIONS Drug: VASOCONSTRICTORS cause severe hypertension; **cyclopropane anesthesia** causes hypotension, maternal bradycardia, arrhythmias. **Herbal: Ephedra, mahuang** may cause hypertension.

PHARMACOKINETICS Duration: 1 h. **Distribution:** Distributed throughout extracellular fluid; small amount may cross placenta. **Metabolism:** Rapidly destroyed in liver and kidneys. **Elimination:** Small amounts excreted unchanged in urine. **Half-Life:** 3–5 min.

CLINICAL IMPLICATIONS
Assessment & Drug Effects
- Start flow charts to record maternal BP and other vital signs, I&O ratio, weight, strength, duration, and frequency of contractions, as well as fetal heart tone and rate, before instituting treatment.
- Monitor fetal heart rate and maternal BP and pulse at least q15min during infusion period; evaluate tonus of myometrium during and between contractions and record on flow chart. Report change in rate and rhythm immediately.
- Stop infusion to prevent fetal anoxia, turn patient on her side, and notify physician if contractions are prolonged (occurring at less than 2-min intervals) and if monitor records contractions about 50 mm Hg or if contractions last 90

Common adverse effects in *italic*, life-threatening effects <u>underlined</u>; generic names in **bold**; classifications in SMALL CAPS; ✦ Canadian drug name; ⊚ Prototype drug

1141

seconds or longer. Stimulation will wane rapidly within 2–3 min. Oxygen administration may be necessary.

- If local or regional (caudal, spinal) anesthesia is being given to the patient receiving oxytocin, be alert to the possibility of hypertensive crisis (sudden intense occipital headache, palpitation, marked hypertension, stiff neck, nausea, vomiting, sweating, fever, photophobia, dilated pupils, bradycardia or tachycardia, constricting chest pain).
- Monitor I&O during labor. If patient is receiving drug by prolonged IV infusion, watch for symptoms of water intoxication (drowsiness, listlessness, headache, confusion, anuria, weight gain). Report changes in alertness and orientation and changes in I&O ratio (i.e., marked decrease in output with excessive intake).
- Check fundus frequently during the first few postpartum hours and several times daily thereafter.
- Incidence of hypersensitivity or allergic reactions is higher when oxytocin is given by IM or IV injection rather than by IV infusion (diluted solution).

Patient & Family Education
- Be aware of purpose and anticipated effect of oxytocin.
- Report sudden, severe headache immediately to health care providers.

PACLITAXEL ℗

(pac-li-tax'el)
Abraxane, Taxol
Classifications: ANTINEOPLASTIC; TAXANE
Therapeutic: ANTINEOPLASTIC
Pregnancy Category: D

AVAILABILITY 6 mg/mL injection; 100 mg powder for injection (with 900 mg human albumin)

ACTION & *THERAPEUTIC EFFECT*
Normal functioning microtubules within a cell are essential for cell shape and organelles present within cells. Paclitaxel is an antimicrotubular agent that interferes with the microtubule network essential for interphase and mitosis. Induces abnormal spindle formation and multiple asters during mitosis. *Interferes with growth of rapidly dividing cells including cancer cells, and eventually causes cell death.*

USES Ovarian cancer, breast cancer, Kaposi's sarcoma, non-small cell lung cancer (NSCLC).
UNLABELED USES Other solid tumors, leukemia, melanoma.

CONTRAINDICATIONS For **Taxol:** hypersensitivity to paclitaxel, or taxane; baseline neutrophil count <1500 cells/mm^3; thrombocytopenia; with AIDS-related Kaposi sarcoma baseline neutrophil count <1000 cells/mm^3. For **Abraxane:** baseline neutrophil count <1500 cells/mm^3; pregnancy (category D), lactation.
CAUTIOUS USE Cardiac arrhythmias, cardiac disease; impaired liver function; alcoholism; older adults; peripheral neuropathy. Safety and efficacy in children are not established.

ROUTE & DOSAGE

Ovarian Cancer, NSCLC
Adult: **IV** 135 mg/m^2 24-h infusion repeated q3w

Breast Cancer
Adult: **IV** 175–250 mg/m^2 over 3 h q3wk

Abraxane: **IV** 260 mg/m^2 over 30 min q3wk

Kaposi's Sarcoma

Adult: **IV** 135 mg/m^2 infused over 3 h q3wk or 100 mg/m^2 infused over 3 h q2wk

ADMINISTRATION

Note: Premedication with dexamethasone, diphenhydramine, and H$_2$ antagonists (or ephedrine) is recommended to reduce hypersensitivity reactions, and consists of dexamethasone 20 mg PO or IV 14 and 7 h prior to Taxol infusion; diphenhydramine 50 mg IV 30 min prior to Taxol; and cimetidine 300 mg or ranitidine 50 mg IV 30 min before Taxol infusion.

Intravenous

Follow institutional or standard guidelines for preparation, handling, and disposal of cytotoxic agents.

- Premedicate (except with Abraxane) before using to avoid severe hypersensitivity.
- Do not administer unless neutrophil count is at least 1500/mm^3 and platelet count is at least 100,000/mm^3.

PREPARE: **IV Infusion: Taxol & Onxol:** Do not use equipment or devices containing polyvinyl chloride (PVC) in preparation of infusion. Dilute to a final concentration of 0.3–1.2 mg/mL in any of the following: D5W, NS, D5/NS, or D5W in Ringer's injection. The prepared solution may be hazy, but this does not indicate a loss of potency. **Abraxane:** Reconstitute vial by slowly injecting 20 mL NS over at least 1 min onto the inside wall of the vial to yield 5 mg/mL. DO NOT inject directly into the cake powder. Allow vial to sit for at least 5 min, then gently swirl for at least 2 min to completely dissolve. If foaming occurs, let stand for at least 15 min until foam subsides. *ADMINISTER:* **IV Infusion:** Because tissue necrosis occurs with extravasation, frequently assess patency of a peripheral IV site. **Taxol & Onxol:** The prepared solution may be hazy. Administer over 3 h through IV tubing containing inline (0.22 micron or less) filter. Do not use equipment containing PVC. **Abraxane:** If particulates or settling are visible, gently invert vial to ensure complete resuspension prior to use. Inject the required dose into an empty, sterile, PVC or non-PVC type IV bag. DO NOT use an inline filter. Infuse over 30 min.

INCOMPATIBILITIES **Solution/additive: PVC bags** and **infusion sets** should be avoided (except with Abraxane) due to leaching of DEHP (plasticizer). Do not mix with any other medications. **Y-site: Amphotericin B, amphotericin B cholesteryl sulfate complex, chlorpromazine, doxorubicin liposome, hydroxyzine, methylprednisolone, mitoxantrone.**

- Solutions diluted for infusion are stable at room temperature (approximately 25° C/77° F) for up to 27 h.

ADVERSE EFFECTS (≥1%) **CV:** Ventricular tachycardia, ventricular ectopy, *transient bradycardia,* chest pain. **CNS:** Fatigue, headaches, *peripheral neuropathy,* weakness, seizures. **GI:** *Nausea, vomiting,* diarrhea, taste changes, *mucositis,* elevations in serum triglycerides. **Hematologic:** <u>Neutropenia</u>, *anemia,* <u>thrombocytopenia</u>. **Body as a Whole:** *Hypersensitivity reactions (Hypotension, dyspnea with <u>bron-</u>*

Common adverse effects in *italic,* life-threatening effects <u>underlined</u>; generic names in **bold**; classifications in SMALL CAPS; ♣ Canadian drug name; ⊕ Prototype drug

1143

chospasm, urticaria, abdominal and extremity pain, diaphoresis, angioedema), myalgias, arthralgias, alopecia. **Skin:** _Alopecia,_ tissue necrosis with extravasation. **Urogenital:** Minor elevations in kidney and liver function tests.

INTERACTIONS Drug: Increased myelosuppression if **cisplatin, doxorubicin** is given before paclitaxel; **ketoconazole** can inhibit metabolism of paclitaxel; additive bradycardia with BETA BLOCKERS, **digoxin, verapamil;** additive risk of bleeding with ANTICOAGULANTS, NSAIDS, PLATELET INHIBITORS (including **aspirin**), THROMBOLYTIC AGENTS.

PHARMACOKINETICS Distribution: >90% protein bound; does not cross CSF. **Metabolism:** In liver (CYP3A4, 2C8). **Elimination:** Feces 70%, urine 14%. **Half-Life:** 1–9 h.

CLINICAL IMPLICATIONS
Assessment & Drug Effects
- Monitor for hypersensitivity reactions, especially during first and second administrations of the paclitaxel. S&S requiring treatment, but not necessarily discontinuation of the drug, include dyspnea, hypotension, and chest pain. Discontinue immediately and manage symptoms aggressively if angioedema and generalized urticaria develop.
- Monitor vital signs frequently, especially during the first hour of infusion. Bradycardia occurs in approximately 12% of patients, usually during infusion. It does not normally require treatment. Cardiac monitoring is indicated for those with severe conduction abnormalities.
- Lab tests: Monitor hematologic status throughout course of treatment. Severe neutropenia is common but usually of short duration (less than

500/mm^3 for less than 7 d) with the nadir occurring about day 11. Thrombocytopenia occurs less often and is less severe with the nadir around day 8 or 9. The incidence and severity of anemia increase with exposure to paclitaxel.
- Monitor for peripheral neuropathy, the severity of which is dose dependent. Severe symptoms occur primarily with higher than recommended doses.

Patient & Family Education
- Immediately report to physician S&S of paclitaxel hypersensitivity: difficulty breathing, chest pain, palpitations, angioedema (subcutaneous swelling usually around face and neck), and skin rashes or itching.
- Be sure to have periodic blood work as prescribed.
- Avoid aspirin, NSAIDS, and alcohol to minimize GI distress.
- Be aware of high probability of developing hair loss (>80%).

PALIFERMIN
(pal-i-fur′men)
Kepivance
Classifications: BIOLOGIC RESPONSE MODIFIER; KERATINOCYTE GROWTH FACTOR; CYTOKINE
Therapeutic: BIOLOGIC RESPONSE MODIFIER; KERATINOCYTE GROWTH FACTOR
Pregnancy Category: C

AVAILABILITY 6.25 mg powder for injection

ACTION & _THERAPEUTIC EFFECT_
Naturally occurring keratinocyte growth factor (KGF) is produced and regulated in response to epithelial tissue injury. Binding of KGF to its receptors in epithelial cells results in proliferation, differentiation, and

repair of injury to epithelial cells. Palifermin is a synthetic form of KCG; thus it enhances replacement of injured cells. *Palifermin reduces the incidence of severe oral mucositis that interferes with food consumption in the cancer patient.*

USES Reduction of the incidence and duration of severe oral mucositis in patients with hematologic malignancies who are receiving myelotoxic therapy requiring hematopoietic stem cell support.

CONTRAINDICATIONS Hypersensitivity to *Escherichia coli*–derived protein, palifermin; nonhematologic malignancies; within 24 h of chemotherapy; pregnancy (category C). Safe use in children not established.

CAUTIOUS USE Use contraception for females of childbearing age; lactation.

ROUTE & DOSAGE

Oral Mucositis

Adult: **IV** 60 mcg/kg/d for 3 d before and 3 d after myelotoxic therapy **Premyelotoxic therapy:** Final dose should be given 24–48 h before therapy. **Postmyelotoxic therapy:** First dose should be given after but on the same day of hematopoietic stem cell infusion, and at least 4 d after the most recent administration of palifermin.

ADMINISTRATION

Intravenous
Do not give within 24 h before/after or during myelotoxic chemotherapy.

PREPARE: **Direct:** Reconstitute powder with 1.2 mL sterile water to yield 5 mg/mL. Gently swirl to dissolve but do not shake. Powder will dissolve in about 3 min. Should be used immediately.

ADMINISTER: **Direct:** Give as a bolus dose. If heparin is used to maintain the IV line, flush before/after with NS. If diluted solution was refrigerated, may warm to room temperature for up to 1 h but protect from light.
INCOMPATIBILITIES **Y-site:** Heparin.

▪Store powder vial at 2°–8° C (36°–46° F). Protect from light. If needed, may store reconstituted solution refrigerated for up to 24 h. Discard any reconstituted solution left at room temperature for longer than 1 h.

ADVERSE EFFECTS (≥5%) **Body as a Whole:** *Edema, fever, pain.* **CNS:** *Dysesthesia.* **GI:** *Mouth/tongue thickness or discoloration, taste alterations.* **Metabolic:** *Elevated serum amylase, elevated serum lipase.* **Musculoskeletal:** *Arthralgia.* **Skin:** *Erythema, pruritus, rash.* **Urogenital:** *Proteinuria.*

INTERACTIONS **Drug:** Administration of palifermin within 24 h of **myelotoxic chemotherapy** increases the severity and duration of oral mucositis.

PHARMACOKINETICS Distribution: Extravascular distribution. **Half-Life:** 4.5 h.

CLINICAL IMPLICATIONS

Assessment & Drug Effects
▪Monitor for improvement in mucositis.
▪Monitor for S&S of oral toxicities and skin toxicities.

Patient & Family Education
▪Report any of the following to a health care provider: alteration of taste, discoloration or enlargement of the tongue, lack of sensation around the mouth, skin rash, itching, or edema.

PALIVIZUMAB

(pal-i-viz'u-mab)

Synagis

Classifications: IMMUNOMODULATOR; MONOCLONAL ANTIBODY; IMMUNOGLOBULIN

Therapeutic: MONOCLONAL ANTIBODY; IMMUNOGLOBULIN (IGG)

Pregnancy Category: C

AVAILABILITY 100 mg vial

ACTION & *THERAPEUTIC EFFECT*
Monoclonal antibody (IgG1$_k$ produced by recombinant DNA technology) to the respiratory syncytial virus (RSV). *Provides passive immunity against respiratory syncytial virus. Indicated by prevention of lower respiratory tract infection.*

USES Prevention of serious lower respiratory tract infections in children susceptible to RSV.

CONTRAINDICATIONS Hypersensitivity to palivizumab; pregnancy (category C), lactation.

CAUTIOUS USE Hypersensitivity to other immunoglobulin preparations, blood products, or other medications; kidney or liver dysfunction; acute RSV infection.

ROUTE & DOSAGE

RSV
Child: **IM** 15 mg/kg qmo during RSV season

ADMINISTRATION

Intramuscular

- Reconstitute solution by gently injecting 1 mL of sterile water for injection (without preservative) toward the sides of the vial. Gently swirl for 30 s to dissolve (do not shake solution). Allow to stand at room temperature for at least 20 min until solution clears.
- Give IM only into the anterolateral aspect of the thigh. Volumes >1 mL should be divided and given in different sites.
- Use reconstituted solution within 6 h. Discard any unused portion of the vial. It contains no preservatives.

ADVERSE EFFECTS (≥1%) **Body as a Whole:** *Otitis media,* pain, hernia. **GI:** Increased AST, diarrhea, nausea, vomiting, gastroenteritis. **Respiratory:** *URI, rhinitis,* pharyngitis, cough, wheeze, bronchiolitis, asthma, croup, dyspnea, sinusitis, apnea. **Skin:** *Rash.*

PHARMACOKINETICS Half-Life: 20 d.

CLINICAL IMPLICATIONS

Assessment & Drug Effects

- Lab tests: Periodic monitoring of liver functions may be warranted.
- Monitor carefully for and immediately report S&S of respiratory illness including fever, cough, wheezing, and retractions.
- Assess for and report erythema or indurations at injection site.

Patient & Family Education

- Contact physician if S&S of respiratory illness, vomiting, diarrhea, or redness develop at injection site.

PALONOSETRON

(pal-o-no'si-tron)

Aloxi

Classifications: 5-HT$_3$ ANTAGONIST; ANTIEMETIC

Therapeutic: ANTIEMETIC; SEROTONIN 5-HT$_3$ RECEPTOR ANTAGONIST

Prototype: Ondansetron
Pregnancy Category: B

AVAILABILITY 0.25 mg/5 mL injection

ACTION & *THERAPEUTIC EFFECT*
Selectively blocks serotonin 5-HT$_3$ receptors found centrally in the chemoreceptor trigger zone (CTZ) in the hypothalamus, and peripherally at vagal nerve endings in the intestines. *Prevents acute chemotherapy-induced nausea and vomiting associated with initial and repeat courses of moderately or highly emetogenic chemotherapy.*

USES Prevention of acute and delayed nausea and vomiting associated with highly emetogenic cancer chemotherapy.
UNLABELED USES Postoperative nausea/vomiting.

CONTRAINDICATIONS Hypersensitivity to palonosetron; lactation, children <18 y.
CAUTIOUS USE Dehydration; cardiac arrhythmias, QT prolongation; electrolyte imbalance; pregnancy (category B).

ROUTE & DOSAGE

Prevention of Chemotherapy-Induced Nausea and Vomiting
Adult: **IV** 0.25 mg infused over 30 sec 30 min prior to chemotherapy; do not repeat for at least 7 d

Hepatic Impairment/Renal Impairment
No adjustment necessary

ADMINISTRATION

Intravenous _____

PREPARE: Direct: Do not dilute and do not mix with other drugs.

ADMINISTER: Direct: Give over 30 sec. Flush IV line with NS before and after administration.

INCOMPATIBILITIES Do not mix with other drugs.

■ Store at room temperature of 15°–30° C (59°–86° F). Protect from light.

ADVERSE EFFECTS (≥1%) **CNS:** Headache, anxiety, dizziness. **GI:** Constipation, diarrhea, abdominal pain. **Dermatologic:** Pruritus.

INTERACTIONS Drug: Can cause profound hypotension with **apomorphine.**

PHARMACOKINETICS Metabolism: In liver (CYP2D6, 1A2, 3A4). **Elimination:** Primarily renal. **Half-Life:** 40 h.

CLINICAL IMPLICATIONS
Assessment & Drug Effects
■ Monitor closely cardiac status especially in those taking diuretics or otherwise at risk for hypokalemia or hypomagnesemia, with congenital QT syndrome, or patients taking antiarrhythmic or other drugs that lead to QT prolongation.

Patient & Family Education
■ Report promptly any of the following: difficulty breathing, wheezing, or shortness of breath; palpitations or chest tightness; skin rash or itching; swelling of the face, tongue, throat, hands, or feet.

PAMIDRONATE DISODIUM

(pa-mi'dro-nate)
Aredia
Classifications: BISPHOSPHONATE (REGULATORY, BONE METABOLISM)
Therapeutic: REGULATORY, BONE METABOLISM
Prototype: Etidronate
Pregnancy Category: X

P

Common adverse effects in *italic*, life-threatening effects <u>underlined</u>; generic names in **bold**; classifications in SMALL CAPS; ◆ Canadian drug name; ☻ Prototype drug

1147

AVAILABILITY 30 mg, 60 mg, 90 mg injection

ACTION & *THERAPEUTIC EFFECT* A bone-resorption inhibitor thought to absorb calcium phosphate crystals into bone. May also inhibit osteoclast activity, thus contributing to inhibition of bone resorption. Does not inhibit bone formation or mineralization. *Reduces bone turnover and, when used in combination with adequate hydration, it increases renal excretion of calcium, thus reducing serum calcium concentrations.*

USES Hypercalcemia of malignancy and Paget's disease, bone metastases in multiple myeloma.
UNLABELED USES Primary hyperparathyroidism, osteoporosis.

CONTRAINDICATIONS Hypersensitivity to pamidronate; breast cancer, severe renal disease, hypercalcemia, hypercholesterolemia, polycythemia, pregnancy (category D), prostatic cancer. Safety and effectiveness in children are not established.
CAUTIOUS USE Heart failure, nephrosis or nephrotic syndrome, moderate renal disease; hepatic disease, cholestasis; peripheral edema, prostate hypertrophy; chronic kidney failure; lactation.

ROUTE & DOSAGE

Moderate Hypercalcemia of Malignancy (corrected calcium 12–13.5 mg/dL)
Adult: **IV** 60–90 mg infused over 4–24 h, may repeat in 7 d
Severe Hypercalcemia of Malignancy (corrected calcium >13.5 mg/dL)
Adult: **IV** 90 mg infused over 4–24 h, may repeat in 7 d

Paget's Disease, Metastases in Multiple Myeloma
Adult: **IV** 30 mg once daily for 3 d (90 mg total)

ADMINISTRATION

Intravenous

PREPARE: **IV Infusion:** Add 10 mL sterile water for injection to reconstitute the 30, 60, or 90 mg vial to produce concentrations of 3, 6, and 9 mg/1 mL, respectively. Withdraw the recommended dose and further dilute with D5W, NS, or 0.45% NaCl.
ADMINISTER: **IV Infusion: For hypercalcemia of malignancy:** Use 1000 mL of IV solution. **For Paget's disease or osteolytic lesions of multiple myeloma:** Use 500 mL of IV solution.
INCOMPATIBILITIES **Solution/additive:** CALCIUM-CONTAINING SOLUTIONS (including LACTATED RINGER'S).

▪Refrigerate reconstituted pamidronate solution at 2°–8° C (36°–46° F); the IV solution may be stored at room temperature. Both are stable for 24 h.

ADVERSE EFFECTS (≥1%) **Body as a Whole:** *Fever with or without rigors* generally occurs within 48 h and subsides within 48 h despite continued therapy; *thrombophlebitis at injection site;* general malaise lasting for several weeks; transient increase in bone pain. **Metabolic:** *Hypocalcemia.* **GI:** Nausea, abdominal pain, *epigastric discomfort.* **CV:** Hypertension. **Skin:** Rash.

INTERACTIONS Drug: Concurrent use of **foscarnet** may further decrease serum levels of ionized calcium.

PHARMACOKINETICS Absorption: 50% of dose is retained in body.

Onset: 24–48 h. **Peak:** 6 d. **Duration:** 2 wk–3 mo. **Distribution:** Accumulates in bone; once deposited, remains bound until bone is remodeled. **Metabolism:** Not metabolized. **Elimination:** 50% excreted in urine unchanged. **Half-Life:** 28 h.

CLINICAL IMPLICATIONS

Assessment & Drug Effects

- Assess IV injection site for thrombophlebitis.
- Lab tests: Monitor serum calcium and phosphate levels, CBC, and kidney function throughout course of therapy.
- Monitor for S&S of hypocalcemia, hypokalemia, hypomagnesemia, and hypophosphatemia.
- Monitor for seizures especially in those with a preexisting seizure disorder.
- Monitor vital signs. Be aware that drug fever, which may occur with pamidronate use, is self-limiting, usually subsiding in 48 hours even with continued therapy.

Patient & Family Education

- Be aware that transient, self-limiting fever with/without chills may develop.
- Generalized malaise, which may last for several weeks following treatment, is an anticipated adverse effect.
- Report to physician immediately perioral tingling, numbness, and paresthesia. These are signs of hypocalcemia.

PANCRELIPASE ⓟ

(pan-kre-li′pase)

Cotazym, Cotazym-S, Festal II, Ilozyme, Ku-Zyme-Hp, Pancrease, Ultrase, Viokase

Classifications: ENZYMES; ENZYME REPLACEMENT THERAPY

Therapeutic: PANCREATIC ENZYME REPLACEMENT THERAPY

Pregnancy Category: C

AVAILABILITY Tablets or capsules containing lipase, protease, and amylase

ACTION & *THERAPEUTIC EFFECT*
Pancreatic enzyme concentrate of porcine origin standardized for lipase content. Similar to pancreatin but on a weight basis has 12 times the lipolytic activity and at least 4 times the trypsin and amylase content of pancreatin. *Facilitates the hydrolysis of fats into glycerol and fatty acids, starches into dextrins and sugars, and proteins into peptides for easier absorption.*

USES Replacement therapy in symptomatic treatment of malabsorption syndrome due to cystic fibrosis and other conditions associated with exocrine pancreatic insufficiency.

CONTRAINDICATIONS History of allergy to porcine protein or enzymes; esophageal strictures; pancreatitis; pregnancy (category C).

CAUTIOUS USE GI disease, Crohn's disease, short bowel syndrome; CF; lactation.

ROUTE & DOSAGE

Pancreatic Insufficiency

Adult: **PO** 1–3 capsules or tablets or 1–2 packets of powder 1–2 h before, during, or 1 h after meals, with an extra dose taken with any food eaten between meals
Child: **PO** 1–2 capsules or tablets 1–2 h before, during, or 1 h after meals, with an extra dose taken with any food eaten between meals

P

Common adverse effects in *italic*, life-threatening effects <u>underlined</u>; generic names in **bold**; classifications in SMALL CAPS; ♣ Canadian drug name; ⓟ Prototype drug

1149

ADMINISTRATION

Oral

- Ensure that enteric-coated preparations are not crushed or chewed.
- Note: For children, powder form may be sprinkled on food.
- Open capsule and sprinkled contents on soft food, which should be swallowed without chewing to prevent mucus membrane irritation. Follow with a full glass of water or juice. Cimetidine, ranitidine, or an antacid may be prescribed to be given before pancrelipase to prevent drug's destruction by gastric pepsin and acid pH.
- Determine dosage in relation to fat content in diet (suggested ratio: 300 mg pancrelipase for each 17 g dietary fat).

ADVERSE EFFECTS (≥1%) **GI:** Anorexia, nausea, vomiting, diarrhea. **Metabolic:** Hyperuricosuria.

INTERACTIONS Drug: Iron absorption may be decreased.

PHARMACOKINETICS Absorption: Not absorbed. **Distribution:** Acts locally in GI tract. **Elimination:** In feces.

CLINICAL IMPLICATIONS

Assessment & Drug Effects

- Monitor I&O and weight. Note appetite and quality of stools, weight loss, abdominal bloating, polyuria, thirst, hunger, itching. Pancreatic insufficiency is frequently associated with steatorrhea, bulky stools, and insulin-dependent diabetes.

Patient & Family Education

- Learn proper timing of medication in relation to meals.

PANCURONIUM BROMIDE

(pan-kyoo-roe'nee-um)

Classifications: SKELETAL MUSCLE RELAXANT, NONDEPOLARIZING
Therapeutic: SKELETAL MUSCLE RELAXANT, NONDEPOLARIZING
Prototype: Atracurium
Pregnancy Category: C

AVAILABILITY 1 mg/mL, 2 mg/mL injection

ACTION & THERAPEUTIC EFFECT
Synthetic curariform nondepolarizing neuromuscular blocking agent that produces little or no histamine release or ganglionic blockade and thus does not cause bronchospasm or hypotension. Produces skeletal muscle relaxation or paralysis by competing with acetylcholine at cholinergic receptor sites on skeletal muscle endplate and thus blocks nerve impulse transmission. *Induces skeletal muscle relaxation or paralysis.*

USES Adjunct to anesthesia to induce skeletal muscle relaxation. Also to facilitate management of patients undergoing mechanical ventilation.

CONTRAINDICATIONS Hypersensitivity to the drug or bromides; tachycardia; pregnancy (category C).
CAUTIOUS USE Debilitated patients; dehydration; myasthenia gravis; neuromuscular disease; pulmonary, liver, or kidney disease; fluid or electrolyte imbalance; lactation.

ROUTE & DOSAGE

Skeletal Muscle Relaxation
Adult/Child: **IV** 0.04–0.1 mg/kg initial dose, may give additional doses of 0.01 mg/kg at 30–60 min intervals

Common adverse effects in *italic*, life-threatening effects underlined; generic names in **bold**, classifications in SMALL CAPS; ♣ Canadian drug name; ⑩ Prototype drug

Neonate: IV 0.02 mg/kg test dose, then 0.03 mg/kg

Obesity
Use IBW

Renal Impairment
Cl_{cr} 10–50 mL/min: use 50% of dose; <10 mL/min: do not use

ADMINISTRATION

Intravenous

Plastic syringe may be used for administration, but drug may adsorb to plastic with prolonged storage.

- Use a test dose of 0.02 mg/kg in infants ≥1 mo.

PREPARE: **Direct:** Give undiluted.
ADMINISTER: **Direct:** Give over 30–90 sec.
INCOMPATIBILITIES **Solution/additive: Furosemide.**

- Refrigerate at 2°–8° C (36°–46° F). Do not freeze.

ADVERSE EFFECTS (≥1%) **CV:** *Increased pulse rate and BP,* ventricular extrasystoles. **Skin:** Transient acneiform rash, burning sensation along course of vein. **Body as a Whole:** Salivation, skeletal muscle weakness, <u>respiratory depression</u>.

DIAGNOSTIC TEST INTERFERENCE Pancuronium may decrease *serum cholinesterase* concentrations.

INTERACTIONS Drug: GENERAL ANESTHETICS increase neuromuscular blocking and duration of action; AMINOGLYCOSIDES, **bacitracin, polymyxin B, clindamycin, lidocaine,** parenteral **magnesium, quinidine, quinine, trimethaphan, verapamil** increase neuromuscular blockade; DIURETICS may increase or decrease neuromuscular blockade; **lithium** prolongs duration of neuromuscular blockade; NARCOTIC ANALGESICS possibly add to respiratory depression; **succinylcholine** increases onset and depth of neuromuscular blockade; **phenytoin** may cause resistance to or reversal of neuromuscular blockade.

PHARMACOKINETICS Onset: 30–45 s. **Peak:** 2–3 min. **Duration:** 60 min. **Distribution:** Well distributed to tissues and extracellular fluids; crosses placenta in small amounts. **Metabolism:** Small amount in liver. **Elimination:** Primarily in urine. **Half-Life:** 2 h.

CLINICAL IMPLICATIONS

Assessment & Drug Effects

- Assess cardiovascular and respiratory status continuously.
- Observe patient closely for residual muscle weakness and signs of respiratory distress during recovery period. Monitor BP and vital signs. Peripheral nerve stimulator may be used to assess the effects of pancuronium and to monitor restoration of neuromuscular function.
- Note: Consciousness is not affected by pancuronium. Patient will be awake and alert but unable to speak.

PANITUMUMAB

(pan-i-tu-mu′mab)
Vectibix
Classifications: ANTINEOPLASTIC AGENT; BIOLOGIC RESPONSE MODIFIER; MONOCLONAL ANTIBODY; EPIDERMAL GROWTH FACTOR RECEPTOR (EGFR) INHIBITOR
Therapeutic: ANTINEOPLASTIC; MONOCLONAL ANTIBODY; EGFR INHIBITOR
Pregnancy Category: C

AVAILABILITY 20 mg/mL solution for injection in 5 mL, 10 mL, and 20 mL vials

P

Common adverse effects in *italic*, life-threatening effects <u>underlined</u>; generic names in **bold**; classifications in SMALL CAPS; ♣ Canadian drug name; ⊘ Prototype drug

1151

ACTION & *THERAPEUTIC EFFECT*

Overexpression of epidermal growth factor receptors (EGFRs) occurs in many human cancers, including those of the colon and rectum. EGFRs control the activity of intracellular tyrosine kinases that regulate transcription of DNA molecules involved in cellular growth, survival, motility, proliferation, and transformation. *Panitumumab inhibits upregulation or overexpression of EGFR in cancer cells, decreasing their capacity for cell proliferation, cell survival, and decreasing their invasive capacity and metastases.*

USES Treatment of EGFR-expressing metastatic colorectal carcinoma in patients with disease progression on or following fluoropyrimidine-, oxaliplatin-, and irinotecan-containing chemotherapy regimens.

CONTRAINDICATIONS Pulmonary fibrosis; interstitial lung disease. Use contraception for females of childbearing age; pregnancy (category C); lactation. Safe use in children not established.

CAUTIOUS USE Photosensitivity with drug use; electrolyte imbalances, especially hypomagnesemia, and hypocalcemia; lung disorders.

ROUTE & DOSAGE

Metastatic Colorectal Carcinoma
Adult: **IV** 6 mg/kg q14d

Dosage Adjustments for Infusion Reactions and Dermatologic Reactions

Mild or moderate infusion reactions (Grade 1 or 2): Reduce infusion rate by 50%
Severe infusion reactions (Grade 3 or 4): DC permanently

Intolerable or severe dermatologic toxicity (greater than Grade 3): Withhold drug. If toxicity does not improve to at least grade 2 within 1 mo, permanently DC. If toxicity improves to at least grade 2 and patient is symptomatically improved after withholding no more than 2 doses, resume at 50% of original dose. If toxicities recur, DC permanently. If toxicities do not recur, subsequent doses may be increased by increments of 25% of original dose until 6 mg/kg is reached.

ADMINISTRATION

Intravenous

PREPARE: **IV Infusion:** Dilute doses up to 1000 mg with NS to a total volume of 100 mL. Dilute higher doses with NS to a total volume of 150 mL. Final concentration should not exceed 10 mg/mL. Mix by gentle inversion and do not shake. Solution will contain small translucent particles that will be removed by filtration during infusion.

ADMINISTER: **IV Infusion:** Infuse doses <1000 mg over 60 min. Infuse doses >1000 mg over 90 min. Use an infusion pump and a 0.2 or 0.22 micron in-line filter. Flush the line before/after infusion with NS. Discontinue infusion immediately if an anaphylactic reaction is suspected (i.e., bronchospasm, fever, chills, hypotension).

■ Store unopened vials at 2°–8° C (36°–46° F). Protect vials from direct sunlight. Use diluted infusion solution within 6 h if stored at room temperature, or within 24 h if stored at 2°–8° C (36°– 46° F).

ADVERSE EFFECTS (≥1%) **Body as a Whole:** *Fatigue,* infectious seque-

P

lae and septic death, infusion reactions, peripheral edema. **GI:** *Abdominal pain, constipation, diarrhea,* mucosal inflammation, *nausea,* stomatitis, *vomiting.* **Metabolic:** *Hypomagnesemia.* **Respiratory:** *Cough,* pulmonary fibrosis. **Skin:** *Acneiform dermatitis, dry skin, erythema, pruritus, skin exfoliation, skin fissures,* nail disorders, paronychia. **Special Senses:** Conjunctivitis, eye/eyelid irritation, increased lacrimation, ocular hyperemia.

PHARMACOKINETICS Half-Life: 7.5 d.

CLINICAL IMPLICATIONS

Assessment & Drug Effects
- Monitor for S&S of a severe infusion reaction; check vital signs q30min during infusion and 30 min post-infusion.
- Monitor for and report S&S of dermatologic toxicity such as acne-like dermatitis, pruritus, erythema, rash, skin exfoliation, dry skin, and skin fissures; inflammatory or infectious sequelae in those who experience severe dermatologic toxicities.
- Withhold drug and notify physician for any signs of drug toxicity.
- Lab tests: Periodic serum electrolytes during and for 8 wk following completion of therapy.

Patient & Family Education
- Immediately report any discomfort experienced during and shortly after drug infusion.
- Wear sunscreen and limit sun exposure while receiving panitumumab.
- Report any of the following to a health care provider: any signs of irritation, inflammation, or infection of the skin, nails, or eyes; shortness of breath or any other breathing difficulty.
- Women of childbearing age should use reliable means of contraception during and for 6 mo after the last dose of panitumumab.

PANTOPRAZOLE SODIUM
(pan-to'pra-zole)
Protonix, Protonix IV
Classifications: PROTON PUMP INHIBITOR
Therapeutic: ANTIULCER; PROTON PUMP INHIBITOR
Prototype: Omeprazole
Pregnancy Category: B

AVAILABILITY 40 mg enteric coated tablets; 40 mg injection

ACTION & THERAPEUTIC EFFECT Gastric acid pump inhibitor; belongs to a class of antisecretory compounds. Gastric acid secretion is decreased by inhibiting the H^+, K^+-ATPase enzyme system responsible for acid production. *Specifically, suppresses gastric acid secretion by inhibiting the acid (proton H^+) pump in the parietal cells.*

USES Short-term treatment of erosive esophagitis associated with gastroesophageal reflux disease (GERD), hypersecretory disease.
UNLABELED USES Peptic ulcer disease.

CONTRAINDICATIONS Hypersensitivity to pantoprazole or other proton pump inhibitors (PPIs); severe hepatic insufficiency, cirrhosis; lactation.
CAUTIOUS USE Mild to moderate hepatic insufficiency; pregnancy (category B). Safety and effectiveness in children <18 y are not established.

Common adverse effects in *italic*, life-threatening effects underlined; generic names in **bold**, classifications in SMALL CAPS; ♦ Canadian drug name; ☺ Prototype drug

1153

ROUTE & DOSAGE

Erosive Esophagitis

Adult: **PO** 40 mg q.d. times 8–16 wks **IV** 40 mg q.d. times 7–10 d

Hypersecretory Disease

Adult: **PO** 40 mg b.i.d. (doses up to 240 mg/d have been used) **IV** 80 mg b.i.d.; adjust based on acid output

Renal Impairment/Hepatic Impairment

Adjustment not needed.
Hemodialysis: Drug not removed.

ADMINISTRATION

Oral

- Do not crush or break in half. Must be swallowed whole.
- Note: Therapy beyond 16 wk is not recommended.
- Store preferably at 20°–25° C (66°–77° F), but room temperature permitted.

Intravenous

PREPARE: IV Infusion: *Two-min infusion:* Reconstitute each 40 mg vial with 10 mL NS. *Fifteen-min infusion:* Reconstitute as for 2-min infusion, then further dilute with 100 mL of D5W, NS, or RL to yield 0.4 mg/mL.

ADMINISTER: IV Infusion: Give through a dedicated line or flushed IV line before and after each dose with D5W, NS, or RL. *Two-min infusion:* Give over at least 2 min. *Fifteen-min infusion:* Infuse over 15 min at a rate of 6 mg/min (7 mL/min). Note: Protonix IV packaged with an in-line filter must be used with the provided filter. A newer formulation does not require an in-line filter.

INCOMPATIBILITIES Solution/additive: Solutions containing **zinc.** **Y-site: Midazolam, zinc.**

- Reconstituted solution may be stored for up to 2 h at 15–30° C (59–86° F) before further dilution. The diluted 100 mL solution may be stored for up to 22 h.

ADVERSE EFFECTS (≥1%) **GI:** Diarrhea, flatulence, abdominal pain. **CNS:** Headache, insomnia. **Skin:** Rash.

INTERACTIONS Drug: May decrease absorption of **ampicillin,** IRON SALTS, **itraconazole, ketoconazole;** increases INR with **warfarin. Herbal: Ginkgo** may decrease plasma levels.

PHARMACOKINETICS Absorption: Well absorbed with 77% bioavailability. **Peak:** 2.4 h. **Distribution:** 98% protein bound. **Metabolism:** In liver (CYP2C19). **Elimination:** 71% in urine, 18% in feces. **Half-Life:** 1 h.

CLINICAL IMPLICATIONS

Assessment & Drug Effects

- Monitor for and immediately report S&S of angioedema or a severe skin reaction.
- Lab tests: Urea breath test 4–6 wk after completion of therapy.

Patient & Family Education

- Contact physician promptly if any of the following occur: Peeling, blistering, or loosening of skin; skin rash, hives, or itching; swelling of the face, tongue, or lips; difficulty breathing or swallowing.

PAPAVERINE HYDROCHLORIDE

(pa-pav'er-een)

Classifications: NONNITRATE VASODILATOR
Therapeutic: NONNITRATE VASODILATOR
Prototype: Hydralazine
Pregnancy Category: C

AVAILABILITY 150 mg sustained release capsule; 30 mg/mL injection

ACTION & *THERAPEUTIC EFFECT*
Exerts nonspecific direct spasmolytic effect on smooth muscles unrelated to innervation. Action is especially pronounced on coronary, cerebral, pulmonary, and peripheral arteries when spasm is present. Acts directly on myocardium, depresses conduction and irritability, and prolongs refractory period. *Relaxes the smooth muscle of the heart as well as produces relaxation of the vascular smooth muscles.*

USES Primarily for relief of cerebral and peripheral ischemia associated with arterial spasm and MI complicated by arrhythmias. Also visceral spasm as in ureteral, biliary, and GI colic.
UNLABELED USES Impotence, cardiac bypass surgery.

CONTRAINDICATIONS Parenteral use in complete AV block; pregnancy (category C); lactation.
CAUTIOUS USE Glaucoma; myocardial depression; glaucoma; QT prolongation, angina pectoris; recent stroke.

ROUTE & DOSAGE

Cerebral and Peripheral Ischemia
Adult: **PO** 150–300 mg q8–12h **IM/IV** 30–120 mg q3h as needed
Child: **IM/IV** 6 mg/kg/d divided into 4 doses

ADMINISTRATION
Oral
- Give with or following meals; give milk or prescribed antacid to reduce possibility of nausea.
- Ensure that sustained release form is not chewed or crushed. Must be swallowed whole.

Intramuscular
- Aspirate carefully before injecting IM to avoid inadvertent entry into blood vessel, and administer slowly.

Intravenous
- IV administration to children: Verify correct IV concentration and rate of infusion with physician.

PREPARE: Direct: Give undiluted or diluted in an equal volume of sterile water for injection.
ADMINISTER: Direct: Give slowly over 1–2 min. AVOID rapid injection.
INCOMPATIBILITIES Solution/additive: Aminophylline, heparin.

ADVERSE EFFECTS (≥1%) **Body as a Whole:** General discomfort, facial flushing, sweating, weakness, coma. **CNS:** Dizziness, drowsiness, headache, sedation. **CV:** Slight rise in BP, paroxysmal tachycardia, transient ventricular ectopic rhythms, AV block, arrhythmias. **GI:** Nausea, anorexia, constipation, diarrhea, abdominal distress, dry mouth and throat, hepatotoxicity (jaundice, eosinophilia, abnormal liver function tests); with rapid IV administration. **Respiratory:** Increased depth of respiration, respiratory depression, fatal apnea. **Skin:** Pruritus, skin rash. **Special Senses:** Diplopia, nystagmus. **Urogenital:** Priapism.

INTERACTIONS Drug: May decrease **levodopa** effectiveness; **morphine** may antagonize smooth muscle relaxation effect of papaverine.

PHARMACOKINETICS Absorption: Readily from GI tract. **Peak:** 1–2 h. **Duration:** 12 h sustained release. **Metabolism:** In liver. **Elimination:** In urine chiefly as metabolites. **Half-Life:** 90 min.

CLINICAL IMPLICATIONS
Assessment & Drug Effects
- Monitor pulse, respiration, and BP in patients receiving drug paren-

P

Common adverse effects in *italic*, life-threatening effects underlined; generic names in **bold**; classifications in SMALL CAPS; ♣ Canadian drug name; Ⓟ Prototype drug

1155

terally. If significant changes are noted, withhold medication and report promptly to physician.

▪ Lab tests: Perform liver function and blood tests periodically. Hepatotoxicity (thought to be a hypersensitivity reaction) is reversible with prompt drug withdrawal.

Patient & Family Education

▪ Notify physician if any adverse effect persists or if GI symptoms, jaundice, or skin rash appear. Liver function tests may be indicated.

▪ Do not drive or engage in potentially hazardous activities until response to drug is known. Alcohol may increase drowsiness and dizziness.

PARALDEHYDE

(par-al'de-hyde)
Paral
Classifications: ANTICONVULSANT; SEDATIVE-HYPNOTIC; BARBITURATE
Therapeutic: ANTICONVULSANT; SEDATIVE-HYPNOTIC
Prototype: Phenobarbital
Pregnancy Category: C
Controlled Substance: Schedule IV

AVAILABILITY 1 g/mL liquid

ACTION & *THERAPEUTIC EFFECT*
Cyclic ether formed by polymerization of acetaldehyde. Potent CNS depressant with sedative and hypnotic actions similar to those of alcohol, barbiturates, and chloral hydrate. *CNS depressant with sedative and hypnotic effects. Also has anticonvulsant properties.*

USES Sedative and hypnotic in acute agitation due to alcohol withdrawal; used to control convulsions arising from tetanus, eclampsia, Status Epilepticus, and drug poisoning. Has been used rectally to

induce basal anesthesia, particularly in children.

CONTRAINDICATIONS Severe hepatic insufficiency; respiratory disease; GI inflammation or ulceration; disulfiram therapy; pregnancy (category C), lactation.

ROUTE & DOSAGE

Hypnotic
Adult: **PO** 10–30 mL prn
Child: **PO** 0.3 mL/kg

Sedative
Adult: **PO** 5–10 mL prn
Child: **PO** 0.15 mL/kg

Seizures Secondary to Tetanus
Adult: **PO** up to 12 mL diluted 1:10 q4h prn

Seizures Secondary to Other Poisons
Adult: **PR** 5–15 mL diluted in 200 mL per rectal tube

Status Epilepticus
Child: **PR** 1 mL/y of age up to 5 mL; may repeat in 1 h if necessary, then change to PO. PO 2–5 mL q2–4h

Alcohol Withdrawal Seizures
Adult: **PO** 5–10 mL q4–6h for 24 h, then q6h prn

ADMINISTRATION

Note: Both oral and rectal doses must be diluted before they are administered.

Oral, Rectal

▪ Note: On exposure to light, air, and heat, drug liberates acetaldehyde, which oxidizes to acetic acid. Do not use solution if it is colored in any way or smells of acetic acid (vinegar odor).

▪ Discard unused contents of any container that has been open for more than 24 h. Decomposed paraldehyde is extremely corrosive to tissues and can cause fatal poisoning.

- Do not use plastics for measuring or administering paraldehyde. Contact with plastic materials can decompose paraldehyde to toxic compounds. Draw parenteral preparation into a glass syringe; use rubber catheter for rectal administration.
- Give oral drug well diluted in iced fruit juice or milk to reduce irritation of GI tract and mask odor and taste.
- When given rectally, dilute drug with at least 2 volumes of olive oil or cottonseed oil or dissolved in 200 mL of NS solution to prevent rectal irritation.
- Do not withdraw rapidly after prolonged use; may produce delirium tremens and hallucinations.
- Preserve in tight, light-resistant containers in amounts not exceeding 30 mL and at temperatures not over 25° C (77° F).

ADVERSE EFFECTS (≥1%) **Body as a Whole:** Occasionally confusion and paradoxical excitement. **CNS:** Hangover, dizziness, ataxia. **CV:** Hypotension, dilation and failure of right heart, cardiovascular collapse. **GI:** *Irritation of mucous membrane (oral and rectal routes),* nausea, vomiting, unpleasant taste and odor, toxic hepatitis, bleeding gastritis, liver damage. **Urogenital:** Nephrosis, renal damage. **Metabolic:** Metabolic acidosis, acidosis. **Respiratory:** Rapid labored breathing, respiratory depression, pulmonary hemorrhage and edema. **Skin:** *Erythematous skin rash.*

DIAGNOSTIC TEST INTERFERENCE Chronic use of alcohol (ethanol) and paraldehyde may cause false-positive *serum ketones (nitroprusside tube dilution method)* and *urine ketones (Acetest)* and may interfere with *urinary steroid (17-OHCS) determinations* by modification of *Reddy, Jenkins, Thorn procedure.*

INTERACTIONS Drug: Disulfiram may increase paraldehyde levels; **alcohol** and other CNS DEPRESSANTS add to CNS depressant effects—fatalities reported with **alcohol.**

PHARMACOKINETICS Absorption: Readily absorbed from GI tract. **Onset:** 10–15 min. **Duration:** 6–8 h. **Distribution:** Distributed into CNS; crosses placenta. **Metabolism:** 80–90% of doses metabolized in liver. **Elimination:** Excreted through lungs (11–28%) and urine. **Half-Life:** 7.5 h.

CLINICAL IMPLICATIONS

Assessment & Drug Effects

- Monitor cardiovascular and respiratory status closely.
- Keep the patient turned on side to prevent aspiration since bronchial secretions may be increased. Suctioning may be necessary.
- Be aware that patient's breath will have a characteristic odor for several hours.

PAREGORIC (CAMPHORATED OPIUM TINCTURE)

(par-e-gor'ik)
Classifications: ANTIDIARRHEAL; NARCOTIC (OPIATE) AGONIST ANALGESIC
Therapeutic: ANTIDIARRHEAL; OPIATE
Prototype: Loperamide
Pregnancy Category: C
Controlled Substance: Schedule III

AVAILABILITY 2 mg/5 mL liquid

Common adverse effects in *italic*, life-threatening effects underlined; generic names in **bold**; classifications in SMALL CAPS; ♣ Canadian drug name; ☺ Prototype drug

1157

ACTION & *THERAPEUTIC EFFECT*
Contains 2 mg anhydrous morphine, alcohol, benzoic acid, camphor, and anise oil. Pharmacologic activity is due to morphine content. Increases smooth muscle tone of GI tract, decreases motility and effective propulsive peristalsis while diminishing digestive secretions. *Delayed transit of intestinal contents results in desiccation of feces and constipation.*

USES Short-term treatment for symptomatic relief of acute diarrhea and abdominal cramps.

CONTRAINDICATIONS Hypersensitivity to opium alkaloids; diarrhea caused by poisons (until eliminated); COPD; pregnancy (category C).

CAUTIOUS USE Asthma; liver disease; GI disease; history of opiate agonist dependence; severe prostatic hypertrophy, lactation.

ROUTE & DOSAGE

Acute Diarrhea
Adult: **PO** 5–10 mL after loose bowel movement, 1–4 times daily if needed
Child: **PO** 0.25–0.5 mL/kg 1–4 times/d

ADMINISTRATION
Oral
- Give paregoric in sufficient water (2 or 3 swallows) to ensure its passage into the stomach (mixture will appear milky).

ADVERSE EFFECTS (≥1%) **GI:** Anorexia, nausea, vomiting, *constipation,* abdominal pain. **Body as a Whole:** Dizziness, faintness, drowsiness, facial flushing, sweating, physical dependence.

INTERACTIONS Drug: Alcohol and other CNS DEPRESSANTS add to CNS effects.

PHARMACOKINETICS Absorption: Readily from GI tract. **Duration:** 4–5 h. **Distribution:** Crosses placenta; distributed into breast milk. **Metabolism:** In liver. **Elimination:** In urine. **Half-Life:** 2–3 h.

CLINICAL IMPLICATIONS
Assessment & Drug Effects
- Paregoric may worsen the course of infection-associated diarrhea by delaying the elimination of pathogens.
- Be aware that adverse effects are primarily due to morphine content. Paregoric abuse results because of the narcotic content of the drug.
- Assess for fluid and electrolyte imbalance until diarrhea has stopped.

Patient & Family Education
- Adhere strictly to prescribed dosage schedule.
- Maintain bed rest if diarrhea is severe with a high level of fluid loss.
- Replace fluids and electrolytes as needed for diarrhea. Drink warm clear liquids and avoid dairy products, concentrated sweets, and cold drinks until diarrhea stops.
- Observe character and frequency of stools. Discontinue drug as soon as diarrhea is controlled. Report promptly to physician if diarrhea persists more than 3 d, if fever is >38.8° C (102° F), abdominal pain develops, or if mucus or blood is passed.
- Understand that constipation is often a consequence of antidiarrheal treatment and a normal elimination pattern is usually established as dietary intake increases.

P

Common adverse effects in *italic*, life-threatening effects underlined; generic names in **bold**; classifications in SMALL CAPS; ✦ Canadian drug name; ☉ Prototype drug

PARICALCITOL

(par-i-cal'ci-tol)
Zemplar
Classifications: HORMONE; VITAMIN D ANALOG
Therapeutic: VITAMIN D ANALOG
Prototype: Calcitriol
Pregnancy Category: C

AVAILABILITY 2 mcg/mL, 5 mcg/mL vial; 1 mcg, 2 mcg, 4 mcg capsules

ACTION & *THERAPEUTIC EFFECT*
Synthetic vitamin D analog that reduces parathyroid hormone (PTH) activity levels in chronic kidney failure (CRF) patients. Lowers serum levels of calcium and phosphate. In addition it decreases the parathyroid hormone as well as bone resorption in some patients. *Effectiveness indicated by iPTH levels <1.5–3 times the nonuremic upper limit of normal.*

USES Prevention and treatment of secondary hyperparathyroidism associated with CRF.

CONTRAINDICATIONS Hypersensitivity to paricalcitol; hypercalcemia; evidence of vitamin D toxicity; concurrent administration of phosphate preparations and vitamin D; pregnancy (category C); children <5 y.
CAUTIOUS USE Lactation; severe liver disease; concurrent administration of digitalis; abnormally low levels of PTH.

ROUTE & DOSAGE

CRF-Associated Secondary Hyperparathyroidism

Adult: **IV** 0.04 mcg/kg–0.1 mcg/kg (max: 0.24 mcg/kg), no more than every other day during dialysis PO iPTH <500 pg/mL, 1 mcg/d or 2 mcg 3 times/wk;

iPTH >500 pg/mL, 2 mcg/d or 4 mcg 3 times/wk
Child: **IV** 5–17 y, 0.04 mcg/kg 3 times/wk during dialysis

ADMINISTRATION

Oral
- Give no more frequently than every other day when dosing 3 times/wk.
- Store at 15–30° C (59–86° F).

Intravenous

PREPARE: Direct: Give undiluted.
ADMINISTER: Direct: Give IV bolus dose anytime during dialysis.

- Store at 25° C (77° F). Discard unused portion of a single dose vial.

ADVERSE EFFECTS (≥1%) **Body as a Whole:** Chills, feeling unwell, fever, flu-like symptoms, sepsis, edema. **CNS:** Lightheadedness. **CV:** Palpitations. **GI:** Dry mouth, <u>GI bleeding</u>, *nausea*, vomiting. **Respiratory:** Pneumonia. **Metabolic:** Hypercalcemia.

INTERACTIONS Drug: Hypercalcemia may increase risk of **digoxin** toxicity; may increase **magnesium** absorption and toxicity in renal failure. **Herbal:** Be cautious of **vitamin D** content in herbal and OTC products.

PHARMACOKINETICS Distribution: >99% protein bound. **Metabolism:** Via CYP3A4. **Elimination:** Primarily in feces (74%). **Half-Life:** 15 h.

CLINICAL IMPLICATIONS
Assessment & Drug Effects
- Monitor for S&S of hypercalcemia (see Appendix F).
- Lab tests: Serum calcium and phosphate 2 times a wk during initiation of therapy; then monthly; serum PTH q3mo; periodic serum magnesium, alkaline phosphatase,

P

Common adverse effects in *italic*, life-threatening effects <u>underlined</u>; generic names in **bold**; classifications in SMALL CAPS; ✦ Canadian drug name; ☻ Prototype drug

1159

24-urinary calcium and phosphate. Increase frequency of lab tests during dosage adjustments.
▪ Withhold drug and notify physician if hypercalcemia occurs.
▪ Coadministered drugs: Monitor for digoxin toxicity if serum calcium level is elevated.

Patient & Family Education
▪ Report immediately any of the following to the physician: Weakness, anorexia, nausea, vomiting, abdominal cramps, diarrhea, muscle or bone pain, or excessive thirst.
▪ Adhere strictly to dietary regimen of calcium supplementation and phosphorus restriction to ensure successful therapy.
▪ Avoid excessive use of aluminum-containing compounds such as antacids/vitamins.

PAROMOMYCIN SULFATE ⊕

(par-oh-moe-mye′sin)
Humatin
Classifications: AMINOGLYCOSIDE ANTIBIOTIC; AMEBICIDE
Therapeutic: ANTIBIOTIC; AMEBICIDE
Pregnancy Category: C

AVAILABILITY 250 mg capsules

ACTION & *THERAPEUTIC EFFECT*
Aminoglycoside antibiotic produced by certain strains of *Streptomyces rimosus* with broad spectrum of antibacterial activity closely paralleling that of kanamycin and neomycin. *Exerts direct bactericidal and amebicidal action, primarily in lumen of GI tract. Ineffective against extraintestinal amebiasis.*

USES Acute and chronic intestinal amebiasis and to rid bowel of nitrogen-forming bacteria in patients with hepatic coma; used preoperatively to suppress intestinal flora. Also tapeworm infestation.

CONTRAINDICATIONS Aminoglycoside hypersensitivity; intestinal obstruction; impaired kidney function; pregnancy (category C).
CAUTIOUS USE GI ulceration; renal failure, renal impairment; older adults; myasthenia gravis; parkinsonism.

ROUTE & DOSAGE

Intestinal Amebiasis
Adult/Child: **PO** 25–35 mg/kg divided in 3 doses for 5–10 d
Hepatic Coma
Adult: **PO** 4 g/d in divided doses for 5–6 d

ADMINISTRATION

Oral
▪ Give after meals to prevent gastric distress.

ADVERSE EFFECTS (≥1%) **CNS:** Headache, vertigo. **GI:** *Diarrhea, abdominal cramps,* steatorrhea, *nausea, vomiting, heartburn,* secondary enterocolitis. **Skin:** Exanthema, rash, pruritus. **Special Senses:** Ototoxicity. **Urogenital:** Nephrotoxicity (in patients with GI inflammation or ulcerations). **Body as a Whole:** Eosinophilia, overgrowth of nonsusceptible organisms.

DIAGNOSTIC TEST INTERFERENCE Prolonged use of paromomycin may cause reduction in ***serum cholesterol.***

INTERACTIONS Drug: May decrease absorption of **cyanocobalamin.**

PHARMACOKINETICS Absorption: Poorly from intact GI tract. **Elimination:** In feces.

P

CLINICAL IMPLICATIONS

Assessment & Drug Effects

- Monitor therapeutic effectiveness. Criterion of cure is absence of amoebae in stool specimens examined at weekly intervals for 6 wk after completion of treatment, and thereafter at monthly intervals for 2 y.
- Monitor for appearance of a superinfection during therapy (see Appendix F).
- Lab test: baseline WBC with differential. Repeat if superinfection is suspected.
- Monitor closely patients with history of GI ulceration for nephrotoxicity and ototoxicity (see Appendix F). Drug absorption can take place through diseased mucosa.

Patient & Family Education

- Do not prepare, process, or serve food until treatment is complete when receiving drug for intestinal amebiasis. Isolation is not required.
- Practice strict personal hygiene, particularly hand washing after defecation and before eating food.

PAROXETINE

(par-ox′e-teen)
Pexeva, Paxil, Paxil CR

Classifications: PSYCHOTHERAPEUTIC AGENT; ANTIDEPRESSANT; SELECTIVE SEROTONIN REUPTAKE INHIBITOR (SSRI)
Therapeutic: ANTIDEPRESSANT; SSRI
Prototype: Fluoxetine
Pregnancy Category: D

AVAILABILITY 10 mg, 20 mg, 30 mg, 40 mg tablets; 12.5 mg, 25 mg, 37.5 mg sustained release tablets; 10 mg/5 mL suspension

ACTION & *THERAPEUTIC EFFECT*

Antidepressant structurally unrelated to other serotonin reuptake inhibitors. Potent and highly selective inhibitor of serotonin reuptake by neurons in CNS. *Efficacious in depression resistant to other antidepressants and in depression complicated by anxiety.*

USES Depression, obsessive-compulsive disorders, panic attacks, excessive social anxiety, generalized anxiety, post-traumatic stress disorder (PTSD), premenstrual dysphoric disorder (PMDD).

UNLABELED USES Diabetic neuropathy, myoclonus, bipolar depression in conjunction with lithium, chronic headache, premature ejaculation, fibromyalgia.

CONTRAINDICATIONS Hypersensitivity to paroxetine; suicidal ideation; concomitant use of MAO inhibitors, pregnancy (category D); alcohol; children or adolescents with major depressive disorder.

CAUTIOUS USE History of mania, suicidal ideation; anorexia nervosa, ECT therapy; seizure disorder, seizures; renal/hepatic impairment, renal failure; history of metabolic disorders; volume-depleted patients, recent MI, unstable cardiac disease; lactation. Safety and efficacy have not been established in children <18 y.

ROUTE & DOSAGE

Depression

Adult: **PO** 10–50 mg/d (max: 80 mg/d); 25 mg sustained release q.d. in morning, may increase by 12.5 mg (max: 62.5 mg/d); use lower starting doses for patients with renal or hepatic insufficiency and geriatric patients

P

Common adverse effects in *italic*, life-threatening effects underlined; generic names in **bold**, classifications in SMALL CAPS; ♣ Canadian drug name; ❷ Prototype drug

1161

Geriatric: **PO** Start with 10 mg/d (12.5 mg/d sustained release), [max: 40 mg/d (50 mg/d sustained release)]

Obsessive-Compulsive Disorder

Adult: **PO** 20–60 mg/d

Panic Attacks

Adult: **PO** 40 mg/d

Social Anxiety Disorder

Adult: **PO** 20–60 mg/d

Generalized Anxiety, PTSD

Adult: **PO** Start with 10 mg once daily, may increase by 10 mg/d at weekly intervals if needed to target dose of 40 mg once daily (max: 60 mg/d)
Geriatric: **PO** Start with 10 mg PO once daily, may increase by 10 mg/d at weekly intervals if needed (max: 40 mg/d)

Premenstrual Dysphoric Disorder

Adult: **PO** 12.5 mg once daily (up to 25 mg once daily) throughout the month or daily for 2 wk before menstrual period

ADMINISTRATION

Oral

- Recommended initial dose with older adult, debilitated, or those with severe renal or hepatic impairment is 10 mg/d.
- Monitor children and adolescents for changes in behavior that may indicate suicidal ideation.
- Ensure that sustained release form is not chewed or crushed. Must be swallowed whole.
- Be aware that at least 14 d should elapse when switching a patient from/to an MAO inhibitor to/from paroxetine.

ADVERSE EFFECTS (≥1%) **CV:** Postural hypotension. **CNS:** *Head-ache,* tremor, agitation or nervousness, anxiety, paresthesias, dizziness, insomnia, *sedation.* **GI:** *Nausea,* constipation, vomiting, anorexia, diarrhea, dyspepsia, flatulence, increased appetite, taste aversion, *dry mouth.* **Urogenital:** Urinary hesitancy or frequency. **Hepatic:** Isolated reports of elevated liver enzymes. **Special Senses:** Blurred vision. **Skin:** Diaphoresis, rash, pruritus. **Metabolic:** Hyponatremia in older adult.

INTERACTIONS Drug: **Activated charcoal** reduces absorption of paroxetine. **Cimetidine** increases paroxetine levels. MAO INHIBITORS, **selegiline** may cause an increased vasopressor response leading to hypertensive crisis or death. **Phenytoin** can cause liver enzyme induction resulting in lower paroxetine levels and shorter half-life. **Warfarin** may increase risk of bleeding and **thioridazine** levels, and prolong QTc interval leading to heart block; increase **ergotamine** toxicity with **dihydroergotamine, ergotamine.** **Herbal:** **St. John's wort** may cause serotonin syndrome (headache, dizziness, sweating, agitation).

PHARMACOKINETICS Absorption: 99% from GI tract. **Onset:** 2 wk. **Peak:** 5–8 h. **Distribution:** Very lipophilic. 95% protein bound. Distributes into breast milk. **Metabolism:** Extensively in the liver to inactive metabolites. **Elimination:** Less than 2% is excreted unchanged in urine. 65% of dose appears in urine as metabolites. Metabolites of paroxetine are also excreted in feces, presumably via bile. **Half-Life:** 24 h.

CLINICAL IMPLICATIONS

Assessment & Drug Effects

- Monitor for worsening of depression or emergence of suicidal ideation.

- Monitor for adverse effects, which include headache, weakness, sedation, dizziness, insomnia; nausea, constipation, or diarrhea; dry mouth; sweating; male ejaculatory disturbance. These occur in more than 10% of all patients and may result in poor compliance with drug regimen.
- Monitor older adult for fluid and sodium imbalances.
- Monitor those <18 y for suicidal ideation.
- Monitor for significant weight loss.
- Monitor patients with history of mania for reactivation of condition.
- Monitor patients with preexisting cardiovascular disease carefully because paroxetine may adversely affect hemodynamic status.

Patient & Family Education
- Use caution when operating hazardous machinery or equipment until response to drug is known.
- Concurrent use of alcohol may increase risk of adverse CNS effects.
- Adaptation to some adverse effects (especially dizziness and nausea) may occur over a period of 4–6 wk.
- Do not stop drug therapy after improvement in emotional status occurs.
- Notify physician of any distressing adverse effects.

PEGFILGRASTIM

(peg-fil-gras'tim)
Neulasta
Classifications: BLOOD FORMER; HEMATOPOIETIC GROWTH FACTOR
Therapeutic: HEMATOPOIETIC GROWTH FACTOR
Prototype: Epoetin alfa
Pregnancy Category: C

AVAILABILITY 10 mg/mL injection

ACTION & *THERAPEUTIC EFFECT*
Human granulocyte colony-stimulating factor (G-CSF) produced by recombinant DNA technology. Endogenous G-CSF regulates the production of neutrophils within the bone marrow; primarily affects neutrophil proliferation, differentiation, and selected end-cell functional activity (including enhanced phagocytic activity, antibody-dependent killing, and the increased expression of some functions associated with cell-surface antigens). *Increases neutrophil proliferation and differentiation within the bone marrow.*

USES To decrease the incidence of infection, as manifested by febrile neutropenia, in patients with non-myeloid malignancies receiving myelosuppressive anticancer drugs associated with a significant incidence of severe neutropenia with fever; to decrease neutropenia associated with bone marrow transplant; to treat chronic neutropenia.

CONTRAINDICATIONS Hypersensitivity to *E. coli*–derived proteins, 14 d before or 24 h after administration of chemotherapy; myeloid cancers; splenomegaly; ARDS; pregnancy (category C); children weighing <45 kg.

CAUTIOUS USE Sickle cell disease. For use in peripheral blood stem cells (PBSC) mobilization; neutropenic patients with sepsis; leukemia; concurrent lithium therapy; lactation.

ROUTE & DOSAGE

Neutropenia
Adult: SC >45 kg, 6 mg once per chemotherapy cycle at least 24 h after chemotherapy.

Common adverse effects in *italic*, life-threatening effects underlined; generic names in **bold**; classifications in SMALL CAPS; ✦ Canadian drug name; ☻ Prototype drug

1163

ADMINISTRATION

Subcutaneous

- Do not administer filgrastim in the period 14 d before or 24 h after cytotoxic chemotherapy.
- Use only one dose per vial; do not reenter the vial.
- Prior to injection, filgrastim may be allowed to reach room temperature for a maximum of 6 h. Discard any vial left at room temperature for >6 h.
- Aspirate prior to injection to avoid injection into a blood vessel. Inject SC; do not inject intradermally. Recommended injection sites include outer area of upper arms, abdomen (excluding 2-in area around navel), front of middle thighs, and upper outer areas of the buttocks.
- Do not recap needle. Slide needle guard over needle until it is completely covered and needle guard clicks into place.
- Store refrigerated at 2°–8° C (36°–46° F). Do not freeze. Avoid shaking.

ADVERSE EFFECTS (≥1%) **Body as a Whole:** *Bone pain,* hyperuricemia, *fever.* **Hematologic:** Anemia. **GI:** Nausea, anorexia, increased LFTs. **Body as a Whole:** *Bone pain,* hyperuricemia, *fever.*

INTERACTIONS Drug: Can interfere with activity of CYTOTOXIC AGENTS; do not use 14 d before or <24 h after CYTOTOXIC AGENTS; **lithium** may increase release of neutrophils.

PHARMACOKINETICS Absorption: Readily absorbed from SC site. **Half-Life:** 15–80 h.

CLINICAL IMPLICATIONS

Assessment & Drug Effects

- Lab tests: Obtain a baseline CBC with differential and platelet count prior to administering drug. Obtain CBC twice weekly during therapy to monitor neutrophil count and leukocytosis. Monitor Hct and platelet count regularly.
- Discontinue filgrastim if absolute neutrophil count exceeds 10,000/mm^3 after the chemotherapy-induced nadir. Neutrophil counts should then return to normal.
- Monitor patients with preexisting cardiac conditions closely. MI and arrhythmias have been associated with a small percent of patients receiving filgrastim.
- Monitor temperature q4h. Incidence of infection should be reduced after administration of filgrastim.
- Assess degree of bone pain if present. Consult physician if nonnarcotic analgesics do not provide relief.

Patient & Family Education

- Report bone pain and, if necessary, request analgesics to control pain.
- Note: Proper drug administration and disposal is important. A puncture-resistant container for the disposal of used syringes and needles should be utilized.

PEGINTERFERON ALFA-2A

(peg-in-ter-fer′on)
Pegasys

Classifications: IMMUNOMODULATOR; INTERFERON
Therapeutic: IMMUNOMODULATOR; INTERFERON
Prototype: Interferon alfa-2a
Pregnancy Category: C

AVAILABILITY 180 mcg/mL vials; 180 mcg prefilled syringes

ACTION & *THERAPEUTIC EFFECT*
Interferon-stimulated genes modulate processes leading to inhibition

of viral replication in infected cells, inhibition of cell proliferation, and immunomodulation. Stimulates production of effector proteins that raise body temperature, and causes reversible decreases in leukocyte and platelet counts. *Induces antiviral effects by activation of macrophages, natural killer cells, and T-cells, thus boosting cellular immunity and suppressing hepatic inflammation and replication of hepatitis C virus.*

USES Chronic hepatitis C with or without **ribavirin** in patients coinfected with HIV; treatment of patients with BHeAg-positive or -negative chronic hepatitis B.

CONTRAINDICATIONS Hypersensitivity to peginterferon alfa-2a or any of its components; severe immunosuppression (e.g., organ transplant, advanced AIDS); autoimmune thyroid diseases (e.g., Graves' disease, thyroiditis); autoimmune hepatitis; dental work; sepsis; *E. coli* hypersensitivity, decompensated hepatic disease prior to or during treatment; in neonates and infants because it contains benzyl alcohol; females of childbearing age; lactation; pregnancy (category C).

CAUTIOUS USE History of neuropsychiatric disorder; alcoholism; substance abuse; bipolar disorder, mania, psychosis; bone marrow suppression; cardiac arrhythmias, history of MI, cardiac disease, heart failure, uncontrolled hypertension; pulmonary disease, including COPD; thyroid dysfunction; diabetes mellitus, diabetic ketoacidosis; older adults; autoimmune disorders; autoimmune hepatitis; ulcerative and hemorrhagic colitis; pancreatitis; pulmonary disorders; HBV or HIV coinfection; retinal disease; renal impairment with creatinine clearance <50 mL/min; organ transplant recipients; lactation; children <18 y.

ROUTE & DOSAGE

Chronic Hepatitis C

Adult: **SC** 180 mcg once weekly times 48 wk, may decrease to 135 mcg once weekly if not tolerated

Renal Impairment

End stage renal disease: Reduce dose to 135 mcg once weekly

Hepatic Impairment

Reduce dose to 90 mcg once weekly if LFTs progressively increase over baseline

ADMINISTRATION

Subcutaneous

- Give dose on the same day of each week. Administer SC in the abdomen or thigh and rotate injection sites.
- Warm refrigerated vial by rolling in hands for about 1 min. Do not use if particulate matter is visible in the vial or product is discolored. Discard any unused portion.
- Note that manufacturer recommends the following: dose reduction to 135 mcg if neutrophil count <750 cells/mm³ and with ANC values <500 cells/mm³, treatment should be suspended until ANC values return to more than 1000 cells/mm³; dose reduction to 90 mcg if the platelet count is <50,000 cells/mm³ and discontinuation of therapy if platelet count <25,000 cells/mm³. Consult physician.
- Store in the refrigerator at 36°–46° F (2°–8° C), do not freeze or shake. Protect from light. Vials are for single use only.

P

ADVERSE EFFECTS (≥1%) **Body as a Whole:** *Musculoskeletal pain, myalgia, arthralgia, fatigue, inflammation at injection site, flu-like symptoms, rigors, fever,* pain, malaise, asthenia, exacerbation of autoimmune disease. **CNS:** *Headache, depression,* anxiety, *irritability, insomnia, dizziness,* impaired concentration, impaired memory, <u>suicidal ideation, suicide attempt</u>. **GI:** *Nausea, diarrhea, abdominal pain, anorexia,* dry mouth. **Hematologic:** Thrombocytopenia, *neutropenia.* **Skin:** *Alopecia, pruritus,* dermatitis, sweating, rash.

INTERACTIONS Drug: May increase **theophylline** levels; increased risk of fetal defects with **ribavirin;** additive myelosuppression with ANTINEO-PLASTICS.

PHARMACOKINETICS Peak: 72–96 h. **Elimination:** 30% in urine. **Half-Life:** 80 h.

CLINICAL IMPLICATIONS

Assessment & Drug Effects

- Monitor for S&S of hypersensitivity (e.g., angioedema, bronchoconstriction) and, if noted, institute appropriate medical action immediately. Note that transient rashes are not an indication to discontinue treatment.
- Withhold drug and notify physician for any of the following: severe neuropsychiatric events (e.g., psychosis, hallucinations, suicidal ideation, depression, bipolar disorders and mania), severe neutropenia or thrombocytopenia, abdominal pain accompanied by bloody diarrhea and fever, S&S of pancreatitis, new or worsening ophthalmologic disorders, or any other severe adverse event (see CAUTIOUS USE).
- Withhold drug and notify physician for any of the following:

Baseline neutrophil counts <1500 cells/mm^3, baseline platelet counts <90,000 cells/mm or baseline hemoglobin <10 g/dL.

- Note that acceptable baseline limits for therapy include: Platelet count ≥90,000 cells/mm^3 (as low as 75,000 cells/mm^3 in patients with cirrhosis or transition to cirrhosis), absolute neutrophil count (ANC) ≥1500 cells/mm^3; serum creatinine <1.5 × upper limit of normal; TSH and T4 within normal limit. Withhold therapy and notify physician for unacceptable baseline values.
- Monitor respiratory and cardiovascular status; report dyspnea, chest pain, and hypotension immediately; perform baseline and periodic ECG and chest X-ray.
- Lab tests: Baseline and periodic creatinine clearance, uric acid, CBC with differential, platelet count, Hct & Hgb, TSH, ALT, AST, bilirubin, blood glucose; retest CBC with differential, platelet count, Hct & Hgb after 2 wk and other blood chemistries after 4 wk. Serum HCV RNA levels after 24 wk of treatment.
- Baseline and periodic ophthalmology exams are recommended.

Patient & Family Education

- If you miss a drug dose and remember within 2 d of the scheduled dose, take the dose and continue with your regular schedule. If more than 2 d have passed, contact physician for instructions.
- Notify physician immediately for any of the following: severe depression or suicidal thoughts, severe chest pain, difficulty breathing, changes in vision, unusual bleeding or bruising, bloody diarrhea, high fever, severe stomach or lower back pain, severe chest pain, development a

new or worsening of a preexisting skin condition.

- Follow up with lab tests; compliance with lab testing is extremely important while taking this drug.
- Do not drive or engage in other potentially hazardous activities until reaction to drug is known.
- Women should use reliable means of contraception while taking this drug and notify physician immediately if they become pregnant.

PEGINTERFERON ALFA-2B

(peg-in-ter-fer'on)
PEG-Intron
Classifications: IMMUNOMODULATOR; INTERFERON
Therapeutic: IMMUNOMODULATOR; INTERFERON
Prototype: Interferon alfa-2a
Pregnancy Category: C

AVAILABILITY 100 mcg/mL, 160 mcg/mL, 240 mcg/mL, 300 mcg/mL powder for injection

ACTION & *THERAPEUTIC EFFECT*
Binds to specific membrane receptors on the cell surface, thereby initiating enzyme induction, suppression of cell proliferation, enhanced phagocytic activity of macrophages, augmentation of specific cytotoxic lymphocytes for target cells, and inhibition of viral replication in virus-infected cells. *Induces antiviral effects by activation of macrophages, natural killer cells, and T-cells, thus boosting cellular immunity and suppressing hepatic inflammation and replication of hepatitis C virus.*

USES Chronic hepatitis C.
UNLABELED USES Renal carcinoma.

CONTRAINDICATIONS Hypersensitivity to peginterferon; autoimmune hepatitis; decompensated liver disease; persistently severe or worsening S&S of life-threatening neuropsychiatric, autoimmune, ischemic, or infectious disorders; pregnancy (category C).

CAUTIOUS USE History of neuropsychiatric disorder; bone marrow suppression; ulcerative and hemorrhagic colitis; pulmonary disorders; HBV or HIV coinfection; thyroid dysfunction; diabetes mellitus; cardiovascular disease; autoimmune disorders; pulmonary disease, COPD; retinal disease; renal impairment with creatinine clearance <50 mL/min; older adults; lactation. Safety and efficacy in children <18 y are not established.

ROUTE & DOSAGE

Chronic Hepatitis C
Adult: **SC** Based on weight and injected once weekly times 1 y: *37–45 kg,* 40 mcg; *46–56 kg,* 50 mcg; *57–72 kg,* 64 mcg; *73–88 kg,* 80 mcg; *89–106 kg,* 96 mcg; *107–136 kg,* 120 mcg; *137–160 kg,* 150 mcg.

ADMINISTRATION

Subcutaneous
- Give dose on the same day of each week.
- Be aware that two Safety Lok™ syringes are provided in the drug package: one for reconstitution and one for injection. Reconstitute with only 0.7 mL of supplied diluent and discard remaining diluent. Enter the vial only once as it does not contain a preservative. Swirl gently to produce a clear, colorless solution. Use solution immediately.
- Serious adverse reactions warrant reduction or discontinuation of dose.
- Store dry vial at 15°–30° C (59°–86° F). If necessary, store reconsti-

Common adverse effects in *italic*, life-threatening effects <u>underlined</u>; generic names in **bold**; classifications in SMALL CAPS; ♦ Canadian drug name; ☺ Prototype drug

1167

tuted solution up to 24 h at 2°–8° C (36°–46° F).

ADVERSE EFFECTS (≥1%) **Body as a Whole:** *Musculoskeletal pain, fatigue, inflammation at injection site, flu-like symptoms, rigors, fever, weight loss, viral infection,* pain, malaise, hypertonia. **CNS:** *Headache, depression, anxiety, emotional lability, irritability, insomnia, dizziness.* **GI:** *Nausea, anorexia, diarrhea, abdominal pain,* vomiting, dyspepsia, hepatomegaly. **Endocrine:** Hypothyroidism. **Hematologic:** Thrombocytopenia, neutropenia. **Respiratory:** *Pharyngitis,* sinusitis, cough. **Skin:** *Alopecia, pruritus, dry skin,* sweating, rash, flushing.

INTERACTIONS Drug: May increase **theophylline** levels; additive myelosuppression with ANTINEOPLASTICS; **zidovudine** may increase hematologic toxicity; increase **doxorubicin** toxicity, increase neurotoxicity with **vinblastine; aldesleukin (IL-2)** may potentiate the risk of kidney failure.

PHARMACOKINETICS Peak: 15–44 h. **Duration:** 48–72 h. **Elimination:** 30% in urine. **Half-Life:** 40 h (22–60 h).

CLINICAL IMPLICATIONS

Assessment & Drug Effects
- Monitor for S&S of hypersensitivity (e.g., angioedema, bronchoconstriction) and, if noted, institute appropriate medical action immediately. Note that transient rashes are not an indication to discontinue treatment.
- Monitor for and report immediately S&S of neuropsychiatric disorders (e.g., psychosis, hallucinations, suicidal ideation, depression).
- Monitor respiratory and cardiovascular status; report dyspnea, chest pain, and hypotension immediately; baseline and periodic ECG and chest X-ray.
- Lab tests: Baseline and periodic creatinine clearance, CBC with differential, platelet count, Hct & Hgb, TSH, ALT, AST, bilirubin, blood glucose; with diabetics or hypertensives. Serum HCV RNA levels are assessed after 24 wk of treatment.
- Withhold drug and notify physician for any of the following: severe neuropsychiatric events, severe neutropenia or thrombocytopenia, abdominal pain accompanied by bloody diarrhea and fever, S&S of pancreatitis, or any other severe adverse event (see CAUTIOUS USE).
- Baseline and periodic ophthalmology exams are recommended.

Patient & Family Education
- Drink fluids liberally while taking this drug, especially during the initial stages of therapy.
- Learn reasons for withholding drug (see ASSESSMENT & DRUG EFFECTS).
- Use effective means of contraception while taking this drug. Women should not become pregnant.
- Follow up with lab tests; compliance with lab testing is extremely important while taking this drug.

PEGVISOMANT
(peg-vis′o-mant)
Somavert
Classifications: HORMONE; GROWTH HORMONE MODIFIER; GROWTH HORMONE RECEPTOR ANTAGONIST
Therapeutic: GROWTH HORMONE RECEPTOR ANTAGONIST
Pregnancy Category: B

AVAILABILITY 10 mg, 15 mg, 20 mg, powder for injection

ACTION & *THERAPEUTIC EFFECT*

A growth hormone (GH) receptor antagonist that binds to GH receptors on cell surfaces where it blocks the binding of GH and interferes with its action and ability to stimulate production of insulin-like growth factor I (IGF-I). *Produces a significant decrease in the level of serum insulin-like growth factor I (IGF-I), the primary mediator of GH effects on body tissues.*

USES Treatment of acromegaly when other treatments have failed or are inappropriate.

CONTRAINDICATIONS Hypersensitivity to pegvisomant; hypersensitivity to latex.

CAUTIOUS USE Pituitary tumors; diabetes mellitus; hepatic and/or renal impairment; pregnancy (category B); lactation; children, elderly.

ROUTE & DOSAGE

Acromegaly
Adult: SC 40 mg loading dose, then 10 mg once daily. Adjust dose in 5 mg increments, up to 30 mg/d, based on serum IGF-I concentrations.

ADMINISTRATION

Subcutaneous

- Allow vials to reach room temperature, then reconstitute by adding 1 mL of supplied diluent (sterile water for injection) to the vial. Direct diluent against the glass wall of vial, then mix by gently rolling between palms of hands to dissolve. DO NOT SHAKE. Solution should be clear and colorless. Use within 6 h of reconstitution.
- Inject SC and exercise caution not to inject IV.
- Rotate injection sites and do not use any site more than once every 1–2 mo.
- Store vials of powder at 2°–8° C (36°–46° F).

ADVERSE EFFECTS (≥1%) **Body as a Whole:** Asthenia, flu-like syndrome, infection, injection site reactions, back pain, paresthesias, peripheral edema. **CNS:** Dizziness. **CV:** Angina, chest pain, hypertension, MI. **GI:** Elevated liver function tests, diarrhea, nausea, vomiting. **Metabolic:** Hypercholesterolemia, hypoglycemia, and low titer nonneutralizing antigrowth hormone antibodies. **Musculoskeletal:** Arthralgia. **Respiratory:** Sinusitis.

DIAGNOSTIC TEST INTERFERENCE Similar to growth hormone and may cross-react with ***growth hormone assays.*** Do not use these assays to monitor pegvisomant therapy.

INTERACTIONS Drug: OPIATE AGONISTS may lead to higher **pegvisomant** dosing requirements; may need to decrease doses of **insulin,** ORAL ANTIDIABETIC AGENTS.

PHARMACOKINETICS Absorption: 57% from SC injection site. **Peak:** 33–77 h. **Half-Life:** 6 d.

CLINICAL IMPLICATIONS

Assessment & Drug Effects

- Montior CV status with baseline and periodic BP measurements.
- Monitor diabetics for loss of glycemic control.
- Withhold drug and notify physician for significant elevation in AST/ALT or S&S of hepatitis.
- Lab tests: IGF-I levels 4–6 wk after initiation of therapy or any dose adjustment, then q6mo after IGF-I levels have normalized; pe-

Common adverse effects in *italic*, life-threatening effects <u>underlined</u>; generic names in **bold**; classifications in SMALL CAPS; ✦ Canadian drug name; ☢ Prototype drug

1169

riodic LFTs and lipid profile; frequent blood glucose monitoring, especially if diabetic.

Patient & Family Education
- Report promptly any of the following: chest pain or tightness, signs of infection (e.g., fever, chills, flu-like symptoms).
- Discontinue drug and notify physician immediately if jaundice appears.
- Do not drive or engage in other hazardous activities until reaction to drug is known.

PEMETREXED

(pe-me-trex'ed)
Alimta
Classifications: ANTINEOPLASTIC AGENT; ANTIMETABOLITE, ANTI-FOLATE
Therapeutic: ANTINEOPLASTIC; ANTI-METABOLITE; ANTIFOLATE
Prototype: Methotrexate
Pregnancy Category: D

AVAILABILITY 500 mg powder for injection

ACTION & *THERAPEUTIC EFFECT*
Suppresses tumor growth by inhibiting both DNA synthesis and folate metabolism at multiple target enzymes. *Appears to arrest the cell cycle, thus inhibiting tumor growth.*

USES Treatment of malignant pleural mesothelioma that is unresectable or in patients that are not surgery candidates in combination with cisplatin; treatment of locally advanced or metastatic non-small cell lung cancer (NSCLC).
UNLABELED USES Solid tumors, including bladder, breast, colorectal, gastric, head and neck, pancreatic, and renal cell cancers.

CONTRAINDICATIONS Mannitol hypersensitivity; creatinine clearance is <45 mL/min, renal failure, moderate or severe renal impairment; active infection; vaccines; children <18 y; pregnancy (category D); lactation.
CAUTIOUS USE Anemia, thrombocytopenia, neutropenia, dental disease; older adults; hepatic disease, hypoalbuminemia, hypovolemia, dehydration, ascites, pleural effusion.

ROUTE & DOSAGE

Malignant Mesothelioma, Non-Small Cell Lung Cancer
Adult: **IV** 500 mg/m^2 on day 1 of each 21-d cycle
Renal Impairment
Not recommended if Cl$_{cr}$ <45 mL/min

ADMINISTRATION

Intravenous
Pre-/posttreatment with folic acid, vitamin B$_{12}$, and dexamethasone are needed to reduce hematologic and gastrointestinal toxicity, and the possibility of severe cutaneous reactions from pemetrexed.

***PREPARE:* IV Infusion:** Reconstitute each 500 mg vial with 20 mL of preservative-free NS. Do not use any other diluent. Swirl gently to dissolve. Each vial will contain 25 mg/mL. Withdraw the needed amount of reconstituted solution and add to 100 mL of preservative-free NS. Discard any unused portion.
***ADMINISTER:* IV Infusion:** Do NOT give a bolus dose. Infuse over 10 min.

***INCOMPATIBILITIES* Solution/additive:** Solutions containing **calcium, Lactated Ringer's. Y-site: Amphotericin B, calcium, cefa-**

zolin, cefotaxime, cefote-tan, cefoxitin, ceftazidime, chlorpromazine, ciprofloxa-cin, dobutamine, doxorubi-cin, doxycycline, droperidol, gemcitabine, gentamicin, irinotecan, metronidazole, minocycline, mitoxantrone, nalbuphine, ondansetron, prochlorperazine, tobramy-cin, topotecan.

▪ Store unopened single-use vials at room temperature between 15°–30° C (59°–86° F). The reconstituted drug is stable for up to 24 h at 2°–8° C (36°–46° F) or at 25° C (77° F).

ADVERSE EFFECTS (≥1%) **Body as a Whole:** *Fatigue, fever,* hypersensi-tivity reaction, edema, myalgia, ar-thralgia. **CNS:** Neuropathy, *mood al-teration, depression.* **CV:** Chest pain, thromboembolism. **GI:** *Nausea, vom-iting, constipation, anorexia, stoma-titis, diarrhea,* dehydration, dys-phagia, esophagitis, odynophagia, increased LFTs. **Hematologic:** *Neu-tropenia, leukopenia, anemia, thrombocytopenia.* **Respiratory:** *Dyspnea.* **Skin:** *Rash, desquamation,* alopecia. **Urogenital:** *Increases se-rum creatinine,* renal failure.

INTERACTIONS Drug: Increased risk of renal toxicity with other nephro-toxic drugs **(acyclovir, adefovir, amphotericin B,** AMINOGLYCOSIDES, **carboplatin, cidofovir, cisplatin, cyclosporine, foscarnet, ganci-clovir, sirolimus, tacrolimus, vancomycin),** NSAIDs may increase risk of renal toxicity in patients with preexisting renal insufficiency; may cause additive risk of bleeding with ANTICOAGULANTS, PLATELET INHIBITORS, **aspirin,** THROMBOLYTIC AGENTS.

PHARMACOKINETICS Metabolism: Not extensively. **Elimination:** Primar-ily in urine. **Half-Life:** 3.5 h.

CLINICAL IMPLICATIONS

Assessment & Drug Effects

▪ Withhold drug and notify physi-cian if the absolute neutrophil count (ANC) is <1500 cells/mm^3 or the platelet count is less than at least 100,000 cells/mm^3, or if the Cl_{cr} is <45 mL/min.

▪ Lab tests: Baseline and periodic CBC with differential; monitor for nadir and recovery before each dose (on day 8 and 15, respec-tively, of each cycle); periodic LFTs, serum creatinine and BUN.

▪ Notify physician for S&S of neu-ropathy (paresthesia) or throm-boembolism.

Patient & Family Education

▪ Report promptly any of the follow-ing to physician: symptoms of ane-mia (e.g., chest pain, unusual weakness or tiredness, fainting spells, lightheadedness, shortness of breath); symptoms of poor blood clotting (e.g., bruising; red spots on skin; black, tarry stools; blood in urine); symptoms of in-fection (e.g., fever or chills, cough, sore throat, pain or difficulty pass-ing urine); symptoms of liver problems (e.g., yellowing of skin).

▪ Do not take nonsteroidal antiin-flammatory drugs (NSAIDs) without first consulting the physician.

PEMIROLAST POTASSIUM

(pem-ir′o-last po-tass′i-um)
Alamast
Pregnancy Category: C
See Appendix A-1.

PENBUTOLOL

(pen-bu′tol-ol)
Levatol

Common adverse effects in *italic*, life-threatening effects underlined; generic names in **bold**; classifications in SMALL CAPS; ✦ Canadian drug name; ❷ Prototype drug

1171

Classifications: BETA-ADRENER-GIC ANTAGONIST; ANTIHYPERTEN-SIVE
Therapeutic: ANTIHYPERTENSIVE
Prototype: Propranolol
Pregnancy Category: C

AVAILABILITY 20 mg tablets

ACTION & *THERAPEUTIC EFFECT*
Synthetic beta₁- and beta₂-adrenergic blocking agent which competes with epinephrine and norepinephrine for available beta receptor sites. Lowers both supine and standing BP in hypertensive patients. Hypotensive effect is associated with decreased cardiac output, suppressed renin activity as well as beta blockage. *Effective in lowering mild to moderate blood pressure.*

USES Mild to moderate hypertension alone or with other antihypertensive agents.

CONTRAINDICATIONS Clients with cardiogenic shock, acute CHF, sinus bradycardia, second and third degree AV block; bronchial asthma, COPD; hypersensitivity to the drug; pregnancy (category C).
CAUTIOUS USE Cardiac failure; chronic bronchitis; diabetes; mental depression; myasthenia gravis; renal disease; lactation. Safety and effectiveness in children is not established.

ROUTE & DOSAGE

Hypertension
Adult: **PO** 10–20 mg daily, may increase to 40–80 mg/d

ADMINISTRATION
Oral
- Discontinue by reducing the dose gradually over 1 to 2 wk.

ADVERSE EFFECTS (≥1%) **CNS:** Dizziness, fatigue, *headache,* insomnia. **CV:** AV block, bradycardia. **GI:** Nausea, diarrhea, dyspepsia. **Respiratory:** Cough, dyspnea. **Urogenital:** Impotence.

INTERACTIONS Drug: DIURETICS and other HYPOTENSIVE AGENTS increase hypotensive effect; effects of **albuterol, metaproterenol, terbutaline, pirbuterol,** and penbutolol are antagonized; NSAIDS blunt hypotensive effect; decreases hypoglycemic effect of **glyburide; amiodarone** increases risk of bradycardia and sinus arrest.

PHARMACOKINETICS Absorption: Readily from GI tract. **Peak:** 2–3 h. **Duration:** 20 h. **Metabolism:** In liver. **Elimination:** In urine. **Half-Life:** 5 h.

CLINICAL IMPLICATIONS
Assessment & Drug Effects
- Take apical pulse before administering drug. If pulse is below 60, or other established parameter, hold the drug and contact physician.
- Take a BP reading before giving drug, if BP is not stabilized. If systolic pressure is ≤90 mm Hg, hold drug and contact physician.
- Check BP near end of dosage interval or before administration of next dose to evaluate effectiveness.
- Monitor therapeutic effectiveness. Full effectiveness of the drug may not be seen for 4–6 wk.
- Watch for S&S of bronchial constriction. Report promptly and withhold drug.
- Monitor diabetics for loss of glycemic control. Drug suppresses clinical signs of hypoglycemia (e.g., BP changes, increased pulse rate) and may prolong hypoglycemic state.
- Monitor carefully for exacerbation of angina during drug withdrawal.

Common adverse effects in *italic*, life-threatening effects underlined; generic names in **bold**; classifications in SMALL CAPS; ✦ Canadian drug name; ☻ Prototype drug

Patient & Family Education

- Do not discontinue the drug without physician's advice because of the possible exacerbation of ischemic heart disease.
- If diabetic, report persistent S&S of hypoglycemia (see Appendix F) to physician (diabetics).
- Avoid driving or other potentially hazardous activities until response to drug is known.
- Make position changes slowly and avoid prolonged standing. Notify physician if dizziness and lightheadedness persist.
- Comply with and do not alter established regimen (i.e., do not omit, increase, or decrease dosage or change dosage interval).
- Avoid prolonged exposure of extremities to cold.
- Avoid excesses of alcohol. Heavy alcohol consumption [i.e., >60 mL (2 oz)/d] may elevate arterial pressure; therefore, to maintain treatment effectiveness, either avoid alcohol or drink moderately (<60 mL/d). Consult physician.

PENCICLOVIR

(pen-cy′clo-vir)
Denavir
Classifications: ANTIVIRAL
Therapeutic: ANTIVIRAL
Pregnancy Category: B

AVAILABILITY 10 mg/g cream

ACTION & *THERAPEUTIC EFFECT*

Antiviral agent active against herpes simplex virus type 1 (HSV-1) and type 2 (HSV-2). HSV-1 and HSV-2 infected cells phosphorylate penciclovir utilizing viral thymidine kinase. Resulting form of penciclovir competes with viral DNA, thus inhibiting both viral DNA synthesis and replication. *Inhibits both viral DNA synthesis and replication. Effectiveness is measured in decreased viral load.*

USES Treatment of recurrent herpes labialis (cold sores).

CONTRAINDICATIONS Hypersensitivity to penciclovir, lactation.
CAUTIOUS USE Pregnancy (category B). Safety and efficacy in children <12 y have not been established. Safety in immunocompromised patients is not established.

ROUTE & DOSAGE

Cold Sores
Adult: **Topical** Apply q2h while awake times 4 d

ADMINISTRATION

Topical
- Apply as soon as possible after developing lesion.
- Do not apply to mucous membranes or near the eyes.
- Store at or below 30° C (86° F). Do not freeze.

ADVERSE EFFECTS (≥1%) **CNS:** Headache. **Skin:** Erythema.

PHARMACOKINETICS Absorption: Minimally absorbed from cold sore.

CLINICAL IMPLICATIONS

Assessment & Drug Effects
- Monitor the extent of lesions and treatment effectiveness.

Patient & Family Education
- Wash hands before and after application. Avoid contact of drug with eyes.
- Apply sunscreen to lips; may minimize recurrence of lesions.

P

Common adverse effects in *italic*, life-threatening effects <u>underlined</u>; generic names in **bold**; classifications in SMALL CAPS; ♦ Canadian drug name; ❷ Prototype drug

1173

PENICILLAMINE

(pen-i-sill'a-meen)
Cuprimine, Depen
Classifications: CHELATING AGENT
Therapeutic: CHELATING AGENT
Pregnancy Category: D

AVAILABILITY 250 mg capsules

ACTION & *THERAPEUTIC EFFECT*
Combines chemically with cystine to form a soluble disulfide complex that prevents stone formation and may even dissolve existing cystic stones. Mechanism of action in rheumatoid arthritis appears to be related to inhibition of collagen formation. Forms stable soluble chelate with copper, zinc, iron, lead, mercury, and possibly other heavy metals and promotes their excretion in urine. *With Wilson's disease, therapeutic effectiveness is indicated by improvement in psychiatric and neurologic symptoms, visual symptoms, and liver function. With rheumatoid arthritis, therapeutic effectiveness is indicated by improvement in grip strength, decrease in stiffness following immobility, reduction of pain, decrease in sedimentation rate and rheumatoid factor.*

USES To promote renal excretion of excess copper in Wilson's disease (hepatolenticular degeneration). Active rheumatoid arthritis in patients who have failed to respond to conventional therapy. Cystinuria.
UNLABELED USES Scleroderma, primary biliary cirrhosis, porphyria cutanea tarda, lead poisoning.

CONTRAINDICATIONS Hypersensitivity to penicillamine or to any penicillin; history of penicillamine-related aplastic anemia or agranulocytosis; patients with rheumatoid arthritis who have renal insufficiency or who are pregnant; pregnancy (category D), lactation; renal failure; concomitant administration with drugs that can cause severe hematologic or renal reactions (e.g., antimalarials, gold salts).
CAUTIOUS USE Allergy-prone individuals; diabetes mellitus.

ROUTE & DOSAGE

Wilson's Disease

Adult: **PO** 250 mg q.i.d., with 3 doses 1 h a.c. and the last dose at least 2 h after the last meal
Child: **PO** 20 mg/kg/d in 2–4 divided doses (max: 1 g/d)

Cystinuria

Adult: **PO** 250–500 mg q.i.d., with doses adjusted to limit urinary excretion of cystine to 100–200 mg/d
Child: **PO** 30 mg/kg/d in 4 divided doses with doses adjusted to limit urinary excretion of cystine to 100–200 mg/d

Rheumatoid Arthritis (RA)

Adult: **PO** 125–250 mg/d; may increase at 1–3 mo intervals up to 1–1.5 g/d
Child: **PO** 3 mg/kg/d (≤250 mg/d) times 3 mo, then 6 mg/kg/d (≤500 mg/d) in 2 divided doses times 3 mo [max: of 10 mg/kg/d (≤1.5 g/d) in 3–4 divided doses]

Lead Poisoning

Child: **PO** 30–40 mg/kg/d in 3–4 divided doses (max: 1.5 g/d); initiate at 25% target dose, gradually increase to full dose over 2–3 wk

Renal Impairment

If Cl_{cr} <50 mL/min, avoid use
Hemodialysis: In RA patients dose may be decreased from 250 mg daily to 250 mg 3 times per wk

ADMINISTRATION

Oral

- Give on empty stomach (60 min before or 2 h after meals) to avoid absorption of metals in foods by penicillamine.
- Give contents in 15–30 mL of chilled fruit juice or pureed fruit (e.g., applesauce) if patient cannot swallow capsules or tablets.

ADVERSE EFFECTS (≥1%) **Body as a Whole:** Fever, arthralgia, lymphadenopathy, thyroiditis, SLE-like syndrome, thrombophlebitis, hyperpyrexia, myasthenia gravis syndrome, tingling of feet, weakness. **GI:** *Anorexia, nausea, vomiting,* epigastric pain, diarrhea, oral lesions, *reduction or loss of taste perception (particularly salt and sweet), metallic taste,* activation of peptic ulcer, pancreatitis. **Urogenital:** Membranous glomerulopathy, *proteinuria,* hematuria. **Hematologic:** Thrombocytopenia, leukopenia, <u>agranulocytosis</u>, thrombotic thrombocytopenic purpura, <u>hemolytic anemia, aplastic anemia</u>. **Metabolic:** Pyridoxine deficiency. **Skin:** *Generalized pruritus, urticaria,* mammary hyperplasia, alveolitis, skin friability, excessive skin wrinkling, *early and late occurring rashes,* pemphigus-like rash, alopecia. **Special Senses:** Tinnitus, optic neuritis, ptosis.

INTERACTIONS Drug: ANTIMALARIALS, CYTOTOXICS, **gold** therapy may potentiate hematologic and renal adverse effects; **iron** may decrease penicillamine absorption.

PHARMACOKINETICS Absorption: Readily from GI tract. **Peak:** 1 h. **Distribution:** Crosses placenta. **Metabolism:** In liver. **Elimination:** In urine. **Half-life:** 1–7 hr.

CLINICAL IMPLICATIONS

Assessment & Drug Effects

- Lab tests: Check WBC with differential, direct platelet counts, Hgb, and urinalyses prior to initiation of therapy and every 3 d during the first month of therapy, then every 2 wk thereafter. Perform liver function tests and eye examinations before start of therapy and at least twice yearly thereafter.
- Withhold drug and contact physician if the patient with rheumatoid arthritis develops proteinuria >1 g (some clinicians accept >2 g) or if platelet count drops to <100,000/mm^3, or platelet count falls below 3500–4000/mm^3, or neutropenia occurs.

Patient & Family Education

- Note: Clinical evidence of therapeutic effectiveness may not be apparent until 1–3 mo of drug therapy.
- Take exactly as prescribed. Allergic reactions occur in about one third of patients receiving penicillamine. Temporary interruptions of therapy increase possibility of sensitivity reactions.
- Take temperature nightly during first few months of therapy. Fever is a possible early sign of allergy.
- Observe skin over pressure sites: knees, elbows, shoulder blades, toes, buttocks. Penicillamine increases skin friability.
- Report unusual bruising or bleeding, sore mouth or throat, fever, skin rash, or any other unusual symptoms to physician.

P

PENICILLIN G BENZATHINE

(pen-i-sill'in)
Bicillin, Bicillin L-A, Permapen
Classifications: BETA-LACTAM ANTIBIOTIC; NATURAL PENICILLIN

Common adverse effects in *italic*, life-threatening effects <u>underlined</u>; generic names in **bold**; classifications in SMALL CAPS; ♦ Canadian drug name; 🅞 Prototype drug

1175

Therapeutic: ANTIBIOTIC; BETA-LAC-
TAM
Prototype: Penicillin G potassium
Pregnancy Category: B

AVAILABILITY 300,000 units/mL,
600,000 units/mL, 1,200,000 units/
2 mL, 2,400,000 units/4 mL injection

ACTION & *THERAPEUTIC EFFECT*
Acid-stable, penicillinase-sensitive,
long-acting form of penicillin G.
Absorbed slowly in body because
of extremely low water solubility.
Produces lower blood concentrations than other penicillin G compounds but has the longest duration of antimicrobial activity of all
other available parenteral or repository penicillins. *Effective against
many strains of* Staphylococcus
aureus, *gram-positive cocci, gram-
negative cocci. Also effective
against gram-positive bacilli and
gram-negative bacilli.*

USES Infections highly susceptible
to penicillin G, such as streptococcal, pneumococcal, and staphylococcal infections, venereal disease
such as syphilis (including early,
late, and congenital forms), and
nonvenereal diseases (e.g., yaws,
bejel, and pinta). Also used in prophylaxis of rheumatic fever.

CONTRAINDICATIONS Hypersensitivity to penicillins or cephalosporins; lactation.
CAUTIOUS USE History of or suspected allergy (eczema, hives, hay
fever, asthma); renal disease, renal
impairment; GI disease; pregnancy
(category B); infants, neonates.

ROUTE & DOSAGE

Mild to Moderate Infections
Adult: **IM** 1,200,000 U once/d

Child: **IM** >27 kg: 900,000 U
once/d; <27 kg: 300,000–
600,000 U once/d

Syphilis
Adult: **IM** <1 y duration:
2,400,000 U as single dose;
>1 y duration: 2,400,000 U/wk
for 3 wk
Child: **IM** Congenital: 50,000 U/
kg as single dose

Prophylaxis for Rheumatic Fever
Adult: **IM** 1,200,000 U q4wk
Child: **IM** 1,200,000 U q3–4wk

ADMINISTRATION

Intramuscular

- Do not confuse penicillin G benz-
athine with preparations containing procaine penicillin G (e.g., Bicillin C-R).
- Make IM injection deep into upper
outer quadrant of buttock. In infants and small children, the preferred site is the midlateral aspect
of the thigh.
- Shake multiple-dose vial vigorously
before withdrawing desired IM
dose. Shake prepared cartridge unit
vigorously before injecting drug.
- Select IM site with care. Injection
into or near a major peripheral
nerve can result in nerve damage.
- Inadvertent IV administration has
resulted in arterial occlusion and
cardiac arrest.
- Make injections at a slow steady
rate to prevent needle blockage.
- Store at 15°–30° C (59°–86° F).

ADVERSE EFFECTS (≥1%) **Body as
a Whole:** *Local pain,* tenderness,
and fever associated with IM injection, chills, fever, wheezing, anaphylaxis, neuropathy, nephrotoxicity;
superinfections, Jarisch-Herxheimer
reaction in patients with syphilis.
Skin: Pruritus, urticaria, and other

skin eruptions. **Hematologic:** Eosinophilia, hemolytic anemia, and other blood abnormalities. Also see PENICILLIN G POTASSIUM.

INTERACTIONS Drug: Probenecid decreases renal elimination; may decrease efficacy of ORAL CONTRACEPTIVES.

PHARMACOKINETICS Absorption: Slowly absorbed from IM site. **Peak:** 12–24 h. **Duration:** 26 d. **Distribution:** Crosses placenta; distributed into breast milk. **Metabolism:** Hydrolyzed to penicillin in body. **Elimination:** Excreted slowly by kidneys.

CLINICAL IMPLICATIONS
Note: See penicillin G potassium for numerous additional clinical implications.

Assessment & Drug Effects
- Determine history of hypersensitivity reactions to penicillins, cephalosporins, or other allergens prior to initiation of drug therapy.
- Lab tests: Perform C&S tests prior to initiation of therapy and periodically thereafter. Perform periodic renal function tests.

Patient & Family Education
- Report immediately to physician the onset of an allergic reaction. There is great risk of severe and prolonged reactions because drug is absorbed so slowly.

PENICILLIN G POTASSIUM ⚪Ⓟ

(pen-i-sill'in)
Megacillin ♦

PENICILLIN G SODIUM

Classifications: BETA-LACTAM ANTIBIOTIC; NATURAL PENICILLIN
Therapeutic: ANTIBIOTIC; BETA-LACTAM
Pregnancy Category: B

AVAILABILITY 1,000,000 units, 5,000,000 units, 10,000,000 units, 20,000,000 units vials; 1,000,000 units/50 mL, 2,000,000 units/50 mL 3,000,000 units/50 mL injection

ACTION & *THERAPEUTIC EFFECT*
Acid-labile, penicillinase-sensitive, natural penicillin. Antimicrobial spectrum is relatively narrow compared to that of the semisynthetic penicillins. Acts by interfering with synthesis of mucopeptides essential to formation and integrity of bacterial cell wall. Action is inhibited by penicillinase. *Highly active against grampositive cocci (e.g., non-penicillinase-producing* Staphylococcus, Streptococcus *groups) and gramnegative cocci. Also effective against gram-positive bacilli and gram-negative bacilli. Penicillin G is effective against some strains of* Salmonella *and* Shigella *and spirochetes.*

USES Moderate to severe systemic infections caused by penicillin-sensitive microorganisms. Certain staphylococcal infections; streptococcal infections. Also used as prophylaxis in patients with rheumatic or congenital heart disease. Since oral preparations are absorbed erratically and thus must be given in comparatively high doses, this route is generally used only for mild or stabilized infections or long-term prophylaxis.

CONTRAINDICATIONS Hypersensitivity to any of the penicillins or cephalosporins; administration of oral drug to patients with severe infections; nausea, vomiting, hypermotility, gastric dilatation; cardiospasm. Use of penicillin G sodium in patients on sodium restriction.
CAUTIOUS USE History of or suspected allergy (asthma, eczema, hay fever, hives); history of allergy to cephalosporins; GI disorders;

P

Common adverse effects in *italic*, life-threatening effects <u>underlined</u>; generic names in **bold**; classifications in SMALL CAPS; ♦ Canadian drug name; Ⓟ Prototype drug

1177

kidney or liver dysfunction, myasthenia gravis, epilepsy, neonates, young infants; pregnancy (category B). Use during lactation may lead to sensitization of infants.

ROUTE & DOSAGE

Moderate to Severe Infections

Adult: **IV/IM** 2–24 million U divided q4h
Child: **IV/IM** 250,000–400,000 U/kg divided q4h

ADMINISTRATION

Note: Check whether physician has prescribed penicillin G potassium or sodium.

Intramuscular

- Do not use the 20,000,000 unit dosage form for IM injection.
- Reconstitute for IM: Loosen powder by shaking bottle before adding diluent (sterile water for injection or sterile NS). Keep the total volume to be injected small. Solutions containing up to 100,000 units/mL cause the least discomfort. Adding 10 mL diluent to the 1,000,000 unit vial = 100,000 units/mL. Shake well to dissolve.
- Select IM site carefully. IM injection is made deep into a large muscle mass. Inject slowly. Rotate injection sites.

Intravenous

PREPARE: **Intermittent/Continuous:** Reconstitute as for IM injection then withdraw the required dose and add to 100–1000 mL of D5W or NS IV solution, depending on length of each infusion.
ADMINISTER: **Intermittent/Continuous:** Give intermittent infusion over at least 1 h and continuous infusion at a rate required to infuse the daily dose in 24 h. With high doses, IV penicillin G

should be administered slowly to avoid electrolyte imbalance from potassium or sodium content. Physician will often prescribe specific flow rate.

INCOMPATIBILITIES **Solution/additive: Dextran 40, fat emulsion, aminophylline, amphotericin B, cephalothin, chlorpromazine, dopamine, hydroxyzine, metaraminol, metoclopramide, pentobarbital, prochlorperazine, promazine, sodium bicarbonate,** TETRACYCLINE, **thiopental.**

- Store dry powder (for parenteral use) at room temperature. After reconstitution (initial dilution), store solutions for 1 wk under refrigeration. Intravenous infusion solutions containing penicillin G are stable at room temperature for at least 24 h.

ADVERSE EFFECTS (≥1%) **Body as a Whole:** Coughing, sneezing, feeling of uneasiness; systemic anaphylaxis, fever, widespread increase in capillary permeability and vasodilation with resulting edema (mouth, tongue, pharynx, larynx), laryngospasm, malaise, serum sickness (fever, malaise, pruritus, urticaria, lymphadenopathy, arthralgia, angioedema of face and extremities, neuritis prostration, eosinophilia), SLE-like syndrome, Injection site reactions (pain, inflammation, abscess, phlebitis), superinfections (especially with *Candida* and gram-negative bacteria), neuromuscular irritability (twitching, lethargy, confusion, stupor, hyperreflexia, multifocal myoclonus, localized or generalized seizures, coma). **CV:** Hypotension, circulatory collapse, cardiac arrhythmias, cardiac arrest. **GI:** Vomiting, diarrhea, severe abdominal cramps, nausea, epigastric distress, diarrhea, flatulence, dark discoloration of

tongue, sore mouth or tongue. **Urogenital:** Interstitial nephritis, Loeffler's syndrome, vasculitis. **Hematologic:** Hemolytic anemia, thrombocytopenia. **Metabolic:** Hyperkalemia (penicillin G potassium); hypokalemia, alkalosis, hypernatremia, CHF (penicillin G sodium). **Respiratory:** Bronchospasm, asthma. **Skin:** Itchy palms or axilla, pruritus, *urticaria,* flushed skin, *delayed skin rashes* ranging from urticaria to exfoliative dermatitis, Stevens-Johnson syndrome, fixed-drug eruptions, contact dermatitis.

DIAGNOSTIC TEST INTERFERENCE *Blood grouping and compatibility tests:* possible interference associated with penicillin doses greater than 20 million units daily. *Urine glucose:* massive doses of penicillin may cause false-positive test results with *Benedict's solution* and possibly *Clinitest* but not with *glucose oxidase methods* (e.g., *Clinistix, Diastix, TesTape*). *Urine protein:* massive doses of penicillin can produce false-positive results when turbidity measures are used (e.g., *acetic acid* and *heat, sulfosalicylic acid*); *Ames reagent* reportedly not affected. *Urinary PSP excretion tests:* false decrease in urinary excretion of PSP. *Urinary steroids:* large IV doses of penicillin may interfere with accurate measurement of *urinary 17-OHCS* (*Glenn-Nelson technique* not affected).

INTERACTIONS Drug: Probenecid decreases renal elimination; penicillin G may decrease efficacy of ORAL CONTRACEPTIVES; **colestipol** decreases penicillin absorption; POTASSIUM-SPARING DIURETICS may cause hyperkalemia with penicillin G potassium. **Food:** Food increases breakdown in stomach.

PHARMACOKINETICS Peak: 15–30 min IM. **Distribution:** Widely distributed; good CSF concentrations with inflamed meninges; crosses placenta; distributed in breast milk. **Metabolism:** 16–30% metabolized. **Elimination:** 60% in urine within 6 h. **Half-Life:** 0.4–0.9 h.

CLINICAL IMPLICATIONS

Assessment & Drug Effects

- Obtain an exact history of patient's previous exposure and sensitivity to penicillins and cephalosporins and other allergic reactions of any kind prior to treatment with penicillin.
- Hypersensitivity reactions are more likely to occur with parenteral penicillin but may also occur with the oral drug. Skin rash is the most common type allergic reaction and should be reported promptly to physician.
- Lab tests: Perform C&S tests prior to initiation of therapy; treatment may be started before results are known. Evaluate renal, hepatic, and hematologic systems at regular intervals in patients on high-dose therapy. Additionally, check electrolyte balance periodically in patients receiving high parenteral doses.
- Observe all patients closely for at least 30 min following administration of parenteral penicillin. The rapid appearance of a red flare or wheal at the IM or IV injection site is a possible sign of sensitivity. Also suspect an allergic reaction if patient becomes irritable, has nausea and vomiting, breathing difficulty, or sudden fever. Report any of the foregoing to physician immediately.
- Be aware that reactions to penicillin may be rapid in onset or

Common adverse effects in *italic,* life-threatening effects <u>underlined</u>; generic names in **bold**; classifications in SMALL CAPS; ✦ Canadian drug name; ◎ Prototype drug

1179

may not appear for days or weeks. Symptoms usually disappear fairly quickly once drug is stopped, but in some patients may persist for 5 d or more and require hospitalization for treatment.

- Allergy to penicillin is unpredictable. It has occurred in patients with a negative history of penicillin allergy and also in patients with no known prior contact with penicillin (sensitization may have occurred from penicillin used commercially in foods and beverages).
- Be alert for neuromuscular irritability in patients receiving parenteral penicillin in excess of 20 million U/d who have renal insufficiency, hyponatremia, or underlying CNS disease, notably myasthenia gravis or epilepsy. Seizure precautions are indicated. Symptoms usually begin with twitching, especially of face and extremities.
- Monitor I&O, particularly in patients receiving high parenteral doses. Report oliguria, hematuria, and changes in I&O ratio. Consult physician regarding optimum fluid intake. Dehydration increases the concentration of drug in kidneys and can cause renal irritation and damage.
- Observe closely for signs of toxicity: Neonates, young infants, the older adult, and patients with impaired kidney function receiving high-dose penicillin therapy. Urinary excretion of penicillin is significantly delayed in these patients.
- Observe patients on high-dose therapy closely for evidence of bleeding, and bleeding time should be monitored. (In high doses, penicillin interferes with platelet aggregation.)

Patient & Family Education

- Understand that hypersensitivity reaction may be delayed. Report skin rashes, itching, fever, malaise, and other signs of a delayed reaction to physician immediately (see ADVERSE EFFECTS).
- Notify physician if following symptoms appear when taking penicillin for treatment of syphilis (i.e., Jarisch-Herxheimer reaction occurs 8–24 h after treatment): Headache, chills, fever, myalgia, arthralgia, malaise, and worsening of syphilitic skin lesions. Reaction is usually self-limiting. Check with physician if symptoms do not improve within a few days or get worse.
- Report S&S of superinfection (see Appendix F).
- Understand importance of medical follow-up; present evidence suggests that glomerulonephritis, a possible complication of streptococcal infection, may not be prevented by penicillin.

PENICILLIN G PROCAINE
(pen-i-sill′in)

Classifications: BETA-LACTAM ANTIBIOTIC; NATURAL PENICILLIN
Therapeutic: ANTIBIOTIC; BETA-LACTAM
Prototype: Penicillin G potassium
Pregnancy Category: B

AVAILABILITY 600,000 units/mL, 300,000 units/mL

ACTION & *THERAPEUTIC EFFECT*
Long-acting form of penicillin G. The procaine salt has low solubility and thus creates a tissue depot from which penicillin is slowly absorbed. Onset of action is

slower and produces lower serum concentrations than penicillin G potassium, but has longer duration of action. It inhibits the final stage of bacterial cell wall synthesis by binding to specific penicillin-binding proteins (PBPs) located in the bacterial cell wall. This results in cell death of bacteria. *Same actions and antibacterial activity as for penicillin G potassium and is similarly inactivated by penicillinase and gastric acid.*

USES Moderately severe infections due to penicillin G-sensitive microorganisms that are susceptible to low but prolonged serum penicillin concentrations. Commonly, uncomplicated pneumococcal pneumonia, uncomplicated gonorrheal infections, and all stages of syphilis. May be used concomitantly with penicillin G or probenecid when more rapid action and higher blood levels are indicated.

CONTRAINDICATIONS History of hypersensitivity to any of the penicillins, or to procaine or any other "caine-type" local anesthetic; lactation.

CAUTIOUS USE History of or suspected allergy, hypersensitivity to cephalosporins, carbapenem; asthmatics; GI disease, renal disease; renal impairment; pregnancy (category B); infants, neonates.

ROUTE & DOSAGE

Moderate to Severe Infections
Adult: **IM** 600,000–1,200,000 U once/d
Child: **IM** 300,000 U once/d

Pneumococcal Pneumonia
Adult: **IM** 600,000 U q12h

Uncomplicated Gonorrhea
Adult: **IM** 4,800,000 U divided between 2 different injection sites at one visit preceded by 1 g of probenecid 30 min before injections

Syphilis
Adult: **IM** Primary, secondary, latent: 600,000 U/d for 8 d; late latent, tertiary, neurosyphilis: 600,000 U/d for 10–15 d
Child: **IM** 500,000–1,000,000 U/m^2 once/d

ADMINISTRATION

Intramuscular

- Shake multiple-dose vial thoroughly before withdrawing medication to ensure uniform suspension of drug.
- Use 20-gauge needle to avoid clogging.
- Give IM deep into upper outer quadrant of gluteus muscle; in infants and small children midlateral aspect of thigh is generally preferred. Select IM site carefully. Accidental injection into or near major peripheral nerves and blood vessels can cause neurovascular damage.
- Aspirate carefully before injecting drug to avoid entry into a blood vessel. Inadvertent IV administration reportedly has resulted in pulmonary infarcts and death.
- Inject drug at a slow, but steady rate to prevent needle blockage. Give in two sites if the dose is very large. Rotate injection sites.

ADVERSE EFFECTS (≥1%) **Body as a Whole:** Procaine toxicity [e.g., mental disturbances (anxiety, confusion, depression, combativeness, hallucinations), expressed fear of impending death, weakness, dizzi-

Common adverse effects in *italic*, life-threatening effects <u>underlined</u>; generic names in **bold**; classifications in SMALL CAPS; ✦ Canadian drug name; ❂ Prototype drug

1181

ness, headache, tinnitus, unusual tastes, palpitation, changes in pulse rate and BP, seizures]. Also see PENICILLIN G POTASSIUM.

INTERACTIONS Drug: Probenecid decreases renal elimination; may decrease efficacy of ORAL CONTRACEPTIVES.

PHARMACOKINETICS Absorption: Slowly from IM site. **Peak:** 1–3 h. **Duration:** 15–20 h. **Distribution:** Crosses placenta; distributed into breast milk. **Metabolism:** Hydrolyzed to penicillin in body. **Elimination:** By kidneys within 24–36 h.

CLINICAL IMPLICATIONS

Assessment & Drug Effects

- Obtain an exact history of patient's previous exposure and sensitivity to penicillins, cephalosporins, and to procaine, and other allergic reactions of any kind prior to treatment.
- Test patient by injecting 0.1 mL of 1–2% procaine hydrochloride intradermally if sensitivity is suspected. Appearance of a wheal, flare, or eruption indicates procaine sensitivity.
- Be alert to the possibility of a transient toxic reaction to procaine, particularly when large single doses are administered. The reaction manifested by mental disturbance and other symptoms (see ADVERSE EFFECTS) occurs almost immediately and usually subsides after 15–30 min.

Patient & Family Education

- Report any skin reaction at the site of injection.
- Report onset of rash, itching, fever, chills or other symptoms of an allergic reaction to physician.

PENICILLIN V
PENICILLIN V POTASSIUM
(pen-i-sill'in)

Apo-Pen-VK ♣, Beepen VK, Betapen-VK, Ledercillin VK, Nadopen-V ♣, Novopen-VK ♣, Penicillin VK, Pen-V, Pen-Vee K, Robicillin VK, V-Cillin K, Veetids

Classifications: BETA-LACTAM ANTIBIOTIC; NATURAL PENICILLIN
Therapeutic: ANTIBIOTIC; BETA-LACTAM
Prototype: Penicillin G potassium
Pregnancy Category: B

AVAILABILITY 250 mg, 500 mg tablets; 125 mg/5 mL, 250 mg/5 mL suspension

ACTION & *THERAPEUTIC EFFECT* Acid-stable analog of penicillin G with which it shares actions. It binds with the necessary penicillin-binding proteins (PBP) in cell wall of bacteria interfering with cell wall synthesis and resulting in cell lysis. *Penicillin V is bactericidal, and is inactivated by penicillinase. Less active than penicillin G against gonococci and other gram-negative microorganisms.*

USES Mild to moderate infections caused by susceptible *Streptococci, Pneumococci,* and *Staphylococci.* Also Vincent's infection and as prophylaxis in rheumatic fever.

CONTRAINDICATIONS Hypersensitivity to any penicillin; lactation. **CAUTIOUS USE** History of or suspected allergy (hay fever, asthma, hives, eczema) reactions; hypersensitivity to cephalosporins, beta-lactamase inhibitors, or carbapenem; GI disease; cystic fibrosis; renal impairment, hepatic impairment; pregnancy (category B).

ROUTE & DOSAGE

Mild to Moderate Infections
Adult: PO 125–500 mg q6h
Child: PO <12 y, 15–50 mg/kg/
d in 3–6 divided doses

Endocarditis Prophylaxis
Adult: PO 2 g 30–60 min before
procedure, then 500 mg q6h for
8 doses
Child: PO <30 kg, 1 g 30–60 min
before procedure, then 250 mg
q6h for 8 doses

ADMINISTRATION

Oral
- Give after a meal rather than on an empty stomach; drug may be better absorbed and result in higher blood levels.
- Do not coadminister with neomycin if both drugs are being used; malabsorption of penicillin V may result.
- Shake well before pouring. Following reconstitution, oral solution is stable for 14 d under refrigeration.

ADVERSE EFFECTS (≥1%) **Body as a Whole:** Nausea, vomiting, *diarrhea*, epigastric distress. *Hypersensitivity reactions* (e.g., flushing, pruritus, urticaria or other skin eruptions, eosinophilia, <u>anaphylaxis</u>; hemolytic anemia, leukopenia, thrombocytopenia, neuropathy, superinfections).

INTERACTIONS Drug: Probenecid decreases renal elimination; may decrease efficacy of ORAL CONTRACEPTIVES; **colestipol** decreases absorption. **Food:** Food increases breakdown in stomach.

PHARMACOKINETICS Absorption: 60–73% absorbed from GI tract. **Peak:** 30–60 min. **Duration:** 6 h. **Dis-**tribution: Highest levels in kidneys; crosses placenta; distributed into breast milk. **Elimination:** In urine. **Half-Life:** 30 min.

CLINICAL IMPLICATIONS

Note: See penicillin G potassium for numerous additional clinical implications.

Assessment & Drug Effects
- Obtain careful history concerning hypersensitivity reactions to penicillins, cephalosporins, and other allergens before therapy begins.
- Lab tests: Perform C&S tests prior to initiation and at regular intervals throughout therapy. Evaluate renal, hepatic, and hematologic systems at regular intervals in patients receiving prolonged therapy.

Patient & Family Education
- Take penicillin V around the clock at specific intervals to maintain a constant blood level.
- Do not miss any doses and continue taking medication until it is all gone unless otherwise directed by the physician.
- Discontinue medication and promptly report to physician the onset of hypersensitivity reactions and superinfections (see Appendix F).
- Use specially marked measuring device to ensure accurate doses of oral liquid preparation.

PENTAMIDINE ISOETHIONATE
(pen-tam′i-deen)
Nebupent, Pentacarinat ✦,
Pentam 300
Classifications: ANTIPROTOZOAL
Therapeutic: ANTIPROTOZOAL
Pregnancy Category: C

AVAILABILITY 300 mg injection; 300 mg aerosol

P

Common adverse effects in *italic*, life-threatening effects <u>underlined</u>; generic names in **bold**; classifications in SMALL CAPS; ✦ Canadian drug name; ❷ Prototype drug

ACTION & *THERAPEUTIC EFFECT*

Aromatic diamide antiprotozoal drug that appears to block parasite reproduction by interfering with nucleotide (DNA, RNA), phospholipid, and protein synthesis. *Effective against the porozoan parasite* Pneumocystis carinii *in AIDS patients.*

USES *P. carinii* pneumonia (PCP).
UNLABELED USES African trypanosomiasis and visceral leishmaniasis. (Drug supplied for the latter uses is through the Centers for Disease Control and Prevention, Atlanta, GA.)

CONTRAINDICATIONS QT prolongation, history of torsades de pointes; pregnancy (category C), lactation.
CAUTIOUS USE Hypertension, hypotension; hyperglycemia; pancreatitis; hypoglycemia; hypocalcemia; blood dyscrasias; liver or kidney dysfunction; diabetes mellitus; asthma; cardiac arrhythmias.

ROUTE & DOSAGE

Treatment of *Pneumocystis carinii* Pneumonia
Adult/Child: **IM/IV** 4 mg/kg/d for 14–21 d; infuse IV over 60 min

Prophylaxis of *Pneumocystis carinii* Pneumonia
Adult: **Inhaled** 300 mg per nebulizer q3–4wk
Child: **IV/IM** 4 mg/kg monthly

ADMINISTRATION

Inhaled

- Reconstitute contents of one vial in 6 mL sterile water (not saline) and administer using nebulizer.
- Do not mix with any other drug.

Intramuscular

- Dissolve contents of 1 vial (300 mg) in 3 mL sterile water for injection.

- Give deep IM into a large muscle.
- The IM injection is painful and frequently causes local reactions (pain, indurations, swelling). Select alternate sites for daily doses and institute local treatment if indicated.

Intravenous

PREPARE: IV Infusion: Dissolve contents of 1 vial in 3–5 mL sterile water for injection or D5W. Further dilute in 50–250 mL of D5W.
ADMINISTER: IV Infusion: Give over 60 min.
INCOMPATIBILITIES Y-site: Aldesleukin, CEPHALOSPORINS, **fluconazole, foscarnet, linezolid.**

- Note: IV solutions are stable at room temperature for up to 24 h. Protect solution from light.

ADVERSE EFFECTS (≥1%) **CNS:** Confusion, hallucinations, neuralgia, dizziness, sweating. **CV:** Sudden, severe hypotension, cardiac arrhythmias, ventricular tachycardia, phlebitis. **GI:** Anorexia, nausea, vomiting, pancreatitis, unpleasant taste. **Urogenital:** Acute kidney failure. **Hematologic:** Leukopenia, thrombocytopenia, anemia. **Metabolic:** Hypoglycemia, hypocalcemia, *hyperkalemia.* **Respiratory:** *Cough, bronchospasm,* laryngitis, shortness of breath, chest pain, pneumothorax. **Skin:** Stevens-Johnson syndrome, facial flush (with IV injection), *local reactions at injection site.*

INTERACTIONS Drug: AMINOGLYCOSIDES, **amphotericin B, cidofovir, cisplatin, ganciclovir, cyclosporine, vancomycin,** other nephrotoxic drugs increase risk of nephrotoxicity.

PHARMACOKINETICS Absorption: Readily after IM injection. **Distribution:** Leaves bloodstream rapidly to bind extensively to body tissues. **Elimination:** 50–66% in urine within

Common adverse effects in *italic*, life-threatening effects underlined; generic names in **bold**; classifications in SMALL CAPS; ✦ Canadian drug name; ⊕ Prototype drug

6 h; small amounts found in urine for as long as 6–8 wk. **Half-Life:** 6.5–13.2 h.

CLINICAL IMPLICATIONS

Assessment & Drug Effects

- Monitor BP closely. Sudden severe hypotension may develop after a single dose. Place patient in supine position while receiving the drug. Monitor BP and HR continuously during the infusion, every half hour for 2 h thereafter, and then every 4 h until BP stabilizes.
- Lab tests: Monitor periodically serum electrolytes, renal function, CBC with differential, platelet count, and blood glucose.
- Measure and record I&O ratio and pattern and check patient's pulse (to detect arrhythmia) at least twice daily.
- Be alert and report promptly S&S of impending kidney dysfunction (e.g., changed I&O ratio, oliguria, edema). Dosage adjustment is indicated in renal failure.
- Characteristics of pneumonia in the immunocompromised patient include constant fever, scanty (if any) sputum, dyspnea, tachypnea, and cyanosis.
- Monitor temperature changes and institute measures to lower the temperature as indicated. Fever is a constant symptom in *P. carinii* pneumonia, but may be rapidly elevated [as high as 40° C (104° F)] shortly after drug infusion.

Patient & Family Education

- Report promptly to physician increasing respiratory difficulty.
- Monitor blood glucose for loss of glycemic control if diabetic.
- Report any unusual bruising or bleeding. Avoid using aspirin or other NSAIDs.
- Increase fluid intake (if not contraindicated) to 2–3 quarts (liters) per day.

PENTAZOCINE HYDROCHLORIDE ℗ᵣ

(pen-taz'oh-seen)

Talwin

Classifications: NARCOTIC (OPIATE) AGONIST-ANTAGONIST; ANALGESIC

Therapeutic: NARCOTIC; ANALGESIC

Pregnancy Category: C

Controlled Substance: Schedule IV

AVAILABILITY 30 mg/mL injection

ACTION & *THERAPEUTIC EFFECT*

Synthetic analgesic with analgesic potency approximately one-third that of morphine. Opiates exert their analgesic effects by stimulating specific opiate receptors that produce analgesia, respiratory depression, and euphoria as well as physical dependence. *Effective for moderate to severe pain relief. Acts as weak narcotic antagonist and has sedative properties.*

USES Relief of moderate to severe pain; also used for preoperative analgesia or sedation, and as supplement to surgical anesthesia.

CONTRAINDICATIONS Hypersensitivity to sulfite; head injury, increased intracranial pressure; seizures; emotionally unstable patients, or history of drug abuse; pregnancy (other than labor) (category C), lactation. Safe use in children <12 y is not established.

CAUTIOUS USE Impaired kidney or liver function; cardiac disease; COPD, asthmas, respiratory depression; GI obstruction; biliary surgery; patients with MI who have nausea and vomiting.

ROUTE & DOSAGE

Moderate to Severe Pain (Excluding Patients in Labor)

Adult: **IM/IV/SC** 30–60 mg q3–4h (max: 360 mg/d)

Common adverse effects in *italic*, life-threatening effects underlined; generic names in **bold**; classifications in SMALL CAPS; ♣ Canadian drug name; ℗ Prototype drug

1185

Child: **IM** 15–30 mg

Women in Labor

Adult: **IM** 20–30 mg; 20 mg may be repeated 1 or 2 times at 2–3 h intervals

Renal Impairment

Cl_{cr} 10–50 mL/min: give 75% of dose; <10 mL/min: give 50% of dose

ADMINISTRATION

Subcutaneous, Intramuscular

- IM is preferred to SC route when frequent injections over an extended period are required.
- Observe injection sites daily for signs of irritation or inflammation.

Intravenous

PREPARE: **Direct:** Give undiluted or diluted with 1 mL sterile water for injection for each 5 mg.
ADMINISTER: **Direct:** Give slowly at a rate of 5 mg over 60 sec.
INCOMPATIBILITIES **Solution/additive: Aminophylline,** BARBITURATES, **sodium bicarbonate, glycopyrrolate, heparin, nafcillin. Y-site: Nafcillin.**

ADVERSE EFFECTS (≥1%) **Body as a Whole:** Flushing, allergic reactions, <u>shock</u>. **CNS:** *Drowsiness,* sweating, *dizziness, light-headedness, euphoria,* psychotomimetic effects, confusion, anxiety, hallucinations, disturbed dreams, bizarre thoughts, euphoria and other mood alterations. **CV:** Hypertension, palpitation, tachycardia. **GI:** *Nausea, vomiting,* constipation, dry mouth, alterations of taste. **Urogenital:** Urinary retention. **Respiratory:** <u>Respiratory depression</u>. **Skin:** Injection-site reactions (induration, nodule formation, sloughing, sclerosis, cutaneous depression), rash, pruritus. **Special Senses:** Visual disturbances.

INTERACTIONS Drug: Alcohol and other CNS DEPRESSANTS add to CNS depression; NARCOTIC ANALGESICS may precipitate narcotic withdrawal syndrome.

PHARMACOKINETICS Onset: 15 min IM, SC; 2–3 min IV. **Peak:** 1 h IM, 15 min IV. **Duration:** 3 h IM, 1 h IV. **Distribution:** Crosses placenta. **Metabolism:** Extensively in liver. **Elimination:** Primarily in urine; small amount in feces. **Half-Life:** 2–3 h.

CLINICAL IMPLICATIONS

Assessment & Drug Effects

- Monitor therapeutic effect. Tolerance to analgesic effect sometimes occurs. Psychologic and physical dependence have been reported in patients with history of drug abuse, but rarely in patients without such history. Addiction liability matches that of codeine.
- Be aware that pentazocine may produce acute withdrawal symptoms in some patients who have been receiving opioids on a regular basis.

Patient & Family Education

- Avoid driving and other potentially hazardous activities until response to drug is known.
- Do not discontinue drug abruptly following extended use; may result in chills, abdominal and muscle cramps, yawning, runny nose, tearing, itching, restlessness, anxiety, drug-seeking behavior.

PENTOBARBITAL

(pen-toe-bar'bi-tal)

PENTOBARBITAL SODIUM

Nembutal Sodium, Novopentobarb ✦

Classifications: ANXIOLYTIC; SEDATIVE-HYPNOTIC; BARBITURATE; ANTICONVULSANT

Common adverse effects in *italic*, life-threatening effects <u>underlined</u>; generic names in **bold**; classifications in SMALL CAPS; ✦ Canadian drug name; ⊙ Prototype drug

Therapeutic: ANTIANXIETY; SEDA-
TIVE-HYPNOTIC; ANTICONVULSANT
Prototype: Secobarbital
Pregnancy Category: D
Controlled Substance: Schedule II

AVAILABILITY 50 mg/mL injection

ACTION & *THERAPEUTIC EFFECT*
Short-acting barbiturate with anticonvulsant properties. Potent respiratory depressant. Initially, barbiturates suppress REM sleep, but with
chronic therapy REM sleep returns
to normal. *Effective as a sedative
and hypnotic and anticonvulsant.
CNS depression may range from
mild sedation to coma, depending
on dosage, degree of nervous system
excitability, and drug tolerance.*

USES Sedative or hypnotic for preanesthetic medication, induction of
general anesthesia, adjunct in ma-
nipulative or diagnostic procedures, and emergency control of
acute convulsions.

CONTRAINDICATIONS History of
sensitivity to barbiturates; parturition, fetal immaturity, uncontrolled
pain; ethanol intoxication; hepatic
encephalopathy; porphyria; pregnancy (category D), lactation.
CAUTIOUS USE COPD, sleep apnea;
heart failure; mental status changes,
suicidality, major depression; neonates; renal impairment, renal failure.

ROUTE & DOSAGE

Preoperative Sedation
Adult: **IM** 150–200 mg in 2
divided doses
Child: **IV** 1–3 mg/kg (max: 100
mg)

Hypnotic
Adult: **IM** 150–200 mg **IV** 100
mg q1–3 min up to 500 mg dose
Child: **IM** 2–6 mg/kg (max: 100
mg)

Status Epilepticus
Adult: **IV** 2–15 mg/kg loading
then 0.5–3 mg/kg/hr
Child: **IM** 5–15 mg/kg loading
then 0.5–5 mg/kg/hr

ADMINISTRATION

Note: Do not give within 14 d of
starting/stopping an MAO inhibitor.

Intramuscular
- Do not use parenteral solutions
that appear cloudy or in which a
precipitate has formed.
- Make IM injections deep into large
muscle mass, preferably upper
outer quadrant of buttock. Aspirate
needle carefully before injecting it
to prevent inadvertent entry into
blood vessel. Inject no more than
5 mL (250 mg) in any one site because of possible tissue irritation.

Intravenous

PREPARE: Direct: Give undiluted
or diluted (preferred) with sterile
water, D5W, NS, or other compatible IV solutions.
ADMINISTER: Direct: Give slowly.
Do not exceed rate of 50 mg/
min.
**INCOMPATIBILITIES Solution/ad-
ditive: Atropine, butorphanol,
chlorpheniramine, chlorpromazine, cimetidine, codeine,
dimenhydrinate, diphenhydramine, droperidol, ephedrine,
fentanyl, glycopyrrolate, hydrocortisone, hydroxyzine, in-
ulin, levorphanol, meperidine, methadone, midazolam,
morphine, nalbuphine, norepinephrine,** TETRACYCLINES,
**penicillin G, pentazocine, per-
phenazine, phenytoin, promazine, prochlorperazine,
promethazine, ranitidine, sodium bicarbonate, streptomycin, succinylcholine, triflupro-**

P

Common adverse effects in *italic*, life-threatening effects <u>underlined</u>; generic names
in **bold**; classifications in SMALL CAPS; ♣ Canadian drug name; ⊘ Prototype drug

mazine, vancomycin. Y-site: Amphotericin B cholesteryl, fenoldopam, TPN.
- Take extreme care to avoid extravasation. Necrosis may result because parenteral solution is highly alkaline. ■ Do not use cloudy or precipitated solution.

ADVERSE EFFECTS (≥1%) **Body as a Whole:** Drowsiness, lethargy, hangover, paradoxical excitement in the older adult patient. **CV:** Hypotension with rapid IV. **Respiratory:** With rapid IV (<u>respiratory depression, laryngospasm</u>, bronchospasm, <u>apnea</u>).

INTERACTIONS Drug: Phenmetrazine antagonizes effects of pentobarbital; CNS DEPRESSANTS, **alcohol**, SEDATIVES add to CNS depression; MAO INHIBITORS cause excessive CNS depression; **methoxyflurane** creates risk of nephrotoxicity. **Herbal: Kava-kava, valerian** may potentiate sedation.

PHARMACOKINETICS Onset: 10–15 min IM; 1 min IV. **Duration:** 15 min IV. **Distribution:** Crosses placenta. **Metabolism:** Primarily in liver. **Elimination:** In urine. **Half-Life:** 4–50 h.

CLINICAL IMPLICATIONS

Assessment & Drug Effects
- Monitor BP, pulse, and respiration q3–5min during IV administration. Observe patient closely; maintain airway. Have equipment for artificial respiration immediately available.
- Observe patient closely for adverse effects for at least 30 min after IM administration of hypnotic dose.

Patient & Family Education
- Exercise caution when driving or operating machinery for the remainder of day after taking drug.

- Avoid alcohol and other CNS depressants for 24 h after receiving this drug.

PENTOXIFYLLINE
(pen-tox-i′fi-leen)
Pentoxil, Trental
Classifications: BLOOD FORMER; HEMORRHEOLOGIC AGENT; ANTIPLATELET AGENT
Therapeutic: RED BLOOD CELL MODIFIER; BLOOD VISCOSITY IMPROVER
Pregnancy Category: C

AVAILABILITY 400 mg sustained release tablets

ACTION & THERAPEUTIC EFFECT
Useful in restoration of blood flow through capillary microcirculation that has been compromised by structural and flow dynamic changes in cerebral and peripheral vascular disorders. Action of pentoxifylline on maintaining the flexibility of RBCs appears to be related to an increase in erythrocyte cAMP activity, thus allowing erythrocyte membranes to maintain its integrity and become more resistant to deformity. Improvement in blood viscosity results in increased blood flow to the microcirculation and enhanced tissue oxygenation. *Decreased blood viscosity and improved blood flow, with consequent reduction of tissue hypoxia in extremities and the cerebrum. Results in increased blood flow to the extremities, reduced pain and paresthesia of intermittent claudication.*

USES Intermittent claudication associated with occlusive peripheral vascular disease; diabetic angiopathies.
UNLABELED USES To improve psychopathologic symptoms in pa-

tient with cerebrovascular insufficiency and to reduce incidence of stroke in the patient with recurrent TIAs.

CONTRAINDICATIONS Intolerance to pentoxifylline or to methylxanthines (caffeine and theophylline); intracranial bleeding; retinal bleeding; pregnancy (category C), lactation. Safety in children <18 y is not established.

CAUTIOUS USE Angina, hypotension, arrhythmias, cerebrovascular disease; peptic ulcer disease; renal failure; renal impairment; risk of bleeding; lactation.

ROUTE & DOSAGE

Intermittent Claudication
Adult: **PO** 400 mg t.i.d. with meals

ADMINISTRATION

Oral
- Give on an empty stomach or with food; be consistent with time of day and relationship to food in establishing the daily regimen.
- Store tablets at 15°–30° C (59°–86° F).

ADVERSE EFFECTS (≥1%) **Body as a Whole:** Fever, flushing, convulsions, somnolence, loss of consciousness. **CNS:** Agitation, nervousness, *dizziness,* drowsiness, headache, insomnia, tremor, confusion. **CV:** Angina, chest pain, dyspnea, arrhythmias, palpitations, hypotension, edema, flushing. **Eye:** Blurred vision, conjunctivitis, scotomas. **GI:** Abdominal discomfort, belching, flatus, bloating, diarrhea, *dyspepsia, nausea, vomiting.* **Skin:** Brittle fingernails, pruritus, rash, urticaria. **Other:** Earache, unpleasant taste, excessive salivation, leukopenia, malaise, sore throat, swollen neck glands, weight change.

INTERACTIONS Drug: Ciprofloxacin, cimetidine may increase levels and toxicity, **warfarin** may have additive effects.

PHARMACOKINETICS Absorption: Readily from GI tract; 10–50% reaches systemic circulation (first pass metabolism). **Peak:** 2–4 h. **Distribution:** Distributed into breast milk. **Metabolism:** In liver and erythrocytes. **Elimination:** Primarily in urine. **Half-Life:** 0.4–0.8 h.

CLINICAL IMPLICATIONS

Assessment & Drug Effects
- Monitor therapeutic effectiveness which is indicated by relief from pain and cramping in calf muscles, buttocks, thighs, and feet during exercise and improves walking performance (time and duration).
- Monitor BP if patient is also on antihypertensive treatment. Drug may slightly decrease an already stabilized BP, necessitating a reduced dose of the hypotensive drug.

Patient & Family Education
- Consult physician to determine CV status and capacity before reestablishing walking as exercise.
- Pay particular attention to care of the feet because of arterial insufficiency (diminished perfusion to feet).
- Be aware that bleeding and prolonged PT/INR associated with this treatment have been reported. Report promptly unexplained bleeding, easy bruising, nose bleed, pinpoint rash to physician.
- Avoid driving or working with hazardous machinery until drug response has stabilized because of potential for tiredness, blurred vision, dizziness.

Common adverse effects in *italic*, life-threatening effects <u>underlined</u>; generic names in **bold**; classifications in SMALL CAPS; ♣ Canadian drug name; ⊘ Prototype drug

1189

PERGOLIDE

(per'go-lide)
Permax
Classifications: ANTICHOLINERGIC; DOPAMINE RECEPTOR AGONIST; ANTI-PARKINSON AGENT
Therapeutic: ANTIPARKINSON AGENT
Prototype: Levodopa
Pregnancy Category: B

AVAILABILITY 0.05 mg, 0.25 mg, 1 mg tablets

ACTION & *THERAPEUTIC EFFECT*
Potent dopamine receptor agonist at both D_1- and D_2-dopamine receptor sites. Parkinsonism involves an excess of acetylcholine and a deficiency of dopamine neurotransmitters in the basal ganglia. The reduced tonic stimulation of dopaminergic D_2 receptors located on cholinergic neurons is most likely the cause of parkinsonian symptoms. *Thought that stimulation of the D_2-dopamine receptor alleviates the majority of parkinsonian symptoms.*

USES Adjunct to levodopa/carbidopa for the treatment of Parkinson's disease.
UNLABELED USES Acromegaly, hyperprolactinemia.

CONTRAINDICATIONS Hypersensitivity to pergolide or other ergot derivatives; history of hallucinations, history of hypotension; lactation.
CAUTIOUS USE Cardiac dysrhythmias, pregnancy (category B); pericarditis, pericardial effusion, valvular heart disease; retroperitoneal fibrosis. Safety and efficacy in children are not established.

ROUTE & DOSAGE

Parkinson's Disease
Adult: **PO** Initiate with 0.05 mg daily for 2 d, then increase by 0.1 or 0.15 mg/d every 3 d for the next 12 d, then dose may be increased by 0.25 mg every third day until the desired therapeutic response is achieved; give in divided doses t.i.d. (max: 5 mg/d)

Acromegaly
Adult: **PO** 0.1–1.5 mg once/d

Hyperprolactinemia
Adult: **PO** 0.025–0.6 mg once/d

ADMINISTRATION

Oral
- Note that dosage increases should occur no more than every 3 d with Parkinson's disease.

ADVERSE EFFECTS (≥1%) **CNS:** *Confusion, anxiety, light-headedness, headache,* transient somnolence (may fall asleep without warning), hallucinations, nightmares. **CV:** Ventricular arrhythmias, PVCs, edema, *orthostatic hypotension.* **GI:** *Nausea, vomiting,* constipation. **Body as a Whole:** Rhinitis, withdrawal symptoms (hallucinations, confusion, paranoid ideations, worsening of parkinsonian symptoms). **Skin:** Rash.

DIAGNOSTIC TEST INTERFERENCE
Suppresses ***prolactin*** levels.

INTERACTIONS Drug: Addition of pergolide to **levodopa** therapy has produced an increased incidence of dyskinesias in patients with Parkinson's disease; **haloperidol,** PHENOTHIAZINES can antagonize therapeutic effects.

PHARMACOKINETICS Absorption: Readily absorbed from GI tract; extensive first-pass metabolism. **Onset:** Prolactin levels decrease within 15–30 min. **Peak:** Prolactin nadir in 15 h. **Duration:** 22–24 h. **Distribution:** 90% protein bound;

crosses placenta; distributed into breast milk. **Metabolism:** In liver. **Elimination:** 55% in urine within 48 h; 40–50% in feces. **Half-Life:** 27 h.

CLINICAL IMPLICATIONS

Assessment & Drug Effects

- Monitor carefully for orthostatic hypotension and syncope when initiating therapy.
- Assess neurologic status; concurrent levodopa and pergolide may increase incidence of dyskinesias. If this occurs, levodopa may need to be reduced.
- Monitor patients with cardiac arrhythmias carefully, as drug may induce certain arrhythmias in persons at risk.

Patient & Family Education

- Note: May fall asleep without warning.
- Learn ways to reduce risk of orthostatic hypertension. Make position changes slowly and in stages.
- Understand all potential adverse effects including hallucinations.
- Report worsening neurologic status to physician.
- Do not discontinue drug abruptly.

PERINDOPRIL ERBUMINE

(per-in'do-pril)

Aceon

Classifications: ANGIOTENSIN-CONVERTING ENZYME (ACE) INHIBITOR; ANTIHYPERTENSIVE
Therapeutic: ANTIHYPERTENSIVE; ACE INHIBITOR
Prototype: Captopril
Pregnancy Category: C first trimester; D second and third trimester

AVAILABILITY 2 mg, 4 mg, 8 mg tablets

ACTION & *THERAPEUTIC EFFECT*

Angiotensin-converting enzyme (ACE) inhibitor. ACE catalyzes the conversion of angiotensin I to angiotensin II, a potent vasoconstrictor substance. Lowers BP by inhibition of ACE. Reduced aldosterone is associated with potassium-sparing effect. In addition, it decreases systemic vascular resistance (afterload) and pulmonary capillary wedge pressure (PCWP), a measure of preload, and improves cardiac output as well as activity tolerance. *Effective in lowering blood pressure by vasodilatation resulting from inhibition of ACE. Improves cardiac output as well as activity tolerance in coronary artery disease.*

USES Hypertension, stable coronary artery disease.

CONTRAINDICATIONS Hypersensitivity to perindopril or any other ACE inhibitor; history of angioedema induced by an ACE inhibitor, pregnancy (category C first trimester, category D second and third trimester); lactation; patients with hypertrophic cardiomyopathy, renal artery stenosis.

CAUTIOUS USE Renal insufficiency, volume-depleted patients, severe liver dysfunction; autoimmune diseases, immunosuppressant drug therapy; hyperkalemia or potassium-sparing diuretics; older adult; surgery; neutropenia; febrile illness.

ROUTE & DOSAGE

Hypertension, Stable Coronary Artery Disease
Adult: **PO** 4 mg once daily, may be increased to 8 mg daily in 1 or 2 divided doses (max: 16 mg/d)

Renal Impairment
Cl_{cr} >30 mL/min: start with 2 mg dose; can increase up to 8 mg

P

Common adverse effects in *italic*, life-threatening effects <u>underlined</u>; generic names in **bold**; classifications in SMALL CAPS; ♣ Canadian drug name; ⊘ Prototype drug

1191

ADMINISTRATION

Oral

- Manufacturer recommends an initial dose of 2–4 mg in 1 or 2 divided doses if concurrently ordered diuretic cannot be discontinued 2–3 d before beginning perinodopril. Consult physician.
- Give on an empty stomach 1 h before meals.
- Dosage adjustments are generally made at intervals of at least 1 wk.
- Store at 20°–25° C (68°–77° F) and protect from moisture.

ADVERSE EFFECTS (≥1%) **CNS:** Dizziness, light-headedness (in the absence of postural hypotension), headache, mood and sleep disorders, fatigue. **CV:** Palpitations. **Endocrine:** Hyperkalemia. **GI:** Nausea, vomiting, epigastric pain, diarrhea, taste disturbances, dyspepsia. **Urogenital:** Proteinuria, impotence, sexual dysfunction. **Special Senses:** Dry eyes, blurred vision. **Body as a Whole:** *Cough,* angioedema, pruritus, muscle cramps, sinusitis, hypertonia, fever. **Skin:** Rash.

INTERACTIONS Drug: POTASSIUM-SPARING DIURETICS (**amiloride, spironolactone, triamterene**) may increase the risk of hyperkalemia. POTASSIUM SUPPLEMENTS increase the risk of hyperkalemia; lithium levels can be increased. **Food:** Food can decrease drug absorption 35%.

PHARMACOKINETICS Absorption: Readily from GI tract, absorption significantly decreased when taken with food. **Peak:** Perindopril: 1 h; perindoprilat: 3–7 h. **Duration:** 24 h. **Metabolism:** Hydrolyzed in the liver to its active form, perindoprilat. **Elimination:** Primarily in urine. **Half-Life: Perindopril:** 0.8–1 h, **perindoprilat:** 30–120 h.

CLINICAL IMPLICATIONS

Assessment & Drug Effects

- Monitor BR and HR carefully following initial dose for several hours until stable, especially in patients using concurrent diuretics, on salt restriction, or volume depleted.
- Place patient immediately in a supine position if excess hypotension develops.
- Lab tests: Monitor serum potassium, serum sodium, BUN and creatinine, ALT, blood glucose, lipid profile, and WBC with differential periodically.
- Monitor kidney function in patients with CHF closely.
- Monitor serum lithium levels and assess for S&S of lithium toxicity frequently when used concurrently; increased caution is needed when diuretic therapy is also used.

Patient & Family Education

- Discontinue drug and immediately report S&S of angioedema (i.e., swelling) of face or extremities to physician. Seek emergency help for swelling of the tongue or any other signs of potential airway obstruction.
- Be aware that light-headedness can occur, especially during early therapy; excess fluid loss of any kind (e.g., vomiting, diarrhea) will increase risk of hypotension and syncope.
- Avoid using potassium supplements unless specifically directed to do so by physician.
- Report S&S of infection (e.g., sore throat, fever) promptly to physician.

PERMETHRIN ℗

(per-meth′rin)

Nix, Elimite, Acticin

Common adverse effects in *italic*, life-threatening effects underlined; generic names in **bold**; classifications in SMALL CAPS; ♣ Canadian drug name; ℗ Prototype drug

Classifications: SCABICIDE;
PEDICULICIDE
Therapeutic: SCABICIDE; PEDICULI-
CIDE
Pregnancy Category: B

AVAILABILITY 5% cream; 1% liquid

ACTION & *THERAPEUTIC EFFECT*
Pediculicidal and ovicidal activity
against *Pediculus humanus* var.
capitis (head louse). Inhibits sodium ion influx through nerve cell
membrane channels, resulting in
delayed repolarization of the action potential and paralysis of the
pest. *It prevents burrowing into
host's skin. Since lice are completely dependent on blood for survival, they die within 24–48 h. Also
active against ticks, mites, and
fleas.*

USES Pediculosis capitis.

CONTRAINDICATIONS Hypersensitivity to pyrethrins, chrysanthe-
mums, sulfites, or other preservatives or dyes; acute inflammation of
the scalp; lactation.
CAUTIOUS USE Children <2 y (liquid), and <2 mo (lotion); asthma;
pregnancy (category B).

ROUTE & DOSAGE

Head Lice

Adult/Child: **Topical** >2 y, Apply
sufficient volume to clean wet hair
to saturate the hair and scalp;
leave on 10 min, then rinse hair
thoroughly

ADMINISTRATION

Topical
- Saturate scalp as well as hair with
the lotion; this is not a shampoo.
- Hair should be washed with regular shampoo before treatment with

permethrin, thoroughly rinsed and
dried.
- Shake lotion well before application. One container holds enough
for at least one treatment, but two
containers may be necessary if patient has long hair.
- Rinse hair and scalp thoroughly
and dry with a clean towel following 10 min exposure to the medication. Head lice are usually eliminated with one treatment.
- Store drug away from heat at 15°–
25° C (59°–77° F) and direct light.
Avoid freezing.

ADVERSE EFFECTS (≥1%) **Skin:**
Pruritus, transient tingling, burning, stinging, numbness; erythema,
edema, rash.

PHARMACOKINETICS Absorption:
<2% of amount applied is absorbed
through intact skin. **Metabolism:**
Rapidly hydrolyzed to inactive metabolites. **Elimination:** Primarily in
urine.

CLINICAL IMPLICATIONS
Assessment & Drug Effects
- Do not attempt therapy if patient
is known to be sensitive to any
pyrethrin or pyrethroid. Stop
treatment if a reaction occurs.

Patient & Family Education
- When hair is dry, comb with a
fine-tooth comb (furnished with
medication) to remove dead lice
and remaining nits or nit shells.
- Be aware that drug remains on
hair shaft up to 14 d; therefore,
recurrence of infestation rarely
occurs (<1%).
- Inspect hair shafts daily for at least
1 wk to determine drug effectiveness. Contact physician if live lice
are observed after 7 d. A renewed
prescription for a second treatment
may be ordered. Signs of inade-

P

Common adverse effects in *italic*, life-threatening effects <u>underlined</u>; generic names
in **bold**; classifications in SMALL CAPS; ✤ Canadian drug name; ⓟ Prototype drug

1193

quate treatment: Itching, redness of skin, skin abrasion, infected scalp areas.
- Resume regular shampooing after treatment; residual deposit of drug on hair is not reduced.
- Be aware that drug is usually irritating to the eyes and mucosa. Flush well with water if medicine accidentally gets into eyes.

PERPHENAZINE

(per-fen′a-zeen)
Classifications: PSYCHOTHERAPEUTIC; PHENOTHIAZINE ANTIPSYCHOTIC; ANTIEMETIC
Therapeutic: ANTIPSYCHOTIC; ANTIEMETIC
Prototype: Chlorpromazine
Pregnancy Category: C

AVAILABILITY 2 mg, 4 mg, 6 mg, 8 mg, 16 mg tablets; 16 mg/5 mL liquid

ACTION & *THERAPEUTIC EFFECT*
Affects all parts of CNS similar to chlorpromazine, particularly the hypothalamus. Antipsychotic effect is due to its ability to antagonize the neurotransmitter dopamine by acting on dopamine receptors in the brain. Antiemetic action results from direct blockade of dopamine in the chemoreceptor trigger zone (CTZ) in the medulla. *Has antipsychotic and antiemetic properties.*

USES Psychotic disorders, symptomatic control of severe nausea and vomiting.

CONTRAINDICATIONS Hypersensitivity to perphenazine and other phenothiazines; preexisting liver damage; suspected or established subcortical brain damage, comatose states, CNS depression; hepatic encephalopathy; QT prolongation;

bone marrow depression; pregnancy (category C), lactation.
CAUTIOUS USE Previously diagnosed breast cancer; liver or kidney dysfunction; cardiovascular disorders; alcohol withdrawal, epilepsy, psychic depression, patients with suicidal tendency; cardiac and pulmonary disease; glaucoma; history of intestinal or GU obstruction; geriatric or debilitated patients; patients who will be exposed to extremes of heat or cold, or to phosphorous insecticides.

ROUTE & DOSAGE

Psychotic Disorders
Adult: **PO** 4–16 mg b.i.d. to q.i.d. (max: 64 mg/d)
Child: **PO** 4 mg b.i.d. to q.i.d. (max:16 mg/d)

Nausea
Adult: **PO** 8–16 mg b.i.d. to q.i.d. (up to 24 mg/d)
Hemodialysis: Not dialyzable

ADMINISTRATION
Oral
- Ensure that sustained release form is not chewed or crushed. Must be swallowed whole.
- Dilute oral concentrate before administration: Dilute each 5 mL (16 mg) to 60 mL water, milk, saline solution, 7-Up, or other compatible carbonated beverages. Do not use liquids that cause color changes or precipitate.

ADVERSE EFFECTS (≥1%) **CNS:** *Extrapyramidal effects (dystonic reactions, akathisia, parkinsonian syndrome, tardive dyskinesia), sedation,* convulsions. **CV:** *Orthostatic hypotension,* tachycardia, bradycardia. **Special Senses:** Mydriasis, blurred vision, corneal and lenticular deposits. **GI:** Constipation, *dry mouth,* increased appetite, adynamic ileus, Abnormal liver function tests, cholestatic jaundice. **Urogenital:** *Urinary retention,* gynecomastia, menstrual irregularities, inhibited ejaculation. **Hematologic:** Agranulocytosis, thrombocytopenic purpura, aplastic or hemolytic anemia. **Body as a Whole:** Photosensitivity, itching, erythema, urticaria, angioneurotic edema, drug fever, anaphylactoid reaction, sterile abscess. Nasal congestion, decreased sweating. **Metabolic:** Hyperprolactinemia, galactorrhea, weight gain.

DIAGNOSTIC TEST INTERFERENCE
Perphenazine may cause falsely abnormal *thyroid function* tests because of elevations of *thyroid globulin.*

INTERACTIONS Drug: Alcohol and other CNS DEPRESSANTS enhance CNS depression; ANTACIDS, ANTIDIARRHEALS may decrease absorption of phenothiazines; ANTICHOLINERGIC AGENTS add to anticholinergic effects including fecal impaction and paralytic ileus; BARBITURATES, ANESTHETICS increase hypotension and excitation. **Herbal: Kava-kava** increased risk and severity of dystonic reactions.

PHARMACOKINETICS Absorption: Poorly absorbed from GI tract; 20% reaches systemic circulation. **Peak:** 4–8 h PO. **Duration:** 6–12 h. **Distribution:** Crosses placenta. **Metabolism:** In liver (CYP2D6) with some metabolism in GI tract. **Elimination:** In urine and feces. **Half-Life:** 9.5 h.

CLINICAL IMPLICATIONS
Assessment & Drug Effects
- Establish baseline BP before initiation of drug therapy and check it at regular intervals, especially during early therapy.

- Report restlessness, weakness of extremities, dystonic reactions (spasms of neck and shoulder muscles, rigidity of back, difficulty swallowing or talking); motor restlessness (akathisia: inability to be still); and parkinsonism syndrome (tremors, shuffling gait, drooling, slow speech). A high incidence of extrapyramidal effects accompanies use of perphenazine, particularly with high doses.
- Withhold medication and report IMMEDIATELY to physician S&S of irreversible tardive dyskinesia (i.e., fine, wormlike movements or rapid protrusions of the tongue, chewing motions, lip smacking). Patients on long-term therapy are at high risk. Teach patients and responsible family members about symptoms because early reporting is essential.
- Lab tests: Obtain differential blood cell counts, liver and kidney function studies.
- ECG and ophthalmologic examination are recommended prior to initiation and periodically during therapy.
- Suspect hypersensitivity, withhold drug, and report to physician if jaundice appears between weeks 2 and 4.
- Monitor and bowel elimination pattern.
- Be alert to potential for altered tolerance to environmental temperature changes. Be cautious with external heat devices. Conditioned avoidance behavior may be depressed, and a severe burn could result.

Patient & Family Education
- Make all position changes slowly and in stages, particularly from recumbent to upright posture, and to lie down or sit down if light-headedness or dizziness occurs.

- Do not drive or engage in potentially hazardous activities until response to drug is known. Drug may produce hypotension (dizziness, light-headedness), and sedation especially during early therapy.
- Discontinue drug and report to physician immediately if jaundice appears between weeks 2 and 4.
- Avoid long exposure to sunlight and to sunlamps. Photosensitivity results in skin color changes from brown to blue-gray.
- Adhere strictly to dosage regimen. Contact physician before changing it for any reason.
- Discontinue gradually over a period of several weeks following prolonged therapy.
- Avoid OTC drugs unless physician prescribes them.
- Be aware that perphenazine may discolor urine reddish brown.

PHENAZOPYRIDINE HYDROCHLORIDE

(fen-az-oh-peer′i-deen)

Azo-Standard, Baridium, Geridium, Phenazo ✦, Phenazodine, Pyridiate, Pyridium, Pyronium ✦, Urodine, Urogesic

Classifications: URINARY TRACT ANALGESIC
Therapeutic: URINARY TRACT ANALGESIC
Pregnancy Category: B

AVAILABILITY 95 mg, 97.2 mg, 100 mg, 150 mg, 200 mg tablets

ACTION & *THERAPEUTIC EFFECT*
Azo dye that has local anesthetic action on urinary tract mucosa, which imparts little or no antibacterial activity. *Effective as a urinary tract analgesic.*

USES Symptomatic relief of pain, burning, frequency, and urgency arising from irritation of urinary tract mucosa, as from infection, trauma, surgery, or instrumentation.

CONTRAINDICATIONS Renal insufficiency, glomerulonephritis, pyelonephritis, renal failure, uremia; hepatic disease; glucose-6-phosphate dehydrogenase deficiency, severe hepatitis.
CAUTIOUS USE GI disturbances; older adults; pregnancy (category B), lactation.

ROUTE & DOSAGE

Cystitis
Adult: **PO** 200 mg t.i.d.
Child: **PO** 12 mg/kg/d in 3 divided doses

ADMINISTRATION

Oral
- Give with or after meals.

ADVERSE EFFECTS (≥1%) **Body as a Whole:** Headache, vertigo. **GI:** Mild GI disturbances. **Urogenital:** Kidney stones, transient acute kidney failure. **Metabolic:** Methemoglobinemia, hemolytic anemia. **Skin:** Skin pigmentation. **Special Senses:** May stain soft contact lenses.

DIAGNOSTIC TEST INTERFERENCE Phenazopyridine may interfere with any urinary test that is based on color reactions or spectrometry: *bromsulphalein* and *phenolsulfonphthalein* excretion tests; urinary *glucose* test using *Clinistix* or *TesTape* (*copper-reduction methods* such as *Clinitest* and *Benedict's test* reportedly not affected); *bilirubin* using "foam test" or *Ictotest; ketones* using *nitroprusside* (e.g., *Acetest, Ketostix,* or *Gerhardt ferric chloride*); *urinary protein* using *Albustix,*

Albutest, or *nitric acid ring test;* urinary *steroids; urobilinogen;* assays for *porphyrins.*

INTERACTIONS Drug: No clinically significant interactions established.

PHARMACOKINETICS Absorption: Readily absorbed from GI tract. **Distribution:** Crosses placenta in trace amounts. **Metabolism:** In liver and other tissues. **Elimination:** Primarily in urine.

CLINICAL IMPLICATIONS

Assessment & Drug Effects

- Lab tests: Obtain periodic blood work and kidney function tests in patients on prolonged therapy or with impaired kidney function.

Patient & Family Education

- Be aware that drug will impart an orange to red color to urine and may stain fabric.
- Discontinue drug report to physician immediately the appearance of yellowish tinge to skin or sclerae may indicate drug accumulation due to renal impairment.
- Discontinue drug when pain and discomfort are relieved (usually 3–15 d). Keep physician informed.

PHENELZINE SULFATE ℗

(fen'el-zeen)

Nardil

Classifications: PSYCHOTHERAPEUTIC; ANTIDEPRESSANT; MONOAMINE OXIDASE (MAO) INHIBITOR

Therapeutic: ANTIDEPRESSANT; MAO INHIBITOR

Pregnancy Category: C

AVAILABILITY 15 mg tablets

ACTION & *THERAPEUTIC EFFECT*
Potent hydrazine (monoamine oxidase) MAO inhibitor. Antidepressant and diverse effects believed to be due to irreversible inhibition of MAO, thereby permitting increased concentrations of endogenous epinephrine, norepinephrine, serotonin, and dopamine within presynaptic neurons and at receptor sites. Also thought to inhibit hepatic microsomal drug-metabolizing enzymes; thus it may intensify and prolong the effects of many drugs. *Antidepressant utilization of the drug is limited to individuals who do not respond well to other classes of antidepressants. Termination of drug action depends on regeneration of MAO inhibitors, which occurs 2–3 wk after discontinuation of therapy.*

USES Management of endogenous depression, depressive phase of manic-depressive psychosis, and severe exogenous (reactive) depression not responsive to more commonly used therapy.

CONTRAINDICATIONS Hypersensitivity to MAO inhibitors; suicidal ideation; pheochromocytoma; hyperthyroidism; CHF, acute MI, cardiac arrhythmias, hypertension, history of angina pectoris; cardiovascular or cerebrovascular disease; increased intracranial pressure; intracranial bleeding; renal failure; impaired kidney function, hypernatremia; atonic colitis; glaucoma; history of frequent or severe headaches; history of liver disease, abnormal liver function tests; alcoholism, alcohol intoxication; depression, accompanying alcoholism or drug addiction; older adult or debilitated patients; paranoid schizophrenia; pregnancy (category C), lactation. Safety in children <6 y of age is not established.

CAUTIOUS USE Epilepsy; pyloric stenosis; diabetes; manic-depressive states; agitated patients; schizophre-

P

Common adverse effects in *italic*, life-threatening effects underlined; generic names in **bold**; classifications in SMALL CAPS; ◆ Canadian drug name; ℗ Prototype drug

1197

nia or psychosis; seizures; suicidal tendencies; chronic brain syndromes.

ROUTE & DOSAGE

Depression
Adult: **PO** 15 mg t.i.d., rapidly increase to at least 60 mg/d, may need up to 90 mg/d

ADMINISTRATION

Oral

- Discontinue at least 10 d before elective surgery to allow time for recovery from MAO before anesthetics are given.
- Avoid rapid withdrawal of MAO inhibitors, particularly after high dosage, since a rebound effect may occur (e.g., headache, excitability, hallucinations, and possibly depression).
- Store in tightly covered containers away from heat and light.

ADVERSE EFFECTS (≥1%) **Body as a Whole:** Dizziness or vertigo, headache, *orthostatic hypotension,* drowsiness or *insomnia,* weakness, fatigue, edema, tremors, twitching, akathisia, ataxia, hyperreflexia, faintness, hyperactivity, marked agitation, anxiety, seizures, trismus, opisthotonos, <u>respiratory depression, coma.</u> **CNS:** Mania, hypomania, confusion, memory impairment, delirium, hallucinations, euphoria, acute anxiety reaction, toxic precipitation of schizophrenia, convulsions, peripheral neuropathy. **CV:** <u>Hypertensive crisis</u> (intense occipital headache, palpitation, marked hypertension, stiff neck, nausea, vomiting, sweating, fever, photophobia, dilated pupils, bradycardia or tachycardia, constricting chest pain, intracranial bleeding), hypotension or hypertension, <u>circulatory collapse.</u> **GI:** *Constipation, dry mouth, nausea,* vomiting, *anorexia,*

weight gain. **Hematologic:** Normocytic and normochromic anemia, leukopenia. **Skin:** Hyperhidrosis, skin rash, photosensitivity. **Special Senses:** Blurred vision.

DIAGNOSTIC TEST INTERFERENCE Phenelzine may cause a slight false increase in *serum bilirubin.*

INTERACTIONS Drug: TRICYCLIC ANTIDEPRESSANTS may cause hyperpyrexia, seizures; **fluoxetine, sertraline, paroxetine** may cause serotonin syndrome (see Appendix F); SYMPATHOMIMETIC AGENTS (e.g., **amphetamine, phenylephrine, phenylpropanolamine**), **guanethidine** and **reserpine** may cause hypertensive crisis; CNS DEPRESSANTS have additive CNS depressive effects; OPIATE ANALGESICS (especially **meperidine**) may cause hypertensive crisis and circulatory collapse; **buspirone,** hypertension; GENERAL ANESTHETICS, prolonged hypotensive and CNS depressant effects; hypertension, headache, hyperexcitability reported with **dopamine, methyldopa, levodopa, tryptophan;** **metrizamide** may increase risk of seizures; HYPOTENSIVE AGENTS and DIURETICS have additive hypotensive effects. **Food:** Aged meats or aged cheeses, protein extracts, sour cream, alcohol, anchovies, liver, sausages, overripe figs, bananas, avocados, chocolate, soy sauce, bean curd, natural yogurt, fava beans—**tyramine**-containing foods—may precipitate hypertensive crisis. Avoid **chocolate** or **caffeine. Herbal: Ginseng, ephedra, ma-huang, St. John's wort** may cause hypertensive crisis.

PHARMACOKINETICS Absorption: Readily absorbed from GI tract. **Onset:** 2 wk. **Metabolism:** Rapidly metabolized. **Elimination:** 79% of metabolites excreted in urine in 96 h.

Common adverse effects in *italic,* life-threatening effects <u>underlined</u>; generic names in **bold**; classifications in SMALL CAPS; ✚ Canadian drug name; ⊘ Prototype drug

CLINICAL IMPLICATIONS

Assessment & Drug Effects

- Evaluate patient's BP in standing and recumbent positions. Prior to initiation of treatment.
- Monitor children, adolescents, and adults for changes in behavior that may indicate suicidality.
- Lab tests: Perform baseline CBC and liver function tests. Also perform periodic CBC and liver function tests during prolonged or high-dose therapy.
- Monitor BP and pulse between doses when titrating initial dosages. Observe closely for evidence of adverse drug effects. Thereafter, monitor at regular intervals throughout therapy.
- Report immediately if hypomania (exaggeration of motility, feelings, and ideas) occurs as depression improves. This reaction may also appear at higher than recommended doses or with long-term therapy.
- Observe for and report therapeutic effectiveness of drug: Improvement in sleep pattern, appetite, physical activity, interest in self and surroundings, as well as lessening of anxiety and bodily complaints.
- Observe patient with diabetes closely for S&S of hypoglycemia (see Appendix F). Patients on prolonged therapy should be checked periodically for altered color perception, changes in fundi or visual fields. Changes in red-green vision may be the first indication of eye damage.

Patient & Family Education

- Drug is usually discontinued if no therapeutic response occurs after 3 or 4 wk. Maximum antidepressant effects generally appear in 2–6 wk and persist several weeks after drug withdrawal.
- Avoid self-medication. OTC preparations containing dextromethorphan, sympathomimetic agents, or antihistamines (e.g., cough, cold, and hay fever remedies, appetite suppressants) can precipitate severe hypertensive reactions if taken during therapy or within 2–3 wk after discontinuation of an MAO inhibitor.
- Report immediately to physician the onset of headache and palpitation, prodromal symptoms of hypertensive crisis or any other unusual effects which may indicate need to discontinue therapy.
- Do not consume foods and beverages containing tyramine or tryptophan or drugs containing pressor agent. These can cause severe hypertensive reactions. Get a list from your care provider.
- Avoid drinking excessive caffeine and chocolate beverages (e.g., coffee, tea, cocoa, or cola).
- Discuss with physician wearing elastic stockings and elevating legs when sitting to minimize hypotensive effects of drug.
- Make position changes slowly, especially from recumbent to upright posture, and dangle legs over bed a few minutes before rising to walk. Avoid standing still for prolonged periods. Also avoid hot showers and baths (resulting vasodilatation may potentiate hypotension); lie down immediately if feeling light-headed or faint.
- Check weight 2 or 3 times per week and report unusual gain.
- Report jaundice. Hepatotoxicity is believed to be a hypersensitivity reaction unrelated to dosage or duration of therapy.
- Avoid overexertion while taking this drug. MAO inhibitors may suppress anginal pain that would otherwise serve as a warning sign of myocardial ischemia.

P

Common adverse effects in *italic*, life-threatening effects underlined; generic names in **bold**; classifications in SMALL CAPS; ♣ Canadian drug name; ♦ Prototype drug

1199

PHENOBARBITAL 🄟

(fee-noe-bar′bi-tal)

Solfoton

PHENOBARBITAL SODIUM

Luminal

Classifications: ANTICONVULSANT; SEDATIVE-HYPNOTIC; BARBITURATE

Therapeutic: ANTICONVULSANT; SEDATIVE-HYPNOTIC

Pregnancy Category: D

Controlled Substance: Schedule IV

AVAILABILITY 15 mg, 16 mg, 30 mg, 60 mg, 90 mg, 100 mg tablets; 16 mg capsules; 15 mg/5 mL, 20 mg/5 mL liquid; 30 mg/mL, 60 mg/mL, 65 mg/mL, 130 mg/mL injection

ACTION & *THERAPEUTIC EFFECT*

Long-acting barbiturate. Sedative and hypnotic effects appear to be due primarily to interference with impulse transmission of cerebral cortex by inhibition of reticular activating system. CNS depression may range from mild sedation to coma, depending on dosage, route of administration, degree of nervous system excitability, and drug tolerance. Initially, barbiturates suppress REM sleep, but with chronic therapy REM sleep returns to normal. *Produces sedative and hypnotic effects with no analgesic properties. Limits spread of seizure activity by increasing threshold for motor cortex stimuli.*

USES Long-term management of tonic-clonic (grand mal) seizures and partial seizures; status epilepticus, eclampsia, febrile convulsions in young children. Also used as a sedative in anxiety or tension states; in pediatrics as preoperative and postoperative sedation and to treat pylorospasm in infants.

UNLABELED USES Treatment and prevention of hyperbilirubinemia in neonates and in the management of chronic cholestasis; benzodiazepine withdrawal.

CONTRAINDICATIONS Hypersensitivity to barbiturates; manifest hepatic or familial history of porphyria; severe respiratory or kidney disease; history of previous addiction to sedative hypnotics; alcohol intoxication; uncontrolled pain; renal failure, anuria; pregnancy (category D), lactation.

CAUTIOUS USE Impaired liver, kidney, cardiac, or respiratory function; sleep apnea; COPD; history of allergies; older adult or debilitated patients; patients with fever; hyperthyroidism; diabetes mellitus or severe anemia; seizure disorders; during labor and delivery; patient with borderline hypoadrenal function; young children and neonates.

ROUTE & DOSAGE

Anticonvulsant

Adult: **PO/IV** 1–3 mg/kg/d in divided doses
Child: **PO/IV** 4–8 mg/kg/d in divided doses

Status Epilepticus

Adult: **IV** 300–800 mg, then 120–240 mg q20min (total max: 1–2 g)
Child: **IV** 10–20 mg/kg in single or divided doses, then 5 mg/kg/dose q15–30 min (total max: 40 mg/kg)
Neonate: **IV** 15–20 mg/kg in single or divided doses

Sedative/Hypnotic

Adult: **PO** 30–120 mg/d **IV/IM/SC** 100–320 mg/d

Common adverse effects in *italic*, life-threatening effects underlined; generic names in **bold**; classifications in SMALL CAPS; ✦ Canadian drug name; 🄟 Prototype drug

Child: **PO** 2 mg/kg/d in 3 divided doses **IV/IM/SC** 3–5 mg/kg

Renal Impairment
Cl_{cr} <10 mL/min: dose q12–16h
Hemodialysis: 20–50% dialyzed

ADMINISTRATION

Oral
- Make sure patient actually swallows pill and does not "cheek" it.
- Give crushed and mixed with a fluid or with food if patient cannot swallow pill. Do not permit patient to swallow dry crushed drug.

Intramuscular
- Give IM deep into large muscle mass; do not exceed 5 mL at any one site.

Intravenous
Note: Verify correct IV concentration and rate of infusion for neonates, infants, children with physician. Use IV route ONLY if other routes are not feasible.

PREPARE: **Direct:** Slowly add at least 10 mL of sterile water for injection to ampule. Rotate ampule to dissolve (may take several minutes). If solution not clear in 5 min or if a precipitate remains, discard.

ADMINISTER: **Direct:** Give 60 mg or fraction thereof over at least 60 sec. Give within 30 min after preparation.

INCOMPATIBILITIES **Solution/additive:** Ampicillin, cephalothin, chlorpromazine, cimetidine, clindamycin, codeine phosphate, dexamethasone, diphenhydramine, erythromycin, ephedrine, hydralazine, hydrocortisone sodium succinate, hydroxyzine, insulin, kanamycin, levorphanol, meperidine, methadone, methylphenidate, morphine, nitrofurantoin, norepinephrine, TETRACYCLINES, **pentazocine, pentobarbital, phytonadione, procaine, prochlorperazine, promazine, promethazine, sodium bicarbonate, streptomycin, vancomycin, warfarin.** **Y-site:** **Amphotericin B cholesteryl complex, hydromorphone, TPN with albumin.**
- Be aware that extravasation of IV phenobarbital may cause necrotic tissue changes that necessitate skin grafting. Check injection site frequently.

ADVERSE EFFECTS (≥1%) **Body as a Whole:** Myalgia, neuralgia, <u>CNS depression, coma, and death</u>. **CNS:** *Somnolence,* nightmares, insomnia, "hangover," headache, anxiety, thinking abnormalities, dizziness, nystagmus, irritability, paradoxic excitement and exacerbation of hyperkinetic behavior (in children); confusion or depression or marked excitement (older adult or debilitated patients); ataxia. **CV:** Bradycardia, syncope, hypotension. **GI:** Nausea, vomiting, constipation, diarrhea, epigastric pain, liver damage. **Hematologic:** Megaloblastic anemia, <u>agranulocytosis</u>, thrombocytopenia. **Metabolic:** Hypocalcemia, osteomalacia, rickets. **Musculoskeletal:** Folic acid deficiency, vitamin D deficiency. **Respiratory:** <u>Respiratory depression</u>. **Skin:** Mild maculopapular, morbilliform rash; erythema multiforme, <u>Stevens-Johnson syndrome, exfoliative dermatitis</u> (rare).

DIAGNOSTIC TEST INTERFERENCE BARBITURATES may affect *bromsulphalein* retention tests (by enhancing liver uptake and excretion of dye) and increase *serum phosphatase.*

INTERACTIONS Drug: Alcohol, CNS DEPRESSANTS compound CNS depression; phenobarbital may decrease absorption and increase metabolism of ORAL ANTICOAGULANTS; increases metabolism of CORTICOSTEROIDS, ORAL CONTRACEPTIVES, ANTICONVULSANTS, **digitoxin,** possibly decreasing their effects; ANTIDEPRESSANTS potentiate adverse effects of phenobarbital; **griseofulvin** decreases absorption of phenobarbital; **quinine** increases plasma levels. **Herbal: Kava-kava, valerian** may potentiate sedation.

PHARMACOKINETICS Absorption: 70–90% slowly from GI tract. **Peak:** 8–12 h PO; 30 min IV. **Duration:** 4–6 h IV. **Distribution:** 20–45% protein bound; crosses placenta; enters breast milk. **Metabolism:** In liver (CYP2C19). **Elimination:** In urine. **Half-Life:** 2–6 d.

CLINICAL IMPLICATIONS
Assessment & Drug Effects
- Observe patients receiving large doses closely for at least 30 min to ensure that sedation is not excessive.
- Chronic use in children or infants requires continuous assessment related to normal cognitive and behavioral functioning.
- Keep patient under constant observation when drug is administered IV, and record vital signs at least every hour or more often if indicated.
- Check IV injection site very frequently to prevent extravasation of phenobarbital. It could result in tissue damage requiring skin grafting.
- Lab tests: Obtain liver function and hematology tests and determinations of serum folate and vitamin D levels during prolonged therapy.
- Monitor serum drug levels. Serum concentrations >50 mcg/mL may cause coma. Therapeutic serum concentrations of 15–40 mcg/mL produce anticonvulsant activity in most patients. These values are usually attained after 2 or 3 wk of

therapy with a dose of 100–200 mg/d.
- Expect barbiturates to produce restlessness when given to patients in pain because these drugs do not have analgesic action.
- Be prepared for paradoxical responses and report promptly in older adult or debilitated patient and children [i.e., irritability, marked excitement (inappropriate tearfulness and aggression in children), depression, and confusion].
- Monitor for drug interactions. Barbiturates increase the metabolism of many drugs, leading to decreased pharmacologic effects of those drugs. Whenever a barbiturate is added to an established regimen of another drug, observe for changes in effectiveness of the first drug at least during early phase of barbiturate use.
- Monitor for and report chronic toxicity symptoms (e.g., ataxia, slurred speech, irritability, poor judgment, slight dysarthria, nystagmus on vertical gaze, confusion, insomnia, somatic complaints).

Patient & Family Education
- Be aware that anticonvulsant therapy may cause drowsiness during first few weeks of treatment, but this usually diminishes with continued use.
- Avoid potentially hazardous activities requiring mental alertness until response to drug is known.
- Do not consume alcohol in any amount when taking a barbiturate; it may severely impair judgment and abilities.
- Increase vitamin D-fortified foods (e.g., milk products) because drug increases vitamin D metabolism. A vitamin D supplement may be prescribed.
- Maintain adequate dietary folate intake: fresh vegetables (especially green leafy), fresh fruits, whole

grains, liver. Long-term therapy may result in nutritional folate (B₉) deficiency. A supplement of folic acid may be prescribed.

- Adhere to drug regimen (i.e., do not change intervals between doses or increase or decrease doses) without contacting physician.
- Do not stop taking drug abruptly because of danger of withdrawal symptoms (8–12 h after last dose), which can be fatal.
- Report to physician the onset of fever, sore throat or mouth, malaise, easy bruising or bleeding, petechiae, jaundice, rash when on prolonged therapy.
- Avoid pregnancy when receiving barbiturates. Use or add barrier device to hormonal contraceptive when taking prolonged therapy.

PHENOXYBENZAMINE HYDROCHLORIDE

(fen-ox-ee-ben′za-meen)

Dibenzyline

Classifications: ALPHA-ADRENERGIC ANTAGONIST; ANTIHYPERTENSIVE AGENT

Therapeutic: ANTIHYPERTENSIVE

Prototype: Prazosin

Pregnancy Category: C

AVAILABILITY 10 mg capsules

ACTION & *THERAPEUTIC EFFECT*
Long-acting alpha-adrenergic antagonist. Apparently produces noncompetitive blockade of alpha-adrenergic receptor sites at postganglionic synapse. Alpha-receptor sites are thus unable to react to the endogenous or exogenous sympathomimetic agents epinephrine and norepinephrine. *Blocks excitatory effects of epinephrine, including vasoconstriction, but does not affect adrenergic cardiac inhibitory actions. It produces a "chemical sympathectomy" and it can maintain it.*

USES Management of pheochromocytoma.

UNLABELED USES To improve circulation in peripheral vasospastic conditions such as Raynaud's acrocyanosis and frostbite sequelae, for adjunctive treatment of shock, hypertensive crisis.

CONTRAINDICATIONS Instances when fall in BP would be dangerous; pregnancy (category C), lactation.

CAUTIOUS USE Marked cerebral or coronary arteriosclerosis, compensated congestive heart failure, coronary artery disease; older adults; renal insufficiency; respiratory infections.

ROUTE & DOSAGE

Management of Pheochromocytoma
Adult: **PO** 10 mg b.i.d., may increase by 10 mg/d at 4-d intervals to desired response (usual range 20–40 mg/d in 2–3 divided doses)
Child: **PO** 0.2 mg/kg/d, may increase by 0.2 mg/kg/d to desired response (usual range 0.4–1.2 mg/kg/q6–8h)

ADMINISTRATION

Oral
- Give with milk or in divided doses to reduce gastric irritation.
- Preserve in airtight containers protected from light.

ADVERSE EFFECTS (≥1%) **Body as a Whole:** *Dizziness,* fainting, drowsiness, sedation, tiredness, weakness, lethargy, confusion, headache, <u>shock</u>. **CNS:** CNS stimulation (large doses). **CV:** *Postural hypotension, tachycardia,* palpitation. **GI:** Dry mouth. **Urogenital:** Inhibition of ejaculation. **Respiratory:** *Nasal congestion.* **Skin:** Allergic contact dermatitis. **Special Senses:** *Miosis,* drooping of eyelids.

INTERACTIONS Drug: Inhibits effects of **methoxamine, norepinephrine, phenylephrine;** additive hypotensive effects with ANTIHYPERTENSIVES.

PHARMACOKINETICS Absorption: Variably (approximately 30%) from GI tract. **Onset:** 2 h. **Peak:** 4–6 h. **Duration:** 3–4 d. **Distribution:** Accumulates in adipose tissue. **Elimination:** 80% in urine and bile within 24 h. **Half-Life:** 24 h.

CLINICAL IMPLICATIONS

Assessment & Drug Effects
- Monitor BP and note pulse quality, rate, and rhythm in recumbent and standing positions during period of dosage adjustment. Observe patient closely for at least 4 d from one dosage increment to the next; hypotension and tachycardia are most likely to occur in standing position.
- Drug has cumulative action, thus onset of therapeutic effects may not occur until after 2 wk of therapy, and full therapeutic effects may not be apparent for several more weeks.

Patient & Family Education
- Make position changes slowly, particularly from reclining to upright posture, and dangle legs and exercise ankles and feet for a few minutes before standing.
- Be aware that light headedness, dizziness, and palpitations usually disappear with continued therapy but may reappear under conditions that promote vasodilation,

such as strenuous exercise or ingestion of a large meal or alcohol.
- Pupil constriction, nasal stuffiness, and inhibition of ejaculation generally decrease with continued therapy.
- Do not take OTC medications for coughs, colds, or allergy without approval of physician. Many contain agents that cause BP elevation.

PHENTERMINE HYDROCHLORIDE

(phen-ter'meen)
Ionamin, Fastin, Zantryl, Adipex-P, Obe-Nix-30
Classifications: ANOREXIANT
Therapeutic: APPETITE SUPPRESSANT
Prototype: Diethylpropion
Pregnancy Category: C
Controlled Substance: Schedule IV

AVAILABILITY 8 mg, 30 mg, 37.5 mg tablets; 15 mg, 18.75 mg, 30 mg, 37.5 mg capsules

ACTION & *THERAPEUTIC EFFECT*
Sympathetic amine with pharmacological similarity to amphetamine. Actions include CNS stimulation and blood pressure elevation. *Appetite suppression or metabolic effects along with diet adjustment result in weight loss in obese individuals.*

USES Short-term (8–12 wk) adjunct for weight loss.

CONTRAINDICATIONS History of hypertension, moderate-to-severe hypertension, advanced arteriosclerosis, cardiovascular disease; hyperthyroidism; known hypersensitivity to sympathetic amines; agitated states; psychosis; schizophrenia; history of drug abuse; during or within

14 d of administration of MAO inhibitor; concurrent administration of serotonin reuptake inhibitors (SSRIs); valvular heart disease; glaucoma; pregnancy (category C), lactation, or children <16 y.
CAUTIOUS USE Mild hypertension, diabetes mellitus.

ROUTE & DOSAGE

Obesity

Adult: **PO** 8 mg t.i.d. 30 min before meals or 15–37.5 mg q.d. before breakfast or 10–14 h before retiring

ADMINISTRATION

Oral

- Ensure that at least 14 d have elapsed between the first dose of phentermine and the last dose of an MAO inhibitor.
- Give 30 min before meals.
- Do not administer if an SSRI is currently prescribed.
- Store in a tight container.

ADVERSE EFFECTS (≥1%) **Body as a Whole:** Hypersensitivity (urticaria, rash, erythema, burning sensation), chest pain, excessive sweating, clamminess, chills, flushing, fever, myalgia. **CV:** Palpitations, tachycardia, arrhythmias, hypertension or hypotension, syncope, precordial pain, pulmonary hypertension. **GI:** Dry mouth, altered taste, nausea, vomiting, abdominal pain, diarrhea, constipation, stomach pain. **Endocrine:** Gynecomastia. **Hematologic:** <u>Bone marrow suppression, agranulocytosis</u>, leukopenia. **Musculoskeletal:** Muscle pain. **CNS:** Overstimulation, nervousness, restlessness, dizziness, insomnia, weakness, fatigue, malaise, anxiety, euphoria, drowsiness, depression, agitation, dysphoria,

tremor, dyskinesia, dysarthria, confusion, incoordination, headache, change in libido. **Skin:** Hair loss, ecchymosis. **Special Senses:** Mydriasis, blurred vision. **Urogenital:** Dysuria, polyuria, urinary frequency, impotence, menstrual upset.

INTERACTIONS Drug: MAO INHIBITORS, **furazolidone** may increase pressor response resulting in hypertensive crisis. TRICYCLIC ANTIDEPRESSANTS may decrease anorectic response. May decrease hypotensive effects of **guanethidine.**

PHARMACOKINETICS Absorption: Absorbed from the small intestine. **Duration:** 4–14 h. **Elimination:** Primarily in urine. **Half-Life:** 19–24 h.

CLINICAL IMPLICATIONS

Assessment & Drug Effects

- Assess for tolerance to the anorectic effect of the drug. Withhold drug and report to physician when this occurs.
- Lab tests: Periodic CBC with differential and blood glucose.
- Monitor periodic cardiovascular status, including BP, exercise tolerance, peripheral edema.
- Monitor weight at least 3 times/wk.

Patient & Family Education

- Do not take this drug late in the evening because it could cause insomnia.
- Report immediately any of the following: Shortness of breath, chest pains, dizziness or fainting, swelling of the extremities.
- Tolerance to the appetite suppression effects of the drug usually develops in a few weeks. Notify physician, but do not increase the drug dose.
- Weigh yourself at least 3 times/wk at the same time of day with the same amount of clothing.

Common adverse effects in *italic*, life-threatening effects <u>underlined</u>; generic names in **bold**; classifications in SMALL CAPS; ♣ Canadian drug name; ⊘ Prototype drug

1205

PHENTOLAMINE MESYLATE

(fen-tole′a-meen)

Regitine, Rogitine ♦

Classifications: ALPHA-ADRENERGIC ANTAGONIST; VASODILATOR

Therapeutic: VASODILATOR

Prototype: Prazosin

Pregnancy Category: C

AVAILABILITY 5 mg injection

ACTION & *THERAPEUTIC EFFECT*

Alpha-adrenergic blocking agent. Competitively blocks alpha-adrenergic receptors, but action is transient and incomplete. Causes vasodilation and decreases general vascular resistance and pulmonary arterial pressure, primarily by direct action on vascular smooth muscle. *Prevents hypertension resulting from elevated levels of circulating epinephrine or norepinephrine.*

USES Diagnosis of pheochromocytoma and to prevent or control hypertensive episodes prior to or during pheochromocytomectomy.

UNLABELED USES Prevention of dermal necrosis and sloughing following IV administration or extravasation of norepinephrine.

CONTRAINDICATIONS MI (previous or present), coronary artery disease; peptic ulcer disease; pregnancy (category C), lactation.

CAUTIOUS USE Gastritis.

ROUTE & DOSAGE

To Prevent Hypertensive Episode during Surgery
Adult: **IV/IM** 5 mg 1–2 h before surgery, repeat as needed
Child: **IV/IM** 0.05–0.1 mg/kg/dose (max: 5 mg/dose)

To Test for Pheochromocytoma
Adult: **IV/IM** 5 mg

Child: **IV/IM** 0.05–0.1 mg/kg (max: 5 mg)

To Treat Extravasation
Adult: **Intradermal** 5–10 mg diluted in 10 mL of normal saline injected into affected area within 12 h of extravasation
Child: **Intradermal** 0.1–0.2 mg/kg diluted with normal saline injected into affected area within 12 h of extravasation

ADMINISTRATION

Note: Place patient in supine position when receiving drug parenterally. Monitor BP and pulse q2min until stabilized.

Intramuscular
- Reconstitute 5 mg vial with 1 mL of sterile water for injection.

Intravenous

PREPARE: **Direct:** Reconstitute as for IM. May be further diluted with up to 10 mL of sterile water. Use immediately.
ADMINISTER: **Direct:** Give a single dose over 60 sec.

ADVERSE EFFECTS (≥1%) **Body as a Whole:** Weakness, dizziness, flushing, *orthostatic hypotension.* **GI:** *Abdominal pain, nausea, vomiting, diarrhea, exacerbation of peptic ulcer.* **CV:** *Acute and prolonged hypotension, tachycardia, anginal pain,* cardiac arrhythmias, MI, cerebrovascular spasm, shock-like state. **Special Senses:** Nasal stuffiness, conjunctival infection.

INTERACTIONS Drug: May antagonize BP raising effects of **epinephrine, ephedrine.**

PHARMACOKINETICS Peak: 2 min IV; 15–20 min IM. **Duration:** 10–15 min IV; 3–4 h IM. **Elimination:** In urine. **Half-Life:** 19 min.

CLINICAL IMPLICATIONS

Assessment & Drug Effects

▪ Test for pheochromocytoma:
(1) Withhold medications not deemed absolutely essential for at least 24 h, preferably 48–72 h; antihypertensive agents withheld until BP returns to pretreatment level (rauwolfia drugs withdrawn at least 4 wk prior to testing). (2) Keep patient at rest in supine position throughout test, preferably in quiet darkened room. (3) Take BP q10min for at least 30 min; when BP stabilizes, (4) IV administration: Record BP immediately after injection and at 30-sec intervals for first 3 min; then at 1-min intervals for next 7 min. IM administration: BP determinations at 5-min intervals for 30–45 min.

Patient & Family Education

▪ Avoid sudden changes in position, particularly from reclining to upright posture and dangle legs and exercise ankles and toes for a few minutes before standing to walk.
▪ Lie down or sit down in head-low position immediately if lightheaded or dizzy.

PHENYLEPHRINE HYDROCHLORIDE

(fen-ill-ef'rin)
AK-Dilate Ophthalmic, Alconefrin, Isopto Frin, Mydfrin, Neo-Synephrine, Nostril, Rhinall, Sinarest Nasal, Sinex
Classifications: EYE AND NOSE PREPARATION; ALPHA-ADRENERGIC AGONIST; MYDRIATIC; DECONGESTANT
Therapeutic: DECONGESTANT; MYDRIATIC; VASOCONSTRICTOR
Prototype: Methoxamine
Pregnancy Category: C

AVAILABILITY 10 mg chewable tablet; 0.125%, 0.16%, 0.5%, 1% nasal solution; 0.12%, 2.5%, 10% ophthalmic solution; 10 mg/mL injection

ACTION & *THERAPEUTIC EFFECT*

Potent, synthetic, direct-acting sympathomimetic with strong alpha-adrenergic and weak beta-adrenergic cardiac stimulant actions. Produces little or no CNS stimulation. Elevates systolic and diastolic pressures through arteriolar constriction. Reduces intraocular pressure by increasing outflow and decreasing rate of aqueous humor secretion. *Topical applications to eye produce vasoconstriction and prompt mydriasis of short duration, usually without causing cycloplegia. Nasal decongestant action qualitatively similar to that of epinephrine but more potent and has longer duration of action.*

USES Parenterally to maintain BP during anesthesia, to treat vascular failure in shock, and to overcome paroxysmal supraventricular tachycardia. Used topically for rhinitis of common cold, allergic rhinitis, and sinusitis; in selected patients with wide-angle glaucoma; as mydriatic for ophthalmoscopic examination or surgery, and for relief of uveitis.

CONTRAINDICATIONS Severe coronary disease, severe hypertension, atrial fibrillation, atrial flutter, cardiac arrhythmias; cardiac disease, cardiomyopathy; uncontrolled hypertension; ventricular fibrillation or tachycardia; acute MI, angina; cerebral arteriosclerosis, MAOI; narrow-angle glaucoma (ophthalmic preparations); labor, delivery; pregnancy (category C).
CAUTIOUS USE Hyperthyroidism; diabetes mellitus; older adult patients; 21 d before or following termination of MAO inhibitor therapy;

P

Common adverse effects in *italic*, life-threatening effects <u>underlined</u>; generic names in **bold**; classifications in SMALL CAPS; ✦ Canadian drug name; ⦿ Prototype drug

1207

lactation. **Ophthalmic solution (10%):** Cardiovascular disease; diabetes mellitus; hypertension; aneurysms; infants.

ROUTE & DOSAGE

Hypotension

Adult: **IM/SC** 1–10 mg (initial dose not to exceed 5 mg) q10–15min as needed **IV** 0.1–0.18 mg/min until BP stabilizes; then 0.04–0.06 mg/min for maintenance

Ophthalmoscopy

See Appendix A

Supraventricular Tachycardia

Adult: **IV** 0.25–0.5 mg bolus, then 0.1–0.2 mg doses (total max: 1 mg)

Vasoconstrictor

Adult: **Ophthalmic** See Appendix A–1 **Intranasal** Small amount of nasal jelly placed into each nostril q3–4h as needed or 2–3 drops or sprays of 0.25–0.5% solution q3–4h as needed
Child: **Intranasal** <6 y, 2–3 drops or sprays of 0.125% solution q3–4h as needed; 6–12 y, 2–3 drops or sprays of 0.25% solution q3–4h as needed

ADMINISTRATION

Instillation

- Nasal preparations: Instruct patient to blow nose gently (with both nostrils open) to clear nasal passages before administration of medication.
- Instillation (drops): Tilt head back while sitting or standing up, or lie on bed and hang head over side. Stay in position a few minutes to permit medication to spread through nose. (Spray): With head upright, squeeze bottle quickly and firmly to produce 1 or 2 sprays into each nostril; wait 3–5 min, blow nose, and repeat dose. (Jelly): Place in each nostril and sniff it well back into nose.

- Clean tips and droppers of nasal solution dispensers with hot water after use to prevent contamination of solution. Droppers of ophthalmic solution bottles should not touch any surface including the eye.
- Ophthalmic preparations: To avoid excessive systemic absorption, apply pressure to lacrimal sac during and for 1–2 min after instillation of drops.

Subcutaneous, Intramuscular

- Give undiluted.

Intravenous

PREPARE: Direct: Dilute each 1 mg in 9 mL of sterile water. **IV Infusion:** Further dilute each 10 mg in 500 mL D5W or NS (concentration: 0.2 mg/mL).

ADMINISTER: Direct: Give a single dose over 60 sec. **IV Infusion:** Titrate to maintain BP.

INCOMPATIBILITIES Solution/additive: Phenytoin Y-site: Propofol, thiopental.

- Protect from exposure to air, strong light, or heat, any of which can cause solutions to change color to brown, form a precipitate, and lose potency.

ADVERSE EFFECTS (≥1%) **Special Senses:** *Transient stinging,* lacrimation, brow ache, headache, blurred vision, allergy (pigmentary deposits on lids, conjunctiva, and cornea with prolonged use), increased sensitivity to light. *Rebound nasal congestion* (hyperemia and edema of mucosa), *nasal burning,* stinging, dryness, *sneezing.* **CV:** Palpitation, tachycardia, bradycardia (overdosage), extrasystoles, hypertension. **Body as a**

P

Whole: Trembling, sweating, pallor, sense of fullness in head, tingling of extremities, sleeplessness, dizziness, light-headedness, weakness, restlessness, anxiety, precordial pain, *tremor,* severe visceral or peripheral vasoconstriction, necrosis if IV infiltrates.

INTERACTIONS Drug: ERGOT ALKA-LOIDS, **guanethidine, reserpine,** TRICYCLIC ANTIDEPRESSANTS increase pressor effects of phenylephrine; **halothane, digoxin** increase risk of arrhythmias; MAO INHIBITORS cause hypertensive crisis; **oxytocin** causes persistent hypertension; AL-PHA BLOCKERS, BETA BLOCKERS antagonize effects of phenylephrine.

PHARMACOKINETICS Onset: Immediate IV; 10–15 min IM/SC. **Duration:** 15–20 min IV; 30–120 min IM/SC; 3–6 h topical. **Metabolism:** In liver and tissues by monoamine oxidase.

CLINICAL IMPLICATIONS

Assessment & Drug Effects

- Monitor pulse, BP, and central venous pressure (q2–5min) during IV administration.
- Control flow rate and dosage to prevent excessive dosage. IV overdoses can induce ventricular dysrhythmias.
- Observe for congestion or rebound miosis after topical administration to eye.

Patient & Family Education

- Be aware that instillation of 2.5–10% strength ophthalmic solution can cause burning and stinging.
- Do not exceed recommended dosage regardless of formulation.
- Inform the physician if no relief is experienced from preparation in 5 d.
- Be aware that systemic absorption from nasal and conjunctival membranes can occur, though infrequently (see ADVERSE EFFECTS). Discontinue drug and report to the physician if adverse effects occur.
- Wear sunglasses in bright light because after instillation of ophthalmic drops, pupils will be large and eyes may be more sensitive to light than usual. Stop medication and notify physician if sensitivity persists beyond 12 h after drug has been discontinued.
- Be aware that some ophthalmic solutions may stain contact lenses.

PHENYTOIN 🅿️

(fen'i-toy-in)
Dilantin-125, Dilantin

PHENYTOIN SODIUM EXTENDED

Dilantin Kapseals, Phentek

PHENYTOIN SODIUM PROMPT

Dilantin

Classifications: ANTICONVULSANT; HYDANTOIN
Therapeutic: ANTICONVULSANT
Pregnancy Category: D

P

AVAILABILITY 100 mg capsule; 100 mg, 200 mg, 300 mg sustained release capsule; 50 mg chewable tablet; 125 mg/5 mL suspension; 50 mg/mL injection

ACTION & *THERAPEUTIC EFFECT*

Anticonvulsant action elevates the seizure threshold and/or limits the spread of seizure discharge. Phenytoin is accompanied by reduced voltage, frequency, and spread of electrical discharges within the motor cortex. Has class IB antiarrhythmic properties. *Inhibits seizure activity. Effective in treating arrhythmias associated with QT prolongation.*

USES To control tonic-clonic (grand mal) seizures, psychomotor and nonepileptic seizures (e.g., Reye's syndrome, after head trauma). Also used to prevent or treat seizures occurring during or after neurosurgery. Is not effective for absence seizures.

UNLABELED USES Antiarrhythmic agent (phenytoin IV) especially in treatment of digitalis-induced arrhythmias; treatment of trigeminal neuralgia (tic douloureux).

CONTRAINDICATIONS Hypersensitivity to hydantoin products; rash; seizures due to hypoglycemia; sinus bradycardia, complete or incomplete heart block; Adams-Stokes syndrome; pregnancy (category D).

CAUTIOUS USE Impaired liver or kidney function; alcoholism; blood dyscrasias; hypotension, severe myocardial insufficiency, impending or frank heart failure; older adult, debilitated, gravely ill patients; pancreatic adenoma; diabetes mellitus, hyperglycemia; respiratory depression; acute intermittent porphyria.

ROUTE & DOSAGE

Anticonvulsant

Adult: **PO** 15–20 mg/kg loading dose, then 300 mg/d in 1–3 divided doses, may be gradually increased by 100 mg/wk until seizures are controlled **IV** 10–15 mg/kg then 300 mg/d in divided doses.
Child: **PO/IV** 15–20 mg/kg loading dose, then 5 mg/kg in 2 divided doses

ADMINISTRATION

Oral

- Ensure that sustained release form is not chewed or crushed. Must be swallowed whole.
- Do not give within 2–3 h of antacid ingestion.
- Shake suspension vigorously before pouring to ensure uniform distribution of drug.
- Note: Prompt release capsules and chewable tablets are not intended for once-a-day dosage since drug is too quickly bioavailable and can therefore lead to toxic serum levels.
- Use sustained release capsules ONLY for once-a-day dosage regimens.

Intravenous

Note: Verify correct rate of IV injection for administration to infants or children with physician.

- Inspect solution prior to use. May use a slightly yellowed injectable solution safely. Precipitation may be caused by refrigeration, but slow warming to room temperature restores clarity.

PREPARE: Direct: Give undiluted. Use only when clear without precipitate.

ADMINISTER: Direct: Give 50 mg or fraction thereof over 1 min (25 mg/min in older adult or when used as antiarrhythmic). Follow with an injection of sterile saline through the same in-place catheter or needle. Do not use solutions containing dextrose.

INCOMPATIBILITIES Solution/additive: 5% dextrose, Ringer's lactated, fat emulsion, sodium chloride, amikacin, aminophylline, bretylium, cephalothin, cephapirin, chloramphenicol, chlordiazepoxide, clindamycin, codeine phosphate, diphenhydramine, dobutamine, hydromorphone, insulin, levorphanol, lidocaine, lincomycin, meperidine, metaraminol, methadone, morphine, nitroglycerin, norepinephrine, penicillin G, pentobarbital,

P

phenylephedrine, phytonadione, procaine, prochlorperazine, secobarbital, streptomycin, warfarin. Y-site: Amikacin, amphotericin B cholesteryl complex, bretylium, cimetidine, ciprofloxacin, clarithromycin, clindamycin, diltiazem, dobutamine, enalaprilat, fenoldopam, gatifloxacin, heparin, hydromorphone, lidocaine, linezolid, methadone, morphine, ondansetron, potassium chloride, propofol, sufentanil, tacrolimus, theophylline, TPN, vitamin B complex with C.

■ Observe injection site frequently during administration to prevent infiltration. Local soft tissue irritation may be serious, leading to erosion of tissues.

ADVERSE EFFECTS (≥1%) **CNS:** Usually dose-related: Nystagmus, *drowsiness,* ataxia, dizziness, mental confusion, tremors, insomnia, headache, seizures. **CV:** Bradycardia, hypotension, <u>cardiovascular collapse</u>, ventricular fibrillation, phlebitis. **Special Senses:** Photophobia, conjunctivitis, diplopia, blurred vision. **GI:** *Gingival hyperplasia,* nausea, vomiting, constipation, epigastric pain, dysphagia, loss of taste, weight loss, hepatitis, liver necrosis. **Hematologic:** Thrombocytopenia, leukopenia, leukocytosis, <u>agranulocytosis</u>, pancytopenia, eosinophilia; megaloblastic, hemolytic, or <u>aplastic anemias</u>. **Metabolic:** Fever, hyperglycemia, glycosuria, weight gain, edema, transient increase in serum thyrotropic (TSH) level, osteomalacia or rickets associated with hypocalcemia and elevated alkaline phosphatase activity. **Skin:** Alopecia, hirsutism (especially in young female); rash: scarlatiniform, maculopapular, urticaria, morbilliform; <u>bullous, exfoliative, or purpuric dermatitis; Stevens-Johnson syndrome, toxic epidermal necrolysis</u>, keratosis, neonatal hemorrhage. **Urogenital:** Acute renal failure, Peyronie's disease. **Respiratory:** Acute pneumonitis, pulmonary fibrosis. **Body as a Whole:** Periarteritis nodosum, acute systemic lupus erythematosus, craniofacial abnormalities (with enlargement of lips); lymphadenopathy.

DIAGNOSTIC TEST INTERFERENCE
Phenytoin (HYDANTOINS) may produce lower than normal values for *dexamethasone* or *metyrapone* tests; may increase serum levels of *glucose, BSP,* and *alkaline phosphatase* and may decrease *PBI* and *urinary steroid* levels.

INTERACTIONS Drug: Alcohol decreases phenytoin effects; OTHER ANTICONVULSANTS may increase or decrease phenytoin levels; phenytoin may decrease absorption and increase metabolism of ORAL ANTICOAGULANTS; phenytoin increases metabolism of CORTICOSTEROIDS, ORAL CONTRACEPTIVES, and **nisoldipine,** decreasing their effectiveness; **amiodarone, chloramphenicol, omeprazole,** and **ticlopidine** increase phenytoin levels; ANTITUBERCULOSIS AGENTS decrease phenytoin levels. **Food: Folic acid, calcium,** and **vitamin D** absorption may be decreased by phenytoin; phenytoin absorption may be decreased by enteral nutrition supplements. **Herbal: Ginkgo** may decrease anticonvulsant effectiveness.

PHARMACOKINETICS Absorption: Completely from GI tract. **Peak:** 1.5–3 h prompt release; 4–12 h sustained release. **Distribution:** 95% protein bound; crosses placenta; small amount in breast milk. **Metabolism:** Oxidized in liver to inactive metabo-

P

Common adverse effects in *italic*, life-threatening effects <u>underlined</u>; generic names in **bold**; classifications in SMALL CAPS; ✦ Canadian drug name; ⊕ Prototype drug

1211

lites. **Elimination:** By kidneys. **Half-Life:** 22 h.

CLINICAL IMPLICATIONS
Assessment & Drug Effects

- Continuously monitor vital signs and symptoms during IV infusion and for an hour afterward. Watch for respiratory depression. Constant observation and a cardiac monitor are necessary with older adults or patients with cardiac disease. Margin between toxic and therapeutic IV doses is relatively small.
- Be aware of therapeutic serum concentration: 10–20 mcg/mL; toxic level: 30–50 mcg/mL; lethal level: 100 mcg/mL. Steady-state therapeutic levels are not achieved for at least 7–10 d.
- Lab tests: Periodic serum phenytoin concentration; CBC with differential, platelet count, and Hct and Hgb; serum glucose, serum calcium, and serum magnesium; and liver funtion tests.
- Observe patient closely for neurologic adverse effects following IV administration. Have on hand oxygen, atropine, vasopressor, assisted ventilation, seizure precaution equipment (mouth gag, nonmetal airway, suction apparatus).
- Be aware that gingival hyperplasia appears most commonly in children and adolescents and never occurs in patients without teeth.
- Make sure patients on prolonged therapy have adequate intake of vitamin D-containing foods and sufficient exposure to sunlight.
- Monitor diabetics for loss of glycemic control.
- Check periodically for decrease in serum calcium levels. Particularly susceptible: patients receiving other anticonvulsants concurrently, as well as those who are inactive, have limited exposure to sun, or whose dietary intake is inadequate.
- Observe for symptoms of folic acid deficiency: neuropathy, mental dysfunction.
- Be alert to symptoms of hypomagnesemia (see Appendix F); neuromuscular symptoms: tetany, positive Chvostek's and Trousseau's signs, seizures, tremors, ataxia, vertigo, nystagmus, muscular fasciculations.

Patient & Family Education

- Be aware that drug may make urine pink or red to red-brown.
- Report symptoms of fatigue, dry skin, deepening voice when receiving long-term therapy because phenytoin can unmask a low thyroid reserve.
- Do not alter prescribed drug regimen. Stopping drug abruptly may precipitate seizures and status epilepticus.
- Do not to request/accept change in drug brand when refilling prescription without consulting physician.
- Understand the effects of alcohol: Alcohol intake may increase phenytoin serum levels, leading to phenytoin toxicity.
- Discontinue drug immediately if a measles-like skin rash or jaundice appears and notify physician.
- Be aware that influenza vaccine during phenytoin treatment may increase seizure activity. Understand that a change in dose may be necessary.

PHYSOSTIGMINE SALICYLATE

(fi-zoe-stig′meen)
Antilirium
Classifications: CHOLINESTERASE INHIBITOR
Therapeutic: ANTICHOLINERGIC ANTIDOTE, CHOLINESTERASE INHIBITOR
Prototype: Neostigmine
Pregnancy Category: C

AVAILABILITY 1 mg/mL injection

ACTION & *THERAPEUTIC EFFECT*
Physostigmine competes with acetylcholine (ACE) for its binding site on acetylcholinesterase, thereby potentiating action of ACE on the skeletal muscle, GI tract and within the CNS. Chief effect is increasing concentration of acetylcholine at cholinergic transmission sites that prolongs and exaggerates its action. *Effective in reversing anticholingeric toxicity.*

USES To reverse anticholinergic toxicity.

CONTRAINDICATIONS Asthma; diabetes mellitus; gangrene, cardiovascular disease; mechanical obstruction of intestinal or urogenital tract; peptic ulcer disease; asthma; any vagotonic state; closed angle glaucoma; secondary glaucoma; inflammatory disease of iris or ciliary body; concomitant use with choline esters (e.g., methacholine, bethanechol) or depolarizing neuromuscular blocking agents (e.g., decamethonium, succinylcholine), pregnancy (category C), lactation.
CAUTIOUS USE Epilepsy; parkinsonism; bradycardia; hyperthyroidism; seizure disorders; hypotension.

ROUTE & DOSAGE

Reversal of Anticholinergic Effects

Adult: **IM/IV** 0.5–2 mg (IV not faster than 1 mg/min), repeat as needed
Child: **IV** 0.02 mg/kg/dose, may repeat q5–10 min (max: total dose of 2 mg)

ADMINISTRATION

Intramuscular, Intravenous
- Give undiluted.

- Use only clear, colorless solutions. Red-tinted solution indicates oxidation, and such solutions should be discarded.

Intravenous
Note: Verify correct rate of IV injection for infants or children with physician.

PREPARE: **Direct:** Give undiluted.
ADMINISTER: **Direct:** Give at a slow rate, no more than 1 mg/min. Rapid administration and overdosage can cause a cholinergic crisis.
INCOMPATIBILITIES **Solution/additive: Phenytoin, ranitidine. Y-site: Dobutamine.**

ADVERSE EFFECTS (≥1%) **Body as a Whole:** *Sweating,* cholinergic crisis (acute toxicity), hyperactivity, respiratory distress, convulsions. **CNS:** Restlessness, hallucinations, twitching, tremors, *sweating,* weakness, ataxia, convulsions, collapse. **GI:** *Nausea, vomiting, epigastric pain, diarrhea, salivation.* **Urogenital:** Involuntary urination or defecation. **Special Senses:** Miosis, *lacrimation,* rhinorrhea. **Respiratory:** Dyspnea, bronchospasm, respiratory paralysis, pulmonary edema. **Cardiovascular:** Irregular pulse, palpitation, bradycardia, rise in BP.

INTERACTIONS Drug: Antagonizes effects of **echothiophate, isoflurophate.**

PHARMACOKINETICS Absorption: Readily from mucous membranes, muscle, subcutaneous tissue; 10–12% absorbed from GI tract. **Onset:** 3–8 min IM/IV. **Duration:** 0.5–5 h IM/IV. **Distribution:** Crosses blood–brain barrier. **Metabolism:** In plasma by cholinesterase. **Elimination:** Small amounts in urine. **Half-Life:** 15–40 min.

Common adverse effects in *italic*, life-threatening effects underlined; generic names in **bold**; classifications in SMALL CAPS; ♣ Canadian drug name; ⊘ Prototype drug

1213

CLINICAL IMPLICATIONS

Assessment & Drug Effects

- Monitor vital signs and state of consciousness closely in patients receiving drug for atropine poisoning. Since physostigmine is usually rapidly eliminated, patient can lapse into delirium and coma within 1 to 2 h; repeat doses may be required.
- Monitor closely for adverse effects related to CNS and for signs of sensitivity to physostigmine. Have atropine sulfate readily available for clinical emergency.
- Discontinue parenteral or oral drug if following symptoms arise: Excessive salivation, emesis, frequent urination, or diarrhea.
- Eliminate excessive sweating or nausea with dose reduction.

PHYTONADIONE (VITAMIN K₁)

(fye-toe-na-dye'one)
Mephyton
Classifications: VITAMIN K; ANTIDOTE
Therapeutic: VITAMIN K, ANTIDOTE
Pregnancy Category: C

AVAILABILITY 5 mg tablets; 2 mg/mL, 10 mg/mL injection

ACTION & *THERAPEUTIC EFFECT*

Fat-soluble substance chemically identical to and with similar activity as naturally occurring vitamin K. Vitamin K is essential for hepatic biosynthesis of blood clotting Factors II, VII, IX, and X. *Promotes liver synthesis of clotting factors.*

USES Drug of choice as antidote for overdosage of coumarin and indandione oral anticoagulants. Also reverses hypoprothrombinemia secondary to administration of oral antibiotics, quinidine, quinine, salicylates, sulfonamides, excessive vitamin A, and secondary to inadequate absorption and synthesis of vitamin K (as in obstructive jaundice, biliary fistula, ulcerative colitis, intestinal resection, prolonged hyperalimentation). Also prophylaxis of and therapy for neonatal hemorrhagic disease.

CONTRAINDICATIONS Hypersensitivity to phytonadione, benzyl alcohol or castor oil; severe liver disease; pregnancy (category C).

CAUTIOUS USE Biliary tract disease, obstructive jaundice.

ROUTE & DOSAGE

Anticoagulant Overdose

Adult: **PO/SC/IM** 2.5–10 mg; rarely up to 50 mg/d, may repeat parenteral dose after 6–8 h if needed or PO dose after 12–24 h **IV** Emergency only: 10–15 mg at a rate of ≤1 mg/min, may be repeated in 4 h if bleeding continues

Hemorrhagic Disease of Newborns

Infant: **IM/SC** 0.5–1 mg immediately after delivery, may repeat in 6–8 h if necessary

Other Prothrombin Deficiencies

Adult: **IM/SC/IV** 2–25 mg
Child/Infant: **IM/SC/IV** 0.5–5 mg

ADMINISTRATION

Intramuscular

Note: Konakion, which contains a phenol preservative, is intended ONLY for IM use. AquaMEPHYTON may be given SC, IM, or IV as prescribed.

- Give IM injection in adults and older children in upper outer quadrant of buttocks. For infants and young children, anterolateral

Common adverse effects in *italic*, life-threatening effects underlined; generic names in **bold**; classifications in SMALL CAPS; ♦ Canadian drug name; ⊙ Prototype drug

aspect of thigh or deltoid region is preferred.

- Aspirate carefully to avoid intravascular injection.
- Apply gentle pressure to site following injection. Swelling (internal bleeding) and pain sometimes occur with SC or IM administration.

Intravenous ————————
Note: Reserve IV route only for emergencies.

PREPARE: Direct: Dilute a single dose in 10 mL D5W, NS, or D5/NS.

ADMINISTER: Direct: Give solution immediately after dilution at a rate not to exceed 1 mg/min.

INCOMPATIBILITIES Solution/additive: Ascorbic acid, cephalothin, dobutamine, doxycycline, magnesium sulfate, nitrofurantoin, phenobarbital, ranitidine, thiopental, vancomycin, warfarin. Y-site: Dobutamine.

- Protect infusion solution from light by wrapping container with aluminum foil or other opaque material. ∎ Discard unused solution and contents in open ampul.

ADVERSE EFFECTS (≥1%) **Body as a Whole:** Hypersensitivity or <u>anaphylaxis-like reaction</u>: facial flushing, cramp-like pains, convulsive movements, chills, fever, diaphoresis, weakness, dizziness, shock, <u>cardiac arrest</u>. **CNS:** Headache (after oral dose), brain damage, <u>death</u>. **GI:** Gastric upset. **Hematologic:** Paradoxic hypoprothrombinemia (patients with severe liver disease), severe hemolytic anemia. **Metabolic:** Hyperbilirubinemia, kernicterus. **Respiratory:** <u>Bronchospasm</u>, dyspnea, sensation of chest constriction, <u>respiratory arrest</u>. **Skin:** Pain at injection site, hematoma, and nodule for-

mation, erythematous skin eruptions (with repeated injections). **Special Senses:** Peculiar taste sensation.

DIAGNOSTIC TEST INTERFERENCE Falsely elevated *urine steroids* (by modifications of *Reddy, Jenkins, Thorn procedure*).

INTERACTIONS Drug: Antagonizes effects of **warfarin; cholestyramine, colestipol, mineral oil** decrease absorption of oral phytonadione.

PHARMACOKINETICS Absorption: Readily from intestinal lymph if bile is present. **Onset:** 6–12 h PO; 1–2 h IM/SC; 15 min IV. **Peak:** Hemorrhage usually controlled within 3–8 h; normal prothrombin time may be obtained in 12–14 h after administration. **Distribution:** Concentrates briefly in liver after absorption; crosses placenta; distributed into breast milk. **Metabolism:** Rapidly in liver. **Elimination:** In urine and bile.

CLINICAL IMPLICATIONS
Assessment & Drug Effects

- Monitor patient constantly. Severe reactions, including fatalities, have occurred during and immediately after IV injection (see ADVERSE EFFECTS).
- Lab tests: Baseline and frequent PT/INR.
- Frequency, dose, and therapy duration are guided by PT/INR clinical response.
- Monitor therapeutic effectiveness which is indicated by shortened PT, INR, bleeding, and clotting times, as well as decreased hemorrhagic tendencies.
- Be aware that patients on large doses may develop temporary resistance to coumarin-type anticoagulants. If oral anticoagulant is reinstituted, larger than former

P

Common adverse effects in *italic*, life-threatening effects <u>underlined</u>; generic names in **bold**; classifications in SMALL CAPS; ✤ Canadian drug name; ❷ Prototype drug

1215

doses may be needed. Some patients may require change to heparin.

Patient & Family Education

▪ Maintain consistency in diet and avoid significant increases in daily intake of vitamin K–rich foods when drug regimen is stabilized. Know sources rich in vitamin K: Asparagus, broccoli, cabbage, lettuce, turnip greens, pork or beef liver, green tea, spinach, watercress, and tomatoes.

PILOCARPINE HYDROCHLORIDE 🅟

PILOCARPINE NITRATE

(pye-loe-kar′peen)

Adsorbocarpine, Isopto Carpine, Minims Pilocarpine ♦, Miocarpine ♦, Ocusert, Pilo, Pilocar, Salagen

Classifications: EYE PREPARATION; MIOTIC (ANTIGLAUCOMA AGENT); DIRECT-ACTING CHOLINERGIC
Therapeutic: ANTIGLAUCOMA
Pregnancy Category: C

AVAILABILITY 0.25%, 0.5%, 1%, 2%, 3%, 4%, 5%, 6%, 8%, 10% ophthalmic solution; 4% ophthalmic gel; 20 mcg/h, 40 mcg/h ocular insert; 5 mg tablets

ACTION & *THERAPEUTIC EFFECT*
In open-angle glaucoma, pilocarpine causes contraction of the ciliary muscle, increasing the outflow of aqueous humor. This reduces intraocular pressure (IOP). In closed-angle glaucoma, it induces miosis by opening the angle of the anterior chamber of the eye, through which aqueous humor exits. *Decrease in IOP results from stimulation of ciliary and papillary sphincter muscles, which pull iris away from filtration angle, thus facilitating outflow of aqueous humor. Pilocarpine also decreases production of aqueous humor.*

USES Open-angle and angle-closure glaucomas; to reduce IOP and to protect the lens during surgery and laser iridotomy; to counteract effects of mydriatics and cycloplegics following surgery or ophthalmoscopic examination; to treat xerostomia.

CONTRAINDICATIONS Secondary glaucoma, acute iritis, acute inflammatory disease of anterior segment of eye; asthma; pregnancy (category C), lactation. **Ocular therapeutic system:** Not used in acute infectious conjunctivitis, keratitis, retinal detachment, or when intense miosis is required, contact lens.

CAUTIOUS USE Bronchial asthma; biliary tract disease; COPD; hypertension.

ROUTE & DOSAGE

Acute Glaucoma

Adult/Child: **Ophthalmic** 1 drop of 1–2% solution in affected eye q5–10min for 3–6 doses, then 1 drop q1–3h until IOP is reduced

Chronic Glaucoma

Adult/Child: **Ophthalmic** 1 drop of 0.5–4% solution in affected eye q4–12h or 1 ocular system (Ocusert) q7d

Miotic

Adult/Child: **Ophthalmic** 1 drop of 1% solution in affected eye

Xerostomia

Adult: **PO** 5 mg t.i.d., may increase up to 10 mg t.i.d.

ADMINISTRATION

Instillation

- Note: During acute phase, physician may prescribe instillation of drug into unaffected eye to prevent bilateral attack of acute glaucoma.
- Apply gentle digital pressure to periphery of nasolacrimal drainage system for 1–2 min immediately after instillation of drops to prevent delivery of drug to nasal mucosa and general circulation.

ADVERSE EFFECTS (≥1%) **CNS:** Oral (asthenia, headaches, dizziness, chills). **Special Senses:** Ciliary spasm with brow ache, twitching of eyelids, eye pain with change in eye focus, miosis, *diminished vision in poorly illuminated areas,* blurred vision, reduced visual acuity, sensitivity, contact allergy, lacrimation, follicular conjunctivitis, conjunctival irritation, cataract, <u>retinal detachment</u>. **GI:** *Nausea,* vomiting, abdominal cramps, diarrhea, epigastric distress, *salivation.* **Respiratory:** Bronchospasm, rhinitis. **CV:** Tachycardia. **Body as a Whole:** Tremors, *increased sweating,* urinary frequency.

INTERACTIONS Drug: The actions of pilocarpine and **carbachol** are additive when used concomitantly. Oral form may cause conduction disturbances with BETA BLOCKERS. Antagonizes the effects of concurrent ANTICHOLINERGIC DRUGS (e.g., **atropine, ipratropium**). **Food:** High-fat meal decreases absorption of pilocarpine.

PHARMACOKINETICS Absorption: Topical penetrates cornea rapidly; readily absorbed from GI tract. **Onset:** Miosis 10–30 min; IOP reduction 60 min; salivary stimulation 20 min. **Peak:** Miosis 30 min; IOP reduction 75 min; salivary stimulation 60 min. **Duration:** Miosis 4–8 h; IOP reduction 4–14 h (7 d with Ocusert); salivary stimulation 3–5 h. **Metabolism:** Inactivated at neuronal synapses and in plasma. **Elimination:** In urine. **Half-Life:** 0.76–1.35 h.

CLINICAL IMPLICATIONS

Assessment & Drug Effects

- Be aware that hourly tonometric tests may be done during early treatment because drug may cause an initial transitory increase in IOP.
- Monitor changes in visual acuity.
- Monitor for adverse effects. Brow pain and myopia tend to be more prominent in younger patients and generally disappear with continued use of drug.

Patient & Family Education

- Understand that therapy for glaucoma is prolonged and that adherence to established regimen is crucial to prevent blindness.
- Do not drive or engage in potentially hazardous activities until vision clears. Drug causes blurred vision and difficulty in focusing.
- Discontinue medication if symptoms of irritation or sensitization persist and report to physician.

Ocular Therapeutic System (Ocusert)

- Review information/directions about inserting the ocular system included in the drug package with health care provider. Demonstrate to establish ability to adjust, insert, and remove the system.
- Unit is placed in the eye cul-de-sac, where it remains for a week. Slow release of drug provides a nonfluctuating concentration of pilocarpine in the ciliary body and iris.

P

- Induced myopia, miosis, and spasm of accommodation are less than that produced by eyedrops. However, since transient blurring and dimness of vision may occur following Ocusert insertion, have patient do so at bedtime; myopia will be at a stable level in the a.m.
- Several hours after Ocusert insertion, induced myopia decreases to a low base level that persists for the life of the therapeutic system.
- Notify physician if following symptoms do not subside: Conjunctival irritation with mild erythema and increase in mucus secretion; generally accompany early use of Ocusert.
- Wash system with cool tap water before replacing it into cul-de-sac if it contacts an unclean surface.
- If retention of the system is a problem, the superior conjunctival cul-de-sac may be a preferred site for insertion. This location is also preferred during sleep.
- To change placement: Ocusert may be transferred from the lower conjunctival sac to the superior sac by closing eyelids, rolling the eye toward the nose and, with gentle digital pressure through the closed eyelid, directly moving the system. Avoid moving it over the colored part of the eye.
- Remove system and replace with a new one if an unexpected increase in drug action occurs (sudden miosis, ciliary spasm, decreased visual acuity).

PIMECROLIMUS

(pim-e-cro-lim′us)
Elidel
Classifications: BIOLOGIC RESPONSE MODIFIER; IMMUNOSUPPRESSANT

Therapeutic: IMMUNOSUPPRESSANT; ANTIINFLAMMATORY
Prototype: Cyclosporine
Pregnancy Category: C

AVAILABILITY 1% cream

ACTION & THERAPEUTIC EFFECT
Pimecrolimus selectively inhibits the inflammatory action of skin cells by blocking T-cell activation and cytokine release. It appears to inhibit the production of IL-2, IL-4, IL-10, and interferon gamma in T-cells. It also prevents release of inflammatory cytokines and mediators from mast cells after activation by antigen and IgE. *Topically applied to the skin, pimecrolimus produces significant antiinflammatory activity without evidence of skin atrophy.*

USES Short-term intermittent treatment of mild to moderate atopic dermatitis.

CONTRAINDICATIONS Hypersensitivity to pimecrolimus or components in the cream; Netherton's syndrome; application to active cutaneous viral infection; occlusive dressing; pregnancy (category C); lactation; children <2 y.
CAUTIOUS USE Infection at topical treatment sites; history of untoward effects with topical cyclosporine or tacrolimus; skin papillomas; immunocompromised patients.

ROUTE & DOSAGE

Atopic Dermatitis
Adult: **Topical** Apply thin layer to affected skin b.i.d.

ADMINISTRATION
Topical
- Do not apply to any skin surface that appears to be infected.

ADVERSE EFFECTS (≥1%) **Body as a Whole:** Flu-like symptoms, infections, fever, increased risk of cancer. **CNS:** Headache. **GI:** Gastroenteritis, abdominal pain, nausea, vomiting, diarrhea, constipation. **Respiratory:** Sore throat, *upper respiratory infection, cough,* nasal congestion, asthma exacerbation, rhinitis, epistaxis. **Skin:** *Burning,* irritation, pruritus, skin infection, impetigo, folliculitis, skin papilloma, Herpes simplex dermatitis, urticaria, acne. **Special Senses:** Ear infection, earache, conjunctivitis.

INTERACTIONS Drug: No clinically significant interactions established.

PHARMACOKINETICS Absorption: Minimal through intact skin. **Metabolism:** No evidence of skin-mediated metabolism, metabolized in liver by CYP3A4. **Elimination:** Primarily in feces.

CLINICAL IMPLICATIONS

Assessment & Drug Effects

- Assess for and report persistent skin irritation that develops following application of the cream and lasts for more than 1 wk.

Patient & Family Education

- Minimize exposure of treated area to natural or artificial sunlight.
- Immediately report a new or changed skin lesion to the physician.
- Stop topical application once signs of dermatitis have disappeared. Resume application at the first sign of recurrence.
- Wash hand thoroughly after application if hands are not the treatment sites.
- Report any significant skin irritation that results from application of the cream.

PIMOZIDE
(pi′moe-zide)
Orap
Classifications: PSYCHOTHERAPEUTIC; ANTIPSYCHOTIC; BUTYROPHENONE
Therapeutic: ANTIPSYCHOTIC
Prototype: Haloperidol
Pregnancy Category: C

AVAILABILITY 2 mg tablet

ACTION & *THERAPEUTIC EFFECT* Potent central dopamine antagonist that alters release and turnover of central dopamine stores; has no effect on turnover of norepinephrine. Blockade of CNS dopaminergic receptors results in suppression of the motor and phonic tics that characterize Tourette's disorder. *Effective in suppressing motor and phonic tics associated with Tourette's disorder.*

USES To suppress severe motor and phonic tics in patient with Tourette's disorder who has failed to respond satisfactorily to standard treatment (e.g., haloperidol).

CONTRAINDICATIONS Treatment of simple tics other than those associated with Tourette's disorder; drug-induced tics; history of cardiac dysrhythmias and conditions marked by prolonged QT syndrome, patient taking drugs that may prolong QT interval (e.g., quinidine); congenital heart defects, cardia arrhythmias; electrolyte imbalance; Parkinson's disease; severe toxic CNS depression; pregnancy (category C), lactation. **CAUTIOUS USE** Kidney and liver dysfunction; patients receiving anticonvulsant therapy; cardiac disease; glaucoma; BPH; urinary retention. Safe use in children <12 y is not known.

P

Common adverse effects in *italic*, life-threatening effects <u>underlined</u>; generic names in **bold**; classifications in SMALL CAPS; ♦ Canadian drug name; ⊙ Prototype drug

1219

ROUTE & DOSAGE

Tourette's Disorder

Adult: **PO** 1–2 mg/d in divided doses, gradually increase dose q.o.d. up to 0.2 mg/kg/d or 7–16 mg/d in divided doses, whichever is less (max: 0.2 mg/kg/d or 10 mg/d)

ADMINISTRATION

Oral

- Increase drug dose gradually, usually over 1–3 wk, until maintenance dose is reached.
- Follow regimen prescribed by physician for withdrawal: Usually slow, gradual changes over a period of days or weeks (drug has a long half-life). Sudden withdrawal may cause reemergence of original symptoms (motor and phonic tics) and of neuromuscular adverse effects of the drug.

ADVERSE EFFECTS (≥1%) Body as a Whole: *Akathisia,* speech disorder, *torticollis, tremor,* handwriting changes, *akinesia,* fainting, hyperpyrexia, tardive dyskinesia, *rigidity, oculogyric crisis,* hyperreflexia; seizures, neuroleptic malignant syndrome; *extrapyramidal dysfunction,* hyperthermia, autonomic dysfunction; diaphoresis, weight changes, asthenia, chest pain, periorbital edema. **CNS:** Headache, *sedation, drowsiness,* insomnia, seizures, stupor. **CV:** Prolongation of QT interval, inverted or flattened T wave, appearance of U wave, labile blood pressure. **Urogenital:** Loss of libido, impotence, nocturia, urinary frequency, amenorrhea, dysmenorrhea, mild galactorrhea, urinary retention, acute renal failure. **Respiratory:** Dyspnea, respiratory failure. **Skin:** Sweating, skin irritation. **Special Senses:** Visual disturbances, photosensitivity, decreased accommodation, blurred vision, cataracts. **GI:** Increased salivation, nausea, vomiting, diarrhea, anorexia, abdominal cramps, constipation.

INTERACTIONS Drug: **Alcohol** and other CNS DEPRESSANTS increase CNS depression; ANTICHOLINERGIC AGENTS (e.g., TRICYCLIC ANTIDEPRESSANTS, **atropine**) increase anticholinergic effects; PHENOTHIAZINES, TRICYCLIC ANTIDEPRESSANTS, ANTIARRHYTHMICS, MACROLIDE ANTIBIOTICS, AZOLE ANTIFUNGALS **(itraconazole, ketoconazole, fluconazole)**, PROTEASE INHIBITORS, **nefazodone, sertraline, zileuton** increase risk of arrhythmias and heart block; pimozide antagonizes effects of ANTICONVULSANTS—there is loss of seizure control. **Food:** Grapefruit juice (>1 qt/day) may increase plasma concentrations and adverse effects.

PHARMACOKINETICS Absorption: Slowly and variably from GI tract (40–50% absorbed). **Peak:** 6–8 h. **Metabolism:** In liver (by CYP3A4). **Elimination:** 80–85% in urine, 15–20% in feces. **Half-Life:** 55 h.

CLINICAL IMPLICATIONS

Note: See haloperidol for additional clinical implications.

Assessment & Drug Effects

- Obtain ECG baseline data at beginning of therapy and check periodically, especially during dosage adjustments.
- Notify physician immediately for widening or prolongation of the QT interval, which suggests developing cardiotoxicity [QT interval (QRS complex and T wave) representing both ventricular depolarization and repolarization].
- Risk of tardive dyskinesia appears to be greatest in women, older adults, and those on high-dose therapy.

- Be aware that extrapyramidal reactions often appear within the first few days of therapy, are dose-related, and usually occur when dose is high.
- Be aware that anticholinergic effects (dry mouth, constipation) may increase as dose is increased.

Patient & Family Education

- Adhere to established drug regimen (i.e., do not change dose or intervals and discontinue only with physician's guidance).
- Use measures to relieve dry mouth (frequent rinsing with water, saliva substitute, increased fluid intake) and constipation (increased dietary fiber, drink 6–8 glasses of water daily).
- Do not drive or engage in potentially hazardous activities because drug-caused hand tremors, drowsiness, and blurred vision may impair alertness and abilities.
- Pseudoparkinsonism symptoms are usually mild and reversible with dose adjustment.
- Be alert to the earliest symptom of tardive dyskinesia ("flycatching"— an involuntary movement of the tongue), and report promptly to the physician.
- Return to physician for periodic assessments of therapy benefit and cardiac status.
- Understand dangers of ingesting alcohol to prevent augmenting CNS depressant effects of pimozide.

PINDOLOL

(pin'doe-lole)
Visken

Classifications: BETA-ADRENERGIC ANTAGONIST; ANTIHYPERTENSIVE
Therapeutic: ANTIHYPERTENSIVE
Prototype: Propranolol
Pregnancy Category: B

AVAILABILITY 5 mg, 10 mg tablets

ACTION & *THERAPEUTIC EFFECT*
Nonselective beta-adrenergic antagonist. Hypotensive mechanism results from its competitively blocking the beta-adrenergic receptors primarily in myocardium, and beta receptors within bronchial and smooth muscle. Lowers blood pressure by also decreasing peripheral vascular resistance. *Exerts vasodilation as well as hypotensive effects.*

USES Management of hypertension concurrently with a thiazide diuretic or as single agent. Used in patient who has failed to respond to diet, exercise, and weight reduction.
UNLABELED USES Stress and exercise-induced chronic stable angina pectoris.

CONTRAINDICATIONS Bronchospastic diseases; severe bradycardia, cardiogenic shock, AV block, sick sinus syndrome; cardiac failure; pulmonary failure; lactation. Safety in children is not established.
CAUTIOUS USE Nonallergic bronchospasm; COPD; CHF; diabetes mellitus; hyperthyroidism; myasthenia gravis; impaired liver and kidney function; pregnancy (category B).

ROUTE & DOSAGE

Hypertension
Adult: **PO** 5 mg b.i.d., may increase by 10 mg/d q2–3wk if needed up (max: 60 mg/d in 2–3 divided doses)
Geriatric: **PO** Start with 5 mg q.d.

Angina Pectoris
Adult: **PO** 15–40 mg/d in 3–4 divided doses

P

ADMINISTRATION

Oral

- Give drug at same time of day each day with respect to time of food intake for most predictable results.
- Withdraw or discontinue treatment gradually over a period of 1–2 wk.

ADVERSE EFFECTS (≥1%) **CNS:** *Fatigue,* dizziness, insomnia, drowsiness, confusion, fainting, decreased libido. **CV:** *Bradycardia,* hypotension, CHF. **GI:** Nausea, *diarrhea, constipation,* flatulence. **Respiratory:** Bronchospasm, pulmonary edema, dyspnea. **Body as a Whole:** Back or joint pain. Sensitivity reactions seen as antinuclear antibodies (ANA) (10–30% of patients). **Hematologic:** Agranulocytosis. **Urogenital:** Impotence. **Metabolic:** Hypoglycemia (may mask symptoms of a hypoglycemic reaction).

INTERACTIONS Drug: DIURETICS and other HYPOTENSIVE AGENTS increase hypotensive effect; effects of **albuterol, metaproterenol, terbutaline, pirbuterol** and pindolol antagonized; NSAIDs blunt hypotensive effect; decreases hypoglycemic effect of **glyburide; amiodarone** increases risk of bradycardia and sinus arrest.

PHARMACOKINETICS Absorption: Rapidly from GI tract; 50–95% reaches systemic circulation (first pass metabolism). **Onset:** 3 h. **Peak:** 1–2 h. **Duration:** 24 h. **Distribution:** Distributed into breast milk. **Metabolism:** 40–60% in liver. **Elimination:** In urine. **Half-Life:** 3–4 h.

CLINICAL IMPLICATIONS

Assessment & Drug Effects

- Monitor HR and BP. Report bradycardia and hypotension. Dosage adjustment may be indicated.

- Note: Hypotensive effect may begin within 7 d but is not at maximum therapeutically until about 2 wk after beginning of treatment.
- Lab test: Periodic CBC with differential, kidney function tests, and blood glucose.

Patient & Family Education

- Pindolol masks the dizziness and sweating symptoms of hypoglycemia. Monitor blood glucose for loss of glycemic control.
- Adhere to the prescribed drug regimen; if a change is desired, consult physician first. Abrupt withdrawal of drug might precipitate a thyroid crisis in a patient with hyperthyroidism, and angina in the patient with ischemic heart disease, leading to an MI.

PIOGLITAZONE HYDROCHLORIDE

(pi-o-glit′a-zone)

Actos

Classifications: THIAZOLIDINEDIONE; ANTIDIABETIC
Therapeutic: ANTIDIABETIC
Prototype: Rosiglitazone maleate
Pregnancy Category: C

AVAILABILITY 15 mg, 30 mg, 45 mg tablets

ACTION & *THERAPEUTIC EFFECT*

Results in insulin sensitivity by affecting insulin receptors. Decreases hepatic glucose output and increases insulin-dependent muscle glucose uptake in skeletal muscle and adipose tissue. Improves glycemic control in noninsulin-dependent diabetic (type 2) patients by enhancing insulin sensitivity of cells without stimulating pancreatic insulin secretion. *Improves glycemic control as indicated by im-*

proved blood glucose levels and decreased HbA$_{1C}$ to 6.5 or lower.

USES Adjunct to diet in the treatment of type 2 diabetes mellitus.

CONTRAINDICATIONS Hypersensitivity to pioglitazone, troglitazone, rosiglitazone, englitazone; type 1 diabetes, or treatment of DKA; active liver disease or ALT levels >2.5 times normal limit; jaundice; pregnancy (category C), lactation.

CAUTIOUS USE Liver dysfunction; cardiovascular disease [New York Heart Association (NYHA)] Class III and Class IV (e.g., CHF); hypertension, edema; renal impairment; older adults. Safety and efficacy in children <18 y are not established.

ROUTE & DOSAGE

Type 2 Diabetes Mellitus
Adult: **PO** 15–30 mg once daily (max: 45 mg q.d.)

ADMINISTRATION

Oral
- Give without regard to food.
- Do not initiate therapy if baseline serum ALT >2.5 times normal.
- Store at 15°–30° C (59°–86° F) in tightly closed container; protect from humidity and moisture.

ADVERSE EFFECTS (≥1%) **Body as a Whole:** Headache, myalgia, edema. **CV:** Edema, fluid retention, exacerbation of heart failure. **GI:** Tooth disorder. **Respiratory:** *Upper respiratory tract infection,* sinusitis, pharyngitis. **Metabolic:** Hypoglycemia, mild anemia.

INTERACTIONS Drug: Pioglitazone may decrease serum levels of ORAL CONTRACEPTIVES; **ketoconazole, gemfibrozil** may increase serum levels of **pioglitazone. Herbal: Garlic,** **ginseng** may potentiate hypoglycemic effects.

PHARMACOKINETICS Absorption: Rapidly absorbed. **Peak:** 2 h; steady state concentrations within 7 d. **Duration:** 24 h. **Distribution:** >99% protein bound. **Metabolism:** In liver to active metabolites. **Elimination:** Primarily in bile and feces. **Half-Life:** 16–24 h.

CLINICAL IMPLICATIONS

Assessment & Drug Effects
- Monitor for S&S hypoglycemia (possible when insulin/sulfonylureas are coadministered).
- Monitor closely for S&S of CHF or exacerbation of symptoms with preexisting CHF.
- Lab tests: Baseline serum ALT, then q2mo for first y, then periodically (more often if elevated); periodic HbA$_{1C}$, Hgb and Hct, and lipid profile.
- Discontinue drug if ALT >3 times ULN or patient has jaundice.
- Monitor weight and notify physician of development of edema.

Patient & Family Education
- Be aware that resumed ovulation is possible in nonovulating premenopausal women.
- Use or add barrier contraceptive if using hormonal contraception.
- Report immediately to physician: Unexplained anorexia, nausea, vomiting, abdominal pain, fatigue, dark urine; or S&S of fluid retention such as weight gain, edema, or activity intolerance.
- Combination therapy: May need adjustment of other antidiabetic drugs to avoid hypoglycemia.
- Learn of and adhere strictly to guideliness for liver function tests. Be sure to have blood tests for liver function every 2 mo for first y; then periodically.

P

Common adverse effects in *italic*, life-threatening effects underlined; generic names in **bold**; classifications in SMALL CAPS; ✦ Canadian drug name; ◑ Prototype drug

1223

PIPERACILLIN SODIUM ℞

(pi-per′a-sill-in)

Classifications: BETA-LACTAM ANTIBIOTIC; ANTIPSEUDOMONAL PENICILLIN
Therapeutic: ANTIBIOTIC, BETA-LACTAM
Pregnancy Category: B

AVAILABILITY 2 g, 3 g, 4 g injection

ACTION & *THERAPEUTIC EFFECT*
Piperacillin is a beta-lactam antibiotic and is mainly bactericidal. It inhibits the final stage of bacterial cell wall synthesis by preferentially binding to specific penicillin-binding proteins (PBPs) located inside the bacterial cell wall. This interferes with bacterial cell wall synthesis promotes loss of membrane integrity and leads to death of the organism. *Extended-spectrum parenteral penicillin with antibiotic activity against most gram-negative and many gram-positive anaerobic and aerobic organisms.*

USES Susceptible organisms that cause gynecologic, skin and skin structure, gonococcal, and streptococcal infections; lower respiratory tract, intraabdominal, and bone and joint infections; septicemia, urinary tract infections. Also used prophylactically prior to and during surgery and as empiric antiinfective therapy in granulocytopenic patients.

CONTRAINDICATIONS Hypersensitivity to penicillins.
CAUTIOUS USE Liver and kidney dysfunction; hypersensitivity to cephalosporins or carbapenem; cystic fibrosis; eczema, asthma; GI disease; pregnancy (category B); children; lactation.

ROUTE & DOSAGE

Uncomplicated Urinary Tract Infection
Adult: **IV/IM** 6–8 g/d divided q6–12h

Complicated UTIs
Adult: **IV** 8–16 g/d divided q6–8h

Mild to Moderate Infections
Child: **IV** 200–300 mg/kg/d divided q4–6h (max: 24 g/d)
Neonate: **IV** 150–200 mg/kg/d divided q6–8h

Moderate to Severe Infections
Adult: **IV/IM** 1–3 g q6–8h

Life-Threatening Infection, *Pseudomonas* Infections
Adult: **IV** 12–18 g/d divided q4–6h)

Uncomplicated Gonococcal Infections
Adult: **IM** 2 g with 1 g oral probenecid given 30 min before

Renal Impairment
Cl_{cr} 20–40 mL/min: use 3–4 g q8h; <20 mL/min: give q12h
Hemodialysis: 20–50% dialyzable

ADMINISTRATION

Note: Patients undergoing hemodialysis usually receive a maximum dosage of 2 g piperacillin q8h and an additional 1 g dose after each dialysis period. Doses and frequency are usually modified if creatinine clearance is <40 mL/min.

Intramuscular
▪Limit IM injections to 2 g/site. Use the gluteal muscle, preferably. Use deltoid muscle only if well developed.

- Diluents for reconstitution include sterile or bacteriostatic water for injection, bacteriostatic NaCl injection, and sterile lidocaine HCl injection 0.5–1.0% without epinephrine for IM. When reconstituted, solution contains 1 g/2.5 mL.

Intravenous
Note: Verify correct IV concentration and rate of infusion for administration to neonates, infants, or children with physician.

PREPARE: **Direct:** (Not preferred): Reconstitute by diluting 1 g with 5 mL sterile water or NS for injection. Shake well until dissolved. **Intermittent:** (Preferred): Further dilute with 50–100 mL NS or D5W.
ADMINISTER: **Direct:** (Not preferred): Give over 3–5 min. Avoid rapid injection. **Intermittent:** (Preferred): Give over 30 min.
INCOMPATIBILITIES **Solution/additive:** AMINOGLYCOSIDES. **Y-site:** AMINOGLYCOSIDES, **amiodarone, amphotericin B cholesteryl complex, cisatracurium, filgrastim, fluconazole, gatifloxacin, gemcitabine, ondansetron, sargramostim, vancomycin, vinorelbine.**

ADVERSE EFFECTS (≥1%) **Body as a Whole:** Coughing, sneezing, feeling of uneasiness; systemic anaphylaxis, fever, widespread increase in capillary permeability and vasodilation with resulting edema (mouth, tongue, pharynx, larynx), laryngospasm, malaise, serum sickness (fever, malaise, pruritus, urticaria, lymphadenopathy, arthralgia, angioedema of face and extremities, neuritis prostration, eosinophilia), SLE-like syndrome, Injection site reactions (pain, inflammation, abscess, phlebitis), superinfections (especially with *Candida* and gram-negative bacteria), neuromuscular irritability (twitching, lethargy, confusion, stupor, hyperreflexia, multifocal myoclonus, localized or generalized seizures, coma). **CV:** Hypotension, circulatory collapse, cardiac arrhythmias, cardiac arrest. **GI:** Vomiting, diarrhea, severe abdominal cramps, nausea, epigastric distress, diarrhea, flatulence, dark discoloration of tongue, sore mouth or tongue. **Urogenital:** Interstitial nephritis, Loeffler's syndrome, vasculitis. **Hematologic:** Hemolytic anemia, thrombocytopenia. **Metabolic:** Hyperkalemia (penicillin G potassium); hypokalemia, alkalosis, hypernatremia, CHF (penicillin G sodium). **Respiratory:** Bronchospasm, asthma. **Skin:** Itchy palms or axilla, pruritus, *urticaria*, flushed skin, *delayed skin rashes* ranging from urticaria to exfoliative dermatitis, Stevens-Johnson syndrome, fixed-drug eruptions, contact dermatitis.

INTERACTIONS Drug: May increase risk of bleeding with ANTICOAGULANTS; **probenecid** decreases elimination of piperacillin.

PHARMACOKINETICS Peak: 45 min IM; 5 min IV. **Distribution:** Widely distributed; highest concentrations in urine and bile; adequate CSF penetration with inflamed meninges; crosses placenta; distributed into breast milk. **Metabolism:** In liver. **Elimination:** Primarily in urine, partly in bile. **Half-Life:** 0.6–1.35 h.

CLINICAL IMPLICATIONS
Assessment & Drug Effects
- Obtain history of hypersensitivity to penicillins, cephalosporins, or other drugs prior to administration.
- Lab tests: C&S prior to first dose of the drug; start drug pending results. Periodic CBC with differential, platelet count, Hgb and Hct, and serum electrolytes.

P

Common adverse effects in *italic*, life-threatening effects underlined; generic names in **bold**; classifications in SMALL CAPS; ✦ Canadian drug name; ⊘ Prototype drug

- Monitor for hypersensitivity response; discontinue drug and notify physician if allergic response noted.
- Lab tests: Periodic CBC with differential, platelet count, Hgb and Hct, and serum electrolytes.
- Monitor for hemorrhagic manifestations because high doses may induce coagulation abnormalities.

Patient & Family Education
- Report significant, unexplained diarrhea.
- Withhold drug and report to physician if signs of an allergic reaction develop (e.g., itching, rash, hives).

PIPERACILLIN/TAZOBACTAM

(pi-per'a-cil-lin/taz-o-bac'tam)
Zosyn
Classifications: BETA-LACTAM ANTIBIOTIC; ANTIPSEUDOMONAL PENICILLIN
Therapeutic: ANTIBIOTIC, BETA-LACTAM
Prototype: Piperacillin sodium
Pregnancy Category: B

AVAILABILITY 2 g, 3 g, 4 g injection

ACTION & *THERAPEUTIC EFFECT*
Antibacterial combination product consisting of the semisynthetic piperacillin and the beta-lactamase inhibitor tazobactam. Tazobactam component does not decrease the activity of the piperacillin component against susceptible organisms. Tazobactam is an inhibitor of a wide variety of bacterial beta-lactamases. It has little antibacterial activity itself; however, in combination with piperacillin, it extends the spectrum of bacteria that are susceptible to piperacillin. *Two-drug combination has antibiotic activity against an extremely broad spectrum of gram-positive, gram-negative, and anaerobic bacteria.*

USES Treatment of moderate to severe appendicitis, uncomplicated and complicated skin and skin structure infections, endometritis, pelvic inflammatory disease, or nosocomial or community-acquired pneumonia caused by beta-lactamase-producing bacteria.

CONTRAINDICATIONS Hypersensitivity to piperacillin, tazobactam, penicillins; coagulopathy.
CAUTIOUS USE Hypersensitivity to cephalosporins, carbapenem or beta-lactamase inhibitors such as clavulanic acid and sulbactam; GI disease, colitis; cystic fibrosis; eczema; kidney failure; complicated urinary tract infections; pregnancy (category B), lactation.

ROUTE & DOSAGE

Moderate to Severe Infections

Adult: **IV** 3.375 g q6h, infused over 30 min, for 7–10 d
Child: **IV** <6 mo, 150–300 mg piperacillin/kg/d divided q6–8h; ≥6 mo, 240 mg piperacillin component/kg/d divided q8h

Nosocomial Pneumonia

Adult: **IV** 4.5 g q6h, infused over 30 min, for 7–10 d

Renal Insufficiency

Cl_{cr} 20–40 mL/min: 2.25 g q6h; <20 mL/min: 2.25 g q8h
Hemodialysis: 2.25 g q12h (for nosocomial pneumonia dose q8h); give additional 0.75 g after dialysis session

ADMINISTRATION

Note: Verify correct IV concentration and rate of infusion for administration to infants or children with physician.

Intravenous

For hemodialysis patients, the maximum dose is 2.25 g q8h; give one extra 0.75-g dose after each dialysis period.

PREPARE: **Intermittent:** Reconstitute powder with 5 mL of diluent (e.g., D5W, NS); shake well until dissolved. Further dilute to at least 50 mL of selected diluent. Use single-dose vials immediately after reconstitution.

ADMINISTER: **Intermittent:** Give over at least 30 min.

INCOMPATIBILITIES **Solution/additive: Aminoglycosides, lactated Ringer's, albumin, blood products, solutions containing sodium bicarbonate.** Y-site: **Acyclovir, aminoglycosides, amiodarone, amphotericin B, amphotericin B cholesteryl complex, azithromycin, chlorpromazine, cisatracurium, cisplatin, dacarbazine, daunorubicin, dobutamine, doxorubicin, doxorubicin liposome, doxycycline, droperidol, famotidine, ganciclovir, gatifloxacin, gemcitabine, haloperidol, hydroxyzine, idarubicin, miconazole, minocycline, mitomycin, mitoxantrone, nalbuphine, prochlorperazine, promethazine, streptozocin, vancomycin.**

ADVERSE EFFECTS (≥1%) **CNS:** Headache, insomnia, fever. **GI:** Diarrhea, constipation, nausea, vomiting, dyspepsia, <u>pseudomembranous colitis</u>. **Skin:** Rash, pruritus, hypersensitivity reactions.

INTERACTIONS Drug: May increase risk of bleeding with ANTICOAGULANTS; **probenecid** decreases elimination of piperacillin.

PHARMACOKINETICS Distribution: Distributes into many tissues, including lung, blister fluid, and bile; crosses placenta; distributed into breast milk. **Metabolism:** In liver. **Elimination:** In urine. **Half-Life:** 0.7–1.2 h.

CLINICAL IMPLICATIONS

Assessment & Drug Effects
- Obtain history of hypersensitivity to penicillins, cephalosporins, or other drugs prior to administration.
- Lab tests: C&S prior to first dose of the drug; start drug pending results. Monitor hematologic status with prolonged therapy (Hct and Hgb, CBC with differential and platelet count).
- Monitor patient carefully during the first 30 min after initiation of the infusion for signs of hypersensitivity (see Appendix F).

Patient & Family Education
- Report rash, itching, or other signs of hypersensitivity immediately.
- Report loose stools or diarrhea as these may indicate pseudomembranous colitis.

P

PIRBUTEROL ACETATE

(pir-bu′ter-ol)
Maxair
Classifications: BETA-ADRENERGIC AGONIST; BRONCHODILATOR
Therapeutic: BRONCHODILATOR
Prototype: Albuterol
Pregnancy Category: C

AVAILABILITY 0.2 mg aerosol

ACTION & *THERAPEUTIC EFFECT*
Exhibits preferential effect on beta$_2$-adrenergic receptors. Stimulation of beta$_2$-adrenoreceptors relaxes bronchospasm and increases ciliary motion. Activates the enzyme that catalyzes the conversion of ATP to cyclic adenosine monophosphate (cAMP).

Common adverse effects in *italic*, life-threatening effects <u>underlined</u>; generic names in **bold**; classifications in SMALL CAPS; ◆ Canadian drug name; ⦿ Prototype drug

1227

Increased cAMP is associated with relaxation of bronchial smooth muscle and inhibition of the release of histamine and other mediators of hypersensitivity from mast cells. *Effective bronchodilator and decreases the release of mediators within the mast cell that cause a hypersensitivity reaction.*

USES Prevention and reversal of bronchospasm associated with asthma.

CONTRAINDICATIONS Hypersensitivity to pirbuterol or any other adrenergic agent such as epinephrine, albuterol, or isoproterenol; pregnancy (category C), lactation, children <12 y.

CAUTIOUS USE Heart disease, irregular heartbeat; QT prolongation, AV block; high blood pressure, history of stroke or seizures; diabetes; Parkinson's disease; thyroid disease; prostate disease; glaucoma.

ROUTE & DOSAGE

Asthma
Adult/Child: **Inhaled** >12 y, 2 inhalations (0.4 mg) q6h (max: 12 inhalations/d)

ADMINISTRATION

Inhalation
- Shake inhaler canister well immediately before using.
- Direct patient to exhale deeply, loosely close lips around mouthpiece, then inhale slowly and deeply through mouthpiece while pressing top of canister.
- Store at 15°–30° C (59°–86° F).

ADVERSE EFFECTS (≥1%) **CNS:** Nervousness, headache, dizziness, tremor. **CV:** Palpitations, tachycardia. **GI:** Dry mouth, nausea, glossitis, abdominal pain, cramps, anorexia, diarrhea, stomatitis. **Other:** Cough, tolerance.

INTERACTIONS Drug: Epinephrine and other SYMPATHOMIMETIC BRONCHODILATORS may have additive effects. BETA BLOCKERS may antagonize the effects.

PHARMACOKINETICS Onset: 5 min. **Peak:** 30 min. **Duration:** 3–4 h. **Metabolism:** In liver. **Elimination:** By kidneys. **Half-Life:** 2–3 h.

CLINICAL IMPLICATIONS

Assessment & Drug Effects
- Monitor arterial blood gases and pulmonary functions periodically.
- Monitor vital signs. Report tachycardia, palpitations, and hypertension or hypotension.

Patient & Family Education
- Learn proper technique for using the inhaler.
- Report palpitations, chest pain, nervousness, tremors, or other bothersome adverse effects promptly to physician.
- Contact physician immediately if symptoms of asthma worsen or you do not respond to the usual dose.
- Adhere rigidly to dosing directions and contact physician if breathing difficulty persists.

PIROXICAM

(peer-ox′i-kam)
Feldene
Classifications: ANALGESIC, NONSTEROIDAL ANTIINFLAMMATORY DRUG (NSAID); ANTIPYRETIC
Therapeutic: NSAID, ANALGESIC; ANTIPYRETIC
Prototype: Ibuprofen
Pregnancy Category: C

AVAILABILITY 10 mg, 20 mg capsules

ACTION & *THERAPEUTIC EFFECT*

Nonsteroidal antiinflammatory agent. Strongly inhibits enzyme cyclooxygenase, both COX1 and COX2, the catalyst of prostaglandin synthesis. Decreased prostaglandin is responsible for its anti-inflammatory properties, analgesic and antipyretic effects. *Drug-induced reduction in prostaglandin levels is associated with decreased inflammatory processes in bone-joint disease, as well as analgesic and antipyretic effects.*

USES Acute and long-term relief of mild to moderate pain and for symptomatic treatment of osteoarthritis and rheumatoid arthritis.

UNLABELED USES Acute and chronic relief of mild to moderate pain.

CONTRAINDICATIONS Hypersensitivity to NSAIDS or salicylates; hemophilia; active peptic ulcer, GI bleeding; CABG perioperative pain; pregnancy (category C). Safety in children is not established.

CAUTIOUS USE History of upper GI disease including ulcerative colitis; SLE; kidney dysfunction; CHF; compromised cardiac function; hypertension or other conditions predisposing to fluid retention; renal disease; coagulation disorders.

ROUTE & DOSAGE

Arthritis, Pain
Adult: **PO** 10–20 mg 1–2 times/d

ADMINISTRATION

Oral

- Give at the same time every day.
- Give capsule with food or fluid to help reduce GI irritation.
- Give older adults (>70 y) $^1/_2$ of the usual adult dose.
- Make dose adjustments on basis of clinical response at intervals of weeks rather than days in order to prevent over dosage.
- Store in tightly closed container at 15°–30° C (59°–86° F) unless otherwise directed.

ADVERSE EFFECTS (≥1%) **CNS:** Somnolence, dizziness, vertigo, depression, insomnia, nervousness. **CV:** Peripheral edema, hypertension, worsening of CHF, exacerbation of angina. **Special Senses:** Tinnitus, hearing loss, blurred vision, reduced visual acuity, changes in color vision, scotomas, corneal deposits, retinal disturbances. **GI:** *Nausea, vomiting, dyspepsia,* GI bleeding, diarrhea, constipation, flatulence, dry mouth, peptic ulceration, anorexia, jaundice, hepatitis. **Hematologic:** Anemia, decreases in Hgb, Hct; leukopenia, eosinophilia, aplastic anemia; thrombocytopenia, *prolonged bleeding time.* **Skin:** Urticaria, erythema multiforme, maculopapular, vesiculobullous rash; photosensitivity, sweating, Stevens-Johnson syndrome, bruising, dermatitis. **Body as a Whole:** Allergic rhinitis, angioedema, fever, palpitations, syncope, muscle cramps, fever, hypersensitivity reactions. **Metabolic:** Hypoglycemia, hyperglycemia, hyperkalemia, weight gain. **Urogenital:** Dysuria, acute kidney failure, papillary necrosis, hematuria, proteinuria, nephrotic syndrome. **Respiratory:** Bronchospasm, dyspnea.

INTERACTIONS Drug: ORAL ANTICOAGULANTS, **heparin** may prolong bleeding time; may increase **lithium** toxicity; **alcohol, aspirin** increase risk of GI hemorrhage. **Herbal: Feverfew, garlic, ginger, ginkgo** may increase bleeding potential.

PHARMACOKINETICS Absorption: Extensively from GI tract. **Onset:** 1 h

P

Common adverse effects in *italic*, life-threatening effects underlined; generic names in **bold**; classifications in SMALL CAPS; ♣ Canadian drug name; ☻ Prototype drug

1229

analgesia; 7 d for rheumatoid arthritis. **Peak:** 3–5 h analgesia; 2–4 wk antirheumatic. **Duration:** 48–72 h analgesia. **Distribution:** Small amount distributed into breast milk. **Metabolism:** Extensively in liver. **Elimination:** Primarily in urine, some in bile (<5%). **Half-Life:** 30–86 h.

CLINICAL IMPLICATIONS

Assessment & Drug Effects

- Wait at least 7 d to evaluate antirheumatic effect.
- Clinical evidence of benefits from drug therapy include pain relief in motion and in rest, reduction in night pain, stiffness, and swelling; increased ROM (range of motion) in all joints.
- Be aware that adverse effects may not appear for 7–10 d after start of therapy (except for an allergic reaction).
- Lab tests: Periodic BUN, ALT, AST, CBC, Hgb and Hct in patient (especially the older adult) receiving drug for an extended period.

Patient & Family Education

- If a dose is missed, take drug when missed dose is discovered if it is 6–8 h before the next scheduled dose. Otherwise, omit dose and reestablish regimen at next scheduled hour.
- Do not self-dose with aspirin or other OTC drug without physician's advice.
- Do not increase dosage beyond prescribed regimen. Understand that long half-life of drug may cause delayed therapeutic effect. Higher than recommended doses are associated with increased incidence of GI irritation and peptic ulcer.
- Incidence of GI bleeding with this drug is relatively high. Report symptoms of GI bleeding (e.g., dark, tarry stools, coffee-colored emesis) or severe gastric pain promptly to physician.
- Be alert to symptoms of drug-induced anemia: Profound fatigue, skin and mucous membrane pallor, lethargy.
- Avoid alcohol since it may increase the risk of GI bleeding.
- Be alert to signs of hypoprothrombinemia including bruises, pinpoint rash, unexplained bleeding, nose bleed, blood in urine, when piroxicam is taken concomitantly with an anticoagulant.
- Do not drive or engage in potentially hazardous activities until response to drug is known.
- Drink at least 6–8 full glasses of water daily and report signs of renal insufficiency (see Appendix F) to physician because most of drug is excreted by kidneys and impaired kidney function increases danger of toxicity.

PLASMA PROTEIN FRACTION

(plas'ma)

Plasmanate, Plasma-Plex, Protenate

Classifications: BLOOD FORMER; PLASMA VOLUME EXPANDER
Therapeutic: PLASMA VOLUME EXPANDER; ALBUMIN
Prototype: Normal serum albumin, human
Pregnancy Category: C

AVAILABILITY 5% injection

ACTION & *THERAPEUTIC EFFECT*
Provides plasma proteins that increase colloidal osmotic pressure within the intravascular compartment equal to human plasma; it shifts water from the extravascular tissues back into the intravascular space, thus expanding plasma volume. It is used to maintain cardiac

output in the treatment of shock due to various causes. No coagulation factors or gamma globulins are provided. *It expands plasma volume in cases of shock, especially when blood is not available. Does not require cross matching.*

USES Emergency treatment of hypovolemic shock due to burns, trauma, surgery, infections; temporary measure in treatment of blood loss when whole blood is not available; to replenish plasma protein in patients with hypoproteinemia (if sodium restriction is not a problem).

CONTRAINDICATIONS Hypersensitivity to albumin; severe anemia; cardiac failure; patients undergoing cardiopulmonary bypass surgery; pregnancy (category C).
CAUTIOUS USE Patients with low cardiac reserve; absence of albumin deficiency; liver or kidney failure.

ROUTE & DOSAGE

Plasma Volume Expansion
Adult: **IV** 250–500 mL at a maximum rate of 10 mL/min
Child: **IV** 6.6–30 mL/kg at a rate of 5–10 mL/min
Hypoproteinemia
Adult: **IV** 1–1.5 L/day infused at a rate not to exceed 5–8 mL/min

ADMINISTRATION

Intravenous
Do not use solutions that show a sediment or appear turbid.

- Do not use solutions that have been frozen.

PREPARE: IV Infusion: Give undiluted. Once container is opened, solution should be used within 4 h because it contains no preservatives. Discard unused portions.

ADMINISTER: IV Infusion: Rate of infusion and volume of total dose will depend on patient's age, diagnosis, degree of venous and pulmonary congestion, Hct, and Hgb determinations. As with any oncotically active solution, infusion rate should be relatively slow. Range may vary from 1–10 mL/min.

INCOMPATIBILITIES Protein hydrolysates or solutions containing alcohol.

ADVERSE EFFECTS (≥1%) **GI:** Nausea, vomiting, hypersalivation, headache. **Body as a Whole:** Tingling, chills, fever, cyanosis, chest tightness, backache, urticaria, erythema, shock (systemic anaphylaxis), circulatory overload, pulmonary edema.

CLINICAL IMPLICATIONS

Assessment & Drug Effects
- Monitor vital signs (BP and pulse). Frequency depends on patient's condition. Flow rate adjustments are made according to clinical response and BP. Slow or stop infusion if patient suddenly becomes hypotensive.
- Report a widening pulse pressure (difference between systolic and diastolic); it correlates with increase in cardiac output.
- Report changes in I&O ratio and pattern.
- Observe patient closely during and after infusion for signs of hypervolemia or circulatory overload (see Appendix F). Report these symptoms immediately to physician.
- Make careful observations of patient who has had either injury or surgery in order to detect bleeding points that failed to bleed at lower BP.

P

PLICAMYCIN

(plik-a-mi'cin)
Mithracin

Classifications: ANTINEOPLASTIC; ANTIBIOTIC
Therapeutic: ANTINEOPLASTIC
Prototype: Doxorubicin
Pregnancy Category: C

AVAILABILITY 2.5 mg injection

ACTION & *THERAPEUTIC EFFECT* Cytotoxic antibiotic produced by *Streptomyces plicatus,* with minimal immunosuppressive activity. Complexes with DNA, thus inhibiting DNA-directed RNA synthesis in cancer cells. May lower serum calcium levels by unclear mechanism. Appears to block hypercalcemic action of vitamin D, and may inhibit parathyroid hormone effect on osteoclasts. Interferes with synthesis of various clotting factors. *Has antineoplastic properties. Also lowers serum calcium levels associated with malignancies.*

USES To treat hospitalized patients with hypercalcemia or hypercalciuria associated with advanced neoplasms and to treat testicular malignancy.

CONTRAINDICATIONS Bleeding and coagulation disorders, myelosuppression; electrolyte imbalance (especially hypocalcemia, hypokalemia, hypophosphatemia); pregnancy (category C), lactation.
CAUTIOUS USE Patients with prior abdominal or mediastinal radiology; liver or renal impairment.

ROUTE & DOSAGE

Neoplasia
Adult: **IV** 25–30 mcg/kg daily for 8–10 d or until toxicity necessitates discontinuing (max: 30 mcg/kg/d for 10 d)

Malignant Hypercalcemia
Adult: **IV** 25 mcg/kg/daily for 3–4 d, may repeat after 1 wk
Obesity
Dose on IBW

ADMINISTRATION

Intravenous
Base drug dose on ideal body weight when edema, ascites, or hydrothorax is present.

***PREPARE:* IV Infusion:** Dilute each 2.5 mg with 4.9 mL of sterile water to yield 500 mcg/mL. Withdraw the calculated dose and further dilute in 1000 mL of D5W or D5/NS.
***ADMINISTER:* IV Infusion:** Give at a rate of 4–6 h per liter. Regulate IV flow rate carefully (established by physician); GI adverse effects increase when rate is too fast. Terminate infusion immediately if extravasation occurs. Apply moderate heat to disperse the drug and to minimize tissue irritation.
***INCOMPATIBILITIES* Y-site: Iron.**

* Discard unused portions of reconstituted solution and prepare new ones daily. *Refrigerate unreconstituted vials at 2°–8° C (36°–46° F).

ADVERSE EFFECTS (≥1%) **CNS:** Drowsiness, irritability, dizziness, weakness, headache, mental depression. **GI:** *Stomatitis, anorexia, nausea, vomiting, diarrhea,* widespread intestinal hemorrhage. **Hematologic:** Thrombocytopenia, <u>bleeding and coagulation disorders</u> (dose related), leukopenia (mild). **Body as a Whole:** Fever, marked facial flushing, hemoptysis, abnormal liver and renal function tests. **Skin:** Nonspecific or acneiform skin rash, phlebitis. **Metabolic:** Hypophosphatemia, hypokalemia, hypocalciuria.

INTERACTIONS Drug: Concomitant administration of **vitamin D** may enhance hypercalcemia.

PHARMACOKINETICS Distribution: Crosses blood–brain barrier; appears to localize in areas of bone active resorption. **Elimination:** In urine.

CLINICAL IMPLICATIONS

Assessment & Drug Effects

- Note: Therapy is usually interrupted if leukocyte count is <4000/mm^3, if platelet count is <150,000/mm^3, or if PT is >4 sec higher than control (normal: 12–14 sec).
- Establish flow chart at beginning of therapy, permitting continuous record of weight and I&O ratio and pattern.
- Lab tests: Perform frequent assessments of liver and hematologic (platelet count, bleeding and prothrombin times) and kidney function throughout therapy and for several days after last dose; periodic serum electrolytes.
- Report marked facial flushing. It is often an early symptom or thrombocytopenia, which frequently is evidenced by a single or persistent episode of epistaxis or hematemesis; may be rapid in onset during or after a course of treatment.
- Inspect skin daily for signs of purpura. Report hemoptysis immediately, which may occur because of bleeding into metastasis.
- Note: Rebound hypercalcemia (normal: 9–10.6 mg/dL) following plicamycin-induced hypocalcemia may persist 2–4 d (see Appendix F).
- Monitor I&O ratio to assure adequate fluid intake; the hypercalcemia patient may be dehydrated.
- Monitor for S&S of adverse effects on the GI mucosal cells (hematemesis, melena) that will necessitate stopping drug use.

- Check patient's bowel function daily to prevent high fecal impaction due to diminished peristalsis.
- Consult physician about dietary calcium intake and coordinate dietary planning with dietitian, patient, and family.

Patient & Family Education

- Use a reliable form of birth control during and for several months following completion of treatment with plicamycin.
- Report easy bruising or bleeding immediately to your physician.

PODOPHYLLUM RESIN (PODOPHYLLIN)

(pode-oh-fill'um)
Podo-ben, Podofin

PODOFILOX

Condylox
Classifications: KERATOLYTIC AGENT
Therapeutic: CYTOTOXIC; KERATO-LYTIC
Pregnancy Category: C

AVAILABILITY Podophyllum 25% liquid; **Podofilox** 0.5% gel, solution

ACTION & *THERAPEUTIC EFFECT*

Potent cytotoxic and keratolytic agent with caustic action, derived from rhizomes and roots of *Podophyllum peltatum* (mandrake, May apple). Directly affects epithelial cell metabolism, causing degeneration and arrest of mitosis. *Slow disruption of cells and tissue erosion as a result of its caustic action. Selectively affects embryonic and tumor cells more than adult cells.*

USES Benign growths including external genital and perianal warts, papillomas, fibroids.

Common adverse effects in *italic*, life-threatening effects underlined; generic names in **bold**; classifications in SMALL CAPS; ♣ Canadian drug name; ❂ Prototype drug

1233

CONTRAINDICATIONS Birthmarks, moles, or warts with hair growth from them; cervical, urethral, oral warts; normal skin and mucous membranes peripheral to treated areas; pregnancy (category C); diabetes mellitus; patient with poor circulation; irritated, friable, or bleeding skin; application of drug over large area.

CAUTIOUS USE Lactation. Safe use in children is not known.

ROUTE & DOSAGE

Condylomata Acuminata

Adult: **Topical** Use 10% solution and repeat 1–2 times/wk for up to 4 applications

Verruca Vulgaris (Common Wart)

Adult: **Topical** Apply 0.5% solution q12h for up to 4 wk

Multiple Superficial Epitheliomatosis, Keratoses

Adult: **Topical** Apply 0.5% solution or gel daily for several days

ADMINISTRATION

Note: Use 10–25% solution for areas <10 cm^2 or 5% solution for areas of 10–20 cm^2, anal, or genital warts; apply drug to dry surface, allowing area to dry between drops, wash off after 1–4 h.

Topical

- Avoid podophyllum resin contact with eyes or similar mucosal surfaces; if it occurs, flush thoroughly with lukewarm water for 15 min and remove film precipitated by the water.
- Avoid application of drug to normal tissue. If it occurs, remove with alcohol. Protect surfaces surrounding area to be treated with a layer of petrolatum or flexible collodion.
- Remove drug thoroughly with soap and water after each treatment of accessible tissue surface.
- Apply a protective coat of talcum powder after treatment and drying of anogenital area.
- Remove drug with alcohol, if application causes extreme pain, pruritus, or swelling.
- Store in a tight, light-resistant container; avoid exposure to excessive heat.

ADVERSE EFFECTS (≥1%) **Body as a Whole:** Severe systemic toxicity (sometimes fatal), sensorimotor neuropathy (reversible), symptomatic orthostatic hypotension, paresthesias and weakness of extremities, stocking-glove sensory loss, absent ankle reflexes, decreased response to painful stimuli. **CNS:** Lethargy, mental confusion, disorientation, delirium, agitation, seizures, progressive stupor, polyneuritis, pyrexia, coma, visual and auditory hallucinations, acute psychotic reaction, ataxia, hypotonia, areflexia, increased CSF protein, paralytic ileus. **CV:** Sinus tachycardia. **Hematologic:** Bone marrow suppression similar to that caused by antineoplastic drug toxicity, leukopenia, thrombocytopenia. **GI:** *Nausea, vomiting, diarrhea, abdominal pain,* hepatotoxicity, increased serum concentrations of LDH, AST, and alkaline phosphatase. **Urogenital:** Renal failure, urinary retention. **Respiratory:** Decreased respirations, apnea, hyperventilation.

CLINICAL IMPLICATIONS

Assessment & Drug Effects

- Warts become blanched, then necrotic within 24–48 h. Sloughing begins after about 72 h with no scarring. Frequently, a mild topi-

Common adverse effects in *italic*, life-threatening effects <u>underlined</u>; generic names in **bold**; classifications in SMALL CAPS; ✦ Canadian drug name; ⊘ Prototype drug

cal antiinfective agent, with or without a dressing, is applied until the healing is complete.

- Monitor neurologic status. Sensorimotor polyneuropathy, if it occurs, appears about 2 wk after application of drug, worsens for 3 mo, and may persist for up to 9 mo. Cerebral effects may persist for 7–10 d; ataxia, hypotonia, and areflexia improve more slowly than effects on sensorium.

Patient & Family Education

- Learn proper technique of treatment if self-administered as treatment of verruca vulgaris (common wart). Also be fully aware of the need to report treatment failure to physician.
- Be aware that as with any STD, the patient's sex partner should be examined.
- Systemic toxicity may be severe and serious and is associated with application of drug to large areas, to tissue that is friable, bleeding, or recently biopsied, or for prolonged time. Toxicity may occur within hours of application. There are significant dangers from overuse or misuse of this drug.
- Learn symptoms of toxicity and report any that appear promptly to physician. (see ADVERSE EFFECTS.)

POLYCARBOPHIL

(pol-i-kar'boe-fil)
Equalactin, FiberNorm
Classifications: BULK LAXATIVE; ANTIDIARRHEAL
Therapeutic: BULK LAXATIVE; ANTIDIARRHEAL
Prototype: Psyllium
Pregnancy Category: C

AVAILABILITY 500 mg, 625 mg tablets; 500 mg, 625 mg chewable tablets

ACTION & *THERAPEUTIC EFFECT*

Hydrophilic agent which absorbs free water in intestinal tract and opposes dehydrating forces of bowel by forming a gelatinous mass. *Restores more normal moisture level and motility in the lower GI tract; produces well-formed stool and reduces diarrhea.*

USES Constipation or diarrhea associated with acute bowel syndrome, diverticulosis, irritable bowel and in patients who should not strain during defecation. Also choleretic diarrhea, diarrhea caused by small-bowel surgery or vagotomy, and disease of terminal ileum.

CONTRAINDICATIONS Partial or complete GI obstruction; fecal impaction; dysphagia; acute abdominal pain; rectal bleeding; undiagnosed abdominal pain, or other symptoms symptomatic of appendicitis; poisonings; before radiologic bowel examination; bowel surgery; pregnancy (category C). Safety in children <3 y is not established.

CAUTIOUS USE Renal failure, renal impairment.

ROUTE & DOSAGE

Constipation or Diarrhea
Adult: **PO** 1 g q.i.d. prn (max: 6 g/d)
Child: **PO** 3–6 y, 500 mg b.i.d. prn (max: 1.5 g/d); 6–12 y, 500 mg t.i.d. prn (max: 3 g/d)

ADMINISTRATION

Oral
- Chewable tablets should be chewed well before swallowing.

Common adverse effects in *italic*, life-threatening effects underlined; generic names in **bold**; classifications in SMALL CAPS; ◆ Canadian drug name; ☉ Prototype drug

1235

- Give each dose with a full glass [240 mL (8 oz)] of water or other liquid.
- Repeat dose every 30 min up to the maximum dose in 24 h with severe diarrhea.
- Store at 15°–30° C (59°–86° F) in tightly closed container unless otherwise directed.

ADVERSE EFFECTS (≥1%) **GI:** Esophageal blockage, intestinal impaction, *abdominal fullness.* **Metabolic:** Low serum potassium, elevated blood glucose levels (with extended use). **Respiratory:** Asthma. **Skin:** Skin rash.

INTERACTIONS Drug: May decrease absorption and clinical effects of ANTIBIOTICS, **warfarin, digoxin, nitrofurantoin,** SALICYLATES.

PHARMACOKINETICS Absorption: Not absorbed from GI tract. **Onset:** 12–24 h. **Peak:** 1–3 d.

CLINICAL IMPLICATIONS

Assessment & Drug Effects
- Determine duration and severity of diarrhea in order to anticipate signs of fluid-electrolyte losses.
- Monitor and record number and consistency of stools per day, presence and location of abdominal discomfort (i.e., tenderness, distension), and bowel sounds.
- Monitor and record I&O ratio and pattern. Dehydration is indicated if output is <30 mL/h.
- Inspect oral cavity for dryness, and be alert to systemic signs of dehydration (e.g., thirst and fever). Dehydration from an episode of diarrhea appears rapidly in young children and older adults.

Patient & Family Education
- Consult physician if sudden changes in bowel habit persist more than 1 wk, action is minimal or ineffective for 1 wk, or if there is no antidiarrheal action within 2 d.
- Be aware that extended use of this drug may cause dependence for normal bowel function.
- Do not discontinue polycarbophil unless physician advises if also taking an oral anticoagulant, digoxin, salicylates, or nitrofurantoin.

POLYMYXIN B SULFATE

(pol-i-mix′in)
Classifications: ANTIBIOTIC
Therapeutic: ANTIBIOTIC
Pregnancy Category: B

AVAILABILITY 500,000 unit injection

ACTION & *THERAPEUTIC EFFECT*
Antibiotic derived from strains of *Bacillus polymyxa.* Binds to lipid phosphates in bacterial membranes and, through cationic detergent action, changes permeability to permit leakage of cytoplasm from the bacterial cell, resulting in cell death. *Bactericidal against susceptible gram-negative but not gram-positive organisms.*

USES Topically and in combination with other anti-infectives or corticosteroids for various superficial infections of eye, ear, mucous membrane, and skin. Concurrent systemic anti-infective therapy may be required for treatment of intraocular infection and severe progressive corneal ulcer. Used parenterally only in hospitalized patients for treatment of severe acute infections of urinary tract, bloodstream, and meninges; and in combination with Neosporin for continuous bladder irrigation to prevent bacteremia associated with use of indwelling catheter.

CONTRAINDICATIONS Hypersensitivity to polymyxin antibiotics; concurrent and sequential use of other nephrotoxic and neurotoxic drugs; concurrent use of skeletal muscle relaxants, ether, or sodium citrate; lactation. Safety in children <2 mo is not established.

CAUTIOUS USE Impaired kidney function, renal failure; myasthenia gravis; pulmonary disease; pregnancy (category B).

ROUTE & DOSAGE

Infections

Adult/Child: IV 15,000–25,000 U/kg/day divided q12h **IM** 25,000–30,000 U/kg/d divided q4–6h **Intrathecal** 50,000 U × 3–4 d then every other day; *child >2 y,* 20,000 U × 3–4 d, then 25,000 U every other day
Infant: **IV/IM** Up to 40,000 U/kg/d

ADMINISTRATION

Intramuscular

- Routine administration by IM routes not recommended because it causes intense discomfort, along the peripheral nerve distribution, 40–60 min after IM injection.
- Make IM injection in adults deep into upper outer quadrant of buttock. Select IM site carefully to avoid injection into nerves or blood vessels. Rotate injection sites. Follow agency policy for IM site used in children.

Intravenous

PREPARE: **Intermittent:** Reconstitute by dissolving 500,000 U in 5 mL sterile water for injection or NS to yield 100,000 U/mL. Withdraw a single dose and then further dilute in 300–500 mL of D5W.

ADMINISTER: **Intermittent:** Infuse over period of 60–90 min. Inspect injection site for signs of phlebitis and irritation.

INCOMPATIBILITIES **Solution/additive: Amphotericin B, cefazolin, cephalothin, cephapirin, chloramphenicol, heparin, nitrofurantoin, prednisolone, tetracycline.**

- Protect unreconstituted product and reconstituted solution from light and freezing. Store in refrigerator at 2°–8° C (36°–46° F). Parenteral solutions are stable for 1 wk when refrigerated. Discard unused portion after 72 h.

ADVERSE EFFECTS (≥1%) **Body as a Whole:** Irritability, facial flushing, ataxia, circumoral, lingual, and peripheral paresthesias (stocking-glove distribution); severe pain (IM site), thrombophlebitis (IV site), superinfections, electrolyte disturbances (prolonged use; also reported in patients with acute leukemia); local irritation and burning (topical use), <u>anaphylactoid reactions</u> (rare). **CNS:** Drowsiness, dizziness, vertigo, convulsions, coma; <u>neuromuscular blockade (generalized muscle weakness, respiratory depression or arrest)</u>; meningeal irritation, increased protein and cell count in cerebrospinal fluid, fever, headache, stiff neck (intrathecal use). **Special Senses:** Blurred vision, nystagmus, slurred speech, dysphagia, ototoxicity (vestibular and auditory) with high doses. **GI:** GI disturbances. **Urogenital:** Albuminuria, cylindruria, azotemia, hematuria.

INTERACTIONS Drug: ANESTHETICS and NEUROMUSCULAR BLOCKING AGENTS may prolong skeletal muscle relax-

Common adverse effects in *italic*, life-threatening effects <u>underlined</u>; generic names in **bold**; classifications in SMALL CAPS; ✚ Canadian drug name; ✪ Prototype drug

1237

ation. AMINOGLYCOSIDES and **amphotericin B** have additive nephrotoxic potential.

PHARMACOKINETICS Peak: 2 h IM. **Distribution:** Widely distributed except to CSF, synovial fluid, and eye; does not cross placenta. **Metabolism:** Unknown. **Elimination:** 60% excreted unchanged in urine. **Half-Life:** 4.3–6 h.

CLINICAL IMPLICATIONS

Assessment & Drug Effects

- Lab tests: Obtain C&S tests prior to first dose and periodically thereafter to determine continuing sensitivity of causative organisms. Perform baseline serum electrolytes and kidney function tests before parenteral therapy. Frequent monitoring of kidney function and serum drug levels is advised during therapy. Monitor electrolytes at regular intervals during prolonged therapy.
- Review electrolyte results. Patients with low serum calcium and low intracellular potassium are particularly prone to develop neuromuscular blockade.
- Inspect tongue every day. Assess for S&S of superinfection (see Appendix F). Polymyxin therapy supports growth of opportunistic organisms. Report symptoms promptly.
- Monitor I&O. Maintain fluid intake sufficient to maintain daily urinary output of at least 1500 mL. Some degree of renal toxicity usually occurs within first 3 or 4 d of therapy even with therapeutic doses. Consult physician.
- Withhold drug and report findings to physician for any of the following: Decreases in urine output (change in I&O ratio), proteinuria, cellular casts, rising BUN, serum creatinine, or serum drug levels

(not associated with dosage increase). All can be interpreted as signs of nephrotoxicity.

- Nephrotoxicity is generally reversible, but it may progress even after drug is discontinued. Therefore, close monitoring of kidney function is essential, even following termination of therapy.
- Be alert for respiratory arrest after the first dose and also as long as 45 d after initiation of therapy. It occurs most commonly in patients with kidney failure and high plasma drug levels and is often preceded by dyspnea and restlessness.

Patient & Family Education

- Report to physician immediately any muscle weakness, shortness of breath, dyspnea, depressed respiration. These symptoms are rapidly reversible if drug is withdrawn.
- Stop drug administration immediately and report to physician if you experience eyelid irritation, itching, and burning with ophthalmic drops.
- Report promptly to physician transient neurologic disturbances (burning or prickling sensations, numbness, dizziness). All occur commonly and usually respond to dosage reduction.
- Report promptly to physician the onset of stiff neck and headache (possible symptoms of neurotoxic reactions, including neuromuscular blockade). This response is usually associated with high serum drug levels or nephrotoxicity.
- Report promptly S&S of superinfection (see Appendix F).

POLYTHIAZIDE

(pol-i-thye'a-zide)
Renese

Classifications: ELECTROLYTIC AND WATER BALANCE AGENT; THIAZIDE DIURETIC
Therapeutic: THIAZIDE DIURETIC; ANTIHYPERTENSIVE
Prototype: Hydrochlorothiazide
Pregnancy Category: D

AVAILABILITY 1 mg, 2 mg, 4 mg

ACTION & *THERAPEUTIC EFFECT*
Thiazide derivative. Diuretic action is associated with drug interference with transport of sodium ions across renal tubular epithelium. Enhances excretion of sodium, chloride, potassium, bicarbonates, and water. *Reduces edema and results in a hypotensive action.*

USES Primary agent in antihypertensive treatment and adjunctively in the management of edema associated with CHF, renal pathology, and hepatic cirrhosis.

CONTRAINDICATIONS Hypersensitivity to other thiazides or sulfonamides; anuria; pregnancy (category D), lactation.
CAUTIOUS USE Kidney and liver dysfunction; SLE; gout; diabetes mellitus.

ROUTE & DOSAGE

Edema
Adult: **PO** 1–4 mg/d or q.o.d.

Hypertension
Adult: **PO** 2–4 mg/d
Child: **PO** 0.02–0.08 mg/kg/d

ADMINISTRATION

Oral
- Give drug early in morning after eating (to reduce gastric irritation) and to prevent interrupted sleep because of diuresis.
- Store drug in tightly closed container.

ADVERSE EFFECTS (≥1%) **Hematologic:** <u>Agranulocytosis</u>, vascular thrombosis. **Metabolic:** *Hyperuricemia, hypokalemia, hyperglycemia.* **Body as a Whole:** Orthostatic hypotension, hepatic encephalopathy, photosensitivity.

INTERACTIONS Drug: Amphotericin B, CORTICOSTEROIDS increase hypokalemic effects; may antagonize hypoglycemic effects of **insulin,** SULFONYLUREAS; **cholestyramine, colestipol** decrease thiazide absorption; intensifies hypoglycemic and hypotensive effects of **diazoxide.** Increased **potassium** and **magnesium** loss may cause **digoxin** toxicity; decreases **lithium** excretion, increasing its toxicity; NSAIDS may attenuate diuresis and increase risk of NSAID-induced kidney failure.

PHARMACOKINETICS Onset: 2 h. **Peak:** 6 h. **Duration:** 24–48 h. **Distribution:** Distributed throughout extracellular tissue; concentrates in kidney; crosses placenta; distributed into breast milk. **Metabolism:** Does not appear to be metabolized. **Elimination:** In urine.

CLINICAL IMPLICATIONS

Assessment & Drug Effects
- Older adult patients may be more sensitive to the average adult therapeutic dose. Excessive diuresis may induce sudden hypotension and serious electrolyte imbalance.
- Be aware that antihypertensive effects may be noted in 3–4 d; maximal effects may require 3–4 wk. Effects persist for at least 1 wk after drug is discontinued.
- Lab tests: Periodic serum electrolytes and blood glucose.
- Monitor for S&S of hypokalemia and hyperglycemia (see Appendix F).

P

Common adverse effects in *italic*, life-threatening effects <u>underlined</u>; generic names in **bold**; classifications in SMALL CAPS; ♣ Canadian drug name; ⊙ Prototype drug

1239

Patient & Family Education

- Change position slowly and in stages, particularly from lying down to upright positions; avoid hot baths or showers, extended exposure to sunlight, and standing still.
- Include specific sources of potassium in daily diet such as a banana (about 370 mg potassium) and at least 180 mL (6 oz) orange juice (about 330 mg potassium).
- Monitor blood glucose for loss of glycemic control of diabetic.
- Be aware of the possibility of photosensitivity reaction and notify physician if it occurs. Thiazide-related photosensitivity is considered a photoallergy and occurs 10–14 d after initial sun exposure. Use sunscreen lotion with a high SPF (12–15).
- Avoid OTC drugs unless approved by the physician. Many preparations contain both potassium and sodium and if misused can induce electrolyte adverse effects.

PORACTANT ALPHA

(por-act'ant)
Curosurf
Classifications: LUNG SURFACTANT
Therapeutic: LUNG SURFACTANT
Prototype: Beractant

AVAILABILITY 120 mg/1.5 mL, 240 mg/3 mL vials

ACTION & *THERAPEUTIC EFFECT*

Lung surfactant obtained from minced porcine lungs. Endogenous pulmonary surfactant lowers the surface tension on alveoli surfaces during respiration, and stabilizes the alveoli against collapse at resting pressures. *Alleviates respiratory distress syndrome (RDS) in premature infants caused by deficiency of surfactant.*

USES Treatment (rescue) of respiratory distress syndrome in premature infants.

CONTRAINDICATIONS Hypersensitivity to porcine products or poractant alpha.

CAUTIOUS USE Infants born >3 wk after ruptured membranes; intraventricular hemorrhage of grade III or IV; major congenital malformations; nosocomial infection; pretreatment of hypothermia or acidosis due to increased risk of intracranial hemorrhage; lactation.

ROUTE & DOSAGE

Respiratory Distress Syndrome
Neonate: **Intratracheal** 2.5 mL/kg birth weight, may repeat with 1.25 mL/kg q12h times 2 more doses if needed (max: 5 mL/kg)

ADMINISTRATION

Note: Correction of acidosis, hypotension, anemia, hypoglycemia, and hypothermia is recommended prior to administration of poractant alfa.

Intratracheal

- Warm vial slowly to room temperature; gently turn upside down to form uniform suspension, but do NOT shake.
- Withdraw slowly the entire contents of a vial (concentration equals 80 mg/mL) into a 3 or 5 mL syringe through a large gauge (>20 gauge) needle.
- Attach a 5 French catheter, precut to 8 cm, to the syringe.
- Fill the catheter with poractant alfa and discard excess through the catheter so that only the total dose to be given remains in the syringe.

- Refer to specific instruction provided by manufacturer for proper dosing technique. Follow instructions carefully regarding installation of drug and ventilation of infant. Note that catheter tip should not extend beyond distal tip of endotracheal tube.
- Store refrigerated at 2°–8° C (36°–46° F) and protect from light. Do not shake vials. Do not warm to room temperature and return to refrigeration more than once.

ADVERSE EFFECTS (≥1%) **CV:** Bradycardia, hypotension. **Respiratory:** Intratracheal tube blockage, oxygen desaturation.

PHARMACOKINETICS Not studied.

CLINICAL IMPLICATIONS
Assessment & Drug Effects
- Stop administration of poractant alfa and take appropriate measures if any of the following occur: Transient episodes of bradycardia, decreased oxygen saturation, reflux of poractant alfa into endotracheal tube, or airway obstruction. Dosing may resume after stabilization.
- Do not suction airway for 1 h after poractant alfa instillation unless there is significant airway obstruction.

POSACONAZOLE

(pos-a-con′a-zole)
Noxafil
Classifications: ANTIBIOTIC; AZOLE ANTIFUNGAL
Therapeutic: ANTIFUNGAL; ANTIBIOTIC
Prototype: Fluconazole
Pregnancy Category: C

AVAILABILITY 200 mg/5 mL oral suspension

ACTION & THERAPEUTIC EFFECT
Azole antifungals inhibit ergosterol synthesis, the principal sterol in the fungal cell membrane, thus interfering with the functions of fungal cell membrane. This results in increased membrane permeability causing leakage of cellular contents. *Azole antifungals have a broad spectrum of antifungal activity against common fungal pathogens, exerting their effect by altering fungal cell membranes.*

USES Prophylactic treatment of invasive *Aspergillus* and *Candida* infections in patients 13 y of age and older who are at high risk due to immunosuppression (e.g., hematopoietic stem cell transplant recipients with graft versus host disease, or patients with hematologic malignancies with prolonged neutropenia from chemotherapy).

UNLABELED USES Treatment of febrile neutropenia or refractory invasive fungal infection; treatment of periorbital cellulitis due to *Rhizopus* sp.; treatment of refractory histoplasmosis; treatment of refractory coccidioidomycosis; treatment of fungal necrotizing fasciitis.

CONTRAINDICATIONS Hypersensitivity to posaconazole; coadministration with ergot alkaloids, or CYP3A4 substrates; history of QT prolongation; abnormal levels of potassium, magnesium, or calcium; pregnancy (category C); lactation; children <13 y.
CAUTIOUS USE Hypersensitivity to other azole antifungal antibiotics; hepatic disease or hepatitis; cardiac arrhythmias; history of proarrhythmic conditions; CHF, myocardial ischemia, atrial fibrillation; AIDS.

ROUTE & DOSAGE

Prophylactic Treatment of Invasive Aspergillus and Candida Infections
Adult: PO 200 mg t.i.d.

ADMINISTRATION

Oral

- Shake well before use. Give with a full meal or liquid nutritional supplement.
- Store at 15°–30° C (59°–86° F).

ADVERSE EFFECTS (≥1%) **Body as a Whole:** Anxiety, *bacteremia, dizziness, edema, fatigue, fever, headache, infection, insomnia, rigors,* weakness. **CNS:** QT/QTc prolongation, tremor. **CV:** *Hypertension, hypotension, tachycardia.* **GI:** *Abdominal pain, anorexia constipation, diarrhea, dyspepsia, mucositis, nausea,* vomiting. **Hematologic:** *Anemia, febrile neutropenia, neutropenia, petechiae, thrombocytopenia.* **Metabolic:** *Bilirubinemia,* creatinine levels increased, elevated liver enzymes, hypocalcemia, *hyperglycemia, hypokalemia, hypomagnesemia.* **Musculoskeletal:** *Arthralgia, back pain, musculoskeletal pain.* **Respiratory:** *Cough, dyspnea, epistaxis, pharyngitis,* upper respiratory tract infection. **Skin:** *Pruritus, rash.* **Special Senses:** Blurred vision, taste disturbances. **Urogenital:** *Vaginal hemorrhage.*

INTERACTIONS Drug: **Rifabutin** and **phenytoin** increase the metabolism of posaconazole resulting in decreased plasma levels. **Cimetidine** decreases the absorption of posaconazole. Posaconazole is known to increase the plasma levels of **cyclosporine, tacrolimus, rifabutin, midazolam,** and **phenytoin.** Coadminstration with other drugs that cause QT prolongation (e.g., **quinidine**) can result in torsades de pointes. Posaconazole may increase the plasma levels of ERGOT ALKALOIDS, VINCA ALKALOIDS, HMG COA REDUCTASE INHIBITORS, and CALCIUM CHANNEL BLOCKERS. **Food:** Administration with food increases absorption of posaconazole.

PHARMACOKINETICS Peak: 3–5 h. **Distribution:** 98% protein bound. **Metabolism:** Conjugated to inactive metabolites. **Elimination:** Primarily fecal elimination (71%) with minor renal elimination. **Half-Life:** 35 h.

CLINICAL IMPLICATIONS

Assessment & Drug Effects

- Monitor for and report S&S of breakthrough fungal infections, especially in those with severe renal impairment, or experiencing vomiting and diarrhea, or who cannot tolerate a full meal or supplement along with posaconazole.
- Monitor and report degree of improvement of oropharyngeal candidiasis.
- Monitor those with proarrhythmic conditions for development of arrhythmias.
- Lab tests: Baseline and periodic LFTs; baseline serum electrolytes.
- Withhold drug and notify physician of abnormal serum potassium, magnesium, or calcium levels.
- Monitor blood levels of phenytoin, cyclosporine, tacrolimus, and sirolimus with concurrent therapy. Monitor for adverse effects of concurrently administered statins or calcium channel blockers.

Patient & Family Education

- Follow directions for taking the drug (see Administration).
- Do not take and prescription or nonprescription drugs without informing your physician.
- Know parameters for withholding drug (i.e., inability to take with a full meal or nutritional supplement).

■ Report immediately any of the following to your health care provider: vomiting, diarrhea, inability to eat, jaundice of skin, yellowing of eyes, itching, or skin rash.

POTASSIUM CHLORIDE

(poe-tass'ee-um)
Apo-K ◆, K-10, Kalium Durules ◆, Kaochlor, Kaochlor-20 Concentrate, Kaon-Cl, KCl 5% and 20%, K-Long ◆, Klor, Klor-10%, Klor-Con, Kloride, Klorvess, Klotrix, K-Dur, K-Lyte/Cl, K-tab, Micro-K Extentabs, SK-Potassium Chloride, Slo-Pot ◆, Slow-K

POTASSIUM GLUCONATE

Kaon, Kaylixir
Classifications: ELECTROLYTIC AND WATER BALANCE AGENT
Therapeutic: ELECTROLYTE REPLACEMENT
Pregnancy Category: C

AVAILABILITY Chloride 6.7 mEq, 8 mEq, 10 mEq, 20 mEq sustained release tablets; 500 mg, 595 mg tablets; 20 mEq, 25 mEq, 50 mEq effervescent tablets; 20 mEq/15 mL, 40 mEq/15 mL, 45 mEq/15 mL liquid; 15 mEq, 20 mEq, 25 mEq powder; 2 mEq/mL injection; 10 mEq, 20 mEq, 30 mEq, 40 mEq, 60 mEq, 90 mEq vials **Gluconate** 20 mEq/ 15 mL liquid

ACTION & *THERAPEUTIC EFFECT*
Principal intracellular cation; essential for maintenance of intracellular isotonicity, transmission of nerve impulses, contraction of cardiac, skeletal, and smooth muscles, maintenance of normal kidney function, and for enzyme activity. Plays a prominent role in both formation and correction of imbalances in acid–base metabolism. *Effective in treatment of hypokalemia. Effectiveness measured by serum potassium concentration greater than 3.5 mEq/ liter.*

USES To prevent and treat potassium deficit secondary to diuretic or corticosteroid therapy. Also indicated when potassium is depleted by severe vomiting, diarrhea; intestinal drainage, fistulas, or malabsorption; prolonged diuresis, diabetic acidosis. Effective in the treatment of hypokalemic alkalosis (chloride, not the gluconate).

CONTRAINDICATIONS Severe renal impairment; severe hemolytic reactions; untreated Addison's disease; crush syndrome; early postoperative oliguria (except during GI drainage); adynamic ileus; acute dehydration; heat cramps, hyperkalemia, patients receiving potassium-sparing diuretics, digitalis intoxication with AV conduction disturbance; pregnancy (category C).
CAUTIOUS USE Cardiac or kidney disease; systemic acidosis; slow-release potassium preparations in presence of delayed GI transit or Meckel's diverticulum; extensive tissue breakdown (such as severe burns); lactation.

ROUTE & DOSAGE

Hypokalemia
Adult: **PO** 10–100 mEq/d in divided doses **IV** 10–60 mEq/h diluted to at least 10–20 mEq/ 100 mL of solution (max: 200– 400 mEq/d, monitor higher doses carefully)
Child: **PO** 1–3 mEq/kg/d in divided doses; sustained release tablets not recommended **IV** Up to 3 mEq/kg/24 h at a rate <0.02 mEq/kg/min

P

Common adverse effects in *italic*, life-threatening effects <u>underlined</u>; generic names in **bold**; classifications in SMALL CAPS; ◆ Canadian drug name; ⊘ Prototype drug

1243

ADMINISTRATION

Oral

- Give while patient is sitting up or standing (never in recumbent position) to prevent drug–induced esophagitis. Some patients find it difficult to swallow the large sized KCl tablet.
- Do not crush or allow to chew any potassium salt tablets. Observe to make sure patient does not suck tablet (oral ulcerations have been reported if tablet is allowed to dissolve in mouth).
- Swallow whole tablet with a large glass of water or fruit juice (if allowed) to wash drug down and to start esophageal peristalsis.
- Follow directions for diluting various liquid forms of KCl exactly. In general, dilute each 20 mEq potassium in at least 90 mL water or juice and allowed to completely before administration.
- Dilute liquid forms as directed before giving it through nasogastric tube.

Intravenous

PREPARE: IV Infusion: Add desired amount to 100–1000 mL IV solution (compatible with all standard solutions). Usual maximum is 80 mEq/1000 mL, however, 40 mEq/L is preferred to lessen irritation to veins. Note: **NEVER** add KCl to an IV bag/bottle which is hanging. After adding KCl invert bag/bottle several times to ensure even distribution.

ADMINISTER: IV Infusion: KCl is **never** given IV push or in concentrated amounts by any route. Infuse at rate not to exceed 10 mEq/h. Adult patients with severe potassium depletion may be able to tolerate 20 mEq/h. Too rapid infusion may cause fatal hyperkalemia.

- Take extreme care to prevent extravasation and infiltration. At first sign, discontinue infusion and select another site.

INCOMPATIBILITIES Solution/additive: Furosemide, pentobarbital, phenobarbital, succinylcholine. Y-site: Amphotericin B cholesteryl complex, azithromycin, chlordiazepoxide, chlorpromazine, diazepam, ergotamine, methylprednisolone, phenytoin.

ADVERSE EFFECTS (≥1%) **GI:** *Nausea, vomiting,* diarrhea, abdominal distention. **Body as a Whole:** Pain, mental confusion, irritability, listlessness, paresthesias of extremities, muscle weakness and heaviness of limbs, difficulty in swallowing, <u>flaccid paralysis</u>. **Urogenital:** Oliguria, anuria. **Hematologic:** Hyperkalemia. **Respiratory:** <u>Respiratory distress</u>. **CV:** Hypotension, bradycardia; <u>cardiac depression, arrhythmias, or arrest</u>; altered sensitivity to digitalis glycosides. *ECG changes in hyperkalemia:* Tenting (peaking) of T wave (especially in right precordial leads), lowering of R with deepening of S waves and depression of RST; prolonged P-R interval, widened QRS complex, decreased amplitude and disappearance of P waves, prolonged Q-T interval, signs of right and left bundle block, <u>deterioration of QRS contour and finally ventricular fibrillation and death</u>.

INTERACTIONS Drug: POTASSIUM-SPARING DIURETICS, ANGIOTENSIN-CONVERTING ENZYME (ACE) INHIBITORS may cause hyperkalemia.

PHARMACOKINETICS Absorption: Readily from upper GI tract. **Elimination:** 90% in urine, 10% in feces.

CLINICAL IMPLICATIONS

Assessment & Drug Effects

- Monitor I&O ratio and pattern in patients receiving the parenteral

Common adverse effects in *italic*, life-threatening effects <u>underlined</u>; generic names in **bold**; classifications in SMALL CAPS; ✦ Canadian drug name; ❍ Prototype drug

drug. If oliguria occurs, stop infusion promptly and notify physician.
- Lab test: Frequent serum electrolytes are warranted.
- Monitor for and report signs of GI ulceration (esophageal or epigastric pain or hematemesis).
- Monitor patients receiving parenteral potassium closely with cardiac monitor. Irregular heartbeat is usually the earliest clinical indication of hyperkalemia.
- Be alert for potassium intoxication (hyperkalemia, see S&S, Appendix F); may result from any therapeutic dosage, and the patient may be asymptomatic.
- The risk of hyperkalemia with potassium supplement increases (1) in older adults because of decremental changes in kidney function associated with aging, (2) when dietary intake of potassium suddenly increases, and (3) when kidney function is significantly compromised.

Patient & Family Education

- Do not be alarmed when the tablet carcass appears in your stool. The sustained release tablet (e.g., Slow-K) utilizes a wax matrix as carrier for KCl crystals that passes through the digestive system.
- Learn about sources of potassium with special reference to foods and OTC drugs.
- Avoid licorice; large amounts can cause both hypokalemia and sodium retention.
- Do not use any salt substitute unless it is specifically ordered by the physician. These contain a substantial amount of potassium and electrolytes other than sodium.
- Do not self-prescribe laxatives. Chronic laxative use has been associated with diarrhea-induced potassium loss.

- Notify physician of persistent vomiting because losses of potassium can occur.
- Report continuing signs of potassium deficit to physician: Weakness, fatigue, polyuria, polydipsia.
- Advise dentist or new physician that a potassium drug has been prescribed as long-term maintenance therapy.
- Do not open foil-wrapped powders and tablets before use.

POTASSIUM IODIDE

(poe-tass'ee-um)
Pima, SSKI, Thyro-Block ♦
Classifications: ANTITHYROID AGENT; EXPECTORANT
Therapeutic: ANTITHYROID; EXPECTORANT
Prototype: Guaifenesin
Pregnancy Category: D

AVAILABILITY 325 mg/5 mL syrup; 1 g/mL solution

ACTION & *THERAPEUTIC EFFECT*

Pharmacologic use primarily related to iodide portion of molecule. Appears to increase secretion of respiratory fluids by direct action on bronchial tissue, thereby decreasing mucus viscosity. If patient is euthyroid, excess iodide ions causes minimal change in thyroid gland mass. Conversely, when the thyroid gland is hyperplastic, excess iodide ions temporarily inhibit secretion of thyroid hormone, foster accumulation in thyroid follicles, and decrease vascularity of gland. *Potassium iodide administration for hyperthyroidism is limited to short-term therapy. As an expectorant, the iodine ion increases mucous secretion formation in the bronchi, and decreases viscosity of the mucus.*

Common adverse effects in *italic*, life-threatening effects <u>underlined</u>; generic names in **bold**; classifications in SMALL CAPS; ♦ Canadian drug name; ❷ Prototype drug

USES To facilitate bronchial drainage and cough in emphysema, asthma, chronic bronchitis, bronchiectasis, and respiratory tract allergies characterized by difficult-to-raise sputum. Also used alone for hyperthyroidism or in conjunction with antithyroid drugs and propranolol in treatment of thyrotoxic crisis; in immediate preoperative period for thyroidectomy to decrease vascularity, fragility, and size of thyroid gland and for treatment of persistent or recurring hyperthyroidism that occurs in Graves' disease patients. Used as a radiation protectant in patients receiving radioactive iodine and to shield the thyroid gland from radiation in the wake of a serious nuclear plant accident. (Use as an expectorant has been largely replaced by other agents.)

CONTRAINDICATIONS Hypersensitivity or idiosyncrasy to iodine; hyperthyroidism; hyperkalemia; acute bronchitis; pregnancy (category D), lactation.
CAUTIOUS USE Renal impairment; cardiac disease; pulmonary tuberculosis; Addison's disease.

ROUTE & DOSAGE

To Reduce Thyroid Vascularity
Adult/Child: **PO** 50–250 mg t.i.d. for 10–14 d before surgery
Expectorant
Adult: **PO** 300–650 mg p.c. b.i.d. or t.i.d.
Child: **PO** 60–250 mg p.c. b.i.d. or t.i.d.
Thyroid Blocking in Radiation Emergency
Adult: **PO** 130 mg/d for 10 d
Child: **PO** <1 y, 65 mg/d for 10 d; >1 y, 130 mg/d for 10 d

ADMINISTRATION
Oral
- Give with meals in a full glass (240 mL) of water or fruit juice and at bedtime with food or juice to disguise salty taste and minimize gastric distress.
- Avoid giving KI with milk; absorption of the drug may be decreased by dairy products.
- Adhere strictly to schedule and accurate dose measurements when iodide is administered to prepare thyroid gland for surgery, particularly at end of treatment period when possibility of "escape" (from iodide) effect on thyroid gland increases.
- Place container in warm water and gently agitating to dissolve if crystals are noted in the solution.
- Discard any solution that has turned a brownish yellow on standing, especially if exposed to light (caused by liberated trace of free iodine).
- Store in airtight, light-resistant container.

ADVERSE EFFECTS (≥1%) **GI:** Diarrhea, nausea, vomiting, stomach pain, nonspecific small bowel lesions (associated with enteric coated tablets). **Body as a Whole:** <u>Angioneurotic edema</u>, cutaneous and mucosal hemorrhage, fever, arthralgias, lymph node enlargement, eosinophilia, paresthesias, periorbital edema, weakness. *Iodine poisoning (iodism):* Metallic taste, stomatitis, salivation, coryza, sneezing; swollen and tender salivary glands (sialadenitis), frontal headache, vomiting (blue vomitus if stomach contained starches, otherwise yellow vomitus); bloody diarrhea. **Metabolic:** Hyperthyroid adenoma, goiter, hypothyroidism, collagen disease–like syndromes. **CV:** Irregular heartbeat. **CNS:** Mental confusion. **Skin:** Acneiform skin lesions (prolonged use), flare-up of adolescent acne. **Respiratory:** Productive cough, pulmonary edema.

DIAGNOSTIC TEST INTERFERENCE
Potassium iodide may alter *thyroid function* test results and may interfere with *urinary 17-OHCS* determinations.

INTERACTIONS Drug: ANTITHYROID DRUGS, **lithium** may potentiate hypothyroid and goitrogenic actions; POTASSIUM-SPARING DIURETICS, POTASSIUM SUPPLEMENTS, ACE INHIBITORS increase risk of hyperkalemia.

PHARMACOKINETICS Absorption: Adequately absorbed from GI tract. **Distribution:** Crosses placenta. **Elimination:** Cleared from plasma by renal excretion or thyroid uptake.

CLINICAL IMPLICATIONS

Assessment & Drug Effects
- Lab tests: Determine serum potassium levels before and periodically during therapy.
- Keep physician informed about characteristics of sputum: quantity, consistency, color.

Patient & Family Education
- Report to physician promptly the occurrence of GI bleeding, abdominal pain, distension, nausea, or vomiting.
- Report clinical S&S of iodism (see ADVERSE EFFECTS). Usually, symptoms will subside with dose reduction and lengthened intervals between doses.
- Avoid foods rich in iodine if iodism develops: Seafood, fish liver oils, and iodized salt.
- Be aware that sudden withdrawal following prolonged use may precipitate thyroid storm.
- Do not use OTC drugs without consulting physician. Many preparations contain iodides and could augment prescribed dose [e.g., cough syrups, gargles, asthma medication, salt substitutes, cod liver oil, multiple vitamins (often suspended in iodide solutions)].
- Be aware that optimum hydration is the best expectorant when taking KI as an expectorant. Increase daily fluid intake.

PRALIDOXIME CHLORIDE

(pra-li-dox′eem)
2-PAM, Protopam Chloride
Classifications: ANTIDOTE
Therapeutic: ANTIDOTE
Pregnancy Category: C

AVAILABILITY 1 g injection

ACTION & *THERAPEUTIC EFFECT*
Reactivates cholinesterase inhibited by phosphate esters by displacing the enzyme from its receptor sites; the free enzyme then can resume its function of degrading accumulated acetylcholine, thereby restoring normal neuromuscular transmission. *More active against effects of anticholinesterases at skeletal neuromuscular junction than at autonomic effector sites or in CNS respiratory center; therefore, atropine must be given concomitantly to block effects of acetylcholine and its accumulation in these sites.*

USES Antidote in treatment of poisoning by organophosphate insecticides and pesticides with anticholinesterase activity (e.g., parathion, TEPP, sarin) and to control overdosage by anticholinesterase drugs used in treatment of myasthenia gravis (cholinergic crisis).
UNLABELED USES To reverse toxicity of echothiophate ophthalmic solution.

P

Common adverse effects in *italic*, life-threatening effects underlined; generic names in **bold**; classifications in SMALL CAPS; ♦ Canadian drug name; ⊘ Prototype drug

1247

CONTRAINDICATIONS Use in poisoning by carbamate; insecticide (Sevin), inorganic phosphates, or organophosphates having no anticholinesterase activity; asthma, peptic ulcer, severe cardiac disease, patients receiving aminophylline, theophylline, morphine, succinylcholine, reserpine, or phenothiazines; pregnancy (category C).

CAUTIOUS USE Myasthenia gravis; renal insufficiency; concomitant use of barbiturates in organophosphorus poisoning; lactation, children.

ROUTE & DOSAGE

Organophosphate Poisoning

Adult: **IV** 1–2 g in 100 mL NS infused over 15–30 min; or 1–2 g as 5% solution in sterile water over not less than 5 min, may repeat after 1 h if muscle weakness not relieved **IM/SC** 1–2 g if IV route is not feasible

Child: **IV** 20–50 mg/kg. May repeat in 1–2 h if needed.

Anticholinesterase Overdose in Myasthenia Gravis

Adult: **IV** 1–2 g in 100 mL NS infused over 15–30 min, followed by increments of 250 mg q5min prn

ADMINISTRATION

Subcutaneous, Intramuscular

- Give only if unable to give IV; NOT preferred routes.
- Reconstitute as for direct IV injection (see below).

Intravenous

PREPARE: Direct: Reconstitute 1-g vial by adding 20 mL NS to yield 50 mg/mL (a 5% solution). If pulmonary edema is present, give without further dilution. **IV Infusion:** Preferred method is to further dilute in 100 mL NS.

ADMINISTER: Direct: In pulmonary edema, 1 g or fraction thereof over 5 min; do not exceed 200 mg/min. **IV Infusion:** Give over 15–30 min (preferred).

- Stop infusion and reduce rate if hypertension occurs.

ADVERSE EFFECTS (≥1%) **CNS:** Dizziness, headache, drowsiness. **GI:** Nausea. **Special Senses:** Blurred vision, diplopia, impaired accommodation. **CV:** Tachycardia, hypertension (dose-related). **Body as a Whole:** Hyperventilation, muscular weakness, laryngospasm, muscle rigidity.

INTERACTIONS Drug: May potentiate the effects of BARBITURATES.

PHARMACOKINETICS Peak: 5–15 min IV; 10–20 min IM. **Distribution:** Distributed throughout extracellular fluids; crosses blood–brain barrier slowly if at all. **Metabolism:** Probably in liver. **Elimination:** Rapidly in urine. **Half-Life:** 0.8–2.7 h.

CLINICAL IMPLICATIONS

Assessment & Drug Effects

- Monitor BP, vital signs, and I&O. Report oliguria or changes in I&O ratio.
- Monitor closely. It is difficult to differentiate toxic effects of organophosphates or atropine from toxic effects of pralidoxime.
- Be alert for and report immediately: Reduction in muscle strength, onset of muscle twitching, changes in respiratory pattern, altered level of consciousness, increases or changes in heart rate and rhythm.
- Observe necessary safety precautions with unconscious patient because excitement and manic behavior reportedly may occur following recovery of consciousness.
- Keep patient under close observation for 48–72 h, particularly when

P

poison was ingested, because of likelihood of continued absorption of organophosphate from lower bowel.

- In patients with myasthenia gravis, overdosage with pralidoxime may convert cholinergic crisis into myasthenic crisis.

PRAMIPEXOLE DIHYDROCHLORIDE

(pra-mi-pex'ole)

Mirapex

Classifications: DOPAMINE AGONIST; ANTIPARKINSON AGENT
Therapeutic: ANTIPARKINSON AGENT
Prototype: Dopamine
Pregnancy Category: C

AVAILABILITY 0.125 mg, 0.25 mg, 1 mg, 1.5 mg tablets

ACTION & *THERAPEUTIC EFFECT*
Nonergot dopamine receptor agonist structurally similar to ropinirole for treatment of Parkinson's disease. Exhibits high affinity for the D_2 subfamily of dopamine receptors in the brain and higher binding affinity to D_3 than to D_2 or D_4 dopamine receptor subtypes. *Effectiveness is indicated by improved control of neuromuscular functioning.*

USES Treatment of idiopathic Parkinson's disease and moderate to severe primary restless legs syndrome (RLS).

CONTRAINDICATIONS Hypersensitivity to pramipexole or ropinirole; lactation; pregnancy (category C).
CAUTIOUS USE Renal and liver function impairment; concomitant use of CNS depressants. Safety and efficacy in children are not established.

ROUTE & DOSAGE

Parkinson's Disease
Adult: **PO** Start with 0.125 mg t.i.d. times 1 wk, then 0.25 mg t.i.d. for 1 wk, continue to increase by 0.25 mg/dose t.i.d. qwk to a target dose of 1.5 mg t.i.d.

Restless Leg Syndrome
Adult: **PO** 0.125 mg taken 2–3 h before bed; dose can be increased every 4–7 d

Renal Impairment
Cl_{cr} 35–60 mL/min: same titration schedule dosed b.i.d. (max: 1.5 mg b.i.d.); 15–35 mL/min: same titration schedule dosed q.d. (max: 1.5 mg q.d.)

ADMINISTRATION

Oral
- Titrate dose increments gradually with at least 4–7 d between increases.
- Reduce doses for creatinine clearance >60 mL/min.
- Give with food if nausea develops.

ADVERSE EFFECTS (≥1%) **Body as a Whole:** *Asthenia,* general edema, malaise, fever, decreased weight. **CNS:** *Dizziness, somnolence, sudden sleep attacks, insomnia, hallucinations, dyskinesia, extrapyramidal syndrome,* headache, confusion, amnesia, hypesthesia, dystonia, akathisia, myoclonus, peripheral edema. **CV:** *Postural hypotension,* chest pain. **GI:** *Nausea, constipation,* anorexia, dysphagia, dry mouth. **Respiratory:** Dyspnea, rhinitis. **Urogenital:** Decreased libido, impotence, urinary frequency or incontinence. **Special Senses:** Vision abnormalities.

INTERACTIONS Drug: Cimetidine decreases clearance; BUTYROPHE-

Common adverse effects in *italic*, life-threatening effects <u>underlined</u>; generic names in **bold**; classifications in SMALL CAPS; ♣ Canadian drug name; ⊘ Prototype drug

1249

NONES, **metoclopramide**, PHENOTHI-AZINES may antagonize effects.

PHARMACOKINETICS Absorption: Rapidly from GI tract, >90% bioavailability. **Peak:** 2 h. **Distribution:** 15% protein bound. **Metabolism:** Minimally in the liver. **Elimination:** Primarily in urine. **Half-Life:** 8–12 h.

CLINICAL IMPLICATIONS

Assessment & Drug Effects

- Monitor for S&S of orthostatic hypotension, especially when the dosage is increased.
- Monitor cardiac status, especially in those with significant orthostatic hypotension.
- Lab tests: Monitor BUN and creatinine periodically; monitor CPK with complaints of muscle pain.
- Monitor for and report signs of tardive dyskinesia (see Appendix F).

Patient & Family Education

- Hallucinations are an adverse effect of this drug and occur more often in older adults.
- Make position changes slowly especially from a lying or sitting to standing.
- Use caution with potentially dangerous activities until response to drug is known; drowsiness is a common adverse effect.
- Avoid alcohol and use extra caution if taking other prescribed CNS depressants; both may exaggerate drowsiness, dizziness, and orthostatic hypotension.
- Do not abruptly stop taking this drug. It should be discontinued over a period of 1 wk.

PRAMLINTIDE

Symlin

Classifications: ANTIDIABETIC AGENT; AMYLIN ANALOG

Therapeutic: ANTIDIABETIC; AMYLIN ANALOG
Pregnancy Category: C

AVAILABILITY 0.6 mg/mL injection.

ACTION & *THERAPEUTIC EFFECT*

Pramlintide is a synthetic analog of human amylin, a hormone secreted by pancreatic beta cells. In type 2 diabetic patients using insulin and in type 1 diabetics, beta cells in the pancreas are either damaged or destroyed, resulting in reduced secretion of both insulin and amylin after meals. Amylin reduces postmeal glucagon levels, thus lowering serum glucose level. *Pramlintide is an antihyperglycemic drug that controls postprandial blood glucose levels.*

USES Adjunct treatment of diabetes mellitus type 1 and type 2 in patients who use mealtime insulin therapy and who have failed to achieve desired glucose control despite optimal insulin therapy.

CONTRAINDICATIONS Hypersensitivity to pramlintide, cresol; noncompliance with insulin regime or medical care; HbA_{1C} >9%; hypoglycemia; gastroparesis; concomitant use of drugs to stimulate GI motility; renal failure or dialysis; pregnancy (category C). Safety and efficacy in children not established.
CAUTIOUS USE Osteoporosis; thyroid disease; lactation, alcohol.

ROUTE & DOSAGE

Type 1 Diabetes Mellitus

Adult: **SC** 15 mcg immediately before each major meal; may increase by 15 mcg increments if no clinically significant nausea for 3–7 d. If nausea or vomiting persists at 45 mcg or 60 mcg, reduce to 30 mcg.

Type 2 Diabetes Mellitus

Adult: **SC** 60 mcg immediately before each major meal; may increase to 120 mcg if no clinically significant nausea for 3–7 d. If nausea or vomiting persists at 120 mcg, reduce to 60 mcg.

ADMINISTRATION

Subcutaneous

- Give SC into the abdomen or thigh (not the arm) immediately before each major meal. Rotate injection sites.
- Never mix pramlintide and insulin in the same syringe. Separate injection sites.
- Use a U100 insulin syringe to administer. One Unit of pramlintide drawn from a 0.6 mg/mL vial contains 6 mcg of medication. Thus, a 30 mcg dose is equal to 5 U in a U100 syringe.
- Do not administer to patients with HbA1C >9% or those taking drugs to stimulate GI motility.
- Note: When initiating pramlintide therapy, insulin dose reduction is required.
- Store at 2°–8° C (36°–46° F), and protect from light. Do not freeze. Discard vials that have been frozen or overheated. Discard open vials after 28 d.

ADVERSE EFFECTS (≥1%) CNS:
Dizziness, fatigue, *headache*. **GI:** Abdominal pain, *anorexia, nausea, vomiting*. **Musculoskeletal:** Arthralgia. **Respiratory:** *Coughing*, pharyngitis. **Body as a Whole:** *Allergic reaction, inflicted injury*.

INTERACTIONS Drugs:
Pramlintide can decrease rate and/or extent of GI absorption of other oral drugs. Significant slowing of gastric motility with ANTIMUSCARINICS.

PHARMACOKINETICS Absorption: 30–40% bioavailability. **Peak:** 20 min. **Distribution:** 40% protein bound. **Metabolism:** Extensive renal metabolism. **Half-Life:** 48 min.

CLINICAL IMPLICATIONS

Assessment & Drug Effects

- Monitor for severe hypoglycemia, which usually occurs within 3 h of injection. Hypoglycemia is worse in type 1 diabetics.
- Monitor diabetics for loss of glycemic control.
- Lab tests: Baseline and periodic HbA1C; frequent pre/post meal plasma glucose levels.
- Withhold drug and notify physician for clinically significant nausea or increased frequency or severity of hypoglycemia.

Patient & Family Education

- Follow directions for taking the drug (see Administration). Use a new needle for each injection.
- Note: Patients should reduce a.c. rapid-acting or short-acting insulin dosages by 50% when pramlintide is initiated. Check with physician.
- Do not drive or engage in potentially hazardous activities until response to drug is known.
- Report any of the following to physician: persistent, significant nausea; episodes of hypoglycemia (e.g., hunger, headache, sweating, tremor, irritability, or difficulty concentrating).

PRAMOXINE HYDROCHLORIDE

(pra-mox'een)

Fleet Relief Anesthetic Hemorrhoidal, Prax, ProctoFoam, Tronolane, Tronothane ◆

Classifications: LOCAL ANESTHETIC (MUCOSAL); ANTIPRURITIC

P

Common adverse effects in *italic*, life-threatening effects <u>underlined</u>; generic names in **bold**; classifications in SMALL CAPS; ◆ Canadian drug name; ☉ Prototype drug

1251

Therapeutic: LOCAL ANESTHETIC; ANTIPRURITIC
Prototype: Procaine
Pregnancy Category: C

AVAILABILITY 1% cream, gel, lotion, spray

ACTION & *THERAPEUTIC EFFECT*
Differs chemically from the amide- or ester-type anesthetics; therefore, it can be used in patients sensitive to these classes of drugs. Produces anesthesia by blocking conduction and propagation of sensory nerve impulses in skin and mucous membranes. Potency matches that of benzocaine as a topical anesthetic. *Provides temporary relief from pain and itching on skin or mucous membrane. Does not abolish gag reflex.*

USES To relieve pain caused by minor burns and wounds; for temporary relief of pruritus secondary to dermatoses, hemorrhoids, and anal fissures; and to facilitate sigmoidoscopic examination.

CONTRAINDICATIONS Application to large areas of skin; prolonged use; preparation for laryngopharyngeal examination, bronchoscopy, or gastroscopy; pregnancy (category C). Safety in children <2 y is not established.
CAUTIOUS USE Extensive skin disorders; lactation.

ROUTE & DOSAGE

Relief of Minor Pain and Itching
Adult/Child: **Topical** >2 y, apply t.i.d. or q.i.d.

ADMINISTRATION
Topical
▪ Clean thoroughly and dry rectal area before use for temporary relief of hemorrhoidal pain and itching.

▪ Administer rectal preparations in the morning and evening and after bowel movement or as directed by physician.
▪ Apply lotion or cream to affected surfaces with a gloved hand. Wash hands thoroughly before and after treatment.
▪ Do not apply to eyes or nasal membranes.

ADVERSE EFFECTS (≥1%) **Skin:** Burning, stinging, sensitization.

INTERACTIONS : No clinically significant interactions established.

PHARMACOKINETICS Onset: 3–5 min. **Duration:** Up to 5 h.

CLINICAL IMPLICATIONS
Patient & Family Education
▪ Drug is usually discontinued if condition being treated does not improve within 2–3 wk or if it worsens, or if rash or condition not present before treatment appears, or if treated area becomes inflamed or infected.
▪ Discontinue and consult physician if rectal bleeding and pain occur during hemorrhoid treatment.

PRAVASTATIN

(pra-vah-stat′in)
Pravachol
Classifications: ANTILIPEMIC; HMG-COA REDUCTASE INHIBITOR (STATIN)
Therapeutic: ANTILIPEMIC; STATIN
Prototype: Lovastatin
Pregnancy Category: X

AVAILABILITY 10 mg, 20 mg, 40 mg, 80 mg tablets

ACTION & *THERAPEUTIC EFFECT*
Competitively inhibits 3-hydroxy-3-methylglutaryl-coenzyme A (HMG-

P

CoA) reductase, the enzyme that catalyzes cholesterol biosynthesis. HMG-CoA reductase inhibitors (statins) increase serum HDL cholesterol, decrease serum LDL cholesterol, VLDL cholesterol, and plasma triglyceride levels. *It is effective in reducing total and LDL cholesterol in various forms of hypercholesterolemia.*

USES Hypercholesterolemia (alone or in combination with bile acid sequestrants) and familial hypercholesterolemia.

CONTRAINDICATIONS Hypersensitivity to pravastatin; active liver disease or unexplained elevated liver function test; hepatic encephalopathy, hepatitis, jaundice, rhabdomyolysis; pregnancy (category X), lactation. Safety and efficacy in children less than 8 y are not established.
CAUTIOUS USE Alcoholics, history of liver disease; renal impairment; renal disease; seizure disorders.

ROUTE & DOSAGE

Hyperlipidemia
Adult: **PO** 10–80 mg q.d.
Child: **PO** 8–13 y, 20 mg q.d.

ADMINISTRATION

Oral
- Give without regard to meals.
- Give in the evening.

ADVERSE EFFECTS (≥1%) **GI:** Nausea, diarrhea, abdominal pain, vomiting, constipation, flatulence, heartburn, transient elevations in serum liver transaminase levels. **Other:** Fatigue, rhinitis, cough, transient elevations in CPK.

INTERACTIONS Drug: May increase PT when administered with **warfarin.**

PHARMACOKINETICS Absorption: Poorly from GI tract; 17% reaches systemic circulation. **Onset:** 2 wk. **Peak:** 4 wk. **Distribution:** 43–55% protein bound; does not cross blood–brain barrier; crosses placenta; distributed into breast milk. **Metabolism:** Extensive first-pass metabolism in liver; has no active metabolites. **Elimination:** 20% of dose excreted in urine, 71% in feces. **Half-Life:** 1.8–2.6 h.

CLINICAL IMPLICATIONS

Assessment & Drug Effects
- Lab tests: Perform liver function tests at start of therapy and then at 12 wk. If normal at 12 wk, may change to semiannual monitoring. Monitor cholesterol levels throughout therapy.
- Monitor coagulation studies with patients receiving concurrent warfarin therapy. PT may be prolonged.
- Monitor CPK levels if patient experiences unexplained muscle pain.

Patient & Family Education
- Report unexplained muscle pain, tenderness, or weakness, especially if accompanied by malaise or fever, to physician promptly.
- Report signs of bleeding to physician promptly when taking concomitant warfarin therapy.

PRAZIQUANTEL

(pray-zi-kwon'tel)
Biltricide
Classifications: ANTHELMINTIC
Therapeutic: ANTHELMINTIC
Prototype: Mebendazole
Pregnancy Category: B

Common adverse effects in *italic*, life-threatening effects underlined; generic names in **bold**; classifications in SMALL CAPS; ♣ Canadian drug name; ⊙ Prototype drug

1253

AVAILABILITY 600 mg tablets

ACTION & *THERAPEUTIC EFFECT*

Synthetic agent with broad-spectrum anthelmintic activity against all developmental stages of schistosomes and other trematodes (flukes) and against cestodes (tapeworm). Increases permeability of parasite cell membrane to calcium. Leads to immobilization of their suckers and dislodgment from their residence in blood vessel walls. *Active against all developmental stages of schistosomes, including cercaria (free-swimming larvae). Activity against other trematodes (flukes) not fully understood; activity against cestodes (tapeworms) not clear but may be similar to that against schistosomes.*

USES All stages of schistosomiasis (bilharziasis) caused by all *Schistosoma* species pathogenic to humans. Other trematode infections caused by Chinese liver fluke.

UNLABELED USES Lung, sheep liver, and intestinal flukes and tapeworm infections.

CONTRAINDICATIONS Hypersensitivity to drug; ocular cysticercosis. Safety in children <4 y is not established; women should not breast feed on day of praziquantel therapy or for 72 h after last dose of drug.

CAUTIOUS USE Hepatic disease; cardiac arrhythmias; pregnancy (category B).

ROUTE & DOSAGE

Schistosomiasis

Adult/Child: **PO** >4 y, 60 mg/kg in 3 equally divided doses at 4–6 h intervals on the same day, may repeat in 2–3 mo after exposure

Other Trematodes

Adult/Child: **PO** >4 y, 75 mg/kg in 3 equally divided doses at 4–6 h intervals on the same day

Cestodiasis (Adult or Intestinal Stage)

Adult: **PO** 10–20 mg/kg as single dose

Cestodiasis (Larval or Tissue Stage)

Adult: **PO** 50 mg/kg in 3 divided doses/d for 14 d

ADMINISTRATION

Oral

- Give dose with food and fluids. Tablets can be broken into quarters but should NOT be chewed.
- Advise patient to take sufficient fluid to wash down the medication. Tablets are soluble in water; gagging or vomiting because of bitter taste may result if tablets are retained in the mouth.
- Treatment for cestodiasis (tapeworm) is followed by gentle purgation 2 h after drug administration to facilitate rapid removal of tapeworms and ova.
- Store tablets in tight containers at <30° C (86° F).

ADVERSE EFFECTS (≥1%) **CNS:** *Dizziness, headache, malaise,* drowsiness, lassitude, <u>CSF reaction syndrome</u> (exacerbation of neurologic signs and symptoms such as seizures, increased CSF protein concentration, increased anticysticercal IgG levels, hyperthermia, intracranial hypertension) in patient treated for cerebral cysticercosis. **GI:** *Abdominal pain or discomfort with or without nausea;* vomiting, anorexia, diarrhea. **Hepatic:** *Increased AST, ALT (slight).* **Skin:** Pruritus, urticaria. **Body as a Whole:** Fever, sweating, symptoms of host-mediated immunologic response to antigen release from worms (fever, eosinophilia).

DIAGNOSTIC TEST INTERFERENCE
Be mindful that selected drugs may interfere with stool studies for ova and parasites: *iron, bismuth, oil* (*mineral* or *castor*), *Metamucil* (if ingested within 1 wk of test), *barium, antibiotics, antiamebic* and *antimalarial drugs,* and *gallbladder dye* (if administered within 3 wk of test).

INTERACTIONS Drug: Phenytoin
can lead to therapeutic failure. **Food:** Grapefruit juice (>1 qt/d) may increase plasma concentrations and adverse effects.

PHARMACOKINETICS Absorption:
Rapidly, 80% reaches systemic circulation. **Peak:** 1–3 h. **Distribution:** Enters cerebrospinal fluid. **Metabolism:** Extensively to inactive metabolites. **Elimination:** Primarily in urine. **Half-Life:** 0.8–1.5 h.

CLINICAL IMPLICATIONS
Assessment & Drug Effects
- Patient is reexamined in 2 or 3 mo to ensure complete eradication of the infections.

Patient & Family Education
- Do not drive or operate other hazardous machinery on day of treatment or the following day because of potential drug-induced dizziness and drowsiness.
- Usually, all schistosomal worms are dead 7 d following treatment.
- Contact physician if you develop a sustained headache or high fever.

PRAZOSIN HYDROCHLORIDE Ⓟⓡ
(pra'zoe-sin)
Minipress

Classifications: ALPHA-ADRENERGIC ANTAGONIST; ANTIHYPERTENSIVE; VASODILATOR
Therapeutic: ANTIHYPERTENSIVE; VASODILATOR
Pregnancy Category: C

AVAILABILITY 1 mg, 2 mg, 5 mg capsules

ACTION & THERAPEUTIC EFFECT
Selective inhibition of alpha$_1$-adrenoceptors; produces vasodilation in both resistance (arterioles) and capacitance (veins) vessels with the result that both peripheral vascular resistance and blood pressure are reduced. *Lowers blood pressure in supine and standing positions with most pronounced effect on diastolic pressure. Infrequently used in monotherapy because of tendency to support sodium and water retention resulting in increased plasma volume.*

USES Treatment of hypertension.
UNLABELED USES Severe refractory congestive heart failure, Raynaud's disease or phenomenon, ergotamine-induced peripheral ischemia, pheochromocytoma, benign prostatic hypertrophy.

CONTRAINDICATIONS Safety during pregnancy (category C) is not established.
CAUTIOUS USE Renal impairment; chronic kidney failure; hypertensive patient with cerebral thrombosis; angina; men with sickle cell trait; lactation.

ROUTE & DOSAGE

Hypertension
Adult: **PO** Start with 1 mg h.s., then 1 mg b.i.d. or t.i.d., may increase to 20 mg/d in divided doses

P

Common adverse effects in *italic*, life-threatening effects underlined; generic names in **bold**; classifications in SMALL CAPS; ✦ Canadian drug name; Ⓟ Prototype drug

1255

Child: **PO** Start with 5 mcg/kg q6h, gradually increase to 25 mcg/kg q6h (max: 15 mg or 0.4 mg/kg/d)

ADMINISTRATION

Oral

- Give initial dose at bedtime to reduce possibility of adverse effects such as postural hypotension and syncope. However, if first dose is taken during the day, advise patient not to drive a car for about 4 h after ingestion of drug.
- Give drug with food to reduce incidence of faintness and dizziness; food may delay absorption but does not affect extent of absorption.
- Store in tightly closed container away from strong light. Do not freeze.

ADVERSE EFFECTS (≥1%) **CNS:** *Dizziness, headache, drowsiness,* nervousness, vertigo, depression, paresthesia, insomnia. **CV:** Edema, dyspnea, syncope *first-dose phenomenon,* postural hypotension, *palpitations,* tachycardia, angina. **Special Senses:** Blurred vision, tinnitus, reddened sclerae. **GI:** Dry mouth, *nausea,* vomiting, diarrhea, constipation, abdominal discomfort, pain. **Urogenital:** Urinary frequency, incontinence, priapism (especially in men with sickle cell anemia), impotence. **Skin:** Rash, pruritus, alopecia, lichen planus. **Body as a Whole:** Diaphoresis, epistaxis, nasal congestion, arthralgia, transient leukopenia, increased serum uric acid, and BUN.

INTERACTIONS Drug: DIURETICS, HYPOTENSIVE AGENTS and alcohol increase hypotensive effects. **Sildenafil, vardenafil,** and **tadalafil** may enhance hypotensive effects.

PHARMACOKINETICS Absorption: Approximately 60% of oral dose reaches the systemic circulation. **Onset:** 2 h. **Peak:** 2–4 h. **Duration:** <24 h. **Distribution:** Widely distributed, including into breast milk. **Metabolism:** Extensively in liver. **Elimination:** 6–10% in urine, rest in bile and feces. **Half-Life:** 2–4 h.

CLINICAL IMPLICATIONS

Assessment & Drug Effects

- Be alert for first-dose phenomenon (rare adverse effect: 0.15% of patients); characterized by a precipitous decline in BP, bradycardia, and consciousness disturbances (syncope) within 90–120 min after the initial dose of prazosin. Recovery is usually within several hours. Preexisting low plasma volume (from diuretic therapy or salt restriction), beta-adrenergic therapy, and recent stroke appear to increase the risk of this phenomenon.
- Monitor blood pressure. If it falls precipitously with first dose, notify physician promptly.
- Full therapeutic effect may not be achieved until 4–6 wk of therapy.

Patient & Family Education

- Avoid situations that would result in injury if you should faint, particularly during early phase of treatment. In most cases, effect does not recur after initial period of therapy; however, it may occur during acute febrile episodes, when drug dose is increased, or when another antihypertensive drug is added to the medication regimen.
- Make position and direction changes slowly and in stages. Dangle legs and move ankles a minute or so before standing when arising in the morning or after a nap.
- Lie down immediately if you experience light-headedness, dizzi-

Common adverse effects in *italic,* life-threatening effects <u>underlined</u>; generic names in **bold**; classifications in SMALL CAPS; ♣ Canadian drug name; ☯ Prototype drug

ness, a sense of impending loss of consciousness, or blurred vision. Attempting to stand or walk may result in a fall.

- Do not drive or engage in other potentially hazardous activities until response to drug is known.
- Take drug at same time(s) each day. Keep a daily record noting BP and time taken, when medication was taken, which arm was used, position (i.e., standing, sitting), and time of day. Take this record to physician for reference at checkup appointment.
- Report priapism or impotence. A change in the drug regimen usually reverses these difficulties. Since acute episodes of priapism followed by impotence spontaneously occur in men with sickle cell anemia, another antihypertensive should be selected. In these patients, drug-induced priapism is frequently irreversible.
- Do not take OTC medications, especially those that may contain an adrenergic agent (e.g., remedies for coughs, colds, allergy), without consulting physician.
- Be aware that adverse effects usually disappear with continuation of therapy, but dosage reduction may be necessary.

PREDNISOLONE

(pred-niss'oh-lone)
Prelone

PREDNISOLONE ACETATE

Pred Forte, Pred Mild

PREDNISOLONE SODIUM PHOSPHATE

AK-Pred, Inflamase Forte, Inflamase Mild

Classifications: ADRENAL CORTICOSTEROID; GLUCOCORTICOID
Therapeutic: CORTICOSTEROID; GLUCOCORTICOID
Prototype: Prednisone
Pregnancy Category: C

AVAILABILITY Prednisolone 1 mg, 2.5 mg, 5 mg tablet; 5 mg/5 mL, 15 mg/5 mL syrup **Acetate** 1% ophthalmic suspension **Sodium Phosphate** 5 mg/5 mL liquid; 0.125%, 1%, 0.9%, 0.11% ophthalmic solution

ACTION & *THERAPEUTIC EFFECT*
Analog of hydrocortisone with 3–5 times greater potency. Mineralocorticoid properties are minimal, and potential for sodium and water retention as well as potassium loss is reduced. *Effective as an antiinflammatory agent.*

USES Principally as an antiinflammatory and immunosuppressant agent.

CONTRAINDICATIONS Fungal infections; GI bleeding; pregnancy (category C).
CAUTIOUS USE Cataracts; coagulopathy; diabetes mellitus; seizure disorders; renal disease; psychosis; emotional instability; GI disorders.

ROUTE & DOSAGE

Antiinflammatory
Adult: **PO** 5–60 mg/d in single or divided doses **Ophthalmic** See Appendix A-1
Child: **PO** 0.1–2 mg/kg/d in divided doses

ADMINISTRATION

Oral
- Give with meals to reduce gastric irritation. If distress continues, consult physician about possible adjunctive antacid therapy.

Common adverse effects in *italic*, life-threatening effects <u>underlined</u>; generic names in **bold**; classifications in SMALL CAPS; ♣ Canadian drug name; ☻ Prototype drug

1257

Alternate-Day Therapy (ADT) for Patient on Long-Term Therapy

- With ADT, the 48-h requirement for steroids is administered as a single dose every other morning.
- Be aware that ADT minimizes adverse effects associated with long-term treatment while maintaining the desired therapeutic effect.
- See **prednisone** for numerous additional clinical implications.

ADVERSE EFFECTS (≥1%) **Endocrine:** Hirsutism (occasional), adverse effects on growth and development of the individual and on sperm. **Special Senses:** Perforation of cornea (with topical drug). **Body as a Whole:** Sensitivity to heat; fat embolism, hypotension and shock-like reactions. **CNS:** Insomnia. **GI:** Gastric irritation or ulceration. **Skin:** Ecchymotic skin lesions; vasomotor symptoms. Also see prednisone.

INTERACTIONS Drug: BARBITURATES, **phenytoin, rifampin** increase steroid metabolism, therefore may need increased doses of prednisolone; **amphotericin B,** DIURETICS add to **potassium** loss; **ambenonium, neostigmine, pyridostigmine** may cause severe muscle weakness in patients with myasthenia gravis; VACCINES, TOXOIDS may inhibit antibody response. **Food:** Licorice may elevate plasma levels and adverse effects.

PHARMACOKINETICS Absorption: Readily from GI tract. **Peak:** 1–2 h. **Duration:** 1–1.5 d. **Distribution:** Crosses placenta; distributed into breast milk. **Metabolism:** In liver. **Elimination:** HPA suppression: 24–36 h; in urine. **Half-Life:** 3.5 h.

CLINICAL IMPLICATIONS

Assessment & Drug Effects

- Be alert to subclinical signs of lack of improvement such as continued drainage, low-grade fever, and interrupted healing. In diseases caused by microorganisms, infection may be masked, activated, or enhanced by corticosteroids. Observe and report exacerbation of symptoms after short period of therapeutic response.
- Be aware that temporary local discomfort may follow injection of prednisolone into bursa or joint.

Patient & Family Education

- Adhere to established dosage regimen (i.e., do not increase, decrease, or omit doses or change dose intervals).
- Report gastric distress or any sign of peptic ulcer.

PREDNISONE 🅟

(pred′ni-sone)

Apo-Prednisone ◆, Deltasone, Meticorten, Orasone, Panasol, Prednicen-M, Sterapred, Winpred ◆

Classifications: ADRENAL CORTICOSTEROID; GLUCOCORTICOID
Therapeutic: CORTICOSTEROID; GLUCOCORTICOID
Pregnancy Category: C

AVAILABILITY 1 mg, 2.5 mg, 5 mg, 10 mg, 20 mg, 50 mg tablets; 5 mg/5 mL, 5 mg/mL solution

ACTION & *THERAPEUTIC EFFECT*
Immediate-acting synthetic analog of hydrocortisone. Effect depends on biotransformation to prednisolone, a conversion that may be impaired in patient with liver dysfunction. Less mineralocorticoid activity than hydrocortisone, but sodium retention and potassium depletion can occur. *Has antiinflammatory properties.*

USES May be used as a single agent or conjunctively with antineoplas-

P

tics in cancer therapy; also used in treatment of myasthenia gravis and inflammatory conditions and as an immunosuppressant.

CONTRAINDICATIONS Systemic fungal infections and known hypersensitivity; cataracts; pregnancy (category C).

CAUTIOUS USE Patients with infections; nonspecific ulcerative colitis; diverticulitis; active or latent peptic ulcer; renal insufficiency; coagulopathy; psychosis; seizure disorders; thromboembolic disease; hypertension; osteoporosis; myasthenia gravis.

ROUTE & DOSAGE

Antiinflammatory
Adult: PO 5–60 mg/d in single or divided doses
Child: PO 0.1–0.15 mg/kg/d in single or divided doses

Acute Asthma
Child: PO <1 y, 1–2 mg/kg/d times 3–5 d or 10 mg q12h; 1–4 y, 20 mg q12h; 5–13 y, 30 mg q12h; >13 y, 40 mg q12h times 3–5 d

ADMINISTRATION

Oral
- Crush tablet and give with fluid of patient's choice if unable to swallow whole.
- Give at mealtimes or with a snack to reduce gastric irritation.
- Dose adjustment may be required if patient is subjected to severe stress (serious infection, surgery, or injury) or if a remission or disease exacerbation occurs.
- Do not abruptly stop drug. Reduce dose gradually by scheduled decrements (various regimens) to prevent withdrawal symptoms and permit adrenals to recover from drug-induced partial atrophy.

Alternate-Day Therapy (ADT) for Patient on Long-Term Therapy
- With ADT, the 48-h requirement for steroids is administered as a single dose every other morning.
- Be aware that ADT minimizes adverse effects associated with long-term treatment while maintaining the desired therapeutic effect.
- See **prednisone** for numerous additional clinical implications.

ADVERSE EFFECTS (≥1%) **CNS:** Euphoria, headache, insomnia, confusion, psychosis. **CV:** CHF, edema. **GI:** Nausea, vomiting, peptic ulcer. **Musculoskeletal:** Muscle weakness, delayed wound healing, muscle wasting, osteoporosis, aseptic necrosis of bone, spontaneous fractures. **Endocrine:** Cushingoid features, growth suppression in children, carbohydrate intolerance, hyperglycemia. **Special Senses:** Cataracts. **Hematologic:** Leukocytosis. **Metabolic:** Hypokalemia.

INTERACTIONS Drug: BARBITURATES, **phenytoin, rifampin** increase steroid metabolism—increased doses of prednisone may be needed; **amphotericin B,** DIURETICS increase **potassium** loss; **ambenonium, neostigmine, pyridostigmine** may cause severe muscle weakness in patients with myasthenia gravis; may inhibit antibody response to VACCINES, TOXOIDS.

PHARMACOKINETICS Absorption: Readily from GI tract. **Peak:** 1–2 h. **Duration:** 1–1.5 d. **Distribution:** Crosses placenta; distributed into breast milk. **Metabolism:** In liver. **Elimination:** Hypothalamus-pituitary axis suppression: 24–36 h; in urine. **Half-Life:** 3.5 h.

P

Common adverse effects in *italic*, life-threatening effects <u>underlined</u>; generic names in **bold**; classifications in SMALL CAPS; ♣ Canadian drug name; ⊘ Prototype drug

1259

CLINICAL IMPLICATIONS

Assessment & Drug Effects

- Establish baseline and continuing data regarding BP, I&O ratio and pattern, weight, fasting blood glucose level, and sleep pattern. Start flow chart as reference for planning individualized pharmacotherapeutic patient care.
- Check and record BP during dose stabilization period at least 2 times daily. Report an ascending pattern.
- Monitor patient for evidence of HPA axis suppression during long-term therapy by determining plasma cortisol levels at weekly intervals.
- Lab tests: Obtain fasting blood glucose, serum electrolytes, and routine laboratory studies at regular intervals during long-term steroid therapy.
- Be aware that older adult patients and patients with low serum albumin are especially susceptible to adverse effects because of excess circulating free glucocorticoids.
- Be alert to signs of hypocalcemia (see Appendix F). Patients with hypocalcemia have increased requirements for pyridoxine (vitamin B₆), vitamins C and D, and folates.
- Be alert to possibility of masked infection and delayed healing (antiinflammatory and immunosuppressive actions). Prednisone suppresses early classic signs of inflammation. When patient is on an extended therapy regimen, incidence of oral *Candida* infection is high. Inspect mouth daily for symptoms: white patches, black furry tongue, painful membranes and tongue.
- Monitor bone density. Compression and spontaneous fractures of long bones and vertebrae present hazards, particularly in long-term corticosteroid treatment of rheumatoid arthritis or diabetes, in immobilized patients, and older adults.
- Be aware of previous history of psychotic tendencies. Watch for changes in mood and behavior, emotional stability, sleep pattern, or psychomotor activity, especially with long-term therapy, that may signal onset of recurrence. Report symptoms to physician.
- If a patient is receiving aspirin concomitantly with a corticosteroid, salicylism may be induced when the corticosteroid dosage is decreased or discontinued.
- Be aware that long-term corticosteroid therapy is ordinarily not interrupted when patient undergoes major surgery, but dosage may be increased.
- Monitor for withdrawal syndrome (e.g., myalgia, fever, arthralgia, malaise) and hypocorticism (e.g., anorexia, vomiting, nausea, fatigue, dizziness, hypotension, hypoglycemia, myalgia, arthralgia) with abrupt discontinuation of corticosteroids after long-term therapy.

Patient & Family Education

- Take drug as prescribed and do not alter dosing regimen or stop medication without consulting physician.
- Be aware that a slight weight gain with improved appetite is expected, but after dosage is stabilized, a sudden slow but steady weight increase [2 kg (5 lb) per wk] should be reported to physician.
- Avoid or minimize alcohol and caffeine may contribute to steroid-ulcer development in long-term therapy.
- Report symptoms of GI distress to physician and do not self-medicate to find relief.

- Do not use aspirin or other OTC drugs unless they are prescribed specifically by the physician.
- Report slow healing, any vague feeling of being sick, or return of pretreatment symptoms.
- Be fastidious about personal hygiene; give special attention to foot care, and be particularly cautious about bruising or abrading the skin.
- Report persistent backache or chest pain (possible symptoms of vertebral or rib fracture) that may occur with long-term therapy.
- Tell dentist or new physician about prednisone therapy.
- Carry medical information at all times. It needs to indicate medical diagnosis, medication(s), physician's name(s), address(es), and telephone number(s).

PREGABALIN

Lyrica

Classifications: ANALGESIC; ANTICONVULSANT; ANXIOLYTIC; GABA-ANALOG
Therapeutic: ANTICONVULSANT; ANTIANXIETY; ANALGESIC
Prototype: Gabapentin
Pregnancy Category: C
Controlled Substance: Schedule V

AVAILABILITY 25 mg, 50 mg, 75 mg, 100 mg, 150 mg, 200 mg, 225 mg, 300 mg capsules

ACTION & *THERAPEUTIC EFFECT*
Pregabalin is an analog of gamma-aminobutyric acid (GABA). It is structurally related to gabapentin, but shows greater potency in pain and seizure disorders (3–10 times greater). The exact mechanism of action of pregabalin as an antiseizure agent is unknown. It increases neuronal GABA levels and reduces calcium currents in the calcium channels of neurons; this may account for its control of pain and anxiety. *Has analgesic, anti-anxiety, and anticonvulsant properties.*

USES Management of neuropathic pain associated with diabetic peripheral neuropathy, adjunctive therapy for adult patients with partial-onset seizures, management of postherpetic neuralgia.
UNLABELED USES Treatment of generalized anxiety disorders, treatment of social anxiety disorder, treatment of moderate pain.

CONTRAINDICATIONS Hypersensitivity to pregabalin or gabapentin; alcohol; pregnancy (category C); lactation. Safety and efficacy in children <12 y have not been established.
CAUTIOUS USE Renal impairment or failure, hemodialysis; elderly; congestive heart failure, NYHA (Class III or IV) cardiac status.

ROUTE & DOSAGE

Neuropathic Pain (Diabetic Peripheral Neuropathy)
Adult: **PO** 50–100 mg t.i.d.

Partial-Onset Seizures
Adult: **PO** Initial dose ≤ 75 mg b.i.d or 50 mg t.i.d.; may increase to 300 mg b.i.d. or 200 mg t.i.d.

Postherpetic Neuralgia
Adult: **PO** Initial dose 75 mg b.i.d. or 50 mg t.i.d; may increase to 150–300 mg b.i.d. or 100–200 mg t.i.d.

Renal Impairment
Cl_{cr} 30–60 mL/min: 75–300 mg/d given in 2 or 3 divided doses. Cl_{cr} 15–30 mL/min: 25–150 mg/d given in 1 or 2 divided doses. Cl_{cr} < 15 mL/min: 25–75 mg once daily.

P

Common adverse effects in *italic*, life-threatening effects underlined; generic names in **bold**; classifications in SMALL CAPS; ♦ Canadian drug name; ⊘ Prototype drug

1261

ADMINISTRATION

Oral

- Dosage reduction is required with renal dysfunction.
- Drug should not be abruptly stopped; discontinue by tapering over a minimum of 1 wk.
- Give a supplemental dose immediately following dialysis.
- Store at 15°–30° C (59°– 86° F).

ADVERSE EFFECTS (≥1%) **Body as a Whole:** *Accidental injury,* flu syndrome, pain. **CNS:** Abnormal gait, amnesia, *ataxia,* confusion, *dizziness,* euphoria, headache, incoordination, myoclonus, nervousness, neuropathy, *somnolence,* speech disorder, abnormal thinking, tremor, twitching, vertigo. **CV:** Chest pain. **GI:** Constipation, dry mouth, flatulence, increased appetite, vomiting. **GU:** Urinary incontinence. **Metabolic/Nutritional:** Edema, facial edema, hypoglycemia, *peripheral edema, weight gain.* **Musculoskeletal:** Back pain, myasthenia. **Respiratory:** Bronchitis, dyspnea. **Special Senses:** Abnormal vision, *blurry vision, diplopia.*

INTERACTIONS Drug: Concomitant use with THIAZOLIDINEDIONES may exacerbate weight gain and fluid retention.

PHARMACOKINETICS Absorption: 90% bioavailability. **Peak:** 1.5 h. **Metabolism:** Negligible. **Elimination:** Primarily in the urine. **Half-Life:** 6 h.

CLINICAL IMPLICATIONS

Assessment & Drug Effects

- Monitor for weight gain, peripheral edema, and S&S of heart failure, especially with concurrent thiazolidinedione (e.g., rosiglitazone) therapy.
- Lab tests: Baseline and periodic kidney function tests; periodic platelet counts; CPK if rhabdomyolysis is suspected.
- Monitor diabetics for increased incidences of hypoglycemia.
- Withhold drug and notify physician if rhabdomyolysis is suspected.
- Supervise ambulation especially when other CNS drugs are used concurrently.

Patient & Family Education

- Do not drive or engage in potentially hazardous activities until response to drug is known.
- Report any of the following to a health care provider: changes in vision (i.e., blurred vision); dizziness and incoordination; unexplained muscle pain, weakness, or tenderness; weight gain and swelling of the extremities.
- Avoid alcohol consumption while taking this drug.
- Inform your physician if you plan to become pregnant or father a child.

PRIMAQUINE PHOSPHATE

(prim'a-kween)
Primaquine
Classifications: ANTIMALARIAL
Therapeutic: ANTIMALARIAL
Prototype: Chloroquine
Pregnancy Category: C

AVAILABILITY 26.3 mg tablets; 5 g, 25 g, 100 g, 500 g powder

ACTION & *THERAPEUTIC EFFECT*

Acts on primary exoerythrocytic forms of *Plasmodium vivax* and *Plasmodium falciparum* by an incompletely known mechanism. Destroys late tissue forms of *P. vivax* and thus effects radical cure (prevents relapse). *Gametocidal activity against all species of* Plasmodia *that infect man; interrupts transmission of malaria.*

USES To prevent relapse ("radical" or "clinical" cure) of *P. vivax* and *P. ovale* malarias and to prevent attacks after departure from areas where *P. vivax* and *P. ovale* malarias are endemic. With clindamycin for the treatment of *Pneumocystis carinii* pneumonia (PCP) in AIDS.

CONTRAINDICATIONS Hypersensitivity to primaquine or iodoquinol; rheumatoid arthritis; lupus erythematosus (SLE); hemolytic drugs, concomitant or recent use of agents capable of bone marrow depression (e.g., quinacrine; patients with G6PD deficiency); pregnancy (category C), lactation.

CAUTIOUS USE Bone marrow depression; hematologic disease; methemoglobin reductase deficiency.

ROUTE & DOSAGE

Malaria Treatment
Adult: **PO** 30 mg daily for 14 d concomitantly or consecutively with chloroquine or hydroxychloroquine on first 3 d of acute attack
Child: **PO** 0.5 mg/kg daily for 14 d concomitantly or consecutively with chloroquine or hydroxychloroquine on first 3 d of acute attack

Malaria Prophylaxis
Adult: **PO** 15 mg daily for 14 d beginning immediately after leaving malarious area
Child: **PO** 0.3 mg/kg daily for 14 d beginning immediately after leaving malarious area

ADMINISTRATION
Oral
- Give drug at mealtime or with an antacid (prescribed); may prevent or relieve gastric irritation. Notify physician if GI symptoms persist.
- Store in tight, light-resistant containers.

ADVERSE EFFECTS (≥1%) **Hematologic:** Hematologic reactions including granulocytopenia and acute hemolytic anemia in patients with G6PD deficiency, moderate leukocytosis or leukopenia, anemia, granulocytopenia, agranulocytosis. **GI:** Nausea, vomiting, epigastric distress, abdominal cramps. **Skin:** Pruritus. **Metabolic:** Methemoglobinemia (cyanosis). **Body as a Whole:** Headache, confusion, mental depression. **Special Senses:** Disturbances of visual accommodation. **CV:** Hypertension, arrhythmias (rare).

INTERACTIONS Drug: Toxicity of both **quinacrine** and primaquine increased.

PHARMACOKINETICS Absorption: Readily from GI tract. **Peak:** 6 h. **Metabolism:** Rapidly in liver to active metabolites. **Elimination:** In urine. **Half-Life:** 3.7–9.6 h.

CLINICAL IMPLICATIONS
Assessment & Drug Effects
- Be aware drug may precipitate acute hemolytic anemia in patients with G6PD deficiency, an inherited error of metabolism carried on the X chromosome, present in about 10% of American black males and certain white ethnic groups: Sardinians, Sephardic Jews, Greeks, and Iranians. Whites manifest more intense expression of hemolytic reaction than do blacks. Screen for prior to initiation of therapy.

Common adverse effects in *italic*, life-threatening effects <u>underlined</u>; generic names in **bold**; classifications in SMALL CAPS; ✚ Canadian drug name; ⊘ Prototype drug

1263

- Lab tests: Perform repeated hematologic studies (particularly blood cell counts and Hgb) and urinalyses during therapy.

Patient & Family Education

- Examine urine after each voiding and to report to physician darkening of urine, red-tinged urine, and decrease in urine volume. Also report chills, fever, precordial pain, cyanosis (all suggest a hemolytic reaction). Sudden reductions in hemoglobin or erythrocyte count suggest an impending hemolytic reaction.

PRIMIDONE

(pri'mi-done)
Apo-Primidone ✦, Mysoline
Classifications: BARBITURATE;
ANTICONVULSANT
Therapeutic: ANTICONVULSANT
Prototype: Phenobarbital
Pregnancy Category: D

AVAILABILITY 50 mg, 250 mg tablets; 250 mg/5 mL suspension

ACTION & *THERAPEUTIC EFFECT* Converted in body to phenobarbital. Impairs vitamin D, calcium, folic acid, and vitamin B_{12} metabolism and utilization. *Antiepileptic properties result from raising the seizure threshold and changing seizure patterns.*

USES Alone or concomitantly with other anticonvulsant agents in the prophylactic management of complex partial (psychomotor) and generalized tonic-clonic (grand mal) seizures.
UNLABELED USES Essential tremor.

CONTRAINDICATIONS Hypersensitivity to barbiturates, porphyria; ethanol intoxication, hepatic encepha-

lopathy, pregnancy (category D), lactation.
CAUTIOUS USE Chronic lung disease, sleep apnea; liver or kidney disease, dialysis; hyperactive children; mental status changes, major depression, suicidal ideation.

ROUTE & DOSAGE

Seizures
Adult/Child: **PO** ≥8 y, 250 mg/ d, increased by 250 mg/wk (max: 2 g in 2–4 divided doses)
Child: **PO** <8 y, 125 mg/d, increased by 125 mg/wk (max: 2 g/d in 2–4 divided doses)

ADMINISTRATION

Oral

- Give whole or crush with fluid of patient's choice.
- Give with food if drug causes GI distress.
- Note: Transition from another anticonvulsant to primidone normally requires at least 21 wk.

ADVERSE EFFECTS (≥1%) **CNS:** *Drowsiness, sedation, vertigo, ataxia, headache,* excitement (children), confusion, unusual fatigue, hyperirritability, emotional disturbances, acute psychoses (usually patients with psychomotor epilepsy). **Special Senses:** Diplopia, nystagmus, swelling of eyelids. **GI:** *Nausea, vomiting, anorexia.* **Hematologic:** Leukopenia, thrombocytopenia, eosinophilia, decreased serum folate levels, megaloblastic anemia (rare). **Skin:** Alopecia, maculopapular or morbilliform rash, edema, lupus erythematosus-like syndrome. **Urogenital:** Impotence. **Body as a Whole:** Lymphadenopathy, osteomalacia.

INTERACTIONS Drug: Alcohol, CNS DEPRESSANTS compound CNS depression; **phenobarbital** may decrease absorption and increase metabolism of ORAL ANTICOAGULANTS; increases metabolism of CORTICOSTEROIDS, ORAL CONTRACEPTIVES, ANTICONVULSANTS, **digitoxin**, possibly decreasing their effects; ANTIDEPRESSANTS potentiate adverse effects of primidone; **griseofulvin** decreases absorption of primidone. **Herbal: Kava-kava, valerian** may potentiate sedation.

PHARMACOKINETICS Absorption: Approximately 60–80% from GI tract. **Peak:** 4 h. **Distribution:** Distributed into breast milk. **Metabolism:** In liver to phenobarbital and PEMA. **Elimination:** In urine. **Half-Life:** Primidone 3–24 h, PEMA 24–48 h; phenobarbital 72–144 h.

CLINICAL IMPLICATIONS

Assessment & Drug Effects
- Lab tests: Perform baseline and periodic CBC, complete blood chemistry (q6mo), and primidone blood levels. (Therapeutic blood level for primidone: 5–10 mcg/mL.)
- Monitor primidone plasma levels (concentrations of primidone >10 mcg/mL are usually associated with significant ataxia and lethargy).
- Therapeutic response may not be evident for several weeks.
- Observe for S&S of folic acid deficiency: Mental dysfunction, psychiatric disorders, neuropathy, megaloblastic anemia. Determine serum folate levels if indicated.
- Be aware that presence of unusual drowsiness in breast fed newborns of primidone-treated mothers is an indication to discontinue breast feeding.

Patient & Family Education
- Avoid driving and other potentially hazardous activities during beginning of treatment because drowsiness, dizziness, and ataxia may be severe. Symptoms tend to disappear with continued therapy; if they persist, dosage reduction or drug withdrawal may be necessary.
- Avoid alcohol and other CNS depressants unless otherwise directed by physician.
- Do not take OTC medications unless approved by physician.
- Pregnant women should receive prophylactic vitamin K therapy for 1 mo prior to and during delivery to prevent neonatal hemorrhage.
- Withdraw primidone gradually to avoid precipitating status epilepticus.
- Carry medical information at all times. It needs to indicate medical diagnosis, medication(s), physician's name(s), address(es), and telephone number(s).

PROBENECID ⓟ

(proe-ben'e-sid)
Benemid, Benuryl ✦, Probalan, SK-Probenecid
Classifications: ANTIGOUT AGENT; SULFONAMIDE; URICOSURIC AGENT
Therapeutic: ANTIGOUT; URICOSURIC AGENT
Pregnancy Category: B

AVAILABILITY 0.5 g tablet

ACTION & _THERAPEUTIC EFFECT_
Sulfonamide-derivative renal tubular blocking agent. In sufficiently high doses, competitively inhibits renal tubular reabsorption of uric acid, thereby promoting its excretion and reducing serum urate levels. _Prevents formation of new tophaceous deposits and causes gradual shrinking of old tophi by preventing uric acid build-up in the serum and tissues. As an additive to_

P

penicillin, it increases the serum concentration of the antibiotic, and also prolongs the serum concentration of the penicillins.

USES Hyperuricemia in chronic gouty arthritis and tophaceous gout. **UNLABELED USES** Adjuvant to therapy with penicillin G and penicillin analogs to elevate and prolong plasma concentrations of these antibiotics; to promote uric acid excretion in hyperuricemia secondary to administration of thiazides and related diuretics, furosemide, ethacrynic acid, pyrazinamide.

CONTRAINDICATIONS Blood dyscrasias; uric acid kidney stones; during or within 2–3 wk of acute gouty attack; overexcretion of uric acid (>1000 mg/d); patients with creatinine clearance <50 mg/min; use with penicillin in presence of known renal impairment; use for hyperuricemia secondary to cancer chemotherapy. Safe use in children <2 y is not established.
CAUTIOUS USE History of peptic ulcer; pregnancy (category B), lactation.

ROUTE & DOSAGE

Gout
Adult: **PO** 250 mg b.i.d. for 1 wk, then 500 mg b.i.d. (max: 3 g/d)

Adjunct for Penicillin or Cephalosporin Therapy
Adult: **PO** 500 mg q.i.d. or 1 g with single dose therapy (e.g., gonorrhea)
Child: **PO** 2–14 y or <50 kg, 25–40 mg/kg/d in 4 divided doses

ADMINISTRATION
Oral
- Therapy is usually not initiated during an acute gouty attack. Consult physician.

- Minimize GI adverse effects by giving after meals, with food, milk, or antacid (prescribed). If symptoms persist, dosage reduction may be required.
- Give with a full glass of water if not contraindicated.
- Be aware that physician may prescribe concurrent prophylactic doses of colchicine for first 3–6 mo of therapy because frequency of acute gouty attacks may increase during first 6–12 mo of therapy.

ADVERSE EFFECTS (≥1%) **Body as a Whole:** Flushing, dizziness, fever, anaphylaxis. **CNS:** *Headache.* **GI:** *Nausea, vomiting, anorexia,* sore gums, hepatic necrosis (rare). **Urogenital:** Urinary frequency. **Hematologic:** Anemia, hemolytic anemia (possibly related to G6PD deficiency), aplastic anemia (rare). **Musculoskeletal:** Exacerbations of gout, uric acid kidney stones. **Skin:** Dermatitis, pruritus. **Respiratory:** Respiratory depression.

DIAGNOSTIC TEST INTERFERENCE False-positive **urine glucose** tests are possible with **Benedict's solution** or **Clinitest** (*glucose oxidase methods* not affected, e.g., **Clinistix, TesTape**).

INTERACTIONS Drug: SALICYLATES may decrease uricosuric activity; may decrease **methotrexate** elimination, causing increased toxicity; decreases **nitrofurantoin** efficacy and increases its toxicity. Decreases clearance of penicillins, cephalosporins, and NSAIDs.

PHARMACOKINETICS Absorption: Readily from GI tract. **Onset:** 30 min. **Peak:** 2–4 h. **Duration:** 8 h. **Distribution:** Crosses placenta. **Metabolism:** In liver. **Elimination:** In urine. **Half-Life:** 4–17 h.

CLINICAL IMPLICATIONS

Assessment & Drug Effects

- Decrease daily dosage with caution by 0.5 g q6mo to lowest effective dosage that maintains stable serum urate levels when gouty attacks have been absent for 6 mo or more and serum urate levels are controlled.
- Lab tests: Periodic serum urate levels, Hct and Hgb, and urinalysis. Determine acid–base balance periodically when urinary alkalinizers are used. Some physicians prescribe acetazolamide at bedtime to keep urine alkaline and dilute throughout night.
- Patients taking sulfonylureas may require dosage adjustment. Probenecid enhances hypoglycemic actions of these drugs (see DIAGNOSTIC TEST INTERFERENCES).
- Expect urate tophaceous deposits to decrease in size. Classic locations are in cartilage of ear pinna and big toe, but they can occur in bursae, tendons, skin, kidneys, and other tissues.

Patient & Family Education

- Drink fluid liberally (approximately 3000 mL/d) to maintain daily urinary output of at least 2000 mL or more. This is important because increased uric acid excretion promoted by drug predisposes to renal calculi.
- Physician may advise restriction of high-purine foods during early therapy until uric acid level stabilizes. Foods high in purine include organ meats (sweetbreads, liver, kidney), meat extracts, meat soups, gravy, anchovies, and sardines. Moderate amounts are present in other meats, fish, seafood, asparagus, spinach, peas, dried legumes, wild game.
- Avoid alcohol because it may increase serum urate levels.

- Do not stop taking drug without consulting physician. Irregular dosage schedule may sharply elevate serum urate level and precipitate acute gout.
- Be aware that lifelong therapy is usually required in patients with symptomatic hyperuricemia. Keep scheduled appointments with physician and for kidney function and hematology lab work.
- Report symptoms of hypersensitivity to physician. Discontinuation of drug is indicated.
- Do not take aspirin or other OTC medications without consulting physician. If a mild analgesic is required, acetaminophen is usually allowed.

PROCAINAMIDE HYDROCHLORIDE ⊕

(proe-kane-a′mide)

Procanbid, Pronestyl, Pronestyl SR

Classifications: ANTIARRHYTHMIC, CLASS IA

Therapeutic: ANTIARRHYTHMIC, CLASS IA

Pregnancy Category: C

AVAILABILITY 250 mg, 375 mg, 500 mg tablets, capsules; 250 mg, 500 mg, 750 mg, 1000 mg sustained release tablets; 100 mg/mL, 500 mg/mL injection

ACTION & *THERAPEUTIC EFFECT*
Class IA antiarrhythmic agent. Depresses excitability of myocardium to electrical stimulation, reduces conduction velocity in atria, ventricles, and His-Purkinje system. Increases duration of refractory period, especially in the atria. *Effectively used for atrial arrhythmias;*

Common adverse effects in *italic*, life-threatening effects <u>underlined</u>; generic names in **bold**; classifications in SMALL CAPS; ♣ Canadian drug name; ⊕ Prototype drug

1267

produces slight change in contractility of cardiac muscle and cardiac output; suppresses automaticity of His-Purkinje ventricular muscle. Produces peripheral vasodilation and hypotension, especially with IV use.

USES Prophylactically to maintain normal sinus rhythm following conversion of atrial flutter or fibrillation by other methods; to prevent recurrence of paroxysmal atrial fibrillation and tachycardia, paroxysmal AV junctional rhythm, ventricular tachycardia, ventricular and atrial premature contractions. Also cardiac arrhythmias associated with surgery and anesthesia.
UNLABELED USES Malignant hyperthermia.

CONTRAINDICATIONS Myasthenia gravis; hypersensitivity to procainamide or procaine; blood dyscrasias; bundle branch block; complete AV block, second and third degree AV block unassisted by pacemaker; QT prolongation; pregnancy (category C).
CAUTIOUS USE Patient who has undergone electrical conversion to sinus rhythm; bone marrow suppression; hypotension, cardiac enlargement, CHF, MI, coronary occlusion, ventricular dysrhythmia from digitalis intoxication; hepatic or renal insufficiency; electrolyte imbalance; bronchial asthma; history of SLE.

ROUTE & DOSAGE

Arrhythmias

Adult: **PO** 50 mg/kg/d in divided doses (b.i.d. for Procanbid); max: 5 g/d **IM** 0.5–1 g q4–8h until able to take PO **IV** 100 mg q5min at a rate of 25–50 mg/min until arrhythmia is controlled or 1 g given, then 2–6 mg/min

Child: **PO** 15–50 mg/kg/d divided q3–6h **IM** 50 mg/kg/d divided q3–6 until PO tolerated **IV** 3–6 mg/kg q 10–30 min (max: 100 mg/dose), then 20–80 mcg/kg/min

Renal Impairment

Oral doses Cl_{cr} 10–50 mL/min: give q6–12h; <10 mL/min: give q8–24h. **IV doses** reduce loading dose to 12 mg/kg, then maintenance by $1/3$ to $2/3$.
Hemodialysis: Give 200 mg supplemental dose post dialysis.

ADMINISTRATION

Oral

- Give first PO dose at least 4 h after last IV dose
- Give oral preparation on empty stomach, 1 h before or 2 h after meals, with a full glass of water to enhance absorption. If drug causes gastric distress, give with food.
- Crush immediate release (but NOT sustained release) tablet if patient is unable to swallow it whole.
- Swallow sustained release tablet whole. It has a wax matrix that is not absorbed but appears in the stool.

Intramuscular

- Assess procainamide blood levels if more than three IM injections are required.

Intravenous

Use IV route for emergency situations.

PREPARE: Direct: When given direct IV, dilute each 100 mg with 5–10 mL of D5W or sterile water for injection. **IV Infusion:** When given by IV infusion, add 1 g of procainamide to 250–500 mL of D5W solution to yield 4 mg/mL in 250 mL or 2 mg/mL in 500 mL.

ADMINISTER: Direct: Usual rate 20 mg/min. Faster rates (up to 50 mg/min) should be used with caution. **IV Infusion:** 2–6 mg/min. **INCOMPATIBILITIES Solution/additive: Bretylium, esmolol, ethacrynate, milrinone, phenytoin. Y-site: Inamrinone (amrinone), milrinone.**

- Control IV administration over several hours by assessment of procainamide plasma levels.
- Use an infusion pump with constant monitoring. Keep patient in supine position. Be alert to signs of too rapid administration of drug (speed shock: irregular pulse, tight feeling in chest, flushed face, headache, loss of consciousness, shock, cardiac arrest).

- Store solution for up to 24 h at room temperature and for 7 d under refrigeration at 2°–8° C (36°–46° F). Slight yellowing does not alter drug potency, but discard solution if it is markedly discolored or precipitated.

ADVERSE EFFECTS (≥1%) CNS: Dizziness, psychosis. **CV:** Severe hypotension, pericarditis, ventricular fibrillation, AV block, tachycardia, flushing. **GI:** Bitter taste, nausea, vomiting, diarrhea, anorexia, (all mostly PO). **Hematologic:** Agranulocytosis with repeated use; thrombocytopenia. **Body as a Whole:** Fever, muscle and joint pain, angioneurotic edema, myalgia, *SLE-like syndrome (50% of patients on large doses for 1 y):* Polyarthralgias, pleuritic pain, pleural effusion. **Skin:** Maculopapular rash, pruritus. erythema, skin rash.

DIAGNOSTIC TEST INTERFERENCE
Procainamide increases the plasma levels of **alkaline phosphatase, bilirubin, lactic dehydrogenase** and **AST.** It may also alter results of the **edrophonium test.**

INTERACTIONS Drug: Other ANTIARRHYTHMICS add to therapeutic and toxic effects; ANTICHOLINERGIC AGENTS compound anticholinergic effects; ANTIHYPERTENSIVES add to hypotensive effects; **cimetidine** may increase levels with increase in toxicity.

PHARMACOKINETICS Absorption: 75–95% from GI tract. **Peak:** 15–60 min IM; 30–60 min PO. **Duration:** 3 h; 8 h with sustained release. **Distribution:** Distributed to CSF, liver, spleen, kidney, brain, and heart; crosses placenta; distributed into breast milk. **Metabolism:** In liver to *N*-acetylprocainamide (NAPA), an active metabolite (30–60% metabolized to NAPA). **Elimination:** In urine. **Half-Life:** 3 h procainamide, 6 h NAPA.

CLINICAL IMPLICATIONS

Assessment & Drug Effects

- Check apical radial pulses before each dose during period of adjustment to the oral route.
- Patients with severe heart, liver, or kidney disease and hypotension are at particular risk for adverse effects.
- Monitor the patient's ECG and BP continuously during IV drug administration.
- Discontinue IV drug temporarily when (1) arrhythmia is interrupted, (2) severe toxic effects are present, (3) QRS complex is excessively widened (greater than 50%), (4) PR interval is prolonged, or (5) BP drops 15 mm Hg or more. Obtain rhythm strip and notify physician.
- Ventricular dysrhythmias are usually abolished within a few minutes after IV dose and within an hour after PO or IM administration.

P

Common adverse effects in *italic*, life-threatening effects <u>underlined</u>; generic names in **bold**; classifications in SMALL CAPS; ♣ Canadian drug name; ⊘ Prototype drug

1269

- Report promptly complaints of chest pain, dyspnea, and anxiety. Digitalization may have preceded procainamide in patients with atrial arrhythmias. Cardiotonic glycosides may induce sufficient increase in atrial contraction to dislodge atrial mural emboli, with subsequent pulmonary embolism.
- Therapeutic procainamide blood levels are reached in approximately 24 h if kidney function is normal but are delayed in presence of renal impairment.

Patient & Family Education

- Keep a record of weekly weight. Notify physician if weight gain of 1 kg (2 lb) or more is accompanied by local edema.
- Record and report date, time, and duration of fibrillation episodes when taking maintenance doses: Light-headedness, giddiness, weakness, or faintness.
- Keep a record of pulse rates. Report to physician changes in rate or quality.
- Report to physician signs of reduced procainamide control: Weakness, irregular pulse, unexplained fatigability, anxiety.
- Do not double dose or change an interval because a previous dose was missed. Take procainamide at evenly spaced intervals around the clock unless otherwise prescribed.

PROCAINE HYDROCHLORIDE ℗⁺

(proe′kane)

Novocain

Classifications: LOCAL ANESTHETIC (ESTER-TYPE)

Therapeutic: LOCAL ANESTHETIC

Pregnancy Category: C

AVAILABILITY 1%, 2%, 10% injection

ACTION & *THERAPEUTIC EFFECT*
Decreases sodium flux into nerve cell, thus depressing initial depolarization and preventing propagation and conduction of the nerve impulse. *Local anesthetic action produces loss of sensation and motor activity in circumscribed areas of the body close to the injection or application site.*

USES Spinal anesthesia and epidural and peripheral nerve block by injection and infiltration methods.

CONTRAINDICATIONS Known hypersensitivity to procaine or to other drugs of similar chemical structure, to PABA, and to parabens; generalized septicemia, inflammation, or sepsis at proposed injection site; cerebrospinal diseases (e.g., meningitis, syphilis); heart block, hypotension, hypertension; bowel pathology, GI hemorrhage; coagulopathy, anticoagulants, thrombocytopenia; pregnancy (category C).

CAUTIOUS USE Debilitated, older adults, or acutely ill patients; obstetric delivery; increased intraabdominal pressure; known drug allergies and sensitivities; impaired cardiac function, dysrhythmias; shock; lactation.

ROUTE & DOSAGE

Spinal Anesthesia
Adult: **SC** 10% solution diluted with NS at 1 mL/5 sec

Infiltration Anesthesia/Peripheral Nerve Block
Adult: **SC** 0.25–0.5% solution

ADMINISTRATION

Subcutaneous

- Reconstitute solution: To prepare 60 mL of a 0.5% solution (5 mg/mL), dilute 30 mL of 1%-solution with 30 mL sterile distilled water. Add 0.5–1 mL epinephrine 1:1000/100 mL anesthetic solution for vasoconstrictive effect (1:200,000–1:100,000).
- Do not use solutions that are cloudy, discolored, or that contain crystals. Discard unused portion of solutions not containing a preservative. Avoid use of solution with preservative for spinal, epidural, or caudal block.
- Inject slowly with frequent aspirations to avoid inadvertent intravascular administration, which can lead to a systemic reaction.

INCOMPATIBILITIES **Solution/additive: Aminophylline, amobarbital, chlorothiazide, magnesium sulfate, phenobarbital, phenytoin, secobarbital, sodium bicarbonate.**

ADVERSE EFFECTS (≥1%) **CNS:** Anxiety, nervousness, dizziness, circumoral paresthesia, tremors, drowsiness, sedation, convulsions, <u>respiratory arrest</u>. With spinal anesthesia: postspinal headache, arachnoiditis, palsies, spinal nerve paralysis, meningism. **Special Senses:** Tinnitus, blurred vision. **CV:** Myocardial depression, arrhythmias including bradycardia (also fetal bradycardia); hypotension. **GI:** Nausea, vomiting. **Skin:** Cutaneous lesions of delayed onset, urticaria, pruritus, angioneurotic edema, sweating, syncope, <u>anaphylactoid reaction</u>. **Urogenital:** Urinary retention, fecal or urinary incontinence, loss of perineal sensation and sexual function, slowing of labor and increased incidence of forceps de-

livery (all with caudal or epidural anesthesia).

INTERACTIONS Drug: May antagonize effects of SULFONAMIDES; increased risk of hypotension with MAOIS, ANTIHYPERTENSIVES.

PHARMACOKINETICS Absorption: Rapidly from injection site. **Onset:** 2–5 min. **Duration:** 1 h. **Metabolism:** Hydrolyzed by plasma pseudocholinesterases. **Elimination:** 80% of metabolites excreted in urine. **Half-Life:** 7.7 min.

CLINICAL IMPLICATIONS

Assessment & Drug Effects

- Be aware that reactions during dental procedure are usually mild, transient, and produced by epinephrine added to local anesthetic (e.g., headache, palpitation, tachycardia, hypertension, dizziness).
- Use procaine with epinephrine with caution in body areas with limited blood supply (e.g., fingers, toes, ears, nose). If used, inspect particular area for evidence of reduced perfusion (vasospasm): Pale, cold, sensitive skin.
- Hypotension is the most important complication of spinal anesthesia. Risk period is during first 30 min after induction and is intensified by changes in position that promote decreased venous return, or by preexisting hypertension, pregnancy, old age, or hypovolemia.

Patient & Family Education

- Understand that that there will be temporary loss of sensation in the area of the injection.
- Do not consume hot liquids or foods until sensation returns when drug used for dental procedure.

Common adverse effects in *italic*, life-threatening effects <u>underlined</u>; generic names in **bold**; classifications in SMALL CAPS; ✚ Canadian drug name; ⊕ Prototype drug

PROCARBAZINE HYDROCHLORIDE

(proe-kar′ba-zeen)
Matulane, Natulan ✦

Classifications: ANTINEOPLASTIC; ALKYLATING AGENT
Therapeutic: ANTINEOPLASTIC
Prototype: Cyclophosphamide
Pregnancy Category: D

AVAILABILITY 50 mg capsules

ACTION & *THERAPEUTIC EFFECT*
Hydrazine derivative with antimetabolite properties; cell cycle–specific for the S phase of cell division. Suppresses mitosis at interphase, and causes chromatin derangement. *Highly toxic to rapidly proliferating tissue. May delay myelosuppression.*

USES Adjunct in palliative treatment of Hodgkin's disease.
UNLABELED USES Solid tumors.

CONTRAINDICATIONS Severe myelosuppression; pheochromocytoma; alcohol ingestion; foods high in tyramine content; sympathomimetic drugs. MAO inhibitors should be discontinued 14 d prior to therapy; tricyclic antidepressants, 7 d before therapy; pregnancy (category D), lactation.
CAUTIOUS USE Concomitant administration with CNS depressants; hepatic or renal impairment; cardiac disease; bipolar disorder, mania, paranoid schizophrenia; G6PD deficiency; parkinsonism; following radiation or chemotherapy before at least 1 mo has elapsed; alcoholism; infection; diabetes mellitus.

ROUTE & DOSAGE

Adjunct for Hodgkin's Disease
Adult: PO 2–4 mg/kg/d in single or divided doses for 1 wk, then 4–6 mg/kg/d until WBC <4000/mm^3 or platelets are <100,000/mm^3 or maximum response obtained; drug is then discontinued until bone marrow recovery is satisfactory; treatment is started again at 1–2 mg/kg/d
Child: PO 50 mg/m^2/d in single or divided doses for 1 wk, then 100 mg/m^2/d until WBC is <4000/mm^3 or platelets are <100,000/mm^3 or maximum response obtained; drug is then discontinued until bone marrow recovery is satisfactory; treatment is started again at 50 mg/m^2/d

ADMINISTRATION
Oral
- Do not give if WBC count <4000/mm^3 or platelet count <100,000/mm^3. Consult physician.
- Store at 15°–30° C (59°–86° F). Protect from freezing, moisture, and light.

ADVERSE EFFECTS (≥1%) **CNS:** Myalgia, arthralgia, paresthesias, weakness, fatigue, lethargy, drowsiness, neuropathies, mental depression, acute psychosis, hallucinations, dizziness, headache, ataxia, nervousness, insomnia, <u>coma</u>, confusion, seizures. **GI:** *Severe nausea and vomiting,* anorexia, stomatitis, dry mouth, dysphagia, diarrhea, constipation, jaundice, ascites. **Hematologic:** <u>Bone marrow suppression (leukopenia, anemia, thrombocytopenia)</u>, hemolysis, bleeding tendencies. **Skin:** Dermatitis, pruritus, herpes, hyperpigmentation, flushing, alopecia. **Respiratory:** *Pleural effusion, cough,* hoarseness. **CV:** Hypotension, tachycardia. **Body as a Whole:** Chills, fever, sweating, photosensitivity; <u>intercurrent infections</u>. **Urogenital:** Gynecomastia, depressed spermatogenesis, atrophy of testes.

Common adverse effects in *italic*, life-threatening effects <u>underlined</u>; generic names in **bold**; classifications in SMALL CAPS; ✦ Canadian drug name; ❷ Prototype drug

DIAGNOSTIC TEST INTERFERENCE
Procarbazine may enhance the effects of **CNS depressants.** A disulfiram-like reaction may occur following ingestion of *alcohol.*

INTERACTIONS Drug: Alcohol, PHENOTHIAZINES, and other CNS DEPRESSANTS add to CNS depression; TRICYCLIC ANTIDEPRESSANTS, MAO INHIBITORS, SYMPATHOMIMETICS, **ephedrine, phenylpropanolamine** may precipitate hypertensive crisis, hyperpyrexia; seizures; or death. **Food: Tyramine**-containing foods may precipitate hypertensive crisis [see **phenelzine sulfate** (MAO INHIBITOR)].

PHARMACOKINETICS Absorption: Readily from GI tract. **Peak:** 1 h. **Distribution:** Widely distributed with high concentrations in liver, kidneys, intestinal wall, and skin. **Metabolism:** In liver. **Elimination:** In urine. **Half-Life:** 1 h.

CLINICAL IMPLICATIONS
Assessment & Drug Effects
▪ Start flow sheet and record baseline BP, weight, temperature, pulse, and I&O ratio and pattern.
▪ Lab tests: Determine hematologic status (Hgb, Hct, WBC, differential, reticulocyte, and platelet counts) initially and at least q3–4d. Hepatic and renal studies (transaminase, alkaline phosphatase, BUN, urinalysis) are also indicated initially and at least weekly during therapy.
▪ Protect patient from exposure to infection and trauma when nadir of leukopenia (<4000/mm^3) is approached. Note and report changes in voiding pattern, hematuria, and dysuria (possible signs of urinary tract infection). Monitor I&O ratio and temperature closely.
▪ Withhold drug and notify physician of any of the following: CNS

S&S (e.g., paresthesias, neuropathies, confusion); leukopenia [WBC count <4000/mm^3; thrombocytopenia (platelet count <100,000/mm^3)]; hypersensitivity reaction, the first small ulceration or persistent spot or soreness in oral cavity, diarrhea, and bleeding.
▪ Monitor for and report any of the following: chills, fever, weakness, shortness of breath, productive cough. Drug will be discontinued.
▪ Assess for signs of liver dysfunction: Jaundice (yellow skin, sclerae, and soft palate), frothy or dark urine, clay-colored stools.
▪ Tolerance to nausea and vomiting (most common adverse effects) usually develops by end of first week of treatment. Doses are kept at a minimum during this time. If vomiting persists, therapy will be interrupted.

Patient & Family Education
▪ Avoid OTC nose drops, cough medicines, and antiobesity preparations containing sympathomimetic drugs (e.g., ephedrine, amphetamine, epinephrine) and tricyclic antidepressants because they may cause hypertensive crises since procarbazine has MAO inhibitory activity. Do not to use OTC preparations without physician's approval.
▪ Report to physician any sign of impending infection.
▪ Do not eat foods high in tyramine content (e.g., aged cheese, beer, wine).
▪ Avoid alcohol; ingestion of any form of alcohol may precipitate a disulfiram-type reaction (see Appendix F).
▪ Report to physician immediately signs of hemorrhagic tendencies: Bleeding into skin and mucosa, epistaxis, hemoptysis, hematemesis, hematuria, melena, ecchy-

Common adverse effects in *italic*, life-threatening effects underlined; generic names in **bold**; classifications in SMALL CAPS; ♣ Canadian drug name; ⊘ Prototype drug

1273

moses, petechiae. Bone marrow depression often occurs 2–8 wk after start of therapy.

- Avoid excessive exposure to the sun because of potential photosensitivity reaction: Cover as much skin area as possible with clothing, and use sunscreen lotion (SPF >12) on all exposed skin surfaces.
- Use caution while driving or performing hazardous tasks until response to drug is known since drowsiness, dizziness, and blurred vision are possible adverse effects.
- Use contraceptive measures during procarbazine therapy.

PROCHLORPERAZINE 🅟

(proe-klor-per′a-zeen)
Compazine, Compro

PROCHLORPERAZINE EDISYLATE

Compazine

PROCHLORPERAZINE MALEATE

Compazine, Stemetil ✦

Classifications: PSYCHOTHERAPEUTIC; ANTIPSYCHOTIC PHENOTHIAZINE; ANTIEMETIC
Therapeutic: ANTIPSYCHOTIC; ANTIEMETIC
Pregnancy Category: C

AVAILABILITY 5 mg, 10 mg, 25 mg tablets; 10 mg, 15 mg, 30 mg sustained release capsule; 2.5 mg, 5 mg, 25 mg suppositories; 5 mg/mL injection **Edisylate** 5 mg/mL injection

ACTION & *THERAPEUTIC EFFECT*
Phenothiazine derivative. Produces strong antipsychotic effects thought to be related to blockade of postsynaptic dopamine receptors in the brain. Action on the hypothalamus and reticular formation results in sedative effects. Antiemetic effect is produced by suppression of the chemoreceptor trigger zone (CTZ). Inhibits dopamine reuptake; may be basis for moderate extrapyramidal symptoms. *Greater extrapyramidal effects and antiemetic potency but fewer sedative, hypotensive, and anticholinergic effects than chlorpromazine.*

USES Management of manifestations of psychotic disorders, of excessive anxiety, tension, and agitation, and to control severe nausea and vomiting.

UNLABELED USES Behavioral syndromes in dementia.

CONTRAINDICATIONS Hypersensitivity to phenothiazines; bone marrow depression; blood dyscrasias, jaundice; comatose or severely depressed states; children <9 kg (20 lb) or 2 y of age; pediatric surgery; short-term vomiting in children or vomiting of unknown etiology; Reye's syndrome or other encephalopathies; history of dyskinetic reactions or epilepsy; pregnancy (category C), lactation.

CAUTIOUS USE Patient with previously diagnosed breast cancer, children with acute illness or dehydration; Parkinson's disease; GI obstruction; hepatic disease; seizure disorders; urinary retention, BPH.

ROUTE & DOSAGE

Severe Nausea, Vomiting

Adult: **PO** 5–10 mg 3–4 times daily; sustained release: 10–15 mg q12h **IM** 5–10 mg q3–4h up to 40 mg/d **IV** 2.5–10 mg q3–4h (max: 40 mg/d) **PR** 25 mg b.i.d.

Common adverse effects in *italic*, life-threatening effects <u>underlined</u>; generic names in **bold**; classifications in SMALL CAPS; ✦ Canadian drug name; 🅟 Prototype drug

Child (over 9 kg): **PO/PR** 2.5 mg 1–3 times/d or 5 mg b.i.d. (max: 15 mg/d) **IM** 0.13 mg/kg q3–4h

Psychotic Disorders

Adult: **PO** 5–10 mg 3–4 times daily; titrate up q2–3 d **IM** 10–20 mg; may repeat q1–4h to gain control, then q4–6h
Child (2–12 years): **PO/PR** 2.5 mg 2–3 times daily (max: 20 mg daily ages 2–5 and 25 mg daily ages 6–12)

ADMINISTRATION

Oral

- Dosages for older adults, emaciated patients and children should be increased slowly.
- Ensure that sustained release form is not chewed or crushed. Must be swallowed whole.
- Do not give oral concentrate to children.
- Avoid skin contact with oral concentrate or injection solution because of possibility of contact dermatitis.

Intramuscular

- Do not inject drug SC.
- Make injection deep into the upper outer quadrant of the buttock in adults. Follow agency policy regarding IM injection site for children.

Intravenous

PREPARE: **Direct:** Dilute each 5 mg (1 mL) in 4 mL of NS or other compatible solution to yield 1 mg/mL. **IV Infusion:** Dilute in 50–100 mL of D5W, NS, D5/0.45% NaCl, RL or other compatible solution.
ADMINISTER: **Direct:** Do not exceed 10 mg for a single dose. Do not give a bolus dose. Give at a maximum rate of 5 mg/min. **IV Infusion:** Give over 15–30 min. Do not exceed direct IV rate.

INCOMPATIBILITIES **Solution/additive:** Aminophylline, amphotericin B, ampicillin, calcium gluconate, cephalothin, chloramphenicol, chlorothiazide, dimenhydrinate, epinephrine, erythromycin, furosemide, hydrocortisone, hydromorphone, kanamycin, ketorolac, methohexital, midazolam, morphine, penicillin G sodium, pentobarbital, phenobarbital, tetracycline, thiopental, vancomycin, warfarin. **Y-site:** Aldesleukin, allopurinol, amifostine, amphotericin B cholesteryl complex, aztreonam, bivalirudin, cefepime, etoposide, fenoldopam, filgrastim, fludarabine, foscarnet, gemcitabine, piperacillin-tazobactam.

- Discard markedly discolored solutions; slight yellowing does not appear to alter potency.

ADVERSE EFFECTS (≥1%) **CNS:** *Drowsiness, dizziness, extrapyramidal reactions (akathisia, dystonia, or parkinsonism),* <u>persistent tardive dyskinesia</u>, acute catatonia. **CV:** Hypotension. **GI:** Cholestatic jaundice. **Skin:** Contact dermatitis, photosensitivity. **Endocrine:** Galactorrhea, amenorrhea. **Special Senses:** Blurred vision. **Hematologic:** Leukopenia, <u>agranulocytosis</u>.

INTERACTIONS Drug: Alcohol, CNS DEPRESSANTS increase CNS depression; ANTACIDS, ANTIDIARRHEALS decrease absorption, therefore, administer 2 h apart; **phenobarbital** increases metabolism of prochlorperazine; GENERAL ANESTHETICS increase excitation and hypotension; antagonizes antihypertensive action of **guanethidine; phenylpropanolamine** poses possibility of sudden death; TRICYCLIC ANTIDEPRESSANTS

Common adverse effects in *italic*, life-threatening effects <u>underlined</u>; generic names in **bold**; classifications in SMALL CAPS; ✦ Canadian drug name; ☻ Prototype drug

1275

intensify hypotensive and anticholinergic effects; decreases seizure threshold—ANTICONVULSANT dosage may need to be increased. **Herbal: Kava-kava** may increase risk and severity of dystonic reactions.

PHARMACOKINETICS Absorption: Readily from GI tract. **Onset:** 30–40 min PO; 60 min PR; 10–20 min IM. **Duration:** 3–4 h PO; 10–12 h sustained release PO; 3–4 h PR; up to 12 h IM. **Distribution:** Crosses placenta; distributed into breast milk. **Metabolism:** In liver. **Elimination:** In urine.

CLINICAL IMPLICATIONS

Assessment & Drug Effects

- Positioned nauseated patients who have received prochlorperazine carefully to prevent aspiration of vomitus; may have depressed cough reflex.
- Most older adult and emaciated patients and children, especially those with dehydration or acute illness, appear to be particularly susceptible to extrapyramidal effects. Be alert to onset of symptoms: Early in therapy watch for pseudoparkinson's and acute dyskinesia. After 1–2 mo, be alert to akathisia.
- Keep in mind that the antiemetic effect may mask toxicity of other drugs or make it difficult to diagnose conditions with a primary symptom of nausea, such as intestinal obstruction and increased intracranial pressure.
- Lab tests: Periodic CBC with differential in long-term therapy.
- Be alert to signs of high core temperature: Red, dry, hot skin; full bounding pulse; dilated pupils; dyspnea; confusion; temperature over 40.6° C (105° F); elevated BP. Exposure to high environmental temperature, to sun's rays, or to a high fever associated with serious illness places this patient at risk for heat stroke. Inform physician and institute measures to reduce body temperature rapidly.

Patient & Family Education

- Take drug only as prescribed and do not alter dose or schedule. Consult physician before stopping the medication.
- Avoid hazardous activities such as driving a car until response to drug is known because drug may impair mental and physical abilities, especially during first few days of therapy.
- Be aware that drug may color urine reddish brown. It also may cause the sun-exposed skin to turn gray-blue.
- Protect skin from direct sun's rays and use a sunscreen lotion (SPF >12) to prevent photosensitivity reaction.
- Withhold dose and report to the physician if the following symptoms persist more than a few hours: Tremor, involuntary twitching, exaggerated restlessness. Other reportable symptoms include light-colored stools, changes in vision, sore throat, fever, rash.

PROCYCLIDINE HYDROCHLORIDE

(proe-sye′kli-deen)
Kemadrin, Procyclid ♦

Classifications: ANTICHOLINERGIC; ANTIMUSCARINIC; ANTISPASMODIC; ANTIPARKINSON AGENT
Therapeutic: ANTIPARKINSON
Prototype: Atropine
Pregnancy Category: C

AVAILABILITY 5 mg tablets

ACTION & *THERAPEUTIC EFFECT*
Centrally acting synthetic anticholin-

P

ergic agent with actions similar to those of atropine. Selectively blocks muscarinic responses to acetylcholine (ACh), whether excitatory or inhibitory. *Diminishes the characteristic tremor of parkinsonism.*

USES To relieve symptoms of parkinsonism syndrome (postencephalitic, arteriosclerotic, and idiopathic), and drug-induced extrapyramidal symptoms.

CONTRAINDICATIONS Angle-closure glaucoma; pregnancy (category C), lactation. Safe use in children not established.

CAUTIOUS USE Hypotension; mental disorders; tachycardia; prostatic hypertrophy.

ROUTE & DOSAGE

Parkinsonism Symptoms
Adult: **PO** 2.5 mg t.i.d. p.c., may be gradually increased to 5 mg t.i.d. if tolerated with an additional 5 mg h.s. (max: 45–60 mg/d)
Geriatric: **PO** Start with 2.5 mg 1–2 times/d

ADMINISTRATION

Oral
- Minimize adverse effects by administration of drug during or after meals.
- Store at 15°–30° C (59°–86° F) in tightly closed containers unless otherwise directed.

ADVERSE EFFECTS (≥1%) **Body as a Whole:** Flushing of skin, decreased sweating, headache, lightheadedness, dizziness, feeling of muscle weakness. **Special Senses:** Blurred vision, mydriasis, photophobia. **CV:** Palpitation, tachycardia, *hypotension.* **GI:** *Dry mouth,*

nausea, vomiting, epigastric distress, constipation, paralytic ileus, acute suppurative parotitis. **Urogenital:** Urinary retention. **Skin:** Skin eruptions (occasionally). **CNS:** Mental confusion, psychotic-like symptoms.

INTERACTIONS Drug: Additive adverse effects with ANTICHOLINERGIC AGENTS. **Herbal: Betel nut** may induce extrapyramidal symptoms.

PHARMACOKINETICS Onset: 35–40 min. **Duration:** 4–6 h.

CLINICAL IMPLICATIONS
Assessment & Drug Effects
- Monitor heart rate and rhythm and BP. Report palpitations, tachycardia, paradoxical bradycardia, or decreasing BP. Dosage adjustment or discontinuation of drug may be indicated.
- Monitor therapeutic effectiveness. Generally more effective in controlling rigidity than tremors. Tremors may temporarily appear to be exaggerated as rigidity is relieved, especially in patients with severe spasticity.
- Observe for and report symptoms of mental confusion, disorientation, agitation, and psychotic-like symptoms, particularly in older adult patients who have low BP, to physician.
- Check for constipation and abdominal distention and provide information for preventing constipation.

Patient & Family Education
- Void before taking drug if urinary hesitancy or retention is a problem.
- Avoid potentially hazardous activities until response to drug is known because drug may cause blurred vision and dizziness.
- Relieve dry mouth by rinsing frequently with water, chewing sug-

Common adverse effects in *italic*, life-threatening effects <u>underlined</u>; generic names in **bold**; classifications in SMALL CAPS; ✦ Canadian drug name; ☺ Prototype drug

1277

arless gum or sucking hard candy, or increasing noncaloric fluid intake. If these measures fail, a saliva substitute, available OTC, may help (e.g., Orex, Xero-Lube).

- Avoid alcohol and do not to take other CNS depressants unless otherwise advised by physician.

PROGESTERONE ⊕

(proe-jess'ter-one)
Crinone Gel, Gesterol 50, Progestaject, Progestasert, Prometrium
Classifications: HORMONE; PROGESTIN
Therapeutic: PROGESTIN
Pregnancy Category: X; vaginal gel in early pregnancy (category B)

AVAILABILITY 100 mg capsules; 50 mg/mL injection; 8% gel

ACTION & *THERAPEUTIC EFFECT*
Steroid hormone synthesized and released by testes, ovary, adrenal cortex, and placenta. Has estrogenic, anabolic, and androgenic activity. Physiologic precursor to estrogens, androgens, and adrenocortical steroids. Transforms endometrium from proliferative to secretory state; suppresses pituitary gonadotropin secretion, thereby blocking follicular maturation and ovulation. Acting with estrogen, promotes mammary gland development without causing lactation and increases body temperature 1° F at time of ovulation. *Relaxes estrogen-primed myometrium and prohibits spontaneous contraction of uterus. Sudden drop in blood levels of progestin (and estradiol) causes "withdrawal bleeding" from endometrium. Intrauterine placement of progesterone (intra-uterine progesterone contraceptive system) hypothetically inhibits sperm survival, and suppresses endometrial proliferation (antiestrogenic effect).*

USES Secondary amenorrhea, functional uterine bleeding, endometriosis, and premenstrual syndrome. As an intrauterine agent (Progestasert) and in combination with estrogens provides fertility control. Largely supplanted by new progestins, which have longer action and oral effectiveness. Treatment of infertile women with progesterone deficiency.

CONTRAINDICATIONS Hypersensitivity to progestins, known or suspected breast or genital malignancy; use as a pregnancy test; thrombophlebitis, thromboembolic disorders; ectopic pregnancy; cerebral apoplexy (or its history); severely impaired liver function or disease; undiagnosed vaginal bleeding, incomplete abortion; use during first 4 mo of pregnancy (category X), other than vaginal gel used for assisted reproductive technology (ART) in early pregnancy. *Progestasert:* Pregnancy or suspicion of pregnancy. *Prometrium* (oral): Patients with peanut allergy.

CAUTIOUS USE Anemia; diabetes mellitus; history of psychic depression; persons susceptible to acute intermittent porphyria or with conditions that may be aggravated by fluid retention (asthma, seizure disorders, cardiac or kidney function, migraine); impaired liver function; previous ectopic pregnancy; presence or history of salpingitis; venereal disease; unresolved abnormal Pap smear; genital bleeding of unknown etiology; previous pelvic surgery.

ROUTE & DOSAGE

Amenorrhea
Adult: **IM** 5–10 mg for 6–8 consecutive days **PO** 400 mg h.s. times 10 d

Uterine Bleeding
Adult: **IM** 5–10 mg/d for 6 d

Premenstrual Syndrome
Adult: **PR** 200–400 mg/d

Intrauterine Contraceptive
Adult: **Intrauterine** Insert in uterus for 1 y

ADMINISTRATION

Intramuscular

- Immerse vial in warm water momentarily to redissolve crystals (if present) and to facilitate aspiration of drug into syringe.
- Inject deeply IM. Injection site may be irritated. Inspect IM sites carefully and rotate areas systematically.
- Do not give oral capsules, which contain peanut oil, to patients allergic to peanuts.
- Store drug at 15°–30° C (59°–86° F) unless otherwise specified by manufacturer. Protect from freezing and light.

ADVERSE EFFECTS (≥1%) **CNS:** Migraine headache, *dizziness,* lethargy, mental depression, somnolence, insomnia. **CV:** <u>Thromboembolic disorder, pulmonary embolism.</u> **Special Senses:** Change in vision, proptosis, diplopia, papilledema, retinal vascular lesions. **GI:** Hepatic disease, cholestatic jaundice; *nausea,* vomiting, *abdominal cramps.* **Urogenital:** Vaginal candidiasis, chloasma, cervical erosion and changes in secretions, *breakthrough bleeding,* dysmenorrhea, amenorrhea, pruritus vulvae. **Metabolic:** Hyperglycemia, decreased libido, transient increase in sodium and chloride excretion, pyrexia. **Skin:** *Acne,* pruritus, allergic rash, photosensitivity, urticaria, hirsutism, alopecia. **Body as a Whole:** *Edema, weight changes;* pain at injection site; fatigue. **Endocrine:** Gynecomastia, galactorrhea.

DIAGNOSTIC TEST INTERFERENCE PROGESTINS may decrease levels of *urinary pregnanediol* and increase levels of *serum alkaline phosphatase, plasma amino acids, urinary nitrogen,* and *coagulation factors VII, VIII, IX,* and *X.* They also decrease *glucose tolerance* (may cause false-positive *urine glucose tests*) and lower *HDL* (high-density lipoprotein) levels.

INTERACTIONS Drug: BARBITURATES, **carbamazepine, phenytoin, rifampin** may alter contraceptive effectiveness; **ketoconazole** may inhibit progesterone metabolism; may antagonize effects of **bromocriptine.**

PHARMACOKINETICS Absorption: Rapid from IM site; PO peaks at 3 h. **Metabolism:** Extensively in liver. **Elimination:** Primarily in urine; excreted in breast milk. **Half-Life:** 5 min.

CLINICAL IMPLICATIONS

Assessment & Drug Effects

- Record baseline data for comparative value about patient's weight, BP, and pulse at onset of progestin therapy. Report deviations promptly.
- Lab tests: Periodic liver function tests, blood glucose, and serum electrolytes.
- Monitor for and report immediately S&S of thrombophlebitis or thromboembolic disease.

P

Common adverse effects in *italic,* life-threatening effects <u>underlined</u>; generic names in **bold**; classifications in SMALL CAPS; ♣ Canadian drug name; ❷ Prototype drug

1279

- Be alert for S&S of acute intermittent porphyria in susceptible patients (e.g., severe, colicky abdominal pain, vomiting, distention, diarrhea, constipation).

Patient & Family Education

- Avoid exposure to UV light and prolonged periods of time in the sun. Photosensitivity severity is related to both time of exposure and dose. A phototoxic drug reaction usually looks like an exaggerated sunburn and occurs within 5–18 h after exposure to sun and is maximal by 36–72 h.
- Use sunscreen lotion (SPF >12) that contains paraaminobenzoic acid (PABA) on exposed skin surfaces whenever outdoors, even on dark days.
- Inform physician promptly if any of the following occur: Sudden severe headache or vomiting, dizziness or fainting, numbness in an arm or leg, pain in calves accompanied by swelling, warmth, and redness; acute chest pain or dyspnea.
- Report to physician promptly unexplained sudden or gradual, partial or complete loss of vision, ptosis, or diplopia.
- Monitor for loss of glycemic control if diabetic.
- Notify physician if you become or suspect pregnancy. Learn the potential risk to the fetus from exposure to progestin.

Intrauterine Progesterone Contraceptive System (Progestasert)

- Use another method of birth control (foam or condom) during the first 2 mo of Progestasert use.
- Regular cyclic pattern of ovulation continues while Progestasert is in place.
- Be prepared for heavier and longer menstrual periods during Progestasert use. Consult physician if increased menstrual bleeding continues.
- Check Progestasert threads frequently during first few months and after menstruation (times when expulsion is most likely to occur). If you cannot feel threads, return to physician for an examination and prescription for another method of birth control.
- Do not pull on threads for any reason. If the IUD is partially expelled, it should be removed; however, do not try to remove it yourself nor allow your partner to attempt to do so.
- Consult physician if a period is missed and pregnancy is suspected. Remove the device during pregnancy.
- Report to the physician for immediate treatment if you experience fever, acute pelvic pain and tenderness, unusual bleeding, or severe cramping. These are symptoms that indicate infection.

PROMAZINE HYDROCHLORIDE

(proe′ma-zeen)

Prozine-50, Sparine

Classifications: PSYCHOTHERAPEUTIC; PHENOTHIAZINE; ANTIPSYCHOTIC

Therapeutic: ANTIPSYCHOTIC

Prototype: Chlorpromazine

Pregnancy Category: C

AVAILABILITY 25 mg, 50 mg tablets; 25 mg/mL, 50 mg/mL injection

ACTION & *THERAPEUTIC EFFECT*
Derivative of phenothiazine. Compared with chlorpromazine has weak antipsychotic activity and extrapyramidal effects occur less fre-

quently. Thought to block the postsynaptic dopamine receptors in the brain, with a higher affinity for D_1 over D_2 dopamine receptors. *Antipsychotic drugs are sometimes called neuroleptics because they tend to reduce initiative and interest in the environment, decrease displays of emotions or affect, suppress spontaneous movements and complex behavior, and decrease psychotic symptoms.*

USES Manifestations of psychotic disorders and for reducing agitation and paranoia associated with alcohol withdrawal.

CONTRAINDICATIONS Hypersensitivity to phenothiazines; myelosuppression; CNS depression; children <2 y of age, Reye's syndrome; pregnancy (category C), lactation.

CAUTIOUS USE Prostatic hypertrophy; cardiovascular or liver disease; paralytic ileus; xerostomia; angle closure glaucoma; persons exposed to extremes in temperature or to organophosphorous insecticides; convulsive disorders.

ROUTE & DOSAGE

Psychotic Disorders
Adult: **PO/IM** 10–200 mg q4–6h up to 1000 mg/d
Adolescent: **PO/IM** *>12 y*, 10–25 mg q4–6h

Dementia Behavior
Geriatric: **PO/IM** Start with 25 mg 1–2 times/d, may increase q4–7d in divided doses (max: 500 mg/d)

ADMINISTRATION

Oral
- Use oral route whenever possible. Reserve parenteral administration for acutely disturbed or uncooperative patients or those who cannot tolerate oral preparation.
- Give 1 h before or 2 h after antacid; absorption is inhibited by antacids.
- Dilute the concentrate immediately before administration with fruit juice, chocolate-flavored drinks, carbonated drinks, or soup (for best taste, 10 mL of diluent for each 25 mg of drug). Avoid coffee or tea ingestion at or near medication times. Explain dosage and dilution to patient if drug is to be self-administered.
- Avoid contact of liquid preparations with skin.

Intramuscular
- Make IM injection deep into upper outer quadrant of buttock. Carefully aspirate before injecting drug slowly. Tissue irritation can occur if given SC. Intraarterial injection can cause arterial or arteriolar spasm and consequent impairment of local circulation. Rotate injection sites.
- Store at 15°–30° C (59°–86° F) in light-resistant container unless otherwise directed.

ADVERSE EFFECTS (≥1%) **Body as a Whole:** *Drowsiness, orthostatic hypotension,* syncope. **Special Senses:** Blurred vision, photosensitivity. **GI:** Constipation, xerostomia. **CNS:** Extrapyramidal effects, tardive dyskinesia, epileptic seizures in susceptible individuals, leukopenia, <u>agranulocytosis</u> (rare). **CV:** Hypotension, sinus tachycardia.

INTERACTIONS Drug: Alcohol, CNS DEPRESSANTS increases CNS depression; **phenobarbital** increases metabolism; GENERAL ANESTHETICS increase excitation and hypotension; antagonizes antihypertensive action

Common adverse effects in *italic*, life-threatening effects <u>underlined</u>; generic names in **bold**; classifications in SMALL CAPS; ✚ Canadian drug name; ⦿ Prototype drug

1281

of **guanethidine;** TRICYCLIC ANTIDEPRESSANTS intensify hypotensive and anticholinergic effects; ANTICONVULSANTS decrease seizure threshold—may need to increase anticonvulsant dose. **Herbal: Kava-kava** may increase risk and severity of dystonic reactions.

PHARMACOKINETICS Absorption: Variable, absorbed from GI tract. **Metabolism:** In liver.

CLINICAL IMPLICATIONS

Assessment & Drug Effects

- Monitor BP and pulse before administration and between doses. Keep patient recumbent for about 1 h after IM dose is given because incidence of postural hypotension and drowsiness is particularly high after parenteral administration.
- Encourage adequate fluid intake as prophylaxis for constipation and xerostomia. The depressed patient may not seek help for either symptom or for urinary retention.
- Report symptoms suggesting agranulocytosis promptly (see Appendix F).

Patient & Family Education

- Make position changes slowly, particularly from lying down to upright positions. Dizziness or faintness may occur on arising.
- Avoid alcohol during therapy.
- Do not spill oral solutions on hands or clothing; wash exposed skin well with soap and water. Drug may cause contact dermatitis.
- Be aware that promazine may color urine pink to red to reddish brown.
- Do not take OTC drugs without physician approval.

PROMETHAZINE HYDROCHLORIDE

(proe-meth′a-zeen)
Histantil ◆, Phenergan
Classifications: ANTIEMETIC; ANTIVERTIGO AGENT; PHENOTHIAZINE
Therapeutic: ANTIEMETIC; ANTIVERTIGO
Prototype: Prochlorperazine
Pregnancy Category: C

AVAILABILITY 12.5 mg, 25 mg, 50 mg tablets; 6.25 mg/5 mL syrup; 12.5 mg, 25 mg, 50 mg suppositories; 25 mg/mL, 50 mg/mL injection

ACTION & *THERAPEUTIC EFFECT* In common with other antihistamines, exerts anti-serotonin, anticholinergic, and local anesthetic action. Antiemetic action thought to be due to depression of CTZ in medulla. *Long-acting derivative of phenothiazine with marked antihistamine activity and prominent sedative, amnesic, antiemetic, and anti–motion-sickness actions.*

USES Symptomatic relief of various allergic conditions, to ameliorate and prevent reactions to blood and plasma, and in prophylaxis and treatment of motion sickness, nausea, and vomiting. Preoperative, postoperative, and obstetric sedation and as adjunct to analgesics for control of pain.

CONTRAINDICATIONS Hypersensitivity to phenothiazines; acute MI; angina, atrial fibrillation, atrial flutter, cardiac arrhythmias, cardiomyopathy coronary artery disease, uncontrolled hypertension, peripheral vascular disease; MAOI therapy; narrowangle glaucoma; stenosing peptic ulcer, pyloroduodenal obstruction; prostatic hypertrophy; bladder neck obstruction; epilepsy; bone marrow depression; comatose or severely depressed states; Reye's syndrome, encephalopathy, hepatic diseases; acutely ill or dehydrated children; children <2 y; pregnancy (category C), lactation, newborn or premature infants.

CAUTIOUS USE Impaired liver function; cardiovascular disease; asthma; acute or chronic respiratory impairment (particularly in children); hypertension; older adult or debilitated patients.

ROUTE & DOSAGE

Motion Sickness
Adult: **PO/PR** 25 mg q12h prn
Child >2 y: **PO/PR** 10.5 mg/kg/dose q12h prn (max: 25 mg/dose)

Nausea
Adult: **PO/PR/IM/IV** 12.5–25 mg q4–6h prn
Child >2 y: **PO/PR/IM/IV** 0.25–0.5 mg/kg q4–6h prn (max: 25 mg/dose)

Allergies
Adult: **PO/PR** 12.5 mg q.i.d. or 25 mg h.s. **IM/IV** 25 mg, repeat in 2 hrs if necessary, switch to PO
Child >2 y: **PO** 0.1 mg/kg q6h and 0.05 mg/kg at bedtime prn

Sedation
Adult: **PO/PR/IM/IV** 25–50 mg/dose
Child >2 y: **PO/PR/IM/IV** 12.5–25 mg/dose (max: 50 mg)

ADMINISTRATION

Oral
- Give with food, milk, or a full glass of water may minimize GI distress.
- Tablets may be crushed and mixed with water or food before swallowing.
- Oral doses for allergy are generally prescribed before meals and on retiring or as single dose at bedtime.

Intramuscular
- Give IM injection deep into large muscle mass. Aspirate carefully before injecting drug. Intraarterial injection can cause arterial or arteriolar spasm, with resultant gangrene. Subcutaneous injection (also contraindicated) can cause chemical irritation and necrosis. Rotate injection sites and observe daily.

Intravenous

PREPARE: Direct: Concentrations of 25 mg/mL or less may be given undiluted. Dilute more concentrated preparations in NS to yield no more than 25 mg/mL (e.g., diluting the 50 mg/mL concentration in 9 mL yields 5 mg/mL). ■ Inspect parenteral drug before preparation. Discard if it is darkened or contains precipitate.

ADMINISTER: Direct: Give each 25 mg over at least 1 min.
INCOMPATIBILITIES Solution/additive: Aminophylline, ampicillin, carbenicillin, cefazolin, cefotetan, ceftizoxime, chloramphenicol, chlordiazepoxide, chlorothiazide, dexamethasone, dimenhydrinate. furosemide, heparin, hydrocortisone, ketorolac, methicillin, methohexital, nalbuphine, nitrofurantoin, penicillin G sodium, pentobarbital, phenobarbital, thiopental. Y-site: Aldesleukin, allopurinol, amphotericin B cholesteryl complex, cefepime, cefmetazole, cefoperazone, cefotetan, doxo-

P

Common adverse effects in *italic*, life-threatening effects <u>underlined</u>; generic names in **bold**; classifications in SMALL CAPS; ✤ Canadian drug name; ☻ Prototype drug

1283

rubicin liposome, foscarnet, furosemide, heparin, methotrexate, piperacillin/tazobactam, TPN.

- Store at 15°–30° C (59°–86° F) in tight, light-resistant container unless otherwise directed.

ADVERSE EFFECTS (≥1%) **Body as a Whole:** Deep sleep, coma, convulsions, cardiorespiratory symptoms, extrapyramidal reactions, nightmares (in children), CNS stimulation, abnormal movements. **Respiratory:** Irregular respirations, <u>respiratory depression, apnea</u>. **CNS:** Sedation *drowsiness,* confusion, dizziness, disturbed coordination, restlessness, tremors. **CV:** Transient mild hypotension or hypertension. **GI:** Anorexia, nausea, vomiting, constipation. **Hematologic:** Leukopenia, <u>agranulocytosis</u>. **Special Senses:** *Blurred vision, dry mouth,* nose, or throat. **Skin:** Photosensitivity. **Urogenital:** Urinary retention.

DIAGNOSTIC TEST INTERFERENCE May interfere with ***blood grouping in ABO system*** and may produce false results with ***urinary pregnancy tests*** (***Gravindex, false-positive; Prepurex*** and ***Dap tests,*** false-negative). Promethazine can cause significant alterations of ***flare response*** in ***intradermal allergen tests*** if performed within 4 d of patient receiving promethazine.

INTERACTIONS Drug: Alcohol and other CNS DEPRESSANTS add to CNS depression and anticholinergic effects.

PHARMACOKINETICS Absorption: Readily from GI tract. **Onset:** 20 min PO/PR/IM; 5 min IV. **Duration:** 2–8 h. **Distribution:** Crosses placenta. **Metabolism:** In liver (CYP2D6, 2B6). **Elimination:** Slowly in urine and feces.

CLINICAL IMPLICATIONS

Assessment & Drug Effects
- Supervise ambulation. Promethazine sometimes produces marked sedation and dizziness.
- Be aware that antiemetic action may mask symptoms of unrecognized disease and signs of drug overdosage as well as dizziness, vertigo, or tinnitus associated with toxic doses of aspirin or other ototoxic drugs.
- Patients in pain may develop involuntary (athetoid) movements of upper extremities following parenteral administration. These symptoms usually disappear after pain is controlled.
- Monitor respiratory function in patients with respiratory problems, particularly children. Drug may suppress cough reflex and cause thickening of bronchial secretions.

Patient & Family Education
- For motion sickness: Take initial dose 30–60 min before anticipated travel and repeat at 8–12 h intervals if necessary. For duration of journey, repeat dose on arising and again at evening meal.
- Do not drive or engage in other potentially hazardous activities requiring mental alertness and normal reaction time until response to drug is known.
- Avoid sunlamps or prolonged exposure to sunlight. Use sunscreen lotion during initial drug therapy.
- Do not take OTC medications without physician's approval.
- Avoid alcohol and other CNS depressants.
- Relieve dry mouth by frequent rinses with water or by increasing noncaloric fluid intake (if allowed), chewing sugarless gum, or sucking hard candy. If these measures fail, add a saliva substitute (e.g., Moi-Stir, Orex, Xero-Lube).

PROPAFENONE

(pro-pa'fen-one)
Rythmol
Classifications: ANTIARRHYTHMIC CLASS IC
Therapeutic: ANTIARRHYTHMIC CLASS IC
Prototype: Flecainide
Pregnancy Category: C

AVAILABILITY 150 mg, 225 mg, 300 mg tablets

ACTION & *THERAPEUTIC EFFECT*

Class IC antiarrhythmic drug with a direct stabilizing action on myocardial membranes. Reduces spontaneous automaticity. Exerts a negative inotropic effect on the myocardium. *Appropriate dose and concentration decreases rate of single and multiple PVCs; additionally, it suppresses ventricular arrhythmias.*

USES Ventricular arrhythmias.
UNLABELED USES Atrial tachyarrhythmias, reentrant arrhythmias, Wolff-Parkinson-White syndrome.

CONTRAINDICATIONS Uncontrolled CHF, cardiogenic shock, sinoatrial, AV or intraventricular disorders (e.g., sick sinus node syndrome, AV block) without a pacemaker; cardiogenic shock; bradycardia, QT prolongation; marked hypotension; bronchospastic disorders; electrolyte imbalances; hypersensitivity to propafenone; nonlife-threatening arrhythmias; chronic bronchitis, emphysema; pregnancy (category C). Safety and efficacy in children are not established.
CAUTIOUS USE CHF, AV block; hepatic/renal impairment; older adult patients; lactation.

ROUTE & DOSAGE

Ventricular Arrhythmias

Adult: **PO** Initiate with 150 mg q8h, may be increased at 3–4 d intervals (max: 300 mg q8h)

ADMINISTRATION

- Dosage increments gradually are usually made with older adults or those with previous extensive myocardial damage.
- Significant dose reduction is warranted with severe liver dysfunction. Consult physician.
- Store at 15°–30° C (59°–86° F).

ADVERSE EFFECTS (≥1%) **CNS:**
Blurred vision, dizziness, paresthesias, fatigue, somnolence, vertigo, headache. **CV:** Arrhythmias, ventricular tachycardia, hypotension, bundle branch block, AV block, complete heart block, sinus arrest, CHF. **Hematologic:** Leukopenia, granulocytopenia (both rare). **GI:** Nausea, abdominal discomfort, constipation, vomiting, dry mouth, *taste alterations,* cholestatic hepatitis. **Skin:** Rash.

INTERACTIONS **Drug: Amiodarone, quinidine** increases the levels and toxicity of propafenone. May increase levels and toxicity of TRICYCLIC ANTIDEPRESSANTS, **cyclosporine, digoxin,** BETA BLOCKERS, **theophylline,** and **warfarin** may increase levels of both **propafenone** and **diltiazem. Phenobarbital** decreases levels of propafenone.

PHARMACOKINETICS **Absorption:** Readily from GI tract. **Peak:** 3.5 h. **Distribution:** 97% protein bound, highest concentrations in the lung. Crosses placenta, distributed into breast milk. **Metabolism:** Exten-

P

Common adverse effects in *italic,* life-threatening effects <u>underlined</u>; generic names in **bold**; classifications in SMALL CAPS; ♣ Canadian drug name; ⊕ Prototype drug

1285

sively metabolized in the liver. **Elimination:** 18.5–38% of dose excreted in urine as metabolites. **Half-Life:** 5–8 h.

CLINICAL IMPLICATIONS

Assessment & Drug Effects

- Monitor cardiovascular status frequently (e.g., ECG, Holter monitor) to determine effectiveness of drug and development of new or worsened arrhythmias.
- Monitor patients with preexisting CHF closely for worsening of this condition. Monitor for digoxin toxicity with concurrent use, because drug may increase serum digoxin levels.
- Report development of second- or third-degree AV block or significant widening of the QRS complex. Dosage adjustment may be warranted.

Patient & Family Education

- Report to physician any of following: Chest pain, palpitations, blurred or abnormal vision, dyspnea, or signs and symptoms of infection.
- Be aware when taking concurrent warfarin of possible increase in plasma levels that increase bleeding risk. Report unusual bleeding or bruising.
- Monitor radial pulse daily and report decreased heart rate or development of an abnormal heartbeat.
- Be aware of possibility of dizziness and need for caution with walking, especially in older adult or debilitated patients.

PROPANTHELINE BROMIDE

(proe-pan′the-leen)
Pro-Banthine, Propanthel ♦
Classifications: ANTICHOLINERGIC; ANTIMUSCARINIC AGENT; ANTISPASMODIC

Therapeutic: ANTISPASMODIC
Prototype: Atropine
Pregnancy Category: C

AVAILABILITY 7.5 mg, 15 mg tablets

ACTION & *THERAPEUTIC EFFECT*
Similar to atropine in peripheral effects. Has potent antimuscarinic activity and ganglionic blocking action. *Decreases motility (smooth muscle tone) in the GI, biliary, and urinary tracts. Results in antispasmodic action.*

USES Adjunct in treatment of peptic ulcer, irritable bowel syndrome, pancreatitis, ureteral and urinary bladder spasm. Also used prior to radiologic diagnostic procedures to reduce duodenal motility.

CONTRAINDICATIONS Pregnancy (category C); narrow-angle glaucoma; tachycardia; MI; paralytic ileus, GI obstructive disease; myasthenia gravis. Safety in children is not established.

CAUTIOUS USE CAD, CHF, cardiac arrhythmias; liver disease, ulcerative colitis, hiatus hernia, esophagitis; kidney disease; prostatic hypertrophy; glaucoma; debilitated patients; hyperthyroidism; autonomic neuropathy; brain damage; Down's syndrome; spastic disorders; lactation.

ROUTE & DOSAGE

Irritable Bowel Syndrome
Adult: **PO** 15 mg 30 min a.c. and 30 mg h.s. (max: 120 mg/d)
Geriatric: **PO** 7.5 mg 2–3 times/ d a.c. (max: 90 mg/d)

ADMINISTRATION

Oral

- Give 30–60 min before meals and at bedtime. Advise not to chew tablet; drug is bitter.

- Give at least 1 h before or 1 h after an antacid (or antidiarrheal agent).
- Store dry powder and tablets at 15°–30° C (59°–86° F); protect from freezing and moisture.

ADVERSE EFFECTS (≥1%) **GI:** *Constipation, dry mouth.* **Special Senses:** Blurred vision, mydriasis, increased intraocular pressure. **CNS:** Drowsiness. **Urogenital:** Decreased sexual activity, difficult urination.

INTERACTIONS Drug: Decreased absorption of **ketoconazole;** ORAL POTASSIUM may increase risk of GI ulcers. **Food:** Food significantly decreases absorption.

PHARMACOKINETICS Absorption: Incompletely from GI tract. **Onset:** 30–45 min. **Duration:** 4–6 h. **Metabolism:** 50% in GI tract before absorption; 50% in liver. **Elimination:** Primarily in urine; some in bile. **Half-Life:** 9 h.

CLINICAL IMPLICATIONS

Assessment & Drug Effects

- Assess bowel sounds, especially in presence of ulcerative colitis, since paralytic ileus may develop, predisposing to toxic megacolon.
- Be aware that older adult or debilitated patients may respond to a usual dose with agitation, excitement, confusion, drowsiness. Stop drug and report to physician if these symptoms are observed.
- Check BP, heart sounds and rhythm periodically in patients with cardiac disease.

Patient & Family Education

- Void just prior to each dose to minimize risk of urinary hesitancy or retention. Record daily urinary volume and report problems to physician.
- Relieve dry mouth by rinsing with water frequently, chewing sugar-free gum or sucking hard candy.

- Maintain adequate fluid and high-fiber food intake to prevent constipation.
- Make all position changes slowly and lie down immediately if faintness, weakness, or palpitations occur. Report symptoms to physician.
- Do not drive or engage in potentially hazardous activities until response to drug is known.

PROPOFOL

(pro′po-fol)
Diprivan
Classifications: GENERAL ANESTHESIA; SEDATIVE-HYPNOTIC
Therapeutic: SEDATIVE-HYPNOTIC; GENERAL ANESTHESIA
Prototype: Thiopental
Pregnancy Category: B

AVAILABILITY 10 mg/mL injection

ACTION & *THERAPEUTIC EFFECT*
Sedative-hypnotic used in the induction and maintenance of anesthesia or sedation. Rapid onset (40 sec) and minimal excitation during induction of anesthesia. *Effectively used for conscious sedation.*

USES Induction or maintenance of anesthesia as part of a balanced anesthesia technique; conscious sedation in mechanically ventilated patients.

CONTRAINDICATIONS Hypersensitivity to propofol or propofol emulsion, which contain soybean oil and egg phosphatide; obstetrical procedures; patients with increased intracranial pressure or impaired cerebral circulation; lactation. Do not use for conscious sedation in children <3 y.
CAUTIOUS USE Patients with severe cardiac or respiratory disorders or

P

Common adverse effects in *italic*, life-threatening effects <u>underlined</u>; generic names in **bold**; classifications in SMALL CAPS; ♣ Canadian drug name; ❷ Prototype drug

1287

history of epilepsy or seizures; pregnancy (category B).

ROUTE & DOSAGE

Induction of Anesthesia

Adult: **IV** 2–2.5 mg/kg q10sec until induction onset
Adult (over 55 years): **IV** 1–1.5 mg/kg q10sec until induction onset
Child: **IV** ≥3 y, 2.5–3.5 mg/kg over 20–30 sec

Maintenance of Anesthesia

Adult: **IV** 100–200 mcg/kg/min
Adult (over 55 years): **IV** 50–100 mcg/kg/min
Child: **IV** ≥3 y, 125–300 mcg/kg/min

Conscious Sedation

Adult: **IV** 5 mcg/kg/min for at least 5 min, may increase by 5–10 mcg/kg/min q5–10 min until desired level of sedation is achieved (may need maintenance rate of 5–80 mcg/kg/min)

ADMINISTRATION

▪ Use strict aseptic technique to prepare propofol for injection; drug emulsion supports rapid growth of microorganisms.
▪ Inspect ampuls and vials for particulate matter and discoloration. Discard if either is noted.
▪ Shake well before use. Inspect for separation of the emulsion. Do not use if there is evidence of separation of phases of the emulsion.

Intravenous

PREPARE: IV Infusion: Give undiluted or diluted in D5W to a concentration not less than 2 mg/mL. Must draw up into a sterile syringe immediately after ampules or vials are opened. Begin drug administration immediately and completed within 6 h.

ADMINISTER: IV Infusion: Use syringe or volumetric pump to control rate. Determine rate by weight. Administer immediately after spiking the vial. Complete infusion within 6 h.

INCOMPATIBILITIES Y-site: Amikacin, amphotericin B, ascorbic acid, atracurium, bretylium, calcium chloride, ciprofloxacin, cisatracurium, diazepam, digoxin, doxorubicin, gentamicin, levofloxacin, methotrexate, methylprednisolone, metoclopramide, minocycline, mitoxantrone, netilmicin, phenytoin, tobramycin, verapamil.

▪ Store unopened between 4° C (40° F) and 22° C (72° F). Refrigeration is not recommended. Protect from light.

ADVERSE EFFECTS (≥1%) **CNS:** Headache, dizziness, *twitching, bucking, jerking, thrashing, clonic/myoclonic movements.* **Special Senses:** Decreased intraocular pressure. **CV:** Hypotension, <u>ventricular asystole</u> (rare). **GI:** Vomiting, abdominal cramping. **Respiratory:** Cough, hiccups, apnea. **Other:** Pain at injection site.

DIAGNOSTIC TEST INTERFERENCE Propofol produces a temporary reduction in ***serum cortisol levels.*** However, propofol does not seem to inhibit adrenal responsiveness to ***ACTH.***

INTERACTIONS Drug: Concurrent continuous infusions of propofol and **alfentanil** produce higher plasma levels of **alfentanil** than expected. CNS DEPRESSANTS cause additive CNS depression.

PHARMACOKINETICS Onset: 9–36 sec. **Duration:** 6–10 min. **Distribution:** Highly lipophilic, crosses placenta, excreted in breast milk. **Metabolism:** Extensively in the liver (CYP 2B6, 2C9). **Elimination:** Approximately 88% of the dose is recovered in the urine as metabolites. **Half-Life:** 5–12 h.

CLINICAL IMPLICATIONS

Assessment & Drug Effects

- Monitor hemodynamic status and assess for dose-related hypotension.
- Take seizure precautions. Tonic-clonic seizures have occurred following general anesthesia with propofol.
- Be alert to the potential for drug induced excitation (e.g., twitching, tremor, hyperclonus) and take appropriate safety measures.
- Provide comfort measures; pain at the injection site is quite common especially when small veins are used.

PROPOXYPHENE HYDROCHLORIDE

(proe-pox′i-feen)
Darvon 642 ♦, Novopropoxyn ♦

PROPOXYPHENE NAPSYLATE

Darvon-N
Classifications: NARCOTIC (OPIATE) AGONIST, ANALGESIC
Therapeutic: NARCOTIC ANALGESIC, AGONIST
Prototype: Morphine
Pregnancy Category: C (D for prolonged use or at term)
Controlled Substance: Schedule IV

AVAILABILITY Napsylate 100 mg tablets **Hydrochloride** 65 mg capsules

ACTION & *THERAPEUTIC EFFECT*

Centrally acting opioid structurally related to methadone. Acts as a weak agonist at opiate receptors within the CNS. Analgesic potency about $^1/_2$–$^2/_3$ that of codeine. *Potent analgesic.*

USES Relief of mild to moderate pain.
UNLABELED USES To suppress narcotic withdrawal symptoms.

CONTRAINDICATIONS Hypersensitivity to drug; suicidal individuals; alcoholism; dependence on opiates; safety during pregnancy [category C (D for prolonged use or at term)] or in children is not established.
CAUTIOUS USE Kidney or liver disease; cardiac disease; biliary tract disease; pulmonary insufficiency.

ROUTE & DOSAGE

Mild to Moderate Pain
Adult: **PO** 65 mg HCl or 100 mg napsylate q4h prn (max: 390 mg HCl/d, 600 mg napsylate/d)

ADMINISTRATION

Note: 100 mg napsylate = 65 mg HCl

- Empty capsules and mix contents with water or food if unable to swallow capsule whole. ■ Be aware that absorption may be delayed by presence of food in stomach.
- Store at 15°–30° C (59°–86° F).

ADVERSE EFFECTS (≥1%) **CNS:** Dizziness, light-headedness, *drowsiness,* sedation, unusual fatigue or weakness, restlessness, tremor, euphoria, dysphoria, headache, paradoxic excitement, mental confusion, toxic psychosis, <u>coma, convulsions</u>. **GI:** Nausea, vomiting, abdominal pain, constipation, liver dysfunction. **Special Senses:** Minor visual

P

Common adverse effects in *italic*, life-threatening effects <u>underlined</u>; generic names in **bold**; classifications in SMALL CAPS; ♦ Canadian drug name; ☻ Prototype drug

1289

disturbances, pinpoint pupils (dilate with advancing hypoxia). **Skin:** Skin eruptions (hypersensitivity). **Metabolic:** Hypoglycemia (patients with impaired kidney function), acidosis, nephrogenic diabetes insipidus. **Respiratory:** <u>Respiratory depression</u>, pulmonary edema. **CV:** <u>Circulatory collapse</u>, ECG abnormalities.

INTERACTIONS Drug: **Alcohol** and other CNS DEPRESSANTS add to CNS depression, also fatalities reported with alcohol use; may increase hypoprothrombinemic effects of **warfarin**; may increase **carbamazepine** toxicity through decreased metabolism; **orphenadrine** increases CNS stimulation, anxiety, tremors, confusion. **Herbal:** **St. John's wort** may increase sedation.

PHARMACOKINETICS Absorption: Readily from upper part of small intestine. **Onset:** 15–60 min. **Peak:** 2–3 h. **Duration:** 4–6 h. **Distribution:** Crosses placenta; distributed into breast milk. **Metabolism:** In liver. **Elimination:** In urine. **Half-Life:** 6–12 h, 30–36 h for metabolite.

CLINICAL IMPLICATIONS

Assessment & Drug Effects
- Evaluate need for drug since abuse potential is high.
- Monitor CNS effects, respiratory status and therapeutic effectiveness.
- Overdose: Prompt action required; fatalities occur commonly within first hour following overdosage.

Patient & Family Education
- Do not drive or engage in potentially hazardous activities until response to drug is known.
- Do not exceed recommended dose; do not use alcohol and

other CNS depressants with propoxyphene.
- Lie down if dizziness, light-headedness, drowsiness, nausea, or vomiting occur while ambulating.
- Be aware that tolerance and physical or psychic dependence of the morphine type can occur with excessive use.

PROPRANOLOL HYDROCHLORIDE 🅟

(proe-pran′oh-lole)

Apo-Propranolol ◆, Inderal, Inderal LA, InnoPran XL, Novopranol ◆

Classifications: BETA-ADRENERGIC ANTAGONIST; ANTIHYPERTENSIVE AGENT; ANTIARRHYTHMIC, CLASS II
Therapeutic: ANTIHYPERTENSIVE; ANTIARRHYTHMIC, CLASS II
Pregnancy Category: C

AVAILABILITY 10 mg, 20 mg, 40 mg, 60 mg, 80 mg, 90 mg tablets; 60 mg, 80 mg, 120 mg, 160 mg sustained release capsules; 4 mg/mL, 8 mg/mL, 80 mg/mL solution; 1 mg/mL injection

ACTION & *THERAPEUTIC EFFECT*
Nonselective beta-blocker of both cardiac and bronchial adrenoreceptors that competes with epinephrine and norepinephrine for available beta-receptor sites. In higher doses, exerts direct quinidine-like effects, that depresses cardiac function including contractility and arrhythmias. Lowers both supine and standing blood pressures in hypertensive patients. Mechanism of antimigraine action unknown but thought to be related to inhibition of cerebral vasodilation and arteriolar spasms. *Blocks cardiac effects of beta-adrenergic stimulation; as a*

P

result, reduces heart rate, myocardial irritability (Class II antiarrhythmic), and force of contraction, depresses automaticity of sinus node and ectopic pacemaker, and decreases AV and intraventricular conduction velocity. Hypotensive effect is associated with decreased cardiac output, suppressed renin activity, as well as beta-blockade; decreases platelet aggregation.

USES Management of cardiac arrhythmias, myocardial infarction, tachyarrhythmias associated with digitalis intoxication, anesthesia, and thyrotoxicosis, hypertrophic subaortic stenosis, angina pectoris due to coronary atherosclerosis, pheochromocytoma, hereditary essential tremor; also treatment of hypertension alone, but generally with a thiazide or other antihypertensives.

UNLABELED USES Anxiety states, migraine prophylaxis, essential tremors, schizophrenia, tardive dyskinesia, acute panic symptoms (e.g., stage fright), recurrent GI bleeding in cirrhotic patients, treatment of aggression and rage.

CONTRAINDICATIONS Greater than first-degree heart block; CHF, right ventricular failure secondary to pulmonary hypertension; ventricular dysfunction; sinus bradycardia, cardiogenic shock, significant aortic or mitral valvular disease; bronchial asthma or bronchospasm, severe COPD, pulmonary edema, allergic rhinitis during pollen season; concurrent use with adrenergic-augmenting psychotropic drugs or within 2 wk of MAO inhibition therapy; abrupt discontinuation; major depression; peripheral vascular disease, Raynaud's disease; pregnancy (category C).
CAUTIOUS USE Peripheral arterial insufficiency; history of systemic insect sting reaction; patients prone to nonallergenic bronchospasm (e.g., chronic bronchitis, emphysema); major surgery; cerebrovascular disease, stroke; renal or hepatic disease; pheochromocytoma, vasospastic angina; older adults; diabetes mellitus; patients prone to hypoglycemia; hyperthyroidism, thyrotoxicosis; surgery; myasthenia gravis; Wolff-Parkinson-White syndrome; lactation.

ROUTE & DOSAGE

Hypertension
Adult: **PO** 40 mg b.i.d., usually need 160–480 mg/d in divided doses; **InnoPran XL** dose 80 mg q hs, may increase to 120 mg hs
Child: **PO** 0.5–1 mg/kg/d in 2 divided doses (max: 16 mg/kg/d)
Neonate: **PO** 0.25 mg/kg q6–8h (max: 5 mg/kg/d) **IV** 0.01 mg/kg slow IV push over 10 min q6–8h prn (max: 0.15 mg/kg q6–8h)

Angina
Adult: **PO** 80–320 mg mg/d in divided doses

Arrhythmias
Adult: **PO** 10–30 mg q6–8h **IV** 0.5–3 mg q4h prn
Child: **PO** 0.5–1 mg/kg/d in divided doses, titrate up to daily dose of 2–6 mg/kg/d (max: 16 mg/kg/d) **IV** 0.01–0.1 mg/kg/min over 10 min (infant max: 1 mg, child max: 3 mg)

Acute MI
Adult: **PO** 180–240 mg/d in divided doses

Migraine Prophylaxis
Adult: **PO** 80 mg/d in divided doses, may need 160–240 mg/d
Hemodialysis: No supplemental dose needed

P

Common adverse effects in *italic*, life-threatening effects <u>underlined</u>; generic names in **bold**; classifications in SMALL CAPS; ✦ Canadian drug name; ⊙ Prototype drug

1291

ADMINISTRATION

- Do not give within 2 wk of a MAO inhibitor.
- Note that InnoPran XL should be given hs.
- Be consistent with regard to giving with food or on an empty stomach to minimize variations in absorption.
- Take apical pulse and BP before administering drug. Withhold drug if heart rate <60 bpm or systolic BP <90 mm Hg. Consult physician for parameters.
- Ensure that sustained release form is not chewed or crushed. Must be swallowed whole.
- Reduce dosage gradually over a period of 1–2 wk and monitor patient closely when discontinued.

Intravenous

Note: Verify correct IV concentration and rate of infusion for neonates with physician.

PREPARE: **Direct:** Give undiluted or dilute each 1 mg in 10 mL of D5W. **Intermittent:** Dilute a single dose in 50 mL of NS.

ADMINISTER: **Direct:** Give each 1 mg over 1 min. **Intermittent:** Give each dose over 15–20 min.

INCOMPATIBILITIES **Y-site: Amphotericin B cholesteryl complex, diazoxide.**

- Store at 15°–30° C (59°–86° F) in tightly closed, light-resistant containers.

ADVERSE EFFECTS (≥1%) **Body as a Whole:** Fever; pharyngitis; respiratory distress, weight gain, LE-like reaction, cold extremities, leg fatigue, arthralgia, <u>anaphylactic/anaphylactoid reactions</u>. **Urogenital:** Impotence or decreased libido. **Skin:** Erythematous, psoriasis-like eruptions; pruritus, <u>Stevens-Johnson syndrome, toxic epidermal necrolysis</u>, erythema multiforme, <u>exfoliative dermatitis</u>, urticaria. Reversible alopecia, hyperkeratoses of scalp, palms, feet; nail changes, dry skin. **CNS:** Drug-induced psychosis, sleep disturbances, depression, *confusion,* agitation, giddiness, light-headedness, *fatigue,* vertigo, syncope, weakness, *drowsiness,* insomnia, vivid dreams, visual hallucinations, delusions, reversible organic brain syndrome. **CV:** Palpitation, profound *bradycardia,* AV heart block, cardiac standstill, hypotension, angina pectoris, tachyarrhythmia, acute CHF, peripheral arterial insufficiency resembling Raynaud's disease, myotonia, paresthesia of *hands.* **Special Senses:** Dry eyes (gritty sensation), visual disturbances, conjunctivitis, tinnitus, hearing loss, nasal stuffiness. **GI:** Dry mouth, nausea, vomiting, heartburn, diarrhea, constipation, flatulence, abdominal cramps, mesenteric arterial thrombosis, ischemic colitis, pancreatitis. **Hematologic:** Transient eosinophilia, thrombocytopenic or nonthrombocytopenic purpura, <u>agranulocytosis</u>. **Metabolic:** Hypoglycemia, hyperglycemia, hypocalcemia (patients with hyperthyroidism). **Respiratory:** Dyspnea, <u>laryngospasm</u>, bronchospasm.

DIAGNOSTIC TEST INTERFERENCE

BETA-ADRENERGIC BLOCKERS may produce false-negative test results in exercise tolerance ECG tests, and elevations in *serum potassium, peripheral platelet count, serum uric acid, serum transaminase, alkaline phosphatase, lactate dehydrogenase, serum creatinine, BUN,* and an increase or decrease in *blood glucose* levels in diabetic patients.

INTERACTIONS Drug: PHENOTHIA-ZINES have additive hypotensive effects. BETA-ADRENERGIC AGONISTS (e.g., **albuterol**) antagonize effects. **Atropine** and TRICYCLIC ANTIDEPRESSANTS block bradycardia. DIURETICS and other HYPOTENSIVE AGENTS increase hypotension. High doses of **tubocurarine** may potentiate neuromuscular blockade. **Cimetidine** decreases clearance, increases effects. ANTACIDS, **ascorbic acid** may decrease absorption. **Herbal: Black pepper** may increase plasma levels.

PHARMACOKINETICS Absorption: Completely from GI tract; undergoes extensive first-pass metabolism. **Peak:** 60–90 min immediate release; 6 h sustained release; 5 min IV. **Distribution:** Widely distributed including CNS, placenta, and breast milk. **Metabolism:** Almost completely in liver (CYP1A2, 2D6). **Elimination:** 90–95% in urine as metabolites; 1–4% in feces. **Half-Life:** 2.3 h.

CLINICAL IMPLICATIONS

Assessment & Drug Effects

- Obtain careful medical history to rule out allergies, asthma, and obstructive pulmonary disease. Propranolol can cause bronchiolar constriction even in normal subjects.
- Monitor apical pulse, respiration, BP, and circulation to extremities closely throughout period of dosage adjustment. Consult physician for acceptable parameters.
- Evaluate adequate control or dosage interval for patients being treated for hypertension by checking blood pressure near end of dosage interval or before administration of next dose.
- Be aware that adverse reactions occur most frequently following IV administration soon after therapy is initiated; however, incidence is also high following oral use in the older adult and in patients with impaired kidney function. Reactions may or may not be dose related.
- Lab tests: Obtain periodic hematologic, kidney, liver, and cardiac functions when propranolol is given for prolonged periods.
- Monitor I&O ratio and daily weight as significant indexes for detecting fluid retention and developing heart failure.
- Consult physician regarding allowable salt intake. Drug plasma volume may increase with consequent risk of CHF if dietary sodium is not restricted in patients not receiving concomitant diuretic therapy.
- Fasting for more than 12 h may induce hypoglycemic effects fostered by propranolol.
- If patient complains of cold, painful, or tender feet or hands, examine carefully for evidence of impaired circulation. Peripheral pulses may still be present even though circulation is impaired. Caution patient to avoid prolonged exposure of extremities to cold.

Patient & Family Education

- Learn usual pulse rate and take radial pulse before each dose. Report to physician if pulse is below the established parameter or becomes irregular.
- Be aware that propranolol suppresses clinical signs of hypoglycemia (e.g., BP changes, increased pulse rate) and may prolong hypoglycemia.
- Understand importance of compliance. Do not alter established regimen (i.e., do not omit, increase, or decrease dosage or change dosage interval).
- Do not discontinue abruptly; can precipitate withdrawal syndrome

P

Common adverse effects in *italic*, life-threatening effects underlined; generic names in **bold**; classifications in SMALL CAPS; ♣ Canadian drug name; ⓟ Prototype drug

1293

(e.g., tremulousness, sweating, severe headache, malaise, palpitation, rebound hypertension, MI, and life-threatening arrhythmias in patients with angina pectoris).

- Be aware that drug may cause mild hypotension (experienced as dizziness or lightheadedness) in normotensive patients on prolonged therapy. Make position changes slowly and avoid prolonged standing. Notify physician if symptoms persist.
- Do not drive or engage in potentially hazardous activities until response to drug is known.
- Consult physician before self-medicating with OTC drugs.
- Inform dentist, surgeon, or ophthalmologist that you are taking propranolol (drug lowers normal and elevated intraocular pressure).

PROPYLTHIOURACIL (PTU) ℗

(proe-pill-thye-oh-yoor'a-sill)
Propyl-Thyracil ✦
Classifications: HORMONE; ANTITHYROID AGENT
Therapeutic: ANTITHYROID
Pregnancy Category: D

AVAILABILITY 50 mg tablets

ACTION & *THERAPEUTIC EFFECT*
Interferes with use of iodine and blocks synthesis of thyroxine (T₄) and triiodothyronine (T₃). Does not interfere with release and utilization of stored thyroid hormone; thus antithyroid action is delayed days and weeks until preformed T₃ and T₄ are degraded. *Drug-induced hormone reduction results in compensatory release of thyrotropin (TSH), which causes marked hyperplasia and vascularization of thyroid gland.*

USES Hyperthyroidism, iodine-induced thyrotoxicosis, and hyperthyroidism associated with thyroiditis; to establish euthyroidism prior to surgery or radioactive iodine treatment; palliative control of toxic nodular goiter.

CONTRAINDICATIONS Hypersensitivity to propylthiouracil; concurrent administration of sulfonamides or coal tar derivatives such as aminopyrine or antipyrine; pregnancy (category D).

CAUTIOUS USE Infection; concomitant administration of anticoagulants or other drugs known to cause agranulocytosis; bone marrow depression; impaired liver function.

ROUTE & DOSAGE

Hyperthyroidism

Adult: **PO** 300–450 mg/d divided q8h, may need 600–1200 mg/d initially
Geriatric: **PO** 150–300 mg/d divided q8h
Child: **PO** 6–10 y, 50–150 mg/d; >10 y, 150–300 mg/d or 150 mg/m²/d
Neonates: **PO** 5–10 mg/kg/d

Thyrotoxic Crisis

Adult: **PO** 200 mg q4–6h until full control achieved

ADMINISTRATION

- Give at the same time each day with relation to meals. Food may alter drug response by changing absorption rate.
- If drug is being used to improve thyroid state before radioactive iodine (RAI) treatment, discontinued 3 or 4 d before treatment to prevent uptake interference. PTU therapy may be resumed if neces-

sary 3–5 d after the RAI administration.

▪ Store drug at 15°–30° C (59°–86° F) in light-resistant container.

ADVERSE EFFECTS (≥1%) **CNS:** Paresthesias, headache, vertigo, drowsiness, neuritis. **GI:** Nausea, vomiting, diarrhea, dyspepsia, loss of taste, sialoadenitis, hepatitis. **Hematologic:** Myelosuppression, lymphadenopathy, periarteritis, hypoprothrombinemia, thrombocytopenia, leukopenia, <u>agranulocytosis</u>. **Metabolic:** Hypothyroidism (goitrogenic): Enlarged thyroid, reduced GI motility, periorbital edema, puffy hands and feet, bradycardia, cool and pale skin, worsening of ophthalmopathy, sleepiness, fatigue, mental depression, dizziness, vertigo, sensitivity to cold, paresthesias, nocturnal muscle cramps, changes in menstrual periods, unusual weight gain. **Skin:** Skin rash, urticaria, pruritus, hyperpigmentation, lightening of hair color, abnormal hair loss. **Body as a Whole:** Drug fever, lupus-like syndrome, arthralgia, myalgia, hypersensitivity vasculitis.

DIAGNOSTIC TEST INTERFERENCE Propylthiouracil may elevate *prothrombin time* and serum *alkaline phosphatase, AST, ALT* levels.

INTERACTIONS Drug: A m i o d a - r o n e, potassium iodide, sodium iodide, THYROID HORMONES can reverse efficacy.

PHARMACOKINETICS Absorption: Rapidly from GI tract. **Peak:** 1–1.5 h. **Distribution:** Appears to concentrate in thyroid gland; crosses placenta; some distribution into breast milk. **Metabolism:** Rapidly to inactive metabolites. **Elimination:** 35% in urine within 24 h. **Half-Life:** 1–2 h.

CLINICAL IMPLICATIONS

Assessment & Drug Effects

▪ Be aware that about 10% of patients with hyperthyroidism have leukopenia <4000 cells/mm^3 and relative granulopenia.

▪ Observe for signs of clinical response to PTU (usually within 2 or 3 wk): Significant weight gain, reduced pulse rate, reduced serum T_4.

▪ Lab tests: Baseline and periodic T_3 and T_4; periodic CBC with differential and platelet count.

▪ Satisfactory euthyroid state may be delayed for several months when thyroid gland is greatly enlarged.

▪ Be alert to signs of hypoprothrombinemia: Ecchymoses, purpura, petechiae, unexplained bleeding. Warn ambulatory patients to report these signs promptly.

▪ Be alert for important diagnostic signs of excess dosage: Contraction of a muscle bundle when pricked, mental depression, hard and nonpitting edema, and need for high thermostat setting and extra blankets in winter (cold intolerance).

▪ Monitor for urticaria (occurs in 3–7% of patients during weeks 2–8 of treatment). Report severe rash.

Patient & Family Education

▪ Note that PTU treatment may be reinstituted if surgery fails to produce normal thyroid gland function.

▪ Be aware that thyroid hormone may be given concomitantly with PTU throughout pregnancy to prevent hypothyroidism in mother with little effect on fetus.

▪ Report severe skin rash or swelling of cervical lymph nodes. Therapy may be discontinued.

▪ Report to physician sore throat, fever, and rash immediately (most apt to occur in first few months of

P

Common adverse effects in *italic*, life-threatening effects <u>underlined</u>; generic names in **bold**; classifications in SMALL CAPS; ♣ Canadian drug name; ⊘ Prototype drug

1295

treatment). Drug will be discontinued and hematologic studies initiated.

- Avoid use of OTC drugs for asthma, or cough treatment without checking with the physician. Iodides sometimes included in such preparations are contraindicated.
- Learn how to take pulse accurately and check daily. Report to physician continued tachycardia.
- Report diarrhea, fever, irritability, listlessness, vomiting, weakness; these are signs of inadequate therapy or thyrotoxicosis.
- Chart weight 2 or 3 times weekly; clinical response is monitored through changes in weight and pulse.
- Continue monitoring and recording weight and pulse rate while in remission. Report onset of tremor, anxiety state, gradual ascending pulse rate, and loss of weight to physician (signs of hormone deficiency).
- Do not alter drug regimen (e.g., increase, decrease, omit doses, change dosage intervals).
- Check with physician about use of iodized salt and inclusion of seafood in the diet.

PROTAMINE SULFATE

(proe′ta-meen)
Classifications: ANTIDOTE
Therapeutic: ANTIDOTE
Pregnancy Category: C

AVAILABILITY 10 mg/mL injection

ACTION & *THERAPEUTIC EFFECT*
Because protamine is strongly basic, it combines with strongly acidic heparin to produce a stable complex; thus anticoagulant effect of both drugs is neutralized. *Effective antidote to heparin overdose.*

USES Antidote for heparin overdosage (after heparin has been discontinued).

UNLABELED USES Antidote for heparin administration during extracorporeal circulation.

CONTRAINDICATIONS Hemorrhage not induced by heparin overdosage; pregnancy (category C); lactation.

CAUTIOUS USE Cardiovascular disease; history of allergy to fish; vasectomized or infertile males; diabetes mellitus; patients who have received protamine-containing insulin.

ROUTE & DOSAGE

Antidote for Heparin Overdose
Adult/Child: **IV** 1 mg for every 100 units of heparin to be neutralized (max: 100 mg in a 2 h period), give the first 25–50 mg by slow direct IV and the rest over 2–3 h

ADMINISTRATION

Note: Titrate dose carefully to prevent excess anticoagulation because protamine has a longer half-life than heparin and also has some anticoagulant effect of its own.

Intravenous
Note: Verify correct IV concentration and rate of infusion for infants or children with physician.

PREPARE: **Direct:** Reconstitute each 50 mg with 5 mL of sterile water for injection. Shake until dissolved. **Continuous:** Further dilute in 50 mL or more of NS or D5W.

ADMINISTER: **Direct:** Give each 50 mg or fraction thereof slowly over 10–15 min. NEVER give more than 50 mg in any 10 min period or 100 mg in any 2 h period. **Continuous:** Do not exceed direct rate. Give over 2–3 h or longer as determined by coagulation studies.

INCOMPATIBILITIES Solution/additive: RADIOCONTRAST MATERIALS, **furosemide.**

■ Store protamine sulfate injection at 2°–8° C (36°–46° F); protamine powder for injection and reconstituted solution at 15°–30° C (59°–86° F). Solutions are stable for 72 h at this temperature.

ADVERSE EFFECTS (≥1%) **CV:** *Abrupt drop in BP* (with rapid IV infusion), bradycardia. **Body as a Whole:** Urticaria, angioedema, pulmonary edema, anaphylaxis, dyspnea, lassitude; transient flushing and feeling of warmth. **GI:** Nausea, vomiting. **Hematologic:** Protamine overdose or "heparin rebound" (hyperheparinemia).

INTERACTIONS No clinically significant interactions established.

PHARMACOKINETICS Onset: 5 min. **Duration:** 2 h.

CLINICAL IMPLICATIONS

Assessment & Drug Effects

■ Do not use protamine if only minor bleeding occurs during heparin therapy because withdrawal of heparin will usually correct minor bleeding within a few hours.

■ Monitor BP and pulse q15–30min, or more often if indicated. Continue for at least 2–3 h after each dose, or longer as dictated by patient's condition. Be prepared to treat patient for shock as well as hemorrhage.

■ Lab tests: Monitor effect of protamine in neutralizing heparin by aPTT or ACT values. Coagulation tests are usually performed 5–15 min after administration of protamine, and again in 2–8 h if desirable.

■ Observe patients undergoing extracorporeal dialysis or patients who have had cardiac surgery carefully for bleeding (heparin rebound). Even with apparent adequate neutralization of heparin by protamine, bleeding may occur 30 min to 18 h after surgery. Monitor vital signs closely. Additional protamine may be required in these patients.

PROTRIPTYLINE HYDROCHLORIDE

(proe-trip′te-leen)

Triptil ♦, **Vivactil**

Classifications: PSYCHOTHERAPEUTIC; TRICYCLIC ANTIDEPRESSANT

Therapeutic: ANTIDEPRESSANT, TRICYCLIC

Prototype: Imipramine

Pregnancy Category: C

AVAILABILITY 5 mg, 10 mg tablets

ACTION & *THERAPEUTIC EFFECT*
Tricyclic antidepressant (TCA) with more rapid onset of action than imipramine. Has little if any sedative properties characteristic of most other TCAs. It is believed that their most important effect is to enhance the actions of norepinephrine and serotonin by blocking their reuptake at the neuronal membrane. *TCAs potentiate both norepinephrine and serotonin in CNS by blocking their reuptake by presynaptic neurons. Effective in the treatment of mentally depressed individuals, particularly those who are withdrawn.*

USES Symptomatic treatment of endogenous depression in patients under close medical supervision.

Particularly effective for depression manifested by psychomotor retardation, apathy, and fatigue.

CONTRAINDICATIONS Hypersensitivity to TCAs; use in children; concurrent use of MAOIS; during acute recovery phase following MI; QT prolongation, bundle branch block; cardiac conduction defects; suicidal ideation; pregnancy (category C).

CAUTIOUS USE Hepatic, cardiovascular, or kidney dysfunction; diabetes mellitus; hyperthyroidism; history of alcoholism; patients with insomnia; asthma; bipolar disorder; suicidal tendencies; lactation.

ROUTE & DOSAGE

Antidepressant
Adult: **PO** 15–40 mg/d in 3–4 divided doses (max: 60 mg/d)
Adolescent: **PO** 15 mg/d in divided doses

ADMINISTRATION

- Give whole or crush and mix with fluid or food.
- Give dosage increases in the morning dose to prevent sleep interference and because this TCA has psychic energizing action.
- Give last dose of day no later than midafternoon; insomnia rather than drowsiness is a frequent adverse effect.
- Store at 15°–30° C (59°–86° F) in tightly closed container.

ADVERSE EFFECTS (≥1%) **Body as a Whole:** Photosensitivity, <u>edema</u> (general or of face and <u>tongue</u>). **GI:** *Xerostomia, constipation,* paralytic ileus. **Special Senses:** Blurred vision. **Urogenital:** *Urinary retention.* **CNS:** Insomnia, headache, confusion. **CV:** Change in heat or cold tolerance; *orthostatic hypotension, tachycardia.*

INTERACTIONS Drug: May decrease some response to ANTIHYPERTENSIVES; CNS DEPRESSANTS, **alcohol,** HYPNOTICS, BARBITURATES, SEDATIVES potentiate CNS depression; ORAL ANTICOAGULANTS may increase hypoprothrombinemic effects; **ethchlorvynol** causes transient delirium; **levodopa** SYMPATHOMIMETICS (e.g., **epinephrine, norepinephrine**) increases possibility of sympathetic hyperactivity with hypertension and hyperpyrexia; MAO INHIBITORS present possibility of severe reactions—toxic psychosis, cardiovascular instability; **methylphenidate** increases plasma TCA levels; THYROID DRUGS may increase possibility of arrhythmias; **cimetidine** may increase plasma TCA levels. **Herbal: Ginkgo** may decrease seizure threshold; **St. John's wort** may cause **serotonin** syndrome (headache, dizziness, sweating, agitation).

PHARMACOKINETICS Absorption: Rapidly from GI tract. **Peak levels:** 24–30 h. **Distribution:** Crosses placenta; distributed into breast milk. **Metabolism:** In liver. **Elimination:** Primarily in urine. **Half-Life:** 54–98 h.

CLINICAL IMPLICATIONS

Assessment & Drug Effects
- Monitor therapeutic effectiveness. Onset of initial effect characterized by increased activity and energy is fairly rapid, usually within 1 wk after therapy is initiated. Maximum effect may not occur for 2 wk or more.
- Monitor adolescents as well as adults for changes in behavior that may indicate suicidality.
- Monitor vital signs closely and CV system responses during early therapy, particularly in patients with cardiovascular disorders and older adults receiving daily doses in excess of 20 mg. Withhold

drug and inform physician if BP falls more than 20 mm Hg or if there is a sudden increase in pulse rate.

- Lab tests: Obtain periodic liver function and blood cell counts in patients receiving large doses for prolonged periods or in combination with other drugs.

- Monitor I&O ratio and question patient about bowel regularity during early therapy and when patient is on large doses.

- Assess and advise physician as indicated for prominent anticholinergic effects (xerostomia, blurred vision, constipation, paralytic ileus, urinary retention, delayed micturition).

- Assess condition of oral membranes frequently; institute symptomatic treatment if necessary. Xerostomia can interfere with appetite, fluid intake, and integrity of tooth surfaces.

- Supervise patient closely during early treatment period. Suicide is an inherent risk with any depressed patient and may remain until there is significant improvement.

- Bear in mind that the potentiation of TCA effects may increase the danger of overdosage or suicide attempt (especially in patients who use excessive amounts of alcohol).

Patient & Family Education

- Consult physician about safe amount of alcohol, if any, that can be taken. Actions of both alcohol and protriptyline are potentiated when used together for up to 2 wk after the TCA is discontinued.

- Stop or to reduce smoking; smoking reduces TCAs effectiveness. Apparent treatment failure may be due to the nicotine effect.

- Consult physician before taking any OTC medications.

- Be aware that effects of barbiturates and other CNS depressants are enhanced by TCAs.

- Avoid potentially hazardous activities requiring alertness and skill until response to drug is known.

- Avoid exposure to the sun without protecting skin with sunscreen lotion (SPF >12). Photosensitivity reactions may occur.

PSEUDOEPHEDRINE HYDROCHLORIDE

(soo-doe-e-fed′rin)
Cenafed, Decongestant Syrup, Dorcol Children's Decongestant, Eltor ◆, Eltor 120 ◆, Halofed, Novafed, PediaCare, Pseudofrin ◆, Robidrine ◆, Sudafed, Sudrin
Classifications: ALPHA- AND BETA-ADRENERGIC AGONIST; DECONGESTANT
Therapeutic: DECONGESTANT
Prototype: Epinephrine
Pregnancy Category: C

AVAILABILITY 30 mg, 60 mg tablets; 120 mg, 240 mg sustained release tablets; 15 mg/5 mL, 30 mg/5 mL liquid; 7.5 mg/0.8 mL drops

ACTION & *THERAPEUTIC EFFECT*
Sympathomimetic amine that produces decongestion of respiratory tract mucosa by stimulating the sympathetic nerve endings including alpha-, beta-1, and beta-2 receptors. Also acts directly on smooth muscle and constricts renal and vertebral arteries. *Effective as a nasal decongestant by causing vasoconstriction and thus increasing nasal airway patency.*

USES Symptomatic relief of nasal congestion associated with rhinitis, coryza, and sinusitis and for eustachian tube congestion.

Common adverse effects in *italic*, life-threatening effects underlined; generic names in **bold**; classifications in SMALL CAPS; ◆ Canadian drug name; ⦿ Prototype drug

1299

CONTRAINDICATIONS Hypersensitivity to sympathomimetic amines; severe hypertension; severe coronary artery disease; use within 14 d of MAOIS; hyperthyroidism; prostatic hypertrophy; pregnancy (category C). Safe use in children <2 y is not established.

CAUTIOUS USE Hypertension, heart disease, renal impairment; acute MI, angina; closed-angle glaucoma; concurrent use of ACE INHIBITOR.

ROUTE & DOSAGE

Nasal Congestion
Adult: **PO** 60 mg q4–6h or 120 mg sustained release q12h
Geriatric: **PO** 30–60 mg q6h prn
Child: **PO** 2–6 y, 15 mg q4–6h (max: 60 mg/d); 6–11 y, 30 mg q4–6h (max: 120 mg/d)

ADMINISTRATION

Oral
- Ensure that sustained release form is not chewed or crushed. Must be swallowed whole.

ADVERSE EFFECTS (≥1%) **Body as a Whole:** *Transient stimulation,* tremulousness, difficulty in voiding. **CV:** Arrhythmias, palpitation, *tachycardia.* **CNS:** *Nervousness,* dizziness, headache, sleeplessness, numbness of extremities. **GI:** Anorexia, dry mouth, nausea, vomiting.

INTERACTIONS Drug: Other SYMPATHOMIMETICS increase pressor effects and toxicity; MAO INHIBITORS may precipitate hypertensive crisis; BETA BLOCKERS may increase pressor effects; may decrease antihypertensive effects of **guanethidine, methyldopa, reserpine.**

PHARMACOKINETICS Absorption: Readily from GI tract. **Onset:** 15–30 min. **Duration:** 4–6 h (8–12 h sustained release). **Distribution:** Crosses placenta; distributed into breast milk. **Metabolism:** Partially metabolized in liver. **Elimination:** In urine.

CLINICAL IMPLICATIONS

Assessment & Drug Effects
- Monitor HR and BP, especially in those with a history of cardiac disease. Report tachycardia or hypertension.

Patient & Family Education
- Avoid taking it within 2 h of bedtime because drug may act as a stimulant.
- Discontinue medication and consult physician if extreme restlessness or signs of sensitivity occur.
- Consult physician before concomitant use of OTC medications; many contain ephedrine or other sympathomimetic amines and might intensify action of pseudoephedrine.

PSYLLIUM HYDROPHILIC MUCILLOID ⊙

(sill'i-um)

Hydrocil, Instant, Karasil ♦, Konsyl, Metamucil, Modane Bulk, Perdiem Plain, Reguloid, Serutan, Siblin, Syllact, V-Lax
Classifications: BULK LAXATIVE
Therapeutic: BULK LAXATIVE
Pregnancy Category: C

AVAILABILITY 3.4 g/dose powder; 2.5 g, 3.4 g, 4.03 g/teaspoon granules

ACTION & *THERAPEUTIC EFFECT*
Bulk-producing laxative that promotes peristalsis and natural elimination. Highly refined colloid of psyllium seed. Absorbs liquid in

Common adverse effects in *italic*, life-threatening effects underlined; generic names in **bold**; classifications in SMALL CAPS; ♦ Canadian drug name; ⊙ Prototype drug

the GI tract, resulting in an alteration in facilitating peristalsis and bowel motility. *Bulk-producing laxative that promotes peristalsis and natural elimination.*

USES Chronic atonic or spastic constipation and constipation associated with rectal disorders or anorectal surgery.

CONTRAINDICATIONS Esophageal and intestinal obstruction, dysphagia; nausea, vomiting, fecal impaction, acute abdomen; undiagnosed abdominal pain, appendicitis; pregnancy (category C), children <2 y.
CAUTIOUS USE Diabetics; pregnancy (category C), lactation.

ROUTE & DOSAGE

Constipation or Diarrhea
Adult: **PO** 1–2 rounded tsp or 1 packet 1–3 times/d prn
Child: **PO** >6 y, 1 tsp in water h.s.

ADMINISTRATION

Oral
- Fill an 8-oz (240-mL) water glass with cool water, milk, fruit juice, or other liquid; sprinkle powder into liquid; stir briskly; and give immediately (if effervescent form is used, add liquid to powder). Granules should not be chewed.
- Follow each dose with an additional glass of liquid to obtain best results.
- Exercise caution with older adult patient who may aspirate the drug.

ADVERSE EFFECTS (≥1%) **Hematologic:** Eosinophilia. **GI:** *Nausea and vomiting, diarrhea* (with excessive use); GI tract strictures when drug used in dry form, abdominal cramps.

INTERACTIONS Drug: Psyllium may decrease absorption and clinical effects of ANTIBIOTICS, **warfarin, digoxin, nitrofurantoin,** SALICYLATES.

PHARMACOKINETICS Absorption: Not absorbed from GI tract. **Onset:** 12–24 h. **Peak:** 1–3 d.

CLINICAL IMPLICATIONS

Assessment & Drug Effects
- Report promptly to physician if patient complains of retrosternal pain after taking the drug. Drug may be lodged as a gelatinous mass (because of poor mixing) in the esophagus.
- Monitor therapeutic effectiveness. When psyllium is used as either a bulk laxative or to treat diarrhea, the expected effect is formed stools. Laxative effect usually occurs within 12–24 h. Administration for 2 or 3 d may be needed to establish regularity.
- Assess for complaints of abdominal fullness. Smaller, more frequent doses spaced throughout the day may be indicated to relieve discomfort of abdominal fullness.
- Monitor warfarin and digoxin levels closely if either is given concurrently.

Patient & Family Education
- Note sugar and sodium content of preparation if on low-sodium or low-calorie diet. Some preparations contain natural sugars, whereas others contain artificial sweeteners.
- Understand that drug works to relieve both diarrhea and constipation by restoring a more normal moisture level to stool.
- Be aware that drug may reduce appetite if it is taken before meals.

P

Common adverse effects in *italic*, life-threatening effects underlined; generic names in **bold**; classifications in SMALL CAPS; ♣ Canadian drug name; ♦ Prototype drug

1301

PYRANTEL PAMOATE

(pi-ran'tel)
Antiminth, Pin-Rid
Classifications: ANTHELMINTIC
Therapeutic: ANTHELMINTIC
Prototype: Mebendazole
Pregnancy Category: C

AVAILABILITY 180 mg capsules; 50 mg/mL suspension

ACTION & *THERAPEUTIC EFFECT*
Exerts selective depolarizing neuromuscular blocking action, which results in spastic paralysis of worm; also inhibits cholinesterase. *Causes evacuation of worms from intestines.*

USES *Enterobius vermicularis* (pinworm) and *Ascaris lumbricoides* (roundworm) infestations.
UNLABELED USES Hookworm infestations; trichostrongylosis.

CONTRAINDICATIONS Safety during pregnancy (category C), lactation.
CAUTIOUS USE Liver dysfunction; malnutrition; dehydration; anemia.

ROUTE & DOSAGE

Pinworm or Roundworm
Adult/Child: **PO 11 mg/kg as a single dose (max: 1 g)**

ADMINISTRATION

Oral
- Shake suspension well before pouring it to ensure accurate dosage.
- Give with milk or fruit juices and without regard to prior ingestion of food or time of day.
- Store below 30° C (86° F). Protect from light.

ADVERSE EFFECTS (≥1%) **CNS:** Dizziness, headache, drowsiness, insomnia. **GI:** Anorexia, *nausea,* vomiting, abdominal distention, diarrhea, *tenesmus,* transient elevation of AST. **Skin:** Skin rashes.

INTERACTIONS Drug: Piperazine and pyrantel may be mutually antagonistic.

PHARMACOKINETICS Absorption: Poorly from GI tract. **Peak:** 1–3 h. **Metabolism:** In liver. **Elimination:** >50% in feces, 7% in urine.

CLINICAL IMPLICATIONS

Assessment & Drug Effects
- Lab tests: Monitor baseline and periodic AST/ALT in individuals with known liver dysfunction.

Patient & Family Education
- Do not drive or engage in other potentially hazardous activities until response to drug is known.

PYRAZINAMIDE

(peer-a-zin'a-mide)
PZA, Tebrazid ♦
Classifications: ANTIBIOTIC; ANTITUBERCULOSIS AGENT
Therapeutic: ANTIBIOTIC; ANTITUBERCULOSIS
Pregnancy Category: C

AVAILABILITY 500 mg tablets

ACTION & *THERAPEUTIC EFFECT*
Pyrazinoic acid amide, analog of nicotinamide. *Bacteriostatic against* Mycobacterium tuberculosis. *Not used as sole agent against TB infection.*

USES Short-term therapy of advanced tuberculosis before surgery and to treat patients unresponsive to primary agents (e.g., isoniazid, streptomycin).

CONTRAINDICATIONS Severe liver damage, acute gout; pregnancy (category C).

CAUTIOUS USE History of gout or diabetes mellitus; impaired kidney function; alcoholism; history of peptic ulcer; acute intermittent porphyria, and lactation.

ROUTE & DOSAGE

Tuberculosis
Adult: **PO** 15–35 mg/kg/d in 3–4 divided doses (max: 2 g/d)
Child: **PO** 20–40 mg/kg/d divided q12–24h (max: 2 g/d)

ADMINISTRATION

Oral
- Discontinue drug if hepatic reactions (jaundice, pruritus, icteric sclerae, yellow skin) or hyperuricemia with acute gout (severe pain in great toe and other joints) occur.
- Store at 15°–30° C (59°–86° F) in tightly closed container.

ADVERSE EFFECTS (≥1%) **Body as a Whole:** *Active gout,* arthralgia, lymphadenopathy. **Urogenital:** Difficulty in urination. **CNS:** Headache. **Skin:** Urticaria. **Hematologic:** Hemolytic anemia, decreased plasma prothrombin. **GI:** Splenomegaly, <u>fatal hemoptysis</u>, aggravation of peptic ulcer, *hepatotoxicity, abnormal liver function tests.* **Metabolic:** *Rise in serum uric acid.*

DIAGNOSTIC TEST INTERFERENCE Pyrazinamide may produce a temporary decrease in **17-ketosteroids** and an increase in ***protein-bound iodine.***

INTERACTIONS Drug: Increase in liver toxicity (including fatal hepatoxicity in when treating latent TB) with **rifampin.**

PHARMACOKINETICS Absorption: Readily from GI tract. **Peak:** 2 h. **Distribution:** Crosses blood–brain barrier. **Metabolism:** In liver. **Elimination:** Slowly in urine. **Half-Life:** 9–10 h.

CLINICAL IMPLICATIONS

Assessment & Drug Effect
- Observe and supervise closely. Patients should receive at least one other effective antituberculosis agent concurrently.
- Examine patients at regular intervals and question about possible signs of toxicity: Liver enlargement or tenderness, jaundice, fever, anorexia, malaise, impaired vascular integrity (ecchymoses, petechiae, abnormal bleeding).
- Hepatic reactions appear to occur more frequently in patients receiving high doses.
- Lab tests: Obtain liver function tests (especially AST, ALT, serum bilirubin) prior to and at 2–4 wk intervals during therapy. Blood uric acid determinations are advised before, during, and following therapy.

Patient & Family Education
- Report to physician onset of difficulty in voiding. Keep fluid intake at 2000 mL/d if possible.
- Monitor blood glucose (diabetics) for possible loss of glycemic control.

PYRETHRINS

(peer′e-thrins)

A-200 Pyrinate, Barc, Blue, Pyrinate, Pyrinyl, R & C, RID, TISIT, Triple X

P

Common adverse effects in *italic*, life-threatening effects <u>underlined</u>; generic names in **bold**; classifications in SMALL CAPS; ♣ Canadian drug name; ⊘ Prototype drug

1303

Classifications: PEDICULICIDE
Therapeutic: ANTIPARASITIC; PEDI-CULICIDE
Prototype: Permethrin
Pregnancy Category: C

AVAILABILITY 0.18%, 0.2%, 0.3% liquid; 0.3% gel; 0.3% shampoo

ACTION & *THERAPEUTIC EFFECT*
Pediculicide solution that contains active chemicals in deodorized kerosene. Acts as a contact poison affecting the parasite's nervous system, causing paralysis and death. *Controls head lice, pubic (crab) lice, and body lice and their eggs (nits).*

USES External treatment of *Pediculus humanus* infestations.

CONTRAINDICATIONS Sensitivity to solution components; skin infections and abrasions; pregnancy (category C), lactation.
CAUTIOUS USE Ragweed-sensitized patient, infants, children.

ROUTE & DOSAGE

Pediculus humanus
Infestations
Adult: **Topical** See Administration for appropriate application

ADMINISTRATION

Topical
- Apply enough solution to completely wet infested area, including hair. Allow to remain on area for 10 min.
- Wash and rinse with large amounts of warm water.
- Use fine-toothed comb to remove lice and eggs from hair.
- Shampoo hair to restore body and luster.

- Repeat treatment once in 24 h if necessary.
- Repeat treatment in 7–10 d to kill newly hatched lice.
- Do not apply to eyebrows or eyelashes without consulting physician.
- Flush eyes with copious amounts of warm water if accidental contact occurs.

ADVERSE EFFECTS (≥1%) **Body as a Whole:** Irritation with repeated use.

CLINICAL IMPLICATIONS

Patient & Family Education
- Do not swallow, inhale, or allow pyrethrins to contact mucosal surfaces or the eyes.
- Discontinue use and consult physician if treated area becomes irritated.
- Examine each family member carefully; if infested, treat immediately to prevent spread or reinfestation of previously treated patient.
- Dry clean, boil, or otherwise treat contaminated clothing. Sterilize (soak in pyrethrins) comb and brushes used by patient.
- Do not share combs, brushes, or other headgear with another person.

PYRIDOSTIGMINE BROMIDE

(peer-id-oh-stig′meen)
Mestinon, Regonol
Classifications: ANTICHOLINERGIC AGENT; CHOLINESTERASE INHIBITOR
Therapeutic: CHOLINESTERASE INHIBITOR
Prototype: Neostigmine
Pregnancy Category: C

AVAILABILITY 60 mg/5 mL syrup; 60 mg tablet; 180 mg extended release tablet; 5 mg/mL injection

ACTION & *THERAPEUTIC EFFECT*

Analog of neostigmine; indirect-acting cholinergic that inhibits cholinesterase activity. Facilitates transmission of impulses across myoneural junctions by blocking destruction of acetylcholine. *Direct stimulant action on voluntary muscle fibers and possibly on autonomic ganglia and CNS neurons. Produces increased tone in skeletal muscles.*

USES Myasthenia gravis and as an antagonist to nondepolarizing skeletal muscle relaxants (e.g., curariform drugs).

CONTRAINDICATIONS Hypersensitivity to anticholinesterase agents or to bromides. Mechanical obstruction of urinary or intestinal tract; bradycardia, hypotension; pregnancy (category C).
CAUTIOUS USE Bronchial asthma; epilepsy; renal impairment; vagotonia; hyperthyroidism; peptic ulcer; cardiac dysrhythmias.

ROUTE & DOSAGE

Myasthenia Gravis

Adult: **PO** 60 mg–1.5 g/d spaced according to response of individual patient; sustained release: 180–540 mg 1–2 times/d at intervals of at least 6 h **IM/IV** Approximately $^1/_{30}$ of PO dose
Child: **PO** 7 mg/kg/d divided into 5–6 doses
Neonates: **PO** 5 mg q4–6h **IM/IV** 0.05–0.15 mg/kg q4–6h

Reversal of Muscle Relaxants

Adult: **IV** 10–20 mg immediately preceded by IV atropine

ADMINISTRATION

Oral
- Give with food or fluid.
- Ensure that sustained release form is not chewed or crushed. Must be swallowed whole.
- Note: A syrup is available. Some patients may not like it because it is sweet; try to make it more palatable by giving it over ice chips. The syrup formulation contains 5% alcohol.

Intramuscular
- Note: Parenteral dose is about $^1/_{30}$ the oral adult dose.
- Give deep IM into a large muscle.

Intravenous

PREPARE: Direct: Give undiluted. Do NOT add to IV solutions.
ADMINISTER: Direct: Give at a rate of 0.5 mg over 1 min for myasthenia gravis; 5 mg over 1 min for reversal of muscle relaxants.

- Store at 15°–30° C (59°–86° F). Protect from light and moisture.

ADVERSE EFFECTS (≥1%) **Skin:** Acneiform rash. **Hematologic:** Thrombophlebitis (following IV administration). **GI:** *Nausea, vomiting, diarrhea.* **Special Senses:** *Miosis.* **Body as a Whole:** *Excessive salivation and sweating,* weakness, fasciculation. **Respiratory:** Increased bronchial secretion, <u>bronchoconstriction</u>. **CV:** Bradycardia, hypotension.

INTERACTIONS Drug: Atropine, NONDEPOLARIZING MUSCLE RELAXANTS antagonize effects of pyridostigmine.

PHARMACOKINETICS Absorption: Poorly from GI tract. **Onset:** 30–45 min PO; 15 min IM; 2–5 min IV. **Duration:** 3–6 h. **Distribution:** Crosses placenta. **Metabolism:** In liver and in serum and tissue by cholinesterases. **Elimination:** In urine.

Common adverse effects in *italic*, life-threatening effects <u>underlined</u>; generic names in **bold**; classifications in SMALL CAPS; ✿ Canadian drug name; ✪ Prototype drug

1305

CLINICAL IMPLICATIONS

Assessment & Drug Effects

- Report increasing muscular weakness, cramps, or fasciculations. Failure of patient to show improvement may reflect either underdosage or overdosage.
- Observe patient closely if atropine is used to abolish GI adverse effects or other muscarinic adverse effects because it may mask signs of overdosage (cholinergic crisis): Increasing muscle weakness, which through involvement of respiratory muscles can lead to death.
- Monitor vital signs frequently, especially respiratory rate.
- Observe for signs of cholinergic reactions (see Appendix F), particularly when drug is administered IV.
- Observe neonates of myasthenic mothers, who have received pyridostigmine, closely for difficulty in breathing, swallowing, or sucking.
- Observe patient continuously when used as muscle relaxant antagonist. Airway and respiratory assistance must be maintained until full recovery of voluntary respiration and neuromuscular transmission is assured. Complete recovery usually occurs within 30 min.

Patient & Family Education

- Be aware that duration of drug action may vary with physical and emotional stress, as well as with severity of disease.
- Report onset of rash to physician. Drug may be discontinued.
- Sustained release tablets may become mottled in appearance; this does not affect their potency.

PYRIDOXINE HYDROCHLORIDE (VITAMIN B₆)

(peer-i-dox'een)

Classifications: VITAMIN

Therapeutic: VITAMIN B₆ REPLACEMENT

Pregnancy Category: A (C if greater than RDA)

AVAILABILITY 25 mg, 50 mg, 100 mg, 250 mg, 500 mg tablets; 100 mg/mL injection

ACTION & THERAPEUTIC EFFECT

Water-soluble complex of three closely related compounds with B₆ activity. Considered essential to human nutrition, although a deficiency syndrome is not well defined. Converted in body to pyridoxal, a coenzyme that functions in protein, fat, and carbohydrate metabolism and in facilitating release of glycogen from liver and muscle. In protein metabolism, participates in many enzymatic transformations of amino acids and conversion of tryptophan to niacin and serotonin. Aids in energy transformation in brain and nerve cells, and is thought to stimulate heme production. *Evaluated by improvement of B₆ deficiency manifestations: Nausea, vomiting, skin lesions resembling those of riboflavin and niacin deficiency, edema, CNS symptoms, hypochromic microcytic anemia.*

USES Prophylaxis and treatment of pyridoxine deficiency, as seen with inadequate dietary intake, drug-induced deficiency (e.g., isoniazid, oral contraceptives), and inborn errors of metabolism (vitamin B₆–dependent convulsions or anemia). Also to prevent chloramphenicol-induced optic neuritis, to treat acute toxicity caused by overdosage of cycloserine, hydralazine, isoniazid (INH); alcoholic polyneuritis; sideroblastic anemia associated with high serum iron concentration. Has been used for management of many other conditions ranging from nausea and vomiting in radiation sickness and pregnancy to suppression of postpartum lactation.

CONTRAINDICATIONS Pregnancy [category A (C if >RDA)].

CAUTIOUS USE Renal impairment; neonatal prematurity with renal impairment; cardiac disease.

ROUTE & DOSAGE

Dietary Deficiency
Adult: **PO/IM/IV** 10–20 mg/d times 2–3 wk
Child: **PO** 5–25 mg/d times 3 wk, then 1.5–2.5 mg/d

Pyridoxine Deficiency Syndrome
Adult: **PO/IM/IV** Initial dose up to 600 mg/d may be required; then up to 50 mg/d

Isoniazid-Induced Deficiency
Adult: **PO/IM/IV** 100 mg/d times 3 wk, then 30 mg/d
Child: **PO** 10–50 mg/d times 3 wk, then 1–2 mg/kg/d

Pyridoxine-Dependent Seizures
Neonate/Infant: **PO/IM/IV** 50–100 mg/d

ADMINISTRATION

Oral
- Ensure that sustained release and enteric forms are not chewed or crushed. Must be swallowed whole.

Intramuscular
- Give deep IM into a large muscle.

Intravenous

PREPARE: Direct: Give undiluted. **Continuous:** May be added to most standard IV solutions.
ADMINISTER: Direct: Give at a rate of 50 mg or fraction thereof over 60 seconds. **Continuous:** Give according to ordered rate for infusion.

- Store at 15°–30° C (59°–86° F) in tight, light-resistant containers. Avoid freezing.

ADVERSE EFFECTS (≥1%) **Body as a Whole:** Paresthesias, slight flushing or feeling of warmth, temporary burning or stinging pain in injection site. **CNS:** Somnolence seizures (particularly following large parenteral doses). **Metabolic:** Low folic acid levels.

INTERACTIONS Drug: Isoniazid, cycloserine, penicillamine, hydralazine and ORAL CONTRACEPTIVES, may increase pyridoxine requirements; may reverse or antagonize therapeutic effects of **levodopa.**

PHARMACOKINETICS Absorption: Readily from GI tract. **Distribution:** Stored in liver; crosses placenta. **Metabolism:** In liver. **Elimination:** In urine.

CLINICAL IMPLICATIONS

Assessment & Drug Effects
- Monitor neurologic status to determine therapeutic effect in deficiency states.
- Record a complete dietary history so poor eating habits can be identified and corrected (a single vitamin deficiency is rare; patient can be expected to have multiple vitamin deficiencies).
- Lab tests: Periodic Hct and Hgb, and serum iron.

Patient & Family Education
- Learn rich dietary sources of vitamin B6: Yeast, wheat germ, whole grain cereals, muscle and glandular meats (especially liver), legumes, green vegetables, bananas.
- Do not self-medicate with vitamin combinations (OTC) without first consulting physician.

P

PYRIMETHAMINE

(peer-i-meth'a-meen)

Daraprim

Classifications: ANTIMALARIAL

Therapeutic: ANTIMALARIAL

Prototype: Chloroquine

Pregnancy Category: C

AVAILABILITY 25 mg tablets

ACTION & *THERAPEUTIC EFFECT*
Long-acting folic acid antagonist. Selectively inhibits action of dehydrofolic reductase in parasites with resulting blockade of folic acid metabolism. *No gametocidal activity but prevents development of fertilized gametes in the mosquito and thus helps to prevent transmission of malaria.*

USES Prophylaxis of malaria due to susceptible strains of plasmodia. May be used conjointly with fast-acting antimalarial (e.g., chloroquine, quinacrine, quinine) to initiate transmission control and suppressive cure. Used with a sulfonamide to provide synergistic action in treatment of toxoplasmosis.

CONTRAINDICATIONS Chloroguanide-resistant malaria; hypersensitivity to sulfonamides; megaloblastic anemia caused by folate deficiency; children <2 mo; pregnancy (category C).

CAUTIOUS USE Convulsive disorders; asthma; bone marrow suppression; folate deficiency; hepatic disease; renal disease.

ROUTE & DOSAGE

Malaria Chemoprophylaxis
Adult: **PO** 25 mg once/wk

Child: **PO** <4 y, 6.25 mg once/wk; 4–10 y, 12.5 mg once/wk; >10 y, 25 mg once/wk

Toxoplasmosis
Adult: **PO** 50–75 mg/d with a sulfonamide for 1–3 wk, then decrease dose by half and continue for 1 mo
Child: **PO** 1 mg/kg/d divided into 2 doses with a sulfonamide for 1–3 wk, then decrease to 0.5 mg/kg/d for 1 mo (max: 25 mg/d)

ADMINISTRATION

Oral

- Minimize GI distress by giving with meals. If symptoms persist, dosage reduction may be necessary.
- Give on same day each week for malaria prophylaxis. Begin when individual enters malarious area and continue for 10 wk after leaving the area.

ADVERSE EFFECTS (≥1%) **GI:** Anorexia, vomiting, atrophic glossitis, abdominal cramps, diarrhea. **Skin:** Skin rashes. **Hematologic:** *Folic acid deficiency (megaloblastic anemia, leukopenia, thrombocytopenia, pancytopenia, diarrhea).* **CNS:** CNS stimulation including convulsions, respiratory failure.

INTERACTIONS Drug: Folic acid, *para*-aminobenzoic acid (PABA) may decrease effectiveness against toxoplasmosis.

PHARMACOKINETICS Absorption: Readily from GI tract. **Peak:** 2 h. **Distribution:** Concentrates in kidneys, lungs, liver, and spleen; distributed into breast milk. **Elimination:** Slowly in urine; excretion may extend over 30 d or longer. **Half-Life:** 54–148 h.

CLINICAL IMPLICATIONS

Assessment & Drug Effects

- Monitor patient response closely. Dosages required for treatment of toxoplasmosis approach toxic levels.
- Lab tests: Perform blood counts, including platelets, twice weekly during therapy.
- Withhold drug and notify physician if hematologic abnormalities appear.

Patient & Family Education

- Be aware that folic acid deficiency may occur with long-term use of pyrimethamine. Report to physician weakness, and pallor (from anemia), ulcerations of oral mucosa, superinfections, glossitis; GI disturbances such as diarrhea and poor fat absorption, fever. Folate (folinic acid) replacement may be prescribed. Increase food sources of folates (if allowed) in diet.

QUAZEPAM

(qua′ze-pam)
Doral
Classifications: BENZODIAZEPINE; ANXIOLYTIC; SEDATIVE-HYPNOTIC
Therapeutic: ANTIANXIETY; SEDATIVE-HYPNOTIC
Prototype: Lorazepam
Pregnancy Category: X
Controlled Substance: Schedule IV

AVAILABILITY 15 mg tablets

ACTION & *THERAPEUTIC EFFECT*

Believed to potentiate gamma-aminobutyric acid (GABA) neuronal inhibition in the limbic, neocortical, and mesencephalic reticular systems. *Significantly decreases sleep latency and total wake time and significantly increases sleep time. REM sleep is essentially unchanged.*

USES Insomnia characterized by difficulty in falling asleep, frequent nocturnal awakenings, or early morning awakenings.

CONTRAINDICATIONS Hypersensitivity to quazepam or benzodiazepines; sleep apnea; pregnancy (category X), lactation.

CAUTIOUS USE Impaired liver and kidney function; compromised respiratory function; history of seizures; elderly; debilitated clients. Safety and effectiveness in children <18 y are not established.

ROUTE & DOSAGE

Insomnia
Adult: PO 7.5–15 mg h.s.

ADMINISTRATION

Oral

- Initial dose is usually 15 mg but can often be effectively reduced after several nights of therapy.
- Use lowest effective dose in older adults as soon as possible.

ADVERSE EFFECTS (≥1%) **CNS:** *Drowsiness, headache,* fatigue, dizziness, dry mouth. **GI:** Dyspepsia.

INTERACTIONS Drug: Alcohol, CNS DEPRESSANTS, ANTICONVULSANTS potentiate CNS depression; **cimetidine** increases quazepam plasma levels, increasing its toxicity; may decrease antiparkinsonism effects of **levodopa;** may increase **phenytoin** levels; **smoking** decreases sedative effects of quazepam. **Herbal: Kava-kava, valerian** may potentiate sedation.

PHARMACOKINETICS Absorption: Readily from GI tract. **Onset:** 30 min. **Peak:** 2 h. **Distribution:** Crosses placenta; distributed into breast milk. **Metabolism:** In liver to active metabolites. **Elimination:** In urine and feces. **Half-Life:** 39 h.

CLINICAL IMPLICATIONS

Assessment & Drug Effects

- Monitor for respiratory depression in patients with chronic respiratory insufficiency.
- Monitor for suicidal tendencies in previously depressed clients.
- Daytime drowsiness is more likely to occur in older adult clients.

Patient & Family Education

- Inform physician about any alcohol consumption and prescription or nonprescription medication that you take. Avoid alcohol use since it potentiates CNS depressant effects.
- Inform physician immediately if you become pregnant. This drug causes birth defects.
- Do not drive or engage in potentially hazardous activities until response to drug is known.
- Do not increase the dose of this drug; inform physician if the drug no longer works.
- This drug may cause daytime sedation, even for several days after drug is discontinued.

QUETIAPINE FUMARATE

(ke-ti-a′peen)
Seroquel
Classifications: PSYCHOTHERAPEU-TIC AGENT; ANTIPSYCHOTIC, ATYPICAL
Therapeutic: ANTIPSYCHOTIC
Prototype: Clozapine
Pregnancy Category: C

AVAILABILITY 25 mg, 100 mg, 200 mg tablets

ACTION & *THERAPEUTIC EFFECT*
Antagonizes multiple neurotransmitter receptors in the brain including serotonin (5-HT$_{1A}$ and 5-HT$_2$) as well as dopamine D$_1$ and D$_2$ receptors. *Therapeutic effectiveness indicated by a reduction in psychotic behavior.*

USES Management of psychotic disorders, management of bipolar disorder.

UNLABELED USES Management of agitation and dementia.

CONTRAINDICATIONS Hypersensitivity to quetiapine; pregnancy (category C), lactation; alcohol use; suicidal ideation.

CAUTIOUS USE Dementia-related psychosis; liver function impairment, older adults, cardiovascular disease (history of MI or ischemic heart disease, heart failure, arrhythmias, CVA, hypotension, dehydration, treatment with antihypertensives; history of seizures or suicide; breast cancer; Alzheimer's, Parkinson's disease; concurrent use of centrally acting drugs; patient at risk for aspiration pneumonia; debilitated patients; cerebrovascular disease; adolescents and children with major depression or psychosis.

ROUTE & DOSAGE

Psychosis, Acute Mania
Adult: **PO** Initiate with 25 mg b.i.d., may increase by 25–50 mg b.i.d. to t.i.d. on the second or third day as tolerated to a target dose of 300–400 mg/d divided b.i.d. to t.i.d., may adjust dose by 25–50 mg b.i.d. q.d. as needed (max: 800 mg/d)
Geriatric: **PO** Initiate with 25 mg b.i.d., titrate more slowly than adult patients, target range 150–200 mg/day in divided doses

Agitation, Dementia
Geriatric: **PO** Initiate with 25 mg b.i.d., may increase by 25–50 mg b.i.d. q 2–7 d if needed (max: 200 mg/d)

ADMINISTRATION

Oral

- Titrate dose over 4 d usually to a target range of 300–400 mg/d. Make further dose adjustments of 25–50 mg 2 times/d at intervals of at least 2 d.
- Retitrate to desired dose when patient has been off the drug for >1 wk.
- Follow recommended lower doses and slower titration for the older adults, the debilitated, and those with hepatic impairment or a predisposition to hypotension.
- Store at 15°–30° C (59°–86° F).

ADVERSE EFFECTS (≥1%) **Body as a Whole:** Asthenia, fever, hypertonia, dysarthria, flu syndrome, weight gain, peripheral edema. **CNS:** *Dizziness, headache, somnolence.* **CV:** Postural hypotension, tachycardia, palpitations. **GI:** Dry mouth, dyspepsia, abdominal pain, constipation, anorexia. **Metabolic:** Hyperglycemia, diabetes mellitus. **Respiratory:** Rhinitis, pharyngitis, cough, dyspnea. **Skin:** Rash, sweating. **Hematologic:** Leukopenia.

INTERACTIONS Drug: BARBITURATES, **carbamazepine, phenytoin, rifampin, thioridazine** may increase clearance of quetiapine. Quetiapine may potentiate the cognitive and motor effects of **alcohol,** enhance the effects of ANTIHYPERTENSIVE AGENTS, antagonize the effects of **levodopa** and DOPAMINE AGONISTS. **Ketoconazole, itraconazole, fluconazole, erythromycin** may decrease clearance of quetiapine. **Herbal:** St. John's wort may cause **serotonin** syndrome (see Appendix F).

PHARMACOKINETICS Absorption: Rapidly and completely absorbed from GI tract. **Peak:** 1.5 h. **Distribution:** 83% protein bound. **Metabolism:** Extensively in the liver by CYP3A4. **Elimination:** 73% in urine, 20% in feces. **Half-Life:** 6 h.

CLINICAL IMPLICATIONS

Assessment & Drug Effects

- Monitor diabetics for loss of glycemic control.
- Monitor for changes in behavior that may indicate suicidality.
- Reassess need for continued treatment periodically.
- Withhold the drug and immediately report S&S of tardive dyskinesia or neuroleptic malignant syndrome (see Appendix F).
- Lab tests: Periodically monitor liver function, lipid profile, thyroid function, blood glucose, CBC with differential.
- Monitor ECG periodically, especially in those with known cardiovascular disease.
- Perform baseline cataract exam when therapy is started and at 6 mo intervals thereafter.
- Monitor patients with a history of seizures for lowering of the seizure threshold.

Patient & Family Education

- Carefully monitor blood glucose levels if diabetic.
- Exercise caution with potentially dangerous activities requiring alertness, especially during the first week of drug therapy or during dose increments.
- Make position changes slowly, especially when changing from lying or sitting to standing to avoid dizziness, palpitations, and fainting.
- Avoid alcohol consumption and activities that may cause overheating and dehydration.
- Inform physician immediately if you become pregnant.

Q

Common adverse effects in *italic*, life-threatening effects underlined; generic names in **bold**; classifications in SMALL CAPS; ✦ Canadian drug name; ✪ Prototype drug

1311

QUINAPRIL HYDROCHLORIDE

(quin'a-pril)

Accupril

Classifications: ANGIOTENSIN-CONVERTING ENZYME (ACE) INHIBITOR; ANTIHYPERTENSIVE

Therapeutic: ANTIHYPERTENSIVE; ACE INHIBITOR

Prototype: Enalapril

Pregnancy Category: C first trimester; D second and third trimester

AVAILABILITY 5 mg, 10 mg, 20 mg, 40 mg tablets

ACTION & *THERAPEUTIC EFFECT*
Potent, long-acting second-generation ACE inhibitor that lowers BP by interrupting the conversion sequences initiated by renin to form angiotensin II, a vasoconstrictor. Inhibition of ACE also decreases circulating aldosterone, a secretory response to angiotensin II stimulation. Reduces pulmonary capillary wedge pressure, systemic vascular resistance, and mean arterial pressure, with concurrent increases in cardiac output, cardiac index, and stroke volume. *Lowers BP by producing vasodilation. Effective in the treatment of CHF because it improves cardiac indicators.*

USES Mild to moderate hypertension, CHF.

CONTRAINDICATIONS Hypersensitivity to quinapril or other ACE inhibitors; children; pregnancy (category C first trimester, category D second and third trimester), lactation.

CAUTIOUS USE Renal insufficiency, severe CHF; autoimmune disease, volume-depleted patients, renal artery stenosis, neutropenia.

ROUTE & DOSAGE

Hypertension, CHF

Adult: **PO** 10–20 mg q.d., may increase up to 80 mg/d in 1–2 divided doses

Geriatric: **PO** Start with 2.5–5 mg q.d.

Renal Insufficiency

Cl_{cr} 30–60 mL/min: 5 mg/q.d. initially; Cl_{cr} <10–30 mL/min: 2.5 mg/d initially

ADMINISTRATION

Oral

- Discontinue diuretics 2–3 d before initiation of quinapril. Do NOT exceed initial dose of 5 mg if diuretics cannot be discontinued.
- Store at 15°–30° C (59°–86° F) and protect from moisture.

ADVERSE EFFECTS (≥1%) **CV:** Edema, hypotension. **CNS:** Dizziness, fatigue, headache. **GI:** Nausea, vomiting, diarrhea. **Hematologic:** Eosinophilia, neutropenia. **Metabolic:** Hyperkalemia, proteinuria. **Respiratory:** Cough. **Body as a Whole:** <u>Angioedema</u>, myalgia.

DIAGNOSTIC TEST INTERFERENCE
May increase ***BUN*** or ***serum creatinine.***

INTERACTIONS Drug: POTASSIUM-SPARING DIURETICS may increase risk of hyperkalemia. May elevate serum **lithium** levels, resulting in **lithium** toxicity.

PHARMACOKINETICS Absorption: Rapidly from GI tract. **Onset:** 1 h. **Peak:** 2–4 h. **Duration:** Up to 24 h. **Distribution:** 97% bound to plasma proteins; crosses placenta; not known if distributed into breast milk. **Metabolism:** Extensively metabolized in liver to its active metabolite, quinaprilat. **Elimination:** 50–60% in urine, primarily as quinaprilat; 30% in feces. **Half-Life:** 2 h.

CLINICAL IMPLICATIONS

Assessment & Drug Effects

- Monitor BP at time of peak effectiveness, 2–4 h after dosing, and at end of dosing interval just before next dose.
- Report diminished antihypertensive effect toward end of dosing interval. Inadequate trough response may indicate need to divide daily dose.
- Monitor for first-dose hypotension, especially in salt- or volume-depleted clients.
- Lab tests: Monitor BUN and serum creatinine periodically. Increases may necessitate dose reduction or discontinuation of drug. Monitor serum potassium values.
- Observe for S&S of hyperkalemia (see Appendix F).

Patient & Family Education

- Discontinue quinapril and report S&S of angioedema (e.g., swelling of face or extremities, difficulty breathing or swallowing) to physician.
- Maintain adequate fluid intake and avoid potassium supplements or salt substitutes unless specifically prescribed by physician.
- Note: A high-fat meal may lessen drug's absorption.

QUINIDINE SULFATE

(kwin′i-deen sul-fate)
Apo-Quinidine ♣, Novoquinidin ♣

QUINIDINE GLUCONATE

Quinaglute Duratabs
Classifications: ANTIARRHYTHMIC CLASS IA

Therapeutic: ANTIARRHYTHMIC CLASS IA
Prototype: Procainamide
Pregnancy Category: C

AVAILABILITY Quinidine sulfate 200 mg, 300 mg tablets; 300 mg sustained release tablets **Quinidine gluconate** 324 mg sustained release tablets; 80 mg/mL injection

ACTION & *THERAPEUTIC EFFECT*

Class IA antiarrhythmic that depresses myocardial excitability, contractility, automaticity, and conduction velocity, and prolongs effective refractory period. Anticholinergic action blocks vagal stimulation of AV node, thus tending to increase ventricular rate, particularly in larger doses. *Depresses myocardial excitability, conduction velocity, and irregularity of nerve impulse conduction.*

USES Premature atrial, AV junctional, and ventricular contraction; paroxysmal atrial tachycardia, chronic ventricular tachycardia (when not associated with complete heart block); maintenance therapy after electrical conversion of atrial fibrillation or flutter; life-threatening malaria.

CONTRAINDICATIONS Hypersensitivity or idiosyncrasy to quinine or quinidine; pregnancy (category C). Thrombocytopenic purpura resulting from prior use of quinidine; intraventricular conduction defects, complete AV block, ectopic impulses and rhythms due to escape mechanisms; thyrotoxicosis; acute rheumatic fever; subacute bacterial endocarditis, extensive myocardial damage, frank CHF, hypotensive states; digitalis intoxication.
CAUTIOUS USE Incomplete heart block; impaired kidney or liver function; bronchial asthma or other

Q

Common adverse effects in *italic*, life-threatening effects <u>underlined</u>; generic names in **bold**; classifications in SMALL CAPS; ♣ Canadian drug name; ❷ Prototype drug

1313

respiratory disorders; myasthenia gravis; potassium imbalance.

ROUTE & DOSAGE

(Dose of Quinidine Base)

Ventricular Arrhythmias
Sulfate

Adult: **PO** 166 mg q6h until arrhythmia terminates, then 200–300 mg 3–4 times/d

Gluconate

Adult: **PO** 202 mg q8–12 h until sinus rhythm restored or toxicity occurs (max: 3–4 g)

Atrial Fibrillation or Flutter
Sulfate

Adult: **PO** 332 mg q6h until sinus rhythm restored or toxicity occurs (max: 3–4 g)

Gluconate

Adult: **PO** 403 mg q8h × 3–4 doses OR 202 mg q8h × 2 d, then 403 mg q12h × 2 d, then 403 mg q8h up to 4 d **IV** 0.25 mg/kg/min; not more than 5–10 mg/kg until converted

Malaria

Adult: **IV** 15 mg/kg loading dose over 4 h, then 7.5 mg/kg q8h for a total of 7 d OR 6.25 mg/kg loading dose, then 12.5 mcg/kg/min for 72 h

Renal Impairment

Cl_{cr} <10 mL/min: give 75% of dose
Hemodialysis: 200 mg supplement dose post-dialysis

ADMINISTRATION

Note: Sulfate contains 83% anhydrous quinidine base; polygalacturonate, 80%; and gluconate, 62%. Examine parenteral solution before preparation; use only if clear and colorless.

Oral

- Note: Test dose is used by some physicians to determine idiosyncrasy before establishing full dosage schedule.
- Take with a full glass of water on an empty stomach for optimum absorption (i.e., 1 h before or 2 h after meals). Administer drug with food if GI symptoms occur (nausea, vomiting, diarrhea are most common).
- Reserve sustained release tablets for maintenance and prophylactic therapy.
- Adjust dosage to maintain plasma concentration between 2–5 mcg/mL. Levels of 8 mcg/mL or more are associated with myocardial toxicity.
- Store in tight, light-resistant containers away from excessive heat.

Intramuscular

- Aspirate carefully before injection to avoid inadvertent entry into blood vessel.

Intravenous

PREPARE: IV Infusion: Dilute 800 mg (10 mL) in at least 40 mL D5W to yield a maximum concentration of 16 mg/mL.

ADMINISTER: IV Infusion: Give via infusion pump at a rate not to exceed 16 mg (1 mL)/min.

INCOMPATIBILITIES Solution/additive: Amiodarone, atracurium, furosemide. Y-site: Furosemide, heparin in dextrose.

- Use supine position during drug administration; severe hypotension is most likely to occur in patients receiving drug via IV. ■ Protect IV solutions from light and heat to prevent brownish discoloration and possibly precipitation.

ADVERSE EFFECTS (≥1%) **CNS:** Headache, fever, tremors, apprehension, delirium, syncope with sudden loss of consciousness, seizures. **CV:** Hypotension, CHF, <u>widened QRS complex</u>, bradycardia, <u>heart block</u>, atrial flutter, <u>ventricular flutter, fibrillation</u> or tachycardia; quinidine syncope, <u>torsades de pointes</u>. **Special Senses:** Mydriasis, blurred vision, disturbed color perception, reduced visual field, photophobia, diplopia, night blindness, scotomas, optic neuritis, disturbed hearing (tinnitus, auditory acuity). **GI:** *Nausea, vomiting, diarrhea, abdominal pain,* hepatic dysfunction. **Hematologic:** <u>Acute hemolytic anemia</u> (especially in patients with G6PD deficiency), hypoprothrombinemia, leukopenia. Thrombocytopenia, <u>agranulocytosis</u> (both rare). **Body as a Whole:** Cinchonism (nausea, vomiting, headache, dizziness, fever, tremors, vertigo, tinnitus, visual disturbances), <u>angioedema</u>, acute asthma, <u>respiratory depression, vascular collapse</u>. **Skin:** Rash, urticaria, cutaneous flushing with intense pruritus, photosensitivity. **Metabolic:** SLE, hypokalemia.

INTERACTIONS Drug: May increase **digoxin** levels by 50%; **amiodarone** may increase quinidine levels, increasing its risk of heart block; other ANTIARRHYTHMICS, PHENOTHIAZINES, **reserpine** add to cardiac depressant effects; ANTICHOLINERGIC AGENTS add to vagolytic effects; CHOLINERGIC AGENTS may antagonize cardiac effects; ANTICONVULSANTS, BARBITURATES, **rifampin** increase the metabolism of quinidine, thus decreasing its efficacy; CARBONIC ANHYDRASE INHIBITORS, **sodium bicarbonate,** CHRONIC ANTACIDS decrease renal elimination of quinidine, thus increasing its toxicity; **verapamil** causes significant hypotension; may increase hypoprothrombinemic effects of **warfarin. Diltiazem** may increase levels and decrease elimination of quinidine. **Food:** Grapefruit juice (>1 qt/d) may decrease absorption.

PHARMACOKINETICS Absorption: Almost completely from GI tract. **Onset:** 1–3 h. **Peak:** 0.5–1 h. **Duration:** 6–8 h. **Distribution:** Widely distributed to most body tissues except the brain; crosses placenta; distributed into breast milk. **Metabolism:** In liver (CYP3A4). **Elimination:** >95% in urine, <5% in feces. **Half-Life:** 6–8 h.

CLINICAL IMPLICATIONS

Assessment & Drug Effects

- Observe cardiac monitor and report immediately the following indications for stopping quinidine: (1) sinus rhythm, (2) widening QRS complex in excess of 25% (i.e., >0.12 sec), (3) changes in QT interval or refractory period, (4) disappearance of P waves, (5) sudden onset of or increase in ectopic ventricular beats (extrasystoles, PVCs), (6) decrease in heart rate to 120 bpm. Also report immediately any worsening of minor side effects.
- Continuous monitoring of ECG and BP is required. Observe patient closely (check sensorium and be alert for any sign of toxicity); determine plasma quinidine concentrations frequently when large doses (more than 2 g/d) are used or when quinidine is given parenterally (i.e., quinidine gluconate).
- Observe patient closely following each parenteral dose. Amount of subsequent dose is gauged by response to preceding dose.
- Monitor vital signs q1–2h or more often as needed during acute treatment. Count apical pulse for a full minute. Report any change

Q

Common adverse effects in *italic*, life-threatening effects <u>underlined</u>; generic names in **bold**; classifications in SMALL CAPS; ♣ Canadian drug name; ⊘ Prototype drug

1315

in pulse rate, rhythm, or quality or any fall in BP.

- Severe hypotension is most likely to occur in patients receiving high oral doses or parenteral quinidine (i.e., quinidine gluconate).

- Be aware: Reversion to sinus rhythm in long-standing fibrillation or when fibrillation is complicated by CHF involves some risk of embolization from dislodgment of atrial mural emboli.

- Quinidine can cause unpredictable rhythm abnormalities in the digitalized heart. Patients with atrial flutter or fibrillation may be pretreated with digitalis (until ventricular rate is 100 bpm) to increase AV nodal block and thus reduce possibility of paradoxic tachycardia.

- Lab tests: Periodic blood counts, serum electrolyte determinations, and kidney and liver function during long-term therapy.

- Monitor I&O. Diarrhea occurs commonly during early therapy; most patients become tolerant to this side effect. Evaluate serum electrolytes, acid-base, and fluid balance when symptoms become severe; dosage adjustment may be required.

Patient & Family Education

- Report feeling of faintness to physician. "Quinidine syncope" is caused by quinidine-induced changes in ventricular rhythm resulting in decreased cardiac output and syncope.

- Note: Hypersensitivity reactions usually appear 3–20 d after drug is started. Fever occurs commonly and may or may not be accompanied by other symptoms. Inform physician if these S&S occur.

- Eat a balanced diet with no excesses in fruit or fruit juices, milk, or a vegetarian diet. A diet high in alkaline ash foods (vegetables, citrus fruit, milk) may prolong half-life of quinidine by decreasing its excretion and increasing danger of toxicity.

- Do not self-medicate with OTC drugs without advice from physician.

- Do not increase, decrease, skip, or discontinue doses without consulting physician.

- Notify physician immediately of disturbances in vision, ringing in ears, sense of breathlessness, onset of palpitations, and unpleasant sensation in chest. Be sure to note the time of occurrence and duration of chest symptoms.

QUININE SULFATE

(kwye'nine)

Novoquinine ♦

Classifications: ANTIMALARIAL
Therapeutic: ANTIMALARIAL
Prototype: Chloroquine
Pregnancy Category: X

AVAILABILITY 325 mg capsules

ACTION & *THERAPEUTIC EFFECT*

Inhibits protein synthesis and depresses many enzyme systems in malaria parasite. Has schizonticidal action and is gametocidal with *Plasmodium vivax* and *Plasmodium malariae* but not *Plasmodium falciparum*. Resembles salicylates in analgesic and antipyretic properties and exerts curare-like skeletal muscle relaxant effect. Also has oxytocic action and hypoprothrombinemic effect. Qualitatively similar to quinidine in cardiovascular effects. Generally replaced by less toxic and more effective agents in treatment of malaria. *Effective against* Plasmodium vivax *and* Plasmodium malariae *but not* Plasmodium falciparum. *Generally replaced by less toxic and more effective agents in treatment of malaria.*

USES Chloroquine-resistant falciparum malaria and in combination with other antimalarials for radical cure of relapsing vivax malaria; also relief of nocturnal recumbency leg cramps.

CONTRAINDICATIONS Hypersensitivity to quinine; tinnitus, optic neuritis; myasthenia gravis; G6PD deficiency; pregnancy (category X). **CAUTIOUS USE** Cardiac arrhythmias. Same precautions as for quinidine sulfate when used in patients with cardiovascular conditions.

ROUTE & DOSAGE

Acute Malaria
Adult: **PO** 650 mg q8h for 3 d
Child: **PO** 25 mg/kg/d in three divided doses q8h for 3 d

Malaria Chemoprophylaxis
Adult: **PO** 325 mg b.i.d. for 6 wk

Nocturnal Leg Cramps
Adult: **PO** 260–300 mg h.s.

ADMINISTRATION
Oral

- Give with or after meals or a snack to minimize gastric irritation. Quinine has potent local irritant effect on gastric mucosa. Do not crush capsule; drug is not only irritating but also extremely bitter.
- Store in tight, light-resistant containers.

ADVERSE EFFECTS (≥1%) **Body as a Whole:** Cinchonism (tinnitus, decreased auditory acuity, dizziness, vertigo, headache, visual impairment, *nausea, vomiting, diarrhea,* fever); hypersensitivity (cutaneous flushing, visual impairment, pruritus, skin rash, fever, gastric distress, dyspnea, tinnitus); hypothermia, coma. **CNS:** Confusion, excitement, apprehension, syncope, delirium, convulsions, blackwater fever (extensive intravascular hemolysis with renal failure), death. **CV:** Angina, hypotension, tachycardia, cardiovascular collapse. **Hematologic:** Leukopenia, thrombocytopenia, agranulocytosis, hypoprothrombinemia, hemolytic anemia. **Respiratory:** Decreased respiration.

DIAGNOSTIC TEST INTERFERENCE Quinine may interfere with determinations of *urinary catecholamines* (*Sobel* and *Henry modification procedure*) and *urinary steroids (17-hydroxycorticosteroids)* (modification of *Reddy, Jenkins, Thorn* method).

INTERACTIONS Drug: May increase **digoxin** levels; ANTICHOLINERGIC AGENTS add to vagolytic effects; CHOLINERGIC AGENTS may antagonize cardiac effects; ANTICONVULSANTS, BARBITURATES, **rifampin** increase the metabolism of quinine, thus decreasing its efficacy; CARBONIC ANHYDRASE INHIBITORS, CHRONIC ANTACIDS decrease renal elimination of quinine, thus increasing its toxicity; **warfarin** may increase hypoprothrombinemic effects. **Amantadine, carbamazepine, phenobarbital** levels may be increased. **Food:** Grapefruit juice (>1 qt/d) may increase plasma concentrations and adverse effects.

PHARMACOKINETICS Absorption: Well from GI tract. **Peak:** 1–3 h. **Duration:** 6–8 h. **Distribution:** Widely distributed to most body tissues except the brain; crosses placenta; distributed into breast milk. **Metabolism:** In liver. **Elimination:** >95% in urine, <5% in feces. **Half-Life:** 8–21 h.

Q

Common adverse effects in *italic*, life-threatening effects underlined; generic names in **bold**; classifications in SMALL CAPS; ✦ Canadian drug name; ✪ Prototype drug

1317

CLINICAL IMPLICATIONS

Assessment & Drug Effects

- Be alert for S&S of rising plasma concentration of quinine marked by tinnitus and hearing impairment, which usually do not occur until concentration is 10 mcg/mL or more.
- Follow the same precautions with quinine as are used with quinidine in patients with atrial fibrillation; quinine may produce cardiotoxicity in these patients.

Patient & Family Education

- Learn possible adverse reactions and report onset of any unusual symptom promptly to physician.

QUINUPRISTIN/DALFOPRISTIN

(quin-u-pris'tin/dal'fo-pris-tin)
Synercid
Classifications: ANTIBIOTIC, STREPTOGRAMIN
Therapeutic: ANTIBIOTIC
Pregnancy Category: B

AVAILABILITY 500 mg vial (150 mg quinupristin/350 mg dalfopristin)

ACTION & *THERAPEUTIC EFFECT*
Streptogramin (cyclic macrolide) antibiotic that is produced by various *Streptomyces* bacteria. The site of action of both quinupristin and dalfopristin is the bacterial ribosome. Dalfopristin inhibits the early phase of protein synthesis of bacteria while quinupristin inhibits the late phase of protein synthesis of bacteria. This leads to death of the bacteria organisms. *Effectiveness indicated by clinical improvement in S&S of infection. Active against gram-positive pathogens including vancomycin-resistant* Enterococcus faecium *(VREF), as well as some gram-negative anaerobes.*

USES Serious or life-threatening infections associated with VREF bacteremia; complicated skin and skin structure infections caused by *Staphylococcus aureus* or *Streptococcus pyogenes*.

CONTRAINDICATIONS Hypersensitivity to quinupristin/dalfopristin, pristinamycin, other streptogramins; children <16 y.

CAUTIOUS USE Renal or hepatic dysfunction; pregnancy (category B); lactation.

ROUTE & DOSAGE

Vancomycin-Resistant *Enterococcus faecium*
Adult: **IV** 7.5 mg/kg infused over 60 min q8h

Complicated Skin and Skin Structure Infections
Adult: **IV** 7.5 mg/kg infused over 60 min q12h times 7 d

ADMINISTRATION

Intravenous

PREPARE: Intermittent: Reconstitute a single vial by adding 5 mL D5W or sterile water for injection to yield 100 mg/mL. Gently swirl to dissolve but do NOT shake. Allow solution to clear. Withdraw the required dose and further dilute by adding to 100 mL (central line) or 250–500 mL (peripheral site) of D5W.

ADMINISTER: Intermittent: Flush line before & after with D5W. Do NOT use saline. Administer over 1 h.

INCOMPATIBILITIES Solution/additive: **Saline solutions** and **lactated Ringer's** solution (flush lines with D5W before infusing other drugs). **Y-site:** Any drugs diluted in **saline.**

Common adverse effects in *italic*, life-threatening effects underlined; generic names in **bold**; classifications in SMALL CAPS; ♦ Canadian drug name; ⊕ Prototype drug

- Refrigerate unopened vials. After reconstitution solution is stable for 5 h at room temperature and 54 h refrigerated.

ADVERSE EFFECTS (≥1%) **Body as a Whole:** Headache, pain, *myalgia, arthralgia.* **GI:** Nausea, diarrhea, vomiting. **Skin:** Rash, pruritus. **Other:** *Inflammation, pain, or edema at infusion site, other infusion site reactions,* thrombophlebitis.

INTERACTIONS Drug: Inhibits CYP3A4 metabolism of **cyclosporine, midazolam, nifedipine,** PROTEASE INHIBITORS, **vincristine, vinblastine, docetaxel, paclitaxel, diazepam, tacrolimus, carbamazepine, quinidine, lidocaine, disopyramide.**

PHARMACOKINETICS Distribution: Moderately protein bound. **Metabolism:** Metabolized to several active metabolites. **Elimination:** Primarily in feces (75–77%). **Half-Life:** 3 h quinupristin, 1 h dalfopristin.

CLINICAL IMPLICATIONS

Assessment & Drug Effects

- Monitor for S&S of infusion site irritation; change infusion site if irritation is apparent.
- Monitor for cutaneous reaction (e.g., pruritus/erythema of neck, face, upper body).
- Lab tests: C&S from site of infection prior to initiating therapy; WBC with differential; and liver function (especially with preexisting hepatic insufficiency).

Patient & Family Education

- Report burning, itching, or pain at infusion site to physician.
- Report any sensation of swelling of face and tongue; difficulty swallowing.

RABEPRAZOLE SODIUM

(rab-e-pra′zole)

AcipHex

Classifications: PROTON PUMP INHIBITOR

Therapeutic: ANTIULCER; PROTON PUMP INHIBITOR

Prototype: Omeprazole

Pregnancy Category: B

AVAILABILITY 20 mg tablets

ACTION & *THERAPEUTIC EFFECT*
Gastric proton pump inhibitor that specifically suppresses gastric acid secretion by inhibiting the H^+, K^+-ATPase enzyme system [the acid (proton H^+) pump] in the parietal cells of the stomach. Produces an antisecretory effect on the hydrogen ion (H+) in the parietal cells. *Effectiveness indicated by a negative urea breath test for* H. pylori *with preexisting gastric ulcer; also by elimination of S&S of GERD or peptic ulcers.*

USES Healing and maintenance of healing of erosive or ulcerative gastroesophageal reflux disease (GERD); healing of duodenal ulcers; treatment of hypersecretory conditions.

CONTRAINDICATIONS Hypersensitivity to rabeprazole, lansoprazole, or omeprazole or proton pump inhibitors (PPIs); lactation.

CAUTIOUS USE Pregnancy (category B); severe hepatic impairment; mild to moderate hepatic disease; Japanese. Safety and efficacy in children <18 are not established.

ROUTE & DOSAGE

Healing of Erosive GERD
Adult: **PO** 20 mg q.d. × 48 wk, may continue up to 16 wk if needed

R

Maintenance Therapy for GERD
Adult: **PO** 20 mg q.d.

Healing Duodenal Ulcer
Adult: **PO** 20 mg q.d. × 4 wk

Hypersecretory Disease
Adult: **PO** 60 mg q.d. in 1–2 divided doses (max: 100 mg q.d. or 60 mg b.i.d.)

ADMINISTRATION

Oral
- Adjust dose as needed with preexisting liver disease.
- Store at 15°–30° C (59°–86° F).

ADVERSE EFFECTS (≥1%) **Body as a Whole:** Headache. **Skin:** (Rare) <u>Stevens-Johnson syndrome, toxic epidermal necrolysis, erythema multiforme</u>.

INTERACTIONS Drug: May decrease absorption of **ketoconazole**; may increase **digoxin** levels. **Herbal: Ginkgo** may decrease plasma levels.

PHARMACOKINETICS Absorption: 52% bioavailability. **Distribution:** 96% protein bound. **Metabolism:** In liver by (CYP3A4, 2C19). **Elimination:** Primarily in urine. **Half-Life:** 1–2 h.

CLINICAL IMPLICATIONS

Assessment & Drug Effects
- Lab tests: Routine serum chemistry; serum gastrin in long-term therapy.
- Coadministered drugs: Monitor for changes in digoxin blood level.

Patient & Family Education
- Report diarrhea, skin rash, other bothersome adverse effects to physician.

RALOXIFENE HYDROCHLORIDE

(ra-lox′i-feen)
Evista

Classifications: HORMONE; SELECTIVE ESTROGEN RECEPTOR ANTAGONIST/AGONIST
Therapeutic: OSTEOPOROSIS PROPHYLACTIC
Prototype: Tamoxifen
Pregnancy Category: X

AVAILABILITY 60 mg tablets

ACTION & *THERAPEUTIC EFFECT*
Tamoxifen analog that exhibits selective estrogen receptor antagonist activity on uterus and breast tissue. Prevents tissue proliferation in both sites. Decreases bone resorption and increases bone density. *Effectiveness indicated by increased bone mineral density.*

USES Prevention and treatment of osteoporosis in postmenopausal women.

CONTRAINDICATIONS Active thromboembolic event; hypersensitivity to raloxifene; pregnancy (category X), lactation, children.
CAUTIOUS USE Concurrent use of raloxifene and estrogen hormone replacement therapy and lipid-lowering agents; hyperlipidemia; hepatic impairment.

ROUTE & DOSAGE

Prevention or Treatment of Osteoporosis
Adult: **PO** 60 mg q.d.

ADMINISTRATION

Oral
- Discontinue 72 h before and during prolonged immobilization.
- Store at 15°–30° C (59°–86° F) in a tightly closed container and protect from light.

ADVERSE EFFECTS (≥1%) **Body as a Whole:** Infection, flu-like syndrome, leg cramps, fever, arthralgia, myalgia, arthritis. **CNS:** Migraine headache, depression, insomnia. **CV:** *Hot flashes*, chest pain, peripheral edema, decreased serum cholesterol. **GI:** Nausea, dyspepsia, vomiting, flatulence, GI disorder, gastroenteritis, weight gain. **Respiratory:** Sinusitis, pharyngitis, cough, pneumonia, laryngitis. **Skin:** Rash, sweating. **Urogenital:** Vaginitis, UTI, cystitis, leukorrhea, endometrial disorder, breast pain, vaginal bleeding.

INTERACTIONS Drug: Use of ESTROGENS not recommended; absorption reduced by **cholestyramine;** use with **warfarin** or other **coumarin** derivatives may result in changes in prothrombin time (PT).

PHARMACOKINETICS Absorption: 60% absorbed, absolute bioavailability 2%. **Metabolism:** Extensive first-pass metabolism in liver. **Elimination:** Primarily in feces. **Half-Life:** 27.7–32.5 h.

CLINICAL IMPLICATIONS
Assessment & Drug Effects
- Lab tests: Periodically monitor bone density, liver function, and plasma lipids; with concurrent oral anticoagulants, carefully monitor PT and INR.
- Monitor carefully for and immediately report S&S of thromboembolic events.
- Do not give drug concurrently with cholestyramine; however, if unavoidable, space the two drugs as widely as possible.

Patient & Family Education
- Contact physician immediately if unexplained calf pain or tenderness occurs.
- Avoid prolonged restriction of movement during travel.
- Drug does not prevent and may induce hot flashes.

- Do not take drug with other estrogen-containing drugs.
- Tell prescriber if you are taking drugs to lower your cholesterol.

RAMELTEON
Rozerem
Classifications: MELATONIN AGONIST; PSYCHOTROPIC AGENT; SEDATIVE-HYPNOTIC
Therapeutic: SEDATIVE-HYPNOTIC
Pregnancy Category: C

AVAILABILITY 8 mg tablets

ACTION & *THERAPEUTIC EFFECT*
Ramelteon is a melatonin receptor agonist with high affinity for melatonin MT_1 and MT_2 receptors and selectivity affinity for the MT_3 receptor in the brain. The activity of ramelteon at MT_1 and MT_2 receptors is believed to promote sleep, as these receptors, in response to endogenous melatonin, are thought to be involved in maintaining the circadian rhythm underlying the normal sleep-wake cycle. *Effective in promoting onset of sleep.*

USES Treatment of insomnia characterized by difficulty with sleep onset.

CONTRAINDICATIONS Hypersensitivity to ramelteon; severe hepatic function impairment (Child-Pugh C class); severe sleep apnea or severe COPD; concurrent use of alcohol, sedative, or CNS depressant drugs; concurrent use of fluvoxamine; severe depression; suicidal ideation; pregnancy (category C); lactation.
CAUTIOUS USE Moderate hepatic function impairment (Child-Pugh B class); depression with suicidal tendencies; elderly.

R

Common adverse effects in *italic*, life-threatening effects <u>underlined</u>; generic names in **bold**; classifications in SMALL CAPS; ♦ Canadian drug name; ☺ Prototype drug

1321

ROUTE & DOSAGE

Insomnia
Adult: **PO** 8 mg within 30 min of h.s.

ADMINISTRATION

Oral
- Give within 30 min of bedtime.
- Do not administer to anyone on concurrent fluvoxamine therapy without alerting physician. This combination causes a dramatic increase in ramelteon blood level.
- Store at 15°–30° C (59°– 86° F).

ADVERSE EFFECTS (≥1%) **CNS:** Depression, dizziness, fatigue, headache, insomnia, somnolence. **GI:** Diarrhea, unpleasant taste, nausea. **Musculoskeletal:** Arthralgia, myalgia. **Respiratory:** Upper respiratory tract infection.

INTERACTIONS Drug: Concurrent use with **ethanol** produces additive CNS depressant effects; **ketoconazole, itraconazole,** and **fluvoxamine** increase ramelteon levels; other CYP1A2 inhibitors (e.g., **ciprofloxacin, enoxacin, mexiletine, norfloxacin, tacrine**) may also increase ramelteon levels; **rifampin** decreases ramelteon levels. **Food:** High fat meal, grapefruit or grapefruit juice increase ramelteon level.

PHARMACOKINETICS Absorption: 84%. **Peak:** 45 min. **Distribution:** 82% protein bound. **Metabolism:** Rapid and extensive first pass hepatic metabolism; one metabolite, M-II, is active. **Elimination:** Primarily renal. **Half-Life:** 1–2.5 h.

CLINICAL IMPLICATIONS

Assessment & Drug Effects
- Monitor for and report worsening insomnia and cognitive or behavioral changes.
- Monitor for S&S of decreased testosterone levels (e.g., loss of libido) or increased prolactin levels (galactorrhea).
- Lab test: Baseline LFTs.

Patient & Family Education
- Follow directions for taking the drug (see Administration).
- Do not take with or immediately after a high fat meal.
- Do not drive or engage in potentially hazardous activities until response to drug is known.
- Do not consume alcohol while taking this drug.
- Report any of the following to physician: worsening insomnia, cognitive or behavioral changes, problem with reproductive function.

RAMIPRIL

(ram′i-pril)
Altace
Classifications: ANGIOTENSIN-CONVERTING ENZYME (ACE) INHIBITOR; ANTIHYPERTENSIVE
Therapeutic: ANTIHYPERTENSIVE; ACE INHIBITOR
Prototype: Enalapril
Pregnancy Category: C first trimester; D second and third trimester

AVAILABILITY 1.25 mg, 2.5 mg, 5 mg, 10 mg capsules

ACTION & *THERAPEUTIC EFFECT*
Reduces peripheral vascular resistance by inhibiting the formation of angiotensin II, a potent vasoconstrictor. Inhibition of ACE also decreases serum aldosterone levels and reduces peripheral arterial resistance (afterload) as well as improves cardiac output and exercise tolerance. *Lowers BP, and improves cardiac output as well as exercise tolerance.*

USES Mild to moderate hypertension, CHF.

CONTRAINDICATIONS Hypersensitivity to ramipril or any other ACE inhibitor, patients with history of angioneurotic edema; jaundice; hyperkalemia; pregnancy (category C first trimester and category D second and third trimester), lactation. **CAUTIOUS USE** Impaired kidney or liver function, surgery or anesthesia; CHF. Safety and effectiveness in children are not established.

ROUTE & DOSAGE

Hypertension, CHF
Adult: **PO** 2.5–5 mg q.d., may increase up to 20 mg/d in 1–2 divided doses

ADMINISTRATION

Oral
- Discontinue diuretics 2–3 d before initiation of drug. Limit initial dose to 1.25 mg if diuretics cannot be discontinued.
- Store at 15°–30° C (59°–86° F) and protect from moisture.

ADVERSE EFFECTS (≥1%) **CNS:** Dizziness, fatigue, headache. **GI:** Nausea, vomiting, diarrhea, eructation. **Metabolic:** Hyperkalemia, hyponatremia. **Skin:** Erythema, pruritus. **Body as a Whole:** <u>Angioedema</u>. **Respiratory:** Cough.

INTERACTIONS Drug: POTASSIUM-SPARING DIURETICS may increase risk of hyperkalemia. May, elevate, serum **lithium** levels, resulting in lithium toxicity. NSAIDS may attenuate antihypertensive effects.

PHARMACOKINETICS Absorption: 60% absorbed from GI tract. **Onset:** 2 h. **Peak:** 6–8 h. **Duration:** Up to 24 h. **Distribution:** Crosses placenta; not known if distributed into breast milk. **Metabolism:** Rapidly metabolized in liver to its active metabolite, ramiprilat. **Elimination:** 40–60% in urine, 40% in feces. **Half-Life:** 2–3 h.

CLINICAL IMPLICATIONS

Assessment & Drug Effects
- Monitor BP at time of peak effectiveness, 3–6 h after dosing and at end of dosing interval just before next dose.
- Report diminished antihypertensive effect.
- Monitor for first-dose hypotension, especially in salt- or volume-depleted persons.
- Lab tests: Monitor BUN and serum creatinine periodically. Increases may necessitate dose reduction or discontinuation of drug. Monitor serum potassium values.
- Observe for S&S of hyperkalemia (see Appendix F).

Patient & Family Education
- Discontinue drug and report S&S of angioedema to physician (e.g., swelling of face or extremities, difficulty breathing or swallowing).
- Maintain adequate fluid intake and avoid potassium supplements or salt substitutes unless specifically prescribed by the physician.

R

RANITIDINE HYDROCHLORIDE

(ra-nye´te-deen)
Zantac, Zantac EFFERdose, Zantac-75

Classifications: ANTISECRETORY (H$_2$-RECEPTOR ANTAGONIST)
Therapeutic: ANTIULCER; H$_2$-RECEPTOR ANTAGONIST
Prototype: Cimetidine
Pregnancy Category: B

AVAILABILITY 75 mg, 150 mg, 300 mg tablets; 25 mg, 150 mg effer-

Common adverse effects in *italic*, life-threatening effects <u>underlined</u>; generic names in **bold**; classifications in SMALL CAPS; ♦ Canadian drug name; ✪ Prototype drug

1323

vescent tablets; 150 mg, 300 mg capsules; 15 mg/mL syrup; 1 mg/mL, 25 mg/mL injection

ACTION & *THERAPEUTIC EFFECT*

Potent anti-ulcer drug that competitively and reversibly inhibits histamine action at H_2-receptor sites on parietal cells, thus blocking gastric acid secretion. Indirectly reduces pepsin secretion but appears to have minimal effect on fasting and postprandial serum gastrin concentrations or secretion of gastric intrinsic factor or mucus. *Blocks daytime and nocturnal basal gastric acid secretion stimulated by histamine and reduces gastric acid release in response to food, pentagastrin, and insulin. Shown to inhibit 50% of the stimulated gastric acid secretion.*

USES Short-term treatment of active duodenal ulcer; maintenance therapy for duodenal ulcer patient after healing of acute ulcer; treatment of gastroesophageal reflux disease; short-term treatment of active, benign gastric ulcer; treatment of pathologic GI hypersecretory conditions (e.g., Zollinger-Ellison syndrome, systemic mastocytosis, and postoperative hypersecretion); heartburn.

CONTRAINDICATIONS Hypersensitivity to ranitidine; acute porphyria; OTC administration in children <12 y.

CAUTIOUS USE Hypersensitivity to H_2-blockers; hepatic and renal dysfunction; renal failure; elderly; PKU; pregnancy (category B), infants <1 mo, lactation.

ROUTE & DOSAGE

Duodenal Ulcer, Gastric Ulcer, Gastroesophageal Reflux

Adult: **PO** 150 mg b.i.d. or 300 mg h.s. **IV** 50 mg q6–8h; 150–300 mg/24 h by continuous infusion

Child: **PO** 4–5 mg/kg/d divided q8–12h (max: 300 mg/d) **IM/IV** 2–4 mg/kg/d divided q6–8h (max: 200 mg/d)

Infant: **PO** <2 wk, 1.5–2 mg/kg/d divided q12h **IV** 1.5 mg/kg/d divided q12h or 0.04 mg/kg/h by continuous infusion

Duodenal Ulcer, Maintenance Therapy

Adult: **PO** 150 mg h.s.

Pathologic Hypersecretory Conditions

Adult: **PO** 150 mg b.i.d. up to 6 g/d **IV** 1 mg/kg/h, adjusted for gastric output

Heartburn

Adult: **PO** 75–150 mg b.i.d.

Renal Impairment

If Cl_{cr} <50 mL/min, use PO dose q24h, use IV dose q18–24h
Hemodialysis: Time dose to administer at the end of dialysis

ADMINISTRATION

Oral

- Give with or without food; simultaneous administration does not appear to reduce absorption or serum concentrations.
- Administer adjunctive antacid treatment 2 h before or after drug.
- Store tablets in light-resistant, tightly capped container at 15°–30° C (59°–86° F) in a dry place.

Intramuscular

- Note: Does not need to be diluted.

Intravenous

Note: Verify correct IV concentration and rate of infusion for infants and children with physician.

PREPARE: **Direct:** Dilute 50 mg NS, D5W, RL, or other compatible IV solution to a total volume of 20 mL. **Intermittent:** Dilute 50 mg in

Common adverse effects in *italic*, life-threatening effects <u>underlined</u>; generic names in **bold**; classifications in SMALL CAPS; ♣ Canadian drug name; ☯ Prototype drug

50–100 mL of NS, D5W, RL, or other compatible IV solution. **Continuous:** Dilute total daily dose in 250 mL of NS, D5W, RL, or other compatible IV solution. Final concentration should be ≤2.5 mg/mL.

ADMINISTER: **Direct:** Give at a rate of 4 mL/min or 20 mL over not less than 5 min. **Intermittent:** Give over 15–30 min. **Continuous:** Give over 24 h.

INCOMPATIBILITIES **Solution/additive:** Amphotericin B, **atracurium, cefazolin, cefoxitin, ceftazidime, cefuroxime, clindamycin, chlorpromazine, diazepam, ethacrynic acid, hydroxyzine, methotrimeprazine, midazolam, pentobarbital, phenobarbital, phytonadione** Y-site: **Amphotericin B cholesteryl complex, hetastarch in normal saline, insulin.**

- Schedule dose to coincide with end of treatment if patient is having hemodialysis.

ADVERSE EFFECTS (≥1%) **CNS:** Headache, malaise, dizziness, somnolence, insomnia, vertigo, mental confusion, agitation, depression, hallucinations in older adults. **CV:** Bradycardia (with rapid IV push). **GI:** Constipation, nausea, abdominal pain, diarrhea. **Skin:** Rash. **Hematologic:** Reversible decrease in WBC count, thrombocytopenia. **Body as a Whole:** Hypersensitivity reactions, <u>anaphylaxis</u> (rare).

DIAGNOSTIC TEST INTERFERENCE
Ranitidine may produce slight elevations in *serum creatinine* (without concurrent increase in *BUN*); (rare) increases in *AST, ALT, alkaline phosphatase, LDH,* and total *bilirubin.* Produces false-positive tests for *urine protein* with *Multistix* (use *sulfosalicylic acid* instead).

INTERACTIONS Drug: may reduce absorption of **cefpodoxime, cefuroxime, delavirdine, ketoconazole, itraconazole.**

PHARMACOKINETICS Absorption: Incompletely from GI tract (50% reaches systemic circulation). **Peak:** 2–3 h PO. **Duration:** 8–12 h. **Distribution:** Distributed into breast milk. **Metabolism:** In liver. **Elimination:** In urine, with some excreted in feces. **Half-Life:** 2–3 h.

CLINICAL IMPLICATIONS

Assessment & Drug Effects
- Potential toxicity results from decreased clearance (elimination) and therefore prolonged action; greatest in the older adult patients or those with hepatic or renal dysfunction.
- Lab tests: Periodic liver functions. Monitor creatinine clearance if renal dysfunction is present or suspected. When clearance is <50 mL/min, manufacturer recommends reduction of the dose to 150 mg once q24h with cautious and gradual reduction of the interval to q12h or less, if necessary.
- Be alert for early signs of hepatotoxicity (though low and thought to be a hypersensitivity reaction): jaundice (dark urine, pruritus, yellow sclera and skin), elevated transaminases (especially ALT) and LDH.
- Long-term therapy may lead to vitamin B_{12} deficiency.

Patient & Family Education
- Note: Long duration of action provides ulcer pain relief that is maintained through the night as well as the day.
- Be aware that even if symptomatic relief is provided by ranitidine, this

R

Common adverse effects in *italic*, life-threatening effects <u>underlined</u>; generic names in **bold**; classifications in SMALL CAPS; ✦ Canadian drug name; ⊙ Prototype drug

1325

should not be interpreted as absence of gastric malignancy. Follow-up examinations will be scheduled after therapy is discontinued.

- Adhere to scheduled periodic laboratory checkups during ranitidine treatment.
- Do not supplement therapy with OTC remedies for gastric distress or pain without physician's advice (e.g., Mylanta II reduces ranitidine absorption).
- Do not smoke; research shows smoking decreases ranitidine efficacy and adversely affects ulcer healing.

RANOLAZINE

(ra-no′la-zeen)
Ranexa
Classifications: ANTIANGINAL AGENT
Therapeutic: ANTIANGINAL; PARTIAL FATTY ACID OXIDATION (PFOX) INHIBITOR
Pregnancy Category: C

AVAILABILITY 500 mg extended release tablets

ACTION & *THERAPEUTIC EFFECT*
Complete mechanism of action is unknown. Ranolazine is a partial fatty-acid oxidation inhibitor that shifts myocardial metabolism away from fatty acids to glucose. This shift in fuel source requires less oxygen for oxidation and results in decreased oxygen demand by the myocardium. *Ranolazine improves exercise tolerance and angina symptoms. It has no effect on heart rate or hemodynamic action of the heart.*

USES Treatment of chronic stable angina in patients who are unresponsive or cannot tolerate other antianginal agents. Used in combination with amlodipine, beta-blockers, or nitrates.

CONTRAINDICATIONS Mild, moderate, or severe hepatic impairment; severe renal impairment, renal failure, hypokalemia, hypomagnesemia; preexisting QT prolongation, history of torsades de pointes, ventricular tachycardia, ventricular arrhythmias, significant bradycardia, acute MI, cardiac arrhythmia; concurrent use with QT prolongation drugs; grapefruit juice; concurrent use of potent or moderately potent CYP3A inhibitors; pregnancy (category C); lactation. Safety and efficacy in children have not been established.
CAUTIOUS USE History of QT prolongation; older adult.

ROUTE & DOSAGE

Chronic Stable Angina
Adult: **PO** 500–1000 mg b.i.d.

ADMINISTRATION

Oral
- Must be swallowed whole. Should not be crushed, broken, or chewed.
- Store at 15°–30° C (59°–86° F).

ADVERSE EFFECTS (≥1%) **Body as a Whole:** Peripheral edema. **CNS:** *Dizziness,* headache. **CV:** Palpitations. **GI:** Abdominal pain, *constipation,* dry mouth, nausea, vomiting. **Respiratory:** Dyspnea. **Special Senses:** Tinnitus, vertigo.

DIAGNOSTIC TEST INTERFERENCE Ranolazine is not known to interfere with any diagnostic laboratory test.

INTERACTIONS Drug: Inhibitors of P-glycoprotein (e.g., **ritonavir, cyclosporine**) may increase ranolazine absorption. Ranolazine increases the plasma concentrations of **digoxin** and **simvastatin.** Inhibitors of CYP3A4 [e.g., **diltiazem,** grapefruit juice, HIV PROTEASE INHIBITORS, **ketoconazole,** MACROLIDE ANTIBIOTICS (especially **ketoconazole**), **verapamil**] can increase plasma levels and QTc elevation. **Paroxetine,** a CYP2D6 inhibitor, increases the plasma levels of ranolazine. CLASS I or III ANTIARRHYTHMICS (e.g., **quinidine, dofetilide, sotalol**), **thioridazine,** and **ziprasidone** can cause additive increases in QTc elevation.

PHARMACOKINETICS Absorption: 73% of PO dose absorbed. **Peak:** 2–5 h. **Distribution:** 62% protein bound. **Metabolism:** Extensive hepatic metabolism. **Elimination:** 75% in urine; 25% in feces. **Half-Life:** 7 h.

CLINICAL IMPLICATIONS

Assessment & Drug Effects
- Monitor ECG at baseline and periodically for prolongation of the QTc interval.
- Lab tests: Baseline and periodic LFTs.
- Monitor blood levels of digoxin with concurrent therapy.
- When coadministered with simvastatin, monitor for and report unexplained muscle weakness or pain.

Patient & Family Education
- Follow directions for taking the drug (see Administration).
- Do not drink grapefruit juice or eat grapefruit while taking this drug.

RASAGILINE

(ras-a-gi′leen)

Azilect

Classifications: MONOAMINE OXIDASE INHIBITOR; ANTIPARKINSON AGENT

Therapeutic: ANTIPARKINSON AGENT

Prototype: Levodopa
Pregnancy Category: C

AVAILABILITY 0.5 mg, 1 mg tablets

ACTION & *THERAPEUTIC EFFECT*
Rasagiline is a potent monoamine oxidase B inhibitor (MAOI-B) that prevents the enzyme monoamine oxidase B from breaking down dopamine in the brain. Rasagiline also interferes with dopamine reuptake at synapses in the brain. *Rasagiline helps to overcome dopaminergic motor dysfunction in Parkinson's disease.*

USES Treatment of Parkinson's disease, either as monotherapy or as an adjunct to levodopa.

CONTRAINDICATIONS Moderate to severe hepatic impairment; alcoholism; biliary cirrhosis; cardiac arrhythmias, cardiac disease, CHF, angina, acute MI; migraine headaches, increased intracranial pressure, cerebrovascular disease, intracranial bleeding, recent head trauma, stroke; hypertension, concurrent use of antihypertensive drugs; concurrent use of MAOI therapy; pregnancy (category C); elective surgery; children.

CAUTIOUS USE Mild hepatic dysfunction; concurrent anticholinergic drugs or CNS depressant drugs; diabetes mellitus; asthma, bronchitis, hyperthyroidism; postural or orthostatic hypotension; moderate to severe renal impairment, anuria; epilepsy or preexisting seizure disorders; lactation.

ROUTE & DOSAGE

Parkinson's Disease

Adult: **PO** 1 mg/d as monotherapy; 0.5–1 mg/d if adjunctive therapy

R

Common adverse effects in *italic*, life-threatening effects underlined; generic names in **bold**; classifications in SMALL CAPS; ✦ Canadian drug name; ⊕ Prototype drug

1327

Hepatic Impairment
Mild Impairment: 0.5 mg/d

ADMINISTRATION

Oral

May be given without regard to food.

- Store at 15–30° C (59–86° F).

ADVERSE EFFECTS (≥1%) **Body as a Whole:** Accidental injury, allergic reaction, alopecia, gingivitis, hernia, infection, neck pain, pruritus. **CNS:** Abnormal dreams, abnormal gait, amnesia, anxiety, asthenia, ataxia, confusion, depression, dizziness, *dyskinesia*, dystonia, *fall*, fever, flu syndrome, hallucinations, *headache*, hyperkinesias, hypertonia, malaise, neuropathy, neck pain, paresthesia, somnolence, syncope, tremor, vertigo. **CV:** Angina pectoris, bundle branch block, cerebrovascular accident, chest pain, postural hypotension. **GI:** Abdominal pain, anorexia, constipation, diarrhea, dry mouth, dyspepsia, dysphagia, gastroenteritis, GI hemorrhage, *nausea,* vomiting. **Hematologic:** Anemia, hemorrhage. **Metabolic:** Abnormal liver function tests, albuminuria, weight loss. **Musculoskeletal:** Arthralgia, arthritis, bursitis, leg cramps, myasthenia, tenosynovitis. **Respiratory:** Asthma, dyspnea, epistaxis, increased cough, rhinitis. **Skin:** Ecchymosis, eczema, skin carcinoma, skin ulcer, sweating, urticaria, vesiculobullous rash. **Special Senses:** Conjunctivitis. **Urogenital:** Decreased libido, hematuria, impotence, urinary incontinence.

INTERACTIONS Drug: Inhibitors of CYP1A2 (e.g., **atazanavir, ciprofloxacin, mexiletine, tacrine**) may increase rasagiline plasma levels. Rasagiline increases the plasma levels of ANESTHETICS; thus it must be discontinued 14 d prior to elective surgery. Rasagiline can cause severe CNS toxicity, including hyperpyrexia and death, with ANTIDEPRESSANTS, SELECTIVE SEROTONIN REUPTAKE-INHIBITORS (SSRI), SEROTONIN-NOREPINEPHRINE REUPTAKE INHIBITORS (SNRI), NONSELECTIVE MAO INHIBITORS, or SELECTIVE MAO-B INHIBITORS. Rasagiline can increase the plasma levels of **cyclobenzaprine** and SYMPATHOMIMETIC AMINES. Rasagiline and **dextromethorphan** can cause brief episodes of psychosis and bizarre behavior. Rasagiline can potentiate the dopaminergic effects of **levodopa.** Rasagiline can increase the plasma levels of **meperidine, methadone, propoxyphene,** and **tramadol,** resulting in coma, severe hypertension or hypotension, severe respiratory depression, convulsions, and death.: **Herbal:** Rasagiline increases the plasma levels of **St. John's wort**.

PHARMACOKINETICS Absorption: Rapidly absorbed with 36% bioavailability. **Peak:** 1 h. **Distribution:** 88–94% protein bound. **Metabolism:** Extensive hepatic metabolism. **Elimination:** Primarily renal (62%) with minor fecal elimination. **Half-Life:** 3 h.

CLINICAL IMPLICATIONS

Assessment & Drug Effects

- Monitor for and report S&S of dopaminergic side effects (e.g., dyskinesia, hallucinations, etc.) with concurrent levodopa.
- Monitor for and report suspicious skin changes suggestive of melanoma or other skin cancers.
- Lab tests: Baseline and periodic LTFs; periodic renal function tests, CBC with Hct & Hgb.
- Note all contraindicated drugs and drug groups and exercise caution not to administer a contraindicated substance.
- Note all drug interactions and monitor for the indicated effects.

Patient & Family Education

- Do not take any prescription or nonprescription drug without consulting physician.
- Periodic skin examinations should be scheduled with a dermatologist. If you notice changes in a skin mole or new skin lesion, contact the dermatologist.
- Avoid foods and beverages containing tyramine (e.g., aged cheeses and meats, tap beer, red wine, soybean products).
- Make position changes slowly, especially when standing from a lying or sitting position.
- Do not drive or engage in potentially hazardous activities until response to drug is known.
- Report immediately any of the following to a health care provider: palpitations, severe headache, blurred vision, difficulty thinking, seizures, chest pain, unexplained nausea or vomiting, or any sudden weakness or paralysis.

RASBURICASE

(ras-bur′i-case)

Elitek, Fasturtec ✦

Classifications: ANTIGOUT AGENT; ANTIMETABOLITE

Therapeutic: ANTIGOUT

Pregnancy Category: C

AVAILABILITY 1.5 mg/vial powder for injection

ACTION & THERAPEUTIC EFFECT

A recombinant urate-oxidase enzyme produced by DNA technology from *Aspergillus flavus*. In humans, uric acid is the final step in the catabolic pathway of purines. Rasburicase catalyzes enzymatic oxidation of uric acid; thus it is only active at the end of the purine catabolic pathway. *Used to manage plasma uric acid levels in pediatric patients with leukemia, lymphoma, and solid tumor malignancies who are receiving anticancer therapy that results in tumor lysis, and therefore elevates plasma uric acid.*

USES Initial management of increased uric acid levels secondary to tumor lysis.

CONTRAINDICATIONS Hypersensitivity to rasburicase; deficiency in glucose-6-phosphate dehydrogenase (G6PD); history of anaphylaxis or hypersensitivity reactions; hemolytic reactions or methemoglobinemia reactions to rasburicase; pregnancy (category C), lactation, children <1 mo.

CAUTIOUS USE Patients at risk for G6PD deficiency (e.g., African or Mediterranean ancestry). Safety and efficacy in adults and elderly are unknown.

ROUTE & DOSAGE

Hyperuricemia

Child: **IV** *>1 mo,* 0.15–0.2 mg/kg/d × 5 d starting 4–24 h before chemotherapy

ADMINISTRATION

Intravenous

PREPARE: IV Infusion: Reconstitute each 1.5 mg vial of ELITEK with 1 mL of the provided diluent and mix by swirling very gently. **Do not shake.** Discard if particulate matter is visible or if product is discolored after reconstitution. Remove the predetermined dose from the reconstituted vials and inject enough NS into an infusion bag to achieve a final total volume of 50 mL. **ADMINISTER: IV Infusion:** Give over 30 min. **DO NOT GIVE BOLUS DOSE.** Infuse through an

R

Common adverse effects in *italic*, life-threatening effects <u>underlined</u>; generic names in **bold**; classifications in SMALL CAPS; ✦ Canadian drug name; ⊘ Prototype drug

1329

unfiltered line used for no other medications. If a separate line is not possible, flush the line with at least 15 mL of saline solution before/after infusion of rasburicase.

▪ Immediately discontinue IV infusion and institute emergency measures for S&S of anaphylaxis including chest pain, dyspnea, hypotension, and/or urticaria.

INCOMPATIBILITIES Do not mix or infuse with other drugs.

ADVERSE EFFECTS (≥1%) **Body as a Whole:** *Fever,* sepsis, severe hypersensitivity reactions including anaphylaxis at any time during treatment. **CNS:** *Headache.* **GI:** *Mucositis, vomiting, nausea, diarrhea, abdominal pain.* **Hematologic:** Neutropenia. **Skin:** *Rash.*

DIAGNOSTIC TEST INTERFERENCE May give false elevations for ***uric acid*** if blood sample is left at room temperature.

PHARMACOKINETICS Half-Life: 18 h.

CLINICAL IMPLICATIONS

Assessment & Drug Effects
▪ Lab tests: Patients at higher risk for G6PD deficiency (e.g., patients of African or Mediterranean ancestry) should be screened prior to starting therapy as this deficiency is a contraindication for this drug.
▪ Lab test special instructions: Blood for uric acid analysis must be collected into prechilled tubes containing heparin anticoagulant and **immediately immersed in an ice water bath.** Plasma samples must be prepared by centrifugation in a precooled centrifuge (4° C) and plasma must be maintained in an ice water bath and analyzed for uric acid within 4 h of collection.
▪ Monitor closely for S&S of hypersensitivity and be prepared to institute emergency measures for anaphylaxis.
▪ Monitor cardiovascular, respiratory, neurologic, and renal status throughout therapy.

Patient & Family Education
▪ Report immediately any distressing S&S to physician.

REMIFENTANIL HYDROCHLORIDE

(rem-i-fent′a-nil)

Ultiva

Classifications: ANALGESIC; NARCOTIC (OPIATE) AGONIST; GENERAL ANESTHESIA
Therapeutic: NARCOTIC (OPIATE) ANALGESIC; GENERAL ANESTHESIA
Prototype: Morphine
Pregnancy Category: C
Controlled Substance: Schedule II

AVAILABILITY 1 mg/mL, 2 mg/mL, 5 mg/mL injection

ACTION & *THERAPEUTIC EFFECT* Synthetic, potent narcotic agonist analgesic similar to fentanyl. Rapidly metabolized; therefore respiratory depression is of shorter duration than fentanyl analogs when discontinued. *Used as the analgesic component of an anesthesia regime.*

USES Analgesic during induction and maintenance of general anesthesia, as the analgesic component of monitored anesthesia care.

CONTRAINDICATIONS Hypersensitivity to fentanyl analogs, epidural or intrathecal administration; pregnancy (category C).
CAUTIOUS USE Head injuries, increased intracranial pressure; older adults, debilitated, morbid obesity,

R

poor-risk patients; COPD, other respiratory problems, bradyarrhythmia; lactation. Safety in labor and delivery has not been demonstrated.

ROUTE & DOSAGE

Adjunct to Anesthesia

Adult: IV 0.5–1 mcg/kg/min or 1 mcg/kg bolus
Child: IV Birth to 2 mo, 0.4–1 mcg/kg/min; 1–12 y, 0.5–1 mcg/kg/min or 1 mcg/kg bolus

Obesity

Dose based on IBW

ADMINISTRATION

Note: See manufacturer's guidelines for reconstitution information and infusion rates.

INCOMPATIBILITIES Solution/additive: Unknown. Y-site: Amphotericin B, amphotericin B cholesteryl, cefoperazone, chlorpromazine, diazepam.

Intravenous
- Reduce starting doses by 50% for patients >65 y. Base doses on ideal body weight for obese patients (>30% over ideal body weight). - Clear IV tubing completely of the drug following discontinuation of remifentanil infusion to ensure that inadvertent administration of the drug will not occur at a later time. - Reconstituted solution is stable for 24 h at room temperature. Store vials of powder at 2°–25° C (36°–77° F).

ADVERSE EFFECTS (≥1%) Body as a Whole: Muscle rigidity, shivering. CNS: Dizziness, headache. CV: Hypotension, hypertension, bradycardia. GI: *Nausea*, vomiting. Respiratory: Respiratory depression, apnea. Skin: Pruritus.

INTERACTIONS Drug: Alcohol and other CNS DEPRESSANTS potentiate effects; MAO INHIBITORS may precipitate hypertensive crisis.

PHARMACOKINETICS Duration: 12 min. Distribution: 70% protein bound. Metabolism: Hydrolyzed by nonspecific esterases in the blood and tissues. Elimination: In urine. Half-Life: 3–10 min.

CLINICAL IMPLICATIONS

Assessment & Drug Effects
- Monitor vital signs during postoperative period; observe for and immediately report any S&S of respiratory distress or respiratory depression, or skeletal and thoracic muscle rigidity and weakness.
- Monitor for adequate postoperative analgesia.

REPAGLINIDE ⊕

(rep-a-gli'nide)
Prandin, GlucoNorm ✦
Classifications: HORMONE; ANTIDIABETIC AGENT; MEGLITINIDE
Therapeutic: ANTIDIABETIC
Pregnancy Category: C

AVAILABILITY 0.5 mg, 1 mg, 2 mg tablets

ACTION & *THERAPEUTIC EFFECT*
Oral hypoglycemic agent that lowers blood glucose levels by stimulating release of insulin from the pancreatic islets. *Significantly reduces postprandial blood glucose in type 2 diabetes [preprandial blood glucose between 80 and 120 mg/dL and HbA_{1c} (glycosylated Hgb <6.5%)]. Minimal effects on fasting blood glucose were observed.*

USES Adjunct to diet and exercise in type 2 diabetes. May also be used in combination with metformin.

Common adverse effects in *italic*, life-threatening effects <u>underlined</u>; generic names in **bold**; classifications in SMALL CAPS; ✦ Canadian drug name; ⊕ Prototype drug

1331

CONTRAINDICATIONS Hypersensitivity to repaglinide; insulin-dependent diabetes, diabetic ketoacidosis, hypoglycemia; severe renal dysfunction; pregnancy (category C), lactation.

CAUTIOUS USE Hypoglycemia; loss of glycemic control due to secondary failure; hepatic impairment; older adults, surgery, fever, systemic infection, trauma. No studies have been done in children.

ROUTE & DOSAGE

Type 2 Diabetes
Adult: **PO** Initial dose: 0.5 mg 15–30 min a.c.; initial dose for patients previously using glucose-lowering agents: 1–2 mg 15–30 min a.c. (2–4 doses/d depending on meal pattern; max: 16 mg/d); dosage range: 0.5–4 mg 15–30 min a.c.

ADMINISTRATION

Oral
- Give within 30 min of beginning a meal.
- Store at 15°–30° C (59°–86° F) in a tightly closed container and protect from moisture.

ADVERSE EFFECTS (≥1%) **Body as a Whole:** Arthralgia, back pain, paresthesia, allergy. **CNS:** Headache. **CV:** Chest pain, angina. **GI:** Nausea, diarrhea, constipation, vomiting, dyspepsia. **Respiratory:** URI, sinusitis, rhinitis, bronchitis. **Metabolic:** *Hypoglycemia.*

INTERACTIONS Drug: Erythromycin, ketoconazole may inhibit metabolism and potentiate hypoglycemia; BARBITURATES, **carbamazepine, rifabutin, rifampin, rifapentine, pioglitazone** may induce metabolism and cause hyperglycemia; **gemfibrozil** may increase risk of hypoglycemia and duration of action. **Herbal: Ginseng, garlic** may increase hypoglycemic effects. **Food:** Grapefruit juice (>1 qt/day) may increase plasma concentrations and adverse effects.

PHARMACOKINETICS Absorption: Rapidly from GI tract, 56% bioavailability. **Peak:** 1 h. **Distribution:** 98% protein bound. **Metabolism:** In liver (CYP3A4). **Elimination:** 90% in feces. **Half-Life:** 1 h.

CLINICAL IMPLICATIONS

Assessment & Drug Effects
- Lab tests: Frequent FBS and postprandial blood glucose monitoring and HbA$_{1C}$ q3mo to determine effective dose.
- Monitor carefully for S&S of hypoglycemia especially during the 1-wk period following transfer from a longer-acting sulfonylurea such as chlorpropamide.

Patient & Family Education
- Take only with meals to lessen the chance of hypoglycemia. If a meal is skipped, skip a dose; if a meal is added, add a dose.
- Start repaglinide the morning after the other agent is stopped when changing from another oral hypoglycemic drug.
- Be alert for S&S of hyperglycemia or hypoglycemia (see Appendix F); report poor blood glucose control to physician.

RESERPINE ⊕

(re-ser'peen)

Serpalan, Sk-Reserpine

Classifications: RAUWOLFIA ALKALOID; ANTIHYPERTENSIVE

Therapeutic: ANTIHYPERTENSIVE

Pregnancy Category: D

AVAILABILITY 0.1 mg, 0.25 mg tablets

ACTION & *THERAPEUTIC EFFECT*
Principal alkaloid of *Rauwolfia serpentina*. Interferes with binding of serotonin at receptor sites, decreases synthesis of norepinephrine by depleting dopamine (its precursor), and competitively inhibits their reuptake in storage granules. Depletes norepinephrine and serotonin in CNS, peripheral nervous system, heart, and other organs and tissues. *Sympathetic inhibition seen in small but persistent decrease in BP, frequently associated with bradycardia, and reduced cardiac output. Central effect results in tranquilization and sedation similar to those produced by chlorpromazine.*

USES Mild essential hypertension and as adjunctive therapy with other antihypertensive agents in the more severe forms of hypertension. Also used in agitated psychotic states, primarily in patients intolerant to phenothiazine or patients who also require antihypertensive medication.

UNLABELED USES Reduce vasospastic attacks in Raynaud's phenomenon and other peripheral vascular disorders, and for short-term symptomatic treatment of thyrotoxicosis.

CONTRAINDICATIONS Hypersensitivity to rauwolfia alkaloids; history of mental depression; acute peptic ulcer, ulcerative colitis; patients receiving electroconvulsive therapy; within 7–14 d of MAO inhibitor therapy; pregnancy (category D), lactation. Safe use in children is not established.

CAUTIOUS USE Renal insufficiency; cardiac arrhythmias; cardiac damage; cerebrovascular accident; history of peptic ulcers; epilepsy; bronchitis; asthma; older adults, de-

bilitated patients; gallstones; obesity; chronic sinusitis; parkinsonism; pheochromocytoma.

ROUTE & DOSAGE

Hypertension
Adult: **PO** 0.5 mg/d initially, reduced to 0.1–0.25 mg/d
Geriatric: **PO** Start with 0.05 mg q.d., increase by 0.05 mg per wk

ADMINISTRATION

Oral
- Give with meals or with milk or other food to minimize possibility of gastric irritation (drug increases gastric secretions).
- Store in tight, light-resistant containers, preferably at 15°–30° C (59°–86° F), unless otherwise directed by manufacturer.

ADVERSE EFFECTS (≥1%) **CNS:** *Drowsiness*, sedation, *lethargy*, mental depression, nervousness, anxiety, nightmares, increased dreaming, headache, dizziness, increased appetite, dull sensorium; prolonged use of large doses: CNS stimulation (parkinsonian syndrome): tremors, muscle rigidity; <u>respiratory depression</u>, convulsions, hypothermia. **CV:** Bradycardia, *edema*, orthostatic hypotension, increased AV conduction time (prolonged therapy); angina-like symptoms, arrhythmias, CHF (rare). **Special Senses:** *Nasal congestion,* epistaxis, lacrimation, blurred vision; miosis, ptosis, conjunctival congestion (acute toxicity). **GI:** Dry mouth or excessive salivation, nausea, vomiting, abdominal cramps, diarrhea, reactivation of peptic ulcer (hypersecretion), heartburn, biliary colic. **Hematologic:** Thrombocytopenic purpura, anemia, prolonged BT. **Body as a Whole:** Hypersensi-

Common adverse effects in *italic*, life-threatening effects <u>underlined</u>; generic names in **bold**; classifications in SMALL CAPS; ♣ Canadian drug name; ● Prototype drug

1333

tivity (Pruritus, rash, asthma), Muscle aches, dysuria, fixed-drug eruptions. **Urogenital:** Menstrual irregularities, breast engorgement, galactorrhea, gynecomastia, feminization (males), impaired sexual function, impotence.

DIAGNOSTIC TEST INTERFERENCE

Possibility of elevated **blood glucose** values; however, it is also reported that reserpine may decrease thiazide-induced hyperglycemia. Increase in **serum prolactin** with chronic administration of **rauwolfia** alkaloids; overdoses may cause initial increase in excretion of **urinary catecholamines;** decreases with chronic administration. Large doses may cause initial rise in **urinary 5 HIAA** excretion. Initial IM doses may increase **urinary VMA** excretion followed by decrease by end of third day of therapy (with oral or parenteral administration). Possible interference with **urinary steroid** colorimetric determinations: **17-OHCS** and **17-KS.**

INTERACTIONS Drug: Diuretics,

other HYPOTENSIVE AGENTS compound hypotensive effects; CARDIAC GLYCOSIDES (**digoxin**) may increase risk of arrhythmias; MAO INHIBITORS may cause excitation and hypertension; CNS DEPRESSANTS compound depression; may decrease response to **levodopa. Herbal: St. John's wort** may antagonize hypotensive effects.

PHARMACOKINETICS Peak: 2 h.

Distribution: Widely distributed, especially to adipose tissue; crosses blood–brain barrier and placenta; distributed in breast milk. **Metabolism:** Extensively metabolized to inactive compounds. **Elimination:** Slowly excreted, 60% in feces within 96 h and 10% in urine. **Half-Life:** 4.5 and 11.3 h.

CLINICAL IMPLICATIONS

Assessment & Drug Effects

- Assess vital signs at intervals prescribed by physician. Compare readings with baseline data and keep physician informed. (Note: Drop in BP may be accompanied by bradycardia.)
- Lab tests: Periodic CBC with differential, platelet count, serum electrolytes, and plasma glucose.
- Supervise ambulation as indicated; postural hypotension occurs rarely with usual PO doses but is not uncommon in patients receiving large parenteral doses.
- Monitor I&O, especially in patients with impaired kidney function. Report changes in I&O ratio and pattern.
- Full therapeutic effect of oral drug for hypertension may not occur until 2–3 wk of therapy, and effects may persist for as long as 4–6 wk after drug is discontinued.
- Take special precautions with older adult and obese patients (half-life is reportedly prolonged in obese patients). Anticipate increased incidence of adverse effects.
- Be aware that mental depression is a serious adverse effect and may be severe. It occurs most commonly in high dosage regimens (e.g., 0.5–1 mg/d or more) and may not appear until 2–8 mo of therapy and may last for several months after drug is withdrawn.

Patient & Family Education

- Take drug at the same time each day, do not skip or double doses, and do not stop therapy without advice of physician.
- Do not drive or engage in potentially hazardous activities until response to drug is known.
- Learn about possible adverse effects and report promptly to physician.

- Report the following possible beginning symptoms of depression: early morning insomnia, anorexia, inability to concentrate, despondency, self-deprecation, attitude of detachment, mood swings, or impotence. Hospitalization may be necessary.
- Make position changes slowly, particularly from recumbent to upright posture, and lie down or sit down (head-low position) if patient feels faint. Do not take hot showers or hot tub baths, and do not to stand still for prolonged periods. Report symptoms of dizziness or lightheadedness to physician.
- Check for edema and record weight daily to help make a distinction between weight gain from edema and that from increased appetite. Consult physician about gain of 1–2 kg (3–5 lb) in 1 wk.
- Do not take OTC medications without consulting physician or pharmacist (many preparations for coughs and colds contain adrenergic agents that affect the actions of rauwolfia alkaloids).

RESPIRATORY SYNCYTIAL VIRUS IMMUNE GLOBULIN (RSV-IVIG)

(res-pir′a-tory sin-cy′ti-al)

RespiGam

Classifications: BIOLOGIC RESPONSE MODIFIER; IMMUNOGLOBULIN
Therapeutic: IMMUNOGLOBULIN
Prototype: Immune globulin
Pregnancy Category: C

AVAILABILITY 2500 mg/50 mL vial

ACTION & THERAPEUTIC EFFECT Contains IgG immune globulin antibodies from human plasma. *The preparation contains large amounts of RSV-neutralizing antibodies.*

USES Prevention of serious lower respiratory tract infection caused by RSV in children <24 mo with bronchopulmonary dysplasia or history of premature birth; hypervolemia.

CONTRAINDICATIONS Previous severe reaction to RespiGam or other human immunoglobulin preparation, selective IgA deficiency; congenital heart disease; fluid overload; hepatic disease, pregnancy (category C).
CAUTIOUS USE Immunodeficiency, AIDS, pulmonary disease; CHF; renal failure.

ROUTE & DOSAGE

RSV

Child/Infant/Neonate: **IV** 750 mg/kg infused at 1.5 mL/kg/h for first 15 min, then 3 mL/kg/h for next 15 min, then 6 mL/kg/h for rest of infusion, may repeat monthly as needed

ADMINISTRATION

Intravenous
PREPARE: IV Infusion: Give undiluted.
ADMINISTER: IV Infusion: Do not shake vial; infuse vial contents undiluted through a separate IV line if possible; if "piggyback" must be used, see manufacturer's directions. DO NOT EXCEED IV INFUSION RATES given in Route & Dosage table! Use a constant infusion pump.
INCOMPATIBILITIES Solution/additive or Y-site: Do not mix with other drugs.

- Store vials at 2°–8° C (35°–46° F). Begin infusion within 6 h after vial is entered and complete within 12 h.

ADVERSE EFFECTS (≥1%) **Body as a Whole:** Fever, pyrexia, fluid over-

Common adverse effects in *italic*, life-threatening effects underlined; generic names in **bold**; classifications in SMALL CAPS; ♦ Canadian drug name; ☻ Prototype drug

1335

load. **CV:** Tachycardia, hypertension. **GI:** Vomiting, diarrhea, gastroenteritis. **Respiratory:** Respiratory distress, wheezing, rales, hypoxia, hypoxemia, tachypnea. **Skin:** Injection site inflammation.

INTERACTIONS Drug: May interfere with immune response to LIVE VIRUS VACCINES (mumps, rubella, measles), may need to repeat vaccine if given within 10 mo of **RespiGam**.

PHARMACOKINETICS Half-Life: 22–28 d.

CLINICAL IMPLICATIONS
Assessment & Drug Effects
- Monitor closely during and after each IV rate change.
- Assess vital signs and respiratory status prior to infusion, during and after each rate change, and at 30-min intervals until 30 min after infusion is completed, and periodically thereafter for 24 h.
- Slow infusion immediately if S&S of fluid overload appear and report to physician.
- Lab tests: Monitor routine blood chemistry, serum electrolytes, blood gases, osmolality.
- Monitor for aseptic meningitis syndrome, which may begin up to 2 d after infusion.

Patient & Family Education
- Be aware of the possibility of aseptic meningitis syndrome; learn S&S to report (headache, drowsiness, fever, photophobia, painful eye movements, muscle rigidity, nausea, vomiting).

RETEPLASE RECOMBINANT

(re'te-plase)
Retavase
Classifications: ANTICOAGULANT; THROMBOLYTIC ENZYME

Therapeutic: THROMBOLYTIC
Prototype: Alteplase
Pregnancy Category: C

AVAILABILITY 10.4 IU vials

ACTION & THERAPEUTIC EFFECT
DNA recombinant human tissue-type plasminogen activator (t-PA) that acts as a catalyst in the cleavage of plasminogen to plasmin. Responsible for degrading the fibrin matrix of a clot. *Has antithrombolytic properties.*

USES Thrombolysis management of acute MI to reduce the incidence of CHF and mortality.

CONTRAINDICATIONS Active internal bleeding, history of CVA, recent neurologic surgery or trauma, intercranial neoplasm, or aneurysm, bleeding disorders, severe uncontrolled hypertension; pregnancy (category C).
CAUTIOUS USE Any condition in which bleeding constitutes a significant hazard (i.e., severe hepatic or renal disease, CVA, hypertension, acute pancreatitis, septic thrombophlebitis); lactation. Safety and efficacy in children are not established.

ROUTE & DOSAGE

Thrombolysis during Acute MI
Adult: **IV** 10 U injected over 2 min. Repeat dose in 30 min (20 U total)

ADMINISTRATION
Intravenous

PREPARE: Direct: Reconstitute using only the diluent, syringe, needle, and dispensing pin provided with reteplase. Withdraw diluent with syringe provided. Remove needle from syringe, replace with dispensing pin and transfer diluent to vial of reteplase. Leave pin and syringe in place in vial and swirl to dissolve. Do NOT shake. When completely dissolved, remove 10 mL solution, replace dispensing pin with a 20-gauge needle.

***ADMINISTER:* Direct:** Flush IV line before & after with 30 mL NS or D5W and do NOT give any other drug simultaneously through the same IV line. Give a single dose evenly over 2 min.

***INCOMPATIBILITIES* Solution/additive: Heparin. Y-site: Bivalirudin, heparin.**

- Store drug kit unopened at 2°–25° C (36°–77° F).

ADVERSE EFFECTS (≥1%) **Hematologic:** *Hemorrhage* (including *intracranial*, GI, genitourinary), anemia. **CV:** Reperfusion arrhythmias.

DIAGNOSTIC TEST INTERFERENCE Causes decreases in plasminogen and fibrinogen, making coagulation and fibrinolytic tests unreliable.

INTERACTIONS Drug: Aspirin, abciximab, dipyridamole, heparin may increase risk of bleeding.

PHARMACOKINETICS Elimination: In urine. **Half-Life:** 13–16 min.

CLINICAL IMPLICATIONS
Assessment & Drug Effects
- Discontinue concomitant heparin immediately if serious bleeding not controllable by local pressure occurs and, if not already given, withhold the second reteplase bolus.
- Monitor carefully all potential bleeding sites; monitor for S&S of internal hemorrhage (e.g., GI, GU, intracranial, retroperitoneal, pulmonary).
- Monitor carefully cardiac status for arrhythmias associated with reperfusion.

- Avoid invasive procedures, arterial and venous punctures, IM injections, and nonessential handling of the patient during reteplase therapy.

Patient & Family Education
- Report changes in consciousness or signs of bleeding to physician immediately.

RH₀(D) IMMUNE GLOBULIN
(row)
RhoGAM, Rhophylac, WinRho SDF

RH₀(D) IMMUNE GLOBULIN MICRO-DOSE
BayRho-D Mini Dose, MICRho-GAM
Classifications: BIOLOGIC RESPONSE MODIFIER; IMMUNOGLOBULIN
Therapeutic: IMMUNOGLOBULIN
Prototype: Immune globulin
Pregnancy Category: C

AVAILABILITY RhoGAM, MICRho-GAM 5% solution in prefilled syringes; **Rhophylac** 300 mcg prefilled syringe; **WinRho SDF** 120 mcg, 300 mcg, 1000 mcg vials

ACTION & *THERAPEUTIC EFFECT* Sterile nonpyrogenic gamma globulin solution containing immunoglobulins (IgG) of at least 90% IgG, which provides passive immunity by suppressing active antibody response and formation of anti-Rh₀(D) in Rh-negative [Rh₀(D)-negative] individuals previously exposed to Rh-positive [Rh₀(D)-positive, Dᵘ-positive] blood. *Effective for exposure in Rh-negative women when Rh-positive fetal RBCs enter maternal circulation during third stage of labor, fetal-maternal hemorrhage (as early as second trimester), amnio-*

R

Common adverse effects in *italic*, life-threatening effects <u>underlined</u>; generic names in **bold**; classifications in SMALL CAPS; ♣ Canadian drug name; ⓒ Prototype drug

1337

centesis, or other trauma during pregnancy, termination of pregnancy, and following transfusion with Rh-positive RBC, whole blood, or components (platelets, WBC) prepared from Rh-positive blood.

USES To prevent isoimmunization in Rh-negative individuals exposed to Rh-positive RBC (see above). $Rh_0(D)$ immune globulin micro-dose is for use only after spontaneous or induced abortion or termination of ectopic pregnancy up to and including 12 wk of gestation. Treatment of idiopathic thrombocytopenia purpura.

CONTRAINDICATIONS $Rh_0(D)$-positive patient; person previously immunized against $Rh_0(D)$ factor, hypersensitivity for thimerosal, severe immune globulin hypersensitivity, bleeding disorders; pregnancy (category C); neonates.
CAUTIOUS USE IgA deficiency.

ROUTE & DOSAGE

Note: Only WinRho SDF can be given IV. BayRho-E and RhoGAM are available in regular and mini-dose vials

Antepartum Prophylaxis

Adult: **IM/IV** 300 mcg at approximately 28 wk gestation; followed by 1 vial of mini-dose or 120 mcg within 72 h of delivery if infant is Rh-positive

Postpartum Prophylaxis

Adult: **IM/IV** 300 mcg preferably within 72 h of delivery if infant is Rh-positive

Following Amniocentesis, Miscarriage, Abortion, Ectopic Pregnancy

Adult: **IM** If over 13 wk gestation, 300 mcg, preferably within 3 h but at least within 72 h; if less than 13 wk, give 50 mcg

Transfusion Accident

Adult: **IM/IV** 300 mcg for each volume of RBCs infused divided by 15, given within at least 72 h of accident
Child: **IV** Administer 600 mcg q8h until total dose given. Exposure to positive whole blood 9 mcg/mL, exposure to positive RBCs 18 mcg/mL. **IM** Administer 1200 mcg q12h until total dose given. Exposure to positive whole blood 12 mcg/mL, exposure to positive RBCs 24 mcg/mL

Idiopathic Thrombocytopenia Purpura

Adult/Child: **IV** 50 mcg/kg, then 25–60 mcg/kg depending on response

ADMINISTRATION

Note: Each vial of $Rh_0(D)$ immune globulin contains enough anti-$Rh_0(D)$ to suppress the immunizing potential of 15 mL Rh-positive packed RBC. Each vial of micro-dose contains enough anti-$Rh_0(D)$ to suppress the immune response to 2.5 mL of Rh-positive packed RBC.

Intramuscular
- Make sure that lot numbers of drug used for the cross-match and the drug to be administered are the same.
- Administer $Rh_0(D)$ immune globulin via IM to the mother only; not to the infant.
- Use the deltoid muscle. Give in divided doses at different sites, all at once or at intervals, as long as the entire dose is given within 72 h after delivery or termination of pregnancy.
- Reconstitute with 1.25 mL of NS (using the same method to dissolve as for IV). Give immediately after reconstitution.

R

- Keep epinephrine immediately available; systemic allergic reactions sometimes occur.

Intravenous

- Note: 5 IU equals 1 mcg.
- Verify correct IV concentration and rate of infusion for a child >3 y with physician.

PREPARE: Direct: Reconstitute each vial with 2.5 ml NS (provided by manufacturer). Direct stream of diluent to side of vial, swirl to dissolve, do not shake. Concentration of reconstituted vials: 600 IU yields 240 IU/mL and 1500 IU vial yields 600 IU/mL.

ADMINISTER: Direct: Give a single dose over 3–5 min.

- Refrigerate commercially prepared solutions, although may remain stable up to 30 d at room temperature according to manufacturers. Discard solutions that have been frozen. Store powder at 2°–8° C (36°–46° F) unless otherwise directed; avoid freezing.

ADVERSE EFFECTS (≥1%) **Body as a Whole:** Injection site irritation, slight fever, myalgia, lethargy.

INTERACTIONS Drug: May interfere with immune response to LIVE VIRUS VACCINE; should delay use of LIVE VIRUS VACCINES for 3 mo after administration of **Rho(D) immune globulin.**

PHARMACOKINETICS Peak: 2 h IV, 5–10 d IM. **Half-Life:** 25 d.

CLINICAL IMPLICATIONS

Assessment & Drug Effects

- Obtain history of systemic allergic reactions to human immune globulin preparations prior to drug administration.
- Send sample of newborn's cord blood to laboratory for cross-match and typing immediately after delivery and before administration of Rho(D) immune globulin. Confirm that mother is Rho(D) and D^u-negative. Infant must be Rh-positive.

Patient & Family Education

- Be aware that administration of Rho(D) immune globulin (antibody) prevents hemolytic disease of the newborn in a subsequent pregnancy.

RIBAVIRIN

(rye-ba-vye′rin)
Virazole, Rebetol, Copegus, Ribasphere
Classifications: ANTIVIRAL AGENT
Therapeutic: ANTIVIRAL
Prototype: Acyclovir
Pregnancy Category: X

AVAILABILITY 6 g/100 mL vial; 200 mg tablets; 200 mg capsules; 40 mg/mL oral solution

ACTION & THERAPEUTIC EFFECT
Synthetic nucleoside with broad-spectrum antiviral activity against DNA and RNA viruses. Mode is believed to involve multiple mechanisms including selective interference with viral ribonucleic protein synthesis. *Active against many RNA and DNA viruses, including respiratory syncytial virus (RSV), influenza A and B, parainfluenza, measles, mumps, Lassa fever, enterovirus 72 (formerly called hepatitis A), yellow fever, HIV, herpes simplex virus (HSV-1 and HSV-2), and vaccinia.*

USES Aerosol treatment of carefully selected hospitalized infants and young children with severe lower respiratory tract infection caused by respiratory syncytial virus (RSV). Oral used in combination with interferon-alfa to treat hepatitis C and in combination with peginterferon alpha for treatment of hepatitis C in patients coinfected with HIV.

R

Common adverse effects in *italic*, life-threatening effects underlined; generic names in **bold**; classifications in SMALL CAPS; ◆ Canadian drug name; ⊕ Prototype drug

1339

UNLABELED USES Prophylaxis and treatment of influenza A and B, pneumonia caused by adenovirus; Lassa fever, measles, HSV-1, HSV-2, hepatitis A, herpes zoster, and for carefully selected patients with AIDS and AIDS-related complex (ARC).

CONTRAINDICATIONS Mild RSV infections of lower respiratory tract; infants requiring simultaneous assisted ventilation; severe cardiovascular disease, congestive heart failure, angina, unstable cardiac disease; pancreatitis, prolonged or multiple courses of ribavirin inhalation therapy; autoimmune hepatitis; renal failure, or Cl_{cr} <50 mL/min; hemoglobinopathy, thalassemia major, sickle cell disease; pregnancy (category X), lactation; tablet form for children <18 y.

CAUTIOUS USE COPD, asthma; anemia; history of MI, cardiac arrhythmias; older adults, decreased renal, hepatic, or cardiac function; respiratory depression; history of depression or suicidal tendencies.

ROUTE & DOSAGE

RSV

Child: **Inhalation** 20 mg via SPAG nebulizer administered over 12–18 h/d for a minimum of 3 d (max: 7 d)

Hepatitis C

(in combination with interferon-alfa)

Adult: **PO** >75 kg, 600 mg b.i.d. for 24–48 wk; <75 kg, 400 mg in a.m., 600 mg in p.m. for 24–48 wk

Child: **PO** >3 y and >75 kg, 600 mg b.i.d.; 62–75 kg, 400 mg in a.m., 600 mg in p.m.; 50–61 kg, 400 mg b.i.d.; 37–49 kg, 200 mg in a.m. and 400 mg in p.m.; 25–36 kg, 200 mg b.i.d. for 24–48 wk

Renal Impairment

Cl_{cr} <50 mL/min: oral ribavirin should not be used

ADMINISTRATION

Note: Aerosol solution is prepared with either sterile water for injection or sterile water for inhalation, without preservatives or any other added substance. See manufacturer's package insert for preparation directions. Inspect solution for discoloration or presence of particulate matter. Discard discolored or cloudy solutions.

Inhalation

- Administer only by SPAG-2 aerosol generator, following manufacturer's directions.
- Caution: Ribavirin has demonstrated teratogenicity in animals. Advise pregnant health care personnel of the potential teratogenic risks associated with exposure during ribavirin administration to patients.
- Do not give other aerosol medication concomitantly with ribavirin.
- Discard solution in the SPAG-2 reservoir at least q24h and whenever liquid level is low before fresh reconstituted solution is added.
- Store unopened vial in a dry place at 15°–25° C (59°–78° F) unless otherwise directed.
- Following reconstitution, store solution at 20°–30° C (68°–86° F) for 24 h.

ADVERSE EFFECTS (≥1%) **CV:** Hypotension (faintness, light-headedness, unusual fatigue), <u>MI, cardiac arrest</u>. **Special Senses:** Conjunctivitis, erythema of eyelids. **Hematologic:** Reticulocytosis, <u>hemolytic anemia</u> (especially in combination with interferon alpha). **Respiratory:** Deterioration of respiratory function, dyspnea, <u>apnea</u>, chest soreness, bacterial pneumonia, ventila-

Common adverse effects in *italic*, life-threatening effects <u>underlined</u>; generic names in **bold**; classifications in SMALL CAPS; ♣ Canadian drug name; ☻ Prototype drug

tor dependence. **GI:** Transient increases in AST, ALT, bilirubin; abdominal cramps, jaundice.

INTERACTIONS Drug: Ribavirin may antagonize the antiviral effects of **zidovudine** against HIV; increased risk of fetal defects with **peginterferon.**

PHARMACOKINETICS Absorption: Rapidly absorbed orally (44%) and systemically from lungs. **Peak:** Inhaled 60–90 min. PO 1.7–3 h. **Distribution:** Crosses placenta; distributed into breast milk. **Metabolism:** In cells to an active metabolite. **Elimination:** 85% in urine, 15% in feces. **Half-Life:** 24 h in plasma, 16–40 d in RBCs.

CLINICAL IMPLICATIONS

Assessment & Drug Effects

- Obtain specimens for rapid diagnosis of RSV infection before therapy is initiated or at least during the first 24 h of ribavirin therapy. Do not continue therapy without laboratory confirmation of RSV infection.
- Treatment efficacy in RSV infections appears greatest if initiated within the first 3 d.
- Monitor respiratory function and fluid status closely during therapy. Note baseline rate and character of respirations and pulse. Observe for signs of labored breathing: dyspnea, apnea; rapid, shallow respirations, intercostal and substernal retraction, nasal flaring, limited excursion of lungs, cyanosis. Auscultate lungs for abnormal breath sounds.
- Observe patients requiring simultaneous assisted ventilation closely for S&S of worsening pulmonary function. Check equipment carefully every 2 h, including endotracheal tube, for malfunction.

Precipitation of ribavirin and accumulation of fluid in tubing can obstruct the apparatus and cause inadequate ventilation and gas exchange.

- Consult physician about management of fluid and food intake and keep an accurate record of I&O.

RIBOFLAVIN (VITAMIN B₂)

(rye′bo-flay-vin)
Riboflavin (Vitamin B₂)
Classifications: VITAMIN
Therapeutic: VITAMIN REPLACEMENT
Pregnancy Category: A (C if >RDA)

AVAILABILITY 50 mg, 100 mg tablets

ACTION & *THERAPEUTIC EFFECT*

Water-soluble vitamin and component of the flavoprotein enzymes, which work together with a wide variety of proteins to catalyze many cellular respiratory reactions by which the body derives its energy. *Evaluated by improvement of clinical manifestations of deficiency: digestive disturbances, headache, burning sensation of skin (especially "burning" feet), cracking at corners of mouth (cheilosis), glossitis, seborrheic dermatitis (and other skin lesions, mental depression, corneal vascularization (with photophobia, burning and itchy eyes, lacrimation, roughness of eyelids), anemia, neuropathy.*

USES To prevent riboflavin deficiency and to treat ariboflavinosis; also to treat microcytic anemia and as a supplement to other B vitamins in treatment of pellagra and beri-beri.

CAUTIOUS USE Pregnancy (category A; category C if >RDA).

Common adverse effects in *italic*, life-threatening effects <u>underlined</u>; generic names in **bold**; classifications in SMALL CAPS; ✦ Canadian drug name; ❷ Prototype drug

1341

ROUTE & DOSAGE

Nutritional Supplement
Adult: **PO** 5–10 mg/d
Child: **PO** 1–4 mg/d

Nutritional Deficiency
Adult: **PO** 5–30 mg/d in divided doses
Child: **PO** 3–10 mg/d

ADMINISTRATION

Oral

▪ Give with food to enhance absorption.
▪ Store in airtight containers protected from light.

ADVERSE EFFECTS (≥1%) **Urogenital:** May discolor urine bright yellow.

DIAGNOSTIC TEST INTERFERENCE

In large doses, riboflavin may produce yellow-green fluorescence in *urine* and thus cause false elevations in certain *fluorometric determinations* of *urinary catecholamines.*

INTERACTIONS Drug: No clinically significant interactions established.

PHARMACOKINETICS Absorption: Readily absorbed from GI tract. **Distribution:** Little is stored; excess amounts are excreted in urine. **Elimination:** In urine. **Half-Life:** 66–84 min.

CLINICAL IMPLICATIONS

Assessment & Drug Effects

▪ Collaborate with physician, dietitian, patient, and responsible family member in planning for diet. A complete dietary history is an essential part of vitamin replacement so that poor eating habits can be identified and corrected. Deficiency in one vitamin is usually associated with other vitamin deficiencies.

Patient & Family Education

▪ Be aware that large doses may cause an intense yellow discoloration of urine.
▪ Note: Rich dietary sources of riboflavin are found in liver, kidney, beef, pork, heart, eggs, milk and milk products, yeast, whole-grain cereals, vitamin A–enriched breakfast cereals, green vegetables, and mushrooms.

RIFABUTIN

(rif-a-bu′tin)
Ansamycin, Mycobutin
Classifications: ANTITUBERCULOSIS AGENT; ANTIBIOTIC
Therapeutic: ANTIBIOTIC; ANTITUBERCULOSIS
Prototype: Rifampin
Pregnancy Category: B

AVAILABILITY 150 mg capsules

ACTION & *THERAPEUTIC EFFECT*

Semisynthetic bacteriostatic antibiotic. Mode of action may be to inhibit DNA-dependent RNA polymerase in susceptible bacterial cells but not in human cells. *Effective against* Mycobacterium avium *complex (MAC) (or* M. avium-intracellulare*) and many strains of* M. tuberculosis.

USES The prevention of disseminated *Mycobacterium avium* complex (MAC) disease in patients with advanced HIV infection.

CONTRAINDICATIONS Hypersensitivity to rifabutin or any other rifamycins; lactation.
CAUTIOUS USE Pregnancy (category B); older adults.

Common adverse effects in *italic*, life-threatening effects underlined; generic names in **bold**; classifications in SMALL CAPS; ♦ Canadian drug name; ◎ Prototype drug

ROUTE & DOSAGE

Prevention of MAC
Adult: **PO** 300 mg q.d., may give 150 mg b.i.d. if nausea is a problem
Child: **PO** 75 mg q.d.

ADMINISTRATION

Oral
- Give as usual dose of 300 mg/d or in two divided doses of 150 mg with food if needed to reduce GI upset.
- Store at room temperature, 15°–30° C (59°–86° F), unless otherwise directed.

ADVERSE EFFECTS (≥1%) **CNS:** Headache, **GI:** *Abdominal pain, dyspepsia, nausea, taste perversion, increased liver enzymes.* **Hematologic:** Thrombocytopenia, eosinophilia, leukopenia, <u>neutropenia</u>. **Skin:** Rash. **Other:** *Turns urine, feces, saliva, sputum, perspiration, and tears orange. Soft contact lenses may be permanently discolored.*

INTERACTIONS Drug: May decrease levels of BENZODIAZEPINES, BETA BLOCKERS, **clofibrate, dapsone,** NARCOTICS, ANTICOAGULANTS, CORTICOSTEROIDS, **cyclosporine, quinidine,** ORAL CONTRACEPTIVES, PROGESTINS, SULFONYLUREAS, **ketoconazole, fluconazole,** BARBITURATES, **theophylline,** and ANTICONVULSANTS, resulting in therapeutic failure.

PHARMACOKINETICS Absorption: 12–20% of oral dose reaches the systemic circulation. **Peak:** 2–3 h. **Distribution:** 85% protein bound. Widely distributed, high concentrations in the lungs, liver, spleen, eyes, and kidney. Crosses placenta, distributed into breast milk. **Metabolism:** In the liver. Causes induction of hepatic enzymes. **Elimination:** Approximately 53% of dose is excreted in urine as metabolites, 30% is excreted in feces. **Half-Life:** 16–96 h (average 45 h).

CLINICAL IMPLICATIONS

Assessment & Drug Effects
- Monitor patients for S&S of active TB. Report immediately.
- Lab tests: Monitor periodic blood work for neutropenia and thrombocytopenia.
- Evaluate patients on concurrent oral hypoglycemic therapy for loss of glycemic control.
- Review patient's complete drug regimen because dosage adjustment of a significant number of drugs may be needed when rifabutin is added to regimen.

Patient & Family Education
- Learn S&S of TB and MAC (e.g., persistent fever, progressive weight loss, anorexia, night sweats, diarrhea) and notify physician if any of these develop.
- Notify physician of following: Muscle or joint pain, eye pain or other discomfort, chest pain with dyspnea, rash, or a flu-like syndrome.
- Be aware that urine, feces, saliva, sputum, perspiration, tears, and skin may be colored brown-or-ange. Soft contact lens may be permanently discolored.
- Rifabutin may reduce the activity of a wide variety of drugs. Provide a complete and accurate list of concurrent drugs to the physician for evaluation.

R

RIFAMPIN ⊕

(rif′am-pin)
Rifadin, Rimactane, Rofact ♦
Classifications: ANTIBIOTIC; ANTITUBERCULOSIS AGENT

Common adverse effects in *italic*; life-threatening effects <u>underlined</u>; generic names in **bold**; classifications in SMALL CAPS; ♦ Canadian drug name; ⊕ Prototype drug

1343

Therapeutic: ANTIBIOTIC; ANTITUBER-
CULOSIS AGENT
Pregnancy Category: C

AVAILABILITY 150 mg, 300 mg
capsules; 600 mg injection

ACTION & *THERAPEUTIC EFFECT*
Semisynthetic derivative of rifamycin B, an antibiotic derived from
Streptococcus mediterranei, with
bacteriostatic and bactericidal actions. Inhibits DNA-dependent RNA
polymerase activity in susceptible
bacterial cells, thereby suppressing
RNA synthesis. *Active against* Mycobacterium tuberculosis, M. leprae, Neisseria meningitidis, *and a
wide range of gram-negative and
gram-positive organisms.*

USES Primarily as adjuvant with
other antituberculosis agents in
initial treatment and retreatment of
clinical tuberculosis; as short-term
therapy to eliminate meningococci
from nasopharynx of asymptomatic carriers of *N. meningitidis*
when risk of meningococcal meningitis is high.
UNLABELED USES Chemoprophylaxis in contacts of patients with
Haemophilus influenzae type B infection; alone or in combination
with dapsone and other antiinfectives in treatment of leprosy (especially dapsone-resistant leprosy).
Also infections caused by susceptible gram-negative and gram-positive bacteria that fail to respond to
other antiinfectives; in combination with erythromycin or tetracycline for treatment of Legionnaire's
disease.

CONTRAINDICATIONS Hypersensitivity to rifampin; obstructive
biliary disease; meningococcal
disease; intermittent rifampin therapy; pregnancy (category C). Safe

use in children <5 y is not established.
CAUTIOUS USE Hepatic disease;
history of alcoholism; concomitant
use of other hepatotoxic agents.

ROUTE & DOSAGE

Pulmonary Tuberculosis
Adult: **PO/IV** 600 mg daily in
conjunction with other antituberculosis agents
Child: **PO/IV** 10–20 mg/kg/d
(max: 600 mg/d)

Meningococcal Carriers
Adult: **PO** 600 mg q12h for 2
consecutive days
Child: **PO** 10–20 mg/kg q12h
for 2 consecutive days (max: 600
mg/d)

**Prophylaxis for *H. influenzae*
Type B**
Adult: **PO** 600 mg/d for 4 d
Child: **PO** 20 mg/kg/d for 4 d
(max: 600 mg/d)

**Dapsone-Sensitive Multibacillary
Leprosy**
Adult: **PO** 600 mg once/mo with
clofazimine and dapsone for a
minimum of 2 y

ADMINISTRATION
Oral
- Give 1 h before or 2 h after a
  meal. Peak serum levels are delayed and may be slightly lower
  when given with food; capsule
  contents may be emptied into fluid
  or mixed with food.
- Note: An oral suspension can be
  prepared from capsules for use
  with pediatric patients. Consult
  pharmacist for directions.
- Keep a desiccant in bottle containing capsules to prevent moisture
  causing instability.

Intravenous

***PREPARE:* IV Infusion:** Dilute by adding 10 mL of sterile water for injection to each 600-mg vial to yield 60 mg/mL. Swirl to dissolve. Withdraw the ordered dose and further dilute in 500 mL (preferred) of D5W. If necessary, 100 mL of D5W may be used.

***ADMINISTER:* IV Infusion:** Infuse 500 mL solution over 3 h and 100 mL solution over 30 min. Note: A less concentrated solution infused over a longer period is preferred.

***INCOMPATIBILITIES* Solution/additive:** Minocycline. **Y-site:** Diltiazem.

■ Use diluted solution within 4 h of preparation.

ADVERSE EFFECTS (≥1%) **CNS:** Fatigue, drowsiness, headache, ataxia, confusion, dizziness, inability to concentrate, generalized numbness, pain in extremities, muscular weakness. **Special Senses:** Visual disturbances, transient low-frequency hearing loss, conjunctivitis. **GI:** *Heartburn, epigastric distress, nausea, vomiting, anorexia, flatulence, cramps, diarrhea,* <u>pseudomembranous colitis,</u> *transient elevations in liver function tests* (bilirubin, BSP, alkaline phosphatase, ALT, AST), pancreatitis. **Hematologic:** Thrombocytopenia, transient leukopenia, anemia, including hemolytic anemia. **Body as a Whole:** Hypersensitivity (fever, pruritus, urticaria, skin eruptions, soreness of mouth and tongue, eosinophilia, hemolysis), flu-like syndrome. **Urogenital:** Hemoglobinuria, hematuria, <u>acute renal failure,</u> light-chain proteinuria, menstrual disorders, <u>hepatorenal syndrome,</u> (with intermittent therapy). **Respiratory:** Hemoptysis. **Other:** Increasing lethargy, liver enlargement and tenderness, jaundice, brownish-red or orange discoloration of skin, sweat, saliva, tears, and feces; unconsciousness.

DIAGNOSTIC TEST INTERFERENCE Rifampin interferes with contrast media used for ***gallbladder study;*** therefore, test should precede daily dose of rifampin. May also cause retention of ***BSP.*** Inhibits standard assays for ***serum folate*** and ***vitamin B₁₂.***

INTERACTIONS Drug: Alcohol, isoniazid, pyrazinamide, ritonavir, saquinavir increase risk of drug-induced hepatotoxicity (including fatal hepatotoxicity when used for latent TB); ***p*-aminosalicylic acid (PAS)** decreases concentrations of rifampin; decreases concentrations of **alfentanil, alosetron, alprazolam, amprenavir,** BARBITURATES, BENZODIAZEPINES, **carbamazepine, atovaquone, cevimeline, chloramphenicol, clofibrate,** CORTICOSTEROIDS, **cyclosporine, dapsone, delavirdine, diazepam, digoxin, diltiazem, disopyramide, estazolam, estramustine, fentanyl, fosphenytoin, fluconazole galantamine, indinavir, itraconazole, ketoconazole, lamotrigine, levobupivacaine, lopinavir, methadone, metoprolol, mexiletine, midazolam, nelfinavir,** ORAL SULFONYLUREAS, ORAL CONTRACEPTIVES, **phenytoin,** PROGESTINS, **propafenone, propranolol, quinidine, quinine, ritonavir, sirolimus, theophylline,** THYROID HORMONES, **tocainide, tramadol, verapamil, warfarin, zaleplon,** and **zonisamide,** leading to potential therapeutic failure.

PHARMACOKINETICS Absorption: Readily from GI tract. **Peak:** 2–4 h. **Distribution:** Widely distributed, including CSF; crosses placenta; distributed into breast milk. **Metabolism:** In liver to active and inactive metabolites; is enterohepatically cycled. **Elimination:** Up to 30% in urine, 60–65% in feces. **Half-Life:** 3 h.

CLINICAL IMPLICATIONS

Assessment & Drug Effects

▪ Lab tests: Periodic liver function tests are advised. Closely monitor patients with hepatic disease.
▪ Check prothrombin time daily or as necessary to establish and maintain required anticoagulant activity when patient is also receiving an anticoagulant.

Patient & Family Education

▪ Do not interrupt prescribed dosage regimen. Hepatorenal reaction with flu-like syndrome has occurred when therapy has been resumed following interruption.
▪ Be aware that drug may impart a harmless red-orange color to urine, feces, sputum, sweat, and tears. Soft contact lenses may be permanently stained.
▪ Report onset of jaundice, hypersensitivity reactions, and persistence of GI adverse effects to physician.
▪ Use or add barrier contraceptive if using hormonal contraception. Concomitant use of rifampin and oral contraceptives leads to decreased effectiveness of the contraceptive and to menstrual disturbances (spotting, breakthrough bleeding).
▪ Keep drug out of reach of children.

RIFAPENTINE

(rif'a-pen-teen)
Priftin
Classifications: ANTIBIOTIC; ANTI-TUBERCULOSIS AGENT

Therapeutic: ANTIBIOTIC; ANTITUBER-CULOSIS AGENT
Prototype: Rifampin
Pregnancy Category: C

AVAILABILITY 150 mg tablets

ACTION & *THERAPEUTIC EFFECT*
Rifamycin derivative similar to rifampin. Inhibits DNA-dependent RNA polymerase activity in susceptible bacterial cells, thereby suppressing RNA synthesis. Inhibits the growth of *Mycobacterium tuberculosis. Effective against* Mycobacterium tuberculosis, *indicated by improvement in clinical S&S (e.g., fever, cough, pleuritic pain, fatigue) and on chest x-ray.*

USES Pulmonary tuberculosis in conjunction with at least one other antitubercular agent.

CONTRAINDICATIONS Hypersensitivity to any rifamycins (e.g., rifampin, rifabutin, rifapentine); porphyria; pregnancy (category C); lactation.

CAUTIOUS USE Patients with abnormal liver function tests or hepatic disease; older adults; HIV disease or concurrent use of protease inhibitors. Safe use in children <12 y not established.

ROUTE & DOSAGE

Tuberculosis: Short-Course Therapy
Adult: **PO** 600 mg twice weekly (at least 72 h apart) times 2 mo, then 600 mg once weekly times 4 mo

ADMINISTRATION

Oral

▪ Give with an interval of NO LESS than 72 h between doses.
▪ Give with food to minimize GI upset.

- Store at 15°–30° C (59°–86° F) in a tightly closed container and protect from excess moisture.

ADVERSE EFFECTS (≥1%) **CNS:** Headache, dizziness. **CV:** Hypertension. **GI:** Increased liver function tests (ALT, AST), anorexia, nausea, vomiting, dyspepsia, diarrhea. **GU:** *Hyperuricemia*, pyuria, proteinuria, hematuria, urinary casts. **Hematologic:** Neutropenia, lymphopenia, anemia, leukopenia, thrombocytosis. **Respiratory:** Hemoptysis. **Skin:** Rash, pruritus, acne. **Body as a Whole:** Arthralgia, pain.

INTERACTIONS Drug: Decreased levels of **indinavir** and possibly other PROTEASE INHIBITORS; increased metabolism and decreased activity of ORAL CONTRACEPTIVES, **phenytoin, disopyramide, mexiletine, quinidine, tocainide, warfarin, fluconazole, itraconazole, ketoconazole, diazepam,** BETA BLOCKERS, CALCIUM CHANNEL BLOCKERS, CORTICOSTEROIDS, **haloperidol,** SULFONYLUREAS, **cyclosporine, tacrolimus, levothyroxine,** NARCOTIC ANALGESICS, **quinine,** REVERSE TRANSCRIPTASE INHIBITORS, TRICYCLIC ANTIDEPRESSANTS, **sildenafil, theophylline.**

PHARMACOKINETICS Absorption: Approximately 70% absorbed. **Peak:** 5–6 h. **Distribution:** 97.7% protein bound. **Metabolism:** Hydrolyzed by esterase enzyme to active metabolite in liver; inducer of cytochromes P450 3A4 and 2C8/9. **Elimination:** 70% in feces, 17% in urine. **Half-Life:** 13.3 h.

CLINICAL IMPLICATIONS

Assessment & Drug Effects

- Lab tests: Sputum smear and culture, CBC, baseline liver functions (especially serum transaminases) to rule out preexisting hepatic disease and serum creatinine and BUN.

- Monitor carefully for S&S of toxicity with concurrent use of oral anticoagulants, digitalis preparations, or anticonvulsants.

Patient & Family Education

- Follow strict adherence to the prescribed dosing schedule to prevent emergence of resistant strains of tuberculosis.
- Be aware that food may be useful in preventing GI upset.
- Report immediately any of the following to the physician: fever, weakness, nausea or vomiting, loss of appetite, dark urine or yellowing of eyes or skin, pain or swelling of the joints, severe or persistent diarrhea.
- Use or add barrier contraceptive if using hormonal contraception.

RIFAXIMIN

(ri-fax′i-min)
Xifaxan
Classifications: RIFAMYCIN ANTIBIOTIC
Therapeutic: ANTIBIOTIC
Prototype: Rifampin
Pregnancy Category: C

R

AVAILABILITY 200 mg tablets

ACTION & THERAPEUTIC EFFECT
A rifamycin antibiotic structurally related to rifampin. Inhibits bacterial RNA synthesis by binding to DNA-dependent RNA polymerase, thereby blocking RNA transcription. *Its spectrum of activity includes gram-positive and gram-negative aerobes and anaerobes.*

USES Treatment of traveler's diarrhea cause by noninvasive strains of *E. coli*.

CONTRAINDICATIONS Hypersensitivity to rifaximin, other rifamycin

Common adverse effects in *italic*, life-threatening effects <u>underlined</u>; generic names in **bold**; classifications in SMALL CAPS; ◆ Canadian drug name; ☻ Prototype drug

1347

antimicrobial agents or to any of its components; ulcerative intestinal disease; dysentery; children <12 y; pregnancy (category C); lactation.
CAUTIOUS USE Diarrhea with fever and/or blood in the stool, or diarrhea due to organisms other than *E. coli;* worsening diarrhea or diarrhea persisting for >24–48 h.

ROUTE & DOSAGE

Traveler's Diarrhea
Adult: **PO** 200 mg t.i.d. for 3 d

ADMINISTRATION

Oral
- May be given without regard to food.
- Store at 15°–30° C (59°–86° F).

ADVERSE EFFECTS (≥1%) **Body as a Whole:** Fever. **CNS:** Headache. **GI:** *Flatulence,* abdominal pain, rectal tenesmus, defecation urgency, nausea, constipation, vomiting.

PHARMACOKINETICS Absorption: <0.4% absorbed orally. **Peak:** 1.21 h. **Elimination:** In feces. **Half-Life:** 5.85 h.

CLINICAL IMPLICATIONS

Assessment & Drug Effects
- Withhold drug and notify physician if symptoms worsen or last >48 h after starting drug; an alternative treatment should be considered.
- Report promptly the appearance of blood in the stool.

Patient & Family Education
- Report promptly any of the following: fever; difficulty breathing; skin rash, itching, or hives; worsening diarrhea during or after treatment or blood in the stool.

RILUZOLE

(ri-lu′zole)
Rilutek
Classifications: AMYOTROPHIC LATERAL SCLEROSIS (ALS) AGENT; GLUTAMATE ANTAGONIST
Therapeutic: ALS AGENT
Pregnancy Category: C

AVAILABILITY 50 mg tablets

ACTION & *THERAPEUTIC EFFECT* Glutamate antagonist used for treating amyotrophic lateral sclerosis (ALS). Inhibits the presynaptic release of glutamic acid in the CNS. Effectiveness based on hypothesis that pathogenesis of ALS is related to injury of motor neurons by glutamate. *Believed to reduce the degeneration of neurons that occurs in ALS.*

USES Treatment of ALS, may extend survival or time to tracheostomy.

CONTRAINDICATIONS Hypersensitivity to riluzole; pregnancy (category C); lactation.
CAUTIOUS USE Hepatic dysfunction, renal impairment; hypertension, history of other CNS disorders. Safe use in children <12 y is not established.

ROUTE & DOSAGE

ALS
Adult: **PO** 50 mg q12h at least 1 h before or 2 h after meals

ADMINISTRATION

Oral
- Give at same time daily and at least 1 h before or 2 h after a meal. Do not give before/after a high-fat meal.
- Store at room temperature; protect from bright light.

ADVERSE EFFECTS (≥1%) **Body as a Whole:** *Asthenia,* headache, back pain, malaise, arthralgia, weight loss, peripheral edema, flu-like syndrome. **CNS:** Hypertonia, depression, dizziness, dry mouth, insomnia, somnolence, circumoral paresthesia. **CV:** Hypertension, tachycardia, phlebitis, palpitation. **GI:** Abdominal pain, *nausea,* vomiting, dyspepsia, anorexia, diarrhea, flatulence, stomatitis. **Respiratory:** *Decreased lung function,* rhinitis, increased cough, apnea, bronchitis, dysphagia, dyspnea. **Skin:** Pruritus, eczema, alopecia, <u>exfoliative dermatitis</u> (rare). **Urogenital:** UTI.

INTERACTIONS Drug: BARBITURATES, **carbamazepine** may increase risk of hepatotoxicity.

PHARMACOKINETICS Absorption: Well absorbed from GI tract, 60% reaches systemic circulation. **Peak:** Steady-state levels by day 5. **Distribution:** 96% protein bound. **Metabolism:** In liver by cytochrome P4501A2 (CYP1A2). **Elimination:** 90% in urine. **Half-Life:** 12 h.

CLINICAL IMPLICATIONS

Assessment & Drug Effects

- Lab tests: Monitor periodically Hct and Hgb, routine blood chemistries, and alkaline phosphatase. If febrile illness develops, monitor WBC count. Monitor liver function before and during course of therapy; evaluate ALT/SGPT every month for first 3 mo, every 3 mo for remainder of first year, and periodically thereafter.
- Withhold drug and notify physician if liver enzymes are elevated.

Patient & Family Education

- Do not increase dose. There is no increased benefit from daily doses >50 mg q12h.
- Report any febrile illness to physician.

- Do not drive or engage in potentially hazardous activities until response to drug is known.
- Learn common adverse effects and possible adverse interaction with alcohol.

RIMANTADINE

(ri-man′ta-deen)
Flumadine
Classifications: ANTIVIRAL
Therapeutic: ANTIVIRAL
Prototype: Amantadine
Pregnancy Category: C

AVAILABILITY 100 mg tablets; 50 mg/5 mL syrup

ACTION & *THERAPEUTIC EFFECT*
Antiviral agent for treatment and prophylaxis of influenza A infections. Thought to exert an inhibitory effect early in the viral replication cycle, probably by interfering with the viral uncoating procedure of the influenza A virus. Inhibits synthesis of both viral RNA and viral protein, thus causing viral destruction. *Prevents or interrupts influenza A infections.*

USES Prophylaxis and treatment of influenza A in adults and prophylaxis of influenza A in children.

CONTRAINDICATIONS Hypersensitivity to rimantadine and amantadine; pregnancy (category C), lactation, children <1 y.
CAUTIOUS USE History of seizures; renal or hepatic impairment; elderly.

ROUTE & DOSAGE

Prophylaxis of Influenza A
Adult/Child: **PO** >10 y, 100 mg b.i.d., reduce to 100 mg daily in older adults or patients with liver disease

R

Common adverse effects in *italic*, life-threatening effects <u>underlined</u>; generic names in **bold**; classifications in SMALL CAPS; ♣ Canadian drug name; ❂ Prototype drug

1349

Child: **PO** <10 y, 5 mg/kg once daily (max: 150 mg/d)

Treatment of Influenza A

Adult: **PO** 100 mg b.i.d., reduce to 100 mg daily in older adults or patients with liver disease, initiate as soon as possible and preferably within 48 h of onset of symptoms and continue for about 7 d

ADMINISTRATION

Oral

- Store at 15°–30° C (59°–86° F).

ADVERSE EFFECTS (≥1%) **CNS:** Nervousness, dizziness, headache, sleep disturbances, fatigue or malaise, drowsiness, anticholinergic effects. **GI:** Nausea, vomiting, diarrhea, dyspepsia, dry mouth, anorexia, abdominal pain.

INTERACTIONS Drug: No clinically significant interactions established.

PHARMACOKINETICS Absorption: Readily absorbed from GI tract. **Peak:** Serum levels 3.2–4.3 h. **Distribution:** Concentrates in respiratory secretions. **Metabolism:** Extensively in liver. **Elimination:** By kidneys. **Half-Life:** 20–36 h.

CLINICAL IMPLICATIONS

Assessment & Drug Effects

- Monitor carefully for seizure activity in patients with a history of seizures. Seizures are an indication to discontinue the drug.
- Monitor cardiac, respiratory, and neurologic status while on drug. Report palpitations, hypertension, dyspnea, or pedal edema.

Patient & Family Education

- Report bothersome adverse effects to physician; especially hallucinations, palpitations, difficulty breathing, and swelling of legs.

- Use caution with hazardous activities until reaction to drug is known.

RIMEXOLONE

(rim-ex'o-lone)
Vexol
Pregnancy Category: C
See Appendix A-1.

RISEDRONATE SODIUM

(ri-se-dron'ate)
Actonel
Classifications: BISPHOSPHONATE; REGULATOR, BONE METABOLISM
Therapeutic: BONE RESORPTION INHIBITOR; OSTEOPOROSIS TREATMENT
Prototype: Etidronate disodium
Pregnancy Category: C

AVAILABILITY 5 mg, 30 mg, 35 mg tablets

ACTION & *THERAPEUTIC EFFECT* Diphosphate preparation with primary action on bone. Mechanism of action not fully understood. Lowers serum alkaline phosphatase, presumably by decreasing release of phosphate from bone and increasing excretion of parathyroid hormone. Slows rate of bone resorption and new bone formation in pagetic bone lesions and in normal remodeling process. *Effectiveness indicated by decreased bone and joint pain and improved bone density.*

USES Paget's disease, prevention and treatment of postmenopausal osteoporosis and steroid-induced osteoporosis.

CONTRAINDICATIONS Hypersensitivity to risedronate or other bisphosphonates; hypocalcemia, vita-

R

min D deficiency; severe renal impairment (creatinine clearance <30 mL/min); pregnancy (category C); lactation.

CAUTIOUS USE Renal impairment; CHF; hyperphosphatemia; hepatic disease; fever related to infection or other causes. Safety and efficacy in children <18 y are not established.

ROUTE & DOSAGE

Paget's Disease

Adult: **PO** 30 mg q.d. at least 30 min before the first food or drink of the day times 2 mo, may repeat after 2 mo rest if necessary

Prevention & Treatment of Osteoporosis

Adult: **PO** 5 mg q.d. 30 min before first food or drink or one dose of 35 mg weekly

ADMINISTRATION

Oral

- Give on an empty stomach (before first food or drink of the day) with at least 6–8 oz plain water.
- Note: Patient should be upright. Maintain upright position and empty stomach for at least 30 min after administration.
- Space calcium supplements and antacids as far as possible from risedronate.
- Store at 15°–30° C (59°–86° F) in a tightly closed container and protect from light.

ADVERSE EFFECTS (≥1%) **Body as a Whole:** Flu-like syndrome, asthenia, arthralgia, bone pain, leg cramps, myasthenia. **CNS:** Headache, dizziness. **CV:** Chest pain, peripheral edema. **GI:** *Diarrhea,* abdominal pain, nausea, constipation, belching, colitis. **Respiratory:** Bronchitis, sinusitis. **Skin:** Rash. **Special**

Senses: Amblyopia, tinnitus, dry eyes.

DIAGNOSTIC TEST INTERFERENCE
May interfere with the use of bone-imaging agents.

INTERACTIONS Drug: C a l c i u m, ANTACIDS significantly decrease absorption.

PHARMACOKINETICS Absorption: Minimally absorbed from GI tract, bioavailability 0.63%. **Peak:** 1 h. **Distribution:** Approximately 60% of dose is distributed to bone. **Metabolism:** Not metabolized. **Elimination:** In urine; unabsorbed drug excreted in feces. **Half-Life:** 220 h.

CLINICAL IMPLICATIONS

Assessment & Drug Effects
- Lab tests: Baseline and periodic serum calcium, phosphorus, and alkaline phosphatase.
- Monitor carefully for and immediately report S&S of GI bleeding and hypocalcemia.

Patient & Family Education
- Learn administration guidelines regarding upright position, empty stomach, and spacing relative to calcium supplements and antacids must be strictly followed.
- Report any of the following to physician: eye irritation, significant GI upset, or flu-like symptoms.

R

RISPERIDONE
(ris-per'i-done)
Risperdal, Risperdal M-TAB, Risperdal Consta
Classifications: PSYCHOTHERAPEUTIC; ANTIPSYCHOTIC, ATYPICAL
Therapeutic: ANTIPSYCHOTIC, ATYPICAL
Prototype: Clozapine
Pregnancy Category: C

Common adverse effects in *italic*, life-threatening effects <u>underlined</u>; generic names in **bold**; classifications in SMALL CAPS; ✦ Canadian drug name; ✪ Prototype drug

1351

AVAILABILITY 0.25 mg, 0.5 mg, 1 mg, 2 mg, 3 mg, 4 mg tablets; 0.5 mg, 1 mg, 2 mg quick-dissolving tablets; 1 mg/mL solution; 25 mg, 37.5 mg, 50 mg injection

ACTION & *THERAPEUTIC EFFECT*
Interferes with binding of dopamine to D_2-interlimbic region of the brain, serotonin (5-HT_2) receptors, and alpha-adrenergic receptors in the occipital cortex. It has low to moderate affinity for the other serotonin (5-HT) receptors. *Effective in controlling symptoms of schizophrenia as well as other psychotic symptoms.*

USES Reduction or elimination of psychotic symptoms in schizophrenia and related psychoses; treatment of bipolar disorder. Seems to improve negative symptoms such as apathy, blunted affect, and emotional withdrawal, irritability in autistic children/adolescents.

UNLABELED USES Management of patients with dementia-related psychotic symptoms. Adjunctive treatment of behavioral disturbances in patients with mental retardation.

CONTRAINDICATIONS Hypersensitivity to risperidone; elderly with dementia-related psychosis; QT prolongation, Reye's syndrome, brain tumor, severe CNS depression, head trauma; suicidal ideation, tardive dyskinesia; sunlight (UV) exposure, tanning beds; pregnancy (category C), lactation, children <15 y.

CAUTIOUS USE Older adults; arrhythmias, hypotension, breast cancer, blood dyscrasia, cardiac disorders, cerebrovascular disease, hypotension, dehydration, diabetes mellitus, diabetic ketoacidosis, hyperglycemia, hypokalemia, hypomagnesemia, hyponatremia, MI, obesity, orthostatic hypotension, mild or moderate CNS depression, coma; GI obstruction, dysphagia; electrolyte imbalance, ethanol intoxication, heart failure, renal or hepatic dysfunction; seizure disorder, seizures, stroke, Parkinson's disease.

ROUTE & DOSAGE

Psychosis
Adult: **PO** 1–6 mg b.i.d., start with 1 mg b.i.d., increase by 1 mg b.i.d. daily to an initial target dose of 3 mg b.i.d. (max: 8 mg/d) **IM** 25 mg once q2wk (max: 50 mg)
Geriatric: **PO** Start with 0.5 mg b.i.d. and increase by 0.5 mg b.i.d. daily to an initial target of 1.5 mg b.i.d. (max: 4 mg/d) **IM** 25 mg once q2wk (max: 25 mg)

Bipolar Disorder
Adult: **PO** 2–3 mg once daily for up to 3 wk
Geriatric: **PO** Start with 0.5 mg b.i.d. and increase by 0.5 mg b.i.d. daily to an initial target of 1.5 mg b.i.d. (max: 4 mg/d). May convert to once daily dosing after stabilized in b.i.d. 2–3 d

Dementia-Related Psychotic Symptoms
Geriatric: **PO** Start with 0.5 mg b.i.d., increase by 0.5 mg b.i.d. daily to an initial target of 1 mg b.i.d. (max: 2 mg/d)

Renal Impairment
Cl_{cr} <30 mL/min: Start with 0.5 mg b.i.d., increase by 0.5 mg b.i.d. daily to an initial target of 1.5 mg b.i.d., may increase by 0.5 mg b.i.d. at weekly intervals (max: 6 mg/d)

Hepatic Impairment
Start with dose of 0.5 mg b.i.d.

ADMINISTRATION

Oral

- Note that quick-dissolving tablets dissolve rapidly when placed on tongue.
- Do not exceed increases/decreases of 1 mg b.i.d. in normal populations or 0.5 mg b.i.d. in older adults or the debilitated during dosage adjustments.
- Make further increases at 1-wk or longer intervals after the target dose of 3 mg b.i.d. in normal populations and 1.5 mg b.i.d. in older adults or the debilitated are reached.
- Store at 15°–30° C (59°–86° F).

Intramuscular

- Reconstitute the 25, 37.5, or 50 mg vial using the supplied 2 mL pre-filled syringe. Shake vigorously for at least 10 sec to produce a uniform, thick, milky suspension. If 2 min or more pass before injection, shake vial again.
- Give deep IM into the upper-outer quadrant of the gluteal muscle with the supplied needle; do not substitute. Follow the manufacturer's instructions for use of the SmartSite Needle-Free Vial Access Device and Needle-Pro device.
- Store unopened vials at 2°–8° C (36°–46° F). Protect from light.

ADVERSE EFFECTS (≥1%) **Body as a Whole:** Orthostatic hypotension with initial doses, sweating, weakness, fatigue. **CNS:** *Sedation, drowsiness, headache,* transient blurred vision, *insomnia,* disinhibition, *agitation,* anxiety, increased dream activity, dizziness, catatonia, *extrapyramidal symptoms* (akathisia, dystonia, pseudoparkinsonism), especially with doses >10 mg/d, <u>neuroleptic malignant syndrome</u> (rare), increased risk of stroke in elderly. **CV:** Prolonged QTc interval, tachy-cardia. **GI:** Dry mouth, dyspepsia, nausea, vomiting, diarrhea, constipation, abdominal pain, elevated liver function tests (AST, ALT). **Endocrine:** Galactorrhea. **Metabolic:** Hyperglycemia, diabetes mellitus. **Respiratory:** Rhinitis, cough, dyspnea. **Skin:** Photosensitivity. **Urogenital:** Urinary retention, menorrhagia, decreased sexual desire, erectile dysfunction, sexual dysfunction male and female.

DIAGNOSTIC TEST INTERFERENCE

Liver function tests (AST, ALT) are elevated.

INTERACTIONS Drug: Risperidone may enhance the effects of certain ANTIHYPERTENSIVE AGENTS. May antagonize the antiparkinson effects of **bromocriptine, cabergoline, levodopa, pergolide, pramipexole, ropinirole. Carbamazepine** may decrease risperidone levels. **Clozapine** may increase risperidone levels.

PHARMACOKINETICS Absorption: Rapidly; not affected by food. **Onset:** Therapeutic effect 1–2 wk. **Peak:** 1–2 h. **Distribution:** 0.7 L/kg; in animal studies, risperidone has been found in breast milk. **Metabolism:** Primarily in liver by cytochrome P450 with an active metabolite, 9-hydroxyrisperidone. **Elimination:** 70% in urine; 14% in feces. **Half-Life:** 20 h for slow metabolizers, 30 h for fast metabolizers.

CLINICAL IMPLICATIONS

Assessment & Drug Effects

- Monitor diabetics for loss of glycemic control.
- Reassess patients periodically and maintain on the lowest effective drug dose.
- Monitor closely neurologic status of older adults.

R

Common adverse effects in *italic*, life-threatening effects <u>underlined</u>; generic names in **bold**; classifications in SMALL CAPS; ✦ Canadian drug name; ☻ Prototype drug

1353

- Monitor cardiovascular status closely; assess for orthostatic hypotension, especially during initial dosage titration.
- Monitor closely those at risk for seizures.
- Assess degree of cognitive and motor impairment, and assess for environmental hazards.
- Lab tests: Monitor periodically blood glucose, serum electrolytes, liver function, and complete blood counts.

Patient & Family Education
- Carefully monitor blood glucose levels if diabetic.
- Do not engage in potentially hazardous activities until the response to drug is known.
- Be aware of the risk of orthostatic hypotension.
- Learn adverse effects and report to physician those that are bothersome.
- Wear sunscreen and protective clothing to avoid photosensitivity.
- Notify physician if you intend to or become pregnant.

RITODRINE HYDROCHLORIDE
(ri'toe-dreen)
Classifications: BETA-ADRENERGIC AGONIST
Therapeutic: DECREASES PRETERM LABOR CONTRACTIONS (TOCOLYTIC EFFECT)
Prototype: Isoproterenol
Pregnancy Category: C

AVAILABILITY 10 mg/mL, 15 mg/mL injection

ACTION & *THERAPEUTIC EFFECT*
Preferentially stimulates beta$_2$-receptors in uterine smooth muscle, reducing intensity and frequency of uterine contractions and lengthening gestation period. Transitory cardiovascular effects include increased cardiac output, increased maternal and fetal heart rates, and widening of maternal pulse pressure. *Clinically effective in preventing or delaying preterm labor (tocolytic effect). Uterine contractions will decrease in frequency and intensity during treatment.*

USES To manage premature labor in selected patients.

CONTRAINDICATIONS Mild to moderate preeclampsia or eclampsia, intrauterine infection, cervix dilated 4 cm or more (in a single pregnancy); pregnancy (category C); hypertension; diabetes mellitus; prior to 20th wk or after 36th wk of pregnancy or if continuation of pregnancy would be hazardous to mother and fetus (e.g., antepartum hemorrhage, eclampsia, intrauterine fetal death, maternal cardiac disease, pulmonary hypertension, maternal hyperthyroidism, severe diabetes mellitus). Also hypovolemia, cardiac arrhythmias associated with tachycardia or digitalis intoxication, uncontrolled hypertension; thyrotoxicosis; bronchial asthma being treated with betamimetics or steroids; lactation.

CAUTIOUS USE Concomitant use of potassium-depleting diuretics, cardiac disease.

ROUTE & DOSAGE

Premature Labor
Adult: **IV** 50 mcg/min, may increase by 50 mcg/min q10min until uterine relaxation is achieved, may continue for 12–24 h after contractions have ceased

ADMINISTRATION

Note: IV solution should be clear. Discard if cloudy or a precipitate is present.

Intravenous

PREPARE: **IV Infusion:** Add 150 mg ritodrine to 500 mL D5W or NS solution to yield 0.3 mg/mL (300 mcg/mL).

ADMINISTER: **IV Infusion:** Begin at 50 mcg/min and increase by 50 mcg q10 min until desired response. Monitor IV infusion flow rate to prevent circulation overload. Use a microdrip and infusion pump.

■ Place patient in left lateral recumbent position throughout the infusion period to reduce risk of hypotension.

■ Store drug below 30° C (86° F). Do not freeze.

ADVERSE EFFECTS (≥1%) **Body as a Whole:** Erythema, *nervousness, restlessness, anxiety, malaise, ana-phylactic shock,* sweating, chills, drowsiness, weakness, myotonic and muscular dystrophies. **CNS:** Tremor, headache. **CV:** *Altered maternal and fetal heart rates and maternal BP* (dose related), *palpitations,* arrhythmias, chest pain, pulmonary edema. **Endocrine:** *Temporary hyperglycemia.* **GI:** Nausea, vomiting, epigastric distress, ileus, bloating, constipation, diarrhea. **Urogenital:** Glycosuria. **Respiratory:** Dyspnea, hyperventilation. **Skin:** Rash.

DIAGNOSTIC TEST INTERFERENCE Ritodrine may produce an increase in *serum* levels of *glucose, insulin,* and *free fatty acids,* and a decrease in *serum potassium.* It temporarily elevates results of *glucose tolerance test.*

INTERACTIONS Drug: CORTICOSTEROIDS may precipitate pulmonary edema; BETA AGONISTS add to cardiovascular adverse effects; effects of both ritodrine and BETA BLOCKERS antagonized.

PHARMACOKINETICS Distribution: Crosses placenta. **Metabolism:** In liver. **Elimination:** In urine. **Half-Life:** 1.7–2.6 h.

CLINICAL IMPLICATIONS

Assessment & Drug Effects

■ Monitor continuously for pronounced dose-related adverse effects to maternal and fetal heart rates and maternal BP while infusion is running.

■ Be alert to S&S of pulmonary edema (see Appendix F).

Patient & Family Education

■ Report immediately any of the following: palpitations, chest pain, dizziness, respiratory distress, weakness, tremors, sweating or chills.

RITONAVIR

(ri-ton'a-vir)

Norvir

Classifications: ANTIRETROVIRAL AGENT; PROTEASE INHIBITOR

Therapeutic: ANTIRETROVIRAL; PROTEASE INHIBITOR

Prototype: Saquinavir

Pregnancy Category: B

AVAILABILITY 100 mg capsules; 80 mg/mL solution

ACTION & THERAPEUTIC EFFECT HIV protease is an enzyme required to produce the polyprotein procurers of functional proteins in infectious HIV. Protease inhibitors prevent cleavage of the viral polyproteins, resulting in the formation of immature noninfectious virus particles. *Protease inhibitor of both HIV-1 and HIV-2 resulting in the formation of noninfectious viral particles.*

R

Common adverse effects in *italic*, life-threatening effects underlined; generic names in **bold**; classifications in SMALL CAPS; ♣ Canadian drug name; ☻ Prototype drug

1355

USES Alone or in combination with other antiretroviral agents or protease inhibitors for treatment of HIV infection. Often used to increase the effect of other ANTIRETROVIRALS.

CONTRAINDICATIONS Hypersensitivity to ritonavir; antimicrobial resistance to protease inhibitors; pancreatitis; lactation. Safe use in children <1 mo has not been established.

CAUTIOUS USE Pregnancy (category B); hepatic diseases, hepatic insufficiency, liver enzyme abnormalities, or hepatitis, jaundice, advanced HIV disease; diabetes mellitus, diabetic ketoacidosis, hyperglycemia, hyperlipidemia, hypertriglyceridemia; hemophilia A or B, renal insufficiency, concurrent administration with HMG-CoA reductase inhibitors.

ROUTE & DOSAGE

HIV
Adult: **PO** 600 mg b.i.d. 1 h before or 2 h after meal (may take with a light snack)
Child: **PO** >1 mo, 300–400 mg/ m^2 b.i.d. (max: 600 mg b.i.d.), start with 250 mg/m^2 b.i.d., increase by 50 mg/m^2 q2–3d

ADMINISTRATION

Oral

- Give preferably with food; oral solution may be mixed with chocolate milk within 1 h of dosing to improve taste.
- Do not give concurrently with any of the following drugs: alprazolam, amiodarone, bepridil, bupropion, clozapine, clorazepate, diazepam, dihydroergotamine, ergotamine, encainide, estazolam, flecainide, flurazepam, meperidine,

midazolam, piroxicam, propafenone, propoxyphene, quinidine, rifabutin, triazolam, zolpidem.

- Store refrigerated at 2°–8° C (36°–46° F). Protect from light in tightly closed container.

ADVERSE EFFECTS (≥1%) **Body as a Whole:** Myalgia, allergic reaction, bronchitis, cough, rhinitis, taste alterations, visual disturbances, dysuria, hyperglycemia, diabetes. **CNS:** *Asthenia,* fatigue, headache, fever, malaise, circumoral or peripheral paresthesia, insomnia, dizziness, somnolence, abnormal thinking, amnesia, agitation, anxiety, confusion, convulsions, aphasia, ataxia, diplopia, emotional lability, euphoria, hallucinations, decreased libido, nervousness, neuralgia, neuropathy, peripheral neuropathy, paralysis, tremor, vertigo. **CV:** Palpitations, vasodilation, hypotension, postural hypotension, syncope, tachycardia. **Hematologic:** Anemia, thrombocytopenia, lymphadenopathy. **GI:** *Nausea, diarrhea, vomiting,* abdominal pain, dyspepsia, stomatitis, anorexia, dry mouth, constipation, flatulence, cholecystitis, cholestasis, abnormal liver function tests, hepatitis. **Skin:** Rash, sweating, acne, contact dermatitis, pruritus, urticaria, skin ulceration, dry skin.

INTERACTIONS Drug: Carbamazepine, dexamethasone, phenobarbital, phenytoin, rifabutin, rifampin, smoking can decrease ritonavir levels. **Ritonavir** may increase serum levels and toxicity of **clarithromycin,** especially in patients with renal insufficiency (reduce **clarithromycin** dose in patients with Cl_{cr} <60 mL/min); **desipramine; saquinavir, amiodarone, bepridil, bupropion, clozapine, dihydroergotamine,**

Common adverse effects in *italic*, life-threatening effects underlined; generic names in **bold**; classifications in SMALL CAPS; ♣ Canadian drug name; ☻ Prototype drug

flecainide, meperidine, pimozide, piroxicam, propoxyphene, quinidine, rifabutin, trazodone, alfuzosin, fluticasone. Ritonavir decreases levels of ORAL CONTRACEPTIVES, theophylline; may increase ergotamine toxicity with dihydroergotamine, ergotamine; may increase systemic steroid exposure with fluticasone. Liquid formulation may cause disulfiram-like reaction with alcohol or metronidazole. See the complete prescribing information for a comprehensive table of potential, but not studied, drug interactions. Herbal: St. John's wort, garlic may decrease ANTIRETROVIRAL activity.

PHARMACOKINETICS Absorption: Rapidly from GI tract. Peak: 2–4 h. Distribution: 98–99% protein bound. Metabolism: In liver (CYP3A4). Elimination: Primarily in feces (>80%).

CLINICAL IMPLICATIONS

Assessment & Drug Effects
▪ Lab tests: Monitor periodically CBC with differential and platelet count, liver function, kidney function, serum albumin, lipid profile, CPK, serum amylase, electrolytes, blood glucose HbA$_{1C}$, and alkaline phosphatase.
▪ Withhold drug and notify physician in the presence of abnormal liver function.
▪ Assess for S&S of GI distress, peripheral neuropathy, and other potential adverse effects.

Patient & Family Education
▪ Learn potential adverse reactions and drug interactions; report to physician use of any OTC or prescription drugs.
▪ Take this drug exactly as prescribed. Do not skip doses. Take at same time each day.

RITUXIMAB
(rit-ux'i-mab)
Rituxan
Classifications: ANTINEOPLASTIC AGENT; IMMUNOMODULATOR
Therapeutic: ANTINEOPLASTIC; MONOCLONAL ANTIBODY; DISEASE-MODIFYING ANTIRHEUMATIC DRUG (DMARD)
Pregnancy Category: C

AVAILABILITY 10 mg/mL injection

ACTION & THERAPEUTIC EFFECT
Genetically engineered monoclonal antibody that binds with the CD20 antigen on the surface of normal and malignant B lymphocytes. Administration of drug results in a rapid and sustained depletion of circulating and tissue-based (e.g., thymus, spleen) B lymphocytes in non-Hodgkin's lymphoma.

USES Relapsed or refractory CD20 positive, B-cell non-Hodgkin's lymphoma, treatment of rheumatoid arthritis (with methotrexate).

CONTRAINDICATIONS Hypersensitivity to murine proteins, rituximab, or abciximab; angina, cardiac arrhythmias, cardiac disease; pulmonary disease, chronic lymphocytic leukemia (CLL), lymphoma, severe hypotension; oliguria, rising serum creatinine; viral hepatitis B (HBV), vaccination; pregnancy (category C), lactation.
CAUTIOUS USE Prior exposure to murine-based monoclonal antibodies; history of allergies; asthma and other pulmonary disease (increased risk of bronchospasm); respiratory insufficiency; older adults; CAD; thrombocytopenia; history of cardiac arrhythmias; hypertension, renal impairment. Safety and efficacy in children are not established.

R

Common adverse effects in *italic*, life-threatening effects underlined; generic names in bold; classifications in SMALL CAPS; ♣ Canadian drug name; ⊘ Prototype drug

1357

ROUTE & DOSAGE

Non-Hodgkin's Lymphoma

Adult: **IV** 375 mg/m² infused at 50 mg/h, may increase infusion rate q30min (max: 400 mg/h if tolerated), repeat dose on days 8, 15, and 22 (total of 4 doses)

Rheumatoid Arthritis

Adult: **IV** 1000 mg on days 1 and 15 (with methotrexate)

ADMINISTRATION

Intravenous

PREPARE: **IV Infusion:** Dilute ordered dose to 1–4 mg/mL by adding to an infusion bag of NS or D5W. Examples: 500 mg in 400 mL yields 1 mg/mL; 500 mg in 75 mL yields 4 mg/mL. Gently invert bag to mix. Discard unused portion left in vial.

ADMINISTER: **IV Infusion:** Infuse first dose at a rate of 50 mg/h; may increase rate at 50 mg/h increments q30min to maximum rate of 400 mg/h. For subsequent doses, infuse at a rate of 100 mg/h and increase by 100 mg/h increments q30min up to maximum rate of 400 mg/h.

▪ Slow or stop infusion if S&S of hypersensitivity appear (see Appendix F).

▪ Store unopened vials at 2°–8° C (36°–46° F) and protect from light.

ADVERSE EFFECTS (≥1%) **Body as a Whole:** Angioedema, *fatigue,* asthenia, night sweats, *fever, chills,* myalgia. **CNS:** Headache, dizziness, depression. **CV:** Hypotension, tachycardia, peripheral edema. **GI:** *Nausea,* vomiting, throat irritation, anorexia, abdominal pain, hepatitis B reactivation with <u>fulminant hepatitis, hepatic failure, and death.</u> **Hemato-**logic: <u>Leukopenia, thrombocytopenia, anemia, neutropenia.</u> **Respiratory:** Bronchospasm, dyspnea, rhinitis. **Skin:** Pruritus, rash urticaria. **Other:** Infusion-related reactions: *Fever, chills, rigors, pruritus, urticaria, pain, flushing,* chest pain, hypotension, hypertension, dyspnea; <u>fatal infusion-related reactions</u> have been reported.

INTERACTIONS Drug: ANTIHYPERTENSIVE AGENTS should be stopped 12 h prior to avoid excessive hypotension; **cisplatin** may cause additive nephrotoxicity.

PHARMACOKINETICS Duration: 6–12 mo. **Half-Life:** 60–174 h (increases with multiple infusions).

CLINICAL IMPLICATIONS

Assessment & Drug Effects

▪ Lab tests: CBC with differential, peripheral CD20+ B lymphocytes.
▪ Monitor carefully BP and ECG status during infusion and immediately report S&S of hypersensitivity (e.g., fever, chills, urticaria, pruritus, hypotension, bronchospasms; see Appendix F for others).

Patient & Family Education

▪ Do not take antihypertensive medication within 12 h of rituximab infusions.
▪ Note: Use effective contraception during and for up to 12 mo following rituximab therapy.
▪ Report any of the following experienced during infusion: itching, difficulty breathing, tightness in throat, dizziness, headache, nausea.

RIVASTIGMINE TARTRATE

(ri-vas′tig-meen)
Exelon

Classifications: CHOLINESTERASE INHIBITOR

Therapeutic: ANTIDEMENTIA; CHOLINESTERASE INHIBITOR
Prototype: Neostigmine bromide
Pregnancy Category: B

AVAILABILITY 2 mg/mL oral solution; 1.5 mg, 3 mg, 4.5 mg, 6 mg capsule

ACTION & THERAPEUTIC EFFECT
Inhibits acetylcholinesterase G_1 form of this enzyme in the cerebral cortex and the hippocampus. The G_1 form of acetylcholinesterase is found in higher levels in the brains of patients with Alzheimer's disease. *Inhibits acetylcholinesterase more specifically in the brain (hippocampus and cortex) than in the heart or skeletal muscle.*

USES Treatment of mild to moderate dementia of the Alzheimer's type.

CONTRAINDICATIONS Hypersensitivity to rivastigmine or carbamate derivatives; lactation.
CAUTIOUS USE History of toxicity to cholinesterase inhibitors (e.g. tacrine); diabetes mellitus, cardiovascular/pulmonary disease; GI disorders including intestinal obstruction/peptic ulcer disease; concurrent use of other cholinergic agents, or anticholinergic agents; urogenital tract obstruction; Parkinson's disease; history of seizures; pregnancy (category B); hepatic or renal insufficiency; concurrent use of NSAIDs.

ROUTE & DOSAGE

Alzheimer's Dementia
Adult/Geriatric: **PO** Start with 1.5 mg b.i.d with food, may increase by 1.5 mg b.i.d. q2wk if tolerated, target dose 3–6 mg b.i.d. (max: 12 mg b.i.d.)

(if discontinued for a few doses, restart at ≤ last dose; if treatment is interrupted for several days, reinitiate with 1.5 mg b.i.d. and titrate q2wk as above)

ADMINISTRATION
Oral
- Give both capsules and liquid with food.
- Give liquid form undiluted or mixed with water, juice, or soda (do not mix with other liquids). Stir completely to dissolve. Ensure that entire mixture is swallowed.
- Discontinue drug for several days if significant anorexia, nausea, or vomiting occur. When adverse effects subside, restart at same or lower dose level (see ROUTE & DOSAGE).
- Store capsules and oral solution below 25° C (77° F). Ensure that bottle of liquid is in an UPRIGHT position.

ADVERSE EFFECTS (≥1%) **Body as a Whole:** Asthenia, increased sweating, syncope, fatigue, malaise, flu-like syndrome. **CV:** Hypertension. **GI:** *Nausea, vomiting, anorexia,* dyspepsia, *diarrhea, abdominal pain,* constipation, flatulence, eructation. **Metabolic:** Weight loss. **CNS:** *Dizziness, headache,* somnolence, tremor, insomnia, confusion, depression, anxiety, hallucination, aggressive reaction. **Respiratory:** Rhinitis.

INTERACTIONS Drug: May exaggerate muscle relations with **succinylcholine** and other NEUROMUSCULAR BLOCKING AGENTS, may attenuate effects of ANTICHOLINERGIC AGENTS.

PHARMACOKINETICS Absorption: Well absorbed, 40% reaches systemic circulation. **Peak:** 1 h. **Duration:** 10 h. **Distribution:** Crosses blood–brain barrier with CSF peak

R

Common adverse effects in *italic*, life-threatening effects underlined; generic names in **bold**; classifications in SMALL CAPS; ✦ Canadian drug name; ⊕ Prototype drug

1359

concentrations in 1.4–2.6 h, 40% protein bound. **Metabolism:** By cholinesterase-mediated hydrolysis. **Elimination:** In urine. **Half-Life:** 1.5 h.

CLINICAL IMPLICATIONS

Assessment & Drug Effects

- Monitor cognitive function and ability to perform ADLs.
- Monitor for and report S&S of GI distress: Anorexia, weight loss, nausea and vomiting.
- Lab tests: Periodic ECG, serum electrolytes, Hgb & Hct, urinalysis, blood glucose HbA$_{1C}$, especially with long-term therapy.
- Monitor ambulation as dizziness is a common adverse effect.
- Monitor diabetics for loss of glycemic control.

Patient & Family Education

- Review instruction sheet provided with liquid form of the drug.
- Monitor weight at least weekly.
- Report any of the following to the physician: Loss of appetite, weight loss, significant nausea and/or vomiting.
- Supervise activity since there is a high potential for dizziness.

RIZATRIPTAN BENZOATE

(ri-za-trip′tan ben′zo-ate)
Maxalt, Maxalt-MLT

Classifications: ADRENERGIC ANTAGONIST; SEROTONIN (5-HT$_1$) RECEPTOR AGONIST
Therapeutic: ANTIMIGRAINE
Prototype: Sumatriptan
Pregnancy Category: C

AVAILABILITY 5 mg, 10 mg tablets; 5 mg, 10 mg disintegrating tablets

ACTION & *THERAPEUTIC EFFECT*
Selective (5-HT$_{1B/1D}$) receptor agonist. The agonist effects at 5-HT$_{1B/1D}$

reverse the vasodilation of cranial blood vessels associated with a migraine. *Activation of the 5-HT$_{1B/1D}$ receptors reduces the pain pathways associated with the migraine headache as well as reversing vasodilation of cranial blood vessels.*

USES Acute migraine headaches with or without aura.

CONTRAINDICATIONS Hypersensitivity to rizatriptan; CAD; Prinzmetal's angina (potential for vasospasm); ischemic heart disease; risk factors for CAD such as hypertension, hypercholesterolemia, obesity, diabetes, smoking, and strong family history; concurrent administration with ergotamine drugs or sumatriptan; concurrent administration with MAOIS; basilar or hemiplegic migraine; pregnancy (category C).
CAUTIOUS USE Hypersensitivity to sumatriptan; renal or hepatic impairment; lactation; hypertension; asthmatic patients. Safety and effectiveness in patients <18 y are not established.

ROUTE & DOSAGE

Acute Migraine
Adult: **PO** 5–10 mg, may repeat in 2 h if necessary (max: 30 mg/ 24 h); 5 mg with concurrent propranolol (max: 15 mg/24 h)

ADMINISTRATION

Oral

- Give any time after symptoms of migraine appear. If symptoms return, a second tablet may be given but no sooner than 2 h after the first.
- Do not exceed 30 mg (three doses) in any 24 h period.
- Do not give within 24 h of an ergot-containing drug or another 5-HT$_1$ agonist.

- Store at 15°–30° C (59°–86° F) and protect from light and moisture.

ADVERSE EFFECTS (≥1%) **Body as a Whole:** Asthenia, fatigue, pain, pressure sensation, paresthesias, throat pressure, warm/cold sensations. **CNS:** Somnolence, dizziness, headache, hypesthesia, decreased mental acuity, euphoria, tremor. **CV:** Coronary artery vasospasm, transient myocardial ischemia, <u>MI</u>, ventricular tachycardia, ventricular fibrillation, chest pain/tightness/heaviness, palpitations. **GI:** Dry mouth, nausea, vomiting, diarrhea. **Respiratory:** Dyspnea. **Skin:** Flushing. **Endocrine:** Hot flashes.

INTERACTIONS Drug: Propranolol may increase concentrations of rizatriptan, use smaller rizatriptan doses; **dihydroergotamine, methysergide,** other 5-HT₁ AGONISTS may cause prolonged vasospastic reactions; SSRIS have rarely caused weakness, hyperreflexia, and incoordination; MAOIS should not be used with 5-HT₁ agonists. **Herbal: St. John's wort** may increase triptan toxicity.

PHARMACOKINETICS Absorption: 45% of oral dose reaches systemic circulation. **Peak:** 1–1.5 h for oral tabs; 1.6–2.5 h for orally disintegrating tablets. **Metabolism:** Via oxidative deamination by monoamine oxidase A. **Elimination:** Primarily in urine (82%). **Half-Life:** 2–3 h.

CLINICAL IMPLICATIONS

Assessment & Drug Effects

- Monitor cardiovascular status carefully following first dose in patients at risk for CAD (e.g., postmenopausal women, men over 40 years old, persons with known CAD risk factors) or coronary artery vasospasms.

- ECG is recommended following first administration of rizatriptan to someone with known CAD risk factors.
- Report immediately to physician: chest pain or tightness in chest or throat that is severe or does not quickly resolve.
- Monitor periodically cardiovascular status with continued rizatriptan use.

Patient & Family Education

- Do not exceed 30 mg (three doses) in 24 h.
- Allow orally disintegrating tablets to dissolve on tongue; no liquid is needed.
- Contact physician immediately if any of the following develop following rizatriptan use: symptoms of angina (e.g., severe and/or persistent pain or tightness in chest or throat), hypersensitivity (e.g., wheezing, facial swelling, skin rash, or hives), abdominal pain.
- Report any other adverse effects (e.g., tingling, flushing, dizziness) at next physician visit.

R

ROPINIROLE HYDROCHLORIDE

(ro-pi'ni-role)
Requip
Classifications: DOPAMINE RECEPTOR AGONIST; ANTIPARKINSON AGENT
Therapeutic: ANTIPARKINSON AGENT
Prototype: Levodopa
Pregnancy Category: C

AVAILABILITY 0.25 mg, 0.5 mg, 1 mg, 2 mg, 5 mg tablets

ACTION & THERAPEUTIC EFFECT
Nonergot dopamine receptor agonist used for treatment of Parkinson's disease. It has high affinity for the D₂ subfamily of dopamine re-

Common adverse effects in *italic*, life-threatening effects <u>underlined</u>; generic names in **bold**; classifications in SMALL CAPS; ◆ Canadian drug name; ⊘ Prototype drug

1361

ceptors and higher binding affinity to D_3 than to D_2 or D_4 receptor subtypes, but its precise mechanism is unknown. *Indicated by improvement in idiopathic Parkinson's disease.*

USES Idiopathic Parkinson's disease, restless legs syndrome.

CONTRAINDICATIONS Hypersensitivity to ropinirole or pramipexole; lactation, pregnancy (category C).

CAUTIOUS USE Hepatic impairment; severe renal impairment; mental instability; concomitant use of CNS depressants. Safety and efficacy in children are not established.

ROUTE & DOSAGE

Parkinson's Disease
Adult: **PO** Start with 0.25 mg t.i.d., titrate up by 0.25 mg/dose t.i.d. qwk to a target dose of 1 mg t.i.d.; if response is still not satisfactory, may continue to increase by 1.5 mg/d qwk to a dose of 9 mg/d, and then by ≤3 mg/d weekly (max: dose of 24 mg/d)

Restless Legs Syndrome
Adult: **PO** Take 0.25 mg 1–3 h before bed × 2 d, increase to 0.5 mg for the first wk, then increase by 0.5 mg qwk to a maximum of 4 mg.

ADMINISTRATION

Oral
- Give with food to reduce occurrence of nausea.
- Titrate dose as needed at weekly intervals (see ROUTE & DOSAGE).
- Discontinue drug gradually over 7 d by decreasing from t.i.d. to b.i.d. dosing for 4 d, and then to q.d. dosing for 3 d.

- Note: Lower initial and maintenance doses with moderate to severe renal impairment.
- Store at 15°–30° C (59°–86° F).

ADVERSE EFFECTS (≥1%) **Body as a Whole:** Increased sweating, dry mouth, flushing, asthenia, *fatigue,* pain, edema, malaise, *viral infection,* UTI, impotence. **CNS:** *Dizziness, somnolence, sudden sleep attacks,* hallucinations, confusion, amnesia, hypesthesia, yawning, hyperkinesia, impaired concentration, vertigo, hallucinations. **CV:** *Syncope,* chest pain, orthostatic symptoms, hypertension, palpitations, atrial fibrillation, extrasystoles, hypotension, tachycardia, peripheral edema, peripheral ischemia. **GI:** *Nausea, vomiting, dyspepsia,* abdominal pain, anorexia, flatulence. **Respiratory:** Pharyngitis, rhinitis, sinusitis, bronchitis, dyspnea. **Special Senses:** Abnormal vision, xerophthalmia, eye abnormality.

INTERACTIONS Drug: Ropinirole levels may be increased by ESTROGENS, QUINOLONE ANTIBIOTICS, **cimetidine, diltiazem, erythromycin, fluvoxamine, mexiletine, tacrine;** effects may be antagonized by PHENOTHIAZINES, BUTYROPHENONES, **metoclopramide.**

PHARMACOKINETICS Absorption: Rapidly from GI tract; 55% bioavailability. **Peak:** 1–2 h. **Distribution:** 30–40% protein bound. **Metabolism:** In liver (CYP1A2). **Elimination:** Primarily in urine. **Half-Life:** 6 h.

CLINICAL IMPLICATIONS

Assessment & Drug Effects
- Lab test: Periodically monitor BUN and creatinine, hepatic function.
- Schedule periodic eye exams and chest x-rays during long-term use.

- Monitor carefully for orthostatic hypotension, especially during dose escalation.

Patient & Family Education
- Be aware that hallucinations are a possible adverse effect and occur more often in older adults.
- Make position changes slowly, especially after long periods of lying or sitting. Postural hypotension is common, especially during early treatment.
- Exercise caution with hazardous activities requiring alertness since drowsiness and sedation are common adverse effects. Effects are additive with alcohol or other CNS depressants.
- Immediately notify physician if you become pregnant.

ROPIVACAINE HYDROCHLORIDE

(ro-piv′i-cane)
Naropin
Classifications: LOCAL ANESTHETIC (ESTER-TYPE)
Therapeutic: LOCAL ANESTHETIC
Prototype: Procaine HCl
Pregnancy Category: B

AVAILABILITY 2 mg/mL, 5 mg/mL, 7.5 mg/mL, 10 mg/mL injection

ACTION & *THERAPEUTIC EFFECT*
Blocks the generation and conduction of nerve impulses, probably by increasing the threshold for electrical excitability. *Local anesthetic action produces loss of sensation and motor activity in areas of the body close to the injection site.*

USES Local and regional anesthesia, postoperative pain management, anesthesia/pain management for obstetric procedures.

CONTRAINDICATIONS Hypersensitivity to ropivacaine or any local anesthetic of the amide type; generalized septicemia, inflammation or sepsis at the proposed injection site; cerebral spinal diseases (e.g., meningitis); heart block, hypotension, hypertension, GI hemorrhage.
CAUTIOUS USE Debilitated, older adult, or acutely ill patients; arrhythmias, shock; pregnancy (category B), lactation.

ROUTE & DOSAGE

Surgical Anesthesia
Adult: **Epidural** 25–200 mg (0.5–1% solution) **Nerve block** 5–250 mg (0.5%, 0.75% solution)

Labor Pain
Adult: **Epidural** 20–40 mg (0.2% solution)

Postoperative Pain Management
Adult: **Epidural** 12–20 mg/h (0.2% solution) **Infiltration** 2–200 mg (0.2–0.5% solution)

ADMINISTRATION

Intrathecal
- Avoid rapid injection of large volumes of ropivacaine. Incremental doses should always be used to achieve the smallest effective dose and concentration.
- Use an infusion concentration of 2 mg/mL (0.2%) for postoperative analgesia.
- Do not use disinfecting agents containing heavy metal ions (e.g., mercury, copper, zinc, etc.) on skin insertion site or to clean the ropivacaine container top.
- Discard continuous infusions solution after 24 h; it contains no preservatives.
- Store unopened at 20°–25° C (68°–77° F).

R

Common adverse effects in *italic*, life-threatening effects <u>underlined</u>; generic names in **bold**; classifications in SMALL CAPS; ◆ Canadian drug name; ◎ Prototype drug

1363

ADVERSE EFFECTS (≥1%) **Body as a Whole:** Pain, fever, rigors, hypoesthesia. **CNS:** Paresthesia, headache, dizziness, anxiety. **CV:** *Hypotension,* bradycardia, hypertension, tachycardia, chest pain, fetal bradycardia. **GI:** Nausea. **Skin:** Pruritus. **Urogenital:** Urinary retention, oliguria. **Hematologic:** Anemia.

INTERACTIONS Drug: Additive adverse effects with other LOCAL ANESTHETICS.

PHARMACOKINETICS Onset: 1–30 min (average 10–20 min) depending on dose/route of administration. **Duration:** 0.5–8 h depending on dose/route of administration. **Distribution:** 94% protein bound. **Metabolism:** In the liver by CYP1A. **Elimination:** In urine. **Half-Life:** 1.8–4.2 h.

CLINICAL IMPLICATIONS

Assessment & Drug Effects

- Monitor carefully cardiovascular and respiratory status throughout treatment period. Assess for hypotension and bradycardia.
- Report immediately S&S of CNS stimulation or CNS depression.

Patient & Family Education

- Report any of the following to physician immediately: restlessness, anxiety, tinnitus, blurred vision, tremors.

ROSIGLITAZONE MALEATE ℗

(ros-i-glit′a-zone)
Avandia
Classifications: HORMONE; ANTIDIABETIC; THIAZOLIDINEDIONES
Therapeutic: ANTIDIABETIC
Pregnancy Category: C

AVAILABILITY 2 mg, 4 mg, 8 mg tablets

ACTION & *THERAPEUTIC EFFECT*
Antidiabetic agent that lowers blood sugar levels by improving target cell response to insulin in Type 2 diabetics. It reduces cellular insulin resistance and decreases hepatic glucose output (gluconeogenesis). *Reduces hyperglycemia and hyperlipidemia, thus improving hyperinsulinemia without stimulating pancreatic insulin secretion. Indicated by decreased HbA$_{1C}$.*

USES Adjunct to diet in the treatment of Type 2 diabetes. May also be used in combination with metformin.

CONTRAINDICATIONS Hypersensitivity to rosiglitazone; cardiovascular disease, particularly hypertensive patients with New York Heart Association Class III and IV cardiac status (e.g., CHF); pregnancy (category C), lactation; active hepatic disease or ALT >2.5 times normal.
CAUTIOUS USE As monotherapy in Type 1 diabetes mellitus or diabetic ketoacidosis; CHF or risk for CHF; hepatic impairment. Safety and efficacy in children <18 y are not established.

ROUTE & DOSAGE

Type 2 Diabetes Mellitus
Adult: **PO** Start at 4 mg q.d. or 2 mg b.i.d., may increase after 12 wk (max: 8 mg/d in 1–2 divided doses)

Hepatic Impairment
Do not use if ALT >2.5 times upper limit of normal

ADMINISTRATION

Oral
- Do not initiate therapy if baseline serum ALT >2.5.
- Store at 15°–30° C (59°–86° F) in tight, light-resistant container.

ADVERSE EFFECTS (≥1%) **Body as a Whole:** Edema, anemia, headache, back pain, fatigue. **CV:** edema, fluid retention, exacerbation of heart failure. **GI:** Diarrhea. **Respiratory:** Upper respiratory tract infection, sinusitis. **Special Senses:** Macular edema. **Other:** Hyperglycemia.

INTERACTIONS Drug: Insulin may increase risk of heart failure or edema; enhance hypoglycemia with ORAL ANTIDIABETIC AGENTS, **ketoconazole, gemfibrozil** may increase effect.. **Herbal: Garlic, ginseng** may potentiate hypoglycemic effects.

PHARMACOKINETICS Absorption: 99% from GI tract. **Peak:** 1 h, food delays time to peak by 1.75 h. **Duration:** >24 h. **Distribution:** >99% protein bound. **Metabolism:** Extensively in liver (CYP2C8) to inactive metabolites. **Elimination:** 64% in urine, 23% in feces. **Half-Life:** 3–4 h. Moderate to severe liver disease increases serum concentrations and increases half-life by 2 h.

CLINICAL IMPLICATIONS

Assessment & Drug Effects

- Monitor for S&S of hypoglycemia (possible when insulin/sulfonylureas are coadministered).
- Monitor for S&S of CHF or exacerbation of symptoms with preexisting CHF.
- Lab tests: Liver function and serum ALT at baseline, then q2mo for first year; then periodically (more often when elevated); periodic HbA1C, Hgb and Hct, and lipid profile.
- Withhold drug and notify physician if ALT >3 times normal or patient jaundiced.
- Monitor weight and notify physician of development of edema.

Patient & Family Education

- Have blood tested for liver function every 2 mo for first year; then periodically.
- Be aware that resumed ovulation is possible in nonovulating premenopausal women.
- Use or add barrier contraceptive if using hormonal contraception.
- Report immediately to physician: S&S of liver dysfunction such as unexplained anorexia, nausea, vomiting, abdominal pain, fatigue, dark urine; or S&S of fluid retention such as weight gain, edema, or activity intolerance.
- Combination therapy: May need adjustment of other antidiabetic drugs to avoid hypoglycemia.

ROSUVASTATIN

(ro-su-va-sta′ten)
Crestor
Classifications: ANTILIPEMIC; HMG-COA REDUCTASE INHIBITOR (STATIN)
Therapeutic: ANTIHYPERLIPEMIC; STATIN
Prototype: Lovastatin
Pregnancy Category: X

AVAILABILITY 5 mg, 10 mg, 20 mg, 40 mg tablets

ACTION & THERAPEUTIC EFFECT
Rosuvastatin is a potent inhibitor of HMG-CoA reductase, an enzyme that catalyzes the conversion of HMG-CoA to mevalonic acid, an early and rate-limiting step in cholesterol biosynthesis. Interference with this enzyme reduces the quantity of mevalonic acid, a precursor of cholesterol. *Reduces total cholesterol and LDL cholesterol; additionally, lowers plasma triglycerides and apolipoprotein B while increasing HDL.*

USES Adjunct to diet for the reduction of LDL cholesterol and triglyc-

R

Common adverse effects in *italic*, life-threatening effects <u>underlined</u>; generic names in **bold**; classifications in SMALL CAPS; ♣ Canadian drug name; ☻ Prototype drug

1365

erides in patients with primary hypercholesterolemia and mixed dyslipidemia.

CONTRAINDICATIONS Hypersensitivity to any component of the product, active liver disease, pregnancy (category X), women of child-bearing potential not using appropriate contraceptive measures, lactation.
CAUTIOUS USE Concomitant use of cyclosporine and gemfibrozil; excessive alcohol use or history of liver disease; renal impairment; advanced age; hypothyroidism.

ROUTE & DOSAGE

Hyperlipidemia
Adult: **PO** 10 mg once daily (5–40 mg/d), max dose 40 mg/d. If taking cyclosporine, start with 5 mg/d
Geriatric: Initial dose of 5 mg/d

Renal Impairment
Cl_{cr} <30 mL/min: 5 mg once daily (max: 10 mg/d)

ADMINISTRATION

Oral
- Persons of Asian descent may be slow metabolizers and may require half the normal dose.
- May give any time of day without regard to food.
- Store at or below 30° C (86° F).

ADVERSE EFFECTS (≥1%) **Body as a Whole:** Asthenia, back pain, flu syndrome, chest pain, infection, pain, peripheral edema. **CNS:** Headache, dizziness, insomnia, hypertonia, paresthesia, depression, anxiety, vertigo, neuralgia. **CV:** Hypertension, angina, vasodilatation, palpitations. **GI:** Diarrhea, dyspepsia, nausea, abdominal pain, constipation, gastroenteritis, vomiting, flatu-

lence, gastritis. **Endocrine:** Diabetes. **Hematologic:** Anemia, ecchymosis. **Musculoskeletal:** Myalgia, arthritis, arthralgia, rhabdomyolysis (especially with dose >40 mg). **Respiratory:** Pharyngitis, rhinitis, sinusitis, bronchitis, increased cough, dyspnea, pneumonia, asthma. **Skin:** Rash, pruritus. **Urogenital:** UTI.

INTERACTIONS Drug: Cyclosporine, gemfibrozil, niacin, may increase risk of rhabdomyolysis; ANTACIDS may decrease rosuvastatin absorption; may cause increase in INR with **warfarin.**

PHARMACOKINETICS Absorption: Well absorbed. **Peak:** 3–5 h. **Metabolism:** Limited metabolism in the liver (not CYP3A4). **Elimination:** Primarily in feces (90%). **Half-Life:** 20 h.

CLINICAL IMPLICATIONS

Assessment & Drug Effects
- Monitor for and report promptly S&S of myopathy (e.g., skeletal muscle pain, tenderness or weakness).
- Withhold drug and notify physician if CPK levels are markedly elevated (≥10 × ULN) or if myopathy is diagnosed or suspected.
- Lab tests: CPK levels for S&S of myopathy; periodic LFTs; more frequent INR values with concomitant warfarin therapy.
- Monitor CV status, especially with a known history of hypertension or heart disease.
- Monitor diabetics for loss of glycemic control.

Patient & Family Education
- Do not take antacids within 2 h of taking this drug.
- Females should use reliable means of contraception while taking this drug to prevent pregnancy.

SALMETEROL XINAFOATE

(sal-me′ter-ol xin′a-fo-ate)
Serevent
Classifications: BETA₂-ADRENERGIC AGONIST; BRONCHODILATOR; RESPIRATORY SMOOTH MUSCLE RELAXANT
Therapeutic: BRONCHODILATOR; SMOOTH MUSCLE RELAXANT
Prototype: Albuterol
Pregnancy Category: C

AVAILABILITY 25 mcg aerosol; 50 mcg powder diskus for inhalation

ACTION & *THERAPEUTIC EFFECT*
Long-acting beta₂-adrenoreceptor agonist and an analog of albuterol. Stimulation of beta₂-adrenoreceptors relaxes bronchospasm and increases ciliary motility, thus facilitating expectoration. Inhibits the release of mediators (i.e., histamine) from mast cells, macrophages, and eosinophils. *Relaxes bronchospasm and increases ciliary motility, thus facilitating expectoration of pulmonary secretions. Salmeterol also decreases airway reaction to allergens.*

USES Maintenance therapy for asthma or bronchospasm. Prevention of exercise-induced bronchospasm. Do not use to treat acute bronchospasm.

CONTRAINDICATIONS Hypersensitivity to salmeterol; other long-acting beta₂-adrenergic agonists; primary treatment of status asthmaticus; acute bronchospasm; MAOI therapy; pregnancy (category C); safety and efficacy in children <4 y not established.
CAUTIOUS USE Cardiovascular disorders, cardiac arrhythmias, hypertension; history of seizures or thyrotoxicosis; liver and renal impairment, older adults, diabetes mellitus, sensitivity to other beta-adrenergic agonists; women in labor; lactation.

ROUTE & DOSAGE

Asthma or Bronchospasm
Adult/Child ≥4 y: **Inhalation** 2 inhalations of aerosol (42 mcg) or 1 powder diskus (50 mcg) b.i.d. approximately 12 h apart

Prevention of Exercise-Induced Bronchospasm
Adult/Child ≥4 y: **Inhaled** 2 inhalations of aerosol (42 mcg) or 1 powder diskus (50 mcg) 30–60 min before exercise

ADMINISTRATION

Inhalation
- Do not use to relieve symptoms of acute asthma.
- Shake canister well before using; close lips tightly around the mouthpiece, and patient inhales deeply during each actuation.
- Store at room temperature, 15°–30° C (59°–86° F).

ADVERSE EFFECTS (≥1%) **CNS:** Dizziness, headache, tremor. **CV:** Palpitations, sinus tachycardia. **Respiratory:** Respiratory arrest (rare). **Skin:** Rash. **Body as a Whole:** Tolerance (tachyphylaxis).

INTERACTIONS Drug: Effects antagonized by BETA BLOCKERS.

PHARMACOKINETICS Onset: 10–20 min. **Peak:** Effect 2 h. **Duration:** Up to 12 h. **Distribution:** 94–95% protein bound. **Metabolism:** Dissociates in solution; salmeterol base and xinafoate salt are metabolized, absorbed, distributed, and excreted independently; salmeterol is extensively metabolized by hydroxylation. **Elimination:** Primarily in feces. **Half-Life:** 3–4 h.

S

Common adverse effects in *italic*, life-threatening effects underlined; generic names in **bold**; classifications in SMALL CAPS; ✦ Canadian drug name; ✪ Prototype drug

1367

CLINICAL IMPLICATIONS

Assessment & Drug Effects

- Withhold drug and notify physician immediately if bronchospasms occur following its use.
- Monitor cardiovascular status; report tachycardia.
- Monitor liver enzymes periodically with long-term therapy.

Patient & Family Education

- Notify physician immediately of worsening asthma or failure to respond to the usual dose of salmeterol.
- Do not use an additional dose prior to exercise if taking twice-daily doses of salmeterol.
- Take the preexercise dose 30–60 min before exercise and wait 12 h before an additional dose.

SALSALATE

(sal′sal-ate)

Artha-G, Mono-Gesic, Salflex, Salsitab

Classifications: ANALGESIC (SALICYLATE); NONSTEROIDAL ANTIINFLAMMATORY DRUG (NSAID)
Therapeutic: NSAID, ANALGESIC; DISEASE-MODIFYING ANTIRHEUMATIC DRUG (DMARD)
Prototype: Aspirin
Pregnancy Category: C

AVAILABILITY 500 mg, 750 mg tablets

ACTION & *THERAPEUTIC EFFECT*
Actions similar to those of other salicylates. Clinical studies suggest that salsalate does not produce significant gastric irritation, and it has not been associated with reactions causing asthmatic attacks in susceptible individuals. Unlike aspirin, it does not appear to inhibit platelet aggregation. Its antiinflammatory and analgesic activity may be mediated through inhibition of the prostaglandin synthetase enzyme complex. *Has analgesic, antiinflammatory, and antirheumatic effects.*

USES Symptomatic treatment, rheumatoid arthritis, osteoarthritis, and related rheumatic disorders.

CONTRAINDICATIONS Hypersensitivity to salicylates or NSAIDs, especially patients with history of asthma, nasal polyposis, or chronic urticaria; chronic renal insufficiency; peptic ulcer; children <12 y; hemophilia; chickenpox, influenza, tinnitus; pregnancy (category C).

CAUTIOUS USE Liver function impairment; older adults; lactation.

ROUTE & DOSAGE

Arthritis

Adult: **PO** 325–3000 mg/d in divided doses (max: 4 g/d)

ADMINISTRATION

Oral

- Give with a full glass of water or food or milk to reduce GI adverse effects.

ADVERSE EFFECTS (≥1%) **GI:** Nausea, dyspepsia, heartburn, vomiting, diarrhea, risk of GI bleed. **Special Senses:** Tinnitus, hearing loss (reversible). **Body as a Whole:** Vertigo, flushing, headache, confusion, hyperventilation, sweating. **CNS:** Drowsiness.

DIAGNOSTIC TEST INTERFERENCE
False-negative results for ***Clinistix***; false positives for ***Clinitest***.

INTERACTIONS Drug: Aminosalicylic acid increases risk of salicylate toxicity. **Ammonium chloride** and other ACIDIFYING AGENTS decrease renal elimination and increase risk of salicylate toxicity. ANTICOAGULANTS increase risk of bleeding. ORAL HYPOGLYCEMIC AGENTS increase hypoglycemic activity with salsalate doses >2 g/d. CARBONIC ANHYDRASE INHIBITORS enhance salicylate toxicity. CORTICOSTEROIDS add to ulcerogenic effects. **Methotrexate** toxicity is increased. Low doses of salicylates may antagonize uricosuric effects of **probenecid** and **sulfinpyrazone**. **Herbal:** Feverfew, garlic, ginger, ginkgo may increase bleeding potential.

PHARMACOKINETICS Absorption: Readily absorbed from small intestine. **Peak:** 1.5–4 h. **Metabolism:** Hydrolyzed in liver, GI mucosa, plasma, whole blood, and other tissues. **Elimination:** In urine. **Half-Life:** 1 h.

CLINICAL IMPLICATIONS

Assessment & Drug Effects
- Symptom relief is gradual (may require 3–4 d to establish steady-state salicylate level).
- Monitor for adverse GI effects, especially in patient with a history of peptic ulcer disease.

Patient & Family Education
- Do not to take another salicylate (e.g., aspirin) while on salsalate therapy.
- Monitor blood glucose for loss of glycemic control in diabetes; drug may induce hypoglycemia when used with sulfonylureas.
- Report tinnitus, hearing loss, vertigo, rash, or nausea.

SAQUINAVIR MESYLATE ℗

(sa-quin′a-vir mes′y-late)
Invirase

Classifications: ANTIRETROVIRAL AGENT; PROTEASE INHIBITOR
Therapeutic: ANTIRETROVIRAL; PROTEASE INHIBITOR
Pregnancy Category: B

AVAILABILITY 200 mg gelatin capsules; 500 mg tablet

ACTION & *THERAPEUTIC EFFECT*
Synthetic peptide that inhibits the activity of HIV protease and prevents the cleavage of viral polyproteins essential for the maturation of HIV. *Effectiveness indicated by reduced viral load (decreased number of RNA copies), and increased number of T helper CD4 cells.*

USES Advanced HIV infection, usually in combination with zidovudine or zalcitabine.

CONTRAINDICATIONS Significant hypersensitivity to saquinavir; severe hepatic impairment; concurrent administration with lovastatin, simvastatin, amiodarone, flecainide, propafenone, quinidine, ergot derivatives, rifampin, cisapride, triazolam, midazolam, antimicrobial resistance to other protease inhibitors, monotherapy, lactation.

CAUTIOUS USE Mild to moderate hepatic insufficiency; severe renal impairment; hepatitis B or C; diabetes mellitus, diabetic ketoacidosis; older adults; hemophilia A or B, pregnancy (category B). Safety and effectiveness in HIV-infected children <16 y are not established.

ROUTE & DOSAGE

HIV
Adult: **PO** Invirase 600 mg (3 × 200 mg) t.i.d. taken 2 h after a full meal; Fortovase 1200 mg (6 × 200 mg) t.i.d. with meals; or 1000 mg b.i.d. with ritonavir 100 mg b.i.d.

Common adverse effects in *italic*, life-threatening effects <u>underlined</u>; generic names in **bold**; classifications in SMALL CAPS; ◆ Canadian drug name; ℗ Prototype drug

ADMINISTRATION

Oral

- Give with or up to 2 h after a full meal to ensure adequate absorption and bioavailability.
- Do not administer to anyone taking rifampin or rifabutin because these drugs significantly decrease the plasma level of saquinavir.
- Store Invirase at 15°–30° C (59°–86° F) in tightly closed bottle. Store Fortovase in refrigerator. Capsules are stable for 3 mo at room temperature ≤25° C (≤77° F).

ADVERSE EFFECTS (≥1%) **CNS:** Headache, paresthesia, numbness, dizziness, peripheral neuropathy, ataxia, confusion, convulsions, hyperreflexia, hyporeflexia, tremor, agitation, amnesia, anxiety, depression, excessive dreaming, hallucinations, euphoria, irritability, lethargy, somnolence. **CV:** Chest pain, hypertension, hypotension, syncope. **Endocrine:** Dehydration, hyperglycemia, diabetes, weight changes. **Hematologic:** Anemia, splenomegaly, thrombocytopenia, <u>pancytopenia</u>. **GI:** *Nausea, diarrhea, abdominal discomfort,* dyspepsia, mucosal damage, change in appetite, dry mouth. **Skin:** Rash, pruritus, acne, erythema, seborrhea, hair changes, photosensitivity, skin ulceration, dry skin. **Body as a Whole:** Myalgia, allergic reaction. **Respiratory:** Bronchitis, cough, dyspnea, epistaxis, hemoptysis, laryngitis, rhinitis. **Special Senses:** Xerophthalmia, ear ache, taste alterations, tinnitus, visual disturbances.

INTERACTIONS Drug: **Rifampin, rifabutin** significantly decrease **saquinavir** levels. **Phenobarbital, phenytoin, dexamethasone, carbamazepine** may also reduce **saquinavir** levels. **Saquinavir** levels may be increased by **delavirdine, ketoconazole, ritonavir, clarithromycin, indinavir.** May increase serum levels of **triazolam, midazolam,** ERGOT DERIVATIVES, **nelfinavir, sildenafil.** May significantly increase **simvastatin** levels and toxicity; may increase risk of **ergotamine** toxicity of **dihydroergotamine, ergotamine. Herbal: St. John's wort, garlic** may decrease antiretroviral activity. **Food:** Grapefruit juice (>1 qt/day) may increase plasma concentrations and adverse effects.

PHARMACOKINETICS Absorption: Rapidly from GI tract; only 4% reaches systemic circulation; food significantly increases bioavailability. **Distribution:** 98% protein bound. **Metabolism:** In liver (CYP3A4), first-pass metabolism. **Elimination:** Primarily in feces (>80%). **Half-life:** 13 h.

CLINICAL IMPLICATIONS

Assessment & Drug Effects

- Lab tests: Monitor serum electrolytes, CBC with differential, liver function, blood glucose and HbA_{1C}, CPK, and serum amylase prior to initiating therapy and periodically thereafter.
- Monitor for and report S&S of peripheral neuropathy.
- Assess for buccal mucosa ulceration or other distressing GI S&S.
- Monitor weight periodically.
- Monitor for toxicity if any of the following drugs is used concomitantly: calcium channel blockers, clindamycin, dapsone, quinidine, triazolam, or simvastatin.

Patient & Family Education

- Take drug within 2 h of a full meal.
- Be aware of all drugs which should not be taken concurrently with saquinavir.
- Be aware that saquinavir is not a cure for HIV infection and that its long-term effects are unknown.
- Report any distressing adverse effects to physician.

SARGRAMOSTIM (GM-CSF)

(sar-gra'mos-tim)

Leukine

Classifications: BLOOD FORMER; HEMATOPOIETIC GROWTH FACTOR; COLONY STIMULATING FACTOR

Therapeutic: HEMATOPOIETIC GROWTH FACTOR

Prototype: Epoetin alfa

Pregnancy Category: C

AVAILABILITY 250 mcg, 500 mcg injection

ACTION & *THERAPEUTIC EFFECT*
Recombinant human granulocyte macrophage colony stimulating factor (GM-CSF) is produced by recombinant DNA technology in a yeast. GM-CSF is a hematopoietic growth factor that stimulates proliferation and differentiation of hematopoietic progenitor cells in the granulocyte-macrophage pathways. *Effectiveness is measured by an increase in the number of mature white blood cells (i.e., neutrophil count).*

USES Myeloid reconstitution after autologous bone marrow transplantation for patients with non-Hodgkin's lymphoma (NHL), acute lymphoblastic leukemia (ALL), and Hodgkin's disease; mobilization of peripheral blood stem cells (PBSCs) for autologous transplantation.

UNLABELED USES To increase WBC counts in AIDS patients; to decrease leukopenia secondary to myelosuppressive chemotherapy; to correct neutropenia in aplastic anemia and in liver and kidney transplantations.

CONTRAINDICATIONS Excessive leukemic myeloid blasts in bone marrow or blood; known hypersensitivity to GM-CSF or yeast products; benzyl alcohol; within 24 h of chemotherapy or radiation treatment; pregnancy (category C); lactation.

CAUTIOUS USE History of cardiac arrhythmias, preexisting cardiac disease, hypoxia, CHF, pulmonary infiltrates; kidney and liver dysfunction.

ROUTE & DOSAGE

Autologous Bone Marrow Transplant

Adult/Child: **IV** 250 mcg/m^2/d infused over 2 h for 21 d, begin 2–4 h after bone marrow transfusion and not less than 24 h after last dose of chemotherapy or 12 h after last radiation therapy

Neutropenia Following Chemotherapy

Adult/Child: **IV** 250 mcg/m^2/d infused over 4 h starting ~day 11

ADMINISTRATION

▪ Note: Do not give within 24 h preceding or following chemotherapy or within 12 h preceding or following radiotherapy.

Subcutaneous

▪ Reconstitute each 250 or 500 mcg vial with 1 mL of sterile water for injection (without preservative). Direct sterile water against side of vial and swirl gently. Avoid excessive or vigorous agitation. Do not shake. Use without further dilution for SC injection.

Intravenous

Note: Verify correct IV concentration and rate of infusion administration in infants and children with physician.

***PREPARE:* IV Infusion:** Reconstitute as for SC, then further dilute reconstituted solution with NS. If the final concentration is <1 mcg/mL, add albumin (human) to NS before addition of sargramostim. Use 1 mg albumin per 1 mL of

NS to give a final concentration of 0.1% albumin. Administer as soon as possible and within 6 h of reconstitution or dilution for IV infusion. Discard after 6 h. Sargramostim vials are single-dose vials, do not reenter or reuse. Discard unused portion.

ADMINISTER: **IV Infusion:** Give over 2 h. Do not use an in-line membrane filter.

INCOMPATIBILITIES **Y-site: Acyclovir, amphotericin B, ampicillin, ampicillin/sulbactam, amsacrine, cefonicid, cefoperazone, ceftazidime, chlorpromazine, ganciclovir, haloperidol, hydrocortisone, hydromorphone, hydroxyzine, idarubicin, imipenem/cilastatin, lorazepam, methylprednisolone, mitomycin, morphine, nalbuphine, ondansetron, piperacillin, sodium bicarbonate, tobramycin.**

- Interrupt administration and reduce the dose by 50% if absolute neutrophil count exceeds 20,000/mm³ or if platelet count exceeds 500,000/mm³. Notify physician. ▪ Reduce the IV rate 50% if patient experiences dyspnea during administration. Discontinue infusion if respiratory symptoms worsen. Notify physician.

- Refrigerate the sterile powder, the reconstituted solution, and store diluted solution at 2°–8° C (36°–46° F). Do not freeze or shake.

ADVERSE EFFECTS (≥1%) **CNS:** Lethargy, malaise, headache, fatigue. **CV:** Abnormal ST segment depression, supraventricular arrhythmias, edema, *hypotension, tachycardia,* pericardial effusion, pericarditis. **Hematologic:** Anemia, *thrombocytopenia.* **GI:** Nausea, vomiting, diarrhea, anorexia. **Body as a Whole:** *Bone pain, myalgia, arthralgias,* weight gain, hyperuricemia, *fever.* **Respiratory:** Pleural effusion. **Skin:** *Rash, pruritus.* **Other:** *First-dose reaction* (some or all of the following symptoms: hypotension, tachycardia, fever, rigors, flushing, nausea, vomiting, diaphoresis, back pain, leg spasms, and dyspnea).

INTERACTIONS Drug: CORTICOSTEROIDS and **lithium** should be used with caution because it may potentiate the myeloproliferative effects.

PHARMACOKINETICS Absorption: Readily from SC site. **Onset:** 3–6 h. **Peak:** 1–2 h. **Duration:** 5–10 d SC. **Elimination:** Probably in urine. **Half-Life:** 80–150 min.

CLINICAL IMPLICATIONS

Assessment & Drug Effects

- Lab tests: Obtain a CBC and platelet count prior to initiation of therapy. Monitor biweekly CBC with differential during therapy. Monitor kidney and liver function biweekly in patients with kidney or liver dysfunction prior to the initiation of therapy.
- Discontinue treatment if WBC 50,000/mm³. Notify the physician.
- Occasional transient supraventricular arrhythmias have occurred during administration, particularly in those with a history of cardiac arrhythmias. Arrhythmias are reversed with discontinuation of drug.
- Give special attention to respiratory symptoms (dyspnea) during and immediately following infusion, especially in patients with preexisting pulmonary disease.
- Use drug with caution in patients with preexisting fluid retention, pulmonary infiltrates, or CHF. Peripheral edema, pleural or peri-

S

cardial effusion has occurred after administration. It is reversible with dose reduction.
- Notify physician of any severe adverse reaction immediately.
- Discontinue therapy and notify physician if disease progression is detected. Potentially, drug can act as a growth factor for myeloid malignancies.

Patient & Family Education
- Notify nurse or physician immediately of any adverse effect (e.g., dyspnea, palpitations, peripheral edema, bone or muscle pain) during or after drug administration.

SCOPOLAMINE

(skoe-pol'a-meen)
Transderm-Scop, Transderm-V ♦

SCOPOLAMINE HYDROBROMIDE

Hyoscine, Isopto-Hyoscine, Scopace, Murocoll, Triptone
Classifications: ANTICHOLINERGIC; ANTIMUSCARINIC; ANTISPASMODIC; ANTIVERTIGO
Therapeutic: ANTISPASMODIC; ANTI-EMETIC; ANTIVERTIGO
Prototype: Atropine
Pregnancy Category: C

AVAILABILITY Scopolamine 1.5 mg transdermal patch **Scopolamine HBr** 0.4 mg tablets; 0.3 mg/mL, 0.4 mg/mL, 0.86 mg/mL, 1 mg/mL injection; 0.25% ophthalmic solution

ACTION & *THERAPEUTIC EFFECT*
Antimuscarinic agent that inhibits the action on acetylcholine (ACh) on postganglionic cholinergic nerves as well as on smooth muscles that lack cholinergic innervation. *More potent than atropine in mydriatic and cycloplegic actions. Produces CNS depression with marked sedative and tranquilizing effects for use in anesthesia. Used as a preanesthetic agent to control bronchial, nasal, pharyngeal, and salivary secretions.*

USES In obstetrics with morphine to produce amnesia and sedation ("twilight sleep") and as preanesthetic medication. To control spasticity (and drooling) in postencephalitic parkinsonism, paralysis agitans, and other spastic states, as prophylactic agent for motion sickness and as mydriatic and cycloplegic in ophthalmology. Therapeutic system (**Transderm-Scop**) is used to prevent nausea and vomiting associated with motion sickness.

CONTRAINDICATIONS Asthma; hepatitis; toxemia of pregnancy; hypersensitivity to anticholinergic drugs; hypersensitive to belladonna or barbiturates; narrow-angle glaucoma; GI or urogenital obstructive diseases; myasthenia gravis; pregnancy (category C).
CAUTIOUS USE Coronary heart disease, CHF, cardiac arrhythmias, tachycardia, hypertension; infants, children, Down's syndrome; patients over 40 y, pyloric obstruction, urinary bladder neck obstruction; autonomic neuropathy; angle-closure glaucoma, thyrotoxicosis, liver disease; paralytic ileus; hiatal hernia, ulcerative colitis, gastric ulcer; older adults, parkinsonism; COPD, asthma or allergies; hyperthyroidism; brain damage, spastic paralysis; tartrazine or sulfite sensitivity.

ROUTE & DOSAGE

Preanesthetic
Adult: **PO** 0.4–0.8 mg **IM/SC/IV** 0.3–0.6 mg q4–6h
Child: **PO/IM/SC/IV** 6 mcg/kg q6–8h (max: 0.3 mg/dose)

S

Common adverse effects in *italic*, life-threatening effects <u>underlined</u>; generic names in **bold**; classifications in SMALL CAPS; ♦ Canadian drug name; ☯ Prototype drug

1373

Motion Sickness

Adult: **Topical** 1 patch q72h starting 12 h before anticipated travel
Child: **PO** 6 mcg/kg 1 h before anticipated travel

Refraction

Adult: **Ophthalmic** 1–2 drops in eye 1 h before refraction

Uveitis

Adult: **Ophthalmic** 1–2 drops in eye up to q.i.d.

ADMINISTRATION

Instillation

- Minimize possibility of systemic absorption by applying pressure against lacrimal sac during and for 1 or 2 min following instillation of eye drops.

Transdermal

- Apply transdermal disc system (Transderm-Scop, a controlled-release system) to dry surface behind the ear.
- Replace with another disc on another site behind the ear if disc system becomes dislodged.

Subcutaneous or Intramuscular

- Give undiluted.

Intravenous

PREPARE: Direct: Dilute required dose in 10 mL of sterile water for injection.

ADMINISTER: Direct: Give a single dose over 1 min.

- Preserve in tight, light-resistant containers.

ADVERSE EFFECTS (≥1%) **Body as a Whole:** Fatigue, dizziness, *drowsiness,* disorientation, restlessness, hallucinations, toxic psychosis. **GI:** *Dry mouth and throat, constipation.* **Urogenital:** Urinary retention. **CV:** Decreased heart rate. **Special Senses:** Dilated pupils, photophobia, blurred vision, *local irritation,* follicular conjunctivitis. **Respiratory:** <u>Depressed respiration.</u> **Skin:** Local irritation from patch adhesive, rash.

INTERACTIONS Drug: Amantadine, ANTIHISTAMINES, TRICYCLIC ANTIDEPRESSANTS, **quinidine, disopyramide, procainamide** add to anticholinergic effects; decreases **levodopa** effects; **methotrimeprazine** may precipitate extrapyramidal effects; decreases antipsychotic effects (decreased absorption) of PHENOTHIAZINES. **Food:** Grapefruit juice (>1 qt/d) may increase plasma concentrations and adverse effects.

PHARMACOKINETICS Absorption: Readily from GI tract and percutaneously. **Peak:** 20–60 min. **Duration:** 5–7 d. **Distribution:** Crosses placenta; distributed to CNS. **Metabolism:** In liver. **Elimination:** In urine.

CLINICAL IMPLICATIONS

Assessment & Drug Effects

- Observe patient closely; some patients manifest excitement, delirium, and disorientation shortly after drug is administered until sedative effect takes hold.
- Use of side rails is advisable, particularly for older adults, because of amnesic effect of scopolamine.
- In the presence of pain, scopolamine may cause delirium, restlessness, and excitement unless given with an analgesic.
- Be aware that tolerance may develop with prolonged use.
- Terminate ophthalmic use if local irritation, edema, or conjunctivitis occur.

Patient & Family Education

- Vision may blur when used as mydriatic or cycloplegic; do not drive or engage in potentially hazardous activities until vision clears.

S

- Place disc on skin site the night before an expected trip or anticipated motion for best therapeutic effect.
- Wash hands carefully after handling scopolamine. Anisocoria (unequal size of pupils, blurred vision can develop by rubbing eye with drug-contaminated finger).

SECOBARBITAL SODIUM ℗

(see-koe-bar′bi-tal)
Seconal Sodium
Classifications: SEDATIVE-HYP-NOTIC; BARBITURATE; ANXIOLYTIC
Therapeutic: SEDATIVE-HYPNOTIC
Pregnancy Category: D
Controlled Substance: Schedule II

AVAILABILITY 50 mg, 100 mg capsules

ACTION & *THERAPEUTIC EFFECT*
Short-acting barbiturate with CNS depressant effects as well as mood alteration from excitation to mild sedation, hypnosis, and deep coma. Depresses the sensory cortex, decreases motor activity, alters cerebellar function and produces drowsiness, sedation, and hypnosis. *Alters cerebellar function and produces drowsiness, sedation, and hypnosis.*

USES Hypnotic for simple insomnia and preoperatively to provide basal hypnosis for general, spinal, or regional anesthesia.

CONTRAINDICATIONS History of sensitivity to barbiturates; porphyria; severe liver function; renal function impairment; severe respiratory disease; nephritic syndrome; parturition, fetal immaturity; uncontrolled pain. Use of sterile injection containing polyethylene glycol vehicle in patients with renal insuffi-ciency; pregnancy (category D); children <6 y.
CAUTIOUS USE Pregnant women with toxemia or history of bleeding; labor and delivery; seizure disorders; aspirin hypersensitivity; liver function impairment; hyperthyroidism; diabetes mellitus; severe anemia; older adults, debilitated individuals.

ROUTE & DOSAGE

Sedative
Adult: **PO** 100–300 mg/d in 3 divided doses
Child: **PO** 4–6 mg/kg/d in 3 divided doses
Preoperative Sedative
Adult: **PO** 100–300 mg 1–2 h before surgery
Child: **PO** 50–100 mg 1–2 h before surgery
Hypnotic
Adult: **PO** 100–200 mg

ADMINISTRATION

Oral
- Give hypnotic dose only after patient retires for the evening.
- Crush and mix with a fluid or with food if patient cannot swallow pill.

ADVERSE EFFECTS (≥1%) **CNS:** Drowsiness, lethargy, hangover, paradoxical excitement in older adults. **Respiratory:** <u>Respiratory depression, laryngospasm.</u>

INTERACTIONS Drug: Phenmetra-zine antagonizes effects of secobarbital; CNS DEPRESSANTS, **alcohol,** SEDA-TIVES compound CNS depression; MAO INHIBITORS cause excessive CNS depression; **methoxyflurane** increases risk of nephrotoxicity. **Herbal: Kava-kava, valerian** may potentiate sedation.

S

Common adverse effects in *italic*, life-threatening effects <u>underlined</u>; generic names in **bold**; classifications in SMALL CAPS; ✦ Canadian drug name; ℗ Prototype drug

1375

PHARMACOKINETICS Absorption: 90% from GI tract. **Onset:** 15–30 min. **Duration:** 1–4 h. **Distribution:** Crosses placenta; distributed into breast milk. **Metabolism:** In liver. **Elimination:** In urine. **Half-Life:** 30 h.

CLINICAL IMPLICATIONS

Assessment & Drug Effects

- Be alert to unexpected responses and report promptly. Older adults or debilitated patients and children sometimes have paradoxical response to barbiturate therapy (i.e., irritability, marked excitement as inappropriate tearfulness and aggression in children, depression, and confusion). Protect older adult patients from falling, irrational behavior, and effects of depression (anorexia, social withdrawal).
- Patient may become irritable, and uncooperative after a subhypnotic dose of a short-acting barbiturate (uncommon response).
- Be aware that barbiturates do not have analgesic action, and may produce restlessness when given to patients in pain.
- Long-term therapy may result in nutritional folate (B₉) and vitamin D deficiency.
- Lab tests: Obtain liver function and hematology tests, serum folate and vitamin D levels during prolonged therapy.
- Observe closely for changes in established drug regimen effectiveness whenever a barbiturate is added, at least during early phase of barbiturate use. Barbiturates increase the metabolism of many drugs, leading to decreased pharmacologic effects of those drugs.
- Be alert for acute toxicity (intoxication) characterized by profound CNS depression, respiratory depression that may progress to Cheyne-Stokes respirations, hypoventilation, cyanosis, cold clammy skin, hypothermia, constricted pupils (but may be dilated in severe intoxication), shock, oliguria, tachycardia, hypotension, respiration arrest, circulatory collapse, and death.

Patient & Family Education

- Do not drive or engage in potentially hazardous activities until response to drug is established.
- Store barbiturates in a safe place; not on the bedside table or other readily accessible places. It is possible to forget having taken the drug, and in half-wakened conditions take more and accidentally overdose.
- Barbiturates are reportedly teratogenic. Do not become pregnant. Use or add barrier contraception if using hormonal contraceptives.
- Report onset of fever, sore throat or mouth, malaise, easy bruising or bleeding, petechiae, jaundice, rash to physician during prolonged therapy.
- Do not consume alcohol in any amount when taking a barbiturate. It may severely impair judgment and abilities.

SELEGILINE HYDROCHLORIDE (L-Deprenyl)

(se-leg′i-leen)

Carbex, Eldepryl, Emsam, Zelapar

Classifications: ANTICHOLINERGIC; ANTIPARKINSON AGENT

Therapeutic: ANTIPARKINSON AGENT; ANTIDEPRESSANT (MAOI)

Prototype: Levodopa (L-dopa)

Pregnancy Category: C

AVAILABILITY 5 mg tablets, capsules; 1.25 mg orally disintegrating tab; 6 mg, 9 mg, 12 mg transdermal patch

ACTION & *THERAPEUTIC EFFECT*

Increase in dopaminergic activity is thought to be primarily due to selective inhibition of MAO type B activity. Ability of selegiline to control parkinsonism is thought to be due to increased dopaminergic activity. It interferes with dopamine reuptake at the synapse of neurons as well as its inhibition of MAO type B dopaminergic activity in the brain. Interference with dopamine reuptake at the MAO type A dopaminergic receptors in the brain is thought to be the mechanism for antidepression. *Effectiveness is measured in decreased tremors, reduced akinesia, improved speech and motor abilities as well as improved walking. At slightly higher doses it is an effective antidepressant.*

USES Adjunctive therapy of Parkinson's disease for patients being treated with levodopa and carbidopa who exhibit deterioration in the quality of their response to therapy, major depressive disorder.
UNLABELED USES Attention deficit/hyperactivity disorder, extrapyramidal symptoms.

CONTRAINDICATIONS Hypersensitivity to selegiline; uncontrolled hypertension; concomitant use with meperidine and other opioids; suidical ideation; pregnancy (category C); lactation.
CAUTIOUS USE Hypertension; history of suicide, bipolar disorder; psychosis. Safety and efficacy in adolescents and children are not established.

ROUTE & DOSAGE

Parkinson's Disease

Adult: **PO** 5 mg b.i.d. with breakfast and lunch (doses >10 mg/d are associated with increased risk of toxicity due to MAO inhibition)

PO (Zelapar) 1.25 mg qd × 6 weeks (max: 2.5 mg qd)
Geriatric: **PO** Start with 5 mg qa.m.

Depression

Adult: **Transdermal** 6 mg/d, may increase by 3 mg/d q2wk up to 12 mg/d

ADMINISTRATION

Oral

- Do not give daily doses exceeding 10 mg/d.
- Note: Concurrent levodopa and carbidopa doses are usually reduced 10–30% after 2–3 d of selegiline therapy.
- Do not use concurrently with opioids (especially meperidine).
- Store at 15°–30° C (59°–86° F).

Transdermal

- Do not cut or trim patch.
- Before application wash the area with soap and warm water. Dry thoroughly.
- Apply to upper torso, upper thigh, or outer surface of upper arm. Do not apply to hairy, oily, irritated, broken, or calloused skin.
- Rotate sites.
- Wash hands after application.

ADVERSE EFFECTS (≥1%) **CNS:** Sleep disturbances, psychosis, agitation, confusion, dyskinesia, dizziness, hallucinations, dystonia, akathisia. **CV:** Hypotension. **GI:** A n o r-exia, *nausea,* vomiting, abdominal pain, constipation, diarrhea.

INTERACTIONS Drug: TRICYCLIC ANTI-DEPRESSANTS may cause hyperpyrexia, seizures; **fluoxetine, sertraline, paroxetine** may cause hyperthermia, diaphoresis, tremors, seizures, delirium; SYMPATHOMIMETIC AGENTS (e.g., **amphetamine, phenylephrine, phenylpropanolamine**), **guanethidine,** and **reser-**

S

pine may cause hypertensive crisis; CNS DEPRESSANTS have additive CNS depressive effects; OPIATE ANALGESICS (especially **meperidine**) may cause hypertensive crisis and circulatory collapse; **buspirone,** hypertension; GENERAL ANESTHETICS—prolonged hypotensive and CNS depressant effects; hypertension, headache, hyperexcitability reported with **dopamine, methyldopa, levodopa, tryptophan; metrizamide** may increase risk of seizures; HYPOTENSIVE AGENTS and DIURETICS have additive hypotensive effects. **Food:** Aged meats or aged cheeses, protein extracts, sour cream, alcohol, anchovies, liver, sausages, overripe figs, bananas, avocados, chocolate, soy sauce, bean curd, natural yogurt, fava beans—**tyramine**-containing foods—may precipitate hypertensive crisis (less frequent with usual doses of **selegiline** than with other MAOIs). **Herbal:** Ginseng, ephedra, ma huang, St. John's wort may cause hypertensive crisis.

PHARMACOKINETICS Absorption: Rapid; 73% reaches systemic circulation. **Onset:** 1 h. **Duration:** 1–3 d. **Distribution:** Crosses placenta; not known if distributed into breast milk. **Metabolism:** In liver to *N*-desmethyldeprenyl-amphetamine and methamphetamine. **Elimination:** In urine. **Half-Life:** 15 min (metabolites 2–20 h).

CLINICAL IMPLICATIONS

Assessment & Drug Effects

- Monitor vital signs, particularly during period of dosage adjustment. Report alterations in BP or pulse. Indications for discontinuation of the drug include orthostatic hypotension, hypertension, and arrhythmias.
- Monitor for changes in behavior that may indicate increase suicidality, especially in adolescents or children being treated for depression.
- Monitor all patients closely for behavior changes (e.g., hallucinations, confusion, depression, delusions).

Patient & Family Education

- Do not exceed the prescribed drug dose.
- Report symptoms of MAO inhibitor-induced hypertension (e.g., severe headache, palpitations, neck stiffness, nausea, vomiting) immediately to physician.
- Do not drive or engage in potentially hazardous activities until response to drug is known.
- Make positional changes slowly and in stages. Orthostatic hypotension is possible as well as dizziness, light-headedness, and fainting.
- If the transdermal patch falls off, apply a new patch to a new area, and resume previous schedule.
- Only one should be worn at a given time. Remove the old transdermal patch.

SELENIUM SULFIDE

(se-lee'nee-um)

Exsel, Selsun, Selsun Blue

Classifications: ANTIBIOTIC; ANTIFUNGAL
Therapeutic: TOPICAL ANTIBIOTIC; TOPICAL ANTIFUNGAL, ANTISEBORRHEIC
Pregnancy Category: C

AVAILABILITY 1% lotion, shampoo

ACTION & *THERAPEUTIC EFFECT*
Has antibacterial and mild antifungal and antiseborrheic activity. Absorption of selenium sulfide into epithelial tissue cells is followed by degradation of compound to selenium and sulfide ions. Selenium

ions block enzyme systems involved in epithelial cell growth. As a result, rate of turnover in cells with normal or higher than normal turnover rates is reduced. *Active against* Pityrosporum ovale, *a yeast-like fungus found in the normal flora of the scalp. Also decreases rate of growth of the epithelial cells of the scalp and other epithelial layers of cells in the body.*

USES Itching and flaking of the scalp associated with dandruff, seborrheic dermatitis of the scalp, and tinea versicolor.

CONTRAINDICATIONS Kidney failure or biliary tract obstruction, GI malfunction; Wilson's disease; application to damaged or inflamed skin surfaces; as treatment of tinea versicolor during pregnancy; pregnancy (category C) as antiseborrheic only when clearly needed; lactation, children <2 y.
CAUTIOUS USE Prolonged skin contact; use in genital area or skin folds.

ROUTE & DOSAGE

Dandruff Control, Seborrheic Dermatitis
Adult/Child: **Topical** Massage 5–10 mL of a 1–2.5% solution into wet scalp and leave on for 2–3 min, rinse thoroughly, then repeat application and rinse well again (initially, shampoo 2 times/wk for 2 wk, then decrease to once q1–4wk prn)

Tinea Versicolor
Adult/Child: **Topical** Apply a 2.5% solution to affected area with a small amount of water to form a lather, leave on for 10 min, then rinse thoroughly, repeat once/d for 7 d

ADMINISTRATION
Topical
- Wash hands thoroughly after application of selenium sulfide to affected areas. Remove jewelry before treatment; drug will damage it.
- Rinse genital areas and skin folds well with water and dry thoroughly after treatment for tinea versicolor to prevent irritation.
- Store at 15°–30° C (59°–86° F) in tight container; protected from heat. Avoid freezing.

ADVERSE EFFECTS (≥1%) **Skin:** *Skin irritation (stinging),* rebound oiliness of scalp, hair discoloration, diffuse hair loss (reversible), systemic toxicity (if applied to abraded, infected skin).

PHARMACOKINETICS Absorption: No percutaneous absorption if skin is intact.

CLINICAL IMPLICATIONS
Assessment & Drug Effects
- Monitor therapeutic effectiveness.

Patient & Family Education
- Rinse thoroughly with water if lotion contacts eyes in order to prevent chemical conjunctivitis.
- Do not use drug more frequently than required to maintain control of dandruff.
- Hair loss is reversible, usually within 2–3 wk after treatment is discontinued.
- Discontinue use if skin is irritated or treatment fails. Systemic toxicity may result from application of lotion to damaged skin (percutaneous absorption) or from prolonged use (overdosage). Toxicity symptoms include tremors, an-

Common adverse effects in *italic*, life-threatening effects <u>underlined</u>; generic names in **bold**; classifications in SMALL CAPS; ♣ Canadian drug name; ☯ Prototype drug

1379

orexia, occasional vomiting, lethargy, weakness, severe perspiration, garlicky breath, lower abdominal pain. Symptoms disappear 10–12 d after treatment is stopped.

SENNA (SENNOSIDES)

(sen'na)

Black-Draught, Gentlax B, Senexon, Senokot, Senolax

Classifications: STIMULANT LAXATIVE

Therapeutic: STIMULANT LAXATIVE
Prototype: Bisacodyl
Pregnancy Category: C

AVAILABILITY 8.6 mg, 15 mg, 25 mg tablets; 8.6 mg/5 mL, 15 mg/5 mL syrup

ACTION & *THERAPEUTIC EFFECT*
Prepared from dried leaflet of *Cassia acutifolia* or *Cassia angustifolia*. Senna glycosides are converted in colon to active aglycone, which stimulates peristalsis. Concentrate is purified and standardized for uniform action and is claimed to produce less colic than crude form. *Peristalsis stimulated by conversion of drug to active chemical.*

USES Acute constipation and preoperative and preradiographic bowel evacuation.

CONTRAINDICATIONS Hypersensitivity; appendicitis, fecal impaction; fluid and electrolyte imbalances; irritable colon, nausea, vomiting, undiagnosed abdominal pain, intestinal obstruction; children <6 y; pregnancy (category C), lactation.
CAUTIOUS USE Diabetes mellitus; children >6 y; fluid and electrolyte imbalances.

ROUTE & DOSAGE

Constipation

Adult: **PO Standard Senna Concentrate** 1–2 tablets or $^1/_2$–1 tsp h.s. (max: 4 tablets or 2 tsp b.i.d.); **Syrup, Liquid** 10–15 mL at h.s.
Child: **PO Standard Senna Concentrate** >27 kg, 1 tablet or $^1/_2$ tsp h.s.; **Syrup, Liquid** 1 mo–1 y, 1.25–2.5 mL h.s.; 1–5 y, 2.5–5 mL h.s.; 5–15 y, 5–10 mL h.s.

ADMINISTRATION

Oral

■ Give at bedtime, generally.
■ Avoid exposing drug to excessive heat; protect fluid extracts from light.

ADVERSE EFFECTS (≥1%) **GI:** Abdominal cramps, flatulence, nausea, watery diarrhea, excessive loss of water and electrolytes, weight loss, melanotic segmentation of colonic mucosa (reversible).

PHARMACOKINETICS Onset: 6–10 h; may take up to 24 h. **Metabolism:** In liver. **Elimination:** In feces.

CLINICAL IMPLICATIONS

Assessment & Drug Effects

■ Reduce dose in patients who experience considerable abdominal cramping.

Patient & Family Education

■ Be aware that drug may alter urine and feces color; yellowish brown (acid), reddish brown (alkaline).
■ Continued use may lead to dependence. Consult physician if constipation persists.
■ See bisacodyl for additional clinical implications.

SERTACONAZOLE NITRATE

(ser-ta-con′a-zole)

Ertaczo

Classifications: ANTIBIOTIC; AZOLE ANTIFUNGAL

Therapeutic: ANTIFUNGAL ANTIBIOTIC

Prototype: Fluconazole

Pregnancy Category: C

AVAILABILITY 2% cream

ACTION & *THERAPEUTIC EFFECT*
Antifungal that belongs to the azole class of antifungals. It is believed that azole antifungals act primarily by inhibiting cytochrome P450–dependent synthesis of ergosterol, a key component of the cell membrane of fungi resulting in fungal cell injury. *Has a broad spectrum of activity against common fungal pathogens.*

USES Treatment of tinea pedis in immunocompetent patients.

CONTRAINDICATIONS Onychomycosis; children <12 y; pregnancy (category C).
CAUTIOUS USE History of hypersensitivity to azole antifungals; lactation.

ROUTE & DOSAGE

Tinea Pedis
Adult/Child: **Topical** *>12 y,* apply thin layer to affected area twice daily for 4 wk

ADMINISTRATION

Topical
- Cleanse the affected area and dry thoroughly before application.
- Apply a thin layer of the cream to affected area between the toes and the immediately surrounding healthy skin. Gently rub into the skin.
- Store at 15°–30° C (57°–86° F).

ADVERSE EFFECTS (≥1%) **Skin:** Contact dermatitis, dry skin, burning, application site reaction, skin tenderness.

PHARMACOKINETICS Absorption: Negligible through intact skin.

CLINICAL IMPLICATIONS

Assessment & Drug Effects
- Monitor for clinical improvement, which should be seen about 2 wk after initiating treatment.

Patient & Family Education
- Report any of the following: severe skin irritation, redness, burning, blistering, or itching.
- Do not stop using this medication prematurely. Athlete's foot takes about 4 wk to clear completely.
- Nursing mothers should ensure that this topical cream does not accidentally get on the breast.

SERTRALINE HYDROCHLORIDE

(ser′tra-leen)

Zoloft

Classifications: PSYCHOTHERAPEUTIC AGENT; ANTIDEPRESSANT; SELECTIVE SEROTONIN REUPTAKE INHIBITOR (SSRI)

Therapeutic: ANTIDEPRESSANT; SSRI

Prototype: Fluoxetine

Pregnancy Category: C

AVAILABILITY 25 mg, 50 mg, 100 mg tablets; 20 mg/mL liquid

ACTION & *THERAPEUTIC EFFECT*
Potent inhibitor of serotonin (5-HT) reuptake in the brain. Chronic administration results in downregulation of norepinephrine, a reaction found with other effective antidepressants. Sertraline does not inhibit MAO. *Effective in controlling*

S

Common adverse effects in *italic*, life-threatening effects <u>underlined</u>; generic names in **bold**; classifications in SMALL CAPS; ✦ Canadian drug name; ⊘ Prototype drug

1381

depression, obsessive-compulsive disorder, anxiety, and panic disorder.

USES Major depression, obsessive-compulsive disorder, panic disorder, social anxiety disorder, premenstrual dysphoric disorder, generalized anxiety, post-traumatic stress disorder.

UNLABELED USES Eating disorders, generalized anxiety disorder.

CONTRAINDICATIONS Patients taking MAO inhibitors or within 14 d of discontinuing MAO inhibitor; concurrent use of Antabuse; suicidal ideation, hyponatremia; mania or hypomania, pregnancy (category C); third trimester of pregnancy. Safety and effectiveness in children <6 y are not established.

CAUTIOUS USE Seizure disorders, major affective disorders, bipolar disorder, history of suicide; liver dysfunction, renal impairment; abrupt discontinuation; anorexia nervosa, recent history of MI or unstable cardiac disease, dehydration; diabetes mellitus; older adults; ECT therapy, seizure disorder, seizures; lactation.

ROUTE & DOSAGE

Depression, Anxiety
Adult: **PO** Begin with 50 mg/d, gradually increase every few weeks according to response (range: 50–200 mg)
Geriatric: **PO** Start with 25 mg/d

Premenstrual Dysphoric Disorder
Adult: **PO** Begin with 50 mg/d for first cycle, may titrate up to 150 mg/d

Obsessive-Compulsive Disorder
Adult: **PO** Begin with 50 mg/d, may titrate at weekly intervals up to 200 mg/d

Child: **PO** 6–12 y, Begin with 25 mg/d, may increase by 50 mg/wk, as tolerated and needed, up to 200 mg/d

ADMINISTRATION

Oral
- Give in the morning or evening.
- Do not give concurrently with an MAO INHIBITOR or within 14 d of discontinuing an MAO INHIBITOR.
- Dilute concentrate before use with 4 oz of water, ginger ale, lemon/lime soda, lemonade, or orange juice ONLY. Give immediately after mixing. Caution with latex sensitivity, as the dropper contains dry natural rubber.

ADVERSE EFFECTS (≥1%) **CV:** Palpitations, chest pain, hypertension, hypotension, edema, syncope, tachycardia. **CNS:** *Agitation, insomnia, headache, dizziness, somnolence, fatigue,* ataxia, incoordination, vertigo, abnormal dreams, aggressive behavior, delusions, hallucinations, emotional lability, paranoia, suicidal ideation, depersonalization. **Endocrine:** Gynecomastia, male sexual dysfunction. **GI:** Nausea, vomiting, diarrhea, constipation, indigestion, anorexia, flatulence, abdominal pain, dry mouth. **Special Senses:** Exophthalmos, blurred vision, dry eyes, diplopia, photophobia, tearing, conjunctivitis, mydriasis. **Skin:** Rash, urticaria, acne, alopecia. **Respiratory:** Rhinitis, pharyngitis, cough, dyspnea, bronchospasm. **Body as a Whole:** Myalgia, arthralgia, muscle weakness. **Metabolic:** Hyponatremia in older adults.

DIAGNOSTIC TEST INTERFERENCE
May cause asymptomatic elevations in *liver function tests.* Slight decrease in *uric acid.*

S

INTERACTIONS Drug: MAOIS (e.g., **selegiline, phenelzine**) should be stopped 14 d before sertraline is started because of serious problems with other SEROTONIN REUPTAKE INHIBITORS (shivering, nausea, diplopia, confusion, anxiety). **Sertraline** may increase levels and toxicity of **diazepam, pimozide, tolbutamide.** Use cautiously with other centrally acting CNS drugs; increase risk of **ergotamine** toxicity with **dihydroergotamine, ergotamine.** Concentrate interacts with **disulfiram. Herbal: St. John's wort** may cause **serotonin** syndrome (headache, dizziness, sweating, agitation). **Food:** Grapefruit juice (>1 qt/d) may increase plasma concentrations and adverse effects.

PHARMACOKINETICS Absorption: Slowly from GI tract. **Onset:** 2–4 wk. **Distribution:** 99% protein bound; distribution into breast milk unknown. **Metabolism:** Extensive first-pass metabolism in liver to inactive metabolites. **Elimination:** 40–45% in urine, 40–45% in feces. **Half-Life:** 24 h.

CLINICAL IMPLICATIONS

Assessment & Drug Effects

- Supervise patients at risk for suicide closely during initial therapy.
- Monitor for worsening of depression or emergence of suicidal ideation.
- Monitor older adults for fluid and sodium imbalances.
- Monitor patients with a history of a seizure disorder closely.
- Lab tests: Monitor PT and INR with patients receiving concurrent warfarin therapy.

Patient & Family Education

- Report diarrhea, nausea, dyspepsia, insomnia, drowsiness, dizzi-

ness, or persistent headache to physician.
- Report signs of bleeding promptly to physician when taking concomitant warfarin.

SEVELAMER HYDROCHLORIDE ℗

(se-vel′a-mer)

Renagel

Classifications: ELECTROLYTE AND WATER BALANCE AGENT; PHOSPHATE BINDER

Therapeutic: PHOSPHATE BINDER

Pregnancy Category: C

AVAILABILITY 403 mg capsules; 400 mg, 800 mg tablets

ACTION & *THERAPEUTIC EFFECT*

Polymer that binds intestinal phosphate; interacts with phosphate by way of ion-exchange and hydrogen binding. Advantageously, does not contain aluminum or calcium in treating hyperphosphatemia in end stage kidney failure. *Indicated by a serum phosphate level ≤6.0 mg/dL.*

USES Reduction of serum phosphorus in patients with end-stage kidney disease.

CONTRAINDICATIONS Hypophosphatemia; hypersensitivity to sevelamer HCl; fecal impaction; bowel obstruction; hypophosphatemia; appendicitis; dysphagia, GI bleeding, major GI surgery; pregnancy (category C), lactation. Safety and efficacy in children <18 y are not established.

CAUTIOUS USE GI motility disorders; vitamin deficiencies (especially vitamins D, E, and K and folic acid).

S

Common adverse effects in *italic*, life-threatening effects underlined; generic names in **bold**; classifications in SMALL CAPS; ♣ Canadian drug name; ℗ Prototype drug

1383

ROUTE & DOSAGE

Hyperphosphatemia

Adult: **PO** 2 capsules or tablets t.i.d. for serum phosphorus >6 and <7.5 mg/dL; 3 capsules or tablets t.i.d. for serum phosphorus >7.5 and <9 mg/dL; 4 capsules or tablets t.i.d. for serum phosphorus ≥9 mg/dL

ADMINISTRATION

Oral

- Give with meals; do not open or chew capsule.
- Give other oral medications 1 h before or 3 h after Renagel.
- Discard capsules after printed expiration date.
- Store at 15°–30° C (59°–86° F); protect from moisture.

ADVERSE EFFECTS (≥1%) **Body as a Whole:** Headache, infection, pain. **CV:** Hypertension, hypotension, thrombosis. **GI:** Diarrhea, dyspepsia, vomiting, nausea, constipation, flatulence. **Respiratory:** Increased cough.

CLINICAL IMPLICATIONS

Assessment & Drug Effects

- Lab tests: Obtain frequent serum phosphate levels.

Patient & Family Education

- Do not use capsules after printed expiration date.
- Take daily multivitamin supplement approved by physician.

SIBUTRAMINE HYDROCHLORIDE MONOHYDRATE

(si-bu'tra-meen)

Meridia

Classifications: SELECTIVE SEROTONIN REUPTAKE INHIBITOR (SSRI); NOREPINEPHRINE REUPTAKE INHIBITOR

Therapeutic: APPETITE SUPPRESSANT
Prototype: Fluoxetine
Pregnancy Category: C
Controlled Substance: Schedule IV

AVAILABILITY 5 mg, 10 mg, 15 mg capsules

ACTION & *THERAPEUTIC EFFECT* Inhibits central reuptake of serotonin (5HT$_3$), monoamine reuptake, as well as norepinephrine and dopamine reuptake, by blocking their receptors. *Appetite suppression by enhancing satiety and raising the metabolic rate. Indicated by a loss of at least 4 lb during the first 4 wk of therapy.*

USES Management of obesity, including weight loss and maintenance of weight loss, in patients with BMI of at least 30 kg/m^2 or BMI of at least 27 kg/m^2 and other risk factors (hypertension, diabetes, dyslipidemia).

CONTRAINDICATIONS Major eating disorders; anorexia nervosa, bulimia; arrhythmias; concurrent administration with other serotonin reuptake inhibitors (e.g., fluoxetine), MAOIS, lithium, tryptophan; severe hepatic or renal impairment; ESRD, dialysis; CHF, stroke, CAD; uncontrolled or poorly controlled hypertension; seizures; pregnancy (category C), lactation.

CAUTIOUS USE History of hypertension; older adults; narrow-angle glaucoma; mild or moderate hepatic disease; renal impairment. Safety and efficacy in patients <16 y are not established.

ROUTE & DOSAGE

Weight Loss

Adult: **PO** 10 mg once daily, preferably in morning, may be increased to 15 mg if inadequate weight loss (<4 lb) in 4 wk

ADMINISTRATION

Oral
- Note: Doses above 15 mg/d are not recommended.
- Allow at least 2 wk to elapse between discontinuing an MAOI and starting sibutramine.
- Store at 15°–30° C (59°–86° F) in a tightly closed container; protect from light.

ADVERSE EFFECTS (≥1%) **Body as a Whole:** Back pain, flu-like syndrome, asthenia, arthralgia. **CNS:** *Headache,* insomnia, migraine headache, dizziness, nervousness, anxiety, depression, paresthesias, seizures (rare). **CV:** Increase in BP, tachycardia, vasodilation, palpitations. **GI:** *Dry mouth,* anorexia, constipation, abdominal pain, increased appetite, nausea, dyspepsia, taste perversion. **Respiratory:** Rhinitis, pharyngitis, sinusitis, cough. **Skin:** Rash, sweating. **Urogenital:** Dysmenorrhea, UTI.

INTERACTIONS Drug: DECONGESTANTS, COUGH AND ALLERGY MEDICATIONS may cause additional increase in BP; MAOIS, ERGOT DERIVATIVES, **sumatriptan, naratriptan, rizatriptan, zolmitriptan, dextromethorphan, meperidine, pentazocine, fentanyl, lithium;** SSRIS may predispose to **serotonin** syndrome (see Appendix F); **ketoconazole, erythromycin** may inhibit metabolism of sibutramine. **Herbal: St. John's wort** may cause **serotonin** syndrome (headache, dizziness, sweating, agitation).

PHARMACOKINETICS Absorption: Rapidly from GI tract. **Peak:** 1.2 h. **Distribution:** 97% protein bound; concentrates in liver and kidneys. **Metabolism:** In liver by cytochrome P450 3A4 to 2 active metabolites. **Elimination:** Primarily in kidneys.

Half-Life: 14–16 h (active metabolites).

CLINICAL IMPLICATIONS

Assessment & Drug Effects
- Monitor weight changes carefully to determine therapeutic effect.
- Lab tests: Periodic liver function, bilirubin, alkaline phosphatases, lipid profile.
- Monitor BR and HR regularly; report sustained increases in BP or HR immediately.
- Monitor for and immediately report S&S of serotonin syndrome (see Appendix F).
- Monitor persons with narrow-angle glaucoma closely for worsening intraocular pressure.

Patient & Family Education
- Notify physician if any of the following develop: Rash, hives, or other S&S of an allergic reaction; signs of hyperstimulation such as restlessness, shivering, profuse sweating, irritability, and tremor.
- Take in the morning; causes less interference with sleep.
- Check with physician before taking any OTC cough, cold, allergy, or weight-loss drugs.
- Maintain strict adherence to prescribed antihypertensives.
- Inform physician of all drugs being taken. Serious adverse effects may be experienced with concomitant use of some drugs used to treat depression.

SILDENAFIL CITRATE ⓟ

(sil-den′a-fil ci′trate)
Revatio, Viagra
Classifications: IMPOTENCE AGENT; PHOSPHODIESTERASE (PDE) INHIBITOR
Therapeutic: IMPOTENCE
Pregnancy Category: B

S

Common adverse effects in *italic*, life-threatening effects <u>underlined</u>; generic names in **bold**; classifications in SMALL CAPS; ◆ Canadian drug name; ⓟ Prototype drug

1385

AVAILABILITY 20 mg, 25 mg, 50 mg, 100 mg tablets

ACTION & *THERAPEUTIC EFFECT* Enhances vasodilation effect of nitric oxide in the corpus cavernosus of the penis, thus sustaining an erection. *Oral treatment for erectile dysfunction, whether organic or psychogenic in origin.*

USES Erectile dysfunction, pulmonary arterial hypertension.

CONTRAINDICATIONS Hypersensitivity to sildenafil; concurrent administration of organic nitrates and nitroglycerin; lactation, children, infants.

CAUTIOUS USE CAD, heart failure, MI, cardiac arrhythmias, stroke within 6 mo of starting drug; nitrate therapy; hypotension and hypertension; risk factors for CVA; aortic stenosis; anatomic deformity of the penis; sickle cell anemia, polycythemia; multiple myeloma; leukemia; active bleeding or a peptic ulcer, GERD, hiatal hernia; coagulopathy; retinitis pigmentosa; hepatic disease, hepatitis, cirrhosis; severe renal impairment (Cl_{cr} <30 mL/min); older adults; concurrent use with other medicines for penile dysfunction; pregnancy (category B).

ROUTE & DOSAGE

Erectile Dysfunction

Adult: **PO** 50 mg 0.5–4 h before sexual activity (dose range: 25 to 100 mg once/d); max dose: 25 mg/d with itraconazole or ketoconazole; max dose: 25 mg/48 h with ritonavir

Geriatric: **PO** 25 mg approximately 1 h before sexual activity

Pulmonary Arterial Hypertension

Adult: **PO** 20 mg t.i.d. (4–6 h apart)

Hepatic or Severe Renal Impairment

Adult: **PO** 25 mg approximately 1 h before sexual activity

ADMINISTRATION

Oral

- For ED: Dose 1 h prior to sexual activity (effective range is 0.5–4 h).
- Do not give within 24 h of taking any medication with nitrates (i.e., nitroglycerin).
- Store at 15°–30° C (59°–86° F) in a tightly closed container; protect from light.

ADVERSE EFFECTS (≥1%) **Body as a Whole:** Face edema, photosensitivity, shock, asthenia, pain, chills, fall, allergic reaction, arthritis, myalgia. **CNS:** *Headache,* dizziness, migraine, syncope, cerebral thrombosis, ataxia, neuralgia, paresthesias, tremor, vertigo, depression, insomnia, somnolence, abnormal dreams. **CV:** Flushing, chest pain, <u>MI</u>, angina, AV block, tachycardia, palpitation, hypotension, postural hypotension, <u>cardiac arrest</u>, <u>sudden cardiac death</u>, heart failure, cardiomyopathy, abnormal ECG, edema. **GI:** Dyspepsia, diarrhea, abdominal pain, vomiting, colitis, dysphagia, gastritis, gastroenteritis, esophagitis, stomatitis, dry mouth, abnormal liver function tests, thirst. **Respiratory:** Nasal congestion, asthma, dyspnea, laryngitis, pharyngitis, sinusitis, bronchitis, cough. **Skin:** Rash, urticaria, pruritus, sweating, <u>exfoliative dermatitis</u>. **Urogenital:** UTI. **Special Senses:** Abnormal vision (color changes, photosensitivity, blurred vision, sudden vision loss). **Hematologic:** Anemia, leukopenia. **Metabolic:** Gout, hyperglycemia, hyperuricemia, hypoglycemia, hypernatremia.

INTERACTIONS Drug: NITRATES increase risk of serious hypotension; if used within 4 h of **doxazosin, prazosin, terazosin, tamsulosin; cimetidine, erythromycin, ketoconazole, itraconazole,** PROTEASE INHIBITORS increase sildenafil levels; **rifampin** can decrease sildenafil levels. **Food:** Grapefruit juice (>1 qt/day) may increase plasma concentrations and adverse effects.

PHARMACOKINETICS Absorption: Rapidly from GI tract. **Peak:** 30–120 min. **Distribution:** 96% protein bound. **Metabolism:** In liver (CYP3A4 and 2C9). **Elimination:** 80% in feces, 12% in urine. **Half-Life:** 4 h.

CLINICAL IMPLICATIONS
Assessment & Drug Effects
- Monitor carefully for and immediately report S&S of cardiac distress.

Patient & Family Education
- Do not take sildenafil within 4 h of taking doxazosin, prazosin, terazosin, or tamsulosin.
- Consuming a high-fat meal before taking drug may cause delay in drug action.
- Report to physician: Headaches, flushing, chest pain, indigestion, blurred vision, sensitivity to light, changes in color vision.

SILVER SULFADIAZINE

(sul-fa-dye′a-zeen)
Silvadene
Classifications: SULFONAMIDE
Therapeutic: TOPICAL ANTIINFECTIVE
Prototype: Sulfisoxazole
Pregnancy Category: B

AVAILABILITY 1%/50 g cream

ACTION & *THERAPEUTIC EFFECT*
Silver salt is released slowly and exerts bactericidal effect only on bacterial cell membrane and wall, rather than by inhibiting folic acid synthesis; antibacterial activity is not inhibited by *p*-aminobenzoic acid (PABA). *Broad antimicrobial activity including many gram-negative and gram-positive bacteria and yeast.*

USES Prevention and treatment of sepsis in second- and third-degree burns.

CONTRAINDICATIONS Hypersensitivity to other sulfonamides; pregnant women at term, premature infants and neonates <1 mo.
CAUTIOUS USE Impaired kidney or liver function; porphyria; impaired respiratory function; G6PD deficiency; thrombocytopenia, leukopenia, hematological disease; pregnancy (category B), lactation.

ROUTE & DOSAGE

Burn Wound Treatment
Adult/Child: **Topical** Apply 1% cream 1–2 times/d to thickness of approximately 1.5 mm ($^1/_{16}$ in.)

ADMINISTRATION
Topical
- Do not use if cream darkens; it is water soluble and white.
- Apply with sterile, gloved hands to cleansed, debrided burned areas. Reapply cream to areas where it has been removed by patient activity; cover burn wounds with medication at all times.
- Bathe patient daily (in whirlpool or shower or in bed) as aid to debridement. Reapply drug.
- Note: Dressings are not required but may be used if necessary. Drug does not stain clothing.
- Store at room temperature away from heat.

S

Common adverse effects in *italic*, life-threatening effects underlined; generic names in **bold**; classifications in SMALL CAPS; ♦ Canadian drug name; ◑ Prototype drug

1387

ADVERSE EFFECTS (≥1%) **Body as a Whole:** Pain (occasionally), burning, itching, rash, reversible leukopenia. Potential for toxicity as for other sulfonamides if applied to extensive areas of the body surface.

INTERACTIONS Drug: PROTEOLYTIC ENZYMES are inactivated by silver in cream.

PHARMACOKINETICS Absorption: Not absorbed through intact skin, however, approximately 10% could be absorbed when applied to second- or third-degree burns. **Distribution:** Distributed into most body tissues. **Metabolism:** In the liver. **Elimination:** In urine.

CLINICAL IMPLICATIONS

Assessment & Drug Effects
- Observe for and report hypersensitivity reaction: Rash, itching, or burning sensation in unburned areas.
- Lab tests: Obtain serum sulfa concentrations, urinalysis, and kidney function tests when drug is applied to extensive areas. Significant quantities of drug may be absorbed.
- Observe patient for reactions attributed to sulfonamides.
- Note: Analgesic may be required. Occasionally, pain is experienced on application; intensity and duration depend on depth of burn.
- Continue treatment until satisfactory healing or burn site is ready for grafting, unless adverse reactions occur.

SIMVASTATIN

(sim-vah-sta'-tin)
Zocor
Classifications: ANTILIPEMIC; HMG-COA REDUCTASE INHIBITOR (STATIN)

Therapeutic: ANTIHYPERLIPEMIC; STATIN
Prototype: Lovastatin
Pregnancy Category: X

AVAILABILITY 5 mg, 10 mg, 20 mg, 40 mg, 80 mg tablets

ACTION & *THERAPEUTIC EFFECT*
Inhibitor of 3-hydroxy-3-methylglutaryl coenzyme A (HMG-CoA) reductase; similar in action to lovastatin but more potent. HMG-CoA reductase inhibitors increase HDL cholesterol, and decrease LDL cholesterol, and total cholesterol synthesis. *Effectiveness indicated by decreased serum triglycerides, decreased LDL, cholesterol, and modest increases in HDL cholesterol.*

USES Hypercholesterolemia (alone or in combination with bile acid sequestrants), familial hypercholesterolemia. Reduces risk of coronary death and nonfatal MI.

CONTRAINDICATIONS Hypersensitivity to simvastatin; active liver disease, hepatic encephalopathy, hepatitis, jaundice, rhabdomyolysis; cholestasis; pregnancy (category X), children <10 y, lactation.
CAUTIOUS USE Homozygous familial hypercholesterolemia, history of liver disease, alcoholics; renal disease, renal impairment; seizure disorder.

ROUTE & DOSAGE

Hypercholesterolemia

Adult: **PO** 5–40 mg q.d. (max: 80 mg q.d.). Patients taking danazol or cyclosporine should not exceed 10 mg q.d.

ADMINISTRATION

Oral
- Adjust dosage usually at 4-wk intervals.

- Give in the evening.
- Store at 15°–30° C (59°–86° F).

ADVERSE EFFECTS (≥1%) **CV:** Angina. **CNS:** Dizziness, headache, vertigo, asthenia, fatigue, insomnia. **GI:** Nausea, diarrhea, vomiting, abdominal pain, constipation, flatulence, heartburn, transient elevations in liver transaminases, transient elevations in CPK. **Body as a Whole:** Fatigue. **Respiratory:** Rhinitis, cough.

INTERACTIONS Drug: May increase PT when administered with **warfarin; cyclosporine, gemfibrozil, fenofibrate, clofibrate,** antilipemic doses of **niacin, fluconazole, itraconazole, ketoconazole, miconazole, nefazodone, nelfinavir, ritonavir, saquinavir, sildenafil, tacrolimus, clarithromycin, erythromycin, telithromycin** may increase serum levels and increase risk of myopathy, rhabdomyolysis and acute kidney failure. **Food:** Grapefruit juice (>1 quart daily) may increase risk of myopathy, rhabdomyolysis. **Herbal: Peppermint oil** may increase plasma concentrations. **St. John's wort** may decrease efficacy.

PHARMACOKINETICS Absorption: Rapidly from GI tract. **Onset:** 2 wk. **Peak:** 4–6 wk. **Distribution:** 95% protein bound; achieves high liver concentrations; crosses placenta. **Metabolism:** Extensive first-pass metabolism in liver to its active metabolite. **Elimination:** 13% in urine, 60% in bile and feces.

CLINICAL IMPLICATIONS

Assessment & Drug Effects
- Lab tests: Obtain baseline and periodic (q6mo) liver function during the first year and yearly thereafter. Monitor cholesterol levels throughout therapy.

- Monitor coagulation studies with patients receiving concurrent warfarin therapy. PT may be prolonged.
- Assess for and report unexplained muscle pain. Determine CPK level at onset of muscle pain.

Patient & Family Education
- Report unexplained muscle pain, tenderness, or weakness, especially if accompanied by malaise or fever, to physician.
- Report signs of bleeding to physician promptly when taking concurrent warfarin.
- Moderate intake of grapefruit juice while taking this medication.

SIROLIMUS

(sir-o-li'mus)
Rapamune
Classifications: IMMUNOMODULATOR; IMMUNOSUPPRESSANT
Therapeutic: IMMUNOSUPPRESSANT
Prototype: Cyclosporine
Pregnancy Category: C

AVAILABILITY 1 mg tablets; 1 mg/mL oral solution

ACTION & THERAPEUTIC EFFECT Macrolide antibiotic structurally related to tacrolimus with immunosuppressive activity. Active in reducing a transplant rejection by inhibiting the response of helper T-lymphocytes and B-lymphocytes to cytokinesis [(interleukin) IL-2, IL-4, and IL-5]. *Inhibits antibody production and acute transplant rejection reaction in autoimmune disorders [e.g., systemic lupus erythematosus (SLE)]. Indicated by nonrejection of transplanted organ.*

USES Prophylaxis of kidney transplant rejection.

S

Common adverse effects in *italic*, life-threatening effects <u>underlined</u>; generic names in **bold**; classifications in SMALL CAPS; ✦ Canadian drug name; ⊙ Prototype drug

1389

UNLABELED USES Treatment of psoriasis.

CONTRAINDICATIONS Hypersensitivity to sirolimus; lung or liver transplant patients; soya lecithin (soy fatty acids) hypersensitivity; lymphoma, neoplastic disease; children <13 y; females of childbearing age; pregnancy (category C); lactation.

CAUTIOUS USE Hypersensitivity to or concurrent administration with tacrolimus; impaired renal function; concurrent use of aminoglycosides, and amphotericin B; renal transplant patients; dialysis patients, UV exposure, retransplant patients, multiorgan transplant recipients, African-American transplant patients; viral or bacterial infection; hypertriglyceridemia, hyperlipidemia, diabetic patients, atrial fibrillation, CHF, hypervolemia, palpitations; mild to moderate hepatic disease; coronary artery disease; myelosuppression; liver disease.

ROUTE & DOSAGE

Kidney Transplant

Adult: **PO** 6 mg loading dose immediately after transplant, then 2 mg/d. Doses will need to be much higher (up to 40 mg/d) if not on cyclosporine

Adolescent: **PO** ≥13 y and <40 kg, 3 mg/m² loading dose immediately after transplant, then 1 mg/m²/d. Doses will need to be much higher (up to 40 mg/d) if not on cyclosporine

Hepatic Impairment

Reduce maintenance dose by 33%

ADMINISTRATION

Oral
- Give 4 h after oral cyclosporine.
- Add prescribed amount of sirolimus to a glass containing ≥2 oz (60 mL) of water or orange juice (do not use any other type of liquid). Stir vigorously and administer immediately. Refill glass with ≥4 oz (120 mL) of water or orange juice. Stir vigorously and administer immediately.
- Give consistently with respect to amount and type of food.
- Refrigerate; protect from light; use multidose bottles within 1 mo of opening.

ADVERSE EFFECTS (≥1%) **Body as a Whole:** *Asthenia, back pain, chest pain, fever, pain, arthralgia;* flu-like syndrome; generalized edema; infection; lymphocele; malaise; <u>sepsis</u>, arthrosis, bone necrosis, leg cramps, myalgia, osteoporosis, tetany, abscess, ascites, cellulitis, chills, face edema, hernia, pelvic pain, peritonitis. **CNS:** *Insomnia, tremor, headache,* anxiety, confusion, depression, dizziness, emotional lability, hypertonia, hyperesthesia, hypotonia, neuropathy, paresthesia, somnolence. **CV:** *Hypertension,* atrial fibrillation, CHF, hypervolemia, hypotension, palpitation, peripheral vascular disorder, postural hypotension, syncope, tachycardia, thrombophlebitis, thrombosis, vasodilation. **GI:** *Constipation, diarrhea, dyspepsia, nausea, vomiting, abdominal pain,* anorexia, dysphagia, eructation, esophagitis, flatulence, gastritis, gastroenteritis, gingivitis, gum hyperplasia, ileus, mouth ulceration, oral moniliasis, stomatitis, abnormal liver function tests. **Hematologic:** *Anemia, thrombocytopenia,* <u>leukopenia</u>, hemorrhage, ecchymosis, leukocytosis, lymphadenopathy, polycythemia, thrombotic, thrombocytopenic purpura. **Metabolic:** *Edema, hypercholesterolemia, hyperkalemia, hyperlipidemia, hypokalemia, hypophosphatemia, peripheral edema, weight gain,* Cushing's

S

syndrome, diabetes, acidosis, hyper-calcemia, hyperglycemia, hyper-phosphatemia, hypocalcemia, hy-poglycemia, hypomagnesemia, hyponatremia; increased LDH, alka-line phosphatase, BUN, creatine phosphokinase, ALT, or AST; weight loss. **Respiratory:** *Dyspnea, pharyngitis, upper respiratory tract infection,* asthma, atelectasis, bronchitis, cough, epistaxis, hypoxia, lung edema, pleural effusion, pneumonia, rhinitis, sinusitis. **Skin:** *Acne, rash,* fungal dermatitis, hirsutism, pruri-tus, skin hypertrophy, skin ulcer, sweating. **Urogenital:** *UTI,* albumin-uria, bladder pain, dysuria, hema-turia, hydronephrosis, impotence, kidney pain, nocturia, renal tubular necrosis, oliguria, pyuria, scrotal edema, incontinence, urinary reten-tion, glycosuria. **Special Senses:** Ab-normal vision, cataract, conjunctivi-tis, deafness, ear pain, otitis media, tinnitus.

INTERACTIONS Drug: Sirolimus concentrations increased by **clari-thromycin, cyclosporine, diltia-zem, erythromycin, ketocona-zole, itraconazole, telithromy-cin;** sirolimus concentrations decreased by **rifabutin, rifampin;** VACCINES may be less effective with sirolimus; **tacrolimus** increases mortality, hepatic artery thrombosis, and graft loss. **Food:** Grapefruit juice significantly increases plasma levels. High fat meals increase levels. **Herbal: St. John's wort** decreases efficacy.

PHARMACOKINETICS Absorption: Rapidly with 14% bioavailability. **Peak:** 2 h. **Distribution:** 92% protein bound, distributes in high concen-trations to heart, intestines, kidneys, liver, lungs, muscle, spleen, and tes-tes. **Metabolism:** In liver (CYP3A4). **Elimination:** 91% in feces, 2.2% in urine. **Half-Life:** 62 h.

CLINICAL IMPLICATIONS

Assessment & Drug Effects
- Monitor for S&S of graft rejection.
- Control hyperlipidemia prior to initiating drug.
- Draw trough whole-blood siroli-mus levels 1 h before a scheduled dose.
- Lab tests: Obtain periodic lipid pro-file, CBC with differential, fasting plasma glucose, blood chemistry, BUN, and creatinine (especially with other drugs known to cause renal impairment).

Patient & Family Education
- Avoid grapefruit juice within 2 h of taking sirolimus.
- Limit exposure to sunlight (UV exposure).
- Note: Decreased effectiveness pos-sible for vaccines during therapy.
- Use or add barrier contraceptive before, during, and for 12 wk af-ter discontinuing therapy.

SITAGLIPTIN
(sit-a-glip'tin)
Januvia
Classifications: HORMONE MODI-FIER; ANTIDIABETIC AGENT; DIPEPTI-DYL PEPTIDASE-4 (DPP-4) INHIBI-TOR; INCRETIN MODIFIER
Therapeutic: ANTIDIABETIC; INCRETIN MODIFIER; DPP-4 INHIBITOR
Pregnancy Category: B

AVAILABILITY 25 mg, 50 mg, and 100 mg tablets

ACTION & THERAPEUTIC EFFECT
Sitagliptin slows inactivation of incretin hormones [e.g., glucagon-like peptide-1 (GLP-1) and glucose-dependent insulinotropic polypep-tide (GIP)] that are released by the intestine. As plasma glucose rises, incretin hormones stimulate release of insulin from the pancreas, and

S

Common adverse effects in *italic*, life-threatening effects <u>underlined</u>; generic names in **bold**; classifications in SMALL CAPS; ♣ Canadian drug name; ⊙ Prototype drug

1391

GLP-1 also lowers glucagon secretion, resulting in reduced hepatic glucose production. *Sitagliptin elevates the level of incretin hormones, thus increasing insulin secretion and reducing glucagon secretion. Sitagliptin lowers both fasting and postprandial plasma glucose levels.*

USES Adjunct treatment of type 2 diabetes mellitus in combination with exercise and diet.

CONTRAINDICATIONS Type I diabetes mellitus, diabetic ketoacidosis. Safety and efficacy in children <18 y are not known.

CAUTIOUS USE Moderate to severe renal impairment, renal failure, hemodialysis; older adults; pregnancy (category B), lactation.

ROUTE & DOSAGE

Type 2 Diabetes Mellitus
Adult: **PO** 100 mg/d
Renal Impairment
Cl_{cr} >30 mL/min and <50 mL/min: 50 mg/d
Cl_{cr} <30 mL/min: 25 mg/d

ADMINISTRATION

Oral
- May be given without regard to meals.
- Note that dosage adjustment is recommended for moderate to severe renal impairment.
- Store at 20°–25° C (68°–77° F).

ADVERSE EFFECTS (≥1%) **CNS:** Headache. **Respiratory:** Nasopharyngitis, upper respiratory tract infection.

INTERACTIONS Drug: Sitagliptin may increase **digoxin** levels.

PHARMACOKINETICS Absorption: 87% absorbed. **Peak:** 1–4 h. **Distribution:** 38% protein bound. **Metabolism:** 20% metabolized in the liver. **Elimination:** Primarily renal (87%) with minor elimination in the kidneys. **Half-Life:** 12.4 h.

CLINICAL IMPLICATIONS
Assessment & Drug Effects
- Monitor for and report S&S of significant GI distress, including NV&D.
- Monitor for S&S of hypoglycemia when used in combination with a sulfonylurea drug or insulin.
- Lab tests: Baseline and periodic Cl_{cr}; periodic fasting and postprandial plasma glucose and HbA_{1C}.
- Monitor blood levels of digoxin with concurrent therapy.

Patient & Family Education
- Follow directions for taking the drug (see Administration).
- Note: When taken alone to control diabetes, sitagliptin is unlikely to cause hypoglycemia because it only works when your blood sugar is rising.

SODIUM BICARBONATE NA(HCO₃)

(sod′i-um bi-car′bon-ate)
Sodium Bicarbonate
Classifications: FLUID AND ELECTROLYTE BALANCE AGENT; ANTACID
Therapeutic: ANTACID
Pregnancy Category: C

AVAILABILITY 325 mg, 520 mg, 650 mg tablets; 4.2%, 5%, 7.5%, 8.4% injection

ACTION & THERAPEUTIC EFFECT
Short-acting, potent systemic antacid and alkalinizing agent. Rapidly neutralizes gastric acid to form sodium chloride, carbon dioxide, and water. After absorption of sodium

bicarbonate, plasma alkali reserve is increased and excess sodium and bicarbonate ions are excreted in urine, thus rendering urine less acid. *Short-acting, potent systemic antacid; rapidly neutralizes gastric acid or systemic acidosis.*

USES Systemic alkalinizer to correct metabolic acidosis (as occurs in diabetes mellitus, shock, cardiac arrest, or vascular collapse), to minimize uric acid crystallization associated with uricosuric agents, to increase the solubility of sulfonamides, and to enhance renal excretion of barbiturate and salicylate overdosage. Commonly used as home remedy for relief of occasional heartburn, indigestion, or sour stomach. Used topically as paste, bath, or soak to relieve itching and minor skin irritations such as sunburn, insect bites, prickly heat, poison ivy, sumac, or oak. Sterile solutions are used to buffer acidic parenteral solutions to prevent acidosis. Also as a buffering agent in many commercial products (e.g., mouthwashes, douches, enemas, ophthalmic solutions).

CONTRAINDICATIONS Prolonged therapy with sodium bicarbonate; patients losing chloride (as from vomiting, GI suction, diuresis); hypocalcemia; metabolic alkalosis; respiratory alkalosis; peptic ulcer; pregnancy (category C).
CAUTIOUS USE Edema, sodium-retaining disorders; heart disease, hypertension; renal disease, renal insufficiency; hypokalemia; children <2 y; lactation; older adults.

ROUTE & DOSAGE

Antacid
Adult: **PO** 0.3–2 g 1–4 times/d or $^1/_2$ tsp of powder in glass of water

Urinary Alkalinizer
Adult: **PO** 4 g initially, then 1–2 g q4h
Child: **PO** 84–840 mg/kg/d in divided doses

Cardiac Arrest
Adult: **IV** 1 mEq/kg initially, then 0.5 mEq/kg q10 min depending on arterial blood gas determinations (8.4% solutions contain 50 mEq/50 mL), give over 1–2 min
Child: **IV** 0.5–1 mEq/kg q10 min depending on arterial blood gas determinations, give over 1–2 min

Metabolic Acidosis
Adult/Child: **IV** Dose adjusted according to pH, base deficit, $PaCO_2$, fluid limits, and patient response.

ADMINISTRATION

Oral
- Do not add oral preparation to calcium-containing solutions.

Topical
- Use manufacturer's directions: Bath or soak, $^1/_2$ cup or more into tub of warm water; footsoak, 4 tbsp/L(qt) warm water; soak 5–10 min; paste, 3 parts sodium bicarbonate to 1 part water
- Note: Solutions in water slowly decompose, decomposition is accelerated by agitating or warming the solution.

Intravenous
PREPARE: IV Infusion: May give 4.2% (0.5 mEq/mL) and 5% (0.595 mEq/mL) $NaHCO_3$ solutions undiluted. Dilute 7.5% (0.892 mEq/mL) and 8.4% (1 mEq/mL) solutions with compatible IV solutions. Dilute to at least 4.2% for infants and children.
ADMINISTER: IV Infusion: Give a bolus dose only in emergency

S

Common adverse effects in *italic*, life-threatening effects <u>underlined</u>; generic names in **bold**; classifications in SMALL CAPS; ♣ Canadian drug name; ⓓ Prototype drug

1393

situations. Usually, the rate is 2–5 mEq/kg over 4–8 h; do not exceed 50 mEq/h. Stop infusion immediately if extravasation occurs. Severe tissue damage has followed tissue infiltration.

INCOMPATIBILITIES **Solution/additive: Alcohol 5%, lactated Ringer's, amoxicillin, ascorbic acid, bupivacaine, carboplatin, carmustine, ciprofloxacin, cisplatin, codeine, corticotropin, dobutamine, dopamine, epinephrine, glycopyrrolate, hydromorphone, imipenem-cilastatin, insulin, isoproterenol, labetalol, levorphanol, magnesium sulfate, meperidine, meropenem, methadone, metoclopramide, morphine, norepinephrine, oxytetracycline, penicillin G, pentazocine, pentobarbital, phenobarbital, procaine, promazine, streptomycin, succinylcholine, tetracycline, thiopental, vancomycin, vitamin B complex with C. Y-site: Allopurinol, amiodarone, amphotericin B cholesteryl complex, calcium chloride, ciprofloxacin, cisatracurium, diltiazem, doxorubicin liposome, fenoldopam, hetastarch, idarubicin, imipenem/cilastatin, inamrinone, leucovorin, lidocaine, midazolam, nalbuphine, ondansetron, oxacillin, sargramostim, verapamil, vincristine, vindesine, vinorelbine.**

▪ Store in airtight containers. ▪ Note expiration date.

ADVERSE EFFECTS (≥1%) **GI:** *Belching, gastric distention,* flatulence. **Metabolic:** Metabolic alkalosis; electrolyte imbalance: sodium overload (pulmonary edema), hypocalcemia (tetany), hypokalemia, milk-alkali syndrome, dehydration. **Other:** Rapid IV in neonates (Hypernatremia, reduction in CSF pressure, <u>intracranial hemorrhage</u>). **Skin:** Severe tissue damage following extravasation of IV solution. **Urogenital:** Renal calculi or crystals, impaired kidney function.

DIAGNOSTIC TEST INTERFERENCE Small increase in ***blood lactate*** levels (following IV infusion of sodium bicarbonate); false-positive ***urinary protein*** determinations (using ***ames reagent, sulfacetic acid,*** heat and ***acetic acid*** or ***nitric acid ring method***); elevated ***urinary urobilinogen*** levels (***urobilinogen*** excretion increases in alkaline urine).

INTERACTIONS Drug: May decrease absorption of **ketoconazole;** may decrease elimination of **dextroamphetamine, ephedrine, pseudoephedrine, quinidine;** may increase elimination of **chlorpropamide, lithium,** SALICYLATES, TETRACYCLINES.

PHARMACOKINETICS Absorption: Readily from GI tract. **Onset:** 15 min. **Duration:** 1–2 h. **Elimination:** In urine within 3–4 h.

CLINICAL IMPLICATIONS

Assessment & Drug Effects

▪ Be aware that long-term use of oral preparation with milk or calcium can cause milk-alkali syndrome: Anorexia, nausea, vomiting, headache, mental confusion, hypercalcemia, hypophosphatemia, soft tissue calcification, renal and ureteral calculi, renal insufficiency, metabolic alkalosis.
▪ Lab tests: Urinary alkalinization: Monitor urinary pH as a guide to dosage (pH testing with nitrazine paper may be done at intervals

throughout the day and dosage adjustments made accordingly).

- Lab tests: Metabolic acidosis: Monitor patient closely by observations of clinical condition; measurements of acid-base status (blood pH, P_{O_2}, P_{CO_2}, HCO_3^-, and other electrolytes, are usually made several times daily during acute period). Observe for signs of alkalosis (over treatment) (see Appendix F).
- Observe for and report S&S of improvement or reversal of metabolic acidosis (see Appendix F).

Patient & Family Education

- Do not use sodium bicarbonate as antacid. A nonabsorbable OTC alternative for repeated use is safer.
- Do not take antacids longer than 2 wk except under advice and supervision of a physician. Self-medication with routine doses of sodium bicarbonate or soda mints may cause sodium retention and alkalosis, especially when kidney function is impaired.
- Be aware that commonly used OTC antacid products contain sodium bicarbonate: Alka-Seltzer, Bromo-Seltzer, Gaviscon.

SODIUM CHLORIDE 20%

(sod'i-um)
Sodium Chloride 20%
Classifications: ABORTIFACIENT
Therapeutic: ABORTIFACIENT
Pregnancy Category: X

AVAILABILITY 20% solution

ACTION & _THERAPEUTIC EFFECT_
Hypertonic saline instillation into the amniotic sac induces abortion and fetal death. Mechanism is unclear, but abortifacient activity may be a response to prostaglandins released by hypertonic NaCl-damaged cells. _Uterine contractions induced by the saline solution are sufficient to cause evacuation of fetus and placenta; however, in 25–40% of the patients, abortion may be incomplete._

USES To induce abortion late in the second trimester of pregnancy. Oxytocin may be used as an adjunct (concurrent) uterine stimulant.

CONTRAINDICATIONS Pregnancy (category X) of less than 15 wk or more than 24 wk; prior uterine surgery (including cervix), pelvic adhesions; sickle cell disease, diabetes mellitus; increased intraamniotic pressure (as in contracting or hypertonic uterus); poor health, blood disorders, coagulation factor deficiencies.

CAUTIOUS USE Malignant hypertension, cardiovascular and kidney disease, thrombocytopenia, fibrinolytic defects.

ROUTE & DOSAGE

Abortion Induction

Adult: **Instillation** Intraamniotic with 20% solution in volumes equal to amount of amniotic fluid removed (max: 200–250 mL) administered slowly over 20–30 min; repeat in 48 h if uterine contractility, cervical effacement, or cervical dilation is inadequate or if labor has not begun

ADMINISTRATION

Instillation

- Prepare skin as for surgery prior to procedure. Withdraw about 1 mL of amniotic fluid by transabdominal tap to confirm location of needle (amniotic fluid has pH 7.4 and ability to fern). If blood is present or if no amniotic fluid is withdrawn, needle is repositioned.

S

Common adverse effects in _italic_, life-threatening effects <u>underlined</u>; generic names in **bold**; classifications in SMALL CAPS; ♣ Canadian drug name; ⓟ Prototype drug

1395

Some clinicians then remove all amniotic fluid (30–250 mL); others wait until NaCl instillation.

▪Instill NaCl through 3-way stopcock with needle and polyethylene catheter inserted into amniotic cavity.

▪Administer IV infusion of dilute solution of oxytocin within 1–2 h after hypertonic solution instillation and after uterine response to the solution has ceased at rate, 20–100 mU/min. Oxytocin action as an adjunctive uterine stimulant shortens the abortifacient-abortion interval.

▪Be prepared to treat extraamniotic injection: Stop procedure promptly. Start IV infusion of D5W; additional support for hypernatremic shock.

ADVERSE EFFECTS (≥1%) **Hematologic:** (Within 12–24 h of instillation) Coagulation changes; increased plasma volume, fibrin levels, thrombin, prothrombin, and partial thromboplastin times; mild self-limiting form of disseminated intravascular coagulation. **Metabolic:** Ascites, hypervolemia, <u>circulation failure, uterine necrosis,</u> severe electrolyte disturbances. **Urogenital:** Cervical lacerations and perforation, uterine rupture, retained placenta, hemorrhagic fever, infection, sepsis. **Respiratory:** <u>Pulmonary embolism.</u> **Body as a Whole:** Fever, flushing, <u>cortical necrosis of kidneys.</u>

INTERACTIONS Drug: Indomethacin may delay onset time of abortion; **terbutaline, ritodrine** inhibit uterine activity induced by hypertonic **NaCl.**

PHARMACOKINETICS Absorption: Some drug diffuses into maternal blood. **Onset:** Within 51 h. **Distribution:** Sodium concentration in amniotic fluid must be at least 2.2 mEq/mL to induce abortion; most of drug concentrates in decidua and fetal part of placenta.

CLINICAL IMPLICATIONS
Assessment & Drug Effects

▪Observe patient for at least 30 min after instillation procedure. Be available for complaints and to check vital signs: temperature, pulse rate, BP.

▪Note: Intraamniotic instillation is a painless procedure. No anesthetic or sedative is needed or given so that patient is able to report early signs of extraamniotic injection including mental confusion, hypotension, severe headache, vague distress, extreme nervousness, pain, sensation of heat, thirst, fingertip numbness, dry mouth, salty taste, tinnitus.

▪Suspect accidental intraperitoneal, intravascular, or myometrial injection if patient begins vomiting. Cardiovascular collapse, seizures, and maternal death may follow.

Patient & Family Education

▪Drink at least 2 L water on day of procedure to promote NaCl excretion.

▪Return promptly to treatment center with onset of labor, signs of rupture of fetal membrane, vaginal bleeding, fever, or any other untoward symptom.

▪Return to physician for evaluation and treatment if labor has not begun within 48 h of hypertonic saline instillation.

SODIUM FERRIC GLUCONATE COMPLEX

(so′di-um fer′ric glu′co-nate)
Ferrlecit
Classifications: BLOOD FORMER; IRON PREPARATION
Therapeutic: ANTIANEMIC; IRON REPLACEMENT
Prototype: Ferrous sulfate
Pregnancy Category: B

AVAILABILITY 62.5 mg elemental iron/5 mL ampule

ACTION & *THERAPEUTIC EFFECT*
Stable iron complex used to restore iron loss in chronic kidney failure patients. The use of erythropoietin therapy and blood loss through hemodialysis require iron replacement. The ferric ion combines with transferrin and is transported to bone marrow where it is incorporated into hemoglobin. *Effectiveness indicated by improved Hgb and Hct, iron saturation, serum ferritin levels.*

USES Treatment of iron deficiency in patients on chronic hemodialysis and receiving erythropoietin therapy.

CONTRAINDICATIONS All anemias not related to iron deficiency; hypersensitivity to sodium ferric gluconate complex, benzyl alcohol; hemochromatosis, hemosiderosis; hemolytic anemia; thalassemia; neonates. **CAUTIOUS USE** Active or suspected infection; cardiac disease; hepatic disease; pregnancy (category B), lactation; older adults. Safety and efficacy in children <6 y are not established.

ROUTE & DOSAGE

Iron Deficiency in Dialysis Patients
Adult: **IV** 125 mg infused over 1 h
Child (>6 years): **IV** 1.5 mg/kg infused over 1 h (max: 125 mg/dose)

ADMINISTRATION
Intravenous
***PREPARE:* IV Infusion:** Dilute 10 mL of Ferrlecit in 100 mL of NS. Use immediately after dilution.
***ADMINISTER:* IV Infusion:** Give over NOT LESS than 60 min. Never administer at a rate greater than 2.1 mg/min.

INCOMPATIBILITIES **Solution/additive:** Do not mix with any other medications or add to parenteral nutrition solutions.

▪ Store unopened ampules at 20°–25° C (68°–77° F).

ADVERSE EFFECTS (≥1%) **Body as a Whole:** Hypersensitivity reaction (cardiovascular collapse, cardiac arrest, bronchospasm, oral/pharyngeal edema, dyspnea, angioedema, urticaria, pruritus). **CV:** Flushing, hypotension.

PHARMACOKINETICS Not studied.

CLINICAL IMPLICATIONS
Assessment & Drug Effects
▪ Monitor closely for S&S of severe hypersensitivity (see Appendix F) during IV administration.
▪ Monitor vital signs periodically during IV administration (transient hypotension possible especially during dialysis).
▪ Stop infusion immediately and notify physician if hypersensitivity is suspected.
▪ Lab tests: Periodic Hgb, Hct, Fe saturation, serum ferritin.

Patient & Family Education
▪ Report to physician immediately: Difficulty breathing, itching, flushing, rash, weakness, light-headedness, pain, or any other discomfort during infusion.

S

SODIUM FLUORIDE
(sod'i-um)
Fluorinse, Fluoritab, Flura-Drops, Karidium, Pediaflor, Point-Two, Thera-Flur-N
Classifications: ELECTROLYTE REPLACEMENT AGENT; DENTAL PROPHYLACTIC

Therapeutic: DENTAL PROPHYLACTIC
Pregnancy Category: B topical, C oral

AVAILABILITY 0.25 mg, 0.5 mg, 1 mg tablets; 0.125 mg, 0.25 mg, 0.5 mg drops; 0.2 mg/mL solution; 0.02%, 0.04%, 0.09%, 2% rinse; 0.5%, 1.2% gel

ACTION & *THERAPEUTIC EFFECT*
Source of the fluorine ion, a trace element. Incorporates into developing tooth enamel, hardens surfaces, and increases resistance to cariogenic microbial processes. Topical application reduces acid production by bacteria in dental plaque and promotes remineralization of acid-damaged enamel. Application to exposed root surfaces supports formation of insoluble materials within dentinal tubules, thereby blocking transport of offending stimuli. Arrests rapid dental decay associated with drug-, radiation-, or age-related xerostomia. Oral form stimulates osteoblastic activity leading to increased bone mass. *Topical application reduces acid production by bacteria in dental plaque and promotes remineralization of enamel.*

USES When fluoride ion concentration in drinking water is 0.7 ppm or less, to prevent periodontal disease and dental caries, to treat dental cervical hypersensitivity, and to control dental caries associated with xerostomia.

UNLABELED USES Adjunctive treatment of osteoporosis; management of bone lesions in multiple myeloma; to reduce bone pain in patient with metastatic prostatic carcinoma; to stabilize progression of hearing loss in a limited number of patients with otosclerosis.

CONTRAINDICATIONS When daily intake of fluoride from drinking water exceeds 0.7 ppm; low-sodium or sodium-free diets; rheumatoid arthritis; hypersensitivity to fluoride; gels or dental rinses by children <6 y, 1 mg tablet or rinse in children <3 y, or 1 mg rinse in children <6 y, pregnancy (topical form category B and oral form category C); lactation (oral form); GI disease.

CAUTIOUS USE Renal dysfunction; rheumatoid arthritis; arthralgia.

ROUTE & DOSAGE

Prevent Periodontal Disease (Drinking Water Concentration <0.3 ppm)
Child: **PO** *Birth–2 y,* 0.25 mg/d; *2–3 y,* 0.5 mg/d; *3–13 y,* 1 mg/d

Prevent Periodontal Disease (Drinking Water Concentration 0.3–0.7 ppm)
Child: **PO** *Birth–2 y,* 0.125 mg/d; *2–3 y,* 0.25 mg/d; *3–13 y,* 0.5 mg/d

Prevent Dental Caries
Child: **Topical** *6–12 y,* 5 mL of 0.2% solution daily; *>12 y,* 10 mL of 0.2% solution daily

Desensitization of Exposed Root Surfaces
Child: **Topical** 0.2% rinsing solution once nightly after brushing and flossing

ADMINISTRATION
Oral
- Avoid giving sodium fluoride with milk or dairy products. Calcium from these products combines with fluorine, decreasing its absorption.
- Give drops preferably after meals. Give undiluted or mixed with fluids or foods.
- Dissolve tablets in the mouth or chew before swallowing. Adminis-

Common adverse effects in *italic*, life-threatening effects underlined; generic names in **bold**; classifications in SMALL CAPS; ♣ Canadian drug name; ⊘ Prototype drug

ter at bedtime (after brushing the teeth).

Topical
- Apply all fluorine preparations after thoroughly brushing and flossing; preferably at bedtime.
- Do not swallow topical or rinse preparations.
- If patient's mouth is sore, the neutral preparation (Thera-Flur N) is better tolerated.
- Use as treatment for dental cervical hypersensitivity: thoroughly brush teeth; then swish PO solution around and between teeth for 1 min; expectorate. If gel is used, apply a few drops to toothbrush and brush gently onto affected surfaces.
- Apply Gel-drops with applicators supplied by the dentist. Spread gel on inner surfaces of applicators, which are placed over lower and upper teeth at the same time. User bites down lightly for 6 min, then removes applicators and rinses mouth thoroughly. Applicators are cleaned with cold water.
- Store all forms in tight plastic or paraffin-lined glass containers (sodium fluoride reacts with ordinary glass at a slow but appreciable rate) at 15°–30° C (59°–86° F). Avoid freezing.

ADVERSE EFFECTS (≥1%) **Skin:** Rash, atopic dermatitis, urticaria, stomatitis. **Body as a Whole:** GI and respiratory allergic reactions, salty or soapy taste, dehydration, thirst, excessive salivation, muscle weakness, tremors, <u>shock, death from cardiac and respiratory failure</u>. **Musculoskeletal:** Dental fluorosis (brown or white mottling of tooth enamel), osseous fluorosis (patchy mineralization and possible decrease in bone strength).

INTERACTIONS Drug: Aluminum, calcium, magnesium-containing products may decrease **fluoride** absorption.

PHARMACOKINETICS Absorption: Readily from GI tract. **Distribution:** Fluoride is stored in bones and teeth; crosses placenta; distributed into breast milk. **Elimination:** Rapidly excreted, primarily in urine with small amounts in feces.

CLINICAL IMPLICATIONS

Assessment & Drug Effect
- Monitor therapeutic effectiveness.

Patient & Family Education
- Do not eat, drink, or rinse mouth for at least 30 min after using the rinsing solution.
- Do not exceed recommended dosage. If mottling of teeth occurs, notify dentist.
- Apply sodium fluoride gel or solution used in orthodontic treatment regimen immediately before attachment or reattachment of the tooth-encircling bands.
- To be effective, fluoride supplementation must be consistent and continuous from infancy until 12–14 y.
- Consult dentist about continuing fluoride therapy if you move or there is a change in water supply (mottling may occur if drinking water has fluorine content >1.5 ppm).

SODIUM OXYBATE (GHB)

(sod'i-um ox'y-bate)

Xyrem

Classifications: CENTRAL NERVOUS SYSTEM (CNS) DEPRESSANT
Therapeutic: CNS DEPRESSANT
Pregnancy Category: B
Controlled Substance: Schedule III

AVAILABILITY 500 mg/mL solution

S

Common adverse effects in *italic*, life-threatening effects <u>underlined</u>; generic names in **bold**; classifications in SMALL CAPS; ✦ Canadian drug name; ⊙ Prototype drug

1399

ACTION & *THERAPEUTIC EFFECT*

CNS depressant; the precise mechanism by which sodium oxybate produces anticataplexy in narcolepsy is unknown. Sodium oxybate is GHB, a known drug of abuse. *Produces anticataplectic effects in narcolepsy and decreases the number of cataplexy events in individuals with narcolepsy. Also has sedative and amnestic properties.*

USES Treatment of cataplexy in patients with narcolepsy.

CONTRAINDICATIONS Alcohol or sedative-hypnotics or other CNS depressants; patients being treated with sedative-hypnotic agents; psychosis; coma; eclampsia; patients with succinic semialdehyde dehydrogenase deficiency; compromised respiratory drive, severe depression, or suicidal tendencies; lactation; children <16 y.

CAUTIOUS USE Hepatic dysfunction; compromised respiratory function; sleep disorders; history of seizures; heart failure, hypertension, impaired renal function; previous history of depressive illness or suicide attempt; elderly; sleep-walking; pregnancy (category B).

ROUTE & DOSAGE

Cataplexy

Adult: **PO** Start with 2.25 g given at bedtime while in bed and repeated 2.5–4 h later. Dose may be increased by 1.5 g/d every 2 wk to a max of 9 g/d in 2 divided doses.

Hepatic Impairment

Reduce dose by 50% in patients with hepatic impairment

ADMINISTRATION

Oral

- Give at bedtime at least 2–3 h after the evening meal.
- Dilute each dose with 2 oz (60 mL) of water in the dosing cups provided.
- Instruct patient to remain in bed after taking sodium oxybate.
- Discard any diluted dose that has not been used within 24 h.
- Store at 15°–30° C (59°–86° F).

ADVERSE EFFECTS (≥1%) **Body as a Whole:** *Pain, infection,* flu-like syndrome, asthenia, allergic reactions, chills. **CNS:** Confusion, depression, sleepwalking, *headache, dizziness, somnolence,* nervousness, abnormal dreams, insomnia, agitation, ataxia, convulsion, stupor, tremor. **CV:** Hypertension. **GI:** *Nausea,* diarrhea, vomiting, dyspepsia, abdominal pain, anorexia, constipation. **Metabolic:** Increased alkaline phosphatase, edema, hypercholesteremia, hypocalcemia, weight gain. **Respiratory:** *Pharyngitis,* rhinitis, sinusitis **Skin:** Increased sweating, acne, alopecia, rash. **Special Senses:** Amblyopia, tinnitus. **Urogenital:** Urinary incontinence, dysmenorrhea, albuminuria, cystitis, hematuria, metrorrhagia, urinary frequency.

INTERACTIONS Drug: Alcohol, SEDATIVE-HYPNOTICS, other CNS DEPRESSANTS may increase CNS depressant effects. **Food:** High-fat meal will significantly reduce absorption.

PHARMACOKINETICS Absorption: Incompletely absorbed, 25% reaches systemic circulation. **Peak:** 0.05–1.25 h. **Metabolism:** Oxidized in the Kreb's cycle to carbon dioxide and water. **Elimination:** Primarily eliminated as carbon dioxide in respiration. **Half-Life:** 0.5–1 h.

CLINICAL IMPLICATIONS

Assessment & Drug Effects

- Monitor for and report immediately any of the following: seizure, respiratory depression, or decreased level of consciousness.
- Monitor closely patients with hepatic insufficiency for adverse events.
- Monitor for and report excessive weight gain and development of edema.
- Lab tests: Perform baseline LFTs; monitor periodically serum electrolytes and lipid profile.

Patient & Family Education

- Do not take sodium oxybate at any time other than at night, immediately before bedtime.
- Be consistent with timing of the evening meal and take this drug at least 2–3 h after eating.
- Prepare both doses prior to bedtime. After ingesting each dose remain in bed.
- Do not consume alcohol or use other sedative hypnotic drugs with sodium oxybate.
- Do not drive or engage in potentially hazardous activities until reaction to drug is known.

SODIUM POLYSTYRENE SULFONATE

(pol-ee-stye′reen)
Kayexalate, SPS Suspension
Classifications: ELECTROLYTE AND WATER BALANCE AGENT; CATION EXCHANGE
Therapeutic: CATION EXCHANGE
Pregnancy Category: C

AVAILABILITY 15 g/60 mL suspension; 100 mg/g powder

ACTION & *THERAPEUTIC EFFECT*

Sulfonic cation-exchange resin that removes potassium from body by exchanging sodium ion for potassium, particularly in large intestine; potassium-containing resin is then excreted through the bowel. Small amounts of other cations such as calcium and magnesium may be lost during treatment. *Removes potassium from body by exchanging sodium ion for potassium through the large intestine.*

USES Hyperkalemia.

CONTRAINDICATIONS Patients with hypokalemia; hypersensitivity to Kayexalate; GI obstruction; hypocalcemia, hypokalemia; pregnancy (category C), lactation.
CAUTIOUS USE Older adults; acute or chronic kidney failure; low birth weight infants; neonates with reduced gut; patients receiving digitalis preparations; patients who cannot tolerate even a small increase in sodium load (e.g., CHF, severe hypertension, and marked edema).

ROUTE & DOSAGE

Hyperkalemia
Adult: **PO** 15 g suspended in 70% sorbitol or 20–100 mL of other fluid 1–4 times/d **PR** 30–50 g/ 100 mL 70% sorbitol q6h as warm emulsion high into sigmoid colon
Child: **PO** Calculate appropriate amount on exchange rate of 1 mEq of potassium per gram of resin and suspend in 70% sorbitol or other appropriate solution (Usual dose: 1 g/kg q6h) **PR** 1 g/kg q2–6h

ADMINISTRATION

Oral

- Give as a suspension in a small quantity of water or in syrup. Usual

Common adverse effects in *italic*, life-threatening effects <u>underlined</u>; generic names in **bold**; classifications in SMALL CAPS; ♣ Canadian drug name; ● Prototype drug

1401

amount of fluid ranges from 20–100 mL or approximately 3–4 mL/g of drug.

Rectal

- Use warm fluid (as prescribed) to prepare the emulsion for enema.
- Administer at body temperature and introduce by gravity, keeping suspension particles in solution by stirring. Flush suspension with 50–100 mL of fluid; then clamp tube and leave it in place.
- Urge patient to retain enema at least 30–60 min but as long as several hours if possible.
- Irrigate colon (after enema solution has been expelled) with 1 or 2 quarts flushing solution (nonsodium containing). Drain returns constantly through a Y-tube connection.
- Store remainder of prepared solution for 24 h; then discard.

ADVERSE EFFECTS (≥1%) **GI:** *Constipation, fecal impaction (in older adults);* anorexia, gastric irritation, nausea, vomiting, diarrhea (with sorbitol emulsions). **Metabolic:** Sodium retention, hypocalcemia, hypokalemia, hypomagnesemia.

INTERACTIONS Drug: ANTACIDS, LAXATIVES containing **calcium** or **magnesium** may decrease potassium exchange capability of the resin.

PHARMACOKINETICS Absorption: Not absorbed systemically. **Onset:** Several hours to days. **Metabolism:** Not metabolized. **Elimination:** In feces.

CLINICAL IMPLICATIONS

Assessment & Drug Effects

- Lab tests: Determine serum potassium levels daily throughout therapy. Monitor acid–base balance, electrolytes, and minerals in patients receiving repeated doses.

- Serum potassium levels do not always reflect intracellular potassium deficiency. Observe patient closely for early clinical signs of severe hypokalemia (see Appendix F). ECGs are also recommended.
- Consult physician about restricting sodium content from dietary and other sources since drug contains approximately 100 mg (4.1 mEq) of sodium per gram (1 tsp, 15 mEq sodium).

Patient & Family Education

- Check bowel function daily. Usually, a mild laxative is prescribed to prevent constipation (common adverse effect). Older adult patients are particularly prone to fecal impaction.

SOLIFENACIN SUCCINATE

(sol-i-fen′a-sin)

VESIcare

Classifications: ANTICHOLINERGIC; ANTIMUSCARINIC; ANTISPASMODIC
Therapeutic: ANTISPASMODIC
Prototype: Atropine
Pregnancy Category: C

AVAILABILITY 5 mg, 10 mg tablets

ACTION & *THERAPEUTIC EFFECT*
Solifenacin is a selective muscarinic antagonist that depresses both voluntary and involuntary bladder contractions caused by detrusor overactivity. *Solifenacin improves the volume of urine per void and reduces the frequency of incontinent and urgency episodes.*

USES Treatment of overactive bladder (OAB) with symptoms of urinary incontinence, urgency, and frequency.

CONTRAINDICATIONS Hypersensitivity to solifenacin or any component of its formulations; severe hepatic impairment; gastric retention; uncontrolled narrow-angle glaucoma; urinary retention; toxic megacolon; GI obstruction; ileus; GERD; pregnancy (category C), lactation.

CAUTIOUS USE Bladder outflow obstruction; concurrent use of ketoconazole or other potent CYP3A4 inhibitors; obstructive disorders; decreased GI motility; hepatic impairment; history of QT prolongation or concurrent use of medications known to prolong the QT interval; controlled narrow-angle glaucoma; renal impairment; renal disease; renal failure; mild to moderate hepatic impairment; older adults.

ROUTE & DOSAGE

Overactive Bladder

Adult: **PO** 5 mg once daily; may be increased to 10 mg once daily if tolerated (max of 5 mg/d if taking drugs that inhibit CYP3A4—see Interactions, Drug)

Hepatic Impairment

If moderate hepatic impairment, does not exceed 5 mg/d. If severe hepatic impairment, do not use.

Renal Impairment

Cl_{cr} <30 mL/min: max dose 5 mg/d

ADMINISTRATION

Oral
- Tablets should be swallowed whole.
- Store at 15–30° C (59–86° F).

ADVERSE EFFECTS (≥1%) **Body as a Whole:** Edema, fatigue. **CNS:** Dizziness, depression. **CV:** Hypertension. **GI:** *Dry mouth, constipation,* nausea, vomiting, dyspepsia, upper abdominal pain. **Respiratory:** Cough. **Special Senses:** Blurred vision, dry eyes. **Urogenital:** Urinary tract infection, urinary retention.

INTERACTIONS Drug: CYP3A4 INHIBITORS (e.g., **clarithromycin, delavirdine, diltiazem, efavirenz, erythromycin, fluconazole, fluvoxamine, itraconazole, nefazodone, norfloxacin, omeprazole,** PROTEASE INHIBITORS, **quinine, verapamil, troleandomycin, voriconazole, zafirlukast**) may increase levels and toxicity (max dose 5 mg/d); **amantadine, amoxapine, bupropion, clozapine, cyclobenzaprine, diphenhydramine, disopyramide, maprotiline, olanzapine, orphenadrine,** PHENOTHIAZINES, TRICYCLIC ANTIDEPRESSANTS have additive anticholinergic adverse effects. **Food:** Grapefruit juice may increase solifenacin levels and toxicity.

PHARMACOKINETICS Absorption: 90% absorbed from GI tract. **Peak:** 3–8 h. **Metabolism:** Extensively metabolized in the liver by CYP3A4. **Elimination:** Primarily in urine, 22% in feces. **Half-Life:** 45–68 h.

CLINICAL IMPLICATIONS

Assessment & Drug Effects
- Monitor ECG in patients with a known history of QT prolongation or patients taking medications that prolong the QT interval.

Patient & Family Education
- Stop taking this drug and report to physician if urinary retention occurs.
- Report promptly any of the following: blurred vision or difficulty focusing vision, palpitations, confusion, or severe dizziness.
- Report to physician problems with bowel elimination, especially constipation lasting 3 or more days.

S

Common adverse effects in *italic*, life-threatening effects <u>underlined</u>; generic names in **bold**; classifications in SMALL CAPS; ✦ Canadian drug name; ⊘ Prototype drug

1403

- Exercise caution in hot environments, as the risk of heat prostration increases with this drug.

SOMATROPIN ℗

(soe-ma-troe′pin)
Bio-Tropin, Genotropin, Humatrope, Norditropin, Nutropin, Nutropin AQ, Nutropin AQ Pen, Serostim, Saizen
Classifications: HORMONE; GROWTH HORMONE
Therapeutic: GROWTH HORMONE
Pregnancy Category: B, C (brand dependent)

AVAILABILITY 1.5 mg, 4 mg, 5 mg, 5.8 mg, 6 mg, 8 mg, 10 mg injection; 5 mg/1.5 mL, 15 mg/1.5 mL prefilled syringe

ACTION & *THERAPEUTIC EFFECT*
New recombinant growth hormone with the natural sequence of 191 amino acids characteristic of endogenous growth hormone (GH). *Induces growth responses similar to those produced in children treated with GH obtained from human pituitary glands.*

USES Growth failure due to GH deficiency; replacement therapy prior to epiphyseal closure in patients with idiopathic GH deficiency; GH deficiency secondary to intracranial tumors or panhypopituitarism; inadequate GH secretion; short stature in girls with Turner's syndrome; AIDS wasting syndrome; short bowel syndrome.

CONTRAINDICATIONS Patient with closed epiphyses; underlying progressive intracranial tumor; cresol hypersensitivity, glycerin hypersensitivity; diabetic retinopathy; respiratory insufficiency; during chemotherapy, radiation therapy, active neoplastic disease; Prader-Willi syndrome; untreated hypothyroidism, obesity; pregnancy (category B or category C depending on the brand).

CAUTIOUS USE Diabetes mellitus or family history of the disease; history of upper airway obstruction, sleep apnea, or unidentified URI; lactation; concomitant or prior use of thyroid or androgens in prepubertal male; hypothyroidism; surgery, trauma; neonates with benzyl alcohol hypersensitivity; neonates; lactation.

ROUTE & DOSAGE

Note: Dosing will vary with specific products

Growth Hormone Deficiency
Adult: **SC Humatrope** 0.006 mg/kg (0.018 IU/kg) q.d., may increase [max: 0.0125 mg/kg/d (0.0375 IU/kg/d)]; **Nutropin, Nutropin AQ** 0.006 mg/kg q.d. (max: *<35 y,* 0.025 mg/kg/d; *>35 y,* 0.0125 mg/kg/d)
Child: **SC Genotropin** 0.16–0.24 mg/kg/wk divided into 6–7 q.d. doses; **Humatrope** 0.18 mg/kg/wk (0.54 IU/kg/wk) divided into equal doses given on either 3 alternate days or 6 times/wk; **Norditropin** 0.024–0.034 mg/kg/d 6–7 times/wk; **Nutropin, Nutropin AQ** 0.3 mg/kg/wk (0.9 IU/kg/wk) divided into 6–7 q.d. doses

Inadequate Growth Hormone Secretion
Child: **SC Nutropin** 0.3 mg/kg every week

AIDS Wasting or Cachexia
Adult: **SC Serostim** *>55 kg,* 6 mg qh.s.; *45–55 kg,* 5 mg qh.s.; *35–45 kg,* 4 mg qh.s.; *<35 kg,* 0.1 mg/kg qh.s.

Short Bowel Syndrome
Adult: SC Zorptive: 0.1 mg/kg once daily for 4 wk (max: 8 mg/d)

ADMINISTRATION

Subcutaneous
- Reconstitute each brand following its manufacturer's instructions (vary from brand to brand).
- Read and carefully follow directions for use supplied with the Nutropin AQ Pen™ Cartridge if this is the product being used.
- Rotate injection sites; abdomen and thighs are preferred sites. Do not use buttocks until the child has been walking for a year or more and the muscle is adequately developed.
- Store lyophilized powder at 2°–8° C (36°–46° F). After reconstitution, most preparations are stable for at least 14 d under refrigeration. DO NOT FREEZE.

ADVERSE EFFECTS (≥1%) Body as a Whole: Pain, swelling at injection site; myalgia. Fatalities reported in patients with Prader-Willi syndrome and one or more of severe obesity, history of respiratory impairment or sleep apnea, or unidentified respiratory infection, especially male patients. **Metabolic:** *Hypercalciuria;* over saturation of bile with cholesterol, hyperglycemia, ketosis. **Endocrine:** High circulating GH antibodies with resulting treatment failure, accelerated growth of intracranial tumor.

INTERACTIONS Drug: ANABOLIC STEROIDS, **thyroid hormone,** ANDROGENS, ESTROGENS may accelerate epiphyseal closure; **ACTH,** CORTICOSTEROIDS may inhibit growth response to somatropin.

PHARMACOKINETICS Metabolism: In liver. **Elimination:** In urine. **Half-Life:** 15–50 min.

CLINICAL IMPLICATIONS
Assessment & Drug Effects
- Assess bone age annually in all patients and especially those also receiving concurrent thyroid or androgen treatment, since these drugs may precipitate early epiphyseal closure. Urge parent to take child for bone age assessment on appointed annual dates.
- Lab test: Periodic serum and urine calcium and plasma glucose.
- Hypercalciuria, a frequent adverse effect in the first 2–3 mo of therapy, may be symptomless; however, it may be accompanied by renal calculi, with these reportable symptoms: flank pain and colic, GI symptoms, urinary frequency, chills, fever, hematuria.
- Test for circulating GH antibodies (antisomatropin antibodies) in patients who respond initially but later fail to respond to therapy.
- Observe diabetics or those with family history of diabetes closely. Obtain regular urine for glycosuria or fasting blood glucose and HbA$_{1C}$.
- Examine patients with GH deficiency secondary to intracranial lesion frequently for progression or recurrence of underlying disease.

Patient & Family Education
- Be aware that during first 6 mo of successful treatment, linear growth rates may be increased 8–16 cm or more per year (average about 7 cm/y or approximately 3 in.). Additionally, SC fat diminishes but returns to pretreatment value later.
- Record accurate height measurements at regular intervals and report to physician if rate is less than expected.

S

Common adverse effects in *italic,* life-threatening effects <u>underlined</u>; generic names in **bold**; classifications in SMALL CAPS; ✦ Canadian drug name; ⊙ Prototype drug

- In general, growth response to somatropin is inversely proportional to duration of treatment.
- Discontinue treatment when patient has reached satisfactory adult height, when epiphyses have fused, or when patient fails to exhibit growth response.

SORAFENIB

(sor-a-fe′nib)
Nexavar
Classifications: ANTINEOPLASTIC AGENT; TYROSINE KINASE INHIBITOR; MULTI-KINASE INHIBITOR
Therapeutic: ANTINEOPLASTIC; MULTI-KINASE INHIBITOR
Prototype: Gefitinib
Pregnancy Category: D

AVAILABILITY 200 mg tablets

ACTION & *THERAPEUTIC EFFECT*
Sorafenib is a multi-kinase inhibitor targeting enzyme systems in both tumor cells and tumor vasculature. The anticancer activity of sorafenib appears to be cytostatic, requiring continued drug exposure for tumor growth inhibition. *Sorafenib inhibits enzymes responsible for uncontrolled tumor cellular proliferation and angiogenesis. Antineoplastic activity of sorafenib inhibits the growth of renal cell cancers.*

USES Treatment of advanced renal cell cancer.
UNLABELED USES Treatment of advanced malignant melanoma. Treatment of metastatic hepatocellular cancer.

CONTRAINDICATIONS Active infection; severe renal impairment (<30 mL/min), or hemodialysis; pregnancy (category D), lactation. Safe use in children <18 y is not established.

CAUTIOUS USE Previous myelosuppressive therapy, either radiation or chemotherapy; mild or moderate renal disease; hepatic disease; heart failure, ventricular dysfunction, cardiac disease, peripheral edema; females of childbearing age.

ROUTE & DOSAGE

Renal Cell Cancer
Adult: **PO** 400 mg b.i.d.

Dosage Adjustments for Skin Toxicity
Grade 2 (1st episode): Continue therapy and treat symptoms. If no improvement in 7 d, DC until toxicity resolves to at least grade 1, then resume with 400 mg/d or 400 mg q.o.d.
Grade 2 (2nd or 3rd episode): DC until toxicity resolves to at least grade 1, then resume with 400 mg/d or 400 mg q.o.d.
Grade 2 (4th episode): DC therapy.
Grade 3 (1st or 2nd episode): DC until toxicity resolves to at least grade 1, then resume with 400 mg/d or 400 mg q.o.d.
Grade 3 (3rd episode): DC therapy

ADMINISTRATION
Oral
- Tablets must be swallowed whole. They should not be crushed, broken, or chewed.
- Give on an empty stomach 1 h before or 2 h after eating.
- Store at 15°–30° C (59°–86° F). Protect from moisture.

ADVERSE EFFECTS (≥1%) **Body as a Whole:** Asthenia, bone pain, decreased appetite, *fatigue,* influenza-like illness, *joint pain,* mouth pain, muscle pain, pyrexia. **CNS:** Depression, *headache, sensory neuropa-*

thy. **CV:** *Hypertension.* **GI:** *Abdominal pain, anorexia, constipation, diarrhea,* dyspepsia, dysphagia, mucositis, *nausea,* stomatitis, *vomiting.* **Hematologic:** *Anemia,* hemorrhage, *leucopenia, lymphopenia, neutropenia, thrombocytopenia.* **Metabolic:** *Amylase elevation, hypophosphatemia, lipase elevation, weight loss.* **Musculoskeletal:** Arthralgia, myalgia. **Respiratory:** *Cough, dyspnea,* hoarseness. **Skin:** Acne, *alopecia, desquamation, dry skin,* erythema, exfoliative dermatitis, flushing, *hand-foot skin reaction, rash.* **Urogenital:** Erectile dysfunction.

INTERACTIONS Drug: Sorafenib may increase levels of drugs requiring glucuronidation by the UGT1A1 and UGT1A9 pathways (e.g., **irinotecan**). Due to thrombocytopenic effects, sorafenib can contribute to increased bleeding from NONSTEROIDAL ANTIINFLAMMATORY DRUGS, PLATELET INHIBITORS (e.g., **aspirin, clopidogrel**), THROMBOLYTIC AGENTS, and **warfarin.** Inducers of CYP3A4 (e.g., **carbamazepine, phenobarbital, phenytoin, rifampin**) may decrease the levels of sorafenib. **Food:** Food decreases the absorption of sorafenib. **Herbal: St. John's wort** may decrease the levels of sorafenib.

PHARMACOKINETICS Absorption: 38–49% absorbed. **Peak:** 3 h. **Distribution:** 99.5% protein bound. **Metabolism:** In the liver. **Elimination:** Primarily fecal (77%) with minor elimination in the urine (19%). **Half-Life:** 25–48 h.

CLINICAL IMPLICATIONS

Assessment & Drug Effects

■ Monitor for and report S&S of skin toxicity (e.g., rash, erythema, dermatitis, paresthesia, swelling, or pain in hands or feet). Severe reactions may require temporary suspension of therapy or dose reduction.
■ Monitor for S&S of bleeding, especially in those on anticoagulation therapy.
■ Monitor BP weekly for the first 6 wk of therapy and periodically thereafter. New-onset hypertension has been associated with sorafenib.
■ Lab tests: Periodic CBC with differential and platelet count, serum electrolytes, LFTs, lipase, amylase, and alkaline phosphatase.
■ Monitor blood levels of warfarin with concurrent therapy

Patient & Family Education

■ Follow directions for taking the drug (see Administration).
■ Report any of the following to a health care provider: skin rash; redness, blisters, pain or swelling of the palms or hands or soles of feet; signs of bleeding; unexplained chest, shoulder, neck and jaw, or back pain.
■ Do not take any prescription or nonprescription drugs without consulting the physician.
■ Male and female patients should use effective birth control during treatment and for at least 2 wk following completion of treatment.

S

SOTALOL

(so-ta'lol)

Betapace, Betapace AF

Classifications: BETA-ADRENERGIC ANTAGONIST; ANTIARRHYTHMIC CLASS II AND III

Therapeutic: ANTIARRHYTHMIC CLASS II AND III

Prototype: Amiodarone

Pregnancy Category: B

Common adverse effects in *italic*, life-threatening effects <u>underlined</u>; generic names in **bold**; classifications in SMALL CAPS; ♣ Canadian drug name; ⊘ Prototype drug

1407

AVAILABILITY **Betapace** 80 mg, 120 mg, 160 mg, 240 mg tablets. **Betapace AF** 80 mg, 120 mg, 160 mg tablets

ACTION & *THERAPEUTIC EFFECT*
Has both class II and class III antiarrhythmic properties. Slows heart rate, decreases AV nodal conduction, and increases AV nodal refractoriness. Produces significant reduction in both systolic and diastolic blood pressure. *Antiarrhythmic properties are effective in controlling ventricular arrhythmias as well as atrial fibrillation/flutter. Regulates blood pressure values.*

USES Treatment of life-threatening ventricular arrhythmias (sustained ventricular tachycardia) and maintenance of normal sinus rhythm in patients with atrial fibrillation/flutter.
UNLABELED USES Hypertension, angina.

CONTRAINDICATIONS Hypersensitivity to sotalol; bronchial asthma, acute bronchospasm; sinus bradycardia, sick sinus syndrome; second and third degree heart block, long QT syndrome, cardiogenic shock, uncontrolled CHF; chronic bronchitis, emphysema; hypokalemia <4 mEq/L; creatinine clearance of <40 mL/min.
CAUTIOUS USE CHF, electrolyte disturbances, recent MI, diabetes, sick sinus rhythm, renal impairment; pregnancy (category B); concomitant use of drugs which prolong the QT segment, and antiarrhythmic drugs; excessive diarrhea, or profuse sweating.

ROUTE & DOSAGE

Ventricular Arrhythmias (Betapace)
Adult: **PO** Initial dose of 80 mg b.i.d. or 160 mg q.d. taken prior to meals, may increase every 3–4 d in 40–160 mg increments (most patients respond to 240–320 mg/d in 2 or 3 divided doses, doses >640 mg/d have not been studied)

Renal Impairment
Cl_{cr} >60 mL/min: q12h; 30–60 mL/min: q24h; 10–30 mL/min: q36–48h; <10 mL/min: Individualize carefully

Atrial Fibrillation/Flutter (Betapace AF)
Adult: **PO** Initial dose of 80 mg b.i.d., may increase every 3–4 d (max: 240 mg/d in 1–2 divided doses)

Renal Impairment
Cl_{cr} >60 mL/min: q12h; 40–60 mL/min: q24h; <40 mL/min contraindicated

ADMINISTRATION

Oral
- Give on an empty stomach 1 h before or 2 h after meals. Do not give with milk or milk products.
- Initiate and increase doses only under close supervision, preferably in a hospital with cardiac rhythm monitoring and frequent assessment.
- Use smallest effective dose for patients with nonallergic bronchospasms.
- Do not discontinue drug abruptly. Gradually reduce dose over 1–2 wk.
- Store at room temperature, 15°–30° C (59°–86° F).

ADVERSE EFFECTS (≥1%) **CV:** AV block, hypotension, aggravation of CHF, although the incidence of heart failure may be lower than for other beta-blockers, <u>life-threatening ventricular arrhythmias, including polymorphous ventricular tachycar-</u>

dia or torsades de pointes, *brady-cardia, dyspnea, chest pain, palpita-tion,* bleeding (<2%). **CNS:** Headache, *fatigue, dizziness,* weakness, lethargy, depression, lassitude. **GI:** Nausea, vomiting, diarrhea, dyspepsia, dry mouth. **Urogenital:** Impotence, decreased libido. **Metabolic:** Hyperglycemia. **Special Senses:** Visual disturbances. **Respiratory:** Respiratory complaints. **Skin:** Rash.

INTERACTIONS Drug: Antagonizes the effects of BETA AGONISTS. **Amiodarone** may lead to symptomatic bradycardia and sinus arrest. The hypoglycemic effects of ORAL HYPOGLYCEMIC AGENTS may be potentiated. May cause resistance to **epinephrine** in anaphylactic reactions. Should be used with caution with other ANTIARRHYTHMIC AGENTS. **Food:** absorption may be reduced by food, especially **milk** and MILK PRODUCTS.

PHARMACOKINETICS Absorption: Slowly and completely from GI tract. Negligible first-pass metabolism. Reduced by food, especially milk and milk products. **Peak:** 2–3 h. **Duration:** 24 h. **Distribution:** Drug is hydrophilic and will enter the CSF slowly (about 10%). Crosses placental barrier. Distributed in breast milk. Not appreciably protein bound. **Metabolism:** Does not undergo significant hepatic enzyme metabolism and no active metabolites have been identified. **Elimination:** In urine with 75% of the drug excreted unchanged within 72 h. **Half-Life:** 7–18 h.

CLINICAL IMPLICATIONS

Assessment & Drug Effects

- Monitor ECG for initial baseline and periodically thereafter (especially when doses are increased) because proarrhythmic events most often occur within 7 d of initiating therapy or increasing dose.

- Lab test: Baseline serum electrolytes. Correct electrolyte imbalances of hypokalemia or hypomagnesemia prior to initiating therapy.
- Monitor cardiac status carefully, including ECG, throughout therapy. Exercise special caution when sotalol is used concurrently with other antiarrhythmics, digoxin, or calcium channel blockers.
- Monitor patients with bronchospastic disease (e.g., bronchitis, emphysema) carefully for inhibition of bronchodilation.
- Monitor diabetics for loss of glycemic control. Beta blockage reduces the release of endogenous insulin in response to hyperglycemia and may blunt symptoms of acute hypoglycemia (e.g., tachycardia, BP changes).

Patient & Family Education

- Be aware of risk for hypotension and syncope, especially with concurrent treatment with catecholamine-depleting drugs (e.g., reserpine, guanethidine).
- Take radial pulse daily and report marked bradycardia (pulse below 60 or other established parameter) to physician.
- Type 2 diabetics are at increased risk for hyperglycemia. All diabetics are at risk of possible masking of symptoms of hypoglycemia.
- Do not abruptly discontinue drug because of the risk of exacerbation of angina, arrhythmias, and possible myocardial infarction.

S

SPECTINOMYCIN HYDROCHLORIDE

(spek-ti-noe-mye′sin)
Trobicin
Classifications: ANTIBIOTIC

Common adverse effects in *italic*, life-threatening effects underlined; generic names in **bold**; classifications in SMALL CAPS; ♣ Canadian drug name; ☉ Prototype drug

1409

Therapeutic: ANTIBIOTIC
Pregnancy Category: B

AVAILABILITY 400 mg injection

ACTION & **THERAPEUTIC EFFECT**
Antibiotic produced by *Streptomyces spectabilis*. Action is usually bacteriostatic. Spectinomycin appears to exert its bacteriostatic effect by binding to the 30S ribosomal subunit, interfering with bacterial protein synthesis. *Variable activity against a wide variety of gram-negative and gram-positive organisms. Inhibits majority of* Neisseria gonorrhoeae *strains; effective for urethral and anorectal infections, but not pharyngeal.*

USES Only for treatment of uncomplicated gonorrhea in patients sensitized or resistant to penicillin or other effective drugs approved by US Centers for Disease Control and Prevention.
UNLABELED USES Disseminated gonococcal infections caused by penicillinase-producing strains of *N. gonorrhoeae* (PPNG) and sexually transmitted epididymoorchitis.

CONTRAINDICATIONS Safe use in infants and children <8 y is not established.
CAUTIOUS USE History of allergies; pregnancy (category B), lactation.

ROUTE & DOSAGE

Uncomplicated Gonorrhea
Adult: IM 2 g as single dose
Child: IM *<45 kg,* 40 mg/kg (max: 2 g); *>45 kg,* use adult dosing

Disseminated Gonorrhea
Adult: IM 2 g q12h for 7 d or until switched to oral medication

Child: IM ≥8 y and ≥45 kg, 2 g q12h for 7 d

ADMINISTRATION
Intramuscular
- Give IM injection deep into upper outer quadrant of gluteus. No more than 5 mL should be injected into single site (using 20-gauge needle). Injection may be painful.
- Reconstitute with supplied diluent (bacteriostatic water for injection with 0.9% benzyl alcohol). Shake vial vigorously immediately after adding diluent and before withdrawing drug.
- Use solution within 24 h of reconstitution.
- Store at 15°–30° C (59°–86° F) unless otherwise directed.

ADVERSE EFFECTS (≥1%) **Skin:**
Pain and soreness at injection site, urticaria, pruritus, transient rash. **Body as a Whole:** Headache, dizziness, chills, fever, insomnia, nervousness. **GI:** Nausea, vomiting. **Metabolic:** Decrease in Hgb, Hct, Cl_{cr}, elevated serum alkaline phosphatase, ALT, BUN.

PHARMACOKINETICS **Absorption:** Readily absorbed from IM site. **Peak:** 1 hr. **Metabolism:** In liver. **Elimination:** In urine. **Half-Life:** 1.2–2.8 h.

CLINICAL IMPLICATIONS
Assessment & Drug Effects
- Observe patient for 45–60 min after injection. Systemic anaphylaxis has been reported (apprehension, pruritus, hypertension, abdominal pain, collapse).
- Obtain serologic tests for syphilis at time of diagnosis in patients with gonorrhea and again after 3 mo.

- Monitor clinical effectiveness of drug to detect antibiotic resistance.
- Culture all gonococcal infection sites 3–7 d after spectinomycin therapy is completed to verify eradication of infection.
- Lab tests: Monitor Hgb and Hct when multiple doses are required.

Patient & Family Education
- Notify sexual partners of their risk of infection.
- Refrain from sexual intercourse until infection is resolved.

SPIRONOLACTONE ⊕

(speer-on-oh-lak′tone)
Aldactone, Novospiroton ♦
Classifications: ELECTROLYTIC AND WATER BALANCE AGENT; POTASSIUM-SPARING DIURETIC
Therapeutic: POTASSIUM-SPARING DIURETIC; ANTIHYPERTENSIVE
Pregnancy Category: D

AVAILABILITY 25 mg, 50 mg, 100 mg tablets

ACTION & *THERAPEUTIC EFFECT*
Steroidal compound and specific pharmacologic antagonist of aldosterone. Presumably acts by competing with aldosterone for cellular receptor sites in distal renal tubule. Promotes sodium and chloride excretion without concomitant loss of potassium. Activity depends on presence of endogenous or exogenous aldosterone. *A diuretic agent that promotes sodium and chloride excretion without concomitant loss of potassium. Lowers systolic and diastolic pressures in hypertensive patients.*

USES Clinical conditions associated with augmented aldosterone production, as in essential hypertension, refractory edema due to CHF, hepatic cirrhosis, nephrotic syndrome, and idiopathic edema. May be used to potentiate actions of other diuretics and antihypertensive agents or for its potassium-sparing effect. Also used for treatment of (and as presumptive test for) primary aldosteronism.
UNLABELED USES Hirsutism in women with polycystic ovary syndrome or idiopathic hirsutism; adjunct in treatment of myasthenia gravis and familial periodic paralysis.

CONTRAINDICATIONS Anuria, severe renal insufficiency; renal failure; diabetic nephropathy; progressing impairment of kidney function, hyperkalemia; pregnancy (category D).
CAUTIOUS USE BUN of 40 mg/dL or greater, mild or moderate renal impairment; liver disease.

ROUTE & DOSAGE

Edema
Adult: **PO** 25–200 mg/d in divided doses, continued for at least 5 d (dose adjusted to optimal response; if no response, a thiazide or loop diuretic may be added)
Child: **PO** 3.3 mg/kg/d in single or divided doses, continued for at least 5 d (dose adjusted to optimal response)
Neonate: **PO** 1–3 mg/kg/d divided q12–24h

Hypertension
Adult: **PO** 25–100 mg/d in single or divided doses, continued for at least 2 wk (dose adjusted to optimal response)

Primary Aldosteronism: Diagnosis
Adult: **PO** Short Test: 400 mg/d for 4 d; long test: 400 mg/d for 3–4 wk

S

Common adverse effects in *italic*, life-threatening effects <u>underlined</u>; generic names in **bold**; classifications in SMALL CAPS; ♦ Canadian drug name; ⊕ Prototype drug

Primary Aldosteronism: Treatment
Adult: **PO** 100–400 mg/d in divided doses

ADMINISTRATION
Oral
- Give with food to enhance absorption.
- Crush tablets and give with fluid of patient's choice if unable to swallow whole.
- Store in tight, light-resistant containers. Suspension is stable for 1 mo under refrigeration.

ADVERSE EFFECTS (≥1%) CNS:
Lethargy, mental confusion, fatigue (with rapid weight loss), headache, drowsiness, ataxia. **Endocrine:** Gynecomastia (both sexes), inability to achieve or maintain erection, androgenic effects (hirsutism, irregular menses, deepening of voice); parathyroid changes, decreased glucose tolerance, SLE. **GI:** Abdominal cramps, nausea, vomiting, anorexia, diarrhea. **Skin:** Maculopapular or erythematous rash, urticaria. **Metabolic:** Fluid and electrolyte imbalance (particularly hyperkalemia and hyponatremia); elevated BUN, mild acidosis, hyperuricemia, gout. **Body as a Whole:** Drug fever. **Hematologic:** Agranulocytosis. **CV:** Hypertension (post-sympathectomy patient).

DIAGNOSTIC TEST INTERFERENCE
May produce marked increases in *plasma cortisol* determinations by *Mattingly fluorometric* method; these may persist for several days after termination of drug (spironolactone metabolite produces fluorescence). There is the possibility of false elevations in measurements of *digoxin serum levels* by *RIA* procedures.

INTERACTIONS Drug:
Combinations of spironolactone and acidifying doses of **ammonium chloride** may produce systemic acidosis; use these combinations with caution. Diuretic effect of spironolactone may be antagonized by **aspirin** and other SALICYLATES. **Digoxin** should be monitored for decreased effect of CARDIAC GLYCOSIDE. Hyperkalemia may result with POTASSIUM SUPPLEMENTS, ACE INHIBITORS, ARBS, **heparin** may decrease **lithium** clearance resulting in increased tenacity; may alter anticoagulant response in **warfarin. Food:** Salt substitutes may increase risk of hyperkalemia.

PHARMACOKINETICS Absorption:
~73% from GI tract. **Onset:** Gradual. **Peak:** 2–3 d; maximum effect may take up to 2 wk. **Duration:** 2–3 d or more. **Distribution:** Crosses placenta, distributed into breast milk. **Metabolism:** In liver and kidneys to active metabolites. **Elimination:** 40–57% in urine, 35–40% in bile. **Half-Life:** 1.3–2.4 h parent compound, 18–23 h metabolites.

CLINICAL IMPLICATIONS
Assessment & Drug Effects
- Check blood pressure before initiation of therapy and at regular intervals throughout therapy.
- Lab tests: Monitor serum electrolytes (sodium and potassium) especially during early therapy; monitor digoxin level when used concurrently.
- Assess for signs of fluid and electrolyte imbalance, and signs of digoxin toxicity.
- Monitor daily I&O and check for edema. Report lack of diuretic response or development of edema; both may indicate tolerance to drug.
- Weigh patient under standard conditions before therapy begins and daily throughout therapy. Weight is a useful index of need for dos-

S

age adjustment. For patients with ascites, physician may want measurements of abdominal girth.

- Observe for and report immediately the onset of mental changes, lethargy, or stupor in patients with liver disease.
- Adverse reactions are generally reversible with discontinuation of drug. Gynecomastia appears to be related to dosage level and duration of therapy; it may persist in some after drug is stopped.

Patient & Family Education

- Be aware that the maximal diuretic effect may not occur until third day of therapy and that diuresis may continue for 2–3 d after drug is withdrawn.
- Report signs of hyponatremia or hyperkalemia (see Appendix F), most likely to occur in patients with severe cirrhosis.
- Avoid replacing fluid losses with large amounts of free water (can result in dilutional hyponatremia).
- Weigh 2–3 times each week. Report gains/loss of ≥5 lb.
- Do not drive or engage in potentially hazardous activities until response to the drug is known.
- Avoid excessive intake of high-potassium foods and salt substitutes.

STAVUDINE (D4T)

(sta'vu-deen)

Zerit

Classifications: ANTIRETROVIRAL; NUCLEOSIDE REVERSE TRANSCRIPTASE INHIBITOR (NRTI)
Therapeutic: ANTIRETROVIRAL; NRTI
Prototype: Lamivudine
Pregnancy Category: C

AVAILABILITY 15 mg, 20 mg, 30 mg, 40 mg capsules; 1 mg/mL solution

ACTION & *THERAPEUTIC EFFECT*
Synthetic analog of thymidine (a major nucleoside in DNA) with antiviral action against HIV, the causative agent of AIDS. Phosphorylated to stavudine triphosphate by endogenous thymidine kinase. Appears to act by being incorporated into the growing DNA chains by viral transcriptase, thus terminating viral replication. *Inhibits the replication of HIV in human cells and decreases the viral load.*

USES Treatment of adults with advanced HIV infection who are intolerant of other antiretroviral agents (zidovudine, didanosine, zalcitabine) or who have deteriorated on the other agents.

CONTRAINDICATIONS Hypersensitivity to stavudine; pregnancy (category C), lactation.
CAUTIOUS USE Previous hypersensitivity to zidovudine, didanosine, or zalcitabine; folic acid or B_{12} deficiency; liver and renal insufficiency; alcoholism; peripheral neuropathy; history of pancreatitis.

ROUTE & DOSAGE

Advanced HIV Infection
Adult: **PO** <60 kg, 30 mg q12h; ≥60 kg, 40 mg q12h
Child: **PO** <30 kg, give 2 mg/kg/d in 2 divided doses; ≥30 kg, same as adult

Renal Impairment
Cl_{cr} 25–50 mL/min: Reduce dose by 50% (also in patients with peripheral neuropathy)

ADMINISTRATION

Oral
- Adhere strictly to 12-h interval between doses.
- Reconstitute powder by adding 202 mL of water to the container.

Common adverse effects in *italic*, life-threatening effects underlined; generic names in **bold**; classifications in SMALL CAPS; ✦ Canadian drug name; ⊙ Prototype drug

1413

Shake vigorously. Yields 200 mL of 1 mg/mL solution.
- Store at room temperature, 15°–30° C (59°–86° F).

ADVERSE EFFECTS (≥1%) **CNS:** *Peripheral neuropathy,* paresthesias. **GI:** *Anorexia, nausea, vomiting, diarrhea,* cramping, pancreatitis, abdominal pain, elevated liver function tests, abdominal pain. **Body as a Whole:** *Headache,* chills/fever, *myalgia.* **Hematologic:** Anemia, neutropenia. **Skin:** *Rash.* **Metabolic:** Lactic acidosis in pregnant women.

INTERACTIONS Drug: Didanosine may increase risk of pancreatitis and hepatotoxicity; **probenecid** can decrease elimination.

PHARMACOKINETICS Absorption: Readily absorbed from GI tract; 82% reaches systemic circulation. **Peak:** Effect 6 wk. **Distribution:** Distributes into CSF; excreted in breast milk of animals. **Metabolism:** Metabolized in liver; in addition to hepatic metabolism, some investigators suggest that degradation and salvage by other pyrimidine pathways may contribute to elimination; intracellularly, stavudine is phosphorylated by cellular enzymes to its active triphosphate form. **Elimination:** Primarily in urine. **Half-Life:** 1–1.6 h.

CLINICAL IMPLICATIONS

Assessment & Drug Effects
- Monitor for peripheral neuropathy and report numbness, tingling, or pain, which may indicate a need to interrupt stavudine.
- Lab tests: Monitor liver enzymes, CBC with differential, PT and INR, and kidney function periodically.
- Monitor for development of opportunistic infection.

Patient & Family Education
- Take drug exactly as prescribed.
- Report to physician any adverse drug effects that are bothersome.
- Report symptoms of peripheral neuropathy to physician immediately.

STREPTOKINASE

(strep-toe-kye′nase)
Streptase
Classifications: ANTICOAGULANT; THROMBOLYTIC ENZYME
Therapeutic: THROMBOLYTIC
Prototype: Alteplase
Pregnancy Category: C

AVAILABILITY 250,000 IU, 750,000 IU, 1,500,000 IU vials

ACTION & *THERAPEUTIC EFFECT* Derivative of the beta-hemolytic streptococci. Promotes thrombolysis by activating the conversion of plasminogen to plasmin, the enzyme that degrades fibrin, fibrinogen, and other procoagulant proteins into soluble fragments. Decreases blood and plasma viscosity and erythrocyte aggregation tendency, thus increasing perfusion of collateral blood vessels. *Promotes thrombolysis. The fibrinolytic activity of streptokinase is effective both outside and within the formed thrombus/embolus.*

USES Acute extensive deep venous thrombosis, acute arterial thrombosis or embolism, acute pulmonary embolus, coronary artery thrombosis, MI, and arteriovenous cannula occlusion.

CONTRAINDICATIONS Active internal bleeding; very recent cardiopulmonary resuscitation; recent (within

2 mo) intraspinal, intracranial, intra-arterial procedures; intracranial neoplasm; CVA, severe uncontrolled hypertension; history of allergic response to SK, recent streptococcal infection; obstetrical delivery; diabetic hemorrhagic retinopathy; ulcerative colitis, diverticulitis; any condition in which bleeding presents a hazard or would be difficult to manage because of location; pregnancy (category C). Safety and efficacy in children are not established.

CAUTIOUS USE Patient with preexisting hemostatic deficits; conditions accompanied by risk of cerebral embolism; atrial flutter, atrial fibrillation; septic thrombophlebitis; anticoagulant therapy; uremia; liver failure; lactation.

ROUTE & DOSAGE

Coronary Artery Thrombosis, MI

Adult: **IV** 1.5 million IU infused over 60 min within 6 h of symptoms **Intracoronary** 20,000 IU bolus, followed by 2000 IU/min for 60 min (total dose 140,000 IU)

Deep Vein Thrombosis, Pulmonary Embolism, Arterial Embolism

Adult: **IV** 250,000 IU over 30 min loading dose, then 100,000 IU/h for 24–72 h

Occluded Cannula

Adult: **IV** 250,000 IU in 2 mL over 25–35 min; clamp for 2 h, then aspirate cannula

ADMINISTRATION

Intravenous

PREPARE: IV Infusion: *All uses except cannula occlusion*—Reconstitute with 5 mL NS (preferred) or 5 mL D5W. Roll or tilt vial to dissolve; avoid shaking to pre-vent foaming or increase in flocculation. Further dilute by carefully adding an additional 40 mL to the vial, avoiding shaking or agitation of the solution. If necessary, may be further diluted in 45 mL increments to approximately 500 mL. Slight flocculation does not interfere with drug action; discard solution with large amount of flocculent.

ADMINISTER: IV Infusion: Start IV infusion as soon as possible after the thrombotic event; thrombi more than 7 d old respond poorly to SK therapy. Give at rate specified under Route & Dosage for specific indication (e.g., 1.5 million IU over 60 min for coronary artery thrombosis). Observe infusion site frequently. If phlebitis occurs, it can usually be controlled by diluting the infusion solution.

INCOMPATIBILITIES Y-site: Bivalirudin.

- Store unopened vials at 15°–30° C (59°–86° F). - Store reconstituted solution at 2°–4° C (36°–39° F). Discard after 24 h.

ADVERSE EFFECTS (≥1%) **Body as a Whole:** *Allergic reactions* (bronchospasm, periorbital swelling, angioneurotic edema, anaphylaxis); urticaria, itching, headache, musculoskeletal pain, flushing, nausea, pyrexia. **Hematologic:** Phlebitis, *bleeding or oozing at sites of percutaneous trauma;* prolonged systemic hypocoagulability; spontaneous bleeding (GI, urogenital, retroperitoneal). **CV:** Unstable blood pressure; reperfusion atrial or ventricular dysrhythmias.

DIAGNOSTIC TEST INTERFERENCE Streptokinase promotes increases in *TT, APTT,* and *PT.*

S

Common adverse effects in *italic*, life-threatening effects <u>underlined</u>; generic names in **bold**; classifications in SMALL CAPS; ✦ Canadian drug name; ◉ Prototype drug

1415

INTERACTIONS Drug: ANTICOAGU-LANTS increase risk of bleeding; **aminocaproic acid** reverses the action of streptokinase.

PHARMACOKINETICS Metabolism: Rapidly cleared from circulation by antibodies. **Elimination:** Does not cross placenta, but antibodies do. **Half-Life:** 83 min.

CLINICAL IMPLICATIONS

Assessment & Drug Effects

- Lab tests: Discontinue heparin and obtain baseline control levels for TT, aPTT, PT, INR, Hct, and platelet count prior to treatment. Treatment is delayed until TT and aPTT are less than 2 times the normal control level. During treatment with SK, TT is generally kept at about 2 times or more baseline value and checked q3–4h.

- Protect patient from invasive procedures: IM injections are contraindicated. Also prevent undue manipulation during thrombolytic therapy to prevent bruising. Spontaneous bleeding occurs about twice as often with SK as with heparin.

- Monitor for excessive bleeding q15min for the first hour of therapy, q30min for second to eighth hour, then q8h.

- Be aware that patient is at risk for postthrombolytic bleeding for 2–4 d after intracoronary SK treatment. Continue monitoring vital signs until laboratory tests confirm anticoagulant control.

- Report signs of potential serious bleeding; gum bleeding, epistaxis, hematoma, spontaneous ecchymoses, oozing at catheter site, increased pulse, pain from internal bleeding. SK infusion should be interrupted, then resumed when bleeding stops.

- Report promptly symptoms of a major allergic reaction; therapy will be discontinued and emergency treatment instituted. Minor symptoms (e.g., itching, nausea) respond to concurrent antihistamine or corticosteroid treatment or both without interruption of SK administration.

- Check cardiac monitor frequently. Be alert to changes in cardiac rhythm, especially during intracoronary instillation. Dysrhythmias signal need to stop therapy at once.

- Monitor BP. Mild changes can be expected, but report substantial changes (greater than ±25 mm Hg). Therapy may be discontinued.

- Check patient's temperature during treatment. A slight elevation, 0.8° C (1.5° F), perhaps with chills, occurs in about one third of the patients. Higher elevations may be treated with acetaminophen.

- Avoid giving aspirin because of its antiplatelet action if an analgesic-antipyretic is indicated.

Patient & Family Education

- Report immediately to physician symptoms of hypersensitivity (e.g., labored, difficult breathing; hives; itching skin).

STREPTOMYCIN SULFATE

(strep-toe-mye′sin)

Streptomycin

Classifications: AMINOGLYCOSIDE ANTIBIOTIC; ANTITUBERCULOSIS AGENT

Therapeutic: ANTIBIOTIC; ANTITUBERCULOSIS AGENT

Prototype: Gentamicin

Pregnancy Category: C

AVAILABILITY 400 mg/mL, 1 g injection

ACTION & *THERAPEUTIC EFFECT*

Aminoglycoside antibiotic derived

from *Streptomyces griseus,* with bactericidal and bacteriostatic actions. It works by inhibiting bacterial protein synthesis through irreversible binding to the 30S ribosomal subunit of susceptible bacteria. Reportedly, it is the least nephrotoxic of the aminoglycosides. *Active against a variety of gram-positive, gram-negative, and acid-fast organisms.*

USES Only in combination with other antitubercular drugs in treatment of all forms of active tuberculosis caused by susceptible organisms. Used alone or in conjunction with tetracycline for tularemia, plague, and brucellosis. Also used with other antibiotics in treatment of subacute bacterial endocarditis due to *Enterococci* and *Streptococci* (viridans group) and *Haemophilus influenzae* and in treatment of peritonitis, respiratory tract infections, granuloma inguinale, and chancroid when other drugs have failed.

CONTRAINDICATIONS History of toxic reaction or hypersensitivity to aminoglycosides; labyrinthine disease; myasthenia gravis; concurrent or sequential use of other neurotoxic or nephrotoxic agents; pregnancy (category C).
CAUTIOUS USE Impaired kidney function (given in reduced dosages); use in older adults and in prematures, neonates, and children.

ROUTE & DOSAGE

Tuberculosis
Adult: **IM** 15 mg/kg up to 1 g/d as single dose
Geriatric: **IM** 10 mg/kg (max: 750 mg/d)
Child: **IM** 20–40 mg/kg/d up to 1 g/d as single dose
Infant: **IM** 10–15 mg/kg q12h
Neonate: **IM** 10–20 mg/kg q24h

Tularemia
Adult: **IM** 1–2 g/d in 1–2 divided doses for 7–10 d
Child: **IM** 20–40 mg/kg/d divided q6–12h

Plague
Adult: **IM** 2 g/d in 2–4 divided doses
Child: **IM** 30 mg/kg/d divided q8–12

ADMINISTRATION

Intramuscular
- Give IM deep into large muscle mass to minimize possibility of irritation. Injections are painful.
- Avoid direct contact with drug; sensitization can occur. Use gloves during preparation of drug.
- Use commercially prepared IM solution undiluted; intended only for IM injection (contains a preservative, and therefore is not suitable for other routes).
- Store ampules at room temperature. Protect from light; exposure to light may slightly darken solution, with no apparent loss of potency.

ADVERSE EFFECTS (≥1%) **CNS:** Paresthesias (peripheral, facial). **Body as a Whole:** Hypersensitivity angioedema, drug fever, enlarged lymph nodes, <u>anaphylactic shock</u>, headache, inability to concentrate, lassitude, muscular weakness, *pain and irritation at IM site,* superinfections, neuromuscular blockade, arachnoiditis. **GI:** Stomatitis, hepatotoxicity. **Hematologic:** Blood dyscrasias (leukopenia, neutropenia, pancytopenia, hemolytic or aplastic anemia, eosinophilia). **Special Senses:** *Labyrinthine damage,* auditory damage, optic nerve toxicity (scotomas). **Urogenital:** Nephrotoxicity. **CNS:** Encephalopathy, <u>CNS depression</u>

S

syndrome in infants (stupor, flaccid-ity, coma, paralysis, cardiac arrest). **Respiratory:** Respiratory depression. **Skin:** Skin rashes, pruritus, exfoliative dermatitis.

DIAGNOSTIC TEST INTERFERENCE
Streptomycin reportedly produces false-positive **urinary glucose** tests using **copper sulfate methods (Benedict's solution, Clinitest)** but not with **glucose oxidase methods** (e.g., **Clinistix, TesTape**). False increases in protein content in **urine** and **CSF** using **Folin-Ciocalteau reaction** and decreased **BUN** readings with **Berthelot reaction** may occur from test interferences. **C&S** tests may be affected if patient is taking salts such as sodium and potassium chloride, sodium sulfate and tartrate, ammonium acetate, calcium and magnesium ions.

INTERACTIONS Drug: May potentiate anticoagulant effects of **warfarin;** additive nephrotoxicity with **acyclovir, amphotericin B,** AMINOGLYCOSIDES, **carboplatin, cidofovir, cisplatin, cyclosporine, foscarnet, ganciclovir,** SALICYLATES, **tacrolimus, vancomycin.**

PHARMACOKINETICS Peak: 1–2 h. **Distribution:** Diffuses into most body tissues and extracellular fluids; crosses placenta; distributed into breast milk. **Elimination:** In urine. **Half-Life:** 2–3 h adults, 4–10 h newborns.

CLINICAL IMPLICATIONS
Assessment & Drug Effects
- Lab tests: Obtain C&S tests prior to and periodically during course of therapy. In patients with impaired kidney function, frequent determinations of serum drug concentrations and periodic kidney and liver function tests are advised (serum concentrations should not exceed 25 mcg/mL in these patients).
- Be alert for and report immediately symptoms of ototoxicity (see Appendix F). Symptoms are most likely to occur in patients with impaired kidney function, patients receiving high doses (1.8–2 g/d) or other ototoxic or neurotoxic drugs, and older adults. Irreversible damage may occur if drug is not discontinued promptly.
- Early damage to vestibular portion of eighth cranial nerve (higher incidence than auditory toxicity) is initially manifested by moderately severe headache, nausea, vomiting, vertigo in upright position, difficulty in reading, unsteadiness, and positive Romberg sign.
- Be aware that auditory nerve damage is usually preceded by vestibular symptoms and high-pitched tinnitus, roaring noises, impaired hearing (especially to high-pitched sounds), sense of fullness in ears. Audiometric test should be done if these symptoms appear, and drug should be discontinued. Hearing loss can be permanent if damage is extensive. Tinnitus may persist several days to weeks after drug is stopped.
- Monitor I&O. Report oliguria or changes in I&O ratio (possible signs of diminishing kidney function). Sufficient fluids to maintain urinary output of 1500 mL/24 h are generally advised. Consult physician.

Patient & Family Education
- Report any unusual symptoms. Review adverse reactions with physician periodically, especially with prolonged therapy.
- Be aware of possibility of ototoxicity and its symptoms (see Appendix F).

- Report to physician immediately any of the following: Nausea, vomiting, vertigo, incoordination, tinnitus, fullness in ears, impaired hearing.

STREPTOZOCIN

(strep-toe-zoe'sin)
Zanosar
Classifications: ANTINEOPLASTIC; ALKYLATING AGENT
Therapeutic: ANTINEOPLASTIC
Prototype: Cyclophosphamide
Pregnancy Category: D

AVAILABILITY 1 g injection

ACTION & *THERAPEUTIC EFFECT*
Streptozocin is highly toxic and has a low therapeutic index; thus a clinically effective response is likely to be accompanied by some evidence of toxicity. Inhibits DNA synthesis in cells and prevents progression of cells into mitosis, affecting all phases of the cell cycle (cell-cycle nonspecific). Appears to have minimal effects on RNA or protein synthesis. Functional islet cell tumors produce and secrete a variety of hormones including glucagon, insulin, calcitonin, serotonin, and others. *Successful therapy with streptozocin (alone or in combination) produces a biochemical response evidenced by decreased secretion of hormones as well as measurable tumor regression. Thus, serial fasting insulin levels during treatment indicate response to this drug.*

USES Metastatic functional and nonfunctional islet cell carcinoma of pancreas, as single agent or in combination with fluorouracil.
UNLABELED USES A variety of other malignant neoplasms including metastatic carcinoid tumor or carcinoid syndrome, refractory advanced Hodgkin's disease, and metastatic colorectal cancer.

CONTRAINDICATIONS Renal disease; pregnancy (category D), lactation. Safety in children is not established.
CAUTIOUS USE Renal impairment; hepatic disease; patients with history of hypoglycemia; diabetes mellitus; hepatic impairment.

ROUTE & DOSAGE

Islet Cell Carcinoma of Pancreas
Adult: **IV** 500 mg/m^2/d for 5 consecutive days q6wk or 1 g/m^2/wk for 2 wk, then increase to 1.5 g/m^2/wk, infuse dose over 15 min to 6 h

Renal Impairment
If Cl$_{cr}$ 10–50 mL/min, use 75% of dose; if less, use 50% of dose

ADMINISTRATION

Intravenous
Use only under constant supervision by physician experienced in therapy with cytotoxic agents and only when the benefit to risk ratio is fully and thoroughly understood by patient and family.

- Wear gloves to protect against topical exposure, which may pose a carcinogen hazard, when handling streptozocin. If solution or powder comes in contact with skin or mucosa, promptly flush the area thoroughly with soap and water.

***PREPARE:* IV Infusion:** Reconstitute with 9.5 mL D5W or NS, to yield 100 mg/mL. Solution will be pale gold. May be further diluted with up to 250 mL of the original diluent. Protect reconsti-

S

Common adverse effects in *italic*, life-threatening effects <u>underlined</u>; generic names in **bold**; classifications in SMALL CAPS; ♣ Canadian drug name; ✪ Prototype drug

1419

tuted solution and vials of drug from light.

ADMINISTER: IV Infusion: Give over 15–60 min. Inspect injection site frequently for signs of extravasation (patient complaints of stinging or burning at site, swelling around site, no blood return or questionable blood return). If extravasation occurs, area requires immediate attention to prevent necrosis. Remove needle, apply ice, and contact physician regarding further treatment to infiltrated tissue.

INCOMPATIBILITIES Y-site: Allopurinol, aztreonam, cefepime, piperacillin/tazobactam.

- Note: An antiemetic given routinely every 4 or 6 h and prophylactically 30 min before a treatment may provide sufficient control to maintain the treatment regimen (even if it reduces but not completely eliminates nausea and vomiting).

- Discard reconstituted solutions after 12 h (contains no preservative and not intended for multidose use).

ADVERSE EFFECTS (≥1%) **CNS:** Confusion, lethargy, depression. **GI:** *Nausea, vomiting,* diarrhea, transient increase in AST, ALT, or alkaline phosphatase; hypoalbuminemia. **Hematologic:** *Mild* to moderate myelosuppression *(leukopenia, thrombocytopenia, anemia).* **Metabolic:** Glucose tolerance abnormalities (moderate and reversible); glycosuria without hyperglycemia; <u>insulin shock</u> (rare). **Urogenital:** <u>Nephrotoxicity: azotemia, anuria, proteinuria, hypophosphatemia, hyperchloremia;</u> *Fanconi-like syndrome* (proximal renal tubular reabsorption defects, alkaline pH of urine, glucosuria, acetonuria, aminoaciduria): Hypokalemia, hypocalcemia. **Other:** Local necrosis following extravasation.

INTERACTIONS Drug: MYELOSUPPRESSIVE AGENTS add to hematologic toxicity; nephrotoxic agents (e.g., AMINOGLYCOSIDES, **vancomycin, amphotericin B, cisplatin**) increase risk of nephrotoxicity; **phenytoin** may reduce cytotoxic effect on pancreatic beta cells.

PHARMACOKINETICS Absorption: Undetectable in plasma within 3 h. **Distribution:** Metabolite enters CSF. **Metabolism:** In liver and kidneys. **Elimination:** 70–80% of dose in urine, 1% in feces, and 5% in expired air. **Half-Life:** 35–40 min.

CLINICAL IMPLICATIONS

Assessment & Drug Effects

- Lab tests: Perform CBC at least weekly, and liver function tests prior to each course of therapy. Dosage adjustment or discontinuation may be required if there is evidence of decreased liver or bone marrow function. Obtain serial urinalyses and determinations of BUN, creatinine clearance, and serum electrolytes prior to and weekly during therapy, then for 4 wk after termination of therapy.
- Ensure that repeat courses of streptozocin treatment are not given until patient's liver, kidney, and hematologic functions are within acceptable limits. Platelet and leukocyte nadirs generally occur 1–2 wk after beginning therapy.
- Report evidence of drug-induced declining kidney function promptly; changes are dose related and cumulative.
- Be alert to early laboratory evidence of kidney dysfunction: Hypophosphatemia, mild proteinuria, and changes in I&O ratio and pattern.
- Mild adverse renal effects may be reversible following discontinuation of streptozocin, but nephro-

toxicity may be irreversible, severe, or fatal.

- Be alert to symptoms of sepsis and superinfections (leukopenia) or increased tendency to bleed (thrombocytopenia). Myelosuppression is severe in 10–20% of patients and may be cumulative and more severe if patient has had prior exposure to radiation or to other antineoplastics.
- Monitor for S&S of superinfection (see Appendix F).
- Monitor and record temperature pattern to promptly recognize impending sepsis.

Patient & Family Education

- Inspect site at weekly intervals and report changes in tissue appearance if extravasation occurred during IV infusion.
- Report symptoms of hypoglycemia (see Appendix F) even though this drug has minimal, if any, diabetogenic action.
- Drink fluids liberally (2000–3000 mL/d). Hydration may protect against drug toxicity effects.
- Report S&S of nephrotoxicity (see Appendix F).
- Do not take aspirin without consulting physician.
- Report to physician promptly any signs of bleeding: Hematuria, epistaxis, ecchymoses, petechial.
- Report symptoms that suggest anemia: Shortness of breath, pale mucous membranes and nail beds, exhaustion, rapid pulse.

SUCCINYLCHOLINE CHLORIDE ℗

(suk-sin-ill-koe'leen)
Anectine, Quelicin
Classifications: DEPOLARIZING SKELETAL MUSCLE RELAXANT

Therapeutic: DEPOLARIZING SKELETAL MUSCLE RELAXANT
Pregnancy Category: C

AVAILABILITY 20 mg/mL, 50 mg/mL, 100 mg/mL injection

ACTION & THERAPEUTIC EFFECT

Synthetic, ultrashort-acting depolarizing neuromuscular blocking agent with high affinity for acetylcholine (ACh) receptor sites. *Initial transient contractions and fasciculations are followed by sustained flaccid skeletal muscle paralysis produced by state of accommodation that develops in adjacent excitable muscle membranes.*

USES To produce skeletal muscle relaxation as adjunct to anesthesia; to facilitate intubation and endoscopy, to increase pulmonary compliance in assisted or controlled respiration, and to reduce intensity of muscle contractions in pharmacologically induced or electroshock convulsions.

CONTRAINDICATIONS Hypersensitivity to succinylcholine; family history of malignant hyperthermia; burns; trauma; pregnancy (category C).
CAUTIOUS USE During delivery by cesarean section; lactation; kidney, liver, pulmonary, metabolic, or cardiovascular disorders; myasthenia gravis; dehydration, electrolyte imbalance, patients taking digitalis, severe burns or trauma, fractures, spinal cord injuries, degenerative or dystrophic neuromuscular diseases, low plasma pseudocholinesterase levels (recessive genetic trait, but often associated with severe liver disease, severe anemia, dehydration, marked changes in body temperature, exposure to neurotoxic insecticides, certain drugs); collagen diseases, porphyria, intraocular surgery, glaucoma; lactation.

S

Common adverse effects in *italic*, life-threatening effects <u>underlined</u>; generic names in **bold**; classifications in SMALL CAPS; ♣ Canadian drug name; ℗ Prototype drug

1421

ROUTE & DOSAGE

Surgical and Anesthetic Procedures

Adult: **IV** 0.3–1.1 mg/kg administered over 10–30 sec, may give additional doses prn **IM** 2.5–4 mg/kg up to 150 mg
Child: **IV** 1–2 mg/kg administered over 10–30 sec, may give additional doses prn **IM** 2.5–4 mg/kg up to 150 mg

Prolonged Muscle Relaxation

Adult: **IV** 0.5–10 mg/min by continuous infusion

Obesity

Dose based on IBW

ADMINISTRATION

Intramuscular

▪ Give IM injections deeply, preferably high into deltoid muscle.

Intravenous

Use only freshly prepared solutions; succinylcholine hydrolyzes rapidly with consequent loss of potency.

▪ Give initial small test dose (0.1 mg/kg) to determine individual drug sensitivity and recovery time.

PREPARE: Direct: Give undiluted. **Intermittent/Continuous:** Dilute 1 g in 500–1000 mL of D5W or NS.

ADMINISTER: Direct: Give a bolus dose over 30 sec. **Intermittent/Continuous:** Preferred. Give at a rate of 0.5–10 mg/min. Do not exceed 10 mg/min.

INCOMPATIBILITIES Solution/additive: Aminophylline, ampicillin, cephalothin, diazepam, epinephrine, hydrocortisone, methicillin, methohexital, nitrofurantoin, oxacillin, oxytet-racycline, sodium bicarbonate, thiopental, warfarin. **Y-site:** Thiopental.

▪ Note: Expiration date and storage before and after reconstitution; varies with the manufacturer.

ADVERSE EFFECTS (≥1%) **CNS:** *Muscle fasciculations,* profound and prolonged muscle relaxation, muscle pain. **CV:** *Bradycardia,* tachycardia, hypotension, hypertension, arrhythmias, sinus arrest. **Respiratory:** <u>Respiratory depression,</u> bronchospasm, hypoxia, <u>apnea.</u> **Body as a Whole:** <u>Malignant hyperthermia,</u> increased IOP, excessive salivation, enlarged salivary glands. **Metabolic:** Myoglobinemia, hyperkalemia. **GI:** Decreased tone and motility of GI tract (large doses).

INTERACTIONS Drug: **Aminoglycosides, colistin, cyclophosphamide, cyclopropane, echothiophate iodide, halothane, lidocaine,** MAGNESIUM SALTS, **methotrimeprazine,** NARCOTIC ANALGESICS, ORGANOPHOSPHAMIDE INSECTICIDES, MAO INHIBITORS, PHENOTHIAZINES, **procaine, procainamide, quinidine, quinine, propranolol** may prolong neuromuscular blockade; DIGITALIS GLYCOSIDES may increase risk of cardiac arrhythmias.

PHARMACOKINETICS Onset: 0.5–1 min IV; 2–3 min IM. **Duration:** 2–3 min IV; 10–30 min IM. **Distribution:** Crosses placenta in small amounts. **Metabolism:** In plasma by pseudocholinesterases. **Elimination:** In urine.

CLINICAL IMPLICATIONS

Assessment & Drug Effects

▪ Lab tests: Obtain baseline serum electrolytes. Electrolyte imbalance (particularly potassium, calcium, magnesium) can potentiate effects of neuromuscular blocking agents.

- Be aware that transient apnea usually occurs at time of maximal drug effect (1–2 min); spontaneous respiration should return in a few seconds or, at most, 3 or 4 min.
- Have immediately available: Facilities for emergency endotracheal intubation, artificial respiration, and assisted or controlled respiration with oxygen.
- Monitor vital signs and keep airway clear of secretions.

Patient & Family Education
- Patient may experience postprocedural muscle stiffness and pain (caused by initial fasciculations following injection) for as long as 24–30 h.
- Be aware that hoarseness and sore throat are common even when pharyngeal airway has not been used.
- Report residual muscle weakness to physician.

SUCRALFATE

(soo-kral'fate)
Carafate, Sulcrate ♦
Classifications: ANTIULCER
Therapeutic: ANTIULCER
Pregnancy Category: B

AVAILABILITY 1 g tablets; 1 g/10 mL suspension

ACTION & *THERAPEUTIC EFFECT*
A complex of aluminum hydroxide and sulfated sucrose. Following oral administration, sucralfate and gastric acid react to form a viscous, adhesive, paste-like substance that resists further reaction with gastric acid. This "paste" adheres to the GI mucosa with a major portion binding electrostatically to the positively charged protein molecules in the damaged mucosa of an ulcer crater or an acute gastric erosion caused by alcohol or other drugs. *Absorbs bile, inhibits the enzyme pepsin, and blocks back diffusion of H^+ ions. These actions plus adherence of the paste-like complex protect damaged mucosa against further destruction from ulcerogenic secretions and drugs.*

USES Short-term (up to 8 wk) treatment of duodenal ulcer.
UNLABELED USES Short-term treatment of gastric ulcer, aspirin-induced erosions, suspension for chemotherapy-induced mucositis.

CONTRAINDICATIONS Pregnancy (category B). Safety and efficacy in children are not established.
CAUTIOUS USE Chronic kidney failure or dialysis due to aluminum accumulation; renal impairment.

ROUTE & DOSAGE

Duodenal Ulcer
Adult: **PO** 1 g q.i.d. 1 h a.c. and h.s. **PO** Maintenance 1 g b.i.d.

ADMINISTRATION

Oral
- Use drug solubilized in an appropriate diluent by a pharmacist when given through nasogastric tube.
- Administer antacids prescribed for pain relief 30 min before or after sucralfate.
- Separate administration of QUINOLONES, digoxin, phenytoin, tetracycline from that of sucralfate by 2 h to prevent sucralfate from binding to these compounds in the intestinal tract and reducing their bioavailability.
- Store in tight container at room temperature, 15°–30° C (59°–86° F). Stable for 2 y after manufacture.

S

Common adverse effects in *italic*, life-threatening effects <u>underlined</u>; generic names in **bold**; classifications in SMALL CAPS; ♦ Canadian drug name; ☺ Prototype drug

1423

ADVERSE EFFECTS (≥1%) **GI:** Nausea, gastric discomfort, *constipation,* diarrhea.

INTERACTIONS Drug: May decrease absorption of QUINOLONES (e.g., **ciprofloxacin, norfloxacin**), **digoxin, phenytoin, tetracycline.**

PHARMACOKINETICS Absorption: Minimally absorbed from GI tract (<5%). **Duration:** Up to 6 h (depends on contact time with ulcer crater). **Elimination:** 90% in feces.

CLINICAL IMPLICATIONS

Assessment & Drug Effects
▪ Be aware of drug interactions and schedule other medications accordingly.

Patient & Family Education
▪ Although healing has occurred within the first 2 wk of therapy, treatment is usually continued 4–8 wk.
▪ Be aware that constipation is a drug-related problem. Follow these measures unless contraindicated: Increase water intake to 8–10 glasses per day; increase physical exercise, increase dietary bulk. Consult physician: a suppository or bulk laxative (e.g., Metamucil) may be prescribed.

SUFENTANIL CITRATE

(soo-fen′ta-nil)
Sufenta
Classifications: NARCOTIC (OPIATE) AGONIST ANALGESIC; GENERAL ANESTHETIC
Therapeutic: NARCOTIC ANALGESIC
Prototype: Morphine
Pregnancy Category: C
Controlled Substance: Schedule II

AVAILABILITY 50 mcg/mL injection

ACTION & *THERAPEUTIC EFFECT*
Synthetic opioid related to fentanyl with similar pharmacologic actions, but about 7 times more potent. Onset of action and recovery from anesthesia occur more rapidly with sufentanil than with fentanyl. In common with other opiate agonists, sufentanil can cause respiratory depression and suppression of cough reflex. *Effective agent for analgesia as a supplement or a primary anesthesia.*

USES Analgesic supplement in maintenance of balanced general anesthesia and also as a primary anesthetic.

CONTRAINDICATIONS Hypersensitivity to opiate agonists; pregnancy (category C).
CAUTIOUS USE Pulmonary disease, reduced respiratory reserve; COPD; cardiac disease; increased intracranial pressure; seizure disorders; impaired liver or kidney function; GI disease; lactation.

ROUTE & DOSAGE

Adjunct to General Anesthesia
Adult: **IV** 1–8 mcg/kg, depending on duration of surgery, may give additional doses of 10–50 mcg if needed

As Primary Anesthetic
Adult: **IV** 1–30 mcg/kg administered with 100% oxygen and a muscle relaxant, may give additional doses of 10–50 mcg if needed
Child: **IV** <12 y, 10–25 mcg/kg administered with 100% oxygen and a muscle relaxant, may give additional doses of 25–50 mcg up to 1–2 mcg/kg/dose if needed

Obesity
Use lean body weight.

ADMINISTRATION

Intravenous

Administer only by qualified personnel, specifically trained in the use of IV anesthesia and in the management of respiratory depression.

- Have available a narcotic antagonist (e.g., naloxone) to reverse respiratory depression.

PREPARE: Direct: Examine solution for particulate matter and discoloration (solution should be clear) before administration. Give undiluted.

ADMINISTER: Direct: Give a bolus dose over 3–5 sec. **Epidural:** Give by slow injection and closely monitor respirations after each injection.

INCOMPATIBILITIES Solution/additive: Diazepam, lorazepam, phenobarbital, phenytoin, sodium bicarbonate, sodium chloride. Y-site: Lorazepam, phenytoin, thiopental.

- Store at 15°–30° C (59°–86° F) unless otherwise directed; protect from light.

ADVERSE EFFECTS (≥1%) **CV:** Bradycardia, tachycardia, hypotension, hypertension, arrhythmias. **GI:** Nausea, vomiting, constipation. **Respiratory:** Bronchospasm, *respiratory depression, apnea.* **Body as a Whole:** *Skeletal muscle rigidity (especially of trunk),* chills, *itching,* spasms of sphincter of Oddi, urinary retention.

INTERACTIONS Drug: BETA-ADRENERGIC ANTAGONISTS increase incidence of bradycardia; **alcohol** and other CNS DEPRESSANTS such as BARBITURATES, TRANQUILIZERS, OPIATES and INHALATION GENERAL ANESTHETICS add to CNS depression; **cimetidine** increases risk of respiratory depression.

PHARMACOKINETICS Onset: 1.5–3 min. **Duration:** 40 min. **Distribution:** Crosses blood–brain barrier. **Metabolism:** In liver (CYP3A4) and small intestine. **Elimination:** In urine and feces. **Half-Life:** 2–3 h.

CLINICAL IMPLICATIONS

Assessment & Drug Effects

- Monitor vital signs. Observe for skeletal muscle rigidity, especially of chest wall, and respiratory depression, particularly in older adults, and in patients who are obese, debilitated, or who have received high doses.
- Bear in mind that if naloxone is given to reverse respiratory depression, the duration of sufentanil-induced respiratory depression may exceed the duration of naloxone.

Patient & Family Education

- Avoid activities which require mental alertness for at least 24 h after receiving this drug.

SULFACETAMIDE SODIUM

(sul-fa-see′ta-mide)
AK-Sulf, Bleph 10, Cetamide, Isopto Cetamide, Ophthacet, Sebizon, Sodium Sulamyd, Sulf-10

SULFACETAMIDE SODIUM/ SULFUR

Sulfacet, Rosula
Classifications: SULFONAMIDE ANTIBIOTIC
Therapeutic: ANTIBIOTIC; SULFONAMIDE
Prototype: Sulfisoxazole
Pregnancy Category: B, D (near term)

AVAILABILITY Sulfacetamide 10% lotion; 1%, 10%, 15%, 30% solu-

Common adverse effects in *italic*, life-threatening effects underlined; generic names in **bold**; classifications in SMALL CAPS; ♣ Canadian drug name; ☺ Prototype drug

1425

tion; 10% ointment **Sulfacetamide/ Sulfur** 10%/5% gel, lotion

ACTION & *THERAPEUTIC EFFECT*
Highly soluble sulfonamide that exerts bacteriostatic effect by interfering with bacterial utilization of PABA, thereby inhibiting folic acid biosynthesis required for bacterial growth. *Effective against a wide range of gram-positive and gram-negative microorganisms.*

USES Ophthalmic preparations are used for conjunctivitis, corneal ulcers, and other superficial ocular infections and as adjunct to systemic sulfonamide therapy for trachoma. The topical lotion is used for scaly dermatoses, seborrheic dermatitis, seborrhea sicca, and other bacterial skin infections.

CONTRAINDICATIONS Hypersensitivity to sulfonamides or to any ingredients in the formulation; neonates, pregnancy (category D near term). Safe use in children not known.
CAUTIOUS USE Application of lotion to denuded or debrided skin; lactation, pregnancy (category B).

ROUTE & DOSAGE

Conjunctivitis
Adult: **Ophthalmic** 1–3 drops of 10%, 15%, or 30% solution into lower conjunctival sac q2–3h, may increase interval as patient responds or use 1.5–2.5 cm (½–1 in) of 10% ointment q6h and at h.s.

Seborrhea, Rosacea
Adult: **Topical** Apply thin film to affected area 1–3 times per day

ADMINISTRATION
Instillation
- Be aware that ophthalmic preparations and skin lotion are not interchangeable.

- Check strength of medication prescribed.
- See patient instructions for instilling eye drops.
- Discard darkened solutions; results when left standing for a long time.
- Store at 8°–15° C (46°–59° F) in tightly closed containers unless otherwise directed.

ADVERSE EFFECTS (≥1%) Special Senses: *Temporary stinging or burning sensation,* retardation of corneal healing associated with long-term use of ophthalmic ointment. **Body as a Whole:** Hypersensitivity reactions (<u>Stevens-Johnson syndrome</u>, lupus-like syndrome), superinfections with nonsusceptible organisms.

INTERACTIONS Drug: Tetracaine and other LOCAL ANESTHETICS DERIVED FROM PABA may antagonize the antibacterial effects of sulfonamides; SILVER PREPARATIONS may precipitate sulfacetamide from solution.

PHARMACOKINETICS Absorption: Minimal systemic absorption, but may be enough to cause sensitization. **Metabolism:** In liver to inactive metabolites. **Elimination:** In urine.

CLINICAL IMPLICATIONS
Assessment & Drug Effects
- Discontinue if symptoms of hypersensitivity appear (erythema, skin rash, pruritus, urticaria).

Patient & Family Education
- Wash hands thoroughly with soap and running water (before and after instillation).
- Examine eye medication; discard if cloudy or dark in color.
- Avoid contaminating any part of eye dropper that is inserted in bottle.
- Tilt head back, pull down lower lid. At the same time, look up

while drop is being instilled into conjunctival sac. Immediately apply gentle pressure just below the eyelid and next to nose for 1 min. Close eyes gently, so as not to squeeze out medication.

- Report purulent eye discharge to physician. Sulfacetamide sodium is inactivated by purulent exudates.

SULFADIAZINE

(sul-fa-dye′a-zeen)
Microsulfon
Classifications: SULFONAMIDE ANTIBIOTIC
Therapeutic: ANTIBIOTIC, SULFON-AMIDE
Prototype: Sulfisoxazole
Pregnancy Category: C

AVAILABILITY 500 mg tablets

ACTION & *THERAPEUTIC EFFECT*
Short-acting sulfonamide, slightly less soluble than sulfisoxazole. Exerts bacteriostatic effect by interfering with bacterial utilization of PABA, thereby inhibiting folic acid biosynthesis required for bacterial growth. *Effective against a wide range of gram-positive and gram-negative microorganisms.*

USES Used in combination with pyrimethamine for treatment of cerebral toxoplasmosis and chloroquine-resistant malaria.

CONTRAINDICATIONS Hypersensitivity to sulfonamides or to any ingredients in the formulation; porphyria; pregnancy (category C); at term pregnancy; lactation.
CAUTIOUS USE Application of lotion to denuded or debrided skin; dehydration; hepatic disease; impaired renal function.

ROUTE & DOSAGE

Mild to Moderate Infections

Adult: **PO Loading Dose** 2–4 g loading dose **PO Maintenance Dose** 2–4 g/d in 4–6 divided doses
Child: **PO Loading Dose** >2 mo, 75 mg/kg **PO Maintenance Dose** 150 mg/kg/d in 4–6 divided doses (max: 6 g/d)

Rheumatic Fever Prophylaxis

Adult: **PO** <30 kg, 500 mg/d; >30 kg, 1 g/d

Toxoplasmosis

Adult: **PO** 2–8 g/d divided q6h
Child: **PO** >2 mo, 100–200 mg/kg/d divided q6h
Neonate: **PO** 50 mg/kg q12h times 12 mo

ADMINISTRATION

Oral

- Maintain sufficient fluid intake to produce urinary output of at least 1500 mL/24 h for children between 3000 and 4000 mL/24 h for adults. Concomitant administration of urinary alkalinizer may be prescribed to reduce possibility of crystalluria and stone formation.
- Store in tight, light-resistant containers.

ADVERSE EFFECTS (≥1%) **CNS:** Headache, peripheral neuritis, peripheral neuropathy, tinnitus, hearing loss, vertigo, insomnia, drowsiness, mental depression, acute psychosis, ataxia, convulsions, kernicterus (newborns). **GI:** *Nausea, vomiting, diarrhea,* abdominal pains, hepatitis, jaundice, pancreatitis, stomatitis. **Hematologic:** Acute hemolytic anemia (especially in patients with G6PD deficiency), <u>aplastic anemia</u>, methemoglobinemia,

S

agranulocytosis, thrombocytopenia, leukopenia, eosinophilia, hypoprothrombinemia. **Body as a Whole:** Headache, *fever,* chills, arthralgia, malaise, allergic myocarditis, serum sickness, anaphylactoid reactions, lymphadenopathy, local reaction following IM injection, fixed drug eruptions, diuresis, overgrowth of nonsusceptible organisms, LE phenomenon. **Skin:** Pruritus, urticaria, rash, erythema multiforme including *Stevens-Johnson syndrome, exfoliative dermatitis,* alopecia, photosensitivity, vascular lesions. **Urogenital:** *Crystalluria,* hematuria, proteinuria, anuria, toxic nephrosis, reduction in sperm count. **Metabolic:** Goiter, hypoglycemia. **Special Senses:** Conjunctivitis, conjunctival or scleral infection, retardation of corneal healing (ophthalmic ointment).

INTERACTIONS Drug: PABA-CONTAINING LOCAL ANESTHETICS may antagonize sulfa's effects; ORAL ANTICOAGULANTS potentiate hypoprothrombinemia; may potentiate SULFONYLUREA-induced hypoglycemia. May decrease concentrations of **cyclosporine;** may increase levels of **phenytoin.**

PHARMACOKINETICS Absorption: Readily absorbed from GI tract. **Peak:** 3–6 h. **Distribution:** Distributed to most tissues, including CSF; crosses placenta. **Metabolism:** In liver. **Elimination:** In urine.

CLINICAL IMPLICATIONS

Assessment & Drug Effects
▪ Lab tests: Baseline and periodic urine C&S to determine drug effectiveness; with long-term therapy, CBC, Hct, and Hgb.
▪ Monitor hydration status.

Patient & Family Education
▪ Take drug exactly as prescribed. Do not alter schedule or dose; take total amount prescribed unless physician changes the regimen.
▪ Drink fluids liberally unless otherwise directed.
▪ Report early signs of blood dyscrasias (sore throat, pallor, fever) promptly to the physician.

SULFAMETHOXAZOLE

(sul-fa-meth-ox′a-zole)
Sulfamethoxazole
Classifications: ANTIBIOTIC, SULFONAMIDE
Therapeutic: ANTIBIOTIC; SULFONAMIDE
Prototype: Sulfisoxazole
Pregnancy Category: B, D (near term)

AVAILABILITY 500 mg tablets

ACTION & *THERAPEUTIC EFFECT*
Intermediate-acting sulfonamide antibiotic. Sulfonamides exert their bacteriostatic action by interfering with folic acid synthesis required for bacterial growth. Intestinal absorption and urinary excretion are slow; therefore, it is rarely used due to the potential of excessive blood level. *Effective against community-acquired* E. coli *strains and other susceptible organisms.*

USES Acute, recurrent, or chronic urinary tract infections, lymphogranuloma venereum, and other infections caused by susceptible organisms.

CONTRAINDICATIONS Hypersensitivity to sulfonamides; use in treatment of group A beta-hemolytic streptococcal infections; infants <2 mo of age; neonates; porphyria; advanced kidney or liver disease; intestinal or urinary obstruction; G6PD deficiency; pregnancy (category D near term); lactation.

Common adverse effects in *italic,* life-threatening effects underlined; generic names in **bold,** classifications in SMALL CAPS; ♣ Canadian drug name; ⊙ Prototype drug

CAUTIOUS USE Impaired kidney or liver function; severe allergy; bronchial asthma; blood dyscrasias.

ROUTE & DOSAGE

Mild to Moderate Infections
Adult: **PO Loading Dose** 2 g **PO Maintenance Dose** 1 g q8–12h
Child: **PO Loading Dose** >2 mo, 50–60 mg/kg **PO Maintenance Dose** 25–30 mg/kg q12h (max: 75 mg/kg/d)

ADMINISTRATION

Oral

- Give with fluid of patient's choice; tablet may be crushed.
- Maintain sufficient fluid intake to produce urinary output of at least 1500 mL/24 h for children and between 3000 and 4000 mL/24 h for adults. Concomitant administration of urinary alkalinizer may be prescribed to reduce possibility of crystalluria and stone formation.
- Store 15°–30° C (59°–86° F) in tight, light-resistant containers. Do not freeze.

ADVERSE EFFECTS (≥1%) **CNS:** Headache, peripheral neuritis, peripheral neuropathy, tinnitus, hearing loss, vertigo, insomnia, drowsiness, mental depression, acute psychosis, ataxia, convulsions, kernicterus (newborns). **GI:** *Nausea, vomiting, diarrhea,* abdominal pains, hepatitis, jaundice, pancreatitis, stomatitis. **Hematologic:** Acute hemolytic anemia (especially in patients with G6PD deficiency), aplastic anemia, methemoglobinemia, agranulocytosis, thrombocytopenia, leukopenia, eosinophilia, hypoprothrombinemia. **Body as a Whole:** Headache, *fever,* chills, arthralgia, malaise, allergic myocarditis, serum sickness, anaphylactoid reactions, lymphadenopathy, local reaction following IM injection, fixed drug eruptions, diuresis, overgrowth of nonsusceptible organisms, LE phenomenon. **Skin:** Pruritus, urticaria, rash, erythema multiforme including Stevens-Johnson syndrome, exfoliative dermatitis, alopecia, photosensitivity, vascular lesions. **Urogenital:** Crystalluria, hematuria, proteinuria, anuria, toxic nephrosis, reduction in sperm count. **Metabolic:** Goiter, hypoglycemia. **Special Senses:** Conjunctivitis, conjunctival or scleral infection, retardation of corneal healing (ophthalmic ointment).

INTERACTIONS Drug: PABA-CONTAINING LOCAL ANESTHETICS may antagonize sulfa's effects; ORAL ANTICOAGULANTS potentiate hypoprothrombinemia; may potentiate SULFONYLUREA-induced hypoglycemia, may decrease concentrations of **cyclosporine;** may increase levels of **phenytoin.**

PHARMACOKINETICS Absorption: Incompletely absorbed from GI tract. **Peak:** 3–4 h. **Distribution:** Distributed to most tissues, including CSF; crosses placenta. **Metabolism:** In liver. **Elimination:** In urine. **Half-Life:** 7–12 h.

CLINICAL IMPLICATIONS

Assessment & Drug Effects

- Lab tests: Baseline and periodic urine C&S to determine drug effectiveness; with long-term therapy, CBC, Hct and Hgb.
- Monitor hydration status.

Patient & Family Education

- Take drug exactly as prescribed. Do not alter schedule or dose; take total amount prescribed unless physician changes the regimen.
- Drink fluids liberally unless otherwise directed.
- Report early signs of blood dyscrasias (sore throat, pallor, fever) promptly to the physician.

S

Common adverse effects in *italic,* life-threatening effects underlined; generic names in **bold**; classifications in SMALL CAPS; ♣ Canadian drug name; ☻ Prototype drug

1429

SULFASALAZINE

(sul-fa-sal'a-zeen)

Azulfidine, PMS Sulfasalazine ✦, PMS Sulfasalazine E.C. ✦, Salazopyrin ✦, SAS Enteric-500 ✦, S.A.S.-500 ✦

Classifications: MUCOUS MEMBRANE AGENT; ANTIINFLAMMATORY; SULFONAMIDE
Therapeutic: GI ANTIINFLAMMATORY; IMMUNOMODULATORY; DISEASE-MODIFYING ANTIRHEUMATIC DRUG (DMARD)
Prototype: Mesalamine
Pregnancy Category: B

AVAILABILITY 500 mg tablets; 500 mg sustained release tablets

ACTION & *THERAPEUTIC EFFECT*
Locally acting sulfonamide. Believed to be converted by intestinal microflora to sulfapyridine (provides antibacterial action) and 5-aminosalicylic acid (5-ASA) or mesalamine, which may exert an antiinflammatory effect. Proposed mechanisms of action include inhibition of prostaglandins known to cause diarrhea and affect mucosal transport and interference with absorption of fluids and electrolytes from colon. *Reduces Clostridium and Escherichia coli in the stools. Antiinflammatory and immunomodulatory properties are effective in controlling the S&S of ulcerative colitis and rheumatoid arthritis.*

USES Ulcerative colitis and relatively mild regional enteritis; rheumatoid arthritis.
UNLABELED USES Granulomatous colitis, Crohn's disease, scleroderma.

CONTRAINDICATIONS Sensitivity to sulfasalazine, other sulfonamides and salicylates; carbonic anhydrase inhibitors, thiazide diuretics; agranulocytosis; children <2 y; intestinal and urinary tract obstruction; porphyria.
CAUTIOUS USE Severe allergy, or bronchial asthma; blood dyscrasias; hepatic or renal impairment; G6PD deficiency; older adults; pregnancy (category B); lactation; children <6 y.

ROUTE & DOSAGE

Ulcerative Colitis, Rheumatoid Arthritis

Adult: **PO** 1–2 g/d in 4 divided doses, may increase up to 8 g/d if needed
Child: **PO** 40–50 mg/kg/d in 4 divided doses (max: 75 mg/kg/d)

Juvenile Rheumatoid Arthritis

Child: **PO** 10 mg/kg/d, increase weekly by 10 mg/kg/d [usual dose: 15–25 mg/kg q12h (max: 2 g/d)]

ADMINISTRATION

Oral
- Give after eating to provide longer intestine transit time.
- Do not crush or chew sustained release tablets; must be swallowed whole.
- Use evenly divided doses over each 24-h period; do not exceed 8-h intervals between doses.
- Consult physician if GI intolerance occurs after first few doses. Symptoms are probably due to irritation of stomach mucosa and may be relieved by spacing total daily dose more evenly over 24 h or by administration of enteric-coated tablets.
- Store at 15°–30° C (59°–86° F) in tight, light-resistant containers.

ADVERSE EFFECTS (≥1%) **Body as a Whole:** *Nausea, vomiting, bloody diarrhea; anorexia,* arthralgia, rash, anemia, oligospermia (reversible),

S

blood dyscrasias, liver injury, infectious mononucleosis–like reaction, *allergic reactions*.

INTERACTIONS Drug: Iron, ANTIBIOTICS may alter absorption of sulfasalazine.

PHARMACOKINETICS Absorption: 10–15% from GI tract unchanged; remaining drug is hydrolyzed in colon to sulfapyridine (most of which is absorbed) and 5-aminosalicylic acid (30% of which is absorbed). **Peak:** 1.5–6 h sulfasalazine; 6–24 h sulfapyridine. **Distribution:** Crosses placenta; distributed into breast milk. **Metabolism:** In intestines and liver. **Elimination:** All metabolites are excreted in urine. **Half-Life:** 5–10 h.

CLINICAL IMPLICATIONS

Assessment & Drug Effects

▪ Monitor for GI distress. GI symptoms that develop after a few days of therapy may indicate need for dosage adjustment. If symptoms persist, physician may withhold drug for 5–7 d and restart it at a lower dosage level.

▪ Be aware that adverse reactions generally occur within a few days to 12 wk after start of therapy; most likely to occur in patients receiving high doses (4 g or more).

▪ Lab tests: Measure RBC folate in patients on high doses (more than 2 g/d); a daily supplement may be prescribed.

Patient & Family Education

▪ Examine stools and report to physician if enteric-coated tablets have passed intact in feces. Some patients lack enzymes capable of dissolving coating; conventional tablet will be ordered.

▪ Be aware that drug may color alkaline urine and skin orange-yellow.

▪ Remain under close medical supervision. Relapses occur in about 40% of patients after initial satisfactory response. Response to therapy and duration of treatment are governed by endoscopic examinations.

SULFINPYRAZONE

(sul-fin-peer'a-zone)

Antazone ◆, Anturan ◆, Anturane, Apo-Sulfinpyrazone ◆, Novopyrazone ◆

Classifications: ANTIGOUT AGENT; URICOSURIC

Therapeutic: ANTIGOUT

Prototype: Probenecid

Pregnancy Category: C

AVAILABILITY 100 mg tablets; 200 mg capsules

ACTION & *THERAPEUTIC EFFECT*
Potent renal tubular blocking agent of uric acid in the kidney that lowers its serum blood level. Like all uricosurics, low doses may inhibit tubular secretion of uric acid and cause urate retention. Inhibits release of adenosine diphosphate and 5-hydroxytryptophan, and thus decreases platelet adhesiveness and increases platelet survival time; has no effect on prothrombin or blood clotting time. *Promotes urinary excretion of uric acid and reduces serum urate levels by competitively inhibiting tubular reabsorption of uric acid in the kidney.*

USES Maintenance therapy in chronic gouty arthritis and tophaceous gout.

UNLABELED USES Drug-induced hyperuricemia, to decrease platelet aggregation and increase their survival in prevention of TIAs and stroke.

CONTRAINDICATIONS Known hypersensitivity to phenylbutazone, or pyrazoline derivatives or salicylates; active peptic ulcer; concurrent ad-

S

Common adverse effects in *italic*, life-threatening effects underlined; generic names in **bold**; classifications in SMALL CAPS; ◆ Canadian drug name; ◒ Prototype drug

1431

ministration of salicylates; blood dyscrasias; patients with creatinine clearance <50 mg/min, treatment of hyperuricemia secondary to neoplastic disease or cancer chemotherapy; bone marrow suppression; hematologic disease; nephrolithiasis.

CAUTIOUS USE NSAID hypersensitivity; impaired kidney function; severe hepatic disease; history of healed peptic ulcer; concurrent use of anticoagulant therapy; thrombocytopenia; use in conjunction with sulfonamides and sulfonylureas; pregnancy (category C), lactation.

ROUTE & DOSAGE

Gout

Adult: **PO** 100–200 mg b.i.d. for 1 wk, then increase to 200–400 mg b.i.d., may reduce to 200 mg/d after serum urate levels are controlled (max: 800 mg/d)

Inhibition of Platelet Aggregation

Adult: **PO** 200 mg t.i.d. or q.i.d.

ADMINISTRATION

Oral

- Give with meals, milk, or antacid (prescribed) to prevent local drug irritant effect. Severity and frequency of symptoms increase with dosage. Persistence of GI symptoms may require discontinuation of drug.
- Ensure fluid intake sufficient to support urinary output of at least 2000–3000 mL/d during early therapy (consult physician). Also alkalinize urine (e.g., with large doses vitamin C) to increase solubility of uric acid and minimize risk of uric acid stones.

ADVERSE EFFECTS (≥1%) **GI:** *Nausea,* vomiting, diarrhea, *epigastric pain, blood loss, reactivation or ag-*

gravation of peptic ulcer, jaundice. **CNS:** Ataxia, dizziness, vertigo, convulsions, coma. **Special Senses:** Tinnitus. **Body as a Whole:** Edema, labored respirations, hypersensitivity, reactions (skin rashes, fever). **Urogenital:** Precipitation of acute gout, urolithiasis, renal colic.

DIAGNOSTIC TEST INTERFERENCE

Sulfinpyrazone decreases urinary excretion of *aminohippuric acid* and *phenolsulfonphthalein.*

INTERACTIONS Drug: May decrease efficacy of **nitrofurantoin** for UTI and increase its systemic toxicity. May displace SULFONYLUREAS from protein binding and increase risk of hypoglycemia; may augment prothrombin time increased by **warfarin; cholestyramine** decreases absorption of sulfinpyrazone; **aspirin** may inhibit uricosuric effects of sulfinpyrazone.

PHARMACOKINETICS Absorption: Readily absorbed from GI tract. **Peak:** 1–2 h. **Duration:** 4–6 h; may persist up to 10 h. **Metabolism:** In liver to active and inactive metabolites. **Elimination:** Slowly in urine; 5% in feces. **Half-Life:** 3 h.

CLINICAL IMPLICATIONS

Assessment & Drug Effects

- Monitor therapy using serum urate levels (lower to about 6 mg/dL) to reduce joint changes, tophi formation, and frequency of acute attacks and to improve kidney function.
- Lab tests: Obtain periodic blood cell counts during prolonged therapy. Also kidney function, particularly with renal impairment. Monitor PT and INR with concurrent warfarin use.
- Frequency of acute gouty attacks may increase during first 6–12 mo

S

of therapy, even when serum urate levels appear to be controlled. Concurrent prophylactic doses of colchicine may be prescribed during first 3–6 mo of treatment to prevent or lessen severity of attacks.

Patient & Family Education
- Remain under close medical supervision; therapy is continued indefinitely.
- Do not experiment with dosage; subtherapeutic doses may enhance urate retention and large doses may increase risk of toxicity.
- Continue medication without interruption even during acute gouty attack. Contact physician for concomitant treatment with full therapeutic doses of colchicine or other antiinflammatory agent.
- Avoid aspirin-containing medications. If an analgesic is required (in patients with normal kidney function), acetaminophen is generally recommended.

SULFISOXAZOLE ⓟ

(sul-fi-sox′a-zole)
Gantrisin
Classifications: SULFONAMIDE ANTIBIOTIC
Therapeutic: ANTIBIOTIC, SULFON-AMIDE
Pregnancy Category: C (D if near term)

AVAILABILITY 500 mg tablets

ACTION & *THERAPEUTIC EFFECT*
Short-acting derivative of sulfanilamide. Bacteriostatic action believed to be by competitive inhibition of p-aminobenzoic acid (PABA), thereby interfering with folic acid biosynthesis required for bacterial growth. *Exhibits broad antimicrobial spectrum against both gram-positive and gram-negative organisms.*

USES Acute, recurrent, and chronic urinary tract infections and chancroid; adjunctive therapy in trachoma, chloroquine-resistant strains of malaria, acute otitis media due to *Haemophilus influenzae,* and meningococcal and *H. influenzae* meningitis. Ophthalmic preparations used in treatment of conjunctivitis, corneal ulcer, and other superficial eye infections and as adjunct to systemic sulfonamide therapy for trachoma. Topical vaginal preparation used for *H. vaginalis* vaginitis.

CONTRAINDICATIONS History of hypersensitivity to sulfonamides, salicylates, or chemically related drugs; use in treatment of group A beta-hemolytic streptococcal infections; infants <2 mo of age (except in treatment of congenital toxoplasmosis); neonates; porphyria; G6PD deficiency; advanced kidney or liver disease; intestinal and urinary obstruction; pregnancy (category C, category D if near term).
CAUTIOUS USE Impaired kidney or liver function; severe allergy; bronchial asthma; blood dyscrasias.

ROUTE & DOSAGE

Infection by Susceptible Organisms
Adult: **PO** 2–4 g initially, followed by 4–8 g/d in 4–6 divided doses
Child: **PO** >2 mo, 75 mg/kg initially, followed by 150 mg/kg/d in 4–6 divided doses (max: 6 g/ d)

ADMINISTRATION

Oral
- Give with full glass of water or other fluid; tablet may be crushed.

S

Common adverse effects in *italic*, life-threatening effects underlined; generic names in **bold**; classifications in SMALL CAPS; ♥ Canadian drug name; ⓟ Prototype drug

1433

- Store at 15°–30° C (59°–86° F) in tight, light-resistant containers.

ADVERSE EFFECTS (≥1%) **CNS:** Headache, peripheral neuritis, peripheral neuropathy, tinnitus, hearing loss, vertigo, insomnia, drowsiness, mental depression, acute psychosis, ataxia, convulsions, kernicterus (newborns). **GI:** *Nausea, vomiting, diarrhea,* abdominal pains, hepatitis, jaundice, pancreatitis, stomatitis. **Hematologic:** Acute hemolytic anemia (especially in patients with G6PD deficiency), <u>aplastic anemia</u>, methemoglobinemia, <u>agranulocytosis</u>, thrombocytopenia, leukopenia, eosinophilia, hypoprothrombinemia. **Body as a Whole:** Headache, *fever,* chills, arthralgia, malaise, allergic myocarditis, serum sickness, <u>anaphylactoid reactions</u>, lymphadenopathy, local reaction following IM injection, fixed drug eruptions, diuresis, overgrowth of nonsusceptible organisms, LE phenomenon. **Skin:** Pruritus, urticaria, rash, erythema multiforme including *Stevens-Johnson syndrome <u>exfoliative, dermatitis,</u>* alopecia, photosensitivity, vascular lesions. **Urogenital:** *Crystalluria,* hematuria, proteinuria, anuria, toxic nephrosis, reduction in sperm count. **Metabolic:** Goiter, hypoglycemia. **Special Senses:** Conjunctivitis, conjunctival or scleral infection, retardation of corneal healing (ophthalmic ointment).

DIAGNOSTIC TEST INTERFERENCE Sulfonamides may interfere with *BSP* retention and *PSP* excretion tests and may affect results of *thyroid function* tests (*I-131* may be decreased for about 7 d). Large doses of sulfonamides reportedly may produce false-positive *urine glucose* determinations with *copper reduction methods* (e.g., *Benedict's* and *Clinitest*). SULFON-

AMIDES may produce false-positive results for *urinary protein* (with *sulfosalicylic acid test*) and may interfere with *urine urobilinogen* determinations using *Ehrlich's reagent* or *Urobilistix.* Follow-up cultures are unreliable unless PABA is added to culture medium.

INTERACTIONS Drug: PABA-CONTAINING LOCAL ANESTHETICS may antagonize sulfa's effects; ORAL ANTICOAGULANTS potentiate hypoprothrombinemia; may potentiate SULFONYLUREA-induced hypoglycemia; may decrease concentrations of **cyclosporine;** may increase levels of **phenytoin.**

PHARMACOKINETICS Absorption: Readily from GI tract. **Peak:** 2–4 h. **Distribution:** Distributed in extracellular space; crosses blood–brain barrier and placenta; detected in breast milk. **Metabolism:** in liver. **Elimination:** 95% in urine in 24 h. **Half-Life:** 4.6–7.8 h.

CLINICAL IMPLICATIONS

Assessment & Drug Effects

- Lab tests: Obtain a specimen for C&S prior to initiation of therapy. Perform frequent kidney function tests and urinalyses; complete blood counts and liver function tests, especially during regimens longer than 2 wk.
- Monitor I&O. Report oliguria and changes in I&O ratio. Fluid intake should be adequate to support urinary output of at least 1500 mL/d to prevent crystalluria and stone formation.
- Check urine pH daily with Nitrazine paper or Labstix; fall in urinary pH (more acidic) increases risk of crystalluria.
- Report increasing urine acidity. If urine is highly acidic, physician may prescribe a urinary alkalinizer.

S

Common adverse effects in *italic*, life-threatening effects <u>underlined</u>; generic names in **bold**; classifications in SMALL CAPS; ✦ Canadian drug name; ⊕ Prototype drug

- Monitor temperature. Sudden appearance of fever may signify sensitization (serum sickness) or hemolytic anemia (frequent in patients with G6PD deficiency, which is most common among black males and Mediterranean ethnic groups). Reactions generally develop within 10 d. Agranulocytosis may develop after 10 d–6 wk of therapy.
- Report early manifestations of blood dyscrasias or hypersensitivity reactions immediately (fever with sore throat, malaise, unusual fatigue, joint pains, pallor, bleeding tendencies, rash, jaundice).
- Be alert for skin lesions, papular or vesiculobullous lesions, especially on sun-exposed areas, Stevens-Johnson syndrome (severe erythema multiforme) may be preceded by high fever, severe headache, stomatitis, conjunctivitis, rhinitis, urticaria, balanitis (inflammation of penis or clitoris). Termination of drug therapy is indicated.
- Observe diabetic patients receiving oral hypoglycemic agents closely for hypoglycemic reactions. Obtain blood glucose and HbA1c levels before and shortly after initiation of therapy.

Patient & Family Education

- Do not take OTC medications without consulting physician. Many analgesic mixtures contain aspirin in combination with *p*-aminobenzoic acid; avoid to prevent crystallization in urine.
- Use or add barrier contraceptives if using hormonal contraceptives, which may be unreliable while taking this drug.
- Avoid exposure to ultraviolet light and excessive sunlight to prevent photosensitivity reaction during therapy and for several months after treatment is discontinued.

- Inform dentist or new physician that you are taking a sulfonamide.

SULINDAC
(sul-in′dak)
Clinoril
Classifications: ANALGESIC, NONSTEROIDAL ANTIINFLAMMATORY DRUG (NSAID); ANTIPYRETIC
Therapeutic: NSAID, ANALGESIC; ANTIPYRETIC
Prototype: Ibuprofen
Pregnancy Category: B (D in third trimester)

AVAILABILITY 150 mg, 200 mg tablets

ACTION & *THERAPEUTIC EFFECT*
Mechanism of antiinflammatory action thought to result from inhibition of prostaglandin synthesis. Comparable to aspirin in antiinflammatory activity with longer half-life. *Exhibits antiinflammatory, analgesic, and antipyretic properties.*

USES Acute and long-term symptomatic treatment of osteoarthritis, rheumatoid arthritis, ankylosing spondylitis; acute painful shoulder (acute subacromial bursitis or supraspinatus tendinitis); acute gouty arthritis.

CONTRAINDICATIONS Hypersensitivity to sulindac; hypersensitivity to aspirin (patients with "aspirin triad": acute asthma, rhinitis, nasal polyps), other NSAIDs, or salicylates; significant kidney or liver dysfunction; CABG perioperative pain; pregnancy (category B; category D in third trimester), lactation. Safety in children is not established.

CAUTIOUS USE History of upper GI tract disorders; anticoagulant therapy; CHF; moderate or mild renal

Common adverse effects in *italic*, life-threatening effects underlined; generic names in **bold**; classifications in SMALL CAPS; ♥ Canadian drug name; ☻ Prototype drug

1435

impairment; compromised cardiac function, hypertension, hemophilia or other bleeding tendencies.

ROUTE & DOSAGE

Arthritis, Ankylosing Spondylitis, Acute Gouty Arthritis
Adult: **PO** 150–200 mg b.i.d. (max: 400 mg/d)

ADMINISTRATION

Oral
- Crush and give mixed with liquid or food if patient cannot swallow tablet.
- Administer with food, milk, or antacid (if prescribed) to reduce possibility of GI upset. Note: Food retards absorption and delays and lowers peak concentrations.

ADVERSE EFFECTS (≥1%) **CNS:** Drowsiness, *dizziness, headache,* anxiety, nervousness. **CV:** Palpitation, peripheral edema, CHF, (patients with marginal cardiac function). **Special Senses:** Blurred vision, amblyopia, vertigo, tinnitus, decreased hearing. **GI:** *Abdominal pain, dyspepsia, nausea, vomiting, constipation,* diarrhea, ulceration, flatulence, anorexia; stomatitis, sore or dry mucous membranes, dry mouth; GI bleeding, gastritis. **Hematologic:** Prolonged bleeding time, aplastic anemia, thrombocytopenia, leukopenia, eosinophilia. **Body as a Whole:** Angioneurotic edema, fever, chills, anaphylaxis. **Skin:** Stevens-Johnson syndrome, toxic epidermal necrolysis syndrome, rash, pruritus. **Urogenital:** Renal impairment.

DIAGNOSTIC TEST INTERFERENCE Abnormalities in *liver function tests* may occur.

INTERACTIONS Drug: Heparin, ORAL ANTICOAGULANTS may prolong bleeding time; may increase **lithium** toxicity; **aspirin,** other NSAIDs add to ulcerogenic effects; may increase **methotrexate** toxicity; **dimethylsulfoxide (DMSO)** may decrease effects of sulindac. **Herbal:** Feverfew, garlic, ginger, ginkgo may increase bleeding potential.

PHARMACOKINETICS Absorption: 90% from GI tract. **Peak:** 2 h without food, 3–4 h with food. **Duration:** 10–12 h. **Distribution:** Minimal passage across placenta; distributed into breast milk. **Metabolism:** In liver to active sulfide metabolite. **Elimination:** 75% in urine, 25% in feces. **Half-Life:** 7.8 h sulindac, 16.4 h sulfide metabolite.

CLINICAL IMPLICATIONS

Assessment & Drug Effects
- Lab tests: Obtain baseline and periodic evaluations of Hgb, kidney and liver function.
- Schedule auditory and ophthalmic examinations in patients receiving prolonged or high-dose therapy.
- Recommend an ophthalmoscopic examination if patient has eye complaints.

Patient & Family Education
- Do not drive or engage in potentially hazardous activities until response to drug is known.
- Report any incidence of unexplained bleeding or bruising immediately to physician (e.g., bleeding gums, black and tarry stools, coffee-colored emesis).
- Report onset of skin rash, itching, hives, jaundice, swelling of feet or hands, sore throat or mouth, shortness of breath, or night cough to physician.
- Be aware that adverse GI effects are relatively common. Report abdominal pain, nausea, dyspepsia, diarrhea, or constipation.

S

- Note: Initial effect may take up to 7 d; peak effect is usually experienced in 2–3 wk (relief of joint pain and stiffness, reduction in joint swelling, increase in grip strength, and improved mobility).
- Avoid alcohol and aspirin as they may increase risk of GI ulceration and bleeding tendencies.
- Inform dentist or surgeon of drug regimen because bleeding time may be prolonged.

SUMATRIPTAN ⓟ

(sum-a-trip'tan)

Imitrex

Classifications: 5-HT$_1$ SEROTONIN AGONIST; ANTIMIGRAINE

Therapeutic: ANTIMIGRAINE; 5-HT$_1$-SEROTONIN AGONIST

Pregnancy Category: C

AVAILABILITY 25 mg, 50 mg tablets; 12 mg/mL injection; 5 mg, 20 mg nasal spray

ACTION & *THERAPEUTIC EFFECT*
Selective agonist for a serotonin receptor (probably 5-HT$_{1D}$) that causes vasoconstriction of cranial carotid arteries. *Causes vasoconstriction of cranial carotid arteries, thus relieving the migraine headache. Also relieves photophobia, phonophobia, nausea and vomiting associated with migraine attacks.*

USES Treatment of acute migraine attacks with or without aura, cluster headache.

CONTRAINDICATIONS Hypersensitivity to sumatriptan; IV use; coronary artery disease (CAD); acute MI, angina, arteriosclerosis; cerebrovascular disease; colitis; older adults; risk factors for CAD such as hypertension, hypercholesterolemia, obesity, diabetes, smoking, and strong family history; concurrent use with ergotamine drugs; concurrent use of oral sumatriptan with MAO INHIBITORS; intracranial bleeding; PVD; Raynaud's disease; stroke; Wolff-Parkinson-White syndrome; basilar or hemiplegic migraine; pregnancy (category C).

CAUTIOUS USE Impaired liver or kidney function; concurrent use of subcutaneous sumatriptan and MAO INHIBITORS. Safety and effectiveness in children are not established.

ROUTE & DOSAGE

Migraine or Cluster Headache

Adult: **SC** 6 mg any time after onset of migraine. If headache returns, may repeat with 6 mg SC at least 1 h after first injection (max: 12 mg/24 h) **PO** 25 mg × 1 dose, if headache returns may repeat once after 2 h (max: 100 mg) **Intranasal** 5, 10, or 20 mg in one nostril. If headache returns, may repeat once after 2 h (max: 40 mg/24 h)

ADMINISTRATION

Note: Do not give within 24 h of an ergot-containing drug.

Oral
- Give any time after symptoms of migraine appear.
- A second tablet may be given if symptoms return but no sooner than 2 h after the first tablet.
- Do not exceed 100 mg in a single oral dose or 300 mg/d.

Intranasal
- Note: A single dose is one spray into ONE nostril.

Subcutaneous
- A second injection may be given 1 h or longer following first injection if initial relief is not obtained or if migraine returns.

S

Common adverse effects in *italic*, life-threatening effects <u>underlined</u>; generic names in **bold**; classifications in SMALL CAPS; ✦ Canadian drug name; ⓟ Prototype drug

1437

- Be aware that if adverse effects are dose limiting, a lower dose may be effective.
- Store all forms at room temperature, 15°–30° C (59°–86° F). Protect from light.

ADVERSE EFFECTS (≥1%) **CV:** Chest pressure and tightness, hypotension or hypertension, hypertensive crisis, syncope, peripheral cyanosis, thromboembolism, heart block, sinus bradycardia, atrial fibrillation, ventricular fibrillation, ventricular tachycardia, coronary artery vasospasm, angina, transient myocardial ischemia, MI, cardiac arrest. **CNS:** *Tingling, warming sensation, pressure, numbness,* headache, *dizziness, vertigo,* drowsiness, sedation, seizure, CNS hemorrhage, subarachnoid hemorrhage, stroke. **Body as a Whole:** Dizziness, lightheadedness, myalgia, or muscle cramps, *pain on injection,* weakness, flushing and a sensation of warmth or burning after injection. **GI:** Abdominal pain, cramping, diarrhea, nausea, vomiting.

INTERACTIONS Drug: Dihydroergotamine, ERGOT ALKALOIDS may cause vasospasm and a slight elevation in blood pressure. MAO INHIBITORS increase sumatriptan levels and toxicity (especially the oral form); do not use concurrently or within 2 wk of stopping MAO INHIBITORS; use with other serotonin altering drugs increases risk of serotonin syndrome (see Appendix F). **Herbal: St. John's wort** may increase triptan toxicity.

PHARMACOKINETICS Onset: 10–30 min after SC administration. **Duration:** 1–2 h. **Distribution:** Widely distributed, 10–20% protein bound. May be excreted in breast milk. **Metabolism:** Hepatically to inactive metabolite. **Elimination:** 57% in urine, 38% in feces. **Half-Life:** 2 h.

CLINICAL IMPLICATIONS

Assessment & Drug Effects

- Monitor cardiovascular status carefully following first dose in patients at relatively high risk for coronary artery disease (e.g., postmenopausal women, men over 40 years old, persons with known CAD risk factors) or who have coronary artery vasospasms.
- Report to physician immediately chest pain or tightness in chest or throat that is severe or does not quickly resolve following a dose of sumatriptan.
- Monitor therapeutic effectiveness. Pain relief usually begins within 10 min of injection, with complete relief in approximately 65% of all patients within 2 h.

Patient & Family Education

- Review patient information leaflet provided by the manufacturer carefully.
- Learn correct use of autoinjector for self-administration of SC dose.
- Pain or redness at injection site is common but usually disappears in less than 1 h.
- Notify physician immediately if symptoms of severe angina (e.g., severe or persistent pain or tightness in chest, back, neck, or throat) or hypersensitivity (e.g., wheezing, facial swelling, skin rash, or hives) occur.
- Do not take any other serotonin receptor agonist (Axert, Maxalt, Zomig, Amerge) within 24 h of taking sumatriptan.
- Check with physician before taking any new OTC or prescription drugs.
- Report any other adverse effects (e.g., tingling, flushing, dizziness) at next physician visit.

Common adverse effects in *italic*, life-threatening effects <u>underlined</u>; generic names in **bold**; classifications in SMALL CAPS; ♣ Canadian drug name; ✪ Prototype drug

SUNITINIB

(sun-i-ti'nib)

Sutent

Classifications: ANTINEOPLASTIC AGENT; GROWTH FACTOR RECEPTOR INHIBITOR; TYROSINE KINASE INHIBITOR

Therapeutic: ANTINEOPLASTIC; GROWTH FACTOR RECEPTOR INHIBITOR; TYROSINE KINASE INHIBITOR

Prototype: Gefitinib

Pregnancy Category: D

AVAILABILITY 12.5 mg, 25 mg, 50 mg capsules

ACTION & *THERAPEUTIC EFFECT*

An antineoplastic agent that is a selective inhibitor of receptor tyrosine kinases (RTKs) in solid tumors. Carcinogenic activity within these tumors is a result of tumor angiogenesis and proliferation. *Sunitinib causes tumor regression and decreased tumor growth.*

USES Treatment of advanced renal cell cancer; treatment of gastrointestinal stromal tumors (GIST) after disease progression on or intolerance to imatinib.

CONTRAINDICATIONS Hypersensitivity to sunitinib; uncontrolled hypertension, acute MI; fever, abnormal bleeding, sore throat; children, pregnancy (category D), lactation.

CAUTIOUS USE Cardiac disease, CHF, history of hypertension, history of MI; CVA; females of childbearing age.

ROUTE & DOSAGE

Advanced Renal Cell Cancer
Adult: PO 50 mg/d for 4 wk, followed by 2 wk off treatment; repeat 6-wk cycle as needed.

Dosage Adjustments with Concurrent Hepatic CYP3A4 Modifiers
CYP3A4 Inducers: Increase to maximum of 87.5 mg/d

CYP3A4 Inhibitors: Decrease to minimum of 37.5 mg/d

ADMINISTRATION

Oral
- Note that this drug is given on a 6-wk cycle: 4 wk on therapy and 2 wk off.
- Incremental dosage changes of 12.5 mg are recommended.
- Store at 15°–30° C (59°–86° F).

ADVERSE EFFECTS (≥1%) **Body as a Whole:** *Alopecia, asthenia, dizziness, fatigue, fever,* hair color change, *headache, peripheral edema.* **CV:** *Hypertension,* <u>myocardial ischemia</u>. **GI:** *Abdominal pain, altered taste, anorexia, constipation, diarrhea, dyspepsia, flatulence, glossodynia, nausea, mucositis, stomatitis, vomiting.* **Hematologic:** *Anemia, bleeding, neutropenia, lymphopenia, thrombocytopenia.* **Metabolic:** *Dehydration, elevated hepatic enzymes (AST/ALT, alkaline phosphatase, pancreatic enzymes, amylasemia, lipasemia), hypothyroidism, hyperbilirubinemia.* **Musculoskeletal:** *Arthralgia, back pain, myalgia/limb pain.* **Respiratory:** *Cough, dyspnea.* **Skin:** *Dry skin, hand-foot syndrome, rash, skin discoloration.*

INTERACTIONS Drug: Coadministration of CYP3A4 inducers (e.g., **carbamazepine, dexamethasone, phenobarbital, phenytoin, rifabutin, rifampin, rifapentine**) may decrease plasma levels of sunitinib. Coadministration of CYP3A4 inhibitors (e.g., **atazanavir, clarithromycin, erythromycin, indinavir, itraconazole, ketoconazole, nefazodone, nelfinavir, ritonavir, saquinavir, telithromycin, voriconazole**) may increase plasma levels of sunitinib. **Food:** Grapefruit and grapefruit juice may increase the plasma levels of sunitinib.

S

Common adverse effects in *italic*, life-threatening effects <u>underlined</u>; generic names in **bold**; classifications in SMALL CAPS; ♣ Canadian drug name; ⊙ Prototype drug

1439

Herbal: St. John's wort may decrease the plasma levels of sunitinib.

PHARMACOKINETICS Peak: 6–12 h. **Distribution:** 95–98% protein bound. **Metabolism:** Extensive hepatic metabolism. **Elimination:** Primarily fecal elimination (61%) with minor renal elimination. **Half-Life:** 40–60 h.

CLINICAL IMPLICATIONS

Assessment & Drug Effects

- Monitor for and report S&S of bleeding (e.g., GI, GU, gingival, etc.).
- Monitor BP regularly and assess regularly for S&S of congestive heart failure. Withhold drug and notify physician if severe hypertension or signs of heart failure develop.
- Lab tests: At the beginning of each treatment cycle, CBC with differential and platelet count; periodic serum electrolytes; thyroid function tests with symptoms suggestive of hypothyroidism.

Patient & Family Education

- Follow directions for taking the drug (see Administration).
- Do not use any prescription or nonprescription drugs without consulting a physician.
- Skin discoloration (yellow color) and/or loss of skin and hair pigmentation may occur with this drug.
- Report any of the following to a health care provider: painful redness of palms and soles of feet; severe abdominal pain, vomiting, and diarrhea; signs of bleeding; chest pain or discomfort; shortness of breath; swelling of feet, legs, or hands; rapid weight gain.
- Women of childbearing age are advised not be become pregnant while taking sunitinib.

TACRINE

(tac'rine)

Cognex

Classifications: CHOLINERGIC; CHOLINESTERASE INHIBITOR; ANTI-DEMENTIA AGENT

Therapeutic: ANTIDEMENTIA; CHOLINESTERASE INHIBITOR

Prototype: Neostigmine

Pregnancy Category: C

AVAILABILITY 10 mg, 20 mg, 30 mg, 40 mg capsules

ACTION & *THERAPEUTIC EFFECT*
Cholinesterase inhibitor, presumably elevates acetylcholine in the cerebral cortex by slowing degradation of acetylcholine release by the remaining intact neurons. Balances pathologic changes in neurons that result in deficiency of acetylcholine in early stages of Alzheimer's disease. *Slows manifestations of Alzheimer's disease.*

USES Improvement of memory in mild to moderate Alzheimer's dementia.

UNLABELED USES HIV infection (severe dementia), tardive dyskinesia, acute anticholinergic syndrome with possible advantage over physostigmine.

CONTRAINDICATIONS Hypersensitivity to tacrine; patients who develop jaundice while taking tacrine; pregnancy (category C).

CAUTIOUS USE Anesthesia, sick sinus rhythm, bradycardia; history of ulcers, GI bleeding, abnormal liver function; patients with asthma, hypotension, hyperthyroidism, urinary tract obstruction, intestinal obstruction; lactation. Safety and efficacy in children are not established.

ROUTE & DOSAGE

Alzheimer's Disease
Adult: **PO** 10 mg q.i.d. (taken between meals if tolerated), increase in 40 mg/d increments not sooner than q6wk (max: 160 mg/d)

Hepatic Impairment
Dose-related hepatotoxic effects have been observed; use with caution or not at all in patients with history of past or current liver disease

ADMINISTRATION

Oral
- Give at least 1 h before meals; bioavailability reduced 30–40% when taken with food. Effectiveness depends on administration at regular intervals.
- Titrate dose upward as long as serum transaminase (ALT) levels remain less than or equal to 3 times upper limit of normal (ULN).
- Reduce daily dose by 40 mg/d when ALT exceeds 3 times but is less than or equal to 5 times ULN. Resume titration when ALT returns to normal.
- Stop treatment if ALT exceeds 5 times ULN.
- Store at room temperature, 15°–30° C (59°–86° F), away from moisture.

ADVERSE EFFECTS (≥1%) **CNS:** Agitation, dizziness and confusion, ataxia, insomnia, somnolence, hallucinations. **GI:** Nausea, *vomiting,* belching, *diarrhea,* abdominal discomfort, anorexia, *hepatotoxicity.* **Skin:** Purpura. **Urogenital:** Excessive micturition and incontinence with UTI infections. **Body as a Whole:** Diaphoresis.

INTERACTIONS Drug: Prolongs action of **succinylcholine** and possibly other NEUROMUSCULAR BLOCKING AGENTS due to inhibition of plasma pseudocholinesterase. Increases **theophylline** concentrations twofold. **Cimetidine** increases concentration of tacrine by 64%. **Herbal: Echinacea** may increase risk of hepatotoxicity.

PHARMACOKINETICS Absorption: Approximately 17% absorbed from GI tract. Food decreases rate and extent of absorption by 30–40%. **Onset:** 30–90 min. **Peak:** 2 h. Steady state in 24–36 h. **Distribution:** Penetrates blood–brain barrier. Protein binding is 55%. **Metabolism:** Metabolized in the liver by cytochrome P-450 system. At least three hydroxylated metabolites have been identified that may be biologically active. Females have lower activity in cytochrome P-450 isoenzymes so plasma levels are approximately 50% higher than men with same dose. **Elimination:** Less than 3% of dose recovered in urine in 24 h. **Half-Life:** 3.5 h.

CLINICAL IMPLICATIONS

Assessment & Drug Effects
- Monitor for clinical improvement (defined as a 4-point improvement in Alzheimer's Disease Assessment Scale/Cognitive Subscale). Improvement has been observed after 1–4 wk; may take 6 mo for maximum benefit.
- Lab tests: Monitor serum transaminase (ALT) levels according to following schedule: Every 2 wk for first 16 wk, then monthly for 2 mo, then every 3 mo thereafter; resume weekly monitoring for 6 wk with each dose increase; continue weekly monitoring if ALT remains more than 2 times normal; if therapy is interrupted more than 4 wk then restarted, resume full ALT monitoring schedule.

T

Common adverse effects in *italic*, life-threatening effects underlined; generic names in **bold**; classifications in SMALL CAPS; ♣ Canadian drug name; ⊙ Prototype drug

1441

- Monitor I&O because tacrine may cause bladder outflow obstruction.
- Monitor for seizure activity and take appropriate precautions.
- Monitor patients with history of angle-closure glaucoma for a worsening of this condition.
- Monitor for GI distress and bleeding, especially in patients with a history of peptic ulcer disease or on concurrent NSAID therapy.
- Supervise ambulation because dizziness occurs in more than 10% of patients.
- Monitor cardiovascular status including periodic ECG monitoring. Assess for fluid retention and worsening of CHF.
- Monitor periodically for development of drug-induced diabetes.

Patient & Family Education
- Be aware of adverse effects related to initiation of therapy or dosage increases (e.g., nausea, vomiting, diarrhea) as well as delayed effects (e.g., rash, GI bleeding, jaundice). Report adverse effects to the physician.
- Do not discontinue or reduce dosage of 80 mg/d or more abruptly because it may precipitate acute deterioration of cognitive function.
- Make sure to have regular follow-up and liver function tests.
- Tacrine may induce seizures, vertigo, and syncope. Use appropriate precautions.
- Understand that tacrine therapy is not a cure and will become ineffective at some point as the disease progresses.

TACROLIMUS

(tac-rol'i-mus)
Prograf, Protopic
Classifications: BIOLOGIC RESPONSE MODIFIER; IMMUNOSUPPRESSANT

Therapeutic: IMMUNOSUPPRESSANT
Prototype: Cyclosporine
Pregnancy Category: C

AVAILABILITY 0.5 mg, 1 mg, 5 mg capsules; 5 mg/mL injection; 0.1%, 0.03% ointment

ACTION & *THERAPEUTIC EFFECT*
Inhibits helper T-lymphocytes by selectively inhibiting secretion of interleukin-2, interleukin-3, and interleukin-gamma; thus reduces transplant rejection. *Inhibits antibody production (thus subduing immune response) by creating an imbalance in favor of suppressor T-lymphocytes.*

USES Liver rejection prophylaxis; rejection prophylaxis for other organ transplants (kidney, heart, bone marrow, pancreas, small bowel), moderate to severe atopic dermatitis (e.g., eczema).
UNLABELED USES Acute organ transplant rejection, severe plaque-type psoriasis.

CONTRAINDICATIONS Hypersensitivity to tacrolimus or castor oil; pregnancy (category C), lactation.
CAUTIOUS USE Renal or hepatic insufficiency, hyperkalemia, QT prolongation; CHF; diabetes mellitus, gout, history of seizures, hypertension.

ROUTE & DOSAGE

Rejection Prophylaxis
Adult: **PO** 0.15–0.2 mg/kg/d in 2 divided doses q12h, start no sooner than 6 h after transplant; give first oral dose 8–12 h after discontinuing IV therapy **IV** 0.01–0.05 mg/kg/d as continuous IV infusion, start no sooner than 6 h after transplant, continue until patient can take oral therapy
Child: **PO** 0.15–0.2 mg/kg/d **IV** 0.03–0.05 mg/kg/d

Atopic Dermatitis

Adult: **Topical** Apply thin layer to affected area b.i.d., continue until clearing of symptoms

Child: **Topical** 2–15 y, Apply thin layer of 0.03% ointment to affected area b.i.d., continue until clearing of symptoms

Severe Plaque-Type Psoriasis

Adult: **PO** Start with 0.05 mg/kg/d, increase to 0.1 mg/kg/d at week 3 and to 0.15 mg/kg/d at week 6 if necessary

Renal Impairment

Start with lower dose.
Hemodialysis: Supplementation not necessary

ADMINISTRATION

Oral

- Discontinue cyclosporine at least 24 h before the first dose of tacrolimus.
- Convert patient from IV to oral therapy as soon as possible.
- Give first oral dose 8–12 h after discontinuing IV infusion.

Topical

- Ensure that skin is clean and completely dry before application.
- Apply a thin layer to the affected area and rub in gently and completely.
- Do not apply occlusive dressing over the site.

Intravenous

PREPARE: **IV Infusion:** Dilute 5 mg/mL ampules with NS or D5W to a concentration of 0.004–0.02 mg/mL; use a less concentrated solution for pediatric patients.

ADMINISTER: **IV Infusion:** Give as continuous IV.

INCOMPATIBILITIES **Y-site: Phenytoin.**

- Store ampules between 5° and 25° C (41° and 77° F); store cap-sules at room temperature, 15°–30° C (59°–86° F). ▪ Store the diluted infusion in glass or polyethylene containers and discard after 24 h.

ADVERSE EFFECTS (≥1%) CNS:
Headache, tremors, insomnia, paresthesia, hyperesthesia and/or sensations of warmth, circumoral numbness. **CV:** *Mild to moderate hypertension.* **Endocrine:** Hirsutism, *hyperglycemia, hyperkalemia, hypokalemia, hypomagnesemia,* hyperuricemia, decreased serum cholesterol. **GI:** *Nausea, abdominal pain, gas,* appetite changes, *vomiting, anorexia, constipation,* diarrhea, ascites. **Hematologic:** *Anemia, leukocytosis, thrombocytopenia purpura.* **Urogenital:** UTI, oliguria, nephrotoxicity. **Respiratory:** *Pleural effusion, atelectasis, dyspnea.* **Special Senses:** Blurred vision, photophobia. **Skin:** *Flushing, rash, pruritus, skin irritation,* alopecia, erythema, folliculitis, hyperesthesia, <u>exfoliative dermatitis</u>, hirsutism, photosensitivity, skin discoloration, skin ulcer, sweating. **Body as a Whole:** *Pain, fever, peripheral edema, increased risk of cancer.*

INTERACTIONS Drug: Use with cyclosporine increases risk of nephrotoxicity. **Erythromycin, metoclopramide** may increase levels; **caspofungin, rifampin** may decrease levels. NSAIDs may lead to oliguria or anuria. **Herbal: St. John's wort** decreases efficacy. **Food:** Grapefruit juice (>1 qt/d) may increase plasma concentrations and adverse effects.

PHARMACOKINETICS Absorption:
Erratic and incompletely from GI tract; absolute bioavailability approximately 14–25%; absorption reduced by food. **Peak:** PO 1–4 h. **Duration:** IV 12 h. **Distribution:** Within plasma, tacrolimus is found primarily in lipoprotein-deficient fraction; 75–97% protein bound; distributed into red

T

blood cells; blood:plasma ratio reported >4; animal studies have demonstrated high concentrations of tacrolimus in lung, kidney, heart, and spleen; distributed into breast milk. **Metabolism:** Extensively in liver (CYP3A4). **Elimination:** Metabolites primarily in bile. **Half-Life:** 8.7–11.3 h.

CLINICAL IMPLICATIONS
Assessment & Drug Effects

- Lab tests: Monitor serum electrolytes, blood glucose, uric acid, BUN, and creatinine clearance periodically.
- Monitor kidney function closely; report elevated serum creatinine or decreased urinary output.
- Monitor for neurotoxicity, and report tremors, changes in mental status, or other signs of toxicity.
- Monitor cardiovascular status and report hypertension.

Patient & Family Education

- Learn complete dosing instructions.
- Be aware of potential adverse effects.
- Minimize exposure to natural or artificial sunlight while using the ointment.
- Notify physician of S&S of neurotoxicity.

TADALAFIL

(ta-dal′a-fil)
Cialis
Classifications: IMPOTENCE AGENT; PHOSPHODIESTERASE (PDE) INHIBITOR; VASODILATOR
Therapeutic: IMPOTENCE; PDE INHIBITOR
Prototype: Sildenafil
Pregnancy Category: B

AVAILABILITY 5 mg, 10 mg, 20 mg tablets

ACTION & THERAPEUTIC EFFECT
Tadalafil is a selective phosphodiesterase (PDE) type 5 inhibitor. PDE type 5 is responsible for degradation of cyclic GMP in the corpus cavernosum of the penis. Cyclic GMP causes smooth muscle relaxation in the corpus cavernosum, thereby allowing inflow of blood into the penis. *Tadalafil promotes sustained erection only in the presence of sexual stimulation.*

USES Treatment of erectile dysfunction.

CONTRAINDICATIONS Hypersensitivity to tadalafil, vardenafil, or sildenafil; concurrent administration of nitrates, nitroglycerin, or any alpha-adrenergic antagonist (other than 0.4 mg qd tamsulosin); MI within last 90 d; Class 2 or greater heart failure within last 6 mo; unstable angina or angina during intercourse; uncontrolled cardiac arrhythmias; nitrate/nitrite therapy; hypotension, uncontrolled hypertension; retinitis pigmentosa; CVA within last 6 mo; left ventricular outflow obstruction, aortic stenosis; not recommended for women; lactation.
CAUTIOUS USE CAD, risk factors for CVA; renal insufficiency; hepatic impairment, hepatic disease; anatomic deformity of the penis; sickle cell anemia; multiple myeloma; leukemia; active bleeding or a peptic ulcer; hiatal hernia, GERD; sickle cell disease; retinitis pigmentosa; hepatitis, cirrhosis; severe renal impairment; older adults; concurrent use with other medicines for penile dysfunction; pregnancy (category B).

ROUTE & DOSAGE

Erectile Dysfunction
Adult: **PO** 10 mg prior to anticipated sexual activity. May increase to max dose 20 mg/d or reduce to 5 mg/d if needed. If taking ritonavir, itraconazole, ketoconazole, or voriconazole, max dose 10 mg q72h.

Hepatic Impairment
Mild to Moderate Impairment: max 10 mg/d; not recommended with severe hepatic impairment

Renal Impairment
Cl_{cr} 30–50 mL/min: start at 5 mg once daily (max: 10 mg q48h); <30 mL/min: max dose 5 mg

ADMINISTRATION

Oral
- Take approximately 1 h before expected intercourse, but preferably not after a heavy or high-fat meal.
- Store at 15°–30° C (59°–86° F).

ADVERSE EFFECTS (≥1%) **Body as a Whole:** Flushing, back pain, asthenia, facial edema, fatigue, pain. **CNS:** *Headache*, dizziness, insomnia, somnolence, vertigo, hypesthesia, paresthesia. **CV:** Angina, chest pain, hypertension, hypotension, MI, orthostatic hypotension, palpitations, syncope, sinus tachycardia. **GI:** Dyspepsia, nausea, vomiting, abdominal pain, abnormal liver function tests, diarrhea, loose stools, dysphagia, esophagitis, gastritis, GERD, xerostomia. **Metabolic:** Increased GGTP. **Musculoskeletal:** Arthralgia, myalgia, neck pain. **Respiratory:** Nasal congestion, dyspnea, epistaxis, pharyngitis. **Skin:** Rash, pruritus, sweating. **Special Senses:** Blurred vision, changes in color vision, conjunctivitis, eye pain, lacrimation, swelling of eyelids, sudden vision loss. **Urogenital:** Spontaneous penile erection.

INTERACTIONS Drug: May potentiate hypotensive effects of ETHANOL, NITRATES, **alfuzosin, doxazosin, prazosin, tamsulosin** (doses >0.4 mg/d), **terazosin; erythromycin** (and other MACROLIDES), **indinavir, intraconazole, ketoconazole,** PROTEASE INHIBITORS, **ritonavir, saquinavir, voriconazole** may increase levels and toxicity of tadalafil; **barbiturates, bosentan, carbamazepine, dexamethasone, fosphenytoin, nevirapine, rifampin phenytoin, rifabutin, troglitazone** may reduce level and effectiveness of tadalafil. **Food:** Grapefruit juice may increase levels and toxicity of tadalafil.

PHARMACOKINETICS Absorption: Rapidly absorbed, 15% reaches systemic circulation. **Onset:** 30–45 min. **Peak:** 2 h. **Duration:** Up to 36 h. **Metabolism:** In liver by CYP3A4. **Elimination:** In feces (61%) and urine (39%). **Half-Life:** 17.5 h.

CLINICAL IMPLICATIONS

Assessment & Drug Effects
- Monitor CV status and report angina or other S&S of cardiac dysfunction.
- Lab tests: Baseline and periodic LFTs.

Patient & Family Education
- Do not take more than once per day.
- Note: With moderate renal insufficiency, the maximum recommended dose is 10 mg not more than once in every 48 h.
- Moderate use of alcohol when taking this drug.
- Do not take this drug without consulting physician if you are taking drugs called "alpha blockers" or "nitrates" or any other drugs for high blood pressure, chest pain, or enlarged prostate.
- Report promptly any of the following: palpitations, chest pain, back pain, difficulty breathing, or shortness of breath; dizziness or fainting; changes in vision; swollen eyelids; muscle aches; painful or prolonged erection (lasting longer than 4 h); skin rash, or itching.

T

Common adverse effects in *italic*, life-threatening effects <u>underlined</u>; generic names in **bold**; classifications in SMALL CAPS; ♣ Canadian drug name; ⊘ Prototype drug

1445

TAMOXIFEN CITRATE 🅟

(ta-mox'i-fen)

Nolvadex, Nolvadex-D ✦, Tamofen ✦

Classifications: ANTINEOPLASTIC AGENT; HORMONE; SELECTIVE ESTROGEN RECEPTOR MODULATOR (SERM)
Therapeutic: ANTINEOPLASTIC; ANTIESTROGEN; SERM
Pregnancy Category: D

AVAILABILITY 10 mg, 20 mg tablets

ACTION & *THERAPEUTIC EFFECT*
Nonsteroidal gonad-stimulating drug with potent antiestrogenic as well as estrogenic activity on various tissues. Competes with estradiol at estrogen receptor (ER-positive) sites in target tissues such as breast, uterus, vagina, anterior pituitary. Estrogen is thought to increase breast cancer in ER-positive tumors. Tamoxifen has no effect on the development of ER-negative breast cancer disease. *Has effects on tumor with high concentration of estrogen receptors. Tamoxifen-receptor complexes move into the cell nucleus, decreasing DNA synthesis and estrogen responses. Ovulation may be induced by stimulation of the release of hypothalamic gonadotropic-releasing factor.*

USES Palliative treatment of advanced with metastatic estrogen receptors (ER)-positive breast cancer in postmenopausal women, adjunctively with surgery in the treatment of breast carcinoma with positive lymph nodes.

UNLABELED USES Investigationally to stimulate ovulation in selected anovulatory women desiring pregnancy.

CONTRAINDICATIONS Anticoagulant therapy, pregnancy (category D), especially during first trimester; preexisting endometrial hyperplasia; intramuscular injections if platelets <50,000/mm³; history of thromboembolic disease; lactation; children.

CAUTIOUS USE Vision disturbances; cataracts, visual disturbance; leukopenia, bone marrow suppression; thrombocytopenia; hypercalcemia; hypercholesterolemia, lipid protein abnormalities.

ROUTE & DOSAGE

Breast Carcinoma
Adult: **PO** 10–20 mg 1–2 times/d (morning and evening)
Stimulation of Ovulation
Adult: **PO** 5–40 mg b.i.d. for 4 d

ADMINISTRATION

Oral
- With severe adverse effects, a simple reduction in dosage gives sufficient relief without losing control of disease. Consult physician.
- Store at 15°–30° C (59°–86° F); protect from light.

ADVERSE EFFECTS (≥1%) **Body as a Whole:** Increased bone pain, and transient local disease flair; loss of hair, weight gain, shortness of breath, photosensitivity, *hot flashes.* **CNS:** Depression, light-headedness, dizziness, headache, mental confusion, sleepiness. **CV:** Thrombosis, pulmonary embolism, increased risk of stroke. **GI:** *Nausea and vomiting (about 25% of patients),* distaste for food, anorexia. **Hematologic:** Leukopenia, thrombocytopenia. **Metabolic:** Hypercalcemia. **Skin:** Skin rash or dryness. **Special Senses:** Retinopathy, decreased visual acuity, blurred vision. **Urogenital:** Changes in menstrual period, milk production and leaking from breasts, vaginal discharge and bleeding, pruritus vulvae, risk of uterine malignancies.

DIAGNOSTIC TEST INTERFERENCE
Tamoxifen may produce transient increase in ***serum calcium.***

INTERACTIONS Drug: May enhance hypoprothrombinemic effects of **warfarin;** may increase risk of thromboembolic events with CYTO-TOXIC AGENTS; **bromocriptine** may elevate tamoxifen levels, SSRI ANTIDE-PRESSANTS may decrease effectiveness of tamoxifen.

PHARMACOKINETICS Absorption: Slowly from GI tract. **Peak:** 3–6 h. **Metabolism:** In liver, enterohepatically cycled. **Elimination:** Primarily in feces. **Half-Life:** 7 d.

CLINICAL IMPLICATIONS

Assessment & Drug Effects

▪ Monitor therapeutic effectiveness. An objective response may require 4–10 wk of therapy, longer if there is bone metastasis.

▪ Administer analgesics for pain relief as necessitated by bone and tumor pain or local disease flair. Reassure patient that this discomfort frequently signals a good tumor response.

▪ Be aware that local swelling and marked erythema over preexisting lesions or the development of new lesions may signal soft-tissue disease response to tamoxifen. These symptoms rapidly subside.

▪ Lab tests: Assess CBC, including platelet counts, periodically. Transient leukopenia and thrombocytopenia ($50,000–100,000/mm^3$) without hemorrhagic tendency have been reported. Monitor serum calcium periodically.

Patient & Family Education

▪ Do not change established dose schedule.

▪ Report to physician occurrence of marked weakness, sleepiness, mental confusion, edema, dyspnea, blurred vision.

▪ Understand the possibility of drug-induced menstrual irregularities before starting treatment.

▪ Avoid prolonged sun exposure, especially if skin is unprotected. Apply sunscreen lotions (SPF 12 or greater) to all exposed skin surfaces.

▪ Avoid OTC drugs unless specifically prescribed by the physician; particularly OTC pain medicines.

▪ Report onset of tenderness or redness in an extremity.

TAMSULOSIN HYDROCHLORIDE

(tam′su-lo-sin)

Flomax

Classifications: ALPHA-ADREN-ERGIC ANTAGONIST

Therapeutic: SMOOTH MUSCLE RE-LAXANT OF BLADDER OUTLET & PROSTATE GLAND

Prototype: Prazosin HCl

Pregnancy Category: B

AVAILABILITY 0.4 mg capsules

ACTION & *THERAPEUTIC EFFECT*

Antagonist of the $alpha_{1A}$-adrenergic receptors located in the prostate. Blockage of $alpha_{1A}$-adrenergic receptors can cause smooth muscles in the bladder outlet and the prostate gland to relax, resulting in improvement in urinary blood flow and a reduction in symptoms of BPH. *Effectiveness is indicated by improved voiding. Improves symptoms related to benign prostatic hypertrophy (BPH) related to bladder outlet obstruction.*

USES Benign prostatic hypertrophy.

CONTRAINDICATIONS Hypersensitivity to tamsulosin; in conjunction with another $alpha_{1A}$-adrenergic blocking agent; women; lactation, pediatric patients.

CAUTIOUS USE History of syncope, hypersensitivity to sulfonamides; hypotension; older adults; renal impairment, renal failure, renal disease; pregnancy (category B).

T

Common adverse effects in *italic*, life-threatening effects underlined; generic names in **bold**; classifications in SMALL CAPS; ◆ Canadian drug name; ⊕ Prototype drug

1447

ROUTE & DOSAGE

Benign Prostatic Hypertrophy
Adult: **PO** 0.4 mg q.d. 30 min after a meal, may increase up to 0.8 mg q.d.

ADMINISTRATION

Oral
- Give 30 min after the same meal each day.
- Instruct to swallow capsules whole; not to crush, chew, or open.
- If dose is interrupted for several days, reinitiate at the lowest dose, 0.4 mg.
- Store at 20°–25° C (68°–77° F).

ADVERSE EFFECTS (≥1%) **Body as a Whole:** Asthenia, back or chest pain. **CNS:** *Headache, dizziness,* insomnia. **CV:** *Orthostatic hypotension (especially with first dose).* **GI:** Diarrhea, nausea. **Respiratory:** *Rhinitis,* pharyngitis, increased cough, sinusitis. **Urogenital:** Decreased libido, *abnormal ejaculation.* **Special Senses:** Amblyopia.

INTERACTIONS Drug: **Cimetidine** may decrease clearance of tamsulosin. **Sildenafil, vardenafil,** and **tadalafil,** and alcohol may enhance hypotensive effects.

PHARMACOKINETICS Absorption: Rapidly from GI tract. >90% bioavailability. **Peak:** 4–5 h fasting, 6–7 h fed. **Distribution:** Widely distributed in body tissues, including kidney and prostate. **Metabolism:** In the liver. **Elimination:** 76% in urine. **Half-Life:** 14–15 h.

CLINICAL IMPLICATIONS

Assessment & Drug Effects
- Monitor for signs of orthostatic hypotension; take BP lying down, then upon standing. Report a systolic pressure drop of ≥15 mm Hg or a HR ≥15 beats upon standing.
- Monitor patients on warfarin therapy closely.

Patient & Family Education
- Make position changes slowly to minimize orthostatic hypotension.
- Report dizziness, vertigo, or fainting to physician. Exercise caution with hazardous activities until response to drug is known.
- Be aware that concurrent use of cimetidine may increase the orthostatic hypotension adverse effect.

TAZAROTENE
(ta-zar′o-teen)
Avage, Tazorac
Classifications: ANTIACNE; RETINOID
Therapeutic: ANTIACNE
Prototype: Isotretinoin
Pregnancy Category: X

AVAILABILITY 0.05%, 0.1% gel, cream

ACTION & *THERAPEUTIC EFFECT*
Retinoid prodrug that blocks epidermal cell proliferation and hyperplasia. *Suppresses inflammation present in the epidermis of psoriasis patients. Effectiveness indicated by improvement in acne or psoriasis.*

USES Topical treatment of plaque psoriasis on up to 20% of the body, mild to moderate acne, facial fine wrinkling, mottled hypo- and hyperpigmentation (blotchy skin discoloration), and benign facial lentigines.

CONTRAINDICATIONS Hypersensitivity to tazarotene; pregnancy (category X), women who are or may become pregnant; lactation. **CAUTIOUS USE** Concurrent administration with drugs that are photosensitizers (e.g., thiazide diuretics, tetracyclines); retinoid hypersensitivity. Safety and efficacy in children <12 y are not established.

ROUTE & DOSAGE

Plaque Psoriasis
Adult: **Topical** Apply thin film to affected area once daily in evening

Acne
Adult: **Topical** After cleansing and drying face, apply thin film to acne lesions once daily in evening

Fine Wrinkles
Adult: **Topical** Apply thin film of cream to affected area once daily

ADMINISTRATION

Topical
- Dry skin completely before application of a thin film of medication.
- Apply medication to no more than 20% of body surface in those with psoriasis.
- Apply only to affected areas; avoid contact with eyes and mucous membranes.

ADVERSE EFFECTS (≥1%) Skin: *Pruritus, burning/stinging, erythema, worsening of psoriasis, irritation, skin pain,* rash, desquamation of skin, irritant contact dermatitis, inflammation, fissuring, bleeding, dry skin, sunburn.

INTERACTIONS Drug: Increased risk of photosensitivity reactions with QUINOLONES (especially **sparfloxacin**), PHENOTHIAZINES, SULFONAMIDES, SULFONYLUREAS, TETRACYCLINES, THIAZIDE DIURETICS.

PHARMACOKINETICS Absorption: Rapidly absorbed through skin. **Distribution:** Active metabolite >99% protein bound; crosses placenta, distributed into breast milk. **Metabolism:** Undergoes esterase hydrolysis to active metabolite AGN 190299. **Elimination:** In both urine and feces. **Half-Life:** 18 h.

CLINICAL IMPLICATIONS

Assessment & Drug Effects
- Monitor for photosensitivity in those concurrently using any of the following: thiazides, tetracyclines, fluoroquinolones, phenothiazines, sulfonamides.

Patient & Family Education
- Understand fully the risk of serious fetal harm. Use reliable forms of effective contraception. Discontinue treatment and notify physician if pregnancy occurs.
- Alert: Immediately rinse thoroughly with water if contact with eyes occurs.
- Avoid all unnecessary exposure to sunlight or artificial UV light. If brief exposure is necessary, cover as much skin surface as possible and use sunscreens (minimum SPF 15).
- Do not apply to sunburned skin.
- Discontinue medication and notify physician if any of the following occur: pruritus, burning, skin redness, excessive peeling, worsening of psoriasis.
- Limit application of topicals with strong skin-drying effects to skin areas being treated with tazarotene.

TEGASEROD MESYLATE

(teg-a-se′rod mes′y-late)
Zelnorm
Classifications: SEROTONIN 5-HT₄ RECEPTOR AGONIST
Therapeutic: GI MOTILITY AGENT; SEROTONIN 5-HT₄ RECEPTOR AGONIST
Pregnancy Category: B

Common adverse effects in *italic*, life-threatening effects <u>underlined</u>; generic names in **bold**; classifications in SMALL CAPS; ✤ Canadian drug name; ◑Prototype drug

1449

AVAILABILITY 2 mg, 6 mg tablets

ACTION & *THERAPEUTIC EFFECT*
A serotonin 5-HT$_4$ receptor agonist that triggers the peristaltic reflex by activating 5-HT$_4$ receptors, thereby normalizing impaired GI motility. *Significantly decreases gastric lag time, accelerates gastric emptying, reduces small bowel transit time, and accelerates colonic transit time; thus, it increases the number of bowel movements and facilitates stool formation.*

USES Short-term treatment of irritable bowel syndrome (IBS) in women whose primary symptom is constipation, chronic idiopathic constipation in males and females <65 y.
UNLABELED USES IBS in men; diabetic gastroparesis.

CONTRAINDICATIONS Hypersensitivity to tegaserod; severe hepatic or renal dysfunction; cirrhosis; renal failure; bowel obstruction; symptomatic gall bladder disease, abdominal pain, colitis, GI bleeding; renal failure; syncope; hypotension; patients who are currently or frequently experiencing diarrhea; lactation; children <18 y.
CAUTIOUS USE Mild to moderate hepatic and renal impairment; MI, cardiac disease; history of ovarian cysts; patients in whom increased diarrhea could have negative effects; pregnancy (category B).

ROUTE & DOSAGE

Irritable Bowel Syndrome
Adult: **PO** 6 mg b.i.d. before meals for 4–6 wk. May extend therapy an additional 4–6 wk if needed and responding.
Chronic Constipation
Adult: **PO** 2–6 mg b.i.d.

ADMINISTRATION
Oral
- Give drug just prior to a meal with a full glass of water.
- Determine duration of therapy prior to drug administration as manufacturer states maximum duration of therapy should be 12 wk.
- Do not initiate therapy with patients experiencing frequent diarrhea. Report to physician.
- Store at 15°–30° C (59°–86° F).

ADVERSE EFFECTS (≥1%) **Body as a Whole:** Leg pain. **CNS:** *Headache,* dizziness, migraine. **GI:** *Abdominal pain,* diarrhea, nausea, flatulence. **Musculoskeletal:** Back pain, arthropathy.

INTERACTIONS Food: Food significantly decreases the bioavailability of tegaserod.

PHARMACOKINETICS Absorption: Poorly absorbed, 10% bioavailability on an empty stomach. **Peak:** 1 h. **Distribution:** 99% protein bound to alpha-1 glycoprotein. **Metabolism:** Presystemic hydrolysis in stomach to an inactive metabolite. Glucuronidation in liver of remaining drug. **Elimination:** $2/3$ in feces, $1/3$ in urine. **Half-Life:** 11 h.

CLINICAL IMPLICATIONS
Assessment & Drug Effects
- Lab tests: Monitor baseline and periodic LFTs and renal functions.
- Monitor symptom relief. Report lack of symptom relief or frequent diarrhea.
- Monitor cardiovascular status especially with preexisting CV disease.

Patient & Family Education
- Report no relief of symptoms after 4 wk of therapy as manufacturer recommends discontinuation of therapy in this case.

T

■ Notify physician if you experience new or worsening abdominal pain unlike your typical IBS symptoms.

TELBIVUDINE

(tel-bi′vu-deen)

Tyzeka

Classifications: ANTIRETROVIRAL AGENT; NUCLEOSIDE REVERSE TRANSCRIPTASE INHIBITOR (NRTI)

Therapeutic: ANTIRETROVIRAL; NRTI

Prototype: Lamivudine

Pregnancy Category: B

AVAILABILITY 600 mg tablets

ACTION & *THERAPEUTIC EFFECT*

Telbivudine is a nucleoside analogue with activity against hepatitis B virus (HBV) DNA polymerase. Its metabolite inhibits HBV DNA polymerase (reverse transcriptase) by competing with the natural nucleoside substrate. Incorporation of the metabolite of telbivudine into HBV viral DNA causes DNA chain termination, resulting in inhibition of HBV replication. *Telbivudine inhibits HBV viral DNA replication, reducing the viral load and preventing infection of new hepatocytes.*

USES Treatment of chronic hepatitis B in patients with evidence of either histologically active disease or evidence of persistent elevations in serum aminotransferases (ALT or AST).

CONTRAINDICATIONS Hypersensitivity to telbivudine; lactation. Safe use in children <16 y not established. **CAUTIOUS USE** Moderate to severe renal impairment, hemodialysis; alcoholism; obesity in females; risk of hepatic disease; individuals with organ transplants; older adults; pregnancy (category B).

ROUTE & DOSAGE

Chronic Hepatitis B

Adults and Adolescents ≥16 y:
PO 600 mg/d

Renal Impairment

Cl_{cr} ≥50 mL/min: No dosage adjustment
Cl_{cr} = 30–49 mL/min: 600 mg q48h
Cl_{cr} <30 mL/min (not requiring dialysis): 600 mg q72h
Cl_{cr} <5–10 mL/min (ESRD): 600 mg q96h

ADMINISTRATION

Oral

■ May be given without regard to food.
■ Note dose adjustment for Cl_{cr} <50 mL/min.
■ Store at 15°–30° C (59°–86° F).

ADVERSE EFFECTS (≥1%) **Body as a Whole:** *Fatigue and malaise, headache, influenza-like syndrome, post-procedural pain,* pyrexia. **CNS:** Dizziness, insomnia. **GI:** *Abdominal pain, diarrhea and loose stools,* dyspepsia, *nausea, vomiting.* **Metabolic:** *Increased CPK levels,* lactic acidosis and severe hepatomegaly with steatosis. **Musculoskeletal:** Arthralgia, back pain, myalgia. **Respiratory:** *Cough, nasopharyngitis,* pharyngolaryngeal pain, *upper respiratory tract infection.* **Skin:** Rash.

INTERACTIONS Drug: Coadministration with drugs that alter renal function may alter plasma concentrations of telbivudine. Anti-HBV activity of telbivudine is additive with **adefovir** and is not antagonized by the HIV NRTIS **didanosine** and **stavudine.** Telbivudine is not antagonistic to anti-HIV activity of

Common adverse effects in *italic*, life-threatening effects underlined; generic names in **bold**; classifications in SMALL CAPS; ♣ Canadian drug name; ☻ Prototype drug

1451

abacavir, didanosine, emtricitabine, lamivudine, stavudine, tenofovir, or zidovudine.

PHARMACOKINETICS Peak: 1–4 h. **Distribution:** Minimal protein binding; widely distributed in tissues. **Elimination:** Primarily unchanged in urine. **Half-Life:** 40–49 h.

CLINICAL IMPLICATIONS

Assessment & Drug Effects

- Monitor for and report S&S of lactic acidosis (e.g., anorexia, nausea, vomiting, bloating, abdominal pain, malaise, tachycardia or other arrhythmia, and difficulty in breathing).
- Withhold drug and notify physician of any of the following: suspected lactic acidosis, steatosis, or markedly elevated liver enzymes.
- Lab tests: LFTs during and for several months after discontinuation of telbivudine; periodic serum bicarbonate.

Patient & Family Education

- Follow directions for taking the drug (see Administration).
- Avoid all alcohol consumption while taking this drug.
- Report any of the following to a health care provider: loss of appetite, nausea and vomiting, abdominal pain, palpitations, or difficulty breathing.

TELITHROMYCIN

(tel-i-thro-my′sin)
Ketek, Ketek Pak
Classifications: ANTIBIOTIC; KETOLIDE
Therapeutic: ANTIBIOTIC; KETOLIDE
Prototype: Erythromycin
Pregnancy Category: C

AVAILABILITY 400 mg tablets

ACTION & *THERAPEUTIC EFFECT*

Telithromycin binds to bacterial ribosomal RNA site of the 50S subunit; this action results in inhibition of RNA-dependent protein synthesis of bacteria, thus resulting in cell death. Telithromycin concentrates in phagocytes where it works against intracellular respiratory pathogens. *Its broad spectrum of activity is effective against respiratory pathogens, including erythromycin- and penicillin-resistant pneumococci.*

USES Treatment of mild to moderate community-acquired pneumonia due to susceptible bacteria.

CONTRAINDICATIONS Macrolide antibiotic hypersensitivity; QT prolongation; ongoing proarrhythmic conditions such as hypokalemia, hypomagnesemia, significant bradycardia, concurrent administration of Class IA or Class III antiarrhythmic drugs; myasthenia gravis, unless no other therapeutic option is available; severe renal impairment or renal failure; concurrent administration with terfenadine or pimozide; viral infections; pregnancy (category C). Safety and efficacy in children <18 y are not established.

CAUTIOUS USE History of GI disease; hepatic disease; history of hepatitis or jaundice; lactation.

ROUTE & DOSAGE

Community-Acquired Pneumonia
Adult: **PO** 800 mg once daily for 7–10 d

ADMINISTRATION

Oral

- Do not administer concurrently with simvastatin, lovastatin, atorvastatin, Class 1A (e.g., quinidine, procainamide) or Class III (e.g., dofetilide) antiarrhythmic agents. See drug interactions for other prohibited drug combinations.

- Store at 15°–30° C (59°–86° F). Keep container tightly closed. Protect from light.

ADVERSE EFFECTS (≥1%) CNS: Headache, dizziness. **CV:** Potential to cause QTc prolongation. **GI:** *Diarrhea,* nausea, vomiting, loose stools, dysgeusia. **Metabolic:** Elevated LFTs, liver failure. **Musculoskeletal:** May exacerbate myasthenia gravis. **Special Senses:** Blurred vision, diplopia, difficulty focusing.

INTERACTIONS Drug: Pimozide may cause life-threatening arrhythmias; may increase concentrations of **atorvastatin, lovastatin, simvastatin,** BENZODIAZEPINES; **rifampin** decreases telithromycin levels; ERGOT DERIVATIVES **(ergotamine, dihydroergotamine)** may cause severe peripheral vasospasm; **theophylline** may exacerbate adverse GI effects. **Food:** Grapefruit juice (>1 qt/d) may increase plasma concentrations and adverse effects.

PHARMACOKINETICS Absorption: 57% bioavailable. **Peak:** 1 h. **Metabolism:** 50% in liver (CYP3A4,) 50% by CYP-independent mechanisms. **Elimination:** In urine and feces. **Half-Life:** 10 h.

CLINICAL IMPLICATIONS

Assessment & Drug Effects

- Monitor ECG in patients at risk for QTc interval prolongation (i.e., bradycardia).
- Withhold drug and notify physician for S&S of QTc interval prolongation such as dizziness or fainting; liver dysfunction.

- Lab tests: baseline LFTs, BUN and creatinine, serum potassium.

Patient & Family Education

- Stop taking drug and notify physician for episodes of dizziness or fainting; jaundice (yellow color of the skin and/or eyes).
- Exercise caution when engaging in potentially hazardous activities; visual disturbances (e.g., blurred vision, difficulty focusing, double vision) are potential side effects of this drug. If visual problems occur, avoid quick changes in viewing between close and distant objects.

TELMISARTAN

(tel-mi-sar′tan)
Micardis
Classifications: ANTIHYPERTENSIVE; ANGIOTENSIN II RECEPTOR ANTAGONIST
Therapeutic: ANTIHYPERTENSIVE; ACE INHIBITOR
Prototype: Losartan potassium
Pregnancy Category: C first trimester; D second and third trimester

AVAILABILITY 40 mg, 80 mg tablets

ACTION & *THERAPEUTIC EFFECT*
Angiotensin II receptor (type AT_1) antagonist. Selectively blocks the binding of angiotensin II to the AT_1 receptors in many tissues (e.g., vascular smooth muscles, adrenal glands). Blocks the vasoconstricting and aldosterone-secreting effects of angiotensin II, thus resulting in an antihypertensive effect. *Effectiveness is indicated by a reduction in BP.*

USES Treatment of hypertension.

CONTRAINDICATIONS Hypersensitivity to telmisartan or other angio-

Common adverse effects in *italic*, life-threatening effects <u>underlined</u>; generic names in **bold**; classifications in SMALL CAPS; ♣ Canadian drug name; ☻ Prototype drug

1453

tensin receptor antagonists (e.g., losartan, eprosartan, etc.); pregnancy (category C first trimester; category D second and third trimester), lactation. **CAUTIOUS USE** Coronary artery disease (CAD); hypertropic cardiomyopathy; CHF; oliguria; hypotension; renal artery stenosis; older adult patients; biliary obstruction; liver dysfunction; renal impairment. Safety and efficacy in children <18 y are not established.

ROUTE & DOSAGE

Hypertension
Adult: **PO** 40 mg q.d., may increase to 80 mg/d

ADMINISTRATION

Oral
- Do not remove tablets from blister pack until immediately before administration.
- Correct volume depletion prior to initial dose.
- Store at 15°–30° C (59°–86° F).

ADVERSE EFFECTS (≥1%) **Body as a Whole:** Back pain, flu-like syndrome, myalgia, headache, fatigue. **CNS:** Dizziness. **CV:** Hypotension, hypertension, chest pain, peripheral edema. **GI:** Diarrhea, dyspepsia, abdominal pain, nausea. **Respiratory:** Sinusitis, pharyngitis.

INTERACTIONS Drug: Telmisartan may increase **digoxin** levels.

PHARMACOKINETICS Absorption: Absorption is dose dependent, 42% of 40 mg dose is absorbed. **Peak:** 0.5–1 h. **Distribution:** >99% protein bound. **Metabolism:** Minimally metabolized. **Elimination:** Primarily in feces as unchanged drug. **Half-Life:** 24 h.

CLINICAL IMPLICATIONS

Assessment & Drug Effects
- Monitor BP carefully after initial dose; and periodically thereafter. Monitor more frequently with preexisting biliary obstructive disorders or hepatic insufficiency.
- Monitor dialysis patients closely for orthostatic hypotension.
- Lab tests: Periodic Hgb, creatinine clearance, liver enzymes.
- Monitor concomitant digoxin levels throughout therapy.

Patient & Family Education
- Report pregnancy to physician immediately.
- Allow between 2–4 wk for maximum therapeutic response.

TEMAZEPAM

(te-maz′e-pam)
Restoril
Classifications: ANXIOLYTIC; SEDATIVE-HYPNOTIC; BENZODIAZEPINE
Therapeutic: ANTIANXIETY; SEDATIVE-HYPNOTIC
Prototype: Lorazepam
Pregnancy Category: X
Controlled Substance: Schedule IV

AVAILABILITY 7.5 mg, 15 mg, 30 mg capsules

ACTION & *THERAPEUTIC EFFECT* Benzodiazepine derivative with hypnotic, anxiolytic, sedative effects. Principal effect is significant improvement in sleep parameters. Minimal change in REM sleep. *Reduces night awakenings and early morning awakenings; increases total sleep times, absence of rebound effects.*

USES To relieve insomnia associated with frequent nocturnal awakenings or early morning awakenings.

CONTRAINDICATIONS Benzodiazepine hypersensitivity; ethanol intoxication; pregnancy (category X); safety in children <18 y is not established; narrow-angle glaucoma; psychoses; lactation. **CAUTIOUS USE** Severely depressed patient or one with suicidal ideation; history of drug abuse or dependence, acute intoxication; alcoholism; COPD; liver or kidney dysfunction; older adults; sleep apnea.

ROUTE & DOSAGE

Insomnia
Adult: **PO** 7.5–30 mg h.s.
Geriatric: **PO** 7.5 mg h.s.

ADMINISTRATION
Oral
▪ Give 20–30 min before patient retires.
▪ Store at 15°–30° C (59°–86° F) in tight container unless otherwise specified by manufacturer.

ADVERSE EFFECTS (≥1%) **CNS:** *Drowsiness,* dizziness, lethargy, confusion, headache, euphoria, relaxed feeling, weakness. **GI:** Anorexia, diarrhea. **CV:** Palpitations.

INTERACTIONS Drug: Alcohol, CNS DEPRESSANTS, ANTICONVULSANTS potentiate CNS depression; **cimetidine** increases temazepam plasma levels, thus increasing its toxicity; may decrease antiparkinsonism effects of **levodopa;** may increase **phenytoin** levels; smoking decreases sedative effects. **Herbal: Kava-kava, valerian** may potentiate sedation.

PHARMACOKINETICS Absorption: Readily from GI tract. **Onset:** 30–50 min. **Peak:** 2–3 h. **Duration:** 10–12 h. **Distribution:** Crosses placenta; distributed into breast milk. **Metabolism:** In liver to oxazepam. **Elimination:** In urine. **Half-Life:** 8–24 h.

CLINICAL IMPLICATIONS
Assessment & Drug Effects
▪ Be alert to signs of paradoxical reaction (excitement, hyperactivity, and disorientation) in older adults. Psychoactive drugs are the most frequent cause of acute confusion in this age group.
▪ CNS adverse effects are more apt to occur in the patient with hypoalbuminemia, liver disease, and in older adults. Report promptly incidence of bradycardia, drowsiness, dizziness, clumsiness, lack of coordination. Supervise ambulation, especially at night.
▪ Lab tests: Obtain liver and kidney function tests during long-term use.
▪ Be alert to S&S of overdose: Weakness, bradycardia, somnolence, confusion, slurred speech, ataxia, coma with reduced or absent reflexes, hypertension, and respiratory depression.

Patient & Family Education
▪ Be aware that improvement in sleep will not occur until after 2–3 doses of drug.
▪ Notify physician if dreams or nightmares interfere with rest. An alternate drug or reduced dose may be prescribed.
▪ Be aware that difficulty getting to sleep may continue. Drug effect is evidenced by the increased amount of rest once asleep.
▪ Consult physician if insomnia continues in spite of medication.
▪ Do not smoke after medication is taken.
▪ Do not use OTC drugs (especially for insomnia) without advice of physician.
▪ Consult physician before discontinuing drug especially after long-term use. Gradual reduction of dose may be necessary to avoid withdrawal symptoms.

T

Common adverse effects in *italic*, life-threatening effects underlined; generic names in **bold**; classifications in SMALL CAPS; ✚ Canadian drug name; ⦿ Prototype drug

- Avoid use of alcohol and other CNS depressants.
- Do not drive or engage in other potentially hazardous activities until response to drug is known. This drug may depress psychomotor skills and cause sedation.

TEMOZOLOMIDE

(tem-o-zol'o-mide)
Temodar
Classifications: ANTINEOPLASTIC; ALKYLATING AGENT
Therapeutic: ANTINEOPLASTIC
Prototype: Cyclophosphamide
Pregnancy Category: D

AVAILABILITY 5 mg, 20 mg, 100 mg, 140 mg, 180 mg, 250 mg capsules

ACTION & *THERAPEUTIC EFFECT* Cytotoxic agent with alkylating properties structurally similar to dacarbazine. Effects are cell cycle nonspecific. Interferes with purine (e.g., guanine) metabolism and thus protein synthesis in rapidly proliferating cells. *Effectiveness is indicated by objective evidence of tumor regression.*

USES Adult patients with refractory anaplastic astrocytoma, glioblastoma multiforme with radiotherapy.

CONTRAINDICATIONS Hypersensitivity to temozolomide, DTIC, or dacarbazine; severe bone marrow suppression; children <3 y; pregnancy (category D), lactation.
CAUTIOUS USE Bacterial or viral infection; older adults; severe hepatic or renal impairment; myelosuppression; prior radiotherapy or chemotherapy.

ROUTE & DOSAGE

Astrocytoma
Adult: **PO** 150 mg/m^2 daily for 5 consecutive days per 28 d treatment cycle; subsequent doses are based on absolute neutrophil count on day 21 or at least 48 h before next scheduled cycle (see prescribing information for dosage adjustments based on neutrophil count)

Glioblastoma Multiforme
Adult: **PO** 75 mg/m^2 daily for 42 d with focal radiotherapy; after 4 wk, maintenance phase of 150 mg/m^2

ADMINISTRATION

Oral
- Give consistently with regard to food.
- Do not administer unless absolute neutrophil count >1500 per microliter and platelet count >100,000 per microliter.
- Do not open capsules. Avoid inhalation or contact with skin or mucous membranes, if accidentally opened/damaged.
- Store at room temperature, 15°–30° C (59°–86° F).

ADVERSE EFFECTS (≥1%) **Body as a Whole:** *Headache, fatigue, asthenia, fever,* back pain, myalgia, weight gain; viral infection. **CNS:** *Convulsions, hemiparesis, dizziness, abnormal coordination, amnesia, insomnia,* paresthesia, somnolence, paresis, ataxia, dysphasia, abnormal gait, confusion, anxiety, depression. **CV:** *Peripheral edema.* **GI:** *Nausea, vomiting, constipation, diarrhea,* abdominal pain, anorexia. **Hematologic:** Anemia, *neutropenia, thrombocytopenia,* leukopenia, lymphopenia. **Respiratory:** Upper respiratory tract infection, pharyngitis, sinusitis, cough. **Skin:** Rash, pruritus. **Meta-**

Common adverse effects in *italic*, life-threatening effects underlined; generic names in **bold**; classifications in SMALL CAPS; ♣ Canadian drug name; ⓟ Prototype drug

bolic: Adrenal hypercorticism. **Urogenital:** Urinary incontinence. **Special Senses:** Diplopia, abnormal vision.

INTERACTIONS Drug: Valproic acid may decrease **temozolomide** levels.

PHARMACOKINETICS Absorption: Rapidly. **Peak:** 1 h. **Metabolism:** Spontaneously metabolized to active metabolite MTIC. **Elimination:** Primarily in urine. **Half-Life:** 1.8 h.

CLINICAL IMPLICATIONS

Assessment & Drug Effects
- Monitor for S&S of toxicity: Infection, bleeding episodes, jaundice, rash, CNS disturbances.
- Lab tests: CBC with differential on day 22 and weekly until absolute neutrophil count (ANC) >1500 per microliter and platelet count >100,000 per microliter; periodic liver function tests & routine serum chemistry, including serum calcium.

Patient & Family Education
- Take consistently with respect to meals.
- Report to physician signs of infection, bleeding, discoloration of skin or skin rash, dizziness, lack of balance, or other bothersome side effects promptly.
- Exercise caution with hazardous activities until response to drug is known.
- Use effective methods of contraception; avoid pregnancy.

TENECTEPLASE RECOMBINANT

(ten-ect′e-plase)

TNKase

Classifications: ANTICOAGULANT; THROMBOLYTIC ENZYME

Therapeutic: THROMBOLYTIC ENZYME

Prototype: Alteplase
Pregnancy Category: C

AVAILABILITY 50 mg vial

ACTION & *THERAPEUTIC EFFECT*
Tenecteplase (TNK-tPA) is a third generation thrombolytic agent with advantages over alteplase: Longer half-life, more rapid thrombolysis, greater fibrin specificity. Additionally, rate of noncerebral bleeding is less than in alteplase. *Effective in producing thrombolysis of a clot involved in a myocardial infarction.*

USES Reduction of mortality associated with acute myocardial infarction (AMI).

CONTRAINDICATIONS Active internal bleeding; history of CVA; intracranial or intraspinal surgery with 2 mo; intracranial neoplasm; arteriovenous malformation, or aneurysm; known bleeding diathesis; brain tumor; increased intracranial pressure; coagulopathy; head trauma; stroke; surgery; severe uncontrolled hypertension; pregnancy (category C), lactation.

CAUTIOUS USE Recent major surgery, previous puncture of compressible vessels, CVA, recent GI or GU bleeding, recent trauma; hypertension, mitral valve stenosis, acute pericarditis, bacterial endocarditis; severe liver or kidney disease; hemorrhagic ophthalmic conditions; septic thrombophlebitis or occluded, infected AV cannula; advanced age; concurrent administration of oral anticoagulants, recent administration of GP IIb/IIIa inhibitors, condition involving bleeding. Safety and efficacy in children are not established.

T

Common adverse effects in *italic*, life-threatening effects underlined; generic names in **bold**; classifications in SMALL CAPS; ♦ Canadian drug name; ⊙ Prototype drug

1457

ROUTE & DOSAGE

Acute Myocardial Infarction
Adult: **IV** Infuse dose over 5 sec, <60 kg, 30 mg; 60–70 kg, 35 mg; 70–80 kg, 40 mg; 80–90 kg, 45 mg; >90 kg, 50 mg

ADMINISTRATION

Intravenous

PREPARE: Direct: Read and follow instructions supplied with Twin-Pak™ Dual Cannula Device. Withdraw 10 mL of sterile water for injection from the supplied vial; inject entire contents into the TNKase vial directing the diluent stream into the powder. Gently swirl until dissolved but do not shake. The resulting solution contains 5 mg/mL. Withdraw the appropriate dose and discard any unused solution. Follow directions supplied with TwinPak™ for proper handling of syringe.

ADMINISTER: Direct: Dextrose-containing IV line must be flushed before and after bolus with NS. Give as a single bolus dose over 5 sec. The total dose given should not exceed 50 mg.

INCOMPATIBILITIES Solution/additive: Dextrose solutions.

- Store unopened TwinPak™ at ≤30° C (86° F) or under refrigeration at 2°–8° C (36°–46° F).

ADVERSE EFFECTS (≥1%) **Hematologic:** <u>Major bleeding</u>, *hematoma*, GI bleed, bleeding at puncture site, hematuria, pharyngeal, epistaxis.

DIAGNOSTIC TEST INTERFERENCE Unreliable results for *coagulation test I* and measures of *fibrinolytic activity*.

PHARMACOKINETICS Metabolism: In liver. **Half-Life:** 90–130 min.

CLINICAL IMPLICATIONS

Assessment & Drug Effects
- Avoid IM injections and unnecessary handling or invasive procedures for the first few hours after treatment.
- Monitor for S&S of bleeding. Should bleeding occur, discontinue concomitant heparin and antiplatelet therapy; notify physician.
- Monitor cardiovascular and neurologic status closely. Persons at increased risk for life-threatening cardiac events include those with: A high potential for bleeding, recent surgery, severe hypertension, mitral stenosis and atrial fibrillation, anticoagulant therapy, and advanced age.
- Lab tests: Baseline and 1 h after administration of drug determine cardiac enzymes, circulating myoglobin, cardiac troponin-1, creatine kinase-MB; Hgb & Hct post-infusion.
- Coagulation parameters may not predict bleeding episodes.

Patient & Family Education
- Notify physician of the following immediately: A sudden, severe headache; any sign of bleeding; signs or symptoms of hypersensitivity (see Appendix F).
- Stay as still as possible and do not attempt to get out of bed until directed to do so.

TENOFOVIR DISOPROXIL FUMARATE
(ten-o-fo'vir di-so-prox'il fum'a-rate)
Viread
Classifications: ANTIRETROVIRAL AGENT; NUCLEOSIDE REVERSE TRANSCRIPTASE INHIBITOR (NRTI)
Therapeutic: ANTIRETROVIRAL; NRTI
Prototype: Zidovudine
Pregnancy Category: B

Common adverse effects in *italic*, life-threatening effects <u>underlined</u>; generic names in **bold**; classifications in SMALL CAPS; ♦ Canadian drug name; ☺ Prototype drug

AVAILABILITY 300 mg tablets

ACTION & *THERAPEUTIC EFFECT*
Tenofovir is a potent inhibitor of retroviruses, including HIV-1. It may be active against nucleoside-resistant HIV strains. The active form of tenofovir persists in HIV-infected cells for prolonged periods, thus, it results in sustained inhibition of HIV replication. *It reduces the viral load (plasma HIV-RNA), and CD4 counts.*

USES In combination with other antiretrovirals for the treatment of HIV.

CONTRAINDICATIONS Hypersensitivity to tenofovir; hepatitis; lactic acidosis; concurrent administration of nephrotoxic agents, renal failure; lactation.
CAUTIOUS USE Hepatic dysfunction, alcoholism; renal impairment; obesity; children, pregnancy (category B).

ROUTE & DOSAGE

HIV Infection
Adult: **PO** 300 mg once daily with meal
Renal Impairment
Cl$_{cr}$ 30–49 mL/min: dose q48h, 10–29 mL/min dose twice weekly
Hemodialysis: Dose weekly or after 12 h of dialysis

ADMINISTRATION
Oral
- Give at the same time each day with a meal.
- Give 2 h before or 1 h after didanosine (if ordered concurrently).
- Store at room temperature; excursions to 15°–30° C (59°–80° F) are permitted.

ADVERSE EFFECTS (≥1%) **Body as a Whole:** Asthenia. **CNS:** Headache. **GI:** *Nausea,* vomiting, diarrhea, flatulence, abdominal pain, anorexia. **Hematologic:** Neutropenia. **Metabolic:** Increased *creatine kinase,* AST, ALT, serum amylase, triglycerides, serum glucose.

INTERACTIONS Drug: May increase **didanosine** toxicity; **acyclovir, amphotericin B, cidofovir, foscarnet, ganciclovir, probenecid, valacyclovir, valganciclovir** may increase tenofovir toxicity by decreasing its renal elimination. **Food:** Food increases absorption.

PHARMACOKINETICS Absorption: Bioavailability 25% fasting, 40% with high fat meal. **Peak:** 1 h. **Distribution:** <7% protein bound. **Metabolism:** Not metabolized by CYP450 enzyme system. **Elimination:** Renally eliminated. **Half-Life:** 11–14 h.

CLINICAL IMPLICATIONS
Assessment & Drug Effects
- Lab tests: Monitor baseline and periodic renal function and LFTs; monitor periodically serum electrolytes, and ABGs if lactic acidosis is suspected.
- Monitor for S&S of bone abnormalities (e.g., bone pain, stress fractures).
- Monitor closely patients receiving other nephrotoxic agents for changes in serum creatinine and phosphorus. Withhold drug and notify physician for creatinine clearance <60 mL/min.
- Withhold drug and notify physician if patient develops clinical or lab findings suggestive of lactic acidosis or pronounced hepatotoxicity (e.g., hepatomegaly and steatosis even in the absence of marked transaminase elevations).

Patient & Family Education
- Take this drug exactly as prescribed. Do not miss any doses. If

T

Common adverse effects in *italic*, life-threatening effects underlined; generic names in **bold**; classifications in SMALL CAPS; ✦ Canadian drug name; ❿ Prototype drug

1459

you miss a dose, take it as soon as possible and then take your next dose at its regular time. If it is almost time for your next dose, do not take the missed dose. Wait and take the next dose at the regular time. Do not double the next dose.

▪ Report any of the following to physician: unexplained anorexia, nausea, vomiting, abdominal pain, fatigue, dark urine.

TERAZOSIN

(ter-ay'zoe-sin)
Hytrin
Classifications: ALPHA-ADRENERGIC ANTAGONIST; ANTIHYPERTENSIVE
Therapeutic: ANTIHYPERTENSIVE; VASODILATOR
Prototype: Prazosin
Pregnancy Category: C

AVAILABILITY 1 mg, 2 mg, 5 mg, 10 mg capsules

ACTION & *THERAPEUTIC EFFECT*
Quinazoline antihypertensive and vasodilator. Selectively blocks alpha$_1$-adrenergic receptors in vascular smooth muscle, producing relaxation that leads to reduction of peripheral vascular resistance and lowered BP. Vasodilation is accompanied by minimal reflex increase in heart rate. *Effectiveness is measured in lowering of blood pressure values and controlling the symptoms of benign prostate hypertrophy.*

USES To treat hypertension alone or in combination with other antihypertensive agents (beta-adrenergic blocking agents, diuretics). To treat benign prostatic hypertrophy (BPH) and urinary flow obstruction.

CONTRAINDICATIONS Hypersensitivity to terazosin; pregnancy (category C). Safe use in children is not established.

CAUTIOUS USE Patients with BPH; prostate cancer; history of hypotensive episodes; angina; renal impairment, renal disease, renal failure; elderly; lactation.

ROUTE & DOSAGE

Hypertension, Benign Prostatic Hypertrophy
Adult: **PO** Start with 1 mg h.s., then 1–5 mg/d (max: 20 mg/d)

ADMINISTRATION

Oral
▪ Give initial dose at bedtime to reduce the potential for severe hypotensive effect, which may occur with first few doses. After the initial dose, give any time of day.

▪ Store at 15°–30° C (59°–86° F) in tightly closed container away from heat and strong light. Do not freeze.

ADVERSE EFFECTS (≥1%) **CNS:** *Asthenia (weakness), dizziness, headache,* drowsiness, weakness. **CV:** Postural hypotension, palpitation, *first-dose phenomenon (syncope).* **Special Senses:** Blurred vision. **GI:** Nausea. **Body as a Whole:** Weight gain, pain in extremities, peripheral edema. **Respiratory:** Nasal congestion, sinusitis, dyspnea. **Urogenital:** Impotence.

INTERACTIONS Drug: Antihypertensive effects may be attenuated by NSAIDS. **Sildenafil, vardenafil,** and **tadalafil** may enhance hypotensive effects.

PHARMACOKINETICS Absorption: Readily from GI tract. **Peak:** 1–2 h. **Metabolism:** In liver. **Elimination:** 60% in feces, 40% in urine. **Half-Life:** 9–12 h.

CLINICAL IMPLICATIONS

Assessment & Drug Effects

- Be alert for possible first-dose phenomenon (precipitous decline in BP with consciousness disturbance). This is rare; occurs within 90–120 min of initial dose.
- Monitor BP at end of dosing interval (just before next dose) to determine level of antihypertensive control. Check BP also 2–3 h after the dose to determine if maximum and minimal responses are similar.
- Be aware that drug-induced decrease in BP appears to be more position dependent (i.e., greater in the erect position) during the first few hours after dosing than at end of 24 h.
- A greatly diminished hypotensive response at end of 24 h indicates need for change in dosage (increased dose or twice daily regimen). Report to physician.

Patient & Family Education

- Avoid situations that would result in injury should syncope (loss of consciousness) occur after first dose. If faintness develops, lie down promptly.
- Make position changes slowly (i.e., change in direction or from recumbent to upright posture). Dangle legs and move ankles a minute or so before standing when arising. Orthostatic hypotension (greatest shortly after dosing) can pose a problem with ambulation.
- Do not drive or engage in potentially hazardous activities for at least 12 h after first dose, after dosage increase, or when treatment is resumed after interruption of therapy. Twelve hours should be sufficient time for serious adverse effects (syncope, orthostatic hypotension, light-headedness, dizziness) to appear if they are going to do so.

- Monitor weight: Report sudden gain of more than 0.5–1 kg (1–2 lb) accompanied by edema in extremities to physician. Dose adjustment may be indicated.
- Do not alter established drug regimen. Consult physician if drug is omitted for several days. Drug will be started with the initial dosing regimen.
- Keep scheduled appointments for assessment of BP control and other clinically significant tests.
- Keep a daily record noting BP and time taken, which arm was used, position (i.e., standing, sitting), and time when medication was taken. Take this record to physician for reference at checkup appointment.
- Do not take OTC medications, particularly those that may contain an adrenergic agent (e.g., remedies for coughs, colds, allergy) without first consulting physician.

TERBINAFINE HYDROCHLORIDE ℗

(ter-bin'a-feen)

Lamisil, Lamisil DermaGel

Classifications: ANTIBIOTIC; ALLYLAMINE ANTIFUNGAL

Therapeutic: ANTIBIOTIC; ANTIFUNGAL

Pregnancy Category: B

AVAILABILITY 250 mg tablets; 1% cream; 1.12% gel

ACTION & *THERAPEUTIC EFFECT*

Synthetic antifungal agent that inhibits sterol biosynthesis in fungi and ultimately causes fungal cell death. *Effective as a topical antifungal treatment as well as in oral form.*

USES Topical treatment of superficial mycoses such as interdigital tinea pedis, tinea cruris, and tinea

Common adverse effects in *italic*, life-threatening effects underlined; generic names in **bold**; classifications in SMALL CAPS; ✤ Canadian drug name; ℗ Prototype drug

1461

corporis due to *Epidermophyton floccosum, Trichophyton mentagrophytes,* or *T. rubrum;* oral treatment of onychomycosis due to tinea unguium.

CONTRAINDICATIONS Hypersensitivity to terbinafine; alcoholism; hepatic disease; hepatitis; jaundice; renal impairment; renal failure; lactation.

CAUTIOUS USE Pregnancy (category B). Safety and efficacy in children <12 y are not established.

ROUTE & DOSAGE

Tinea Pedis, Tinea Cruris, or Tinea Corporis
Adult: **Topical** Apply q.d. or b.i.d. to affected and immediately surrounding areas until clinical signs and symptoms are significantly improved (1–7 wk)

Onychomycosis
Adult: **PO** 250 mg q.d. times 6 wk for fingernails or times 12 wk for toenails

ADMINISTRATION

Topical
- Apply externally. Avoid application to mucous membranes and avoid contact with eyes.
- Do not use occlusive dressings unless specifically directed to do so by physician.
- Store at 15°–30° C (59°–86° F).

ADVERSE EFFECTS (≥1%) **Skin:** Pruritus, local burning, dryness, rash, vesiculation, redness, contact dermatitis at application site. **CNS:** *Headache.* **GI:** Diarrhea, dyspepsia, abdominal pain, liver test abnormalities, liver failure (rare). **Hematologic:** Neutropenia (rare). **Special Senses:** Taste disturbances.

INTERACTIONS Drug: May increase **theophylline** levels; may decrease **cyclosporine** levels; **rifampin** may decrease **terbinafine** levels.

PHARMACOKINETICS Absorption: 70% PO; approximately 3.5% of topical dose is absorbed systemically. **Elimination:** In urine. **Half-Life:** 36 h.

CLINICAL IMPLICATIONS
Assessment & Drug Effects
- Monitor for and report increased skin irritation.

Patient & Family Education
- Learn correct technique for application of cream.
- Notify physician if drug causes increased skin irritation or sensitivity.
- Be aware that medication must be used for full treatment time to be effective.

TERBUTALINE SULFATE
(ter-byoo'te-leen)
Brethaire, Brethine, Bricanyl
Classifications: BRONCHODILATOR; BETA-ADRENERGIC AGONIST
Therapeutic: BRONCHODILATOR; RESPIRATORY SMOOTH MUSCLE RELAXANT; BETA-ADRENERGIC AGONIST
Prototype: Albuterol
Pregnancy Category: B

AVAILABILITY 2.5 mg, 5 mg tablets; 0.2 mg aerosol; 1 mg/mL injection

ACTION & *THERAPEUTIC EFFECT*
Synthetic adrenergic stimulant with selective beta$_2$- and negligible beta$_1$-agonist (cardiac) activity. Exerts preferential effect on beta$_2$ receptors in bronchial smooth muscles, inhibits histamine release from mast cells, and increases ciliary motility. *Relieves bronchospasm in chronic obstructive pulmonary disease (COPD) and significantly in-*

creases vital capacity. Promotes relaxation of vascular smooth muscle, contraction of GI and urinary sphincters, increase in renin, pancreatic beta-cell secretion, and serum HDL-cholesterol concentration. Increases uterine relaxation (thereby preventing or abolishing high intrauterine pressure).

USES Orally or subcutaneously as a bronchodilator in bronchial asthma and for reversible airway obstruction associated with bronchitis and emphysema.

UNLABELED USES To delay delivery in preterm labor.

CONTRAINDICATIONS Known hypersensitivity to sympathomimetic amines; severe hypertension and coronary artery disease; tachycardia with digitalis intoxication; within 14 d of MAO inhibitor therapy; angle-closure glaucoma.

CAUTIOUS USE Angina, stroke, hypertension; diabetes mellitus; thyrotoxicosis; history of seizure disorders; MAOI therapy; cardiac arrhythmias; QT prolongation; thyroid disease; older adults; kidney and liver dysfunction; pregnancy (category B). Use further caution in second and third trimester (may inhibit uterine contractions and labor).

ROUTE & DOSAGE

Bronchodilator

Adult: **PO** 2.5–5 mg t.i.d. at 6 h intervals (max: 15 mg/d) **SC** 0.25 mg q15–30min up to 0.5 mg in 4 h **Inhaled** 2 inhalations separated by 60 sec q4–6h
Adolescent: **PO** 12–15 y, 2.5 mg t.i.d. at 6 h intervals (max: 7.5 mg/d) **SC** 0.25 mg q15–30min up to 0.5 mg in 4 h **Inhaled** 2 inhalations separated by 60 sec q4–6h

Child: **PO** <12 y, 0.05 mg/kg q8h, gradually increase up to 0.15 mg/kg q8h (max: 5 mg/d) **SC** 0.005–0.01 mg/kg (max: 0.4 mg) q15–20min times 2 doses

Premature Labor

Adult: **PO** 2.5 mg q4–6h

ADMINISTRATION

Oral

- Give with fluid of patient's choice; tablets may be crushed.
- Be certain about recommended doses: PO preparation, 2.5 mg; SC, 0.25 mg. A decimal point error can be fatal.
- Give with food if GI symptoms occur.

Subcutaneous

- Give SC injection into lateral deltoid area.
- Store all forms at 15°–30° C (59°–86° F); protect from light. Do not freeze.

ADVERSE EFFECTS (≥1%) **CNS:** *Nervousness, tremor,* headache, *lightheadedness,* drowsiness, fatigue, seizures. **CV:** *Tachycardia,* hypotension or hypertension, *palpitation,* maternal and fetal tachycardia. **GI:** Nausea, vomiting. **Body as a Whole:** Sweating, muscle cramps.

DIAGNOSTIC TEST INTERFERENCE Terbutaline may increase **blood glucose** and free **fatty acids.**

INTERACTIONS Drug: Epinephrine, other SYMPATHOMIMETIC BRONCHODILATORS may add to effects; MAO INHIBITORS, TRICYCLIC ANTIDEPRESSANTS potentiate action on vascular system; effects of both BETA-ADRENERGIC BLOCKERS and terbutaline antagonized.

PHARMACOKINETICS Absorption: 33–50% from GI tract. **Onset:** 30 min

T

Common adverse effects in *italic*, life-threatening effects <u>underlined</u>; generic names in **bold**; classifications in SMALL CAPS; ✚ Canadian drug name; ⊘ Prototype drug

1463

PO; <15 min SC; 5–30 min inhaled. **Peak:** 2–3 h PO; 30–60 min SC; 1–2 h inhaled. **Duration:** 4–8 h PO; 1.5–4 h SC; 3–4 h inhaled. **Distribution:** Into breast milk. **Metabolism:** In liver. **Elimination:** Primarily in urine, 3% in feces. **Half-Life:** 3–4 h.

CLINICAL IMPLICATIONS

Assessment & Drug Effects

- Assess vital signs: Baseline pulse and BP and before each dose. If significantly altered from baseline level, consult physician. Cardiovascular adverse effects are more apt to occur when drug is given by SC route or it is used by a patient with cardiac arrhythmia.
- Most adverse effects are transient, however, rapid heart rate may persist for a relatively long time.
- Be aware that onset and degree of effect and incidence and severity of adverse effects of SC formulation resemble those of epinephrine.
- Aerosolized drug produces minimal cardiac stimulation or tremors.
- Be aware that muscle tremor is a fairly common adverse effect that appears to subside with continued use.
- Monitor for symptoms of hypoglycemia in neonates born of a mother who used terbutaline during pregnancy.
- Monitor patient being treated for premature labor for CV S&S for 12 h after drug is discontinued. Report tachycardia promptly.
- Monitor I&O ratio. Fluid restriction may be necessary. Consult physician.

Patient & Family Education

- Adhere to established dosage regimen (i.e., do not change dose intervals or omit, increase, or decrease the dose).
- Inhalator therapy: Review instructions for use of inhalator (included in the package).
- Learn how to take your own pulse and the limits of change that indicate need to notify the physician.
- Consult physician if breathing difficulty is not relieved or if it becomes worse within 30 min after an oral dose.
- Keep appointments with physician for evaluation of continued drug effectiveness and clinical condition. Terbutaline appears to have a short clinical period for sustained effectiveness.
- Consult physician if symptomatic relief wanes; tolerance can develop with chronic use. Usually, a substitute agent will be prescribed.
- Do not self-dose this drug, particularly during long-term therapy. In the face of waning response, increasing the dose will not improve the clinical condition and may cause overdosage. Understand that decreasing relief with continued treatment indicates need for another bronchodilator, not an increase in dose.
- Do not puncture container, use or store it near heat or open flame, or expose to temperatures above 49° C (120° F), which may cause bursting. Contents of the aerosol (inhalator) are under pressure.
- Do not use any other aerosol bronchodilator while being treated with aerosol terbutaline. Do not self-medicate with an OTC aerosol.
- Do not use OTC drugs without physician approval. Many cold and allergy remedies, for example, contain a sympathomimetic agent that when combined with terbutaline may cause harmful adverse effects.

T

Common adverse effects in *italic*, life-threatening effects <u>underlined</u>; generic names in **bold**; classifications in SMALL CAPS; ✦ Canadian drug name; ⊘ Prototype drug

TERCONAZOLE

(ter-con'a-zole)
Terazol₇, Terazol₃
Classifications: AZOLE ANTIFUNGAL
Therapeutic: ANTIFUNGAL
Prototype: Fluconazole
Pregnancy Category: C

AVAILABILITY 0.4%, 0.8% vaginal cream; 80 mg vaginal suppositories

ACTION & *THERAPEUTIC EFFECT*
Terconazole is thought to exert antifungal activity by disruption of normal fungal cell membrane permeability. *Exhibits fungicidal activity against* Candida albicans.

USES Local treatment of vulvovaginal candidiasis.

CONTRAINDICATIONS Hypersensitivity to terconazole or azole antifungals; use of tampons; lactation.
CAUTIOUS USE Pregnancy (category C). Safety and efficacy in children <18 y are not established.

ROUTE & DOSAGE

Candidiasis

Adult: **Intravaginal** One suppository (2.5 g) q.h.s. times 3 d; one applicator full of 0.4% cream q.h.s. times 7 d; one applicator full of 0.8% cream q.h.s. times 3 d

ADMINISTRATION

Intravaginal
- Insert applicator high into the vagina (except during pregnancy).
- Wash applicator before and after each use.
- Store away from direct heat and light.

ADVERSE EFFECTS (≥1%) **CNS:** *Headache.* **Urogenital:** Vaginal itching, burning, irritation. **Body as a Whole:** Rash, flu-like syndrome (fever, chills, headache, hypotension).

INTERACTIONS Drug: May inactivate **nonoxynol-9** spermicides.

PHARMACOKINETICS Absorption: Slow minimal absorption from vagina. **Onset:** Within 3 d. **Metabolism:** In liver. **Elimination:** Half in urine, half in feces. **Half-Life:** 4–11 h.

CLINICAL IMPLICATIONS

Assessment & Drug Effects
- Do not use if patient has a history of allergic reaction to other antifungal agents, such as miconazole.
- Monitor for sensitization and irritation; these may indicate need to discontinue drug.

Patient & Family Education
- Use correct application technique.
- Do not use tampons concurrently with terconazole.
- Learn potential adverse reactions, including sensitization and allergic response.
- Be aware that terconazole may interact with diaphragms and latex condoms; avoid concurrent use within 72 h.
- Refrain from sexual intercourse while using terconazole.
- Wear only cotton underwear; change daily.

TERIPARATIDE

(ter-i-par'a-tide)
Forteo
Classifications: HORMONE; PARATHYROID HORMONE AGONIST
Therapeutic: PARATHYROID HORMONE AGONIST
Pregnancy Category: C

AVAILABILITY 750 mcg/3 mL injection

Common adverse effects in *italic*, life-threatening effects underlined; generic names in **bold**; classifications in SMALL CAPS; ♣ Canadian drug name; ⊙ Prototype drug

ACTION & *THERAPEUTIC EFFECT*

Parathyroid hormone (PTH) is the primary regulator of calcium and phosphate metabolism in bone and kidney. Actions of PTH include regulation of bone metabolism, renal reabsorption of calcium and phosphate, and intestinal calcium absorption. Biological actions of PTH and teriparatide are similar in bone and the kidneys. *Stimulates new bone formation by preferential stimulation of osteoblastic activity over osteoclastic activity; improves bone microarchitecture, and increases bone mass and strength by stimulating new bone formation.*

USES Treatment of osteoporosis in postmenopausal women at high risk for fracture; increase bone mass in men with primary or hypogonadal osteoporosis who are at high risk for fracture.

CONTRAINDICATIONS Hypersensitivity to teriparatide; osteosarcoma; Paget's disease; unexplained elevations of alkaline phosphatase; bone metastases or a history of skeletal malignancies; metabolic bone diseases other than osteoporosis; preexisting hypercalcemia; prior history of radiation therapy involving the skeleton; pediatric patients or young adults with open epiphyses; children 18 y and younger; lactation; pregnancy (category C).

CAUTIOUS USE Active or recent urolithiasis, hypercalciuria; hypotension; concurrent use of digitalis; hepatic, renal, and cardiac disease.

ROUTE & DOSAGE

Osteoporosis
Adult: **SC** 20 mcg q.d.

ADMINISTRATION

Subcutaneous

- Do not administer to anyone with hypercalcemia. Consult physician.
- Rotate SC injection sites.

ADVERSE EFFECTS (≥1%) **Body as a Whole:** *Pain,* asthenia, neck pain. **CNS:** Headache, dizziness, depression, insomnia, vertigo. **CV:** Hypertension, angina, syncope. **GI:** Nausea, constipation, dyspepsia, vomiting. **Metabolic:** *Transient increase in calcium levels,* increase in serum uric acid, antibodies to teriparatide after 12 mo therapy. **Musculoskeletal:** *Arthralgia,* leg cramps. **Respiratory:** Rhinitis, cough, pharyngitis, dyspnea, pneumonia. **Skin:** Rash, sweating.

INTERACTIONS Drug: May increase risk of **digoxin** toxicity.

PHARMACOKINETICS Absorption: Extensively absorbed from SC site. **Onset:** 2 h for calcium concentration increase. **Peak:** Max. calcium concentrations 4–6 h. **Duration:** 16–24 h. **Metabolism:** Parathyroid hormone is metabolized non-specific enzymes. **Elimination:** Primarily in urine. **Half-Life:** 1 h SC.

CLINICAL IMPLICATIONS

Assessment & Drug Effects

- Monitor cardiovascular status including BP and subjective reports of angina.
- Lab tests: Monitor periodically serum calcium, alkaline phosphatase, uric acid and bone density levels.
- Concurrent drugs: Monitor closely for digoxin toxicity with concurrent use.

Patient & Family Education

- Report unexplained leg cramps and bone pain.
- Learn correct technique for SC injection.

Common adverse effects in *italic*, life-threatening effects <u>underlined</u>; generic names in **bold**; classifications in SMALL CAPS; ✦ Canadian drug name; Ⓟ Prototype drug

TESTOLACTONE

(tess-toe-lak'tone)
Teslac
Classifications: ANTINEOPLASTIC;
HORMONE; ANABOLIC STEROID
Therapeutic: ANTINEOPLASTIC; ANA-
BOLIC STEROID
Pregnancy Category: C
Controlled Substance: Schedule III

AVAILABILITY 50 mg tablets

ACTION & *THERAPEUTIC EFFECT*
Chemotherapeutic agent with
chemical configuration similar to
certain androgens but devoid of
androgenic activity (virilization) in
therapeutic doses. In breast cancer, effect may result from depression of ovarian function by inhibition of synthesis of pituitary
gonadotropin. *Effectiveness indi-*
cated by decrease in size of tumor;
more than 50% of nonosseous le-
sions decrease in size even though
all bone lesions remain static.

USES Adjunctive treatment in palliation of breast carcinoma in postmenopausal women when hormone therapy is indicated. Also
effective in women diagnosed before menopause in whom ovarian
function has been subsequently terminated.

CONTRAINDICATIONS Premenopausal women; breast cancer in
males; pregnancy (category C), lactation.
CAUTIOUS USE Hypercalcemia; cardiorenal disease.

ROUTE & DOSAGE

Adjunctive Therapy for Breast Cancer
Adult: **PO** 250 mg q.i.d.

ADMINISTRATION

Oral
- Note: If anticoagulants are concurrently ordered, dose is usually
reduced when testolactone is initiated.
- Store at 15°–30° C (59°–86° F) unless otherwise directed. Protect
from freezing.

ADVERSE EFFECTS (≥1%) **CNS:**
Paresthesias. **Endocrine:** Deepening
of the voice, acne, facial hair
growth, clitoral enlargement. **GI:**
Glossitis, anorexia; nausea, vomiting. **CV:** Hypertension, edema in
extremities.

DIAGNOSTIC TEST INTERFERENCE
Urinary 17-OHCS determinations
may be elevated.

INTERACTIONS Drug: May enhance
hypoprothrombinemic effects of
ORAL ANTICOAGULANTS.

PHARMACOKINETICS Absorption:
Readily from GI tract. **Metabo-**
lism: In liver. **Elimination:** In urine.

CLINICAL IMPLICATIONS

Assessment & Drug Effects
- Monitor therapeutic effectiveness.
Clinical response usually occurs
in 6–12 wk.
- Lab tests: Check plasma calcium
levels periodically (normal serum
calcium: 8.5–10.6 mg/dL).
- Monitor PT and INR carefully with
concurrent anticoagulant therapy.
- Report S&S that suggest impending hypercalcemia (see Appendix F).
- Monitor I&O ratio and pattern.
- Encourage patient mobility if feasible; if not, assist with passive
exercises.

Patient & Family Education
- Drug treatment is usually continued for a minimum of 3 mo to

T

Common adverse effects in *italic*, life-threatening effects <u>underlined</u>; generic names
in **bold**; classifications in SMALL CAPS; ♣ Canadian drug name; ⊘ Prototype drug

1467

evaluate response (unless there is active progression of the disease).

- Be aware that hypercalcemia represents active remission of bone metastasis; if it occurs, appropriate therapy is instituted.

TESTOSTERONE 🔴

(tess-toss′ter-one)

Androderm, AndroGel, Striant, Testim

TESTOSTERONE CYPIONATE

Andro-Cyp, Depo-Testosterone, Depotest

TESTOSTERONE ENANTHATE

Delatest, Delatestryl, Malogex ✦

Classifications: HORMONE; ANDROGEN/ANABOLIC STEROID; ANTINEOPLASTIC

Therapeutic: ANTINEOPLASTIC; ANABOLIC STEROID

Pregnancy Category: X

Controlled Substance: Schedule III

AVAILABILITY Testosterone 75 mg implantable pellets; 2.5 mg/24 h, 4 mg/24 h, 5 mg/24 h, 6 mg/24 h, transdermal patch; 1% gel; 2.5 g, 5 g gel packets; 30 mg buccal patch **Testosterone Cypionate** 100 mg/mL, 200 mg/mL injection **Testosterone Enanthate** 100 mg/mL, 200 mg/mL injection

ACTION & *THERAPEUTIC EFFECT*

Synthetic steroid compound with both androgenic and anabolic activity (1:1). Controls development and maintenance of secondary sexual characteristics. **Androgenic activity:** Responsible for the growth spurt of the adolescent and for growth termination by epiphyseal closure. In males and some females, reduces excretion of phosphorus, nitrogen, potassium, sodium, and chloride. In-creases erythropoiesis, possibly by stimulating production of renal or extrarenal erythropoietin, and promotes vascularization and darkening of skin. **Anabolic activity:** Increases protein metabolism and decreases its catabolism. Large doses suppress spermatogenesis, thereby causing testicular atrophy. *Antagonizes effects of estrogen excess on female breast and endometrium. Responsible for the growth spurt of the adolescent male and onset of puberty.*

USES Androgen replacement therapy, delayed puberty (male), palliation of female mammary cancer (1–5 y postmenopausal), and to treat postpartum breast engorgement. Available in fixed combination with estrogens in many preparations.

CONTRAINDICATIONS Hypersensitivity or toxic reactions to androgens; serious cardiac, liver, or kidney disease; hypercalcemia; known or suspected prostatic or breast cancer in male; benign prostatic hypertrophy with obstruction; patients easily stimulated sexually; older adults; asthenic males who may react adversely to androgenic overstimulation; conditions aggravated by fluid retention; hypertension; pregnancy (category X), possibility of virilization of external genitalia of female fetus, lactation.

CAUTIOUS USE Cardiac, liver, and kidney disease; prepubertal males; diabetes mellitus; history of MI; CAD; BPH; geriatric patients, acute intermittent porphyria.

ROUTE & DOSAGE

Male Hypogonadism

Adult: **IM Cypionate, Enanthate** 50–400 mg q2–4wk **Topical** Start with 6 mg/d system applied daily, if scrotal area inadequate, use 4 mg/d system

Androderm Apply to torso; **AndroGel** Apply one packet to upper arms, shoulders, or abdomen once daily; **Striant** Apply one patch to the gum region just above the incisor tooth q12h

Delayed Puberty

Adult: **IM Cypionate, Enanthate** 50–200 mg q2–4wk

Metastatic Breast Cancer

Adult: **IM Cypionate, Enanthate** 200–400 mg q2–4wk

ADMINISTRATION

Buccal

- Apply buccal patch to gum just above the incisor tooth.

Transdermal

- Apply transdermal system on clean, dry scrotal skin. Dry shave scrotal hair for optimal skin contact. Do not use chemical depilatories. Wear patch for 22–24 h.
- Apply Androderm patches to abdomen, back, thigh, or upper arm. Alternate application site q24h with ≥7 d between same site.
- Store at 15°–30° C (59°–86° F).

Intramuscular

- Give IM injections deep into gluteal musculature.
- Store IM formulations prepared in oil at room temperature. Warming and shaking vial will redisperse precipitated crystals.

ADVERSE EFFECTS (≥1%) **CNS:** Excitation, insomnia. **CV:** Skin flushing and vascularization. **GI:** Nausea, vomiting, anorexia, diarrhea, gastric pain, jaundice. **Hematologic:** Leukopenia. **Metabolic:** Hypercalcemia, hypercholesterolemia, *sodium and water retention (especially in older adults) with edema.* **Renal:** Renal calculi (especially in the immobilized patient), bladder irritability. **Urogeni**-tal: *Increased libido.* **Skin:** *Acne,* injection site irritation and sloughing. **Body as a Whole:** Hypersensitivity to testosterone, <u>anaphylactoid reactions</u> (rare). **Hematologic:** Precipitation of acute intermittent porphyria. **Endocrine:** Female—suppression of ovulation, lactation, or menstruation; hoarseness or deepening of voice (often irreversible); hirsutism; oily skin; clitoral enlargement; regression of breasts; male-pattern baldness (in disseminated breast cancer); flushing, sweating; vaginitis with pruritus, drying, bleeding; menstrual irregularities. Male—prepubertal-premature epiphyseal closure, phallic enlargement, priapism. Postpubertal—testicular atrophy, decreased ejaculatory volume, azoospermia, oligospermia (after prolonged administration or excessive dosage), impotence, epididymitis, priapism, *gynecomastia.*

DIAGNOSTIC TEST INTERFERENCE

Testosterone alters **glucose tolerance** tests; decreases **thyroxine-binding globulin concentration** (resulting in decreased **total T_4** serum levels and increased **resin of T_3** and **T_4**). Increases **creatinine** and **creatinine** excretion (lasting up to 2 wk after therapy is discontinued) and alters response to **metyrapone test.** It suppresses **clotting factors II, V, VII, X** and decreases excretion of **17-ketosteroids.** May increase or decrease **serum cholesterol.**

INTERACTIONS Drug: ORAL ANTICOAGULANTS may potentiate hypoprothrombinemia. May decrease **insulin** requirements.

PHARMACOKINETICS Absorption: **Cypionate** and **enanthate** are slowly absorbed from lipid tissue. **Duration:** 2–4 wk **cypionate** and **enanthate. Distribution:** 98% bound

Common adverse effects in *italic*, life-threatening effects <u>underlined</u>; generic names in **bold**; classifications in SMALL CAPS; ♣ Canadian drug name; ⊕ Prototype drug

1469

to sex hormone-binding globulin. **Metabolism:** Primarily in liver. **Elimination:** 90% in urine, 6% in feces. **Half-Life:** 10–100 min.

CLINICAL IMPLICATIONS

Assessment & Drug Effects

- Therapeutic response from testosterone therapy is slow; breast cancer, usually apparent within 3 mo after regimen begins. Terminate therapy if signs of disease progression appear.
- Check I&O and weigh patient daily during dose adjustment period. Weight gain (due to sodium and water retention) suggests need for decreased dosage. When dosage is stabilized, urge patient to check weight at least twice weekly and to report increases, particularly if accompanied by edema in dependent areas. Dose adjustment and diuretic therapy may be started.
- Lab tests: Periodic serum cholesterol, serum electrolytes as well as liver function tests throughout therapy.
- Monitor serum calcium closely. Androgenic therapy is usually terminated if serum calcium rises above 14 mg/dL.
- Report S&S of hypercalcemia (see Appendix F) promptly. The immobilized patient is particularly prone to develop hypercalcemia, which indicates progression of bone metastasis in patients with metastatic breast cancer. Treatment includes withdrawing testosterone and checking calcium, phosphate, and BUN levels daily.
- Instruct diabetic to report sweating, tremor, anxiety, vertigo. Testosterone-induced anabolic action enhances hypoglycemia (hyperinsulinism). Dosage adjustment of antidiabetic agent may be required.

- Observe patients on concomitant anticoagulant treatment for signs of overdosage (e.g., ecchymoses, petechiae). Report promptly to physician; anticoagulant dose may need to be reduced.
- Monitor prepubertal or adolescent males throughout therapy to avoid precocious sexual development and premature epiphyseal closure. Skeletal stimulation may continue 6 mo beyond termination of therapy.

Patient & Family Education

- Review directions for application of transdermal patches.
- Report soreness at injection site, because postinjection furunculosis may be an associated adverse reaction.
- Report priapism (sustained and often painful erections occurring especially in early replacement therapy), reduced ejaculatory volume, and gynecomastia to physician. Symptoms indicate necessity for temporary withdrawal or discontinuation of testosterone therapy.
- Notify physician promptly if pregnancy is suspected or planned. Masculinization of the fetus is most likely to occur if testosterone (androgen) therapy is provided during first trimester of pregnancy.
- Androgens may cause virilism in women at dosage required to treat carcinoma. Report increase in libido (early sign of toxicity), growth of facial hair, deepening of voice, male-pattern baldness. The onset of hoarseness can easily be overlooked unless its significance as an early and possibly irreversible sign of virilism is appreciated. Reevaluation of treatment plan is indicated.

TETRACAINE HYDROCHLORIDE

(tet'ra-kane)

Pontocaine

Classifications: LOCAL ANES-
THETIC (ESTER TYPE)
Therapeutic: LOCAL ANESTHETIC
Prototype: Procaine HCl
Pregnancy Category: C

AVAILABILITY 1%, 0.2%, 0.3% injection; 20 mg powder; 2% solution; 1%, 2% cream; 2% gel; 1% ointment; 0.5% ophthalmic solution

ACTION & *THERAPEUTIC EFFECT*

A potent and toxic local anesthetic
that depresses the initial depolarization phase of the action potential, thus preventing propagation
and conduction of the nerve impulse. *Effectiveness indicated by
loss of sensation and motor activity
in circumscribed body areas close
to injection or application site.*

USES Spinal anesthesia (high, low,
saddle block) and topically to produce surface anesthesia. **Eye:** To
anesthetize conjunctiva and cornea prior to superficial procedures
(including tonometry, gonioscopy,
removal of foreign bodies or su-
tures, corneal scraping). **Nose and
Throat:** To abolish laryngeal and
esophageal reflexes prior to bronchoscopy, esophagoscopy. **Skin:**
To relieve pruritus, pain, burning.

CONTRAINDICATIONS Older adult
and debilitated patients; prolonged use of ophthalmic preparations; known hypersensitivity to
tetracaine or other local anesthetics of ester type (e.g., procaine,
chloroprocaine, cocaine), sulfite,
or to PABA or its derivatives; coagulopathy; anticoagulant therapy;
thrombocytopenia; increased
bleeding time; infection at application or injection site; pregnancy
(category C).
CAUTIOUS USE Shock; cachexia,
cardiac decompensation; QT prolongation; lactation; elderly; children <16 y.

ROUTE & DOSAGE

Local Anesthesia

Adult: **Topical** Before procedure,
1–2 drops of 0.5% solution or
1.25–2.5 cm of ointment in lower
conjunctival fornix or 0.5% solution or ointment to nose or throat
Spinal 1% solution diluted with
equal volume of 10% dextrose
injected in subarachnoid space

ADMINISTRATION

Topical
- Avoid use of solutions that are
  cloudy, discolored, or crystallized.
- When tetracaine is used on mucosa of larynx, trachea, or esophagus, the manufacturer recommends adding 0.06 mL of a 0.1%
  epinephrine solution to each mL
  tetracaine solution to slow absorption of the anesthetic.
- Store ophthalmic solution and ointment at 15°–30° C (59°–86° F); refrigerate topical. Avoid freezing.
  Use tight, light-resistant containers.

ADVERSE EFFECTS (≥1%) **Body as
a Whole:** <u>Anaphylactic reactions</u>,
convulsions, faintness, syncope.
CNS: Postspinal headache, headache, spinal nerve paralysis, anxiety,
nervousness, seizures. **CV:** Bradycardia, arrhythmias, hypotension.
Special Senses: Stinging; corneal
erosion, retardation or prevention of
healing of corneal abrasion, transient pitting and sloughing of corneal surface, dry corneal epithelium;
dry mucous membranes, prolonged
depression of cough reflex.

T

Common adverse effects in *italic*, life-threatening effects <u>underlined</u>; generic names
in **bold**; classifications in SMALL CAPS; ✚ Canadian drug name; ⓟ Prototype drug

INTERACTIONS Drug: May antagonize effects of SULFONAMIDES.

PHARMACOKINETICS Onset: 1 min eye; 3 min mucosal surface; 3 min spinal. **Duration:** Up to 15 min eye; 30–60 min mucosal surface; 1.5–3 h spinal. **Metabolism:** In liver and plasma. **Elimination:** In urine.

CLINICAL IMPLICATIONS

Assessment & Drug Effects

- Recovery from anesthesia to the pharyngeal area is complete when patient has feeling in the hard and soft palates and when muscles in the faucial (tonsillar) pillars contract with stimulation.
- Do not give food or liquids until these normal pharyngeal responses are present (usually about 1 h after anesthetic administration). The first small amount of liquid (water) should be given under supervision of care provider.
- Be aware that increased blood concentration of the drug may result from excess application of tetracaine to the skin (to relieve pruritus or burning), application to debrided or infected skin surfaces, or too rapid injection rate.
- High blood concentrations of tetracaine can lead to adverse systemic effects involving CNS and CV systems: Convulsions, respiratory arrest, dysrhythmias, cardiac arrest.

Patient & Family Education

- Do not use ophthalmic drug longer than prescribed period. Prolonged use to eye surface may cause corneal epithelial erosions and retard healing of corneal surface.
- Natural barriers to eye infection and injury are removed by the anesthesia. Do not rub eye after drug instillation until anesthetic effect has dissipated (evidenced by return of blink reflex). Patching for

temporary protection of the corneal epithelium may be ordered.
- Wash or disinfect hands before and after self-administration of solutions or ointment.

TETRACYCLINE HYDROCHLORIDE ℗ℝ

(tet-ra-sye′kleen)
Novotetra ✦, Sumycin
Classifications: ANTIBIOTIC; TETRACYCLINE
Therapeutic: ANTIBIOTIC
Pregnancy Category: D

AVAILABILITY 100 mg, 125 mg, 250 mg, 500 mg capsules; 125 mg/ 5 mL suspension

ACTION & *THERAPEUTIC EFFECT*
Tetracyclines usually are bacteriostatic but may be bactericidal in high concentrations. Exerts antiacne action by suppressing growth of *Propionibacterium acnes* within sebaceous follicles, thereby reducing free fatty acid content in sebum. Free fatty acids are thought to be largely responsible for inflammatory skin lesions (papules, pustules, cysts) and comedones of acne. *Effective against a variety of gram-positive and gram-negative bacteria and against most chlamydiae, mycoplasmas, rickettsiae, and certain protozoa (e.g., amebae). Exerts antiacne action by suppressing growth of* Propionibacterium acnes *within sebaceous follicles.*

USES Chlamydial infections (e.g., lymphogranuloma venereum, psittacosis, trachoma, inclusion conjunctivitis, nongonococcal urethritis); mycoplasmal infections (e.g., *Mycoplasma pneumoniae*); rickettsial infections (e.g., Q fever, Rocky Mt spotted fever, typhus); spirochetal

T

infections: relapsing fever (*Borrelia*), leptospirosis, syphilis (penicillin-hypersensitive patients); amebiases; uncommon gram-negative bacterial infections [e.g., brucellosis, shigellosis, cholera, gonorrhea (penicillin-hypersensitive patients), granuloma inguinale, tularemia]; gram-positive infections (e.g., tetanus). Also used orally and topically (solution) for inflammatory acne vulgaris; topical ointment is used for superficial skin infections. See tetracycline HCl, ophthalmic, for ophthalmic uses.

UNLABELED USES Actinomycosis, acute exacerbations of chronic bronchitis; Lyme disease; pericardial effusion (metastatic); acute PID; sexually transmitted epididymoorchitis; with quinine for multidrug-resistant strains of *Plasmodium falciparum* malaria; antiinfective prophylaxis for rape victims; recurrent cystic thyroid nodules; melioidosis; and as fluorescence test for malignancy.

CONTRAINDICATIONS Hypersensitivity to tetracyclines or to any ingredient in the formulation; severe renal or hepatic impairment, common bile duct obstruction; concurrent corticosteroid therapy; UV exposure. Use during tooth development [last half of pregnancy (category D)], during infancy and childhood to the 8th year. Safety of topical tetracycline preparations in children <8 y is not established.

CAUTIOUS USE History of kidney or liver dysfunction; myasthenia gravis; history of allergy, asthma, hay fever, urticaria; undernourished patients.

ROUTE & DOSAGE

Systemic Infection
Adult: **PO** 250–500 mg b.i.d.–q.i.d. (1–2 g/d) **IM** 250 mg once/d or 300 mg/d in 2–3 divided doses

Child: **PO** >8 y, 25–50 mg/kg/d in 2–4 divided doses **IM** >8 y, 15–25 mg/kg/d in 2–3 divided doses (max: 250 mg/injection)

Acne
Adult/Child: **PO** >8 y, 500–1000 mg/d in 4 divided doses **Topical** Apply to cleansed areas twice daily

ADMINISTRATION

Oral
- Give with a full glass of water on an empty stomach at least 1 h before or 2 h after meals (food, milk, and milk products can reduce absorption by 50% or more).
- Do not give immediately before bed.
- Give with food if patient is having GI symptoms (e.g., nausea, vomiting, anorexia); do not give with foods high in calcium such as milk or milk products.
- Shake suspension well before pouring to ensure uniform distribution of drug. Use calibrated liquid measure to dispense.
- Consult physician about ordering the oral suspension formulation if patient cannot swallow pills.
- Check expiration date for all tetracyclines. Fanconi-like syndrome (renal tubular dysfunction) and also an LE-like syndrome have been attributed to outdated tetracycline preparations.
- Tetracycline decomposes with age, exposure to light, and when improperly stored under conditions of extreme humidity, heat, or cold. The resultant product may be toxic.
- Store at 15°–30° C (59°–86° F) in tightly covered container in dry place. Protect from light.

Intramuscular
- Ask patient if he or she is allergic to any of the "caine" local anesthet-

Common adverse effects in *italic*, life-threatening effects underlined; generic names in **bold**; classifications in SMALL CAPS; ✚ Canadian drug name; ◎ Prototype drug

1473

ics. (Tetracycline for IM use contains 40 mg procaine HCl per vial.)

- Reconstitute powder by adding 2 mL sterile water for injection or NS injection to 100- or 250-mg vial.
- Give injection deep into body of a relatively large muscle mass (e.g., gluteus maximus or midlateral thigh). Alternate injection sites and observe daily for irritation and swelling.
- Forewarn patient that IM administration may cause local irritation and is extremely painful.
- Store solution at room temperature. Discard after 24 h (directions may vary with manufacturer).

ADVERSE EFFECTS (≥1%) **CNS:** Headache, intracranial hypertension (rare). **Special Senses:** Pigmentation of conjunctiva due to drug deposit. **GI:** Reported mostly for oral administration, but also may occur with parenteral tetracycline (*nausea, vomiting,* epigastric distress, heartburn, *diarrhea,* bulky loose stools, steatorrhea, *abdominal discomfort, flatulence,* dry mouth); dysphagia, retrosternal pain, esophagitis, esophageal ulceration with oral administration, abnormally high liver function test values, decrease in serum cholesterol, fatty degeneration of liver [jaundice, increasing nitrogen retention (azotemia), hyperphosphatemia, acidosis, irreversible shock]; foul-smelling stools or vaginal discharge, stomatitis, glossitis; black hairy tongue (lingua nigra), diarrhea; staphylococcal enterocolitis. **Body as a Whole:** Drug fever, angioedema, serum sickness, anaphylaxis. **Urogenital:** Particularly in patients with kidney disease; increase in BUN/serum creatinine, renal impairment even with therapeutic doses; Fanconi-like syndrome (outdated tetracycline) (characterized by polyuria, polydipsia, nau-

sea, vomiting, glycosuria, proteinuria acidosis, aminoaciduria); vulvovaginitis, pruritus vulvae or ani (possibly hypersensitivity). **Skin:** Dermatitis, *phototoxicity:* discoloration of nails, onycholysis (loosening of nails); cheilosis; fixed drug eruptions particularly on genitalia; thrombocytopenic purpura; Urticaria, rash, exfoliative dermatitis; With topical applications: skin irritation, dry scaly skin, transient stinging or burning sensation, slight yellowing of skin at application site, acute contact dermatitis. **Other:** Pancreatitis, local reactions: pain and irritation (IM site), Jarisch-Herxheimer reaction (see Clinical Implications).

DIAGNOSTIC TEST INTERFERENCE

TETRACYCLINES may cause false increases in *urinary catecholamines* (by *fluorometric methods*), and false decreases in *urinary urobilinogen.* Parenteral TETRACYCLINES containing *ascorbic acid* reportedly may produce false-positive *urinary glucose* determinations by *copper reduction methods* (e.g., *Benedict's reagent, Clinitest*); TETRACYCLINES may cause false-negative results with *glucose oxidase methods* (e.g., *Clinistix, TesTape*).

INTERACTIONS Drug: ANTACIDS, **calcium,** and **magnesium** bind tetracycline in gut and decrease absorption. ORAL ANTICOAGULANTS potentiate hypoprothrombinemia. ANTIDIARRHEAL AGENTS with **kaolin** and pectin may decrease absorption. Effectiveness of ORAL CONTRACEPTIVES decreased. **Methoxyflurane** may produce fatal nephrotoxicity. **Food:** Dairy products and **iron, zinc** supplements decrease tetracycline absorption.

PHARMACOKINETICS Absorption: 75–80% of dose absorbed. **Peak:** 2–4 h. **Distribution:** Widely distrib-

T

uted, preferentially binds to rapid growing tissues; crosses placenta; enters breast milk. **Metabolism:** Not metabolized; enterohepatic cycling. **Elimination:** 50–60% in urine within 72 h. **Half-Life:** 6–12 h.

CLINICAL IMPLICATIONS
Assessment & Drug Effects
- Lab tests: Obtain baseline and periodic C&S tests to confirm susceptibility of infecting organism to tetracycline. Also, preform initial and periodic kidney, liver, and hematopoietic function tests, particularly during high-dose, long-term therapy. Determine serum tetracycline levels in patients at-risk for hepatotoxicity (sometimes associated with pancreatitis and occurs most frequently in patients receiving other hepatotoxic drugs or with history of renal or hepatic impairment).
- Report GI symptoms (e.g., nausea, vomiting, diarrhea) to physician. These are generally dose-dependent, occurring mostly with oral forms in patients receiving 2 g/d or more and during prolonged therapy. Frequently, symptoms are controlled by reducing dosage or administering with compatible foods.
- Be alert to evidence of superinfections (see Appendix F). Regularly inspect tongue and mucous membrane of mouth for candidiasis (thrush). Suspect superinfection if patient complains of irritation or soreness of mouth, tongue, throat, vagina, or anus, or persistent itching of any area, diarrhea, or foul-smelling excreta or discharge.
- Withhold drug and notify physician if superinfection develops. Superinfections occur most frequently in patients receiving prolonged therapy, the debilitated, or

those who have diabetes, leukemia, systemic LE, or lymphoma. Women taking oral contraceptives reportedly are more susceptible to vaginal candidiasis.
- Obtain follow-up cultures from all gonococcal infection sites 3–7 d after completion of tetracycline therapy to verify eradication of infection.
- Monitor I&O in patients receiving parenteral tetracycline. Report oliguria or any changes in appearance of urine or in I&O.

Patient & Family Education
- Report onset of diarrhea to physician. It is important to determine whether diarrhea is due to irritating drug effect or superinfections or pseudomembranous colitis (caused by overgrowth of toxin-producing bacteria: *Clostridium difficile*) (see Appendix F). The latter two conditions can be **LIFE THREATENING** and require immediate withdrawal of tetracycline and prompt initiation of symptomatic and supportive therapy.
- Reduce incidence of superinfection (see Appendix F) by meticulous care of mouth, skin, and perineal area. Rinse mouth of food debris after eating; floss daily and use a soft-bristled toothbrush. Wash hands several times a day, particularly after each bowel movement and before eating.
- Avoid direct exposure to sunlight during and for several days after therapy is terminated to reduce possibility of photosensitivity reaction (appearing like an exaggerated sunburn, it begins a few minutes to hours following sun exposure, often with tingling, burning sensation).
- Report onset of severe headache or visual disturbances immediately. These are possible symp-

T

Common adverse effects in *italic*, life-threatening effects <u>underlined</u>; generic names in **bold**; classifications in SMALL CAPS; ✦ Canadian drug name; ⊙ Prototype drug

1475

toms of increased intracranial pressure and necessitate prompt withdrawal of tetracycline to prevent irreversible loss of vision.

- Note: Tetracycline therapy for brucellosis or spirochetal infections may cause a Jarisch-Herxheimer reaction. The reaction is usually mild and appears abruptly within 6–24 h after initiation of therapy. It is manifested by malaise, fever, chills, headache, adenopathy, leukocytosis, exacerbation of skin lesions, arthralgia, transient hypotension. Treatment is symptomatic; recovery generally occurs within 24 h.

- Report immediately sudden onset of painful or difficult swallowing (dysphagia) to physician. Esophagitis and esophageal ulceration have been associated with bedtime administration of tetracycline capsules or tablets with insufficient fluid, particularly to patients with hiatal hernia or esophageal problems.

- Do not allow topical medication to contact eyes, nose, or mouth. Be aware that tetracycline may stain clothing.

- Clean affected skin area with soap and water; rinse and dry well before application of topical drug.

- Report a worsening infection or stinging and burning sensation with topical applications to physician if pronounced.

- Skin treated with topical drug will exhibit bright yellow to green fluorescence under ultraviolet light and "black light."

- Be aware that topicycline contains a sulfite that can cause an allergic reaction (itching, wheezing, anaphylaxis) in susceptible persons (e.g., asthmatics or allergic individuals).

- Response to acne therapy usually requires 2–8 wk, maximal results may not be apparent for up to 12 wk.

TETRAHYDROZOLINE HYDROCHLORIDE

(tet-ra-hye-drozz'a-leen)
Collyrium, Mallazine, Murine Plus, Optigene, Soothe, Tyzine, Visine
Classifications: EYE, EAR, NOSE, AND THROAT PREPARATION; VASO-CONSTRICTOR; DECONGESTANT
Therapeutic: NASAL DECONGESTANT; VASOCONSTRICTOR
Prototype: Naphazoline
Pregnancy Category: C

AVAILABILITY 0.05% ophthalmic solution; 0.05%, 0.1% nasal solution

ACTION & *THERAPEUTIC EFFECT*
Alpha-adrenergic agonist that causes intense vasoconstriction when applied topically to mucous membranes. Also causes vasoconstriction when applied as eye drops. *Ophthalmic solution is effective for allergic reactions of the eye; nasal solution is antiinflammatory and also decreases allergic congestion.*

USES Symptomatic relief of minor eye irritation and allergies and for nasopharyngeal congestion of allergic or inflammatory origin.

CONTRAINDICATIONS Hypersensitivity to any component; use of ophthalmic preparation in glaucoma or other serious eye diseases; use within 14 d of MAO inhibitor therapy. Use in children <2 y; use of 0.1% or higher strengths in children <6 y; pregnancy (category C).
CAUTIOUS USE Hypertension; cardiovascular disease; hyperthyroidism; diabetes mellitus; young children; lactation.

ROUTE & DOSAGE

Decongestant

Adult: **Ophthalmic** See Appendix A-1. **Nasal** 2–4 drops of 0.1% solution or spray in each nostril q3h prn
Child: **Nasal** 2–6 y, 2–4 drops of 0.05% solution or spray in each nostril q3h prn; ≥6 y, same as adult

ADMINISTRATION

Instillation

- Make sure interval between doses is at least 4–6 h since drug action lasts 4–8 h.
- Place patient in upright position when using nasal spray. (If patient is reclining, a stream rather than a spray may be ejected, with consequent overdosage.)
- Use lateral, head-low position to administer nasal drops.

ADVERSE EFFECTS (≥1%) Special

Senses: *Transient stinging,* irritation, *sneezing,* dryness, headache, tremors, drowsiness, light-headedness, insomnia, palpitation. **Body as a Whole:** With overdose: marked drowsiness, sweating, <u>coma</u>, hypotension, <u>shock</u>, bradycardia.

PHARMACOKINETICS Absorption:

May be absorbed from nasal mucosa. **Duration:** 4–8 h.

CLINICAL IMPLICATIONS

Patient & Family Education

- Discontinue medication and consult physician if relief is not obtained within 48 h or if symptoms persist or increase.
- Do not exceed recommended dosage. Rebound congestion and rhinitis may occur with frequent or prolonged use of nasal preparation.

THALIDOMIDE

(tha-lid'o-mide)
Thalomid
Classifications: IMMUNOMODULATOR; TUMOR NECROSIS FACTOR (TNF) MODIFIER
Therapeutic: IMMUNOSUPPRESSIVE; TNF MODIFIER
Pregnancy Category: X

AVAILABILITY 50 mg capsules

ACTION & *THERAPEUTIC EFFECT*

Has several antiinflammatory and immunologic actions. Antiinflammatory effects may be due to its inhibition of neutrophil chemotaxis and decrease of monocyte phagocytosis. Immunosuppressive effect may result from suppression of excessive tumor necrosis factor-alpha (TNF-alpha) production. Also, reduces helper T cells and increases suppressor T cells. *Has both antiinflammatory and immunosuppressive actions. Effectiveness indicated by control of cutaneous manifestations of erythema nodosum leprosum.*

USES Acute and maintenance treatment of cutaneous manifestations of moderate to severe erythema nodosum leprosum. Refractory Crohn's disease.

UNLABELED USES Stimulate appetite in patients with HIV-associated cachexia, lupus, multiple myeloma.

CONTRAINDICATIONS Hypersensitivity to thalidomide; peripheral neuropathy; pregnancy (category X), lactation, children <12 y.

CAUTIOUS USE Liver and kidney disease; CHF or hypertension; constipation or other GI disorders; neurologic disorders or history of neuritis.

T

Common adverse effects in *italic*, life-threatening effects <u>underlined</u>; generic names in **bold**; classifications in SMALL CAPS; ♣ Canadian drug name; ⊘ Prototype drug

1477

ROUTE & DOSAGE

Erythema Nodosum Leprosum

Adult: **PO** 100–300 mg q.d. (max: 400 mg/d) times at least 2 wk
Child: **PO** *11–17 y,* 100 mg q.d.

Refractory Crohn's Disease

Adult: **PO** 50–100 mg q.d. (doses up to 300 mg studied)

ADMINISTRATION

Oral

- Give at bedtime and at least 1 h after the evening meal.
- Give this drug only to persons who understand and have signed the required consent form.
- Verify, prior to administration, that this drug was prescribed and dispensed only by persons registered by the STEPS (System for Thalidomide Education and Prescribing Safety) program.
- Store at 15°–30° C (59°–86° F); protect from light.

ADVERSE EFFECTS (≥1%) **Body as a Whole:** Asthenia, back pain, chills, facial edema, *fever,* malaise, pain. **CNS:** Drowsiness, *somnolence,* peripheral neuropathy (possibly irreversible), *dizziness,* orthostatic hypotension, headache, agitation, insomnia, nervousness, paresthesia, tremor, vertigo, seizures. **CV:** Bradycardia, peripheral edema, hyperlipidemia. **GI:** Abdominal pain, anorexia, constipation, *diarrhea,* dry mouth, flatulence, abnormal liver function tests, nausea, oral moniliasis. **Hematologic:** Neutropenia, anemia, *leukopenia,* lymphadenopathy. **Respiratory:** Pharyngitis, rhinitis, sinusitis. **Skin:** *Rash,* acne, nail disorder, fungal dermatitis, pruritus, sweating, <u>toxic epiderma necroly-</u> sis. **Body as a Whole:** Hypersensitivity reaction (rash, fever, tachycardia, hypotension), HIV viral load increase, infection. **Urogenital:** Teratogenicity, albuminuria, hematuria, impotence.

INTERACTIONS Drug: Enhances sedation associated with BARBITURATES, **alcohol, chlorpromazine, reserpine.**

PHARMACOKINETICS Absorption: Slowly absorbed from GI tract. **Peak:** 2.9–5.7 h. **Distribution:** Crosses placenta; present in ejaculate in males. **Metabolism:** Does not appear to be hepatically metabolized. **Half-Life:** 6–7.5 h.

CLINICAL IMPLICATIONS

Assessment & Drug Effects

- Lab tests: Monitor WBC with differential prior to therapy and periodically thereafter.
- Monitor carefully for and immediately report S&S of peripheral neuropathy. Discontinue drug and notify prescriber if peripheral neuropathy is suspected.

Patient & Family Education

- Do not share this medication with anyone else under any circumstances.
- Use effective methods of birth control (both women and men); starting 1 mo before, during, and 1 mo following discontinuation of thalidomide therapy. Men **MUST** use condoms when engaging in sexual activity.
- Exercise caution while driving or engaging in potentially hazardous activities because drug may cause dizziness.
- Report pain, numbness, or tingling in the hands or feet to physician immediately.

T

Common adverse effects in *italic,* life-threatening effects <u>underlined</u>; generic names in **bold**; classifications in SMALL CAPS; ✚ Canadian drug name; ⊘ Prototype drug

THEOPHYLLINE ℗

(thee-off'i-lin)

Elixophyllin, Lanophyllin, PMS Theophylline ✦, Pulmophylline ✦, Theo-24, Theolair, Theophylline Ethylenediamine, Theospan-SR, Uniphyl

Classifications: BRONCHODILATOR (RESPIRATORY SMOOTH MUSCLE RELAXANT); XANTHINE

Therapeutic: BRONCHODILATOR

Pregnancy Category: C

AVAILABILITY 100 mg, 125 mg, 200 mg, 250 mg, 300 mg tablets; 100 mg, 200 mg capsules; 80 mg/15 mL, 150 mg/15 mL liquid; 100 mg, 200 mg, 250 mg, 300 mg, 450 mg, 500 mg, 600 mg sustained release tablets; 50 mg, 75 mg, 100 mg, 125 mg, 200 mg, 250 mg, 260 mg, 300 mg sustained release capsules; 200 mg, 400 mg, 800 mg injection

ACTION & *THERAPEUTIC EFFECT*
Xanthine derivative that relaxes smooth muscle by direct action, particularly of bronchi and pulmonary vessels, and stimulates medullary respiratory center with resulting increase in vital capacity. Also relaxes smooth muscles of biliary and GI tracts. Stimulates myocardium, thereby increasing force of contractions and cardiac output, and stimulates all levels of CNS, but to a lesser degree than caffeine. *Effective for relief of bronchospasm in asthmatics, chronic bronchitis, and emphysema.*

USES Prophylaxis and symptomatic relief of bronchial asthma, as well as bronchospasm associated with chronic bronchitis and emphysema. Also used for emergency treatment of paroxysmal cardiac dyspnea and edema of CHF.

UNLABELED USES Treatment of apnea and bradycardia of premature infants and to reduce severe bronchospasm associated with cystic fibrosis and acute descending respiratory infection.

CONTRAINDICATIONS Hypersensitivity to xanthines; coronary artery disease or angina pectoris when myocardial stimulation might be harmful; severe renal or liver impairment; pregnancy (category C).

CAUTIOUS USE Children; compromised cardiac or circulatory function, hypertension; acute pulmonary edema; multiple organ failure; CF; hyperthyroidism; peptic ulcer; prostatic hypertrophy; glaucoma; diabetes mellitus; older adults and neonates.

ROUTE & DOSAGE

Bronchospasm
Adult/Child: **PO/IV Loading Dose** 5 mg/kg
Adult: **PO/IV Maintenance Dose*** Nonsmoker, 0.4 mg/kg/h [*IV by continuous infusion, PO divided q6h (immediate release) or q8–12h (sustained release)]; Smoker, 0.6 mg/kg/h; with CHF or cirrhosis, 0.2 mg/kg/h
Child: **PO/IV Maintenance Dose*** 1–9 y, 0.8 mg/kg/h; 10–12 y, 0.6 mg/kg/h
Infant: **PO/IV Maintenance Dose*** 0.5–0.7 mg/kg/h
Neonate: **PO/IV Maintenance Dose*** 0.13 mg/kg/h
Obesity
Dose on IBW

ADMINISTRATION

Note: All doses based on ideal body weight.

Common adverse effects in *italic*, life-threatening effects <u>underlined</u>; generic names in **bold**; classifications in SMALL CAPS; ✦ Canadian drug name; ℗ Prototype drug

1479

Oral

- Wait 4–6 h after the last IV dose, when switching from IV to oral dosing.
- Give with a full glass of water and after meals to minimize gastric irritation.
- Give sustained-release forms and enteric-coated tablets whole. Chewable tablets must be chewed thoroughly before swallowing. Sustained-release granules from capsules can be taken on an empty stomach or mixed with applesauce or water.
- Note: Timing of dose is critical. Be certain patient understands necessity to adhere to the correct intervals between doses.

Intravenous

Give *prediluted solutions* at a rate not to exceed 20 mg/min.

PREPARE: **IV Infusion:** Give IV theophylline ethylenediamine solution with a concentration of 25 mg/mL undiluted by direct IV or diluted (preferred) in up to 200 mL of D5W.

ADMINISTER: **IV Infusion:** Give at a rate not to exceed 20 mg/min.

INCOMPATIBILITIES **Solution/additive: Ascorbic acid, ceftriaxone, cimetidine, hetastarch. Y-site: Hetastarch, phenytoin.**

ADVERSE EFFECTS (≥1%) **CNS:** Stimulation (Irritability, restlessness, insomnia, dizziness, headache, tremor, hyperexcitability, muscle twitching, <u>drug-induced seizures</u>). **CV:** Palpitation, *tachycardia,* extrasystoles, flushing, marked hypotension, <u>circulatory failure</u>. **GI:** *Nausea,* vomiting, anorexia, epigastric or abdominal pain, diarrhea, activation of peptic ulcer. **Urogenital:** Transient urinary frequency, albuminuria, kidney irritation. **Respiratory:** Tachypnea, <u>respiratory arrest</u>. **Body as a Whole:** Fever, dehydration.

DIAGNOSTIC TEST INTERFERENCE False-positive elevations of *serum uric acid* (*Bittner* or colorimetric methods). *Probenecid* may cause false high *serum theophylline* readings, and spectrophotometric methods of determining *serum theophylline* are affected by a furosemide, sulfathiazole, phenylbutazone, probenecid, theobromine.

INTERACTIONS Drug: Increases **lithium** excretion, lowering lithium levels; **cimetidine,** high-dose **allopurinol** (600 mg/d), **tacrine,** QUINOLONES, MACROLIDE ANTIBIOTICS, and **zileuton** can significantly increase theophylline levels; **tobacco** use significantly decreases levels. **Herbal:** **St. John's wort** may decrease theophylline efficacy. **Daidzein** (in soy), **black pepper** increase serum concentrations and adverse effects.

PHARMACOKINETICS Absorption: Most products are 100% absorbed from GI tract. **Peak:** IV 30 min; uncoated tablet 1 h; sustained release 4–6 h. **Duration:** 4–8 h; varies with age, smoking, and liver function. **Distribution:** Crosses placenta. **Metabolism:** Extensively in liver. **Elimination:** Parent drug and metabolites excreted by kidneys; excreted in breast milk.

CLINICAL IMPLICATIONS

Assessment & Drug Effects

- Monitor vital signs. Improvement in respiratory status is the expected outcome.
- Observe and report early signs of possible toxicity: Anorexia, nausea, vomiting, dizziness, shakiness, restlessness, abdominal discomfort, irritability, palpitation, tachycardia, marked hypotension, cardiac arrhythmias, seizures.
- Monitor for tachycardia, which may be worse in patients with severe

Common adverse effects in *italic*, life-threatening effects <u>underlined</u>; generic names in **bold**; classifications in SMALL CAPS; ✦ Canadian drug name; ⊙ Prototype drug

cardiac disease. Conversely, theophylline toxicity may be masked in patients with tachycardia.

- Lab tests: Monitor plasma level of theophylline. Be aware that therapeutic plasma level ranges from 10–20 mcg/mL (a narrow therapeutic range). Levels exceeding 20 mcg/mL are associated with toxicity.
- Monitor drug levels closely in heavy smokers. Cigarette smoking induces hepatic microsomal enzyme activity, decreasing serum half-life and increasing body clearance of theophylline. An increase of dosage from 50–100% is usual in heavy smokers.
- Monitor plasma drug level closely in patients with heart failure, kidney or liver dysfunction, alcoholism, high fever. Plasma clearance of xanthines may be reduced.
- Take necessary safety precautions and forewarn older adult patients of possible dizziness during early therapy.
- Monitor patients on sustained release preparations for S&S of overdosage. Continued slow absorption leads to high plasma concentrations for a prolonged period.
- Note: Neonates of mothers using this drug have exhibited slight tachycardia, jitteriness, and apnea.
- Monitor CLOSELY for adverse effects in infants <6 mo and prematures; theophylline metabolism is prolonged as is the half-life in this age group.

Patient & Family Education

- Take medication at the same time every day.
- Avoid charcoal-broiled foods (high in polycyclic carbon content); may increase theophylline elimination and reduce the half-life as much as 50%.
- Limit caffeine intake because it may increase incidence of adverse effects.
- Cigarette smoking may significantly lower theophylline plasma concentration.
- Be aware that a low-carbohydrate, high-protein diet increases theophylline elimination, and a high-carbohydrate, low-protein diet decreases it.
- Drink fluids liberally (2000–3000 mL/d) if not contraindicated to decrease viscosity of airway secretions.
- Avoid self-dosing with OTC medications, especially cough suppressants, which may cause retention of secretions and CNS depression.

THIABENDAZOLE
(thye-a-ben′da-zole)
Mintezol
Classifications: ANTHELMINTIC
Therapeutic: ANTHELMINTIC
Prototype: Mebendazole
Pregnancy Category: C

AVAILABILITY 500 mg chewable tablets

ACTION & *THERAPEUTIC EFFECT*
Has a wide spectrum of anthelmintic activity. Inhibits helminth-specific enzyme fumarate reductase. *Suppresses production of eggs or larvae by some parasites and may inhibit subsequent development of eggs or larvae passed in feces. Demonstrates antiinflammatory, antipyretic, and analgesic effects.*

USES Enterobiasis (pinworm infestation), ascariasis (roundworm), strongyloidiasis (threadworm), cutaneous larva migrans (creeping eruption), and hookworm infesta-

T

Common adverse effects in *italic*, life-threatening effects <u>underlined</u>; generic names in **bold**; classifications in SMALL CAPS; ♣ Canadian drug name; ⊕ Prototype drug

1481

tions caused by *Ancyclostoma duodenale* or *Necator americanus*. Used during invasive stage of trichinosis to relieve symptoms and for mixed helminthic infestations.

CONTRAINDICATIONS Hypersensivity to thiabendazole; pregnancy (category C); lactation.

CAUTIOUS USE Liver or kidney dysfunction; when vomiting can be dangerous, severe dehydration or malnutrition; anemia; children weighing <15 kg.

ROUTE & DOSAGE

Enterobiasis, Ascariasis, Strongyloidiasis, Hookworm

Adult: PO <70 kg, 25 mg/kg b.i.d. times 2 d; >70 kg, 1.5 g b.i.d. (max: 3 g/d) times 2 d
Child: PO 14–70 kg, 25 mg/kg b.i.d. times 2 d

ADMINISTRATION

Oral
- Give after meals. Chewable tablets must be chewed thoroughly before swallowing.
- Shake suspension well before pouring.

ADVERSE EFFECTS (≥1%) **CNS:** Weariness, *dizziness,* drowsiness, headache. **CV:** Hypotension, bradycardia. **GI:** *Anorexia, nausea, vomiting,* epigastric distress, jaundice, cholestasis, parenchymal liver damage, diarrhea, perianal rash. **Urogenital:** Malodor of urine, crystalluria, hematuria, nephrotoxicity, enuresis. **Metabolic:** Transient rise in AST, transient leukopenia, hypersensitivity, hyperglycemia. **Skin:** Pruritus.

PHARMACOKINETICS Absorption: Readily from GI tract. **Peak:** 1–2 h. **Metabolism:** In liver. **Elimination:** >90% in urine; 5% in feces.

CLINICAL IMPLICATIONS
Assessment & Drug Effects
- Provide supportive treatment prior to therapy if patient is anemic, dehydrated, or malnourished.
- Adverse effects generally occur 3–4 h after administration, are mild, and last for 2–8 h. Incidence tends to be related to dose and duration of treatment.
- Discontinued immediately with S&S of hypersensitivity: Fever, facial flush, chills, conjunctival infection, skin rashes, or erythema multiforme (including Stevens-Johnson syndrome), which can be fatal.

Patient & Family Education
- Do not drive or engage in potentially hazardous activities until response to drug is known. CNS adverse effects occur frequently.

THIAMINE HYDROCHLORIDE (VITAMIN B₁)

(thye'a-min)
Classifications: VITAMIN B₁
Therapeutic: VITAMIN B₁ REPLACEMENT THERAPY
Pregnancy Category: A, C if dose is above RDA

AVAILABILITY 50 mg, 100 mg, 250 mg tablets; 20 mg enteric-coated tablet; 100 mg/mL injection

ACTION & THERAPEUTIC EFFECT
Water-soluble B₁ vitamin and member of B-complex group used for thiamine replacement therapy. Functions as an essential coenzyme in carbohydrate metabolism and has a role in conversion of tryptophan to nicotinamide. *Effectiveness is evidenced by improvement of clinical manifestations of thiamine deficiency: Anorexia, gastric distress, depression, irritability, insomnia, palpitations, tachycardia, loss of memory,*

paresthesias, muscle weakness and pain, elevated blood pyruvic acid level (diagnostic test for thiamine deficiency), and elevated lactic acid level.

USES Treatment and prophylaxis of beriberi, to correct anorexia due to thiamine deficiency states, and in treatment of neuritis associated with pregnancy, pellagra, and alcoholism, including Wernicke-Korsakoff syndrome. Therapy generally includes other members of vitamin B complex, since thiamine deficiency rarely occurs alone. Severe deficiency is characterized by ophthalmoplegia, polyneuropathy, muscle wasting ("dry" beriberi), edema, serous effusions, and CHF ("wet" beriberi).

CONTRAINDICATIONS Pregnancy (category C if dose is above RDA). **CAUTIOUS USE** Pregnancy (category A).

ROUTE & DOSAGE

Thiamine Deficiency
Adult: IV/IM 50–100 mg t.i.d. then 5–10 mg PO for one month
Child: IV/IM 10–25 mg t.i.d. then 5–10 mg PO for 1 mo

Alcohol Withdrawal
Adult: IV/IM 100 mg/d until PO 50–100 mg/d as tolerated

Wernicke's Encephalopathy
Adult: IV/IM 100 mg/d then 50–100 mg/d until on normal diet

Dietary Supplement
Adult: PO 15–30 mg/d
Child: PO 10–50 mg/d

ADMINISTRATION

Oral
- Do not crush or chew enteric-coated tablets. These must be swallowed whole.

Intramuscular
- Give deep IM into a large muscle; may be painful. Rotate sites and apply cold compresses to area if necessary for relief of discomfort.

Intravenous
Note: Intradermal test dose is recommended prior to administration in suspected thiamine sensitivity. Deaths have occurred following IV use.

PREPARE: **Direct:** Give undiluted. **IV Infusion:** Diluted in 1000 mL of most IV solutions.

ADMINISTER: **Direct:** Give at a rate of 100 mg over 5 min. **IV Infusion:** Give at the ordered rate.

INCOMPATIBILITIES **Solution/additive: Amobarbital, diazepam, furosemide, phenobarbital.**
- Preserve in tight, light-resistant, nonmetallic containers. Thiamine is unstable in alkaline solutions (e.g., solutions of acetates, barbiturates, bicarbonates, carbonates, citrates) and neutral solutions.

ADVERSE EFFECTS (≥1%) **Body as a Whole:** Feeling of warmth, weakness, sweating, restlessness, tightness of throat, angioneurotic edema, anaphylaxis. **Respiratory:** Cyanosis, pulmonary edema. **CV:** Cardiovascular collapse, slight fall in BP following rapid IV administration. **GI:** GI hemorrhage, nausea. **Skin:** Urticaria, pruritus.

INTERACTIONS Drug: No clinically significant interactions established.

PHARMACOKINETICS Absorption: Limited from GI tract. **Distribution:** Widely distributed, including into breast milk. **Elimination:** In urine.

CLINICAL IMPLICATIONS

Assessment & Drug Effects
- Record patient's dietary history carefully as an essential part of vi-

T

Common adverse effects in *italic*, life-threatening effects underlined; generic names in **bold**; classifications in SMALL CAPS; ✦ Canadian drug name; ⊙ Prototype drug

1483

tamin replacement therapy. Collaborate with physician, dietitian, patient, and responsible family member in developing a diet teaching plan that can be sustained by patient.

▪ Note: Body requirement of thiamine is directly proportional to carbohydrate intake and metabolic rate; requirement increases when diet consists predominantly of carbohydrates. Total absence of dietary thiamine produce deficiency state in about 3 wk.

Patient & Family Education

▪ Food–drug relationships: Learn about rich dietary sources of thiamine (e.g., yeast, pork, beef, liver, wheat and other whole grains, nutrient-added breakfast cereals, fresh vegetables, especially peas and dried beans).

THIMEROSAL

(thye-mer'oh-sal)
Mersol, Merthiolate
Classifications: ANTIINFECTIVE, TOPICAL; ANTISEPTIC, TOPICAL
Therapeutic: TOPICAL ANTISEPTIC
Pregnancy Category: C

AVAILABILITY 1:1000 solution, tincture, spray

ACTION & *THERAPEUTIC EFFECT*
Topical organic mercurial with sustained bacteriostatic and fungistatic activity. Ineffective against spore-forming organisms. *Utilized as a topical antiseptic because it is both a bacteriostatic and fungistatic agent.*

USES First-aid treatment of contaminated wounds, in antisepsis of intact skin, before surgery, and in pustular dermatosis; as antifungal agent in athlete's foot for wound irrigations. Ophthalmic preparation is used to treat conjunctivitis and corneal ulcer and for prevention of infection following removal of foreign bodies. Used as preservative in most solutions sold for cleaning, wetting, soaking, and storage of contact lenses; also used as preservative for biologic and pharmaceutical products.

CONTRAINDICATIONS History of sensitivity to thio or mercurial compounds; prolonged use; pregnancy (category C).
CAUTIOUS USE Lactation.

ROUTE & DOSAGE

Antiseptic
Adult: **Topical** 1:1000 solution, apply locally 1–3 times/d

ADMINISTRATION
Topical
▪ Clean before applying antiseptic for first-aid treatment.
▪ Do not apply bandage or other occlusive dressing until tincture application has completely dried in order to prevent skin irritation.
▪ Store in tightly covered, light-resistant containers. Avoid exposure to excessive heat.

ADVERSE EFFECTS (≥1%) **Skin:** Itching erythema, papular or vesicular eruptions. **Body as a Whole:** Mercury poisoning with prolonged use (metallic taste, salivation, stomatitis, lethargy, peripheral neuropathy).

PHARMACOKINETICS Absorption: May have mercury absorption with prolonged use over large areas.

T

CLINICAL IMPLICATIONS

Assessment & Drug Effects

- Be aware that Aqueous Merthiolate contains thimerosal and borate (0.14%). Both are toxic if absorbed systemically.

THIOGUANINE (TG, 6-THIOGUANINE)

(thye-oh-gwah'neen)

Lanvis ✦, Tabloid

Classifications: ANTINEOPLASTIC; ANTIMETABOLITE; PURINE ANTAGONIST
Therapeutic: ANTINEOPLASTIC; ANTI-METABOLITE
Prototype: Mercaptopurine
Pregnancy Category: D

AVAILABILITY 40 mg tablets

ACTION & *THERAPEUTIC EFFECT*

Antimetabolite and purine antagonist with immunosuppressive activity. Highly toxic. Drug is incorporated into the DNA and RNA of human bone marrow cells. *Delays myelosuppression; has potential mutagenic and carcinogenic properties.*

USES In combination with other antineoplastics for remission induction in acute myelogenous leukemia and as treatment of chronic myelogenous leukemia. Has little advantage over mercaptopurine.

CONTRAINDICATIONS Patients with prior resistance to this drug; severe bone marrow depression; pregnancy (category D), lactation.
CAUTIOUS USE Hepatic disease.

ROUTE & DOSAGE

Leukemia
Adult: **PO** 2 mg/kg/d, may increase to 3 mg/kg/d if no response after 4 wk

ADMINISTRATION

Oral

- Withhold drug and notify physician if toxicity develops. There is no known antagonist; prompt discontinuation of the drug is essential to avoid irreversible myelosuppression from toxicity.
- Store at 15°–30° C (59°–86° F) in airtight container.

ADVERSE EFFECTS (≥1%) **Hematologic:** Leukopenia, thrombocytopenia, anemia. **GI:** Jaundice, nausea, vomiting, anorexia, stomatitis, diarrhea. **Urogenital:** *Hyperuricemia.* **Other:** Hepatotoxicity (risk increased with long-term use).

INTERACTIONS Drug: Severe hepatotoxicity with **busulfan;** may decrease immune response to VACCINES; increase risk of bleeding with ANTICOAGULANTS; NSAIDS, SALICYLATES; PLATELET INHIBITORS, THROMBOLYTIC AGENTS; effects may be reversed by **filgrastim, sargramostim.**

PHARMACOKINETICS Absorption: Variable and incomplete absorption from GI tract. **Peak:** 8 h. **Distribution:** Crosses placenta. **Metabolism:** In liver. **Elimination:** In urine. **Half-Life:** 11 h.

CLINICAL IMPLICATIONS

Assessment & Drug Effects

- Lab tests: Monitor blood counts weekly (CBC with differential and platelet count); periodic LFTs with long-term use.
- Determine hematologic parameters for withholding drug.
- Monitor I&O ratio and report oliguria.
- Observe patient's skin and sclera for jaundice. It should be reported promptly as a symptom of toxicity; drug will be discontinued promptly.

Common adverse effects in *italic*, life-threatening effects underlined; generic names in **bold**; classifications in SMALL CAPS; ✦ Canadian drug name; ❂ Prototype drug

1485

- Expect that the drop in leukocyte count may be slow over a period of 2–4 wk. Treatment is interrupted if there is a rapid fall within a few days.

Patient & Family Education
- Maintenance doses are continued throughout remissions.

THIOPENTAL SODIUM ⓟ

(thye-oh-pen'tal)
Pentothal
Classifications: GENERAL ANESTHETIC; SEDATIVE-HYPNOTIC; BARBITURATE
Therapeutic: GENERAL ANESTHETIC; SEDATIVE-HYPNOTIC
Pregnancy Category: C
Controlled Substance: Schedule III

AVAILABILITY 20 mg/mL, 25 mg/mL injection

ACTION & *THERAPEUTIC EFFECT*
Ultrashort-acting barbiturate; induces brief general anesthesia without analgesia by depression of CNS. Loss of consciousness is rapid. Reduction in cardiac output and peripheral vasodilation frequently accompany anesthesia. Rapid redistribution of agent out of brain reduces anesthesia level and increases reflex airway hyperactivity to mechanical stimulation. *Muscle relaxation is slight, and reflexes are poorly controlled. Since analgesia is slight, thiopental is seldom used alone except for brief minor procedures.*

USES To induce hypnosis and anesthesia prior to or as supplement to other anesthetic agents or as sole agent for brief (15-min) operative procedures. Also used as an anticonvulsant and sedative-hypnotic and for narcoanalysis and narcosynthesis in psychiatric disorders.

CONTRAINDICATIONS Hypersensitivity to barbiturates; history of paradoxic excitation; absence of suitable veins for IV administration; status asthmaticus; acute intermittent or other hepatic porphyrias; pregnancy (category C).

CAUTIOUS USE Coronary artery disease, hypotension, shock; conditions that may potentiate or prolong hypnotic effect including excessive premedication, liver or kidney dysfunction, myxedema, Addison's disease, severe anemia, increased BUN; increased intracranial pressure; myasthenia gravis; asthma and other respiratory diseases.

ROUTE & DOSAGE

Induction
Adult: **IV Test Dose** 25–75 mg, then 50–75 mg at 20–40 sec intervals, an additional 50 mg may be given if needed
Child: **IV** 5–6 mg/kg initially, followed by 1 mg/kg if needed
Infant: **IV** 5–8 mg/kg

Convulsions
Adult: **IV** 75–250 mg, repeat as needed
Child: **IV** 2–3 mg/kg/dose, repeat as needed

Narcoanalysis
Adult: **IV** 100 mg/min until confusion occurs

Renal Impairment
If Cl_{cr} <10 mL/min, give 75% of dose

ADMINISTRATION

Note: Verify correct IV concentration and rate of infusion to neonates, infants, children with physician.

Intravenous

Test dose: May be given to assess unusual sensitivity to drug. Following administration, observe patient for at least 1 min for unexpected deep anesthesia or respiratory depression.

PREPARE: **Direct:** Reconstitute each 500 mg of powder by adding at least 20 mL of sterile water for injection to yield a 2.5% solution (25 mg/1 mL). Add 20 mL of reconstituted solution to at least 100 mL of NS or D5W. Prepare solution freshly and use promptly. If a precipitate is present, discard solution. Unused portions should be discarded within 24 h.

ADMINISTER: **Direct:** Infuse each 25 mg over 1 min or more. Do not infuse solution with a concentration <2.5% (concentration <2% causes hemolysis).

INCOMPATIBILITIES **Solution/additive: Dextrose Ringer's lactate, 10% dextrose, fructose 10%, lactated Ringer's injection, amikacin, calcium chloride, calcium gluconate, cephalothin, cephapirin, chloramphenicol, chlorpromazine, cimetidine, clindamycin, codeine phosphate, dimenhydrinate, diphenhydramine, doxapram, ephedrine, fibrinolysin, glycopyrrolate, heparin, hydromorphone, insulin, levorphanol, meperidine, metaraminol, methadone, methicillin, morphine, norepinephrine, penicillin G, prochlorperazine, promazine, promethazine, sodium bicarbonate, succinylcholine, tetracycline, vancomycin. Y-site: Alfentanil, ascorbic acid, atracurium, atropine, cisatracurium, diltiazem, dobutamine, dopamine, ephedrine, epinephrine, fenoldopam, furosemide, hydromorphone, labetalol, lidocaine, lorazepam, midazolam, morphine, nicardipine, norepinephrine, pancuronium, phenylephrine, succinylcholine, sufentanil, vecuronium.**

■ Consult physician if intraarterial injection or extravasation occurs. The site will require particular attention to prevent arteritis, neuritis, and skin slough. An intraarterial injection usually causes extreme pain before patient loses consciousness.

■ Store at 15°–30° C (59°–86° F). Avoid excessive heat; protect from freezing.

ADVERSE EFFECTS (≥1%) **CNS:** Headache, retrograde amnesia, emergence delirium, prolonged somnolence and recovery. **CV:** Myocardial depression, arrhythmias, <u>circulatory depression</u>. **GI:** Nausea, vomiting, regurgitation of gastric contents, rectal irritation, cramping, rectal bleeding, diarrhea. **Respiratory:** <u>Respiratory depression with apnea</u>; hiccups, sneezing, coughing, bronchospasm, <u>laryngospasm</u>. **Body as a Whole:** Hypersensitivity reactions, <u>anaphylaxis</u> (rare), hypothermia, thrombosis and sloughing (with extravasation); salivation, shivering, skeletal muscle hyperactivity.

DIAGNOSTIC TEST INTERFERENCE *Thiopental* may cause decrease in I^{123} and I^{131} *thyroidal uptake* test results.

INTERACTIONS Drug: CNS DEPRESSANTS, **alcohol** potentiate CNS and respiratory depression. PHENOTHIAZINES increase risk of hypotension. **Probenecid** may prolong anesthesia. **Herbal: Kava-kava, valerian** may potentiate sedation.

Common adverse effects in *italic*, life-threatening effects <u>underlined</u>; generic names in **bold**; classifications in SMALL CAPS; ✤ Canadian drug name; ⊚ Prototype drug

1487

PHARMACOKINETICS Onset: 30–60 sec. **Duration:** 10–30 min. **Distribution:** Distributed into muscle and liver; crosses placenta. **Metabolism:** In liver. **Elimination:** In urine. **Half-Life:** 12 min.

CLINICAL IMPLICATIONS

Assessment & Drug Effects

- Monitor vital signs q3–5min before, during, and after anesthetic administration until recovery and into postoperative period, if necessary.
- Report increases in pulse rate or drop in blood pressure. Hypovolemia, cranial trauma, or premedication with opioids increases potential for apnea and symptoms of myocardial depression (decreased cardiac output and arterial pressure).
- Shivering, excitement, muscle twitching may develop during recovery period if patient is in pain.

Patient & Family Education

- Onset of drug effect is rapid, with loss of consciousness within 30–60 sec.

THIORIDAZINE HYDROCHLORIDE

(thye-or-rid′a-zeen)
Novoridazine ✦

Classifications: PSYCHOTHERAPEUTIC; PHENOTHIAZINE ANTIPSYCHOTIC
Therapeutic: ANTIPSYCHOTIC
Prototype: Chlorpromazine
Pregnancy Category: C

AVAILABILITY 10 mg, 15 mg, 25 mg, 50 mg, 100 mg, 150 mg, 200 mg tablets; 30 mg/mL, 100 mg/mL solution; 25 mg/5 mL suspension

ACTION & *THERAPEUTIC EFFECT*
A phenothiazine that rarely produces extrapyramidal effects. Thioridazine blocks postsynaptic dopamine receptors in the mesolimbic system of the brain. The decrease in dopamine neurotransmission has been found to correlate to the antipsychotic effects. *Effective in reducing excitement, hypermotility, abnormal initiative, affective tension, and agitation by inhibiting psychomotor functions. Also effective as an antipsychotic agent, and for behavioral disorders in children.*

USES Management of nonpsychotic behavioral disturbances of senility, manifestations of psychotic disorders, alcohol withdrawal; symptomatic treatment of organic brain disease. Short-term treatment of moderate to marked depression and for management of hyperkinetic behavior syndrome (attention deficit disorder).

CONTRAINDICATIONS Hypersensitivity to phenothiazines. Severe CNS depression; CV disease; family history of QT prolongation; suicidal ideation; children <2 y; pregnancy (category C), lactation.

CAUTIOUS USE Premature ventricular contractions; previously diagnosed breast cancer; patients exposed to extremes in heat or to organophosphorus insecticides; history of suicidal ideation; Parkinson's disease; seizure disorders; closed-angle glaucoma; respiratory disorders.

ROUTE & DOSAGE

Psychotic Disorders
Adult: **PO** 50–100 mg t.i.d., may increase up to 800 mg/d as needed or tolerated

---

Common adverse effects in *italic*, life-threatening effects underlined; generic names in **bold**; classifications in SMALL CAPS; ✦ Canadian drug name; ⊘ Prototype drug

Geriatric: **PO** 10 mg t.i.d., may increase up to 200 mg/d
Child: **PO** >2 y, 0.5–3 mg/kg/d in divided doses; if hospitalized, may start at 25 mg t.i.d.

Moderate to Marked Depression
Adult: **PO** 25 mg t.i.d., may increase up to 200 mg/d in divided doses

Dementia Behavior
Geriatric: **PO** 10–25 mg 1–2 times/d, may increase q4–7d (max: 400 mg/d in divided doses)

ADMINISTRATION

Oral

- Give with fluid of patient's choice; tablet may be crushed.
- Schedule phenothiazine at least 1 h before or 1 h after an antacid or antidiarrheal medication.
- Dilute liquid concentrate just prior to administration with $^1/_2$ glass of fruit juice, milk, water, carbonated beverage, or soup.
- Add increases in dose to the first dose of the day to prevent sleep disturbance.
- Store at 15°–30° C (59°–86° F) in tightly covered, light-resistant containers unless otherwise indicated.

ADVERSE EFFECTS (≥1%) **CNS:** *Sedation,* dizziness, drowsiness, lethargy, extrapyramidal syndrome, nocturnal confusion, hyperactivity. **Special Senses:** Nasal congestion, blurred vision, pigmentary retinopathy. **GI:** Xerostomia, *constipation,* paralytic ileus. **Urogenital:** Amenorrhea, breast engorgement, gynecomastia, galactorrhea, *urinary retention.* **CV:** Ventricular dysrhythmias, hypotension, prolonged QTc interval.

INTERACTIONS Drug: Alcohol, ANXIOLYTICS, SEDATIVE-HYPNOTICS, other CNS DEPRESSANTS add to CNS depression; additive adverse effects with other PHENOTHIAZINES; **amiodarone, amoxapine, arsenic trioxide, bepridil, clarithromycin, daunorubicin, diltiazem, disopyramide, dofetilide, dolasetron, doxorubicin, encainide, erythromycin, flecainide, fluoxetine, fluvoxamine gatifloxacin, grepafloxacin, haloperidol, ibutilide, indapamide, local anesthetics, maprotiline, moxifloxacin, octreotide, paroxetine, pentamidine, pimozide, procainamide, probucol, quinidine, risperidone, sotalol, sertraline, sparfloxacin, terodiline, tocainide, tricyclic antidepressants, venlafaxine, verapamil, ziprasidone** can prolong QTc interval resulting in arrhythmias. **Herbal: Kava-kava** may increase risk and severity of dystonic reactions.

PHARMACOKINETICS Absorption: Well absorbed from GI tract. **Onset:** Days to weeks. **Distribution:** Crosses placenta; distributed into breast milk. **Metabolism:** In liver. **Elimination:** In urine. **Half-Life:** 26–36 h.

CLINICAL IMPLICATIONS

Assessment & Drug Effects

- Monitor for changes in behavior that may indicate increased possibility of suicidality.
- Orthostatic hypotension may occur in early therapy. Female patients appear to be more susceptible than males.
- Be aware that patients may be unable to adjust to extremes of temperature because drug effects heat regulatory center in the hypothalamus. Patient may complain of being cold even at average room temperature; older adults are particularly susceptible.
- Monitor I&O ratio and bowel elimination pattern. Check for abdominal distension and pain. En-

T

Common adverse effects in *italic,* life-threatening effects <u>underlined</u>; generic names in **bold**; classifications in SMALL CAPS; ♣ Canadian drug name; ⊘ Prototype drug

1489

courage adequate fluid intake as prophylaxis for constipation and xerostomia. The depressed patient may not seek help for either symptom or for urinary retention.
- Lab tests: Obtain periodic CBC and liver function tests during therapy.
- Supervise patient closely during early course of therapy. Suicide is an inherent risk with any depressed patient and may remain a problem until there is significant clinical improvement.

Patient & Family Education
- Exercise care not to spill drug on skin because of danger of contact dermatitis. Wash skin well in soap and water if liquid drug is spilled.
- Take drug as prescribed and do not alter dosing regimen or stop medication without consulting physician.
- Avoid alcohol during phenothiazine therapy. Concomitant use enhances CNS depression effects.
- Be aware that marked drowsiness generally subsides with continued therapy or reduction in dosage.
- Do not drive or engage in potentially hazardous activities until response to drug is known.
- Make position changes slowly, particularly from lying down to upright posture; dangle legs a few minutes before standing.
- Vasodilation produced by hot showers or baths or by long exposure to environmental heat may accentuate hypotensive effect.
- Do not apply heating pad or hot water bottles to the body for external heat. Because of depressed conditioned avoidance behaviors, a severe burn may result.
- Report the onset of any change in visual acuity, brownish coloring of vision, or impairment of night vision to physician. Symptoms suggest pigmentary retinopathy (observed primarily in patients re-

ceiving extremely high doses). An ophthalmic consultation may be indicated.
- Note: Thioridazine may color urine pink-red to reddish brown.
- Do not use any OTC drugs unless approved by the physician.

THIOTEPA
(thye-oh-tep′a)
Classifications: ANTINEOPLASTIC; ALKYLATING AGENT
Therapeutic: ANTINEOPLASTIC
Prototype: Cyclophosphamide
Pregnancy Category: D

AVAILABILITY 15 mg, 30 mg injection

ACTION & *THERAPEUTIC EFFECT*
Cell-cycle nonspecific alkylating agent that selectively reacts with DNA phosphate groups to produce chromosome cross-linkage and consequent blocking of nucleoprotein synthesis. Nonvesicant, highly toxic hematopoietic agent. *Myelosuppression is cumulative and unpredictable and may be delayed. Has some immunosuppressive activity.*

USES To produce remissions in malignant lymphomas, including Hodgkin's disease, and adenocarcinoma of breast and ovary. Also in chronic granulocytic and lymphocytic leukemia, superficial papillary carcinoma of urinary bladder, bronchogenic carcinoma, and in malignant effusions secondary to neoplastic disease of serosal cavities.
UNLABELED USES Prevention of pterygium recurrences following postoperative beta-irradiation; leukemia, malignant meningeal neoplasms.

CONTRAINDICATIONS Hypersensitivity to drug; acute leukemia; acute

Common adverse effects in *italic*, life-threatening effects <u>underlined</u>; generic names in **bold**; classifications in SMALL CAPS; ◆ Canadian drug name; ⓟ Prototype drug

infection; pregnancy (category D), lactation.

CAUTIOUS USE Chronic lymphocytic leukemia; myelosuppression produced by radiation; with other antineoplastics; bone marrow invasion by tumor cells; impaired kidney or liver function.

ROUTE & DOSAGE

Malignant Lymphomas

Adult: **IV** 0.3–0.4 mg/kg q1–4wk **IM/SC** 30–60 mg/m² once weekly **Intracavitary** 0.6–0.8 mg/kg instilled through same tubing used for paracentesis at intervals of at least 1 wk **Intravesicular** 60 mg in 30–60 mL of distilled water instilled into bladder to be retained for 2 h once/wk for 4 wk **Intrathecal** 1–11.5 mg/m² 1–2 times/wk
Child: **IV** 25–65 mg/m²/dose every 21 d

ADMINISTRATION

Intravenous

Use only under constant supervision by physicians experienced in therapy with cytotoxic agents.

- Avoid exposure of skin and respiratory tract to particles of thiotepa during solution preparation.

PREPARE: **Direct:** Reconstitute each 15 mg vial with 1.5 mL sterile water for injection (supplied) to yield 10 mg/mL. Further dilute with 50–100 mL NS. Filter solution through a 0.22 micron filter to eliminate haze. Use immediately.
ADMINISTER: **Direct:** Give 60 mg or fraction thereof over 1 min.
INCOMPATIBILITIES **Solution/additive:** Cisplatin. **Y-site:** Cisplatin, **filgrastim, minocycline, vinorelbine.**

- Store powder for injection and reconstituted solutions at 2°–8° C (35°–46° F); protect from light. Solutions reconstituted with sterile water only are stable for 8 h under refrigeration.

ADVERSE EFFECTS (≥1%) **GI:** Anorexia, nausea, vomiting, stomatitis, ulceration of intestinal mucosa. **Hematologic:** <u>Leukopenia, thrombocytopenia, anemia, pancytopenia.</u> **Skin:** Hives, rash, pruritus. **Urogenital:** Amenorrhea, interference with spermatogenesis. **Body as a Whole:** Headache, febrile reactions, pain and weeping of injection site, hyperuricemia, slowed or lessened response in heavily irradiated area, sensation of throat tightness. **Other:** Reported with intravesical administration (lower abdominal pain, hematuria, hemorrhagic chemical cystitis, vesical irritability).

INTERACTIONS Drug: May prolong muscle paralysis with **mivacurium;** ANTICOAGULANTS, NSAIDS, SALICYLATES, ANTIPLATELET AGENTS may increase risk of bleeding.

PHARMACOKINETICS Absorption: Rapidly cleared from plasma. **Onset:** Gradual response over several wk. **Metabolism:** In liver. **Elimination:** 60% in urine within 24–72 h.

CLINICAL IMPLICATIONS

Assessment & Drug Effects

- Monitor closely because most patients will manifest some evidence of toxicity.
- Be aware that because of cumulative effects, maximum myelosuppression may be delayed 3–4 wk after termination of therapy.
- Discontinue therapy (per manufacturer) if leukocyte count falls to 3000/mm³ or below or if platelet count falls below 150,000/mm³.

Common adverse effects in *italic*, life-threatening effects <u>underlined</u>; generic names in **bold**; classifications in SMALL CAPS; ♣ Canadian drug name; ⊚ Prototype drug

1491

- Lab tests: Determine Hgb level, WBC with differential, and thrombocyte (i.e., platelet) counts at least weekly during therapy and for at least 3 wk after therapy is discontinued.
- Monitor leukocyte and thrombocyte counts as indicators for adaptations in nursing and drug regimens.

Patient & Family Education
- Be aware of possibility of amenorrhea (usually reversible in 6–8 mo).
- Report onset of fever, bleeding, a cold or illness, no matter how mild to physician; medical supervision may be necessary.

THIOTHIXENE HYDROCHLORIDE

(thye-oh-thix'een)
Navane
Classifications: PSYCHOTHERAPEUTIC; PHENOTHIAZINE ANTIPSYCHOTIC
Therapeutic: ANTIPSYCHOTIC
Prototype: Chlorpromazine
Pregnancy Category: C

AVAILABILITY 1 mg, 2 mg, 5 mg, 10 mg, 20 mg capsules; 5 mg/mL solution

ACTION & THERAPEUTIC EFFECT
Xanthene derivative and a phenothiazine. Mechanism of antipsychotic effects is thought to be related to blockade of postsynaptic dopamine receptors in the brain. *Possesses antipsychotic, sedative, adrenolytic, and antiemetic activity.*

USES Manifestations of psychotic disorders.
UNLABELED USES Antidepressant.

CONTRAINDICATIONS Hypersensitivity to thioxanthenes and phenothiazines; children <12 y; comatose states; CNS depression; circulatory collapse; blood dyscrasias; pregnancy (category C), lactation.
CAUTIOUS USE History of convulsive disorders; alcohol withdrawal; glaucoma; prostatic hypertrophy; cardiovascular disease; patients who might be exposed to organophosphorus insecticides or to extreme heat; concomitant use of atropine or related drugs or ototoxic medications (especially ototoxic antibiotics); previously diagnosed breast cancer.

ROUTE & DOSAGE

Psychotic Disorders
Adult: **PO** 2 mg t.i.d., may increase up to 15 mg/d as needed or tolerated (max: 60 mg/d) **IM** 4 mg b.i.d. to q.i.d. (max: 30 mg/d)
Dementia Behavior
Geriatric: **PO** 1–2 mg 1–2 times/ d, may increase q4–7d (max: 30 mg/d in divided doses)

ADMINISTRATION

Oral
- Avoid contact between oral concentrate and skin or clothing to prevent contact dermatitis. If concentrate spills, wash skin promptly with water.
- Give oral concentrate (contains 7% alcohol) diluted in a cupful of water, fruit juice, carbonated beverage, milk, or soup.
- Empty capsule and give with water or mix with food; useful if patient unable or unwilling to swallow the capsule.

Intramuscular
- Give IM injection deep into upper outer quadrant of buttock. Aspirate carefully before injection. Rotate injection sites.
- Do not permit access to more than one dose of medication if patient

has suicidal tendency; supervise ingestion to prevent hoarding.

- Store at 15°–30° C (59°–86° F) in light-resistant containers unless otherwise indicated.

ADVERSE EFFECTS (≥1%) **CNS:** *Drowsiness,* insomnia, dizziness, cerebral edema, convulsions, *extrapyramidal symptoms (dose related),* paradoxical exaggeration of psychotic symptoms; <u>sudden death, neuroleptic malignant syndrome</u>, tardive dyskinesia, depressed cough reflex. **GI:** Xerostomia, constipation. **CV:** Tachycardia, *orthostatic hypotension* (especially with IM). **Urogenital:** Impotence, gynecomastia, galactorrhea, amenorrhea. **Skin:** Rash, contact dermatitis, photosensitivity. **Special Senses:** Blurred vision, pigmentary retinopathy. **Metabolic:** Decreased serum uric acid levels.

INTERACTIONS Drug: Alcohol, ANXIOLYTICS, SEDATIVE-HYPNOTICS, other CNS DEPRESSANTS add to CNS depression; additive adverse effects with other PHENOTHIAZINES; **Herbal: Kava-kava** may increase risk and severity of dystonic reactions.

PHARMACOKINETICS Absorption: Slowly absorbed from GI tract. **Onset:** Days to weeks PO; 1–6 h IM. **Duration:** Up to 12 h. **Distribution:** May remain in body for several weeks; crosses placenta. **Metabolism:** In liver. **Elimination:** In bile and feces. **Half-Life:** 34 h.

CLINICAL IMPLICATIONS
Assessment & Drug Effects

- Monitor for therapeutic response. Although therapeutic response can be observed 1–6 h following IM injection, it may be days or several weeks before there is a response with oral drug.
- Keep patient recumbent for at least 1 h following IM because of

possibility of orthostatic hypotension. Check BP periodically.

- Monitor BP for excessive hypotensive response when thiothixene is added to drug regimen of patient on hypertensive treatment until therapy is stabilized.
- Monitor response when patient is changed from IM to PO forms (capsules, concentrate). Dosage adjustment may be necessary.
- Monitor infants delivered from mothers who have received thiothixene. Hyperreflexia has been reported.
- Lab tests: Periodic blood chemistry and liver function tests with prolonged therapy.
- Report extrapyramidal effects (pseudoparkinsonism, akathisia, dystonia) to physician; dose adjustment or short-term therapy with an antiparkinsonism agent may provide relief.
- Be alert to first symptoms of tardive dyskinesia (see Appendix F). Discontinue drug immediately and inform physician.

Patient & Family Education

- Make position changes slowly, particularly from lying down to upright because of danger of light-headedness; sit a few minutes before walking.
- Do not drive or engage in potentially hazardous activities until response to drug is known.
- Avoid alcohol and other depressants during therapy.
- Take drug as prescribed; do not alter dosing regimen or stop medication without consulting physician. Abrupt discontinuation can cause delirium.
- Do not use any OTC drugs without approval of physician.
- Note: Hyperhidrosis, while an uncomfortable adverse effect, does not indicate need to terminate therapy.

T

Common adverse effects in *italic*, life-threatening effects <u>underlined</u>; generic names in **bold**; classifications in SMALL CAPS; ♣ Canadian drug name; ❂ Prototype drug

- Avoid excessive exposure to sunlight to prevent a photosensitivity reaction. If sun exposure is expected, protect skin with sunscreen lotion (SPF 12 or above).
- Schedule periodic eye exams and report blurred vision to physician.

THROMBIN

(throm'bin)

Thrombinar, Thrombostat

Classifications: COAGULATOR; HEMOSTATIC

Therapeutic: COAGULATOR; HEMOSTATIC

Prototype: Aminocaproic acid

Pregnancy Category: C

AVAILABILITY 1,000, 5,000, 10,000, 20,000, 50,000 unit vials

ACTION & *THERAPEUTIC EFFECT*
Plasma protein prepared from prothrombin of bovine origin. Induces clotting of whole blood or fibrinogen solution without addition of other substances. *Facilitates conversion of fibrinogen to fibrin resulting in clotting of whole blood.*

USES When oozing of blood from capillaries and small venules is accessible, as in dental extraction, plastic surgery, grafting procedures, and epistaxis; also to shorten bleeding time at puncture sites in heparinized patient (i.e., following hemodialysis).

CONTRAINDICATIONS Known hypersensitivity to any of drug components or to material of bovine origin; parenteral use; entry or infiltration into large blood vessels; pregnancy (category C).
CAUTIOUS USE Children and infants.

ROUTE & DOSAGE

Oozing Blood

Adult: **Topical** 100–2000 NIH U/mL, depending on extent of bleeding, may be used as solution, in dry form, by mixing thrombin with blood plasma to form a fibrin "glue," or in conjunction with absorbable gelatin sponge

ADMINISTRATION

Topical
- Ensure that sponge recipient area is free of blood before applying thrombin.
- Prepare solutions in sterile distilled water or isotonic saline.
- Use solutions within a few hours of preparation. If several hours are to elapse between time of preparation and use, solution should be refrigerated, or preferably frozen, and used within 48 h.
- Store lyophilized preparation at 2°–8° C (36°–46° F).

ADVERSE EFFECTS (≥1%) **Body as a Whole:** Sensitivity, allergic and febrile reactions, intravascular clotting and death when thrombin is allowed to enter large blood vessels.

THYROID

(thye'roid)

Armour Thyroid, Thyrar

Classifications: HORMONE; THYROID AGENT

Therapeutic: THYROID HORMONE REPLACEMENT

Prototype: Levothyroxine sodium

Pregnancy Category: A

AVAILABILITY 15 mg ($^1/_4$ grain), 30 mg ($^1/_2$ grain), 60 mg (1 grain),

1494

Common adverse effects in *italic*, life-threatening effects underlined; generic names in **bold**; classifications in SMALL CAPS; ♣ Canadian drug name; ⑩ Prototype drug

90 mg (1$^1/_2$ grain), 120 mg (2 grain), 180 mg (3 grain), 240 mg (4 grain), 300 mg (5 grain) tablets

ACTION & *THERAPEUTIC EFFECT*

Preparation of desiccated animal thyroid gland containing active thyroid hormones, *l*-thyroxine (T$_4$) and *l*-triiodothyronine (T$_3$). Action mechanism unknown; T$_4$ is largely converted to T$_3$, which exerts the principal effects. Influences growth and maturation of various tissues (including skeletal and CNS) at critical periods. Promotes a generalized increase in metabolic rate of body tissues. *Effectiveness indicated by diuresis, accompanied by loss of weight and puffiness, followed by sense of well-being, increased pulse rate, increased pulse pressure, increased appetite, increased psychomotor activity, loss of constipation, normalization of skin texture and hair, and increased T$_3$ and T$_4$ serum levels.*

USES Replacement or substitution therapy in primary hypothyroidism (cretinism, myxedema, simple goiter, deficiency states in pregnancy and older adults) and secondary hypothyroidism caused by surgery, excess radiation, or antithyroid drug therapy. May be given as adjunct to antithyroid agents when it is desirable to limit release of thyrotropic hormones and to prevent goitrogenesis and hypothyroidism.

CONTRAINDICATIONS Thyrotoxicosis; acute MI not associated with hypothyroidism, cardiovascular disease; morphologic hypogonadism; nephrosis; uncorrected hypoadrenalism.

CAUTIOUS USE Angina pectoris, hypertension, older adults who may have occult cardiac disease; renal insufficiency; concomitant administration of catecholamines; diabetes

mellitus; hyperthyroidism (history of); malabsorption states; pregnancy (category A).

ROUTE & DOSAGE

Mild to Moderate Hypothyroidism
Adult: **PO** 60 mg/d, may increase q30d to 60–180 mg/d
Severe Hypothyroidism
Adult: **PO** 15 mg/d, increased q2wk to 60 mg/d, then may increase q30d if needed
Child: **PO** 15 mg/d, may increase by 15 mg q2wk if needed

ADMINISTRATION

Oral

- Give as a single dose, preferably on an empty stomach.
- Initiate dosage generally at low level and systematically increase in small increments to desired maintenance dose.
- Store in dark bottle to minimize spontaneous deiodination. Keep desiccated thyroid dry.

ADVERSE EFFECTS (≥1%) **Endocrine:** Hyperthyroidism, thyroid storm [high temperature (as high as 41° C [106° F])], tachycardia, vomiting, <u>shock, coma</u>. **Special Senses:** Staring expression in eyes. **CV:** CHF, angina, cardiac arrhythmias, palpitation, tachycardia. **Body as a Whole:** Weight loss, tremors, headache, nervousness, fever, insomnia, warm and moist skin, heat intolerance, leg cramps, menstrual irregularities, <u>shock</u>, changes in appetite. **GI:** Diarrhea or abdominal cramps. **Metabolic:** Hyperglycemia (usually offset by increased tissue oxidation of sugar).

DIAGNOSTIC TEST INTERFERENCE

Thyroid increases *basal metabolic rate;* may increase *blood*

T

glucose levels, creatine phos-phokinase, AST, LDH, PBI. It may decrease *serum uric acid, cholesterol, thyroid-stimulating hormone (TSH), iodine 131* uptake. Many medications may produce false results in *thyroid function tests.*

INTERACTIONS Drug: ORAL ANTICOAGULANTS potentiate hypoprothrombinemia; may increase requirements for **insulin,** SULFONYLUREAS; **epinephrine** may precipitate coronary insufficiency; **cholestyramine** may decrease thyroid absorption.

PHARMACOKINETICS Absorption: Variably absorbed from GI tract. **Peak:** 1–3 wk. **Distribution:** Does not readily cross placenta; minimal amounts in breast milk. **Metabolism:** Deiodination in thyroid gland. **Elimination:** In urine and feces. **Half-Life:** T_3, 1–2 d; T_4, 6–7 d.

CLINICAL IMPLICATIONS

Assessment & Drug Effects

- Observe patient carefully during initial treatment for untoward reactions such as angina, palpitations, cardiac pain.
- Be alert for symptoms of overdosage (see ADVERSE EFFECTS) that may occur 1–3 wk after therapy is started. If they develop, interrupt treatment for several days and restart with reduced dosage.
- Monitor response until regimen is stabilized to prevent iatrogenic hyperthyroidism. In drug-induced hyperthyroidism, there may also be increased bone loss. Such a patient is vulnerable to pathologic fractures.
- Monitor vital signs: Pulse rate is an important clue to drug effectiveness. Assess pulse before each dose during period of dosage adjustment. Consult physician if rate is 100 or more or if there has been a marked change in rate or rhythm.
- Lab tests: Monitor thyroid function q3mo during dose adjustment period. Monitor prothrombin time closely if patient is receiving concurrent anticoagulant therapy. A decrease in requirement usually develops within 1–4 wk after starting treatment with thyroid.
- Be aware that toxic effects of thyroid develop slowly and disappear gradually. T_4 effects require up to 3–6 wk to dissipate; T_3 effects last 6–14 d after drug withdrawal.

Patient & Family Education

- Adhere to established dosage regimen; do not change dose intervals without approval of the physician.
- Be aware that replacement therapy for hypothyroidism is lifelong; continued follow-up care is important.
- Do not change brands of thyroid unless physician approves. Hormone content varies among brands.
- Monitor pulse rate and report increases greater than parameter set by physician.
- Report onset of chest pain or other signs of aggravated CV disease (dyspnea, tachycardia) to physician promptly.
- Report evidence of any unexplained bleeding to physician when taking concomitant anticoagulant.
- Use serial height and weight measurement to monitor growth in juvenile undergoing treatment.

T

TIAGABINE HYDROCHLORIDE

(ti-a′ga-been)
Gabitril Filmtabs
Classifications: ANTICONVULSANT; GABA INHIBITOR
Therapeutic: ANTICONVULSANT
Prototype: Valproic acid sodium (sodium valproate)
Pregnancy Category: C

AVAILABILITY 2 mg, 4 mg, 12 mg, 16 mg, 20 mg tablets

ACTION & *THERAPEUTIC EFFECT*

GABA inhibitor for the treatment of partial epilepsy. Potent and selective inhibitor of GABA uptake into presynaptic neurons; allows more GABA to bind to the surfaces of postsynaptic neurons in the CNS. *Effectiveness indicated by reduction in seizure activity.*

USES Adjunctive therapy for partial seizures.

CONTRAINDICATIONS Hypersensitivity to tiagabine; pregnancy (category C); lactation; children <12 y.
CAUTIOUS USE Liver function impairment; history of spike and wave discharge on EEG; status epilepticus.

ROUTE & DOSAGE

Seizures

Adult: **PO** Start with 4 mg q.d., may increase dose by 4–8 mg/d qwk (max: 56 mg/d in 2–4 divided doses)
Adolescent: **PO** 12–18 y, Start with 4 mg q.d., after 2 wk may increase dose by 4–8 mg/d qwk (max: 32 mg/d in 2–4 divided doses)

ADMINISTRATION

Oral
- Give with food.

- Make dosage increases, when needed, at weekly intervals.
- Store at 15°–30° C (59°–86° F) in a tightly closed container and protect from light.

ADVERSE EFFECTS (≥1%) **Body as a Whole:** Infection, flu-like syndrome, pain, myasthenia, allergic reactions, chills, malaise, arthralgia. **CNS:** *Dizziness, asthenia, tremor, somnolence, nervousness,* difficulty concentrating, ataxia, depression, insomnia, abnormal gait, hostility, confusion, speech disorder, difficulty with memory, paresthesias, emotional lability, agitation, dysarthria, euphoria, hallucinations, hyperkinesia, hypertonia, hypotonia, myoclonus, twitching, vertigo. Risk of new-onset seizures. **CV:** Vasodilation, hypertension, palpitations, tachycardia, syncope, edema, peripheral edema. **GI:** Abdominal pain, diarrhea, nausea, vomiting, increased appetite, mouth ulcers. **Respiratory:** Pharyngitis, cough, bronchitis, dyspnea, epistaxis, pneumonia. **Skin:** Rash, pruritus, alopecia, dry skin, sweating, ecchymoses. **Special Senses:** Amblyopia, nystagmus, tinnitus. **Urogenital:** Dysmenorrhea, dysuria, metrorrhagia, incontinence, vaginitis, UTI.

INTERACTIONS Drug: carbamazepine, phenytoin, phenobarbital decrease levels of tiagabine. Use with ANTIDEPRESSANTS, ANTIPSYCHOTICS, STIMULANTS, and NARCOTICS may increase seizure risk. **Herbal: Ginkgo** may decrease anticonvulsant effectiveness. **Evening primrose** oil may affect seizure threshold.

PHARMACOKINETICS Absorption: Rapidly absorbed; 90% bioavailability. **Peak:** 45 min. **Distribution:** 96% protein bound. **Metabolism:** In liver, probably by cytochrome P450 3A isoform. **Elimination:** 25% in urine,

T

Common adverse effects in *italic*, life-threatening effects underlined; generic names in **bold**; classifications in SMALL CAPS; ♣ Canadian drug name; ✦ Prototype drug

1497

63% in feces. **Half-Life:** 7–9 h (4–7 h with other enzyme-inducing drugs).

CLINICAL IMPLICATIONS

Assessment & Drug Effects

- Lab tests: Measure plasma levels of tiagabine before and after changes are made in the drug regimen.
- Be aware that concurrent use of other anticonvulsants may decrease effectiveness of tiagabine or increase the potential for adverse effects.
- Monitor carefully for S&S of CNS depression.

Patient & Family Education

- Do not stop taking drug abruptly; may cause sudden onset of seizures.
- Exercise caution while engaging in potentially hazardous activities because drug may cause dizziness.
- Use caution when taking other prescription or OTC drugs that can cause drowsiness.
- Report any of the following to the physician: Rash or hives; red, peeling skin; dizziness; drowsiness; depression; GI distress; nervousness or tremors; difficulty concentrating or talking.

TICARCILLIN DISODIUM/ CLAVULANATE POTASSIUM

(tye-kar-sill′in/clav-yoo′la-nate)

Timentin

Classifications: ANTIBIOTIC; ANTIPSEUDOMONAL PENICILLIN
Therapeutic: ANTIBIOTIC
Prototype: Piperacillin
Pregnancy Category: B

AVAILABILITY 3.1 g injection

ACTION & *THERAPEUTIC EFFECT*

Injectable extended-spectrum penicillin and fixed combination of ticarcillin disodium with the potassium salt of clavulanic acid, a beta-lactamase inhibitor. Used alone, clavulanic acid antibacterial activity is weak, but in combination with ticarcillin prevents degradation by beta-lactamase and extends ticarcillin spectrum of activity against many strains of beta-lactamase-producing bacteria (synergistic effect). Synergism between the two drugs does not occur against organisms susceptible to ticarcillin alone. *Extends ticarcillin spectrum of activity against many strains of beta-lactamase–producing bacteria (synergistic effect).*

USES Infections of lower respiratory tract and urinary tract and skin and skin structures, infections of bone and joint, and septicemia caused by susceptible organisms. Also mixed infections and as presumptive therapy before identification of causative organism.

CONTRAINDICATIONS Hypersensitivity to penicillins or to cephalosporins, coagulopathy.
CAUTIOUS USE Pregnancy (category B); diabetes mellitus; GI disease; asthma; history of allergies; renal impairment.

ROUTE & DOSAGE

Moderate to Severe Infections

Adult: **IV** >60 kg, 3.1 g q4–6h
Child: **IV** >3 mo, 200–300 mg/kg/d divided q4–6h (based on ticarcillin)
Infant: **IV** <3 mo, 200–300 mg/kg/d divided q6–8h (based on ticarcillin)

Renal Impairment

Cl_{cr} 30–60 mL/min: give 2 g q4h or 3.1 g q8h; 10–30 mL/min: give 2 g q8h or 3.1 g q12h; <10 mL/min: give 2 g q12h

Hemodialysis: 2 g q12h, supplement with 3.1 g after dialysis

ADMINISTRATION

Intravenous

Note: Verify correct IV concentration and rate of infusion for administration to infants and children with physician.

PREPARE: **Intermittent:** Reconstitute by adding to 3.1 g of powder 13 mL sterile water for injection or NS injection to yield 200 mg/mL ticarcillin with 6.7 mg/mL clavulanic acid. Shake until dissolved. Further dilute with NS, D5W, or RL. Do not use if discoloration or particulate matter is present.

ADMINISTER: **Intermittent:** Give over 30 min.

INCOMPATIBILITIES **Solution/additive:** AMINOGLYCOSIDES, **sodium bicarbonate. Y-site:** AMINOGLYCOSIDES, **amphotericin B cholesteryl complex, azithromycin, vancomycin.**

- Store vial with sterile powder at 21°–24° C (69°–75° F) or colder. If exposed to higher temperature, powder will darken, indicating degradation of clavulanate potassium and loss of potency. Discard vial. See package insert for information about storage and stability of reconstituted and diluted IV solutions of drug.

ADVERSE EFFECTS (≥1%) **Body as a Whole:** Hypersensitivity reactions, pain, burning, swelling at injection site; phlebitis, thrombophlebitis; superinfections. **CNS:** Headache, blurred vision, mental deterioration, convulsions, hallucinations, seizures, giddiness, neuromuscular hyperirritability. **GI:** *Diarrhea, nausea,* vomiting, disturbances of taste or smell, stomatitis, flatulence. **Hematologic:** Eosinophilia, thrombocytopenia, leukopenia, neutropenia, hemolytic anemia. **Metabolic:** Hypernatremia, transient increases in serum AST, ALT, BUN, and alkaline phosphatase; increases in serum LDH, bilirubin, and creatinine and decreased serum uric acid.

DIAGNOSTIC TEST INTERFERENCE

May interfere with test methods used to determine ***urinary proteins*** except for tests for urinary protein that use ***bromphenol blue.*** ***Positive direct antiglobulin (Coombs') test*** results, apparently caused by clavulanic acid, have been reported. This test may interfere with ***transfusion crossmatching procedures.***

INTERACTIONS **Drugs:** May increase risk of bleeding with ANTICOAGULANTS; **probenecid** decreases elimination of ticarcillin.

PHARMACOKINETICS **Distribution:** Widely distributed with highest concentrations in urine and bile; crosses placenta; distributed into breast milk. **Metabolism:** In liver. **Elimination:** In urine. **Half-Life:** 1.1–1.2 h ticarcillin, 1.1–1.5 h clavulanate.

CLINICAL IMPLICATIONS

Assessment & Drug Effects

- Lab tests: Obtain baseline C&S tests before initiating therapy; drug may be started pending results. Monitor kidney and liver functions, CBC, platelet count, and serum electrolytes during prolonged treatment.

- Be aware that serious and sometimes fatal anaphylactoid reactions have been reported in patients with penicillin hypersensitivity or history of sensitivity to multiple allergens. Reported incidence is low with this combination drug.

T

Common adverse effects in *italic*, life-threatening effects <u>underlined</u>; generic names in **bold**; classifications in SMALL CAPS; ♣ Canadian drug name; ⦿ Prototype drug

- Monitor cardiac status because of high sodium content of drug.
- Overdose symptoms: This drug may cause neuromuscular hyper-irritability or seizures.

Patient & Family Education
- Report urticaria, rashes, or pruritus to physician immediately.
- Report frequent loose stools, diarrhea, or other possible signs of pseudomembranous colitis (see Appendix F) to physician.

TICLOPIDINE
(ti-clo'pi-deen)
Ticlid
Classifications: ANTICOAGULANT; ANTIPLATELET AGENT
Therapeutic: ANTIPLATELET
Prototype: Clopidogrel
Pregnancy Category: B

AVAILABILITY 250 mg tablets

ACTION & *THERAPEUTIC EFFECT*
Platelet aggregation inhibitor that interferes with platelet membrane functioning and therefore platelet interactions. *Prevents release of platelet constituents and prolongs bleeding time.*

USES Reduction of the risk of thrombotic stroke in patients intolerant to aspirin.
UNLABELED USES Prevention of venous thromboembolic disorders; maintenance of bypass graft patency and of vascular access sites in hemodialysis patients; improvement of exercise performance in patients with ischemic heart disease and intermittent claudication; prevention of postoperative deep venous thrombosis (DVT).

CONTRAINDICATIONS Hypersensitivity to ticlopidine; hematopoietic disease, coagulopathy; leukemia; pathologic bleeding; severe liver impairment; lactation.
CAUTIOUS USE Hepatic function impairment, renal impairment; patients at risk for bleeding from trauma, surgery, or a bleeding disorder; GI bleeding; pregnancy (category B). Safe use in children <18 y not established.

ROUTE & DOSAGE

Stroke Prevention
Adult: **PO** 250 mg b.i.d. with food

ADMINISTRATION
Oral
- Give with food or just after eating to minimize GI irritation.
- Discontinue anticoagulants or fibrinolytic drugs before ticlopidine administration.
- Store at 15°–30° C (59°–86° F).

ADVERSE EFFECTS (≥1%) **CNS:** Dizziness. **GI:** Nausea, vomiting, abdominal cramps; dyspepsia, flatulence, anorexia; abnormal liver function tests (few cases of hepatotoxicity reported). **Hematologic:** Neutropenia (resolves in 1–3 wk), thrombocytopenia, leukopenia, agranulocytosis (usually within first 3 mo), and pancytopenia; hemorrhage (ecchymosis, epistaxis, menorrhagia, GI bleeding), thrombotic thrombocytopenia purpura (usually within first month). **Skin:** Urticaria, maculopapular rash, erythema nodosum (generally occur within the first 3 mo of therapy, with most occurring within the first 3–6 wk).

DIAGNOSTIC TEST INTERFERENCE Increases *total serum cholesterol* by 8–10% within 4 wk of beginning therapy. *Lipoprotein ratios* remain unchanged. Elevates *alka-*

line phosphatase and *serum transaminases.*

INTERACTIONS Drug: ANTACIDS decrease bioavailability of ticlopidine. ANTICOAGULANTS increase risk of bleeding. **Cimetidine** decreases clearance of ticlopidine. CORTICOSTEROIDS counteract increased bleeding time associated with ticlopidine. May decrease **cyclosporine** levels (one case report). Increases **theophylline** half-life by 42%, possibly increasing **theophylline** serum levels. May increase **phenytoin** levels. **Food:** Food may increase bioavailability of ticlopidine.

PHARMACOKINETICS Absorption: 90% absorbed from GI tract; increased absorption when taken with food. **Onset:** Antiplatelet activity, 24–48 h; maximal effect at 3–5 d. **Peak:** Peak serum levels at 2 h. **Duration:** Bleeding times return to baseline within 4–10 d. **Distribution:** 90% bound to plasma proteins. **Metabolism:** Rapidly and extensively metabolized in liver. **Elimination:** Only 1% excreted unchanged; 60% of metabolites excreted in urine, 23% in feces. **Half-Life:** 12.6 h; terminal half-life is 4–5 d with repeated dosing.

CLINICAL IMPLICATIONS

Assessment & Drug Effects

- Lab tests: Monitor platelet count and bleeding time periodically. Monitor CBC with differentials q2wk from second week to end of third month of therapy and thereafter if S&S of infection develop.
- Report promptly laboratory values indicative of neutropenia, thrombocytopenia, or agranulocytosis.
- Monitor for signs of bleeding (e.g., ecchymosis, epistaxis, hematuria, GI bleeding).

Patient & Family Education

- Report promptly to physician any of the following: Nausea, diarrhea, rash, sore throat, or other signs of infection, signs of bleeding, or signs of cholestasis (e.g., yellow skin or sclera, dark urine or clay-colored stools).
- Understand risk of GI bleeding; do not take aspirin along with ticlopidine.
- Do not take antacids within 2 h of ticlopidine.
- Keep appointments for regularly scheduled blood tests.

TIGECYCLINE
(ti-ge-cy′cline)
Tygacil
Classifications: ANTIBIOTIC; GLYCYLCYCLINE
Therapeutic: ANTIBIOTIC
Prototype: Tetracycline
Pregnancy Category: D

AVAILABILITY 50 mg injection

ACTION & *THERAPEUTIC EFFECT*
Tigecycline inhibits protein production in bacteria by binding to the 30S ribosomal subunit and blocking entry of transfer RNA molecules into the ribosome of the bacteria. This prevents formation of peptide chains in bacteria, thus interfering with their growth. *Tigecycline is active against a broad spectrum of bacterial pathogens and is bacteriostatic.*

USES Treatment of complicated skin and skin structure infections and complicated intraabdominal infections.

CONTRAINDICATIONS Hypersensitivity to tigecycline; pregnancy (category D) and during tooth de-

Common adverse effects in *italic*, life-threatening effects <u>underlined</u>; generic names in **bold**; classifications in SMALL CAPS; ♣ Canadian drug name; ⊘ Prototype drug

1501

velopment of the fetus; viral infections.

CAUTIOUS USE Severe hepatic impairment (Child-Pugh class C); hypersensitivity to tetracycline, intestinal perforations, intraabdominal infections; GI disorders; lactation; children <18 y.

ROUTE & DOSAGE

Complicated Skin and Intra-abdominal Infections

Adult: **IV** 100 mg initially, followed by 50 mg q12h over 30–60 min × 5–14 d

Hepatic Impairment

Child-Pugh class C: Initial dose 100 mg, followed by 25 mg q12h

ADMINISTRATION

- Note that dosage adjustment is required with severe hepatic impairment.

Intravenous

PREPARE: **Intermittent:** Reconstitute each vial (50 mg) with 5.3 mL of NS or D5W to yield 10 mg/mL. Swirl gently to dissolve; reconstituted solution should be yellow to orange in color. After reconstitution, immediately withdraw the solution and add to 100 mL IV bag of NS or D5W for infusion. The maximum concentration in the IV bag should be 1 mg/mL.

ADMINISTER: **Intermittent:** Give over 30–60 min; when using Y-site, flush IV line with NS or D5W before/after infusion.

INCOMPATIBILITIES **Y-site:** **Amphotericin B, chlorpromazine, methylprednisolone, voriconazole.**

- Store in the IV bag at room temperature for up to 6 h, or refrigerated at 2°–8° C (36°–46° F) for up to 24 h.

ADVERSE EFFECTS (≥1%) **CNS:** Asthenia, dizziness, headache, insomnia. **CV:** Hypertension, hypotension, peripheral edema, phlebitis. **GI:** Abdominal pain, constipation, diarrhea, dyspepsia, *nausea, vomiting.* **Hepatologic/Lymphatic:** Abnormal healing, anemia, infection, leukocytosis, thrombocythemia. **Metabolic/Nutritional:** Alkaline phosphatase increased, ALT increased, amylase increased, AST increased, bilirubinemia, BUN increased, hyperglycemia, hypokalemia, hypoproteinemia, lactic dehydrogenase increased. **Musculoskeletal:** Back pain. **Respiratory:** Dyspnea, increased cough, pulmonary physical findings. **Skin:** Pruritus, rash, sweating. **Body as a Whole:** Abscess, fever, local reaction to injection, pain.

INTERACTIONS Drug: Increased concentrations of **warfarin** required close monitoring of INR. Efficacy of ORAL CONTRACEPTIVES may be decreased when used in combination with tigecycline.

PHARMACOKINETICS Distribution: 71–89% protein bound. **Metabolism:** Negligible. **Elimination:** Fecal (major) and renal. **Half-Life:** 27 h (single dose); 42 h (multiple doses).

CLINICAL IMPLICATIONS

Assessment & Drug Effects

- Monitor for hypersensitivity reaction in those with reported tetracycline allergy.
- Monitor for and report S&S of superinfection (see Appendix F) or pseudomembranous enterocolitis (see Appendix F).
- Lab tests: C&S prior to initiation of therapy; periodic serum electro-

lytes, LFTs and kidney function tests; PT and INT with concurrent anticoagulant therapy.
- Monitor diabetics for loss of glycemic control.

Patient & Family Education
- Avoid direct exposure to sunlight during and for several days after therapy is terminated to reduce risk of photosensitivity reaction.
- Report to physician loose stools or diarrhea either during or shortly after termination of therapy.
- Use a barrier contraceptive in addition to oral contraceptives if trying to avoid pregnancy.

TILUDRONATE DISODIUM

(til-u′dro-nate)
Skelid
Classifications: REGULATOR, BONE METABOLISM (BISPHOSPHONATE)
Therapeutic: BONE METABOLISM REGULATOR
Prototype: Etidronate disodium
Pregnancy Category: C

AVAILABILITY 240 mg tablets

ACTION & THERAPEUTIC EFFECT
Mechanism of action of this diphosphate is to inhibit osteoclastic activity, which leads to resorption of the bone matrix. Acts primarily by inhibiting normal or abnormal bone resorption, thus reducing bone formation. *Reduces bone formation and effectiveness indicated by decreasing levels of alkaline phosphatase.*

USES Treatment of Paget's disease.

CONTRAINDICATIONS Hypersensitivity to diphosphonates (e.g., alendronate, etidronate, pamidronate, tiludronate); severe kidney failure (Cl$_{cr}$ <30 mL/min); pregnancy (category C); lactation.

CAUTIOUS USE Hypocalcemia, renal impairment; active UGI problems (e.g., gastritis, dysphagia, ulcer, esophageal disease); vitamin D deficiency; CHF. Safety and efficacy in children are not established.

ROUTE & DOSAGE

Paget's Disease
Adult: **PO** 400 mg/d with 6–8 oz of water times 3 mo

ADMINISTRATION
Oral
- Give with 6–8 oz of plain water 2 h before or after food.
- Do not give within 2 h of drugs containing calcium, aspirin, or indomethacin. Give aluminum- or magnesium-containing antacids no sooner than 2 h after tiludronate.
- Store in manufacturer's packaging at 15°–30° C (59°–86° F).

ADVERSE EFFECTS (≥1%) **Body as a Whole:** *Pain,* flu-like syndrome, edema. **CNS:** Headache, dizziness, paresthesias. **CV:** Chest pain. **GI:** *Nausea, diarrhea,* dyspepsia, vomiting, flatulence. **Special Senses:** Cataract, conjunctivitis, glaucoma. **Respiratory:** Rhinitis, sinusitis, coughing, pharyngitis. **Skin:** Rash. **Metabolic:** Hyperparathyroidism, vitamin D deficiency, **Musculoskeletal:** Arthralgia, arthrosis.

INTERACTIONS Drug: Absorption decreased by CALCIUM, ALUMINUM- or MAGNESIUM-CONTAINING ANTACIDS, **aspirin.** Absorption increased by **indomethacin.**

PHARMACOKINETICS Absorption: Poorly absorbed from GI tract. **Steady-State:** 30 d. **Metabolism:** Not metabolized. **Elimination:** Primarily in urine. **Half-Life:** 150 h.

T

Common adverse effects in *italic,* life-threatening effects underlined; generic names in **bold**; classifications in SMALL CAPS; ♣ Canadian drug name; ⊘ Prototype drug

1503

CLINICAL IMPLICATIONS

Assessment & Drug Effects

- Monitor for S&S of upper GI dysfunction or ulceration.
- Lab tests: Periodic serum calcium and serum phosphate.

Patient & Family Education

- Do not remove tablets from foil strips until time to be taken.
- Wait at least 2 h after taking tiludronate to take aluminum- and magnesium-containing antacids.
- Consult physician to determine appropriate daily intake of vitamin D and calcium.

TIMOLOL MALEATE

(tye'moe-lole)

Betimol, Blocadren, Istalol, Timoptic, Timoptic XE

Classifications: BETA-ADRENERGIC ANTAGONIST; EYE PREPARATION; MIOTIC

Therapeutic: MIOTIC
Prototype: Propranolol
Pregnancy Category: C

AVAILABILITY 5 mg, 10 mg, 20 mg tablets; 0.25%, 0.5% ophthalmic solution or gel

ACTION & *THERAPEUTIC EFFECT*

Nonselective beta-adrenergic antagonist. Demonstrates antihypertensive, antiarrhythmic, and antianginal properties, and suppresses plasma renin activity. When applied topically, lowers elevated and normal intraocular pressure (IOP) by reducing formation of aqueous humor and possibly by increasing outflow. *Topically, lowers elevated and normal intraocular pressure (IOP). Orally, therapeutically useful for mild hypertension and migraine headaches.*

USES Topically (ophthalmic solution) to reduce elevated IOP in chronic, open-angle glaucoma, aphakic glaucoma, secondary glaucoma, and ocular hypertension. May be used alone or in conjunction with epinephrine, pilocarpine, or a carbonic anhydrase inhibitor such as acetazolamide. Oral preparation is used as monotherapy or in combination with a thiazide diuretic to prevent reinfarction after MI and to treat mild hypertension.

UNLABELED USES Prophylactic management of stable, uncomplicated angina pectoris and migraine headaches.

CONTRAINDICATIONS Bronchospasm; severe COPD; bronchial asthma; heart failure; pregnancy (category C), abrupt discontinuation, acute bronchospasm, AV block, bradycardia, cardiogenic shock, acute pulmonary edema, compromised left ventricular dysfunction, Raynaud's disease. Safety in children is not established.

CAUTIOUS USE Bronchitis, patients subject to bronchospasm, asthma; sinus bradycardia, greater than first-degree heart block, heart failure; renal impairment; hepatic disease; vasospastic angina, peripheral vascular disease; pheochromocytoma; thyrotoxicosis, hyperthyroidism; right ventricular failure secondary to pulmonary hypertension, COPD; stroke, cerebrovascular disease; depression; older adults; psoriasis; myasthenia gravis; concomitant use with adrenergic augmenting drugs, e.g., MAO inhibitors.

ROUTE & DOSAGE

Glaucoma

See Appendix A-1.

Hypertension

Adult: **PO** 10 mg b.i.d., may increase to 60 mg/d in 2 divided doses

Angina

Adult: **PO** 15–45 mg in 3 divided doses

ADMINISTRATION

Oral

- Give with fluid of patient's choice; tablet may be crushed.
- Make dosage increases for hypertension at weekly intervals.

ADVERSE EFFECTS (≥1%) **CNS:** Fatigue, lethargy, weakness, somnolence, anxiety, headache, dizziness, confusion, psychic dissociation, depression. **CV:** Palpitation, bradycardia, hypotension, syncope, AV conduction disturbances, CHF, aggravation of peripheral vascular insufficiency. **Special Senses:** *Eye irritation* including conjunctivitis, blepharitis, keratitis, superficial punctate keratopathy. **GI:** Anorexia, dyspepsia, nausea. **Skin:** Rash, urticaria. **Respiratory:** Difficulty in breathing, bronchospasm. **Body as a Whole:** Fever. **Metabolic:** Hypoglycemia, hypokalemia.

INTERACTIONS Drug: ANTIHYPERTENSIVE AGENTS, DIURETICS, SELECTIVE SEROTONIN REUPTAKE INHIBITORS potentiate hypotensive effects; NSAIDS may antagonize hypotensive effects.

PHARMACOKINETICS Absorption: 90% absorbed from GI tract; 50% reaches systemic circulation; some systemic absorption from topical application. **Peak:** 1–2 h PO; 1–5 h topical. **Distribution:** Distributed into breast milk. **Metabolism:** 80% metabolized in liver to inactive metabolites. **Elimination:** In urine.

CLINICAL IMPLICATIONS

Assessment & Drug Effects

- Check pulse before administering timolol, topical or oral. If there are extremes (rate or rhythm), withhold medication and call the physician.
- Assess pulse rate and BP at regular intervals and more often in patients with severe heart disease.
- Note: Some patients develop tolerance during long-term therapy.

Patient & Family Education

- Be aware that drug may cause slight reduction in resting heart rate. Learn how to assess pulse rate and report significant changes. Consult physician for parameters.
- Do not stop drug abruptly; angina may be exacerbated. Dosage is reduced over a period of 1–2 wk.
- Report difficulty in breathing promptly to physician. Drug withdrawal may be indicated.

TINIDAZOLE

(tin′i-da-zole)
Tindamax
Classifications: AZOLE ANTIBIOTIC; ANTIPROTOZOAL; AMEBICIDE
Therapeutic: AZOLE ANTIBIOTIC; ANTIPROTOZOAL; AMEBICIDE
Prototype: Metronidazole
Pregnancy Category: D first trimester; C second and third trimester

AVAILABILITY 250 mg, 500 mg tablets

ACTION & *THERAPEUTIC EFFECT*

Made from cell extracts of *Trichomonas*. Tinidazole is effective against dividing and nondividing cells of targeted bacteria and protozoa. It inhibits formation of their DNA helix and thus inhibits DNA synthesis of these organisms. This leads to bacterial and protozoal cell

T

Common adverse effects in *italic*, life-threatening effects underlined; generic names in **bold**; classifications in SMALL CAPS; ♣ Canadian drug name; ⊕ Prototype drug

1505

death. *Demonstrates activity against infections caused by protozoa and anaerobic bacteria.*

USES Treatment of trichomoniasis, giardiasis, amebiasis, and amebic liver abscess.

CONTRAINDICATIONS First trimester of pregnancy (category D), second and third trimesters pregnancy (category C); known hypersensitivity to tinidazole or other azole antibiotics (e.g., metronidazole); lactation within 72 h of tinidazole use; children <3 y.

CAUTIOUS USE CNS diseases, liver dysfunction, alcoholism, ethanol intoxication; hematologic disease; neurologic disease; bone marrow depression; dialysis; candidiasis.

ROUTE & DOSAGE

Giardiasis
Adult: **PO** 2 g as single dose with food
Child: **PO** ≥3 y 50 mg/kg (up to 2 g) as single dose with food

Intestinal Amebiasis
Adult: **PO** 2 g once daily for 3 d
Child: **PO** ≥3 y 50 mg/kg/d (up to 2 g/d) once daily for 3 d

Amebic Liver Abscess
Adult: **PO** 2 g once daily for 3–5 d
Child: **PO** ≥3 y 50 mg/kg/d (up to 2 g/d) once daily for 3–5 d

Trichomoniasis
Adult: **PO** 2 g as single dose

ADMINISTRATION
Oral
- Give with food to minimize GI distress; may be crushed in artificial cherry syrup if tablets cannot be swallowed whole.
- If given on a dialysis day, add a 50% dose of tinidazole at the end of hemodialysis.

- Separate the dosing of cholestyramine and tinidazole by 2–4 h when used concurrently.
- Do not give within 2 wk of the last dose of disulfiram.
- Store at 15°–30° C (59°–86° F). Protect from light.

ADVERSE EFFECTS (≥1%) **Body as a Whole:** Weakness, fatigue, malaise. **CNS:** Dizziness, headache. **GI:** Metallic/bitter taste, nausea, anorexia, dyspepsia, cramps, epigastric discomfort, vomiting, constipation.

INTERACTIONS Drug: May increase INR with **warfarin; alcohol** may cause abdominal cramps, nausea, vomiting, headache, flushing; psychotic reactions with **disulfiram;** may increase the half-life of **fosphenytoin, phenytoin;** may increase levels and toxicity of **lithium, fluorouracil, cyclosporine, tacrolimus; cholestyramine** may decrease absorption of tinidazole.

PHARMACOKINETICS Peak: 2 h. **Distribution:** Crosses blood–brain barrier and placenta and is excreted in breast milk. **Metabolism:** In the liver by CYP3A4. **Elimination:** Primarily in urine. **Half-Life:** 12–14 h.

CLINICAL IMPLICATIONS
Assessment & Drug Effects
- Withhold drug and notify physician for S&S of CNS dysfunction (e.g., seizures, numbness or paresthesia of extremities). Drug should be discontinued if abnormal neurologic signs appear.
- Lab tests: baseline LTFs; CBC with differential, if retreatment is required.
- Monitor INR/PT frequently with concomitant oral anticoagulants. Continue monitoring for at least 8 d after discontinuation of tinidazole.
- Monitor serum lithium levels with concurrent use.

▪ Monitor for phenytoin toxicity with concurrent IV phenytoin.

Patient & Family Education
▪ Stop taking the drug and report promptly: convulsions, numbness, tingling, pain, or weakness in the hands or feet; dizziness or unsteadiness; fever.
▪ Harmless urine discoloration may occur while taking this drug.

TINZAPARIN SODIUM

(tinz′a-par-in)
Innohep
Pregnancy Category: B
See Appendix A-2.

TIOCONAZOLE

(ti-o-con′a-zole)
Vagistat-1
Classifications: ANTIBIOTIC; AZOLE ANTIFUNGAL
Therapeutic: AZOLE ANTIFUNGAL
Prototype: Fluconazole
Pregnancy Category: C

AVAILABILITY 6.5% vaginal ointment

ACTION & *THERAPEUTIC EFFECT*
Broad-spectrum antifungal agent that inhibits growth of human pathogenic yeasts by disrupting normal fungal cell membrane permeability. *Effective against* Candida albicans, *other species of* Candida, *and* Torulopsis glabrata.

USES Local treatment of vulvovaginal candidiasis.

CONTRAINDICATIONS Hypersensitivity to tioconazole or other imidazole antifungal agents; pregnancy (category C), children <12 y; lactation.
CAUTIOUS USE Diabetes mellitus; HIV infections; immunosuppression.

ROUTE & DOSAGE

Candidiasis
Adult: **Intravaginal** One applicator full h.s. times 1 d

ADMINISTRATION

Instillation
▪ Insert applicator high into the vagina (except during pregnancy).
▪ Wash applicator before and after each use.
▪ Store away from direct heat and light.

ADVERSE EFFECTS (≥1%) **Urogenital:** Mild erythema, burning, discomfort, rash, itching.

INTERACTIONS Drug: May inactivate spermicidal effects of **nonoxynol-9.**

PHARMACOKINETICS Absorption: Minimal absorption from vagina.

CLINICAL IMPLICATIONS

Assessment & Drug Effects
▪ Do not use for patient with a history of allergic reaction to other antifungal agents, such as miconazole.
▪ Monitor for sensitization and irritation; these may be an indication to discontinue drug.

Patient & Family Education
▪ Learn correct application technique.
▪ Understand potential adverse reactions, including sensitization and allergic response.
▪ Tioconazole may interact with diaphragms and latex condoms; avoid concurrent use within 72 h.
▪ Refrain from sexual intercourse while using tioconazole.
▪ Wear only cotton underwear; change daily.

T

Common adverse effects in *italic*, life-threatening effects underlined; generic names in **bold**; classifications in SMALL CAPS; ♣ Canadian drug name; ❽ Prototype drug

1507

TIOTROPIUM BROMIDE

(ti-o-tro'pi-um)
Spiriva
Classifications: ANTICHOLINERGIC;
ANTIMUSCARINIC; ANTISPASMODIC;
BRONCHODILATOR
Therapeutic: BRONCHODILATOR;
ANTISPASMODIC
Prototype: Ipratropium
Pregnancy Category: C

AVAILABILITY 18 mcg capsules
with powder for inhalation

ACTION & *THERAPEUTIC EFFECT*
A long-acting, antispasmodic agent.
In the bronchial airways, it exhibits
inhibition of muscarinic receptors of
the smooth muscle resulting in
bronchodilation. The drug effect
can last up to 24 h. *Bronchodilation after inhalation of tiotropium is
predominantly a site-specific effect.*

USES Maintenance treatment of bronchospasm associated with chronic
obstructive pulmonary disease
(COPD).

CONTRAINDICATIONS Hypersensitivity to tiotropium, atropine, or ipratropium; acute bronchospasm; pregnancy (category C); children <18 y.
CAUTIOUS USE Decreased renal
function; BPH, urinary bladder neck
obstruction; narrow-angle glaucoma;
older adults; lactation.

ROUTE & DOSAGE

COPD

Adult: **Inhaled** Inhale the contents
of one capsule once daily using
hand inhaler device provided.

ADMINISTRATION

Inhalation

- Place capsule in HandiHaler® and
press button to puncture. Instruct
patient to exhale deeply then

put the mouthpiece to the lips
and breathe in the dose deeply and
slowly; remove HandiHaler® and
hold breath for at least 10 sec,
and then exhale slowly; rinse
mouth with water to minimize dry
mouth.
- Ensure that drug does not contact
the eyes.
- Store at 15°–30° C (59°–86° F).

ADVERSE EFFECTS (≥1%) **Body as
a Whole:** Nonspecific chest pain,
dependent edema, infection, moniliasis, flu-like syndrome, cough, allergic reactions. **CNS:** Dysphonia,
paresthesia, depression. **GI:** Abdominal pain, constipation, *dry mouth,*
dyspepsia, vomiting, reflux, stomatitis. **Metabolic:** Hypercholesterolemia, hyperglycemia. **Musculoskeletal:** Myalgia, skeletal pain. **Respiratory:** Epistaxis, pharyngitis, rhinitis,
laryngitis, *sinusitis, upper respiratory
tract infection.* **Skin:** Rash. **Special
Senses:** Cataract. **Urogenital:** Urinary tract infection.

INTERACTIONS Drug: May cause
additive anticholinergic effects with
other ANTICHOLINERGIC AGENTS.

PHARMACOKINETICS Absorption:
19.5% absorbed from the lungs.
Peak: 5 min. **Metabolism:** <25% of
dose is metabolized in liver by
CYP2D6 and 3A4. **Elimination:** 14%
of dose excreted in urine; remaining
is excreted in feces as nonabsorbed
drug. **Half-Life:** 5–6 d.

CLINICAL IMPLICATIONS

Assessment & Drug Effects

- Withhold drug and notify physician if S&S of angioedema occurs.
- Monitor for anticholinergic effects
(e.g., tachycardia, urinary retention).

Patient & Family Education

- Do not allow powdered medication to contact the eyes, as this

may cause blurring of vision and pupil dilation.

- Tiotropium bromide is intended as a once-daily maintenance treatment. It is not useful for treatment of acute episodes of bronchospasm (i.e., rescue therapy).
- Withhold drug and notify physician if swelling around the face, mouth, or neck occurs.
- Report any of the following: constipation, increased heart rate, blurred vision, urinary difficulty.

TIPRANAVIR

(ti-pra'na-vir)
Aptivus
Classifications: ANTIRETROVIRAL AGENT; HIV PROTEASE INHIBITOR
Therapeutic: ANTIRETROVIRAL; PROTEASE INHIBITOR
Prototype: Saquinavir
Pregnancy Category: C

AVAILABILITY 250 mg capsules

ACTION & THERAPEUTIC EFFECT
A non-peptide protease inhibitor. It inhibits virus-specific processing of the viral polyproteins in HIV-1 infected cells, thus preventing the formation of mature viral particles. *Helps decrease viral load of HIV-1 strains resistant to other protease inhibitors.*

USES Treatment of HIV-1 infection in adults with evidence of viral replication who are highly treatment-experienced or have HIV-1 strains resistant to multiple protease inhibitors. Tipranavir should be used in combination with ritonavir 200 mg and other antiretroviral agents.

CONTRAINDICATIONS Known hypersensitivity to any of the ingredients in tipranavir; moderate to severe (Child-Pugh class B and C, respectively) hepatic insufficiency; pancreatitis; pregnancy (category C); lactation. Safety and efficacy in children have not been established.
CAUTIOUS USE Hypersensitivity to sulfonamides; patients with chronic hepatitis B or hepatitis C coinfection; hemophilia; coagulopathy; elevated liver enzymes; diabetes mellitus or hyperglycemia; hyperlipidemia; concurrent administration with HMG-CoA inhibitors.

ROUTE & DOSAGE

HIV-1 Infection
Adult: **PO** 500 mg (with 200 mg ritonavir) b.i.d.

ADMINISTRATION

Oral
- Coadminister with 200 mg ritonavir. Give with food.
- Store at 15°–30° C (59°–86° F). Once opened, use contents of bottle within 60 d.

ADVERSE EFFECTS (≥1%) **Body as a Whole:** Fatigue, pyrexia. **CNS:** Asthenia, depression, headache, insomnia. **GI:** Abdominal pain, *diarrhea,* nausea, vomiting. **Hematologic:** Decreased white blood cell levels, risk of hemorrhage. **Hepatic:** *Elevated liver enzymes (amylase, ALT, AST).* **Metabolic:** *Increased cholesterol, increased triglycerides.* **Respiratory:** Bronchitis, cough. **Skin:** Rash.

INTERACTIONS Drug: Aluminum- and **magnesium-**based ANTACIDS may decrease tipranavir absorption. AZOLE ANTIFUNGAL AGENTS, **clarithromycin, erythromycin,** and other inhibitors of CYP3A4 may increase tipranavir levels. **Efavirenz, loperamide,** NRTIS, and RIFAMYCINS (e.g., **rifampin**) may decrease tipranavir

T

Common adverse effects in *italic*, life-threatening effects underlined; generic names in **bold**; classifications in SMALL CAPS; ♣ Canadian drug name; ⓟ Prototype drug

1509

levels. Tipranavir increases **rifabutin** levels. Coadministration of tipranavir and **tenofovir** decreases the levels of both compounds. Tipranavir increases the concentration of BENZODIAZEPINES, **desipramine**, ERGOT ALKALOIDS, and numerous ANTIARRHYTHMIC AGENTS **(amiodarone, flecainide, propafenone, quinidine)**. Tipranavir may decrease **ethinyl estradiol** levels by 50%. Combination use of tipranavir and HMG COA REDUCTASE INHIBITORS increases the risk of myopathy. Tipranavir capsules contain **alcohol** that can produce disulfiram-like reactions with **metronidazole** and **disulfiram. Food:** Food enhances the bioavailability of tipranavir. **Herbal: St. John's wort** decreases the levels of tipranavir.

PHARMACOKINETICS Peak: 3 h. **Distribution:** >99.9% protein bound. **Metabolism:** Extensive hepatic oxidation to inactive metabolites (when given alone); minimal metabolism (when given with ritonavir). **Elimination:** Fecal (primary) and renal (minimal). **Half-Life:** 6 h.

CLINICAL IMPLICATIONS

Assessment & Drug Effects

- Monitor for and report immediately S&S of liver toxicity.
- Monitor for S&S of adverse drug reactions and toxicity from concurrently administered drugs. Many drugs interact with tipranavir.
- Monitor diabetics for loss of glycemic control.
- Use barrier contraceptive if using hormonal contraceptive.
- Lab tests: Baseline and frequent LFTs, especially in those with hepatitis B or C; periodic lipid profile and fasting plasma glucose.
- Monitor blood levels of anticoagulants with concurrent therapy.

Patient & Family Education

- Follow directions for taking the drug (see Administration). If a dose is missed, take it as soon as possible and then return to the normal schedule. Never double a dose.
- Inform physician of all medications and herbal products you are taking.
- Protect against sunlight exposure to minimize risk of photosensitivity.
- Report any of the following to physician: fatigue, weakness, loss of appetite, nausea, jaundice, dark urine, or clay colored stools.

TIROFIBAN HYDROCHLORIDE

(tir-o-fi'ban)

Aggrastat

Classifications: ANTICOAGULANT; ANTIPLATELET AGENT; GLYCOPROTEIN IIB/IIIA RECEPTOR INHIBITOR
Therapeutic: ANTIPLATELET
Prototype: Abciximab
Pregnancy Category: B

AVAILABILITY 250 mcg/mL, 50 mcg/mL injection

ACTION & *THERAPEUTIC EFFECT*
Antiplatelet agent that binds to the glycoprotein IIb/IIIa receptor of platelets inhibiting platelet aggregation. *Effectiveness indicated by minimizing thrombotic events during treatment of acute coronary syndrome.*

USES Acute coronary syndromes (unstable angina, MI).

CONTRAINDICATIONS Active internal bleeding within 30 d; acute pericarditis; aortic dissection; intracranial aneurysm, intracranial mass, coagulopathy; concurrent use with another glycoprotein IIb/IIIa receptor inhibitor (e.g., eptifibatide, abciximab), or heparin; history of aneurysm or AV malformation; history of intracranial hemorrhage or neoplasm; hypersensitivity to tirofiban; active abnormal bleeding; retinal bleeding; hemorrhagic retinopathy; major surgery or trauma within 3 d; stroke within 30 d; history of hemorrhagic stroke; thrombocytopenia following administration of tirofiban; within 4 h of percutaneous coronary intervention (PCI); lactation. **CAUTIOUS USE** Concomitant use with thrombolytic agents or drugs that cause hemolysis; platelet count <150,000 mm^3; severe renal insufficiency; pregnancy (category B). Safety and efficacy in children <18 y are unknown.

ROUTE & DOSAGE

Acute Coronary Syndromes
Adult: **IV** 0.4 mcg/kg/min for 30 min, then 0.1 mcg/kg/min for 12–24 h after angioplasty or arteriectomy
Renal Impairment
Cl$_{cr}$ <30 mL/min: Reduce rate of infusion 50%

ADMINISTRATION

Intravenous

PREPARE: **IV Infusion:** Withdraw 100 mL from a 500-mL bag of NS or D5W and replace with 100 mL of tirofiban HCl injection. If a 250-mL IV bag is used, withdraw 50 mL of IV solution and replace with 50 mL of tirofiban injection. Either preparation yields 50 mcg/mL. Mix well before infusing. Note: Commercially premixed IV tirofiban solutions are available. *ADMINISTER:* **IV Infusion:** An initial loading dose of 0.4 mcg/kg/min for 30 min is usually followed by a maintenance infusion of 0.1 mcg/kg/min.

INCOMPATIBILITIES Y-site: **Diazepam, tenecteplase.**

• Discard unused IV solution 24 h following start of infusion. • Store unopened containers at 15°–30° C (59°–86° F). Do not freeze and protect from light.

ADVERSE EFFECTS (≥1%) **Body as a Whole:** Edema, swelling, pelvic pain, vasovagal reaction, leg pain. **CNS:** Dizziness. **CV:** Bradycardia, coronary artery dissection. **GI:** GI bleeding. **Hematologic:** *Bleeding* (major bleeding), anemia, thrombocytopenia. **Skin:** Sweating.

INTERACTIONS Drug: Increased risk of bleeding with ANTICOAGULANTS, NSAIDS, SALICYLATES, ANTIPLATELET AGENTS. **Herbal: Feverfew, garlic, ginger, ginkgo, horse chestnut** may increase risk of bleeding.

PHARMACOKINETICS Duration: 4–8 h after stopping infusion. **Distribution:** 65% protein bound. **Metabolism:** Minimally metabolized. **Elimination:** 65% in urine, 25% in feces. **Half-Life:** 2 h.

CLINICAL IMPLICATIONS

Assessment & Drug Effects
• Lab tests: Monitor platelet count, Hgb and Hct before treatment, (within 6 h of infusing loading dose), and frequently throughout treatment; monitor aPTT, INR, and ACT.
• Withhold drug and notify physician if thrombocytopenia (platelets <100,000) is confirmed.
• Monitor carefully for and immediately report S&S of internal or external bleeding.
• Wait at least 3–4 h after heparin is stopped and until ACT <180 sec and aPPT <45 sec before removing the femoral catheter sheath.

Common adverse effects in *italic*, life-threatening effects underlined; generic names in **bold**; classifications in SMALL CAPS; ♣ Canadian drug name; ⊙ Prototype drug

1511

- Minimize unnecessary invasive procedures and devices to reduce the risk of bleeding.

Patient & Family Education
- Report unexplained pelvic or abdominal pain.

TIZANIDINE HYDROCHLORIDE

(ti-zan'i-deen)
Zanaflex
Classifications: SKELETAL MUSCLE RELAXANT, CENTRAL-ACTING
Therapeutic: SKELETAL MUSCLE RELAXANT, CENTRAL-ACTING; ANTISPASMODIC
Prototype: Cyclobenzaprine
Pregnancy Category: C

AVAILABILITY 4 mg tablets; 2 mg, 4 mg, 6 mg capsules

ACTION & *THERAPEUTIC EFFECT*
Centrally acting alpha-adrenergic agonist that reduces spasticity by increasing presynaptic inhibition of motor neurons. Greatest effect on polysynaptic afferent reflex activity at the spinal cord level. No effect on skeletal muscle fibers, the neuromuscular junction, or monosynaptic spinal reflexes. *Site of action is the spinal cord; reduces skeletal muscle spasms. Effectiveness indicated by decreased muscle tone.*

USES Acute and intermittent management of increased muscle tone associated with spasticity.

CONTRAINDICATIONS Hypersensitivity to tizanidine; pregnancy (category C). Safety in labor and delivery is unknown.
CAUTIOUS USE Patients with hepatic impairment, hepatic disease; renal insufficiency (Cl_{cr} <25 mL/min), or renal failure; concurrent use of antihypertensive therapy; psychosis; women taking oral contraceptives; older adults because of renal impairment; lactation. Safety and efficacy in children are not established.

ROUTE & DOSAGE

Spasticity
Adult: **PO** Start with 4 mg and gradually increase to 8 mg q6–8h prn (max: 3 doses or 36 mg/24 h)
Renal Impairment
Cl_{cr} <25 mL/min: Use lower dose

ADMINISTRATION

Oral
- Make dose increments gradually in 2- to 4-mg steps.
- Store at 15°–30° C (59°–86° F).

ADVERSE EFFECTS (≥1%) **Body as a Whole:** *Asthenia (tiredness),* flu-like syndrome, fever, myasthenia, back pain, infection. **CNS:** *Somnolence, dizziness,* dyskinesia, nervousness, depression, anxiety, paresthesia. **CV:** *Hypotension, bradycardia.* **GI:** *Dry mouth,* constipation, abnormal liver function tests, vomiting, abdominal pain, diarrhea, dyspepsia. **Respiratory:** Pharyngitis, rhinitis. **Skin:** Rash, sweating, skin ulcer. **Urogenital:** *UTI,* urinary frequency. **Special Senses:** Speech disorder, blurred vision.

INTERACTIONS Drug: ORAL CONTRACEPTIVES decrease clearance of **tizanidine. Alcohol** will increase peak levels and decrease clearance of tizanidine. Increases levels and toxicity of **fluvoxamine, amiodarone, ketoconazole, norfloxacin, ciprofloxacin,** and **ofloxacin. Herbal: Kava-kava, valerian** may potentiate sedation.

PHARMACOKINETICS Absorption: Rapidly absorbed from GI tract; 40%

bioavailability. **Peak:** 1–2 h. **Duration:** 3–6 h. **Distribution:** Crosses placenta, distributed into breast milk. **Metabolism:** In the liver. **Elimination:** 60% in urine, 20% in feces. **Half-Life:** 2.5 h.

CLINICAL IMPLICATIONS

Assessment & Drug Effects

- Lab tests: Monitor liver function tests (AST, ALT) during the first 6 mo of treatment (baseline, 1, 3, and 6 mo) and periodically thereafter.
- Monitor cardiovascular status and report orthostatic hypotension or bradycardia.
- Monitor closely older adults, those with renal impairment, and women taking oral contraceptives for adverse effects because drug clearance is reduced.

Patient & Family Education

- Exercise caution with potentially hazardous activities requiring alertness since sedation is a common adverse effect. Effects are additive with alcohol or other CNS depressants.
- Make position changes slowly because of the risk of orthostatic hypotension.
- Report unusual sensory experiences; hallucinations and delusions have occurred with tizanidine use.

TOBRAMYCIN SULFATE

(toe-bra-mye′sin)

AKTob, TobraDex, Tobrex, TOBI
Classifications: AMINOGLYCOSIDE ANTIBIOTIC
Therapeutic: ANTIBIOTIC, AMINO-GLYCOSIDE
Prototype: Gentamicin sulfate
Pregnancy Category: D

AVAILABILITY 10 mg/mL, 40 mg/mL injection; 300 mg/5 mL inhalation solution; 0.1%, 0.3% ophthalmic solution; 0.1%, 0.3% ophthalmic ointment

ACTION & *THERAPEUTIC EFFECT*

Broad-spectrum, aminoglycoside antibiotic derived from *Streptomyces tenebrarius*. Tobramycin binds irreversibly to one of two aminoglycoside binding sites on the 30S ribosomal subunit of the bacteria, thus inhibiting protein synthesis. This results in bacterial cell death. *Exhibits greater antibiotic activity against* Pseudomonas aeruginosa *than other aminoglycosides*.

USES Treatment of severe infections caused by susceptible organisms.

CONTRAINDICATIONS History of hypersensitivity to tobramycin and other aminoglycoside antibiotics; pregnancy (category D).

CAUTIOUS USE Impaired kidney function; renal disease; dehydration; hearing impairment; myasthenia gravis; parkinsonism; concurrent use with other neurotoxic or nephrotoxic agents or potent diuretics; premature and neonatal infants; older adults; lactation.

ROUTE & DOSAGE

Moderate to Severe Infections

Adult: **IV/IM** 3 mg/kg/d divided q8h up to 5 mg/kg/d OR 4–7 mg/kg/d single dose **Topical** 1–2 drops in affected eye q1–4h
Child: **IM/IV** <5 y, 2.5 mg/kg q8h **IV/IM** ≥5 y, 2–2.5 mg/kg/d divided q8h
Neonate: **IM/IV** 2.5 mg/kg q12–24h

Cystic Fibrosis

Adult/Child: **IM/IV** 2.5–3.5 mg/kg q6–8h **Nebulized** 300 mg inhaled b.i.d. times 28 d, may repeat after 28 d drug-free period

T

Common adverse effects in *italic*, life-threatening effects underlined; generic names in **bold**; classifications in SMALL CAPS; ✚ Canadian drug name; ⊙ Prototype drug

1513

Renal Impairment
Increase interval
Hemodialysis: Administer dose after dialysis and monitor levels
Obesity
Dose on IBW; in morbid obesity, use dosing weight of IBW + 0.4 (Weight – IBW)

ADMINISTRATION

Note: All doses based on ideal body weight.

Instillation

▪Wash hands before and after instillation of eye medication. Apply gentle finger pressure to lacrimal sac (under inside of eyelid) for 1 min after drug has been instilled in eye.

Intramuscular

▪Give deep IM into a large muscle. Rotate injection sites.

Intravenous

Note: Verify correct IV concentration and rate of infusion to neonates, infants, or children with physician.

PREPARE: **Intermittent:** Dilute each dose in 50–100 mL or more of D5W, NS or D5/NS. Final concentration should not exceed 1 mg/mL.

ADMINISTER: **Intermittent:** Infuse diluted solution over 20–60 min.

INCOMPATIBILITIES **Solution/additive: Alcohol 5% in dextrose, cefamandole, cefepime, cefoperazone, cefoxitin, clindamycin, heparin. Y-site: Allopurinol, amphotericin B cholesteryl complex, azithromycin, cefoperazone, heparin, hetastarch, indomethacin, propofol, sargramostim.**

▪Store at 15°–30° C (59°–86° F) prior to reconstitution. After reconstitution, solution may be refrigerated and used within 96 h. If kept at room temperature, use within 24 h.

ADVERSE EFFECTS (≥1%) **CNS:** Neurotoxicity (including ototoxicity), *nephrotoxicity,* increased AST, ALT, LDH, serum bilirubin; anemia, fever, rash, pruritus, urticaria, nausea, vomiting, headache, lethargy, superinfections; hypersensitivity. **Special Senses:** *Burning, stinging of eye after drug instillation;* lid itching and edema.

INTERACTIONS Drug: ANESTHETICS, SKELETAL MUSCLE RELAXANTS add to neuromuscular blocking effects; **acyclovir, amphotericin B, bacitracin, capreomycin,** CEPHALOSPORINS, **colistin, cisplatin, carboplatin, methoxyflurane, polymyxin B, vancomycin, furosemide, ethacrynic acid** increased risk of ototoxicity, nephrotoxicity.

PHARMACOKINETICS Peak: 30–90 min IM. **Duration:** Up to 8 h. **Distribution:** Crosses placenta; accumulates in renal cortex. **Elimination:** In urine. **Half-Life:** 2–3 h in adults.

CLINICAL IMPLICATIONS

Assessment & Drug Effects

▪Weigh patient before treatment for calculation of dosage.
▪Obtain bacterial C&S tests prior to and during therapy.
▪Observe patient receiving tobramycin closely because of the high potential for toxicity, even in conventional doses.
▪Lab tests: Baseline and periodic kidney function; monitor serum drug concentrations to minimize rise of toxicity. Prolonged peak serum concentrations >10 mcg/mL or trough concentrations >2 mcg/mL are not recommended.
▪Monitor auditory, and vestibular functions closely, particularly in patients with known or suspected

renal impairment and patients receiving high doses.

- Be aware that drug-induced auditory changes are irreversible (partial or total); usually bilateral. In cochlear damage, patient may be asymptomatic, and partial or bilateral deafness may continue to develop even after therapy discontinued.
- Evidence of renal insufficiency, ototoxicity (see Appendix F), or vestibular damage indicates need for dosage adjustment or withdrawal of drug.
- Monitor I&O. Report oliguria, changes in I&O ratio, and cloudy or frothy urine (may indicate proteinuria). Keep patient well hydrated to prevent chemical irritation in renal tubules; older adults are especially susceptible to renal toxicity.
- Monitor patient with neuromuscular disorder (e.g., myasthenia gravis) for muscular weakness. Observe ambulation and assist if necessary.
- Be aware that prolonged use of ophthalmic solution may encourage superinfection with nonsusceptible organisms including fungi.
- Report overdose symptoms for eye medication: Increased lacrimation, keratitis, edema and itching of eyelids.

Patient & Family Education
- Report symptoms of superinfections (see Appendix F) to physician. Prompt treatment with an antibiotic or antifungal medication may be necessary.
- Report S&S of hearing loss, tinnitus, or vertigo to physician.

TOLAZAMIDE
(tole-az'a-mide)
Tolinase

Classifications: HORMONE; SULFO-NYLUREA ANTIDIABETIC
Therapeutic: ANTIDIABETIC, SULFO-NYLUREA
Prototype: Glyburide
Pregnancy Category: C

AVAILABILITY 100 mg, 250 mg, 500 mg tablets

ACTION & THERAPEUTIC EFFECT
Orally effective sulfonylurea hypoglycemic structurally and pharmacologically related to tolbutamide but about 5 times more potent. Lowers blood glucose primarily by stimulating pancreatic beta cells to secrete insulin. *Antidiabetic action is a result of stimulation of the pancreas to secrete more insulin in the presence of blood sugar; it requires functioning beta cells.*

USES Mild to moderately severe type 2 diabetes mellitus that cannot be controlled by diet and weight reduction and that is uncomplicated by acidosis, ketosis, coma. Effective in primary or secondary failures to other sulfonylurea

CONTRAINDICATIONS Known sensitivity to sulfonylureas and to sulfonamides; type 1 diabetes complicated by ketoacidosis; infection; trauma; pregnancy (category C). Safety in lactation or children is not established.
CAUTIOUS USE Older adults; renal disease; renal failure, renal impairment.

ROUTE & DOSAGE

Type 2 Diabetes Mellitus
Adult: **PO** 100 mg–1 g q.d. to b.i.d. a.c., may adjust dose by 100–250 mg/d at weekly intervals (max: 1 g/d)

T

Common adverse effects in *italic*, life-threatening effects underlined; generic names in **bold**; classifications in SMALL CAPS; ♣ Canadian drug name; ☻ Prototype drug

1515

ADMINISTRATION

Oral
- Give in the morning with or before meals.
- Divide dose of more than 500 mg and give b.i.d.
- Crush tablet if patient is unable to swallow it whole. Be sure to give with an allowable fluid, not dry.
- Store at 15°–30° C (59°–86° F) in a tightly closed container unless otherwise directed. Keep drug out of the reach of children.

ADVERSE EFFECTS (≥1%) **GI:** Nausea, vomiting, cholestatic jaundice. **Metabolic:** Hypoglycemia. **CNS:** Vertigo. **Skin:** Photosensitivity. **Hematologic:** Agranulocytosis.

INTERACTIONS Drug: Alcohol elicits disulfiram-type reaction in some patients; ORAL ANTICOAGULANTS, **chloramphenicol, clofibrate, phenylbutazone,** MAO INHIBITORS, SALICYLATES, **probenecid,** SULFONAMIDES may potentiate hypoglycemic actions; THIAZIDES may antagonize hypoglycemic effects; **cimetidine** may increase tolazamide levels, causing hypoglycemia. **Herbal: Ginseng, karela** may potentiate hypoglycemic effects.

PHARMACOKINETICS Absorption: Slowly from GI tract. **Onset:** 60 min. **Peak:** 4–6 h. **Duration:** 10–15 h (up to 20 h in some patients). **Distribution:** Distributed in highest concentrations in liver, kidneys, and intestines; crosses placenta; distributed into breast milk. **Metabolism:** Extensively in liver. **Elimination:** 85% in urine, 15% in feces. **Half-Life:** 7 h.

CLINICAL IMPLICATIONS

Assessment & Drug Effects
- Be aware that reduction of dose frequently alleviates most mild to moderately severe hypoglycemic symptoms.
- Observe patients with a history of ketoacidosis or coma closely, especially during the early adjustment period.

Patient & Family Education
- Check blood glucose and urine daily for sugar and acetone. Important to continue close medical supervision for first 6 wk of treatment.
- Be aware that doses >1000 mg/d rarely provide improvement in diabetic control.
- Do not take OTC preparations unless approved or prescribed by physician.
- Understand that alcohol can precipitate a disulfiram-type reaction.

TOLBUTAMIDE
(tole-byoo′ta-mide)
Mobenol ✦, Novobutamide ✦, Orinase

TOLBUTAMIDE SODIUM
Orinase Diagnostic
Classifications: HORMONE; SULFONYLUREA ANTIDIABETIC
Therapeutic: ANTIDIABETIC, SULFONYLUREA
Prototype: Glyburide
Pregnancy Category: C

AVAILABILITY 500 mg tablets; 1 g vial

ACTION & *THERAPEUTIC EFFECT* Short-acting sulfonylurea that lowers blood glucose concentration by stimulating pancreatic beta cells to synthesize and release insulin. No action demonstrated if functional beta cells are absent. *Lowers blood glucose concentration by stimulating pancreatic beta cells to synthesize and release insulin.*

USES Management of mild to moderately severe, stable type 2 diabetes that is not controlled by diet and weight reduction alone. Also used in treatment of patients who are unresponsive to other sulfonylureas and adjunctively with insulin to stabilize certain cases of labile diabetes. Used as diagnostic agent to rule out pancreatic islet cell adenoma or diabetes.

CONTRAINDICATIONS Hypersensitivity to sulfonylureas or to sulfonamides; history of repeated episodes of diabetic ketoacidosis (with or without coma); type 1 diabetes as sole therapy; diabetic coma; severe stress, infection, trauma, or major surgery; severe renal insufficiency, liver or endocrine disease; pregnancy (category C). Safe use in children is not established.

CAUTIOUS USE Cardiac, thyroid, pituitary, or adrenal dysfunction; severe hepatic disease, renal disease, renal impairment, renal failure; history of peptic ulcer; alcoholism; infection; older adults, debilitated, malnourished, or uncooperative patient; lactation.

ROUTE & DOSAGE

Type 2 Diabetes
Adult: **PO** 250 mg to 3 g/d in 1–2 divided doses

Diagnosis of Functioning Insulinoma
Adult: **IV** 1 g over 2–3 min

ADMINISTRATION

Oral
- Give total dose before breakfast but preferably in divided doses after meals.
- Crush tablet and give with full glass of water if patient desires.
- Do not give at bedtime because of danger of nocturnal hypoglycemia, unless specifically prescribed.

- Discontinue at least 2 wk before the expected delivery date to prevent prolonged severe hypoglycemia (4–10 d) in the neonate if used during pregnancy.
- Store below 40° C (104° F), preferably between 15°–30° C (59°–86° F) in well-closed container. Avoid freezing.

ADVERSE EFFECTS (≥1%) **GI:** Nausea, epigastric fullness, heartburn, anorexia, constipation, diarrhea, cholestatic jaundice (rare). **Hematologic:** Agranulocytosis, thrombocytopenia, leukopenia, hemolytic anemia, aplastic anemia, pancytopenia. **Metabolic:** Hepatic porphyria, disulfiram-like reactions, SIADH, hypoglycemia without loss of consciousness or neurologic symptoms (unusual fatigue, tremulousness, hunger, drowsiness, GI distress, sweating, anxiety, headache) severe hypoglycemia (visual disturbances, ataxia, paresthesias, confusion, tachycardia, seizures, coma). **Skin:** Allergic skin reactions: pruritus, erythema, urticaria, morbilliform or maculopapular eruptions; porphyria cutanea tarda, photosensitivity. **Special Senses:** Taste alterations. **CNS:** Headache.

DIAGNOSTIC TEST INTERFERENCE The SULFONYLUREAS may produce abnormal *thyroid function test* results and reduced *RAI uptake* (after long-term administration). A tolbutamide metabolite may cause false-positive *urinary protein* values when turbidity procedures are used (such as heat and *acetic acid* or *sulfosalicylic acid*); *Ames reagent* strips reportedly not affected.

INTERACTIONS Drug: Phenylbutazone increases hypoglycemic effects; THIAZIDE DIURETICS may attenuate hypoglycemic effects; **alcohol** may produce disulfiram reaction;

Common adverse effects in *italic*, life-threatening effects underlined; generic names in **bold**; classifications in SMALL CAPS; ✦ Canadian drug name; ⊙ Prototype drug

1517

BETA BLOCKERS may mask symptoms of a hypoglycemic reaction. **Herbal: Ginseng, karela** may potentiate hypoglycemic effects.

PHARMACOKINETICS Absorption: Readily from GI tract. **Peak:** 3–5 h. **Distribution:** Into extracellular fluids. **Metabolism:** Principally in liver. **Elimination:** 75–85% in urine; some in feces. **Half-Life:** 7 h.

CLINICAL IMPLICATIONS

Assessment & Drug Effects

- Supervise closely during initial period of therapy until dosage is established. One or 2 wk of therapy may be required before full therapeutic effect is achieved.
- Give low initial dose before breakfast to older adults, who may be hyperresponsive to oral antidiabetic therapy. If blood and urine glucose tests are negative during first 24 h of therapy, initial dose may be continued on a daily basis.
- Monitor closely during adjustment period, watching for S&S of impending hypoglycemia (see Appendix F). Detection of a hypoglycemic reaction in a diabetic patient also receiving a beta blocker, especially older adults, is difficult.
- Evaluate nondefinitive vague complaints; hypoglycemic symptoms may be especially vague in older adults. Observe patient carefully, especially 2–3 h after eating, check urine for sugar and ketone bodies and capillary blood glucose.
- Lab tests: Baseline liver and kidney function tests; periodic HbA_{1C}, serum electrolytes, CBC with differential, and platelet counts.
- Report repetitive complaints of headache and weakness a few hours after eating; may signal incipient hypoglycemia.
- Be aware that pruritus and rash, frequently reported adverse effects, may clear spontaneously; if these persist, drug will be discontinued.

Patient & Family Education

- Understand need to inform physician promptly of symptoms of hyperglycemia and ketoacidosis: flushed, dry skin, weight loss, fatigue, Kussmaul respiration, double or blurred vision, soft eyeballs, irritability, fruity-smelling breath, abdominal cramps, nausea, vomiting, diarrhea, dyspnea, polydipsia, polyphagia, polyuria, headache, hypotension, weak and rapid pulse, positive ketonuria and glycosuria.
- Hypoglycemia is frequently caused by overdosage of hypoglycemic drug, inadequate or irregular food intake, nausea, vomiting, diarrhea, and added exercise without caloric supplement or dose adjustment. Its occurrence indicates need for immediate reevaluation of patient's diet, medication regimen, and compliance. It is most likely to appear in patients >50 y of age.
- Report any illness promptly. Physician may want to evaluate need for insulin.
- Do not self-medicate with OTC drugs unless approved or prescribed by physician.
- Be aware that alcohol, even in moderate amounts, can precipitate a disulfiram-type reaction (see Appendix F). A hypoglycemic response after ingesting alcohol requires emergency treatment.
- Protect exposed skin areas from the sun with a sunscreen lotion (SPF 12–15) because of potential photosensitivity (especially in the alcoholic).
- Weigh at least weekly and report a progressive gain, especially if edema is present. These signs indicate the necessity to discontinue tolbutamide.

- Be alert to added danger of loss of control (hyperglycemia) when a drug that affects the hypoglycemic action of sulfonylureas (see DRUG INTERACTIONS) is withdrawn or added to the tolbutamide regimen. Monitor blood glucose carefully.
- Use or add barrier contraceptive if using hormonal contraceptives.
- Carry medical identification at all times. It needs to indicate medical diagnosis, medication(s) and doses, patient's and physician's names, addresses, and telephone numbers.
- Potential for hypoglycemia in breast fed infants presents the necessity to decide whether to discontinue breast feeding or temporarily transfer to insulin (if diet alone is inadequate for blood sugar control).

TOLCAPONE ⓟ

(tol′ca-pone)
Tasmar
Classifications: ANTICHOLINERGIC; CATECHOLAMINE-O-METHYLTRANS-FERASE (COMT) INHIBITOR
Therapeutic: ANTICHOLINERGIC; ANTI-PARKINSON
Pregnancy Category: C

AVAILABILITY 100 mg, 200 mg tablets

ACTION & *THERAPEUTIC EFFECT*
Selective and reversible inhibitor of catecholamine-O-methyltransferase (COMT). COMT is the enzyme responsible for metabolizing catecholamines and, therefore, levodopa. *Concurrent administration of tolcapone and levodopa increases the amount of levodopa available to control Parkinson's disease by increasing dopaminergic brain stimulation.*

USES Idiopathic Parkinson's disease as adjunct to levodopa/carbidopa.

CONTRAINDICATIONS Hypersensitivity to tolcapone; liver disease; pregnancy (category C); MAOI therapy.
CAUTIOUS USE History of hypersensitivity to other COMT inhibitors (e.g., entacapone, nitecapone); anorexia nervosa; hematuria; hypotension; syncopy; renal disease; renal impairment; lactation.

ROUTE & DOSAGE

Parkinson's Disease
Adult: **PO** 100 mg t.i.d. (max: 200 mg t.i.d.)

ADMINISTRATION

Oral
- Give with food if GI upset occurs.
- Give only in conjunction with levodopa/carbidopa therapy.
- Note: Doses >100 mg t.i.d. are not recommended with moderate to severe liver impairment.
- Store at 20°–25° C (68°–77° F) in a tightly closed container.

ADVERSE EFFECTS (≥1%) **Body as a Whole:** Muscle cramps, orthostatic complaints, fatigue, falling, balance difficulties, hyperkinesia, stiffness, arthritis, hypokinesia. **CNS:** *Dyskinesia, sleep disorder, dystonia, excessive dreaming,* somnolence, confusion, dizziness, headache, hallucination, syncope, paresthesias. **CV:** Chest pain, hypotension. **GI:** *Nausea,* anorexia, diarrhea, vomiting, constipation, <u>fulminant liver failure, severe hepatocellular injury,</u> dry mouth, abdominal pain, dyspepsia, flatulence. **Respiratory:** URI, dyspnea, sinus congestion. **Skin:** Sweating. **Urogenital:** UTI, urine discoloration, micturition disorder.

INTERACTIONS Drug: Will increase **levodopa** levels when taken simultaneously; CNS DEPRESSANTS may

---

Common adverse effects in *italic*, life-threatening effects <u>underlined</u>; generic names in **bold**; classifications in SMALL CAPS; ♣ Canadian drug name; ⓟ Prototype drug

cause additive sedation; do not give with non-selective MAOIS **(isocarboxazid, phenelzine, or tranylcypromine furazolidone, linezolid, procarbazine).**

PHARMACOKINETICS Absorption: Rapidly absorbed from GI tract, bioavailability 65%; food decreases bioavailability. **Peak:** 2 h. **Distribution:** >99% protein bound. **Metabolism:** Extensively metabolized by COMT and glucuronidation. **Elimination:** 60% in urine, 40% in feces; clearance is reduced by 50% in patients with moderate cirrhotic liver disease. **Half-Life:** 2–3 h.

CLINICAL IMPLICATIONS

Assessment & Drug Effects

- Lab tests: Monitor liver functions monthly for first 3 mo, every 6 wk for the next 3 mo, and periodically thereafter.
- Monitor PT and INR carefully when given concurrently with warfarin.
- Monitor carefully for and immediately report S&S of hepatic impairment (e.g., jaundice, dark urine).

Patient & Family Education

- Do not engage in hazardous activities until response to drug is known. Avoid use of alcohol or sedative drugs while on tolcapone.
- Rise slowly from a sitting or lying position to avoid a rapid drop in BP with possible weakness or fainting.
- Nausea is a common possible adverse effect especially at the beginning of therapy.
- Do not suddenly stop taking this drug. Doses must be gradually reduced over time.
- Notify physician promptly about any of following: Increased loss of muscle control, fainting, yellowing of skin or eyes, darkening of urine, severe diarrhea, hallucinations.

TOLMETIN SODIUM

(tole′met-in)

Tolectin, Tolectin DS

Classifications: ANALGESIC, NONSTEROIDAL ANTIINFLAMMATORY (NSAID); ANTIPYRETIC

Therapeutic: NSAID, ANALGESIC; ANTIPYRETIC; DISEASE-MODIFYING ANTIRHEUMATIC DRUG (DMARD)

Prototype: Ibuprofen

Pregnancy Category: C first and second trimester; D third trimester

AVAILABILITY 200 mg, 600 mg tablets; 400 mg capsules

ACTION & *THERAPEUTIC EFFECT*

Nonsteroidal antiinflammatory analgesic that competitively inhibits both cyclooxygenase (COX) isoenzymes, COX-1 and COX-2, by blocking arachidonate binding to prostaglandin sites, and thus inhibits prostaglandin synthesis. *Possesses analgesic, antiinflammatory, and antipyretic and antirheumatic activity.*

USES In acute flares and management of chronic rheumatoid arthritis. May be used alone or in combination with gold or corticosteroids.

CONTRAINDICATIONS History of intolerance or hypersensitivity to tolmetin, aspirin, and other NSAIDs; active peptic ulcer, patients with asthma, nasal polyps, rhinitis, "aspirin triad," CABG perioperative pain; in patients with functional class IV rheumatoid arthritis (severely incapacitated, bedridden, or confined to a wheelchair); Safety during pregnancy (category C in first and second trimester, and category D in third trimester), lactation, or children <2 y is not established.

CAUTIOUS USE History of upper GI tract disease; impaired kidney function; SLE; compromised cardiac function.

ROUTE & DOSAGE

Arthritis

Adult: **PO** 400 mg t.i.d. (max: 2 g/d)
Child: **PO** ≥2 y, 20 mg/kg/d in 3–4 divided doses (max: 30 mg/kg/d)

ADMINISTRATION

Oral

- Schedule treatment (preferred) to include a morning dose (on arising) and a bedtime dose.
- Give with fluid of patient's choice; crush tablet or empty capsule to mix with water or food if patient cannot swallow tablet/capsule.
- Store at 15°–30° C (59°–86° F) in tightly capped and light-resistant container unless otherwise instructed.

ADVERSE EFFECTS (≥1%) CNS:
Headache, dizziness, vertigo, lightheadedness, mood elevation or depression, tension, nervousness, weakness, drowsiness, insomnia, tinnitus. **CV:** Mild edema (about 7% patients), sodium and water retention, mild to moderate hypertension. **GI:** Epigastric or abdominal pain, dyspepsia, *nausea,* vomiting, heartburn, constipation, peptic ulcer, <u>GI bleeding</u>. **Hematologic:** Transient and small decreases in hemoglobin and hematocrit, purpura, petechiae, granulocytopenia, leukopenia. **Urogenital:** Hematuria, proteinuria, increased BUN. **Skin:** <u>Toxic epidermal necrolysis</u>, morbilliform eruptions, urticaria, pruritus. **Body as a Whole:** <u>Anaphylaxis</u> (especially after drug is discontinued and then reinstituted).

DIAGNOSTIC TEST INTERFERENCE

Tolmetin prolongs *bleeding time,* inhibits *platelet aggregation,* elevates *BUN, alkaline phosphatase,* and *AST* levels; may decrease *hemoglobin* and *hematocrit* values. Metabolites may produce false-positive results for *proteinuria* (with tests that rely on acid precipitation, e.g., *sulfosalicylic acid*).

INTERACTIONS Drug: ORAL ANTICOAGULANTS, **heparin** may prolong bleeding time; may increase **lithium** toxicity; **aspirin,** other NSAIDS add to ulcerogenic effects; may increase **methotrexate** toxicity. **Herbal:** **Feverfew, garlic, ginger, ginkgo** may increase bleeding potential.

PHARMACOKINETICS Absorption:
Rapidly from GI tract. **Peak:** 30–60 min. **Distribution:** Crosses blood–brain barrier and placenta; distributed into breast milk. **Metabolism:** In liver. **Elimination:** In urine. **Half-Life:** 60–90 min.

CLINICAL IMPLICATIONS

Assessment & Drug Effects

- Monitor therapeutic effect. Therapeutic response for rheumatoid arthritis or osteoarthritis generally occurs within 1 wk with progressive improvement in succeeding week: Reduced joint pain and swelling, reduction in duration of morning stiffness, improved functional capacity (increase in grip strength, delayed onset of fatigue).
- Monitor patients with kidney damage closely. Evaluate I&O ratio and encourage patient to increase fluid intake to at least 8 full glasses per day.
- Lab tests: Obtain periodic kidney function tests (routine urinalysis, creatinine clearance, and serum creatinine) for patient on long-term therapy.
- Check self-medicating habits of the patient. Sodium bicarbonate alkalinizes the urine, which in-

T

Common adverse effects in *italic*, life-threatening effects <u>underlined</u>; generic names in **bold**; classifications in SMALL CAPS; ♣ Canadian drug name; ⓟ Prototype drug

1521

creases urinary excretion of tolmetin and may reduce degree and duration of effectiveness.

Patient & Family Education

- Take drug with meals or milk if GI disturbances occur. Notify physician if symptoms persist; dosage reduction may be necessary, or antacid added.
- Monitor weight and report an increase >2 kg (4 lb)/wk with impaired kidney or cardiac function; check for swelling in ankles, tibiae, hands, and feet.
- Inform surgeon or dentist before treatment if you are taking tolmetin because of possible enhanced bleeding.
- Report promptly signs of abnormal bleeding (ecchymosis, epistaxis, melena, petechiae), itching, skin rash, persistent headache, edema.
- Avoid potentially hazardous activities until response to drug is known because dizziness and drowsiness are common adverse effects.

TOLNAFTATE

(tole-naf′tate)

Aftate, Pitrex ♣, Tinactin

Classifications: ANTIFUNGAL ANTIBIOTIC

Therapeutic: ANTIFUNGAL ANTIBIOTIC

Pregnancy Category: C

AVAILABILITY 1% cream, solution, gel, powder, spray

ACTION & *THERAPEUTIC EFFECT*
Synthetic topical antifungal agent. Tolnaftate distorts hyphae and stunts mycelial growth on susceptible fungi. *Fungistatic or fungicidal as well as antiinfective against bacteria, protozoa, and viruses.*

USES Tinea pedis (athlete's foot), tinea cruris (jock itch), tinea cor-poris (body ringworm); also tinea capitis and tinea unguium if infection is superficial, plantar or palmar lesions adjunctively with keratolytic agents, and tinea versicolor (caused by *Malassezia furfur*).

CONTRAINDICATIONS Skin irritations prior to therapy, nail and scalp infections; immunosuppressed patients, diabetes mellitus, peripheral vascular disease. Hypersensitivity to tolnaftate; lactation; occlusive dressing over drug; pregnancy (category C). Safe use in children <2 y is not established.

CAUTIOUS USE Excoriated skin.

ROUTE & DOSAGE

Tinea Infestations

Adult/Child: **Topical** Apply 0.5–1 cm ($^1/_4$–$^1/_2$ in) of cream or 3 drops of solution b.i.d. in morning and evening; powder may be used prophylactically in normally moist areas

ADMINISTRATION

Topical

- Cleanse site thoroughly with water and dry completely before applying. Massage thin layer gently into skin. Make sure area is not wet from excess drug after application.
- Shake aerosol powder container well before use.
- Note: Cream and powder are not recommended for nail or scalp infection.
- Use liquids (solutions) for scalp infection or to treat hairy areas.
- Store cream, gel, powder, and topical solution in light-resistant containers at 15°–30° C (59°–86° F); store aerosol container at 2°–30° C (38°–86° F). Avoid freezing and exposure to light.

ADVERSE EFFECTS (≥1%) **Skin:** Local irritation, stinging of skin from aerosol formulation.

CLINICAL IMPLICATIONS

Patient & Family Education
- Expect relief from pruritus, soreness, and burning within 24–72 h after start of treatment.
- Continue treatment for 2–3 wk after disappearance of all symptoms to prevent recurrence.
- Return to physician for reevaluation in absence of improvement within 4 wk.
- Note: If skin has thickened as a result of the infection, desired clinical response may be delayed for 4–6 wk.
- Avoid contact with eyes of all drug forms.
- Place container in warm water to liquify contents if solution solidifies. Potency is unaffected.

TOLTERODINE TARTRATE

(tol-ter′o-deen tar′trate)
Detrol, Detrol LA
Classifications: ANTICHOLINERGIC AGENT; MUSCARINIC RECEPTOR ANTAGONIST
Therapeutic: ANTICHOLINERGIC AGENT; ANTIMUSCARINIC AGENT; MUSCARINIC RECEPTOR ANTAGONIST
Prototype: Atropine
Pregnancy Category: C

AVAILABILITY 1 mg, 2 mg tablets; 2 mg, 4 mg sustained release

ACTION & *THERAPEUTIC EFFECT*
Selective muscarinic urinary bladder receptor antagonist. Reduces urinary incontinence, urgency, and frequency. *Controls urinary bladder incontinence by controlling contractions.*

USES Overactive bladder (urinary frequency, urgency, urge incontinence).

CONTRAINDICATIONS Gastric retention; hypersensitivity to tolterodine; uncontrolled narrow-angle glaucoma; urinary retention; pregnancy (category C); lactation.
CAUTIOUS USE Cardiovascular disease; liver disease; controlled narrow-angle glaucoma; urinary retention; severe hepatic impairment; obstructive GI disease; obstructive uropathy; paralytic ileus or intestinal atony; renal impairment; ulcerative colitis.

ROUTE & DOSAGE

Overactive Bladder
Adult: **PO** 2 mg b.i.d. or 4 mg sustained release q.d.
Hepatic Impairment
May decrease to 1 mg b.i.d. or 2 mg sustained release q.d. in those with significantly reduced liver function

ADMINISTRATION

Oral
- Do not crush or chew sustained release tablets. These must be swallowed whole.
- Do not give doses >1 mg b.i.d. to those with significantly reduced liver function or concurrently receiving macrolide antibiotics, azole antifungal agents, or other cytochrome P450 3A4 inhibitors.
- Store at 20°–25° C (68°–77° F) in a tightly closed container.

ADVERSE EFFECTS (≥1%) **Body as a Whole:** Back pain, fatigue, flu-like syndrome, falls, arthralgia, weight gain. **CNS:** Headache, pares-

---

Common adverse effects in *italic*, life-threatening effects underlined; generic names in **bold**; classifications in SMALL CAPS; ♣ Canadian drug name; ⊕ Prototype drug

1523

thesias, vertigo, dizziness, nervousness, somnolence. **CV:** Chest pain, hypertension. **GI:** *Dry mouth,* dyspepsia, constipation, abdominal pain, diarrhea, flatulence, nausea, vomiting. **Urogenital:** Dysuria, micturition frequency, urinary retention, UTI. **Respiratory:** Bronchitis, cough, pharyngitis, rhinitis, sinusitis, URI. **Skin:** Pruritus, rash, erythema, dry skin. **Special Senses:** Dry eyes, vision abnormalities.

INTERACTIONS Drug: Additive anticholinergic effects with **amantadine, amoxapine, bupropion, clozapine, cyclobenzaprine, disopyramide, maprotiline, olanzapine, orphenadrine,** SEDATING H₁-BLOCKERS, PHENOTHIAZINES, TRICYCLIC ANTIDEPRESSANTS. Increased effects with **clarithromycin, cyclosporine, erythromycin, itraconazole,** or **ketoconazole. Food:** Grapefruit juice may increase **tolterodine** levels in some patients.

PHARMACOKINETICS Absorption: 77% absorbed, significantly decreased with food. **Peak:** 1–2 h. **Distribution:** 96% protein bound. **Metabolism:** In liver by cytochrome P450 2D6 enzymes to active metabolite. **Elimination:** 77% in urine, 17% in feces. **Half-Life:** 1.9–3.7 h.

CLINICAL IMPLICATIONS

Assessment & Drug Effects
- Monitor intraocular pressure more frequently with glaucoma patients.
- Monitor vital signs carefully (HR and BP), especially in those with cardiovascular disease.

Patient & Family Education
- Notify physician promptly if you experience eye pain, rapid heartbeat, difficulty breathing, skin rash or hives, confusion, or incoordination.

- Report blurred vision, sensitivity to light, and dry mouth (all common adverse effects) to physician if bothersome.
- Avoid the use of alcohol or OTC antihistamines.

TOPIRAMATE
(to-pir′a-mate)
Topamax
Classifications: GAMMA-AMINO-BUTYRATE (GABA) ENHANCER; ANTICONVULSANT
Therapeutic: ANTICONVULSANT
Pregnancy Category: C

AVAILABILITY 25 mg, 100 mg, 200 mg tablets; 15 mg, 25 mg, 50 mg capsules

ACTION & *THERAPEUTIC EFFECT*
Sulfamate-substituted monosaccharide with a broad spectrum of anticonvulsant activity. Exhibits sodium channel-blocking action, as well as enhancing the ability of GABA to induce a flux of chloride ions into the neurons, thus potentiating the activity of this inhibitory neurotransmitter (GABA). *Effectiveness indicated by a decrease in seizure activity. Effectively controls partial onset seizures in adults and children.*

USES Adjunctive therapy for partial-onset seizures in adults and children age 2–16 y; generalized tonic-clonic seizures; migraine prophylaxis.
UNLABELED USES Cluster headache, bulimia nervosa, neuropathic pain, infantile spasms, weight loss.

CONTRAINDICATIONS Hypersensitivity to topiramate; metabolic acidosis; epilepsy, pregnancy (category C); children <2 y. Effect on labor and delivery is unknown.

CAUTIOUS USE Moderate and severe renal impairment, hepatic impairment; COPD; severe pulmonary disease; lactation.

ROUTE & DOSAGE

Partial-Onset Seizures

Adult: **PO** Initiate with 25 mg b.i.d., increase by 50 mg/wk to efficacy **PO Maintenance Dose** 200–400 mg/d divided b.i.d. (max: 1600 mg/d)
Child: **PO** 2–16 y, Initiate with 1–3 mg/kg h.s. × 1 wk, then increase by 1–3 mg/kg/d in 2 divided doses q1–2wk to a target range of 5–9 mg/kg/d

Generalized Tonic-Clonic

Child: **PO** Initiate with 1–3 mg/kg h.s.; titrate to 6 mg/kg/d by the end of 8 wk

Migraine Prophylaxis

Adult: **PO** Initiate with 25 mg b.i.d., increase by 25 mg/wk to 200 mg/d or max tolerated dose

Renal Impairment

Cl_{cr} <70 mL/min: decrease dose by 50%

ADMINISTRATION

Oral

- Make dosage increments of 50 mg at weekly intervals to the recommended dose, usually 400 mg/d.
- Do not break tablets unless absolutely necessary because of bitter taste.
- Store at 15°–30° C (59°–86° F) in a tightly closed container. Protect from light and moisture.

ADVERSE EFFECTS (≥1%) **Body as a Whole:** *Fatigue, speech problems,* weight loss; decreased sweating and hyperthermia in children; metabolic acidosis. **CNS:** *Somnolence, dizzi-*ness, ataxia, psychomotor slowing, confusion, nystagmus, paresthesia, memory difficulty, difficulty concentrating, nervousness, depression, anxiety, tremor. **GI:** Anorexia. **Special Senses:** Angle closure glaucoma (rare).

INTERACTIONS Drug: Increased CNS depression with **alcohol** and other CNS DEPRESSANTS; may increase **phenytoin** concentrations; may decrease ORAL CONTRACEPTIVE, **valproate** concentrations; may increase risk of kidney stone formation with other CARBONIC ANHYDRASE INHIBITORS. **Carbamazepine, phenytoin, valproate** may decrease topiramate concentrations. **Herbal: Ginkgo** may decrease anticonvulsant effectiveness.

PHARMACOKINETICS Absorption: Rapidly absorbed from GI tract; 80% bioavailability. **Peak:** 2 h. **Distribution:** 13–17% protein bound. **Metabolism:** Minimally metabolized in the liver. **Elimination:** Primarily in urine. **Half-Life:** 21 h.

CLINICAL IMPLICATIONS

Assessment & Drug Effects

- Monitor mental status and report significant cognitive impairment.
- Lab tests: Periodically monitor CBC with Hgb and Hct.

Patient & Family Education

- Do not stop drug abruptly; discontinue gradually to minimize seizures.
- To minimize risk of kidney stones, drink at least 6–8 full glasses of water each day.
- Exercise caution with potentially hazardous activities. Sedation is common, especially with concurrent use of alcohol or other CNS depressants.
- Use or add barrier contraceptive if using hormonal contraceptives.

T

Common adverse effects in *italic*, life-threatening effects underlined; generic names in **bold**; classifications in SMALL CAPS; ♣ Canadian drug name; ⊕ Prototype drug

1525

- Be aware that psychomotor slowing and speech/language problems may develop while on topiramate therapy.
- Report adverse effects that interfere with activities of daily living.

TOPOTECAN HYDROCHLORIDE Ⓟ

(toe-po-tee'can)

Hycamtin

Classifications: ANTINEOPLASTIC AGENT; CAMPTOTHECIN; TOPOISOMERASE I INHIBITOR

Therapeutic: ANTINEOPLASTIC; CAMPTOTHECIN; TOPOISOMERASE I INHIBITOR

Pregnancy Category: D

AVAILABILITY 4 mg injection

ACTION & *THERAPEUTIC EFFECT*
Antitumor mechanism is related to inhibition of activity of topoisomerase I, an enzyme required for DNA replication. Topoisomerase I is essential for the relaxation of supercoiled double-stranded DNA, which enables replication and transcription to proceed. Topotecan binds to the DNA-topoisomerase I complex. *Permits uncoiling but prevents recoiling of the two strands of DNA, resulting in a permanent break in the DNA strands.*

USES Metastatic ovarian cancer, small cell lung cancer.

CONTRAINDICATIONS Previous hypersensitivity to topotecan, irinotecan, or other camptothecin analogs; acute infection; severe bone marrow depression; severe thrombocytopenia; pregnancy (category D), lactation.

CAUTIOUS USE Myelosuppression; severe renal impairment or renal failure; history of bleeding disorders; previous cytotoxic or radiation therapy.

ROUTE & DOSAGE

Metastatic Ovarian Cancer and Small Cell Lung Cancer

Adult: **IV** 1.5 mg/m^2 daily for 5 d starting on day 1 of a 21 d course. Four courses of therapy recommended. Subsequent doses can be adjusted by 0.25 mg/m^2 depending on toxicity

Renal Impairment

Cl_{cr} 20–39 mL/min: use 0.75 mg/m^2
Hemodialysis: Supplementation not needed

ADMINISTRATION

Intravenous
Initiate therapy only if baseline neutrophil count ≥1500/mm^3 and platelet count ≥100,000/mm^3. Do not give subsequent doses until neutrophils >1000/mm^3, platelets ≥100,000/mm^3, and Hgb = 9.0 mg/dL.

- Note: Dosage adjustments to 0.75 mg/m^2 are recommended with moderate renal impairment.

PREPARE: IV Infusion: Reconstitute each 4-mg vial with 4 mL sterile water for injection to yield 1 mg/mL. Withdraw the required dose and inject into 50–100 mL of NS or D5W. If skin contacts drug during preparation, wash immediately with soap and water.

ADMINISTER: IV Infusion: Give over 30 min immediately after preparation.

INCOMPATIBILITIES Y-site: Dexamethasone, fluorouracil, mitomycin.

■ Store vials at 20°–25° C (68°–77° F); protect from light. Reconstituted vials are stable for 24 h.

ADVERSE EFFECTS (≥1%) **Body as a Whole:** *Asthenia, fever, fatigue.* **GI:** *Nausea, vomiting, diarrhea, constipation, abdominal pain, stomatitis, anorexia,* transient elevations in liver function tests. **Hematologic:** <u>Leukopenia, neutropenia,</u> anemia, thrombocytopenia. **Respiratory:** *Dyspnea.* **Skin:** *Alopecia.*

INTERACTIONS Drug: Increased risk of bleeding with ANTICOAGULANTS, NSAIDS, SALICYLATES, ANTIPLATELET AGENTS.

PHARMACOKINETICS Distribution: 35% bound to plasma proteins. **Metabolism:** Undergoes pH-dependent hydrolysis. **Elimination:** ~30% in urine. **Half-Life:** 2–3 h.

CLINICAL IMPLICATIONS

Assessment & Drug Effects
■ Lab tests: Obtain CBC counts with differential frequently; periodically monitor ALT.
■ Assess for GI distress, respiratory distress, neurosensory symptoms, and S&S of infection throughout therapy.

Patient & Family Education
■ Learn common adverse effects and measures to control or minimize when possible. Immediately report any distressing adverse effects to physician.
■ Avoid pregnancy during therapy.

TOREMIFENE CITRATE

(tor-em'i-feen ci'trate)
Fareston
Classifications: ANTINEOPLASTIC; HORMONE, ANTIESTROGEN

Therapeutic: ANTINEOPLASTIC; ANTI-ESTROGEN
Prototype: Tamoxifen
Pregnancy Category: D

AVAILABILITY 60 mg tablets

ACTION & *THERAPEUTIC EFFECT*
Nonsteroidal antiestrogen chemical derivative of tamoxifen. Antitumor activity thought to be due to ability to compete with estrogen for binding sites in the cancer cells. *Depresses growth in estrogen receptor–positive tumors in postmenopausal women.*

USES Metastatic breast cancer in postmenopausal women who are estrogen receptor positive.

CONTRAINDICATIONS Hypersensitivity to toremifene; history of thromboembolic disease; pregnancy (category D); lactation.
CAUTIOUS USE Preexisting endometrial hyperplasia; bone metastases (may result in hypercalcemia); geriatric patients; leukopenia and thrombocytopenia; liver disease; history of thrombolytic disease.

ROUTE & DOSAGE

Breast Cancer
Adult: **PO** 60 mg q.d.

ADMINISTRATION

Oral
■ Withhold drug and notify physician if severe hypercalcemia develops.
■ Store at 15°–30° C (59°–86° F) in a tightly closed container and protect from light.

ADVERSE EFFECTS (≥1%) **Body as a Whole:** *Hot flashes, sweating,* edema. **CNS:** Dizziness. **GI:** *Nausea,* vomiting, abnormal liver func-

T

Common adverse effects in *italic*, life-threatening effects <u>underlined</u>; generic names in **bold**; classifications in SMALL CAPS; ✚ Canadian drug name; ◎ Prototype drug

1527

tion tests. **Respiratory:** Pulmonary embolism. **Urogenital:** *Vaginal discharge,* vaginal bleeding. **Special Senses:** Cataracts, dry eyes, corneal keratopathy.

INTERACTIONS Drug: THIAZIDE DIURETICS increase risk of hypercalcemia; increased PT on **warfarin; carbamazepine, phenobarbital, phenytoin** may increase toremifene metabolism.

PHARMACOKINETICS Absorption: Rapidly absorbed from GI tract. **Peak:** 3 h. **Distribution:** >99% protein bound; crosses placenta. **Metabolism:** In liver by cytochrome P450 3A4. **Elimination:** Primarily in feces. **Half-Life:** 5 d.

CLINICAL IMPLICATIONS

Assessment & Drug Effects

- Lab tests: Periodically monitor CBC with differential, serum calcium, liver and kidney functions.
- Monitor patients carefully with bone metastases or those on drugs that decrease calcium excretion (e.g., thiazide diuretics) for S&S of hypercalcemia (see Appendix F).
- Monitor PT and INR carefully when given concurrently with warfarin.

Patient & Family Education

- Report to physician promptly any of the following: Unexplained weakness or fatigue, musculoskeletal pain or calf pain and tenderness, sudden chest pain, vaginal bleeding.
- Schedule periodic eye exams with long-term therapy.

TORSEMIDE

(tor'se-mide)

Demadex

Classifications: ELECTROLYTE AND WATER BALANCE AGENT; LOOP DIURETIC
Therapeutic: LOOP DIURETIC; ANTIHYPERTENSIVE
Prototype: Furosemide
Pregnancy Category: B

AVAILABILITY 5 mg, 10 mg, 20 mg, 100 mg tablets; 10 mg/mL injection

ACTION & *THERAPEUTIC EFFECT*
Long-acting potent sulfonamide "loop" diuretic that inhibits reabsorption of sodium and chloride primarily in the loop of Henle and also in the proximal and distal renal tubules. Binds to the sodium/potassium/chloride carrier in the loop of Henle and in the renal tubules. *Long-acting potent sulfonamide "loop" diuretic and antihypertensive agent.*

USES Management of edema associated with CHF, chronic kidney failure, hepatic cirrhosis; hypertension.

CONTRAINDICATIONS Hypersensitivity to torsemide or sulfonamides; anuria, fluid and electrolyte depletion states; acute MI; hepatic coma.

CAUTIOUS USE Renal impairment; ventricular arrhythmias; concurrent use of other ototoxic drugs; gout or hyperuricemia; diabetes mellitus or history of pancreatitis; liver disease; hearing impairment; pregnancy (category B); lactation.

ROUTE & DOSAGE

Edema of CHF, Chronic Kidney Failure
Adult: **PO/IV** 10–20 mg once daily, may increase up to 200 mg/d as needed

Common adverse effects in *italic*, life-threatening effects underlined; generic names in **bold**; classifications in SMALL CAPS; ◆ Canadian drug name; ⊙ Prototype drug

Hepatic Cirrhosis

Adult: **PO/IV** 5–10 mg once daily administered with an aldosterone antagonist or potassium-sparing diuretic, may increase up to 40 mg/d as needed

Hypertension

Adult: **PO** 2.5–5 mg once daily, may increase to 10 mg/d if no response after 4–6 wk

ADMINISTRATION

▪ Note: With hepatic cirrhosis, use an aldosterone antagonist concomitantly to prevent hypokalemia and metabolic alkalosis.

Oral

▪ Be aware that oral and IV doses are therapeutically equivalent; patients may be switched between the two forms with no change in dosage.

Intravenous

PREPARE: **Direct:** Given undiluted.
ADMINISTER: **Direct:** Give slowly over 2 min.

INCOMPATIBILITIES **Solution/additive: Dobutamine.**

▪ Store at 15°–30° C (59°–86° F).

ADVERSE EFFECTS (≥1%) **CNS:** Headache, dizziness, fatigue, insomnia. **CV:** Orthostatic hypotension. **Endocrine:** *Hypokalemia,* hyponatremia, hyperuricemia. **GI:** Nausea, diarrhea. **Skin:** Rash, pruritus. **Body as a Whole:** Muscle cramps, rhinitis.

INTERACTIONS Drug: NSAIDS may reduce diuretic effects. Also see furosemide for potential drug interactions such as increased risk of **digoxin** toxicity due to hypokalemia, prolonged neuromuscular blockade with NEUROMUSCULAR BLOCKING AGENTS, and decreased **lithium** elimination with increased toxicity. **Herbal: Ginseng** may decrease efficacy.

PHARMACOKINETICS Absorption: Readily from GI tract. **Onset:** IV 10 min; PO 60 min. **Peak:** IV within 60 min; PO 60–120 min. **Duration:** 6–8 h. **Metabolism:** In liver (CYP system). **Elimination:** 80% in bile; 20% in urine. **Half-Life:** 210 min.

CLINICAL IMPLICATIONS

Assessment & Drug Effects

▪ Monitor BP often and assess for orthostatic hypotension; periodically assess weight as an index of fluid retention.
▪ Lab tests: Monitor serum electrolytes, uric acid, blood glucose, BUN, and creatinine periodically throughout the course of therapy.
▪ Monitor coagulation parameters and lithium levels in patients on concurrent anticoagulant and/or lithium therapy.

Patient & Family Education

▪ Check weight at least weekly and report abrupt gains or losses to physician.
▪ Understand the risk of orthostatic hypotension.
▪ Report symptoms of hypokalemia (see Appendix F) or hearing loss immediately to physician.
▪ Monitor blood glucose for loss of glycemic control if diabetic.

TRAMADOL HYDROCHLORIDE

(tra′ma-dol)

Ultram, Zydol ♦

Classifications: ANALGESIC; NARCOTIC (OPIATE) AGONIST
Therapeutic: NARCOTIC ANALGESIC; OPIATE AGONIST
Prototype: Morphine sulfate
Pregnancy Category: C

AVAILABILITY 50 mg tablets; 50 mg orally disintegrating tablets

T

Common adverse effects in *italic*, life-threatening effects underlined; generic names in **bold**; classifications in SMALL CAPS; ♣ Canadian drug name; ❍ Prototype drug

1529

ACTION & *THERAPEUTIC EFFECT*

Centrally acting opiate receptor agonist that inhibits the uptake of norepinephrine and serotonin, suggesting both opioid and nonopioid mechanisms of pain relief. May produce opioid-like effects, but causes less respiratory depression than morphine. *Effective agent for control of moderate to moderately severe pain.*

USES Management of moderate to moderately severe pain.

CONTRAINDICATIONS Hypersensitivity to tramadol or other opioid analgesics; patients on MAO inhibitors; patients acutely intoxicated with alcohol, hypnotics, centrally acting analgesics, opioids, or psychotropic drugs; substance abuse; patients on obstetric preoperative medication; abrupt discontinuation; alcohol intoxication; pregnancy (category C); lactation; children <16 y.

CAUTIOUS USE Debilitated patients; chronic respiratory disorders; respiratory depression; older adults; liver disease; renal impairment; myxedema, hypothyroidism, or hypoadrenalism; GI disease; acute abdominal conditions; increased ICP or head injury, increased intracranial pressure; history of seizures; patients >75 y.

ROUTE & DOSAGE

Pain
Adult: **PO** 50–100 mg q4–6h prn (max: 400 mg/d), may start with 25 mg/d if not well tolerated, and increase by 25 mg q3d up to 200 mg/d
Geriatric: **PO** 50–100 mg q4–6h prn (max: 300 mg/d), may start with 25 mg/d if not well tolerated, and increase by 25 mg q3d up to 200 mg/d

Renal Impairment
Cl_{cr} <30 mL/min: decrease to 50–100 mg q12h
Hepatic Impairment
Cirrhosis decrease to 50–100 mg q12h

ADMINISTRATION

Oral

- Note: Dosage reduction is recommended for patients with renal insufficiency and hepatic impairment.
- Store at 15°–30° C (59°–86° F).

ADVERSE EFFECTS (≥1%) **CNS:** Drowsiness, *dizziness, vertigo, fatigue, headache, somnolence,* restlessness, euphoria, confusion, anxiety, coordination disturbance, sleep disturbances, seizures. **CV:** Palpitations, vasodilation. **GI:** *Nausea, constipation,* vomiting, xerostomia, dyspepsia, diarrhea, abdominal pain, anorexia, flatulence. **Body as a Whole:** Sweating, <u>anaphylactic reaction</u> (even with first dose), withdrawal syndrome (anxiety, sweating, nausea, tremors, diarrhea, piloerection, panic attacks, paresthesia, hallucinations) with abrupt discontinuation. **Skin:** Rash. **Special Senses:** Visual disturbances. **Urogenital:** Urinary retention/frequency, menopausal symptoms.

DIAGNOSTIC TEST INTERFERENCE Increased *creatinine, liver enzymes;* decreased *hemoglobin; proteinuria.*

INTERACTIONS Drug: Carbamazepine significantly decreases tramadol levels (may need up to twice usual dose). Tramadol may increase adverse effects of MAO INHIBITORS. TRICYCLIC ANTIDEPRESSANTS, **cyclobenzaprine,** PHENOTHIAZINES, SELECTIVE SEROTONIN-REUPTAKE INHIBI-

T

TORS (SSRIS), MAO INHIBITORS may enhance seizure risk with tramadol. May increase CNS adverse effects when used with other CNS DEPRESSANTS. **Herbal: St. John's wort** may increase sedation.

PHARMACOKINETICS Absorption: Rapidly absorbed from GI tract; 75% reaches systemic circulation. **Onset:** 30–60 min. **Peak:** 2 h. **Duration:** 3–7 h. **Distribution:** Approximately 20% bound to plasma proteins; probably crosses blood–brain barrier; crosses placenta; 0.1% excreted into breast milk. **Metabolism:** Extensively in liver by cytochrome P450 system. **Elimination:** Primarily in urine. **Half-Life:** 6–7 h.

CLINICAL IMPLICATIONS

Assessment & Drug Effects

- Assess for level of pain relief and administer prn dose as needed but not to exceed the recommended total daily dose.
- Monitor vital signs and assess for orthostatic hypotension or signs of CNS depression.
- Discontinue drug and notify physician if S&S of hypersensitivity occur.
- Assess bowel and bladder function; report urinary frequency or retention.
- Use seizure precautions for patients who have a history of seizures or who are concurrently using drugs that lower the seizure threshold.
- Monitor ambulation and take appropriate safety precautions.

Patient & Family Education

- Exercise caution with potentially hazardous activities until response to drug is known.
- Understand potential adverse effects and report problems with bowel and bladder function, CNS

impairment, and any other bothersome adverse effects to physician.

TRANDOLAPRIL

(tran-do'la-pril)
Mavik
Classifications: ANGIOTENSIN-CONVERTING ENZYME (ACE) INHIBITOR; ANTIHYPERTENSIVE
Therapeutic: ANTIHYPERTENSIVE; ACE INHIBITOR
Prototype: Enalapril
Pregnancy Category: C first trimester; D second and third trimester

AVAILABILITY 1 mg, 2 mg, 4 mg tablets

ACTION & *THERAPEUTIC EFFECT*
Inhibits ACE and interrupts conversion sequences initiated by renin which leads to the formation of angiotensin II from angiotensin I. Angiotensin II is a potent endogenous vasoconstrictor. Inhibition of ACE leads to vasodilation and also to decreased circulating aldosterone. Decreased aldosterone leads to diuresis and a slight increase in serum potassium. *Lowers blood pressure by specific inhibition of ACE. Unlike other ACE inhibitors, all racial groups respond to trandolapril, including low-renin hypertensives.*

USES Treatment of hypertension, alone or in combination with other antihypertensive agents.
UNLABELED USES CHF.

CONTRAINDICATIONS Hypersensitivity to trandolapril or ACE inhibitors; history of angioedema related to previous treatment with an ACE inhibitor; pregnancy (category C, first trimester; category D, second and third trimesters), lactation.

T

Common adverse effects in *italic*, life-threatening effects underlined; generic names in **bold**; classifications in SMALL CAPS; ✦ Canadian drug name; ⊙ Prototype drug

1531

CAUTIOUS USE Renal impairment, hepatic insufficiency; patients prone to hypotension (e.g., CHF, ischemic heart disease, aortic stenosis, CVA, dehydration); SLE, scleroderma. Safety and effectiveness in children <18 y are not established.

ROUTE & DOSAGE

Note: Discontinue diuretics 2–3 d before starting trandolapril.

Hypertension
Adult: **PO** 1 mg in nonblack patients, 2 mg in black patients once daily, may increase weekly to 2–4 mg once daily (max: 8 mg/d)

Renal Impairment
Cl_{cr} <30 mL/min: start with 0.5 mg once daily

Hepatic Impairment
Hepatic cirrhosis: start with 0.5 mg once daily

ADMINISTRATION

Oral
- Note: If concurrently ordered diuretic cannot be discontinued 2–3 d before beginning trandolapril therapy, reduce initial dose to 0.5 mg.
- Make dosage adjustments generally at intervals of at least 1 wk.
- Store at 15°–30° C (59°–86° F).

ADVERSE EFFECTS (≥1%) **Body as a Whole:** Fatigue, <u>angioedema</u>. **CNS:** Dizziness, headache. **CV:** Hypotension. **GI:** Diarrhea. **Respiratory:** Cough. **Skin:** Rash, pruritus. **Metabolic:** Hyperkalemia.

INTERACTIONS Drug: DIURETICS may enhance hypotensive effects. POTASSIUM-SPARING DIURETICS (amiloride, spironolactone, triamterene), POTASSIUM SUPPLEMENTS, POTASSIUM-CONTAINING SALT SUBSTITUTES may increase risk of hyperkalemia. May increase serum levels and toxicity of **lithium**.

PHARMACOKINETICS Absorption: Rapidly absorbed from GI tract and converted to active form, trandolaprilat, in liver; 70% of dose reaches systemic circulation as trandolaprilat. **Peak:** 4–10 h. **Distribution:** 80% protein bound; crosses placenta, secreted into breast milk of animals (human secretion unknown). **Metabolism:** In liver to active metabolite, trandolaprilat. **Elimination:** 33% in urine, 66% in feces. **Half-Life:** 6 h trandolapril, 10 h trandolaprilat.

CLINICAL IMPLICATIONS

Assessment & Drug Effects
- Monitor BP carefully for 1–3 h following initial dose, especially in patients using concurrent diuretics, on salt restriction, or volume depleted.
- Lab tests: Monitor BP and cardiac status; serum potassium, sodium, creatinine, and ALT/SGTP; and WBC with differential periodically.
- Monitor serum lithium levels frequently with concurrent use and assess for S&S of lithium toxicity; increase caution when diuretic therapy is also used.

Patient & Family Education
- Discontinue drug and immediately report S&S of angioedema of face or extremities to physician. Advise to seek emergency help for swelling of the tongue or any other sign of potential airway obstruction.
- Be aware that light-headedness can occur, especially during early therapy. Excess fluid loss of any kind will increase risk of hypotension and syncope.

TRANYLCYPROMINE SULFATE

(tran-ill-sip′roe-meen)
Parnate
Classifications: PSYCHOTHERAPEU-
TIC; ANTIDEPRESSANT; MONOAMINE
OXIDASE INHIBITOR (MAOI)
Therapeutic: ANTIDEPRESSANT; MAOI
Prototype: Phenelzine
Pregnancy Category: C

AVAILABILITY 10 mg tablets

ACTION & *THERAPEUTIC EFFECT*

Potent nonhydrazine MAO inhibitor. Antidepressant activity arises
from the increased availability of
monoamines resulting from the inhibition of the enzyme MAO. Reduction of MAO activity results in
an increased concentration of neurotransmitters, such as epinephrine,
norepinephrine, and dopamine in
the CNS. *Drug of last choice for severe depression unresponsive to other
MAO inhibitors.*

USES Severe depression.

CONTRAINDICATIONS Patients >60
y; confirmed or suspected cerebrovascular defect, cardiovascular
disease, CHF; history of hepatic disease; hypertension, pheochromocytoma, history of severe or recurrent
headaches; acute MI; alcoholism; angina; renal failure; suicidal ideation;
anuria; pregnancy (category C); lactation.

CAUTIOUS USE Bipolar disorder; Parkinson's disease; psychosis; schizophrenia; seizure disorders; history of
suicidal attempts.

ROUTE & DOSAGE

Severe Depression
Adult: **PO** 30 mg/d in 2 divided
doses (20 mg in a.m., 10 mg in
p.m.), may increase by 10 mg/d
at 3 wk intervals (max: 60 mg/d)

ADMINISTRATION

Oral
- Crush tablet and give with fluid or
  mix with food if patient cannot
  swallow pill.
- Note: Usually not given in the
  evening because of possibility of
  insomnia.

ADVERSE EFFECTS (≥1%) **CNS:** Vertigo, dizziness, tremors, muscle
twitching, headache, blurred vision.
CV: *Orthostatic hypotension,* arrhythmias, hypertensive crisis. **GI:** D r y
mouth, anorexia, constipation, diarrhea, abdominal discomfort. **Skin:**
Rash. **Urogenital:** Impotence. **Body
as a Whole:** Peripheral edema,
sweating.

INTERACTIONS Drug: TRICYCLIC ANTI-
DEPRESSANTS, **fluoxetine,** AMPHETA-
MINES, **ephedrine, reserpine,
guanethidine, buspirone, methyldopa, dopamine, levodopa,
tryptophan** may precipitate hypertensive crisis, headache, or hyperexcitability; **alcohol** and other CNS DE-
PRESSANTS add to CNS depressant
effects; **meperidine** can cause fatal
cardiovascular collapse; ANESTHETICS
exaggerate hypotensive and CNS
depressant effects; **metrizamide** increases risk of seizures; DIURETICS
and other ANTIHYPERTENSIVE AGENTS
add to hypotensive effects. **Food:
Tyramine**-containing foods may
precipitate hypertensive crisis
(e.g., aged cheeses, processed
cheeses, sour cream, wine, champagne, beer, pickled herring, anchovies, caviar, shrimp, liver, dry
sausage, figs, raisins, overripe bananas or avocados, chocolate, soy
sauce, bean curd, yeast extracts,
yogurt, papaya products, meat
tenderizers, broad beans). **Herbal:
Ginseng, ephedra, ma huang, St.
John's wort** may lead to hypertensive crisis; **ginseng** may lead to
manic episodes.

T

Common adverse effects in *italic*, life-threatening effects underlined; generic names
in **bold**; classifications in SMALL CAPS; ♣ Canadian drug name; ⓹ Prototype drug

1533

PHARMACOKINETICS Absorption:
Completely absorbed from GI tract.
Onset: 10 d. **Metabolism:** Rapidly
metabolized in liver to active metabolite. **Elimination:** Primarily in urine.
Half-Life: 2.5 h (but may take 120 h
for urinary tryptamine levels to return to normal).

CLINICAL IMPLICATIONS

Assessment & Drug Effects

- Monitor BP closely. Incidence of
  severe hypertensive reactions appears to be greater with tranylcypromine than with other MAO
  inhibitors.
- Monitor for changes in behavior
  that could indicate increased suicidality.
- Expect therapeutic response within
  3 d, but full antidepressant effects
  may not be obtained until 2–3 wk
  of drug therapy.

Patient & Family Education

- Do not eat tyramine-containing
  foods (see FOOD–DRUG INTERAC-
  TIONS).
- Be aware that excessive use of
  caffeine-containing beverages
  (chocolate, coffee, tea, cola) can
  contribute to development of
  rapid heartbeat, arrhythmias, and
  hypertension.
- Make position changes slowly,
  particularly from recumbent to
  upright posture.
- Avoid potentially hazardous activities until response to drug is
  known.
- Avoid alcohol or other CNS depressants because of their possible additive effects.

TRASTUZUMAB

(tra-stu'zu-mab)
Herceptin

Classifications: IMMUNOMODU-
LATOR; MONOCLONAL ANTIBODY;
ANTINEOPLASTIC; ANTI-HUMAN EPI-
DERMAL GROWTH FACTOR (ANTI-HER)
Therapeutic: ANTINEOPLASTIC; IMMU-
NOMODULATOR; ANTI-HER
Pregnancy Category: B

AVAILABILITY 21 mg/mL injection

ACTION & *THERAPEUTIC EFFECT*
Recombinant DNA monoclonal antibody (I_gG_1 kappa) that selectively
binds to the human epidermal
growth factor receptor-2 protein
(HER_2). *Inhibits growth of human
tumor cells that overexpress HER_2
proteins.*

USES Metastatic breast cancer in
those whose tumors overexpress
the HER_2 protein. HER_2-positive
breast cancer after surgery.

CONTRAINDICATIONS Concurrent
administration of anthracycline or
radiation; lactation during and for
6 mo following administration of
trastuzumab.
CAUTIOUS USE Preexisting cardiac
dysfunction; pulmonary disease; previous administration of cardiotoxic
therapy (e.g., anthracycline or radiation); pregnancy (category B); older
adults; hypersensitivity to benzyl alcohol (preservative in bacteriostatic
water).

ROUTE & DOSAGE

Metastatic Breast Cancer
Adult: **IV** 4 mg/kg, then 2 mg/kg qwk

ADMINISTRATION

Intravenous ───────

PREPARE: **IV Infusion:** Reconstitute each vial with 20 mL of supplied diluent (bacteriostatic water) to produce a multidose vial
containing 21 mg/mL. Note: For

patients with a hypersensitivity to benzyl alcohol, reconstitute with sterile water for injection; this solution must be used immediately with any unused portion discarded. Withdraw the ordered dose and add to a 250-mL of NS and invert bag to mix. Do not give or mix with dextrose solutions. *ADMINISTER:* **IV Infusion:** Infuse loading dose (4 mg/kg) over 90 min; infuse subsequent doses (2 mg/kg) over 30 min. Do not give IV push or as a bolus dose. *INCOMPATIBILITIES* **Solution/additive:** Dextrose solution; do not mix or coadminister with other drugs.

▪ Store unopened vials and reconstituted vials at 2°–8° C (36°–46° F). Discard reconstituted vials 28 days after reconstitution.

ADVERSE EFFECTS (≥1%) **Body as a Whole:** *Pain, asthenia, fever, chills,* flu syndrome, allergic reaction, bone pain, arthralgia, hypersensitivity (anaphylaxis, urticaria, bronchospasm, angioedema, or hypotension), increased incidence of infections, infusion reaction (*chills, fever,* nausea, vomiting, pain, rigors, headache, dizziness, dyspnea, hypotension, rash). **CNS:** *Headache, insomnia, dizziness, paresthesias,* depression, peripheral neuritis, neuropathy. **CV:** CHF, cardiac dysfunction (dyspnea, cough, paroxysmal nocturnal dyspnea, peripheral edema, S3 gallop, reduced ejection fraction), tachycardia, edema, cardiotoxicity. **GI:** *Diarrhea, abdominal pain, nausea, vomiting,* anorexia. **Hematologic:** *Anemia, leukopenia.* **Respiratory:** *Cough, dyspnea,* rhinitis, pharyngitis, sinusitis. **Skin:** *Rash,* herpes simplex, acne.

INTERACTIONS Drug: Paclitaxel may increase trastuzumab levels and toxicity.

PHARMACOKINETICS Half-Life: 5.8 d.

CLINICAL IMPLICATIONS
Assessment & Drug Effects
▪ Lab tests: Periodically monitor CBC with differential, platelet count, and Hgb and Hct.
▪ Monitor for chills and fever during the first IV infusion; these adverse events usually respond to prompt treatment without the need to discontinue the infusion. Notify physician immediately.
▪ Monitor carefully cardiovascular status at baseline and throughout course of therapy, assessing for S&S of heart failure (e.g., dyspnea, increased cough, PND, edema, S3 gallop). Those with preexisting cardiac dysfunction are at high risk for cardiotoxicity.

Patient & Family Education
▪ Report promptly any unusual symptoms (e.g., chills, nausea, fever) during infusion.
▪ Report promptly any of the following: Shortness of breath, swelling of feet or legs, persistent cough, difficulty sleeping, loss of appetite, abdominal bloating.

TRAVOPROST
(tra'-vo-prost)
Travatan
Pregnancy Category: C
See Appendix A-1.

TRAZODONE HYDROCHLORIDE
(tray'zoe-done)
Classifications: PSYCHOTHERAPEUTIC AGENT; ANTIDEPRESSANT
Therapeutic: ANTIDEPRESSANT
Prototype: Imipramine
Pregnancy Category: C

T

Common adverse effects in *italic*, life-threatening effects underlined; generic names in **bold**; classifications in SMALL CAPS; ◆ Canadian drug name; ⊙ Prototype drug

1535

AVAILABILITY 50 mg, 100 mg, 150 mg, 300 mg tablets

ACTION & *THERAPEUTIC EFFECT* Centrally acting antidepressant chemically and structurally unrelated to tricyclic, tetracyclic, or other antidepressants. Potentiates serotonin effects by selectively blocking its reuptake at presynaptic membranes in CNS. Produces varying degrees of sedation in normal and mentally depressed patient. *Increases total sleep time, decreases number and duration of awakenings in depressed patient, and decreases REM sleep. Has antianxiety effect in severely depressed patient.*

USES Both inpatient and outpatient with major depression with or without prominent anxiety.

UNLABELED USES Adjunctive treatment of alcohol dependence, anxiety neuroses, drug-induced dyskinesias, insomnia.

CONTRAINDICATIONS Initial recovery phase of MI; ventricular ectopy; electroshock therapy; suicidal ideation; pregnancy (category C). Safe use in children <6 y is not established.

CAUTIOUS USE Bipolar disorder, older adults; history of suicidal tendencies; cardiac arrhythmias or disease; hepatic disease, renal impairment; lactation.

ROUTE & DOSAGE

Depression
Adult: PO 150 mg/d in divided doses, may increase by 50 mg/d q3–4d (max: 400–600 mg/d)
Geriatric: PO 25–50 mg h.s., may increase q3–7d to usual range of 75–150 mg/d
Child: PO 6–18 y, 1.5–2 mg/kg/d in divided doses, increase q3–4d prn (max: 6 mg/kg/d)

ADMINISTRATION
Oral
- Give drug with food; increases amount of absorption by 20% and appears to decrease incidence of dizziness or light-headedness. Maintain the same schedule for food-drug intake throughout treatment period to prevent variations in serum concentration.
- Store in tightly closed, light-resistant container at 15°–30° C (59°–86° F).

ADVERSE EFFECTS (≥1%) **CNS:** *Drowsiness,* light-headedness, tiredness, dizziness, insomnia, headache, agitation, impaired memory and speech, disorientation. **CV:** *Hypotension (including orthostatic hypotension),* hypertension, syncope, shortness of breath, chest pain, tachycardia, palpitations, bradycardia, PVCs, ventricular tachycardia (short episodes of 3–4 beats). **Special Senses:** Nasal and sinus congestion, blurred vision, eye irritation, sweating or clamminess, tinnitus. **GI:** *Dry mouth,* anorexia, constipation, abdominal distress, nausea, vomiting, dysgeusia, flatulence, diarrhea. **Urogenital:** Hematuria, increased frequency, delayed urine flow, early or absent menses, male priapism, ejaculation inhibition. **Hematologic:** Anemia. **Musculoskeletal:** Skeletal aches and pains, muscle twitches. **Skin:** Skin eruptions, rash, pruritus, acne, photosensitivity. **Body as a Whole:** Weight gain or loss.

INTERACTIONS Drug: ANTIHYPERTENSIVE AGENTS may potentiate hypotensive effects; **alcohol** and other CNS DEPRESSANTS add to depressant effects; may increase **digoxin** or **phenytoin** levels; MAO INHIBITORS may precipitate hypertensive crisis; **ketoconazole, indinavir, ritonavir** may

T

increase levels and toxicity. **Herbal: Ginkgo** may increase sedation.

PHARMACOKINETICS Absorption: Readily from GI tract. **Onset:** 1–2 wk. **Peak:** 1–2 h. **Distribution:** Distributed into breast milk. **Metabolism:** In liver. **Elimination:** 75% in urine, 25% in feces. **Half-Life:** 5–9 h.

CLINICAL IMPLICATIONS

Assessment & Drug Effects

- Monitor pulse rate and regularity before administration if patient has preexisting cardiac disease.
- Note: Adverse effects generally are mild and tend to decrease and disappear after the first few weeks of treatment.
- Monitor children and adolescents for changes in behavior that indicate increased suicidality.
- Observe patient's level of activity. If it appears to be increasing toward sleeplessness and agitation with changes in reality orientation, report to physician. Manic episodes have been reported.
- Check patient for symptoms of hypotension. If orthostatic hypotension is troublesome, suggest measures to reduce danger of falling and help patient to tolerate the effects. Discuss with physician; reduction of dose or discontinuation of the drug may be prescribed.
- Male patient should report inappropriate or prolonged penile erections. The drug may be discontinued.
- Be aware that overdose is characterized by an extension of common adverse effects: Vomiting, lethargy, drowsiness, and exaggerated anticholinergic effects. Seizures or arrhythmias are unusual.

Patient & Family Education

- Expect therapeutic response to begin in 1 wk; may require 2–4 wk to reach maximum levels. Adhere to regimen.
- Do not alter dose or intervals between doses.
- Consult physician if drowsiness becomes a distressing adverse effect. Dose regimen may be changed so that largest dose is at bedtime.
- Limit or abstain from alcohol use. The depressant effects of CNS depressants and alcohol may be potentiated by this drug.
- Do not self-medicate with OTC drugs for colds, allergy, or insomnia treatment without advice of physician. Many of these drugs contain CNS depressants.
- Keep follow-up appointments to permit dose adjustment or discontinuation, as indicated.
- Alert dentist, surgeon, or emergency personnel that drug is being used. Trazodone is discontinued as long as possible prior to elective surgery.

TREPROSTINIL SODIUM

(tre-pros′tin-il)
Remodulin
Classifications: PROSTAGLANDIN; PULMONARY ANTIHYPERTENSIVE
Therapeutic: PULMONARY ANTIHYPERTENSIVE
Prototype: Epoprostenol
Pregnancy Category: B

T

AVAILABILITY 1 mg/mL, 2.5 mg/mL, 5 mg/mL, 10 mg/mL injection

ACTION & *THERAPEUTIC EFFECT*

Causes direct vasodilation of the pulmonary and systemic arterial vascular beds, and inhibition of platelet aggregation. The vasodilatory effects reduce right and left ventricular afterload, and increase cardiac output and stroke volume. Also improves dyspnea, fatigue, and signs and

Common adverse effects in *italic*, life-threatening effects underlined; generic names in **bold**; classifications in SMALL CAPS; ◆ Canadian drug name; ⊙ Prototype drug

1537

symptoms of pulmonary arterial hypertension (PAH). *Vasodilation of the arteries in the pulmonary system results in lowering of pulmonary arterial hypertension (PAH).*

USES Treatment of pulmonary arterial hypertension (PAH) in patients with severe heart failure.

UNLABELED USES Severe intermittent claudication

CONTRAINDICATIONS Severe hepatic insufficiency; hypersensitivity to treprostinil.

CAUTIOUS USE Mild or moderate hepatic insufficiency; bleeding disorders; concurrent use of anticoagulants, NSAIDS, hypotensive drugs (e.g., diuretics, antihypertensive agents, etc.); renal disease, renal impairment, renal failure; lactation, pregnancy (category B); elderly. Safety and efficacy in children <16 y are not established.

ROUTE & DOSAGE

Pulmonary Arterial Hypertension
Adult: **SC** >16 y, 1.25 ng/kg/min. If dose is not tolerated, reduce to 0.625 ng/kg/min. Then increase rate by no more than 1.25 ng/kg/min/wk for first 4 wk, then by 2.5 ng/kg/min/wk until achieve desired response. There is little experience with doses >40 ng/kg/min

Transition from Epoprostenol to Treprostinil
Adult: **SC** >16 y, While still receiving IV epoprostenol, initiate a dose of SC treprostinil no greater than one-half of the current epoprostenol dose (generally ≤5 ng/kg/min). Maintain treprostinil at this dose for at least 6 h. During this time, reduce the epoprostenol dose in no greater than 2 ng/kg/min decrements, based on appearance of prostacyclin-related signs and symptoms. Continue to increase treprostinil dose by no more than one-half of the current dose and maintain for 6 h while reducing epoprostenol dose by no greater than 2 ng/kg/min decrements until epoprostenol is discontinued.

ADMINISTRATION

Subcutaneous
- Initiate therapy only in a setting with adequate personnel and equipment for physiological monitoring and emergency.
- Administer Remodulin undiluted.
- Avoid abrupt withdrawal or sudden large reductions in dosage as these may lead to worsening of PAH symptom.
- Note that in patients with mild to moderate hepatic insufficiency, the initial dose of should be 0.625 ng/kg/min ideal body weight and should be increased cautiously.
- Store at 15°–25° C (59°–77° F).

ADVERSE EFFECTS (≥1%) **Body as a Whole:** *Jaw pain,* flushing, syncope. **CNS:** *Headache,* dizziness. **CV:** *Vasodilation,* edema, hypotension. **GI:** *Diarrhea, nausea, vomiting.* **Skin:** *Rash,* pruritus. **Other:** *Infusion site reactions (erythema, hematoma, induration, pruritus, rash, injection site pain).*

INTERACTIONS Drug: NSAIDS, ANTICOAGULANTS may increase risk of bleeding; ANTIHYPERTENSIVE AGENTS, DIURETICS, VASODILATORS may exacerbate hypotension; **ephedrine, pseudoephedrine** may antagonize antihypertensive effects. **Herbal: Ephedra, ma huang** may antagonize antihypertensive effects.

PHARMACOKINETICS Absorption: Completely absorbed from SC site. **Onset:** Steady state reached in 10 h. **Metabolism:** Extensively in liver by unknown enzyme system. **Elimination:** 79% in urine, 13% in feces. **Half-Life:** 2–4 h.

CLINICAL IMPLICATIONS

Assessment & Drug Effects

- Monitor for therapeutic effectiveness indicated by less dyspnea and fatigue, increased activity tolerance, and improved hemodynamic parameters.
- Monitor for and report symptoms of excessive response to the drug including: headache, nausea, emesis, restlessness, anxiety and infusion site pain or reaction (e.g., erythema, induration or rash). If these occur, the rate of SC infusion should be slowed.
- Monitor BP closely, especially if taking concurrent antihypertensive drugs (e.g., diuretics, vasodilators).
- Lab tests: Baseline and periodic LFTs and renal function tests. Monitor periodically coagulation parameters (more often if on concurrent anticoagulation therapy).

Patient & Family Education

- Note: Therapy with this drug may be needed for prolonged periods, possibly years.
- Report any of the following: headache, nausea, vomiting, restlessness, anxiety and infusion site pain.

TRETINOIN

(tret'i-noyn)

Avita, Renova, Retin-A, Retin-A Micro, Retinoic Acid, Vesanoid, Vitamin A Acid

Classifications: ANTIACNE (RETINOID); ANTIPSORIATIC

Therapeutic: ANTIACNE
Prototype: Isotretinoin
Pregnancy Category: C

AVAILABILITY 0.025%, 0.05%, 0.1% cream; 0.025%, 0.01% gel; 0.05% liquid; 10 mg capsules

ACTION & THERAPEUTIC EFFECT
Contact irritant containing retinoic acid and vitamin A acid. Reverses retention hyperkeratosis and comedo formation, primary events in acne pathology. Suggests that keratinocytes in the sebaceous follicle become less adherent and turnover of follicular epithelial cells is increased; two processes that promote easy extrusion of the comedo and prevent it from reformation. Also increases permeability of skin and supports conversion of follicular epithelium into a less sturdy and almost fragile condition. *Effective in early treatment and control of acne vulgaris grades I–III.*

USES Topical treatment of acne vulgaris grades I–III, especially during early stages when number of comedones is greatest; adjunctively in management of associated comedones and in treatment of flat warts; oral for remission induction treatment of acute promyelocytic leukemia; cream as adjunctive therapy for mitigation of fine wrinkles. **UNLABELED USES** Psoriasis, senile keratosis, ichthyosis vulgaris, keratosis palmaris and plantaris, basal cell carcinoma, photodamaged skin (photoaging), and other skin conditions. **Orphan drug:** For squamous metaplasia of conjunctiva or cornea with mucous deficiency and keratinization.

CONTRAINDICATIONS Eczema; exposure to sunlight or ultraviolet rays (as with sunlamp), sunburn;

T

Common adverse effects in *italic*, life-threatening effects underlined; generic names in **bold**; classifications in SMALL CAPS; ♣ Canadian drug name; ◯ Prototype drug

1539

pregnancy (category C); lactation; children <12 y.

CAUTIOUS USE Patient in an occupation necessitating considerable sun exposure or weather extremes; hepatic disease.

ROUTE & DOSAGE

Acne
Adult: **Topical** Apply once/d h.s.

Acute Promyelocytic Leukemia
Adult: **PO** 45 mg/m^2/d

Antiwrinkle Cream
Adult: **Topical** (0.05% cream) Apply to face once daily h.s.

ADMINISTRATION

Topical

- Wait long enough for recovery if patient has been using a desquamative agent before starting treatment.
- Cleanse using a mild bland soap, and thoroughly dry areas being treated before applying drug. Avoid use of medicated, drying, or abrasive soaps and cleansers.
- Wash hands before and after treatment. Apply lightly over affected areas. Do not apply to nonaffected skin area.
- Avoid contact of drug with eyes, mouth, angles of nose, open wounds, mucous membranes.
- Store gel and liquid formulations below 30° C (86° F) and solution below 27° C (80° F).

ADVERSE EFFECTS (≥1%) **Body as a Whole: Note:** Listed adverse effects occur primarily with oral administration; only skin effects with topical administration. *Bone pain, malaise, shivering, hemorrhage, peripheral edema, pain, chest discomfort, weight gain or loss,* <u>DIC</u>. **CNS:** *Dizziness, paresthesias, anxiety, in-* *somnia, depression, headache, fever, weakness, fatigue,* cerebral hemorrhage, intracranial hypertension, hallucinations. **CV:** *Arrhythmias, flushing, hypotension, hypertension,* CHF. **Special Senses:** Visual disturbances, ocular disturbances, change in visual acuity, earache. **GI:** *Nausea, vomiting, abdominal pain, diarrhea, constipation, dyspepsia,* <u>GI hemorrhage</u>. **Respiratory:** *Dyspnea, respiratory insufficiency, pneumonia, rales, pleural effusion, wheezing.* **Skin:** Local inflammatory reactions, transient stinging or warmth on site, *redness, scaling, severe erythema,* blistering, crusting and peeling, temporary hypopigmentation or hyperpigmentation, *increased sweating.* **Urogenital:** Renal insufficiency, dysuria, acute kidney failure.

INTERACTIONS Drug: TOPICAL ACNE MEDICATIONS (including **sulfur, resorcinol, benzoyl peroxide,** and **salicylic acid**) may increase inflammation and peeling; topical products containing **alcohol** or **menthol** may cause stinging.

PHARMACOKINETICS Absorption: Minimally absorbed from intact skin, Topical; 60% absorbed, PO. **Elimination:** About 0.1% of topical dose is excreted in urine within 24 h; 63% excreted in urine and 31% in feces, PO. **Half-Life:** 45 min, Topical; 2–2.5 h, PO.

CLINICAL IMPLICATIONS

Assessment & Drug Effects

- Be aware that treatment to dark-skinned individuals may cause unsightly postinflammatory hyperpigmentation; that is reversible with termination of drug treatment.
- Clinical response should be evident in 2–3 wk; complete and satisfactory response (in 75% of the patients) may require 3–4 mo.

Common adverse effects in *italic*, life-threatening effects <u>underlined</u>; generic names in **bold**; classifications in SMALL CAPS; ✦ Canadian drug name; ⊕ Prototype drug

Once achieved, control is maintained by less frequent applications or a change in formulation or dosage.

Patient & Family Education

- Be aware that erythema and desquamation during the first 1–3 wk of treatment do not represent exacerbation of the skin problem but a probable response to the drug from deep previously unseen lesions.
- As treatment is continued, lesions gradually disappear, leaving an inflammatory background; scaling and redness decrease after 8–10 wk of therapy.
- Wash face no more often than 2–3 times daily.
- Do not use topical preparations with high concentrations of alcohol, astringents, spices or lime, perfumes and shaving lotions during treatment period.
- Be aware that drug is not curative; relapses commonly occur within 3–6 wk after treatment has been discontinued.
- Remove nonmedicated cosmetics thoroughly before drug is applied.
- Avoid exposure to sun; when cannot be avoided, use a SPF 15 or higher sunscreen.
- Do not self-medicate with additional acne treatment because of danger of drug interactions.

TRIAMCINOLONE

(trye-am-sin'oh-lone)
Aristocort, Atolone, Kenacort, Kenalog-E

TRIAMCINOLONE ACETONIDE

Azmacort, Cenocort A₂, Kenalog, Nasacort HFA, Triam-A, Triamonide, Tri-kort, Trilog, Tri-Nasal

TRIAMCINOLONE DIACETATE

Aristocort Forte, Kenacort

TRIAMCINOLONE HEXACETONIDE

Aristospan

Classifications: HORMONE; ADRENAL CORTICOSTEROID; GLUCOCORTICOID; ANTIINFLAMMATORY
Therapeutic: ADRENAL CORTICOSTEROID; ANTIINFLAMMATORY; IMMUNOSUPPRESSANT
Prototype: Prednisone
Pregnancy Category: C

AVAILABILITY Triamcinolone 4 mg, 8 mg tablets; 4 mg/5 mL syrup **Triamcinolone acetonide** 3 mg/mL, 10 mg/mL, 40 mg/mL injection; 100 mcg aerosol; 55 mcg inhaler; 55 mcg spray; 0.5 mg/mL nasal spray; 0.025%, 0.1%, 0.5% cream, ointment, lotion; 10.3% topical spray **Triamcinolone diacetate** 4 mg tablet **Triamcinolone hexacetonide** 5 mg/mL, 20 mg/mL injection.

ACTION & *THERAPEUTIC EFFECT* Immediate-acting synthetic fluorinated adrenal corticosteroid with glucocorticoid properties. Possesses minimal sodium and water retention properties in therapeutic doses. *Antiinflammatory and immunosuppressant drug that is effective in the treatment of bronchial asthma.*

USES An antiinflammatory or immunosuppressant agent. Orally inhaled: bronchial asthma in patient who has not responded to conventional inhalation treatment. Therapeutic doses do not appear to suppress HPA (hypothalamic-pituitary-adrenal) axis.

CONTRAINDICATIONS Kidney dysfunction; glaucoma; pregnancy (category C), lactation, children <6 y. Also see hydrocortisone.
CAUTIOUS USE Coagulopathy, hemophilia, diabetes mellitus, GI dis-

T

Common adverse effects in *italic*, life-threatening effects underlined; generic names in **bold**; classifications in SMALL CAPS; ◆ Canadian drug name; ⊙ Prototype drug

1541

ease; congestive heart failure; herpes infection; infection; inflammatory bowel disease; myasthenia gravis; MI; ocular exposure, ocular infection; osteoporosis; peptic ulcer disease; PVD; skin abrasion.

ROUTE & DOSAGE

Inflammation, Immunosuppression

Adult: PO/IM/SC 4–48 mg/d in divided doses Intraarticular/Intradermal 4–48 mg/d Inhaled 2–4 inhalations q.i.d. Topical See Appendix A
Child: PO/IM/SC 3.3–50 mg/m²/d in divided doses Intraarticular/Intradermal 3.3–50 mg/m²/d

Acetonide

Adult: IM 60 mg, may repeat with 20–100 mg q6wk Intradermal 1 mg per injection site (max: 30 mg total) Intraarticular 2.5–4.0 mg Inhalation See Appendix A.
Child: IM 6–12 y, 0.03–0.2 mg q1–7d Inhalation See Appendix A.

Diacetate

Adult: PO 4–48 mg/d in 1–4 divided doses IM 40 mg once/wk Intradermal 5–48 mg (max: 75 mg/wk), may repeat q1–2wk if needed Intraarticular 2–40 mg q1–8wk
Child: PO 0.117–1.66 mg/kg/d

Hexacetonide

Adult: Intralesional Up to 0.5 mg/in² of skin Intraarticular 2–20 mg q3–4wk

ADMINISTRATION

Oral

▪ Give with fluid of patient's choice; tablet may be crushed.

Subcutaneous, Intramuscular

▪ Do not give triamcinolone injection IV.

▪ See hydrocortisone for additional administration information.
▪ Store at 15°–30° C (59°–86° F). Protect from light.

ADVERSE EFFECTS (≥1%) CNS:
Euphoria, headache, insomnia, confusion, psychosis. **CV:** CHF, edema. **GI:** Nausea, vomiting, peptic ulcer. **Musculoskeletal:** Muscle weakness, delayed wound healing, muscle wasting, osteoporosis, aseptic necrosis of bone, spontaneous fractures. **Endocrine:** Cushingoid features, growth suppression in children, carbohydrate intolerance, hyperglycemia. **Special Senses:** Cataracts. **Hematologic:** Leukocytosis. **Metabolic:** Hypokalemia. **Skin:** Burning, itching, folliculitis, hypertrichosis, hypopigmentation.

INTERACTIONS Drug: BARBITURATES, phenytoin, rifampin increase steroid metabolism—may need increased doses of triamcinolone; amphotericin B, DIURETICS add to potassium loss; ambenonium, neostigmine, pyridostigmine may cause severe muscle weakness in patients with myasthenia gravis; may inhibit antibody response to VACCINES, TOXOIDS.

PHARMACOKINETICS Absorption:
Readily absorbed from all routes. **Onset:** 24–48 h PO, IM. **Peak:** 1–2 h PO; 8–10 h IM. **Duration:** 2.25 d PO; 1–6 wk IM. **Metabolism:** In liver. **Elimination:** In urine. **Half-Life:** 2–5 h; HPA suppression, 18–36 h.

CLINICAL IMPLICATIONS

Assessment & Drug Effects

▪ Discuss adequate diet with dietitian, patient, and physician to counter natriuresis, negative nitrogen balance, with weight loss in most patients (along with headache, fatigue, and dizziness) and sodium retention with weight gain and moon facies in others. High-protein, high-potassium diet is often needed.

- Lab tests: Periodic serum electrolytes and blood glucose.
- Discontinue occlusive dressing and start appropriate antimicrobial treatment if a local infection develops at site of application. Consult physician.
- Report symptoms of hypercortisolism or Cushing's syndrome (see Appendix F), hyperglycemia (see Appendix F), and glucosuria (e.g., polyuria). These may arise from systemic absorption after topical application, especially in children and if used over extensive areas for prolonged periods or if occlusive dressings are used.

Patient & Family Education
- Be aware that postural hypotension may accompany sodium loss and weight loss.
- Adhere to drug regimen; do not increase or decrease established regimen and do not discontinue abruptly.

TRIAMTERENE

(trye-am'ter-een)
Dyrenium
Classifications: ELECTROLYTE AND WATER BALANCE AGENT; POTASSIUM-SPARING DIURETIC
Therapeutic: POTASSIUM-SPARING DIURETIC
Prototype: Spironolactone
Pregnancy Category: D

AVAILABILITY 50 mg, 100 mg capsules

ACTION & *THERAPEUTIC EFFECT*
Structurally related to folic acid. Like spironolactone, has weak diuretic action and a potassium-sparing effect. Promotes excretion of sodium, chloride (to lesser extent), and carbonate. Unlike spironolactone, blocks potassium excretion by direct action on distal renal tubule rather than by inhibiting aldosterone. Decreased glomerular filtration rate and elevated BUN are associated with daily administration. *Has a diuretic action and a potassium-sparing effect.*

USES Adjunct in the management of edema associated with CHF, hepatic cirrhosis, nephrotic syndrome, idiopathic edema, steroid-induced edema, and edema due to secondary hyperaldosteronism. Also alone or in conjunction with a thiazide or loop diuretic in patients with hypertension because of its potassium-sparing activity.

CONTRAINDICATIONS Hypersensitivity to drug; anuria, severe or progressive kidney disease or dysfunction; severe liver disease; diabetic neuropathy; elevated serum potassium; severe electrolyte or acid-base imbalance; pregnancy (category D).
CAUTIOUS USE Impaired kidney or liver function; gout; history of gouty arthritis; diabetes mellitus, older adults; history of kidney stones; lactation.

ROUTE & DOSAGE

Edema
Adult: **PO** 100 mg b.i.d. (max: 300 mg/d), may be able to decrease to 100 mg/d or q.o.d.
Geriatric: **PO** 50 mg/d (max: 100 mg/d in 1–2 divided doses)
Child: **PO** 2–4 mg/kg/d in divided doses or q.o.d. (max: 300 mg/d)

Common adverse effects in *italic*, life-threatening effects underlined; generic names in **bold**; classifications in SMALL CAPS; ♣ Canadian drug name; ⊘ Prototype drug

1543

ADMINISTRATION

Oral

- Empty capsule and give with fluid or mix with food, if patient cannot swallow capsule.
- Give drug with or after meals to prevent or minimize nausea.
- Schedule doses to prevent interruption of sleep from diuresis (e.g., with or after breakfast if a single dose is taken, or no later than 6 p.m. if more than one dose is prescribed). Consult physician.
- Withdraw drug gradually in patients on prolonged or high-dose therapy in order to prevent rebound increased urinary excretion of potassium.
- Store in tight, light-resistant containers at 15°–30° C (59°–86° F) unless otherwise directed.

ADVERSE EFFECTS (≥1%) **GI:** Diarrhea, nausea, vomiting, and other GI disturbances. **CNS:** Dizziness, headache, dry mouth, <u>anaphylaxis</u>, weakness, muscle cramps. **Skin:** Pruritus, rash, photosensitivity. **CV:** Hypotension (large doses). **Metabolic:** *Hyperkalemia* and other electrolyte imbalances, elevated BUN, elevated uric acid (patients predisposed to gouty arthritis), hyperchloremic acidosis. **Hematologic:** Blood dyscrasias: granulocytopenia, eosinophilia, megaloblastic anemia in patients with reduced folic acid stores (e.g., hepatic cirrhosis).

DIAGNOSTIC TEST INTERFERENCE Pale blue fluorescence in urine interferes with *fluorometric assay* of *quinidine* and *lactic dehydrogenase activity.* Triamterene may cause increases in *blood glucose* levels (diabetic patients), *BUN, serum potassium, magnesium,* and *uric acid* and *urinary calcium excretion.*

INTERACTIONS Drug: May increase **lithium** levels, thus increasing its toxicity; **indomethacin** may decrease renal elimination of triamterene; ANGIOTENSIN-CONVERTING ENZYME (ACE) INHIBITORS, other POTASSIUM-SPARING DIURETICS may cause hyperkalemia. **Food:** High potassium foods may increase risk of hyperkalemia.

PHARMACOKINETICS Absorption: Rapidly but variably from GI tract. **Onset:** 2–4 h. **Duration:** 7–9 h. **Metabolism:** In liver to active and inactive metabolites. **Elimination:** In urine. **Half-Life:** 100–150 min.

CLINICAL IMPLICATIONS

Assessment & Drug Effects

- Monitor BP during periods of dosage adjustment. Hypotensive reactions, although rare, have been reported. Take care with ambulation, particularly for older adults.
- Weigh patient under standard conditions, prior to drug initiation and daily during therapy.
- Diuretic response usually occurs on first day of therapy; maximum effect may not occur for several days.
- Monitor and report oliguria and unusual changes in I&O ratio. Consult physician regarding allowable fluid intake.
- Be alert for S&S of kidney stone formation; reported in patients taking high doses or who have low urine volume and increased urine acidity.
- Lab tests: Obtain baseline and periodic determinations of serum potassium and other electrolytes. Obtain periodic kidney function (BUN, serum creatinine) in patients with known or suspected renal insufficiency. Obtain periodic blood studies in patients on prolonged therapy or with cirrho-

sis since both are prone to develop megaloblastic anemia.

- Observe for S&S of hyperkalemia (see Appendix F), particularly in patients with renal insufficiency, on high-dose or prolonged therapy, older adults, and those with diabetes.
- Do not give to a diabetic patient unless blood glucose is controlled because triamterene may increase blood glucose. Monitor patients closely.

Patient & Family Education

- Do not take potassium supplements, potassium-rich diet, and salt substitutes; unlike most diuretics, triamterene promotes potassium retention.
- Do not restrict salt; there is a possibility of low-salt syndrome (hyponatremia). Consult physician.
- Report overpowering fatigue or weakness, malaise, fever, sore throat, or mouth (possible symptoms of granulocytopenia) and unusual bleeding or bruising (thrombocytopenia) to physician.
- Be aware that drug may cause photosensitivity; avoid exposure to sun and sunlamps.
- Drug may impart a harmless pale blue fluorescence to urine.

TRIAZOLAM

(trye-ay'zoe-lam)

Halcion

Classifications: BENZODIAZEPINE; ANXIOLYTIC; SEDATIVE-HYPNOTIC

Therapeutic: SEDATIVE-HYPNOTIC; ANTIANXIETY

Prototype: Lorazepam

Pregnancy Category: X

Controlled Substance: Schedule IV

AVAILABILITY 0.125 mg, 0.25 mg tablets

ACTION & *THERAPEUTIC EFFECT*

Benzodiazepine derivative with hypnotic effects with fewer residual daytime effects. Its blockade of cortical and limbic arousal results in hypnotic activity. *Drug-induced effects on sleep include decreased sleep latency and number of nocturnal awakenings, decreased total nocturnal wake time, and increased duration of sleep.*

USES Short-term management of insomnia characterized by difficulty in falling asleep, frequent wakeful periods. Following long-term use, tolerance or adaptation may develop.

CONTRAINDICATIONS Hypersensitivity to triazolam and benzodiazepines; pregnancy (category X), lactation; ethanol intoxication; suicidal ideations; concurrent administration with the following medications that impair cytochrome P450 3A (e.g., ketoconazole, itraconazole, and nefazodone).

CAUTIOUS USE Depression; bipolar disorder; dementia; psychosis; myasthenia gravis; Parkinson's disease; older adults and debilitated patients; patients with suicidal tendency; impaired kidney or liver function; chronic pulmonary insufficiency; sleep apnea.

ROUTE & DOSAGE

Insomnia
Adult: **PO** 0.125–0.25 mg h.s. (max: 0.5 mg/d)
Geriatric: **PO** 0.0625–0.125 mg h.s.

ADMINISTRATION

Oral

- Give immediately before bed; onset of drug action is rapid.
- Do not exceed recommended doses.
- Store at 15°–30° C (59°–86° F).

T

Common adverse effects in *italic*, life-threatening effects underlined; generic names in **bold**; classifications in SMALL CAPS; ♣ Canadian drug name; ● Prototype drug

1545

ADVERSE EFFECTS (≥1%) **CNS:** *Drowsiness,* light-headedness, headache, dizziness, ataxia, visual disturbances, confusional states, *memory impairment, "rebound insomnia," anterograde amnesia,* paradoxical reactions, minor changes in EEG patterns. **GI:** Nausea, vomiting, constipation.

INTERACTIONS Drug: Alcohol, CNS DEPRESSANTS, ANTICONVULSANTS, **nefazodone,** BENZODIAZEPINES potentiate CNS depression; **cimetidine** increases triazolam plasma levels, thus increasing its toxicity; may decrease antiparkinsonism effects of **levodopa. Herbal: Kava-kava, valerian** may potentiate sedation. **St. John's wort** may decrease efficacy. **Food:** Grapefruit juice (>1 qt/d) may increase plasma concentrations and adverse effects.

PHARMACOKINETICS Absorption: Readily from GI tract. **Onset:** 15–30 min. **Peak:** 1–2 h. **Duration:** 6–8 h. **Distribution:** Crosses placenta; distributed into breast milk. **Elimination:** In urine. **Half-Life:** 2–3 h.

CLINICAL IMPLICATIONS

Assessment & Drug Effects
▪ Be aware that signs of developing tolerance or adaptation (with long-term use) include increased daytime anxiety, increased wakefulness during last one third of the night.
▪ Lab tests: Obtain periodic blood counts, urinalysis, and blood chemistries during long-term use.
▪ Do not use with addiction-prone patients (drug addicts, alcoholics) unless careful surveillance by health personnel is available. Habituation and dependence can occur.
▪ Evaluate smoking habit. As with other benzodiazepines, smoking may decrease hypnotic effects.

▪ Monitor for symptoms of overdosage: Slurred speech, somnolence, confusion, impaired coordination, and coma.

Patient & Family Education
▪ Do not drive or engage in potentially hazardous activities until response to drug is known.
▪ Avoid use of alcohol or other CNS depressants while on this drug; they may increase sedative effects.
▪ Do not stop taking drug suddenly, especially if you are subject to seizures. Withdrawal symptoms may occur and range from mild dysphoria to more serious symptoms (e.g., tremors, abdominal and muscle cramps, convulsions). Consult physician for schedule to discontinue therapy.
▪ Do not increase dose without physician's advice because of toxic potential of drug.

TRIFLUOPERAZINE HYDROCHLORIDE

(trye-floo-oh-per′a-zeen)
Novoflurazine ✦, **Solazine** ✦, **Stelazine, Terfluzine** ✦

Classifications: PSYCHOTHERAPEUTIC; ANTIPSYCHOTIC, PHENOTHIAZIDE
Therapeutic: ANTIPSYCHOTIC
Prototype: Chlorpromazine
Pregnancy Category: C

AVAILABILITY 1 mg, 2 mg, 5 mg, 10 mg tablets; 10 mg/mL liquid; 2 mg/mL injection

ACTION & *THERAPEUTIC EFFECT*
Phenothiazine with antipsychotic effects thought to be related to blockade of postsynaptic dopamine receptors in the brain. *Effectiveness indicated by increase in mental and physical activity. Strong antipsychotic drug with prolonged action.*

Common adverse effects in *italic*, life-threatening effects underlined; generic names in **bold**; classifications in SMALL CAPS; ✦ Canadian drug name; ☯ Prototype drug

USES Management of manifestations of psychotic disorders; "possibly effective" control of excessive anxiety and tension associated with neuroses or somatic conditions.

CONTRAINDICATIONS Hypersensitivity to phenothiazines or sulfites; comatose states; CNS depression; ethanol intoxication; blood dyscrasias; children <6 y; bone marrow depression; preexisting liver disease; pregnancy (category C), lactation.

CAUTIOUS USE Previously detected breast cancer; history of QT prolongation; significant cardiac disease or pulmonary disease; compromised respiratory function; seizure disorders.

ROUTE & DOSAGE

Psychotic Disorders

Adult: PO 1–2 mg b.i.d., may increase up to 20 mg/d in hospitalized patients IM 1–2 mg q4–6h (max: 10 mg/d)
Child: PO 6–12 y, 1 mg 1–2 times/d, may increase up to 15 mg/d in hospitalized patients IM 6–12 y, 1 mg 1–2 times/d, may increase up to 15 mg/d

Dementia Behavior

Geriatric: PO 0.5–1 mg 1–2 times/d, may increase q4–7d (max: 40 mg in divided doses) IM 1 mg q4–6h (max: 6 mg/d)

ADMINISTRATION

Oral

- Separate antacid and phenothiazine doses by at least 2 h.
- Dilute oral concentrate just before administration with about 60–120 mL suitable diluent (e.g., water, fruit juices, carbonated beverage, milk, soups, puddings). Avoid coffee or tea near time of taking oral preparation. Explain dosage and dilution to patient if drug is to be self-administered.
- Crush tablet and give with fluid or mix with food if patient will not or cannot swallow pill.
- Monitor ingestion of tablet to ensure that patient does not hoard medication.

Intramuscular

- Give IM injection deep into upper outer quadrant of buttock.
- Note: Slight yellow discoloration of injectable drug reportedly does not alter potency. If color is markedly changed, discard solution.
- Wash hands if undiluted concentrate is spilled on skin to prevent contact dermatosis.
- Store in light-resistant container at 15°–30° C (59°–86° F) unless otherwise directed.

ADVERSE EFFECTS (≥1%) **CNS:** *Drowsiness*, insomnia, dizziness, agitation, *extrapyramidal effects*, neuroleptic malignant syndrome. **Special Senses:** Nasal congestion, *dry mouth*, blurred vision, pigmentary retinopathy. **Hematologic:** Agranulocytosis. **Skin:** Photosensitivity, skin rash, sweating. **GI:** Constipation. **CV:** Tachycardia, *hypotension*. **Respiratory:** Depressed cough reflex. **Endocrine:** Gynecomastia, galactorrhea.

INTERACTIONS Drug: Alcohol and other CNS DEPRESSANTS add to CNS depression. **Herbal: Kava-kava** may increase risk and severity of dystonic reactions.

PHARMACOKINETICS Absorption: Well absorbed from GI tract. **Onset:** Rapid onset. **Peak:** 2–3 h. **Duration:** Up to 12 h. **Metabolism:** In liver. **Elimination:** In bile and feces.

CLINICAL IMPLICATIONS

Assessment & Drug Effects

- Monitor HR and BP. Hypotension is a common adverse effect.

T

Common adverse effects in *italic*, life-threatening effects underlined; generic names in **bold**; classifications in SMALL CAPS; ♣ Canadian drug name; ⓟ Prototype drug

1547

- Hypotension and extrapyramidal effects (especially akathisia and dystonia) are most likely to occur in patients receiving high doses or parenteral administration and in older adults. Withhold drug and notify physician if patient has dysphagia, neck muscle spasm, or if tongue protrusion occurs.
- Monitor I&O ratio and bowel elimination pattern. Check for abdominal distention and pain. Encourage adequate fluid intake as prophylaxis for constipation and xerostomia. The depressed patient may not seek help for either symptom or for urinary retention.
- Be aware that since trifluoperazine potentiates analgesics, its use may reduce amount of narcotic required in painful long-term illness such as cancer.
- Agitation, jitteriness, and sometimes insomnia may simulate original neurotic or psychotic symptoms. These adverse effects may disappear spontaneously.
- Expect maximum therapeutic response within 2–3 wk after initiation of therapy.

Patient & Family Education

- Take drug as prescribed; do not alter dosing regimen or stop medication without consulting physician.
- Consult physician about use of any OTC drugs during therapy.
- Do not take alcohol and other depressants during therapy.
- Avoid potentially hazardous activities such as driving or operating machinery, until response to drug is known. Drowsiness and dizziness may be prominent during this time.
- Cover as much skin surface as possible with clothing when you must be in direct sunlight. Use a SPF >12 sunscreen on exposed skin.
- Urine may be discolored or reddish brown and this is harmless.

TRIFLURIDINE

(trye-flure'i-deen)
Viroptic

Classifications: ANTIVIRAL
Therapeutic: ANTIVIRAL
Pregnancy Category: C

AVAILABILITY 1% ophthalmic solution

ACTION & *THERAPEUTIC EFFECT*
Pyrimidine nucleoside whose mechanism of antiviral action is not completely known but appears to involve inhibition of viral DNA synthesis and viral replication. *Active against herpes simplex virus (HSV) types 1 and 2, vaccinia virus, and certain strains of adenovirus.*

USES Topically to eyes for treatment of primary keratoconjunctivitis and recurring epithelial keratitis caused by herpes simplex virus types 1 and 2. Also for other herpetic ophthalmic infections including stromal keratitis, uveitis, and for infections caused by vaccinia and *Adenovirus,* but clinical effectiveness has not been established.

CONTRAINDICATIONS Pregnancy (category C), lactation; children <6 y.
CAUTIOUS USE Dry eye syndrome.

ROUTE & DOSAGE

Viral Infections of Eye

Adult: **Ophthalmic** 1 drop 1% ophthalmic solution into affected eye q2h during waking hours until healing (reepithelialization) has occurred (max: 9 drops/d); when healing appears to be complete, dosage reduced to 1 drop q4h during waking hours for an additional 7 d (max: 5 drops/d); continuous administration beyond 21 d not recommended

ADMINISTRATION

Instillation

- Wait several minutes between applications when used concurrently with other eye drops.
- Store refrigerated at 2°–8° C (36°–46° F) unless otherwise directed.

ADVERSE EFFECTS (≥1%) **Special Senses:** Mild transient burning or stinging, mild irritation of conjunctiva or cornea, photophobia, edema of eyelids and cornea, punctal occlusion, superficial punctate keratopathy, epithelial keratopathy, stromal edema, keratitis sicca, hyperemia, increased intraocular pressure.

INTERACTIONS Drug: No clinically significant interactions established.

PHARMACOKINETICS Absorption: Following topical application to eye, trifluridine penetrates cornea and aqueous humor (inflammation enhances penetration). Systemic absorption does not appear to be significant.

CLINICAL IMPLICATIONS

Assessment & Drug Effects

- Expect epithelial eye infections to respond to therapy within 2–7 d, with complete healing occurring in 1–2 wk.

Patient & Family Education

- Inform physician of progress and keep follow-up appointments. Herpetic eye infections have a tendency to recur and can lead to corneal damage if not adequately treated.

TRIHEXYPHENIDYL HYDROCHLORIDE

(trye-hex-ee-fen′i-dill)
Aparkane ♦, **Apo-Trihex ♦**,
Novohexidyl ♦

Classifications: ANTICHOLINERGIC; ANTIPARKINSON AGENT; ANTI-MUSCARINIC; ANTISPASMODIC
Therapeutic: ANTIPARKINSON; ANTISPASMODIC
Prototype: Atropine
Pregnancy Category: C

AVAILABILITY 2 mg, 5 mg tablets; 2 mg/5 mL elixir

ACTION & *THERAPEUTIC EFFECT*

Synthetic tertiary amine anticholinergic agent similar to atropine. Thought to act by blocking excess of acetylcholine at certain cerebral synaptic sites. Relaxes smooth muscle by direct effect and by atropinelike blocking action on the parasympathetic nervous system. *Anticholinergic agent diminishes the characteristic tremor of Parkinson's disease. Antispasmodic action appears to be one-half that of atropine.*

USES Symptomatic treatment of all forms of parkinsonism (arteriosclerotic, idiopathic, postencephalitic). Also to prevent or control drug-induced extrapyramidal disorders.
UNLABELED USES Huntington's chorea, spasmodic torticollis.

CONTRAINDICATIONS Narrow-angle glaucoma; tardive dyskinesia; pregnancy (category C), lactation. Safe use in children is not established.
CAUTIOUS USE History of drug hypersensitivities; arteriosclerosis; hypertension; cardiac disease, kidney or liver disorders; myasthenia gravis; alcoholism; obstructive diseases of GI or genitourinary tracts; older adults with prostatic hypertrophy.

ROUTE & DOSAGE

Parkinsonism
Adult: **PO** 1 mg day 1, 2 mg day 2, then increase by 2 mg q3–5d

Common adverse effects in *italic*, life-threatening effects underlined; generic names in **bold**; classifications in SMALL CAPS; ♦ Canadian drug name; ⓟ Prototype drug

1549

up to 6–10 mg/d in 3 or more divided doses (max: 15 mg/d)

Extrapyramidal Effects

Adult: **PO** 5–15 mg/d in divided doses

ADMINISTRATION

Oral

- Give before or after meals, depending on how patient reacts. Older adults and patients prone to excessive salivation (e.g., postencephalitic parkinsonism) may prefer to take drug after meals. If drug causes excessive mouth dryness, it may be better given before meals, unless it causes nausea.
- Once stabilized on conventional dosage forms, patient may be switched to sustained release capsules to permit once- or twice-a-day dosing.
- Do not crush or chew sustained release capsules. These must be swallowed whole.
- Store at 15°–30° C (59°–86° F) in tight container unless otherwise directed.

ADVERSE EFFECTS (≥1%) **GI:** *Dry mouth, nausea,* constipation. **Special Senses:** *Blurred vision,* mydriasis, photophobia, angle-closure glaucoma. **Urogenital:** Urinary hesitancy or retention. **CNS:** *Dizziness, nervousness,* insomnia, drowsiness, confusion, agitation, delirium, psychotic manifestations, euphoria. **CV:** Tachycardia, palpitations, hypotension, orthostatic hypotension. **Body as a Whole:** Hypersensitivity reactions.

INTERACTIONS Drug: Reduces therapeutic effects of **chlorpromazine, haloperidol,** PHENOTHIAZINES; increases bioavailability of **digoxin;** MAO INHIBITORS potentiate actions of trihexyphenidyl. **Herbal: Betel nut**

may increase risk of extrapyramidal symptoms.

PHARMACOKINETICS Absorption: Readily from GI tract. **Onset:** Within 1 h. **Peak:** 2–3 h. **Duration:** 6–12 h. **Elimination:** In urine.

CLINICAL IMPLICATIONS

Assessment & Drug Effects

- Be aware that incidence and severity of adverse effects are usually dose related and may be minimized by dosage reduction. Older adults appear more sensitive to usual adult doses.
- Monitor vital signs. Pulse is a particularly sensitive indicator of response to drug. Report tachycardia, palpitations, paradoxical bradycardia, or fall in BP.
- Assess for and report severe CNS stimulation (see ADVERSE EFFECTS) that occurs with high doses, and in patients with arteriosclerosis, or those with history of hypersensitivity to other drugs.
- In patients with severe rigidity, tremors may appear to be accentuated during therapy as rigidity diminishes.
- Monitor daily I&O if patient develops urinary hesitancy or retention. Voiding before taking drug may relieve problem.
- Check for abdominal distention and bowel sounds if constipation is a problem.
- Monitor intraocular pressure at regular intervals.
- Provide close follow-up care. Tolerance may develop, necessitating dosage adjustment or use of combination therapy. Patients ≥60 y frequently develop sensitivity to drug action.

Patient & Family Education

- Learn measures to relieve drug-induced dry mouth; rinse mouth frequently with water and suck

T

ice chips, sugarless gum, or hard candy. Maintain adequate total daily fluid intake.

- Avoid excessive heat because drug suppresses perspiration and, therefore, heat loss.
- Do not to engage in potentially hazardous activities requiring alertness and skill. Drug causes dizziness, drowsiness, and blurred vision. Help walking may be indicated.

TRIMETHOBENZAMIDE HYDROCHLORIDE

(trye-meth-oh-ben′za-mide)
Arrestin, Ticon, Tigan, T-Gen
Classifications: ANTIEMETIC
Therapeutic: ANTIEMETIC
Prototype: Prochlorperazine
Pregnancy Category: C

AVAILABILITY 100 mg, 250 mg, 300 mg capsules; 100 mg, 200 mg suppositories; 100 mg/mL injection

ACTION & THERAPEUTIC EFFECT
Antiemetic actions less effective than phenothiazine antiemetics but produces fewer adverse effects. Must be used with other agents when vomiting is severe. Primary locus of action is thought to be the chemoreceptor trigger zone (CTZ) in medulla. *Less effective than phenothiazine antiemetics but produces fewer adverse effects.*

USES Control of nausea and vomiting.

CONTRAINDICATIONS Uncomplicated vomiting in viral illness; parenteral use in children or infants; rectal administration in prematures and newborns; known sensitivity to benzocaine (in suppository) or

to similar local anesthetics; pregnancy (category C). Safe use in lactation is not established.

CAUTIOUS USE Patients who have recently received other centrally acting drugs; in presence of high fever, dehydration, electrolyte imbalance.

ROUTE & DOSAGE

Nausea and Vomiting
Adult: **PO** 250–300 mg t.i.d. or q.i.d. **Rectal/IM** 200 mg t.i.d. or q.i.d.
Child: **PO/Rectal** 15–45 kg, 100–200 mg t.i.d. or q.i.d. **Rectal** <15 kg, 100 mg t.i.d. or q.i.d.

ADMINISTRATION

Oral
- Empty capsule and give with water or mix with food if patient cannot swallow capsule.

Intramuscular
- Give IM deep into upper outer quadrant of buttock.
- Minimize possibility of irritation and pain by avoiding escape of solution along needle track. Use Z-track technique. Rotate injection sites.

ADVERSE EFFECTS (≥1%) **Body as a Whole:** Hypersensitivity reactions (including allergic skin eruptions), muscle cramps, pain, stinging, burning, redness, irritation at IM site; local irritation following rectal administration. **CNS:** Pseudoparkinsonism. **CV:** Hypotension. **GI:** Diarrhea, exaggeration of nausea, acute hepatitis, jaundice.

INTERACTIONS Drug: Alcohol and other CNS DEPRESSANTS add to depressant activity; BELLADONNA ALKALOIDS may intensify anticholinergic effects; PHENOTHIAZINES may precipitate extrapyramidal syndrome.

T

Common adverse effects in *italic*, life-threatening effects underlined; generic names in **bold**; classifications in SMALL CAPS; ✦ Canadian drug name; ⊘ Prototype drug

1551

PHARMACOKINETICS Onset: 10–40 min PO; 15 min IM. **Duration:** 3–4 h PO; 2–3 h IM. **Elimination:** 30–50% of dose excreted unchanged in urine within 48–72 h.

CLINICAL IMPLICATIONS
Assessment & Drug Effects
- Monitor BP. Hypotension may occur particularly in surgical patients receiving drug parenterally.
- Report promptly and stop drug therapy if an acute febrile illness accompanies or begins during therapy.
- Antiemetic effect of drug may obscure diagnoses of GI or other pathologic conditions or signs of toxicity from other drugs.

Patient & Family Education
- Report promptly to physician onset of rash or other signs of hypersensitivity (see Appendix F). Discontinue drug immediately.
- Do not drive or engage in potentially hazardous activities until response to drug is known.
- Do not drink alcohol or alcoholic beverages during therapy with this drug.

TRIMETHOPRIM ⊕

(trye-meth′oh-prim)
Primsol, Proloprim
Classifications: ANTIINFECTIVE, URINARY TRACT
Therapeutic: ANTIINFECTIVE, URINARY TRACT
Pregnancy Category: C

AVAILABILITY 100 mg, 200 mg tablets; 50 mg/5 mL liquid

ACTION & *THERAPEUTIC EFFECT*
Antiinfective and folic acid antagonist with slow bactericidal action. Binding and interference with bacterial cell growth. *Effective against most common UTI pathogens. Most pathogens causing UTI are in normal vaginal and fecal flora.*

USES Initial episodes of acute uncomplicated UTIs, acute otitis media in children.
UNLABELED USES Treatment and prophylaxis of chronic and recurrent UTI in both men and women; treatment in conjunction with dapsone of initial episodes of *Pneumocystis carinii* pneumonia; treatment of travelers' diarrhea.

CONTRAINDICATIONS Megaloblastic anemia secondary to folate deficiency; creatinine clearance <15 mL/min, impaired kidney or liver function; possible folate deficiency; pregnancy (category C), or in children with fragile X chromosome associated with mental retardation. Safety in infants <2 mo has not been established.
CAUTIOUS USE Renal disease; mild or moderate renal impairment; lactation.

ROUTE & DOSAGE

Urinary Tract Infection
Adult: **PO** 100 mg b.i.d. or 200 mg once/d
Child: **PO** 2–3 mg/kg q12h times 10 d

Acute Otitis Media
Child: **PO** >6 mo, 10 mg/kg divided q12 h times 10 d

Travelers' Diarrhea
Adult: **PO** 200 mg b.i.d.

ADMINISTRATION
Oral
- Give with 240 mL (8 oz) of fluid if not contraindicated.
- Store at 15°–30° C (59°–86° F) in dry, light-protected place.

ADVERSE EFFECTS (≥1%) **GI:** Epigastric discomfort, nausea, vomiting, glossitis, abnormal taste sensation. **Hematologic:** Neutropenia, *megaloblastic anemia,* methemoglobinemia, leukopenia, thrombocytopenia (rare). **Skin:** *Rash, pruritus,* <u>exfoliative dermatitis</u>, photosensitivity. **Body as a Whole:** Fever. **Metabolic:** Increased serum transaminases (ALT, AST), bilirubin, creatinine, BUN.

DIAGNOSTIC TEST INTERFERENCE Interferes with serum *methotrexate assays* that use a competitive binding protein technique with a bacterial dihydrofolate reductase as the binding protein. May cause falsely elevated *creatinine* values when *Jaffe reaction* is used.

INTERACTIONS Drug: May inhibit **phenytoin** metabolism causing increased levels.

PHARMACOKINETICS Absorption: Almost completely absorbed from GI tract. **Peak:** 1–4 h. **Distribution:** Widely distributed, including lung, saliva, middle ear fluid, bile, bone, CSF; crosses placenta; appears in breast milk. **Metabolism:** In liver. **Elimination:** 80% in urine unchanged. **Half-Life:** 8–11 h.

CLINICAL IMPLICATIONS

Assessment & Drug Effects

- Lab tests: Obtain C&S tests before trimethoprim therapy is initiated; therapy may be started before results are received. Obtain periodic urine cultures, BUN, creatinine clearance, CBC, Hgb, and Hct. Follow-up cultures may be ordered at end of treatment to verify elimination of causative organism.
- Reinforce necessity to adhere to established drug regimen. Recurrent infection after terminating prophylactic treatment of UTI

may occur even after 6 mo of therapy.

- Assess urinary pattern during treatment. Altered pattern (frequency, urgency, nocturia, retention, polyuria) may reflect emerging drug resistance, necessitating change of drug regimen. Periodically check for bladder distention.
- Be alert for toxic effects on bone marrow, particularly in older adults, malnourished, alcoholic, pregnant, or debilitated patients. Recognize and report signs of infection or anemia.
- Drug-induced rash, a common adverse effect, is usually maculopapular, pruritic, or morbilliform and appears 7–14 d after start of therapy with daily doses of 200 mg or less.
- Watch for overdose symptoms: Nausea, vomiting, diarrhea, mental depression, confusion, facial swelling, elevated serum transaminases.

Patient & Family Education

- Take all prescribed medication; uncomplicated UTIs usually respond to treatment.
- Drink fluids liberally (2000–3000 mL/d, if not contraindicated) to help flush out urinary bacteria.
- Take urinary analgesic for pain and discomfort with voiding before full drug effects are experienced. Report pain and hematuria to physician immediately.
- Do not postpone voiding even though increases in fluid intake may cause more frequent urination.
- Do not use douches or sprays during treatment periods; practice careful perineal hygiene to prevent reinfection.
- Report to physician promptly any symptoms of a hematologic disorder (fever, sore throat, pallor, purpura, ecchymosis).

T

Common adverse effects in *italic*, life-threatening effects <u>underlined</u>; generic names in **bold**; classifications in SMALL CAPS; ✦ Canadian drug name; ⊘ Prototype drug

1553

- Consult physician if severe traveler's diarrhea does not respond to 3–5 d therapy (i.e., persistence of symptoms of severe nausea, abdominal pain, diarrhea with mucus or blood, and dehydration).

TRIMETHOPRIM-SULFAMETHOXAZOLE (TMP-SMZ)

(tri-meth'o-prim-sul-fa-meth'ox-a-zole)

Bactrim, Bactrim DS, Co-Trim, Septra, Septra DS

Classifications: URINARY TRACT AGENT; SULFONAMIDE
Therapeutic: URINARY TRACT ANTIINFECTIVE
Prototype: Trimethoprim
Pregnancy Category: C

AVAILABILITY 80 mg TMP/400 mg SMZ, 160 mg TMP/800 mg SMZ tablets; 40 mg TMP/200 mg SMZ/5 ml suspension; 16 mg TMP/80 mg SMZ/5 ml, 80 mg TMP/400 mg SMZ/5 ml injection

ACTION & *THERAPEUTIC EFFECT*
Fixed combination of sulfamethoxazole (SMZ), an intermediate-acting antiinfective sulfonamide, and trimethoprim (TMP), a synthetic antiinfective. Both components of the combination are synthetic folate antagonist antiinfectives. Mechanism of action is principally enzyme inhibition that prevents bacterial synthesis of essential nucleic acids and proteins. *Effective against* Pneumocystis carinii *pneumonitis,* Shigellosis *enteritis, and severe complicated UTIs due to most strains of the Enterobacteriaceae.*

USES *Pneumocystis carinii* pneumonitis, *Shigellosis* enteritis, and severe complicated UTIs. Also children with acute otitis media due to susceptible strains of *Haemophilus influenzae,* and acute episodes of chronic bronchitis in adults.

UNLABELED USES Isosporiasis; prevention of traveler's diarrhea; cholera; genital ulcers caused by *Haemophilus ducreyi;* prophylaxis for *P. carinii* pneumonia in neutropenic patients.

CONTRAINDICATIONS Hypersensitivity to TMP, SMZ, sulfonamides, or bisulfites, carbonic anhydrase inhibitors; group A beta-hemolytic streptococcal pharyngitis; megaloblastic anemia due to folate deficiency; creatinine clearance <15 mL/min; G6PD deficiency; hyperkalemia; porphyria; pregnancy (category C), lactation. Not recommended for infants <2 mo.

CAUTIOUS USE Impaired kidney or liver function; bone marrow depression; possible folate deficiency; severe allergy or bronchial asthma; hypersensitivity to sulfonamide derivative drugs (e.g., acetazolamide, thiazides, tolbutamide).

ROUTE & DOSAGE

Systemic Infections

Adult: **PO** 160 mg TMP/800 mg SMZ q12h **IV** 8–10 mg/kg/d TMP divided q6–12h infused over 60–90 min
Child: **PO** >2 mo & <40 kg, 4 mg/kg/d TMP q12h; >40 kg, 160 mg TMP/800 mg SMZ q12h **IV** >2 mo, 8–10 mg/kg/d TMP divided q6–12h infused over 60–90 min

Pneumocystis carinii Pneumonia

Adult: **IV/PO** 15–20 mg/kg/d TMP divided q6h infused over 60–90 min

Prophylaxis for *Pneumocystis carinii* **Pneumonia**

Adult: **PO** 160 mg TMP/800 mg SMZ q24h
Child: **PO** 150 mg/m^2 TMP/750 mg/m^2 SMZ b.i.d. 3 consecutive d/wk (max: 320 mg TMP/d)

Renal Impairment
Cl$_{cr}$ 10–30 mL/min: reduce dose by 50%

ADMINISTRATION

Oral
- Give with a full glass of desired fluid.
- Maintain adequate fluid intake (at least 1500 mL/d) during therapy.

Intravenous

PREPARE: **Intermittent:** Add contents of 5-mL ampul to 125 mL D5W. Use within 6 h. If less fluid is desired, dilute in 75 or 100 mL and use within 2 h or 4 h, respectively. Do not refrigerate.

ADMINISTER: **Intermittent:** Give over 60–90 min. Avoid bolus or rapid injection. Do not mix other drugs or solutions with IV infusion. Discard solution if cloudy or if crystallization appears after mixing.

INCOMPATIBILITIES **Solution/additive:** Stability in **dextrose** and **normal saline** is concentration dependent; **fluconazole, linezolid, verapamil.** Y-site: **Cisatracurium, fluconazole, foscarnet, midazolam, vinorelbine.**

- Store at 15°–30° C (59°–86° F) in dry place protected from light. Avoid freezing.

ADVERSE EFFECTS (≥1%) **Skin:**
Mild to moderate rashes (including fixed drug eruptions), <u>toxic epidermal necrolysis</u>. **GI:** *Nausea, vomiting,* diarrhea, *anorexia,* hepatitis, <u>pseudomembranous enterocolitis</u>, stomatitis, glossitis, abdominal pain. **Uro-**

genital: Kidney failure, oliguria, anuria, crystalluria. **Hematologic:** <u>Agranulocytosis</u> (rare), <u>aplastic anemia</u> (rare), megaloblastic anemia, hypoprothrombinemia, thrombocytopenia (rare). **Body as a Whole:** Weakness, arthralgia, myalgia, photosensitivity, <u>allergic myocarditis</u>.

DIAGNOSTIC TEST INTERFERENCE
May elevate levels of serum creatinine, transaminase, bilirubin, alkaline phosphatase.

INTERACTIONS Drug: May enhance hypoprothrombinemic effects of ORAL ANTICOAGULANTS; may increase **methotrexate** toxicity. **Alcohol** may cause disulfiram reaction.

PHARMACOKINETICS Absorption: Readily from GI tract. **Peak:** 1–4 h PO. **Distribution:** Widely distributed, including CNS; crosses placenta; distributed into breast milk. **Metabolism:** In liver. **Elimination:** In urine. **Half-Life:** 8–10 h TMP, 10–13 h SMZ.

CLINICAL IMPLICATIONS

Assessment & Drug Effects
- Be aware that IV Septra contains sodium metabisulfite, which produces allergic-type reactions in susceptible patients: Hives, itching, wheezing, anaphylaxis. Susceptibility (low in general population) is seen most frequently in asthmatics or atopic nonasthmatic persons.
- Lab tests: Baseline and followup urinalysis; CBC with differential, platelet count, BUN and creatinine clearance with prolonged therapy.
- Monitor coagulation tests and prothrombin times in patient also receiving warfarin. Change in warfarin dosage may be indicated.
- Monitor I&O volume and pattern. Report significant changes to forestall renal calculi formation. Also report failure of treatment (i.e., continued UTI symptoms).

T

Common adverse effects in *italic*, life-threatening effects <u>underlined</u>; generic names in **bold**; classifications in SMALL CAPS; ✚ Canadian drug name; ⊘ Prototype drug

1555

- Older adult patients are at risk for severe adverse reactions, especially if liver or kidney function is compromised or if certain other drugs are given. Most frequently observed: thrombocytopenia (with concurrent thiazide diuretics); severe decrease in platelets (with or without purpura); bone marrow suppression; severe skin reactions.
- Be alert for overdose symptoms (no extensive experience has been reported): nausea, vomiting, anorexia, headache, dizziness, mental depression, confusion, and bone marrow depression.

Patient & Family Education

- Report immediately to physician if rash appears. Other reportable symptoms are sore throat, fever, purpura, jaundice; all are early signs of serious reactions.
- Monitor for and report fixed eruptions to physician. This drug can cause fixed eruptions at the same sites each time the drug is administered. Every contact with drug may not result in eruptions; therefore, patient may overlook the relationship.
- Drink 2.5–3 liters (1 liter is approximately equal to 1 quart) daily, unless otherwise directed.

TRIMETREXATE

(tri-me-trex′ate)
Neutrexin

Classifications: ANTINEOPLASTIC AGENT; ANTIMETABOLITE; ANTIFOLATE ANTAGONIST
Therapeutic: ANTINEOPLASTIC AGENT; ANTIMETABOLITE; ANTIFOLATE ANTAGONIST
Prototype: Methotrexate
Pregnancy Category: D

AVAILABILITY 25 mg, 200 mg injection

ACTION & *THERAPEUTIC EFFECT*

Antimetabolite and folic acid antagonist. Blocks folinic acid (active form of folic acid) participation in nucleic acid synthesis, thereby interfering with miotic process. Acts as a dihydrofolate reductase (DHFR) inhibitor in a similar manner to methotrexate. *Disrupts DNA, RNA, and protein synthesis, with consequent cell death.*

USES Used with concurrent leucovorin administration, as an alternate therapy for moderate to severe *Pneumocystis carinii* pneumonia (PCP) in immunocompromised patients, including AIDS patients.
UNLABELED USES Advanced non-small cell lung cancer, metastatic cancer of the head and neck, metastatic colorectal adenocarcinoma, pancreatic carcinoma.

CONTRAINDICATIONS Hypersensitivity to trimetrexate, leucovorin, or methotrexate; profound myelosuppression; pregnancy (category D), lactation.
CAUTIOUS USE Seizures; mild myelosuppression; severe kidney or liver dysfunction; hypoalbuminemia or hypoproteinemia; concomitant use of myelosuppressive, hepatotoxic, or renal toxic drugs; previous radiation of bone marrow or extensive chemotherapy with myelotoxic agents. Safety and efficacy in children <18 y are not established.

ROUTE & DOSAGE

Pneumocystis carinii Pneumonia

Adult: **IV** 45 mg/m^2 once daily by IV infusion over 60–90 min with concurrent leucovorin 20 mg/m^2 q6h (IV or PO, trimetrexate times 21 d and leucovorin times 24 d)

ADMINISTRATION

Intravenous

PREPARE: **IV Infusion:** Reconstitute 25 mg with 2 mL of D5W or sterile water for injection to yield 12.5 mg/mL. Allow 30 s for complete dissolution. Manufacturer recommends filtering (0.22 micron) reconstituted solution prior to dilution. Further dilute with 10–100 mL of D5W to a final concentration of 0.25–2 mg/mL. *ADMINISTER:* **IV Infusion:** Give over 60–90 min. Flush IV line with at least 10 mL of D5W before and after administering trimetrexate. *INCOMPATIBILITIES* **Solution/additive:** CHLORIDE-CONTAINING SOLUTIONS (including **sodium chloride**), **leucovorin. Y-site: Foscarnet, indomethacin.**

▪ Wash with soap and water immediately if drug contacts skin.

▪ Store reconstituted solution at room temperature or refrigerated for 24 h.

ADVERSE EFFECTS (≥1%) **Hematologic:** *Myelosuppression, granulocytopenia, thrombocytopenia.* **GI:** *Nausea, vomiting, stomatitis.* **Skin:** Erythematous rash with posteruption hyperpigmentation. **Metabolic:** Mild transient elevations in serum creatinine and liver function tests.

DIAGNOSTIC TEST INTERFERENCE

Mild increases in *serum creatinine* and *liver function tests.*

INTERACTIONS Drug: Cimetidine, erythromycin, fluconazole

(and other AZOLE ANTIFUNGAL AGENTS) may increase trimetrexate levels and toxicity. **Rifabutin, rifampin** may decrease trimetrexate levels. **Zidovudine** may cause additive hematologic toxicity.

PHARMACOKINETICS Absorption:

Approximately 44% from GI tract. **Onset:** 3 d. **Distribution:** Very low CSF concentrations; distributes into lung tissue; 98% protein bound. **Metabolism:** Extensively in liver. **Elimination:** In urine and feces. **Half-Life:** 15–17 h.

CLINICAL IMPLICATIONS

Assessment & Drug Effects

▪ Lab tests: Monitor CBC at least twice a week during therapy. Myelosuppression nadir occurs around day 8. Monitor kidney and liver functions; impaired functioning may indicate need for dosage reduction.

Patient & Family Education

▪ Learn potential adverse effects and report those that are bothersome.
▪ Understand that myelosuppression is the primary dose-limiting adverse effect.

TRIMIPRAMINE MALEATE

(tri-mip′ra-meen)
Surmontil
Classifications: PSYCHOTHERAPEUTIC; TRICYCLIC ANTIDEPRESSANT
Therapeutic: TRICYCLIC ANTIDEPRESSANT
Prototype: Imipramine
Pregnancy Category: C

T

AVAILABILITY 25 mg, 50 mg, 100 mg capsules

ACTION & THERAPEUTIC EFFECT

Tricyclic antidepressant (TCA) with moderate anticholinergic and strong sedative effects; useful in depression associated with anxiety and sleep disturbances. Recent studies suggest strong, active H_2-receptor antagonism is a characteristic of TCAs. *More effective in alle-*

Common adverse effects in *italic*, life-threatening effects <u>underlined</u>; generic names in **bold**; classifications in SMALL CAPS; ♣ Canadian drug name; ☺ Prototype drug

1557

viation of endogenous depression than other depressive states.

USES Treatment of major depression.
UNLABELED USES Peptic ulcer disease.

CONTRAINDICATIONS Hypersensitivy to tricyclic antidepressants; prostatic hypertrophy; during recovery period after MI; AV block; bundle-branch block; ileus; MAOI therapy; QT prolongation; pregnancy (category C).
CAUTIOUS USE Schizophrenia, electroshock therapy, psychosis; Parkinson's disease; seizure disorders; suicidal tendency; cardiovascular, liver, thyroid, kidney disease; lactation.

ROUTE & DOSAGE

Depression
Adult: **PO** 75–100 mg/d in divided doses, may increase gradually up to 300 mg/d if needed **PO Maintenance Dose** Usually 50–150 mg/d
Geriatric: **PO** 25 mg h.s., may increase q3d (max: 100 mg/d)

ADMINISTRATION

Oral
- Give with food to decrease gastric distress.
- Store in tightly closed container at 15°–30° C (59°–86° F) unless otherwise specified.

ADVERSE EFFECTS (≥1%) **CNS:** Seizures, tremor, confusion, *sedation.* **Special Senses:** Blurred vision. **CV:** Tachycardia, *orthostatic hypotension,* hypertension. **GI:** *Xerostomia, constipation,* paralytic ileus. **Urogenital:** *Urinary retention.* **Skin:** Photosensitivity, sweating.

INTERACTIONS Drug: May decrease some antihypertensive response to ANTIHYPERTENSIVES; CNS DEPRESSANTS, **alcohol,** HYPNOTICS, BARBITURATES, SEDATIVES potentiate CNS depression; may increase hypoprothrombinemic effect of ORAL ANTICOAGULANTS; **ethchlorvynol** may cause transient delirium; with **levodopa,** SYMPATHOMIMETICS (e.g., **epinephrine, norepinephrine**), possibility of sympathetic hyperactivity with hypertension and hyperpyrexia; with MAO INHIBITORS, possibility of severe reactions, toxic psychosis, cardiovascular instability; **methylphenidate increases plasma TCA levels;** THYROID AGENTS may increase possibility of arrhythmias; **cimetidine** may increase plasma TCA levels. **Herbal: Ginkgo** may decrease seizure threshold; **St. John's wort** may cause **serotonin** syndrome.

PHARMACOKINETICS Absorption: Rapidly absorbed from GI tract. **Peak:** 2 h. **Metabolism:** In liver. **Elimination:** In urine and feces. **Half-Life:** 9.1 h.

CLINICAL IMPLICATIONS
Assessment & Drug Effects
- Assess vital signs (BP and pulse rate) during adjustment period of tricyclic antidepressant (TCA) therapy. If BP falls more than 20 mm Hg or if there is a sudden increase in pulse rate, withhold medication and notify physician.
- Orthostatic hypotension may be sufficiently severe to require protective assistance when patient is ambulating. Instruct patient to change position from recumbency to standing slowly and in stages.
- Monitor for changes in behavior that may indicate increased incidence of suicidality.
- Report signs of liver dysfunction: Yellow skin and sclerae, light-colored stools, pruritus, abdominal discomfort.
- Report fine tremors, a distressing extrapyramidal adverse effect, to physician.

- Monitor bowel elimination pattern and I&O ratio. Severe constipation and urinary retention are potential problems, especially in older adults. Advise increased fluid intake to at least 1500 mL/d (if allowed).
- Monitor patient carefully during initial drug therapy when therapeutic "lag period" may foster noncompliance.
- Inspect oral membranes daily with high-dose therapy. Urge outpatient to report symptoms of stomatitis or xerostomia.
- Regulate environmental temperature and patient's clothing carefully; drug may cause intolerance to heat or cold.
- Excessive alcohol may potentiate TCA effects and increase the danger of overdosage or suicide attempt.

Patient & Family Education

- Be aware that your ability to perform tasks requiring alertness and skill may be impaired.
- Do not use OTC drugs unless approved by physician.
- Understand that the actions of both alcohol and trimipramine are increased when used together during therapy and for up to 2 wk after the TCA is discontinued. Consult physician about safe amounts of alcohol, if any, that can be taken.
- Be aware that the effects of barbiturates and other CNS depressants may also be enhanced by trimipramine.
- Expect that therapeutic response will be delayed because TCAs have a "lag period" of 2–4 wk. Increased dosage does not shorten period but rather increases incidence of adverse reactions. Keep physician advised and do not interrupt therapy.

TRIPELENNAMINE HYDROCHLORIDE

(tri-pel-enn'a-meen)
PBZ-SR, Pelamine, Pyribenzamine ◆

Classifications: ANTIHISTAMINE; H_1-RECEPTOR ANTAGONIST
Therapeutic: ANTIHISTAMINE; H_1-RECEPTOR ANTAGONIST
Prototype: Diphenhydramine
Pregnancy Category: B

AVAILABILITY 25 mg, 50 mg tablets; 100 mg sustained release tablets

ACTION & *THERAPEUTIC EFFECT*
Antihistamine with mild CNS depressant effects. Antagonizes histamine action (i.e., increased capillary permeability, edema formation, itching, and constriction of respiratory, GI, and vascular smooth muscle). *Has antihistamine, antitussive, anticholinergic, and local anesthetic action.*

USES To relieve symptoms of various allergic conditions, to ameliorate reactions to blood or plasma, and in anaphylaxis as adjunct to epinephrine and other standard measures after acute symptoms have been controlled. Also to provide oral mucous membrane analgesia in young children with herpetic gingiva-stomatitis.

CONTRAINDICATIONS Narrow-angle glaucoma; symptomatic prostatic hypertrophy; bladder neck obstruction; GI obstruction or stenosis; lower respiratory tract symptoms, including asthma; within 14 d of MAO inhibitor therapy. Safe use in neonates and premature infants is not established.

T

Common adverse effects in *italic*, life-threatening effects underlined; generic names in **bold**; classifications in SMALL CAPS; ◆ Canadian drug name; ❷ Prototype drug

1559

CAUTIOUS USE History of asthma; convulsive disorders; increased intraocular pressure; hyperthyroidism; cardiovascular disease; hypertension; diabetes mellitus; pregnancy (category B), lactation.

ROUTE & DOSAGE

Allergic Conditions

Adult: **PO** 25–50 mg q4–6h or 100 mg sustained release q8–12h (max: 600 mg/d)
Child: **PO** 5 mg/kg/d in 4–6 divided doses (max: 300 mg/d)

ADMINISTRATION

Oral

- Give with or immediately after meals or food or with a glass of milk or water to lessen GI adverse effects.
- Do not use sustained release formulation (100 mg) with children of any age.
- Do not crush, break, or chew sustained release tablets. These must be swallowed whole.
- Store in tight, light-resistant containers.

ADVERSE EFFECTS (≥1%) **Respiratory:** Thickened bronchial secretions, wheezing, sensation of chest tightness. **Special Senses:** Blurred vision, diplopia. **Urogenital:** Urinary hesitancy or retention; dysuria. **CV:** Palpitation, tachycardia, mild hypotension or hypertension, <u>cardiovascular collapse</u>. **CNS:** *Drowsiness,* dizziness, tinnitus, vertigo, fatigue, headache; disturbed coordination, tingling, tremors, euphoria, nervousness, restlessness, insomnia, hallucinations, excitement. **GI:** *Epigastric distress, anorexia, nausea, vomiting, constipation* or diarrhea, *dry mouth, nose,* and *throat.* **Hemato-**logic: Leukopenia, hemolytic anemia. **Skin:** Skin rash, urticaria, photosensitivity. **Body as a Whole:** <u>Anaphylactic shock</u>, fever, ataxia, athetosis, convulsions, <u>coma</u>.

INTERACTIONS Drug: Alcohol and other CNS DEPRESSANTS add to CNS depression; MAO INHIBITORS may intensify anticholinergic effects.

PHARMACOKINETICS Absorption: Readily from GI tract. **Onset:** 15–30 min. **Peak:** 2–3 h. **Duration:** 4–6 h (up to 8 h with sustained-release). **Distribution:** Crosses placenta; distributed into breast milk. **Metabolism:** In liver. **Elimination:** In urine.

CLINICAL IMPLICATIONS

Assessment & Drug Effects

- Assist older adults during ambulation; dizziness, sedation, and hypotension are more likely to occur in this age group.
- Lab tests: Obtain periodic blood cell counts during long-term therapy with antihistamines.

Patient & Family Education

- Void just before taking drug if urinary hesitancy is a problem.
- Do not drive or engage in potentially hazardous activities until response to drug is known. Mild to moderate drowsiness, blurred vision, and dizziness occur in some patients.
- Be aware that the effects of antihistamines may be augmented by concomitant use of alcohol or other CNS depressants.
- Do not take OTC preparations without consulting physician.
- Discontinue antihistamines within 4 d before skin testing procedure for allergy because drug may interfere with reactions and obscure test results.

TRIPTORELIN PAMOATE

(trip-tor′e-lyn)
Trelstar Depot
Classifications: HORMONE; GONA-
DOTROPIN-RELEASING HORMONE AG-
ONIST ANALOG
Therapeutic: GONADOTROPIN-RELEAS-
ING HORMONE AGONIST ANALOG
Prototype: Leuprolide acetate
Pregnancy Category: X

AVAILABILITY 3.75 mg injection

ACTION & *THERAPEUTIC EFFECT*
Synthetic luteinizing releasing hormone agonist (LHRH or GnRH)
with greater potency than naturally
occurring luteinizing hormone. Potent inhibitor of gonadotropin secretion. It causes decreased formation of testosterone. *In men, the
level of serum testosterone is equivalent to a surgically castrated man.*

USES Palliative treatment of advanced prostate cancer.

CONTRAINDICATIONS Hypersensitivity to triptorelin, other LHRH agonists, or LHRH; dysfunctional uterine bleeding; pregnancy (category
X), lactation; children.
CAUTIOUS USE Prostatic carcinoma;
hepatic or renal dysfunction; patients with impending spinal cord
compression or severe urogenital
disorder; premenstrual syndrome;
renal insufficiency.

ROUTE & DOSAGE

Prostate Cancer
Adult: **IM** 3.75 mg q mo

ADMINISTRATION

Intramuscular
- Give deep into a large muscle.

ADVERSE EFFECTS (≥1%) **Body
as a Whole:** *Hot flushes,* pain, leg
pain, fatigue. **CV:** Hypertension. **GI:**
Diarrhea, vomiting. **Hematologic:**
Anemia. **Musculoskeletal:** Skeletal
pain. **CNS:** Headache, dizziness, insomnia, impotence, emotional lability. **Skin:** Pruritus. **Urogenital:** Urinary retention, UTI. **Other:** Pain at
injection site.

DIAGNOSTIC TEST INTERFERENCE
May interfere with tests for *pitu-
itary-gonadal function.*

PHARMACOKINETICS Peak: 1–3 h.
Duration: 1 mo. **Metabolism:** Unknown. **Elimination:** Eliminated by
liver and kidneys. **Half-Life:** 3 h.

CLINICAL IMPLICATIONS
Assessment & Drug Effects
- Monitor for S&S of disease flare,
especially during the first 1–2 wk
of therapy: Increased bone pain,
blood in urine, urinary obstruction, or symptoms of spinal compression.
- Lab tests: Periodic serum testosterone, PSA, acid phosphatase
levels; urinary and serum calcium;
urinary calcium/creatinine ratio;
lipid profile in those at risk for
atherosclerosis.

Patient & Family Education
- Disease flare (see ASSESSMENT &
DRUG EFFECTS) is a common, temporary adverse effect of therapy;
however, symptoms may be-
come serious enough to report to
the physician.
- Notify physician promptly of the
following: S&S of an allergic reaction (itching, hives, swelling of
face, arms, or legs; tingling in
mouth or throat, tightness in chest
or trouble breathing); weakness
or loss of muscle control; rapid
weight gain.

T

Common adverse effects in *italic*, life-threatening effects underlined; generic names
in **bold**; classifications in SMALL CAPS; ♣ Canadian drug name; ⊙ Prototype drug

1561

TROLEANDOMYCIN

(troe-lee-an-doe-mye′sin)
Tao
Classifications: MACROLIDE ANTIBIOTIC
Therapeutic: ANTIBIOTIC, MACROLIDE
Prototype: Erythromycin
Pregnancy Category: C

AVAILABILITY 250 mg capsules

ACTION & *THERAPEUTIC EFFECT*

Binds to the 50S ribosomal subunit, resulting in inhibition of bacterial protein synthesis. Action is mainly bacteriostatic but can be bacteriocidal depending on bacterial sensitivity. *Effective against susceptible strains of* Clostridium, Haemophilus, Neisseria, Staphylococcus, Streptococcus, *and* Pneumonia.

USES Acute, severe infections of upper respiratory tract caused by susceptible strains of pneumococci and group A beta-hemolytic streptococci.

CONTRAINDICATIONS History of hypersensitivity to any of the macrolide antibiotics; bacteriemia; concurrent use with ergot derivatives, pimozide, astemizole, or cisapride; use for prophylaxis or for minor infections; pregnancy (category C); porphyria.
CAUTIOUS USE Impaired liver function; lactation.

ROUTE & DOSAGE

Upper Respiratory Tract Infections
Adult: **PO** 250–500 mg q6h
Child: **PO** 6.6–11 mg/kg (125–250 mg) q6h

ADMINISTRATION

Oral
- Give on an empty stomach (1 h before or 2 h after meals).
- Give in evenly spaced intervals throughout the day, preferably around the clock, in order to maintain effective blood levels.

ADVERSE EFFECTS (≥1%) **GI:** *Abdominal cramps and discomfort, nausea,* vomiting, diarrhea, cholestatic jaundice. **Body as a Whole:** Allergic reactions (urticaria, skin rash, <u>anaphylaxis</u>); superinfections.

DIAGNOSTIC TEST INTERFERENCE

Troleandomycin may cause false elevations of *urinary 17-ketosteroids (Drekter),* and *17-hydroxycorticosteroids (Porter-Silver method).*

INTERACTIONS Drug: May increase levels of **carbamazepine,** CYCLOSPORINES, and **theophylline** and their toxicity; ORAL CONTRACEPTIVES may cause cholestatic jaundice; **warfarin** may increase **prothrombin time (PT); ergotamine** may induce ischemia and peripheral vasospasm. **Food:** Grapefruit juice (>1 qt/d) may increase plasma concentrations and adverse effects.

PHARMACOKINETICS Absorption: Incompletely from GI tract. **Peak:** 2 h. **Distribution:** Distributed throughout body fluids; diffusion into CSF is poor unless meninges are inflamed. **Metabolism:** In liver. **Elimination:** In bile and urine.

CLINICAL IMPLICATIONS

Assessment & Drug Effects
- Lab tests: Obtain periodic liver function tests in patients receiving drug longer than 10 d or in repeated courses.

■ Some patients develop an allergic type of hepatitis with right upper quadrant pain, fever, nausea, vomiting, jaundice, eosinophilia, and leukocytosis. Liver changes are reversible if drug is discontinued immediately.

■ Be aware that superinfections are most likely to occur in patients on prolonged or repeated therapy. Withdraw if symptoms present (see Appendix F), and start appropriate therapy.

Patient & Family Education

■ Report signs of jaundice: Clay-colored stools, pruritus, yellow sclerae.

■ Do not stop drug before full course of therapy is completed. Do not interrupt and then restart therapy or increase or decrease dose or interval.

TROMETHAMINE

(troe-meth′a-meen)
Tham
Classifications: ELECTROLYTIC BALANCE AGENT; SYSTEMIC ALKALINIZER
Therapeutic: SYSTEMIC ALKALINIZER
Pregnancy Category: C

AVAILABILITY 3.6 g/100 mL injection

ACTION & *THERAPEUTIC EFFECT*
A proton acceptor that binds cations of fixed or metabolic acids and hydrogen ions of carbonic acid, thus increasing bicarbonate anion (HCO_3^-). It also penetrates the cell membrane to combine with intracellular acid. *Acts as a weak osmotic diuretic, increasing urine pH and excretion of fixed acids, CO_2, and electrolytes. Corrects and prevents metabolic acidosis.*

USES To prevent or correct metabolic acidosis associated with cardiac bypass surgery and cardiac arrest and to correct excess acidity of stored blood [preserved with acid citrate dextrose (CD)] and used in cardiac bypass surgery. (Stored blood has a pH range of 6.8–6.22.)
UNLABELED USES Metabolic acidosis of status asthmaticus and neonatal respiratory distress syndrome.

CONTRAINDICATIONS Anuria, uremia; chronic respiratory acidosis; pregnancy (category C).
CAUTIOUS USE Renal impairment; >1 d of therapy.

ROUTE & DOSAGE

Note: Dosage may be estimated from buffer base deficit of extracellular fluid using the following formula as a guide: mL of 0.3 M tromethamine solution = body weight (kg) × base deficit (mEq/L)

Metabolic Acidosis Associated with Cardiac Arrest
Adult: **IV** 3.5–6 mL/kg (126–216 mg/kg) of a 0.3 M solution into large peripheral vein; if chest is open, 55–165 mL (2–6 g) 0.3 M solution into ventricular cavity

Systemic Acidosis during Cardiac Bypass Surgery
Adult: **IV** 9 mL/kg or approximately 500 mL (18 g) 0.3 M solution; a single dose of up to 1000 mL (36 g) may be necessary in severe acidosis

Excess Acidity of ACD Priming Blood
Adult: **IV** 14–70 mL (0.5–2.5 g) 0.3 M solution added to each 500 mL blood

ADMINISTRATION
Intravenous

PREPARE: IV Infusion: Maximum allowable concentration is 0.3 M.

T

Common adverse effects in *italic*, life-threatening effects <u>underlined</u>; generic names in **bold**; classifications in SMALL CAPS; ♣ Canadian drug name; ☯ Prototype drug

1563

Available premixed as a 0.3 M solution or may be prepared by adding 36 g to 1 L of sterile water.

ADMINISTER: **IV Infusion:** Give undiluted by slow IV infusion or added to pump-oxygenator blood or other priming fluid. Give over a period of no less than 1 h.

- Observe entry site carefully. Perivascular infiltration of the highly alkaline solution may lead to vasospasm, necrosis, and tissue sloughing. Stop infusion if extravasation occurs. ■ Treat extravasation with a procaine and hyaluronidase infiltration to reduce vasospasm and to dilute tromethamine remaining in tissues. If necessary, local infiltration of an alpha-adrenergic blocking agent (e.g., phentolamine) into the area may be ordered.

- Discard solution 24 h after reconstitution; solution is highly alkaline and can erode glass. ■ Store drug (available as solution or powder) away from extreme heat. Do not freeze.

ADVERSE EFFECTS (≥1%) **Body as a Whole:** *Local irritation,* tissue inflammation, *chemical phlebitis,* extravasation. **Respiratory:** <u>Respiratory depression</u>. **Metabolic:** Transient decrease in blood glucose, hypervolemia, hyperkalemia (with depressed kidney function).

PHARMACOKINETICS Metabolism: No appreciable metabolism. **Elimination:** Rapidly by kidneys; 75% within 8 h.

CLINICAL IMPLICATIONS
Assessment & Drug Effects
- Watch for signs of hypoxia (see Appendix F). Hypoxia and hypoventilation may result from drug-induced reduction of CO_2 tension (a potent stimulus to breathing), particularly if respiratory acidosis is also present.
- Drug-induced hypoxia is a particular risk when concomitant use of other respiratory depressants or with COPD or impaired kidney function.
- Lab tests: Monitor blood pH, Pco_2, Po_2, bicarbonate, glucose, and electrolytes before, during, and after treatment. Dosage is controlled to raise blood pH to normal limits (arterial: 7.35–7.45) and to correct acid–base imbalance.
- Monitor ECG and serum potassium if drug is given to patient with impaired kidney function (reduced drug elimination). Since hyperkalemia is often associated with metabolic acidosis, be alert to early signs (see Appendix F).
- Be alert for overdose symptoms (from total drug or too rapid administration): Alkalosis, overhydration, prolonged hypoglycemia, solute overload.

TROPICAMIDE
(troe-pik′a-mide)
Pregnancy Category: C
See Appendix A-1.

TROSPIUM CHLORIDE
(tro-spi′um)
Sanctura

Classifications: ANTICHOLINERGIC; ANTIMUSCARINIC; ANTISPASMODIC
Therapeutic: ANTICHOLINERGIC; ANTISPASMODIC; URINARY SMOOTH MUSCLE RELAXANT
Prototype: Ipratropium bromide
Pregnancy Category: C

AVAILABILITY 20 mg tablets

ACTION & *THERAPEUTIC EFFECT*
Antagonizes the effect of acetylcholine on muscarinic receptors in smooth muscle. Its parasympatholytic action reduces the tonus of the smooth muscle of the bladder. *Trospium decreases urinary frequency, urgency, and urge incontinence in patients with overactive bladders.*

USES Treatment of overactive (neurogenic) bladder with symptoms of urgency, frequency, and urge urinary incontinence.

CONTRAINDICATIONS Hypersensitivity to trospium; patients with or at risk for urinary retention; uncontrolled narrow-angle glaucoma; gastric tension, GI obstruction, ileus, pyloric stenosis, toxic megacolon, severe ulcerative colitis; pregnancy (category C). Safety and effectiveness in children have not been established.

CAUTIOUS USE Significant bladder obstruction, closed-angle glaucoma; BPH; ulcerative colitis, GERD, intestinal atony; myasthenia gravis, autonomic neuropathy; moderate or severe hepatic dysfunction; severe renal insufficiency, renal failure; glaucoma; older adults; lactation.

ROUTE & DOSAGE

Overactive Bladder
Adult: **PO** 20 mg twice daily on empty stomach
Geriatric: **PO** 20 mg twice daily on empty stomach, may decrease to 20 mg once daily at bedtime if anticholinergic adverse effects are intolerable

Renal Impairment
Cl_{cr} < 30 mL/min: reduce dose to 20 mg once daily at bedtime.

ADMINISTRATION

Oral
- Give at least 1 h before meals or on an empty stomach.
- Store at 20°–25° C (66°–77° F).

ADVERSE EFFECTS (≥1%) **Body as a Whole:** Fatigue. **CNS:** Headache. **GI:** *Dry mouth, constipation,* abdominal pain, dyspepsia, flatulence. **Special Senses:** Dry eyes. **Urogenital:** Urinary retention.

INTERACTIONS Drug: Increased anticholinergic adverse effects with ANTICHOLINERGIC AGENTS.

PHARMACOKINETICS Absorption: <10% absorbed orally. **Peak:** 5–6 h. **Elimination:** Primarily in feces (unabsorbed dose), renal tubular secretion of absorbed dose. **Half-Life:** 20 h.

CLINICAL IMPLICATIONS

Assessment & Drug Effects
- Monitor bowel and bladder function. Report urinary hesitancy or significant constipation.
- Withhold drug and notify physician if urinary retention develops.
- Monitor for and report worsening of GI symptoms in those with GERD.
- Frequent monitoring of IOP is required in those with controlled narrow-angle glaucoma.

Patient & Family Education
- Report promptly any of the following: signs of an allergic reaction, (e.g., itching or hives), blurred vision or difficulty focusing, confusion, dizziness, difficulty passing urine.
- Moderate intake of tea, coffee, caffeinated sodas, and alcohol to minimize side effects of this drug.
- Avoid situations in which overheating is likely, as drug may im-

Common adverse effects in *italic*, life-threatening effects <u>underlined</u>; generic names in **bold**; classifications in SMALL CAPS; ♣ Canadian drug name; ⊘ Prototype drug

1565

pair sweating, which is a normal cooling mechanism.
- Do not engage in hazardous activities until response to the drug is known.

VACCINIA IMMUNE GLOBULIN (VIG-IV)

(vac-cin′i-a)

Classifications: BIOLOGIC RESPONSE MODIFIER; IMMUNOGLOBULIN
Therapeutic: IMMUNOGLOBULIN
Prototype: Immune globulin intravenous
Pregnancy Category: C

AVAILABILITY 50 mg/mL injection

ACTION & *THERAPEUTIC EFFECT*
Vaccinia immune globulin, VIG (VIG-IV) is a purified human immunoglobulin G (IgG) with trace amounts of IgA and IgM. It is derived from adult human plasma collected from donors who received booster immunizations with the smallpox vaccine. VIG (VIG-IV) contains high titers of antivaccinia antibodies. *VIG is effective in the treatment of smallpox vaccine adverse reactions secondary to continued vaccinia virus replication after vaccination.*

USES Prevention of serious complications of smallpox vaccine; treatment of progressive vaccinia; severe generalized vaccinia; eczema vaccinatum; vaccinia infection in patients with skin conditions (e.g., burns, impetigo, varicella-zoster, poison ivy, or eczematous skin lesions); treatment or modification of aberrant infections induced by vaccinia virus.

CONTRAINDICATIONS Predisposition to acute renal failure (i.e., preexisting renal insufficiency, diabetes mellitus, volume depletion, sepsis, patients >65 y); AIDS; chronic skin conditions (e.g., burn, atopy); bone marrow suppression; chemotherapy; radiation therapy; corticosteroid therapy, eczema; hematologic disease; herpes infection; postvaccinal encephalitis; pregnancy (category C); lactation; infants <12 mo.
CAUTIOUS USE Concurrent administration of known nephrotoxic drugs; autoimmune disease; cardiomyopathy, cardiac disease.

ROUTE & DOSAGE

Vaccinia
Adults: IV 100–500 mg/kg
Renal Impairment
Maximum dose: 400 mg/kg

ADMINISTRATION

Intravenous

PREPARE: **IV Infusion:** No dilution required. Use solution as supplied.
ADMINISTER: **IV Infusion:** Begin infusion within 6 h of entering the vial. Complete infusion within 12 h of entering the vial. Use in-line filter (0.22 microns), infusion pump, and dedicated IV line [may infuse into a preexisting catheter if it contains NS, D2.5W, D5W, D10W, or D20W (or any combination of these)]. Infuse at 1.0 mL/kg/h the first 30 min, increase to 2.0 mL/kg/h the next 30 min, and then increase to 3.0 mL/kg/h until infused.

ADVERSE EFFECTS (≥1%) **Body as a Whole:** Injection site reaction. **CNS:** Dizziness, *headache*. **GI:** Abdominal pain, nausea, vomiting. **Musculoskeletal:** Arthralgia, back pain. **Respiratory:** Upper respira-

V

tory infection. **Skin:** Erythema, flushing.

INTERACTIONS Drug: May interfere with the immune response to live virus VACCINES. Vaccination with live virus VACCINES should be deferred until approximately 6 mo after administration of VIG-IV.

PHARMACOKINETICS Half-Life: 22 d.

CLINICAL IMPLICATIONS

Assessment & Drug Effects
- Monitor vital signs continuously during infusion, especially after infusion rate changes.
- Slow infusion rate for any of the following: flushing, chills, muscle cramps, back pain, fever, nausea, vomiting, arthralgia, and wheezing.
- DC infusion, institute supportive measures, and notify physician for any of the following: increase in heart rate, increase in respiratory rate, shortness of breath, rales or other signs of anaphylaxis.
- Have loop diuretic available for management of fluid overload.

Patient & Family Education
- Promptly report any discomfort that develops while drug is being infused.

VALACYCLOVIR HYDROCHLORIDE

(val-a-cy'clo-vir)
Valtrex
Classifications: ANTIVIRAL
Therapeutic: ANTIVIRAL
Prototype: Acyclovir
Pregnancy Category: B

AVAILABILITY 500 mg tablets

ACTION & *THERAPEUTIC EFFECT*
An antiviral agent hydrolyzed in the intestinal wall or liver to acyclovir; interferes with viral DNA synthesis. Because of increased GI absorption, the plasma level of this drug is substantially higher than that of acyclovir when both are taken orally. *Active against herpes simplex virus types 1 (HSV-1) and 2 (HSV-2), varicella zoster virus, and cytomegalovirus. Inhibits viral replication.*

USES Herpes zoster (shingles) in immunocompetent adults. Treatment and suppression of recurrent genital herpes; suppression of recurrent herpes in HIV-positive patients; treatment of cold sores.

CONTRAINDICATIONS Hypersensitivity to or intolerance of valacyclovir or acyclovir; children <2 y.
CAUTIOUS USE Renal impairment, patients receiving nephrotoxic drugs, advanced HIV disease, allogeneic bone marrow transplant and renal transplant recipients, treatment of disseminated herpes zoster, immunocompromised patients, pregnancy (category B); lactation.

ROUTE & DOSAGE

Herpes Zoster
Adult: **PO** 1 g (2 × 500 mg) t.i.d. for 7 d, start within 48 h of onset of zoster rash

Renal Impairment
Cl$_{cr}$ 30–49 mL/min: 1 g q12h 10–29 mL/min: 1 g q24h <10 mL/min: 500 mg q24h

Treatment of Recurrent Genital Herpes
Adult: **PO** 500 mg b.i.d. × 3 d

Renal Impairment
Cl$_{cr}$ ≤29 mL/min: 500 mg q.d.

V

Common adverse effects in *italic*, life-threatening effects <u>underlined</u>; generic names in **bold**; classifications in SMALL CAPS; ♣ Canadian drug name; ⓟ Prototype drug

1567

Suppression of Recurrent Genital Herpes
Adult: **PO** 1 g q.d.

Treatment of Cold Sores
Adult: **PO** 2 g 12 h × 2 doses

ADMINISTRATION

Oral

- Start drug as soon as possible after diagnosis of herpes zoster, preferably within 48 h of onset of rash.
- Note: Dosage reduction is recommended for patients with renal impairment.
- Give valacyclovir after hemodialysis.
- Store at 15°–30° C (59°–86° F).

ADVERSE EFFECTS (≥1%) **CNS:** *Headache,* weakness, somnolence, dizziness, fatigue, lethargy, confusion. **GI:** *Nausea, vomiting, diarrhea,* abdominal pain, dyspepsia, flatulence. **Urogenital:** Glomerulonephritis, renal tubular damage, acute renal failure. **Skin:** Rash, urticaria, pruritus.

INTERACTIONS Drug: Probenecid, cimetidine decrease valacyclovir elimination. **Zidovudine** may cause increased drowsiness and lethargy.

PHARMACOKINETICS Absorption: Rapidly absorbed from GI tract; 54% reaches systemic circulation as acyclovir. **Peak:** 1.5 h. **Distribution:** 13.5–17.9% bound to plasma proteins; distributes into plasma, cerebrospinal fluid, saliva, and major body organs; crosses placenta; excreted in breast milk. **Metabolism:** Rapidly converted to acyclovir during first pass through intestine and liver. **Elimination:** 40–50% in urine. **Half-Life:** 2.5–3.3 h.

CLINICAL IMPLICATIONS

Assessment & Drug Effects

- Monitor kidney function in patients with kidney impairment or those receiving potentially nephrotoxic drugs.
- Monitor for S&S of hypersensitivity; if present, withhold drug and notify physician.

Patient & Family Education

- Be aware of potential adverse effects and do not discontinue drug until full course is completed.
- Note: Post-herpes pain is likely to be present for several months after completion of therapy.

VALGANCICLOVIR HYDROCHLORIDE

(val-gan-ci′clo-vir)

Valcyte

Classifications: ANTIVIRAL AGENT
Therapeutic: ANTIVIRAL
Prototype: Acyclovir
Pregnancy Category: C

AVAILABILITY 450 mg tablets

ACTION & *THERAPEUTIC EFFECT* Rapidly converted to ganciclovir by intestinal and hepatic enzymes. In cells infected with cytomegalovirus (CMV), ganciclovir is phosphorylated to ganciclovir triphosphate, which inhibits viral DNA synthesis. *Antiviral drug active against cytomegalovirus (CMV). Prevents replication of viral CMV DNA.*

USES Treatment of CMV retinitis; prevention of CMV disease in high-risk kidney, kidney-pancreas, and heart transplant patients (not effective in liver transplants).

CONTRAINDICATIONS Hypersensitivity to valganciclovir, ganciclovir, or acyclovir. Not recommended for persons on hemodialysis; renal failure; dental work; antimicrobial resistance; neutropenia, thrombocytopenia; pregnancy (category C), females of childbearing age; lactation.

CAUTIOUS USE Impaired kidney function; older adults; dental disease; anemia; leukopenia; bone marrow depression; concomitant use of myelosuppressive drugs; irradiation. Safety and efficacy in children are not established.

ROUTE & DOSAGE

Cytomegalovirus Prophylaxis

Adult: PO 900 mg once daily with food, starting within 10 d of transplantation until 100 d posttransplantation

Cytomegalovirus Retinitis Induction

Adult: PO 900 mg b.i.d. with food times 21 d

Cytomegalovirus Retinitis Maintenance

Adult: PO 900 mg q.d. with food

Renal Impairment

Cl_{cr} 40–59 mL/min: 450 mg b.i.d. (induction) or q.d. (maintenance) 25–39 mL/min: 450 mg q.d. (induction) or q2d (maintenance) 10–24 mL/min: 450 mg q2d (induction) or twice weekly (maintenance)

ADMINISTRATION

Oral

- Exercise caution in handling tablets. Do not crush or break tablets. Avoid direct contact of crushed or broken tablets with skin or mucous membranes.
- Give with food.
- Do not give to patients on hemodialysis.
- Store at 25°–30° C (77°–86° F).

ADVERSE EFFECTS (≥1%) **Body as a Whole:** *Fever,* local and systemic infections, hypersensitivity reactions. **CNS:** *Headache, insomnia,* peripheral neuropathy, paresthesia, convulsions, psychosis, confusion, hallucinations, agitation. **GI:** *Diarrhea, nausea, vomiting, abdominal pain.* **Hematologic:** *Neutropenia, anemia,* thrombocytopenia, pancytopenia, bone marrow suppression, aplastic anemia. **Special Senses:** *Retinal detachment.*

INTERACTIONS Drug: ANTINEOPLASTIC AGENTS, **amphotericin B, didanosine, trimethoprim-sulfamethoxazole (TMP-SMZ), dapsone, pentamidine, probenecid, zidovudine** may increase bone marrow suppression and other toxic effects of valganciclovir; may increase risk of nephrotoxicity from **cyclosporine;** ANTIRETROVIRAL AGENTS may decrease valganciclovir levels; valganciclovir may increase levels and toxicity of ANTIRETROVIRAL AGENTS; may increase risk of seizures due to **imipenem-cilastatin.**

PHARMACOKINETICS Absorption: Well absorbed from GI tract, 60% reaches systemic circulation as ganciclovir. **Onset:** 3–8 d. **Peak:** 1–3 h. **Duration:** Clinical relapse can occur 14 d to 3.5 mo after stopping therapy; positive blood and urine cultures recur 12–60 d after therapy. **Distribution:** Distributes throughout body including CSF, eye, lungs, liver, and kidneys; crosses placenta in animals; not known if distributed into breast milk. **Metabolism:** Metabolized in intestinal wall to ganciclovir, ganciclovir is not metabolized. **Elimination:** 94–99% of dose is excreted unchanged in urine. **Half-Life:** 4 h.

CLINICAL IMPLICATIONS

Assessment & Drug Effects

- Withhold drug and notify physician for any of the following: Ab-

V

Common adverse effects in *italic*, life-threatening effects underlined; generic names in **bold**; classifications in SMALL CAPS; ✦ Canadian drug name; ⊘ Prototype drug

1569

solute neutrophil count <500 cells/mm^3, platelet count <25,000/mm^3, hemoglobin <8 g/dL, declining creatinine clearance.

- Monitor for S&S of bronchospasm in asthma patients; notify physician immediately.
- Lab tests: Baseline and frequent serum creatinine or creatinine clearance, CBC with differential, platelet count, Hct & Hgb.

Patient & Family Education

- Schedule ophthalmologic follow-up examinations at least every 4–6 wk while being treated with valganciclovir.
- Keep all scheduled appointments for laboratory tests.
- Do not drive or engage in potentially hazardous activities until response to drug is known.
- Report any of the following immediately: unexpected bleeding, infection.
- Use effective methods of contraception (barrier and other types) during and for at least 90 d following treatment.
- Discontinue drug and notify physician immediately in the event of pregnancy.

VALPROIC ACID (DIVALPROEX SODIUM, SODIUM VALPROATE) ℗

(val-proe'ic)

Depacon, Depakene, Depakote, Depakote ER, Depakote Sprinkle, Epival ♦, Zalkote

Classifications: ANTICONVULSANT; GABA INHIBITOR
Therapeutic: ANTICONVULSANT
Pregnancy Category: D

AVAILABILITY 250 mg capsules; 125 mg sprinkle capsules; 125 mg, 250 mg, 500 mg delayed release tablets; 500 mg sustained release tablets; 250 mg/5 mL syrup; 100 mg/mL injection

ACTION & THERAPEUTIC EFFECT
Anticonvulsant whose mechanism of action is believed to be related to increased bioavailability of the inhibitory neurotransmitter gamma-aminobutyric acid (GABA) to brain neurons. It may also suppress repetitive neuronal firing through inhibition of voltage-sensitive sodium channels. *Depresses abnormal neuron discharges in the CNS, thus decreasing seizure activity.*

USES Alone or with other anticonvulsants in management of absence (petit mal) and mixed seizures; mania; migraine headache prophylaxis.

UNLABELED USES Status epilepticus refractory to IV diazepam, petit mal variant seizures, febrile seizures in children, other types of seizures including psychomotor (temporal lobe), myoclonic, akinetic and tonic-clonic seizures, photosensitivity seizures, and those refractory to other anticonvulsants.

CONTRAINDICATIONS Hypersensitivity to valproate sodium; thrombocytopenia, patient with bleeding disorders or liver dysfunction or disease; cirrhosis, pancreatitis; congenital metabolic disorders, those with severe seizures, or on multiple anticonvulsant drugs; encephalopathy; AIDS; pregnancy (category D); child <2 y; children <18 y for treatment of mania.

CAUTIOUS USE History of kidney disease, renal impairment or failure; adjunctive treatment with other anticonvulsants; congenital metabolic disorders, those with severe epilepsy, use as sole anticonvulsant drug; HIV; hypoalbuminemia; organic brain syndrome.

ROUTE & DOSAGE

Note: May need to increase dose when converting from immediate release to extended release products

Management of Seizures, Mania

Adult/Child: **PO/IV** 10–15 mg/kg/d in divided doses when total daily dose >250 mg, increase at 1 wk intervals by 5–10 mg/kg/d until seizures are controlled or adverse effects develop (max: 60 mg/kg/d)

Migraine Headache Prophylaxis

Adult: **PO** 250 mg b.i.d. (max: 1000 mg/d) or **Depakote ER** 500 mg q.d. × 1 wk, may increase to 1000 mg q.d.

Mania

Adult: **PO** 250 mg t.i.d. (max: 60 mg/kg/d)

Hepatic Impairment

Dose reduction recommended

ADMINISTRATION

Oral

- Give tablets and capsules whole; instruct patient to swallow whole & not to chew. Instruct to swallow sprinkle capsules whole or sprinkle entire contents on teaspoonful of soft food, and instruct to not chew food.
- Avoid using a carbonated drink as diluent for the syrup because it will release drug from delivery vehicle; free drug painfully irritates oral and pharyngeal membranes.
- Reduce gastric irritation by administering drug with food because serious GI adverse effects can lead to discontinuation of therapy. Enteric-coated tablet or syrup formulation is usually well tolerated.

Intravenous

***PREPARE:* IV Infusion:** Dilute each dose in 50 mL or more of D5W, NS, or RL.

***ADMINISTER:* IV Infusion:** Give a single dose over at least 60 min (≤20 mg/min). Avoid rapid infusion.

***INCOMPATIBILITIES* Solution/additive:** Should avoid mixing with other drugs.

ADVERSE EFFECTS (≥1%) **CNS:** Breakthrough seizures, *sedation, drowsiness,* dizziness, increased alertness, hallucinations, emotional upset, aggression; deep coma, death (with overdose). **GI:** *Nausea, vomiting, indigestion (transient),* hypersalivation, anorexia with weight loss, increased appetite with weight gain, abdominal cramps, diarrhea, constipation, liver failure, pancreatitis. **Hematologic:** *Prolonged bleeding time,* leukopenia, lymphocytosis, thrombocytopenia, hypofibrinogenemia, bone marrow depression, anemia. **Skin:** Skin rash, photosensitivity, transient hair loss, curliness or waviness of hair. **Endocrine:** Irregular menses, secondary amenorrhea. **Metabolic:** Hyperammonemia (usually asymptomatic) hyperammonemic encephalopathy in patients with urea cycle disorders. **Respiratory:** Pulmonary edema (with overdose).

DIAGNOSTIC TEST INTERFERENCE Valproic acid produces false-positive results for **urine ketones,** elevated **AST, ALT, LDH,** and **serum alkaline phosphatase,** prolonged **bleeding time,** altered **thyroid function tests.**

INTERACTIONS Drug: Alcohol and other CNS DEPRESSANTS potentiate depressant effects; other ANTICONVULSANTS, BARBITURATES increase or de-

Common adverse effects in *italic*, life-threatening effects underlined; generic names in **bold**; classifications in SMALL CAPS; ♣ Canadian drug name; ⊕ Prototype drug

V

1571

crease anticonvulsant and BARBITU-RATE levels; **haloperidol, loxapine, maprotiline,** MAOIS, PHENOTHIAZINES, THIOXANTHENES, TRICYCLIC ANTIDEPRESSANTS can increase CNS depression or lower seizure threshold; **aspirin, dipyridamole, warfarin** increase risk of spontaneous bleeding and decrease clotting; **clonazepam** may precipitate absence seizures; SALICYLATES, **cimetidine,** isoniazid may increase valproic acid levels and toxicity. **Mefloquine** can decrease valproic acid levels; **meropenem** may decrease valproic acid levels; **cholestyramine** may decrease absorption. **Herbal: Ginkgo** may decrease anticonvulsant effectiveness.

PHARMACOKINETICS Absorption: Readily from GI tract. **Peak:** 1–4 h valproic acid; 3–5 h divalproex. **Therapeutic Range:** 50–100 mcg/mL. **Distribution:** Crosses placenta; distributed into breast milk. **Metabolism:** In liver. **Elimination:** Primarily in urine; small amount in feces and expired air. **Half-Life:** 5–20 h.

CLINICAL IMPLICATIONS

Assessment & Drug Effects

- Monitor for therapeutic effectiveness achieved with serum levels of valproic acid at 50–100 mcg/mL.
- Monitor patient alertness especially with multiple drug therapy for seizure control. Evaluate plasma levels of the adjunctive anticonvulsants periodically as indicators for possible neurologic toxicity.
- Monitor patient carefully during dose adjustments and promptly report presence of adverse effects. Increased dosage is associated with frequency of adverse effects.
- Lab tests: Perform baseline platelet counts, bleeding time, and serum ammonia, then repeat at least q2mo, especially during the first 6 mo of therapy.

- Multiple drugs for seizure control increase the risk of hyperammonemia, marked by lethargy, anorexia, asterixis, increased seizure frequency, and vomiting. Report such symptoms promptly to physician. If they persist with decreased dosage, the drug will be discontinued.

Patient & Family Education

- Do not discontinue therapy abruptly; such action could result in loss of seizure control. Consult physician before you stop or alter dosage regimen.
- Note to diabetic patients: Drug may cause a false-positive test for urine ketones. Notify physician if this occurs; a differential diagnostic blood test may be indicated.
- Notify physician promptly if spontaneous bleeding or bruising occurs (e.g., petechiae, ecchymotic areas, otorrhagia, epistaxis, melena).
- Withhold dose and notify physician for following symptoms: visual disturbances, rash, jaundice, light-colored stools, protracted vomiting, diarrhea. Fatal liver failure has occurred in patients receiving this drug.
- Avoid alcohol and self-medication with other depressants during therapy.
- Consult physician before using any OTC drugs during anticonvulsant therapy. Combination drugs containing aspirin, sedatives, and medications for hay fever or other allergies are particularly UNSAFE.
- Do not drive or engage in potentially hazardous activities until response to drug is known.
- Inform doctor or dentist before any kind of surgery that you are taking valproic acid.
- Carry medical identification card at all times. It needs to indicate medical diagnosis, medication(s), physician's name, address, and telephone number.

VALRUBICIN

(val-roo'bi-sin)
Valstar
Classifications: ANTINEOPLASTIC; ANTIBIOTIC
Therapeutic: ANTINEOPLASTIC
Prototype: Doxorubicin hydrochloride
Pregnancy Category: C

AVAILABILITY 40 mg/mL solution

ACTION & THERAPEUTIC EFFECT
Semisynthetic analog of doxorubicin. It is a cytotoxic antibiotic agent that inhibits the incorporation of nucleosides in DNA and RNA, resulting in extensive chromosomal damage. Valrubicin interferes with DNA topoisomerase II, which is responsible for the normal DNA separation of strands and the resealing of those DNA strands. *Valrubicin has higher antitumor efficacy and lower toxicity than doxorubicin.*

USES Intravesical therapy of BCG-refractory carcinoma *in situ* of the urinary bladder.

CONTRAINDICATIONS Hypersensitivity to valrubicin, doxorubicin, anthracyclines, or castor oil; patients with a perforated bladder, concurrent UTI, active infection; severe irritable bladder symptoms; severe myelosuppression; pregnancy (category C); lactation.

CAUTIOUS USE Within 2 wk of a transureteral resection; compromised bladder mucosa; mild-to-moderate myelosuppression; concurrent use of anticoagulants, or history of bleeding disorders; GI disorders, renal impairment.

ROUTE & DOSAGE

BCG-Refractory Bladder Carcinoma *in situ*
Adult: **Intravesically** 800 mg once per wk × 6 wk

ADMINISTRATION

Instillation
Avoid skin reactions by using gloves during preparation/administration.

- Use only glass, polypropylene, or polyolefin containers and tubing.

PREPARE: Slowly warm 4 vials (5 mL each) to room temperature. When a precipitate is initially present, warm vials in hands until solution clears. Add contents of 4 vials to 55 mL of 0.9% NaCl injection to yield 75 mL of diluted solution.

INSTILL: Aseptically insert a urethral catheter and drain the bladder. Use gravity drainage to instill valrubicin slowly over several min. Withdraw catheter; instruct patient not to void for 2 h. Note: Do not leave a clamped catheter in place.
- Refrigerate. Do not freeze.

ADVERSE EFFECTS (≥1%) **Body as a Whole:** Abdominal pain, asthenia, back pain, fever, headache, malaise, myalgia. **CNS:** Dizziness. **CV:** Vasodilation. **GI:** Diarrhea, flatulence, nausea, vomiting. **Urogenital:** *Urinary frequency, urgency, dysuria, bladder spasm, hematuria, bladder pain, incontinence, cystitis, UTI,* nocturia, local burning, urethral pain, pelvic pain, gross hematuria, urinary retention. **Respiratory:** Pneumonia. **Skin:** Rash. **Other:** Anemia, hyperglycemia, peripheral edema.

V

Common adverse effects in *italic*, life-threatening effects underlined; generic names in **bold**; classifications in SMALL CAPS; ✦ Canadian drug name; ◯ Prototype drug

1573

PHARMACOKINETICS Absorption: Not absorbed. **Distribution:** Penetrates bladder wall. **Metabolism:** Not metabolized. **Elimination:** Almost completely excreted by voiding the instillate.

CLINICAL IMPLICATIONS

Assessment & Drug Effects

- Therapeutic effectiveness: Indicated by regression of the bladder tumor.
- Notify physician if bladder spasms with spontaneous discharge of valrubicin occur during/shortly after instillation.

Patient & Family Education

- Expect red-tinged urine during the first 24 h after administration.
- Report prolonged passage of red-colored urine or prolonged bladder irritation.
- Drink plenty of fluids during 48 h period following administration.
- Use reliable contraception during therapy period (approximately 6 wk).

VALSARTAN

(val-sar'tan)

Diovan

Classifications: ANGIOTENSIN II (ACE) RECEPTOR ANTAGONIST; ANTIHYPERTENSIVE
Therapeutic: ANTIHYPERTENSIVE; ACE INHIBITOR
Prototype: Losartan
Pregnancy Category: C first trimester; D second and third trimester

AVAILABILITY 40 mg, 80 mg, 160 mg capsules

ACTION & *THERAPEUTIC EFFECT*

An angiotensin II receptor (type AT_1) antagonist that blocks the angiotensin converting enzyme (ACE); it inhibits the binding of angiotensin II to the AT_1 receptors found in many tissues (e.g., vascular smooth muscle, adrenal glands). Angiotensin II is a potent vasoconstrictor and primary vasoactive hormone of the renin–angiotensin–aldosterone system. *Blocking the angiotensin II receptor results in vasodilation and blocking of the aldosterone-secreting effects of angiotensin II, thus resulting in an antihypertensive effect.*

USES Treatment of hypertension, heart failure.

CONTRAINDICATIONS Hypersensitivity to valsartan or losartan; pregnancy [(category C) first trimester, (category D) second and third trimesters], lactation; severe heart failure with compromised renal function.
CAUTIOUS USE Severe renal or hepatic impairment; renal artery stenosis; hypovolemia; congestive heart failure. Safety and efficacy in children <18 y are not established.

ROUTE & DOSAGE

Hypertension
Adult: **PO** 80 mg q.d. (max: 320 mg q.d.)
Heart Failure
Adult: **PO** Start with 40 mg b.i.d. and titrate up to 160 mg b.i.d. *Hemodialysis:* Adjustment not needed

ADMINISTRATION

Oral

- Give on an empty stomach.
- Correct volume depletion prior to initiation of therapy to prevent hypotension.
- Reduce dosage with severe hepatic or renal impairment.

- Note: Daily dose may be titrated up to 320 mg.
- Store at 15°–30° C (59°–86° F).

ADVERSE EFFECTS (≥1%) **Body as a Whole:** Arthralgia. **CNS:** Headache, dizziness. **GI:** Diarrhea, nausea. **Respiratory:** Cough, sinusitis. **Metabolic:** Hyperkalemia.

PHARMACOKINETICS Absorption: Rapidly from GI tract, 25% bioavailability. **Onset:** Blood pressure decreased in 2 wk. **Peak:** Plasma levels, 2–4 h; blood pressure effect 4 wk. **Distribution:** 99% protein bound. **Metabolism:** In the liver. **Elimination:** Primarily in feces. **Half-Life:** 6 h.

CLINICAL IMPLICATIONS

Assessment & Drug Effects

- Monitor BP periodically; take trough readings, just prior to the next scheduled dose, when possible.
- Lab tests: Monitor liver function tests, BUN and creatinine, serum potassium, and CBC with differential, periodically.

Patient & Family Education

- Inform physician immediately if you become pregnant.
- Note: Maximum pressure lowering effect is usually evident between 2 and 4 wk after initiation of therapy.
- Notify physician of episodes of dizziness, especially those that occur when making position changes.

VANCOMYCIN HYDROCHLORIDE
(van-koe-mye′sin)
Vancocin
Classifications: ANTIBIOTIC; GLYCOPEPTIDE

Therapeutic: ANTIBIOTIC
Pregnancy Category: B

AVAILABILITY 125 mg, 250 mg capsules; 1 g, 10 g oral powder; 500 mg, 1 g, 5 g, 10 g injection

ACTION & THERAPEUTIC EFFECT
Bactericidal action is due to inhibition of cell-wall biosynthesis and alteration of bacterial cell-membrane permeability and ribonucleic acid (RNA) synthesis. *Active against many gram-positive organisms.*

USES Parenterally for potentially life-threatening infections in patients allergic, nonsensitive, or resistant to other less toxic antimicrobial drugs. Used orally only in *Clostridium difficile* colitis (not effective by oral route for treatment of systemic infections).

CONTRAINDICATIONS Known hypersensitivity to vancomycin, allergy to corn or corn products, previous hearing loss, concurrent or sequential use of other ototoxic or nephrotoxic agents, IM administration.

CAUTIOUS USE Neonates; children; older adults; impaired kidney function, renal failure, renal impairment, concomitant administration of aminoglycosides; hearing impairment; colitis, inflammatory disorders of the intestine; pregnancy (category B), lactation.

ROUTE & DOSAGE

Systemic Infections
Adult: **IV** 500 mg q6h or 1 g q12h, infuse over 60–90 min
Child: **IV** 10 mg/kg q6h, infuse over 60–90 min
Neonate: **IV** 15 mg/kg, then 10 mg/kg/d divided q8–12h, infuse over 60–90 min

V

Common adverse effects in *italic*, life-threatening effects underlined; generic names in **bold**; classifications in SMALL CAPS; ◆ Canadian drug name; ⊙ Prototype drug

1575

Clostridium difficile Colitis

Adult: **PO** 125–500 mg q6h
Child: **PO** 40 mg/kg/d divided q6h (max: 2 g/d)
Neonate: **PO** 10 mg/kg/d in divided doses

Renal Impairment

Cl_{cr} 40–60 mL/min: dose q24h; <40 mL/min: extend interval based on monitoring levels
Hemodialysis: Not dialyzed

ADMINISTRATION

Oral

- Oral solution is prepared by adding to 10 g oral powder 115 mL of distilled water. The solution may be further diluted in 10 g of water.

Intravenous

PREPARE: Intermittent: Reconstitute 500 mg vial or 1 g vial with 10 mL or 20 mL, respectively, of sterile water for injection to yield 50 mg/mL. Further dilute each 1 g with at least 200 mL of D5W, NS, or RL.

ADMINISTER: Intermittent: Give a single dose at a rate of 10 mg/min or over NOT LESS than 60 min. Avoid rapid infusion, which may cause sudden hypotension. Monitor IV site closely; necrosis and tissue sloughing will result from extravasation.

INCOMPATIBILITIES Solution/additive: Aminophylline, BARBITURATES, **aztreonam** (high concentration), **calcium chloride, chloramphenicol, chlorothiazide, dexamethasone, erythromycin, heparin, methicillin, sodium bicarbonate, warfarin. Y-site: Albumin, amphotericin B cholesteryl, aztreonam, bivalirudin, cefazolin, cefepime, cefotaxime, cefotetan, cefoxitin, ceftazidime, cef-triaxone, cefuroxime, foscarnet, gatifloxacin, heparin, idarubicin, nafcillin, omeprazole, piperacillin/tazobactam, sargramostim, ticarcillin, ticarcillin/clavulanate, warfarin.**

- Store oral and parenteral solutions in refrigerator for up to 14 d; after further dilution, parenteral solution is stable 24 h at room temperature.

ADVERSE EFFECTS (≥1%) **Special Senses:** Ototoxicity (auditory portion of eighth cranial nerve). **Urogenital:** <u>Nephrotoxicity leading to uremia</u>. **Body as a Whole:** Hypersensitivity reactions (chills, fever, skin rash, urticaria, <u>shock-like state</u>), <u>anaphylactoid reaction with vascular collapse</u>, superinfections, severe pain, thrombophlebitis at injection site, generalized tingling following rapid IV infusion. **Hematologic:** Transient leukopenia, eosinophilia. **GI:** Nausea, warmth. **Other:** Injection reaction that includes *hypotension accompanied by flushing and erythematous rash on face and upper body* ("red-neck syndrome") following rapid IV infusion.

INTERACTIONS Drug: Adds to toxicity of OTOTOXIC and NEPHROTOXIC DRUGS (AMINOGLYCOSIDES, **amphotericin B, colistin, capreomycin; cidofovir; cisplatin; cyclosporine; foscarnet; ganciclovir; IV pentamidine; polymyxin B; streptozocin; tacrolimus**). **Cholestyramine, colestipol** can decrease absorption of oral vancomycin; may increase risk of lactic acidosis with **metformin.**

PHARMACOKINETICS Absorption: Not absorbed. **Peak:** 30 min after end of infusion. **Distribution:** Diffuses into pleural, ascitic, pericardial, and synovial fluids; small amount

V

penetrates CSF if meninges are inflamed; crosses placenta. **Elimination:** 80–90% of IV dose excreted in urine within 24 h; PO dose excreted in feces. **Half-Life:** 4–8 h.

CLINICAL IMPLICATIONS

Assessment & Drug Effects

- Monitor BP and heart rate continuously through period of drug administration.
- Lab tests: Monitor urinalysis, kidney & liver functions, and hematologic studies periodically.
- Monitor serial tests of vancomycin blood levels (peak and trough) in patients with borderline kidney function, in infants and neonates, and in patients >60 y.
- Assess hearing. Drug may cause damage to auditory branch (not vestibular branch) of eighth cranial nerve, with consequent deafness, which may be permanent.
- Be aware that serum levels of 60–80 mcg/mL are associated with ototoxicity. Tinnitus and high-tone hearing loss may precede deafness, which may progress even after drug is withdrawn. Older adults and those on high doses are especially susceptible.
- Monitor I&O: Report changes in I&O ratio and pattern. Oliguria or cloudy or pink urine may be a sign of nephrotoxicity (also manifested by transient elevations in BUN, albumin, and hyaline and granular casts in urine).

Patient & Family Education

- Notify physician promptly of ringing in ears.
- Adhere to drug regimen (i.e., do not increase, decrease, or interrupt dosage. The full course of prescribed drug therapy must be completed).

VARDENAFIL HYDROCHLORIDE

(var-den′a-fil hy-dro-chlo′ride)

Levitra

Classifications: IMPOTENCE AGENT; PHOSPHODIESTERASE (PDE) INHIBITOR; VASODILATOR

Therapeutic: IMPOTENCE; PDE INHIBITOR; VASODILATOR

Prototype: Sildenafil

Pregnancy Category: B

AVAILABILITY 2.5 mg, 5 mg, 10 mg, 20 mg tablets

ACTION & *THERAPEUTIC EFFECT*

Phosphodiesterases-5 (PDE5) is an enzyme that speeds up the degradation of cyclic guanosine monophosphate (cGMP), an enzyme needed to cause and maintain increased blood flow into the penis necessary for an erection. Vardenafil is a PDE5 inhibitor. *It enhances erectile function by increasing the amount of cGMP in the penis.*

USES Treatment of erectile dysfunction.

CONTRAINDICATIONS Hypersensitivity to vardenafil or sildenafil; concurrent administration of nitrates or nitroglycerin; QT prolongation, renal failure, severe renal impairment; retinitis pigmentosa; not recommended for women or children; lactation.

CAUTIOUS USE CAD, MI, or stroke within 6 mo; hypotension, or hypertension; risk factors for CVA; anatomic deformity of the penis; subaortic stenosis; sickle cell anemia, leukemia; multiple myeloma; leukemia; coagulopathy; active bleeding or a peptic ulcer; coagulopathy; GERD; hepatitis, cirrhosis; older adults; concurrent use with other medicines for penile dysfunction; pregnancy (category B).

V

ROUTE & DOSAGE

Erectile Dysfunction

Adult: **PO** 10 mg approximately 60 min before sexual activity. May increase to max 20 mg/d if needed. If taking ritonavir, max dose is 2.5 mg/72 h. If taking erythromycin, indinavir, itraconazole, ketoconazole, max dose is 2.5–5 mg/24 h.
Geriatric: **PO** Start with 5 mg 60 min before sexual activity (max: 20 mg/d)

Hepatic Impairment

Moderate impairment: reduce dose to 5 mg (max: 10 mg/d)

ADMINISTRATION

Oral

- Take approximately 1 h before expected intercourse, but preferably not after a heavy or high-fat meal.
- Store at 15°–30° C (59°–86° F).

ADVERSE EFFECTS (≥1%) **Body as a Whole:** *Flushing,* flu-like syndrome, back pain, anaphylactoid reactions, asthenia, facial edema, pain, paresthesias. **CNS:** *Headache,* dizziness, insomnia, somnolence, vertigo. **CV:** Angina, hypertension, hypotension, MI, orthostatic hypotension, palpitations, syncope, sinus tachycardia. **GI:** Dyspepsia, nausea, vomiting, abdominal pain, abnormal liver function tests, diarrhea, dysphagia, esophagitis, gastritis, GERD, xerostomia. **Metabolic:** Increased creatine kinase. **Musculoskeletal:** Arthralgia, myalgia, hypertonia, hyperesthesia. **Respiratory:** Rhinitis, sinusitis, dyspnea, epistaxis, pharyngitis. **Skin:** Photosensitivity, rash, pruritus, sweating. **Special Senses:** Tinnitus, sudden vision loss, blurred vision, changes in color vision. **Urogenital:** Ejaculation dysfunction.

INTERACTIONS Drug: May potentiate hypotensive effects of NITRATES, **alfuzosin, doxazosin, prazosin, tamsulosin, terazosin; amiodarone, dofetilide, procainamide, quinidine, sotalol** may increase QTc interval leading to arrhythmias; **erythromycin** (and other MACROLIDES), **indinavir, itraconazole, ketoconazole,** PROTEASE INHIBITORS, **ritonavir, voriconazole** may increase level and toxicity of vardenafil.

PHARMACOKINETICS Absorption: Rapidly absorbed, 15% reaches systemic circulation. **Onset:** Within 1 h. **Peak:** 0.5–2 h. **Metabolism:** In liver by CYP3A4. **Elimination:** Primarily in feces (90–95%). **Half-Life:** 4–5 h.

CLINICAL IMPLICATIONS

Assessment & Drug Effects

- Monitor CV status and report angina or other S&S of cardiac dysfunction.
- Lab tests: Baseline and periodic LFTs.

Patient & Family Education

- Do not take more than once a day and never take more than the prescribed dose.
- Do not take this drug without consulting physician if you are taking drugs called "alpha blockers" or "nitrates" or any other drugs for high blood pressure, chest pain, or enlarged prostate.
- Report promptly any of the following: palpitations, chest pain, back pain, difficulty breathing, or shortness of breath; dizziness or fainting; changes in vision; dizziness; swollen eyelids; muscle aches; painful or prolonged erection (lasting longer than 4 h); skin rash, or itching.

V

VARENICLINE

(var-en'i-cline)

Chantix

Classifications: SMOKING DETERRENT AGENT; NICOTINIC PARTIAL AGONIST

Therapeutic: SMOKING CESSATION AGENT; NICOTINIC RECEPTOR AGONIST

Prototype: Nicotine
Pregnancy Category: C

AVAILABILITY 0.5 mg, 1 mg capsules

ACTION & *THERAPEUTIC EFFECT*

Nicotine increases dopamine release in the brain and cravings for nicotine are stimulated by low levels of dopamine during periods of abstinence. Varenicline is a partial agonist at nicotinic acetylcholine receptors (nAChRs), the sites responsible for the dopamine effects of nicotine. It partially stimulates these receptors to produce a modest level of dopamine but blocks nicotine from binding to many of the nicotinic receptor sites. *Varenicline binds to nicotinic receptors more potently than nicotine itself. By blocking these receptors, it reduces effects of nicotine in cases where patient relapses and uses tobacco.*

USES Adjunct for smoking cessation in patients experiencing nicotine withdrawal.

CONTRAINDICATIONS Pregnancy (category C), lactation. Safe use in children or adolescents <18 y is not known.

CAUTIOUS USE Renal disease, impaired renal function, renal failure, older adults

ROUTE & DOSAGE

Smoking Cessation

Adult: **PO** Begin with 0.5 mg/d for 3 d, increase to 0.5 mg b.i.d. for 4 d, then increase to 1 mg b.i.d. on day 8. Treatment duration is 12 wk and may be repeated an additional 12 wk for patients who respond.

Renal Impairment

$Cl_{cr} \leq 50$ mL/min: Titrate to 0.5 mg b.i.d. (max)

ADMINISTRATION

Oral

- Give after a meal with a full glass of water.
- Dose titration over 8 d (from 0.5 mg to 2 mg daily) is recommended to minimize adverse effects.
- Store at 15°–30° C (59°–86° F).

ADVERSE EFFECTS (≥1%) **Body as a Whole:** Fatigue, flushing, gingivitis, headache, influenza-like symptoms, lethargy, malaise, thirst. **CNS:** *Abnormal dreams,* anorexia, anxiety, asthenia, disturbance in attention, depression, dizziness, drowsiness, emotional lability, *insomnia,* irritability, *nightmares,* restlessness, sensory disturbance, *sleep disorder.* **CV:** Chest pain, hypertension. **GI:** Abdominal pain, *constipation,* diarrhea, dyspepsia, *flatulence,* gastroesophageal reflux, *nausea, vomiting.* **Metabolic:** Abnormal liver function test, appetite stimulation, weight gain. **Musculoskeletal:** Arthralgia, back pain, muscle cramps, musculoskeletal pain, myalgia. **Respiratory:** Dyspnea, epistaxis, respiratory disorder, rhinorrhea. **Skin:** Hyperhidrosis, pruritus, rash. **Special Senses:** Dysgeusia, xerostomia. **Urogenital:** Menstrual irregularity, polyuria.

V

Common adverse effects in *italic,* life-threatening effects underlined; generic names in **bold**; classifications in SMALL CAPS; ♣ Canadian drug name; ⊘ Prototype drug

1579

INTERACTIONS Drug: Cimetidine increases systemic exposure to varenicline by 29%.

PHARMACOKINETICS Absorption: Complete absorption from GI tract. **Peak:** 3–4 h. **Distribution:** <20% protein bound. **Metabolism:** Minimal. **Elimination:** Primarily eliminated unchanged in the urine. **Half-Life:** 24 h.

CLINICAL IMPLICATIONS

Assessment & Drug Effects

- Monitor smoking cessation behavior and adverse effects.
- Monitor BP for new-onset hypertension.
- Monitor diabetics for loss of glycemic control.

Patient & Family Education

- Follow directions for taking the drug (see Administration).
- Report persistent nausea, vomiting, or insomnia to a health care provider.

VARICELLA VACCINE

(var-i-cel′la)

Varivax

Classifications: VACCINE, VIRAL
Therapeutic: VIRAL VACCINE
Prototype: Hepatitis B
Pregnancy Category: C

AVAILABILITY 1350 PFU/vial

ACTION & *THERAPEUTIC EFFECT*

A live attenuated vaccine that acts against both chickenpox and shingles, both of which are caused by *Varicella zoster* infection. *Effective in protecting healthy children and adults from varicella.*

USES Vaccination against varicella in individuals ≥12 mo.

CONTRAINDICATIONS Hypersensitivity to any component of the vaccine; history of anaphylactoid reaction to neomycin; individuals with blood dyscrasia, leukemia, lymphomas, bone marrow or lymphatic system malignancies, concomitant immunosuppression therapy; individuals with primary or acquired immunodeficient states; active untreated tuberculosis; any febrile respiratory illness or other febrile infections; pregnancy (category C); children <1 y.

CAUTIOUS USE Acute lymphoblastic leukemia in remission; IgA deficiency; lactation.

ROUTE & DOSAGE

Varicella Protection

Adult: **SC** Primary immunization of 0.5 mL followed by 0.5 mL 4–8 wk after first dose, may need to revaccinate 3 mo after initial series if patient fails to seroconvert

Child: **SC** 12 mo–12 y, Single dose of 0.5 mL

ADMINISTRATION

Subcutaneous

- Reconstitute vaccine with 0.7 mL of supplied diluent; gently agitate the vial to mix. Withdraw entire contents of vial (0.5 mL) into syringe for injection. Change needle on syringe and administer immediately or within 30 min of reconstitution.
- Give SC into the outer aspect of the deltoid. Exercise caution not to inject IV.
- Store powder vaccine in frost-free freezer at –15° C (+5° F) or colder. Store diluent separately at room temperature or in the refrigerator.

ADVERSE EFFECTS (≥1%) **CNS:** Headache, fever. **Hematologic:** Mild thrombocytopenia. **Skin:** *Redness,*

V

swelling, or rash at injection site. **Other:** Herpes zoster infection (rare).

INTERACTIONS Drug: Acyclovir decreases vaccine's effectiveness. It is recommended that **yellow fever vaccine** be given at least 1 mo apart from varicella or any other live virus vaccine. Avoid **salicylates** for 6 wk after vaccination to decrease risk of developing Reye's syndrome.

PHARMACOKINETICS Onset: Seroconversion approximately 42 d after vaccination. **Duration:** >5–10 y in healthy children. **Distribution:** Crosses placenta; distributed into breast milk.

CLINICAL IMPLICATIONS

Assessment & Drug Effects
- Withhold vaccine and notify physician if patient has a history of hypersensitivity to neomycin or a current febrile infection.
- Monitor for signs and symptoms of hypersensitivity (see Appendix F) and administer epinephrine if an anaphylactoid reaction occurs.

Patient & Family Education
- Avoid use of salicylates (e.g., acetylsalicylic acid) for 6 wk after vaccination, especially with children and adolescents.
- Notify physician about all adverse reactions (i.e., fever, rash, respiratory illness).

VASOPRESSIN INJECTION 🅟🅡

(vay-soe-press′in)
Classifications: HORMONE; PITUITARY, ANTIDIURETIC HORMONE (ADH)
Therapeutic: ADH REPLACEMENT
Pregnancy Category: C

AVAILABILITY 20 pressor units/mL injection

ACTION & *THERAPEUTIC EFFECT*
Polypeptide hormone extracted from animal posterior pituitaries. Possesses pressor and antidiuretic (ADH) properties, but is relatively free of oxytocic properties. Produces concentrated urine by increasing tubular reabsorption of water, preserving up to 90% of water in the renal tubules. *Effective in reversing diuresis caused by diabetes insipidus.*

USES Antidiuretic to treat diabetes insipidus, to dispel gas shadows in abdominal roentgenography, and as prevention and treatment of postoperative abdominal distension. Also given to treat transient polyuria due to ADH deficiency (related to head injuries or to neurosurgery).
UNLABELED USES Test for differential diagnosis of nephrogenic, psychogenic, and neurohypophyseal diabetes insipidus; test to elevate ability of kidney to concentrate urine, and provocative test for pituitary release of corticotropin and growth hormone; emergency and adjunct pressor agent in the control of massive GI hemorrhage (e.g., esophageal varices).

CONTRAINDICATIONS Chronic nephritis accompanied by nitrogen retention; ischemic heart disease, PVCs, advanced arteriosclerosis; pregnancy (category C); during first stage of labor; lactation.
CAUTIOUS USE Epilepsy; migraine; asthma; heart failure, angina pectoris; any state in which rapid addition to extracellular fluid may be hazardous; vascular disease; preoperative and postoperative polyuric patients, kidney disease; goiter with cardiac complications; older adult patients, children.

V

Common adverse effects in *italic*, life-threatening effects underlined; generic names in **bold**; classifications in SMALL CAPS; ✦ Canadian drug name; 🅟 Prototype drug

1581

ROUTE & DOSAGE

Diabetes Insipidus
Adult: **IM/SC** 5–10 U aqueous solution 2–4 times/d (5–60 U/d) or 1.25–2.5 U in oil q2–3d
Intranasal Apply to cotton pledget or intranasal spray
Child: **IM/SC** 2.5–10 U aqueous solution 2–4 times/d

Abdominal Distention, Abdominal Radiographic Procedures
Adult: **IM/SC** 5 U with 5–10 U q3–4h prn or 5–15 U 2 h and 30 min prior to procedure

GI Hemorrhage
Adult: **IV** 0.2–0.4 U/min up to 0.9 U/min

ADMINISTRATION

Intramuscular, Subcutaneous
- Give 1–2 glasses of water with vasopressin to reduce adverse effects of tannate and improve therapeutic response.
- Do NOT administer vasopressin tannate via IV. Warm ampule to body temperature and shake vigorously to disperse active principle before withdrawing drug for IM administration.
- The tannate injection is often painful, and allergic reactions may develop. It is preferred for use in chronic therapy because of its longer duration of action.

Intravenous

PREPARE: IV Infusion: Give vasopressin aqueous injection by continuous IV. Dilute with NS or D5W to a concentration of 0.1–1 U/mL.

ADMINISTER: IV Infusion: Titrate dose and rate to patient's response.

ADVERSE EFFECTS (≥1%) **Skin:** Rash, urticaria. **Body as a Whole:** <u>Anaphylaxis</u>; *tremor,* sweating, bronchoconstriction, *circumoral and facial pallor,* angioneurotic edema, *pounding in head, water intoxication* (especially with tannate), gangrene at injection site with intraarterial infusion. **GI:** *Eructations, passage of gas, nausea, vomiting,* heartburn, abdominal cramps, increased bowel movements secondary to excessive use. **CV:** Angina (in patient with coronary vascular disease); <u>cardiac arrest</u>, hypertension, bradycardia, minor arrhythmias, premature atrial contraction, heart block, peripheral vascular collapse, coronary insufficiency, <u>MI</u>; cardiac arrhythmia, pulmonary edema, bradycardia (with intraarterial infusion). **Urogenital:** Uterine cramps. **Respiratory:** Congestion, rhinorrhea, irritation, mucosal ulceration and pruritus, postnasal drip. **Special Senses:** Conjunctivitis.

DIAGNOSTIC TEST INTERFERENCE
Vasopressin increases *plasma cortisol* levels.

INTERACTIONS Drug: **Alcohol, demeclocycline, epinephrine, heparin, lithium, phenytoin** may decrease antidiuretic effects of vasopressin; **guanethidine, neostigmine** increase vasopressor actions; **chlorpropamide, clofibrate, carbamazepine,** THIAZIDE DIURETICS may increase antidiuretic activity.

PHARMACOKINETICS Duration: 2–8 h in aqueous solution, 48–72 h in oil, 30–60 min IV infusion. **Distribution:** Extracellular fluid. **Metabolism:** In liver and kidneys. **Elimination:** In urine. **Half-Life:** 10–20 min.

CLINICAL IMPLICATIONS
Assessment & Drug Effects
- Monitor infants and children closely. They are more suscepti-

ble to volume disturbances (such as sudden reversal of polyuria) than adults.

- Establish baseline data of BP, weight, I&O pattern and ratio. Monitor BP and weight throughout therapy. (Dose used to stimulate diuresis has little effect on BP.) Report sudden changes in pattern to physician.

- Be alert to the fact that even small doses of vasopressin may precipitate MI or coronary insufficiency, especially in older adult patients. Keep emergency equipment and drugs (antiarrhythmics) readily available.

- Check patient's alertness and orientation frequently during therapy. Lethargy and confusion associated with headache may signal onset of water intoxication, which, although insidious in rate of development, can lead to convulsions and terminal coma.

- Monitor urine output, specific gravity, and serum osmolality while patient is hospitalized.

- Withhold vasopressin, restrict fluid intake, and notify physician if urine-specific gravity is <1.015.

Patient & Family Education

- Be prepared for possibility of anginal attack and have coronary vasodilator available (e.g., nitroglycerin) if there is a history of coronary artery disease. Report to physician.

- Measure and record data related to polydipsia and polyuria. Learn how to determine specific gravity and how to keep an accurate record of output. Understand that treatment should diminish intense thirst and restore undisturbed normal sleep.

- Avoid concentrated fluids (e.g., undiluted syrups), since these increase urine volume.

VECURONIUM
(vek-yoo-roe'nee-um)

Classifications: ACETYLCHOLINE ANTAGONIST; NONDEPOLARIZING SKELETAL MUSCLE RELAXANT
Therapeutic: SKELETAL MUSCLE RELAXANT, NONDEPOLARIZING
Prototype: Atracurium
Pregnancy Category: C

AVAILABILITY 4 mg, 10 mg, 20 mg vials

ACTION & *THERAPEUTIC EFFECT*
Intermediate-acting nondepolarizing skeletal muscle relaxant structurally similar to pancuronium. Inhibits neuromuscular transmission by competitively binding with acetylcholine to motor endplate receptors that result in skeletal muscular relaxation. *Inhibits neuromuscular transmission by competitively binding with acetylcholine to motor endplate receptors resulting in skeletal muscular relaxation.*

USES Adjunct for general anesthesia to produce skeletal muscle relaxation during surgery. Especially useful for patients with severe kidney disease, limited cardiac reserve, and history of asthma or allergy. Also to facilitate endotracheal intubation.

UNLABELED USES Continuous infusion for facilitation of mechanical ventilation.

CONTRAINDICATIONS Hypersensitivity to bromide; pregnancy (category C).

CAUTIOUS USE Severe liver disease; impaired acid–base, fluid and electrolyte balance; severe obesity; adrenal or neuromuscular disease (myasthenia gravis, Eaton-Lambert

Common adverse effects in *italic*, life-threatening effects underlined; generic names in **bold**; classifications in SMALL CAPS; ♣ Canadian drug name; ⊘ Prototype drug

1583

syndrome); patients with slow circulation time (cardiovascular disease, old age, edematous states); malignant hyperthermia; lactation.

ROUTE & DOSAGE

Skeletal Muscle Relaxation

Adult/Child: **IV** ≥1 y, 0.04–0.1 mg/kg initially, then after 25–40 min, 0.01–0.15 mg/kg q12–15 min or 0.001 mg/kg/min by continuous infusion
Infant: **IV** 0.08–0.1 mg/kg, then 0.05–0.1 mg/kg q1h prn
Neonate: **IV** 0.1 mg/kg, followed by 0.03–0.15 mg/kg q1–2h prn

Obesity
Dose on IBW

ADMINISTRATION

Note: Vecuronium is administered only by qualified clinicians.

Intravenous

PREPARE: **Direct:** Dilute 10–20 mg with 50 mL sterile water for injection (supplied). **Continuous:** Further dilute with up to 100 mL D5W, NS, or RL to yield 0.1–0.2 mg/mL.

ADMINISTER: **Direct:** Give a bolus dose over 30 sec. **Continuous:** Give at the required rate.

INCOMPATIBILITIES Y-site: **Amphotericin B cholesteryl complex, diazepam, etomidate, furosemide, thiopental.**

- Refrigerate after reconstitution below 30° C (86° F), unless otherwise directed. Discard solution after 24 h.

ADVERSE EFFECTS (≥1%) **Body as a Whole:** Skeletal muscle weakness, <u>malignant hyperthermia</u>. **Respiratory:** <u>Respiratory depression</u>.

INTERACTIONS Drug: GENERAL ANESTHETICS increase neuromuscular blockade and duration of action; AMINOGLYCOSIDES, **bacitracin, polymyxin B, clindamycin, lidocaine, parenteral magnesium, quinidine, quinine, trimethaphan, verapamil** increase neuromuscular blockade; DIURETICS may increase or decrease neuromuscular blockade; **lithium** prolongs duration of neuromuscular blockade; NARCOTIC ANALGESICS increase possibility of additive respiratory depression; **succinylcholine** increases onset and depth of neuromuscular blockade; **phenytoin** may cause resistance to or reversal of neuromuscular blockade.

PHARMACOKINETICS Onset: <1 min. **Peak:** 3–5 min. **Duration:** 25–40 min. **Distribution:** Well distributed to tissues and extracellular fluids; crosses placenta; distribution into breast milk unknown. **Metabolism:** Rapid nonenzymatic degradation in bloodstream. **Elimination:** 30–35% in urine, 30–35% in bile. **Half-Life:** 30–80 min.

CLINICAL IMPLICATIONS

Assessment & Drug Effects

- Lab tests: Baseline serum electrolytes, acid–base balance, and kidney & liver functions.
- Use peripheral nerve stimulator during and following drug administration to avoid risk of overdosage and to identify residual paralysis during recovery period. This is especially indicated when cautious use of drug is specified.
- Monitor vital signs at least q15 min until stable, then every 30 min for the next 2 h. Also monitor airway patency until assured that patient has fully recovered from drug effects. Note rate, depth, and pattern of respirations. Obese patients and patients with myasthenia gravis or other neuromuscular

disease may have ventilation problems.

- Evaluate patients for recovery from neuromuscular blocking (curare-like) effects as evidenced by ability to breathe naturally or take deep breaths and cough, to keep eyes open, and to lift head keeping mouth closed and by adequacy of hand grip strength. Notify physician if recovery is delayed.
- Note: Recovery time may be delayed in patients with cardiovascular disease, edematous states, and in older adults.

VENLAFAXINE ⓟ

(ven-la-fax′een)

Effexor, Effexor XR

Classifications: PSYCHOTHERAPEUTIC; ANTIDEPRESSANT; SEROTONIN NOREPINEPHRINE REUPTAKE INHIBITOR (SNRI)

Therapeutic: ANTIDEPRESSANT (SNRI)

Pregnancy Category: C

AVAILABILITY 25 mg, 37.5 mg, 50 mg, 75 mg, 100 mg tablets; 37.5 mg, 75 mg, 150 mg sustained release capsules

ACTION & *THERAPEUTIC EFFECT*

Potent inhibitor of neuronal serotonin and norepinephrine reuptake and weak inhibitor of dopamine reuptake. *Antidepressant effect presumed to be due to potentiation of neurotransmitter activity in the CNS.*

USES Depression, generalized anxiety disorder; social anxiety disorder.
UNLABELED USES Obsessive-compulsive disorder.

CONTRAINDICATIONS Hypersensitivity to venlafaxine, or other SNRI drugs; concurrent administration with MAO inhibitors; abrupt discontinuation; neonates; pregnancy (category C), lactation.

CAUTIOUS USE Renal and hepatic impairment, renal failure; anorexia nervosa, history of mania, suicidal ideations; elevated intraocular pressure, acute closed-angle glaucoma; cardiac disorders, recent MI, heart failure; hypertension; hyperthyroidism; concomitant administration with CNS drugs, CNS depression; history of seizures or seizure disorders; older adults. Safety in children <18 y is not established.

ROUTE & DOSAGE

Depression

Adult: **PO** 25–125 mg t.i.d.
Geriatric: **PO** Start with lower doses in older adults

Anxiety

Adult: **PO** Start with 37.5 mg sustained release q.d. and increase to 75–225 mg sustained release per day

Renal Impairment

Cl_{cr} 10–70 mL/min: reduce total daily dose by 25–50%; <10 mL/min: reduce total daily dose by 50%

ADMINISTRATION

Oral

- Give with food. Sustained release capsules must be swallowed whole, must not be opened or chewed.
- Dosage increments of up to 75 mg/d are usually made at 4 d or longer intervals.
- Allow 14 d interval after discontinuing an MAO inhibitor before starting venlafaxine.
- Do not abruptly withdraw drug after 1 wk or more of therapy.

V

Common adverse effects in *italic*, life-threatening effects <u>underlined</u>; generic names in **bold**, classifications in SMALL CAPS; ♣ Canadian drug name; ⓟ Prototype drug

1585

- Store at room temperature, 15°–30° C (59°–86° F).

ADVERSE EFFECTS (≥1%) **CV:** *Increased blood pressure and heart rate,* palpitations. **CNS:** *Dizziness,* fatigue, headache, anxiety, insomnia, *somnolence.* **Endocrine:** Small but statistically significant increase in serum cholesterol, weight loss (approximately 3 lb). **GI:** *Nausea, vomiting, dry mouth,* constipation. **Urogenital:** Sexual dysfunction, erectile failure, delayed orgasm, anorgasmia, impotence, abnormal ejaculation. **Special Senses:** Blurred vision. **Body as a Whole:** *Sweating,* asthenia.

INTERACTIONS Drug: Cimetidine, MAO INHIBITORS, **desipramine, haloperidol** may increase venlafaxine levels and toxicity. Should not use in combination with MAO INHIBITORS: do not start until >14 d after stopping MAO INHIBITOR; do not start MAO INHIBITOR until 7 d after stopping venlafaxine. **Trazodone** may lead to **serotonin** syndrome. **Herbal: St. John's wort**, sour date nut may cause **serotonin** syndrome.

PHARMACOKINETICS Absorption: Well absorbed from GI tract. **Onset:** 2 wk. **Peak:** Venlafaxine 1–2 h; metabolite 3–4 h. **Duration:** Approximately 30% protein bound, but extensively tissue bound. **Metabolism:** Undergoes substantial first-pass metabolism to its major active metabolite, O-desmethylvenlafaxine, with similar activity to venlafaxine. **Elimination:** ~60% in urine as parent compound and metabolites. **Half-Life:** Venlafaxine 3–4 h, O-desmethylvenlafaxine 10 h.

CLINICAL IMPLICATIONS
Assessment & Drug Effects
- Monitor for worsening of depression or emergence of suicidal ideation.

- Monitor cardiovascular status periodically with measurements of HR and BP.
- Lab tests: Periodic lipid profile.
- Monitor neurologic status and report excessive anxiety, nervousness, and insomnia.
- Monitor weight periodically and report excess weight loss.
- Assess safety, as dizziness and sedation are common.

Patient & Family Education
- Be aware of potential adverse effects and notify physician of those that are bothersome.
- Do not drive or engage in potentially hazardous activities until response to drug is known.
- Avoid using alcohol while on venlafaxine.
- Do not use herbal medications without consulting physician.

VERAPAMIL HYDROCHLORIDE ℗

(ver-ap'a-mill)

Calan, Calan SR, Covera-HS, Isoptin, Isoptin SR, Verelan, Verelan PM

Classifications: CALCIUM CHANNEL BLOCKER; ANTIARRHYTHMIC CLASS IV; ANTIHYPERTENSIVE
Therapeutic: ANTIARRHYTHMIC, CLASS IV; CALCIUM CHANNEL BLOCKER, ANTIHYPERTENSIVE
Pregnancy Category: C

AVAILABILITY 40 mg, 80 mg, 120 mg tablets; 120 mg, 180 mg, 240 mg sustained release tablets; 100 mg, 120 mg, 180 mg, 200 mg, 240 mg, 300 mg sustained release capsules; 5 mg/2 mL injection

ACTION & *THERAPEUTIC EFFECT*
Inhibits calcium ion influx through slow channels into cells

V

of myocardial and arterial smooth muscle. Dilates coronary arteries and arterioles and inhibits coronary artery spasm. Decreases and slows SA and AV node conduction without affecting normal arterial action potential or intraventricular conduction. *Decreases angina attacks by dilating coronary arteries and inhibiting coronary vasospasms. Decreases nodal conduction, resulting in an antiarrhythmic effect. Dilates peripheral arterioles, causing decreased total peripheral vascular resistance with reduction in BP.*

USES Supraventricular tachyarrhythmias; Prinzmetal's (variant) angina, chronic stable angina; unstable, crescendo or preinfarctive angina and essential hypertension.

UNLABELED USES Paroxysmal supraventricular tachycardia, atrial fibrillation; prophylaxis of migraine headache; and as alternate therapy in manic depression.

CONTRAINDICATIONS Severe hypotension (systolic <90 mm Hg), cardiogenic shock, cardiomegaly, digitalis toxicity, second- or third-degree AV block; Wolff-Parkinson-White syndrome including atrial flutter and fibrillation; accessory AV pathway, left ventricular dysfunction, severe CHF, sinus node disease, sick sinus syndrome (except in patients with functioning ventricular pacemaker); pregnancy (category C); children <18 y (extended release tablets).

CAUTIOUS USE Duchenne's muscular dystrophy; hepatic and renal impairment; MI followed by coronary occlusion, aortic stenosis; GI obstruction, GERD, hiatal hernia, ileus; IV form in neonates or infants.

ROUTE & DOSAGE

Angina
Adult: **PO** 80 mg q6–8h, may increase up to 320–480 mg/d in divided doses (Note: Covera-HS must be given once daily h.s.)

Hypertension
Adult: **PO** 80 mg t.i.d. or 90–240 mg sustained release 1–2 times/d up to 480 mg/d (Note: Covera-HS must be given once daily h.s.)

Supraventricular Tachycardia, Atrial Fibrillation
Adult: **IV** 2.5–5 mg initial dose, then 5–10 mg after 15–30 min (max total dose: 20 mg)
Child: **IV** <1 y, 0.1–0.2 mg/kg q30min prn; *1–15 y*, 0.1–0.3 mg/kg (max dose: 5 mg)

Renal Impairment
Cl_{cr} <10 mL/min: give 50–75% of dose
Hemodialysis: Supplemental dose not necessary

Hepatic Impairment
In cirrhosis, use 20–50% of normal dose

ADMINISTRATION

Oral
- Give with food to reduce gastric irritation.
- Capsules can be opened and contents sprinkled on food. DO NOT dissolve or chew capsule contents.
- Give Covera-HS once a day in the evening.
- Do not withdraw abruptly; may increase and extend duration of pain in the angina patient.

Intravenous
PREPARE: **IV Direct:** Given undiluted or diluted in 5 mL of sterile

V

Common adverse effects in *italic*, life-threatening effects underlined; generic names in **bold**; classifications in SMALL CAPS; ♣ Canadian drug name; ⊘ Prototype drug

1587

water for injection. Inspect parenteral drug preparation before administration. Make sure solution is clear and colorless.

ADMINISTER: **Direct:** Give a single dose over 2–3 min.

INCOMPATIBILITIES **Solution/additive: Albumin, aminophylline, amphotericin B, hydralazine, trimethoprim/sulfamethoxazole.** Y-site: **Albumin, amphotericin B cholesteryl complex, ampicillin, mezlocillin, nafcillin, oxacillin, propofol, sodium bicarbonate.**

- Store at 15°–30° C (59°–86° F) and protect from light.

ADVERSE EFFECTS (≥1%) **CNS:** Dizziness, vertigo, *headache,* fatigue, sleep disturbances, depression, syncope. **CV:** *Hypotension,* congestive heart failure, bradycardia, severe tachycardia, peripheral edema, <u>AV block</u>. **GI:** Nausea, abdominal discomfort, *constipation,* elevated liver enzymes. **Body as a Whole:** Flushing, pulmonary edema, muscle fatigue, diaphoresis. **Skin:** Pruritus.

DIAGNOSTIC TEST INTERFERENCE Verapamil may cause elevations of serum *AST, ALT, alkaline phosphatase.*

INTERACTIONS Drug: BETA BLOCKERS increase risk of CHF, bradycardia, or heart block; significantly increased levels of **digoxin** and **carbamazepine** and toxicity; potentiates hypotensive effects of HYPOTENSIVE AGENTS; levels of **lithium** and **cyclosporine** may be increased, increasing their toxicity; **calcium salts** (IV) may antagonize verapamil effects. **Food:** Grapefruit juice may increase verapamil levels. **Herbal: Hawthorne** may have additive hypotensive effects. **St. John's wort** may decrease efficacy.

PHARMACOKINETICS Absorption: 90% absorbed, but only 25–30% reaches systemic circulation (first pass metabolism). **Peak:** 1–2 h PO; 4–8 h sustained release; 5 min IV. **Distribution:** Widely distributed, including CNS; crosses placenta; present in breast milk. **Metabolism:** In liver (CYP3A4). **Elimination:** 70% in urine; 16% in feces. **Half-Life:** 2–8 h.

CLINICAL IMPLICATIONS

Assessment & Drug Effects

- Monitor therapeutic effectiveness. Drug should decrease angina frequency, nitroglycerin consumption, and episodes of ST segment deviation.
- Establish baseline data and periodically monitor: BP and pulse.
- Lab tests: Baseline and periodic liver and kidney functions.
- Instruct patient to remain in recumbent position for at least 1 h after dose is given to diminish subjective effects of transient asymptomatic hypotension that may accompany infusion.
- Monitor for AV block or excessive bradycardia when infusion is given concurrently with digitalis.
- Monitor I&O ratio during IV and early oral maintenance therapy. Renal impairment prolongs duration of action, increasing potential for toxicity and incidence of adverse effects. Advise patient to report gradual weight gain and evidence of edema.
- Monitor ECG continuously during IV administration. Essential because drug action may be prolonged and incidence of adverse reactions is highest during IV administration in older adults, patients with impaired kidney function, and patients of small stature.

Common adverse effects in *italic,* life-threatening effects <u>underlined</u>; generic names in **bold**; classifications in SMALL CAPS; ✦ Canadian drug name; ⊙ Prototype drug

- Check BP shortly before administration of next dose to evaluate degree of control during early treatment for hypertension.

Patient & Family Education

- Monitor radial pulse before each dose, notify physician of an irregular pulse or one slower than established guideline.
- Adhere to established guidelines for exercise program.
- Do not drive or engage in potentially hazardous activities until response to drug is known.
- Decrease intake of caffeine-containing beverage (i.e., coffee, tea, chocolate).
- Change positions slowly from lying down to standing to prevent falls because of drug-related vertigo until tolerance to reduced BP is established.
- Notify physician of easy bruising, petechiae, unexplained bleeding.
- Do not use OTC drugs, especially aspirin, unless they are specifically prescribed by physician.

VINBLASTINE SULFATE

(vin-blast'een)
Classifications: ANTINEOPLASTIC; MITOTIC INHIBITOR
Therapeutic: ANTINEOPLASTIC
Prototype: Vincristine
Pregnancy Category: D

AVAILABILITY 10 mg powder for injection; 1 mg/mL vial

ACTION & *THERAPEUTIC EFFECT*
Cell cycle–specific drug that interferes with microtubules that form the mitotic spindle fibers required to complete the process of mitosis. Has an effect on cell energy production needed for mitosis and interferes with nucleic acid synthe-

sis. *Interrupts the cell cycle in metaphase, thus preventing cell replication.*

USES Palliative treatment of Hodgkin's disease and non-Hodgkin's lymphomas, choriocarcinoma, lymphosarcoma, neuroblastoma, mycosis fungoides, advanced testicular germinal cell cancer, histiocytosis, and other malignancies resistant to other chemotherapy. Used singly or in combination with other chemotherapeutic drugs.

CONTRAINDICATIONS Severe bone marrow suppression, leukopenia, bacterial infection, adynamic ileus; pregnancy (category D), lactation, men and women of childbearing potential, older adult patients with cachexia or skin ulcers.
CAUTIOUS USE Malignant cell infiltration of bone marrow; obstructive jaundice, hepatic impairment; history of gout; use of small amount of drug for long periods; use in eyes.

ROUTE & DOSAGE

Antineoplastic
Adult: **IV** 3.7 mg/m² infused over 1 min q wk, may increase up to 18.5 mg/m² if tolerated
Child: **IV** 2.5 mg/m² infused over 1 min q wk, may increase up to 12.5 mg/m² if tolerated

ADMINISTRATION
Intravenous
PREPARE: **Direct:** Add 10 mL NS to 10 mg of drug (yields 1 mg/mL). Do not use other diluents. Avoid contact with eyes. Severe irritation and persisting corneal changes may occur. Flush immediately and thoroughly with copious amounts of water. Wash

V

Common adverse effects in *italic*, life-threatening effects underlined; generic names in **bold**; classifications in SMALL CAPS; ◆ Canadian drug name; ⓟ Prototype drug

1589

both eyes; do not assume one eye escaped contamination.

***ADMINISTER:* Direct:** Drug is usually injected into tubing of running IV infusion of NS or D5W over period of 1 min. Stop injection promptly if extravasation occurs. Use applications of moderate heat and local injection of hyaluronidase to help disperse extravasated drug. Restart infusion in another vein. Observe injection site for sloughing.

***INCOMPATIBILITIES* Solution/additive: Furosemide, heparin. Y-site: Cefepime, doxorubicin, furosemide.**

■Refrigerate reconstituted solution in tight, light-resistant containers up to 30 d without loss of potency.

ADVERSE EFFECTS (≥1%) **Body as a Whole:** Fever, weight loss, muscular pains, weakness, parotid gland pain and tenderness, tumor site pain, Raynaud's phenomenon. **CNS:** Mental depression, peripheral neuritis, numbness and paresthesias of tongue and extremities, loss of deep tendon reflexes, headache, convulsions. **GI:** Vesiculation of mouth, stomatitis, pharyngitis, anorexia, *nausea, vomiting,* diarrhea, ileus, abdominal pain, constipation, rectal bleeding, <u>hemorrhagic enterocolitis</u>, <u>bleeding of old peptic ulcer</u>. **Hematologic:** <u>Leukopenia</u>, thrombocytopenia, and anemia. **Skin:** *Alopecia (reversible),* vesiculation, photosensitivity, phlebitis, cellulitis, and sloughing following extravasation (at injection site). **Urogenital:** Urinary retention, *hyperuricemia,* aspermia. **Respiratory:** <u>Bronchospasm</u>.

INTERACTIONS Drug: Mitomycin may cause acute shortness of breath and severe bronchospasm; may decrease **phenytoin** levels; ALFA INTERFERONS, **erythromycin, itracona-**zole may increase vinblastine toxicity.

PHARMACOKINETICS Distribution: Concentrates in liver, platelets, and leukocytes; poor penetration of blood–brain barrier. **Metabolism:** Partially in liver. **Elimination:** In feces and urine. **Half-Life:** 24 h.

CLINICAL IMPLICATIONS

Assessment & Drug Effects

■Lab tests: Monitor WBC count. Recovery from leukopenic nadir occurs usually within 7–14 d. With high doses, total leukocyte count may not return to normal for 3 wk.

■Do not administer drug unless WBC count has returned to at least 4000/mm³, even if 7 d have passed.

■Monitor for unexplained bruising or bleeding, which should be promptly reported, even though thrombocyte reduction seldom occurs unless patient has had prior treatment with other antineoplastics.

■Adverse reactions seldom persist beyond 24 h with exception of epilation, leukopenia, and neurologic adverse effects.

■Monitor bowel elimination pattern and bowel sounds to recognize severe constipation or paralytic ileus. A stool softener may be necessary.

■Inspect skin surfaces over pressure areas daily if patient is not ambulating. Note condition of skin of older adults especially.

■Stop drug if oral tissues break down.

Patient & Family Education

■Keep all appointments so that course of treatment is not interrupted.

■Be aware that temporary mental depression sometimes occurs on second or third day after treatment begins.

V

- Avoid exposure to infection, injury to skin or mucous membranes, and excessive physical stress, especially during leukocyte nadir period.
- Notify physician promptly about onset of symptoms of agranulocytosis (see Appendix F). Do not delay seeking appropriate treatment.
- Avoid exposure to sunlight unless protected with sunscreen lotion (SPF >12) and clothing.

VINCRISTINE SULFATE ℗

(vin-kris′teen)

Classifications: ANTINEOPLASTIC; MITOTIC INHIBITOR
Therapeutic: ANTINEOPLASTIC
Pregnancy Category: D

AVAILABILITY 1 mg/mL injection

ACTION & *THERAPEUTIC EFFECT*

Cell cycle–specific vinca alkaloid (obtained from periwinkle plant *Vinca rosea*); analog of vinblastine. Arrests mitosis at metaphase by inhibition of mitotic spindle function, thereby inhibiting cell division. *Induction of metaphase arrest in 50% of cells results in inhibition of cancer cell proliferation.*

USES Acute lymphoblastic and other leukemias, Hodgkin's disease, lymphosarcoma, neuroblastoma, Wilms' tumor, lung and breast cancer, reticular cell carcinoma, and osteogenic and other sarcomas.

UNLABELED USES Idiopathic thrombocytopenic purpura, alone or adjunctively with other antineoplastics.

CONTRAINDICATIONS Obstructive jaundice; pregnancy (category D), lactation, men and women of childbearing potential; active infection; adynamic ileus; radiation of the liver; patient with demyelinating

form of Charcot-Marie-Tooth syndrome.
CAUTIOUS USE Leukopenia; preexisting neuromuscular or neurological disease; hypertension; hepatic or biliary tract disease; elderly; patients receiving drugs with neurotoxic potential.

ROUTE & DOSAGE

Antineoplastic

Adult: **IV** 1.4 mg/m² (max: 2 mg/m²) at weekly intervals
Child: **IV** >10 kg, 1–2 mg/m² at weekly intervals; <10 kg, 0.05 mg/kg initial weekly dose, then titrate

Hepatic Impairment

Bilirubin 1.5–3 mg/dL: use 50% of dose; bilirubin 3–5: use 25% of dose; bilirubin >5: skip dose

ADMINISTRATION

Intravenous

PREPARE: Direct: Reconstitute with provided solution (bacteriostatic NaCl), sterile water, or NS to concentrations of 0.01 to 1.0 mg/mL. Note: Vincristine is available in solution form, which does not require reconstitution. Avoid contact with eyes. Severe irritation and persisting corneal changes may occur. Flush immediately and thoroughly with copious amounts of water. Wash both eyes; do not assume one eye escaped contamination.
ADMINISTER: Direct: Drug is usually injected into tubing of running infusion over a 1 min period. Stop injection promptly if extravasation occurs. Use applications of moderate heat and local injection of hyaluronidase to help disperse extravasated drug. Restart infusion in another vein. Observe injection site for sloughing.

V

Common adverse effects in *italic*, life-threatening effects underlined; generic names in **bold**; classifications in SMALL CAPS; ♣ Canadian drug name; ℗ Prototype drug

1591

INCOMPATIBILITIES Solution/additive: **Furosemide.** Y-site: **Cefepime, furosemide, idarubicin, sodium bicarbonate.**

■ Store solution in the refrigerator.

ADVERSE EFFECTS (≥1%) **CNS:** *Peripheral neuropathy,* neuritic pain, *paresthesias, especially of hands and feet;* foot and hand drop, sensory loss, athetosis, ataxia, loss of deep tendon reflexes, muscle atrophy, dysphagia, weakness in larynx and extrinsic eye muscles, ptosis, diplopia, mental depression. **Special Senses:** Optic atrophy with blindness; transient cortical blindness, ptosis, diplopia, photophobia. **GI:** Stomatitis, pharyngitis, anorexia, nausea, vomiting, diarrhea, abdominal cramps, *severe constipation (upper-colon impaction), paralytic ileus (especially in children),* rectal bleeding; <u>hepatotoxicity</u>. **Urogenital:** Urinary retention, polyuria, dysuria, SIADH (high urinary sodium excretion, hyponatremia, dehydration, hypotension); uric acid nephropathy. **Skin:** Urticaria, rash, *alopecia,* cellulitis and phlebitis following extravasation (at injection site). **Body as a Whole:** Convulsions with hypertension, malaise, fever, headache, pain in parotid gland area, weight loss. **Metabolic:** Hyperuricemia, hyperkalemia. **CV:** Hypertension, hypotension. **Respiratory:** Bronchospasm.

INTERACTIONS Drug: Mitomycin may cause acute shortness of breath and severe bronchospasm; may decrease **digoxin, phenytoin** levels.

PHARMACOKINETICS Distribution: Concentrates in liver, platelets, and leukocytes; poor penetration of blood–brain barrier. **Metabolism:** Partially in liver (CYP3A4). **Elimination:** Primarily in feces. **Half-Life:** 10–155 h.

CLINICAL IMPLICATIONS
Assessment & Drug Effects

■ Monitor I&O ratio and pattern, BP, and temperature daily.

■ Weigh patient under standard conditions weekly or more often if ordered. In the presence of edema or ascites, patient's ideal weight is used to determine dosage. Report a steady gain or sudden weight change to physician.

■ Lab tests: Monitor serum electrolytes and CBC with differential. Complete bone marrow remission in leukemia varies widely and may not occur for as long as 100 d after therapy is started.

■ Be aware that neuromuscular adverse effects, most apt to appear in the patient with preexisting neuromuscular disease, usually disappear after 6 wk of treatment. Children are especially susceptible to neuromuscular adverse effects.

■ Assess for hand muscular weakness, and check deep tendon reflexes (depression of Achilles reflex is the earliest sign of neuropathy). Also observe for and report promptly: Mental depression, ptosis, double vision, hoarseness, paresthesias, neuritic pain, and motor difficulties.

■ Provide special protection against infection or injury during leukopenic days. Leukopenia occurs in a significant number of patients; leukocyte count in children usually reaches nadir on fourth day and begins to rise on fifth day after drug administration.

■ Avoid use of rectal thermometer or intrusive tubing to prevent injury to rectal mucosa.

■ Check patient's ability to ambulate and supply support if necessary. Walking may be impaired.

■ Take care to distinguish between the depression associated with re-

V

alization of neoplastic disease and that which is drug-induced.

Patient & Family Education

- Notify physician promptly of stomach, bone, or joint pain, and swelling of lower legs and ankles.
- Start a prophylactic regimen against constipation and paralytic ileus (adequate fluids, high-fiber diet, laxatives) at beginning of treatment and report changes in bowel habit to health care providers as soon as manifested (paralytic ileus is most likely to occur in young children).
- Reversible hair loss is reportedly the most common adverse reaction and may persist for the duration of therapy. Regrowth may start before end of treatment. This is a distressing adverse effect because the scalp hair will drop out in large clumps.

VINORELBINE TARTRATE

(vin-o-rel'been)
Navelbine
Classifications: ANTINEOPLASTIC AGENT; MITOTIC INHIBITOR
Therapeutic: ANTINEOPLASTIC
Prototype: Vincristine
Pregnancy Category: D

AVAILABILITY 10 mg/mL injection

ACTION & *THERAPEUTIC EFFECT*
A semisynthetic vinca alkaloid with antineoplastic activity. Inhibits polymerization of tubules into microtubules, which disrupts mitotic spindle formation. *Arrests mitosis at metaphase, thereby inhibiting cell division in cancer cells.*

USES Non-small cell lung cancer.
UNLABELED USES Breast cancer, ovarian cancer, Hodgkin's disease.

CONTRAINDICATIONS Hypersensitivity to vinorelbine, infection; severe bone marrow suppression; pregnancy (category D), lactation.
CAUTIOUS USE Hypersensitivity to vincristine or vinblastine; leukopenia or other indicator(s) of bone marrow suppression; chickenpox or herpes zoster infection; hepatic insufficiency; pulmonary disease; pre-existing neurologic or neuromuscular disorders. Safety and efficacy in children are not established.

ROUTE & DOSAGE

Non-Small Cell Lung Cancer, Breast Cancer
Adult: IV 30 mg/m^2 weekly
Hepatic Impairment
Bilirubin 2.1–3 mg/dL: use 50% of dose; bilirubin >3 mg/dL: use 25% of dose

ADMINISTRATION

Intravenous
Use caution to prevent contact with skin, mucous membranes, or eyes during preparation.

***PREPARE:* Direct:** Dilute each 10 mg in a syringe with either 2 or 5 mL of D5W or NS to yield 3 mg/mL or 1.5 mg/L, respectively. **IV Infusion:** Dilute the 10 mg/mL dose in an IV bag with D5W, NS, or RL to a final concentration of 0.5–2 mg/mL (example: 10 mg diluted in 19 mL yields 0.5 mg/mL).
***ADMINISTER:* IV Infusion:** Give diluted solution over 6–10 min into the side port closest to an IV bag with free-flowing IV solution; follow by flushing with at least 75–125 mL of IV solution over 10 min. Take every precaution to avoid extravasation. If suspected, discontinue IV immediately and begin in a different site.

V

Common adverse effects in *italic*, life-threatening effects <u>underlined</u>; generic names in **bold**; classifications in SMALL CAPS; ✦ Canadian drug name; ⊕ Prototype drug

INCOMPATIBILITIES Solution/additive: Acyclovir, aminophylline, amphotericin B, ampicillin, cefazolin, cefoperazone, ceforanide, cefotaxime, cefotetan, ceftazidime, ceftriaxone, cefuroxime, fluorouracil, furosemide, ganciclovir, methylprednisolone, mitomycin, piperacillin, sodium bicarbonate, thiotepa, trimethoprim-sulfamethoxazole. Y-site: Acyclovir, allopurinol, aminophylline, amphotericin B, amphotericin B cholesteryl complex, ampicillin, cefazolin, cefoperazone, cefotetan, ceftriaxone, cefuroxime, fluorouracil, furosemide, ganciclovir, methylprednisolone, mitomycin, piperacillin, sodium bicarbonate, thiotepa, trimethoprim-sulfamethoxazole.

▪ Store at 2°–8° C (36°–46° F).

ADVERSE EFFECTS (≥1%) **CNS:** *Decreased deep tendon reflexes, paresthesia, fatigue, asthenia, peripheral neuropathy,* myalgia, jaw pain. **Hematologic:** *Anemia, neutropenia, granulocytopenia,* thrombocytopenia. **GI:** Paralytic ileus, *constipation, nausea, vomiting, diarrhea,* stomatitis, mucositis, hepatotoxicity *(elevated LFT).* **Body as a Whole:** *Pain on injection,* venous pain, thrombophlebitis, *alopecia,* myalgia, muscle weakness.

INTERACTIONS Drug: Increased severity of granulocytopenia in combination with **cisplatin;** increased risk of acute pulmonary reactions in combination with **mitomycin; paclitaxel** may increase neuropathy.

PHARMACOKINETICS Distribution: 60–80% bound to plasma proteins (including platelets and lymphocytes); sequestered in tissues, especially lung, spleen, liver, and kidney, and released slowly. **Metabolism:** In liver (CYP3A4). **Elimination:** Primarily in bile and feces (50%), 10% in urine. **Half-Life:** 42–45 h.

CLINICAL IMPLICATIONS

Assessment & Drug Effects
▪ Lab tests: Monitor CBC with differential throughout therapy and on the day of treatment prior to each infusion. Monitor kidney & liver functions and serum electrolytes periodically.
▪ Withhold drug and notify physician if the granulocyte count is below 1000 cells/mm^3.
▪ Monitor for S&S of infection, especially during period of granulocyte nadir 7–10 d after dosing.

Patient & Family Education
▪ Be aware of potential and inevitable adverse effects.
▪ Notify physician of distressing adverse effects, especially symptoms of leukopenia (e.g., chills, fever, cough) and peripheral neuropathy.

VITAMIN A
(vye'ta-min)
Aquasol A, Del-Vi-A
Classifications: VITAMIN
Therapeutic: VITAMIN A REPLACEMENT
Pregnancy Category: A (X if >RDA)

AVAILABILITY 5,000 IU tablets 10,000 IU, 15,000 IU, 25,000 IU capsules; 50,000 IU/mL injection

ACTION & *THERAPEUTIC EFFECT*
Vitamin A, a fat-soluble vitamin, acts as a cofactor in mucopolysaccharide synthesis, cholesterol synthesis, and the metabolism of hydroxysteroids. *Essential for normal growth and development of bones and teeth, for integrity of epi-*

thelial and mucosal surfaces, and for synthesis of visual purple necessary for visual adaptation to the dark. Has antioxidant properties.

USES Vitamin A deficiency and as dietary supplement during periods of increased requirements, such as pregnancy, lactation, infancy, and infections. Used as replacement therapy in conditions that affect absorption, mobilization, or storage of vitamin A (e.g., steatorrhea, severe biliary obstruction, liver cirrhosis, total gastrectomy). Used in skin disorders [e.g., folliculosis keratosis (Darier's disease), psoriasis]; however, other retinoids are being preferentially selected. Also used as a screening test for fat malabsorption.

CONTRAINDICATIONS History of sensitivity to vitamin A or to any ingredient in formulation, hypervitaminosis A, oral administration to patients with malabsorption syndrome. Safe use in amounts exceeding 6000 IU during pregnancy [category A (category X if >RDA)] is not established.

CAUTIOUS USE Pregnancy (category A at RDA value); women on oral contraceptives, children, hepatic disease, hepatic dysfunction, hepatitis; low-birth-weight infants; renal disease; lactation.

ROUTE & DOSAGE

Severe Deficiency

Adult: PO 500,000 IU/d for 3 d followed by 50,000 IU/d for 2 wk, then 10,000–20,000 IU/d for 2 mo IM 100,000 IU/d for 3 d followed by 50,000 IU/d for 2 wk
Child: PO/IM <1 y, 10,000 IU/kg/d for 3 d followed by 7500–15,000 IU/d for 10 d; 1–8 y, 10,000 IU/kg/d for 3 d followed by 17,000–35,000 IU/d for 2 wk; >8 y, same as for adult

Dietary Supplement

Child: PO <4 y, 10,000 IU/d; 4–8 y, 15,000 IU/d

ADMINISTRATION

Oral
- Give on an empty stomach or following food or milk if GI upset occurs.
- Store in tight, light-resistant containers.

ADVERSE EFFECTS (≥1%) **CNS:** Irritability, headache, intracranial hypertension (pseudotumor cerebri), increased intracranial pressure, bulging fontanelles, papilledema, exophthalmos, miosis, nystagmus. **Metabolic:** Hypervitaminosis A syndrome (malaise, lethargy, abdominal discomfort, anorexia, vomiting), hypercalcemia. **Musculoskeletal:** Slow growth; deep, tender, hard lumps (subperiosteal thickening) over radius, tibia, occiput; migratory arthralgia; retarded growth; premature closure of epiphyses. **Skin:** Gingivitis, lip fissures, excessive sweating, drying or cracking of skin, pruritus, increase in skin pigmentation, massive desquamation, brittle nails, alopecia. **Urogenital:** Hypomenorrhea. **GI:** Hepatosplenomegaly, jaundice. **Endocrine:** Polydipsia, polyurea. **Hematologic:** Leukopenia, hypoplastic anemias, vitamin A plasma levels >1200 IU/dL, elevations of sedimentation rate and prothrombin time. **Body as a Whole:** <u>Anaphylaxis, death</u> (after IV use).

DIAGNOSTIC TEST INTERFERENCE Vitamin A may falsely increase *serum cholesterol* determinations *(Zlatkis-Zak reaction);* may falsely elevate *bilirubin* determination (with *Ehrlich's reagent*).

V

Common adverse effects in *italic*, life-threatening effects underlined; generic names in **bold**; classifications in SMALL CAPS; ✦ Canadian drug name; ⊕ Prototype drug

1595

INTERACTIONS Drug: Mineral oil, cholestyramine may decrease absorption of vitamin A.

PHARMACOKINETICS Absorption: Readily absorbed from GI tract in presence of bile salts, pancreatic lipase, and dietary fat. **Distribution:** Stored mainly in liver; small amounts also found in kidney and body fat; distributed into breast milk. **Metabolism:** In liver. **Elimination:** In feces and urine.

CLINICAL IMPLICATIONS

Assessment & Drug Effects

- Evaluate dosage with consideration of patient's average daily intake of vitamin A. Take dietary and drug history (e.g., intake of fortified foods, dietary supplements, self-administration or prescription drug sources). Women taking oral contraceptives tend to have significantly high plasma vitamin A levels.
- Monitor therapeutic effectiveness. Vitamin A deficiency is often associated with protein malnutrition as well as other vitamin deficiencies. It may manifest as night blindness, restriction of growth and development, epithelial alterations, susceptibility to infection, abnormal dryness of skin, mouth, and eyes (xerophthalmia) progressing to keratomalacia (ulceration and necrosis of cornea and conjunctiva), and urinary tract calculi.

Patient & Family Education

- Avoid use of mineral oil while on vitamin A therapy.
- Notify physician of symptoms of overdosage (e.g., nausea, vomiting, anorexia, drying and cracking of skin or lips, headache, loss of hair).

VITAMIN B₁
See Thiamine HCl.

VITAMIN B₂
See Riboflavin.

VITAMIN B₃
See Niacin.

VITAMIN B₆
See Pyridoxine.

VITAMIN B₉
See Folic acid.

VITAMIN B₁₂
See Cyanocobalamin.

VITAMIN B₁₂ₐ
See Hydroxocobalamin.

VITAMIN C
See Ascorbic acid.

VITAMIN D
See Calcitriol, Ergocalciferol.

VITAMIN E (TOCOPHEROL)
(vit′a-min E)

Aquasol E, Vita-Plus E, Vitec
Classifications: VITAMIN
Therapeutic: VITAMIN E
Pregnancy Category: A within RDA

AVAILABILITY 100 IU, 200 IU, 400 IU, 500 IU, 800 IU tablets; 100 IU, 200 IU, 400 IU, 1000 IU capsules; 15 IU/0.3 mL, 15 IU/30 mL liquid

ACTION & *THERAPEUTIC EFFECT*

A group of naturally occurring fat-soluble substances known as tocopherols. Alpha tocopherol, comprising 90% of the tocopherols, is the most biologically potent. An antioxidant, it prevents peroxidation, a process that gives rise to free radicals (highly reactive chemical structures that damage cell membranes and alter nuclear proteins). *Prevents cell membrane and protein damage, protects against blood clot formation by decreasing platelet aggregation, enhances vitamin A utilization, and promotes normal growth, development, and tone of muscles.*

USES To treat and prevent hemolytic anemia due to vitamin E deficiency in premature neonates; to prevent retrolental fibroplasia secondary to oxygen treatment in neonates, and in treatment of diseases with secondary erythrocyte membrane abnormalities (e.g., sickle cell anemia, and G6PD deficiency and as supplement in malabsorption syndromes). Used in patients on diets containing large amounts of polyunsaturated fats for long periods and in the patient who abruptly discontinues such a diet. Also used topically for dry or chapped skin and minor skin disorders.

UNLABELED USES Muscular dystrophy and a number of other conditions with no conclusive evidence of value. A component of many multivitamin formulations and of topical deodorant preparations as an antioxidant.

CONTRAINDICATIONS Bleeding disorders; thrombocytopenia; concurrent administration with Coumadin.
CAUTIOUS USE Pregnancy (category A within RDA). Large doses may exacerbate iron deficiency anemia.

ROUTE & DOSAGE

Vitamin E Deficiency
Adult: **PO/IM** 60–75 IU/d
Child: **PO** 1 IU/kg/d
Prophylaxis for Vitamin E Deficiency
Adult: **PO** 12–15 IU/d
Child: **PO** 7–10 IU/d
Neonate: **PO** 5 IU/d

ADMINISTRATION

Oral

- Give on an empty stomach or following food or milk if GI upset occurs.
- Store in tight containers protected from light.

ADVERSE EFFECTS (≥1%) **Body as a Whole:** Skeletal muscle weakness, headache, fatigue (with excessive doses). **GI:** Nausea, diarrhea, intestinal cramps. **Urogenital:** Gonadal dysfunction. **Metabolic:** Increased serum creatine kinase, cholesterol, triglycerides; decreased serum thyroxine and triiodothyronine; increased urinary estrogens, androgens; creatinuria. **Skin:** Sterile abscess, thrombophlebitis, contact dermatitis. **Special Senses:** Blurred vision.

INTERACTIONS Herbal: Mineral oil, cholestyramine may decrease absorption of vitamin E; may enhance anticoagulant activity of **warfarin.**

PHARMACOKINETICS Absorption: 20–60% absorbed from GI tract if fat absorption is normal; enters blood via lymph. **Distribution:** Stored mainly in adipose tissue; crosses placenta. **Metabolism:** In liver. **Elimination:** Primarily in bile.

CLINICAL IMPLICATIONS

Patient & Family Education

- If taking a large dose of iron, the RDA of vitamin E may be increased.

V

Common adverse effects in *italic*, life-threatening effects <u>underlined</u>; generic names in **bold**; classifications in SMALL CAPS; ✦ Canadian drug name; ⊕ Prototype drug

1597

- Natural sources of vitamin E are found in wheat germ (the richest source) as well as in vegetable oils (sunflower, corn, soybean, cottonseed), green leafy vegetables, nuts, dairy products, eggs, cereals, meat, and liver.

VORICONAZOLE

(vor-i-con'a-zole)
Vfend
Classifications: ANTIBIOTIC; AZOLE ANTIFUNGAL
Therapeutic: ANTIBIOTIC; AZOLE ANTIFUNGAL
Prototype: Fluconazole
Pregnancy Category: D

AVAILABILITY 50 mg, 200 mg tablets; 200 mg injection

ACTION & *THERAPEUTIC EFFECT*
Inhibits fungal cytochrome P-450 enzymes used for an essential step in fungal ergosterol biosynthesis. The subsequent loss of ergosterol in the fungal cell wall is thought to be responsible for the antifungal activity of voriconazole. *Voriconazole is active against* Aspergillus *and* Candida.

USES Treatment of invasive *Aspergillosis,* esophageal candidiasis, candidemia in nonneutropenic patients and disseminated skin infections, and abdomen, kidney, bladder wall, and wound infections due to *Candida.*

CONTRAINDICATIONS Known hypersensitivity to voriconazole; intravenous voriconazole should be avoided in moderate or severe renal impairment (Cl_{cr} <50 mL/min); severe hepatic impairment; history of galactose intolerance; Lapp lactase deficiency or glucose-galactose malabsorption; concurrent use of sirolimus; coadministration of the CYP3A4 substrates pimozide or quin-idine; concurrent use of rifampin, rifabutin, carbamazepine and long-acting barbiturates, ergot alkaloids; sunlight (UV) exposure; pregnancy (category D); lactation.

CAUTIOUS USE Mild to moderate hepatic cirrhosis, hepatitis, hepatic disease; renal disease, mild renal impairment; ocular disease; hypersensitivity to other azole antifungal agents such as fluconazole; children <12 y.

ROUTE & DOSAGE

Aspergillosis

Adult: **IV** 6 mg/kg q12h day 1, then 4 mg/kg q12h. May reduce to 3 mg/kg q12h if not tolerated **PO** *>40 kg,* 400 mg q12h day 1, then 200 mg q12h. May increase to 300 mg q12h if inadequate response. *<40 kg,* 400 mg q12h day 1, then 100 mg q12h. May increase to 150 mg q12h if inadequate response.

Esophageal Candidiasis

Adult: **PO** *>40 kg,* 200 mg q12h for a minimum of 14 d and for at least 7 d after resolution of symptoms; *<40 kg,* 100 mg q12h for a minimum of 14 d and for at least 7 d after resolution of symptoms.

Dose Adjustment for Concomitant Fosphenytoin or Phenytoin

Adult: **IV** 6 mg/kg q12h day 1, then 5 mg/kg q12h. **PO** *>40 kg,* 400 mg q12h day 1, then 400 mg q12h. *<40 kg,* 400 mg q12h day 1, then 200 mg q12h

Renal Impairment

Cl_{cr} <50 mL/min: switch to PO therapy after loading dose

Hepatic Impairment

Child-Pugh Class A or B: reduce maintenance dose by 50%

Common adverse effects in *italic,* life-threatening effects <u>underlined</u>; generic names in **bold**; classifications in SMALL CAPS; ♣ Canadian drug name; ⓟ Prototype drug

ADMINISTRATION

Oral

- Give at least 1 h before or 1 h following a meal.
- Manufacturer recommendation: maintenance dose to be halved in patients with mild to moderate hepatic cirrhosis. Consult physician.
- Store tablets at 15°–30° C (59°–86° F).

Intravenous

IV voriconazole should be avoided in patients with moderate or severe renal impairment.

PREPARE: **Intermittent:** Use a 20 mL syringe to reconstitute powder with exactly 19 mL of sterile water for injection to yield 10 mg/mL. Discard vial if a vacuum does not pull the diluent into vial. Shake until completely dissolved. From an IV infusion bag of NS, D5W, D5/NS, D5/.45NS, RL or other suitable diluent withdraw and discard a volume of IV solution adequate to produce final voriconazole concentration within the range of 0.5–5 mg/mL. Inject the calculated dose of voriconazole into the IV bag. Discard unused voriconazole. Infuse IV solution immediately.

ADMINISTER: **Intermittent:** Infuse over 1–2 h at a maximum rate of 3 mg/kg per h. DO NOT give a bolus dose.

INCOMPATIBILITIES **Solution/additive:** Do not dilute with **sodium bicarbonate;** do not mix with any other drugs. **Y-site:** Do not infuse with other drugs.

- Store unreconstituted vials at 15°–30° C (59°–86° F).

ADVERSE EFFECTS (≥1%) **Body as a Whole:** Peripheral edema, fever, chills. **CNS:** Headache, hallucinations, dizziness. **CV:** Tachycardia, hypotension, hypertension, vasodilation. **GI:** Nausea, vomiting, abdominal pain, abnormal LFTs, diarrhea, cholestatic jaundice, dry mouth. **Metabolic:** Increased alkaline phosphatase, AST, ALT, hypokalemia, hypomagnesemia. **Skin:** Rash, pruritus. **Special Senses:** *Abnormal vision (enhanced brightness, blurred vision, or color vision changes),* photophobia.

INTERACTIONS Drug: Due to significant increased toxicity or decreased activity, the following drugs are <u>contraindicated</u> with voriconazole: BARBITURATES, **carbamazepine, efavirenz,** ERGOT ALKALOIDS, **pimozide, quinidine, rifabutin, sirolimus; fosphenytoin, phenytoin, rifampin, ritonavir** may significantly decrease voriconazole levels. PROTEASE INHIBITORS (except **indinavir**) may increase voriconazole toxicity; voriconazole may increase the toxicity of BENZODIAZEPINES, **cyclosporine,** PROTEASE INHIBITORS (except **indinavir**), NONNUCLEOSIDE REVERSE TRANSCRIPTASE INHIBITORS, **omeprazole, tacrolimus, vinblastine, vincristine, warfarin;** NONNUCLEOSIDE REVERSE TRANSCRIPTASE INHIBITORS may increase or decrease voriconazole levels. **Food:** Absorption reduced with high-fat meals. **Herbal: St. John's wort** may decrease efficacy.

PHARMACOKINETICS Absorption: 96% absorbed. Has a non-linear pharmacokinetic profile, a small change in dose may cause a large change in serum levels. Steady state not achieved until day 5–6 if no loading dose is given. **Peak:** 1–2 h. **Metabolism:** In liver by (and inhibits) CYP3A4, 2C9 and 2C19. **Elimination:** Primarily in urine. **Half-Life:** 6 h–6 d depending on dose.

V

Common adverse effects in *italic*, life-threatening effects <u>underlined</u>; generic names in **bold**; classifications in SMALL CAPS; ♣ Canadian drug name; ⦿ Prototype drug

1599

CLINICAL IMPLICATIONS

Assessment & Drug Effects

- Monitor visual acuity, visual field, and color perception if treatment continues beyond 28 d.
- Withhold drug and notify physician if skin rash develops.
- Monitor cardiovascular status especially with preexisting CV disease.
- Lab tests: Monitor baseline and periodic LFTs including bilirubin; patients who develop abnormal liver function tests during therapy should be monitored for the development of more severe hepatic injury. Monitor frequently renal function tests, especially serum creatinine. Monitor periodic CBC with platelet count, Hct & Hgb, serum electrolytes, alkaline phosphatase, blood glucose, and lipid profile.
- Concurrent drugs: Monitor PT/INR closely with warfarin as dose adjustments of warfarin may be needed. Monitor frequently blood glucose levels with sulfonylurea drugs as reduction in the sulfonylurea dosage may be needed. Monitor for and report any of the following: S&S of rhabdomyolysis in patient receiving a statin drug; prolonged sedation in patient receiving a benzodiazepine; S&S of heart block, bradycardia, or CHF in patient receiving a calcium channel blocker.

Patient & Family Education

- Use reliable means of birth control to prevent pregnancy. If you suspect you are pregnant, contact physician immediately.
- Do not drive at night while taking voriconazole as the drug may cause blurred vision and photophobia.
- Do not drive or engage in other potentially hazardous activities until reaction to drug is known.
- Avoid strong, direct sunlight while taking voriconazole.

WARFARIN SODIUM

(war'far-in)

Coumadin Sodium, Warfilone ◆

Classifications: ANTICOAGULANT
Therapeutic: ANTICOAGULANT

Pregnancy Category: X

AVAILABILITY 1 mg, 2 mg, 2.5 mg, 3 mg, 4 mg, 5 mg, 6 mg, 7.5 mg, 10 mg tablets; 2.5 mg/mL injection

ACTION & THERAPEUTIC EFFECT
Indirectly interferes with blood clotting by depressing hepatic synthesis of vitamin K-dependent coagulation factors: II, VII, IX, and X. *Deters further extension of existing thrombi and prevents new clots from forming. Has no effect on already synthesized circulating coagulation factors or on circulating thrombi.*

USES Prophylaxis and treatment of deep vein thrombosis and its extension, pulmonary embolism; treatment of atrial fibrillation with embolization. Also used as adjunct in treatment of coronary occlusion, cerebral transient ischemic attacks (TIAs), and as a prophylactic in patients with prosthetic cardiac valves. Used extensively as rodenticide.

CONTRAINDICATIONS Hemorrhagic tendencies, vitamin C or K deficiency, hemophilia, coagulation factor deficiencies, dyscrasias; active bleeding; open wounds, active peptic ulcer, visceral carcinoma, esophageal varices, malabsorption syndrome; hypertension (diastolic BP >110 mm Hg), cerebral vascular disease; heparin-induced thrombocytopenia (HIT); pericarditis with acute MI; severe hepatic or renal disease; continuous tube drainage of any orifice; subacute bacterial endocarditis; recent surgery of brain, spinal cord,

or eye; regional or lumbar block anesthesia; threatened abortion; unreliable patients; pregnancy (category X).
CAUTIOUS USE Alcoholism, allergic disorders, during menstruation, older adults, senility, psychosis; debilitated patients. Endogenous factors that may increase prothrombin time response (enhance anticoagulant effect): carcinoma, CHF, collagen diseases, hepatic and renal insufficiency, diarrhea, fever, pancreatic disorders, malnutrition, vitamin K deficiency. Endogenous factors that may decrease prothrombin time response (decrease anticoagulant response): edema, hypothyroidism, hyperlipidemia, hypercholesterolemia, chronic alcoholism, hereditary resistance to coumarin therapy.

ROUTE & DOSAGE

Anticoagulant

Adult: **PO/IV** Usual dose 2–10 mg daily with dose adjusted to maintain a PT 1.2–2 times control or INR of 2–3
Child: **PO** 0.1–0.3 mg/kg/d, adjust to maintain INR of 2–3

ADMINISTRATION

Note: Antidote for bleeding—anticoagulant effect usually is reversed by omitting 1 or more doses of warfarin and by administration of specific antidote phytonadione (vitamin K1) 2.5–10 mg orally. Physician may advise patient to carry vitamin K1 at all times, but not to take it until after consultation. If bleeding persists or progresses to a severe level, vitamin K 15–25 mg IV is given, or a fresh whole blood transfusion may be necessary.

Oral

- Give tablet whole or crushed with fluid of patient's choice.

Intravenous

PREPARE: **Direct:** Add 2 mL of supplied diluent to 50 mg of warfarin powder.
ADMINISTER: **Direct:** Give immediately by direct IV at a rate of 25 mg (1 mL)/min.
INCOMPATIBILITIES **Solution/additive: Ammonium chloride, 5% dextrose, Ringer's lactate, atropine, calcium chloride, calcium gluconate, chloramphenicol, chlorothiazide, chlortetracycline, erythromycin, methicillin, nitrofurantoin, oxacillin, oxytetracycline, penicillin, pentobarbital, phenobarbital, promethazine, sodium bicarbonate, succinyl chloride, vitamin B with C. Y-site: Aminophylline, ammonium chloride, bretylium, ceftazidime, cephalothin, cimetidine, ciprofloxacin, dobutamine, esmolol, gentamicin, labetalol, metronidazole, promazine, vancomycin.**

- Store at 15°–30° C (59°–86° F). Discard discolored or precipitated solutions. Protect all preparations from light and moisture.

ADVERSE EFFECTS (≥1%) **Body as a Whole:** Major or minor hemorrhage from any tissue or organ; hypersensitivity (dermatitis, urticaria, pruritus, fever). **GI:** Anorexia, nausea, vomiting, abdominal cramps, diarrhea, steatorrhea, stomatitis. **Other:** Increased serum transaminase levels, hepatitis, jaundice, burning sensation of feet, transient hair loss. **Overdosage:** Internal or external bleeding, paralytic ileus; skin necrosis of toes (purple toes syndrome), tip of nose, buttocks, thighs, calves, female breast, abdomen, and other fat-rich areas.

W

Common adverse effects in *italic*, life-threatening effects underlined; generic names in **bold**; classifications in SMALL CAPS; ♣ Canadian drug name; ⊘ Prototype drug

1601

DIAGNOSTIC TEST INTERFERENCE

Warfarin (coumarins) may cause alkaline urine to be red-orange; may enhance *uric acid* excretion, cause elevation of *serum transaminases,* and may increase *lactic dehydrogenase* activity.

INTERACTIONS Drug: In addition to the drugs listed below, many other drugs have been reported to alter the expected response to warfarin; however, clinical importance of these reports has not been substantiated. The addition or withdrawal of any drug to an established drug regimen should be made cautiously, with more frequent INR determinations than usual and with careful observation of the patient and dose adjustment as indicated. The following may enhance the anticoagulant effects of warfarin: **Acetohexamide, acetaminophen,** ALKYLATING AGENTS, **allopurinol,** AMINOGLYCOSIDES, **aminosalicylic acid, amiodarone,** ANABOLIC STEROIDS, ANTIBIOTICS (ORAL), ANTIMETABOLITES, ANTIPLATELET DRUGS, **aspirin, asparaginase, capecitabine, celecoxib, chloramphenicol, chlorpropamide, chymotrypsin, cimetidine, clofibrate, co-trimoxazole, danazol, dextran, dextrothyroxine, diazoxide, disulfiram, erythromycin, ethacrynic acid, fluconazole, glucagons, guanethidine,** HEPATOTOXIC DRUGS, **influenza vaccine, isoniazid, itraconazole, ketoconazole,** MAO INHIBITORS, **meclofenamate, mefenamic acid, methyldopa, methylphenidate, metronidazole, miconazole, mineral oil, nalidixic acid, neomycin (oral),** NONSTEROIDAL ANTI-INFLAMMATORY DRUGS, **oxandrolone, plicamycin,** POTASSIUM PRODUCTS, **propoxyphene, propylthiouracil, quinidine, quinine, rofecoxib, salicylates, streptokinase,** **sulindac,** SULFONAMIDES, SULFONYLUREAS, TETRACYCLINES, THIAZIDES, THYROID DRUGS, **tolbutamide, tricyclic antidepressants, urokinase, vitamin E, zileuton.** The following may increase or decrease the anticoagulant effects of warfarin: **Alcohol** (acute intoxication may increase, chronic alcoholism may decrease effects), **chloral hydrate,** DIURETICS. The following may decrease the anticoagulant effects of warfarin: **barbiturates, carbamazepine, cholestyramine,** CORTICOSTEROIDS, **corticotropin, ethchlorvynol, glutethimide, griseofulvin,** LAXATIVES, **mercaptopurine,** ORAL CONTRACEPTIVES, **rifampin, spironolactone, vitamin C, vitamin K. Herbal: Boldo, capsicum, celery, chamomile, clove, coenzyme Q10, danshen, devil's claw, dong quai, echinacea, fenugreek, feverfew, fish oil, garlic, ginger, ginkgo, horse chestnut, licorice root, passionflower herb, tumeric, willow bark** may increase risk of bleeding; **avocado, ginseng, green tea, seaweed, soy, St. John's wort** may decrease effectiveness of warfarin. **Food: Cranberry juice** may increase INR. Green leafy vegetables may affect efficacy.

PHARMACOKINETICS Absorption:

Well absorbed from GI tract. **Onset:** 2–7 d. **Peak:** 0.5–3 d. **Distribution:** 97% protein bound; crosses placenta. **Metabolism:** In liver (CYP2C9). **Elimination:** In urine and bile. **Half-Life:** 0.5–3 d.

CLINICAL IMPLICATIONS

Assessment & Drug Effects

- Determine PT/INP prior to initiation of therapy and then daily until maintenance dosage is established.
- Obtain a CAREFUL medication history prior to start of therapy and whenever altered responses to therapy

require interpretation; extremely IM-PORTANT since many drugs interfere with the activity of anticoagulant drugs (see INTERACTIONS).

- Adjust dose to maintain PT at $1^1/_2$–$2^1/_2$ times the control (12–15 sec), or 15–35% of normal prothrombin activity, or an INR of 2–4 depending on diagnosis.

- Lab tests: For maintenance dosage, PT/INR determinations at 1–4-wk intervals depending on patient's response; periodic urinalyses, stool guaiac, and liver function tests. Blood samples should be drawn at 12–18 h after last dose (optimum).

- Monitor closely older adult, psychotic, or alcoholic patients because they present serious noncompliance problems.

- Note: Patients at greatest risk of hemorrhage include those whose PT/INR are difficult to regulate, who have an aortic valve prosthesis, who are receiving long-term anticoagulant therapy, and older adult and debilitated patients.

Patient & Family Education

- Understand that bleeding can occur even though PT/INR are within therapeutic range. Stop drug and notify physician immediately if bleeding or signs of bleeding appear: Blood in urine, bright red or black tarry stools, vomiting of blood, bleeding with tooth brushing, blue or purple spots on skin or mucous membrane, round pinpoint purplish red spots (often occur in ankle areas), nosebleed, bloody sputum; chest pain; abdominal or lumbar pain or swelling, profuse menstrual bleeding, pelvic pain; severe or continuous headache, faintness or dizziness; prolonged oozing from any minor injury (e.g., nicks from shaving).

- Stop drug and report immediately any symptoms of hepatitis (dark urine, itchy skin, jaundice, abdominal pain, light stools) or hypersensitivity reaction (see Appendix F).

- Avoid brand interchange, take drug at same time each day, and do NOT alter dose.

- Notify physician if there is an unusual increase in menstrual bleeding (slightly increased or prolonged). Note: PT/INR are checked at least monthly in menstruating women.

- Risk of bleeding is increased for up to 1 mo after receiving the influenza vaccine.

- Fever, prolonged hot weather, malnutrition, and diarrhea lengthen PT/INR (enhanced anticoagulant effect).

- A high-fat diet, sudden increase in vitamin K–rich foods (cabbage, cauliflower, broccoli, asparagus, lettuce, turnip greens, onions, spinach, kale, fish, liver), coffee or green tea (caffeine), or by tube feedings with high vitamin K content shorten PT/INR.

- Maintain a well-balanced diet and avoid excess intake of alcohol.

- Inform dentist or any new physician about anticoagulant therapy and duration of treatment.

- Use a soft toothbrush and floss teeth gently with waxed floss.

- Use barrier contraceptive measures; if you become pregnant while on anticoagulant therapy the fetus is at great potential risk of congenital malformations.

- Do not take any other prescription or OTC drug unless specifically approved by physician or pharmacist. Carry medical identification at all times. It needs to indicate medical diagnosis, medication(s), physician's name, address, and telephone number.

W

Common adverse effects in *italic*, life-threatening effects underlined; generic names in **bold**; classifications in SMALL CAPS; ✦ Canadian drug name; Ⓟ Prototype drug

1603

XYLOMETAZOLINE HYDROCHLORIDE

(zye-loe-met-az'oh-leen)

Neo-Synephrine 12 Hour, Otrivin

Classifications: NASAL DECONGESTANT; VASOCONSTRICTOR
Therapeutic: NASAL DECONGESTANT
Prototype: Naphazoline
Pregnancy Category: C

AVAILABILITY 0.05%, 0.1% nasal solution

ACTION & *THERAPEUTIC EFFECT*
Markedly constricts dilated arterioles of nasal membrane. Has little or no beta-adrenergic activity. *Decreases fluid exudate and mucosal engorgement associated with rhinitis and may open up obstructed eustachian tubes.*

USES
Temporary relief of nasal congestion associated with common cold, sinusitis, acute and chronic rhinitis, and hay fever and other allergies.

CONTRAINDICATIONS
Sensitivity to adrenergic substances; angle-closure glaucoma; concurrent therapy with MAO inhibitors or tricyclic antidepressants; lactation, and infants; pregnancy (category C).

CAUTIOUS USE
Hypertension; hyperthyroidism; heart disease, including angina; advanced arteriosclerosis, older adults, and children.

ROUTE & DOSAGE

Nasal Congestion
Adult: **Nasal** 1–2 sprays or 1–2 drops of 0.1% solution in each nostril q8–10h (max: 3 doses/d)

Child: **Nasal** <6 *mo*, 1 drop of 0.05% solution in each nostril q6h (max: 3 doses/d); *6 mo–12 y*, 1 spray or 2–3 drops of 0.05% solution in each nostril q8–10h (max: 3 doses/d)

ADMINISTRATION

Instillation
- Have patient clear each nostril gently before administering spray or drops.
- Spray: Do not shake container. Hold tube vertically (spray end up) so that solution is delivered in a fine spray. Head should be erect; spray into each nostril; 3–5 min later, clear (blow) nose thoroughly.
- Drops: Patient should be in a lateral, head-low position to permit application of drops to lower nostril surface. Have patient remain in this position for 5 min, then apply drops to opposite nostril surface in same manner; or drops may be instilled with patient in reclining position with head tilted back as far as possible.
- Store at 15°–30° C (59°–86° F) in a tight, light-resistant container.

ADVERSE EFFECTS (≥1%)
All: Usually mild and infrequent; local stinging, burning, dryness and ulceration, sneezing, headache, insomnia, drowsiness. **With excessive use:** *Rebound nasal congestion* and vasodilation, tremulousness, hypertension, palpitations, tachycardia, arrhythmia, somnolence, sedation, coma.

INTERACTIONS Drug:
May cause increase BP with **guanethidine, methyldopa,** MAO INHIBITORS; PHENOTHIAZINES may decrease effectiveness of nasal decongestant.

PHARMACOKINETICS Onset:
5–10 min. **Duration:** 5–6 h.

CLINICAL IMPLICATIONS

Assessment & Drug Effects

- Evaluate for development of rebound congestion (see ADVERSE EFFECTS).

Patient & Family Education

- Prevent contamination of nasal solution and spread of infection by rinsing dropper and tip of nasal spray in hot water after each use; restrict use to the individual patient.
- Note: Prolonged use can cause rebound congestion and chemical rhinitis. Do NOT exceed prescribed dosage and report to physician if drug fails to provide relief within 3–4 d.
- Do NOT self-medicate with OTC drugs, sprays, or drops without physician's approval.
- Note: Excessive use by a child may lead to CNS depression.

ZAFIRLUKAST ℗

(za-fir-lu′kast)

Accolate

Classifications: BRONCHODILATOR (RESPIRATORY SMOOTH MUSCLE RELAXANT); LEUKOTRIENE RECEPTOR ANTAGONIST
Therapeutic: BRONCHODILATOR; LEUKOTRIENE RECEPTOR ANTAGONIST
Pregnancy Category: B

AVAILABILITY 10 mg, 20 mg tablets

ACTION & THERAPEUTIC EFFECT

Selective leukotriene receptor antagonist (LTRA) that inhibits binding of leukotriene D_4 and E_4, thus inhibiting inflammation and bronchoconstriction. Leukotriene production and receptor affinity have been correlated with the pathogenesis of asthma. *Zafirlukast helps to prevent the signs and symptoms of asthma, including airway edema, smooth muscle constriction, and altered cellular activity due to inflammation.*

USES Prophylaxis and chronic treatment of asthma in adults and children >5 y (not for acute bronchospasm).

CONTRAINDICATIONS Hypersensitivity to zafirlukast; acute asthma attacks, including status asthmaticus, acute bronchospasm; lactation, children <5 y.
CAUTIOUS USE Hepatic impairment, hepatic disease; concurrent administration with warfarin; corticosteroid withdrawal or reduction in dose; patients ≥65 y, pregnancy (category B).

ROUTE & DOSAGE

Asthma
Adult: **PO** 20 mg b.i.d. 1 h before or 2 h after meals
Child: **PO** >5 y, 10 mg b.i.d.

ADMINISTRATION

Oral

- Give 1 h before or 2 h after meals.
- Store at 20°–25° C (68°–77° F); protect from light and moisture.

ADVERSE EFFECTS (≥1%) **Body as a Whole:** Generalized pain, asthenia, myalgia, fever, back pain. **CNS:** *Headache,* dizziness. **GI:** Nausea, diarrhea, abdominal pain, vomiting, dyspepsia; liver dysfunction, increased liver function tests, hepatic failure. **Other:** Churg-Strauss syndrome (fever, muscle aches and pains, weight loss).

INTERACTIONS Drug: May increase prothrombin time (PT) in patients on **warfarin. Erythromycin** decreases bioavailability of zafirlukast.

Z

Common adverse effects in *italic*, life-threatening effects underlined; generic names in **bold**; classifications in SMALL CAPS; ✦ Canadian drug name; ℗ Prototype drug

1605

PHARMACOKINETICS Absorption: Rapidly from GI tract, bioavailability significantly reduced by food. **Onset:** 1 wk. **Peak:** 3 h. **Distribution:** >99% protein bound; secreted into breast milk. **Metabolism:** In liver (CYP2C9). **Elimination:** 90% in feces, 10% in urine. **Half-Life:** 10 h.

CLINICAL IMPLICATIONS

Assessment & Drug Effects

- Assess respiratory status and airway function regularly.
- Lab tests: Periodic liver function tests.
- Monitor closely PT and INR with concurrent warfarin therapy.
- Monitor closely phenytoin level with concurrent phenytoin therapy.

Patient & Family Education

- Taking medication regularly, even during symptom-free periods.
- Note: Drug is not intended to treat acute episodes of asthma.
- Report S&S of hepatic toxicity (see Appendix F) or flu-like symptoms to physician. Follow-up lab work is very important.
- Notify physician immediately if condition worsens while using prescribed doses of all antiasthmatic medications.

ZALCITABINE (DDC, DIDEOXYCYTIDINE)

(zal-cit'a-been)
Hivid

Classifications: ANTIVIRAL; NUCLEOSIDE REVERSE TRANSCRIPTASE INHIBITOR (NRTI)
Therapeutic: ANTIVIRAL; NRTI
Prototype: Lamivudine
Pregnancy Category: C

AVAILABILITY 0.375 mg, 0.75 mg tablets

ACTION & *THERAPEUTIC EFFECT*

A synthetic pyrimidine nucleotide that inhibits the replication of HIV by inhibition of viral DNA synthesis. It appears to act by becoming incorporated into the DNA chains of the HIV virus during viral replication. *Zalcitabine is able to decrease the HIV viral load by its antiviral properties.*

USES Combination therapy with zidovudine for AIDS. Second-line monotherapy for AIDS.

UNLABELED USES Can be used in children.

CONTRAINDICATIONS Hypersensitivity to zalcitabine; lactic acidosis; pancreatitis; peripheral neuropathy; pregnancy (category C), lactation. Safe use in infants <6 mo has not been established.

CAUTIOUS USE History of pancreatitis; CHF, cardiomyopathy; renal impairment, hepatic impairment, alcohol abuse; diabetes mellitus.

ROUTE & DOSAGE

Combination Therapy for HIV

Adult: **PO** 0.75 mg q8h given with zidovudine 200 mg q8h
Child: **PO** 0.015 to 0.04 mg/kg q6h for 8 wk, after 8 wk of monotherapy an alternating regimen of zalcitabine and zidovudine is begun (4-wk cycle of zidovudine for 3 wk and zalcitabine for 1 wk)

Monotherapy for HIV

Adult: **PO** 0.01 mg/kg q8h

ADMINISTRATION

Oral

- Give on an empty stomach.
- Store at 15°–30° C (56°–86° F).

ADVERSE EFFECTS (≥1%) **CV:** May exacerbate existing CHF and cardiomyopathy. **CNS:** *Peripheral neu-*

Z

ropathy, numbness. **GI:** Diarrhea, mouth and esophageal ulcers, <u>pancreatitis</u>, may exacerbate existing hepatic dysfunction. **Hematologic:** Neutropenia, thrombocytopenia. **Skin:** *Transient symptom complex of cutaneous eruptions (maculovesicular in nature), fever, malaise, and aphthous mouth ulcers,* arthralgia, urticaria, <u>anaphylaxis</u>.

INTERACTIONS Drug: May cause additive peripheral neuropathy with **didanosine.**

PHARMACOKINETICS Absorption: Readily absorbed from GI tract. **Onset:** 2 wk. **Distribution:** Distributes somewhat into CSF. **Metabolism:** Does not appear to be metabolized. **Elimination:** 62% excreted unchanged in urine. **Half-Life:** 1.2–1.8 h.

CLINICAL IMPLICATIONS

Assessment & Drug Effects

- Discontinue drug and promptly notify physician if patient experiences numbness, tingling, burning, or pain in extremities.
- Lab tests: Baseline and periodic tests for serum amylase, serum glucose, triglycerides, and serum calcium levels; monitor closely in patients with history of pancreatitis or elevated serum amylase.

Patient & Family Education

- Report to physician promptly S&S of pancreatitis and peripheral neuropathy (see Appendix F).
- Use contraception while taking zalcitabine.

ZALEPLON

(zal′ep-lon)
Sonata
Classifications: ANXIOLYTIC; SEDATIVE-HYPNOTIC; NONBENZODIAZEPINE

Therapeutic: SEDATIVE-HYPNOTIC; ANTIANXIETY
Prototype: Zolpidem
Pregnancy Category: C
Controlled Substance: Schedule IV

AVAILABILITY 5 mg, 10 mg capsules.

ACTION & *THERAPEUTIC EFFECT*
Short-acting nonbenzodiazepine with sedative-hypnotic, muscle relaxant, and anticonvulsant activity. *Reduces difficulty in initially falling asleep. Preserves deep sleep (stage 3 through stage 4) at hypnotic dose with minimal-to-absent rebound insomnia when discontinued.*

USES Short-term treatment of insomnia.

CONTRAINDICATIONS Hypersensitivity to zaleplon, or tartrazine dye (Yellow 5); suicidal ideation; pregnancy (category C); lactation. Safe use in children not established.

CAUTIOUS USE Hypersensitivity to salicylates; concurrent use of other CNS depressants (e.g., benzodiazepines, alcohol); chronic depression; history of drug abuse; COPD; respiratory insufficiency; hepatic or renal impairment; pulmonary disease.

ROUTE & DOSAGE

Insomnia
Adult: **PO** 10 mg h.s. (max: 20 mg h.s.)
Geriatric: **PO** 5 mg h.s. (max: 10 mg h.s.)

ADMINISTRATION

Oral

- Give immediately before bedtime; not while patient is still ambulating.
- Give lower dose of 5 mg to older adult or debilitated patients.
- Store at 20°–25° C (68°–77° F).

Z

Common adverse effects in *italic,* life-threatening effects <u>underlined;</u> generic names in **bold;** classifications in SMALL CAPS; ✦ Canadian drug name; ⊘ Prototype drug

1607

ADVERSE EFFECTS (≥1%) **Body as a Whole:** Asthenia, fever, *headache*, migraine, myalgia, back pain. **CNS:** Amnesia, dizziness, paresthesia, somnolence, tremor, vertigo, depression, hypertonia, nervousness, difficulty concentrating. **GI:** Abdominal pain, dyspepsia, nausea, constipation, dry mouth. **Respiratory:** Bronchitis. **Skin:** Pruritus, rash. **Special Senses:** Eye pain, hyperacusis, conjunctivitis. **Urogenital:** Dysmenorrhea.

INTERACTIONS Drug: **Alcohol, imipramine, thioridazine** may cause additive CNS impairment; **rifampin** increases metabolism of **zaleplon; cimetidine** increases serum levels of **zaleplon. Herbal: Valerian, melatonin** may produce additive sedative effects. **Food:** High-fat meals may delay absorption.

PHARMACOKINETICS Absorption: Rapidly and completely absorbed, 30% reaches systemic circulation. **Onset:** 15–20 min. **Peak:** 1 h. **Duration:** 3–4 h. **Distribution:** 60% protein bound. **Metabolism:** Extensively in liver (CYP3A4) to inactive metabolites. **Elimination:** 70% in urine, 17% in feces. **Half-Life:** 1 h.

CLINICAL IMPLICATIONS
Assessment & Drug Effects
- Monitor behavior and notify physician for significant changes. Use extra caution with preexisting clinical depression.
- Provide safe environment and monitor ambulation after drug is ingested.
- Monitor respiratory status with preexisting compromised pulmonary function.

Patient & Family Education
- Exercise caution when walking; avoid all hazardous activities after taking zaleplon.

- Do not take in combination with alcohol or any other sleep medication.
- Note: Exhibits altered effectiveness if taken with/immediately after high-fat meal.
- Do not use longer than 2–3 wk.
- Expect possible mild/brief rebound insomnia after discontinuing regimen.
- Report use of OTC medications to physician (e.g., cimetidine).
- Report pregnancy to physician immediately.

ZANAMIVIR

(zan'a-mi-vir)
Relenza
Classifications: ANTIVIRAL
Therapeutic: ANTIVIRAL; ANTIINFLUENZA
Pregnancy Category: C

AVAILABILITY 5 mg/Rotadisk blister

ACTION & *THERAPEUTIC EFFECT*
Inhibitor of influenza A and B viral enzyme; does not permit the release of newly formed viruses from the surface of the infected cells. *Prevents viral spread across the mucus lining of the respiratory tract, and inhibits the replication of influenza A and B virus. Relieves flu-like symptoms.*

USES Uncomplicated acute influenza in patients symptomatic <2 d.

CONTRAINDICATIONS Hypersensitivity to zanamivir or milk protein; severe renal impairment, renal failure; pregnancy (category C); COPD; severe asthma.

CAUTIOUS USE Concurrent use of inhaled medication with inhaled zanamivir; renal impairment; cardiac disease; older adults; severe metabolic

Z

Common adverse effects in *italic*, life-threatening effects underlined; generic names in **bold**; classifications in SMALL CAPS; ♣ Canadian drug name; ⊕Prototype drug

disease; lactation. Safety and efficacy in children <7 y are unknown. Safe use in prophylactic treatment for children <5 y unknown.

ROUTE & DOSAGE

Acute Influenza
Adult/Child >7 y: **Inhaled** 2 inhalations (one 5 mg blister/inhalation) b.i.d. (approximately 12 h apart) times 5 d

Influenza Prophylaxis
Adult/Child >5 y: **Inhaled** 2 inhalations daily for 10 d (household prophylaxis) or 2 inhalations daily for 28 d (community outbreak)

ADMINISTRATION

Inhalation
- Initiate within 48 h of onset of flu-like symptoms.
- Give any scheduled inhaled bronchodilator before zanamivir.
- Store at 25° C (77° F).

ADVERSE EFFECTS (≥1%) **Body as a Whole:** Headache. **CNS:** Dizziness. **GI:** Nausea, diarrhea, vomiting. **Respiratory:** Nasal symptoms, bronchitis, cough, sinusitis; ear, nose, throat infection.

INTERACTIONS Drug: No clinically significant interactions established.

PHARMACOKINETICS Absorption: 4–17% of inhaled dose is systemically absorbed. **Peak:** 1–2 h. **Distribution:** <10% protein bound. **Metabolism:** Not metabolized. **Elimination:** In urine. **Half-Life:** 2.5–5.1 h.

CLINICAL IMPLICATIONS

Patient & Family Education
- Start within 48 h of onset of flu-like symptoms for most effective response.
- Use any scheduled inhaled bronchodilator first; then use zanamivir.

ZICONOTIDE
zi-con'o-tide
Prialt
Classifications: NONNARCOTIC ANALGESIC; N-TYPE CALCIUM CHANNEL BLOCKER
Therapeutic: NONNARCOTIC ANALGESIC
Pregnancy Category: C

AVAILABILITY 25 mcg/mL, 100 mcg/mL injection

ACTION & *THERAPEUTIC EFFECT*
Ziconotide binds to N-type calcium channels located on the afferent nerves in the dorsal horn in the spinal cord. It is thought that these binding blocks of N-type calcium channels lead to a blockade of excitatory neurotransmitter release in the afferent nerve endings. *Ziconotide is effective in controlling severe chronic pain that is intractable to other analgesics.*

USES Management of severe chronic pain in patients for whom intrathecal (IT) therapy is warranted.
UNLABELED USES Spasticity associated with spinal cord trauma.

CONTRAINDICATIONS Hypersensitivity to ziconotide; epidural or intravenous administration; preexisting history of psychosis; sepsis; depression with suicidal ideation; cognitive impairment; bipolar disorder; schizophrenia; dementia; presence of infection at the injection site, uncontrolled bleeding, or spinal canal obstruction that impairs circulation of CSF; coagulopathy; seizures; pregnancy (category C); lactation. Safety and efficacy in children or infants are not established.
CAUTIOUS USE Elderly; renal, hepatic, and cardiac impairment; concurrent use of CNS depressant(s); older adults.

Common adverse effects in *italic*, life-threatening effects underlined; generic names in **bold**; classifications in SMALL CAPS; ♣ Canadian drug name; ⊕ Prototype drug

1609

Z

ROUTE & DOSAGE

Severe Chronic Pain

Adult: **Intrathecal** Initial 0.1 mcg/h; may titrate up ≤ 0.1 mcg/h q2–3d to 0.8 mcg/h (19.2 mcg/d)

ADMINISTRATION

Intrathecal

- May be administered undiluted (25 mcg/mL in 20 mL vial) or diluted using the 100 mcg/mL vials. Diluted ziconotide is prepared with NS without preservatives.
- Administer using an implanted variable-rate microinfusion device or an external microinfusion device and catheter.
- Note: Due to serious adverse events, 19.2 mcg/d (0.8 mcg/h) is the maximum recommended dose.
- Doses should normally be titrated upward by no more than 2.4 mcg/d (0.1 mcg/h) at intervals of 2–3 times/wk.
- Refrigerate all ziconotide solutions after preparation and begin infusion within 24 h. Discard any unused portion left in a vial.

ADVERSE EFFECTS (≥1%) **Body as a Whole:** Accidental injury, back pain, catheter complication, catheter-site pain, cellulitis, chest pain, chills, *fever,* flu syndrome, infection, malaise, neck pain, neck rigidity, *pain,* pump-site complication, pump-site mass, pump-site pain, viral infection. **CNS:** Abnormal dreams, *abnormal gait,* agitation, *anxiety, aphasia, asthenia, ataxia,* CSF abnormal, *confusion,* depression, difficulty concentrating, *dizziness,* dry mouth, *dysesthesia,* emotional lability, *headache,* hostility, hyperesthesia, *hypertonia,* incoordination, insomnia, *memory impairment,* mental slowing, meningitis, *nervousness,* neuralgia, paranoid reaction, *paresthesia,* reflexes decreased, *somnolence, speech disorder,* stupor, abnormal thinking, tremor, twitching, *vertigo.* **CV:** Hypertension, hypotension, postural hypotension, syncope, tachycardia, vasodilation. **GI:** Abdominal pain, *anorexia,* constipation, *diarrhea,* dyspepsia, gastrointestinal disorder, *nausea, vomiting.* **GU:** Dysuria, urinary incontinence, *urinary retention,* urinary tract infection, impaired urination. **Hematologic:** Anemia, ecchymosis. **Metabolic/Nutritional:** Creatinine phosphokinase increased, dehydration, edema, hypokalemia, peripheral edema, weight loss. **Musculoskeletal:** Arthralgia, arthritis, leg cramps, myalgia, myasthenia. **Respiratory:** Bronchitis, cough increased, dyspnea, lung disorder, pharyngitis, pneumonia, rhinitis, sinusitis. **Skin:** Cutaneous surgical complication, dry skin, pruritus, rash, skin disorder, sweating. **Special Senses:** *Abnormal vision,* diplopia, *nystagmus,* photophobia, taste perversion, tinnitus.

INTERACTIONS Drug: Ethanol and other CNS DEPRESSANTS may increase drowsiness, dizziness, and confusion.

PHARMACOKINETICS Distribution: 50% protein bound. **Metabolism:** Hydrolyzed by peptidases. **Half-Life:** 4.6 h.

CLINICAL IMPLICATIONS

Assessment & Drug Effects

- Monitor for and report S&S of meningitis, cognitive impairment, hallucinations, changes in mood or consciousness, or other psychiatric symptoms.
- Lab tests: Serum creatine kinase every other week for first month and monthly thereafter.

Patient & Family Education

- Report any of the following to physician: muscle pain, soreness,

Z

or weakness, confusion, unusual behavior, symptoms of depression or suicidal thoughts, fever, headache, stiff neck, nausea or vomiting, seizures.

- Note: Taking this drug with other depressants (e.g., alcohol, sedatives, tranquilizers) will increase the risk of side effects.

ZIDOVUDINE (FORMERLY AZIDOTHYMIDINE, AZT)

(zye-doe'vyoo-deen)
Retrovir

Classifications: ANTIVIRAL; NUCLEOSIDE REVERSE TRANSCRIPTASE INHIBITOR
Therapeutic: ANTIVIRAL; NRTI
Prototype: Lamivudine
Pregnancy Category: C

AVAILABILITY 300 mg tablets; 100 mg capsules; 50 mg/5 mL syrup; 10 mg/mL injection

ACTION & *THERAPEUTIC EFFECT*

Appears to act by being incorporated into growing DNA chains by viral reverse transcriptase, thereby terminating viral replication. *Zidovudine has antiviral action against HIV, LAV (lymphadenopathy-associated virus), and ARV (AIDS-associated retrovirus).*

USES Patients who are HIV positive and have a CD4 count ≤500/mm^3, asymptomatic HIV infection, early and late symptomatic HIV disease, prevention of perinatal transfer of HIV during pregnancy.

UNLABELED USES Pediatric patients, postexposure chemoprophylaxis.

CONTRAINDICATIONS Life-threatening allergic reactions to any of the components of the drug; lactic

acidosis; pregnancy (category C), lactation.

CAUTIOUS USE Impaired renal or hepatic function, alcoholism; anemia; chemotherapy; radiation therapy; bone marrow depression.

ROUTE & DOSAGE

Symptomatic HIV Infection
Adult: **PO** 300 mg b.i.d. OR 200 mg t.i.d. **IV** 1–2 mg/kg q4h (1200 mg/d)
Child: **PO** *3 mo–13 y*, 160 mg/m^2 q8h **IV** 120 mg/m^2 q6h

Prevention of Maternal-Fetal Transmission
Neonate: **PO** *Full term:* 2 mg/kg q6h for 6 wk beginning within 12 h after birth; *30–35 wk gestation:* 2 mg/kg q12h for 2 wk, then q8h for 4 wk; *<30 wk gestation:* 2 mg/kg q12h for 4 wk, then q8h for 2 wk **IV** *Full term:* 1.5 mg/kg q6h × 6 wk
Maternal: **PO** 100 mg five times daily OR 300 mg b.i.d. from 14 wk gestation until delivery **IV** During labor, 2 mg/kg loading dose, then 1 mg/kg/h

ADMINISTRATION

Oral
- Do not expose capsules and syrup to light during drug preparation.

Intravenous

PREPARE: **Intermittent:** Withdraw required dose from vial and dilute with D5W to a concentration not to exceed 4 mg/mL.
ADMINISTER: **Intermittent:** Give calculated dose at a constant rate over 60 min; avoid rapid infusion.
INCOMPATIBILITIES **Solution/additive: Meropenem. Y-site: Meropenem.**

Common adverse effects in *italic*, life-threatening effects <u>underlined</u>; generic names in **bold**; classifications in SMALL CAPS; ♣ Canadian drug name; ⊙ Prototype drug

1611

Z

■Store at 15°–25° C (59°–77° F) and protected from light unless otherwise directed.

ADVERSE EFFECTS (≥1%) **Body as a Whole:** *Fever,* dyspnea, *malaise,* weakness, *myalgia,* myopathy. **CNS:** *Headache,* insomnia, dizziness, paresthesias, mild confusion, anxiety, restlessness, agitation. **GI:** *Nausea,* diarrhea, *vomiting, anorexia,* GI pain. **Hematologic:** <u>*Bone marrow depression, granulocytopenia, anemia.*</u> **Respiratory:** *Cough, wheezing.* **Skin:** *Rash,* itching, diaphoresis.

INTERACTIONS Drug: Acetaminophen ganciclovir, interferon-alfa may enhance bone marrow suppression; **atovaquone, amphotericin B, aspirin, dapsone, doxorubicin, fluconazole, flucytosine, indomethacin, interferon alfa, methadone, pentamidine, vincristine, valproic acid** may increase risk of AZT toxicity; **probenecid** will decrease AZT elimination, resulting in increased serum levels and thus toxicity. **Nelfinavir, rifampin, ritonavir** may decrease zidovudine (AZT) concentrations; other ANTIRETROVIRAL AGENTS may cause lactic acidosis and severe hepatomegaly with steatosis; **stavudine, doxorubicin** may antagonize AZT effects.

PHARMACOKINETICS Absorption: Readily from GI tract; 60–70% reaches systemic circulation (first-pass metabolism). **Peak:** 0.5–1.5 h. **Distribution:** Crosses blood–brain barrier and placenta. **Metabolism:** In liver. **Elimination:** 63–95% in urine. **Half-Life:** 1 h.

CLINICAL IMPLICATIONS

Assessment & Drug Effects

■Evaluate patient at least weekly during the first month of therapy.

■Lab tests: Baseline and frequent (at least q2wk) blood counts, CD4 (T_4) lymphocyte count, Hgb, and granulocyte count to detect hematologic toxicity.

■Myelosuppression results in anemia, which commonly occurs after 4–6 wk of therapy, and granulocytopenia in 6–8 wk. Frequently, both respond to dosage adjustment. Significant anemia (Hgb <7.5 g/dL or reduction >25% of baseline value), or granulocyte count <750/mm^3 (or reduction >50% of baseline) may require temporary interruption of therapy and transfusions.

■Monitor for common adverse effects, especially severe headache, nausea, insomnia, and myalgia.

Patient & Family Education

■Contact physician promptly if health status worsens or any unusual symptoms develop.

■Understand that this drug is not a cure for HIV infection; you will continue to be at risk for opportunistic infections.

■Do not share drug with others; take drug exactly as prescribed.

■Drug does NOT reduce the risk of transmission of HIV infection through body fluids.

ZILEUTON

(zi-leu'ton)

Zyflo

Classifications: BRONCHODILATOR (RESPIRATORY SMOOTH MUSCLE RELAXANT); LEUKOTRIENE RECEPTOR ANTAGONIST

Therapeutic: BRONCHODILATOR; LEUKOTRIENE RECEPTOR ANTAGONIST

Prototype: Zafirlukast

Pregnancy Category: C

AVAILABILITY 600 mg tablets

Z

ACTION & *THERAPEUTIC EFFECT*

Inhibits 5-lipoxygenase, the enzyme needed to start the conversion of arachidonic acid to leukotrienes, which are important inflammatory agents that induce bronchoconstriction and mucus production. *Zileuton helps to prevent the signs and symptoms of asthma including airway edema, smooth muscle constriction, and altered cellular activity due to inflammation.*

USES Prophylaxis and chronic treatment of asthma in adults and children <12 y.

CONTRAINDICATIONS Hypersensitivity to zileuton or zafirlukast, active liver disease, status asthmaticus; QT prolongation; lactation, pregnancy (category C).
CAUTIOUS USE Hepatic insufficiency; alcoholism; older adults; older females; fever; infection; history of QT prolongation. Safety and effectiveness in children <12 y are not established.

ROUTE & DOSAGE

Asthma
Adult/Child: **PO** >12 y, 600 mg q.i.d.

ADMINISTRATION

Oral
- Give at meals and bedtime.
- Store at room temperature, 15°–30° C (59°–86° F); protect from light.

ADVERSE EFFECTS (≥1%) Body as a Whole: Pain, asthenia, myalgia, arthralgia, fever, malaise, neck pain/rigidity. **CNS:** *Headache,* dizziness, insomnia, nervousness, somnolence. **CV:** Chest pain. **GI:** Abdominal pain, *dyspepsia,* nausea, constipation, flatulence, vomiting, elevated liver function tests, asymptomatic hepatitis. **Skin:** Pruritus. **Other:** Conjunctivitis, hypertonia, lymphadenopathy, vaginitis, UTI, leukopenia.

INTERACTIONS Drug: May double **theophylline** levels and increase toxicity. Increases hypoprothrombinemic effects of **warfarin.** May increase levels of BETA BLOCKERS (especially **propranolol**), leading to hypotension and bradycardia.

PHARMACOKINETICS Absorption: Rapidly from GI tract. **Peak:** 1.7 h. **Duration:** 5–8 h. **Distribution:** 93% protein bound; secreted in the breast milk of rats. **Metabolism:** In liver primarily via glucuronide conjugation. **Elimination:** Primarily in urine (94%). **Half-Life:** 2.5 h.

CLINICAL IMPLICATIONS

Assessment & Drug Effects

- Assess respiratory status and airway function regularly.
- Lab tests: Periodic CBC and routine blood chemistry; monthly liver function tests for 3 mo, then every 2–3 mo for rest of first year, then periodically.
- Instructions for CONCURRENT THERAPIES: Reduce theophylline dose and closely monitor theophylline levels; closely monitor PT and INR with warfarin therapy; closely monitor phenytoin level with phenytoin therapy; closely monitor HR and BP for excessive beta blockade with propranolol therapy.

Patient & Family Education

- Take medication regularly even during symptom-free periods.
- Drug is not intended to treat acute episodes of asthma.
- Report to physician promptly S&S of hepatic toxicity (see Appendix F) or flu-like symptoms. Follow-up lab work is very important.

Common adverse effects in *italic*, life-threatening effects <u>underlined</u>; generic names in **bold**; classifications in SMALL CAPS; ♣ Canadian drug name; ⊙ Prototype drug

1613

Z

■ Notify physician if condition worsens while using prescribed doses of all antiasthmatic medications.

ZIPRASIDONE HYDROCHLORIDE

(zip-ra-si′done)
Geodon

Classifications: PSYCHOTHERAPEUTIC; ANTIPSYCHOTIC, ATYPICAL
Therapeutic: ANTIPSYCHOTIC, ATYPICAL
Prototype: Clozapine
Pregnancy Category: C

AVAILABILITY 20 mg, 40 mg, 60 mg, 80 mg capsules; 20 mg/mL injection; 10 mg/mL suspension

ACTION & *THERAPEUTIC EFFECT*
Exerts antischizophrenic effects through dopamine (D_2) and serotonin ($5HT_{2A}$) receptor antagonist. Exerts antidepressant effects through $5HT_1A$ agonism, $5HT_1D$ antagonism, and serotonin/norepinephrine reuptake inhibition. *Improves symptoms of schizophrenia, schizoaffective disorder, and psychotic depression.*

USES Treatment of schizophrenia, acute bipolar mania.
UNLABELED USES Tourette's syndrome.

CONTRAINDICATIONS Hypersensitivity to ziprasidone; history of QT prolongation including congenital long QT syndrome or with other drugs known to prolong the QT interval; AV block, bundle branch block, cardiac arrhythmias, congenital heart disease, recent MI or uncompensated heart failure; bradycardia, hypokalemia or hypomagnesemia; intravenous administration; neuroleptic malignant syndrome and tardive dyskinesia; dehydration or hypovolemia; UV exposure and tanning beds; pregnancy (category C), lactation. Safety and efficacy in children or adolescents are not established.
CAUTIOUS USE History of seizures, CVA, dementia, Parkinson's disease, or Alzheimer disease; known cardiovascular disease, conduction abnormalities, treatment with antihypertensive drugs; cerebrovascular disease; hepatic impairment; seizure disorder, seizures; breast cancer; risk factors for elevated core body temperature; esophageal motility disorders and risk of aspiration pneumonia; schizophrenia; suicide potential; children >7 y for use in Tourette's syndrome only.

ROUTE & DOSAGE

Schizophrenia
Adult: **PO** Start with 20 mg b.i.d. with food, may increase q2d up to 80 mg b.i.d. if needed **IM** 10 mg q2h or 20 mg q4h up to max of 40 mg/d

Acute Mania
Adult: **PO** Start with 40 mg b.i.d. with food; may increase q2d up to 80 mg b.i.d. if needed

ADMINISTRATION

Note: CONTRAINDICATIONS for this drug. Do NOT administer to anyone with a history of cardiac arrhythmias or other cardiac disease, hypokalemia, hypomagnesemia, prolonged QT/QTc interval, or to anyone on other drugs known to prolong the QTc interval. Withhold drug and consult physician if any of the foregoing conditions are present.

Common adverse effects in *italic*, life-threatening effects underlined; generic names in **bold**; classifications in SMALL CAPS; ✦ Canadian drug name; ⊘ Prototype drug

Z

Oral
- Give with food.
- Make dosage adjustments at intervals of ≥2 d.

Intramuscular
- Give deep IM into a large muscle.
- Store at 15°–30° C (59°–86° F).

ADVERSE EFFECTS (≥1%) **Body as a Whole:** Asthenia, myalgia, weight gain, flu-like syndrome, face edema, chills, hypothermia. **CNS:** *Somnolence,* akathisia, dizziness, extrapyramidal effects, dystonia, hypertonia, agitation, tremor, dyskinesias, hostility, paresthesia, confusion, vertigo, hypokinesia, hyperkinesias, abnormal gait, oculogyric crisis, hypesthesia, ataxia, amnesia, cogwheel rigidity, delirium, hypotonia, akinesia, dysarthria, withdrawal syndrome, buccoglossal syndrome, choreoathetosis, diplopia, incoordination, neuropathy. **CV:** Tachycardia, postural hypotension, prolonged QTc interval, hypertension. **GI:** *Nausea,* constipation, dyspepsia, diarrhea, dry mouth, anorexia, abdominal pain, vomiting. **Metabolic:** Hyperglycemia, diabetes mellitus. **Respiratory:** Rhinitis, increased cough, dyspnea. **Skin:** Rash, fungal dermatitis, photosensitivity. **Special Senses:** Abnormal vision.

INTERACTIONS Drug: Carbamazepine may decrease **ziprasidone** levels; **ketoconazole** may increase **ziprasidone** levels; may enhance hypotensive effects of ANTIHYPERTENSIVE AGENTS; may antagonize effects of **levodopa;** increased risk of arrhythmias and heart block due to prolonged QTc interval with ANTIARRHYTHMIC AGENTS, **amoxapine, arsenic trioxide, chlorpromazine, clarithromycin, daunorubicin, diltiazem, dolasetron, doxorubicin, droperidol, erythromycin, halofantrine, indapamide, levomethadyl,** LOCAL ANESTHETICS, **maprotiline, mefloquine, mesoridazine, octreotide, pentamidine, pimozide, probucol, gatifloxacin, grepafloxacin, levofloxacin, moxifloxacin, sparfloxacin,** TRICYCLIC ANTIDEPRESSANTS, **tacrolimus, thioridazine, troleandomycin;** additive CNS depression with SEDATIVE-HYPNOTICS, ANXIOLYTICS, **ethanol,** OPIATE AGONISTS.

PHARMACOKINETICS Absorption: Well absorbed with 60% reaching systemic circulation. **Peak:** 6–8 h. **Metabolism:** Extensively in the liver. **Elimination:** 20% of metabolites in urine, 66% of metabolites in bile. **Half-Life:** 7 h.

CLINICAL IMPLICATIONS
Assessment & Drug Effects
- Lab tests: Baseline and periodic ECG, serum potassium and serum magnesium, especially with concomitant diuretic therapy. Periodically monitor blood glucose.
- Monitor diabetics for loss of glycemic control.
- Monitor for S&S of torsade de pointes (e.g., dizziness, palpitations, syncope), tardive dyskinesia (see Appendix F) especially in older adult women and with prolonged therapy, and the appearance of an unexplained rash. Withhold drug and report to physician immediately if any of these develop.
- Monitor for signs and symptoms of suicidality.
- Monitor I&O ratio and pattern: Notify physician if diarrhea, vomiting or any other conditions develops which may cause electrolyte imbalance.
- Monitor BP lying, sitting, and standing. Report orthostatic hypotension to physician.
- Monitor cognitive status and take appropriate precautions.

Z

Common adverse effects in *italic*, life-threatening effects underlined; generic names in **bold**; classifications in SMALL CAPS; ✦ Canadian drug name; ❂ Prototype drug

1615

▪Monitor for loss of seizure control, especially with a history of seizures or dementia.

Patient & Family Education

▪Carefully monitor blood glucose levels if diabetic.

▪Be aware that therapeutic effect may not be evident for several weeks.

▪Report any of the following to a health care provider immediately: Palpitations, faintness or loss of consciousness, rash, abnormal muscle movements, vomiting or diarrhea.

▪Do not drive or engage in potentially hazardous activities until response to drug is known.

▪Make position changes slowly and in stages to prevent dizziness upon arising.

▪Avoid strenuous exercise, exposure to extreme heat, or other activities that may cause dehydration.

ZOLEDRONIC ACID

(zo-le-dron′ic)

Zometa

Classifications: BISPHOSPHONATE; REGULATOR, BONE METABOLISM

Therapeutic: BONE METABOLISM REGULATOR

Prototype: Etidronate disodium

Pregnancy Category: D

AVAILABILITY 4 mg injection

ACTION & *THERAPEUTIC EFFECT*

Zoledronic acid inhibits various stimulatory factors of osteoclastic activity produced by bone tumors. It also induces osteoclast apoptosis. *Zoledronic acid blocks osteoclastic resorption of bone, thus reducing the amount of calcium released from bone.*

USES Treatment of hypercalcemia of malignancy, multiple myeloma, and bony metastases from solid tumors.

UNLABELED USES Paget's disease.

CONTRAINDICATIONS Hypersensitivity to zoledronic acid or other bisphosphonates; preexisting hypocalcemia; serum creatinine of 0.5 mg/dL; pregnancy (category D); lactation.

CAUTIOUS USE Aspirin-sensitive asthma; cancer chemotherapy, corticosteroid therapy; renal and/or hepatic impairment; renal failure; dental work; concurrent administration of aminoglycosides, or loop diuretics; multiple myeloma; older adults. Safety and effectiveness of zoledronic acid in children have not been established.

ROUTE & DOSAGE

Hypercalcemia of Malignancy

Adult: **IV** 4 mg over a minimum of 15 min. May consider retreatment if serum calcium has not returned to normal, may repeat after 7 d

Multiple Myeloma and Bony Metastases from Solid Tumors

Adult: **IV** 4 mg over a minimum of 15 min q 3–4 wk

Paget's Disease

Adult: **IV** A single dose of 100–400 mcg

Renal Impairment

Cl_{cr} >60 mL/min: 4 mg; 50–60 mL/min 3.5 mg; 40–49 mL/min: 3.3 mg; 30–39 mL/min: 3.0 mg

ADMINISTRATION

Intravenous

Do not administer to anyone who is dehydrated or suspected

of being dehydrated. Consult physician.

- Do not administer zoledronic acid unless patient is adequately rehydrated.
- Do not administer until serum creatinine values have been evaluated by the physician.

PREPARE: **IV Infusion:** Reconstitute by adding 5 mL of sterile water for injection to each vial. Withdraw the entire contents of the vial (4 mg) and further dilute in 100 mL of D5W or NS. Do not use lactated Ringer's solution. If not used immediately, refrigerate. The total time between reconstitution and end of infusion must not exceed 24 h.

ADMINISTER: **IV Infusion:** Infuse 4 mg or less (NEVER MORE) over NO LESS than 15 min.

INCOMPATIBILITIES **Solution/additive and Y-site:** Do not mix or infuse with **calcium**-containing solutions (e.g., **Ringer's lactate**).

- Store at 2°–8° C (36°–46° F) follow reconstitution. Must be completely infused within 24 h of reconstitution.

ADVERSE EFFECTS (≥1%) **Body as a Whole:** *Fever,* flu-like syndrome, redness and swelling at injection site, asthenia, chest pain, leg edema, mucositis, rigors. **CNS:** *Insomnia, anxiety, confusion, agitation,* headache, somnolence. **CV:** *Hypotension.* **GI:** *Nausea, vomiting, constipation, abdominal pain, anorexia,* dysphagia. **Hematologic:** *Anemia,* granulocytopenia, thrombocytopenia, <u>pancytopenia</u>. **Metabolic:** *Hypophosphatemia, hypokalemia, hypomagnesemia,* hypocalcemia, dehydration. **Musculoskeletal:** Skeletal pain, arthralgias, osteonecrosis of the jaw in cancer pa-

tients. **Respiratory:** *Dyspnea, cough,* pleural effusion. **Skin:** Alopecia, dermatitis. **Urogenital:** Renal deterioration (increase in S_{cr}).

INTERACTIONS Drug: LOOP DIURETICS may increase risk of hypocalcemia; **thalidomide** and other NEPHROTOXIC DRUGS may increase risk of renal toxicity.

PHARMACOKINETICS Onset: 4–10 d. **Duration:** 3–4 wk. **Metabolism:** Not metabolized. **Elimination:** In urine. **Half-Life:** 146 h.

CLINICAL IMPLICATIONS

Assessment & Drug Effects

- Lab tests: Baseline renal function tests prior to each dose and periodically thereafter; periodic ionized calcium or corrected serum calcium levels, serum phosphate and magnesium, electrolytes, CBC with differential, Hct and Hgb.
- Notify physician immediately of deteriorating renal function as indicated by rising serum creatinine levels over baseline value.
- Withhold subsequent doses of zoledronic acid if serum creatinine is not within 10% of the baseline value. Consult physician.
- Monitor closely patient's hydration status. Note that loop diuretics should be used with caution due to the risk of hypocalcemia.
- Monitor for S&S of bronchospasm in aspirin-sensitive asthma patients; notify physician immediately.

Patient & Family Education

- Maintain adequate daily fluid intake. Consult with physician for guidelines.
- Report unexplained weakness, tiredness, irritation, muscle pain, insomnia, or flu-like symptoms.

Z

Common adverse effects in *italic*, life-threatening effects <u>underlined</u>; generic names in **bold**; classifications in SMALL CAPS; ✚ Canadian drug name; ⊘ Prototype drug

ZOLMITRIPTAN

(zol-mi-trip'tan)
Zomig, Zomig ZMT, Zomig Nasal Spray
Classifications: ALPHA-ADRENERGIC ANTAGONIST; SEROTONIN 5-HT$_{1B/1D}$ RECEPTOR AGONIST; ERGOT ALKALOID; ANTIMIGRAINE
Therapeutic: ANTIMIGRAINE; ERGOT ALKALOID
Prototype: Sumatriptan
Pregnancy Category: C

AVAILABILITY 2.5 mg, 5 mg tablets orally disintegrating tablets; 5 mg nasal spray

ACTION & *THERAPEUTIC EFFECT*
Selective serotonin (5-HT$_{1B/1D}$) receptor agonist. The agonist effects at 5-HT$_{1B/1D}$ reverse the vasodilation of cranial blood vessels and inhibit release of pro-inflammatory neuropeptides. *Vasoconstricts dilated cranial blood vessels and decreased neuropeptide release relieve the pain of a migraine headache.*

USES Acute migraine headaches with or without aura.

CONTRAINDICATIONS Hypersensitivity to zolmitriptan; ischemic heart disease (angina pectoris, arteriosclerosis, ECG changes, history of MI or Prinzmetal's angina); cardiac arrhythmias, symptomatic Wolff-Parkinson-White syndrome, uncontrolled hypertension; hemiplegia or basilar migraine; concurrent administration of ergotamine or sumatriptan; PKU; adults >65 y; pregnancy (category C); children <18 y.

CAUTIOUS USE Men >40 y; postmenopausal women; patients with other cardiac risk factors, such as diabetes, obesity, cigarette smoking, high cholesterol levels, strong family history of CAD; concurrent adminis-

tration of MAOIs; GI disease, PVD, ischemic colitis, Raynaud's disease, cerebrovascular disease, stroke, intracranial bleeding; renal failure or renal disease; lactation.

ROUTE & DOSAGE

Acute Migraine
Adult: **PO** 2.5–5 mg, may repeat in 2 h if necessary (max: 10 mg/24 h) **Nasal Spray** One spray into one nostril

ADMINISTRATION
Oral
- Give any time after symptoms of migraine appear. Give ≤2.5 mg by breaking a 5 mg tablet in half. If headache returns, may repeat q2h up to 10 mg in 24 h.
- Do NOT give zolmitriptan within 24 h of an ergot-containing drug or other 5-HT$_1$ agonist.
- Discard unused tablets that have been removed from the packaging.

Intranasal
- Unit-dose spray device delivers a 5 mg dose. Do not exceed the maximum dose of 10 mg in 24 h.
- Store at 2°–25° C (36°–77° F) and protect from light.

ADVERSE EFFECTS (≥1%) **Body as a Whole:** Asthenia, fatigue, malaise, pain, pressure sensation, paresthesia, throat pressure, warm/cold sensations, hypesthesia. **CNS:** Somnolence, dizziness, drowsiness, headache, hypesthesia, decreased mental acuity, euphoria, tremor. **CV:** Coronary artery vasospasm, transient myocardial ischemia, <u>MI</u>, ventricular tachycardia, ventricular fibrillation, chest pain/tightness/heaviness, palpitations. **GI:** Dry mouth, nausea, vomiting. **Respiratory:** Dyspnea. **Skin:** Flushing. **Other:** Hot flushes.

Z

INTERACTIONS Drug: Dihydroergotamine, methysergide, other 5-HT$_1$ AGONISTS may cause prolonged vasospastic reactions; SSRIS have rarely caused weakness, hyperreflexia, and incoordination; MAOIS should not be used with 5-HT$_1$ agonists; **cimetidine** increases half-life of zolmitriptan. **Herbal: St. John's wort** may increase triptan toxicity.

PHARMACOKINETICS Absorption: Rapidly absorbed, 40% bioavailability. **Peak:** 2–3 h. **Distribution:** 25% protein bound. **Metabolism:** In liver to active metabolite. **Elimination:** Primarily in urine (65%), 30% in feces. **Half-Life:** 3 h.

CLINICAL IMPLICATIONS
Assessment & Drug Effects
- Monitor for therapeutic effectiveness: Relief or reduction of migraine pain within 1–4 h.
- Monitor cardiovascular status carefully following first dose in patients at risk for CAD (e.g., postmenopausal women, men >40 y, persons with known CAD risk factors) or coronary artery vasospasms.
- Perform periodic cardiovascular evaluation and ECG with long-term use.
- Report to physician immediately chest pain, nausea, or tightness in chest or throat that is severe or does not quickly resolve.

Patient & Family Education
- Carefully review patient information insert and guidelines for taking drug.
- Do NOT take zolmitriptan during the aura phase, but as early as possible after onset of migraine.
- Concurrent oral contraceptive use may increase incidence of adverse effects.
- Contact physician immediately if any of the following occur after zolmitriptan use: Symptoms of angina (e.g., severe or persistent pain or tightness in chest or throat, sudden nausea), hypersensitivity (e.g., wheezing, facial swelling, skin rash, hives), fainting, or abdominal pain.
- Report any other adverse effects (e.g., tingling, flushing, dizziness) at next physician visit.

ZOLPIDEM ℗
(zol'-pi-dem)
Ambien, Ambien CR
Classifications: ANXIOLYTIC; SEDATIVE-HYPNOTIC, NON-BENZODIAZEPINE
Therapeutic: SEDATIVE-HYPNOTIC; ANTIANXIETY
Pregnancy Category: C
Controlled Substance: Schedule IV

AVAILABILITY 5 mg, 10 mg tablets; 6.25 mg, 12.5 mg extended release tablets

ACTION & *THERAPEUTIC EFFECT*
An agonist that binds to the BZD1 subunit on the gamma-aminobutyric acid (GABA)-A receptor chloride channel, thus inhibiting the action potential. *Sedative, anticonvulsant, and antianxiety effects thought to be due to GABA-A agonism.*

USES Short-term treatment of insomnia.

CONTRAINDICATIONS Suicidal ideation; labor or obstetric delivery; pregnancy (category C), children <18 y.
CAUTIOUS USE Depressed patients, hepatic/renal impairment, older adults, alcohol or drug abuse; patients with compromised respiratory status, COPD, sleep apnea; chronic depression.

Z

Common adverse effects in *italic*, life-threatening effects <u>underlined</u>; generic names in **bold**; classifications in SMALL CAPS; ♣ Canadian drug name; ℗ Prototype drug

1619

ROUTE & DOSAGE

Short-Term Treatment of Insomnia

Adult: **PO** 5–10 mg h.s. limited to 7–10 d
Geriatric: **PO** Start with 5 mg h.s. limited to 7–10 d

ADMINISTRATION

Oral

- Give immediately before bedtime; for more rapid sleep onset, do NOT give with or immediately after a meal.
- Extended release tablets should be swallowed whole. Ensure that they are not crushed or chewed.
- Use reduced dosage of 5 mg in older adult or debilitated patients.
- Store at room temperature, 15°–30° C (59°–86° F).

ADVERSE EFFECTS (≥1%) **CNS:** Headache on awakening, drowsiness or fatigue, lethargy, drugged feeling, depression, anxiety, irritability, dizziness, double vision. Confusion and falls reported in elderly. Doses >10 mg may be associated with anterograde amnesia or memory impairment. **GI:** Dyspepsia, nausea, vomiting. **Other:** Myalgia.

INTERACTIONS Drug: CNS DEPRESSANTS, **alcohol,** PHENOTHIAZINES by augmenting CNS depression. **Food:** Extent and rate of absorption of zolpidem are significantly decreased.

PHARMACOKINETICS Absorption: Readily from GI tract. 70% reaches systemic circulation. Food decreases rate and extent of absorption. **Onset:** 7–27 min. **Peak:** 0.5–2.3 h. **Duration:** 6–8 h. **Distribution:** Highly protein bound. Lowest concentrations in CNS, highest concentrations in glandular tissue and fat.

Crosses placenta, very small amounts (<0.02%) distributed into breast milk. **Metabolism:** In the liver to 3 inactive metabolites. **Elimination:** 79–96% of dose appears as metabolites in the bile, urine, and feces. **Half-Life:** 1.7–2.5 h.

CLINICAL IMPLICATIONS

Assessment & Drug Effects

- Assess respiratory function in patients with compromised respiratory status. Report immediately to physician significantly depressed respiratory rate (<12/min).
- Monitor patients for S&S of depression (see Appendix F); zolpidem may increase level of depression.
- Monitor older adult or debilitated patients closely for impaired cognitive or motor function and unusual sensitivity to the drug's effects.

Patient & Family Education

- Avoid taking alcohol or other CNS depressants while on zolpidem.
- Do not drive or engage in other potentially hazardous activities until response to drug is known.
- Report vision changes to physician.
- Note: Onset of drug is more rapid when taken on an empty stomach.

ZONISAMIDE ℗

(zon-i'sa-mide)
Zonegran
Classifications: ANTICONVULSANT; SULFONAMIDE
Therapeutic: ANTICONVULSANT; SULFONAMIDE
Pregnancy Category: C

AVAILABILITY 25 mg, 50 mg, 100 mg capsules

Z

ACTION & *THERAPEUTIC EFFECT*

A broad-spectrum anticonvulsant that facilitates dopaminergic and serotonergic neurotransmission but does not potentiate the activity of gamma-aminobutyric acid (GABA) in the synapses of the neurons. *Suppresses focal spike discharges and electroshock seizures. Effective against a variety of seizure types.*

USES Adjunctive therapy for partial seizures in adults.
UNLABELED USES Bipolar disorder.

CONTRAINDICATIONS Hypersensitivity to sulfonamides or zonisamide; pregnancy (category C), lactation; children <16 y.
CAUTIOUS USE Renal or hepatic insufficiency, dehydration, hypovolemia; renal impairment; concomitant administration of drugs that induce or inhibit CYP3A4; older adults.

ROUTE & DOSAGE

Partial Seizures
Adult: **PO** Start at 100 mg q.d., may increase after 2 wk to 200 mg/d, may then increase q2wk, if necessary (max: 400 mg/d in 1–2 divided doses)

ADMINISTRATION

Oral

- Do not crush or break capsules; ensure capsules are swallowed whole with adequate fluid.
- Withdraw drug gradually when discontinued to minimize seizure potential.
- Store at 25° C (77° F); room temperature permitted. Protect from light and moisture.

ADVERSE EFFECTS (≥1%) **Body as a Whole:** Flu-like syndrome, weight loss. **CNS:** Agitation, irritability, anxiety, ataxia, confusion, depression, difficulty concentrating, difficulty with memory, *dizziness,* fatigue, *headache,* insomnia, mental slowing, nervousness, nystagmus, paresthesia, schizophrenic behavior, *somnolence,* tiredness, tremor, convulsion, abnormal gait, hyperesthesia, incoordination. **GI:** Abdominal pain, *anorexia,* constipation, diarrhea, dyspepsia, nausea, dry mouth, flatulence, gingivitis, gum hyperplasia, gastritis, stomatitis, cholelithiasis, glossitis, melena, rectal hemorrhage, ulcerative stomatitis, ulcer, dysphagia. **Metabolic:** Oligohidrosis, sometimes resulting in heat stroke and hyperthermia in children. **Respiratory:** Rhinitis, pharyngitis, cough. **Skin:** Ecchymosis, rash, pruritus. **Special Senses:** Difficulties in verbal expression, diplopia, speech abnormalities, taste perversion, amblyopia, tinnitus. **Urogenital:** Kidney stones.

INTERACTIONS Drug: Phenytoin, carbamazepine, phenobarbital, valproic acid may decrease half-life of zonisamide.

PHARMACOKINETICS Peak: 2–6 h. **Distribution:** 40% protein bound, extensively binds to erythrocytes. **Metabolism:** Acetylated in liver by CYP3A4. **Elimination:** Primarily in urine. **Half-Life:** 63–105 h.

CLINICAL IMPLICATIONS

Assessment & Drug Effects

- Withhold drug and notify physician if an unexplained rash or S&S of hypersensitivity appear (see Appendix F).
- Monitor for and report S&S of CNS impairment (somnolence, excessive fatigue, cognitive deficits, speech or language problems, incoordination, gait disturbances); oligohidrosis (lack of sweating) and hyperthermia in pediatric patients.

Z

Common adverse effects in *italic*, life-threatening effects <u>underlined</u>; generic names in **bold**; classifications in SMALL CAPS; ♣ Canadian drug name; ⊘ Prototype drug

- Lab tests: Periodic BUN and serum creatinine, and CBC with differential.

Patient & Family Education
- Do not abruptly stop taking this medication.
- Increase daily fluid intake to minimize risk of renal stones. Notify physician immediately of S&S of renal stones: sudden back or abdominal pain, and blood in urine.

- Report any of the following: dizziness, excess drowsiness, frequent headaches, malaise, double vision, lack of coordination, persistent nausea, sore throat, fever, mouth ulcers, or easy bruising.
- Exercise special caution with concurrent use of alcohol or CNS depressants.
- Do not drive or engage in other potentially hazardous activities until response to drug is known.

Appendixes

(Generic names are in **bold**)

APPENDIX A-1
OCULAR MEDICATIONS:

BETA-ADRENERGIC BLOCKERS **Prototype for classification: Propranolol HCl** **Use:** Intraocular hypertension and chronic open-angle glaucoma.

Betaxolol HCl 0.25%, 0.5% soln Betoptic, Betoptic S	*Adult:* **Topical** 1 drop of 0.5% solution or 0.25% suspension in affected eye twice daily.
Carteolol HCl 1% soln Ocupress	*Adult:* **Topical** 1 drop b.i.d.
Levobetaxolol 0.5% susp Betaxon	*Adult:* **Topical** 1 drop b.i.d.
Levobunolol 0.25%, 0.5% soln Betagan	*Adult:* **Topical** 1–2 drops 1–2 times/d.
Metipranolol HCl 0.3% soln OptiPranolol	*Adult:* **Topical** 1 drop b.i.d.
Timolol maleate 0.25%, 0.5% soln Betimol, Timoptic, Timoptic XE, Istalol	*Adult:* **Topical** 1 drop of 0.25–0.5% solution b.i.d.; may decrease to q.d. Apply gel q.d. Apply Istalol solution once daily.

Adverse Effects/Clinical Implications: May cause *mild ocular stinging* and discomfort; tearing; may also have the adverse effects of systemic beta blockers. May mask symptoms of acute hypoglycemia in diabetic patients (tachycardia, tremor, but not sweating). May precipitate thyroid storm in patients with hyperthyroidism. Patients with impaired cardiac function and the elderly should report to physician signs and symptoms of CHF (see Appendix G). Monitor BP for hypotension and heart rate for bradycardia.

MIOTICS **Prototype for classification: Pilocarpine HCl** **Use:** Open-angle and angle-closure glaucomas; to reduce IOP and to protect the lens during surgery and laser iridotomy; to counteract effects of mydriatics and cycloplegics following surgery or ophthalmoscopic examination.

Apraclonidine HCl Iopidine, 0.5%, 1% solution	**Intraoperative and Post-surgical Increase in IOP:** *Adult:* **Topical** 1 drop of 1% solution in affected eye 1 h before surgery and 1 drop in same eye immediately after surgery. **Open-angle Glaucoma:** *Adult:* **Topical** 1 drop of 0.5% solution in affected eye q12h.

Brimonidine tartrate Alphagan P, 0.1%, 0.15% solution	**Glaucoma:** *Adult:* **Topical** 1 drop in affected eye(s) t.i.d. approximately 8 h apart.
Brinzolamide Azopt, 1% suspension	**Ocular Hypertension or Open-angle Glaucoma:** *Adult:* **Topical** 1 drop in affected eye(s) t.i.d.
Carbachol Carbastat, Miostat, 0.01% solution	*Adult:* **Intraocular** 0.5 ml of 0.01% solution injected into anterior chamber of eye.
Dorzolamide Trusopt, 2% solution	**Ocular Hypertension or Open-angle Glaucoma:** *Adult/Child:* **Topical** 1 drop in affected eye(s) t.i.d.
Echothiophate iodide Phospholine Iodide, 0.125% solution	**Glaucoma:** *Adult:* **Topical** 1 drop of 0.03–0.25% solution in conjunctival sac 1–2 times/d. **Accommodative Esotropia:** *Adult:* **Topical** *Diagnosis:* 1 drop of 0.125% solution in both eyes once/d at bedtime for 2–3 wk. *Treatment:* 1 drop of 0.125% solution q.o.d. or 1 drop of 0.06% solution daily (max: 1 drop 0.125% solution daily).
Pilocarpine HCl Isopto Carpine, Miocarpine, Pilopine HS, 0.5%, 1%, 2%, 3%, 4%, 6% solution	**Acute Glaucoma:** *Adult:* **Topical** 1 drop of 1–2% solution in affected eye q5–10min for 3–6 doses, then 1 drop q1–3h until IOP is reduced. **Chronic Glaucoma:** *Adult:* **Topical** 1 drop of 0.5–4% solution in affected eye q4–12h or 1 ocular system (Ocusert) q7d **Miotic:** *Adult:* **Topical** 1 drop of 1% solution in affected eye.

Adverse Effects/Clinical Implications: Ocular: Ciliary spasm with browache, twitching of eyelids, eye pain with change in eye focus, miosis, *diminished vision in poorly illuminated areas,* blurred vision, reduced visual acuity, sensitivity, contact allergy, lacrimation, follicular conjunctivitis, conjunctival irritation, cataract, retinal detachment. **CNS:** *Headache, drowsiness,* depression, syncope. **GI:** Abnormal taste, dry mouth. **Clinical Implications:** Wait 15 min after instillation before inserting soft contact lenses to avoid staining the lenses. Use with MAO inhibitors may have increased risk of hypertensive emergency. May increase the effects of beta blockers and other antihypertensives on blood pressure and heart rate. TCAs may reduce the effects of **brimonidine. Brinzolamide** is a carbonic anhydrase inhibitor (prototype: acetazolamide) and is a sulfonamide. It should not be used by patients with sulfa allergies. Reconstituted solutions of **echothiophate** remain stable for 1 mo at room temperature. Expiration date should appear on label. The length of time solutions remain stable under refrigeration varies with manufacturer. **Echothiophate** therapy is generally discontinued 2–6 wk before surgery. If necessary, alternate miotic therapy is substituted. Medication should be given in the evening. Give at least 5 min apart from other topical ophthalmic drugs. The patient with brown or hazel eyes may require a stronger ophthalmic solution or more frequent instillation of **physostigmine** for desired effects than the patient with blue eyes.

PROSTAGLANDINS **Prototype for classification: Latanoprost**
Use: Open-angle glaucoma and intraocular hypertension.

Bimatoprost Lumigan, 0.03% solution	*Adult:* **Topical** 1 drop in affected eye(s) once daily in the evening.
Latanoprost Xalatan, 0.005% solution	*Adult:* **Topical** 1 drop (1.5 mcg) in affected eye(s) once daily in the evening.
Travoprost Travatan, 0.004% solution	*Adult:* **Topical** 1 drop in affected eye(s) once daily in the evening.

Adverse Effects: Ocular: *Conjunctival hyperemia, growth of eyelashes, ocular pruritus,* ocular dryness, visual disturbance, ocular burning, foreign body sensation, eye pain, pigmentation of the periocular skin, blepharitis, cataract, superficial punctate keratitis, eyelid erythema, ocular irritation, eyelash darkening, eye discharge, tearing, photophobia, allergic conjunctivitis, increases in iris pigmentation (brown pigment), conjunctival edema. **Body as a Whole:** Headaches, abnormal liver function tests, asthenia, and hirsutism. **Clinical Implications:** Should instill in the evening. Wait 15 min after instillation before inserting soft contact lenses to avoid staining the lenses. Give at least 5 min apart from other topical ophthalmic drugs.

MYDRIATIC **Prototype for classification: Homatropine HBr**
Use: Mydriatic for ocular examination and as cycloplegic to measure errors of refraction. Also inflammatory conditions of uveal tract, ciliary spasm, as a cycloplegic and mydriatic in preoperative and postoperative conditions, and as an optical aid in select patients with axial lens opacities.

Cyclopentolate HCl AK-Pentolate, Cyclogyl, Pentalair, 0.5%, 1%, 2% solution	**Cycloplegic Refraction:** *Adult:* **Topical** 1 drop of 1% solution in eye 40–50 min before procedure, followed by 1 drop in 5 min; may need 2% solution in patients with darkly pigmented eyes. *Child:* **Topical** 1 drop of 0.5–1% solution in eye 40–50 min before procedure, followed by 1 drop in 5 min; may need 2% solution in patients with darkly pigmented eyes.
Dipivefrin HCl Propine, 0.1% solution	**Glaucoma:** *Adult:* **Topical** 1 drop in eye q12h.

Homatropine HBr
AK-Homatropine,
Homatrine,
Homatroptine, Isopto
Homatropine, 2%,
5% solution

Cycloplegic Refraction: *Adult:* **Topical** 1–2 drops of 2% or 5% solution in eye repeated in 5–10 min if necessary. **Ocular Inflammation:** *Adult:* **Topical** 1–2 drops of 2% or 5% solution in eye up to q3–4h.

Hydroxyam-phetamine HBr/ Tropicamide
Paremyd, 0.25%, 1% solution

Dilation of pupil: *Adult:* **Topical** 1–2 drops in conjunctival sac.

Phenylephrine HCl
AK-Dilate
Ophthalmic,
Alconefrin,
Mydfrin,
Neo-Synephrine,
0.12%, 0.125%,
0.16%, 0.25%, 0.5%,
1%, 1.5%, 10% solution

Ophthalmoscopy: *Adult:* **Topical** 1 drop of 2.5% or 10% solution before examination. *Child:* **Topical** 1 drop of 2.5% solution before examination.
Vasoconstrictor: *Adult:* **Topical** 2 drops of 0.12–0.15% solution q3–4h as necessary.

Tropicamide
Mydriacyl,
Tropicacyl, 0.5%, 1% solution

Refraction: *Adult:* **Topical** 1–2 drops of 1% solution in each eye, repeat in 5 min; if patient is not seen within 20–30 min, an additional drop may be instilled. **Examination of Fundus:** *Adult:* **Topical** 1–2 drops of 0.5% solution in each eye 15–20 min prior to examination; may repeat q30min if necessary.

Contraindicated in: Primary (narrow-angle) glaucoma or predisposition to glaucoma; children <6 y. **Cautious Use in:** Increased IOP, infants, children, pregnancy (category C), the elderly or debilitated; hypertension; hyperthyroidism; diabetes; cardiac disease. **Adverse Effects:** Increased IOP, *blurred vision, photophobia.* **Prolonged Use:** Local irritation, congestion, edema, eczema, follicular conjunctivitis. **Excessive Dosage/Systemic Absorption:** Symptoms of atropine poisoning (flushing, dry skin, mouth, nose; decreased sweating; fever, rash, rapid/irregular pulse; abdominal and bladder distension; hallucinations, confusion). **CNS:** Psychotic reaction, behavior disturbances, ataxia, incoherent speech, restlessness, hallucinations, somnolence, disorientation, failure to recognize people, grand mal seizures. **Clinical Implications:** Carefully monitor **cyclopentolate** patients with seizure disorders, since systemic absorption may precipitate a seizure. Photophobia associated with mydriasis may require patient to wear dark glasses. Since drug causes blurred vision, supervision of activity may be indicated.

VASOCONSTRICTOR; DECONGESTANT   Prototype for classification: Naphazoline HCl   Use: Ocular vasoconstrictor.

Naphazoline HCl
AK-Con, Albalon,
Allerest, Clear Eyes,
Comfort, Degest-2,
Nafazair, Naphcon,
Privine, VasoClear,
Vasocon, 0.012%,
0.02%, 0.03%, 0.1%
solution

Adult: **Topical** 1–3 drops of 0.1% solution q3–4h prn or 1–2 drops of a 0.01–0.03% solution q4h prn.

Tetrahydrozoline HCl
Collyrium, Mallazine,
Murine Plus,
Optigene, Soothe,
Tyzine, Visine, 0.05%
solution

Adult: **Topical** 1–2 drops of 0.05% solution in eye b.i.d. or t.i.d.

Contraindicated in: Narrow-angle glaucoma; concomitant use with MAO INHIBITORS or TRICYCLIC ANTIDEPRESSANTS **Cautious Use in:** Hypertension, cardiac irregularities, advanced arteriosclerosis; diabetes; hyperthyroidism; elderly patients. **Adverse Effects:** Pupillary dilation, increased intraocular pressure, rebound redness of the eye, headache, hypertension, nausea, weakness, sweating. **Overdosage:** Drowsiness, hypothermia, bradycardia, shocklike hypotension, coma.

CORTICOSTEROID, ANTI-INFLAMMATORY   Prototype for classification:
Hydrocortisone   Use: Inflammation. **Unlabeled Use:** Anterior uveitis.

Dexamethasone sodium phosphate
Maxidex
Ophthalmic, 0.1%
suspension

Adult: **Topical** 1–2 drops in conjunctival sac up to 4–6 times/d; may instill hourly for severe disease.

Fluorometholone
Fluor-Op,
FML Forte,
FML Liquifilm,
FML S.O.P.,
0.1%, 0.25% suspension; 0.1% ointment

Adult and Child >2 y: **Topical** 1–2 drops of suspension in conjunctival sac q.h. for the first 24–48 h; then b.i.d. to q.i.d.; or a thin strip of ointment q4h for the first 24–48 h; then 1–3 times/d.

Loteprednol etabonate
Alrex, Lotemax, 0.2%,
0.5% suspension

Adult: **Topical** 1–2 drops in conjunctival sac q.i.d. during initial treatment, may increase to q1h if necessary.

Prednisolone sodium phosphate
Inflamase Mild,
Pred Mild, Prednisol,
Inflamase Forte,
0.11%, 0.12%, 0.9%
suspension

Adult: **Topical** 1–2 drops in conjunctival sac q.h. during the day; then q2h at night; may decrease to 1 drop t.i.d. or q.i.d.

Rimexolone Vexol, 1% solution	**Postoperative Ocular Inflammation:** *Adult:* **Topical** 1–2 drops q.i.d. beginning 24 h after surgery, continue through first 2 wk postoperatively. **Anterior Uveitis:** *Adult:* **Topical** 1–2 drops in affected eye every hour while awake for first week, then q2h for second week, then taper frequency until uveitis resolves.

Contraindicated in: Ocular fungal diseases, *herpes simplex* keratitis, ocular infections, ocular mycobacterial infections, viral disease of cornea or conjunctiva such as vaccina, varicella. **Adverse Effects: Ocular:** Blurred vision, photophobia, conjunctival edema, corneal edema, erosion, eye discharge, dryness, irritation, pain; prolonged use: glaucoma, ocular hypertension, damage to optic nerve, defects in visual acuity and visual fields, posterior subcapsular cataract formation, secondary ocular infections. **Other:** Headache, taste perversion. **Clinical Implications:** Shake all products well before use.

OCULAR ANTIHISTAMINES   Prototype for classification: Emedastine
Use: Relief of signs and symptoms of allergic conjunctivitis.

Azelastine HCl OPTIVAR, 0.05% solution	*Adult and Child >3 y:* **Topical** 1 drop in affected eye(s) b.i.d.
Cromolyn sodium Crolom, Opticrom, 4% solution	*Adult:* **Topical** 1–2 drops in each eye 4–6 times/d.
Emedastine difumarate Emadine, 0.05% solution	*Adult and Child >3 y:* **Topical** 1 drop in affected eye(s) up to q.i.d.
Epinastine hydrochloride Elestat, 0.05% solution	*Adult and Child >3 y:* **Topical** 1 drop in affected eye(s) up to b.i.d.
Ketotifen fumarate Zaditor, 0.025% solution	*Adult:* **Topical** 1 drop in affected eye(s) q8–12h.
Lodoxamide Alomide, 0.1% solution	*Adult and Child >2 mo:* **Topical** 1–2 drop in affected eye(s) q.i.d. for up to 3 mo.
Nedocromil sodium Alocril, 2% solution	*Adult and Child >3 y:* **Topical** 1–2 drops in affected eye(s) b.i.d.
Olopatadine HCl Patanol, 0.1% solution	*Adult and Child >3 y:* **Topical** 1–2 drops in affected eye(s) b.i.d. at least 6–8 h apart.
Pemirolast potassium Alamast, 0.1% solution	*Adult:* **Topical** 1–2 drops in affected eye(s) q.i.d.

Adverse Effects: Ocular: Allergic reactions, *burning, stinging,* discharge, dry eyes, eye pain, eyelid disorder, itching keratitis, lacrimation disorder, mydriasis, photophobia, rash. **CNS:** Drowsiness, fatigue, headache. **Other:** Dry mouth, cold syndrome, pharyngitis, rhinitis, sinusitis, taste perversion. **Clinical Implications:** Wait 10 min after instilling **emedastine** before inserting soft contact lenses; do not use **olopatadine** with soft contact lenses.

OCULAR NONSTEROIDAL ANTIINFLAMMATORY DRUGS:

Prototype for classification: Ibuprofen **Use:** Treatment of ocular pain and inflammation associated with cataract surgery.

Bromfenac Xibrom, 0.09% solution	*Adult:* **Topical** 1 drop into affected eye(s) b.i.d. beginning 24 h after cataract surgery and continuing for 14 d.
Nepafenac Nevanac, 0.1% suspension	*Adult and Child >10 y:* **Topical** 1 drop into affected eye(s) t.i.d. beginning 24 h after cataract surgery and continuing for 14 d.

Adverse Effects: Ocular: Conjunctival hyperemia, ocular hypertension, foreign body sensation, decreased visual acuity, headache, iritis, ocular inflammation (e.g., edema, erythema), ocular irritation (burning/stinging), ocular pruritus, ocular pain, photophobia, lacrimation, abnormal sensation in the eye, delayed wound healing, keratitis, lid margin crusting, corneal erosion, corneal perforation, corneal thinning, and epithelial breakdown. Continued use can lead to ulceration or perforation.

Clinical Implications: Nepafenac suspension must be shaken well prior to use.

APPENDIX A-2

LOW MOLECULAR WEIGHT HEPARINS:

ANTICOAGULANT, LOW MOLECULAR WEIGHT HEPARIN Prototype for classification: Enoxaparin Use: Prevention and treatment of DVT following hip or knee replacement or abdominal surgery, unstable angina, acute coronary syndromes.

Dalteparin sodium Fragmin, 10,000 IU/mL, 25,000 IU/mL	**DVT Prophylaxis, Abdominal Surgery:** *Adult:* SC 2500 IU q.d. starting 1–2 h prior to surgery and continuing for 5–10 d postoperatively **DVT Prophylaxis, Total Hip Arthroplasty:** *Adult:* SC 2500–5000 IU q.d. starting 1–2 h prior to surgery and continuing for 5–14 d postoperatively **Acute Thromboembolism:** *Adult:* SC 120 IU/kg b.i.d. for at least 5 d. **Recurrent Thromboembolism:** *Adult:* SC 5000 IU b.i.d. for 3–6 mo. **Unstable angina/non Q-wave MI:** *Adult:* SC 120 IU/kg (max 10,000 IU) q12h. **DVT prophylaxis with risk of PE:** *Adult:* SC 5000 IU once daily for 12–14 d.
Enoxaparin Lovenox, 100 mg/mL	**Prevention of DVT after Hip or Knee Surgery:** *Adult:* SC 30 mg SC b.i.d. for 10–14 d starting 12–24 h post-surgery. **Prevention of DVT after Abdominal Surgery:** *Adult:* SC 40 mg q.d. starting 2 h before surgery and continuing for 7–10 d (max 12 d) **Treatment of DVT and Pulmonary Embolus:** *Adult:* SC 1 mg/kg b.i.d.; monitor anti-Xa activity to determine appropriate dose. **Acute Coronary Syndrome:** *Adult:* SC 1 mg/kg q12h × 2–8 d. Give concurrently with aspirin 100–325 mg/d.

Tinzaparin sodium Innohep, 20,000 IU/ mL	Treatment of DVT: *Adult:* SC 175 anti-Xa IU/kg q.d. × at least 6 d.

Contraindicated in: Hypersensitivity to ardeparin, other low molecular weight heparins, pork products, or parabens; active major bleeding, thrombocytopenia that is positive for antiplatelet antibodies with ardeparin; uncontrolled hypertension; nursing mothers. **Cautious Use in:** Hypersensitivity to heparin; history of heparin-induced thrombocytopenia; bacterial endocarditis; severe and uncontrolled hypertension, cerebral aneurysm or hemorrhagic stroke, bleeding disorders, recent GI bleeding or associated GI disorders (e.g., ulcerative colitis), thrombocytopenia, or platelet disorders; severe liver or renal disease, diabetic retinopathy, hypertensive retinopathy, invasive procedures; pregnancy (category C). **Adverse Effects: Body as a Whole:** Allergic reactions (rash, urticaria), arthralgia, pain and inflammation at injection site, peripheral edema, fever. **CNS:** *CVA,* dizziness, headache, insomnia. **CV:** Chest pain. **GI:** Nausea, vomiting. **Hematologic:** *Hemorrhage,* thrombocytopenia, ecchymoses, anemia. **Respiratory:** Dyspnea. **Skin:** Rash, pruritus. **Drug Interactions:** Aspirin, NSAIDs, **warfarin** can increase risk of hemorrhage **Clinical Implications:** Alternate injection sites using the abdomen, anterior thigh, or outer aspect of upper arms. **Lab tests:** CBC with platelet count, urinalysis, and stool for occult blood should be tested throughout therapy. Routine coagulation tests are not required. Carefully monitor for and immediately report S&S of excessive anticoagulation (e.g., bleeding at venipuncture sites or surgical site) or hemorrhage (e.g., drop in BP or Hct). Patients on oral anticoagulants, platelet inhibitors, or with impaired renal function must be very carefully monitored for hemorrhage. Patient should be sitting or lying supine for injection. Inject deep SC with entire length of needle inserted into skin fold. Hold skin fold gently throughout injection and do not rub site after injection.

APPENDIX A-3
INHALED CORTICOSTEROIDS (ORAL AND NASAL INHALATIONS):

CORTICOSTEROID, ANTIINFLAMMATORY Prototype for classification: Hydrocortisone Use: Oral inhalation to treat steroid-dependent asthma, nasal inhalation for the management of the symptoms of seasonal or perennial rhinitis.

Beclomethasone diproprionate Beconase AQ, QVAR, Vancenase AQ	**Asthma:** *Adult:* **Oral inhaler** 2 inhalations t.i.d. or q.i.d. up to 20 inhalations/d; may try to reduce systemic steroids after 1 wk of concomitant therapy; QVAR 40–80 mcg b.i.d. (max 320 mcg/d). *Child 6–12 y:* **Oral inhaler** 1–2 inhalations t.i.d. or q.i.d. up to 10 inhalations/d; QVAR 5–11 y, 40–80 mcg b.i.d. (max 160 mcg/d). **Allergic Rhinitis:** *Adult:* **Nasal inhaler** 1 spray in each nostril b.i.d. to q.i.d. *Child >6 y:* spray q.d.

Budesonide
Pulmicort,
Turbuhaler,
Pulmicort,
Respules,
Rhinocort,
Rhinocort Aqua,
Rhinocort,
Turbuhaler,

Asthma, Maintenance Therapy: *Adult:* **Oral inhalation** 1 or 2 inhalations (200 mcg/inhalation) q.d.–b.i.d. (max 800 mcg b.i.d.). *Child ≥6 y:* **Oral inhalation** 1 inhalation (200 mcg/inhalation) q.d.–b.i.d. (max 400 mcg b.i.d.) *Child 12 mo–8 y:* **Nebulization** 0.5 mg/d in 1–2 divided doses. **Rhinitis:** *Adult, Child ≥6 y:* **Intranasal** 2 sprays in each nostril in the morning and evening or 4 sprays in each nostril in the morning. Each actuation releases 32 mcg from the nasal adapter.

Ciclesonide
Omnaris, 50 mcg/
spray

Intranasal: *Adult, child >12 y:* **Intranasal** 2 sprays in each nostril once daily (200 mcg/d).

Dexamethasone
Decadron,
Decaspray, 0.04%
solution

Adult: **Oral Inhalation** Up to 3 inhalations t.i.d. or q.i.d. (max 12 inhalations/d). **Intranasal** 2 sprays in each nostril b.i.d. or t.i.d. (max 12 sprays/d) *Child:* **Oral Inhalation** Up to 2 inhalations q.i.d. (max 8 inhalations/d). **Intranasal** 1 or 2 sprays in each nostril b.i.d. (max 8 sprays/d).

Flunisolide
AeroBid,
Nasalide,
Nasarel, 250 mcg/
spray

Allergic Rhinitis: *Adult:* **Inhaled/Intranasal** 2 sprays orally, or intranasally in each nostril, b.i.d.; may increase to t.i.d., if needed. *Child:* **Inhaled/Intranasal** 6–14 y, 1 spray orally, or intranasally in each nostril t.i.d. or 2 sprays b.i.d.

Fluticasone
Flonase,
Flovent,
Flovent HFA, 44
mcg, 110 mcg, 220
mcg aerosol

Seasonal Allergic Rhinitis: *Adult:* **Intranasal** 100 mcg (1 inhalation) in each nostril 1–2 times daily (max 4 times daily). **Inhalation** 1–2 inhalations b.i.d. *Child ≥4 y:* **Intranasal** 1 spray in each nostril once daily. May increase to 2 sprays in each nostril once daily if inadequate response, then decrease to 1 spray in each nostril once daily when control is achieved.

**Mometasone
furoate**
Asmanex, Nasonex,
Twisthaler, 220
mcg/inhalation, 50
mcg/inhalation

Adult: **Intranasal** 2 sprays (50 mcg each) in each nostril once daily. *Child ≥2 y:* **Intranasal** 1 spray in each nostril once daily. *Child >12 y and Adult:* **Powder for Inhalation** 1 inhalation (220 mcg) once daily (max: 1 inhalation b.i.d.).

**Triamcinolone
acetonide**
Azmacort, 100
mcg/inhalation

Adult: **Inhalation** 2 puffs 3–4 times/d (max 16 puffs/d) or 4 puffs b.i.d. **Nasal spray** 2 spray/nostril once daily (max 8 sprays/d) *Child 6–12 y:* **Inhalation** 1–2 sprays t.i.d. or q.i.d. (max 12 sprays/d) or 2–4 sprays b.i.d.

Contraindicated in: Nonasthmatic bronchitis, primary treatment of status asthmaticus, acute attack of asthma. **Cautious Use in:** Patients receiving systemic corticosteroids; use with extreme caution if at all in respiratory tuberculosis, untreated fungal, bacterial, or viral infections, and ocular herpes simplex; nasal inhalation therapy for nasal septal ulcers, nasal trauma, or surgery. **Adverse Effects: Oral inha-**

lation: *Candidal infection of oropharynx* and occasionally larynx, hoarseness, dry mouth, sore throat, sore mouth. **Nasal (inhaler):** *Transient nasal irritation, burning, sneezing,* epistaxis, bloody mucous, nasopharyngeal itching, dryness, crusting, and ulceration; headache, nausea, vomiting. **Other:** With excessive doses, symptoms of hypercorticism. Increase risk of adverse effects if Advair is used with other long-acting beta-agonists. **Clinical Implications:** Note that oral inhalation and nasal inhalation products are not to be used interchangeably. **Oral inhaler:** Emphasize the following: (1) Shake inhaler well before using. (2) After exhaling fully, place mouthpiece well into mouth with lips closed firmly around it. (3) Inhale slowly through mouth while activating the inhaler. (4) Hold breath 5–10 sec, if possible, then exhale slowly. (5) Wait 1 min between puffs. Clean inhaler daily. Separate parts as directed in package insert, rinse them with warm water, and dry them thoroughly. Rinsing mouth and gargling with warm water after each oral inhalation removes residual medication from oropharyngeal area. Mouth care may also delay or prevent onset of oral dryness, hoarseness, and candidiasis. **Nasal inhaler:** Directions for use of nasal inhaler provided by manufacturer should be carefully reviewed with patient. Emphasize the following points: (1) Gently blow nose to clear nostrils. (2) Shake inhaler well before using. (3) If 2 sprays in each nostril are prescribed, direct one spray toward upper, and the other toward lower part of nostril. (4) Wash cap and plastic nosepiece daily with warm water; dry thoroughly. Inhaled steroids do not provide immediate symptomatic relief and are not prescribed for this purpose.

APPENDIX A-4
TOPICAL CORTICOSTEROIDS:

CORTICOSTEROID, ANTI-INFLAMMATORY Prototype for classification: Hydrocortisone Use: As a topical corticosteroid, the drug is used for the relief of the inflammatory and pruritic manifestations of corticosteroid-responsive dermatoses.

Hydrocortisone
Aeroseb-HC, Alphaderm, Cetacort, Cortaid, Cortenema, Dermolate, Hytone, Rectocort, Synacort Anusol HC, CaldeCort, 0.5%, 1%, 2.5% cream, lotion, ointment, spray

Hydrocortisone acetate
Carmol HC, Colifoam, Cortaid, Cortamed, Cort-Dome, Corticaine, Cortifoam, Cortiment A, Epifoam, 0.5%, 1% ointment, cream

Adult: **Topical** Apply a small amount to the affected area 1–4 times/d. **PR** Insert 1% cream, 10% foam, 10–25 mg suppository, or 100 mg enema nightly.

Alclometasone diproprionate
Aclovate, 0.05% cream, ointment

Adult: **Topical** 0.05% cream or ointment applied sparingly b.i.d. or t.i.d.; may use occlusive dressing for resistant dermatoses.

Amcinonide
Cyclocort, 0.1% cream, lotion, ointment

Adult: **Topical** Apply thin film b.i.d. or t.i.d.

Betamethasone dipropionate
Diprolene, Diprolene AF, Diprosone, Maxivate, 0.05% cream, gel, lotion, ointment

Adult: **Topical** Apply thin film b.i.d.

Betamethasone valerate
Luxiq, Valisone, Psorion, Beta-Val, 0.1% cream, ointment, lotion; 0.12% aerosol foam

Adult: **Topical** Apply sparingly b.i.d.

Clobetasol propionate
Clobex, Cormax, Embeline, Olux, Temovate, 0.05% cream, gel, ointment, lotion, aerosol foam

Adult: **Topical** Apply sparingly b.i.d. (max 50 g/wk), or b.i.d. 3 d/wk or 1–2 times/wk for up to 6 mo.

Clocortolone pivalate
Cloderm, 0.1% cream

Adult: **Topical** Apply thin layer 1–4 times/d.

Desonide
DesOwen, Tridesilon, 0.05% cream, ointment, lotion

Adult: **Topical** Apply thin layer b.i.d. to q.i.d.

Desoximetasone
Topicort, Topicort-LP, 0.05% cream, ointment

Adult: **Topical** Apply thin layer b.i.d.

Diflorasone diacetate
Florone, Florone E, Maxiflor, Psorcon E, Psorcon, 0.05% cream, ointment

Adult: **Topical** Apply thin layer of ointment 1–3 times/d or cream 2–4 times/d.

Fluocinolone acetonide
Fluoderm, Synalar, 0.025% ointment, cream 0.2% cream; 0.01% cream, solution, shampoo, oil; 0.59 mg ophthalmic insert

Adult: **Topical** Apply thin layer b.i.d. to q.i.d.

Fluocinonide
Lidemol, Lidex, Lidex-E, Lyderm, Topsyn, Vanos, 0.05% cream, ointment, solution, gel; 0.1% cream

Adult: **Topical** Apply thin layer b.i.d. to q.i.d.

Flurandrenolide
Cordran, Cordran SP, Drenison, 0.025% ointment, cream; 0.05% ointment, cream, lotion

Adult: **Topical** Apply thin layer b.i.d. or t.i.d.; apply tape 1–2 times/d at 12 h intervals. *Child:* **Topical** Apply thin layer 1–2 times/d; apply tape once/d.

Fluticasone
Cutivate, 0.05%, 0.005% cream; 0.005% ointment

Adult, Child >3 mo: **Topical** Apply a thin film of cream or ointment to affected area once or twice daily.

Halcinonide
Halog, 0.1% cream, ointment, solution

Adult: **Topical** Apply thin layer b.i.d. or t.i.d. *Child:* **Topical** Apply thin layer once/d.

Halobetasol
Ultravate, 0.05% cream, ointment

Adult: **Topical** Apply sparingly b.i.d.

Mometasone furoate
Elocon, 0.1% cream, lotion, ointment

Adult: **Topical** Apply a thin film of cream or ointment or a few drops of lotion to affected area once/d.

Triamcinolone
Aristocort, Kenacort, Kenalog, Triderm, 0.025%, 0.5%, 0.1% cream; 0.025%, 0.5%, 0.1% ointment; 0.025%, 0.1% lotion

Adult: **Topical** Apply sparingly b.i.d. or t.i.d.

Contraindicated in: Topical steroids contraindicated in presence of varicella, vaccinia, on surfaces with compromised circulation, and in children <2 y. **Cautious Use in:** Children; diabetes mellitus; stromal *herpes simplex;* glaucoma, tuberculosis of eye; osteoporosis; untreated fungal, bacterial, or viral infections **Adverse Effects: Skin:** Skin thinning and atrophy, *acne, impaired wound healing;* petechiae, ecchymosis, easy bruisings; suppression of skin test reaction; hypopigmentation or hyperpigmentation, hirsutism, acneiform eruptions, subcutaneous fat atrophy; allergic dermatitis, urticaria, angioneurotic edema, increased sweating. **Clinical Implications:** Administer retention enema preferably after a bowel movement. The enema should be retained at least 1 h or all night if possible. If an occlusive dressing is to be used, apply medication sparingly, rub until it disappears, and then reapply, leaving a thin coat over lesion. Completely cover area with transparent plastic or other occlusive device or vehicle. Avoid covering a weeping or exudative lesion. Usually, occlusive dressings are not applied to face, scalp, scrotum, axilla, and groin. Inspect skin carefully between applications for ecchymotic, petechial, and purpuric signs, maceration, secondary infection, skin atrophy, striae or milaria; if present, stop medication and notify physician. Warn patient not to self-dose with OTC topical preparations of a corticosteroid more than 7 d. They should not be used for children <2 y. If symptoms do not abate, consult physician. Usually, topical preparations are applied after a shower or bath when skin is damp or wet. Cleansing and application of prescribed preparation should be done with extreme gentleness because of fragility, easy bruisability, and poor-healing skin. Hazard of systemic toxicity is higher in small children because of the greater ratio of skin surface area to body weight. Apply sparingly. Urge patient on long-term therapy with topical corticosterone to check expiration date.

Schedule I

High potential for abuse and of no currently accepted medical use. Examples: heroin, LSD, marijuana, mescaline, peyote. Not obtainable by prescription but may be legally procured for research, study, or instructional use.

Schedule II

High abuse potential and high liability for severe psychological or physical dependence. Prescription required and cannot be renewed.[a] Includes opium derivatives, other opioids, and short-acting barbiturates. Examples: amphetamine, cocaine, meperidine, morphine, secobarbital.

Schedule III

Potential for abuse is less than that for drugs in Schedules I and II. Moderate to low physical dependence and high psychological dependence. Includes certain stimulants and depressants not included in the above schedules and preparations containing limited quantities of certain opioids. Examples: chlorphentermine, glutethimide, mazindol, paregoric, phendimetrazine. Prescription required.[b]

Schedule IV

Lower potential for abuse than Schedule III drugs. Examples: certain psychotropics (tranquilizers), chloral hydrate, chlordiazepoxide, diazepam, meprobamate, phenobarbital. Prescription required.[a]

Schedule V

Abuse potential less than that for Schedule IV drugs. Preparations contain limited quantities of certain narcotic drugs; generally intended for antitussive and antidiarrheal purposes and may be distributed without a prescription provided that:

1. Such distribution is made only by a pharmacist.
2. Not more than 240 mL or not more than 48 solid dosage units of any substance containing opium, nor more than 120 mL or not more than 24 solid dosage units of any other controlled substance may be distributed at retail to the same purchaser in any given 48-hour period without a valid prescription order.
3. The purchaser is at least 18 years old.
4. The pharmacist knows the purchaser or requests suitable identification.
5. The pharmacist keeps an official written record of: name and address of purchaser, name and quantity of controlled substance purchased, date of sale, initials of dispensing pharmacist. This record is to be made available for inspection and copying by U.S. officers authorized by the Attorney General.

6. Other federal, state, or local law does not require a prescription order.

Under jurisdiction of the Federal Controlled Substances Act:

[a]Except when dispensed directly by a practitioner, other than a pharmacist, to an ultimate user, no controlled substance in Schedule II may be dispensed without a *written* prescription, except that in emergency situations such drug may be dispensed upon oral prescription and a written prescription must be obtained within the time frame prescribed by law. No prescription for a controlled substance in Schedule II may be refilled.

[b]Refillable up to 5 times within 6 mo, but only if so indicated by physician.

The FDA requires that all prescription drugs absorbed systemically or known to be potentially harmful to the fetus be classified according to one of five pregnancy categories (A, B, C, D, X). The identifying letter signifies the level of risk to the fetus and is to appear in the precautions section of the package insert. The categories described by the FDA are as follows:

Category A

Controlled studies in women fail to demonstrate a risk to the fetus in the first trimester (and there is no evidence of risk in later trimesters), and the possibility of fetal harm appears remote.

Category B

Either animal-reproduction studies have not demonstrated a fetal risk but there are no controlled studies in pregnant women, or animal-reproduction studies have shown an adverse effect (other than a decrease in fertility) that was not confirmed in controlled studies in women in the first trimester (and there is no evidence of a risk in later trimesters).

Category C

Either studies in animals have revealed adverse effects on the fetus (teratogenic or embryocidal effects or other) and there are no controlled studies in women, or studies in women and animals are not available. Drugs should be given only if the potential benefit justifies the potential risk to the fetus.

Category D

There is positive evidence of human fetal risk, but the benefits from use in pregnant women may be acceptable despite the risk (e.g., if the drug is needed in a life-threatening situation or for a serious disease for which safer drugs cannot be used or are ineffective). There will be an appropriate statement in the "warnings" section of the labeling.

Category X

Studies in animals or human beings have demonstrated fetal abnormalities or there is evidence of fetal risk based on human experience, or both, and the risk of the use of the drug in pregnant women clearly outweighs any possible benefit. The drug is contraindicated in women who are or may become pregnant. There will be an appropriate statement in the "contraindications" section of the labeling.

Some oral dosage forms should not be crushed or chewed. These dosage forms have been specially designed to release the drug slowly over several hours, to protect the drug from the low pH of the stomach, and/or to protect the stomach from the irritating effects of the drug.

Drugs may have an **enteric coating** which is designed to allow the drug to pass through the stomach intact with the drug being released in the intestines. This protects the stomach from the irritating effects of the drug, protects the drug from being destroyed by the acid pH of the stomach, and can delay the onset of action.

Extended release (slow release, SR) formulations are designed to release the drug over an extended period of time. These formulations can include multiple-layer compressed tablets where drug is released as each layer dissolves, mixed-release pellets that dissolve at different time intervals, and special tablets that are themselves inert but are designed to release drug slowly from the formulation. Some extended release dosage forms are scored and may be broken in half without affecting the release mechanism but still should not be crushed or chewed. Some mixed-release capsule formulations can be opened and the contents sprinkled on food. However, the pellets should not be crushed or chewed. Some extended release formulations can be identified by common abbreviations used in their brand names. These abbreviations include: CR (controlled release), CRT (controlled release tablet), LA (long acting), SR (sustained release), TR (time release), SA (sustained action), and XL or XR (extended release).

Occasionally, drugs should not be crushed because they are oral mucosa irritants, are extremely bitter, or contain dyes that may stain teeth or mucosal tissue.

The table contains a list of drugs found in the Guide that should not be crushed or chewed. A liquid dosage form may be available for many of these drugs. However, the dose or frequency of administration may be different from the slow-release product. Check with your pharmacist for liquid availability and dosing conversions.

	Generic Name	Comments
Accutane	isotretinoin	mucous membrane irritant
Aciphex	rabeprazole	slow release
Adalat CC	nifedipine	slow release
Adderall XR	amphetamine	slow release
Advicor	niacin/lovastatin	slow release
Aggrenox	aspirin/dipyridamole	slow release; may be opened and contents taken without crushing

	Generic Name	Comments
Allegra D	fexofenadine/ pseudoephedrine	slow release
Arthrotec	diclofenac/misoprostol	enteric coated
Asacol	mesalamine	slow release
Augmentin XR	amoxicillin/clavulanic acid	slow release; may be scored and broken
Avinza	morphine	slow release; capsule may be opened
Avodart	dutasteride	skin contact may cause tumor production
Azulfidine En-tabs	sulfasalazine	enteric coated
Bayer Extra Strength Enteric 500	aspirin, enteric coated	enteric coated; slow release
Bayer Low Adult 81 mg	aspirin, enteric coated	enteric coated
Bayer Caplet	aspirin, enteric coated	enteric coated
Biaxin XL	clarithromycin	slow release
Bisacodyl	bisacodyl	enteric coated
BiscoLax	bisacodyl	enteric coated
Calan SR	verapamil	slow release; may break tablet
Cama Arthritis Strength	aspirin, magnesium oxide, aluminum hydroxide	special tablet formulation
Cardizem, Cardizem CD, Cardizem SR, Cardizem LA	diltiazem	slow release; capsules may be opened and contents taken without chewing or crushing
Ceftin	cefuroxime	taste; use liquid formulation
Chloral Hydrate	chloral hydrate	liquid-filled capsule
Chlor-Trimeton Repetab	chlorpheniramine	slow release
Choledyl SA	oxtriphylline	slow release
Cipro	ciprofloxacin	taste
Compazine Spansule	prochlorperazine	slow release; capsules may be opened and contents taken without chewing or crushing
Concerta	methylphenidate	slow release

	Generic Name	Comments
Constant T	theophylline	slow release; capsules may be opened and contents taken without chewing or crushing
Cotazym S	pancrelipase	enteric coated; capsules may be opened and contents taken without chewing or crushing
Covera-HS	verapamil	slow release
Cymbalta	duloxetine	enteric coated
Deconamine SR	chlorpheniramine, pseudoephedrine	slow release
Depakene	valproic acid	slow release; mucous membrane irritant
Depakote	valproate disodium	enteric coated
Desoxyn Gradumets	methamphetamine	slow release
Detrol LA	tolterodine	slow release
Dexedrine Spansule	dextroamphetamine	slow release
Diamox Sequels	acetazolamide	slow release
Dilacor XR	diltiazem	slow release
Dilatrate-SR	isosorbide dinitrate	slow release
Disophrol Chronotab	dexbrompheniramine, pseudoephedrine	slow release
Donnatal Extentab	atropine, scopolamine, hyoscyamine, phenobarbital	slow release
Donnazyme	pancreatin, pepsin, bile salts, atropine, scopolamine, hyoscyamine, phenobarbital	slow release
Drixoral	dexbrompheniramine, pseudoephedrine	slow release
Dulcolax	bisacodyl	enteric coated
Duratuss	phenylephrine, guaifenesin	slow release
Easprin	aspirin	enteric coated
Ecotrin	aspirin	enteric coated
E.E.S. 400	erythromycin ethylsuccinate	enteric coated
Effexor XR	venlafaxine	slow release

	Generic Name	Comments
Elixophyllin SR	theophylline	slow release; capsules may be opened and contents taken without chewing or crushing
E-Mycin	erythromycin	enteric coated
Ergostat	ergotamine	sublingual tablet
Eryc	erythromycin	enteric coated; capsules may be opened and contents taken without chewing or crushing
Ery-tab	erythromycin	enteric coated
Erythrocin Stearate	erythromycin	enteric coated
Erythromycin Base	erythromycin	enteric coated
Eskalith CR	lithium	slow release
Fedahist Timecaps	chlorpheniramine, pseudoephedrine	slow release
Feldene	piroxicam	mucous membrane irritant
Feosol	ferrous sulfate	enteric coated
Feosol Spansule	ferrous sulfate	slow release; capsules may be opened and contents taken without chewing or crushing
Fergon	ferrous gluconate	slow release; capsules may be opened and contents taken without chewing or crushing
Ferro-Sequels	ferrous fumarate, docusate	slow release
Fero-Gradumet	ferrous sulfate	slow release
Festal II	pancrelipase	enteric coated
Glucophage XR	metformin	slow release
Glucotrol XL	glipizide	slow release
Gris-Peg	griseofulvin ultramicrosize	crushing may result in precipitation of drug as larger particles
Ilotycin	erythromycin	enteric coated
Imdur	isosorbide mononitrate	slow release
Inderal LA	propranolol	slow release
Indocin SR	indomethacin	slow release; capsules may be opened and contents taken without chewing or crushing

	Generic Name	Comments
Isoptin SR	verapamil	slow release
Iso-Bid	isosorbide dinitrate	slow release
Isosorbide Dinitrate SR	isosorbide dinitrate	slow release
Isuprel Glossets	isoproterenol	sublingual
Kadian	morphine	slow release
Kaon CL 10	potassium chloride	slow release
Klor-Con	potassium chloride	slow release
Klotrix	potassium chloride	slow release
K-Tab	potassium chloride	slow release
Levsinex Timecaps	hyoscyamine	slow release
Lithobid	lithium	slow release
Meprospan	meprobamate	slow release; capsules may be opened and contents taken without chewing or crushing
Mestinon Timespan	pyridostigmine	slow release
Micro K	potassium chloride	slow release
MS Contin	morphine	slow release
Mucinex	guaifenesin	slow release
Nico-400	niacin	slow release
Nicobid	niacin	slow release
Nitro Bid	nitroglycerin	slow release; capsules may be opened and contents taken without chewing or crushing
Nitroglyn	nitroglycerin	slow release; capsules may be opened and contents taken without chewing or crushing
Nitrong SR	nitroglycerin	slow release
Norflex	orphenadrine	slow release
Norpace CR	disopyramide	slow release
Novafed A	pseudoephedrine, chlorpheniramine	slow release
Oramorph SR	morphine	slow release
Pancrease	pancrelipase	enteric coated
Papaverine Sustained Action	papaverine	slow release

	Generic Name	Comments
PBZ-SR	tripelennamine hydrochloride	slow release
Perdiem	psyllium hydrophilic mucilloid	wax coated
Peritrate SA	pentaerythritol tetranitrate	slow release
Permitil Chronotab	fluphenazine	slow release
Phazyme, Phazyme 95	simethicone	slow release
Phyllocontin	aminophylline	slow release
Plendil	felodipine	slow release
Polaramine Repetabs	dexchlorpheniramine	slow release
Prevacid	lansoprazole	slow release; capsules may be opened and contents taken without chewing or crushing
Prilosec	omeprazole	slow release
Procainamide HCl SR	procainamide	slow release
Procan SR	procainamide	slow release
Procardia XL	nifedipine	slow release
Pronestyl SR	procainamide	slow release
Proventil Repetabs	albuterol	slow release
Quibron-T SR	theophylline	slow release
Quinaglute Dura Tabs	quinidine gluconate	slow release
Quinidex Extentabs	quinidine sulfate	slow release
Respid	theophylline	slow release
Ritalin SR	methylphenidate	slow release
Robimycin Robitab	erythromycin	enteric coated
Rondec TR	pseudoephedrine, carbinoxamine	slow release
Roxanol SR	morphine	slow release
Sinemet CR	levodopa, carbidopa	slow release; tablet is scored and may be broken in half

	Generic Name	Comments
Slo-Bid Gyrocaps	theophylline	slow release; capsules may be opened and contents taken without chewing or crushing
Slo-Phyllin Gyrocaps	theophylline	slow release; capsules may be opened and contents taken without chewing or crushing
Slow-Fe	ferrous sulfate	slow release
Slow-K	potassium chloride	slow release
Sorbitrate SA	isosorbide dinitrate	slow release
Strattera	atomoxetine	slow release
Sudafed 12 hour	pseudoephedrine	slow release
Tarka	trandolapril, verapamil	slow release
Teldrin	chlorpheniramine	slow release; capsules may be opened and contents taken without chewing or crushing
Tepanil Ten-Tab	diethylpropion	slow release
Tessalon Perles	benzonatate	slow release
Theo-24	theophylline	slow release
Thorazine Spansule	chlorpromazine	slow release
Toprol XL	metoprolol	slow release
Trental	pentoxifylline	slow release
Trilafon Repetabs	perphenazine	slow release
Triptone Caplets	scopolamine	slow release
Uniphyl	theophylline	slow release
Valrelease	diazepam	slow release
Verelan	verapamil	slow release; capsules may be opened and contents taken without chewing or crushing
Volmax	albuterol	slow release
Wellbutrin SR, Wellbutrin XL	bupropion	slow release; mucous membrane irritant
ZORprin	aspirin	slow release
Zyban	buproprion	slow release

Note: This listing is not comprehensive. Please check with your pharmacist for additional questions.

Information from The Institute for Safe Medication Practices available at: http://www.ismp.org/tools/DoNotCrush.pdf

Accuretic (ANTIHYPERTENSIVE) *tablet:* 10 mg quinapril (see p. 1312)/12.5 mg hydrochlorothiazide (see p. 741); 20 mg quinapril/12.5 mg hydrochlorothiazide; 20 mg quinapril/25 mg hydrochlorothiazide.

Activella (HORMONE REPLACEMENT THERAPY) *tablet:* estradiol (see p. 584) 1 mg/norethindrone acetate (see p. 1092) 0.5 mg.

Actonel with Calcium (BISPHOSPHONATE) *tablet:* risedronate (see p. 1350) 35 mg/1250 calcium carbonate (see p. 217).

ACTOplus Met (ANTIDIABETIC) *tablet:* pioglitazone (see p. 1222) 15 mg/metformin (see p. 956) 500 mg; pioglitazone 15 mg/metformin 850 mg.

Advair Diskus (BRONCHODILATOR) *Inhalation powder:* fluticasone propionate (see p. 665) 100 mcg/salmeterol (see p. 1367) 50 mcg; fluticasone propionate 250 mcg/salmeterol 50 mcg.

Advicor (ANTILIPEMIC) *tablets, sustained release:* niacin (see p. 1067) 500 mg/lovastatin (see p. 905) 20 mg; niacin 1000 mg/lovastatin 20 mg.

Aggrenox (ANTIPLATELET) *extended release capsule:* dipyridamole (see p. 489) 200 mg/aspirin (see p. 117) 25 mg.

Aldactazide 25/25 (DIURETIC) *tablet:* spironolactone (see p. 1411) 25 mg/hydrochlorothiazide (see p. 741) 25 mg.

Aldactazide 50/50 (DIURETIC) *tablet:* spironolactone (see p. 1411) 50 mg/hydrochlorothiazide (see p. 741) 50 mg.

Allegra D 12 hour (ANTIHISTAMINE, DECONGESTANT) *tablet, extended release:* fexofenadine (see p. 635) 60 mg/pseudoephedrine (see p. 1299) 120 mg.

Allegra D 24 hour (ANTIHISTAMINE, DECONGESTANT) *tablet, extended release:* fexofenadine (see p. 635) 180 mg/pseudoephedrine (see p. 1299) 240 mg.

Anexsia (NARCOTIC ANALGESIC [schedule III]) *tablet:* hydrocodone (see p. 743) 5 mg/acetaminophen (see p. 9) 500 mg.

Anexsia 5/325 (NARCOTIC ANALGESIC [schedule III]) *tablet:* hydrocodone (see p. 743) 5 mg/acetaminophen (see p. 9) 325 mg.

Anexsia 7.5/325 (NARCOTIC ANALGESIC [schedule III]) *tablet:* hydrocodone (see p. 743) 7.5 mg/acetaminophen (see p. 9) 325 mg.

Anexsia 7.5/650 (NARCOTIC ANALGESIC [schedule III]) *tablet:* hydrocodone (see p. 743) 7.5 mg/acetaminophen (see p. 9) 650 mg.

Angeliq (HORMONE) *tablet:* drospirenone 0.5 mg/estradiol (see p. 584) 1 mg.

Antrocol (GASTROINTESTINAL ANTICHOLINERGIC, SEDATIVE) *capsule, tablet:* atropine sulfate (see p. 132) 0.195 mg/phenobarbital (see p. 1200) 16 mg.

Apresazide 25/25 (ANTIHYPERTENSIVE) *capsule:* hydralazine hydrochloride (see p. 740) 25 mg/hydrochlorothiazide (see p. 741) 25 mg.

Apresazide 50/50 (ANTIHYPERTENSIVE) *capsule:* hydralazine hydrochloride (see p. 740) 50 mg/hydrochlorothiazide (see p. 741) 50 mg.

Apresodex (ANTIHYPERTENSIVE) *tablet:* hydralazine hydrochloride (see p. 740) 25 mg/hydrochlorothiazide (see p. 741) 15 mg.

Apresoline-Esidrex (ANTIHYPERTENSIVE) *tablet:* hydralazine hydrochloride (see p. 740) 25 mg/ hydrochlorothiazide (see p. 741) 15 mg.

Aralen Phosphate with Primaquine Phosphate (ANTIMALARIAL) *tablet:* chloroquine phosphate (see p. 303) 500 mg (300 mg base)/primaquine phosphate (see p. 1262) 79 mg (45 mg base).

Arthrotec 50 (NSAID) *tablet:* diclofenac sodium (see p. 461) 50 mg/misoprostol (see p. 1008) 200 mcg.

Arthrotec 75 (NSAID) *tablet:* diclofenac sodium (see p. 461) 75 mg/misoprostol (see p. 1008) 200 mcg.

Atacand HCT (ANTIHYPERTENSIVE) *tablet:* candesartan (see p. 225) 32 mg/hydrochlorothiazide (see p. 741) 12.5 mg; candesartan 16 mg/hydrochlorothiazide 12.5 mg.

Atripla (ANTIRETROVIRAL) *tablet:* 600 mg efavirenz (see p. 535)/ 200 mg emtricitabine (see p. 541)/300 mg tenofovir (see p. 1458).

Augmentin (ANTIBIOTIC) *tablet:* amoxicillin (see p. 82) 250 mg/ clavulanic acid 125 mg; amoxicillin 500 mg/clavulanic acid 125 mg; amoxicillin 875 mg/ clavulanic acid 125 mg; amoxicillin 1000 mg/clavulanic acid 125 mg; *chewable tablet:* amoxicillin 125 mg/clavulanic acid 31.25 mg; amoxicillin 200 mg/ clavulanic acid 28.5 mg; amoxicillin 250 mg/clavulanic acid 62.5 mg; amoxicillin 400 mg/ clavulanic acid 57 mg; *suspension (per 5 mL):* amoxicillin 125 mg/clavulanic acid 31.25 mg; amoxicillin 200 mg/clavulanic acid 28.5 mg; amoxicillin 250 mg/clavulanic acid 62.5 mg; amoxicillin 400 mg/clavulanic acid 57 mg; amoxcillin 600 mg/ clavulanic acid 42.9 mg.

Auralgan Otic (OTIC PREPARATION: DECONGESTANT, ANALGESIC) *solution:* benzocaine (see p. 159) 1.4%/antipyrine 5.4%.

Avalide (ANTIHYPERTENSIVE) *tablet:* irbesartan (see p. 815) 150 mg/ hydrochlorothiazide (see p. 741) 12.5 mg; irbesartan 300 mg/hydrochlorothiazide 12.5 mg; irbesartan 300 mg/hydrochlorothiazide 25 mg.

Avandamet (HYPOGLYCEMIC AGENT) *tablet:* 1 mg rosiglitazone maleate (see p. 1364)/500 mg metformin HCl (see p. 956); 2 mg rosiglitazone/500 mg metformin; 4 mg rosiglitazone/500 mg metformin; 2 mg rosiglitazone/1000 mg metformin; 4 mg rosiglitazone/1000 mg metformin.

Avandaryl (HYPOGLYCEMIC AGENT) *tablet:* rosiglitazone (see p. 1364) 4 mg/glimepiride (see p. 706) 1 mg; rosiglitazone 4 mg/ glimepiride 2 mg; rosiglitazone 4 mg/glimepiride 4 mg.

Azdone (NARCOTIC AGONIST ANALGESIC [schedule III]) *tablet:* hydrocodone bitartrate (see p. 743) 5 mg/aspirin (see p. 117) 500 mg.

Azo Gantanol (URINARY ANTIINFECTIVE, ANALGESIC) *tablet:* sulfamethoxazole (see p. 1428) 500 mg, phenazopyridine hydrochloride (see p. 1196) 100 mg.

Azo Gantrisin (URINARY ANTIINFECTIVE, ANALGESIC) *tablet:* sulfisoxazole (see p. 1433) 500 mg/ phenazopyridine hydrochloride (see p. 1196) 50 mg.

B-A-C (ANALGESIC) acetaminophen (see p. 9) 650 mg/caffeine (see p. 211) 40 mg/butalbital 50 mg.

Bacticort Ophthalmic (ANTIINFLAMMATORY) *suspension:* hydrocortisone (see p. 744) 1%/neomycin sulfate (see p. 1061) 0.35%/polymyxin B (see p. 1236) 10,000 units.

Bactrim (URINARY TRACT AGENT) *tablet:* sulfamethoxazole (see p. 1428) 400 mg/trimethoprim (see p. 1552) 80 mg.

Bactrim DS (URINARY TRACT AGENT) *tablet:* sulfamethoxazole (see p. 1428) 800 mg/trimethoprim (see p. 1552) 160 mg.

Bancap HC (NARCOTIC AGONIST ANALGESIC [schedule III]) *capsule:* hydrocodone bitartrate (see p. 743) 5 mg/acetaminophen (see p. 9) 500 mg.

Benicar HCT (ANTIHYPERTENSIVE) *tablet:* 20 mg olmesartan medoxomil (see p. 1107)/12.5 mg hydrochlorothiazide (see p. 741); 40 mg olmesartan medoxomil/12.5 mg hydrochlorothiazide; 40 mg olmesartan medoxomil/25 mg hydrochlorothiazide.

Betoptic Pilo Suspension (ANTIGLAUCOMA) *suspension:* betaxolol (see p. 168) 0.25%/pilocarpine (see p. 1216) 1.75%.

BiDil (ANTIHYPERTENSIVE) *tablet:* isosorbide dinitrate (see p. 829) 20 mg/hydralazine (see p. 740) 37.5 mg.

Blephamide (OPHTHALMIC STEROID, SULFONAMIDE) *suspension:* prednisolone acetate (see p. 1257) 0.2%/sulfacetamide sodium (see p. 1425) 10%.

Blephamide S.O.P. (OPHTHALMIC STEROID, SULFONAMIDE) *ointment:* prednisolone acetate (see p. 1257) 0.2%/sulfacetamide sodium (see p. 1425) 10%.

Brevicon (MONOPHASIC ORAL CONTRACEPTIVE [ESTROGEN, PROGESTIN]) *tablet:* ethinyl estradiol (see p. 606) 35 mcg/norethindrone (see p. 1092) 0.5 mg.

Bromfed (DECONGESTANT, ANTIHISTAMINE) *sustained release capsule:* pseudoephedrine hydrochloride (see p. 1299) 120 mg/brompheniramine maleate (see p. 191) 12 mg.

Bromfed-PD (DECONGESTANT, ANTIHISTAMINE) *sustained release capsule:* pseudoephedrine hydrochloride (see p. 1299) 60 mg/brompheniramine maleate (see p. 191) 6 mg.

Bronchial Capsules (ANTIASTHMATIC) *capsule:* theophylline (see p. 1479) 150 mg/guaifenesin (see p. 721) 90 mg.

Butibel (GASTROINTESTINAL ANTICHOLINERGIC, SEDATIVE) *elixir (per 5 mL):* belladonna extract (see p. 156) 15 mg/butabarbital sodium (see p. 205) 15 mg/alcohol 7%; *tablet:* belladonna extract 15 mg/butabarbital sodium 15 mg.

Caduet (ANTIHYPERTENSIVE/ANTILIPEMIC) *tablet:* 2.5 mg amlodipine (see p. 77)/10 mg atorvastatin (see p. 127); 2.5 mg amlodipine/20 mg atorvastatin; 2.5 mg amlodipine/40 mg atorvastatin; 5 mg amlodipine/10 mg atorvastatin; 10 mg amlodipine/10 mg atorvastatin; 5 mg amlodipine/20 mg atorvastatin; 10 mg amlodipine/20 mg atorvastatin; 5 mg amlodipine/40 mg atorvastatin; 10 mg amlodipine/40 mg atorvastatin; 5 mg amlodipine/80 mg atorvastatin; 10 mg amlodipine/80 mg atorvastatin.

Cafergot Suppositories (ANTIMIGRAINE) *suppository:* ergotamine tartrate (see p. 569) 2 mg/caffeine (see p. 211) 100 mg.

Cam-ap-es (ANTIHYPERTENSIVE) *suspension, tablet:* hydrochlorothiazide (see p. 741) 15 mg/reserpine (see p. 1332) 0.1 mg/hydralazine hydrochloride (see p. 740) 25 mg.

Capital with Codeine (NARCOTIC ANALGESIC [schedule V]) *suspension (per 5 mL):* codeine phosphate (see p. 367) 12 mg/acetaminophen (see p. 9) 120 mg.

Capozide 25/15 (ANTIHYPERTEN-SIVE) *tablet:* captopril (see p. 230) 25 mg, hydrochlorothiazide (see p. 741) 15 mg.

Capozide 25/25 (ANTIHYPERTEN-SIVE) *tablet:* captopril (see p. 230) 25 mg/hydrochlorothiazide (see p. 741) 25 mg.

Capozide 50/15 (ANTIHYPER-TENSIVE) *tablet:* captopril (see p. 230) 50 mg/hydrochlorothiazide (see p. 741) 15 mg.

Capozide 50/25 (ANTIHYPER-TENSIVE) *tablet:* captopril (see p. 230) 50 mg/hydrochlorothiazide (see p. 741) 25 mg.

Carisoprodol Compound (SKEL-ETAL MUSCLE RELAXANT, ANALGE-SIC) *tablet:* carisoprodol (see p. 242) 200 mg/aspirin (see p. 117) 325 mg.

Carmol HC (ANTIINFLAMMATORY) *cream:* hydrocortisone acetate (see p. 744) 1%/urea 10%.

Celestone-Soluspan (GLUCOCORTI-COID) *injection (suspension) (per mL):* beta-methasone acetate (see p. 165) 3 mg/betamethasone sodium phosphate (see p. 165) 3 mg.

Cetacaine (TOPICAL ANESTHETIC) *gel, liquid, ointment, aerosol:* benzocaine (see p. 159) 14%/tetracaine hydrochloride (see p. 1471) 2%/butamben 2%/benzalkonium chloride (see p. 158) 0.5%.

Cheracol Syrup (NARCOTIC ANTI-TUSSIVE, EXPECTORANT [schedule V]) *syrup (per 5 mL):* codeine phosphate (see p. 367) 10 mg/guaifenesin (see p. 721) 100 mg/alcohol 4.75%.

Chloroserpine (ANTIHYPERTEN-SIVE) *tablet:* chlorothiazide (see p. 306) 500 mg/reserpine (see p. 1332) 0.125 mg.

Cipro HC Otic (ANTIINFECTIVE/ANTIINFLAMMATORY) *topical:* ciprofloxacin (see p. 331) 2

mg/dexamethasone (see p. 441) 10 mg otic suspension.

Ciprodex Otic (ANTIINFECTIVE/ANTIINFLAMMATORY) *topical:* ciprofloxacin (see p. 331) 0.3%/dexamethasone (see p. 441) 0.1% otic suspension.

Claritin D (ANTIHISTAMINE, DECON-GESTANT) loratadine (see p. 901), 5 mg/pseudoephedrine (see p. 1299) 120 mg; loratadine 10 mg/pseudoephedrine 240 mg.

Clarinex D 24 hr (ANTIHISTAMINE, DECONGESTANT) *tablet:* desloratadine (see p. 437) 5 mg/pseudoephedrine (see p. 1299) 240 mg.

Climara Pro (HORMONE REPLACE-MENT THERAPY) *transdermal patch:* estradiol (see p. 584) 0.045 mg/levonorgestrel acetate 0.015 mg.

Codiclear DH Syrup (ANTITUS-SIVE [schedule III]) *syrup (per 5 mL):* hydrocodone (see p. 743) 5 mg/guaifenesin (see p. 721) 100 mg/alcohol 10%.

Codimal DH (ANTITUSSIVE [schedule III]) *syrup (per 5 mL):* phenylephrine hydrochloride (see p. 1207) 5 mg/pyrilamine maleate 8.33 mg/hydrocodone bitartrate (see p. 743) 1.66 mg.

Codimal PH (ANTITUSSIVE [schedule III]) *syrup (per 5 mL):* codeine (see p. 367) 10 mg/pyrilamine maleate 8.33 mg/phenylephrine (see p. 1207) 5 mg.

Co-Gesic (NARCOTIC ANALGESIC [schedule V]) *tablet:* hydrocodone (see p. 743) 5 mg/acetaminophen (see p. 9) 500 mg.

Coly-Mycin S Otic (OTIC: STEROID, ANTIBIOTIC) *suspension (per mL):* hydrocortisone acetate (see p. 744) 1%/neomycin sulfate (see p. 1061) 3.3 mg/colistin sulfate 3 mg/thonzonium bromide 0.05%.

Combipatch (HORMONE REPLACEMENT THERAPY) *transdermal patch:* estradiol (see p. 584) 0.05 mg/norethindrone acetate (see p. 1092) 0.14 mg; estradiol 0.05 mg/norethindrone acetate 0.25 mg.

Combivir (ANTIVIRAL) *tablet:* zidovudine (see p. 1611) 300 mg/lamivudine (see p. 852) 150 mg.

Cortisporin (OPHTHALMIC STEROID, ANTIBIOTIC) *suspension (per mL):* hydrocortisone (see p. 744) 1%/neomycin sulfate (see p. 1061) (equivalent to 0.35% neomycin base)/polymyxin B sulfate (see p. 1236) 10,000 units.

Cortisporin Ointment (OPHTHALMIC STEROID, ANTIBIOTIC) *ointment:* hydrocortisone (see p. 744) 1%/neomycin sulfate (see p. 1061) (equivalent to 0.35% neomycin base)/bacitracin zinc (see p. 147) 400 units, polymyxin B sulfate (see p. 1236) 10,000 units/g.

Corzide 40/5 (ANTIHYPERTENSIVE) *tablet:* nadolol (see p. 1034) 40 mg/bendroflumethiazide 5 mg.

Corzide 80/5 (ANTIHYPERTENSIVE) *tablet:* nadolol (see p. 1034) 80 mg/bendroflumethiazide 5 mg.

Cosopt (OPHTHALMIC, GLAUCOMA) *ophthalamic solution:* dorzolamide (see p. 508) 2%/timolol (see p. 1504) 0.5%.

Cotrim (ANTIINFECTIVE) *tablet:* trimethoprim (see p. 1552) 80 mg/sulfamethoxazole (see p. 1428) 400 mg.

Cotrim DS (Double Strength) (ANTIINFECTIVE) *tablet:* trimethoprim (see p. 1552) 160 mg/sulfamethoxazole (see p. 1428) 800 mg.

Cotrim Pediatric (ANTIINFECTIVE) *suspension:* trimethoprim (see p. 1552) 40 mg/sulfamethoxazole (see p. 1428) 200 mg/5 mL.

Cyclomydril (OPHTHALMIC DECONGESTANT) *ophthalmic solution:* cyclopentolate hydrochloride (see p. 391) 0.2%/phenylephrine hydrochloride (see p. 1207) 1%.

Darvocet-A 500 (NARCOTIC AGONIST ANALGESIC [schedule IV]) *tablet:* propoxyphene napsylate (see p. 1289) 100 mg/acetaminophen (see p. 9) 500 mg.

Darvocet-N 50 (NARCOTIC AGONIST ANALGESIC [schedule IV]) *tablet:* propoxyphene napsylate (see p. 1289) 50 mg/acetaminophen (see p. 9) 325 mg.

Darvocet-N 100 (NARCOTIC AGONIST ANALGESIC [schedule IV]) *tablet:* propoxyphene napsylate (see p. 1289) 100 mg/acetaminophen (see p. 9) 650 mg.

Darvon Compound-65 (NARCOTIC AGONIST ANALGESIC [schedule IV]) *pulvule (capsule):* propoxyphene hydrochloride (see p. 1289) 65 mg/aspirin (see p. 117) 389 mg/caffeine (see p. 211) 32.4 mg.

Decadron with Xylocaine (GLUCOCORTICOID) *injection (per mL):* dexamethasone sodium phosphate (see p. 441) 4 mg/lidocaine hydrochloride (see p. 879) 10 mg.

Deconamine (DECONGESTANT, ANTIHISTAMINE) *syrup (per 5 mL):* pseudoephedrine hydrochloride (see p. 1299) 30 mg/chlorpheniramine maleate (see p. 308) 2 mg; *tablet:* pseudoephedrine hydrochloride 60 mg/chlorpheniramine maleate 4 mg.

Deconamine SR (DECONGESTANT, ANTIHISTAMINE) *sustained release capsule:* pseudoephedrine hydrochloride (see p. 1299) 120 mg/chlorpheniramine maleate (see p. 308) 8 mg.

Demulen 1/50 (ORAL CONTRACEPTIVE) *tablet:* ethinyl estradiol (see p. 606) 50 mcg/norethindrone (see p. 1092) 1 mg.

Depo-Testadiol (ESTROGEN, AN-DROGEN) *injection (per mL):* estradiol cypionate (see p. 584) 2 mg/testosterone cypionate (see p. 1468) 50 mg.

Dilaudid Cough Syrup (NARCOTIC ANTITUSSIVE [schedule II]) *syrup:* hydromorphone (see p. 748) 1 mg/guaifenesin (see p. 721) 100 mg/alcohol 5%.

Dilor G (ANTIASTHMATIC) *liquid (per 5 mL):* dyphylline (see p. 528) 100 mg/guaifenesin (see p. 721) 100 mg.

Diovan HCT (ANTIHYPERTENSIVE) *tablet:* hydrochlorothiazide (see p. 741) 12.5 mg/valsartan (see p. 1574) 80 mg; hydrochlorothiazide 12.5 mg/valsartan 160 mg; hydrochlorothiazide 25 mg/valsartan 160 mg; hydrochlorothiazide 12.5 mg/valsartan 320 mg; hydrochlorothiazide 25 mg/valsartan 320 mg.

Diutensin-R (ANTIHYPERTENSIVE) *tablet:* methyclothiazide (see p. 973) 2.5 mg/reserpine (see p. 1332) 0.1 mg.

Donnatal (GASTROINTESTINAL ANTICHOLINERGIC, SEDATIVE) *capsule, tablet, elixir:* atropine sulfate (see p. 132) 0.0194 mg/scopolamine hydrobromide (see p. 1373) 0.0065 mg/hyoscyamine hydrobromide or sulfate (see p. 757) 0.1037 mg/phenobarbital (see p. 1200) 16.2 mg. The elixir contains alcohol 23%/5 mL.

Donnatal Extentab (GASTROINTESTINAL ANTICHOLINERGIC, SEDATIVE) *tablet:* atropine sulfate (see p. 132) 0.0582 mg/scopolamine hydrobromide (see p. 1373) 0.0195 mg/hyoscyamine sulfate (see p. 757) 0.3111 mg/phenobarbital (see p. 1200) 48.6 mg.

Donnatal No. 2 (GASTROINTESTINAL ANTICHOLINERGIC, SEDATIVE) *tablet:* atropine sulfate (see p. 132) 0.0194 mg/scopolamine hydrobromide (see p. 1373) 0.0065 mg/hyoscyamine hydrobromide or sulfate (see p. 757) 0.1037 mg/phenobarbital (see p. 1200) 32.4 mg.

Duac (ANTIACNE) *gel:* clindamycin (see p. 344) 1%/benzoyl peroxide 5%.

Duo-Medihaler (BRONCHODILATOR [ADRENERGIC]) *aerosol:* each valve actuation delivers isoproterenol hydrochloride (see p. 827) 0.16 mg/phenylephrine bitartrate (see p. 1207) 0.24 mg.

DuoNeb (BETA-AGONIST/ANTICHOLINERGIC BRONCHODILATOR) *inhalation solution:* 3 mg albuterol sulfate (see p. 30)/0.5 mg ipratropium bromide (see p. 814) per 3 mL.

Dyazide (DIURETIC) *capsule:* triamterene (see p. 1543) 37.5 mg/hydrochlorothiazide (see p. 741) 25 mg.

Endocet (NARCOTIC ANALGESIC [schedule II]) *tablet:* oxycodone (see p. 1133) 7.5 mg/acetaminophen (see p. 9) 325 mg; oxycodone 7.5 mg/acetaminophen 500 mg; oxycodone 10 mg/acetaminophen 325 mg; oxycodone 10 mg/acetaminophen 650 mg.

Epzicom (ANTIRETROVIRAL AGENT) *tablet:* abacavir (see p. 1) 600 mg/lamivudine (see p. 852) 300 mg.

Estratest (ESTROGEN, ANDROGEN) *tablet:* esterified estrogens (see p. 595) 1.25 mg/methyltestosterone (see p. 982) 2.5 mg.

Estratest H.S. (ESTROGEN, ANDROGEN) *tablet:* esterified estrogens (see p. 595) 0.625 mg/methyltestosterone (see p. 982) 1.25 mg.

Femhrt (HORMONES) *tablet:* ethinyl estradiol (see p. 606) 5 mcg/norethindrone acetate (see p. 1092) 1 mg; ethinyl estradiol 2.5 mcg/norethindrone acetate 0.5 mg.

Fioricet (NONNARCOTIC AGONIST AN-ALGESIC) *tablet:* acetaminophen (see p. 9) 325 mg/butalbital 50 mg/caffeine (see p. 211) 40 mg.

Fiorinal (NONNARCOTIC AGONIST ANALGESIC [schedule III]) *capsule, tablet:* aspirin (see p. 117) 325 mg/butalbital 50 mg/caffeine (see p. 211) 40 mg.

Fiorinal with Codeine (NARCOTIC AGONIST ANALGESIC [schedule III]) *capsule:* codeine phosphate (see p. 367) 30 mg/aspirin (see p. 117) 325 mg/caffeine (see p. 211) 40 mg/butalbital 50 mg.

Fluress (OPHTHALMIC ANESTHETIC) *ophthalmic solution:* benoxinate hydrochloride 0.4%/fluorescein sodium (see p. 650) 0.25%.

Fosamax Plus D (BISPHOSPHONATE) *tablet:* 70 mg alendronate (see p. 35)/2800 IU vitamin D (see p. 1596).

Glucovance (ANTIDIABETIC) *tablet:* glyburide (see p. 710) 1.25 mg/metformin (see p. 956) 250 mg; glyburide 2.5 mg/metformin 500 mg; glyburide 5 mg/metformin 500 mg.

Helidac (ANTIULCER, ANTIBIOTIC) *tablet:* bismuth subsalicylate (see p. 177) 262.4 mg/metronidazole (see p. 990) 250 mg/tetracycline (see p. 1472) 500 mg.

Hycodan (ANTITUSSIVE [schedule III]) *tablet, syrup:* hydrocodone bitartrate (see p. 743) 5 mg/homatropine methylbromide 1.5 mg.

Hycotuss Expectorant (ANTITUSSIVE [schedule III]) guaifenesin (see p. 721) 100 mg/hydrocodone (see p. 743) 5 mg.

Hydrocet (NARCOTIC ANALGESIC [schedule III]) *capsule:* hydrocodone (see p. 743) 5 mg/acetaminophen (see p. 9) 500 mg.

Hyzaar (ANTIHYPERTENSIVE) *tablet:* losartan (see p. 904) 50 mg/hydrochlorothiazide (see p. 741) 12.5 mg/losartan 100 mg/hydrochlorothiazide 12.5 mg/losartan 100 mg/hydrochlorothiazide 25 mg.

Inderide 40/25 (ANTIHYPERTENSIVE) *tablet:* propranolol hydrochloride (see p. 1290) 40 mg/hydrochlorothiazide (see p. 741) 25 mg.

Levlen (ORAL CONTRACEPTIVE) *tablet:* ethinyl estradiol (see p. 606) 30 mcg/levonorgestrel 0.15 mg.

Lexxel (ANTIHYPERTENSIVE) *tablet:* enalapril (see p. 543) 5 mg/felodipine (see p. 625) 5 mg/enalapril 5 mg/felodipine 2.5 mg.

LidoSite (LOCAL ANESTHETIC) *transdermal patch:* lidocaine (see p. 879) 100 mg/epinephrine (see p. 553) 1.05 mg.

Limbitrol (PSYCHOTHERAPEUTIC [schedule IV]) *tablet:* chlordiazepoxide (see p. 299) 5 mg/amitriptyline (see p. 74) 12.5 mg.

Limbitrol DS (PSYCHOTHERAPEUTIC [schedule IV]) *tablet:* chlordiazepoxide (see p. 299) 10 mg/amitriptyline (see p. 74) 25 mg.

Loestrin 1/20 (ORAL CONTRACEPTIVE) *tablet:* ethinyl estradiol (see p. 606) 20 mcg/norethindrone acetate (see p. 1092) 1 mg.

Loestrin 1/20 Fe (ORAL CONTRACEPTIVE) *tablet:* ethinyl estradiol (see p. 606) 20 mcg/norethindrone acetate (see p. 1092) 1 mg/ferrous fumarate 75 mg in last 7 tablets.

Loestrin 1.5/30 (ORAL CONTRACEPTIVE) *tablet:* ethinyl estradiol (see p. 606) 30 mcg/norethindrone acetate (see p. 1092) 1.5 mg.

Loestrin 1.5/30 Fe (ORAL CONTRACEPTIVE) *tablet:* ethinyl estradiol (see p. 606) 30 mcg/norethindrone acetate (see p. 1092) 1.5 mg/ferrous fumarate 75 mg in last 7 tablets.

Lomotil (ANTIDIARRHEAL) *tablet:* diphenoxylate (see p. 488) 2.5 mg/atropine (see p. 132) 0.025 mg

Lo/Ovral (ORAL CONTRACEPTIVE) *tablet:* ethinyl estradiol (see p. 606) 30 mcg/norgestrel (see p. 1096) 0.3 mg.

Lopressor HCT 50/25 (ANTIHYPERTENSIVE) *tablet:* metoprolol tartrate (see p. 987) 50 mg/hydrochlorothiazide (see p. 741) 25 mg.

Lopressor HCT 100/25 (ANTIHYPERTENSIVE) *tablet:* metoprolol tartrate (see p. 987) 100 mg/hydrochlorothiazide (see p. 741) 25 mg.

Lopressor HCT 100/50 (ANTIHYPERTENSIVE) *tablet:* metoprolol tartrate (see p. 987) 100 mg/hydrochlorothiazide (see p. 741) 50 mg.

Lorcet (NARCOTIC ANALGESIC [schedule III]) *tablet:* hydrocodone (see p. 743) 5 mg/acetaminophen (see p. 9) 500 mg.

Lorcet 10/650 (NARCOTIC ANALGESIC [schedule III]) *tablet:* hydrocodone (see p. 743) 10 mg/acetaminophen (see p. 9) 650 mg.

Lorcet-HD (NARCOTIC ANALGESIC [schedule III]) *tablet:* hydrocodone (see p. 743) 5 mg/acetaminophen (see p. 9) 500 mg.

Lortab 5 (NARCOTIC ANALGESIC [schedule III]) *tablet:* hydrocodone (see p. 743) 5 mg/acetaminophen (see p. 9) 500 mg.

Lortab 7.5/500 (NARCOTIC ANALGESIC [schedule III]) *tablet:* hydrocodone (see p. 743) 7.5 mg/acetaminophen (see p. 9) 500 mg.

Lotensin HCT 20/25 (ANTIHYPERTENSIVE) *tablet:* hydrochlorothiazide (see p. 741) 25 mg/benazepril (see p. 157) 20 mg.

Lotensin HCT 20/12.5 (ANTIHYPERTENSIVE) *tablet:* hydrochlorothiazide (see p. 741) 12.5/benazepril (see p. 157) 20 mg.

Lotensin HCT 10/12.5 (ANTIHYPERTENSIVE) *tablet:* hydrochlorothiazide (see p. 741) 12.5 mg/benazepril (see p. 157) 10 mg.

Lotrel (ANTIHYPERTENSIVE) *tablet:* amlodipine (see p. 77) 2.5 mg/benazepril (see p. 157) 10 mg; amlodipine 5 mg/benazepril 10 mg; amlodipine 5 mg/benazepril 20 mg; amlodipine 10 mg/benazepril 20 mg.

Lotrisone (CORTICOSTEROID, ANTIFUNGAL) *cream:* betamethasone (see p. 165) (as dipropionate) 0.05%/clotrimazole (see p. 362) 1%.

Malarone (ANTIMALARIAL) *tablet:* atovaquone 250 mg/proguanil HCl (see p. 129) 100 mg; atovaquone 62.5 mg/proguanil HCl 25 mg.

Maxitrol (OPHTHALMIC STEROID, ANTIBIOTIC) *ophthalmic ointment, ophthalmic suspension:* dexamethasone (see p. 441) 0.1%/neomycin sulfate (see p. 1061) (equivalent to 0.35% neomycin base)/polymyxin B sulfate (see p. 1236) 10,000 units.

Maxzide (DIURETIC) *tablet:* triamterene (see p. 1543) 75 mg/hydrochlorothiazide (see p. 741) 50 mg.

Maxzide 25 (DIURETIC) *tablet:* triamterene (see p. 1543) 37.5 mg/hydrochlorothiazide (see p. 741) 25 mg.

Metaglip (HYPOGLYCEMIC AGENT) *tablet:* glipizide (see p. 707) 2.5 mg/metformin HCl (see p. 956) 250 mg; glipizide 2.5 mg/metformin 500 mg; glipizide 5 mg/metformin 500 mg.

Micardis HCT (ANTIHYPERTENSIVE) *tablet:* telmisartan (see p. 1453) 40 mg/hydrochlorothiazide (see

p. 741) 12.5 mg; telmisartan 80 mg/hydrochlorothiazide 12.5 mg; telmisartan 80 mg/hydrochlorothiazide 25 mg.

Minizide (ANTIHYPERTENSIVE) *capsule:* polythiazide (see p. 1238) 0.5 mg/prazosin hydrochloride (see p. 1255) 1 mg; polythiazide 0.5 mg/prazosin hydrochloride 2 mg; polythiazide 0.5 mg/prazosin hydrochloride 5 mg.

Modicon (ORAL CONTRACEPTIVE) *tablet:* ethinyl estradiol (see p. 606) 35 mcg/norethindrone (see p. 1092) 0.5 mg.

Moduretic (DIURETIC) *tablet:* amiloride hydrochloride (see p. 62) 5 mg/hydrochlorothiazide (see p. 741) 50 mg.

Mycitracin (OPHTHALMIC ANTIBIOTIC) *ophthalmic ointment:* polymyxin B sulfate (see p. 1236) 10,000 units/neomycin sulfate (see p. 1061) 3.5 mg/bacitracin (see p. 147) 500 units/g.

Mycodone (NARCOTIC ANALGESIC [schedule III]) *syrup (per 5 mL):* homotropine methylbromide 1.5 mg/hydrocodone (see p. 743) 5 mg.

Mycolog II (CORTICOSTEROID, ANTIFUNGAL) *cream, ointment:* triamcinolone acetonide (see p. 1541) 0.1%/nystatin (see p. 1100) 100,000 units/g.

Neo-Cortef (CORTICOSTEROID ANTIBIOTIC) *water-soluble cream, topical ointment:* hydrocortisone acetate (see p. 744) 1%/neomycin sulfate (see p. 1061) 0.5%.

Neosporin (OPHTHALMIC ANTIBIOTIC) *ophthalmic drops:* polymyxin B sulfate (see p. 1236) 10,000 units/neomycin sulfate (see p. 1061) 1.75 mg/gramicidin 0.025 mg/mL; *ophthalmic ointment:* polymyxin B sulfate 10,000 units/neomycin sulfate 3.5 mg/bacitracin zinc (see p. 147) 400 units/g.

Neosporin G.U. Irrigant (ANTIBIOTIC) *solution:* neomycin sulfate (see p. 1061) 40 mg/polymyxin B sulfate (see p. 1236) 200,000 units/mL.

Neutra-Phos (PHOSPHORUS REPLACEMENT) *capsule, powder:* phosphorus 250 mg/potassium (see p. 1243) 278 mg/sodium (see p. 1395) 164 mg/combination of monobasic, dibasic, sodium, and potassium phosphate.

Norco (NARCOTIC AGONIST ANALGESIC [schedule III]) *tablet:* hydrocodone bitartrate (see p. 743) 10 mg/acetaminophen (see p. 9) 325 mg; hydrocodone bitartrate 7.5 mg/acetaminophen 325 mg.

Nordette (ORAL CONTRACEPTIVE) *tablet:* ethinyl estradiol (see p. 606) 30 mcg/levonorgestrel 0.15 mg.

Norethin 1/35 E (ORAL CONTRACEPTIVE) *tablet:* ethinyl estradiol (see p. 606) 35 mcg/norethindrone (see p. 1092) 1 mg.

Norethin 1/50 M (ORAL CONTRACEPTIVE) *tablet:* mestranol 50 mcg/norethindrone (see p. 1092) 1 mg.

Norgesic (SKELETAL MUSCLE RELAXANT) *tablet:* orphenadrine citrate (see p. 1118) 25 mg/aspirin (see p. 117) 385 mg/caffeine (see p. 211) 30 mg.

Norgesic Forte (SKELETAL MUSCLE RELAXANT, ANALGESIC) *tablet:* orphenadrine citrate (see p. 1118) 50 mg/aspirin (see p. 117) 770 mg/caffeine (see p. 211) 60 mg.

Norinyl 1+35 (ORAL CONTRACEPTIVE) *tablet:* ethinyl estradiol (see p. 606) 35 mcg/norethindrone (see p. 1092) 1 mg.

Norinyl 1+50 (ORAL CONTRACEPTIVE) *tablet:* mestranol 50 mcg/norethindrone (see p. 1092) 1 mg.

Ortho Evra (CONTRACEPTIVE) *transdermal patch:* norelgestromin 0.15 mg/ethinyl estradiol (see p. 606) 0.02 mg.

Paremyd (MYDRIATIC/CYCLOPLEGIC) *ophthalmic solution:* 1% hydroxy-amphetamine/0.25% tropicamide (see p. 1564).

P$_1$E$_1$, P$_2$E$_1$, P$_4$E$_1$, P$_6$E$_1$ (ANTIGLAU-COMA) *ophthalmic solution:* epinephrine bitartrate (see p. 553) 1%/pilocarpine hydrochloride (see p. 1216) 1%, 2%, 4%, or 6%/benzalkonium chloride (see p. 158) 0.01%/polyethylene glycol, sodium bisulfite.

Paremyd (MYDRIATIC) *ophthalmic solution:* 1% hydroxyamphetamine hydrobromide, 0.25% tropicamide (see p. 1564).

Percocet (NARCOTIC ANALGESIC [schedule II]) *tablet:* oxycodone (see p. 1133) 2.5 mg/acetaminophen (see p. 9) 325 mg; oxycodone 7.5 mg/acetaminophen 325 mg; oxycodone 10 mg/acetaminophen 325 mg; oxycodone 10 mg/acetaminophen 650 mg.

Percodan (NARCOTIC ANALGESIC [schedule II]) *tablet:* oxycodone hydrochloride (see p. 1133) 4.5 mg/oxycodone terephthalate 0.38 mg/aspirin (see p. 117) 325 mg.

Phrenilin (NONNARCOTIC AGONIST ANALGESIC) *tablet:* acetaminophen (see p. 9) 325 mg/butalbital 50 mg.

Phrenilin Forte (NONNARCOTIC AGONIST ANALGESIC) *capsule:* acetaminophen (see p. 9) 650 mg/butalbital 50 mg.

Polysporin Ointment (ANTIINFECTIVE [OPHTHALMIC]) *ophthalmic ointment:* polymyxin B sulfate (see p. 1236) 10,000 units/bacitracin zinc (see p. 147) 500 units/g.

Pravigard Pac (LIPID-LOWERING AGENT) *tablet:* pravastatin (see p. 1252) 20 mg/buffered aspirin (see p. 117) 81 mg; pravastatin 20 mg/buffered aspirin 325 mg; pravastatin 40 mg/aspirin 81 mg; pravastatin 40 mg/buffered aspirin 325 mg; pravastatin 80 mg/buffered aspirin 81 mg; pravastatin 80 mg/buffered aspirin 325 mg.

Premarin with Methyltestosterone (ESTROGEN, ANDROGEN) *tablet:* conjugated estrogens (see p. 593) 0.625 mg/methyltestosterone (see p. 982) 5 mg.

Premphase (ESTROGEN, PROGESTERONE) *tablet:* conjugated estrogens (see p. 593) 0.625 mg/medroxyprogesterone acetate (see p. 932) 5 mg.

PremPro (ESTROGEN, PROGESTIN) *tablet:* conjugated estrogens (see p. 593) 0.3 mg/medroxyprogesterone (see p. 932) 1.5 mg; conjugated estrogen 0.45 mg/medroxyprogesterone 1.5 mg; conjugated estrogen 0.625 mg/medroxyprogesterone 2.5 mg; conjugated estrogen 0.625 mg/medroxyprogesterone 5 mg.

Prevacid NapraPac (PROTON PUMP INHIBITOR/ANTIINFLAMMATORY) *capsules & tablets:* lansoprazole (see p. 856) 15 mg capsule/naproxen sodium (see p. 1049) 375 mg table; lansoprazole 15 mg capsule/naproxen sodium 500 mg tablet.

Prevpac (ANTIBIOTIC/ANTISECRETORY) *capsules & tablets:* amoxicillin (see p. 82) 500 mg capsules, clarithromycin (see p. 341) 500 mg tablets, lansoprazole (see p. 856) 30 mg capsules.

Prinzide (ANTIHYPERTENSIVE) *tablet:* hydrochlorothiazide (see p. 741) 12.5 mg/lisinopril (see p.

890) 10 mg; hydrochlorothiazide 12.5 mg/lisinopril 20 mg; hydrochlorothiazide 25 mg/lisinopril 20 mg.

Probenecid and Colchicine (ANTIGOUT) *tablet:* probenecid (see p. 1265) 500 mg/colchicine (see p. 369) 0.5 mg.

Pyridium Plus (ANALGESIC) *tablet:* phenazopyridine hydrochloride (see p. 1196) 150 mg/hyoscyamine hydrobromide (see p. 757) 0.3 mg/butalbital 15 mg.

Rebetron (INTERFERON, ANTIVIRAL) ribavirin (see p. 1339) 200 mg capsule, interferon alfa-2b recombinant (see p. 804) 3 mU/0.5 mL injection.

Renese-R (ANTIHYPERTENSIVE) *tablet:* polythiazide (see p. 1238) 2 mg/reserpine (see p. 1332) 0.25 mg.

Rifamate (ANTITUBERCULOSIS) *capsule:* isoniazid (see p. 825) 150 mg/rifampin (see p. 1343) 300 mg.

Rifater (ANTITUBERCULOSIS) *tablet:* rifampin (see p. 1343) 120 mg/isoniazid (see p. 825) 50 mg/pyrazinamide (see p. 1302) 300 mg.

Rimactane/INH Dual Pack (ANTITUBERCULOSIS) *pack:* thirty isoniazid (see p. 825) 300 mg tablets, sixty rifampin (see p. 1343) 300 mg capsules.

Robitussin A-C (ANTITUSSIVE, EXPECTORANT) [schedule V]) *syrup (per 5 mL):* codeine phosphate (see p. 367) 10 mg/guaifenesin (see p. 721) 100 mg/alcohol 3.5%.

Rondec (DECONGESTANT, ANTIHISTAMINE) *tablet:* pseudoephedrine hydrochloride (see p. 1299) 60 mg/carbinoxamine maleate 4 mg; *drops (per mL):* pseudoephedrine hydrochloride 25 mg/carbinoxamine maleate 2 mg; *syrup (per mL):* pseudoephedrine hydrochloride 60 mg/carbinoxamine maleate 4 mg.

Roxicet (NARCOTIC ANALGESIC [schedule II]) *tablet:* oxycodone (see p. 1133) 5 mg/acetaminophen (see p. 9) 325 mg; *syrup (per 5 mL):* oxycodone 5 mg/acetaminophen 325 mg.

Soma Compound (SKELETAL MUSCLE RELAXANT) *tablet:* carisoprodol (see p. 242) 200 mg/aspirin (see p. 117) 325 mg.

Soma Compound with Codeine (SKELETAL MUSCLE RELAXANT [schedule III]) *tablet:* carisoprodol (see p. 242) 200 mg, aspirin (see p. 117) 325 mg/codeine phosphate (see p. 367) 16 mg.

Stalevo (ANTIPARKINSON AGENT) *tablet:* 12.5 mg carbidopa (see p. 236)/50 mg levodopa (see p. 870)/200 mg entacapone (see p. 548); 25 mg carbidopa/100 mg levodopa/200 mg entacapone; 37.5 mg carbidopa/150 mg levodopa/200 mg entacapone.

Suboxone (ANALGESIC) *sublingual tablet:* 2 mg buprenorphine (see p. 198)/0.5 mg naloxone (see p. 1044); 8 mg buprenorphine/2 mg naloxone.

Symbicort (MINERALOCORTICOID/BRONCHODILATOR) *inhaler:* budesonide (see p. 193) 0.08 mg/formoterol (see p. 670) 0.045 mg; budesonide 0.16 mg/formoterol 0.045 mg.

Symbyax (ATYPICAL ANTIPSYCHOTIC/SSRI) *capsule:* olanzapine (see p. 1105) 6 mg/fluoxetine (see p. 654) 25 mg; olanzapine 6 mg/fluoxetine 50 mg; olanzapine 12 mg/fluoxetine 25 mg; olanzapine 12 mg/fluoxetine 50 mg.

Symprex-D (ANTIHISTAMINE/DECONGESTANT) *capsule:* acrivastine 8 mg/pseudoephedrine (see p. 18) 60 mg.

Synalgos-DC (NARCOTIC AGONIST ANALGESIC [schedule III]) *capsule:* dihydrocodeine bitartrate 16 mg/aspirin (see p. 117) 356.4 mg/caffeine (see p. 211) 30 mg.

Synera (LOCAL ANESTHETIC) *transdermal patch:* lidocaine (see p. 879) 70 mg/tetracycline (see p. 1472) 70 mg.

Syntest D.S. (ESTROGEN, ANDROGEN) *tablet:* esterified estrogens (see p. 595) 1.25 mg/methyltestosterone (see p. 982) 2.5 mg.

Syntest H.S. (ESTROGEN, ANDROGEN) *tablet:* esterified estrogens (see p. 595) 0.625 mg/methyltestosterone (see p. 982) 1.25 mg.

Talacen (NARCOTIC AGONIST-ANTAGONIST ANALGESIC [schedule IV]) *tablet:* pentazocine hydrochloride (see p. 1185) 25 mg/acetaminophen (see p. 9) 625 mg.

Talwin NX (NARCOTIC ANALGESIC [schedule IV]) *tablet:* pentazocine (see p. 1185) 50 mg/naloxone (see p. 1044) 0.5 mg.

Tanafed DP (DECONGESTANT, ANTIHISTAMINE) *suspension:* pseudoephedrine (see p. 1299) 75 mg/chlorpheniramine tannate 4.5 mg.

Tarka (ANTIHYPERTENSIVE) *tablet:* trandolapril (see p. 1531) 2 mg/verapamil HCl (see p. 1586) 180 mg; trandolapril 4 mg/verapamil HCl 240 mg; trandolapril 1 mg/verapamil HCl 240 mg, trandolapril 2 mg/verapamil HCl 240 mg.

Tenoretic 50 (ANTIHYPERTENSIVE) *tablet:* chlorthalidone (see p. 316) 25 mg/atenolol (see p. 123) 50 mg.

Tenoretic 100 (ANTIHYPERTENSIVE) *tablet:* chlorthalidone (see p. 316) 25 mg/atenolol (see p. 123) 100 mg.

Terra-Cortril Suspension (OCULAR STEROID AND ANTIBIOTIC) *suspension:* hydrocortisone acetate (see p. 744) 1.5%/oxytetracycline (see p. 1138) 0.5%.

Teveten HCT (ANTIHYPERTENSIVE) *tablet:* eprosartan mesylate (see p. 564) 600 mg/hydrochlorothiazide (see p. 741) 12.5 mg; eprosartan 600 mg/hydrochlorothiazide 25 mg.

Timolide (ANTIHYPERTENSIVE) *tablet:* hydrochlorothiazide (see p. 741) 25 mg/timolol maleate (see p. 1504) 10 mg.

Triacin-C Cough Syrup (ANTITUSSIVE [schedule V]) *syrup:* pseudoephedrine (see p. 1299) 30 mg/triprolidine 1.25 mg/codeine (see p. 367) 10 mg.

Tri-Hydroserpine (ANTIHYPERTENSIVE) *tablet:* hydrochlorothiazide (see p. 741) 15 mg/reserpine (see p. 1332) 0.1 mg/hydralazine hydrochloride (see p. 740) 25 mg.

Tri-Levlen (ORAL CONTRACEPTIVE) *tablet:* ethinyl estradiol (see p. 606) 30 mcg/levonorgestrel 0.05 mg × 6 d, ethinyl estradiol 40 mcg/levonorgestrel 0.075 mg × 5 d, ethinyl estradiol 30 mcg/levonorgestrel 0.125 mg × 10 d.

Tri-Luma Cream (STEROID) *cream:* 4% hydroquinone (see p. 750)/0.05% tretinoin (see p. 1539)/0.01% fluocinolone acetonide (see p. 650).

Tri-Norinyl (ORAL CONTRACEPTIVE) *tablet:* ethinyl estradiol (see p. 606) 35 mcg/norethindrone (see p. 1092) 0.5 mg × 7 d, ethinyl estradiol 35 mcg/norethindrone 1 mg × 9 d, ethinyl estradiol 35 mcg/norethindrone 0.5 mg × 5 d.

Triphasil (ORAL CONTRACEPTIVE) *tablet:* ethinyl estradiol (see p. 606) 30 mcg/levonorgestrel 0.05 mg × 6 d, ethinyl estradiol 40

mcg/levonorgestrel 0.075 mg ×
5 d, ethinyl estradiol 30 mcg/
levonorgestrel 0.125 mg × 10 d.

Triple Antibiotic (OPHTHALMIC
ANTBIOTIC) *ophthalmic ointment:* hydrocortisone (see p.
744) 1%/neomycin sulfate (see
p. 1061) 0.5%/bacitracin zinc
(see p. 147) 400 units/poly-
myxin B sulfate (see p. 1236)
10,000 units/g.

Trizivir (REVERSE TRANSCRIPTASE
INHIBITOR) *tablet:* abacavir (see
p. 1) 300 mg/lamivudine (see p.
852) 150 mg/zidovudine (see p.
1611) 300 mg.

Truvada (NUCLEOSIDE REVERSE
TRANSCRIPTASE INHIBITOR) *tablet:* emtricitabine (see p. 541)
200 mg/tenofovir disoproxil
fumarate (see p. 1458) 300 mg.

Tussigon (ANTITUSSIVE [schedule
III]) *tablet:* homotropine methylbromide 1.5 mg/hydrocodone
(see p. 743) 5 mg.

Tussionex (ANTITUSSIVE [schedule
III]) *tablet:* chlorpheniramine
(see p. 308) 8 mg/hydrocodone
(see p. 743) 10 mg.

Twinrix (VACCINE) *injection:* hepatitis A vaccine (see p. 733) 720
ELU/hepatitis B recombinant
vaccine (see p. 736) 20 mcg per
single dose vial.

Tylenol with Codeine Elixir (NAR-
COTIC AGONIST ANALGESIC [sched-
ule V]) *elixir (per 5 mL)* acetaminophen (see p. 9) 120 mg/codeine
phosphate (see p. 367) 12 mg/al-
cohol 7%.

Tylenol with Codeine No. 1 (NAR-
COTIC AGONIST ANALGESIC [sched-
ule III]) *tablet:* acetaminophen
(see p. 9) 300 mg/codeine phosphate (see p. 367) 7.5 mg.

Tylenol with Codeine No. 2 (NAR-
COTIC AGONIST ANALGESIC [sched-
ule III]) *tablet:* acetaminophen
(see p. 9) 300 mg/codeine phosphate (see p. 367) 15 mg.

Tylenol with Codeine No. 3 (NAR-
COTIC AGONIST ANALGESIC [sched-
ule III]) *tablet:* acetaminophen
(see p. 9) 300 mg/codeine phosphate (see p. 367) 30 mg.

Tylenol with Codeine No. 4 (NAR-
COTIC AGONIST ANALGESIC [sched-
ule III]) *tablet:* acetaminophen
(see p. 9) 300 mg/codeine phosphate (see p. 367) 60 mg.

Tylox (NARCOTIC AGONIST ANAL-
GESIC [schedule II]) *capsule:* oxycodone hydrochloride (see p.
1133) 5 mg/acetaminophen (see
p. 9) 500 mg.

Ultracet (ANALGESIC/ANTIPYRETIC)
tablet: tramadol (see p. 1529)
37.5 mg/acetaminophen (see p.
9) 325 mg.

Uniretic (ANTIHYPERTENSIVE) *tablet:* moexipril (see p. 1017) 7.5
mg/hydrochlorothiazide (see p.
741) 12.5 mg; moexipril 15 mg/
hydrochlorothiazide 12.5 mg,
moexipril 15 mg/hydrochloro-
thiazide 25 mg.

Urised (URINARY ANTIINFECTIVE)
tablet: methenamine (see p.
962) 40.8 mg/phenyl salicylate
18.1 mg/atropine sulfate (see p.
132) 0.03 mg/hyoscyamine (see
p. 757) 0.03 mg/benzoic acid
4.5 mg/methylene blue 5.4 mg.

Vaseretic (ANTIHYPERTENSIVE) *tablet:* enalapril maleate (see p. 543)
5 mg/hydrochlorothiazide (see p.
741) 12.5 mg; enalapril maleate
10 mg/hydrochlorothiazide 25
mg.

Vasocidin (OPHTHALMIC CORTICO-
STEROID, ANTIINFECTIVE) *ophthalmic solution:* prednisolone sodium phosphate (see p. 1257)
0.23%/sulfacetamide sodium (see
p. 1425) 10%.

Vasocon-A (OPHTHALMIC DECON-
GESTANT) *ophthalmic solution:*
naphazoline hydrochloride (see
p. 1048) 0.05%/antazoline phosphate 0.5%.

Vicodin (NARCOTIC AGONIST ANALGESIC [schedule III]) *tablet:* hydrocodone bitartrate (see p. 743) 5 mg/acetaminophen (see p. 9) 500 mg.

Vicodin ES (NARCOTIC AGONIST ANALGESIC [schedule III]) *tablet:* hydrocodone (see p. 743) 7.5 mg/acetaminophen (see p. 9) 750 mg.

Vicodin HP (NARCOTIC AGONIST ANALGESIC [schedule III]) *tablet:* hydrocodone (see p. 743) 10 mg/acetaminophen (see p. 9) 660 mg.

Vicoprofen (NARCOTIC AGONIST ANALGESIC [schedule III]) *tablet:* hydrocodone bitartrate (see p. 743) 7.5 mg/ibuprofen (see p. 760) 200 mg.

Vytorin (ANTILIPEMIC AGENT) *tablet:* ezetimibe (see p. 617) 10 mg/simvastatin (see p. 1388) 10 mg; ezetimibe 10 mg/simvastatin 20 mg; ezetimibe 10 mg/ simvastatin 40 mg; ezetimibe 10 mg/simvastatin 80 mg.

Wygesic (NARCOTIC AGONIST ANALGESIC [schedule IV]) *tablet:* propoxyphene hydrochloride (see p. 1289) 65 mg/acetaminophen (see p. 9) 650 mg.

Yasmin (ORAL CONTRACEPTIVE) *tablet:* ethinyl estradiol (see p. 606) 30 mcg/drospirenone 3 mg.

Zestoretic (ANTIHYPERTENSIVE) *tablet:* hydrochlorothiazide (see p. 741) 12.5 mg/lisinopril (see p. 890) 10 mg; hydrochlorothiazide 12.5 mg/lisinopril 20 mg; hydrochlorothiazide 25 mg/lisinopril 20 mg.

Ziac (ANTIHYPERTENSIVE) *tablet:* bisoprolol (see p. 179) 2.5 mg/ hydrochlorothiazide (see p. 741) 6.25 mg; bisoprolol 5 mg/hydrochlorothiazide 6.25 mg; bisoprolol 10 mg/hydrochlorothiazide 6.25 mg.

Zylet (OPHTHALMIC ANTIBIOTIC) *solution:* loteprednol etabonate (see p. 905) 0.5%/tobramycin (see p. 1513) 0.3%.

Zyrtec-D (ANTIHISTAMINE/DECONGESTANT) *tablet, sustained release:* cetirizine (see p. 287) 5 mg/pseudoephedrine (see p. 1299) 120 mg.

acute dystonia extrapyramidal symptom manifested by abnormal posturing, grimacing, spastic torticollis (neck torsion), and oculogyric (eyeball movement) crisis.

adverse effect unintended, unpredictable, and nontherapeutic response to drug action. Adverse effects occur at doses used therapeutically or for prophylaxis or diagnosis. They generally result from drug toxicity, idiosyncrasies, or hypersensitivity reactions caused by the drug itself or by ingredients added during manufacture, e.g., preservatives, dyes, or vehicles.

afterload resistance that ventricles must work against to eject blood into the aorta during systole.

agranulocytosis sudden drop in leukocyte count; often followed by a severe infection manifested by high fever, chills, prostration, and ulcerations of mucous membrane such as in the mouth, rectum, or vagina.

akathisia extrapyramidal symptom manifested by a compelling need to move or pace, without specific pattern, and an inability to be still.

analeptic restorative medication that enhances excitation of the CNS without affecting inhibitory impulses.

anaphylactoid reaction excessive allergic response manifested by wheezing, chills, generalized pruritic urticaria, diaphoresis, sense of uneasiness, agitation, flushing, palpitations, coughing, difficulty breathing, and cardiovascular collapse.

anticholinergic actions inhibition of parasympathetic response manifested by dry mouth, decreased peristalsis, constipation, blurred vision, and urinary retention.

bioavailability fraction of active drug that reaches its action sites after administration by any route. Following an IV dose, bioavailability is 100%; however, such factors as first-pass effect, enterohepatic cycling, and biotransformation reduce bioavailability of an orally administered drug.

blood dyscrasia pathological condition manifested by fever, sore mouth or throat, unexplained fatigue, easy bruising or bleeding.

cardiotoxicity impairment of cardiac function manifested by one or more of the following: hypotension, arrhythmias, precordial pain, dyspnea, electrocardiogram (ECG) abnormalities, cardiac dilation, congestive failure.

cholinergic response stimulation of the parasympathetic response manifested by lacrimation, diaphoresis, salivation, abdominal cramps, diarrhea, nausea, and vomiting.

circulatory overload excessive vascular volume manifested by increased central venous pressure (CVP), elevated blood pressure, tachycardia, distended neck veins, peripheral edema, dyspnea, cough, and pulmonary rales.

CNS stimulation excitement of the CNS manifested by hyperactivity, excitement, nervousness, insomnia, and tachycardia.

CNS toxicity impairment of CNS function manifested by ataxia, tremor, incoordination, paresthesias, numbness, impairment of pain or touch sensation, drowsiness, confusion, headache, anxiety, tremors, and behavior changes.

congestive heart failure (CHF) impaired pumping ability of the heart manifested by paroxysmal nocturnal dyspnea, cough, fatigue or dyspnea on exertion, tachycardia, peripheral or pulmonary edema, and weight gain.

Cushing's syndrome fatty swellings in the interscapular area (buffalo hump) and in the facial area (moon face), distension of the abdomen, ecchymoses following even minor trauma, impotence, amenorrhea, high blood pressure, general weakness, loss of muscle mass, osteoporosis, and psychosis.

dehydration decreased intracellular or extracellular fluid manifested by elevated temperature, dry skin and mucous membranes, decrease tissue turgor, sunken eyes, furrowed tongue, low blood pressure, diminished or irregular pulse, muscle or abdominal cramps, thick secretions, hard feces and impaction, scant urinary output, urine specific gravity above 1.030, an elevated hemoglobin.

disulfiram-type reaction Antabuse-type reaction manifested by facial flushing, pounding headache, sweating, slurred speech, abdominal cramps, nausea, vomiting, tachycardia, fever, palpitations, drop in blood pressure, dyspnea, and sense of chest constriction. Symptoms may last up to 24 hours.

enzyme induction stimulation of microsomal enzymes by a drug resulting in its accelerated metabolism and decreased activity. If reactive intermediates are formed, drug-mediated toxicity may be exacerbated.

first-pass effect reduced bioavailability of an orally administered drug due to metabolism in GI epithelial cells and liver or to biliary excretion. Effect may be avoided by use of sublingual tablets or rectal suppositories.

fixed drug eruption drug-induced circumscribed skin lesion that persists or recurs in the same site. Residual pigmentation may remain following drug withdrawal.

half-life ($t_{1/2}$) time required for concentration of a drug in the body to decrease by 50%. Half-life also represents the time necessary to reach steady state or to decline from steady state after a change (i.e., starting or stopping) in the dosing regimen. Half-life may be affected by a disease state and age of the drug user.

heat stroke a life-threatening condition manifested by absence of sweating; red, dry, hot skin; dilated pupils; dyspnea; full bounding pulse; temperature above 40° C (105° F); and mental confusion.

hepatic toxicity impairment of liver function manifested by jaundice, dark urine, pruritus, lightcolored stools, eosinophilia, itchy skin or rash, and persistently high elevations of alanine amino-transferase (ALT) and aspartate aminotransferase (AST).

hyperammonemia elevated level of ammonia or ammonium in the blood manifested by lethargy, decreased appetite, vomiting, asterixis (flapping tremor), weak pulse, irritability, decreased responsiveness, and seizures.

hypercalcemia elevated serum calcium manifested by deep bone and flank pain, renal calculi, anorexia, nausea, vomiting, thirst, constipation, muscle hypotonicity, pathologic fracture, bradycardia, lethargy, and psychosis.

hyperglycemia elevated blood glucose manifested by flushed, dry skin, low blood pressure and elevated pulse, tachypnea, Kussmaul's respirations, polyuria, polydipsia; polyphagia, lethargy, and drowsiness.

hyperkalemia excessive potassium in blood, which may produce lifethreatening cardiac arrhythmias, including bradycardia and heart block, unusual fatigue, weakness or heaviness of limbs, general muscle weakness, muscle cramps, paresthesias, flaccid paralysis of extremities, shortness of breath, nervousness, confusion, diarrhea, and GI distress.

hypermagnesemia excessive magnesium in blood, which may produce cathartic effect, profound thirst, flushing, sedation, confusion, depressed deep tendon reflexes (DTRs), muscle weakness, hypotension, and depressed respirations.

hypernatremia excessive sodium in blood, which may produce confusion, neuromuscular excitability, muscle weakness, seizures, thirst, dry and flushed skin, dry mucous membranes, pyrexia, agitation, and oliguria or anuria.

hypersensitivity reactions excessive and abnormal sensitivity to given agent manifested by urticaria, pruritus, wheezing, edema, redness, and anaphylaxis.

hyperthyroidism excessive secretion by the thyroid glands, which increases basal metabolic rate, resulting in warm, flushed, moist skin; tachycardia, exophthalmos; infrequent lid blinking; lid edema; weight loss despite increased appetite; frequent urination; menstrual irregularity; breathlessness; hypoventilation; congestive heart failure; excessive sweating.

hyperuricemia excessive uric acid in blood, resulting in pain in flank; stomach, or joints, and changes in intake and output ratio and pattern.

hypocalcemia abnormally low calcium level in blood, which may result in depression; psychosis; hyperreflexia; diarrhea; cardiac arrhythmias; hypotension; muscle spasms; paresthesias of feet, fingers, tongue; positive Chvostek's sign. Severe deficiency (tetany) may result in carpopedal spasms, spasms of face muscle, laryngospasm, and generalized convulsions.

hypoglycemia abnormally low glucose level in the blood, which may result in acute fatigue, restlessness, malaise, marked irritability and weakness, cold sweats, excessive hunger, headache, dizziness, confusion, slurred speech, loss of consciousness, and death.

hypokalemia abnormally low level of potassium in blood, which may result in malaise, fatigue, paresthesias, depressed reflexes, muscle weakness and cramps, rapid, irregular pulse, arrhythmias, hypotension, vomiting, paralytic ileus, mental confusion, depression, delayed thought process, abdominal distension, polyuria, shallow breathing, and shortness of breath.

hypomagnesemia abnormally low level of magnesium in

blood, resulting in nausea, vomiting, cardiac arrhythmias, and neuromuscular symptoms (tetany, positive Chvostek's and Trousseau's signs, seizures, tremors, ataxia, vertigo, nystagmus, muscular fasciculations).

hypophosphatemia abnormally low level of phosphates in blood, resulting in muscle weakness, anorexia, malaise, absent deep tendon reflexes, bone pain, paresthesias, tremors, negative calcium balance, osteomalacia, osteoporosis.

hypothyroidism condition caused by thyroid hormone deficiency that lowers basal metabolic rate and may result in periorbital edema, lethargy, puffy hands and feet, cool, pale skin, vertigo, nocturnal cramps, decreased GI motility, constipation, hypotension, slow pulse, depressed muscular activity, and enlarged thyroid gland.

hypoxia insufficient oxygenation in the blood manifested by dyspnea, tachypnea, headache, restlessness, cyanosis, tachycardia, dysrhythmias, confusion, decreased level of consciousness, and euphoria or delirium.

international normalizing ratio measurement that normalizes for the differences obtained from various laboratory readings in the value for thromboplastin blood level.

leukopenia abnormal decrease in number of white blood cells, usually below 5000 per cubic millimeter, resulting in fever, chills, sore mouth or throat, and unexplained fatigue.

liver toxicity manifested by anorexia, nausea, fatigue, lethargy, itching, jaundice, abdominal pain, dark-colored urine, and flu-like symptoms.

metabolic acidosis decrease in pH value of the extracellular fluid caused by either an increase in hydrogen ions or a decrease in bicarbonate ions. It may result in one or more of the following: lethargy, headache, weakness, abdominal pain, nausea, vomiting, dyspnea, hyperpnea progressing to Kussmaul breathing, dehydration, thirst, weakness, flushed face, full bounding pulse, progressive drowsiness, mental confusion, combativeness.

metabolic alkalosis increase in pH value of the extracellular fluid caused by either a loss of acid from the body (e.g., through vomiting) or an increased level of bicarbonate ions (e.g., through ingestion of sodium bicarbonate). It may result in muscle weakness, irritability, confusion, muscle twitching, slow and shallow respirations, and convulsive seizures.

microsomal enzymes drug-metabolizing enzymes located in the endoplasmic reticulum of the liver and other tissues chiefly responsible for oxidative drug metabolism, e.g., cytochrome P450.

myopathy any disease or abnormal condition of striated muscles manifested by muscle weakness, myalgia, diaphoresis, fever, and reddish-brown urine (myoglobinuria) or oliguria.

nephrotoxicity impairment of the nephrons of the kidney manifested by one or more of the following: oliguria, urinary frequency, hematuria, cloudy urine, rising BUN and serum creatinine, fever, graft tenderness or enlargement.

neuroleptic malignant syndrome (NMS) potentially fatal complication associated with antipsychotic drugs manifested by hyperpyrexia, altered mental status, muscle rigidity, irregular pulse, fluctuating BP, diaphoresis, and tachycardia.

orphan drug (as defined by the Orphan Drug Act, an amendment of the Federal Food, Drug, and Cosmetic Act which took effect in January 1983): drug or biological product used in the treatment, diagnosis, or prevention of a rare disease. A rare disease or condition is one that affects fewer than 200,000 persons in the United States, or affects more than 200,000 persons but for which there is no reasonable expectation that drug research and development costs can be recovered from sales within the United States.

ototoxicity impairment of the ear manifested by one or more of the following: headache, dizziness or vertigo, nausea and vomiting with motion, ataxia, nystagmus.

prodrug inactive drug form that becomes pharmacologically active through biotransformation.

protein binding reversible interaction between protein and drug resulting in a drug-protein complex (bound drug) which is in equilibrium with free (active) drug in plasma and tissues. Since only free drug can diffuse to action sites, factors that influence drug-binding (e.g., displacement of bound drug by another drug, or decreased albumin concentration) may potentiate pharmacological effect.

pseudomembranous enterocolitis life-threatening superinfection characterized by severe diarrhea and fever.

pseudoparkinsonism extrapyramidal symptom manifested by slowing of volitional movement (akinesia), mask facies, rigidity and tremor at rest (especially of upper extremities); and pill rolling motion.

pulmonary edema excessive fluid in the lung tissue manifested by one or more of the following: shortness of breath, cyanosis, persistent productive cough (frothy sputum may be blood tinged), expiratory rales, restlessness, anxiety, increased heart rate, sense of chest pressure.

renal insufficiency reduced capacity of the kidney to perform its functions as manifested by one or more of the following: dysuria, oliguria, hematuria, swelling of lower legs and feet.

serotonin syndrome manifested by restlessness, myoclonus, mental status changes, hyperreflexia, diaphoresis, shivering, and tremor.

Somogyi effect rebound phenomenon clinically manifested by fasting hyperglycemia and worsening of diabetic control due to unnecessarily large p.m. insulin doses. Hormonal response to unrecognized hypoglycemia (i.e., release of epinephrine, glucagon, growth hormone, cortisol) causes insensitivity to insulin. Increasing the amount of insulin required to treat the hyperglycemia intensifies the hypoglycemia.

superinfection new infection by an organism different from the initial infection being treated by antimicrobial therapy manifested by one or more of the following: black, hairy tongue; glossitis, stomatitis; anal itching; loose, foul-smelling stools; vaginal itching or discharge; sudden fever; cough.

tachyphylaxis rapid decrease in response to a drug after administration of a few doses. Initial drug response cannot be restored by an increase in dose.

tardive dyskinesia extrapyramidal symptom manifested by involuntary rhythmic, bizarre movements of face, jaw, mouth, tongue, and sometimes extremities.

vasovagal symptoms transient vascular and neurogenic reaction marked by pallor, nausea, vomiting, bradycardia, and rapid fall in arterial blood pressure.

water intoxication (dilutional hyponatremia) less than normal concentration of sodium in the blood resulting from excess extracellular and intracellular fluid and producing one or more of the following: lethargy, confusion, headache, decreased skin turgor, tremors, convulsions, coma, anorexia, nausea, vomiting, diarrhea, sternal fingerprinting, weight gain, edema, full bounding pulse, jugular vein distension, rales, signs and symptoms of pulmonary edema.

ABGs	arterial blood gases
a.c.	before meals (*ante cibum*)
ACD	acid–citrate–dextrose
ACE	angiotensin-converting enzyme
ACh	acetylcholine
ACIP	Advisory Committee on Immunization Practices
ACLS	advanced cardiac life support
ACS	acute coronary syndrome
ACT	activated clotting time
ACTH	adrenocorticotropic hormone
AD	Alzheimer's disease
ADD	attention deficit disorder
ADH	antidiuretic hormone
ADLs	activities of daily living
ad lib	as desired (*ad libitum*)
ADP	adenosine diphosphate
ADT	alternate-day drug (administration)
AIDS	acquired immunodeficiency syndrome
alpha1-PI	alpha1-proteinase inhibitor
ALS	amyotrophic lateral sclerosis
ALT	alanine aminotransferase (formerly SGPT)
AML	acute myelogenous leukemia
AMP	adenosine monophosphate
ANA	antinuclear antibody(ies)
ANC	acid neutralizing capacity
aPTT	activated partial thromboplastin time
ARC	AIDS related complex
ARDS	adult respiratory distress syndrome
ASHD	arteriosclerotic heart disease
AST	aspartate aminotransferase (formerly SGOT)
AT$_1$	angiotensin II receptor subtype I
AT$_2$	angiotensin II receptor subtype II
ATP	adenosine triphosphate
AV	atrioventricular
b.i.d.	two times a day
BMD	bone mineral density
BMI	body mass index
BMR	basal metabolic rate
BP	blood pressure
BPH	benign prostatic hypertrophy
bpm	beats per minute
BSA	body surface area
BSE	breast self-exam
BSP	bromsulphalein
BT	bleeding time
BUN	blood urea nitrogen
C	centigrade, Celsius

CAD	coronary artery disease
cAMP	cyclic adenosine monophosphate
CBC	complete blood count
cc	cubic centimeter
CDC	Centers for Disease Control and Prevention
CF	cystic fibrosis
cGMP	cyclic guanosine monophosphate
CHF	congestive heart failure
Cl_{cr}	creatinine clearance
CLL	chronic lymphocytic leukemia
cm	centimeter
CMV	cytomegalovirus-I
CNS	central nervous system
Coll	collyrium (eye wash)
COMT	catecholamine-*o*-methyl transferase
COPD	chronic obstructive pulmonary disease
COX-2	cyclooxygenase-2
CPK	creatinine phosphokinase
CPR	cardiopulmonary resuscitation
CRF	chronic renal failure
CRFD	chronic renal failure disease
C&S	culture and sensitivity
CSF	cerebrospinal fluid
CSP	cellulose sodium phosphate
CT	clotting time
CTZ	chemoreceptor trigger zone
CV	cardiovascular
CVA	cerebrovascular accident
CVP	central venous pressure
CYP	cytochrome P450 system of enzymes
d	day
D5W	5% dextrose in water
D&C	dilation and curettage
DIC	disseminated intravascular coagulation
DKA	diabetic ketoacidosis
dL	deciliter (100 mL or 0.1 liter)
DM	diabetes mellitus
DMARD	disease-modifying antirheumatic drug
DNA	deoxyribonucleic acid
DPD	dihydropyrimidine dehydrogenase
DTRs	deep tendon reflexes
DVT	deep venous thrombosis
ECG, EKG	electrocardiogram
ECT	electroconvulsive therapy
EEG	electroencephalogram
EENT	eye, ear, nose, throat
e.g.	for example (*exempli gratia*)
EGFR	epidermal growth factor receptor
ENT	ear, nose, throat
EPS	extrapyramidal symptoms (or syndrome)

ER	estrogen receptor
ESRF	end-stage renal failure
F	Fahrenheit
FBS	fasting blood sugar
FDA	Food and Drug Administration
FSH	follicle-stimulating hormone
FTI	free thyroxine index
5-FU	5-fluorouracil
FUO	fever of unknown origin
g	gram
G6PD	glucose-6-phosphate dehydrogenase
GABA	gamma-aminobutyric acid
GERD	gastroesophageal reflux disease
GM-CSF	granulocyte-macrophage colony-stimulating factor
GnRH	gonadotropic releasing hormone
GFR	glomerular filtration rate
GH	growth hormone
GI	gastrointestinal
GPIIb/IIIa	glycoprotein IIb/IIIa
GU	genitourinary
h	hour
HACA	human antichimeric antibody
HbA$_{1c}$	glycosylated hemoglobin
HBV	viral hepatitis B
HCG	human chorionic gonadotropin
Hct	hematocrit
HDL	high density lipoprotein
HDL-C	high-density-lipoprotein cholesterol
HER	human epidermal growth factor
Hgb	hemoglobin
5-HIAA	5-hydroxyindoleacetic acid
HIT	heparin-induced thrombocytopenia
HIV	human immunodeficiency virus
HMG-CoA	3-hydroxy-3-methyl-glutaryl coenzyme A
HPA	hypothalamic–pituitary–adrenocortical (axis)
HPV	human papillomavirus
HR	heart rate
h.s.	nightly or at bedtime (*hora somni*)
HSV-1	herpes simplex virus type 1
HSV-2	herpes simplex virus type 2
5-HT	5-hydroxytryptamine (serotonin receptor)
IBW	ideal body weight
IC	intracoronary
ICP	intracranial pressure
ICU	intensive care unit
ID	intradermal
IFN	interferon
Ig	immunoglobulin
IGF-1	insulin-like growth factor 1
IL	interleukin

IM	intramuscular
INR	international normalized ratio
IOP	intraocular pressure
IPPB	intermittent positive pressure breathing
iPTH	idiopathic parathyroid hormone
IT	intrathecal
ITP	idiopathic thrombocytopenic purpura
IU	international unit
IV	intravenous
JRA	juvenile rheumatoid arthritis
kg	kilogram
17-KGS	17-ketogenic steroids
17-KS	17-ketosteroids
KVO	keep vein open
L	liter
LDH	lactic dehydrogenase
LDL	low density lipoprotein
LDL-C	low-density-lipoprotein cholesterol
LE	lupus erythematosus
LFT	liver function test
LH	luteinizing hormone
LSD	lysergic acid diethylamide
LTRA	leukotriene receptor antagonist
LVEDP	left ventricular end diastolic pressure
M	molar (strength of a solution)
m^2	square meter (of body surface area)
MAO	monoamine oxidase
MAOI	monoamine oxidase inhibitor
MBD	minimal brain dysfunction
MCH	mean corpuscular hemoglobin
MCHC	mean corpuscular hemoglobin concentration
mCi	millicurie
mcg	microgram (1/1000 of a milligram)
μm	micrometer
MDI	metered dose inhaler
MDR	minimum daily requirements
mEq	milliequivalent
mg	milligram
min	minute
MI	myocardial infarction
MIC	minimum inhibitory concentration
mL	milliliter (0.001 liter)
mm	millimeter
mo	month
MPS I	mucopolysaccharidosis I
MRSA	methicillin-resistant *Staphylococcus aureus*
MS	multiple sclerosis
N	normal (strength of a solution)
NADH	reduced form of nicotine adenine dinucleotide
NAPA	*N*-acetyl procainamide

nb	note well (*nota bene*)
ng	nanogram (1/1000 of a microgram)
NMS	neuroleptic malignant syndrome
NNRTI	nonnucleoside reverse transcriptase inhibitor
NPN	nonprotein nitrogen
NPO	nothing by mouth
NRTI	nucleoside reverse transcriptase inhibitor
NS	normal saline
NSAID	nonsteroidal antiinflammatory drug
NSCLC	non-small cell lung cancer
NSR	normal sinus rhythm
NYHA Class I, II, III, IV	New York Heart Association classes of heart failure
OAB	overactive bladder
OC	oral contraceptive
ODT	oral disintegrating tablet
17-OHCS	17-hydroxycorticosteroids
OTC	over the counter (nonprescription)
P450	cytochrome P450 system of enzymes
PABA	*para*-aminobenzoic acid
PAS	*para*-aminosalicylic acid
PAWP	pulmonary artery wedge pressure
PBI	protein-bound iodine
PBP	penicillin-binding protein
p.c.	after meals (*post cibum*)
PCI	percutaneous coronary intervention
PCWP	pulmonary capillary wedge pressure
PE	pulmonary embolism
PDE	phosphodiesterase
PERLA	pupils equal, react to light and accommodation
PG	prostaglandin
PGE$_2$	prostaglandin E$_2$
pH	hydrogen ion concentration
PID	pelvic inflammatory disease
PKU	phenylketonuria
PMDD	premenstrual dysphoric disorder
PND	paroxysmal nocturnal dyspnea
PO	by mouth or orally (*per os*)
PPI	proton pump inhibitor
PPM	parts per million
PR	rectally (*per rectum*)
prn	when required (*pro re nata*)
PSA	prostate-specific antigen
PSP	phenolsulfonphthalein
PSVT	paroxysmal supraventricular tachycardia
PT	prothrombin time
PTH	parathyroid hormone
PTT	partial thromboplastin time
PUD	peptic ulcer disease
PVC	premature ventricular contraction

PVD	peripheral vascular disease
PZI	protamine zinc insulin
q.d.	every day
q.i.d.	four times daily
q.o.d.	every other day
RA	rheumatoid arthritis
RAI	radioactive iodine
RAST	radioallergosorbent test
RBC	red blood (cell) count
RDA	recommended (daily) dietary allowance
RDS	respiratory distress syndrome
REM	rapid eye movement
rem	radiation equivalent man
RES	reticuloendothelial system
RIA	radioimmunoassay
RL	Ringer's lactate
RNA	ribonucleic acid
ROM	range of motion
RSV	respiratory syncytial virus
RT	reverse transcriptase
RT_3U	total serum thyroxine concentration
sec	second
S&S	signs and symptoms
SA	sinoatrial
SBE	subacute bacterial endocarditis
SC	subcutaneous
S_{cr}	serum creatinine
SGGT	serum gamma-glutamyl transferase
SGOT	serum glutamic–oxaloacetic transaminase (*see* AST)
SGPT	serum glutamic–pyruvic transaminase (*see* ALT)
SIADH	syndrome of inappropriate antidiuretic hormone
SI Units	International System of Units
SK	streptokinase
SL	sublingual
SLE	systemic lupus erythematosus
SMA	sequential multiple analysis
SNRI	serotonin norepinephrine reuptake inhibitor
SOS	if necessary (*si opus cit*)
sp	species
SPF	sun protection factor
sq	square
SR	sedimentation rate
SRS-A	slow-reactive substance of anaphylaxis
SSRI	selective serotonin reuptake inhibitor
stat	immediately
STD	sexually transmitted disease
SVT	supraventricular tachyarrhythmias
$t_{1/2}$	half-life
T_3	triiodothyronine
T_4	thyroxine

TCA	tricyclic antidepressant
TG	total triglycerides
TIA	transient ischemic attack
t.i.d.	three times a day (*ter in die*)
TNF	tumor necrosis factor
tPA	tissue plasminogen activator
TPN	total parenteral nutrition
TPR	temperature, pulse, respirations
TSH	thyroid-stimulating hormone
TSS	toxic shock syndrome
TT	thrombin time
URI	upper respiratory infection
USP	United States Pharmacopeia
USPHS	United States Public Health Service
UTI	urinary tract infection
UV-A, UVA	ultraviolet A wave
VDRL	Venereal Disease Research Laboratory
VEGF	vascular endothelial growth factor
VLDL	very low density lipoprotein
VMA	vanillylmandelic acid
VREF	vancomycin-resistant *Enterococcus faecium*
VRSA	vancomycin-resistant *Staphylococcus aureus*
VS	vital signs
wk	week
WBC	white blood (cell) count
WBCT	whole blood clotting time
y	year

As patient interest in dietary supplements and other natural products increases, there continues to be an elevated need for information on this topic. These products are not standardized or regulated by FDA guidelines; therefore, caution should be used when discussing these products. Consumers should note that since rigid quality control standards are not required for these products, substantial variability can occur in both potency and purity of a given product, especially between different commercial companies.

Many of these products have limited research on safety; thus, side effects and potential drug interactions are not well understood. Dietary supplements may either increase or decrease the level of a drug in the patient's body.

This table provides basic information on some of the most commonly sold dietary supplements. For additional information, a specialty resource on herbal and/or dietary supplements should be consulted.

Name	Most Common Use	Significant Safety Concerns
Bilberry	Eye health	Long-term, high-dose use can cause liver problems
Black cohosh	Menopausal symptoms	Should be avoided in pregnant patients
Cranberry	Urinary tract infections	Considered safe at usual doses
Echinacea	Infections	May cause allergic reactions; should be used only short-term
Eleuthera (Siberian ginseng)	Energy	Avoid use with digoxin
Evening primrose	Menopausal symptoms	May affect seizure threshold
Garlic	Cholesterol	Potentially significant drug interactions with drugs metabolized by CYP system
Ginkgo	Memory enhancement	Potential increased bleeding risk
Ginger	Nausea	Overdoses may cause cardiac arrhythmias
Ginseng (American ginseng)	Energy	Should not be used with MAO inhibitors; may affect anticoagulants

Name	Most Common Use	Significant Safety Concerns
Glucosamine	Osteoarthritis	Considered safe at usual doses; at higher doses, possible interaction with warfarin and other coumarin anticoagulants
Green tea	Energy, weight loss	High doses may cause cardiovascular side effects
Horny goat weed	Sexual function	Should be avoided in pregnant/lactating women
Horse chestnut	Congestive heart failure	Potential hepatotoxicity
Milk thistle	Liver function	May affect CYP metabolism and interact with drugs metabolized by this system
Saw palmetto	Benign prostatic hyperplasia	Adverse effects appear mild
Soy	Menopausal symptoms	GI-related side effects may be significant for some patients
St. John's wort	Depression	Significant drug interactions with several drugs metabolized by CYP system
Valerian	Sleep disorder	Potentially hepatotoxic
Yohimbe	Sexual function	Do not use with drugs affecting serotonin system

BIBLIOGRAPHY

American Academy of Pediatrics Committee on Drugs. The transfer of drugs and other chemicals into human milk. *Pediatrics*. 2001;108:776–89.

American Hospital Formulary Service (AHFS) Drug Information. 07. Bethesda, MD: American Society of Health-System Pharmacists. 2007.

Bell MS, Nolt DH. Visual compatibility of doxapram hydrochloride with drugs commonly administered via a Y-site in the intensive care nursery. *American Journal of Health System Pharmacy*. 2003;60:193–194.

Bindler R, Howry L. *Prentice Hall Pediatric Drug Guide with Nursing Implications*. Upper Saddle River, NJ: Prentice Hall Health. 2005.

Chalmers JR, Bobek MB, Militello MA. Visual compatibility of amiodarone hydrochloride injection with various intravenous drugs. *American Journal of Health System Pharmacy*. 2001;58:504–506.

Clinical Pharmacology. http://www.gsm.com. Gold Standard Media. 2007.

Drug Facts and Comparisons. http://factsandcomparisons.com. Version 4.0 online. St. Louis: Wolters Kluwer Health. 2007.

King Guide to Parenteral Admixtures. Napa, CA: King Guide Publications, Inc. 2005.

Lacy CF, Armstrong LL, Goldman MP, Lance LL. *Drug Information Handbook*. 13th ed. Hudson, OH: Lexi-Comp. 2005.

Micromedex Healthcare Series. Greenwood Village, NJ: Thompson Healthcare. 2007.

Physicians' Desk Reference. 60th ed. Montvale, NJ: Thompson Healthcare. 2007.

Semla TP, Beizer JL, Higbee MD. *Geriatric Dosage Handbook*. 10th ed. Hudson, OH: Lexi-Comp. 2005.

Seto W, Trope A, Carfrae L, Walker S. Visual compatibility of sodium nitroprusside with other injectable medications given to pediatric patients. *American Journal of Health System Pharmacy*. 2001;58:1422–1426.

Trissel LA, *Handbook of Injectable Drugs*. 13th ed. Bethesda, MD: American Society of Health-System Pharmacists. 2005.

USP DI: Advice to Patients. Rockville, MD: US Pharmacopeial Convention. 2007.

USP DI: Drug Information for the Health Care Professional. Rockville, MD: US Pharmacopeial Convention. 2007.

Veltri MA, Conner KG. Physical compatibility of milrinone lactate injection with intravenous drugs commonly used in the pediatric intensive care unit. *American Journal of Health System Pharmacy*. 2002;59:452–454.

Voytilla KL, Tyler LS, Rusho WJ. Visual compatibility of azithromycin with 24 commonly used drugs during simulated Y-site delivery. *American Journal of Health System Pharmacy*. 2002;59:853–855.

INDEX

Drug categories are in SMALL CAPS. Prototypes in **bold.**
Generic drug names are given in parentheses.

ritodrine hydrochloride, 1354–1355
salmeterol xinafoate, 1367–1368
terbutaline sulfate, 1462–1464

ADRENERGIC AGONIST, SEROTONIN 5-HT$_1$ RECEPTOR AGONIST
almotriptan, 42–44

ADRENERGIC ANTAGONISTS, ALPHA-
alfuzosin, 38–39
carvedilol, 247–249
dihydroergotamine mesylate, 475–476
doxazosin mesylate, 512–513
ergoloid mesylate, 568–569
ergotamine tartrate, 569–571
labetalol hydrochloride, 848–851
methylergonovine maleate, 977–978
phenoxybenzamine hydrochloride, 1203–1204
phentolamine mesylate, 1206–1207
prazosin hydrochloride, 1255–1257
tamsulosin hydrochloride, 1447–1448
terazosin, 1460–1461

ADRENERGIC ANTAGONISTS, BETA-. *See also* EYE PREPARATIONS, BETA-ADRENERGIC BLOCKER
acebutolol hydrochloride, 7–9
atenolol, 123–125
betaxolol hydrochloride, 168–169, 1624
bisoprolol fumarate, 179–180
carteolol hydrochloride, 245–247, 1624
carvedilol, 247–249
esmolol hydrochloride, 580–582
labetalol hydrochloride, 848–851
levobetaxolol hydrochloride, 1624
levobunolol, 1624
metipranolol hydrochloride, 1624
metoprolol tartrate, 987–990
nadolol, 1034–1035
penbutolol, 1171–1173
pindolol, 1221–1222
propranolol hydrochloride, 1290–1294, 1624
sotalol, 1407–1409
timolol maleate, 1504–1505, 1624

ADRENERGIC ANTAGONISTS, ERGOT ALKALOID
bromocriptine mesylate, 189–191
cabergoline, 210
dihydroergotamine mesylate, 475–476
ergoloid mesylate, 568–569

ergotamine tartrate, 569–571
methylergonovine maleate, 977–978
zolmitriptan, 1618–1619

ADRENERGIC ANTAGONISTS, SEROTONIN 5-HT$_1$ RECEPTOR AGONIST
eletriptan hydrobromide, 537–539
frovatriptan, 679–681
naratriptan, 1051–1052
rizatriptan benzoate, 1360–1361
sumatriptan, 1437–1438
zolmitriptan, 1618–1619

Adriamycin (doxorubicin hydrochloride), 516–518

ADSORBENTS
activated charcoal, 292–293
aluminum carbonate, 54–55
aluminum hydroxide, 54–55
aluminum phosphate, 54–55

ADSORBENT, ANTIDIARRHEAL
bismuth subsalicylate, 177–178

Adsorbocarpine (pilocarpine hydrochloride/nitrate), 1216–1218
Advair Diskus (combination drug), 1647
Advicor (combination drug), 1640, 1647
Advil (ibuprofen), 760–762
AeroBid (flunisolide), 1632
Aeroseb-HC (hydrocortisone), 744–748, 1633
Afrin (oxymetazoline hydrochloride), 1135–1136
Aftate (tolnaftate), 1522–1523
agalsidase beta, 27–28
Agenerase (amprenavir), 96–97
Aggrastat (tirofiban hydrochloride), 1510–1512
Aggrenox (combination drug), 1640, 1647
Agrylin (anagrelide hydrochloride), 99–100
A-HydroCort (hydrocortisone sodium succinate), 744–748
Airbron (acetylcysteine), 15–16
Ak-Con (naphazoline hydrochloride), 1048–1049, 1628
AK-Dilate Ophthalmic (phenylephrine hydrochloride), 1207–1209, 1627
AK-Homatropine (homatropine hydrobromide), 1627
Akineton (biperiden hydrochloride), 175–176

Drug categories are in SMALL CAPS. Prototypes in **bold.**
Generic drug names are given in parentheses.

1679

Drug categories are in SMALL CAPS. Prototypes in **bold.**
Generic drug names are given in parentheses.

Drug categories are in SMALL CAPS. Prototypes in **bold.**
Generic drug names are given in parentheses.

1681

Drug categories are in SMALL CAPS. Prototypes in **bold.**
Generic drug names are given in parentheses.

Drug categories are in SMALL CAPS. Prototypes in **bold.**
Generic drug names are given in parentheses.

INDEX

Drug categories are in SMALL CAPS. Prototypes in **bold**.
Generic drug names are given in parentheses.

Drug categories are in SMALL CAPS. Prototypes in **bold.**
Generic drug names are given in parentheses.

Drug categories are in SMALL CAPS. Prototypes in **bold.**
Generic drug names are given in parentheses.

Drug categories are in SMALL CAPS. Prototypes in **bold.**
Generic drug names are given in parentheses.

1687

Drug categories are in SMALL CAPS. Prototypes in **bold.**
Generic drug names are given in parentheses.

Drug categories are in SMALL CAPS. Prototypes in **bold**.
Generic drug names are given in parentheses.

1689

Drug categories are in SMALL CAPS. Prototypes in **bold.**
Generic drug names are given in parentheses.

Drug categories are in SMALL CAPS. Prototypes in **bold.**
Generic drug names are given in parentheses.

1691

Drug categories are in SMALL CAPS. Prototypes in **bold.**
Generic drug names are given in parentheses.

Drug categories are in SMALL CAPS. Prototypes in **bold.**
Generic drug names are given in parentheses.

1693

Drug categories are in SMALL CAPS. Prototypes in **bold.**
Generic drug names are given in parentheses.

Drug categories are in SMALL CAPS. Prototypes in **bold.**
Generic drug names are given in parentheses.

1695

Drug categories are in SMALL CAPS. Prototypes in **bold.**
Generic drug names are given in parentheses.

Drug categories are in SMALL CAPS. Prototypes in **bold.**
Generic drug names are given in parentheses.

Drug categories are in SMALL CAPS. Prototypes in **bold.**
Generic drug names are given in parentheses.

Drug categories are in SMALL CAPS. Prototypes in **bold.**
Generic drug names are given in parentheses.

1699

Drug categories are in SMALL CAPS. Prototypes in **bold.**
Generic drug names are given in parentheses.

Drug categories are in SMALL CAPS. Prototypes in **bold.**
Generic drug names are given in parentheses.

1701

Drug categories are in SMALL CAPS. Prototypes in **bold.**
Generic drug names are given in parentheses.

Drug categories are in SMALL CAPS. Prototypes in **bold.**
Generic drug names are given in parentheses.

1703

INDEX

Drug categories are in SMALL CAPS. Prototypes in **bold.**
Generic drug names are given in parentheses.

Drug categories are in SMALL CAPS. Prototypes in **bold.**
Generic drug names are given in parentheses.

1705

Drug categories are in SMALL CAPS. Prototypes in **bold.**
Generic drug names are given in parentheses.

Drug categories are in SMALL CAPS. Prototypes in **bold.**
Generic drug names are given in parentheses.

1707

Drug categories are in SMALL CAPS. Prototypes in **bold.**
Generic drug names are given in parentheses.

Drug categories are in SMALL CAPS. Prototypes in **bold.**
Generic drug names are given in parentheses.
1709

Drug categories are in SMALL CAPS. Prototypes in **bold.**
Generic drug names are given in parentheses.

Drug categories are in SMALL CAPS. Prototypes in **bold.**
Generic drug names are given in parentheses.

1711

Drug categories are in SMALL CAPS. Prototypes in **bold.**
Generic drug names are given in parentheses.

Drug categories are in SMALL CAPS. Prototypes in **bold.**
Generic drug names are given in parentheses.

1713

Drug categories are in SMALL CAPS. Prototypes in **bold.**
Generic drug names are given in parentheses.

Drug categories are in SMALL CAPS. Prototypes in **bold.**
Generic drug names are given in parentheses.

1715

Drug categories are in SMALL CAPS. Prototypes in **bold.**
Generic drug names are given in parentheses.

Drug categories are in SMALL CAPS. Prototypes in **bold.**
Generic drug names are given in parentheses.

Drug categories are in SMALL CAPS. Prototypes in **bold.**
Generic drug names are given in parentheses.

1719

Drug categories are in SMALL CAPS. Prototypes in **bold.**
Generic drug names are given in parentheses.

Drug categories are in SMALL CAPS. Prototypes in **bold.**
Generic drug names are given in parentheses.

1721

Drug categories are in SMALL CAPS. Prototypes in **bold.**
Generic drug names are given in parentheses.

Drug categories are in SMALL CAPS. Prototypes in **bold.**
Generic drug names are given in parentheses.

1723

Drug categories are in SMALL CAPS. Prototypes in **bold.**
Generic drug names are given in parentheses.

Drug categories are in SMALL CAPS. Prototypes in **bold.**
Generic drug names are given in parentheses.

1727

Drug categories are in SMALL CAPS. Prototypes in **bold.**
Generic drug names are given in parentheses.

1729

Drug categories are in SMALL CAPS. Prototypes in **bold.**
Generic drug names are given in parentheses.

Drug categories are in SMALL CAPS. Prototypes in **bold.**
Generic drug names are given in parentheses.

Drug categories are in SMALL CAPS. Prototypes in **bold.**
Generic drug names are given in parentheses.

Drug categories are in SMALL CAPS. Prototypes in **bold.**
Generic drug names are given in parentheses.

1733

Drug categories are in SMALL CAPS. Prototypes in **bold.**
Generic drug names are given in parentheses.

Drug categories are in SMALL CAPS. Prototypes in **bold.**
Generic drug names are given in parentheses.

1735

1736
Drug categories are in SMALL CAPS. Prototypes in **bold.**
Generic drug names are given in parentheses.

Drug categories are in SMALL CAPS. Prototypes in **bold.**
Generic drug names are given in parentheses.

1737

Drug categories are in SMALL CAPS. Prototypes in **bold.**
Generic drug names are given in parentheses.

Drug categories are in SMALL CAPS. Prototypes in **bold.**
Generic drug names are given in parentheses.

1739

INDEX

Drug categories are in SMALL CAPS. Prototypes in **bold.**
Generic drug names are given in parentheses.

Drug categories are in SMALL CAPS. Prototypes in **bold.**
Generic drug names are given in parentheses.

1741

Drug categories are in SMALL CAPS. Prototypes in **bold.**
Generic drug names are given in parentheses.

Drug categories are in SMALL CAPS. Prototypes in **bold.**
Generic drug names are given in parentheses.

1743

1744

Drug categories are in SMALL CAPS. Prototypes in **bold.**
Generic drug names are given in parentheses.

Drug categories are in SMALL CAPS. Prototypes in **bold.**
Generic drug names are given in parentheses.

1745

Drug categories are in SMALL CAPS. Prototypes in **bold.**
Generic drug names are given in parentheses.

1747

Drug categories are in SMALL CAPS. Prototypes in **bold.**
Generic drug names are given in parentheses.

Drug categories are in SMALL CAPS. Prototypes in **bold.**
Generic drug names are given in parentheses.

1749

Drug categories are in SMALL CAPS. Prototypes in **bold.**
Generic drug names are given in parentheses.

Drug categories are in SMALL CAPS. Prototypes in **bold.**
Generic drug names are given in parentheses.

Drug categories are in SMALL CAPS. Prototypes in **bold.**
Generic drug names are given in parentheses.

Drug categories are in SMALL CAPS. Prototypes in **bold.**
Generic drug names are given in parentheses.

1753

Drug categories are in SMALL CAPS. Prototypes in **bold.**
Generic drug names are given in parentheses.

1755

Drug categories are in SMALL CAPS. Prototypes in **bold.**
Generic drug names are given in parentheses.

Drug categories are in SMALL CAPS. Prototypes in **bold.**
Generic drug names are given in parentheses.

1757

Drug categories are in SMALL CAPS. Prototypes in **bold.**
Generic drug names are given in parentheses.

Drug categories are in SMALL CAPS. Prototypes in **bold.**
Generic drug names are given in parentheses.

1759

Drug categories are in SMALL CAPS. Prototypes in **bold.**
Generic drug names are given in parentheses.

Drug categories are in SMALL CAPS. Prototypes in **bold.**
Generic drug names are given in parentheses.

Drug categories are in SMALL CAPS. Prototypes in **bold.**
Generic drug names are given in parentheses.

Drug categories are in SMALL CAPS. Prototypes in **bold.**
Generic drug names are given in parentheses.

1763

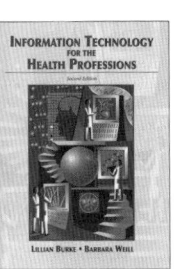

	AMINO-PHYLLINE	DOBUTA-MINE	DOPAMINE	HEPARIN	MEPERIDINE	MORPHINE	NITRO-GLYCERIN	ONDAN-SETRON	POTASSIUM IN D5W OR NS
acyclovir				C	I/C	I/C		I	C
alteplase							—		
amikacin	C	C	—	—		C		C	
amino acids (TPN)	C	—	—	—	C	C		—	C
aminophylline	—	C	I/C	C	C	C		I	C
amiodarone		C	C	C	—	C	C	—	C
ampicillin			—	—		C	C	—	
ampicillin/sulbactam				C				—	C
amrinone	C	C	C	C	C	C	C		
aztreonam	C		C	C	C	C		C	C
bretylium		I/C	C				C		
bumetanide	—	—	C		C				
calcium chloride	C		C	C					C
cefamandole	C		C		—				C
cefazolin	C	—	C		C	C		C	
cefoperazone	C			C	—	C		—	
cefotaxime	C		C		C	C		C	
cefotetan	C		C		C	C			
cefoxitin	C		C	—	C	C			C
ceftazidime	C			C	C	C		C	
ceftizoxime	C				C	C		C	
ceftriaxone	C				C	C		C	
cefuroxime	C			C	C	C			C
chloramphenicol	C		C		C	C		C	C
cimetidine	—	C	C	C	C	C			C
ciprofloxacin	—	C		—	C			C	C
clindamycin	—			C	C	C		C	C
dexamethasone	C			C	C	C		C	C

	AMINO-PHYLLINE	DOBUTA-MINE	DOPAMINE	HEPARIN	MEPERIDINE	MORPHINE	NITRO-GLYCERIN	ONDAN-SETRON	POTASSIUM IN D5W OR NS
diazepam	C	I		I	I				I
digoxin	I		C	C	C	C			C
diltiazem	C	C		C	C	C	C	C	C
diphenydramine	I	C	C	I/C	C	C	C		C
dobutamine	I		I	C	C	C	C		C
dopamine	I	C	C	C	C	C	C	C	C
doxycycline									
enalapril/enalaprilat	C	C			C	C			C
epinephrine	I	C	C	I			C		C
eptifibatide				C	C	C			
erythromycin	I	C	C	I	C	C	C	C	C
esmolol	C		C	C	C	C	C	C	C
famotidine	C	C	C	C	C	C		C	C
filgrastim	C							C	C
fluconazole	C	C	C	I	C	C			
foscarnet	C	I	C	C			C		C
fosphenytoin									
furosemide	C	I/C	I	C	I/C	I	C	I	C
ganciclovir			I/C					I	
gentamicin	C	I/C	I/C	C	C	C		I	C
heparin	C		C	C	C	C		C	C
hydrocortisone	C			C				C	C
hydromorphone				C				C	
imipenem/cilastatin				C	I	C		C	
insulin		C		C	I			C	C
isoproterenol	C	C	C	C	C	C	C		C
labetolol	C	C	C	C	C	C	C		C
lidocaine									
lorazepam								I	